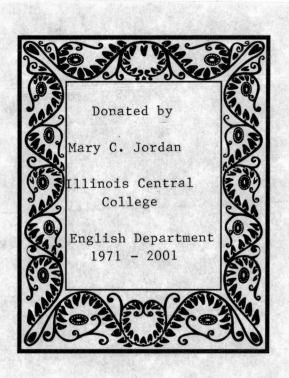

THE STORY
AND ITS WRITER

FOURTH EDITION

THE STORY AND ITS WRITER

An Introduction to Short Fiction

Ann Charters

UNIVERSITY OF CONNECTICUT

Bedford Books *of* **St. Martin's Press**
BOSTON

For Bedford Books

President and Publisher: Charles H. Christensen
General Manager and Associate Publisher: Joan E. Feinberg
Managing Editor: Elizabeth M. Schaaf
Developmental Editor: Stephen A. Scipione
Production Editor: John Amburg
Production Assistants: Karen Baart, Jonathan Burns
Copyeditor: Nancy Bell Scott
Text Design: Anna George
Cover Design: Hannus Design
Cover Painting: Henry Varnum Poor, *The Writer at Window*, c. 1930. Bornick
Fine Art.

Acknowledgments

Chinua Achebe. "Civil Peace" from *Girls at War and Other Stories* by Chinua Achebe. Copy-
right © 1972, 1973 by Chinua Achebe. "An Image of Africa: Conrad's 'Heart of
Darkness'" from *Hopes and Impediments* by Chinua Achebe. Copyright © 1988 by
Chinua Achebe. Used by permission of Doubleday, a division of Bantam Doubleday
Dell Publishing Group, Inc. and Harold Ober Associates.
Alice Adams. "The Last Lovely City" from *Best American Short Stories*, eds. Robert Stone and
Katrina Kenison. Copyright © 1992 by Houghton Mifflin Company. Reprinted by
permission of the author.

*Acknowledgments and copyrights are continued at the back of the book on pages 1659–1666, which
constitute an extension of the copyright page. It is a violation of the law to reproduce these selections
by any means whatsoever without the written permission of the copyright holder.*

PREFACE

A true work of fiction is a wonderfully simple thing—so simple that most so-called serious writers avoid trying it, feeling they ought to do something more important and ingenious, never guessing how incredibly difficult it is. A true work of fiction does all of the following things, and does them elegantly, efficiently: it creates a vivid and continuous dream in the reader's mind; it is implicitly philosophical; it fulfills or at least deals with all of the expectations it sets up; and it strikes us, in the end, not simply as a thing done but as a shining performance.

John Gardner, "What Writers Do"

If John Gardner's description summarizes what writers of fiction do, then this anthology was created to enable readers of short fiction to experience their "shining performance" as elegantly and efficiently as possible. *The Story and Its Writer* grew out of my desire to teach from an anthology filled as much as possible with writer talk about short stories, after years of dissatisfaction using textbooks filled with too much editor talk. The books available tended to be of two types: textbooks with a limited number of stories and a bothersome, often prescriptive, abundance of editorial material; or large anthologies with many stories and very little discussion by anyone about matters sure to be perplexing to students. The first type made the editor the authority; the second type made the teacher assume that role. In neither case were those most qualified to speak about fiction — the storytellers — given space to express *their* authority about their craft. *The Story and Its Writer* seeks to redress these imbalances. The gratifying success the book has enjoyed over three editions confirms the appeal and usefulness of its premise.

Those looking for good fiction will find it in abundance in *The Story and Its Writer*: 124 stories in this edition, arranged alphabetically by author. The stories range from classic tales by Nathaniel Hawthorne and Edgar Allan Poe through modern masterpieces by Flannery O'Connor and William Faulkner to contemporary selections from the work of writers such as Raymond Carver, Louise Erdrich, and Isabel Allende. The sheer number and variety of stories should offer plenty of choice and teaching flexibility.

Editorial material is amply provided as well, but all of it is designed to support students without getting in the way of their reading. Most of the editor talk is packed discreetly at the back of the book, to be consulted when appropriate, if appropriate. It includes a history of the short story, an outline of the elements of fiction, an extensive section on writing about fiction, a glossary of more than 100 literary terms, and a chronological listing of authors and stories. The stories themselves appear with substantial biographical headnotes, but no other apparatus that might constrain a student's response — no interpretive introductions, no directive questions or assignments.

Those interested in more editor talk may want to examine the instructor's manual. *Resources for Teaching The Story and Its Writer* contains discussions of each story, questions and writing assignments for students, short bibliographies, a thematic index of the stories, a chronological guide to authors and stories in the anthology, and a listing of short stories on film.

Finally, the most distinctive feature of *The Story and Its Writer* is the section of commentaries that immediately follows the anthology of stories. These commentaries — seventy-five in this edition — justify the title of the book. In most of the commentaries, writers discuss their stories and the stories of fellow writers that appear in the anthology, and more generally remark on the form of the story and vocation of storyteller. I, and the many instructors who have used the earlier editions, find these commentaries to be just the ingredient to stimulate class discussion and give rise to lively writing.

New to This Edition

The Story and Its Writer has grown significantly, with more stories and more commentaries than ever before. Those familiar with the book from earlier editions will notice that the representation of women writers, contemporary American and minority writers, and international writers, both Western and non-Western, is greater than ever before. All told, the 124 selections are about equally divided between "classic stories by classic writers" and fine, fresh stories that may someday make — or perhaps break — that canon. The number of commentaries has grown by about a third and includes commentaries by literary critics reading individual stories from different critical perspectives (psychological, feminist, gender, deconstructionist, and others). In sampling these perspectives, students may learn something about how to deploy, in their reading and writing, the strategies of various critical schools. For the first time, the anthology includes "Casebooks" on three important writers — Raymond Carver, Flannery O'Connor, and Leslie Marmon Silko, each of whom is represented by three stories in Part One. Each casebook includes comments by, and about, the author, background and source information about the stories, and numerous critical commentaries. No other anthology enables students to examine in such depth the work of exemplary writers.

Compact Edition

The Story and Its Writer is also available in a Compact Fourth Edition containing sixty stories by fifty-three writers, forty-one commentaries, and a new casebook on Raymond Carver. This shorter edition retains all of the longer book's widely praised editorial features, for those who want a smaller, less expensive book.

Acknowledgments

I wish to acknowledge the help of many people in the preparation and revision of the anthology and the instructor's manual. I want to thank William Sheidley of the University of Southern Colorado, whose insightful commentaries on many stories that appear in *The Story and Its Writer* can be found in the instructor's manual. Thanks also to past and present graduate students whose work helped shape the manual from edition to edition: Martha Ramsey, Robert Gaspar, Dennis Lazor, Maureen Grogan, Patricia Vincent and Ning Yu. My colleagues in the English Department at the University of Connecticut — Lee Jacobus, Scott Bradfield, Compton Rees, William Curtin, Milton Stern, Jack Davis, Jack Manning, Michael Meyer, David Benson, and Feenie Ziner — generously contributed suggestions and advice. The staff at the Homer Babbidge Library, especially Leanne Pander, Pamela Skinner, David McChesney, and Carol Abramson, gave unflagging assistance. Students in my short story classes diligently drafted the sample essays illustrating the various ways to write about stories. Charles Flynn of the Rockefeller Library and Emily Meideros and Clare Durst of the Dean of the College Office at Brown University were also particularly helpful. In addition, professors who used the third edition of the anthology and generously took time to share their ideas about it include Dirk Aardsma, Carol Abate, Iska Alter, Dr. G. M. Andersen, Ronald G. Ashcroft, James S. Bass, Charlotte Bill, Robert Boswell, Sara Braut, Ronald R. Butters, Eve La Salle Caram, Maxine Clair, Anne Clifford, Gladys M. Clifton, Linda R. Cooler, David Crowe, Virginia Cyrus, Lisa Denbleyker, Marvin Diogenes, Joanne Drechsel, Rainey Duke, Jenni Dyman, Mara Faulkner, Arnold Gordenstein, Richard Grande, Joseph Green, Susan G. Hall, Susan Hardebeck, Sydney Morgan Harrison, E. Havazelet, Roseanne Hoefel, Christopher Howell, Ann Iles, Geri Jacobs, Rich Johnson, Hilda Johnston, Andrew Levy, Laurie Litchford, Patricia Lorimer Lyndberg, Cecilia Machesla, Marni L. Magda, MaryJo Mahoney, Lawrence W. Manglitz, Barbara McClure, Donovan McDonough, Bruce McNallie, Jane Melnick, Jeanne Montague, Patricia O'Donnell, Carol Orlock, Helen Orman, Ted Otteson, JHE Paine, Morton D. Rich, Dana Ringuette, Elizabeth Robertson, Paula Robison, Zelda Jeanne Rouillard, M. Craig Sanders, Deborah Simpson, Clifton Snider, Hao Sun, Susan Swan, Claire Taft, Donn E. Taylor, Herbert K. Tjessem, Linda

Jorclan Tucker, Wasserburg, Jean Weber, Margaret Whitt, Salaam Yousif, and Jane Zunkel. I thank them for their help and encouragement, which made the task of revising *The Story and Its Writer* an interesting and enjoyable one.

In preparing the fourth edition of *The Story and Its Writer*, I am especially grateful to my intelligent and resourceful editor, Stephen Scipione, whose assistance was invaluable. My publisher, Charles Christensen, was an untiring source of suggestions and practical advice. Others at Bedford Books who helped with this edition include associate publisher Joan Feinberg, managing editor Elizabeth Schaaf, Karen Baart, Jonathan Burns, Adrian Harris, Mark Reimold, and especially associate editor Laura Arcari and my conscientious production editor, John Amburg. Last, but by no means least, I want to thank my husband, Samuel Charters, my daughters, Mallay and Nora, and my friends Jennifer Hartig, Mel and Bob Chatain, Suzie Staubach and Jenny Schuessler for sharing their ideas about short fiction during the preparation of all four editions of this book.

Ann Charters
Storrs, Connecticut

CONTENTS

LINDA L. DANIELSON

Part Four   APPENDICES

THE STORY AND ITS WRITER

CHINUA ACHEBE *(b. 1930) was born and grew up in Ogidi in eastern Nigeria, the son of devout Christian parents. He has recalled that in his childhood "the bounties of the Christian God were not to be taken lightly — education, paid jobs, and many other advantages that nobody in his right senses could underrate." As a member of the Ibo tribe, his first language was Igbo, which he remembers was "spoken with such eloquence by the old men of the village"; he learned English at the age of eight. After graduating from the University College of Ibadan, Achebe began a career in radio. In 1966 he resigned as director of external broadcasting in Nigeria and joined the Biafran Ministry of Information to help raise funds for his compatriots in the upheaval of the Biafran War. When Nigeria was put under military rule, he left the country to teach, and he is currently at the University of Massachusetts, Amherst. There he gave a controversial chancellor's lecture titled "Racism in Conrad's 'Heart of Darkness,'" which was later published in his collection of essays* Hopes and Impediments *(1988).*

Achebe says he began to think about becoming a writer after reading "some appalling novels about Africa" written by European authors. These made him decide, while still a student, "that the story we had to tell could not be told for us by anyone else no matter how gifted or well-intentioned." He won acclaim with his first novel, Things Fall Apart *(1958), a brilliant depiction of the decay of an African state under the impact of Europe. More recent books include the short story collection* Girls at War *(1973) and the novel* Anthills of the Savannah *(1988). Achebe was also the founding editor of the distinguished African Writers Series of novels, stories, poetry, and plays published by Heinemann in London, Ibadan, and Nairobi.*

The story "Civil Peace" dramatizes Achebe's awareness of catastrophic disturbances in the lives of ordinary people in war-torn Nigeria. He believes that Africans have always lived in what he calls "the crossroads of cultures."

> *We still do today, but when I was a boy one could see and sense the peculiar quality and atmosphere of it more clearly. I am not talking about all that rubbish we hear of the spiritual void and mental stresses that Africans are supposed to have, or the evil forces and irrational passions prowling through Africa's heart of darkness. We know the racist mystique behind a lot of that stuff. . . . What I do remember is a fascination for the ritual and the life on the other arm of the crossroads.*

RELATED COMMENTARY: *Chinua Achebe, "An Image of Africa: Conrad's 'Heart of Darkness,'" page 1373.*

CHINUA ACHEBE

Civil Peace

Jonathan Iwegbu counted himself extraordinarily lucky. "Happy survival!" meant so much more to him than just a current fashion of greeting old friends in the first hazy days of peace. It went deep to his heart. He had come out of the war with five inestimable blessings — his head, his wife Maria's head, and the heads of three out of their four children. As a bonus he also had his old bicycle — a miracle too but naturally not to be compared to the safety of five human heads.

The bicycle had a little history of its own. One day at the height of the war it was commandeered "for urgent military action." Hard as its loss would have been to him he would still have let it go without a thought had he not had some doubts about the genuineness of the officer. It wasn't his disreputable rags, nor the toes peeping out of one blue and one brown canvas shoes, nor yet the two stars of his rank done obviously in a hurry in biro, that troubled Jonathan; many good and heroic soldiers looked the same or worse. It was rather a certain lack of grip and firmness in his manner. So Jonathan, suspecting he might be amenable to influence, rummaged in his raffia bag and produced the two pounds with which he had been going to buy firewood which his wife, Maria, retailed to camp officials for extra stock-fish and corn meal, and got his bicycle back. That night he buried it in the little clearing in the bush where the dead of the camp, including his own youngest son, were buried. When he dug it up again a year later after the surrender all it needed was a little palm-oil greasing. "Nothing puzzles God," he said in wonder.

He put it to immediate use as a taxi and accumulated a small pile of Biafran money ferrying camp officials and their families across the four-mile stretch to the nearest tarred road. His standard charge per trip was six pounds and those who had the money were only glad to be rid of some of it in this way. At the end of a fortnight he had made a small fortune of one hundred and fifteen pounds.

Then he made the journey to Enugu and found another miracle waiting for him. It was unbelievable. He rubbed his eyes and looked again and it was still standing there before him. But, needless to say, even that monumental blessing must be accounted also totally inferior to the five heads in the family. This newest miracle was his little house in Ogui Overside. Indeed nothing puzzles God! Only two houses away a huge concrete edifice some wealthy contractor had put up just before the war was a mountain of rubble. And here was Jonathan's little zinc house of no regrets built with mud blocks quite intact! Of course the doors and windows were missing and five sheets off the roof. But what was that? And anyhow he had returned to Enugu early enough to pick up bits of old zinc and wood and soggy sheets of cardboard lying around the neighbourhood before thousands more came out of their forest holes looking for the same things. He got a destitute carpenter with one old hammer, a blunt plane, and a few bent and rusty nails in his tool bag to turn this assortment of wood, paper, and metal into door and window shutters for five Nigerian shillings or fifty Biafran pounds. He paid the pounds, and moved in with his overjoyed family carrying five heads on their shoulders.

His children picked mangoes near the military cemetery and sold them to soldiers' wives for a few pennies — real pennies this time — and his wife started making breakfast akara balls for neighbours in a hurry to start life again. With his family earnings he took his bicycle to the villages around and bought fresh palm-wine which he mixed generously in his rooms with the water which had recently started running again in the public tap down the road, and opened up a bar for soldiers and other lucky people with good money.

At first he went daily, then every other day, and finally once a week, to the offices of the Coal Corporation where he used to be a miner, to find out what was what. The only thing he did find out in the end was that that little house of his was even a greater blessing than he had thought. Some of his fellow ex-miners who had nowhere to return at the end of the day's waiting just slept outside the doors of the offices and cooked what meal they could scrounge together in Bournvita tins. As the weeks lengthened and still nobody could say what was what Jonathan discontinued his weekly visits altogether and faced his palm-wine bar.

But nothing puzzles God. Came the day of the windfall when after five days of endless scuffles in queues and counter-queues in the sun outside the Treasury he had twenty pounds counted into his palms as ex-gratia award for the rebel money he had turned in. It was like Christmas for him and for many others like him when the payments began. They called it (since few could manage its proper official name) *egg-rasher.*

As soon as the pound notes were placed in his palm Jonathan simply closed it tight over them and buried fist and money inside his trouser pocket. He had to be extra careful because he had seen a man a couple of days earlier collapse into near-madness in an instant before that oceanic crowd because no sooner had he got his twenty pounds than some heartless ruffian picked it off him. Though it was not right that a man in such an extremity of agony should be blamed yet many in the queues that day were able to remark quietly on the victim's carelessness, especially after he pulled out the innards of his pocket and revealed a hole in it big enough to pass a thief's head. But of course he had insisted that the money had been in the other pocket, pulling it out too to show its comparative wholeness. So one had to be careful.

Jonathan soon transferred the money to his left hand and pocket so as to leave his right free for shaking hands should the need arise, though by fixing his gaze at such an elevation as to miss all approaching human faces he made sure that the need did not arise, until he got home.

He was normally a heavy sleeper but that night he heard all the neighbourhood noises die down one after another. Even the night watchman who knocked the hour on some metal somewhere in the distance had fallen silent after knocking one o'clock. That must have been the last thought in Jonathan's mind before he was finally carried away himself. He couldn't have been gone for long, though, when he was violently awakened again.

"Who is knocking?" whispered his wife lying beside him on the floor.

"I don't know," he whispered back breathlessly.

The second time the knocking came it was so loud and imperious that the rickety old door could have fallen down.

"Who is knocking?" he asked then, his voice parched and trembling.

"Na tief-man and him people," came the cool reply. "Make you hopen de door." This was followed by the heaviest knocking of all.

Maria was the first to raise the alarm, then he followed and all their children.

"Police-o! Thieves-o! Neighbours-o! Police-o! We are lost! We are dead! Neighbours, are you asleep? Wake up! Police-o!"

This went on for a long time and then stopped suddenly. Perhaps they had scared the thief away. There was total silence. But only for a short while.

"You done finish?" asked the voice outside. "Make we help you small. Oya, everybody!"

"Police-o! Tief-man-o! Neighbours-o! we done loss-o! Police-o! . . ."

There were at least five other voices besides the leader's.

Jonathan and his family were now completely paralysed by terror. Maria and the children sobbed inaudibly like lost souls. Jonathan groaned continuously.

The silence that followed the thieves' alarm vibrated horribly. Jonathan all but begged their leader to speak again and be done with it.

"My frien," said he at long last, "we don try our best for call dem but I tink say dem all done sleep-o . . . So wetin we go do now? Sometaim you wan call soja? Or you wan make we call dem for you? Soja better pass police. No be so?"

"Na so!" replied his men. Jonathan thought he heard even more voices now than before and groaned heavily. His legs were sagging under him and his throat felt like sandpaper.

"My frien, why you no de talk again. I de ask you say you wan make we call soja?"

"No."

"Awrighto. Now make we talk business. We no be bad tief. We no like for make trouble. Trouble done finish. War done finish and all the katakata wey de for inside. No Civil War again. This time na Civil Peace. No be so?"

"Na so!" answered the horrible chorus.

"What do you want from me? I am a poor man. Everything I had went with this war. Why do you come to me? You know people who have money. We . . ."

"Awright! We know say you no get plenty money. But we sef no get even anini. So derefore make you open dis window and give us one hundred pound and we go commot. Orderwise we de come for inside now to show you guitar-boy like dis . . ."

A volley of automatic fire rang through the sky. Maria and the children began to weep aloud again.

"Ah, missisi de cry again. No need for dat. We done talk say we na good tief. We just take our small money and go nwayorly. No molest. Abi we de molest?"

"At all!" sang the chorus.

"My friends," began Jonathan hoarsely. "I hear what you say and I thank you. If I had one hundred pounds . . ."

"Lookia my frien, no be play we come play for your house. If we make mistake and step for inside you no go like am-o. So derefore . . ."

"To God who made me; if you come inside and find one hundred pounds, take it and shoot me and shoot my wife and children. I swear to God. The only money I have in this life is this twenty pounds *egg-rasher* they gave me today . . ."

"OK. Time de go. Make you open dis window and bring the twenty pound. We go manage am like dat."

There were now loud murmurs of dissent among the chorus: "Na lie de man de lie; e get plenty money . . . Make we go inside and search properly well . . . Wetin be twenty pound? . . ."

"Shurrup!" rang the leader's voice like a lone shot in the sky and silenced the murmuring at once. "Are you dere? Bring the money quick!"

"I am coming," said Jonathan fumbling in the darkness with the key of the small wooden box he kept by his side on the mat.

At the first sign of light as neighbours and others assembled to commiserate with him he was already strapping his five-gallon demijohn to his bicycle carrier and his wife, sweating in the open fire, was turning over akara balls in a wide clay bowl of boiling oil. In the corner his eldest son was rinsing out dregs of yesterday's palm-wine from old beer bottles.

"I count it as nothing," he told his sympathizers, his eyes on the rope he was tying. "What is *egg-rasher*? Did I depend on it last week? Or is it greater than other things that went with the war? I say, let *egg-rasher* perish in the flames! Let it go where everything else has gone. Nothing puzzles God."

[1971]

ALICE ADAMS (b. 1926) was born in Fredericksburg, Virginia. Her parents were interested in literature, although she remembers she never saw her father "read a book for pleasure." As a young girl Adams wrote poetry and had her work published in school magazines. Then she went to Radcliffe College, where she took a short story class and "fell totally and permanently in love" with the works of James Joyce, Katherine Mansfield, Katherine Anne Porter, John Cheever, and many other writers. She graduated from Radcliffe in 1945, married, had children, and then was divorced, all the time continuing to write fiction. Her first novel, Careless Love (1966), was published when she was forty.

Living in San Francisco, Adams now publishes regularly and no longer works the succession of office jobs she used to support herself and her family until she could make a living from her writing. She is a frequent contributor of short stories to the Atlantic Monthly, The New Yorker, and the Paris Review. To date she has published several novels, including Families and Survivors (1975), Listening to Billie (1978) — its title referring to the blues singer Billie Holiday — and Rich Rewards (1980). She has also published two collections of short stories, Beautiful Girl (1979) and To See You Again (1982). In 1982 she won the O. Henry Award for Continuing Achievement as a short story writer. Adams's recent books are Second Chances (1988), After You've Gone (1989), and Almost Perfect (1993).

In her essay "Why I Write," Adams revealed that she writes "mainly because it is what I most enjoy doing." "The Last Lovely City" is a recent story that first appeared in The New Yorker and was later included in The Best American Short Stories of 1992.

A L I C E   A D A M S

The Last Lovely City

Old and famous, an acknowledged success both in this country and in his native Mexico, though now a sadhearted widower, Dr. Benito Zamora slowly and unskillfully navigates the high, sharp curves on the road to Stinson Beach, California — his destination. From time to time, barely moving his heavy, white-maned head, he glances at the unfamiliar young woman near him on the seat — the streaky-haired, underweight woman in a very short skirt and green sandals (her name is Carla) who has somewhat inexplicably invited him to come along to this party. What old hands, Benito thinks, of his own, on the wheel, an old beggar's hands. What can this girl want of me? he wonders. Some new heaviness around the doctor's neck and chin makes him look both strong and fierce, and his deep-set black eyes are powerful, still, and unrelenting in their judgmental gaze, beneath thick, uneven, white brows.

"We're almost there," he tells the girl, this Carla.

"I don't care; I love the drive," she says, and moves her head closer to the window, so her long hair fans out across her shoulders. "Do you go back to Mexico very often?" she turns now to ask him.

"Fairly. My very old mother still lives there. Near Oaxaca."

"Oh, I've been to Oaxaca. So beautiful." She beams. "The hotel — "

"My mother's not in the Presidente."

She grins, showing small, white, even teeth. "Well, you're right. I did stay there. But it is a very nice hotel."

"Very nice," he agrees, not looking at her.

His mother is not the doctor's only reason for going to Oaxaca. His interests are actually in almost adjacent Chiapas, where he oversees and has largely funded two large, free clinics — hence his fame, and his nickname, Dr. Do-Good (to Benito, an epithet replete with irony, and one that he much dislikes).

They have now emerged from the dark, tall, covering woods, the groves of redwood, eucalyptus, occasional laurel, and they are circling down the western slope, as the two-lane road forms wide arcs. Ahead of them is the sea, the white curve of beach, and strung-out Stinson, the strange, small coastal town of rich retirees; weekenders, also rich; and a core population of former hippies, now just plain poor, middle-aged people with too many children. In his palmier days, his early, successful years, Dr. Zamora often came to Stinson from San Francisco on Sundays for lunch parties, first as a semi-sought-after bachelor ("But would you want your daughter actually to marry . . . ?" Benito thought he felt this question), and later, less often, with his bride, the fairest of them all, his wife, his lovely blonde. His white soul. Elizabeth.

After Elizabeth died, now some five months ago, in April, friends and colleagues were predictably kind — many invitations, too many solicitious phone calls. And then, just as predictably (he had seen this happen with relatives of patients), all the attention fell off, and he was often alone. And at a time impossible for trips to Mexico: rains made most of the roads in Chiapas impassable, and he feared that he was now too old for the summer heat. Besides, these days the clinics actually ran quite well without him; he imagined that all they really needed was the money that came regularly from his banks. (Had that always been the case? he wondered. Were all those trips to Chiapas unnecessary, ultimately self-serving?) And his mother, in her tiny stucco villa, near Oaxaca, hardly recognized her oldest living son.

Too much time alone, then, and although he had always known that would happen, was even in a sense prepared, the doctor is sometimes angry: Why must they leave him now, when he is so vulnerable? Is no one able to imagine the daily lack, the loss with which he lives?

And then this girl, this Carla, whom the doctor had met at a dinner a month or so before, called and asked him to the lunch, at Stinson Beach. "I hope you don't mind a sort of last-minute invitation," she said, "but I really loved our talk, and I'd wanted to see you again, and this seemed a good excuse." He gratefully accepted, although he remembered very little of her, really, except for her hair, which was very long and silky-looking, streaked all shades of brown, with yellow. He remembered her hair, and that she seemed nice, a little shy; she was quiet, and so he had talked too much. ("Not too unusual, my darling," Elizabeth might have said.) He thinks she said she worked for a newspaper; it now seems too late to ask. He believes she is intelligent, and serious. Curious about his clinics.

But in the short interval between her call and this drive a host of fantasies has crowded old Benito's imagination. She looked about thirty, this girl did, but these days most women look young; she could be forty-two. Still a long way from his own age, but such things did happen. One read of them.

Or was it possible that Carla meant to write about him for her paper? The doctor had refused most interviews for years; had refused until he noticed that no one had asked, not for years.

"What did you say the name of our hostess was?" he thinks to ask her as they round the last curve and approach the first buildings of the town.

"Posey Pendergast. You've never met her?"

"I don't think so, but the name — something goes off in my head."

"Everyone knows Posey; I really thought you would. She's quite marvelous."

"Quite marvelous" is a phrase that Benito (Elizabeth used to agree) finds cautionary; those marvelous people are almost as bad as "characters." All those groups he is sure not to like, how they do proliferate, thinks old Benito sourly, aware of the cruel absence of Elizabeth, with her light laugh, agreeing.

"I'm sure you'll know some of her friends," adds Carla.

Posey Pendergast is a skinny old wreck of a woman, in a tattered straw sun hat and a red, Persian-looking outfit. She breathes heavily. Emphysema and some problems with her heart, the doctor thinks, automatically noting the pink-white skin, faintly bluish mouth, and arthritic hands — hugely blue-veined, rings buried in finger flesh. "I've been hearing of you for years," she tells Benito, in her raspy, classy voice. Is she English? No, more like Boston, or somewhere back there, the doctor decides. She goes on. "I can't believe we've never met. I'm *so* glad Carla brought you."

"This is some house," he says solemnly (using what Elizabeth called his innocent-Indian pose, which is one of his tricks).

It is some house, and the doctor now remembers walking past it, with Elizabeth, marveling at its size and opulence. It was right out there on the beach, not farther along, in Seadrift, with the other big, expensive houses, but out in public — a huge house built up on pilings, all enormous beams, and steel and glass, and diagonal boards.

"My son designed it for me," Posey Pendergast is saying. "Carla's friend," she adds, just as some remote flash is going off in the doctor's mind: he used to hear a lot about this Posey, he recalls, something odd and somewhat scandalous, but from whom? Not Elizabeth, he is sure of that, although she was fond of gossip and used to lament his refusal to talk about patients. Did he hear of Posey from some patient? Some old friend?

This large room facing the sea is now fairly full of people. Women in short, silk, flowered dresses or pastel pants, men in linen or cashmere coats. Rich old gringos is Benito's instant assessment. He notes what seems an unusual number of hearing aids.

He and Carla are introduced around by Posey, although Carla seems already to know a number of the guests. People extend their hands; they all say how nice it is to meet the doctor; several people say that they have heard so much about him. And then, from that roster of Anglo-Saxon names, all sounding somewhat alike, from those voices, nasal Eastern to neutral Californian, Benito hears a familiar sound: "Oh." (It is the drawn-out "Oh" that he recognizes.) "Oh, but I've known Dr. Zamora *very* well, for a *very* long time."

He is confronted by an immense (she must weigh two hundred pounds), short woman, with a huge puff of orange hair, green eyeshadow, and the pinkish spots that skin cancer leaves marking her pale, lined forehead. It is Dolores. Originally Dolores Gutierrez — then Osborne, then Graham, and then he lost track. But here she is before him, her doughy face tightened into a mask, behind which he can indistinctly see the beauty that she was.

"Benito Zamora. Benny Zamora. What an absolutely awful name, my darling. So *spic*," said Dolores, almost fifty years ago.

"How about Dolores Gutierrez?"

"I can marry out of it, and I certainly plan to. Why else would I even think of Boy Osborne, or for that matter Whitey Satterfield? But you, you simply have to change yours. How about Benjamin Orland? That keeps some of the sound, you see? I really don't like names to begin with 'Z.'"

"This is an extremely ugly room," he told her.

She laughed. "I know, but poor dear Norman thinks it's the cat's pajamas, and it's costing him a fortune."

"When you laugh I feel ice on my back." He shivered.

"Pull the sheet up. There. My, you are a gorgeous young man. You really are. Too bad about your name. You don't look so terribly spic."

They were in the pink and gold suite of a lesser Nob Hill hotel, definitely not the Mark or the Fairmont, but still no doubt costing poor Norman a lot. Heavy, gold-threaded, rose-colored draperies, barely parted, yielded a narrow, blue view of the San Francisco Bay, the Bay Bridge, a white slice of Oakland. The bedspread, a darker rose, also gold-threaded, lay in a heavy, crumpled mass on the floor. The sheets were pink, and the shallow buttocks of Dolores Gutierrez were ivory — cool and smooth. Her hair, even then, was false gold.

"You know what I'd really like you to do? Do you want to know?" Her voice was like scented oil, the young doctor thought, light and insidious and finally dirty, making stains.

"I do want to know," he told her.

"Well, this is really perverse. *Really*. It may be a little too much for you."

She was suddenly almost breathless with wanting to tell him what she really wanted, what was so terrifically exciting.

"Tell me." His breath caught, too, although in a rational way he believed that they had surely done everything. He stroked her smooth, cool bottom.

"I want you to pay me," she said. "I know you don't have much money, so that will make it all the more exciting. I want you to pay me a lot. And I might give it back to you, but then again I might not."

After several minutes, during which he took back his hand, Benito told her, "I don't want to do that. I don't think it would be fun."

And now this new Dolores, whose laugh is deeper, tells him, his is a classic situation, isn't it, my angel? Famous man runs into an old lady friend, who's run to fat?" She laughs, and, as before, Benito shivers. "But wherever did you meet my darling old Posey?"

"Just now, actually. I never saw her before."

"The love of my life," Dolores declaims, as the doctor reflects that this could well be true, for he has just remembered a few more lines from their past. "I really don't like men at all," Dolores confided back then. "I only need them, although I'm terrified of them. And now I've fallen in love with this beautiful girl, who is very rich, of course. Even thinner than I am. With the most delicious name. Posey Pendergast. You must meet her one day. She would like you, too."

Wishing no more of this, and wishing no more of Dolores, ever, Benito turns in search of Carla, who seems to have vanished or hidden herself in the crowd that now populates this oversized room, milling around the long bar table and spilling out onto the broad deck that faces the sea. As he catches sight of the deck, the doctor instinctively moves toward it, even as Dolores is saying, "You must come back and tell me how you made all that money, Dr. Do-Good."

"Excuse me," he mutters, stiffly, making for the door. He is not at all graceful in the usual way of Latins; Elizabeth said that from time to time.

From the deck San Francisco is still invisible; it lurks there behind the great cliffs of land, across the surging, dark-streaked sea. The tall, pale city, lovely and unreal. Benito thinks of his amazement at that city, years back, when he roamed its streets as an almost indigent medical student — at Stanford, in those days a city medical school, at Clay and Webster streets, in Pacific Heights. How lonely he used to feel as he walked across those hills and stared at massive apartment houses, at enormous family houses — how isolated and full of greed. He wanted the city, both to possess and to immerse himself in. It is hardly surprising, he now thinks — with a small, wry, private smile — that he ended in bed with Dolores Gutierrez, and that a few years later he found himself the owner of many sleazy blocks of hotels in the Tenderloin.

But that is not how he ended up, the doctor tells himself, in a fierce interior whisper. He ended up with Elizabeth, who was both beautiful and good, a serious woman, with whom he lived harmoniously, if sometimes sadly (they had no children, and Elizabeth was given to depression), near St.

Francis Woods, in a house with a view of everything — the city and the sea, the Farallon Islands.

Nor is that life with Elizabeth how he ended up, actually. The actual is now, of course, and he has ended up alone. Childless and without Elizabeth.

The doctor takes deep breaths, inhaling the cool, fresh wind, and exhaling, he hopes and believes, the germs of self-pity that sometimes enter and threaten to invade his system. He looks back to the great Marin headlands, those steep, sweeping hills of green. Far out at sea he sees two small, hopeful white boats, sails bobbing against the dark horizon.

Looking back inside the house, he sees Carla in intimate-seeming conversation with withered old Posey. Fresh from the intimations of Dolores, he shudders: Posey must be even older than he is, and quite unwell. But before he has time for speculation along those lines, he is jolted by a face, suddenly glimpsed behind the glass doors: bright-eyed and buck-toothed, thinner and grayer but otherwise not much aged, in a starched white embroidered shirt (Why on earth? Does he want to look Mexican?), that lawyer, Herman Tolliver.

"Well, of course they should be condemned; half this town should be condemned, are you crazy?" Tolliver grinned sideways, hiding his teeth. "The point is, they're not going to be condemned. Somebody's going to make a bundle off them. And from where I'm sitting it looks like you could be the guy. Along with me." Another grin, which was then extinguished as Tolliver tended to the lighting of a new cigar.

In that long-ago time (about forty years back) the doctor had just opened his own office and begun his cardiology practice. And had just met a young woman with straw-blond hair, clear, dark-blue eyes, and a sexy overbite — Carole Lombard with a Gene Tierney mouth. A young woman of class and style, none of which he could ever afford. Elizabeth Montague: her very name was defeating. Whoever would exchange Montague for Zamora?

None of which excused Benito's acquiescence in Tolliver's scheme. (Certain details as to the precise use of Tolliver's "hotels" Benito arranged not quite to know, but he had, of course, his suspicions.) It ended in making the doctor and his wife, Elizabeth Montague Zamora, very rich. And in funding the clinics for the indigent of Chiapas.

After that first encounter with Herman Tolliver, the doctor almost managed never to see him again. They talked on the phone, or, in the later days of success and busyness, through secretaries. Benito was aware of Tolliver, aware that they were both making a great deal of money, but otherwise he was fairly successful in dismissing the man from his mind.

One morning, not long before Elizabeth died, she looked up from the paper at breakfast (Benito only scanned the *New York Times*, did not read local news at all) and said, "Didn't you used to know this scandalous lawyer, this Tolliver?"

"We've met." But how did Elizabeth know that? Benito, shaken, wondered, and then remembered: some time back there had been phone calls, a secretary saying that Mr. Tolliver wanted to get in touch (fortunately, nothing urgent). Just enough to fix the name in Elizabeth's mind. "Is he scandalous?" Benito then asked his wife, very lightly.

"Well, some business with tax evasion. Goodness, do all lawyers do things like that these days?"

Aware of his own relief (he certainly did not want public scandals connected with Tolliver), Benito told her, "I very much doubt it, my darling."

And that was the end of that, it seemed.

Carla is now talking to both old Posey and Herman Tolliver, but the doctor can see from her posture that she doesn't really like him much, does not really want to talk to Tolliver. She is barely giving him the time of day, holding her glass out in front of her like a shield, or a weapon. She keeps glancing about, not smiling, as Tolliver goes on talking.

Is she looking for him? the doctor wonders. Does she ask herself what has happened to old Benito? He smiles to himself at this notion — and then, almost at the same moment, is chilled with longing for Elizabeth.

A problem with death, the doctor has more than once thought, is its removal of all the merciful dross of memory: he no longer remembers any petty annoyance, ever, or even moments of boredom, irritation, or sad, failed acts of love. All that is erased, and he only recalls, with the most cruel, searing accuracy, the golden peaks of their time together. Beautiful days, long nights of love. He sees Elizabeth at their dining table, on a rare warm summer night. Her shoulders bare and white, a thin gold necklace that he brought her from Oaxaca shines in the candlelight; she is bending toward their guest, old Dr. McPherson, from med-school days. Benito sees, too, McPherson's wife, and other colleague guests with their wives — all attractive, pale, and well dressed. But none so attractive as his own wife, his pale Elizabeth.

"Oh, there you are," Carla says, coming up to him suddenly.

"You couldn't see me out here? I could see you quite clearly," he tells her, in his sober, mechanical voice.

"I was busy fending off that creep, Tolliver. Mr. Slime." She tosses her hair, now gleaming in the sunlight. "I can't imagine what Posey sees in him. Do you know him?"

"We've met," the doctor admits. "But how do you know him?"

"I'm a reporter, remember? I meet everyone."

"And Posey Pendergast? You know her because — "

But that question and its possible answer are interrupted, cut off by the enormous, puffing arrival of Dolores. "Oh, here's where you've got to," she tells Benito and Carla, as though she had not seen them from afar and headed directly to where they stand, leaning together against the balcony's railing. "Carla, I'm absolutely in love with your hair," says Dolores.

Carla giggles — out of character for her, the doctor thinks — and then, another surprise, she takes his arm for a moment and laughs as she asks him, "Why don't you ever say such flattering things to me?"

Is she flirting with him, seriously flirting? Well, she could be. Such things do happen, the doctor reminds himself. And she seems a very honest young woman, and kind. She could brighten my life, he thinks, and lighten my home, all those rooms with their splendid views that seem to have darkened.

"Don't you want some lunch?" she is asking. "Can't I get you something?"

Before he can answer (and he had very much liked the idea of her bringing him food), Dolores, again interrupting, has stated, "He never eats. Can't you tell? Dr. Abstemious, I used to call him."

"Well, I'm really hungry, I'll see you two later." And with an uncertain smile (from shyness? annoyance? and if annoyance, at which of them?), Carla has left. She is pushing back into the room, through the crowds; she has vanished behind the glass.

Looking at Dolores then, the old doctor is seized with rage; he stares at that puffy, self-adoring face, those dark and infinitely self-pitying eyes. How he longs to push her against the railing, down into the sand! How he despises her!

"My darling, I believe you're really hungry after all" is what Dolores says, but she may have felt some of his anger, for she deftly steps sideways, on her high, thin, dangerous heels, just out of his reach.

"Not in the least," says Benito rigidly. "In fact, I think I'll go for a walk on the beach."

Down on the sand, though, as he walks along the dark, packed strip that is nearest to the sea, Benito's confusion increases. He feels the presence of those people in that rather vulgar, glassed-in house behind him — of Dolores Gutierrez and Herman Tolliver, and God knows who else, what other ghosts from his past whom he simply failed to see. As though they were giants, he feels their looming presences, and feels their connection to some past year or years of his own life. He no longer knows where he is. What place is this, what country? What rolling gray-green ocean does he walk beside? What year is this, and what is his own true age?

Clearly, some derangement has taken hold of him, or nearly, and Benito is forced to fight back with certain heavy and irrefutable facts: this is September, 1990, the last year of a decade, and the year in which Elizabeth died. He is in Stinson Beach, and if he continues walking far enough along the coast — he is heading south, toward the Golden Gate — he will be in sight of beautiful, mythical San Francisco, the city and the center of all his early dreams, the city where everything, finally, happened: Dolores Gutierrez and his medical degree; Herman Tolliver and those hotels. His (at last) successful medical practice. Elizabeth, and all that money, and his house with its fabulous views. His fame as Dr. Do-Good.

His whole San Francisco history seems to rise up then and to break his heart. The city itself is still pale and distant and invisible, and he stands absolutely still, a tall figure on the sand, next to an intricate, crumbling sandcastle that some children have recently abandoned.

Hearing running feet behind him, at that moment the doctor turns in fright (expecting what? some dangerous stranger?) — but it is Carla, out of breath, her hair streaming backward in the wind. His savior.

"Ah, you," he says to her. "You ran."

"And these aren't the greatest running shoes." She laughs, pointing down to her sandals, now sand-streaked and damp.

"You came after me — "

She looks down, and away. "Well. It was partly an excuse to get out of there. It was getting a little claustrophobic, and almost everyone I talked to was hard of hearing."

"Oh, right."

"Well, shall we walk for a while?"

"*Yes.*"

Walking along with Carla, the doctor finds that those giants from his dark and tangled past have quite suddenly receded: Dolores and Tolliver have shrunk down to human size, the size of people accidentally encountered at a party. Such meetings can happen to anyone, easily, especially at a certain age.

Benito even finds that he can talk about them. o tell you the truth" — an ominous beginning, he knows, but it is what he intends to do — "I did some business with Herman Tolliver a long time ago, maybe forty years. It came out very well, financially, but I'm still a little ashamed of it. It seems to me now that I was pretending to myself not to know certain things that I really did know."

"You mean about his hotels?"

"Well, yes. Hotels. But how do you — Does everyone know all that?"

"I'm a reporter, remember? Investigative." She laughs, then sniffles a little in the hard, cold ocean wind. "He had an idea a few years back about running for supervisor, but I'm sure he was really thinking mayor, ultimately. But we dug up some stuff."

"Here, take my handkerchief — "

"Thanks. Anyway, he was persuaded to forget it. There were really ugly things about preteen-age Asian girls. We made a bargain: the papers would print only the stuff about his 'tax problems' if he'd bow out." She sighs, a little ruefully. "I don't know. It might have been better to let him get into politics; he might have done less harm that way."

This walk, and the conversation, are serving both to calm and to excite the doctor. Simultaneously. Most peculiar. He feels a calm, and at the same time a strange, warm, quiet excitement. "How do you mean?" he asks Carla.

"Oh, he got in deeper and deeper. Getting richer and richer."

"I got richer and richer, too, back then. Sometimes I felt like I owned the whole goddam city." Benito is paying very little attention to what he is saying; it is now all he can do to prevent himself from speaking his heart, from saying, "When will you marry me? How soon can that be?"

"But that's great that you made so much money," Carla says. hat way you could start those clinics, and do so much good."

Barely listening, Benito murmurs, "I suppose . . ."

She could redecorate the house any way she would like to, he thinks. Throw things out, repaint, reupholster, add mirrors. His imagination sees, all completed, a brilliant house, with Carla its brilliant, shining center.

"How did you happen to know Dolores?" Carla is asking.

By now they have reached the end of the beach: a high mass of rocks left there by mammoth storms the year before. Impassable. Beyond lie more beach, more cliffs, more headlands, all along the way to the sight of the distant city.

"Actually, Dolores was an old girlfriend, you might say." Since he cares so much for this girl, Benito will never lie to her, he thinks. "You might not believe this, but she was quite a beauty in her day."

"Oh, I believe you. She's still so vain. That hair."

Benito laughs, feeling pleased, and wondering, Can this adorable girl be, even slightly, jealous? "You're right there," he tells Carla. "Very vain, always was. Of course, she's a few years older than I am."

"I guess we have to turn around now," says Carla.

"And now Dolores tells me that she and that Posey Pendergast were at one time, uh, lovers," Benito continues, in his honest mode.

"I guess they could have been," Carla muses. "On the other hand, it's my impression that Dolores lies a lot. And Posey I'm just not sure about. Nor any of that group, for that matter. Tolliver, all those people. It's worrying." She laughs. "I guess I sort of hoped you might know something about them. Sort of explain them to me."

Not having listened carefully to much of this, Benito rephrases the question he does not remember having begun to ask before, which Dolores interrupted: "How do you know Posey?" he asks Carla.

"It's mostly her son I know. Patrick. He's my fiancé, I guess you could say. We keep planning to make it legal, and I guess we will. Any day now." And she goes on. "Actually, Patrick was supposed to come today, and then he couldn't, and then I thought — I thought of you."

The sun has sunk into the ocean, and Benito's heart has sunk with it, drowned. He shudders, despising himself. How could he possibly have imagined, how not have guessed?

"How nice," Benito remarks, without meaning, and then he babbles on, "You know, the whole city seems so corrupt these days. It's all real estate, and deals."

"Get real," she chides him, in her harsh young voice. hat's what it's like all over."

"Well, I'll be awfully glad to get back to Mexico. At least I more or less understand the corruption there."

"Are you going back for long?"

The wind is really cold now. Benito sniffs, wishing he had his handkerchief back, and unable to ask for it. "Oh, permanently," he tells Carla. "A permanent move. I want to be near my clinics. See how they're doing. Maybe help."

The doctor had no plan to say (much less to do) any of this before he spoke, but he knows that he is now committed to this action. This permanent move. He will buy a house in San Cristóbal de las Casas, and will bring his mother there, from Oaxaca, to live in that house for as long as she lasts. And he, for as long as he lasts, will work in his clinics, with his own poor.

"Well, that's great. Maybe we could work out a little interview before you go."

"Well, maybe."

"I wonder if we couldn't just bypass the party for now," says Carla. "I'm just not up to going in again, going through all that, with those people."

"Nor I," the doctor tells her. "Good idea."

"I'll call Posey as soon as we get back. Did she tell you the house was up for sale? She may have sold it today — all those people . . ."

Half hearing her, the doctor is wrestling with the idea of a return to the city, which is suddenly unaccountably terrible to him; he dreads the first pale, romantic view of it from the bridge, and then the drive across town to his empty house, after dropping Carla off on Telegraph Hill. His house with its night views of city hills and lights. But he braces himself with the thought that he won't be in San Francisco long this time. That as soon as he can arrange things he will be back in Chiapas, in Mexico. For the rest of his life.

And thus he manages to walk on, following Carla past the big, fancy house, for sale — and all those people, the house's rich and crazily corrupt population. He manages to walk across the sand toward his car, and the long, circuitous, and risky drive to the city. [1991]

JACK AGUEROS (b. 1934) was born and raised in East Harlem, New York City. He grew up in a multicultural neighborhood and attended local schools, where a Jewish friend taught him about the prevalence of prejudice in the world by talking about Hitler's efforts to exterminate the Jews during World War II. "I had thought that prejudice meant discrimination against Puerto Ricans . . . ," he remembers. "[My friend] made me think it wasn't so bad to be Puerto Rican, even though I definitely did not look American."

In the 1960s Agueros was a political activist ("rabble-rouser" is his term) for Puerto Rican rights, serving as New York City deputy commissioner of the Community Development Agency, appointed by then-mayor John Lindsay. In 1967 he resigned his position and began a hunger strike, vowing to fast until the city government changed its practice of excluding Puerto Ricans from advisory and decision-making boards. From 1976 to 1986 Agueros was the director of El Museo del Barrio in New York, the oldest Puerto Rican cultural institution in the United States. During these years he thought of himself as "working the other side of the cultural angle" in his efforts to promote working-class art and to make visual arts more accessible to the Puerto Rican community.

Agueros has written television dramas for children about Puerto Rican life that were produced on "Sesame Street," but in recent years he has concentrated on writing autobiographical essays, short fiction, and poetry, including a translation of the early-twentieth-century Puerto Rican poet Julia de Burgos. Dominoes and Other Stories from the Puerto Rican, Agueros's first collection of stories, was published in 1993. Commenting on "Dominoes," he has compared the rules of the game to the social rules that bind the men playing it: "I've seen it happen many times — over a game of stickball or asking a girl to dance. These men are not depraved or crazy. They're trapped in the culture. It's very systematic. You mention my mother and we have to go to blows. Just the way the double-six domino has to lead to the Dead Man's Box." Agueros portrays his working-class characters sympathetically, but he is skeptical of the writer's role in stimulating significant social change: "I don't know how the role of a writer relates to the advancement of his community. A lot of people think that when they're doing better, it means that the community is doing better. I don't believe that at all."

Dominoes

DOUBLE SIX: THE BOX OF TEETH

Ebarito liked to hold six dominoes in his left hand. And he wished his hands were larger so that he might span all seven at once. But even Paco with his large hands could not hold seven dominoes.

He tapped the single domino he held in his right hand once on the board. It was a signal that meant he passed. It was irritating to pass at his first turn in the first game.

Paco, sitting to Ebarito's right, laughed a simple "ha," and said nothing.

Tito, the next player, played his domino at a right angle to the double six that Paco had led with. And he also kept another domino spinning at his right hand by periodically snapping his index finger and his thumb.

Wilson, the fourth player, liked to lay his dominoes on their sides in one semicircle. He took one and placed it on the board, then tightened the semicircle.

Paco laughed two loud "ha's" and slapped his domino down on the board. When he took his hand away Ebarito could see he would have to pass again since the game was at sixes at both ends.

"*No voy*," he said in Spanish, without tapping his domino.

Paco laughed one "ha."

Tito, playing one and spinning one, said, "Remember, many of one, few of another."

Ebarito took a long drink from his can of beer.

Wilson looked at his little round wall and played a domino. Then he said, "Only three of those."

Paco played and said, "You know how to count, but the game was invented by a mute."

Another round had gone by and Ebarito saw that he was controlling the threes. But it was too late in this game. He had passed twice and might have to pass once more. There was no doubt about it — Paco had the luck and the skill. It was very hard to beat him in a game of dominoes. And especially when he teamed up with Tito — or even worse when he teamed up with Wilson. Luckily today Wilson was Ebarito's partner and so Ebarito had expectations of making a decent showing — perhaps even coming in under the one hundred point handicap that Paco had offered. If Paco had teamed with Wilson, Ebarito could have gotten a handicap of 200 points — but so what — nobody could beat Paco and Wilson, not even with a 250 point handicap. And with a handicap that large there was no purpose to the game. A handicap only meant something if it was the element that wobbled the wheel of fortune.

Ebarito finished his beer. Decided he would not drink another one. None of them drank, why should he? Or maybe they just wouldn't drink with him.

DOUBLE FIVE

Alma leaned on the ledge of her second floor window. With a cushion under her elbows she could sit like this for hours, enjoying the street life. The boys were not yet playing stoop ball. But by the *bodega*, near the empty yard, she could see her uncle Paco playing dominoes with of all people, Ebarito. Most of the men disliked Ebarito. And even though he had a reputation as a good barber the men avoided him. And as he also had a reputation as a lousy domino player it was strange to see him sitting there teamed up with Wilson. Her uncle Paco had told her once, "Ebarito is nothing but a barber and a pretty boy. He can't play dominoes and he's always trying. In the merchant marine we were all barbers."

She had learned the game out of curiosity — she couldn't see what was in it that kept the men sitting there day and night playing and playing. In the summer in the street and in the winter in her kitchen.

She had begged uncle Paco to teach her the game and one Saturday evening, when her old boyfriend Sammy had stood her up, he took the dominoes out and said, "Sit down." He was a man like that — couldn't express too many things and yet he was smart. For twenty years he sailed around the world visiting many interesting places, reading when he was not playing. But he just didn't talk very much.

Dominoes seemed to Alma a ridiculous game. Whoever got the double six played first if you were just starting. Once you played the first game whoever won started the second game. Then it was just a matter of following the numbers. Your opponent put down a six, you played a six. Your opponent put down a two, you put down a two. If you didn't have something you passed. But her uncle said it wasn't like that at all. He said there was strategy. If you had a two-five and a four-five and you could play a five, which one would you play? Well, that was strategy. You looked over the board, you counted all the fours, you counted all the twos, you looked at your own hand, and you decided which one to play. That wasn't luck, that was skill. That was how you controlled the game.

But Alma didn't like the game — if she wanted to kill time she preferred looking out the window, and in the winter she liked cards now and then — especially a game called "Casino." For the moment she was more interested in her new boyfriend PeeWee. She was hoping he would come over from 112th Street, where he lived near Third Avenue. And perhaps he would invite her for a walk in Central Park or better still, to a movie. She hadn't been to a movie in a few weeks, and the Star Theater on 107th and Lexington was playing two good films. But PeeWee did not come around the corner.

DOUBLE FOUR

Paco shifted his weight on the milk crate he was sitting on.

Ebarito played one of his threes.

Tito knocked on the board, close to where his domino was spinning.

"Oh, oh, somebody's got no threes or sixes," said Wilson.

Ebarito said, "I believe Paco said this was a game invented by a mute."

Paco slapped down his domino with great force, and when he removed his ham-sized hand he said, "*Lo tranque*. I locked it at sixes — let's go, count up."

Tito took everyone's dominoes and counted forty-two points, then turned them all face down.

Paco mixed the dominoes driving his left hand clockwise, and his right hand counterclockwise, slightly out of synchronization.

Tito said, "I like a hand where I have four of something and they don't come out until the second or third play."

"Take your dominoes," said Paco leaving his hands at the side of the board. This meant he would take last — take whatever remained. It was like a boxer dropping his gloves to his sides and daring his opponent to hit him.

Ebarito took his seven, skipping around hoping to get a better selection. But he was feeling worse and worse. He had no business in this foursome. This was strictly a losing proposition for him. His game was women; the barber shop. His hand was terrible, three doubles. "*La caja de muerto*," the dead man's box, meaning the double blank, and "*La caja de dientes*," meaning the box of teeth, or the double six, and the double three. This was going to be another painful and embarrassing loss. He could see that he would lose by 250 points — the 100 point handicap would be just another humiliation.

"*No voy*," said Tito furiously spinning his domino.

"Already?" said Wilson.

By the next play Ebarito had to pass and he struck his domino down with a hard sharp blow — like an angry gaveling. And he wished it were a nail that he could drive through the board and into the ground. He knew he was going to lose, knew he had but one recourse now — to lose gracefully — be a good sport — offer to buy everyone a beer, a cigar or a drink — say the obvious out loud — "You are too good for me" — but Goddammit he couldn't do it — it stuck in his craw like a thing he could not swallow, could not spit.

DOUBLE THREE

Of all the sounds on the street the sharp blow of a domino on a wooden board caught Alma's attention. It was a sound she had heard many times before, and which she disliked. When she looked over at the game Ebarito looked angry, but she still couldn't see Paco's face. She could see Wilson, whom she didn't like although she had known him all her life. He was her uncle's best friend. A master domino player and a very hard man. He believed in fate. "Men who are real men can live their lives anyway they like — because their destiny is clear. To be a *macho* is the destiny. The trouble for you Alma is that you fool around with men who are not *machos*," he had told her once in her kitchen. "And for a woman, Wilson, what is the fate for a woman?" "I don't know," he had answered, "I don't know anything about women. For women I recommend an *espiritista* and the church. One will tell you the future and the other will console you about it. But I'm not sure which does what."

After that pronouncement both Wilson and Paco had broken into very heavy prolonged laughter. Tito was not like that. He was kinder and he talked more, but he was not as strong as they were. They could make him do the opposite of what he believed. But they genuinely liked him — not because they influenced him, but because they seemed to enjoy his company — he was what they were not — social and friendly, fun loving and relaxed. But he had not left Puerto Rico to join the merchant marine when he was sixteen — like Wilson or Paco. They were just *jibaro* kids — country boys suddenly with mean men and dangerous work and thirty years at sea always looking to see who was standing behind you. Tito had steady legs, like a man used to walking on the earth. Wilson and Paco had a strange gait, always waiting for the sea to pitch!

Double Two

Tito played and was talking. "You know my father used to say when we were watching the baseball games — 'The ball is round, son, the game is not over until the last out.' But in dominoes, especially in double-six, the game is over as soon as you get your hand. Isn't it?"

Paco grimaced. He believed in skill.

"I know, I know, the game was invented by a mute. But I can't be like you Paco — I can't sit through a whole game and not say a word — to me part of this game is talking — about this about that."

"Oh yeah — some people even say that that is your strategy as a team. You yak yak to distract them while Paco . . ." Ebarito let his voice trail off.

"While Paco what?" asked Tito and Wilson at the same time.

"Yeah, while Paco what, little barber?" asked Paco.

"Something the matter with being a barber?" asked Ebarito while playing his double six.

Paco stared at the board.

"Apparently barbers can't count," said Paco.

"Right," said Tito, the domino perfectly still under his right index finger, "you passed on six before — it's called reneging."

"You calling me a cheater?" asked Ebarito standing up.

"No," said Paco, "but then you better admit you can't count."

"Perhaps your mother can't count," said Ebarito. And in the moment that his words were being formed in his mouth he bent over, picked up the metal milk crate he had been sitting on and swung it at Paco's head.

Paco was already rising, his straightening legs upending the board, the dominoes scattering, and with his left arm he grabbed the milk crate and pushed it back into Ebarito's chest. And Ebarito went backward, losing his balance, down. And Paco was on top of him, both massive hands tightly around Ebarito's throat.

Tito went to break it up, but Wilson pulled him by the arm, and hissed, "Fuck the pretty boy barber," and Tito just stopped, as if Wilson's venom had paralyzed him.

Then Paco started to lift Ebarito's head and strike it against the sidewalk at the same time that he tightened his hands ever more around his neck. Ebarito reached into his jacket and pulled out the long thin trimming scissor with the loop that cradles the pinky and adds balance and control to the tool. He began to drive the scissor into Paco's rib cage with a circular motion from the elbow, for the rest of his arm was immobilized by Paco's knee.

"They are killing each other," gasped Tito to Wilson who was still holding him.

DOUBLE ONE

Alma broke out of a reverie to see PeeWee across the street calling her and yelling and pointing over to the vacant lot. When Alma looked she let go a scream and yelled, "Paco, Paco, stop it, stop it, Wilson stop them. Tito for God's sake do something. PeeWee call the police." And she screamed again. But no one moved.

She screamed again, her hands covering her ears as if she could not tolerate her own penetrating wail. And then she turned into the apartment. When she was no longer visible in the window PeeWee came to life again, for he had been more startled by the screaming than by the fight. The screaming turned the fight into something more serious than he had at first thought.

He looked in two directions trying to remember where the nearest phone was. And then he headed for the corner drugstore, before he could see Alma come screaming out of her hallway like a train out of a tunnel onto the street.

Wilson still held Tito's arm in a vice-like grip. "They are *machos*," said Wilson, seeming to speak through clenched teeth, "they know what they want."

But at the sight of Alma pulling at Paco, Tito broke loose and kicked the scissor from Ebarito's hand and pulled at Paco too.

Paco stood up thinking Ebarito was dead. He took a few staggering steps and then found his balance, and began walking off in no particular direction. But his left rib cage looked like a colander with blood pouring out of twelve scissor holes, some spurting, some just trickling down over the already forming clots. And when he reached the fire hydrant Paco crumbled down into a pile like a pneumatic tire that had a blow out.

He was dead.

He was dead before he fell.

He was dead even before he stood up and walked.

The body had its habits and in a man who spoke very little, his body had spoken last — it had refused to die where fate had ordained — he didn't want to be near Ebarito. Death wanted him there, but he would go here.

Alma in tears, in terror and hysteria was on her knees crying and screaming next to the body of the wrong man, for it was inconceivable to her that Ebarito could be alive and her uncle dead. She screamed over the bloody head, face and body of Ebarito, "You killed him, you let him be killed, you killers." She screamed at everyone. She screamed at no one.

DOUBLE BLANK
THE DEAD MAN'S BOX

Ebarito awoke. Pain played over his body head to throat to arm. And he realized he had his eyes closed.

He tried to open his eyes and found it difficult to do. He could not turn his head and his neck seemed very stiff. As he tried to feel his body beyond the pain he discovered that he could not lift his head, and while he did not seem to be tied down, he couldn't shift his weight at all. He could curl his fingers and wiggle his toes. His tongue felt huge in his mouth: as if he had a washcloth stuffed there rather than a tongue. His left arm was more mobile but he could only raise it somewhat. He tried to open his eyes again.

And when he opened them everything seemed to be clouded and out of focus. And there was nothing but white to see, but there was the unmistakable smell of hospital — like there was the unmistakable smell of barbershop, of dentist, of laundry.

Then he heard a squeaky wheel, footsteps, and heard someone speaking. The doctor was asking, "Do you understand English? — Do you speak English? English?"

Painfully he tried to shake his head yes, as he could not find his voice. He could not move the wash rag in his mouth, nor spit it out. And he could not shake his head either.

The doctor was saying, "Lucky boy you are to be alive — your skull was cracked — do you remember?"

"No," said the doctor, "you can't speak — he wrecked your trachea, larynx? — you know — voice box? Adam's apple? With a little oxygen deprivation — maybe asphyxia. Drove your cricoid up against the 7th in the neck — you understand? You have cracks in your trachea. Severe damage to the vocal cords from bone and cartilage pushing up against them, tearing through them. You may never be able to speak — maybe growl. I did some marvelous work in there — you understand — *vida* — life? Serious concussion, on your *cabeza* — you know — head, *cabeza*? One eye is fine — a matter of a few days, maybe two weeks and we will know the whole story on the eyes. There is a little infection there now — *infección*, you know?"

Ebarito tried to point to his mouth, but his left arm was manacled to the bed.   [1993]

WOODY ALLEN *was born Allen Stewart Konigsberg in 1935 and grew up in what he calls "a typical, noisy ethnic family" in Brooklyn, New York. "Probably if my parents had pushed me along more cultural lines, I might have started out being a serious writer, because that's what has always interested me. But I had no cultural background whatsoever. . . . I didn't go to a play until I was about eighteen years old, almost never went to a museum, listened only to popular music, and never read at all." After graduating from high school, Allen attended and dropped out of both New York University and the City College of New York. While still a student he sold jokes to newspaper columnists, and at the age of seventeen, in 1952, he joined the National Broadcasting Corporation as a staff writer.*

In 1964 Allen wrote his first screenplay, What's New Pussycat? *Since then he has written, directed, and often starred in more than twenty films. He is one of the few major American filmmakers to insist on total control over his productions, which he equates with artistic freedom. "I'm only making films because I'm as free there as if I were writing novels. You can't create unless you're completely free." Writing was important to Allen even as a child. "From the first grade, I was always the class writer. I remember very distinctly, I'd buy those little black and white notebooks and say, 'Today I'll write a mystery story.' I'd go home and write, and invariably they'd come out funny. I certainly couldn't care less if I ever performed again, and don't care much if I ever direct another film, but I would not like to be in a position not to write."*

In addition to screenplays, Allen has published three books of comic stories and sketches: Getting Even *(1971),* Without Feathers *(1975), and* Side Effects *(1980).* The Complete Prose of Woody Allen *appeared in 1991. Like his films, his short fiction reveals a humorously skeptical, yet romantic, mind at work. He is also an astute analyzer of his own work: "If it's successful, the laughs don't come from jokes, they come from characters in emotionally desperate circumstances." "The Kugelmass Episode," which first appeared in* The New Yorker, *won the O. Henry Award as one of the best stories of 1978. As the critic Sanford Pinsker has noted, in this story Allen "has written a comic fantasy that is a worthy successor to James Thurber's 'The Secret Life of Walter Mitty' . . . [Allen's] story reveals as much about our cultural moment as Thurber's tale did about his."*

WOODY ALLEN

The Kugelmass Episode

Kugelmass, a professor of humanities at City College, was unhappily married for the second time. Daphne Kugelmass was an oaf. He also had two dull sons by his first wife, Flo, and was up to his neck in alimony and child support.

"Did I know it would turn out so badly?" Kugelmass whined to his analyst one day. "Daphne had promised. Who suspected she'd let herself go and swell up like a beach ball? Plus she had a few bucks, which is not in itself a healthy reason to marry a person, but it doesn't hurt, with the kind of operating nut I have. You see my point?"

Kugelmass was bald and as hairy as a bear, but he had soul.

"I need to meet a new woman," he went on. "I need to have an affair. I may not look the part, but I'm a man who needs romance. I need softness, I need flirtation. I'm not getting younger, so before it's too late I want to make love in Venice, trade quips at '21,'[1] and exchange coy glances over red wine and candlelight. You see what I'm saying?"

Dr. Mandel shifted in his chair and said, "An affair will solve nothing. You're so unrealistic. Your problems run much deeper."

"And also this affair must be discreet," Kugelmass continued. "I can't afford a second divorce. Daphne would really sock it to me."

"Mr. Kugelmass — "

"But it can't be anyone at City College, because Daphne also works there. Not that anyone on the faculty at C.C.N.Y. is any great shakes, but some of those coeds . . ."

"Mr. Kugelmass — "

"Help me. I had a dream last night. I was skipping through a meadow holding a picnic basket and the basket was marked 'Options.' And then I saw there was a hole in the basket."

"Mr. Kugelmass, the worst thing you could do is act out. You must simply express your feelings here, and together we'll analyze them. You have been in treatment long enough to know there is no overnight cure. After all, I'm an analyst, not a magician."

"Then perhaps what I need is a magician," Kugelmass said, rising from his chair. And with that he terminated his therapy.

A couple of weeks later, while Kugelmass and Daphne were moping around in their apartment one night like two pieces of old furniture, the phone rang.

"I'll get it," Kugelmass said. "Hello."

"Kugelmass?" a voice said. "Kugelmass, this is Persky."

"Who?"

"Persky. Or should I say The Great Persky?"

"Pardon me?"

"I hear you're looking all over town for a magician to bring a little exotica into your life? Yes or no?"

"Sh-h-h," Kugelmass whispered. "Don't hang up. Where are you calling from, Persky?"

Early the following afternoon, Kugelmass climbed three flights of stairs in a broken-down apartment house in the Bushwick section of Brooklyn. Peering through the darkness of the hall, he found the door he was looking for and pressed the bell. I'm going to regret this, he thought to himself.

---

[1] A famous restaurant in New York City.

Seconds later, he was greeted by a short, thin, waxy-looking man.

"*You're* Persky the Great?" Kugelmass said.

"The Great Persky. You want a tea?"

"No, I want romance. I want music. I want love and beauty."

"But not tea, eh? Amazing. O.K., sit down."

Persky went to the back room, and Kugelmass heard the sounds of boxes and furniture being moved around. Persky reappeared, pushing before him a large object on squeaky roller-skate wheels. He removed some old silk handkerchiefs that were lying on its top and blew away a bit of dust. It was a cheap-looking Chinese cabinet, badly lacquered.

"Persky," Kugelmass said, "what's your scam?"

"Pay attention," Persky said. "This is some beautiful effect. I developed it for a Knights of Pythias date last year, but the booking fell through. Get into the cabinet."

"Why, so you can stick it full of swords or something?"

"You see any swords?"

Kugelmass made a face and, grunting, climbed into the cabinet. He couldn't help noticing a couple of ugly rhinestones glued onto the raw plywood just in front of his face. "If this is a joke," he said.

"Some joke. Now, here's the point. If I throw any novel into this cabinet with you, shut the doors, and tap it three times, you will find yourself projected into that book."

Kugelmass made a grimace of disbelief.

"It's the emess,"[2] Persky said. "My hand to God. Not just a novel, either. A short story, a play, a poem. You can meet any of the women created by the world's best writers. Whoever you dreamed of. You could carry on all you like with a real winner. Then when you've had enough you give a yell, and I'll see you're back here in a split second."

"Persky, are you some kind of outpatient?"

"I'm telling you it's on the level," Persky said.

Kugelmass remained skeptical. "What are you telling me — that this cheesy homemade box can take me on a ride like you're describing?"

"For a double sawbuck."[3]

Kugelmass reached for his wallet. "I'll believe this when I see it," he said.

Persky tucked the bills in his pants pocket and turned toward his bookcase. "So who do you want to meet? Sister Carrie? Hester Prynne? Ophelia? Maybe someone by Saul Bellow? Hey, what about Temple Drake?[4] Although for a man your age she'd be a workout."

"French, I want to have an affair with a French lover."

---

[2] The truth.

[3] $20.

[4] Carrie Meeber is the heroine of Theodore Dreiser's novel *Sister Carrie* (1900); Hester Prynne is in Nathaniel Hawthorne's *The Scarlet Letter* (1850); Ophelia is in *Hamlet* (c. 1600); and Temple Drake is a character in William Faulkner's novel *Sanctuary* (1931).

"Nana?"[5]

"I don't want to have to pay for it."

"What about Natasha in 'War and Peace'?"

"I said French. I know! What about Emma Bovary?[6] That sounds to me perfect."

"You got it, Kugelmass. Give me a holler when you've had enough." Persky tossed in a paperback copy of Flaubert's novel.

"You sure this is safe?" Kugelmass asked as Persky began shutting the cabinet doors.

"Safe. Is anything safe in this crazy world?" Persky rapped three times on the cabinet and then flung open the doors.

Kugelmass was gone. At the same moment, he appeared in the bedroom of Charles and Emma Bovary's house at Yonville. Before him was a beautiful woman standing alone with her back turned to him as she folded some linen. I can't believe this, thought Kugelmass, staring at the doctor's ravishing wife. This is uncanny. I'm here. It's her.

Emma turned in surprise. "Goodness, you startled me," she said. "Who are you?" She spoke in the same fine English translation as the paperback.

It's simply devastating, he thought. Then, realizing that it was he whom she had addressed, he said, "Excuse me, I'm Sidney Kugelmass. I'm from City College. A professor of humanities. C.C.N.Y.? Uptown. I — oh, boy!"

Emma Bovary smiled flirtatiously and said, "Would you like a drink? A glass of wine, perhaps?"

She is beautiful, Kugelmass thought. What a contrast with the troglodyte who shared his bed! He felt a sudden impulse to take this vision into his arms and tell her she was the kind of woman he had dreamed of all his life.

"Yes, some wine," he said hoarsely. "White. No, red. No, white. Make it white."

"Charles is out for the day," Emma said, her voice full of playful implication.

After the wine, they went for a stroll in the lovely French countryside. "I've always dreamed that some mysterious stranger would appear and rescue me from the monotony of this crass rural existence," Emma said, clasping his hand. They passed a small church. "I love what you have on," she murmured. "I've never seen anything like it around here. It's so . . . so modern."

"It's called a leisure suit," he said romantically. "It was marked down." Suddenly he kissed her. For the next hour they reclined under a tree and whispered together and told each other deeply meaningful things with their eyes. Then Kugelmass sat up. He had just remembered he had to meet Daphne at Bloomingdale's. "I must go," he told her. "But don't worry. I'll be back."

"I hope so," Emma said.

---

[5] Nana is in Emile Zola's *Nana* (1880).

[6] Emma Bovary is the heroine of Gustave Flaubert's novel *Madame Bovary* (1865).

He embraced her passionately, and the two walked back to the house. He held Emma's face cupped in his palms, kissed her again, and yelled, "O.K., Persky! I got to be at Bloomingdale's by three-thirty."

There was an audible pop, and Kugelmass was back in Brooklyn.

"So? Did I lie?" Persky asked triumphantly.

"Look, Persky, I'm right now late to meet the ball and chain at Lexington Avenue, but when can I go again? Tomorrow?"

"My pleasure. Just bring a twenty. And don't mention this to anybody."

"Yeah. I'm going to call Rupert Murdoch."[7]

Kugelmass hailed a cab and sped off to the city. His heart danced on point. I am in love, he thought, I am the possessor of a wonderful secret. What he didn't realize was that at this very moment students in various classrooms across the country were saying to their teachers, "Who is this character on page 100? A bald Jew is kissing Madame Bovary?" A teacher in Sioux Falls, South Dakota, sighed and thought, Jesus, these kids, with their pot and acid. What goes through their minds!

Daphne Kugelmass was in the bathroom-accessories department at Bloomingdale's when Kugelmass arrived breathlessly. "Where've you been?" she snapped. "It's four-thirty."

"I got held up in traffic," Kugelmass said.

Kugelmass visited Persky the next day, and in a few minutes was again passed magically to Yonville. Emma couldn't hide her excitement at seeing him. The two spent hours together, laughing and talking about their different backgrounds. Before Kugelmass left, they made love. "My God, I'm doing it with Madame Bovary!" Kugelmass whispered to himself. "Me, who failed freshman English."

As the months passed, Kugelmass saw Persky many times and developed a close and passionate relationship with Emma Bovary. "Make sure and always get me into the book before page 120," Kugelmass said to the magician one day. "I always have to meet her before she hooks up with this Rodolphe character."

"Why?" Persky asked. "You can't beat his time?"

"Beat his time. He's landed gentry. Those guys have nothing better to do than flirt and ride horses. To me, he's one of those faces you see in the pages of *Women's Wear Daily*. With the Helmut Berger hairdo. But to her he's hot stuff."

"And her husband suspects nothing?"

"He's out of his depth. He's a lack-lustre little paramedic who's thrown in his lot with a jitterbug. He's ready to go to sleep by ten, and she's putting on her dancing shoes. Oh, well . . . See you later."

And once again Kugelmass entered the cabinet and passed instantly to the Bovary estate at Yonville. "How you doing, cupcake?" he said to Emma.

---

[7] Rupert Murdoch (b. 1931) is an Australian newspaper tycoon.

"Oh, Kugelmass," Emma sighed. "What I have to put up with. Last night at dinner, Mr. Personality dropped off to sleep in the middle of the dessert course. I'm pouring my heart out about Maxim's and the ballet, and out of the blue I hear snoring."

"It's O.K., darling, I'm here now," Kugelmass said, embracing her. I've earned this, he thought, smelling Emma's French perfume and burying his nose in her hair. I've suffered enough. I've paid enough analysts. I've searched till I'm weary. She's young and nubile, and I'm here a few pages after Léon and just before Rodolphe. By showing up during the correct chapters, I've got the situation knocked.

Emma, to be sure, was just as happy as Kugelmass. She had been starved for excitement, and his tales of Broadway night life, of fast cars and Hollywood and TV stars, enthralled the young French beauty.

"Tell me again about O. J. Simpson," she implored that evening, as she and Kugelmass strolled past Abbé Bournisien's church.

"What can I say? The man is great. He sets all kinds of rushing records. Such moves. They can't touch him."

"And the Academy Awards?" Emma said wistfully. "I'd give anything to win one."

"First you've got to be nominated."

"I know. You explained it. But I'm convinced I can act. Of course, I'd want to take a class or two. With Strasberg maybe. Then, if I had the right agent —"

"We'll see, we'll see. I'll speak to Persky."

That night, safely returned to Persky's flat, Kugelmass brought up the idea of having Emma visit him in the big city.

"Let me think about it," Persky said. "Maybe I could work it. Stranger things have happened." Of course, neither of them could think of one.

"Where the hell do you go all the time?" Daphne Kugelmass barked at her husband as he returned home late that evening. "You got a chippie stashed somewhere?"

"Yeah, sure, I'm just the type," Kugelmass said wearily. "I was with Leonard Popkin. We were discussing Socialist agriculture in Poland. You know Popkin. He's a freak on the subject."

"Well, you've been very odd lately," Daphne said. "Distant. Just don't forget about my father's birthday. On Saturday?"

"Oh, sure, sure," Kugelmass said, heading for the bathroom.

"My whole family will be there. We can see the twins. And Cousin Hamish. You should be more polite to Cousin Hamish — he likes you."

"Right, the twins," Kugelmass said, closing the bathroom door and shutting out the sound of his wife's voice. He leaned against it and took a deep breath. In a few hours, he told himself, he would be back in Yonville again, back with his beloved. And this time, if all went well, he would bring Emma back with him.

At three-fifteen the following afternoon, Persky worked his wizardry again. Kugelmass appeared before Emma, smiling and eager. The two spent a few hours at Yonville with Binet and then remounted the Bovary carriage. Following Persky's instructions, they held each other tightly, closed their eyes, and counted to ten. When they opened them, the carriage was just drawing up at the side door of the Plaza Hotel, where Kugelmass had optimistically reserved a suite earlier in the day.

"I love it! It's everything I dreamed it would be," Emma said as she whirled joyously around the bedroom, surveying the city from their window. "There's F. A. O. Schwarz. And there's Central Park, and the Sherry is which one? Oh, there — I see. It's too divine."

On the bed there were boxes from Halston and Saint Laurent. Emma unwrapped a package and held up a pair of black velvet pants against her perfect body.

"The slacks suit is by Ralph Lauren," Kugelmass said. "You'll look like a million bucks in it. Come on, sugar, give us a kiss."

"I've never been so happy!" Emma squealed as she stood before the mirror. "Let's go out on the town. I want to see *Chorus Line* and the Guggenheim and this Jack Nicholson character you always talk about. Are any of his flicks showing?"

"I cannot get my mind around this," a Stanford professor said. "First a strange character named Kugelmass, and now she's gone from the book. Well, I guess the mark of a classic is that you can reread it a thousand times and always find something new."

The lovers passed a blissful weekend. Kugelmass had told Daphne he would be away at a symposium in Boston, and would return Monday. Savoring each moment, he and Emma went to the movies, had dinner in Chinatown, passed two hours at a discothèque, and went to bed with a TV movie. They slept till noon on Sunday, visited SoHo, and ogled celebrities at Elaine's. They had caviar and champagne in their suite on Sunday night and talked until dawn. That morning, in the cab taking them to Persky's apartment, Kugelmass thought, It was hectic, but worth it. I can't bring her here too often, but now and then it will be a charming contrast with Yonville.

At Persky's, Emma climbed into the cabinet, arranged her new boxes of clothes neatly around her, and kissed Kugelmass fondly. "My place next time," she said with a wink. Persky rapped three times on the cabinet. Nothing happened.

"Hmm," Persky said, scratching his head. He rapped again, but still no magic. "Something must be wrong," he mumbled.

"Persky, you're joking!" Kugelmass cried. "How can it not work?"

"Relax, relax. Are you still in the box, Emma?"

"Yes."

Persky rapped again — harder this time.

"I'm still here, Persky."

"I know, darling. Sit tight."

"Persky, we *have* to get her back," Kugelmass whispered. "I'm a married man, and I have a class in three hours. I'm not prepared for anything more than a cautious affair at this point."

"I can't understand it," Persky muttered. "It's such a reliable little trick."

But he could do nothing. "It's going to take a little while," he said to Kugelmass. "I'm going to have to strip it down. I'll call you later."

Kugelmass bundled Emma into a cab and took her back to the Plaza. He barely made it to his class on time. He was on the phone all day, to Persky and to his mistress. The magician told him it might be several days before he got to the bottom of the trouble.

"How was the symposium?" Daphne asked him that night.

"Fine, fine," he said, lighting the filter end of a cigarette.

"What's wrong? You're as tense as a cat."

"Me? Ha, that's a laugh. I'm as calm as a summer night. I'm just going to take a walk." He eased out the door, hailed a cab, and flew to the Plaza.

"This is no good," Emma said. "Charles will miss me."

"Bear with me, sugar," Kugelmass said. He was pale and sweaty. He kissed her again, raced to the elevators, yelled at Persky over a pay phone in the Plaza lobby, and just made it home before midnight.

"According to Popkin, barley prices in Kraków have not been this stable since 1971," he said to Daphne, and smiled wanly as he climbed into bed.

The whole week went by like that. On Friday night, Kugelmass told Daphne there was another symposium he had to catch, this one in Syracuse. He hurried back to the Plaza, but the second weekend there was nothing like the first. "Get me back into the novel or marry me," Emma told Kugelmass. "Meanwhile, I want to get a job or go to class, because watching TV all day is the pits."

"Fine. We can use the money," Kugelmass said. "You consume twice your weight in room service."

"I met an Off Broadway producer in Central Park yesterday, and he said I might be right for a project he's doing," Emma said.

"Who is this clown?" Kugelmass asked.

"He's not a clown. He's sensitive and kind and cute. His name's Jeff Something-or-Other, and he's up for a Tony."

Later that afternoon, Kugelmass showed up at Persky's drunk.

"Relax," Persky told him. "You'll get a coronary."

"Relax. The man says relax. I've got a fictional character stashed in a hotel room, and I think my wife is having me tailed by a private shamus."[8]

"O.K., O.K. We know there's a problem." Persky crawled under the cabinet and started banging on something with a large wrench.

"I'm like a wild animal," Kugelmass went on. "I'm sneaking around town, and Emma and I have had it up to here with each other. Not to mention a hotel tab that reads like the defense budget."

---

[8] Detective.

"So what should I do? This is the world of magic," Persky said. "It's all nuance."

"Nuance, my foot. I'm pouring Dom Pérignon and black eggs into this little mouse, plus her wardrobe, plus she's enrolled at the Neighborhood Playhouse and suddenly needs professional photos. Also, Persky, Professor Fivish Kopkind, who teaches Comp Lit and who has always been jealous of me, has identified me as the sporadically appearing character in the Flaubert book. He's threatened to go to Daphne. I see ruin and alimony; jail. For adultery with Madame Bovary, my wife will reduce me to beggary."

"What do you want me to say? I'm working on it night and day. As far as your personal anxiety goes, that I can't help you with. I'm a magician, not an analyst."

By Sunday afternoon, Emma had locked herself in the bathroom and refused to respond to Kugelmass's entreaties. Kugelmass stared out the window at the Wollman Rink and contemplated suicide. Too bad this is a low floor, he thought, or I'd do it right now. Maybe if I ran away to Europe and started life over . . . Maybe I could sell the *International Herald Tribune*, like those young girls used to.

The phone rang. Kugelmass lifted it to his ear mechanically.

"Bring her over," Persky said. "I think I got the bugs out of it."

Kugelmass's heart leaped. "You're serious?" he said. "You got it licked?"

"It was something in the transmission. Go figure."

"Persky, you're a genius. We'll be there in a minute. Less than a minute."

Again the lovers hurried to the magician's apartment, and again Emma Bovary climbed into the cabinet with her boxes. This time there was no kiss. Persky shut the doors, took a deep breath, and tapped the box three times. There was the reassuring popping noise, and when Persky peered inside, the box was empty. Madame Bovary was back in her novel. Kugelmass heaved a great sigh of relief and pumped the magician's hand.

"It's over," he said. "I learned my lesson. I'll never cheat again, I swear it." He pumped Persky's hand again and made a mental note to send him a necktie.

Three weeks later, at the end of a beautiful spring afternoon, Persky answered his doorbell. It was Kugelmass, with a sheepish expression on his face.

"O.K., Kugelmass," the magician said. "Where to this time?"

"It's just this once," Kugelmass said. "The weather is so lovely, and I'm not getting any younger. Listen, you've read *Portnoy's Complaint*? Remember The Monkey?"[9]

"The price is now twenty-five dollars, because the cost of living is up, but I'll start you off with one freebie, due to all the trouble I caused you."

---

[9] The Monkey is the sexually liberated heroine of Philip Roth's novel *Portnoy's Complaint* (1969).

"You're good people," Kugelmass said, combing his few remaining hairs as he climbed into the cabinet again. "This'll work all right?"

"I hope. But I haven't tried it much since all that unpleasantness."

"Sex and romance," Kugelmass said from inside the box. "What we go through for a pretty face."

Persky tossed in a copy of *Portnoy's Complaint* and rapped three times on the box. This time, instead of a popping noise there was a dull explosion, followed by a series of crackling noises and a shower of sparks. Persky leaped back, was seized by a heart attack, and dropped dead. The cabinet burst into flames, and eventually the entire house burned down.

Kugelmass, unaware of this catastrophe, had his own problems. He had not been thrust into *Portnoy's Complaint*, or into any other novel, for that matter. He had been projected into an old textbook, *Remedial Spanish*, and was running for his life over a barren, rocky terrain as the word *tener* ("to have") — a large and hairy irregular verb — raced after him on its spindly legs.

[1977]

ISABEL ALLENDE (b. 1942) was born in Peru, the daughter of a Chilean diplomat. After her parents' divorce, she spent her childhood in her maternal grandparents' household; she was especially close to her grandmother, a believer in the occult. When Allende's mother remarried another diplomat, Isabel left Chile to live during her adolescence in Bolivia, the Middle East, and Europe. She began her career by working as a journalist in Chile, writing articles for a radical women's magazine and eventually creating her own television program. In 1970 her father's first cousin Dr. Salvador Allende Gossens became the first Marxist-Leninist to be freely elected as president of Chile. Three years later he was assassinated by Augusto Pinochet Ugarte, who instituted a repressive military dictatorship backed by the United States until 1990. Allende and her family fled to Venezuela; she felt that "my life had been cut into pieces, and that I had to start over again."

In 1981, after the death of her grandparents, Allende began to write her first work of long fiction. This was the internationally acclaimed novel The House of the Spirits (1982), a chronicle of several generations of an imaginary family in Chile based on her memories of her own family. She has said that "in Latin America, we value dreams, passions, obsessions, emotions, and all that which is very important to our lives has a place in literature — our sense of family, our sense of religion, of superstition too. . . . Fantastic things happen every day in Latin America — it's not that we make them up."

Allende followed the success of her first book with two other novels — Of Love and Shadows (1986) and Eva Luna (1988) — and a volume of short stories, The Stories of Eva Luna (1991). "And of Clay Are We Created" is an autobiographical story that concludes the book, which begins with a prologue by her friend Rolf Carlé. In his opening statement Carlé compared the author's skill as a storyteller to the prowess of Scheherazade in The Thousand and One Nights: "You think in words; for you, language is an inexhaustible thread you weave as if life were created as you tell it."

ISABEL ALLENDE

And of Clay Are We Created

Translated by Margaret Sayers Peden

They discovered the girl's head protruding from the mudpit, eyes wide open, calling soundlessly. She had a First Communion name, Azucena. Lily. In that vast cemetery where the odor of death was already attracting vultures from far away, and where the weeping of orphans and wails of the injured filled the air, the little girl obstinately clinging to life became the symbol of the tragedy. The television cameras transmitted so often the unbearable image of the head budding like a black squash from the clay that there was no one who did not recognize her and know her name. And every time we saw her on the screen, right behind her was Rolf Carlé, who had gone there on assignment, never suspecting that he would find a fragment of his past, lost thirty years before.

First a subterranean sob rocked the cotton fields, curling them like waves of foam. Geologists had set up their seismographs weeks before and knew that the mountain had awakened again. For some time they had predicted that the heat of the eruption could detach the eternal ice from the slopes of the volcano, but no one heeded their warnings; they sounded like the tales of frightened old women. The towns in the valley went about their daily life, deaf to the moaning of the earth, until that fateful Wednesday night in November when a prolonged roar announced the end of the world, and walls of snow broke loose, rolling in an avalanche of clay, stones, and water that descended on the villages and buried them beneath unfathomable meters of telluric vomit. As soon as the survivors emerged from the paralysis of that first awful terror, they could see that houses, plazas, churches, white cotton plantations, dark coffee forests, cattle pastures — all had disappeared. Much later, after soldiers and volunteers had arrived to rescue the living and try to assess the magnitude of the cataclysm, it was calculated that beneath the mud lay more than twenty thousand human beings and an indefinite number of animals putrefying in a viscous soup. Forests and rivers had also been swept away, and there was nothing to be seen but an immense desert of mire.

When the station called before dawn, Rolf Carlé and I were together. I crawled out of bed, dazed with sleep, and went to prepare coffee while he hurriedly dressed. He stuffed his gear in the green canvas backpack he always carried, and we said goodbye, as we had so many times before. I had no presentiments. I sat in the kitchen, sipping my coffee and planning the long hours without him, sure that he would be back the next day.

He was one of the first to reach the scene, because while other reporters were fighting their way to the edges of that morass in jeeps, bicycles, or on foot, each getting there however he could, Rolf Carlé had the advantage of the television helicopter, which flew him over the avalanche. We watched on our screens the footage captured by his assistant's camera, in which he was up to his knees in muck, a microphone in his hand, in the midst of a bedlam of lost children, wounded survivors, corpses, and devastation. The story came to us in his calm voice. For years he had been a familiar figure in newscasts, reporting live at the scene of battles and catastrophes with awesome tenacity. Nothing could stop him, and I was always amazed at his equanimity in the face of danger and suffering; it seemed as if nothing could shake his fortitude or deter his curiosity. Fear seemed never to touch him, although he had confessed to me that he was not a courageous man, far from it. I belive that the lens of the camera had a strange effect on him; it was as if it transported him to a different time from which he could watch events without actually participating in them. When I knew him better, I came to realize that this fictive distance seemed to protect him from his own emotions.

Rolf Carlé was in on the story of Azucena from the beginning. He filmed the volunteers who discovered her, and the first persons who tried to reach her; his camera zoomed in on the girl, her dark face, her large desolate eyes, the plastered-down tangle of her hair. The mud was like quicksand around her, and anyone attempting to reach her was in danger of sinking. They threw a rope to her that she made no effort to grasp until they shouted to her to catch it; then she pulled a hand from the mire and tried to move, but immediately sank a little deeper. Rolf threw down his knapsack and the rest of his equipment and waded into the quagmire, commenting for his assistant's microphone that it was cold and that one could begin to smell the stench of corpses.

"What's your name?" he asked the girl, and she told him her flower name. "Don't move, Azucena," Rolf Carlé directed, and kept talking to her, without a thought for what he was saying, just to distract her, while slowly he worked his way forward in mud up to his waist. The air around him seemed as murky as the mud.

It was impossible to reach her from the approach he was attempting, so he retreated and circled around where there seemed to be firmer footing. When finally he was close enough, he took the rope and tied it beneath her arms, so they could pull her out. He smiled at her with that smile that crinkles his eyes and makes him look like a little boy; he told her that everything was fine, that he was here with her now, that soon they would have her out. He signaled the others to pull, but as soon as the cord tensed, the girl screamed. They tried again, and her shoulders and arms appeared, but they could move her no farther; she was trapped. Someone suggested that her legs might be caught in the collapsed walls of her house, but she said it was not just rubble, that she was also held by the bodies of her brothers and sisters clinging to her legs.

"Don't worry, we'll get you out of here," Rolf promised. Despite the quality of the transmission, I could hear his voice break, and I loved him more than ever. Azucena looked at him, but said nothing.

During those first hours Rolf Carlé exhausted all the resources of his ingenuity to rescue her. He struggled with poles and ropes, but every tug was an intolerable torture for the imprisoned girl. It occurred to him to use one of the poles as a lever but got no result and had to abandon the idea. He talked a couple of soldiers into working with him for a while, but they had to leave because so many other victims were calling for help. The girl could not move, she barely could breathe, but she did not seem desperate, as if an ancestral resignation allowed her to accept her fate. The reporter, on the other hand, was determined to snatch her from death. Someone brought him a tire, which he placed beneath her arms like a life buoy, and then laid a plank near the hole to hold his weight and allow him to stay closer to her. As it was impossible to remove the rubble blindly, he tried once or twice to dive toward her feet, but emerged frustrated, covered with mud, and spitting gravel. He concluded that he would have to have a pump to drain the water, and radioed a request for one, but received in return a message that there was no available transport and it could not be sent until the next morning.

"We can't wait that long!" Rolf Carlé shouted, but in the pandemonium no one stopped to commiserate. Many more hours would go by before he accepted that time had stagnated and reality had been irreparably distorted.

A military doctor came to examine the girl, and observed that her heart was functioning well and that if she did not get too cold she could survive the night.

"Hang on, Azucena, we'll have the pump tomorrow," Rolf Carlé tried to console her.

"Don't leave me alone," she begged.

"No, of course I won't leave you."

Someone brought him coffee, and he helped the girl drink it, sip by sip. The warm liquid revived her and she began telling him about her small life, about her family and her school, about how things were in that little bit of world before the volcano had erupted. She was thirteen, and she had never been outside her village. Rolf Carlé, buoyed by a premature optimism, was convinced that everything would end well: the pump would arrive, they would drain the water, move the rubble, and Azucena would be transported by helicopter to a hospital where she would recover rapidly and where he could visit her and bring her gifts. He thought, She's already too old for dolls, and I don't know what would please her; maybe a dress. I don't know much about women, he concluded, amused, reflecting that although he had known many women in his lifetime, none had taught him these details. To pass the hours he began to tell Azucena about his travels and adventures as a newshound, and when he exhausted his memory, he called upon imagination, inventing things he thought might entertain her. From time to time she dozed, but he kept talking in the darkness, to assure her that he was still there and to overcome the menace of uncertainty.

That was a long night.

Many miles away, I watched Rolf Carlé and the girl on a television screen. I could not bear the wait at home, so I went to National Television, where I often spent entire nights with Rolf editing programs. There, I was near his world, and I could at least get a feeling of what he lived through during those three decisive days. I called all the important people in the city, senators, commanders of the armed forces, the North American ambassador, and the president of National Petroleum, begging them for a pump to remove the silt, but obtained only vague promises. I began to ask for urgent help on radio and television, to see if there wasn't *someone* who could help us. Between calls I would run to the newsroom to monitor the satellite transmissions that periodically brought new details of the catastrophe. While reporters selected scenes with most impact for the news report, I searched for footage that featured Azucena's mudpit. The screen reduced the disaster to a single plane and accentuated the tremendous distance that separated me from Rolf Carlé; nonetheless, I was there with him. The child's every suffering hurt me as it did him; I felt his frustration, his impotence. Faced with the impossibility of communicating with him, the fantastic idea came to me that if I tried, I could reach him by force of mind and in that way give him encouragement.

I concentrated until I was dizzy — a frenzied and futile activity. At times I would be overcome with compassion and burst out crying; at other times, I was so drained I felt as if I were staring through a telescope at the light of a star dead for a million years.

I watched that hell on the first morning broadcast, cadavers of people and animals awash in the current of new rivers formed overnight from the melted snow. Above the mud rose the tops of trees and the bell towers of a church where several people had taken refuge and were patiently awaiting rescue teams. Hundreds of soldiers and volunteers from the Civil Defense were clawing through rubble searching for survivors, while long rows of ragged specters awaited their turn for a cup of hot broth. Radio networks announced that their phones were jammed with calls from families offering shelter to orphaned children. Drinking water was in scarce supply, along with gasoline and food. Doctors, resigned to amputating arms and legs without anesthesia, pled that at least they be sent serum and painkillers and antibiotics; most of the roads, however, were impassable, and worse were the bureaucratic obstacles that stood in the way. To top it all, the clay contaminated by decomposing bodies threatened the living with an outbreak of epidemics.

Azucena was shivering inside the tire that held her above the surface. Immobility and tension had greatly weakened her, but she was conscious and could still be heard when a microphone was held out to her. Her tone was humble, as if apologizing for all the fuss. Rolf Carlé had a growth of beard, and dark circles beneath his eyes; he looked near exhaustion. Even from that enormous distance I could sense the quality of his weariness, so different from the fatigue of other adventures. He had completely forgotten the camera; he could not look at the girl through a lens any longer. The pictures we were receiving were not his assistant's but those of other reporters who had appropriated Azucena, bestowing on her the pathetic responsibility of embodying the horror of what had happened in that place. With the first light Rolf tried again to dislodge the obstacles that held the girl in her tomb, but he had only his hands to work with; he did not dare use a tool for fear of injuring her. He fed Azucena a cup of the cornmeal mush and bananas the Army was distributing, but she immediately vomited it up. A doctor stated that she had a fever, but added that there was little he could do: antibiotics were being reserved for cases of gangrene. A priest also passed by and blessed her, hanging a medal of the Virgin around her neck. By evening a gentle, persistent drizzle began to fall.

"The sky is weeping," Azucena murmured, and she, too, began to cry.

"Don't be afraid," Rolf begged. "You have to keep your strength up and be calm. Everything will be fine. I'm with you, and I'll get you out somehow."

Reporters returned to photograph Azucena and ask her the same questions, which she no longer tried to answer. In the meanwhile, more television and movie teams arrived with spools of cable, tapes, film, videos, precision lenses, recorders, sound consoles, lights, reflecting screens, auxiliary motors, cartons of supplies, electricians, sound technicians, and cameramen: Azucena's face was beamed to millions of screens around the world. And all the while Rolf Carlé kept pleading for a pump. The improved technical facilities bore results, and National Television began receiving sharper pictures and clearer sound; the distance seemed suddenly compressed, and I had the horrible sensation that Azucena and Rolf were by my side, separated from me by impenetrable glass. I was able to follow events hour by hour; I knew everything my love did to wrest the girl from her prison and help her endure her suffering; I overheard fragments of what they said to one another and could guess the rest; I was present when she taught Rolf to pray, and when he distracted her with the stories I had told him in a thousand and one nights beneath the white mosquito netting of our bed.

When darkness came on the second day, Rolf tried to sing Azucena to sleep with old Austrian folk songs he had learned from his mother, but she was far beyond sleep. They spent most of the night talking, each in a stupor of exhaustion and hunger, and shaking with cold. That night, imperceptibly, the unyielding floodgates that had contained Rolf Carlé's past for so many years began to open, and the torrent of all that had lain hidden in the deepest and most secret layers of memory poured out, leveling before it the obstacles that had blocked his consciousness for so long. He could not tell it all to Azucena; she perhaps did not know there was a world beyond the sea or time previous to her own; she was not capable of imagining Europe in the years of the war. So he could not tell her of defeat, nor of the afternoon the Russians had led them to the concentration camp to bury prisoners dead from starvation. Why should he describe to her how the naked bodies piled like a mountain of firewood resembled fragile china? How could he tell this dying child about ovens and gallows? Nor did he mention the night that he had seen his mother naked, shod in stiletto-heeled red boots, sobbing with humiliation. There was much he did not tell, but in those hours he relived for the first time all the things his mind had tried to erase. Azucena had surrendered her fear to him and so, without wishing it, had obliged Rolf to confront his own. There, beside that hellhole of mud, it was impossible for Rolf to flee from himself any longer, and the visceral terror he had lived as a boy suddenly invaded him. He reverted to the years when he was the age of Azucena, and younger, and, like her, found himself trapped in a pit without escape, buried in life, his head barely above ground; he saw before his eyes the boots and legs of his father, who had removed his belt and was whipping it in the air with the never-forgotten hiss of a viper coiled to strike. Sorrow flooded through him, intact and precise, as if it had lain always in his mind, waiting. He was once again in the armoire where his father locked him to punish him for imagined misbehavior, there where for eternal hours he had crouched with his eyes closed, not to see the darkness, with his hands over his ears, to shut out the beating of his heart, trembling, huddled like a cornered animal. Wandering in the mist of his memories he found his sister Katharina, a sweet, retarded child who spent her life hiding, with the hope that her father would forget the disgrace of her having been born. With Katharina, Rolf crawled beneath the dining room table, and with her hid there under the long white tablecloth, two children forever embraced, alert to footsteps and voices. Katharina's scent melded with his own sweat, with aromas of cooking, garlic, soup, freshly baked bread, and the unexpected odor of putrescent clay. His sister's hand in his, her frightened breathing, her silk hair against his cheek, the candid gaze of her eyes. Katharina . . . Katharina materialized before him, floating on the air like a flag, clothed in the white tablecloth, now a winding sheet, and at last he could weep for her death and for the guilt of having abandoned her. He understood then that all his exploits as a reporter, the feats that had won him such recognition and fame, were merely an attempt to keep his most ancient fears at bay, a stratagem for taking refuge behind a lens to test whether reality was more tolerable from that perspective. He took excessive risks as an exercise of courage, training by day to conquer the monsters that tormented him by night. But he had come face to face with the moment of truth; he could not continue to escape his past. He *was* Azucena; he was buried in the clayey mud; his terror was not the distant emotion of an almost forgotten childhood, it was a claw sunk in his throat. In the flush of his tears he saw his mother, dressed in black and clutching her imitation-crocodile pocketbook to her bosom, just as he had last seen her on the dock when she had come to put him on the boat to South America. She had not come to dry his tears, but to tell him to pick up a shovel: the war was over and now they must bury the dead.

"Don't cry. I don't hurt anymore. I'm fine," Azucena said when dawn came.

"I'm not crying for you," Rolf Carlé smiled. "I'm crying for myself. I hurt all over."

The third day in the valley of the cataclysm began with a pale light filtering through storm clouds. The President of the Republic visited the area in his tailored safari jacket to confirm that this was the worst catastrophe of the century; the country was in mourning; sister nations had offered aid; he had ordered a state of siege; the Armed Forces would be merciless, anyone caught stealing or committing other offenses would be shot on sight. He added that it was impossible to remove all the corpses or count the thousands who had disappeared; the entire valley would be declared holy ground, and bishops would come to celebrate a solemn mass for the souls of the victims. He went to the Army field tents to offer relief in the form of vague promises to crowds of the rescued, then to the improvised hospital to offer a word of encouragement to doctors and nurses worn down from so many hours of tribulations. Then he asked to be taken to see Azucena, the little girl the whole world had seen. He waved to her with a limp statesman's hand, and microphones recorded his emotional voice and paternal tone as he told her that her courage had served as an example to the nation. Rolf Carlé interrupted to ask for a pump, and the President assured him that he personally would attend to the matter. I caught a glimpse of Rolf for a few seconds kneeling beside the mudpit. On the evening news broadcast, he was still in the same position; and I, glued to the screen like a fortuneteller to her crystal ball, could tell that something fundamental had changed in him. I knew somehow that during the night his defenses had crumbled and he had given in to grief; finally he was vulnerable. The girl had touched a part of him that he himself had no access to, a part he had never shared with me. Rolf had wanted to console her, but it was Azucena who had given him consolation.

I recognized the precise moment at which Rolf gave up the fight and surrendered to the torture of watching the girl die. I was with them, three days and two nights, spying on them from the other side of life. I was there when she told him that in all her thirteen years no boy had ever loved her and that it was a pity to leave this world without knowing love. Rolf assured her that he loved her more than he could ever love anyone, more than he loved his mother, more than his sister, more than all the women who had slept in his arms, more than he loved me, his life companion, who would have given anything to be trapped in that well in her place, who would have exchanged her life for Azucena's, and I watched as he leaned down to kiss her poor forehead, consumed by a sweet, sad emotion he could not name. I felt how in that instant both were saved from despair, how they were freed from the clay, how they rose above the vultures and helicopters, how together they flew above the vast swamp of corruption and laments. How, finally, they were able to accept death. Rolf Carlé prayed in silence that she would die quickly, because such pain cannot be borne.

By then I had obtained a pump and was in touch with a general who had agreed to ship it the next morning on a military cargo plane. But on the night of that third day, beneath the unblinking focus of quartz lamps and the lens of a hundred cameras, Azucena gave up, her eyes locked with those of the friend who had sustained her to the end. Rolf Carlé removed the life buoy, closed her eyelids, held her to his chest for a few moments, and then let her go. She sank slowly, a flower in the mud.

You are back with me, but you are not the same man. I often accompany you to the station and we watch the videos of Azucena again; you study them intently, looking for something you could have done to save her, something you did not think of in time. Or maybe you study them to see yourself as if in a mirror, naked. Your cameras lie forgotten in a closet; you do not write or sing; you sit long hours before the window, staring at the mountains. Beside you, I wait for you to complete the voyage into yourself, for the old wounds to heal. I know that when you return from your nightmares, we shall again walk hand in hand, as before.   [1989]

SHERWOOD ANDERSON *(1876–1941) was born the son of a jack-of-all-trades father in Camden, Ohio. He did not publish his first book until he was over forty years old, after working for many years as a newsboy, farm laborer, stable boy, factory hand, and advertising copywriter. Dissatisfied with the commercial spirit of the advertising business, Anderson made friends with writers in Chicago and began to publish his own poetry and fiction. The poet Carl Sandburg encouraged him, but Anderson's literary style was most influenced by* Three Lives *(1909), an experimental book by the expatriate American writer Gertrude Stein, which he felt revolutionized the language of narrative.*

In 1916 Anderson published his first novel, Windy McPherson's Son. *He followed it with another novel and a volume of poetry, but he did not receive wide recognition until 1919, with the book* Winesburg, Ohio. *This was a collection of related stories, including "Hands," about life in a small town that explored the devastating consequences of the repressive conventions of a provincial society. It was followed by other important collections of stories:* The Triumph of the Egg *(1921),* Horses and Men *(1923), and* Death in the Woods and Other Stories *(1933). In his time Anderson was a strong influence on Ernest Hemingway, William Faulkner, Richard Wright, and John Steinbeck. The editor Martha Foley wrote in 1941 that*

> *Sherwood Anderson set out on new paths at a time when the American short story seemed doomed to a formula-ridden, conventionalized, mechanized, and commercialized concept. When* Winesburg, Ohio, *appeared in 1919 it was intensely influential on writers who either had lost heart or had not yet found their way. His vision was his own; his characters were people into whose hearts and minds he seemed intuitively to peer; his prose was simple, deceptively simple, sensuous, rich, and evocative.*

As literary critics have observed, the characteristic tone of Anderson's short fiction is melancholy reminiscence. In an understated fashion, he wove carefully selected realistic details into a narrative like "Death in the Woods" that moves by apparently formless associations of thought and feeling but is actually a controlled progression of fully dramatized situations. Anderson's importance in our literature is suggested by Richard Wright's acknowledgment that Anderson's stories made him see that through the powers of fiction, "America could be shaped nearer to the hearts of those who lived in it."

RELATED COMMENTARY: *Sherwood Anderson, "Form, Not Plot, in the Short Story," page 1379.*

SHERWOOD ANDERSON

Death in the Woods

I

She was an old woman and lived on a farm near the town in which I lived. All country and small-town people have seen such old women, but no one knows much about them. Such an old woman comes into town driving an old worn-out horse or she comes afoot carrying a basket. She may own a few hens and have eggs to sell. She brings them in a basket and takes them to a grocer. There she trades them in. She gets some salt pork and some beans. Then she gets a pound or two of sugar and some flour.

Afterwards she goes to the butcher's and asks for some dog-meat. She may spend ten or fifteen cents, but when she does she asks for something. Formerly the butchers gave liver to any one who wanted to carry it away. In our family we were always having it. Once one of my brothers got a whole cow's liver at the slaughter-house near the fairgrounds in our town. We had it until we were sick of it. It never cost a cent. I have hated the thought of it ever since.

The old farm woman got some liver and a soup-bone. She never visited with any one, and as soon as she got what she wanted she lit out for home. It made quite a load for such an old body. No one gave her a lift. People drive right down a road and never notice an old woman like that.

There was such an old woman who used to come into town past our house one Summer and Fall when I was a young boy and was sick with what was called inflammatory rheumatism. She went home later carrying a heavy pack on her back. Two or three large gaunt-looking dogs followed at her heels.

The old woman was nothing special. She was one of the nameless ones that hardly anyone knows, but she got into my thoughts. I have just suddenly now, after all these years, remembered her and what happened. It is a story. Her name was Grimes, and she lived with her husband and son in a small unpainted house on the bank of a small creek four miles from town.

The husband and son were a tough lot. Although the son was but twenty-one, he had already served a term in jail. It was whispered about that the woman's husband stole horses and ran them off to some other county. Now and then, when a horse turned up missing, the man had also disappeared. No one ever caught him. Once, when I was loafing at Tom White-head's livery-barn, the man came there and sat on the bench in front. Two or three other men were there, but no one spoke to him. He sat for a few minutes and then got up and went away. When he was leaving he turned around and stared at the men. There was a look of defiance in his eyes. "Well, I have tried to be friendly. You don't want to talk to me. It has been so wherever I have gone in this town. If, some day, one of your fine horses turns up missing, well, then what?" He did not say anything actually. "I'd like to bust one of you on the jaw," was about what his eyes said. I remember how the look in his eyes made me shiver.

The old man belonged to a family that had had money once. His name was Jake Grimes. It all comes back clearly now. His father, John Grimes, had owned a sawmill when the country was new, and had made money. Then he got to drinking and running after women. When he died there wasn't much left.

Jake blew in the rest. Pretty soon there wasn't any more lumber to cut and his land was nearly all gone.

He got his wife off a German farmer, for whom he went to work one June day in the wheat harvest. She was a young thing then and scared to death. You see, the farmer was up to something with the girl — she was, I think, a bound girl and his wife had her suspicions. She took it out on the girl when the man wasn't around. Then, when the wife had to go off to town for supplies, the farmer got after her. She told young Jake that nothing really ever happened, but he didn't know whether to believe it or not.

He got her pretty easy himself, the first time he was out with her. He wouldn't have married her if the German farmer hadn't tried to tell him where to get off. He got her to go riding with him in his buggy one night when he was threshing on the place, and then he came for her the next Sunday night.

She managed to get out of the house without her employer's seeing, but when she was getting into the buggy he showed up. It was almost dark, and he just popped up suddenly at the horse's head. He grabbed the horse by the bridle and Jake got out his buggy-whip.

They had it out all right! The German was a tough one. Maybe he didn't care whether his wife knew or not. Jake hit him over the face and shoulders with the buggy-whip, but the horse got to acting up and he had to get out.

Then the two men went for it. The girl didn't see it. The horse started to run away and went nearly a mile down the road before the girl got him stopped. Then she managed to tie him to a tree beside the road. (I wonder how I know all this. It must have stuck in my mind from small-town tales when I was a boy.) Jake found her there after he got through with the German. She was huddled up in the buggy seat, crying, scared to death. She told Jake a lot of stuff, how the German had tried to get her, how he chased her once into the barn, how another time, when they happened to be alone in the house together, he tore her dress open clear down the front. The German, she said, might have got her that time if he hadn't heard his old woman drive in at the gate. She had been off to town for supplies. Well, she would be putting the horse in the barn. The German managed to sneak off to the fields without his wife seeing. He told the girl he would kill her if she told. What could she do? She told a lie about ripping her dress in the barn when she was feeding the stock. I remember now that she was a bound girl and did not know where her father and mother were. Maybe she did not have any father. You know what I mean.

Such bound children were often enough cruelly treated. They were children who had no parents, slaves really. There were very few orphan homes then. They were legally bound into some home. It was a matter of pure luck how it came out.

II

She married Jake and had a son and daughter, but the daughter died.

Then she settled down to feed stock. That was her job. At the German's place she had cooked the food for the German and his wife. The wife was a strong woman with big hips and worked most of the time in the fields with her husband. She fed them and fed the cows in the barn, fed the pigs, the horses and the chickens. Every moment of every day, as a young girl, was spent feeding something.

Then she married Jake Grimes and he had to be fed. She was a slight thing, and when she had been married for three or four years, and after the two children were born, her slender shoulders became stooped.

Jake always had a lot of big dogs around the house, that stood near the unused sawmill near the creek. He was always trading horses when he wasn't stealing something and had a lot of poor bony ones about. Also he kept three or four pigs and a cow. They were all pastured in the few acres left of the Grimes place and Jake did little enough work.

He went into debt for a threshing outfit and ran it for several years, but it did not pay. People did not trust him. They were afraid he would steal the grain at night. He had to go a long way off to get work and it cost too much to get there. In the Winter he hunted and cut a little firewood, to be sold in some nearby town. When the son grew up he was just like the father. They got drunk together. If there wasn't anything to eat in the house when they came home the old man gave his old woman a cut over the head. She had a few chickens of her own and had to kill one of them in a hurry. When they were all killed she wouldn't have any eggs to sell when she went to town, and then what would she do?

She had to scheme all her life about getting things fed, getting the pigs fed so they would grow fat and could be butchered in the Fall. When they were butchered her husband took most of the meat off to town and sold it. If he did not do it first the boy did. They fought sometimes and when they fought the old woman stood aside trembling.

She had got the habit of silence anyway — that was fixed. Sometimes, when she began to look old — she wasn't forty yet — and when the husband and son were both off, trading horses or drinking or hunting or stealing, she went around the house and the barnyard muttering to herself.

How was she going to get everything fed? — that was her problem. The dogs had to be fed. There wasn't enough hay in the barn for the horses and the cow. If she didn't feed the chickens how could they lay eggs? Without eggs to sell how could she get things in town, things she had to have to keep the life of the farm going? Thank heaven, she did not have to feed her husband — in a certain way. That hadn't lasted long after their marriage and after the babies came. Where he went on his long trips she did not know.

Sometimes he was gone from home for weeks, and after the boy grew up they went off together.

They left everything at home for her to manage and she had no money. She knew no one. No one ever talked to her in town. When it was Winter she had to gather sticks of wood for her fire, had to try to keep the stock fed with very little grain.

The stock in the barn cried to her hungrily, the dogs followed her about. In the Winter the hens laid few enough eggs. They huddled in the corners of the barn and she kept watching them. If a hen lays an egg in the barn in the Winter and you do not find it, it freezes and breaks.

One day in Winter the old woman went off to town with a few eggs and the dogs followed her. She did not get started until nearly three o'clock and the snow was heavy. She hadn't been feeling very well for several days and so she went muttering along, scantily clad, her shoulders stooped. She had an old grain bag in which she carried her eggs, tucked away down in the bottom. There weren't many of them, but in Winter the price of eggs is up. She would get a little meat in exchange for the eggs, some salt pork, a little sugar, and some coffee perhaps. It might be the butcher would give her a piece of liver.

When she had got to town and was trading in her eggs the dogs lay by the door outside. She did pretty well, got the things she needed, more than she had hoped. Then she went to the butcher and he gave her some liver and some dog-meat.

It was the first time any one had spoken to her in a friendly way for a long time. The butcher was alone in his shop when she came in and was annoyed by the thought of such a sick-looking old woman out on such a day. It was bitter cold and the snow, that had let up during the afternoon, was falling again. The butcher said something about her husband and her son, swore at them, and the old woman stared at him, a look of mild surprise in her eyes as he talked. He said that if either the husband or the son were going to get any of the liver or the heavy bones with scraps of meat hanging to them that he had put into the grain bag, he'd see him starve first.

Starve, eh? Well, things had to be fed. Men had to be fed, and horses that weren't any good but maybe could be traded off, and the poor thin cow that hadn't given any milk for three months.

Horses, cows, pigs, dogs, men.

III

The old woman had to get back before darkness came if she could. The dogs followed at her heels, sniffing at the heavy grain bag she had fastened on her back. When she got to the edge of town she stopped by a fence and tied the bag on her back with a piece of rope she had carried in her dress-pocket for just that purpose. It was hard when she had to crawl over fences and once she fell over and landed in the snow. The dogs went frisking about. She had to struggle to get to her feet again, but she made it. The point of climbing over the fences was that there was a short cut over a hill and through a woods. She might have gone around by the road, but it was a mile farther that way. She was afraid she couldn't make it. And then, besides, the stock had to be fed. There was a little hay left and a little corn. Perhaps her husband and son would bring some home when they came. They had driven off in the only buggy the Grimes family had, a rickety thing, a rickety horse hitched to the buggy, two other rickety horses led by halters. They were going to trade horses, get a little money if they could. They might come home drunk. It would be well to have something in the house when they came back.

The son had an affair on with a woman at the county seat, fifteen miles away. She was a rough enough woman, a tough one. Once, in the Summer, the son had brought her to the house. Both she and the son had been drinking. Jake Grimes was away and the son and his woman ordered the old woman about like a servant. She didn't mind much; she was used to it. Whatever happened she never said anything. That was her way of getting along. She had managed that way when she was a young girl at the German's and ever since she had married Jake. That time her son brought his woman to the house they stayed all night, sleeping together just as though they were married. It hadn't shocked the old woman, not much. She had got past being shocked early in life.

With the pack on her back she went painfully along across an open field, wading in the deep snow, and got into the woods.

There was a path, but it was hard to follow. Just beyond the top of the hill, where the woods was thickest, there was a small clearing. Had some one once thought of building a house there? The clearing was as large as a building lot in town, large enough for a house and a garden. The path ran along the side of the clearing, and when she got there the old woman sat down to rest at the foot of a tree.

It was a foolish thing to do. When she got herself placed, the pack against the tree's trunk, it was nice, but what about getting up again? She worried about that for a moment and then quietly closed her eyes.

She must have slept for a time. When you are about so cold you can't get any colder. The afternoon grew a little warmer and the snow came thicker than ever. Then after a time the weather cleared. The moon even came out.

There were four Grimes dogs that had followed Mrs. Grimes into town, all tall gaunt fellows. Such men as Jake Grimes and his son always keep just such dogs. They kick and abuse them, but they stay. The Grimes dogs, in order to keep from starving, had to do a lot of foraging for themselves, and they had been at it while the old woman slept with her back to the tree at the side of the clearing. They had been chasing rabbits in the woods and in adjoining fields and in their ranging had picked up three other farm dogs.

After a time all the dogs came back to the clearing. They were excited about something. Such nights, cold and clear and with a moon, do things to dogs. It may be that some old instinct, come down from the time when they were wolves, and ranged the woods in packs on Winter nights, comes back to them.

The dogs in the clearing, before the old woman, had caught two or three rabbits and their immediate hunger had been satisfied. They began to play, running in circles in the clearing. Round and round they ran, each dog's nose at the tail of the next dog. In the clearing, under the snow-laden trees and under the wintry moon they made a strange picture, running thus silently, in a circle their running had beaten in the soft snow. The dogs made no sound. They ran around and around in the circle.

It may have been that the old woman saw them doing that before she died. She may have awakened once or twice and looked at the strange sight with dim old eyes.

She wouldn't be very cold now, just drowsy. Life hangs on a long time. Perhaps the old woman was out of her head. She may have dreamed of her girlhood at the German's, and before that, when she was a child and before her mother lit out and left her.

Her dreams couldn't have been very pleasant. Not many pleasant things had happened to her. Now and then one of the Grimes dogs left the running circle and came to stand before her. The dog thrust his face to her face. His red tongue was hanging out.

The running of the dogs may have been a kind of death ceremony. It may have been that the primitive instinct of the wolf, having been aroused in the dogs by the night and the running, made them somehow, afraid.

"Now we are no longer wolves. We are dogs, the servants of men. Keep alive, man! When man dies we become wolves again." When one of the dogs came to where the old woman sat with her back against the tree and thrust his nose close to her face he seemed satisfied and went back to run with the pack. All the Grimes dogs did it at some time during the evening, before she died. I knew all about it afterward, when I grew to be a man, because once in a woods in Illinois, on another Winter night, I saw a pack of dogs act just like that. The dogs were waiting for me to die as they had waited for the old woman that night when I was a child, but when it happened to me I was a young man and had no intention whatever of dying.

The old woman died softly and quietly. When she was dead and when one of the Grimes dogs had come to her and had found her dead all the dogs stopped running.

They gathered about her.

Well, she was dead now. She had fed the Grimes dogs when she was alive, what about now?

There was the pack on her back, the grain bag containing the piece of salt pork, the liver the butcher had given her, the dog-meat, the soup bones. The butcher in town, having been suddenly overcome with a feeling of pity, had loaded her grain bag heavily. It had been a big haul for the old woman.

It was a big haul for the dogs now.

IV

One of the Grimes dogs sprang suddenly out from among the others and began worrying the pack on the old woman's back. Had the dogs really been wolves that one would have been the leader of the pack. What he did, all the others did.

All of them sank their teeth into the grain bag the old woman had fastened with ropes to her back. When she got back to

They dragged the old woman's body out into the open clearing. The worn-out dress was quickly torn from her shoulders. When she was found, a day or two later, the dress had been torn from her body clear to the hips, but the dogs had not touched her body. They had got the meat out of the grain bag, that was all. Her body was frozen stiff when it was found, and the shoulders were so narrow and the body so slight that in death it looked like the body of some charming young girl.

Such things happened in towns of the Middle West, on farms near town, when I was a boy. A hunter out after rabbits found the old woman's body and did not touch it. Something, the beaten round path in the little snow-covered clearing, the silence of the place, the place where the dogs had worried the body trying to pull the grain bag away or tear it open — something startled the man and he hurried off to town.

I was in Main Street with one of my brothers who was town newsboy and who was taking the afternoon papers to the stores. It was almost night.

The hunter came into a grocery and told his story. Then he went into a hardware-shop and into a drugstore. Men began to gather on the sidewalks. Then they started out along the road to the place in the woods.

My brother should have gone on about his business of distributing papers but he didn't. Every one was going to the woods. The undertaker went and the town marshal. Several men got on a dray and rode out to where the path left the road and went into the woods, but the horses weren't very sharply shod and slid about on the slippery roads. They made no better time than those of us who walked.

The town marshal was a large man whose leg had been injured in the Civil War. He carried a heavy cane and limped rapidly along the road. My brother and I followed at his heels, and as we went other men and boys joined the crowd.

It had grown dark by the time we got to where the old woman had left the road but the moon had come out. The marshal was thinking there might have been a murder. He kept asking the hunter questions. The hunter went along with his gun across his shoulders, a dog following at his heels. It isn't often a rabbit hunter has a chance to be so conspicuous. He was taking full advantage of it, leading the procession with the town marshal. "I didn't see any wounds. She was a beautiful young girl. Her face was buried in the snow. No, I didn't know her." As a matter of fact, the hunter had not looked closely at the body. He had been frightened. She might have been murdered and some one might spring out from behind a tree and murder him. In a woods, in the late afternoon, when the trees are all bare and there is white snow on the ground, when all is silent, something creepy steals over the mind and body. If something strange or uncanny has happened in the neighborhood all you think about is getting away from there as fast as you can.

The crowd of men and boys had got to where the old woman had crossed the field and went, following the marshal and the hunter, up the slight incline and into the woods.

My brother and I were silent. He had his bundle of papers in a bag slung across his shoulder. When he got back to town he would have to go on distributing his papers before he went home to supper. If I went along, as he had no doubt already determined I should, we would both be late. Either mother or our older sister would have to warm our supper.

Well, we would have something to tell. A boy did not get such a chance very often. It was lucky we just happened to go into the grocery when the hunter came in. The hunter was a country fellow. Neither of us had ever seen him before.

Now the crowd of men and boys had got to the clearing. Darkness comes quickly on such Winter nights, but the full moon made everything clear. My brother and I stood near the tree, beneath which the old woman had died.

She did not look old, lying there in that light, frozen and still. One of the men turned her over in the snow and I saw everything. My body trembled with some strange mystical feeling and so did my brother's. It might have been the cold.

Neither of us had ever seen a woman's body before. It may have been the snow, clinging to the frozen flesh, that made it look so white and lovely, so like marble. No woman had come with the party from town; but one of the men, he was the town blacksmith, took off his overcoat and spread it over her. Then he gathered her into his arms and started off to town, all the others following silently. At that time no one knew who she was.

V

I had seen everything, had seen the oval in the snow, like a miniature race-track, where the dogs had run, had seen how the men were mystified, had seen the white bare young-looking shoulders, had heard the whispered comments of the men.

The men were simply mystified. They took the body to the undertaker's, and when the blacksmith, the hunter, the marshal, and several others had got inside they closed the door. If father had been there perhaps he could have got in, but we boys couldn't.

I went with my brother to distribute the rest of his papers and when we got home it was my brother who told the story.

I kept silent and went to bed early. It may have been I was not satisfied with the way he told it.

Later, in the town, I must have heard other fragments of the old woman's story. She was recognized the next day and there was an investigation.

The husband and son were found somewhere and brought to town and there was an attempt to connect them with the woman's death, but it did not work. They had perfect enough alibis.

However, the town was against them. They had to get out. Where they went I never heard.

I remember only the picture there in the forest, the men standing about, the naked girlish-looking figure, face down in the snow, the tracks made by the running dogs and the clear cold Winter sky above. White fragments of clouds were drifting across the sky. They went racing across the little open space among the trees.

The scene in the forest had become for me, without my knowing it, the foundation for the real story I am now trying to tell. The fragments, you see, had to be picked up slowly, long afterwards.

Things happened. When I was a young man I worked on the farm of a German. The hired-girl was afraid of her employer. The farmer's wife hated her.

I saw things at that place. Once later, I had a half-uncanny, mystical adventure with dogs in an Illinois forest on a clear, moon-lit Winter night. When I was a schoolboy, and on a Summer day, I went with a boy friend out along a creek some miles from town and came to the house where the old woman had lived. No one had lived in the house since her death. The doors were broken from the hinges; the window lights were all broken. As the boy and I stood in the road outside, two dogs, just roving farm dogs no doubt, came running around the corner of the house. The dogs were tall, gaunt fellows and came down to the fence and glared through at us, standing in the road.

The whole thing, the story of the old woman's death, was to me as I grew older like music heard from far off. The notes had to be picked up slowly one at a time. Something had to be understood.

The woman who died was one destined to feed animal life. Anyway, that is all she ever did. She was feeding animal life before she was born, as a child, as a young woman working on the farm of the German, after she married, when she grew old and when she died. She fed animal life in cows, in chickens, in pigs, in horses, in dogs, in men. Her daughter had died in childhood and with her one son she had no articulate relations. On the night when she died she was hurrying homeward, bearing on her body food for animal life.

She died in the clearing in the woods and even after her death continued feeding animal life.

You see it is likely that, when my brother told the story, that night when we got home and my mother and sister sat listening, I did not think he got the point. He was too young and so was I. A thing so complete has its own beauty.

I shall not try to emphasize the point. I am only explaining why I was dissatisfied then and have been ever since. I speak of that only that you may understand why I have been impelled to try to tell the simple story over again.

[1933]

Hands

Upon the half decayed veranda of a small frame house that stood near the edge of a ravine near the town of Winesburg, Ohio, a fat little old man walked nervously up and down. Across a long field that had been seeded for clover but that had produced only a dense crop of yellow mustard weeds, he could see the public highway along which went a wagon filled with berry pickers returning from the fields. The berry pickers, youths and maidens, laughed and shouted boisterously. A boy clad in a blue shirt leaped from the wagon and attempted to drag after him one of the maidens who screamed and protested shrilly. The feet of the boy in the road kicked up a cloud of dust that floated across the face of the departing sun. Over the long field came a thin girlish voice. "Oh, you Wing Biddlebaum, comb your hair, it's falling into your eyes," commanded the voice to the man, who was bald and whose nervous little hands fiddled about the bare white forehead as though arranging a mass of tangled locks.

Wing Biddlebaum, forever frightened and beset by a ghostly band of doubts, did not think of himself as in any way a part of the life of the town where he had lived for twenty years. Among all the people of Winesburg but one had come close to him. With George Willard, son of Tom Willard, the proprietor of the new Willard House, he had formed something like a friendship. George Willard was the reporter on the *Winesburg Eagle* and sometimes in the evenings he walked out along the highway to Wing Biddlebaum's house. Now as the old man walked up and down on the veranda, his hands moving nervously about, he was hoping that George Willard would come and spend the evening with him. After the wagon containing the berry pickers had passed, he went across the field through the tall mustard weeds and climbing a rail fence peered anxiously along the road to the town. For a moment he stood thus, rubbing his hands together and looking up and down the road, and then, fear overcoming him, ran back to walk again upon the porch of his own house.

In the presence of George Willard, Wing Biddlebaum, who for twenty years had been the town mystery, lost something of his timidity, and his shadowy personality, submerged in a sea of doubts, came forth to look at the world. With the young reporter at his side, he ventured in the light of day into Main Street or strode up and down on the rickety front porch of his own house, talking excitedly. The voice that had been low and trembling became shrill and loud. The bent figure straightened. With a kind of wriggle, like a fish returned to the brook by the fisherman, Biddlebaum the silent began to talk, striving to put into words the ideas that had been accumulated by his mind during long years of silence.

Wing Biddlebaum talked much with his hands. The slender expressive fingers, forever active, forever striving to conceal themselves in his pockets or behind his back, came forth and became the piston rods of his machinery of expression.

The story of Wing Biddlebaum is a story of hands. Their restless activity, like unto the beating of the wings of an imprisoned bird, had given him his name. Some obscure poet of the town had thought of it. The hands alarmed their owner. He wanted to keep them hidden away and looked with amazement at the quiet inexpressive hands of other men who worked beside him in the fields, or passed, driving sleepy teams on country roads.

When he talked to George Willard, Wing Biddlebaum closed his fists and beat with them upon a table or on the walls of his house. The action made him more comfortable. If the desire to talk came to him when the two were walking in the fields, he sought out a stump or the top board of a fence and with his hands pounding busily talked with renewed ease.

The story of Wing Biddlebaum's hands is worth a book itself. Sympathetically set forth it would tap many strange, beautiful qualities in obscure men. It is a job for a poet. In Winesburg the hands had attracted attention merely because of their activity. With them Wing Biddlebaum had picked as high as a hundred and forty quarts of strawberries in a day. They became his distinguishing feature, the source of his fame. Also they made more grotesque an already grotesque and elusive individuality. Winesburg was proud of the hands of Wing Biddlebaum in the same spirit in which it was proud of Banker White's new stone house and Wesley Moyer's bay stallion, Tony Tip, that had won the two-fifteen trot at the fall races in Cleveland.

As for George Willard, he had many times wanted to ask about the hands. At times an almost overwhelming curiosity had taken hold of him. He felt that there must be a reason for their strange activity and their inclination to keep hidden away and only a growing respect for Wing Biddlebaum kept him from blurting out the questions that were often in his mind.

Once he had been on the point of asking. The two were walking in the fields on a summer afternoon and had stopped to sit upon a grassy bank. All afternoon Wing Biddlebaum had talked as one inspired. By a fence he had stopped and beating like a giant woodpecker upon the top board had shouted at George Willard, condemning his tendency to be too much influenced by the people about him. "You are destroying yourself," he cried.

"You have the inclination to be alone and to dream and you are afraid of dreams. You want to be like others in town here. You hear them talk and you try to imitate them."

On the grassy bank Wing Biddlebaum had tried again to drive his point home. His voice became soft and reminiscent, and with a sigh of contentment he launched into a long rambling talk, speaking as one lost in a dream.

Out of the dream Wing Biddlebaum made a picture for George Willard. In the picture men lived again in a kind of pastoral golden age. Across a green open country came clean-limbed young men, some afoot, some mounted upon horses. In crowds the young men came to gather about the feet of an old man who sat beneath a tree in a tiny garden and who talked to them.

Wing Biddlebaum became wholly inspired. For once he forgot the hands. Slowly they stole forth and lay upon George Willard's shoulders. Something new and bold came into the voice that talked. "You must try to forget all you have learned," said the old man. "You must begin to dream. From this time on you must shut your ears to the roaring of the voices."

Pausing in his speech, Wing Biddlebaum looked long and earnestly at George Willard. His eyes glowed. Again he raised the hands to caress the boy and then a look of horror swept over his face.

With a convulsive movement of his body, Wing Biddlebaum sprang to his feet and thrust his hands deep into his trousers pockets. Tears came to his eyes. "I must be getting along home. I can talk no more with you," he said nervously.

Without looking back, the old man had hurried down the hillside and across a meadow, leaving George Willard perplexed and frightened upon the grassy slope. With a shiver of dread the boy arose and went along the road toward town. "I'll not ask him about his hands," he thought, touched by the memory of the terror he had seen in the man's eyes. "There's something wrong, but I don't want to know what it is. His hands have something to do with his fear of me and of everyone."

And George Willard was right. Let us look briefly into the story of the hands. Perhaps our talking of them will arouse the poet who will tell the hidden wonder story of the influence for which the hands were but fluttering pennants of promise.

In his youth Wing Biddlebaum had been a school teacher in a town in Pennsylvania. He was not then known as Wing Biddlebaum, but went by the less euphonic name of Adolph Myers. As Adolph Myers he was much loved by the boys of his school.

Adolph Myers was meant by nature to be a rare teacher of youth. He was one of those rare, little-understood men who rule by a power so gentle that it passes as a lovable weakness. In their feeling for the boys under their charge such men are not unlike the finer sort of women in their love of men.

And yet that is but crudely stated. It needs the poet there. With the boys of his school, Adolph Myers had walked in the evening or had sat talking until dusk upon the schoolhouse steps lost in a kind of dream. Here and there went his hands, caressing the shoulders of the boys, playing about the tousled heads. As he talked his voice became soft and musical. There was a caress in that also. In a way the voice and the hands, the stroking of the shoulders and the touching of the hair was a part of the schoolmaster's effort to carry a dream into the young minds. By the caress that was in his fingers he expressed himself. He was one of those men in whom the force that creates life is diffused, not centralized. Under the caress of his hands doubt and disbelief went out of the minds of the boys and they began also to dream.

And then the tragedy. A half-witted boy of the school became enamored of the young master. In his bed at night he imagined unspeakable things and in the morning went forth to tell his dreams as facts. Strange, hideous accusations fell from his loose-hung lips. Through the Pennsylvania town went a shiver. Hidden, shadowy doubts that had been in men's minds concerning Adolph Myers were galvanized into beliefs.

The tragedy did not linger. Trembling lads were jerked out of bed and questioned. "He put his arms about me," said one. "His fingers were always playing in my hair," said another.

One afternoon a man of the town, Henry Bradford, who kept a saloon, came to the schoolhouse door. Calling Adolph Myers into the school yard he began to beat him with his fists. As his hard knuckles beat down into the frightened face of the schoolmaster, his wrath became more and more terrible. Screaming with dismay, the children ran here and there like disturbed insects. "I'll teach you to put your hands on my boy, you beast," roared the saloon keeper, who, tired of beating the master, had begun to kick him about the yard.

Adolph Myers was driven from the Pennsylvania town in the night. With lanterns in their hands a dozen men came to the door of the house where he lived alone and commanded that he dress and come forth. It was raining and one of the men had a rope in his hands. They had intended to hang the schoolmaster, but something in his figure, so small, white, and pitiful, touched their hearts and they let him escape. As he ran away into the darkness they repented of their weakness and ran after him, swearing and throwing sticks and great balls of soft mud at the figure that screamed and ran faster and faster into the darkness.

For twenty years Adolph Myers had lived alone in Winesburg. He was but forty but looked sixty-five. The name Biddlebaum he got from a box of goods seen at a freight station as he hurried through an eastern Ohio town. He had an aunt in Winesburg, a black-toothed old woman who raised chickens, and with her he lived until she died. He had been ill for a year after the experience in Pennsylvania, and after his recovery worked as a day laborer in the fields, going timidly about and striving to conceal his hands. Although he did not understand what had happened he felt that the hands must be to blame. Again and again the fathers of the boys had talked of the hands. "Keep your hands to yourself," the saloon keeper had roared, dancing with fury in the schoolhouse yard.

Upon the veranda of his house by the ravine, Wing Biddlebaum continued to walk up and down until the sun had disappeared and the road beyond the field was lost in the grey shadows. Going into his house he cut slices of bread and spread honey upon them. When the rumble of the evening train that took away the express cars loaded with the day's harvest of berries had passed and restored the silence of the summer night, he went again to walk upon the veranda. In the darkness he could not see the hands and they became quiet. Although he still hungered for the presence of the boy, who was the medium through which he expressed his love of man, the hunger became again a part of his loneliness and his waiting. Lighting a lamp, Wing Biddlebaum washed the few dishes soiled by his simple meal and, setting up a folding cot by the screen door that led to the porch, prepared to undress for the night. A few stray white bread crumbs lay on the cleanly washed floor by the table; putting the lamp upon a low stool he began to pick up the crumbs, carrying them to his mouth one by one with unbelievable rapidity. In the dense blotch of light beneath the table, the kneeling figure looked like a priest engaged in some service of his church. The nervous expressive fingers, flashing in and out of the light, might well have been mistaken for the fingers of the devotee going swiftly through decade after decade of his rosary.   [1919]

MARGARET ATWOOD (b. 1939) is a Canadian writer of poetry and fiction. Born in Ottawa, Ontario, she spent the first eleven years of her life in the sparsely settled "bush" country of northern Ontario and Quebec, where her father, an entomologist, did research. She remembers that

> I did not spend a full year in school until I was in Grade Eight. I began to write at the age of five — poems, "novels," comic books, and plays — but I had no thought of being a professional writer until I was sixteen. I entered Victoria College, University of Toronto, when I was seventeen and graduated in 1961. I won a Woodrow Wilson Fellowship to Harvard, where I studied Victorian Literature, and spent the next ten years in one place after another: Boston, Montreal, Edmonton, Toronto, Vancouver, England, and Italy, alternately teaching and writing.

Atwood's first poem was published when she was nineteen. To date she has published two collections of short stories, several novels — including the best-sellers Surfacing (1972), The Handmaid's Tale (1986), Cat's Eye (1989), and The Robber Bride (1993) — and more than a dozen books of poetry. She was encouraged to write as a young author because Canadians of her generation felt a strong need to develop a national literature.

Atwood has compared writing stories to telling riddles and jokes, all three requiring "the same mystifying buildup, the same surprising twist, the same impeccable sense of timing." She took pleasure in writing "Happy Endings," but she was puzzled by the form the story took. She has said,

> When I wrote "Happy Endings" — the year was, I think, 1982, and I was writing a number of short fictions then — I did not know what sort of creature it was. It was not a poem, a short story, or a prose poem. It was not quite a condensation, a commentary, a questionnaire, and it missed being a parable, a proverb, a paradox. It was a mutation. Writing it gave me a sense of furtive glee, like scribbling anonymously on a wall with no one looking.
>
> This summer I saw a white frog. It would not have been startling if I didn't know that this species of frog is normally green. This is the way such a mutant literary form unsettles us. We know what is expected, in a given arrangement of words; we know what is supposed to come next. And then it doesn't.
>
> It was a little disappointing to learn that other people had a name for such aberrations [metafiction], and had already made up rules.

RELATED COMMENTARY: Margaret Atwood, "Reading Blind," page 1381.

65

Happy Endings

John and Mary meet.
What happens next?
If you want a happy ending, try A.

A

John and Mary fall in love and get married. They both have worthwhile and remunerative jobs which they find stimulating and challenging. They buy a charming house. Real estate values go up. Eventually, when they can afford live-in help, they have two children, to whom they are devoted. The children turn out well. John and Mary have a stimulating and challenging sex life and worthwhile friends. They go on fun vacations together. They retire. They both have hobbies which they find stimulating and challenging. Eventually they die. This is the end of the story.

B

Mary falls in love with John but John doesn't fall in love with Mary. He merely uses her body for selfish pleasure and ego gratification of a tepid kind. He comes to her apartment twice a week and she cooks him dinner, you'll notice that he doesn't even consider her worth the price of a dinner out, and after he's eaten the dinner he fucks her and after that he falls asleep, while she does the dishes so he won't think she's untidy, having all those dirty dishes lying around, and puts on fresh lipstick so she'll look good when he wakes up, but when he wakes up he doesn't even notice, he puts on his socks and his shorts and his pants and his shirt and his tie and his shoes, the reverse order from the one in which he took them off. He doesn't take off Mary's clothes, she takes them off herself, she acts as if she's dying for it every time, not because she likes sex exactly, she doesn't, but she wants John to think she does because if they do it often enough surely he'll get used to her, he'll come to depend on her and they will get married, but John goes out the door with hardly so much as a good-night and three days later he turns up at six o'clock and they do the whole thing over again.

Mary gets run-down. Crying is bad for your face, everyone knows that and so does Mary but she can't stop. People at work notice. Her friends tell her John is a rat, a pig, a dog, he isn't good enough for her, but she can't believe it. Inside John, she thinks, is another John, who is much nicer. This other John will emerge like a butterfly from a cocoon, a Jack from a box, a pit from a prune, if the first John is only squeezed enough.

One evening John complains about the food. He has never complained about the food before. Mary is hurt.

Her friends tell her they've seen him in a restaurant with another woman, whose name is Madge. It's not even Madge that finally gets to Mary: it's the restaurant. John has never taken Mary to a restaurant. Mary collects all the sleeping pills and aspirins she can find, and takes them and a half a bottle of sherry. You can see what kind of a woman she is by the fact that it's not even whiskey. She leaves a note for John. She hopes he'll discover her and get her to the hospital in time and repent and then they can get married, but this fails to happen and she dies.

John marries Madge and everything continues as in A.

C

John, who is an older man, falls in love with Mary, and Mary, who is only twenty-two, feels sorry for him because he's worried about his hair falling out. She sleeps with him even though she's not in love with him. She met him at work. She's in love with someone called James, who is twenty-two also and not yet ready to settle down.

John on the contrary settled down long ago: this is what is bothering him. John has a steady, respectable job and is getting ahead in his field, but Mary isn't impressed by him, she's impressed by James, who has a motorcycle and a fabulous record collection. But James is often away on his motorcycle, being free. Freedom isn't the same for girls, so in the meantime Mary spends Thursday evenings with John. Thursdays are the only days John can get away.

John is married to a woman called Madge and they have two children, a charming house which they bought just before the real estate values went up, and hobbies which they find stimulating and challenging, when they have the time. John tells Mary how important she is to him, but of course he can't leave his wife because a commitment is a commitment. He goes on about this more than is necessary and Mary finds it boring, but older men can keep it up longer so on the whole she has a fairly good time.

One day James breezes in on his motorcycle with some top-grade California hybrid and James and Mary get higher than you'd believe possible and they climb into bed. Everything becomes very underwater, but along comes John, who has a key to Mary's apartment. He finds them stoned and entwined. He's hardly in any position to be jealous, considering Madge, but nevertheless he's overcome with despair. Finally he's middle-aged, in two years he'll be bald as an egg and he can't stand it. He purchases a handgun, saying he needs it for target practice — this is the thin part of the plot, but it can be dealt with later — and shoots the two of them and himself.

Madge, after a suitable period of mourning, marries an understanding man called Fred and everything continues as in A, but under different names.

D

Fred and Madge have no problems. They get along exceptionally well and are good at working out any little difficulties that may arise. But their charming house is by the seashore and one day a giant tidal wave approaches. Real estate values go down. The rest of the story is about what caused the tidal wave and how they escape from it. They do, though thousands drown, but Fred and Madge are virtuous and lucky. Finally on high ground they clasp each other, wet and dripping and grateful, and continue as in A.

E

Yes, but Fred has a bad heart. The rest of the story is about how kind and understanding they both are until Fred dies. Then Madge devotes herself to charity work until the end of A. If you like, it can be "Madge," "cancer," "guilty and confused," and "bird watching."

F

If you think this is all too bourgeois, make John a revolutionary and Mary a counterespionage agent and see how far that gets you. Remember, this is Canada. You'll still end up with A, though in between you may get a lustful brawling saga of passionate involvement, a chronicle of our times, sort of.

You'll have to face it, the endings are the same however you slice it. Don't be deluded by any other endings, they're all fake, either deliberately fake, with malicious intent to deceive, or just motivated by excessive optimism if not by downright sentimentality.
The only authentic ending is the one provided here:
John and Mary die. John and Mary die. John and Mary die.

So much for endings. Beginnings are always more fun. True connoisseurs, however, are known to favor the stretch in between, since it's the hardest to do anything with.
That's about all that can be said for plots, which anyway are just one thing after another, a what and a what and a what.
Now try How and Why.   [1983]

ISAAC BABEL *(1894–1939?) was born in the Moldavanka district of Odessa, in Russia. His father, a Jewish businessman, made him study Yiddish, the Bible, and the Talmud, but his favorite subject was French literature. By the time Babel was fifteen he began to write stories in French "à la Maupassant," and his later story "Guy de Maupassant" (1932) is a tribute to the influence of this writer. In 1915 Babel moved to St. Petersburg and tried unsuccessfully to publish his stories. His only encouragement came from the Russian writer Maxim Gorky, who advised him to get more life experience: "Go to the people." For six years Babel took Gorky at his word. He became a soldier on the Romanian Front in World War I, worked as a press correspondent attached to the Soviet Cavalry, and found other jobs as a reporter and a printer during the chaotic period of civil war that followed the Russian Revolution of 1917. In 1924 he began to publish his stories in* Left, *a Soviet avant-garde literary magazine devoted to revolution in politics and the arts. A year later he published a collection of his tales,* The Story of My Dove-Cote, *and in 1925 his best work appeared —* Red Cavalry, *thirty-four sketches depicting scenes of bravery and suffering during the Polish campaign of 1920, when Babel was with the Soviet Cavalry.*

Babel's literary style has been called "as terse as algebra," but its lyricism is also unmistakable. He juxtaposed poetic and natural details in his descriptions, often stressing the grotesque and sensual, as in "My First Goose." Critics have noted that these tactics are Babel's way of catching us off guard and breaking down our defenses so we will be more receptive to his main theme as a writer, the complex relation between our illusions about life and the truth of life.

Babel often revised his stories several times before he was satisfied. When his books first appeared, he was hailed in the Soviet Union as a master prose stylist, but during Stalin's purges in the 1930s he was attacked for his ideological shortcomings. In 1937 he told his Soviet critics, who asked him why he wrote so little, that he could manage only short things: "Let me put it this way; the point is that Tolstoy was able to describe what happened to him minute by minute, he remembered it all, whereas I, evidently, only have it in me to describe the most interesting five minutes I've experienced in twenty-four hours." The tone of Babel's reply is joking, but underneath is a sense of his bitterness and frustration. He also wrote, "No steel can pierce the human heart so chillingly as a period at the right moment," a pun on Stalin's name as "the man of steel." Babel's brave affirmation of individuality was unacceptable to the Soviet authorities, and in May 1939 he was arrested and disappeared into a concentration camp.

Isaac Babel

My First Goose

Translated by Walter Morison

Savitsky, Commander of the VI Division, rose when he saw me, and I wondered at the beauty of his giant's body. He rose, the purple of his riding-breeches and the crimson of his little tilted cap and the decorations stuck on his chest cleaving the hut as a standard cleaves the sky. A smell of scent and sickly sweet freshness of soap emanated from him. His long legs were like girls sheathed to the neck in shining riding-boots.

He smiled at me, struck his riding-whip on the table, and drew toward him an order that the Chief of Staff had just finished dictating. It was an order for Ivan Chesnokov to advance on Chugunov-Dobryvodka with the regiment entrusted to him, to make contact with the enemy and destroy the same.

"For which destruction," the Commander began to write, smearing the whole sheet, "I make this same Chesnokov entirely responsible, up to and including the supreme penalty, and will if necessary strike him down on the spot; which you, Chesnokov, who have been working with me at the front for some months now, cannot doubt."

The Commander signed the order with a flourish, tossed it to his orderlies, and turned upon me grey eyes that danced with merriment.

I handed him a paper with my appointment to the Staff of the Division.

"Put it down in the Order of the Day," said the Commander. "Put him down for every satisfaction save the front one. Can you read and write?"

"Yes, I can read and write," I replied, envying the flower and iron of that youthfulness. "I graduated in law from St. Petersburg University."

"Oh, are you one of those grinds?" he laughed. "Specs on your nose, too! What a nasty little object! They've sent you along without making any inquiries; and this is a hot place for specs. Think you'll get on with us?"

"I'll get on all right," I answered, and went off to the village with the quartermaster to find a billet for the night.

The quartermaster carried my trunk on his shoulder. Before us stretched the village street. The dying sun, round and yellow as a pumpkin, was giving up its roseate ghost to the skies.

We went up to a hut painted over with garlands. The quartermaster stopped, and said suddenly, with a guilty smile:

"Nuisance with specs. Can't do anything to stop it, either. Not a life for the brainy type here. But you go and mess up a lady, and a good lady too, and you'll have the boys patting you on the back."

He hesitated, my little trunk on his shoulder; then he came quite close to me, only to dart away again despairingly and run to the nearest yard. Cossacks were sitting there, shaving one another.

"Here, you soldiers," said the quartermaster, setting my little trunk down on the ground. "Comrade Savitsky's orders are that you're to take this chap in your billets, so no nonsense about it, because the chap's been through a lot in the learning line."

The quartermaster, purple in the face, left us without looking back. I raised my hand to my cap and saluted the Cossacks. A lad with long straight flaxen hair and the handsome face of the Ryazan Cossacks went over to my little trunk and tossed it out at the gate. Then he turned his back on me and with remarkable skill emitted a series of shameful noises.

"To your guns — number double-zero!" an older Cossack shouted at him, and burst out laughing. "Running fire!"

His guileless art exhausted, the lad made off. Then, crawling over the ground, I began to gather together the manuscripts and tattered garments that had fallen out of the trunk. I gathered them up and carried them to the other end of the yard. Near the hut, on a brick stove, stood a cauldron in which pork was cooking. The steam that rose from it was like the far-off smoke of home in the village, and it mingled hunger with desperate loneliness in my head. Then I covered my little broken trunk with hay, turning it into a pillow, and lay down on the ground to read in *Pravda* Lenin's speech at the Second Congress of the Comintern. The sun fell upon me from behind the toothed hillocks, the Cossacks trod on my feet, the lad made fun of me untiringly, the beloved lines came toward me along a thorny path and could not reach me. Then I put aside the paper and went out to the landlady, who was spinning on the porch.

"Landlady," I said, "I've got to eat."

The old woman raised to me the diffused whites of her purblind eyes and lowered them again.

"Comrade," she said, after a pause, "what with all this going on, I want to go and hang myself."

"Christ!" I muttered, and pushed the old woman in the chest with my fist. "You don't suppose I'm going to go into explanations with you, do you?"

And turning around I saw somebody's sword lying within reach. A severe-looking goose was waddling about the yard, inoffensively preening its feathers. I overtook it and pressed it to the ground. Its head cracked beneath my boot, cracked and emptied itself. The white neck lay stretched out in the dung, the wings twitched.

"Christ!" I said, digging into the goose with my sword. "Go and cook it for me, landlady."

Her blind eyes and glasses glistening, the old woman picked up the slaughtered bird, wrapped it in her apron, and started to bear it off toward the kitchen.

"Comrade," she said to me, after a while. "I want to go and hang myself." And she closed the door behind her.

The Cossacks in the yard were already sitting around their cauldron. They sat motionless, stiff as heathen priests at a sacrifice, and had not looked at the goose.

"The lad's all right," one of them said, winking and scooping up the cabbage soup with his spoon.

The Cossacks commenced their supper with all the elegance and re- straint of peasants who respect one another. And I wiped the sword with sand, went out at the gate, and came in again, depressed. Already the moon hung above the yard like a cheap earring.

"Hey, you," suddenly said Surovkov, an older Cossack. "Sit down and feed with us till your goose is done."

He produced a spare spoon from his boot and handed it to me. We supped up the cabbage soup they had made, and ate the pork.

"What's in the newspaper?" asked the flaxen-haired lad, making room for me.

"Lenin writes in the paper," I said, pulling out *Pravda*. "Lenin writes that there's a shortage of everything."

And loudly, like a triumphant man hard of hearing, I read Lenin's speech out to the Cossacks.

Evening wrapped about me the quickening moisture of its twilight sheets; evening laid a mother's hand upon my burning forehead. I read on and rejoiced, spying out exultingly the secret curve of Lenin's straight line.

"Truth tickles everyone's nostrils," said Surovkov, when I had come to the end. "The question is, how's it to be pulled from the heap. But he goes and strikes at it straight off like a hen pecking at a grain!"

This remark about Lenin was made by Surovkov, platoon commander of the Staff Squadron; after which we lay down to sleep in the hayloft. We slept, all six of us, beneath a wooden roof that let in the stars, warming one another, our legs intermingled. I dreamed: and in my dreams saw women. But my heart, stained with bloodshed, grated and brimmed over.   [1925]

JAMES BALDWIN *(1924–1987) was born the son of a clergyman in Harlem, where he attended Public School 24, Frederick Douglass Junior High School, and DeWitt Clinton High School. While still a high school student he preached at the Fireside Pentecostal Assembly, but when he was seventeen he renounced the ministry. Two years later, living in Greenwich Village, he met Richard Wright, who encouraged him to be a writer and helped him win a Eugene Saxton Fellowship. Soon afterward Baldwin moved to France, as Wright had, to escape the stifling racial oppression he found in the United States. Although France was his more or less permanent residence until his death from cancer nearly forty years later, Baldwin regarded himself as a "commuter" rather than an expatriate. He said,*

> *Only white Americans can consider themselves to be expatriates. Once I found myself on the other side of the ocean, I could see where I came from very clearly, and I could see that I carried myself, which is my home, with me. You can never escape that. I am the grandson of a slave, and I am a writer. I must deal with both.*

Baldwin began his career by publishing novels and short stories. In 1953 Go Tell It on the Mountain, *his first novel, was highly acclaimed. It was based on his childhood in Harlem and his fear of his tyrannical father. Baldwin's frank depiction of homosexuality in the novels* Giovanni's Room *(1956) and* Another Country *(1962) drew criticism, but during the civil rights movement a few years later, he established himself as a brilliant essayist. In his lifetime Baldwin published several collections of essays, three more novels, and a book of five short stories,* Going to Meet the Man *(1965).*

"Sonny's Blues," from that collection, is one of Baldwin's strongest psychological dramatizations of the frustrations of African American life in our times. Like Wright's autobiographical books, Baldwin's work is an inspiration to young writers struggling to express their experience of racism. The African writer Chinua Achebe has said that "as long as injustice exists . . . the words of James Baldwin will be there to bear witness and to inspire and elevate the struggle for human freedom."

RELATED COMMENTARY: *James Baldwin, "Autobiographical Notes," page 1385.*

JAMES BALDWIN

Sonny's Blues

I read about it in the paper, in the subway, on my way to work. I read it, and I couldn't believe it, and I read it again. Then perhaps I just stared at it, at the newsprint spelling out his name, spelling out the story. I stared at it in the swinging lights of the subway car, and in the faces and bodies of the people, and in my own face, trapped in the darkness which roared outside.

It was not to be believed and I kept telling myself that, as I walked from the subway station to the high school. And at the same time I couldn't doubt it. I was scared, scared for Sonny. He became real to me again. A great block of ice got settled in my belly and kept melting there slowly all day long, while I taught my classes algebra. It was a special kind of ice. It kept melting, sending trickles of ice water all up and down my veins, but it never got less. Sometimes it hardened and seemed to expand until I felt my guts were going to come spilling out or that I was going to choke or scream. This would always be at a moment when I was remembering some specific thing Sonny had once said or done.

When he was about as old as the boys in my classes his face had been bright and open, there was a lot of copper in it; and he'd had wonderfully direct brown eyes, and great gentleness and privacy. I wondered what he looked like now. He had been picked up, the evening before, in a raid on an apartment downtown, for peddling and using heroin.

I couldn't believe it: but what I mean by that is that I couldn't find any room for it anywhere inside me. I had kept it outside me for a long time. I hadn't wanted to know. I had had suspicions, but I didn't name them, I kept putting them away. I told myself that Sonny was wild, but he wasn't crazy. And he'd always been a good boy, he hadn't ever turned hard or evil or disrespectful, the way kids can, so quick, so quick, especially in Harlem. I didn't want to believe that I'd ever see my brother going down, coming to nothing, all that light in his face gone out, in the condition I'd already seen so many others. Yet it had happened and here I was, talking about algebra to a lot of boys who might, every one of them for all I knew, be popping off needles every time they went to the head. Maybe it did more for them than algebra could.

I was sure that the first time Sonny had ever had horse, he couldn't have been much older than these boys were now. These boys, now, were living as we'd been living then, they were growing up with a rush and their heads bumped abruptly against the low ceiling of their actual possibilities. They were filled with rage. All they really knew were two darknesses, the darkness of their lives, which was now closing in on them, and the darkness of the movies, which had blinded them to that other darkness, and in which they now, vindictively, dreamed, at once more together than they were at any other time, and more alone.

When the last bell rang, the last class ended, I let out my breath. It seemed I'd been holding it for all that time. My clothes were wet — I may have looked as though I'd been sitting in a steam bath, all dressed up, all afternoon. I sat alone in the classroom a long time. I listened to the boys outside, downstairs, shouting and cursing and laughing. Their laughter struck me for perhaps the first time. It was not the joyous laughter which — God knows why — one associates with children. It was mocking and insular, its intent to denigrate. It was disenchanted, and in this, also, lay the authority of their curses. Perhaps I was listening to them because I was thinking about my brother and in them I heard my brother. And myself.

One boy was whistling a tune, at once very complicated and very simple, it seemed to be pouring out of him as though he were a bird, and it sounded very cool and moving through all that harsh, bright air, only just holding its own through all those other sounds.

I stood up and walked over to the window and looked down into the courtyard. It was the beginning of the spring and the sap was rising in the boys. A teacher passed through them every now and again, quickly, as though he or she couldn't wait to get out of that courtyard, to get those boys out of their sight and off their minds. I started collecting my stuff. I thought I'd better get home and talk to Isabel.

The courtyard was almost deserted by the time I got downstairs. I saw this boy standing in the shadow of a doorway, looking just like Sonny. I almost called his name. Then I saw that it wasn't Sonny, but somebody we used to know, a boy from around our block. He'd been Sonny's friend. He'd never been mine, having been too young for me, and, anyway, I'd never liked him. And now, even though he was a grown-up man, he still hung around that block, still spent hours on the street corners, was always high and raggy. I used to run into him from time to time and he'd often work around to asking me for a quarter or fifty cents. He always had some real good excuse, too, and I always gave it to him, I don't know why.

But now, abruptly, I hated him. I couldn't stand the way he looked at me, partly like a dog, partly like a cunning child. I wanted to ask him what the hell he was doing in the school courtyard.

He sort of shuffled over to me, and he said, "I see you got the papers. So you already know about it."

"You mean about Sonny? Yes, I already know about it. How come they didn't get you?"

He grinned. It made him repulsive and it also brought to mind what he'd looked like as a kid. "I wasn't there. I stay away from them people."

"Good for you." I offered him a cigarette and I watched him through the smoke. "You come all the way down here just to tell me about Sonny?"

"That's right." He was sort of shaking his head and his eyes looked strange, as though they were about to cross. The bright sun deadened his damp dark brown skin and it made his eyes look yellow and showed up the dirt in his kinked hair. He smelled funky. I moved a little away from him and I said, "Well, thanks. But I already know about it and I got to get home."

"I'll walk you a little ways," he said. We started walking. There were a couple of kids still loitering in the courtyard and one of them said goodnight to me and looked strangely at the boy beside me.

"What're you going to do?" he asked me. "I mean, about Sonny?"

"Look. I haven't seen Sonny for over a year. I'm not sure I'm going to do anything. Anyway, what the hell *can* I do?"

"That's right," he said quickly, "ain't nothing you can do. Can't much help old Sonny no more, I guess."

It was what I was thinking and so it seemed to me he had no right to say it.

"I'm surprised at Sonny, though," he went on — he had a funny way of talking, he looked straight ahead as though he were talking to himself — "I thought Sonny was a smart boy, I thought he was too smart to get hung."

"I guess he thought so too," I said sharply, "and that's how he got hung. And now about you? You're pretty goddamn smart, I bet."

Then he looked directly at me, just for a minute. "I ain't smart," he said. "If I was smart, I'd have reached for a pistol a long time ago."

"Look. Don't tell *me* your sad story, if it was up to me, I'd give you one." Then I felt guilty — guilty, probably, for never having supposed that the poor bastard *had* a story of his own, much less a sad one, and I asked, quickly, "What's going to happen to him now?"

He didn't answer this. He was off by himself some place. "Funny thing," he said, and from his tone we might have been discussing the quickest way to get to Brooklyn, "when I saw the papers this morning, the first thing I asked myself was if I had anything to do with it. I felt sort of responsible."

I began to listen more carefully. The subway station was on the corner, just before us, and I stopped. He stopped, too. We were in front of a bar and he ducked slightly, peering in, but whoever he was looking for didn't seem to be there. The juke box was blasting away with something black and bouncy and I half watched the barmaid as she danced her way from the juke box to her place behind the bar. And I watched her face as she laughingly responded to something someone said to her, still keeping time to the music. When she smiled one saw the little girl, one sensed the doomed, still-struggling woman beneath the battered face of the semi-whore.

"I never *give* Sonny nothing," the boy said finally, "but a long time ago I come to school high and Sonny asked me how it felt." He paused, I couldn't bear to watch him, I watched the barmaid, and I listened to the music which seemed to be causing the pavement to shake. "I told him it felt great." The music stopped, the barmaid paused and watched the juke box until the music began again. "It did."

All this was carrying me some place I didn't want to go. I certainly didn't want to know how it felt. It filled everything, the people, the houses, the music, the dark, quicksilver barmaid, with menace; and this menace was their reality.

"What's going to happen to him now?" I asked again.

"They'll send him away some place and they'll try to cure him." He shook his head. "Maybe he'll even think he's kicked the habit. Then they'll let him loose" — he gestured, throwing his cigarette into the gutter. "That's all."

"What do you mean, that's *all*?"

But I knew what he meant.

"I *mean*, that's *all*." He turned his head and looked at me, pulling down the corners of his mouth. "Don't you know what I mean?" he asked, softly.

"How the hell *would* I know what you mean?" I almost whispered it, I don't know why.

"That's right," he said to the air, "how would *he* know what I mean?" He turned toward me again, patient and calm, and yet I somehow felt him shaking, shaking as though he were going to fall apart. I felt that ice in my guts again, the dread I'd felt all afternoon; and again I watched the barmaid, moving about the bar, washing glasses, and singing. "Listen. They'll let him out and then it'll just start all over again. That's what I mean."

"You mean — they'll let him out. And then he'll just start working his way back in again. You mean he'll never kick the habit. Is that what you mean?"

"That's right," he said, cheerfully. "*You* see what I mean."

"Tell me," I said at last, "why does he want to die? He must want to die, he's killing himself, why does he want to die?"

He looked at me in surprise. He licked his lips. "He don't want to die. He wants to live. Don't nobody want to die, ever."

Then I wanted to ask him — too many things. He could not have answered, or if he had, I could not have borne the answers. I started walking. "Well, I guess it's none of my business."

"It's going to be rough on old Sonny," he said. We reached the subway station. "This is your station?" he asked. I nodded. I took one step down. "Damn!" he said, suddenly. I looked up at him. He grinned again. "Damn it if I didn't leave all my money home. You ain't got a dollar on you, have you? Just for a couple of days, is all."

All at once something inside gave and threatened to come pouring out of me. I didn't hate him any more. I felt that in another moment I'd start crying like a child.

"Sure," I said. "Don't sweat." I looked in my wallet and didn't have a dollar, I only had a five. "Here," I said. "That hold you?"

He didn't look at it — he didn't want to look at it. A terrible closed look came over his face, as though he were keeping the number on the bill a secret from him and me. "Thanks," he said, and now he was dying to see me go. "Don't worry about Sonny. Maybe I'll write him or something."

"Sure," I said. "You do that. So long."

"Be seeing you," he said. I went on down the steps.

And I didn't write Sonny or send him anything for a long time. When I finally did, it was just after my little girl died, he wrote me back a letter which made me feel like a bastard.

Here's what he said:

> Dear brother,
> You don't know how much I needed to hear from you. I wanted
> to write you many a time but I dug how much I must have hurt you
> and so I didn't write. But now I feel like a man who's been trying to
> climb up out of some deep, real deep and funky hole and just saw the
> sun up there, outside. I got to get outside.
> I can't tell you much about how I got here. I mean I don't know
> how to tell you. I guess I was afraid of something or I was trying to
> escape from something and you know I have never been very strong
> in the head (smile). I'm glad Mama and Daddy are dead and can't see
> what's happened to their son and I swear if I'd known what I was
> doing I would never have hurt you so, you and a lot of other fine
> people who were nice to me and who believed in me.
> I don't want you to think it had anything to do with me being a
> musician. It's more than that. Or maybe less than that. I can't get
> anything straight in my head down here and I try not to think about
> what's going to happen to me when I get outside again. Sometime I
> think I'm going to flip and *never* get outside and sometime I think I'll
> come straight back. I tell you one thing, though, I'd rather blow my
> brains out than go through this again. But that's what they all say, so
> they tell me. If I tell you when I'm coming to New York and if you
> could meet me, I sure would appreciate it. Give my love to Isabel and
> the kids and I was sure sorry to hear about little Gracie. I wish I could
> be like Mama and say the Lord's will be done, but I don't know it
> seems to me that trouble is the one thing that never does get stopped
> and I don't know what good it does to blame it on the Lord. But
> maybe it does some good if you believe it.
>
> > Your brother,
> > Sonny

Then I kept in constant touch with him and I sent him whatever I could
and I went to meet him when he came back to New York. When I saw him
many things I thought I had forgotten came flooding back to me. This was
because I had begun, finally, to wonder about Sonny, about the life that Sonny
lived inside. This life, whatever it was, had made him older and thinner and
it had deepened the distant stillness in which he had always moved. He
looked very unlike my baby brother. Yet, when he smiled, when we shook
hands, the baby brother I'd never known looked out from the depths of his
private life, like an animal waiting to be coaxed into the light.

"How you been keeping?" he asked me.

"All right. And you?"

"Just fine." He was smiling all over his face. "It's good to see you again."

"It's good to see you."

The seven years' difference in our ages lay between us like a chasm: I
wondered if these years would ever operate between us as a bridge. I was
remembering, and it made it hard to catch my breath, that I had been there
when he was born; and I had heard the first words he had ever spoken. When

he started to walk, he walked from our mother straight to me. I caught him just before he fell when he took the first steps he ever took in this world.

"How's Isabel?"

"Just fine. She's dying to see you."

"And the boys?"

"They're fine, too. They're anxious to see their uncle."

"Oh, come on. You know they don't remember me."

"Are you kidding? Of course they remember you."

He grinned again. We got into a taxi. We had a lot to say to each other, far too much to know how to begin.

As the taxi began to move, I asked, "You still want to go to India?"

He laughed. "You still remember that. Hell, no. This place is Indian enough for me."

"It used to belong to them," I said.

And he laughed again. "They damn sure knew what they were doing when they got rid of it."

Years ago, when he was around fourteen, he'd been all hipped on the idea of going to India. He read books about people sitting on rocks, naked, in all kinds of weather, but mostly bad, naturally, and walking barefoot through hot coals and arriving at wisdom. I used to say that it sounded to me as though they were getting away from wisdom as fast as they could. I think he sort of looked down on me for that.

"Do you mind," he asked, "if we have the driver drive alongside the park? On the west side — I haven't seen the city in so long."

"Of course not," I said. I was afraid that I might sound as though I were humoring him, but I hoped he wouldn't take it that way.

So we drove along, between the green of the park and the stony, lifeless elegance of hotels and apartment buildings, toward the vivid, killing streets of our childhood. These streets hadn't changed, though housing projects jutted up out of them now like rocks in the middle of a boiling sea. Most of the houses in which we had grown up had vanished, as had the stores from which we had stolen, the basements in which we had first tried sex, the rooftops from which we had hurled tin cans and bricks. But houses exactly like the houses of our past yet dominated the landscape, boys exactly like the boys we once had been found themselves smothering in these houses, came down into the streets for light and air and found themselves encircled by disaster. Some escaped the trap, most didn't. Those who got out always left something of themselves behind, as some animals amputate a leg and leave it in the trap. It might be said, perhaps, that I had escaped, after all, I was a school teacher; or that Sonny had, he hadn't lived in Harlem for years. Yet, as the cab moved uptown through streets which seemed, with a rush, to darken with dark people, and as I covertly studied Sonny's face, it came to me that what we both were seeking through our separate cab windows was that part of ourselves which had been left behind. It's always at the hour of trouble and confrontation that the missing member aches.

We hit 110th Street and started rolling up Lenox Avenue. And I'd known this avenue all my life, but it seemed to me again, as it had seemed on the day I'd first heard about Sonny's trouble, filled with a hidden menace which was its very breath of life.

"We almost there," said Sonny.

"Almost." We were both too nervous to say anything more.

We live in a housing project. It hasn't been up long. A few days after it was up it seemed uninhabitably new, now, of course, it's already rundown. It looks like a parody of the good, clean, faceless life — God knows the people who live in it do their best to make it a parody. The beat-looking grass lying around isn't enough to make their lives green, the hedges will never hold out the streets, and they know it. The big windows fool no one, they aren't big enough to make space out of no space. They don't bother with the windows, they watch the TV screen instead. The playground is most popular with the children who don't play at jacks, or skip rope, or roller skate, or swing, and they can be found in it after dark. We moved in partly because it's not too far from where I teach, and partly for the kids; but it's really just like the houses in which Sonny and I grew up. The same things happen, they'll have the same things to remember. The moment Sonny and I started into the house I had the feeling that I was simply bringing him back into the danger he had almost died trying to escape.

Sonny has never been talkative. So I don't know why I was sure he'd be dying to talk to me when supper was over the first night. Everything went fine, the oldest boy remembered him, and the youngest boy liked him, and Sonny had remembered to bring something for each of them; and Isabel, who is really much nicer than I am, more open and giving, had gone to a lot of trouble about dinner and was genuinely glad to see him. And she's always been able to tease Sonny in a way that I haven't. It was nice to see her face so vivid again and to hear her laugh and watch her make Sonny laugh. She wasn't, or, anyway, she didn't seem to be, at all uneasy or embarrassed. She chatted as though there were no subject which had to be avoided and she got Sonny past his first, faint stiffness. And thank God she was there, for I was filled with that icy dread again. Everything I did seemed awkward to me, and everything I said sounded freighted with hidden meaning. I was trying to remember everything I'd heard about dope addiction and I couldn't help watching Sonny for signs. I wasn't doing it out of malice. I was trying to find out something about my brother. I was dying to hear him tell me he was safe.

"Safe!" my father grunted, whenever Mama suggested trying to move to a neighborhood which might be safer for children. "Safe, hell! Ain't no place safe for kids, nor nobody."

He always went on like this, but he wasn't, ever, really as bad as he sounded, not even on weekends, when he got drunk. As a matter of fact, he was always on the lookout for "something a little better," but he died before he found it. He died suddenly, during a drunken weekend in the middle of the war, when Sonny was fifteen. He and Sonny hadn't ever got on too well. And this was partly because Sonny was the apple of his father's eye. It was because he loved Sonny so much and was frightened for him, that he was always fighting with him. It doesn't do any good to fight with Sonny. Sonny just moves back, inside himself, where he can't be reached. But the principal reason that they never hit it off is that they were so much alike. Daddy was big and rough and loud-talking, just the opposite of Sonny, but they both had — that same privacy.

Mama tried to tell me something about this, just after Daddy died. I was home on leave from the army.

This was the last time I ever saw my mother alive. Just the same, this picture gets all mixed up in my mind with pictures I had of her when she was younger. The way I always see her is the way she used to be on a Sunday afternoon, say, when the old folks were talking after the big Sunday dinner. I always see her wearing pale blue. She'd be sitting on the sofa. And my father would be sitting in the easy chair, not far from her. And the living room would be full of church folks and relatives. There they sit, in chairs all around the living room, and the night is creeping up outside, but nobody knows it yet. You can see the darkness growing against the windowpanes and you hear the street noises every now and again, or maybe the jangling beat of a tambourine from one of the churches close by, but it's real quiet in the room. For a moment nobody's talking, but every face looks darkening, like the sky outside. And my mother rocks a little from the waist, and my father's eyes are closed. Everyone is looking at something a child can't see. For a minute they've forgotten the children. Maybe a kid is lying on the rug, half asleep. Maybe somebody's got a kid in his lap and is absent-mindedly stroking the kid's head. Maybe there's a kid, quiet and big-eyed, curled up in a big chair in the corner. The silence, the darkness coming, and the darkness in the faces frightens the child obscurely. He hopes that the hand which strokes his forehead will never stop — will never die. He hopes that there will never come a time when the old folks won't be sitting around the living room, talking about where they've come from, and what they've seen, and what's happened to them and their kinfolk.

But something deep and watchful in the child knows that this is bound to end, is already ending. In a moment someone will get up and turn on the light. Then the old folks will remember the children and they won't talk any more that day. And when light fills the room, the child is filled with darkness. He knows that everytime this happens he's moved just a little closer to that darkness outside. The darkness outside is what the old folks have been talking about. It's what they've come from. It's what they endure. The child knows that they won't talk any more because if he knows too much about what's happened to *them*, he'll know too much too soon, about what's going to happen to *him*.

The last time I talked to my mother, I remember I was restless. I wanted to get out and see Isabel. We weren't married then and we had a lot to straighten out between us.

There Mama sat, in black, by the window. She was humming an old church song, *Lord, you brought me from a long ways off.* Sonny was out somewhere. Mama kept watching the streets.

"I don't know," she said, "if I'll ever see you again, after you go off from here. But I hope you'll remember the things I tried to teach you."

"Don't talk like that," I said, and smiled. "You'll be here a long time yet."

She smiled, too, but she said nothing. She was quiet for a long time. And I said, "Mama, don't you worry about nothing. I'll be writing all the time, and you be getting the checks. . . ."

"I want to talk to you about your brother," she said, suddenly. "If anything happens to me he ain't going to have nobody to look out for him."

"Mama," I said, "ain't nothing going to happen to you *or* Sonny. Sonny's all right. He's a good boy and he's got good sense."

"It ain't a question of his being a good boy," Mama said, "nor of his having good sense. It ain't only the bad ones, nor yet the dumb ones that gets sucked under." She stopped, looking at me. "Your Daddy once had a brother," she said, and she smiled in a way that made me feel she was in pain. "You didn't never know that, did you?"

"No," I said, "I never knew that," and I watched her face.

"Oh, yes," she said, "your Daddy had a brother." She looked out of the window again. "I know you never saw your Daddy cry. But *I* did — many a time, through all these years."

I asked her, "What happened to his brother? How come nobody's ever talked about him?"

This was the first time I ever saw my mother look old.

"His brother got killed," she said, "when he was just a little younger than you are now. I knew him. He was a fine boy. He was maybe a little full of the devil, but he didn't mean nobody no harm."

Then she stopped and the room was silent, exactly as it had sometimes been on those Sunday afternoons. Mama kept looking out into the streets.

"He used to have a job in the mill," she said, "and, like all young folks, he just liked to perform on Saturday nights. Saturday nights, him and your father would drift around to different places, go to dances and things like that, or just sit around with people they knew, and your father's brother would sing, he had a fine voice, and play along with himself on his guitar. Well, this particular Saturday night, him and your father was coming home from some place, and they were both a little drunk and there was a moon that night, it was bright like day. Your father's brother was feeling kind of good, and he was whistling to himself, and he had his guitar slung over his shoulder. They was coming down a hill and beneath them was a road that turned off from the highway. Well, your father's brother, being always kind of frisky, decided to run down this hill, and he did, with that guitar banging and clanging behind him, and he ran across the road, and he was making water behind a tree. And your father was sort of amused at him and he was still coming down the hill, kind of slow. Then he heard a car motor and that same minute his brother stepped from behind the tree, into the road, in the moonlight. And he started to cross the road. And your father started to run down the hill, he says he don't know why. This car was full of white men. They was all drunk, and when they seen your father's brother they let out a great whoop and holler and they aimed the car straight at him. They was having fun, they just wanted to scare him, the way they do sometimes, you know. But they was drunk. And

I guess the boy, being drunk, too, and scared, kind of lost his head. By the time he jumped it was too late. Your father says he heard his brother scream when the car rolled over him, and he heard the wood of that guitar when it give, and he heard them strings go flying, and he heard them white men shouting, and the car kept on a-going and it ain't stopped till this day. And, time your father got down the hill, his brother weren't nothing but blood and pulp."

Tears were gleaming on my mother's face. There wasn't anything I could say.

"He never mentioned it," she said, "because I never let him mention it before you children. Your Daddy was like a crazy man that night and for many a night thereafter. He says he never in his life seen anything as dark as that road after the lights of that car had gone away. Weren't nothing, weren't nobody on that road, just your Daddy and his brother and that busted guitar. Oh, yes. Your Daddy never did really get right again. Till the day he died he weren't sure but that every white man he saw was the man that killed his brother."

She stopped and took out her handkerchief and dried her eyes and looked at me.

"I ain't telling you all this," she said, "to make you scared or bitter or to make you hate nobody. I'm telling you this because you got a brother. And the world ain't changed."

I guess I didn't want to believe this. I guess she saw this in my face. She turned away from me, toward the window again, searching those streets.

"But I praise my Redeemer," she said at last, "that He called your Daddy home before me. I ain't saying it to throw no flowers at myself, but, I declare, it keeps me from feeling too cast down to know I helped your father get safely through this world. Your father always acted like he was the roughest, strongest man on earth. And everybody took him to be like that. But if he hadn't had *me* there — to see his tears!"

She was crying again. Still, I couldn't move. I said, "Lord, Lord, Mama, I didn't know it was like that."

"Oh, honey," she said, "there's a lot that you don't know. But you are going to find it out." She stood up from the window and came over to me. "You got to hold on to your brother," she said, "and don't let him fall, no matter what it looks like is happening to him and no matter how evil you gets with him. You going to be evil with him many a time. But don't you forget what I told you, you hear?"

"I won't forget," I said. "Don't you worry, I won't forget. I won't let nothing happen to Sonny."

My mother smiled as though she were amused at something she saw in my face. Then, "You may not be able to stop nothing from happening. But you got to let him know you's *there*."

Two days later I was married, and then I was gone. And I had a lot of things on my mind and I pretty well forgot my promise to Mama until I got shipped home on a special furlough for her funeral.

And, after the funeral, with just Sonny and me alone in the empty kitchen, I tried to find out something about him.

"What do you want to do?" I asked him.

"I'm going to be a musician," he said.

For he had graduated, in the time I had been away, from dancing to the juke box to finding out who was playing what, and what they were doing with it, and he had bought himself a set of drums.

"You mean, you want to be a drummer?" I somehow had the feeling that being a drummer might be all right for other people but not for my brother Sonny.

"I don't think," he said, looking at me very gravely, "that I'll ever be a good drummer. But I think I can play a piano."

I frowned. I'd never played the role of the older brother quite so seriously before, had scarcely ever, in fact, *asked* Sonny a damn thing. I sensed myself in the presence of something I didn't really know how to handle, didn't understand. So I made my frown a little deeper as I asked: "What kind of musician do you want to be?"

He grinned. "How many kinds do you think there are?"

"Be *serious*," I said.

He laughed, throwing his head back, and then looked at me. "I *am* serious."

"Well, then, for Christ's sake, stop kidding around and answer a serious question. I mean, do you want to be a concert pianist, you want to play classical music and all that, or — or what?" Long before I finished he was laughing again. "For Christ's *sake*, Sonny!"

He sobered, but with difficulty. "I'm sorry. But you sound so — *scared!*" and he was off again.

"Well, you may think it's funny now, baby, but it's not going to be so funny when you have to make your living at it, let me tell you *that*." I was furious because I knew he was laughing at me and I didn't know why.

"No," he said, very sober now, and afraid, perhaps, that he'd hurt me, "I don't want to be a classical pianist. That isn't what interests me. I mean" — he paused, looking hard at me, as though his eyes would help me to understand, and then gestured helplessly, as though perhaps his hand would help — "I mean, I'll have a lot of studying to do, and I'll have to study *everything*, but, I mean, I want to play *with* — jazz musicians." He stopped. "I want to play jazz," he said.

Well, the word had never before sounded as heavy, as real, as it sounded that afternoon in Sonny's mouth. I just looked at him and I was probably frowning a real frown by this time. I simply couldn't see why on earth he'd want to spend his time hanging around nightclubs, clowning around on bandstands, while people pushed each other around a dance floor. It seemed — beneath him, somehow. I had never thought about it before, had never been forced to, but I suppose I had always put jazz musicians in a class with what Daddy called "good-time people."

"Are you *serious*?"

"Hell, *yes*, I'm serious."

He looked more helpless than ever, and annoyed, and deeply hurt.

I suggested, helpfully: "You mean — like Louis Armstrong?"

His face closed as though I'd struck him. "No. I'm not talking about none of that old-time, down home crap."

"Well, look, Sonny, I'm sorry, don't get mad. I just don't altogether get it, that's all. Name somebody — you know, a jazz musician you admire."

"Bird."

"Who?"

"Bird! Charlie Parker! Don't they teach you nothing in the goddamn army?"

I lit a cigarette. I was surprised and then a little amused to discover that I was trembling. "I've been out of touch," I said. "You'll have to be patient with me. Now. Who's this Parker character?"

"He's just one of the greatest jazz musicians alive," said Sonny, sullenly, his hands in his pockets, his back to me. "Maybe *the* greatest," he added, bitterly, "that's probably why *you* never heard of him."

"All right," I said, "I'm ignorant. I'm sorry. I'll go out and buy all the cat's records right away, all right?"

"It don't," said Sonny, with dignity, "make any difference to me. I don't care what you listen to. Don't do me no favors."

I was beginning to realize that I'd never seen him so upset before. With another part of my mind I was thinking that this would probably turn out to be one of those things kids go through and that I shouldn't make it seem important by pushing it too hard. Still, I didn't think it would do any harm to ask: "Doesn't all this take a lot of time? Can you make a living at it?"

He turned back to me and half leaned, half sat, on the kitchen table. "Everything takes time," he said, "and — well, yes, sure, I can make a living at it. But what I don't seem to be able to make you understand is that it's the only thing I want to do."

"Well, Sonny," I said, gently, "you know people can't always do exactly what they *want* to do — "

"*No*, I don't know that," said Sonny, surprising me. "I think people *ought* to do what they want to do, what else are they alive for?"

"You getting to be a big boy," I said desperately, "it's time you started thinking about your future."

"I'm thinking about my future," said Sonny, grimly. "I think about it all the time."

I gave up. I decided, if he didn't change his mind, that we could always talk about it later. "In the meantime," I said, "you got to finish school." We had already decided that he'd have to move in with Isabel and her folks. I knew this wasn't the ideal arrangement because Isabel's folks are inclined to be dicty and they hadn't especially wanted Isabel to marry me. But I didn't know what else to do. "And we have to get you fixed up at Isabel's."

There was a long silence. He moved from the kitchen table to the window. "That's a terrible idea. You know it yourself."

"Do you have a *better* idea?"

He just walked up and down the kitchen for a minute. He was as tall as I was. He had started to shave. I suddenly had the feeling that I didn't know him at all.

He stopped at the kitchen table and picked up my cigarettes. Looking at me with a kind of mocking, amused defiance, he put one between his lips. "You mind?"

"You smoking already?"

He lit the cigarette and nodded, watching me through the smoke. "I just wanted to see if I'd have the courage to smoke in front of you." He grinned and blew a great cloud of smoke to the ceiling. "It was easy." He looked at my face. "Come on, now. I bet you was smoking at my age, tell the truth."

I didn't say anything but the truth was on my face, and he laughed. But now there was something very strained in his laugh. "Sure. And I bet that ain't all you was doing."

He was frightening me a little. "Cut the crap," I said. "We already decided that you was going to go and live at Isabel's. Now what's got into you all of a sudden?"

"*You* decided it," he pointed out. "*I* didn't decide nothing." He stopped in front of me, leaning against the stove, arms loosely folded. "Look, brother. I don't want to stay in Harlem no more, I really don't." He was very earnest. He looked at me, then over toward the kitchen window. There was something in his eyes I'd never seen before, some thoughtfulness, some worry all his own. He rubbed the muscle of one arm. "It's time I was getting out of here."

"Where do you want to *go*, Sonny?"

"I want to join the army. Or the navy, I don't care. If I say I'm old enough, they'll believe me."

Then I got mad. It was because I was so scared. "You must be crazy. You goddamn fool, what the hell do you want to go and join the *army* for?"

"I just told you. To get out of Harlem."

"Sonny, you haven't even finished *school*. And if you really want to be a musician, how do you expect to study if you're in the *army*?"

He looked at me, trapped, and in anguish. "There's ways. I might be able to work out some kind of deal. Anyway, I'll have the G.I. Bill when I come out."

"*If* you come out." We stared at each other. "Sonny, please. Be reasonable. I know the setup is far from perfect. But we got to do the best we can."

"I ain't learning nothing in school," he said. "Even when I go." He turned away from me and opened the window and threw his cigarette out into the narrow alley. I watched his back. "At least, I ain't learning nothing you'd want me to learn." He slammed the window so hard I thought the glass would fly out, and turned back to me. "And I'm sick of the stink of these garbage cans!"

"Sonny," I said, "I know how you feel. But if you don't finish school now, you're going to be sorry later that you didn't." I grabbed him by the shoulders. "And you only got another year. It ain't so bad. And I'll come back and I swear I'll help you do *whatever* you want to do. Just try to put up with it till I come back. Will you please do that? For me?"

He didn't answer and he wouldn't look at me.

"Sonny. You hear me?"

He pulled away. "I hear you. But you never hear anything *I* say."

I didn't know what to say to that. He looked out of the window and then back at me. "OK," he said, and sighed. "I'll try."

Then I said, trying to cheer him up a little, "They got a piano at Isabel's. You can practice on it."

And as a matter of fact, it did cheer him up for a minute. "That's right," he said to himself. "I forgot that." His face relaxed a little. But the worry, the thoughtfulness, played on it still, the way shadows play on a face which is staring into the fire.

But I thought I'd never hear the end of that piano. At first, Isabel would write me, saying how nice it was that Sonny was so serious about his music and how, as soon as he came in from school, or wherever he had been when he was supposed to be at school, he went straight to that piano and stayed there until suppertime. And, after supper, he went back to that piano and stayed there until everybody went to bed. He was at the piano all day Saturday and all day Sunday. Then he bought a record player and started playing records. He'd play one record over and over again, all day long sometimes, and he'd improvise along with it on the piano. Or he'd play one section of the record, one chord, one change, one progression, then he'd do it on the piano. Then back to the record. Then back to the piano.

Well, I really don't know how they stood it. Isabel finally confessed that it wasn't like living with a person at all, it was like living with sound. And the sound didn't make any sense to her, didn't make any sense to any of them — naturally. They began, in a way, to be afflicted by this presence that was living in their home. It was as though Sonny were some sort of god, or monster. He moved in an atmosphere which wasn't like theirs at all. They fed him and he ate, he washed himself, he walked in and out of their door; he certainly wasn't nasty or unpleasant or rude, Sonny isn't any of those things; but it was as though he were all wrapped up in some cloud, some fire, some vision all his own; and there wasn't any way to reach him.

At the same time, he wasn't really a man yet, he was still a child, and they had to watch out for him in all kinds of ways. They certainly couldn't throw him out. Neither did they dare to make a great scene about that piano because even they dimly sensed, as I sensed, from so many thousands of miles away, that Sonny was at that piano playing for his life.

But he hadn't been going to school. One day a letter came from the school board and Isabel's mother got it — there had, apparently, been other letters but Sonny had torn them up. This day, when Sonny came in, Isabel's mother showed him the letter and asked where he'd been spending his time. And she finally got it out of him that he'd been down in Greenwich Village, with musicians and other characters, in a white girl's apartment. And this scared her and she started to scream at him and what came up, once she began — though she denies it to this day — was what sacrifices they were making to give Sonny a decent home and how little he appreciated it.

Sonny didn't play the piano that day. By evening, Isabel's mother had calmed down but then there was the old man to deal with, and Isabel herself. Isabel says she did her best to be calm but she broke down and started crying. She says she just watched Sonny's face. She could tell, by watching him, what was happening with him. And what was happening was that they penetrated his cloud, they had reached him. Even if their fingers had been a thousand times more gentle than human fingers ever are, he could hardly help feeling that they had stripped him naked and were spitting on that nakedness. For he also had to see that his presence, that music, which was life or death to him, had been torture for them and that they had endured it, not at all for his sake, but only for mine. And Sonny couldn't take that. He can take it a little better today than he could then but he's still not very good at it and, frankly, I don't know anybody who is.

The silence of the next few days must have been louder than the sound of all the music ever played since time began. One morning, before she went to work, Isabel was in his room for something and she suddenly realized that all of his records were gone. And she knew for certain that he was gone. And he was. He went as far as the navy would carry him. He finally sent me a postcard from some place in Greece and that was the first I knew that Sonny was still alive. I didn't see him any more until we were both back in New York and the war had long been over.

He was a man by then, of course, but I wasn't willing to see it. He came by the house from time to time, but we fought almost every time we met. I didn't like the way he carried himself, loose and dreamlike all the time, and I didn't like his friends, and his music seemed to be merely an excuse for the life he led. It sounded just that weird and disordered.

Then we had a fight, a pretty awful fight, and I didn't see him for months. By and by I looked him up, where he was living, in a furnished room in the Village, and I tried to make it up. But there were lots of people in the room and Sonny just lay on his bed, and he wouldn't come downstairs with me, and he treated these other people as though they were his family and I weren't. So I got mad and then he got mad, and then I told him that he might just as well be dead as live the way he was living. Then he stood up and he told me not to worry about him any more in life, that he *was* dead as far as I was concerned. Then he pushed me to the door and the other people looked on as though nothing were happening, and he slammed the door behind me. I stood in the hallway, staring at the door. I heard somebody laugh in the room and then the tears came to my eyes. I started down the steps, whistling to keep from crying, I kept whistling to myself, *You going to need me, baby, one of these cold, rainy days.*

I read about Sonny's trouble in the spring. Little Grace died in the fall. She was a beautiful little girl. But she only lived a little over two years. She died of polio and she suffered. She had a slight fever for a couple of days, but it didn't seem like anything and we just kept her in bed. And we would certainly have called the doctor, but the fever dropped, she seemed to be all right. So we thought it had just been a cold. Then, one day, she was up, playing, Isabel was in the kitchen fixing lunch for the two boys when they'd come in from school, and she heard Grace fall down in the living room. When you have a lot of children you don't always start running when one of them falls, unless they start screaming or something. And, this time, Grace was quiet. Yet, Isabel says that when she heard that *thump* and then that silence, something happened in her to make her afraid. And she ran to the living room and there was little Grace on the floor, all twisted up, and the reason she hadn't screamed was that she couldn't get her breath. And when she did scream, it was the worst sound, Isabel says, that she'd ever heard in all her life, and she still hears it sometimes in her dreams. Isabel will sometimes wake me up with a low, moaning, strangled sound and I have to be quick to awaken her and hold her to me and where Isabel is weeping against me seems a mortal wound.

I think I may have written Sonny the very day that little Grace was buried. I was sitting in the living room in the dark, by myself, and I suddenly thought of Sonny. My trouble made his real.

One Saturday afternoon, when Sonny had been living with us, or, anyway, been in our house, for nearly two weeks, I found myself wandering aimlessly about the living room, drinking from a can of beer, and trying to work up the courage to search Sonny's room. He was out, he was usually out whenever I was home, and Isabel had taken the children to see their grand-parents. Suddenly I was standing still in front of the living room window, watching Seventh Avenue. The idea of searching Sonny's room made me still. I scarcely dared to admit to myself what I'd be searching for. I didn't know what I'd do if I found it. Or if I didn't.

On the sidewalk across from me, near the entrance to a barbecue joint, some people were holding an old-fashioned revival meeting. The barbecue cook, wearing a dirty white apron, his conked hair reddish and metallic in the pale sun, and a cigarette between his lips, stood in the doorway, watching them. Kids and older people paused in their errands and stood there, along with some older men and a couple of very tough-looking women who watched everything that happened on the avenue, as though they owned it, or were maybe owned by it. Well, they were watching this, too. The revival was being carried on by three sisters in black, and a brother. All they had were their voices and their Bibles and a tambourine. The brother was testifying and while he testified two of the sisters stood together, seeming to say, amen, and the third sister walked around with the tambourine outstretched and a couple of people dropped coins into it. Then the brother's testimony ended and the sister who had been taking up the collection dumped the coins into her palm and transferred them to the pocket of her long black robe. Then she raised both hands, striking the tambourine against the air, and then against one hand, and she started to sing. And the two other sisters and the brother joined in.

It was strange, suddenly, to watch, though I had been seeing these street meetings all my life. So, of course, had everybody else down there. Yet, they paused and watched and listened and I stood still at the window. *"Tis the old ship of Zion,"* they sang, and the sister with the tambourine kept a steady, jangling beat, *"it has rescued many a thousand!"* Not a soul under the sound of their voices was hearing this song for the first time, not one of them had been rescued. Nor had they seen much in the way of rescue work being done around them. Neither did they especially believe in the holiness of the three sisters and the brother, they knew too much about them, knew where they lived, and how. The woman with the tambourine, whose voice dominated the air, whose face was bright with joy, was divided by very little from the woman who stood watching her, a cigarette between her heavy, chapped lips, her hair a cuckoo's nest, her face scarred and swollen from many beatings, and her black eyes glittering like coal. Perhaps they both knew this, which was why, when, as rarely, they addressed each other, they addressed each other as Sister. As the singing filled the air the watching, listening faces underwent a change, the eyes focusing on something within; the music seemed to soothe a poison out of them; and time seemed, nearly, to fall away from the sullen, belligerent, battered faces, as though they were fleeing back to their first condition, while dreaming of their last. The barbecue cook half shook his head and smiled, and dropped his cigarette and disappeared into his joint. A man fumbled in his pockets for change and stood holding it in his hand impatiently, as though he had just remembered a pressing appointment further up the avenue. He looked furious. Then I saw Sonny, standing on the edge of the crowd. He was carrying a wide, flat notebook with a green cover, and it made him look, from where I was standing, almost like a schoolboy. The coppery sun brought out the copper in his skin, he was very faintly smiling, standing very still. Then the singing stopped, the tambourine turned into a collection plate again. The furious man dropped in his coins and vanished, so did a couple of the women, and Sonny dropped some change in the plate, looking directly at the woman with a little smile. He started across the avenue, toward the house. He has a slow, loping walk, something like the way Harlem hipsters walk, only he's imposed on this his own half-beat. I had never really noticed it before.

I stayed at the window, both relieved and apprehensive. As Sonny disappeared from my sight, they began singing again. And they were still singing when his key turned in the lock.

"Hey," he said.

"Hey, yourself. You want some beer?"

"No. Well, maybe." But he came up to the window and stood beside me, looking out. "What a warm voice," he said.

They were singing *If I could only hear my mother pray again!*

"Yes," I said, "and she can sure beat that tambourine."

"But what a terrible song," he said, and laughed. He dropped his notebook on the sofa and disappeared into the kitchen. "Where's Isabel and the kids?"

"I think they went to see their grandparents. You hungry?"

"No." He came back into the living room with his can of beer. "You want to come some place with me tonight?"

I sensed, I don't know how, that I couldn't possibly say no. "Sure. Where?"

He sat down on the sofa and picked up his notebook and started leafing through it. "I'm going to sit in with some fellows in a joint in the Village."

"You mean, you're going to play, tonight?"

"That's right." He took a swallow of his beer and moved back to the window. He gave me a sidelong look. "If you can stand it."

"I'll try," I said.

He smiled to himself and we both watched as the meeting across the way broke up. The three sisters and the brother, heads bowed, were singing *God be with you till we meet again*. The faces around them were very quiet. Then the song ended. The small crowd dispersed. We watched the three women and the lone man walk slowly up the avenue.

"When she was singing before," said Sonny, abruptly, "her voice reminded me for a minute of what heroin feels like sometimes — when it's in your veins. It makes you feel sort of warm and cool at the same time. And distant. And — and sure." He sipped his beer, very deliberately not looking at me. I watched his face. "It makes you feel — in control. Sometimes you've got to have that feeling."

"Do you?" I sat down slowly in the easy chair.

"Sometimes." He went to the sofa and picked up his notebook again. "Some people do."

"In order," I asked, "to play?" And my voice was very ugly, full of contempt and anger.

"Well" — he looked at me with great, troubled eyes, as though, in fact, he hoped his eyes would tell me things he could never otherwise say — "they *think* so. And *if* they think so — !"

"And what do *you* think?" I asked.

He sat on the sofa and put his can of beer on the floor. "I don't know," he said, and I couldn't be sure if he were answering my question or pursuing his thoughts. His face didn't tell me. "It's not so much to *play*. It's to *stand* it, to be able to make it at all. On any level." He frowned and smiled: "In order to keep from shaking to pieces."

"But these friends of yours," I said, "they seem to shake themselves to pieces pretty goddamn fast."

"Maybe." He played with the notebook. And something told me that I should curb my tongue, that Sonny was doing his best to talk, that I should listen. "But of course you only know the ones that've gone to pieces. Some don't — or at least they haven't *yet* and that's just about all *any* of us can say." He paused. "And then there are some who just live, really, in hell, and they know it and they see what's happening and they go right on. I don't know." He sighed, dropped the notebook, folded his arms. "Some guys, you can tell from the way they play, they on something *all* the time. And you can see that, well, it makes something real for them. But of course," he picked up his beer from the floor and sipped it and put the can down again, "they *want* to, too, you've got to see that. Even some of them that say they don't — *some*, not all."

"And what about you?" I asked — I couldn't help it. "What about you? Do *you* want to?"

He stood up and walked to the window and remained silent for a long time. Then he sighed. "Me," he said. Then: "While I was downstairs before, on my way here, listening to that woman sing, it struck me all of a sudden how much suffering she must have had to go through — to sing like that. It's *repulsive* to think you have to suffer that much."

I said: "But there's no way not to suffer — is there, Sonny?"

"I believe not," he said and smiled, "but that's never stopped anyone from trying." He looked at me. "Has it?" I realized, with this mocking look, that there stood between us, forever, beyond the power of time or forgiveness, the fact that I had held silence — so long! — when he had needed human speech to help him. He turned back to the window. "No, there's no way not to suffer. But you try all kinds of ways to keep from drowning in it, to keep on top of it, and to make it seem — well, like *you*. Like you did something, all right, and now you're suffering for it. You know?" I said nothing. "Well you know," he said, impatiently, "why *do* people suffer? Maybe it's better to do something to give it a reason, *any* reason."

"But we just agreed," I said "that there's no way not to suffer. Isn't it better, then, just to — take it?"

"But nobody just takes it," Sonny cried, "that's what I'm telling you! *Everybody* tries not to. You're just hung up on the *way* some people try — it's not *your* way!"

The hair on my face began to itch, my face felt wet. "That's not true," I said, "that's not true. I don't give a damn what other people do, I don't even care how they suffer. I just care how *you* suffer." And he looked at me. "Please believe me," I said, "I don't want to see you — die — trying not to suffer."

"I won't," he said, flatly, "die trying not to suffer. At least, not any faster than anybody else."

"But there's no need," I said, trying to laugh, "is there? in killing yourself."

I wanted to say more, but I couldn't. I wanted to talk about will power and how life could be — well, beautiful. I wanted to say that it was all within; but was it? or, rather, wasn't that exactly the trouble? And I wanted to promise that I would never fail him again. But it would all have sounded — empty words and lies.

So I made the promise to myself and prayed that I would keep it.

"It's terrible sometimes, inside," he said, "that's what's the trouble. You walk these streets, black and funky and cold, and there's not really a living ass to talk to, and there's nothing shaking, and there's no way of getting it out — that storm inside. You can't talk it and you can't make love with it, and when you finally try to get with it and play it, you realize *nobody's* listening. So *you've* got to listen. You got to find a way to listen."

And then he walked away from the window and sat on the sofa again, as though all the wind had suddenly been knocked out of him. "Sometimes you'll do *anything* to play, even cut your mother's throat." He laughed and looked at me. "Or your brother's." Then he sobered. "Or your own." Then: "Don't worry. I'm all right now and I think I'll *be* all right. But I can't forget — where I've been. I don't mean just the physical place I've been, I mean where I've *been*. And *what* I've been."

"What have you been, Sonny?" I asked.

He smiled — but sat sideways on the sofa, his elbow resting on the back, his fingers playing with his mouth and chin, not looking at me. "I've been something I didn't recognize, didn't know I could be. Didn't know anybody could be." He stopped, looking inward, looking helplessly young, looking old. "I'm not talking about it now because I feel *guilty* or anything like that — maybe it would be better if I did, I don't know. Anyway, I can't really talk about it. Not to you, not to anybody," and now he turned and faced me. "Sometimes, you know, and it was actually when I was most *out* of the world, I felt that I was in it, that I was *with* it, really, and I could play or I didn't really have to *play*, it just came out of me, it was there. And I don't know how I played, thinking about it now, but I know I did awful things, those times, sometimes, to people. Or it wasn't that I *did* anything to them — it was that they weren't real." He picked up the beer can; it was empty; he rolled it between his palms: "And other times — well, I needed a fix, I needed to find a place to lean, I needed to clear a space to *listen* — and I couldn't find it, and I — went crazy, I did terrible things to *me*, I was terrible *for* me." He began pressing the beer can between his hands, I watched the metal begin to give. It glittered, as he played with it, like a knife, and I was afraid he would cut himself, but I said nothing. "Oh well. I can never tell you. I was all by myself at the bottom of something, stinking and sweating and crying and shaking, and I smelled it, you know? *my* stink, and I thought I'd die if I couldn't get away from it and yet, all the same, I knew that everything I was doing was just locking me in with it. And I didn't know," he paused, still flattening the beer can, "I didn't know, I still *don't* know, something kept telling me that maybe it was good to smell your own stink, but I didn't think that *that* was what I'd been trying to do — and — who can stand it?" and he abruptly dropped the ruined beer can, looking at me with a small, still smile, and then rose, walking to the window as though it were the lodestone rock. I watched his face, he watched the avenue. "I couldn't tell you when Mama died — but the reason I wanted to leave Harlem so bad was to get away from drugs. And then, when I ran away, that's what I was running from — really. When I came back, nothing had changed, *I* hadn't changed, I was just — older." And he stopped, drumming with his fingers on the windowpane. The sun had vanished, soon darkness would fall. I watched his face. "It can come again," he said, almost as though speaking to himself. Then he turned to me. "It can come again," he repeated. "I just want you to know that."

"All right," I said, at last. "So it can come again, All right."

He smiled, but the smile was sorrowful. "I had to try to tell you," he said.

"Yes," I said. "I understand that."

"You're my brother," he said, looking straight at me, and not smiling at all.

"Yes," I repeated, "yes. I understand that."

He turned back to the window, looking out. "All that hatred down there," he said, "all that hatred and misery and love. It's a wonder it doesn't blow the avenue apart."

We went to the only nightclub on a short, dark street, downtown. We squeezed through the narrow, chattering, jam-packed bar to the entrance of the big room, where the bandstand was. And we stood there for a moment, for the lights were very dim in this room and we couldn't see. Then, "Hello, boy," said a voice and an enormous black man, much older than Sonny or myself, erupted out of all that atmospheric lighting and put an arm around Sonny's shoulder. "I been sitting right here," he said, "waiting for you."

He had a big voice, too, and heads in the darkness turned toward us.

Sonny grinned and pulled a little away, and said, "Creole, this is my brother. I told you about him."

Creole shook my hand. "I'm glad to meet you, son," he said, and it was clear that he was glad to meet me *there,* for Sonny's sake. And he smiled, "You got a real musician in *your* family," and he took his arm from Sonny's shoulder and slapped him, lightly, affectionately, with the back of his hand.

"Well. Now I've heard it all," said a voice behind us. This was another musician, and a friend of Sonny's, a coal-black, cheerful-looking man, built close to the ground. He immediately began confiding to me, at the top of his lungs, the most terrible things about Sonny, his teeth gleaming like a light-house and his laugh coming up out of him like the beginning of an earth-quake. And it turned out that everyone at the bar knew Sonny, or almost everyone; some were musicians, working there, or nearby, or not working, some were simply hangers-on, and some were there to hear Sonny play. I was introduced to all of them and they were all very polite to me. Yet, it was clear that, for them, I was only Sonny's brother. Here, I was in Sonny's world. Or, rather: his kingdom. Here, it was not even a question that his veins bore royal blood.

They were going to play soon and Creole installed me, by myself, at a table in a dark corner. Then I watched them, Creole, and the little black man, and Sonny, and the others, while they horsed around, standing just below the bandstand. The light from the bandstand spilled just a little short of them and, watching them laughing and gesturing and moving about, I had the feeling that they, nevertheless, were being most careful not to step into that circle of light too suddenly: that if they moved into the light too suddenly, without thinking, they would perish in flame. Then, while I watched, one of them, the small, black man, moved into the light and crossed the bandstand and started fooling around with his drums. Then — being funny and being, also, ex-tremely ceremonious — Creole took Sonny by the arm and led him to the piano. A woman's voice called Sonny's name and a few hands started clap-ping. And Sonny, also being funny and being ceremonious, and so touched, I think, that he could have cried, but neither hiding it nor showing it, riding it like a man, grinned, and put both hands to his heart and bowed from the waist.

Creole then went to the bass fiddle and a lean, very bright-skinned brown man jumped up on the bandstand and picked up his horn. So there they were, and the atmosphere on the bandstand and in the room began to change and tighten. Someone stepped up to the microphone and announced them. Then there were all kinds of murmurs. Some people at the bar shushed others. The waitress ran around, frantically getting in the last orders, guys and chicks got closer to each other, and the lights on the bandstand, on the quartet, turned to a kind of indigo. Then they all looked different there. Creole looked about him for the last time, as though he were making certain that all his chickens were in the coop, and then he — jumped and struck the fiddle. And there they were.

All I know about music is that not many people ever really hear it. And even then, on the rare occasions when something opens within, and the music enters, what we mainly hear, or hear corroborated, are personal, private, vanishing evocations. But the man who creates the music is hearing something else, is dealing with the roar rising from the void and imposing order on it as it hits the air. What is evoked in him, then, is of another order, more terrible because it has no words, and triumphant, too, for that same reason. And his triumph, when he triumphs, is ours. I just watched Sonny's face. His face was troubled, he was working hard, but he wasn't with it. And I had the feeling that, in a way, everyone on the bandstand was waiting for him, both waiting for him and pushing him along. But as I began to watch Creole, I realized that it was Creole who held them all back. He had them on a short rein. Up there, keeping the beat with his whole body, wailing on the fiddle, with his eyes half closed, he was listening to everything, but he was listening to Sonny. He was having a dialogue with Sonny. He wanted Sonny to leave the shoreline and strike out for the deep water. He was Sonny's witness that deep water and drowning were not the same thing — he had been there, and he knew. And he wanted Sonny to know. He was waiting for Sonny to do the things on the keys which would let Creole know that Sonny was in the water.

And, while Creole listened, Sonny moved, deep within, exactly like someone in torment. I had never before thought of how awful the relationship must be between the musician and his instrument. He has to fill it, this instrument, with the breath of life, his own. He has to make it do what he wants it to do. And a piano is just a piano. It's made out of so much wood and wires and little hammers and big ones, and ivory. While there's only so much you can do with it, the only way to find this out is to try; to try and make it do everything.

And Sonny hadn't been near a piano for over a year. And he wasn't on much better terms with his life, not the life that stretched before him now. He and the piano stammered, started one way, got scared, stopped; started another way, panicked, marked time, started again; then seemed to have found a direction, panicked again, got stuck. And the face I saw on Sonny I'd never seen before. Everything had been burned out of it, and, at the same time, things usually hidden were being burned in, by the fire and fury of the battle which was occurring in him up there.

Yet, watching Creole's face as they neared the end of the first set, I had the feeling that something had happened, something I hadn't heard. Then they finished, there was scattered applause, and then, without an instant's warning, Creole started into something else, it was almost sardonic, it was *Am I Blue*. And, as though he commanded, Sonny began to play. Something began to happen. And Creole let out the reins. The dry, low, black man said something awful on the drums, Creole answered, and the drums talked back. Then the horn insisted, sweet and high, slightly detached perhaps, and Creole listened, commenting now and then, dry, and driving, beautiful and calm and old. Then they all came together again, and Sonny was part of the family again. I could tell this from his face. He seemed to have found, right there beneath his fingers, a damn brand-new piano. It seemed that he couldn't get over it. Then, for awhile, just being happy with Sonny, they seemed to be agreeing with him that brand-new pianos certainly were a gas.

Then Creole stepped forward to remind them that what they were playing was the blues. He hit something in all of them, he hit something in me, myself, and the music tightened and deepened, apprehension began to beat the air. Creole began to tell us what the blues were all about. They were not about anything very new. He and his boys up there were keeping it new, at the risk of ruin, destruction, madness, and death, in order to find new ways to make us listen. For, while the tale of how we suffer, and how we are delighted, and how we may triumph is never new, it always must be heard. There isn't any other tale to tell, it's the only light we've got in all this darkness.

And this tale, according to that face, that body, those strong hands on those strings, has another aspect in every country, and a new depth in every generation. Listen, Creole seemed to be saying, listen. Now these are Sonny's blues. He made the little black man on the drums know it, and the bright, brown man on the horn. Creole wasn't trying any longer to get Sonny in the water. He was wishing him Godspeed. Then he stepped back, very slowly, filling the air with the immense suggestion that Sonny speak for himself.

Then they all gathered around Sonny and Sonny played. Every now and again one of them seemed to say, amen. Sonny's fingers filled the air with life, his life. But that life contained so many others. And Sonny went all the way back, he really began with the spare, flat statement of the opening phrase of the song. Then he began to make it his. It was very beautiful because it wasn't hurried and it was no longer a lament. I seemed to hear with what burning he had made it his, with what burning we had yet to make it ours, how we could cease lamenting. Freedom lurked around us and I understood, at last, that he could help us to be free if we would listen, that he would never be free until we did. Yet, there was no battle in his face now. I heard what he had gone through, and would continue to go through until he came to rest in earth. He had made it his: that long line, of which we knew only Mama and Daddy. And he was giving it back, as everything must be given back, so that, passing through death, it can live forever. I saw my mother's face again, and felt, for the first time, how the stones of the road she had walked on must have bruised her feet. I saw the moonlit road where my father's brother died. And it brought something else back to me, and carried me past it. I saw my little girl again and felt Isabel's tears again, and I felt my own tears begin to rise. And I was yet aware that this was only a moment, that the world waited outside, as hungry as a tiger, and that trouble stretched above us, longer than the sky.

Then it was over. Creole and Sonny let out their breath, both soaking wet, and grinning. There was a lot of applause and some of it was real. In the dark, the girl came by and I asked her to take drinks to the bandstand. There was a long pause, while they talked up there in the indigo light and after awhile I saw the girl put a Scotch and milk on top of the piano for Sonny. He didn't seem to notice it, but just before they started playing again, he sipped from it and looked toward me, and nodded. Then he put it back on top of the piano. For me, then, as they began to play again, it glowed and shook above my brother's head like the very cup of trembling. [1957]

TONI CADE BAMBARA (b. 1939) was born in New York City and grew up in Harlem and Bedford-Stuyvesant. As a child she began scribbling stories on the margins of her father's copies of the New York Daily News and the squares of thin white cardboard her mother's stockings came wrapped around. She has said of herself,

> I was raised by my family and community to be a combatant. Forays to the Apollo [Theater in Harlem] with my daddy and hanging tough on Speakers Corner with my mama taught me the power of the word, the importance of the resistance tradition, and the high standards our [black] community had regarding verbal performance. While my heart is a laughing gland and my favorite thing to be doing is laughing so hard I have to lower myself on the wall to keep from falling down, near that chamber is a blast furnace where a rifle pokes from the ribs.

In high school and at Queens College, Bambara remembers that she "hogged the lit journal." She took writing courses and wrote novels, stories, plays, film scripts, operas, "you-name-its." After her college graduation, she worked various jobs and studied for her M.A. at City College of New York while she wrote fiction in "the predawn in-betweens." She began to publish her stories, and in 1972 she collected them in her first book, Gorilla, My Love. It wasn't until Bambara returned from a trip to Cuba in 1973 that she thought of herself as a writer: "There I learned what Langston Hughes and others, most especially my colleagues in the Neo-Black Arts Movement, had been teaching for years — that writing is a legitimate way, an important way, to participate in the empowerment of the community that names me." Her books include The Black Woman (1970), Tales and Stories for Black Folks (1971), The Sea Birds Are Still Alive: Collected Stories (1977), and a novel, The Salt Eaters (1980).

Like Zora Neale Hurston, whom Bambara credits with giving her new ways to consider literary material (folkways as the basis of art) and new categories of perception (women's images), Bambara often uses humor in her fiction. She has said that "what I enjoy most in my work is the laughter and the outrage and the attention to language." Her stories, like "The Lesson," are often about children, but Bambara tries to avoid sentimentality. She attempts to keep her torrents of language and feeling in control by remembering the premises from which she proceeds as a black writer: "One, we are at war. Two, the natural response to oppression, ignorance, evil, and mystification is wide-awake resistance. Three, the natural response to stress and crisis is not breakdown and capitulation, but transformation and renewal."

TONI CADE BAMBARA

The Lesson

Back in the days when everyone was old and stupid or young and foolish and me and Sugar were the only ones just right, this lady moved on our block with nappy hair and proper speech and no makeup. And quite naturally we laughed at her, laughed the way we did at the junk man who went about his business like he was some big-time president and his sorry-ass horse his secretary. And we kinda hated her too, hated the way we did the winos who cluttered up our parks and pissed on our handball walls and stank up our hallways and stairs so you couldn't halfway play hide-and-seek without a goddamn gas mask. Miss Moore was her name. The only woman on the block with no first name. And she was black as hell, cept for her feet, which were fish-white and spooky. And she was always planning these boring-ass things for us to do, us being my cousin, mostly, who lived on the block cause we all moved North the same time and to the same apartment then spread out gradual to breathe. And our parents would yank our heads into some kinda shape and crisp up our clothes so we'd be presentable for travel with Miss Moore, who always looked like she was going to church, though she never did. Which is just one of the things the grownups talked about when they talked behind her back like a dog. But when she came calling with some sachet she'd sewed up or some gingerbread she'd made or some book, why then they'd all be too embarrassed to turn her down and we'd get handed over all spruced up. She'd been to college and said it was only right that she should take responsibility for the young ones' education, and she not even related by marriage or blood. So they'd go for it. Specially Aunt Gretchen. She was the main gofer in the family. You got some ole dumb shit foolishness you want somebody to go for, you send for Aunt Gretchen. She been screwed into the go-along for so long, it's a blood-deep natural thing with her. Which is how she got saddled with me and Sugar and Junior in the first place while our mothers were in a la-de-da apartment up the block having a good ole time.

So this one day, Miss Moore rounds us all up at the mailbox and it's puredee hot and she's knockin herself out about arithmetic. And school suppose to let up in summer I heard, but she don't never let up. And the starch in my pinafore scratching the shit outta me and I'm really hating this nappy-head bitch and her goddamn college degree. I'd much rather go to the pool or to the show where it's cool. So me and Sugar leaning on the mailbox being surly, which is a Miss Moore word. And Flyboy checking out what everybody brought for lunch. And Fat Butt already wasting his peanut-but-ter-and-jelly sandwich like the pig he is. And Junebug punchin on Q.T.'s arm for potato chips. And Rosie Giraffe shifting from one hip to the other waiting for somebody to step on her foot or ask her if she from Georgia so she can

99

kick ass, preferably Mercedes'. And Miss Moore asking us do we know what money is, like we a bunch of retards. I mean real money, she say, like it's only poker chips or monopoly papers we lay on the grocer. So right away I'm tired of this and say so. And would much rather snatch Sugar and go to the Sunset and terrorize the West Indian kids and take their hair ribbons and their money too. And Miss Moore files that remark away for next week's lesson on brotherhood, I can tell. And finally I say we oughta get to the subway cause it's cooler and besides we might meet some cute boys. Sugar done swiped her mama's lipstick, so we ready.

So we heading down the street and she's boring us silly about what things cost and what our parents make and how much goes for rent and how money ain't divided up right in this country. And then she gets to the part about we all poor and live in the slums, which I don't feature. And I'm ready to speak on that, but she steps out in the street and hails two cabs just like that. Then she hustles half the crew in with her and hands me a five-dollar bill and tells me to calculate 10 percent tip for the driver. And we're off. Me and Sugar and Junebug and Flyboy hangin out the window and hollering to everybody, putting lipstick on each other cause Flyboy a faggot anyway, and making farts with our sweaty armpits. But I'm mostly trying to figure how to spend this money. But they all fascinated with the meter ticking and Junebug starts laying bets as to how much it'll read when Flyboy can't hold his breath no more. Then Sugar lays bets as to how much it'll be when we get there. So I'm stuck. Don't nobody want to go for my plan, which is to jump out at the next light and run off to the first bar-b-que we can find. Then the driver tells us to get the hell out cause we there already. And the meter reads eighty-five cents. And I'm stalling to figure out the tip and Sugar say give him a dime. And I decide he don't need it bad as I do, so later for him. But then he tries to take off with Junebug foot still in the door so we talk about his mama something ferocious. Then we check out that we on Fifth Avenue and everybody dressed up in stockings. One lady in a fur coat, hot as it is. White folks crazy.

"This is the place," Miss Moore say, presenting it to us in the voice she uses at the museum. "Let's look in the windows before we go in."

"Can we steal?" Sugar asks very serious like she's getting the ground rules squared away before she plays. "I beg your pardon," say Miss Moore, and we fall out. So she leads us around the windows of the toy store and me and Sugar screamin, "This is mine, that's mine, I gotta have that, that was made for me, I was born for that," till Big Butt drowns us out.

"Hey, I'm going to buy that there."

"That there? You don't even know what it is, stupid."

"I do so," he say punchin on Rosie Giraffe. "It's a microscope."

"Whatcha gonna do with a microscope, fool?"

"Look at things."

"Like what, Ronald?" ask Miss Moore. And Big Butt ain't got the first notion. So here go Miss Moore gabbing about the thousands of bacteria in a drop of water and the somethinorother in a speck of blood and the million and one living things in the air around us is invisible to the naked eye. And what she say that for? Junebug go to town on that "naked" and we rolling. Then Miss Moore ask what it cost. So we all jam into the window smudgin it up and the price tag say $300. So then she ask how long'd take for Big Butt and Junebug to save up their allowances. "Too long," I say. "Yeh," adds Sugar, "outgrown it by that time." And Miss Moore say no, you never outgrow learning instruments. "Why, even medical students and interns and," blah, blah, blah. And we ready to choke Big Butt for bringing it up in the first damn place.

"This here costs four hundred eighty dollars," say Rosie Giraffe. So we pile up all over her to see what she pointin out. My eyes tell me it's a chunk of glass cracked with something heavy, and different-color inks dripped into the splits, then the whole thing put into a oven or something. But for $480 it don't make sense.

"That's a paperweight made of semi-precious stones fused together under tremendous pressure," she explains slowly, with her hands doing the mining and all the factory work.

"So what's a paperweight?" ask Rosie Giraffe.

"To weigh paper with, dumbbell," say Flyboy, the wise man from the East.

"Not exactly," say Miss Moore, which is what she say when you warm or way off too. "It's to weigh paper down so it won't scatter and make your desk untidy." So right away me and Sugar curtsy to each other and then to Mercedes who is more the tidy type.

"We don't keep paper on top of the desk in my class," say Junebug, figuring Miss Moore crazy or lyin one.

"At home, then," she say. "Don't you have a calendar and a pencil case and a blotter and a letter-opener on your desk at home where you do your homework?" And she know damn well what our homes look like cause she nosys around in them every chance she gets.

"I don't even have a desk," say Junebug. "Do we?"

"No. And I don't get no homework neither," says Big Butt.

"And I don't even have a home," says Flyboy like he do at school to keep the white folks off his back and sorry for him. Send this poor kid to camp posters, is his specialty.

"I do," says Mercedes. "I have a box of stationery on my desk and a picture of my cat. My godmother bought the stationery and the desk. There's a big rose on each sheet and the envelopes smell like roses."

"Who wants to know about your smelly-ass stationery," say Rosie Giraffe fore I can get my two cents in.

"It's important to have a work area all your own so that . . ."

"Will you look at this sailboat, please," say Flyboy, cutting her off and pointin to the thing like it was his. So once again we tumble all over each other to gaze at this magnificent thing in the toy store which is just big enough to maybe sail two kittens across the pond if you strap them to the posts tight. We all start reciting the price tag like we in assembly. "Handcrafted sailboat of fiberglass at one thousand one hundred ninety-five dollars."

"Unbelievable," I hear myself say and am really stunned. I read it again for myself just in case the group recitation put me in a trance. Same thing. For some reason this pisses me off. We look at Miss Moore and she lookin at us, waiting for I dunno what.

"Who'd pay all that when you can buy a sailboat set for a quarter at Pop's, a tube of glue for a dime, and a ball of string for eight cents? It must have a motor and a whole lot else besides," I say. "My sailboat cost me about fifty cents."

"But will it take water?" say Mercedes with her smart ass.

"Took mine to Alley Pond Park once," say Flyboy. "String broke. Lost it. Pity."

"Sailed mine in Central Park and it keeled over and sank. Had to ask my father for another dollar."

"And you got the strap," laugh Big Butt. "The jerk didn't even have a string on it. My old man wailed on his behind."

Little Q.T. was staring hard at the sailboat and you could see he wanted it bad. But he too little and somebody'd just take it from him. So what the hell. "This boat for kids, Miss Moore?"

"Parents silly to buy something like that just to get all broke up," say Rosie Giraffe.

"That much money it should last forever," I figure.

"My father'd buy it for me if I wanted it."

"Your father, my ass," say Rosie Giraffe getting a chance to finally push Mercedes.

"Must be rich people shop here," say Q.T.

"You are a very bright boy," say Flyboy. "What was your first clue?" And he rap him on the head with the back of his knuckles, since Q.T. the only one he could get away with. Though Q.T. liable to come up behind you years later and get his licks in when you half expect it.

"What I want to know is," I says to Miss Moore though I never talk to her, I wouldn't give the bitch that satisfaction, "is how much a real boat costs? I figure a thousand'd get you a yacht any day."

"Why don't you check that out," she says, "and report back to the group?" Which really pains my ass. If you gonna mess up a perfectly good swim day least you could do is have some answers. "Let's go in," she say like she got something up her sleeve. Only she don't lead the way. So me and Sugar turn the corner to where the entrance is, but when we get there I kinda hang back. Not that I'm scared, what's there to be afraid of, just a toy store. But I feel funny, shame. But what I got to be shamed about? Got as much right to go in as anybody. But somehow I can't seem to get hold of the door, so I step away from Sugar to lead. But she hangs back too. And I look at her and she looks at me and this is ridiculous. I mean, damn, I have never been shy about doing nothing or going nowhere. But then Mercedes steps up and then Rosie Giraffe and Big Butt crowd in behind and shove, and next thing we all stuffed into the doorway with only Mercedes squeezing past us, smoothing out her jumper and walking right down the aisle. Then the rest of us tumble in like a glued-together jigsaw done all wrong. And people lookin at us. And it's like the time me and Sugar crashed into the Catholic church on a dare. But once we got in there and everything so hushed and holy and the candles and the bowin and the handkerchiefs on all the drooping heads, I just couldn't go through with the plan. Which was for me to run up to the altar and do a tap dance while Sugar played the nose flute and messed around in the holy water. And Sugar kept given me the elbow. Then later teased me so bad I tied her up in the shower and turned it on and locked her in. And she'd be there till this day if Aunt Gretchen hadn't finally figured I was lying about the boarder takin a shower.

Same thing in the store. We all walkin on tiptoe and hardly touchin the games and puzzles and things. And I watched Miss Moore who is steady watchin us like she waitin for a sign. Like Mama Drewery watches the sky and sniffs the air and takes note of just how much slant is in the bird formation. Then me and Sugar bump smack into each other, so busy gazing at the toys, 'specially the sailboat. But we don't laugh and go into our fat-lady bump-stomach routine. We just stare at that price tag. Then Sugar run a finger over the whole boat. And I'm jealous and want to hit her. Maybe not her, but I sure want to punch somebody in the mouth.

"Watcha bring us here for, Miss Moore?"

"You sound angry, Sylvia. Are you mad about something?" Givin me one of them grins like she tellin a grown-up joke that never turns out to be funny. And she's lookin very closely at me like maybe she plannin to do my portrait from memory. I'm mad, but I won't give her that satisfaction. So I slouch around the store being very bored and say, "Let's go."

Me and Sugar at the back of the train watchin the tracks whizzin by large then small then getting gobbled up in the dark. I'm thinkin about this tricky toy I saw in the store. A clown that somersaults on a bar then does chin-ups just cause you yank lightly at his leg. Cost $35. I could see me askin my mother for a $35 birthday clown. "You wanna who that costs what?" she'd say, cocking her head to the side to get a better view of the hole in my head. Thirty-five dollars could buy new bunk beds for Junior and Gretchen's boy. Thirty-five dollars and the whole household could go visit Grand-daddy Nelson in the country. Thirty-five dollars would pay for the rent and the piano bill too. Who are these people that spend that much for performing clowns and $1000 for toy sailboats? What kinda work they do and how they live and how come we ain't in on it? Where we are is who we are, Miss Moore always pointin out. But it don't necessarily have to be that way, she always adds then waits for somebody to say that poor people have to wake up and demand their share of the pie and don't none of us know what kind of pie she talking about in the first damn place. But she ain't so smart cause I still got her four dollars from the taxi and she sure ain't gettin it. Messin up my day with this shit. Sugar nudges me in my pocket and winks.

Miss Moore lines us up in front of the mailbox where we started from, seem like years ago, and I got a headache for thinkin so hard. And we lean all over each other so we can hold up under the draggy-ass lecture she always finishes us off with at the end before we thank her for borin us to tears. But she just looks at us like she readin tea leaves. Finally she say, "Well, what did you think of F.A.O. Schwarz?"

Rosie Giraffe mumbles, "White folks crazy."

"I'd like to go there again when I get my birthday money," says Mercedes, and we shove her out the pack so she has to lean on the mailbox by herself.

"I'd like a shower. Tiring day," say Flyboy.

Then Sugar surprises me by sayin, "You know, Miss Moore, I don't think all of us here put together eat in a year what that sailboat costs." And Miss Moore lights up like somebody goosed her "And?" she say, urging Sugar on. Only I'm standin on her foot so she don't continue.

"Imagine for a minute what kind of society it is in which some people can spend on a toy what it would cost to feed a family of six or seven. What do you think?"

"I think," say Sugar pushing me off her feet like she never done before, cause I whip her ass in a minute, "that this is not much of a democracy if you ask me. Equal chance to pursue happiness means an equal crack at the dough, don't it?" Miss Moore is besides herself and I am disgusted with Sugar's treachery. So I stand on her foot one more time to see if she'll shove me. She shuts up, and Miss Moore looks at me, sorrowfully I'm thinkin. And somethin weird is goin on, I can feel it in my chest.

"Anybody else learn anything today?" lookin dead at me. I walk away and Sugar has to run to catch up and don't even seem to notice when I shrug her arm off my shoulder.

"Well, we got four dollars anyway," she says.

"Uh, hunh."

"We could go to Hascombs and get half a chocolate layer and then go to the Sunset and still have plenty money for potato chips and ice cream sodas."

"Uh, hunh."

"Race you to Hascombs," she say.

We start down the block and she gets ahead which is O.K. by me cause I'm going to the West End and then over to the Drive to think this day through. She can run if she want to and even run faster. But ain't nobody gonna beat me at nuthin.   [1972]

JOHN BARTH (b. 1930) *was born in Cambridge, Maryland, on the Eastern Shore of the Chesapeake Bay. Music was Barth's first vocation. He was a student of orchestration for a year at the Juilliard School before he enrolled as a journalism major on a scholarship at Johns Hopkins University. His job as a book filer in the university library stacks developed his taste for fiction: "I was permanently impressed with the size of literature and its wild variety; likewise, as I explored the larger geography of the stacks, with the variety of temperaments, histories, and circumstances from which came the literature I came to love." In his undergraduate writing class he began but did not finish a cycle of one hundred stories about Dorchester County, Maryland, his own version of the* Arabian Nights.

Barth's early fiction is conventional in form and language, but The Sot-Weed Factor *(1960) and* Giles Goat-Boy *(1966) are very long, experimental comic novels, indebted to the fiction of Jorge Luis Borges and Vladimir Nabokov. Reviewers praised both of these novels for their display of erudition and bawdy wit. Barth's talent for parody is evident in all his works. "At heart I'm an arranger still, whose chiefest literary pleasure is to take a received melody — an old narrative poem, a classical myth, a shopworn literary convention, a shard of my experience . . . and, improvising like a jazzman within its constraints, reorchestrate it to present purpose." His recent publications include* The Literature of Exhaustion *(1982), Barth's analysis of postmodernist literary aesthetics, and the novels* Tidewater Tales *(1987) and* Last Voyage of Somebody the Sailor *(1991).*

Barth has published only one book of short stories so far, Lost in the Funhouse *(1968), subtitled* Fiction for Print, Tape, Live Voice. *It was influenced by his friendships with the philosopher Marshall McLuhan and the scholar and critic Leslie Fiedler. The title story, "Lost in the Funhouse," like his other short experimental pieces in the collection, suggests that Barth is self-consciously concerned with what happens when a writer writes, and what happens when a reader reads — "the metaphysical plight of imagination engaging with imagination." As John Updike has observed, Barth "hit the floor of nihilism hard and returns to us covered with coal dust. . . . [He] seems to me a very strongminded and inventive and powerful voice from another planet."*

JOHN BARTH

Lost in the Funhouse

For whom is the funhouse fun? Perhaps for lovers. For Ambrose it is *a place of fear and confusion.* He has come to the seashore with his family for the holiday, *the occasion of their visit is Independence Day, the most important secular holiday of the United States of America.* A single straight underline is the manuscript mark for italic type, *which in turn* is the printed equivalent to oral emphasis of words and phrases as well as the customary type for titles of complete works, not to mention. Italics are also employed, in fiction stories especially, for "outside," intrusive, or artificial voices, such as radio announcements, the texts of telegrams and newspaper articles, et cetera. They should be used *sparingly*. If passages originally in roman type are italicized by someone repeating them, it's customary to acknowledge the fact. *Italics mine.*

Ambrose was "at that awkward age." His voice came out high-pitched as a child's if he let himself get carried away; to be on the safe side, therefore, he moved and spoke with *deliberate calm* and *adult gravity*. Talking soberly of unimportant or irrelevant matters and listening consciously to the sound of your own voice are useful habits for maintaining control in this difficult interval. *En route* to Ocean City he sat in the back seat of the family car with his brother Peter, age fifteen, and Magda G ——, age fourteen, a pretty girl and exquisite young lady, who lived not far from them on B —— Street in the town of D ——, Maryland. Initials, blanks, or both were often substituted for proper names in nineteenth-century fiction to enhance the illusion of reality. It is as if the author felt it necessary to delete the names for reasons of tact or legal liability. Interestingly, as with other aspects of realism, it is an *illusion* that is being enhanced, by purely artificial means. Is it likely, does it violate the principle of verisimilitude, that a thirteen-year-old boy could make such a sophisticated observation? A girl of fourteen is *the psychological coeval* of a boy of fifteen or sixteen; a thirteen-year-old boy, therefore, even one precocious in some other respects, might be three years *her emotional junior*.

Thrice a year — on Memorial, Independence, and Labor Days — the family visits Ocean City for the afternoon and evening. When Ambrose and Peter's father was their age, the excursion was made by train, as mentioned in the novel *The 42nd Parallel* by John Dos Passos. Many families from the same neighborhood used to travel together, with dependent relatives and often with Negro servants; schoolfuls of children swarmed through the railway cars; everyone shared everyone else's Maryland fried chicken, Virginia ham, deviled eggs, potato salad, beaten biscuits, iced tea. Nowadays (that is, in 19 ——, the year of our story) the journey is made by automobile — more comfortably and quickly though without the extra fun though without the *camaraderie* of a general excursion. It's all part of the deterioration of American life, their father declares; Uncle Karl supposes that when the boys take *their* families to Ocean City for the holidays they'll fly in Autogiros. Their mother, sitting in the middle of the front seat like Magda in the second, only with her arms on the seat-back behind the men's shoulders, wouldn't want the good old days back again, the steaming trains and stuffy long dresses; on the other hand she can do without Autogiros, too, if she has to become a grandmother to fly in them.

Description of physical appearance and mannerisms is one of several standard methods of characterization used by writers of fiction. It is also important to "keep the senses operating"; when a detail from one of the five senses, say visual, is "crossed" with a detail from another, say auditory, the reader's imagination is oriented to the scene, perhaps unconsciously. This procedure may be compared to the way surveyors and navigators determine their positions by two or more compass bearings, a process known as triangulation. The brown hair on Ambrose's mother's forearms gleamed in the sun like. Though right-handed, she took her left arm from the seat-back to press the dashboard cigar lighter for Uncle Karl. When the glass bead in its handle glowed red, the lighter was ready for use. The smell of Uncle Karl's cigar smoke reminded one of. The fragrance of the ocean came strong to the picnic ground where they always stopped for lunch, two miles inland from Ocean City. Having to pause for a full hour almost within sound of the breakers was difficult for Peter and Ambrose when they were younger; even at their present age it was not easy to keep their anticipation, *stimulated by the briny spume*, from turning into short temper. The Irish author James Joyce, in his unusual novel entitled *Ulysses*, now available in this country, uses the adjectives *snot-green* and *scrotum-tightening* to describe the sea. Visual, auditory, tactile, olfactory, gustatory. Peter and Ambrose's father, while steering their black 1936 LaSalle sedan with one hand, could with the other remove the first cigarette from a white pack of Lucky Strikes and, more remarkably, light it with a match forefingered from its book and thumbed against the flint paper without being detached. The matchbook cover merely advertised U.S. War Bonds and Stamps. A fine metaphor, simile, or other figure of speech, in addition to its obvious "first-order" relevance to the thing it describes, will be seen upon reflection to have a second order of significance: it may be drawn from the *milieu* of the action, for example, or be particularly appropriate to the sensibility of the narrator, even hinting to the reader things of which the narrator is unaware; or it may cast further and subtler lights upon the things it describes, sometimes ironically qualifying the more evident sense of the comparison.

To say that Ambrose's and Peter's mother was *pretty* is to accomplish nothing; the reader may acknowledge the proposition, but his imagination is not engaged. Besides, Magda was also pretty, yet in an altogether different way. Although she lived on B —— Street she had very good manners and did better than average in school. Her figure was very well developed for her age. Her right hand lay casually on the plush upholstery of the seat, very near Ambrose's left leg, on which his own hand rested. The space between their legs, between her right and his left leg, was out of the line of sight of anyone sitting on the other side of Magda, as well as anyone glancing into the rear-view mirror. Uncle Karl's face resembled Peter's — rather, vice versa. Both had dark hair and eyes, short husky statures, deep voices. Magda's left hand was probably in a similar position on her left side. The boys' father is difficult to describe; no particular feature of his appearance or manner stood out. He wore glasses and was principal of a T —— County grade school. Uncle Karl was a masonry contractor.

Although Peter must have known as well as Ambrose that the latter, because of his position in the car, would be first to see the electrical towers of the power plant at V ——, the halfway point of their trip, he leaned forward and slightly toward the center of the car and pretended to be looking for them through the flat pinewoods and tuckahoe creeks along the highway. For as long as the boys could remember, "looking for the Towers" had been a feature of the first half of their excursions to Ocean City, "looking for the standpipe" of the second. Though the game was childish, their mother preserved the tradition of rewarding the first to see the Towers with a candy-bar or piece of fruit. She insisted now that Magda play the game; the prize, she said, was "something hard to get nowadays." Ambrose decided not to join in; he sat far back in his seat. Magda, like Peter, leaned forward. Two sets of straps were discernible through the shoulders of her sun dress; the inside right one, a brassiere-strap, was fastened or shortened with a small safety pin. The right armpit of her dress, presumably the left as well, was damp with perspiration. The simple strategy for being first to espy the Towers, which Ambrose had understood by the age of four, was to sit on the right-hand side of the car. Whoever sat there, however, had also to put up with the worst of the sun, and so Ambrose, without mentioning the matter, chose sometimes the one and sometimes the other. Not impossibly Peter had never caught on to the trick, or thought that his brother hadn't simply because Ambrose on occasion preferred shade to a Baby Ruth or tangerine.

The shade-sun situation didn't apply to the front seat, owing to the windshield; if anything the driver got more sun, since the person on the passenger side not only was shadowed below by the door and dashboard but might swing down his sunvisor all the way too.

"Is that them?" Magda asked. Ambrose's mother teased the boys for letting Magda win, insinuating that "somebody [had] a girlfriend." Peter and Ambrose's father reached a long thin arm across their mother to butt his cigarette in the dashboard ashtray, under the lighter. The prize this time for seeing the Towers first was a banana. Their mother bestowed it after chiding their father for wasting a half-smoked cigarette when everything was so scarce. Magda, to take the prize, moved her hand from so near Ambrose's that he could have touched it as though accidentally. She offered to share the prize, things like that were so hard to find; but everyone insisted it was hers alone. Ambrose's mother sang an iambic trimeter couplet from a popular song, femininely rhymed:

> "What's good is in the Army;
> What's left will never harm me."

Uncle Karl tapped his cigar ash out the ventilator window; some particles were sucked by the slipstream back into the car through the rear window on the passenger side. Magda demonstrated her ability to hold a banana in one hand and peel it with her teeth. She still sat forward; Ambrose pushed his glasses back onto the bridge of his nose with his left hand, which he then negligently let fall to the seat cushion immediately behind her. He even permitted the single hair, gold, on the second joint of his thumb to brush the fabric of her skirt. Should she have sat back at that instant, his hand would have been caught under her.

Plush upholstery prickles uncomfortably through gabardine slacks in the July sun. The function of the *beginning* of a story is to introduce the principal characters, establish their initial relationships, set the scene for the main action, expose the background of the situation if necessary, plant motifs and foreshadowings where appropriate, and initiate the first complication or whatever of the "rising action." Actually, if one imagines a story called "The Funhouse," or "Lost in the Funhouse," the details of the drive to Ocean City don't seem especially relevant. The *beginning* should recount the events between Ambrose's first sight of the funhouse early in the afternoon and his entering it with Magda and Peter in the evening. The *middle* would narrate all relevant events from the time he goes in to the time he loses his way; middles have the double and contradictory function of delaying the climax while at the same time preparing the reader for it and fetching him to it. Then the *ending* would tell what Ambrose does while he's lost, how he finally finds his way out, and what everybody makes of the experience. So far there's been no real dialogue, very little sensory detail, and nothing in the way of a *theme*. And a long time has gone by already without anything happening; it makes a person wonder. We haven't even reached Ocean City yet: we will never get out of the funhouse.

The more closely an author identifies with the narrator, literally or metaphorically, the less advisable it is, as a rule, to use the first-person narrative viewpoint. Once three years previously the young people *aforementioned* played Niggers and Masters in the backyard; when it was Ambrose's turn to be Master and theirs to be Niggers Peter had to go serve his evening papers; Ambrose was afraid to punish Magda alone, but she led him to the whitewashed Torture Chamber between the woodshed and the privy in the Slaves Quarters; there she knelt sweating among bamboo rakes and dusty Mason jars, pleadingly embraced his knees, and while bees droned in the lattice as if on an ordinary summer afternoon, purchased clemency at a surprising price set by herself. Doubtless she remembered nothing of this event; Ambrose on the other hand seemed unable to forget the least detail of his life. He even recalled how, standing beside himself with awed impersonality in the reeky heat, he'd stared the while at an empty cigar box in which Uncle Karl kept stone-cutting chisels: beneath the words *El Producto*, a laureled, loose-toga'd lady regarded the sea from a marble bench; beside her, forgotten or not yet turned to, was a five-stringed lyre. Her chin reposed on the back of her right hand; her left depended negligently from the bench-arm. The lower half of scene and lady was peeled away; the words EXAMINED BY — were inked there into the wood. Nowadays cigar boxes are made of pasteboard. Ambrose wondered what Magda would have done, Ambrose wondered what Magda would do when she sat back on his hand as he resolved she should. Be angry. Make a teasing joke of it. Give no sign at all. For a long time she leaned forward, playing cow-poker with Peter against Uncle Karl and Mother and watching for the first sign of Ocean City. At nearly the same instant, picnic ground and Ocean City standpipe hove into view; an Amoco filling station on their side of the road cost Mother and Uncle Karl fifty cows and the game; Magda bounced back, clapping her right hand on Mother's right arm; Ambrose moved clear "in the nick of time."

At this rate our hero, at this rate our protagonist will remain in the funhouse forever. Narrative ordinarily consists of alternating dramatization and summarization. One symptom of nervous tension, paradoxically, is repeated and violent yawning; neither Peter nor Magda nor Uncle Karl nor Mother reacted in this manner. Although they were no longer small children, Peter and Ambrose were each given a dollar to spend on boardwalk amusements in addition to what money of their own they'd brought along. Magda too, though she protested she had ample spending money. The boys' mother made a little scene out of distributing the bills; she pretended that her sons and Magda were small children and cautioned them not to spend the sum too quickly or in one place. Magda promised with a merry laugh and, having both hands free, took the bill with her left. Peter laughed also and pledged in a falsetto to be a good boy. His imitation of a child was not clever. The boys' father was tall and thin, balding, fair-complexioned. Assertions of that sort are not effective; the reader may acknowledge the proposition, but. We should be much farther along than we are; something has gone wrong; not much of the preliminary rambling seems relevant. Yet everyone begins in the same place; how is it that most go along without difficulty but a few lose their way?

"Stay out from under the boardwalk," Uncle Karl growled from the side of his mouth. The boys' mother pushed his shoulder *in mock annoyance.* They were all standing before Fat May the Laughing Lady who advertised the funhouse. Larger than life, Fat May mechanically shook, rocked on her heels, slapped her thighs while recorded laughter — uproarious, female — came amplified from a hidden loudspeaker. It chuckled, wheezed, wept; tried in vain to catch its breath; tittered, groaned, exploded raucous and anew. You couldn't hear it without laughing yourself, no matter how you felt. Father came back from talking to a Coast-Guardsman on duty and reported that the surf was spoiled with crude oil from tankers recently torpedoed offshore. Lumps of it, difficult to remove, made tarry tidelines on the beach and stuck on swimmers. Many bathed in the surf nevertheless and came out speckled; others paid to use a municipal pool and only sunbathed on the beach. We would do the latter. We would do the latter. We would do the latter.

Under the boardwalk, matchbook covers, grainy other things. What is the story's theme? Ambrose is ill. He perspires in the dark passages, candied apples-on-a-stick, delicious-looking, disappointing to eat. Funhouses need men's and ladies' rooms at intervals. Others perhaps have also vomited in corners and corridors; may even have had bowel movements liable to be stepped in in the dark. The word *fuck* suggests suction and/or and/or flatulence. Mother and Father; grandmothers and grandfathers on both sides; great-grandmothers and great-grandfathers on four sides, et cetera. Count a generation as thirty years: in approximately the year when Lord Baltimore was granted charter to the province of Maryland by Charles I, five hundred twelve women — English, Welsh, Bavarian, Swiss — of every class and character, received into themselves the penises the intromittent organs of five hundred twelve men, ditto, in every circumstance and posture, to conceive the five hundred twelve ancestors of the two hundred fifty-six ancestors of the et cetera et cetera et cetera et cetera et cetera et cetera et cetera et cetera of the author, of the narrator, of this story, *Lost in the Funhouse.* In alleyways, ditches, canopy beds, pinewoods, bridal suites, ship's cabins, coach-and-fours, coaches-and-four, sultry toolsheds; on the cold sand under boardwalks, littered with *El Producto* cigar butts, treasured with Lucky Strike cigarette stubs, Coca-Cola caps, gritty turds, cardboard lollipop sticks, matchbook covers warning that A Slip of the Lip Can Sink a Ship. The shluppish whisper, continuous as seawash round the globe, tidelike falls and rises with the circuit of dawn and dusk.

Magda's teeth. She *was* left-handed. Perspiration. They've gone all the way, through, Magda and Peter, they've been waiting for hours with Mother and Uncle Karl while Father searches for his lost son; they draw french-fried potatoes from a paper cup and shake their heads. They've named the children they'll one day have and bring to Ocean City on holidays. Can spermatozoa properly be thought of as male animalcules when there are no female spermatozoa? They grope through hot, dark windings, past Love's Tunnel's fearsome obstacles. Some perhaps lose their way.

Peter suggested then and there that they do the funhouse; he had been through it before, so had Magda, Ambrose hadn't and suggested, his voice cracking on account of Fat May's laughter, that they swim first. All were chuckling, couldn't help it; Ambrose's father, Ambrose's and Peter's father came up grinning like a lunatic with two boxes of syrup-coated popcorn, one for Mother, one for Magda; the men were to help themselves. Ambrose walked on Magda's right; being by nature left-handed, she carried the box in her left hand. Up front the situation was reversed.

"What are you limping for?" Magda inquired of Ambrose. He supposed in a husky tone that his foot had gone to sleep in the car. Her teeth flashed. "Pins and needles?" It was the honeysuckle on the lattice of the former privy that drew the bees. Imagine being stung there. How long is this going to take?

The adults decided to forgo the pool; but Uncle Karl insisted they change into swimsuits and do the beach. "He wants to watch the pretty girls," Peter teased, and ducked behind Magda from Uncle Karl's pretended wrath. "You've got all the pretty girls you need right here," Magda declared, and Mother said: "Now that's the gospel truth." Magda scolded Peter, who reached over her shoulder to sneak some popcorn. "Your brother and father aren't getting any." Uncle Karl wondered if they were going to have fireworks that night, what with the shortages. It wasn't the shortages, Mr. M —— replied; Ocean City had fireworks from pre-war. But it was too risky on account of the enemy submarines, some people thought.

"Don't seem like Fourth of July without fireworks," said Uncle Karl. The inverted tag in dialogue writing is still considered permissible with proper names or epithets, but sounds old-fashioned with personal pronouns. "We'll have 'em again soon enough," predicted the boys' father. Their mother declared she could do without fireworks: they reminded her too much of the real thing. Their father said all the more reason to shoot off a few now and again. Uncle Karl asked *rhetorically* who needed reminding, just look at people's hair and skin.

"The oil, yes," said Mrs. M ——.

Ambrose had a pain in his stomach and so didn't swim but enjoyed watching the others. He and his father burned red easily. Magda's figure was exceedingly well developed for her age. She too declined to swim, and got mad, and became angry when Peter attempted to drag her into the pool. She always swam, he insisted; what did she mean not swim? Why did a person come to Ocean City?

"Maybe I want to lay here with Ambrose," Magda teased.

Nobody likes a pedant.

"Aha," said Mother. Peter grabbed Magda by one ankle and ordered Ambrose to grab the other. She squealed and rolled over on the beach blanket. Ambrose pretended to help hold her back. Her tan was darker than even Mother's and Peter's. "Help out, Uncle Karl!" Peter cried. Uncle Karl went to seize the other ankle. Inside the top of her swimsuit, however, you could see the line where the sunburn ended and, when she hunched her shoulders and squealed again, one nipple's auburn edge. Mother made them behave themselves. "*You* should certainly know," she said to Uncle Karl. Archly. "That when a lady says she doesn't feel like swimming, a gentleman doesn't ask questions." Uncle Karl said excuse *him*; Mother winked at Magda; Ambrose blushed; stupid Peter kept saying "Phooey on *feel like!*" and tugging at Magda's ankle; then even he got the point, and cannonballed with a holler into the pool.

"I swear," Magda said, in mock *in feigned* exasperation.

The diving would make a suitable literary symbol. To go off the high board you had to wait in a line along the poolside and up the ladder. Fellows tickled girls and goosed one another and shouted to the ones at the top to hurry up, or razzed them for bellyfloppers. Once on the springboard some took a great while posing or clowning or deciding on a dive or getting up their nerve; others ran right off. Especially among the younger fellows the idea was to strike the funniest pose or do the craziest stunt as you fell, a thing that got harder to do as you kept on and kept on. But whether you hollered *Geronimo!* or *Sieg heil!*, held your nose or "rode a bicycle," pretended to be shot or did a perfect jackknife or changed your mind halfway down and ended up with nothing, it was over in two seconds, after all that wait. Spring, pose, splash. Spring, neat-o, splash, Spring, aw fooey, splash.

The grown-ups had gone on; Ambrose wanted to converse with Magda; she was remarkably well developed for her age; it was said that that came from rubbing with a turkish towel, and there were other theories. Ambrose could think of nothing to say except how good a diver Peter was, who was showing off for her benefit. You could pretty well tell by looking at their bathing suits and arm muscles how far along the different fellows were. Ambrose was glad he hadn't gone in swimming, the cold water shrank you up so. Magda pretended to be uninterested in the diving; she probably weighed as much as he did. If you knew your way around in the funhouse like your own bedroom, you could wait until a girl came along and then slip away without ever getting caught, even if her boyfriend was right with her. She'd think *he* did it! It would be better to be the boyfriend, and act outraged, and tear the funhouse apart.

Not act; *be*.

"He's a master diver," Ambrose said. In feigned admiration. "You really have to slave away at it to get that good." What would it matter anyhow if he asked her right out whether she remembered, even teased her with it as Peter would have?

There's no point in going farther; this isn't getting anybody anywhere; they haven't even come to the funhouse yet. Ambrose is off the track, in some new or old part of the place that's not supposed to be used; he strayed into it by some one-in-a-million chance, like the time the roller-coaster car left the tracks in the nineteen-teens against all the laws of physics and sailed over the boardwalk in the dark. And they can't locate him because they don't know where to look. Even the designer and operator have forgotten this other part, that winds around on itself like a whelk shell. That winds around the right part like the snakes on Mercury's caduceus. Some people, perhaps, don't "hit their stride" until their twenties, when the growing-up business is over and women appreciate other things besides wisecracks and teasing and strutting. Peter didn't have one-tenth the imagination *he* had, not one-tenth. Peter did this naming-their-children thing as a joke, making up names like Aloysius and Murgatroyd, but Ambrose knew *exactly* how it would feel to be married and have children of your own, and be a loving husband and father, and go comfortably to work in the mornings and to bed with your wife at night, and wake up with her there. With a breeze coming through the sash and birds and mockingbirds singing in the Chinese-cigar trees. His eyes watered, there aren't enough ways to say that. He would be quite famous in his line of work. Whether Magda was his wife or not, one evening when he was wise-lined and gray at the temples he'd smile gravely, at a fashionable dinner party and remind her of his youthful passion. The time they went with his family to Ocean City; the *erotic fantasies* he used to have about her. How long ago it seemed, and childish! Yet tender, too, *n'est-ce pas?* Would she have imagined that the world-famous whatever remembered how many strings were on the lyre on the bench beside the girl on the label of the cigar box he'd stared at in the toolshed at age ten while, she, age eleven. Even then he had felt *wise beyond his years;* he'd stroked her hair and said in his deepest voice and correctest English, as to a dear child: "I shall never forget this moment."

But though he had breathed heavily, groaned as if ecstatic, what he'd really felt throughout was an odd detachment, as though someone else were Master. Strive as he might to be transported, he heard his mind take notes upon the scene: *This is what they call* passion. *I am experiencing it.* Many of the digger machines were out of order in the penny arcades and could not be repaired or replaced for the duration. Moreover the prizes, made now in USA, were less interesting than formerly, pasteboard items for the most part, and some of the machines wouldn't work on white pennies. The gypsy fortune-teller machine might have provided a foreshadowing of the climax of this story if Ambrose had operated it. It was even dilapidateder than most: the silver coating was worn off the brown metal handles, the glass windows around the dummy were cracked and taped, her kerchiefs and silks long-faded. If a man lived by himself, he could take a department-store mannequin with flexible joints and modify her in certain ways. *However*: by the time he was that old he'd have a real woman. There was a machine that stamped your

name around a white-metal coin with a star in the middle: A ——. His son
would be the second, and when the lad reached thirteen or so he would put
a strong arm around his shoulder and tell him calmly: "It is perfectly normal.
We have all been through it. It will not last forever." Nobody knew how to
be what they were right. He'd smoke a pipe, teach his son how to fish and
softcrab, assure him he needn't worry about himself. Magda would certainly
give, Magda would certainly yield a great deal of milk, although guilty of
occasional solecisms. It don't taste so bad. Suppose the lights came on now!

The day wore on. You think you're yourself, but there are other persons
in you. Ambrose gets hard when Ambrose doesn't want to, *and obversely.*
Ambrose watches them disagree; Ambrose watches him watch. In the funhouse mirror room you can't see yourself go on forever, because no matter
how you stand, your head gets in the way. Even if you had a glass periscope,
the image of your eye would cover up the thing you really wanted to see.
The police will come; there'll be a story in the papers. That must be where it
happened. Unless he can find a surprise exit, an unofficial backdoor or escape
hatch opening on an alley, say, and then stroll up to the family in front of the
funhouse and ask where everybody's been; *he's* been out of the place for ages.
That's just where it happened, in that last lighted room: Peter and Magda
found the right exit; he found one that you weren't supposed to find and
strayed off into the works somewhere. In a perfect funhouse you'd be able to
go only one way, like the divers off the highboard; getting lost would be
impossible; the doors and halls would work like minnow traps on the valves
in veins.

On account of German U-boats, Ocean City was "browned out":
streetlights were shaded on the seaward side; shop-windows and boardwalk
amusement places were kept dim, not to silhouette tankers and Liberty ships
for torpedoing. In a short story about Ocean City, Maryland, during World
War II, the author could make use of the image of sailors on leave in the penny
arcades and shooting galleries, sighting through the crosshairs of toy machine
guns at swastika'd subs, while out in the black Atlantic a U-boat skipper
squints through his periscope at real ships outlined by the glow of penny
arcades. After dinner the family strolled back to the amusement end of the
boardwalk. The boys' father had burnt red as always and was masked with
Noxzema, a minstrel in reverse. The grownups stood at the end of the boardwalk where the Hurricane of '33 had cut an inlet from the ocean to Assawoman Bay.

"Pronounced with a long *o*," Uncle Karl reminded Magda with a wink.
His shirt sleeves were rolled up; Mother punched his brown biceps with the
arrowed heart on it and said his mind was naughty. Fat May's laugh came
suddenly from the funhouse, as if she'd just got the joke; the family laughed
too at the coincidence. Ambrose went under the boardwalk to search for
out-of-town matchbook covers with the aid of his pocket flashlight; he looked
out from the edge of the North American continent and wondered how far
their laughter carried over the water. Spies in rubber rafts; survivors in
lifeboats. If the joke had been beyond his understanding, he could have said:

"The laughter was over his head." And let the reader see the serious wordplay on second reading.

He turned the flashlight on and then off at once even before the woman whooped. He sprang away, heart athud, dropping the light. What had the man grunted? Perspiration drenched and chilled him by the time he scrambled up to the family. "See anything?" his father asked. His voice wouldn't come; he shrugged and violently brushed sand from his pants legs.

"Let's ride the old flying horses!" Magda cried. I'll never be an author. It's been forever already, everybody's gone home, Ocean City's deserted, the ghost-crabs are tickling across the beach and down the littered cold streets. And the empty halls of clapboard hotels and abandoned funhouses. A tidal wave; an enemy air raid; a monster-crab swelling like an island from the sea. *The inhabitants fled in terror.* Magda clung to his trouser leg; he alone knew the maze's secret. "He gave his life that we might live," said Uncle Karl with a scowl of pain, as he. The fellow's hands had been tattooed; the woman's legs, the woman's fat white legs had. *An astonishing coincidence.* He yearned to tell Peter. He wanted to throw up for excitement. They hadn't even chased him. He wished he were dead.

One possible ending would be to have Ambrose come across another lost person in the dark. They'd match their wits together against the funhouse, struggle like Ulysses past obstacle after obstacle, help and encourage each other. Or a girl. By the time they found the exit they'd be closest friends, sweethearts if it were a girl; they'd know each other's inmost souls, be bound together *by the cement of shared adventure*; then they'd emerge into the light and it would turn out that his friend was a Negro. A blind girl. President Roosevelt's son. Ambrose's former archenemy.

Shortly after the mirror room he'd groped along a musty corridor, his heart already misgiving him at the absence of phosphorescent arrows and other signs. He'd found a crack of light — not a door, it turned out, but a seam between the plyboard wall panels — and squinting up to it, espied a small old man, *in appearance not unlike* the photographs at home of Ambrose's late grandfather, nodding upon a stool beneath a bare, speckled bulb. A crude panel of toggle- and knife-switches hung beside the open fuse box near his head; elsewhere in the little room were wooden levers and ropes belayed to boat cleats. At the time, Ambrose wasn't lost enough to rap or call; later he couldn't find that crack. Now it seemed to him that he'd possibly dozed off for a few minutes somewhere along the way; certainly he was exhausted from the afternoon's sunshine and the evening's problems; he couldn't be sure he hadn't dreamed part or all of the sight. Had an old black wall fan droned like bees and shimmied two flypaper streamers? Had the funhouse operator — gentle, somewhat sad and tired-appearing, in expression not unlike the photographs at home of Ambrose's late Uncle Konrad — murmured in his sleep? Is there really such a person as Ambrose, or is he a figment of the author's imagination? Was it Assawoman Bay or Sinepuxent? Are there other errors of fact in this fiction? Was there another sound besides the little slap slap of thigh on ham, like water sucking at the chine-boards of a skiff?

When you're lost, the smartest thing to do is stay put till you're found, hollering if necessary. But to holler guarantees humiliation as well as rescue; keeping silent permits some saving of face — you can act surprised at the fuss when your rescuers find you and swear you weren't lost, if they do. What's more you might find your own way yet, *however belatedly.*

"Don't tell me your foot's still asleep!" Magda exclaimed as the three young people walked from the inlet to the area set aside for ferris wheels, carrousels, and other carnival rides, they having decided in favor of the vast and ancient merry-go-round instead of the funhouse. What a sentence, everything was wrong from the outset. People don't know what to make of him, he doesn't know what to make of himself, he's only thirteen, *athletically and socially inept,* not astonishingly bright, but there are antennae; he has . . . some sort of receivers in his head; things speak to him, he understands more than he should, the world winks at him through its objects, grabs grinning at his coat. Everybody else is in on some secret he doesn't know; they've forgotten to tell him. Through simple *procrastination* his mother put off his baptism until this year. Everyone else had it done as a baby; he'd assumed the same of himself, as had his mother, so she claimed, until it was time for him to join Grace Methodist-Protestant and the oversight came out. He was mortified, but pitched sleepless through his private catechizing, intimidated by the ancient mysteries, a thirteen year old would never say that, resolved to experience conversion like St. Augustine. When the water touched his brow and Adam's sin left him, he contrived by a strain like defecation to bring tears into his eyes — but felt nothing. There was some simple, radical difference about him; he hoped it was genius, feared it was madness, devoted himself to amiability and inconspicuousness. Alone on the seawall near his house he was seized by the terrifying transports he'd thought to find in toolshed, in Communion-cup. The grass was alive! The town, the river, himself, were not imaginary; time roared in his ears like wind; the world was *going on!* This part ought to be dramatized. The Irish author James Joyce once wrote. Ambrose M —— is going to scream.

There is no *texture of rendered sensory detail,* for one thing. The faded distorting mirrors beside Fat May; the impossibility of choosing a mount when one had but a single ride on the great carrousel; the *vertigo attendant on his recognition* that Ocean City was worn out, the place of fathers and grandfathers, straw-boatered men and parasoled ladies survived by their amusements. Money spent, the three paused at Peter's insistence beside Fat May to watch the girls get their skirts blown up. The object was to tease Magda, who said: "I swear, Peter M ——, you've got a one-track mind! Amby and me aren't *interested* in such things." In the tumbling-barrel, too, just inside the Devil's-mouth entrance to the funhouse, the girls were upended and their boyfriends and others could see up their dresses if they cared to. Which was the whole point, Ambrose realized. Of the entire funhouse! If you looked around, you noticed that almost all the people on the boardwalk were paired off into couples except the small children; in a way, that was the whole point of Ocean City! If you had X-ray eyes and could see everything going on at that instant under the boardwalk and in all the hotel rooms and cars and alleyways, you'd realize that all that normally *showed,* like restaurants and dance halls and clothing and test-your-strength machines, was merely preparation and intermission. Fat May screamed.

Because he watched the going-ons from the corner of his eye, it was Ambrose who spied the half-dollar on the boardwalk near the tumbling-barrel. Losers weepers. The first time he'd heard some people moving through a corridor not far away, just after he'd lost sight of the crack of light, he'd decided not to call to them, for fear they'd guess he was scared and poke fun; it sounded like roughnecks; he'd hoped they'd come by and he could follow in the dark without their knowing. Another time he'd heard just one person, unless he imagined it, bumping along as if on the other side of the plywood; perhaps Peter coming back for him, or Father, or Magda lost too. Or the owner and operator of the funhouse. He'd called out once, as though merrily: "Anybody know where the heck we are?" But the query was too stiff, his voice cracked, when the sounds stopped he was terrified: maybe it was a queer who waited for fellows to get lost, or a longhaired filthy monster that lived in some cranny of the funhouse. He stood rigid for hours it seemed like, scarcely respiring. His future was shockingly clear, in outline. He tried holding his breath to the point of unconsciousness. There ought to be a button you could push to end your life absolutely without pain; disappear in a flick, like turning out a light. He would push it instantly! He despised Uncle Karl. But he despised his father too, for not being what he was supposed to be. Perhaps his father hated *his* father, and so on, and his son would hate him, and so on. Instantly!

Naturally he didn't have nerve enough to ask Magda to go through the funhouse with him. With incredible nerve and to everyone's surprise he invited Magda, quietly and politely, to go through the funhouse with him. "I warn you, I've never been through it before," he added, *laughing easily;* "but I reckon we can manage somehow. The important thing to remember, after all, is that it's meant to be a *fun*house; that is, a place of amusement. If people really got lost or injured or too badly frightened in it, the owner'd go out of business. There'd even be lawsuits. No character in a work of fiction can make a speech this long without interruption or acknowledgment from the other characters."

Mother teased Uncle Karl: "Three's a crowd, I always heard." But actually Ambrose was relieved that Peter now had a quarter too. Nothing was what it looked like. Every instant, under the surface of the Atlantic Ocean, millions of living animals devoured one another. Pilots were falling in flames over Europe; women were being forcibly raped in the South Pacific. His father should have taken him aside and said: "There is a simple secret to getting through the funhouse, as simple as being first to see the Towers. Here it is. Peter does not know it; neither does your Uncle Karl. You and I are different. Not surprisingly, you've often wished you weren't. Don't think I haven't noticed how unhappy your childhood has been! But you'll understand, when I tell you, why it had to be kept secret until now. And you won't regret not being like your brother and your uncle. *On the contrary!*" If you knew all the stories behind all the people on the boardwalk, you'd see that *nothing* was what it looked like. Husbands and wives often hated each other; parents didn't necessarily love their children; et cetera. A child took things for granted because he had nothing to compare his life to and everybody acted as if things were as they should be. Therefore each saw himself as the hero of the story, when the truth might turn out to be that he's the villain, or the coward. And there wasn't one thing you could do about it!

Hunchbacks, fat ladies, fools — that no one chose what he was was unbearable. In the movies he'd meet a beautiful young girl in the funhouse; they'd have hairs-breadth escapes from real dangers; he'd do and say the right things; she also; in the end they'd be lovers; their dialogue lines would match up; he'd be perfectly at ease; she'd not only like him well enough, she'd think he was *marvelous*; she'd lie awake thinking about *him*, instead of vice versa — the way *his* face looked in different lights and how he stood and exactly what he'd said — and yet that would be only one small episode in his wonderful life, among many many others. Not a *turning point* at all. What had happened in the toolshed was nothing. He hated, he loathed his parents! One reason for not writing a lost-in-the-funhouse story is that either everybody's felt what Ambrose feels, in which case it goes without saying, or else no normal person feels such things, in which case Ambrose is a freak. "Is anything more tiresome, in fiction, than the problems of sensitive adolescents?" And it's all too long and rambling, as if the author. For all a person knows the first time through, the end could be just around any corner; perhaps, *not impossibly* it's been within reach any number of times. On the other hand he may be scarcely past the start, with everything yet to get through, an intolerable idea.

Fill in: His father's raised eyebrows when he announced his decision to do the funhouse with Magda. Ambrose understands now, but didn't then, that his father was wondering whether he knew what the funhouse was *for* — especially since he didn't object, as he should have, when Peter decided to come along too. The ticket-woman, witchlike, mortifying him when inadvertently he gave her his name-coin instead of the half-dollar, then unkindly calling Magda's attention to the birthmark on his temple: "Watch out for him, girlie, he's a marked man!" She wasn't even cruel, he understood, only vulgar and insensitive. Somewhere in the world there was a young woman with such splendid understanding that she'd see him entire, like a poem or story, and find his words so valuable after all that when he confessed his apprehensions she would explain why they were in fact the very things that made him precious to her . . . and to Western Civilization! There was no such girl, the simple truth being. Violent yawns as they approached the mouth. Whispered advice from an old-timer on a bench near the barrel: "Go crabwise and ye'll get an eyeful without upsetting!" Composure vanished at the first pitch: Peter hollered joyously, Magda tumbled, shrieked, clutched her skirt; Ambrose scrambled crabwise, tight-lipped with terror, was soon out, watched his dropped name-coin slide among the couples. Shame-faced he saw that to get through expeditiously was not the point; Peter feigned assistance in order to trip Magda up, shouted "I see Christmas!" when her legs went flying. The old man, his latest betrayer, cackled approval. A dim hall then of black-thread cobwebs and recorded gibber: he took Magda's elbow to steady her against revolving discs set in the slanted floor to throw your feet out from under, and explained to her in a calm, deep voice his theory that each phase of the funhouse was triggered either automatically, by a series of photoelectric devices, or else manually by operators stationed at peepholes. But he lost his voice thrice as the discs unbalanced him; Magda was anyhow squealing; but at one point she clutched him about the waist to keep from falling, and her right cheek pressed for a moment against his belt-buckle. Heroically he drew her up, it was his chance to clutch her close as if for support and say: "I love you." He even put an arm lightly about the small of her back before a sailor-and-girl pitched into them from behind, sorely treading his left big toe and knocking Magda asprawl with them. The sailor's girl was a string-haired hussy with a loud laugh and light blue drawers; Ambrose realized that he wouldn't have said "I love you" anyhow, and was smitten with self-contempt. How much better it would be to be that common sailor! A wiry little Seaman 3rd, the fellow squeezed a girl to each side and stumbled hilarious into the mirror room, closer to Magda in thirty seconds than Ambrose had got in thirteen years. She giggled at something the fellow said to Peter; she drew her hair from her eyes with a movement so womanly it struck Ambrose's heart; Peter's smacking her backside then seemed particularly coarse. But Magda made a pleased indignant face and cried, "All right for *you*, mister!" and pursued Peter into the maze without a backward glance. The sailor followed after, leisurely, drawing his girl against his hip; Ambrose understood not only that they were all so relieved to be rid of his burdensome company that they didn't even notice his absence, but that he himself shared their relief. Stepping from the treacherous passage at last into the mirror-maze, he saw once again, more clearly than ever, how readily he deceived himself into supposing he was a person. He even foresaw, wincing at his dreadful self-knowledge, that he would repeat the deception, at ever-rarer intervals, all his wretched life, so fearful were the alternatives. Fame, madness, suicide; perhaps all three. It's not believable that so young a boy could articulate that reflection, and in fiction the merely true must always yield to the plausible. Moreover, the symbolism is in places heavy-footed. Yet Ambrose M —— understood, as few adults do, that the famous loneliness of the great was no popular myth but a general truth — furthermore, that it was as much cause as effect.

All the preceding except the last few sentences is exposition that should've been done earlier or interspersed with the present action instead of lumped together. No reader would put up with so much with such *prolixity*. It's interesting that Ambrose's father, though presumably an intelligent man (as indicated by his role as grade-school principal), neither encouraged nor discouraged his sons at all in any way — as if he either didn't care about them or cared all right but didn't know how to act. If this fact should contribute to one of them's becoming a celebrated but wretchedly unhappy scientist, was it a good thing or not? He too might someday face the question; it would be useful to know whether it had tortured his father for years, for example, or never once crossed his mind.

In the maze two important things happened. First, our hero found a name-coin someone else had lost or discarded: AMBROSE, suggestive of the famous lightship and of his late grandfather's favorite dessert, which his mother used to prepare on special occasions out of coconut, oranges, grapes, and what else. Second, as he wondered at the endless replication of his image in the mirrors, second, as he *lost himself in the reflection* that the necessity for an observer makes perfect observation impossible, better make him eighteen at least, yet that would render other things unlikely, he heard Peter and Magda chuckling somewhere together in the maze. "Here!" "No, here!" they shouted to each other; Peter said, "Where's Amby?" Magda murmured, "Amb?" Peter called. In a pleased, friendly voice. He didn't reply. The truth was, his brother was a *happy-go-lucky youngster* who'd've been better off with a regular brother of his own, but who seldom complained of his lot and was generally cordial. Ambrose's throat ached; there aren't enough different ways to say that. He stood quietly while the two young people giggled and thumped through the glittering maze, hurrah'd their discovery of its exit, cried out in joyful alarm at what next beset them. Then he set his mouth and followed after, as he supposed, took a wrong turn, strayed into the pass *wherein he lingers yet.*

The action of conventional dramatic narrative may be represented by a diagram called Freitag's Triangle:

or more accurately by a variant of that diagram:

in which *AB* represents the exposition, *B* the introduction of conflict, *BC* the "rising action," complication, or development of the conflict, *C* the climax, or turn of the action, *CD* the dénouement, or resolution of the conflict. While there is no reason to regard this pattern as an absolute necessity, like many other conventions it became conventional because great numbers of people over many years learned by trial and error that it was effective; one ought not to forsake it, therefore, unless one wishes to forsake as well the effect of drama or has clear cause to feel that deliberate violation of the "normal" pattern can better can better effect that effect. This can't go on much longer; it can go on forever. He died telling stories to himself in the dark; years later, when that vast unsuspected area of the funhouse came to light, the first expedition found his skeleton in one of its labyrinthine corridors and mistook it for part of the entertainment. He died of starvation telling himself stories in the dark; but unbeknownst unbeknownst to him, an assistant operator of the funhouse, happening to overhear him, crouched just behind the plyboard partition and wrote down his every word. The operator's daughter, an exquisite young woman with a figure unusually well developed for her age, crouched just behind the partition and transcribed his every word. Though she had never laid eyes on him, she recognized that here was one of Western Culture's truly great imaginations, the eloquence of whose suffering would be an inspiration to unnumbered. And her heart was torn between her love for the misfortunate young man (yes, she loved him, though she had never laid though she knew him only — but how well! — through his words, and the deep, calm voice in which he spoke them) between her love et cetera and her womanly intuition that only in suffering and isolation could he give voice et cetera. Lone dark dying. Quietly she kissed the rough plyboard, and a tear fell upon the page. Where she had written in shorthand *Where she had written in shorthand* Where she had written in shorthand *Where she* et cetera. A long time ago we should have passed the apex of Freitag's Triangle and made brief work of the *dénouement*; the plot doesn't rise by meaningful steps but winds upon itself, digresses, retreats, hesitates, sighs, collapses, expires. The climax of the story must be its protagonist's discovery of a way to get through the funhouse. But he had found none, may have ceased to search.

What relevance does the war have to the story? Should there be fireworks outside or not?

Ambrose wandered, languished, dozed. Now and then he fell into his habit of rehearsing to himself the unadventurous story of his life, narrated from the third-person point of view, from his earliest memory parenthesis of maple leaves stirring in the summer breath of tidewater Maryland end of parenthesis to the present moment. Its principal events, on this telling, would appear to have been A, B, C, and D.

He imagined himself years hence, successful, married, at ease in the world, the trials of his adolescence far behind him. He has come to the seashore with his family for the holiday: how Ocean City has changed! But at one seldom at one ill-frequented end of the boardwalk a few derelict amusements survive from times gone by: the great carrousel from the turn of the century, with its monstrous griffins and mechanical concert band; the roller coaster rumored since 1916 to have been condemned; the mechanical shooting gallery in which only the image of our enemies changed. His own son laughs with Fat May and wants to know what a funhouse is; Ambrose hugs the sturdy lad close and smiles around his pipestem at his wife.

The family's going home. Mother sits between Father and Uncle Karl, who teases him good-naturedly who chuckles over the fact that the comrade with whom he'd fought his way shoulder to shoulder through the funhouse had turned out to be a blind Negro girl — to their mutual discomfort, as they'd opened their souls. But such are the walls of custom, which even. Whose arm is where? How must it feel. He dreams of a funhouse vaster by far than any yet constructed; but by then they may be out of fashion, like steamboats and excursion trains. Already quaint and seedy: the draperied ladies on the frieze of the carrousel are his father's father's mooncheeked dreams; if he thinks of it more he will vomit his apple-on-a-stick.

He wonders: will he become a regular person? Something has gone wrong; his vaccination didn't take; at the Boy-Scout initiation campfire he only pretended to be deeply moved, as he pretends to this hour that it is not so bad after all in the funhouse, and that he has a little limp. How long will it last? He envisions a truly astonishing funhouse, incredibly complex yet utterly controlled from a great central switchboard like the console of a pipe organ. Nobody had enough imagination. He could design such a place himself, wiring and all, and he's only thirteen years old. He would be its operator: panel lights would show what was up in every cranny of its cunning of its multivarious vastness; a switch-flick would ease this fellow's way, complicate that's, to balance things out; if anyone seemed lost or frightened, all the operator had to do was.

He wishes he had never entered the funhouse. But he has. Then he wishes he were dead. But he's not. Therefore he will construct funhouses for others and be their secret operator — though he would rather be among the lovers for whom funhouses are designed.   [1968]

DONALD BARTHELME *(1931–1989) was born in Philadelphia and raised in Texas, where his father was a prominent architect. While a high school student he won awards for his stories and poetry, and at the University of Houston he edited the campus newspaper and wrote film criticism for the* Houston Post. *At age thirty he became director of the Contemporary Arts Museum in Houston. In 1962 he moved to New York City, where he lived when he was not teaching at the University of Houston as Cullen Distinguished Professor of English.*

During the twenty years that Barthelme contributed short fiction to The New Yorker, *his minimalist style was often imitated. His stories amused some readers as magazine fiction, but they intrigued others who sensed the heavier substance beneath their light narrative surface, as in "The Indian Uprising," written after the French New Left students rioted in Paris in 1968. Barthelme compared his style of writing short fiction with that of collage, saying that "the principle of collage is the central principle of all art in the twentieth century." Literary critics have noted that Barthelme, like the French poet Stéphane Mallarmé, whom he admired, plays with the meanings of words, relying on poetic intuition to spark new connections of ideas buried in trite expressions and conventional responses.*

Readers sometimes criticized Barthelme's stories — along with those of other authors in the group he called "the alleged postmodernists," such as John Barth and Italo Calvino, for being too obscure. Barthelme replied, "Art is not difficult because it wishes to be difficult, rather because it wishes to be art. However much the writer might long to be straight-forward, these virtues are no longer available to him. He discovers that in being simple, honest, straight-forward, nothing much happens." Barthelme published two novels, Snow White *(1967) and* The Dead Father *(1975), and left a third novel,* The King, *ready for publication in 1992 after his death from cancer. Of his eight volumes of short stories,* Sixty Stories *(1981), which won the PEN/Faulkner Award for fiction, is the most representative.*

DONALD BARTHELME

The Indian Uprising

We defended the city as best we could. The arrows of the Comanches came in clouds. The war clubs of the Comanches clattered on the soft, yellow pavements. There were earthworks along the Boulevard Mark Clark and the hedges had been laced with sparkling wire. People were trying to understand. I spoke to Sylvia. "Do you think this is a good life?" The table held apples, books, long-playing records. She looked up. "No."

Patrols of paras and volunteers with armbands guarded the tall, flat buildings. We interrogated the captured Comanche. Two of us forced his head back while another poured water into his nostrils. His body jerked, he choked and wept. Not believing a hurried, careless, and exaggerated report of the number of casualties in the outer districts where trees, lamps, swans had been reduced to clear fields of fire we issued entrenching tools to those who seemed trustworthy and turned the heavy-weapons companies so that we could not be surprised from that direction. And I sat there getting drunker and drunker and more in love and more in love. We talked.

"Do you know Fauré's 'Dolly'?"

"Would that be Gabriel Fauré?"

"It would."

"Then I know it,"she said. "May I say that I play it at certain times, when I am sad, or happy, although it requires four hands."

"How is that managed?"

"I accelerate,"she said, "ignoring the time signature."

And when they shot the scene in the bed I wondered how you felt under the eyes of the cameramen, grips, juicers, men in the mixing booth: excited? stimulated? And when they shot the scene in the shower I sanded a hollow-core door working carefully against the illustrations in texts and whispered instructions from one who had already solved the problem. I had made after all other tables, one while living with Nancy, one while living with Alice, one while living with Eunice, one while living with Marianne.

Red men in waves like people scattering in a square startled by something tragic or a sudden, loud noise accumulated against the barricades we had made of window dummies, silk, thoughtfully planned job descriptions (including scales for the orderly progress of other colors), wine in demijohns, and robes. I analyzed the composition of the barricade nearest me and found two ashtrays, ceramic, one dark brown and one dark brown with an orange blur at the lip; a tin frying pan; two-litre bottles of red wine; three-quarter-litre bottles of Black & White, aquavit, cognac, vodka, gin, Fad #6 sherry; a hollow-core door in birch veneer on black wrought-iron legs; a blanket, red-orange with faint blue stripes; a red pillow and a blue pillow; a woven straw wastebasket; two glass jars for flowers; corkscrews and can openers; two plates and two cups, ceramic, dark brown; a yellow-and-purple poster; a Yugoslavian carved flute, wood, dark brown; and other items. I decided I knew nothing.

The hospitals dusted wounds with powders the worth of which was not quite established, other supplies having been exhausted early in the first day. I decided I knew nothing. Friends put me in touch with a Miss R., a teacher, unorthodox they said, excellent they said, successful with difficult cases, steel shutters on the windows made the house safe. I had just learned via an International Distress Coupon that Jane had been beaten up by a dwarf in a bar on Tenerife but Miss R. did not allow me to speak of it. "You know nothing," she said, "you feel nothing, you are locked in a most savage and terrible ignorance, I despise you, my boy, *mon cher*, my heart. You may attend but you must not attend now, you must attend later, a day or a week or an hour, you are making me ill . . ." I nonevaluated these remarks as Korzybski instructed. But it was difficult. Then they pulled back in a feint near the river and we rushed into that sector with a reinforced battalion hastily formed among the Zouaves and cabdrivers. This unit was crushed in the afternoon of a day that began with spoons and letters in hallways and under windows where men tasted the history of the heart, cone-shaped muscular organ that maintains *circulation of the blood*.

But it is you I want now, here in the middle of this Uprising, with the streets yellow and threatening, short, ugly lances with fur at the throat and inexplicable shell money lying in the grass. It is when I am with you that I am happiest, and it is for you that I am making this hollow-core door table with black wrought-iron legs. I held Sylvania by her bear-claw necklace. "Call off your braves," I said. "We have many years left to live." There was a sort of muck running in the gutters, yellowish, filthy stream suggesting excrement, or nervousness, a city that does not know what it has done to deserve baldness, errors, infidelity. "With luck you will survive until matins," Sylvia said. She ran off down the Rue Chester Nimitz, uttering shrill cries.

Then it was learned that they had infiltrated our ghetto and that the people of the ghetto instead of resisting had joined the smooth, well-coordinated attack with zipguns, telegrams, lockets, causing that portion of the line held by the IRA to swell and collapse. We sent more heroin into the ghetto, and hyacinths, ordering another hundred thousand of the pale, delicate flowers. On the map we considered the situation with its strung-out inhabitants and merely personal emotions. Our parts were blue and their parts were green. I showed the blue-and-green map to Sylvia. "Your parts are green," I said. "You gave me heroin first a year ago," Sylvia said. She ran off down George C. Marshall Allée, uttering shrill cries. Miss R. pushed me into a large room painted white (jolting and dancing in the soft light, and I was excited! and there were people watching!) in which there were two chairs. I sat in one chair and Miss R. sat in the other. She wore a blue dress containing a red figure. There was nothing exceptional about her. I was disappointed by her plainness, by the bareness of the room, by the absence of books.

The girls of my quarter wore long blue mufflers that reached to their knees. Sometimes the girls hid Comanches in their rooms, the blue mufflers together in a room creating a great blue fog. Block opened the door. He was carrying weapons, flowers, loaves of bread. And he was friendly, kind, enthusiastic, so I related a little to the history of torture, reviewing the technical literature quoting the best modern sources, French, German, and American, and pointing out the flies which had gathered in anticipation of some new, cool color.

"What is the situation?" I asked.

"The situation is liquid," he said. "We hold the south quarter and they hold the north quarter. The rest is silence."

"And Kenneth?"

"That girl is not in love with Kenneth," Block said frankly. "She is in love with his coat. When she is not wearing it she is huddling under it. Once I caught it going down the stairs by itself. I looked inside. Sylvia."

Once I caught Kenneth's coat going down the stairs by itself but the coat was a trap and inside a Comanche who made a thrust with his short, ugly knife at my leg which buckled and tossed me over the balustrade through a window and into another situation. Not believing that your body brilliant as it was and your fat, liquid spirit distinguished and angry as it was were stable quantities to which one could return on wires more than once, twice, or another number of times I said: "See the table?"

In Skinny Wainwright Square the forces of green and blue swayed and struggled. The referees ran out on the field trailing chains. And then the blue part would be enlarged, the green diminished. Miss R. began to speak. "A former king of Spain, a Bonaparte, lived for a time in Bordentown, New Jersey. But that's no good." She paused. "The ardor aroused in men by the beauty of women can only be satisfied by God. That is *very* good (it is Valéry) but it is not what I have to teach you, goat, muck, filth, heart of my heart." I showed the table to Nancy. "See the table?" She stuck out her tongue red as a cardinal's hat. "I made such a table once," Block said frankly. "People all over America have made such tables. I doubt very much whether one can enter an American home without finding at least one such table, or traces of its having been there, such as faded places in the carpet." And afterward in the garden the men of the 7th Cavalry played Gabrieli, Albinoni, Marcello, Vivaldi, Boccherini. I saw Sylvia. She wore a yellow ribbon, under a long blue muffler. "Which side are you on," I cried, "after all?"

"The only form of discourse of which I approve," Miss R. said in her dry, tense voice, "is the litany. I believe our masters and teachers as well as plain citizens should confine themselves to what can safely be said. Thus when I hear the words *pewter, snake, tea, Fad #6 sherry, serviette, fenestration, crown, blue* coming from the mouth of some public official, or some raw youth, I am not disappointed. Vertical organization is also possible," Miss R. said, "as in

pewter
snake
tea
Fad #6 sherry
serviette
fenestration
crown
blue.

I run to liquids and colors," she said, "but you, you may run to something else, my virgin, my darling, my thistle, my poppet, my own. Young people," Miss R. said, "run to more and more unpleasant combinations as they sense the nature of our society. Some people," Miss R. said, "run to conceits or wisdom but I hold to the hard, brown, nutlike word. I might point out that there is enough aesthetic excitement here to satisfy anyone but a damned fool." I sat in solemn silence.

Fire arrows lit my way to the post office in Patton Place where members of the Abraham Lincoln Brigade offered their last, exhausted letters, postcards, calendars. I opened a letter but inside was a Comanche flint arrowhead played by Frank Wedekind in an elegant gold chain and congratulations. Your earring rattled against my spectacles when I leaned forward to touch the soft, ruined place where the hearing aid had been. "Pack it in! Pack it in!" I urged, but the men in charge of the Uprising refused to listen to reason or to understand that it was real and that our water supply had evaporated and that our credit was no longer what it had been, once.

We attached wires to the testicles of the captured Comanche. And I sat there getting drunker and drunker and more in love and more in love. When we threw the switch he spoke. His name, he said, was Gustave Aschenbach. He was born at L ——, a country town in the province of Silesia. He was the son of an upper official in the judicature, and his forebears had all been officers, judges, departmental functionaries . . . And you can never touch a girl in the same way more than once, twice, or another number of times however much you may wish to hold, wrap, or otherwise fix her hand, or look, or some other quality, or incident, known to you previously. In Sweden the little Swedish children cheered when we managed nothing more remarkable than getting off a bus burdened with packages, bread and liver-paste and beer. We went to an old church and sat in the royal box. The organist was practising. And then into the graveyard next to the church. Here lies Anna Pederson, a good woman. I threw a mushroom on the grave. The officer commanding the garbage dump reported by radio that the garbage had begun to move.

Jane! I heard via an International Distress Coupon that you were beaten up by a dwarf in a bar on Tenerife. That doesn't sound like you, Jane. Mostly you kick the dwarf in his little dwarf groin before he can get his teeth into your tasty and nice-looking leg, don't you, Jane? Your affair with Harold is reprehensible, you know that, don't you, Jane? Harold is married to Nancy. And there is Paula to think about (Harold's kid), and Billy (Harold's other kid). I think your values are peculiar, Jane! Strings of language extend in every direction to bind the world into a rushing, ribald whole.

And you can never return to felicities in the same way, the brilliant body, the distinguished spirit recapitulating moments that occur once, twice, or another number of times in rebellions, or water. The rolling consensus of the Comanche nation smashed our inner defenses on three sides. Block was firing a greasegun from the upper floor of a building designed by Emery Roth & Sons. "See the table?" "Oh, pack it in with your bloody table!" The city officials were tied to trees. Dusky warriors padded with their forest tread into the mouth of the mayor. "Who do you want to be?" I asked Kenneth and he said he wanted to be Jean-Luc Godard but later when time permitted conversations in large, lighted rooms, whispering galleries with black-and-white Spanish rugs and problematic sculpture on calm, red catafalques. The sickness of the quarrel lay thick in the bed. I touched your back, the white, raised scars.

We killed a great many in the south suddenly with helicopters and rockets but we found that those we had killed were children and more came from the north and from the east and from other places where there are children preparing to live. "Skin," Miss R. said softly in the white, yellow room. "This is the Clemency Committee. And would you remove your belt and shoelaces." I removed my belt and shoelaces and looked (rain shattering from a great height the prospects of silence and clear, neat rows of houses in the subdivisions) into their savage black eyes, paint, feathers, beads.   [1968]

ANN BEATTIE (b. 1947) was born in Washington, D.C. She grew up in Chevy Chase, Maryland, the only child of parents who sent her to a suburban school that she called "a civilized concentration camp" because of its strict dress code and stern disciplinary system. She rebelled by bleaching her hair, wearing fishnet stockings, smoking cigarettes, and graduating in the bottom tenth of her class: "That took a little effort on my part." In 1969 she received a B.A. from American University, and the following year she went on to the University of Connecticut as a graduate student in English literature. Her short stories attracted the interest of Professor J. D. O'Hara there.

> He said that he heard that I wrote, and if I was so good at it, why didn't I let him see what I was doing? So I took one of the few stories I had and put it in his mailbox, and it came back with comments all over it — more comments than I'd ever seen, more words than there were in the story. I would put something in his mailbox every few days and he would return it. He taught me a lot . . . about the technical process of writing.

Beattie began to send her stories to magazines, and her first publication, "A Rose for Judy Garland's Casket," appeared in the Western Humanities Review in 1972. The next year another story won an Atlantic Monthly "first" award, and shortly thereafter she began publishing in The New Yorker. Beattie estimates that she sent thirteen stories to that magazine before one was accepted. "You see, I was living in Eastford, Connecticut, at the time and I was bored. You either wrote a story every night or watched television. I wrote a story every night."

Her first book of nineteen stories, Distortions, was published in 1976, the same year as her first novel, Chilly Scenes of Winter, which was later made into a film. In 1978 she published her second collection of stories, Secrets and Surprises, and a third collection, The Burning House, appeared in 1982. Her most recent collection of stories is What Was Mine (1991). Critics have compared Beattie's fiction to work of John Cheever and John Updike for its exploration of American suburban life and its "weird domesticities." Beattie herself sees little resemblance: "I think they're fine writers, but I don't see any comparison in the world between us. . . . Updike's style, that learned elegance, that intrusion of self into the material, and that very careful way he orchestrates everything, and the same thing with Cheever — they're writing traditionally well-made stories." In stories such as "Janus," Beattie says she writes about chaos, "and many of the simple flat statements that I bring together are usually non sequiturs or bordering on being non sequiturs — which reinforces the chaos. I write in these flat simple sentences because that's the way I think."

ANN BEATTIE

Janus

The bowl was perfect. Perhaps it was not what you'd select if you faced a shelf of bowls, and not the sort of thing that would inevitably attract a lot of attention at a crafts fair, yet it had real presence. It was as predictably admired as a mutt who has no reason to suspect he might be funny. Just such a dog, in fact, was often brought out (and in) along with the bowl.

Andrea was a real-estate agent, and when she thought that some prospective buyers might be dog lovers, she would drop off her dog at the same time she placed the bowl in the house that was up for sale. She would put a dish of water in the kitchen for Mondo, take his squeaking plastic frog out of her purse and drop it on the floor. He would pounce delightedly, just as he did every day at home, batting around his favorite toy. The bowl usually sat on a coffee table, though recently she had displayed it on top of a pine blanket chest and on a lacquered table. It was once placed on a cherry table beneath a Bonnard still life, where it held its own.

Everyone who has purchased a house or who has wanted to sell a house must be familiar with some of the tricks used to convince a buyer that the house is quite special: a fire in the fireplace in early evening; jonquils in a pitcher on the kitchen counter, where no one ordinarily has space to put flowers; perhaps the slight aroma of spring, made by a single drop of scent vaporizing from a lamp bulb.

The wonderful thing about the bowl, Andrea thought, was that it was both subtle and noticeable — a paradox of a bowl. Its glaze was the color of cream and seemed to glow no matter what light it was placed in. There were a few bits of color in it — tiny geometric flashes — and some of these were tinged with flecks of silver. They were as mysterious as cells seen under a microscope; it was difficult not to study them, because they shimmered, flashing for a split second, and then resumed their shape. Something about the colors and their random placement suggested motion. People who liked country furniture always commented on the bowl, but then it turned out that people who felt comfortable with Biedermeier loved it just as much. But the bowl was not at all ostentatious, or even so noticeable that anyone would suspect that it had been put in place deliberately. They might notice the height of the ceiling on first entering a room, and only when their eye moved down from that, or away from the refraction of sunlight on a pale wall, would they see the bowl. Then they would go immediately to it and comment. Yet they always faltered when they tried to say something. Perhaps it was because they were in the house for a serious reason, not to notice some object.

Once Andrea got a call from a woman who had not put in an offer on a house she had shown her. That bowl, she said — would it be possible to find out where the owners had bought that beautiful bowl? Andrea pretended that she did not know what the woman was referring to. A bowl, somewhere in the house? Oh, on a table under the window. Yes, she would ask, of course. She let a couple of days pass, then called back to say that the bowl had been a present and the people did not know where it had been purchased.

When the bowl was not being taken from house to house, it sat on Andrea's coffee table at home. She didn't keep it carefully wrapped (although she transported it that way, in a box); she kept it on the table, because she liked to see it. It was large enough so that it didn't seem fragile or particularly vulnerable if anyone sideswiped the table or Mondo blundered into it at play. She had asked her husband to please not drop his house key in it. It was meant to be empty.

When her husband first noticed the bowl, he had peered into it and smiled briefly. He always urged her to buy things she liked. In recent years, both of them had acquired many things to make up for all the lean years when they were graduate students, but now that they had been comfortable for quite a while, the pleasure of new possessions dwindled. Her husband had pronounced the bowl "pretty," and he had turned away without picking it up to examine it. He had no more interest in the bowl than she had in his new Leica.

She was sure that the bowl brought her luck. Bids were often put in on houses where she had displayed the bowl. Sometimes the owners, who were always asked to be away or to step outside when the house was being shown, didn't even know that the bowl had been in their house. Once — she could not imagine how — she left it behind, and then she was so afraid that something might have happened to it that she rushed back to the house and sighed with relief when the woman owner opened the door. The bowl, Andrea explained — she had purchased a bowl and set it on the chest for safekeeping while she toured the house with the prospective buyers, and she . . . She felt like rushing past the frowning woman and seizing her bowl. The owner stepped aside, and it was only when Andrea ran to the chest that the lady glanced at her a little strangely. In the few seconds before Andrea picked up the bowl, she realized that the owner must have just seen that it had been perfectly placed, that the sunlight struck the bluer part of it. Her pitcher had been moved to the far side of the chest, and the bowl predominated. All the way home, Andrea wondered how she could have left the bowl behind. It was like leaving a friend at an outing — just walking off. Sometimes there were stories in the paper about families forgetting a child somewhere and driving to the next city. Andrea had only gone a mile down the road before she remembered.

In time, she dreamed of the bowl. Twice, in a waking dream — early in the morning, between sleep and a last nap before rising — she had a clear vision of it. It came into sharp focus and startled her for a moment — the same bowl she looked at every day.

She had a very profitable year selling real estate. Word spread, and she had more clients than she felt comfortable with. She had the foolish thought that if only the bowl were an animate object she could thank it. There were times when she wanted to talk to her husband about the bowl. He was a stockbroker, and sometimes told people that he was fortunate to be married to a woman who had such a fine aesthetic sense and yet could also function in the real world. They were a lot alike, really — they had agreed on that. They were both quiet people — reflective, slow to make value judgments, but almost intractable once they had come to a conclusion. They both liked details, but while ironies attracted her, he was more impatient and dismissive when matters became many-sided or unclear. They both knew this, and it was the kind of thing they could talk about when they were alone in the car together, coming home from a party or after a weekend with friends. But she never talked to him about the bowl. When they were at dinner, exchanging their news of the day, or while they lay in bed at night listening to the stereo and murmuring sleepy disconnections, she was often tempted to come right out and say that she thought that the bowl in the living room, the cream-colored bowl, was responsible for her success. But she didn't say it. She couldn't begin to explain it. Sometimes in the morning, she would look at him and feel guilty that she had such a constant secret.

Could it be that she had some deeper connection with the bowl — a relationship of some kind? She corrected her thinking: how could she imagine such a thing, when she was a human being and it was a bowl? It was ridiculous. Just think of how people lived together and loved each other . . . But was that always so clear, always a relationship? She was confused by these thoughts, but they remained in her mind. There was something within her now, something real, that she never talked about.

The bowl was a mystery, even to her. It was frustrating, because her involvement with the bowl contained a steady sense of unrequited good fortune; it would have been easier to respond if some sort of demand were made in return. But that only happened in fairy tales. The bowl was just a bowl. She did not believe that for one second. What she believed was that it was something she loved.

In the past, she had sometimes talked to her husband about a new property she was about to buy or sell — confiding some clever strategy she had devised to persuade owners who seemed ready to sell. Now she stopped doing that, for all her strategies involved the bowl. She became more deliberate with the bowl, and more possessive. She put it in houses only when no one was there, and removed it when she left the house. Instead of just moving a pitcher or a dish, she would remove all the other objects from a table. She had to force herself to handle them carefully, because she didn't really care about them. She just wanted them out of sight.

She wondered how the situation would end. As with a lover, there was no exact scenario of how matters would come to a close. Anxiety became the operative force. It would be irrelevant if the lover rushed into someone else's arms, or wrote her a note and departed to another city. The horror was the possibility of the disappearance. That was what mattered.

She would get up at night and look at the bowl. It never occurred to her that she might break it. She washed and dried it without anxiety, and she moved it often, from coffee table to mahogany corner table or wherever, without fearing an accident. It was clear that she would not be the one who would do anything to the bowl. The bowl was only handled by her, set safely on one surface or another; it was not very likely that anyone would break it. A bowl was a poor conductor of electriciity: it would not be hit by lightning. Yet the idea of damage persisted. She did not think beyond that — to what her life would be without the bowl. She only continued to fear that some accident would happen. Why not, in a world where people set plants where they did not belong, so that visitors touring a house would be fooled into thinking that dark corners got sunlight — a world full of tricks?

She had first seen the bowl several years earlier, at a crafts fair she had visited half in secret, with her lover. He had urged her to buy the bowl. She didn't *need* any more things, she told him. But she had been drawn to the bowl, and they had lingered near it. Then she went on to the next booth, and he came up behind her, tapping the rim against her shoulder as she ran her fingers over a wood carving. "You're still insisting that I buy that?" she said. "No," he said. "I bought it for you." He had bought her other things before this — things she liked more, at first — the child's ebony-and-turquoise ring that fitted her little finger; the wooden box, long and thin, beautifully dove-tailed, that she used to hold paper clips; the soft gray sweater with a pouch pocket. It was his idea that when he could not be there to hold her hand she could hold her own — clasp her hands inside the lone pocket that stretched across the front. But in time she became more attached to the bowl than to any of his other presents. She tried to talk herself out of it. She owned other things that were more striking or valuable. It wasn't an object whose beauty jumped out at you; a lot of people must have passed it by before the two of them saw it that day.

Her lover had said that she was always too slow to know what she really loved. Why continue with her life the way it was? Why be two-faced, he asked her. He had made the first move toward her. When she would not decide in his favor, would not change her life and come to him, he asked her what made her think she could have it both ways. And then he made the last move and left. It was a decision meant to break her will, to shatter her intransigent ideas about honoring previous commitments.

Time passed. Alone in the living room at night, she often looked at the bowl sitting on the table, still and safe, unilluminated. In its way, it was perfect: the world cut in half, deep and smoothly empty. Near the rim, even in dim light, the eye moved toward one small flash of blue, a vanishing point on the horizon.   [1985]

AMBROSE BIERCE *(1842–1914?), the youngest of nine children, was born in a log cabin in Horse Cave Creek, Ohio. His father was a farmer, and Bierce had only one year of formal education at the Kentucky Military Institute when he was seventeen. During the Civil War he enlisted with the Ninth Indiana Infantry as a drummer boy. Wounded in 1864, he left the army and went to live with a brother in San Francisco. There he began his career as a newspaper writer, publishing his first story, "The Haunted Valley," in the* Overland Magazine *in 1871. When Bierce married the daughter of a wealthy Nevada miner, his father-in-law gave the young couple a wedding gift of $10,000, enabling them to live in London for five years. Homesick for California, Bierce returned with his wife and wrote for various newspapers, including William Randolph Hearst's* San Francisco Examiner. *In the 1880s he became very influential in his profession, although in literary circles outside California he was not widely known. Then his wife separated from him, his two sons died tragically, and he became embittered. In his seventies Bierce supervised publication of the twelve volumes of his* Collected Works, *revisited the Civil War battlefields of his youth, and then disappeared across the Mexican border. The Mexican writer Carlos Fuentes imagined Bierce's last months in the novel* The Old Gringo *(1985), which was made into a film.*

Bierce is known as the author of the philosophical epigrams in The Devil's Dictionary *(1906), but his two volumes of short stories are his finest achievement as a writer. He is considered a notable forerunner of American realists such as Stephen Crane. "An Occurrence at Owl Creek Bridge" was included in Bierce's first story collection,* In the Midst of Life, *published privately in San Francisco under the title* Tales of Soldiers and Civilians *(1891). His second collection,* Can Such Things Be? *was published two years later.*

Bierce preferred the short story to the novel, defining the novel as a "short story padded." He modeled his creation of suspense leading up to a dramatic crisis after the stories of Edgar Allan Poe, but Bierce described more realistic situations in his fiction. Dreams, flashbacks, and hallucinations, as in "An Occurrence at Owl Creek Bridge," provided vivid images but no escape from the violent death that was Bierce's obsession.

AMBROSE BIERCE

An Occurrence at Owl Creek Bridge

I

A man stood upon a railroad bridge in Northern Alabama, looking down into the swift waters twenty feet below. The man's hands were behind his back, the wrists bound with a cord. A rope loosely encircled his neck. It was attached to a stout cross-timber above his head, and the slack fell to the level of his knees. Some loose boards laid upon the sleepers supporting the metals of the railway supplied a footing for him and his executioners — two private soldiers of the Federal army, directed by a sergeant, who in civil life may have been a deputy sheriff. At a short remove upon the same temporary platform was an officer in the uniform of his rank, armed. He was a captain. A sentinel at each end of the bridge stood with his rifle in the position known as "support," that is to say, vertical in front of the left shoulder, the hammer resting on the forearm thrown straight across the chest — a formal and unnatural position, enforcing an erect carriage of the body. It did not appear to be the duty of these two men to know what was occurring at the centre of the bridge; they merely blockaded the two ends of the foot plank which traversed it.

Beyond one of the sentinels nobody was in sight; the railroad ran straight away into a forest for a hundred yards, then, curving, was lost to view. Doubtless there was an outpost further along. The other bank of the stream was open ground — a gentle acclivity crowned with a stockade of vertical tree trunks, loop-holed for rifles, with a single embrasure through which protruded the muzzle of a brass cannon commanding the bridge. Midway of the slope between bridge and fort were the spectators — a single company of infantry in line, at "parade rest," the butts of the rifles on the ground, the barrels inclining slightly backward against the right shoulder, the hands crossed upon the stock. A lieutenant stood at the right of the line, the point of his sword upon the ground, his left hand resting upon his right. Excepting the group of four at the centre of the bridge not a man moved. The company faced the bridge, staring stonily, motionless. The sentinels, facing the banks of the stream, might have been statues to adorn the bridge. The captain stood with folded arms, silent, observing the work of his subordinates but making no sign. Death is a dignitary who, when he comes announced, is to be received with formal manifestations of respect, even by those most familiar with him. In the code of military etiquette silence and fixity are forms of deference.

The man who was engaged in being hanged was apparently about thirty-five years of age. He was a civilian, if one might judge from his dress, which was that of a planter. His features were good — a straight nose, firm mouth, broad forehead, from which his long, dark hair was combed straight back, falling behind his ears to the collar of his well-fitted frock coat. He wore a moustache and pointed beard, but no whiskers; his eyes were large and dark grey and had a kindly expression which one would hardly have expected in one whose neck was in the hemp. Evidently this was no vulgar assassin. The liberal military code makes provision for hanging many kinds of people, and gentlemen are not excluded.

The preparations being complete, the two private soldiers stepped aside and each drew away the plank upon which he had been standing. The sergeant turned to the captain, saluted and placed himself immediately behind that officer, who in turn moved apart one pace. These movements left the condemned man and the sergeant standing on the two ends of the same plank, which spanned three of the cross-ties of the bridge. The end upon which the civilian stood almost, but not quite, reached a fourth. This plank had been held in place by the weight of the captain; it was now held by that of the sergeant. At a signal from the former, the latter would step aside, the plank would tilt and the condemned man go down between two ties. The arrangement commended itself to his judgment as simple and effective. His face had not been covered nor his eyes bandaged. He looked a moment at his "unsteadfast footing," then let his gaze wander to the swirling water of the stream racing madly beneath his feet. A piece of dancing driftwood caught his attention and his eyes followed it down the current. How slowly it appeared to move! What a sluggish stream!

He closed his eyes in order to fix his last thoughts upon his wife and children. The water, touched to gold by the early sun, the brooding mists under the banks at some distance down the stream, the fort, the soldiers, the piece of drift — all had distracted him. And now he became conscious of a new disturbance. Striking through the thought of his dear ones was a sound which he could neither ignore nor understand, a sharp, distinct, metallic percussion like the stroke of a blacksmith's hammer upon the anvil; it had the same ringing quality. He wondered what it was, and whether immeasurably distant or near by — it seemed both. Its recurrence was regular, but as slow as the tolling of a death knell. He awaited each stroke with impatience and — he knew not why — apprehension. The intervals of silence grew progressively longer; the delays became maddening. With their greater infrequency the sounds increased in strength and sharpness. They hurt his ear like the thrust of a knife; he feared he would shriek. What he heard was the ticking of his watch.

He unclosed his eyes and saw again the water below him. "If I could free my hands," he thought, "I might throw off the noose and spring into the stream. By diving I could evade the bullets, and, swimming vigorously, reach the bank, take to the woods, and get away home. My home, thank God, is as yet outside their lines; my wife and little ones are still beyond the invader's farthest advance."

As these thoughts, which have here to be set down in words, were flashed into the doomed man's brain rather than evolved from it, the captain nodded to the sergeant. The sergeant stepped aside.

II

Peyton Farquhar was a well-to-do planter, of an old and highly-re-spected Alabama family. Being a slave owner, and, like other slave owners, a politician, he was naturally an original secessionist and ardently devoted to the Southern cause. Circumstances of an imperious nature which it is unnec-essary to relate here, had prevented him from taking service with the gallant army which had fought the disastrous campaigns ending with the fall of Corinth, and he chafed under the inglorious restraint, longing for the release of his energies, the larger life of the soldier, the opportunity for distinction. That opportunity, he felt, would come, as it comes to all in war time. Mean-while he did what he could. No service was too humble for him to perform in aid of the South, no adventure too perilous for him to undertake if consis-tent with the character of a civilian who was at heart a soldier, and who in good faith and without too much qualification assented to at least a part of the frankly villainous dictum that all is fair in love and war.

One evening while Farquhar and his wife were sitting on a rustic bench near the entrance to his grounds, a grey-clad soldier rode up to the gate and asked for a drink of water. Mrs. Farquhar was only too happy to serve him with her own white hands. While she was gone to fetch the water, her husband approached the dusty horseman and inquired eagerly for news from the front.

"The Yanks are repairing the railroads," said the man, "and are getting ready for another advance. They have reached the Owl Creek bridge, put it in order, and built a stockade on the other bank. The commandant has issued an order, which is posted everywhere, declaring that any civilian caught interfering with the railroad, its bridges, tunnels, or trains, will be summarily hanged. I saw the order."

"How far is it to the Owl Creek bridge?" Farquhar asked.

"About thirty miles."

"Is there no force on this side the creek?"

"Only a picket post half a mile out, on the railroad, and a single sentinel at this end of the bridge."

"Suppose a man — a civilian and student of hanging — should elude the picket post and perhaps get the better of the sentinel," said Farquhar, smiling, "what could he accomplish?"

The soldier reflected. "I was there a month ago," he replied. "I observed that the flood of last winter had lodged a great quantity of driftwood against the wooden pier at this end of the bridge. It is now dry and would burn like tow."

The lady had now brought the water, which the soldier drank. He thanked her ceremoniously, bowed to her husband, and rode away. An hour later, after nightfall, he repassed the plantation, going northward in the direc-tion from which he had come. He was a Federal scout.

III

As Peyton Farquhar fell straight downward through the bridge, he lost consciousness and was as one already dead. From this state he was awakened — ages later, it seemed to him — by the pain of a sharp pressure upon his throat, followed by a sense of suffocation. Keen, poignant agonies seemed to shoot from his neck downward through every fibre of his body and limbs. These pains appeared to flash along well-defined lines of ramification, and to beat with an inconceivably rapid periodicity. They seemed like streams of pulsating fire heating him to an intolerable temperature. As to his head, he was conscious of nothing but a feeling of fullness — of congestion. These sensations were unaccompanied by thought. The intellectual part of his nature was already effaced; he had power only to feel, and feeling was torment. He was conscious of motion. Encompassed in a luminous cloud, of which he was now merely the fiery heart, without material substance, he swung through unthinkable arcs of oscillation, like a vast pendulum. Then all at once, with terrible suddenness, the light about him shot upward with the noise of a loud plash; a frightful roaring was in his ears, and all was cold and dark. The power of thought was restored; he knew that the rope had broken and he had fallen into the stream. There was no additional strangulation; the noose about his neck was already suffocating him, and kept the water from his lungs. To die of hanging at the bottom of a river — the idea seemed to him ludicrous. He opened his eyes in the blackness and saw above him a gleam of light, but how distant, how inaccessible! He was still sinking, for the light became fainter and fainter until it was a mere glimmer. Then it began to grow and brighten, and he knew that he was rising toward the surface — knew it with reluctance, for he was now very comfortable. "To be hanged and drowned," he thought, "that is not so bad; but I do not wish to be shot. No; I will not be shot; that is not fair."

He was not conscious of an effort, but a sharp pain in his wrist apprised him that he was trying to free his hands. He gave the struggle his attention, as an idler might observe the feat of a juggler, without interest in the outcome. What splendid effort! — what magnificent, what superhuman strength! Ah, that was a fine endeavor! Bravo! The cord fell away; his arms parted and floated upward, the hands dimly seen on each side in the growing light. He watched them with a new interest as first one and then the other pounced upon the noose at his neck. They tore it away and thrust it fiercely aside, its undulations resembling those of a water-snake. "Put it back, put it back!" He thought he shouted these words to his hands, for the undoing of the noose had been succeeded by the direst pang which he had yet experienced. His neck arched horribly; his brain was on fire; his heart, which had been fluttering faintly, gave a great leap, trying to force itself out at his mouth. His whole body was racked and wrenched with an insupportable anguish! But his disobedient hands gave no heed to the command. They beat the water vigorously with quick, downward strokes, forcing him to the surface. He felt his head emerge; his eyes were blinded by the sunlight; his chest expanded convulsively, and with a supreme and crowning agony his lungs engulfed a great draught of air, which instantly he expelled in a shriek!

He was now in full possession of his physical senses. They were, indeed, preternaturally keen and alert. Something in the awful disturbance of his organic system had so exalted and refined them that they made record of things never before perceived. He felt the ripples upon his face and heard their separate sounds as they struck. He looked at the forest on the bank of the stream, saw the individual trees, the leaves and the veining of each leaf — saw the very insects upon them, the locusts, the brilliant-bodied flies, the grey spiders stretching their webs from twig to twig. He noted the prismatic colors in all the dewdrops upon a million blades of grass. The humming of the gnats that danced above the eddies of the stream, the beating of the dragon flies' wings, the strokes of the water spiders' legs, like oars which had lifted their boat — all these made audible music. A fish slid along beneath his eyes and he heard the rush of its body parting the water.

He had come to the surface facing down the stream; in a moment the visible world seemed to wheel slowly round, himself the pivotal point, and he saw the bridge, the fort, the soldiers upon the bridge, the captain, the sergeant, the two privates, his executioners. They were in silhouette against the blue sky. They shouted and gesticulated, pointing at him; the captain had drawn his pistol, but did not fire; the others were unarmed. Their movements were grotesque and horrible, their forms gigantic.

Suddenly he heard a sharp report and something struck the water smartly within a few inches of his head, spattering his face with spray. He heard a second report, and saw one of the sentinels with his rifle at his shoulder, a light cloud of blue smoke rising from the muzzle. The man in the water saw the eye of the man on the bridge gazing into his own through the sights of the rifle. He observed that it was a grey eye, and remembered having read that grey eyes were keenest and that all famous marksmen had them. Nevertheless, this one had missed.

A counter swirl had caught Farquhar and turned him half round; he was again looking into the forest on the bank opposite the fort. The sound of a clear, high voice in a monotonous singsong now rang out behind him and came across the water with a distinctness that pierced and subdued all other sounds, even the beating of the ripples in his ears. Although no soldier, he had frequented camps enough to know the dread significance of that deliberate, drawling, aspirated chant; the lieutenant on shore was taking a part in the morning's work. How coldly and pitilessly — with what an even, calm intonation, presaging and enforcing tranquility in the men — with what accurately-measured intervals fell those cruel words:

"Attention, company. . . . Shoulder arms. . . . Ready. . . . Aim. . . . Fire."

Farquhar dived — dived as deeply as he could. The water roared in his ears like the voice of Niagara, yet he heard the dulled thunder of the volley, and rising again toward the surface, met shining bits of metal, singularly flattened, oscillating slowly downward. Some of them touched him on the face and hands, then fell away, continuing their descent. One lodged between his collar and neck; it was uncomfortably warm, and he snatched it out.

As he rose to the surface, gasping for breath, he saw that he had been a long time under water; he was perceptibly farther down stream — nearer to safety. The soldiers had almost finished reloading; the metal ramrods flashed all at once in the sunshine as they were drawn from the barrels, turned in the air, and thrust into their sockets. The two sentinels fired again, independently and ineffectually.

The hunted man saw all this over his shoulder; he was now swimming vigorously with the current. His brain was as energetic as his arms and legs; he thought with the rapidity of lightning.

"The officer," he reasoned, "will not make the martinet's error a second time. It is as easy to dodge a volley as a single shot. He has probably already given the command to fire at will. God help me, I cannot dodge them all!"

An appalling plash within two yards of him, followed by a loud rushing sound, *diminuendo*, which seemed to travel back through the air to the fort and died in an explosion which stirred the very river to its deeps! A rising sheet of water, which curved over him, fell down upon him, blinded him, strangled him! The cannon had taken a hand in the game. As he shook his head free from the commotion of the smitten water, he heard the deflected shot humming through the air ahead, and in an instant it was cracking and smashing the branches in the forest beyond.

"They will not do that again," he thought; "the next time they will use a charge of grape. I must keep my eye upon the gun; the smoke will apprise me — the report arrives too late; it lags behind the missile. It is a good gun."

Suddenly he felt himself whirled round and round — spinning like a top. The water, the banks, the forest, the now distant bridge, fort, and men — all were commingled and blurred. Objects were represented by their colors only; circular horizontal streaks of color — that was all he saw. He had been caught in a vortex and was being whirled on with a velocity of advance and gyration which made him giddy and sick. In a few moments he was flung upon the gravel at the foot of the left bank of the stream — the southern bank — and behind a projecting point which concealed him from his enemies. The sudden arrest of his motion, the abrasion of one of his hands on the gravel, restored him and he wept with delight. He dug his fingers into the sand, threw it over himself in handfuls and audibly blessed it. It looked like gold, like diamonds, rubies, emeralds; he could think of nothing beautiful which it did not resemble. The trees upon the bank were giant garden plants; he noted a definite order in their arrangement, inhaled the fragrance of their blooms. A strange, roseate light shone through the spaces among their trunks, and the wind made in their branches the music of æolian harps. He had no wish to perfect his escape, was content to remain in that enchanting spot until retaken.

A whizz and rattle of grapeshot among the branches high above his head roused him from his dream. The baffled cannoneer had fired him a random farewell. He sprang to his feet, rushed up the sloping bank, and plunged into the forest.

All that day he travelled, laying his course by the rounding sun. The forest seemed interminable; nowhere did he discover a break in it, not even a woodman's road. He had not known that he lived in so wild a region. There was something uncanny in the revelation.

By nightfall he was fatigued, footsore, famishing. The thought of his wife and children urged him on. At last he found a road which led him in what he knew to be the right direction. It was as wide and straight as a city street, yet it seemed untravelled. No fields bordered it, no dwelling anywhere. Not so much as the barking of a dog suggested human habitation. The black bodies of the great trees formed a straight wall on both sides, terminating on the horizon in a point, like a diagram in a lesson in perspective. Overhead, as he looked up through this rift in the wood, shone great golden stars looking unfamiliar and grouped in strange constellations. He was sure they were arranged in some order which had a secret and malign significance. The wood on either side was full of singular noises, among which — once, twice, and again — he distinctly heard whispers in an unknown tongue.

His neck was in pain, and, lifting his hand to it, he found it horribly swollen. He knew that it had a circle of black where the rope had bruised it. His eyes felt congested; he could no longer close them. His tongue was swollen with thirst; he relieved its fever by thrusting it forward from between his teeth into the cool air. How softly the turf had carpeted the untravelled avenue! He could no longer feel the roadway beneath his feet!

Doubtless, despite his suffering, he fell asleep while walking, for now he sees another scene — perhaps he has merely recovered from a delirium. He stands at the gate of his own home. All is as he left it, and all bright and beautiful in the morning sunshine. He must have travelled the entire night. As he pushes open the gate and passes up the wide white walk, he sees a flutter of female garments; his wife, looking fresh and cool and sweet, steps down from the verandah to meet him. At the bottom of the steps she stands waiting, with a smile of ineffable joy, an attitude of matchless grace and dignity. Ah, how beautiful she is! He springs forward with extended arms. As he is about to clasp her, he feels a stunning blow upon the back of the neck; a blinding white light blazes all about him, with a sound like a shock of a cannon — then all is darkness and silence!

Peyton Farquhar was dead; his body, with a broken neck, swung gently from side to side beneath the timbers of the Owl Creek bridge.   [1891]

AMY BLOOM (*b. 1953*), *a psychotherapist who divides her time between writing and her practice, recalls that she "started writing stories when I started reading, and stopped when I was sixteen. I could barely make sense of my life, let alone write about it." After high school graduation, she left home and worked a series of casual jobs in different parts of the United States, attended college, married, and went on to graduate school. She was about to begin her own psychoanalysis as a therapist when, driving home after her first meeting with her training analyst, she found the urge to write fiction suddenly resurfaced: "My unconscious nudged me so sharply . . . [that an] entire plot for a story came tumbling at me and I took notes. By the time I was home, I knew that my relationship to stories and secrets, the telling and the listening, had altered."*

Bloom took the material for her stories from her own life and that of her friends and family. She felt that her commitment to confidentiality with her patients undergoing analysis meant that no one she had ever treated should "have the experience of seeing themselves or their remarks reproduced in my work. This means that there are a lot of wonderful stories and turns of phrase that I can't use, but I sleep soundly at night and don't worry that I've inadvertently betrayed my clients' trust." Highly conscious of her multiple roles as wife, mother, daughter, sister, and therapist, Bloom understands that "all the roles affect my writing. I see a lot of different points of view because I live a lot of different points of view. Understanding has always mattered more to me than assessing, and my writing reflects that."

Bloom's short fiction was published in Antaeus, Story, *and* The Best American Short Stories *of 1991 and 1992. The following year, twelve stories were collected in her first book of short fiction,* Come to Me. *Reviewing the book, Ursula Le Guin commented that Bloom "can handle unspeakable pain with the quiet authority of a Chekhov." "Silver Water" is the last of three linked stories in the collection tracing a complex web of family relationships over nearly half a century. The first two stories are told from the point of view of the father and the mother, the last by the younger daughter of the Silverstein family. Bloom has said that "the grief, love, and exhaustion of life with schizophrenics is so close to unbearable that I can only admire, and want to sing for, the afflicted and their families."*

AMY BLOOM

Silver Water

My sister's voice was like mountain water in a silver pitcher; the clear, blue beauty of it cools you and lifts you up beyond your heat, beyond your body. After we went to see *La Traviata*, when she was fourteen and I was twelve, she elbowed me in the parking lot and said, "Check this out." And she opened her mouth unnaturally wide and her voice came out, so crystalline and bright, that all the departing operagoers stood frozen by their cars, unable to take out their keys or open their doors until she had finished and then they cheered like hell.

That's what I like to remember and that's the story I told to all of her therapists. I wanted them to know her, to know that who they saw was not all there was to see. That before the constant tinkling of commercials and fast-food jingles, there had been Puccini and Mozart and hymns so sweet and mighty, you expected Jesus to come down off his cross and clap. That before there was a mountain of Thorazined fat, swaying down the halls in nylon maternity tops and sweatpants, there had been the prettiest girl in Arrandale Elementary School, the belle of Landmark Junior High. Maybe there were other pretty girls, but I didn't see them. To me, Rose, my beautiful blond defender, my guide to Tampax and my mother's moods, was perfect.

She had her first psychotic break when she was fifteen. She had been coming home moody and tearful, then quietly beaming, then she stopped coming home. She would go out into the woods behind our house and not come in until my mother would go out at dusk, and step gently into the briars and saplings and pull her out, blank-faced, her pale blue pullover covered with crumbled leaves, her white jeans smeared with dirt. After three weeks of this, my mother, who is a musician and widely regarded as eccentric, said to my father, who is a psychiatrist and a kind, sad man, "She's going off."

"What is that, your professional opinion?" He picked up the newspaper and put it down again, sighing. "I'm sorry, I didn't mean to snap at you. I know something's bothering her. Have you talked to her?"

"What's there to say? David, she's going crazy, she doesn't need a heart-to-heart talk with Mom, she needs a hospital."

They went back and forth and my father sat down with Rose for a few hours and she sat there, licking the hairs on her forearm, first one way, then the other. My mother stood in the hallway, dry-eyed and pale, watching the two of them. She had already packed Rose's bag and when three of my father's friends dropped by to offer free consultations and recommendations, my mother and Rose's suitcase were already in the car. My mother hugged me and told me that they would be back that night, but not with Rose. She also said, divining my worst fear, "It won't happen to you, honey. Some people go crazy and some people never do. You never will." She smiled and stroked my hair. "Not even when you want to."

Rose was in hospitals, great and small, for the next ten years. She had lots of terrible therapists and a few good ones. One place had no pictures on the walls, no windows, and the patients all wore slippers with the hospital crest on them. My mother didn't even bother to go to Admissions. She turned Rose around and the two of them marched out, my father, trailing behind them, apologizing to his colleagues. My mother ignored the psychiatrists, the social workers and the nurses and she played Handel and Bessie Smith for the patients on whatever piano was available. At some places, she had a Steinway donated by a grateful, or optimistic, family; at others, she banged out "Gimme a Pigfoot" on an old, scarred box that hadn't been tuned since there'd been English-speaking physicians on the grounds. My father talked in serious, appreciative voices to the administrators and unit chiefs and tried to be friendly with whoever was managing Rose's case. We all hated the family therapists.

The worst family therapist we ever had sat in a pale green room with us, visibly taking stock of my mother's ethereal beauty and her faded blue T-shirt and girl-sized jeans, my father's rumpled suit and stained tie and my own unreadable, sixteen-year-old fashion statement. Rose was beyond fashion that year, in one of her dancing teddy-bear smocks and extra-extra-large Celtics sweatpants. Mr. Walker read Rose's file in front of us and then watched, in alarm, as Rose began crooning, beautifully, and slowly massaging her breasts. My mother and I started to laugh and even my father started to smile. This was Rose's usual opening salvo for new therapists.

Mr. Walker said, "I wonder why it is that everyone is so entertained by Rose behaving inappropriately."

Rose burped and then we all laughed. This was the seventh family therapist we had seen and none of them had lasted very long. Mr. Walker, unfortunately, was determined to do right by us.

"What do you think of Rose's behavior, Violet?" They did this sometimes. In their manual, it must say, if you think the parents are too weird, try talking to the sister.

"I don't know. Maybe she's trying to get you to stop talking about her in the third person."

"Nicely put," my father said.

"Indeed," my mother said.

"Fuckin' A," Rose said.

"Well, this is something that the whole family agrees upon," Mr. Walker said, trying to act as if he understood, or even liked us.

"That was not a successful intervention, Ferret Face." Rose tended to function better when she was angry. He did look like a blond ferret and we all laughed again. Even my father, who tried to give these people a chance out of some sense of collegiality, had given it up.

Mr. Walker decided, after fourteen minutes, that our time was up and walked out, leaving us grinning at each other. Rose was still nuts, but at least we'd all had a little fun.

Our best family therapist started out almost as badly. We scared off a resident and then scared off her supervisor, who sent us Dr. Thorne. Three hundred pounds of Texas chili, cornbread and Lone Star beer, finished off with big black cowboy boots and a little string tie around the area of his neck.

"Oh, frabjous day, it's Big Nut." Rose was in heaven and stopped massaging her breasts immediately.

"Hey, Little Nut." You have to understand how big a man would have to be to call my sister "little." He christened us all, right away. "And it's the good Doctor Nut, and Madame Hickory Nut, 'cause they are the hardest damn nuts to crack, and over here in the overalls and not much else, is No One's Nut" — a name which summed up both my sanity and my loneliness. We all relaxed.

Dr. Thorne was good for us. Rose moved into a halfway house, whose director loved Big Nut so much she kept Rose even when Rose went through a period of having sex with everyone who passed her door. She was in a fever for a while, trying to still the voices by fucking her brains out.

Big Nut said, "Darlin', I can't. I cannot make love to every beautiful woman I meet and, furthermore, I can't do that and be your therapist, too. It's a great shame, but I think you might be able to find a really nice guy, someone who treats you just as sweet and kind as I would, if I were lucky enough to be your beau. I don't want you to settle for less." And she stopped propositioning the crack addicts and the alcoholics and the guys at the shelter. We loved Dr. Thorne.

My father cut back on seeing rich neurotics and helped out one day a week at Dr. Thorne's walk-in clinic. My mother finished a record of Mozart concerti and played at fund-raisers for Rose's halfway house. I went back to college and found a wonderful linebacker from Texas to sleep with. In the dark, I would make him call me "darlin'." Rose took her meds, lost about fifty pounds and began singing at the A.M.E. Zion Church, down the street from the halfway house.

At first, they didn't know what to do with this big, blonde lady, dressed funny and hovering wistfully in the doorway during their rehearsals, but she gave them a few bars of "Precious Lord" and the choir director felt God's hand and saw that, with the help of His sweet child, Rose, the Prospect Street Choir was going all the way to the Gospel Olympics.

Amidst a sea of beige, umber, cinnamon and espresso faces, there was Rose, bigger, blonder and pinker than any two white women could be. And Rose and the choir's contralto, Addie Robicheaux, laid out their gold and silver voices and wove them together in strands as fine as silk, as strong as steel. And we wept as Rose and Addie, in their billowing garnet robes, swayed together, clasping hands until the last perfect note floated up to God and then they smiled down at us.

Rose would still go off from time to time and the voices would tell her to do bad things, but Dr. Thorne or Addie or my mother could usually bring her back. After five good years, Big Nut died. Stuffing his face with a chili dog, sitting in his un-air-conditioned office in the middle of July, he had one big, Texas-sized aneurism and died.

Rose held on tight for seven days; she took her meds, went to choir practice and rearranged her room about a hundred times. His funeral was a Lourdes for the mentally ill. If you were psychotic, borderline, bad-off neurotic, or just very hard to get along with, you were there. People shaking so bad from years of heavy meds that they fell out of the pews. People holding hands, crying, moaning, talking to themselves; the crazy and the not-so-crazy were all huddled together, like puppies at the pound.

Rose stopped taking her meds and the halfway house wouldn't keep her after she pitched another patient down the stairs. My father called the insurance company and found out that Rose's new, improved psychiatric coverage wouldn't begin for forty-five days. I put all of her stuff in a garbage bag and we walked out of the halfway house, Rose winking at the poor, drooling boy on the couch.

"This is going to be difficult — not all bad, but difficult — for the whole family and I thought we should discuss everybody's expectations. I know I have some concerns." My father had convened a family meeting as soon as Rose had finished putting each one of her thirty stuffed bears in its own special place.

"No meds," Rose said, her eyes lowered, her stubby fingers, those fingers that had braided my hair and painted tulips on my cheeks, pulling hard on the hem of her dirty smock.

My father looked in despair at my mother.

"Rosie, do you want to drive the new car?" my mother asked.

Rose's face lit up. "I'd love to drive that car. I'd drive to California, I'd go see the bears at the San Diego Zoo. I would take you, Violet, but you always hated the zoo. Remember how she cried at the Bronx Zoo when she found out that the animals didn't get to go home at closing?" Rose put her damp hand on mine and squeezed it, sympathetically. "Poor Vi."

"If you take your medication, after a while, you'll be able to drive the car. That's the deal. Meds, car." My mother sounded accommodating but unenthusiastic, careful not to heat up Rose's paranoia.

"You got yourself a deal, darlin'."

I was living about an hour away then, teaching English during the day, writing poetry at night. I went home every few days, for dinner. I called every night.

My father said, quietly, "It's very hard. We're doing all right, I think. Rose has been walking in the mornings with your mother and she watches a lot of TV. She won't go to the day hospital and she won't go back to the choir. Her friend, Mrs. Robicheaux, came by a couple of times. What a sweet woman. Rose wouldn't even talk to her; she just sat there, staring at the wall and humming. We're not doing all that well, actually, but I guess we're getting by. I'm sorry, sweetheart, I don't mean to depress you."

My mother said, emphatically, "We're doing fine. We've got our routine and we stick to it and we're fine. You don't need to come home so often, you know. Wait till Sunday, just come for the day. Lead your life, Vi. She's leading hers."

I stayed away until Sunday, afraid to pick up my phone, grateful to my mother for her harsh calm and her reticence, the qualities that had enraged me throughout my childhood.

I came on a Sunday, in the early afternoon, to help my father garden, something we had always enjoyed together. We weeded and staked tomatoes and killed aphids while my mother and Rose were down at the lake. I didn't even get into the house until four, when I needed a glass of water.

Someone had broken the piano bench into five neatly stacked pieces and placed them where the piano bench usually was.

"We were having such a nice time, I couldn't bear to bring it up," my father said, standing in the doorway, carefully keeping his gardening boots out of the kitchen.

"What did Mommy say?"

"She said, 'Better the bench than the piano.' And your sister lay down on the floor and just wept. Then, your mother took her down to the lake. This can't go on, Vi. We have twenty-seven days left, your mother gets no sleep because Rose doesn't sleep and if I could just pay twenty-seven thousand dollars to keep her in the hospital until the insurance takes over, I'd do it."

"All right. Do it. Pay the money and take her back to Hartley-Rees. It was the prettiest place and she liked that art therapy there."

"I would if I could. The policy states that she must be symptom-free for at least forty-five days before her coverage begins. Symptom-free means no hospitalization."

"Jesus, Daddy, how could you get that kind of policy? She hasn't been symptom-free for forty-five minutes."

"It's the only one I could get for long-term psychiatric." He put his hand over his mouth to block whatever he was about to say and went back out to the garden. I couldn't see if he was crying.

He stayed outside and I stayed inside, until Rose and my mother came home from the lake, Rose's soggy sweatpants were rolled up to her knees and she had a bucketful of shells and gray stones, which my mother persuaded her to leave on the back porch. My mother kissed me lightly and told Rose to go up to her room and change out of her wet pants.

Rose's eye grew very wide. "Never. I will never . . ." she began banging her head with rhythmic intensity, against the kitchen floor, throwing all of her weight behind each attack. My mother put her arms around Rose's waist and tried to hold her back. Rose shook her off, not even looking around to see what was slowng her down. My mother crumpled next to the refrigerator.

"Violet, please . . ."

I threw myself onto the kitchen floor, becoming the spot that Rose was smacking her head against. She stopped a fraction of an inch short of my stomach.

"Oh, Vi, Mommy, I'm sorry. I'm sorry, don't hate me." She staggered to her feet and ran, wailing, to her room.

My mother got up and washed her face, brusquely, rubbing it dry with a dishcloth. My father heard the wailing and came running in, slipping his long bare feet out of his rubber boots.

"Galen, Galen, let me see." He held her head and looked closely for bruises on her pale, small face. "What happened?" My mother looked at me. "Violet, what happened? Where's Rose?"

"Rose got upset and when she went running upstairs, she pushed Mommy out of the way." I've only told three lies in my life and that was my second.

"She must feel terrible, pushing you, of all people. It would have to be you, but I know she didn't want it to be." He made my mother a cup of tea and all the love he had for her, despite her silent rages and her vague stares, came pouring through the teapot, warming her cup, filling her small, long-fingered hands. He stood by her and she rested her head against his hip. I looked away.

"Let's make dinner, then I'll call her. Or you call her, David, maybe she'd rather see your face first."

Dinner was filled with all of our starts and stops and Rose's desperate efforts to control herself. She could barely eat and hummed the McDonald's theme song over and over again, pausing only to spill her juice down the front of her smock and begin weeping. My father looked at my mother and handed Rose his napkin. She dabbed at herself, listlessly, but the tears stopped.

"I want to go to bed. I want to go to bed and be in my head. I want to go to bed and be in my bed and in my head and just wear red. For red is the color that my baby wore and once more, it's true, yes, it is, it's true. Please don't wear red tonight, ohh, ohh, please don't wear red tonight, for red is the color — "

"Okay, okay, Rose. It's okay. I'll go upstairs with you and you can get ready for bed. Then, Mommy will come up and say good night, too. It's okay, Rose." My father reached out his hand and Rose grasped it and they walked out of the dining room together, his long arm around her middle.

My mother sat at the table for a moment, her face in her hands and then she began clearing the table. We cleared without talking, my mother humming Schubert's "Schlummerlied," a lullaby about the woods and the river calling to the child to go to sleep. She sang it to us every night, when we were small.

My father came back into the kitchen and signaled to my mother. She went upstairs and they came back down together, a few minutes later.

"She's asleep," they said and we went to sit on the porch and listen to the crickets. I don't remember the rest of the evening, but I remember it as quietly sad and I remember the rare sight of my parents holding hands, sitting on the picnic table, watching the sunset.

I woke up at three o'clock in the morning, feeling the cool night air through my sheet. I went down the hall for another blanket and looked into Rose's room, for no reason. She wasn't there. I put on my jeans and a sweater and went downstairs. I could feel her absence. I went outside and saw her wide, draggy footprints darkening the wet grass, into the woods.

"Rosie," I called, too softly, not wanting to wake my parents, not wanting to startle Rose. "Rosie, it's me. Are you here? Are you all right?"

I almost fell over her. Huge and white in the moonlight, her flowered smock bleached in the light and shadow, her sweatpants now completely wet. Her head was flung back, her white, white neck exposed like a lost Greek column.

"Rosie, Rosie — " Her breathing was very slow and her lips were not as pink as they usually were. Her eyelids fluttered.

"Closing time," she whispered. I believe that's what she said.

I sat with her, uncovering the bottle of white pills by her hand, and watched the stars fade.

When the stars were invisible and the sun was warming the air, I went back to the house. My mother was standing on the porch, wrapped in a blanket, watching me. Every step I took overwhelmed me; I could picture my mother slapping me, shooting me for letting her favorite die.

"Warrior queens," she said, wrapping her thin strong arms around me.

"I raised warrior queens." She kissed me fiercely and went into the woods by herself.

A little later, she woke my father, who could not go into the woods, and still later she called the police and the funeral parlor. She hung up the phone, lay down, and didn't get back out of bed until the day of the funeral. My father fed us both and called the people who needed to be called and picked out Rose's coffin by himself.

My mother played the piano and Addie sang her pure gold notes and I closed my eyes and saw my sister, fourteen years old, lion's mane thrown back and her eyes tightly closed against the glare of the parking lot lights. That sweet sound held us tight, flowing around us, eddying through our hearts, rising, still rising.   [1991]

JORGE LUIS BORGES *(1899–1986), the Argentinean writer of fiction, poetry, and criticism, was born in Buenos Aires. His father, a professor of psychology, amused him in childhood with various philosophical puzzles that continued to intrigue Borges when he grew up. Educated in Europe, he began to write as a member of a Spanish avant-garde literary movement called* ultráisme, *a development of expressionism in which image and metaphor were exaggerated to become more important than plot, character, or theme. Borges rejected this extreme view when he matured as an artist, but he remained an antirealist whose fiction influenced a generation of postmodernist writers. After his return to Buenos Aires in 1921, he worked in the National Library, rising to be its director before the dictator Juan Perón hounded him out of the job for political reasons. Borges published his first book in 1923, but in the 1930s he was most active as an essayist and editor; he also wrote detective stories under other names. Then came* Fictions *(1944), a collection of short, often playful prose pieces in which Borges examined various ideas to show that every human effort is a "fiction."* Labyrinths *(1962),* The Aleph and Other Stories *(1970), and* Doctor Brodie's Report *(1972) are more collections of sketches and stories.* Borges on Writing *(1973) contains his views on fiction, poetry, and translation. Until his death Borges lived in Buenos Aires, where his progressive blindness circumscribed his activities.*

Borges said that he wrote stories for the "sheer fun of it. . . . I'm fond of short stories, but I'm far too lazy for novel writing. I'd get tired of the whole thing after writing ten or fifteen pages." He wrote his first story, "Streetcorner Man," as a literary experiment after seeing a gangster film by Josef von Sternberg. He wanted to write a vivid, visual story, not a realistic one: "I knew quite well it was all unreal, but as I wasn't striving after reality I didn't mind." An erudite man, Borges often based his stories on ideas that interested him, as in "The Garden of Forking Paths."

A repeated image in this story is the labyrinth, representing the central paradox that "the rich symmetries" of the mind, of history, and of time can end only in confusion or mystery. Less concerned with character than with plot or situation, Borges worked into every story the idea that he, as author, was not sure of all things, "because that's the way reality is." He was equally undogmatic when he speculated on his practices as a writer. From Ralph Waldo Emerson he got the idea that all literary works are one work and that all writers are one impersonal writer. Wondering if he had ever created a single original line in his writing, Borges said that if the reader looks long enough, a source might be found for everything he wrote. To him invention was just "mixing up memories. I don't think we're capable of creation in the way that God created the world."

RELATED COMMENTARIES: *Jorge Luis Borges, "The Labyrinth in 'The Garden of Forking Paths,'" page 1391; Peter Brooks, "A Narratological Analysis of Borges's 'The Garden of Forking Paths,'" page 1393.*

JORGE LUIS BORGES

The Garden of Forking Paths

Translated by Donald A. Yates

For Victoria Ocampo

On page 22 of Liddell Hart's *History of World War I* you will read that an attack against the Serre-Montauban line by thirteen British divisions (supported by 1,400 artillery pieces), planned for the 24th of July, 1916, had to be postponed until the morning of the 29th. The torrential rains, Captain Liddell Hart comments, caused this delay, an insignificant one, to be sure.

The following statement, dictated, reread, and signed by Dr. Yu Tsun, former professor of English at the *Hochschule*[1] at Tsingtao, throws an unsuspected light over the whole affair. The first two pages of the document are missing.

". . . and I hung up the receiver. Immediately afterwards, I recognized the voice that had answered in German. It was that of Captain Richard Madden. Madden's presence in Viktor Runeberg's apartment meant the end of our anxieties and — but this seemed, *or should have seemed,* very secondary to me — also the end of our lives. It meant that Runeberg had been arrested or murdered.[2] Before the sun set on that day, I would encounter the same fate. Madden was implacable. Or rather, he was obliged to be so. An Irishman at the service of England, a man accused of laxity and perhaps of treason, how could he fail to seize and be thankful for such a miraculous opportunity: the discovery, capture, maybe even the death of two agents of the German Reich? I went up to my room; absurdly I locked the door and threw myself on my back on the narrow iron cot. Through the window I saw the familiar roofs and the cloud-shaded six o'clock sun. It seemed incredible to me that that day without premonitions or symbols should be the one of my inexorable death. In spite of my dead father, in spite of having been a child in a symmetrical garden of Hai Feng, was I — now — going to die? Then I reflected that everything happens to a man precisely, precisely *now.* Centuries of centuries and only in the present do things happen; countless men in the air, on the face of the earth and the sea, and all that really is happening is happening to me . . . The almost intolerable recollection of Madden's horselike face banished these wanderings. In the midst of my hatred and terror (it means nothing to me now to speak of terror, now that I have mocked Richard Madden, now that my throat yearns for the noose) it occurred to me that that tumultuous and doubtless happy warrior did not suspect that I possessed the Secret. The name of the exact location of the new British artillery park on the

---

[1] College or university (German).

[2] An hypothesis both hateful and odd. The Prussian spy Hans Rabener, alias Viktor Runeberg, attacked with drawn automatic the bearer of the warrant for his arrest, Captain Richard Madden. The latter, in self-defense, inflicted the wound which brought about Runeberg's death. [Borges's note]

River Ancre. A bird streaked across the gray sky and blindly I translated it into an airplane and that airplane into many (against the French sky) annihilating the artillery station with vertical bombs. If only my mouth, before a bullet shattered it, could cry out that secret name so it could be heard in Germany . . . My human voice was very weak. How might I make it carry to the ear of the Chief? To the ear of that sick and hateful man who knew nothing of Runeberg and me save that we were in Staffordshire and who was waiting in vain for our report in his arid office in Berlin, endlessly examining newspapers . . . I said out loud: *I must flee.* I sat up noiselessly, in a useless perfection of silence, as if Madden were already lying in wait for me. Something — perhaps the mere vain ostentation of proving my resources were nil — made me look through my pockets. I found what I knew I would find. The American watch, the nickel chain and the square coin, the key ring with the incriminating useless keys to Runeberg's apartment, the notebook, a letter which I resolved to destroy immediately (and which I did not destroy), a crown, two shillings and a few pence, the red and blue pencil, the handkerchief, the revolver with one bullet. Absurdly, I took it in my hand and weighed it in order to inspire courage within myself. Vaguely I thought that a pistol report can be heard at a great distance. In ten minutes my plan was perfected. The telephone book listed the name of the only person capable of transmitting the message; he lived in a suburb of Fenton, less than a half hour's train ride away.

I am a cowardly man. I say it now, now that I have carried to its end a plan whose perilous nature no one can deny. I know its execution was terrible. I didn't do it for Germany, no. I care nothing for a barbarous country which imposed upon me the abjection of being a spy. Besides, I know of a man from England — a modest man — who for me is no less great than Goethe. I talked with him for scarcely an hour, but during that hour he was Goethe . . . I did it because I sensed that the Chief somehow feared people of my race — for the innumerable ancestors who merge within me. I wanted to prove to him that a yellow man could save his armies. Besides, I had to flee from Captain Madden. His hands and his voice could call at my door at any moment. I dressed silently, bade farewell to myself in the mirror, went downstairs, scrutinized the peaceful street and went out. The station was not far from my home, but I judged it wise to take a cab. I argued that in this way I ran less risk of being recognized; the fact is that in the deserted street I felt myself visible and vulnerable, infinitely so. I remember that I told the cab driver to stop a short distance before the main entrance. I got out with voluntary, almost painful slowness; I was going to the village of Ashgrove but I bought a ticket for a more distant station. The train left within a very few minutes, at eight-fifty. I hurried; the next one would leave at nine-thirty. There was hardly a soul on the platform. I went through the coaches; I remember a few farmers, a woman dressed in mourning, a young boy who was reading with fervor the *Annals* of Tacitus,[3] a wounded and happy soldier. The coaches

---

[3] The *Annals* (c. 116) is a history of the Roman emperors from Tiberius through Nero by Cornelius Tacitus (56–c.120).

jerked forward at last. A man whom I recognized ran in vain to the end of the platform. It was Captain Richard Madden. Shattered, trembling, I shrank into the far corner of the seat, away from the dreaded window.

From this broken state I passed into an almost abject felicity. I told myself that the duel had already begun and that I had won the first encounter by frustrating, even if for forty minutes, even if by a stoke of fate, the attack of my adversary. I argued that this slightest of victories foreshadowed a total victory. I argued (no less fallaciously) that my cowardly felicity proved that I was a man capable of carrying out the adventure successfully. From this weakness I took strength that did not abandon me. I foresee that man will resign himself each day to more atrocious undertakings; soon there will be no one but warriors and brigands; I give them this counsel: *The author of an atrocious undertaking ought to imagine that he has already accomplished it, ought to impose upon himself a future as irrevocable as the past.* Thus I proceeded as my eyes of a man already dead registered the elapsing of that day, which was perhaps the last, and the diffusion of the night. The train ran gently along, amid ash trees. It stopped, almost in the middle of the fields. No one announced the name of the station. "Ashgrove?" I asked a few lads on the platform. "Ashgrove," they replied. I got off.

A lamp enlightened the platform but the faces of the boys were in shadow. One questioned me, "Are you going to Dr. Stephen Albert's house?" Without waiting for my answer, another said, "The house is a long way from here, but you won't get lost if you take this road to the left and at every crossroads turn again to your left." I tossed them a coin (my last), descended a few stone steps, and started down the solitary road. It went downhill, slowly. It was of elemental earth; overhead the branches were tangled; the low, full moon seemed to accompany me.

For an instant, I thought that Richard Madden in some way had penetrated my desperate plan. Very quickly, I understood that that was impossible. The instructions to turn always to the left reminded me that such was the common procedure for discovering the central point of certain labyrinths. I have some understanding of labyrinths: not for nothing am I the great grandson of that Ts'ui Pên who was governor of Yunnan and who renounced worldly power in order to write a novel that might be even more populous than the *Hung Lu Meng*[4] and to construct a labyrinth in which all men would become lost. Thirteen years he dedicated to these heterogeneous tasks, but the hand of a stranger murdered him — and his novel was incoherent and no one found the labyrinth. Beneath English trees I meditated on that lost maze: I imagined it inviolate and perfect at the secret crest of a mountain; I imagined it erased by rice fields or beneath the water; I imagined it infinite, no longer composed of octagonal kiosks and returning paths, but of rivers and provinces and kingdoms . . . I thought of a labyrinth of labyrinths, of one sinuous spreading labyrinth that would encompass the past and the future

---

[4]*Dream of the Red Chamber* by Ts'ao Chan contains over four hundred characters. Published in 1791, its faithful representation of upper-class life and character profiles is considered unsurpassed in Chinese literature.

and in some way involve the stars. Absorbed in these illusory images, I forgot my destiny of one pursued. I felt myself to be, for an unknown period of time, an abstract perceiver of the world. The vague, living countryside, the moon, the remains of the day worked on me, as well as the slope of the road which eliminated any possibility of weariness. The afternoon was intimate, infinite. The road descended and forked among the now confused meadows. A high-pitched, almost syllabic music approached and receded in the shifting of the wind, dimmed by leaves and distance. I thought that a man can be an enemy of other men, of the moments of other men, but not of a country: not of fireflies, words, gardens, streams of water, sunsets. Thus I arrived before a tall, rusty gate. Between the iron bars I made out a poplar grove and a pavilion. I understood suddenly two things, the first trivial, the second almost unbelievable: the music came from the pavilion, and the music was Chinese. For precisely that reason I had openly accepted it without paying it any heed. I do not remember whether there was a bell or whether I knocked with my hand. The sparkling of the music continued.

From the rear of the house within a lantern approached: a lantern that the trees sometimes striped and sometimes eclipsed, a paper lantern that had the form of a drum and the color of the moon. A tall man bore it. I didn't see his face for the light blinded me. He opened the door and said slowly, in my own language: "I see that the pious Hsi P'êng persists in correcting my solitude. You no doubt wish to see the garden?"

I recognized the name of one of our consuls and I replied, disconcerted, "The garden?"

"The garden of forking paths."

Something stirred in my memory and I uttered with incomprehensible certainty, "The garden of my ancestor Ts'ui Pên."

"Your ancestor? Your illustrious ancestor? Come in."

The damp path zigzagged like those of my childhood. We came to a library of Eastern and Western books. I recognized bound in yellow silk several volumes of the Lost Encyclopedia, edited by the Third Emperor of the Luminous Dynasty but never printed. The record on the phonograph revolved next to a bronze phoenix. I also recall a *famille rose*[5] vase and another, many centuries older, of that shade of blue which our craftsmen copied from the potters of Persia . . .

Stephen Albert observed me with a smile. He was, as I have said, very tall, sharp-featured, with gray eyes and a gray beard. He told me that he had been a missionary in Tientsin "before aspiring to become a Sinologist."

We sat down — I on a long, low divan, he with his back to the window and a tall circular clock. I calculated that my pursuer, Richard Madden, could not arrive for at least an hour. My irrevocable determination could wait.

"An astounding fate, that of Ts'ui Pên," Stephen Albert said. "Governor of his native province, learned in astronomy, in astrology, and in the tireless interpretation of the canonical books, chess player, famous poet and calligra-

---

[5] Chinese porcelain decorated primarily with the color rose.

pher — he abandoned all this in order to compose a book and a maze. He renounced the pleasures of both tyranny and justice, of his populous couch, of his banquets, and even of erudition — all to close himself up for thirteen years in the Pavilion of the Limpid Solitude. When he died, his heirs found nothing save chaotic manuscripts. His family, as you may be aware, wished to condemn them to the fire; but his executor — a Taoist or Buddhist monk — insisted on their publication."

"We descendants of Ts'ui Pên," I replied, "continue to curse that monk. Their publication was senseless. The book is an indeterminate heap of contradictory drafts. I examined it once: in the third chapter the hero dies, in the fourth he is alive. As for the other undertaking of Ts'ui Pên, his labyrinth . . ."

"Here is Ts'ui Pên's labyrinth," he said, indicating a tall lacquered desk.

"An ivory labyrinth!" I exclaimed. "A minimum labyrinth."

"A labyrinth of symbols," he corrected. "An invisible labyrinth of time. To me, a barbarous Englishman, has been entrusted the revelation of this diaphanous mystery. After more than a hundred years, the details are irretrievable; but it is not hard to conjecture what happened. Ts'ui Pên must have said once: *I am withdrawing to write a book.* And another time: *I am withdrawing to construct a labyrinth.* Every one imagined two works; to no one did it occur that the book and the maze were one and the same thing. The Pavilion of the Limpid Solitude stood in the center of a garden that was perhaps intricate; that circumstance could have suggested to the heirs a physical labyrinth. Ts'ui Pên died; no one in the vast territories that were his came upon the labyrinth; the confusion of the novel suggested to me that *it* was the maze. Two circumstances gave me the correct solution of the problem. One: the curious legend that Ts'ui Pên had planned to create a labyrinth which would be strictly infinite. The other: a fragment of a letter I discovered."

Albert rose. He turned his back on me for a moment; he opened a drawer of the black and gold desk. He faced me and in his hands he held a sheet of paper that had once been crimson, but was now pink and tenuous and cross-sectioned. The fame of Ts'ui Pên as a calligrapher had been justly won. I read, uncomprehendingly and with fervor, these words written with a minute brush by a man of my blood: *I leave to the various futures (not to all) my garden of forking paths.* Wordlessly, I returned the sheet. Albert continued:

"Before unearthing this letter, I had questioned myself about the ways in which a book can be infinite. I could think of nothing other than a cyclic volume, a circular one. A book whose last page was identical with the first, a book which had the possibility of continuing indefinitely. I remembered too that night which is at the middle of the Thousand and One Nights[6] when Scheherazade (through a magical oversight of the copyist) begins to relate word for word the story of the Thousand and One Nights, establishing the risk of coming once again to the night when she must repeat it, and thus on

---

[6]Or *Arabian Nights* is a collection of tales supposedly narrated by Scheherazade to her husband, the sultan, each night in exchange for another day of life.

to infinity. I imagined as well a Platonic, hereditary work, transmitted from father to son, in which each new individual adds a chapter or corrects with pious care the pages of his elders. These conjectures diverted me; but none seemed to correspond, not even remotely, to the contradictory chapters of Ts'ui Pên. In the midst of this perplexity, I received from Oxford the manuscript you have examined. I lingered, naturally, on the sentence: *I leave to the various futures (not to all) my garden of forking paths.* Almost instantly, I understood: 'the garden of forking paths' was the chaotic novel; the phrase 'the various futures (not to all)' suggested to me the forking in time, not in space. A broad rereading of the work confirmed the theory. In all fictional works, each time a man is confronted with several alternatives, he chooses one and eliminates the others; in the fiction of Ts'ui Pên, he chooses — simultaneously — all of them. *He creates,* in this way, diverse futures, diverse times which themselves also proliferate and fork. Here, then, is the explanation of the novel's contradictions. Fang, let us say, has a secret; a stranger calls at his door; Fang resolves to kill him. Naturally, there are several possible outcomes: Fang can kill the intruder, the intruder can kill Fang, they both can escape, they both can die, and so forth. In the work of Ts'ui Pên, all possible outcomes occur; each one is the point of departure for other forkings. Sometimes, the paths of this labyrinth converge: for example, you arrive at this house, but in one of the possible pasts you are my enemy, in another, my friend. If you will resign yourself to my incurable pronunciation, we shall read a few pages."

His face, within the vivid circle of the lamplight, was unquestionably that of an old man, but with something unalterable about it, even immortal. He read with slow precision two versions of the same epic chapter. In the first, an army marches to a battle across a lonely mountain; the horror of the rocks and shadows makes the men undervalue their lives and they gain an easy victory. In the second, the same army traverses a palace where a great festival is taking place; the resplendent battle seems to them a continuation of the celebration and they win the victory. I listened with proper veneration to these ancient narratives, perhaps less admirable in themselves than the fact that they had been created by my blood and were being restored to me by a man of a remote empire, in the course of a desperate adventure, on a Western isle. I remember the last words, repeated in each version like a secret commandment: *Thus fought the heroes, tranquil their admirable hearts, violent their swords, resigned to kill and to die.*

From that moment on, I felt about me and within my dark body an invisible, intangible swarming. Not the swarming of the divergent, parallel, and finally coalescent armies, but a more inaccessible, more intimate agitation that they in some manner prefigured. Stephen Albert continued:

"I don't believe that your illustrious ancestor played idly with these variations. I don't consider it credible that he would sacrifice thirteen years to the infinite execution of a rhetorical experiment. In your country, the novel is a subsidiary form of literature; in Ts'ui Pên's time it was a despicable form. Ts'ui Pên was a brilliant novelist, but he was also a man of letters who doubtless did not consider himself a mere novelist. The testimony of his contemporaries proclaims — and his life fully confirms — his metaphysical and mystical interests. Philosophic controversy usurps a good part of the novel. I know that of all problems, none disturbed him so greatly nor worked upon him so much as the abysmal problem of time. Now then, the latter is the only problem that does not figure in the pages of the *Garden*. He does not even use the word that signifies *time*. How do you explain this voluntary omission?"

I proposed several solutions — all unsatisfactory. We discussed them. Finally, Stephen Albert said to me:

"In a riddle whose answer is chess, what is the only prohibited word?"

I thought a moment and replied: "The word *chess*."

"Precisely," said Albert. "*The Garden of Forking Paths* is an enormous riddle, or parable, whose theme is time; this recondite cause prohibits its mention. To omit a word always, to resort to inept metaphors and obvious periphrases, is perhaps the most emphatic way of stressing it. That is the tortuous method preferred, in each of the meanderings of his indefatigable novel, by the oblique Ts'ui Pên. I have compared hundreds of manuscripts, I have corrected the errors that the negligence of the copyists has introduced, I have guessed the plan of this chaos, I have re-established — I believe I have re-established — the primordial organization, I have translated the entire work: it is clear to me that not once does he employ the word 'time.' The explanation is obvious: *The Garden of Forking Paths* is an incomplete, but not false, image of the universe as Ts'ui Pên conceived it. In contrast to Newton and Schopenhauer, your ancestor did not believe in a uniform, absolute time. He believed in an infinite series of times, in a growing, dizzying net of divergent, convergent, and parallel times. This network of times which approached one another, forked, broke off, or were unaware of one another for centuries, embraces *all* possibilities of time. We do not exist in the majority of these times; in some you exist, and not I; in others I, and not you; in others, both of us. In the present one, which a favorable fate has granted me, you have arrived at my house; in another, while crossing the garden, you found me dead; in still another, I utter these same words, but I am a mistake, a ghost."

"In every one," I pronounced, not without a tremble to my voice, "I am grateful to you and revere you for your re-creation of the garden of Ts'ui Pên."

"Not in all," he murmured with a smile. "Time forks perpetually toward innumerable futures. In one of them I am your enemy."

Once again I felt the swarming sensation of which I have spoken. It seemed to me that the humid garden that surrounded the house was infinitely saturated with invisible persons. Those persons were Albert and I, secret, busy, and multiform in other dimensions of time. I raised my eyes and the tenuous nightmare dissolved. In the yellow and black garden there was only one man; but this man was as strong as a statue . . . this man was approaching along the path and he was Captain Richard Madden.

"The future already exists," I replied, "but I am your friend. Could I see the letter again?"

Albert rose. Standing tall, he opened the drawer of the tall desk; for the moment his back was to me. I had readied the revolver. I fired with extreme caution. Albert fell uncomplainingly, immediately. I swear his death was instantaneous — a lightning stroke.

The rest is unreal, insignificant. Madden broke in, arrested me. I have been condemned to the gallows. I have won out abominably; I have communicated to Berlin the secret name of the city they must attack. They bombed it yesterday; I read it in the same papers that offered to England the mystery of the learned Sinologist Stephen Albert who was murdered by a stranger, one Yu Tsun. The Chief had deciphered this mystery. He knew my problem was to indicate (through the uproar of the war) the city called Albert, and that I had found no other means to do so than to kill a man of that name. He does not know (no one can know) my innumerable contrition and weariness.

[1941]

T ADEUSZ BOROWSKI *(1922–1951), Polish short story writer and poet, created stories about his experiences in the concentration camp at Auschwitz during World War II that constitute one of the most harrowing literary statements of our century. Borowski was acquainted early with suffering and deprivation. His father was sent from the family's home in the Soviet Ukraine to an Arctic labor camp in 1926; his mother was also transported to Siberia four years later, leaving Borowski to be raised by an aunt. In 1939 the family was reunited in Poland, but shortly afterward the Nazis occupied that country. Unable to attend school because the Nazis prohibited education for Poles, Borowski studied on his own and began to write poetry. He published his first mimeographed collection in 1942. Arrested soon after, he was transported to Auschwitz and tattooed with a camp serial number. As his friend Jan Kott has said, Borowski was lucky: "Three weeks earlier 'Aryans' had stopped being sent to the gas chambers — except for special cases. From then on only Jews were gassed en masse."*

Borowski remained in Auschwitz and Dachau for two years. At the end of the war, he was released and then repatriated to Poland in 1946. In 1948 he joined the Communist Party, working for them as a journalist in Warsaw until his suicide three years later. He is chiefly remembered for the hundred pages of short stories written a year after his release from the concentration camp; they are collected in the book This Way for the Gas, Ladies and Gentlemen *(1967).*

As Jan Kott has realized, Borowski's writing is unique in the "literature of atrocity" produced by Holocaust survivors. "Among the tens of thousands of pages written about the Holocaust and the death camps, Borowski's slender book continues to occupy, for more than a quarter century now, a place apart. The book is one of the cruelest of testimonies to what men did to men, and a pitiless verdict that anything can be done to a human being." In his stories Borowski identified with his first person narrator, Vorarbeiter Tadeusz. Thus he assumed full moral responsibility for the terms of his survival at Auschwitz: following the orders of the Nazi directors. The detached, almost scientific descriptions in "This Way for the Gas, Ladies and Gentlemen" reflect all of existence turned into a concentration camp. In these stories Borowski grappled with his own question: "What will the world know of us if the Germans win?"

Tadeusz Borowski

This Way for the Gas, Ladies and Gentlemen

Translated by Barbara Vedder

All of us walk around naked. The delousing is finally over, and our striped suits are back from the tanks of Cyclone B solution, an efficient killer of lice in clothing and of men in gas chambers. Only the inmates in the blocks cut off from ours by the "Spanish goats"[1] still have nothing to wear. But all the same, all of us walk around naked: the heat is unbearable. The camp has been sealed off tight. Not a single prisoner, not one solitary louse, can sneak through the gate. The labour Kommandos have stopped working. All day, thousands of naked men shuffle up and down the roads, cluster around the squares, or lie against the walls and on top of the roofs. We have been sleeping on plain boards, since our mattresses and blankets are still being disinfected. From the rear blockhouses we have a view of the F.K.L. — *Frauen Konzentration Lager;* [2] there too the delousing is in full swing. Twenty-eight thousand women have been stripped naked and driven out of the barracks. Now they swarm around the large yard between the blockhouses.

The heat rises, the hours are endless. We are without even our usual diversion: the wide roads leading to the crematoria are empty. For several days now, no new transports have come in. Part of "Canada"[3] has been liquidated and detailed to a labour Kommando — one of the very toughest — at Harmenz. For there exists in the camp a special brand of justice based on envy: when the rich and mighty fall, their friends see to it that they fall to the very bottom. And Canada, our Canada, which smells not of maple forests but of French perfume, has amassed great fortunes in diamonds and currency from all over Europe.

Several of us sit on the top bunk, our legs dangling over the edge. We slice the neat loaves of crisp, crunchy bread. It is a bit coarse to the taste, the kind that stays fresh for days. Sent all the way from Warsaw — only a week ago my mother held this white loaf in her hands . . . dear Lord, dear Lord . . .

We unwrap the bacon, the onion, we open a can of evaporated milk. Henri, the fat Frenchman, dreams aloud of the French wine brought by the transports from Strasbourg, Paris, Marseille . . . Sweat streams down his body.

---

[1] Crossed wooden beams wrapped in barbed wire.

[2] Women's concentration camp. (Unless otherwise indicated, all foreign phrases are in German.)

[3] A designation of wealth and well-being in the camp. More specifically, the members of the labour gang, or Kommando, who helped to unload the incoming transports of people destined for the gas chambers.

"Listen, *mon ami,*[4] next time we go up on the loading ramp, I'll bring you real champagne. You haven't tried it before, eh?"

"No. But you'll never be able to smuggle it through the gate, so stop teasing. Why not try and 'organize' some shoes for me instead — you know, the perforated kind, with a double sole, and what about that shirt you promised me long ago?"

"*Patience, patience.* When the new transports come, I'll bring all you want. We'll be going on the ramp again!"

"And what if there aren't any more 'cremo' transports?" I say spitefully. "Can't you see how much easier life is becoming around here: no limit on packages, no more beatings? You even write letters home . . . One hears all kind of talk, and, dammit, they'll run out of people!"

"Stop talking nonsense." Henri's serious fat face moves rhythmically, his mouth is full of sardines. We have been friends for a long time, but I do not even know his last name. "Stop talking nonsense," he repeats, swallowing with effort. "They can't run out of people, or we'll starve to death in this blasted camp. All of us live on what they bring."

"All? We have our packages . . ."

"Sure, you and your friend, and ten other friends of yours. Some of you Poles get packages. But what about us, and the Jews, and the Russkis? And what if we had no food, no 'organization' from the transports, do you think you'd be eating those packages of yours in peace? We wouldn't let you!"

"You would, you'd starve to death like the Greeks. Around here, whoever has grub, has power."

"Anyway, you have enough, we have enough, so why argue?"

Right, why argue? They have enough, I have enough, we eat together and we sleep on the same bunks. Henri slices the bread, he makes a tomato salad. It tastes good with the commissary mustard.

Below us, naked sweat-drenched men crowd the narrow barracks aisles or lie packed in eights and tens in the lower bunks. Their nude, withered bodies stink of sweat and excrement; their cheeks are hollow. Directly beneath me, in the bottom bunk, lies a rabbi. He has covered his head with a piece of rag torn off a blanket and reads from a Hebrew prayer book (there is no shortage of this type of literature at the camp), wailing loudly, monotonously.

"Can't somebody shut him up? He's been raving as if he'd caught God himself by the feet."

"I don't feel like moving. Let him rave. They'll take him to the oven that much sooner."

"Religion is the opium of the people," Henri, who is a Communist and a *rentier,* says sententiously. "If they didn't believe in God and eternal life, they'd have smashed the crematoria long ago."

"Why haven't you done it then?"

The question is rhetorical; the Frenchman ignores it.

---

[4]My friend (French).

"Idiot," he says simply, and stuffs a tomato in his mouth.

Just as we finish our snack, there is a sudden commotion at the door. The Muslims[5] scurry in fright to the safety of their bunks, a messenger runs into the Block Elder's shack. The Elder, his face solemn, steps out at once.

"Canada! *Antreten!*[6] But fast! There's a transport coming!"

"Great God!" yells Henri, jumping off the bunk. He swallows the rest of his tomato, snatches his coat, screams *"Raus"*[7] at the men below, and in a flash is at the door. We can hear a scramble in the other bunks. Canada is leaving for the ramp.

"Henri, the shoes!" I call after him.

"*Keine Angst!*"[8] he shouts back, already outside.

I proceed to put away the food. I tie a piece of rope around the suitcase where the onions and the tomatoes from my father's garden in Warsaw mingle with Portuguese sardines, bacon from Lublin (that's from my brother), and authentic sweetmeats from Salonica. I tie it all up, pull on my trousers, and slide off the bunk.

"*Platz!*"[9] I yell, pushing my way through the Greeks. They step aside. At the door I bump into Henri.

"*Was ist los?*"[10]

"Want to come with us on the ramp?"

"Sure, why not?"

"Come along then, grab your coat! We're short a few men. I've already told the Kapo," and he shoves me out of the barracks door.

We line up. Someone has marked down our numbers, someone up ahead yells, "March, march," and now we are running towards the gate, accompanied by the shouts of a multilingual throng that is already being pushed back to the barracks. Not everybody is lucky enough to be going on the ramp . . . We have almost reached the gate. *Links, zwei, drei, vier! Mützen ab!*[11] Erect, arms stretched stiffly along our hips, we march past the gate briskly, smartly, almost gracefully. A sleepy S.S. man with a large pad in his hand checks us off, waving us ahead in groups of five.

"*Hundert!*" he calls after we have all passed.

"*Stimmt!*"[12] comes a hoarse answer from out front.

We march fast, almost at a run. There are guards all around, young men with automatics. We pass camp II B, then some deserted barracks and a clump of unfamiliar green — apple and pear trees. We cross the circle of watchtowers

---

[5] The camp name for a prisoner who had been destroyed physically and spiritually, and who had neither the strength nor the will to go on living — a man ripe for the gas chamber.

[6] Get going.

[7] "Get out."

[8] "Don't worry."

[9] "Place!" (In the sense of "Take your place!")

[10] "What's the matter?"

[11] "Left, two, three, four! Hats off!"

[12] "One hundred! . . . "OK!"

and, running, burst on to the highway. We have arrived. Just a few more yards. There, surrounded by trees, is the ramp.

A cheerful little station, very much like any other provincial railway stop: a small square framed by tall chestnuts and paved with yellow gravel. Not far off, beside the road, squats a tiny wooden shed, uglier and more flimsy than the ugliest and flimsiest railway shack; farther along lie stacks of old rails, heaps of wooden beams, barracks parts, bricks, paving stones. This is where they load freight for Birkenau: supplies for the construction of the camp, and people for the gas chambers. Trucks drive around, load up lumber, cement, people — a regular daily routine.

And now the guards are being posted along the rails, across the beams, in the green shade of the Silesian chestnuts, to form a tight circle around the ramp. They wipe the sweat from their faces and sip out of their canteens. It is unbearably hot; the sun stands motionless at its zenith.

"Fall out!"

We sit down in the narrow streaks of shade along the stacked rails. The hungry Greeks (several of them managed to come along, God only knows how) rummage underneath the rails. One of them finds some pieces of mildewed bread, another a few half-rotten sardines. They eat.

"*Schweinedreck,*"[13] spits a young, tall guard with corn-coloured hair and dreamy blue eyes. "For God's sake, any minute you'll have so much food to stuff down your guts, you'll bust!" He adjusts his gun, wipes his face with a handkerchief.

"Hey you, fatso!" His boot lightly touches Henri's shoulder. "*Pass mal auf,*[14] want a drink?"

"Sure, but I haven't got any marks," replies the Frenchman with a professional air.

"*Schade,* too bad."

"Come, come, Herr Posten, isn't my word good enough any more? Haven't we done business before? How much?"

"One hundred. *Gemacht?*"[15]

"*Gemacht.*"

We drink the water, lukewarm and tasteless. It will be paid for by the people who have not yet arrived.

"Now you be careful," says Henri, turning to me. He tosses away the empty bottle. It strikes the rails and bursts into tiny fragments. "Don't take any money, they might be checking. Anyway, who the hell needs money? You've got enough to eat. Don't take suits, either, or they'll think you're planning to escape. Just get a shirt, silk only, with a collar. And a vest. And if you find something to drink, don't bother calling me. I know how to shift for myself, but you watch your step or they'll let you have it."

"Do they beat you up here?"

---

[13] "Filthy pigs."
[14] Pay attention.
[15] Done.

"Naturally. You've got to have eyes in your ass. *Arschaugen.*"[16]

Around us sit the Greeks, their jaws working greedily, like huge human insects. They munch on stale lumps of bread. They are restless, wondering what will happen next. The sight of the large beams and the stacks of rails has them worried. They dislike carrying heavy loads.

"*Was wir arbeiten?*"[17] they ask.

"*Niks. Transport kommen, alles Krematorium, compris?*"[18]

"*Alles verstehen,*"[19] they answer in crematorium Esperanto. All is well — they will not have to move the heavy rails or carry the beams.

In the meantime, the ramp has become increasingly alive with activity, increasingly noisy. The crews are being divided into those who will open and unload the arriving cattle cars and those who will be posted by the wooden steps. They receive instructions on how to proceed most efficiently. Motor cycles drive up, delivering S.S. officers, bemedalled, glittering with brass, beefy men with highly polished boots and shiny, brutal faces. Some have brought their briefcases, others hold thin, flexible whips. This gives them an air of military readiness and agility. They walk in and out of the commissary — for the miserable little shack by the road serves as their commissary, where in the summertime they drink mineral water, *Studentenquelle,* and where in winter they can warm up with a glass of hot wine. They greet each other in the state-approved way, raising an arm Roman fashion, then shake hands cordially, exchange warm smiles, discuss mail from home, their children, their families. Some stroll majestically on the ramp. The silver squares on their collars glitter, the gravel crunches under their boots, their bamboo whips snap impatiently.

We lie against the rails in the narrow streaks of shade, breathe unevenly, occasionally exchange a few words in our various tongues, and gaze listlessly at the majestic men in green uniforms, at the green trees, and at the church steeple of a distant village.

"The transport is coming," somebody says. We spring to our feet, all eyes turn in one direction. Around the bend, one after another, the cattle cars begin rolling in. The train backs into the station, a conductor leans out, waves his hand, blows a whistle. The locomotive whistles back with a shrieking noise, puffs, the train rolls slowly alongside the ramp. In the tiny barred windows appear pale, wilted, exhausted human faces, terror-stricken women with tangled hair, unshaven men. They gaze at the station in silence. And then, suddenly, there is a stir inside the cars and a pounding against the wooden boards.

"Water! Air!" — weary, desperate cries.

Heads push through the windows, mouths gasp frantically for air. They draw a few breaths, then disappear; others come in their place, then also disappear. The cries and moans grow louder.

---

[16] Ass eyes.
[17] "What will we be working on?"
[18] "Nothing. Transport coming, all Crematorium, understand?"
[19] "We understand."

A man in a green uniform covered with more glitter than any of the others jerks his head impatiently, his lips twist in annoyance. He inhales deeply, then with a rapid gesture throws his cigarette away and signals to the guard. The guard removes the automatic from his shoulder, aims, sends a series of shots along the train. All is quiet now. Meanwhile, the trucks have arrived, steps are being drawn up, and the Canada men stand ready at their posts by the train doors. The S.S. officer with the briefcase raises his hand.

"Whoever takes gold, or anything at all besides food, will be shot for stealing Reich property. Understand? *Verstanden?*"

"*Jawohl!*"[20] we answer eagerly.

"*Also los!* Begin!"

The bolts crack, the doors fall open. A wave of fresh air rushes inside the train. People . . . inhumanly crammed, buried under incredible heaps of luggage, suitcases, trunks, packages, crates, bundles of every description (everything that had been their past and was to start their future). Monstrously squeezed together, they have fainted from heat, suffocated, crushed one another. Now they push towards the opened doors, breathing like fish cast out on the sand.

"Attention! Out, and take your luggage with you! Take out everything. Pile all your stuff near the exits. Yes, your coats too. It is summer. March to the left. Understand?"

"Sir, what's going to happen to us?" They jump from the train on to the gravel, anxious, worn-out.

"Where are you people from?"

"Sosnowiec-Będzin. Sir, what's going to happen to us?" They repeat the question stubbornly, gazing into our tired eyes.

"I don't know. I don't understand Polish."

It is the camp law: people going to their death must be deceived to the very end. This is the only permissible form of charity. The heat is tremendous. The sun hangs directly over our heads, the white, hot sky quivers, the air vibrates, an occasional breeze feels like a sizzling blast from a furnace. Our lips are parched, the mouth fills with the salty taste of blood, the body is weak and heavy from lying in the sun. Water!

A huge, multicoloured wave of people loaded down with luggage pours from the train like a blind, mad river trying to find a new bed. But before they have a chance to recover, before they can draw a breath of fresh air and look at the sky, bundles are snatched from their hands, coats ripped off their backs, their purses and umbrellas taken away.

"But please, sir, it's for the sun, I cannot . . . ."

"*Verboten!*"[21] one of us barks through clenched teeth. There is an S.S. man standing behind your back, calm, efficient, watchful.

"*Meine Herrschaften,*[22] this way, ladies and gentlemen, try not to throw

---

[20] "Yes, indeed!"

[21] "Forbidden!"

[22] Distinguished ladies and gentlemen.

your things around, please. Show some goodwill," he says courteously, his restless hands playing with the slender whip.

"Of course, of course," they answer as they pass, and now they walk alongside the train somewhat more cheerfully. A woman reaches down quickly to pick up her handbag. The whip flies, the woman screams, stumbles, and falls under the feet of the surging crowd. Behind her, a child cries in a thin little voice "Mamele!" — a very small girl with tangled black curls.

The heaps grow. Suitcases, bundles, blankets, coats, handbags that open as they fall, spilling coins, gold, watches; mountains of bread pile up at the exits, heaps of marmalade, jams, masses of meat, sausages; sugar spills on the gravel. Trucks, loaded with people, start up with a deafening roar and drive off amidst the wailing and screaming of the women separated from their children, and the stupefied silence of the men left behind. They are the ones who had been ordered to step to the right — the healthy and the young who will go to the camp. In the end, they too will not escape death, but first they must work.

Trucks leave and return, without interruption, as on a monstrous conveyor belt. A Red Cross van drives back and forth, back and forth, incessantly: it transports the gas that will kill these people. The enormous cross on the hood, red as blood, seems to dissolve in the sun.

The Canada men at the trucks cannot stop for a single moment, even to catch their breath. They shove the people up the steps, pack them in tightly, sixty per truck, more or less. Near by stands a young, cleanshaven "gentleman," an S.S. officer with a notebook in his hand. For each departing truck he enters a mark; sixteen gone means one thousand people, more or less. The gentleman is calm, precise. No truck can leave without a signal from him, or a mark in his notebook: *Ordnung muss sein.*[23] The marks swell into thousands, the thousands into whole transports, which afterwards we shall simply call "from Salonica," "from Strasbourg," "from Rotterdam." This one will be called "Sosnowiec-Będzin." The new prisoners from Sosnowiec-Będzin will receive serial numbers 131–2 — thousand, of course, though afterwards we shall simply say 131–2, for short.

The transports swell into weeks, months, years. When the war is over, they will count up the marks in their notebooks — all four and a half million of them. The bloodiest battle of the war, the greatest victory of the strong, united Germany. *Ein Reich, ein Volk, ein Führer*[24] — and four crematoria.

The train has been emptied. A thin, pock-marked S.S. man peers inside, shakes his head in disgust, and motions to our group, pointing his finger at the door.

"*Rein.* Clean it up!"

We climb inside. In the corners amid human excrement and abandoned wrist-watches lie squashed, trampled infants, naked little monsters with enormous heads and bloated bellies. We carry them out like chickens, holding several in each hand.

---

[23] There must be order.
[24] One Empire, one People, one Leader.

"Don't take them to the trucks, pass them on to the women," says the S.S. man, lighting a cigarette. His cigarette lighter is not working properly; he examines it carefully.

"Take them, for God's sake!" I explode as the women run from me in horror, covering their eyes.

The name of God sounds strangely pointless, since the women and the infants will go on the trucks, every one of them, without exception. We all know what this means, and we look at each other with hate and horror.

"What, you don't want to take them?" asks the pock-marked S.S. man with a note of surprise and reproach in his voice, and reaches for his revolver.

"You mustn't shoot, I'll carry them." A tall, grey-haired woman takes the little corpses out of my hands and for an instant gazes straight into my eyes.

"My poor boy," she whispers and smiles at me. Then she walks away, staggering along the path. I lean against the side of the train. I am terribly tired. Someone pulls at my sleeve.

"*En avant*, to the rails, come on!"

I look up, but the face swims before my eyes, dissolves, huge and transparent, melts into the motionless trees and the sea of people . . . I blink rapidly: Henri.

"Listen, Henri, are we good people?"

"That's stupid. Why do you ask?"

"You see, my friend, you see, I don't know why, but I am furious, simply furious with these people — furious because I must be here because of them. I feel no pity. I am not sorry they're going to the gas chamber. Damn them all! I could throw myself at them, beat them with my fists. It must be pathological, I just can't understand . . ."

"Ah, on the contrary, it is natural, predictable, calculated. The ramp exhausts you, you rebel — and the easiest way to relieve your hate is to turn against someone weaker. Why, I'd even call it healthy. It's simple logic, *compris*?" He props himself up comfortably against the heap of rails. "Look at the Greeks, they know how to make the best of it! They stuff their bellies with anything they find. One of them has just devoured a full jar of marmalade."

"Pigs! Tomorrow half of them will die of the shits."

"Pigs? You've been hungry."

"Pigs!" I repeat furiously. I close my eyes. The air is filled with ghastly cries, the earth trembles beneath me, I can feel sticky moisture on my eyelids. My throat is completely dry.

The morbid procession streams on and on — trucks growl like mad dogs. I shut my eyes tight, but I can still see corpses dragged from the train, trampled infants, cripples piled on top of the dead, wave after wave . . . freight cars roll in, the heaps of clothing, suitcases, and bundles grow, people climb out, look at the sun, take a few breaths, beg for water, get into the trucks, drive away. And again freight cars roll in, again people . . . The scenes become confused in my mind — I am not sure if all of this is actually happening, or if I am dreaming. There is a humming inside my head; I feel that I must vomit.

Henri tugs at my arm.

"Don't sleep, we're off to load up the loot."

All the people are gone. In the distance, the last few trucks roll along the road in clouds of dust, the train has left, several S.S. officers promenade up and down the ramp. The silver glitters on their collars. Their boots shine, their red, beefy faces shine. Among them there is a woman — only now I realize she has been here all along — withered, flat-chested, bony, her thin, colourless hair pulled back and tied in a "Nordic" knot; her hands are in the pockets of her wide skirt. With a rat-like, resolute smile glued on her thin lips she sniffs around the corners of the ramp. She detests feminine beauty with the hatred of a woman who is herself repulsive, and knows it. Yes, I have seen her many times before and I know her well: she is the commandant of the F.K.L. She has come to look over the new crop of women, for some of them, instead of going on the trucks, will go on foot — to the concentration camp. There our boys, the barbers from Zauna, will shave their heads and will have a good laugh at their "outside world" modesty.

We proceed to load the loot. We lift huge trunks, heave them on to the trucks. There they are arranged in stacks, packed tightly. Occasionally somebody slashes one open with a knife, for pleasure or in search of vodka and perfume. One of the crates falls open; suits, shirts, books drop out on the ground . . . I pick up a small, heavy package. I unwrap it — gold, about two handfuls, bracelets, rings, brooches, diamonds . . .

"*Gib hier*,"[25] an S.S. man says calmly, holding up his briefcase already full of gold and colourful foreign currency. He locks the case, hands it to an officer, takes another, an empty one, and stands by the next truck, waiting. The gold will go to the Reich.

It is hot, terribly hot. Our throats are dry, each word hurts. Anything for a sip of water! Faster, faster, so that it is over, so that we may rest. At last we are done, all the trucks have gone. Now we swiftly clean up the remaining dirt: there must be "no trace left of the *Schweinerei*."[26] But just as the last truck disappears behind the trees and we walk, finally, to rest in the shade, a shrill whistle sounds around the bend. Slowly, terribly slowly, a train rolls in, the engine whistles back with a deafening shriek. Again weary, pale faces at the windows, flat as though cut out of paper, with huge, feverishly burning eyes. Already trucks are pulling up, already the composed gentleman with the notebook is at his post, and the S.S. men emerge from the commissary carrying briefcases for the gold and money. We unseal the train doors.

It is impossible to control oneself any longer. Brutally we tear suitcases from their hands, impatiently pull off their coats. Go on, go on, vanish! They go, they vanish. Men, women, children. Some of them know.

Here is a woman — she walks quickly, but tries to appear calm. A small child with a pink cherub's face runs after her and, unable to keep up, stretches out his little arms and cries: "Mama! Mama!"

"Pick up your child, woman!"

---

[25] "Give it here."
[26] Obscenity.

"It's not mine, sir, not mine!" she shouts hysterically and runs on, covering her face with her hands. She wants to hide, she wants to reach those who will not ride the trucks, those who will go on foot, those who will stay alive. She is young, healthy, good-looking, she wants to live.

But the child runs after her, wailing loudly: "Mama, mama, don't leave me!"

"It's not mine, not mine, no!"

Andrei, a sailor from Sevastopol, grabs hold of her. His eyes are glassy from vodka and the heat. With one powerful blow he knocks her off her feet, then, as she falls, takes her by the hair and pulls her up again. His face twitches with rage.

"Ah, you bloody Jewess! So you're running from your own child! I'll show you, you whore!" His huge hand chokes her, he lifts her in the air and heaves her on to the truck like a heavy sack of grain.

"Here! And take this with you, bitch!" and he throws the child at her feet.

"*Gut gemacht*, good work. That's the way to deal with degenerate mothers," says the S.S. man standing at the foot of the truck. "*Gut, gut, Russki.*"

"Shut your mouth," growls Andrei through clenched teeth, and walks away. From under a pile of rags he pulls out a canteen, unscrews the cork, takes a few deep swallows, passes it to me. The strong vodka burns the throat. My head swims, my legs are shaky, again I feel like throwing up.

And suddenly, above the teeming crowd pushing forward like a river driven by an unseen power, a girl appears. She descends lightly from the train, hops on to the gravel, looks around inquiringly, as if somewhat surprised. Her soft, blonde hair has fallen on her shoulders in a torrent, she throws it back impatiently. With a natural gesture she runs her hands down her blouse, casually straightens her skirt. She stands like this for an instant, gazing at the crowd, then turns and with a gliding look examines our faces, as though searching for someone. Unknowingly, I continue to stare at her, until our eyes meet.

"Listen, tell me, where are they taking us?"

I look at her without saying a word. Here, standing before me, is a girl, a girl with enchanting blonde hair, with beautiful breasts, wearing a little cotton blouse, a girl with a wise, mature look in her eyes. Here she stands, gazing straight into my face, waiting. And over there is the gas chamber: communal death, disgusting and ugly. And over in the other direction is the concentration camp: the shaved head, the heavy Soviet trousers in sweltering heat, the sickening, stale odour of dirty, damp female bodies, the animal hunger, the inhuman labour, and later the same gas chamber, only an even more hideous, more terrible death . . .

Why did she bring it? I think to myself, noticing a lovely gold watch on her delicate wrist. They'll take it away from her anyway.

"Listen, tell me," she repeats.

I remain silent. Her lips tighten.

"I know," she says with a shade of proud contempt in her voice, tossing her head. She walks off resolutely in the direction of the trucks. Someone tries to stop her; she boldly pushes him aside and runs up the steps. In the distance I can only catch a glimpse of her blonde hair flying in the breeze.

I go back inside the train; I carry out dead infants; I unload luggage. I touch corpses, but I cannot overcome the mounting, uncontrollable terror. I try to escape from the corpses, but they are everywhere: lined up on the gravel, on the cement edge of the ramp, inside the cattle cars. Babies, hideous naked women, men twisted by convulsions. I run off as far as I can go, but immediately a whip slashes across my back. Out of the corner of my eye I see an S.S. man, swearing profusely. I stagger forward and run, lose myself in the Canada group. Now, at last, I can once more rest against the stack of rails. The sun has leaned low over the horizon and illuminates the ramp with a reddish glow; the shadows of the trees have become elongated, ghostlike. In the silence that settles over nature at this time of day, the human cries seem to rise all the way to the sky.

Only from this distance does one have a full view of the inferno on the teeming ramp. I see a pair of human beings who have fallen to the ground locked in a last desperate embrace. The man has dug his fingers into the woman's flesh and has caught her clothing with his teeth. She screams hysterically, swears, cries, until at last a large boot comes down over her throat and she is silent. They are pulled apart and dragged like cattle to the truck. I see four Canada men lugging a corpse: a huge, swollen female corpse. Cursing, dripping wet from the strain, they kick out of their way some stray children who have been running all over the ramp, howling like dogs. The men pick them up by the collars, heads, arms, and toss them inside the trucks, on top of the heaps. The four men have trouble lifting the fat corpse on to the car, they call others for help, and all together they hoist up the mound of meat. Big, swollen, puffed-up corpses are being collected from all over the ramp; on top of them are piled the invalids, the smothered, the sick, the unconscious. The heap seethes, howls, groans. The driver starts the motor, the truck begins rolling.

"Halt! Halt!" an S.S. man yells after them. "Stop, damn you!"

They are dragging to the truck an old man wearing tails and a band around his arm. His head knocks against the gravel and pavement; he moans and wails in an uninterrupted monotone: *"Ich will mit dem Herrn Kommandanten sprechen* — I wish to speak with the commandant . . ."* With senile stubbornness he keeps repeating these words all the way. Thrown on the truck, trampled by others, choked, he still wails: *"Ich will mit dem . . ."*

"Look here, old man!" a young S.S. man calls, laughing jovially. "In half an hour you'll be talking with the top commandant! Only don't forget to greet him with a *Heil Hitler!*"

Several other men are carrying a small girl with only one leg. They hold her by the arms and the one leg. Tears are running down her face and she whispers faintly: "Sir, it hurts, it hurts . . ." They throw her on the truck on top of the corpses. She will burn alive along with them.

The evening has come, cool and clear. The stars are out. We lie against the rails. It is incredibly quiet. Anaemic bulbs hang from the top of the high lamp-posts; beyond the circle of light stretches an impenetrable darkness. Just one step, and a man could vanish for ever. But the guards are watching, their automatics ready.

"Did you get the shoes?" asks Henri.

"No."

"Why?"

"My God, man, I am finished, absolutely finished!"

"So soon? After only two transports? Just look at me, I . . . since Christmas, at least a million people have passed through my hands. The worst of all are the transports from around Paris — one is always bumping into friends."

"And what do you say to them?"

"That first they will have a bath, and later we'll meet at the camp. What would you say?"

I do not answer. We drink coffee with vodka; somebody opens a tin of cocoa and mixes it with sugar. We scoop it up by the handful, the cocoa sticks to the lips. Again coffee, again vodka.

"Henri, what are we waiting for?"

"There'll be another transport."

"I'm not going to unload it! I can't take any more."

"So, it's got you down? Canada is nice, eh?" Henri grins indulgently and disappears into the darkness. In a moment he is back again.

"All right. Just sit here quietly and don't let an S.S. man see you. I'll try to find you your shoes."

"Just leave me alone. Never mind the shoes." I want to sleep. It is very late.

Another whistle, another transport. Freight cars emerge out of the darkness, pass under the lamp-posts, and again vanish in the night. The ramp is small, but the circle of lights is smaller. The unloading will have to be done gradually. Somewhere the trucks are growling. They back up against the steps, black, ghostlike, their searchlights flash across the trees. *Wasser! Luft!* The same all over again, like a late showing of the same film: a volley of shots, the train falls silent. Only this time a little girl pushes herself halfway through the small window and, losing her balance, falls out on to the gravel. Stunned, she lies still for a moment, then stands up and begins walking around in a circle, faster and faster, waving her rigid arms in the air, breathing loudly and spasmodically, whining in a faint voice. Her mind has given way in the inferno inside the train. The whining is hard on the nerves: an S.S. man approaches calmly, his heavy boot strikes between her shoulders. She falls. Holding her down with his foot, he draws his revolver, fires once, then again. She remains face down, kicking the gravel with her feet, until she stiffens. They proceed to unseal the train.

I am back on the ramp, standing by the doors. A warm, sickening smell gushes from inside. The mountain of people filling the car almost halfway up to the ceiling is motionless, horribly tangled, but still steaming.

"Ausladen!"[27] comes the command. An S.S. man steps out from the darkness. Across his chest hangs a portable searchlight. He throws a stream of light inside.

---

[27] "Unload."

"Why are you standing about like sheep? Start unloading!" His whip flies and falls across our backs. I seize a corpse by the hand; the fingers close tightly around mine. I pull back with a shriek and stagger away. My heart pounds, jumps up to my throat. I can no longer control the nausea. Hunched under the train I begin to vomit. Then, like a drunk, I weave over to the stack of rails.

I lie against the cool, kind metal and dream about returning to the camp, about my bunk, on which there is no mattress, about sleep among comrades who are not going to the gas tonight. Suddenly I see the camp as a haven of peace. It is true, others may be dying, but one is somehow still alive, one has enough food, enough strength to work . . .

The lights on the ramp flicker with a spectral glow, the wave of people — feverish, agitated, stupefied people — flows on and on, endlessly. They think that now they will have to face a new life in the camp, and they prepare themselves emotionally for the hard struggle ahead. They do not know that in just a few moments they will die, that the gold, money, and diamonds which they have so prudently hidden in their clothing and on their bodies are now useless to them. Experienced professionals will probe into every recess of their flesh, will pull the gold from under the tongue and the diamonds from the uterus and the colon. They will rip out gold teeth. In tightly sealed crates they will ship them to Berlin.

The S.S. men's black figures move about, dignified, businesslike. The gentleman with the notebook puts down his final marks, rounds out the figures: fifteen thousand.

Many, very many, trucks have been driven to the crematoria today.

It is almost over. The dead are being cleared off the ramp and piled into the last truck. The Canada men, weighed down under a load of bread, marmalade, and sugar, and smelling of perfume and fresh linen, line up to go. For several days the entire camp will live off this transport. For several days the entire camp will talk about "Sosnowiec-Będzin." "Sosnowiec-Będzin" was a good, rich transport.

The stars are already beginning to pale as we walk back to the camp. The sky grows translucent and opens high above our heads — it is getting light.

Great columns of smoke rise from the crematoria and merge up above into a huge black river which very slowly floats across the sky over Birkenau and disappears beyond the forests in the direction of Trzebinia. The "Sosnowiec-Będzin" transport is already burning.

We pass a heavily armed S.S. detachment on its way to change guard. The men march briskly, in step, shoulder to shoulder, one mass, one will.

"*Und morgen die ganze Welt* . . ."[28] they sing at the top of their lungs.

"*Rechts ran!* To the right march!" snaps a command from up front. We move out of their way.   [1948]

---

[28] "And tomorrow the whole world . . ."

PAUL BOWLES *(b. 1910) was born in New York City, the son of a dentist. When he was very young, his parents encouraged his interest in music, art, and literature, and he began to compose his first opera at the age of eight. After a year at the University of Virginia, he studied music with Aaron Copland in New York and Berlin from 1930 to 1932, and with Virgil Thomson in Paris from 1933 to 1934. In 1938 Bowles married Jane Sydney Auer, who later published fiction under the name Jane Bowles.*

As the critic Paul Gray has noted, Bowles is a Renaissance man born into an age that applauds specialization. He has been a distinguished composer, writing music for the plays of his friend Tennessee Williams; he has translated the works of Jean-Paul Sartre and founded Antaeus, *a literary quarterly; he has been a collector of folklore and legends from North Africa (he has lived in Tangier on and off since the early 1930s); and he has published novels, collections of poetry, travel essays, and an autobiography,* Without Stopping *(1972). In 1992 appeared* The Collected Stories of Paul Bowles, *a volume that secured his place as one of the most accomplished contemporary American writers of short fiction.*

"The Eye" is a story that has contributed to Bowles's reputation as a pitiless chronicler of bizarre and sadistic situations. Bowles used North Africa for its setting and religious context, yet there is a classical tone to the literary style here that is characteristic of his best work. In Without Stopping *he made clear his attitude toward the difference between his life and his fiction:*

> *Telling what happened [in autobiography] does not necessarily make a good story. In my tale, for instance, there are no dramatic victories because there was no struggle. I hung on and waited. It seems to me that this must be what most people do; the occasions when there is the possibility of doing more than that are becoming rare indeed.*

PAUL BOWLES

The Eye

Ten or twelve years ago there came to live in Tangier a man who would have done better to stay away. What happened to him was in no way his fault, notwithstanding the whispered innuendos of the English-speaking residents. These people often have reactions similar to those of certain primitive groups: when misfortune overtakes one of their number, the others by mutual consent refrain from offering him aid, and merely sit back to watch, certain that he has called his suffering down upon himself. He has become taboo, and is incapable of receiving help. In the case of this particular man, I suppose no one could have been of much comfort; still, the tacit disapproval called forth by his bad luck must have made the last months of his life harder to bear.

His name was Duncan Marsh, and he was said to have come from Vancouver. I never saw him, nor do I know anyone who claims to have seen him. By the time his story reached the cocktail-party circuit he was dead, and the more irresponsible residents felt at liberty to indulge their taste for myth-making.

He came alone to Tangier, rented a furnished house on the slopes of Djamaa el Mokra — they were easy enough to find in those days, and correspondingly inexpensive — and presently installed a teenage Moroccan on the premises to act as night-watchman. The house provided a resident cook and gardener, but both of these were discharged from their duties, the cook being replaced by a woman brought in at the suggestion of the watchman. It was not long after this that Marsh felt the first symptoms of a digestive illness which over the months grew steadily worse. The doctors in Tangier advised him to go to London. Two months in hospital there helped him somewhat. No clear diagnosis was made, however, and he returned here only to become bedridden. Eventually he was flown back to Canada on a stretcher, and succumbed there shortly after his arrival.

In all this there was nothing extraordinary; it was assumed that Marsh had been one more victim of slow poisoning by native employees. There have been several such cases during my five decades in Tangier. On each occasion it has been said that the European victim had only himself (or herself) to blame, having encouraged familiarity on the part of a servant. What strikes the outsider as strange is that no one ever takes the matter in hand and inaugurates a search for the culprit, but in the total absence of proof there is no point in attempting an investigation.

Two details complete the story. At some point during his illness, Marsh told an acquaintance of the arrangements he had made to provide financial aid for his night-watchman in the event that he himself should be obliged to leave Morocco; he had given him a notarized letter to that effect, but apparently the boy never tried to press his claim. The other report came from Dr. Halsey, the physician who arranged for Marsh's removal from the house to the airport. It was this bit of information which, for me at least, made the story take on life. According to the doctor, the soles of Marsh's feet had been systematically marked with deep incisions in the form of crude patterns; the cuts were recent, but there was some infection. Dr. Halsey called in the cook and the watchman: they showed astonishment and dismay at the sight of their employer's feet, but were unable to account for the mutilations. Within a few days after Marsh's departure, the original cook and gardener returned to take up residence, the other two having already left the house.

The slow poisoning was classical enough, particularly in the light of Marsh's remark about his provision for the boy's well-being, but the knife-drawn designs on the feet somehow got in the way of whatever combinations of motive one could invent. I thought about it. There could be little doubt that the boy was guilty. He had persuaded Marsh to get rid of the cook that came with the house, even though her wages had to continue to be paid, and to hire another woman (very likely from his own family) to do the cooking. The poisoning process lasts many months if it is to be undetectable, and no one is in a better position to take charge of it than the cook herself. Clearly she knew about the financial arrangement that had been made for the boy, and expected to share in it. At the same time, the crosses and circles slashed in the feet were inexplicable. The slow poisoner is patient, careful, methodical; his principal concerns are to keep the dosage effective and to avoid leaving any visible marks. Bravado is unknown to him.

The time came when people no longer told the story of Duncan Marsh. I myself thought of it less often, having no more feasible hypotheses to supply. One evening perhaps five years ago, an American resident here came to me with the news that he had discovered a Moroccan who claimed to have been Marsh's night-watchman. The man's name was Larbi; he was a waiter at Le Fin Bec, a small back-street restaurant. Apparently he spoke poor English, but understood it without difficulty. This information was handed me for what it was worth, said the American, in the event that I felt inclined to make use of it.

I turned it over in my mind, and one night a few weeks later I went down to the restaurant to see Larbi for myself. The place was dimly lit and full of Europeans. I studied the three waiters. They were interchangeable, with wide black moustaches, blue jeans, and sport shirts. A menu was handed me; I could scarcely read it, even directly under the glow of the little table lamp. When the man who had brought it returned, I asked for Larbi.

He pulled the menu from my hand and left the table. A moment later another of the triumvirate came up beside me and handed me the menu he carried under his arm. I ordered in Spanish. When he brought the soup I murmured that I was surprised to find him working there. This brought him up short; I could see him try to remember me.

"Why wouldn't I be working here?" His voice was level, without inflection.

"Of course! Why not? It was just that I thought by now you'd have a bazaar or some sort of shop."

His laugh was a snort. "Bazaar!"

When he arrived with the next course, I begged his pardon for meddling in his affairs. But I was interested, I said, because for several years I had been under the impression that he had received a legacy from an English gentleman.

"You mean Señor Marsh?" His eyes were at last wide open.

"Yes, that was his name. Didn't he give you a letter? He told his friends he had."

He looked over my head as he said: "He gave me a letter."

"Have you ever showed it to anyone?" This was tactless, but sometimes it is better to drive straight at the target.

"Why? What good is it? Señor Marsh is dead." He shook his head with an air of finality, and moved off to another table. By the time I had finished my crème caramel, most of the diners had left, and the place seemed even darker. He came over to the table to see if I wanted coffee. I asked for the check. When he brought it I told him I should like very much to see the letter if he still had it.

"You can come tomorrow night or any night, and I'll show it to you. I have it at home."

I thanked him and promised to return in two or three days. I was confused as I left the restaurant. It seemed clear that the waiter did not consider himself to be incriminated in Duncan Marsh's troubles. When, a few nights later, I saw the document, I no longer understood anything.

It was not a letter; it was a *papier timbré* of the kind on sale at tobacconists. It read, simply: *To Whom It May Concern: I, Duncan Whitelow Marsh, do hereby agree to deposit the sum of One Hundred Pounds to the account of Larbi Lairini, on the first of each month, for as long as I live.* It was signed and notarized in the presence of two Moroccan witnesses and bore the date June 11, 1966. As I handed it back to him I said: "And it never did you any good."

He shrugged and slipped the paper into his wallet. "How was it going to? The man died."

"It's too bad."

"*Suerte.*" In the Moroccan usage of the word, it means *fate*, rather than simple luck.

At that moment I could have pressed on, and asked him if he had any idea as to the cause of Marsh's illness, but I wanted time for considering what I had just learned. As I rose to leave I said: "I'm sorry it turned out that way. I'll be back in a few days." He held out his hand and I shook it. I had no intentions then. I might return soon or I might never go back.

For as long as I live. The phrase echoed in my mind for several weeks. Possibly Marsh had worded it that way so it would be readily understandable to the *adoul* of Tangier who had affixed their florid signatures to the sheet; yet I could not help interpreting the words in a more melodramatic fashion. To me the document represented the officializing of a covenant already in existence between master and servant: Marsh wanted the watchman's help, and the watchman had agreed to give it. There was nothing upon which to base such an assumption, nevertheless I thought I was on the right track. Slowly I came to believe that if only I could talk to the watchman, in Arabic and inside the house itself, I might be in a position to see things more clearly.

One evening I walked to Le Fin Bec and without taking a seat motioned to Larbi to step outside for a moment. There I asked him if he could find out whether the house Señor Marsh had lived in was occupied at the moment or not.

"There's nobody living there now." He paused and added: "It's empty. I know the guardian."

I had decided, in spite of my deficient Arabic, to speak to him in his own language, so I said: "Look. I'd like to go with you to the house and see where everything happened. I'll give you fifteen thousand francs for your trouble."

He was startled to hear the Arabic; then his expression shifted to one of satisfaction. "He's not supposed to let anyone in," he said.

I handed him three thousand francs. "You arrange that with him. And fifteen for you when we leave the house. Could we do it Thursday?"

The house had been built, I should say, in the fifties, when good construction was still possible. It was solidly embedded in the hillside, with the forest towering behind it. We had to climb three flights of stairs through the garden to get to the entrance. The guardian, a squinting Djibli in a brown djellaba, followed close on our footsteps, eyeing me with mistrust.

There was a wide terrace above, with a view to the southeast over the town and the mountains. Behind the terrace a shadowed lawn ended where the forest began. The living room was large and bright, with French doors giving onto the lawn. Odors of damp walls and mildew weighted the air. The absurd conviction that I was about to understand everything had taken possession of me; I noticed that I was breathing more quickly. We wandered into the dining room. There was a corridor beyond, and the room where Marsh had slept, shuttered and dark. A wide, curving stairway led down to a level where there were two more bedrooms and continued its spiral to the kitchen and servants' rooms below. The kitchen door opened onto a small flagstoned patio where high philodendron covered the walls.

Larbi looked out and shook his head. "That's the place where all the trouble began," he said glumly.

I pushed through the doorway and sat down on a wrought-iron bench in the sun. "It's damp inside. Why don't we stay out here?"

The guardian left us and locked up the house. Larbi squatted comfortably on his heels near the bench.

There would have been no trouble at all, he said, if only Marsh had been satisfied with Yasmina, the cook whose wages were included in the rent. But she was a careless worker and the food was bad. He asked Larbi to find him another cook.

"I told him ahead of time that this woman Meriam had a little girl, and some days she could leave her with friends and some days she would have to bring her with her when she came to work. He said it didn't matter, but he wanted her to be quiet."

The woman was hired. Two or three days a week she came accompanied by the child, who would play in the patio where she could watch her. From the beginning Marsh complained that she was noisy. Repeatedly he sent messages down to Meriam, asking her to make the child be still. And one day he went quietly around the outside of the house and down to the patio. He got on all fours, put his face close to the little girl's face, and frowned at her so fiercely that she began to scream. When Meriam rushed out of the kitchen he stood up smiling and walked off. The little girl continued to scream and wail in a corner of the kitchen until Meriam took her home. That night, still sobbing, she came down with a high fever. For several weeks she hovered between life and death, and when she was finally out of danger she could no longer walk.

Meriam, who was earning relatively high wages, consulted one *faqih* after another. They agreed that "the eye" had been put on the child; it was equally clear that the Nazarene for whom she worked had done it. What they told her she must do, Larbi explained, was to administer certain substances to Marsh which eventually would make it possible to counteract the spell. This was absolutely necessary, he said, staring at me gravely. Even if the señor had agreed to remove it (and of course she never would have mentioned it to him) he would not have been able to. What she gave him could not harm him; it was merely medicine to relax him so that when the time came to undo the spell he would not make any objections.

At some point Marsh confided to Larbi that he suspected Meriam of slipping soporifics into his food, and begged him to be vigilant. The provision for Larbi's well-being was signed as an inducement to enlisting his active support. Since to Larbi the mixtures Meriam was feeding her master were relatively harmless, he reassured him and let her continue to dose him with her concoctions.

Tired of squatting, Larbi suddenly stood up and began to walk back and forth, stepping carefully in the center of each flagstone. "When he had to go to the hospital in London, I told her, 'Now you've made him sick. Suppose he doesn't come back? You'll never break it.' She was worried about it. 'I've done what I could,' she said. 'It's in the hands of Allah.'"

When Marsh did return to Tangier, Larbi urged her to be quick about bringing things to a head, now that she had been fortunate enough to get him back. He was thinking, he said, that it might be better for the señor's health if her treatment were not continued for too long a time.

I asked no questions while he talked; I made a point of keeping my face entirely expressionless, thinking that if he noticed the least flicker of disapproval he might stop. The sun had gone behind the trees and the patio was chilly. I had a strong desire to get up and walk back and forth as he was doing, but I thought even that might interrupt him. Once stopped, the flow might not resume.

Soon Marsh was worse than ever, with racking pains in his abdomen and kidneys. He remained in bed then, and Larbi brought him his food. When Meriam saw that he was no longer able to leave the bed, even to go into the bathroom, she decided that the time had come to get rid of the spell. On the same night that a *faqih* held a ceremony at her house in the presence of the crippled child, four men from Meriam's family came up to Djamaa el Mokra.

"When I saw them coming, I got onto my motorcycle and went into the city. I didn't want to be here when they did it. It had nothing to do with me."

He stood still and rubbed his hands together. I heard the southwest wind beginning to sound in the trees; it was that time of afternoon. "Come. I'll show you something," he said.

We climbed steps around the back of the house and came out onto a terrace with a pergola over it. Beyond this lay the lawn and the wall of trees.

"He was very sick for the next two days. He kept asking me to telephone the English doctor."

"Didn't you do it?"

Larbi stopped walking and looked at me. "I had to clean everything up first. Meriam wouldn't touch him. It was during the rains. He had mud and blood all over him when I got back here and found him. The next day I gave him a bath and changed the sheets and blankets. And I cleaned the house, because they got mud everywhere when they brought him back in. Come on. You'll see where they had to take him."

We had crossed the lawn and were walking in the long grass that skirted the edge of the woods. A path led off to the right through the tangle of undergrowth, and we followed it, climbing across boulders and fallen tree trunks until we came to an old stone well. I leaned over the wall of rocks around it and saw the small circle of sky far below.

"They had to drag him all the way here, you see, and hold him steady right over the well while they made the signs on his feet, so the blood would fall into the water. It's no good if it falls on the side of the well. And they had to make the same signs the *faqih* drew on paper for the little girl. That's hard to do in the dark and in the rain. But they did it. I saw the cuts when I bathed him."

Cautiously I asked him if he saw any connection between all this and Marsh's death. He ceased staring into the well and turned around. We started to walk back toward the house.

"He died because his hour had come."

And had the spell been broken? I asked him. Could the child walk afterward? But he had never heard, for Meriam had gone to Kenitra not much later to live with her sister.

When we were in the car, driving back down to the city, I handed him the money. He stared at it for several seconds before slipping it into his pocket.

I let him off in town with a vague sense of disappointment, and I saw that I had not only expected, but actually hoped, to find someone on whom the guilt might be fixed. What constitutes a crime? There was no criminal intent — only a mother moving in the darkness of ancient ignorance. I thought about it on my way home in the taxi.   [1981]

KAY BOYLE (1902–1992), *author of almost forty volumes of fiction, poetry, essays, and translations, was born in St. Paul, Minnesota, and studied as a teenager at the Cincinnati Conservatory of Music. At the age of twenty she fell in love with the French engineer Richard Brault, a veteran of World War I, who graduated from the University of Cincinnati and, as she later wrote in her memoir, shared her hope that "our life together was going to be a confirmation of our impatience with conventions and our commitment to something called freedom in which we believed so passionately."*

After her marriage, Boyle moved to Greenwich Village with her husband, saving money to live in France, a country she revered because she believed it "did not put its socialists in jail, as Eugene Debs was jailed in America, and did not harass its writers." In New York City she worked as a secretary in the office of the experimental literary magazine Broom *for a year before sailing to France, where she published her first short story in an avant-garde literary magazine in 1925. In Paris she became acquainted with such expatriate modernists as Gertrude Stein, James Joyce, Djuna Barnes, Ernest Hemingway, and Robert McAlmon. The memoir Boyle coauthored with McAlmon,* Being Geniuses Together 1920–1930 *(1984) — he wrote an earlier version of the book by himself — is one of our most vivid accounts of the experimental writers' lives in Paris.*

Boyle lived in Europe and published steadily for thirty years, returning to the United States to teach in various colleges. Thrice married, with six children, she was also a political activist deeply committed to pacifist and feminist causes. Reflecting at the end of her long life, she said that "the older I grow, the more I feel that all writers should be more committed to their times and write of their times and of the issues of their times." Boyle's volumes of short stories include The White Horses of Vienna and Other Stories *(1936),* The Smoking Mountain: Stories of Postwar Germany *(1951),* Nothing Ever Breaks Except the Heart *(1966), and* Fifty Stories *(1980). The critic Marilyn Elkins has noted that "the political and personal consequences of patriarchal ideology undergird much of Boyle's short fiction," as in "Black Boy," an early story that dramatizes Boyle's concern for social justice and human suffering.*

KAY BOYLE

Black Boy

At that time, it was the forsaken part, it was the other end of the city, and on early spring mornings there was no one about. By soft words, you could woo the horse into the foam, and ride her with the sea knee-deep around her. The waves came in and out there, as indolent as ladies, gathered up their skirts in their hands and, with a murmur, came tiptoeing in across the velvet sand.

The wooden promenade was high there, and when the wind was up the water came running under it like wild. On such days, you had to content yourself with riding the horse over the deep white drifts of dry sand on the other side of the walks; the horse's hoofs here made no sound and the sparks of sand stung your face in fury. It had no body to it, like the mile or two of sand packed hard that you could open out on once the tide was down.

My little grandfather, Puss, was alive then, with his delicate gait and ankles, and his belly pouting in his dove-gray clothes. When he saw from the window that the tide was sidling out, he put on his pearl fedora and came stepping down the street. For a minute, he put one foot on the sand, but he was not at ease there. On the boardwalk over our heads was some other kind of life in progress. If you looked up, you could see it in motion through the cracks in the timber: rolling chairs, and women in high heels proceeding, if the weather were fair.

"You know," my grandfather said, "I think I might like to have a look at a shop or two along the boardwalk." Or: "I suppose you don't feel like leaving the beach for a minute," or: "If you would go with me, we might take a chair together, and look at the hats and the dresses and roll along in the sun."

He was alive then, taking his pick of the broad easy chairs and the black boys.

"There's a nice skinny boy," he'd say. "He looks as though he might put some action into it. Here you are, sonny. Push me and the little girl down to the Million Dollar Pier and back."

The cushions were red velvet with a sheen of dew over them. And Puss settled back on them and took my hand in his. In his mind there was no hesitation about whether he would look at the shops on one side, or out on the vacant side where there was nothing shining but the sea.

"What's your name, Charlie?" Puss would say without turning his head to the black boy pushing the chair behind our shoulders.

"Charlie's my name, sir," he'd answer with his face dripping down like tar in the sun.

"What's your name, sonny?" Puss would say another time, and the black boy answered:

"Sonny's my name, sir."

"What's your name, Big Boy?"

"Big Boy's my name."

He never wore a smile on his face, the black boy. He was thin as a shadow but darker, and he was pushing and sweating, getting the chair down to the Million Dollar Pier and back again, in and out through the people. If you turned toward the sea for a minute, you could see his face out of the corner of your eye, hanging black as a bat's wing, nodding and nodding like a dark heavy flower.

But in the early morning, he was the only one who came down onto the sand and sat under the beams of the boardwalk, sitting idle there with a languor fallen on every limb. He had long bones. He sat idle there, with his clothes shrunk up from his wrists and his ankles, with his legs drawn up, looking out at the sea.

"I might be a king if I wanted to be," was what he said to me.

Maybe I was twelve years old, or maybe I was ten when we used to sit eating dog biscuits together. Sometimes when you broke them in two, a worm fell out and the black boy lifted his sharp finger and flicked it carelessly from off his knee.

"I seen kings," he said, "with a kind of cloth over they heads, and kind of jewels-like around here and here. They weren't any blacker than me, if as black," he said. "I could be almost anything I made up my mind to be."

"King Nebuchadnezzar," I said. "He wasn't a white man."

The wind was off the ocean and was filled with alien smells. It was early in the day, and no human sign was given. Overhead were the green beams of the boardwalk and no wheel or step to sound it.

"If I was a king," said the black boy with his biscuit in his fingers, "I wouldn't put much stock in hanging around here."

Great crystal jelly beasts were quivering in a hundred different colors on the wastes of sand around us. The dogs came, jumping them, and when they saw me still sitting still, they wheeled like gulls and sped back to the sea.

"I'd be traveling around," he said, "here and there. Now here, now there. I'd change most of my habits."

His hair grew all over the top of his head in tight dry rosettes. His neck was longer and more shapely than a white man's neck, and his fingers ran in and out of the sand like the blue feet of a bird.

"I wouldn't have much to do with pushing chairs around under them circumstances," he said. "I might even give up sleeping out here on the sand."

Or if you came out when it was starlight, you could see him sitting there in the clear white darkness. I could go and come as I liked, for whenever I went out the door, I had the dogs shouldering behind me. At night, they shook the taste of the house out of their coats and came down across the sand. There he was, with his knees up, sitting idle.

"They used to be all kinds of animals come down here to drink in the dark," he said. "They was a kind of a mirage came along and gave that impression. I seen tigers, lions, lambs, deer; I seen ostriches drinking down there side by side with each other. They's the Northern Lights gets crossed some way and switches the wrong picture down."

It may be that the coast has changed there, for even then it was changing. The lighthouse that had once stood far out on the white rocks near the outlet was standing then like a lighted torch in the heart of the town. And the deep currents of the sea may have altered so that the clearest water runs in another direction, and houses may have been built down as far as where the brink used to be. But the brink was so perilous then that every word the black boy spoke seemed to fall into a cavern of beauty.

"I seen camels; I seen zebras," he said. "I might have caught any of one of them if I'd felt inclined."

The street was so still and wide then that when Puss stepped out of the house, I could hear him clearing his throat of the sharp salty air. He had no intention of soiling the soles of his boots, but he came down the street to find me.

"If you feel like going with me," he said, "we'll take a chair and see the fifty-seven varieties changing on the electric sign."

And then he saw the black boy sitting quiet. His voice drew up short on his tongue and he touched his white mustache.

"I shouldn't think it a good idea," he said, and he put his arm through my arm. "I saw another little oak not three inches high in the Jap's window yesterday. We might roll down the boardwalk and have a look at it. You know," said Puss, and he put his kid gloves carefully on his fingers, "that black boy might do you some kind of harm."

"What kind of harm could he do me?" I said.

"Well," said Puss with the garlands of lights hanging around him, "he might steal some money from you. He might knock you down and take your money away."

"How could he do that?" I said. "We just sit and talk there." Puss looked at me sharply.

"What do you find to sit and talk about?" he said.

"I don't know," I said. "I don't remember. It doesn't sound like much to tell it."

The burden of his words was lying there on my heart when I woke up in the morning. I went out by myself to the stable and led the horse to the door and put the saddle on her. If Puss were ill at ease for a day or two, he could look out the window in peace and see me riding high and mighty away. The day after tomorrow, I thought, or the next day, I'll sit down on the beach again and talk to the black boy. But when I rode out, I saw him seated idle there, under the boardwalk, heedless, looking away to the cool wide sea. He had been eating peanuts and the shells lay all around him. The dogs came running at the horse's heels, nipping the foam that lay along the tide.

The horse was as shy as a bird that morning, and when I drew her up beside the black boy, she tossed her head on high. Her mane went back and forth, from one side to the other, and a flight of joy in her limbs sent her forelegs like rockets into the air. The black boy stood up from the cold smooth sand, unsmiling, but a spark of wonder shone in his marble eyes. He put out his arm in the short tight sleeve of his coat and stroked her shivering shoulder.

"I was going to be a jockey once," he said, "but I changed my mind."

I slid down on one side while he climbed up the other.

"I don't know as I can ride him right," he said as I held her head. "The kind of saddle you have, it gives you nothing to grip your heels around. I ride them with their bare skin."

The black boy settled himself on the leather and put his feet in the stirrups. He was quiet and quick with delight, but he had no thought of smiling as he took the reins in his hands.

I stood on the beach with the dogs beside me, looking after the horse as she ambled down to the water. The black boy rode easily and straight, letting the horse stretch out and sneeze and canter. When they reached the jetty, he turned her casually and brought her loping back.

"Some folks licks hell out of their horses," he said. "I'd never raise a hand to one, unless he was to bite me or do something I didn't care for."

He sat in the saddle at ease, as though in a rocker, stroking her shoulder with his hand spread open, and turning in the stirrups to smooth her shining flank.

"Jockeys make a pile of money," I said.

"I wouldn't care for the life they have," said the black boy. "They have to watch their diet so careful."

His fingers ran delicately through her hair and laid her mane back on her neck.

When I was up on the horse again, I turned her toward the boardwalk.

"I'm going to take her over the jetty," I said. "You'll see how she clears it. I'll take her up under the boardwalk to give here a good start."

I struck her shoulder with the end of my crop, and she started toward the tough black beams. She was under it, galloping, when the dogs came down the beach like mad. They had chased a cat out of cover and were after it, screaming as they ran, with a wing of sand blowing wide behind them, and when the horse saw them under her legs, she jumped sidewise in sprightliness and terror and flung herself against an iron arch.

For a long time I heard nothing at all in my head except the melody of someone crying, whether it was my dead mother holding me in comfort, or the soft wind grieving over me where I had fallen. I lay on the sand asleep; I could feel it running with my tears through my fingers. I was rocked in a cradle of love, cradled and rocked in sorrow.

"Oh, my little lamb, my little lamb pie!" Oh, sorrow, sorrow, wailed the wind, or the tide, or my own kin about me. "Oh, lamb, oh, lamb!"

I could feel the long swift fingers of love untying the terrible knot of pain that bound my head. And I put my arms around him and lay close to his heart in comfort.

Puss was alive then, and when he met the black boy carrying me up to the house, he struck him square across the mouth.   [1932]

T. CORAGHESSAN BOYLE *(b. 1948) was born in Peekskill, New York. Growing up he wasn't interested at all in literature — "I don't think I ever read a book until I was eighteen" — although he attended college and even taught high school for a short time. Until 1972, he says, he "was just hanging out." As "a way out of a dead end," he applied and was admitted to the Iowa Writers Workshop program on the basis of a short story he had published in the* North American Review. *"The sole criterion for admittance to the workshop is the work itself; they didn't look at my grades, which were so bad I couldn't have gotten into graduate school."*

At the University of Iowa, Boyle's talent flourished. He resumed writing and publishing short stories, passed his courses and preliminary examinations, and completed his doctorate with a story collection instead of a dissertation. Hired to teach at the University of Southern California, he earned tenure by publishing four books in seven years: Descent of Man: Stories *(1979),* Water Music *(1981),* Budding Prospects *(1984), and* Greasy Lake and Other Stories *(1985). He also received several literary awards and a National Endowment for the Arts Creative Writing Fellowship. What he called his "wild and woolly days" were well behind him. In 1994 he published* Without a Hero and Other Stories.

Boyle continues to produce short stories as a relief from the concentration required by his novels. Descent of Man *made his reputation as an experimental writer, an inventor of literary parodies in the "playful" tradition of John Barth, Richard Brautigan, and Thomas Pynchon. Boyle believes that "humor resides in exaggeration, and humor is a quick cover for alarm and bewilderment." "Stones in My Passway, Hellhound on My Trail" is a story about the brief life of the legendary Mississippi blues musician, Robert Johnson, whom the blues historian Samuel Charters has described as being "on fire with his music." The story's title is also the title of one of Johnson's most riveting blues compositions.*

T. Coraghessan Boyle

Stones in My Passway, Hellhound on My Trail

> I got stones in my passway
> and my road seems black as night.
> I have pains in my heart,
> they have taken my appetite.
>
> *Robert Johnson (1914?–1938)*

Saturday night. He's playing the House Party Club in Dallas, singing his blues, picking notes with a penknife. His voice rides up to a reedy falsetto that gets the men hooting and then down to the cavernous growl that chills the women, the hard chords driving behind it, his left foot beating like a hammer. The club's patrons — field hands and laborers — pound over the floorboards like the start of the derby, stamping along with him. Skirts fly, straw hats slump over eyebrows, drinks spill, ironed hair goes wiry. Overhead two dim yellow bulbs sway on their cords; the light is suffused with cigarette smoke, dingy and brown. The floor is wet with spittle and tobacco juice. From the back room, a smell of eggs frying. And beans.

Huddie Doss, the proprietor, has set up a bar in the corner: two barrels of roofing nails and a pine plank. The plank supports a cluster of gallon jugs, a bottle of Mexican rum, a pewter jigger, and three lemons. Robert sits on a stool at the far end of the room, boxed in by men in kerchiefs, women in calico. The men watch his fingers, the women look into his eyes.

It is 1938, dust bowl, New Deal. FDR is on the radio, and somebody in Robinsonville is naming a baby after Jesse Owens. Once, on the road to Natchez, Robert saw a Pierce Arrow and talked about it for a week. Another time he spent six weeks in Chicago and didn't know the World's Fair was going on. Now he plays his guitar up and down the Mississippi, and in Louisiana, Texas, and Arkansas. He's never heard of Hitler and he hasn't eaten in two days.

When he was fifteen he watched a poisoned dog tear out its entrails. It was like this:

They were out in the fields when a voice shouted, "Loup's gone mad!" and then he was running with the rest of them, down the slope and across the red dust road, past the shanties and into the gully where they dumped their trash, the dog crying high over the sun and then baying deep as craters in the moon. It was a coonhound, tawny, big-boned, the color of a lion. Robert pushed through the gathering crowd and stood watching as the animal dragged its hindquarters along the ground like a birthing bitch, the ropy testicles strung out behind. It was mewling now, the high-pitched cries sawing away at each breath, and then it was baying again, howling death until the day was filled with it, their ears and the pits of their stomachs soured with it. One of the men said in a terse, angry voice, "Go get Turkey Nason to come on down here with his gun," and a boy detached himself from the crowd and darted up the rise.

It was then that the dog fell heavily to its side, ribs heaving, and began to dig at its stomach with long racing thrusts of the rear legs. There was yellow foam on the black muzzle, blood bright in the nostrils. The dog screamed and dug, dug until the flesh was raw and its teeth could puncture the cavity to get at the gray intestine, tugging first at a bulb of it and then fastening on a lank strand like dirty wash. There was no sign of the gun. The woman beside Robert began to cry, a sound like crumpling paper. Then one of the men stepped in with a shovel in his hand. He hit the dog once across the eyes and the animal lunged for him. The shovel fell twice more and the dog stiffened, its yellow eyes gazing round the circle of men, the litter of bottles and cans and rusted machinery, its head lolling on the lean, muscular neck, poised for one terrible moment, and then it was over. Afterward Robert came close: to look at the frozen teeth, the thin, rigid limbs, the green flies on the pink organs.

Between sets Robert has been out back with a girl named Beatrice, and Ida Mae Doss, Huddie's daughter, is not happy about it. As he settles back down on the stool and reaches for his guitar, he looks up at the pine plank, the barrels, Ida Mae stationed behind the bar. She is staring at him — cold, hard, her eyes like razors. What can he do? He grins, sheepish. But then Beatrice steams in, perfumed in sweat, the blue print shift clinging like a wet sheet. She sashays through the knot of men milling around Robert and says, "Why don't you play something sweet?" Robert pumps the neck of the guitar, strikes the strings twice, and then breaks into "Phonograph Blues":

> And we played it on the sofa and we played it 'side the wall,
> But, boys, my needle point got rusty and it will not play at all.

The men nudge one another. Ida Mae looks daggers. Beatrice flounces to the center of the floor, raises her arms above her head, and begins a slow grinding shuffle to the pulse of the guitar.

No one knows how Robert got his guitar. He left Letterman's farm when he was sixteen, showed up a year and a half later with a new Harmony Sovereign. He walked into the Rooster Club in Robinsonville, Mississippi, and leaned against the wall while Walter Satter finished out his set. When Satter stepped up to the bar, Robert was at his elbow. "I heard your record," Robert said. He was short, skinny, looked closer to twelve than eighteen.

"You like it?"

"Taught me a lot."

Satter grinned.

"Mind if I sit in on the next set?"

"Sure — if you think you can go on that thing."

Robert sat in. His voice was a shower, his guitar a storm. The sweet slide leads cut the atmosphere like lightning at dusk. Satter played rhythm behind him for a while, then stepped down.

The lemons are pulp, the rum decimated, jugs lighter. Voices drift through the open door, fireflies perforate the dark rafters. It is hot as a jungle, dark as a cave. The club's patrons are quieter now — some slouched against the walls, others leaning on the bar, their fingers tapping like batons. Beatrice is an exception. She's still out in the center of the floor, head swaying to the music, heels kicking, face bright with perspiration — dancing. A glass in her hand. But suddenly she lurches to the left, her leg buckles, and she goes down. There is the shrill of breaking glass, and then silence. Robert has stopped playing. The final chord rings in the air, decapitated; a sudden unnatural silence filters through the smoke haze, descending like a judgment. Robert sets the guitar across the stool and shuffles out to where Beatrice lies on the floor. She rolls heavily to her side, laughing, muttering to herself. Robert catches her under the arms, helps her up, and guides her to a chair in the corner — and then it's over. The men start joking again, the bar gets busy, women tell stories, laugh.

Beatrice slumps in the chair, chin to chest, and begins to snore — delicate, jagged, the purr of a cat. Robert grins and pats her head — then turns to the bar. Ida Mae is there, measuring out drinks. Her eyes are moist. Robert squeezes the husk of a lemon over his glass, half fills it with rum, and presses a nickel into her palm. "What you got cooking, Ida Mae?" he says.

A thin silver chain hangs between her breasts, beneath the neckline of her cotton dress. It is ornamented with a wooden guitar pick, highly varnished, the shape of a seed.

"Got eggs," she says. "And beans."

Lubbock, Natchez, Pascagoula, Dallas, Eudora, Rosedale, Baton Rouge, Memphis, Friars Point, Vicksburg, Jonesboro, Mooringsport, Edwards, Chattanooga, Rolling Fork, Commerce, Itta Bena. Thelma, Betty Mae, Adeline, Harriet, Bernice, Ida Bell, Bertha Lee, Winifred, Maggie, Willie Mae. "Robert been driving too hard," people said. "Got to stumble."

In 1937 Franco laid siege to Madrid, the Japanese invaded Nanking, Amelia Earhart lost herself in the Pacific, and Robert made a series of recordings for Victrix Records. He was twenty-three at the time. Or twenty-two. A man from Victrix sent him train fare to New Orleans in care of the High Times Club in Biloxi. Robert slit the envelope with his penknife and ran his thumb over the green-and-silver singles while the bartender read him the letter. Robert was ecstatic. He kissed women, danced on the tables, bought a Havana cigar — but the bills whispered in his palm and he never made it to the station. A week later the man sent him a nonrefundable one-way ticket.

The man was waiting for him when the train pulled into the New Orleans station. Robert stepped off the day coach with his battered Harmony Sovereign and a cardboard valise. The stink of kerosene and coal blistered the air. Outside, automobiles stood at the curb like a dream of the twentieth century. "Walter Fagen," the man said, holding out his hand. Robert looked up at the wisps of white-blond hair, the pale irises, the red tie, and then down at a torn ticket stub on the platform. "Pleased to meet you," he mumbled. One hand was on the neck of the guitar, the other in his pocket: "Go ahead, shake," Fagen said. Robert shook.

Fagen took him to a boardinghouse, paid the big kerchief-headed woman at the door, instructed Robert to come around to the Arlington Hotel in the morning. Then he gave him a two-dollar advance. Three hours later Fagen's dinner was interrupted by a phone call from the New Orleans police: Robert was being held for disorderly conduct. Fagen hired a taxi, drove to the jailhouse, laid five silver dollars on the desk, and walked out with his recording artist. Robert's right eye was swollen closed; the guitar was gone. Robert had nothing to say. When the taxi stopped in front of the boardinghouse, Fagen gave him thirty-five cents for breakfast and told him to get a good night's sleep.

Back at the Arlington, Fagen took a seat in the dining room and reordered. He was sipping a gimlet when a boy paged him to the phone. It was Robert. "I'm lonesome," he said.

"Lonesome?"

"Yeah — there's a woman here wants forty cents and I'm a nickel short."

The voices wash around her like birds at dawn, a Greek chorus gone mad. Smoke and stale sweat, the smell of lemon. She grits her teeth. "Give me a plate of it, then, girl," he is saying. "Haven't eat in two days." Then she's in the back room, stirring beans, cracking eggs, a woman scorned. The eggs, four of them, stare up at her like eyes. Tiny embryos. On the shelf above the stove: can of pepper, saltcellar, a knife, the powder they use for rats and roaches.

Agamemnon, watch out!

Robert's dream is thick with the thighs of women, the liquid image of songs sung and songs to come, bright wire wheels and sloping fenders, swamps, trees, power lines, and the road, the road spinning out like string from a spool, like veins, blood and heart, distance without end, without horizon.

It is the last set. Things are winding down. Beatrice sags in the chair, skirt pulled up over her knees, her chest rising and falling with the soft rhythm of sleep. Beside her, a man in red suspenders presses a woman against the wall. Robert watches the woman's hands like dark animals on the man's hips. Earlier, a picker had been stabbed in the neck after a dispute over dice or women or liquor, and an old woman had fallen, drunk, and cut her head on the edge of a bench. But now things are winding down. Voices are hushed, cigarettes burn unattended, moonlight limns the windows.

Robert rests the guitar on his knee and does a song about a train station, a suitcase, and the eyes of a woman. His voice is mournful, sad as a steady rain, the guitar whining above it like a cry in the distance. "Yes!" they call out. "Robert!" Somebody whistles. Then they applaud, waves on the rocks, smoke rising as if from a rent in the earth. In response, the guitar reaches low for the opening bars of Robert's signature tune, his finale, but there is something wrong — the chords staggering like a seizure, stumbling, finally breaking off cold.

Cramps. A spasm so violent it jerks his fingers from the strings. He begins again, his voice quavering, shivered: "Got to keep moving, got to keep moving, / Hellhound on my trail." And then suddenly the voice chokes off, gags, the guitar slips to the floor with a percussive shock. His bowels are on fire. He stands, clutches his abdomen, drops to hands and knees. "Boy's had too much of that Mexican," someone says. He looks up, a sword run through him, panting, the shock waves pounding through his frame, looks up at the pine plank, the barrels, the cold, hard features of the girl with the silver necklace in her hand. Looks up, and snarls.   [1979]

ROBERT OLEN BUTLER (b. 1944) grew up in Granite City, Illinois, the son of a professor at St. Louis University. Butler attended Northwestern University and the University of Iowa, where he earned an M.A. in playwriting. In 1969 he enlisted in the army and studied the Vietnamese language for a year in Washington, D.C., before being sent to Saigon, where he served as assistant to the Foreign Service officer who was adviser to the mayor of Saigon. Butler's knowledge of the language facilitated his immersion in Vietnamese culture, which fascinated him.

After leaving the army in 1973, Butler took a job editing a business newspaper in New York City. For the next eight years he wrote novels and tried to get them published. After twenty-one rejections, Alleys of Eden, the first in a trilogy of novels about Vietnam, came out in 1981. Five more novels followed in the 1980s; all were widely praised by critics but had negligible sales. Finally Butler left New York to take a job teaching fiction writing at McNeese State University in Lake Charles, Louisiana. As Butler told the interviewer Sybil Steinberg, when he flew to the area for the first time, he looked out the plane window and saw what looked to him like the landscape of the Mekong Delta: "There was the same calligraphy of waterways, the rice paddies, the subtropical climate, the French influence." Vietnamese immigrants had settled in the towns of Gretna and Versailles near Lake Charles, and Butler began to work on the short stories that would make up the collection A Good Scent from a Strange Mountain, a volume that won the 1993 Pulitzer Prize and a Tu Do Chinh Kien Award given by the Vietnam Veterans of America for outstanding creative work by a Vietnam veteran.

The story "A Good Scent from a Strange Mountain," placed last in the collection, was also included in The Best American Short Stories of 1992, where Butler explained that the facts in the story about Ho Chi Minh's career as a young man in London and Paris are all true.

> I carried them in my head for a long time. . . . These images then awaited the aesthetic dialectic that eventually came from an old man in a back alley in Saigon who translated for me the four Chinese characters on the Buddhist shrine in his tiny sleeping room. This, he said, is the mystery of life, all that we need ever to consider: "A good scent from a strange mountain." It took nearly twenty years for me to put all of this together, to understand the vision of a peace that struggled to harmonize these two men, and, happily, that articulated the everarching vision of the book of short fiction that this eponymous story completed.

ROBERT OLEN BUTLER

A Good Scent from a Strange Mountain

Hô Chí Minh came to me again last night, his hands covered with confectioners' sugar. This was something of a surprise to me, the first time I saw him beside my bed, in the dim light from the open shade. My oldest daughter leaves my shades open, I think so that I will not forget that the sun has risen again in the morning. I am a very old man. She seems to expect that one morning I will simply forget to keep living. This is very foolish. I will one night rise up from my bed and slip into her room and open the shade there. Let *her* see the sun in the morning. She is sixty-four years old and she should worry for herself. I could never die from forgetting.

But the light from the street was enough to let me recognize Hô when I woke, and he said to me, "Đạo, my old friend, I have heard it is time to visit you." Already on that first night there was a sweet smell about him, very strong in the dark, even before I could see his hands. I said nothing, but I stretched to the nightstand beside me and I turned on the light to see if he would go away. And he did not. He stood there beside the bed — I could even see him reflected in the window — and I knew it was real because he did not appear as he was when I'd known him but as he was when he'd died. This was Uncle Hô before me, the thin old man with the dewlap beard wearing the dark clothes of a peasant and the rubber sandals, just like in the news pictures I studied with such a strange feeling for all those years. Strange because when I knew him, he was not yet Hô Chí Minh. It was 1917 and he was Nguyễn Ái Quôc and we were both young men with clean-shaven faces, the best of friends, and we worked at the Carlton Hotel in London, where I was a dishwasher and he was a pastry cook under the great Escoffier. We were the best of friends and we saw snow for the first time together. This was before we began to work at the hotel. We shoveled snow and Hô would stop for a moment and blow his breath out before him and it would make him smile, to see what was inside him, as if it was the casting of bones to tell the future.

On that first night when he came to me in my house in New Orleans, I finally saw what it was that smelled so sweet and I said to him, "Your hands are covered with sugar."

He looked at them with a kind of sadness.

I have received that look myself in the past week. It is time now for me to see my family, and the friends I have made who are still alive. This is our custom from Vietnam. When you are very old, you put aside a week or two to receive the people of your life so that you can tell one another your feelings, or try at last to understand one another, or simply say good-bye. It is a formal leave-taking, and with good luck you can do this before you have your final illness. I have lived almost a century and perhaps I should have called them

191

all to me sooner, but at last I felt a deep weariness and I said to my oldest daughter that it was time.

They look at me with sadness, some of them. Usually the dull-witted ones, or the insincere ones. But Hô's look was, of course, not dull-witted or insincere. He considered his hands and said, "The glaze. Maestro's glaze."

There was the soft edge of yearning in his voice and I had the thought that perhaps he had come to me for some sort of help. I said to him, "I don't remember. I only washed dishes." As soon as the words were out of my mouth, I decided it was foolish for me to think he had come to ask me about the glaze.

But Hô did not treat me as foolish. He looked at me and shook his head. "It's all right," he said. "I remember the temperature now. Two hundred and thirty degrees, when the sugar is between the large thread stage and the small orb stage. The Maestro was very clear about that and I remember." I knew from his eyes, however, that there was much more that still eluded him. His eyes did not seem to move at all from my face, but there was some little shifting of them, a restlessness that perhaps only I could see, since I was his close friend from the days when the world did not know him.

I am nearly one hundred years old, but I can still read a man's face. Perhaps better than I ever have. I sit in the overstuffed chair in my living room and I receive my visitors and I want these people, even the dull-witted and insincere ones — please excuse an old man's ill temper for calling them that — I want them all to be good with one another. A Vietnamese family is extended as far as the bloodline strings us together, like so many paper lanterns around a village square. And we all give off light together. That's the way it has always been in our culture. But these people who come to visit me have been in America for a long time and there are very strange things going on that I can see in their faces.

None stranger than this morning. I was in my overstuffed chair and with me there were four of the many members of my family: my son-in-law Thắng, a former colonel in the Army of the Republic of Vietnam and one of the insincere ones, sitting on my Castro convertible couch; his youngest son, Lợi, who had come in late, just a few minutes earlier, and had thrown himself down on the couch as well, youngest but a man old enough to have served as a lieutenant under his father as our country fell to the Communists more than a decade ago; my daughter Lâm, who is Thắng's wife, hovering behind the both of them and refusing all invitations to sit down; and my oldest daughter, leaning against the door frame, having no doubt just returned from my room, where she had opened the shade that I had closed when I awoke.

It was Thắng who gave me the sad look I have grown accustomed to, and I perhaps seemed to him at that moment a little weak, a little distant. I had stopped listening to the small talk of these people and I had let my eyes half close, though I could still see them clearly and I was very alert. Thắng has a steady face and the quick eyes of a man who is ready to come under fire, but I have always read much more there, in spite of his efforts to show nothing. So after he thought I'd faded from the room, it was with slow eyes, not quick, that he moved to his son and began to speak of the killing.

You should understand that Mr. Nguyễn Bích Lê had been shot dead in our community here in New Orleans just last week. There are many of us Vietnamese living in New Orleans and one man, Mr. Lê, published a little newspaper for all of us. He had recently made the fatal error — though it should not be that in America — of writing that it was time to accept the reality of the communist government in Vietnam and begin to talk with them. We had to work now with those who controlled our country. He said that he remained a patriot to the Republic of Vietnam, and I believed him. If anyone had asked an old man's opinion on this whole matter, I would not have been afraid to say that Mr. Lê was right.

But he was shot dead last week. He was forty-five years old and he had a wife and three children and he was shot as he sat behind the wheel of his Chevrolet pickup truck. I find a detail like that especially moving, that this man was killed in his Chevrolet, which I understand is a strongly American thing. We knew this in Saigon. In Saigon it was very American to own a Chevrolet, just as it was French to own a Citroën.

And Mr. Lê had taken one more step in his trusting embrace of this new culture. He had bought not only a Chevrolet but a Chevrolet pickup truck, which made him not only American but also a man of Louisiana, where there are many pickup trucks. He did not, however, also purchase a gun rack for the back window, another sign of this place. Perhaps it would have been well if he had, for it was through the back window that the bullet was fired. Someone had hidden in the bed of his truck and had killed him from behind in his Chevrolet and the reason for this act was made very clear in a phone call to the newspaper office by a nameless representative of the Vietnamese Party for the Annihilation of Communism and for the National Restoration.

And Thắng, my son-in-law, said to his youngest son, Lợi, "There is no murder weapon." What I saw was a faint lift of his eyebrows as he said this, like he was inviting his son to listen beneath his words. Then he said it again, more slowly, like it was code. "There is *no weapon*." My grandson nodded his head once, a crisp little snap. Then my daughter Lâm said in a very loud voice, with her eyes on me, "That was a terrible thing, the death of Mr. Lê." She nudged her husband and son, and both men turned their faces sharply to me and they looked at me squarely and said, also in very loud voices, "Yes, it was terrible."

I am not deaf, and I closed my eyes further, having seen enough and wanting them to think that their loud talk had not only failed to awake me but had put me more completely to sleep. I did not like to deceive them, however, even though I have already spoken critically of these members of my family. I am a Hòa Hảo Buddhist and I believe in harmony among all living things, especially the members of a Vietnamese family.

After Hô had reassured me, on that first visit, about the temperature needed to heat Maestro Escoffier's glaze, he said, "Đạo, my old friend, do you still follow the path you chose in Paris?"

He meant by this my religion. It was in Paris that I embraced the Buddha and disappointed Hô. We went to France in early 1918, with the war still on, and we lived in the poorest street of the poorest part of the Seventeenth Arrondissement. Number nine, Impasse Compoint, a blind alley with a few crumbling houses, all but ours rented out for storage. The cobblestones were littered with fallen roof tiles and Quôc and I each had a tiny single room with only an iron bedstead and a crate to sit on. I could see my friend Quôc in the light of the tallow candle and he was dressed in a dark suit and a bowler hat and he looked very foolish. I did not say so, but he knew it himself and he kept seating and reseating the hat and shaking his head very slowly, with a loudly silent anger. This was near the end of our time together, for I was visiting daily with a Buddhist monk and he was drawing me back to the religion of my father. I had run from my father, gone to sea, and that was where I had met Nguyễn Aí Quôc and we had gone to London and to Paris and now my father was calling me back, through a Vietnamese monk I met in the Tuileries.

Quôc, on the other hand, was being called not from his past but from his future. He had rented the dark suit and bowler and he would spend the following weeks in Versailles, walking up and down the mirrored corridors of the Palace trying to gain an audience with Woodrow Wilson. Quôc had eight requests for the Western world concerning Indochina. Simple things. Equal rights, freedom of assembly, freedom of the press. The essential things that he knew Wilson would understand, based as they were on Wilson's own Fourteen Points. And Quôc did not even intend to ask for independence. He wanted Vietnamese representatives in the French Parliament. That was all he would ask. But his bowler made him angry. He wrenched out of the puddle of candlelight, both his hands clutching the bowler, and I heard him muttering in the darkness and I felt that this was a bad sign already, even before he had set foot in Versailles. And as it turned out, he never saw Wilson, or Lloyd George either, or even Clemenceau. But somehow his frustration with his hat was what made me sad, even now, and I reached out from my bedside and said "Uncle Hô, it's all right."

He was still beside me. This was not an awakening, as you might expect, this was not a dream ending with the bowler in Paris and I awaking to find that Hô was never there. He was still beside my bed, though he was just beyond my outstretched hand and he did not move to me. He smiled on one side of his mouth, a smile full of irony, as if he, too, was thinking about the night he'd tried on his rented clothes. He said, "Do you remember how I worked in Paris?"

I thought about this and I did remember, with the words of his advertisement in the newspaper "La Vie Ouvrière": "If you would like a lifelong memento of your family, have your photos retouched at Nguyễn Aí Quôc's." This was his work in Paris; he retouched photos with a very delicate hand, the same fine hand that Monsieur Escoffier had admired in London. I said, "Yes, I remember."

Hô nodded gravely. "I painted the blush into the cheeks of Frenchmen."

I said, "A lovely portrait in a lovely frame for forty francs," another phrase from his advertisement.

"Forty-five," Hô said.

I thought now of his question that I had not answered. I motioned to the far corner of the room where the prayer table stood. "I still follow the path."

He looked and said, "At least you became a Hòa Hảo."

He could tell this from the simplicity of the table. There was only a red cloth upon it and four Chinese characters: Bao So'n Kỳ Hu'o'ng. This is the saying of the Hòa Hảos. We follow the teachings of a monk who broke away from the fancy rituals of the other Buddhists. We do not need elaborate pagodas or rituals. The Hòa Hảo believes that the maintenance of our spirits is very simple, and the mystery of joy is simple, too. The four characters mean "A good scent from a strange mountain."

I had always admired the sense of humor of my friend Quốc, so I said, "You never did stop painting the blush into the faces of Westerners."

Hô looked back to me but he did not smile. I was surprised at this but more surprised at my little joke seeming to remind him of his hands. He raised them and studied them and said, "After the heating, what was the surface for the glaze?"

"My old friend," I said, "you worry me now."

But Hô did not seem to hear. He turned away and crossed the room and I knew he was real because he did not vanish from my sight but opened the door and went out and closed the door behind him with a loud click.

I rang for my daughter. She had given me a porcelain bell, and after allowing Hô enough time to go down the stairs and out the front door, if that was where he was headed, I rang the bell, and my daughter, who is a very light sleeper, soon appeared.

"What is it, Father?" she asked with great patience in her voice. She is a good girl. She understands about Vietnamese families and she is a smart girl.

"Please feel the doorknob," I said.

She did so without the slightest hesitation and this was a lovely gesture on her part, a thing that made me wish to rise up and embrace her, though I was very tired and did not move.

"Yes?" she asked after touching the knob.

"Is it sticky?"

She touched it again. "Ever so slightly," she said. "Would you like to me to clean it?"

"In the morning," I said.

She smiled and crossed the room and kissed me on the forehead. She smelled of lavender and fresh bedclothes and there are so many who have gone on before me into the world of spirits and I yearn for them all, yearn to find them all together in a village square, my wife there smelling of lavender and our own sweat, like on a night in Saigon soon after the terrible fighting in 1968 when we finally opened the windows onto the night and there were sounds of bombs falling on the horizon and there was no breeze at all, just the heavy stillness of the time between the dry season and the wet, and Saigon smelled of tar and motorcycle exhaust and cordite but when I opened the window and turned to my wife, the room was full of a wonderful scent, a sweet smell that made her sit up, for she sensed it, too. This was a smell that had nothing to do with flowers but instead reminded us that flowers were always ready to fall into dust, while this smell was as if a gemstone had begun to give off a scent, as if a mountain of emerald had found its own scent. I crossed the room to my wife and we were already old, we had already buried children and grandchildren that we prayed waited for us in that village square at the foot of the strange mountain, but when I came near the bed, she lifted her silk gown and threw it aside and I pressed close to her and our own sweat smelled sweet on that night. I want to be with her in that square and with the rest of those we'd buried, the tiny limbs and the sullen eyes and the gray faces of the puzzled children and the surprised adults and the weary old people who have gone before us, who know the secrets now. And the sweet smell of the glaze on Hô's hands reminds me of others that I would want in the square, the people from the ship, too, the Vietnamese boy from a village near my own who died of a fever in the Indian Ocean and the natives in Dakar who were forced by colonial officials to swim out to our ship in shark-infested waters to secure the moorings and two were killed before our eyes without a French regret. Hô was very moved by this, and I want those men in our square and I want the Frenchman, too, who called Hô "monsieur" for the first time. A man on the dock in Marseilles. Hô spoke of him twice more during our years together and I want that Frenchman there. And, of course, Hô. Was he in the village square even now, waiting? Heating his glaze fondant? My daughter was smoothing my covers around me and the smell of lavender on her was still strong.

"He was in this room," I said to her to explain the sticky doorknob.

"Who was?"

But I was very sleepy and I could say no more, though perhaps she would not have understood anyway, in spite of being the smart girl that she is.

The next night I left my light on to watch for Hô's arrival, but I dozed off and he had to wake me. He was sitting in a chair that he'd brought from across the room. He said to me, "Đạo. Wake up, my old friend."

I must have awakened when he pulled the chair near to me, for I heard each of these words. "I am awake," I said. "I was thinking of the poor men who had to swim out to our ship."

"They are already among those I have served," Hô said. "Before I forgot." And he raised his hands and they were still covered with sugar.

I said, "Wasn't it a marble slab?" I had a memory, strangely clear after these many years, as strange as my memory of Hô's Paris business card.

"A marble slab," Hô repeated, puzzled.

"That you poured the heated sugar on."

"Yes." Hô's sweet-smelling hands came forward but they did not quite touch me. I thought to reach out from beneath the covers and take them in my own hands, but Hô leaped up and paced about the room. "The marble slab, moderately oiled. Of course. I am to let the sugar half cool and then use the spatula to move it about in all directions, every bit of it, so that it doesn't harden and form lumps."

I asked, "Have you seen my wife?"

Hô had wandered to the far side of the room, but he turned and crossed back to me at this. "I'm sorry, my friend. I never knew her."

I must have shown some disappointment in my face, for Hô sat down and brought his own face near mine. "I'm sorry," he said. "There are many other people that I must find here."

"Are you very disappointed in me?" I asked. "For not having traveled the road with you?"

"It's very complicated," Hô said softly "You felt that you'd taken action. I am no longer in a position to question another soul's choice."

"Are you at peace, where you are?" I asked this knowing of his worry over the recipe for the glaze, but I hoped that this was only a minor difficulty in the afterlife, like the natural anticipation of the good cook expecting guests when everything always turns out fine in the end.

But Hô said, "I am not at peace."

"Is Monsieur Escoffier over there?"

"I have not seen him. This has nothing to do with him, directly."

"What is it about?"

"I don't know."

"You won the country. You know that, don't you?"

Hô shrugged. "There are no countries here."

I should have remembered Hô's shrug when I began to see things in the faces of my son-in-law and grandson this morning. But something quickened in me, a suspicion. I kept my eyes shut and laid my head to the side, as if I was fast asleep, encouraging them to talk more.

My daughter said, "This is not the place to speak."

But the men did not regard her. "How?" Lợi asked his father, referring to the missing murder weapon.

"It's best not to know too much," Thắng said.

Then there was a silence. For all the quickness I'd felt at the first suspicion, I was very slow now. In fact, I did think of Hô from that second night. Not his shrug. He had fallen silent for a long time and I had closed my eyes, for the light seemed very bright. I listened to his silence just as I listened to the silence of these two conspirators before me.

And then Hô said, "They were fools, but I can't bring myself to grow angry anymore."

I opened my eyes in the bedroom and the light was off. Hô had turned it off, knowing that it was bothering me. "Who were fools?" I asked.

"We had fought together to throw out the Japanese. I had very good friends among them. I smoked their lovely Salem cigarettes. They had been repressed by colonialists themselves. Did they not know their own history?"

"Do you mean the Americans?"

"There are a million souls here with me, the young men of our country, and they are all dressed in black suits and bowler hats. In the mirrors they are made ten million, a hundred million."

"I chose my path, my dear friend Quốc, so that there might be harmony."

And even with that yearning for harmony I could not overlook what my mind made of what my ears had heard this morning. Thắng was telling Lợi that the murder weapon had been disposed of. Thắng and Lợi both knew the killers, were in sympathy with them, perhaps were part of the killing. The father and son had been airborne rangers and I had several times heard them talk bitterly of the exile of our people. We were fools for trusting the Americans all along, they said. We should have taken matters forward and disposed of the infinitely corrupt Thiệu and done what needed to be done. Whenever they spoke like this in front of me, there was soon a quick exhange of sideways glances at me and then a turn and an apology. "We're sorry, Grandfather. Old times often bring old anger. We are happy our family is living a new life."

I would wave my hand at this, glad to have the peace of the family restored. Glad to turn my face and smell the dogwood tree or even smell the coffee plant across the highway. These things had come to be the new smells of our family. But then a weakness often came upon me. The others would drift away, the men, and perhaps one of my daughters would come to me and stroke my head and not say a word and none of them ever would ask why I was weeping. I would smell the rich blood smells of the afterbirth and I would hold our first son, still slippery in my arms, and there was the smell of dust from the square and the smell of the South China Sea just over the rise of the hill and there was the smell of the blood and of the inner flesh from my wife as my son's own private sea flowed from this woman that I loved, flowed and carried him into the life that would disappear from him so soon. In the afterlife would he stand before me on unsteady child's legs? Would I have to bend low to greet him or would he be a man now?

My grandson said, after the silence had nearly carried me into real sleep, troubled sleep, my grandson Lợi said to his father, "I would be a coward not to know."

Thắng laughed and said, "You have proved yourself no coward."

And I wished then to sleep, I wished to fall asleep and let go of life somewhere in my dreams and seek my village square. I have lived too long, I thought. My daughter was saying, "Are you both mad?" And then she changed her voice, making the words very precise. "Let Grandfather sleep."

So when Hô came tonight for the third time, I wanted to ask his advice. His hands were still covered with sugar and his mind was, as it had been for the past two nights, very much distracted. "There's something still wrong with the glaze," he said to me in the dark, and I pulled back the covers and swung my legs around to get up. He did not try to stop me, but he did draw back quietly into the shadows.

"I want to pace the room with you," I said. "As we did in Paris, those tiny rooms of ours. We would talk about Marx and about Buddha and I must pace with you now."

"Very well," he said. "Perhaps it will help me remember."

I slipped on my sandals and I stood up and Hô's shadow moved past me, through the spill of streetlight and into the dark near the door. I followed him, smelling the sugar on his hands, first before me and then moving past me as I went on into the darkness he'd just left. I stopped as I turned and I could see Hô outlined before the window and I said, "I believe my son-in-law and grandson are involved in the killing of a man. A political killing."

Hô stayed where he was, a dark shape against the light, and he said nothing and I could not smell his hands from across the room and I smelled only the sourness of Lợi as he laid his head on my shoulder. He was a baby and my daughter Lâm retreated to our balcony window after handing him to me and the boy turned his head and I turned mine to him and I could smell his mother's milk, sour on his breath, he had a sour smell and there was incense burning in the room, jasmine, the smoke of souls, and the boy sighed on my shoulder, and I turned my face away from the smell of him. Thắng was across the room and his eyes were quick to find his wife and he was waiting for her to take the child from me.

"You have never done the political thing," Hô said.

"Is this true?"

"Of course."

I asked, "Are there politics where you are now, my friend?"

I did not see him moving toward me, but the smell of the sugar on his hands grew stronger, very strong, and I felt Hô Chí Minh very close to me, though I could not see him. He was very close and the smell was strong and sweet and it was filling my lungs as if from the inside, as if Hô was passing through my very body, and I heard the door open behind me and then close softly shut.

I moved across the room to the bed. I turned to sit down but I was facing the window, the scattering of a streetlamp on the window like a nova in some far part of the universe. I stepped to the window and touched the reflected light there, wondering if there was a great smell when a star explodes, a great burning smell of gas and dust. Then I closed the shade and slipped into bed, quite gracefully, I felt, I was quite wonderfully graceful, and I lie here now waiting for sleep. Hô is right, of course. I will never say a word about my grandson. And perhaps I will be as restless as Hô when I join him. But that will be all right. He and I will be together again and perhaps we can help each other. I know now what it is that he has forgotten. He has used confectioners' sugar for his glaze fondant and he should be using granulated sugar. I was only a washer of dishes but I did listen carefully when Monsieur Escoffier spoke. I wanted to understand everything. His kitchen was full of such smells that you knew you had to understand everything or you would be incomplete forever.   [1992]

ITALO CALVINO (1923–1985) *was born in Cuba but grew up in Italy, where his father was a professor of agronomy at the University of Turin. Encouraged to study science, Calvino was more excited by novels of adventure. During World War II he participated in the Resistance against Fascism in Italy; his early novel* The Path to the Nest of Spiders *(1947) and his first story collection,* Adam, One Afternoon and Other Stories *(1949), were based on this experience.*

Calvino is perhaps best known to American readers for his brilliant collection Italian Folktales *(1956), which gathered different versions of tales from the oral tradition of his country. "The Feathered Ogre" is from this book. Like that of Jorge Luis Borges, Calvino's erudition was profound, and it entered his fiction seamlessly.* Cosmicomics, *translated from the Italian by William Weaver, won the National Book Award in 1965 for literary translation. Seven years later Calvino's experimental prose poems in the collection* Invisible Cities *won the most important literary prize in Italy. A prolific author, Calvino lived in Paris for fifteen years, during which time he was influenced by the literary theorists Claude Lévi-Strauss and Roland Barthes and enjoyed speculating about the origins of literature.*

> *It all began with the first storyteller of the tribe. He began to put forth words . . . to test the extent to which words could fit with one another, give birth to one another — in order to extract an explanation of the world from the thread of every possible spoken narrative and from the arabesque that nouns and verbs, subjects and predicates performed as they unfolded from one another.*

Shortly before his death, Calvino began writing stories based on the five senses. The three he completed — on the tongue, ear, and nose — were published in 1988 with the title Under the Jaguar Sun. *A book of lectures on literature for Harvard University,* Six Memos for the Next Millennium, *appeared in 1992.*

RELATED COMMENTARY: *Italo Calvino, "On 'Quickness' in Narrative," page* 1396.

ITALO CALVINO

The Feathered Ogre

Translated by George Martin

A king fell ill and was told by his doctors, "Majesty, if you want to get well, you'll have to obtain one of the ogre's feathers. That will not be easy, since the ogre eats every human he sees."

The king passed the word on to everybody, but no one was willing to go to the ogre. Then he asked one of his most loyal and courageous attendants, who said, "I will go."

The man was shown the road and told, "On a mountaintop are seven caves, in one of which lives the ogre."

The man set out and walked until dark, when he stopped at an inn. When the innkeeper learned of his mission, he said, "How about bringing me a feather too on your way back, since they are so beneficial."

"I'll be glad to," replied the king's man.

"And should you talk to the ogre, try and find out something about my daughter. She disappeared years ago and is now goodness knows where."

In the morning the man continued on his way. He came to a river and called the ferryman to row him to the other side. During the crossing, they got into conversation.

"Will you bring me a feather too?" asked the ferryman. "I know they bring luck."

"Yes, of couse I'll bring you one."

"And if you have the chance, ask the ogre how come I've been at this job for so many years and can't get off the ferry."

"I'll certainly ask him."

The king's man disembarked and continued his journey on foot. At a fountain he sat down to eat a bite of lunch. Two well-dressed noblemen came by and also sat down, and the three of them got to talking.

"Why don't you bring us a feather too," they said.

"I certainly will."

"Also, would you ask the ogre something? In our garden is a fountain that once spewed gold and silver, but it has since dried up."

"I'll ask him why, without fail."

He moved on and walked until dark, when he knocked at a monastery. Friars answered the door, and he requested shelter.

"Come in, come in."

After hearing his story, the friars inquired, "But do you know what you are getting into?"

"I was told there are seven caves. At the back of one of them is a door I'm to knock on and be greeted by the ogre."

"My poor man," said the prior, "if you are unmindful of all the danger, you'll certainly lose your life. This is no laughing matter. I'll tell you about the ogre, in hopes you'll do us a favor."

"Of course I will."

"Listen to me, then. When you get to the mountaintop, you'll see seven caves. The seventh is the ogre's. Go down into that one, all the way to the end, where it will be pitch-dark. We'll give you a candle and matches to light your way. But be sure to go in right at noon, when the ogre is out. You'll find his wife there, a bright girl who will tell you exactly what to do. Beware of the ogre, who would eat you up in a minute."

"How good of you to tell me all these things I didn't know."

"Now here's what you are to find out for us. We lived here in peace for no telling how many years. But for the last ten, we've done nothing but wrangle. Some want one thing, others another, there is bickering, and things are always in turmoil. What is the meaning of it?"

The next morning the man scaled the mountain. He was at the top by eleven o'clock and sat down to rest. At the stroke of noon he slipped into the seventh cave. It was pitch-dark, but he lit the candle and discovered a door. The minute he knocked, a beautiful girl opened and asked, "Who are you? What brings you here? You don't know my husband! He eats every human being he sees!"

"I came for some feathers. Since I'm already here, I'll stay and try my luck. If I get eaten, that's that."

"Listen, I've been here for years and years and can't stand it any longer. Be very careful, and we'll both flee. He must under no circumstances see you, or he'll eat you. I'll hide you under the bed and when he retires for the night, I'll pull out the feathers. How many do you want?"

"Four." And he told her about king, innkeeper, ferryman, noblemen, friars, and the queries of each.

They talked as they ate their dinner. As it had grown late in the meantime, the young lady began getting the ogre's meal ready. "When he's hungry, he smells humans right away. After eating he no longer notices, luckily for you!"

At six o'clock a great clatter was heard at the door, and the man disappeared under the bed in a flash. In stormed the ogre sniffing and saying:

"Here, here,
There're stinking humans here.
There were, there are, they're hiding;
My nose informs me they are near!"

"Nonsense!" replied his wife. "Your hunger is making you imagine things. Sit down and eat."

The ogre ate, but he could still smell a man and went all through the house after dinner looking for him. It was at last bedtime, so they undressed, got under the covers, and the ogre went to sleep at once.

The man under the bed held his breath. "Listen closely," whispered the woman. "I'm going to pretend to be dreaming and pull out one of his fathers." She plucked a feather and slipped it under the bed to him.

"Ouch! What do you mean by plucking me?" yelled the ogre.

"Oh, dear, I was dreaming . . ."

"What were you dreaming?"

"I was dreaming about the monastery down below us. For the last ten years the friars have been so much at odds with one another that it's pure torture to be under one roof together."

"That's no dream but a fact," answered the ogre. "The friars are ill-tempered because ten years ago the Devil got into their monastery dressed as a priest."

"How could they get rid of him?"

"The real friars would have to start doing good deeds. Then they'd spot the Devil in their midst." At that, the ogre went back to sleep.

A quarter of an hour later, his wife pulled out another feather and passed it to the man under the bed.

"Ouch! That hurt!"

"I was dreaming."

"Again? What were you dreaming this time?"

"You know the fountain down below us in the garden of those two noblemen, which used to spew gold and silver? I dreamt it had gone dry. What on earth could that mean?"

"All of your dreams are true tonight. The fountain is stopped up and can't spew any more gold and silver. They would have to dig gently down to the mouth of the fountain, where they'd find a ball entwined with a sleeping snake. They would have to crush the snake's head beneath the ball before the snake awakened, and the fountain would spew gold and silver anew."

Again in a quarter of an hour she plucked another feather. "Ouch! I believe you've made up your mind to pluck me clean tonight."

"I'm sorry, I was dreaming."

"What now?"

"A ferryman down there on the river hasn't been able to leave his ferry for years."

"True. He doesn't realize that he should ferry a man across the river, collect his fare, and disembark before his passenger can. The traveler will then have to remain on the ferry."

The wife pulled out the fourth feather. "Confound it! What are you about?"

"I'm sorry. I keep on dreaming. I was dreaming of an innkeeper still looking for his daughter, years after her disappearance."

"You mean your father, because you are that innkeeper's daughter."

In the morning at six o'clock, the ogre rose, bid his wife goodbye, and went off. The man came out from under the bed with the four feathers wrapped in a package, took the young lady by the arm, and together they fled.

They stopped at the monastery to tell the friars, "The ogre said that one of you is the Devil. You must start doing all the good you can, and he will flee."

The friars all did one good deed after another until the Devil finally fled.

The couple next stopped by the garden to give the two noblemen a feather and explain to them about the snake. And it wasn't long before the fountain was again spewing gold and silver.

They came to the ferryman. "Here's your feather!"

"Thank you. And what did the ogre say concerning me?"

"I'll have to wait until I'm on the other bank to tell you."

Once the couple was safely on the opposite shore, they told the ferryman what to do.

Upon arriving at the inn, the king's man cried, "Innkeeper, here I am with your feather and your daughter!" Right away the innkeeper wanted to give his daughter to the man in marriage.

"Let me first take the king his feather and ask his permission."

He carried the feather to the king, who got well and rewarded him. The man said, "Now if Your Majesty permits, I'll be off to my wedding." The king doubled the reward, and the man took leave of him and returned to the inn.

What about the ogre? Discovering his wife gone, he set out in pursuit, fully intending to devour her and whoever was involved in her escape. He came to the river and jumped on the ferry. "Pay your fare," said the ferryman. The ogre paid, never dreaming the ferryman knew the secret. Before landing on the opposite shore, off jumped the ferryman, and the ogre could no longer leave the boat.   [1956]

imminent cessation of being; the year, in turning, turns in on itself. Introspective weather, a sickroom hush.

The woods enclose. You step between the first trees and then you are no longer in the open air; the wood swallows you up. There is no way through the wood any more, this wood has reverted to its original privacy. Once you are inside it, you must stay there until it lets you out again for there is no clue to guide you through in perfect safety; grass grew over the track years ago and now the rabbits and the foxes make their own runs in the subtle labyrinth and nobody comes. The trees stir with a noise like taffeta skirts of women who have lost themselves in the woods and hunt round hopelessly for the way out. Tumbling crows play tig in the branches of the elms they clotted with their nests, now and then raucously cawing. A little stream with soft margins of marsh runs through the wood but it has grown sullen with the time of the year; the silent, blackish water thickens, now, to ice. All will fall still, all lapse.

A young girl would go into the wood as trustingly as Red Riding Hood to her granny's house but this light admits of no ambiguities and, here, she will be trapped in her own illusion because everything in the wood is exactly as it seems.

The woods enclose and then enclose again, like a system of Chinese boxes opening one into another; the intimate perspectives of the wood changed endlessly around the interloper, the imaginary traveller walking towards an invented distance that perpetually receded before me. It is easy to lose yourself in these woods.

The two notes of the song of a bird rose on the still air, as if my girlish and delicious loneliness had been made into a sound. There was a little tangled mist in the thickets, mimicking the tufts of old man's beard that flossed the lower branches of the trees and bushes; heavy bunches of red berries as ripe and delicious as goblin or enchanted fruit hung on the hawthorns but the old grass withers, retreats. One by one, the ferns have curled up their hundred eyes and curled back into the earth. The trees threaded a cat's cradle of half-stripped branches over me so that I felt I was in a house of nets and though the cold wind that always heralds your presence, had I but known it then, blew gentle around me, I thought that nobody was in the wood but me.

Erl-King will do you grievous harm.

Piercingly, now, there came again the call of the bird, as desolate as if it came from the throat of the last bird left alive. That call, with all the melancholy of the failing year in it, went directly to my heart.

I walked through the wood until all its perspectives converged upon a darkening clearing; as soon as I saw them, I knew at once that all its occupants had been waiting for me from the moment I first stepped into the wood, with the endless patience of wild things, who have all the time in the world.

It was a garden where all the flowers were birds and beasts; ash-soft doves, diminutive wrens, freckled thrushes, robins in their tawny bibs, huge, helmeted crows that shone like patent leather, a blackbird with a yellow bill, voles, shrews, fieldfares, little brown bunnies with their ears laid together along their backs like spoons, crouching at his feet. A lean, tall, reddish hare, up on its great hind legs, nose a-twitch. The rusty fox, its muzzle sharpened to a point, laid its head upon his knee. On the trunk of a scarlet rowan a squirrel clung, to watch him; a cock pheasant delicately stretched his shimmering neck from a brake of thorn to peer at him. There was a goat of uncanny whiteness, gleaming like a goat of snow, who turned her mild eyes towards me and bleated softly, so that he knew I had arrived.

He smiles. He lays down his pipe, his elder bird-call. He lays upon me his irrevocable hand.

His eyes are quite green, as if from too much looking at the wood.

There are some eyes can eat you.

The Erl-King lives by himself all alone in the heart of the wood in a house which has only the one room. His house is made of sticks and stones and has grown a pelt of yellow lichen. Grass and weeds grow in the mossy roof. He chops fallen branches for his fire and draws his water from the stream in a tin pail.

What does he eat? Why, the bounty of the woodland! Stewed nettles; savoury messes of chickweed sprinkled with nutmeg; he cooks the foliage of shepherd's purse as if it were cabbage. He knows which of the frilled, blotched, rotted fungi are fit to eat; he understands their eldritch ways, how they spring up overnight in lightless places and thrive on dead things. Even the homely wood blewits, that you cook like tripe, with milk and onions, and the egg-yolk yellow chanterelle with its fan-vaulting and faint scent of apricots, all spring up overnight like bubbles of earth, unsustained by nature, existing in a void. And I could believe that it has been the same with him; he came alive from the desire of the woods.

He goes out in the morning to gather his unnatural treasures, he handles them as delicately as he does pigeons' eggs, he lays them in one of the baskets he weaves from osiers. He makes salads of the dandelion that he calls rude names, "bum-pipes" or "piss-the-beds", and flavours them with a few leaves of wild strawberry but he will not touch the brambles, he says the Devil spits on them at Michaelmas.

His nanny goat, the colour of whey, gives him her abundant milk and he can make soft cheese that has a unique, rank, amniotic taste. Sometimes he traps a rabbit in a snare of string and makes a soup or stew, seasoned with wild garlic. He knows all about the wood and the creatures in it. He told me about the grass snakes, how the old ones open their mouths wide when they smell danger and the thin little ones disappear down the old ones' throats until the fright is over and out they come again, to run around as usual. He told me how the wise toad who squats among the kingcups by the stream in summer has a very precious jewel in his head. He said the owl was a baker's daughter; then he smiled at me. He showed me how to thread mats from reeds and weave osier twigs into baskets and into the little cages in which he keeps his singing birds.

His kitchen shakes and shivers with birdsong from cage upon cage of singing birds, larks and linnets, which he piles up one on another against the wall, a wall of trapped birds. How cruel it is, to keep wild birds in cages! But he laughs at me when I say that; laughs, and shows his white, pointed teeth with the spittle gleaming on them.

He is an excellent housewife. His rustic home is spick and span. He puts his well-scoured saucepan and skillet neatly on the hearth side by side, like a pair of polished shoes. Over the hearth hang bunches of drying mushrooms, the thin, curling kind they call jew's-ears, which have grown on the elder trees since Judas hanged himself on one; this is the kind of lore he tells me, tempting my half-belief. He hangs up herbs in bunches to dry, too — thyme, marjoram, sage, vervain, southernwood, yarrow. The room is musical and aromatic and there is always a wood fire crackling in the gate, a sweet, acrid smoke, a bright, glancing flame. But you cannot get a tune out of the old fiddle hanging on the wall beside the birds because all its strings are broken.

Now, when I go for walks, sometimes in the mornings when the frost has put its shiny thumbprint on the undergrowth or sometimes, though less frequently, yet more enticingly, in the evenings when the cold darkness settles down, I always go to the Erl-King and he lays me down on his bed of rustling straw where I lie at the mercy of his huge hands.

He is the tender butcher who showed me how the price of flesh is love; skin the rabbit, he says! Off come all my clothes.

When he combs his hair that is the colour of dead leaves, dead leaves fall out of it; they rustle and drift to the ground as though he were a tree and he can stand as still as a tree, when he wants the doves to flutter softly, crooning as they come, down upon his shoulders, those silly, fat, trusting woodies with the pretty wedding rings round their necks. He makes his whistles out of an elder twig and that is what he uses to call the birds out of the air — all the birds come; and the sweetest singers he will keep in cages.

The wind stirs the dark wood; it blows through the bushes. A little of the cold air that blows over graveyards always goes with him, it crisps the hairs on the back of my neck but I am not afraid of him; only, afraid of vertigo, of the vertigo with which he seizes me. Afraid of falling down.

Falling as a bird would fall through the air if the Erl-King tied up the winds in his handkerchief and knotted the ends together so they could not get out. Then the moving currents of the air would no longer sustain them and all the birds would fall at the imperative of gravity, as I fall down for him, and I know it is only because he is kind to me that I do not fall still further. The earth with its fragile fleece of last summer's dying leaves and grasses supports me only out of complicity with him, because his flesh is of the same substance as those leaves that are slowly turning into earth.

He could thrust me into the seed-bed of next year's generation and I would have to wait until he whistled me up from my darkness before I could come back again.

Yet, when he shakes out those two clear notes from his bird call, I come, like any other trusting thing that perches on the crook of his wrist.

I found the Erl-King sitting on an ivy-covered stump winding all the birds in the wood to him on a diatonic spool of sound, one rising note, one falling note; such a sweet piercing call that down there came a soft, chirruping jostle of birds. The clearing was cluttered with dead leaves, some the colour of honey, some the colour of cinders, some the colour of earth. He seemed so much the spirit of the place I saw without surprise how the fox laid its muzzle fearlessly upon his knee. The brown light of the end of the day drained into the moist, heavy earth; all silent, all still and the cool smell of night coming. The first drops of rain fell. In the wood, no shelter but his cottage.

That was the way I walked into the bird-haunted solitude of the Erl-King, who keeps his feathered things in little cages he has woven out of osier twigs and there they sit and sing for him.

Goat's milk to drink, from a chipped tin mug; we shall eat the oatcakes he has baked on the hearthstone. Rattle of the rain on the roof. The latch clanks on the door; we are shut up inside with one another, in the brown room crisp with the scent of burning logs that shiver with tiny flame, and I lie down on the Erl-King's creaking palliasse of straw. His skin is the tint and texture of sour cream, he has stiff, russet nipples ripe as berries. Like a tree that bears bloom and fruit on the same bough together, how pleasing, how lovely.

And now — ach! I feel your sharp teeth in the subaqueous depths of your kisses. The equinoctial gales seize the bare elms and make them whizz and whirl like dervishes; you sink your teeth into my throat and make me scream.

The white moon above the clearing coldly illuminates the still tableaux of our embracements. How sweet I roamed, or, rather, used to roam; once I was the perfect child of the meadows of summer, but then the year turned, the light clarified and I saw the gaunt Erl-King, tall as a tree with birds in its branches, and he drew me towards him on this magic lasso of inhuman music.

If I strung that old fiddle with your hair, we could waltz together to the music as the exhausted daylight founders among the trees; we should have better music than the shrill prothalamions of the larks stacked in their pretty cages as the roof creaks with the freight of birds you've lured to it while we engaged in your profane mysteries under the leaves.

He strips me to my last nakedness, that underskin of mauve, pearlized satin, like a skinned rabbit; then dresses me again in an embrace so lucid and encompassing it might be made of water. And shakes over me dead leaves as if into the stream I have become.

Sometimes the birds, at random, all singing, strike a chord.

His skin covers me entirely; we are like two halves of a seed, enclosed in the same integument. I should like to grow enormously small, so that you could swallow me, like those queens in fairy tales who conceive when they swallow a grain of corn or a sesame seed. Then I could lodge inside your body and you would bear me.

The candle flutters and goes out. His touch both consoles and devastates me; I feel my heart pulse, then wither, naked as a stone on the roaring mattress while the lovely, moony night slides through the window to dapple the flanks of this innocent who makes cages to keep the sweet birds in. Eat me, drink me; thirsty, cankered, goblin-ridden, I go back and back to him to have his fingers strip the tattered skin away and clothe me in his dress of water, this garment that drenches me, its slithering odour, its capacity for drowning.

Now the crows drop winter from their wings, invoke the harshest season with their cry.

It is growing colder. Scarcely a leaf left on the trees and the birds come to him in even greater numbers because, in this hard weather, it is lean pickings. The blackbirds and thrushes must hunt the snails from hedge bottoms and crack the shells on stones. But the Erl-King gives them corn and when he whistles to them, a moment later you cannot see him for the birds that have covered him like a soft fall of feathered snow. He spreads out a goblin feast of fruit for me, such appalling succulence; I lie above him and see the light from the fire sucked into the black vortex of his eye, the omission of light at the centre, there, that exerts on me such a tremendous pressure, it draws me inwards.

Eyes green as apples. Green as dead sea fruit.

A wind rises; it makes a singular, wild, low, rushing sound.

What big eyes you have. Eyes of an incomparable luminosity, the numinous phosphorescence of the eyes of lycanthropes. The gelid green of your eyes fixes my reflective face. It is a preservative, like a green liquid amber; it catches me. I am afraid I will be trapped in it forever like the poor little ants and flies that stuck their feet in resin before the sea covered the Baltic. He winds me into the circle of his eye on a reel of birdsong. There is a black hole in the middle of both your eyes; it is their still centre, looking there makes me giddy, as if I might fall into it.

Your green eye is a reducing chamber. If I look into it long enough, I will become as small as my own reflection, I will diminish to a point and vanish. I will be drawn down into that black whirlpool and be consumed by you. I shall become so small you can keep me in one of your osier cages and mock my loss of liberty. I have seen the cage you are weaving for me; it is a very pretty one and I shall sit, hereafter, in my cage among the other singing birds but I — I shall be dumb, from spite.

When I realized what the Erl-King meant to do to me, I was shaken with a terrible fear and I did not know what to do for I loved him with all my heart and yet I had no wish to join the whistling congregation he kept in his cages although he looked after them very affectionately, gave them fresh water every day and fed them well. His embraces were his enticements and yet, oh yet! they were the branches of which the trap itself was woven. But in his innocence he never knew he might be the death of me, although I knew from the first moment I saw him how Erl-King would do me grievous harm.

Although the bow hangs beside the old fiddle on the wall, all the strings are broken so you cannot play it. I don't know what kind of tunes you might play on it, if it were strung again; lullabies for foolish virgins, perhaps, and now I know the birds don't sing, they only cry because they can't find their way out of the wood, have lost their flesh when they were dipped in the corrosive pools of his regard and now must live in cages.

Sometimes he lays his head on my lap and lets me comb his lovely hair for him; his combings are leaves of every tree in the wood and dryly susurrate around my feet. His hair falls down over my knees. Silence like a dream in front of the spitting fire while he lies at my feet and I comb the dead leaves out of his languorous hair. The robin has built his nest in the thatch again, this year; he perches on an unburnt log, cleans his beak, ruffles his plumage. There is a plaintive sweetness in his song and a certain melancholy, because the year is over — the robin, the friend of man, in spite of the wound in his breast from which Erl-King tore out his heart.

Lay your head on my knee so that I can't see the greenish inward-turning suns of your eyes any more.

My hands shake.

I shall take two huge handfuls of his rustling hair as he lies half dreaming, half waking, and wind them into ropes, very softly, so he will not wake up, and, softly, with hands as gentle as rain, I shall strangle him with them.

Then she will open all the cages and let the birds free; they will change back into young girls, every one, each with the crimson imprint of his love-bite on their throats.

She will carve off his great mane with the knife he uses to skin the rabbits; she will string the old fiddle with five single strings of ash-brown hair.

Then it will play discordant music without a hand touching it. The bow will dance over the new strings of its own accord and they will cry out: "Mother, mother, you have murdered me!"   [1979]

RAYMOND CARVER (1938–1988) grew up in a logging town in Oregon, where his father worked in a sawmill and his mother held odd jobs. After graduating from high school, Carver married at the age of nineteen and had two children. Working hard to support his wife and family, he managed to enroll briefly in 1958 as a student at Chico State College in California, where he took a creative writing course from a then unknown young novelist named John Gardner. Carver remembered that he decided to try to become a writer because he liked to read pulp novels and magazines about hunting and fishing. He credited Gardner for giving him a strong sense of direction as a writer: "A writer's values and craft. This is what the man taught and what he stood for, and this is what I've kept by me in the years since that brief but all-important time."

In 1963 Carver received his B.A. degree from Humboldt State College in northern California. The following year he studied writing at the University of Iowa. But the 1960s were difficult for him and his wife.

> I learned a long time ago when my kids were little and we had no money, and we were working our hearts out and weren't getting anywhere, even though we were giving it our best, my wife and I, that there were more important things than writing a poem or a story. That was a very hard realization for me to come to. But it came to me, and I had to accept it or die. Getting milk and food on the table, getting the rent paid, if a choice had to be made, then I had to forgo writing.

Carver's desire to be a writer was so strong that he kept on writing long after the "cold facts" of his life told him he ought to quit. His first collection of stories, Will You Please Be Quiet, Please? was nominated for a National Book Award in 1976. Four more collections of stories followed, along with five books of poetry, before his death from lung cancer.

Critics have noted that the rapid evolution of Carver's style causes his fiction to fall into three distinct periods. The tentative writing in his first book of stories — many of which he subsequently revised and republished — was followed by a paring down of his prose. This resulted in the hard-edged, detached minimalist style of his middle period, exemplified by the stories in his collection What We Talk About When We Talk About Love (1981). In his final period Carver developed a more expansive style, as in the collection Cathedral (1983) and the new stories in his last collection, Where I'm Calling From: New and Selected Stories (1988), from which "Errand" is taken.

Influenced by the cadence of Ernest Hemingway's sentences, Carver also believed in simplicity. He wrote:

> It's possible, in a poem or a short story, to write about commonplace things and objects using commonplace but precise language, and to endow those things — a chair, a window curtain, a fork, a stone, a woman's earring — with immense, even startling power. . . . If the words are heavy with the writer's own unbridled emotions, or if they are imprecise and inaccurate for some other reason — if the words are in any way blurred — the reader's eyes will slide right over them and nothing will be achieved. The reader's own artistic sense will simply not be engaged.

RELATED COMMENTARIES: See Casebook on Raymond Carver, pages 1523–1540, including Raymond Carver's "On Writing," page 1524; "Creative Writing

RAYMOND CARVER

Cathedral

This blind man, an old friend of my wife's, he was on his way to spend the night. His wife had died. So he was visiting the dead wife's relatives in Connecticut. He called my wife from his in-laws'. Arrangements were made. He would come by train, a five-hour trip, and my wife would meet him at the station. She hadn't seen him since she worked for him one summer in Seattle ten years ago. But she and the blind man had kept in touch. They made tapes and mailed them back and forth. I wasn't enthusiastic about his visit. He was no one I knew. And his being blind bothered me. My idea of blindness came from the movies. In the movies, the blind moved slowly and never laughed. Sometimes they were led by seeing-eye dogs. A blind man in my house was not something I looked forward to.

That summer in Seattle she had needed a job. She didn't have any money. The man she was going to marry at the end of the summer was in officers' training school. He didn't have any money, either. But she was in love with the guy, and he was in love with her, etc. She'd seen something in the paper: HELP WANTED — *Reading to Blind Man,* and a telephone number. She phoned and went over, was hired on the spot. She'd worked with this blind man all summer. She read stuff to him, case studies, reports, that sort of thing. She helped him organize his little office in the county social-service department. They'd become good friends, my wife and the blind man. How do I know these things? She told me. And she told me something else. On her last day in the office, the blind man asked if he could touch her face. She agreed to this. She told me he touched his fingers to every part of her face, her nose — even her neck! She never forgot it. She even tried to write a poem about it. She was always trying to write a poem. She wrote a poem or two every year, usually after something really important had happened to her.

When we first started going out together, she showed me the poem. In the poem, she recalled his fingers and the way they had moved around over her face. In the poem, she talked about what she had felt at the time, about what went through her mind when the blind man touched her nose and lips. I can remember I didn't think much of the poem. Of course, I didn't tell her that. Maybe I just don't understand poetry. I admit it's not the first thing I reach for when I pick up something to read.

Anyway, this man who'd first enjoyed her favors, the officer-to-be, he'd been her childhood sweetheart. So okay. I'm saying that at the end of the summer she let the blind man run his hands over her face, said goodbye to him, married her childhood etc., who was now a commissioned officer, and she moved away from Seattle. But they'd kept in touch, she and the blind man. She made the first contact after a year or so. She called him up one night from an Air Force base in Alabama. She wanted to talk. They talked. He asked her to send him a tape and tell him about her life. She did this. She sent the tape. On the tape, she told the blind man about her husband and about their life together in the military. She told the blind man she loved her husband but she didn't like it where they lived and she didn't like it that he was a part of the military-industrial thing. She told the blind man she'd written a poem and he was in it. She told him that she was writing a poem about what it was like to be an Air Force officer's wife. The poem wasn't finished yet. She was still writing it. The blind man made a tape. He sent her the tape. She made a tape. This went on for years. My wife's officer was posted to one base and then another. She sent tapes from Moody AFB, McGuire, McConnell, and finally Travis, near Sacramento, where one night she got to feeling lonely and cut off from people she kept losing in that moving-around life. She got to feeling she couldn't go it another step. She went in and swallowed all the pills and capsules in the medicine chest and washed them down with a bottle of gin. Then she got into a hot bath and passed out.

But instead of dying, she got sick. She threw up. Her officer — why should he have a name? he was the childhood sweetheart, and what more does he want? — came home from somewhere, found her, and called the ambulance. In time, she put it all on a tape and sent the tape to the blind man. Over the years, she put all kinds of stuff on tapes and sent the tapes off lickety-split. Next to writing a poem every year, I think it was her chief means of recreation. On one tape, she told the blind man she'd decided to live away from her officer for a time. On another tape, she told him about her divorce. She and I began going out, and of course she told her blind man about it. She told him everything, or so it seemed to me. Once she asked me if I'd like to hear the latest tape from the blind man. This was a year ago. I was on the tape, she said. So I said okay, I'd listen to it. I got us drinks and we settled down in the living room. We made ready to listen. First she inserted the tape into the player and adjusted a couple of dials. Then she pushed a lever. The tape squeaked and someone began to talk in this loud voice. She lowered the volume. After a few minutes of harmless chitchat, I heard my own name in the mouth of this stranger, this blind man I didn't even know! And then this: "From all you've said about him, I can only conclude —" But we were interrupted, a knock at the door, something, and we didn't ever get back to the tape. Maybe it was just as well. I'd heard all I wanted to.

Now this same blind man was coming to sleep in my house.

"Maybe I could take him bowling," I said to my wife. She was at the draining board doing scalloped potatoes. She put down the knife she was using and turned around.

"If you love me," she said," "you can do this for me. If you don't love me, okay. But if you had a friend, any friend, and the friend came to visit, I'd make him feel comfortable." She wiped her hands with the dish towel.

"I don't have any blind friends," I said.

"You don't have *any* friends," she said. "Period. Besides," she said, "goddamn it, his wife's just died! Don't you understand that? The man's lost his wife!"

I didn't answer, She'd told me a little about the blind man's wife. Her name was Beulah. Beulah! That's a name for a colored woman.

"Was his wife Negro?" I asked.

"Are you crazy?" my wife said. "Have you just flipped or something?" She picked up a potato. I saw it hit the floor, then roll under the stove. "What's wrong with you?" she said. "Are you drunk?"

"I'm just asking," I said.

Right then my wife filled me in with more detail than I cared to know. I made a drink and sat at the kitchen table to listen. Pieces of the story began to fall into place.

Beulah had gone to work for the blind man the summer after my wife had stopped working for him. Pretty soon Beulah and the blind man had themselves a church wedding. It was a little wedding — who'd want to go to such a wedding in the first place? — just the two of them, plus the minister and the minister's wife. But it was a church wedding just the same. It was what Beulah had wanted, he'd said. But even then Beulah must have been carrying the cancer in her glands. After they had been inseparable for eight years — my wife's word, *inseparable* — Beulah's health went into a rapid decline. She died in a Seattle hospital room, the blind man sitting beside the bed and holding on to her hand. They'd married, lived and worked together, slept together — had sex, sure — and then the blind man had to bury her. All this without his having ever seen what the goddamned woman looked like. It was beyond my understanding. Hearing this, I felt sorry for the blind man for a little bit. And then I found myself thinking what a pitiful life this woman must have led. Imagine a woman who could never see herself as she was seen in the eyes of her loved one. A woman who could go on day after day and never receive the smallest compliment from her beloved. A woman whose husband could never read the expression on her face, be it misery or something better. Someone who could wear makeup or not — what difference to him? She could, if she wanted, wear green eye-shadow around one eye, a straight pin in her nostril, yellow slacks and purple shoes, no matter. And then to slip off into death, the blind man's hand on her hand, his blind eyes streaming tears — I'm imagining now — her last thought maybe this: that he never even knew what she looked like, and she on an express to the grave. Robert was left with a small insurance policy and half of a twenty-peso Mexican coin. The other half of the coin went into the box with her. Pathetic.

So when the time rolled around, my wife went to the depot to pick him up. With nothing to do but wait — sure, I blamed him for that — I was having a drink and watching the TV when I heard the car pull into the drive. I got up from the sofa with my drink and went to the window to have a look.

I saw my wife laughing as she parked the car. I saw her get out of the car and shut the door. She was still wearing a smile. Just amazing. She went around to the other side of the car to where the blind man was already starting to get out. This blind man, feature this, he was wearing a full beard! A beard on a blind man! Too much, I say. The blind man reached into the back seat and dragged out a suitcase. My wife took his arm, shut the car door, and, talking all the way, moved him down the drive and then up the steps to the front porch. I turned off the TV. I finished my drink, rinsed the glass, dried my hands. Then I went to the door.

My wife said, "I want you to meet Robert. Robert, this is my husband. I've told you all about him." She was beaming. She had this blind man by his coat sleeve.

The blind man let go of his suitcase and up came his hand.

I took it. He squeezed hard, held my hand, and then he let it go.

"I feel like we've already met," he boomed.

"Likewise," I said. I didn't know what else to say. Then I said, "Welcome. I've heard a lot about you." We began to move then, a little group, from the porch into the living room, my wife guiding him by the arm. The blind man was carrying his suitcase in his other hand. My wife said things like, "To your left here, Robert. That's right. Now watch it, there's a chair. That's it. Sit down right here. This is the sofa. We just bought this sofa two weeks ago."

I started to say something about the old sofa. I'd liked that old sofa. But I didn't say anything. Then I wanted to say something else, small-talk, about the scenic ride along the Hudson. How going *to* New York, you should sit on the right-hand side of the train, and coming *from* New York, the left-hand side.

"Did you have a good train ride?" I said. "Which side of the train did you sit on, by the way?"

"What a question, which side!" my wife said. "What's it matter which side?" she said.

"I just asked," I said.

"Right side," the blind man said. "I hadn't been on a train in nearly forty years. Not since I was a kid. With my folks. That's been a long time. I'd nearly forgotten the sensation. I have winter in my beard now," he said. "So I've been told, anyway. Do I look distinguished, my dear?" the blind man said to my wife.

"You look distinguished, Robert," she said. "Robert," she said. "Robert, it's just so good to see you."

My wife finally took her eyes off the blind man and looked at me. I had the feeling she didn't like what she saw. I shrugged.

I've never met, or personally known, anyone who was blind. This blind man was late forties, a heavy-set, balding man with stooped shoulders, as if he carried a great weight there. He wore brown slacks, brown shoes, a light-brown shirt, a tie, a sports coat. Spiffy. He also had this full beard. But he didn't use a cane and he didn't wear dark glasses. I'd always thought dark glasses were a must for the blind. Fact was, I wished he had a pair. At first glance, his eyes looked like anyone else's eyes. But if you look close, there was something different about them. Too much white in the iris, for one thing, and the pupils seemed to move around in the sockets without his knowing it or being able to stop it. Creepy. As I stared at his face, I saw the left pupil turn in toward his nose while the other made an effort to keep in one place. But it was only an effort, for that eye was on the roam without his knowing it or wanting it to be.

I said, "Let me get you a drink. What's your pleasure? We have a little of everything. It's one of our pastimes."

"Bub, I'm a Scotch man myself," he said fast enough in this big voice.

"Right," I said. Bub! "Sure you are, I knew it."

He let his fingers touch his suitcase, which was sitting alongside the sofa. He was taking his bearings. I didn't blame him for that.

"I'll move that up to your room," my wife said.

"No, that's fine," the blind man said loudly. "It can go up when I go up."

"A little water with the Scotch?" I said.

"Very little," he said.

"I knew it," I said.

He said, "Just a tad. The Irish actor, Barry Fitzgerald? I'm like that fellow. When I drink water, Fitzgerald said, I drink water. When I drink whiskey, I drink whiskey." My wife laughed. The blind man brought his hand up under his beard. He lifted his beard slowly and let it drop.

I did the drinks, three big glasses of Scotch with a splash of water in each. Then we made ourselves comfortable and talked about Robert's travels. First the long flight from the West Coast to Connecticut, we covered that. Then from Connecticut up here by train. We had another drink concerning that leg of the trip.

I remembered having read somewhere that the blind didn't smoke because, as speculation had it, they couldn't see the smoke they exhaled. I thought I knew that much and that much only about blind people. But this blind man smoked his cigarette down to the nubbin and then lit another one. This blind man filled his ashtray and my wife emptied it.

When we sat down at the table for dinner, we had another drink. My wife heaped Robert's plate with cube steak, scalloped potatoes, green beans. I buttered him up two slices of bread. I said, "Here's bread and butter for you." I swallowed some of my drink. "Now let us pray," I said, and the blind man lowered his head. My wife looked at me, her mouth agape. "Pray the phone won't ring and the food doesn't get cold," I said.

We dug in. We ate everything there was to eat on the table. We ate like there was no tomorrow. We didn't talk. We ate. We scarfed. We grazed that table. We were into serious eating. The blind man had right away located his foods, he knew just where everything was on his plate. I watched with admiration as he used his knife and fork on the meat. He'd cut two pieces of meat, fork the meat into his mouth, and then go all out for the scalloped potatoes, the beans next, and then he'd tear off a hunk of buttered bread and eat that. He'd follow this up with a big drink of milk. It didn't seem to bother him to use his fingers once in a while, either.

We finished everything, including half a strawberry pie. For a few moments, we sat as if stunned. Sweat beaded on our faces. Finally, we got up from the table and left the dirty plates. We didn't look back. We took ourselves into the living room and sank into our places again. Robert and my wife sat on the sofa. I took the big chair. We had us two or three more drinks while they talked about the major things that had come to pass for them in the past ten years. For the most part, I just listened. Now and then I joined in. I didn't want him to think I'd left the room, and I didn't want her to think I was feeling left out. They talked of things that had happened to them — to them! — these past ten years. I waited in vain to hear my name on my wife's sweet lips: "And then my dear husband came into my life" — something like that. But I heard nothing of the sort. More talk of Robert. Robert had done a little of everything, it seemed, a regular blind jack-of-all-trades. But most recently he and his wife had had an Amway distributorship, from which, I gathered, they'd earned their living, such as it was. The blind man was also a ham radio operator. He talked in his loud voice about conversations he'd had with fellow operators in Guam, in the Philippines, in Alaska, and even in Tahiti. He said he'd have a lot of friends there if he ever wanted to go visit those places. From time to time, he'd turn his blind face toward me, put his hand under his beard, ask me something. How long had I been in my present position? (Three years.) Did I like my work? (I didn't.) Was I going to stay with it? (What were the options?) Finally, when I thought he was beginning to run down, I got up and turned on the TV.

My wife looked at me with irritation. She was heading toward a boil. Then she looked at the blind man and said, "Robert, do you have a TV?"

The blind man said, "My dear, I have two TVs. I have a color set and a black-and-white thing, an old relic. It's funny, but if I turn the TV on, and I'm always turning it on, I turn on the color set. It's funny, don't you think?"

I didn't know what to say to that. I had absolutely nothing to say to that. No opinions. So I watched the news program and tried to listen to what the announcer was saying.

"This is a color TV," the blind man said. "Don't ask me how, but I can tell."

"We traded up a while ago," I said.

The blind man had another taste of his drink. He lifted his beard, sniffed it, and let it fall. He leaned forward on the sofa. He positioned his ashtray on the coffee table, then put the lighter to his cigarette. He leaned back on the sofa and crossed his legs at the ankles.

My wife covered her mouth, and then she yawned. She stretched. She said, "I think I'll go upstairs and put on my robe. I think I'll change into something else. Robert, you make yourself comfortable," she said.

"I'm comfortable," the blind man said.

"I want you to feel comfortable in this house," she said.

"I am comfortable," the blind man said.

After she'd left the room, he and I listened to the weather report and then to the sports roundup. By that time, she'd been gone so long I didn't know if she was going to come back. I thought she might have gone to bed. I wished she'd come back downstairs. I didn't want to be left alone with a blind man. I asked him if he wanted another drink, and he said sure. Then I asked if he wanted to smoke some dope with me. I said I'd just rolled a number. I hadn't, but I planned to do so in about two shakes.

"I'll try some with you," he said.

"Damn right," I said. "That's the stuff."

I got our drinks and sat down on the sofa with him. Then I rolled us two fat numbers. I lit one and passed it. I brought it to his fingers. He took it and inhaled.

"Hold it as long as you can," I said. I could tell he didn't know the first thing.

My wife came back downstairs wearing her pink robe and her pink slippers.

"What do I smell?" she said.

"We thought we'd have us some cannabis," I said.

My wife gave me a savage look. Then she looked at the blind man and said, "Robert, I didn't know you smoked."

He said, "I do now, my dear. There's a first time for everything. But I don't feel anything yet."

"This stuff is pretty mellow," I said. "This stuff is mild. It's dope you can reason with," I said. "It doesn't mess you up."

"Not much it doesn't, bub," he said, and laughed.

My wife sat on the sofa between the blind man and me. I passed her the number. She took it and toked and then passed it back to me. "Which way is this going?" she said. Then she said, "I shouldn't be smoking this. I can hardly keep my eyes open as it is. That dinner did me in. I shouldn't have eaten so much."

"It was the strawberry pie," the blind man said. "That's what did it," he said, and he laughed his big laugh. Then he shook his head.

"There's more strawberry pie," I said.

"Do you want some more, Robert?" my wife said.

"Maybe in a little while," he said.

We gave our attention to the TV. My wife yawned again. She said, "Your bed is made up when you feel like going to bed, Robert. I know you must have had a long day. When you're ready to go to bed, say so." She pulled his arm. "Robert?"

He came to and said, "I've had a real nice time. This beats tapes, doesn't it?"

I said. "Coming at you," and I put the number between his fingers. He inhaled, held the smoke, and then let it go. It was like he'd been doing it since he was nine years old.

"Thanks, bub," he said. "But I think this is all for me. I think I'm beginning to feel it," he said. He held the burning roach out for my wife.

"Same here," she said. "Ditto. Me, too." She took the roach and passed it to me. "I may just sit here for a while between you two guys with my eyes closed. But don't let me bother you, okay? Either one of you. If it bothers you, say so. Otherwise, I may just sit here with my eyes closed until you're ready to go to bed," she said. "Your bed's made up, Robert, when you're ready. It's right next to our room at the top of the stairs. We'll show you up when you're ready. You wake me up now, you guys, if I fall asleep." She said that and then she closed her eyes and went to sleep.

The news program ended. I got up and changed the channel. I sat back down on the sofa. I wished my wife hadn't pooped out. Her head lay across the back of the sofa, her mouth open. She'd turned so that her robe had slipped away from her legs, exposing a juicy thigh. I reached to draw her robe back over her, and it was then that I glanced at the blind man. What the hell! I flipped the robe open again.

"You say when you want some strawberry pie," I said.

"I will," he said.

I said, "Are you tired? Do you want me to take you up to your bed? Are you ready to hit the hay?"

"Not yet," he said. "No, I'll stay up with you, bub. If that's all right. I'll stay up until you're ready to turn in. We haven't had a chance to talk. Know what I mean? I feel like me and her monopolized the evening." He lifted his beard and he let it fall. He picked up his cigarettes and his lighter.

"That's all right," I said. Then I said, "I'm glad for the company."

And I guess I was. Every night I smoked dope and stayed up as long as I could before I fell asleep. My wife and I hardly ever went to bed at the same time. When I did go to sleep, I had these dreams. Sometimes I'd wake up from one of them, my heart going crazy.

Something about the church and the Middle Ages was on the TV. Not your run-of-the-mill TV fare. I wanted to watch something else. I turned to the other channels. But there was nothing on them, either. So I turned back to the first channel and apologized.

"Bub, it's all right," the blind man said. "It's fine with me. Whatever you want to watch is okay. I'm always learning something. Learning never ends. It won't hurt me to learn something tonight. I got ears," he said.

We didn't say anything for a time. He was leaning forward with his head turned at me, his right ear aimed in the direction of the set. Very disconcerting. Now and then his eyelids drooped and then they snapped open again. Now and then he put his fingers into his beard and tugged, like he was thinking about something he was hearing on the television.

On the screen, a group of men wearing cowls was being set upon and tormented by men dressed in skeleton costumes and men dressed as devils. The men dressed as devils wore devil masks, horns, and long tails. This pageant was part of a procession. The Englishman who was narrating the thing said it took place in Spain once a year. I tried to explain to the blind man what was happening.

"Skeletons," he said. "I know about skeletons," he said, and he nodded.

The TV showed this one cathedral. Then there was a long, slow look at another one. Finally, the picture switched to the famous one in Paris, with its flying buttresses and its spires reaching up to the clouds. The camera pulled away to show the whole of the cathedral rising above the skyline.

There were times when the Englishman who was telling the thing would shut up, would simply let the camera move around over the cathedrals. Or else the camera would tour the countryside, men in fields walking behind oxen. I waited as long as I could. Then I felt I had to say something. I said, "They're showing the outside of this cathedral now. Gargoyles. Little statues carved to look like monsters. Now I guess they're in Italy. Yeah, they're in Italy. There's paintings on the walls of this one church."

"Are those fresco paintings, bub?" he asked, and he sipped from his drink.

I reached for my glass. But it was empty. I tried to remember what I could remember. "You're asking me are those frescoes?" I said. "That's a good question. I don't know."

The camera moved to a cathedral outside Lisbon. The differences in the Portuguese cathedral compared with the French and Italian were not that great. But they were there. Mostly the interior stuff. Then something occurred to me, and I said, "Something has occurred to me. Do you have any idea what a cathedral is? What they look like, that is? Do you follow me? If somebody says cathedral to you, do you have any notion what they're talking about? Do you know the difference between that and a Baptist church, say?"

He let the smoke dribble from his mouth. "I know they took hundreds of workers fifty or a hundred years to build," he said. "I just heard the man say that, of course. I know generations of the same families worked on a cathedral. I heard him say that too. The men who began their life's work on them, they never lived to see the completion of their work. In that wise, bub, they're no different from the rest of us, right?" He laughed. Then his eyelids drooped again. His head nodded. He seemed to be snoozing. Maybe he was imagining himself in Portugal. The TV was showing another cathedral now. This one was in Germany. The Englishman's voice droned on. "Cathedrals," the blind man said. He sat up and rolled his head back and forth. "If you want the truth, bub, that's about all I know. What I just said. What I heard him say. But maybe you could describe one to me? I wish you'd do it. I'd like that. If you want to know, I really don't have a good idea."

I stared hard at the shot of the cathedral on the TV. How could I even begin to describe it? But say my life depended on it. Say my life was being threatened by an insane guy who said I had to do it or else.

I stared some more at the cathedral before the picture flipped off into the countryside. There was no use. I turned to the blind man and said, "To begin with, they're very tall." I was looking around the room for clues. "They reach way up. Up and up. Toward the sky. They're so big, some of them, they have to have these supports. To help hold them up, so to speak. These supports are called buttresses. They remind me of viaducts, for some reason. But maybe you don't know viaducts, either? Sometimes the cathedrals have devils and such carved into the front. Sometimes lords and ladies. Don't ask me why this is," I said.

He was nodding. The whole upper part of his body seemed to be moving back and forth.

"I'm not doing so good, am I?" I said.

He stopped nodding and leaned forward on the edge of the sofa. As he listened to me, he was running his fingers through his beard. I wasn't getting through to him, I could see that. But he waited for me to go on just the same. He nodded, like he was tryng to encourage me. I tried to think what else to say. "They're really big," I said. "They're massive. They're built of stone. Marble, too, sometimes. In those olden days, when they built cathedrals, men wanted to be close to God. In those olden days, God was an important part of everyone's life. You could tell this from their cathedral-building. I'm sorry," I said, "but it looks like that's the best I can do for you. I'm just no good at it."

"That's all right, bub," the blind man said. "Hey, listen. I hope you don't mind my asking you. Can I ask you something? Let me ask you a simple question, yes or no. I'm just curious and there's no offense. You're my host. But let me ask if you are in any way religious? You don't mind my asking?"

I shook my head. He couldn't see that, though. A wink is the same as a nod to a blind man. "I guess I don't believe in it. In anything. Sometimes it's hard. You know what I'm saying?"

"Sure I do," he said.

"Right," I said.

The Englishman was still holding forth. My wife sighed in her sleep. She drew a long breath and went on with her sleeping.

"You'll have to forgive me," I said. "But I can't tell you what a cathedral looks like. It just isn't in me to do it. I can't do any more than I've done."

The blind man sat very still, his head down, as he listened to me.

I said, "The truth is, cathedrals don't mean anything special to me. Nothing. Cathedrals. They're something to look at on late-night TV. That's all they are."

It was then that the blind man cleared his throat. He brought something up. He took a handkerchief from his back pocket. Then he said, "I get it, bub. It's okay. It happens. Don't worry about it," he said. "Hey, listen to me. Will you do me a favor? I got an idea. Why don't you find us some heavy paper? And a pen. We'll do something. We'll draw one together. Get us a pen and some heavy paper. Go on, bub, get the stuff," he said.

So I went upstairs. My legs felt like they didn't have any strength in them. They felt like they did after I'd done some running. In my wife's room, I looked around. I found some ballpoints in a little basket on her table. And then I tried to think where to look for the kind of paper he was talking about.

Downstairs, in the kitchen, I found a shopping bag with onion skins in the bottom of the bag. I emptied the bag and shook it. I brought it into the living room and sat down with it near his legs. I moved some things, smoothed the wrinkles from the bag, spread it out on the coffee table.

The blind man got down from the sofa and sat next to me on the carpet.

He ran his fingers over the paper. He went up and down the sides of the paper. The edges, even the edges. He fingered the corners.

"All right," he said. "All right, let's do her."

He found my hand, the hand with the pen. He closed his hand over my hand. "Go ahead, bub, draw," he said. "Draw. You'll see. I'll follow along with you. It'll be okay. Just begin now like I'm telling you. You'll see. Draw," the blind man said.

So I began. First I drew a box that looked like a house. It could have been the house I lived in. Then I put a roof on it. At either end of the roof, I drew spires. Crazy.

"Swell," he said. "Terrific. You're doing fine," he said.

"Never thought anything like this could happen in your lifetime, did you, bub? Well, its a strange life, we all know that. Go on now. Keep it up."

I put in windows with arches. I drew flying buttresses. I hung great doors. I couldn't stop. The TV station went off the air. I put down the pen and closed and opened my fingers. The blind man felt round over the paper. He moved the tips of his fingers over the paper, all over what I had drawn, and he nodded.

"Doing fine," the blind man said.

I took up the pen again, and he found my hand. I kept at it. I'm no artist. But I kept drawing just the same.

My wife opened up her eyes and gazed at us. She sat up on the sofa, her robe hanging open. She said, "What are you doing? Tell me, I want to know."

I didn't answer her.

The blind man said, "We're drawing a cathedral. Me and him are working on it. Press hard," he said to me. "That's right. That's good," he said. "Sure. You got it, bub. I can tell. You didn't think you could. But you can, can't you? You're cooking with gas now. You know what I'm saying? We're going to really have us something here in a minute. How's the old arm?" he said. "Put some people in there now. What's a cathedral without people?"

My wife said, "What's going on? Robert, what are you doing? What's going on?"

"It's all right," he said to her. "Close your eyes now," the blind man said to me.

I did it. I closed them just like he said.

"Are they closed? he said. "Don't fudge."

"They're closed," I said.

"Keep them that way," he said. He said, "Don't stop now. Draw."

So we kept on with it. His fingers rode my fingers as my hand went over the paper. It was like nothing else in my life up to now.

Then he said, "I think that's it. I think you got it," he said. "Take a look. What do you think?"

But I had my eyes closed. I thought I'd keep them that way for a little longer. I thought it was something I ought to do.

"Well?" he said. "Are you looking?"

My eyes were still closed. I was in my house. I knew that. But I didn't feel like I was inside anything.

"It's really something," I said.   [1981]

RAYMOND CARVER

Errand

Chekhov. On the evening of March 22, 1897, he went to dinner in Moscow with his friend and confidant Alexei Suvorin. This Suvorin was a very rich newspaper and book publisher, a reactionary, a self-made man whose father was a private at the battle of Borodino. Like Chekhov, he was the grandson of a serf. They had that in common: each had peasant's blood in his veins. Otherwise, politically and temperamentally, they were miles apart. Nevertheless, Suvorin was one of Chekhov's few intimates, and Chekhov enjoyed his company.

Naturally, they went to the best restaurant in the city, a former town house called the Hermitage — a place where it could take hours, half the night even, to get through a ten-course meal that would, of course, include several wines, liqueurs, and coffee. Chekhov was impeccably dressed, as always — a dark suit and waistcoat, his usual pince-nez. He looked that night very much as he looks in the photographs taken of him during this period. He was relaxed, jovial. He shook hands with the maître d', and with a glance took in the large dining room. It was brilliantly illuminated by ornate chandeliers, the tables occupied by elegantly dressed men and women. Waiters came and went ceaselessly. He had just been seated across the table from Suvorin when suddenly, without warning, blood began gushing from his mouth. Suvorin and two waiters helped him to the gentlemen's room and tried to stanch the flow of blood with ice packs. Suvorin saw him back to his own hotel and had a bed prepared for Chekhov in one of the rooms of the suite. Later, after another hemorrhage, Chekhov allowed himself to be moved to a clinic that specialized in the treatment of tuberculosis and related respiratory infections. When Suvorin visited him there, Chekhov apologized for the "scandal" at the restaurant three nights earlier but continued to insist there was nothing seriously wrong. "He laughed and jested as usual," Suvorin noted in his diary, "while spitting blood into a large vessel."

Maria Chekhov, his younger sister, visited Chekhov in the clinic during the last days of March. The weather was miserable; a sleet storm was in progress, and frozen heaps of snow lay everywhere. It was hard for her to wave down a carriage to take her to the hospital. By the time she arrived she was filled with dread and anxiety.

"Anton Pavlovich lay on his back," Maria wrote in her *Memoirs*. "He was not allowed to speak. After greeting him, I went over to the table to hide my emotions." There, among bottles of champagne, jars of caviar, bouquets of flowers from well-wishers, she saw something that terrified her: a freehand drawing, obviously done by a specialist in these matters, of Chekhov's lungs. It was the kind of sketch a doctor often makes in order to show his patient what he thinks is taking place. The lungs were outlined in blue, but the upper parts were filled in with red. "I realized they were diseased," Maria wrote.

Leo Tolstoy was another visitor. The hospital staff were awed to find themselves in the presence of the country's greatest writer. The most famous man in Russia? Of course they had to let him in to see Chekhov, even though "nonessential" visitors were forbidden. With much obsequiousness on the part of the nurses and resident doctors, the bearded, fierce-looking old man was shown into Chekhov's room. Despite his low opinion of Chekhov's abilities as a playwright (Tolstoy felt the plays were static and lacking in any moral vision. "Where do your characters take you?" he once demanded of Chekhov. "From the sofa to the junk room and back"), Tolstoy liked Chekhov's short stories. Furthermore, and quite simply, he loved the man. He told Gorky, "What a beautiful, magnificent man: modest and quiet, like a girl. He even walks like a girl. He's simply wonderful." And Tolstoy wrote in his journal (everyone kept a journal or a diary in those days), "I am glad I love . . . Chekhov."

Tolstoy removed his woollen scarf and bearskin coat, then lowered himself into a chair next to Chekhov's bed. Never mind that Chekhov was taking medication and not permitted to talk, much less carry on a conversation. He had to listen, amazedly, as the Count began to discourse on his theories of the immortality of the soul. Concerning that visit, Chekhov later wrote, "Tolstoy assumes that all of us (humans and animals alike) will live on in a principle (such as reason or love) the essence and goals of which are a mystery to us. . . . I have no use for that kind of immortality. I don't understand it, and Lev Nikolayevich [Tolstoy] was astonished I didn't."

Nevertheless, Chekhov was impressed with the solicitude shown by Tolstoy's visit. But, unlike Tolstoy, Chekhov didn't believe in an afterlife and never had. He didn't believe in anything that couldn't be apprehended by one or more of his five senses. And as far as his outlook on life and writing went, he once told someone that he lacked "a political, religious, and philosophical world view. I change it every month, so I'll have to limit myself to the description of how my heroes love, marry, give birth, die, and how they speak."

Earlier, before his t.b. was diagnosed, Chekhov had remarked, "When a peasant has consumption, he says, 'There's nothing I can do. I'll go off in the spring with the melting of the snows.'" (Chekhov himself died in the summer, during a heat wave.) But once Chekhov's own tuberculosis was discovered he continually tried to minimize the seriousness of his condition. To all appearances, it was as if he felt, right up to the end, that he might be able to throw off the disease as he would a lingering catarrh. Well into his final days, he spoke with seeming conviction of the possibility of an improvement. In fact, in a letter written shortly before his end, he went so far as to tell his sister that he was "getting fat" and felt much better now that he was in Badenweiler.

Badenweiler is a spa and resort city in the western area of the Black Forest, not far from Basel. The Vosges are visible from nearly anywhere in the city, and in those days the air was pure and invigorating. Russians had been going there for years to soak in the hot mineral baths and promenade on the boulevards. In June, 1904, Chekhov went there to die.

Earlier that month, he'd made a difficult journey by train from Moscow to Berlin. He traveled with his wife, the actress Olga Knipper, a woman he'd met in 1898 during rehearsals for "The Seagull." Her contemporaries describe her as an excellent actress. She was talented, pretty, and almost ten years younger than the playwright. Chekhov had been immediately attracted to her, but was slow to act on his feelings. As always, he preferred a flirtation to marriage. Finally, after a three-year courtship involving many separations, letters, and the inevitable misunderstandings, they were at last married, in a private ceremony in Moscow, on May 25, 1901. Chekhov was enormously happy. He called Olga his "pony," and sometimes "dog" or "puppy." He was also fond of addressing her as "little turkey" or simply as "my joy."

In Berlin, Chekhov consulted with a renowned specialist in pulmonary disorders, a Dr. Karl Ewald. But, according to an eyewitness, after the doctor examined Chekhov he threw up his hands and left the room without a word. Chekhov was too far gone for help: this Dr. Ewald was furious with himself for not being able to work miracles, and with Chekhov for being so ill.

A Russian journalist happened to visit the Chekhovs at their hotel and sent back this dispatch to his editor: "Chekhov's days are numbered. He seems mortally ill, is terribly thin, coughs all the time, gasps for breath at the slightest movement, and is running a high temperature." This same journalist saw the Chekhovs off at Potsdam Station when they boarded their train for Badenweiler. According to his account, "Chekhov had trouble making his way up the small staircase at the station. He had to sit down for several minutes to catch his breath." In fact, it was painful for Chekhov to move: his legs ached continually and his insides hurt. The disease had attacked his intestines and spinal cord. At this point he had less than a month to live. When Chekhov spoke of his condition now, it was, according to Olga, "with an almost reckless indifference."

Dr. Schwöhrer was one of the many Badenweiler physicians who earned a good living by treating the well-to-do who came to the spa seeking relief from various maladies. Some of his patients were ill and infirm, others simply old and hypochondriacal. But Chekhov's was a special case: he was clearly beyond help and in his last days. He was also very famous. Even Dr. Schwöhrer knew his name: he'd read some of Chekhov's stories in a German magazine. When he examined the writer early in June, he voiced his appreciation of Chekhov's art but kept his medical opinions to himself. Instead, he prescribed a diet of cocoa, oatmeal drenched in butter, and strawberry tea. This last was supposed to help Chekhov sleep at night.

On June 13, less than three weeks before he died, Chekhov wrote a letter to his mother in which he told her his health was on the mend. In it he said, "It's likely that I'll be completely cured in a week." Who knows why he said this? What could he have been thinking? He was a doctor himself, and he knew better. He was dying, it was as simple and as unavoidable as that. Nevertheless, he sat out on the balcony of his hotel room and read railway timetables. He asked for information on sailings of boats bound for Odessa from Marseilles. But he *knew*. At this stage he had to have known. Yet in one of the last letters he ever wrote he told his sister he was growing stronger by the day.

He no longer had any appetite for literary work, and hadn't for a long time. In fact, he had very nearly failed to complete *The Cherry Orchard* the year before. Writing that play was the hardest thing he'd ever done in his life. Toward the end, he was able to manage only six or seven lines a day. "I've started losing heart," he wrote Olga. "I feel I'm finished as a writer, and every sentence strikes me as worthless and of no use whatever." But he didn't stop. He finished his play in October, 1903. It was the last thing he ever wrote, except for letters and a few entries in his notebook.

A little after midnight on July 2, 1904, Olga sent someone to fetch Dr. Schwöhrer. It was an emergency: Chekhov was delirious. Two young Russians on holiday happened to have the adjacent room, and Olga hurried next door to explain what was happening. One of the youths was in his bed asleep, but the other was still awake, smoking and reading. He left the hotel at a run to find Dr. Schwöhrer. "I can still hear the sound of the gravel under his shoes in the silence of that stifling July night," Olga wrote later on in her memoirs. Chekhov was hallucinating, talking about sailors, and there were snatches of something about the Japanese. "You don't put ice on an empty stomach," he said when she tried to place an ice pack on his chest.

Dr. Schwöhrer arrived and unpacked his bag, all the while keeping his gaze fastened on Chekhov, who lay gasping in the bed. The sick man's pupils were dilated and his temples glistened with sweat. Dr. Schwöhrer's face didn't register anything. He was not an emotional man, but he knew Chekhov's end was near. Still, he was a doctor, sworn to do his utmost, and Chekhov held on to life, however tenuously. Dr. Schwöhrer prepared a hypodermic and administered an injection of camphor, something that was supposed to speed up the heart. But the injection didn't help — nothing, of course, could have helped. Nevertheless, the doctor made known to Olga his intention of sending for oxygen. Suddenly, Chekhov roused himself, became lucid, and said quietly, "What's the use? Before it arrives I'll be a corpse."

Dr. Schwöhrer pulled on his big moustache and stared at Chekhov. The writer's cheeks were sunken and gray, his complexion waxen; his breath was raspy. Dr. Schwöhrer knew the time could be reckoned in minutes. Without a word, without conferring with Olga, he went over to an alcove where there was a telephone on the wall. He read the instructions for using the device. If he activated it by holding his finger on a button and turning a handle on the side of the phone, he could reach the lower regions of the hotel — the kitchen. He picked up the receiver, held it to his ear, and did as the instructions told him. When someone finally answered, Dr. Schwöhrer ordered a bottle of the hotel's best champagne. "How many glasses?" he was asked. "Three glasses!" the doctor shouted into the mouthpiece. "And hurry, do you hear?" It was one of those rare moments of inspiration that can easily enough be overlooked later on, because the action is so entirely appropriate it seems inevitable.

The champagne was brought to the door by a tired-looking young man

whose blond hair was standing up. The trousers of his uniform were wrinkled, the creases gone, and in his haste he'd missed a loop while buttoning
his jacket. His appearance was that of someone who'd been resting (slumped
in a chair, say, dozing a little), when off in the distance the phone had
clamored in the early-morning hours — great God in Heaven! — and the next
thing he knew he was being shaken awake by a superior and told to deliver
a bottle of Moët to Room 211. "And hurry, do you hear?"

The young man entered the room carrying a silver ice bucket with the
champagne in it and a silver tray with three cut-crystal glasses. He found a
place on the table for the bucket and glasses, all the while craning his neck,
trying to see into the other room, where someone panted ferociously for
breath. It was a dreadful, harrowing sound, and the young man lowered his
chin into his collar and turned away as the ratchety breathing worsened.
Forgetting himself, he stared out the open window toward the darkened city.
Then this big imposing man with a thick moustache pressed some coins into
his hand — a large tip, by the feel of it — and suddenly the young man saw
the door open. He took some steps and found himself on the landing, where
he opened his hand and looked at the coins in amazement.

Methodically, the way he did everything, the doctor went about the
business of working the cork out of the bottle. He did it in such a way as to
minimize, as much as possible, the festive explosion. He poured three glasses
and, out of habit, pushed the cork back into the neck of the bottle. He then
took the glasses of champagne over to the bed. Olga momentarily released
her grip on Chekhov's hand — a hand, she said later, that burned her fingers.
She arranged another pillow behind his head. Then she put the cool glass of
champagne against Chekhov's palm and made sure his fingers closed around
the stem. They exchanged looks — Chekhov, Olga, Dr. Schwöhrer. They didn't
touch glasses. There was no toast. What on earth was there to drink to? To
death? Chekhov summoned his remaining strength and said, "It's been so
long since I've had champagne." He brought the glass to his lips and drank.
In a minute or two Olga took the empty glass from his hand and set it on the
nightstand. Then Chekhov turned onto his side. He closed his eyes and
sighed. A minute later, his breathing stopped.

Dr. Schwöhrer picked up Chekhov's hand from the bedsheet. He held
his fingers to Chekhov's wrist and drew a gold watch from his vest pocket,
opening the lid of the watch as he did so. The second hand on the watch
moved slowly, very slowly. He let it move around the face of the watch three
times while he waited for signs of a pulse. It was three o'clock in the morning
and still sultry in the room. Badenweiler was in the grip of its worst heat wave
in years. All the windows in both rooms stood open, but there was no sign
of a breeze. A large, black-winged moth flew through a window and banged
wildly against the electric lamp. Dr. Schwöhrer let go of Chekhov's wrist. "It's
over," he said. He closed the lid of his watch and returned it to his vest pocket.

At once Olga dried her eyes and set about composing herself. She
thanked the doctor for coming. He asked if she wanted some medication —
laudanum, perhaps, or a few drops of valerian. She shook her head. She did

have one request, though: before the authorities were notified and the news-papers found out, before the time came when Chekhov was no longer in her keeping, she wanted to be alone with him for a while. Could the doctor help with this? Could he withhold, for a while anyway, news of what had just occurred?

Dr. Schwöhrer stroked his moustache with the back of a finger. Why not? After all, what difference would it make to anyone whether this matter became known now or a few hours from now? The only detail that remained was to fill out a death certificate, and this could be done at his office later on in the morning, after he'd slept a few hours. Dr. Schwöhrer nodded his agreement and prepared to leave. He murmured a few words of condolence. Olga inclined her head. "An honor," Dr. Schwöhrer said. He picked up his bag and left the room and, for that matter, history.

It was at this moment that the cork popped out of the champagne bottle; foam spilled down onto the table. Olga went back to Chekhov's bedside. She sat on a footstool, holding his hand, from time to time stroking his face. "There were no human voices, no everyday sounds," she wrote. "There was only beauty, peace, and the grandeur of death."

She stayed with Chekhov until daybreak, when thrushes began to call from the garden below. Then came the sound of tables and chairs being moved about down there. Before long, voices carried up to her. It was then a knock sounded at the door. Of course she thought it must be an official of some sort — the medical examiner, say, or someone from the police who had questions to ask and forms for her to fill out, or maybe, just maybe, it could be Dr. Schwöhrer returning with a mortician to render assistance in embalming and transporting Chekhov's remains back to Russia.

But, instead, it was the same blond young man who'd brought the champagne a few hours earlier. This time, however, his uniform trousers were neatly pressed, with stiff creases in front, and every button on his snug green jacket was fastened. He seemed quite another person. Not only was he wide awake but his plump cheeks were smooth-shaven, his hair was in place, and he appeared anxious to please. He was holding a porcelain vase with three long-stemmed yellow roses. He presented these to Olga with a smart click of his heels. She stepped back and let him into the room. He was there, he said, to collect the glasses, ice bucket, and tray, yes. But he also wanted to say that, because of the extreme heat, breakfast would be served in the garden this morning. He hoped this weather wasn't too bothersome; he apologized for it.

The woman seemed distracted. While he talked, she turned her eyes away and looked down at something in the carpet. She crossed her arms and held her elbows. Meanwhile, still holding his vase, waiting for a sign, the young man took in the details of the room. Bright sunlight flooded through the open windows. The room was tidy and seemed undisturbed, almost untouched. No garments were flung over chairs, no shoes, stockings, braces, or stays were in evidence, no open suitcases. In short, there was no clutter, nothing but the usual heavy pieces of hotel-room furniture. Then, because the woman was still looking down, he looked down, too, and at once spied a cork near the toe of his shoe. The woman did not see it — she was looking somewhere else. The young man wanted to bend over and pick up the cork, but he was still holding the roses and was afraid of seeming to intrude even more by drawing any further attention to himself. Reluctantly, he left the cork where it was and raised his eyes. Everything was in order except for the uncorked, half-empty bottle of champagne that stood alongside two crystal glasses over on the little table. He cast his gaze about once more. Through an open door he saw that the third glass was in the bedroom, on the nightstand. But someone still occupied the bed! He couldn't see a face, but the figure under the covers lay perfectly motionless and quiet. He noted the figure and looked elsewhere. Then, for a reason he couldn't understand, a feeling of uneasiness took hold of him. He cleared his throat and moved his weight to the other leg. The woman still didn't look up or break her silence. The young man felt his cheeks grow warm. It occurred to him, quite without his having thought it through, that he should perhaps suggest an alternative to breakfast in the garden. He coughed, hoping to focus the woman's attention, but she didn't look at him. The distinguished foreign guests could, he said, take breakfast in their rooms this morning if they wished. The young man (his name hasn't survived, and it's likely he perished in the Great War) said he would be happy to bring up a tray. Two trays, he added, glancing uncertainly once again in the direction of the bedroom.

He fell silent and ran a finger around the inside of his collar. He didn't understand. He wasn't even sure the woman had been listening. He didn't know what else to do now; he was still holding the vase. The sweet odor of the roses filled his nostrils and inexplicably caused a pang of regret. The entire time he'd been waiting, the woman had apparently been lost in thought. It was as if all the while he'd been standing there, talking, shifting his weight, holding his flowers, she had been someplace else, somewhere far from Baden-weiler. But now she came back to herself, and her face assumed another expression. She raised her eyes, looked at him, and then shook her head. She seemed to be struggling to understand what on earth this young man could be doing there in the room holding a vase with three yellow roses. Flowers? She hadn't ordered flowers.

The moment passed. She went over to her handbag and scooped up some coins. She drew out a number of banknotes as well. The young man touched his lips with his tongue; another large tip was forthcoming, but for what? What did she want him to do? He'd never before waited on such guests. He cleared his throat once more.

No breakfast, the woman said. Not yet, at any rate. Breakfast wasn't the important thing this morning. She required something else. She needed him to go out and bring back a mortician. Did he understand her? Herr Chekhov was dead, you see. *Comprenez-vous?* Young man? Anton Chekhov was dead. Now listen carefully to me, she said. She wanted him to go downstairs and ask someone at the front desk where he could go to find the most respected mortician in the city. Someone reliable, who took great pains in his work and whose manner was appropriately reserved. A mortician, in short, worthy of a great artist. Here, she said, and pressed the money on him. Tell them downstairs that I have specifically requested you to perform this duty for me. Are you listening? Do you understand what I'm saying to you?

The young man grappled to take in what she was saying. He chose not to look again in the direction of the other room. He had sensed the something was not right. He became aware of his heart beating rapidly under his jacket, and he felt perspiration break out on his forehead. He didn't know where he should turn his eyes. He wanted to put the vase down.

Please do this for me, the woman said. I'll remember you with gratitude. Tell them downstairs that I insist. Say that. But don't call any unnecessary attention to yourself or to the situation. Just say that this is necessary, that I request it — and that's all. Do you hear me? Nod if you understand. Above all, don't raise an alarm. Everything else, all the rest, the commotion — that'll come soon enough. The worst is over. Do we understand each other?

The young man's face had grown pale. He stood rigid, clasping the vase. He managed to nod his head.

After securing permission to leave the hotel he was to proceed quietly and resolutely, though without any unbecoming haste, to the mortician's. He was to behave exactly as if he were engaged on a very important errand, nothing more. He *was* engaged on an important errand, she said. And if it would help keep his movements purposeful he should imagine himself as someone moving down the busy sidewalk carrying in his arms a porcelain vase of roses that he had to deliver to an important man. (She spoke quietly, almost confidentially, as if to a relative or a friend.) He could even tell himself that the man he was going to see was expecting him, was perhaps impatient for him to arrive with his flowers. Nevertheless, the young man was not to become excited and run, or otherwise break his stride. Remember the vase he was carrying! He was to walk briskly, comporting himself at all times in as dignified a manner as possible. He should keep walking until he came to the mortician's house and stood before the door. He would then raise the brass knocker and let it fall, once, twice, three times. In a minute the mortician himself would answer.

This mortician would be in his forties, no doubt, or maybe early fifties — bald, solidly built, wearing steel-frame spectacles set very low on his nose. He would be modest, unassuming, a man who would ask only the most direct and necessary questions. An apron. Probably he would be wearing an apron. He might even be wiping his hands on a dark towel while he listened to what was being said. There'd be a faint whiff of formaldehyde on his clothes. But it was all right, and the young man shouldn't worry. He was nearly a grown-up now and shouldn't be frightened or repelled by any of this. The mortician would hear him out. He was a man of restraint and bearing, this mortician, someone who could help allay people's fears in this situation, not increase them. Long ago he'd acquainted himself with death in all its various guises and forms; death held no surprises for him any longer, no hidden secrets. It was this man whose services were required this morning.

The mortician takes the vase of roses. Only once while the young man is speaking does the mortician betray the least flicker of interest, or indicate that he's heard anything out of the ordinary. But the one time the young man mentions the name of the deceased, the mortician's eyebrows rise just a little. Chekhov, you say? Just a minute, and I'll be with you.

Do you understand what I'm saying, Olga said to the young man. Leave the glasses. Don't worry about them. Forget about crystal wineglasses and such. Leave the room as it is. Everything is ready now. We're ready. Will you go?

But at that moment the young man was thinking of the cork still resting near the toe of his shoe. To retrieve it he would have to bend over, still gripping the vase. He would do this. He leaned over. Without looking down, he reached out and closed it into his hand. [1987]

R AYMOND   C ARVER

What We Talk About When We Talk About Love

My friend Mel McGinnis was talking. Mel McGinnis is a cardiologist, and sometimes that gives him the right.

The four of us were sitting around his kitchen table drinking gin. Sunlight filled the kitchen from the big window behind the sink. There were Mel and me and his second wife, Teresa — Terri, we called her — and my wife, Laura. We lived in Albuquerque then. But we were all from somewhere else.

There was an ice bucket on the table. The gin and the tonic water kept going around, and we somehow got on the subject of love. Mel thought real love was nothing less than spiritual love. He said he'd spent five years in a seminary before quitting to go to medical school. He said he still looked back on those years in the seminary as the most important years in his life.

Terri said the man she lived with before she lived with Mel loved her so much he tried to kill her. Then Terri said, "He beat me up one night. He dragged me around the living room by my ankles. He kept saying, 'I love you, I love you, you bitch.' He went on dragging me around the living room. My head kept knocking on things." Terri looked around the table. "What do you do with love like that?"

She was a bone-thin woman with a pretty face, dark eyes, and brown hair that hung down her back. She liked necklaces made of turquoise, and long pendant earrings.

"My God, don't be silly. That's not love, and you know it," Mel said. "I don't know what you'd call it, but I sure know you wouldn't call it love."

"Say what you want to, but I know it was," Terri said. "It may sound crazy to you, but it's true just the same. People are different, Mel. Sure, sometimes he may have acted crazy. Okay. But he loved me. In his own way maybe, but he loved me. There was love there, Mel. Don't say there wasn't."

Mel let out his breath. He held his glass and turned to Laura and me. "The man threatened to kill me," Mel said. He finished his drink and reached for the gin bottle. "Terri's a romantic. Terri's of the kick-me-so-I'll-know-you-love-me school. Terri, hon, don't look that way." Mel reached across the table and touched Terri's cheek with his fingers. He grinned at her.

"Now he wants to make up," Terri said.

"Make up what?" Mel said. "What is there to make up? I know what I know. That's all."

"How'd we get started on this subject, anyway?" Terri said. She raised her glass and drank from it. "Mel always has love on his mind," she said. "Don't you, honey?" She smiled, and I thought that was the last of it.

"I just wouldn't call Ed's behavior love. That's all I'm saying, honey," Mel said. "What about you guys?" Mel said to Laura and me. "Does that sound like love to you?"

"I'm the wrong person to ask," I said. "I didn't even know the man. I've only heard his name mentioned in passing. I wouldn't know. You'd have to know the particulars. But I think what you're saying is that love is an absolute."

Mel said, "The kind of love I'm talking about is. The kind of love I'm talking about, you don't try to kill people."

Laura said, "I don't know anything about Ed, or anything about the situation. But who can judge anyone else's situation?"

I touched the back of Laura's hand. She gave me a quick smile. I picked up Laura's hand. It was warm, the nails polished, perfectly manicured. I encircled the broad wrist with my fingers, and I held her.

"When I left, he drank rat poison," Terri said. She clasped her arms with her hands. "They took him to the hospital in Sante Fe. That's where we lived then, about ten miles out. They saved his life. But his gums went crazy from it. I mean they pulled away from his teeth. After that, his teeth stood out like fangs. My God," Terri said. She waited a minute, then let go of her arms and picked up her glass.

"What people won't do!" Laura said.

"He's out of the action now," Mel said. "He's dead."

Mel handed me the saucer of limes. I took a section, squeezed it over my drink, and stirred the ice cubes with my finger.

"It gets worse," Terri said. "He shot himself in the mouth. But he bungled that too. Poor Ed," she said. Terri shook her head.

"Poor Ed nothing," Mel said. "He was dangerous."

Mel was forty-five years old. He was tall and rangy with curly soft hair. His face and arms were brown from the tennis he played. When he was sober, his gestures, all his movements, were precise, very careful.

"He did love me though, Mel. Grant me that," Terri said. "That's all I'm asking. He didn't love me the way you love me. I'm not saying that. But he loved me. You can grant me that, can't you?"

"What do you mean, he bungled it?" I said.

Laura leaned forward with her glass. She put her elbows on the table and held her glass in both hands. She glanced from Mel to Terri and waited with a look of bewilderment on her open face, as if amazed that such things happened to people you were friendly with.

"How'd he bungle it when he killed himself?" I said.

"I'll tell you what happened," Mel said. "He took this twenty-two pistol he'd bought to threaten Terri and me with. Oh, I'm serious, the man was always threatening. You should have seen the way we lived in those days. Like fugitives. I even bought a gun myself. Can you believe it? A guy like me? But I did. I bought one for self-defense and carried it in the glove compartment. Sometimes I'd have to leave the apartment in the middle of the night. To go to the hospital, you know? Terri and I weren't married then, and my first wife had the house and kids, the dog, everything, and Terri and I were living in this apartment here. Sometimes, as I say, I'd get a call in the middle of the night and have to go in to the hospital at two or three in the morning. It'd be dark out there in the parking lot, and I'd break into a sweat before I could even get to my car. I never knew if he was going to come up out of the shrubbery or from behind a car and start shooting. I mean, the man was crazy. He was capable of wiring a bomb, anything. He used to call my service at all hours and say he needed to talk to the doctor, and when I'd return the call, he'd say, 'Son of a bitch, your days are numbered.' Little things like that. It was scary, I'm telling you."

"I still feel sorry for him," Terri said.

"It sounds like a nightmare," Laura said. "But what exactly happened after he shot himself?"

Laura is a legal secretary. We'd met in a professional capacity. Before we knew it, it was a courtship. She's thirty-five, three years younger than I am. In addition to being in love, we like each other and enjoy one another's company. She's easy to be with.

"What happened?" Laura said.

Mel said, "He shot himself in the mouth in his room. Someone heard the shot and told the manager. They came in with a passkey, saw what had happened, and called an ambulance. I happened to be there when they brought him in, alive but past recall. The man lived for three days. His head swelled up to twice the size of a normal head. I'd never seen anything like it, and I hope I never do again. Terri wanted to go in and sit with him when she found out about it. We had a fight over it. I didn't think she should see him like that. I didn't think she should see him, and I still don't."

"Who won the fight?" Laura said.

"I was in the room with him when he died," Terri said. "He never came up out of it. But I sat with him. He didn't have anyone else."

"He was dangerous," Mel said. "If you call that love, you can have it."

"It was love," Terri said. "Sure, it's abnormal in most people's eyes. But he was willing to die for it. He did die for it."

"I sure as hell wouldn't call it love," Mel said. "I mean, no one knows what he did it for. I've seen a lot of suicides, and I couldn't say anyone ever knew what they did it for."

Mel put his hands behind his neck and tilted his chair back. "I'm not interested in that kind of love," he said. "If that's love, you can have it."

Terri said, "We were afraid. Mel even made a will out and wrote to his brother in California who used to be a Green Beret. Mel told him who to look for if something happened to him."

Terri drank from her glass. She said, "But Mel's right — we lived like fugitives. We were afraid. Mel was, weren't you, honey? I even called the police at one point, but they were no help. They said they couldn't do anything until Ed actually did something. Isn't that a laugh?" Terry said.

She poured the last of the gin into her glass and waggled the bottle. Mel got up from the table and went to the cupboard. He took down another bottle.

"Well, Nick and I know what love is," Laura said. "For us, I mean," Laura said. She bumped my knee with her knee. "You're supposed to say something now," Laura said, and turned her smile on me.

For an answer, I took Laura's hand and raised it to my lips. I made a big production out of kissing her hand. Everyone was amused.

"We're lucky," I said.

"You guys," Terri said. "Stop that now. You're making me sick. You're still on the honeymoon, for God's sake. You're still gaga, for crying out loud. Just wait. How long have you been together now? How long has it been? A year? Longer than a year?"

"Going on a year and a half," Laura said, flushed and smiling.

"Oh, now," Terri said. "Wait awhile."

She held her drink and gazed at Laura.

"I'm only kidding," Terri said.

Mel opened the gin and went around the table with the bottle.

"Here, you guys," he said. "Let's have a toast. I want to propose a toast. A toast to love. To true love," Mel said.

We touched glasses.

"To love," we said.

Outside in the backyard, one of the dogs began to bark. The leaves of the aspen that leaned past the window ticked against the glass. The afternoon sun was like a presence in this room, the spacious light of ease and generosity. We could have been anywhere, somewhere enchanted. We raised our glasses again and grinned at each other like children who had agreed on something forbidden.

"I'll tell you what real love is," Mel said. "I mean, I'll give you a good example. And then you can draw your own conclusions." He poured more gin into his glass. He added an ice cube and a sliver of lime. We waited and sipped our drinks. Laura and I touched knees again. I put a hand on her warm thigh and left it there.

"What do any of us really know about love?" Mel said. "It seems to me we're just beginners at love. We say we love each other and we do, I don't doubt it. I love Terri and Terri loves me, and you guys love each other too. You know the kind of love I'm talking about now. Physical love, that impulse that drives you to someone special, as well as love of the other person's being, his or her essence, as it were. Carnal love and, well, call it sentimental love, the day-to-day caring about the other person. But sometimes I have a hard time accounting for the fact that I must have loved my first wife too. But I did, I know I did. So I suppose I am like Terri in that regard. Terri and Ed." He thought about it and then he went on. "There was a time when I thought I loved my first wife more than life itself. But now I hate her guts. I do. How do you explain that? What happened to that love? What happened to it, is what I'd like to know. I wish someone could tell me. Then there's Ed. Okay, we're back to Ed. He loves Terri so much he tries to kill her and he winds up killing himself." Mel stopped talking and swallowed from his glass. "You guys have been together eighteen months and you love each other. It shows all over you. You glow with it. But you both loved other people before you met each other. You've both been married before, just like us. And you probably loved other people before that too, even. Terri and I have been together five years, been married for four. And the terrible thing, the terrible thing is, but the good thing too, the saving grace, you might say, is that if something happened to one of us — excuse me for saying this — but if something happened to one of us tomorrow I think the other one, the other person, would grieve for a while, you know, but then the surviving party would go out and love again, have someone else soon enough. All this, all of this love we're talking about, it would just be a memory. Maybe not even a memory. Am I wrong? Am I way off base? Because I want you to set me straight if you think I'm wrong. I want to know. I mean, I don't know anything, and I'm the first one to admit it."

"Mel, for God's sake," Terri said. She reached out and took hold of his wrist. "Are you getting drunk? Honey? Are you drunk?"

"Honey, I'm just talking," Mel said. "All right? I don't have to be drunk to say what I think. I mean, we're all just talking, right?" Mel said. He fixed his eyes on her.

"Sweetie, I'm not criticizing," Terri said.

She picked up her glass.

"I'm not on call today," Mel said. "Let me remind you of that. I am not on call," he said.

"Mel, we love you," Laura said.

Mel looked at Laura. He looked at her as if he could not place her, as if she was not the woman she was.

"Love you too, Laura," Mel said. "And you, Nick, love you too. You know something?" Mel said. "You guys are our pals," Mel said.

He picked up his glass.

Mel said, "I was going to tell you about something. I mean, I was going to prove a point. You see, this happened a few months ago, but it's still going on right now, and it ought to make us feel ashamed when we talk like we know what we're talking about when we talk above love."

"Come on now," Terri said. "Don't talk like you're drunk if you're not drunk."

"Just shut up for once in your life," Mel said very quietly. "Will you do me a favor and do that for a minute? So as I was saying, there's this old couple who had this car wreck out on the interstate. A kid hit them and they were all torn to shit and nobody was giving them much chance to pull through."

Terri looked at us and then back at Mel. She seemed anxious, or maybe that's too strong a word.

Mel was handing the bottle around the table.

"I was on call that night," Mel said. "It was May or maybe it was June. Terri and I had just sat down to dinner when the hospital called. There'd been this thing out on the interstate. Drunk kid, teenager, plowed his dad's pickup into this camper with this old couple in it. They were up in their mid-seventies, that couple. The kid — eighteen, nineteen, something — he was DOA. Taken the steering wheel through his sternum. The old couple, they were alive, you understand. I mean, just barely. But they had everything. Multiple fractures, internal injuries, hemorrhaging, contusions, lacerations, the works, and they each of them had themselves concussions. They were in a bad way, believe me. And, of course, their age was two strikes against them. I'd say she was worse off than he was. Ruptured spleen along with everything else. Both kneecaps broken. But they'd been wearing their seatbelts and, God knows, that's what saved them for the time being."

"Folks, this is an advertisement for the National Safety Council," Terri said. "This is your spokesman, Dr. Melvin R. McGinnis, talking." Terri laughed. "Mel," she said, "sometimes you're just too much. But I love you, hon," she said.

"Honey, I love you," Mel said.

He leaned across the table. Terri met him halfway. They kissed.

"Terri's right," Mel said as he settled himself again. "Get those seatbelts on. But seriously, they were in some shape, those oldsters. By the time I got down there, the kid was dead, as I said. He was off in a corner, laid out on a gurney. I took one look at the old couple and told the ER nurse to get me a neurologist and an orthopedic man and a couple of surgeons down there right away."

He drank from his glass. "I'll try to keep this short," he said. "So we took the two of them up to the OR and worked like fuck on them most of the night. They had these incredible reserves, those two. You see that once in a while. So we did everything that could be done, and toward morning we're giving them a fifty-fifty chance, maybe less than that for her. So here they are, still alive the next morning. So, okay, we move them into the ICU, which is where they both kept plugging away at it for two weeks, hitting it better and better on all the scopes. So we transfer them out to their own room."

Mel stopped talking. "Here," he said, "let's drink this cheapo gin the hell up. Then we're going to dinner, right? Terri and I know a new place.

That's where we'll go, to this new place we know about. But we're not going until we finish up this cut-rate, lousy gin."

Terri said, "We haven't actually eaten there yet. But it looks good. From the outside, you know."

"I like food," Mel said. "If I had it to do all over again, I'd be a chef, you know? Right, Terri?" Mel said.

He laughed. He fingered the ice in his glass.

"Terri knows," he said. "Terri can tell you. But let me say this. If I could come back again in a different life, a different time and all, you know what? I'd like to come back as a knight. You were pretty safe wearing all that armor. It was all right being a knight until gunpowder and muskets and pistols came along."

"Mel would like to ride a horse and carry a lance," Terri said.

"Carry a woman's scarf with you everywhere," Laura said.

"Or just a woman," Mel said.

"Shame on you," Laura said.

Terri said, "Suppose you came back as a serf. The serfs didn't have it so good in those days," Terri said.

"The serfs never had it good," Mel said. "But I guess even the knights were vessels to someone. Isn't that the way it worked? But then everyone is always a vessel to someone. Isn't that right? Terri? But what I liked about knights, besides their ladies, was that they had that suit of armor, you know, and they couldn't get hurt very easy. No cars in those days, you know? No drunk teenagers to tear into your ass."

"Vassals," Terri said.

"What?" Mel said.

"Vassals," Terri said. "They were called vassals, not vessels."

"Vassals, vessels," Mel said, "what the fuck's the difference? You knew what I meant anyway. All right," Mel said. "So I'm not educated. I learned my stuff. I'm a heart surgeon, sure, but I'm just a mechanic. I go in and I fuck around and I fix things. Shit," Mel said.

"Modesty doesn't become you," Terri said.

"He's just a humble sawbones," I said. "But sometimes they suffocated in all that armor, Mel. They'd even have heart attacks if it got too hot and they were too tired and worn out. I read somewhere that they'd fall off their horses and not be able to get up because they were too tired to stand with all that armor on them. They got trampled by their own horses sometimes."

"That's terrible," Mel said. "That's a terrible thing, Nicky. I guess they'd just lay there and wait until somebody came along and made a shish kebab out of them."

"Some other vessel," Terri said.

"That's right," Mel said. "Some vassal would come along and spear the bastard in the name of love. Or whatever the fuck it was they fought over in those days."

"Same things we fight over these days," Terri said.

Laura said, "Nothing's changed."

The color was still high in Laura's cheeks. Her eyes were bright. She brought her glass to her lips.

Mel poured himself another drink. He looked at the label closely as if studying a long row of numbers. Then he slowly put the bottle down on the table and slowly reached for the tonic water.

"What about the old couple?" Laura said. "You didn't finish that story you started."

Laura was having a hard time lighting her cigarette. Her matches kept going out.

The sunshine inside the room was different now, changing, getting thinner. But the leaves outside the window were still shimmering, and I stared at the pattern they made on the panes and on the Formica counter. They weren't the same patterns, of course.

"What about the old couple?" I said.

"Older but wiser," Terri said.

Mel stared at her.

Terri said, "Go on with your story, hon. I was only kidding. Then what happened?"

"Terri, sometimes," Mel said.

"Please, Mel," Terri said. "Don't always be so serious, sweetie. Can't you take a joke?"

"Where's the joke?" Mel said.

He held his glass and gazed steadily at his wife.

"What happened?" Laura said.

Mel fastened his eyes on Laura. He said, "Laura, if I didn't have Terri and if I didn't love her so much, and if Nick wasn't my best friend, I'd fall in love with you, I'd carry you off, honey," he said.

"Tell your story," Terri said. "Then we'll go to that new place, okay?"

"Okay," Mel said. "Where was I?" he said. He stared at the table and then he began again.

"I dropped in to see each of them every day, sometimes twice a day if I was up doing other calls anyway. Casts and bandages, head to foot, the both of them. You know, you've seen it in the movies. That's just the way they looked, just like in the movies. Little eye-holes and nose-holes and mouth-holes. And she had to have her legs slung up on top of it. Well, the husband was very depressed for the longest while. Even after he found out that his wife was going to pull through, he was still very depressed. Not about the accident, though. I mean, the accident was one thing, but it wasn't everything. I'd get up to his mouth-hole, you know, and he'd say no, it wasn't the accident exactly but it was because he couldn't see her through his eye-holes. He said that was what was making him feel so bad. Can you imagine? I'm telling you, the man's heart was breaking because he couldn't turn his goddamn head and *see* his goddamn wife."

Mel looked around the table and shook his head at what he was going to say.

"I mean, it was killing the old fart just because he couldn't *look* at the fucking woman."

We all looked at Mel.

"Do you see what I'm saying?" he said.

Maybe we were a little drunk by then. I know it was hard keeping things in focus. The light was draining out of the room, going back through the window where it had come from. Yet nobody made a move to get up from the table to turn on the overhead light.

"Listen," Mel said. "Let's finish this fucking gin. There's about enough left here for one shooter all around. Then let's go eat. Let's go to the new place."

"He's depressed," Terri said. "Mel, why don't you take a pill?"

Mel shook his head. "I've taken everything there is."

"We all need a pill now and then," I said.

"Some people are born needing them," Terri said.

She was using her finger to rub at something on the table. Then she stopped rubbing.

"I think I want to call my kids," Mel said. "Is that all right with everybody? I'll call my kids," he said.

Terri said, "What if Marjorie answers the phone? You guys, you've heard us on the subject of Marjorie? Honey, you know you don't want to talk to Marjorie. It'll make you feel even worse."

"I don't want to talk to Marjorie," Mel said. "But I want to talk to my kids."

"There isn't a day goes by that Mel doesn't say he wishes she'd get married again. Or else die," Terri said. "For one thing," Terri said, "she's bankrupting us. Mel says it's just to spite him that she won't get married again. She has a boyfriend who lives with her and the kids, so Mel is supporting the boyfriend too."

"She's allergic to bees," Mel said. "If I'm not praying she'll get married again, I'm praying she'll get herself stung to death by a swarm of fucking bees."

"Shame on you," Laura said.

"Bzzzzzzz," Mel said, turning his fingers into bees and buzzing them at Terri's throat. Then he let his hands drop all the way to his sides.

"She's vicious," Mel said. "Sometimes I think I'll go up there dressed like a beekeeper. You know, that hat that's like a helmet with the plate that comes down over your face, the big gloves, and the padded coat? I'll knock on the door and let loose a hive of bees in the house. But first I'd make sure the kids were out, of course."

He crossed one leg over the other. It seemed to take him a lot of time to do it. Then he put both feet on the floor and leaned forward, elbows on the table, his chin cupped in his hands.

"Maybe I won't call the kids, after all. Maybe it isn't such a hot idea. Maybe we'll just go eat. How does that sound?"

"Sounds fine to me," I said. "Eat or not eat. Or keep drinking. I could head right on out into the sunset."

"What does that mean, honey?" Laura said.

"It just means what I said," I said. "It means I could just keep going. That's all it means."

"I could eat something myself," Laura said. "I don't think I've ever been so hungry in my life. Is there something to nibble on?"

"I'll put out some cheese and crackers," Terri said.

But Terri just sat there. She did not get up to get anything.

Mel turned his glass over. He spilled it out on the table.

"Gin's gone," Mel said.

Terri said, "Now what?"

I could hear my heart beating. I could hear everyone's heart. I could hear the human noise we sat there making, not one of us moving, not even when the room went dark.   [1981]

WILLA CATHER (1873–1947) *once wrote that "a creative writer can do his best only with what lies within the range and character of his deepest sympathies." She was thirty-nine before she found her true subject. The oldest of seven children, Cather was raised in a loving home, but she hated the frontier prairie village of Red Cloud, Nebraska, where her family finally settled after leaving Virginia. She went to a preparatory school in Lincoln and continued at the University of Nebraska, studying classics. After her graduation in 1895, she moved to Pittsburgh, where she worked as a journalist for seven years before teaching English and Latin in high schools. At this time her stories and poems began to appear in popular magazines. Her first book was a volume of poetry,* April Twilights *(1903), followed in 1905 by* The Troll Gardens, *the first of four collections of short stories.*

The most important influence on Cather's work was Sarah Orne Jewett, who taught her that beautiful writing is a consequence of steady concentration on a thoroughly understood subject. Cather met Jewett in Boston, and Jewett urged her to develop her talent, advising her to "find your own quiet center of life and write to the human heart, the great consciousness that all humanity goes to make up." It was not until 1912 that Cather found her subject, after a trip home to Red Cloud. When she no longer saw her adolescence on the prairie as deprived and stifling, she was able to feel that her own experience was significant enough to write about. O Pioneers! *(1913), the first of her three novels about immigrant life on the western frontier, was followed in 1915 by* The Song of the Lark *and in 1918 by* My Ántonia, *a portrait of a pioneer woman that is generally regarded as her masterpiece.*

Cather went on to publish a total of twelve novels and several collections of stories, many about artists, but she did not value her forty-four stories as highly as her novels, including only three of them in the definitive "Library Edition" that represents her final judgment of her work. She wrote "Paul's Case" (1905), a story about a sensitive boy who hungers for art and feels oppressed by everyday life, while she was still a high school teacher in Pittsburgh. Many critics have commented on the purity of Cather's prose style. Her early study of classical languages and her admiration of Flaubert helped form her attitudes toward rigorous control in her realistic fiction, but she later realized that as a young writer she had been inhibited by her awe of great writers: "Life began for me when I ceased to admire and began to remember." Cather was also a perceptive literary critic. She published a collection of essays, On Writing *(1949), in which she analyzed the subtle magic of the storyteller's art: "Whatever is felt on the page without being specifically named there — that, one might say, is created."*

RELATED COMMENTARY: *Willa Cather, "The Stories of Katherine Mansfield,"* page 1398.

WILLA CATHER

Paul's Case

It was Paul's afternoon to appear before the faculty of the Pittsburgh High School to account for his various misdemeanors. He had been suspended a week ago, and his father had called at the Principal's office and confessed his perplexity about his son. Paul entered the faculty room suave and smiling. His clothes were a trifle outgrown and the tan velvet on the collar of his open overcoat was frayed and worn; but for all that there was something of the dandy about him, and he wore an opal pin in his neatly knotted black four-in-hand, and a red carnation in his buttonhole. This latter adornment the faculty somehow felt was not properly significant of the contrite spirit befitting a boy under the ban of suspension.

Paul was tall for his age and very thin, with high, cramped shoulders and a narrow chest. His eyes were remarkable for a certain hysterical brilliancy and he continually used them in a conscious, theatrical sort of way, peculiarly offensive in a boy. The pupils were abnormally large, as though he were addicted to belladonna, but there was a glassy glitter about them which that drug does not produce.

When questioned by the Principal as to why he was there, Paul stated, politely enough, that he wanted to come back to school. This was a lie, but Paul was quite accustomed to lying; found it, indeed, indispensable for overcoming friction. His teachers were asked to state their respective charges against him, which they did with such a rancor and aggrievedness as evinced that this was not a usual case. Disorder and impertinence were among the offenses named, yet each of his instructors felt that it was scarcely possible to put into words the real cause of the trouble, which lay in a sort of hysterically defiant manner of the boy's; in the contempt which they all knew he felt for them, and which he seemingly made not the least effort to conceal. Once, when he had been making a synopsis of a paragraph at the blackboard, his English teacher had stepped to his side and attempted to guide his hand. Paul had started back with a shudder and thrust his hands violently behind him. The astonished woman could scarcely have been more hurt and embarrassed had he struck at her. The insult was so involuntary and definitely personal as to be unforgettable. In one way and another, he had made all his teachers, men and women alike, conscious of the same feeling of physical aversion. In one class he habitually sat with his hand shading his eyes; in another he always looked out of the window during the recitation; in another he made a running commentary on the lecture, with humorous intention.

His teachers felt this afternoon that his whole attitude was symbolized by his shrug and his flippantly red carnation flower, and they fell upon him without mercy, his English teacher leading the pack. He stood through it smiling, his pale lips parted over his white teeth. (His lips were continually twitching, and he had a habit of raising his eyebrows that was contemptuous and irritating to the last degree.) Older boys than Paul had broken down and shed tears under that baptism of fire, but his set smile did not once desert him, and his only sign of discomfort was the nervous trembling of the fingers that toyed with the buttons of his overcoat, and an occasional jerking of the other hand that held his hat. Paul was always smiling, always glancing about him, seeming to feel that people might be watching him and trying to detect something. This conscious expression, since it was as far as possible from boyish mirthfulness, was usually attributed to insolence or "smartness."

As the inquisition proceeded, one of his instructors repeated an impertinent remark of the boy's, and the Principal asked him whether he thought that a courteous speech to make to a woman. Paul shrugged his shoulders slightly and his eyebrows twitched.

"I don't know," he replied. "I didn't mean to be polite or impolite, either. I guess it's a sort of way I have of saying things regardless."

The Principal, who was a sympathetic man, asked him whether he didn't think that a way it would be well to get rid of. Paul grinned and said he guessed so. When he was told that he could go, he bowed gracefully and went out. His bow was but a repetition of the scandalous red carnation.

His teachers were in despair, and his drawing master voiced the feeling of them all when he declared there was something about the boy which none of them understood. He added: "I don't really believe that smile of his comes altogether from insolence; there's something sort of haunted about it. The boy is not strong, for one thing. I happen to know that he was born in Colorado, only a few months before his mother died out there of a long illness. There is something wrong about the fellow."

The drawing master had come to realize that, in looking at Paul, one saw only his white teeth and the forced animation of his eyes. One warm afternoon the boy had gone to sleep at his drawing-board, and his master had noted with amazement what a white, blue-veined face it was; drawn and wrinkled like an old man's about the eyes, the lips twitching even in his sleep, and stiff with a nervous tension that drew them back from his teeth.

His teachers left the building dissatisfied and unhappy; humiliated to have felt so vindictive toward a mere boy, to have uttered this feeling in cutting terms, and to have set each other on, as it were, in the gruesome game of intemperate reproach. Some of them remembered having seen a miserable street cat set at bay by a ring of tormentors.

As for Paul, he ran down the hill whistling the Soldiers' Chorus from *Faust*, looking wildly behind him now and then to see whether some of his teachers were not there to writhe under this light-heartedness. As it was now late in the afternoon and Paul was on duty that evening as usher at Carnegie Hall, he decided that he would not go home to supper. When he reached the concert hall the doors were not yet open and, as it was chilly outside, he decided to go up into the picture gallery — always deserted at this hour — where there were some of Raffelli's gay studies of Paris streets and an airy blue Venetian scene or two that always exhilarated him. He was delighted to find no one in the gallery but the old guard, who sat in one corner, a newspaper on his knee, a black patch over one eye and the other closed. Paul possessed himself of the place and walked confidently up and down, whistling under his breath. After a while he sat down before a blue Rico and lost himself. When he bethought him to look at his watch, it was after seven o'clock, and he rose with a start and ran downstairs, making a face at Augustus, peering out from the cast-room, and an evil gesture at the Venus of Milo as he passed her on the stairway.

When Paul reached the ushers' dressing-room half-a-dozen boys were there already, and he began excitedly to tumble into his uniform. It was one of the few that at all approached fitting, and Paul thought it very becoming — though he knew that the tight, straight coat accentuated his narrow chest, about which he was exceedingly sensitive. He was always considerably excited while he dressed, twanging all over to the tuning of the strings and the preliminary flourishes of the horns in the music-room; but tonight he seemed quite beside himself, and he teased and plagued the boys until, telling him that he was crazy, they put him down on the floor and sat on him.

Somewhat calmed by his suppression, Paul dashed out to the front of the house to seat the early comers. He was a model usher; gracious and smiling he ran up and down the aisles; nothing was too much trouble for him; he carried messages and brought programmes as though it were his greatest pleasure in life, and all the people in his section thought him a charming boy, feeling that he remembered and admired them. As the house filled, he grew more and more vivacious and animated, and the color came to his cheeks and lips. It was very much as though this were a great reception and Paul were the host. Just as the musicians came out to take their places, his English teacher arrived with checks for the seats which a prominent manufacturer had taken for the season. She betrayed some embarrassment when she handed Paul the tickets, and a *hauteur* which subsequently made her feel very foolish. Paul was startled for a moment, and had the feeling of wanting to put her out; what business had she here among all these fine people and gay colors? He looked her over and decided that she was not appropriately dressed and must be a fool to sit downstairs in such togs. The tickets had probably been sent her out of kindness, he reflected as he put down a seat for her, and she had about as much right to sit there as he had.

When the symphony began Paul sank into one of the rear seats with a long sigh of relief, and lost himself as he had done before the Rico. It was not that symphonies, as such, meant anything in particular to Paul, but the first sigh of the instruments seemed to free some hilarious and potent spirit within him; something that struggled there like the Genius in the bottle found by the Arab fisherman. He felt a sudden zest of life; the lights danced before his eyes and the concert hall blazed into unimaginable splendor. When the soprano soloist came on, Paul forgot even the nastiness of his teacher's being there and gave himself up to the peculiar stimulus such personages always had for him. The soloist chanced to be a German woman, by no means in her first youth, and the mother of many children; but she wore an elaborate gown and a tiara, and above all she had that indefinable air of achievement, that world-shine upon her, which, in Paul's eyes, made her a veritable queen of Romance.

After a concert was over Paul was always irritable and wretched until he got to sleep, and tonight he was even more than usually restless. He had the feeling of not being able to let down, of its being impossible to give up this delicious excitement which was the only thing that could be called living at all. During the last number he withdrew and, after hastily changing his clothes in the dressing-room, slipped out to the side door where the soprano's carriage stood. Here he began pacing rapidly up and down the walk, waiting to see her come out.

Over yonder the Schenley, in its vacant stretch, loomed big and square through the fine rain, the windows of its twelve stories glowing like those of a lighted cardboard house under a Christmas tree. All the actors and singers of the better class stayed there when they were in the city, and a number of the big manufacturers of the place lived there in the winter. Paul had often hung about the hotel, watching the people go in and out, longing to enter and leave school-masters and dull care behind him forever.

At last the singer came out, accompanied by the conductor, who helped her into her carriage and closed the door with a cordial *auf wiedersehen* which set Paul to wondering whether she were not an old sweetheart of his. Paul followed the carriage over to the hotel, walking so rapidly as not to be far from the entrance when the singer alighted and disappeared behind the swinging glass doors that were opened by a negro in a tall hat and a long coat. In the moment that the door was ajar it seemed to Paul that he, too, entered. He seemed to feel himself go after her up the steps, into the warm, lighted building, into an exotic, a tropical world of shiny, glistening surfaces and basking ease. He reflected upon the mysterious dishes that were brought into the dining-room, the green bottles in buckets of ice, as he had seen them in the supper party pictures of the *Sunday World* supplement. A quick gust of wind brought the rain down with sudden vehemence, and Paul was startled to find that he was still outside in the slush of the gravel driveway; that his boots were letting in the water and his scanty overcoat was clinging wet about him; that the lights in front of the concert hall were out, and that the rain was driving in sheets between him and the orange glow of the windows above him. There it was, what he wanted — tangibly before him, like the fairy world of a Christmas pantomime, but mocking spirits stood guard at the doors, and, as the rain beat in his face, Paul wondered whether he were destined always to shiver in the black night outside, looking up at it.

He turned and walked reluctantly toward the car tracks. The end had to come sometime; his father in his night-clothes at the top of the stairs, explanations that did not explain, hastily improvised fictions that were for-ever tripping him up, his upstairs room and its horrible yellow wall-paper, the creaking bureau with the greasy plush collar-box, and over his painted wooden bed the pictures of George Washington and John Calvin, and the framed motto, "Feed my Lambs," which had been worked in red worsted by his mother.

Half an hour later, Paul alighted from his car and went slowly down one of the side streets off the main thoroughfare. It was a highly respectable street, where all the houses were exactly alike, and where businessmen of moderate means begot and reared large families of children, all of whom went to Sabbath-school and learned the shorter catechism, and were interested in arithmetic; all of whom were as exactly alike as their homes, and of a piece of the monotony in which they lived. Paul never went up Cordelia Street without a shudder of loathing. His home was next to the house of the Cumberland minister. He approached it tonight with the nerveless sense of defeat, the hopeless feeling of sinking back forever into ugliness and commonness that he had always had when he came home. The moment he turned into Cordelia Street he felt the waters close above his head. After each of these orgies of living, he experienced all the physical depression which follows a debauch; the loathing of respectable beds, of common food, of a house penetrated by kitchen odors; a shuddering repulsion for the flavorless, colorless mass of every-day existence; a morbid desire for cool things and soft lights and fresh flowers.

The nearer he approached the house, the more absolutely unequal Paul felt to the sight of it all; his ugly sleeping chamber; the cold bathroom with the grimy zinc tub, the cracked mirror, the dripping spiggots; his father, at the top of the stairs, his hairy legs sticking out from his night-shirt, his feet thrust into carpet slippers. He was so much later than usual that there would certainly be inquiries and reproaches. Paul stopped short before the door. He felt that he could not be accosted by his father tonight; that he could not toss again on that miserable bed. He would not go in. He would tell his father that he had no car fare, and it was raining so hard he had gone home with one of the boys and stayed all night.

Meanwhile, he was wet and cold. He went around to the back of the house and tried one of the basement windows, found it open, raised it cautiously, and scrambled down the cellar wall to the floor. There he stood, holding his breath, terrified by the noise he had made, but the floor above him was silent, and there was no creak on the stairs. He found a soap-box, and carried it over to the soft ring of light that streamed from the furnace door, and sat down. He was horribly afraid of rats, so he did not try to sleep, but sat looking distrustfully at the dark, still terrified lest he might have awakened his father. In such reactions, after one of the experiences which made days and nights out of the dreary blanks of the calendar, when his senses were deadened, Paul's head was always singularly clear. Suppose his father had heard him getting in at the window and had come down and shot him for a burglar? Then, again, suppose his father had come down, pistol in hand, and he had cried out in time to save himself, and his father had been horrified to think how nearly he had killed him? Then, again, suppose a day should come when his father would remember that night, and wish there had been no warning cry to stay his hand? With this last supposition Paul entertained himself until daybreak.

The following Sunday was fine; the sodden November chill was broken by the last flash of autumnal summer. In the morning Paul had to go to church and Sabbath-school, as always. On seasonable Sunday afternoons the burghers of Cordelia Street always sat out on their front "stoops," and talked to their neighbors on the next stoop, or called to those across the street in neighborly fashion. The men usually sat on gay cushions placed upon the steps that led down to the sidewalk, while the women, in their Sunday "waists," sat in rockers on the cramped porches, pretending to be greatly at their ease. The children played in the streets; there were so many of them that the place resembled the recreation grounds of a kindergarten. The men on the steps — all in their shirt sleeves, their vests unbuttoned — sat with their legs well apart, their stomachs comfortably protruding, and talked of the prices of things, or told anecdotes of the sagacity of their various chiefs and overlords. They occasionally looked over the multitude of squabbling children, listened affectionately to their high-pitched, nasal voices, smiling to see their own proclivities reproduced in their offspring, and interspersed their legends of the iron kings with remarks about their sons' progress at school, their grades in arithmetic, and the amounts they had saved in their toy banks.

On this last Sunday of November, Paul sat all the afternoon on the lowest step of his "stoop," staring into the street, while his sisters, in their rockers, were talking to the minister's daughters next door about how many shirt-waists they had made in the last week, and how many waffles some one had eaten at the last church supper. When the weather was warm, and his father was in a particularly jovial frame of mind, the girls made lemonade, which was always brought out in a red-glass pitcher, ornamented with for-get-me-nots in blue enamel. This the girls thought very fine, and the neighbors always joked about the suspicious color of the pitcher.

Today Paul's father sat on the top step, talking to a young man who shifted a restless baby from knee to knee. He happened to be the young man who was daily held up to Paul as a model, and after whom it was his father's dearest hope that he would pattern. This young man was of a ruddy complexion, with a compressed, red mouth, and faded, near-sighted eyes, over which he wore thick spectacles, with gold bows that curved about his ears. He was clerk to one of the magnates of a great steel corporation, and was looked upon in Cordelia Street as a young man with a future. There was a story that, some five years ago — he was now barely twenty-six — he had been a trifle dissipated but in order to curb his appetites and save the loss of time and strength that a sowing of wild oats might have entailed, he had taken his chief's advice, oft reiterated to his employees, and at twenty-one had married the first woman whom he could persuade to share his fortunes. She happened to be an angular school-mistress, much older than he, who also wore thick glasses, and who had now borne him four children, all near-sighted, like herself.

The young man was relating how his chief, now cruising in the Mediterranean, kept in touch with all the details of the business, arranging his office hours on his yacht just as though he were at home, and "knocking off work enough to keep two stenographers busy." His father told, in turn, the plan his corporation was considering, of putting in an electric railway plant at Cairo. Paul snapped his teeth; he had an awful apprehension that they might spoil it all before he got there. Yet he rather liked to hear these legends of the iron kings, that were told and retold on Sundays and holidays; these stories of palaces in Venice, yachts on the Mediterranean, and high play at

Monte Carlo appealed to his fancy, and he was interested in the triumphs of these cash boys who had become famous, though he had no mind for the cash-boy stage.

After supper was over, and he had helped to dry the dishes, Paul nervously asked his father whether he could go to George's to get some help in his geometry, and still more nervously asked for car fare. This latter request he had to repeat, as his father, on principle, did not like to hear requests for money, whether much or little. He asked Paul whether he could not go to some boy who lived nearer, and told him that he ought not to leave his school work until Sunday; but he gave him the dime. He was not a poor man, but he had a worthy ambition to come up in the world. His only reason for allowing Paul to usher was, that he thought a boy ought to be earning a little.

Paul bounded upstairs, scrubbed the greasy odor of the dish-water from his hands with the ill-smelling soap he hated, and then shook over his fingers a few drops of violet water from the bottle he kept hidden in his drawer. He left the house with his geometry conspicuously under his arm, and the moment he got out of Cordelia Street and boarded a downtown car, he shook off the lethargy of two deadening days, and began to live again.

The leading juvenile of the permanent stock company which played at one of the downtown theatres was an acquaintance of Paul's, and the boy had been invited to drop in at the Sunday-night rehearsals whenever he could. For more than a year Paul had spent every available moment loitering about Charley Edward's dressing-room. He had won a place among Edward's following not only because the young actor, who could not afford to employ a dresser, often found him useful, but because he recognized in Paul something akin to what churchmen term "vocation."

It was at the theatre and at Carnegie Hall that Paul really lived; the rest was but a sleep and a forgetting. This was Paul's fairy tale, and it had for him all the allurement of a secret love. The moment he inhaled the gassy, painty, dusty odor behind the scenes, he breathed like a prisoner set free, and felt within him the possibility of doing or saying splendid, brilliant, poetic things. The moment the cracked orchestra beat out the overture from *Martha*, or jerked at the serenade from *Rigoletto*, all stupid and ugly things slid from him, and his senses were deliciously, yet delicately fired.

Perhaps it was because, in Paul's world, the natural nearly always wore the guise of ugliness, that a certain element of artificiality seemed to him necessary in beauty. Perhaps it was because his experience of life elsewhere was so full of Sabbath-school picnics, petty economies, wholesome advice as to how to succeed in life, and the unescapable odors of cooking, that he found this existence so alluring, these smartly-clad men and women so attractive, that he was so moved by these starry apple orchards that bloomed perennially under the lime-light.

It would be difficult to put it strongly enough how convincingly the stage entrance of that theatre was for Paul the actual portal of Romance. Certainly none of the company ever suspected it, least of all Charley Edwards. It was very like the old stories that used to float about London of fabulously rich Jews, who had subterranean halls there, with palms, and fountains, and soft lamps and richly apparelled women who never saw the disenchanting light of London day. So, in the midst of that smoke-palled city, enamored of figures and grimy toil, Paul had his secret temple, his wishing carpet, his bit of blue-and-white Mediterranean shore bathed in perpetual sunshine.

Several of Paul's teachers had a theory that his imagination had been perverted by garish fiction, but the truth was that he scarcely ever read at all. The books at home were not such as would either tempt or corrupt a youthful mind, and as for reading the novels that some of his friends urged upon him — well, he got what he wanted much more quickly from music; any sort of music, from an orchestra to a barrel organ. He needed only the spark, the indescribable thrill that made his imagination master of his senses, and he could make plots and pictures enough of his own. It was equally true that he was not stage struck — not, at any rate, in the usual acceptation of that expression. He had no desire to become an actor, any more than he had to become a musician. He felt no necessity to do any of these things; what he wanted was to see, to be in the atmosphere, float on the wave of it, to be carried out, blue league after blue league, away from everything.

After a night behind the scenes, Paul found the school-room more than ever repulsive; the bare floors and naked walls; the prosy men who never wore frock coats, or violets in their buttonholes; the women with their dull gowns, shrill voices, and pitiful seriousness about prepositions that govern the dative. He could not bear to have the other pupils think, for a moment, that he took these people seriously; he must convey to them that he considered it all trivial, and was there only by way of a jest, anyway. He had autographed pictures of all the members of the stock company which he showed his classmates, telling them the most incredible stories of his familiarity with these people, of his acquaintance with the soloists who came to Carnegie Hall, his suppers with them and the flowers he sent them. When these stories lost their effect, and his audience grew listless, he became desperate and would bid all the boys good-bye, announcing that he was going to travel for a while; going to Naples, to Venice, to Egypt. Then, next Monday, he would slip back, conscious and nervously smiling; his sister was ill, and he should have to defer his voyage until spring.

Matters went steadily worse with Paul at school. In the itch to let his instructors know how heartily he despised them and their homilies, and how thoroughly he was appreciated elsewhere, he mentioned once or twice that he had no time to fool with theorems; adding — with a twitch of the eyebrows and a touch of that nervous bravado which so perplexed them — that he was helping the people down at the stock company; they were old friends of his.

The upshot of the matter was that the Principal went to Paul's father, and Paul was taken out of school and put to work. The manager at Carnegie Hall was told to get another usher in his stead; the door-keeper at the theatre was warned not to admit him to the house; and Charley Edwards remorsefully promised the boy's father not to see him again.

The members of the stock company were vastly amused when some of Paul's stories reached them — especially the women. They were hard-working women, most of them supporting indigent husbands or brothers, and they laughed rather bitterly at having stirred the boy to such fervid and florid inventions. They agreed with the faculty and with his father that Paul's was a bad case.

The east-bound train was ploughing through a January snow-storm; the dull dawn was beginning to show grey when the engine whistled a mile out of Newark. Paul started up from the seat where he had lain curled in uneasy slumber, rubbed the breath-misted window glass with his hand, and peered out. The snow was whirling in curling eddies above the white bottom lands, and the drifts lay already deep in the fields and along the fences, while here and there the long dead grass and dried weed stalks protruded black above it. Lights shone from the scattered houses, and a gang of laborers who stood beside the track waved their lanterns.

Paul had slept very little, and he felt grimy and uncomfortable. He had made the all-night journey in a day coach, partly because he was ashamed, dressed as he was, to go into a Pullman, and partly because he was afraid of being seen there by some Pittsburgh businessman, who might have noticed him in Denny & Carson's office. When the whistle awoke him, he clutched quickly at his breast pocket, glancing about him with an uncertain smile. But the little, clay-bespattered Italians were still sleeping, the slatternly women across the aisle were in open-mouthed oblivion, and even the crumby, crying babies were for the nonce stilled. Paul settled back to struggle with his impatience as best he could.

When he arrived at the Jersey City station, he hurried through his breakfast, manifestly ill at ease and keeping a sharp eye about him. After he reached the Twenty-third Street station, he consulted a cabman, and had himself driven to a men's furnishing establishment that was just opening for the day. He spent upward of two hours there, buying with endless reconsidering and great care. His new street suit he put on in the fitting-room; the frock coat and dress clothes he had bundled into the cab with his linen. Then he drove to a hatter's and a shoe house. His next errand was at Tiffany's, where he selected his silver and a new scarf-pin. He would not wait to have his silver marked, he said. Lastly, he stopped at a trunk shop on Broadway, and had his purchases packed into various travelling bags.

It was a little after one o'clock when he drove up to the Waldorf, and after settling with the cabman, went into the office. He registered from Washington; said his mother and father had been abroad, and that he had come down to await the arrival of their steamer. He told his story plausibly and had no trouble, since he volunteered to pay for them in advance, in engaging his rooms; a sleeping-room, sitting-room, and bath.

Not once, but a hundred times Paul had planned this entry into New York. He had gone over every detail of it with Charley Edwards, and in his scrap book at home there were pages of description about New York hotels, cut from the Sunday papers. When he was shown to his sitting-room on the eighth floor, he saw at a glance that everything was as it should be; there was but one detail in his mental picture that the place did not realize, so he rang for the bell boy and sent him down for flowers. He moved about nervously until the boy returned, putting away his new linen and fingering it delight-edly as he did so. When the flowers came, he put them hastily into water, and then tumbled into a hot bath. Presently he came out of his white bath-room, resplendent in his new silk underwear, and playing with the tassels of his red robe. The snow was whirling so fiercely outside his windows that he could scarcely see across the street, but within the air was deliciously soft and fragrant. He put the violets and jonquils on the taboret beside the couch, and threw himself down, with a long sigh, covering himself with a Roman blanket. He was thoroughly tired; he had been in such haste, he had stood up to such a strain, covered so much ground in the last twenty-four hours, that he wanted to think how it had all come about. Lulled by the sound of the wind, the warm air, and the cool fragrance of the flowers, he sank into deep, drowsy retrospection.

It had been wonderfully simple; when they had shut him out of the theatre and concert hall, when they had taken away his bone, the whole thing was virtually determined. The rest was a mere matter of opportunity. The only thing that at all surprised him was his own courage — for he realized well enough that he had always been tormented by fear, a sort of apprehen-sive dread that, of late years, as the meshes of the lies he had told closed about him, had been pulling the muscles of his body tighter and tighter. Until now, he could not remember the time when he had not been dreading something. Even when he was a little boy, it was always there — behind him, or before, or on either side. There had always been the shadowed corner, the dark place into which he dared not look, but from which something seemed always to be watching him — and Paul had done things that were not pretty to watch, he knew.

But now he had a curious sense of relief, as though he had at last thrown down the gauntlet to the thing in the corner.

Yet it was but a day since he had been sulking in the traces; but yesterday afternoon that he had been sent to the bank with Denny & Carson's deposit, as usual — but this time he was instructed to leave the book to be balanced. There was above two thousand dollars in checks, and nearly a thousand in the bank notes which he had taken from the book and quietly transferred to his pocket. At the bank he had made out a new deposit slip. His nerves had been steady enough to permit of his returning to the office, where he had finished his work and asked for a full day's holiday tomorrow, Saturday, giving a perfectly reasonable pretext. The bank book, he knew, would not be returned before Monday or Tuesday, and his father would be out of town for the next week. From the time he slipped the bank notes into his pocket until he boarded the night train for New York, he had not known a moment's hesitation. It was not the first time Paul had steered through treacherous waters.

How astonishingly easy it had all been; here he was, the thing done; and this time there would be no awakening, no figure at the top of the stairs. He watched the snow flakes whirling by his window until he fell asleep.

When he awoke, it was three o'clock in the afternoon. He bounded up with a start; half of one of his precious days gone already! He spent more than an hour in dressing, watching every stage of his toilet carefully in the mirror. Everything was quite perfect; he was exactly the kind of boy he had always wanted to be.

When he went downstairs, Paul took a carriage and drove up Fifth Avenue toward the Park. The snow had somewhat abated; carriages and tradesmen's wagons were hurrying soundlessly to and fro in the winter twilight; boys in woollen mufflers were shovelling off the doorsteps; the avenue stages made fine spots of color against the white street. Here and there on the corners were stands, with whole flower gardens blooming under glass cases, against the sides of which the snow flakes stuck and melted; violets, roses, carnations, lilies of the valley — somewhat vastly more lovely and alluring that they blossomed thus unnaturally in the snow. The Park itself was a wonderful stage winterpiece.

When he returned, the pause of the twilight had ceased, and the tune of the streets had changed. The snow was falling faster, lights streamed from the hotels that reared their dozen stories fearlessly up into the storm, defying the raging Atlantic winds. A long, black stream of carriages poured down the avenue, intersected here and there by other streams, tending horizontally. There were a score of cabs about the entrance of his hotel, and his driver had to wait. Boys in livery were running in and out of the awning stretched across the sidewalk, up and down the red velvet carpet laid from the door to the street. Above, about, within it all was the rumble and roar, the hurry and toss of thousands of human beings as hot for pleasure as himself, and on every side of him towered the glaring affirmation of the omnipotence of wealth.

The boy set his teeth and drew his shoulders together in a spasm of realization: the plot of all dramas, the text of all romances, the nerve-stuff of all sensations was whirling about him like the snow flakes. He burnt like a faggot in a tempest.

When Paul went down to dinner, the music of the orchestra came floating up the elevator shaft to greet him. His head whirled as he stepped into the thronged corridor, and he sank back into one of the chairs against the wall to get his breath. The lights, the chatter, the perfumes, the bewildering medley of color — he had, for a moment, the feeling of not being able to stand it. But only for a moment; these were his own people, he told himself. He went slowly about the corridors, through the writing-rooms, smoking-rooms, reception-rooms, as though he were exploring the chambers of an enchanted palace, built and peopled for him alone.

When he reached the dining-room he sat down at a table near a window. The flowers, the white linen, the many-colored wine glasses, the gay toilettes of the women, the low popping of corks, the undulating repetitions of the *Blue Danube* from the orchestra, all flooded Paul's dream with bewildering radiance. When the roseate tinge of his champagne was added — that cold, precious, bubbling stuff that creamed and foamed in his glass — Paul wondered that there were honest men in the world at all. This was what all the world was fighting for, he reflected; this was what all the struggle was about. He doubted the reality of his past. Had he ever known a place called Cordelia Street, a place where fagged-looking businessmen got on the early car; mere rivets in a machine they seemed to Paul — sickening men, with combings of children's hair always hanging to their coats, and the smell of cooking in their clothes. Cordelia Street — Ah! that belonged to another time and country; had he not always been thus, had he not sat here night after night, from as far back as he could remember, looking pensively over just such shimmering textures, and slowly twirling the stem of a glass like this one between his thumb and middle finger? He rather thought he had.

He was not in the least abashed or lonely. He had no especial desire to meet or to know any of these people; all he demanded was the right to look on and conjecture, to watch the pageant. The mere stage properties were all he contended for. Nor was he lonely later in the evening, in his loge at the Metropolitan. He was now entirely rid of his nervous misgivings, of his forced aggressiveness, of the imperative desire to show himself different from his surroundings. He felt now that his surroundings explained him. Nobody questioned the purple; he had only to wear it passively. He had only to glance down at his attire to reassure himself that here it would be impossible for anyone to humiliate him.

He found it hard to leave his beautiful sitting-room to go to bed that night, and sat long watching the raging storm from his turret window. When he went to sleep it was with the lights turned on in his bedroom; partly because of his old timidity, and partly so that, if he should wake in the night, there would be no wretched moment of doubt, no horrible suspicion of yellow wall-paper, or of Washington or Calvin above his bed.

Sunday morning the city was practically snow-bound. Paul breakfasted late, and in the afternoon he fell in with a wild San Francisco boy, a freshman at Yale, who said he had run down for a "little flyer" over Sunday. The young man offered to show Paul the night side of the town, and the two boys went out together after dinner, not returning to the hotel until seven o'clock the next morning. They had started out in the confiding warmth of a champagne friendship, but their parting in the elevator was singularly cool. The freshman pulled himself together to make his train, and Paul went to bed. He awoke at two o'clock in the afternoon, very thirsty and dizzy, and rang for ice-water, coffee, and the Pittsburgh papers.

On the part of the hotel management, Paul excited no suspicion. There was this to be said for him, that he wore his spoils with dignity and in no way made himself conspicuous. Even under the glow of his wine he was never boisterous, though he found the stuff like a magician's wand for won-der-building. His chief greediness lay in his ears and eyes, and his excesses were not offensive ones. His dearest pleasures were the grey winter twilights in his sitting-room; his quiet enjoyment of his flowers, his clothes, his wide divan, his cigarette, and his sense of power. He could not remember a time when he had felt so at peace with himself. The mere release from the necessity of petty lying, lying every day and every day, restored his self-respect. He had never lied for pleasure, even at school; but to be noticed and admired, to assert his difference from other Cordelia Street boys; and he felt a good deal more manly, more honest, even, now that he had no need for boastful preten-sions, now that he could, as his actor friends used to say, "dress the part." It was characteristic that remorse did not occur to him. His golden days went by without a shadow, and he made each as perfect as he could.

On the eighth day after his arrival in New York, he found the whole affair exploited in the Pittsburgh papers, exploited with a wealth of detail which indicated that local news of a sensational nature was at a low ebb. The firm of Denny & Carson announced that the boy's father had refunded the full amount of the theft, and that they had no intention of prosecuting. The Cumberland minister had been interviewed, and expressed his hope of yet reclaiming the motherless lad, and his Sabbath-school teacher declared that she would spare no effort to that end. The rumor had reached Pittsburgh that the boy had been seen in a New York hotel, and his father had gone East to find him and bring him home.

Paul had just come in to dress for dinner; he sank into a chair, weak to the knees, and clasped his head in his hands. It was to be worse than jail, even; the tepid waters of Cordelia Street were to close over him finally and forever. The grey monotony stretched before him in hopeless, unrelieved years; Sabbath-school, Young People's Meeting, the yellow-papered room, the damp dish-towels; it all rushed back upon him with a sickening vividness. He had the old feeling that the orchestra had suddenly stopped, the sinking sensation that the play was over. The sweat broke out on his face, and he sprang to his feet, looked about him with his white, conscious smile, and winked at himself in the mirror. With something of the old childish belief in miracles with which he had so often gone to class, all his lessons unlearned, Paul dressed and dashed whistling down the corridor to the elevator.

He had no sooner entered the dining-room and caught the measure of the music than his remembrance was lightened by his old elastic power of claiming the moment, mounting with it, and finding it all sufficient. The glare and glitter about him, the mere scenic accessories had again, and for the last time, their old potency. He would show himself that he was game, he would finish the thing splendidly. He doubted, more than ever, the existence of Cordelia Street, and for the first time he drank his wine recklessly. Was he not, after all, one of those fortunate beings born to the purple, was he not still himself and in his own place? He drummed a nervous accompaniment to the Pagliacci music and looked about him, telling himself over and over that it had paid.

He reflected drowsily, to the swell of the music and the chill sweetness of his wine, that he might have done it more wisely. He might have caught an outboard steamer and been well out of their clutches before now. But the other side of the world had seemed too far away and too uncertain then; he could not have waited for it; his need had been too sharp. If he had to choose over again, he would do the same thing tomorrow. He looked affectionately about the dining-room, now gilded with a soft mist. Ah, it had paid indeed!

Paul was awakened next morning by a painful throbbing in his head and feet. He had thrown himself across the bed without undressing, and had slept with his shoes on. His limbs and hands were lead heavy, and his tongue and throat were parched and burnt. There came upon him one of those fateful attacks of clear-headedness that never occurred except when he was physically exhausted and his nerves hung loose. He lay still and closed his eyes and let the tide of things wash over him.

His father was in New York; "stopping at some joint or other," he told himself. The memory of successive summers on the front stoop fell upon him like a weight of black water. He had not a hundred dollars left; and he knew now, more than ever, that money was everything, the wall that stood between all he loathed and all he wanted. The thing was winding itself up; he had thought of that on his first glorious day in New York, and had even provided a way to snap the thread. It lay on his dressing-table now; he had got it out last night when he came blindly up from dinner, but the shiny metal hurt his eyes, and he disliked the looks of it.

He rose and moved about with a painful effort, succumbing now and again to attacks of nausea. It was the old depression exaggerated; all the world had become Cordelia Street. Yet somehow he was not afraid of anything, was absolutely calm; perhaps because he had looked into the dark corner at last and knew. It was bad enough, what he saw there, but somehow not so bad as his long fear of it had been. He saw everything clearly now. He had a feeling that he had made the best of it, that he had lived the sort of life he was meant to live, and for half an hour he sat staring at the revolver. But he told himself that was not the way, so he went downstairs and took a cab to the ferry.

When Paul arrived at Newark, he got off the train and took another cab, directing the driver to follow the Pennsylvania tracks out of the town. The snow lay heavy on the roadways and had drifted deep in the open fields. Only here and there the dead grass or dried weed stalks projected, singularly black, above it. Once well into the country, Paul dismissed the carriage and walked, floundering along the tracks, his mind a medley of irrelevant things. He seemed to hold in his brain an actual picture of everything he had seen that morning. He remembered every feature of both his drivers, of the tooth-less old woman from whom he had bought the red flowers in his coat, the agent from whom he had got his ticket, and all of his fellow-passengers on the ferry. His mind, unable to cope with vital matters near at hand, worked feverishly and deftly at sorting and grouping these images. They made for him a part of the ugliness of the world, of the ache in his head, and the bitter burning on his tongue. He stopped and put a handful of snow into his mouth as he walked, but that, too, seemed hot. When he reached a little hillside, where the tracks ran through a cut some twenty feet below him, he stopped and sat down.

The carnations in his coat were drooping with the cold, he noticed; their red glory all over. It occurred to him that all the flowers he had seen in the glass cases that first night must have gone the same way, long before this. It was only one splendid breath they had, in spite of their brave mockery at the winter outside the glass; and it was a losing game in the end, it seemed, this revolt against the homilies by which the world is run. Paul took one of the blossoms carefully from his coat and scooped a little hole in the snow, where he covered it up. Then he dozed a while, from his weak condition, seemingly insensible to the cold.

The sound of an approaching train awoke him, and he started to his feet, remembering only his resolution, and afraid lest he should be too late. He stood watching the approaching locomotive, his teeth chattering, his lips drawn away from them in a frightened smile; once or twice he glanced nervously sidewise, as though he were being watched. When the right moment came, he jumped. As he fell, the folly of his haste occurred to him with merciless clearness, the vastness of what he had left undone. There flashed through his brain, clearer than ever before, the blue of Adriatic water, the yellow of Algerian sands.

He felt something strike his chest, and that his body was being thrown swiftly through the air, on and on, immeasurably far and fast, while his limbs were gently relaxed. Then, because the picture making mechanism was crushed, the disturbing visions flashed into black, and Paul dropped back into the immense design of things.   [1905]

JOHN CHEEVER *(1912–1982), the leading exponent of the kind of carefully fashioned story of modern suburban manners that* The New Yorker *popularized, has been called by the reviewer John Leonard "the Chekhov of the suburbs." Cheever spent most of his life in New York City and in suburban towns similar to the ones he described in much of his fiction. Born in Quincy, Massachusetts, he was raised by parents who owned a prosperous business that failed after the 1929 stock market crash. His parents enjoyed reading literature to him, so at an early age he was acquainted with the fiction of Charles Dickens, Jack London, and Robert Louis Stevenson. He started his career at an unusually young age. Expelled from Thayer Academy for being, by his own account, a "quarrelsome, intractable . . . and lousy student," he moved to New York City, lived in a cell of a room on a bread-and-buttermilk diet, and wrote stories. When his first one, "Expelled," was accepted for publication by Malcolm Cowley, then editor of the* New Republic, *Cheever was launched as a teenager into a career as a writer of fiction. Earlier Cowley had told him that his stories were too long to get published by magazines that paid, so he made Cheever write a story of not more than a thousand words every day for four days to encourage discipline.*

Cheever's first collection of stories, The Way Some People Live, *appeared in 1942, while he was completing a four-year stint of army duty. In 1953 he strengthened his literary reputation with the book* The Enormous Radio and Other Stories, *a collection of fourteen of his* New Yorker *pieces. Six years later appeared another story collection,* The Housebreaker of Shady Hill. *In the 1960s and 1970s he published three more books of short stories and two widely acclaimed novels,* Bullet Park *(1969) and* Falconer *(1977).* The Stories of John Cheever, *published in 1978, won both the Pulitzer Prize and the National Book Critics Circle Award and became one of the few collections of short stories ever to make the* New York Times *best-seller list. In more than fifty years, Cheever published over 200 magazine stories; he figured that he earned "enough money to feed the family and buy a new suit every other year."*

Usually a rapid writer, Cheever said he liked best the stories that he wrote in less than a week, although he spent months working on "The Swimmer" (1964). He originally wrote a draft of the plot as "a perfectly good" novel, but then he burned it. "I could very easily have sold the book," he said, "but the trick was to get the winter constellations in the midsummer sky without anyone knowing about it, and it didn't take 250 pages to do that."

RELATED COMMENTARY: *John Cheever, "Why I Write Short Stories," page 1403.*

JOHN CHEEVER

The Swimmer

It was one of those midsummer Sundays when everyone sits around saying, "I *drank* too much last night." You might have heard it whispered by the parishioners leaving church, heard it from the lips of the priest himself, struggling with his cassock in the *vestiarium*, heard it from the golf links and the tennis courts, heard it from the wild-life preserve where the leader of the Audubon group was suffering from a terrible hangover. "I *drank* too much," said Donald Westerhazy. "We all *drank* too much," said Lucinda Merrill. "It must have been the wine," said Helen Westerhazy. "I *drank* too much of that claret."

This was the edge of the Westerhazys' pool. The pool, fed by an artesian well with a high iron content, was a pale shade of green. It was a fine day. In the west there was a massive stand of cumulus cloud so like a city seen from a distance — from the bow of an approaching ship — that it might have had a name. Lisbon. Hackensack. The sun was hot. Neddy Merrill sat by the green water, one hand in it, one around a glass of gin. He was a slender man — he seemed to have the especial slenderness of youth — and while he was far from young he had slid down his banister that morning and given the bronze backside of Aphrodite on the hall table a smack, as he jogged toward the smell of coffee in his dining room. He might have been compared to a summer's day, particularly the last hours of one, and while he lacked a tennis racket or a sail bag the impression was definitely one of youth, sport, and clement weather. He had been swimming and now he was breathing deeply, stertorously as if he could gulp into his lungs the components of that moment, the heat of the sun, the intenseness of his pleasure. It all seemed to flow into his chest. His own house stood in Bullet Park, eight miles to the south, where his four beautiful daughters would have had their lunch and might be playing tennis. Then it occurred to him that by taking a dogleg to the southwest he could reach his home by water.

His life was not confining and the delight he took in this observation could not be explained by its suggestion of escape. He seemed to see, with a cartographer's eye, that string of swimming pools, that quasi-subterranean stream that curved across the county. He had made a discovery, a contribution to modern geography; he would name the stream Lucinda after his wife. He was not a practical joker nor was he a fool but he was determinedly original and had a vague and modest idea of himself as a legendary figure. The day was beautiful and it seemed to him that a long swim might enlarge and celebrate its beauty.

He took off a sweater that was hung over his shoulders and dove in. He had an inexplicable contempt for men who did not hurl themselves into pools. He swam a choppy crawl, breathing either with every stroke or every fourth stroke and counting somewhere well in the back of his mind the one-two one-two of a flutter kick. It was not a serviceable stroke for long distances but the domestication of swimming had saddled the sport with some customs and in his part of the world a crawl was customary. To be embraced and sustained by the light green water was less a pleasure, it seemed, than the resumption of a natural condition, and he would have liked to swim without trunks, but this was not possible, considering his project. He hoisted himself up on the far curb — he never used the ladder — and started across the lawn. When Lucinda asked where he was going he said he was going to swim home.

The only maps and charts he had to go by were remembered or imaginary but these were clear enough. First there were the Grahams, the Hammers, the Lears, the Howlands, and the Crosscups. He would cross Ditmar Street to the Bunkers and come, after a short portage, to the Levys, the Welchers, and the public pool in Lancaster. Then there were the Hallorans, the Sachses, the Biswangers, Shirley Adams, the Gilmartins, and the Clydes. The day was lovely, and he lived in a world so generously supplied with water seemed like a clemency, a beneficence. His heart was high and he ran across the grass. Making his way home by an uncommon route gave him the feeling that he was a pilgrim, an explorer, a man with a destiny, and he knew that he would find friends all along the way; friends would line the banks of the Lucinda River.

He went through a hedge that separated the Westerhazys' land from the Grahams', walked under some flowering apple trees, passed the shed that housed their pump and filter, and came out at the Grahams' pool. "Why, Neddy," Mrs. Graham said, "what a marvelous surprise. I've been trying to get you on the phone all morning. Here, let me get you a drink." He saw then, like any explorer, that the hospitable customs and traditions of the natives would have to be handled with diplomacy if he was ever going to reach his destination. He did not want to mystify or seem rude to the Grahams nor did he have the time to linger there. He swam the length of their pool and joined them in the sun and was rescued, a few minutes later, by the arrival of two carloads of friends from Connecticut. During the uproarious reunions he was able to slip away. He went down by the front of the Grahams' house, stepped over a thorny hedge, and crossed a vacant lot to the Hammers'. Mrs. Hammer, looking up from her roses, saw him swim by although she wasn't quite sure who it was. The Lears heard him splashing past the open windows of their living room. The Howlands and the Crosscups were away. After leaving the Howlands' he crossed Ditmar Street and started for the Bunkers', where he could hear, even at that distance, the noise of a party.

The water refracted the sound of voices and laughter and seemed to suspend it in midair. The Bunkers' pool was on a rise and he climbed some stairs to a terrace where twenty-five or thirty men and women were drinking. The only person in the water was Rusty Towers, who floated there on a rubber raft. Oh, how bonny and lush were the banks of the Lucinda River! Prosperous men and women gathered by the sapphire-colored waters while caterer's men in white coats passed them cold gin. Overhead a red de Haviland trainer was circling around and around and around in the sky with something like the glee of a child in a swing. Ned felt a passing affection for the scene, a tenderness for the gathering, as if it was something he might touch. In the distance he heard thunder. As soon as Enid Bunker saw him she began to scream: "Oh, look who's here! What a marvelous surprise! When Lucinda said you couldn't come I thought I'd *die*." She made her way to him through the crowd, and when they had finished kissing she led him to the bar, a progress that was slowed by the fact that he stopped to kiss eight or ten other women and shake the hands of as many men. A smiling bartender he had seen at a hundred parties gave him a gin and tonic and he stood by the bar for a moment, anxious not to get stuck in any conversation that would delay his voyage. When he seemed about to be surrounded he dove in and swam close to the side to avoid colliding with Rusty's raft. At the far end of the pool he bypassed the Tomlinsons with a broad smile and jogged up the garden path. The gravel cut his feet but this was only unpleasantness. The party was confined to the pool, and as he went toward the house he heard the brilliant, watery sound of voices fade, heard the noise of a radio from the Bunkers' kitchen, where someone was listening to a ball game. Sunday afternoon. He made his way through the parked cars and down the grassy border of their driveway to Alewives Lane. He did not want to be seen on the road in his bathing trunks but there was no traffic and he made the short distance to the Levys' driveway, marked with a PRIVATE PROPERTY sign and a green tube for the *New York Times*. All the doors and windows of the big house were open but there were no signs of life; not even a dog barked. He went around the side of the house to the pool and saw that the Levys had only recently left. Glasses and bottles and dishes of nuts were on a table at the deep end, where there was a bathhouse or gazebo, hung with Japanese lanterns. After swimming the pool he got himself a glass and poured a drink. It was his fourth or fifth drink and he had swum nearly half the length of the Lucinda River. He felt tired, clean, and pleased at that moment to be alone; pleased with everything.

It would storm. The stand of cumulus cloud — that city — had risen and darkened, and while he sat there he heard the percussiveness of thunder again. The de Haviland trainer was still circling overhead and it seemed to Ned that he could almost hear the pilot laugh with pleasure in the afternoon; but when there was another peal of thunder he took off for home. A train whistle blew and he wondered what time it had gotten to be. Four? Five? He thought of the provincial station at that hour, where a waiter, his tuxedo concealed by a raincoat, a dwarf with some flowers wrapped in newspaper, and a woman who had been crying would be waiting for the local. It was suddenly growing dark; it was that moment when the pin-headed birds seemed to organize their song into some acute and knowledgeable recognition of the storm's approach. Then there was a fine noise of rushing water from the crown of an oak at his back, as if a spigot there had been turned. Then the noise of fountains came from the crowns of all the tall trees. Why did he love storms, what was the meaning of his excitement when the door sprang open and the rain wind fled rudely up the stairs, why had the simple task of shutting the windows of an old house seemed fitting and urgent, why did the first watery notes of a storm wind have for him the unmistakable sound of good news, cheer, glad tidings? Then there was an explosion, a smell of cordite, and rain lashed the Japanese lanterns that Mrs. Levy had bought in Kyoto the year before last, or was it the year before that?

He stayed in the Levys' gazebo until the storm had passed. The rain had cooled the air and he shivered. The force of the wind had stripped a maple of its red and yellow leaves and scattered them over the grass and the water. Since it was midsummer the tree must be blighted, and yet he felt a peculiar sadness at this sign of autumn. He braced his shoulders, emptied his glass, and started for the Welchers' pool. This meant crossing the Lindleys' riding ring and he was surprised to find it overgrown with grass and all the jumps dismantled. He wondered if the Lindleys had sold their horses or gone away for the summer and put them out to board. He seemed to remember having heard something about the Lindleys and their horses but the memory was unclear. On he went, barefoot through the wet grass, to the Welchers', where he found their pool was dry.

This breach in his chain of water disappointed him absurdly, and he felt like some explorer who seeks a torrential headwater and finds a dead stream. He was disappointed and mystified. It was common enough to go away for the summer but no one ever drained his pool. The Welchers had definitely gone away. The pool furniture was folded, stacked, and covered with a tarpaulin. The bathhouse was locked. All the windows of the house were shut, and when he went around to the driveway in front he saw a FOR SALE sign nailed to a tree. When had he last heard from the Welchers — when, that is, had he and Lucinda last regretted an invitation to dine with them? It seemed only a week or so ago. Was his memory failing or had he so disciplined it in the repression of unpleasant facts that he had damaged his sense of the truth? Then in the distance he heard the sound of a tennis game. This cheered him, cleared away all his apprehensions and let him regard the overcast sky and the cold air with indifference. This was the day that Neddy Merrill swam across the county. That was the day! He started off then for his most difficult portage.

Had you gone for a Sunday afternoon ride that day you might have seen him, close to naked, standing on the shoulders of Route 424, waiting for a chance to cross. You might have wondered if he was the victim of foul play, had his car broken down, or was he merely a fool. Standing barefoot in the deposits of the highway — beer cans, rags, and blowout patches — exposed to all kinds of ridicule, he seemed pitiful. He had known when he started that this was a part of his journey — it had been on his maps — but confronted with the lines of traffic, worming through the summery light, he found himself unprepared. He was laughed at, jeered at, a beer can was thrown at him, and he had no dignity or humor to bring to the situation. He could have gone back, back to the Westerhazys', where Lucinda would still be sitting in the sun. He had signed nothing, vowed nothing, pledged nothing, not even to himself. Why, believing as he did, that all human obduracy was susceptible to common sense, was he unable to turn back? Why was he determined to complete his journey even if it meant putting his life in danger? At what point had this prank, this joke, this piece of horseplay become serious? He could not go back, he could not even recall with any clearness the green water at the Westerhazys', the sense of inhaling the day's components, the friendly and relaxed voices saying that they had *drunk* too much. In the space of an hour, more or less, he had covered a distance that made his return impossible.

An old man, tooling down the highway at fifteen miles an hour, let him get to the middle of the road, where there was a grass divider. Here he was exposed to the ridicule of the northbound traffic, but after ten or fifteen minutes he was able to cross. From here he had only a short walk to the Recreation Center at the edge of the village of Lancaster, where there were some handball courts and a public pool.

The effect of the water on voices, the illusion of brilliance and suspense, was the same here as it had been at the Bunkers' but the sounds here were louder, harsher, and more shrill, and as soon as he entered the crowded enclosure he was confronted with regimentation. "ALL SWIMMERS MUST TAKE A SHOWER BEFORE USING THE POOL. ALL SWIMMERS MUST USE THE FOOTBATH. ALL SWIMMERS MUST WEAR THEIR IDENTIFICATION DISKS." He took a shower, washed his feet in a cloudy and bitter solution, and made his way to the edge of the water. It stank of chlorine and looked to him like a sink. A pair of lifeguards in a pair of towers blew police whistles at what seemed to be regular intervals and abused the swimmers through a public address system. Neddy remembered the sapphire water at the Bunkers' with longing and thought that he might contaminate himself — damage his own prosperousness and charm — by swimming in this murk, but he reminded himself that he was an explorer, a pilgrim, and that this was merely a stagnant bend in the Lucinda River. He dove, scowling with distaste, into the chlorine and had to swim with his head above water to avoid collisions, but even so he was bumped into, splashed, and jostled. When he got to the shallow end both lifeguards were shouting at him: "Hey, you, you without the identification disk, get outa the water." He did, but they had no way of pursuing him and he went through the reek of suntan oil and chlorine out through the hurricane fence and passed the handball courts. By crossing the road he entered the wooded part of the Halloran estate. The woods were not cleared and the footing was treacherous and difficult until he reached the lawn and the clipped beech hedge that encircled their pool.

The Hallorans were friends, an elderly couple of enormous wealth who seemed to bask in the suspicion that they might be Communists. They were zealous reformers but they were not Communists, and yet when they were accused, as they sometimes were, of subversion, it seemed to gratify and excite them. Their beech hedge was yellow and he guessed this had been blighted like the Levys' maple. He called hullo, hullo, to warn the Hallorans of his approach, to palliate his invasion of their privacy. The Hallorans, for reasons that had never been explained to him, did not wear bathing suits. No explanations were in order, really. Their nakedness was a detail in their uncompromising zeal for reform and he stepped politely out of his trunks before he went through the opening in the hedge.

Mrs. Halloran, a stout woman with white hair and a serene face, was reading the *Times*. Mr. Halloran was taking beech leaves out of the water with a scoop. They seemed not surprised or displeased to see him. Their pool was perhaps the oldest in the country, a fieldstone rectangle, fed by a brook. It had no filter or pump and its waters were the opaque gold of the stream.

"I'm swimming across the county," Ned said.

"Why, I didn't know one could," exclaimed Mrs. Halloran.

"Well, I've made it from the Westerhazys'," Ned said. "That must be about four miles."

He left his trunks at the deep end, walked to the shallow end, and swam this stretch. As he was pulling himself out of the water he heard Mrs. Halloran say, "We've been *terribly* sorry to hear about all your misfortunes, Neddy."

"My misfortunes?" Ned asked. "I don't know what you mean."

"Why we heard that you'd sold the house and that your poor children. . . ."

"I don't recall having sold the house," Ned said, "and the girls are at home."

"Yes," Mrs. Halloran sighed. "Yes. . . ." Her voice filled the air with an unseasonable melancholy and Ned spoke briskly. "Thank you for the swim."

"Well, have a nice trip," said Mrs. Halloran.

Beyond the hedge he pulled on his trunks and fastened them. They were loose and he wondered if, during the space of an afternoon, he could have lost some weight. He was cold and he was tired and the naked Hallorans and their dark water had depressed him. The swim was too much for his strength but how could he have guessed this, sliding down the banister that morning and sitting in the Westerhazys' sun? His arms were lame. His legs felt rubbery and ached at the joints. The worst of it was the cold in his bones and the feeling that he might never be warm again. Leaves were falling down around him and he smelled wood smoke on the wind. Who would be burning wood at this time of the year?

He needed a drink. Whiskey would warm him, pick him up, carry him through the last of his journey, refresh his feeling that it was original and valorous to swim across the county. Channel swimmers took brandy. He needed a stimulant. He crossed the lawn in front of the Hallorans' house and went down a little path to where they had built a house for their only daughter, Helen, and her husband, Eric Sachs. The Sachses' pool was small and he found Helen and her husband there.

"Oh, *Neddy*," Helen said. "Did you lunch at Mother's?"

"Not *really*," Ned said. "I *did* stop to see your parents." This seemed to be explanation enough. "I'm terribly sorry to break in on you like this but I've taken a chill and I wonder if you'd give me a drink."

"Why, I'd *love* to," Helen said, "but there hasn't been anything in this house to drink since Eric's operation. That was three years ago."

Was he losing his memory, had his gift for concealing painful facts let him forget that he had sold his house, that his children were in trouble, and that his friend had been ill? His eyes slipped from Eric's face to his abdomen, where he saw three pale, sutured scars, two of them at least a foot long. Gone was his navel, and what, Neddy thought, would the roving hand, bed-checking one's gifts at 3 A.M., make of a belly with no navel, no link to birth, this breach in the succession?

"I'm sure you can get a drink at the Biswangers'," Helen said. "They're having an enormous do. You can hear it from here. Listen!"

She raised her head and from across the road, the lawns, the gardens, the woods, the fields, he heard again the brilliant noise of voices over water. "Well, I'll get wet," he said, still feeling that he had no freedom of choice about his means of travel. He dove into the Sachses' cold water, and gasping, close to drowning, made his way from one end of the pool to the other. "Lucinda and I want *terribly* to see you," he said over his shoulder, his face set toward the Biswangers'. "We're sorry it's been so long and we'll call you *very* soon."

He crossed some fields to the Biswangers' and the sounds of revelry there. They would be honored to give him a drink, they would be happy to give him a drink. The Biswangers invited him and Lucinda for dinner four times a year, six weeks in advance. They were always rebuffed and yet they continued to send out their invitations, unwilling to comprehend the rigid and undemocratic realities of their society. They were the sort of people who discussed the price of things at cocktails, exchanged market tips during dinner, and after dinner told dirty stories to mixed company. They did not belong to Neddy's set — they were not even on Lucinda's Christmas card list. He went toward their pool with feelings of indifference, charity, and some unease, since it seemed to be getting dark and these were the longest days of the year. The party when he joined it was noisy and large. Grace Biswanger was the kind of hostess who asked the optometrist, the veterinarian, the real-estate dealer, and the dentist. No one was swimming and the twilight, reflected on the water of the pool, had a wintry gleam. There was a bar and he started for this. When Grace Biswanger saw him she came toward him, not affectionately as he had every right to expect, but bellicosely.

"Why, this party has everything," she said loudly, "including a gate crasher."

She could not deal him a social blow — there was no question about this and he did not flinch. "As a gate crasher," he asked politely, "do I rate a drink?"

"Suit yourself," she said. "You don't seem to pay much attention to invitations."

She turned her back on him and joined some guests, and he went to the bar and ordered a whiskey. The bartender served him but he served him rudely. His was a world in which the caterer's men kept the social score, and to be rebuffed by a part-time barkeep meant that he had suffered some loss of social esteem. Or perhaps the man was new and uninformed. Then he heard Grace at his back say: "They went for broke overnight — nothing but income — and he showed up drunk one Sunday and asked us to loan him five thousand dollars. . . ." She was always talking about money. It was worse than eating your peas off a knife. He dove into the pool, swam its length, and went away.

The next pool on his list, the last but two, belonged to his old mistress, Shirley Adams. If he had suffered any injuries at the Biswangers' they would be cured here. Love — sexual roughhouse in fact — was the supreme elixir, the pain killer, the brightly colored pill that would put the spring back into his step, the joy of life in his heart. They had had an affair last week, last month, last year. He couldn't remember. It was he who had broken it off, his was the upper hand, and he stepped through the gate of the wall that surrounded her pool with nothing so considered as self-confidence. It seemed in a way to be his pool, as the lover, particularly the illicit lover, enjoys the possessions of his mistress with an authority unknown to holy matrimony. She was there, her hair the color of brass, but her figure, at the edge of the lighted, cerulean water, excited in him no profound memories. It had been, he thought, a lighthearted affair, although she had wept when he broke it off. She seemed confused to see him and he wondered if she was still wounded. Would she, God forbid, weep again?

"What do you want?" she asked.

"I'm swimming across the county."

"Good Christ. Will you ever grow up?"

"What's the matter?"

"If you've come here for money," she said, "I won't give you another cent."

"You could give me a drink."

"I could but I won't. I'm not alone."

"Well, I'm on my way."

He dove in and swam the pool, but when he tried to haul himself up onto the curb he found that the strength in his arms and shoulders had gone, and he paddled to the ladder and climbed out. Looking over his shoulder he saw, in the lighted bathhouse, a young man. Going out onto the dark lawn he smelled chrysanthemums or marigolds — some stubborn autumnal fragrance — on the night air, strong as gas. Looking overhead he saw that the stars had come out, but why should he seem to see Andromeda, Cepheus, and Cassiopeia? What had become of the constellations of midsummer? He began to cry.

It was probably the first time in his adult life that he had ever cried, certainly the first time in his life that he had ever felt so miserable, cold, tired, and bewildered. He could not understand the rudeness of the caterer's barkeep or the rudeness of a mistress who had come to him on her knees and showered his trousers with tears. He had swum too long, he had been immersed too long, and his nose and his throat were sore from the water. What he needed then was a drink, some company, and some clean, dry clothes, and while he could have cut directly across the road to his home he went on to the Gilmartins' pool. Here, for the first time in his life, he did not dive but went down the steps into the icy water and swam a hobbled sidestroke that he might have learned as a youth. He staggered with fatigue on his way to the Clydes' and paddled the length of their pool, stopping again and again with his hand on the curb to rest. He climbed up the ladder and wondered if he had the strength to get home. He had done what he wanted, he had swum the county, but he was so stupefied with exhaustion that his triumph seemed vague. Stooped, holding on to the gateposts for support, he turned up the driveway of his own house.

The place was dark. Was it so late that they had all gone to bed? Had Lucinda stayed at the Westerhazys' for supper? Had the girls joined her there or gone someplace else? Hadn't they agreed, as they usually did on Sunday, to regret all their invitations and stay at home? He tried the garage doors to see what cars were in but the doors were locked and rust came off the handles onto his hands. Going toward the house, he saw the force of the thunderstorm had knocked one of the rain gutters loose. It hung down over the front door like an umbrella rib, but it could be fixed in the morning. The house was locked, and he thought that the stupid cook or the stupid maid must have locked the place up until he remembered that it had been some time since they had employed a maid or a cook. He shouted, pounded on the door, tried to force it with his shoulder, and then, looking in at the windows, saw that the place was empty. [1964]

ANTON CHEKHOV (1860–1904), *the short story writer and playwright, wrote his first stories while he was a medical student at Moscow University, to help his family pay off debts. His grandfather had been a serf who had bought his freedom. His father was an unsuccessful grocer in Taganrog, in southwestern Russia. After completing medical school, Chekhov became an assistant to the district doctor in a small provincial town. His early sketches were mostly humorous stories that he first published in newspapers under different pen names, keeping his own name for his medical articles. But the popularity of these sketches made him decide to become a writer.*

Chekhov's first two collections of short stories, published in 1886 and 1887, were acclaimed by readers, and from that time on he was able to give all his time to writing. He bought a small estate near Moscow, where he lived with his family and treated sick peasants at no charge. Chekhov's kindness and good works were not a matter of any political program or religious impulse but rather "the natural coloration of his talent," as Vladimir Nabokov put it. He was extremely modest about his extraordinary ability to empathize with the characters he created. Once he said to a visitor, "Do you know how I write my stories? Here's how!" And he glanced at his table, took up the first object that he saw — it was an ashtray — and said, "If you want it, you'll have a story tomorrow. It will be called 'The Ashtray.'" And it seemed to the visitor that Chekhov was conjuring up a story in front of his eyes: "Certain indefinite situations, adventures which had not yet found concrete form, were already beginning to crystallize about the ashtray."

In his stories Chekhov's technique appears disarmingly simple. Yet, as Virginia Woolf recognized, "as we read these little stories about nothing at all, the horizon widens; the soul gains an astonishing sense of freedom." Chekhov's remarkable absence of egotism can be seen in masterpieces such as "The Darling" and "The Lady with the Pet Dog," both of which he wrote toward the end of his life. He once sent a sketch describing himself to the editor who first encouraged him in which he gave a sense of the depth of his self-knowledge:

> Write a story, do, about a young man, the son of a serf, a former grocery boy, a choir singer, a high school pupil and university student, brought up to respect rank, to kiss the hands of priests, to truckle to the ideas of others — a young man who expressed thanks for every piece of bread, who was whipped many times, who went without galoshes to do his tutoring, who used his fists, tortured animals, was fond of dining with rich relatives, was a hypocrite in his dealings with God and men, needlessly, solely out of a realization of his own insignificance — write how this young man squeezes the slave out of himself, drop by drop, and how, on awaking one fine morning, he feels that the blood coursing through his veins is no longer that of a slave but that of a real human being.

Chekhov's more than 800 stories have immensely influenced writers of short fiction. Unconcerned with giving a social or ethical message in his work, he championed what he called "the holy of holies" — "love and absolute freedom — freedom from violence and lies, whatever their form."

RELATED COMMENTARIES: *Raymond Carver, "The Ashtray," page 1531; Anton Chekhov, "Technique in Writing the Short Story," page 1405; Vladimir Nabokov, "A Reading of Chekhov's 'The Lady with the Little Dog,'" page 1471; Leo*

Tolstoy, "Chekhov's Intent in 'The Darling,'" page 1497; Henri Troyat, *From Chekhov*, page 1534; Eudora Welty, "Plot and Character in Chekhov's 'The Darling,'" page 1510, and "Reality in Chekhov's Stories," page 1512.

ANTON CHEKHOV

The Darling

Translated by Constance Garnett

Olenka, the daughter of the retired collegiate assessor, Plemyanniakov, was sitting in her back porch, lost in thought. It was hot, the flies were persistent and teasing, and it was pleasant to reflect that it would soon be evening. Dark rainclouds were gathering from the east, and bringing from time to time a breath of moisture in the air.

Kukin, who was the manager of an open-air theatre called the Tivoli, and who lived in the lodge, was standing in the middle of the garden looking at the sky.

"Again!" he observed despairingly. "It's going to rain again! Rain every day, as though to spite me. I might as well hang myself! It's ruin! Fearful losses every day."

He flung up his hands, and went on, addressing Olenka:

"There! that's the life we lead, Olga Semyonovna. It's enough to make one cry. One works and does one's utmost; one wears oneself out, getting no sleep at night, and racks one's brain what to do for the best. And then what happens? To begin with, one's public is ignorant, boorish. I give them the very best operetta, a dainty masque, first rate music-hall artists. But do you suppose that's what they want! They don't understand anything of that sort. They want a clown; what they ask for is vulgarity. And then look at the weather! Almost every evening it rains. It started on the tenth of May, and it's kept it up all May and June. It's simply awful! The public doesn't come, but I've to pay the rent just the same, and pay the artists."

The next evening the clouds would gather again, and Kukin would say with an hysterical laugh:

"Well, rain away, then! Flood the garden, drown me! Damn my luck in this world and the next! Let the artists have me up! Send me to prison! — to Siberia! — the scaffold! Ha, ha, ha!"

And next day the same thing.

Olenka listened to Kukin with silent gravity, and sometimes tears came into her eyes. In the end his misfortunes touched her; she grew to love him. He was a small thin man, with a yellow face, and curls combed forward on his forehead. He spoke in a thin tenor; as he talked his mouth worked on one side, and there was always an expression of despair on his face; yet he aroused a deep and genuine affection in her. She was always fond of some one, and could not exist without loving. In earlier days she had loved her papa, who now sat in a darkened room, breathing with difficulty; she had loved her aunt who used to come every other year from Bryansk; and before that, when she was at school, she had loved her French master. She was a gentle, soft-hearted, compassionate girl, with mild, tender eyes and very good health. At the sight of her full rosy cheeks, her soft white neck with a little dark mole on it, and the kind, naïve smile, which came into her face when she listened to anything pleasant, men thought, "Yes, not half bad," and smiled too, while lady visitors could not refrain from seizing her hand in the middle of a conversation, exclaiming in a gush of delight, "You darling!"

The house in which she had lived from her birth upwards, and which was left her in her father's will, was at the extreme end of the town, not far from the Tivoli. In the evenings and at night she could hear the band playing, and the crackling and banging of fireworks, and it seemed to her that it was Kukin struggling with his destiny, storming the entrenchments of his chief foe, the indifferent public; there was a sweet thrill at her heart, she had no desire to sleep, and when he returned home at daybreak, she tapped softly at her bedroom window, and showing him only her face and one shoulder through the curtain, she gave him a friendly smile. . . .

He proposed to her, and they were married. And when he had a closer view of her neck and her plump, fine shoulders, he threw up his hands, and said:

"You darling!"

He was happy, but as it rained on the day and night of his wedding, his face still retained an expression of despair.

They got on very well together. She used to sit in his office, to look after things in the Tivoli, to put down the accounts and pay the wages. And her rosy cheeks, her sweet, naïve, radiant smile, were to be seen now at the office window, now in the refreshment bar or behind the scenes of the theatre. And already she used to say to her acquaintances that the theatre was the chief and most important thing in life, and that it was only through the drama that one could derive true enjoyment and become cultivated and humane.

"But do you suppose the public understands that?" she used to say. "What they want is a clown. Yesterday we gave 'Faust Inside Out,' and almost all the boxes were empty; but if Vanitchka and I had been producing some vulgar thing, I assure you the theatre would have been packed. Tomorrow Vanitchka and I are doing 'Orpheus in Hell.' Do come."

And what Kukin said about the theatre and the actors she repeated. Like him she despised the public for their ignorance and their indifference to art; she took part in the rehearsals, she corrected the actors, she kept an eye on the behavior of the musicians, and when there was an unfavorable notice in the local paper, she shed tears, and then went to the editor's office to set things right.

The actors were fond of her and used to call her "Vanitchka and I," and "the darling"; she was sorry for them and used to lend them small sums of money, and if they deceived her, she used to shed a few tears in private, but did not complain to her husband.

They got on well in the winter too. They took the theatre in the town for the whole winter, and let it for short terms to a Little Russian company, or to a conjurer, or to a local dramatic society. Olenka grew stouter, and was always beaming with satisfaction, while Kukin grew thinner and yellower, and continually complained of their terrible losses, although he had not done badly all the winter. He used to cough at night, and she used to give him hot raspberry tea or lime-flower water, to rub him with eau-de-Cologne and to wrap him in her warm shawls.

"You're such a sweet pet!" she used to say with perfect sincerity, stroking his hair. "You're such a pretty dear!"

Towards Lent he went to Moscow to collect a new troupe, and without him she could not sleep, but sat all night at her window, looking at the stars, and she compared herself with the hens, who are awake all night and uneasy when the cock is not in the hen-house. Kukin was detained in Moscow, and wrote that he would be back at Easter, adding some instructions about the Tivoli. But on the Sunday before Easter, late in the evening, came a sudden ominous knock at the gate; some one was hammering on the gate as though on a barrel — boom, boom, boom! The drowsy cook went flopping with her bare feet through the puddles, as she ran to open the gate.

"Please open," said some one outside in a thick bass. "There is a telegram for you."

Olenka had received telegrams from her husband before, but this time for some reason she felt numb with terror. With shaking hands she opened the telegram and read as follows:

> "Ivan Petrovitch died suddenly to-day. Awaiting immate instructions fufuneral Tuesday."

That was how it was written in the telegram — "fufuneral," and the utterly incomprehensible word "immate." It was signed by the stage manager of the operatic company.

"My darling!" sobbed Olenka. "Vanitchka, my precious, my darling! Why did I ever meet you! Why did I know you and love you! Your poor heart-broken Olenka is all alone without you!"

Kukin's funeral took place on Tuesday in Moscow, Olenka returned home on Wednesday, and as soon as she got indoors she threw herself on her bed and sobbed so loudly that it could be heard next door, and in the street.

"Poor darling!" the neighbors said, as they crossed themselves. "Olga Semyonovna, poor darling! How she does take on!"

Three months later Olenka was coming home from mass, melancholy and in deep mourning. It happened that one of her neighbors, Vassily Andreitch Pustovalov, returning home from church, walked back beside her. He was the manager at Babakayev's, the timber merchant's. He wore a straw hat, a white waistcoat, and a gold watch-chain, and looked more like a country gentleman than a man in trade.

"Everything happens as it is ordained, Olga Semyonovna," he said gravely, with a sympathetic note in his voice; "and if any of our dear ones die, it must be because it is the will of God, so we ought to have fortitude and bear it submissively."

After seeing Olenka to her gate, he said good-bye and went on. All day afterwards she heard his sedately dignified voice, and whenever she shut her eyes she saw his dark beard. She liked him very much. And apparently she had made an impression on him too, for not long afterwards an elderly lady, with whom she was only slightly acquainted, came to drink coffee with her, and as soon as she was seated at table began to talk about Pustovalov, saying that he was an excellent man whom one could thoroughly depend upon, and that any girl would be glad to marry him. Three days later Pustovalov came himself. He did not stay long, only about ten minutes, and he did not say much, but when he left, Olenka loved him — loved him so much that she lay awake all night in a perfect fever, and in the morning she sent for the elderly lady. The match was quickly arranged, and then came the wedding.

Pustovalov and Olenka got on very well together when they were married.

Usually he sat in the office till dinner-time, then he went out on business, while Olenka took his place, and sat in the office till evening, making up accounts and booking orders.

"Timber gets dearer every year; the price rises twenty per cent," she would say to her customers and friends. "Only fancy we used to sell local timber, and now Vassitchka always has to go for wood to the Mogilev district. And the freight!" she would add, covering her cheeks with her hands in horror. "The freight!"

It seemed to her that she had been in the timber trade for ages and ages, and that the most important and necessary thing in life was timber; and there was something intimate and touching to her in the very sound of words such as "baulk," "post," "beam," "pole," "scantling," "batten," "lath," "plank," etc.

At night when she was asleep she dreamed of perfect mountains of planks and boards, and long strings of wagons, carting timber somewhere far away. She dreamed that a whole regiment of six-inch beams forty feet high, standing on end, was marching upon the timber-yard; that logs, beams, and boards knocked together with the resounding crash of dry wood, kept falling and getting up again, piling themselves on each other. Olenka cried out in her sleep, and Pustovalov said to her tenderly: "Olenka, what's the matter, darling? Cross yourself!"

Her husband's ideas were hers. If he thought the room was too hot, or that business was slack, she thought the same. Her husband did not care for entertainments, and on holidays he stayed at home. She did likewise.

"You are always at home or in the office," her friends said to her. "You should go to the theatre, darling, or to the circus."

"Vassitchka and I have no time to go to theatres," she would answer sedately. "We have no time for nonsense. What's the use of these theatres?"

On Saturdays Pustovalov and she used to go to the evening service; on holidays to early mass, and they walked side by side with softened faces as they came home from church. There was a pleasant fragrance about them both, and her silk dress rustled agreeably. At home they drank tea, with fancy bread and jams of various kinds, and afterwards they ate pie. Every day at twelve o'clock there was a savory smell of beet-root soup and of mutton or duck in their yard, and on fast-days of fish, and no one could pass the gate without feeling hungry. In the office the samovar was always boiling, and customers were regaled with tea and cracknels. Once a week the couple went to the baths and returned side by side, both red in the face.

"Yes, we have nothing to complain of, thank God," Olenka used to say to her acquaintances. "I wish every one were as well off as Vassitchka and I."

When Pustovalov went away to buy wood in the Mogilev district, she missed him dreadfully, lay awake and cried. A young veterinary surgeon in the army, called Smirnin, to whom they had let their lodge, used sometimes to come in in the evening. He used to talk to her and play cards with her, and this entertained her in her husband's absence. She was particularly interested in what he told her of his home life. He was married and had a little boy, but was separated from his wife because she had been unfaithful to him, and now he hated her and used to send her forty rubles a month for the maintenance of their son. And hearing of all this, Olenka sighed and shook her head. She was sorry for him.

"Well, God keep you," she used to say to him at parting, as she lighted him down the stairs with a candle. "Thank you for coming to cheer me up, and may the Mother of God give you health."

And she always expressed herself with the same sedateness and dignity, the same reasonableness, in imitation of her husband. As the veterinary surgeon was disappearing behind the door below, she would say:

"You know, Vladimir Platonitch, you'd better make it up with your wife. You should forgive her for the sake of your son. You may be sure the little fellow understands."

And when Pustovalov came back, she told him in a low voice about the veterinary surgeon and his unhappy home life, and both sighed and shook their heads and talked about the boy, who, no doubt, missed his father, and by some strange connection of ideas, they went up to the holy icons, bowed to the ground before them, and prayed that God would give them children.

And so the Pustovalovs lived for six years quietly and peaceably in love and complete harmony.

But behold! one winter day after drinking hot tea in the office, Vassily Andreitch went out into the yard without his cap on to see about sending off some timber, caught cold, and was taken ill. He had the best doctors, but he grew worse and died after four months' illness. And Olenka was a widow once more.

"I've nobody, now you've left me, my darling," she sobbed, after her husband's funeral. "How can I live without you, in wretchedness and misery! Pity me, good people, all alone in the world!"

She went about dressed in black with long "weepers," and gave up wearing hat and gloves for good. She hardly ever went out, except to church, or to her husband's grave, and led the life of a nun. It was not till six months later that she took off the weepers and opened the shutters of the windows. She was sometimes seen in the mornings, going with her cook to market for provisions, but what went on in her house and how she lived now could only be surmised. People guessed, from seeing her drinking tea in her garden with the veterinary surgeon, who read the newspaper aloud to her, and from the fact that, meeting a lady she knew at the post-office, she said to her:

"There is no proper veterinary inspection in our town, and that's the cause of all sorts of epidemics. One is always hearing of people's getting infection from the milk supply, or catching diseases from horses and cows. The health of domestic animals ought to be as well cared for as the health of human beings."

She repeated the veterinary surgeon's words, and was of the same opinion as he about everything. It was evident that she could not live a year without some attachment, and had found new happiness in the lodge. In any one else this would have been censured, but no one could think ill of Olenka; everything she did was so natural. Neither she nor the veterinary surgeon said anything to other people of the change in their relations, and tried, indeed, to conceal it, but without success, for Olenka could not keep a secret. When he had visitors, men serving in his regiment, and she poured out tea or served the supper, she would begin talking of the cattle plague, of the foot and mouth disease, and of the municipal slaughter-houses. He was dreadfully embarrassed, and when the guests had gone, he would seize her by the hand and hiss angrily:

"I've asked you before not to talk about what you don't understand. When we veterinary surgeons are talking among ourselves, please don't put your word in. It's really annoying."

And she would look at him with astonishment and dismay, and ask him in alarm: "But, Voloditchka, what *am* I to talk about?"

And with tears in her eyes she would embrace him, begging him not to be angry, and they were both happy.

But this happiness did not last long. The veterinary surgeon departed, departed for ever with his regiment, when it was transferred to a distant place — to Siberia, it may be. And Olenka was left alone.

Now she was absolutely alone. Her father had long been dead, and his armchair lay in the attic, covered with dust and lame of one leg. She got thinner and plainer, and when people met her in the street they did not look at her as they used to, and did not smile to her; evidently her best years were over and left behind, and now a new sort of life had begun for her, which did not bear thinking about. In the evening Olenka sat in the porch, and heard the band playing and the fireworks popping in the Tivoli, but now the sound stirred no response. She looked into her yard without interest, thought of nothing, wished for nothing, and afterwards, when night came on she went to bed and dreamed of her empty yard. She ate and drank as it were unwillingly.

And what was worst of all, she had no opinions of any sort. She saw the objects about her and understood what she saw, but could not form any opinion about them, and did not know what to talk about. And how awful it is not to have any opinions! One sees a bottle, for instance, or the rain, or a peasant driving in his cart, but what the bottle is for, or the rain, or the peasant, and what is the meaning of it, one can't say, and could not even for a thousand rubles. When she had Kukin, or Pustovalov, or the veterinary surgeon, Olenka could explain everything, and give her opinion about anything you like, but now there was the same emptiness in her brain and in her heart as there was in her yard outside. And it was as harsh and as bitter as wormwood in the mouth.

Little by little the town grew in all directions. The road became a street, and where the Tivoli and the timber-yard had been, there were new turnings and houses. How rapidly time passes! Olenka's house grew dingy, the roof got rusty, the shed sank on one side, and the whole yard was overgrown with docks and stinging-nettles. Olenka herself had grown plain and elderly; in summer she sat in the porch, and her soul, as before, was empty and dreary and full of bitterness. In winter she sat at her window and looked at the snow. When she caught the scent of spring, or heard the chime of the church bells, a sudden rush of memories from the past came over her, there was a tender ache in her heart, and her eyes brimmed over with tears; but this was only for a minute, and then came emptiness again and the sense of the futility of life. The black kitten, Briska, rubbed against her and purred softly, but Olenka was not touched by these feline caresses. That was not what she needed. She wanted a love that would absorb her whole being, her whole soul and reason — that would give her ideas and an object in life, and would warm her old blood. And she would shake the kitten off her skirt and say with vexation:

"Get along; I don't want you!"

And so it was, day after day and year after year, and no joy, and no opinions. Whatever Mavra, the cook, said she accepted.

One hot July day, towards evening, just as the cattle were being driven away, and the whole yard was full of dust, some one suddenly knocked at the gate. Olenka went to open it herself and was dumbfounded when she looked out; she saw Smirnin, the veterinary surgeon, grey-headed, and dressed as a civilian. She suddenly remembered everything. She could not help crying and letting her head fall on his breast without uttering a word, and in the violence of her feeling she did not notice how they both walked into the house and sat down to tea.

"My dear Vladimir Platonitch! What fate has brought you?" she muttered, trembling with joy.

"I want to settle here for good, Olga Semyonovna," he told her. "I have resigned my post, and have come to settle down and try my luck on my own account. Besides, it's time for my boy to go to school. He's a big boy. I am reconciled with my wife, you know."

"Where is she?" asked Olenka.

"She's at the hotel with the boy, and I'm looking for lodgings."

"Good gracious, my dear soul! Lodgings? Why not have my house? Why shouldn't that suit you? Why, my goodness, I wouldn't take any rent!"

cried Olenka in a flutter, beginning to cry again. "You live here, and the lodge will do nicely for me. Oh dear! how glad I am!"

Next day the roof was painted and the walls were whitewashed, and Olenka, with her arms akimbo, walked about the yard giving directions. Her face was beaming with her old smile, and she was brisk and alert as though she had waked from a long sleep. The veterinary's wife arrived — a thin, plain lady, with short hair and a peevish expression. With her was her little Sasha, a boy of ten, small for his age, blue-eyed, chubby, with dimples in his cheeks. And scarcely had the boy walked into the yard when he ran after the cat, and at once there was the sound of his gay, joyous laugh.

"Is that your puss, auntie?" he asked Olenka. "When she has little ones, do give us a kitten. Mamma is awfully afraid of mice."

Olenka talked to him, and gave him tea. Her heart warmed and there was a sweet ache in her bosom, as though the boy had been her own child. And when he sat at the table in the evening, going over his lessons, she looked at him with deep tenderness and pity as she murmured to herself:

"You pretty pet! . . . my precious! . . . Such a fair little thing, and so clever."

"'An island is a piece of land which is entirely surrounded by water,'" he read aloud.

"An island is a piece of land," she repeated, and this was the first opinion to which she gave utterance with positive conviction after so many years of silence and dearth of ideas.

Now she had opinions of her own, and at supper she talked to Sasha's parents, saying how difficult the lessons were at the high schools, but that yet the high school was better than a commercial one, since with a high-school education all careers were open to one, such as being a doctor or an engineer.

Sasha began going to the high school. His mother departed to Harkov to her sister's and did not return; his father used to go off every day to inspect cattle, and would often be away from home for three days together, and it seemed to Olenka as though Sasha was entirely abandoned, that he was not wanted at home, that he was being starved, and she carried him off to her lodge and gave him a little room there.

And for six months Sasha had lived in the lodge with her. Every morning Olenka came into his bedroom and found him fast asleep, sleeping noiselessly with his hand under his cheek. She was sorry to wake him.

"Sashenka," she would say mournfully, "get up, darling. It's time for school."

He would get up, dress and say his prayers, and then sit down to breakfast, drink three glasses of tea, and eat two large cracknels and half a buttered roll. All this time he was hardly awake and a little ill-humored in consequence.

"You don't quite know your fable, Sashenka," Olenka would say, looking at him as though he were about to set off on a long journey. "What a lot of trouble I have with you! You must work and do your best, darling, and obey your teachers."

"Oh, do leave me alone!" Sasha would say.

Then he would go down the street to school, a little figure, wearing a big cap and carrying a satchel on his shoulder. Olenka would follow him noiselessly.

"Sashenka!" she would call after him, and she would pop into his hand a date or a caramel. When he reached the street where the school was, he would feel ashamed of being followed by a tall, stout woman; he would turn round and say:

"You'd better go home, auntie. I can go the rest of the way alone."

She would stand still and look after him fixedly till he had disappeared at the school-gate.

Ah, how she loved him! Of her former attachments not one had been so deep; never had her soul surrendered to any feeling so spontaneously, so disinterestedly, and so joyously as now that her maternal instincts were aroused. For this little boy with the dimple in his cheek and the big school cap, she would have given her whole life, she would have given it with joy and tears of tenderness. Why? Who can tell why?

When she had seen the last of Sasha, she returned home, contented and serene, brimming over with love; her face, which had grown younger during the last six months, smiled and beamed; people meeting her looked at her with pleasure.

"Good-morning, Olga Semyonovna, darling. How are you, darling?"

"The lessons at the high school are very difficult now," she would relate at the market. "It's too much; in the first class yesterday they gave him a fable to learn by heart, and a Latin translation and a problem. You know it's too much for a little chap."

And she would begin talking about the teachers, the lessons, and the school books, saying just what Sasha said.

At three o'clock they had dinner together: in the evening they learned their lessons together and cried. When she put him to bed, she would stay a long time making the Cross over him and murmuring a prayer; then she would go to bed and dream of that far-away misty future when Sasha would finish his studies and become a doctor or an engineer, would have a big house of his own with horses and a carriage, would get married and have children. . . . She would fall asleep still thinking of the same thing, and tears would run down her cheeks from her closed eyes, while the black cat lay purring beside her: "Mrr, mrr, mrr."

Suddenly there would come a loud knock at the gate.

Olenka would wake up breathless with alarm, her heart throbbing. Half a minute later would come another knock.

"It must be a telegram from Harkov," she would think, beginning to tremble from head to foot. "Sasha's mother is sending for him from Harkov. . . . Oh, mercy on us!"

She was in despair. Her head, her hands, and her feet would turn chill, and she would feel that she was the most unhappy woman in the world. But another minute would pass, voices would be heard: it would turn out to be the veterinary surgeon coming home from the club.

"Well, thank God!" she would think.

And gradually the load in her heart would pass off, and she would feel at ease. She would go back to bed thinking of Sasha, who lay sound asleep in the next room, sometimes crying out in his sleep:

"I'll give it you! Get away! Shut up!" [1899]

ANTON CHEKHOV

The Lady with the Pet Dog

Translated by Avrahm Yarmolinsky

I

A new person, it was said, had appeared on the esplanade: a lady with a pet dog. Dmitry Dmitrich Gurov, who had spent a fortnight at Yalta and had got used to the place, had also begun to take an interest in new arrivals. As he sat in Vernet's confectionery shop, he saw, walking on the esplanade, a fair-haired young woman of medium height, wearing a beret; a white Pomeranian was trotting behind her.

And afterwards he met her in the public garden and in the square several times a day. She walked alone, always wearing the same beret and always with the white dog; no one knew who she was and everyone called her simply "the lady with the pet dog."

"If she is here alone without husband or friends," Gurov reflected, "it wouldn't be a bad thing to make her acquaintance."

He was under forty, but he already had a daughter twelve years old, and two sons at school. They had found a wife for him when he was very young, a student in his second year, and by now she seemed half as old again as he. She was a tall, erect woman with dark eyebrows, stately and dignified and, as she said of herself, intellectual. She read a great deal, used simplified spelling in her letters, called her husband, not Dmitry, but Dimitry, while he privately considered her of limited intelligence, narrow-minded, dowdy, was afraid of her, and did not like to be at home. He had begun being unfaithful to her long ago — had been unfaithful to her often and, probably for that reason, almost always spoke ill of women, and when they were talked of in his presence used to call them "the inferior race."

It seemed to him that he had been sufficiently tutored by bitter experience to call them what he pleased, and yet he could not have lived without "the inferior race" for two days together. In the company of men he was bored and ill at ease, he was chilly and uncommunicative with them;

but when he was among women he felt free, and knew what to speak to them about and how to comport himself; and even to be silent with them was no strain on him. In his appearance, in his character, in his whole make-up there was something attractive and elusive that disposed women in his favor and allured them. He knew that, and some force seemed to draw him to them, too.

Oft-repeated and really bitter experience had taught him long ago that with decent people — particularly Moscow people — who are irresolute and slow to move, every affair which at first seems a light and charming adventure inevitably grows into a whole problem of extreme complexity, and in the end a painful situation is created. But at every new meeting with an interesting woman this lesson of experience seemed to slip from his memory, and he was eager for life, and everything seemed so simple and diverting.

One evening while he was dining in the public garden the lady in the beret walked up without haste to take the next table. Her expression, her gait, her dress, and the way she did her hair told him that she belonged to the upper class, that she was married, that she was in Yalta for the first time and alone, and that she was bored there. The stories told of the immorality in Yalta are to a great extent untrue; he despised them, and knew that such stories were made up for the most part by persons who would have been glad to sin themselves if they had had the chance; but when the lady sat down at the next table three paces from him, he recalled these stories of easy conquests, of trips to the mountains, and the tempting thought of a swift, fleeting liaison, a romance with an unknown woman of whose very name he was ignorant, suddenly took hold of him.

He beckoned invitingly to the Pomeranian, and when the dog approached him, shook his finger at it. The Pomeranian growled; Gurov threatened it again.

The lady glanced at him and at once dropped her eyes.

"He doesn't bite," she said and blushed.

"May I give him a bone?" he asked; and when she nodded he inquired affably, "Have you been in Yalta long?"

"About five days."

"And I am dragging out the second week here."

There was a short silence.

"Time passes quickly, and yet it is so dull here!" she said, not looking at him.

"It's only the fashion to say it's dull here. A provincial will live in Belyov or Zhizdra and not be bored, but when he comes here it's 'Oh, the dullness! Oh, the dust!' One would think he came from Granada."

She laughed. Then both continued eating in silence, like strangers, but after dinner they walked together and there sprang up between them the light banter of people who are free and contented, to whom it does not matter where they go or what they talk about. They walked and talked of the strange light on the sea: the water was a soft, warm, lilac color, and there was a golden band of moonlight upon it. They talked of how sultry it was after a hot day.

Gurov told her that he was a native of Moscow, that he had studied languages and literature at the university, but had a post in a bank; that at one time he had trained to become an opera singer but had given it up, that he owned two houses in Moscow. And he learned from her that she had grown up in Petersburg, but had lived in S—— since her marriage two years previously, that she was going to stay in Yalta for about another month, and that her husband, who needed a rest, too, might perhaps come to fetch her. She was not certain whether her husband was a member of a Government Board or served on a Zemstvo Council,[1] and this amused her. And Gurov learned too that her name was Anna Sergeyevna.

Afterwards in his room at the hotel he thought about her — and was certain that he would meet her the next day. It was bound to happen. Getting into bed he recalled that she had been a schoolgirl only recently, doing lessons like his own daughter; he thought how much timidity and angularity there was still in her laugh and her manner of talking with a stranger. It must have been the first time in her life that she was alone in a setting in which she was followed, looked at, and spoken to for one secret purpose alone, which she could hardly fail to guess. He thought of her slim, delicate throat, her lovely gray eyes.

"There's something pathetic about her, though," he thought, and dropped off.

II

A week had passed since they had struck up an acquaintance. It was a holiday. It was close indoors, while in the street the wind whirled the dust about and blew people's hats off. One was thirsty all day, and Gurov often went into the restaurant and offered Anna Sergeyevna a soft drink or ice cream. One did not know what to do with oneself.

In the evening when the wind had abated they went out on the pier to watch the steamer come in. There were a great many people walking about the dock; they had come to welcome someone and they were carrying bunches of flowers. And two peculiarities of a festive Yalta crowd stood out: the elderly ladies were dressed like young ones and there were many generals.

Owing to the choppy sea, the steamer arrived late, after sunset, and it was a long time tacking about before it put in at the pier. Anna Sergeyevna peered at the steamer and the passengers through her lorgnette as though looking for acquaintances, and whenever she turned to Gurov her eyes were shining. She talked a great deal and asked questions jerkily, forgetting the next moment what she had asked; then she lost her lorgnette in the crush.

The festive crowd began to disperse; it was now too dark to see people's faces; there was no wind any more, but Gurov and Anna Sergeyevna still stood as though waiting to see someone else come off the steamer. Anna Sergeyevna was silent now, and sniffed her flowers without looking at Gurov.

---

[1] County council.

"The weather has improved this evening," he said. "Where shall we go now? Shall we drive somewhere?"

She did not reply.

Then he looked at her intently, and suddenly embraced her and kissed her on the lips, and the moist fragrance of her flowers enveloped him; and at once he looked round him anxiously, wondering if anyone had seen them.

"Let us go to your place," he said softly. And they walked off together rapidly.

The air in her room was close and there was the smell of the perfume she had bought at the Japanese shop. Looking at her, Gurov thought: "What encounters life offers!" From the past he preserved the memory of carefree, good-natured women whom love made gay and who were grateful to him for the happiness he gave them, however brief it might be; and of women like his wife who loved without sincerity, with too many words, affectedly, hysterically, with an expression that it was not love or passion that engaged them but something more significant; and of two or three others, very beautiful, frigid women, across whose faces would suddenly flit a rapacious expression — an obstinate desire to take from life more than it could give, and these were women no longer young, capricious, unreflecting, domineering, unintelligent, and when Gurov grew cold to them their beauty aroused his hatred, and the lace on their lingerie seemed to him to resemble scales.

But here there was the timidity, the angularity of inexperienced youth, a feeling of awkwardness; and there was a sense of embarrassment, as though someone had suddenly knocked at the door. Anna Sergeyevna, "the lady with the pet dog," treated what had happened in a peculiar way, very seriously, as though it were her fall — so it seemed, and this was odd and inappropriate. Her features drooped and faded, and her long hair hung down sadly on either side of her face; she grew pensive and her dejected pose was that of a Magdalene in a picture by an old master.

"It's not right," she said. "You don't respect me now, you first of all."

There was a watermelon on the table. Gurov cut himself a slice and began eating it without haste. They were silent for at least half an hour.

There was something touching about Anna Sergeyevna; she had the purity of a well-bred, naive woman who has seen little of life. The single candle burning on the table barely illumined her face, yet it was clear that she was unhappy.

"Why should I stop respecting you, darling?" asked Gurov. "You don't know what you're saying."

"God forgive me," she said, and her eyes filled with tears. "It's terrible."

"It's as though you were trying to exonerate yourself."

"How can I exonerate myself? No. I am a bad, low woman; I despise myself and I have no thought of exonerating myself. It's not my husband but myself I have deceived. And not only just now; I have been deceiving myself for a long time. My husband may be a good, honest man, but he is a flunkey! I don't know what he does, what his work is, but I know he is a flunkey! I was twenty when I married him. I was tormented by curiosity; I wanted something better. 'There must be a different sort of life,' I said to myself. I wanted to live! To live, to live! Curiosity kept eating at me — you don't understand it, but I swear to God I could no longer control myself; something was going on in me; I could not be held back. I told my husband I was ill, and came here. And here I have been walking about as though in a daze, as though I were mad; and now I have become a vulgar, vile woman whom anyone may despise."

Gurov was already bored with her; he was irritated by her naive tone, by her repentance, so unexpected and so out of place, but for the tears in her eyes he might have thought she was joking or play-acting.

"I don't understand, my dear," he said softly. "What do you want?"

She hid her face on his breast and pressed close to him.

"Believe me, believe me, I beg you," she said, "I love honesty and purity, and sin is loathsome to me; I don't know what I'm doing. Simple people say, 'The Evil One has led me astray.' And I may say of myself now that the Evil One has led me astray."

"Quiet, quiet," he murmured.

He looked into her fixed, frightened eyes, kissed her, spoke to her softly and affectionately, and by degrees she calmed down, and her gaiety returned; both began laughing.

Afterwards when they went out there was not a soul on the esplanade. The town with its cypresses looked quite dead, but the sea was still sounding as it broke upon the beach; a single launch was rocking on the waves and on it a lantern was blinking sleepily.

They found a cab and drove to Oreanda.

"I found out your surname in the hall just now: it was written on the board — von Dideritz," said Gurov. "Is your husband German?"

"No; I believe his grandfather was German, but he is Greek Orthodox himself."

At Oreanda they sat on a bench not far from the church, looked down at the sea, and were silent. Yalta was barely visible through the morning mist; white clouds rested motionlessly on the mountaintops. The leaves did not stir on the trees, cicadas twanged, and the monotonous muffled sound of the sea that rose from below spoke of the peace, the eternal sleep awaiting us. So it rumbled below when there was no Yalta, no Oreanda here; so it rumbles now, and it will rumble as indifferently and as hollowly when we are no more. And in this constancy, in this complete indifference to the life and death of each of us, there lies, perhaps, a pledge of our eternal salvation, of the unceasing advance of life upon earth, of unceasing movement towards perfection. Sitting beside a young woman who in the dawn seemed so lovely, Gurov, soothed and spellbound by these magical surroundings — the sea, the mountains, the clouds, the wide sky — thought how everything is really beautiful in this world when one reflects: everything except what we think or do ourselves when we forget the higher aims of life and our own human dignity.

A man strolled up to them — probably a guard — looked at them, and walked away. And this detail, too, seemed so mysterious and beautiful. They saw a steamer arrive from Feodosia, its lights extinguished in the glow of dawn.

"There is dew on the grass," said Anna Sergeyevna, after a silence.

"Yes, it's time to go home."

They returned to the city.

Then they met every day at twelve o'clock on the esplanade, lunched and dined together, took walks, admired the sea. She complained that she slept badly, that she had palpitations, asked the same questions, troubled now by jealousy and now by the fear that he did not respect her sufficiently. And often in the square or the public garden, when there was no one near them, he suddenly drew her to him and kissed her passionately. Complete idleness, these kisses in broad daylight exchanged furtively in dread of someone's seeing them, the heat, the smell of the sea, and the continual flitting before his eyes of idle, well-dressed, well-fed people, worked a complete change in him; he kept telling Anna Sergeyevna how beautiful she was, how seductive, was urgently passionate; he would not move a step away from her, while she was often pensive and continually pressed him to confess that he did not respect her, did not love her in the least, and saw in her nothing but a common woman. Almost every evening rather late they drove somewhere out of town, to Oreanda or to the waterfall; and the excursion was always a success, the scenery invariably impressed them as beautiful and magnificent.

They were expecting her husband, but a letter came from him saying that he had eye-trouble, and begging his wife to return home as soon as possible. Anna Sergeyevna made haste to go.

"It's a good thing I am leaving," she said to Gurov. "It's the hand of Fate!"

She took a carriage to the railway station, and he went with her. They were driving the whole day. When she had taken her place in the express, and when the second bell had rung, she said, "Let me look at you once more — let me look at you again. Like this."

She was not crying but was so sad that she seemed ill and her face was quivering.

"I shall be thinking of you — remembering you," she said. "God bless you; be happy. Don't remember evil against me. We are parting forever — it has to be, for we ought never to have met. Well, God bless you."

The train moved off rapidly, its lights soon vanished, and a minute later there was no sound of it, as though everything had conspired to end as quickly as possible that sweet trance, that madness. Left alone on the platform, and gazing into the dark distance, Gurov listened to the twang of the grasshoppers and the hum of the telegraph wires, feeling as though he had just waked up. And he reflected, musing, that there had now been another episode or adventure in his life, and it, too, was at an end, and nothing was left of it but a memory. He was moved, sad, and slightly remorseful: this young woman whom he would never meet again had not been happy with him; he had been warm and affectionate with her, but yet in his manner, his tone, and his caresses there had been a shade of light irony, the slightly coarse arrogance of a happy male who was, besides, almost twice her age. She had constantly called him kind, exceptional, high-minded; obviously he had seemed to her different from what he really was, so he had involuntarily deceived her.

Here at the station there was already a scent of autumn in the air; it was a chilly evening.

"It is time for me to go north, too," thought Gurov as he left the platform. "High time!"

III

At home in Moscow the winter routine was already established; the stoves were heated, and in the morning it was still dark when the children were having breakfast and getting ready for school, and the nurse would light the lamp for a short time. There were frosts already. When the first snow falls, on the first day the sleighs are out, it is pleasant to see the white earth, the white roofs; one draws easy, delicious breaths, and the season brings back the days of one's youth. The old limes and birches, white with hoar-frost, have a good-natured look; they are closer to one's heart than cypresses and palms, and near them one no longer wants to think of mountains and the sea.

Gurov, a native of Moscow, arrived there on a fine frosty day, and when he put on his fur coat and warm gloves and took a walk along Petrovka, and when on Saturday night he heard the bells ringing, his recent trip and the places he had visited lost all charm for him. Little by little he became immersed in Moscow life, greedily read three newspapers a day, and declared that he did not read the Moscow papers on principle. He already felt a longing for restaurants, clubs, formal dinners, anniversary celebrations, and it flattered him to entertain distinguished lawyers and actors, and to play cards with a professor at the physicians' club. He could eat a whole portion of meat stewed with pickled cabbage and served in a pan, Moscow style.

A month or so would pass and the image of Anna Sergeyevna, it seemed to him, would become misty in his memory, and only from time to time he would dream of her with her touching smile as he dreamed of others. But more than a month went by, winter came into its own, and everything was still clear in his memory as though he had parted from Anna Sergeyevna only yesterday. And his memories glowed more and more vividly. When in the evening stillness the voices of his children preparing their lessons reached his study, or when he listened to a song or to an organ playing in a restaurant, or when the storm howled in the chimney, suddenly everything would rise up in his memory; what had happened on the pier and the early morning with the mist on the mountains, and the steamer coming from Feodosia, and the kisses. He would pace about his room a long time, remembering and smiling; then his memories passed into reveries, and in his imagination the past would mingle with what was to come. He did not dream of Anna Sergeyevna, but she followed him about everywhere and watched him. When he shut his eyes he saw her before him as though she were there in the flesh, and she seemed to him lovelier, younger, tenderer than she had been, and he imagined himself a finer man than he had been in Yalta. Of evenings she peered out at him from the bookcase, from the fireplace, from the corner — he heard her breathing, the caressing rustle of her clothes. In the street he followed the women with his eyes, looking for someone who resembled her.

Already he was tormented by a strong desire to share his memories with someone. But in his home it was impossible to talk of his love, and he had no one to talk to outside; certainly he could not confide in his tenants or in anyone at the bank. And what was there to talk about? He hadn't loved her then, had he? Had there been anything beautiful, poetical, edifying, or simply interesting in his relations with Anna Sergeyevna? And he was forced to talk vaguely of love, of women, and no one guessed what he meant; only his wife would twitch her black eyebrows and say, "The part of a philanderer does not suit you at all, Dimitry."

One evening, coming out of the physicians' club with an official with whom he had been playing cards, he could not resist saying:

"If you only knew what a fascinating woman I became acquainted with at Yalta!"

The official got into his sledge and was driving away, but turned suddenly and shouted:

"Dmitry Dmitrich!"

"What is it?"

"You were right this evening: the sturgeon was a bit high."

These words, so commonplace, for some reason moved Gurov to indignation, and struck him as degrading and unclean. What savage manners, what mugs! What stupid nights, what dull, humdrum days! Frenzied gambling, gluttony, drunkenness, continual talk always about the same thing! Futile pursuits and conversations always about the same topics take up the better part of one's time, the better part of one's strength, and in the end there is left a life clipped and wingless, an absurd mess, and there is no escaping or getting away from it — just as though one were in a madhouse or a prison.

Gurov, boiling with indignation, did not sleep all night. And he had a headache all the next day. And the following nights too he slept badly; he sat up in bed, thinking, or paced up and down his room. He was fed up with his children, fed up with the bank; he had no desire to go anywhere or to talk of anything.

In December during the holidays he prepared to take a trip and told his wife he was going to Petersburg to do what he could for a young friend — and he set off for S——. What for? He did not know, himself. He wanted to see Anna Sergeyevna and talk with her, to arrange a rendezvous if possible.

He arrived at S—— in the morning, and at the hotel took the best room, in which the floor was covered with gray army cloth, and on the table there was an inkstand, gray with dust and topped by a figure on horseback, its hat in its raised hand and its head broken off. The porter gave him the necessary information: von Dideritz lived in a house of his own on Staro-Goncharnaya Street, not far from the hotel: he was rich and lived well and kept his own horses; everyone in the town knew him. The porter pronounced the name: "Dridiritz."

Without haste Gurov made his way to Staro-Goncharnaya Street and found the house. Directly opposite the house stretched a long gray fence studded with nails.

"A fence like that would make one run away," thought Gurov, looking now at the fence, now at the windows of the house.

He reflected: this was a holiday, and the husband was apt to be at home. And in any case, it would be tactless to go into the house and disturb her. If he were to send her a note, it might fall into her husband's hands, and that might spoil everything. The best thing was to rely on chance. And he kept walking up and down the street and along the fence, waiting for the chance. He saw a beggar go in at the gate and heard the dogs attack him; then an hour later he heard a piano, and the sound came to him faintly and indistinctly. Probably it was Anna Sergeyevna playing. The front door opened suddenly, and an old woman came out, followed by the familiar white Pomeranian. Gurov was on the point of calling to the dog, but his heart began beating violently, and in his excitement he could not remember the Pomeranian's name.

He kept walking up and down, and hated the gray fence more and more, and by now he thought irritably that Anna Sergeyevna had forgotten him, and was perhaps already diverting herself with another man, and that that was very natural in a young woman who from morning till night had to look at that damn fence. He went back to his hotel room and sat on the couch for a long while, not knowing what to do, then he had dinner and a long nap.

"How stupid and annoying all this is!" he thought when he woke and looked at the dark windows: it was already evening. "Here I've had a good sleep for some reason. What am I going to do at night?"

He sat on the bed, which was covered with a cheap gray blanket of the kind seen in hospitals, and he twitted himself in his vexation:

"So there's your lady with the pet dog. There's your adventure. A nice place to cool your heels in."

That morning at the station a playbill in large letters had caught his eye. *The Geisha* was to be given for the first time. He thought of this and drove to the theater.

"It's quite possible that she goes to first nights," he thought.

The theater was full. As in all provincial theaters, there was a haze above the chandelier, the gallery was noisy and restless; in the front row, before the beginning of the performance the local dandies were standing with their hands clasped behind their backs; in the Governor's box the Governor's daughter, wearing a boa, occupied the front seat, while the Governor himself hid modestly behind the portiere and only his hands were visible; the curtain swayed; the orchestra was a long time tuning up. While the audience was coming in and taking their seats, Gurov scanned the faces eagerly.

Anna Sergeyevna, too, came in. She sat down in the third row, and when Gurov looked at her his heart contracted, and he understood clearly that in the whole world there was no human being so near, so precious, and so important to him; she, this little, undistinguished woman, lost in a provincial crowd, with a vulgar lorgnette in her hand, filled his whole life now, was his sorrow and his joy, the only happiness that he now desired for himself, and to the sounds of the bad orchestra, of the miserable local violins, he thought how lovely she was. He thought and dreamed.

A young man with small side-whiskers, very tall and stooped, came in with Anna Sergeyevna and sat down beside her; he nodded his head at every step and seemed to be bowing continually. Probably this was the husband whom at Yalta, in an access of bitter feeling, she had called a flunkey. And there really was in his lanky figure, his side-whiskers, his small bald patch, something of a flunkey's retiring manner; his smile was mawkish, and in his buttonhole there was an academic badge like a waiter's number.

During the first intermission the husband went out to have a smoke; she remained in her seat. Gurov, who was also sitting in the orchestra, went up to her and said in a shaky voice, with a forced smile:

"Good evening!"

She glanced at him and turned pale, then looked at him again in horror, unable to believe her eyes, and gripped the fan and the lorgnette tightly together in her hands, evidently trying to keep herself from fainting. Both were silent. She was sitting, he was standing, frightened by her distress and not daring to take a seat beside her. The violins and the flute that were being tuned up sang out. He suddenly felt frightened: it seemed as if all the people in the boxes were looking at them. She got up and went hurriedly to the exit; he followed her, and both of them walked blindly along the corridors and up and down stairs, and figures in the uniforms prescribed for magistrates, teachers, and officials of the Department of Crown Lands, all wearing badges, flitted before their eyes, as did also ladies, and fur coats on hangers; they were conscious of drafts and the smell of stale tobacco. And Gurov, whose heart was beating violently, thought:

"Oh, Lord! Why are these people here and this orchestra!"

And at that instant he suddenly recalled how when he had seen Anna Sergeyevna off at the station he had said to himself that all was over between them and that they would never meet again. But how distant the end still was!

On the narrow, gloomy staircase over which it said "To the Amphitheatre," she stopped.

"How you frightened me!" she said, breathing hard, still pale and stunned. "Oh, how you frightened me! I am barely alive. Why did you come? Why?"

"But do understand, Anna, do understand — " he said hurriedly, under his breath. "I implore you, do understand — "

She looked at him with fear, with entreaty, with love; she looked at him intently, to keep his features more distinctly in her memory.

"I suffer so," she went on, not listening to him. "All this time I have been thinking of nothing but you; I live only by the thought of you. And I wanted to forget, to forget; but why, oh, why have you come?"

On the landing above them two high school boys were looking down and smoking, but it was all the same to Gurov; he drew Anna Sergeyevna to him and began kissing her face and hands.

"What are you doing, what are you doing!" she was saying in horror, pushing him away. "We have lost our senses. Go away today; go away at once — I conjure you by all that is sacred, I implore you — People are coming this way!"

Someone was walking up the stairs.

"You must leave," Anna Sergeyevna went on in a whisper. "Do you hear, Dmitry Dmitrich? I will come and see you in Moscow. I have never been happy; I am unhappy now, and I never, never shall be happy, never! So don't make me suffer still more! I swear I'll come to Moscow. But now let us part. My dear, good, precious one, let us part!"

She pressed his hand and walked rapidly downstairs, turning to look round at him, and from her eyes he could see that she really was unhappy. Gurov stood for a while, listening, then when all grew quiet, he found his coat and left the theater.

IV

And Anna Sergeyevna began coming to see him in Moscow. Once every two or three months she left S—— telling her husband that she was going to consult a doctor about a woman's ailment from which she was suffering — and her husband did and did not believe her. When she arrived in Moscow she would stop at the Slavyansky Bazar Hotel, and at once send a man in a red cap to Gurov. Gurov came to see her, and no one in Moscow knew of it.

Once he was going to see her in this way on a winter morning (the messenger had come the evening before and not found him in). With him walked his daughter, whom he wanted to take to school; it was on the way. Snow was coming down in big wet flakes.

"It's three degrees above zero,[2] and yet it's snowing," Gurov was saying to his daughter. "But this temperature prevails only on the surface of the earth; in the upper layers of the atmosphere there is quite a different temperature."

"And why doesn't it thunder in winter, papa?"

He explained that, too. He talked, thinking all the while that he was on his way to a rendezvous, and no living soul knew of it, and probably no one would ever know. He had two lives, an open one, seen and known by all who needed to know it, full of conventional truth and conventional falsehood, exactly like the lives of his friends and acquaintances; and another life that went on in secret. And through some strange, perhaps accidental, combination of circumstances, everything that was of interest and importance to him, everything that was essential to him, everything about which he felt sincerely and did not deceive himself, everything that constituted the core of his life, was going on concealed from others; while all that was false, the shell in

---

[2]On the Celsius scale — about thirty-seven degrees Fahrenheit.

which he hid to cover the truth — his work at the bank, for instance, his discussions at the club, his references to the "inferior race," his appearances at anniversary celebrations with his wife — all that went on in the open. Judging others by himself, he did not believe what he saw, and always fancied that every man led his real, most interesting life under cover of secrecy as under cover of night. The personal life of every individual is based on secrecy, and perhaps it is partly for that reason that civilized man is so nervously anxious that personal privacy should be respected.

Having taken his daughter to school, Gurov went on to the Slavyansky Bazar Hotel. He took off his fur coat in the lobby, went upstairs, and knocked gently at the door. Anna Sergeyevna, wearing his favorite gray dress, exhausted by the journey and by waiting, had been expecting him since the previous evening. She was pale, and looked at him without a smile, and he had hardly entered when she flung herself on his breast. That kiss was a long, lingering one, as though they had not seen one another for two years.

"Well, darling, how are you getting on there?" he asked. "What news?"

"Wait; I'll tell you in a moment — I can't speak."

She could not speak; she was crying. She turned away from him, and pressed her handkerchief to her eyes.

"Let her have her cry; meanwhile I'll sit down," he thought, and he seated himself in an armchair.

Then he rang and ordered tea, and while he was having his tea she remained standing at the window with her back to him. She was crying out of sheer agitation, in the sorrowful consciousness that their life was so sad; that they could only see each other in secret and had to hide from people like thieves! Was it not a broken life?

"Come, stop now, dear!" he said.

It was plain to him that this love of theirs would not be over soon, that the end of it was not in sight. Anna Sergeyevna was growing more and more attached to him. She adored him, and it was unthinkable to tell her that their love was bound to come to an end some day; besides, she would not have believed it!

He went up to her and took her by the shoulders, to fondle her and say something diverting, and at that moment he caught sight of himself in the mirror.

His hair was already beginning to turn gray. And it seemed odd to him that he had grown so much older in the last few years, and lost his looks. The shoulders on which his hands rested were warm and heaving. He felt compassion for this life, still so warm and lovely, but probably already about to begin to fade and wither like his own. Why did she love him so much? He always seemed to women different from what he was, and they loved in him not himself, but the man whom their imagination created and whom they had been eagerly seeking all their lives; and afterwards, when they saw their mistake, they loved him nevertheless. And not one of them had been happy with him. In the past he had met women, come together with them, parted from them, but he had never once loved; it was anything you please, but not love. And only now when his head was gray he had fallen in love, really, truly — for the first time in his life.

Anna Sergeyevna and he loved each other as people do who are very close and intimate, like man and wife, like tender friends; it seemed to them that Fate itself had meant them for one another, and they could not understand why he had a wife and she a husband; and it was as though they were a pair of migratory birds, male and female, caught and forced to live in different cages. They forgave each other what they were ashamed of in their past, they forgave everything in the present, and felt that this love of theirs had altered them both.

Formerly in moments of sadness he had soothed himself with whatever logical arguments came into his head, but now he no longer cared for logic; he felt profound compassion, he wanted to be sincere and tender.

"Give it up now, my darling," he said. "You've had your cry; that's enough. Let us have a talk now, we'll think up something."

Then they spent a long time taking counsel together, they talked of how to avoid the necessity for secrecy, for deception, for living in different cities, and not seeing one another for long stretches of time. How could they free themselves from these intolerable fetters?

"How? How?" he asked, clutching his head. "How?"

And it seemed as though in a little while the solution would be found, and then a new and glorious life would begin; and it was clear to both of them that the end was still far off, and that what was to be most complicated and difficult for them was only just beginning.   [1899]

CHARLES WADDELL CHESNUTT (1858–1932), *writer of short stories, novels, and a pioneering biography of the abolitionist Frederick Douglass, is generally considered, as Joyce Carol Oates has noted, to be "the first black writer to find a white readership in America." Chesnutt was born in Cleveland, Ohio, and moved with his family to Fayetteville, North Carolina, when he was eight years old. Educated at local schools, he became a schoolteacher and then a lawyer before his short stories began to appear regularly in newspapers and magazines. The quality of his fiction was recognized by William Dean Howells, one of the most influential American writers of the time, who compared Chesnutt's stories to the work of Henry James and Guy de Maupassant.*

Two collections of Chesnutt's short fiction, The Conjure Woman *and* The Wife of His Youth and Other Stories of the Color Line, *appeared in 1899. After publishing three novels a few years later, Chesnutt abandoned his career as a writer and spent the remaining years of his life as a businessman. Committed in his fiction to the theme of the dehumanizing effects of racial prejudice in the United States, he expressed his ideas with characteristic irony when he stated that "the object of my writings would not be so much the elevation of the colored people as the elevation of the whites — for I consider the unjust spirit of caste which is so insidious as to pervade a whole nation . . . as a barrier to the moral progress of the American people."*

Chesnutt's stories in The Conjure Woman *belong to the genre of local color fiction with their dramatization of the exotic folkways and dialect of characters living in backwater poverty and superstition. "The Sheriff's Children," from* The Wife of His Youth, *is a more mainstream, realistic story about the daunting challenges faced by African Americans after the Civil War. This was a period of white supremacy and black suppression in the South extolled in novels such as Thomas Dixon's* The Clansman *(1905), the best-seller later turned into the popular silent film* The Birth of a Nation. *As the critic William L. Howard recognized, a common thread running throughout Chesnutt's compassionate stories is "the search for identity and the ambivalences a person of mixed blood experiences on such a search."*

CHARLES CHESNUTT

The Sheriff's Children

Branson County, North Carolina, is in a sequestered district of one of the staidest and most conservative States of the Union. Society in Branson County is almost primitive in its simplicity. Most of the white people own the farms they till, and even before the war there were no very wealthy families to force their neighbors, by comparison, into the category of "poor whites."

To Branson County, as to most rural communities in the South, the war is the one historical event that overshadows all others. It is the era from which all local chronicles are dated — births, deaths, marriages, storms, freshets. No description of the life of any Southern community would be perfect that failed to emphasize the all pervading influence of the great conflict.

Yet the fierce tide of war that had rushed through the cities and along the great highways of the country had comparatively speaking but slightly disturbed the sluggish current of life in this region, remote from railroads and navigable streams. To the north in Virginia, to the west in Tennessee, and all along the seaboard the war had raged; but the thunder of its cannon had not disturbed the echoes of Branson County, where the loudest sounds heard were the crack of some hunter's rifle, the baying of some deep-mouthed hound, or the yodel of some tuneful negro on his way through the pine forest. To the east, Sherman's army had passed on its march to the sea; but no straggling band of "bummers" had penetrated the confines of Branson County. The war, it is true, had robbed the county of the flower of its young manhood; but the burden of taxation, the doubt and uncertainty of the conflict, and the sting of ultimate defeat, had been borne by the people with an apathy that robbed misfortune of half its sharpness.

The nearest approach to town life afforded by Branson County is found in the little village of Troy, the county seat, a hamlet with a population of four or five hundred.

Ten years make little difference in the appearance of these remote Southern towns. If a railroad is built through one of them, it infuses some enterprise; the social corpse is galvanized by the fresh blood of civilization that pulses along the farthest ramifications of our great system of commercial highways. At the period of which I write, no railroad had come to Troy. If a traveler, accustomed to the bustling life of cities, could have ridden through Troy on a summer day, he might easily have fancied himself in a deserted village. Around him he would have seen weather-beaten houses, innocent of paint, the shingled roofs in many instances covered with a rich growth of moss. Here and there he would have met a razor-backed hog lazily rooting his way along the principal thoroughfare; and more than once he would probably have had to disturb the slumbers of some yellow dog, dozing away the hours in the ardent sunshine, and reluctantly yielding up his place in the middle of the dusty road.

On Saturdays the village presented a somewhat livelier appearance, and the shade trees around the court-house square and along Front Street served as hitching-posts for a goodly number of horses and mules and stunted oxen, belonging to the farmer-folk who had come in to trade at the two or three local stores.

A murder was a rare event in Branson County. Every well-informed citizen could tell the number of homicides committed in the county for fifty years back, and whether the slayer, in any given instance, had escaped, either by flight or acquittal, or had suffered the penalty of the law. So, when it became known in Troy early one Friday morning in summer, about ten years after the war, that old Captain Walker, who had served in Mexico under Scott, and had left an arm on the field of Gettysburg, had been foully murdered during the night, there was intense excitement in the village. Business was practically suspended, and the citizens gathered in little groups to discuss the murder, and speculate upon the identity of the murderer. It transpired from testimony at the coroner's inquest, held during the morning, that a strange mulatto had been seen going in the direction of Captain Walker's house the night before, and had been met going away from Troy early Friday morning, by a farmer on his way to town. Other circumstances seemed to connect the stranger with the crime. The sheriff organized a posse to search for him, and early in the evening, when most of the citizens of Troy were at supper, the suspected man was brought in and lodged in the county jail.

By the following morning the news of the capture had spread to the farthest limits of the county. A much larger number of people than usual came to town that Saturday, — bearded men in straw hats and blue homespun shirts, and butternut trousers of great amplitude of material and vagueness of outline: women in homespun frocks and slat-bonnets, with faces as expressionless as the dreary sandhills which gave them a meagre sustenance.

The murder was almost the sole topic of conversation. A steady stream of curious observers visited the house of mourning, and gazed upon the rugged face of the old veteran, now stiff and cold in death; and more than one eye dropped a tear at the remembrance of the cheery smile, and the joke — sometimes superannuated, generally feeble, but always good-natured — with which the captain had been wont to greet his acquaintances. There was a growing sentiment of anger among these stern men, toward the murderer who had thus cut down their friend, and a strong feeling that ordinary justice was too slight a punishment for such a crime.

Toward noon there was an informal gathering of citizens in Dan Tyson's store.

"I hear it 'lowed that Square Kyahtah's too sick ter hol' co'te this evenin'," said one, "an' that the purlim'nary hearin' 'll haf ter go over 'tel nex' week."

A look of disappointment went round the crowd.

"Hit 's the durndes', meanes' murder ever committed in this caounty," said another, with moody emphasis.

"I s'pose the nigger 'lowed the Cap'n had some greenbacks," observed a third speaker.

"The Cap'n," said another, with an air of superior information, "has left two bairls of Confedrit money, which he 'spected 'ud be good some day er nuther."

This statement gave rise to a discussion of the speculative value of Confederate money; but in a little while the conversation returned to the murder.

"Hangin' air too good fer the murderer," said one; "he oughter be burnt, stidier bein' hung."

There was an impressive pause at this point, during which a jug of moonlight whiskey went the round of the crowd.

"Well," said a round-shouldered farmer, who, in spite of his peaceable expression and faded gray eye, was known to have been one of the most daring followers of a rebel guerrilla chieftain, "what air yer gwine ter do about it? Ef you fellers air gwine ter set down an' let a wuthless nigger kill the bes' white man in Branson, an' not say nuthin' ner do nuthin', *I'll* move outen the caounty."

This speech gave tone and direction to the rest of the conversation. Whether the fear of losing the round-shouldered farmer operated to bring about the result or not is immaterial to this narrative; but, at all events, the crowd decided to lynch the negro. They agreed that this was the least that could be done to avenge the death of their murdered friend, and that it was a becoming way in which to honor his memory. They had some vague notions of the majesty of the law and the rights of the citizen, but in the passion of the moment these sunk into oblivion; a white man had been killed by a negro.

"The Cap'n was an ole sodger," said one of his friends solemnly. "He'll sleep better when he knows that a co'te-martial has be'n hilt an' jestice done."

By agreement the lynchers were to meet at Tyson's store at five o'clock in the afternoon, and proceed thence to the jail, which was situated down the Lumberton Dirt Road (as the old turnpike antedating the plank-road was called), about half a mile south of the court-house. When the preliminaries of the lynching had been arranged, and a committee appointed to manage the affair, the crowd dispersed, some to go to their dinners, and some to secure recruits for the lynching party.

It was twenty minutes to five o'clock, when an excited negro, panting and perspiring, rushed up to the back door of Sheriff Campbell's dwelling, which stood at a little distance from the jail and somewhat farther than the latter building from the court-house. A turbaned colored woman came to the door in response to the negro's knock.

"Hoddy, Sis' Nance."

"Hoddy, Brer Sam."

"Is de shurff in," inquired the negro.

"Yas, Brer Sam, he's eatin' his dinner," was the answer.

"Will yer ax 'im ter step ter de do' a minute, Sis' Nance?"

The woman went into the dining-room, and a moment later the sheriff came to the door. He was a tall, muscular man, of a ruddier complexion than is usual among Southerners. A pair of keen, deep-set gray eyes looked out from under bushy eyebrows, and about his mouth was a masterful expression, which a full beard, once sandy in color, but now profusely sprinkled with gray, could not entirely conceal. The day was hot; the sheriff had discarded his coat and vest, and had his white shirt open at the throat.

"What do you want, Sam?" he inquired of the negro, who stood hat in hand, wiping the moisture from his face with a ragged shirtsleeve.

"Shurff, dey gwine ter hang de pris'ner w'at's lock' up in de jail. Dey're comin' dis a-way now. I wuz layin' down on a sack er corn down at de sto', behine a pile er flour-bairls, w'en I hearn Doc' Cain en Kunnel Wright talkin' erbout it. I slip' outen de back do', en run here as fas' as I could. I hearn you say down ter de sto' once't dat you would n't let nobody take a pris'ner 'way fum you widout walkin' over yo' dead body, en I though I'd let you know 'fo' dey come, so yer could pertec' de pris'ner."

The sheriff listened calmly, but his face grew firmer, and a determined gleam lit up his gray eyes. His frame grew more erect, and he unconsciously assumed the attitude of a soldier who momentarily expects to meet the enemy face to face.

"Much obliged, Sam," he answered. "I'll protect the prisoner. Who's coming?"

"I dunno who-all *is* comin'," replied the negro. "Dere's Mistah McSwayne, en Doc' Cain, en Maje' McDonal', en Kunnel Wright, en a heap er yuthers. I wuz so skeered I done furgot mo' d'n half un em. I spec' dey mus' be mos' here by dis time, so I'll git outen de way, fer I don' want nobody fer ter think I wuz mix' up in dis business." The negro glanced nervously down the road toward the town, and made a movement as if to go away.

"Won't you have some dinner first?" asked the sheriff.

The negro looked longingly in at the open door, and sniffed the appetizing odor of boiled pork and collards.

"I ain't got no time fer ter tarry, Shurff," he said, "but Sis' Nance mought gin me sump'n I could kyar in my han' en eat on de way."

A moment later Nancy brought him a huge sandwich of split corn-pone, with a thick slice of fat bacon inserted between the halves, and a couple of baked yams. The negro hastily replaced his ragged hat on his head, dropped the yams in the pocket of his capacious trousers, and, taking the sandwich in his hand, hurried across the road and disappeared in the woods beyond.

The sheriff reëntered the house, and put on his coat and hat. He then took down a double-barreled shotgun and loaded it with buckshot. Filling the chambers of a revolver with fresh cartridges, he slipped it into the pocket of the sack-coat which he wore.

A comely young woman in a calico dress watched these proceedings with anxious surprise.

"Where are you going, father?" she asked. She had not heard the conversation with the negro.

"I am goin' over to the jail," responded the sheriff. "There's a mob comin' this way to lynch the nigger we've got locked up. But they won't do it," he added, with emphasis.

"Oh, father! don't go!" pleaded the girl, clinging to his arm; "they'll shoot you if you don't give him up."

"You never mind me, Polly," said her father reassuringly, as he gently unclasped her hands from his arm. "I'll take care of myself and the prisoner, too. There ain't a man in Branson County that would shoot me. Besides, I have faced fire too often to be scared away from my duty. You keep close in the house," he continued, "and if any one disturbs you just use the old horse-pistol in the top bureau drawer. It's a little old-fashioned, but it did good work a few years ago."

The young girl shuddered at this sanguinary allusion, but made no further objection to her father's departure.

The sheriff of Branson was a man far above the average of the community in wealth, education, and social position. His had been one of the few families in the county that before the war had owned large estates and numerous slaves. He had graduated at the State University at Chapel Hill, and had kept up some acquaintance with current literature and advanced thought. He had traveled some in his youth, and was looked up to in the county as an authority on all subjects connected with the outer world. At first an ardent supporter of the Union, he had opposed the secession movement in his native State as long as opposition availed to stem the tide of public opinion. Yielding at last to the force of circumstances, he had entered the Confederate service rather late in the war, and served with distinction through several campaigns, rising in time to the rank of colonel. After the war he had taken the oath of allegiance, and had been chosen by the people as the most available candidate for the office of sheriff, to which he had been elected without opposition. He had filled the office for several terms, and was universally popular with his constituents.

Colonel or Sheriff Campbell, as he was indifferently called, as the military or civil title happened to be most important in the opinion of the person addressing him, had a high sense of the responsibility attaching to his office. He had sworn to do his duty faithfully, and he knew what his duty was, as sheriff, perhaps more clearly than he had apprehended it in other passages of his life. It was, therefore, with no uncertainty in regard to his course that he prepared his weapons and went over to the jail. He had no fears for Polly's safety.

The sheriff had just locked the heavy front door of the jail behind him when a half dozen horsemen, followed by a crowd of men on foot, came round a bend in the road and drew near the jail. They halted in front of the picket fence that surrounded the building, while several of the committee of arrangements rode on a few rods farther to the sheriff's house. One of them dismounted and rapped on the door with his riding-whip.

"Is the sheriff at home?" he inquired.

"No, he has just gone out," replied Polly, who had come to the door.

"We want the jail keys," he continued.

"They are not here," said Polly. "The sheriff has them himself." Then she added, with assumed indifference. "He is at the jail now."

The man turned away, and Polly went into the front room, from which she peered anxiously between the slats of the green blinds of a window that looked toward the jail. Meanwhile the messenger returned to his companions and announced his discovery. It looked as though the sheriff had learned of their design and was preparing to resist it.

One of them stepped forward and rapped on the jail door.

"Well, what is it?" said the sheriff, from within.

"We want to talk to you, Sheriff," replied the spokesman.

There was a little wicket in the door: this the sheriff opened, and answered through it.

"All right, boys, talk away. You are all strangers to me, and I don't know what business you can have." The sheriff did not think it necessary to recognize anybody in particular on such an occasion; the question of identity sometimes comes up in the investigation of these extra-judicial executions.

"We're a committee of citizens and we want to get into the jail."

"What for? It ain't much trouble to get into jail. Most people want to keep out."

The mob was in no humor to appreciate a joke, and the sheriff's witticism fell dead upon an unresponsive audience.

"We want to have a talk with the nigger that killed Cap'n Walker."

"You can talk to that nigger in the courthouse, when he's brought out for trial. Court will be in session here next week. I know what you fellows want, but you can't get my prisoner to-day. Do you want to take the bread out of a poor man's mouth? I get seventy-five cents a day for keeping this prisoner, and he's the only one in jail. I can't have my family suffer just to please you fellows."

One or two young men in the crowd laughed at the idea of Sheriff Campbell's suffering for want of seventy-five cents a day; but they were frowned into silence by those who stood near them.

"Ef yer don't let us in," cried a voice, "we'll bu's' the do' open."

"Bust away," answered the sheriff, raising his voice so that all could hear. "But I give you fair warning. The first man that tries it will be filled with buckshot. I'm sheriff of this county; I know my duty, and I mean to do it."

"What's the use of kicking, Sheriff?" argued one of the leaders of the mob. "The nigger is sure to hang anyhow; he richly deserves it; and we've got to do something to teach the niggers their places, or white people won't be able to live in the county."

"There's no use talking, boys," responded the sheriff. "I'm a white man outside, but in this jail I'm sheriff; and if this nigger's to be hung in this county, I propose to do the hanging. So you fellows might as well right-about-face, and march back to Troy. You've had a pleasant trip, and the exercise will be good for you. You know *me.* I've got powder and ball, and I've faced fire before now, with nothing between me and the enemy, and I don't mean to surrender this jail while I'm able to shoot." Having thus announced his determination, the sheriff closed and fastened the wicket, and looked around for the best position from which to defend the building.

The crowd drew off a little, and the leaders conversed together in low tones.

The Branson County jail was a small, two-story brick building, strongly constructed, with no attempt at architectural ornamentation. Each story was divided into two large cells by a passage running from front to rear. A grated iron door gave entrance from the passage to each of the four cells. The jail seldom had many prisoners in it, and the lower windows had been boarded up. When the sheriff had closed the wicket, he ascended the steep wooden stairs to the upper floor. There was no window at the front of the upper passage, and the most available position from which to watch the movements of the crowd below was the front window of the cell occupied by the solitary prisoner.

The sheriff unlocked the door and entered the cell. The prisoner was crouched in a corner, his yellow face, blanched with terror, looking ghastly in the semi-darkness of the room. A cold perspiration had gathered on his forehead, and his teeth were chattering with affright.

"For God's sake, Sheriff," he murmured hoarsely, "don't let 'em lynch me; I did n't kill the old man."

The sheriff glanced at the cowering wretch with a look of mingled contempt and loathing.

"Get up," he said sharply. "You will probably be hung sooner or later, but it shall not be to-day, if I can help it. I'll unlock your fetters, and if I can't hold the jail, you'll have to make the best fight you can. If I'm shot, I'll consider my responsibility at an end."

There were iron fetters on the prioner's ankles, and handcuffs on his wrists. These the sheriff unlocked, and they fell clanking to the floor.

"Keep back from the window," said the sheriff. "They might shoot if they saw you."

The sheriff drew toward the window a pine bench which formed a part of the scanty furniture of the cell, and laid his revolver upon it. Then he took his gun in hand, and took his stand at the side of the window where he could with least exposure of himself watch the movements of the crowd below.

The lynchers had not anticipated any determined resistance. Of course they had looked for a formal protest, and perhaps a sufficient show of opposition to excuse the sheriff in the eye of any stickler for legal formalities. They had not however come prepared to fight a battle, and no one of them seemed willing to lead an attack upon the jail. The leaders of the party conferred together with a good deal of animated gesticulation, which was visible to the sheriff from his outlook, though the distance was too great for him to hear what was said. At length one of them broke away from the group, and rode back to the main body of the lynchers, who were restlessly awaiting orders.

"Well, boys," said the messenger, "we'll have to let it go for the present. The sheriff says he'll shoot, and he's got the drop on us this time. There ain't any of us that want to follow Cap'n Walker jest yet. Besides, the sheriff is a good fellow, and we don't want to hurt 'im. But," he added, as if to reassure the crowd, which began to show signs of disappointment, "the nigger might as well say his prayers, for he ain't got long to live."

There was a murmur of dissent from the mob, and several voices insisted that an attack be made on the jail. But pacific counsels finally prevailed, and the mob sullenly withdrew.

The sheriff stood at the window until they had disappeared around the bend in the road. He did not relax his watchfulness when the last one was out of sight. Their withdrawal might be a mere feint, to be followed by a further attempt. So closely, indeed, was his attention drawn to the outside, that he neither saw nor heard the prisoner creep stealthily across the floor, reach out his hand and secure the revolver which lay on the bench behind the sheriff, and creep as noiselessly back to his place in the corner of the room.

A moment after the last of the lynching party had disappeared there was a shot fired from the woods across the road; a bullet whistled by the window and buried itself in the wooden casing a few inches from where the sheriff was standing. Quick as thought, with the instinct born of a semi-guerrilla army experience, he raised his gun and fired twice at the point from which a faint puff of smoke showed the hostile bullet to have been sent. He stood a moment watching, and then rested his gun against the window, and reached behind him mechanically for the other weapon. It was not on the bench. As the sheriff realized this fact, he turned his head and looked into the muzzle of the revolver.

"Stay where you are, Sheriff," said the prisoner, his eyes glistening, his face almost ruddy with excitement.

The sheriff mentally cursed his own carelessness for allowing him to be caught in such a predicament. He had not expected anything of the kind. He had relied on the negro's cowardice and subordination in the presence of an armed white man as a matter of course. The sheriff was a brave man, but realized that the prisoner had him at an immense disadvantage. The two men stood thus for a moment, fighting a harmless duel with their eyes.

"Well, what do you mean to do?" asked the sheriff with apparent calmness.

"To get away, of course," said the prisoner, in a tone which caused the sheriff to look at him more closely, and with an involuntary feeling of apprehension; if the man was not mad, he was in a state of mind akin to madness, and quite as dangerous. The sheriff felt that he must speak the prisoner fair, and watch for a chance to turn the tables on him. The keen-eyed, desperate man before him was a different being altogether from the groveling wretch who had begged so piteously for life a few minutes before.

At length the sheriff spoke: —

"Is this your gratitude to me for saving your life at the risk of my own? If I had not done so, you would now be swinging from the limb of some neighboring tree."

"True," said the prisoner, "you saved my life, but for how long? When you came in, you said Court would sit next week. When the crowd went away they said I had not long to live. It is merely a choice of two ropes."

"While there's life there's hope," replied the sheriff. He uttered this commonplace mechanically, while his brain was busy in trying to think out some way of escape. "If you are innocent you can prove it."

The mulatto kept his eye upon the sheriff. "I didn't kill the old man," he replied; "but I shall never be able to clear myself. I was at his house at nine o'clock. I stole from it the coat that was on my back when I was taken. I would be convicted, even with a fair trial, unless the real murderer were discovered beforehand."

The sheriff knew this only too well. While he was thinking what argument next to use, the prisoner continued: —

"Throw me the keys — no, unlock the door."

The sheriff stood a moment irresolute. The mulatto's eyes glittered ominously. The sheriff crossed the room and unlocked the door leading into the passage.

"Now go down and unlock the outside door."

The heart of the sheriff leaped within him. Perhaps he might make a dash for liberty, and gain the outside. He descended the narrow stairs, the prisoner keeping close behind him.

The sheriff inserted the huge iron key into the lock. The rusty bolt yielded slowly. It still remained for him to pull the door open.

"Stop!" thundered the mulatto, who seemed to divine the sheriff's purpose. "Move a muscle, and I'll blow your brains out."

The sheriff obeyed; he realized that his chance had not yet come.

"Now keep on that side of the passage, and go back upstairs."

Keeping the sheriff under cover of the revolver, the mulatto followed him up the stairs. The sheriff expected the prisoner to lock him into the cell and make his own escape. He had about come to the conclusion that the best thing he could do under the circumstances was to submit quietly, and take his chances of recapturing the prisoner after the alarm had been given. The sheriff had faced death more than once upon the battlefield. A few minutes before, well armed, and with a brick wall between him and them he had dared a hundred men to fight; but he felt instinctively that the desperate man confronting him was not to be trifled with, and he was too prudent a man to risk his life against such heavy odds. He had Polly to look after, and there was a limit beyond which devotion to duty would be quixotic and even foolish.

"I want to get away," said the prisoner, "and I don't want to be captured; for if I am I know I will be hung on the spot. I am afraid," he added somewhat reflectively, "that in order to save myself I shall have to kill you."

"Good God!" exclaimed the sheriff in involuntary terror: "you would not kill the man to whom you owe your own life."

"You speak more truly than you know," replied the mulatto. "I indeed owe my life to you."

The sheriff started. He was capable of surprise, even in that moment of extreme peril. "Who are you?" he asked in amazement.

"Tom, Cicely's son," returned the other. He had closed the door and stood talking to the sheriff through the grated opening. "Don't you remember Cicely — Cicely whom you sold, with her child, to the speculator on his way to Alabama?"

The sheriff did remember. He had been sorry for it many a time since. It had been the old story of debts, mortgages, and bad crops. He had quarreled with the mother. The price offered for her and her child had been unusually large, and he had yielded to the combination of anger and pecuniary stress.

"Good God!" he gasped, "you would not murder your own father?"

"My father?" replied the mulatto. "It were well enough for me to claim the relationship, but it comes with poor grace from you to ask anything by reason of it. What father's duty have you ever performed for me? Did you give me your name, or even your protection? Other white men gave their colored sons freedom and money, and sent them to the free States. *You* sold *me* to the rice swamps."

"I at least gave you the life you cling to," murmured the sheriff.

"Life?" said the prisoner, with a sarcastic laugh. "What kind of a life? You gave me your own blood, your features, — no man need look at us together twice to see that, — and you gave me a black mother. Poor wretch! She died under the lash, because she had enough womanhood to call her soul her own. You gave me a white man's spirit, and you made me a slave, and crushed it out."

"But you are free now," said the sheriff. He had not doubted, could not doubt, the mulatto's word. He knew whose passions coursed beneath that swarthy skin and burned in the black eyes opposite his own. He saw in this mulatto what he himself might have become had not the safeguards of parental restraint and public opinion been thrown around him.

"Free to do what?" replied the mulatto. "Free in name, but despised and scorned and set aside by the people to whose race I belong far more than to my mother's."

"There are schools," said the sheriff. "You have been to school." He had noticed that the mulatto spoke more eloquently and used better language than most Branson County people.

"I have been to school, and dreamed when I went that it would work some marvelous change in my condition. But what did I learn? I learned to feel that no degree of learning or wisdom will change the color of my skin and that I shall always wear what in my own country is a badge of degradation. When I think about it seriously I do not care particularly for such a life. It is the animal in me, not the man, that flees the gallows. I owe you nothing," he went on, "and expect nothing of you; and it would be no more than justice if I should avenge upon you my mother's wrongs and my own. But still I hate to shoot you; I have never yet taken human life — for I did *not* kill the old captain. Will you promise to give no alarm and make no attempt to capture me until morning, if I do not shoot?"

So absorbed were the two men in their colloquy and their own tumultuous thoughts that neither of them had heard the door below move upon its hinges. Neither of them had heard a light step come stealthily up the stairs, nor seen a slender form creep along the darkening passage toward the mulatto.

The sheriff hesitated. The struggle between his love of life and his sense of duty was a terrific one. It may seem strange that a man who could sell his own child into slavery should hesitate at such a moment, when his life was trembling in the balance. But the baleful influence of human slavery poisoned the very fountains of life, and created new standards of right. The sheriff was conscientious: his conscience had merely been warped by his environment. Let no one ask what his answer would have been: he was spared the necessity of a decision.

"Stop," said the mulatto, "you need not promise. I could not trust you if you did. It is your life for mine: there is but one safe way for me; you must die."

He raised his arm to fire, when there was a flash — a report from the passage behind him. His arm fell heavily at his side, and the pistol dropped at his feet.

The sheriff recovered first from his surprise, and throwing open the door secured the fallen weapon. Then seizing the prisoner he thrust him into the cell and locked the door upon him: after which he turned to Polly, who leaned half-fainting against the wall, her hands clasped over her heart.

"Oh, father. I was just in time!" she cried hysterically, and, wildly sobbing, threw herself into her father's arms.

"I watched until they all went away," she said. "I heard the shot from the woods and I saw you shoot. Then when you did not come out I feared something had happened, that perhaps you had been wounded. I got out the other pistol and ran over here. When I found the door open, I knew something was wrong and when I heard voices I crept upstairs, and reached the top just in time to hear him say he would kill you. Oh, it was a narrow escape!"

When she had grown somewhat calmer, the sheriff left her standing there and went back into the cell. The prisoner's arm was bleeding from a flesh wound. His bravado had given place to a stony apathy. There was no sign in his face of fear or disappointment or feeling of any kind. The sheriff sent Polly to the house for cloth, and bound up the prisoner's wound with a rude skill acquired during his army life.

"I'll have a doctor come and dress the wound in the morning," he said to the prisoner. "It will do very well until then, if you will keep quiet. If the doctor asks you how the wound was caused, you can say that you were struck by the bullet fired from the woods. It would do you no good to have it known that you were shot while attempting to escape."

The prisoner uttered no word of thanks or apology, but sat in sullen silence. When the wounded arm had been bandaged, Polly and her father returned to the house.

The sheriff was in an unusually thoughtful mood that evening. He put salt in his coffee at super, and poured vinegar over his pancakes. To many of Polly's questions he returned random answers. When he had gone to bed he lay awake for several hours.

In the silent watches of the night, when he was alone with God, there came into his mind a flood of unaccustomed thoughts. An hour or two before, standing face to face with death, he had experienced a sensation similar to that which drowning men are said to feel — a kind of clarifying of the moral faculty, in which the veil of the flesh, with its obscuring passions and prejudices, is pushed aside for a moment, and all the acts of one's life stand out, in the clear light of truth, in their correct proportions and relations, — a state of mind in which one sees himself as God may be supposed to see him. In the reaction following his rescue, this feeling had given place for a time to far different emotions. But now, in the silence of midnight, something of this clearness of spirit returned to the sheriff. He saw that he had owed some duty to this son of his, — that neither law nor custom could destroy a responsibility inherent in the nature of mankind. He could not thus, in the eyes of God at least, shake off the consequences of his sin. Had he never sinned, this wayward spirit would never have come back from the vanished past to haunt him. As these thoughts came, his anger against the mulatto died away, and in its place there sprang up a great pity. The hand of parental authority might have restrained the passions he had seen burning in the prisoner's eyes when the desperate man spoke the words which had seemed to doom his father to death. The sheriff felt that he might have saved this fiery spirit from the slough of slavery; that he might have sent him to the free North, and given him there, or in some other land, an opportunity to turn to usefulness and honorable pursuits the talents that had run to crime, perhaps to madness; he might, still less, have given this son of his the poor simulacrum of liberty which men of his caste could possess in a slave-holding community; or least of all, but still something, he might have kept the boy on the plantation, where the burdens of slavery would have fallen lightly upon him.

The sheriff recalled his own youth. He had inherited an honored name to keep untarnished; he had had a future to make; the picture of a fair young bride had beckoned him on to happiness. The poor wretch now stretched upon a pallet of straw between the brick walls of the jail had had none of these things, — no name, no father, no mother — in the true meaning of motherhood, — and until the past few years no possible future, and then one vague and shadowy in its outline, and dependent for form and substance upon the slow solution of a problem in which there were many unknown quantities.

From what he might have done to what he might yet do was an easy transition for the awakened conscience of the sheriff. It occurred to him, purely as a hypothesis, that he might permit his prisoner to escape; but his oath of office, his duty as sheriff, stood in the way of such a course, and the sheriff dismissed the idea from his mind. He could, however, investigate the circumstances of the murder, and move Heaven and earth to discover the real criminal, for he no longer doubted the prisoner's innocence; he could employ counsel for the accused, and perhaps influence public opinion in his favor. An acquittal once secured, some plan could be devised by which the sheriff might in some degree atone for his crime against this son of his — against society — against God.

When the sheriff had reached this conclusion he fell into an unquiet slumber, from which he awoke late the next morning.

He went over to the jail before breakfast and found the prisoner lying on his pallet, his face turned to the wall; he did not move when the sheriff rattled the door.

"Good-morning," said the latter, in a tone intended to waken the prisoner.

There was no response. The sheriff looked more keenly at the recumbent figure; there was an unnatural rigidity about its attitude.

He hastily unlocked the door and, entering the cell, bent over the prostrate form. There was no sound of breathing; he turned the body over — it was cold and stiff. The prisoner had torn the bandage from his wound and bled to death during the night. He had evidently been dead several hours.

[1899]

KATE CHOPIN *(1851–1904) was born in St. Louis. Her father died when she was four, and she was raised by her Creole mother's family. In 1870 she married Oscar Chopin, a cotton broker. They lived in Louisiana, first in New Orleans and then on a large plantation among the French-speaking Acadians. When her husband died in 1882, Chopin moved with her six children back to St. Louis. Friends encouraged her to write, and when she was nearly forty years old she published her first novel,* At Fault *(1890). Her stories began to appear in* Century *and* Harper's Magazine, *and two collections followed:* Bayou Folk *(1894) and* A Night in Arcadie *(1897). Her last major work, the novel* The Awakening *(1899), is her masterpiece, but its sympathetic treatment of adultery shocked reviewers and readers throughout America. In St. Louis the novel was taken out of the libraries, and Chopin was denied membership in the St. Louis Fine Arts Club. When her third collection of stories was rejected by her publisher at the end of 1899, Chopin felt herself a literary outcast; she wrote very little in the last years of her life.*

What affronted the genteel readers of the 1890s was Chopin's attempt to write frankly about women's emotions in their relations with men, children, and their own sexuality. After her mother's death in 1885, she stopped being a practicing Catholic and accepted the Darwinian view of human evolution. Seeking God in nature rather than through the church, Chopin wrote freely on the subjects of sex and love, but she said she learned to her sorrow that for American authors, "the limitations imposed upon their art by their environment hamper a full and spontaneous expression." Magazine editors turned down her work if it challenged conventional social behavior, as does "The Story of an Hour," which feminist critics championed more than half a century after Chopin's death.

Chopin adopted Guy de Maupassant as a model after translating his stories from the French. She felt, "Here was life, not fiction; for where were the plots, the old fashioned mechanism and stage trappings that in a vague, unthinking way I had fancied were essential to the art of story making?" If her fiction is sometimes marred by stilted language or improbable coincidence, at her best, as in "Désirée's Baby," Chopin subtly emphasized character rather than plot in her dramatization of the tragic repercussions of racial prejudice.

RELATED COMMENTARY: *Kate Chopin, "How I Stumbled upon Maupassant," page 1407.*

KATE CHOPIN

Désirée's Baby

As the day was pleasant, Madame Valmondé drove over to L'Abri to see Désirée and the baby.

It made her laugh to think of Désirée with a baby. Why, it seemed but yesterday that Désirée was little more than a baby herself; when Monsieur in riding through the gateway of Valmondé had found her lying asleep in the shadow of the big stone pillar.

The little one awoke in his arms and began to cry for "Dada." That was as much as she could do or say. Some people thought she might have strayed there of her own accord, for she was of the toddling age. The prevailing belief was that she had been purposely left by a party of Texans, whose canvas-covered wagon, late in the day, had crossed the ferry that Coton Maïs kept, just below the plantation. In time Madame Valmondé abandoned every speculation but the one that Désirée had been sent to her by a beneficent Providence to be the child of her affection, seeing that she was without child of the flesh. For the girl grew to be beautiful and gentle, affectionate and sincere, — the idol of Valmondé.

It was no wonder, when she stood one day against the stone pillar in whose shadow she had lain asleep, eighteen years before, that Armand Aubigny riding by and seeing her there, had fallen in love with her. That was the way all the Aubignys fell in love, as if struck by a pistol shot. The wonder was that he had not loved her before; for he had known her since his father brought him home from Paris, a boy of eight, after his mother died there. The passion that awoke in him that day, when he saw her at the gate, swept along like an avalanche, or like a prairie fire, or like anything that drives headlong over all obstacles.

Monsieur Valmondé grew practical and wanted things well considered: that is, the girl's obscure origin. Armand looked into her eyes and did not care. He was reminded that she was nameless. What did it matter about a name when he could give her one of the oldest and proudest in Louisiana? He ordered the *corbeille* from Paris, and contained himself with what patience he could until it arrived; then they were married.

Madame Valmondé had not seen Désirée and the baby for four weeks. When she reached L'Abri she shuddered at the first sight of it, as she always did. It was a sad looking place, which for many years had not known the gentle presence of a mistress, old Monsieur Aubigny having married and buried his wife in France, and she having loved her own land too well ever to leave it. The roof came down steep and black like a cowl, reaching out beyond the wide galleries that encircled the yellow stuccoed house. Big, solemn oaks grew close to it, and their thick-leaved, far-reaching branches shadowed it like a pall. Young Aubigny's rule was a strict one, too, and under it his negroes had forgotten how to be gay, as they had been during the old master's easy-going and indulgent lifetime.

The young mother was recovering slowly, and lay full length, in her soft white muslins and laces, upon a couch. The baby was beside her, upon her arm, where he had fallen sleep, at her breast. The yellow nurse woman sat beside a window fanning herself.

Madame Valmondé bent her portly figure over Désirée and kissed her, holding her an instant tenderly in her arms. Then she turned to the child.

"This is not the baby!" she exclaimed, in startled tones. French was the language spoken at Valmondé in those days.

"I knew you would be astonished," laughed Désirée, "at the way he has grown. The little *cochon de lait!* Look at his legs, mamma, and his hands and fingernails, — real finger-nails. Zandrine had to cut them this morning. Is n't it true, Zandrine?"

The woman bowed her turbaned head majestically, "Mais si, Madame."

"And the way he cries," went on Désirée, "is deafening. Armand heard him the other day as far away as La Blanche's cabin."

Madame Valmondé had never removed her eyes from the child. She lifted it and walked with it over to the window that was lightest. She scanned the baby narrowly, then looked as searchingly at Zandrine, whose face was turned to gaze across the fields.

"Yes, the child has grown, has changed," said Madame Valmondé, slowly, as she replaced it beside its mother. "What does Armand say?"

Désirée's face became suffused with a glow that was happiness itself.

"Oh, Armand is the proudest father in the parish, I believe, chiefly because it is a boy, to bear his name; though he says not, — that he would have loved a girl as well. But I know it is n't true. I know he says that to please me. And mamma," she added, drawing Madame Valmondé's head down to her and speaking in a whisper, "he has n't punished one of them — not one of them — since baby is born. Even Négrillon, who pretended to have burnt his leg that he might rest from work — he only laughed, and said Négrillon was a great scamp. Oh, mamma, I'm so happy; it frightens me."

What Désirée said was true. Marriage, and later the birth of his son had softened Armand Aubigny's imperious and exacting nature greatly. This was what made the gentle Désirée so happy, for she loved him desperately. When he frowned she trembled, but loved him. When he smiled, she asked no greater blessing of God. But Armand's dark, handsome face had not often been disfigured by frowns since the day he fell in love with her.

When the baby was about three months old, Désirée awoke one day to the conviction that there was something in the air menacing her peace. It was at first too subtle to grasp. It had only been a disquieting suggestion; an air of mystery among the blacks; unexpected visits from far-off neighbors who could hardly account for their coming. Then a strange, an awful change in her husband's manner, which she dared not ask him to explain. When he spoke to her, it was with averted eyes, from which the old love-light seemed to have gone out. He absented himself from home; and when there, avoided her presence and that of her child, without excuse. And the very spirit of Satan seemed suddenly to take hold of him in his dealings with the slaves. Désirée was miserable enough to die.

She sat in her room, one hot afternoon, in her *peignoir*, listlessly drawing through her fingers the strands of her long, silky brown hair that hung about her shoulders. The baby, half naked, lay asleep upon her own great mahogany bed, that was like a sumptuous throne, with its satin-lined half-canopy. One of La Blanche's little quadroon boys — half naked too — stood fanning the child slowly with a fan of peacock feathers. Désirée's eyes had been fixed absently and sadly upon the baby, while she was striving to penetrate the threatening mist that she felt closing about her. She looked from her child to the boy who stood beside him, and back again; over and over. "Ah!" It was a cry that she could not help; which she was not conscious of having uttered. The blood turned like ice in her veins, and a clammy moisture gathered upon her face.

She tried to speak to the little quadroon boy; but no sound would come, at first. When he heard his name uttered, he looked up, and his mistress was pointing to the door. He laid aside the great, soft fan, and obediently stole away, over the polished floor, on his bare tiptoes.

She stayed motionless, with gaze riveted upon her child, and her face the picture of fright.

Presently her husband entered the room, and without noticing her, went to a table and began to search among some papers which covered it.

"Armand," she called to him, in a voice which must have stabbed him, if he was human. But he did not notice. "Armand," she said again. Then she rose and tottered towards him. "Armand," she panted once more, clutching his arm, "look at our child. What does it mean? tell me."

He coldly but gently loosened her fingers from about his arm and thrust the hand away from him. "Tell me what it means!" she cried despairingly.

"It means," he answered lightly, "that the child is not white; it means that you are not white."

A quick conception of all that this accusation meant for her nerved her with unwonted courage to deny it. "It is a lie; it is not true, I am white! Look at my hair, it is brown; and my eyes are gray, Armand, you know they are gray. And my skin is fair," seizing his wrist. "Look at my hand; whiter than yours, Armand," she laughed hysterically.

"As white as La Blanche's," he returned cruelly; and went away leaving her alone with their child.

When she could hold a pen in her hand, she sent a despairing letter to Madame Valmondé.

"My mother, they tell me I am not white. Armand has told me I am not white. For God's sake tell them it is not true. You must know it is not true. I shall die. I must die. I cannot be so unhappy, and live."

The answer that came was as brief:

"My own Désirée: Come home to Valmondé; back to your mother who loves you. Come with your child."

When the letter reached Désirée she went with it to her husband's study, and laid it open upon the desk before which he sat. She was like a stone image: silent, white, motionless after she placed it there.

In silence he ran his cold eyes over the written words. He said nothing. "Shall I go, Armand?" she asked in tones sharp with agonized suspense.

"Yes, go."

"Do you want me to go?"

"Yes, I want you to go."

He thought Almighty God had dealt cruelly and unjustly with him; and felt, somehow, that he was paying Him back in kind when he stabbed thus into his wife's soul. Moreover he no longer loved her, because of the unconscious injury she had brought upon his home and his name.

She turned away like one stunned by a blow, and walked slowly towards the door, hoping he would call her back.

"Good-by, Armand," she moaned.

He did not answer her. That was his last blow at fate.

Désirée went in search of her child. Zandrine was pacing the sombre gallery with it. She took the little one from the nurse's arms with no word of explanation, and descending the steps, walked away, under the live-oak branches.

It was an October afternoon; the sun was just sinking. Out in the still fields the negroes were picking cotton.

Désirée had not changed the thin white garment nor the slippers which she wore. Her hair was uncovered and the sun's rays brought a golden gleam from its brown meshes. She did not take the broad, beaten road which led to the far-off plantation of Valmondé. she walked across a deserted field, where the stubble bruised her tender feet, so delicately shod, and tore her thin gown to shreds.

She disappeared among the reeds and willows that grew thick along the banks of the deep, sluggish bayou; and she did not come back again.

Some weeks later there was a curious scene enacted at L'Abri. In the centre of the smoothly swept back yard was a great bonfire. Armand Aubigny sat in the wide hallway that commanded a view of the spectacle; and it was he who dealt out to a half dozen negroes the material which kept this fire ablaze.

A graceful cradle of willow, with all its dainty furbishings, was laid upon the pyre, which had already been fed with the richness of a priceless *layette*. Then there were silk gowns, and velvet and satin ones added to these; laces, too, and embroideries; bonnets and gloves; for the *corbeille* had been of rare quality.

The last thing to go was a tiny bundle of letters; innocent little scribblings that Désirée had sent to him during the days of their espousal. There was the remnant of one back in the drawer from which he took them. But it was not Désirée's; it was part of an old letter from his mother to his father. He read it. She was thanking God for the blessing of her husband's love: —

"But, above all," she wrote, "night and day, I thank the good God for having so arranged our lives that our dear Armand will never know that his mother, who adores him, belongs to the race that is cursed with the brand of slavery." [1892]

KATE CHOPIN

The Story of an Hour

Knowing that Mrs. Mallard was afflicted with a heart trouble, great care was taken to break to her as gently as possible the news of her husband's death.

It was her sister Josephine who told her, in broken sentences; veiled hints that revealed in half concealing. Her husband's friend Richards was there, too, near her. It was he who had been in the newspaper office when intelligence of the railroad disaster was received, with Brently Mallard's name leading the list of "killed." He had only taken the time to assure himself of its truth by a second telegram, and had hastened to forestall any less careful, less tender friend in bearing the sad message.

She did not hear the story as many women have heard the same, with a paralyzed inability to accept its significance. She wept at once, with sudden, wild abandonment, in her sister's arms. When the storm of grief had spent itself she went away to her room alone. She would have no one follow her.

There stood, facing the open window, a comfortable, roomy armchair. Into this she sank, pressed down by a physical exhaustion that haunted her body and seemed to reach into her soul.

She could see in the open square before her house the tops of trees that were all aquiver with the new spring life. The delicious breath of rain was in the air. In the street below a peddler was crying his wares. The notes of a distant song which some one was singing reached her faintly, and countless sparrows were twittering in the eaves.

There were patches of blue sky showing here and there through the clouds that had met and piled one above the other in the west facing her window.

She sat with her head thrown back upon the cushion of the chair, quite motionless, except when a sob came up into her throat and shook her, as a child who had cried itself to sleep continues to sob in its dreams.

She was young, with a fair, calm face, whose lines bespoke repression and even a certain strength. But now there was a dull stare in her eyes, whose gaze was fixed away off yonder on one of those patches of blue sky. It was not a glance of reflection, but rather indicated a suspension of intelligent thought.

There was something coming to her and she was waiting for it, fearfully. What was it? She did not know; it was too subtle and elusive to name. But she felt it, creeping out of the sky, reaching toward her through the sounds, the scents, the color that filled the air.

Now her bosom rose and fell tumultuously. She was beginning to recognize this thing that was approaching to possess her, and she was striving to beat it back with her will — as powerless as her two white slender hands would have been.

When she abandoned herself a little whispered word escaped her slightly parted lips. She said it over and over under her breath: "free, free, free!" The vacant stare and the look of terror that had followed it went from her eyes. They stayed keen and bright. Her pulses beat fast, and the coursing blood warmed and relaxed every inch of her body.

She did not stop to ask if it were or were not a monstrous joy that held her. A clear and exalted perception enabled her to dismiss the suggestion as trivial.

She knew that she would weep again when she saw the kind, tender hands folded in death; the face that had never looked save with love upon her, fixed and gray and dead. But she saw beyond that bitter moment a long procession of years to come that would belong to her absolutely. And she opened and spread her arms out to them in welcome.

There would be no one to live for her during those coming years: she would live for herself. There would be no powerful will bending hers in that blind persistence with which men and women believe they have a right to impose a private will upon a fellow-creature. A kind intention or a cruel intention made the act seem no less a crime as she looked upon it in that brief moment of illumination.

And yet she had loved him — sometimes. Often she had not. What did it matter! What could love, the unsolved mystery, count for in face of this possession of self-assertion which she suddenly recognized as the strongest impulse of her being!

"Free! Body and soul free!" she kept whispering.

Josephine was kneeling before the closed door with her lips to the keyhole, imploring for admission. "Louise, open the door! I beg; open the door — you will make yourself ill. What are you doing, Louise? For heaven's sake open the door."

"Go away. I am not making myself ill." No; she was drinking in a very elixir of life through that open window.

Her fancy was running riot along those days ahead of her. Spring days, and summer days, and all sorts of days that would be her own. She breathed a quick prayer that life might be long. It was only yesterday she had thought with a shudder that life might be long.

She arose at length and opened the door to her sister's importunities. There was a feverish triumph in her eyes, and she carried herself unwittingly like a goddess of Victory. She clasped her sister's waist, and together they descended the stairs. Richards stood waiting for them at the bottom.

Some one was opening the front door with a latchkey. It was Brently Mallard who entered, a little travel-stained, composedly carrying his gripsack and umbrella. He had been far from the scene of accident, and did not even know there had been one. He stood amazed at Josephine's piercing cry; at Richards' quick motion to screen him from the view of his wife.

But Richards was too late.

When the doctors came they said she had died of heart disease — of joy that kills.   [1894]

SANDRA CISNEROS (*b. 1954*), *the daughter of a Mexican father and a Chicana mother, grew up in ghetto neighborhoods in Chicago and began writing poetry when she was ten years old. Her six brothers so dominated the household that she remembers that she felt she had "seven fathers." Cisneros spoke Spanish at home with her father and on her frequent trips to Mexico to visit her grandmother, but she didn't think of herself as a Chicana writer until she began a series of autobiographical sketches as a graduate student in the M.A. program at the University of Iowa's Writers' Workshop in 1977. Then she discovered her literary voice, realizing the uniqueness of her experience growing up as a poor Latina in Chicago:*

> Everyone seemed to have some communal knowledge which I did not have. . . . This caused me to question myself, to become defensive. What did I, Sandra Cisneros, know? What could I know? My classmates were from the best schools in the country. They had been bred as fine hothouse flowers. I was a yellow weed among the city's cracks.

Cisneros says that she became a writer because she was "determined to fill a literary void . . . trying to write the stories that haven't been written." These early sketches developed into the book published as The House on Mango Street *(1983), over forty short narratives that were highly praised by critics and won the 1985 Before Columbus American Book Award. Cisneros had found a way to write stories*

> that were a cross between poetry and fiction. . . . [I] wanted to write a collection which could be read at any random point without having any knowledge of what came before or after. Or, that could be read in a series to tell one big story. I wanted stories like poems, compact and lyrical and ending with reverberation.

As Joyce Carol Oates has observed, Cisneros's "emotionally rich subject is the Latino community, specifically the experience of growing up female in a male-dominated society; her work . . . might be as readily classified as prose poetry as prose fiction." To date Cisneros has published three books of poetry in addition to her short stories.

"Little Miracles, Kept Promises" is from Woman Hollering Creek and Other Stories *(1991), a collection of more than twenty lyrical narratives about Mexican Americans in San Antonio who have different experiences living on both sides of the border with Mexico. The form of this experimental story consists entirely of letters to patron saints that have been left with small charms or presents as offerings alongside religious statues. Here Cisneros's growing mastery of the short story form ensures, as one reviewer observed, that her "irony defers to her powers of observation so that feminism and cultural imperialism, while important issues here, do not overwhelm the narrative."*

Little Miracles, Kept Promises

Exvoto Donated as Promised

On the 20th of December of 1988 we suffered a terrible disaster on the road to Corpus Christi. The bus we were riding skidded and overturned near Robstown and a lady and her little girl were killed. Thanks to La Virgen de Guadalupe we are alive, all of us miraculously unharmed, and with no visible scars, except we are afraid to ride buses. We dedicate this retablo to La Virgencita with our affection and gratitude and our everlasting faith.

> Familia Arteaga
> Alice, Texas
> G.R. (Gracias Recibido/Thanks Given)

Blessed Santo Niño de Atocha,

Thank you for helping us when Chapa's truck got stolen. We didn't know how we was going to make it. He needs it to get to work, and this job, well, he's been on probation since we got him to quit drinking. Raquel and the kids are hardly ever afraid of him anymore, and we are proud parents. We don't know how we can repay you for everything you have done for our family. We will light a candle to you every Sunday and never forget you.

> Sidronio Tijerina
> Brenda A. Camacho de Tijerina
> San Angelo, Texas

Dear San Martín de Porres,

Please send us clothes, furniture, shoes, dishes. We need anything that don't eat. Since the fire we have to start all over again and Lalo's disability check ain't much and don't go far. Zulema would like to finish school but I says she can just forget about it now. She's our oldest and her place is at home helping us out I told her. Please make her see some sense. She's all we got.

> Thanking you,
> Adelfa Vásquez
> Escobas, Texas

Dear San Antonio de Padua,

Can you please help me find a man who isn't a pain in the nalgas. There aren't any in Texas, I swear. Especially not in San Antonio.

Can you do something about all the educated Chicanos who have to go to California to find a job. I guess what my sister Irma says is true: "If you didn't get a husband when you were in college, you don't get one."

I would appreciate it very much if you sent me a man who speaks Spanish, who at least can pronounce his name the way it's supposed to be pronounced. Someone please who never calls himself "Hispanic" unless he's applying for a grant from Washington, D.C.

Can you send me a man man. I mean someone who's not ashamed to be seen cooking or cleaning or looking after himself. In other words, a man who acts like an adult. Not one who's never lived alone, never bought his own underwear, never ironed his own shirts, never even heated his own tortillas. In other words, don't send me someone like my brothers who my mother ruined with too much chichi, or I'll throw him back.

I'll turn your statue upside down until you send him to me. I've put up with too much too long, and now I'm just too intelligent, too powerful, too beautiful, too sure of who I am finally to deserve anything less.

Ms. Barbara Ybañez

San Antonio, TX

Dear Niño Fidencio,

I would like for you to help me get a job with good pay, benefits, and retirement plan. I promise you if you help me I will make a pilgrimage to your tomb in Espinazo and bring you flowers. Many thanks.

César Escandón

Pharr, Tejas

DEAR DON PEDRITO JARAMILLO HEALER OF LOS OLMOS

MY NAME IS ENRIQUETA ANTONIA SANDOVAL I LIVE IN SAN MARCOS TX I AM SICK THEY OPERATED ME FROM A KIDNEY AND A TUMOR OF CANCER BUT THANKS TO GOD I AM ALIVE BUT I HAVE TO GET TREATMENTS FOR A YEAR THE KIMO I AM 2 1/2 YEARS OLD BUT MY GRANDMA BROUGHT ME THAT YOU AND OUR LORD WHO IS IN THE HEAVENS WILL CURE ME WITH THIS LETTER THAT I AM DEPOSITING HERE ITS MY GRANDMA WHO IS WRITING THIS I HOPE EVERY-BODY WHO SEES THIS LETTER WILL TAKE A MINUTE TO ASK FOR MY HEALTH

ENRIQUETA ANTONIA SANDOVAL

2 AND A HALF YEARS OLD

I LEOCADIA DIMAS VDA. DE CORDERO OF SAN MARCOS TX HAVE COME TO PAY THIS REQUEST TO DON PEDRITO THAT MY GRANDDAUGHTER WILL COME OUT FINE FROM HER OPERATION THANKS TO GOD AND THOSE WHO HELPED SUCH GOOD DOCTORS THAT DID THEIR JOB WELL THE REST IS IN GODS HANDS THAT HE DO HIS WILL MANY THANKS WITH ALL MY HEART.

YOUR VERY RESPECTFUL SERVANT

LEOCADIA

Oh Mighty Poderosos, Blessed Powerful Ones,

You who are crowned in heaven and who are so close to our Divine Savior, I implore your intercession before the Almighty on my behalf. I ask for peace of spirit and prosperity, and that the demons in my path that are the cause of all my woes be removed so that they no longer torment me. Look favorably on this petition and bless me, that I may continue to glorify your deeds with all my heart — santísimo Niño Fidencio, gran General Pancho

Villa, bendito Don Pedrito Jaramillo, virtuoso John F. Kennedy, and blessed Pope John Paul. Amen.

Gertrudis Parra
Uvalde, Tejas

Father Almighty,
Teach me to love my husband again. Forgive me.

s.
Corpus Christi

Seven African Powers that surround our Savior — Obatala, Yemaya, Ochún, Orunla, Ogun, Elegua, and Shango — why don't you behave and be good to me? Oh Seven African Powers, come on, don't be bad. Let my Illinois lottery ticket win, and if it does, don't let my cousin Cirilo in Chicago cheat me out of my winnings, since I'm the one who pays for the ticket and all he does is buy it for me each week — if he does even that. He's my cousin, but like the Bible says, better to say nothing than to say nothing nice.

Protect me from the evil eye of the envious and don't let my enemies do me harm, because I've never done a thing wrong to anyone first. Save this good Christian who the wicked have taken advantage of.

Seven Powers, reward my devotion with good luck. Look after me, why don't you? And don't forget me because I never forget you.

Moises Ildefonso Mata
San Antonio, Texas

Virgencita de Guadalupe,
I promise to walk to your shrine on my knees the very first day I get back, I swear, if you will only get the Tortillería la Casa de la Masa to pay me the $253.72 they owe me for two weeks' work. I put in $67 \frac{1}{2}$ hours that first week and 79 hours the second, and I don't have anything to show for it yet. I calculated with the taxes deducted, I have $253.72 coming to me. That's all I'm asking for. The $253.72 I have coming to me.

I have asked the proprietors Blanquita and Rudy Mondragón, and they keep telling me next week, next week, next week. And it's almost the middle of the third week already and I don't know how I'm going to do it to pay this week's rent, since I'm already behind, and the other guys have loaned me as much as they're able, and I don't know what I'm going to do, I don't know what I'm going to do.

My wife and the kids and my in-laws all depend on what I send home. We are humble people, Virgencita. You know I'm not full of vices. That's how I am. It's been hard for me to live here so far away without seeing my wife, you know. And sometimes one gets tempted, but no, and no, and no. I'm not like that. Please, Virgencita, all I'm asking for is my $253.72. There is no one else I can turn to here in this country, and well, if you can't help me, well, I just don't know.

Arnulfo Contreras
San Antonio, Tejas

Saint Sebastian who was persecuted with arrows and then survived, thank you for answering my prayers! All them arrows that had persecuted me — my brother-in-law Ernie and my sister Alba and their kids — el Junior, la Gloria, and el Skyler — all gone. And now my home sweet home is mine again, and my Dianita bien lovey-dovey, and my kids got something to say to me besides who hit who.

Here is the little gold milagrito I promised you, a little house, see? And it ain't that cheap gold-plate shit either. So now that I paid you back, we're even, right? Cause I don't like for no one to say Victor Lozano don't pay his debts. I pays cash on the line, bro. And Victor Lozano's word like his deeds is solid gold.

> Victor A. Lozano
> Houston, TX

Dear San Lázaro,

My mother's comadre Demetria said if I prayed to you that like maybe you could help me because you were raised from the dead and did a lot of miracles and maybe if I lit a candle every night for seven days and prayed, you might maybe could help me with my face breaking out with so many pimples. Thank you.

> Rubén Ledesma
> Hebbronville, Texas

Santísima Señora de San Juan de los Lagos,

We came to see you twice when they brought you to San Antonio, my mother and my sister Yolanda and two of my aunts, Tía Enedina and my Tía Perla, and we drove all the way from Beeville just to visit you and make our requests.

I don't know what my Tía Enedina asked for, she's always so secretive, but probably it had to do with her son Beto who doesn't do anything but hang around the house and get into trouble. And my Tía Perla no doubt complained about her ladies' problems — her ovaries that itch, her tangled fallopians, her uterus that makes her seasick with all its flipping and flopping. And Mami who said she only came along for the ride, lit three candles so you would bless us all and sweep jealousy and bitterness from our hearts because that's what she says every day and every night. And my sister Yoli asked that you help her lose weight because I don't want to wind up like Tía Perla, embroidering altar cloths and dressing saints.

But that was a year ago, Virgencita, and since then my cousin Beto was fined for killing the neighbor's rooster with a flying Big Red bottle, and my Tía Perla is convinced her uterus has fallen because when she walks something inside her rattles like a maraca, and my mother and my aunts are arguing and yelling at each other same as always. And my stupid sister Yoli is still sending away for even stupider products like the Grasa Fantástica, guaranteed to burn away fat — It really works, Tere, just rub some on while you're watching TV— only she's fatter than ever and just as sad.

What I realize is that we all made the trip to San Antonio to ask something of you, Virgencita, we all needed you to listen to us. And of all of us, my mama and sister Yoli, and my aunts Enedina and Perla, of all of us, you granted me my petition and sent, just like I asked, a guy who would love only me because I was tired of looking at girls younger than me walking along the street or riding in cars or standing in front of the school with a guy's arm hooked around their neck.

So what is it I'm asking for? Please, Virgencita. Lift this heavy cross from my shoulders and leave me like I was before, wind on my neck, my arms swinging free, and no one telling me how I ought to be.

Teresa Galindo
Beeville, Texas

Miraculous Black Christ of Esquipulas,
Please make our grandson to be nice to us and stay away from drugs. Save him to find a job and move away from us. Thank you.

Grandma y Grandfather
Harlingen

M3r1c5l45s Bl1ck Chr3st 4f 2sq53p5l1s,
3 1sk y45, L4rd, w3th 1ll my h21rt pl21s2 w1tch 4v2r M1nny B2n1v3d2s wh4 3s 4v2rs21s. 3 l4v2 h3m 1nd 3 d4n't kn4w wh1t t4 d4 1b45t 1ll th3s l4v2 s1dn2ss 1nd sh1m2 th1t f3lls m2.

B2nj1m3n T.
D21 R34 TX

Milagroso Cristo Negro de Esquipulas,
Te ofrezco este retrato de mis niños. Wáchelos, Dios Santo, y si le quitas el trago a mi hijo te prometo prender velitas. Ayúdanos con nuestras cuentas, Señor, y que el cheque del income tax nos llegue pronto para pagar los biles. Danos una buena vida y que les ayudes a mis hijos a cambiar sus modos. Tú que eres tan bondadoso escucha estas peticiones que te pido con todo mi corazón y con toda la fe de mi alma. Ten piedad, Padre mio. Mi nombre es Adela O.

Elizondo.
Cotulla TX

Milagroso Cristo Negro,
Thank you por el milagro de haber graduado de high school. Aquí le regalo mi retrato de graduation.

Fito Moroles
Rockport, Texas

Cristo Negro,
Venimos desde muy lejos. Infinitas gracias, Señor. Gracias por habernos escuchado.

Familia Armendáriz G.
Matamoros, Tamps. México

Jesus Christ,
    Please keep Deborah Abrego and Ralph S. Urrea together forever.

Love,
Deborah Abrego
Sabinal, Texas

Blessed Virgen de los Remedios,
    Señora Dolores Alcalá de Corchado finds herself gravely ill from a complication that resulted after a delicate operation she underwent Thursday last, and from which she was recovering satisfactorily until suffering a hemmorhage Tuesday morning. Please intercede on her behalf. We leave her in the hands of God, that His will be done, now that we have witnessed her suffering and don't know whether she should die or continue this life. Her husband of forty-eight years offers this request with all his heart.

Señor Gustavo Corchado B.
Laredo, Tejas

Madrecita de Dios,
    Thank you. Our child is born healthy!

Rene y Janie Garza
Hondo, TX

Saint Jude, patron saint of lost causes,
    Help me pass my English 320, British Restoration Literature class and everything to turn out ok.

Eliberto González
Dallas

. . .

Virgencita . . .
    I've cut off my hair just like I promised I would and pinned my braid here by your statue. Above a Toys "Я" Us name tag that says IZAURA. Along several hospital bracelets. Next to a business card for Sergio's Casa de la Belleza Beauty College. Domingo Reyna's driver's license. Notes printed on the flaps of envelopes. Silk roses, plastic roses, paper roses, roses crocheted out of fluorescent orange yarn. Photo button of a baby in a *charro* hat. Caramel-skinned woman in a white graduation cap and gown. Mean dude in bandanna and tattoos. Oval black-and-white passport portrait of the sad uncle who never married. A mama in a sleeveless dress watering the porch plants. Sweet boy with new mustache and new soldier uniform. Teenager with a little bit of herself sitting on her lap. Blurred husband and wife leaning one into the other as if joined at the hip. Black-and-white photo of the cousins *la* Josie *y la* Mary Helen, circa 1942. Polaroid of Sylvia Rios, First Holy Communion, age nine years.
    So many *milagritos* safety-pinned here, so many little miracles dangling from red thread — a gold Sacred Heart, a tiny copper arm, a kneeling man in silver, a bottle, a brass truck, a foot, a house, a hand, a baby, a cat, a breast,

a tooth, a belly button, an evil eye. So many petititons, so many promises made and kept. And there is nothing I can give you except this braid of hair the color of coffee in a glass.

Chayo, what have you done! All that beautiful hair.
Chayito, how could you ruin in one second what your mother took years to create?
You might as well've plucked out your eyes like Saint Lucy. All that hair!

My mother cried, did I tell you? All that beautiful hair . . .

I've cut off my hair. Which I've never cut since the day I was born. The donkey tail in a birthday game. Something shed like a snakeskin.

My head as light as if I'd raised it from water. My heart buoyant again, as if before I'd worn *el* Sagrado Corazón in my open chest. I could've lit this entire church with my grief.

I'm a bell without a clapper. A woman with one foot in this world and one foot in that. A woman straddling both. This thing between my legs, this unmentionable.

I'm a snake swallowing its tail. I'm my history and my future. All my ancestors' ancestors inside my own belly. All my futures and all my pasts.

I've had to steel and hoard and hone myself. I've had to push the furniture against the door and not let you in.

What you doing sitting in there in the dark?

I'm thinking.

Thinking of what?

Just . . . thinking.

You're nuts. Chayo, ven a saludar. All the relatives are here. You come out of there and be sociable.

Do boys think, and girls daydream? Do only girls have to come out and greet the relatives and smile and be nice and *quedar bien*?

It's not good to spend so much time alone.
What she do in there all by herself? It don't look right.
Chayito, when you getting married? Look at your cousin Leticia. She's younger than you.
How many kids you want when you grow up?
When I become a mommy . . .
You'll change. You'll see. Wait till you meet Mr. Right.
Chayo, tell everybody what it is you're studying again.
Look at our Chayito. She likes making her little pictures. She's gonna be a painter.
A painter! Tell her I got five rooms that need painting.
When you become a mother . . .

Thank you for making all those months I held my breath not a child in my belly, but a thyroid problem in my throat.

I can't be a mother. Not now. Maybe never. Not for me to choose, like I didn't choose being female. Like I didn't choose being artist — it isn't something you choose. It's something you are, only I can't explain it.

I don't want to be a mother.

I wouldn't mind being a father. At least a father could still be artist, could love some*thing* instead of some*one*, and no one would call that selfish.

I leave my braid here and thank you for believing what I do is important. Though no one else in my family, no other woman, neither friend nor relative, no one I know, not even the heroine in the *telenovelas*, no woman wants to live alone.

I do.

Virgencita de Guadalupe. For a long time I wouldn't let you in my house. I couldn't see you without seeing my ma each time my father came home drunk and yelling, blaming everything that ever went wrong in his life on her.

I couldn't look at your folded hands without seeing my *abuela* mumbling, "My son, my son, my son . . ." Couldn't look at you without blaming you for all the pain my mother and her mother and all our mothers' mothers have put up with in the name of God. Couldn't let you in my house.

I wanted you bare-breasted, snakes in your hands. I wanted you leaping and somersaulting the backs of bulls. I wanted you swallowing raw hearts and rattling volcanic ash. I wasn't going to be my mother or my grandma. All that self-sacrifice, all that silent suffering. Hell no. Not here. Not me.

Don't think it was easy going without you. Don't think I didn't get my share of it from everyone. Heretic. Atheist. *Malinchista. Hocicona.* But I wouldn't shut my yap. My mouth always getting me in trouble. *Is that what they teach you at the university? Miss High-and-Mighty. Miss Thinks-She's-Too-Good-for-Us.* Acting like a *bolilla*, a white girl. *Malinche.* Don't think it didn't hurt being called a traitor. Trying to explain to my ma, to my *abuela*, why I didn't want to be like them.

I don't know how it all fell in place. How I finally understood who you are. No longer Mary the mild, but our mother Tonantzín. Your church at Tepeyac built on the site of her temple. Sacred ground no matter whose goddess claims it.

That you could have the power to rally a people when a country was born, and again during civil war, and during a farmworkers' strike in California made me think maybe there is power in my mother's patience, strength in my grandmother's endurance. Because those who suffer have a special power, don't they? The power of understanding someone else's pain. And understanding is the beginning of healing.

When I learned your real name is Coatlaxopeuh, She Who Has Dominion over Serpents, when I recognized you as Tonantzín, and learned your names are Teteoinnan, Toci, Xochiquetzal, Tlazolteotl, Coatlicue, Chalchiuhtlicue, Coyolxauhqui, Huixtocihuatl, Chicomecoatl, Cihuacoatl, when I could see you as Nuestra Señora de la Soledad, Nuestra Señora de los Remedios, Nuestra Señora del Perpetuo Socorro, Nuestra Señora de San Juan de los Lagos, Our Lady of Lourdes, Our Lady of Mount Carmel, Our Lady of the

Rosary, Our Lady of Sorrows, I wasn't ashamed, then, to be my mother's daughter, my grandmother's granddaughter, my ancestors' child.

When I could see you in all your facets, all at once the Buddha, the Tao, the true Messiah, Yahweh, Allah, the Heart of the Sky, the Heart of the Earth, the Lord of the Near and Far, the Spirit, the Light, the Universe, I could love you, and, finally, learn to love me.

· · ·

Mighty Guadalupana Coatlaxopeuh Tonantzín,

What "little miracle" could I pin here? Braid of hair in its place and know that I thank you.

Rosario (Chayo) De Leon
Austin, Tejas

[1990]

JOSEPH CONRAD *(1857–1924) was born Jozef Teodore Konrad Nalecz Korzeniowski near Kiev, in what was then Russian Poland. His parents died when he was young, and he was raised by his uncle. At the age of seventeen Conrad went to sea, and for many years he sailed in the French and British navies. He then took a job as steamboat captain on the Congo River, an experience that matured him: "Before I went to the Congo I was just a mere animal," he later wrote. After leaving Africa he settled in England to become a professional writer. Conrad did not learn English until after he was twenty (Polish was his first language, French his second), but he is considered one of the supreme English stylists despite having complained that writing in English was like throwing mud at a wall. In 1895 he published his first novel,* Almayer's Folly, *followed by a stream of others:* An Outcast of the Islands *(1896),* The Nigger of the "Narcissus" *(1897),* Lord Jim *(1902), and* Nostromo *(1904). His later novels included* The Secret Agent *(1907),* Chance *(1913), and* Victory *(1915).*

Conrad believed that his imagination was his most precious possession as a writer, and he did not consider himself bound by what he called the "fettering dogmas of some romantic, realistic, or naturalistic creed." He said that the avowed aim of his fiction was "to make you hear, to make you feel, above all to make you see." The epic sweep of his descriptions of nature often suggests a disquieting sense of the larger world's indifference to the fates of the mortal men and women whose stories he unfolds. In his use of rich symbolism and his subtle exploration of human psychology, he anticipated the direction modern fiction would take.

Conrad structured "Heart of Darkness" as a "frame story" to conform to a formula often used in Blackwood's, *the English magazine for which he wrote it. But the depth of his psychological insight and the grandeur of his prose lifts "Heart of Darkness" far above a formula story. In Marlow's identification with Kurtz, Conrad explored another twist to the "double" theme, the idea that an honorable man might be attracted to his opposite. As the critic Tony Tanner has said, Conrad showed "that a hidden part of a man committed to order and the rules of society might suddenly embrace and identify itself with a being, a presence, an apparition which seems most antithetic to his own conscious self, a walking reminder of all that inner darkness and weakness which civilized man has suppressed in order to make group life possible."*

Conrad felt that he might have made Kurtz "too symbolic" and that his story "pushed a little (but only very little)" beyond the actual facts of his four-month experience in the Congo. He justified his exaggeration, however, by his strong desire to give a political dimension to "Heart of Darkness." When the story was published, in 1902, it gave literary expression to an entire age's perception of the Congo as a place of horror and human degradation resulting from ruthless colonialism. In the story, the "Company" collecting "ivory" from the natives is a thinly disguised reference to the Anglo-Belgium India-Rubber Company. During the twenty years of King Leopold of Belgium's control of the company (he personally owned 50 percent of its stock), its agents killed an estimated 5 million people in the Congo, terrorizing and murdering the natives who failed to meet rubber quotas. Leopold himself cleared at least $20 million in profit before he lost his monopoly control of the trade as a result of the reform movement sparked by "Heart of Darkness" and other eyewitness reports.

RELATED COMMENTARIES: *Chinua Achebe, "An Image of Africa: Conrad's 'Heart of Darkness,'" page 1373; Lionel Trilling, "The Greatness of Conrad's 'Heart of Darkness,'" page 1501.*

JOSEPH CONRAD

Heart of Darkness

I

The *Nellie,* a cruising yawl, swung to her anchor without a flutter of the sails, and was at rest. The flood had made, the wind was nearly calm, and being bound down the river, the only thing for it was to come to and wait for the turn of the tide.

The sea-reach of the Thames stretched before us like the beginning of an interminable waterway. In the offing the sea and the sky were welded together without a joint, and in the luminous space the tanned sails of the barges drifting up with the tide seemed to stand still in red clusters of canvas sharply peaked, with gleams of varnished sprits. A haze rested on the low shores that ran out to sea in vanishing flatness. The air was dark above Gravesend, and farther back still seemed condensed into a mournful gloom, brooding motionless over the biggest, and the greatest, town on earth.

The Director of Companies was our captain and our host. We four affectionately watched his back as he stood in the bows looking to seaward. On the whole river there was nothing that looked half so nautical. He resembled a pilot, which to a seaman is trustworthiness personified. It was difficult to realize his work was not out there in the luminous estuary, but behind him, within the brooding gloom.

Between us there was, as I have already said somewhere, the bond of the sea. Besides holding our hearts together through long periods of separation, it had the effect of making us tolerant of each other's yarns — and even convictions. The Lawyer — the best of old fellows — had, because of his many years and many virtues, the only cushion on deck, and was lying on the only rug. The accountant had brought out already a box of dominoes, and was toying architecturally with the bones. Marlow sat cross-legged right aft, leaning against the mizzen-mast. He had sunken cheeks, a yellow complexion, a straight back, and ascetic aspect, and, with his arms dropped, the palms of hands outwards, resembled an idol. The director, satisfied the anchor had good hold, made his way aft and sat down amongst us. We exchanged a few words lazily. Afterwards there was silence on board the yacht. For some reason or other we did not begin that game of dominoes. We felt meditative, and fit for nothing but placid staring. The day was ending in a serenity of still and exquisite brilliance. The water shone pacifically; the sky, without a speck, was a benign immensity of unstained light; the very mist on the Essex marshes was like a gauzy and radiant fabric, hung from the wooded rises inland, and draping the low shores in diaphanous folds. Only the gloom to the west, brooding over the upper reaches, became more somber every minute, as if angered by the approach of the sun.

And at last, in its curved and imperceptible fall, the sun sank low, and from glowing white changed to a dull red without rays and without heat, as if about to go out suddenly, stricken to death by the touch of that gloom brooding over a crowd of men.

Forthwith a change came over the water, and the serenity became less brilliant but more profound. The old river in its broad reach rested unruffled at the decline of day, after ages of good service done to the race that peopled its banks, spread out in the tranquil dignity of a waterway leading to the uttermost ends of the earth. We looked at the venerable stream not in the vivid flush of a short day that comes and departs forever, but in the august light of abiding memories. And indeed nothing is easier for a man who has, as the phrase goes, "followed the sea" with reverence and affection, than to evoke the great spirit of the past upon the lower reaches of the Thames. The tidal current runs to and fro in its unceasing service, crowded with memories of men and ships it had borne to the rest of home or to the battles of the sea. It had known and served all the men of whom the nation is proud, from Sir Francis Drake[1] to Sir John Franklin,[2] knights all, titled and untitled — the knights-errant of the sea. It had borne all the ships whose names are like jewels flashing in the night of time, from the *Golden Hind* returning with her round flanks full of treasure, to be visited by the Queen's Highness and thus pass out of the gigantic tale, to the *Erebus* and *Terror,* bound on other conquests — and that never returned. It had known the ships and the men. They had sailed from Deptford, from Greenwich, from Erith — the adventurers and the settlers; kings' ships and the ships of men on 'Change;[3] captains, admirals, the dark "interlopers" of the Eastern trade, and the commissioned "Generals" of East India fleets. Hunters for gold or pursuers of fame, they all had gone out on that stream, bearing the sword, and often the torch, messengers of the night within the land, bearers of a spark from the sacred fire. What greatness had not floated on the ebb of that river into the mystery of an unknown earth! . . . The dreams of men, the seed of commonwealths, the germs of empires.

The sun set; the dusk fell on the stream, and lights began to appear along the shore. The Chapman lighthouse, a three-legged thing erect on a mud-flat,

---

[1] Sir Francis Drake (1540–1596), English navigator and pirate who sailed around the world (1577–1580) and led the fleet that defeated the Spanish Armada in 1588. The *Golden Hind* was his ship.

[2] Sir John Franklin (1786–1847), English explorer of the Arctic. His ships the *Erebus* and the *Terror* were lost in an expedition to find the Northwest Passage from the Atlantic to the Pacific.

[3] Investors at the London Stock Exchange.

shone strongly. Lights of ships moved in the fairway — a great stir of lights going up and going down. And farther west on the upper reaches the place of the monstrous town was still marked ominously on the sky, a brooding gloom in sunshine, a lurid glare under the stars.

"And this also," said Marlow suddenly, "has been one of the dark places on the earth."

He was the only man of us who still "followed the sea." The worst that could be said of him was that he did not represent his class. He was a seaman, but he was a wanderer, too, while most seamen lead, if one may so express it, a sedentary life. Their minds are of the stay-at-home order, and their home is always with them — the ship; and so is their country — the sea. One ship is very much like another, and the sea is always the same. In the immutability of their surroundings the foreign shores, the foreign faces, the changing immensity of life, glide past, veiled not by a sense of mystery but by a slightly disdainful ignorance; for there is nothing mysterious to a seaman unless it be the sea itself, which is the mistress of his existence and as inscrutable as Destiny. For the rest, after his hours of work, a casual stroll or a casual spree on shore suffices to unfold for him the secret of a whole continent, and generally he finds the secret not worth knowing. The yarns of seamen have a direct simplicity, the whole meaning of which lies within the shell of a cracked nut. But Marlow was not typical (if his propensity to spin yarns be excepted), and to him the meaning of an episode was not inside like a kernel but outside, enveloping the tale which brought it out only as a glow brings out a haze, in the likeness of one of these misty halos that sometimes are made visible by the special illumination of moonshine.

His remark did not seem at all surprising. It was just like Marlow. It was accepted in silence. No one took the trouble to grunt even; and presently he said, very slow —

"I was thinking of very old times, when the Romans first came here, nineteen hundred years ago — the other day. . . . Light came out of this river since — you say Knights? Yes; but it is like a running blaze on a plain, like a flash of lightning in the clouds. We live in the flicker — may it last as long as the old earth keeps rolling! But darkness was here yesterday. Imagine the feelings of a commander of a fine — what d'ye call 'em? — trireme in the Mediterranean, ordered suddenly to the north; run overland across the Gauls in a hurry; put in charge of one of these craft the legionaries — a wonderful lot of handy men they must have been, too — used to build, apparently by the hundred, in a month or two, if we may believe what we read. Imagine him here — the very end of the world, a sea the color of lead, a sky the color of smoke, a kind of ship about as rigid as a concertina — and going up this river with stores, or orders, or what you like. Sandbanks, marshes, forests, savages — precious little to eat fit for a civilized man, nothing but Thames water to drink. No Falernian wine[4] here, no going ashore. Here and there a military camp lost in a wilderness, like a needle in a bundle of hay — cold,

---

[4]Legendary Roman wine.

fog, tempests, disease, exile, and death — death skulking in the air, in the water, in the bush. They must have been dying like flies here. Oh, yes — he did it. Did it very well, too, no doubt, and without thinking much about it either, except afterwards to brag of what he had gone through in his time, perhaps. They were men enough to face the darkness. And perhaps he was cheered by keeping his eye on a chance of promotion to the fleet at Ravenna by and by, if he had good friends in Rome and survived the awful climate. Or think of a decent young citizen in a toga — perhaps too much dice, you know — coming out here in the train of some prefect, or taxgatherer, or trader even, to mend his fortunes. Land in a swamp, march through the woods, and in some inland post feel the savagery, the utter savagery, had closed round him — all that mysterious life of the wilderness that stirs in the forest, in the jungles, in the hearts of wild men. There's no initiation either into such mysteries. He has to live in the midst of the incomprehensible, which is also detestable. And it has a fascination, too, that goes to work upon him. The fascination of the abomination — you know, imagine the growing regrets, the longing to escape, the powerless disgust, the surrender, the hate."

He paused.

"Mind," he began again, lifting one arm from the elbow, the palm of the hand outwards, so that, with his legs folded before him, he had the pose of a Buddha preaching in European clothes and without a lotus-flower — "Mind, none of us would feel exactly like this. What saves us is efficiency — the devotion to efficiency. But these chaps were not much account, really. They were no colonists; their administration was merely a squeeze, and nothing more, I suspect. They were conquerors, and for that you want only brute force — nothing to boast of, when you have it, since your strength is just an accident arising from the weakness of others. They grabbed what they could get for the sake of what was to be got. It was just robbery with violence, aggravated murder on a great scale, and men going at it blind — as is very proper for those who tackle a darkness. The conquest of the earth, which mostly means the taking it away from those who have a different complexion or slightly flatter noses than ourselves, is not a pretty thing when you look into it too much. What redeems it is the idea only. An idea at the back of it; not a sentimental pretense but an idea; and an unselfish belief in the idea — something you can set up, and bow down before, and offer a sacrifice to. . . ."

He broke off. Flames glided in the river, small green flames, red flames, white flames, pursuing, overtaking, joining, crossing each other — then separating slowly or hastily. The traffic of the great city went on in the deepening night upon the sleepless river. We looked on, waiting patiently — there was nothing else to do till the end of the flood; but it was more after a long silence, when he said, in a hesitating voice, "I suppose you fellows remember I did once turn fresh-water sailor for a bit," that we knew we were fated, before the ebb began to run, to hear one of Marlow's inconclusive experiences.

"I don't want to bother you much with what happened to me personally," he began, showing in this remark the weakness of many tellers of tales who seem so often unaware of what their audience would best like to hear;

"yet to understand the effect of it on me you ought to know how I got out there, what I saw, how I went up that river to the place where I first met the poor chap. It was the farthest point of navigation and the culminating point of my experience. It seemed somehow to throw a kind of light on everything about me — and into my thoughts. It was somber enough, too — and pitiful — not extraordinary in any way — not very clear either. No, not very clear. And yet it seemed to throw a kind of light.

"I had then, as you remember, just returned to London after a lot of Indian Ocean, Pacific, China Seas — a regular dose of the East — six years or so, and I was loafing about, hindering you fellows in your work and invading your homes, just as though I had got a heavenly mission to civilize you. It was very fine for a time, but after a bit I did get tired of resting. Then I began to look for a ship — I should think the hardest work on earth. But the ships wouldn't even look at me. And I got tired of that game, too.

"Now when I was a little chap I had a passion for maps. I would look for hours at South America, or Africa, or Australia, and lose myself in all the glories of exploration. At that time there were many blank spaces on the earth, and when I saw one that looked particularly inviting on a map (but they all look that) I would put my finger on it and say, When I grow up I will go there. The North Pole was one of these places, I remember. Well, I haven't been there yet, and shall not try now. The glamour's off. Other places were scattered about the Equator, and in every sort of latitude all over the two hemispheres. I have been in some of them, and . . . well, we won't talk about that. But there was one yet — the biggest, the most blank, so to speak — that I had a hankering after.

"True, by this time it was not a blank space any more. It had got filled since my childhood with rivers and lakes and names. It had ceased to be a blank space of delightful mystery — a white patch for a boy to dream gloriously over. It had become a place of darkness. But there was in it one river especially, a mighty big river, that you could see on the map, resembling an immense snake uncoiled, with its head in the sea, its body at rest curving afar over a vast country, and its tail lost in the depths of the land. And as I looked at the map of it in a shop-window, it fascinated me as a snake would a bird — a silly little bird. Then I remembered there was a big concern, a Company for trade on that river. Dash it all! I thought to myself, they can't trade without using some kind of craft on that lot of fresh water — steamboats! Why shouldn't I try to get charge of one? I went on along Fleet Street, but could not shake off the idea. The snake had charmed me.

"You understand it was a Continental concern, that Trading society; but I have a lot of relations living on the Continent, because it's cheap and not so nasty as it looks, they say.

"I am sorry to own I began to worry them. This was already a fresh departure for me. I was not used to getting things that way, you know. I always went my own road and on my own legs where I had a mind to go. I wouldn't have believed it of myself; but, then — you see — I felt somehow I must get there by hook or by crook. So I worried them. The men said 'My dear fellow,' and did nothing. Then — would you believe it? — I tried the women. I, Charlie Marlow, set the women to work — to get a job. Heavens! Well, you see, the notion drove me. I had an aunt, a dear enthusiastic soul. She wrote: 'It will be delightful. I am ready to do anything, anything for you. It is a glorious idea. I know the wife of a very high personage in the Administration, and also a man who has lots of influence with,' etc., etc. She was determined to make no end of fuss to get me appointed skipper of a river steamboat, if such was my fancy.

"I got my appointment — of course; and I got it very quick. It appears the Company had received news that one of their captains had been killed in a scuffle with the natives. This was my chance, and it made me the more anxious to go. It was only months and months afterwards, when I made the attempt to recover what was left of the body, that I heard the original quarrel arose from a misunderstanding about some hens. Yes, two black hens. Fresleven — that was the fellow's name, a Dane — thought himself wronged somehow in the bargain, so he went ashore and started to hammer the chief of the village with a stick. Oh, it didn't suprise me in the least to hear this, and at the same time to be told that Fresleven was the gentlest, quietest creature that ever walked on two legs. No doubt he was; but he had been a couple of years already out there engaged in the noble cause, you know, and he probably felt the need at last of asserting his self-respect in some way. Therefore he whacked the old nigger mercilessly, while a big crowd of his people watched him, thunderstruck, till some man — I was told the chief's son — in desperation at hearing the old chap yell, made a tentative jab with a spear at the white man — and of course it went quite easy between the shoulder blades. Then the whole population cleared into the forest, expecting all kinds of calamities to happen, while, on the other hand, the steamer Fresleven commanded left also in a bad panic, in charge of the engineer, I believe. Afterwards nobody seemed to trouble much about Fresleven's remains, till I got out and stepped into his shoes. I couldn't let it rest, though; but when an opportunity offered at last to meet my predecessor, the grass growing through his ribs was tall enough to hide his bones. They were all there. The supernatural being had not been touched after he fell. And the village was deserted, the huts gaped black, rotting, all askew within the fallen enclosures. A calamity had come to it, sure enough. The people had vanished. Mad terror had scattered them, men, women, and children, through the bush, and they had never returned. What became of the hens I don't know either. I should think the cause of progress got them, anyhow. However, through this glorious affair I got my appointment, before I had fairly begun to hope for it.

"I flew around like mad to get ready, and before forty-eight hours I was crossing the Channel to show myself to my employers, and sign the contract. In a very few hours I arrived in a city that always makes me think of a whited sepulcher. Prejudice no doubt. I had no difficulty in finding the Company's offices. It was the biggest thing in the town, and everybody I met was full of it. They were going to run an over-sea empire, and make no end of coin by trade.

"A narrow and deserted street in deep shadow, high houses, innumerable windows with venetian blinds, a dead silence, grass sprouting between the stones, imposing carriage archways right and left, immense double doors standing ponderously ajar. I slipped through one of these cracks, went up a swept and ungarnished staircase, as arid as a desert, and opened the first door I came to. Two women, one fat and the other slim, sat on straw-bottomed chairs, knitting black wool. The slim one got up and walked straight at me — still knitting with downcast eyes — and only just as I began to think of getting out of her way, as you would for a somnambulist, stood still, and looked up. Her dress was as plain as an umbrella-cover, and she turned round without a word and preceded me into a waiting-room. I gave my name, and looked about. Deal table in the middle, plain chairs all around the walls, on one end a large shining map, marked with all the colors of a rainbow. There was a vast amount of red — good to see at any time, because one knows that some real work is done in there, a deuce of a lot of blue, a little green, smears of orange, and, on the East Coast, a purple patch, to show where the jolly pioneers of progress drink the jolly lagerbeer. However, I wasn't going into any of these. I was going into the yellow. Dead in the center. And the river was there — fascinating — deadly — like a snake. Ough! A door opened, a white-haired secretarial head, but wearing a compassionate expression, appeared, and a skinny forefinger beckoned me into the sanctuary. Its light was dim, and a heavy writing-desk squatted in the middle. From behind that structure came out an impression of pale plumpness in a frock-coat. The great man himself. He was five feet six, I should judge, and had his grip on the handle-end of ever so many millions. He shook hands, I fancy, murmured vaguely, was satisfied with my French. *Bon voyage.*

"In about forty-five seconds I found myself again in the waiting-room with the compassionate secretary, who, full of desolation and sympathy, made me sign some document. I believe I undertook amongst other things not to disclose any trade secrets. Well, I am not going to.

"I began to feel slightly uneasy. You know I am not used to such ceremonies, and there was something ominous in the atmosphere. It was just as though I had been let into some conspiracy — I don't know — something not quite right; and I was glad to get out. In the outer room the two women knitted black wool feverishly. People were arriving, and the younger one was walking back and forth introducing them. The old one sat on her chair. Her flat cloth slippers were propped up on a footwarmer, and a cat reposed on her lap. She wore a starched white affair on her head, had a wart on one cheek, and silver-rimmed spectacles hung on the tip of her nose. She glanced at me above the glasses. The swift and indifferent placidity of that look troubled me. Two youths with foolish and cheery countenances were being piloted over, and she threw at them the same quick glance of unconcerned wisdom. She seemed to know all about them and about me, too. An eerie feeling came over me. She seemed uncanny and fateful. Often far away there I thought of these two, guarding the door of Darkness, knitting black wool as for a warm pall, one introducing, introducing continuously to the unknown, the other scrutinizing the cheery and foolish faces with unconcerned old eyes. *Ave!* Old knitter of black wool. *Morituri te salutant.*[5] Not many of those she looked at ever saw her again — not half, by a long way.

"There was yet a visit to the doctor. 'A simple formality,' assured me the secretary, with an air of taking an immense part in all my sorrows. Accordingly a young chap wearing his hat over the left eyebrow, some clerk I suppose — there must have been clerks in the business, though the house was as still as a house in a city of the dead — came from somewhere upstairs, and led me forth. He was shabby and careless, with inkstains on the sleeves of his jacket, and his cravat was large and billowy, under a chin shaped like the toe of an old boot. It was a little too early for the doctor, so I proposed a drink, and thereupon he developed a vein of joviality. As we sat over our vermouths he glorified the Company's business, and by and by I expressed casually my surprise at him not going out there. He became very cool and collected all at once. 'I am not such a fool as I look, quoth Plato to his disciples,' he said sententiously, emptied his glass with great resolution, and we rose.

"The old doctor felt my pulse, evidently thinking of something else the while. 'Good, good for there,' he mumbled, and then with a certain eagerness asked me whether I would let him measure my head. Rather surprised, I said Yes, when he produced a thing like calipers and got the dimensions back and front and every way, taking notes carefully. He was an unshaven little man in a threadbare coat like a gaberdine, with his feet in slippers, and I thought him a harmless fool. 'I always ask leave, in the interests of science, to measure the crania of those going out there,' he said. 'And when they come back, too?' I asked, 'Oh, I never see them,' he remarked; 'and, moreover, the changes take place inside, you know.' He smiled, as if at some quiet joke. 'So you are going out there. Famous. Interesting, too.' He gave me a searching glance, and made another note. 'Ever any madness in your family?' he asked, in a matter-of-fact tone. I felt very annoyed. 'Is that question in the interests of science, too?' 'It would be,' he said, without taking notice of my irritation, 'interesting for science to watch the mental changes of individuals, on the spot, but. . . .' 'Are you an alienist?' I interrupted. 'Every doctor should be — a little,' answered that original, imperturbably. 'I have a little theory which you Messieurs who go out there must help me to prove. This is my share in the advantages my country shall reap from the possession of such a magnificent dependency. The mere wealth I leave to others. Pardon my questions, but you are the first Englishman coming under my observation. . . .' I hastened to assure him I was not in the least typical. 'If I were,' said I 'I wouldn't be talking like this with you.' 'What you say is rather profound, and probably erroneous,' he said, with a laugh. 'Avoid irritation more than exposure to the sun. Adieu. How do you English say, eh? Good-by. Ah! Good-by. Adieu. In the tropics one must before everything keep calm.' . . . He lifted a warning forefinger. . . . '*Du calme, du calme. Adieu.*'

---

[5] "Those who are about to die salute you" (Latin).

"One thing more remained to do — say good-by to my excellent aunt. I found her triumphant. I had a cup of tea — the last decent cup of tea for many days — and in a room that most soothingly looked just as you would expect a lady's drawing-room to look, we had a long quiet chat by the fireside. In the course of these confidences it became quite plain to me I had been represented to the wife of the high dignitary, and goodness knows to how many more people besides, as an exceptional and gifted creature — a piece of good fortune for the Company — a man you don't get hold of every day. Good heavens! and I was going to take charge of a two-penny-half-penny river-steamboat with a penny whistle attached! It appeared, however, I was also one of the Workers, with a capital — you know. Something like an emissary of light, something like a lower sort of apostle. There had been a lot of such rot let loose in print and talk just about that time, and the excellent woman, living right in the rush of all that humbug, got carried off her feet. She talked about 'weaning those ignorant millions from their horrid ways,' till, upon my word, she made me quite uncomfortable. I ventured to hint that the Company was run for profit.

"'You forget, dear Charlie, that the laborer is worthy of his hire,' she said, brightly. It's queer how out of touch with truth women are. They live in a world of their own, and there has never been anything like it, and never can be. It is too beautiful altogether, and if they were to set it up it would go to pieces before the first sunset. Some confounded fact we men have been living contentedly with ever since the day of creation would start up and knock the whole thing over.

"After this I got embraced, told to wear flannel, be sure to write often, and so on — and I left. In the street — I don't know why — a queer feeling came to me that I was an impostor. Odd thing that I, who used to clear out for any part of the world at twenty-four hours' notice, with less thought than most men give to the crossing of a street, had a moment — I won't say of hesitation, but of startled pause, before this commonplace affair. The best way I can explain it to you is by saying that, for a second or two, I felt as though, instead of going to the center of a continent, I were about to set off for the center of the earth.

"I left in a French steamer, and she called in every blamed port they have out there, for, as far as I could see, the sole purpose of landing soldiers and custom-house officers. I watched the coast. Watching a coast as it slips by the ship is like thinking about an enigma. There it is before you — smiling, frowning, inviting, grand, mean, insipid, or savage, and always mute with an air of whispering, Come and find out. This one was almost featureless, as if still in the making, with an aspect of monotonous grimness. The edge of a colossal jungle, so dark-green as to be almost black, fringed with white surf, ran straight, like a ruled line, far, far away along a blue sea whose glitter was blurred by a creeping mist. The sun was fierce, the land seemed to glisten and drip with steam. Here and there grayish-whitish specks showed up clustered inside the white surf, with a flag flying above them perhaps. Settlements some centuries old, and still no bigger than pinheads on the untouched expanse of their background. We pounded along, stopped, landed soldiers; went on, landed custom-house clerks to levy toll in what looked like a God-forsaken wilderness, with a tin shed and a flag-pole lost in it; landed more soldiers — to take care of the custom-house clerks, presumably. Some, I heard, got drowned in the surf; but whether they did or not, nobody seemed particularly to care. They were just flung out there, and on we went. Every day the coast looked the same, as though we had not moved; but we passed various places — trading places — with names like Gran' Bassam, Little Popo; names that seemed to belong to some sordid farce acted in front of a sinister backcloth. The idleness of a passenger, my isolation amongst all these men with whom I had no point of contact, the oily and languid sea, the uniform somberness of the coast, seemed to keep me away from the truth of things, within the toil of a mournful and senseless delusion. The voice of the surf heard now and then was a positive pleasure, like the speech of a brother. It was something natural, that had its reason, that had a meaning. Now and then a boat from the shore gave one a momentary contact with reality. It was paddled by black fellows. You could see from afar the white of their eyeballs glistening. They shouted, sang; their bodies streamed with perspiration; they had faces like grotesque masks — these chaps; but they had bone, muscle, a wild vitality, an intense energy of movement, that was as natural and true as the surf along their coast. They wanted no excuse for being there. They were a great comfort to look at. For a time I would feel I belonged still to a world of straightforward facts; but the feeling would not last long. Something would turn up to scare it away. Once, I remember, we came upon a man-of-war anchored off the coast. There wasn't even a shed there, and she was shelling the bush. It appears the French had one of their wars going on thereabouts. Her ensign dropped limp like a rag; the muzzles of the long six-inch guns stuck out all over the low hull; the greasy, slimy swell swung her up lazily and let her down, swaying her thin masts. In the empty immensity of earth, sky, and water, there she was, incomprehensible, firing into a continent. Pop, would go one of the six-inch guns; a small flame would dart and vanish, a little white smoke would disappear, a tiny projectile would give a feeble screech — and nothing happened. Nothing could happen. There was a touch of insanity in the proceeding, a sense of lugubrious drollery in the sight; and it was not dissipated by somebody on board assuring me earnestly there was a camp of natives — he called them enemies! — hidden out of sight somewhere.

"We gave her her letters (I heard the men in that lonely ship were dying of fever at the rate of three a day) and went on. We called at some more places with farcical names, where the merry dance of death and trade goes on in a still and earthy atmosphere as of an overheated catacomb; all along the formless coast bordered by dangerous surf, as if Nature herself had tried to ward off intruders; in and out of rivers, streams of death in life, whose banks were rotting into mud, whose waters, thickened into slime, invaded the contorted mangroves, that seemed to writhe at us in the extremity of an impotent despair. Nowhere did we stop long enough to get a particularized impression, but the general sense of vague and oppressive wonder grew upon me. It was like a weary pilgrimage amongst hints for nightmares.

"It was upward of thirty days before I saw the mouth of the big river.

We anchored off the seat of the government. But my work would not begin till some two hundred miles farther on. So as soon as I could I made a start for a place thirty miles higher up.

"I had my passage on a little sea-going steamer. Her captain was a Swede, and knowing me for a seaman, invited me on the bridge. He was a young man, lean, fair, and morose, with lanky hair and a shuffling gait. As we left the miserable little wharf, he tossed his head contemptuously at the shore. 'Been living there?' he asked. I said, 'Yes.' 'Fine lot these government chaps — are they not?' he went on, speaking English with great precision and considerable bitterness. 'It is funny what some people will do for a few francs a month. I wonder what becomes of that kind when it goes upcountry?' I said to him I expected to see that soon. 'So-o-o!' he exclaimed. He shuffled athwart, keeping one eye ahead vigilantly. 'Don't be too sure,' he continued. 'The other day I took up a man who hanged himself on the road. He was a Swede, too.' 'Hanged himself! Why, in God's name?' I cried. I kept on looking out watchfully. 'Who knows? The sun was too much for him, or the country perhaps.'

"At last we opened a reach. A rocky cliff appeared, mounds of turned-up earth by the shore, houses on a hill, others with iron roofs, amongst a waste of excavations, or hanging to the declivity. A continuous noise of the rapids above hovered over this scene of inhabited devastation. A lot of people, mostly black and naked, moved about like ants. A jetty projected into the river. A blinding sunlight drowned all this at times in a sudden recrudescence of glare. 'There's your Company's station,' said the Swede, pointing to three wooden barrack-like structures on the rocky slope. 'I will send your things up. Four boxes did you say? So. Farewell.'

"I came upon a boiler wallowing in the grass, then found a path leading up the hill. It turned aside for the boulders, and also for an undersized railway-truck lying there on its back with its wheels in the air. One was off. The thing looked as dead as the carcass of some animal. I came upon more pieces of decaying machinery, a stack of rusty rails. To the left a clump of trees made a shady spot, where dark things seemed to stir feebly. I blinked, the path was steep. A horn tooted to the right, and I saw the black people run. A heavy and dull detonation shook the ground, a puff of smoke came out of the cliff, and that was all. No change appeared on the face of the rock. They were building a railway. The cliff was not in the way of anything; but the objectless blasting was all the work going on.

"A slight clinking behind me made me turn my head. Six black men advanced in a file, toiling up the path. They walked erect and slow, balancing small baskets full of earth on their heads, and the clink kept time with their footsteps. Black rags were wound round their loins, and the short ends behind waggled to and fro like tails. I could see every rib, the joints of their limbs were like knots in a rope; each had an iron collar on his neck, and all were connected together with a chain whose bights[6] swung between them, rhythmically clinking. Another report from the cliff made me think suddenly of

---

[6] Loops.

that ship of war I had seen firing into a continent. It was the same kind of ominous voice; but these men could by no stretch of imagination be called enemies. They were called criminals, and the outraged law, like the bursting shells, had come to them, an insoluble mystery from the sea. All their meager breasts panted together, the violently dilated nostrils quivered, the eyes stared stonily uphill. They passed me within six inches, without a glance, with that complete, deathlike indifference of unhappy savages. Behind this raw matter one of the reclaimed, the product of the new forces at work, strolled despondently, carrying a rifle by its middle. He had a uniform jacket with one button off, and seeing a white man on the path, hoisted his weapon to his shoulder with alacrity. This was simple prudence, white men being so much alike at a distance that he could not tell who I might be. He was speedily reassured, and with a large, white, rascally grin, and a glance at his charge, seemed to take me into partnership in his exalted trust. After that, I also was a part of the great cause of these high and just proceedings.

"Instead of going up, I turned and descended to the left. My idea was to let that chain-gang get out of sight before I climbed the hill. You know I am not particularly tender, I've had to strike and to fend off. I've had to resist and to attack sometimes — that's only one way of resisting — without counting the exact cost, according to the demands of such sort of life as I had blundered into. I've seen the devil of violence, and the devil of greed, and the devil of hot desire; but, by all the stars! these were strong, lusty, red-eyed devils, that swayed and drove men — men, I tell you. But as I stood on this hillside, I foresaw that in the blinding sunshine of that land I would become acquainted with a flabby, pretending, weak-eyed devil of a rapacious and pitiless folly. How insidious he could be, too, I was only to find out several months later and a thousand miles farther. For a moment I stood appalled, as though by a warning. Finally I descended the hill, obliquely, towards the trees I had seen.

"I avoided a vast artificial hole somebody had been digging on the slope, the purpose of which I found it impossible to divine. It wasn't a quarry or a sandpit, anyhow. It was just a hole. It might have been connected with the philanthropic desire of giving the criminals something to do. I don't know. Then I nearly fell into a very narrow ravine, almost no more than a scar in the hillside. I discovered that a lot of imported drainage-pipes for the settlement had been tumbled in there. There wasn't one that was not broken. It was a wanton smash-up. At last I got under the trees. My purpose was to stroll into the shade for a moment; but no sooner within than it seemed to me I had stepped into the gloomy circle of some Inferno. The rapids were near, and an uninterrupted, uniform, headlong, rushing noise filled the mournful stillness of the grove, where not a breath stirred, not a leaf moved, with a mysterious sound — as though the tearing pace of the launched earth had suddenly become audible.

"Black shapes crouched, lay, sat between the trees leaning against the trunks, clinging to the earth, half coming out, half effaced within the dim light, in all the attitudes of pain, abandonment, and despair. Another mine on the cliff went off, followed by a slight shudder of the soil under my feet. The work was going on. The work! and this was the place where some of the helpers had withdrawn to die.

"They were dying slowly — it was very clear. They were not enemies, they were not criminals, they were nothing earthly now — nothing but black shadows of disease and starvation, lying confusedly in the greenish gloom. Brought from all the recesses of the coast in all the legality of time contracts, lost in uncongenial surroundings, fed on unfamiliar food, they sickened, became inefficient, and were then allowed to crawl away and rest. These moribund shapes were free as air — and nearly as thin. I began to distinguish the gleam of the eyes under the trees. Then, glancing down, I saw a face near my hand. The black bones reclined at full length with one shoulder against the tree, and slowly the eyelids rose and the sunken eyes looked up at me, enormous and vacant, a kind of blind, white flicker in the depths of the orbs, which died out slowly. The man seemed young — almost a boy — but you know with them it's hard to tell. I found nothing else to do but to offer him one of my good Swede's ship's biscuits I had in my pocket. The fingers closed slowly on it and held — there was no other movement and no other glance. He had tied a bit of white worsted round his neck — Why? Where did he get it? Was it a badge — an ornament — a charm — a propitiatory act? Was there any idea at all connected with it? It looked startling round his black neck, this bit of white thread from beyond the seas.

"Near the same tree two more bundles of acute angles sat with their legs drawn up. One, with his chin propped on his knees, stared at nothing, in an intolerable and appalling manner: his brother phantom rested its forehead, as if overcome with a great weariness; and all about others were scattered in every pose of contorted collapse, as in some picture of a massacre or a pestilence. While I stood horror-struck, one of these creatures rose to his hands and knees, and went off on all-fours towards the river to drink. He lapped out of his hand, then sat up in the sunlight, crossing his shins in front of him, and after a time let his woolly head fall on his breastbone.

"I didn't want any more loitering in the shade, and I made haste towards the station. When near the buildings I met a white man, in such an unexpected elegance of get-up that in the first moment I took him for a sort of vision. I saw a high starched collar, white cuffs, a light alpaca jacket, snowy trousers, a clean necktie, and varnished boots. No hat. Hair parted, brushed, oiled, under a green-lined parasol held in a big white hand. He was amazing, and had a penholder behind his ear.

"I shook hands with this miracle, and I learned he was the Company's chief accountant, and that all the bookkeeping was done at this station. He had come out for a moment, he said, 'to get a breath of fresh air.' The expression sounded wonderfully odd, with its suggestion of sedentary desk life. I wouldn't have mentioned the fellow to you at all, only it was from his lips that I first heard the name of the man who is so indissolubly connected with the memories of that time. Moreover, I respected the fellow. Yes; I respected his collars, his vast cuffs, his brushed hair. His appearance was certainly that of a hairdresser's dummy; but in the great demoralization of the land he kept up his appearance. That's backbone. His starched collars and got-up shirt-fronts were achievements of character. He had been out nearly three years; and, later, I could not help asking him how he managed to sport such linen. He had just the faintest blush, and said modestly, 'I've been teaching one of the native women about the station. It was difficult. She had a distaste for the work.' Thus this man had verily accomplished something. And he was devoted to his books, which were in apple-pie order.

"Everything else in the station was in a muddle — heads, things, buildings. Strings of dusty niggers with splay feet arrived and departed; a stream of manufactured goods, rubbishy cottons, beads, and brass-wire sent into the depths of darkness, and in return came a precious trickle of ivory.

"I had to wait in the station for ten days — an eternity. I lived in a hut in the yard, but to be out of the chaos I would sometimes get into the accountant's office. It was built of horizontal planks, and so badly put together that, as he bent over his high desk, he was barred from neck to heels with narrow strips of sunlight. There was no need to open the big shutter to see. It was hot there, too; big flies buzzed fiendishly, and did not sting, but stabbed. I sat generally on the floor, while, of faultless appearance (and even slightly scented), perching on a high stool, he wrote, he wrote. Sometimes he stood up for exercise. When a trucklebed with a sick man (some invalid agent from up-country) was put in there, he exhibited a gentle annoyance. 'The groans of this sick person,' he said, 'distract my attention. And without that it is extremely difficult to guard against clerical errors in this climate.'

"One day he remarked, without lifting his head, 'In the interior you will no doubt meet Mr. Kurtz.' On my asking who Mr. Kurtz was, he said he was a first-class agent; and seeing my disappointment at this information, he added slowly, laying down his pen, 'He is a very remarkable person.' Further questions elicited from him that Mr. Kurtz was at present in charge of a trading-post, a very important one, in the true ivory-country, at 'the very bottom of there. Sends in as much ivory as all the others put together. . . .' He began to write again. The sick man was too ill to groan. The flies buzzed in a great peace.

"Suddenly there was a growing murmur of voices and a great tramping of feet. A caravan had come in. A violent babble of uncouth sounds burst out on the other side of the planks. All the carriers were speaking together, and in the midst of the uproar the lamentable voice of the chief agent was heard 'giving it up' tearfully for the twentieth time that day. . . . He rose slowly. 'What a frightful row,' he said. He crossed the room gently to look at the sick man, and returning, said to me, 'He does not hear.' 'What! Dead?' I asked, startled. 'No, not yet,' he answered, with great composure. Then, alluding with a toss of the head to the tumult in the station-yard, 'When one has got to make correct entries, one comes to hate those savages — hate them to the death.' He remained thoughtful for a moment. 'When you see Mr. Kurtz,' he went on, 'tell him for me that everything here' — he glanced at the desk — 'is very satisfactory. I don't like to write to him — with those messengers of ours you never know who may get hold of your letter — at that Central Station.' He stared at me for a moment with his mild, bulging eyes. 'Oh, he will go far, very far,' he began again. 'He will be a somebody in the Administration before long. They, above — the Council in Europe, you know — mean him to be.'

"He turned to his work. The noise outside had ceased, and presently in going out I stopped at the door. In the steady buzz of flies the homeward-bound agent was lying flushed and insensible; the other, bent over his books, was making correct entries of perfectly correct transactions; and fifty feet below the doorstep I could see the still tree-tops of the grove of death.

"Next day I left the station at last, with a caravan of sixty men, for a two-hundred-mile tramp.

"No use telling you much about that. Paths, paths, everywhere; a stamped-in network of paths spreading over the empty land, through long grass, through burnt grass, through thickets, down and up chilly ravines, up and down stony hills ablaze with heat; and a solitude, a solitude, nobody, not a hut. The population had cleared out a long time ago. Well, if a lot of mysterious niggers armed with all kinds of fearful weapons suddenly took to traveling on the road between Deal and Gravesend, catching the yokels right and left to carry heavy loads for them, I fancy every farm and cottage thereabouts would get empty very soon. Only here the dwellings were gone, too. Still I passed through several abandoned villages. There's something pathetically childish in the ruins of grass walls. Day after day, with the stamp and shuffle of sixty pair of bare feet behind me, each pair under a sixty-pound load. Camp, cook, sleep, strike camp, march. Now and then a carrier dead in harness, at rest in the long grass near the path, with an empty water-gourd and his long staff lying by his side. A great silence around and above. Perhaps on some quiet night the tremor of far-off drums, sinking, swelling, a tremor vast, faint; a sound weird, appealing, suggestive, and wild — and perhaps with as profound a meaning as the sound of bells in a Christian country. Once a white man in an unbuttoned uniform, camping on the path with an armed escort of lank Zanzibaris, very hospitable and festive — not to say drunk. Was looking after the upkeep of the road, he declared. Can't say I saw any road or any upkeep, unless the body of a middle-aged Negro, with a bullet-hole in the forehead, upon which I absolutely stumbled three miles farther on, may be considered as a permanent improvement. I had a white companion, too, not a bad chap, but rather too fleshy and with the exasperating habit of fainting on the hot hillsides, miles away from the least bit of shade and water. Annoying, you know, to hold your own coat like a parasol over a man's head while he is coming to. I couldn't help asking him once what he meant by coming there at all. 'To make money, of course. What do you think?' he said, scornfully. Then he got fever, and had to be carried in a hammock slung under a pole. As he weighed sixteen stone[7] I had no end of rows with the carriers. They jibbed, ran away, sneaked off with their loads in the night — quite a mutiny. So, one evening, I made a speech in English with gestures, not one of which was lost to the sixty pairs of eyes before me, and the next morning I started the hammock off in front all right. An hour afterwards I came upon

---

[7]224 pounds (a *stone* is the equivalent of fourteen pounds).

the whole concern wrecked in a bush — man, hammock, groans, blankets, horrors. The heavy pole had skinned his poor nose. He was very anxious for me to kill somebody, but there wasn't the shadow of a carrier near. I remember the old doctor — 'It would be interesting for science to watch the mental changes of individuals, on the spot.' I felt I was becoming scientifically interesting. However, all that is to no purpose. On the fifteenth day I came in sight of the big river again, and hobbled into the Central Station. It was a backwater surrounded by scrub and forest, with a pretty border of smelly mud on one side, and on the three others enclosed by a crazy fence of rushes. A neglected gap was all the gate it had, and the first glance at the place was enough to let you see the flabby devil was running that show. White men with long staves in their hands appeared languidly from amongst the buildings, strolling up to take a look at me, and then retired out of sight somewhere. One of them, a stout, excitable chap with black mustaches, informed me with great volubility and many digressions, as soon as I told him who I was, that my steamer was at the bottom of the river. I was thunderstruck. What, how, why? Oh, it was 'all right.' The 'manager himself' was there. All quite correct. 'Everybody had behaved splendidly! splendidly!' — 'you must,' he said in agitation, 'go and see the general manager at once. He is waiting!'

"I did not see the real significance of that wreck at once. I fancy I see it now, but I am not sure — not at all. Certainly the affair was too stupid — when I think of it — to be altogether natural. Still. . . . But at the moment it presented itself simply as a confounded nuisance. The steamer was sunk. They had started two days before in a sudden hurry up the river with the manager on board, in charge of some volunteer skipper, and before they had been out three hours they tore the bottom out of her on stones, and she sank near the south bank. I asked myself what I was to do there, now my boat was lost. As a matter of fact, I had plenty to do in fishing my command out of the river. I had to set about it the very next day. That, and the repairs when I brought the pieces to the station, took some months.

"My first interview with the manager was curious. He did not ask me to sit down after my twenty-mile walk that morning. He was commonplace in complexion, in feature, in manners, and in voice. He was of middle size and of ordinary build. His eyes, of the usual blue, were perhaps remarkably cold, and he certainly could make his glance fall on one as trenchant and heavy as an ax. But even at these times the rest of his person seemed to disclaim the intention. Otherwise there was only an indefinable, faint expression of his lips, something stealthy — a smile — not a smile — I remember it, but I can't explain. It was unconscious, this smile was, though just after he had said something it got intensified for an instant. It came at the end of his speeches like a seal applied on the words to make the meaning of the commonest phrase appear absolutely inscrutable. He was a common trader, from his youth up employed in these parts — nothing more. He was obeyed, yet he inspired neither love nor fear, nor even respect. He inspired uneasiness. That was it! Uneasiness. Not a definite mistrust — just uneasiness — nothing more. You have no idea how effective such a . . . a . . . faculty can be. He had no genius for organizing, for initiative, or for order even. That was evident in such things as the deplorable state of the station. He had no learning, and no intelligence. His position had come to him — why? Perhaps because he was never ill. . . . He had served three terms of three years out there. . . . Because triumphant health in the general rout of constitutions is a kind of power in itself. When he went home on leave he rioted on a large scale — pompously. Jack ashore — with a difference — in externals only. This one could gather from his casual talk. He originated nothing, he could keep the routine going — that's all. But he was great. He was great by this little thing that it was impossible to tell what could control such a man. He never gave the secret away. Perhaps there was nothing within him. Such a suspicion made one pause — for out there there were no external checks. Once when various tropical diseases had laid low almost every 'agent' in the station, he was heard to say, 'Men who come out here should have no entrails.' He sealed the utterance with that smile of his, as though it had been a door opening into a darkness he had in his keeping. You fancied you had seen things — but the seal was on. When annoyed at meal-times by the constant quarrels of the white men about precedence, he ordered an immense round table to be made, for which a special house had to be built. This was the station's messroom. Where he sat was the first place — the rest were nowhere. One felt this to be his unalterable conviction. He was neither civil nor uncivil. He was quiet. He allowed his 'boy' — an overfed young Negro from the coast — to treat the white men, under his very eyes, with provoking insolence.

"He began to speak as soon as he saw me. I had been very long on the road. He could not wait. Had to start without me. The upriver stations had to be relieved. There had been so many delays already that he did not know who was dead and who was alive, and how they got on — and so on, and so on. He paid no attention to my explanations, and, playing with a stick of sealing-wax, repeated several times that the situation was 'very grave, very grave.' There were rumors that a very important station was in jeopardy, and its chief, Mr. Kurtz, was ill. Hoped it was not true. Mr. Kurtz was. . . . I felt weary and irritable. Hang Kurtz, I thought. I interrupted him by saying I had heard of Mr. Kurtz on the coast. 'Ah! So they talk of him down there,' he murmured to himself. Then he began again, assuring me Mr. Kurtz was the best agent he had, an exceptional man, of the greatest importance to the Company; therefore I could understand his anxiety. He was, he said, 'very, very uneasy.' Certainly he fidgeted on his chair a good deal, exclaimed, 'Ah, Mr. Kurtz!' broke the stick of sealing-wax and seemed dumfounded by the accident. Next thing he wanted to know 'how long it would take to. . . .' I interrupted him again. Being hungry, you know, and kept on my feet too, I was getting savage. 'How can I tell?' I said. 'I haven't even seen the wreck yet — some months, no doubt.' All this talk seemed to me so futile. 'Some months,' he said. 'Well, let us say three months before we can make a start. Yes. That ought to do the affair.' I flung out of his hut (he lived all alone in a clay hut with a sort of veranda) muttering to myself my opinion of him. He was a chattering idiot. Afterwards I took it back when it was borne in upon me startlingly with what extreme nicety he had estimated the time requisite for the 'affair.'

"I went to work the next day, turning, so to speak, my back on that station. In that way only it seemed to me I could keep my hold on the redeeming facts of life. Still, one must look about sometimes; and then I saw this station, these men strolling aimlessly about in the sunshine of the yard. I asked myself sometimes what it all meant. They wandered here and there with their absurd long staves in their hands, like a lot of faithless pilgrims bewitched inside a rotten fence. The word 'ivory' rang in the air, was whispered, was sighed. You would think they were praying to it. A taint of imbecile rapacity blew through it all, like a whiff from some corpse. By Jove! I've never seen anything so unreal in my life. And outside, the silent wilderness surrounding this cleared speck on the earth struck me as something great and invincible, like evil or truth, waiting patiently for the passing away of this fantastic invasion.

"Oh, these months! Well, never mind. Various things happened. One evening a grass shed full of calico, cotton prints, beads, and I don't know what else, burst into a blaze so suddenly that you would have thought the earth had opened to let an avenging fire consume all the trash. I was smoking my pipe quietly by my dismantled steamer, and saw them all cutting capers in the light, with their arms lifted high, when the stout man with mustaches came tearing down to the river, a tin pail in his hand, assured me that everybody was 'behaving splendidly, splendidly,' dipped about a quart of water, and tore back again. I noticed there was a hole in the bottom of his pail.

"I strolled up. There was no hurry. You see the thing had gone off like a box of matches. It had been hopeless from the very first. The flame had leaped high, driven everybody back, lighted up everything — and collapsed. The shed was already a heap of embers glowing fiercely. A nigger was being beaten near by. They said he had caused the fire in some way; be that as it may, he was screeching most horribly. I saw him, later, for several days, sitting in a bit of shade looking very sick and trying to recover himself: afterwards he arose and went out — and the wilderness without a sound took him into its bosom again. As I approached the glow from the dark I found myself at the back of two men, talking. I heard the name of Kurtz pronounced, then the words, 'take advantage of this unfortunate accident.' One of the men was the manager. I wished him a good evening. 'Did you ever see anything like it — eh? it is incredible,' he said, and walked off. The other man remained. He was a first-class agent, young, gentlemanly, a bit reserved, with a forked little beard and a hooked nose. He was standoffish with the other agents, and they on their side said he was the manager's spy among them. As to me, I had hardly ever spoken to him before. We got into talk, and by and by we strolled away from the hissing ruins. Then he asked me to his room, which was in the main building of the station. He struck a match, and I perceived that this young aristocrat had not only a silver-mounted dressing-case but also a whole candle all to himself. Just at that time the manager was the only man supposed to have any right to candles. Native mats covered the clay walls; a collection of spears, assegais, shields, knives was hung up in trophies. The business intrusted to this fellow was the making of bricks — so I had been informed; but there wasn't a fragment of a brick anywhere in the station, and he had been there more than a year — waiting. It seems he could not make bricks without something, I don't know what — straw, maybe. Anyways, it could not be found there, and as it was not likely to be sent from Europe, it did not appear clear to me what he was waiting for. An act of special creation perhaps. However, they were all waiting — all the sixteen or twenty pilgrims of them — for something; and upon my word it did not seem an uncongenial occupation, from the way they took it, though the only thing that ever came to them was disease — as far as I could see. They beguiled the time by backbiting and intriguing against each other in a foolish kind of way. There was an air of plotting about that station, but nothing came of it, of course. It was as unreal as everything else — as the philanthropic pretense of the whole concern, as their talk, as their government, as their show of work. The only real feeling was a desire to get appointed to a trading-post where ivory was to be had, so that they could earn percentages. They intrigued and slandered and hated each other only on that account — but as to effectually lifting a little finger — oh, no. By heavens! there is something after all in the world allowing one man to steal a horse while another must not look at the halter. Steal a horse straight out. Very well. He has done it. Perhaps he can ride. But there is a way of looking at a halter that would provoke the most charitable of saints into a kick.

"I had no idea why he wanted to be sociable, but as we chatted in there it suddenly occurred to me the fellow was trying to get at something — in fact, pumping me. He alluded constantly to Europe, to the people I was supposed to know there — putting leading questions as to my acquaintances in the sepulchral city, and so on. His little eyes glittered like mica discs — with curiosity — though he tried to keep up a bit of superciliousness. At first I was astonished, but very soon I became awfully curious to see what he would find out from me. I couldn't possibly imagine what I had in me to make it worth his while. It was very pretty to see how he baffled himself, for in truth my body was full only of chills, and my head had nothing in it but that wretched steamboat business. It was evident he took me for a perfectly shameless prevaricator. At last he got angry, and, to conceal a movement of furious annoyance, he yawned. I rose. Then I noticed a small sketch in oils, on a panel, representing a woman, draped and blindfolded, carrying a lighted torch. The background was somber — almost black. The movement of the woman was stately, and the effect of the torchlight on the face was sinister.

"It arrested me, and he stood by civilly, holding an empty half-pint champagne bottle (medical comforts) with the candle stuck in it. To my question he said Mr. Kurtz had painted this — in this very station more than a year ago — while waiting for means to go to his trading-post. 'Tell me, pray,' said I, 'who is this Mr. Kurtz?'

"'The chief of the Inner Station,' he answered in a short tone, looking away. 'Much obliged,' I said, laughing. 'And you are the brickmaker of the Central Station. Everyone knows that.' He was silent for a while. 'He is a prodigy,' he said at last. 'He is an emissary of pity, and science, and progress, and devil knows what else. We want,' he began to declaim suddenly, 'for the guidance of the cause intrusted to us by Europe, so to speak, higher intelligence, wide sympathies, a singleness of purpose.' 'Who says that?' I asked. 'Lots of them,' he replied. 'Some even write that; and so *he* comes here, a special being, as you ought to know.' 'Why ought I to know?' I interrupted, really surprised. He paid no attention. 'Yes. Today he is chief of the best station, next year he will be assistant-manager, two years more and . . . but I daresay you know what he will be in two years' time. You are of the new gang — the gang of virtue. The same people who sent him specially also recommended you. Oh, don't say no. I've my own eyes to trust.' Light dawned upon me. My dear aunt's influential acquaintances were producing an unexpected effect upon that young man. I nearly burst into a laugh. 'Do you read the Company's confidential correspondence?' I asked. He hadn't a word to say. It was great fun. 'When Mr. Kurtz,' I continued, severely, 'is General Manager, you won't have the opportunity.'

"He blew the candle out suddenly, and we went outside. The moon had risen. Black figures strolled about listlessly, pouring water on the glow, whence proceeded a sound of hissing; steam ascended in the moonlight, the beaten nigger groaned somewhere. 'What a row the brute makes!' said the indefatigable man with the mustaches, appearing near us. 'Serves him right. Transgression — punishment — bang! Pitiless, pitiless. That's the only way. This will prevent all conflagrations for the future. I was just telling the manager. . . .' He noticed my companion, and became crestfallen all at once. 'Not in bed yet,' he said, with a kind of servile heartiness; 'it's so natural. Ha! Danger — agitation.' He vanished. I went on to the riverside, and the other followed me. I heard a scathing murmur at my ear, 'Heap of muffs — go to.' The pilgrims could be seen in knots gesticulating, discussing. Several had still their staves in their hands. I verily believe they took these sticks to bed with them. Beyond the fence the forest stood up spectrally in the moonlight, and through the dim stir, through the faint sounds of that lamentable courtyard, the silence of the land went home to one's very heart — its mystery, its greatness, the amazing reality of its concealed life. The hurt nigger moaned feebly somewhere near by, and then fetched a deep sigh that made me mend my pace away from there. I felt a hand introducing itself under my arm. 'My dear sir,' said the fellow, 'I don't want to be misunderstood, and especially by you, you will see Mr. Kurtz long before I can have that pleasure. I wouldn't like him to get a false idea of my disposition. . . .'

"I let him run on, this papier-mâché Mephistopheles, and it seemed to me that if I tried I could poke my forefinger through him, and would find nothing inside but a little loose dirt, maybe. He, don't you see, had been planning to be assistant-manager by and by under the present man, and I could see that the coming of that Kurtz had upset them both not a little. He talked precipitately, and I did not try to stop him. I had my shoulders against the wreck of my steamer, hauled up on the slope like a carcass of some big river animal. The smell of mud, of primeval mud, by Jove! was in my nostrils, the high stillness of primeval forest was before my eyes; there were shiny patches on the black creek. The moon had spread over everything a thin layer of silver — over the rank grass, over the mud, upon the wall of matted vegetation standing higher than the wall of a temple, over the great river I could see through a somber gap glittering, glittering, as it flowed broadly by without a murmur. All this was great, expectant, mute, while the man jabbered about himself. I wondered whether the stillness on the face of the immensity looking at us two were meant as an appeal or as a menace. What were we who had strayed in here? Could we handle that dumb thing, or would it handle us? I felt how big, how confoundedly big, was that thing that couldn't talk, and perhaps was deaf as well. What was in there? I could see a little ivory coming out from there, and I had heard Mr. Kurtz was in there. I had heard enough about it, too — God knows! Yet somehow it didn't bring any image with it — no more than if I had been told an angel or a fiend was in there. I believed it in the same way one of you might believe there are inhabitants in the planet Mars. I knew once a Scotch sailmaker who was certain, dead sure, there were people in Mars. If you asked him for some idea how they looked and behaved, he would get shy and mutter something about 'walking on all-fours.' If you as much as smiled, he would — though a man of sixty — offer to fight you. I would not have gone so far as to fight for Kurtz, but I went for him near enough to a lie. You know I hate, detest, and can't bear a lie, not because I am straighter than the rest of us, but simply because it appalls me. There is a taint of death, a flavor of mortality in lies — which is exactly what I hate and detest in the world — what I want to forget. It makes me miserable and sick, like biting something rotten would do. Temperament, I suppose. Well, I went near enough to it by letting the young fool there believe anything he liked to imagine as to my influence in Europe. I became in an instant as much of a pretense as the rest of the bewitched pilgrims. This simply because I had a notion it somehow would be of help to that Kurtz whom at the time I did not see — you understand. He was just a word for me. I did not see the man in the name any more than you do. Do you see him? Do you see the story? Do you see anything? It seems to me I am trying to tell you a dream — making a vain attempt, because no relation of a dream can convey the dream-sensation, that commingling of absurdity, surprise, and bewilderment in a tremor of struggling revolt, that notion of being captured by the incredible which is of the very essence of dreams. . . ."

He was silent for a while.

". . . No, it is impossible; it is impossible to convey the life-sensation of any given epoch of one's existence — that which makes its truth, its meaning — its subtle and penetrating essence. It is impossible. We live, as we dream — alone. . . ."

He paused again as if reflecting, then added —

"Of course in this you fellows see more than I could then. You see me, whom you know. . . ."

It had become so pitch dark that we listeners could hardly see one another. For a long time already he, sitting apart, had been no more to us than a voice. There was not a word from anybody. The others might have been asleep, but I was awake. I listened, I listened on the watch for the sentence, for the word, that would give me the clew of the faint uneasiness inspired by this narrative that seemed to shape itself without human lips in the heavy night-air of the river.

". . . Yes — I let him run on," Marlow began again, "and think what he pleased about the powers that were behind me. I did! And there was nothing behind me! There was nothing but that wretched, old, mangled steamboat I was leaning against, while he talked fluently about 'the necessity for every man to get on.' 'And when one comes out here, you conceive, it is not to gaze at the moon.' Mr. Kurtz was a 'universal genius,' but even a genius would find it easier to work with 'adequate tools — intelligent men.' He did not make bricks — why, there was a physical impossibility in the way — as I was well aware; and if he did secretarial work for the manager, it was because 'no sensible man rejects wantonly the confidence of his superiors.' Did I see it? I saw it. What more did I want? What I really wanted was rivets, by heavens! Rivets. To get on with the work — to stop the hole. Rivets I wanted. There were cases of them down at the coast — cases — piled up — burst — split! You kicked a loose rivet at every second step in that station yard on the hillside. Rivets had rolled into the grove of death. You could fill your pockets with rivets for the trouble of stooping down — and there wasn't one rivet to be found where it was wanted. We had plates that would do, but nothing to fasten them with. And every week the messenger, a lone Negro, letter-bag on shoulder and staff in hand, left our station for the coast. And several times a week a coast caravan came in with trade goods — ghastly glazed calico that made you shudder only to look at it; glass beads, valued about a penny a quart, confounded spotted cotton handkerchiefs. And no rivets. Three carriers could have brought all that was wanted to set that steamboat afloat.

"He was becoming confidential now, but I fancy my unresponsive attitude must have exasperated him at last, for he judged it necessary to inform me he feared neither God nor devil, let alone any mere man. I said I could see that very well, but what I wanted was a certain quantity of rivets — and rivets were what really Mr. Kurtz wanted, if he had only known it. Now letters went to the coast every week. . . . 'My dear sir,' he cried, 'I write from dictation.' I demanded rivets. There was a way — for an intelligent man. He changed his manner; became very cold, and suddenly began to talk about a hippopotamus; wondered whether sleeping on board the steamer (I stuck to my salvage night and day) I wasn't disturbed. There was an old hippo that had the bad habit of getting out on the bank and roaming at night over the station grounds. The pilgrims used to turn out in a body and empty every rifle they could lay hands on at him. Some even had sat up o' nights for him. All this energy was wasted, though. 'That animal had a charmed life,' he said; 'but you can say this only of brutes in this country. No man — you apprehend me? — no man here bears a charmed life.' He stood there for a moment in the moonlight with his delicate hooked nose set a little askew, and his mica eyes glittering without a wink, then, with a curt good night, he strode off. I could see he was disturbed and considerably puzzled, which made me feel more hopeful than I had been for days. It was a great comfort to turn from that chap to my influential friend, the battered, twisted, ruined, tin-pot steamboat. I clambered on board. She rang under my feet like an empty Huntley & Palmer biscuit-tin kicked along a gutter; she was nothing so solid in make, and rather less pretty in shape, but I had expended enough hard work on her to make me love her. No influential friend would have served me better. She had given me a chance to come out a bit — to find out what I could do. No, I don't like work. I had rather laze about and think of all the fine things that can be done. I don't like work — no man does — but I like what is in the work — the chance to find yourself. Your own reality — for yourself, not for others — what no other man can ever know. They can only see the mere show, and never tell me what it really means.

"I was not surprised to see somebody sitting aft, on the deck, with his legs dangling over the mud. You see I rather chummed with the few mechanics there were in that station, whom the other pilgrims naturally despised — on account of their imperfect manners, I suppose. This was the foreman — a boiler-maker by trade — a good worker. He was a lank, bony, yellow-faced man, with big intense eyes. His aspect was worried, and his head was as bald as the palm of my hand; but his hair in falling seemed to have stuck to his chin; and had prospered in the new locality, for his beard hung down to his waist. He was a widower with six young children (he had left them in charge of a sister of his to come out there), and the passion of his life was pigeon-flying. He was an enthusiast and a connoisseur. He would rave about pigeons. After work hours he used sometimes to come over from his hut for a talk about his children and his pigeons; at work, when he had to crawl in the mud under the bottom of the steamboat, he would tie up that beard of his in a kind of white serviette he brought for the purpose. It had loops to go over his ears. In the evening he could be seen squatted on the bank rinsing that wrapper in the creek with great care, then spreading it solemnly on a bush to dry.

"I slapped him on the back and shouted, 'We shall have rivets!' He scrambled to his feet exclaiming, 'No! Rivets!' as though he couldn't believe his ears. Then in a low voice, 'You . . . eh?' I don't know why we behaved like lunatics. I put my finger to the side of my nose and nodded mysteriously. 'Good for you!' he cried, snapped his fingers above his head, lifting one foot. I tried a jig. We capered on the iron deck. A frightful clatter came out of that hulk, and the virgin forest on the other bank of the creek sent it back in a thundering roll upon the sleeping station. It must have made some of the pilgrims sit up in their hovels. A dark figure obscured the lighted doorway of the manager's hut, vanished, then, a second or so after, the doorway itself vanished, too. We stopped, and the silence driven away by the stamping of our feet flowed back again from the recesses of the land. The great wall of vegetation, an exuberant and entangled mass of trunks, branches, leaves, boughs, festoons, motionless in the moonlight, was like a rioting invasion of soundless life, a rolling wave of plants, piled up, crested, ready to topple over the creek, to sweep every little man of us out of his little existence. And it moved not. A deadened burst of mighty splashes and snorts reached us from afar as though an ichthyosaurus[8] had been taking a bath of glitter in the great

---

[8] Water-dwelling dinosaur.

river. 'After all,' said the boiler-maker in a reasonable tone, 'why shouldn't we get the rivets?' Why not, indeed! I did not know of any reason why we shouldn't. 'They'll come in three weeks,' I said confidently.

"But they didn't. Instead of rivets there came an invasion, an infliction, a visitation. It came in sections during the next three weeks, each section headed by a donkey carrying a white man in new clothes and tan shoes, bowing from that elevation right and left to the impressed pilgrims. A quarrelsome band of footsore sulky niggers trod on the heels of the donkeys; a lot of tents, campstools, tin boxes, white cases, brown bales would be shot down in the courtyard, and the air of mystery would deepen a little over the muddle of the station. Five such installments came, with their absurd air of disorderly flight with the loot of innumerable outfit shops and provision stores, that, one would think, they were lugging, after a raid, into the wilderness for equitable division. It was an extricable mess of things decent in themselves but that human folly made look like the spoils of thieving.

"This devoted band called itself the Eldorado Exploring Expedition, and I believe they were sworn to secrecy. Their talk, however, was the talk of sordid buccaneers: it was reckless without hardihood, greedy without audacity, and cruel without courage; there was not an atom of foresight or of serious intention in the whole batch of them, and they did not seem aware these things are wanted for the work of the world. To tear treasure out of the bowels of the land was their desire, with no more moral purpose at the back of it than there is in burglars breaking into a safe. Who paid the expenses of the noble enterprise I don't know; but the uncle of our manager was leader of that lot.

"In exterior he resembled a butcher in a poor neighborhood, and his eyes had a look of sleepy cunning. He carried his fat paunch with ostentation on his short legs, and during the time his gang infested the station spoke to no one but his nephew. You could see these two roaming about all day long with their heads close together in an everlasting confab.

"I had given up worrying myself about the rivets. One's capacity for that kind of folly is more limited than you would suppose. I said Hang! — and let things slide. I had plenty of time for meditation, and now and then I would give some thought to Kurtz. I wasn't very interested in him. No. Still, I was curious to see whether this man, who had come out equipped with moral ideas of some sort, would climb to the top after all and how he would set about his work when there."

II

"One evening as I was lying flat on the deck of my steamboat, I heard voices approaching — and there were the nephew and the uncle strolling along the bank. I laid my head on my arm again, and had nearly lost myself in a doze, when somebody said in my ear, as it were: 'I am as harmless as a little child, but I don't like to be dictated to. Am I the manager — or am I not? I was ordered to send him there. It's incredible.' . . . I became aware that the two were standing on the shore alongside the forepart of the steamboat, just below my head. I did not move; it did not occur to me to move: I was sleepy.

'It *is* unpleasant,' grunted the uncle. 'He has asked the Administration to be sent there,' said the other, 'with the idea of showing what he could do; and I was instructed accordingly. Look at the influence that man must have. Is it not frightful?' They both agreed it was frightful, then made several bizarre remarks: 'Make rain and fine weather — one man — the Council — by the nose' — bits of absurd sentences that got the better of my drowsiness, so that I had pretty near the whole of my wits about me when the uncle said, 'The climate may do away with this difficulty for you. Is he alone there?' 'Yes,' answered the manager; 'he sent his assistant down the river with a note to me in these terms: "Clear this poor devil out of the country, and don't bother sending more of that sort. I had rather be alone than have the kind of men you can dispose of with me." It was more than a year ago. Can you imagine such impudence!' 'Anything since then?' asked the other, hoarsely. 'Ivory,' jerked the nephew; 'lots of it — prime sort — lots — most annoying, from him.' 'And with that?' questioned the heavy rumble. 'Invoice,' was the reply fired out, so to speak. Then silence. They had been talking about Kurtz.

"I was broad awake by this time, but, lying perfectly at east, remained still, having no inducement to change my position. 'How did that ivory come all this way?' growled the elder man, who seemed very vexed. The other explained that it had come with a fleet of canoes in charge of an English half-caste clerk Kurtz had with him; that Kurtz had apparently intended to return himself, the station being by that time bare of goods and stores, but after coming three hundred miles, he suddenly decided to go back, which he started to do alone in a small dugout with four paddlers, leaving the half-caste to continue down the river with the ivory. The two fellows there seemed astounded at anybody attempting such a thing. They were at a loss for an adequate motive. As to me, I seemed to see Kurtz for the first time. It was a distinct glimpse: the dugout, four paddling savages, and the lone white man turning his back suddenly on the headquarters, on relief, on thoughts of home — perhaps; setting his face towards the depths of the wilderness, towards his empty and desolate station. I did not know the motive. Perhaps he was just simply a fine fellow who stuck to his work for its own sake. His name, you understand, had not been pronounced once. He was 'that man.' The half-caste, who, as far as I could see, had conducted a difficult trip with great prudence and pluck, was invariably alluded to as 'that scoundrel.' The 'scoundrel' had reported that the 'man' had been very ill — had recovered imperfectly. . . . The two below me moved away then a few paces, and strolled back and forth at some little distance. I heard: 'Military post — doctor — two hundred miles — quite alone now — unavoidable delays — nine months — no news — strange rumors.' They approached again, just as the manager was saying, 'No one, as far as I know, unless a species of wandering trader — a pestilential fellow, snapping ivory from the natives.' Who was it they were talking about now? I gathered in snatches that this was some man supposed to be in Kurtz's district, and of whom the manager did not approve. 'We will not be free from unfair competition till one of these fellows is hanged for an example,' he said. 'Certainly,' grunted the other; 'get him hanged! Why not? Anything — anything can be done in this country. That's what I say; nobody here, you understand, *here*, can endanger your position. And why? You stand the climate — you outlast them all. The danger is in Europe; but there before I left I took care to —' They moved off and whispered, then their voices rose again. 'The extraordinary series of delays is not my fault. I did my best.' The fat man sighed. 'Very sad.' 'And the pestiferous absurdity of his talk,' continued the other; 'he bothered me enough when he was here. "Each station should be like a beacon on the road towards better things, a center for trade, of course, but also for humanizing, improving, instructing." Conceive you — that ass! And he wants to be manager! No it's —' Here he got choked by excessive indignation, and I lifted my head the least bit. I was surprised to see how near they were — right under me. I could have spat upon their hats. They were looking on the ground, absorbed in thought. The manager was switching his leg with a slender twig: his sagacious relative lifted his head. 'You have been well since you came out this time?' he asked. The other gave a start. 'Who? I? Oh! Like a charm — like a charm. But the rest — oh, my goodness! All sick. They die so quick, too, that I haven't the time to send them out of the country — it's incredible!' 'H'm. Just so,' grunted the uncle. 'Ah! my boy, trust to this — I say, trust to this.' I saw him extend his short flipper of an arm for a gesture that took in the forest, the creek, the mud, the river — seemed to beckon with a dishonoring flourish before the sunlit face of the land a treacherous appeal to the lurking death, to the hidden evil, to the profound darkness of its heart. It was so startling that I leaped to my feet and looked back at the edge of the forest, as though I had expected an answer of some sort to that black display of confidence. You know the foolish notions that come to one sometimes. The high stillness confronted these two figures with its ominous patience, waiting for the passing away of a fantastic invasion.

"They swore aloud together — out of sheer fright, I believe — then pretending not to know anything of my existence, turned back to the station. The sun was low; and leaning forward side by side, they seemed to be tugging painfully uphill their two ridiculous shadows of unequal length, that trailed behind them slowly over the tall grass without bending a single blade.

"In a few days the Eldorado Expedition went into the patient wilderness, that closed upon it as the sea closes over a diver. Long afterwards the news came that all the donkeys were dead. I know nothing as to the fate of the less valuable animals. They, no doubt, like the rest of us, found what they deserved. I did not inquire. I was then rather excited at the prospect of meeting Kurtz very soon. When I say very soon I mean it comparatively. It was just two months from the day we left the creek when we came to the bank below Kurtz's station.

"Going up that river was like traveling back to the earliest beginnings of the world, when vegetation rioted on the earth and the big trees were kings. An empty stream, a great silence, an impenetrable forest. The air was warm, thick, heavy, sluggish. There was no joy in the brilliance of sunshine. The long stretches of the waterway ran on, deserted, into the gloom of overshadowed distances. On silvery sandbanks hippos and alligators sunned themselves side by side. The broadening waters flowed through a mob of wooded islands; you lost your way on that river as you would in a desert, and butted all day long against shoals, trying to find the channel, till you thought yourself bewitched and cut off forever from everything you had known once — somewhere — far away — in another existence perhaps. There were moments when one's past came back to one, as it will sometimes when you have not a moment to spare to yourself; but it came in the shape of an unrestful and noisy dream, remembered with wonder amongst the overwhelming realities of this strange world of plants, and water, and silence. And this stillness of life did not in the least resemble a peace. It was the stillness of an implacable force brooding over an inscrutable intention. It looked at you with a vengeful aspect. I got used to it afterwards; I did not see it any more; I had no time. I had to keep guessing at the channel; I had to discern, mostly by inspiration, the signs of hidden banks; I watched for sunken stones; I was learning to clap my teeth smartly before my heart flew out, when I shaved by a fluke some infernal sly old snag that would have ripped the life out of the tin-pot steamboat and drowned all the pilgrims; I had to keep a lookout for the signs of dead wood we could cut up in the night for next day's steaming. When you have to attend to things of that sort, to the mere incidents of the surface, the reality — the reality, I tell you — fades. The inner truth is hidden — luckily, luckily. But I felt it all the same; I felt often its mysterious stillness watching me at my monkey tricks, just as it watches you fellows performing on your respective tightropes for — what is it? half-a-crown a tumble —"

"Try to be civil, Marlow," growled a voice, and I knew there was at least one listener awake besides myself.

"I beg your pardon. I forgot the heartache which makes up the rest of the price. And indeed what does the price matter, if the trick be well done? You do your tricks very well. And I didn't do badly either, since I managed not to sink that steamboat on my first trip. It's a wonder to me yet. Imagine a blindfolded man set to drive a van over a bad road. I sweated and shivered over the business considerably, I can tell you. After all, for a seaman, to scrape the bottom of the thing that's supposed to float all the time under his care is the unpardonable sin. No one may know of it, but you never forget the thump — eh? A blow on the very heart. You remember it, you dream of it, you wake up at night and think of it — years after — and go hot and cold all over. I don't pretend to say that steamboat floated all the time. More than once she had to wade for a bit, with twenty cannibals splashing around and pushing. We had enlisted some of these chaps on the way for a crew. Fine fellows — cannibals — in their place. They were men one could work with, and I am grateful to them. And, after all, they did not eat each other before my face: they had brought along a provision of hippo-meat which went rotten, and made the mystery of the wilderness stink in my nostrils. Phoo! I can sniff it now. I had the manager on board and three or four pilgrims with their staves — all complete. Sometimes we came upon a station close by the bank, clinging to the skirts of the unknown, and the white men rushing out of a tumble-down hovel, with great gestures of joy and surprise and welcome, seemed very strange — had the appearance of being held there captive by a spell. The word ivory would ring in the air for a while — and on we went again into the silence, along empty reaches, round the still bends, between the high walls of our winding way, reverberating in hollow claps the ponderous beat of the stern-wheel. Trees, trees, millions of trees, massive, immense, running up high; and at their foot, hugging the bank against the stream, crept the little begrimed steamboat, like a sluggish beetle crawling on the floor of a lofty portico. It made you feel very small, very lost, and yet it was not altogether depressing, that feeling. After all, if you were small, the grimy beetle crawled on — which was just what you wanted it to do. Where the pilgrims imagined it crawled to I don't know. To some place where they expected to get something, I bet! For me it crawled towards Kurtz — exclusively; but when the steam-pipes started leaking we crawled very slow. The reaches opened before us and closed behind, as if the forest had stepped leisurely across the water to bar the way for our return. We penetrated deeper and deeper into the heart of darkness. It was very quiet there. At night sometimes the roll of drums behind the curtain of trees would run up the river and remain sustained faintly, as if hovering in the air over our heads, till the first break of day. Whether it meant war, peace, or prayer we could not tell. The dawns were heralded by the descent of a chill stillness; the wood-cutters slept, their fires burned low; the snapping of a twig would make you start. We were wanderers on a prehistoric earth, on an earth that wore the aspect of an unknown planet. We could have fancied ourselves the first men taking possession of an accursed inheritance, to be subdued at the cost of profound anguish and of excessive toil. But suddenly, as we struggled round a bend, there would be a glimpse of rush walls, of peaked grass-roofs, a burst of yells, a whirl of black limbs, a mass of hands clapping, of feet stamping, of bodies swaying, of eyes rolling, under the droop of heavy and motionless foliage. The steamer toiled along slowly on the edge of a black and incomprehensible frenzy. The prehistoric man was cursing us, praying to us, welcoming us — who could tell? We were cut off from the comprehension of our surroundings; we glided past like phantoms, wondering and secretly appalled, as sane men would be before an enthusiastic outbreak in a madhouse. We could not understand because we were too far and could not remember, because we were traveling in the night of first ages, of those ages that are gone, leaving hardly a sign — and no memories.

"The earth seemed unearthly. We are accustomed to look upon the shackled form of a conquered monster, but there — there you could look at a thing monstrous and free. It was unearthly, and the men were — No, they were not inhuman. Well, you know, that was the worst of it — this suspicion of their not being inhuman. It would come slowly to one. They howled and leaped, and spun, and made horrid faces; but what thrilled you was just the thought of their humanity — like yours — the thought of your remote kinship with this wild and passionate uproar. Ugly. Yes, it was ugly enough; but if you were man enough you would admit to yourself that there was in you just the faintest trace of a response to the terrible frankness of that noise, a dim suspicion of there being a meaning in it which you — you so remote from the night of first ages — could comprehend. And why not? The mind of man is capable of anything — because everything is in it, all the past as well as all the future. What was there after all? Joy, fear, sorrow, devotion, valor, rage —

who can tell? — but truth — truth stripped of its cloak of time. Let the fool gape and shudder — the man knows, and can look on without a wink. But he must at least be as much of a man as these on the shore. He must meet the truth with his own true stuff — with his own inborn strength. Principles won't do. Acquisitions, clothes, pretty rags — rags that would fly off at the first good shake. No; you want a deliberate belief. An appeal to me in this fiendish row — is there? Very well; I hear; I admit, but I have a voice, too, and for good or evil mine is the speech that cannot be silenced. Of course, a fool, what with sheer fright and fine sentiments, is always safe. Who's that grunting? You wonder I didn't go ashore for a howl and a dance? Well, no — I didn't. Fine sentiments, you say? Fine sentiments, be hanged! I had no time. I had to mess about with white-lead and strips of woolen blanket helping to put bandages on those leaky steam-pipes — I tell you. I had to watch the steering, and circumvent those snags, and get the tin-pot along by hook or by crook. There was surface-truth enough in these things to save a wiser man. And between whiles I had to look after the savage who was fireman. He was an improved specimen; he could fire up a vertical boiler. He was there below me, and, upon my word, to look at him was as edifying as seeing a dog in a parody of breeches and a feather hat, walking on his hindlegs. A few months of training had done for that really fine chap. He squinted at the steam-gauge and at the water-gauge with an evident effort of intrepidity — and he had filed teeth, too, the poor devil, and the wool of his pate shaved into queer patterns, and three ornamental scars on each of his cheeks. He ought to have been clapping his hands and stamping his feet on the bank, instead of which he was hard at work, a thrall to strange witchcraft, full of improving knowledge. He was useful because he had been instructed; and what he knew was this — that should the water in that transparent thing disappear, the evil spirit inside the boiler would get angry through the greatness of his thirst, and take a terrible vengeance. So he sweated and fired up and watched the glass fearfully (with an impromptu charm, made of rags, tied to his arm, and a piece of polished bone, as big as a watch, stuck flatways through his lower lip), while the wooden banks slipped past us slowly, the short noise was left behind, the interminable miles of silence — and we crept on, towards Kurtz. But the snags were thick, the water was treacherous and shallow, the boiler seemed indeed to have a sulky devil in it, and thus neither that fireman nor I had any time to peer into our creepy thoughts.

"Some fifty miles below the Inner Station we came upon a hut of reeds, an inclined and melancholy pole, with the unrecognizable tatters of what had been a flag of some sort flying from it, and a neatly stacked woodpile. This was unexpected. We came to the bank, and on the stack of firewood found a flat piece of board with some faded pencil-writing on it. When deciphered it said: 'Wood for you. Hurry up. Approach cautiously.' There was a signature, but it was illegible — not Kurtz — a much longer word. 'Hurry up.' Where? Up the river? 'Approach cautiously.' We had not done so. But the warning could not have been meant for the place where it could be only found after approach. Something was wrong above. But what — and how much? That was the question. We commented adversely upon the imbecility of that telegraphic style. The bush around said nothing, and would not let us look very far, either. A torn curtain of red twill hung in the doorway of the hut, and flapped sadly in our faces. The dwelling was dismantled; but we could see a white man had lived there not very long ago. There remained a rude table — a plank on two posts; a heap of rubbish reposed in a dark corner, and by the door I picked up a book. It had lost its covers, and the pages had been thumbed into a state of extremely dirty softness; but the back had been lovingly stitched afresh with white cotton thread, which looked clean yet. It was an extraordinary find. Its title was, *An Inquiry into Some Points of Seamanship,* by a man Towser, Towson — some such name — Master in his Majesty's Navy. The matter looked dreary reading enough, with illustrative diagrams and repulsive tables of figures, and the copy was sixty years old. I handled this amazing antiquity with the greatest possible tenderness, lest it should dissolve in my hands. Within, Towson or Towser was inquiring earnestly into the breaking strain of ships' chains and tackle, and other such matters. Not a very enthralling book; but at the first glance you could see there a singleness of intention, an honest concern for the right way of going to work, which made these humble pages, thought out so many years ago, luminous with another than a professional light. The simple old sailor, with his talk of chains and purchases, made me forget the jungle and the pilgrims in a delicious sensation of having come upon something unmistakably real. Such a book being there was wonderful enough; but still more astounding were the notes penciled in the margin, and plainly referring to the text. I couldn't believe my eyes! They were in cipher! Yes, it looked like cipher. Fancy a man lugging with him a book of that description into this nowhere and studying it — and making notes — in cipher at that! It was an extravagant mystery.

"I had been dimly aware for some time of a worrying noise, and when I lifted my eyes I saw the woodpile was gone, and the manager, aided by all the pilgrims, was shouting at me from the riverside. I slipped the book into my pocket. I assure you to leave off reading was like tearing myself away from the shelter of an old and solid friendship.

"I started the lame engine ahead. 'It must be this miserable trader — this intruder,' exclaimed the manager, looking back malevolently at the place we had left. 'He must be English,' I said. 'It will not save him from getting into trouble if he is not careful,' muttered the manager darkly. I observed with assumed innocence that no man was safe from trouble in this world.

"The current was more rapid now, the steamer seemed at her last gasp, the stern-wheel flopped languidly, and I caught myself listening on tiptoe for the next beat of the float, for in sober truth I expected the wretched thing to give up every moment. It was like watching the last flickers of a life. But still we crawled. Sometimes I would pick out a tree a little way ahead to measure our progress towards Kurtz by, but I lost it invariably before we got abreast. To keep the eyes so long on one thing was too much for human patience. The manager displayed a beautiful resignation. I fretted and fumed and took to arguing with myself whether or not I would talk openly with Kurtz; but before I could come to any conclusion it occurred to me that my speech or my silence, indeed any action of mine, would be a mere futility. What did it matter what anyone knew or ignored? What did it matter who was manager? One gets sometimes such a flash of insight. The essentials of this affair lay deep under the surface, beyond my reach, and beyond my power of meddling.

"Towards the evening of the second day we judged ourselves about eight miles from Kurtz's station. I wanted to push on; but the manager looked grave, and told me the navigation up there was so dangerous that it would be advisable, the sun being very low already, to wait where we were till next morning. Moreover, he pointed out that if the warning to approach cautiously were to be followed, we must approach in daylight — not at dusk, or in the dark. This was sensible enough. Eight miles meant nearly three hours' steaming for us, and I could also see suspicious ripples at the upper end of the reach. Nevertheless, I was annoyed beyond expression at the delay, and most unreasonably, too, since one night more could not matter much after so many months. As we had plenty of wood, and caution was the word, I brought up in the middle of the stream. The reach was narrow, straight, with high sides like a railway cutting. The dusk came gliding into it long before the sun had set. The current ran smooth and swift, but a dumb immobility sat on the banks. The living trees, lashed together by the creepers and every living bush of the undergrowth, might have been changed into stone, even to the slenderest twig, to the lightest leaf. It was not sleep — it seemed unnatural, like a state of trance. Not the faintest sound of any kind could be heard. You looked on amazed, and began to suspect yourself of being deaf — then the night came suddenly, and struck you blind as well. About three in the morning some large fish leaped, and the loud splash made me jump as though a gun had been fired. When the sun rose there was a white fog, very warm and clammy, and more blinding than the night. It did not shift or drive; it was just there, standing all around you like something solid. At eight or nine, perhaps, it lifted as a shutter lifts. We had a glimpse of the towering multitude of trees, of the immense matted jungle, with the blazing little ball of the sun hanging over it — all perfectly still — and then the white shutter came down again, smoothly, as if sliding in greased grooves. I ordered the chain, which we had begun to heave in, to be paid out again. Before it stopped running with a muffled rattle, a cry, a very loud cry, as of infinite desolation, soared slowly in the opaque air. It ceased. A complaining clamor, modulated in savage discords, filled our ears. The sheer unexpectedness of it made my hair stir under my cap. I don't know how it struck the others: to me it seemed as though the mist itself had screamed, so suddenly, and apparently from all sides at once, did this tumultuous and mournful uproar arise. It culminated in a hurried outbreak of almost intolerably excessive shrieking, which stopped short, leaving us stiffened in a variety of silly attitudes, and obstinately listening to the nearly as appalling and excessive silence. 'Good God! What is the meaning —' stammered at my elbow one of the pilgrims — a little fat man, with sandy hair and red whiskers, who wore side-spring boots, and pink pajamas tucked into his socks. Two others remained open-mouthed a whole minute, then dashed into the little cabin, to rush out incontinently and stand darting scared glances, with Winchesters at 'ready' in their hands.

What we could see was just the steamer we were on, her outlines blurred as though she had been on the point of dissolving, and a misty strip of water, perhaps two feet broad, around her — and that was all. The rest of the world was nowhere, as far as our eyes and ears were concerned. Just nowhere. Gone, disappeared; swept off without leaving a whisper or a shadow behind.

"I went forward, and ordered the chain to be hauled in short, so as to be ready to trip the anchor and move the steamboat at once if necessary. 'Will they attack?' whispered an awed voice. 'We will be all butchered in this fog,' murmured another. The faces twitched with the strain, the hands trembling slightly, the eyes forgot to wink. It was very curious to see the contrast of expressions of the white men and of the black fellows of our crew, who were as much strangers to that part of the river as we, though their homes were only eight hundred miles away. The whites, of course, greatly discomposed, had besides a curious look of being painfully shocked by such an outrageous row. The others had an alert, naturally interested expression; but their faces were essentially quiet, even those of the one or two who grinned as they hauled at the chain. Several exchanged short, grunting phrases, which seemed to settle the matter to their satisfaction. Their headman, a young, broad-chested black, severely draped in dark-blue fringed cloths, with fierce nostrils and his hair all done up artfully in oily ringlets, stood near me. 'Aha!' I said, just for good fellowship's sake. 'Catch 'em,' he snapped, with a bloodshot widening of his eyes and a flash of sharp teeth — 'catch 'im. Give 'im to us.' 'To you, eh?' I asked; 'what would you do with them?' 'Eat 'em!' he said, curtly, and, leaning his elbow on the rail, looked out into the fog in a dignified and profoundly pensive attitude. I would no doubt have been properly horrified, had it not occurred to me that he and his chaps must be very hungry: that they must have been growing increasingly hungry for at least this month past. They had been engaged for six months (I don't think a single one of them had any clear idea of time, as we at the end of countless ages have. They still belonged to the beginnings of time — had no inherited experience to teach them as it were), and of course, as long as there was a piece of paper written over in accordance with some farcical law or other made down the river, it didn't enter anybody's head to trouble how they would live. Certainly they had brought with them some rotten hippo-meat, which couldn't have lasted very long, anyway, even if the pilgrims hadn't, in the midst of a shocking hullabaloo, thrown a considerable quantity of it overboard. It looked like a high-handed proceeding; but it was really a case of legitimate self-defense. You can't breathe dead hippo waking, sleeping, and eating, and at the same time keep your precarious grip on existence. Besides that, they had given them every week three pieces of brass wire, each about nine inches long; and the theory was they were to buy their provisions with that currency in riverside villages. You can see how *that* worked. There were either no villages, or the people were hostile, or the director, who like the rest of us fed out of tins, with an occasional old he-goat thrown in, didn't want to stop the steamer for some more or less recondite reason. So, unless they swallowed the wire itself, or made loops of it to snare the fishes with, I don't see what good their extravagant salary could be to them. I must say it was paid with a regularity worthy of a large and honorable trading company. For the rest, the only thing to eat — though it didn't look eatable in the least — I saw in their possession was a few lumps of some stuff like half-cooked dough, of a dirty lavender color, they kept wrapped in leaves, and now and then swallowed a piece of, but so small that it seemed done more for the looks of the thing than for any serious purpose of sustenance. Why in the name of all the gnawing devils of hunger they didn't go for us — they were thirty to five — and have a good tuck-in for once, amazes me now when I think of it. They were big powerful men, with not much capacity to weigh the consequences, with courage, with strength, even yet, though their skins were no longer glossy and their muscles no longer hard. And I saw that something restraining, one of those human secrets that baffle probability, had come into play there. I looked at them with a swift quickening of interest — not because it occurred to me I might be eaten by them before very long, though I own to you that just then I perceived — in a new light, as it were — how unwholesome the pilgrims looked, and I hoped, yes, I positively hoped, that my aspect was not so — what shall I say? — so — unappetizing: a touch of fantastic vanity which fitted well with the dream-sensation that pervaded all my days at that time. Perhaps I had a little fever, too. One can't live with one's finger everlastingly on one's pulse. I had often 'a little fever,' or a little touch of other things — the playful paw-strokes of the wilderness, the preliminary trifling before the more serious onslaught which came in due course. Yes; I looked at them as you would on any human being, with a curiosity of their impulses, motives, capacities, weaknesses, when brought to the test of an inexorable physical necessity. Restraint! What possible restraint! Was it superstition, disgust, patience, fear — or some kind of primitive honor? No fear can stand up to hunger, no patience can wear it out, disgust simply does not exist where hunger is; and as to superstition, beliefs, and what you may call principles, they are less than chaff in a breeze. Don't you know the devilry of lingering starvation, its exasperating torment, its black thoughts, its somber and brooding ferocity? Well, I do. It takes a man all his inborn strength to fight hunger properly. It's really easier to face bereavement, dishonor, and the perdition of one's soul — than this kind of prolonged hunger. Sad, but true. And these chaps, too, had no earthly reason for any kind of scruple. Restraint! I would just as soon have expected restraint from a hyena prowling amongst the corpses of a battlefield. But there was the fact facing me — the fact dazzling, to be seen, like the foam on the depths of the sea, like a ripple on an unfathomable enigma, a mystery greater — when I thought of it — than the curious, inexplicable note of desperate grief in this savage clamor that had swept by us on the riverbank, behind the blind whiteness of the fog.

'Two pilgrims were quarreling in hurried whispers as to which bank, 'Left.' 'No, no; how can you? Right, right, of course.' 'It is very serious,' said the manager's voice behind me; 'I would be desolated if anything should happen to Mr. Kurtz before we came up.' I looked at him, and had not the slightest doubt he was sincere. He was just the kind of man who would wish to preserve appearances. That was his restraint. But when he muttered something about going on at once, I did not even take the trouble to answer him.

I knew, and he knew, that it was impossible. Were we to let go our hold of the bottom, we would be absolutely in the air — in space. We wouldn't be able to tell where we were going to — whether up or down stream, or across — till we fetched against one bank or the other — and then we wouldn't know at first which it was. Of course I made no move. I had no mind for a smash-up. You couldn't imagine a more deadly place for a shipwreck. Whether drowned at once or not, we were sure to perish speedily in one way or another. 'I authorize you to take all the risks,' he said, after a short silence. 'I refuse to take any,' I said, shortly; which was just the answer he expected, though its tone might have surprised him. 'Well, I must defer to your judgment. You are captain,' he said, with marked civility. I turned my shoulder to him in sign of my appreciation, and looked into the fog. How long would it last? It was the most hopeless lookout. The approach to this Kurtz grubbing for ivory in the wretched bush was beset by as many dangers as though he had been an enchanted princess sleeping in a fabulous castle. 'Will they attack, do you think?' asked the manager, in a confidential tone.

"I did not think they would attack, for several obvious reasons. The thick fog was one. If they left the bank in their canoes they would get lost in it, as we would be if we attempted to move. Still, I had also judged the jungle of both banks quite impenetrable — and yet eyes were in it, eyes that had seen us. The riverside bushes were certainly very thick; but the undergrowth behind was evidently penetrable. However, during the short lift I had seen no canoes anywhere in the reach — certainly not abreast of the steamer. But what made the idea of attack inconceivable to me was the nature of the noise — of the cries we had heard. They had not the fierce character boding immediate hostile intention. Unexpected, wild, and violent as they had been, they had given me an irresistible impression of sorrow. The glimpse of the steamboat had for some reason filled those savages with unrestrained grief. The danger, if any, I expounded, was from our proximity to a great human passion let loose. Even extreme grief may ultimately vent itself in violence — but more generally takes the form of apathy. . . .

"You should have seen the pilgrims stare! They had no heart to grin, or even to revile me: but I believe they thought me gone mad — with fright, maybe. I delivered a regular lecture. My dear boys, it was no good bothering. Keep a lookout? Well, you may guess I watched the fog for the signs of lifting as a cat watches a mouse; but for anything else our eyes were of no more use to us than if we had been buried miles deep in a heap of cotton-wool. It felt like it, too — choking, warm, stifling. Besides, all I said, though it sounded extravagant, was absolutely true to fact. What we afterwards alluded to as an attack was really an attempt at repulse. The action was very far from being aggressive — it was not even defensive, in the usual sense: it was undertaken under the stress of desperation, and in its essence was purely protective.

"It developed itself, I should say, two hours after the fog lifted, and its commencement was at a spot, roughly speaking, about a mile and a half below Kurtz's station. We had just floundered and flopped round a bend, when I saw an islet, a mere grassy hummock of bright green, in the middle of the stream. It was the only thing of the kind; but as we opened the reach more, I perceived it was the head of a long sandbank, or rather of a chain of shallow patches stretching down the middle of the river. They were discolored, just awash, and the whole lot was seen just under the water, exactly as a man's backbone is seen running down the middle of his back under the skin. Now, as far as I did see, I could go to the right or to the left of this. I didn't know either channel, of course. The banks looked pretty well alike, the depth appeared the same; but as I had been informed the station was on the west side, I naturally headed for the western passage.

"No sooner had we fairly entered it than I became aware it was much narrower than I had supposed. To the left of us there was the long uninterrupted shoal, and to the right a high, steep bank heavily overgrown with bushes. Above the bush the trees stood in serried ranks. The twigs overhung the current thickly, and from distance to distance a large limb of some tree projected rigidly over the stream. It was then well on in the afternoon, the face of the forest was gloomy, and a broad strip of shadow had already fallen on the water. In this shadow we steamed up — very slowly, as you may imagine. I sheered her well inshore — the water being deepest near the bank, as the sounding-pole informed me.

"One of my hungry and forbearing friends was sounding in the bows just below me. This steamboat was exactly like a decked scow. On the deck, there were two little teak-wood houses, with doors and windows. The boiler was in the fore-end, and the machinery right astern. Over the whole there was a light roof, supported on stanchions. The funnel projected through that roof, and in front of the funnel a small cabin built of light planks served for a pilot-house. It contained a couch, two campstools, a loaded Martini-Henry[9] leaning in one corner, a tiny table, and the steering-wheel. It had a wide door in front and a broad shutter at each side. All these were always thrown open, of course. I spent my days perched up there on the extreme fore-end of that roof, before the door. At night I slept, or tried to, on the couch. An athletic black belonging to some coast tribe, and educated by my poor predecessor, was the helmsman. He sported a pair of brass earrings, wore a blue cloth wrapper from the waist to the ankles, and thought all the world of himself. He was the most unstable kind of fool I had ever seen. He steered with no end to a swagger while you were by; but if he lost sight of you, he became instantly the prey of an abject funk, and would let that cripple of a steamboat get the upper hand of him in a minute.

"I was looking down at the sounding-pole, and feeling much annoyed to see at each try a little more of it stick out that river, when I saw my poleman give up the business suddenly, and stretch himself flat on the deck, without even taking the trouble to haul his pole in. He kept hold on it though, and it trailed in the water. At the same time the fireman, whom I could also see below me, sat down abruptly before his furnace and ducked his head. I was amazed. Then I had to look at the river mighty quick, because there was a snag in the fairway. Sticks, little sticks, were flying about — thick: they were

---

[9] A heavy military rifle.

whizzing before my nose, dropping below me, striking behind me against my pilot-house. All this time the river, the shore, the woods, were very quiet — perfectly quiet. I could only hear the heavy splashing thump of the stern-wheel and the patter of these things. We cleared the snag clumsily. Arrows, by Jove! We were being shot at! I stepped in quickly to close the shutter on the land-side. That fool-helmsman, his hands on the spokes, was lifting his knees high, stamping his feet, champing his mouth, like a reined-in horse. Confound him! And we were staggering within ten feet of the bank. I had to lean right out to swing the heavy shutter, and I saw a face amongst the leaves on the level with my own, looking at me very fierce and steady; and then suddenly, as though a veil had been removed from my eyes, I made out, deep in the tangled gloom, naked breasts, arms, legs, glaring eyes — the bush was swarming with human limbs in movement, glistening, of bronze color. The twigs shook, swayed, and rustled, the arrows flew out of them, and then the shutter came to. 'Steer her straight,' I said to the helmsman. He held his head rigid, face forward; but his eyes rolled, he kept on lifting and setting down his feet gently, his mouth foamed a little. 'Keep quiet!' I said in a fury. I might just as well have ordered a tree not to sway in the wind. I darted out. Below me there was a great scuffle of feet on the iron deck; confused exclamations; a voice screamed, 'Can you turn back?' I caught sight of a V-shaped ripple on the water ahead. What? Another snag! A fusillade burst out under my feet. The pilgrims had opened with their Winchesters, and were simply squirting lead into that bush. A deuce of a lot of smoke came up and drove slowly forward. I swore at it. Now I couldn't see the ripple or the snag either. I stood in the doorway, peering, and the arrows came in swarms. They might have been poisoned, but they looked as though they wouldn't kill a cat. The bush began to howl. Our wood-cutters raised a war-like whoop; the report of a rifle just at my back deafened me. I glanced over my shoulder, and the pilot-house was yet full of noise and smoke when I made a dash at the wheel. The fool-nigger had dropped everything to throw the shutter open and let off that Martini-Henry. He stood before the wide opening, glaring, and I yelled at him to come back, while I straightened the sudden twist out of that steamboat. There was no room to turn even if I had wanted to, the snag was somewhere very near ahead in that confounded smoke, there was no time to lose, so I just crowded her into the bank — right into the bank, where I knew the water was deep.

"We tore slowly along the overhanging bushes in a whirl of broken twigs and flying leaves. The fusillade below stopped short, as I had foreseen it would when the squirts got empty. I threw my head back to a glinting whizz that traversed the pilot-house, in at one shutter-hole and out at the other. Looking past that mad helmsman, who was shaking the empty rifle and yelling at the shore, I saw vague forms of men running bent double, leaping, gliding, distinct, incomplete, evanescent. Something big appeared in the air before the shutter, the rifle went overboard, and the man stepped back swiftly, looked at me over his shoulder in an extraordinary, profound, familiar manner, and fell upon my feet. The side of his head hit the wheel twice, and the end of what appeared a long cane clattered round and knocked over a little campstool. It looked as though after wrenching that thing from somebody ashore he had lost his balance in the effort. The thin smoke had blown away, we were clear of the snag, and looking ahead I could see that in another hundred yards or so I would be free to sheer off, away from the bank; but my feet felt so very warm and wet that I had to look down. The man had rolled on his back and stared straight up at me; both his hands clutched that cane. It was the shaft of a spear that, either thrown or lunged through the opening, had caught him in the side just below the ribs; the blade had gone in out of sight, after making a frightful gash; my shoes were full; a pool of blood lay very still, gleaming dark-red under the wheel; his eyes shone with an amazing luster. The fusillade burst out again. He looked at me anxiously, gripping the spear like something precious, with an air of being afraid I would try to take it away from him. I had to make an effort to free my eyes from his gaze and attend to steering. With one hand I felt above my head for the line of the steam-whistle, and jerked out screech after screech hurriedly. The tumult of angry and warlike yells was checked instantly, and then from the depths of the woods went out such a tremulous and prolonged wail of mournful fear and utter despair as may be imagined to follow the flight of the last hope from the earth. There was a great commotion in the bush; the shower of arrows stopped, a few dropping shots rang out sharply — then silence, in which the languid beat of the stern-wheel came plainly to my ears. I put the helm hard a-starboard at the moment when the pilgrim in pink pajamas, very hot and agitated, appeared in the doorway. 'The manager sends me — ' he began in an official tone, and stopped short. 'Good God!' he said, glaring at the wounded man.

"We two whites stood over him, and his lustrous and inquiring glance enveloped us both. I declare it looked as though he would presently put to us some question in an understandable language; but he died without uttering a sound, without moving a limb, without twitching a muscle. Only in the very last moment, as though in response to some sign we could not see, to some whisper we could not hear, he frowned heavily, and that frown gave to his black death-mask an inconceivably somber, brooding, and menacing expression. The luster of inquiring glance faded swiftly into vacant glassiness. 'Can you steer?' I asked the agent eagerly. He looked very dubious; but I made a grab at his arm, and he understood at once I meant him to steer whether or no. To tell you the truth, I was morbidly anxious to change my shoes and socks. 'He is dead,' murmured the fellow, immensely impressed. 'No doubt about it,' said I tugging like mad at the shoe-laces. 'And by the way, I suppose Mr. Kurtz is dead as well by this time.'

"For the moment that was the dominant thought. There was a sense of extreme disappointment, as though I had found out I had been striving after something altogether without a substance. I couldn't have been more disgusted if I had traveled all this way for the sole purpose of talking with Mr. Kurtz. Talking with. . . . I flung one shoe overboard, and became aware that that was exactly what I had been looking forward to — a talk with Kurtz. I made the strange discovery that I had never imagined him as doing, you know, but as discoursing. I didn't say to myself, 'Now I will never see him,' or 'Now I will never shake him by the hand,' but, 'Now I will never hear him.' The man presented himself as a voice. Not of course that I did not connect him with some sort of action. Hadn't I been told in all the tones of jealousy and admiration that he had collected, bartered, swindled, or stolen more ivory than all the other agents together? That was not the point. The point was in his being a gifted creature, and that of all his gifts the one that stood out preeminently, that carried with it a sense of real presence, was his ability to talk, his words — the gift of expression, the bewildering, the illuminating, the most exalted and the most contemptible, the pulsating stream of light, or the deceitful flow from the heart of an impenetrable darkness.

"The other shoe went flying unto the devil-god of that river. I thought, by Jove! it's all over. We are too late; he has vanished — the gift has vanished, by means of some spear, arrow, or club. I will never hear that chap speak after all — and my sorrow had a startling extravagance of emotion, even such as I had noticed in the howling sorrow of these savages in the bush. I couldn't have felt more lonely desolation somehow, had I been robbed of a belief or had missed my destiny in life. . . . Why do you sigh in this beastly way, somebody? Absurd? Well, absurd. Good Lord! mustn't a man ever — Here, give me some tobacco." . . .

There was a pause of profound stillness, then a match flared, and Marlow's lean face appeared, worn, hollow, with downward folds and drooped eyelids, with an aspect of concentrated attention; and as he took vigorous draws at his pipe, it seemed to retreat and advance out of the night in the regular flicker of the tiny flame. The match went out.

"Absurd!" he cried. "This is the worst of trying to tell. . . . Here you all are, each moored with two good addresses, like a hulk with two anchors, a butcher round one corner, a policeman round another, excellent appetites, and temperature normal — you hear — normal from year's end to year's end. And you say, Absurd! Absurd be — exploded! Absurd! My dear boys, what can you expect from a man who out of sheer nervousness had just flung overboard a pair of new shoes! Now I think of it, it is amazing I did not shed tears. I am, upon the whole, proud of my fortitude. I was cut to the quick at the idea of having lost the inestimable privilege of listening to the gifted Kurtz. Of course I was wrong. The privilege was waiting for me. Oh, yes, I heard more than enough. And I was right, too. A voice. He was very little more than a voice. And I heard — him — it — this voice — other voices — all of them were so little more than voices — and the memory of that time itself lingers around me, impalpable, like a dying vibration of one immense jabber, silly, atrocious, sordid, savage, or simply mean, without any kind of sense. Voices, voices — even the girl herself — now — "

He was silent for a long time.

"I laid the ghost of his gifts at last with a lie," he began, suddenly. "Girl! What? Did I mention a girl? Oh, she is out of it — completely. They — the women I mean — are out of it — should be out of it. We must help them to stay in that beautiful world of their own, lest ours gets worse. Oh, she had to be out of it. You should have heard the disinterred body of Mr. Kurtz saying, 'My Intended.' You would have perceived directly then how completely she was out of it. And the lofty frontal bone of Mr. Kurtz! They say the hair goes on growing sometimes, but this — ah — specimen, was impressively bald. The wilderness had patted him on the head, and, behold, it was like a ball — an ivory ball; it had caressed him, and — lo! — he had withered; it had taken him, loved him, embraced him, got into his veins, consumed his flesh, and sealed his soul to its own by the inconceivable ceremonies of some devilish initiation. He was its spoiled and pampered favorite. Ivory? I should think so. Heaps of it, stacks of it. The old mud shanty was bursting with it. You would think there was not a single tusk left either above or below the ground in the whole country. 'Mostly fossil,' the manager had remarked, disparagingly. It was no more fossil than I am; but they call it fossil when it is dug up. It appears these niggers do bury the tusks sometimes — but evidently they couldn't bury this parcel deep enough to save the gifted Mr. Kurtz from his fate. We filled the steamboat with it, and had to pile a lot on the deck. Thus he could see and enjoy as long as he could see, because the appreciation of this favor had remained with him to the last. You should have heard him say, 'My ivory.' Oh, yes, I heard him. 'My Intended, my ivory, my station, my river, my — ' everything belonged to him. It made me hold my breath in expectation of hearing the wilderness burst into a prodigious peal of laughter that would shake the fixed stars in their places. Everything belonged to him — but that was a trifle. The thing was to know what he belonged to, how many powers of darkness claimed him for their own. That was the reflection that made you creepy all over. It was impossible — it was not good for one either — trying to imagine. He had taken a high seat amongst the devils of the land — I mean literally. You can't understand. How could you? — with solid pavement under your feet, surrounded by kind neighbors ready to cheer you or to fall on you, stepping delicately between the butcher and the policeman, in the holy terror of scandal and gallows and lunatic asylums — how can you imagine what particular region of the first ages a man's untrammeled feet may take him into by the way of solitude — utter solitude without a policeman — by the way of silence — utter silence, where no warning voice of a kind neighbor can be heard whispering of public opinion? These little things make all the great difference. When they are gone you must fall back upon your own innate strength, upon your own capacity for faithfulness. Of course you may be too much of a fool to go wrong — too dull even to know you are being assaulted by the powers of darkness. I take it, no fool ever made a bargain for his soul with the devil: the fool is too much of a fool, or the devil too much of a devil — I don't know which. Or you may be such a thunderingly exalted creature as to be altogether deaf and blind to anything but heavenly sights and sounds. Then the earth for you is only a standing place — and whether to be like this is your loss or your gain I won't pretend to say. But most of us are neither one nor the other. The earth for us is a place to live in, where we must put up with sights, with sounds, with smells, too, by Jove! — breathe dead hippo, so to speak and not be contaminated. And there, don't you see? your strength comes in, the faith in your ability for the digging of unostentatious holes to bury the stuff in — your power of devotion, not to yourself, but to an obscure, back-breaking business. And that's difficult enough. Mind, I am not trying to excuse or even explain — I am trying to account to myself for — for — Mr. Kurtz — for the shade of Mr. Kurtz. This initiated wraith from the back of Nowhere honored me with its amazing confidence before it vanished altogether. This was because it could speak English to me. The original Kurtz had been educated partly in England, and — as he was good enough to say himself — his sympathies were in the right place. His mother was half-English, his father was half-French. All Europe contributed to the making of Kurtz; and by and by I learned that, most appropriately, the International Society for the Suppression of Savage Customs had intrusted him with the making of a report, for its future guidance. And he had written it, too. I've seen it. I've read it. It was eloquent, vibrating with eloquence, but too high-strung, I think. Seventeen pages of close writing he had found time for! But this must have been before his — let us say — nerves, went wrong, and caused him to preside at certain midnight dances ending with unspeakable rites, which — as far as I reluctantly gathered from what I heard at various times — were offered up to him — do you understand? — to Mr. Kurtz himself. But it was a beautiful piece of writing. The opening paragraph, however, in the light of later information, strikes me now as ominous. He began with the argument that we whites, from the point of development he had arrived at, 'must necessarily appear to them [savages] in the nature of supernatural beings — we approach them with the might as of a deity,' and so on, and so on. 'By the simple exercise of our will we can exert a power for good practically unbounded,' etc., etc. From that point he soared and took me with him. The peroration was magnificent, though difficult to remember, you know. It gave me the notion of an exotic Immensity ruled by an august Benevolence. It made me tingle with enthusiasm. This was the unbounded power of eloquence — of words — of burning noble words. There were no practical hints to interrupt the magic current of phrases, unless a kind of note at the foot of the last page, scrawled evidently much later, in an unsteady hand, may be regarded as the exposition of a method. It was very simple, and at the end of that moving appeal to every altruistic sentiment it blazed at you, luminous and terrifying, like a flash of lightning in a serene sky: 'Exterminate all the brutes!' The curious part was that he had apparently forgotten all about that valuable postscriptum, because, later on, when he in a sense came to himself, he repeatedly entreated me to take good care of 'my pamphlet' (he called it), as it was sure to have in the future a good influence upon his career. I had full information about all these things, and, besides, as it turned out, I was to have the care of his memory. I've done enough for it to give me the indisputable right to lay it, if I choose, for an everlasting rest in the dust-bin of progress, amongst all the sweepings and, figuratively speaking, all the dead cats of civilization. But then, you see, I can't choose. He won't be forgotten. Whatever he was, he was not common. He had the power to charm or frighten rudimentary souls into an aggravated witch-dance in his honor; he could also fill the small souls of the pilgrims with bitter misgivings: he had one devoted friend at least, and he had conquered one soul in the world that was neither rudimentary nor tainted with self-seeking. No; I can't forget him, though I am not prepared to affirm the fellow was exactly worth the life we lost in getting to him. I missed my late helmsman awfully — I missed him even while his body was still lying in the pilot-house. Perhaps you will think it passing strange this regret for a savage who was no more account than a grain of sand in a black Sahara. Well, don't you see, he had done something, he had steered; for months I had him at my back — a help — an instrument. It was a kind of partnership. He steered for me — I had to look after him, I worried about his deficiencies, and thus a subtle bond had been created, of which I only became aware when it was suddenly broken. And the intimate profundity of that look he gave me when he received his hurt remains to this day in my memory — like a claim of distant kinship affirmed in a supreme moment.

"Poor fool! If he had only left that shutter alone. He had no restraint, no restraint — just like Kurtz — a tree swayed by the wind. As soon as I had put on a dry pair of slippers, I dragged him out, after first jerking the spear out of his side, which operation I confess I performed with my eyes shut tight. His heels leaped together over the little door-step; his shoulders were pressed to my breast; I hugged him from behind desperately. Oh! he was heavy, heavy; heavier than any man on earth, I should imagine. Then without more ado I tipped him overboard. The current snatched him as though he had been a wisp of grass, and I saw the body roll over twice before I lost sight of it forever. All the pilgrims and the manager were then congregated on the awning-deck about the pilot-house, chattering at each other like a flock of excited magpies, and there was a scandalized murmur at my heartless promptitude. What they wanted to keep that body hanging about for I can't guess. Embalm it, maybe. But I had also heard another, and a very ominous, murmur on the deck below. My friends the woodcutters were likewise scandalized, and with a better show of reason — though I admit that the reason itself was quite inadmissible. Oh, quite! I had made up my mind that if my late helmsman was to be eaten, the fishes alone should have him. He had been a very second-rate helmsman while alive, but now he was dead he might have become a first-class temptation, and possibly cause some startling trouble. Besides, I was anxious to take the wheel, the man in pink pajamas showing himself a hopeless duffer at the business.

"This I did directly the simple funeral was over. We were going half-speed, keeping right in the middle of the stream, and I listened to the talk about me. They had given up Kurtz, they had given up the station; Kurtz was dead, and the station had been burnt — and so on — and so on. The red-haired pilgrim was beside himself with the thought that at least this poor Kurtz had been properly avenged. 'Say! We must have made a glorious slaughter of them in the bush. Eh? What do you think? Say?' He positively danced, the blood-thirsty little gingery beggar. And he had nearly fainted when he saw the wounded man! I could not help saying, 'You made a glorious lot of smoke, anyhow.' I had seen, from the way the tops of the bushes rustled and flew, that almost all the shots had gone too high. You can't hit anything unless you take aim and fire from the shoulder; but these chaps fired from the hip with their eyes shut. The retreat, I maintained — and I was right — was caused by the screeching of the steam-whistle. Upon this they forgot Kurtz, and began to howl at me with indignant protests.

"The manager stood by the wheel murmuring confidentially about the necessity of getting well away down the river before dark at all events, when I saw in the distance a clearing on the riverside and the outlines of some sort of building. 'What's this?' I asked. He clapped his hands in wonder. 'The station!' he cried. I edged in at once, still going half-speed.

"Through my glasses I saw the slope of a hill interspersed with rare trees and perfectly free from undergrowth. A long decaying building on the summit was half buried in the high grass; the large holes in the peaked roof gaped black from afar; the jungle and the woods made a background. There was no enclosure or fence of any kind; but there had been one apparently, for near the house half-a-dozen slim posts remained in a row, roughly trimmed, and with their upper ends ornamented with round carved balls. The rails, or whatever there had been between, had disappeared. Of course the forest surrounded all that. The riverbank was clear, and on the waterside I saw a white man under a hat like a cart-wheel beckoning persistently with his whole arm. Examining the edge of the forest above and below, I was almost certain I could see movements — human forms gliding here and there. I steamed past prudently, then stopped the engines and let her drift down. The man on the shore began to shout, urging us to land. 'We have been attacked,' screamed the manager. 'I know — I know. It's all right,' yelled back the other, as cheerful as you please. 'Come along. It's all right, I am glad.'

"His aspect reminded me of something I had seen — something funny I had seen somewhere. As I maneuvered to get alongside, I was asking myself, 'What does this fellow look like?' Suddenly I got it. He looked like a harlequin. His clothes had been made of some stuff that was brown holland probably, but it was covered with patches all over, with bright patches, blue, red, and yellow — patches on the back, patches on the front, patches on elbows, on knees; colored binding around his jacket, scarlet edging at the bottom of his trousers; and the sunshine made him look extremely gay and wonderfully neat withal, because you could see how beautifully all this patching had been done. A beardless, boyish face, very fair, no features to speak of, nose peeling, little blue eyes, smiles and frowns chasing each other over that open countenance like sunshine and shadow on a windswept plain. 'Look out, captain!' he cried; 'there's a snag lodged in here last night.' What! Another snag? I confess I swore shamefully. I had nearly holed my cripple, to finish off that charming trip. The harlequin on the bank turned his little pug-nose up to me. 'You English?' he asked, all smiles. 'Are you?' I shouted from the wheel. The smiles vanished, and he shook his head as if sorry for my disappointment. Then he brightened up. 'Never mind!' he cried, encouragingly. 'Are we in time?' I asked. 'He is up there,' he replied with a toss of the head up the hill, and becoming gloomy all of a sudden. His face was like the autumn sky, overcast one moment and bright the next.

"When the manager, escorted by the pilgrims, all of them armed to the teeth, had gone to the house this chap came on board. 'I say, I don't like this. These natives are in the bush,' I said. He assured me earnestly it was all right. 'They are simple people,' he added; 'well, I am glad you came. It took me all my time to keep them off.' 'But you said it was all right,' I cried. 'Oh, they meant no harm,' he said; and as I stared he corrected himself, 'Not exactly.'

Then vivaciously, 'My faith, your pilot-house wants a clean-up!' In the next breath he advised me to keep enough steam on the boiler to blow the whistle in case of any trouble. 'One good screech will do more for you than all your rifles. They are simple people,' he repeated. He rattled away at such a rate he quite overwhelmed me. He seemed to be trying to make up for lots of silence, and actually hinted, laughing, that such was the case. 'Don't you talk with Mr. Kurtz?' I said. 'You don't talk with that man — you listen to him,' he exclaimed with severe exaltation. 'But now — ' He waved his arm, and in the twinkling of an eye was in the uttermost depths of despondency. In a moment he came up again with a jump, possessed himself of both my hands, and shook them continuously, while he gabbled: 'Brother sailor . . . honor . . . pleasure . . . delight . . . introduce myself . . . Russian . . . son of an arch-priest . . . Government of Tambov . . . What? Tobacco! English tobacco; the excellent English tobacco! Now, that's brotherly. Smoke? Where's a sailor that does not smoke?'

"The pipe soothed him, and gradually I made out he had run away from school, had gone to sea in a Russian ship; ran away again; served some time in English ships; was now reconciled with the arch-priest. He made a point of that. 'But when one is young one must see things, gather experience, ideas; enlarge the mind.' 'Here!' I interrupted. 'You can never tell! Here I met Mr. Kurtz,' he said, youthfully solemn and reproachful. I held my tongue after that. It appears he had persuaded a Dutch trading-house on the coast to fit him out with stores and goods, and had started for the interior with a light heart, and no more idea of what would happen to him than a baby. He had been wandering about that river for nearly two years alone, cut off from everybody and everything. 'I am not so young as I look. I am twenty-five,' he said. 'At first old Van Shuyten would tell me to go to the devil,' he narrated with keen enjoyment; 'but I stuck to him, and talked and talked, till at last he got afraid I would talk the hind-leg off his favorite dog, so he gave me some cheap things and a few guns, and told me he hoped he would never see my face again. Good old Dutchman, Van Shuyten. I've sent him one small lot of ivory a year ago, so that he can't call me a little thief when I get back. I hope he got it. And for the rest I don't care. I had some wood stacked for you. That was my old house. Did you see?'

"I gave him Towson's book. He made as though he would kiss me, but restrained himself. 'The only book I had left, and I thought I had lost it,' he said, looking at it ecstatically. 'So many accidents happen to a man going about alone, you know. Canoes get upset sometimes — and sometimes you've got to clear out so quick when the people get angry.' He thumbed the pages. 'You made notes in Russian?' I asked. He nodded. 'I thought they were written in cipher,' I said. He laughed, then became serious. 'I had lots of trouble to keep these people off,' he said. 'Did they want to kill you?' I asked. 'Oh, no!' he cried, and checked himself. 'Why did they attack us?' I pursued. He hesitated, then said shamefacedly, 'They don't want him to go.' 'Don't they?' I said, curiously. He nodded a nod full of mystery and wisdom. 'I tell you,' he cried, 'this man has enlarged my mind.' He opened his arms wide, staring at me with his little blue eyes that were perfectly round."

III

"I looked at him, lost in astonishment. There he was before me, in motley, as though he had absconded from a troupe of mimes, enthusiastic, fabulous. His very existence was improbable, inexplicable, and altogether bewildering. He was an insoluble problem. It was inconceivable how he had existed, how he had succeeded in getting so far, how he had managed to remain — why he did not instantly disappear. 'I went a little farther,' he said, 'then still a little farther — till I had gone so far that I don't know how I'll ever get back. Never mind. Plenty time. I can manage. You take Kurtz away quick — quick — I tell you.' The glamour of youth enveloped his parti-colored rags, his destitution, his loneliness, the essential desolation of his futile wanderings. For months — for years — his life hadn't been worth a day's purchase; and there he was gallantly, thoughtlessly alive, to all appearance indestructible solely by the virtue of his few years and of his unreflecting audacity. I was seduced into something like admiration — like envy. Glamour urged him on, glamour kept him unscathed. He surely wanted nothing from the wilderness but space to breathe in and to push on through. His need was to exist, and to move onwards at the greatest possible risk, and with a maximum of privation. If the absolutely pure, uncalculating, unpractical spirit of adventure had ever ruled a human being, it ruled this be-patched youth. I almost envied him the possession of this modest and clear flame. It seemed to have consumed all thought of self so completely, that even while he was talking to you, you forgot that it was he — the man before your eyes — who had gone through these things. I did not envy him his devotion to Kurtz, though. He had not meditated over it. It came to him and he accepted it with a sort of eager fatalism. I must say that to me it appeared about the most dangerous thing in every way he had come upon so far.

"They had come together unavoidably, like two ships becalmed near each other, and lay rubbing sides at last. I suppose Kurtz wanted an audience, because on a certain occasion, when encamped in the forest, they had talked all night, or more probably Kurtz had talked. 'We talked of everything,' he said, quite transported at the recollection. 'I forgot there was such a thing as sleep. The night did not seem to last an hour. Everything! Everything! . . . Of love, too.' 'Ah, he talked to you of love!' I said, much amused. 'It isn't what you think,' he cried, almost passionately. 'It was in general. He made me see things — things.'

"He threw his arms up. We were on deck at the time, and the head-man of my wood-cutters, lounging near by, turned upon him his heavy and glittering eyes. I looked around, and I don't know why, but I assure you that never, never before, did this land, this river, this jungle, the very arch of this blazing sky, appear to me so hopeless and so dark, so impenetrable to human thought, so pitiless to human weakness. 'And, ever since, you have been with him, of course?' I said.

"On the contrary. It appears their intercourse had been very much broken by various causes. He had, as he informed me proudly, managed to nurse Kurtz through two illnesses (he alluded to it as you would to some risky feat), but as a rule Kurtz wandered alone far in the depths of the forest. 'Very often coming to this station, I had to wait days and days before he would turn up,' he said. 'Ah, it was worth waiting for! — sometimes.' 'What was he doing? exploring or what?' I asked. 'Oh, yes, of course'; he had discovered lots of villages, a lake, too — he did not know exactly in what direction; it was dangerous to inquire too much — but mostly his expeditions had been for ivory. 'But he had no goods to trade with by that time,' I objected. 'There's a good lot of cartridges left even yet,' he answered, looking away. 'To speak plainly, he raided the country,' I said. He nodded. 'Not alone, surely!' He muttered something about the villages round that lake. 'Kurtz got the tribe to follow him, did he?' I suggested. He fidgeted a little. 'They adored him,' he said. The tone of these words was so extraordinary that I looked at him searchingly. It was curious to see his mingled eagerness and reluctance to speak of Kurtz. The man filled his life, occupied his thoughts, swayed his emotions. 'What can you expect?' he burst out; 'he came to them with thunder and lightning, you know — and they had never seen anything like it — and very terrible. He could be very terrible. You can't judge Mr. Kurtz as you would an ordinary man. No, no, no! Now — just to give you an idea — I don't mind telling you, he wanted to shoot me, too, one day — but I don't judge him.' 'Shoot you!' I cried. 'What for?' 'Well, I had a small lot of ivory the chief of that village near my house gave me. You see I used to shoot game for them. Well, he wanted it, and wouldn't hear reason. He declared he would shoot me unless I gave him the ivory and then cleared out of the country, because he could do so, and had a fancy for it, and there was nothing on earth to prevent him killing whom he jolly well pleased. And it was true, too. I gave him the ivory. What did I care! But I didn't clear out. No, no. I couldn't leave him. I had to be careful, of course, till we got friendly again for a time. He had his second illness then. Afterwards I had to keep out of the way; but I didn't mind. He was living for the most part in those villages on the lake. When he came down to the river, sometimes he would take to me, and sometimes it was better for me to be careful. This man suffered too much. He hated all this, and somehow he couldn't get away. When I had a chance I begged him to try and leave while there was time; I offered to go back with him. And he would say yes, and then he would remain; go off on another ivory hunt; disappear for weeks; forget himself amongst these people — forget himself — you know.' 'Why! he's mad,' I said. He protested indignantly. Mr. Kurtz couldn't be mad. If I had heard him talk, only two days ago, I wouldn't dare hint at such a thing. . . . I had taken up my binoculars while we talked, and was looking at the shore, sweeping the limit of the forest at each side and at the back of the house. The consciousness of there being people in that bush, so silent, so quiet — as silent and quiet as the ruined house on the hill — made me uneasy. There was no sign on the face of nature of this amazing tale that was not so much told as suggested to me in desolate exclamations, completed by shrugs, in interrupted phrases, in hints ending in deep sighs. The woods were unmoved, like a mask — heavy, like the closed door of a prison — they looked with their air of hidden knowledge, of patient expectation, of unapproachable silence. The Russian was explaining to me that it was only lately that Mr. Kurtz had come down to the river, bringing along with him all the fighting men of that lake tribe. He had been absent for several months — getting himself adored, I suppose — and had come down unexpectedly, with the intention to all appearance of making a raid either across the river or down stream. Evidently the appetite for more ivory had got the better of the — what shall I say? — less material aspirations. However he had got much worse suddenly. 'I heard he was lying helpless, and so I came up — took my chance,' said the Russian. 'Oh, he is bad, very bad.' I directed my glass to the house. There were no signs of life, but there was the ruined roof, the long mud wall peeping above the grass, with three little square window-holes, no two of the same size; all this brought within reach of my hand, as it were. And then I made a brusque movement, and one of the remaining posts of that vanished fence leaped up in the field of my glass. You remember I told you I had been struck at the distance by certain attempts at ornamentation, rather remarkable in the ruinous aspect of the place. Now I had suddenly a nearer view, and its first result was to make me throw my head back as if before a blow. Then I went carefully from post to post with my glass, and I saw my mistake. These round knobs were not ornamental but symbolic; they were expressive and puzzling, striking and disturbing — food for thought and also for vultures if there had been any looking down from the sky; but at all events for such ants as were industrious enough to ascend the pole. They would have been even more impressive, those heads on the stakes, if their faces had not been turned to the house. Only one, the first I had made out, was facing my way. I was not so shocked as you may think. The start back I had given was really nothing but a movement of surprise. I had expected to see a knob of wood there, you know. I returned deliberately to the first I had seen — and there it was, black, dried, sunken, with closed eyelids — a head that seemed to sleep at the top of that pole, and with the shrunken dry lips showing a narrow white line of the teeth, was smiling, too, smiling continuously at some endless and jocose dream of that eternal slumber.

"I am not disclosing any trade secrets. In fact, the manager said afterwards that Mr. Kurtz's methods had ruined the district. I have no opinion on that point, but I want you clearly to understand that there was nothing exactly profitable in these heads being there. They only showed that Mr. Kurtz lacked restraint in the gratification of his various lusts, that there was something wanting in him — some small matter which, when the pressing need arose, could not be found under his magnificent eloquence. Whether he knew of this deficiency himself I can't say. I think the knowledge came to him at last — only at the very last. But the wilderness had found him out early, and had taken on him a terrible vengeance for the fantastic invasion. I think it had whispered to him things about himself which he did not know, things of which he had no conception till he took counsel with this great solitude — and the whisper had proved irresistibly fascinating. It echoed loudly within him because he was hollow at the core. . . . I put down the glass, and the head that had appeared near enough to be spoken to seemed at once to have leaped away from me into inaccessible distance.

"The admirer of Mr. Kurtz was a bit crestfallen. In a hurried indistinct voice he began to assure me he had not dared to take these — say, symbols — down. He was not afraid of the natives; they would not stir till Mr. Kurtz gave the word. His ascendancy was extraordinary. The camps of these people surrounded the place, and the chiefs came every day to see him. They would crawl. . . . 'I don't want to know anything of the ceremonies used when approaching Mr. Kurtz,' I shouted. Curious, this feeling that came over me that such details would be more intolerable than those heads drying on the stakes under Mr. Kurtz's windows. After all, that was only a savage sight, while I seemed at one bound to have been transported into some lightless region of subtle horrors, where pure, uncomplicated savagery was a positive relief, being something that had a right to exist — obviously — in the sunshine. The young man looked at me with surprise. I suppose it did not occur to him that Mr. Kurtz was no idol of mine. He forgot I hadn't heard any of these splendid monologues on, what was it? on love, justice, conduct of life — or what not. If it had come to crawling before Mr. Kurtz, he crawled as much as the veriest savage of them all. I had no idea of the conditions, he said: these heads were the heads of rebels. I shocked him excessively by laughing. Rebels! What would be the next definition I was to hear? There had been enemies, criminals, workers — and these were rebels. Those rebellious heads looked very subdued to me on their sticks. 'You don't know how such a life tries a man like Kurtz,' cried Kurtz's last disciple. 'Well, and you?' I said. 'I! I! I am a simple man. I have no great thoughts. I want nothing from anybody. How can you compare me to . . . ?' His feelings were too much for speech, and suddenly he broke down. 'I don't understand,' he groaned. 'I've been doing my best to keep him alive, and that's enough. I had no hand in all this. I have no abilities. There hasn't been a drop of medicine or a mouthful of invalid food for months here. He was shamefully abandoned. A man like this, with such ideas. Shamefully! Shamefully! I — I — haven't slept for the last ten nights. . . .'

"His voice lost itself in the calm of the evening. The long shadows of the forest had slipped downhill while we talked, had gone far beyond the ruined hovel, beyond the symbolic row of stakes. All this was in the gloom, while we down there were yet in the sunshine, and the stretch of the river abreast of the clearing glittered in a still and dazzling splendor, with a murky and overshadowed bend above and below. Not a living soul was seen on the shore. The bushes did not rustle.

"Suddenly round the corner of the house a group of men appeared, as though they had come up from the ground. They waded waist-deep in the grass, in a compact body, bearing an improvised stretcher in their midst. Instantly, in the emptiness of the landscape, a cry arose while shrillness pierced the still air like a sharp arrow flying straight to the very heart of the land; and, as if by enchantment, streams of human beings — of naked human beings — with spears in their hands, with bows, with shields, with wild glances and savage movements, were poured into the clearing by the dark-faced and pensive forest. The bushes shook, the grass swayed for a time, and then everything stood still in attentive immobility.

"'Now, if he does not say the right thing to them we are all done for,' said the Russian at my elbow. The knot of men with the stretcher had stopped, too, halfway to the steamer, as if petrified. I saw the man on the stretcher sit up, lank and with an uplifted arm, above the shoulders of the bearers. 'Let us hope that the man who can talk so well of love in general will find some particular reason to spare us this time,' I said. I resented bitterly the absurd danger of our situation, as if to be at the mercy of that atrocious phantom had been a dishonoring necessity. I could not hear a sound, but through my glasses I saw the thin arm extended commandingly, the lower jaw moving, the eyes of that apparition shining darkly far in its bony head that nodded with grotesque jerks. Kurtz — Kurtz — that means short in German — don't it? Well, the name was as true as everything else in his life — and death. He looked at least seven feet long. His covering had fallen off, and his body emerged from it pitiful and appalling as from a winding-sheet. I could see the cage of his ribs all astir, the bones of his arm waving. It was as though an animated image of death carved out of old ivory had been shaking its hand with menaces at a motionless crowd of men made of dark and glittering bronze. I saw him open his mouth wide — it gave him a weirdly voracious aspect, as though he had wanted to swallow all the air, all the earth, all the men before him. A deep voice reached me faintly. He must have been shouting. He fell back suddenly. The stretcher shook as the bearers staggered forward again, and almost at the same time I noticed that the crowd of savages was vanishing without any perceptible movement of retreat, as if the forest that had ejected these beings so suddenly had drawn them in again as the breath is drawn in a long aspiration.

"Some of the pilgrims behind the stretcher carried his arms — two shotguns, a heavy rifle, and a light revolver-carbine — the thunderbolts of that pitiful Jupiter. The manager bent over him murmuring as he walked beside his head. They laid him down in one of the little cabins — just a room for a bedplace and a campstool or two, you know. We had brought his belated correspondence, and a lot of torn envelopes and open letters littered his bed. His hand roamed feebly amongst these papers. I was struck by the fire in his eyes and the composed languor of his expression. It was not so much the exhaustion of disease. He did not seem in pain. This shadow looked satiated and calm, as though for the moment it had had its fill of all the emotions.

"He rustled one of the letters, and looking straight in my face said, 'I am glad.' Somebody had been writing to him about me. These special recommendations were turning up again. The volume of tone he emitted without effort, almost without the trouble of moving his lips, amazed me. A voice! a voice! It was grave, profound, vibrating, while the man did not seem capable of a whisper. However, he had enough strength in him — factitious no doubt — to very nearly make an end of us, as you shall hear directly.

"The manager appeared silently in the doorway; I stepped out at once and he drew the curtain after me. The Russian, eyed curiously by the pilgrims, was staring at the shore. I followed the direction of his glance.

"Dark human shapes could be made out in the distance, flitting indistinctly against the gloomy border of the forest, and near the river two bronze figures, leaning on tall spears, stood in the sunlight under fantastic headdresses of spotted skins, war-like and still in statuesque repose. And from right to left along the lighted shore moved a wild and gorgeous apparition of a woman.

"She walked with measured steps, draped in striped and fringed cloths, treading the earth proudly, with a slight jingle and flash of barbarous orna- ments. She carried her head high; her hair was done in the shape of a helmet; she had brass leggings to the knee, brass wire gauntlets to the elbow, a crimson spot on her tawny cheek, innumerable necklaces of glass beads on her neck; bizarre things, charms, gifts of witchmen, that hung about her, glittered and trembled at every step. She must have had the value of several elephant tusks upon her. She was savage and superb, wild-eyed and mag- nificent; there was something ominous and stately in her deliberate progress. And in the hush that had fallen suddenly upon the whole sorrowful land, the immense wilderness, the colossal body of the fecund and mysterious life seemed to look at her, pensive, as though it had been looking at the image of its own tenebrous and passionate soul.

"She came abreast of the steamer, stood still, and faced us. Her long shadow fell to the water's edge. Her face had a tragic and fierce aspect of wild sorrow and of dumb pain mingled with the fear of some struggling, half-shaped resolve. She stood looking at us without a stir, and like the wilderness itself, with an air of brooding over an inscrutable purpose. A whole minute passed, and then she made a step forward. There was a low jingle, a glint of yellow metal, a sway of fringed draperies, and she stopped as if her heart had failed her. The young fellow by my side growled. The pilgrims murmured at my back. She looked at us all as if her life had depended upon the unswerving steadiness of her glance. Suddenly she opened her bared arms and threw them up rigid above her head, as though in an uncontrollable desire to touch the sky, and at the same time the swift shadows darted out on the earth, swept around on the river, gathering the steamer into a shadowy embrace. A formidable silence hung over the scene.

"She turned away slowly, walked on, followed the bank, and passed into the bushes to the left. Once only her eyes gleamed back at us in the dusk of the thickets before she disappeared.

"'If she had offered to come aboard I really think I would have tried to shoot her,' said the man of patches, nervously. 'I have been risking my life every day for the last fortnight to keep her out of the house. She got in one day and kicked up a row about those miserable rags I picked up in the storeroom to mend my clothes with. I wasn't decent. At least it must have been that, for she talked like a fury to Kurtz for an hour, pointing at me now and then. I don't understand the dialect of this tribe. Luckily for me, I fancy Kurtz felt too ill that day to care, or there would have been mischief. I don't understand. . . . No — it's too much for me. Ah, well, it's all over now.'

"At this moment I heard Kurtz's deep voice behind the curtain: 'Save me! — save the ivory, you mean. Don't tell me. Save *me!* Why, I've had to save you. You are interrupting my plans now. Sick! Sick! Not so sick as you would like to believe. Never mind. I'll carry my ideas out yet — I will return. I'll show you what can be done. You with your little peddling notions — you are intefering with me. I will return. I . . .'

"The manager came out. He did me the honor to take me under the arm and lead me aside. 'He is very low, very low,' he said. He considered it necessary to sigh, but neglected to be consistently sorrowful. 'We have done all we could for him — haven't we? But there is no disguising the fact, Mr. Kurtz has done more harm than good to the Company. He did not see the time was not ripe for vigorous action. Cautiously, cautiously — that's my principle. We must be cautious yet. The district is closed to us for a time. Deplorable! Upon the whole, the trade will suffer. I don't deny there is a remarkable quantity of ivory — mostly fossil. We must save it, at all events — but look how precarious the position is — and why? Because the method is unsound.' 'Do you,' said I, looking at the shore, 'call it "unsound method"?' 'Without doubt,' he exclaimed, hotly. 'Don't you?' . . . 'No method at all,' I murmured after a while. 'Exactly,' he exulted. 'I anticipated this. Shows a complete want of judgment. It is my duty to point it out in the proper quarter.' 'Oh,' said I, 'that fellow — what's his name? — the brick-maker, will make a readable report for you.' He appeared confounded for a moment. It seemed to me I had never breathed an atmosphere so vile, and I turned mentally to Kurtz for relief — positively for relief. 'Nevertheless I think Mr. Kurtz is a remarkable man,' I said with emphasis. He started, dropped on me a cold heavy glance, said very quietly, 'he *was*,' and turned his back on me. My hour of favor was over; I found myself lumped along with Kurtz as a partisan of methods for which the time was not ripe: I was unsound! Ah! but it was something to have at least a choice of nightmares.

"I had turned to the wilderness really, not to Mr. Kurtz, who, I was ready to admit, was as good as buried. And for a moment it seemed to me as if I also were buried in a vast grave full of unspeakable secrets. I felt an intolerable weight oppressing my breast, the smell of the damp earth, the unseen presence of victorious corruption, the darkness of an impenetrable night. . . . The Russian tapped me on the shoulder. I heard him mumbling and stammering something about 'brother seaman — couldn't conceal — knowledge of matters that would affect Mr. Kurtz's reputation.' I waited. For him evidently Mr. Kurtz was not in his grave; I suspect that for him Mr. Kurtz was one of the immortals. 'Well,' said I at last, 'speak out. As it happens, I am Mr. Kurtz's friend — in a way.'

"He stated with a good deal of formality that had we not been 'of the same profession,' he would have kept the matter to himself without regard to consequences. 'He suspected there was an active ill will towards him on the part of these white men that — ' 'You are right,' I said, remembering a certain conversation I had overheard. 'The manager thinks you ought to be hanged.' He showed a concern at this intelligence which amused me at first. 'I had better get out of the way quietly,' he said, earnestly. 'I can do no more for Kurtz now, and they would soon find some excuse. What's to stop them? There's a military post three hundred miles from here.' 'Well, upon my word,' said I, 'perhaps you had better go if you have any friends amongst the savages near by.' 'Plenty,' he said. 'They are simple people — and I want nothing, you know.' He stood biting his lip, then: 'I don't want any harm to happen to these whites here, but of course I was thinking of Mr. Kurtz's reputation — but you are a brother seaman and — ' 'All right,' said I, after a time. 'Mr. Kurtz's reputation is safe with me.' I did not know how truly I spoke.

"He informed me, lowering his voice, that it was Kurtz who had ordered the attack to be made on the steamer. 'He hated sometimes the idea of being taken away — and then again. . . . But I don't understand these matters. I am a simple man. He thought it would scare you away — that you would give it up, thinking him dead. I could not stop him. Oh, I had an awful time of it this last month.' 'Very well,' I said. 'He is all right now.' 'Ye-e-es,' he muttered, not very convinced apparently. 'Thanks,' said I; 'I shall keep my eyes open.' 'But quiet — eh?' he urged, anxiously. 'It would be awful for his reputation if anybody here — ' I promised a complete discretion with great gravity. 'I have a canoe and three black fellows waiting not very far. I am off. Could you give me a few Martini-Henry cartridges?' I could, and did, with proper secrecy. He helped himself, with a wink at me, to a handful of my tobacco. 'Between sailors — you know — good English tobacco.' At the door of the pilot-house he turned round — 'I say, haven't you a pair of shoes you could spare?' He raised one leg. 'Look.' The soles were tied with knotted strings sandal-wise under his bare feet. I rooted out an old pair, at which he looked with admiration before tucking them under his left arm. One of his pockets (bright red) was bulging with cartridges, from the other (dark blue) peeped 'Towson's Inquiry,' etc., etc. He seemed to think himself excellently well equipped for a renewed encounter with the wilderness. 'Ah! I'll never, never meet such a man again. You ought to have heard him recite poetry — his own, too, it was, he told me. Poetry!' He rolled his eyes at the recollection of these delights. 'Oh, he enlarged my mind!' 'Good-by,' said I. He shook hands and vanished in the night. Sometimes I ask myself whether I had ever really seen him — whether it was possible to meet such a phenomenon! . . .

"When I woke up shortly after midnight his warning came to my mind with its hint of danger that seemed, in the starred darkness, real enough to make me get up for the purpose of having a look around. On the hill a big fire burned, illuminating fitfully a crooked corner of the station-house. One of the agents with a picket of a few of our blacks, armed for the purpose, was keeping guard over the ivory; but deep within the forest, red gleams that wavered, that seemed to sink and rise from the ground amongst confused columnar shapes of intense blackness, showed the exact position of the camp where Mr. Kurtz's adorers were keeping their uneasy vigil. The monotonous beating of a big drum filled the air with muffled shocks and a lingering vibration. A steady droning sound of many men chanting each to himself some weird incantation came out from the black, flat wall of the wood as the humming of bees comes out of a hive, and had a strange narcotic effect upon my half-awake senses. I believe I dozed off leaning over the rail, till an abrupt burst of yells, an overwhelming outbreak of a pent-up and mysterious frenzy, woke me up in a bewildered wonder. It was cut short all at once, and the low droning went on with an effect of audible and soothing silence. I glanced casually into the little cabin. A light was burning within, but Mr. Kurtz was not there.

"I think I would have raised an outcry if I had believed my eyes. But I didn't believe them at first — the thing seemed so impossible. The fact is I was completely unnerved by a sheer blank fright, pure abstract terror, unconnected with any distinct shape of physical danger. What made this emotion so overpowering was — how shall I define it? — the moral shock I received, as if something altogether monstrous, intolerable to thought and odious to the soul, had been thrust upon me unexpectedly. This lasted of course the merest fraction of a second, and then the usual sense of commonplace, deadly danger, the possibility of a sudden onslaught and massacre, or something of the kind, which I saw impending, was positively welcome and composing. It pacified me, in fact, so much, that I did not raise an alarm.

"There was an agent buttoned up inside an ulster and sleeping on a chair on deck within three feet of me. The yells had not awakened him; he snored very slightly; I left him to his slumbers and leaped ashore. I did not betray Mr. Kurtz — it was ordered I should never betray him — it was written I should be loyal to the nightmare of my choice. I was anxious to deal with this shadow by myself alone — and to this day I don't know why I was so jealous of sharing with anyone the peculiar blackness of that experience.

"As soon as I got on the bank I saw a trail — a broad trail through the grass. I remember the exultation with which I said to myself, 'He can't walk — he is crawling on all-fours — I've got him.' The grass was wet with dew. I strode rapidly with clenched fists. I fancy I had some vague notion of falling upon him and giving him a drubbing. I don't know. I had some imbecile thoughts. The knitting old woman with the cat obtruded herself upon my memory as a most improper person to be sitting at the other end of such an affair. I saw a row of pilgrims squirting lead in the air out of Winchesters held to the hip. I thought I would never get back to the steamer, and imagined myself living alone and unarmed in the woods to an advanced age. Such silly things — you know. And I remember I confounded the beat of the drum with the beating of my heart, and was pleased at its calm regularity.

"I kept to the track though — then stopped to listen. The night was very clear; a dark blue space, sparkling with dew and starlight, in which black things stood very still. I thought I could see a kind of motion ahead of me. I was strangely cocksure of everything that night. I actually left the track and ran in a wide semicircle (I verily believe chuckling to myself) so as to get in front of that stir, of that motion I had seen — if indeed I had seen anything. I was circumventing Kurtz as though it had been a boyish game.

"I came upon him, and, if he had not heard me coming, I would have fallen over him, too, but he got up in time. He rose, unsteady, long, pale, indistinct, like a vapor exhaled by the earth, and swayed slightly, misty and silent before me; while at my back the fires loomed between the trees, and the murmur of many voices issued from the forest. I had cut him off cleverly; but when actually confronting him I seemed to come to my senses, I saw the danger in its right proportion. It was by no means over yet. Suppose he began to shout? Though he could hardly stand, there was still plenty of vigor in his voice. 'Go away — hide yourself,' he said, in that profound tone. It was very awful. I glanced back. We were within thirty yards from the nearest fire. A black figure stood up, strode on long black legs, waving long black arms, across the glow. It had horns — antelope horns, I think — on its head. Some sorcerer, some witchman, no doubt: it looked fiend-like enough. 'Do you know what you are doing?' I whispered. 'Perfectly,' he answered, raising his voice for that single word: it sounded to me far off and yet loud, like a hail through a speaking-trumpet. If he makes a row we are lost, I thought to myself. This clearly was not a case for fisticuffs, even apart from the very natural aversion I had to beat that Shadow — this wandering and tormented thing. 'You will be lost,' I said — 'utterly lost.' One gets sometimes such a flash of inspiration, you know. I did say the right thing, though indeed he could not have been more irretrievably lost than he was at this very moment, when the foundations of our intimacy were being laid — to endure — to endure — even to the end — even beyond.

"'I had immense plans,' he muttered irresolutely. 'Yes,' said I; 'but if you try to shout I'll smash your head with — ' There was not a stick or a stone near. 'I will throttle you for good,' I corrected myself. 'I was on the threshold of great things,' he pleaded, in a voice of longing, with a wistfulness of tone that made my blood run cold. 'And now for this stupid scoundrel — ' 'Your success in Europe is assured in any case,' I affirmed, steadily. I did not want to have the throttling of him, you understand — and indeed it would have been very little use for any practical purpose. I tried to break the spell — the heavy, mute spell of the wilderness — that seemed to draw him to its pitiless breast by the awakening of forgotten and brutal instincts, by the memory of gratified and monstrous passions. This alone, I was convinced, had driven him out to the edge of the forest, to the bush, towards the gleam of fires, the throb of drums, the drone of weird incantations; this alone had beguiled his unlawful soul beyond the bounds of permitted aspirations. And, don't you see, the terror of the position was not in being knocked on the head — though I had a very lively sense of that danger, too — but in this, that I had to deal with a being to whom I could not appeal in the name of anything high or low. I had, even like the niggers, to invoke him — himself — his own exalted and incredible degradation. There was nothing either above or below him, and I knew it. He had kicked himself loose of the earth. Confound the man! he had kicked the very earth to pieces. He was alone, and I before him did not know whether I stood on the ground or floated in the air. I've been telling you what we said — repeating the phrases we pronounced — but what's the good? They were common everyday words — the familiar, vague sounds exchanged on every waking day of life. But what of that? They had behind them, to my mind, the terrific suggestiveness of words heard in dreams, of phrases spoken in nightmares. Soul! If anybody had ever struggled with a soul, I am the man. And I wasn't arguing with a lunatic either. Believe me or not, his intelligence was perfectly clear — concentrated, it is true, upon himself with horrible intensity, yet clear; and therein was my only chance — barring, of course, the killing him there and then, which wasn't so good, on account of unavoidable noise. But his soul was mad. Being alone in the wilderness, it had looked within itself, and, by heavens! I tell you, it had gone mad. I had — for my sins, I suppose — to go through the ordeal of looking into it myself. No eloquence could have been so withering to one's belief in mankind as his final burst of sincerity. He struggled with himself, too. I saw it — I heard it. I saw the inconceivable mystery of a soul that knew no restraint, no faith, and no fear, yet struggling blindly with itself. I kept my head pretty well; but when I had him at last stretched on the couch, I wiped my forehead, while my legs shook under me as though I had carried half a ton on my back down that hill. And yet I had only supported him, his bony arm clasped round my neck — and he was not much heavier than a child.

"When next day we left at noon, the crowd, of whose presence behind the curtain of trees I had been acutely conscious all the time, flowed out of the woods again, filled the clearing, covered the slope with a mass of naked, breathing, quivering, bronze bodies. I steamed up a bit, then swung downstream, and two thousand eyes followed the evolutions of the splashing, thumping, fierce river-demon beating the water with its terrible tail and breathing black smoke into the air. In front of the first rank, along the river, three men, plastered with bright red earth from head to foot, strutted to and fro restlessly. When we came abreast again, they faced the river, stamped their feet, nodded their horned heads, swayed their scarlet bodies; they shook towards the fierce river-demon a bunch of black feathers, a mangy skin with a pendant tail — something that looked like a dried gourd; they shouted periodically together strings of amazing words that resembled no sounds of human language; and the deep murmurs of the crowd, interrupted suddenly, were like the responses of some satanic litany.

"We had carried Kurtz into the pilot-house: there was more air there. Lying on the couch, he stared through the open shutter. There was an eddy in the mass of human bodies, and the woman with helmeted head and tawny cheeks rushed out to the very brink of the stream. She put out her hands, shouted something, and all that wild mob took up the shout in a roaring chorus of articulated, rapid, breathless utterance.

"'Do you understand this?' I asked.

"He kept on looking out past me with fiery, longing eyes, with a mingled expression of wistfulness and hate. He made no answer, but I saw a smile, a smile of indefinable meaning, appear on his colorless lips that a moment after twitched convulsively. 'Do I not?' he said slowly, gasping, as if the words had been torn out of him by a supernatural power.

"I pulled the string of the whistle, and I did this because I saw the pilgrims on deck getting out their rifles with an air of anticipating a jolly lark. At the sudden screech there was a movement of abject terror through that wedged mass of bodies. 'Don't! don't you frighten them away,' cried someone on deck disconsolately. I pulled the string time after time. They broke and ran, they leaped, they crouched, they swerved, they dodged the flying terror of the sound. The three red chaps had fallen flat, face down on the shore, as though they had been shot dead. Only the barbarous and superb woman did not so much as flinch, and stretched tragically her bare arms after us over the somber and glittering river.

"And then that imbecile crowd down on the deck started their little fun, and I could see nothing more for smoke.

"The brown current ran swiftly out of the heart of darkness, bearing us down towards the sea with twice the speed of our upward progress; and Kurtz's life was running swiftly, too, ebbing out of his heart into the sea of inexorable time. The manager was very placid, he had no vital anxieties now, he took us both in with a comprehensive and satisfied glance: the 'affair' had come off as well as could be wished. I saw the time approaching when I would be left alone of the party of 'unsound method.' The pilgrims looked upon me with disfavor. I was, so to speak, numbered with the dead. It is strange how I accepted this unforeseen partnership, this choice of nightmares forced upon me in the tenebrous land invaded by these mean and greedy phantoms.

"Kurtz discoursed. A voice! a voice! It rang deep to the very last. It survived his strength to hide in the magnificent folds of eloquence the barren darkness of his heart. Oh, he struggled! he struggled! The wastes of his weary brain were haunted by shadowy images now — images of wealth and fame revolving obsequiously round his unextinguishable gift of noble and lofty expression. My Intended, my station, my career, my ideas — these were the objects for the occasional utterances of elevated sentiments. The shade of the original Kurtz frequented the bedside of the hollow sham, whose fate it was to be buried presently in the mold of primeval earth. But both the diabolic love and the unearthly hate of the mysteries it had penetrated fought for the possession of that soul satiated with primitive emotions, avid of lying fame, of sham distinction, of all the appearances of success and power.

"Sometimes he was contemptibly childish. He desired to have kings meet him at railway stations on his return from some ghastly Nowhere, where he intended to accomplish great things. 'You show them you have in you something that is really profitable, and then there will be no limits to the recognition of your ability,' he would say. 'Of course you must take care of the motives — right motives — always.' The long reaches that were like one and the same reach, monotonous bends that were exactly alike, slipped past the steamer with their multitude of secular trees looking patiently after this grimy fragment of another world, the forerunner of change, of conquest, of trade, of massacres, of blessings. I looked ahead — piloting. 'Close the shutter,' said Kurtz suddenly one day; 'I can't bear to look at this.' I did so. There was a silence. 'Oh, but I will wring your heart yet!' he cried at the invisible wilderness.

"We broke down — as I had expected — and had to lie up for repairs at the head of an island. This delay was the first thing that shook Kurtz's confidence. One morning he gave me a packet of papers and a photograph — the lot tied together with a shoestring. 'Keep this for me,' he said, 'This noxious fool' (meaning the manager) 'is capable of prying into my boxes when I am not looking.' In the afternoon I saw him. He was lying on his back with closed eyes, and I withdrew quietly, but I heard him mutter, 'Live rightly, die, die. . . .' I listened. There was nothing more. Was he rehearsing some speech in his sleep, or was it a fragment of a phrase from some newspaper article? He had been writing for the papers and meant to do so again, 'for the furthering of my ideas. It's a duty.'

"His was an impenetrable darkness. I looked at him as you peer down at a man who is lying at the bottom of a precipice where the sun never shines. But I had not much time to give him, because I was helping the engine-driver to take to pieces the leaky cylinders, to straighten a bent connecting-rod, and in other such matters. I lived in an infernal mess of rust, filings, nuts, bolts, spanners, hammers, ratchet-drills — things I abominate, because I don't get on with them. I tended the little forge we fortunately had aboard; I toiled wearily in a wretched scrap-heap — unless I had the shakes too bad to stand.

"One evening coming in with a candle I was startled to hear him say a little tremulously, 'I am lying here in the dark waiting for death.' The light was within a foot of his eyes. I forced myself to murmur, 'Oh, nonsense!' and stood over him as if transfixed.

"Anything approaching the change that came over his features I have never seen before, and hope never to see again. Oh, I wasn't touched. I was fascinated. It was as though a veil had been rent. I saw on that ivory face the expression of somber pride, of ruthless power, of craven terror — of an intense and hopeless despair. Did he live his life again in every detail of desire, temptation, and surrender during that supreme moment of complete knowledge? He cried in a whisper at some image, at some vision — he cried out twice, a cry that was no more than a breath —

"'The horror! The horror!'

"I blew the candle out and left the cabin. The pilgrims were dining in the messroom, and I took my place opposite the manager, who lifted his eyes to give me a questioning glance, which I successfully ignored. He leaned back, serene, with that peculiar smile of his sealing the unexpressed depths of his meanness. A continuous shower of small flies streamed upon the lamp, upon the cloth, upon our hands and faces. Suddenly the manager's boy put his insolent black head in the doorway, and said in a tone of scathing contempt —

"'Mistah Kurtz — he dead.'

"All the pilgrims rushed out to see. I remained, and went on with my dinner. I believe I was considered brutally callous. However, I did not eat much. There was a lamp in there — light, don't you know — and outside it was so beastly, beastly dark. I went no more near the remarkable man who had pronounced a judgment upon the adventures of his soul on this earth. The voice was gone. What else had been there? But I am of course aware that next day the pilgrims buried something in a muddy hole.

"And then they very nearly buried me.

"However, as you see, I did not go to join Kurtz there and then. I did not. I remained to dream the nightmare out to the end, and to show my loyalty to Kurtz once more. Destiny. My destiny! Droll thing life is — that mysterious arrangement of merciless logic for a futile purpose. The most you can hope from it is some knowledge of yourself — that comes too late — a crop of unextinguishable regrets. I have wrestled with death. It is the most unexciting contest you can imagine. It takes place in an impalpable grayness, with nothing underfoot, with nothing around, without spectators, without clamor, without glory, without the great desire of victory, without the great fear of defeat, in a sickly atmosphere of tepid skepticism, without much belief in your own right, and still less in that of your adversary. If such is the form of ultimate wisdom, then life is a greater riddle than some of us think it to be. I was within a hair's breadth of the last opportunity for pronouncement, and I found with humiliation that probably I would have nothing to say. This is the reason why I affirm that Kurtz was a remarkable man. He had something to say. He said it. Since I had peeped over the edge myself, I understand better the meaning of his stare, that could not see the flame of the candle, but was wide enough to embrace the whole universe, piercing enough to penetrate all the hearts that beat in the darkness. He had summed up — he had judged. 'The horror!' He was a remarkable man. After all, this was the expression of some sort of belief; it had candor, it had conviction, it had a vibrating note of revolt in its whisper, it had the appalling face of a glimpsed truth — the strange commingling of desire and hate. And it is not my own extremity I remember best — a vision of grayness without form filled with physical pain, and a careless contempt for the evanescence of all things — even of this pain itself. No! It is his extremity that I seem to have lived through. True, he had made that last stride, he had stepped over the edge, while I had been permitted to draw back my hesitating foot. And perhaps in this is the whole difference; perhaps all the wisdom, and all truth, and all sincerity, are just compressed into that inappreciable moment of time in which we step over the threshold of the invisible. Perhaps! I like to think my summing-up would not have been a word of careless contempt. Better his cry — much better. It was an affirmation, a moral victory paid for by innumerable defeats, by abominable terrors, by abominable satisfactions. But it was a victory! That is why I have remained loyal to Kurtz to the last, and even beyond, when a long time after I heard once more, not his own choice, but the echo of his magnificent eloquence thrown to me from a soul as translucently pure as a cliff of crystal.

"No, they did not bury me, though there is a period of time which I remember mistily, with a shuddering wonder, like a passage through some inconceivable world that had no hope in it and no desire. I found myself back in the sepulchral city resenting the sight of people hurrying through the streets to filch a little money from each other, to devour their infamous cookery, to gulp their unwholesome beer, to dream their insignificant and silly dreams. They trespassed upon my thoughts. They were intruders whose knowledge of life was to me an irritating pretense, because I felt so sure they could not possibly know the things I knew. Their bearing, which was simply the bearing of commonplace individuals going about their business in the assurance of perfect safety, was offensive to me like the outrageous flauntings of folly in the face of a danger it is unable to comprehend. I had no particular desire to enlighten them, but I had some difficulty in restraining myself from laughing in their faces, so full of stupid importance. I daresay I was not very well at that time. I tottered about the streets — there were various affairs to settle — grinning bitterly at perfectly respectable persons. I admit my behavior was inexcusable, but then my temperature was seldom normal in these days. My dear aunt's endeavors to 'nurse up my strength' seemed altogether beside the mark. It was not my strength that wanted nursing, it was my imagination that wanted soothing. I kept the bundle of papers given me by Kurtz, not knowing exactly what to do with it. His mother had died lately, watched over, as I was told, by his Intended. A clean-shaven man, with an official manner and wearing gold-rimmed spectacles, called on me one day and made inquiries, at first circuitous, afterwards suavely pressing, about what he was pleased to denominate certain 'documents.' I was not surprised, because I had had two rows with the manager on the subject out there. I had refused to give up the smallest scrap out of that package, and I took the same attitude with the spectacled man. He became darkly menacing at last, and with much heat argued that the Company had the right to every bit of information about its 'territories.' And he said, 'Mr. Kurtz's knowledge of unexplored regions must have been necessarily extensive and peculiar — owing to his great abilities and to the deplorable circumstances in which he had been placed: therefore — ' I assured him Mr. Kurtz's knowledge, however extensive, did not bear upon the problems of commerce or administration. He invoked then the name of science. 'It would be an incalculable loss if,' etc., etc. I offered him the report on the 'Suppression of Savage Customs,' with the postscriptum torn off. He took it up eagerly, but ended by sniffing at it with an air of contempt. 'This is not what we had a right to expect,' he remarked. 'Expect nothing else,' I said. 'There are only private letters.' He withdrew upon some threat of legal proceedings, and I saw him no more; but another fellow, calling himself Kurtz's cousin, appeared two days later, and was anxious to hear all the details about his dear relative's last moments. Incidentally he gave me to understand that Kurtz had been essentially a great musician. 'There was the making of an immense success,' said the man, who was an organist, I believe, with lank gray hair flowing over a greasy coat-collar. I had no reason to doubt his statement; and to this day I am unable to say what was Kurtz's profession, whether he ever had any — which was the greatest of his talents. I had taken him for a painter who wrote for the papers, or else for a journalist who could paint — but even the cousin (who took snuff during the interview) could not tell me what he had been — exactly. He was a universal genius — on that point I agreed with the old chap, who thereupon blew his nose noisily into a large cotton handkerchief and withdrew in senile agitation, bearing off some family letters and memoranda without importance. Ultimately a journalist anxious to know something of the fate of his 'dear colleague' turned up. This visitor informed me Kurtz's proper sphere ought to have been politics 'on the popular side.' He had furry straight eyebrows, bristly hair cropped short, an eye-glass on a broad ribbon, and, becoming expansive, confessed his opinion that Kurtz really couldn't write a bit — 'But heavens! how that man could talk. He electrified large meetings. He had faith — don't you see? — he had the faith. He could get himself to believe anything — anything. He would have been a splendid leader of an extreme party.' 'What party?' I asked. 'Any party,' answered the other. 'He was an — an — extremist.' Did I not think so? I assented. Did I know, he asked, with a sudden flash of curiosity, 'what it was that had induced him to go out there?' 'Yes,' said I, and forthwith handed him the famous Report for publication, if he thought fit. He glanced through it hurriedly, mumbling all the time, judged 'it would do,' and took himself off with this plunder.

"Thus I was left at last with a slim packet of letters and the girl's portrait. She struck me as beautiful — I mean she had a beautiful expression. I know that the sunlight can be made to lie, too, yet one felt that no manipulation of light and pose could have conveyed the delicate shade of truthfulness upon those features. She seemed ready to listen without mental reservation, without suspicion, without a thought for herself. I concluded I would go and give her back her portrait and those letters myself. Curiosity? Yes; and also some other feeling perhaps. All that had been Kurtz's had passed out of my hands: his soul, his body, his station, his plans, his ivory, his career. There remained only this memory and his Intended — and I wanted to give that up, too, to the past; in a way — to surrender personally all that remained of him with me to that oblivion which is the last word of our common fate. I don't defend myself. I had no clear perception of what it was I really wanted. Perhaps it was an impulse of unconscious loyalty, or the fulfillment of one of those ironic necessities, that lurk in the facts of human existence. I don't know. I can't tell. But I went.

"I thought his memory was like the other memories of the dead that accumulate in every man's life — a vague impress on the brain of shadows that had fallen on it in their swift and final passage; but before the high and ponderous door, between the tall houses of a street as still and decorous as a well-kept alley in a cemetery, I had a vision of him on the stretcher, opening his mouth voraciously, as if to devour all the earth with all its mankind. He lived then before me; he lived as much as he had ever lived — a shadow insatiable of splendid appearances, of frightful realities; a shadow darker than the shadow of the night, and draped nobly in the folds of a gorgeous eloquence. The vision seemed to enter the house with me — the stretcher, the phantom-bearers, the wild crowd of obedient worshipers, the gloom of the forests, the glitter of the reach between the murky bends, the beat of the drum, regular and muffled like the beating of a heart — the heart of a conquering darkness. It was a moment of triumph for the wilderness, an invading and vengeful rush which, it seemed to me, I would have to keep back alone for the salvation of another soul. And the memory of what I had heard him say afar there, with the honored shapes stirring at my back, in the glow of fires, within the patient woods, those broken phrases came back to me, were heard again in their ominous and terrifying simplicity. I remembered his abject peading, his abject threats, the colossal scale of his vile desires, the meanness, the torment, the tempestuous anguish of his soul. And later on I seem to see his collected languid manner, when he said one day, 'This lot of ivory now is really mine. The Company did not pay for it. I collected it myself at a very great personal risk. I am afraid they will try to claim it as theirs though. H'm. It is a difficult case. What do you think I ought to do — resist? Eh? I want no more than justice.' . . . He wanted no more than justice — no more than justice. I rang the bell before a mahogany door on the first floor, and while I waited he seemed to stare at me out of the glassy panel — stare with that wide and immense stare embracing, condemning, loathing all the universe. I seemed to hear the whispered cry, 'The horror! The horror!'

"The dusk was falling. I had to wait in a lofty drawing-room with three long windows from floor to ceiling that were like three luminous and bedraped columns. The bent gilt legs and backs of the furniture shone in indistinct curves. The tall marble fireplace had a cold and monumental whiteness. A grand piano stood massively in a corner; with dark gleams on the flat surfaces like a somber and polished sarcophagus. A high door opened — closed. I rose.

"She came forward, all in black, with a pale head, floating towards me in the dusk. She was in mourning. It was more than a year since his death, more than a year since the news came; she seemed as though she would remember and mourn forever. She took both my hands in hers and murmured, 'I had heard you were coming.' I noticed she was not very young — I mean not girlish. She had a mature capacity for fidelity, for belief, for suffering. The room seemed to have grown darker, as if all the sad light of the cloudy evening had taken refuge on her forehead. This fair hair, this pale visage, this pure brow, seemed surrounded by an ashy halo from which the dark eyes looked out at me. Their glance was guileless, profound, confident, and trustful. She carried her sorrowful head as though she were proud of that sorrow, as though she would say, I — I alone know how to mourn him as he deserves. But while we were still shaking hands, such a look of awful desolation came upon her face that I perceived she was one of those creatures that are not the playthings of Time. For her he had died only yesterday. And, by Jove! the impression was so powerful that for me, too, he seemed to have died only yesterday — nay, this very minute. I saw her and him in the same instant of time — his death and her sorrow — I saw her sorrow in the very moment of his death. Do you understand? I saw them together — I heard them together. She had said, with a deep catch of the breath, 'I have survived' while my strained ears seemed to hear distinctly, mingled with her tone of despairing regret, the summing up whisper of his eternal condemnation. I asked myself what I was doing there, with a sensation of panic in my heart as though I had blundered into a place of cruel and absurd mysteries not fit for a human being to behold. She motioned me to a chair. We sat down. I laid the packet gently on the little table, and she put her hand over it. . . . 'You knew him well,' she murmured, after a moment of mourning silence.

"'Intimacy grows quickly out there,' I said. 'I knew him as well as it is possible for one man to know another.'

"'And you admired him,' she said. 'It was impossible to know him and not to admire him. Was it?'

"'He was a remarkable man,' I said, unsteadily. Then before the appealing fixity of her gaze, that seemed to watch for more words on my lips, I went on, 'It was impossible not to —

"'Love him,' she finished eagerly, silencing me into an appalled dumbness. 'How true! how true! But when you think that no one knew him so well as I! I had all his noble confidence. I knew him best.'

"'You knew him best,' I repeated. And perhaps she did. But with every word spoken the room was growing darker, and only her forehead, smooth and white, remained illumined by the unextinguishable light of belief and love.

"'You were his friend,' she went on. 'His friend,' she repeated, a little louder. 'You must have been, if he had given you this, and sent you to me. I feel I can speak to you — and oh! I must speak. I want you — you have heard his last words — to know I have been worthy of him. . . . It is not pride. . . . Yes! I am proud to know I understood him better than anyone on earth — he told me so himself. And since his mother died I have had no one — no one — to — to —

"I listened. The darkness deepened. I was not even sure he had given me the right bundle. I rather suspect he wanted me to take care of another batch of his papers which, after his death, I saw the manager examining under the lamp. And the girl talked, easing her pain in the certitude of my sympathy; she talked as thirsty men drink. I had heard that her engagement with Kurtz had been disapproved by her people. He wasn't rich enough or something. And indeed I don't know whether he had not been a pauper all his life. He had given me some reason to infer that it was his impatience of comparative poverty that drove him out there.

"'. . . Who was not his friend who had heard him speak once?' she was saying. 'He drew men towards him by what was best in them.' She looked at me with intensity. 'It is the gift of the great,' she went on, and the sound of her low voice seemed to have the accompaniment of all the other sounds, full of mystery, desolation, and sorrow, I had ever heard — the ripple of the river, the soughing of the trees swayed by the wind, the murmurs of the crowds, the faint ring of incomprehensible words cried from afar, the whisper of a voice speaking from beyond the threshold of an external darkness. 'But you have heard him! You know!' she cried.

"'Yes, I know,' I said with something like despair in my heart, but bowing my head before the faith that was in her, before that great and saving illusion that shone with an unearthly glow in the darkness, in the triumphant darkness from which I could not have defended her — from which I could not even defend myself.

"'What a loss to me — to us!' — she corrected herself with beautiful generosity; then added in a murmur, 'To the world.' By the last gleams of twilight I could see the glitter of her eyes, full of tears — of tears that would not fall.

"'I have been very happy — very fortunate — very proud,' she went on. 'Too fortunate. Too happy for a little while. And now I am unhappy for — for life.'

"She stood up; her fair hair seemed to catch all the remaining light in a glimmer of gold. I rose, too.

"'And of all this,' she went on, mournfully, 'of all his promise, and of all his greatness, of his generous mind, of his noble heart, nothing remains — nothing but a memory. You and I —

"'We shall always remember him,' I said, hastily.

"'No!' she cried. 'It is impossible that all this should be lost — that such a life should be sacrificed to leave nothing — but sorrow. You know what vast plans he had. I knew of them, too — I could not perhaps understand — but others knew of them. Something must remain. His words, at least, have not died.'

"'His words will remain,' I said.

"'And his example,' she whispered to herself. 'Men looked up to him — his goodness shone in every act. His example —

"'True,' I said; 'his example, too. Yes, his example. I forgot that.'

"'But I do not. I cannot — I cannot believe — not yet. I cannot believe that I shall never see him again, that nobody will see him again, never, never, never.'

"She put out her arms as if after a retreating figure, stretching them black and with clasped pale hands across the fading and narrow sheen of the window. Never see him! I saw him clearly enough then. I shall see this eloquent phantom as long as I live, and I shall see her, too, a tragic and familiar Shade, resembling in this gesture another one, tragic also, and bedecked with powerless charms, stretching bare brown arms over the glitter of the infernal stream, the stream of darkness. She said suddenly very low, 'He died as he lived.'

"'His end,' said I, with dull anger stirring in me, 'was in every way worthy of his life.'

"'And I was not with him,' she murmured. My anger subsided before a feeling of infinite pity.

"'Everything that could be done — ' I mumbled.

"'Ah, but I believed in him more than anyone on earth — more than his own mother, more than — himself. He needed me! Me! I would have treasured every sigh, every word, every sign, every glance.'

"I felt like a chill grip on my chest. 'Don't,' I said, in a muffled voice.

"'Forgive me. I — I have mourned so long in silence — in silence. . . . You were with him — to the last? I think of his loneliness. Nobody near to understand him as I would have understood. Perhaps no one to hear. . . .'

"'To the very end,' I said shakily. 'I heard his very last words. . . .' I stopped in a fright.

"'Repeat them,' she murmured in a heart-broken tone. 'I want — I want — something — something — to — live with.'

"I was on the point of crying at her, 'Don't you hear them?' The dusk was repeating them in a persistent whisper all around us, in a whisper that seemed to swell menacingly like the first whisper of a rising wind. 'The horror! The horror!'

"'His last word — to live with,' she insisted. 'Don't you understand I loved him — I loved him — I loved him!'

"I pulled myself together and spoke slowly.

"'The last word he pronounced was — your name.'

"I heard a light sigh and then my heart stood still, stopped dead short by an exulting and terrible cry, by the cry of inconceivable triumph and of unspeakable pain. 'I knew it — I was sure!' . . . She knew. She was sure. I heard her weeping, she had hidden her face in her hands. It seemed to me that the house would collapse before I could escape, that the heavens would fall upon my head. But nothing happened. The heavens do not fall for such a trifle. Would they have fallen, I wonder, if I had rendered Kurtz that justice which was his due? Hadn't he said he wanted only justice? But I couldn't. I could not tell her. It would have been too dark — too dark altogether. . . ."

Marlow ceased, and sat apart, indistinct and silent, in the pose of a meditating Buddha. Nobody moved for a time. "We have lost the first of the ebb," said the Director, suddenly. I raised my head. The offing was barred by a black bank of clouds, and the tranquil waterway leading to the uttermost ends of the earth flowed somber under an overcast sky — seemed to lead into the heart of an immense darkness.   [1902]

JULIO CORTÁZAR *(1914–1984), the Argentinean short story writer, novelist, and translator, was born in Brussels but grew up in Buenos Aires. After a short time studying at the university, he taught school until he resigned after clashing with the Peronist government. In 1951 he moved to Paris, where he lived for the rest of his life, working as a translator for UNESCO.*

Influenced as a young writer by the work of Jorge Luis Borges, Cortázar published his first collection of stories, Bestiary, *the year he left Argentina. Seven more books of short fiction followed, including the collections* The End of the Game *(1965) and* We Love Glenda So Much *(1980). A prolific author, Cortázar also published poetry, essays, and novels, the most famous of which —* Hopscotch *(1963) — he called "the imperfect and desperate denunciation of the establishment of letters." His political engagement became more radical after he left Argentina, and in the last half of his life he worked for causes such as the Cuban Revolution and gave his royalties to support the Sandinistas in Nicaragua.*

As the critic Jason Wilson has noted, Cortázar "learnt from the French Surrealists how to shake the lazy reader into an awareness that something threatens behind the conventions of everyday life without ever defining this elusive, often hostile otherness." The story "Axolotl" conveys an atmosphere of disorientation verging on hallucination as the narrator fixates on the fish in an aquarium. Suddenly what he sees offers him an opportunity for what Cortázar called "openings onto estrangement, instances of a dislocation in which the ordinary ceases to be tranquilizing because nothing is ordinary when submitted to a silent and sustained scrutiny."

Cortázar felt that he was possessed by the stories he had to tell:

> *I refer to my own experience as a story writer, and I see a relatively happy and unremarkable man, caught up in the same trivialities and trips to the dentist as any inhabitant of a large city . . . who suddenly, instantaneously, in the subway, in a café, in a dream, in the office while revising a doubtful translation about Tanzanian illiteracy, stops being him-and-his-circumstances and, for no reason, without warning . . . without anything that gives him a chance to clench his teeth and take a deep breath,* he is a story, *a shapeless mass without words or faces or beginning or end, but still a story, something that can only be a story, and then, suddenly, Tanzania can go to hell, because he puts a paper in the typewriter and begins to write, even if his bosses and the whole United Nations scream in his ears.*

JULIO CORTÁZAR

Axolotl

Translated by Paul Blackburn

There was a time when I thought a great deal about the axolotls. I went to see them in the aquarium at the Jardin des Plantes and stayed for hours watching them, observing their immobility, their faint movements. Now I am an axolotl.

I got to them by chance one spring morning when Paris was spreading its peacock tail after a wintry Lent. I was heading down the boulevard Port-Royal, then I took Saint-Marcel and L'Hôpital and saw green among all that grey and remembered the lions. I was friend of the lions and panthers, but had never gone into the dark, humid building that was the aquarium. I left my bike against the gratings and went to look at the tulips. The lions were sad and ugly and my panther was asleep. I decided on the aquarium, looked obliquely at banal fish until, unexpectedly, I hit it off with the axolotls. I stayed watching them for an hour and left, unable to think of anything else.

In the library at Sainte-Geneviève, I consulted a dictionary and learned that axolotls are the larval stage (provided with gills) of a species of salamander of the genus Ambystoma. That they were Mexican I knew already by looking at them and their little pink Aztec faces and the placard at the top of the tank. I read that specimens of them had been found in Africa capable of living on dry land during the periods of drought, and continuing their life under water when the rainy season came. I found their Spanish name, *ajolote*, and the mention that they were edible, and that their oil was used (no longer used, it said) like cod-liver oil.

I didn't care to look up any of the specialized works, but the next day I went back to the Jardin des Plantes. I began to go every morning, morning and afternoon some days. The aquarium guard smiled perplexedly taking my ticket. I would lean up against the iron bar in front of the tanks and set to watching them. There's nothing strange in this, because after the first minute I knew that we were linked, that something infinitely lost and distant kept pulling us together. It had been enough to detain me that first morning in front of the sheet of glass where some bubbles rose through the water. The axolotls huddled on the wretched narrow (only I can know how narrow and wretched) floor of moss and stone in the tank. There were nine specimens, and the majority pressed their heads against the glass, looking with their eyes of gold at whoever came near them. Disconcerted, almost ashamed, I felt it a lewdness to be peering at these silent and immobile figures heaped at the bottom of the tank. Mentally I isolated one, situated on the right and some-what apart from the others, to study it better. I saw a rosy little body, trans-lucent (I thought of those Chinese figurines of milky glass), looking like a small lizard about six inches long, ending in a fish's tail of extraordinary delicacy, the most sensitive part of our body. Along the back ran a transparent fin which joined with the tail, but what obsessed me was the feet, of the slenderest nicety, ending in tiny fingers with minutely human nails. And then I discovered its eyes, its face. Inexpressive features, with no other trait save the eyes, two orifices, like brooches, wholly of transparent gold, lacking any life but looking, letting themselves be penetrated by my look, which seemed to travel past the golden level and lose itself in a diaphanous interior mystery. A very slender black halo ringed the eye and etched it onto the pink flesh, onto the rosy stone of the head, vaguely triangular, but with curved and irregular sides which gave it a total likeness to a statuette corroded by time. The mouth was masked by the triangular plane of the face, its considerable size would be guessed only in profile; in front a delicate crevice barely slit the lifeless stone. On both sides of the head where the ears should have been, there grew three tiny sprigs red as coral, a vegetal outgrowth, the gills, I suppose. And they were the only thing quick about it; every ten or fifteen seconds the sprigs pricked up stiffly and again subsided. Once in a while a foot would barely move, I saw the diminutive toes poise mildly on the moss. It's that we don't enjoy moving a lot, and the tank is so cramped — we barely move in any direction and we're hitting one of the others with our tail or our head — difficulties arise, fights, tiredness. The time feels like it's less if we stay quietly.

It was their quietness that made me lean toward them fascinated the first time I saw the axolotls. Obscurely I seemed to understand their secret will, to abolish space and time with an indifferent immobility. I knew better later; the gill contraction, the tentative reckoning of the delicate feet on the stones, the abrupt swimming (some of them swim with a simple undulation of the body) proved to me that they were capable of escaping that mineral lethargy in which they spent whole hours. Above all else, their eyes obsessed me. In the standing tanks on either side of them, different fishes showed me the simple stupidity of their handsome eyes so similar to our own. The eyes of the axolotls spoke to me of the presence of a different life, of another way of seeing. Glueing my face to the glass (the guard would cough fussily once in a while), I tried to see better those diminutive golden points, that entrance to the infinitely slow and remote world of these rosy creatures. It was useless to tap with one finger on the glass directly in front of their faces; they never gave the least reaction. The golden eyes continued burning with their soft, terrible light; they continued looking at me from an unfathomable depth which made me dizzy.

And nevertheless they were close. I knew it before this, before being an axolotl. I learned it the day I came near them for the first time. The anthropomorphic features of a monkey reveal the reverse of what most people believe, the distance that is traveled from them to us. The absolute lack of similarity between axolotls and human beings proved to me that my recognition was valid, that I was not propping myself up with easy analogies. Only the little hands . . . But an eft, the common newt, has such hands also, and we are not at all alike. I think it was the axolotls' heads, that triangular pink shape with the tiny eyes of gold. That looked and knew. That laid the claim. They were not *animals*.

It would seem easy, almost obvious, to fall into mythology. I began seeing in the axolotls a metamorphosis which did not succeed in revoking a mysterious humanity. I imagined them aware, slaves of their bodies, condemned infinitely to the silence of the abyss, to a hopeless meditation. Their blind gaze, the diminutive gold disc without expression and nonetheless terribly shining, went through me like a message: "Save us, save us." I caught myself mumbling words of advice, conveying childish hopes. They continued to look at me, immobile; from time to time the rosy branches of the gills stiffened. In that instant I felt a muted pain; perhaps they were seeing me, attracting my strength to penetrate into the impenetrable thing of their lives. They were not human beings, but I had found in no animal such a profound relation with myself. The axolotls were like witnesses of something, and at times like horrible judges. I felt ignoble in front of them; there was such a terrifying purity in those transparent eyes. They were larvas, but larva means disguise and also phantom. Behind those Aztec faces, without expression but of an implacable cruelty, what semblance was awaiting its hour?

I was afraid of them. I think that had it not been for feeling the proximity of other visitors and the guard, I would not have been bold enough to remain alone with them. "You eat them alive with your eyes, hey," the guard said, laughing; he likely thought I was a little cracked. What he didn't notice was that it was they devouring me slowly with their eyes, in a cannibalism of gold. At any distance from the aquarium, I had only to think of them, it was as though I were being affected from a distance. It got to the point that I was going every day, and at night I thought of them immobile in the darkness, slowly putting a hand out which immediately encountered another. Perhaps their eyes could see in the dead of night, and for them the day continued indefinitely. The eyes of axolotls have no lids.

I know now that there was nothing strange, that that had to occur. Leaning over in front of the tank each morning, the recognition was greater. They were suffering, every fiber of my body reached toward that stifled pain, that stiff torment at the bottom of the tank. They were lying in wait for something, a remote dominion destroyed, an age of liberty when the world had been that of the axolotls. Not possible that such a terrible expression which was attaining the overthrow of that forced blankness on their stone faces should carry any message other than one of pain, proof of that eternal sentence, of that liquid hell they were undergoing. Hopelessly, I wanted to prove to myself that my own sensibility was projecting a nonexistent consciousness upon the axolotls. They and I knew. So there was nothing strange in what happened. My face was pressed against the glass of the aquarium, my eyes were attempting once more to penetrate the mystery of those eyes of gold without iris, without pupil. I saw from very close up the face of an axolotl immobile next to the glass. No transition and no surprise, I saw my face against the glass, I saw it on the outside of the tank, I saw it on the other side of the glass. Then my face drew back and I understood.

Only one thing was strange: to go on thinking as usual, to know. To realize that was, for the first moment, like the horror of a man buried alive awaking to his fate. Outside, my face came close to the glass again, I saw my mouth, the lips compressed with the effort of understanding the axolotls. I was an axolotl and now I knew instantly that no understanding was possible. He was outside the aquarium, his thinking was a thinking outside the tank. Recognizing him, being him himself, I was an axolotl and in my world. The horror began — I learned in the same moment — of believing myself prisoner in the body of an axolotl, metamorphosed into him with my human mind intact, buried alive in an axolotl, condemned to move lucidly among unconcious creatures. But that stopped when a foot just grazed my face, when I moved just a little to one side and saw an axolotl next to me who was looking at me, and understood that he knew also, no communication possible, but very clearly. Or I was also in him, or all of us were thinking humanlike, incapable of expression, limited to the golden splendor of our eyes looking at the face of the man pressed against the aquarium.

He returned many times, but he comes less often now. Weeks pass without his showing up. I saw him yesterday, he looked at me for a long time and left briskly. It seemed to me that he was not so much interested in us any more, that he was coming out of habit. Since the only thing I do is think, I could think about him a lot. It occurs to me that at the beginning we continued to communicate, that he felt more than ever one with the mystery which was claiming him. But the bridges were broken between him and me, because what was his obsession is now an axolotl, alien to his human life. I think that at the beginning I was capable of returning to him in a certain way — ah, only in a certain way — and of keeping awake his desire to know us better. I am an axolotl for good now, and if I think like a man it's only because every axolotl thinks like a man inside his rosy stone semblance. I believe that all this succeeded in communicating something to him in those first days, when I was still he. And in this final solitude to which he no longer comes, I console myself by thinking that perhaps he is going to write a story about us, that, believing he's making up a story, he's going to write all this about axolotls.

[1967]

STEPHEN CRANE *(1871–1900) wrote some of the most memorable fiction and poetry ever created by an American, publishing fourteen books in his short lifetime. The poet John Berryman, who wrote a biography of Crane, observed the essential truth about him: "Crane was a writer and nothing else: a man alone in a room with the English language, trying to get human feelings right." Crane's style in his short stories is as intensely personal as Edgar Allan Poe's or Nathaniel Hawthorne's, but he did not use the techniques of fantasy and allegory. "His eyes remained wide open on his world. He was almost illusionless, whether about his subjects or himself. Perhaps his sole illusion was the heroic one; and not even this, especially if he was concerned in it himself as a man, escaped his irony."*

Crane was born in Newark, New Jersey, the youngest of fourteen children. His father, a Methodist minister, died when Crane was just a boy, and his mother supported the family by writing articles for Methodist papers and reporting for the New York Tribune *and the* Philadelphia Press. *Crane briefly attended Lafayette College and Syracuse University before going to work in New York City as a freelance journalist. He became interested in life along the Bowery, one of the worst slums in New York, and he used this setting for his novel* Maggie: A Girl of the Streets, *a work so grimly naturalistic in its portrayal of slum life and so frank in its treatment of sex that Crane had to publish it at his own expense in 1893. Two years later he sold a long story about the Civil War to a syndicate for less than a hundred dollars. That work,* The Red Badge of Courage, *was such a vivid account of wartime experience — even though Crane had never been in a battle himself — that it established his literary reputation.*

In the last five years of his life, before he died of tuberculosis in Germany, Crane traveled extensively as a reporter, first to the American West, then to Florida. He couldn't keep away from scenes of war or revolution, believing — as did Ernest Hemingway after him — that "the nearer a writer gets to life, the greater he becomes as an artist." Crane was en route to Florida on the steamship Commodore *when the ship was wrecked on New Year's Day, 1897. He based one of his finest short stories, "The Open Boat," on what happened to him in a lifeboat with the other survivors. He had first reported the disaster in an article for his newspaper shortly after the shipwreck. Joseph Conrad admired Crane's writing and said of "The Open Boat" that "by the deep and simple humanity of its presentation [the story] seems somehow to illustrate the essentials of life itself, like a symbolic tale."*

RELATED COMMENTARY: *Stephen Crane, "The Sinking of the* Commodore," page 1408.

STEPHEN CRANE

The Open Boat

**A Tale Intended to Be after the Fact,
Being the Experience of Four Men from
the Sunk Steamer *Commodore***

I

None of them knew the color of the sky. Their eyes glanced level, and were fastened upon the waves that swept toward them. These waves were of the hue of slate, save for the tops, which were of foaming white, and all of the men knew the colors of the sea. The horizon narrowed and widened, and dipped and rose, and at all times its edge was jagged with waves that seemed thrust up in points like rocks.

Many a man ought to have a bath-tub larger than the boat which here rode upon the sea. These waves were most wrongfully and barbarously abrupt and tall, and each froth-top was a problem in small boat navigation.

The cook squatted in the bottom and looked with both eyes at the six inches of gunwale which separated him from the ocean. His sleeves were rolled over his fat forearms, and the two flaps of his unbuttoned vest dangled as he bent to bail out the boat. Often he said: "Gawd! That was a narrow clip." As he remarked it he invariably gazed eastward over the broken sea.

The oiler, steering with one of the two oars in the boat, sometimes raised himself suddenly to keep clear of water that swirled in over the stern. It was a thin little oar and it seemed often ready to snap.

The correspondent, pulling at the other oar, watched the waves and wondered why he was there.

The injured captain, lying in the bow, was at this time buried in that profound dejection and indifference which comes, temporarily at least, to even the bravest and most enduring when, willy nilly, the firm fails, the army loses, the ship goes down. The mind of the master of a vessel is rooted deep in the timbers of her, though he command for a day or a decade, and this captain had on him the stern impression of a scene in the grays of dawn of seven turned faces, and later a stump of a top-mast with a white ball on it that slashed to and fro at the waves, went low and lower, and down. Thereafter there was something strange in his voice. Although steady, it was deep with mourning, and of a quality beyond oration or tears.

"Keep 'er a little more south, Billie," said he.

"'A little more south,' sir," said the oiler in the stern.

A seat in this boat was not unlike a seat upon a bucking broncho, and, by the same token, a broncho is not much smaller. The craft pranced and reared, and plunged like an animal. As each wave came, and she rose for it, she seemed like a horse making at a fence outrageously high. The manner of her scramble over these walls of water is a mystic thing, and, moreover, at the top of them were ordinarily these problems in white water, the foam racing down from the summit of each wave, requiring a new leap, and a leap from the air. Then, after scornfully bumping a crest, she would slide, and race, and splash down a long incline and arrive bobbing and nodding in front of the next menace.

A singular disadvantage of the sea lies in the fact that after successfully surmounting one wave you discover that there is another behind it just as important and just as nervously anxious to do something effective in the way of swamping boats. In a ten-foot dingey one can get an idea of the resources of the sea in the line of waves that is not probable to the average experience, which is never at sea in a dingey. As each slaty wall of water approached, it shut all else from the view of the men in the boat, and it was not difficult to imagine that this particular wave was the final outburst of the ocean, the last effort of the grim water. There was a terrible grace in the move of the waves, and they came in silence, save for the snarling of the crests.

In the wan light, the faces of the men must have been gray. Their eyes must have glinted in strange ways as they gazed steadily astern. Viewed from a balcony, the whole thing would doubtlessly have been weirdly picturesque. But the men in the boat had no time to see it, and if they had had leisure there were other things to occupy their minds. The sun swung steadily up the sky, and they knew it was broad day because the color of the sea changed from slate to emerald-green, streaked with amber lights, and the foam was like tumbling snow. The process of the breaking day was unknown to them. They were aware only of this effect upon the color of the waves that rolled toward them.

In disjointed sentences the cook and the correspondent argued as to the difference between a life-saving station and a house of refuge. The cook had said: "There's a house of refuge just north of the Mosquito Inlet Light, and as soon as they see us, they'll come off in their boat and pick us up."

"As soon as who see us?" said the correspondent.

"The crew," said the cook.

"Houses of refuge don't have crews," said the correspondent. "As I understand them, they are only places where clothes and grub are stored for the benefit of shipwrecked people. They don't carry crews."

"Oh, yes, they do," said the cook.

"No, they don't," said the correspondent.

"Well, we're not there yet, anyhow," said the oiler, in the stern.

"Well," said the cook, "perhaps it's not a house of refuge that I'm thinking of as being near Mosquito Inlet Light. Perhaps it's a life-saving station."

"We're not there yet," said the oiler, in the stern.

II

As the boat bounced from the top of each wave, the wind tore through the hair of the hatless men, and as the craft plopped her stern down again the spray slashed past them. The crest of each of these waves was a hill, from the top of which the men surveyed, for a moment, a broad tumultuous expanse, shining and wind-riven. It was probably splendid. It was probably glorious, this play of the free sea, wild with lights of emerald and white and amber.

"Bully good thing it's an on-shore wind," said the cook. "If not where would we be? Wouldn't have a show."

"That's right," said the correspondent.

The busy oiler nodded his assent.

Then the captain, in the bow, chuckled in a way that expressed humor, contempt, tragedy, all in one. "Do you think we've got a show, now, boys?" said he.

Whereupon the three went silent, save for a trifle of hemming and hawing. To express any particular optimism at this time they felt to be childish and stupid, but they all doubtless possessed this sense of the situation in their mind. A young man thinks doggedly at such times. On the other hand, the ethics of their condition was decidedly against any open suggestion of hopelessness. So they were silent.

"Oh, well," said the captain, soothing his children, "we'll get ashore all right."

But there was that in his tone which made them think, so the oiler quoth: "Yes! If this wind holds!"

The cook was bailing. "Yes! If we don't catch hell in the surf."

Canton flannel gulls flew near and far. Sometimes they sat down on the sea, near patches of brown sea-weed that rolled over the waves with a movement like carpets on a line in a gale. The birds sat comfortably in groups, and they were envied by some in the dingey, for the wrath of the sea was no more to them than it was to a covey of prairie chickens a thousand miles inland. Often they came very close and stared at the men with black bead-like eyes. At these times they were uncanny and sinister in their unblinking scrutiny, and the men hooted angrily at them, telling them to be gone. One came, and evidently decided to alight on the top of the captain's head. The bird flew parallel to the boat and did not circle, but made short sidelong jumps in the air in chicken-fashion. His black eyes were wistfully fixed upon the captain's head. "Ugly brute," said the oiler to the bird. "You look as if you were made with a jack-knife." The cook and the correspondent swore darkly at the creature. The captain naturally wished to knock it away with the end of the heavy painter, but he did not dare do it, because anything resembling an emphatic gesture would have capsized this freighted boat, and so with his open hand, the captain gently and carefully waved the gull away. After it had been discouraged from the pursuit the captain breathed easier on account of his hair, and others breathed easier because the bird struck their minds at this time as being somehow gruesome and ominous.

In the meantime the oiler and the correspondent rowed. And also they rowed.

They sat together in the same seat, and each rowed an oar. Then the oiler took both oars; then the correspondent took both oars; then the oiler; then the correspondent. They rowed and they rowed. The very ticklish part of the business was when the time came for the reclining one in the stern to take his turn at the oars. By the very last star of truth, it is easier to steal eggs from under a hen than it was to change seats in the dingey. First the man in the stern slid his hand along the thwart and moved with care, as if he were of Sèvres.[1] Then the man in the rowing seat slid his hand along the other thwart. It was all done with the most extraordinary care. As the two sidled past each other, the whole party kept watchful eyes on the coming wave, and the captain cried: "Look out now! Steady there!"

The brown mats of sea-weed that appeared from time to time were like islands, bits of earth. They were travelling, apparently, neither one way nor the other. They were, to all intents, stationary. They informed the men in the boat that it was making progress slowly toward the land.

The captain, rearing cautiously in the bow, after the dingey soared on a great swell, said that he had seen the light-house at Mosquito Inlet. Presently the cook remarked that he had seen it. The correspondent was at the oars, then, and for some reason he too wished to look at the light-house, but his back was toward the far shore and the waves were important, and for some time he could not seize an opportunity to turn his head. But at last there came a wave more gentle than the others, and when at the crest of it he swiftly scoured the western horizon.

"See it?" said the captain.

"No," said the correspondent, slowly, "I didn't see anything."

"Look again," said the captain. He pointed. "It's exactly in that direction."

At the top of another wave, the correspondent did as he was bid, and this time his eyes chanced on a small still thing on the edge of the swaying horizon. It was precisely like the point of a pin. It took an anxious eye to find a light-house so tiny.

"Think we'll make it, Captain?"

"If this wind holds and the boat don't swamp, we can't do much else," said the captain.

The little boat, lifted by each towering sea, and splashed viciously by the crests, made progress that in the absence of sea-weed was not apparent to those in her. She seemed just a wee thing wallowing, miraculously, top-up, at the mercy of five oceans. Occasionally, a great spread of water, like white flames, swarmed into her.

"Bail her, cook," said the captain, serenely.

"All right, Captain," said the cheerful cook.

III

It would be difficult to describe the subtle brotherhood of men that was here established on the seas. No one said that it was so. No one mentioned it. But it dwelt in the boat, and each man felt it warm him. They were a

---

[1] A delicate French porcelain.

captain, an oiler, a cook, and a correspondent, and they were friends, friends in a more curiously iron-bound degree than may be common. The hurt captain, lying against the water-jar in the bow, spoke always in a low voice and calmly, but he could never command a more ready and swiftly obedient crew than the motley three of the dingey. It was more than a mere recognition of what was best for the common safety. There was surely in it a quality that was personal and heartfelt. And after this devotion to the commander of the boat there was this comradeship that the correspondent, for instance, who had been taught to be cynical of men, knew even at the time was the best experience of his life. But no one said that it was so. No one mentioned it.

"I wish we had a sail," remarked the captain. "We might try my overcoat on the end of an oar and give you two boys a chance to rest." So the cook and the correspondent held the mast and spread wide the overcoat. The oiler steered, and the little boat made good way with her new rig. Sometimes the oiler had to scull sharply to keep a sea from breaking into the boat, but otherwise sailing was a success.

Meanwhile the light-house had been growing slowly larger. It had now almost assumed color, and appeared like a little gray shadow on the sky. The man at the oars could not be prevented from turning his head rather often to try for a glimpse of this little gray shadow.

At last, from the top of each wave the men in the tossing boat could see land. Even as the light-house was an upright shadow on the sky, this land seemed but a long black shadow on the sea. It certainly was thinner than paper. "We must be about opposite New Smyrna," said the cook, who had coasted this shore often in schooners. "Captain, by the way, I believe they abandoned that life-saving station there about a year ago."

"Did they?" said the captain.

The wind slowly died away. The cook and the correspondent were not now obliged to slave in order to hold high the oar. But the waves continued their old impetuous swooping at the dingey, and the little craft, no longer under way, struggled woundily over them. The oiler or the correspondent took the oars again.

Shipwrecks are *apropos* of nothing. If men could only train for them and have them occur when the men had reached pink condition, there would be less drowning at sea. Of the four in the dingey none had slept any time worth mentioning for two days and two nights previous to embarking in the dingey, and in the excitement of clambering about the deck of a foundering ship they had also forgotten to eat heartily.

For these reasons, and for others, neither the oiler nor the correspondent was fond of rowing at this time. The correspondent wondered ingenuously how in the name of all that was sane could there be people who thought it amusing to row a boat. It was not an amusement; it was a diabolical punishment, and even a genius of mental aberrations could never conclude that it was anything but a horror to the muscles and a crime against the back. He mentioned to the boat in general how the amusement of rowing struck him, and the weary-faced oiler smiled in full sympathy. Previously to the foundering, by the way, the oiler had worked double-watch in the engine-room of the ship.

"Take her easy, now, boys," said the captain. "Don't spend yourselves. If we have to run a surf you'll need all your strength, because we'll sure have to swim for it. Take your time."

Slowly the land arose from the sea. From a black line it became a line of black and a line of white — trees and sand. Finally, the captain said that he could make out a house on the shore. "That's the house of refuge, sure," said the cook. "They'll see us before long, and come out after us."

The distant light-house reared high. "The keeper ought to be able to make us out now, if he's looking through a glass," said the captain. "He'll notify the life-saving people."

"None of those other boats could have got ashore to give word of the wreck," said the oiler, in a low voice. "Else the life-boat would be out hunting us."

Slowly and beautifully the land loomed out of the sea. The wind came again. It had veered from the northeast to the southeast. Finally, a new sound struck the ears of the men in the boat. It was the low thunder of the surf on the shore. "We'll never be able to make the light-house now," said the captain. "Swing her head a little more north, Billie."

"'A little more north,' sir," said the oiler.

Whereupon the little boat turned her nose once more down the wind, and all but the oarsman watched the shore grow. Under the influence of this expansion doubt and direful apprehension were leaving the minds of the men. The management of the boat was still most absorbing, but it could not prevent a quiet cheerfulness. In an hour, perhaps, they would be ashore.

Their back-bones had become thoroughly used to balancing in the boat and they now rode this wild colt of a dingey like circus men. The correspondent thought that he had been drenched to the skin, but happening to feel in the top pocket of his coat, he found therein eight cigars. Four of them were soaked with sea-water; four were perfectly scatheless. After a search, somebody produced three dry matches, and thereupon the four waifs rode impudently in their little boat, and with an assurance of an impending rescue shining in their eyes, puffed at the big cigars and judged well and ill of all men. Everybody took a drink of water.

IV

"Cook," remarked the captain, "there don't seem to be any signs of life about your house of refuge."

"No," replied the cook. "Funny they don't see us!"

A broad stretch of lowly coast lay before the eyes of the men. It was of dunes topped with dark vegetation. The roar of the surf was plain, and sometimes they could see the white lip of a wave as it spun up the beach. A tiny house was blocked out black upon the sky. Southward, the slim light-house lifted its little gray length.

Tide, wind, and waves were swinging the dingey northward. "Funny they don't see us," said the men.

The surf's roar was here dulled, but its tone was, nevertheless, thunderous and mighty. As the boat swam over the great rollers, the men sat listening to this roar. "We'll swamp sure," said everybody.

It is fair to say here that there was not a life-saving station within twenty miles in either direction, but the men did not know this fact and in consequence they made dark and opprobrious remarks concerning the eyesight of the nation's life-savers. Four scowling men sat in the dingey and surpassed records in the invention of epithets.

"Funny they don't see us."

The light-heartedness of a former time had completely faded. To their sharpened minds it was easy to conjure pictures of all kinds of incompetency and blindness and, indeed, cowardice. There was the shore of the populous land, and it was bitter and bitter to them that from it came no sign.

"Well," said the captain, ultimately, "I suppose we'll have to make a try for ourselves. If we stay out here too long, we'll none of us have strength left to swim after the boat swamps."

And so the oiler, who was at the oars, turned the boat straight for the shore. There was a sudden tightening of muscles. There was some thinking.

"If we don't all get ashore —" said the captain. "If we don't all get ashore, I suppose you fellows know where to send news of my finish?"

They then briefly exchanged some addresses and admonitions. As for the reflections of the men, there was a great deal of rage in them. Perchance they might be formulated thus: "If I am going to be drowned — if I am going to be drowned — if I am going to be drowned, why, in the name of the seven mad gods who rule the sea, was I allowed to come thus far and contemplate sand and trees? Was I brought here merely to have my nose dragged away as I was about to nibble the sacred cheese of life? It is preposterous. If this old ninny-woman, Fate, cannot do better than this, she should be deprived of the management of men's fortunes. She is an old hen who knows not her intention. If she has decided to drown me, why did she not do it in the beginning and save me all this trouble. The whole affair is absurd. . . . But, no, she cannot mean to drown me. She dare not drown me. She cannot drown me. Not after all this work." Afterward the man might have had an impulse to shake his fist at the clouds. "Just you drown me, now, and then hear what I call you!"

The billows that came at this time were more formidable. They seemed always just about to break and roll over the little boat in a turmoil of foam. There was a preparatory and long growl in the speech of them. No mind unused to the sea would have concluded that the dingey could ascend these sheer heights in time. The shore was still afar. The oiler was a wily surfman. "Boys," he said, swiftly, "she won't live three minutes more and we're too far out to swim. Shall I take her to sea again, Captain?"

"Yes! Go ahead!" said the captain.

This oiler, by a series of quick miracles, and fast and steady oarsmanship, turned the boat in the middle of the surf and took her safely to sea again.

There was a considerable silence as the boat bumped over the furrowed sea to deeper water. Then somebody in gloom spoke. "Well, anyhow, they must have seen us from the shore by now."

The gulls went in slanting flight up the wind toward the gray desolate east. A squall, marked by dingy clouds, and clouds brick-red, like smoke from a burning building, appeared from the southeast.

"What do you think of those life-saving people? Ain't they peaches?"

"Funny they haven't seen us."

"Maybe they think we're out here for sport! Maybe they think we're fishin'. Maybe they think we're damned fools."

It was a long afternoon. A changed tide tried to force them southward, but wind and wave said northward. Far ahead, where coast-line, sea, and sky formed their mighty angle, there were little dots which seemed to indicate a city on the shore.

"St. Augustine?"

The captain shook his head. "Too near Mosquito Inlet."

And the oiler rowed, and then the correspondent rowed. Then the oiler rowed. It was a weary business. The human back can become the seat of more aches and pains than are registered in books for the composite anatomy of a regiment. It is a limited area, but it can become the theatre of innumerable muscular conflicts, tangles, wrenches, knots, and other comforts.

"Did you ever like to row, Billie?" asked the correspondent.

"No," said the oiler, "Hang it."

When one exchanged the rowing-seat for a place in the bottom of the boat, he suffered a bodily depression that caused him to be careless of everything save an obligation to wiggle one finger. There was cold sea-water swashing to and fro in the boat, and he lay in it. His head, pillowed on a thwart, was within an inch of the swirl of a wave crest, and sometimes a particularly obstreperous sea came in-board and drenched him once more. But these matters did not annoy him. It is almost certain that if the boat had capsized he would have tumbled comfortably out upon the ocean as if he felt sure that it was a great soft mattress.

"Look! There's a man on the shore!"

"Where?"

"There! See 'im? See 'im?"

"Yes, sure! He's walking along."

"Now he's stopped. Look! He's facing us!"

"He's waving at us!"

"So he is! By thunder!"

"Ah, now, we're all right! There'll be a boat out here for us in half an hour."

"He's going on. He's running. He's going up to that house there."

The remote beach seemed lower than the sea, and it required a searching glance to discern the little black figure. The captain saw a floating stick and they rowed to it. A bath-towel was by some weird chance in the boat, and, tying this on the stick, the captain waved it. The oarsman did not dare turn his head, so he was obliged to ask questions.

"What's he doing now?"

"He's standing still again. He's looking, I think. . . . There he goes again. Toward the house. . . . Now he's stopped again."

"Is he waving at us?"

"No, not now! He was, though."

"Look! There comes another man!"

"He's running."

"Look at him go, would you."

"Why, he's on a bicycle. Now he's met the other man. They're both waving at us. Look!"

"There comes something up the beach."

"What the devil is that thing?"

"Why, it looks like a boat."

"Why, certainly it's a boat."

"No, it's on wheels."

"Yes, so it is. Well, that must be the life-boat. They drag them along shore on a wagon."

"That's the life-boat, sure."

"No, by, it's — it's an omnibus."

"I tell you it's a life-boat."

"It is not! It's an omnibus. I can see it plain. See? One of those big hotel omnibuses."

"By thunder, you're right. It's an omnibus, sure as fate. What do you suppose they are doing with an omnibus? Maybe they are going around collecting the life-crew, hey?"

"That's it, likely. Look! There's a fellow waving a little black flag. He's standing on the steps of the omnibus. There come those other two fellows. Now they're all talking together. Look at the fellow with the flag. Maybe he ain't waving it!"

"That ain't a flag, is it? That's his coat. Why, certainly, that's his coat."

"So it is. It's his coat. He's taken it off and is waving it around his head. But would you look at him swing it!"

"Oh, say, there isn't any life-saving station there. That's just a winter resort hotel omnibus that has brought over some of the boarders to see us drown."

"What's that idiot with the coat mean? What's he signaling, anyhow?"

"It looks as if he were trying to tell us to go north. There must be a life-saving station up there."

"No! He thinks we're fishing. Just giving us a merry hand. See? Ah, there, Willie."

"Well, I wish I could make something out of those signals. What do you suppose he means?"

"He don't mean anything. He's just playing."

"Well, if he'd just signal us to try the surf again, or to go to sea and wait, or go north, or go south, or go to hell — there would be some reason in it. But look at him. He just stands there and keeps his coat revolving like a wheel. The ass!"

"There come more people."

"Now there's quite a mob. Look! Isn't that a boat?"

"Where? Oh, I see where you mean. No, that's no boat."

"That fellow is still waving his coat."

"He must think we like to see him do that. Why don't he quit it. It don't mean anything."

"I don't know. I think he is trying to make us go north. It must be that there's a life-saving station there somewhere."

"Say, he ain't tired yet. Look at 'im wave."

"Wonder how long he can keep that up. He's been revolving his coat ever since he caught sight of us. He's an idiot. Why aren't they getting men to bring a boat out. A fishing boat — one of those big yawls — could come out here all right. Why don't he do something?"

"Oh, it's all right, now."

"They'll have a boat out here for us in less than no time, now that they've seen us."

A faint yellow tone came into the sky over the low land. The shadows on the sea slowly deepened. The wind bore coldness with it, and the men began to shiver.

"Holy smoke!" said one, allowing his voice to express his impious mood, "if we keep on monkeying out here! If we've got to flounder out here all night!"

"Oh, we'll never have to stay here all night! Don't you worry. They've seen us now, and it won't be long before they'll come chasing out after us."

The shore grew dusky. The man waving a coat blended gradually into this gloom, and it swallowed in the same manner the omnibus and the group of people. The spray, when it dashed uproariously over the side, made the voyagers shrink and swear like men who were being branded.

"I'd like to catch the chump who waved the coat. I feel like soaking him one, just for luck."

"Why? What did he do?"

"Oh, nothing, but then he seemed so damned cheerful."

In the meantime the oiler rowed, and then the correspondent rowed, and then the oiler rowed. Gray-faced and bowed forward, they mechanically, turn by turn, plied the leaden oars. The form of the light-house had vanished from the southern horizon, but finally a pale star appeared, just lifting from the sea. The streaked saffron in the west passed before the all-merging darkness, and the sea to the east was black. The land had vanished, and was expressed only by the low and drear thunder of the surf.

"If I am going to be drowned — if I am going to be drowned — if I am going to be drowned, why, in the name of the seven mad gods who rule the sea, was I allowed to come thus far and contemplate sand and trees? Was I brought here merely to have my nose dragged away as I was about to nibble the sacred cheese of life?"

The patient captain, drooped over the water-jar, was sometimes obliged to speak to the oarsman.

"Keep her head up! Keep her head up!"

"'Keep her head up,' sir." The voices were weary and low.

This was surely a quiet evening. All save the oarsman lay heavily and listlessly in the boat's bottom. As for him, his eyes were just capable of noting the tall black waves that swept forward in a most sinister silence, save for an occasional subdued growl of a crest.

The cook's head was on a thwart, and he looked without interest at the water under his nose. He was deep in other scenes. Finally he spoke. "Billie," he murmured, dreamfully, "what kind of pie do you like best?"

V

"Pie," said the oiler and the correspondent, agitatedly. "Don't talk about those things, blast you!"

"Well," said the cook, "I was just thinking about ham sandwiches, and —"

A night on the sea in an open boat is a long night. As darkness settled finally, the shine of the light, lifting from the sea in the south, changed to full gold. On the northern horizon a new light appeared, a small bluish gleam on the edge of the waters. These two lights were the furniture of the world. Otherwise there was nothing but waves.

Two men huddled in the stern, and distances were so magnificent in the dingey that the rower was enabled to keep his feet partly warmed by thrusting them under his companions. Their legs indeed extended far under the rowing-seat until they touched the feet of the captain forward. Sometimes, despite the efforts of the tired oarsman, a wave came piling into the boat, an icy wave of the night, and the chilling water soaked them anew. They would twist their bodies for a moment and groan, and sleep the dead sleep once more, while the water in the boat gurgled about them as the craft rocked.

The plan of the oiler and the correspondent was for one to row until he lost the ability, and then arouse the other from his sea-water couch in the bottom of the boat.

The oiler plied the oars until his head drooped forward, and the overpowering sleep blinded him. And he rowed yet afterward. Then he touched a man in the bottom of the boat, and called his name. "Will you spell me for a little while?" he said, meekly.

"Sure, Billie," said the correspondent, awakening and dragging himself to a sitting position. They exchanged places carefully, and the oiler, cuddling down in the sea-water at the cook's side, seemed to go to sleep instantly.

The particular violence of the sea had ceased. The waves came without snarling. The obligation of the man at the oars was to keep the boat headed so that the tilt of the rollers would not capsize her, and to preserve her from filling when the crests rushed past. The black waves were silent and hard to be seen in the darkness. Often one was almost upon the boat before the oarsman was aware.

In a low voice the correspondent addressed the captain. He was not sure that the captain was awake, although this iron man seemed to be always awake. "Captain, shall I keep her making for that light north, sir?"

The same steady voice answered him. "Yes. Keep it about two points off the port bow."

The cook had tied a life-belt around himself in order to get even the warmth which this clumsy cork contrivance could donate, and he seemed almost stove-like when a rower, whose teeth invariably chattered wildly as soon as he ceased his labor, dropped down to sleep.

The correspondent, as he rowed, looked down at the two men sleeping under foot. The cook's arm was around the oiler's shoulders, and, with their fragmentary clothing and haggard faces, they were the babes of the sea, a grotesque rendering of the old babes in the wood.

Later he must have grown stupid at his work, for suddenly there was a growling of water, and a crest came with a roar and a swash into the boat, and it was a wonder that it did not set the cook afloat in his life-belt. The cook continued to sleep, but the oiler sat up, blinking his eyes and shaking with the new cold.

"Oh, I'm awful sorry, Billie," said the correspondent, contritely.

"That's all right, old boy," said the oiler, and lay down again and was asleep.

Presently it seemed that even the captain dozed, and the correspondent thought that he was the one man afloat on all the oceans. The wind had a voice as it came over the waves, and it was sadder than the end.

There was a long, loud swishing astern of the boat, and a gleaming trail of phosphorescence, like blue flame, was furrowed on the black waters. It might have been made by a monstrous knife.

Then there came a stillness, while the correspondent breathed with the open mouth and looked at the sea.

Suddenly there was another swish and another long flash of bluish light, and this time it was alongside the boat, and might almost have been reached with an oar. The correspondent saw an enormous fin speed like a shadow through the water, hurling the crystalline spray and leaving the long glowing trail.

The correspondent looked over his shoulder at the captain. His face was hidden, and he seemed to be asleep. He looked at the babes of the sea. They certainly were asleep. So, being bereft of sympathy, he leaned a little way to one side and swore softly into the sea.

But the thing did not then leave the vicinity of the boat. Ahead or astern, on one side or the other, at intervals long or short, fled the long sparkling streak, and there was to be heard the whirroo of the dark fin. The speed and power of the thing were greatly to be admired. It cut the water like a gigantic and keen projectile.

The presence of this biding thing did not affect the man with the same horror that it would if he had been a picnicker. He simply looked at the sea dully and swore in an undertone.

Nevertheless, it is true that he did not wish to be alone with the thing. He wished one of his companions to awaken by chance and keep him company with it. But the captain hung motionless over the water-jar and the oiler and the cook in the bottom of the boat were plunged in slumber.

VI

"If I am going to be drowned — if I am going to be drowned — if I am going to be drowned, why, in the name of the seven mad gods who rule the sea, was I allowed to come thus far and contemplate sand and trees?"

During this dismal night, it may be remarked that a man would conclude that it was really the intention of the seven mad gods to drown him, despite the abominable injustice of it. For it was certainly an abominable injustice to drown a man who had worked so hard, so hard. The man felt it would be a crime most unnatural. Other people had drowned at sea since galleys swarmed with painted sails, but still —

When it occurs to a man that nature does not regard him as important, and that she feels she would not maim the universe by disposing of him, he at first wishes to throw bricks at the temple, and he hates deeply the fact that there are no bricks and no temples. Any visible expression of nature would surely be pelleted with his jeers.

Then, if there be no tangible thing to hoot he feels, perhaps, the desire to confront a personification and indulge in pleas, bowed to one knee, and with hands supplicant, saying: "Yes, but I love myself."

A high cold star on a winter's night is the word he feels that she says to him. Thereafter he knows the pathos of his situation.

The men in the dingey had not discussed these matters, but each had, no doubt, reflected upon them in silence and according to his mind. There was seldom any expression upon their faces save the general one of complete weariness. Speech was devoted to the business of the boat.

To chime the notes of his emotion, a verse mysteriously entered the correspondent's head. He had even forgotten that he had forgotten this verse, but it suddenly was in his mind.

> *A soldier of the Legion lay dying in Algiers,*
> *There was lack of woman's nursing, there was dearth of woman's tears;*
> *But a comrade stood beside him, and he took that comrade's hand,*
> *And he said: "I never more shall see my own, my native land."*

In his childhood, the correspondent had been made acquainted with the fact that a soldier of the Legion lay dying in Algiers, but he had never regarded it as important. Myriads of his school-fellows had informed him of the soldier's plight, but the dinning had naturally ended by making him perfectly indifferent. He had never considered it his affair that a soldier of the Legion lay dying in Algiers, nor had it appeared to him as a matter for sorrow. It was less to him than the breaking of a pencil's point.

Now, however, it quaintly came to him as a human, living thing. It was no longer merely a picture of a few throes in the breast of a poet, meanwhile drinking tea and warming his feet at the grate; it was an actuality — stern, mournful, and fine.

The correspondent plainly saw the soldier. He lay on the sand with his feet out straight and still. While his pale left hand was upon his chest in an attempt to thwart the going of his life, the blood came between his fingers. In the far Algerian distance, a city of low square forms was set against a sky that was faint with the last sunset hues. The correspondent, plying the oars and dreaming of the slow and slower movements of the lips of the soldier, was moved by a profound and perfectly impersonal comprehension. He was sorry for the soldier of the Legion who lay dying in Algiers.

The thing which had followed the boat and waited had evidently grown bored at the delay. There was no longer to be heard the slash of the cut-water, and there was no longer the flame of the long trail. The light in the north still glimmered, but it was apparently no nearer to the boat. Sometimes the boom of the surf rang in the correspondent's ears, and he turned the craft seaward then and rowed harder. Southward, some one had evidently built a watch-fire on the beach. It was too low and too far to be seen, but it made a shimmering, roseate reflection upon the bluff back of it, and this could be discerned from the boat. The wind came stronger, and sometimes a wave suddenly raged out like a mountain-cat and there was to be seen the sheen and sparkle of a broken crest.

The captain, in the bow, moved on his water-jar and sat erect. "Pretty long night," he observed to the correspondent. He looked at the shore. "Those life-saving people take their time."

"Did you see that shark playing around?"

"Yes, I saw him. He was a big fellow, all right."

"Wish I had known you were awake."

Later the correspondent spoke into the bottom of the boat.

"Billie!" There was a slow and gradual disentanglement. "Billie, will you spell me?"

"Sure," said the oiler.

As soon as the correspondent touched the cold comfortable sea-water in the bottom of the boat, and had huddled close to the cook's life-belt he was deep in sleep, despite the fact that his teeth played all the popular airs. This sleep was so good to him that it was but a moment before he heard a voice call his name in a tone that demonstrated the last stages of exhaustion. "Will you spell me?"

"Sure, Billie."

The light in the north had mysteriously vanished, but the correspondent took his course from the wide-awake captain.

Later in the night they took the boat farther out to sea, and the captain directed the cook to take one oar at the stern and keep the boat facing the seas. He was to call out if he should hear the thunder of the surf. This plan enabled the oiler and the correspondent to get respite together. "We'll give those boys a chance to get into shape again," said the captain. They curled down and, after a few preliminary chatterings and trembles, slept once more the dead sleep. Neither knew they had bequeathed to the cook the company of another shark, or perhaps the same shark.

As the boat caroused on the waves, spray occasionally bumped over the side and gave them a fresh soaking, but this had no power to break their repose. The ominous slash of the wind and the water affected them as it would have affected mummies.

"Boys," said the cook, with the notes of every reluctance in his voice, "she's drifted in pretty close. I guess one of you had better take her to sea again." The correspondent, aroused, heard the crash of the toppled crests.

As he was rowing, the captain gave him some whiskey and water, and this steadied the chills out of him. "If I ever get ashore and anybody shows me even a photograph of an oar —"

At last there was a short conversation.

"Billie. . . . Billie, will you spell me?"

"Sure," said the oiler.

VII

When the correspondent again opened his eyes, the sea and the sky were each of the gray hue of the dawning. Later, carmine and gold was painted upon the waters. The morning appeared finally, in its splendor, with a sky of pure blue, and the sunlight flamed on the tips of the waves.

On the distant dunes were set many little black cottages, and a tall white wind-mill reared above them. No man, nor dog, nor bicycle appeared on the beach. The cottages might have formed a deserted village.

The voyagers scanned the shore. A conference was held in the boat. "Well," said the captain, "if no help is coming, we might better try a run through the surf right away. If we stay out here much longer we will be too weak to do anything for ourselves at all." The others silently acquiesced in this reasoning. The boat was headed for the beach. The correspondent wondered if none ever ascended the tall wind-tower, and if then they never looked seaward. This tower was a giant, standing with its back to the plight of the ants. It represented in a degree, to the correspondent, the serenity of nature amid the struggles of the individual — nature in the wind, and nature in the vision of men. She did not seem cruel to him then, nor beneficent, nor treacherous, nor wise. But she was indifferent, flatly indifferent. It is, perhaps, plausible that a man in this situation, impressed with the unconcern of the universe, should see the innumerable flaws of his life and have them taste wickedly in his mind and wish for another chance. A distinction between right and wrong seems absurdly clear to him, then, in this new ignorance of the grave-edge, and he understands that if he were given another opportunity he would mend his conduct and his words, and be better and brighter during an introduction, or at a tea.

"Now, boys," said the captain, "she is going to swamp sure. All we can do is to work her in as far as possible, and then when she swamps, pile out and scramble for the beach. Keep cool now, and don't jump until she swamps sure."

The oiler took the oars. Over his shoulders he scanned the surf. "Captain," he said, "I think I'd better bring her about, and keep her head-on to the seas and back her in."

"All right, Billie," said the captain. "Back her in." The oiler swung the boat then and, seated in the stern, the cook and the correspondent were obliged to look over their shoulders to contemplate the lonely and indifferent shore.

The monstrous inshore rollers heaved the boat high until the men were again enabled to see the white sheets of water scudding up the slanted beach. "We won't get in very close," said the captain. Each time a man could wrest his attention from the rollers, he turned his glance toward the shore, and in the expression of the eyes during this contemplation there was a singular quality. The correspondent, observing the others, knew that they were not afraid, but the full meaning of their glances was shrouded.

As for himself, he was too tired to grapple fundamentally with the fact. He tried to coerce his mind into thinking of it, but the mind was dominated at this time by the muscles, and the muscles said they did not care. It merely occurred to him that if he should drown it would be a shame.

There were no hurried words, no pallor, no plain agitation. The men simply looked at the shore. "Now, remember to get well clear of the boat when you jump," said the captain.

Seaward the crest of a roller suddenly fell with a thunderous crash, and the long white comber came roaring down upon the boat.

"Steady now," said the captain. The men were silent. They turned their eyes from the shore to the comber and waited. The boat slid up the incline, leaped at the furious top, bounced over it, and swung down the long back of the wave. Some water had been shipped and the cook bailed it out.

But the next crest crashed also. The tumbling boiling flood of white water caught the boat and whirled it almost perpendicular. Water swarmed in from all sides. The correspondent had his hands on the gunwale at this time, and when the water entered at that place he swiftly withdrew his fingers, as if he objected to wetting them.

The little boat, drunken with this weight of water, reeled and snuggled deeper into the sea.

"Bail her out, cook! Bail her out," said the captain.

"All right, Captain," said the cook.

"Now boys, the next one will do for us, sure," said the oiler. "Mind to jump clear of the boat."

The third wave moved forward, huge, furious, implacable. It fairly swallowed the dingey, and almost simultaneously the men tumbled into the sea. A piece of life-belt had lain in the bottom of the boat, and as the correspondent went overboard he held this to his chest with his left hand.

The January water was icy, and he reflected immediately that it was colder than he had expected to find it off the coast of Florida. This appeared to his dazed mind as a fact important enough to be noted at the time. The coldness of the water was sad; it was tragic. This fact was somehow so mixed and confused with his opinion of his own situation that it seemed almost a proper reason for tears. The water was cold.

When he came to the surface he was conscious of little but the noisy water. Afterward he saw his companions in the sea. The oiler was ahead in the race. He was swimming strongly and rapidly. Off to the correspondent's left, the cook's great white and corked back bulged out of the water, and in the rear the captain was hanging with his one good hand to the keel of the overturned dingey.

There is a certain immovable quality to a shore, and the correspondent wondered at it amid the confusion of the sea.

It seemed also very attractive, but the correspondent knew that it was a long journey, and he paddled leisurely. The piece of life-preserver lay under him, and sometimes he whirled down the incline of a wave as if he were on a hand-sled.

But finally he arrived at a place in the sea where travel was beset with difficulty. He did not pause swimming to inquire what manner of current had caught him, but there his progress ceased. The shore was set before him like a bit of scenery on a stage, and he looked at it and understood with his eyes each detail of it.

As the cook passed, much farther to the left, the captain was calling to him, "Turn over on your back, cook! Turn over on your back and use the oar."

"All right, sir." The cook turned on his back, and, paddling with an oar, went ahead as if he were a canoe.

Presently the boat also passed to the left of the correspondent with the captain clinging with one hand to the keel. He would have appeared like a man raising himself to look over a board fence, if it were not for the extraordinary gymnastics of the boat. The correspondent marvelled that the captain could still hold to it.

They passed on, nearer to shore — the oiler, the cook, the captain — and following them went the water-jar, bouncing gayly over the seas.

The correspondent remained in the grip of this strange new enemy — a current. The shore, with its white slope of sand and its green bluff, topped with little silent cottages, was spread like a picture before him. It was very near to him then, but he was impressed as one who in a gallery looks at a scene from Brittany or Holland.

He thought: "I am going to drown? Can it be possible? Can it be possible? Can it be possible?" Perhaps an individual must consider his own death to be the final phenomenon of nature.

But later a wave perhaps whirled him out of his small deadly current, for he found suddenly that he could again make progress toward the shore. Later still, he was aware that the captain, clinging with one hand to the keel of the dingey, had his face turned away from the shore and toward him, and was calling his name. "Come to the boat! Come to the boat!"

In his struggle to reach the captain and the boat, he reflected that when one gets properly wearied, drowning must really be a comfortable arrangement, a cessation of hostilities accompanied by a large degree of relief, and he was glad of it, for the main thing in his mind for some moments had been the horror of the temporary agony. He did not wish to be hurt.

Presently he saw a man running along the shore. He was undressing with most remarkable speed. Coat, trousers, shirt, everything flew magically off him.

"Come to the boat," called the captain.

"All right, Captain." As the correspondent paddled, he saw the captain let himself down to bottom and leave the boat. Then the correspondent performed his one little marvel of the voyage. A large wave caught him and flung him with ease and supreme speed completely over the boat and far beyond it. It struck him even then as an event in gymnastics, and a true miracle of the sea. An overturned boat in the surf is not a plaything to a swimming man.

The correspondent arrived in water that reached only to his waist, but his condition did not enable him to stand for more than a moment. Each wave knocked him into a heap, and the under-tow pulled at him.

Then he saw the man who had been running and undressing, and undressing and running, come bounding into the water. He dragged ashore the cook, and then waded toward the captain, but the captain waved him away, and sent him to the correspondent. He was naked, naked as a tree in winter, but a halo was about his head, and he shone like a saint. He gave a strong pull, and a long drag, and a bully heave at the correspondent's hand. The correspondent, schooled in the minor formulae, said: "Thanks, old man." But suddenly the man cried: "What's that?" He pointed a swift finger. The correspondent said: "Go."

In the shallows, face downward, lay the oiler. His forehead touched sand that was periodically, between each wave, clear of the sea.

The correspondent did not know all that transpired afterward. When he achieved safe ground he fell, striking the sand with each particular part of his body. It was as if he had dropped from a roof, but the thud was grateful to him.

It seems that instantly the beach was populated with men with blankets, clothes, and flasks, and women with coffee-pots and all the remedies sacred to their minds. The welcome of the land to the men from the sea was warm and generous, but a still and dripping shape was carried slowly up the beach, and the land's welcome for it could only be the different and sinister hospitality of the grave.

When it came night, the white waves paced to and fro in the moonlight, and the wind brought the sound of the great sea's voice to the men on shore, and they felt that they could then be interpreters.   [1897]

ISAK DINESEN *is the name under which Baroness Karen Blixen of Denmark (1885–1962) published her writings. She was born Karen Christentze Dinesen near Elsinore, Denmark, and grew up in her family's ancestral home close to the sea. When she was a child her father committed suicide, and she felt that a part of herself had also died. Dinesen had such an "intuitive fear of being trapped" that she decided not to become a professional writer after publishing some short stories at the age of twenty. She felt that every profession invariably assigns a definite role in life, which would cut her off from the infinite possibilities of her life itself. In 1914 she married her cousin, Baron Bror Blixen, and went with him to British East Africa (now Kenya) to manage a large coffee plantation. In 1921 she and her husband divorced and she took over the management of the plantation. When coffee prices dropped in 1931 she had to give it up — a severe blow, because the seventeen years she spent in Africa had been the happiest of her life. She also lost her lover, the Englishman Denys Finch-Hatton, in a plane crash at this time. With a sense that her life was over, she returned to Denmark.*

Grief over having lost her farm and her lover in Africa made Karen Blixen a writer. She decided that the chief trap in life was not a single profession but rather a single identity, so she created another one for herself as a writer. "Slowly the center of gravity of my being will shift over from the world of day . . . into the world of Imagination." She chose to write in English out of loyalty to her dead lover, and she took the male pseudonym Isak, meaning "the one who laughs," in the spirit of the saying "God loves a joke." Her first collection of short stories, Seven Gothic Tales *— published in 1934 when she was nearly fifty years old — was followed by* Out of Africa *(1937), a reminiscence of her years in Africa, and a second book of stories,* Winter's Tales *(1942). In the final years of her life she published* Last Tales *(1957) and* Anecdotes of Destiny *(1958).*

As Eudora Welty has recognized, Dinesen's tales are "glimpses out of, rather than into, an extraordinary mind." Dinesen spun her stories out of the impulse to bring to life a world of marvels and enchantments, as in "The Sailor-Boy's Tale." Discovering that "all sorrows can be borne if you put them into a story or tell a story about them," she showed that the storyteller can make meaning out of what otherwise would remain an unbearable sequence of events or unrelated happenings. In the selection performed by the imagination, happenings become part of a pattern, what she called a "destiny." Her creation of that destiny in a work of fiction reveals meaning in life without committing the error of defining it. For Dinesen, the answer to the question "Who are you?" was given in the reply "Let me tell you a story."

ISAK DINESEN

The Sailor-Boy's Tale

The barque *Charlotte* was on her way from Marseille to Athens, in grey weather, on a high sea, after three days' heavy gale. A small sailor-boy, named Simon, stood on the wet, swinging deck, held on to a shroud, and looked up towards the drifting clouds, and to the upper top-gallant yard of the main-mast.

A bird, that had sought refuge upon the mast, had got her feet entangled in some loose tackle-yarn of the halliard, and, high up there, struggled to get free. The boy on the deck could see her wings flapping and her head turning from side to side.

Through his own experience of life he had come to the conviction that in this world everyone must look after himself, and expect no help from others. But the mute, deadly fight kept him fascinated for more than an hour. He wondered what kind of bird it would be. These last days a number of birds had come to settle in the barque's rigging: swallows, quails, and a pair of peregrine falcons; he believed that this bird was a peregrine falcon. He remembered how, many years ago, in his own country and near his home, he had once seen a peregrine falcon quite close, sitting on a stone and flying straight up from it. Perhaps this was the same bird. He thought: "That bird is like me. Then she was there, and now she is here."

At that a fellow-feeling rose in him, a sense of common tragedy; he stood looking at the bird with his heart in his mouth. There were none of the sailors about to make fun of him; he began to think out how he might go up by the shrouds to help the falcon out. He brushed his hair back and pulled up his sleeves, gave the deck round him a great glance, and climbed up. He had to stop a couple of times in the swaying rigging.

It was indeed, he found when he got to the top of the mast, a peregrine falcon. As his head was on a level with hers, she gave up her struggle, and looked at him with a pair of angry, desperate yellow eyes. He had to take hold of her with one hand while he got his knife out, and cut off the tackle-yarn. He was scared as he looked down, but at the same time he felt that he had been ordered up by nobody, but that this was his own venture, and this gave him a proud, steadying sensation, as if the sea and the sky, the ship, the bird, and himself were all one. Just as he had freed the falcon, she hacked him in the thumb, so that the blood ran, and he nearly let her go. He grew angry with her, and gave her a clout on the head, then he put her inside his jacket, and climbed down again.

When he reached the deck the mate and the cook were standing there, looking up; they roared to him to ask what he had had to do in the mast. He was so tired that the tears were in his eyes. He took the falcon out and showed her to them, and she kept still within his hands. They laughed and walked off. Simon set the falcon down, stood back and watched her. After a while he reflected that she might not be able to get up from the slippery deck, so he caught her once more, walked away with her and placed her upon a bolt of canvas. A little after she began to trim her feathers, made two or three sharp jerks forward, and then suddenly flew off. The boy could follow her flight above the troughs of the grey sea. He thought: "There flies my falcon."

When the *Charlotte* came home, Simon signed aboard another ship, and two years later he was a light hand on the schooner *Hebe* lying at Bodø, high up on the coast of Norway, to buy herrings.

To the great herring-markets of Bodø ships came together from all corners of the world; here were Swedish, Finnish and Russian boats, a forest of masts, and on shore a turbulent, irregular display of life, with many languages spoken, and mighty fights. On the shore booths had been set up, and the Lapps, small yellow people, noiseless in their movements, with watchful eyes, whom Simon had never seen before, came down to sell bead-embroidered leather-goods. It was April, the sky and the sea were so clear that it was difficult to hold one's eyes up against them — salt, infinitely wide, and filled with bird-shrieks — as if someone were incessantly whetting invisible knives, on all sides, high up in Heaven.

Simon was amazed at the lightness of these April evenings. He knew no geography, and did not assign it to the latitude, but he took it as a sign of an unwonted good-will in the Universe, a favour. Simon had been small for his age all his life, but this last winter he had grown, and had become strong of limb. That good luck, he felt, must spring from the very same source as the sweetness of the weather, from a new benevolence in the world. He had been in need of such encouragement, for he was timid by nature; now he asked for no more. The rest he felt to be his own affair. He went about slowly, and proudly.

One evening he was ashore with land-leave, and walked up to the booth of a small Russian trader, a Jew who sold gold watches. All the sailors knew that his watches were made from bad metal, and would not go, still they bought them, and paraded them about. Simon looked at these watches for a long time, but did not buy. The old Jew had divers goods in his shop, and amongst others a case of oranges. Simon had tasted oranges on his journeys; he bought one and took it with him. He meant to go up on a hill, from where he could see the sea, and suck it there.

As he walked on, and had got to the outskirts of the place, he saw a little girl in a blue frock, standing at the other side of a fence and looking at him. She was thirteen or fourteen years old, as slim as an eel, but with a round, clear, freckled face, and a pair of long plaits. The two looked at one another.

"Who are you looking out for?" Simon asked, to say something. The girl's face broke into an ecstatic presumptuous smile. "For the man I am going to marry, of course," she said. Something in her countenance made the boy confident and happy; he grinned a little at her. "That will perhaps be me," he said. "Ha, ha," said the girl, "he is a few years older than you, I can tell you." "Why," said Simon, "you are not grown up yourself." The little girl shook her head solemnly. "Nay," she said, "but when I grow up I will be exceedingly beautiful, and wear brown shoes with heels, and a hat." "Will you have an orange?" asked Simon, who could give her none of the things she had named. She looked at the orange and at him. "They are very good to eat," said he. "Why do you not eat it yourself then?" she asked. "I have eaten so many already," said he, "when I was in Athens. Here I had to pay a mark for it." "What is your name?" asked she. "My name is Simon," said he. "What is yours?" "Nora," said the girl. "What do you want for your orange now, Simon?"

When he heard his name in her mouth Simon grew bold. "Will you give me a kiss for the orange?" he asked. Nora looked at him gravely for a moment. "Yes," she said, "I should not mind giving you a kiss." He grew as warm as if he had been running quickly. When she stretched out her hand for the orange he took hold of it. At that moment somebody in the house called out for her. "That is my father," said she, and tried to give him back the orange, but he would not take it. "Then come again tomorrow," she said quickly, "then I will give you a kiss." At that she slipped off. He stood and looked after her, and a little later went back to his ship.

Simon was not in the habit of making plans for the future, and now he did not know whether he would be going back to her or not.

The following evening he had to stay aboard, as the other sailors were going ashore, and he did not mind that either. He meant to sit on the deck with the ship's dog, Balthasar, and to practise upon a concertina that he had purchased some time ago. The pale evening was all round him, the sky was faintly roseate, the sea was quite calm, like milk-and-water, only in the wake of the boats going inshore it broke into streaks of vivid indigo. Simon sat and played; after a while his own music began to speak to him so strongly that he stopped, got up and looked upwards. Then he saw that the full moon was sitting high on the sky.

The sky was so light that she hardly seemed needed there; it was as if she had turned up by a caprice of her own. She was round, demure, and presumptuous. At that he knew that he must go ashore, whatever it was to cost him. But he did not know how to get away, since the others had taken the yawl with them. He stood on the deck for a long time, a small lonely figure of a sailor-boy on a boat, when he caught sight of a yawl coming in from a ship farther out, and hailed her. He found that it was the Russian crew from a boat named *Anna*, going ashore. When he could make himself understood to them, they took him with them; they first asked him for money for his fare, then, laughing, gave it back to him. He thought: "These people will be believing that I am going in to town, wenching." And then he felt, with some pride, that they were right, although at the same time they were infinitely wrong, and knew nothing about anything.

When they came ashore they invited him to come in and drink in their company, and he would not refuse, because they had helped him. One of the Russians was a giant, as big as a bear; he told Simon that his name was Ivan. He got drunk at once, and then fell upon the boy with a bear-like affection, pawed him, smiled and laughed into his face, made him a present of a gold watch-chain, and kissed him on both cheeks. At that Simon reflected that he also ought to give Nora a present when they met again, and as soon as he could get away from the Russians he walked up to a booth that he knew of, and bought a small blue silk handkerchief, the same colour as her eyes.

It was Saturday evening, and there were many people amongst the houses; they came in long rows, some of them singing, all keen to have some fun that night. Simon, in the midst of this rich, bawling life under the clear moon, felt his head light with the flight from the ship and the strong drinks. He crammed the handkerchief in his pocket; it was silk, which he had never touched before, a present for his girl.

He could not remember the path up to Nora's house, lost his way, and came back to where he had started. Then he grew deadly afraid that he should be too late, and began to run. In a small passage between two wooden huts he ran straight into a big man, and found that it was Ivan once more. The Russian folded his arms round him and held him. "Good! Good!" he cried in high glee, "I have found you, my little chicken. I have looked for you everywhere, and poor Ivan has wept because he lost his friend." "Let me go, Ivan," cried Simon. "Oho," said Ivan, "I shall go with you and get you what you want. My heart and my money are all yours, all yours; I have been seventeen years old myself, a little lamb of God, and I want to be so again tonight." "Let me go," cried Simon, "I am in a hurry." Ivan held him so that it hurt, and patted him with his other hand. "I feel it, I feel it," he said. "Now trust to me, my little friend. Nothing shall part you and me. I hear the others coming; we will have such a night together as you will remember when you are an old grandpapa."

Suddenly he crushed the boy to him, like a bear that carries off a sheep. The odious sensation of male bodily warmth and the bulk of a man close to him made the lean boy mad. He thought of Nora waiting, like a slender ship in the dim air, and of himself, here, in the hot embrace of a hairy animal. He struck Ivan with all his might. "I shall kill you, Ivan," he cried out, "if you do not let me go." "Oh, you will be thankful to me later on," said Ivan, and began to sing. Simon fumbled in his pocket for his knife, and got it opened. He could not lift his hand, but he drove the knife, furiously, in under the big man's arm. Almost immediately he felt the blood spouting out, and running down in his sleeve. Ivan stopped short in the song, let go his hold of the boy, and gave two long deep grunts. The next second he tumbled down on his knees. "Poor Ivan, poor Ivan," he groaned. He fell straight on his face. At that moment Simon heard the other sailors coming along, singing, in the by-street.

He stood still for a minute, wiped his knife, and watched the blood spread into a dark pool underneath the big body. Then he ran. As he stopped for a second to choose his way, he heard the sailors behind him scream out over their dead comrade. He thought: "I must get down to the sea, where I can wash my hand." But at the same time he ran the other way. After a little while he found himself on the path that he had walked on the day before, and it seemed as familiar to him, as if he had walked it many hundred times in his life.

He slackened his pace to look round, and suddenly saw Nora standing on the other side of the fence; she was quite close to him when he caught sight of her in the moonlight. Wavering and out of breath he sank down on his knees. For a moment he could not speak. The little girl looked down at him. "Good evening, Simon," she said in her small coy voice. "I have waited for you a long time," and after a moment she added: "I have eaten your orange."

"Oh, Nora," cried the boy. "I have killed a man." She stared at him, but did not move. "Why did you kill a man?" she asked after a moment. "To get here," said Simon. "Because he tried to stop me. But he was my friend." Slowly he got on to his feet. "He loved me!" the boy cried out, and at that burst into tears. "Yes," said she slowly and thoughtfully. "Yes, because you must be here in time." "Can you hide me?" he asked. "For they are after me." "Nay," said Nora, "I cannot hide you. For my father is the parson here at Bodø, and he would be sure to hand you over to them, if he knew that you had killed a man." "Then," said Simon, "give me something to wipe my hands on." "What is the matter with your hands?" she asked, and took a little step forward. He stretched out his hands to her. "Is that your own blood?" she asked. "No," said he, "it is his." She took the step back again. "Do you hate me now?" he asked. "No, I do not hate you," said she. "But do put your hands at your back."

As he did so she came up close to him, at the other side of the fence, and clasped her arms round his neck. She pressed her young body to his, and kissed him tenderly. He felt her face, cool as the moonlight, upon his own, and when she released him, his head swam, and he did not know if the kiss had lasted a second or an hour. Nora stood up straight, her eyes wide open. "Now," she said slowly and proudly, "I promise you that I will never marry anybody, as long as I live." The boy kept standing with his hands on his back, as if she had tied them there. "And now," she said, "you must run, for they are coming." They looked at one another. "Do not forget Nora," said she. He turned and ran.

He leapt over a fence, and when he was down amongst the houses he walked. He did not know at all where to go. As he came to a house, from where music and noise streamed out, he slowly went through the door. The room was full of people; they were dancing in here. A lamp hung from the ceiling, and shone down on them; the air was thick and brown with the dust rising from the floor. There were some women in the room, but many of the men danced with each other, and gravely or laughingly stamped the floor. A moment after Simon had come in the crowd withdrew to the walls to clear the floor for two sailors, who were showing a dance from their own country.

Simon thought: "Now, very soon, the men from the boat will come round to look for their comrade's murderer, and from my hands they will know that I have done it." These five minutes during which he stood by the wall of the dancing-room, in the midst of the gay, sweating dancers, were of great significance to the boy. He himself felt it, as if during this time he grew up, and became like other people. He did not entreat his destiny, nor complain. Here he was, he had killed a man, and had kissed a girl. He did not demand any more from life, nor did life now demand more from him. He was Simon, a man like the men round him, and going to die, as all men are going to die.

He only became aware of what was going on outside him, when he saw that a woman had come in, and was standing in the midst of the cleared floor, looking round her. She was a short, broad old woman, in the clothes of the Lapps, and she took her stand with such majesty and fierceness as if she owned the whole place. It was obvious that most of the people knew her, and were a little afraid of her, although a few laughed; the din of the dancing-room stopped when she spoke.

"Where is my son?" she asked in a high shrill voice, like a bird's. The next moment her eyes fell on Simon himself, and she steered through the crowd, which opened up before her, stretched out her old skinny, dark hand, and took him by the elbow. "Come home with me now," she said. "You need not dance here tonight. You may be dancing a high enough dance soon."

Simon drew back, for he thought that she was drunk. But as she looked him straight in the face with her yellow eyes, it seemed to him that he had met her before, and that he might do well in listening to her. The old woman pulled him with her across the floor, and he followed her without a word. "Do not birch your boy too badly, Sunniva," one of the men in the room cried to her. "He has done no harm, he only wanted to look at the dance."

At the same moment as they came out through the door, there was an alarm in the street, a flock of people came running down it, and one of them, as he turned into the house, knocked against Simon, looked at him and the old woman, and ran on.

While the two walked along the street, the old woman lifted up her skirt, and put the hem of it into the boy's hand. "Wipe your hand on my skirt," she said. They had not gone far before they came to a small wooden house, and stopped; the door to it was so low that they must bend to get through it. As the Lapp-woman went in before Simon, still holding on to his arm, the boy looked up for a moment. The night had grown misty; there was a wide ring round the moon.

The old woman's room was narrow and dark, with but one small window to it; a lantern stood on the floor and lighted it up dimly. It was all filled with reindeer skins and wolf skins, and with reindeer horn, such as the Lapps use to make their carved buttons and knife-handles, and the air in here was rank and stifling. As soon as they were in, the woman turned to Simon, took hold of his head, and with her crooked fingers parted his hair and combed it down in Lapp fashion. She clapped a Lapp cap on him and stood back to glance at him. "Sit down on my stool, now," she said. "But first take out your knife." She was so commanding in voice and manner that the boy could not but choose to do as she told him; he sat down on the stool, and he could not take his eyes off her face, which was flat and brown, and as if smeared with dirt in its net of fine wrinkles. As he sat there he heard many people come along outside, and stop by the house; then someone knocked at the door, waited a moment and knocked again. The old woman stood and listened, as still as a mouse.

"Nay," said the boy and got up. "This is no good, for it is me that they are after. It will be better for you to let me go out to them." "Give me your knife," said she. When he handed it to her, she stuck it straight into her thumb, so that the blood spouted out, and she let it drip all over her skirt. "Come in, then," she cried.

The door opened, and two of the Russian sailors came and stood in the opening; there were more people outside. "Has anybody come in here?" they asked. "We are after a man who has killed our mate, but he has run away from us. Have you seen or heard anybody this way?" The old Lapp-woman turned upon them, and her eyes shone like gold in the lamplight. "Have I seen or heard anyone?" she cried, "I have heard you shriek murder all over the town. You frightened me, and my poor silly boy there, so that I cut my thumb as I was ripping the skin-rug that I sew. The boy is too scared to help me, and the rug is all ruined. I shall make you pay me for that. If you are looking for a murderer, come in and search my house for me, and I shall know you when we meet again." She was so furious that she danced where she stood, and jerked her head like an angry bird of prey.

The Russian came in, looked round the room, and at her and her bloodstained hand and skirt. "Do not put a curse on us now, Sunniva," he said timidly. "We know that you can do many things when you like. Here is a mark to pay you for the blood you have spilled." She stretched out her hand, and he placed a piece of money in it. She spat on it. "Then go, and there shall be no bad blood between us," said Sunniva, and shut the door after them. She stuck her thumb in her mouth, and chuckled a little.

The boy got up from his stool, stood straight up before her and stared into her face. He felt as if he were swaying high up in the air, with but a small hold. "Why have you helped me?" he asked her. "Do you not know?" she answered. "Have you not recognised me yet? But you will remember the peregrine falcon which was caught in the tackle-yarn of your boat, the *Charlotte*, as she sailed in the Mediterranean. That day you climbed up by the shrouds of the top-gallant-mast to help her out, in a stiff wind, and with a high sea. That falcon was me. We Lapps often fly in such a manner, to see the world. When I first met you I was on my way to Africa, to see my younger sister and her children. She is a falcon too, when she chooses. By that time she was living at Takaunga, within an old ruined tower, which down there they call a minaret." She swathed a corner of her skirt round her thumb, and bit at it. "We do not forget," she said. "I hacked your thumb, when you took hold of me; it is only fair that I should cut my thumb for you tonight."

She came close to him, and gently rubbed her two brown, claw-like fingers against his forehead. "So you are a boy," she said, "who will kill a man rather than be late to meet your sweetheart? We hold together, the females of this earth. I shall mark your forehead now, so that the girls will know of that, when they look at you, and they will like you for it." She played with the boy's hair, and twisted it round her finger.

"Listen now, my little bird," said she. "My great grandson's brother-in-law is lying with his boat by the landing-place at this moment; he is to take a consignment of skins out to a Danish boat. He will bring you back to your boat, in time, before your mate comes. The *Hebe* is sailing tomorrow morning, is it not so? But when you are aboard, give him back my cap for me." She took up his knife, wiped it in her skirt, and handed it to him. "Here is your knife," she said. "You will stick it into no more men; you will not need to, for from now you will sail the seas like a faithful seaman. We have enough trouble with our sons as it is."

The bewildered boy began to stammer his thanks to her. "Wait," said she, "I shall make you a cup of coffee, to bring back your wits, while I wash your jacket." She went and rattled an old copper kettle upon the fireplace. After a while she handed him a hot, strong, black drink in a cup without a handle to it. "You have drunk with Sunniva now," she said; "you have drunk down a little wisdom, so that in the future all your thoughts shall not fall like raindrops into the salt sea."

When he had finished and set down the cup, she led him to the door and opened it for him. He was surprised to see that it was almost clear morning. The house was so high up that the boy could see the sea from it, and a milky mist about it. He gave her his hand to say good-bye.

She stared into his face. "We do not forget," she said. "And you, you knocked me on the head there, high up in the mast. I shall give you that blow back." With that she smacked him on the ear as hard as she could, so that his head swam. "Now we are quits," she said, gave him a great, mischievous, shining glance, and a little push down the doorstep, and nodded to him.

In this way the sailor-boy got back to his ship, which was to sail the next morning, and lived to tell the story.   [1942]

RALPH ELLISON (1914–1994) was born in Oklahoma City, Oklahoma. When he was three his father, a small-time vendor of ice and coal, died, and thereafter his mother worked as a domestic servant to support herself and her son. Ellison later credited his mother, who recruited black votes for the Socialist Party, for turning him into an activist. She also brought home discarded books and phonograph records from the white households where she worked, and as a boy Ellison developed an interest in literature and music. He played trumpet in his high school band, at the same time that he began to relate the works of fiction he was reading to real life. "I began to look at my own life through the lives of fictional characters. When I read Stendhal, I would search until I began to find patterns of a Stendhalian novel within the Negro communities in which I grew up. I began, in other words, quite early to connect the worlds projected in literature . . . with the life in which I found myself."

In 1933 Ellison entered Tuskegee Institute in Alabama, where he studied music for three years. Then he went to New York City and met the black writers Langston Hughes and Richard Wright, whose encouragement helped him to become a writer. Wright turned Ellison's attention to writing short stories and reading "those works in which writing was discussed as a craft . . . to Henry James's prefaces, to Conrad," and to other authors. In 1939 Ellison's short stories, essays, and reviews began to appear in periodicals. After World War II, he settled down to work on the novel Invisible Man. Published in 1952, it received the National Book Award for fiction; and, in 1965, a Book Week poll listed it as the most distinguished American novel of the preceding twenty years. As the critic Richard D. Lyons recognized, the novel was "a chronicle of a young black man's awakening to racial discrimination and his battle against the refusal of Americans to see him apart from his ethnic background, which in turn leads to humiliation and disillusionment." "Battle Royal," an excerpt from Invisible Man, is often anthologized. It appears after the prologue describing the underground chamber in which the nameless protagonist has retreated from the chaos of life aboveground.

Insisting that "art by its nature is social," Ellison began Invisible Man with the words, "I am an invisible man. No, I am not a spook like those who haunted Edgar Allan Poe; nor am I one of your Hollywood-movie ectoplasms. I am a man of substance, of flesh and bone, fiber and liquids — and I might even be said to possess a mind. I am invisible, understand, simply because people refuse to see me." At the time of his death from cancer, Ellison left an unfinished novel started in the late 1950s. His initial work on the manuscript was destroyed in a fire, and it was difficult for him to complete the book. In addition to Invisible Man, Ellison published a few early short stories, including "King of the Bingo Game," and two collections of essays, Shadow and Act (1964) and Going to the Territory (1986). He also held a chair as Albert Schweitzer Professor of Contemporary Literature and Culture at New York University.

RELATED COMMENTARY: Ralph Ellison, "The Influence of Folklore on 'Battle Royal,'" page 1412.

RALPH ELLISON

Battle Royal

It goes a long way back, some twenty years. All my life I had been looking for something, and everywhere I turned someone tried to tell me what it was. I accepted their answers too, though they were often in contradiction and even self-contradictory. I was naïve. I was looking for myself and asking everyone except myself questions which I, and only I, could answer. It took me a long time and much painful boomeranging of my expectations to achieve a realization everyone else appears to have been born with: That I am nobody but myself. But first I had to discover that I am an invisible man!

And yet I am no freak of nature, nor of history. I was in the cards, other things having been equal (or unequal) eighty-five years ago. I am not ashamed of my grandparents for having been slaves. I am only ashamed of myself for having at one time been ashamed. About eighty-five years ago they were told that they were free, united with others of our country in everything pertaining to the common good, and, in everything social, separate like the fingers of the hand. And they believed it. They exulted in it. They stayed in their place, worked hard, and brought up my father to do the same. But my grandfather is the one. He was an odd old guy, my grandfather, and I am told I take after him. It was he who caused the trouble. On his deathbed he called my father to him and said, "Son, after I'm gone I want you to keep up the good fight. I never told you, but our life is a war and I have been a traitor all my born days, a spy in the enemy's country ever since I give up my gun back in the Reconstruction. Live with your head in the lion's mouth. I want you to overcome 'em with yeses, undermine 'em with grins, agree 'em to death and destruction, let 'em swoller you till they vomit or bust wide open." They thought the old man had gone out of his mind. He had been the meekest of men. The younger children were rushed from the room, the shades drawn, and the flame of the lamp turned so low that it sputtered on the wick like the old man's breathing. "Learn it to the younguns," he whispered fiercely; then he died.

But my folks were more alarmed over his last words than over his dying. It was as though he had not died at all, his words caused so much anxiety. I was warned emphatically to forget what he had said and, indeed, this is the first time it has been mentioned outside the family circle. It had a tremendous effect upon me, however. I could never be sure of what he meant. Grandfather had been a quiet old man who never made any trouble, yet on his deathbed he had called himself a traitor and a spy, and he had spoken of his meekness as a dangerous activity. It became a constant puzzle which lay unanswered in the back of my mind. And whenever things went well for me I remembered my grandfather and felt guilty and uncomfortable. It was as though I was carrying out his advice in spite of myself. And to make it worse, everyone loved me for it. I was praised by the most lily-white men of the town. I was considered an example of desirable conduct — just as my grandfather had been. And what puzzled me was that the old man had defined it as *treachery*. When I was praised for my conduct I felt a guilt that in some way I was doing something that was really against the wishes of the white folks, that if they had understood they would have desired me to act just the opposite, that I should have been sulky and mean, and that that really would have been what they wanted, even though they were fooled and thought they wanted me to act as I did. It made me afraid that some day they would look upon me as a traitor and I would be lost. Still I was more afraid to act any other way because they didn't like that at all. The old man's words were like a curse. On my graduation day I delivered an oration in which I showed that humility was the secret, indeed, the very essence of progress. (Not that I believed this — how could I, remembering my grandfather? — I only believed that it worked.) It was a great success. Everyone praised me and I was invited to give the speech at a gathering of the town's leading white citizens. It was a triumph for our whole community.

It was in the main ballroom of the leading hotel. When I got there I discovered that it was on the occasion of a smoker, and I was told that since I was to be there anyway I might as well take part in the battle royal to be fought by some of my schoolmates as part of the entertainment. The battle royal came first.

All of the town's big shots were there in their tuxedoes, wolfing down the buffet foods, drinking beer and whiskey and smoking black cigars. It was a large room with a high ceiling. Chairs were arranged in neat rows around three sides of a portable boxing ring. The fourth side was clear, revealing a gleaming space of polished floor. I had some misgivings over the battle royal, by the way. Not from a distaste for fighting, but because I didn't care too much for the other fellows who were to take part. They were tough guys who seemed to have no grandfather's curse worrying their minds. No one could mistake their toughness. And besides, I suspected that fighting a battle royal might detract from the dignity of my speech. In those pre-invisible days I visualized myself as a potential Booker T. Washington. But the other fellows didn't care too much for me either, and there were nine of them. I felt superior to them in my way, and I didn't like the manner in which we were all crowded together into the servants' elevator. Nor did they like my being there. In fact, as the warmly lighted floors flashed past the elevator we had words over the fact that I, by taking part in the fight, had knocked one of their friends out of a night's work.

We were led out of the elevator through a rococo hall into an anteroom and told to get into our fighting togs. Each of us was issued a pair of boxing gloves and ushered out into the big mirrored hall, which we entered looking cautiously about us and whispering, lest we might accidentally be heard above the noise of the room. It was foggy with cigar smoke. And already the whiskey was taking effect. I was shocked to see some of the most important men of the town quite tipsy. They were all there — bankers, lawyers, judges, doctors, fire chiefs, teachers, merchants. Even one of the more fashionable pastors. Something we could not see was going on up front. A clarinet was vibrating sensuously and the men were standing up and moving eagerly forward. We were a small tight group, clustered together, our bare upper bodies touching and shining with anticipatory sweat; while up front the big shots were becoming increasingly excited over something we still could not see. Suddenly I heard the school superintendent, who had told me to come, yell, "Bring up the shines, gentlemen! Bring up the little shines!"

We were rushed up to the front of the ballroom, where it smelled even more strongly of tobacco and whiskey. Then we were pushed into place. I almost wet my pants. A sea of faces, some hostile, some amused, ringed around us, and in the center, facing us, stood a magnificent blonde — stark naked. There was dead silence. I felt a blast of cold air chill me. I tried to back away, but they were behind me and around me. Some of the boys stood with lowered heads, trembling. I felt a wave of irrational guilt and fear. My teeth chattered, my skin turned to goose flesh, my knees knocked. Yet I was strongly attracted and looked in spite of myself. Had the price of looking been blindness, I would have looked. The hair was yellow like that of a circus kewpie doll, the face heavily powdered and rouged, as though to form an abstract mask, the eyes hollow and smeared a cool blue, the color of a baboon's butt. I felt a desire to spit upon her as my eyes brushed slowly over her body. Her breasts were firm and round as the domes of East Indian temples, and I stood so close as to see the fine skin texture and beads of pearly perspiration glistening like dew around the pink and erected buds of her nipples. I wanted at one and the same time to run from the room, to sink through the floor, or go to her and cover her from my eyes and the eyes of the others with my body; to feel the soft thighs, to caress her and destroy her, to love her and murder her, to hide from her, and yet to stroke where below the small American flag tattooed upon her belly her thighs formed a capital V. I had a notion that of all in the room she saw only me with her impersonal eyes.

And then she began to dance, a slow sensuous movement; the smoke of a hundred cigars clinging to her like the thinnest of veils. She seemed like a fair bird-girl girdled in veils calling to me from the angry surface of some gray and threatening sea. I was transported. Then I became aware of the clarinet playing and the big shots yelling at us. Some threatened us if we looked and others if we did not. On my right I saw one boy faint. And now a man grabbed a silver pitcher from a table and stepped close as he dashed ice water upon him and stood him up and forced two of us to support him as his head hung and moans issued from his thick bluish lips. Another boy began to plead to go home. He was the largest of the group, wearing dark red fighting trunks much too small to conceal the erection which projected from him as though in answer to the insinuating low-registered moaning of the clarinet. He tried to hide himself with his boxing gloves.

And all the while the blonde continued dancing, smiling faintly at the big shots who watched her with fascination, and faintly smiling at our fear. I noticed a certain merchant who followed her hungrily, his lips loose and drooling. He was a large man who wore diamond studs in a shirtfront which swelled with the ample paunch underneath, and each time the blonde swayed her undulating hips he ran his hand through the thin hair of his bald head and, with his arms upheld, his posture clumsy like that of an intoxicated panda, wound his belly in a slow and obscene grind. This creature was completely hypnotized. The music had quickened. As the dancer flung herself about with a detached expression on her face, the men began reaching out to touch her. I could see their beefy fingers sink into her soft flesh. Some of the others tried to stop them and she began to move around the floor in graceful circles, as they gave chase, slipping and sliding over the polished floor. It was mad. Chairs went crashing, drinks were spilt, as they ran laughing and howling after her. They caught her just as she reached a door, raised her from the floor, and tossed her as college boys are tossed at a hazing, and above her red fixed-smiling lips I saw the terror and disgust in her eyes, almost like my own terror and that which I saw in some of the other boys. As I watched, they tossed her twice and her soft breasts seemed to flatten against the air and her legs flung wildly as she spun. Some of the more sober ones helped her to escape. And I started off the floor, heading for the anteroom with the rest of the boys.

Some were still crying and in hysteria. But as we tried to leave we were stopped and ordered to get into the ring. There was nothing to do but what we were told. All ten of us climbed under the ropes and allowed ourselves to be blindfolded with broad bands of white cloth. One of the men seemed to feel a bit sympathetic and tried to cheer us up as we stood with our backs against the ropes. Some of us tried to grin. "See that boy over there?" one of the men said. "I want you to run across at the bell and give it to him right in the belly. If you don't get him, I'm going to get you. I don't like his looks." Each of us was told the same. The blindfolds were put on. Yet even then I had been going over my speech. In my mind each word was as bright as flame. I felt the cloth pressed into place, and frowned so that it would be loosened when I relaxed.

But now I felt a sudden fit of blind terror. I was unused to darkness. It was as though I had suddenly found myself in a dark room filled with poisonous cottonmouths. I could hear the bleary voices yelling insistently for the battle royal to begin.

"Get going in there!"

"Let me at that big nigger!"

I strained to pick up the school superintendent's voice, as though to squeeze some security out of that slightly more familiar sound.

"Let me at those black sonsabitches!" someone yelled.

"No, Jackson, no!" another voice yelled. "Here, somebody, help me hold Jack."

"I want to get at that ginger-colored nigger. Tear him limb from limb," the first voice yelled.

I stood against the ropes trembling. For in those days I was what they called ginger-colored, and he sounded as though he might crunch me between his teeth like a crisp ginger cookie.

Quite a struggle was going on. Chairs were being kicked about and I could hear voices grunting as with a terrific effort. I wanted to see, to see more desperately than ever before. But the blindfold was as tight as a thick skin-puckering scab and when I raised my gloved hands to push the layers of white aside a voice yelled, "Oh, no you don't, black bastard! Leave that alone!"

"Ring the bell before Jackson kills him a coon!" someone boomed in the sudden silence. And I heard the bell clang and the sound of the feet scuffling forward.

A glove smacked against my head. I pivoted, striking out stiffly as someone went past, and felt the jar ripple along the length of my arm to my shoulder. Then it seemed as though all nine of the boys had turned upon me at once. Blows pounded me from all sides while I struck out as best I could. So many blows landed upon me that I wondered if I were not the only blindfolded fighter in the ring, or if the man called Jackson hadn't succeeded in getting me after all.

Blindfolded, I could no longer control my motions. I had no dignity. I stumbled about like a baby or a drunken man. The smoke had become thicker and with each new blow it seemed to sear and further restrict my lungs. My saliva became like hot bitter glue. A glove connected with my head, filling my mouth with warm blood. It was everywhere. I could not tell if the moisture I felt upon my body was sweat or blood. A blow landed hard against the nape of my neck. I felt myself going over, my head hitting the floor. Streaks of blue light filled the black world behind the blindfold. I lay prone, pretending that I was knocked out, but felt myself seized by hands and yanked to my feet. "Get going, black boy! Mix it up!" My arms were like lead, my head smarting from blows. I managed to feel my way to the ropes and held on, trying to catch my breath. A glove landed in my midsection and I went over again, feeling as though the smoke had become a knife jabbed into my guts. Pushed this way and that by the legs milling around me, I finally pulled erect and discovered that I could see the black, sweat-washed forms weaving in the smoky-blue atmosphere like drunken dancers weaving to the rapid drum-like thuds of blows.

Everyone fought hysterically. It was complete anarchy. Everybody fought everybody else. No group fought together for long. Two, three, four, fought one, then turned to fight each other, were themselves attacked. Blows landed below the belt and in the kidney, with the gloves open as well as closed, and with my eye partly opened now there was not so much terror. I moved carefully, avoiding blows, although not too many to attract attention, fighting from group to group. The boys groped about like blind, cautious crabs crouching to protect their mid-sections, their heads pulled in short against their shoulders, their arms stretched nervously before them, with their fists testing the smoke-filled air like the knobbed feelers of hypersensitive snails. In one corner I glimpsed a boy violently punching the air and heard him scream in pain as he smashed his hand against a ring post. For a second I saw him bent over holding his hand, then going down as a blow caught his unprotected head. I played one group against the other, slipping in and throwing a punch then stepping out of range while pushing the others into the melee to take the blows blindly aimed at me. The smoke was agonizing and there were no rounds, no bells at three minute intervals to relieve our exhaustion. The room spun round me, a swirl of lights, smoke, sweating bodies surrounded by tense white faces. I bled from both nose and mouth, the blood spattering upon my chest.

The men kept yelling, "Slug him, black boy! Knock his guts out!"

"Uppercut him! Kill him! Kill that big boy!"

Taking a fake fall, I saw a boy going down heavily beside me as though we were felled by a single blow, saw a sneaker-clad foot shoot into his groin as the two who had knocked him down stumbled upon him. I rolled out of range, feeling a twinge of nausea.

The harder we fought the more threatening the men became. And yet, I had begun to worry about my speech again. How would it go? Would they recognize my ability? What would they give me?

I was fighting automatically and suddenly I noticed that one after another of the boys was leaving the ring. I was surprised, filled with panic, as though I had been left alone with an unknown danger. Then I understood. The boys had arranged it among themselves. It was the custom for the two men left in the ring to slug it out for the winner's prize. I discovered this too late. When the bell sounded two men in tuxedoes leaped into the ring and removed the blindfold. I found myself facing Tatlock, the biggest of the gang. I felt sick at my stomach. Hardly had the bell stopped ringing in my ears than it clanged again and I saw him moving swiftly toward me. Thinking of nothing else to do I hit him smash on the nose. He kept coming, bringing the rank sharp violence of stale sweat. His face was a black blank of a face, only his eyes alive — with hate of me and aglow with a feverish terror from what had happened to us all. I became anxious. I wanted to deliver my speech and he came at me as though he meant to beat it out of me. I smashed him again and again, taking his blows as they came. Then on a sudden impulse I struck him lightly and as we clinched, I whispered, "Fake like I knocked you out, you can have the prize."

"I'll break your behind," he whispered hoarsely.

"For *them*?"

"For *me*, sonofabitch!"

They were yelling for us to break it up and Tatlock spun me half around with a blow, and as a joggled camera sweeps in a reeling scene, I saw the howling red faces crouching tense beneath the cloud of blue-gray smoke. For a moment the world wavered, unraveled, flowed, then my head cleared and Tatlock bounced before me. That fluttering shadow before my eyes was his jabbing left hand. Then falling forward, my head against his damp shoulder, I whispered,

"I'll make it five dollars more."

"Go to hell!"

But his muscles relaxed a trifle beneath my pressure and I breathed, "Seven!"

"Give it to your ma," he said, ripping me beneath the heart.

And while I still held him I butted him and moved away. I felt myself bombarded with punches. I fought back with hopeless desperation. I wanted to deliver my speech more than anything else in the world, because I felt that only these men could judge truly my ability, and now this stupid clown was ruining my chances. I began fighting carefully now, moving in to punch him and out again with my greater speed. A lucky blow to his chin and I had him going too — until I heard a loud voice yell, "I got my money on the big boy."

Hearing this, I almost dropped my guard. I was confused: Should I try to win against the voice out there? Would not this go against my speech, and was not this a moment for humility, for nonresistance? A blow to my head as I danced about sent my right eye popping like a jack-in-the-box and settled my dilemma. The room went red as I fell. It was a dream fall, my body languid and fastidious as to where to land, until the floor became impatient and smashed up to meet me. A moment later I came to. An hypnotic voice said FIVE emphatically. And I lay there, hazily watching a dark red spot of my own blood shaping itself into a butterfly, glistening and soaking into the soiled gray world of the canvas.

When the voice drawled TEN I was lifted up and dragged to a chair. I sat dazed. My eye pained and swelled with each throb of my pounding heart and I wondered if now I would be allowed to speak. I was wringing wet, my mouth still bleeding. We were grouped along the wall now. The other boys ignored me as they congratulated Tatlock and speculated as to how much they would be paid. One boy whimpered over his smashed hand. Looking up front, I saw attendants in white jackets rolling the portable ring away and placing a small square rug in the vacant space surrounded by chairs. Perhaps, I thought, I will stand on the rug to deliver my speech.

Then the M.C. called to us, "Come on up here boys and get your money."

We ran forward to where the men laughed and talked in their chairs, waiting. Everyone seemed friendly now.

"There it is on the rug," the man said. I saw the rug covered with coins of all dimensions and a few crumpled bills. But what excited me, scattered here and there, were the gold pieces.

"Boys, it's all yours," the man said. "You get all you grab."

"That's right, Sambo," a blond man said, winking at me confidentially.

I trembled with excitement, forgetting my pain. I would get the gold and the bills, I thought. I would use both hands. I would throw my body against the boys nearest me to block them from the gold.

"Get down around the rug now," the man commanded, "and don't anyone touch it until I give the signal."

"This ought to be good," I heard.

As told, we got around the square rug on our knees. Slowly the man raised his freckled hand as we followed it upward with our eyes.

I heard, "These niggers look like they're about to pray!"

Then, "Ready," the man said. "Go!"

I lunged for a yellow coin lying on the blue design of the carpet, touching it and sending a surprised shriek to join those rising around me. I tried frantically to remove my hand but could not let go. A hot, violent force tore through my body, shaking me like a wet rat. The rug was electrified. The hair bristled up on my head as I shook myself free. My muscles jumped, my nerves jangled, writhed. But I saw that this was not stopping the other boys. Laughing in fear and embarrassment, some were holding back and scooping up the coins knocked off by the painful contortions of the others. The men roared above us as we struggled.

"Pick it up, goddamnit, pick it up!" someone called like a bass-voiced parrot. "Go on, get it!"

I crawled rapidly around the floor, picking up the coins, trying to avoid the coppers and to get greenbacks and the gold. Ignoring the shock by laughing, as I brushed the coins off quickly, I discovered that I could contain the electricity — a contradiction, but it works. Then the men began to push us onto the rug. Laughing embarrassedly, we struggled out of their hands and kept after the coins. We were all wet and slippery and hard to hold. Suddenly I saw a boy lifted into the air, glistening with sweat like a circus seal, and dropped, his wet back landing flush upon the charged rug, heard him yell and saw him literally dance upon his back, his elbows beating a frenzied tatoo upon the floor, his muscles twitching like the flesh of a horse stung by many flies. When he finally rolled off, his face was gray and no one stopped him when he ran from the floor amid booming laughter.

"Get the money," the M.C. called. "That's good hard American cash!"

And we snatched and grabbed, snatched and grabbed. I was careful not to come too close to the rug now, and when I felt the hot whiskey breath descend upon me like a cloud of foul air I reached out and grabbed the leg of a chair. It was occupied and I held on desperately.

"Leggo, nigger! Leggo!"

The huge face wavered down to mine as he tried to push me free. But my body was slippery and he was too drunk. It was Mr. Colcord, who owned a chain of movie houses and "entertainment palaces." Each time he grabbed me I slipped out of his hands. It became a real struggle. I feared the rug more than I did the drunk, so I held on, surprising myself for a moment by trying to topple *him* upon the rug. It was such an enormous idea that I found myself actually carrying it out. I tried not to be obvious, yet when I grabbed his leg, trying to tumble him out of the chair, he raised up roaring with laughter, and, looking at me with soberness dead in the eye, kicked me viciously in the chest. The chair leg flew out of my hand. I felt myself going and rolled. It was as though I had rolled through a bed of hot coals. It seemed a whole century would pass before I would roll free, a century in which I was seared through the deepest levels of my body to the fearful breath within me and the breath seared and heated to the point of explosion. It'll all be over in a flash, I thought as I rolled clear. It'll all be over in a flash.

But not yet, the men on the other side were waiting, red faces swollen as though from apoplexy as they bent forward in their chairs. Seeing their fingers coming toward me I rolled away as a fumbled football rolls off the receiver's fingertips, back into the coals. That time I luckily sent the rug sliding out of place and heard the coins ringing against the floor and the boys scuffling to pick them up and the M.C. calling, "All right, boys, that's all. Go get dressed and get your money."

I was limp as a dish rag. My back felt as though it had been beaten with wires.

When we had dressed the M.C. came in and gave us each five dollars, except Tatlock, who got ten for being last in the ring. Then he told us to leave. I was not to get a chance to deliver my speech, I thought. I was going out into the dim alley in despair when I was stopped and told to go back. I returned to the ballroom, where the men were pushing back their chairs and gathering in groups to talk.

The M.C. knocked on a table for quiet. "Gentlemen," he said, "we almost forgot an important part of the program. A most serious part, gentlemen. This boy was brought here to deliver a speech which he made at his graduation yesterday. . . ."

"Bravo!"

"I'm told that he is the smartest boy we've got out there in Greenwood. I'm told that he knows more big words than a pocket-sized dictionary."

Much applause and laughter.

"So now, gentlemen, I want you to give him your attention."

There was still laughter as I faced them, my mouth dry, my eye throbbing. I began slowly, but evidently my throat was tense, because they began shouting, "Louder! Louder!"

"We of the younger generation extol the wisdom of that great leader and educator," I shouted, "who first spoke these flaming words of wisdom: 'A ship lost at sea for many days suddenly sighted a friendly vessel. From the mast of the unfortunate vessel was seen a signal: "Water, water; we die of thirst!" The answer from the friendly vessel came back: "Cast down your bucket where you are." The captain of the distressed vessel, at last heeding the injunction, cast down his bucket, and it came up full of fresh sparkling water from the mouth of the Amazon River.' And like him I say, and in his words, 'To those of my race who depend upon bettering their condition in a foreign land, or who underestimate the importance of cultivating friendly relations with the Southern white man, who is his next-door neighbor, I would say: "Cast down your bucket where you are" — cast it down in making friends in every manly way of the people of all races by whom we are surrounded. . . .'"

I spoke automatically and with such fervor that I did not realize that the men were still talking and laughing until my dry mouth, filling up with blood from the cut, almost strangled me. I coughed, wanting to stop and go to one of the tall brass, sand-filled spittoons to relieve myself, but a few of the men, especially the superintendent, were listening and I was afraid. So I gulped it down, blood, saliva, and all, and continued. (What powers of endurance I had during those days! What enthusiasm! What a belief in the rightness of things!) I spoke even louder in spite of the pain. But still they talked and still they laughed, as though deaf with cotton in dirty ears. So I spoke with greater emotional emphasis. I closed my ears and swallowed blood until I was nauseated. The speech seemed a hundred times as long as before, but I could not leave out a single word. All had to be said, each memorized nuance considered, rendered. Nor was that all. Whenever I uttered a word of three or more syllables a group of voices would yell for me to repeat it. I used the phrase "social responsibility" and they yelled:

"What's the word you say, boy?"

"Social responsibility," I said.

"What?"

"Social . . ."

"Louder."

". . . responsibility."

"More!"

"Respon — "

"Repeat!"

" — sibility."

The room filled with the uproar of laughter until, no doubt, distracted by having to gulp down my blood, I made a mistake and yelled a phrase I had often seen denounced in newspaper editorials, heard debated in private.

"Social . . ."

"What?" they yelled.

". . . equality — "

The laughter hung smokelike in the sudden stillness. I opened my eyes, puzzled. Sounds of displeasure filled the room. The M.C. rushed forward. They shouted hostile phrases at me. But I did not understand.

A small dry mustached man in the front row blared out, "Say that slowly, son!"

"What sir?"

"What you just said!"

"Social responsibility, sir," I said.

"You weren't being smart, were you, boy?" he said, not unkindly.

"No, sir!"

"You sure that about 'equality' was a mistake?"

"Oh, yes, sir," I said. "I was swallowing blood."

"Well, you had better speak more slowly so we can understand. We mean to do right by you, but you've got to know your place at all times. All right, now, go on with your speech."

I was afraid. I wanted to leave but I wanted also to speak and I was afraid they'd snatch me down.

"Thank you, sir," I said, beginning where I had left off, and having them ignore me as before.

Yet when I finished there was a thunderous applause. I was surprised to see the superintendent come forth with a package wrapped in white tissue paper, and, gesturing for quiet, address the men.

"Gentlemen, you see that I did not overpraise this boy. He makes a good speech and some day he'll lead his people in the proper paths. And I don't have to tell you that that is important in these days and times. This is a good, smart boy, and so to encourage him in the right direction, in the name of the Board of Education I wish to present him a prize in the form of this . . ."

He paused, removing the tissue paper and revealing a gleaming calfskin brief case.

"... in the form of this first-class article from Shad Whitmore's shop."

"Boy," he said, addressing me, "take this prize and keep it well. Consider it a badge of office. Prize it. Keep developing as you are and some day it will be filled with important papers that will help shape the destiny of your people."

I was so moved that I could hardly express my thanks. A rope of bloody saliva forming a shape like an undiscovered continent drooled upon the leather and I wiped it quickly away. I felt an importance that I had never dreamed.

"Open it and see what's inside," I was told.

My fingers a-tremble, I complied, smelling the fresh leather and finding an official-looking document inside. It was a scholarship to the state college for Negroes. My eyes filled with tears and I ran awkwardly off the floor.

I was overjoyed; I did not even mind when I discovered that the gold pieces I had scrambled for were brass pocket tokens advertising a certain make of automobile.

When I reached home everyone was excited. Next day the neighbors came to congratulate me. I even felt safe from grandfather, whose deathbed curse usually spoiled my triumphs. I stood beneath his photograph with my brief case in hand and smiled triumphantly into his stolid black peasant's face. It was a face that fascinated me. The eyes seemed to follow everywhere I went.

That night I dreamed I was at a circus with him and that he refused to laugh at the clowns no matter what they did. Then later he told me to open my brief case and read what was inside and I did, finding an official envelope stamped with the state seal; and inside the envelope I found another and another, endlessly, and I thought I would fall of weariness. "Them's years," he said. "Now open that one." And I did and in it I found an engraved document containing a short message in letters of gold. "Read it," my grandfather said. "Out loud."

"To Whom It May Concern," I intoned. "Keep This Nigger-Boy Running."

I awoke with the old man's laughter ringing in my ears.

(It was a dream I was to remember and dream again for many years after. But at the time I had no insight into its meaning. First I had to attend college.)   [1952]

RALPH ELLISON

King of the Bingo Game

The woman in front of him was eating roasted peanuts that smelled so good that he could barely contain his hunger. He could not even sleep and wished they'd hurry and begin the bingo game. There, on his right, two fellows were drinking wine out of a bottle wrapped in a paper bag, and he could hear soft gurgling in the dark. His stomach gave a low, gnawing growl. "If this was down South," he thought, "all I'd have to do is lean over and say, 'Lady, gimme a few of those peanuts, please ma'am,' and she'd pass me the bag and never think nothing of it." Or he could ask the fellows for a drink in the same way. Folks down South stuck together that way; they didn't even have to know you. But up here it was different. Ask somebody for something, and they'd think you were crazy. Well, I ain't crazy. I'm just broke, 'cause I got no birth certificate to get a job, and Laura 'bout to die 'cause we got no money for a doctor. But I ain't crazy. And yet a pinpoint of doubt was focused in his mind as he glanced toward the screen and saw the hero stealthily entering a dark room and sending the beam of a flashlight along a wall of bookcases. This is where he finds the trapdoor, he remembered. The man would pass abruptly through the wall and find the girl tied to a bed, her legs and arms spread wide, and her clothing torn to rags. He laughed softly to himself. He had seen the picture three times, and this was one of the best scenes.

On his right the fellow whispered wide-eyed to his companion, "Man, look a-yonder!"

"Damn!"

"Wouldn't I like to have her tied up like that . . ."

"Hey! That fool's letting her loose!"

"Aw, man, he loves her."

"Love or no love!"

The man moved impatiently beside him, and he tried to involve himself in the scene. But Laura was on his mind. Tiring quickly of watching the picture he looked back to where the white beam filtered from the projection room above the balcony. It started small and grew large, specks of dusk dancing in its whiteness as it reached the screen. It was strange how the beam always landed right on the screen and didn't mess up and fall somewhere else. But they had it all fixed. Everything was fixed. Now suppose when they showed that girl with her dress torn the girl started taking off the rest of her clothes, and when the guy came in he didn't untie her but kept her there and went to taking off his own clothes? *That* would be something to see. If a picture got out of hand like that those guys up there would go nuts. Yeah, and there'd be so many folks in here you couldn't find a seat for nine months! A strange sensation played over his skin. He shuddered. Yesterday he'd seen a bedbug on a woman's neck as they walked out into the bright street. But exploring his thigh through a hole in his pocket he found only goose pimples and old scars.

The bottle gurgled again. He closed his eyes. Now a dreamy music was accompanying the film and train whistles were sounding in the distance, and he was a boy again walking along a railroad trestle down South, and seeing the train coming, and running back as fast as he could go, and hearing the whistle blowing, and getting off the trestle to solid ground just in time, with the earth trembling beneath his feet, and feeling relieved as he ran down the cinder-strewn embankment onto the highway, and looking back and seeing with terror that the train had left the track and was following him right down the middle of the street, and all the white people laughing as he ran screaming . . .

"Wake up there, buddy! What the hell do you mean hollering like that? Can't you see we trying to enjoy this here picture?"

He stared at the man with gratitude.

"I'm sorry, old man," he said. "I musta been dreaming."

"Well, here, have a drink. And don't be making no noise like that, damn!"

His hands trembled as he tilted his head. It was not wine, but whiskey. Cold rye whiskey. He took a deep swoller, decided it was better not to take another, and handed the bottle back to its owner.

"Thanks, old man," he said.

Now he felt the cold whiskey breaking a warm path straight through the middle of him, growing hotter and sharper as it moved. He had not eaten all day, and it made him light-headed. The smell of the peanuts stabbed him like a knife, and he got up and found a seat in the middle aisle. But no sooner did he sit than he saw a row of intense-faced young girls, and got up again, thinking, "You chicks musta been Lindy-hopping somewhere." He found a seat several rows ahead as the lights came on, and he saw the screen disappear behind a heavy red and gold curtain; then the curtain rising, and the man with the microphone and a uniformed attendant coming on the stage.

He felt for his bingo cards, smiling. The guy at the door wouldn't like it if he knew about his having *five* cards. Well, not everyone played the bingo game; and even with five cards he didn't have much of a chance. For Laura, though, he had to have faith. He studied the cards, each with its different numerals, punching the free center hole in each and spreading them neatly across his lap; and when the lights faded he sat slouched in his seat so that he could look from his cards to the bingo wheel with but a quick shifting of his eyes.

Ahead, at the end of the darkness, the man with the microphone was pressing a button attached to a long cord and spinning the bingo wheel and calling out the number each time the wheel came to rest. And each time the voice rang out his finger raced over the cards for the number. With five cards he had to move fast. He became nervous; there were too many cards, and the man went too fast with his grating voice. Perhaps he should just select one and throw the others away. But he was afraid. He became warm. Wonder how much Laura's doctor would cost? Damn that, watch the cards! And with despair he heard the man call three in a row which he missed on all five cards. This way he'd never win . . .

When he saw the row of holes punched across the third card, he sat paralyzed and heard the man call three more numbers before he stumbled forward, screaming,

"Bingo! Bingo!"

"Let that fool up there," someone called.

"Get up there, man!"

He stumbled down the aisle and up the steps to the stage into a light so sharp and bright that for a moment it blinded him, and he felt that he had moved into the spell of some strange, mysterious power. Yet it was as familiar as the sun, and he knew it was the perfectly familiar bingo.

The man with the microphone was saying something to the audience as he held out his card. A cold light flashed from the man's finger as the card left his hand. His knees trembled. The man stepped closer, checking the card against the numbers chalked on the board. Suppose he had made a mistake? The pomade on the man's hair made him feel faint, and he backed away. But the man was checking the card over the microphone now, and he had to stay. He stood tense, listening.

"Under the O, forty-four," the man chanted. "Under the I, seven. Under the G, three. Under the B, ninety-six. Under the N, thirteen!"

His breath came easier as the man smiled at the audience.

"Yessir, ladies and gentlemen, he's one of the chosen people!"

The audience rippled with laughter and applause.

"Step right up to the front of the stage."

He moved slowly forward, wishing that the light was not so bright.

"To win tonight's jackpot of $36.90 the wheel must stop between the double zero, understand?"

He nodded, knowing the ritual from the many days and nights he had watched the winners march across the stage to press the button that controlled the spinning wheel and receive the prizes. And now he followed the instructions as though he'd crossed the slippery stage a million prize-winning times.

The man was making some kind of a joke, and he nodded vacantly. So tense had he become that he felt a sudden desire to cry and shook it away. He felt vaguely that his whole life was determined by the bingo wheel; not only that which would happen now that he was at last before it, but all that had gone before, since his birth, and his mother's birth and the birth of his father. It had always been there, even though he had not been aware of it, handing out the unlucky cards and numbers of his days. The feeling persisted, and he started quickly away. I better get down from here before I make a fool of myself, he thought.

"Here, boy," the man called. "You haven't started yet."

Someone laughed as he went hesitantly back.

"Are you all reet?"

He grinned at the man's jive talk, but no words would come, and he knew it was not a convincing grin. For suddenly he knew that he stood on the slippery brink of some terrible embarrassment.

"Where you from boy?" the man asked.

"Down South."

"He's from down South, ladies and gentlemen," the man said. "Where from? Speak right into the mike."

"Rocky Mont," he said. "Rock' Mont, North Car'lina."

"So you decided to come down off that mountain to the U.S.," the man laughed. He felt that the man was making a fool of him, but then something cold was placed in his hand, and the lights were no longer behind him.

Standing before the wheel he felt alone, but that was somehow right, and he remembered his plan. He would give the wheel a short quick twirl. Just a touch of the button. He had watched it many times, and always it came close to double zero when it was short and quick. He steeled himself; the fear had left, and he felt a profound sense of promise, as though he were about to be repaid for all the things he'd suffered all his life. Trembling, he pressed the button. There was a whirl of lights, and in a second he realized with finality that though he wanted to, he could not stop. It was as though he held a high-powered line in his naked hand. His nerves tightened. As the wheel increased its speed it seemed to draw him more and more into its power, as though it held his fate; and with it came a deep need to submit, to whirl, to lose himself in its swirl of color. He could not stop it now, he knew. So let it be.

The button rested snugly in his palm where the man had placed it. And now he became aware of the man beside him, advising him through the microphone, while behind the shadowy audience hummed with noisy voices. He shifted his feet. There was still that feeling of helplessness within him, making part of him desire to turn back, even now that the jackpot was right in his hand. He squeezed the button until his fist ached. Then, like the sudden shriek of a subway whistle, a doubt tore through his head. Suppose he did not spin the wheel long enough? What could he do, and how could he tell? And then he knew, even as he wondered, that as long as he pressed the button, he could control the jackpot. He and only he could determine whether or not it was to be his. Not even the man with the microphone could do anything about it now. He felt drunk. Then, as though he had come down from a high hill into a valley of people, he heard the audience yelling.

"Come down from there, you jerk!"

"Let somebody else have a chance. . . ."

"Ole Jack thinks he done found the end of the rainbow. . . ."

The last voice was not unfriendly, and he turned and smiled dreamily into the yelling mouths. Then he turned his back squarely on them.

"Don't take too long, boy," a voice said.

He nodded. They were yelling behind him. Those folks did not understand what had happened to him. They had been playing the bingo game day and night for years, trying to win rent money or hamburger change. But not one of those wise guys had discovered this wonderful thing. He watched the wheel whirling past the numbers and experienced a burst of exaltation: This is God! This is the really truly God! He said it aloud, "This is God!"

He said it with such absolute conviction that he feared he would fall fainting into the footlights. But the crowd yelled so loud that they could not hear. These fools, he thought. I'm here trying to tell them the most wonderful secret in the world, and they're yelling like they gone crazy. A hand fell upon his shoulder.

"You'll have to make a choice now, boy. You've taken too long."

He brushed the hand violently away.

"Leave me alone, man. I know what I'm doing!"

The man looked surprised and held on to the microphone for support. And because he did not wish to hurt the man's feelings he smiled, realizing with a sudden pang that there was no way of explaining to the man just why he had to stand there pressing the button forever.

"Come here," he called tiredly.

The man approached, rolling the heavy microphone across the stage.

"Anybody can play this bingo game, right?" he said.

"Sure, but . . ."

He smiled, feeling inclined to be patient with this slick looking white man with his blue sport shirt and his sharp gabardine suit.

"That's what I thought," he said. "Anybody can win the jackpot as long as they get the lucky number, right?"

"That's the rule, but after all . . ."

"That's what I thought," he said. "And the big prize goes to the man who knows how to win it?"

The man nodded speechlessly.

"Well, then, go on over there and watch me win like I want to. I ain't going to hurt nobody," he said, "and I'll show you how to win. I mean to show the whole world how it's got to be done."

And because he understood, he smiled again to let the man know that he held nothing against him for being white and impatient. Then he refused to see the man any longer and stood pressing the button, the voices of the crowd reaching him like sounds in distant streets. Let them yell. All the Negroes down there were just ashamed because he was black like them. He smiled inwardly, knowing how it was. Most of the time he was ashamed of what Negroes did himself. Well, let them be ashamed for something this time. Like him. He was like a long thin black wire that was being stretched and wound upon the bingo wheel; wound until he wanted to scream; wound, but this time himself controlling the winding and the sadness and the shame, and because he did, Laura would be all right. Suddenly the lights flickered. He staggered backwards. Had something gone wrong? All this noise. Didn't they know that although he controlled the wheel, it also controlled him, and unless he pressed the button forever and forever and ever it would stop, leaving him high and dry, dry and high on this hard high slippery hill and Laura dead? There was only one chance; he had to do whatever the wheel demanded. And gripping the button in despair, he discovered with surprise that it imparted a nervous energy. His spine tingled. He felt a certain power.

Now he faced the raging crowd with defiance, its screams penetrating his eardrums like trumpets shrieking from a juke-box. The vague faces growing in the bingo lights gave him a sense of himself that he had never known before. He was running the show, by God! They had to read to him, for he was their luck. This is *me*, he thought. Let the bastards yell. Then someone was laughing inside him, and he realized that somehow he had forgotten his own name. It was a sad, lost feeling to lose your name, and a crazy thing to do. That name had been given him by the white man who had owned his grandfather a long time ago down South. But maybe those wise guys knew his name.

"Who am I?" he screamed.

"Hurry up and bingo, you jerk!"

They didn't know either, he thought sadly. They didn't even know their own names, they were all poor nameless bastards. Well, he didn't need that old name; he was reborn. For as long as he pressed the button he was The-man-who-pressed-the-button-who-held-the-prize-who-was-the-King-of-Bingo. That was the way it was, and he'd have to press the button even if nobody understood, even though Laura did not understand.

"Live!" he shouted.

The audience quited like the dying of a huge fan.

"Live, Laura, baby. I got holt of it now, sugar. Live!"

He screamed it, tears streaming down his face. "I got nobody but you!"

The screams tore from his very guts. He felt as though the rush of blood to his head would burst out in baseball seams of small red droplets, like a head beaten by police clubs. Bending over he saw a trickle of blood splashing the toe of his shoe. With his free hand he searched his head. It was his nose. God, suppose something has gone wrong? He felt that the whole audience had somehow entered him and was stamping its feet in his stomach and he was unable to throw them out. They wanted the prize, that was it. They wanted the secret for themselves. But they'd never get it; he would keep the bingo wheel whirling forever, and Laura would be safe in the wheel. But would she? It had to be, because if she were not safe the wheel would cease to turn; it could not go on. He had to get away, *vomit* all, and his mind formed an image of himself running with Laura in his arms down the tracks of the subway just ahead of an A train, running desperately *vomit* with people screaming for him to come out but knowing no way of leaving the tracks because to stop would bring the train crushing down upon him and to attempt to leave across the other tracks would mean to run into a hot third rail as high as his waist which threw blue sparks that blinded his eyes until he could hardly see.

He heard singing and the audience was clapping its hands.

> Shoot the liquor to him, Jim, boy!
> Clap-clap-clap
> Well a-calla the cop
> He's blowing his top!
> Shoot the liquor to him, Jim, boy!

Bitter anger grew within him at the singing. They think I'm crazy. Well let 'em laugh. I'll do what I got to do.

He was standing in an attitude of intense listening when he saw that they were watching something on the stage behind him. He felt weak. But when he turned he saw no one. If only his thumb did not ache so. Now they were applauding. And for a moment he thought that the wheel had stopped. But that was impossible, his thumb still pressed the button. Then he saw them. Two men in uniform beckoned from the end of the stage. They were coming toward him, walking in step, slowly, like a tap-dance team returning for a third encore. But their shoulders shot forward, and he backed away, looking wildly about. There was nothing to fight them with. He had only the long black cord which led to a plug somewhere back stage, and he couldn't use that because it operated the bingo wheel. He backed slowly, fixing the men with his eyes as his lips stretched over his teeth in a tight, fixed grin; moved toward the end of the stage and realizing that he couldn't go much further, for suddenly the cord became taut and he couldn't afford to break the cord. But he had to do something. The audience was howling. Suddenly he stopped dead, seeing the men halt, their legs lifted as in an interrupted step of a slow-motion dance. There was nothing to do but run in the other direction and he dashed forward, slipping and sliding. The men fell back, surprised. He struck out violently going past.

"Grab him!"

He ran, but all too quickly the cord tightened, resistingly, and he turned and ran back again. This time he slipped them, and discovered by running in a circle before the wheel he could keep the cord from tightening. But this way he had to flail his arms to keep the men away. Why couldn't they leave a man alone? He ran, circling.

"Ring down the curtain," someone yelled. But they couldn't do that. If they did the wheel flashing from the projection room would be cut off. But they had him before he could tell them so, trying to pry open his fist, and he was wrestling and trying to bring his knees into the fight and holding on to the button, for it was his life. And now he was down, seeing a foot coming down, crushing his wrist cruelly, down, as he saw the wheel whirling serenely above.

"I can't give it up," he screamed. Then quietly, in a confidential tone, "Boys, I really can't give it up."

It landed hard against his head. And in the blank moment they had it away from him, completely now. He fought them trying to pull him up from the stage as he watched the wheel spin slowly to a stop. Without surprise he saw it rest at double-zero.

"You see," he pointed bitterly.

"Sure, boy, sure, it's O.K.," one of the men said smiling.

And seeing the man bow his head to someone he could not see, he felt very, very happy; he would receive what all the winners received.

But as he warmed in the justice of the man's tight smile he did not see the man's slow wink, nor see the bow-legged man behind him step clear of the swiftly descending curtain and set himself for a blow. He only felt the dull pain exploding in his skull, and he knew even as it slipped out of him that his luck had run out on the stage.   [1944]

LOUISE ERDRICH *(b. 1954) is of German and Chippewa Indian descent. She grew up in Wahpeton, North Dakota, as a member of the Turtle Mountain Band of Chippewa. For many years her grandfather was tribal chair of the reservation. At Dartmouth College, Erdrich won several prizes for her fiction and poetry, including the American Academy of Poets Prize. After graduating in 1976, she returned to North Dakota, where she taught in the Poetry in the Schools Program. In 1979 she received her M.A. in creative writing from Johns Hopkins University. Erdrich is married to Michael Dorris, a professor of Native American studies at Dartmouth College who is also a writer. They collaborated on the novel* The Crown of Columbus *(1992).*

Erdrich has been an editor of the Boston Indian Council newspaper, The Circle. *Her stories have appeared in* Redbook, *the* New England Review, *and* Mississippi Valley Review *and have been included in* Earth Power Coming, *an anthology of Native American literature, as well as* That's What She Said: Contemporary Poetry and Fiction by Native American Women. *In 1984 a collection of her poetry,* Jacklight, *was published and her first work of fiction,* Love Medicine, *won the National Book Critics Circle Award. Recent novels continuing the* Love Medicine *series of stories are* Beet Queen *(1986) and* Tracks *(1988), which involve the parents and grandparents of characters in the first novel, and* The Bingo Palace *(1994).*

"The Red Convertible" is a chapter from Love Medicine. *Each chapter is a self-enclosed narrative that also functions as a separate short story about the lives of two families, the Kashpaws and the Lamartines, on a North Dakota reservation between 1934 and 1984. "The Red Convertible" takes place in 1974.*

Erdrich's work has won praise for its psychological depth and its literary excellence; it is a landmark achievement in its depiction of the lives of contemporary Native Americans. As the novelist Peter Matthiessen has recognized, Love Medicine *is "quick with agile prose, taut speech, poetry, and power, conveying unflinchingly the funkiness, humor, and great unspoken sadness of the Indian reservations, and a people exiled to a no-man's-land between two worlds."*

LOUISE ERDRICH

The Red Convertible

Lyman Lamartine

I was the first one to drive a convertible on my reservation. And of course it was red, a red Olds. I owned that car along with my brother Henry Junior. We owned it together until his boots filled with water on a windy night and he bought out my share. Now Henry owns the whole car, and his younger brother Lyman (that's myself), Lyman walks everywhere he goes.

How did I earn enough money to buy my share in the first place? My own talent was I could always make money. I had a touch for it, unusual in a Chippewa. From the first I was different that way, and everyone recognized it. I was the only kid they let in the American Legion Hall to shine shoes, for example, and one Christmas I sold spiritual bouquets for the mission door to door. The nuns let me keep a percentage. Once I started, it seemed the more money I made the easier the money came. Everyone encouraged it. When I was fifteen I got a job washing dishes at the Joliet Café, and that was where my first big break happened.

It wasn't long before I was promoted to busing tables, and then the short-order cook quit and I was hired to take her place. No sooner than you know it I was managing the Joliet. The rest is history. I went on managing. I soon became part owner, and of course there was no stopping me then. It wasn't long before the whole thing was mine.

After I'd owned the Joliet for one year, it blew over in the worst tornado ever seen around here. The whole operation was smashed to bits. A total loss. The fryalator was up in a tree, the grill torn in half like it was paper. I was only sixteen. I had it all in my mother's name, and I lost it quick, but before I lost it I had every one of my relatives, and their relatives, to dinner, and I also bought that red Olds I mentioned, along with Henry.

The first time we saw it! I'll tell you when we first saw it. We had gotten a ride up to Winnipeg, and both of us had money. Don't ask me why, because we never mentioned a car or anything, we just had all our money. Mine was cash, a big bankroll from the Joliet's insurance. Henry had two checks — a week's extra pay for being laid off, and his regular check from the Jewel Bearing Plant.

We were walking down Portage anyway, seeing the sights, when we saw it. There it was, parked, large as life. Really as *if* it was alive. I thought of the word *repose*, because the car wasn't simply stopped, parked, or whatever. That car reposed, calm and gleaming, a FOR SALE sign in its left front window. Then, before we had thought it over at all, the car belonged to us and our pockets were empty. We had just enough money for gas back home.

We went places in that car, me and Henry. We took off driving all one whole summer. We started off toward the Little Knife River and Mandaree in Fort Berthold and then we found ourselves down in Wakpala somehow, and then suddenly we were over in Montana on the Rocky Boy, and yet the summer was not even half over. Some people hang on to details when they travel, but we didn't let them bother us and just lived our everyday lives here to there.

I do remember this one place with willows. I remember I laid under those trees and it was comfortable. So comfortable. The branches bent down all around me like a tent or a stable. And quiet, it was quiet, even though there was a powwow close enough so I could see it going on. The air was not too still, not too windy either. When the dust rises up and hangs in the air around the dancers like that, I feel good. Henry was asleep with his arms thrown wide. Later on, he woke up and we started driving again. We were somewhere in Montana, or maybe on the Blood Reserve — it could have been anywhere. Anyway it was where we met the girl.

All her hair was in buns around her ears, that's the first thing I noticed about her. She was posed alongside the road with her arm out, so we stopped. That girl was short, so short her lumber shirt looked comical on her, like a nightgown. She had jeans on and fancy moccasins and she carried a little suitcase.

"Hop on in," says Henry. So she climbs in between us.

"We'll take you home," I says. "Where do you live?"

"Chicken," she says.

"Where the hell's that?" I ask her.

"Alaska."

"Okay," says Henry, and we drive.

We got up there and never wanted to leave. The sun doesn't truly set there in summer, and the night is more a soft dusk. You might doze off, sometimes, but before you know it you're up again, like an animal in nature. You never feel like you have to sleep hard or put away the world. And things would grow up there. One day just dirt or moss, the next day flowers and long grass. The girl's name was Susy. Her family really took to us. They fed us and put us up. We had our own tent to live in by their house, and the kids would be in and out of there all day and night. They couldn't get over me and Henry being brothers, we looked so different. We told them we knew we had the same mother, anyway.

One night Susy came in to visit us. We sat around in the tent talking of this and that. The season was changing. It was getting darker by that time, and the cold was even getting just a little mean. I told her it was time for us to go. She stood up on a chair.

"You never seen my hair," Susy said.

That was true. She was standing on a chair, but still, when she unclipped her buns the hair reached all the way to the ground. Our eyes opened. You couldn't tell how much hair she had when it was rolled up so neatly. Then my brother Henry did something funny. He went up to the chair and said, "Jump on my shoulders." So she did that, and her hair reached down past his waist, and he started twirling, this way and that, so her hair was flung out from side to side.

"I always wondered what it was like to have long pretty hair," Henry says. Well we laughed. It was a funny sight, the way he did it. The next morning we got up and took leave of those people.

On to greener pastures, as they say. It was down through Spokane and across Idaho then Montana and very soon we were racing the weather right along under the Canadian border through Columbus, Des Lacs, and then we were in Bottineau County and soon home. We'd made most of the trip, that summer, without putting up the car hood at all. We got home just in time, it turned out, for the army to remember Henry had signed up to join it.

I don't wonder that the army was so glad to get my brother that they turned him into a Marine. He was built like a brick outhouse anyway. We liked to tease him that they really wanted him for his Indian nose. He had a nose big and sharp as a hatchet, like the nose on Red Tomahawk, the Indian who killed Sitting Bull, whose profile is on signs all along the North Dakota highways. Henry went off to training camp, came home once during Christmas, then the next thing you know we got an overseas letter from him. It was 1970, and he said he was stationed up in the northern hill country. Whereabouts I did not know. He wasn't such a hot letter writer, and only got off two before the enemy caught him. I could never keep it straight, which direction those good Vietnam soldiers were from.

I wrote him back several times, even though I didn't know if those letters would get through. I kept him informed all about the car. Most of the time I had it up on blocks in the yard or half taken apart, because that long trip did a hard job on it under the hood.

I always had good luck with numbers, and never worried about the draft myself. I never even had to think about what my number was. But Henry was never lucky in the same way as me. It was at least three years before Henry came home. By then I guess the whole war was solved in the government's mind, but for him it would keep on going. In those years I'd put his car into almost perfect shape. I always thought of it as his car while he was gone, even though when he left he said, "Now it's yours," and threw me his key.

"Thanks for the extra key," I'd said. "I'll put it up in your drawer just in case I need it." He laughed.

When he came home, though, Henry was very different, and I'll say this: the change was no good. You could hardly expect him to change for the better, I know. But he was quiet, so quiet, and never comfortable sitting still anywhere but always up and moving around. I thought back to times we'd sat still for whole afternoons, never moving a muscle, just shifting our weight along the ground, talking to whoever sat with us, watching things. He'd always had a joke, then, too, and now you couldn't get him to laugh, or when he did it was more the sound of a man choking, a sound that stopped up the throats of other people around him. They got to leaving him alone most of the time, and I didn't blame them. It was a fact: Henry was jumpy and mean.

I'd bought a color TV set for my mom and the rest of us while Henry was away. Money still came very easy. I was sorry I'd ever bought it though, because of Henry. I was also sorry I'd bought color, because with black-and-white the pictures seem older and farther away. But what are you going to do? He sat in front of it, watching it, and that was the only time he was completely still. But it was the kind of stillness that you see in a rabbit when it freezes and before it will bolt. He was not easy. He sat in his chair gripping the armrests with all his might, as if the chair itself was moving at a high speed and if he let go at all he would rocket forward and maybe crash right through the set.

Once I was in the room watching TV with Henry and I heard his teeth click at something. I looked over, and he'd bitten through his lip. Blood was going down his chin. I tell you right then I wanted to smash that tube to pieces. I went over to it but Henry must have known what I was up to. He rushed from his chair and shoved me out of the way, against the wall. I told myself he didn't know what he was doing.

My mom came in, turned the set off real quiet, and told us she had made something for supper. So we went and sat down. There was still blood going down Henry's chin, but he didn't notice it and no one said anything, even though every time he took a bit of his bread his blood fell onto it until he was eating his own blood mixed in with the food.

While Henry was not around we talked about what was going to happen to him. There were no Indian doctors on the reservation, and my mom was afraid of trusting the old man, Moses Pillager, because he courted her long ago and was jealous of her husbands. He might take revenge through her son. We were afraid that if we brought Henry to a regular hospital they would keep him.

"They don't fix them in those places," Mom said; "they just give them drugs."

"We wouldn't get him there in the first place," I agreed, "so let's just forget about it."

Then I thought about the car.

Henry had not even looked at the car since he'd gotten home, though like I said, it was in tip-top condition and ready to drive. I thought the car might bring the old Henry back somehow. So I bided my time and waited for my chance to interest him in the vehicle.

One night Henry was off somewhere. I took myself a hammer. I went out to that car and I did a number on its underside. Whacked it up. Bent the tail pipe double. Ripped the muffler loose. By the time I was done with the car it looked worse than any typical Indian car that has been driven all its life on reservation roads, which they always say are like government promises — full of holes. It just about hurt me, I'll tell you that! I threw dirt in the carburetor and I ripped all the electric tape off the seats. I made it look just as beat up as I could. Then I sat back and waited for Henry to find it.

Still, it took him over a month. That was all right, because it was just getting warm enough, not melting, but warm enough to work outside.

"Lyman," he says, walking in one day, "that red car looks like shit."

"Well it's old," I says. "You got to expect that."

"No way!" says Henry. "That car's a classic! But you went and ran the piss right out of it, Lyman, and you know it don't deserve that. I kept that car in A-one shape. You don't remember. You're too young. But when I left, that car was running like a watch. Now I don't even know if I can get it to start again, let alone get it anywhere near its old condition."

"Well you try," I said, like I was getting mad, "but I say it's a piece of junk."

Then I walked out before he could realize I knew he'd strung together more than six words at once.

After that I thought he'd freeze himself to death working on that car. He was out there all day, and at night he rigged up a little lamp, ran a cord out the window, and had himself some light to see by while he worked. He was better than he had been before, but that's still not saying much. It was easier for him to do the things the rest of us did. He ate more slowly and didn't jump up and down during the meal to get this or that or look out the window. I put my hand in the back of the TV set, I admit, and fiddled around with it good, so that it was almost impossible now to get a clear picture. He didn't look at it very often anyway. He was always out with that car or going off to get parts for it. By the time it was really melting outside, he had it fixed.

I had been feeling down in the dumps about Henry around this time. We had always been together before. Henry and Lyman. But he was such a loner now that I didn't know how to take it. So I jumped at the chance one day when Henry seemed friendly. It's not that he smiled or anything. He just said, "Let's take that old shitbox for a spin." Just the way he said it made me think he could be coming around.

We went out to the car. It was spring. The sun was shining very bright. My only sister, Bonita, who was just eleven years old, came out and made us stand together for a picture. Henry leaned his elbow on the red car's windshield, and he took his other arm and put it over my shoulder, very carefully, as though it was heavy for him to lift and he didn't want to bring the weight down all at once.

"Smile," Bonita said, and he did.

That picture, I never look at it anymore. A few months ago, I don't know why, I got his picture out and tacked it on the wall. I felt good about Henry at the time, close to him. I felt good having his picture on the wall, until one night when I was looking at television. I was a little drunk and stoned. I looked up at the wall and Henry was staring at me. I don't know what it was, but his smile had changed, or maybe it was gone. All I know is I couldn't stay in the same room with that picture. I was shaking. I got up, closed the door, and went into the kitchen. A little later my friend Ray came over and we both went back into that room. We put the picture in a brown bag, folded the bag over and over tightly, then put it way back in a closet.

I still see that picture now, as if it tugs at me, whenever I pass that closet door. The picture is very clear in my mind. It was so sunny that day Henry had to squint against the glare. Or maybe the camera Bonita held flashed like a mirror, blinding him, before she snapped the picture. My face is right out in the sun, big and round. But he might have drawn back, because the shadows on his face are deep as holes. There are two shadows curved like little hooks around the ends of his smile, as if to frame it and try to keep it there — that one, first smile that looked like it might have hurt his face. He has his field jacket on and the worn-in clothes he'd come back in and kept wearing ever since. After Bonita took the picture, she went into the house and we got into the car. There was a full cooler in the trunk. We started off, east, toward Pembina and the Red River because Henry said he wanted to see the high water.

The trip over there was beautiful. When everything starts changing, drying up, clearing off, you feel like your whole life is starting. Henry felt it, too. The top was down and the car hummed like a top. He'd really put it back in shape, even the tape on the seats was very carefully put down and glued back in layers. It's not that he smiled again or even joked, but his face looked to me as if it was clear, more peaceful. It looked as though he wasn't thinking of anything in particular except the bare fields and windbreaks and houses we were passing.

The river was high and full of winter trash when we got there. The sun was still out, but it was colder by the river. There were still little clumps of dirty snow here and there on the banks. The water hadn't gone over the banks yet, but it would, you could tell. It was just at its limit, hard swollen glossy like an old gray scar. We made ourselves a fire, and we sat down and watched the current go. As I watched it I felt something squeezing inside me and tightening and trying to let go all at the same time. I knew I was not just feeling it myself; I knew I was feeling what Henry was going through at that moment. Except that I couldn't stand it, the closing and opening. I jumped to my feet. I took Henry by the shoulders and I started shaking him. "Wake up," I says, "wake up, wake up, wake up!" I didn't know what had come over me. I sat down beside him again.

His face was totally white and hard. Then it broke, like stones break all of a sudden when water boils up inside them.

"I know it," he says. "I know it. I can't help it. It's no use."

We start talking. He said he knew what I'd done with the car. It was obvious it had been whacked out of shape and not just neglected. He said he wanted to give the car to me for good now, it was no use. He said he'd fixed it just to give it back and I should take it.

"No way," I says, "I don't want it."

"That's okay," he says, "you take it."

"I don't want it, though," I says back to him, and then to emphasize, just to emphasize, you understand, I touch his shoulder. He slaps my hand off.

"Take that car," he says.

"No," I say. "Make me," I say, and then he grabs my jacket and rips the arm loose. That jacket is a class act, suede with tags and zippers. I push Henry backwards, off the log. He jumps up and bowls me over. We go down in a clinch and come up swinging hard, for all we're worth, with our fists. He socks my jaw so hard I feel like it swings loose. Then I'm at his rib cage and land a good one under his chin so his head snaps back. He's dazzled. He looks at me and I look at him and then his eyes are full of tears and blood and at first I think he's crying. But no, he's laughing. "Ha! Ha!" he says. "Ha! Ha! Take good care of it."

"Okay," I says, "okay, no problem. Ha! Ha!"

I can't help it, and I start laughing, too. My face feels fat and strange, and after a while I get a beer from the cooler in the trunk, and when I hand it to Henry he takes his shirt and wipes my germs off. "Hoof-and-mouth disease," he says. For some reason this cracks me up, and so we're really laughing for a while, and then we drink all the rest of the beers one by one and throw them in the river and see how far, how fast, the current takes them before they fill up and sink.

"You want to go on back?" I ask after a while. "Maybe we could snag a couple nice Kashpaw girls."

He says nothing. But I can tell his mood is turning again.

"They're all crazy, the girls up here, every damn one of them."

"You're crazy too," I say, to jolly him up. "Crazy Lamartine boys!"

He looks as though he will take this wrong at first. His face twists, then clears, and he jumps up on his feet. "That's right!" he says. "Crazier 'n hell. Crazy Indians!"

I think it's the old Henry again. He throws off his jacket and starts swinging his legs out from the knees like a fancy dancer. He's down doing something between a grass dance and a bunny hop, no kind of dance I ever saw before, but neither has anyone else on all this green growing earth. He's wild. He wants to pitch whoopee! He's up and at me and all over. All this time I'm laughing so hard, so hard my belly is getting tied up in a knot.

"Got to cool me off!" he shouts all of a sudden. Then he runs over to the river and jumps in.

There's boards and other things in the current. It's so high. No sound comes from the river after the splash he makes, so I run right over. I look around. It's getting dark. I see he's halfway across the water already, and I know he didn't swim there but the current took him. It's far. I hear his voice, though, very clearly across it.

"My boots are filling," he says.

He says this in a normal voice, like he just noticed and he doesn't know what to think of it. Then he's gone. A branch comes by. Another branch. And I go in.

By the time I get out of the river, off the snag I pulled myself onto, the sun is down. I walk back to the car, turn on the high beams, and drive it up the bank. I put it in first gear and then I take my foot off the clutch. I get out, close the door, and watch it plow softly into the water. The headlights reach in as they go down, searching, still lighted even after the water swirls over the back end. I wait. The wires short out. It is all finally dark. And then there is only the water, the sound of it going and running and going and running and running.   [1984]

WILLIAM FAULKNER *(1897–1962) was born in New Albany, Mississippi, into an old southern family. When he was a child, his parents moved to the isolated town of Oxford, Mississippi, and except for his service in World War I and some time in New Orleans and Hollywood, he spent the rest of his life there. "I discovered my own little postage stamp of native soil was worth writing about, and that I would never live long enough to exhaust it." His literary career began in New Orleans, where he lived for six months and wrote newspaper sketches and stories for the* Times-Picayune. *He met Sherwood Anderson in New Orleans, and Anderson helped him publish his first novel,* Soldier's Pay, *in 1926. Faulkner's major work was written in the late 1920s and the 1930s, when he created an imaginary county adjacent to Oxford, calling it Yoknapatawpha County and chronicling its history in a series of experimental novels, including* The Sound and the Fury *(1929),* As I Lay Dying *(1930),* Sanctuary *(1931),* Light in August *(1932),* Absalom, Absalom! *(1936), and* The Hamlet *(1940). In these works he showed himself to be a writer of genius, although "a willfully and perversely chaotic one," as Jorge Luis Borges noted, whose "labyrinthine world" required a no less labyrinthine prose technique to describe in epic manner the disintegration of the South through many generations. Faulkner was awarded the Nobel Prize for Literature in 1952.*

Faulkner experimented with using a child's point of view in "That Evening Sun," but he rarely included poetic imagery or stream-of-consciousness narration in his stories, which he wrote, he often said, to help him pay his rent. His biographer Frederick Karl has noted that he used short fiction "as a means of working through, or toward, larger ideas." He wrote nearly a hundred stories, often revising them later to fit as sections into a novel. Four books of his stories were published in his lifetime, and Faulkner thought of each as a collection possessing a discernible internal organization. He wrote his editor Malcolm Cowley that "even to a collection of short stories, form, integration, is as important as to a novel — an entity of its own, single, set for one pitch, contrapuntal in integration, toward one end, one finale."

Although some readers found symbolism in "A Rose for Emily" that suggested he was implying a battle between the North (the character Homer Barron) and the South (Miss Emily herself), Faulkner denied a schematic interpretation. He said he had intended to write a ghost story, and "I think that the writer is too busy trying to create flesh-and-blood people that will stand up and cast a shadow to have time to be conscious of all the symbolism that he may put into what he does or what people may read into it."

RELATED COMMENTARY: *William Faulkner, "The Meaning of 'A Rose for Emily,'" page 1416.*

WILLIAM FAULKNER

A Rose for Emily

I

When Miss Emily Grierson died, our whole town went to her funeral: the men through a sort of respectful affection for a fallen monument, the women mostly out of curiosity to see the inside of her house, which no one save an old manservant — a combined gardener and cook — had seen in at least ten years.

It was a big, squarish frame house that had once been white, decorated with cupolas and spires and scrolled balconies in the heavily lightsome style of the seventies, set on what had once been our most select street. But garages and cotton gins had encroached and obliterated even the august names of that neighborhood; only Miss Emily's house was left, lifting its stubborn and coquettish decay above the cotton wagons and the gasoline pumps — an eyesore among eyesores. And now Miss Emily had gone to join the representatives of those august names where they lay in the cedar-bemused cemetery among the ranked and anonymous graves of Union and Confederate soldiers who fell at the battle of Jefferson.

Alive, Miss Emily had been a tradition, a duty, and a care; a sort of hereditary obligation upon the town, dating from that day in 1894 when Colonel Sartoris, the mayor — he who fathered the edict that no Negro woman should appear on the streets without an apron — remitted her taxes, the dispensation dating from the death of her father on into perpetuity. Not that Miss Emily would have accepted charity. Colonel Sartoris invented an involved tale to the effect that Miss Emily's father had loaned money to the town, which the town, as a matter of business, preferred this way of repaying. Only a man of Colonel Sartoris' generation and thought could have invented it, and only a woman could have believed it.

When the next generation, with its more modern ideas, became mayors and aldermen, this arrangement created some little dissatisfaction. On the first of the year they mailed her a tax notice. February came, and there was no reply. They wrote her a formal letter, asking her to call at the sheriff's office at her convenience. A week later the mayor wrote her himself, offering to call or to send his car for her, and received in reply a note on paper of an archaic shape, in a thin, flowing calligraphy in faded ink, to the effect that she no longer went out at all. The tax notice was also enclosed, without comment.

They called a special meeting of the Board of Aldermen. A deputation waited upon her, knocked at the door through which no visitor had passed since she ceased giving china-painting lessons eight or ten years earlier. They were admitted by the old Negro into a dim hall from which a stairway mounted into still more shadow. It smelled of dust and disuse — a close, dank smell. The Negro led them into the parlor. It was furnished in heavy, leather-covered furniture. When the Negro opened the blinds of one window, they could see that the leather was cracked; and when they sat down, a faint dust rose sluggishly about their thighs, spinning with slow motes in the single sun-ray. On a tarnished gilt easel before the fireplace stood a crayon portrait of Miss Emily's father.

They rose when she entered — a small, fat woman in black, with a thin gold chain descending to her waist and vanishing into her belt, leaning on an ebony cane with a tarnished gold head. Her skeleton was small and spare; perhaps that was why what would have been merely plumpness in another was obesity in her. She looked bloated, like a body long submerged in motionless water, and of that pallid hue. Her eyes, lost in the fatty ridges of her face, looked like two small pieces of coal pressed into a lump of dough as they moved from one face to another while the visitors stated their errand.

She did not ask them to sit. She just stood in the door and listened quietly until the spokesman came to a stumbling halt. Then they could hear the invisible watch ticking at the end of the gold chain.

Her voice was dry and cold. "I have no taxes in Jefferson. Colonel Sartoris explained it to me. Perhaps one of you can gain access to the city records and satisfy yourselves."

"But we have. We are the city authorities, Miss Emily. Didn't you get a notice from the sheriff, signed by him?"

"I received a paper, yes," Miss Emily said. "Perhaps he considers himself the sheriff. . . . I have no taxes in Jefferson."

"But there is nothing on the books to show that, you see. We must go by the — "

"See Colonel Sartoris. I have no taxes in Jefferson."

"But, Miss Emily — "

"See Colonel Sartoris." (Colonel Sartoris had been dead almost ten years.) "I have no taxes in Jefferson. Tobe!" The Negro appeared. "Show these gentlemen out."

II

So she vanquished them, horse and foot, just as she had vanquished their fathers thirty years before about the smell. That was two years after her father's death and a short time after her sweetheart — the one we believed would marry her — had deserted her. After her father's death she went out very little; after her sweetheart went away, people hardly saw her at all. A few of the ladies had the temerity to call, but were not received, and the only sign of life about the place was the Negro man — a young man then — going in and out with a market basket.

"Just as if a man — any man — could keep a kitchen properly," the ladies said; so they were not surprised when the smell developed. It was another link between the gross, teeming world and the high and mighty Griersons.

A neighbor, a woman, complained to the mayor, Judge Stevens, eighty years old.

"But what will you have me do about it, madam?" he said.

"Why, send her word to stop it," the woman said. "Isn't there a law?"

"I'm sure that won't be necessary," Judge Stevens said. "It's probably just a snake or a rat that nigger of hers killed in the yard. I'll speak to him about it."

The next day he received two more complaints, one from a man who came in diffident deprecation. "We really must do something about it, Judge. I'd be the last one in the world to bother Miss Emily, but we've got to do something." That night the Board of Aldermen met — three graybeards and one younger man, a member of the rising generation.

"It's simple enough," he said. "Send her word to have her place cleaned up. Give her a certain time to do it in, and if she don't. . . ."

"Dammit, sir," Judge Stevens said, "will you accuse a lady to her face of smelling bad?"

So the next night, after midnight, four men crossed Miss Emily's lawn and slunk about the house like burglars, sniffing along the base of the brick-work and at the cellar openings while one of them performed a regular sowing motion with his hand out of a sack slung from his shoulder. They broke open the cellar door and sprinkled lime there, and in all the outbuild-ings. As they recrossed the lawn, a window that had been dark was lighted and Miss Emily sat in it, the light behind her, and her upright torso motionless as that of an idol. They crept quietly across the lawn and into the shadow of the locusts that lined the street. After a week or two the smell went away.

That was when people had begun to feel really sorry for her. People in our town, remembering how old lady Wyatt, her great-aunt, had gone com-pletely crazy at last, believed that the Griersons held themselves a little too high for what they really were. None of the young men were quite good enough for Miss Emily and such. We had long thought of them as a tableau, Miss Emily a slender figure in white in the background, her father a spraddled silhouette in the foreground, his back to her and clutching a horsewhip, the two of them framed by the backflung front door. So when she got to be thirty and was still single, we were not pleased exactly, but vindicated; even with insanity in the family she wouldn't have turned down all of her chances if they had really materialized.

When her father died, it got about that the house was all that was left to her; and in a way, people were glad. At last they could pity Miss Emily. Being left alone, and a pauper, she had become humanized. Now she too would know the old thrill and the old despair of a penny more or less.

The day after his death all the ladies prepared to call at the house and offer condolence and aid, as is our custom. Miss Emily met them at the door, dressed as usual and with no trace of grief on her face. She told them that her father was not dead. She did that for three days, with the ministers calling on her, and the doctors, trying to persuade her to let them dispose of the body. Just as they were about to resort to law and force, she broke down, and they buried her father quickly.

We did not say she was crazy then. We believed she had to do that. We remembered all the young men her father had driven away, and we knew that with nothing left, she would have to cling to that which had robbed her, as people will.

III

She was sick for a long time. When we saw her again, her hair was cut short, making her look like a girl, with a vague resemblance to those angels in colored church windows — sort of tragic and serene.

The town had just let the contracts for paving the sidewalks, and in the summer after her father's death they began the work. The construction company came with niggers and mules and machinery, and a foreman named Homer Barron, a Yankee — a big, dark, ready man, with a big voice and eyes lighter than his face. The little boys would follow in groups to hear him cuss the niggers, and the niggers singing in time to the rise and fall of picks. Pretty soon he knew everybody in town. Whenever you heard a lot of laughing anywhere about the square, Homer Barron would be in the center of the group. Presently, we began to see him and Miss Emily on Sunday afternoons driving in the yellow-wheeled buggy and the matched team of bays from the livery stable.

At first we were glad that Miss Emily would have an interest, because the ladies all said, "Of course a Grierson would not think seriously of a Northerner, a day laborer." But there were still others, older people, who said that even grief could not cause a real lady to forget *noblesse oblige* — without calling it *noblesse oblige*. They just said, "Poor Emily. Her kinsfolk should come to her." She had some kin in Alabama; but years ago her father had fallen out with them over the estate of old lady Wyatt, the crazy woman, and there was no communication between the two families. They had not even been represented at the funeral.

And as soon as the old people said, "Poor Emily," the whispering began. "Do you suppose it's really so?" they said to one another. "Of course it is. What else could. . . ." This behind their hands; rustling of craned silk and satin behind jalousies closed upon the sun of Sunday afternoon as the thin, swift clop-clop-clop of the matched team passed: "Poor Emily."

She carried her head high enough — even when we believed that she was fallen. It was as if she demanded more than ever the recognition of her dignity as the last Grierson; as if it had wanted that touch of earthiness to reaffirm her imperviousness. Like when she bought the rat poison, the arsenic. That was over a year after they had begun to say "Poor Emily," and while the two female cousins were visiting her.

"I want some poison," she said to the druggist. She was over thirty then, still a slight woman, though thinner than usual, with cold, haughty black eyes in a face the flesh of which was strained across the temples and about the eyesockets as you imagine a lighthouse-keeper's face ought to look. "I want some poison," she said.

"Yes, Miss Emily. What kind? For rats and such? I'd recom ———"

"I want the best you have. I don't care what kind."

The druggist named several. "They'll kill anything up to an elephant. But what you want is ———"

"Arsenic," Miss Emily said. "Is that a good one?"

"Is . . . arsenic? Yes, ma'am. But what you want ———"

"I want arsenic."

The druggist looked down at her. She looked back at him, erect, her face like a strained flag. "Why, of course," the druggist said. "If that's what you want. But the law requires you to tell what you are going to use it for."

Miss Emily just stared at him, her head tilted back in order to look him eye for eye, until he looked away and went and got the arsenic and wrapped it up. The Negro delivery boy brought her the package; the druggist didn't come back. When she opened the package at home there was written on the box, under the skull and bones: "For rats."

IV

So the next day we all said, "She will kill herself"; and we said it would be the best thing. When she had first begun to be seen with Homer Barron, we had said, "She will marry him." Then we said, "She will persuade him yet," because Homer himself had remarked — he liked men, and it was known that he drank with the younger men in the Elks' Club — that he was not a marrying man. Later we said, "Poor Emily" behind the jalousies as they passed on Sunday afternoon in the glittering buggy, Miss Emily with her head high and Homer Barron with his hat cocked and a cigar in his teeth, reins and whip in a yellow glove.

Then some of the ladies began to say that it was a disgrace to the town and a bad example to the young people. The men did not want to interfere, but at last the ladies forced the Baptist minister — Miss Emily's people were Episcopal — to call upon her. He would never divulge what happened during that interview, but he refused to go back again. The next Sunday they again drove about the streets, and the following day the minister's wife wrote to Miss Emily's relations in Alabama.

So she had blood-kin under her roof again and we sat back to watch developments. At first nothing happened. Then we were sure that they were to be married. We learned that Miss Emily had been to the jeweler's and ordered a man's toilet set in silver, with the letters H.B. on each piece. Two days later we learned that she had bought a complete outfit of men's clothing, including a nightshirt, and we said, "They are married." We were really glad. We were glad because the two female cousins were even more Grierson than Miss Emily had ever been.

So we were not surprised when Homer Barron — the streets had been finished some time since — was gone. We were a little disappointed that there was not a public blowing-off, but we believed that he had gone on to prepare for Miss Emily's coming, or to give her a chance to get rid of the cousins. (By that time it was a cabal, and we were all Miss Emily's allies to help circumvent the cousins.) Sure enough, after another week they departed. And, as we had expected all along, within three days Homer Barron was back in town. A neighbor saw the Negro man admit him at the kitchen door at dusk one evening.

And that was the last we saw of Homer Barron. And of Miss Emily for some time. The Negro man went in and out with the market basket, but the front door remained closed. Now and then we would see her at the window for a moment, as the men did that night when they sprinkled the lime, but for almost six months she did not appear on the streets. Then we knew that this was to be expected too; as if that quality of her father which had thwarted her woman's life so many times had been too virulent and too furious to die.

When we next saw Miss Emily, she had grown fat and her hair was turning gray. During the next few years it grew grayer and grayer until it attained an even pepper-and-salt iron-gray, when it ceased turning. Up to the day of her death at seventy-four it was still that vigorous iron-gray, like the hair of an active man.

From that time on her front door remained closed, save during a period of six or seven years, when she was about forty, during which she gave lessons in china-painting. She fitted up a studio in one of the downstairs rooms, where the daughters and granddaughters of Colonel Sartoris' contemporaries were sent to her with the same regularity and in the same spirit that they were sent to church on Sundays with a twenty-five-cent piece for the collection plate. Meanwhile her taxes had been remitted.

Then the newer generation became the backbone and the spirit of the town, and the painting pupils grew up and fell away and did not send their children to her with boxes of color and tedious brushes and pictures cut from the ladies' magazines. The front door closed upon the last one and remained closed for good. When the town got free postal delivery, Miss Emily alone refused to let them fasten the metal numbers above her door and attach a mailbox to it. She would not listen to them.

Daily, monthly, yearly we watched the Negro grow grayer and more stooped, going in and out with the market basket. Each December we sent her a tax notice, which would be returned by the post office a week later, unclaimed. Now and then we would see her in one of the downstairs win-dows — she had evidently shut up the top floor of the house — like the carven torso of an idol in a niche, looking or not looking at us, we could never tell which. Thus she passed from generation to generation — dear, inescap-able, impervious, tranquil, and perverse.

And so she died. Fell ill in the house filled with dust and shadows, with only a doddering Negro man to wait on her. We did not even know she was sick; we had long since given up trying to get any information from the Negro. He talked to no one, probably not even to her, for his voice had grown harsh and rusty, as if from disuse.

She died in one of the downstairs rooms, in a heavy walnut bed with a curtain, her gray head propped on a pillow yellow and moldy with age and lack of sunlight.

V

The Negro met the first of the ladies at the front door and let them in, with their hushed, sibilant voices and their quick, curious glances, and then he disappeared. He walked right through the house and out the back and was not seen again.

The two female cousins came at once. They held the funeral on the second day, with the town coming to look at Miss Emily beneath a mass of bought flowers, with the crayon face of her father musing profoundly above the bier and the ladies sibilant and macabre; and the very old men — some in their brushed Confederate uniforms — on the porch and the lawn, talking of Miss Emily as if she had been a contemporary of theirs, believing that they had danced with her and courted her perhaps, confusing time with its mathematical progression, as the old do, to whom all the past is not a diminishing road but, instead, a huge meadow which no winter ever quite touches, divided from them now by the narrow bottleneck of the most recent decade of years.

Already we knew that there was one room in that region above stairs which no one had seen in forty years, and which would have to be forced. They waited until Miss Emily was decently in the ground before they opened it.

The violence of breaking down the door seemed to fill this room with pervading dust. A thin, acrid pall as of the tomb seemed to lie everywhere upon this room decked and furnished as for a bridal: upon the valance curtains of faded rose color, upon the rose-shaded lights, upon the dressing table, upon the delicate array of crystal and the man's toilet things backed with tarnished silver, silver so tarnished that the monogram was obscured. Among them lay a collar and tie, as if they had just been removed, which, lifted, left upon the surface a pale crescent in the dust. Upon a chair hung the suit, carefully folded; beneath it the two mute shoes and the discarded socks.

The man himself lay in the bed.

For a long while we just stood there, looking down at the profound and fleshless grin. The body had apparently once lain in the attitude of an embrace, but now the long sleep that outlasts love, that conquers even the grimace of love, had cuckolded him. What was left of him, rotted beneath what was left of the nightshirt, had become inextricable from the bed in which he lay; and upon him and upon the pillow beside him lay that even coating of the patient and biding dust.

Then we noticed that in the second pillow was the indentation of a head. One of us lifted something from it, and leaning forward, that faint and invisible dust dry and acrid in the nostrils, we saw a long strand of iron-gray hair.   [1931]

WILLIAM FAULKNER

That Evening Sun

I

Monday is no different from any other weekday in Jefferson now. The streets are paved now, and the telephone and electric companies are cutting down more and more of the shade trees — the water oaks, the maples and locusts and elms — to make room for iron poles bearing clusters of bloated and ghostly and bloodless grapes, and we have a city laundry which makes the rounds on Monday morning, gathering the bundles of clothes into bright-colored, specially-made motor cars: the soiled wearing of a whole week now flees apparitionlike behind alert and irritable electric horns, with a long diminishing noise of rubber and asphalt like tearing silk, and even the Negro women who still take in white people's washing after the old custom, fetch and deliver it in automobiles.

But fifteen years ago, on Monday morning the quiet, dusty, shady streets would be full of Negro women with, balanced on their steady, turbaned heads, bundles of clothes tied up in sheets, almost as large as cotton bales, carried so without touch of hand between the kitchen door of the white house and the blackened washpot beside a cabin door in Negro Hollow.

Nancy would set her bundle on the top of her head, then upon the bundle in turn she would set the black straw sailor hat which she wore winter and summer. She was tall, with a high, sad face sunken a little where her teeth were missing. Sometimes we would go a part of the way down the lane and across the pasture with her, to watch the balanced bundle and the hat that never bobbed nor wavered, even when she walked down into the ditch and up the other side and stooped through the fence. She would go down on her hands and knees and crawl through the gap, her head rigid, uptilted, the bundle steady as a rock or a balloon, and rise to her feet again and go on.

Sometimes the husbands of the washing women would fetch and deliver the clothes, but Jesus never did that for Nancy, even before father told him to stay away from our house, even when Dilsey was sick and Nancy would come to cook for us.

And then about half the time we'd have to go down the lane to Nancy's cabin and tell her to come on and cook breakfast. We would stop at the ditch, because father told us to not have anything to do with Jesus — he was a short black man, with a razor scar down his face — and we would throw rocks at Nancy's house until she came to the door, leaning her head around it without any clothes on.

"What yawl mean, chunking my house?" Nancy said. "What you little devils mean?"

"Father says for you to come on and get breakfast," Caddy said. "Father says it's over a half an hour now, and you've got to come this minute."

"I aint studying no breakfast," Nancy said. "I going to get my sleep out."

"I bet you're drunk," Jason said. "Father says you're drunk. Are you drunk, Nancy?"

"Who says I is?" Nancy said. "I got to get my sleep out. I ain't studying no breakfast."

So after a while we quit chunking the cabin and went back home. When she finally came, it was too late for me to go to school. So we thought it was whisky until that day they arrested her again and they were taking her to jail and they passed Mr Stovall. He was the cashier in the bank and a deacon in the Baptist church, and Nancy began to say:

"When you going to pay me, white man? When you going to pay me, white man? It's been three times now since you paid me a cent — " Mr Stovall knocked her down, but she kept on saying, "When you going to pay me, white man? It's been three times now since —" until Mr Stovall kicked her in the mouth with his heel and the marshal caught Mr Stovall back, and Nancy lying in the street, laughing. She turned her head and spat out some blood and teeth and said, "It's been three times now since he paid me a cent."

That was how she lost her teeth, and all that day they told about Nancy and Mr Stovall, and all that night the ones that passed the jail could hear Nancy singing and yelling. They could see her hands holding to the window bars, and a lot of them stopped along the fence, listening to her and to the jailer trying to make her stop. She didn't shut up until almost daylight, when the jailer began to hear a bumping and scraping upstairs and he went up there and found Nancy hanging from the window bar. He said that it was cocaine and not whisky, because no nigger would try to commit suicide unless he was full of cocaine, because a nigger full of cocaine wasn't a nigger any longer.

The jailer cut her down and revived her; then he beat her, whipped her. She had hung herself with her dress. She had fixed it all right, but when they arrested her she didn't have on anything except a dress and so she didn't have anything to tie her hands with and she couldn't make her hands let go of the window ledge. So the jailer heard the noise and ran up there and found Nancy hanging from the window, stark naked, her belly already swelling out a little, like a little balloon.

When Dilsey was sick in her cabin and Nancy was cooking for us, we could see her apron swelling out; that was before father told Jesus to stay away from the house. Jesus was in the kitchen, sitting behind the stove, with his razor scar on his black face like a piece of dirty string. He said it was a watermelon that Nancy had under her dress.

"It never come off of your vine, though," Nancy said.

"Off of what vine?" Caddy said.

"I can cut down the vine it did come off of," Jesus said.

"What makes you want to talk like that before these chillen?" Nancy said. "Whyn't you go on to work? You done et. You want Mr Jason to catch you hanging around his kitchen, talking that way before these chillen?"

"Talking what way?" Caddy said. "What vine?"

"I cant hang around white man's kitchen," Jesus said. "But white man can hang around mine. White man can come in my house, but I cant stop him. When white man want to come in my house, I aint got no house. I cant stop him, but he cant kick me outen it. He cant do that."

Dilsey was still sick in her cabin. Father told Jesus to stay off our place. Dilsey was still sick. It was a long time. We were in the library after supper.

"Isn't Nancy through in the kitchen yet?" mother said. "It seems to me that she has had plenty of time to have finished the dishes."

"Let Quentin go and see," father said. "Go and see if Nancy is through, Quentin. Tell her she can go on home."

I went to the kitchen. Nancy was through. The dishes were put away and the fire was out. Nancy was sitting in a chair, close to the cold stove. She looked at me.

"Mother wants to know if you are through," I said.

"Yes," Nancy said. She looked at me. "I done finished." She looked at me.

"What is it?" I said, "What is it?"

"I aint nothing but a nigger," Nancy said. "It aint none of my fault."

She looked at me, sitting in the chair before the cold stove, the sailor hat on her head. I went back to the library. It was the cold stove and all, when you think of a kitchen being warm and busy and cheerful. And with a cold stove and the dishes all put away, and nobody wanting to eat at that hour.

"Is she through?" mother said.

"Yessum," I said.

"What is she doing?" mother said.

"She's not doing anything. She's through."

"I'll go and see," father said.

"Maybe she's waiting for Jesus to come and take her home," Caddy said.

"Jesus is gone," I said. Nancy told us how one morning she woke up and Jesus was gone.

"He quit me," Nancy said. "Done gone to Memphis, I reckon. Dodging them city *po*-lice for a while, I reckon."

"And a good riddance," father said. "I hope he stays there."

"Nancy's scaired of the dark," Jason said.

"So are you," Caddy said.

"I'm not," Jason said.

"Scairy cat," Caddy said.

"I'm not," Jason said.

"You, Candace!" mother said. Father came back.

"I am going to walk down the lane with Nancy," he said. "She says that Jesus is back."

"Has she seen him?" mother said.

"No. Some Negro sent her word that he was back in town. I wont be long."

"You'll leave me alone, to take Nancy home?" mother said. "Is her safety more precious to you than mine?"

"I wont be long," father said.

"You'll leave these children unprotected, with that Negro about?"

"I'm going too," Caddy said. "Let me go, Father."

"What would he do with them, if he were unfortunate enough to have them?" father said.

"I want to go, too," Jason said.

"Jason!" mother said. She was speaking to father. You could tell that by the way she said the name. Like she believed that all day father had been trying to think of doing the thing she wouldn't like the most, and that she knew all the time that after a while he would think of it. I stayed quiet, because father and I both knew that mother would want him to make me stay with her if she just thought of it in time. So father didn't look at me. I was the oldest. I was nine and Caddy was seven and Jason was five.

"Nonsense," father said. "We wont be long."

Nancy had her hat on. We came to the lane. "Jesus always been good to me," Nancy said. "Whenever he had two dollars, one of them was mine." We walked in the lane. "If I can just get through the lane," Nancy said, "I be all right then."

The lane was always dark. "This is where Jason got scared on Hallowe'en," Caddy said.

"I didn't," Jason said.

"Cant Aunt Rachel do anything with him?" father said. Aunt Rachel was old. She lived in a cabin beyond Nancy's, by herself. She had white hair and she smoked a pipe in the door, all day long; she didn't work any more. They said she was Jesus' mother. Sometimes she said she was and sometimes she said she wasn't any kin to Jesus.

"Yes, you did," Caddy said. "You were scairder than Frony. You were scairder than T.P. even. Scairder than niggers."

"Cant nobody do nothing with him," Nancy said. "He say I done woke up the devil in him and aint but one thing going to lay it down again."

"Well, he's gone now," father said. "There's nothing for you to be afraid of now. And if you'd just let white men alone."

"Let what white men alone?" Caddy said. "How let them alone?"

"He aint gone nowhere," Nancy said. "I can feel him. I can feel him now, in this lane. He hearing us talk, every word, hid somewhere, waiting. I aint seen him, and I aint going to see him again but once more, with that razor in his mouth. That razor on that string down his back, inside his shirt. And then I aint going to be even surprised."

"I wasn't scaired," Jason said.

"If you'd behave yourself, you'd have kept out of this," father said. "But it's all right now. He's probably in St. Louis now. Probably got another wife by now and forgot all about you."

"If he has, I better not find out about it," Nancy said. "I'd stand there right over them, and every time he wropped her, I'd cut that arm off. I'd cut his head off and I'd slit her belly and I'd shove —"

"Hush," father said.

"Slit whose belly, Nancy?" Caddy said.

"I wasn't scaired," Jason said. "I'd walk right down this lane by myself."

"Yah," Caddy said. "You wouldn't dare to put your foot down in it if we were not here too."

II

Dilsey was still sick, so we took Nancy home every night until mother said, "How much longer is this going on? I to be left alone in this big house while you take home a frightened Negro?"

We fixed a pallet in the kitchen for Nancy. One night we waked up, hearing the sound. It was not singing and it was not crying, coming up the dark stairs. There was a light in mother's room and we heard father going down the hall, down the back stairs, and Caddy and I went into the hall. The floor was cold. Our toes curled away from it while we listened to the sound. It was like singing and it wasn't like singing, like the sounds that Negroes make.

Then it stopped and we heard father going down the back stairs, and we went to the head of the stairs. Then the sound began again, in the stairway, not loud, and we could see Nancy's eyes halfway up the stairs, against the wall. They looked like cat's eyes do, like a big cat against the wall, watching us. When we came down the steps to where she was, she quit making the sound again, and we stood there until father came back up from the kitchen, with his pistol in his hand. He went back down with Nancy and they came back with Nancy's pallet.

We spread the pallet in our room. After the light in mother's room went off, we could see Nancy's eyes again. "Nancy," Caddy whispered, "are you asleep, Nancy?"

Nancy whispered something. It was oh or no, I dont know which. Like nobody had made it, like it came from nowhere and went nowhere, until it was like Nancy was not there at all; that I had looked so hard at her eyes on the stairs that they had got printed on my eyeballs, like the sun does when you have closed your eyes and there is no sun. "Jesus," Nancy whispered. "Jesus."

"Was it Jesus?" Caddy said. "Did he try to come into the kitchen?"

"Jesus," Nancy said. Like this: Jeeeeeeeeeeeeeeeeesus, until the sound went out, like a match or a candle does.

"It's the other Jesus she means," I said.

"Can you see us, Nancy?" Caddy whispered. "Can you see our eyes too?"

"I aint nothing but a nigger," Nancy said. "God knows. God knows."

"What did you see down there in the kitchen?" Caddy whispered. "What tried to get in?"

"God knows," Nancy said. We could see her eyes. "God knows."

Dilsey got well. She cooked dinner. "You'd better stay in bed a day or two longer," father said.

"What for?" Dilsey said. "If I had been a day later, this place would be to rack and ruin. Get on out of here now, and let me get my kitchen straight again."

Disley cooked supper too. And that night, just before dark, Nancy came into the kitchen.

"How do you know he's back?" Dilsey said. "You aint seen him."

"Jesus is a nigger," Jason said.

"I can feel him," Nancy said. "I can feel him laying yonder in the ditch."

"Tonight?" Dilsey said. "Is he there tonight?"

"Dilsey's a nigger too," Jason said.

"You try to eat something," Dilsey said.

"I dont want nothing," Nancy said.

"I aint a nigger," Jason said.

"Drink some coffee," Dilsey said. She poured a cup of coffee for Nancy. "Do you know he's out there tonight? How come you know it's tonight?"

"I know," Nancy said. "He's there, waiting. I know. I done lived with him too long. I know what he is fixing to do fore he know it himself."

"Drink some coffee," Dilsey said. Nancy held the cup to her mouth and blew into the cup. Her mouth pursed out like a spreading adder's, like a rubber mouth, like she had blown all the color out of her lips with blowing the coffee.

"I aint a nigger," Jason said. "Are you a nigger, Nancy?"

"I hellborn, child," Nancy said. "I wont be nothing soon. I going back where I come from soon."

III

She began to drink the coffee. While she was drinking, holding the cup in both hands, she began to make the sound again. She made the sound into the cup and the coffee sploshed out onto her hands and her dress. Her eyes looked at us and she sat there, her elbows on her knees, holding the cup in both hands, looking at us across the wet cup, making the sound. "Look at Nancy," Jason said. "Nancy cant cook for us now. Dilsey's got well now."

"You hush up," Dilsey said. Nancy held the cup in both hands, looking at us, making the sound, like there were two of them: one looking at us and the other making the sound. "Whyn't you let Mr Jason telefoam the marshal?" Dilsey said. Nancy stopped then, holding the cup in her long brown hands. She tried to drink some coffee again, but it sploshed out of the cup, onto her hands and her dress, and she put the cup down. Jason watched her.

"I cant swallow it," Nancy said. "I swallows but it wont go down me."

"You go down to the cabin," Dilsey said. "Frony will fix you a pallet and I'll be there soon."

"Wont no nigger stop him," Nancy said.

"I aint a nigger," Jason said. "Am I, Dilsey?"

"I reckon not," Dilsey said. She looked at Nancy. "I dont reckon so. What you going to do, then?"

Nancy looked at us. Her eyes went fast, like she was afraid there wasn't time to look, without hardly moving at all. She looked at us, at all three of us at one time. "You member that night I stayed in yawls' room?" she said. She told about how we waked up early the next morning, and played. We had to play quiet, on her pallet, until father woke up and it was time to get breakfast. "Go and ask your maw to let me stay here tonight," Nancy said. "I wont need no pallet. We can play some more."

Caddy asked mother. Jason went too. "I cant have Negroes sleeping in the bedrooms," mother said. Jason cried. He cried until mother said he couldn't have any dessert for three days if he didn't stop. Then Jason said he would stop if Dilsey would make a chocolate cake. Father was there.

"Why dont you do something about it?" mother said. "What do we have officers for?"

"Why is Nancy afraid of Jesus?" Caddy said. "Are you afraid of father, mother?"

"What could the officers do?" father said. "If Nancy hasn't seen him, how could the officers find him?"

"Then why is she afraid?" mother said.

"She says he is there. She says she knows he is there tonight."

"Yet we pay taxes," mother said. "I must wait here alone in this big house while you take a Negro woman home."

"You know that I am not lying outside with a razor," father said.

"I'll stop if Dilsey will make a chocolate cake," Jason said. Mother told us to go out and father said he didn't know if Jason would get a chocolate cake or not, but he knew what Jason was going to get in about a minute. We went back to the kitchen and told Nancy.

"Father said for you to go home and lock the door, and you'll be all right," Caddy said. "All right from what, Nancy? Is Jesus mad at you?" Nancy was holding the coffee cup in her hands again, her elbows on her knees and her hands holding the cup between her knees. She was looking into the cup. "What have you done that made Jesus mad?" Caddy said. Nancy let the cup go. It didn't break on the floor, but the coffee spilled out, and Nancy sat there with her hands still making the shape of the cup. She began to make the sound again, not loud. Not singing and not unsinging. We watched her.

"Here," Dilsey said. "You quit that, now. You get aholt of yourself. You wait here. I going to get Versh to walk home with you." Dilsey went out.

We looked at Nancy. Her shoulders kept shaking, but she quit making the sound. We watched her. "What's Jesus going to do to you?" Caddy said. "He went away."

Nancy looked at us. "We had fun that night I stayed in yawls' room, didn't we?"

"I didn't," Jason said. "I didn't have any fun."

"You were asleep in mother's room," Caddy said. "You were not there."

"Let's go down to my house and have some more fun," Nancy said.

"Mother wont let us," I said. "It's too late now."

"Dont bother her," Nancy said. "We can tell her in the morning. She wont mind."

"She wouldn't let us," I said.

"Dont ask her now," Nancy said. "Dont bother her now."

"She didn't say we couldn't go," Caddy said.

"We didn't ask," I said.

"If you go, I'll tell," Jason said.

"We'll have fun," Nancy said. hey won't mind, just to my house. I been working for yawl a long time. They won't mind."

"I'm not afraid to go," Caddy said. "Jason is the one that's afraid. He'll tell."

"I'm not," Jason said.

"Yes, you are," Caddy said. "You'll tell."

"I won't tell," Jason said. "I'm not afraid."

"Jason ain't afraid to go with me," Nancy said. "Is you, Jason?"

"Jason is going to tell," Caddy said. The lane was dark. We passed the pasture gate. "I bet if something was to jump out from behind that gate, Jason would holler."

"I wouldn't," Jason said. We walked down the lane. Nancy was talking loud.

"What are you talking so loud for, Nancy?" Caddy said.

"Who; me?" Nancy said. "Listen at Quentin and Caddy and Jason saying I'm talking loud."

"You talk like there was five of us here," Caddy said. "You talk like father was here too."

"Who; me talking loud, Mr Jason?" Nancy said.

"Nancy called Jason 'Mister,'" Caddy said.

"Listen how Caddy and Quentin and Jason talk," Nancy said.

"We're not talking loud," Caddy said. "You're the one that's talking like father — "

"Hush," Nancy said; "hush, Mr Jason."

"Nancy called Jason 'Mister' aguh —"

"Hush," Nancy said. She was talking loud when we crossed the ditch and stooped through the fence where she used to stoop through with the clothes on her head. Then we came to her house. We were going fast then. She opened the door. The smell of the house was like the lamp and the smell of Nancy was like the wick, like they were waiting for one another to begin to smell. She lit the lamp and closed the door and put the bar up. Then she quit talking loud, looking at us.

"What're we going to do?" Caddy said.

"What do yawl want to do?" Nancy said.

"You said we would have some fun," Caddy said.

There was something about Nancy's house; something you could smell besides Nancy and the house. Jason smelled it, even. "I don't want to stay here," he said. "I want to go home."

"Go home, then," Caddy said.

"I don't want to go by myself," Jason said.

"We're going to have some fun," Nancy said.

"How?" Caddy said.

Nancy stood by the door. She was looking at us, only it was like she had emptied her eyes, like she had quit using them. "What do you want to do?" she said.

"Tell us a story," Caddy said. "Can you tell a story?"

"Yes," Nancy said.

"Tell it," Caddy said. We looked at Nancy. "You don't know any stories."

"Yes," Nancy said. "Yes, I do."

She came and sat in a chair before the hearth. There was a little fire there. Nancy built it up, when it was already hot inside. She built a good blaze. She told a story. She talked like her eyes looked, like her eyes watching us and her voice talking to us did not belong to her. Like she was living somewhere else, waiting somewhere else. She was outside the cabin. Her voice was inside and the shape of her, the Nancy that could stoop under a barbed wire fence with a bundle of clothes balanced on her head as though without weight, like a balloon, was there. But that was all. "And so this here queen come walking up to the ditch, where that bad man was hiding. She was walking up to the ditch, and she say, 'If I can just get past this here ditch,' was what she say . . ."

"What ditch?" Caddy said. "A ditch like that one out there? Why did a queen want to go into a ditch?"

"To get to her house," Nancy said. She looked at us. "She had to cross the ditch to get into her house quick and bar the door."

"Why did she want to go home and bar the door?" Caddy said.

IV

Nancy looked at us. She quit talking. She looked at us. Jason's legs stuck straight out of his pants where he sat on Nancy's lap. "I don't think that's a good story," he said. "I want to go home."

"Maybe we had better," Caddy said. She got up from the floor. "I bet they are looking for us right now." She went toward the door.

"No," Nancy said. "Don't open it." She got up quick and passed Caddy. She didn't touch the door, the wooden bar.

"Why not?" Caddy said.

"Come back to the lamp," Nancy said. "We'll have fun. You don't have to go."

"We ought to go," Caddy said. "Unless we have a lot of fun." She and Nancy came back to the fire, the lamp.

"I want to go home," Jason said. "I'm going to tell."

"I know another story," Nancy said. She stood close to the lamp. She looked at Caddy, like when your eyes look up at a stick balanced on your nose. She had to look down to see Caddy, but her eyes looked like that, like when you are balancing a stick.

"I won't listen to it," Jason said. "I'll bang on the floor."

"It's a good one," Nancy said. "It's better than the other one."

"What's it about?" Caddy said. Nancy was standing by the lamp. Her hand was on the lamp, against the light, long and brown.

"Your hand is on that hot globe," Caddy said. "Don't it feel hot to your hand?"

Nancy looked at her hand on the lamp chimney. She took her hand away, slow. She stood there, looking at Caddy, wringing her long hand as though it were tied to her wrist with a string.

"Let's do something else," Caddy said.

"I want to go home," Jason said.

"I got some popcorn," Nancy said. She looked at Caddy and then at Jason and then at me and then at Caddy again. "I got some popcorn."

"I don't like popcorn," Jason said. "I'd rather have candy."

Nancy looked at Jason. "You can hold the popper." She was still wringing her hand; it was long and limp and brown.

"All right," Jason said. "I'll stay a while if I can do that. Caddy can't hold it. I'll want to go home again if Caddy holds the popper."

Nancy built up the fire. "Look at Nancy putting her hands in the fire," Caddy said. "What's the matter with you, Nancy?"

"I got popcorn," Nancy said. "I got some." She took the popper from under the bed. It was broken. Jason began to cry.

"Now we can't have any popcorn," he said.

"We ought to go home, anyway," Caddy said. "Come on, Quentin."

"Wait," Nancy said; "wait. I can fix it. Don't you want to help me fix it?"

"I don't think I want any," Caddy said. "It's too late now."

"You help me, Jason," Nancy said. "Don't you want to help me?"

"No," Jason said. "I want to go home."

"Hush," Nancy said; "hush. Watch. Watch me. I can fix it so Jason can hold it and pop the corn." She got a piece of wire and fixed the popper.

"It won't hold good," Caddy said.

"Yes, it will," Nancy said. "Yawl watch. Yawl help me shell some corn."

The popcorn was under the bed too. We shelled it into the popper and Nancy helped Jason hold the popper over the fire.

"It's not popping," Jason said. "I want to go home."

"You wait," Nancy said. "It'll begin to pop. We'll have fun then." She was sitting close to the fire. The lamp was turned up so high it was beginning to smoke.

"Why don't you turn it down some?" I said.

"It's all right," Nancy said. "I'll clean it. Yawl wait. The popcorn will start in a minute."

"I don't believe it's going to start," Caddy said. "We ought to start home, anyway. They'll be worried."

"No," Nancy said. "It's going to pop. Dilsey will tell um yawl with me. I been working for yawl long time. They won't mind if yawl at my house. You wait, now. It'll start popping any minute now."

Then Jason got some smoke in his eyes and he began to cry. He dropped the popper into the fire. Nancy got a wet rag and wiped Jason's face, but he didn't stop crying.

"Hush," she said. "Hush." But he didn't hush. Caddy took the popper out of the fire.

"It's burned up," she said. "You'll have to get some more popcorn, Nancy."

"Did you put all of it in?" Nancy said.

"Yes," Caddy said. Nancy looked at Caddy. Then she took the popper and opened it and poured the cinders into her apron and began to sort the grains, her hands long and brown, and we watching her.

"Haven't you got any more?" Caddy said.

"Yes," Nancy said; "yes. Look. This here ain't burnt. All we need to do is —"

"I want to go home," Jason said. "I'm going to tell."

"Hush," Caddy said. We all listened. Nancy's head was already turned toward the barred door, her eyes filled with red lamplight. "Somebody is coming," Caddy said.

Then Nancy began to make that sound again, not loud, sitting there above the fire, her long hands dangling between her knees; all of a sudden water began to come out on her face in big drops, running down her face, carrying in each one a little turning ball of firelight like a spark until it dropped off her chin. "She's not crying," I said.

"I ain't crying," Nancy said. Her eyes were closed. "I ain't crying. Who is it?"

"I don't know," Caddy said. She went to the door and looked out. "We've got to go now," she said. "Here comes father."

"I'm going to tell," Jason said. "Yawl made me come."

The water still ran down Nancy's face. She turned in her chair. "Listen. Tell him. Tell him we going to have fun. Tell him I take good care of yawl until in the morning. Tell him to let me come home with yawl and sleep on the floor. Tell him I won't need no pallet. We'll have fun. You member last time how we had so much fun?"

"I didn't have fun," Jason said. "You hurt me. You put smoke in my eyes. I'm going to tell."

V

Father came in. He looked at us. Nancy did not get up.

"Tell him," she said.

"Caddy made us come down here," Jason said. "I didn't want to."

Father came to the fire. Nancy looked up at him. "Can't you go to Aunt Rachel's and stay?" he said. Nancy looked up at father, her hands between her knees. "He's not here," father said. "I would have seen him. There's not a soul in sight."

"He in the ditch," Nancy said. "He waiting in the ditch yonder."

"Nonsense," father said. He looked at Nancy. "Do you know he's there?"

"I got the sign," Nancy said.

"What sign?"

"I got it. It was on the table when I come in. It was a hogbone, with blood meat still on it, laying by the lamp. He's out there. When yawl walk out that door, I gone."

"Gone where, Nancy?" Caddy said.

"I'm not a tattletale," Jason said.

"Nonsense," father said.

"He out there," Nancy said. "He looking through that window this minute, waiting for yawl to go. Then I gone."

"Nonsense," father said. "Lock up your house and we'll take you on to Aunt Rachel's."

"'Twont do no good," Nancy said. She didn't look at father now, but he looked down at her, at her long, limp, moving hands. "Putting it off wont do no good."

"Then what do you want to do?" father said.

"I don't know," Nancy said. "I can't do nothing. Just put it off. And that don't do no good. I reckon it belong to me. I reckon what I going to get ain't no more than mine."

"Get what?" Caddy said. "What's yours?"

"Nothing," father said. "You all must get to bed."

"Caddy made me come," Jason said.

"Go on to Aunt Rachel's," father said.

"It won't do no good," Nancy said. She sat before the fire, her elbows on her knees, her long hands between her knees. "When even your own kitchen wouldn't do no good. When even if I was sleeping on the floor in the room with your chillen, and the next morning there I am, and blood —"

"Hush," father said. "Lock the door and put out the lamp and go to bed."

"I scared of the dark," Nancy said. "I scared for it to happen in the dark."

"You mean you're going to sit right here with the lamp lighted?" father said. Then Nancy began to make the sound again, sitting before the fire, her long hands between her knees. "Ah, damnation," father said. "Come along, chillen. It's past bedtime."

"When yawl go home, I gone," Nancy said. She talked quieter now, and her face looked quiet, like her hands. "Anyway, I got my coffin money saved up with Mr. Lovelady." Mr. Lovelady was a short, dirty man who collected the Negro insurance, coming around to the cabins or the kitchens every Saturday morning, to collect fifteen cents. He and his wife lived at the hotel. One morning his wife committed suicide. They had a child, a little girl. He and the child went away. After a week or two he came back alone. We would see him going along the lanes and the back streets on Saturday mornings.

"Nonsense," father said. "You'll be the first thing I'll see in the kitchen tomorrow morning."

"You'll see what you'll see, I reckon," Nancy said. "But it will take the Lord to say what that will be."

VI

"Come and put the bar up," father said. But she didn't move. She didn't look at us again, sitting quietly there between the lamp and the fire. From some distance down the lane we could look back and see her through the open door.

"What, Father?" Caddy said. "What's going to happen?"

"Nothing," father said. Jason was on father's back, so Jason was the tallest of all of us. We went down into the ditch. I looked at it, quiet. I couldn't see much where the moonlight and the shadows tangled.

"If Jesus is hid here, he can see us, cant he?" Caddy said.

"He's not there," father said. "He went away a long time ago."

"You made me come," Jason said, high; against the sky it looked like father had two heads, a little one and a big one. "I didn't want to."

We went up out of the ditch. We could still see Nancy's house and the open door, but we couldn't see Nancy now, sitting before the fire with the door open, because she was tired. "I just done got tired," she said. "I just a nigger. It ain't no fault of mine."

But we could hear her, because she began just after we came up out of the ditch, the sound that was not singing and not unsinging. "Who will do our washing now, Father?" I said.

"I'm not a nigger," Jason said, high and close above father's head.

"You're worse," Caddy said, "you are a tattletale. If something was to jump out, you'd be scairder than a nigger."

"I wouldn't," Jason said.

"You'd cry," Caddy said.

"Caddy," father said.

"I wouldn't!" Jason said.

"Scairy cat," Caddy said.

"Candace!" father said.

[1931]

F. SCOTT FITZGERALD (1896–1940), *regarded as the literary spokesman for the "Lost Generation" of the 1920s in America, was born in St. Paul, Minnesota. His family had some social standing but little money, and it was only with help from a maiden aunt that he was able to go to an eastern preparatory school and then on to Princeton, where he said his family hoped that he would attend to his studies and stop "wasting his time scribbling." He left college before graduating to accept a commission as a second lieutenant in the Regular Army during World War I, but he spent most of his time in the service writing his first novel, which he revised several times before it was published in 1920 as* This Side of Paradise. *The novel was such a success that magazines were eager to print Fitzgerald's stories, and his first story collection,* Flappers and Philosophers, *was rushed into print later the same year to take advantage of the novel's popularity. Another story collection,* Tales of the Jazz Age, *followed in 1922. Years later Fitzgerald would say, writing in the third person, that he was grateful to the Jazz Age because "it bore him up, flattered him, and gave him more money than he had dreamed of, simply for telling people that he felt as they did, that something had to be done with all the nervous energy stored up and unexpended in the War."*

In 1925, with the publication of his novel The Great Gatsby, *Fitzgerald reached the peak of his fame as a writer. His reputation declined rapidly in the harsher years of the 1930s. The Great Depression in the United States and around the world coincided with his own emotional and physical collapse, as his marriage and career fell apart because of his wife's mental illness and his alcoholism. Gertrude Stein had coined the term "Lost Generation" to describe the young men who had served in World War I and were forced to grow up "to find all Gods dead, all wars fought, all faiths in man shaken." But Fitzgerald's last years were truly lost, as he confronted the "waste and horror" of his dissipated talent, writing Hollywood screenplays and struggling unsuccessfully to finish his novel* The Last Tycoon.

At the time of his death Fitzgerald had written about 160 stories. As one of his editors, Malcolm Cowley, has said, the exact number is hard to set because some of his work was on the borderline between fiction and the informal essay or "magazine piece." Simple and clear in style, Fitzgerald's stories make up an informal history of his career, dating from before the publication of his first novel to after his final crack-up. "Babylon Revisited" (1931) is one of his later stories, perhaps one of his best. It is more complicated emotionally than his earlier short fiction. As Cowley realized, it embodies "less regret for the past and more dignity in the face of real sorrow."

F. SCOTT FITZGERALD

Babylon Revisited

I

"And where's Mr. Campbell?" Charlie asked.

"Gone to Switzerland. Mr. Campbell's a pretty sick man, Mr. Wales."

"I'm sorry to hear that. And George Hardt?" Charlie inquired.

"Back in America, gone to work."

"And where is the Snow Bird?"

"He was in here last week. Anyway, his friend, Mr. Schaeffer, is in Paris."

Two familiar names from the long list of a year and a half ago. Charlie scribbled an address in his notebook and tore out the page.

"If you see Mr. Schaeffer, give him this," he said. "It's my brother-in-law's address. I haven't settled on a hotel yet."

He was not really disappointed to find Paris was so empty. But the stillness in the Ritz bar was strange and portentous. It was not an American bar any more — he felt polite in it, and not as if he owned it. It had gone back into France. He felt the stillness from the moment he got out of the taxi and saw the doorman, usually in a frenzy of activity at this hour, gossiping with a *chasseur*[1] by the servants' entrance.

Passing through the corridor, he heard only a single, bored voice in the once-clamorous women's room. When he turned into the bar he traveled the twenty feet of green carpet with his eyes fixed straight ahead by old habit; and then, with his foot firmly on the rail, he turned and surveyed the room, encountering only a single pair of eyes that fluttered up from a newspaper in the corner. Charlie asked for the head barman, Paul, who in the latter days of the bull market had come to work in his own custom-built car — disembarking, however, with due nicety at the nearest corner. But Paul was at his country house today and Alix giving him information.

"No, no more," Charlie said, "I'm going slow these days."

Alix congratulated him: "You were going pretty strong a couple of years ago."

"I'll stick to it all right," Charlie assured him. "I've stuck to it for over a year and a half now."

"How do you find conditions in America?"

"I haven't been to America for months. I'm in business in Prague, representing a couple of concerns there. They don't know about me down there."

Alix smiled.

"Remember the night of George Hardt's bachelor dinner here?" said Charlie. "By the way, what's become of Claude Fessenden?"

---

[1] Bellhop.

Alix lowered his voice confidentially: "He's in Paris, but he doesn't come here any more. Paul doesn't allow it. He ran up a bill of thirty thousand francs, charging all his drinks and his lunches, and usually his dinner, for more than a year. And when Paul finally told him he had to pay, he gave him a bad check."

Alix shook his head sadly.

"I don't understand it, such a dandy fellow. Now he's all bloated up —" He made a plump apple of his hands.

Charlie watched a group of strident queens installing themselves in a corner.

"Nothing affects them," he thought. "Stocks rise and fall, people loaf or work, but they go on forever." The place oppressed him. He called for the dice and shook with Alix for the drink.

"Here for long, Mr. Wales?"

"I'm here for four or five days to see my little girl."

"Oh-h! You have a little girl?"

Outside, the fire-red, gas-blue, ghost-green signs shone smokily through the tranquil rain. It was late afternoon and the streets were in movement; the *bistros* gleamed. At the corner of the Boulevard des Capucines he took a taxi. The Place de la Concorde moved by in pink majesty; they crossed the logical Seine, and Charlie felt the sudden provincial quality of the Left Bank.

Charlie directed his taxi to the Avenue de l'Opera, which was out of his way. But he wanted to see the blue hour spread over the magnificent façade, and imagine that the cab horns, playing endlessly the first few bars of *La Plus que Lente*,[2] were the trumpets of the Second Empire.[3] They were closing the iron grill in front of Brentano's Book-store, and people were already at dinner behind the trim little bourgeois hedge of Duval's. He had never eaten at a really cheap restaurant in Paris. Five-course dinner, four francs fifty, eighteen cents, wine included. For some odd reason he wished that he had.

As they rolled on to the Left Bank and he felt its sudden provincialism, he thought, "I spoiled this city for myself. I didn't realize it, but the days came along one after another, and then two years were gone, and everything was gone, and I was gone."

He was thirty-five, and good to look at. The Irish mobility of his face was sobered by a deep wrinkle between his eyes. As he rang his brother-in-law's bell in the Rue Palatine, the wrinkle deepened till it pulled down his brows; he felt a cramping sensation in his belly. From behind the maid who opened the door darted a lovely little girl of nine who shrieked "Daddy!" and flew up, struggling like a fish, into his arms. She pulled his head around by one ear and set her cheek against his.

"My old pie," he said.

"Oh, daddy, daddy, daddy, daddy, dads, dads, dads!"

She drew him into the salon, where the family waited, a boy and a girl

[2] "Slower than Slow," whimsical piano piece by Claude Debussy (1862–1918).
[3] The reign of Napoleon III, 1852–1871.

his daughter's age, his sister-in-law and her husband. He greeted Marion with his voice pitched carefully to avoid either feigned enthusiasm or dislike, but her response was more frankly tepid, though she minimized her expression of unalterable distrust by directing her regard toward his child. The two men clasped hands in a friendly way and Lincoln Peters rested his for a moment on Charlie's shoulder.

The room was warm and comfortably American. The three children moved intimately about, playing through the yellow oblongs that led to other rooms; the cheer of six o'clock spoke in the eager smacks of the fire and the sounds of French activity in the kitchen. But Charlie did not relax; his heart sat up rigidly in his body and he drew confidence from his daughter, who from time to time came close to him, holding in her arms the doll he had brought.

"Really extremely well," he declared in answer to Lincoln's question. "There's a lot of business there that isn't moving at all, but we're doing even better than ever. In fact, damn well. I'm bringing my sister over from America next month to keep house for me. My income last year was bigger than it was when I had money. You see, the Czechs ——"

His boasting was for a specific purpose; but after a moment, seeing a faint restiveness in Lincoln's eye, he changed the subject:

"Those are fine children of yours, well brought up, good manners."

"We think Honoria's a great little girl too."

Marion Peters came back from the kitchen. She was a tall woman with worried eyes, who had once possessed a fresh American loveliness. Charlie had never been sensitive to it and was always surprised when people spoke of how pretty she had been. From the first there had been an instinctive antipathy between them.

"Well, how do you find Honoria?" she asked.

"Wonderful. I was astonished how much she's grown in ten months. All the children are looking well."

"We haven't had a doctor for a year. How do you like being back in Paris?"

"It seems very funny to see so few Americans around."

"I'm delighted," Marion said vehemently. "Now at least you can go into a store without their assuming you're a millionaire. We've suffered like everybody, but on the whole it's a good deal pleasanter."

"But it was nice while it lasted," Charlie said. "We were a sort of royalty, almost infallible, with a sort of magic around us. In the bar this afternoon" — he stumbled, seeing his mistake — "there wasn't a man I knew."

She looked at him keenly. "I should think you'd have had enough of bars."

"I only stayed a minute. I take one drink every afternoon, and no more."

"Don't you want a cocktail before dinner?" Lincoln asked.

"I take only one drink every afternoon, and I've had that."

"I hope you keep to it," said Marion.

Her dislike was evident in the coldness with which she spoke, but Charlie only smiled; he had larger plans. Her very aggressiveness gave him an advantage, and he knew enough to wait. He wanted them to initiate the discussion of what they knew had brought him to Paris.

At dinner he couldn't decide whether Honoria was most like him or her mother. Fortunate if she didn't combine the traits of both that had brought them to disaster. A great wave of protectiveness went over him. He thought he knew what to do for her. He believed in character; he wanted to jump back a whole generation and trust in character again as the eternally valuable element. Everything else wore out.

He left soon after dinner, but not to go home. He was curious to see Paris by night with clearer and more judicious eyes than those of other days. He bought a *strapontin*[4] for the Casino and watched Josephine Baker go through her chocolate arabesques.

After an hour he left and strolled toward Montmartre, up the Rue Pigalle into the Place Blanche. The rain had stopped and there were a few people in evening clothes disembarking from taxis in front of cabarets, and *cocottes*[5] prowling singly or in pairs, and many Negroes. He passed a lighted door from which issued music, and stopped with the sense of familiarity; it was Bricktop's, where he had parted with so many hours and so much money. A few doors farther on he found another ancient rendezvous and incautiously put his head inside. Immediately an eager orchestra burst into sound, a pair of professional dancers leaped to their feet and a maître d'hôtel swooped toward him, crying, "Crowd just arriving, sir!" But he withdrew quickly.

"You have to be damn drunk," he thought.

Zelli's was closed, the bleak and sinister cheap hotels surrounding it were dark; up in the Rue Blanche there was more light and a local, colloquial French crowd. The Poet's Cave had disappeared, but the two great mouths of the Café of Heaven and the Café of Hell still yawned — even devoured, as he watched, the meager contents of a tourist bus — a German, a Japanese, and an American couple who glanced at him with frightened eyes.

So much for the effort and ingenuity of Montmartre. All the catering to vice and waste was on an utterly childish scale, and he suddenly realized the meaning of the word "dissipate" — to dissipate into thin air; to make nothing out of something. In the little hours of the night every move from place to place was an enormous human jump, an increase of paying for the privilege of slower and slower motion.

He remembered thousand-franc notes given to an orchestra for playing a single number, hundred-franc notes tossed to a doorman for calling a cab.

But it hadn't been given for nothing.

It had been given, even the most wildly squandered sum, as an offering to destiny that he might not remember the things most worth remembering, the things that now he would always remember — his child taken from his control, his wife escaped to a grave in Vermont.

---

[4]Cheap seat in the aisle. Josephine Baker was an American black entertainer who gained fame in Paris in the 1920s and 1930s.

[5]Prostitutes.

In the glare of a *brasserie*[6] a woman spoke to him. He bought her some eggs and coffee, and then, eluding her encouraging stare, gave her a twenty-franc note and took a taxi to his hotel.

II

He woke upon a fine fall day — football weather. The depression of yesterday was gone and he liked the people on the streets. At noon he sat opposite Honoria at Le Grand Vatel, the only restaurant he could think of not reminiscent of champagne dinners and long luncheons that began at two and ended in a blurred and vague twilight.

"Now, how about vegetables? Oughtn't you to have some vegetables?"

"Well, yes."

"Here's *épinards* and *chou-fleur* and carrots and *haricots*."[7]

"I'd like *chou-fleur*."

"Wouldn't you like to have two vegetables?"

"I usually only have one at lunch."

The waiter was pretending to be inordinately fond of children. *"Qu'elle est mignonne la petite! Elle parle exactement comme une Française."*[8]

"How about dessert? Shall we wait and see?"

The waiter disappeared. Honoria looked at her father expectantly.

"What are we going to do?"

"First, we're going to that toy store in the Rue Saint-Honoré and buy you anything you like. And then we're going to the vaudeville at the Empire."

She hesitated. "I like it about the vaudeville, but not the toy store."

"Why not?"

"Well, you brought me this doll." She had it with her. "And I've got lots of things. And we're not rich any more, are we?"

"We never were. But today you are to have anything you want."

"All right," she agreed resignedly.

When there had been her mother and a French nurse he had been inclined to be strict; now he extended himself, reached out for a new tolerance; he must be both parents to her and not shut any of her out of communication.

"I want to get to know you," he said gravely. "First let me introduce myself. My name is Charles J. Wales, of Prague."

"Oh, daddy!" her voice cracked with laughter.

"And who are you, please?" he persisted, and she accepted a rôle immediately: "Honoria Wales, Rue Palatine, Paris."

"Married or single?"

"No, not married. Single."

---

[6]Small, informal restaurant.

[7]Spinach, cauliflower, beans.

[8]"What a cute little girl! She speaks exactly like a French girl."

He indicated the doll. "But I see you have a child, madame."

Unwilling to disinherit it, she took it to her heart and thought quickly: "Yes, I've been married, but I'm not married now. My husband is dead."

He went on quickly, "And the child's name?"

"Simone. That's after my best friend at school."

"I'm very pleased that you're doing so well at school."

"I'm third this month," she boasted. "Elsie" — that was her cousin — "is only about eighteenth, and Richard is at the bottom."

"You like Richard and Elsie, don't you?"

"Oh, yes. I like Richard quite well and I like her all right."

Cautiously and casually he asked: "And Aunt Marion and Uncle Lincoln — which do you like best?"

"Oh, Uncle Lincoln, I guess."

He was increasingly aware of her presence. As they came in, a murmur of ". . . adorable" followed them, and now the people at the next table bent all their silences upon her, staring as if she were something no more conscious than a flower.

"Why don't I live with you?" she asked suddenly. "Because mamma's dead?"

"You must stay here and learn more French. It would have been hard for daddy to take care of you so well."

"I don't really need much taking care of any more. I do everything for myself."

Going out of the restaurant, a man and a woman unexpectedly hailed him.

"Well, the old Wales!"

"Hello there, Lorraine. . . . Dunc."

Sudden ghosts out of the past: Duncan Schaeffer, a friend from college. Lorraine Quarrles, a lovely, pale blonde of thirty; one of a crowd who had helped them make months into days in the lavish times of three years ago.

"My husband couldn't come this year," she said, in answer to his question. "We're poor as hell. So he gave me two hundred a month and told me I could do my worst on that. . . . This your little girl?"

"What about coming back and sitting down?" Duncan asked.

"Can't do it." He was glad for an excuse. As always, he felt Lorraine's passionate, provocative attraction, but his own rhythm was different now.

"Well, how about dinner?" she asked.

"I'm not free. Give me your address and let me call you."

"Charlie, I believe you're sober," she said judicially. "I honestly believe he's sober, Dunc. Pinch him and see if he's sober."

Charlie indicated Honoria with his head. They both laughed.

"What's your address?" said Duncan skeptically.

He hesitated, unwilling to give the name of his hotel.

"I'm not settled yet. I'd better call you. We're going to see the vaudeville at the Empire."

"There! That's what I want to do," Lorraine said. "I want to see some clowns and acrobats and jugglers. That's just what we'll do, Dunc."

"We've got to do an errand first," said Charlie. "Perhaps we'll see you there."

"All right, you snob. . . . Good-by, beautiful little girl."

"Good-by."

Honoria bobbed politely.

Somehow, an unwelcome encounter. They liked him because he was functioning, because he was serious; they wanted to see him, because he was stronger than they were now, because they wanted to draw a certain sustenance from his strength.

At the Empire, Honoria proudly refused to sit upon her father's folded coat. She was already an individual with a code of her own, and Charlie was more and more absorbed by the desire of putting a little of himself into her before she crystallized utterly. It was hopeless to try to know her in so short a time.

Between the acts they came upon Duncan and Lorraine in the lobby where the band was playing.

"Have a drink?"

"All right, but not up at the bar. We'll take a table."

"The perfect father."

Listening abstractedly to Lorraine, Charlie watched Honoria's eyes leave their table, and he followed them wistfully about the room, wondering what they saw. He met her glance and she smiled.

"I liked that lemonade," she said.

What had she said? What had he expected? Going home in a taxi afterward, he pulled her over until her head rested against his chest.

"Darling, do you ever think of your mother?"

"Yes, sometimes," she answered vaguely.

"I don't want you to forget her. Have you got a picture of her?"

"Yes, I think so. Anyhow, Aunt Marion has. Why don't you want me to forget her?"

"She loved you very much."

"I loved her too."

They were silent for a moment.

"Daddy, I want to come and live with you," she said suddenly.

His heart leaped; he had wanted it to come like this.

"Aren't you perfectly happy?"

"Yes, but I love you better than anybody. And you love me better than anybody, don't you, now that mummy's dead?"

"Of course I do. But you won't always like me best, honey. You'll grow up and meet somebody your own age and go marry him and forget you ever had a daddy."

"Yes, that's true," she agreed tranquilly.

He didn't go in. He was coming back at nine o'clock and he wanted to keep himself fresh and new for the thing he must say then.

"When you're safe inside, just show yourself in that window."

"All right. Good-by, dads, dads, dads, dads."

He waited in the dark street until she appeared, all warm and glowing, in the window above and kissed her fingers out into the night.

III

They were waiting. Marion sat behind the coffee service in a dignified black dinner dress that just faintly suggested mourning. Lincoln was walking up and down with the animation of one who had already been talking. They were as anxious as he was to get into the question. He opened it almost immediately:

"I suppose you know what I want to see you about — why I really came to Paris."

Marion played with the black stars on her necklace and frowned.

"I'm awfully anxious to have a home," he continued. "And I'm awfully anxious to have Honoria in it. I appreciate your taking in Honoria for her mother's sake, but things have changed now" — he hesitated and then continued more forcibly — "changed radically with me, and I want to ask you to reconsider the matter. It would be silly for me to deny that about three years ago I was acting badly ——"

Marion looked up at him with hard eyes.

"— but all that's over. As I told you, I haven't had more than a drink a day for over a year, and I take that drink deliberately, so that the idea of alcohol won't get too big in my imagination. You see the idea?"

"No," said Marion succinctly.

"It's a sort of stunt I set myself. It keeps the matter in proportion."

"I get you," said Lincoln. "You don't want to admit it's got any attraction for you."

"Something like that. Sometimes I forget and don't take it. But I try to take it. Anyhow, I couldn't afford to drink in my position. The people I represent are more than satisfied with what I've done, and I'm bringing my sister over from Burlington to keep house for me, and I want awfully to have Honoria too. You know that even when her mother and I weren't getting along well we never let anything that happened touch Honoria. I know she's fond of me and I know I'm able to take care of her and — well, there you are. How do you feel about it?"

He knew that now he would have to take a beating. It would last an hour or two hours, and it would be difficult, but if he modulated his inevitable resentment to the chastened attitude of the reformed sinner, he might win his point in the end.

Keep your temper, he told himself. You don't want to be justified. You want Honoria.

Lincoln spoke first: "We've been talking it over ever since we got your letter last month. We're happy to have Honoria here. She's a dear little thing, and we're glad to be able to help her, but of course that isn't the question ——"

Marion interrupted suddenly. "How long are you going to stay sober, Charlie?" she asked.

"Permanently, I hope."

"How can anybody count on that?"

"You know I never did drink heavily until I gave up business and came over here with nothing to do. Then Helen and I began to run around with ——"

"Please leave Helen out of it. I can't bear to hear you talk about her like that."

He stared at her grimly; he had never been certain how fond of each other the sisters were in life.

"My drinking only lasted about a year and a half — from the time we came over until I — collapsed."

"It was time enough."

"It was time enough," he agreed.

"My duty is entirely to Helen," she said. "I try to think what she would have wanted me to do. Frankly, from the night you did that terrible thing you haven't really existed for me. I can't help that. She was my sister."

"Yes."

"When she was dying she asked me to look out for Honoria. If you hadn't been in a sanitarium then, it might have helped matters."

He had no answer.

"I'll never in my life be able to forget the morning when Helen knocked at my door, soaked to the skin and shivering and said you'd locked her out."

Charlie gripped the sides of the chair. This was more difficult than he expected; he wanted to launch out into a long expostulation and explanation, but he only said: "The night I locked her out —" and she interrupted, "I don't feel up to going over that again."

After a moment's silence Lincoln said: "We're getting off the subject. You want Marion to set aside her legal guardianship and give you Honoria. I think the main point for her is whether she has confidence in you or not."

"I don't blame Marion," Charlie said slowly, "but I think she can have entire confidence in me. I had a good record up to three years ago. Of course, it's within human possibilities I might go wrong any time. But if we wait much longer I'll lose Honoria's childhood and my chance for a home." He shook his head, "I'll simply lose her, don't you see?"

"Yes, I see," said Lincoln.

"Why didn't you think of all this before?" Marion asked.

"I suppose I did, from time to time, but Helen and I were getting along badly. When I consented to the guardianship, I was flat on my back in a sanitarium and the market had cleaned me out. I knew I'd acted badly, and I thought if it would bring any peace to Helen, I'd agree to anything. But now it's different. I'm functioning, I'm behaving damn well, so far as ——"

"Please don't swear at me," Marion said.

He looked at her, startled. With each remark the force of her dislike became more and more apparent. She had built up all her fear of life into one wall and faced it toward him. This trivial reproof was possibly the result of some trouble with the cook several hours before. Charlie became increasingly alarmed at leaving Honoria in this atmosphere of hostility against himself; sooner or later it would come out, in a word here, a shake of the head there, and some of that distrust would be irrevocably implanted in Honoria. But he pulled his temper down out of his face and shut it up inside him; he had won a point, for Lincoln realized the absurdity of Marion's remark and asked her lightly since when she had objected to the word "damn."

"Another thing," Charlie said: "I'm able to give her certain advantages now. I'm going to take a French governess to Prague with me. I've got a lease on a new apartment ——"

He stopped, realizing that he was blundering. They couldn't be expected to accept with equanimity the fact that his income was again twice as large as their own.

"I suppose you can give her more luxuries than we can," said Marion. "When you were throwing away money we were living along watching every ten francs. . . . I suppose you'll start doing it again."

"Oh, no," he said. "I've learned. I worked hard for ten years, you know — until I got lucky in the market, like so many people. Terribly lucky. It won't happen again."

There was a long silence. All of them felt their nerves straining, and for the first time in a year Charlie wanted a drink. He was sure now that Lincoln Peters wanted him to have his child.

Marion shuddered suddenly; part of her saw that Charlie's feet were planted on the earth now, and her own maternal feeling recognized the naturalness of his desire; but she had lived for a long time with a prejudice — a prejudice founded on a curious disbelief in her sister's happiness, and which, in the shock of one terrible night, had turned to hatred for him. It had all happened at a point in her life where the discouragement of ill health and adverse circumstances made it necessary for her to believe in tangible villainy and a tangible villain.

"I can't help what I think!" she cried out suddenly. "How much you were responsible for Helen's death, I don't know. It's something you'll have to square with your own conscience."

An electric current of agony surged through him; for a moment he was almost on his feet, an unuttered sound echoing in his throat. He hung on to himself for a moment, another moment.

"Hold on there," said Lincoln uncomfortably. "I never thought you were responsible for that."

"Helen died of heart trouble," Charlie said dully.

"Yes, heart trouble." Marion spoke as if the phrase had another meaning for her.

Then, in the flatness that followed her outburst, she saw him plainly and she knew he had somehow arrived at control over the situation. Glancing at her husband, she found no help from him, and as abruptly as if it were a matter of no importance, she threw up the sponge.

"Do what you like!" she cried, springing up from her chair. "She's your child. I'm not the person to stand in your way. I think if it were my child I'd rather see her —" She managed to check herself. "You two decide it. I can't stand this. I'm sick. I'm going to bed."

She hurried from the room; after a moment Lincoln said:

"This has been a hard day for her. You know how strongly she feels —" His voice was almost apologetic: "When a woman gets an idea in her head."

"Of course."

"It's going to be all right. I think she sees now that you — can provide for the child, and so we can't very well stand in your way or Honoria's way."

"Thank you, Lincoln."

"I'd better go along and see how she is."

"I'm going."

He was still trembling when he reached the street, but a walk down the Rue Bonaparte to the *quais* set him up, and as he crossed the Seine, fresh and new by the *quai* lamps, he felt exultant. But back in his room he couldn't sleep. The image of Helen haunted him. Helen whom he had loved so until they had senselessly begun to abuse each other's love, tear it into shreds. On that terrible February night that Marion remembered so vividly, a slow quarrel had gone on for hours. There was a scene at the Florida, and then he attempted to take her home, and then she kissed young Webb at a table; after that there was what she had hysterically said. When he arrived home alone he turned the key in the lock in wild anger. How could he know she would arrive an hour later alone, that there would be a snowstorm in which she wandered about in slippers, too confused to find a taxi? Then the aftermath, her escaping pneumonia by a miracle, and all the attendant horror. They were "reconciled," but that was the beginning of the end, and Marion, who had seen with her own eyes and who imagined it to be one of many scenes from her sister's martyrdom, never forgot.

Going over it again brought Helen nearer, and in the white, soft light that steals upon half sleep near morning he found himself talking to her again. She said that he was perfectly right about Honoria and that she wanted Honoria to be with him. She said she was glad he was being good and doing better. She said a lot of other things — very friendly things — but she was in a swing in a white dress, and swinging faster and faster all the time, so that at the end he could not hear clearly all that she said.

IV

He woke up feeling happy. The door of the world was open again. He made plans, vistas, futures for Honoria and himself, but suddenly he grew sad, remembering all the plans he and Helen had made. She had not planned to die. The present was the thing — work to do and someone to love. But not to love too much, for he knew the injury that a father can do to a daughter or a mother to a son by attaching them too closely: afterward, out in the world, the child would seek in the marriage partner the same blind tenderness and, failing probably to find it, turn against love and life.

It was another bright, crisp day. He called Lincoln Peters at the bank where he worked and asked if he could count on taking Honoria when he left for Prague. Lincoln agreed that there was no reason for delay. One thing — the legal guardianship. Marion wanted to retain that a while longer. She was upset by the whole matter, and it would oil things if she felt that the situation was still in her control for another year. Charlie agreed, wanting only the tangible, visible child.

Then the question of a governess. Charles sat in a gloomy agency and talked to a cross Béarnaise and to a buxom Breton peasant, neither of whom he could have endured. There were others whom he would see tomorrow.

He lunched with Lincoln Peters at Griffons, trying to keep down his exultation.

"There's nothing quite like your own child," Lincoln said. "But you understand how Marion feels too."

"She's forgotten how hard I worked for seven years there," Charlie said. "She just remembers one night."

"There's another thing." Lincoln hesitated. "While you and Helen were tearing around Europe throwing money away, we were just getting along. I didn't touch any of the prosperity because I never got ahead enough to carry anything but my insurance. I think Marion felt there was some kind of injustice in it — you not even working toward the end, and getting richer and richer."

"It went just as quick as it came," said Charlie.

"Yes, a lot of it stayed in the hands of *chasseurs* and saxophone players and maîtres d'hôtel — well, the big party's over now. I just said that to explain Marion's feeling about those crazy years. If you drop in about six o'clock tonight before Marion's too tired, we'll settle the details on the spot."

Back at his hotel, Charlie found a *pneumatique*[9] that had been redirected from the Ritz bar where Charlie had left his address for the purpose of finding a certain man.

> Dear Charlie: You were so strange when we saw you the other day that I wondered if I did something to offend you. If so, I'm not conscious of it. In fact, I have thought about you too much for the last year, and it's always been in the back of my mind that I might see you if I came over here. We *did* have such good times that crazy spring, like the night you and I stole the butcher's tricycle, and the time we tried to call on the president and you had the old derby rim and the wire cane. Everybody seems so old lately, but I don't feel old a bit. Couldn't we get together some time today for old time's sake? I've got a vile hang-over for the moment, but will be feeling better this afternoon and will look for you about five in the sweatshop at the Ritz.
>
> Always devotedly,
> Lorraine

His first feeling was one of awe that he had actually, in his mature years, stolen a tricycle and pedaled Lorraine all over the étoile between the small hours and dawn. In retrospect it was a nightmare. Locking out Helen didn't fit in with any other act of his life, but the tricycle incident did — it was one of many. How many weeks or months of dissipation to arrive at that condition of utter irresponsibility?

He tried to picture how Lorraine had appeared to him then — very

---

[9]Message delivered through a citywide system of pneumatic tubes.

attractive; Helen was unhappy about it, though she said nothing. Yesterday, in the restaurant, Lorraine had seemed trite, blurred, worn away. He emphatically did not want to see her, and he was glad Alix had not given away his hotel address. It was a relief to think, instead, of Honoria, to think of Sundays spent with her and of saying good morning to her and of knowing she was there in his house at night, drawing her breath in the darkness.

At five he took a taxi and bought presents for all the Peters — a piquant cloth doll, a box of Roman soldiers, flowers for Marion, big linen handkerchiefs for Lincoln.

He saw, when he arrived in the apartment, that Marion had accepted the inevitable. She greeted him now as though he were a recalcitrant member of the family, rather than a menacing outsider. Honoria had been told she was going; Charlie was glad to see that her tact made her conceal her excessive happiness. Only on his lap did she whisper her delight and the question "When?" before she slipped away with the other children.

He and Marion were alone for a minute in the room, and on an impulse he spoke out boldly:

"Family quarrels are bitter things. They don't go according to any rules. They're not like aches or wounds; they're more like splits in the skin that won't heal because there's not enough material. I wish you and I could be on better terms."

"Some things are hard to forget," she answered. "It's a question of confidence." There was no answer to this and presently she asked, "When do you propose to take her?"

"As soon as I can get a governess. I hoped the day after tomorrow."

"That's impossible. I've got to get her things in shape. Not before Saturday."

He yielded. Coming back into the room, Lincoln offered him a drink.

"I'll take my daily whisky," he said.

It was warm here, it was a home, people together by a fire. The children felt very safe and important; the mother and father were serious, watchful. They had things to do for the children more important than his visit here. A spoonful of medicine was, after all, more important than the strained relations between Marion and himself. They were not dull people, but they were very much in the grip of life and circumstances. He wondered if he couldn't do something to get Lincoln out of his rut at the bank.

A long peal at the door-bell; the *bonne à tout faire*[10] passed through and went down the corridor. The door opened upon another long ring, and then voices, and the three in the salon looked up expectantly; Richard moved to bring the corridor within his range of vision, and Marion rose. Then the maid came back along the corridor, closely followed by the voices, which developed under the light into Duncan Schaeffer and Lorraine Quarrles.

They were gay, they were hilarious, they were roaring with laughter. For

---

[10] Maid.

a moment Charlie was astounded; unable to understand how they ferreted out the Peters' address.

"Ah-h-h!" Duncan wagged his finger roguishly at Charlie. "Ah-h-h!"

They both slid down another cascade of laughter. Anxious and at a loss, Charlie shook hands with them quickly and presented them to Lincoln and Marion. Marion nodded, scarcely speaking. She had drawn back a step toward the fire; her little girl stood beside her, and Marion put an arm about her shoulder.

With growing annoyance at the intrusion, Charlie waited for them to explain themselves. After some concentration Duncan said:

"We came to invite you out to dinner. Lorraine and I insist that all this shishi, cagy business 'bout your address got to stop."

Charlie came closer to them, as if to force them backward down the corridor.

"Sorry, but I can't. Tell me where you'll be and I'll phone you in half an hour."

This made no impression. Lorraine sat down suddenly on the side of a chair, and focusing her eyes on Richard, cried, "Oh, what a nice little boy! Come here, little boy." Richard glanced at his mother, but did not move. With a perceptible shrug of her shoulders, Lorraine turned back to Charlie:

"Come and dine. Sure your cousins won' mine. See you so sel'om. Or solemn."

"I can't," said Charlie sharply. "You two have dinner and I'll phone you."

Her voice became suddenly unpleasant. "All right, we'll go. But I remember once when you hammered on my door at four A.M. I was enough of a good sport to give you a drink. Come on, Dunc."

Still in slow motion, with blurred, angry faces, with uncertain feet, they retired along the corridor.

"Good night," Charlie said.

"Good night!" responded Lorraine emphatically.

When he went back into the salon Marion had not moved, only now her son was standing in the circle of her other arm. Lincoln was still swinging Honoria back and forth like a pendulum from side to side.

"What an outrage!" Charlie broke out. "What an absolute outrage!"

Neither of them answered. Charlie dropped into an armchair, picked up his drink, set it down again and said:

"People I haven't seen for two years having the colossal nerve ——"

He broke off. Marion had made the sound "Oh!" in one swift, furious breath, turned her body from him with a jerk and left the room.

Lincoln set down Honoria carefully.

"You children go in and start your soup," he said, and when they obeyed, he said to Charlie:

"Marion's not well and she can't stand shocks. That kind of people make her really physically sick."

"I didn't tell them to come here. They wormed your name out of somebody. They deliberately ——"

"Well, it's too bad. It doesn't help matters. Excuse me a minute."

Left alone, Charlie sat tense in his chair. In the next room he could hear the children eating, talking in monosyllables, already oblivious to the scene between their elders. He heard a murmur of conversation from a farther room and then the ticking bell of a telephone receiver picked up, and in a panic he moved to the other side of the room and out of earshot.

In a minute Lincoln came back. "Look here, Charlie. I think we'd better call off dinner for tonight. Marion's in bad shape."

"Is she angry with me?"

"Sort of," he said, almost roughly. "She's not strong and ——"

"You mean she's changed her mind about Honoria?"

"She's pretty bitter right now. I don't know. You phone me at the bank tomorrow."

"I wish you'd explain to her I never dreamed these people would come here. I'm just as sore as you are."

"I couldn't explain anything to her now."

Charlie got up. He took his coat and hat and started down the corridor. Then he opened the door of the dining room and said in a strange voice, "Good night, children."

Honoria rose and ran around the table to hug him.

"Good night, sweetheart," he said vaguely, and then trying to make his voice more tender, trying to conciliate something, "Good night, dear children."

V

Charlie went directly to the Ritz bar with the furious idea of finding Lorraine and Duncan, but they were not there, and he realized that in any case there was nothing he could do. He had not touched his drink at the Peters', and now he ordered a whisky-and-soda. Paul came over to say hello.

"It's a great change," he said sadly. "We do about half the business we did. So many fellows I hear about back in the States lost everything, maybe not in the first crash, but then in the second. Your friend George Hardt lost every cent, I hear. Are you back in the States?"

"No, I'm in business in Prague."

"I heard that you lost a lot in the crash."

"I did," and he added grimly, "but I lost everything I wanted in the boom."

"Selling short."

"Something like that."

Again the memory of those days swept over him like a nightmare — the people they had met travelling; then people who couldn't add a row of figures or speak a coherent sentence. The little man Helen had consented to dance with at the ship's party, who had insulted her ten feet from the table;

the women and girls carried screaming with drink or drugs out of public places ——

—— The men who locked their wives out in the snow, because the snow of twenty-nine wasn't real snow. If you didn't want it to be snow, you just paid some money.

He went to the phone and called the Peters' apartment; Lincoln answered.

"I called up because this thing is on my mind. Has Marion said anything definite?"

"Marion's sick," Lincoln answered shortly. "I know this thing isn't altogether your fault, but I can't have her go to pieces about it. I'm afraid we'll have to let it slide for six months; I can't take the chance of working her up to this state again."

"I see."

"I'm sorry, Charlie."

He went back to his table. His whisky glass was empty, but he shook his head when Alix looked at it questioningly. There wasn't much he could do now except send Honoria some things; he would send her a lot of things tomorrow. He thought rather angrily that this was just money — he had given so many people money. . . .

"No, no more," he said to the waiter. "What do I owe you?"

He would come back some day; they couldn't make him pay forever. But he wanted his child, and nothing was much good now, beside that fact. He wasn't young any more, with a lot of nice thoughts and dreams to have by himself. He was absolutely sure Helen wouldn't have wanted him to be so alone.   [1931]

GUSTAVE FLAUBERT *(1821–1880) said that in writing, everything is a matter of style, of the distinctive way one expresses oneself. Flaubert's life was remarkable mostly for the way he devoted himself to writing fiction. He once told a friend, "I have more imagination than heart." Born into a thrifty, prosperous family in Rouen, Flaubert was the son of a surgeon. His mother encouraged him to read literature and write plays while he was still a child. He attended school in Rouen and began to study law in Paris, but in 1844 he suffered the first of many attacks of unconsciousness — possibly epilepsy — so he gave up law and returned home to live with his widowed mother. Like many of his contemporaries, including the poet Charles Baudelaire and his relative Guy de Maupassant, Flaubert was afflicted with syphilis. In his* Dictionary of Accepted Opinions *(1881), Flaubert defined syphilis as being in his time as common as the cold.*

Flaubert's most famous novel is Madame Bovary *(1857), which he worked on for more than four years, struggling to rewrite and polish it. He knew that "the public wants works which flatter its illusions," yet he insisted on telling the truth: "You don't make art out of good intentions." After his mother's death, he wrote "A Simple Heart" for the pleasure of remembering his own childhood in a provincial household. He later said he intended the story to be the legend of a modern saint. It was one of the* Three Tales *he published in 1877. By taking a housemaid as his heroine, he wanted to show that "there are no noble subjects or ignoble subjects; from the standpoint of pure Art one might almost establish the axiom that there is no such thing as subject — style in itself being an absolute manner of seeing things." In his fiction he included no detail that did not have an idea behind it and no physical fact that did not help to establish a psychological mood. Letting the tale speak for itself, Flaubert believed that "the artist ought not to appear in the work any more than God in nature."*

Although Flaubert wrote few short stories, he experimented with different prose forms during his lifetime. He always sought the most exact use of language, trying to make his prose "as rhythmical as verse and as precise as the language of science." His devotion to perfecting his literary craft became an example to later writers, his self-discipline teaching what the novelist Julian Barnes has called "the virtue of being able to remain by yourself in your own room." Flaubert died of a sudden cerebral hemorrhage and was buried in the cemetery at Rouen.

GUSTAVE FLAUBERT

A Simple Heart

Translated by Robert Baldick

I

For half a century the women of Pont-l'Évêque envied Mme Aubain her maidservant Félicité.

In return for a hundred francs a year she did all the cooking and the housework, the sewing, the washing, and the ironing. She could bridle a horse, fatten poultry, and churn butter, and she remained faithful to her mistress, who was by no means an easy person to get on with.

Mme Aubain had married a young fellow who was good-looking but badly-off, and who died at the beginning of 1809, leaving her with two small children and a pile of debts. She then sold all her property except for the farms of Toucques and Geffosses, which together brought in five thousand francs a year at the most, and left her house at Saint-Melaine for one behind the covered market which was cheaper to run and had belonged to her family.

This house had a slate roof and stood between the alley-way and a lane leading down to the river. Inside there were differences in level which were the cause of many a stumble. A narrow entrance-hall separated the kitchen from the parlor, where Mme Aubain sat all day long in a wicker easy-chair by the window. Eight mahogany chairs were lined up against the white-painted wainscoting, and under the barometer stood an old piano loaded with a pyramid of boxes and cartons. On either side of the chimney-piece, which was carved out of yellow marble in the Louis Quinze style, there was a tapestry-covered arm-chair, and in the middle was a clock designed to look like a temple of Vesta.[1] The whole room smelt a little musty, as the floor was on a lower level than the garden.

On the first floor was "Madame's" bedroom — very spacious, with a patterned wallpaper of pale flowers and a portrait of "Monsieur" dressed in what had once been the height of fashion. It opened into a smaller room in which there were two cots, without mattresses. Then came the drawing-room, which was always shut up and full of furniture covered with dust-sheets. Next there was a passage leading to the study, where books and papers filled the shelves of a book-case in three sections built round a big writing-table of dark wood. The two end panels were hidden under pen-and-ink drawings, landscapes in gouache, and etchings by Audran,[2] souvenirs of better days and bygone luxury. On the second floor a dormer window gave light to Félicité's room, which looked out over the fields.

---

[1] Roman goddess of the hearth.
[2] Family name of several famous French engravers.

Every day Félicité got up at dawn, so as not to miss Mass, and worked until evening without stopping. Then, once dinner was over, the plates and dishes put away, and the door bolted, she piled ashes on the log fire and went to sleep in front of the hearth, with her rosary in her hands. Nobody could be more stubborn when it came to haggling over prices, and as for cleanliness, the shine on her saucepans was the despair of all the other servants. Being of a thrifty nature, she ate slowly, picking up from the table the crumbs from her loaf of bread — a twelve pound loaf which was baked specially for her and lasted twenty days.

All the year round she wore a kerchief of printed calico fastened behind with a pin, a bonnet which covered her hair, grey stockings, a red skirt, and over her jacket a bibbed apron such as hospital nurses wear.

Her face was thin and her voice was sharp. At twenty-five she was often taken for forty; once she reached fifty, she stopped looking any age in particular. Always silent and upright and deliberate in her movements, she looked like a wooden doll driven by clock-work.

II

Like everyone else, she had had her love-story.

Her father, a mason, had been killed when he fell off some scaffolding. Then her mother died, and when her sisters went their separate ways, a farmer took her in, sending her, small as she was, to look after the cows out in the fields. She went about in rags, shivering with cold, used to lie flat on the ground to drink water out of the ponds, would be beaten for no reason at all, and was finally turned out of the house for stealing thirty sous, a theft of which she was innocent. She found work at another farm, looking after the poultry, and as she was liked by her employers the other servants were jealous of her.

One August evening — she was eighteen at the time — they took her off to the fête at Colleville. From the start she was dazed and bewildered by the noise of the fiddles, the lamps in the trees, the medley of gaily colored dresses, the gold crosses and lace, and the throng of people jigging up and down. She was standing shyly on one side when a smart young fellow, who had been leaning on the shaft of a cart, smoking his pipe, came up and asked her to dance. He treated her to cider, coffee, griddle-cake, and a silk necker-chief, and imagining that she knew what he was after, offered to see her home. At the edge of a field of oats, he pushed her roughly to the ground. Thoroughly frightened, she started screaming for help. He took to his heels.

Another night, on the road to Beaumont, she tried to get past a big, slow-moving wagon loaded with hay, and as she was squeezing by she recognized Théodore.

He greeted her quite calmly, saying that she must forgive him for the way he had behaved to her, as "it was the drink that did it."

She did not know what to say in reply and felt like running off.

Straight away he began talking about the crops and the notabilities of the commune, saying that his father had left Colleville for the farm at Les Écots, so that they were now neighbors.

"Ah!" she said.

He added that his family wanted to see him settle but that he was in no hurry and was waiting to find a wife to suit his fancy. She lowered her head. Then he asked her if she was thinking of getting married. She answered with a smile that it was mean of him to make fun of her.

"But I'm not making fun of you!" he said. "I swear I'm not!"

He put his left arm round her waist, and she walked on supported by his embrace. Soon they slowed down. There was a gentle breeze blowing, the stars were shining, the huge load of hay was swaying about in front of them, and the four horses were raising clouds of dust as they shambled along. Then, without being told, they turned off to the right. He kissed her once more and she disappeared into the darkness.

The following week Théodore got her to grant him several rendezvous.

They would meet at the bottom of a farm-yard, behind a wall, under a solitary tree. She was not ignorant of life as young ladies are, for the animals had taught her a great deal; but her reason and an instinctive sense of honor prevented her from giving way. The resistance she put up inflamed Théodore's passion to such an extent that in order to satisfy it (or perhaps out of sheer naïveté) he proposed to her. At first she refused to believe him, but he swore that he was serious.

Soon afterwards he had a disturbing piece of news to tell her: the year before, his parents had paid a man to do his military service for him, but now he might be called up again any day, and the idea of going into the army frightened him. In Félicité's eyes this cowardice of his appeared to be a proof of his affection, and she loved him all the more for it. Every night she would steal out to meet him, and every night Théodore would plague her with his worries and entreaties.

In the end he said that he was going to the Prefecture himself to make inquiries, and that he would come and tell her how matters stood the following Sunday, between eleven and midnight.

At the appointed hour she hurried to meet her sweetheart, but found one of his friends waiting for her instead.

He told her that she would not see Théodore again. To make sure of avoiding conscription, he had married a very rich old woman, Mme Lehoussais of Toucques.

Her reaction was an outburst of frenzied grief. She threw herself on the ground, screaming and calling on God, and lay moaning all alone in the open until sunrise. Then she went back to the farm and announced her intention of leaving. At the end of the month, when she had received her wages, she wrapped her small belongings up in a kerchief and made her way to Pont-l'Évêque.

In front of the inn there, she sought information from a woman in a widow's bonnet, who, as it happened, was looking for a cook. The girl did not know much about cooking, but she seemed so willing and expected so little that finally Mme Aubain ended up by saying: "Very well, I will take you on."

A quarter of an hour later Félicité was installed in her house.

At first she lived there in a kind of fearful awe caused by "the style of the house" and the memory of "Monsieur" brooding over everything. Paul and Virginie, the boy aged seven and the girl barely four, seemed to her to be made of some precious substance. She used to carry them about pick-a-back, and when Mme Aubain told her not to keep on kissing them she was cut to the quick. All the same, she was happy now, for her pleasant surroundings had dispelled her grief.

On Thursdays, a few regular visitors came in to play Boston, and Félicité got the cards and the foot-warmers ready beforehand. They always arrived punctually at eight, and left before the clock struck eleven.

Every Monday morning the second-hand dealer who lived down the alley put all his junk out on the pavement. Then the hum of voices began to fill the town, mingled with the neighing of horses, the bleating of lambs, the grunting of pigs, and the rattle of carts in the streets.

About midday, when the market was in full swing, a tall old peasant with a hooked nose and his cap on the back of his head would appear at the door. This was Robelin, the farmer from Geffosses. A little later, and Liébard, the farmer from Toucques, would arrive — a short, fat, red-faced fellow in a grey jacket and leather gaiters fitted with spurs.

Both men had hens or cheeses they wanted to sell to "Madame." But Félicité was up to all their tricks and invariably outwitted them, so that they went away full of respect for her.

From time to time Mme Aubain had a visit from an uncle of hers, the Marquis de Grémanville, who had been ruined by loose living and was now living at Falaise on his last remaining scrap of property. He always turned up at lunch-time, accompanied by a hideous poodle who dirtied all the furniture with its paws. However hard he tried to behave like a gentleman, even going so far as to raise his hat every time he mentioned "my late father," the force of habit was usually too much for him, for he would start pouring himself one glass after another and telling bawdy stories. Félicité used to push him gently out of the house, saying politely: "You've had quite enough, Monsieur de Grémanville. See you another time!" and shutting the door on him.

She used to open it with pleasure to M. Bourais, who was a retired solicitor. His white tie and his bald head, his frilled shirt-front and his ample brown frock-coat, the way he had of rounding his arm to take a pinch of snuff, and indeed everything about him made an overwhelming impression on her such as we feel when we meet some outstanding personality.

As he looked after "Madame's" property, he used to shut himself up with her for hours in "Monsieur's" study. He lived in dread of compromising his reputation, had a tremendous respect for the Bench, and laid claim to some knowledge of Latin.

To give the children a little painless instruction, he made them a present of a geography book with illustrations. These represented scenes in different parts of the world, such as cannibals wearing feather head-dresses, a monkey carrying off a young lady, Bedouins in the desert, a whale being harpooned, and so on.

Paul explained these pictures to Félicité, and that indeed was all the education she ever had. As for the children, they were taught by Guyot, a poor devil employed at the Town Hall, who was famous for his beautiful handwriting, and who had a habit of sharpening his penknife on his boots.

When the weather was fine the whole household used to set off early for a day on the Geffosses farm.

The farm-yard there was on a slope, with the house in the middle; and the sea, in the distance, looked like a streak of grey. Félicité would take some slices of cold meat out of her basket, and they would have their lunch in a room adjoining the dairy. It was all that remained of a country house which had fallen into ruin, and the wallpaper hung in shreds, fluttering in the draught. Mme Aubain used to sit with bowed head, absorbed in her memories, so that the children were afraid to talk. "Why don't you run along and play?" she would say, and away they went.

Paul climbed up into the barn, caught birds, played ducks and drakes on the pond, or banged with a stick on the great casks, which sounded just like drums.

Virginie fed the rabbits, or scampered off to pick cornflowers, showing her little embroidered knickers as she ran.

One autumn evening they came home through the fields. The moon, which was in its first quarter, lit up part of the sky, and there was some mist floating like a scarf over the winding Toucques. The cattle, lying out in the middle of the pasture, looked peacefully at the four people walking by. In the third field a few got up and made a half circle in front of them.

"Don't be frightened!" said Félicité, and crooning softly, she stroked the back of the nearest animal. It turned about and the others did the same. But while they were crossing the next field they suddenly heard a dreadful bellowing. It came from a bull which had been hidden by the mist, and which now came towards the two women.

Mme Aubain started to run.

"No! No!" said Félicité. "Not so fast!"

All the same they quickened their pace, hearing behind them a sound of heavy breathing which came nearer and nearer. The bull's hooves thudded like hammers on the turf, and they realized that it had broken into a gallop. Turning round, Félicité tore up some clods of earth and flung them at its eyes. It lowered its muzzle and thrust its horns forward, trembling with rage and bellowing horribly.

By now Mme Aubain had got to the end of the field with her two children and was frantically looking for a way over the high bank. Félicité was still backing away from the bull, hurling clods of turf which blinded it, and shouting: "Hurry! Hurry!"

Mme Aubain got down into the ditch, pushed first Virginie and then Paul up the other side, fell once or twice trying to climb the bank, and finally managed it with a valiant effort.

The bull had driven Félicité back against a gate, and its slaver was spurting into her face. In another second it would have gored her, but she just had time to slip between two of the bars, and the great beast halted in amazement.

This adventure was talked about at Pont-l'Évêque for a good many years, but Félicité never prided herself in the least on what she had done, as it never occurred to her that she had done anything heroic.

Virginie claimed all her attention, for the fright had affected the little girl's nerves, and M. Poupart, the doctor, recommended sea-bathing at Trouville.

In those days the resort had few visitors. Mme Aubain made inquiries, consulted Bourais, and got everything ready as though for a long journey.

Her luggage went off in Liébard's cart the day before she left. The next morning he brought along two horses, one of which had a woman's saddle with a velvet back, while the other carried a cloak rolled up to make a kind of seat on its crupper. Mme Aubain sat on this, with Liébard in front. Félicité looked after Virginie on the other horse, and Paul mounted M. Lechaptois's donkey, which he had lent them on condition they took great care of it.

The road was so bad that it took two hours to travel the five miles to Toucques. The horses sank into the mud up to their pasterns and had to jerk their hind-quarters to get out; often they stumbled in the ruts, or else they had to jump. In some places, Liébard's mare came to a sudden stop, and while he waited patiently for her to move off again, he talked about the people whose properties bordered the road, adding moral reflections to each story. For instance, in the middle of Toucques, as they were passing underneath some windows set in a mass of nasturtiums, he shrugged his shoulders and said:

"There's a Madame Lehoussais lives here. Now instead of taking a young man, she . . ."

Félicité did not hear the rest, for the horses had broken into a trot and the donkey was galloping along. All three turned down a bridle-path, a gate swung open, a couple of boys appeared, and everyone dismounted in front of a manure-heap right outside the farm-house door.

Old Mother Liébard welcomed her mistress with every appearance of pleasure. She served up a sirloin of beef for lunch, with tripe and black pudding, a fricassee of chicken, sparkling cider, a fruit tart and brandy-plums, garnishing the whole meal with compliments to Madame, who seemed to be enjoying better health, to Mademoiselle, who had turned into a "proper little beauty," and to Monsieur Paul, who had "filled out a lot." Nor did she forget their deceased grandparents, whom the Liébards had known personally, having been in the family's service for several generations.

Like its occupants, the farm had an air of antiquity. The ceiling-beams were worm-eaten, the walls black with smoke, and the window-panes grey with dust. There was an oak dresser laden with all sorts of odds and ends — jugs, plates, pewter bowls, wolf-traps, sheep-shears, and an enormous syringe which amused the children. In the three yards outside there was not a single tree without either mushrooms at its base or mistletoe in its branches. Several had been blown down and had taken root again in the middle; all of them were bent under the weight of their apples. The thatched roofs, which looked like brown velvet and varied in thickness, weathered the fiercest winds, but the cart-shed was tumbling down. Mme Aubain said that she would have it seen to, and ordered the animals to be reharnessed.

It took them another half-hour to reach Trouville. The little caravan dismounted to make their way along the Écores, a cliff jutting right out over the boats moored below; and three minutes later they got to the end of the quay and entered the courtyard of the Golden Lamb, the inn kept by Mère David.

After the first few days Virginie felt stronger, as a result of the change of air and the sea-bathing. Not having a costume, she went into the water in her chemise and her maid dressed her afterwards in a customs officer's hut which was used by the bathers.

In the afternoons they took the donkey and went off beyond the Roches-Noires, in the direction of Hennequeville. To begin with, the path went uphill between gentle slopes like the lawns in a park, and then came out on a plateau where pastureland and ploughed fields alternated. On either side there were holly-bushes standing out from the tangle of brambles, and here and there a big dead tree spread its zigzag branches against the blue sky.

They almost always rested in the same field, with Deauville on their left, Le Havre on their right, and the open sea in front. The water glittered in the sunshine, smooth as a mirror, and so still that the murmur it made was scarcely audible; unseen sparrows could be heard twittering, and the sky covered the whole scene with its huge canopy. Mme Aubain sat doing her needlework, Virginie plaited rushes beside her, Félicité gathered lavender, and Paul, feeling profoundly bored, longed to get up and go.

Sometimes they crossed the Toucques in a boat and hunted for shells. When the tide went out, sea-urchins, ormers, and jelly-fish were left behind; and the children scampered around, snatching at the foam-flakes carried on the wind. The sleepy waves, breaking on the sand, spread themselves out along the shore. The beach stretched as far as the eye could see, bounded on the land side by the dunes which separated it from the Marais, a broad meadow in the shape of an arena. When they came back that way, Trouville, on the distant hillside, grew bigger at every step, and with its medley of oddly assorted houses seemed to blossom out in gay disorder.

On exceptionally hot days they stayed in their room. The sun shone in dazzling bars of light between the slats of the blind. There was not a sound to be heard in the village, and not a soul to be seen down in the street. Everything seemed more peaceful in the prevailing silence. In the distance caulkers were hammering away at the boats, and the smell of tar was wafted along by a sluggish breeze.

The principal amusement consisted in watching the fishingboats come in. As soon as they had passed the buoys, they started tacking. With their canvas partly lowered and their foresails blown out like balloons they glided through the splashing waves as far as the middle of the harbor, where they suddenly dropped anchor. Then each boat came alongside the quay, and the crew threw ashore their catch of quivering fish. A line of carts stood waiting, and women in cotton bonnets rushed forward to take the baskets and kiss their men.

One day one of these women spoke to Félicité, who came back to the inn soon after in a state of great excitement. She explained that she had found one of her sisters — and Nastasie Barette, now Leroux, made her appearance, with a baby at her breast, another child holding her right hand, and on her left a little sailor-boy, his arms akimbo and his cap over one ear.

Mme Aubain sent her off after a quarter of an hour. From then on they were forever hanging round the kitchen or loitering about when the family went for a walk, though the husband kept out of sight.

Félicité became quite attached to them. She bought them a blanket, several shirts, and a stove; and it was clear that they were bent on getting all they could out of her.

This weakness of hers annoyed Mme Aubain, who in any event disliked the familiar way in which the nephew spoke to Paul. And so, as Virginie had started coughing and the good weather was over, she decided to go back to Pont-l'Évêque.

M. Bourais advised her on the choice of a school; Caen was considered the best, so it was there that Paul was sent. He said good-bye bravely, feeling really rather pleased to be going to a place where he would have friends of his own.

Mme Aubain resigned herself to the loss of her son, knowing that it was unavoidable. Virginie soon got used to it. Félicité missed the din he used to make, but she was given something new to do which served as a distraction; from Christmas onwards she had to take the little girl to catechism every day.

III

After genuflecting at the door, she walked up the center aisle under the nave, opened the door of Mme Aubain's pew, sat down, and started looking about her.

The choir stalls were all occupied, with the boys on the right and the girls on the left, while the curé stood by the lectern. In one of the stained-glass windows in the apse the Holy Ghost looked down on the Virgin; another window showed her kneeling before the Infant Jesus; and behind the tabernacle there was a wood-carving of St. Michael slaying the dragon.

The priest began with a brief outline of sacred history. Listening to him, Félicité saw in imagination the Garden of Eden, the Flood, the Tower of Babel, cities burning, peoples dying, and idols being overthrown; and his dazzling vision left her with a great respect for the Almighty and profound fear of His wrath.

Then she wept as she listened to the story of the Passion. Why had they crucified Him, when He loved children, fed the multitudes, healed the blind, and had chosen out of humility to be born among the poor, on the litter of a stable? The sowing of the seed, the reaping of the harvest, the pressing of the grapes — all those familiar things of which the Gospels speak had their place in her life. God had sanctified them in passing, so that she loved the lambs more tenderly for love of the Lamb of God, and the doves for the sake of the Holy Ghost.

She found it difficult, however, to imagine what the Holy Ghost looked like, for it was not just a bird but a fire as well, and sometimes a breath. She wondered whether that was its light she had seen flitting about the edge of the marshes at night, whether that was its breath she had felt driving the clouds across the sky, whether that was its voice she had heard in the sweet music of the bells. And she sat in silent adoration, delighting in the coolness of the walls and the quiet of the church.

Of dogma she neither understood nor even tried to understand anything. The curé discoursed, the children repeated their lesson, and she finally dropped off to sleep, waking up suddenly at the sound of their sabots[3] clattering across the flagstones as they left the church.

It was in this manner, simply by hearing it expounded, that she learnt her catechism, for her religious education had been neglected in her youth. From then on she copied all Virginie's observances, fasting when she did and going to confession with her. On the feast of Corpus Christi the two of them made an altar of repose together.

The preparations for Virginie's first communion caused her great anxiety. She worried over her shoes, her rosary, her missal, and her gloves. And how she trembled as she helped Mme Aubain to dress the child!

All through the Mass her heart was in her mouth. One side of the choir was hidden from her by M. Bourais, but directly opposite her she could see the flock of maidens, looking like a field of snow with their white crowns perched on top of their veils; and she recognized her little darling from a distance by her dainty neck and her rapt attitude. The bell tinkled. Every head bowed low, and there was a silence. Then, to the thunderous accompaniment of the organ, choir and congregation joined in singing the *Agnus Dei*. Next the boys' procession began, and after that the girls got up from their seats. Slowly, their hands joined in prayer, they went towards the brightly lit altar, knelt on the first step, received the Host one by one, and went back to their places in the same order. When it was Virginie's turn, Félicité leant forward to see her, and in one of those imaginative flights born of real affection, it seemed to her that she herself was in the child's place. Virginie's face became her own, Virginie's dress clothed her, Virginie's heart was beating in her breast; and as she closed her eyes and opened her mouth, she almost fainted away.

Early next morning she went to the sacristy and asked M. le Curé to give her communion. She received the sacrament with all due reverence, but did not feel the same rapture as she had the day before.

Mme Aubain wanted her daughter to possess every accomplishment, and since Guyot could not teach her English or music, she decided to send her as a boarder to the Ursuline Convent at Honfleur.

Virginie raised no objection, but Félicité went about sighing at Madame's lack of feeling. Then she thought that perhaps her mistress was right: such matters, after all, lay outside her province.

Finally the day arrived when an old wagonette stopped at their door, and a nun got down from it who had come to fetch Mademoiselle. Félicité

---

[3] Wooden shoes.

hoisted the luggage up on top, gave the driver some parting instructions, and put six pots of jam, a dozen pears, and a bunch of violets in the boot.

At the last moment Virginie burst into a fit of sobbing. She threw her arms round her mother, who kissed her on the forehead, saying: "Come now, be brave, be brave." The step was pulled up and the carriage drove away.

Then Mme Aubain broke down, and that evening all her friends, M. and Mme Lormeau, Mme Lechaptois, the Rochefeuille sisters, M. de Houppeville, and Bourais, came in to console her.

To begin with she missed her daughter badly. But she had a letter from her three times a week, wrote back on the other days, walked around her garden, did a little reading, and thus contrived to fill the empty hours.

As for Félicité, she went into Virginie's room every morning from sheer force of habit and looked round it. It upset her not having to brush the child's hair any more, tie her bootlaces, or tuck her up in bed; and she missed seeing her sweet face all the time and holding her hand when they went out together. For want of something to do, she tried making lace, but her fingers were too clumsy and broke the threads. She could not settle to anything, lost her sleep, and, to use her own words, was "eaten up inside."

To "occupy her mind," she asked if her nephew Victor might come and see her, and permission was granted.

He used to arrive after Mass on Sunday, his cheeks flushed, his chest bare, and smelling of the countryside through which he had come. She laid a place for him straight away, opposite hers, and they had lunch together. Eating as little as possible herself, in order to save the expense, she stuffed him so full of food that he fell asleep after the meal. When the first bell for vespers rang, she woke him up, brushed his trousers, tied his tie, and set off for church, leaning on his arm with all a mother's pride.

His parents always told him to get something out of her — a packet of brown sugar perhaps, some soap, or a little brandy, sometimes even money. He brought her his clothes to be mended, and she did the work gladly, thankful for anything that would force him to come again.

In August his father took him on a coasting trip. The children's holidays were just beginning, and it cheered her up to have them home again. But Paul was turning capricious and Virginie was getting too old to be addressed familiarly — a state of affairs which put a barrier of constraint between them.

Victor went to Morlaix, Dunkirk, and Brighton in turn, and brought her a present after each trip. The first time it was a box covered with shells, the second a coffee cup, the third a big gingerbread man. He was growing quite handsome, with his trim figure, his little moustache, his frank open eyes, and the little leather cap that he wore on the back of his head like a pilot. He kept her amused by telling her stories full of nautical jargon.

One Monday — it was the fourteenth of July 1819, a date she never forgot — Victor told her that he had signed on for an ocean voyage, and that on the Wednesday night he would be taking the Honfleur packet to join his schooner, which was due to sail shortly from Le Havre. He might be away, he said, for two years.

The prospect of such a long absence made Félicité extremely unhappy, and she felt she must bid him godspeed once more. So on the Wednesday evening, when Madame's dinner was over, she put on her clogs and swiftly covered the ten miles between Pont-l'Évêque and Honfleur.

When she arrived at the Calvary she turned right instead of left, got lost in the shipyards, and had to retrace her steps. Some people she spoke to advised her to hurry. She went right round the harbor, which was full of boats, constantly tripping over moorings. Then the ground fell away, rays of light criss-crossed in front of her, and for a moment, she thought she was going mad, for she could see horses up in the sky.

On the quayside more horses were neighing, frightened by the sea. A derrick was hoisting them into the air and dropping them into one of the boats, which was already crowded with passengers elbowing their way between barrels of cider, baskets of cheese, and sacks of grain. Hens were cackling and the captain swearing, while a cabin-boy stood leaning on the cats-head, completely indifferent to it all. Félicité, who had not recognized him, shouted: "Victor!" and he raised his head. She rushed forward, but at that very moment the gangway was pulled ashore.

The packet moved out of the harbor with women singing as they hauled it along, its ribs creaking and heavy waves lashing its bows. The sail swung round, hiding everyone on board from view, and against the silvery, moonlit sea the boat appeared as a dark shape that grew ever fainter, until at last it vanished in the distance.

As Félicité was passing the Calvary, she felt a longing to commend to God's mercy all that she held most dear; and she stood there praying for a long time, her face bathed in tears, her eyes fixed upon the clouds. The town was asleep, except for the customs officers walking up and down. Water was pouring ceaselessly through the holes in the sluice-gate, making as much noise as a torrent. The clocks struck two.

The convent parlor would not be open before daybreak, and Madame would be annoyed if she were late; so, although she would have liked to give a kiss to the other child, she set off for home. The maids at the inn were just waking up as she got to Pont-l'Évêque.

So the poor lad was going to be tossed by the waves for months on end! His previous voyages had caused her no alarm. People came back from England and Brittany; but America, the Colonies, the Islands, were all so far away, somewhere at the other end of the world.

From then on Félicité thought of nothing but her nephew. On sunny days she hoped he was not too thirsty, and when there was a storm she was afraid he would be struck by lightning. Listening to the wind howling in the chimney or blowing slates off the roof, she saw him being buffeted by the very same storm, perched on the top of a broken mast, with his whole body bent backwards under a sheet of foam; or again — and these were reminiscences of the illustrated geography book — he was being eaten by savages, captured by monkeys in the forest, or dying on a desert shore. But she never spoke of her worries.

Mme Aubain had worries of her own about her daughter. The good nuns said that she was an affectionate child, but very delicate. The slightest emotion upset her, and she had to give up playing the piano.

Her mother insisted on regular letters from the convent. One morning when the postman had not called, she lost patience and walked up and down the room, between her chair and the window. It was really extraordinary! Four days without any news!

Thinking her own example would comfort her, Félicité said:

"I've been six months, Madame, without news."

"News of whom?"

The servant answered gently:

"Why — of my nephew."

"Oh, your nephew!" And Mme Aubain started pacing up and down again, with a shrug of her shoulders that seemed to say: "I wasn't thinking of him — and indeed, why should I? Who cares about a young, good-for-nothing cabin-boy? Whereas my daughter — why, just think!"

Although she had been brought up the hard way, Félicité was indignant with Madame, but she soon forgot. It struck her as perfectly natural to lose one's head where the little girl was concerned. For her, the two children were of equal importance; they were linked together in her heart by a single bond, and their destinies should be the same.

The chemist told her that Victor's ship had arrived at Havana: he had seen this piece of information in a newspaper.

Because of its association with cigars, she imagined Havana as a place where nobody did anything but smoke, and pictured Victor walking about among crowds of Negroes in a cloud of tobacco-smoke. Was it possible, she wondered, "in case of need" to come back by land? And how far was it from Pont-l'Évêque? To find out she asked M. Bourais.

He reached for his atlas, and launched forth into an explanation of latitudes and longitudes, smiling like the pedant he was at Félicité's bewilderment. Finally he pointed with his pencil at a minute black dot inside a ragged oval patch, saying:

"There it is."

She bent over the map, but the network of colored lines meant nothing to her and only tired her eyes. So when Bourais asked her to tell him what was puzzling her, she begged him to show her the house where Victor was living. He threw up his hands, sneezed, and roared with laughter, delighted to come across such simplicity. And Félicité — whose intelligence was so limited that she probably expected to see an actual portrait of her nephew — could not make out why he was laughing.

It was a fortnight later that Liébard came into the kitchen at market-time, as he usually did, and handed her a letter from her brother-in-law. As neither of them could read, she turned to her mistress for help.

Mme Aubain, who was counting the stitches in her knitting, put it down and unsealed the letter. She gave a start, and, looking hard at Félicité, said quietly:

"They have some bad news for you. . . . Your nephew. . . ."

He was dead. That was all the letter had to say.

Félicité dropped on to a chair, leaning her head against the wall and closing her eyelids, which suddenly turned pink. Then, with her head bowed, her hands dangling, and her eyes set, she kept repeating:

"Poor little lad! Poor little lad!"

Liébard looked at her and sighed. Mme Aubain was trembling slightly. She suggested that she should go and see her sister at Trouville, but Félicité shook her head to indicate that there was no need for that.

There was a silence. Old Liébard thought it advisable to go.

Then Félicité said:

"It doesn't matter a bit, not to them it doesn't."

Her head fell forward again, and from time to time she unconsciously picked up the knitting needles lying on the work table.

Some women went past carrying a tray full of dripping linen.

Catching sight of them through the window, she remembered her own washing; she had passed the lye through it the day before and today it needed rinsing. So she left the room.

Her board and tub were on the bank of the Toucques. She threw a pile of chemises down by the water's edge, rolled up her sleeves, and picked up her battledore. The lusty blows she gave with it could be heard in all the neighboring gardens.

The fields were empty, the river rippling in the wind; at the bottom long weeds were waving to and fro, like the hair of corpses floating in the water. She held back her grief, and was very brave until the evening; but in her room she gave way to it completely, lying on her mattress with her face buried in the pillow and her fists pressed against her temples.

Long afterwards she learnt the circumstances of Victor's death from the captain of his ship. He had gone down with yellow fever, and they had bled him too much at the hospital. Four doctors had held him at once. He had died straight away, and the chief doctor had said:

"Good! There goes another!"

His parents had always treated him cruelly. She preferred not to see them again, and they made no advances, either because they had forgotten about her or out of the callousness of the poor.

Meanwhile Virginie was growing weaker. Difficulty in breathing, fits of coughing, protracted bouts of fever, and mottled patches on the cheekbones all indicated some deepseated complaint. M. Poupart had advised a stay in Provence. Mme Aubain decided to follow this suggestion, and, if it had not been for the weather at Pont-l'Évêque, she would have brought her daughter home at once.

She arranged with a jobmaster to drive her out to the convent every Tuesday. There was a terrace in the garden, overlooking the Seine, and there Virginie, leaning on her mother's arm, walked up and down over the fallen vineleaves. Sometimes, while she was looking at the sails in the distance, or at the long stretch of horizon from the Château de Tancarville to the lighthouses of Le Havre, the sun would break through the clouds and make her blink. Afterwards they would rest in the arbor. Her mother had secured a little cask of excellent Malaga, and, laughing at the idea of getting tipsy, Virginie used to drink a thimbleful, but no more.

Her strength revived. Autumn slipped by, and Félicité assured Mme Aubain that there was nothing to fear. But one evening, coming back from some errand in the neighborhood, she found M. Poupart's gig standing at the door. He was in the hall, and Mme Aubain was tying on her bonnet.

"Give me my foot-warmer, purse, gloves. Quickly now!"

Virginie had pneumonia and was perhaps past recovery.

"Not yet!" said the doctor; and the two of them got into the carriage with snowflakes swirling around them. Night was falling and it was very cold.

Félicité rushed into the church to light a candle, and then ran after the gig. She caught up with it an hour later, jumped lightly behind, and hung on to the fringe. But then a thought struck her: the courtyard had not been locked up, the burglars might get in. So she jumped down again.

At dawn the next day she went to the doctor's. He had come home and gone out again on his rounds. Then she waited at the inn, thinking that somebody who was a stranger to the district might call there with a letter. Finally, when it was twilight, she got into the coach for Lisieux.

The convent was at the bottom of a steep lane. When she was halfway down the hill, she heard a strange sound which she recognized as a death-bell tolling.

"It's for somebody else," she thought, as she banged the door-knocker hard.

After a few minutes she heard the sound of shuffling feet, the door opened a little way, and a nun appeared.

The good sister said with an air of compunction that "she had just passed away." At that moment the bell of Saint-Léonard was tolled more vigorously than ever.

Félicité went up to the second floor. From the doorway of the room she could see Virginie lying on her back, her hands clasped together, her mouth open, her head tilted back under a black crucifix that leant over her, her face whiter than the curtains that hung motionless on either side. Mme Aubain was clinging to the foot of the bed and sobbing desperately. The Mother Superior stood on the right. Three candlesticks on the chest of drawers added touches of red to the scene, and fog was whitening the windows. Some nuns led Mme Aubain away.

For two nights Félicité never left the dead girl. She said the same prayers over and over again, sprinkled holy water on the sheets, then sat down again to watch. At the end of her first vigil she noticed that the child's face had gone yellow, the lips were turning blue, the nose looked sharper, and the eyes were sunken. She kissed them several times, and would not have been particularly surprised if Virginie had opened them again: to minds like hers the supernatural is a simple matter. She laid her out, wrapped her in a shroud, put her in her coffin, placed a wreath on her, and spread out her hair. It was fair and amazingly long for her age. Félicité cut off a big lock, half of which she slipped into her bosom, resolving never to part with it.

The body was brought back to Pont-l'Évêque at the request of Mme Aubain, who followed the hearse in a closed carriage.

After the Requiem Mass, it took another three-quarters of an hour to reach the cemetery. Paul walked in front, sobbing. Then came M. Bourais, and after him the principal inhabitants of the town, the women all wearing long black veils, and Félicité. She was thinking about her nephew; and since she had been unable to pay him these last honors, she felt an added grief, just as if they were burying him with Virginie.

Mme Aubain's despair passed all bounds. First of all she rebelled against God, considering it unfair of Him to have taken her daughter from her — for she had never done any harm, and her conscience was quite clear. But was it? She ought to have taken Virginie to the south; other doctors would have saved her life. She blamed herself, wished she could have joined her daughter, and cried out in anguish in her dreams. One dream in particular obsessed her. Her husband, dressed like a sailor, came back from a long voyage, and told her amid tears that he had been ordered to take Virginie away — whereupon they put their heads together to discover somewhere to hide her.

One day she came in from the garden utterly distraught. A few minutes earlier — and she pointed to the spot — father and daughter had appeared to her, doing nothing, but simply looking at her.

For several months she stayed in her room in a kind of stupor. Félicité scolded her gently, telling her that she must take care of herself for her son's sake, and also in remembrance of "her."

"Her?" repeated Mme Aubain, as if she were waking from a sleep. "Oh, yes, of course! You don't forget her, do you!" This was an allusion to the cemetery, where she herself was strictly forbidden to go.

Félicité went there every day. She would set out on the stroke of four, going past the houses, up the hill, and through the gate, until she came to Virginie's grave. There was a little column of pink marble with a tablet at its base, and a tiny garden enclosed by chains. The beds were hidden under a carpet of flowers. She watered their leaves and changed the sand, going down on her knees to fork the ground thoroughly. The result was that when Mme Aubain was able to come here, she experienced a feeling of relief, a kind of consolation.

Then the years slipped by, each one like the last, with nothing to vary the rhythm of the great festivals: Easter, the Assumption, All Saints' Day. Domestic events marked dates that later served as points of reference. Thus in 1825 a couple of glaziers whitewashed the hall; in 1827 a piece of the roof fell into the courtyard and nearly killed a man; and in the summer of 1828 it was Madame's turn to provide the bread for consecration. About this time Bourais went away in a mysterious fashion; and one by one the old acquaintances disappeared: Guyot, Liébard, Mme Lechaptois, Robelin, and Uncle Grémanville, who had been paralyzed for a long time.

One night the driver of the mail-coach brought Pont-l'Évêque news of the July Revolution.[4] A few days later a new subprefect was appointed. This

---

[4]Popular rebellion of July and August 1830 in response to the attempt of King Charles X to dissolve the elected Chamber of Deputies and repeal certain freedoms granted in the Charter of 1814. It took just over a week for the rebels to force Charles to abdicate and to replace him with Louis-Philippe, the duke of Orleans.

was the Baron de Larsonnière, who had been a consul in America, and who brought with him, besides his wife, his sister-in-law and three young ladies who were almost grown-up. They were to be seen on their lawn, dressed in loose-fitting smocks; and they had a Negro servant and a parrot. They paid a call on Mme Aubain, who made a point of returning it. As soon as Félicité saw them coming, she would run and tell her mistress. But only one thing could really awaken her interest, and that was her son's letters.

He seemed to be incapable of following any career and spent all his time in taverns. She paid his debts, but he contracted new ones, and the sighs Mme Aubain heaved as she knitted by the window reached Félicité at her spinning wheel in the kitchen.

The two women used to walk up and down together beside the espalier,[5] forever talking of Virginie and debating whether such a thing would have appealed to her, or what she would have said on such and such an occasion.

All her little belongings were in a cupboard in the children's bedroom. Mme Aubain went through them as seldom as possible. One summer day she resigned herself to doing so, and the moths were sent fluttering out of the cupboard.

Virginie's frocks hung in a row underneath a shelf containing three dolls, a few hoops, a set of toy furniture, and the wash-basin she had used. Besides the frocks, they took out her petticoats, her stockings, and her handkerchiefs, and spread them out on the two beds before folding them up again. The sunlight streamed in on these pathetic objects, bringing out the stains and showing up the creases made by the child's movements. The air was warm, the sky was blue, a blackbird was singing, and everything seemed to be utterly at peace.

They found a little chestnut-colored hat, made of plush with a long nap; but the moths had ruined it. Félicité asked if she might have it. The two women looked at each other and their eyes filled with tears. Then the mistress opened her arms, the maid threw herself into them, and they clasped each other in a warm embrace, satisfying their grief in a kiss which made them equal.

It was the first time that such a thing had happened, for Mme Aubain was not of a demonstrative nature. Félicité was as grateful as if she had received a great favor, and henceforth loved her mistress with dog-like devotion and religious veneration.

Her heart grew softer as time went by.

When she heard the drums of a regiment coming down the street she stood at the door with a jug of cider and offered the soldiers a drink. She looked after the people who went down with cholera. She watched over the Polish refugees, and one of them actually expressed a desire to marry her. But they fell out, for when she came back from the Angelus one morning, she found that he had got into her kitchen and was calmly eating an oil-and-vinegar salad.

---

[5] A trellis against which shrubs and fruit trees grow flat.

After the Poles it was Père Colmiche, an old man who was said to have committed fearful atrocities in '93.[6] He lived by the river in a ruined pig-sty. The boys of the town used to peer at him through the cracks in the walls, and threw pebbles at him which landed on the litter where he lay, constantly shaken by fits of coughing. His hair was extremely long, his eyelids inflamed, and on one arm there was a swelling bigger than his head. Félicité brought him some linen, tried to clean out his filthy hovel, and even wondered if she could install him in the wash-house without annoying Madame. When the tumor had burst, she changed his dressings every day, brought him some cake now and then, and put him out in the sun on a truss of hay. The poor old fellow would thank her in a faint whisper, slavering and trembling all the while, fearful of losing her and stretching his hands out as soon as he saw her moving away.

He died, and she had a Mass said for the repose of his soul.

The same day a great piece of good fortune came her way. Just as she was serving dinner, Mme de Larsonnière's Negro appeared carrying the parrot in its cage, complete with perch, chain, and padlock. The Baroness had written a note informing Mme Aubain that her husband had been promoted to a Prefecture and they were leaving that evening; she begged her to accept the parrot as a keepsake and a token of her regard.

This bird had engrossed Félicité's thoughts for a long time, for it came from America, and that word reminded her of Victor. So she had asked the Negro all about it, and once she had even gone so far as to say:

"How pleased Madame would be if it were hers!"

The Negro had repeated this remark to his mistress, who, unable to take the parrot with her, was glad to get rid of it in this way.

IV

His name was Loulou. His body was green, the tips of his wings were pink, his poll blue, and his breast golden.

Unfortunately he had a tiresome mania for biting his perch, and also used to pull his feathers out, scatter his droppings everywhere, and upset his bath water. He annoyed Mme Aubain, and so she gave him to Félicité for good.

Félicité started training him, and soon he could say: "Nice boy! Your servant, sir! Hail, Mary!" He was put near the door, and several people who spoke to him said how strange it was that he did not answer to the name of Jacquot, as all parrots were called Jacquot. They likened him to a turkey or a block of wood, and every sneer cut Félicité to the quick. How odd, she thought, that Loulou should be so stubborn, refusing to talk whenever anyone looked at him!

For all that, he liked having people around him, because on Sundays, while the Rochefeuille sisters, M. Houppeville, and some new friends — the apothecary Onfroy, M. Varin, and Captain Mathieu — were having their game

---

[6] In 1793, during the Reign of Terror in the French Revolution.

of cards, he would beat on the window-panes with his wings and make such a din that it was impossible to hear oneself speak.

Bourais's face obviously struck him as terribly funny, for as soon as he saw it he was seized with uncontrollable laughter. His shrieks rang round the courtyard, the echo repeated them, and the neighbors came to their windows and started laughing too. To avoid being seen by the bird, M. Bourais used to creep along by the wall, hiding his face behind his hat, until he got to the river, and then come into the house from the garden. The looks he gave the parrot were far from tender.

Loulou had once been cuffed by the butcher's boy for poking his head into his basket; and since then he was always trying to give him a nip through his shirt. Fabu threatened to wring his neck, although he was not a cruel fellow, in spite of his tattooed arms and bushy whiskers. On the contrary, he rather liked the parrot, so much so indeed that in a spirit of jovial camaraderie he tried to teach him a few swear-words. Félicité, alarmed at this development, put the bird in the kitchen. His little chain was removed and he was allowed to wander all over the house.

Coming downstairs, he used to rest the curved part of his beak on each step and then raise first his right foot, then his left; and Félicité was afraid that this sort of gymnastic performance would make him giddy. He fell ill and could neither talk nor eat for there was a swelling under his tongue such as hens sometimes have. She cured him by pulling this pellicule[7] out with her finger-nails. One day M. Paul was silly enough to blow the smoke of his cigar at him; another time Mme Lormeau started teasing him with the end of her parasol, and he caught hold of the ferrule with his beak. Finally he got lost.

Félicité had put him down on the grass in the fresh air, and left him there for a minute. When she came back, the parrot had gone. First of all she looked for him in the bushes, by the river, and on the rooftops, paying no attention to her mistress's shouts of: "Be careful, now! You must be mad!" Next she went over all the gardens in Pont-l'Évêque, stopping passersby and asking them: "You don't happen to have seen my parrot by any chance?" Those who did not know him already were given a description of the bird. Suddenly she thought she could make out something green flying about behind the mills at the foot of the hill. But up on the hill there was nothing to be seen. A pedlar told her that he had come upon the parrot a short time before in Mère Simon's shop at Saint-Melaine. She ran all the way there, but no one knew what she was talking about. Finally she came back home, worn out, her shoes falling to pieces, and death in her heart. She was sitting beside Madame on the garden-seat and telling her what she had been doing, when she felt something light drop on her shoulder. It was Loulou! What he had been up to, no one could discover: perhaps he had just gone for a little walk round the town.

Félicité was slow to recover from this fright, and indeed never really got over it.

---

[7] A thin skin or piece of skin.

As the result of a chill she had an attack of quinsy, and soon after that her ears were affected. Three years later she was deaf, and she spoke at the top of her voice, even in church. Although her sins could have been proclaimed over the length and breadth of the diocese without dishonor to her or offense to others, M. le Curé thought it advisable to hear her confession in the sacristy.

Imaginary buzzings in the head added to her troubles. Often her mistress would say: "Heavens, how stupid you are!" and she would reply: "Yes, Madame," at the same time looking all around her for something.

The little circle of her ideas grew narrower and narrower, and the pealing of bells and the lowing of cattle went out of her life. Every living thing moved about in a ghostly silence. Only one sound reached her ears now, and that was the voice of the parrot.

As if to amuse her, he would reproduce the click-clack of the turn-spit, the shrill call of a man selling fish, and the noise of the saw at the joiner's across the way; and when the bell rang he would imitate Mme Aubain's "Félicité! The door, the door!"

They held conversations with each other, he repeating *ad nauseam* the three phrases in his repertory, she replying with words which were just as disconnected but which came from the heart. In her isolation, Loulou was almost a son or a lover to her. He used to climb up her fingers, peck at her lips, and hang on to her shawl; and as she bent over him, wagging her head from side to side as nurses do, the great wings of her bonnet and the wings of the bird quivered in unison.

When clouds banked up in the sky and there was a rumbling of thunder, he would utter piercing cries, no doubt remembering the sudden downpours in his native forests. The sound of the rain falling roused him to frenzy. He would flap excitedly around, shoot up to the ceiling, knocking everything over, and fly out of the window to splash about in the garden. But he would soon come back to perch on one of the firedogs, hopping about to dry his feathers and showing tail and beak in turn.

One morning in the terrible winter of 1837, when she had put him in front of the fire because of the cold she found him dead in the middle of his cage, hanging head down with his claws caught in the bars. He had probably died of a stroke, but she thought he had been poisoned with parsley, and despite the absence of any proof, her suspicions fell on Fabu.

She wept so much that her mistress said to her: "Why don't you have him stuffed?"

Félicité asked the chemist's advice, remembering that he had always been kind to the parrot. He wrote to Le Havre, and a man called Fellacher agreed to do the job. As parcels sometimes went astray on the mail-coach, she decided to take the parrot as far as Honfleur herself.

On either side of the road stretched an endless succession of apple trees, all stripped of their leaves, and there was ice in the ditches. Dogs were barking around the farms; and Félicité, with her hands tucked under her mantlet, her little black sabots, and her basket, walked briskly along the middle of the road.

She crossed the forest, passed Le Haut-Chêne, and got as far as Saint-Gatien.

Behind her, in a cloud of dust, and gathering speed as the horses galloped downhill, a mail-coach swept along like a whirlwind. When he saw this woman making no attempt to get out of the way, the driver poked his head out above the hood, and he and the postilion shouted at her. His four horses could not be held in and galloped faster, the two leaders touching her as they went by. With a jerk of the reins the driver threw them to one side, and then, in a fury, he raised his long whip and gave her such a lash, from head to waist, that she fell flat on her back.

The first thing she did on regaining consciousness was to open her basket. Fortunately nothing had happened to Loulou. She felt her right cheek burning, and when she touched it her hand turned red; it was bleeding.

She sat down on a heap of stones and dabbed her face with her hand-kerchief. Then she ate a crust of bread which she had taken the precaution of putting in her basket, and tried to forget her wound by looking at the bird.

As she reached the top of the hill at Ecquemauville, she saw the lights of Honfleur twinkling in the darkness like a host of stars, and the shadowy expanse of the sea beyond. Then a sudden feeling of faintness made her stop; and the misery of her childhood, the disappointment of her first love, the departure of her nephew, and the death of Virginie all came back to her at once like the waves of a rising tide, and, welling up in her throat, choked her.

When she got to the boat she insisted on speaking to the captain, and without telling him what was in her parcel, asked him to take good care of it.

Fellacher kept the parrot a long time. Every week he promised it for the next; after six months he announced that a box had been sent off, and nothing more was heard of it. It looked as though Loulou would never come back, and Félicité told herself: "They've stolen him for sure!"

At last he arrived — looking quite magnificent, perched on a branch screwed into a mahogany base, one foot in the air, his head cocked to one side, and biting a nut which the taxidermist, out of love of the grandiose, had gilded.

Félicité shut him up in her room.

This place, to which few people were ever admitted, contained such a quantity of religious bric-à-brac and miscellaneous oddments that it looked like a cross between a chapel and a bazaar.

A big wardrobe prevented the door from opening properly. Opposite the window that overlooked the garden was a little round one looking on to the courtyard. There was a table beside the bed, with a water-jug, a couple of combs, and a block of blue soap in a chipped plate. On the walls there were rosaries, medals, several pictures of the Virgin, a holy-water stoup made out of a coconut. On the chest of drawers, which was draped with a cloth just like an altar, was the shell box Victor had given her, and also a watering-can and a ball, some copy-books, the illustrated geography book, and a pair of ankle-boots. And on the nail supporting the looking-glass, fastened by its ribbons, hung the little plush hat.

Félicité carried this form of veneration to such lengths that she even kept one of Monsieur's frock-coats. All the old rubbish Mme Aubain had no more use for, she carried off to her room. That was how there came to be artificial flowers along the edge of the chest of drawers, and a portrait of the Comte d'Artois in the window-recess.

With the aid of a wall-bracket, Loulou was installed on a chimney-breast that jutted out into the room. Every morning when she awoke, she saw him in the light of the dawn, and then she remembered the old days, and the smallest details of insignificant actions, not in sorrow but in absolute tranquility.

Having no intercourse with anyone, she lived in the torpid state of a sleep-walker. The Corpus Christi processions roused her from this condition, for she would go round the neighbors collecting candlesticks and mats to decorate the altar of repose which they used to set up in the street.

In church she was forever gazing at the Holy Ghost, and one day she noticed that it had something of the parrot about it. This resemblance struck her as even more obvious in a colorprint depicting the baptism of Our Lord. With its red wings and its emerald-green body, it was the very image of Loulou.

She bought the print and hung it in the place of the Comte d'Artois, so that she could include them both in a single glance. They were linked together in her mind, the parrot being sanctified by this connection with the Holy Ghost, which itself acquired new life and meaning in her eyes. God the Father could not have chosen a dove as a means of expressing Himself, since doves cannot talk, but rather one of Loulou's ancestors. And although Félicité used to say her prayers with her eyes on the picture, from time to time she would turn slightly towards the bird.

She wanted to join the Children of Mary, but Mme Aubain dissuaded her from doing so.

An important event now loomed up — Paul's wedding.

After starting as a lawyer's clerk, he had been in business, in the Customs, and in Inland Revenue, and had even begun trying to get into the Department of Woods and Forests, when, at the age of thirty-six, by some heaven-sent inspiration, he suddenly discovered his real vocation — in the Wills and Probate Department. There he proved so capable that one of the auditors had offered him his daughter in marriage and promised to use his influence on his behalf.

Paul, grown serious-minded, brought her to see his mother. She criticized the way things were done at Pont-l'Évêque, put on airs, and hurt Félicité's feelings. Mme Aubain was relieved to see her go.

The following week came news of M. Bourais's death in an inn in Lower Brittany. Rumors that he had committed suicide were confirmed, and doubts arose as to his honesty. Mme Aubain went over her accounts and was soon conversant with the full catalogue of his misdeeds — embezzlement of interest, secret sales of timber, forged receipts, etc. Besides all this, he was the father of an illegitimate child, and had had "relations with a person at Dozule."

These infamies upset Mme Aubain greatly. In March 1853 she was afflicted with a pain in the chest; her tongue seemed to be covered with a film; leeches failed to make her breathing any easier; and on the ninth evening of her illness she died. She had just reached the age of seventy-two.

She was thought to be younger because of her brown hair, worn in bandeaux round her pale, pock-marked face. There were few friends to mourn her, for she had a haughty manner which put people off. Yet Félicité wept for her as servants rarely weep for their masters. That Madame should die before her upset her ideas, seemed to be contrary to the order of things, monstrous and unthinkable.

Ten days later — the time it took to travel hot-foot from Besançon — the heirs arrived. The daughter-in-law ransacked every drawer, picked out some pieces of furniture, and sold the rest; and then back they went to the Wills and Probate Department.

Madame's arm-chair, her pedestal table, her foot-warmer, and the eight chairs had all gone. Yellow squares in the center of the wall-panels showed where the pictures had hung. They had carried off the two cots with their mattresses, and no trace remained in the cupboard of all Virginie's things. Félicité climbed the stairs to her room, numbed with sadness.

The next day there was a notice on the door, and the apothecary shouted in her ear that the house was up for sale.

She swayed on her feet, and was obliged to sit down.

What distressed her most of all was the idea of leaving her room, which was so suitable for poor Loulou. Fixing an anguished look on him as she appealed to the Holy Ghost, she contracted the idolatrous habit of kneeling in front of the parrot to say her prayers. Sometimes the sun, as it came through the little window, caught his glass eye, so that it shot out a great luminous ray which sent her into ecstasies.

She had a pension of three hundred and eighty francs a year which her mistress had left her. The garden kept her in vegetables. As for clothes, she had enough to last her till the end of her days, and she saved on lighting by going to bed as soon as darkness fell.

She went out as little as possible, to avoid the second-hand dealer's shop where some of the old furniture was on display. Ever since her fit of giddiness, she had been dragging one leg; and as her strength was failing, Mère Simon, whose grocery business had come to grief, came in every morning to chop wood and pump water for her.

Her eyes grew weaker. The shutters were not opened any more. Years went by, and nobody rented the house and nobody bought it.

For fear of being evicted, Félicité never asked for any repairs to be done. The laths in the roof rotted, and all through one winter her bolster was wet. After Easter she began spitting blood.

When this happened Mère Simon called in the doctor. Félicité wanted to know what was the matter with her, but she was so deaf that only one word reached her: "Pneumonia." It was a word she knew, and she answered gently: "Ah! like Madame," thinking it natural that she should follow in her mistress's footsteps.

The time to set up the altars of repose was drawing near.

The first altar was always at the foot of the hill, the second in front of the post office, the third about halfway up the street. There was some argument as to the siting of this one, and finally the women of the parish picked on Mme Aubain's courtyard.

The fever and the tightness of the chest grew worse. Félicité fretted over not doing anything for the altar. If only she could have something put on it! Then she thought of the parrot. The neighbors protested that it would not be seemly, but the curé gave his permission, and this made her so happy that she begged him to accept Loulou, the only thing of value she possessed, when she died.

From Tuesday to Saturday, the eve of Corpus Christi, she coughed more and more frequently. In the evening her face looked pinched and drawn, her lips stuck to her gums, and she started vomiting. At dawn the next day, feeling very low, she sent for a priest.

Three good women stood by her while she was given extreme unction. Then she said that she had to speak to Fabu.

He arrived in his Sunday best, very ill at ease in this funereal atmosphere.

"Forgive me," she said, making an effort to stretch out her arm. "I thought it was you who had killed him."

What could she mean by such nonsense? To think that she had suspected a man like him of murder! He got very indignant and was obviously going to make a scene.

"Can't you see," they said, "that she isn't in her right mind any more?"

From time to time Félicité would start talking to shadows. The women went away. Mère Simon had her lunch.

A little later she picked Loulou up and held him out to Félicité, saying: "Come now, say good-bye to him."

Although the parrot was not a corpse, the worms were eating him up. One of his wings was broken, and the stuffing was coming out of his stomach. But she was blind by now, and she kissed him on the forehead and pressed him against her cheek. Mère Simon took him away from her to put him on the altar.

V

The scents of summer came up from the meadows; there was a buzzing of flies; the sun was glittering in the river and warming the slates of the roof. Mère Simon had come back into the room and was gently nodding off to sleep.

The noise of church bells woke her up; the congregation was coming out from vespers. Félicité's delirium abated. Thinking of the procession, she could see it as clearly as if she had been following it.

All the school-children, the choristers, and the firemen were walking along the pavements, while advancing up the middle of the street came the church officer armed with his halberd, the beadle carrying a great cross, the schoolmaster keeping an eye on the boys, and the nun fussing over her little girls — three of the prettiest, looking like curly-headed angels, were throwing rose-petals into the air. Then came the deacon, with both arms outstretched, conducting the band, and a couple of censor-bearers who turned round at every step to face the Holy Sacrament, which the curé, wearing his splendid chasuble, was carrying under a canopy of poppy-red velvet held aloft by four churchwardens. A crowd of people surged along behind, between the white cloths covering the walls of the houses, and eventually they got to the bottom of the hill.

A cold sweat moistened Félicité's temples. Mère Simon sponged it up with a cloth, telling herself that one day she would have to go the same way.

The hum of the crowd increased in volume, was very loud for a moment, then faded away.

A fusillade shook the window-panes. It was the postilions saluting the monstrance. Félicité rolled her eyes and said as loud as she could: "Is he all right?" — worrying about the parrot.

She entered into her death-agony. Her breath, coming ever faster, with a rattling sound, made her sides heave. Bubbles of froth appeared at the corners of her mouth, and her whole body trembled.

Soon the booming of the ophicleides,[8] the clear voices of the children, and the deep voices of the men could be heard near at hand. Now and then everything was quiet, and the tramping of feet, deadened by a carpet of flowers, sounded like a flock moving across pasture-land.

The clergy appeared in the courtyard. Mère Simon climbed on to a chair to reach the little round window, from which she had a full view of the altar below.

It was hung with green garlands and adorned with a flounce in English needlepoint lace. In the middle was a little frame containing some relics, there were two orange-trees at the corners, and all the way along stood silver candlesticks and china vases holding sunflowers, lilies, peonies, foxgloves, and bunches of hydrangea. This pyramid of bright colors stretched from the first floor right down to the carpet which was spread out over the pavement. Some rare objects caught the eye: a silver-gilt sugar-basin wreathed in violets, some pendants of Alençon gems gleaming on a bed of moss, and two Chinese screens with landscape decorations. Loulou, hidden under roses, showed nothing but his blue poll, which looked like a plaque of lapis lazuli.

The churchwardens, the choristers, and the children lined up along the three sides of the courtyard. The priest went slowly up the steps and placed his great shining gold sun on the lace altar-cloth. Everyone knelt down. There was a deep silence. And the censers, swinging at full tilt, slid up and down their chains.

A blue cloud of incense was wafted up into Félicité's room. She opened her nostrils wide and breathed it in with a mystical, sensuous fervor. Then she closed her eyes. Her lips smiled. Her heart-beats grew slower and slower, each a little fainter and gentler, like a fountain running dry, an echo fading away. And as she breathed her last, she thought she could see, in the opening heavens, a gigantic parrot hovering above her head.   [1877]

---

[8] An early brass wind instrument.

MAVIS GALLANT (b. 1924) was born in Montreal, Quebec, the daughter of a painter who died when she was ten years old. Educated in a French convent school in Montreal, Gallant moved to New York City as a teenager after her mother's remarriage but returned to Montreal when she finished her schooling. During World War II she worked as a journalist and started to publish short stories, although her first ambition was to be a poet. At the age of twenty-six she sold her first story to The New Yorker magazine and decided to move to Paris and become a writer. Years later she recalled that "I didn't know [if I could make a living from my writing]. I had not completed a story to my satisfaction. I didn't bring much — a couple of notebooks with stories — I destroyed most of what I'd already done, destroyed most of my journals. I must have been crazy. There's no other explanation."

Since 1950 Gallant has lived in Paris and often travels in Europe, experiencing no difficulty as an expatriate. "The only place I was ever lonely was when I went to Finland. I couldn't understand the language, it didn't resemble anything . . . and I turned right around. I went to Germany, where I knew some friends, and started on a collection of stories about Germany." To date she has published eleven books, including eight collections of short fiction, among them Across the Bridge (1993), from which the story "1933" was taken.

Literary critics have noted that many of Gallant's short stories revolve around memory and evoke a clear sense of the past. Gallant dramatizes her stories with an elegant restraint that often suggests a strong emotional undercurrent of loss. She told an interviewer from the New York Times, "I think it's very true that in many, many of the things I write, someone has vanished. And it's often the father. And there is often a sense that nothing is very safe, and you're walking on a very thin crust."

RELATED COMMENTARY: Mavis Gallant, "What Is Style?" page 1418.

MAVIS GALLANT

1933

About a year after the death of M. Carette, his three survivors — Berthe and her little sister, Marie, and their mother — had to leave the comfortable flat over the furniture store in Rue Saint-Denis and move to a smaller place. They were not destitute: there was the insurance and the money from the sale of the store, but the man who had bought the store from the estate had not yet paid and they had to be careful.

Some of the lamps and end tables and upholstered chairs were sent to relatives, to be returned when the little girls grew up and got married. The rest of their things were carried by two small, bent men to the second floor of a stone house in Rue Cherrier near the Institute for the Deaf and Dumb. The men used an old horse and an open cart for the removal. They told Mme.

Carette that they had never worked outside that quarter; they knew only some forty streets of Montreal but knew them thoroughly. On moving day, soft snow, like graying lace, fell. A patched tarpaulin protected the Carettes' wine-red sofa with its border of silk fringe, the children's brass bedstead, their mother's walnut bed with the carved scallop shells, and the round oak table, smaller than the old one, at which they would now eat their meals. Mme. Carette told Berthe that her days of entertaining and cooking for guests were over. She was just twenty-seven.

They waited for the moving men in their new home, in scrubbed, empty rooms. They had already spread sheets of *La Presse* over the floors, in case the men tracked in snow. The curtains were hung, the cream-colored blinds pulled halfway down the sash windows. Coal had been delivered and was piled in the lean-to shed behind the kitchen. The range and the squat, round heater in the dining room issued tidal waves of dense metallic warmth.

The old place was at no distance. Parc Lafontaine, where the children had often been taken to play, was just along the street. By walking an extra few minutes, Mme. Carette could patronize the same butcher and grocer as before. The same horse-drawn sleighs would bring bread, milk, and coal to the door. Still, the quiet stone houses, the absence of heavy traffic and shops made Rue Cherrier seem like a foreign country.

Change, death, absence — the adult mysteries — kept the children awake. From their new bedroom they heard the clang of the first streetcar at dawn — a thrilling chord, metal on metal, that faded slowly. They would have jumped up and dressed at once, but to their mother this was still the middle of the night. Presently, a new, continuous sound moved in the waking streets, like a murmur of leaves. From the confused rustle broke distinct impressions: an alarm clock, a man speaking, someone's radio. Marie wanted to talk and sing. Berthe had to invent stories to keep her quiet. Once she had placed her hand over Marie's mouth and been cruelly bitten.

They slept on a horsehair mattress, which had a summer and a winter side, and was turned twice a year. The beautiful stitching at the edge of the sheets and pillows was their mother's work. She had begun to sew her trousseau at the age of eleven; her early life was spent in preparation for a wedding. Above the girls' bed hung a gilt crucifix with a withered spray of box hedge that passed for the Easter palms of Jerusalem.

Marie was afraid to go to the bathroom alone after dark. Berthe asked if she expected to see their father's ghost, but Marie could not say: she did not yet know whether a ghost and the dark meant the same thing. Berthe was obliged to get up at night and accompany her along the passage. The hall light shone out of a blue glass tulip set upon a column painted to look like marble. Berthe could just reach it on tiptoe; Marie not at all.

Marie would have left the bathroom door open for company, but Berthe knew that such intimacy was improper. Although her First Communion was being delayed because Mme. Carette wanted the two sisters to come to the altar together, she had been to practice confession. Unfortunately, she had soon run out of invented sins. Her confessor seemed to think there should be more: he asked if she and her little sister had ever been in a bathroom with the door shut, and warned her of grievous fault.

On their way back to bed, Berthe unhooked a calendar on which was a picture of a family of rabbits riding a toboggan. She pretended to read stories about the rabbits and presently both she and Marie fell asleep.

They never saw their mother wearing a bathrobe. As soon as Mme. Carette got up she dressed herself in clothes that were in the colors of half-mourning — mauve, dove-gray. Her fair hair was brushed straight and sub-dued under a net. She took a brush to everything — hair, floors, the children's elbows, the kitchen chairs. Her scent was of Baby's Own soap and Florida Water. When she bent to kiss the children, a cameo dangled from a chain. She trained the girls not to lie, or point, or gobble their food, or show their legs above the knee, or leave fingerprints on windowpanes, or handle the parlor curtains — the slightest touch could crease the lace, she said. They learned to say in English, "I don't understand" and "I don't know" and "No, thank you." That was all the English anyone needed between Rue Sant-Denis and Parc Lafontaine.

In the dining room, where she kept her sewing machine, Mme. Carette held the treadle still, rested a hand on the stopped wheel. "What are you doing in the parlor?" she called. "Are you touching the curtains?" Marie had been spitting on the window and drawing her finger through the spit. Berthe, trying to clean the mess with her flannelette petticoat, said, "Marie's just been standing here saying 'Saint Marguerite, pray for us.'"

Downstairs lived M. Grosjean, the landlord, with his Irish wife and an Airedale named Arno. Arno understood English and French; Mme. Grosjean could only speak English. She loved Arno and was afraid he would run away: he was a restless dog who liked to be doing something all the time. Sometimes M. Grosjean took him to Parc Lafontaine and they played at retrieving a collapsed and bitten tennis ball. Arno was trained to obey both *"Cherchez!"* and "Go fetch it!" but he paid attention to neither. He ran with the ball and Mme. Grosjean had to chase him.

Mme. Grosjean stood outside the house on the back step, just under the Carettes' kitchen window, holding Arno's supper. She wailed, "Arno, where have you got to?" M. Grosjean had probably taken Arno for a walk. He made it a point never to say where he was going: he did not think it a good thing to let women know much.

Mme. Grosjean and Mme. Carette were the same age, but they never became friends. Mme. Carette would say no more than a few negative things in English ("No, thank you" and "I don't know" and "I don't understand") and Mme. Grosjean could not work up the conversation. Mme. Carette had a word with Berthe about Irish marriages: An Irish marriage, while not to be sought, need not be scorned. The Irish were not English. God had sent them to Canada to keep people from marrying Protestants.

That winter the girls wore white leggings and mittens, knitted by their mother, and coats and hats of white rabbit fur. Each of them carried a rabbit muff. Marie cried when Berthe had to go to school. On Sunday afternoons they played with Arno and M. Grosjean. He tried to take their picture but it wasn't easy. The girls stood on the front steps, hand-in-hand, mitten-to-mitten, while Arno was harnessed to a sled with curved runners. The red harness had once been worn by another Airedale, Ruby, who was smarter even than Arno.

M. Grosjean wanted Marie to sit down on the sled, hold the reins and look sideways at the camera. Marie clung to Berthe's coat. She was afraid that Arno would bolt into the Rue Saint-Denis, where there were streetcars. M. Grosjean lifted her off the sled and tried the picture a different way, with Berthe pretending to drive and Marie standing face-to-face with Arno. As soon as he set Marie on her feet, she began to scream. Her feet were cold. She wanted to be carried. Her nose ran; she felt humiliated. He got out his handkerchief, checked green and white, and wiped her whole face rather hard.

Just then his wife came to the front door with a dish of macaroni and cut-up sausages for Arno. She had thrown a sweater over her cotton housecoat; she was someone who never felt the cold. A gust of wind lifted her loose hair. M. Grosjean told her that the kid was no picnic. Berthe, picking up English fast, could not have repeated his exact words, but she knew what they meant.

Mme. Carette was still waiting for the money from the sale of the store. A brother-in-law helped with the rent, sending every month a generous postal order from Fall River. It was Mme. Carette's belief that God would work a miracle, allowing her to pay it all back. In the meantime, she did fine sewing. Once she was hired to sew a trousseau, working all day in the home of the bride-to-be. As the date of the wedding drew near she had to stay overnight.

Mme. Grosjean looked after the children. They sat in her front parlor, eating fried-egg sandwiches and drinking cream soda (it did not matter if they dropped crumbs) while she played a record of a man singing, "Dear one, the world is waiting for the sunrise."

Berthe asked, in French, "What is he saying?" Mme. Grosjean answered in English, "A well-known Irish tenor."

When Mme. Carette came home the next day, she gave the girls a hot bath, in case Mme. Grosjean had neglected their elbows and heels. She took Berthe in her arms and said she must never tell anyone their mother had left the house to sew for strangers. When she grew up, she must not refer to her mother as a seamstress, but say instead, "My mother was clever with her hands."

That night, when they were all three having supper in the kitchen, she looked at Berthe and said, "You have beautiful hair." She sounded so tired and stern that Marie, eating mashed potatoes and gravy, with a napkin under her chin, thought Berthe must be getting a scolding. She opened her mouth wide and started to howl. Mme. Carette just said, "Marie, don't cry with your mouth full."

Downstairs, Mme. Grosjean set up her evening chant, calling for Arno. "Oh, where have you got to?" she wailed to the empty backyard.

"The dog is the only thing keeping those two together," said Mme. Carette. "But a dog isn't the same as a child. A dog doesn't look after its masters in their old age. We shall see what happens to the marriage after Arno dies." No sooner had she said this than she covered her mouth and spoke through her fingers: "God forgive my unkind thoughts." She propped her arms on each side of her plate, as the girls were forbidden to do, and let her face slide into her hands.

Berthe took this to mean that Arno was doomed. Only a calamity about to engulf them all could explain her mother's elbows on the table. She got down from her chair and tried to pull her mother's hands apart, and kiss her face. Her own tears ran into her long hair, down onto her starched piqué collar. She felt tears along her nose and inside her ears. Even while she sobbed out words of hope and comfort (Arno would never die) and promises of reassuring behavior (she and Marie would always be good) she wondered how tears could flow in so many directions at once.

Of course, M. Grosjean did not know that all the female creatures in his house were frightened and lonely, calling and weeping. He was in Parc Lafontaine with Arno, trying to play go-fetch-it in the dark.   [1987]

GABRIEL GARCÍA MÁRQUEZ *(b. 1928) was born in the remote small town of Aracataca in Magdalena province, near the Caribbean seacoast of Colombia. The oldest of twelve children of a poverty-stricken telegraph operator and his wife, he was raised by his maternal grandparents. When he was eight years old, he was sent to school near Bogotá, and after his graduation in 1946 he studied law. A writer from childhood, García Márquez published his first book,* Leaf Storm and Other Stories, *which includes "A Very Old Man with Enormous Wings," in 1955. He spent the next few years in Paris, where he wrote two short novels. After the Cuban Revolution, he returned to Central America and worked as a journalist and screenwriter. His great comic masterpiece, the novel* One Hundred Years of Solitude *(1967), was written while he lived in Mexico City.* The Autumn of the Patriarch *(1975), a novel about the life of a Latin American dictator, and the best-seller* Love in the Time of Cholera *(1988) are more recent works. In 1982 he received the Nobel Prize for Literature.*

García Márquez mingles realistic and fantastic details in all his fiction, including "A Very Old Man with Enormous Wings." He has said that the origin of his stories is always an image, "not an idea or a concept. The image grows in my head until the whole story takes shape as it might in real life." Leaf Storm *was written after García Márquez returned from visiting the place where he grew up. As he later explained to an interviewer from the* Paris Review:

> *The atmosphere, the decadence, the heat in the village were roughly the same as what I had felt in Faulkner. It was a banana plantation region inhabited by a lot of Americans from the fruit companies which gave it the same sort of atmosphere I had found in the writers of the Deep South. Critics have spoken of the literary influence of Faulkner but I see it as a coincidence: I had simply found material that had to be dealt with in the same way that Faulkner had treated similar material. . . .*
>
> *What really happened to me in that trip to Aracataca was that I realized that everything that had occurred in my childhood had a literary value that I was only now appreciating. From the moment I wrote* Leaf Storm *I realized I wanted to be a writer and that nobody could stop me and that the only thing left for me to do was to be the best writer in the world.*

Other collections of short fiction by García Márquez are No One Writes to the Colonel and Other Stories *(1968),* Innocent Eréndira and Other Stories *(1978),* Collected Stories, *(1984), and* Strange Pilgrims *(1993).*

GABRIEL GARCÍA MÁRQUEZ

A Very Old Man with Enormous Wings

Translated by Gregory Rabassa

On the third day of rain they had killed so many crabs inside the house that Pelayo had to cross his drenched courtyard and throw them into the sea, because the newborn child had a temperature all night and they thought it was due to the stench. The world had been sad since Tuesday. Sea and sky were a single ash-gray thing and the sands of the beach, which on March nights glimmered like powdered light, had become a stew of mud and rotten shellfish. The light was so weak at noon that when Pelayo was coming back to the house after throwing away the crabs, it was hard for him to see what it was that was moving and groaning in the rear of the courtyard. He had to go very close to see that it was an old man, a very old man, lying face down in the mud, who, in spite of his tremendous efforts, couldn't get up, impeded by his enormous wings.

Frightened by that nightmare, Pelayo ran to get Elisenda, his wife, who was putting compresses on the sick child, and he took her to the rear of the courtyard. They both looked at the fallen body with mute stupor. He was dressed like a ragpicker. There were only a few faded hairs left on his bald skull and very few teeth in his mouth, and his pitiful condition of a drenched great-grandfather had taken away any sense of grandeur he might have had. His huge buzzard wings, dirty and half-plucked, were forever entangled in the mud. They looked at him so long and so closely that Pelayo and Elisenda very soon overcame their surprise and in the end found him familiar. Then they dared speak to him, and he answered in an incomprehensible dialect with a strong sailor's voice. That was how they skipped over the inconvenience of the wings and quite intelligently concluded that he was a lonely castaway from some foreign ship wrecked by the storm. And yet, they called in a neighbor woman who knew everything about life and death to see him, and all she needed was one look to show them their mistake.

"He's an angel," she told them. "He must have been coming for the child, but the poor fellow is so old that the rain knocked him down."

On the following day everyone knew that a flesh-and-blood angel was held captive in Pelayo's house. Against the judgment of the wise neighbor woman, for whom angels in those times were the fugitive survivors of a celestial conspiracy, they did not have the heart to club him to death. Pelayo watched over him all afternoon from the kitchen, armed with his bailiff's club, and before going to bed he dragged him out of the mud and locked him up with the hens in the wire chicken coop. In the middle of the night, when the rain stopped, Pelayo and Elisenda were still killing crabs. A short time afterward the child woke up without a fever and with a desire to eat. Then they felt magnanimous and decided to put the angel on a raft with fresh water and provisions for three days and leave him to his fate on the high seas. But when they went out into the courtyard with the first light of dawn, they found the whole neighborhood in front of the chicken coop having fun with the angel, without the slightest reverence, tossing him things to eat through the openings in the wire as if he weren't a supernatural creature but a circus animal.

Father Gonzaga arrived before seven o'clock, alarmed at the strange news. By that time onlookers less frivolous than those at dawn had already arrived and they were making all kinds of conjectures concerning the captive's future. The simplest among them thought that he should be named mayor of the world. Others of sterner mind felt that he should be promoted to the rank of five-star general in order to win all wars. Some visionaries hoped that he could be put to stud in order to implant on earth a race of winged wise men who could take charge of the universe. But Father Gonzaga, before becoming a priest, had been a robust woodcutter. Standing by the wire, he reviewed his catechism in an instant and asked them to open the door so that he could take a close look at that pitiful man who looked more like a huge decrepit hen among the fascinated chickens. He was lying in a corner drying his open wings in the sunlight among the fruit peels and breakfast leftovers that the early risers had thrown him. Alien to the impertinences of the world, he only lifted his antiquarian eyes and murmured something in his dialect when Father Gonzaga went into the chicken coop and said good morning to him in Latin. The parish priest had his first suspicion of an impostor when he saw that he did not understand the language of God or know how to greet His ministers. Then he noticed that seen close up he was much too human: he had an unbearable smell of the outdoors, the back side of his wings was strewn with parasites and his main feathers had been mistreated by terrestrial winds, and nothing about him measured up to the proud dignity of angels. Then he came out of the chicken coop and in a brief sermon warned the curious against the risks of being ingenuous. He reminded them that the devil had the bad habit of making use of carnival tricks in order to confuse the unwary. He argued that if wings were not the essential element in determining the difference between a hawk and an airplane, they were even less so in the recognition of angels. Nevertheless, he promised to write a letter to his bishop so that the latter would write to his primate so that the latter would write to the Supreme Pontiff in order to get the final verdict from the highest courts.

His prudence fell on sterile hearts. The news of the captive angel spread with such rapidity that after a few hours the courtyard had the bustle of a marketplace and they had to call in troops with fixed bayonets to disperse the mob that was about to knock the house down. Elisenda, her spine all twisted from sweeping up so much marketplace trash, then got the idea of fencing in the yard and charging five cents admission to see the angel.

The curious came from far away. A traveling carnival arrived with a flying acrobat who buzzed over the crowd several times, but no one paid any attention to him because his wings were not those of an angel but, rather, those of a sidereal[1] bat. The most unfortunate invalids on earth came in search of health: a poor woman who since childhood had been counting her heartbeats and had run out of numbers; a Portuguese man who couldn't sleep because the noise of the stars disturbed him; a sleep-walker who got up at night to undo the things he had done while awake; and many others with less serious ailments. In the midst of that shipwreck disorder that made the earth tremble, Pelayo and Elisenda were happy with fatigue, for in less than a week they had crammed their rooms with money and the line of pilgrims waiting their turn to enter still reached beyond the horizon.

The angel was the only one who took no part in his own act. He spent his time trying to get comfortable in his borrowed nest, befuddled by the hellish heat of the oil lamps and sacramental candles that had been placed along the wire. At first they tried to make him eat some mothballs, which, according to the wisdom of the wise neighbor woman, were the food prescribed for angels. But he turned them down, just as he turned down the papal lunches that the penitents brought him, and they never found out whether it was because he was an angel or because he was an old man that in the end he ate nothing but eggplant mush. His only supernatural virtue seemed to be patience. Especially during the first days, when the hens pecked at him, searching for the stellar parasites that proliferated in his wings, and the cripples pulled out feathers to touch their defective parts with, and even the most merciful threw stones at him, trying to get him to rise so they could see him standing. The only time they succeeded in arousing him was when they burned his side with an iron for branding steers, for he had been motionless for so many hours that they thought he was dead. He awoke with a start, ranting in his hermetic language and with tears in his eyes, and he flapped his wings a couple of times, which brought on a whirlwind of chicken dung and lunar dust and a gale of panic that did not seem to be of this world. Although many thought that his reaction had been one not of rage but of pain, from then on they were careful not to annoy him, because the majority understood that his passivity was not that of a hero taking his ease but that of a cataclysm in repose.

Father Gonzaga held back the crowd's frivolity with formulas of maidservant inspiration while awaiting the arrival of a final judgment on the nature of the captive. But the mail from Rome showed no sense of urgency. They spent their time finding out if the prisoner had a navel, if his dialect had any connection with Aramaic, how many times he could fit on the head of a pin, or whether he wasn't just a Norwegian with wings. Those meager letters might have come and gone until the end of time if a providential event had not put an end to the priest's tribulations.

It so happened that during those days, among so many other carnival attractions, there arrived in town the traveling show of the woman who had been changed into a spider for having disobeyed her parents. The admission to see her was not only less than the admission to see the angel, but people

---

[1] Coming from the stars.

were permitted to ask her all manner of questions about her absurd state and to examine her up and down so that no one would ever doubt the truth of her horror. She was a frightful tarantula the size of a ram and with the head of a sad maiden. What was most heart-rending, however, was not her outlandish shape but the sincere affliction with which she recounted the details of her misfortune. While still practically a child she had sneaked out of her parents' house to go to a dance, and while she was coming back through the woods after having danced all night without permission, a fearful thunderclap rent the sky in two and through the crack came the lightning bolt of brimstone that changed her into a spider. Her only nourishment came from the meatballs that charitable souls chose to toss into her mouth. A spectacle like that, full of so much human truth and with such a fearful lesson, was bound to defeat without even trying that of a haughty angel who scarcely deigned to look at mortals. Besides, the few miracles attributed to the angel showed a certain mental disorder, like the blind man who didn't recover his sight but grew three new teeth, or the paralytic who didn't get to walk but almost won the lottery, and the leper whose sores sprouted sunflowers. Those consolation miracles, which were more like mocking fun, had already ruined the angel's reputation when the woman who had been changed into a spider finally crushed him completely. That was how Father Gonzaga was cured forever of his insomnia and Pelayo's courtyard went back to being as empty as during the time it had rained for three days and crabs walked through the bedrooms.

The owners of the house had no reason to lament. With the money they saved they built a two-story mansion with balconies and gardens and high netting so that crabs wouldn't get in during the winter, and with iron bars on the windows so that angels wouldn't get in. Pelayo also set up a rabbit warren close to town and gave up his job as bailiff for good, and Elisenda bought some satin pumps with high heels and many dresses of iridescent silk, the kind worn on Sunday by the most desirable women in those times. The chicken coop was the only thing that didn't receive any attention. If they washed it down with creolin and burned tears of myrrh inside it every so often, it was not in homage to the angel but to drive away the dungheap stench that still hung everywhere like a ghost and was turning the new house into an old one. At first, when the child learned to walk, they were careful that he not get too close to the chicken coop. But then they began to lose their fears and got used to the smell, and before the child got his second teeth he'd gone inside the chicken coop to play, where the wires were falling apart. The angel was no less standoffish with him than with other mortals, but he tolerated the most ingenious infamies with the patience of a dog who had no illusions. They both came down with chicken pox at the same time. The doctor who took care of the child couldn't resist the temptation to listen to the angel's heart, and he found so much whistling in the heart and so many sounds in his kidneys that it seemed impossible for him to be alive. What surprised him most, however, was the logic of his wings. They seemed so natural on that completely human organism that he couldn't understand why other men didn't have them too.

When the child began school it had been some time since the sun and rain had caused the collapse of the chicken coop. The angel went dragging himself about here and there like a stray dying man. They would drive him out of the bedroom with a broom and a moment later find him in the kitchen. He seemed to be in so many places at the same time that they grew to think that he'd been duplicated, that he was reproducing himself all through the house, and the exasperated and unhinged Elisenda shouted that it was awful living in that hell full of angels. He could scarcely eat and his antiquarian eyes had also become so foggy that he went about bumping into posts. All he had left were the bare cannulae[2] of his last feathers. Pelayo threw a blanket over him and extended him the charity of letting him sleep in the shed, and only then did they notice that he had a temperature at night, and was delirious with the tongue twisters of an old Norwegian. That was one of the few times they became alarmed, for they thought he was going to die and not even the wise neighbor woman had been able to tell them what to do with dead angels.

And yet he not only survived his worst winter, but seemed improved with the first sunny days. He remained motionless for several days in the farthest corner of the courtyard, where no one would see him, and at the beginning of December some large, stiff feathers began to grow on his wings, the feathers of a scarecrow, which looked more like another misfortune of decrepitude. But he must have known the reason for those changes, for he was quite careful that no one should notice them, that no one should hear the sea chanteys that he sometimes sang under the stars. One morning Elisenda was cutting some bunches of onions for lunch when a wind that seemed to come from the high seas blew into the kitchen. Then she went to the window and caught the angel in his first attempts at flight. They were so clumsy that his fingernails opened a furrow in the vegetable patch and he was on the point of knocking the shed down with the ungainly flapping that slipped on the light and couldn't get a grip on the air. But he did manage to gain altitude. Elisenda let out a sigh of relief, for herself and for him, when she saw him pass over the last houses, holding himself up in some way with the risky flapping of a senile vulture. She kept watching him even when she was through cutting the onions and she kept on watching until it was no longer possible for her to see him, because then he was no longer an annoyance in her life but an imaginary dot on the horizon of the sea.   [1955]

---

[2]The tubular pieces by which feathers are attached to a body.

CHARLOTTE PERKINS GILMAN (1860–1935) was born in Hartford, Connecticut. Her father deserted the family shortly after she was born and provided her mother with only meager support. As a teenager Gilman attended the Rhode Island School of Design for a brief period and worked as a commercial artist and teacher. Like her great-aunt Harriet Beecher Stowe, she was concerned at an early age with social injustice and wrote poetry about the hardship of women's lives.

In 1884 she married the artist Charles Walter Stetson. Suffering extreme depression after the birth of a daughter, she left her husband and moved to California in 1888. They were divorced, and she later married George Houghton Gilman, with whom she lived for thirty-four years. In the 1890s Gilman established her reputation as a lecturer and writer of feminist tracts. Her book Women and Economics (1898) is considered one of the most important works of the early years of the women's movement in the United States. Gilman's later books — Concerning Children (1900), The Home (1904), and Human Work (1904) — argue that women should be educated to become financially independent; then they could contribute more to the amelioration of systems of justice and the improvement of society. From 1909 to 1917 Gilman published her own journal, The Forerunner, for which she wrote voluminously. At the end of her life, suffering from cancer, she committed suicide with chloroform.

Today Gilman's best-known work is her early story "The Yellow Wallpaper," written around 1890, shortly after her own nervous breakdown. It is part fantasy and part autobiography, a vivid account of her illness and treatment by the physician S. Weir Mitchell, who forbade her any activity, especially writing, the thing she most wanted to do. In setting the story Gilman used elements of the conventional gothic romances that were a staple in women's popular fiction — an isolated mansion, a distant but dominating male figure, and a mysterious household — all of which force the heroine into the role of passive victim of circumstances. But Gilman gave her own twist to the form. Using the brief paragraphs and simple sentences of popular fiction, she narrated her story with a clinical precision that avoided the trite language of typical romances.

RELATED COMMENTARIES: Sandra M. Gilbert and Susan Gubar, "A Feminist Reading of Gilman's 'The Yellow Wallpaper,'" page 1420; Charlotte Perkins Gilman, "Undergoing the Cure for Nervous Prostration," page 1423.

CHARLOTTE PERKINS GILMAN

The Yellow Wallpaper

It is very seldom that mere ordinary people like John and myself secure ancestral halls for the summer.

A colonial mansion, a hereditary estate, I would say a haunted house and reach the height of romantic felicity — but that would be asking too much of fate!

Still I will proudly declare that there is something queer about it.

Else, why should it be let so cheaply? And why have stood so long untenanted?

John laughs at me, of course, but one expects that.

John is practical in the extreme. He has no patience with faith, an intense horror of superstition, and he scoffs openly at any talk of things not to be felt and seen and put down in figures.

John is a physician, and *perhaps* — (I would not say it to a living soul, of course, but this is dead paper and a great relief to my mind) — *perhaps* that is one reason I do not get well faster.

You see, he does not believe I am sick! And what can one do?

If a physician of high standing, and one's own husband, assures friends and relatives that there is really nothing the matter with one but temporary nervous depression — a slight hysterical tendency — what is one to do?

My brother is also a physician, and also of high standing, and he says the same thing.

So I take phosphates or phosphites — whichever it is — and tonics, and air and exercise, and journeys, and am absolutely forbidden to "work" until I am well again.

Personally, I disagree with their ideas.

Personally, I believe that congenial work, with excitement and change, would do me good.

But what is one to do?

I did write for a while in spite of them; but it *does* exhaust me a good deal — having to be so sly about it, or else meet with heavy opposition.

I sometimes fancy that in my condition, if I had less opposition and more society and stimulus — but John says the very worst thing I can do is to think about my condition, and I confess it always makes me feel bad.

So I will let it alone and talk about the house.

The most beautiful place! It is quite alone, standing well back from the road, quite three miles from the village. It makes me think of English places that you read about, for there are hedges and walls and gates that lock, and lots of separate little houses for the gardeners and people.

There is a *delicious* garden! I never saw such a garden — large and shady, full of box-bordered paths, and lined with long grape-covered arbors with seats under them.

There were greenhouses, but they are all broken now.

There was some legal trouble, I believe, something about the heirs and co-heirs; anyhow, the place has been empty for years.

That spoils my ghostliness, I am afraid, but I don't care — there is something strange about the house — I can feel it.

I even said so to John one moonlight evening, but he said what I felt was a draught, and shut the window.

I get unreasonably angry with John sometimes. I'm sure I never used to be so sensitive. I think it is due to this nervous condition.

But John says if I feel so I shall neglect proper self-control; so I take pains to control myself — before him, at least, and that makes me very tired.

I don't like our room a bit. I wanted one downstairs that opened onto the piazza and had roses all over the window, and such pretty old-fashioned chintz hangings! But John would not hear of it.

He said there was only one window and not room for two beds, and no near room for him if he took another.

He is very careful and loving, and hardly lets me stir without special direction.

I have a schedule prescription for each hour in the day; he takes all care from me, and so I feel basely ungrateful not to value it more.

He said he came here solely on my account, that I was to have perfect rest and all the air I could get. "Your exercise depends on your strength, my dear," said he, "and your food somewhat on your appetite; but air you can absorb all the time." So we took the nursery at the top of the house.

It is a big, airy room, the whole floor nearly, with windows that look all ways, and air and sunshine galore. It was nursery first, and then playroom and gymnasium, I should judge, for the windows are barred for little children, and there are rings and things in the walls.

The paint and paper look as if a boys' school had used it. It is stripped off — the paper — in great patches all around the head of my bed, about as far as I can reach, and in a great place on the other side of the room low down. I never saw a worse paper in my life. One of those sprawling, flamboyant patterns committing every artistic sin.

It is dull enough to confuse the eye in following, pronounced enough constantly to irritate and provoke study, and when you follow the lame uncertain curves for a little distance they suddenly commit suicide — plunge off at outrageous angles, destroy themselves in unheard-of contradictions.

The color is repellent, almost revolting: a smouldering unclean yellow, strangely faded by the slow-turning sunlight. It is a dull yet lurid orange in some places, a sickly sulphur tint in others.

No wonder the children hated it! I should hate it myself if I had to live in this room long.

There comes John, and I must put this away — he hates to have me write a word.

We have been here two weeks, and I haven't felt like writing before, since that first day.

I am sitting by the window now, up in this atrocious nursery, and there is nothing to hinder my writing as much as I please, save lack of strength.

John is away all day, and even some nights when his cases are serious.

I am glad my case is not serious!

But these nervous troubles are dreadfully depressing.

John does not know how much I really suffer. He knows there is no reason to suffer, and that satisfies him.

Of course it is only nervousness. It does weigh on me so not to do my duty in any way!

I meant to be such a help to John, such a real rest and comfort, and here I am a comparative burden already!

Nobody would believe what an effort it is to do what little I am able — to dress and entertain, and order things.

It is fortunate Mary is so good with the baby. Such a dear baby!

And yet I *cannot* be with him, it makes me so nervous.

I suppose John never was nervous in his life. He laughs at me so about this wallpaper!

At first he meant to repaper the room, but afterward he said that I was letting it get the better of me, and that nothing was worse for a nervous patient than to give way to such fancies.

He said that after the wallpaper was changed it would be the heavy bedstead, and then the barred windows, and then that gate at the head of the stairs, and so on.

"You know the place is doing you good," he said, "and really, dear, I don't care to renovate the house just for a three months' rental."

"Then do let us go downstairs," I said. "There are such pretty rooms there."

Then he took me in his arms and called me a blessed little goose, and said he would go down cellar, if I wished, and have it whitewashed into the bargain.

But he is right enough about the beds and windows and things.

It is as airy and comfortable a room as anyone need wish, and, of course, I would not be so silly as to make him uncomfortable just for a whim.

I'm really getting quite fond of the big room, all but that horrid paper.

Out of one window I can see the garden — those mysterious deep-shaded arbors, the riotous old-fashioned flowers, and bushes and gnarly trees.

Out of another I get a lovely view of the bay and a little private wharf belonging to the estate. There is a beautiful shaded lane that runs down there from the house. I always fancy I see people walking in these numerous paths and arbors, but John has cautioned me not to give way to fancy in the least. He says that with my imaginative power and habit of story-making, a nervous weakness like mine is sure to lead to all manner of excited fancies, and that I ought to use my will and good sense to check the tendency. So I try.

I think sometimes that if I were only well enough to write a little it would relieve the press of ideas and rest me.

But I find I get pretty tired when I try.

It is so discouraging not to have any advice and companionship about my work. When I get really well, John says we will ask Cousin Henry and Julia down for a long visit; but he says he would as soon put fireworks in my pillow-case as to let me have those stimulating people about now.

I wish I could get well faster.

But I must not think about that. This paper looks to me as if it *knew* what a vicious influence it had!

There is a recurrent spot where the pattern lolls like a broken neck and two bulbous eyes stare at you upside down.

I get positively angry with the impertinence of it and the everlastingness. Up and down and sideways they crawl, and those absurd unblinking eyes are everywhere. There is one place where two breadths didn't match, and the eyes go all up and down the line, one a little higher than the other.

I never saw so much expression in an inanimate thing before, and we all know how much expression they have! I used to lie awake as a child and get more entertainment and terror out of blank walls and plain furniture than most children could find in a toy-store.

I remember what a kindly wink the knobs of our big old bureau used to have, and there was one chair that always seemed like a strong friend.

I used to feel that if any of the other things looked too fierce I could always hop into that chair and be safe.

The furniture in this room is no worse than inharmonious, however, for we had to bring it all from downstairs. I suppose when this was used as a playroom they had to take the nursery things out, and no wonder! I never saw such ravages as the children have made here.

The wallpaper, as I said before, is torn off in spots, and it sticketh closer than a brother — they must have had perseverance as well as hatred.

Then the floor is scratched and gouged and splintered, the plaster itself is dug out here and there, and this great heavy bed, which is all we found in the room, looks as if it had been through the wars.

But I don't mind it a bit — only the paper.

There comes John's sister. Such a dear girl as she is, and so careful of me! I must not let her find me writing.

She is a perfect and enthusiastic housekeeper, and hopes for no better profession. I verily believe she thinks it is the writing which made me sick!

But I can write when she is out, and see her a long way off from these windows.

There is one that commands the road, a lovely shaded winding road, and one that just looks off over the country. A lovely country, too, full of great elms and velvet meadows.

This wallpaper has a kind of subpattern in a different shade, a particularly irritating one, for you can only see it in certain lights, and not clearly then.

But in the places where it isn't faded and where the sun is just so — I can see a strange, provoking, formless sort of figure that seems to skulk about behind that silly and conspicuous front design.

There's sister on the stairs!

Well, the Fourth of July is over! The people are all gone, and I am tired out. John thought it might do me good to see a little company, so we just had Mother and Nellie and the children down for a week.

Of course I didn't do a thing. Jennie sees to everything now.

But it tired me all the same.

John says if I don't pick up faster he shall send me to Weir Mitchell[1] in the fall.

But I don't want to go there at all. I had a friend who was in his hands once, and she says he is just like John and my brother, only more so!

Besides, it is such an undertaking to go so far.

I don't feel as if it was worthwhile to turn my hand over for anything, and I'm getting dreadfully fretful and querulous.

I cry at nothing, and cry most of the time.

Of course I don't when John is here, or anybody else, but when I am alone.

And I am alone a good deal just now. John is kept in town very often by serious cases, and Jennie is good and lets me alone when I want her to.

So I walk a little in the garden or down that lovely lane, sit on the porch under the roses, and lie down up here a good deal.

I'm getting really fond of the room in spite of the wallpaper. Perhaps *because* of the wallpaper.

It dwells in my mind so!

I lie here on this great immovable bed — it is nailed down, I believe — and follow that pattern about by the hour. It is as good as gymnastics, I assure you. I start, we'll say, at the bottom, down in the corner over there where it has not been touched, and I determine for the thousandth time that I *will* follow that pointless pattern to some sort of a conclusion.

I know a little of the principle of design, and I know this thing was not arranged on any laws of radiation, or alternation, or repetition, or symmetry, or anything else that I ever heard of.

It is repeated, of course, by the breadths, but not otherwise.

Looked at in one way, each breadth stands alone; the bloated curves and flourishes — a kind of "debased Romanesque" with delirium tremens go waddling up and down in isolated columns of fatuity.

But, on the other hand, they connect diagonally, and the sprawling outlines run off in great slanting waves of optic horror, like a lot of wallowing sea-weeds in full chase.

The whole thing goes horizontally, too, at least it seems so, and I exhaust myself trying to distinguish the order of its going in that direction.

---

[1] Dr. S. Weir Mitchell (1829–1914) was an eminent Philadelphia neurologist who advocated "rest cures" for nervous disorders. He was the author of *Diseases of the Nervous System, Especially of Women* (1881).

They have used a horizontal breadth for a frieze, and that adds wonderfully to the confusion.

There is one end of the room where it is almost intact, and there, when the crosslights fade and the low sun shines directly upon it, I can almost fancy radiation after all — the interminable grotesque seems to form around a common center and rush off in headlong plunges of equal distraction.

It makes me tired to follow it. I will take a nap, I guess.

I don't know why I should write this.

I don't want to.

I don't feel able.

And I know John would think it absurd. But I *must* say what I feel and think in some way — it is such a relief!

But the effort is getting to be greater than the relief.

Half the time now I am awfully lazy, and lie down ever so much. John says I mustn't lose my strength, and has me take cod liver oil and lots of tonics and things, to say nothing of ale and wines and rare meat.

Dear John! He loves me very dearly, and hates to have me sick. I tried to have a real earnest reasonable talk with him the other day, and tell him how I wish he would let me go and make a visit to Cousin Henry and Julia.

But he said I wasn't able to go, nor able to stand it after I got there; and I did not make out a very good case for myself, for I was crying before I had finished.

It is getting to be a great effort for me to think straight. Just this nervous weakness, I suppose.

And dear John gathered me up in his arms, and just carried me upstairs and laid me on the bed, and sat by me and read to me till it tired my head.

He said I was his darling and his comfort and all he had, and that I must take care of myself for his sake, and keep well.

He says no one but myself can help me out of it, that I must use my will and self-control and not let any silly fancies run away with me.

There's one comfort — the baby is well and happy, and does not have to occupy this nursery with the horrid wallpaper.

If we had not used it, that blessed child would have! What a fortunate escape! Why, I wouldn't have a child of mine, an impressionable little thing, live in such a room for worlds.

I never thought of it before, but it is lucky that John kept me here after all; I can stand it so much easier than a baby, you see.

Of course I never mention it to them any more — I am too wise — but I keep watch for it all the same.

There are things in the wallpaper that nobody knows about but me, or ever will.

Behind that outside pattern the dim shapes get clearer every day.

It is always the same shape, only very numerous.

And it is like a woman stooping down and creeping about behind that pattern. I don't like it a bit. I wonder — I begin to think — I wish John would take me away from here!

It is so hard to talk with John about my case, because he is so wise, and because he loves me so.

But I tried it last night.

It was moonlight. The moon shines in all around just as the sun does.

I hate to see it sometimes, it creeps so slowly, and always comes in by one window or another.

John was asleep and I hated to waken him, so I kept still and watched the moonlight on that undulating wallpaper till I felt creepy.

The faint figure behind seemed to shake the pattern, just as if she wanted to get out.

I got up softly and went to feel and see if the paper *did* move, and when I came back John was awake.

"What is it, little girl?" he said. "Don't go walking about like that — you'll get cold."

I thought it was a good time to talk, so I told him that I really was not gaining here, and that I wished he would take me away.

"Why, darling!" said he. "Our lease will be up in three weeks, and I can't see how to leave before.

"The repairs are not done at home, and I cannot possibly leave town just now. Of course, if you were in any danger, I could and would, but you really are better, dear, whether you can see it or not. I am a doctor, dear, and I know. You are gaining flesh and color, your appetite is better, I feel really much easier about you."

"I don't weigh a bit more," said I, "nor as much; and my appetite may be better in the evening when you are here but it is worse in the morning when you are away!"

"Bless her little heart!" said he with a big hug. "She shall be as sick as she pleases! But now let's improve the shining hours by going to sleep, and talk about it in the morning!"

"And you won't go away?" I asked gloomily.

"Why, how can I, dear? It is only three weeks more and then we will take a nice little trip for a few days while Jennie is getting the house ready. Really, dear, you are better!"

"Better in body perhaps —" I began, and stopped short, for he sat up straight and looked at me with such a stern, reproachful look that I could not say another word.

"My darling," said he, "I beg you, for my sake and for our child's sake, as well as for your own, that you will never for one instant let that idea enter your mind! There is nothing so dangerous, so fascinating, to a temperament like yours. It is a false and foolish fancy. Can you trust me as a physician when I tell you so?"

So of course I said no more on that score, and we went to sleep before long. He thought I was asleep first, but I wasn't, and lay there for hours trying to decide whether that front pattern and the back pattern really did move together or separately.

On a pattern like this, by daylight, there is a lack of sequence, a defiance of law, that is a constant irritant to a normal mind.

The color is hideous enough, and unreliable enough, and infuriating enough, but the pattern is torturing.

You think you have mastered it, but just as you get well under way in following, it turns a back-somersault and there you are. It slaps you in the face, knocks you down, and tramples upon you. It is like a bad dream.

The outside pattern is a florid arabesque, reminding one of a fungus. If you can imagine a toadstool in joints, an interminable string of toadstools, budding and sprouting in endless convolutions — why, that is something like it.

That is, sometimes!

There is one marked peculiarity about this paper, a thing nobody seems to notice but myself, and that is that it changes as the light changes.

When the sun shoots in through the east window — I always watch for that first long, straight ray — it changes so quickly that I never can quite believe it.

That is why I watch it always.

By moonlight — the moon shines in all night when there is a moon — I wouldn't know it was the same paper.

At night in any kind of light, in twilight, candlelight, lamplight, and worst of all by moonlight, it becomes bars! The outside pattern, I mean, and the woman behind it is as plain as can be.

I didn't realize for a long time what the thing was that showed behind, that dim subpattern, but now I am quite sure it is a woman.

By daylight she is subdued, quiet. I fancy it is the pattern that keeps her so still. It is so puzzling. It keeps me quiet by the hour.

I lie down ever so much now. John says it is good for me, and to sleep all I can.

Indeed he started the habit by making me lie down for an hour after each meal.

It is a very bad habit, I am convinced, for you see, I don't sleep.

And that cultivates deceit, for I don't tell them I'm awake — oh, no!

The fact is I am getting a little afraid of John.

He seems very queer sometimes, and even Jennie has an inexplicable look.

It strikes me occasionally, just as a scientific hypothesis, that perhaps it is the paper!

I have watched John when he did not know I was looking, and come into the room suddenly on the most innocent excuses, and I've caught him several times *looking at the paper!* And Jennie too. I caught Jennie with her hand on it once.

She didn't know I was in the room, and when I asked her in a quiet, a very quiet voice, with the most restrained manner possible, what she was doing with the paper, she turned around as if she had been caught stealing, and looked quite angry — asked me why I should frighten her so!

Then she said that the paper stained everything it touched, that she had found yellow smooches on all my clothes and John's and she wished we would be more careful!

Did not that sound innocent? But I know she was studying that pattern, and I am determined that nobody shall find it out but myself!

Life is very much more exciting now than it used to be. You see, I have something more to expect, to look forward to, to watch. I really do eat better, and am more quiet than I was.

John is so pleased to see me improve! He laughed a little the other day, and said I seemed to be flourishing in spite of my wallpaper.

I turned it off with a laugh. I had no intention of telling him it was *because* of the wallpaper — he would make fun of me. He might even want to take me away.

I don't want to leave now until I have found it out. There is a week more, and I think that will be enough.

I'm feeling so much better!

I don't sleep much at night, for it is so interesting to watch developments; but I sleep a good deal during the daytime.

In the daytime it is tiresome and perplexing.

There are always new shoots on the fungus, and new shades of yellow all over it. I cannot keep count of them, though I have tried conscientiously.

It is the strangest yellow, that wallpaper! It makes me think of all the yellow things I ever saw — not beautiful ones like buttercups, but old, foul, bad yellow things.

But there is something else about that paper — the smell! I noticed it the moment we came into the room, but with so much air and sun it was not bad. Now we have had a week of fog and rain, and whether the windows are open or not, the smell is here.

It creeps all over the house.

I find it hovering in the dining-room, skulking in the parlor, hiding in the hall, lying in wait for me on the stairs.

It gets into my hair.

Even when I go to ride, if I turn my head suddenly and surprise it — there is that smell!

Such a peculiar odor, too! I have spent hours in trying to analyze it, to find what it smelled like.

It is not bad — at first — and very gentle, but quite the subtlest, most enduring odor I ever met.

In this damp weather it is awful. I wake up in the night and find it hanging over me.

It used to disturb me at first. I thought seriously of burning the house — to reach the smell.

But now I am used to it. The only thing I can think of that it is like is the *color* of the paper! A yellow smell.

There is a very funny mark on this wall, low down, near the mopboard. A streak that runs round the room. It goes behind every piece of furniture, except the bed, a long, straight, even *smooch*, as if it had been rubbed over and over.

I wonder how it was done and who did it, and what they did it for.

Round and round and round — round and round and round — it makes me dizzy!

I really have discovered something at last.

Through watching so much at night, when it changes so, I have finally found out.

The front pattern *does* move — and no wonder! The woman behind shakes it!

Sometimes I think there are a great many women behind, and sometimes only one, and she crawls around fast, and her crawling shakes it all over.

Then in the very bright spots she keeps still, and in the very shady spots she just takes hold of the bars and shakes them hard.

And she is all the time trying to climb through. But nobody could climb through that pattern — it strangles so; I think that is why it has so many heads.

They get through and then the pattern strangles them off and turns them upside down, and makes their eyes white!

If those heads were covered or taken off it would not be half so bad.

I think that woman gets out in the daytime!

And I'll tell you why — privately — I've seen her!

I can see her out of every one of my windows!

It is the same woman, I know, for she is always creeping, and most women do not creep by daylight.

I see her in that long shaded lane, creeping up and down. I see her in those dark grape arbors, creeping all round the garden.

I see her on that long road under the trees, creeping along, and when a carriage comes she hides under the blackberry vines.

I don't blame her a bit. It must be very humiliating to be caught creeping by daylight!

I always lock the door when I creep by daylight. I can't do it at night, for I know John would suspect something at once.

And John is so queer now that I don't want to irritate him. I wish he would take another room! Besides, I don't want anybody to get that woman out at night but myself.

I often wonder if I could see her out of all the windows at once.

But, turn as fast as I can, I can only see out of one at one time.

And though I always see her, she *may* be able to creep faster than I can turn! I have watched her sometimes away off in the open country, creeping as fast as a cloud shadow in a wind.

If only that top pattern could be gotten off from the under one! I mean to try it, little by little.

I have found out another funny thing, but I shan't tell it this time! It does not do to trust people too much.

There are only two more days to get this paper off, and I believe John is beginning to notice. I don't like the look in his eyes.

And I heard him ask Jennie a lot of professional questions about me. She had a very good report to give.

She said I slept a good deal in the daytime.

John knows I don't sleep very well at night, for all I'm so quiet!

He asked me all sorts of questions too, and pretended to be very loving and kind.

As if I couldn't see through him!

Still, I don't wonder he acts so, sleeping under this paper for three months.

It only interests me, but I feel sure John and Jennie are affected by it.

Hurrah! This is the last day, but it is enough. John is to stay in town over night, and won't be out until this evening.

Jennie wanted to sleep with me — the sly thing; but I told her I should undoubtedly rest better for a night all alone.

That was clever, for really I wasn't alone a bit! As soon as it was moonlight and that poor thing began to crawl and shake the pattern, I got up and ran to help her.

I pulled and she shook. I shook and she pulled, and before morning we had peeled off yards of that paper.

A strip about as high as my head and half around the room.

And then when the sun came and that awful pattern began to laugh at me, I declared I would finish it today!

We go away tomorrow, and they are moving all my furniture down again to leave things as they were before.

Jennie looked at the wall in amazement, but I told her merrily that I did it out of pure spite at the vicious thing.

She laughed and said she wouldn't mind doing it herself, but I must not get tired.

How she betrayed herself that time!

But I am here, and no person touches this paper but Me — not *alive!*

She tried to get me out of the room — it was too patent! But I said it was so quiet and empty and clean now that I believed I would lie down again and sleep all I could, and not to wake me even for dinner — I would call when I woke.

So now she is gone, and the servants are gone, and the things are gone, and there is nothing left but that great bedstead nailed down, with the canvas mattress we found on it.

We shall sleep downstairs tonight, and take the boat home tomorrow.

I quite enjoy the room, now it is bare again.

How those children did tear about here!

This bedstead is fairly gnawed!

But I must get to work.

I have locked the door and thrown the key down into the front path.

I don't want to go out, and I don't want to have anybody come in, till John comes.

I want to astonish him.

I've got a rope up here that even Jennie did not find. If that woman does get out, and tries to get away, I can tie her!

But I forgot I could not reach far without anything to stand on!

This bed will *not* move!

I tried to lift and push it until I was lame, and then I got so angry I bit off a little piece at one corner — but it hurt my teeth.

Then I peeled off all the paper I could reach standing on the floor. It sticks horribly and the pattern just enjoys it! All those strangled heads and bulbous eyes and waddling fungus growths just shriek with derision!

I am getting angry enough to do something desperate. To jump out of the window would be admirable exercise, but the bars are too strong even to try.

Besides I wouldn't do it. Of course not. I know well enough that a step like that is improper and might be misconstrued.

I don't like to *look* out of the windows even — there are so many of those creeping women, and they creep so fast.

I wonder if they all come out of that wallpaper as I did!

But I am securely fastened now by my well-hidden rope — you don't get *me* out in the road there!

I suppose I shall have to get back behind the pattern when it comes night, and that is hard!

It is so pleasant to be out in this great room and creep around as I please!

I don't want to go outside. I won't, even if Jennie asks me to.

For outside you have to creep on the ground, and everything is green instead of yellow.

But here I can creep smoothly on the floor, and my shoulder just fits in that long smooch around the wall, so I cannot lose my way.

Why, there's John at the door!

It is no use, young man, you can't open it!

How he does call and pound!

Now he's crying to Jennie for an axe.

It would be a shame to break down that beautiful door!

"John, dear!" said I in the gentlest voice. "The key is down by the front steps, under a plantain leaf!"

That silenced him for a few moments.

Then he said, very quietly indeed, "Open the door, my darling!"

"I can't," said I. "The key is down by the front door under a plantain leaf!" And then I said it again, several times, very gently and slowly, and said it so often that he had to go and see, and he got it of course, and came in. He stopped short by the door.

"What is the matter?" he cried. "For God's sake, what are you doing!"

I kept on creeping just the same, but I looked at him over my shoulder.

"I've got out at last," said I, "in spite of you and Jane. And I've pulled off most of the paper, so you can't put me back!"

Now why should that man have fainted? But he did, and right across my path by the wall, so that I had to creep over him every time!   [1892]

NIKOLAI GOGOL *(1809–1852) broke through the eighteenth-century literary conventions that prevailed in his time. He is considered the father of Russian realism — "We all came out from under Gogol's 'Overcoat'" is a remark attributed to the novelists Ivan Turgenev, Leo Tolstoy, and Fyodor Dostoevsky, each of whom is supposed to have said it as a tribute to the story's importance. As today's readers can agree, Gogol used romanticism and fantasy in his fiction as well.*

Born in Sorochintsky in the Russian Ukraine, Gogol was sent away to a boarding school as a boy; he was so physically unattractive that the other students gave him the name "the mysterious dwarf." In 1828, after he left school, Gogol moved to St. Petersburg (then the capital of Russia), passed the civil service examinations, and held various government jobs; he also became a friend of Alexander Pushkin, the great Russian poet. In 1831 and 1832 Gogol published a two-volume collection of stories, Evenings on a Farm near Dikanka, *and in 1835 a historical novel about the Ukrainian Cossacks,* Taras Bulba. *In 1836 his play* The Inspector General, *a satire ridiculing Russian officials, was considered so scandalous that Gogol was forced into exile in Rome. In 1840 he published "The Overcoat," and two years later the novel* Dead Souls, *which he considered his most important book. In his last years his health declined, and he died, insane, at the age of forty-three.*

In The Lonely Voice *(1963), his study of the short story, Frank O'Connor maintained that the expression "We all came out from under Gogol's 'Overcoat'" has a validity beyond its relevance for Russian writers. O'Connor identified this story as "the first appearance in fiction of the Little Man." He went on to define the special impact of the short story as a literary form that offers an intense awareness of human isolation. To O'Connor, the short story (unlike the novel) never features a true hero. Instead, it portrays "a submerged population group," which changes character from writer to writer and generation to generation: "It may be Gogol's officials . . . Maupassant's prostitutes, Chekhov's doctors and teachers, Sherwood Anderson's provincials, always dreaming of escape." Everything about Akaky Akakievich in "The Overcoat" — his absurd name, his absurd family, his absurd job — is on the same level of mediocrity, yet something about the little clerk moves us to pity and sympathy. When others torment him, we seem to hear him say, "Leave me alone! Why do you insult me? I am your brother."*

RELATED COMMENTARY: *Vladimir Nabokov, "Gogol's Genius in 'The Overcoat,'" page 1469.*

Nikolai Gogol

The Overcoat

Translated by Constance Garnett

In the department of . . . but I had better not mention which department. There is nothing in the world more touchy than a department, a regiment, a government office, and, in fact, any sort of official body. Nowadays every private individual considers all society insulted in his person. I have been told that very lately a complaint was lodged by a police inspector of which town I don't remember, and that in this complaint he set forth clearly that the institutions of the State were in danger and that his sacred name was being taken in vain; and, in proof thereof, he appended to his complaint an enormously long volume of some romantic work in which a police inspector appeared on every tenth page, occasionally, indeed, in an intoxicated condition. And so, to avoid any unpleasantness, we had better call the department of which we are speaking "a certain department."

And so, in a *certain department* there was a *certain clerk;* a clerk of whom it cannot be said that he was very remarkable; he was short, somewhat pockmarked, with rather reddish hair and rather dim, bleary eyes, with a small bald patch on the top of his head, with wrinkles on both sides of his cheeks and the sort of complexion which is usually described as hemorrhoidal . . . nothing can be done about that, it is the Petersburg climate. As for his grade in the civil service (for among us a man's rank is what must be established first) he was what is called a perpetual titular councilor, a class at which, as we all know, various writers who indulge in the praiseworthy habit of attacking those who cannot defend themselves jeer and jibe to their hearts' content. This clerk's surname was Bashmachkin. From the very name it is clear that it must have been derived from a shoe (*bashmak*); but when and under what circumstances it was derived from a shoe, it is impossible to say. Both his father and his grandfather and even his brother-in-law, and all the Bashmachkins without exception wore boots, which they simply resoled two or three times a year. His name was Akaky Akakievich. Perhaps it may strike the reader as a rather strange and contrived name, but I can assure him that it was not contrived at all, that the circumstances were such that it was quite out of the question to give him any other name. Akaky Akakievich was born toward nightfall, if my memory does not deceive me, on the twenty-third of March. His mother, the wife of a government clerk, a very good woman, made arrangements in due course to christen the child. She was still lying in bed, facing the door, while on her right hand stood the godfather, an excellent man called Ivan Ivanovich Yeroshkin, one of the head clerks in the Senate, and the godmother, the wife of a police official and a woman of rare qualities, Arina Semeonovna Belobriushkova. Three names were offered to the happy mother for selection — Mokky, Sossy, or the name of the martyr Khozdazat. "No," thought the poor lady, "they are all such names!" To satisfy her, they opened the calendar at another page, and the names which turned up were: Trifily, Dula, Varakhasy. "What an infliction!" said the mother. "What names they all are! I really never heard such names. Varadat or Varukh would be bad enough, but Trifily and Varakhasy!" They turned over another page and the names were: Pavsikakhy and Vakhisy. "Well, I see," said the mother, "it is clear that it is his fate. Since that is how it is, he had better be named after his father; his father is Akaky; let the son be Akaky, too." This was how he came to be Akaky Akakievich. The baby was christened and cried and made sour faces during the ceremony, as though he foresaw that he would be a titular councilor. So that was how it all came to pass. We have reported it here so that the reader may see for himself that it happened quite inevitably and that to give him any other name was out of the question.

No one has been able to remember when and how long ago he entered the department, nor who gave him the job. Regardless of how many directors and higher officials of all sorts came and went, he was always seen in the same place, in the same position, at the very same duty, precisely the same copying clerk, so that they used to declare that he must have been born a copying clerk, uniform, bald patch, and all. No respect at all was shown him in the department. The porters, far from getting up from their seats when he came in, took no more notice of him than if a simple fly had flown across the reception room. His superiors treated him with a sort of despotic aloofness. The head clerk's assistant used to throw papers under his nose without even saying "Copy this" or "Here is an interesting, nice little case" or some agreeable remark of the sort, as is usually done in well-bred offices. And he would take it, gazing only at the paper without looking to see who had put it there and whether he had the right to do so; he would take it and at once begin copying it. The young clerks jeered and made jokes at him to the best of their clerkly wit, and told before his face all sorts of stories of their own invention about him; they would say of his landlady, an old woman of seventy, that she beat him, would ask when the wedding was to take place, and would scatter bits of paper on his head, calling them snow. Akaky Akakievich never answered a word, however, but behaved as though there were no one there. It had no influence on his work; in the midst of all this teasing, he never made a single mistake in his copying. It was only when the jokes became too unbearable, when they jolted his arm, and prevented him from going on with his work, that he would say: "Leave me alone! Why do you insult me?" and there was something touching in the words and in the voice in which they were uttered. There was a note in it of something that aroused compassion, so that one young man, new to the office, who, following the example of the rest, had allowed himself to tease him, suddenly stopped as though cut to the heart, and from that time on, everything was, as it were, changed and appeared in a different light to him. Some unseen force seemed to repel him from the companions with whom he had become acquainted because he thought they were well-bred and decent men. And long afterward, during moments of the greatest gaiety, the figure of the humble little clerk with a bald patch on his head appeared before him with his heart-rending words: "Leave me alone! Why do you insult me?" and within those moving words he heard others: "I am your brother." And the poor young man hid his face in his hands, and many times afterward in his life he shuddered, seeing how much inhumanity there is in man, how much savage brutality lies hidden under refined, cultured politeness, and, my God! even in a man whom the world accepts as a gentleman and a man of honor. . . .

It would be hard to find a man who lived for his work as did Akaky Akakievich. To say that he was zealous in his work is not enough; no, he loved his work. In it, in that copying, he found an interesting and pleasant world of his own. There was a look of enjoyment on his face; certain letters were favorites with him, and when he came to them he was delighted; he chuckled to himself and winked and moved his lips, so that it seemed as though every letter his pen was forming could be read in his face. If rewards had been given according to the measure of zeal in the service, he might to his amazement have even found himself a civil councilor; but all he gained in the service, as the wits, his fellow clerks, expressed it, was a button in his buttonhole[1] and hemorrhoids where he sat. It cannot be said, however, that no notice had ever been taken of him. One director, being a good-natured man and anxious to reward him for his long service, sent him something a little more important than his ordinary copying; he was instructed to make some sort of report from a finished document for another office; the work consisted only of altering the headings and in places changing the first person into the third. This cost him so much effort that he was covered with perspiration: he mopped his brow and said at last, "No, I'd rather copy something."

From that time on they left him to his copying forever. It seemed as though nothing in the world existed for him except his copying. He gave no thought at all to his clothes; his uniform was — well, not green but some sort of rusty, muddy color. His collar was very low and narrow, so that, although his neck was not particularly long, yet, standing out of the collar, it looked as immensely long as those of the dozens of plaster kittens with nodding heads which foreigners carry about on their heads and peddle in Russia. And there were always things sticking to his uniform, either bits of hay or threads; moreover, he had a special knack of passing under a window at the very moment when various garbage was being flung out into the street, and so was continually carrying off bits of melon rind and similar litter on his hat. He had never once in his life noticed what was being done and what was going on in the street, all those things at which, as we all know, his colleagues, the young clerks, always stare, utilizing their keen sight so well that they notice anyone on the other side of the street with a strap hanging loose — an observation which always calls forth a sly grin. Whatever Akaky Akakievich looked at, he saw nothing but his clear, evenly written lines, and it was only perhaps when a horse suddenly appeared from nowhere and placed its head

---

[1]Whereas most clerks of long service wore a medal of achievement. (Leonard J. Kent, ed., *The Complete Tales of Nikolai Gogol*, vol. 2 [Chicago: University of Chicago Press, 1985].)

on his shoulder, and with its nostrils blew a real gale upon his cheek, that he would notice that he was not in the middle of his writing, but rather in the middle of the street.

On reaching home, he would sit down at once at the table, hurriedly eat his soup and a piece of beef with an onion; he did not notice the taste at all but ate it all with the flies and anything else that Providence happened to send him. When he felt that his stomach was beginning to be full, he would get up from the table, take out a bottle of ink, and begin copying the papers he had brought home with him. When he had none to do, he would make a copy especially for his own pleasure, particularly if the document were remarkable not for the beauty of its style but because it was addressed to some new or distinguished person.

Even at those hours when the gray Petersburg sky is completely overcast and the whole population of clerks have dined and eaten their fill, each as best he can, according to the salary he receives and his personal tastes; when they are all resting after the scratching of pens and bustle of the office, their own necessary work and other people's, and all the tasks that an overzealous man voluntarily sets himself even beyond what is necessary; when the clerks are hastening to devote what is left of their time to pleasure; some more enterprising are flying to the theater, others to the street to spend their leisure staring at women's hats, some to spend the evening paying compliments to some attractive girl, the star of a little official circle, while some — and this is the most frequent of all — go simply to a fellow clerk's apartment on the third or fourth story, two little rooms with a hall or a kitchen, with some pretensions to style, with a lamp or some such article that has cost many sacrifices of dinners and excursions — at the time when all the clerks are scattered about the apartments of their friends, playing a stormy game of whist, sipping tea out of glasses, eating cheap biscuits, sucking in smoke from long pipes, telling, as the cards are dealt, some scandal that has floated down from higher circles, a pleasure which the Russian can never by any possibility deny himself, or, when there is nothing better to talk about, repeating the everlasting anecdote of the commanding officer who was told that the tail had been cut off the horse on the Falconet monument[2] — in short, even when everyone was eagerly seeking entertainment, Akaky Akakievich did not indulge in any amusement. No one could say that they had ever seen him at an evening party. After working to his heart's content, he would go to bed, smiling at the thought of the next day and wondering what God would send him to copy. So flowed on the peaceful life of a man who knew how to be content with his fate on a salary of four hundred rubles, and so perhaps it would have flowed on to extreme old age, had it not been for the various disasters strewn along the road of life, not only of titular, but even of privy, actual court, and all other councilors, even those who neither give counsel to others nor accept it themselves.

There is in Petersburg a mighty foe of all who receive a salary of about

---

[2] Famous statue of Peter the First. (Kent, ed.)

four hundred rubles. That foe is none other than our northern frost, although it is said to be very good for the health. Between eight and nine in the morning, precisely at the hour when the streets are filled with clerks going to their departments, the frost begins indiscriminately giving such sharp and stinging nips at all their noses that the poor fellows don't know what to do with them. At that time, when even those in the higher grade have a pain in their brows and tears in their eyes from the frost, the poor titular councilors are sometimes almost defenseless. Their only protection lies in running as fast as they can through five or six streets in a wretched, thin little overcoat and then warming their feet thoroughly in the porter's room, till all their faculties and talents for their various duties thaw out again after having been frozen on the way. Akaky Akakievich had for some time been feeling that his back and shoulders were particularly nipped by the cold, although he did try to run the regular distance as fast as he could. He wondered at last whether there were any defects in his overcoat. After examining it thoroughly in the privacy of his home, he discovered that in two or three places, on the back and the shoulders, it had become a regular sieve; the cloth was so worn that you could see through it and the lining was coming out. I must note that Akaky Akakievich's overcoat had also served as a butt for the jokes of the clerks. It had even been deprived of the honorable name of overcoat and had been referred to as the "dressing gown."[3] It was indeed of rather a peculiar make. Its collar had been growing smaller year by year as it served to patch the other parts. The patches were not good specimens of the tailor's art, and they certainly looked clumsy and ugly. On seeing what was wrong, Akaky Akakievich decided that he would have to take the overcoat to Petrovich, a tailor who lived on the fourth floor up a back staircase, and, in spite of having only one eye and being pockmarked all over his face, was rather successful in repairing the trousers and coats of clerks and others — that is, when he was sober, be it understood, and had no other enterprise on his mind. Of this tailor I ought not, of course, say much, but since it is now the rule that the character of every person in a novel must be completely described, well, there's nothing I can do but describe Petrovich too. At first he was called simply Grigory, and was a serf belonging to some gentleman or other. He began to be called Petrovich[4] from the time that he got his freedom and began to drink rather heavily on every holiday, at first only on the main holidays, but afterward, on all church holidays indiscriminately, wherever there was a cross in the calendar. In this he was true to the customs of his forefathers, and when he quarreled with his wife he used to call her a worldly woman and a German. Since we have now mentioned the wife, it will be necessary to say a few words about her, too, but unfortunately not much is known about her, except indeed that Petrovich had a wife and that she wore a cap and not a kerchief, but apparently she could not boast of beauty; anyway, none but

---

[3] *Kapot*, usually a woman's garment. (Kent, ed.)

[4] Customarily, serfs were addressed by first name only, while free men were addressed either by first name and patronymic or just the patronymic. (Kent, ed.)

soldiers of the guard peered under her cap when they met her, and they twitched their mustaches and gave vent to a rather peculiar sound.

As he climbed the stairs leading to Petrovich's — which, to do them justice, were all soaked with water and slops and saturated through and through with that smell of ammonia which makes the eyes smart, and is, as we all know, inseparable from the backstairs of Petersburg houses — Akaky Akakievich was already wondering how much Petrovich would ask for the job, and inwardly resolving not to give more than two rubles. The door was open, because Petrovich's wife was frying some fish and had so filled the kitchen with smoke that you could not even see the cockroaches. Akaky Akakievich crossed the kitchen unnoticed by the good woman, and walked at last into a room where he saw Petrovich sitting on a big, wooden, unpainted table with his legs tucked under him like a Turkish pasha. The feet, as is usual with tailors when they sit at work, were bare; and the first object that caught Akaky Akakievich's eye was the big toe, with which he was already familiar, with a misshapen nail as thick and strong as the shell of a tortoise. Around Petrovich's neck hung a skein of silk and another of thread and on his knees was a rag of some sort. He had for the last three minutes been trying to thread his needle, but could not get the thread into the eye and so was very angry with the darkness and indeed with the thread itself, muttering in an undertone: "She won't go in, the savage! You wear me out, you bitch." Akaky Akakievich was unhappy that he had come just at the minute when Petrovich was in a bad humor; he liked to give him an order when he was a little "elevated," or, as his wife expressed it, "had fortified himself with vodka, the one-eyed devil." In such circumstances Petrovich was as a rule very ready to give way and agree, and invariably bowed and thanked him. Afterward, it is true, his wife would come wailing that her husband had been drunk and so had asked too little, but adding a single ten-kopek piece would settle that. But on this occasion Petrovich was apparently sober and consequently curt, unwilling to bargain, and the devil knows what price he would be ready to demand. Akaky Akakievich realized this, and was, as the saying is, beating a retreat, but things had gone too far, for Petrovich was screwing up his solitary eye very attentively at him and Akaky Akakievich involuntarily said: "Good day, Petrovich!"

"I wish you a good day, sir," said Petrovich, and squinted at Akaky Akakievich's hands, trying to discover what sort of goods he had brought.

"Here I have come to you, Petrovich, do you see . . . .!"

It must be noticed that Akaky Akakievich for the most part explained himself by apologies, vague phrases, and meaningless parts of speech which have absolutely no significance whatever. If the subject were a very difficult one, it was his habit indeed to leave his sentences quite unfinished, so that very often after a sentence had begun with the words, "It really is, don't you know . . ." nothing at all would follow and he himself would be quite oblivious to the fact that he had not finished his thought, supposing he had said all that was necessary.

"What is it?" said Petrovich, and at the same time with his solitary eye he scrutinized his whole uniform from the collar to the sleeves, the back, the skirts, the buttonholes — with all of which he was very familiar since they were all his own work. Such scrutiny is habitual with tailors; it is the first thing they do on meeting one.

"It's like this, Petrovich . . . the overcoat, the cloth . . . you see everywhere else it is quite strong; it's a little dusty and looks as though it were old, but it is new and it is only in one place just a little . . . on the back, and just a little worn on one shoulder and on this shoulder, too, a little . . . do you see? that's all, and it's not much work . . ."

Petrovich took the "dressing gown," first spread it out over the table, examined it for a long time, shook his head, and put his hand out to the window sill for a round snuffbox with a portrait on the lid of some general — which general I can't exactly say, for a finger had been thrust through the spot where a face should have been, and the hole had been pasted over with a square piece of paper. After taking a pinch of snuff, Petrovich held the "dressing gown" up in his hands and looked at it against the light, and again he shook his head; then he turned it with the lining upward and once more shook his head; again he took off the lid with the general pasted up with paper and snuffed a pinch into his nose, shut the box, put it away, and at last said: "No, it can't be repaired; a wretched garment!" Akaky Akakievich's heart sank at those words.

"Why can't it, Petrovich?" he said, almost in the imploring voice of a child. "Why, the only thing is, it is a bit worn on the shoulders; why, you have got some little pieces . . ."

"Yes, the pieces will be found all right," said Petrovich, "but it can't be patched, the stuff is rotten; if you put a needle in it, it would give way."

"Let it give way, but you just put a patch on it."

"There is nothing to put a patch on. There is nothing for it to hold on to; there is a great strain on it; it is not worth calling cloth; it would fly away at a breath of wind."

"Well, then, strengthen it with something — I'm sure, really, this is . . ."

"No," said Petrovich resolutely, "there is nothing that can be done, the thing is no good at all. You had far better, when the cold winter weather comes, make yourself leg wrappings out of it, for there is no warmth in stockings; the Germans invented them just to make money." (Petrovich enjoyed a dig at the Germans occasionally.) "And as for the overcoat, it is obvious that you will have to have a new one."

At the word "new" there was a mist before Akaky Akakievich's eyes, and everything in the room seemed blurred. He could see nothing clearly but the general with the piece of paper over his face on the lid of Petrovich's snuffbox.

"A new one?" he said, still feeling as though he were in a dream; "why, I haven't the money for it."

"Yes, a new one," Petrovich repeated with barbarous composure.

"Well, and if I did have a new one, how much would it . . . ?"

"You mean what will it cost?"

"Yes."

"Well, at least one hundred and fifty rubles," said Petrovich, and he compressed his lips meaningfully. He was very fond of making an effect; he was fond of suddenly disconcerting a man completely and then squinting sideways to see what sort of a face he made.

"A hundred and fifty rubles for an overcoat!" screamed poor Akaky Akakievich — it was perhaps the first time he had screamed in his life, for he was always distinguished by the softness of his voice.

"Yes," said Petrovich, "and even then it depends on the coat. If I were to put marten on the collar, and add a hood with silk linings, it would come to two hundred."

"Petrovich, please," said Akaky Akakievich in an imploring voice, not hearing and not trying to hear what Petrovich said, and missing all his effects, "repair it somehow, so that it will serve a little longer."

"No, that would be wasting work and spending money for nothing," said Petrovich, and after that Akaky Akakievich went away completely crushed, and when he had gone Petrovich remained standing for a long time with his lips pursed up meaningfully before he began his work again, feeling pleased that he had not demeaned himself or lowered the dignity of the tailor's art.

When he got into the street, Akaky Akakievich felt as though he was in a dream. "So that is how it is," he said to himself. "I really did not think it would be this way . . ." and then after a pause he added, "So that's it! So that's how it is at last! and I really could never have supposed it would be this way. And there . . ." There followed another long silence, after which he said: "So that's it! well, it really is so utterly unexpected . . . who would have thought . . . what a circumstance . . ." Saying this, instead of going home he walked off in quite the opposite direction without suspecting what he was doing. On the way a clumsy chimney sweep brushed the whole of his sooty side against him and blackened his entire shoulder; a whole hatful of plaster scattered upon him from the top of a house that was being built. He noticed nothing of this, and only after he had jostled against a policeman who had set his halberd down beside him and was shaking some snuff out of his horn into his rough fist, he came to himself a little and then only because the policeman said: "Why are you poking yourself right in one's face, haven't you enough room on the street?" This made him look around and turn homeward; only there he began to collect his thoughts, to see his position in a clear and true light, and began talking to himself no longer incoherently but reasonably and openly as with a sensible friend with whom one can discuss the most intimate and vital matters. "No," said Akaky Akakievich, "it is no use talking to Petrovich now; just now he really is . . . his wife must have been giving it to him. I had better go to him on Sunday morning; after Saturday night he will have a crossed eye and be sleepy, so he'll want a little drink and his wife won't give him a kopek. I'll slip ten kopeks into his hand and then he will be more accommodating and maybe take the overcoat . . ."

So reasoning with himself, Akaky Akakievich cheered up and waited until the next Sunday; then, seeing from a distance Petrovich's wife leaving the house, he went straight in. Petrovich certainly had a crossed eye after

Saturday. He could hardly hold his head up and was very drowsy; but, despite all that, as soon as he heard what Akaky Akakievich was speaking about, it seemed as though the devil had nudged him. "I can't," he said, "you must order a new one." Akaky Akakievich at once slipped a ten-kopek piece into his hand. "I thank you, sir, I will have just a drop to your health, but don't trouble yourself about the overcoat; it is no good for anything. I'll make you a fine new coat; you can have faith in me for that."

Akaky Akakievich would have said more about repairs, but Petrovich, without listening, said: "A new one I'll make you without fail; you can rely on that; I'll do my best. It could even be like the fashion that is popular, with the collar to fasten with silver-plated hooks under a flap."

Then Akaky Akakievich saw that there was no escape from a new overcoat and he was utterly depressed. How indeed, for what, with what money could he get it? Of course he could to some extent rely on the bonus for the coming holiday, but that money had long been appropriated and its use determined beforehand. It was needed for new trousers and to pay the cobbler an old debt for putting some new tops on some old boots, and he had to order three shirts from a seamstress as well as two items of undergarments which it is indecent to mention in print; in short, all that money absolutely must be spent, and even if the director were to be so gracious as to give him a holiday bonus of forty-five or even fifty, instead of forty rubles, there would be still left a mere trifle, which would be but a drop in the ocean compared to the fortune needed for an overcoat. Though, of course, he knew that Petrovich had a strange craze for suddenly demanding the devil knows what enormous price, so that at times his own wife could not help crying out: "Why, you are out of your wits, you idiot! Another time he'll undertake a job for nothing, and here the devil has bewitched him to ask more than he is worth himself." Though, of course, he knew that Petrovich would undertake to make it for eighty rubles, still where would he get those eighty rubles? He might manage half of that sum; half of it could be found, perhaps even a little more; but where could he get the other half? . . . But, first of all, the reader ought to know where that first half was to be found. Akaky Akakievich had the habit every time he spent a ruble of putting aside two kopeks in a little box which he kept locked, with a slit in the lid for dropping in the money. At the end of every six months he would inspect the pile of coppers there and change them for small silver. He had done this for a long time, and in the course of many years the sum had mounted up to forty rubles and so he had half the money in his hands, but where was he to get the other half; where was he to get another forty rubles? Akaky Akakievich thought and thought and decided at last that he would have to diminish his ordinary expenses, at least for a year; give up burning candles in the evening, and if he had to do any work he must go into the landlady's room and work by her candle; that as he walked along the streets he must walk as lightly and carefully as possible, almost on tiptoe, on the cobbles and flagstones, so that his soles might last a little longer than usual; that he must send his linen to the wash less frequently, and that, to preserve it from being worn, he must take it off every day when he came home and sit in a thin cotton dressing gown, a very

ancient garment which Time itself had spared. To tell the truth, he found it at
first rather difficult to get used to these privations, but after a while it became
a habit and went smoothly enough — he even became quite accustomed to
being hungry in the evening; on the other hand, he had spiritual nourishment,
for he carried ever in his thoughts the idea of his future overcoat. His whole
existence had in a sense become fuller, as though he had married, as though
some other person were present with him, as though he were no longer alone
but an agreeable companion had consented to walk the path of life hand in
hand with him, and that companion was none other than the new overcoat
with its thick padding and its strong, durable lining. He became, as it were,
more alive, even more strong-willed, like a man who has set before himself a
definite goal. Uncertainty, indecision, in fact all the hesitating and vague
characteristics, vanished from his face and his manners. At times there was a
gleam in his eyes; indeed, the most bold and audacious ideas flashed through
his mind. Why not really have marten on the collar? Meditation on the subject
always made him absent-minded. On one occasion when he was copying a
document, he very nearly made a mistake, so that he almost cried out "ough"
aloud and crossed himself. At least once every month he went to Petrovich
to talk about the overcoat: where it would be best to buy the cloth, and what
color it should be, and what price; and, though he returned home a little
anxious, he was always pleased at the thought that at last the time was at
hand when everything would be bought and the overcoat would be made.
Things moved even faster than he had anticipated. Contrary to all expectations, the director bestowed on Akaky Akakievich a bonus of no less than
sixty rubles. Whether it was that he had an inkling that Akaky Akakievich
needed a coat, or whether it happened by luck, owing to this he found he
had twenty rubles extra. This circumstance hastened the course of affairs.
Another two or three months of partial starvation and Akaky Akakievich had
actually saved up nearly eighty rubles. His heart, as a rule very tranquil,
began to throb.

The very first day he set out with Petrovich for the shops. They bought
some very good cloth, and no wonder, since they had been thinking of it for
more than six months, and scarcely a month had passed without their going
out to the shop to compare prices; now Petrovich himself declared that there
was no better cloth to be had. For the lining they chose calico, but of such
good quality, that in Petrovich's words it was even better than silk, and
actually as strong and handsome to look at. Marten they did not buy, because
it was too expensive, but instead they chose cat fur, the best to be found in
the shop — cat which in the distance might almost be taken for marten.
Petrovich was busy making the coat for two weeks, because there was a great
deal of quilting; otherwise it would have been ready sooner. Petrovich
charged twelve rubles for the work; less than that it hardly could have been;
everything was sewn with silk, with fine double seams, and Petrovich went
over every seam afterwards with his own teeth, imprinting various patterns
with them. It was . . . it is hard to say precisely on what day, but probably on
the most triumphant day in the life of Akaky Akakievich, that Petrovich at
last brought the overcoat. He brought it in the morning, just before it was

time to set off for the department. The overcoat could not have arrived at a more opportune time, because severe frosts were just beginning and seemed threatening to become even harsher. Petrovich brought the coat himself as a good tailor should. There was an expression of importance on his face, such as Akaky Akakievich had never seen there before. He seemed fully conscious of having completed a work of no little importance and of having shown by his own example the gulf that separates tailors who only put in linings and do repairs from those who make new coats. He took the coat out of the huge handkerchief in which he had brought it (the handkerchief had just come home from the wash); he then folded it up and put it in his pocket for future use. After taking out the overcoat, he looked at it with much pride and holding it in both hands, threw it very deftly over Akaky Akakievich's shoulders, then pulled it down and smoothed it out behind with his hands; then draped it about Akaky Akakievich somewhat jauntily. Akaky Akakievich, a practical man, wanted to try it with his arms in the sleeves. Petrovich helped him to put it on, and it looked splendid with his arms in the sleeves, too. In fact, it turned out that the overcoat was completely and entirely successful. Petrovich did not let slip the occasion for observing that it was only because he lived in a small street and had no signboard, and because he had known Akaky Akakievich so long, that he had done it so cheaply, and that on Nevsky Prospekt they would have asked him seventy-five rubles for the tailoring alone. Akaky Akakievich had no inclination to discuss this with Petrovich; besides he was frightened of the big sums that Petrovich was fond of flinging airily about in conversation. He paid him, thanked him, and went off, with his new overcoat on, to the department. Petrovich followed him out and stopped in the street, staring for a long time at the coat from a distance and then purposely turned off and, taking a short cut through a side street, came back into the street, and got another view of the coat from the other side, that is, from the front.

Meanwhile Akaky Akakievich walked along in a gay holiday mood. Every second he was conscious that he had a new overcoat on his shoulders, and several times he actually laughed from inward satisfaction. Indeed, it had two advantages: one that it was warm and the other that it was good. He did not notice how far he had walked at all and he suddenly found himself in the department; in the porter's room he took off the overcoat, looked it over, and entrusted it to the porter's special care. I cannot tell how it happened, but all at once everyone in the department learned that Akaky Akakievich had a new overcoat and that the "dressing gown" no longer existed. They all ran out at once into the cloakroom to look at Akaky Akakievich's new overcoat; they began welcoming him and congratulating him so that at first he could do nothing but smile and then felt positively embarrassed. When, coming up to him, they all began saying that he must "sprinkle" the new overcoat and that he ought at least to buy them all a supper, Akaky Akakievich lost his head completely and did not know what to do, how to get out of it, nor what to answer. A few minutes later, flushing crimson, he even began assuring them with great simplicity that it was not a new overcoat at all, that it wasn't much, that it was an old overcoat. At last one of the clerks, indeed the assistant of the head clerk of the room, probably in order to show that he wasn't too proud to mingle with those beneath him, said: "So be it, I'll give a party instead of Akaky Akakievich and invite you all to tea with me this evening; as luck would have it, it is my birthday." The clerks naturally congratulated the assistant head clerk and eagerly accepted the invitation. Akaky Akakievich was beginning to make excuses, but they all declared that it was uncivil of him, that it would be simply a shame and a disgrace that he could not possibly refuse. So, he finally relented, and later felt pleased about it when he remembered that through this he would have the opportunity of going out in the evening, too, in his new overcoat. That whole day was for Akaky Akakievich the most triumphant and festive day in his life. He returned home in the happiest frame of mind, took off the overcoat, and hung it carefully on the wall, admiring the cloth and lining once more, and then pulled out his old "dressing gown," now completely falling apart, and put it next to his new overcoat to compare the two. He glanced at it and laughed: the difference was enormous! And long afterwards he went on laughing at dinner, as the position in which the "dressing gown" was placed recurred to his mind. He dined in excellent spirits and after dinner wrote nothing, no papers at all, but just relaxed for a little while on his bed, till it got dark; then, without putting things off, he dressed, put on his overcoat, and went out into the street. Where precisely the clerk who had invited him lived we regret to say we cannot tell; our memory is beginning to fail sadly, and everything there in Petersburg, all the streets and houses, are so blurred and muddled in our head that it is a very difficult business to put anything in orderly fashion. Regardless of that, there is no doubt that the clerk lived in the better part of the town and consequently a very long distance from Akaky Akakievich. At first Akaky Akakievich had to walk through deserted streets, scantily lighted, but as he approached his destination the streets became more lively, more full of people, and more brightly lighted; passers-by began to be more frequent, ladies began to appear, here and there beautifully dressed, and beaver collars were to be seen on the men. Cabmen with wooden, railed sledges, studded with brass-topped nails, were less frequently seen; on the other hand, jaunty drivers in raspberry-colored velvet caps, with lacquered sledges and bearskin rugs, appeared and carriages with decorated boxes dashed along the streets, their wheels crunching through the snow.

Akaky Akakievich looked at all this as a novelty; for several years he had not gone out into the streets in the evening. He stopped with curiosity before a lighted shop window to look at a picture in which a beautiful woman was represented in the act of taking off her shoe and displaying as she did so the whole of a very shapely leg, while behind her back a gentleman with whiskers and a handsome imperial on his chin was sticking his head in at the door. Akaky Akakievich shook his head and smiled and then went on his way. Why did he smile? Was it because he had come across something quite unfamiliar to him, though every man retains some instinctive feeling on the subject, or was it that he reflected, like many other clerks, as follows: "Well, those Frenchmen! It's beyond anything! If they go in for anything of the sort, it really is . . . !" Though possibly he did not even think that; there is no creeping into a man's soul and finding out all that he thinks. At last he reached the house in which the assistant head clerk lived in fine style; there was a lamp burning on the stairs, and the apartment was on the second floor. As he went into the hall Akaky Akakievich saw rows of galoshes. Among them in the middle of the room stood a hissing samovar puffing clouds of steam. On the walls hung coats and cloaks among which some actually had beaver collars or velvet lapels. From the other side of the wall there came noise and talk, which suddenly became clear and loud when the door opened and the footman came out with a tray full of empty glasses, a jug of cream, and a basket of biscuits. It was evident that the clerks had arrived long before and had already drunk their first glass of tea. Akaky Akakievich, after hanging up his coat with his own hands, went into the room, and at the same moment there flashed before his eyes a vision of candles, clerks, pipes, and card tables, together with the confused sounds of conversation rising up on all sides and the noise of moving chairs. He stopped very awkwardly in the middle of the room, looking about and trying to think of what to do, but he was noticed and received with a shout and they all went at once into the hall and again took a look at his overcoat. Though Akaky Akakievich was somewhat embarrassed, yet, being a simple-hearted man, he could not help being pleased at seeing how they all admired his coat. Then of course they all abandoned him and his coat, and turned their attention as usual to the tables set for whist. All this — the noise, the talk, and the crowd of people — was strange and wonderful to Akaky Akakievich. He simply did not know how to behave, what to do with his arms and legs and his whole body; at last he sat down beside the players, looked at the cards, stared first at one and then at another of the faces, and in a little while, feeling bored, began to yawn — especially since it was long past the time at which he usually went to bed. He tried to say goodbye to his hosts, but they would not let him go, saying that he absolutely must have a glass of champagne in honor of the new coat. An hour later supper was served, consisting of salad, cold veal, pastry and pies from the bakery, and champagne. They made Akaky Akakievich drink two glasses, after which he felt that things were much more cheerful, though he could not forget that it was twelve o'clock, and that he ought to have been home long ago. That his host might not take it into his head to detain him, he slipped out of the room, hunted in the hall for his coat, which he found, not without regret, lying on the floor, shook it, removed some fluff from it, put it on, and went down the stairs into the street. It was still light in the streets. Some little grocery shops, those perpetual clubs for servants and all sorts of people, were open; others which were closed showed, however, a long streak of light at every crack of the door, proving that they were not yet deserted, and probably maids and menservants were still finishing their conversation and discussion, driving their masters to utter perplexity as to their whereabouts. Akaky Akakievich walked along in a cheerful state of mind; he was even on the point of running, goodness knows why, after a lady of some sort who passed by like lightning with every part of her frame in violent motion. He checked himself at once, however, and again walked along very gently, feeling positively surprised at the inexplicable impulse that had seized him. Soon the deserted streets, which are not particularly cheerful by day and even less so in the evening, stretched before him. Now they were still more dead and deserted; the light of street lamps was scantier, the oil evidently running low; then came wooden houses and fences; not a soul anywhere; only the snow gleamed on the streets and the low-pitched slumbering hovels looked black and gloomy with their closed shutters. He approached the spot where the street was intersected by an endless square, which looked like a fearful desert with its houses scarcely visible on the far side.

In the distance, goodness knows where, there was a gleam of light from some sentry box which seemed to be at the end of the world. Akaky Akakievich's lightheartedness faded. He stepped into the square, not without uneasiness, as though his heart had a premonition of evil. He looked behind him and to both sides — it was as though the sea were all around him. "No, better not look," he thought, and walked on, shutting his eyes, and when he opened them to see whether the end of the square was near, he suddenly saw standing before him, almost under his very nose, some men with mustaches; just what they were like he could not even distinguish. There was a mist before his eyes, and a throbbing in his chest. "Why, that overcoat is mine!" said one of them in a voice like a clap of thunder, seizing him by the collar. Akaky Akakievich was on the point of shouting "Help" when another put a fist the size of a clerk's head against his lips, saying: "You just shout now." Akaky Akakievich felt only that they took the overcoat off, and gave him a kick with their knees, and he fell on his face in the snow and was conscious of nothing more. A few minutes later he recovered consciousness and got up on his feet, but there was no one there. He felt that it was cold on the ground and that he had no overcoat, and began screaming, but it seemed as though his voice would not carry to the end of the square. Overwhelmed with despair and continuing to scream, he ran across the square straight to the sentry box beside which stood a policeman leaning on his halberd and, so it seemed, looking with curiosity to see who the devil the man was who was screaming and running toward him from the distance. As Akaky Akakievich reached him, he began breathlessly shouting that he was asleep and not looking after his duty not to see that a man was being robbed. The policeman answered that he had seen nothing, that he had only seen him stopped in the middle of the square by two men, and supposed that they were his friends, and that, instead of abusing him for nothing, he had better go the next day to the police inspector, who would certainly find out who had taken the overcoat. Akaky Akakievich ran home in a terrible state: his hair, which was still comparatively abundant on his temples and the back of his head, was completely disheveled; his sides and chest and his trousers were all covered with snow. When his old landlady heard a fearful knock at the door, she jumped hurriedly out of bed and, with only one slipper on, ran to open it, modestly holding her chemise over her bosom; but when she opened it she stepped back, seeing in what a state Akaky Akakievich was. When he told her what had happened, she clasped her hands in horror and said that he must go straight to the district commissioner, because the local police inspector would deceive him, make promises, and lead him a dance; that it would be best of all to go to the district commissioner, and that she knew him, because Anna, the Finnish girl who was once her cook, was now in service as a nurse at the commissioner's; and that she often saw him himself when he passed by their house, and that he used to be every Sunday at church too, saying his prayers and at the same time looking good-humoredly at everyone, and that therefore by every token he must be a kindhearted man. After listening to this advice, Akaky Akakievich made his way very gloomily to his room, and how he spent that night I leave to the imagination of those who are in the least able to picture the position of others.

Early in the morning he set off to the police commissioner's but was told that he was asleep. He came at ten o'clock, he was told again that he was asleep; he came at eleven and was told that the commissioner was not at home; he came at dinnertime, but the clerks in the anteroom would not let him in, and insisted on knowing what was the matter and what business had brought him and exactly what had happened; so that at last Akaky Akakievich for the first time in his life tried to show the strength of his character and said curtly that he must see the commissioner himself, and they dare not refuse to admit him, that he had come from the department on government business, and that if he made complaint of them they would see. The clerks dared say nothing to this, and one of them went to summon the commissioner. The latter received his story of being robbed of his overcoat in an extremely peculiar manner. Instead of attending to the main point, he began asking Akaky Akakievich questions: why had he been coming home so late? wasn't he going, or hadn't he been, to some bawdy house? so that Akaky Akakievich was overwhelmed with confusion, and went away without knowing whether or not the proper measures would be taken regarding his overcoat. He was absent from the office all that day (the only time that it had happened in his life). Next day he appeared with a pale face, wearing his old "dressing gown," which had become a still more pitiful sight. The news of the theft of the overcoat — though there were clerks who did not let even this chance slip of jeering at Akaky Akakievich — touched many of them. They decided on the spot to get up a collection for him, but collected only a very trifling sum, because the clerks had already spent a good deal contributing to the director's portrait and on the purchase of a book, at the suggestion of the head of their department, who was a friend of the author, and so the total realized was very insignificant. One of the clerks, moved by compassion, ventured at any rate to assist Akaky Akakievich with good advice, telling him not to go to the local police inspector, because, though it might happen that the latter might succeed in finding his overcoat because he wanted to impress his superiors, it would remain in the possession of the police unless he presented legal proofs that it belonged to him; he urged that by far the best thing would be to appeal to a Person of Consequence; that the Person of Consequence, by writing and getting into communication with the proper authorities, could push the matter through more successfully. There was nothing else to do. Akaky Akakievich made up his mind to go to the Person of Consequence. What precisely was the nature of the functions of the Person of Consequence has remained a matter of uncertainty. It must be noted that this Person of

Consequence had only lately become a person of consequence, and until recently had been a person of no consequence. Though, indeed, his position even now was not reckoned of consequence in comparison with others of still greater consequence. But there is always to be found a circle of persons to whom a person of little consequence in the eyes of others is a person of consequence. It is true that he did his utmost to increase the consequence of his position in various ways, for instance by insisting that his subordinates should come out onto the stairs to meet him when he arrived at his office; that no one should venture to approach him directly but all proceedings should follow the strictest chain of command; that a collegiate registrar should report the matter to the governmental secretary; and the governmental secretary to the titular councilors or whomsoever it might be, and that business should only reach him through this channel. Everyone in Holy Russia has a craze for imitation; everyone apes and mimics his superiors. I have actually been told that a titular councilor who was put in charge of a small separate office, immediately partitioned off a special room for himself, calling it the head office, and posted lackeys at the door with red collars and gold braid, who took hold of the handle of the door and opened it for everyone who went in, though the "head office" was so tiny that it was with difficulty that an ordinary writing desk could be put into it. The manners and habits of the Person of Consequence were dignified and majestic, but hardly subtle. The chief foundation of his system was strictness; "strictness, strictness, and — strictness!" he used to say, and at the last word he would look very significantly at the person he was addressing, though, indeed, he had no reason to do so, for the dozen clerks who made up the whole administrative mechanism of his office stood in appropriate awe of him; any clerk who saw him in the distance would leave his work and remain standing at attention till his superior had left the room. His conversation with his subordinates was usually marked by severity and almost confined to three phrases: "How dare you? Do you know to whom you are speaking? Do you understand who I am?" He was, however, at heart a good-natured man, pleasant and obliging with his colleagues; but his advancement to a high rank had completely turned his head. When he received it, he was perplexed, thrown off his balance, and quite at a loss as to how to behave. If he chanced to be with his equals, he was still quite a decent man, a very gentlemanly man, in fact, and in many ways even an intelligent man; but as soon as he was in company with men who were even one grade below him, there was simply no doing anything with him: he sat silent and his position excited compassion, the more so as he himself felt that he might have been spending his time to so much more advantage. At times there could be seen in his eyes an intense desire to join in some interesting conversation, but he was restrained by the doubt whether it would not be too much on his part, whether it would not be too great a familiarity and lowering of his dignity, and in consequence of these reflections he remained everlastingly in the same mute condition, only uttering from time to time monosyllabic sounds, and in this way he gained the reputation of being a terrible bore.

So this was the Person of Consequence to whom our friend Akaky

Akakievich appealed, and he appealed to him at a most unpropitious moment, very unfortunate for himself, though fortunate, indeed, for the Person of Consequence. The latter happened to be in his study, talking in the very best of spirits with an old friend of his childhood who had only just arrived and whom he had not seen for several years. It was at this moment that he was informed that a man called Bashmachkin was asking to see him. He asked abruptly, "What sort of man is he?" and received the answer, "A government clerk." "Ah! he can wait. I haven't time now," said the Person of Consequence. Here I must observe that this was a complete lie on the part of the Person of Consequence; he had time; his friend and he had long ago said all they had to say to each other and their conversation had begun to be broken by very long pauses during which they merely slapped each other on the knee, saying, "So that's how things are, Ivan Abramovich!" — "So that's it, Stepan Varlamovich!" but, despite that, he told the clerk to wait in order to show his friend, who had left the civil service some years before and was living at home in the country, how long clerks had to wait for him. At last, after they had talked or rather been silent, to their heart's content and had smoked a cigar in very comfortable armchairs with sloping backs, he seemed suddenly to recollect, and said to the secretary, who was standing at the door with papers for his signature: "Oh, by the way, there is a clerk waiting, isn't there? tell him he can come in." When he saw Akaky Akakievich's meek appearance and old uniform, he turned to him at once and said: "What do you want?" in a firm and abrupt voice, which he had purposely rehearsed in his own room in solitude before the mirror for a week before receiving his present post and the grade of a general. Akaky Akakievich, who was overwhelmed with appropriate awe beforehand, was somewhat confused and, as far as his tongue would allow him, explained to the best of his powers, with even more frequent "ers" than usual, that he had had a perfectly new overcoat and now he had been robbed of it in the most inhuman way, and that now he had come to beg him by his intervention either to correspond with his honor, the head police commissioner, or anybody else, and find the overcoat. This mode of proceeding struck the general for some reason as too familiar. "What next, sir?" he went on abruptly. "Don't you know the way to proceed? To whom are you addressing yourself? Don't you know how things are done? You ought first to have handed in a petition to the office; it would have gone to the head clerk of the room, and to the head clerk of the section; then it would have been handed to the secretary and the secretary would have brought it to me . . ."

"But, your Excellency," said Akaky Akakievich, trying to gather the drop of courage he possessed and feeling at the same time that he was perspiring all over, "I ventured, your Excellency, to trouble you because secretaries . . . er . . . are people you can't depend on . . ."

"What? what? what?" said the Person of Consequence, "where did you get hold of that attitude? where did you pick up such ideas? What insubordination is spreading among young men against their superiors and their chiefs!" The Person of Consequence did not apparently observe that Akaky Akakievich was well over fifty, and therefore if he could have been called a young man it would only have been in comparison to a man of seventy. "Do you know to whom you are speaking? Do you understand who I am? Do you understand that, I ask you?" At this point he stamped, and raised his voice to such a powerful note that Akaky Akakievich was not the only one to be terrified. Akaky Akakievich was positively petrified; he staggered, trembling all over, and could not stand; if the porters had not run up to support him, he would have flopped on the floor; he was led out almost unconscious. The Person of Consequence, pleased that the effect had surpassed his expectations and enchanted at the idea that his words could even deprive a man of consciousness, stole a sideway glance at his friend to see how he was taking it, and perceived not without satisfaction that his friend was feeling very uncertain and even beginning to be a little terrified himself.

How he got downstairs, how he went out into the street — of all that Akaky Akakievich remembered nothing; he had no feeling in his arms or his legs. In all his life he had never been so severely reprimanded by a general, and this was by one of another department, too. He went out into the snowstorm that was whistling through the streets, with his mouth open, and as he went he stumbled off the pavement; the wind, as its way is in Petersburg, blew upon him from all points of the compass and from every side street. In an instant it had blown a quinsy into his throat, and when he got home he was not able to utter a word; he went to bed with a swollen face and throat. That's how violent the effects of an appropriate reprimand can be!

Next day he was in a high fever. Thanks to the gracious assistance of the Petersburg climate, the disease made more rapid progress than could have been expected, and when the doctor came, after feeling his pulse he could find nothing to do but prescribe a poultice, and that simply so that the patient might not be left without the benefit of medical assistance; however, two days later he informed him that his end was at hand, after which he turned to Akaky Akakievich's landlady and said: "And you had better lose no time, my good woman, but order him now a pine coffin, for an oak one will be too expensive for him." Whether Akaky Akakievich heard these fateful words or not, whether they produced a shattering effect upon him, and whether he regretted his pitiful life, no one can tell, for he was constantly in delirium and fever. Apparitions, each stranger than the one before, were continually haunting him: first he saw Petrovich and was ordering him to make an overcoat trimmed with some sort of traps for robbers, who were, he believed, continually under the bed, and he was calling his landlady every minute to pull out a thief who had even got under the quilt; then he kept asking why his old "dressing gown" was hanging before him when he had a new overcoat; then he thought he was standing before the general listening to the appropriate reprimand and saying, "I am sorry, your Excellency"; then finally he became abusive, uttering the most awful language, so that his old landlady positively crossed herself, having never heard anything of the kind from him before, and the more horrified because these dreadful words followed immediately upon the phrase "your Excellency." Later on, his talk was merely a medley of nonsense, so that it was quite unintelligible; all that was evident was that his incoherent words and thoughts were concerned with nothing but the overcoat. At last poor Akaky Akakievich gave up the ghost. No seal was put upon his room nor upon his things, because, in the first place, he had no heirs and, in the second, the property left was very small, to wit, a bundle of quills, a quire of white government paper, three pairs of socks, two or three buttons that had come off his trousers, and the "dressing gown" with which the reader is already familiar. Who came into all his wealth God only knows; even I who tell the tale must admit that I have not bothered to inquire. And Petersburg carried on without Akaky Akakievich, as though, indeed, he had never been in the city. A creature had vanished and departed whose cause no one had championed, who was dear to no one, of interest to no one, who never attracted the attention of a naturalist, though the latter does not disdain to fix a common fly upon a pin and look at him under the microscope — a creature who bore patiently the jeers of the office and for no particular reason went to his grave, though even he at the very end of his life was visited by an exalted guest in the form of an overcoat that for one instant brought color into his poor, drab life — a creature on whom disease fell as it falls upon the heads of the mighty ones of this world . . . !

Several days after his death, a messenger from the department was sent to his lodgings with instructions that he should go at once to the office, for his chief was asking for him; but the messenger was obliged to return without him, explaining that he could not come, and to the inquiry "Why?" he added, "Well, you see, the fact is he is dead; he was buried three days ago." This was how they learned at the office of the death of Akaky Akakievich, and the next day there was sitting in his seat a new clerk who was very much taller and who wrote not in the same straight handwriting but made his letters more slanting and crooked.

But who could have imagined that this was not all there was to tell about Akaky Akakievich, that he was destined for a few days to make his presence felt in the world after his death, as though to make up for his life having been unnoticed by anyone? But so it happened, and our little story unexpectedly finishes with a fantastic ending.

Rumors were suddenly floating about Petersburg that in the neighborhood of the Kalinkin Bridge and for a little distance beyond, a corpse[5] had begun appearing at night in the form of a clerk looking for a stolen overcoat, and stripping from the shoulders of all passers-by, regardless of grade and calling, overcoats of all descriptions — trimmed with cat fur or beaver or padded, lined with raccoon, fox, and bear — made, in fact of all sorts of skin which men have adapted for the covering of their own. One of the clerks of the department saw the corpse with his own eyes and at once recognized it as Akaky Akakievich; but it excited in him such terror that he ran away as fast as his legs could carry him and so could not get a very clear view of him, and only saw him hold up his finger threateningly in the distance.

---

[5]Mrs. Garnett excepted, this is often translated "ghost," but there is no doubt of Gogol's intention. He uses the word mertverts ("corpse") and not prividenye ("ghost"). To confuse the two is damaging to Gogol's delight in the fantastic, and seriously alters the tone of the story. (Kent, ed.)

From all sides complaints were continually coming that backs and shoulders, not of mere titular councilors, but even of upper court councilors, had been exposed to catching cold, as a result of being stripped of their overcoats. Orders were given to the police to catch the corpse regardless of trouble or expense, dead or alive, and to punish him severely, as an example to others, and, indeed, they very nearly succeeded in doing so. The policeman of one district in Kiryushkin Alley snatched a corpse by the collar on the spot of the crime in the very act of attempting to snatch a frieze overcoat from a retired musician, who used, in his day, to play the flute. Having caught him by the collar, he shouted until he had brought two other policemen whom he ordered to hold the corpse while he felt just a minute in his boot to get out a snuffbox in order to revive his nose which had six times in his life been frostbitten, but the snuff was probably so strong that not even a dead man could stand it. The policeman had hardly had time to put his finger over his right nostril and draw up some snuff in the left when the corpse sneezed violently right into the eyes of all three. While they were putting their fists up to wipe their eyes, the corpse completely vanished, so that they were not even sure whether he had actually been in their hands. From that time forward, the policemen had such a horror of the dead that they were even afraid to seize the living and confined themselves to shouting from the distance: "Hey, you! Move on!" and the clerk's body began to appear even on the other side of the Kalinkin Bridge, terrorizing all timid people.

We have, however, quite neglected the Person of Consequence, who may in reality almost be said to be the cause of the fantastic ending of this perfectly true story. To begin with, my duty requires me to do justice to the Person of Consequence by recording that soon after poor Akaky Akakievich had gone away crushed to powder, he felt something not unlike regret. Sympathy was a feeling not unknown to him; his heart was open to many kindly impulses, although his exalted grade very often prevented them from being shown. As soon as his friend had gone out of his study, he even began brooding over poor Akaky Akakievich, and from that time forward, he was almost every day haunted by the image of the poor clerk who had been unable to survive the official reprimand. The thought of the man so worried him that a week later he actually decided to send a clerk to find out how he was and whether he really could help him in any way. And when they brought him word that Akaky Akakievich had died suddenly in a delirium and fever, it made a great impression on him; his conscience reproached him and he was depressed all day. Anxious to distract his mind and to forget the unpleasant incident, he went to spend the evening with one of his friends, where he found respectable company, and what was best of all, almost everyone was of the same grade so that he was able to be quite uninhibited. This had a wonderful effect on his spirits. He let himself go, became affable and genial — in short, spent a very agreeable evening. At supper he drank a couple of glasses of champagne — a proceeding which we all know is not a bad recipe for cheerfulness. The champagne made him inclined to do something unusual, and he decided not to go home yet but to visit a lady of his acquaintance, a certain Karolina Ivanovna — a lady apparently of German extraction, for whom he entertained extremely friendly feelings. It must be noted that the Person of Consequence was a man no longer young. He was an excellent husband, and the respectable father of a family. He had two sons, one already serving in an office, and a nice-looking daughter of sixteen with a rather turned-up, pretty little nose, who used to come every morning to kiss his hand, saying: *"Bon jour, Papa."* His wife, who was still blooming and decidedly good-looking, indeed, used first to give him her hand to kiss and then turning his hand over would kiss it. But though the Person of Consequence was perfectly satisfied with the pleasant amenities of his domestic life, he thought it proper to have a lady friend in another quarter of the town. This lady friend was not a bit better looking nor younger than his wife, but these puzzling things exist in the world and it is not our business to criticize them. And so the Person of Consequence went downstairs, got into his sledge, and said to his coachman, "To Karolina Ivanovna." While luxuriously wrapped in his warm fur coat he remained in that agreeable frame of mind sweeter to a Russian than anything that could be invented, that is, when one thinks of nothing while thoughts come into the mind by themselves, one pleasanter than the other, without your having to bother following them or looking for them. Full of satisfaction, he recalled all the amusing moments of the evening he had spent, all the phrases that had started the intimate circle of friends laughing; many of them he repeated in an undertone and found them as amusing as before, and so, very naturally, laughed very heartily at them again. From time to time, however, he was disturbed by a gust of wind which, blowing suddenly, God knows why or where from, cut him in the face, pelting him with flakes of snow, puffing out his coat collar like a sail, or suddenly flinging it with unnatural force over his head and giving him endless trouble to extricate himself from it. All at once, the Person of Consequence felt that someone had clutched him very tightly by the collar. Turning around he saw a short man in a shabby old uniform, and not without horror recognized him as Akaky Akakievich. The clerk's face was white as snow and looked like that of a corpse, but the horror of the Person of Consequence was beyond all bounds when he saw the mouth of the corpse distorted into speech, and breathing upon him the chill of the grave, it uttered the following words: "Ah, so here you are at last! At last I've . . . er . . . caught you by the collar. It's your overcoat I want; you refused to help me and abused me in the bargain! So now give me yours!" The poor Person of Consequence very nearly dropped dead. Resolute and determined as he was in his office and before subordinates in general, and though anyone looking at his manly air and figure would have said: "Oh, what a man of character!" yet in this situation he felt, like very many persons of heroic appearance, such terror that not without reason he began to be afraid he would have some sort of fit. He actually flung his overcoat off his shoulders as far as he could and shouted to his coachman in an unnatural voice: "Drive home! Let's get out of here!" The coachman, hearing the tone which he had only heard in critical moments and then accompanied by something even more tangible, hunched his shoulders up to his ears in case of worse following, swung his whip, and flew on like an arrow. In a little over six minutes, the Person of Consequence was at the entrance of his own house. Pale, panic-stricken, and without his overcoat, he arrived home instead of at Karolina Ivanovna's, dragged himself to his own room, and spent the night in great distress, so that next morning his daughter said to him at breakfast, "You look very pale today, Papa"; but her papa remained mute and said not a word to anyone of what had happened to him, where he had been, and where he had been going. The incident made a great impression upon him. Indeed, it happened far more rarely that he said to his subordinates, "How dare you? Do you understand who I am?" and he never uttered those words at all until he had first heard all the facts of the case.

What was even more remarkable is that from that time on the apparition of the dead clerk ceased entirely; apparently the general's overcoat had fitted him perfectly; anyway nothing more was heard of overcoats being snatched from anyone. Many restless and anxious people refused, however, to be pacified, and still maintained that in remote parts of the town the dead clerk went on appearing. One policeman, in Kolomna, for instance, saw with his own eyes an apparition appear from behind a house; but, being by natural constitution somewhat frail — so much so that on one occasion an ordinary grown-up suckling pig, making a sudden dash out of some private building, knocked him off his feet to the great amusement of the cabmen standing around, whom he fined two kopeks each for snuff for such disrespect — he did not dare to stop it, and so followed it in the dark until the apparition suddenly looked around and, stopping, asked him: "What do you want?" displaying a huge fist such as you never see among the living. The policeman said: "Nothing," and turned back on the spot. This apparition, however, was considerably taller and adorned with immense mustaches, and, directing its steps apparently toward Obukhov Bridge, vanished into the darkness of the night.   [1840]

NADINE GORDIMER (b. 1923), the recipient of the 1991 Nobel Prize for Literature, was born in the small town of Springs, near Johannesburg, South Africa. Her mother was English, and her father, a Jewish watchmaker, emigrated to Africa from the Baltic states. Gordimer attended a convent school and studied at the University of the Witwatersrand, getting what she has called "a scrappy and uninspiring minimal education." Growing up in South Africa, she never recognized herself in any of the English books she read until she encountered the stories of the New Zealand writer Katherine Mansfield. Then, Gordimer says, "I realized here was somebody who was writing about this other world, whose seasons at least I shared. Then I understood it was possible to be a writer even if you didn't live in England."

Gordimer began to write stories before she attempted a novel. She acknowledges three writers as her guides: D. H. Lawrence, who influenced her way of looking at the natural world; Henry James, who gave her a consciousness of form; and Ernest Hemingway, who taught her to hear what is essential in dialogue. Her early stories appeared in The New Yorker, Harper's, and other American magazines, and were first collected in Face to Face (1949) and The Soft Voice of the Serpent (1952). Since her first novel, The Lying Days, was published in 1953, she has continued alternating books of long and short fiction. She rarely experiments beyond the realistic rendering of her subject in her stories, but her decision to write in the form of the short story or the novel depends on the shape the material takes as a narrative.

> Whether it sprawls or neatly bites its own tail, a short story is a concept that the writer can "hold" fully realized in his imagination at one time. A novel is, by comparison, staked out, and must be taken possession of stage by stage; it is impossible to contain, all at once, the proliferation of concepts it ultimately may use. For this reason I cannot understand how people can suppose one makes a conscious choice, after knowing what one wants to write about, between writing a novel or a short story. A short story occurs, in the imaginative sense. To write one is to express from a situation in the exterior or interior world the life-giving drop — sweat, tear, semen, saliva — that will spread an intensity on the page; burn a hole in it.

The pair of linked stories in "Town and Country Lovers" demonstrates Gordimer's use of fiction over the last forty years to mirror complex social attitudes in her beleaguered country. She feels herself "selected" by her subject as she continues to explore the ramifications of racial strife in South Africa. In 1988 she published an essay collection, The Essential Gesture: Writing, Politics, and Places. In 1993 appeared Why Haven't You Written? Selected Stories 1950–1970. Gordimer's achievement as a writer is further proof of Flaubert's insight "One is not at all free to write this or that. One does not choose one's subject. This is what the public and the critics do not understand. The secret of masterpieces lies in the concordance between the subject and the temperament of the author."

RELATED COMMENTARY: Nadine Gordimer, "The Flash of Fireflies," page 1425.

NADINE GORDIMER

Town and Country Lovers

I

Dr. Franz-Josef von Leinsdorf is a geologist absorbed in his work; wrapped up in it, as the saying goes — year after year the experience of this work enfolds him, swaddling him away from the landscapes, the cities, and the people, wherever he lives: Peru, New Zealand, the United States. He's always been like that, his mother could confirm from their native Austria. There, even as a handsome small boy he presented only his profile to her: turned away to his bits of rock and stone. His few relaxations have not changed much since then. An occasional skiing trip, listening to music, reading poetry — Rainer Maria Rilke once stayed in his grandmother's hunting lodge in the forests of Styria and the boy was introduced to Rilke's poems while very young.

Layer upon layer, country after country, wherever his work takes him — and now he has been almost seven years in Africa. First the Côte d'Ivoire, and for the past five years, South Africa. The shortage of skilled manpower brought about his recruitment here. He has no interest in the politics of the countries he works in. His private preoccupation-within-the-preoccupation of his work has been research into underground watercourses, but the mining company that employs him in a senior though not executive capacity is interested only in mineral discovery. So he is much out in the field — which is the veld, here — seeking new gold, copper, platinum, and uranium deposits. When he is at home — on this particular job, in this particular country, this city — he lives in a two-roomed flat in a suburban block with a landscaped garden, and does his shopping at a supermarket conveniently across the street. He is not married — yet. That is how his colleagues, and the typists and secretaries at the mining company's head office, would define his situation. Both men and women would describe him as a good-looking man, in a foreign way, with the lower half of his face dark and middle-aged (his mouth is thin and curving, and no matter how close-shaven his beard shows like fine shot embedded in the skin round mouth and chin) and the upper half contradictorily young, with deep-set eyes (some would say grey, some black), thick eyelashes and brows. A tangled gaze: through which concentration and gleaming thoughtfulness perhaps appear as fire and languor. It is this that the women in the office mean when they remark he's not unattractive. Although the gaze seems to promise, he has never invited any one of them to go out with him. There is the general assumption he probably has a girl who's been picked for him, he's bespoken by one of his own kind, back home in Europe where he comes from. Many of these well-educated Europeans have no intention of becoming permanent immigrants; neither the remnant of white colonial life nor idealistic involvement with Black Africa appeals to them.

One advantage, at least, of living in underdeveloped or half-developed countries is that flats are serviced. All Dr. von Leinsdorf has to do for himself is buy his own supplies and cook an evening meal if he doesn't want to go to a restaurant. It is simply a matter of dropping in to the supermarket on his way from his car to his flat after work in the afternoon. He wheels a trolley up and down the shelves, and his simple needs are presented to him in the form of tins, packages, plastic-wrapped meat, cheeses, fruit and vegetables, tubes, bottles . . . At the cashier's counters where customers must converge and queue there are racks of small items uncategorized, for last-minute purchase. Here, as the coloured girl cashier punches the adding machine, he picks up cigarettes and perhaps a packet of salted nuts or a bar of nougat. Or razor-blades, when he remembers he's running short. One evening in winter he saw that the cardboard display was empty of the brand of blades he preferred, and he drew the cashier's attention to this. These young coloured girls are usually pretty unhelpful, taking money and punching their machines in a manner that asserts with the time-serving obstinacy of the half-literate the limit of any responsibility towards customers, but this one ran an alert glance over the selection of razor-blades, apologized that she was not allowed to leave her post, and said she would see that the stock was replenished "next time." A day or two later she recognized him, gravely, as he took his turn before her counter — "I ahssed them, but it's out of stock. You can't get it. I did ahss about it." He said this didn't matter. "When it comes in, I can keep a few packets for you." He thanked her.

He was away with the prospectors the whole of the next week. He arrived back in town just before nightfall on Friday, and was on his way from car to flat with his arms full of briefcase, suitcase, and canvas bags when someone stopped him by standing timidly in his path. He was about to dodge round unseeingly on the crowded pavement but she spoke. "We got the blades in now. I didn't see you in the shop this week, but I kept some for when you come. So . . ."

He recognized her. He had never seen her standing before, and she was wearing a coat. She was rather small and finely-made, for one of them. The coat was skimpy but no big backside jutted. The cold brought an apricot-graining of warm colour to her cheekbones, beneath which a very small face was quite delicately hollowed, and the skin was smooth, the subdued satiny colour of certain yellow wood. That crêpey hair, but worn drawn back flat and in a little knot pushed into one of the cheap wool chignons that (he recognized also) hung in the miscellany of small goods along with the razor-blades, at the supermarket. He said thanks, he was in a hurry, he'd only just got back from a trip — shifting the burdens he carried, to demonstrate. "Oh shame." She acknowledged his load. "But if you want I can run in and get it for you quickly. If you want."

He saw at once it was perfectly clear that all the girl meant was that she would go back to the supermarket, buy the blades, and bring the packet to him there where he stood, on the pavement. And it seemed that it was this certainty that made him say, in the kindly tone of assumption used for an obliging underling, "I live just across there — *Atlantis* — that flat building.

Could you drop them by, for me — number seven-hundred-and-eighteen, seventh floor —"

She had not before been inside one of these big flat buildings near where she worked. She lived a bus- and train-ride away to the West of the city, but this side of the black townships, in a township for people her tint. There was a pool with ferns, not plastic, and even a little waterfall pumped electrically over rocks, in the entrance of the building *Atlantis;* she didn't wait for the lift marked GOODS but took the one meant for whites and a white woman with one of those sausage-dogs on a lead got in with her but did not pay her any attention. The corridors leading to the flats were nicely glassed-in, not draughty.

He wondered if he should give her a twenty-cent piece for her trouble — ten cents would be right for a black; but she said, "Oh no — please, here —" standing outside his open door and awkwardly pushing back at his hand the change from the money he'd given her for the razor-blades. She was smiling, for the first time, in the dignity of refusing a tip. It was difficult to know how to treat these people, in this country; to know what they expected. In spite of her embarrassing refusal of the coin, she stood there, completely unassuming, fists thrust down the pockets of her cheap coat against the cold she'd come in from, rather pretty thin legs neatly aligned, knee to knee, ankle to ankle.

"Would you like a cup of coffee or something?"

He couldn't very well take her into his study-cum-living-room and offer her a drink. She followed him to his kitchen, but at the sight of her pulling out the single chair to drink her cup of coffee at the kitchen table, he said, "No — bring it in here —" and led the way into the big room where, among his books and his papers, his files of scientific correspondence (and the cigar boxes of stamps from the envelopes), his racks of records, his specimens of minerals and rocks, he lived alone.

It was no trouble to her; she saved him the trips to the supermarket and brought him his groceries two or three times a week. All he had to do was to leave a list and the key under the doormat, and she would come up in her lunch-hour to collect them, returning to put his supplies in the flat after work. Sometimes he was home and sometimes not. He bought a box of chocolates and left it, with a note, for her to find; and that was acceptable, apparently, as a gratuity.

Her eyes went over everything in the flat although her body tried to conceal its sense of being out of place by remaining as still as possible, holding its contours in the chair offered her as a stranger's coat is set aside and remains exactly as left until the owner takes it up to go. "You collect?"

"Well, these are specimens — connected with my work."

"My brother used to collect. Miniatures. With brandy and whisky and that, in them. From all over. Different countries."

The second time she watched him grinding coffee for the cup he had offered her she said, "You always do that? Always when you make coffee?"

"But of course. It is no good, for you. Do I make it too strong?"

"Oh it's just I'm not used to it. We buy it ready — you know, it's in a bottle, you just add a bit to the milk or water."

He laughed, instructive: "That's not coffee, that's a synthetic flavouring. In my country we drink only real coffee, fresh, from the beans — you smell how good it is as it's being ground?"

She was stopped by the caretaker and asked what she wanted in the building? Heavy with the *bona fides* of groceries clutched to her body, she said she was working at number 718, on the seventh floor. The caretaker did not tell her not to use the whites' lift; after all, she was not black; her family was very light-skinned.

There was the item "grey button for trousers" on one of his shopping lists. She said as she unpacked the supermarket carrier, "Give me the pants, so long, then," and sat on his sofa that was always gritty with fragments of pipe tobacco, sewing in and out through the four holes of the button with firm, fluent movements of the right hand, gestures supplying the articulacy missing from her talk. She had a little yokel's, peasant's (he thought of it) gap between her two front teeth when she smiled that he didn't much like, but, face ellipsed to three-quarter angle, eyes cast down in concentration with soft lips almost closed, this didn't matter. He said, watching her sew, "You're a good girl"; and touched her.

She remade the bed every late afternoon when they left it and she dressed again before she went home. After a week there was a day when late afternoon became evening, and they were still in the bed.

"Can't you stay the night?"

"My mother," she said.

"Phone her. Make an excuse." He was a foreigner. He had been in the country five years, but he didn't understand that people don't usually have telephones in their houses, where she lived. She got up to dress. He didn't want that tender body to go out in the night cold and kept hindering her with the interruption of his hands; saying nothing. Before she put on her coat, when the body had already disappeared, he spoke, "But you must make some arrangement."

"Oh my mother!" Her face opened to fear and vacancy he could not read.

He was not entirely convinced the woman would think of her daughter as some pure and unsullied virgin . . . "Why?"

The girl said, "S'e'll be scared. S'e'll be scared we get caught."

"Don't tell her anything. Say I'm employing you." In this country he was working in now there were generally rooms on the roofs of flat buildings for tenants' servants.

She said: "That's what I told the caretaker."

She ground fresh coffee beans every time he wanted a cup while he was working at night. She never attempted to cook anything until she had watched in silence while he did it the way he liked, and she learned to reproduce exactly the simple dishes he preferred. She handled his pieces of rock and stone, at first admiring the colours — "It'd make a beautiful ring or necklace, ay." Then he showed her the striations, the formation of each piece, and explained what each was, and how, in the long life of the earth, it had been formed. He named the mineral it yielded, and what that was used for. He worked at his papers, writing, writing, every night, so it did not matter that they could not go out together to public places. On Sundays she got into his car in the basement garage and they drove to the country and picnicked away up in the Magaliesberg, where there was no one. He read or poked about among the rocks; they climbed together, to the mountain pools. He taught her to swim. She had never seen the sea. She squealed and shrieked in the water, showing the gap between her teeth, as — it crossed his mind — she must do when among her own people. Occasionally he had to go out to dinner at the houses of colleagues from the mining company; she sewed and listened to the radio in the flat and he found her in the bed, warm and already asleep, by the time he came in. He made his way into her body without speaking; she made him welcome without a word. Once he put on evening dress for a dinner at his country's consulate; watching him brush one or two fallen hairs from the shoulders of the dark jacket that sat so well on him, she saw a huge room, all chandeliers and people dancing some dance from a costume film — stately, hand-to-hand. She supposed he was going to fetch, in her place in the car, a partner for the evening. They never kissed when either left the flat; he said, suddenly, kindly, pausing as he picked up cigarettes and keys, "Don't be lonely." And added, "Wouldn't you like to visit your family sometimes, when I have to go out?"

He had told her he was going home to his mother in the forests and mountains of his country near the Italian border (he showed her on the map) after Christmas. She had not told him how her mother, not knowing there was any other variety, assumed he was a medical doctor, so she had talked to her about the doctor's children and the doctor's wife who was a very kind lady, glad to have someone who could help out in the surgery as well as the flat.

She remarked wonderingly on his ability to work until midnight or later, after a day at work. She was so tired when she came home from her cash register at the supermarket that once dinner was eaten she could scarcely keep awake. He explained in a way she could understand that while the work she did was repetitive, undemanding of any real response from her intelligence, requiring little mental or physical effort and therefore unrewarding, his work was his greatest interest, it taxed his mental capacities to their limit, exercised all his concentration, and rewarded him constantly as much with the excitement of a problem presented as with the satisfaction of a problem solved. He said later, putting away his papers, speaking out of a silence: "Have you done other kinds of work?" She said, "I was in a clothing factory before. Sportbeau shirts; you know? But the pay's better in the shop."

Of course. Being a conscientious newspaper-reader in every country he lived in, he was aware that it was only recently that the retail consumer trade in this one had been allowed to employ coloureds as shop assistants; even punching a cash register represented advancement. With the continuing shortage of semi-skilled whites a girl like this might be able to edge a little farther into the white-collar category. He began to teach her to type. He was aware that her English was poor, even though, as a foreigner, in his ears her pronunciation did not offend, nor categorize her as it would in those of someone of his education whose mother tongue was English. He corrected her grammatical mistakes but missed the less obvious ones because of his own sometimes exotic English usage — she continued to use the singular pronoun "it" when what was required was the plural "they." Because he was a foreigner (although so clever, as she saw) she was less inhibited than she might have been by the words she knew she misspelled in her typing. While she sat at the typewriter she thought how one day she would type notes for him, as well as making coffee the way he liked it, and taking him inside her body without saying anything, and sitting (even if only through the empty streets of quiet Sundays) beside him in his car, like a wife.

On a summer night near Christmas — he had already bought and hidden a slightly showy but nevertheless good watch he thought she would like — there was a knocking at the door that brought her out of the bathroom and him to his feet, at his work-table. No one ever came to the flat at night; he had no friends intimate enough to drop in without warning. The summons was an imperious banging that did not pause and clearly would not stop until the door was opened.

She stood in the open bathroom doorway gazing at him across the passage into the living-room; her bare feet and shoulders were free of a big bath-towel. She said nothing, did not even whisper. The flat seemed to shake with the strong unhurried blows.

He made as if to go to the door, at last, but now she ran and clutched him by both arms. She shook her head wildly; her lips drew back but her teeth were clenched, she didn't speak. She pulled him into the bedroom, snatched some clothes from the clean laundry laid out on the bed, and got into the wall-cupboard, thrusting the key at his hand. Although his arms and calves felt weakly cold he was horrified, distastefully embarrassed at the sight of her pressed back crouching there under his suits and coat; it was horrible and ridiculous. *Come out!* he whispered. *No! Come out!* She hissed: *Where? Where can I go?*

Never mind! Get out of there!

He put out his hand to grasp her. At bay, she said with all the force of her terrible whisper, baring the gap in her teeth: *I'll throw myself out the window.*

She forced the key into his hand like the handle of a knife. He closed the door on her face and drove the key home in the lock, then dropped it among coins in his trouser pocket.

He unslotted the chain that was looped across the flat door. He turned the serrated knob of the Yale lock. The three policemen, two in plain clothes, stood there without impatience although they had been banging on the door for several minutes. The big dark one with an elaborate moustache held out in a hand wearing a plaited gilt ring some sort of identity card.

Dr. von Leinsdorf said quietly, the blood coming strangely back to legs and arms, "What is it?"

The sergeant told him they knew there was a coloured girl in the flat. They had had information; "I been watching this flat three months, I know."

"I am alone here." Dr. von Leinsdorf did not raise his voice.

"I know, I know who is here. Come —" And the sergeant and his two assistants went into the living-room, the kitchen, the bathroom (the sergeant picked up a bottle of after-shave cologne, seemed to study the French label), and the bedroom. The assistants removed the clean laundry that was laid upon the bed and then turned back the bedding, carrying the sheets over to be examined by the sergeant under the lamp. They talked to one another in Afrikaans, which the Doctor did not understand. The sergeant himself looked under the bed, and lifted the long curtains at the window. The wall-cupboard was of the kind that has no knobs; he saw that it was locked and began to ask in Afrikaans, then politely changed to English, "Give us the key."

Dr. von Leinsdorf said, "I'm sorry, I left it at my office — I always lock and take my keys with me in the mornings."

"It's no good, man, you better give me the key."

He smiled a little, reasonably. "It's on my office desk."

The assistants produced a screwdriver and he watched while they inserted it where the cupboard doors met, gave it quick, firm but not forceful leverage. He heard the lock give.

She had been naked, it was true, when they knocked. But now she was wearing a long-sleeved T-shirt with an appliquéd butterfly motif on one breast, and a pair of jeans. Her feet were still bare; she had managed, by feel, in the dark, to get into some of the clothing she had snatched from the bed, but she had no shoes. She had perhaps been weeping behind the cupboard door (her cheeks looked stained) but now her face was sullen and she was breathing heavily, her diaphragm contracting and expanding exaggeratedly and her breasts pushing against the cloth. It made her appear angry; it might simply have been that she was half-suffocated in the cupboard and needed oxygen. She did not look at Dr. von Leinsdorf. She would not reply to the sergeant's questions.

They were taken to the police station where they were at once separated and in turn led for examination by the district surgeon. The man's underwear was taken away and examined, as the sheets had been, for signs of his seed. When the girl was undressed, it was discovered that beneath her jeans she was wearing a pair of men's briefs with his name on the neatly-sewn laundry tag; in her haste, she had taken the wrong garment to her hiding-place.

Now she cried, standing there before the district surgeon in a man's underwear.

He courteously pretended not to notice. He handed briefs, jeans, and T-shirt round the door, and motioned her to lie on a white-sheeted high table where he placed her legs apart, resting in stirrups, and put into her where the other had made his way so warmly a cold hard instrument that expanded wider and wider. Her thighs and knees trembled uncontrollably while the doctor looked into her and touched her deep inside with more hard instruments, carrying wafers of gauze.

When she came out of the examining room back to the charge office, Dr. von Leinsdorf was not there; they must have taken him somewhere else. She spent what was left of the night in a cell, as he must be doing; but early in the morning she was released and taken home to her mother's house in the coloured township by a white man who explained he was the clerk of the lawyer who had been engaged for her by Dr. von Leinsdorf. Dr. von Leinsdorf, the clerk said, had also been bailed out that morning. He did not say when, or if she would see him again.

A statement made by the girl to the police was handed in to Court when she and the man appeared to meet charges of contravening the Immorality Act in a Johannesburg flat on the night of — December, 19 — . *I lived with the white man in his flat. He had intercourse with me sometimes. He gave me tablets to take to prevent me becoming pregnant.*

Interviewed by the Sunday papers, the girl said, "I'm sorry for the sadness brought to my mother." She said she was one of nine children of a female laundry worker. She had left school in Standard Three because there was no money at home for gym clothes or a school blazer. She had worked as a machinist in a factory and a cashier in a supermarket. Dr. von Leinsdorf taught her to type his notes.

Dr. Franz-Josef von Leinsdorf, described as the grandson of a baroness, a cultured man engaged in international mineralogical research, said he accepted social distinctions between people but didn't think they should be legally imposed. "Even in my own country it's difficult for a person from a higher class to marry one from a lower class."

The two accused gave no evidence. They did not greet or speak to each other in Court. The Defence argued that the sergeant's evidence that they had been living together as man and wife was heresay. (The woman with the dachshund, the caretaker?) The magistrate acquitted them because the State failed to prove carnal intercourse had taken place on the night of — December, 19—.

The girl's mother was quoted, with photograph, in the Sunday papers: "I won't let my daughter work as a servant for a white man again."

II

The farm children play together when they are small; but once the white children go away to school they soon don't play together any more, even in the holidays. Although most of the black children get some sort of schooling, they drop every year farther behind the grades passed by the white children; the childish vocabulary, the child's exploration of the adventurous possibilities of dam, koppies, mealie lands, and veld — there comes a time when the white children have surpassed these with the vocabulary of boarding-school and the possibilities of inter-school sports matches and the kind of adventures seen at the cinema. This usefully coincides with the age of twelve or thirteen;

so that by the time early adolescence is reached, the black children are making, along with the bodily changes common to all, an easy transition to adult forms of address, beginning to call their old playmates *missus* and *baasie* — little master.

The trouble was Paulus Eysendyck did not seem to realize that Thebedi was now simply one of the crowd of farm children down at the kraal, recognizable in his sisters' old clothes. The first Christmas holidays after he had gone to boarding-school he brought home for Thebedi a painted box he had made in his wood-work class. He had to give it to her secretly because he had nothing for the other children at the kraal. And she gave him, before he went back to school, a bracelet she had made of thin brass wire and the grey-and-white beans of the castor-oil crop his father cultivated. (When they used to play together, she was the one who had taught Paulus how to make clay oxen for their toy spans.) There was a craze, even in the *platteland* towns like the one where he was at school, for boys to wear elephant-hair and other bracelets beside their watch-straps; his was admired, friends asked him to get similar ones for them. He said the natives made them on his father's farm and he would try.

When he was fifteen, six feet tall, and tramping round at school dances with the girls from the "sister" school in the same town; when he had learnt how to tease and flirt and fondle quite intimately these girls who were the daughters of prosperous farmers like his father; when he had even met one who, at a wedding he had attended with his parents on a nearby farm, had let him do with her in a locked storeroom what people did when they made love — when he was as far from his childhood as all this, he still brought home from a shop in town a red plastic belt and gilt hoop ear-rings for the black girl, Thebedi. She told her father the missus had given these to her as a reward for some work she had done — it was true she sometimes was called to help out in the farmhouse. She told the girls in the kraal that she had a sweetheart nobody knew about, far away, away on another farm, and they giggled, and teased, and admired her. There was a boy in the kraal called Njabulo who said he wished he could have brought her a belt and ear-rings.

When the farmer's son was home for the holidays she wandered far from the kraal and her companions. He went for walks alone. They had not arranged this; it was an urge each followed independently. He knew it was she, from a long way off. She knew that his dog would not bark at her. Down at the dried-up river-bed where five or six years ago the children had caught a leguaan one great day — a creature that combined ideally the size and ferocious aspect of the crocodile with the harmlessness of the lizard — they squatted side by side on the earth bank. He told her traveller's tales: about school, about the punishments at school, particularly, exaggerating both their nature and his indifference to them. He told her about the town of Middleburg, which she had never seen. She had nothing to tell but she prompted with many questions, like any good listener. While he talked he twisted and tugged at the roots of white stinkwood and Cape willow trees that looped out of the eroded earth around them. It had always been a good spot for children's games, down there hidden by the mesh of old, ant-eaten trees held in place by vigorous ones, wild asparagus bushing up between the trunks, and here and there prickly-pear cactus sunken-skinned and bristly, like an old man's face, keeping alive sapless until the next rainy season. She punctured the dry hide of a prickly-pear again and again with a sharp stick while she listened. She laughed a lot at what he told her, sometimes dropping her face on her knees, sharing amusement with the cool shady earth beneath her bare feet. She put on her pair of shoes — white sandals, thickly Blanco-ed against the farm dust — when he was on the farm, but these were taken off and laid aside, at the river-bed.

One summer afternoon when there was water flowing there and it was very hot she waded in as they used to do when they were children, her dress bunched modestly and tucked into the legs of her pants. The schoolgirls he went swimming with at dams or pools on neighbouring farms wore bikinis but the sight of their dazzling bellies and thighs in the sunlight had never made him feel what he felt now, when the girl came up the bank and sat beside him, the drops of water beading off her dark legs the only points of light in the earth-smelling, deep shade. They were not afraid of one another, they had known one another always; he did with her what he had done that time in the storeroom at the wedding, and this time it was so lovely, so lovely, he was surprised . . . and she was surprised by it, too — he could see in her dark face that was part of the shade, with her big dark eyes, shiny as soft water, watching him attentively: as she had when they used to huddle over their teams of mud oxen, as she had when he told her about detention weekends at school.

They went to the river-bed often through those summer holidays. They met just before the light went, as it does quite quickly, and each returned home with the dark — she to her mother's hut, he to the farmhouse — in time for the evening meal. He did not tell her about school or town any more. She did not ask questions any longer. He told her, each time, when they would meet again. Once or twice it was very early in the morning; the lowing of the cows being driven to graze came to them where they lay, dividing them with unspoken recognition of the sound read in their two pairs of eyes, opening so close to each other.

He was a popular boy at school. He was in the second, then the first soccer team. The head girl of the "sister" school was said to have a crush on him; he didn't particularly like her, but there was a pretty blonde who put up her long hair into a kind of doughnut with a black ribbon round it, whom he took to see films when the schoolboys and girls had a free Saturday afternoon. He had been driving tractors and other farm vehicles since he was ten years old, and as soon as he was eighteen he got a driver's licence and in the holidays, this last year of his school life, he took neighbours' daughters to dances and to the drive-in cinema that had just opened twenty kilometers from the farm. His sisters were married, by then; his parents often left him in charge of the farm over the weekend while they visited the young wives and grandchildren.

When Thebedi saw the farmer and his wife drive away on a Saturday afternoon, the boot of their Mercedes filled with fresh-killed poultry and vegetables from the garden that it was part of her father's work to tend, she knew that she must come not to the river-bed but up to the house. The house was an old one, thick-walled, dark against the heat. The kitchen was its lively thoroughfare, with servants, food supplies, begging cats and dogs, pots boiling over, washing being damped for ironing, and the big deep-freezer the missus had ordered from town, bearing a crocheted mat and a vase of plastic irises. But the dining-room with the bulging-legged heavy table was shut up in its rich, old smell of soup and tomato sauce. The sitting-room curtains were drawn and the T.V. set silent. The door of the parents' bedroom was locked and the empty rooms where the girls had slept had sheets of plastic spread over the beds. It was in one of these that she and the farmer's son stayed together whole nights — almost: she had to get away before the house servants, who knew her, came in at dawn. There was a risk someone would discover her or traces of her presence if he took her to his own bedroom, although she had looked into it many times when she was helping out in the house and knew well, there, the row of silver cups he had won at school.

When she was eighteen and the farmer's son nineteen and working with his father on the farm before entering a veterinary college, the young man Njabulo asked her father for her. Njabulo's parents met with hers and ·the money he was to pay in place of the cows it is customary to give a prospective bride's parents was settled upon. He had no cows to offer; he was a labourer on the Eysendyck farm, like her father. A bright youngster; old Eysendyck had taught him brick-laying and was using him for odd jobs in construction, around the place. She did not tell the farmer's son that her parents had arranged for her to marry. She did not tell him, either, before he left for his first term at the veterinary college, that she thought she was going to have a baby. Two months after her marriage to Njabulo, she gave birth to a daughter. There was no disgrace in that; among her people it is customary for a young man to make sure, before marriage, that the chosen girl is not barren, and Njabulo made love to her then. But the infant was very light and did not quickly grow darker as most African babies do. Already at birth there was on its head a quantity of straight, fine floss, like that which carries the seeds of certain weeds in the veld. The unfocused eyes it opened were grey flecked with yellow. Njabulo was the matt, opaque coffee-grounds colour that has always been called black; the colour of Thebedi's legs on which beaded water looked oyster-shell blue, the same colour as Thebedi's face, where the black eyes, with their interested gaze and clear whites, were so dominant.

Njabulo made no complaint. Out of his farm labourer's earnings he bought from the Indian store a cellophane-windowed pack containing a pink plastic bath, six napkins, a card of safety pins, a knitted jacket, cap and bootees, a dress, and a tin of Johnson's Baby Powder, for Thebedi's baby.

When it was two weeks old Paulus Eysendyck arrived home from the veterinary college for the holidays. He drank a glass of fresh, still-warm milk in the childhood familiarity of his mother's kitchen and heard her discussing with the old house-servant where they could get a reliable substitute to help out now that the girl Thebedi had had a baby. For the first time since he was a small boy he came right into the kraal. It was eleven o'clock in the morning. The men were at work in the lands. He looked about him, urgently; the women turned away, each not wanting to be the one approached to point out where Thebedi lived. Thebedi appeared, coming slowly from the hut Njabulo had built in white man's style, with a tin chimney, and a proper window with glass panes set in straight as walls made of unfired bricks would allow. She greeted him with hands brought together and a token movement representing the respectful bob with which she was accustomed to acknowledge she was in the presence of his father or mother. He lowered his head under the doorway of her home and went in. He said, "I want to see. Show me."

She had taken the bundle off her back before she came out into the light to face him. She moved between the iron bedstead made up with Njabulo's checked blankets and the small wooden table where the pink plastic bath stood among food and kitchen pots, and picked up the bundle from the snugly-blanketed grocer's box where it lay. The infant was asleep; she revealed the closed, pale, plump tiny face, with a bubble of spit at the corner of the mouth, the spidery pink hands stirring. She took off the woollen cap and the straight fine hair flew up after it in static electricity, showing gilded strands here and there. He said nothing. She was watching him as she had done when they were little, and the gang of children had trodden down a crop in their games or trangressed in some other way for which he, as the farmer's son, the white one among them, must intercede with the farmer. She disturbed the sleeping face by scratching or tickling gently at a cheek with one finger, and slowly the eyes opened, saw nothing, were still asleep, and then, awake, no longer narrowed, looked out at them, grey with yellowish flecks, his own hazel eyes.

He struggled for a moment with a grimace of tears, anger, and self-pity. She could not put out her hand to him. He said, "You haven't been near the house with it?"

She shook her head.

"Never?"

Again she shook her head.

"Don't take it out. Stay inside. Can't you take it away somewhere. You must give it to someone —"

She moved to the door with him.

He said, "I'll see what I will do. I don't know." And then he said: "I feel like killing myself."

Her eyes began to glow, to thicken with tears. For a moment there was the feeling between them that used to come when they were alone down at the river-bed.

He walked out.

Two days later, when his mother and father had left the farm for the day, he appeared again. The women were away on the lands, weeding, as they were employed to do as casual labour in the summer; only the very old remained, propped up on the ground outside the huts in the flies and the sun. Thebedi did not ask him in. The child had not been well; it had diarrhoea. He asked where its food was. She said, "The milk comes from me." He went into Njabulo's house, where the child lay; she did not follow but stayed outside the door and watched without seeing an old crone who had lost her mind, talking to herself, talking to the fowls who ignored her.

She thought she heard small grunts from the hut, the kind of infant grunt that indicates a full stomach, a deep sleep. After a time, long or short she did not know, he came out and walked away with plodding stride (his father's gait) out of sight, towards his father's house.

The baby was not fed during the night and although she kept telling Njabulo it was sleeping, he saw for himself in the morning that it was dead. He comforted her with words and caresses. She did not cry but simply sat, staring at the door. Her hands were cold as dead chickens' feet to his touch.

Njabulo buried the little baby where farm workers were buried, in the place in the veld the farmer had given them. Some of the mounds had been left to weather away unmarked, others were covered with stones and a few had fallen wooden crosses. He was going to make a cross but before it was finished the police came and dug up the grave and took away the dead baby: someone — one of the other labourers? their women? — had reported that the baby was almost white, that, strong and healthy, it had died suddenly after a visit by the farmer's son. Pathological tests on the infant corpse showed intestinal damage not always consistent with death by natural causes.

Thebedi went for the first time to the country town where Paulus had been to school, to give evidence at the preparatory examination into the charge of murder brought against him. She cried hysterically in the witness box, saying yes, yes (the gilt hoop ear-rings swung in her ears), she saw the accused pouring liquid into the baby's mouth. She said he had threatened to shoot her if she told anyone.

More than a year went by before, in that same town, the case was brought to trial. She came to Court with a new-born baby on her back. She wore gilt hoop ear-rings; she was calm; she said she had not seen what the white man did in the house.

Paulus Eysendyck said he had visited the hut but had not poisoned the child.

The Defence did not contest that there had been a love relationship between the accused and the girl, or that intercourse had taken place, but submitted there was no proof that the child was the accused's.

The judge told the accused there was strong suspicion against him but not enough proof that he had committed the crime. The Court could not accept the girl's evidence because it was clear she had committed perjury either at this trial or at the preparatory examination. There was the suggestion in the mind of the Court that she might be an accomplice in the crime; but, again, insufficient proof.

The judge commended the honourable behaviour of the husband (sitting in court in a brown-and-yellow-quartered golf cap bought for Sundays) who had not rejected his wife and had "even provided clothes for the unfortunate infant out of his slender means."

The verdict on the accused was "not guilty."

The young white man refused to accept the congratulations of press and public and left the Court with his mother's raincoat shielding his face from photographers. His father said to the press, "I will try and carry on as best I can to hold up my head in the district."

Interviewed by the Sunday papers, who spelled her name in a variety of ways, the black girl, speaking in her own language, was quoted beneath her photograph: "It was a thing of our childhood, we don't see each other anymore."   [1980]

NATHANIEL HAWTHORNE (1804–1864), *writer of short stories and novels, was born in Salem, Massachusetts, into an eminent family who traced their lineage back to the Puritans. After his graduation from Bowdoin College in 1825, Hawthorne lived at home while he wrote works of short fiction he called "tales" or "articles" that he tried to sell to periodicals. American magazines of the time were mostly interested in publishing ghost stories, Indian legends, and "village tales" based on historical anecdotes. Hawthorne (like his contemporary Edgar Allan Poe) created stories that transcended the limitations of these conventions; his imagination was stirred by what he called "an inveterate love of allegory."*

Hawthorne published his first collection of stories, Twice-Told Tales, *in 1837; a second book of stories,* Mosses from an Old Manse, *appeared in 1846. That year he stopped writing to earn a better living for his family as surveyor of customs for the port of Salem. This was a political appointment, and after the Whigs won the presidency three years later, Hawthorne — a Democrat — was out of a job. He returned to writing fiction, sketching his "official life" at the Custom House in the introduction to his novel* The Scarlet Letter *in 1850. During the last decade of his career as a writer he published three other novels, several books for children, and another collection of tales. In "The Custom House," Hawthorne humorously suggested that his profession would not have impressed his Puritan ancestors:*

> *"What is he?" murmurs one grey shadow of my forefathers to the other. "A writer of story-books! What kind of business in life, what manner of glorifying God, or being serviceable to mankind in his day and generation, may that be? Why, the degenerate fellow might as well have been a fiddler!" Such are the compliments bandied between my great-grandsires and myself across the gulf of time! And yet, let them scorn me as they will, strong traits of their nature have intertwined themselves with mine.*

Despite Hawthorne's portrait of himself as an unappreciated artist, he was recognized by contemporaries such as Herman Melville and Edgar Allan Poe as a "genius of a very lofty order." Hawthorne wrote about 120 short tales and sketches in addition to his novels. His notebooks are filled with ideas for stories, more often jottings of abstract ideas than detailed observations of "real" individuals. "My Kinsman, Major Molineux" and "Young Goodman Brown" are two of his most famous moral tales set in the early years of the New England colonies.

RELATED COMMENTARIES: *Simon O. Lesser, "A Psychological Reading of Hawthorne's 'My Kinsman, Major Molineux,'" page 1450; Herman Melville, "Blackness in Hawthorne's 'Young Goodman Brown,'" page 1458; Edgar Allan Poe, "The Importance of the Single Effect in a Prose Tale," page 1488.*

NATHANIEL HAWTHORNE

My Kinsman, Major Molineux

After the kings of Great Britain had assumed the right of appointing the colonial governors, the measures of the latter seldom met with the ready and general approbation, which had been paid to those of their predecessors, under the original charters. The people looked with most jealous scrutiny to the exercise of power, which did not emanate from themselves, and they usually rewarded the rulers with slender gratitude, for the compliances, by which, in softening their instructions from beyond the sea, they had incurred the reprehension of those who gave them. The annals of Massachusetts Bay will inform us, that of six governors, in the space of about forty years from the surrender of the old charter, under James II., two were imprisoned by a popular insurrection; a third, as Hutchinson inclines to believe, was driven from the province by the whizzing of a musket ball; a fourth, in the opinion of the same historian, was hastened to his grave by continual bickerings with the House of Representatives; and the remaining two, as well as their successors, till the Revolution, were favored with few and brief intervals of peaceful sway. The inferior members of the court party, in times of high political excitement, led scarcely a more desirable life. These remarks may serve as preface to the following adventures, which chanced upon a summer night, not far from a hundred years ago. The reader, in order to avoid a long and dry detail of colonial affairs, is requested to dispense with an account of the train of circumstances, that had caused much temporary inflammation of the popular mind.

It was near nine o'clock of a moonlight evening, when a boat crossed the ferry with a single passenger, who had obtained his conveyance, at that unusual hour, by the promise of an extra fare. While he stood on the landing-place, searching in either pocket for the means of fulfilling his agreement, the ferryman lifted a lantern, by the aid of which, and the newly risen moon, he took a very accurate survey of the stranger's figure. He was a youth of barely eighteen years, evidently country-bred, and now, as it should seem, upon his first visit to town. He was clad in a coarse grey coat, well worn, but in excellent repair; his under garments were durably constructed of leather, and sat tight to a pair of serviceable and well-shaped limbs; his stockings of blue yarn, were the incontrovertible handiwork of a mother or a sister; and on his head was a three-cornered hat, which in its better days had perhaps sheltered the graver brow of the lad's father. Under his left arm was a heavy cudgel, formed of an oak sapling, and retaining a part of the hardened root; and his equipment was completed by a wallet, not so abundantly stocked as to incommode the vigorous shoulders on which it hung. Brown, curly hair, well-shaped features, and bright, cheerful eyes, were nature's gifts, and worth all that art could have done for his adornment.

The youth, one of whose names was Robin, finally drew from his pocket the half of a little province-bill of five shillings, which, in the depreciation of that sort of currency, did but satisfy the ferryman's demand, with the surplus of a sexangular piece of parchment valued at three pence. He then walked forward into the town, with as light a step, as if his day's journey had not already exceeded thirty miles, and with as eager an eye, as if he were entering London city, instead of the little metropolis of a New England colony. Before Robin had proceeded far, however, it occurred to him, that he knew not whither to direct his steps; so he paused, and looked up and down the narrow street, scrutinizing the small and mean wooden buildings, that were scattered on either side.

"This low hovel cannot be my kinsman's dwelling," thought he, "nor yonder old house, where the moonlight enters at the broken casement; and truly I see none hereabouts that might be worthy of him. It would have been wise to inquire my way of the ferryman, and doubtless he would have gone with me, and earned a shilling from the Major for his pains. But the next man I meet will do as well."

He resumed his walk, and was glad to perceive that the street now became wider, and the houses more respectable in their appearance. He soon discerned a figure moving on moderately in advance, and hastened his steps to overtake it. As Robin drew nigh, he saw that the passenger was a man in years, with a full periwig of grey hair, a wide-skirted coat of dark cloth, and silk stockings rolled about his knees. He carried a long and polished cane, which he struck down perpendicularly before him, at every step; and at regular intervals he uttered two successive hems, of a peculiarly solemn and sepulchral intonation. Having made these observations, Robin laid hold of the skirt of the old man's coat, just when the light from the open door and windows of a barber's shop, fell upon both their figures.

"Good evening to you, honored Sir," said he, making a low bow, and still retaining his hold of the skirt. "I pray you to tell me whereabouts is the dwelling of my kinsman, Major Molineux?"

The youth's question was uttered very loudly; and one of the barbers, whose razor was descending on a well-soaped chin, and another who was dressing a Ramillies wig, left their occupations, and came to the door. The citizen, in the meantime, turned a long favored countenance upon Robin, and answered him in a tone of excessive anger and annoyance. His two sepulchral hems, however, broke into the very centre of his rebuke, with most singular effect, like a thought of the cold grave obtruding among wrathful passions.

"Let go my garment, fellow! I tell you, I know not the man you speak of. What! I have authority, I have — hem, hem — authority; and if this be the respect you show your betters, your feet shall be brought acquainted with the stocks, by daylight, tomorrow morning!"

Robin released the old man's skirt, and hastened away, pursued by an ill-mannered roar of laughter from the barber's shop. He was at first considerably surprised by the result of his question, but, being a shrewd youth, soon thought himself able to account for the mystery.

"This is some country representative," was his conclusion, "who has never seen the inside of my kinsman's door, and lacks the breeding to answer a stranger civilly. The man is old, or verily — I might be tempted to turn back and smite him on the nose. Ah, Robin, Robin! even the barber's boys laugh at you, for choosing such a guide! You will be wiser in time, friend Robin."

He now became entangled in a succession of crooked and narrow streets, which crossed each other, and meandered at no great distance from the water-side. The smell of tar was obvious to his nostrils, the masts of vessels pierced the moonlight above the tops of the buildings, and the numerous signs, which Robin paused to read, informed him that he was near the centre of business. But the streets were empty, the shops were closed, and lights were visible only in the second stories of a few dwelling-houses. At length, on the corner of a narrow lane, through which he was passing, he beheld the broad countenance of a British hero swinging before the door of an inn, whence proceeded the voices of many guests. The casement of one of the lower windows was thrown back, and a very thin curtain permitted Robin to distinguish a party at supper, round a well-furnished table. The fragrance of the good cheer steamed forth into the outer air, and the youth could not fail to recollect, that the last remnant of his travelling stock of provision had yielded to his morning appetite, and that noon had found, and left him, dinnerless.

"Oh, that a parchment three-penny might give me a right to sit down at yonder table," said Robin, with a sigh. "But the Major will make me welcome to the best of his victuals; so I will even step boldly in, and inquire my way to his dwelling."

He entered the tavern, and was guided by the murmur of voices, and fumes of tobacco, to the public room. It was a long and low apartment, with oaken walls, grown dark in the continual smoke, and a floor, which was thickly sanded, but of no immaculate purity. A number of persons, the larger part of whom appeared to be mariners, or in some way connected with the sea, occupied the wooden benches, or leather-bottomed chairs, conversing on various matters, and occasionally lending their attention to some topic of general interest. Three or four little groups were draining as many bowls of punch, which the great West India trade had long since made a familiar drink in the colony. Others, who had the aspect of men who lived by regular and laborious handicraft, preferred the insulated bliss of an unshared potation, and became more taciturn under its influence. Nearly all, in short, evinced a predilection for the Good Creature in some of its various shapes, for this is a vice, to which, as the Fast-day sermons of a hundred years ago will testify, we have a long hereditary claim. The only guests to whom Robin's sympathies inclined him, were two or three sheepish countrymen, who were using the inn somewhat after the fashion of a Turkish Caravansary; they had gotten themselves into the darkest corner of the room, and, heedless of the Nicotian atmosphere, were supping on the bread of their own ovens, and the bacon cured in their own chimney-smoke. But though Robin felt a sort of brotherhood with these strangers, his eyes were attracted from them, to a person who stood near the door, holding whispered conversation with a group of ill-dressed associates. His features were separately striking almost to grotesqueness, and the whole face left a deep impression in the memory. The forehead bulged out into a double prominence, with a vale between; the nose came boldly forth in an irregular curve, and its bridge was of more than a finger's breadth; the eye-brows were deep and shaggy, and the eyes glowed beneath them like fire in a cave.

While Robin deliberated of whom to inquire respecting his kinsman's dwelling, he was accosted by the innkeeper, a little man in a stained white apron, who had come to pay his professional welcome to the stranger. Being in the second generation from a French Protestant, he seemed to have inherited the courtesy of his parent nation; but no variety of circumstance was ever known to change his voice from the one shrill note in which he now addressed Robin.

"From the country, I presume, Sir?" said he, with a profound bow. "Beg to congratulate you on your arrival, and trust you intend a long stay with us. Fine town here, Sir, beautiful buildings, and much that may interest a stranger. May I hope for the honor of your commands in respect to supper?"

"The man sees a family likeness! the rogue has guessed that I am related to the Major!" thought Robin, who had hitherto experienced little superfluous civility.

All eyes were now turned on the country lad, standing at the door, in his worn three-cornered hat, grey coat, leather breeches, and blue yarn stockings, leaning on an oaken cudgel, and bearing a wallet on his back.

Robin replied to the courteous innkeeper, with such an assumption of consequence, as befitted the Major's relative.

"My honest friend," he said, "I shall make it a point to patronize your house on some occasion, when — " here he could not help lowering his voice — "I may have more than a parchment three-pence in my pocket. My present business," continued he, speaking with lofty confidence, "is merely to inquire the way to the dwelling of my kinsman, Major Molineux."

There was a sudden and general movement in the room, which Robin interpreted as expressing the eagerness of each individual to become his guide. But the innkeeper turned his eyes to a written paper on the wall, which he read, or seemed to read, with occasional recurrences to the young man's figure.

"What have we here?" said he, breaking his speech into little dry fragments. "'Left the house of the subscriber, bounden servant, Hezekiah Mudge — had on, when he went away, grey coat, leather breeches, master's third best hat. One pound currency reward to whoever shall lodge him in any jail in the province.' Better trudge, boy, better trudge!"

Robin had begun to draw his hand towards the lighter end of the oak cudgel, but a strange hostility in every countenance, induced him to relinquish his purpose of breaking the courteous innkeeper's head. As he turned to leave the room, he encountered a sneering glance from the bold-featured personage whom he had before noticed; and no sooner was he beyond the door, than he heard a general laugh, in which the innkeeper's voice might be distinguished, like the dropping of small stones into a kettle.

"Now is it not strange," thought Robin, with his usual shrewdness, "is it not strange, that the confession of an empty pocket, should outweigh the name of my kinsman, Major Molineux? Oh, if I had one of these grinning rascals in the woods, where I and my oak sapling grew up together, I would teach him that my arm is heavy, though my purse be light!"

On turning the corner of the narrow lane, Robin found himself in a spacious street, with an unbroken line of lofty houses on each side, and a steepled building at the upper end, whence the ringing of a bell announced the hour of nine. The light of the moon, and the lamps from numerous shop windows, discovered people promenading on the pavement, and amongst them, Robin hoped to recognize his hitherto inscrutable relative. The result of his former inquiries made him unwilling to hazard another, in a scene of such publicity, and he determined to walk slowly and silently up the street, thrusting his face close to that of every elderly gentleman, in search of the Major's lineaments. In his progress, Robin encountered many gay and gallant figures. Embroidered garments, and showy colors, enormous periwigs, gold-laced hats, and silver hilted swords, glided past him and dazzled his optics. Travelled youths, imitators of the European fine gentlemen of the period, trod jauntily along, half-dancing to the fasionable tunes which they hummed, and making poor Robin ashamed of his quiet and natural gait. At length, after many pauses to examine the gorgeous display of goods in the shop windows, and after suffering some rebukes for the impertinence of his scrutiny into people's faces, the Major's kinsman found himself near the steepled building, still unsuccessful in his search. As yet, however, he had seen only one side of the thronged street; so Robin crossed, and continued the same sort of inquisition down the opposite pavement, with stronger hopes than the philosopher seeking an honest man,[1] but with no better fortune. He had arrived about midway towards the lower end, from which his course began, when he overheard the approach of some one, who struck down a cane on the flagstones at every step, uttering, at regular intervals, two sepulchral hems.

"Mercy on us!" quoth Robin, recognizing the sound.

Turning a corner, which chanced to be close at his right hand, he hastened to pursue his researches, in some other part of the town. His patience was now wearing low, and he seemed to feel more fatigue from his rambles since he crossed the ferry, than from his journey of several days on the other side. Hunger also pleaded loudly within him, and Robin began to balance the propriety of demanding, violently and with lifted cudgel, the necessary guidance from the first solitary passenger, whom he should meet. While a resolution to this effect was gaining strength, he entered a street of mean appearance, on either side of which, a row of ill-built houses was straggling towards the harbor. The moonlight fell upon no passenger along the whole extent, but in the third domicile which Robin passed, there was a half-opened door, and his keen glance detected a woman's garment within.

"My luck may be better here," said he to himself.

Accordingly, he approached the door, and beheld it shut closer as he did

---

[1] Diogenes (412?–323 B.C.) was a Greek philosopher and the founder of the Cynics, a sect that emphasized self-sufficiency and abstention from luxuries. The subject of numerous tales, he is purported to have conducted a search for an honest man while using a lighted lantern in broad daylight.

so; yet an open space remained, sufficing for the fair occupant to observe the stranger, without a corresponding display on her part. All that Robin could discern was a strip of scarlet petticoat, and the occasional sparkle of an eye, as if the moonbeams were trembling on some bright thing.

"Pretty mistress," — for I may call her so with a good conscience, thought the shrewd youth, since I know nothing to the contrary — "my sweet pretty mistress, will you be kind enough to tell me whereabouts I must seek the dwelling of my kinsman, Major Molineux?"

Robin's voice was plaintive and winning, and the female, seeing nothing to be shunned in the handsome country youth, thrust open the door, and came forth into the moonlight. She was a dainty little figure, with a white neck, round arms, and a slender waist, at the extremity of which her scarlet petticoat jutted out over a hoop, as if she were standing in a balloon. Moreover, her face was oval and pretty, her hair dark beneath the little cap, and her bright eyes possessed a sly freedom, which triumphed over those of Robin.

"Major Molineux dwells here," said this fair woman.

Now her voice was the sweetest Robin had heard that night, the airy counterpart of a stream of melted silver; yet he could not help doubting whether that sweet voice spoke Gospel truth. He looked up and down the mean street, and then surveyed the house before which they stood. It was a small, dark edifice of two stories, the second of which projected over the lower floor; and the front apartment had the aspect of a shop for petty commodities.

"Now truly I am in luck," replied Robin, cunningly, "and so indeed is my kinsman, the Major, in having so pretty a housekeeper. But I prithee trouble him to step to the door; I will deliver him a message from his friends in the country, and then go back to my lodgings at the inn."

"Nay, the Major has been a-bed this hour or more," said the lady of the scarlet petticoat; "and it would be to little purpose to disturb him to-night, seeing his evening draught was of the strongest. But he is a kind-hearted man, and it would be as much as my life's worth, to let a kinsman of his turn away from the door. You are the good old gentleman's very picture, and I could swear that was his rainy-weather hat. Also, he has garments very much resembling those leather — But come in, I pray, for I bid you hearty welcome in his name."

So saying, the fair and hospitable dame took our hero by the hand; and though the touch was light, and the force was gentleness, and though Robin read in her eyes what he did not hear in her words, yet the slender waisted woman, in the scarlet petticoat, proved stronger than the athletic country youth. She had drawn his half-willing footsteps nearly to the threshold, when the opening of a door in the neighborhood, startled the Major's housekeeper, and, leaving the Major's kinsman, she vanished speedily into her own domicile. A heavy yawn preceded the appearance of a man, who, like the Moonshine of Pyramus and Thisbe,[2] carried a lantern, needlessly aiding his sister

---

[2]In Shakespeare's *A Midsummer Night's Dream*, a band of rustics perform an inept version of the tragedy of Pyramus and Thisbe in which the moon is a character represented by an actor with a lantern (Act V, Scene i).

luminary in the heavens. As he walked sleepily up the street, he turned his broad, dull face on Robin, and displayed a long staff, spiked at the end.

"Home, vagabond, home!" said the watchman, in accents that seemed to fall asleep as soon as they were uttered. "Home, or we'll set you in the stocks by peep of day!"

"This is the second hint of the kind," thought Robin. "I wish they would end my difficulties, by setting me there tonight."

Nevertheless, the youth felt an instinctive antipathy towards the guardian of midnight order, which at first prevented him from asking his usual question. But just when the man was about to vanish behind the corner, Robin resolved not to lose the opportunity, and shouted lustily after him —

"I say, friend! will you guide me to the house of my kinsman, Major Molineux?"

The watchman made no reply, but turned the corner and was gone; yet Robin seemed to hear the sound of drowsy laughter stealing along the solitary street. At that moment, also, a pleasant titter saluted him from the open window above his head; he looked up, and caught the sparkle of a saucy eye; a round arm beckoned to him, and next he heard light footsteps descending the staircase within. But Robin, being of the household of a New England clergyman, was a good youth, as well as a shrewd one; so he resisted temptation, and fled away.

He now roamed desperately, and at random, through the town, almost ready to believe that a spell was on him, like that, by which a wizard of his country, had once kept three pursuers wandering, a whole winter night, within twenty paces of the cottage which they sought. The streets lay before him, strange and desolate, and the lights were extinguished in almost every house. Twice, however, little parties of men, among whom Robin distinguished individuals in outlandish attire, came hurrying along, but though on both occasions they paused to address him, such intercourse did not at all enlighten his perplexity. They did but utter a few words in some language of which Robin knew nothing, and perceiving his inability to answer, bestowed a curse upon him in plain English, and hastened away. Finally, the lad determined to knock at the door of every mansion that might appear worthy to be occupied by his kinsman, trusting that perseverance would overcome the fatality which had hitherto thwarted him. Firm in this resolve, he was passing beneath the walls of a church, which formed the corner of two streets, when, as he turned into the shade of its steeple, he encountered a bulky stranger, muffled in a cloak. The man was proceeding with the speed of earnest business, but Robin planted himself full before him, holding the oak cudgel with both hands across his body, as a bar to further passage.

"Halt, honest man, and answer me a question," said he, very resolutely. "Tell me, this instant, whereabouts is the dwelling of my kinsman, Major Molineux?"

"Keep your tongue between your teeth, fool, and let me pass," said a deep, gruff voice, which Robin partly remembered. "Let me pass, I say, or I'll strike you to the earth!"

"No, no, neighbor!" cried Robin, flourishing his cudgel, and then thrusting its larger end close to the man's muffled face. "No, no, I'm not the fool you take me for, nor do you pass, till I have an answer to my question. Whereabouts is the dwelling of my kinsman, Major Molineux?"

The stranger, instead of attempting to force his passage, stept back into the moonlight, unmuffled his own face, and stared full into that of Robin.

"Watch here an hour, and Major Molineux will pass by," said he.

Robin gazed with dismay and astonishment, on the unprecedented physiognomy of the speaker. The forehead with its double prominence, the broad-hooked nose, the shaggy eyebrows, and fiery eyes, were those which he had noticed at the inn, but the man's complexion had undergone a singular, or, more properly, a two-fold change. One side of the face blazed of an intense red, while the other was black as midnight, the division line being in the broad bridge of the nose; and a mouth, which seemed to extend from ear to ear, was black or red, in contrast to the color of the cheek. The effect was as if two individual devils, a fiend of fire and a fiend of darkness, had united themselves to form this infernal visage. The stranger grinned in Robin's face, muffled his parti-colored features, and was out of sight in a moment.

"Strange things we travellers see!" ejaculated Robin.

He seated himself, however, upon the steps of the church-door, resolving to wait the appointed time for his kinsman's appearance. A few moments were consumed in philosophical speculations, upon the species of the *genus homo*, who had just left him, but having settled this point shrewdly, rationally, and satisfactorily, he was compelled to look elsewhere for amusement. And first he threw his eyes along the street; it was of more respectable appearance than most of those into which he had wandered, and the moon, "creating, like the imaginative power, a beautiful strangeness in familiar objects," gave something of romance to a scene, that might not have possessed it in the light of day. The irregular, and often quaint architecture of the houses, some of whose roofs were broken into numerous little peaks; while others ascended, steep and narrow, into a single point; and others again were square; the pure milk-white of some of their complexions, the aged darkness of others, and the thousand sparklings, reflected from bright substances in the plastered walls of many; these matters engaged Robin's attention for awhile, and then began to grow wearisome. Next he endeavored to define the forms of distant objects, starting away with almost ghostly indistinctness, just as his eye appeared to grasp them; and finally he took a minute survey of an edifice, which stood on the opposite side of the street, directly in front of the church-door, where he was stationed. It was a large square mansion, distinguished from its neighbors by a balcony, which rested on tall pillars, and by an elaborate Gothic window, communicating therewith.

"Perhaps this is the very house I have been seeking," thought Robin.

Then he strove to speed away the time, by listening to a murmur, which swept continually along the street, yet was scarcely audible, except to an unaccustomed ear like his; it was a low, dull, dreamy sound, compounded of many noises, each of which was at too great a distance to be separately heard. Robin marvelled at this snore of a sleeping town, and marvelled more, whenever its continuity was broken, by now and then a distant shout, apparently loud where it originated. But altogether it was a sleep-inspiring sound, and to shake off its drowsy influence, Robin arose, and climbed a window-frame, that he might view the interior of the church. There the moonbeams came trembling in, and fell down upon the deserted pews, and extended along the quiet aisles. A fainter, yet more awful radiance, was hovering round the pulpit, and one solitary ray had dared to rest upon the opened page of the great Bible. Had Nature, in that deep hour, become a worshipper in the house, which man had builded? Or was that heavenly light the visible sanctity of the place, visible because no earthly and impure feet were within the walls? The scene made Robin's heart shiver with a sensation of loneliness, stronger than he had ever felt in the remotest depths of his native woods; so he turned away, and sat down again before the door. There were graves around the church, and now an uneasy thought obtruded into Robin's breast. What if the object of his search, which had been so often and so strangely thwarted, were all the time mouldering in his shroud? What if his kinsman should glide through yonder gate, and nod and smile to him in passing dimly by?

"Oh, that any breathing thing were here with me!" said Robin.

Recalling his thoughts from this uncomfortable track, he sent them over forest, hill, and stream, and attempted to imagine how that evening of ambiguity and weariness, had been spent by his father's household. He pictured them assembled at the door, beneath the tree, the great old tree, which had been spared for its huge twisted trunk, and venerable shade, when a thousand leafy brethren fell. There, at the going down of the summer sun, it was his father's custom to perform domestic worship, that the neighbors might come and join with him like brothers of the family, and that the wayfaring man might pause to drink at that fountain, and keep his heart pure by freshening the memory of home. Robin distinguished the seat of every individual of the little audience; he saw the good man in the midst, holding the Scriptures in the golden light that shone from the western clouds; he beheld him close the book, and all rise up to pray. He heard the old thanksgivings for daily mercies, the old supplications for their continuance, to which he had so often listened in weariness, but which were now among his dear remembrances. He perceived the slight inequality of his father's voice when he came to speak of the Absent One; he noted how his mother turned her face to the broad and knotted trunk; how his elder brother scorned, because the beard was rough upon his upper lip, to permit his features to be moved; how his younger sister drew down a low hanging branch before her eyes; and how the little one of all, whose sports had hitherto broken the decorum of the scene, understood the prayer for her playmate, and burst into clamorous grief. Then he saw them go in at the door; and when Robin would have entered also, the latch tinkled into its place, and he was excluded from his home.

"Am I here, or there?" cried Robin, starting; for all at once, when his thoughts had become visible and audible in a dream, the long, wide, solitary street shone out before him.

He aroused himself, and endeavored to fix his attention steadily upon the large edifice which he had surveyed before. But still his mind kept vibrating between fancy and reality; by turns, the pillars of the balcony lengthened into the tall, bare stems of pines, dwindled down to human figures, settled again in their true shape and size, and then commenced a new succession of changes. For a single moment, when he deemed himself awake, he could have sworn that a visage, one which he seemed to remember, yet could not absolutely name as his kinsman's, was looking towards him from the Gothic window. A deeper sleep wrestled with, and nearly overcame him, but fled at the sound of footsteps along the opposite pavement. Robin rubbed his eyes, discerned a man passing at the foot of the balcony, and addressed him in a loud, peevish, and lamentable cry.

"Halloo, friend! must I wait here all night for my kinsman, Major Molineux?"

The sleeping echoes awoke, and answered the voice; and the passenger, barely able to discern a figure sitting in the oblique shade of the steeple, traversed the street to obtain a nearer view. He was himself a gentleman in his prime, of open, intelligent, cheerful, and altogether prepossessing countenance. Perceiving a country youth, apparently homeless and without friends, he accosted him in a tone of real kindness, which had become strange to Robin's ears.

"Well, my good lad, why are you sitting here?" inquired he. "Can I be of service to you in any way?"

"I am afraid not, Sir," replied Robin, despondingly; "yet I shall take it kindly, if you'll answer me a single question. I've been searching half the night for one Major Molineux; now, Sir, is there really such a person in these parts, or am I dreaming?"

"Major Molineux! The name is not altogether strange to me," said the gentleman, smiling. "Have you any objection to telling me the nature of your business with him?"

Then Robin briefly related that his father was a clergyman, settled on a small salary, at a long distance back in the country, and that he and Major Molineux were brothers' children. The Major, having inherited riches, and acquired civil and military rank, had visited his cousin in great pomp a year or two before; had manifested much interest in Robin and an elder brother, and, being childless himself, had thrown out hints respecting the future establishment of one of them in life. The elder brother was destined to succeed to the farm, which his father cultivated, in the interval of sacred duties; it was therefore determined that Robin should profit by his kinsman's generous intentions, especially as he had seemed to be rather the favorite, and was thought to possess other necessary endowments.

"For I have the name of being a shrewd youth," observed Robin, in this part of his story.

"I doubt not you deserve it," replied his new friend, good naturedly; "but pray proceed."

"Well, Sir, being nearly eighteen years old, and well-grown, as you see," continued Robin, raising himself to his full height, "I thought it high time to begin the world. So my mother and sister put me in handsome trim, and my father gave me half the remnant of his last year's salary, and five days ago I started for this place, to pay the Major a visit. But would you believe it, Sir? I crossed the ferry a little after dusk, and have yet found nobody that would show me the way to his dwelling; only an hour or two since, I was told to wait here, and Major Molineux would pass by."

"Can you describe the man who told you this?" inquired the gentleman.

"Oh, he was a very ill-favored fellow, Sir," replied Robin, "with two great bumps on his forehead, a hook nose, fiery eyes, and, what struck me as the strangest, his face was of two different colors. Do you happen to know such a man, Sir?"

"Not intimately," answered the stranger, "but I chanced to meet him a little time previous to your stopping me. I believe you may trust his word, and that the Major will very shortly pass through this street. In the mean time, as I have a singular curiosity to witness your meeting, I will sit down here upon the steps, and bear you company."

He seated himself accordingly, and soon engaged his companion in animated discourse. It was but a brief continuance, however, for a noise of shouting, which had long been remotely audible, drew so much nearer, that Robin inquired its cause.

"What may be the meaning of this uproar?" asked he. "Truly, if your town be always as noisy, I shall find little sleep, while I am an inhabitant."

"Why, indeed, friend Robin, there do appear to be three or four riotous fellows abroad to-night," replied the gentleman. "You must not expect all the stillness of your native woods, here in our streets. But the watch will shortly be at the heels of these lads, and —"

"Aye, and set them in the stocks by peep of day," interrupted Robin, recollecting his own encounter with the drowsy lantern-bearer. "But, dear Sir, if I may trust my ears, an army of watchmen would never make head against such a multitude of rioters. There were at least a thousand voices went to make up that one shout."

"May not one man have several voices, Robin, as well as two complexions?" said his friend.

"Perhaps a man may; but Heaven forbid that a woman should!" responded the shrewd youth, thinking of the seductive tones of the Major's housekeeper.

The sounds of a trumpet in some neighboring street now became so evident and continual, that Robin's curiosity was strongly excited. In addition to the shouts, he heard frequent bursts from many instruments of discord, and a wild and confused laughter filled up the intervals. Robin rose from the steps, and looked wistfully towards a point, whither several people seemed to be hastening.

"Surely some prodigious merrymaking is going on," exclaimed he. "I have laughed very little since I left home, Sir, and should be sorry to lose an opportunity. Shall we just step round the corner by that darkish house, and take our share of the fun?"

"Sit down again, sit down, good Robin," replied the gentleman, laying his hand on the skirt of the grey coat. "You forget that we must wait here for your kinsman; and there is reason to believe that he will pass by, in the course of a very few moments."

The near approach of the uproar had now disturbed the neighborhood; windows flew open on all sides; and many heads, in the attire of the pillow, and confused by sleep suddenly broken, were protruded to the gaze of whoever had leisure to observe them. Eager voices hailed each other from house to house, all demanding the explanation, which not a soul could give. Half-dressed men hurried towards the unknown commotion, stumbling as they went over the stone steps, that thrust themselves into the narrow foot-walk. The shouts, the laughter, and the tuneless bray, the antipodes of music, came onward with increasing din, till scattered individuals, and then denser bodies, began to appear round a corner, at the distance of a hundred yards.

"Will you recognize your kinsman, Robin, if he passes in this crowd?" inquired the gentleman.

"Indeed, I can't warrant it, Sir; but I'll take my stand here, and keep a bright look out," answered Robin, descending to the outer edge of the pavement.

A mighty stream of people now emptied into the street, and came rolling slowly towards the church. A single horseman wheeled the corner in the midst of them, and close behind him came a band of fearful wind-instruments, sending forth a fresher discord, now that no intervening buildings kept it from the ear. Then a redder light disturbed the moonbeams, and a dense multitude of torches shone along the street, concealing by their glare whatever object they illuminated. The single horseman, clad in a military dress, and bearing a drawn sword, rode onward as the leader, and, by his fierce and variegated countenance, appeared like war personified; the red of one cheek was an emblem of fire and sword; the blackness of the other betokened the mourning which attends them. In his train, were wild figures in the Indian dress, and many fantastic shapes without a model, giving the whole march a visionary air, as if a dream had broken forth from some feverish brain, and were sweeping visibly through the midnight streets. A mass of people, inactive, except as applauding spectators, hemmed the procession in, and several women ran along the sidewalks, piercing the confusion of heavier sounds, with their shrill voices of mirth or terror.

"The double-faced fellow has his eye upon me," muttered Robin, with an indefinite but uncomfortable idea, that he was himself to bear a part in the pageantry.

The leader turned himself in the saddle, and fixed his glance full upon the country youth, as the steed went slowly by. When Robin had freed his eyes from those fiery ones, the musicians were passing before him, and the torches were close at hand; but the unsteady brightness of the latter formed a veil which he could not penetrate. The rattling of wheels over the stones sometimes found its way to his ear, and confused traces of a human form appeared at intervals, and then melted into the vivid light. A moment more, and the leader thundered a command to halt; the trumpets vomited a horrid breath, and held their peace; the shouts and laughter of the people died away, and there remained only a universal hum, nearly allied to silence. Right before

Robin's eyes was an uncovered cart. There the torches blazed the brightest, there the moon shone out like day, and there, in tar-and-feathery dignity, sate his kinsman, Major Molineux!

He was an elderly man, of large and majestic person, and strong, square features, betokening a steady soul; but steady as it was, his enemies had found the means to shake it. His face was pale as death, and far more ghastly; the broad forehead was contracted in his agony, so that his eyebrows formed one grizzled line; his eyes were red and wild, and the foam hung white upon his quivering lip. His whole frame was agitated by a quick, and continual tremor, which his pride strove to quell, even in those circumstances of overwhelming humiliation. But perhaps the bitterest pang of all was when his eyes met those of Robin; for he evidently knew him on the instant, as the youth stood witnessing the foul disgrace of a head that had grown grey in honor. They stared at each other in silence, and Robin's knees shook, and his hair bristled, with a mixture of pity and terror. Soon, however, a bewildering excitement began to seize upon his mind; the preceding adventures of the night, the unexpected appearance of the crowd, the torches, the confused din, and the hush that followed, the spectre of his kinsman reviled by that great multitude, all this, and more than all, a perception of tremendous ridicule in the whole scene, affected him with a sort of mental inebriety. At that moment a voice of sluggish merriment saluted Robin's ears; he turned instinctively, and just behind the corner of the church stood the lantern-bearer, rubbing his eyes, and drowsily enjoying the lad's amazement. Then he heard a peal of laughter like the ringing of silvery bells; a woman twitched his arm, a saucy eye met his, and he saw the lady of the scarlet petticoat. A sharp, dry cachinnation appealed to his memory, and, standing on tiptoe in the crowd, with his white apron over his head, he beheld the courteous little innkeeper. And lastly, there sailed over the heads of the multitude a great, broad laugh, broken in the midst by two sepulchral hems; thus —

"Haw, haw, haw — hem, hem — haw, haw, haw, haw!"

The sound proceeded from the balcony of the opposite edifice, and thither Robin turned his eyes. In front of the Gothic window stood the old citizen, wrapped in a wide gown, his grey periwig exchanged for a nightcap, which was thrust back from his forehead, and his silk stockings hanging down about his legs. He supported himself on his polished cane in a fit of convulsive merriment, which manifested itself on his solemn old features, like a funny inscription on a tomb-stone. Then Robin seemed to hear the voices of the barbers; of the guests of the inn; and of all who had made sport of him that night. The contagion was spreading among the multitude, when, all at once, it seized upon Robin, and he sent forth a shout of laughter that echoed through the street; every man shook his sides, every man emptied his lungs, but Robin's shout was the loudest there. The cloud-spirits peeped from their silvery islands, as the congregated mirth went roaring up the sky! The Man in the Moon heard the far bellow; "Oho," quoth he, "the old Earth is frolicsome to-night!"

When there was a momentary calm in that tempestuous sea of sound, the leader gave the sign, the procession resumed its march. On they went, like fiends that throng in mockery round some dead potentate, mighty no more, but majestic still in his agony. On they went, in counterfeited pomp, in senseless uproar, in frenzied merriment, trampling all on an old man's heart. On swept the tumult, and left a silent street behind.

"Well, Robin, are you dreaming?" inquired the gentleman, laying his hand on the youth's shoulder.

Robin started, and withdrew his arm from the stone post, to which he had instinctively clung, while the living stream rolled by him. His cheek was somewhat pale, and his eyes not quite so lively as in the earlier part of the evening.

"Will you be kind enough to show me the way to the ferry?" said he, after a moment's pause.

"You have then adopted a new subject of inquiry?" observed his companion, with a smile.

"Why, yes, Sir," replied Robin, rather dryly. "Thanks to you, and to my other friends, I have at last met my kinsman, and he will scarce desire to see my face again. I begin to grow weary of a town life, Sir. Will you show me the way to the ferry?"

"No, my good friend Robin, not to-night, at least," said the gentleman. "Some few days hence, if you continue to wish it, I will speed you on your journey. Or, if you prefer to remain with us, perhaps, as you are a shrewd youth, you may rise in the world, without the help of your kinsman, Major Molineux." [1832]

NATHANIEL HAWTHORNE

Young Goodman Brown

Young Goodman Brown came forth at sunset into the street at Salem village; but put his head back, after crossing the threshold, to exchange a parting kiss with his young wife. And Faith, as the wife was aptly named, thrust her own pretty head into the street, letting the wind play with the pink ribbons of her cap while she called to Goodman Brown.

"Dearest heart," whispered she, softly and rather sadly, when her lips were close to his ear, "prithee put off your journey until sunrise and sleep in your own bed to-night. A lone woman is troubled with such dreams and such thoughts that she's afeared of herself sometimes. Pray tarry with me this night, dear husband, of all nights in the year."

"My love and my Faith," replied young Goodman Brown, "of all nights in the year, this one night must I tarry away from thee. My journey, as thou callest it, forth and back again, must needs be done 'twixt now and sunrise. What, my sweet, pretty wife, dost thou doubt me already, and we but three months married?"

"Then God bless you!" said Faith, with the pink ribbons; "and may you find all well when you come back."

"Amen!" cried Goodman Brown. "Say thy prayers, dear Faith, and go to bed at dusk, and no harm will come to thee."

So they parted; and the young man pursued his way until, being about to turn the corner by the meeting-house, he looked back and saw the head of Faith still peeping after him with a melancholy air, in spite of her pink ribbons.

"Poor little Faith!" thought he, for his heart smote him. "What a wretch am I to leave her on such an errand! She talks of dreams, too. Methought as she spoke there was trouble in her face, as if a dream had warned her what work is to be done to-night. But no, no; 't would kill her to think it. Well, she's a blessed angel on earth, and after this one night I'll cling to her skirts and follow her to heaven."

With this excellent resolve for the future, Goodman Brown felt himself justified in making more haste on his present evil purpose. He had taken a dreary road, darkened by all the gloomiest trees of the forest, which barely stood aside to let the narrow path creep through, and closed immediately behind. It was all as lonely as could be; and there is this peculiarity in such a solitude, that the traveller knows not who may be concealed by the innumerable trunks and the thick boughs overhead; so that with lonely footsteps he may yet be passing through an unseen multitude.

"There may be a devilish Indian behind every tree," said Goodman Brown to himself; and he glanced fearfully behind him as he added, "What if the devil himself should be at my very elbow!"

His head being turned back, he passed a crook of the road, and, looking forward again, beheld the figure of a man, in grave and decent attire, seated at the foot of an old tree. He arose at Goodman Brown's approach and walked onward side by side with him.

"You are late, Goodman Brown," said he. "The clock of the Old South was striking as I came through Boston, and that is full fifteen minutes agone."

"Faith kept me back a while," replied the young man, with a tremor in his voice, caused by the sudden appearance of his companion, though not wholly unexpected.

It was now deep dusk in the forest, and deepest in that part of it where these two were journeying. As nearly as could be discerned, the second traveller was about fifty years old, apparently in the same rank of life as Goodman Brown, and bearing a considerable resemblance to him, though perhaps more in expression than features. Still they might have been taken for father and son. And yet, though the elder person was as simply clad as the younger, and as simple in manner too, he had an indescribable air of one who knew the world, and who would not have felt abashed at the governor's dinner table or in King William's court, were it possible that his affairs should call him thither. But the only thing about him that could be fixed upon as remarkable was his staff, which bore the likeness of a great black snake, so curiously wrought that it might almost be seen to twist and wriggle itself like a living serpent. This, of course, must have been an ocular deception, assisted by the uncertain light.

"Come, Goodman Brown," cried his fellow-traveller, "this is a dull pace for the beginning of a journey. Take my staff, if you are so soon weary."

"Friend," said the other, exchanging his slow pace for a full stop, "having kept covenant by meeting thee here, it is my purpose now to return whence I came. I have scruples touching the matter thou wot'st of."

"Sayest thou so?" replied he of the serpent, smiling apart. "Let us walk on, nevertheless, reasoning as we go; and if I convince thee not thou shalt turn back. We are but a little way in the forest yet."

"Too far! too far!" exclaimed the goodman, unconsciously resuming his walk. "My father never went into the woods on such an errand, nor his father before him. We have been a race of honest men and good Christians since the days of the martyrs; and shall I be the first of the name of Brown that ever took this path and kept" —

"Such company, thou wouldst say," observed the elder person, interpreting his pause. "Well said, Goodman Brown! I have been as well acquainted with your family as with ever a one among the Puritans; and that's no trifle to say. I helped your grandfather, the constable, when he lashed the Quaker woman so smartly through the streets of Salem; and it was I that brought your father a pitch-pine knot, kindled at my own hearth, to set fire to an Indian village, in King Philip's war. They were my good friends, both; and many a pleasant walk have we had along this path, and returned merrily after midnight. I would fain be friends with you for their sake."

"If it be as thou sayest," replied Goodman Brown, "I marvel they never spoke of these matters; or, verily, I marvel not, seeing that the least rumor of the sort would have driven them from New England. We are a people of prayer, and good works to boot, and abide no such wickedness."

"Wickedness or not," said the traveller with the twisted staff, "I have a very general acquaintance here in New England. The deacons of many a church have drunk the communion wine with me; the selectmen of divers towns make me their chairman; and a majority of the Great and General Court are firm supporters of my interest. The governor and I, too — But these are state secrets."

"Can this be so?" cried Goodman Brown, with a stare of amazement at his undisturbed companion. "Howbeit, I have nothing to do with the governor and council; they have their own ways, and are no rule for a simple husbandman like me. But, were I to go on with thee, how should I meet the eye of that good old man, our minister, at Salem village? Oh, his voice would make me tremble both Sabbath day and lecture day."

Thus far the elder traveller had listened with due gravity; but now burst into a fit of irrepressible mirth, shaking himself so violently that his snake-like staff actually seemed to wriggle in sympathy.

"Ha! ha! ha!" shouted he again and again; then composing himself, "Well, go on, Goodman Brown, go on; but, prithee, don't kill me with laughing."

"Well, then, to end the matter at once," said Goodman Brown, considerably nettled, "there is my wife, Faith. It would break her dear little heart; and I'd rather break my own."

"Nay, if that be the case," answered the other, "e'en go thy ways, Goodman Brown. I would not for twenty old women like the one hobbling before us that Faith should come to any harm."

As he spoke he pointed his staff at a female figure on the path, in whom Goodman Brown recognized a very pious and exemplary dame, who had taught him his catechism in youth, and was still his moral and spiritual adviser, jointly with the minister and Deacon Gookin.

"A marvel, truly that Goody Cloyse should be so far in the wilderness at nightfall," said he. "But with your leave, friend, I shall take a cut through the woods until we have left this Christian woman behind. Being a stranger to you, she might ask whom I was consorting with and whither I was going."

"Be it so," said his fellow-traveller. "Betake you to the woods, and let me keep the path."

Accordingly the young man turned aside, but took care to watch his companion, who advanced softly along the road until he had come within a staff's length of the old dame. She, meanwhile, was making the best of her way, with singular speed for so aged a woman, and mumbling some indistinct words — a prayer, doubtless — as she went. The traveller put forth his staff and touched her withered neck with what seemed the serpent's tail.

"The devil!" screamed the pious old lady.

"Then Goody Cloyse knows her old friend?" observed the traveller, confronting her and leaning on his writhing stick.

"Ah, forsooth, and is it your worship indeed?" cried the good dame. "Yea, truly is it, and in the very image of my old gossip, Goodman Brown, the grandfather of the silly fellow that now is. But — would your worship believe it? — my broomstick hath strangely disappeared, stolen, as I suspect, by that unhanged witch, Goody Cory, and that, too, when I was all anointed with the juice of smallage, and cinquefoil, and wolf's bane" —

"Mingled with fine wheat and the fat of a new-born babe," said the shape of old Goodman Brown.

"Ah, your worship knows the recipe," cried the old lady, cackling aloud. "So, as I was saying, being all ready for the meeting, and no horse to ride on, I made up my mind to foot it; for they tell me there is a nice young man to be taken into communion to-night. But now your good worship will lend me your arm, and we shall be there in a twinkling."

"That can hardly be," answered her friend. "I may not spare you my arm, Goody Cloyse; but here is my staff, if you will."

So saying, he threw it down at her feet, where, perhaps, it assumed life, being one of the rods which its owner had formerly lent to the Egyptian magi. Of this fact, however, Goodman Brown could not take cognizance. He had cast up his eyes in astonishment, and, looking down again, beheld neither Goody Cloyse nor the serpentine staff, but his fellow-traveller alone, who waited for him as calmly as if nothing had happened.

"That old woman taught me my catechism," said the young man; and there was a world of meaning in this simple comment.

They continued to walk onward, while the elder traveller exhorted his companion to make good speed and persevere in the path, discoursing so aptly that his arguments seemed rather to spring up in the bosom of his auditor than to be suggested by himself. As they went, he plucked a branch of maple to serve for a walking stick, and began to strip it of the twigs and little boughs, which were wet with evening dew. The moment his fingers touched them they became strangely withered and dried up as with a week's sunshine. Thus the pair proceeded, at a good free pace, until suddenly, in a gloomy hollow of the road, Goodman Brown sat himself down on the stump of a tree and refused to go any farther.

"Friend," he said, stubbornly, "my mind is made up. Not another step will I budge on this errand. What if a wretched old woman do choose to go to the devil when I thought she was going to heaven: is that any reason why I should quit my dear Faith and go after her?"

"You will think better of this by and by," said his acquaintance, composedly. "Sit here and rest yourself a while; and when you feel like moving again, there is my staff to help you along."

Without more words, he threw his companion the maple stick, and was as speedily out of sight as if he had vanished into the deepening gloom. The young man sat a few moments by the roadside, applauding himself greatly, and thinking with how clear a conscience he should meet the minister in his morning walk, nor shrink from the eye of good old Deacon Gookin. And what calm sleep would be his that very night, which was to have been spent so wickedly, but so purely and sweetly now, in the arms of Faith! Amidst these pleasant and praiseworthy meditations, Goodman Brown heard the tramp of horses along the road, and deemed it advisable to conceal himself within the verge of the forest, conscious of the guilty purpose that had brought him thither, though now so happily turned from it.

On came the hoof tramps and the voices of the riders, two grave old voices, conversing soberly as they drew near. These mingled sounds appeared to pass along the road, within a few yards of the young man's hiding-place; but, owing doubtless to the depth of the gloom at that particular spot, neither the travellers nor their steeds were visible. Though their figures brushed the small boughs by the wayside, it could not be seen that they intercepted, even for a moment, the faint gleam from the strip of bright sky athwart which they must have passed. Goodman Brown alternately crouched and stood on tiptoe, pulling aside the branches and thrusting forth his head as far as he durst without discerning so much as a shadow. It vexed him the more, because he could have sworn, were such a thing possible, that he recognized the voices of the minister and Deacon Gookin, jogging along quietly, as they were wont to do, when bound to some ordination or ecclesiastical council. While yet within hearing, one of the riders stopped to pluck a switch.

"Of the two, reverend sir," said the voice like the deacon's, "I had rather miss an ordination dinner than to-night's meeting. They tell me that some of our community are to be here from Falmouth and beyond, and others from Connecticut and Rhode Island, besides several of the Indian powwows, who, after their fashion, know almost as much deviltry as the best of us. Moreover, there is a goodly young woman to be taken into communion."

"Mighty well, Deacon Gookin!" replied the solemn old tones of the minister. "Spur up, or we shall be late. Nothing can be done, you know, until I get on the ground."

The hoofs clattered again; and the voices, talking so strangely in the empty air, passed on through the forest, where no church had ever been gathered or solitary Christian prayed. Whither, then, could these holy men be journeying so deep into the heathen wilderness? Young Goodman Brown caught hold of a tree for support, being ready to sink down on the ground, faint and overburdened with the heavy sickness of his heart. He looked up to the sky, doubting whether there really was a heaven above him. Yet there was the blue arch, and the stars brightening in it.

"With heaven above and Faith below, I will yet stand firm against the devil!" cried Goodman Brown.

While he still gazed upward into the deep arch of the firmament and had lifted his hands to pray, a cloud, though no wind was stirring, hurried across the zenith and hid the brightening stars. The blue sky was still visible, except directly overhead, where this black mass of cloud was sweeping swiftly northward. Aloft in the air, as if from the depths of the cloud, came a confused and doubtful sound of voices. Once the listener fancied that he could distinguish the accents of towns-people of his own, men and women, both pious and ungodly, many of whom he had met at the communion table, and had seen others rioting at the tavern. The next moment, so indistinct were the sounds, he doubted whether he had heard aught but the murmur of the old forest, whispering without a wind. Then came a stronger swell of those familiar tones, heard daily in the sunshine at Salem village, but never until now from a cloud of night. There was one voice, of a young woman, uttering lamentations, yet with an uncertain sorrow, and entreating for some favor, which, perhaps, it would grieve her to obtain; and all the unseen multitude, both saints and sinners, seemed to encourage her onward.

"Faith!" shouted Goodman Brown, in a voice of agony and desperation; and the echoes of the forest mocked him, crying, "Faith! Faith!" as if bewildered wretches were seeking her all through the wilderness.

The cry of grief, rage, and terror was yet piercing the night, when the unhappy husband held his breath for a response. There was a scream, drowned immediately in a louder murmur of voices, fading into far-off laughter, as the dark cloud swept away, leaving the clear and silent sky above Goodman Brown. But something fluttered lightly down through the air and caught on the branch of a tree. The young man seized it, and beheld a pink ribbon.

"My Faith is gone!" cried he after one stupefied moment. "There is no good on earth; and sin is but a name. Come, devil; for to thee is this world given."

And, maddened with despair, so that he laughed loud and long, did

Goodman Brown grasp his staff and set forth again, at such a rate that he seemed to fly along the forest path rather than to walk or run. The road grew wilder and drearier and more faintly traced, and vanished at length, leaving him in the heart of the dark wilderness, still rushing onward with the instinct that guides mortal man to evil. The whole forest was peopled with frightful sounds — the creaking of the trees, the howling of wild beasts, and the yell of Indians; while sometimes the wind tolled like a distant church bell, and sometimes gave a broad roar around the traveller, as if all Nature were laughing him to scorn. But he was himself the chief horror of the scene, and shrank not from its other horrors.

"Ha! ha! ha!" roared Goodman Brown when the wind laughed at him. "Let us hear which will laugh loudest. Think not to frighten me with your deviltry. Come witch, come wizard, come Indian powwow, come devil himself, and here comes Goodman Brown. You may as well fear him as he fear you."

In truth, all through the haunted forest there could be nothing more frightful than the figure of Goodman Brown. On he flew among the black pines, brandishing his staff with frenzied gestures, now giving vent to an inspiration of horrid blasphemy, and now shouting forth such laughter as set all the echoes of the forest laughing like demons around him. The fiend in his own shape is less hideous than when he rages in the breast of man. Thus sped the demoniac on his course, until, quivering among the trees, he saw a red light before him, as when the felled trunks and branches of a clearing have been set on fire, and throw up their lurid blaze against the sky, at the hour of midnight. He paused, in a lull of the tempest that had driven him onward, and heard the swell of what seemed a hymn, rolling solemnly from a distance with the weight of many voices. He knew the tune; it was a familiar one in the choir of the village meeting-house. The verse died heavily away, and was lengthened by a chorus, not of human voices, but of all the sounds of the benighted wilderness pealing in awful harmony together. Goodman Brown cried out, and his cry was lost to his own ear by its unison with the cry of the desert.

In the interval of silence he stole forward until the light glared full upon his eyes. At one extremity of an open space, hemmed in by the dark wall of the forest, arose a rock, bearing some rude, natural resemblance either to an alter or a pulpit, and surrounded by four blazing pines, their tops aflame, their stems untouched, like candles at an evening meeting. The mass of foliage that had overgrown the summit of the rock was all on fire, blazing high into the night and fitfully illuminating the whole field. Each pendent twig and leafy festoon was in a blaze. As the red light arose and fell, a numerous congregation alternately shone forth, then disappeared in shadow, and again grew, as it were, out of the darkness, peopling the heart of the solitary woods at once.

"A grave and dark-clad company," quoth Goodman Brown.

In truth they were such. Among them, quivering to and fro between gloom and splendor, appeared faces that would be seen next day at the council board of the province, and others which, Sabbath after Sabbath, looked devoutly heavenward, and benignantly over the crowded pews, from the holiest pulpits in the land. Some affirm that the lady of the governor was there. At least there were high dames well known to her, and wives of honored husbands, and widows, a great multitude, and ancient maidens, all of excellent repute, and fair young girls, who trembled lest their mothers should espy them. Either the sudden gleams of light flashing over the obscure field bedazzled Goodman Brown, or he recognized a score of the church members of Salem village famous for their especial sanctity. Good old Deacon Gookin had arrived, and waited at the skirts of that venerable saint, his revered pastor. But, irreverently consorting with these grave, reputable, and pious people, these elders of the church, these chaste dames and dewy virgins, there were men of dissolute lives and women of spotted fame, wretches given over to all mean and filthy vice, and suspected even of horrid crimes. It was strange to see that the good shrank not from the wicked, nor were the sinners abashed by the saints. Scattered also among their pale-faced enemies were the Indian priests, or powwows, who had often scared their native forest with more hideous incantations than any known to English witchcraft.

"But where is Faith?" thought Goodman Brown; and, as hope came into his heart, he trembled.

Another verse of the hymn arose, a slow and mournful strain, such as the pious love, but joined to words which expressed all that our nature can conceive of sin, and darkly hinted at far more. Unfathomable to mere mortals is the lore of fiends. Verse after verse was sung; and still the chorus of the desert swelled between like the deepest tone of a mighty organ; and with the final peal of that dreadful anthem there came a sound, as if the roaring wind, the rushing streams, the howling beasts, and every other voice of the uncon-certed wilderness were mingling and according with the voice of guilty man in homage to the prince of all. The four blazing pines threw up a loftier flame, and obscurely discovered shapes and visages of horror on the smoke wreaths above the impious assembly. At the same moment the fire on the rock shot redly forth and formed a flowing arch above its base, where now appeared a figure. With reverence be it spoken, the figure bore no slight similitude, both in garb and manner, to some grave divine of the New England churches.

"Bring forth the converts!" cried a voice that echoed through the field and rolled into the forest.

At the word, Goodman Brown stepped forth from the shadow of the trees and approached the congregation, with whom he felt a loathful broth-erhood by the sympathy of all that was wicked in his heart. He could have well-nigh sworn that the shape of his own dead father beckoned him to advance, looking downward from a smoke wreath, while a woman, with dim features of despair, threw out her hand to warn him back. Was it his mother? But he had no power to retreat one step, nor to resist, even in thought, when the minister and good old Deacon Gookin seized his arms and led him to the blazing rock. Thither came also the slender form of a veiled female, led between Goody Cloyse, that pious teacher of the catechism, and Martha

Carrier, who had received the devil's promise to be queen of hell. A rampant hag was she. And there stood the proselytes beneath the canopy of fire.

"Welcome, my children," said the dark figure, "to the communion of your race. Ye have found thus young your nature and your destiny. My children, look behind you!"

They turned; and flashing forth, as it were, in a sheet of flame, the fiend worshippers were seen; the smile of welcome gleamed darkly on every visage.

"There," resumed the sable form, "are all whom ye have reverenced from youth. Ye deemed them holier than yourselves and shrank from your own sin, contrasting it with their lives of righteousness and prayerful aspirations heavenward. Yet here are they all in my worshipping assembly. This night it shall be granted you to know their secret deeds: how hoary-bearded elders of the church have whispered wanton words to the young maids of their households; how many a woman, eager for widows' weeds, has given her husband a drink at bedtime and let him sleep his last sleep in her bosom; how beardless youths have made haste to inherit their fathers' wealth; and how fair damsels — blush not, sweet ones — have dug little graves in the garden, and bidden me, the sole guest, to an infant's funeral. By the sympathy of your human hearts for sin ye shall scent out all the places — whether in church, bedchamber, street, field, or forest — where crime has been committed, and shall exult to behold the whole earth one stain of guilt, one mighty blood spot. Far more than this. It shall be yours to penetrate, in every bosom, the deep mystery of sin, the fountain of all wicked arts, and which inexhaustibly supplies more evil impulses than human power — than my power at its utmost — can make manifest in deeds. And now, my children, look upon each other."

They did so; and, by the blaze of the hell-kindled torches, the wretched man beheld his Faith, and the wife her husband, trembling before that unhallowed altar.

"Lo, there ye stand, my children," said the figure, in a deep and solemn tone, almost sad with its despairing awfulness, as if his once angelic nature could yet mourn for our miserable race. "Depending upon one another's hearts, ye had still hoped that virtue were not all a dream. Now are ye undeceived. Evil is the nature of mankind. Evil must be your only happiness. Welcome again, my children, to the communion of your race."

"Welcome," repeated the fiend worshippers, in one cry of despair and triumph.

And there they stood, the only pair, as it seemed, who were yet hesitating on the verge of wickedness in this dark world. A basin was hallowed, naturally, in the rock. Did it contain water, reddened by the lurid light? or was it blood? or, perchance, a liquid flame? Herein did the shape of evil dip his hand and prepare to lay the mark of baptism upon their foreheads, that they might be partakers of the mystery of sin, more conscious of the secret guilt of others, both in deed and thought, than they could now be of their own. The husband cast one look at his pale wife, and Faith at him. What polluted wretches would the next glance show them to each other, shuddering alike at what they disclosed and what they saw!

"Faith! Faith!" cried the husband, "look up to heaven, and resist the wicked one."

Whether Faith obeyed he knew not. Hardly had he spoken when he found himself amid calm night and solitude, listening to a roar of the wind which died heavily away through the forest. He staggered against the rock, and felt it chill and damp; while a hanging twig, that had been all on fire, besprinkled his cheek with the coldest dew.

The next morning young Goodman Brown came slowly into the street of Salem village, staring around him like a bewildered man. The good old minister was taking a walk along the graveyard to get an appetite for breakfast and meditate his sermon, and bestowed a blessing, as he passed, on Goodman Brown. He shrank from the venerable saint as if to avoid an anathema. Old Deacon Gookin was at domestic worship, and the holy words of his prayer were heard through the open window. "What God doth the wizard pray to?" quoth Goodman Brown. Goody Cloyse, that excellent old Christian, stood in the early sunshine at her own lattice, catechizing a little girl who had brought her a pint of morning's milk. Goodman Brown snatched away the child as from the grasp of the fiend himself. Turning the corner by the meeting-house, he spied the head of Faith, with the pink ribbons, gazing anxiously forth, and bursting into such joy at sight of him that she skipped along the street and almost kissed her husband before the whole village. But Goodman Brown looked sternly and sadly into her face, and passed on without a greeting.

Had Goodman Brown fallen asleep in the forest and only dreamed a wild dream of a witch-meeting?

Be it so if you will; but, alas! it was a dream of evil omen for young Goodman Brown. A stern, a sad, a darkly meditative, a distrustful, if not a desperate man did he become from the night of that fearful dream. On the Sabbath day, when the congregation were singing a holy psalm, he could not listen because an anthem of sin rushed loudly upon his ear and drowned all the blessed strain. When the minister spoke from the pulpit with power and fervid eloquence, and, with his hand on the open Bible, of the sacred truths of our religion, and of saint-like lives and triumphant deaths, and of future bliss or misery unutterable, then did Goodman Brown turn pale, dreading lest the roof should thunder down upon the gray blasphemer and his hearers. Often, awaking suddenly at midnight, he shrank from the bosom of Faith; and at morning or eventide, when the family knelt down at prayer, he scowled and muttered to himself, and gazed sternly at his wife, and turned away. And when he had lived long, and was borne to his grave a hoary corpse, followed by Faith, an aged woman, and children and grandchildren, a goodly procession, besides neighbors not a few, they carved no hopeful verse upon his tombstone, for his dying hour was gloom. [1835]

BESSIE HEAD *(1937–1986) was born in Pietermaritzburg, South Africa, the daughter of a white mother and a black father. Raised by foster parents, she was placed in a mission orphanage at the age of thirteen. A lonely child, she was comforted by reading, which invited her into what she called "a world of magic beyond your own." In her early twenties she taught in an elementary school and wrote stories for a local newspaper. After her marriage in 1961, she left South Africa, seeking political refuge from apartheid on an agricultural commune in Serowe in Botswana.*

The journalist Betty Fradkin described Head's life as a refugee: "There is no electricity yet. At night Bessie types by the light of six candles. Fruit trees and vegetables surround the house. Bessie makes guava jam to sell, and will sell vegetables when the garden is enlarged." Despite the devastating experiences of racial oppression, and the dislocation and economic hardship of exile, Head found the peace of mind necessary to create her works of fiction: "In South Africa, all my life I lived in shattered little bits. All those shattered bits began to grow together here. . . . I have a peace against which all the turmoil is worked out." In 1969 she published her first novel, When Rain Clouds Gather. *Two other novels followed, along with a collection of related stories titled* The Collector of Treasures and Other Botswana Village Tales *(1977) and a history of her village,* Serowe: Village of the Rain Wind *(1981). Her last novel,* A Bewitched Crossroad *(1984), is a chronicle combining history and folklore. Two years later, Head died of hepatitis while working on her autobiography.*

Highly sensitive to the enduring power of ritual and tradition in contemporary African life, Head was also concerned with the often precarious role of women in the patriarchal systems of African tribal society. "Life" dramatizes the conflict between traditional and contemporary codes of behavior in the villages and cities she had known.

BESSIE HEAD

Life

In 1963, when the borders were first set up between Botswana and South Africa, pending Botswana's independence in 1966, all Botswana-born citizens had to return home. Everything had been mingled up in the old colonial days, and the traffic of people to and fro between the two countries had been a steady flow for years and years. More often, especially if they were migrant labourers working in the mines, their period of settlement was brief, but many people had settled there in permanent employment. It was these settlers who were disrupted and sent back to village life in a mainly rural country. On their return they brought with them bits and pieces of a foreign culture and city habits which they had absorbed. Village people reacted in their own way; what they liked, and was beneficial to them, they absorbed — for instance, the faith-healing cult churches which instantly took hold like wildfire; what was harmful to them, they rejected. The murder of Life had this complicated undertone of rejection.

Life had left the village as a little girl of ten years old with her parents for Johannesburg. They had died in the meanwhile, and on Life's return, seventeen years later, she found, as was village custom, that she still had a home in the village. On mentioning that her name was Life Morapedi, the villagers immediately and obligingly took her to the Morapedi yard in the central part of the village. The family yard had remained intact, just as they had left it, except that it looked pathetic in its desolation. The thatch of the mud huts had patches of soil over them where the ants had made their nests; the wooden poles that supported the rafters of the huts had tilted to an angle as their base had been eaten through by the ants. The rubber hedge had grown to a disproportionate size and enclosed the yard in a gloom of shadows that kept out the sunlight. Weeds and grass of many seasonal rains entangled themselves in the yard.

Life's future neighbours, a group of women, continued to stand near her.

"We can help you to put your yard in order," they said kindly. "We are very happy that a child of ours has returned home."

They were impressed with the smartness of this city girl. They generally wore old clothes and kept their very best things for special occasions like weddings, and even then those best things might just be ordinary cotton prints. The girl wore an expensive cream costume of linen material, tailored to fit her tall, full figure. She had a bright, vivacious, friendly manner and laughed freely and loudly. Her speech was rapid and a little hysterical but that was in keeping with her whole personality.

"She is going to bring us a little light," the women said among themselves, as they went off to fetch their work tools. They were always looking "for the light" and by that they meant that they were ever alert to receive new ideas that would freshen up the ordinariness and everydayness of village life.

A woman who lived near the Morapedi yard had offered Life hospitality until her own yard was set in order. She picked up the shining new suitcases and preceded Life to her own home, where Life was immediately surrounded with all kinds of endearing attentions — a low stool was placed in a shady place for her to sit on; a little girl came shyly forward with a bowl of water for her to wash her hands; and following on this, a tray with a bowl of meat and porridge was set before her so that she could revive herself after her long journey home. The other women briskly entered her yard with hoes to scratch out the weeds and grass, baskets of earth and buckets of water to re-smear the mud walls, and they had found two idle men to rectify the precarious tilt of the wooden poles of the mud hut. These were the sort of gestures people always offered, but they were pleased to note that the newcomer seemed to have an endless stream of money which she flung around generously. The work party in her yard would suggest that the meat of a goat, slowly simmering in a great iron pot, would help the work to move with a swing, and

Life would immediately produce the money to purchase the goat and also tea, milk, sugar, pots of porridge, or anything the workers expressed a preference for, so that those two weeks of making Life's yard beautiful for her seemed like one long wedding-feast; people usually only ate that much at weddings.

"How is it you have so much money, our child?" one of the women at last asked, curiously.

"Money flows like water in Johannesburg," Life replied, with her gay and hysterical laugh. "You just have to know how to get it."

The women received this with caution. They said among themselves that their child could not have lived a very good life in Johannesburg. Thrift and honesty were the dominant themes of village life and everyone knew that one could not be honest and rich at the same time; they counted every penny and knew how they had acquired it — with hard work. They never imagined money as a bottomless pit without end; it always had an end and was hard to come by in this dry, semi-desert land. They predicted that she would soon settle down — intelligent girls got jobs in the post office sooner or later.

Life had had the sort of varied career that a city like Johannesburg offered a lot of black women. She had been a singer, beauty queen, advertising model, and prostitute. None of these careers were available in the village — for the illiterate women there was farming and housework; for the literate, teaching, nursing, and clerical work. The first wave of women Life attracted to herself were the farmers and housewives. They were the intensely conservative hard-core centre of village life. It did not take them long to shun her completely because men started turning up in an unending stream. What caused a stir of amazement was that Life was the first and the only woman in the village to make a business out of selling herself. The men were paying her for her services. People's attitude to sex was broad and generous — it was recognized as a necessary part of human life, that it ought to be available whenever possible like food and water, or else one's life would be extinguished or one would get dreadfully ill. To prevent these catastrophes from happening, men and women generally had quite a lot of sex but on a respectable and human level, with financial considerations coming in as an afterthought. When the news spread around that this had now become a business in Life's yard, she attracted to herself a second wave of women — the beer-brewers of the village.

The beer-brewing women were a gay and lovable crowd who had emancipated themselves some time ago. They were drunk every day and could be seen staggering around the village, usually with a wide-eyed, illegitimate baby hitched on to their hips. They also talked and laughed loudly and slapped each other on the back and had developed a language all their own:

"Boyfriends, yes. Husbands, uh, uh, no. Do this! Do that! We want to rule ourselves."

But they too were subject to the respectable order of village life. Many men passed through their lives but they were all for a time steady boyfriends. The usual arrangement was:

"Mother, you help me and I'll help you."

This was just so much eye-wash. The men hung around, lived on the resources of the women, and during all this time they would part with about two rand of their own money. After about three months a tally-up would be made:

"Boyfriend," the woman would say, "love is love and money is money. You owe me money." And he'd never be seen again, but another scoundrel would take his place. And so the story went on and on. They found their queen in Life and like all queens, they set her activities apart from themselves; they never attempted to extract money from the constant stream of men because they did not know how, but they liked her yard. Very soon the din and riot of a Johannesburg township was duplicated, on a minor scale, in the central part of the village. A transistor radio blared the day long. Men and women reeled around drunk and laughing and food and drink flowed like milk and honey. The people of the surrounding village watched this phenomenon with pursed lips and commented darkly:

"They'll all be destroyed one day like Sodom and Gomorrah."

Life, like the beer-brewing women, had a language of her own too. When her friends expressed surprise at the huge quantities of steak, eggs, liver, kidneys, and rice they ate in her yard — the sort of food they too could now and then afford but would not dream of purchasing — she replied in a carefree, off-hand way: "I'm used to handling big money." They did not believe it; they were too solid to trust to this kind of luck which had such shaky foundations, and as though to offset some doom that might be just around the corner they often brought along their own scraggy, village chickens reared in their yards, as offerings for the day's round of meals. And one of Life's philosophies on life, which they were to recall with trembling a few months later, was: "My motto is: live fast, die young, and have a good-looking corpse." All this was said with the bold, free joy of a woman who had broken all the social taboos. They never followed her to those dizzy heights.

A few months after Life's arrival in the village, the first hotel with its pub opened. It was initially shunned by all the women and even the beer-brewers considered they hadn't fallen *that* low yet — the pub was also associated with the idea of selling oneself. It became Life's favourite business venue. It simplified the business of making appointments for the following day. None of the men questioned their behaviour, nor how such an unnatural situation had been allowed to develop — they could get all the sex they needed for free in the village, but it seemed to fascinate them that they should pay for it for the first time. They had quickly got to the stage where they communicated with Life in short-hand language:

"When?" And she would reply: "Ten o'clock." "When?" "Two o'clock." "When?" "Four o'clock," and so on.

And there would be the roar of cheap small talk and much buttock slapping. It was her element and her feverish, glittering, brilliant black eyes swept around the bar, looking for everything and nothing at the same time.

Then one evening death walked quietly into the bar. It was Lesego, the cattle-man, just come in from his cattle-post, where he had been occupied for a period of three months. Men built up their own, individual reputations in the village and Lesego's was one of the most respected and honoured. People said of him: "When Lesego has got money and you need it, he will give you what he has got and he won't trouble you about the date of payment . . ." He was honoured for another reason also — for the clarity and quiet indifference of his thinking. People often found difficulty in sorting out issues or the truth in any debatable matter. He had a way of keeping his head above water, listening to an argument and always pronouncing the final judgement: "Well, the truth about this matter is . . ." He was also one of the most successful cattle-men with a balance of seven thousand rand in the bank, and whenever he came into the village he lounged around and gossiped or attended village kgotla[1] meetings, so that people had a saying: "Well, I must be getting about my business. I'm not like Lesego with money in the bank."

As usual, the brilliant radar eyes swept feverishly around the bar. They did the rounds twice that evening in the same manner, each time coming to a dead stop for a full second on the thin, dark, concentrated expression of Lesego's face. There wasn't any other man in the bar with that expression; they all had sheepish, inane-looking faces. He was the nearest thing she had seen for a long time to the Johannesburg gangsters she had associated with — the same small, economical gestures, the same power and control. All the men near him quietened down and began to consult with him in low earnest voices; they were talking about the news of the day which never reached the remote cattle-posts. Whereas all the other men had to approach her, the third time her radar eyes swept round he stood his ground, turned his head slowly, and then jerked it back slightly in a silent command:

"Come here."

She moved immediately to his end of the bar.

"Hullo," he said, in an astonishingly tender voice and a smile flickered across his dark, reserved face. That was the sum total of Lesego, that basically he was a kind and tender man, that he liked women and had been so successful in that sphere that he took his dominance and success for granted. But they looked at each other from their own worlds and came to fatal conclusions — she saw in him the power and maleness of the gangsters; he saw the freshness and surprise of an entirely new kind of woman. He had left all his women after a time because they bored him, and like all people who live an ordinary humdrum life, he was attracted to that undertone of hysteria in her.

Very soon they stood up and walked out together. A shocked silence fell upon the bar. The men exchanged looks with each other and the way these things communicate themselves, they knew that all the other appointments had been cancelled while Lesego was there. And as though speaking their thoughts aloud, Sianana, one of Lesego's friends, commented, "Lesego just wants to try it out like we all did because it is something new. He won't stay there when he finds out that it is rotten to the core."

[1] Tribal court.

But Sianana was to find out that he did not fully understand his friend. Lesego was not seen at his usual lounging-places for a week and when he emerged again it was to announce that he was to marry. The news was received with cold hostility. Everyone talked of nothing else; it was as impossible as if a crime was being committed before their very eyes. Sianana once more made himself the spokesman. He waylaid Lesego on his way to the village kgotla:

"I am much surprised by the rumours about you, Lesego," he said bluntly. "You can't marry that woman. She's a terrible fuck-about!"

Lesego stared back at him steadily, then he said in his quiet, indifferent way, "Who isn't here?"

Sianana shrugged his shoulders. The subtleties were beyond him; but whatever else was going on it wasn't commercial, it was human, but did that make it any better? Lesego liked to bugger up an argument like that with a straightforward point. As they walked along together Sianana shook his head several times to indicate that something important was eluding him, until at last, with a smile, Lesego said, "She has told me all about her bad ways. They are over."

Sianana merely compressed his lips and remained silent.

Life made the announcement too, after she was married, to all her beer-brewing friends: "All my old ways are over," she said. "I have now become a woman."

She still looked happy and hysterical. Everything came to her too easily, men, money, and now marriage. The beer-brewers were not slow to point out to her with the same amazement with which they had exclaimed over the steak and eggs, that there were many women in the village who had cried their eyes out over Lesego. She was very flattered.

Their lives, at least Lesego's, did not change much with marriage. He still liked lounging around the village; the rainy season had come and life was easy for the cattle-men at this time because there was enough water and grazing for the animals. He wasn't the kind of man to fuss about the house and during this time he only made three pronouncements about the household. He took control of all the money. She had to ask him for it and state what it was to be used for. Then he didn't like the transistor radio blaring the whole day long.

"Women who keep that thing going the whole day have nothing in their heads," he said.

Then he looked down at her from a great height and commented finally and quietly: "If you go with those men again, I'll kill you."

This was said so indifferently and quietly, as though he never really expected his authority and dominance to encounter any challenge.

She hadn't the mental equipment to analyse what had hit her, but something seemed to strike her a terrible blow behind the head. She instantly succumbed to the blow and rapidly began to fall apart. On the surface, the everyday round of village life was deadly dull in its even, unbroken monotony; one day slipped easily into another, drawing water, stamping corn, cooking food. But within this there were enormous tugs and pulls between people. Custom demanded that people care about each other, and all day long there was this constant traffic of people in and out of each other's lives. Someone had to be buried; sympathy and help were demanded for this event — there were money loans, new-born babies, sorrow, trouble, gifts. Lesego had long been the king of this world; there was, every day, a long string of people, wanting something or wanting to give him something in gratitude for a past favour. It was the basic strength of village life. It created people whose sympathetic and emotional responses were always fully awakened, and it rewarded them by richly filling in a void that was one big, gaping yawn. When the hysteria and cheap rowdiness were taken away, Life fell into the yawn; she had nothing inside herself to cope with this way of life that had finally caught up with her. The beer-brewing women were still there; they still liked her yard because Lesego was casual and easy-going and all that went on in it now — like the old men squatting in corners with gifts: "Lesego, I had good luck with my hunting today. I caught two rabbits and I want to share one with you . . ." — was simply the Tswana way of life they too lived. In keeping with their queen's new status, they said:

"We are women and must do something."

They collected earth and dung and smeared and decorated Life's court-yard. They drew water for her, stamped her corn, and things looked quite ordinary on the surface because Lesego also liked a pot of beer. No one noticed the expression of anguish that had crept into Life's face. The boredom of the daily round was almost throttling her to death and no matter which way she looked, from the beer-brewers to her husband to all the people who called, she found no one with whom she could communicate what had become an actual physical pain. After a month of it, she was near collapse. One morning she mentioned her agony to the beer-brewers: "I think I have made a mistake. Married life doesn't suit me."

And they replied sympathetically, "You are just getting used to it. After all it's a different life in Johannesburg."

The neighbours went further. They were impressed by a marriage they thought could never succeed. They started saying that one never ought to judge a human being who was both good and bad, and Lesego had turned a bad woman into a good woman which was something they had never seen before. Just as they were saying this and nodding their approval, Sodom and Gomorrah started up all over again. Lesego had received word late in the evening that the new-born calves at his cattle-post were dying, and early the next morning he was off again in his truck.

The old, reckless wild woman awakened from a state near death with a huge sigh of relief. The transistor blared, the food flowed again, the men and women reeled around dead drunk. Simply by their din they beat off all the unwanted guests who nodded their heads grimly. When Lesego came back they were going to tell him this was no wife for him.

Three days later Lesego unexpectedly was back in the village. The calves were all anaemic and they had to be brought in to the vet for an injection. He drove his truck straight through the village to the vet's camp. One of the beer-brewers saw him and hurried in alarm to her friend.

"The husband is back," she whispered fearfully, pulling Life to one side.
"Agh," she replied irritably.

She did dispel the noise, the men, and the drink, but a wild anger was driving her to break out of a way of life that was like death to her. She told one of the men she'd see him at six o'clock. At about five o'clock Lesego drove into the yard with the calves. There was no one immediately around to greet him. He jumped out of the truck and walked to one of the huts, pushing open the door. Life was sitting on the bed. She looked up silently and sullenly. He was a little surprised but his mind was still distracted by the calves. He had to settle them in the yard for the night.

"Will you make some tea," he said. "I'm very thirsty."

"There's no sugar in the house," she said. "I'll have to get some."

Something irritated him but he hurried back to the calves and his wife walked out of the yard. Lesego had just settled the calves when a neighbour walked in, he was very angry.

"Lesego," he said bluntly, "we told you not to marry that woman. If you go to the yard of Radithobolo now you'll find her in bed with him. Go and see for yourself that you may leave that bad woman!"

Lesego stared quietly at him for a moment, then at his own pace as though there were no haste or chaos in his life, he went to the hut they used as a kitchen. A tin full of sugar stood there. He turned and found a knife in the corner, one of the large ones he used for slaughtering cattle, and slipped it into his shirt. Then at his own pace he walked to the yard of Radithobolo. It looked deserted, except that the door of one of the huts was partially open and one closed. He kicked open the door of the closed hut and the man within shouted out in alarm. On seeing Lesego he sprang cowering into a corner. Lesego jerked his head back indicating that the man should leave the room. But Radithobolo did not run far. He wanted to enjoy himself so he pressed himself into the shadows of the rubber hedge. He expected the usual husband-and-wife scene — the irate husband cursing at the top of his voice; the wife, hysterical in her lies and self-defence. Only Lesego walked out of the yard and he held in his hand a huge, blood-stained knife. On seeing the knife Radithobolo immediately fell to the ground in a dead faint. There were a few people on the footpath and they shrank into the rubber hedge at the sight of that knife.

Very soon a wail arose. People clutched at their heads and began running in all directions crying yo! yo! yo! in their shock. It was some time before anyone thought of calling the police. They were so disordered because murder, outright and violent, was a most uncommon and rare occurrence in village life. It seemed that only Lesego kept cool that evening. He was sitting quietly in his yard when the whole police force came tearing in. They looked at him in horror and began to thoroughly upbraid him for looking so unperturbed.

"You have taken a human life and you are cool like that!" they said angrily. "You are going to hang by the neck for this. It's a serious crime to take a human life."

He did not hang by the neck. He kept that cool, head-above-water indifferent look, right up to the day of his trial. Then he looked up at the judge and said calmly, "Well, the truth about this matter is, I had just returned from the cattle-post. I had had trouble with my calves that day. I came home late and being thirsty, asked my wife to make me tea. She said there was no sugar in the house and left to buy some. My neighbour, Mathata, came in after this and said that my wife was not at the shops but in the yard of Radithobolo. He said I ought to go and see what she was doing in the yard of Radithobolo. I thought I would check up about the sugar first and in the kitchen I found a tin full of it. I was sorry and surprised to see this. Then a fire seemed to fill my heart. I thought that if she was doing a bad thing with Radithobolo as Mathata said, I'd better kill her because I cannot understand a wife who could be so corrupt . . ."

Lesego had been doing this for years, passing judgement on all aspects of life in his straightforward, uncomplicated way. The judge, who was a white man, and therefore not involved in Tswana custom and its debates, was as much impressed by Lesego's manner as all the village men had been.

"This is a crime of passion," he said sympathetically, "so there are extenuating circumstances. But it is still a serious crime to take a human life so I sentence you to five years' imprisonment . . ."

Lesego's friend, Sianana, who was to take care of his business affairs while he was in jail, came to visit Lesego still shaking his head. Something was eluding him about the whole business, as though it had been planned from the very beginning.

"Lesego," he said, with deep sorrow, "why did you kill that fuck-about? You had legs to walk away. You could have walked away. Are you trying to show us that rivers never cross here? There are good women and good men but they seldom join their lives together. It's always this mess and foolishness . . ."

A song by Jim Reeves was very popular at that time: *That's What Happens When Two Worlds Collide*. When they were drunk, the beer-brewing women used to sing it and start weeping. Maybe they had the last word on the whole affair. [1977]

ERNEST HEMINGWAY *(1898–1961) was born in Oak Park, Illinois, but he spent most of his boyhood in Michigan, where his father, a doctor, encouraged his enthusiasm for camping and hunting. Active as a reporter for his high school news-paper, Hemingway decided not to go on to college. Instead he worked as a reporter on the* Kansas City Star *for a few months before volunteering to serve in an American ambulance unit in France during World War I. Then he went to Italy, served at the front, and was severely wounded in action just before his nineteenth birthday. After the war he was too restless to settle down in the United States, so he lived in Paris and supported himself and his wife as a newspaper correspondent. He worked hard at learning how to write fiction; as he later said, "I found the greatest difficulty, aside from knowing what you really felt, rather than what you were supposed to feel, or had been taught to feel, was to put down what really happened in action: what the actual things were which produced the emotion that you experienced."*

In America Hemingway had admired the work of Sherwood Anderson, espe-cially the colloquial, "unliterary" tone of his stories, and in Paris he came under the influence of Gertrude Stein, telling Anderson in a letter of 1922 that "Gertrude Stein and me are just like brothers." As the critic A. Walton Litz and many others have recognized, Hemingway was receptive to several diverse influences as a young writer forging his literary style. He was also aware of the work of the experimental poet Ezra Pound, whose advice in essays written in 1913 on the composition of Imagist poetry is suggested in the style developed in Hemingway's early fiction:

1. *Direct treatment of the "thing," without evasion or cliché.*
2. *The use of absolutely no word that does not contribute to the general design.*
3. *Fidelity to the rhythms of natural speech.*
4. *The natural object is always the adequate symbol.*

Hemingway's first book, In Our Time *(1925), is a collection of stories and sketches. His early novels,* The Sun Also Rises *(1926) and* A Farewell to Arms *(1929), established him as a master stylist, probably the most influential writer of English prose in the first half of the twentieth century. In 1938 he collected what he considered his best short fiction, forty-nine stories. After publication of* The Old Man and the Sea, *he was awarded the Nobel Prize for Literature in 1954. Seven years later, in poor health and haunted by the memory of the suicide of his father, who had shot himself with a Civil War pistol in 1929, Hemingway killed himself with a shotgun in his Idaho hunting lodge.*

Hemingway's concise way of developing a plot through dialogue, as in "Hills Like White Elephants," attracted many imitators. He once explained how he achieved an intense compression by comparing his method to the principle of the iceberg: "There is seven-eighths of it under water for every part that shows. Anything you know you can eliminate and it only strengthens your iceberg. It is the part that doesn't show. If a writer omits something because he does not know it then there is a hole in the story." The most authoritative collection of Hemingway's stories, The Complete Short Stories of Ernest Hemingway: The Finca-Vigia Edition, *was published in 1991.*

ERNEST HEMINGWAY

Hills Like White Elephants

The hills across the valley of the Ebro were long and white. On this side there was no shade and no trees and the station was between two lines of rails in the sun. Close against the side of the station there was the warm shadow of the building and a curtain, made of strings of bamboo beads, hung across the open door into the bar, to keep out flies. The American and the girl with him sat at a table in the shade, outside the building. It was very hot and the express from Barcelona would come in forty minutes. It stopped at this junction for two minutes and went on to Madrid.

"What should we drink?" the girl asked. She had taken off her hat and put it on the table.

"It's pretty hot," the man said.

"Let's drink beer."

"*Dos cervezas,*" the man said into the curtain.

"Big ones?" a woman asked from the doorway.

"Yes. Two big ones."

The woman brought two glasses of beer and two felt pads. She put the felt pads and the beer glasses on the table and looked at the man and the girl. The girl was looking off at the line of hills. They were white in the sun and the country was brown and dry.

"They look like white elephants," she said.

"I've never seen one," the man drank his beer.

"No, you wouldn't have."

"I might have," the man said. "Just because you say I wouldn't have doesn't prove anything."

The girl looked at the bead curtain. "They've painted something on it," she said. "What does it say?"

"Anis del Toro. It's a drink,"

"Could we try it?"

The man called "Listen" through the curtain. The woman came out from the bar.

"Four reales."

"We want two Anis del Toro."

"With water?"

"Do you want it with water?"

"I don't know," the girl said. "Is it good with water?"

"It's all right."

"You want them with water?" asked the woman.

"Yes, with water."

"It tastes like licorice," the girl said and put the glass down.

"That's the way with everything."

"Yes," said the girl. "Everything tastes of licorice. Especially all the things you've waited so long for, like absinthe."

"Oh, cut it out."

"You started it," the girl said. "I was being amused. I was having a fine time."

"Well, let's try and have a fine time."

"All right. I was trying. I said the mountains looked like white elephants. Wasn't that bright?"

"That was bright."

"I wanted to try this new drink: That's all we do, isn't it — look at things and try new drinks?"

"I guess so."

The girl looked across at the hills.

"They're lovely hills," she said. "They don't really look like white elephants. I just meant the coloring of their skin through the trees."

"Should we have another drink?"

"All right."

The warm wind blew the bead curtain against the table.

"The beer's nice and cool," the man said.

"It's lovely," the girl said.

"It's really an awfully simple operation, Jig," the man said. "It's not really an operation at all."

The girl looked at the ground the table legs rested on.

"I know you wouldn't mind it, Jig. It's really not anything. It's just to let the air in."

The girl did not say anything.

"I'll go with you and I'll stay with you all the time. They just let the air in and then it's all perfectly natural."

"Then what will we do afterward?"

"We'll be fine afterward. Just like we were before."

"What makes you think so?"

"That's the only thing that bothers us. It's the only thing that's made us unhappy."

The girl looked at the bead curtain, put her hand out, and took hold of two of the strings of beads.

"And you think then we'll be all right and be happy."

"I know we will. You don't have to be afraid. I've known lots of people that have done it."

"So have I," said the girl. "And afterward they were all so happy."

"Well," the man said, "if you don't want to you don't have to. I wouldn't have you do it if you didn't want to. But I know it's perfectly simple."

"And you really want to?"

"I think it's the best thing to do. But I don't want you to do it if you don't really want to."

"And if I do it you'll be happy and things will be like they were and you'll love me?"

"I love you now. You know I love you."

"I know. But if I do it, then it will be nice again if I say things are like white elephants, and you'll like it?"

"I'll love it. I love it now but I just can't think about it. You know how I get when I worry."

"If I do it you won't ever worry?"

"I won't worry about that because it's perfectly simple."

"Then I'll do it. Because I don't care about me."

"What do you mean?"

"I don't care about me."

"Well, I care about you."

"Oh, yes. But I don't care about me. And I'll do it and then everything will be fine."

"I don't want you to do it if you feel that way."

The girl stood up and walked to the end of the station. Across, on the other side, were fields of grain and trees along the banks of the Ebro. Far away, beyond the river, were mountains. The shadow of a cloud moved across the field of grain and she saw the river through the trees.

"And we could have all this," she said. "And we could have everything and every day we make it more impossible."

"What did you say?"

"I said we could have everything."

"We can have everything."

"No, we can't."

"We can have the whole world."

"No, we can't."

"We can go everywhere."

"No, we can't. It isn't ours any more."

"It's ours."

"No, it isn't. And once they take it away, you never get it back."

"But they haven't taken it away."

"We'll wait and see."

"Come on back in the shade," he said. "You mustn't feel that way."

"I don't feel any way," the girl said. "I just know things."

"I don't want you to do anything that you don't want to do ——"

"Nor that isn't good for me," she said. "I know. Could we have another beer?"

"All right. But you've got to realize ——"

"I realize," the girl said. "Can't we maybe stop talking?"

They sat down at the table and the girl looked across at the hills on the dry side of the valley and the man looked at her and at the table.

"You've got to realize," he said, "that I don't want you to do it if you don't want to. I'm perfectly willing to go through with it if it means anything to you."

"Doesn't it mean anything to you? We could get along."

"Of course it does. But I don't want anybody but you. I don't want any one else. And I know it's perfectly simple."

"Yes, you know it's perfectly simple."

"It's all right for you to say that, but I do know it."

"Would you do something for me now?"

"I'd do anything for you."

"Would you please please please please please please please stop talking?"

He did not say anything but looked at the bags against the wall of the station. There were labels on them from all the hotels where they had spent nights.

"But I don't want you to," he said, "I don't care anything about it."

"I'll scream," the girl said.

The woman came out through the curtains with two glasses of beer and put them down on the damp felt pads. "The train comes in five minutes," she said.

"What did she say?" asked the girl.

"That the train is coming in five minutes."

The girl smiled brightly at the woman, to thank her.

"I'd better take the bags over to the other side of the station," the man said. She smiled at him.

"All right. Then come back and we'll finish the beer."

He picked up the two heavy bags and carried them around the station to the other tracks. He looked up the tracks but could not see the train. Coming back, he walked through the barroom, where people waiting for the train were drinking. He drank an Anis at the bar and looked at the people. They were all waiting reasonably for the train. He went out through the bead curtain. She was sitting at the table and smiled at him.

"Do you feel better?" he asked.

"I feel fine," she said. "There's nothing wrong with me. I feel fine."

[1927]

ZORA NEALE HURSTON *(1901?–1960) was born in 1901 or 1902 (the records are lost and she gave different birth dates in her writing) in Eatonville, Florida, a town founded by African Americans. When her mother died in 1912, her father, a Baptist minister, couldn't raise their eight children, so Hurston was forced to move from one relative's home to another. She never finished grade school, but when she was old enough to support herself, she attended Howard University in Washington, D.C. In 1921 she published her first story, "John Redding Goes to Sea," in the student literary magazine.*

In 1925 Hurston went to New York City and became active in the cultural renaissance in Harlem, collaborating with Langston Hughes on a folk comedy, Mule Bone. *Like Hughes, she was deeply interested in the abiding folk spirit inherent in southern life. With several other writers of that time, she tried to express her cultural heritage. After Hurston studied with the famous anthropologist Franz Boas at Barnard College, she returned to Florida to record the oral traditions of her native community. As critics have noted, from this time to the end of her life she tried to achieve a balance in her literary work between the folk culture of her racial background and herself as a developing artist. Realizing that average white people used stereotypes to keep African Americans, Asian Americans, Hispanic Americans, and Native Americans in their "place," Hurston insisted that it was*

> urgent to realize that minorities do think, and think about something other than the race problem. That they are very human and internally, according to natural endowment, are just like everybody else. So long as this is not conceived, there must remain that feeling of unsurmountable difference, and difference to the average man means something bad. If people were made right, they would be just like him.

During the Great Depression of the 1930s, Hurston turned all her energies to writing. She published Mules and Men *(1935), based on material from her field trips to Florida, and* Their Eyes Were Watching God *(1937), a novel about a woman's search for love and personal identity, in addition to several other books, including an autobiography. Although she published more than any other African American woman writer of her time, in the last two decades of her life she earned very little from her writing, and she died penniless in Florida. Fifteen years after Hurston's death, her work was rediscovered by the women's movement, and she is now regarded as an important American writer. "The Gilded Six-Bits" and "Spunk" are from* The Eatonville Anthology *(1927), the collection that brought Hurston to the attention of a national audience.*

RELATED COMMENTARIES: *Robert Bone, "A Folkloric Analysis of Hurston's 'Spunk' and 'The Gilded Six-Bits,'" page 1389; Zora Neale Hurston, "What White Publishers Won't Print," page 1430; Alice Walker, "Zora Neale Hurston: A Cautionary Tale and a Partisan View," page 1505.*

The Gilded Six-Bits

It was a Negro yard around a Negro house in a Negro settlement that looked to the payroll of the G and G Fertilizer works for its support.

But there was something happy about the place. The front yard was parted in the middle by a sidewalk from gate to doorstep, a sidewalk edged on either side by quart bottles driven neck down to the ground on a slant. A mess of homey flowers planted without a plan but blooming cheerily from their helter-skelter places. The fence and house were whitewashed. The porch and steps scrubbed white.

The front door stood open to the sunshine so that the floor of the front room could finish drying after its weekly scouring. It was Saturday. Everything clean from the front gate to the privy house. Yard raked so that the strokes of the rake would make a pattern. Fresh newspaper cut in fancy-edge on the kitchen shelves.

Missie May was bathing herself in the galvanized washtub in the bedroom. Her dark-brown skin glistened under the soapsuds that skittered down from her wash rag. Her stiff young breasts thrust forward aggressively like broad-based cones with the tips lacquered in black.

She heard men's voices in the distance and glanced at the dollar clock on the dresser.

"Humph! Ah'm way behind time t'day! Joe gointer be heah 'fore Ah git mah clothes on if Ah don't make haste."

She grabbed the clean meal sack at hand and dried herself hurriedly and began to dress. But before she could tie her slippers, there came the ring of singing metal on wood. Nine times.

Missie May grinned with delight. She had not seen the big tall man come stealing in the gate and creep up the walk grinning happily at the joyful mischief he was about to commit. But she knew that it was her husband throwing silver dollars in the door for her to pick up and pile beside her plate at dinner. It was this way every Saturday afternoon. The nine dollars hurled into the open door, he scurried to a hiding place behind the cape jasmine bush and waited.

Missie May promptly appeared at the door in mock alarm.

"Who dat chunkin' money in mah do'way?" she demanded. No answer from the yard. She leaped off the porch and began to search the shrubbery. She peeped under the porch and hung over the gate to look up and down the road. While she did this, the man behind the jasmine darted to the chinaberry tree. She spied him and gave chase.

"Nobody ain't gointer be chunkin' money at me and Ah not do'em nothin'," she shouted in mock anger. He ran around the house with Missie May at his heels. She overtook him at the kitchen door. He ran inside but could not close it after him before she crowded in and locked with him in a rough and tumble. For several minutes the two were a furious mass of male and female energy. Shouting, laughing, twisting, turning, and Joe trying, but not too hard, to get away.

"Missie May, take yo' hand out mah pocket!" Joe shouted out between laughs.

"Ah ain't, Joe, not lessen you gwine gimme whateve' it is good you got in yo' pocket. Turn it go Jo, do Ah'll tear yo' clothes."

"Go on tear 'em. You de one dat pushes de needles round heah. Move yo' hand Missie May."

"Lemme git dat paper sack out yo' pocket. Ah bet its candy kisses."

"Tain't. Move yo' hand. Woman ain't got no business in a man's clothes nowhow. Go 'way."

Missie May gouged way down and gave an upward jerk and triumphed.

"Unhhunh! Ah got it. It 'tis so candy kisses. Ah knowed you had somethin' for me in yo' clothes. Now Ah got to see whut's in every pocket you got."

Joe smiled indulgently and let his wife go through all of his pockets and take out the things that he had hidden there for her to find. She bore off the chewing gum, the cake of sweet soap, the pocket handkerchief as if she had wrested them from him, as if they had not been bought for the sake of this friendly battle.

"Whew! dat play-fight done got me all warmed up," Joe exclaimed. "Got me some water in de kittle?"

"Yo' water is on de fire and yo' clean things is cross de bed. Hurry up and wash yo'self and git changed so we kin eat. Ah'm hongry." As Missie said this, she bore the steaming kettle into the bedroom.

"You ain't hongry, sugar," Joe contradicted her. "Youse jes's little empty. Ah'm de one whut's hongry. Ah could eat up camp meetin', back off 'ssociation, and drink Jurdan dry. Have it on de table when Ah git out de tub."

"Don't you mess wid mah business, man. You git in yo' clothes. Ah'm a real wife, not no dress and breath. Ah might not look lak one, but if you burn me, you won't git a thing but wife ashes."

Joe splashed in the bedroom and Missie May fanned around in the kitchen. A fresh red and white checked cloth on the table. Big pitcher of buttermilk beaded with pale drops of butter from the churn. Hot fried mullet, crackling bread, ham hocks atop a mound of string beans and new potatoes, and perched on the window-sill a pone of spicy potato pudding.

Very little talk during the meal but that little consisted of banter that pretended to deny affection but in reality flaunted it. Like when Missie May reached for a second helping of the tater pone. Joe snatched it out of her reach. After Missie May had made two or three unsuccessful grabs at the pan, she begged, "Aw, Joe gimme some mo' dat tater pone."

"Nope, sweetenin' is for us men-folks. Y'all pretty li'l frail eels don't need nothin' lak dis. You too sweet already."

"Please, Joe."

"Naw, naw. Ah don't want you to get no sweeter than whut you is already. We goin' down de road al li'l piece t'night so you go put on yo' Sunday-go-to-meetin' things."

Missie May looked at her husband to see if he was playing some prank. "Sho' nuff, Joe?"

"Yeah. We goin' to de ice cream parlor."

"Where de ice cream parlor at, Joe?"

"A new man done come heah from Chicago and he done got a place and took and opened it up for a ice cream parlor, and bein' as it's real swell, Ah wants you to be one de first ladies to walk in dere and have some set down."

"Do Jesus, Ah ain't knowed nothin' 'bout it. Who de man done it?"

"Mister Otis D. Slemmons, of spots and places — Memphis, Chicago, Jacksonville, Philadelphia, and so on."

"Dat heavy-set man wid his mouth full of gold teethes?"

"Yeah. Where did you see 'im at?"

"Ah went down to de sto' tuh git a box of lye and Ah seen 'im standin' on de corner talkin' to some of de mens, and Ah come on back and went to scrubbin' de floor, and he passed and tipped his hat whilst Ah was scourin' de steps. Ah thought never Ah seen *him* befo'."

Joe smiled pleasantly. "Yeah, he's up to date. He got de finest clothes Ah ever seen on a colored man's back."

"Aw, he don't look no better in his clothes than you do in yourn. He got a puzzlegut on 'im and he so chuckle-headed, he got a pone behind his neck."

Joe looked down at his own abdomen and said wistfully, "Wisht Ah had a build on me lak he got. He ain't puzzle-gutted, honey. He jes' got a corperation. Dat make 'm look lak a rich white man. All rich mens is got some belly on 'em."

"Ah seen de pitchers of Henry Ford and he's a spare-built man and Rockefeller look lak he ain't got but one gut. But Ford and Rockefeller and dis Slemmons and all de rest kin be as many-gutted as dey please, ah'm satisfied wid you jes' lak you is, baby. God took pattern after a pine tree and built you noble. Youse a pritty still man, and if Ah knowed any way to make you mo' pritty still Ah'd take and do it."

Joe reached over gently and toyed with Missie May's ear. "You jes' say dat cause you love me, but Ah know Ah can't hold no light to Otis D. Slemmons. Ah ain't never been nowhere and Ah ain't got nothin' but you."

"How you know dat, Joe."

"He tole us so hisself."

"Dat don't make it so. His mouf is cut cross-ways, ain't it? Well, he kin lie jes' lak anybody els."

"Good Lawd, Missie! You womens sho' is hard to sense into things. He's got a five-dollar gold piece for a stick-pin and he got a ten-dollar gold piece on his watch chain and his mouf is jes' crammed full of gold teethes. Sho' wisht it wuz mine. And whut make it so cool, he got money 'cumulated. And womens give it all to 'im."

"Ah don't see whut de womens see on 'im. Ah wouldn't give 'im a wind if de sherff wuz after 'im."

"Well, he tole us how de white womens in Chicago give 'im all dat gold money. So he don't 'low nobody to touch it at all. Not even put dey finger on it. Dey tole 'im not to. You kin make 'miration at it, but don't tetch it."

"Whyn't he stay up dere where dey so crazy 'bout 'im?"

"Ah reckon dey done made 'im vast-rich and he wants to travel some. He say dey wouldn't leave 'im hit a lick of work. He got mo' lady people crazy 'bout him than he kin shake a stick at."

"Joe, Ah hates to see you so dumb. Dat stray nigger jes' tell y'all anything and y'all b'lieve it."

"Go 'head on now, honey and put on yo' clothes. He talkin' 'bout his pritty womens — Ah want 'im to see *mine*."

Missie May went off to dress and Joe spent the time trying to make his stomach punch out like Slemmons' middle. He tried the rolling swagger of the stranger, but found that his tall bone-and-muscle stride fitted ill with it. He just had time to drop back into his seat before Missie May came in dressed to go.

On the way home that night Joe was exultant. "Didn't Ah say ole Otis was swell? Can't he talk Chicago talk? Wuzn't dat funny whut he said when great big fat ole Ida Armstrong come in? He asted me, 'Who is dat broad wid de forty shake?' Dat's a new word. Us always thought forty was a set of figgers but he showed us where it means a whole heap of things. Sometimes he don't say forty, he jes' say thirty-eight and two and dat mean de same thing. Know whut he tole me when Ah was payin' for our ice cream? He say, 'Ah have to hand it to you, Joe. Dat wife of yours is jes' thirty-eight and two. Yessuh, she's forty!' Ain't he killin?"

"He'll do in case of a rush. But he sho' is got uh heap uh gold on 'im. Dat's de first time Ah ever seed gold money. It lookted good on him sho' nuff, but it'd look a whole heap better on you."

"Who, me? Missie May was youse crazy! Where would a po' man lak me git gold money from?"

Missie May was silent for a minute, then she said, "Us might find some goin' long de road some time. Us could."

"Who would be losin' gold money 'round heah? We ain't even seen none dese white folks wearin' no gold money on dey watch chain. You must be figgeren' Mister Packard or Mister Cadillac goin' pass through heah . . ."

"You don't know whut been lost 'round heah. Maybe somebody way back in memorial times lost they gold money and went on off and it ain't never been found. And then if we wuz to find it, you could wear some 'thout havin' no gang of womens lak dat Slemmons say he got."

Joe laughed and hugged her. "Don't be so wishful 'bout me. Ah'm satisfied de way Ah is. So long as Ah be yo' husband, ah don't keer 'bout nothin' else. Ah'd ruther all de other womens in de world to be dead than for you to have de toothache. Less we go to bed and git our night rest."

It was Saturday night once more before Joe could parade his wife in

Slemmons' ice cream parlor again. He worked the night shift and Saturday was his only night off. Every other evening around six o'clock he left home, and dying dawn saw him hustling home around the lake where the challenging sun flung a flaming sword from east to west across the trembling water.

That was the best part of life — going home to Missie May. Their whitewashed house, the mock battle on Saturday, the dinner and ice cream parlor afterwards, church on Sunday nights when Missie outdressed any woman in town — all, everything was right.

One night around eleven the acid ran out at the G and G. The foreman knocked off the crew and let the steam die down. As Joe rounded the lake on his way home, a lean moon rode the lake in a silver boat. If anybody had asked Joe about the moon on the lake, he would have said he hadn't paid it any attention. But he saw it with his feelings. It made him yearn painfully for Missie. Creation obsessed him. He thought about children. They had been married for more than a year now. They had money put away. They ought to be making little feet for shoes. A little boy child would be about right.

He saw a dim light in the bedroom and decided to come in through the kitchen door. He could wash the fertilizer dust off himself before presenting himself to Missie May. It would be nice for her not to know that he was there until he slipped into his place in bed and hugged her back. She always liked that.

He eased the kitchen door open slowly and silently, but when he went to set his dinner bucket on the table he bumped it into a pile of dishes, and something crashed to the floor. He heard his wife gasp in fright and hurried to reassure her.

"Iss me, honey. Don't get skeered."

There was a quick, large movement in the bedroom. A rustle, a thud, and a stealthy silence. The light went out.

What? Robbers? Murderers? Some varmint attacking his helpless wife, perhaps. He struck a match, threw himself on guard, and stepped over the door-sill into the bedroom.

The great belt on the wheel of Time slipped and eternity stood still. By the match light he could see the man's legs fighting with his breeches in his frantic desire to get them on. He had both chance and time to kill the intruder in his helpless condition — half-in and half-out of his pants — but he was too weak to take action. The shapeless enemies of humanity that live in the hours of Time had waylaid Joe. He was assaulted in his weakness. Like Samson awakening after his haircut. So he just opened his mouth and laughed.

The match went out and he struck another and lit the lamp. A howling wind raced across his heart, but underneath its fury he heard his wife sobbing and Slemmons pleading for his life. Offering to buy it with all that he had. "Please, suh, don't kill me. Sixty-two dollars at de sto' gold money."

Joe just stood. Slemmons looked at the window, but it was screened. Joe stood out like a rough-backed mountain between him and the door. Barring him from escape, from sunrise, from life.

He considered a surprise attack upon the big clown that stood there laughing like a chessy cat. But before his fist could travel an inch, Joe's own rushed out to crush him like a battering ram. Then Joe stood over him.

"Git into yo' damn rags, Slemmons, and dat quick."

Slemmons scrambled to his feet and into his vest and coat. As he grabbed his hat, Joe's fury overrode his intentions and he grabbed at Slemmons with his left hand and struck at him with his right. The right landed. The left grazed the front of his vest. Slemmons was knocked a somersault into the kitchen and fled through the open door. Joe found himself alone with Missie May, with the golden watch charm clutched in his left fist. A short bit of broken chain dangled between his fingers.

Missie May was sobbing. Wails of weeping without words. Joe stood, and after awhile she found out that he had something in his hand. And then he stood and felt without thinking and without seeing with his natural eyes. Missie May kept on crying and Joe kept on feeling so much and not knowing what to do with all his feelings, he put Slemmons' watch charm in his pants pocket and took a good laugh and went to bed.

"Missie May, whut you crying for?"

"Cause Ah love you so hard and Ah know you don't love *me* no mo'."

Joe sank his face into the pillow for a spell then he said huskily, "You don't know de feelings of dat yet, Missie May."

"Oh Joe, honey, he said he wuz gointer gimme dat gold money and he jes' kept on after me —"

Joe was very still and silent for a long time. Then he said, "Well, don't cry no mo', Missie May. Ah got yo' gold piece for you."

The hours went past on their rusty ankles. Joe still and quiet on one bed-rail and Missie May wrung dry of sobs on the other. Finally the sun's tide crept upon the shore of night and drowned all its hours. Missie May with her face stiff and streaked towards the window saw the dawn come into her yard. It was day. Nothing more. Joe wouldn't be coming home as usual. No need to fling open the front door and sweep off the porch, making it nice for Joe. Never no more breakfast to cook; no more washing and starching of Joe's jumper-jackets and pants. No more nothing. So why get up?

With this strange man in her bed, she felt embarrassed to get up and dress. She decided to wait till he had dressed and gone. Then she would get up, dress quickly, and be gone forever beyond reach of Joe's looks and laughs. But he never moved. Red light turned to yellow, then white.

From beyond the no-man's land between them came a voice. A strange voice that yesterday had been Joe's.

"Missie May, ain't you gonna fix me no breakfus'?"

She sprang out of bed. "Yeah, Joe. Ah didn't reckon you wuz hongry."

No need to die today. Joe needed her for a few more minutes anyhow.

Soon there was a roaring fire in the cook stove. Water bucket full and two chickens killed. Joe loved fried chicken and rice. She didn't deserve a thing and good Joe was letting her cook him some breakfast. She rushed hot biscuits to the table as Joe took his seat.

He ate with his eyes on his plate. No laughter, no banter.

"Missie May, you ain't eatin' yo' breakfus'."

"Ah don't choose none, Ah thank yuh."

His coffee cup was empty. She sprang to refill it. When she turned from the stove and bent to set the cup beside Joe's plate, she saw the yellow coin on the table between them.

She slumped into her seat and wept into her arms.

Presently Joe said calmly, "Missie May, you cry too much. Don't look back lak Lot's wife and turn to salt."

The sun, the hero of every day, the impersonal old man that beams as brightly on death as on birth, came up every morning and raced across the blue dome and dipped into the sea of fire every evening. Water ran down hill and birds nested.

Missie knew why she didn't leave Joe. She couldn't. She loved him too much. But she couldn't understand why Joe didn't leave her. He was polite, even kind at times, but aloof.

There were no more Saturday romps. No ringing silver dollars to stack beside her plate. No pockets to rifle. In fact the yellow coin in his trousers was like a monster hiding in the cave of his pockets to destroy her.

She often wondered if he still had it, but nothing could have induced her to ask nor yet to explore his pockets to see for herself. Its shadow was in the house whether or no.

One night Joe came home around midnight and complained of pains in the back. He asked Missie to rub him down with liniment. It had been three months since Missie had touched his body and it all seemed strange. But she rubbed him. Grateful for the chance. Before morning, youth triumphed and Missie exulted. But the next day, as she joyfully made up their bed, beneath her pillow she found the piece of money with the bit of chain attached.

Alone to herself, she looked at the thing with loathing, but look she must. She took it into her hands with trembling and saw first thing that it was no gold piece. It was a gilded half-dollar. Then she knew why Slemmons had forbidden anyone to touch his gold. He trusted village eyes at a distance not to recognize his stick-pin as a gilded quarter, and his watch charm as a four-bit piece.

She was glad at first that Joe had left it there. Perhaps he was through with her punishment. They were man and wife again. Then another thought came clawing at her. He had come home to buy from her as if she were any woman in the long house. Fifty cents for her love. As if to say that he could pay as well as Slemmons. She slid the coin into his Sunday pants pocket and dressed herself and left his house.

Halfway between her house and the quarters she met her husband's mother, and after a short talk she turned and went back home. If she had not the substance of marriage, she had the outside show. Joe must leave *her*. She let him see she didn't want his old gold four-bits too.

She saw no more of the coin for some time though she knew that Joe could not help finding it in his pocket. But his health kept poor, and he came home at least every ten days to be rubbed.

The sun swept around the horizon, trailing its robes of weeks and days.

One morning as Joe came in from work, he found Missie May chopping wood. Without a word he took the ax and chopped a huge pile before he stopped.

"You ain't got no business choppin' wood, and you know it."

"How come? Ah been choppin' it for de last longest."

"Ah ain't blind. You makin' feet for shoes."

"Won't you be glad to have a li'l baby chile, Joe?"

"You know dat 'thout astin' me."

"Iss gointer be a boy chile and de very spit of you."

"You reckon, Missie May?"

"Who else could it look lak?"

Joe said nothing, but he thrust his hand deep into his pocket and fingered something there.

It was almost six months later Missie May took to bed and Joe went and got his mother to come wait on the house.

Missie May delivered a fine boy. Her travail was over when Joe came in from work one morning. His mother and the old women were drinking great bowls of coffee around the fire in the kitchen.

The minute Joe came into the room his mother called him aside.

"How did Missie May make out?" he asked quickly.

"Who, dat gal? She strong as a ox. She gointer have plenty mo'. We done fixed her wid de sugar and lard to sweeten her for de nex' one."

Joe stood silent awhile.

"You ain't ast 'bout de baby, Joe. You oughter be mighty proud cause he sho' is de spittin' image of yuh, son. Dat's yourn all right, if you never git another one, dat un is yourn. And you know Ah'm mighty proud too, son, cause Ah never thought well of you marryin' Missie May cause her ma used tuh fan her foot 'round right smart and Ah been mighty skeered dat Missie May wuz gointer git misput on her road."

Joe said nothing. He fooled around the house till late in the day then just before he went to work, he went and stood at the foot of the bed and asked his wife how she felt. He did this every day during the week.

On Saturday he went to Orlando to make his market. It had been a long time since he had done that.

Meat and lard, meal and flour, soap and starch. Cans of corn and tomatoes. All the staples. He fooled around town for awhile and bought bananas and apples. Way after while he went around to the candy store.

"Hellow, Joe," the clerk greeted him. "Ain't seen you in a long time."

"Nope, Ah ain't been heah. Been 'round spots and places."

"Want some of them molasses kisses you always buy?"

"Yessuh." He threw the gilded half-dollar on the counter. "Will dat spend?"

"Whut is it, Joe? Well, I'll be doggone! A gold-plated four-bit piece. Where'd you git it, Joe?"

"Offen a stray nigger dat come through Eatonville. He had it on his watch chain for a charm — goin' 'round making out iss gold money. Ha ha! He had a quarter on his tie pin and it wuz all golded up too. Tryin' to fool people. Makin' out he so rich and everything. Ha! Ha! Trying' to tole off folkses wives from home."

"How did you git it, Joe? Did he fool you, too?"

"Who, me? Naw suh! He ain't fooled me none. Know whut Ah done? He come 'round me wid his smart talk. Ah hauled off and knocked 'im down and took his old four-bits 'way from 'im. Gointer buy my wife some good ole 'lasses kisses wid it. Gimme fifty cents worth of dem candy kisses."

"Fifty cents buys a mightly lot of candy kisses, Joe. Why don't you split it up and take some chocolate bars, too. They eat good, too."

"Yessuh, de do, but Ah wants all dat in kisses. Ah got a li'l boy chile home now. Tain't a week old yet, but he kin suck a sugar tit and maybe eat one them kisses hisself."

Joe got his candy and left the store. The clerk turned to the next customer. "Wisht I could be like these darkies. Laughin' all the time. Nothin' worries 'em."

Back in Eatonville, Joe reached his own front door. There was the ring of singing metal on wood. Fifteen times. Missie May couldn't run to the door, but she crept there as quickly as she could.

"Joe Banks, Ah hear you chunkin' money in mah do'way. You wait till Ah got mah strength back and Ah'm gointer fix you for dat."   [1933]

ZORA   NEALE   HURSTON

Spunk

I

A giant of a brown-skinned man sauntered up the one street of the village and out into the palmetto thickets with a small pretty woman clinging lovingly to his arm.

"Looka theah, folkses!" cried Elijah Mosley, slapping his leg gleefully. "Theah they go, big as life an' brassy as tacks."

All the loungers in the store tried to walk to the door with an air of nonchalance but with small success.

"Now pee-eople!" Walter Thomas gasped. "Will you look at 'em!"

"But that's one thing Ah likes about Spunk Banks — he ain't skeered of nothin' on God's green footstool — *nothin'!* He rides that log down at saw-mill jus' like he struts 'round wid another man's wife — jus' don't give a kitty. When Tes' Miller got cut to giblets on that circle-saw, Spunk steps right up and starts ridin'. The rest of us was skeered to go near it."

A round-shouldered figure in overalls much too large came nervously in the door and the talking ceased. The men looked at each other and winked.

"Gimme some soda-water. Sass'prilla Ah reckon," the newcomer ordered, and stood far down the counter near the open pickled pig-feet tub to drink it.

Elijah nudged Walter and turned with mock gravity to the new-comer.

"Say, Joe, how's everything up yo' way? How's yo' wife?"

Joe started and all but dropped the bottle he was holding. He swallowed several times painfully and his lips trembled.

"Aw 'Lige, you oughtn't to do nothin' like that," Walter grumbled. Elijah ignored him.

"She jus' passed heah a few minutes ago goin' thata way," with a wave of his hand in the direction of the woods.

Now Joe knew his wife had passed that way. He knew that the men lounging in the general store had seen her, moreover, he knew that the men knew *he* knew. He stood there silent for a long moment staring blankly, with his Adam's apple twitching nervously up and down his throat. One could actually *see* the pain he was suffering, his eyes, his face, his hands, and even the dejected slump of his shoulders. He set the bottle down upon the counter. He didn't bang it, just eased it out of his hand silently and fiddled with his suspender buckle.

"Well, Ah'm goin' after her to-day. Ah'm goin' an' fetch her back. Spunk's done gone too fur."

He reached deep down into his trouser pocket and drew out a hollow ground razor, large and shiny, and passed his moistened thumb back and forth over the edge.

"Talkin' like a man, Joe. 'Course that's yo' fambly affairs, but Ah like to see grit in anybody."

Joe Kanty laid down a nickel and stumbled out into the street.

Dusk crept in from the woods. Ike Clarke lit the swinging oil lamp that was almost immediately surrounded by candle-flies. The men laughed boisterously behind Joe's back as they watched him shamble woodward.

"You oughtn't to said whut you said to him, 'Lige — look how it worked him up," Walter chided.

"And Ah hope it did work him up. Tain't even decent for a man to take and take like he do."

"Spunk will sho' kill him."

"Aw, Ah doan know. You never kin tell. He might turn him up an' spank him fur gettin' in the way, but Spunk wouldn't shoot no unarmed man. Dat razor he carried outa heah ain't gonna run Spunk down an' cut him, an' Joe ain't got the nerve to go to Spunk with it knowing he totes that Army .45. He makes that break outa heah to bluff us. He's gonna hide that razor behind the first palmetto root an' sneak back home to bed. Don't tell me nothin' 'bout that rabbit-foot colored man. Didn't he meet Spunk an' Lena face to face one day las' week an' mumble sumthin' to Spunk 'bout lettin' his wife alone?"

"What did Spunk say?" Walter broke in. "Ah like him fine but tain't right the way he carries on wid Lena Kanty, jus' 'cause Joe's timid 'bout fightin'."

"You wrong theah, Walter. Tain't 'cause Joe's timid at all, it's 'cause Spunk wants Lena. If Joe was a passle of wile cats Spunk would tackle the job just the same. He'd go after *anything* he wanted the same way. As Ah wuz sayin' a minute ago, he tole Joe right to his face that Lena was his. 'Call her and see if she'll come. A woman knows her boss an' she answers when he calls.' 'Lena, ain't I yo' husband?' Joe sorter whines out. Lena looked at him real disgusted but she don't answer and she don't move outa her tracks. Then Spunk reaches out an' takes hold of her arm an' says: 'Lena, youse mine. From now on Ah works for you an' fights for you an' Ah never wants you to look to nobody for a crumb of bread, a stitch of close or a shingle to go over yo' head, but *me* long as Ah live. Ah'll git the lumber foh owah house to-morrow. Go home an' git yo' things together!'"

"'Thass mah house,' Lena speaks up. 'Papa gimme that.'

"'Well,' says Spunk, 'doan give up whut's yours, but when youse inside doan forgit youse mine, an' let no other man git outa his place wid you!'

"Lena looked up at him with her eyes so full of love that they wuz runnin' over, an' Spunk seen it an' Joe seen it too, and his lip started to tremblin' and his Adam's apple was galloping up and down his neck like a race horse. Ah bet he's wore out half a dozen Adam's apples since Spunk's been on the job with Lena. That's all he'll do. He'll be back heah after while swallowin' an' workin' his lips like he wants to say somethin' an' can't."

"But didn't he do *nothin'* to stop 'em?"

"Nope, not a frazzlin' thing — jus' stood there. Spunk took Lena's arm and walked off jus' like nothin' ain't happened and he stood there gazin' after them till they was outa sight. Now you know a woman don't want no man like that. I'm jus' waitin' to see whut he's goin' to say when he gits back."

II

But Joe Kanty never came back, never. The men in the store heard the sharp report of a pistol somewhere distant in the palmetto thicket and soon Spunk came walking leisurely, with his big black Stetson set at the same rakish angle and Lena clinging to his arm, came walking right into the general store. Lena wept in a frightened manner.

"Well," Spunk announced calmly, "Joe came out there wid a meat axe an' made me kill him."

He sent Lena home and led the men back to Joe — crumpled and limp with his right hand still clutching his razor.

"See mah back? Mah close cut clear through. He sneaked up an' tried to kill me from the back, but Ah got him, an' got him good, first shot," Spunk said.

The men glared at Elijah, accusingly.

"Take him up an' plant him in Stony Lonesome," Spunk said in a careless voice. "Ah didn't wanna shoot him but he made me do it. He's a dirty coward, jumpin' on a man from behind."

Spunk turned on his heel and sauntered away to where he knew his love wept in fear for him and no man stopped him. At the general store later on, they all talked of locking him up until the sheriff should come from Orlando, but no one did anything but talk.

A clear case of self-defense, the trial was a short one, and Spunk walked out of the court house to freedom again. He could work again, ride the dangerous log-carriage that fed the singing, snarling, biting circle-saw; he could stroll the soft dark lanes with his guitar. He was free to roam the woods again; he was free to return to Lena. He did all of these things.

III

"Whut you reckon, Walt?" Elijah asked one night later. "Spunk's gittin' ready to marry Lena!"

"Naw! Why, Joe ain't had time to git cold yit. Nohow Ah didn't figger Spunk was the marryin' kind."

"Well, he is," rejoined Elijah. "He done moved most of Lena's things — and her along wid 'em — over to the Bradley house. He's buying it. Jus' like Ah told yo' all right in heah the night Joe was kilt. Spunk's crazy 'bout Lena. He don't want folks to keep on talkin' 'bout her — thass reason he's rushin' so. Funny thing 'bout that bob-cat, wan't it?"

"What bob-cat, 'Lige? Ah ain't heered 'bout none."

"Ain't cher? Well, night befo' las' as they was goin' to bed, a big black bob-cat, black all over, you hear me, *black*, walked round and round that house and howled like forty, an' when Spunk got his gun an' went to the winder to shoot it, he says it stood right still an' looked him in the eye, an' howled right at him. The thing got Spunk so nervoused up he couldn't shoot. But Spunk says twan't no bob-cat nohow. He says it was Joe done sneaked back from Hell!"

"Humph!" sniffed Walter, "he oughter be nervous after what he done. Ah reckon Joe come back to dare him to marry Lena, or to come out an' fight. Ah bet he'll be back time and again, too. Know what Ah think? Joe wuz a braver man than Spunk."

There was a general shout of derision from the group.

"Thass a fact," went on Walter. "Lookit whut he done; took a razor an' went out to fight a man he knowed toted a gun an' wuz a crack shot, too; 'nother thing Joe wuz skeered of Spunk, skeered plumb stiff! But he went jes' the same. It took him a long time to get his nerve up. Tain't nothin' for Spunk to fight when he ain't skeered of nothin'. Now, Joe's done come back to have it out wid the man that's got all he ever had. Y'all know Joe ain't never had nothin' nor wanted nothin' besides Lena. It musta been a h'ant cause ain't nobody never seen no black bob-cat."

"'Nother thing," cut in one of the men, "Spunk was cussin' a blue streak to-day 'cause he 'lowed dat saw wuz wobblin' — almos' got 'im once. The machinist come, looked it over an said it wuz alright. Spunk musta been leanin' t'wards it some. Den he claimed somebody pushed 'im but twan't nobody close to 'im. Ah wuz glad when knockin' off time came. I'm skeered of dat man when he gits hot. He'd beat you full of button holes as quick as he's look atcher."

IV

The men gathered the next evening in a different mood, no laughter. No badinage this time.

"Look, 'Lige, you goin' to set up wid Spunk?"

"Naw, Ah reckon not, Walter. Tell yuh the truth, Ah'm a li'l bit skittish. Spunk died too wicket — died cussin' he did. You know he thought he was done outa life."

"Good Lawd, who'd he think done it?"

"Joe."

"Joe Kanty? How come?"

"Walter, Ah b'leeve Ah will walk up thata way an' set. Lena would like it Ah reckon."

"But whut did he say, 'Lige?"

Elijah did not answer until they had left the lighted store and were strolling down the dark street.

"Ah wuz loadin' a wagon wid scantlin' right near the saw when Spunk fell on the carriage but 'fore Ah could git to him the saw got him in the body — awful sight. Me an' Skint Miller got him off but it was too late. Anybody could see that. The fust thing he said wuz: 'He pushed me, 'Lige — the dirty hound pushed me in the back!' — he was spittin' blood at ev'ry breath. We laid him on the sawdust pile with his face to the East so's he could die easy. He helt mah han' till the last, Walter, and said: 'It was Joe, 'Lige . . . the dirty sneak shoved me . . . he didn't dare come to mah face . . . but Ah'll git the son-of-a-wood louse soon's Ah get there an' make hell too hot for him . . . Ah felt him shove me . . . !' Thass how he died."

"If spirits kin fight, there's a powerful tussle goin' on somewhere ovah Jordan 'cause Ah b'leeve Joe's ready for Spunk an' ain't skeered any more — yas, Ah b'leeve Joe pushed 'im mahself."

They had arrived at the house. Lena's lamentations were deep and loud. She had filled the room with magnolia blossoms that gave off a heavy sweet odor. The keepers of the wake tipped about whispering in frightened tones. Everyone in the village was there, even old Jeff Kanty, Joe's father, who a few hours before would have been afraid to come within ten feet of him, stood leering triumphantly down upon the fallen giant as if his fingers had been the teeth of steel that laid him low.

The cooling board consisted of three sixteen-inch boards on saw horses, a dingy sheet was his shroud.

The women ate heartily of the funeral baked meats and wondered who would be Lena's next. The men whispered coarse conjectures between guzzles of whiskey.   [1927]

SHIRLEY JACKSON *(1919–1965) was born in San Francisco, California, her mother a housewife and her father an employee of a lithographing company. Most of her early life was spent in Burlingame, California, which she later used as the setting for her first novel,* The Road Through the Wall *(1948). As a child she was interested in writing; she won a poetry prize at age twelve, and in high school she began keeping a diary to record her writing progress. After high school she briefly attended the University of Rochester, but left because of an attack of the mental depression that was to recur periodically in her later years. She recovered her health by living quietly at home and writing, conscientiously turning out 1,000 words of prose a day. In 1937 she entered Syracuse University, where she published stories in the student literary magazine. There she met Stanley Edgar Hyman, who was to become a noted literary critic. They were married in 1940, the year she received her degree. They had four children while both continued active literary careers, settling to raise their family in a large Victorian house in Vermont, where Hyman taught literature at Bennington College.*

Jackson's first national publication was a humorous story written after a job at a department store during the Christmas rush: "My Life with R. H. Macy" appeared in The New Republic *in 1941. Her first child was born the next year, but she wrote every day on a disciplined schedule, selling her stories to magazines and publishing three novels. She refused to take herself too seriously as a writer: "I can't persuade myself that writing is honest work. It is a very personal reaction, but 50 percent of my life is spent washing and dressing the children, cooking, washing dishes and clothes, and mending. After I get it all to bed, I turn around to my typewriter and try to — well, to create concrete things again. It's great fun, and I love it. But it doesn't tie any shoes."*

Jackson's best-known work, "The Lottery," is often anthologized, dramatized, and televised. She regarded it as a tale *in the sense that Nathaniel Hawthorne used the term — a moral allegory revealing the hidden evil of the human soul. She wrote later that "explaining just what I had hoped the story to say is very difficult. I supposed, I hoped, by setting a particularly brutal ancient rite in the present and in my own village, to shock the story's readers with a graphic dramatization of the pointless violence and general inhumanity in their own lives."*

RELATED COMMENTARY: *Shirley Jackson, "The Morning of June 28, 1948, and 'The Lottery,'" page 1434.*

SHIRLEY JACKSON

The Lottery

The morning of June 27th was clear and sunny, with the fresh warmth of a full-summer day; the flowers were blossoming profusely and the grass was richly green. The people of the village began to gather in the square, between the post office and the bank, around ten o'clock; in some towns there were so many people that the lottery took two days and had to be started on June 26th, but in this village, where there were only about three hundred people, the whole lottery took less than two hours, so it could begin at ten o'clock in the morning and still be through in time to allow the villagers to get home for noon dinner.

The children assembled first, of course. School was recently over for the summer, and the feeling of liberty sat uneasily on most of them; they tended to gather together quietly for a while before they broke into boisterous play, and their talk was still of the classroom and teacher, of books and reprimands. Bobby Martin had already stuffed his pockets full of stones, and the other boys soon followed his example, selecting the smoothest and roundest stones; Bobby and Harry Jones and Dickie Delacroix — the villagers pronounced this name "Dellacroy" — eventually made a great pile of stones in one corner of the square and guarded it against the raids of the other boys. The girls stood aside, talking among themselves, looking over their shoulders at the boys, and the very small children rolled in the dust or clung to the hands of their older brothers or sisters.

Soon the men began to gather, surveying their own children, speaking of planting and rain, tractors and taxes. They stood together, away from the pile of stones in the corner, and their jokes were quiet and they smiled rather than laughed. The women, wearing faded house dresses and sweaters, came shortly after their menfolk. They greeted one another and exchanged bits of gossip as they went to join their husbands. Soon the women, standing by their husbands, began to call to their children, and the children came reluctantly, having to be called four or five times. Bobby Martin ducked under his mother's grasping hand and ran, laughing, back to the pile of stones. His father spoke up sharply, and Bobby came quickly and took his place between his father and his oldest brother.

The lottery was conducted — as were the square dances, the teen-age club, the Halloween program — by Mr. Summers, who had time and energy to devote to civic activities. He was a round-faced, jovial man and he ran the coal business, and people were sorry for him, because he had no children and his wife was a scold. When he arrived in the square, carrying the black wooden box, there was a murmur of conversation among the villagers, and he waved and called, "Little late today, folks." The postmaster, Mr. Graves, followed him, carrying a three-legged stool, and the stool was put in the center of the square and Mr. Summers set the black box down on it. The villagers kept their distance, leaving a space between themselves and the stool, and when Mr. Summers said, "Some of you fellows want to give me a hand?" there was a hesitation before two men, Mr. Martin and his oldest son, Baxter, came forward to hold the box steady on the stool while Mr. Summers stirred up the papers inside it.

The original paraphernalia for the lottery had been lost long ago, and the black box now resting on the stool had been put into use even before Old Man Warner, the oldest man in town, was born. Mr. Summers spoke frequently to the villagers about making a new box, but no one liked to upset even as much tradition as was represented by the black box. There was a story that the present box had been made with some pieces of the box that had preceded it, the one that had been constructed when the first people settled down to make a village here. Every year, after the lottery, Mr. Summers began talking again about a new box, but every year the subject was allowed to fade off without anything's being done. The black box grew shabbier each year; by now it was no longer completely black but splintered badly along one side to show the original wood color, and in some places faded or stained.

Mr. Martin and his oldest son, Baxter, held the black box securely on the stool until Mr. Summers had stirred the papers thoroughly with his hand. Because so much of the ritual had been forgotten or discarded, Mr. Summers had been successful in having slips of paper substituted for the chips of wood that had been used for generations. Chips of wood, Mr. Summers had argued, had been all very well when the village was tiny, but now that the population was more than three hundred and likely to keep on growing, it was necessary to use something that would fit more easily into the black box. The night before the lottery, Mr. Summers and Mr. Graves made up the slips of paper and put them in the box, and it was then taken to the safe of Mr. Summers's coal company and locked up until Mr. Summers was ready to take it to the square next morning. The rest of the year, the box was put away, sometimes one place, sometimes another; it had spent one year in Mr. Graves's barn and another year underfoot in the post office, and sometimes it was set on a shelf in the Martin grocery and left there.

There was a great deal of fussing to be done before Mr. Summers declared the lottery open. There were the lists to make up — of heads of families, heads of households in each family, members of each household in each family. There was the proper swearing-in of Mr. Summers by the postmaster, as the official of the lottery; at one time, some people remembered, there had been a recital of some sort, performed by the official of the lottery, a perfunctory, tuneless chant that had been rattled off duly each year; some people believed that the official of the lottery used to stand just so when he said or sang it, others believed that he was supposed to walk among the people, but years and years ago this part of the ritual had been allowed to lapse. There had been, also, a ritual salute, which the official of the lottery had had to use in addressing each person who came up to draw from the box, but this also had changed with time, until now it was felt necessary only for the official to speak to each person approaching. Mr. Summers was very good at all this; in his clean white shirt and blue jeans, with one hand resting carelessly on the black box, he seemed very proper and important as he talked interminably to Mr. Graves and the Martins.

Just as Mr. Summers finally left off talking and turned to the assembled villagers, Mrs. Hutchinson came hurriedly along the path to the square, her sweater thrown over her shoulders, and slid into place in the back of the crowd. "Clean forgot what day it was," she said to Mrs. Delacroix, who stood next to her, and they both laughed softly. "Thought my old man was out back stacking wood," Mrs. Hutchinson went on, "and then I looked out the window and the kids was gone, and then I remembered it was the twenty-seventh and came a-running." She dried her hands on her apron, and Mrs. Delacroix said, "You're in time, though. They're still talking away up there."

Mrs. Hutchinson craned her neck to see through the crowd and found her husband and children standing near the front. She tapped Mrs. Delacroix on the arm as a farewell and began to make her way through the crowd. The people separated good-humoredly to let her through; two or three people said, in voices just loud enough to be heard across the crowd, "Here comes your Missus, Hutchinson," and "Bill, she made it after all." Mrs. Hutchinson reached her husband, and Mr. Summers, who had been waiting, said cheerfully, "Thought we were going to have to get on without you, Tessie." Mrs. Hutchinson said, grinning, "Wouldn't have me leave m'dishes in the sink, now, would you, Joe?" and soft laughter ran through the crowd as the people stirred back into position after Mrs. Hutchinson's arrival.

"Well, now," Mr. Summers said soberly, "guess we better get started, get this over with, so's we can go back to work. Anybody ain't here?"

"Dunbar," several people said. "Dunbar, Dunbar."

Mr. Summers consulted his list. "Clyde Dunbar," he said. "That's right. He's broke his leg, hasn't he? Who's drawing for him?"

"Me, I guess," a woman said, and Mr. Summers turned to look at her. "Wife draws for her husband," Mr. Summers said. "Don't you have a grown boy to do it for you, Janey?" Although Mr. Summers and everyone else in the village knew the answer perfectly well, it was the business of the official of the lottery to ask such questions formally. Mr. Summers waited with an expression of polite interest while Mrs. Dunbar answered.

"Horace's not but sixteen yet," Mrs. Dunbar said regretfully. "Guess I gotta fill in for the old man this year."

"Right," Mr. Summers said. He made a note on the list he was holding. Then he asked, "Watson boy drawing this year?"

A tall boy in the crowd raised his hand. "Here," he said. "I'm drawing for m'mother and me." He blinked his eyes nervously and ducked his head as several voices in the crowd said things like "Good fellow, Jack," and "Glad to see your mother's got a man to do it."

"Well," Mr. Summers said, "guess that's everyone. Old Man Warner make it?"

"Here," a voice said, and Mr. Summers nodded.

A sudden hush fell on the crowd as Mr. Summers cleared his throat and looked at the list. "All ready?" he called. "Now, I'll read the names — heads of families first — and the men come up and take a paper out of the box. Keep the paper folded in your hand without looking at it until everyone has had a turn. Everything clear?"

The people had done it so many times that they only half listened to the directions; most of them were quiet, wetting their lips, not looking around. Then Mr. Summers raised one hand high and said, "Adams." A man disengaged himself from the crowd and came forward. "Hi, Steve," Mr. Summers said, and Mr. Adams said, "Hi, Joe." They grinned at one another humorlessly and nervously. Then Mr. Adams reached into the black box and took out a folded paper. He held it firmly by one corner as he turned and went hastily back to his place in the crowd, where he stood a little apart from his family, not looking down at his hand.

"Allen," Mr. Summers said, "Anderson. . . . Bentham."

"Seems like there's no time at all between lotteries any more," Mrs. Delacroix said to Mrs. Graves in the back row. "Seems like we got through with the last one only last week."

"Time sure goes fast," Mrs. Graves said.

"Clark. . . . Delacroix."

"There goes my old man," Mrs. Delacroix said. She held her breath while her husband went forward.

"Dunbar," Mr. Summers said, and Mrs. Dunbar went steadily to the box while one of the women said, "Go on, Janey," and another said, "There she goes."

"We're next," Mrs. Graves said. She watched while Mr. Graves came around from the side of the box, greeted Mr. Summers gravely, and selected a slip of paper from the box. By now, all through the crowd there were men holding the small folded papers in their large hands, turning them over and over nervously. Mrs. Dunbar and her two sons stood together, Mrs. Dunbar holding the slip of paper.

"Harburt. . . . Hutchinson."

"Get up there, Bill," Mrs. Hutchinson said, and the people near her laughed.

"Jones."

"They do say," Mr. Adams said to Old Man Warner, who stood next to him, "that over in the north village they're talking of giving up the lottery."

Old Man Warner snorted. "Pack of crazy fools," he said "Listening to the young folks, nothing's good enough for *them*. Next thing you know, they'll be wanting to go back to living in caves, nobody work any more, live *that* way for a while. Used to be a saying about 'Lottery in June, corn be heavy soon.' First thing you know, we'd all be eating stewed chickweed and acorns. There's *always* been a lottery," he added petulantly. "Bad enough to see young Joe Summers up there joking with everybody."

"Some places have already quit lotteries," Mrs. Adams said.

"Nothing but trouble in *that*," Old Man Warner said stoutly. "Pack of young fools."

"Martin." And Bobby Martin watched his father go forward. "Overdyke. . . . Percy."

"I wish they'd hurry," Mrs. Dunbar said to her older son. "I wish they'd hurry."

"They're almost through," her son said.

"You get ready to run tell Dad," Mrs. Dunbar said.

Mr. Summers called his own name and then stepped forward precisely and selected a slip from the box. Then he called, "Warner."

"Seventy-seventh year I been in the lottery," Old Man Warner said as he went through the crowd. "Seventy-seventh time."

"Watson." The tall boy came awkwardly through the crowd. Someone said. "Don't be nervous, Jack," and Mr. Summers said, "Take your time, son."

"Zanini."

After that, there was a long pause, a breathless pause, until Mr. Summers, holding his slip of paper in the air, said, "All right, fellows." For a minute, no one moved, and then all the slips of paper were opened. Suddenly, all the women began to speak at once, saying, "Who is it?" "Who's got it?" "Is it the Dunbars?" "Is it the Watsons?" Then the voices began to say, "It's Hutchinson. It's Bill," "Bill Hutchinson's got it."

"Go tell your father," Mrs. Dunbar said to her older son.

People began to look around to see the Hutchinsons. Bill Hutchinson was standing quiet, staring down at the paper in his hand. Suddenly, Tessie Hutchinson shouted to Mr. Summers, "You didn't give him time enough to take any paper he wanted. I saw you. It wasn't fair!"

"Be a good sport, Tessie," Mrs. Delacroix called, and Mrs. Graves said, "All of us took the same chance."

"Shut up, Tessie," Bill Hutchinson said.

"Well, everyone," Mr. Summers said, "that was done pretty fast, and now we've got to be hurrying a little more to get done in time." He consulted his next list. "Bill," he said, "you draw for the Hutchinson family. You got any other households in the Hutchinsons?"

"There's Don and Eva," Mrs. Hutchinson yelled. "Make *them* take their chance!"

"Daughters drew with their husbands' families, Tessie," Mr. Summers said gently. "You know that as well as anyone else."

"It wasn't *fair*," Tessie said.

"I guess not, Joe," Bill Hutchinson said regretfully. "My daughter draws with her husband's family, that's only fair. And I've got no other family except the kids."

"Then, as far as drawing for families is concerned, it's you," Mr. Summers said in explanation, "and as far as drawing for households is concerned, that's you, too. Right?"

"Right," Bill Hutchinson said.

"How many kids, Bill?" Mr. Summers asked formally.

"Three," Bill Hutchinson said. "There's Bill, Jr., and Nancy, and little Dave. And Tessie and me."

"All right, then," Mr. Summers said. "Harry, you got their tickets back?"

Mr. Graves nodded and held up the slips of paper. "Put them in the box, then," Mr. Summers directed. "Take Bill's and put it in."

"I think we ought to start over," Mrs. Hutchinson said, as quietly as she could. "I tell you it wasn't *fair*. You didn't give him time enough to choose. *Every*body saw that."

Mr. Graves had selected the five slips and put them in the box, and he dropped all the papers but those onto the ground, where the breeze caught them and lifted them off.

"Listen, everybody," Mrs. Hutchinson was saying to the people around her.

"Ready, Bill?" Mr. Summers asked, and Bill Hutchinson, with one quick glance around at his wife and children, nodded.

"Remember," Mr. Summers said, "take the slips and keep them folded until each person has taken one. Harry, you help little Dave." Mr. Graves took the hand of the little boy, who came willingly with him up to the box. "Take a paper out of the box, Davy," Mr. Summers said. Davy put his hand into the box and laughed. "Take just *one* paper," Mr. Summers said. "Harry, you hold it for him." Mr. Graves took the child's hand and removed the folded paper from the tight fist and held it while little Dave stood next to him and looked up at him wonderingly.

"Nancy next," Mr. Summers said. Nancy was twelve, and her school friends breathed heavily as she went forward, switching her skirt, and took a slip daintily from the box. "Bill, Jr.," Mr. Summers said, and Billy, his face red and his feet overlarge, nearly knocked the box over as he got a paper out. "Tessie," Mr. Summers said. She hesitated for a minute, looking around defiantly, and then set her lips and went up to the box. She snatched a paper out and held it behind her.

"Bill," Mr. Summers said, and Bill Hutchinson reached into the box and felt around, bringing his hand out at last with the slip of paper in it.

The crowd was quiet. A girl whispered, "I hope it's not Nancy," and the sound of the whisper reached the edges of the crowd.

"It's not the way it used to be," Old Man Warner said clearly. "People ain't the way they used to be."

"All right," Mr. Summers said. "Open the papers. Harry, you open little Dave's."

Mr. Graves opened the slip of paper and there was a general sigh through the crowd as he held it up and everyone could see that it was blank. Nancy and Bill, Jr., opened theirs at the same time, and both beamed and laughed, turning around to the crowd and holding their slips of paper above their heads.

"Tessie," Mr. Summers said. There was a pause, and then Mr. Summers looked at Bill Hutchinson, and Bill unfolded this paper and showed it. It was blank.

"It's Tessie," Mr. Summers said, and his voice was hushed. "Show us her paper, Bill."

Bill Hutchinson went over to his wife and forced the slip of paper out of her hand. It had a black spot on it, the black spot Mr. Summers had made the night before with the heavy pencil in the coal-company office. Bill Hutchinson held it up and there was a stir in the crowd.

"All right, folks," Mr. Summers said. "Let's finish quickly."

Although the villagers had forgotten the ritual and lost the original black box, they still remembered to use stones. The pile of stones the boys had made earlier was ready; there were stones on the ground with the blowing scraps of paper that had come out of the box. Mrs. Delacroix selected a stone so large she had to pick it up with both hands and turned to Mrs. Dunbar. "Come on," she said. "Hurry up."

Mrs. Dunbar had small stones in both hands, and she said, gasping for breath, "I can't run at all. You'll have to go ahead and I'll catch up with you."

The children had stones already, and someone gave little Davy Hutchinson a few pebbles.

Tessie Hutchinson was in the center of a cleared space by now, and she held her hands out desperately as the villagers moved in on her. "It isn't fair," she said. A stone hit her on the side of the head.

Old Man Warner was saying, "Come on, come on, everyone." Steve Adams was in the front of the crowd of villagers, with Mrs. Graves beside him.

"It isn't fair, it isn't right," Mrs. Hutchinson screamed and then they were upon her.   [1948]

HENRY JAMES *(1843–1916) was born in New York City. His father was a philosopher of religion, and his brother William James was a noted physician, philosopher, and psychologist. Educated mostly by tutors in the United States and Europe, James published his first story at the age of twenty-one. In 1875 he chose to live permanently in England. He formed friendships with several European writers, including Gustave Flaubert and Guy de Maupassant. During the first phase of James's long career, he explored personal relationships, most notably in the novel* The Portrait of a Lady *(1881). Then he turned to themes of social reform, as in* The Bostonians *(1886). He constantly experimented with ways to refine his writing and commented on his "art of fiction" in many essays, prefaces, letters, and notebooks. The dense, symbolic style of his later work can be seen in his last three novels,* The Wings of the Dove *(1902),* The Ambassadors *(1903), and* The Golden Bowl *(1904).*

James wrote more than seventy stories. He felt that experience assumes meaning only when the proper form for its expression is found. One of his favorite words was "awareness," and he tried to make his own awareness encompass everything he could observe, relate, weigh, and judge. In the essay "The Art of Fiction," he said that the source of fiction is not mere raw experience but "the power to guess the unseen from the seen, to trace the implication of things, to judge the whole piece by the pattern, the condition of feeling life in general so completely that you are well on your way to knowing any particular corner of it."

James's stories lack the characteristic compression and dramatic action typical of this literary form. Instead, using the device he called a "central intelligence," he revealed the world through the silent thought of one of his characters, proceeding at a stately pace, through constant self-examination and self-analysis, as in "The Beast in the Jungle." James felt this story dramatized "a great negative adventure," the life of the only "man in the world to whom nothing whatever was to happen," because of his "sterilizing habit" of analyzing his experience and failing "to find it good enough and thence to appropriate it."

Struck by the remarkable construction of Henry James's sentences, the essayist William Gass has commented in On Being Blue*:*

> *If any of us were as well taken care of as the sentences of Henry James, we'd never long for another, never wander away; where else would we receive such constant attention, our thoughts anticipated, our feelings understood? Who else would robe us so richly, take us to the best places, or guard our virtue as his own and defend our character in every situation? If we were his sentences, we'd sing ourselves though we were dying and about to be extinguished, since the silence which would follow our passing would not be like the pause left behind by a noisy train. It would be a memorial, well-remarked grave, just as the Master has assured us death itself is: the distinguished thing.*

RELATED COMMENTARIES: *Henry James, "The Subject of 'The Beast in the Jungle,'" page 1437; Eve Kosofsky Sedgwick, "The Beast in the Closet: A Gender Critic Reads James's 'The Beast in the Jungle,'" page 1491.*

HENRY JAMES

The Beast in the Jungle

I

What determined the speech that startled him in the course of their encounter scarcely matters, being probably but some words spoken by himself quite without intention — spoken as they lingered and slowly moved together after their renewal of acquaintance. He had been conveyed by friends an hour or two before to the house at which she was staying; the party of visitors at the other house, of whom he was one, and thanks to whom it was his theory, as always, that he was lost in the crowd, had been invited over to luncheon. There had been after luncheon much dispersal, all in the interest of the original motive, a view of Weatherend itself and the fine things, intrinsic features, pictures, heirlooms, treasures of all the arts, that made the place almost famous; and the great rooms were so numerous that guests could wander at their will, hang back from the principal group, and in cases where they took such matters with the last seriousness give themselves up to mysterious appreciations and measurements. There were persons to be observed, singly or in couples, bending toward objects in out-of-the-way corners with their hands on their knees and their heads nodding quite as with the emphasis of an excited sense of smell. When they were two they either mingled their sounds of ecstasy or melted into silences of even deeper import, so that there were aspects of the occasion that gave it for Marcher much the air of the "look round," previous to a sale highly advertised, that excites or quenches, as may be, the dream of acquisition. The dream of acquisition at Weatherend would have had to be wild indeed, and John Marcher found himself, among such suggestions, disconcerted almost equally by the presence of those who knew too much and by that of those who knew nothing. The great rooms caused so much poetry and history to press upon him that he needed some straying apart to feel in a proper relation with them, though this impulse was not, as happened, like the gloating of some of his companions, to be compared to the movements of a dog sniffing a cupboard. It had an issue promptly enough in a direction that was not to have been calculated.

It led, briefly, in the course of the October afternoon, to his closer meeting with May Bartram, whose face, a reminder, yet not quite a remembrance, as they sat much separated at a very long table, had begun merely by troubling him rather pleasantly. It affected him as the sequel of something of which he had lost the beginning. He knew it, and for the time quite welcomed it, as a continuation, but didn't know what it continued, which was an interest or an amusement the greater as he was also somehow aware — yet without a direct sign from her — that the young woman herself hadn't lost the thread. She hadn't lost it, but she wouldn't give it back to him, he saw, without some putting forth of his hand for it; and he not only saw that, but saw several things more, things odd enough in the light of the fact at the moment some accident of grouping brought them face to face he was still merely fumbling with the idea that any contact between them in the past would have had no importance. If it had had no importance he scarcely knew why his actual impression of her should so seem to have so much; the answer to which, however, was that in such a life as they all appeared to be leading for the moment one could but take things as they came. He was satisfied, without in the least being able to say why, that this young lady might roughly have ranked in the house as a poor relation; satisfied also that she was not there on a brief visit, but was more or less a part of the establishment — almost a working, a remunerated part. Didn't she enjoy at periods a protection that she paid for by helping, among other services, to show the place and explain it, deal with the tiresome people, answer questions about the dates of the building, the styles of the furniture, the authorship of the pictures, the favourite haunts of the ghost? It wasn't that she looked as if you could have given her shillings — it was impossible to look less so. Yet when she finally drifted toward him, distinctly handsome, though ever so much older — older than when he had seen her before — it might have been as an effect of her guessing that he had, within the couple of hours, devoted more imagination to her than to all the others put together, and had thereby penetrated to a kind of truth that the others were too stupid for. She *was* there on harder terms than any one; she was there as a consequence of things suffered, one way and another, in the interval of years; and she remembered him very much as she was remembered — only a good deal better.

By the time they at last thus came to speech they were alone in one of the rooms — remarkable for a fine portrait over the chimney-place — out of which their friends had passed, and the charm of it was that even before they had spoken they had practically arranged with each other to stay behind for talk. The charm, happily, was in other things too — partly in there being scarce a spot at Weatherend without something to stay behind for. It was in the way the autumn day looked into the high windows as it waned; the way the red light, breaking at the close from under a low sombre sky, reached out in a long shaft and played over old wainscots, old tapestry, old gold, old colour. It was most of all perhaps in the way she came to him as if, since she had been turned on to deal with the simpler sort, he might, should he choose to keep the whole thing down, just take her mild attention for a part of her general business. As soon as he heard her voice, however, the gap was filled up and the missing link supplied; the slight irony he divined in her attitude lost its advantage. He almost jumped at it to get there before her. "I met you years and years ago in Rome. I remember all about it." She confessed to disappointment — she had been so sure he didn't; and to prove how well he did he began to pour forth the particular recollections that popped up as he called for them. Her face and her voice, all at his service now, worked the miracle — the impression operating like the torch of a lamplighter who touches into flame, one by one, a long row of gas-jets. Marcher flattered himself the illumination was brilliant, yet he was really still more pleased on her showing him, with amusement, that in his haste to make everything right he had got most things rather wrong. It hadn't been at Rome — it had been at Naples; and it hadn't been eight years before — it had been more nearly ten. She hadn't been, either, with her uncle and aunt, but with her mother and her brother; in addition to which it was not with the Pembles *he* had been, but with the Boyers, coming down in their company from Rome — a point on which she insisted, a little to his confusion, and as to which she had her evidence in hand. The Boyers she had known, but didn't know the Pembles, though she had heard of them, and it was the people he was with who had made them acquainted. The incident of the thunderstorm that had raged round them with such violence as to drive them for refuge into an excavation — this incident had not occurred at the Palace of the Caesars, but at Pompeii, on an occasion when they had been present there at an important find.

He accepted her amendments, he enjoyed her corrections, though the moral of them was, she pointed out, that he *really* didn't remember the least thing about her; and he only felt it as a drawback that when all was made strictly historic there didn't appear much of anything left. They lingered together still, she neglecting her office — for from the moment he was so clever she had no proper right to him — and both neglected the house, just waiting as to see if a memory or two more wouldn't again breathe on them. It hadn't taken them many minutes, after all, to put down on the table, like the cards of a pack, those that constituted their respective hands; only what came out was that the pack was unfortunately not perfect — that the past, invoked, invited, encouraged, could give them, naturally, no more than it had. It had made them anciently meet — her at twenty, him at twenty-five; but nothing was so strange, they seemed to say to each other, as that, while so occupied, it hadn't done a little more for them. They looked at each other as with the feeling of an occasion missed; the present would have been so much better if the other, in the far distance, in the foreign land, hadn't been so stupidly meagre. There weren't apparently, all counted, more than a dozen little old things that had succeeded in coming to pass between them; trivialities of youth, simplicities of freshness, stupidities of ignorance, small possible germs, but too deeply buried — too deeply (didn't it seem?) to sprout after so many years. Marcher could only feel he ought to have rendered her some service — saved her from a capsized boat in the Bay or at least recovered her dressing-bag, filched from her cab in the streets of Naples by a lazzarone[1] with a stiletto. Or it would have been nice if he could have been taken with fever all alone at his hotel, and she could have come to look after him, to write to his people, to drive him out in convalescence. *Then* they would be in possession of the something or other that their actual show seemed to lack. It yet somehow presented itself, this show, as too good to be spoiled; so that they were reduced for a few minutes more to wondering a little helplessly why — since they seemed to know a certain number of the same people — their reunion had been so long averted. They didn't use that name for it, but their

---

[1] Beggar.

delay from minute to minute to join the others was a kind of confession that they didn't quite want it to be a failure. Their attempted supposition of reasons for their not having met but showed how little they knew of each other. There came in fact a moment when Marcher felt a positive pang. It was vain to pretend she was an old friend, for all the communities were wanting, in spite of which it was as an old friend that he saw she would have suited him. He had new ones enough — was surrounded with them for instance on the stage of the other house; as a new one he probably wouldn't have so much as noticed her. He would have liked to invent something, get her to make-believe with him that some passage of a romantic or critical kind *had* originally occurred. He was really almost reaching out in imagination — as against time — for something that would do, and saying to himself that if it didn't come this sketch of a fresh start would show for quite awkwardly bungled. They would separate, and now for no second or third chance. They would have tried and not succeeded. Then it was, just at the turn, as he afterwards made it out to himself, that, everything else failing, she herself decided to take up the case and, as it were, save the situation. He felt as soon as she spoke that she had been consciously keeping back what she said and hoping to get on without it; a scruple in her that immensely touched him when, by the end of three or four minutes more, he was able to measure it. What she brought out, at any rate, quite cleared the air and supplied the link — the link it was so odd he should frivolously have managed to lose.

"You know you told me something I've never forgotten and that again and again has made me think of you since; it was that tremendously hot day when we went to Sorrento, across the bay, for the breeze. What I allude to was what you said to me, on the way back, as we sat under the awning of the boat enjoying the cool. Have you forgotten?"

He had forgotten and was even more surprised than ashamed. But the great thing was that he saw in this no vulgar reminder of any "sweet" speech. The vanity of women had long memories, but she was making no claim on him of a compliment or a mistake. With another woman, a totally different one, he might have feared the recall possibly even of some imbecile "offer." So, in having to say that he had indeed forgotten, he was conscious rather of a loss than of a gain; he already saw an interest in the matter of her mention. "I try to think — but I give it up. Yet I remember the Sorrento day."

"I'm not very sure you do," May Bartram after a moment said; "and I'm not very sure I ought to want you to. It's dreadful to bring a person back at any time to what he was ten years before. If you've lived away from it," she smiled, "so much the better."

"Ah if *you* haven't why should I?" he asked.

"Lived away, you mean, from what I myself was?"

"From what *I* was. I was of course an ass," Marcher went on; "but I would rather know from you just the sort of ass I was than — from the moment you have something in your mind — not know anything."

Still, however, she hesitated. "But if you've completely ceased to be that sort —"?

"Why I can then all the more bear to know. Besides, perhaps I haven't."

"Perhaps. Yet if you haven't," she added, "I should suppose you'd remember. Not indeed that *I* in the least connect with my impression the invidious name you use. If I had only thought you foolish," she explained, "the thing I speak of wouldn't so have remained with me. It was about yourself." She waited as if it might come to him; but as, only meeting her eyes in wonder, he gave no sign, she burnt her ships. "Has it ever happened?"

Then it was that, while he continued to stare, a light broke for him and the blood slowly came to his face, which began to burn with recognition. "Do you mean I told you — ?" But he faltered, lest what came to him shouldn't be right, lest he should only give himself away.

"It was something about yourself that it was natural one shouldn't forget — that is if one remembered you at all. That's why I ask you," she smiled, "if the thing you then spoke of has ever come to pass?"

Oh then he saw, but he was lost in wonder and found himself embarrassed. This, he also saw, made her sorry for him, as if her allusion had been a mistake. It took him but a moment, however, to feel it hadn't been, much as it had been a surprise. After the first little shock of it her knowledge on the contrary began, even if rather strangely, to taste sweet to him. She was the only other person in the world then who would have it, and she had had it all these years, while the fact of his having so breathed his secret had unaccountably faded from him. No wonder they couldn't have met as if nothing had happened. "I judge," he finally said, "that I know what you mean. Only I had strangely enough lost any sense of having taken you so far into my confidence."

"Is it because you've taken so many others as well?"

"I've taken nobody. Not a creature since then."

"So that I'm the only person who knows?"

"The only person in the world."

"Well," she quickly replied, "I myself have never spoken. I've never, never repeated of you what you told me." She looked at him so that he perfectly believed her. Their eyes met over it in such a way that he was without a doubt. "And I never will."

She spoke with an earnestness that, as if almost excessive, put him at ease about her possible derision. Somehow the whole question was a new luxury to him — that is from the moment she was in possession. If she didn't take the sarcastic view she clearly took the sympathetic, and that was what he had had, in all the long time, from no one whomsoever. What he felt was that he couldn't at present have begun to tell her, and yet could profit perhaps exquisitely by the accident of having done so of old. "Please don't then. We're just right as it is."

"Oh I am," she laughed, "if you are!" To which she added: "Then you do still feel in the same way?"

It was impossible he shouldn't take to himself that she was really interested, though it all kept coming as perfect surprise. He had thought of himself so long as abominably alone, and lo he wasn't alone a bit. He hadn't been, it appeared, for an hour — since those moments on the Sorrento boat. It was *she* who had been, he seemed to see as he looked at her — she who had been made so by the graceless fact of his lapse of fidelity. To tell her what he had told her — what had it been but to ask something of her? something that she had given, in her charity, without his having, by a remembrance, by a return of the spirit, failing another encounter, so much as thanked her. What he had asked of her had been simply at first not to laugh at him. She had beautifully not done so for ten years, and she was not doing so now. So he had endless gratitude to make up. Only for that he must see just how he had figured to her. "What, exactly, was the account I gave —?"

"Of the way you did feel? Well, it was very simple. You said you had had from your earliest time, as the deepest thing within you, the sense of being kept for something rare and strange, possibly prodigious and terrible, that was sooner or later to happen to you, that you had in your bones the foreboding and the conviction of, and that would perhaps overwhelm you."

"Do you call that very simple?" John Marcher asked.

She thought a moment. "It was perhaps because I seemed, as you spoke, to understand it."

"You do understand it?" he eagerly asked.

Again she kept her kind eyes on him. "You still have the belief?"

"Oh!" he exclaimed helplessly. There was too much to say.

"Whatever it's to be," she clearly made out, "it hasn't yet come."

He shook his head in complete surrender now. "It hasn't yet come. Only, you know, it isn't anything I'm to *do*, to achieve in the world, to be distinguished or admired for. I'm not such an ass as *that*. It would be much better, no doubt, if I were."

"It's to be something you're merely to suffer?"

"Well, say to wait for — to have to meet, to face, to see suddenly break out in my life; possibly destroying all further consciousness, possibly annihilating me; possibly, on the other hand, only altering everything, striking at the root of all my world and leaving me to the consequences, however they shape themselves."

She took this in, but the light in her eyes continued for him not to be that of mockery. "Isn't what you describe perhaps but the expectation — or at any rate the sense of danger, familiar to so many people — of falling in love?"

John Marcher wondered. "Did you ask me that before?"

"No — I wasn't so free-and-easy then. But it's what strikes me now."

"Of course," he said after a moment, "it strikes you. Of course it strikes *me*. Of course what's in store for me may be no more than that. The only thing is," he went on, "that I think if it had been that I should by this time know."

"Do you mean because you've *been* in love?" And then as he but looked at her in silence: "You've been in love, and it hasn't meant such a cataclysm, hasn't proved the great affair?"

"Here I am, you see. It hasn't been overwhelming."

"Then it hasn't been love," said May Bartram.

"Well, I at least thought it was. I took it for that — I've taken it till now. It was agreeable, it was delightful, it was miserable," he explained. "But it wasn't strange. It wasn't what *my* affair's to be."

"You want something all to yourself — something that nobody else knows or *has* known?"

"It isn't a question of what I 'want' — God knows I don't want anything. It's only a question of the apprehension that haunts me — that I live with day by day."

He said this so lucidly and consistently that he could see it further impose itself. If she hadn't been interested before she'd have been interested now. "Is it a sense of coming violence?"

Evidently now too again he liked to talk of it. "I don't think of it as — when it does come — necessarily violent. I only think of it as natural and as of course above all unmistakeable. I think of it simply as *the* thing. *The* thing will of itself appear natural."

"Then how will it appear strange?"

Marcher bethought himself. "It won't — to *me*."

"To whom then?"

"Well," he replied, smiling at last, "say to you."

"Oh then I'm to be present?"

"Why you *are* present — since you know."

"I see." She turned it over. "But I mean at the catastrophe."

At this, for a minute, their lightness gave way to their gravity; it was as if the long look they exchanged held them together. "It will only depend on yourself — if you'll watch with me."

"Are you afraid?" she asked.

"Don't leave me *now*," he went on.

"Are you afraid?" she repeated.

"Do you think me simply out of my mind?" he pursued instead of answering. "Do I merely strike you as a harmless lunatic?"

"No," said May Bartram. "I understand you. I believe you."

"You mean you feel how my obsession — poor old thing! — may correspond to some possible reality?"

"To some possible reality."

"Then you *will* watch with me?"

She hesitated, then for the third time put her question. "Are you afraid?"

"Did I tell you I was — at Naples?"

"No, you said nothing about it."

"Then I don't know. And I should *like* to know," said John Marcher. "You'll tell me yourself whether you think so. If you'll watch with me you'll see."

"Very good then." They had been moving by this time across the room, and at the door, before passing out, they paused as for the full wind-up of their understanding. "I'll watch with you," said May Bartram.

II

The fact that she "knew" — knew and yet neither chaffed him nor betrayed him — had in a short time begun to constitute between them a goodly bond, which became more marked when, within the year that followed their afternoon at Weatherend, the opportunities for meeting multiplied. The event that thus promoted these occasions was the death of the ancient lady her great-aunt, under whose wing, since losing her mother, she had to such an extent found shelter, and who, though but the widowed mother of the new successor to the property, had succeeded — thanks to a high tone and a high temper — in not forfeiting the supreme position at the great house. The deposition of this personage arrived but with her death, which, followed by many changes, made in particular a difference for the young woman in whom Marcher's expert attention had recognised from the first a dependent with a pride that might ache though it didn't bristle. Nothing for a long time had made him easier than the thought that the aching must have been much soothed by Miss Bartram's now finding herself able to set up a small home in London. She had acquired property, to an amount that made that luxury just possible, under her aunt's extremely complicated will, and when the whole matter began to be straightened out, which indeed took time, she let him know that the happy issue was at last in view. He had seen her again before that day, both because she had more than once accompanied the ancient lady to town and because he had paid another visit to the friends who so conveniently made of Weatherend one of the charms of their own hospitality. These friends had taken him back there; he had achieved there again with Miss Bartram some quiet detachment; and he had in London succeeded in persuading her to more than one brief absence from her aunt. They went together, on these latter occasions, to the National Gallery and the South Kensington Museum, where, among vivid reminders, they talked of Italy at large — not now attempting to recover, as at first, the taste of their youth and their ignorance. That recovery, the first day at Weatherend, had served its purpose well, had given them quite enough; so that they were, to Marcher's sense, no longer hovering about the headwaters of their stream, but had felt their boat pushed sharply off and down the current.

They were literally afloat together; for our gentleman this was marked, quite as marked as that the fortunate cause of it was just the buried treasure of her knowledge. He had with his own hands dug up this little hoard, brought to light — that is to within reach of the dim day constituted by their discretions and privacies — the object of value the hiding-place of which he had, after putting it into the ground itself, so strangely, so long forgotten. The rare luck of his having again just stumbled on the spot made him indifferent to any other question; he would doubtless have devoted more time to the odd accident of his lapse of memory if he hadn't been moved to devote so much to the sweetness, the comfort, as he felt, for the future, that this accident itself had helped to keep fresh. It had never entered into his plan that any one should "know," and mainly for the reason that it wasn't in him to tell any one. That would have been impossible, for nothing but the amusement of a cold world would have waited on it. Since, however, a mysterious fate had opened his mouth betimes, in spite of him, he would count that a compensation and profit by it to the utmost. That the right person *should* know tempered the asperity of his secret more even than his shyness had permitted him to imagine; and May Bartram was clearly right, because — well, because there she was. Her knowledge simply settled it; he would have been sure enough by this time had she been wrong. There was that in his situation, no doubt, that disposed him too much to see her as a mere confidant, taking all her light for him from the fact — the fact only — of her interest in his predicament; from her mercy, sympathy, seriousness, her consent not to regard him as the funniest of the funny. Aware, in fine, that her price for him was just in her giving him this constant sense of his being admirably spared, he was careful to remember that she had also a life of her own, with things that might happen to *her*, things that in friendship one should likewise take account of. Something fairly remarkable came to pass with him, for that matter, in this connexion — something represented by a certain passage of his consciousness, in the suddenest way, from one extreme to the other.

He had thought himself, so long as nobody knew, the most disinterested person in the world, carrying his concentrated burden, his perpetual suspense, ever so quietly, holding his tongue about it, giving others no glimpse of it nor of its effect upon his life, asking of them no allowance and only making on his side all those that were asked. He hadn't disturbed people with the queerness of their having to know a haunted man, though he had had moments of rather special temptation on hearing them say they were forsooth "unsettled." If they were as unsettled as he was — he who had never been settled for an hour in his life — they would know what it meant. Yet it wasn't, all the same, for him to make them, and he listened to them civilly enough. This was why he had such good — though possibly such rather colourless — manners; this was why, above all, he could regard himself, in a greedy world, as decently — as in fact perhaps even a little sublimely — unselfish. Our point is accordingly that he valued this character quite sufficiently to measure his present danger of letting it lapse, against which he promised himself to be much on his guard. He was quite ready, none the less, to be selfish just a little, since surely no more charming occasion for it had come to him. "Just a little," in a word, was just as much as Miss Bartram, taking one day with another, would let him. He never would be in the least coercive, and would keep well before him the lines on which consideration for her — the very highest — ought to proceed. He would thoroughly establish the heads under which her affairs, her requirements, her peculiarities — he went so far as to give them the latitude of that name — would come into their intercourse. All this naturally was a sign of how much he took the intercourse itself for granted. There was nothing more to be done about *that*. It simply existed; had sprung into being with her first penetrating question to him in the autumn light there at Weatherend. The real form it should have taken on the basis that stood out large was the form of their marrying. But the devil in this was that the very basis itself put marrying out of the question. His conviction, his apprehension, his obsession, in short, wasn't a privilege he could invite a woman to share; and that consequence of it was precisely what was the matter with him. Something or other lay in wait for him, amid the twists and the turns of the months and the years, like a crouching beast in the jungle. It signified little whether the crouching beast were destined to slay him or to be slain. The definite point was the inevitable spring of the creature; and the definite lesson from that was that a man of feeling didn't cause himself to be accompanied by a lady on a tiger-hunt. Such was the image under which he had ended by figuring his life.

They had at first, none the less, in the scattered hours spent together, made no allusion to that view of it; which was a sign he was handsomely alert to give that he didn't expect, that he in fact didn't care, always to be talking about it. Such a feature in one's outlook was really like a hump on one's back. The difference it made every minute of the day existed quite independently of discussion. One discussed of course *like* a hunchback, for there was always, if nothing else, the hunchback face. That remained, and she was watching him; but people watched best, as a general thing, in silence, so that such would be predominantly the manner of their vigil. Yet he didn't want, at the same time, to be tense and solemn; tense and solemn was what he imagined he too much showed for with other people. The thing to be, with the one person who knew, was easy and natural — to make the reference rather than be seeming to avoid it, to avoid it rather than be seeming to make it, and to keep it, in any case, familiar, facetious even, rather than pedantic and portentous. Some such consideration as the latter was doubtless in his mind for instance when he wrote pleasantly to Miss Bartram that perhaps the great thing he had so long felt as in the lap of the gods was no more than this circumstance, which touched him so nearly, of her acquiring a house in London. It was the first allusion they had yet again made, needing any other hitherto so little; but when she replied, after having given him the news, that she was by no means satisfied with such a trifle as the climax to so special a suspense, she almost set him wondering if she hadn't even a larger conception of singularity for him than he had for himself. He was at all events destined to become aware little by little, as time went by, that she was all the while looking at his life, judging it, measuring it, in the light of the thing she knew, which grew to be at last, with the consecration of the years, never mentioned between them save as "the real truth" about him. That had always been his own form of reference to it, but she adopted the form so quietly that, looking back at the end of a period, he knew there was no moment at which it was traceable that she had, as he might say, got inside his idea, or exchanged the attitude of beautifully indulging for that of still more beautifully believing him.

It was always open to him to accuse her of seeing him but as the most harmless of maniacs, and this, in the long run — since it covered so much ground — was his easiest description of their friendship. He had a screw loose for her, but she liked him in spite of it and was practically, against the rest of the world, his kind wise keeper, unremunerated but fairly amused and, in the absence of other near ties, not disreputably occupied. The rest of the world of course thought him queer, but she, she only, knew how, and above all why, queer; which was precisely what enabled her to dispose the concealing veil in the right folds. She took his gaiety from him — since it had to pass with them for gaiety — as she took everything else; but she certainly so far justified by her unerring touch his finer sense of the degree to which he had ended by convincing her. *She* at least never spoke of the secret of his life except as "the real truth about you," and she had in fact a wonderful way of making it seem, as such, the secret of her own life too. That was in fine how he so constantly felt her as allowing for him; he couldn't on the whole call it anything else. He allowed himself, but she, exactly, allowed still more; partly because, better placed for a sight of the matter, she traced his unhappy perversion through reaches of its course into which he could scarce follow it. He knew how he felt, but, besides knowing that, she knew how he *looked* as well; he knew each of the things of importance he was insidiously kept from doing, but she could add up the amount they made, understand how much, with a lighter weight on his spirit, he might have done, and thereby established how, clever as he was, he fell short. Above all she was in the secret of the difference between the forms he went through — those of his little office under Government, those of caring for his modest patrimony, for his library, for his garden in the country, for the people in London whose invitations he accepted and repaid — and the detachment that reigned beneath them and that made of all behaviour, all that could in the least be called behaviour, a long act of dissimulation. What it had come to was that he wore a mask painted with the social simper, out of the eyeholes of which there looked eyes of an expression not in the least matching the other features. This the stupid world, even after years, had never more than half-discovered. It was only May Bartram who had, and she achieved, by an art indescribable, the feat of at once — or perhaps it was only alternately — meeting the eyes from in front and mingling her own vision, as from over his shoulder, with their peep through the apertures.

So while they grew older together she did watch with him, and so she let this association give shape and colour to her own existence. Beneath *her* forms as well detachment had learned to sit, and behaviour had become for her, in the social sense, a false account of herself. There was but one account of her that would have been true all the while and that she could give straight to nobody, least of all to John Marcher. Her whole attitude was a virtual statement, but the perception of that only seemed called to take its place for him as one of the many things necessarily crowded out of his consciousness. If she had moreover, like himself, to make sacrifices to their real truth, it was to be granted that her compensation might have affected her as more prompt and more natural. They had long periods, in this London time, during which, when they were together, a stranger might have listened to them without in the least pricking up his ears; on the other hand the real truth was equally liable at any moment to rise to the surface, and the auditor would then have wondered indeed what they were talking about. They had from an early hour made up their mind that society was, luckily, unintelligent, and the margin allowed them by this had fairly become one of their commonplaces. Yet there were still moments when the situation turned almost fresh — usually under the effect of some expression drawn from herself. Her expressions doubtless repeated themselves, but her intervals were generous. "What saves us, you know, is that we answer so completely to so usual an appearance: that of the man and woman whose friendship had become such a daily habit — or almost — as to be at last indispensable." That for instance was a remark she had frequently enough had occasion to make, though she had given it at different times different developments. What we are especially concerned with is the turn it happened to take from her one afternoon when he had come to see her in honour of her birthday. This anniversary had fallen on a Sunday, at a season of thick fog and general outward gloom; but he had brought her his customary offering, having known her now long enough to have established a hundred small traditions. It was one of his proofs to himself, the present he made her on her birthday, that he hadn't sunk into real selfishness. It was mostly nothing more than a small trinket, but it was always fine of its kind, and he was regularly careful to pay for it more than he thought he could afford. "Our habit saves you at least, don't you see? Because it makes you, after all, for the vulgar, indistinguishable from other men. What's the most inveterate mark of men in general? Why the capacity to spend endless time with dull women — to spend it I won't say without being bored, but without minding that they are, without being driven off at a tangent by it; which comes to the same thing. I'm your dull woman, a part of the daily bread for which you pray at church. That covers your tracks more than anything."

"And what covers yours?" asked Marcher, whom his dull woman could mostly to this extent amuse. "I see of course what you mean by your saving me, in this way and that, so far as other people are concerned — I've seen it all along. Only what is it that saves *you?* I often think, you know, of that."

She looked as if she sometimes thought of that too, but rather in a different way. "Where other people, you mean, are concerned?"

"Well, you're really so in with me, you know — as a sort of result of my being so in with yourself. I mean of my having such an immense regard for you, being so tremendously mindful of all you've done for me. I sometimes ask myself if it's quite fair. Fair I mean to have so involved and — since one may say it — interested you. I almost feel as if you hadn't really had time to do anything else."

"Anything else but be interested?" she asked. "Ah what else does one ever want to be? If I've been 'watching' with you, as we long ago agreed I was to do, watching's always in itself an absorption."

"Oh certainly," John Marcher said, "if you hadn't had your curiosity —! Only doesn't it sometimes come to you as time goes on that your curiosity isn't being particularly repaid?"

May Bartram had a pause. "Do you ask that, by any chance, because you feel at all that yours isn't? I mean because you have to wait so long."

Oh he understood what she meant! "For the thing to happen that never does happen? For the beast to jump out? No, I'm just where I was about it. It isn't a matter as to which I can *choose,* I can decide for a change. It isn't one as to which there *can* be a change. It's in the lap of the gods. One's in the hands of one's law — there one is. As to the form the law will take, the way it will operate, that's its own affair."

"Yes," Miss Bartram replied; "of course one's fate's coming, of course it *has* come in its own form and its own way, all the while. Only, you know, the form and the way in your case were to have been — well, something so exceptional and, as one may say, so particularly *your* own."

Something in this made him look at her with suspicion. "You say 'were to *have* been,' as if in your heart you had begun to doubt."

"Oh!" she vaguely protested.

"As if you believed," he went on, "that nothing will now take place."

She shook her head slowly but rather inscrutably. "You're far from my thought."

He continued to look at her. "What then is the matter with you?"

"Well," she said after another wait, "the matter with me is simply that I'm more sure than ever my curiosity, as you call it, will be but too well repaid."

They were frankly grave now; he had got up from his seat, had turned once more about the little drawing-room to which, year after year, he brought his inevitable topic; in which he had, as he might have said, tasted their intimate community with every sauce, where every object was as familiar to him as the things of his own house and the very carpets were worn with his fitful walk very much as the desks in old counting-houses are worn by the elbows of generations of clerks. The generations of his nervous moods had been at work there, and the place was the written history of his whole middle life. Under the impression of what his friend had just said he knew himself, for some reason, more aware of these things; which made him, after a moment, stop again before her. "Is it possibly that you've grown afraid?"

"Afraid?" He thought, as she repeated the word, that his question had made her, a little, change colour; so that, lest he should have touched on a truth, he explained very kindly: "You remember that that was what you asked *me* long ago — that first day at Weatherend."

"Oh yes, and you told me you didn't know — that I was to see for myself. We've said little about it since, even in so long a time."

"Precisely," Marcher interposed — "quite as if it were too delicate a matter for us to make free with. Quite as if we might find, on pressure, that I *am* afraid. For then," he said, "we shouldn't, should we? quite know what to do."

She had for the time no answer to this question. "There have been days when I thought you were. Only, of course," she added, "there have been days when we have thought almost anything."

"Everything. Oh!" Marcher softly groaned as with a gasp, half-spent, at the face, more uncovered just then than it had been for a long while, of the imagination always with them. It had always had its incalculable moments of glaring out, quite as with the very eyes of the very Beast, and, used as he was to them, they could still draw from him the tribute of a sigh that rose from the depths of his being. All they had thought, first and last, rolled over him; the past seemed to have been reduced to mere barren speculation. This in fact was what the place had just struck him as so full of — the simplification of everything but the state of suspense. That remained only by seeming to hang in the void surrounding it. Even his original fear, if fear it had been, had lost itself in the desert. "I judge, however," he continued, "that you see I'm not afraid now."

"What I see, as I make it out, is that you've achieved something almost unprecedented in the way of getting used to danger. Living with it so long and so closely you've lost your sense of it; you know it's there, but you're indifferent, and you cease even, as of old, to have to whistle in the dark. Considering what the danger is," May Bartram wound up, "I'm bound to say I don't think your attitude could well be surpassed."

John Marcher faintly smiled. "It's heroic?"

"Certainly — call it that."

It was what he would have liked indeed to call it. "I *am* then a man of courage?"

"That's what you were to show me."

He still, however, wondered. "But doesn't the man of courage know what he's afraid of — or *not* afraid of? I don't know *that*, you see. I don't focus it. I can't name it. I only know I'm exposed."

"Yes, but exposed — how shall I say? — so directly. So intimately. That's surely enough."

"Enough to make you feel then — as what we may call the end and the upshot of our watch — that I'm not afraid?"

"You're not afraid. But it isn't," she said, "the end of our watch. That is it isn't the end of yours. You've everything still to see."

"Then why haven't *you?*" he asked. He had had, all along, today, the sense of her keeping something back, and he still had it. As this was his first impression of that it quite made a date. The case was the more marked as she didn't at first answer; which in turn made him go on. "You know something I don't." Then his voice, for that of a man of courage, trembled a little. "You know what's to happen." Her silence, with the face she showed, was almost a confession — it made him sure. "You know, and you're afraid to tell me. It's so bad that you're afraid I'll find out."

All this might be true, for she did look as if, unexpectedly to her, he had crossed some mystic line that she had secretly drawn round her. Yet she might, after all, not have worried; and the real climax was that he himself, at all events, needn't. "You'll never find out."

III

It was all to have made, none the less, as I have said, a date; which came out in the fact that again and again, even after long intervals, other things that passed between them wore in relation to this hour but the character of recalls and results. Its immediate effect had been indeed rather to lighten insistence — almost to provoke a reaction; as if their topic had dropped by its own weight and as if moreover, for that matter, Marcher had been visited by one of his occasional warnings against egotism. He had kept up, he felt, and very decently on the whole, his consciousness of the importance of not being selfish, and it was true that he had never sinned in that direction without promptly enough trying to press the scales the other way. He often repaired his fault, the season permitting, by inviting his friend to accompany him to the opera; and it not infrequently thus happened that, to show he didn't wish her to have but one sort of food for her mind, he was the cause of her appearing there with him a dozen nights in the month. It even happened that, seeing her home at such times, he occasionally went in with her to finish, as he called it, the evening, and, the better to make his point, sat down to the frugal but always careful little supper that awaited his pleasure. His point was made, he thought, by his not eternally insisting with her on himself; made for instance, at such hours, when it befell that, her piano at hand and each of them familiar with it, they went over passages of the opera together. It chanced to be on one of these occasions, however, that he reminded her of her not having answered a certain question he had put to her during the talk that had taken place between them on her last birthday. "What is it that saves *you?*" — saved her, he meant, from that appearance of variation from the usual human type. If he had practically escaped remark, as she pretended, by doing, in the most important particular, what most men do — find the answer to life in patching up an alliance of a sort with a woman no better than himself — how had she escaped it, and how could the alliance, such as it was, since they must suppose it had been more or less noticed, have failed to make her rather positively talked about?

"I never said," May Bartram replied, "that it hadn't made me a good deal talked about."

"Ah well then you're not 'saved.'"

"It hasn't been a question for me. If you've had your woman I've had," she said, "my man."

"And you mean that makes you all right?"

Oh it was always as if there were so much to say! "I don't know why it shouldn't make me — humanly, which is what we're speaking of — as right as it makes you."

"I see," Marcher returned. "'Humanly,' no doubt, as showing that you're living for something. Not, that is, just for me and my secret."

May Bartram smiled. "I don't pretend it exactly shows that I'm not living for you. It's my intimacy with you that's in question."

He laughed as he saw what she meant. "Yes, but since, as you say, I'm only, so far as people make out, ordinary, you're — aren't you? — no more than ordinary either. You help me to pass for a man like another. So if I *am*, as I understand you, you're not compromised. Is that it?"

She had another of her waits, but she spoke clearly enough. "That's it. It's all that concerns me — to help you to pass for a man like another."

He was careful to acknowledge the remark handsomely. "How kind, how beautiful, you are to me! How shall I ever repay you?"

She had her last grave pause, as if there might be a choice of ways. But she chose. "By going on as you are."

It was into this going on as he was that they relapsed, and really for so long a time that the day inevitably came for a further sounding of their depths. These depths, constantly bridged over by a structure firm enough in spite of its lightness and of its occasional oscillation in the somewhat vertiginous air, invited on occasion, in the interest of their nerves, a dropping of the plummet and a measurement of the abyss. A difference had been made moreover, once for all, by the fact that she had all the while not appeared to feel the need of rebutting his charge of an idea within her that she didn't dare to express — a charge uttered just before one of the fullest of their later discussions ended. It had come up for him then that she "knew" something and that what she knew was bad — too bad to tell him. When he had spoken of it as visibly so bad that she was afraid he might find it out, her reply had left the matter too equivocal to be let alone and yet, for Marcher's special sensibility, almost too formidable again to touch. He circled about it at a distance that alternately narrowed and widened and that still wasn't much affected by the conscious-ness in him that there was nothing she could "know," after all, any better than he did. She had no source of knowledge he hadn't equally — except of course that she might have finer nerves. That was what women had where they were interested; they made out things, where people were concerned, that the people often couldn't have made out for themselves. Their nerves, their sensibility, their imagination, were conductors and revealers, and the beauty of May Bartram was in particular that she had given herself so to his case. He felt in these days what, oddly enough, he had never felt before, the growth of a dread of losing her by some catastrophe — some catastrophe that yet wouldn't at all be *the* catastrophe: partly because she had almost of a sudden begun to strike him as more useful to him than ever yet, and partly by reason of an appearance of uncertainty in her health, coincident and equally new. It was characteristic of the inner detachment he had hitherto so successfully cultivated and to which our whole account of him is a reference, it was characteristic that his complications, such as they were, had never yet seemed so as at this crisis to thicken about him, even to the point of making him ask himself if he were, by any chance, of a truth, within sight or sound, within touch or reach, within the immediate jurisdiction, of the thing that waited.

When the day came, as come it had to, that his friend confessed to him her fear of a deep disorder in her blood, he felt somehow the shadow of a change and the chill of a shock. He immediately began to imagine aggrava-tions and disasters, and above all to think of her peril as the direct menace for himself of personal privation. This indeed gave him one of those partial recoveries of equanimity that were agreeable to him — it showed him that what was still first in his mind was the loss she herself might suffer. "What if she should have to die before knowing, before seeing —?" It would have been brutal, in the early stages of her trouble, to put that question to her; but it had immediately sounded for him to his own concern, and the possibility was what most made him sorry for her. If she did "know," moreover, in the sense of her having had some — what should he think? — mystical irresistible light, this would make the matter not better, but worse, inasmuch as her original adoption of his own curiosity had quite become the basis of her life. She had been living to see what would *be* to be seen, and it would quite lacerate her to have to give up before the accomplishment of the vision. These reflexions, as I say, quickened his generosity; yet, make them as he might, he saw himself, with the lapse of the period, more and more disconcerted. It lapsed for him with a strange steady sweep, and the oddest oddity was that it gave him, independently of the threat of much inconvenience, almost the only positive surprise his career, if career it could be called, had yet offered him. She kept the house as she had never done; he had to go to her to see her — she could meet him nowhere now, though there was scarce a corner of their loved old London in which she hadn't in the past, at one time or another, done so; and he found her always seated by her fire in the deep old-fashioned chair she was less and less able to leave. He had been struck one day, after an absence exceeding his usual measure, with her suddenly looking much older to him than he had ever thought of her being; then he recognised that the suddenness was all on his side — he had just simply and suddenly noticed. She looked older because inevitably, after so many years, she *was* old, or almost; which was of course true in still greater measure of her companion. If she was old, or almost, John Marcher assuredly was, and yet it was her showing of the lesson, not his own, that brought the truth home to him. His surprises began here; when once they had begun they multiplied; they came rather with a rush: it was as if, in the oddest way in the world, they had all been kept back, sown in a thick cluster, for the late afternoon of life, the time at which for people in general the unexpected has died out.

One of them was that he should have caught himself — for he *had* so done — *really* wondering if the great accident would take form now as nothing more than his being condemned to see this charming woman, this admirable friend, pass away from him. He had never so unreservedly qualified her as while confronted in thought with such a possibility; in spite of which there was small doubt for him that as an answer to his long riddle the mere effacement of even so fine a feature of his situation would be an abject anti-climax. It would represent, as connected with his past attitude, a drop of dignity under the shadow of which his existence could only become the most grotesque of failures. He had been far from holding it a failure — long as he had waited for the appearance that was to make it a success. He had waited for quite another thing, not for such a thing as that. The breath of his good faith came short, however, as he recognised how long he had waited, or how long at least his companion had. That she, at all events, might be recorded as having waited in vain — this affected him sharply, and all the more because of his at first having done little more than amuse himself with the idea. It grew more grave as the gravity of her condition grew, and the state of mind it produced in him, which he himself ended by watching as if it had been some definite disfigurement of his outer person, may pass for another of his surprises. This conjoined itself still with another, the really stupefying consciousness of a question that he would have allowed to shape itself had he dared. What did everything mean — what, that is, did *she* mean, she and her vain waiting and her probable death and the soundless admonition of it all — unless that, at this time of day, it was simply, it was overwhelmingly too late? He had never at any stage of his queer consciousness admitted the whisper of such a correction; he had never till within these last few months been so false to his conviction as not to hold that what was to come to him had time, whether *he* struck himself as having it or not. That at last, at last, he certainly hadn't it, to speak of, or had it but in the scantiest measure — such, soon enough, as things went with him, became the inference with which his old obsession had to reckon: and this it was not helped to do by the more and more confirmed appearance that the great vagueness casting the long shadow in which he had lived had, to attest itself, almost no margin left. Since it was in Time that he was to have met his fate, so it was in Time that his fate was to have acted; and as he waked up to the sense of no longer being young, which was exactly the sense of being stale, just as that, in turn, was the sense of being weak, he waked up to another matter beside. It all hung together; they were subject, he and the great vagueness, to an equal and indivisible law. When the possibilities themselves had accordingly turned stale, when the secret of the gods had grown faint, had perhaps even quite evaporated, that, and that only, was failure. It wouldn't have been failure to be bankrupt, dishonoured, pilloried, hanged; it was failure not to be anything. And so, in the dark valley into which his path had taken its unlooked-for twist, he wondered not a little as he groped. He didn't care what awful crash might overtake him, and what ignominy or what monstrosity he might yet be associated — since he wasn't after all too utterly old to suffer — if it would only be decently proportionate to the posture he had kept, all his life, in the threatened presence of it. He had but one desire left — that he shouldn't have been "sold."

IV

Then it was that, one afternoon, while the spring of the year was young and new she met all in her own way his frankest betrayal of these alarms. He had gone in late to see her, but evening hadn't settled and she was presented to him in that long fresh light of waning April days which affects us often with a sadness sharper than the greyest hours of autumn. The week had been warm, the spring was supposed to have begun early, and May Bartram sat, for the first time in the year, without a fire; a fact that, to Marcher's sense, gave the scene of which she formed part a smooth and ultimate look, an air of knowing, in its immaculate order and cold meaningless cheer, that it would never see a fire again. Her own aspect — he could scarce have said why — intensified this note. Almost as white as wax, with the marks and signs in her face as numerous and as fine as if they had been etched by a needle, with soft white draperies relieved by a faded green scarf on the delicate tone of which the years had further refined, she was the picture of a serene and exquisite but impenetrable sphinx, whose head, or indeed all whose person, might have been powdered with silver. She was a sphinx, yet with her white petals and green fronds she might have been a lily too — only an artificial lily, wonderfully imitated and constantly kept, without dust or stain, though not exempt from a slight droop and a complexity of faint creases, under some clear glass bell. The perfection of household care, of high polish and finish, always reigned in her rooms, but they now looked most as if everything had been wound up, tucked in, put away, so that she might sit with folded hands and with nothing more to do. She was "out of it," to Marcher's vision; her work was over; she communicated with him as across some gulf or from some island of rest that she had already reached, and it made him feel strangely abandoned. Was it — or rather wasn't it — that if for so long she had been watching with him the answer to their question must have swum into her ken and taken on its name, so that her occupation was verily gone? He had as much as charged her with this in saying to her, many months before, that she even then knew something she was keeping from him. It was a point he had never since ventured to press, vaguely fearing as he did that it might become a difference, perhaps a disagreement, between them. He had in this later time turned nervous, which was what he in all the other years had never been; and the oddity was that his nervousness should have waited till he had begun to doubt, should have held off so long as he was sure. There was something, it seemed to him, that the wrong word would bring down on his head, something that would so at least ease off his tension. But he wanted not to speak the wrong word; that would make everything ugly. He wanted the knowledge he lacked to drop on him, if drop it could, by its own august weight. If she was to forsake him it was surely for her to take leave. This was why he didn't directly ask her again what she knew; but it was also why, approaching the matter from another side, he said to her in the course of his visit: "What do you regard as the very worst that at this time of day *can* happen to me?"

He had asked her that in the past often enough; they had, with the odd irregular rhythm of their intensities and avoidances, exchanged ideas about it and then had seen the ideas washed away by cool intervals, washed like figures traced in sea-sand. It had ever been the mark of their talk that the oldest allusions in it required but a little dismissal and reaction to come out again, sounding for the hour as new. She could thus at present meet his enquiry quite freshly and patiently. "Oh yes, I've repeatedly thought, only it always seemed to me of old that I couldn't quite make up my mind. I thought of dreadful things, between which it was difficult to choose; and so must you have done."

"Rather! I feel now as if I had scarce done anything else. I appear to myself to have spent my life in thinking of nothing *but* dreadful things. A great many of them I've at different times named to you, but there were others I couldn't name."

"They were too, too dreadful?"

"Too, too dreadful — some of them."

She looked at him a minute, and there came to him as he met it an inconsequent sense that her eyes, when one got their full clearness, were still as beautiful as they had been in youth, only beautiful with a strange cold light — a light that somehow was a part of the effect, if it wasn't rather a part of the cause, of the pale hard sweetness of the season and the hour. "And yet," she said at last, "there are horrors we've mentioned."

It deepened the strangeness to see her, as such a figure in such a picture, talk of "horrors," but she was to do in a few minutes something stranger yet — though even of this he was to take the full measure but afterwards — and the note of it already trembled. It was, for the matter of that, one of the signs that her eyes were having again the high flicker of their prime. He had to admit, however, what she said. "Oh yes, there were times when we did go far." He caught himself in the act of speaking as if it all were over. Well, he wished it were; and the consummation depended for him clearly more and more on his friend.

But she had now a soft smile. "Oh far —!"

It was oddly ironic. "Do you mean you're prepared to go further?"

She was frail and ancient and charming as she continued to look at him, yet it was rather as if she had lost the thread. "Do you consider that we went far?"

"Why I thought it the point you were just making — that we *had* looked most things in the face."

"Including each other?" She still smiled. "But you're quite right. We've had together great imaginations, often great fears; but some of them have been unspoken."

"Then the worst — we haven't faced that. I *could* face it, I believe, if I knew what you think it. I feel," he explained, "as if I had lost my power to conceive such things." And he wondered if he looked as blank as he sounded. "It's spent."

"Then why do you assume," she asked, "that mine isn't?"

"Because you've given me signs to the contrary. It isn't a question for you of conceiving, imagining, comparing. It isn't a question now of choosing." At last he came out with it. "You know something I don't. You've shown me that before."

These last words had affected her, he made out in a moment, exceedingly, and she spoke with firmness. "I've shown you, my dear, nothing."

He shook his head. "You can't hide it."

"Oh, oh!" May Bartram sounded over what she couldn't hide. It was almost a smothered groan.

"You admitted it months ago, when I spoke of it to you as of something you were afraid I should find out. Your answer was that I couldn't, that I wouldn't, and I don't pretend I have. But you had something therefore in mind, and I now see how it must have been, how it still is, the possibility that, of all possibilities, has settled itself for you as the worst. This," he went on, "is why I appeal to you. I'm only afraid of ignorance today — I'm not afraid of knowledge." And then as for a while she said nothing: "What makes me sure is that I see in your face and feel here, in this air and amid these appearances, that you're out of it. You've done. You've had your experience. You leave me to my fate."

Well, she listened, motionless and white in her chair, as on a decision to be made, so that her manner was fairly an avowal, though still, with a small fine inner stiffness, an imperfect surrender. "It *would* be the worst," she finally let herself say. "I mean the thing I've never said."

It hushed him a moment. "More monstrous than all the monstrosities we've named?"

"More monstrous. Isn't that what you sufficiently express," she asked, "in calling it the worst?"

Marcher thought. "Assuredly — if you mean, as I do, something that includes all the loss and all the shame that are thinkable."

"It would if it *should* happen," said May Bartram. "What we're speaking of, remember, is only my idea."

"It's your belief," Marcher returned. "That's enough for me. I feel your beliefs are right. Therefore if, having this one, you give me no more light on it, you abandon me."

"No, no!" she repeated. "I'm with you — don't you see? — still." And as to make it more vivid to him she rose from her chair — a movement she seldom risked in these days — and showed herself, all draped and all soft, in her fairness and slimness. "I haven't forsaken you."

It was really, in its effort against weakness, a generous assurance, and had the success of the impulse not, happily, been great, it would have touched him to pain more than to pleasure. But the cold charm in her eyes had spread, as she hovered before him, to all the rest of her person, so that it was for the minute almost a recovery of youth. He couldn't pity her for that; he could only take her as she showed — as capable even yet of helping him. It was as if, at the same time, her light might at any instant go out; wherefore he must make the most of it. There passed before him with intensity the three or four things he wanted most to know; but the question that came of itself to his lips really covered the others. "Then tell me if I shall consciously suffer."

She promptly shook her head. "Never!"

It confirmed the authority he imputed to her, and it produced on him an extraordinary effect. "Well, what's better than that? Do you call that the worst?"

"You think nothing is better?" she asked.

She seemed to mean something so special that he again sharply wondered, though still with the dawn of a prospect of relief. "Why not, if one doesn't *know?*" After which, as their eyes, over his question, met in a silence, the dawn deepened and something to his purpose came prodigiously out of her very face. His own, as he took it in, suddenly flushed to the forehead, and he gasped with the force of a perception to which, on the instant, everything fitted. The sound of his gasp filled the air; then he became articulate. "I see — if I don't suffer!"

In her own look, however, was doubt. "You see what?"

"Why what you mean — what you've always meant."

She again shook her head. "What I mean isn't what I've always meant. It's different."

"It's something new?"

She hung back from it a little. "Something new. It's not what you think. I see what you think."

His divination drew breath then; only her correction might be wrong. "It isn't that I *am* a blockhead?" he asked between faintness and grimness. "It isn't that it's all a mistake?"

"A mistake?" she pityingly echoed. *That* possibility, for her, he saw, would be monstrous; and if she guaranteed him the immunity from pain it would accordingly not be what she had in mind. "Oh no," she declared; "it's nothing of that sort. You've been right."

Yet he couldn't help asking himself if she weren't, thus pressed, speaking but to save him. It seemed to him he should be most in a hole if his history should prove all a platitude. "Are you telling me the truth, so that I shan't have been a bigger idiot than I can bear to know? I *haven't* lived with a vain imagination, in the most besotted illusion? I haven't waited but to see the door shut in my face?"

She shook her head again. "However the case stands *that* isn't the truth. Whatever the reality, it *is* a reality. The door isn't shut. The door's open," said May Bartram.

"Then something's to come?"

She waited once again, always with her cold sweet eyes on him. "It's never too late." She had, with her gliding step, diminished the distance between them, and she stood nearer to him, close to him, a minute, as if still charged with the unspoken. Her movement might have been for some finer emphasis of what she was at once hesitating and deciding to say. He had been standing by the chimney-piece, fireless and sparely adorned, a small perfect old French clock and two morsels of rosy Dresden[2] constituting all its furniture; and her hand grasped the shelf while she kept him waiting, grasped it a little as for support and encouragement. She only kept him waiting, however; that is he only waited. It had become suddenly, from her movement and attitude, beautiful and vivid to him that she had something more to give him; her wasted face delicately shone with it — it glittered almost as with the white lustre of silver in her expression. She was right, incontestably, for what he saw in her face was the truth, and strangely, without consequence, while their talk of it as dreadful was still in the air, she appeared to present it as inordinately soft. This, prompting bewilderment, made him but gape the more gratefully for her revelation, so that they continued for some minutes silent, her face shining at him, her contact imponderably pressing, and his stare all kind but all expectant. The end, none the less, was that what he had expected failed to come to him. Something else took place instead, which seemed to consist at first in the mere closing of her eyes. She gave way at the same instant to a slow fine shudder, and though he remained staring — though he stared in fact but the harder — turned off and regained her chair. It was the end of what she had been intending, but it left him thinking only of that.

"Well, you don't say —?"

She had touched in her passage a bell near the chimney and had sunk back strangely pale. "I'm afraid I'm too ill."

"Too ill to tell me?" It sprang up sharp to him, and almost to his lips, the fear she might die without giving him light. He checked himself in time from so expressing his question, but she answered as if she had heard the words.

---

[2] Dresden china.

"Don't you know — now?"

"'Now' —?" She had spoken as if some difference had been made within the moment. But her maid, quickly obedient to her bell, was already with them. "I know nothing." And he was afterwards to say to himself that he must have spoken with odious impatience, such an impatience as to show that, supremely disconcerted, he washed his hands of the whole question.

"Oh!" said May Bartram.

"Are you in pain?" he asked as the woman went to her.

"No," said May Bartram.

Her maid, who had put an arm round her as if to take her to her room, fixed on him eyes that appealingly contradicted her; in spite of which, however, he showed once more his mystification. "What then has happened?"

She was once more, with her companion's help, on her feet, and, feeling withdrawal imposed on him, he had blankly found his hat and gloves and had reached the door. Yet he waited for her answer. "What *was* to," she said.

V

He came back the next day, but she was then unable to see him, and as it was literally the first time this had occurred in the long stretch of their acquaintance he turned away, defeated and sore, almost angry — or feeling at least that such a break in their custom was really the beginning of the end — and wandered alone with his thoughts, especially with the one he was least able to keep down. She was dying and he would lose her; she was dying and his life would end. He stopped in the Park, into which he had passed, and stared before him at his recurrent doubt. Away from her the doubt pressed again; in her presence he had believed her, but as he felt his forlornness he threw himself into the explanation that, nearest at hand, had most of a miserable warmth for him and least of a cold torment. She had deceived him to save him — to put him off with something in which he should be able to rest. What could the thing that was to happen to him be, after all, but just this thing that had begun to happen? Her dying, her death, his consequent solitude — *that* was what he had figured as the Beast in the Jungle, that was what had been in the lap of the gods. He had had her word for it as he left her — what else on earth could she have meant? It wasn't a thing of a monstrous order; not a fate rare and distinguished; not a stroke of fortune that overwhelmed and immortalised; it had only the stamp of the common doom. But poor Marcher at this hour judged the common doom sufficient. It would serve his turn, and even as the consummation of infinite waiting he would bend his pride to accept it. He sat down on a bench in the twilight. He hadn't been a fool. Something had *been*, as she had said, to come. Before he rose indeed it had quite struck him that the final fact really matched with the long avenue through which he had had to reach it. As sharing his suspense and as giving herself all, giving her life, to bring it to an end, she had come with him every step of the way. He had lived by her aid, and to leave her behind would be cruelly, damnably to miss her. What could be more overwhelming than that?

Well, he was to know within the week, for though she kept him a while at bay, left him restless and wretched during a series of days on each of which he asked about her only again to have to turn away, she ended his trial by receiving him where she had always received him. Yet she had been brought out at some hazard into the presence of so many of the things that were, consciously, vainly, half their past, and there was scant service left in the gentleness of her mere desire, all too visible, to check his obsession and wind up his long trouble. That was clearly what she wanted, the one thing more for her own peace while she could still put out her hand. He was so affected by her state that, once seated by her chair, he was moved to let everything go; it was she herself therefore who brought him back, took up again, before she dismissed him, her last word of the other time. She showed how she wished to leave their business in order. "I'm not sure you understood. You've nothing to wait for more. It *has* come."

Oh how he looked at her! "Really?"

"Really."

"The thing that, as you said, *was* to?"

"The thing that we began in our youth to watch for."

Face to face with her once more he believed her; it was a claim to which he had so abjectly little to oppose. "You mean that it has come as a positive definite occurrence, with a name and a date?"

"Positive. Definite. I don't know about the 'name,' but oh with a date!"

He found himself again too helplessly at sea. "But come in the night — come and passed me by?"

May Bartram had her strange faint smile. "Oh no, it hasn't passed you by!"

"But if I haven't been aware of it and it hasn't touched me —?"

"Ah your not being aware of it" — and she seemed to hesitate an instant to deal with this — "your not being aware of it is the strangeness *in* the strangeness. It's the wonder *of* the wonder." She spoke as with the softness almost of a sick child, yet now at last, at the end of all, with the perfect straightness of a sibyl. She visibly knew that she knew, and the effect on him was of something co-ordinate, in its high character, with the law that had ruled him. It was the true voice of the law; so on her lips would the law itself have sounded. "It *has* touched you," she went on. "It has done its office. It has made you all its own."

"So utterly without my knowing it?"

"So utterly without your knowing it." His hand, as he leaned to her, was on the arm of her chair, and, dimly smiling always now, she placed her own on it. "It's enough if *I* know it."

"Oh!" he confusedly breathed, as she herself of late so often had done.

"What I long ago said is true. You'll never know now, and I think you ought to be content. You've *had* it," said May Bartram.

"But had what?"

"Why what was to have marked you out. The proof of your law. It has acted. I'm too glad," she then bravely added, "to have been able to see what it's *not*."

He continued to attach his eyes to her, and with the sense that it was all beyond him, and that *she* was too, he would still have sharply challenged her hadn't he so felt it an abuse of her weakness to do more than take devoutly what she gave him, take it hushed as to a revelation. If he did speak, it was out of the foreknowledge of his loneliness to come. "If you're glad of what it's 'not' it might then have been worse?"

She turned her eyes away, she looked straight before her; with which after a moment: "Well, you know our fears."

He wondered. "It's something then we never feared?"

On this slowly she turned to him. "Did we ever dream, with all our dreams, that we should sit and talk of it thus?"

He tried for a little to make out that they had; but it was as if their dreams, numberless enough, were in solution in some thick cold mist through which thought lost itself. "It might have been that we couldn't talk?"

"Well" — she did her best for him — "not from this side. This, you see," she said, "is the *other* side."

"I think," poor Marcher returned, "that all sides are the same to me." Then, however, as she gently shook her head in correction: "We mightn't, as it were, have got across —?"

"To where we are — no. We're *here*" — she made her weak emphasis.

"And much good does it do us!" was her friend's frank comment.

"It does us the good it can. It does us the good that *it* isn't here. It's past. It's behind," said May Bartram. "Before — " but her voice dropped.

He had got up, not to tire her, but it was hard to combat his yearning. She after all told him nothing but that his light had failed — which he knew well enough without her. "Before — ?" he blankly echoed.

"Before, you see, it was always to *come*. That kept it present."

"Oh I don't care what comes now! Besides," Marcher added, "it seems to me I liked it better present, as you say, than I can like it absent with *your* absence."

"Oh mine!" — and her pale hands made light of it.

"With the absence of everything." He had a dreadful sense of standing there before her for — so far as anything but this proved, this bottomless drop was concerned — the last time of their life. It rested on him with a weight he felt he could scarce bear, and this weight it apparently was that still pressed out what remained in him of speakable protest. "I believe you; but I can't begin to pretend I understand. *Nothing*, for me, is past; nothing *will* pass till I pass myself, which I pray my stars may be as soon as possible. Say, however," he added, "that I've eaten my cake, as you contend, to the last crumb — how can the thing I've never felt at all be the thing I was marked out to feel?"

She met him perhaps less directly, but she met him unperturbed. "You take your 'feelings' for granted. You were to suffer your fate. That was not necessarily to know it."

"How in the world — when what is such knowledge but suffering?"

She looked up at him a while in silence. "No — you don't understand."

"I suffer," said John Marcher.

"Don't, don't!"

"How can I help at least *that*?"

"*Don't!*" May Bartram repeated.

She spoke it in a tone so special, in spite of her weakness, that he stared an instant — stared as if some light, hitherto hidden, had shimmered across his vision. Darkness again closed over it, but the gleam had already become for him an idea. "Because I haven't the right —?"

"Don't *know* — when you needn't," she mercifully urged. "You needn't — for we shouldn't."

"Shouldn't?" If he could but know what she meant!

"No — it's too much."

"Too much?" he still asked but, with a mystification that was the next moment of a sudden to give way. Her words, if they meant something, affected him in this light — the light also of her wasted face — as meaning *all*, and the sense of what knowledge had been for herself came over him with a rush which broke through into a question. "Is it of that then you're dying?"

She but watched him, gravely at first, as to see, with this, where he was, and she might have seen something or feared something that moved her sympathy. "I would live for you still — if I could." Her eyes closed for a little, as if, withdrawn into herself, she were for a last time trying. "But I can't!" she said as she raised them again to take leave of him.

She couldn't indeed, as but too promptly and sharply appeared, and he had no vision of her after this that was anything but darkness and doom. They had parted for ever in that strange talk; access to her chamber of pain, rigidly guarded, was almost wholly forbidden him; he was feeling now moreover, in the face of doctors, nurses, the two or three relatives attracted doubtless by the presumption of what she had to "leave," how few were the rights, as they were called in such cases, that he had to put forward, and how odd it might even seem that their intimacy shouldn't have given him more of them. The stupidest fourth cousin had more, even though she had been nothing in such a person's life. She had been a feature of features in *his*, for what else was it to have been so indispensable? Strange beyond saying were the ways of existence, baffling for him the anomaly of his lack, as he felt it to be, of producible claim. A woman might have been, as it were, everything to him, and it might yet present him in no connexion that any one seemed held to recognise. If this was the case in these closing weeks it was the case more sharply on the occasion of the last offices rendered, in the great grey London cemetery, to what had been mortal, to what had been precious, in his friend. The concourse at her grave was not numerous, but he saw himself treated as scarce more nearly concerned with it than if there had been a thousand others. He was in short from this moment face to face with the fact that he was to profit extraordinarily little by the interest May Bartram had taken in him. He couldn't quite have said what he expected, but he hadn't surely expected this approach to a double privation. Not only had her interest failed him, but he seemed to feel himself unattended — and for a reason he couldn't seize — by the distinction, the dignity, the propriety, if nothing else, of the man markedly bereaved. It was as if in the view of society he had not *been* markedly bereaved, as if there still failed some sign or proof of it, and as if none the less his character could never be affirmed nor the deficiency ever made up. There were moments as the weeks went by when he would have liked, by some almost aggressive act, to take his stand on the intimacy of his loss, in order that it *might* be questioned and his retort, to the relief of his spirit, so recorded; but the moments of an irritation more helpless followed fast on these, the moments during which, turning things over with a good conscience but with a bare horizon, he found himself wondering if he oughtn't to have begun, so to speak, further back.

He found himself wondering indeed at many things, and this last speculation had others to keep it company. What could he have done, after all, in her lifetime, without giving them both, as it were, away? He couldn't have made known she was watching him, for that would have published the superstition of the Beast. This was what closed his mouth now — now that the Jungle had been threshed to vacancy and that the Beast had stolen away. It sounded too foolish and too flat; the difference for him in this particular, the extinction in his life of the element of suspense, was such as in fact to surprise him. He could scarce have said what the effect resembled; the abrupt cessation, the positive prohibition, of music perhaps, more than anything else, in some place all adjusted and all accustomed to sonority and to attention. If he could at any rate have conceived lifting the veil from his image at some moment of the past (what had he done, after all, if not lift it to *her*?) so to do this today, to talk to people at large of the Jungle cleared and confide to them that he now felt it as safe, would have been not only to see them listen as to a goodwife's tale, but really to hear himself tell one. What it presently came to in truth was that poor Marcher waded through his beaten grass, where no life stirred, where no breath sounded, where no evil eye seemed to gleam from a possible lair, very much as if vaguely looking for the Beast, and still more as if acutely missing it. He walked about in an existence that had grown strangely more spacious, and, stopping fitfully in places where the undergrowth of life struck him as closer, asked himself yearningly, wondered secretly and sorely, if it would have lurked here or there. It would have at all events *sprung*; what was at least complete was his belief in the truth itself of the assurance given him. The change from his old sense to his new was absolute and final: what was to happen *had* so absolutely and finally happened that he was as little able to know a fear for his future as to know a hope; so absent in short was any question of anything still to come. He was to live entirely with the other question, that of his unidentified past, that of his having to see his fortune impenetrably muffled and masked.

The torment of this vision became then his occupation; he couldn't perhaps have consented to live but for the possibility of guessing. She had told him, his friend, not to guess; she had forbidden him, so far as he might, to know, and she had even in a sort denied the power in him to learn: which were so many things, precisely, to deprive him of rest. It wasn't that he wanted, he argued for fairness, that anything past and done should repeat itself; it was only that he shouldn't, as an anticlimax, have been taken sleeping so sound as not to be able to win back by an effort of thought the lost stuff of consciousness. He declared to himself at moments that he would either win it back or have done with consciousness for ever; he made this idea his one motive in fine, made it so much his passion that none other, to compare with it, seemed ever to have touched him. The lost stuff of consciousness became thus for him as a strayed or stolen child to an unappeasable father; he hunted it up and down very much as if he were knocking at doors and enquiring of the police. This was the spirit in which, inevitably, he set himself to travel; he started on a journey that was to be as long as he could make it; it danced before him that, as the other side of the globe couldn't possibly have less to say to him, it might, by a possibility of suggestion, have more. Before he quitted London, however, he made a pilgrimage to May Bartram's grave, took his way to it through the endless avenues of the grim suburban metropolis, sought it out in the wilderness of tombs, and, though he had come but for the renewal of the act of farewell, found himself, when he had at last stood by it, beguiled into long intensities. He stood for an hour, powerless to turn away and yet powerless to penetrate the darkness of death; fixing with his eyes her inscribed name and date, beating his forehead against the fact of the secret they kept, drawing his breath, while he waited, as if some sense would in pity of him rise from the stones. He kneeled on the stones, however, in vain; they kept what they concealed; and if the face of the tomb did become a face for him it was because her two names became a pair of eyes that didn't know him. He gave them a last long look, but no palest light broke.

VI

He stayed away, after this, for a year; he visited the depths of Asia, spending himself on scenes of romantic interest, of superlative sanctity; but what was present to him everywhere was that for a man who had known what *he* had known the world was vulgar and vain. The state of mind in which he had lived for so many years shone out to him, in reflexion, as a light that coloured and refined, a light beside which the glow of the East was garish and cheap and thin. The terrible truth was that he had lost — with everything else — a distinction as well; the things he saw couldn't help being common when he had become common to look at them. He was simply now one of them himself — he was in the dust, without a peg for the sense of difference; and there were hours when, before the temples of gods and the sepulchres of kings, his spirit turned for nobleness of association to the barely discriminated slab in the London suburb. That had become for him, and more intensely with time and distance, his one witness of a past glory. It was all that was left to him for proof or pride, yet the past glories of Pharaohs were nothing to him as he thought of it. Small wonder then that he came back to it on the morrow of his return. He was drawn there this time as irresistibly as the other, yet with a confidence, almost, that was doubtless the effect of the many months that had elapsed. He had lived, in spite of himself, into his change of feeling, and in wandering over the earth had wandered, as might be said, from the circumference to the centre of his desert. He had settled to his safety and accepted perforce his extinction; figuring to himself, with some colour, in the likeness of certain little old men he remembered to have seen, of whom, all meagre and wizened as they might look, it was related that they had in their time fought twenty duels or been loved by ten princesses. They indeed had been wondrous for others while he was but wondrous for himself; which, however, was exactly the cause of his haste to renew the wonder by getting back, as he might put it, into his own presence. That had quickened his steps and checked his delay. If his visit was prompt it was because he had been separated so long from the part of himself that alone he now valued.

It's accordingly not false to say that he reached his goal with a certain elation and stood there again with a certain assurance. The creature beneath the sod *knew* of his rare experience, so that, strangely now, the place had lost for him its mere blankness of expression. It met him in mildness — not, as before, in mockery; it wore for him the air of conscious greeting that we find, after absence, in things that have closely belonged to us and which seem to confess of themselves to the connexion. The plot of ground, the graven tablet, the tended flowers affected him so as belonging to him that he resembled for the hour a contented landlord reviewing a piece of property. Whatever had happened — well, had happened. He had not come back this time with the vanity of that question, his former worrying "what, *what?*" now practically so spent. Yet he would none the less never again so cut himself off from the spot; he would come back to it every month, for if he did nothing else by its aid he at least held up his head. It thus grew for him, in the oddest way, a positive resource; he carried out his idea of periodical returns, which took their place at last among the most inveterate of his habits. What it all amounted to, oddly enough, was that in his finally so simplified world this garden of death gave him the few square feet of earth on which he could still most live. It was as if, being nothing anywhere else for any one, nothing even for himself, he were just everything here, and if not for a crowd of witnesses or indeed for any witness but John Marcher, then by clear right of the register that he could scan like an open page. The open page was the tomb of his friend, and *there* were the facts of the past, there the truth of his life, there the backward reaches in which he could lose himself. He did this from time to time with such effect that he seemed to wander through the old years with his hand in the arm of a companion who was, in the most extraordinary manner, his other, his younger self; and to wander, which was more extraordinary yet, round and round a third presence — not wandering she, but stationary, still, whose eyes, turning with his revolution, never ceased to follow him, and whose seat was his point, so to speak, of orientation. Thus in short he settled to live — feeding all on the sense that he once *had* lived, and dependent on it not alone for a support but for an identity.

It sufficed him in its way for months and the year elapsed; it would doubtless even have carried him further but for an accident, superficially slight, which moved him, quite in another direction, with a force beyond any of his impressions of Egypt or of India. It was a thing of the merest chance — the turn, as he afterwards felt, of a hair, though he was indeed to live to believe that if light hadn't come to him in this particular fashion it would still have come in another. He was to live to believe this, I say, though he was not to live, I may not less definitely mention, to do much else. We allow him at any rate the benefit of the conviction, struggling up for him at the end, that, whatever might have happened or not happened, he would have come round of himself to the light. The incident of an autumn day had put the match to the train laid from of old by his misery. With the light before him he knew that even of late his ache had only been smothered. It was stragely drugged, but it throbbed; at the touch it began to bleed. And the touch, in the event, was the face of a fellow mortal. This face, one grey afternoon when the leaves were thick in the alleys, looked into Marcher's own, at the cemetery, with an expression like the cut of a blade. He felt it, that is, so deep down that he winced at the steady thrust. The person who so mutely assaulted him was a figure he had noticed, on reaching his own goal, absorbed by a grave a short distance away, a grave apparently fresh, so that the emotion of the visitor would probably match it for frankness. This fact alone forbade further attention, though during the time he stayed he remained vaguely conscious of his neighbour, a middle-aged man apparently, in mourning, whose bowed back, among the clustered monuments and mortuary yews, was constantly presented. Marcher's theory that these were elements in contact with which he himself revived, had suffered, on this occasion, it may be granted, a marked, an excessive check. The autumn day was dire for him as none had recently been, and he rested with a heaviness he had not yet known on the low stone table that bore May Bartram's name. He rested without power to move, as if some spring in him, some spell vouchsafed, had suddenly been broken for ever. If he could have done that moment as he wanted he would simply have stretched himself on the slab that was ready to take him, treating it as a place prepared to receive his last sleep. What in all the wide world had he now to keep awake for? He stared before him with the question, and it was then that, as one of the cemetery walks passed near him, he caught the shock of the face.

His neighbour at the other grave had withdrawn, as he himself, with force enough in him, would have done by now, and was advancing along the path on his way to one of the gates. This brought him close, and his pace was slow, so that — and all the more as there was a kind of hunger in his look — the two men were for a minute directly confronted. Marcher knew him at once for one of the deeply stricken — a perception so sharp that nothing else in the picture comparatively lived, neither his dress, his age, nor his presumable character and class; nothing lived but the deep ravage of the features he showed. He *showed* them — that was the point; he was moved, as he passed, by some impulse that was either a signal for sympathy or, more possibly, a challenge to an opposed sorrow. He might already have been aware of our friend, might at some previous hour have noticed in him the smooth habit of the scene, with which the state of his own senses so scantly consorted, and might thereby have been stirred as by an overt discord. What Marcher was at all events conscious of was in the first place that the image of scarred passion presented to him was conscious too — of something that profaned the air; and in the second that, roused, startled, shocked, he was yet the next moment looking after it, as it went, with envy. The most extraordinary thing that had happened to him — though he had given that name to other matters as well — took place, after his immediate vague stare, as a consequence of this impression. The stranger passed, but the raw glare of his grief remained, making our friend wonder in pity what wrong, what wound it expressed, what injury not to be healed. What had the man *had*, to make him by the loss of it so bleed and yet live?

Something — and this reached him with a pang — that *he*, John Marcher, hadn't; the proof of which was precisely John Marcher's arid end. No passion had ever touched him, for this was what passion meant; he had survived and maundered and pined, but where had been *his* deep ravage? The extraordinary thing we speak of was the sudden rush of the result of this question. The sight that had just met his eyes named to him, as in letters of quick flame, something he had utterly, insanely missed, and what he had missed made these things a train of fire, made them mark themselves in an anguish of inward throbs. He had seen *outside* of his life, not learned it within, the way a woman was mourned when she had been loved for herself: such was the force of his conviction of the meaning of the stranger's face, which still flared for him as a smoky torch. It hadn't come to him, the knowledge, on the wings of experience; it had brushed him, jostled him, upset him, with the disrespect of chance, the insolence of accident. Now that the illumination had begun, however, it blazed to the zenith, and what he presently stood there gazing at was the sounded void of his life. He gazed, he drew breath, in pain; he turned in his dismay, and, turning, he had before him in sharper incision than ever the open page of his story. The name on the table smote him as the passage of his neighbour had done, and what it said to him, full in the face, was that *she* was what he had missed. This was the awful thought, the answer to all the past, the vision at the dread clearness of which he grew as cold as the stone beneath him. Everything fell together, confessed, explained, over-whelmed; leaving him most of all stupefied at the blindness he had cherished. The fate he had been marked for he had met with a vengeance — he had emptied the cup to the lees; he had been the man of his time, *the* man, to whom nothing on earth was to have happened. That was the rare stroke — that was his visitation. So he saw it, as we say, in pale horror, while the pieces fitted and fitted. So *she* had seen it while he didn't, and so she served at this hour to drive the truth home. It was the truth, vivid and monstrous, that all the while he had waited the wait was itself his portion. This the companion of his vigil had at a given moment made out, and she had then offered him the chance to baffle his doom. One's doom, however, was never baffled, and on the day she told him his own had come down she had seen him but stupidly stare at the escape she offered him.

The escape would have been to love her; then, *then* he would have lived. *She* had lived — who could say now with what passion? — since she had loved him for himself; whereas he had never thought of her (ah how it hugely glared at him!) but in the chill of his egotism and the light of her use. Her spoken words came back to him — the chain stretched and stretched. The Beast had lurked indeed, and the Beast, at its hour, had sprung it; it had sprung in that twilight of the cold April when, pale, ill, wasted, but all beautiful, and perhaps even then recoverable, she had risen from her chair to stand before him and let him imaginably guess. It had sprung as he didn't guess; it had sprung as she hopelessly turned from him, and the mark, by the time he left her, had fallen where it *was* to fall. He had justified his fear and achieved his fate; he had failed, with the last exactitude, of all he was to fail of; and a moan now rose to his lips as he remembered she had prayed he mightn't know. This horror of waking — *this* was knowledge, knowledge under the breath of which the very tears in his eyes seemed to freeze. Through them, none the less, he tried to fix it and hold it; he kept it there before him so that he might feel the pain. That at least, belated and bitter, had something of the taste of life. But the bitterness suddenly sickened him, and it was as if, horribly, he saw, in the truth, in the cruelty of his image, what had been appointed and done. He saw the Jungle of his life and saw the lurking Beast; then, while he looked, perceived it, as by a stir of the air, rise, huge and hideous, for the leap that was to settle him. His eyes darkened — it was close; and, instinctively turning, in his hallucination, to avoid it, he flung himself, face down, on the tomb.   [1903]

SARAH ORNE JEWETT *(1849–1909) was born in South Berwick, Maine. Her father was a country doctor, and she often accompanied him on his horse-and-buggy rounds among sick people on the local farms. She later said that she got her real education from these trips, rather than from her classes at Miss Rayne's School and the Berwick Academy. She had a fine ear for local speech and the native idiom, which she used to good effect in her stories. Impressed as a girl by the sympathetic depiction of local color (the people and life of a particular geographical setting) in the fiction of Harriet Beecher Stowe, Jewett began to write stories herself, publishing her earliest one, "Jenny Garrow's Lovers," in a Boston weekly when she was eighteen years old. Shortly after her twentieth birthday, her work was accepted by the prestigious* Atlantic Monthly, *and her career was launched. Jewett published her first collection of stories,* Deephaven, *in 1877. She read the work of Gustave Flaubert, Émile Zola, Leo Tolstoy, and Henry James, and her style gradually matured, as is evident in the stories that make up the 1886 volume* A White Heron and Other Stories. *Jewett took her favorite motto from Flaubert, "One should write of ordinary life as if one were writing history." Her masterpiece,* The Country of the Pointed Firs *(1896), is a book of scrupulously observed short sketches linked by the narrator's account of her stay in a Maine seacoast village and her growing involvement in the quiet lives of its people.*

Many stories were written about New England in Jewett's time, but hers have a unique quality stemming from her deep sympathy for the native characters and her ear for local speech. Once she laughingly told the younger writer Willa Cather that her head was full of dear old houses and dear old women, and when an old house and an old woman came together in her brain with a click, she knew a story was under way.

Although it is true that Jewett's realism heightens the attractive aspects of the rural New England character at the same time that it diminishes the harsher qualities, her literary technique is so candid and true to the larger aspects of human nature that the darker undercurrents of deprivation, both physical and psychological, are evident beneath the surface of her descriptions. Henry James recognized that Jewett was "surpassed only by Hawthorne as producer of the most finished and penetrating of the numerous 'short stories' that have the domestic life of New England for their general and their doubtless somewhat lean subject." In her time she was lauded for possessing an exquisitely simple, natural, and graceful style; more recently, readers have responded to the serenity and honesty in stories such as "A White Heron."

RELATED COMMENTARY: *Sarah Orne Jewett, "Looking Back on Girlhood,"* page 1441.

SARAH ORNE JEWETT

A White Heron

I

The woods were already filled with shadows one June evening, just before eight o'clock, though a bright sunset still glimmered faintly among the trunks of the trees. A little girl was driving home her cow, a plodding, dilatory, provoking creature in her behavior, but a valued companion for all that. They were going away from the western light, and striking deep into the dark woods, but their feet were familiar with the path, and it was no matter whether their eyes could see it or not.

There was hardly a night the summer through when the old cow could be found waiting at the pasture bars; on the contrary, it was her greatest pleasure to hide herself away among the high huckleberry bushes, and though she wore a loud bell she had made the discovery that if one stood perfectly still it would not ring. So Sylvia had to hunt for her until she found her and call Co'! Co'! with never an answering Moo, until her childish patience was quite spent. If the creature had not given good milk and plenty of it, the case would have seemed very different to her owners. Besides, Sylvia had all the time there was, and very little use to make of it. Sometimes in pleasant weather it was a consolation to look upon the cow's pranks as an intelligent attempt to play hide and seek, and as the child had no playmates she lent herself to this amusement with a good deal of zest. Though this chase had been so long that the wary animal herself had given an unusual signal of her whereabouts, Sylvia had only laughed when she came upon Mistress Moolly at the swamp-side, and urged her affectionately homeward with a twig of birch leaves. The old cow was not inclined to wander farther, she even turned in the right direction for once as they left the pasture, and stepped along the road at a good pace. She was quite ready to be milked now, and seldom stopped to browse. Sylvia wondered what her grandmother would say because they were so late. It was a great while since she had left home at half past five o'clock, but everybody knew the difficulty of making this errand a short one. Mrs. Tilley had chased the horned torment too many summer evenings herself to blame any one else for lingering, and was only thankful as she waited that she had Sylvia, nowadays, to give such valuable assistance. The good woman suspected that Sylvia loitered occasionally on her own account; there never was such a child for straying about out-of-doors since the world was made! Everybody said that it was a good change for a little maid who had tried to grow for eight years in a crowded manufacturing town, but, as for Sylvia herself, it seemed as if she never had been alive at all before she came to live at the farm. She thought often with wistful compassion of a wretched dry geranium that belonged to a town neighbor.

"'Afraid of folks,'" old Mrs. Tilley said to herself, with a smile, after she had made the unlikely choice of Sylvia from her daughter's houseful of children, and was returning to the farm. "'Afraid of folks,' they said! I guess she won't be troubled no great with 'em up to the old place!" When they reached the door of the lonely house and stopped to unlock it, and the cat came to purr loudly, and rub against them, a deserted pussy, indeed, but fat with young robins, Sylvia whispered that this was a beautiful place to live in, and she never should wish to go home.

The companions followed the shady wood-road, the cow taking slow steps, and the child very fast ones. The cow stopped long at the brook to drink, as if the pasture were not half a swamp, and Sylvia stood still and waited, letting her bare feet cool themselves in the shoal water, while the great twilight moths struck softly against her. She waded on through the brook as the cow moved away, and listened to the thrushes with a heart that beat fast with pleasure. There was a stirring in the great boughs overhead. They were full of little birds and beasts that seemed to be wide-awake, and going about their world, or else saying good-night to each other in sleepy twitters. Sylvia herself felt sleepy as she walked along. However, it was not much farther to the house, and the air was soft and sweet. She was not often in the woods so late as this, and it made her feel as if she were a part of the gray shadows and the moving leaves. She was just thinking how long it seemed since she first came to the farm a year ago, and wondering if everything went on in the noisy town just the same as when she was there; the thought of the great red-faced boy who used to chase and frighten her made her hurry along the path to escape from the shadow of the trees.

Suddenly this little woods-girl is horror-stricken to hear a clear whistle not very far away. Not a bird's whistle, which would have a sort of friendliness, but a boy's whistle, determined, and somewhat aggressive. Sylvia left the cow to whatever sad fate might await her, and stepped discreetly aside into the bushes, but she was just too late. The enemy had discovered her, and called out in a very cheerful and persuasive tone, "Halloa, little girl, how far is it to the road?" and trembling Sylvia answered almost inaudibly, "A good ways."

She did not dare to look boldly at the tall young man, who carried a gun over his shoulder, but she came out of her bush and again followed the cow, while he walked alongside.

"I have been hunting for some birds," the stranger said kindly, "and I have lost my way, and need a friend very much. Don't be afraid," he added gallantly. "Speak up and tell me what your name is, and whether you think I can spend the night at your house, and go out gunning early in the morning."

Sylvia was more alarmed than before. Would not her grandmother consider her much to blame? But who could have foreseen such an accident as this? It did not appear to be her fault, and she hung her head as if the stem of it were broken, but managed to answer, "Sylvy," with much effort when her companion again asked her name.

Mrs. Tilley was standing in the doorway when the trio came into view. The cow gave a loud moo by way of explanation.

"Yes, you'd better speak up for yourself, you old trial! Where'd she tucked herself away this time, Sylvy?" Sylvia kept an awed silence; she knew by instinct that her grandmother did not comprehend the gravity of the situation. She must be mistaking the stranger for one of the farmer-lads of the region.

The young man stood his gun beside the door, and dropped a heavy game-bag beside it; then he bade Mrs. Tilley good-evening, and repeated his wayfarer's story, and asked if he could have a night's lodging.

"Put me anywhere you like," he said. "I must be off early in the morning, before day; but I am very hungry, indeed. You can give me some milk at any rate, that's plain."

"Dear sakes, yes," responded the hostess, whose long slumbering hospitality seemed to be easily awakened. "You might fare better if you went out on the main road a mile or so, but you're welcome to what we've got. I'll milk right off, and you make yourself at home. You can sleep on husks or feathers," she proffered graciously. "I raised them all myself. There's good pasturing for geese just below here towards the ma'sh. Now step round and set a plate for the gentleman, Sylvy!" And Sylvia promptly stepped. She was glad to have something to do, and she was hungry herself.

It was a surprise to find so clean and comfortable a little dwelling in this New England wilderness. The young man had known the horrors of its most primitive housekeeping, and the dreary squalor of that level of society which does not rebel at the companionship of hens. This was the best thrift of an old-fashioned farmstead, though on such a small scale that it seemed like a hermitage. He listened eagerly to the old woman's quaint talk, he watched Sylvia's pale face and shining gray eyes with ever growing enthusiasm, and insisted that this was the best supper he had eaten for a month; then, afterward, the new-made friends sat down in the doorway together while the moon came up.

Soon it would be berry-time, and Sylvia was a great help at picking. The cow was a good milker, though a plaguy thing to keep track of, the hostess gossiped frankly, adding presently that she had buried four children, so that Sylvia's mother, and a son (who might be dead) in California were all the children she had left. "Dan, my boy, was a great hand to go gunning," she explained sadly. "I never wanted for pa'tridges or gray squer'ls while he was to home. He's been a great wand'rer, I expect, and he's no hand to write letters. There, I don't blame him, I'd ha' seen the world myself if it had been so I could.

"Sylvia takes after him," the grandmother continued affectionately, after a minute's pause. "There ain't a foot o' ground she don't know her way over, and the wild creatur's counts her one o' themselves. Squer'ls she'll tame to come an' feed right out o' her hands, and all sorts o' birds. Last winter she got the jay-birds to bangeing here, and I believe she'd 'a' scanted herself of her own meals to have plenty to throw out amongst 'em, if I hadn't kep' watch. Anything but crows, I tell her, I'm willin' to help support, — though Dan he went an' tamed one o' them that did seem to have reason same as folks. It was round here a good spell after he went away. Dan an' his father they didn't hitch, — but he never held up his head ag'in after Dan had dared him an' gone off."

The guest did not notice this hint of family sorrows in his eager interest in something else.

"So Sylvy knows all about birds, does she?" he exclaimed, as he looked round at the little girl who sat, very demure but increasingly sleepy, in the moonlight. "I am making a collection of birds myself. I have been at it ever since I was a boy." (Mrs. Tilley smiled.) "There are two or three very rare ones I have been hunting for these five years. I mean to get them on my own ground if they can be found."

"Do you cage 'em up?" asked Mrs. Tilley doubtfully, in response to this enthusiastic announcement.

"Oh, no, they're stuffed and preserved, dozens and dozens of them," said the ornithologist, "and I have shot or snared every one myself. I caught a glimpse of a white heron three miles from here on Saturday, and I have followed it in this direction. They have never been found in this district at all. The little white heron, it is," and he turned again to look at Sylvia with the hope of discovering that the rare bird was one of her acquaintances.

But Sylvia was watching a hop-toad in the narrow footpath.

"You would know the heron if you saw it," the stranger continued eagerly. "A queer tall white bird with soft feathers and long thin legs. And it would have a nest perhaps in the top of a high tree, made of sticks, something like a hawk's nest."

Sylvia's heart gave a wild beat; she knew that strange white bird, and had once stolen softly near where it stood in some bright green swamp grass, away over at the other side of the woods. There was an open place where the sunshine always seemed strangely yellow and hot, where tall, nodding rushes grew, and her grandmother had warned her that she might sink in the soft black mud underneath and never be heard of more. Not far beyond were the salt marshes and beyond those was the sea, the sea which Sylvia wondered and dreamed about, but never had looked upon, though its great voice could often be heard above the noise of the woods on stormy nights.

"I can't think of anything I should like so much as to find that heron's nest," the handsome stranger was saying. "I would give ten dollars to anybody who could show it to me," he added desperately, "and I mean to spend my whole vacation hunting for it if need be. Perhaps it was only migrating, or had been chased out of its own region by some bird of prey."

Mrs. Tilley gave amazed attention to all this, but Sylvia still watched the toad, not divining, as she might have done at some calmer time, that the creature wished to get to its hole under the doorstep, and was much hindered by the unusual spectators at that hour of the evening. No amount of thought, that night, could decide how many wished-for treasures the ten dollars, so lightly spoken of, would buy.

The next day the young sportsman hovered about the woods, and Sylvia kept him company, having lost her first fear of the friendly lad, who proved to be most kind and sympathetic. He told her many things about the birds and what they knew and where they lived and what they did with themselves. And he gave her a jack-knife, which she thought as great a treasure as if she were a desert-islander. All day long he did not once make her troubled or afraid except when he brought down some unsuspecting singing creature from its bough. Sylvia would have liked him vastly better without his gun; she could not understand why he killed the very birds he seemed to like so much. But as the day waned, Sylvia still watched the young man with loving admiration. She had never seen anybody so charming and delightful; the woman's heart, asleep in the child, was vaguely thrilled by a dream of love. Some premonition of that great power stirred and swayed these young foresters who traversed the solemn woodlands with soft-footed silent care. They stopped to listen to a bird's song; they pressed forward again eagerly, parting the branches — speaking to each other rarely and in whispers; the young man going first and Sylvia following, fascinated, a few steps behind, with her gray eyes dark with excitement.

She grieved because the longed-for white heron was elusive, but she did not lead the guest, she only followed, and there was no such thing as speaking first. The sound of her own unquestioned voice would have terrified her — it was hard enough to answer yes or no when there was need of that. At last evening began to fall, and they drove the cow home together, and Sylvia smiled with pleasure when they came to the place where she heard the whistle and was afraid only the night before.

II

Half a mile from home, at the farther edge of the woods, where the land was highest, a great pine-tree stood, the last of its generation. Whether it was left for a boundary mark, or for what reason, no one could say; the woodchoppers who had felled its mates were dead and gone long ago, and a whole forest of sturdy trees, pines and oaks and maples, had grown again. But the stately head of this old pine towered above them all and made a landmark for sea and shore miles and miles away. Sylvia knew it well. She had always believed that whoever climbed to the top of it could see the ocean; and the little girl had often laid her hand on the great rough trunk and looked up wistfully at those dark boughs that the wind always stirred, no matter how hot and still the air might be below. Now she thought of the tree with a new excitement, for why, if one climbed it at break of day, could not one see all the world, and easily discover whence the white heron flew, and mark the place, and find the hidden nest?

What a spirit of adventure, what wild ambition! What fancied triumph and delight and glory for the later morning when she could make known the secret! It was almost too real and too great for the childish heart to bear.

All night the door of the little house stood open, and the whippoorwills came and sang upon the very step. The young sportsman and his old hostess were sound asleep, but Sylvia's great design kept her broad awake and watching. She forgot to think of sleep. The short summer night seemed as long as the winter darkness, and at last when the whippoorwills ceased, and she was afraid the morning would after all come too soon, she stole out of the house and followed the pasture path through the woods, hastening toward the open ground beyond, listening with a sense of comfort and companionship to the drowsy twitter of a half-awakened bird, whose perch she had jarred in passing. Alas, if the great wave of human interest which flooded for the first time this dull little life should sweep away the satisfactions of an existence heart to heart with nature and the dumb life of the forest!

There was the huge tree asleep yet in the paling moonlight, and small and hopeful Sylvia began with utmost bravery to mount to the top of it, with tingling, eager blood coursing the channels of her whole frame, with her bare feet and fingers, that pinched and held like bird's claws to the monstrous ladder reaching up, up, almost to the sky itself. First she must mount the white oak tree that grew alongside, where she was almost lost among the dark branches and the green leaves heavy and wet with dew; a bird fluttered off its nest, and a red squirrel ran to and fro and scolded pettishly at the harmless housebreaker. Sylvia felt her way easily. She had often climbed there, and knew that higher still one of the oak's upper branches chafed against the pine trunk, just where its lower boughs were set close together. There, when she made the dangerous pass from one tree to the other, the great enterprise would really begin.

She crept out along the swaying oak limb at last, and took the daring step across into the old pine-tree. The way was harder than she thought; she must reach far and hold fast, the sharp dry twigs caught and held her and scratched her like angry talons, the pitch made her thin little fingers clumsy and stiff as she went round and round the tree's great stem, higher and higher upward. The sparrows and robins in the woods below were beginning to wake and twitter to the dawn, yet it seemed much lighter there aloft in the pine-tree, and the child knew that she must hurry if her project were to be of any use.

The tree seemed to lengthen itself out as she went up, and to reach farther and farther upward. It was like a great main-mast to the voyaging earth; it must truly have been amazed that morning through all its ponderous frame as it felt this determined spark of human spirit creeping and climbing from higher branch to branch. Who knows how steadily the least twigs held themselves to advantage this light, weak creature on her way! The old pine must have loved his new dependent. More than all the hawks, and bats, and moths, and even the sweet-voiced thrushes, was the brave, beating heart of the solitary gray-eyed child. And the tree stood still and held away the winds that June morning while the dawn grew bright in the east.

Sylvia's face was like a pale star, if one had seen it from the ground, when the last thorny bough was past, and she stood trembling and tired but wholly triumphant, high in the tree-top. Yes, there was the sea with the dawning sun making a golden dazzle over it, and toward that glorious east flew two hawks with slow-moving pinions. How low they looked in the air from that height when before one had only seen them far up, and dark against the blue sky. Their gray feathers were as soft as moths; they seemed only a little way from the tree, and Sylvia felt as if she too could go flying away among the clouds. Westward, the woodlands and farms reached miles and miles into the distance; here and there were church steeples, and white villages; truly it was a vast and awesome world.

The birds sang louder and louder. At last the sun came up bewilderingly bright. Sylvia could see the white sails of ships out at sea, and the clouds that were purple and rose-colored and yellow at first began to fade away. Where was the white heron's nest in the sea of green branches, and was this wonderful sight and pageant of the world the only reward for having climbed to such a giddy height? Now look down again, Sylvia, where the green marsh is set among the shining birches and dark hemlocks; there where you saw the white heron once you will see him again; look, look! a white spot of him like a single floating feather comes up from the dead hemlock and grows larger, and rises, and comes close at last, and goes by the landmark pine with steady sweep of wing and outstretched slender neck and crested head. And wait! wait! do not move a foot or a finger, little girl, do not send an arrow of light and consciousness from your two eager eyes, for the heron has perched on a pine bough not far beyond yours, and cries back to his mate on the nest, and plumes his feathers for the new day!

The child gives a long sigh a minute later when a company of shouting cat-birds comes also to the tree, and vexed by their fluttering and lawlessness the solemn heron goes away. She knows his secret now, the wild, light, slender bird that floats and wavers, and goes back like an arrow presently to his home in the green world beneath. Then Sylvia, well satisfied, makes her perilous way down again, not daring to look far below the branch she stands on, ready to cry sometimes because her fingers ache and her lamed feet slip. Wondering over and over again what the stranger would say to her, and what he would think when she told him how to find his way straight to the heron's nest.

"Sylvy, Sylvy!" called the busy old grandmother again and again, but nobody answered, and the small husk bed was empty, and Sylvia had disappeared.

The guest waked from a dream, and remembering his day's pleasure hurried to dress himself that it might sooner begin. He was sure from the way the shy little girl looked once or twice yesterday that she had at least seen the white heron, and now she must really be persuaded to tell. Here she comes now, paler than ever, and her worn old frock is torn and tattered, and smeared with pine pitch. The grandmother and the sportsman stand in the door together and question her, and the splendid moment had come to speak of the dead hemlock-tree by the green marsh.

But Sylvia does not speak after all, though the old grandmother fretfully rebukes her, and the young man's kind appealing eyes are looking straight in her own. He can make them rich with money; he has promised it, and they are poor now. He is so well worth making happy, and he waits to hear the story she can tell.

No, she must keep silence! What is it that suddenly forbids her and makes her dumb? Has she been nine years growing, and now, when the great world for the first time puts out a hand to her, must she thrust it aside for a bird's sake? The murmur of the pine's green branches is in her ears, she remembers how the white heron came flying through the golden air and how they watched the sea and the morning together, and Sylvia cannot speak; she cannot tell the heron's secret and give its life away.

Dear loyalty, that suffered a sharp pang as the guest went away disappointed later in the day, that could have served and followed him and loved him as a dog loves! Many a night Sylvia heard the echo of his whistle haunting the pasture path as she came home with the loitering cow. She forgot even her sorrow at the sharp report of his gun and the piteous sight of thrushes and sparrows dropping silent to the ground, their songs hushed and their pretty feathers stained and wet with blood. Were the birds better friends than their hunter might have been, — who can tell? Whatever treasures were lost to her, woodlands and summer-time, remember! Bring your gifts and graces and tell your secrets to this lonely country child! [1886]

CHARLES R. JOHNSON *(b. 1948) was born in Evanston, Illinois, the son of a construction worker. His mother encouraged his early interest in drawing, and at the age of seventeen he published his first book of cartoons. Six years later he created, coproduced, and hosted the PBS series "Charlie's Pad." He also found the time to complete a B.A. in journalism at Southern Illinois University in Carbondale, where he was inspired by the visit to campus of the black activist poet Amiri Baraka (LeRoi Jones). Johnson, who was still drawing cartoons, took Baraka's words to heart: "Baraka said a black artist should bring his talent back home to black people. I cut classes for a week and just drew, all day, all night." Johnson went on to earn an M.A. in philosophy at Southern Illinois University while studying creative writing with the novelist John Gardner, who had been Raymond Carver's teacher fifteen years before.*

According to the critic Mayemma Graham, it was Gardner who helped Johnson "to draw the connection between the Afro-American historical experience and various philosophical ideas — African, Eastern and Western — by appropriating different fictional modes." During this time Johnson devoted himself to developing what he calls "a genuinely philosophical black American fiction, which I don't think existed before the work of Jean Toomer, Richard Wright, and Ralph Ellison." Johnson's first novel, Faith and the Good Thing *(1974), reflects this stage of his development. His second novel,* Oxherding Tale *(1982), is a modern slave narrative, influenced in part by Frederick Douglass's autobiography and Herman Melville's story "Benito Cereno." In 1988 he published a book of essays,* Being and Race: Black Writing Since 1970, *and two years later he won the National Book Award for his novel* Middle Passage.

In the late 1970s Johnson began to publish short fiction in various periodicals. "Menagerie, A Child's Fable" appeared in the Indiana Review *in 1984. It was later collected in his volume of short stories,* The Sorcerer's Apprentice *(1986). Currently Johnson teaches creative writing at the University of Washington and martial arts at a Seattle kung fu club, and he makes frequent public appearances around the country as a lecturer, encouraging what he calls "ambitious, carefully wrought, innovative, intelligent fiction by writers who exhibit what Northrop Frye once called 'an educated imagination.'" Despite his demanding schedule, he says: "I should work twice as hard as I do. You create your essence through what you do. I really believe that work is prayer."*

CHARLES JOHNSON

Menagerie, A Child's Fable

Among watchdogs in Seattle, Berkeley was known generally as one of the best. Not the smartest, but steady. A pious German shepherd (Black Forest origins, probably) with big shoulders, black gums, and weighing more than some men, he sat guard inside the glass door of Tilford's Pet Shoppe, watching the pedestrians scurry along First Avenue, wondering at the derelicts who slept ever so often inside the foyer at night, and sometimes he nodded when things were quiet in the cages behind him, lulled by the bubbling of the fishtanks, dreaming of an especially fine meal he'd once had, or the little female poodle, a real flirt, owned by the aerobic dance teacher (who was no saint herself) a few doors down the street; but Berkeley was, for all his woolgathering, never asleep at the switch. He took his work seriously. Moreover, he knew exactly where he was at every moment, what he was doing, and why he was doing it, which was more than can be said for most people, like Mr. Tilford, a real gumboil, whose ways were mysterious to Berkeley. Sometimes he treated the animals cruelly, or taunted them; he saw them not as pets but profit. Nevertheless, no vandals, or thieves, had ever brought trouble through the doors or windows of Tilford's Pet Shoppe, and Berkeley, confident of his power but never flaunting it, faithful to his master though he didn't deserve it, was certain that none ever would.

At closing time, Mr. Tilford, who lived alone, as most cruel men do, always checked the cages, left a beggarly pinch of food for all the animals, and a single biscuit for Berkeley. The watchdog always hoped for a pat on his head, or for Tilford to play with him, some sign of approval to let him know he was appreciated, but such as this never came. Mr. Tilford had thick glasses and a thin voice, was stubborn, hot-tempered, a drunkard and a loner who, sliding toward senility, sometimes put his shoes in the refrigerator, and once — Berkeley winced at the memory — put a Persian he couldn't sell in the Mix Master during one of his binges. Mainly, the owner drank and watched television, which was something else Berkeley couldn't understand. More than once he'd mistaken gunfire on screen for the real thing (a natural error, since no one told him violence was entertainment for some), howled loud enough to bring down the house, and Tilford booted him outside. Soon enough, Berkeley stopped looking for approval; he didn't bother to get up from biting fleas behind the counter when he heard the door slam.

But it seemed one night too early for closing time. His instincts on this had never been wrong before. He trotted back to the darkened storeroom; then his mouth snapped shut. His feeding bowl was as empty as he'd last left it.

"Say, Berkeley," said Monkey, whose cage was near the storeroom. "What's goin' on? Tilford didn't put out the food."

Berkeley didn't care a whole lot for Monkey, and usually he ignored him. He was downright wicked, a comedian always grabbing his groin to get a laugh, throwing feces, or fooling with the other animals, a clown who'd do anything to crack up the iguana, Frog, Parrot, and the Siamese, even if it meant aping Mr. Tilford, which he did well, though Berkeley found this parody frightening, like playing with fire, or literally biting the hand that fed you. But he, too, was puzzled by Tilford's abrupt departure.

"I don't know," said Berkeley. "He'll be back, I guess."

Monkey, his head through his cage, held onto the bars like a movie inmate. "Wanna bet?"

"What're you talking about?"

"Wake *up*," said Monkey. "Tilford's sick. I seen better faces on dead guppies in the fishtank. You ever see a pulmonary embolus?" Monkey ballooned his cheeks, then started breathing hard enough to hyperventilate, rolled up both red-webbed eyes, then crashed back into his cage, howling.

Not thinking this funny at all, Berkeley padded over to the front door, gave Monkey a grim look, then curled up against the bottom rail, waiting for Tilford's car to appear. Cars of many kinds, and cars of different sizes, came and went, but that Saturday night the owner did not show. Nor the next morning, or the following night, and on the second day it was not only Monkey but every beast, bird, and fowl in the Shoppe that shook its cage or tank and howled at Berkeley for an explanation — an ear-shattering babble of tongues, squawks, trills, howls, mewling, bellows, hoots, blorting, and belly growls because Tilford had collected everything from baby alligators to zebra-striped fish, an entire federation of cultures, with each animal having its own distinct, inviolable nature (so they said), the rows and rows of counters screaming with a plurality of so many backgrounds, needs, and viewpoints that Berkeley, his head splitting, could hardly hear his own voice above the din.

"Be patient!" he said. "Believe me, he's comin' back!"

"Come *off* it," said one of three snakes. "Monkey says Tilford's *dead*. Question is, what're we gonna *do* about it?"

Berkeley looked, witheringly, toward the front door. His empty stomach gurgled like a sewer. It took a tremendous effort to untangle his thoughts. "If we can just hold on a —"

"We're *hungry!*" shouted Frog. "We'll starve before old Tilford comes back!"

Throughout this turmoil, the shouting, beating of wings, which blew feathers everywhere like confetti, and an angry slapping of fins that splashed water to the floor, Monkey simply sat quietly, taking it all in, stroking his chin as a scholar might. He waited for a space in the shouting, then pushed his head through the cage again. His voice was calm, studied, like an old-time barrister before the bar. "Berkeley? Don't get mad now, but I think it's obvious that there's only one solution."

"What?"

"Let us out," said Monkey. "Open the cages."

"No!"

"We've got a crisis situation here." Monkey sighed like one of the elderly, tired lizards, as if his solution bothered even him. "It calls for courage, radical decisons. You're in charge until Tilford gets back. That means you gotta feed us, but you can't do that, can you? Only one here with hands is *me*. See, we all have different talents, unique gifts. If you let us out, we can pool our resources. I can *open* the feed bags!"

"You can?" The watchdog swallowed.

"Uh-huh." He wiggled his fingers dexterously, then the digits on his feet. "But somebody's gotta throw the switch on this cage. I can't reach it. Dog, I'm asking you to be democratic! Keeping us locked up is fascist!"

The animals clamored for release; they took up Monkey's cry, "Self-determination!" But everything within Berkeley resisted this idea, the possibility of chaos it promised, so many different, quarrelsome creatures uncaged, set loose in a low-ceilinged Shoppe where even he had trouble finding room to turn around between the counters, pens, displays of paraphernalia, and heavy, bubbling fishtanks. The chances for mischief were incalculable, no question of that, but slow starvation was certain if he didn't let them in the storeroom. Furthermore, he didn't want to be called a fascist. It didn't seem fair, Monkey saying that, making him look bad in front of the others. It was the one charge you couldn't defend yourself against. Against his better judgment, the watchdog rose on his hindlegs and, praying this was the right thing, forced open the cage with his teeth. For a moment Monkey did not move. He drew breath loudly and stared at the open door. Cautiously, he stepped out, stood up to his full height, rubbed his bony hands together, then did a little dance and began throwing open the other cages one by one.

Berkeley cringed. "The tarantula, too?"

Monkey gave him a cold glance over one shoulder. "You should get to know him, Berkeley. Don't be a bigot."

Berkeley shrank back as Tarantula, an item ordered by a Hell's Angel who never claimed him, shambled out — not so much an insect, it seemed to Berkeley, as Pestilence on legs. ("Be fair!" he scolded himself. "He's okay, I'm okay, we're all okay.") He watched helplessly as Monkey smashed the ant farm, freed the birds, and then the entire troupe, united by the spirit of a bright, common future, slithered, hopped, crawled, bounded, flew, and clawed its way into the storeroom to feed. All except crankled, old Tortoise, whom Monkey hadn't freed, who, in fact, didn't want to be released and snapped at Monkey's fingers when he tried to open his cage. No one questioned it. Tortoise had escaped the year before, remaining at large for a week, and then he returned mysteriously on his own, his eyes strangely unfocused, as if he'd seen the end of the world, or a vision of the world to come. He hadn't spoken in a year. Hunched inside his shell, hardly eating at all, Tortoise lived in the Shoppe, but you could hardly say he was part of it, and even the watchdog was a little leery of him. Berkeley, for his part, had lost his hunger. He dragged himself, wearily, to the front door, barked frantically when a woman walked by, hoping she would stop, but after seeing the window sign, which read–CLOSED–from his side, she stepped briskly on. His tail between his legs, he went slowly back to the storeroom, hoping for the best, but what he found there was no sight for a peace-loving watchdog.

True to his word, Monkey had broken open the feed bags and boxes of food, but the animals, who had always been kept apart by Tilford, discovered as they crowded into the tiny storeroom and fell to eating that sitting down to table with creatures so different in their gastronomic inclinations took the edge off their appetites. The birds found the eating habits of the reptiles, who thought eggs were a delicacy, disgusting and drew away in horror; the reptiles, who were proud of being cold-blooded, and had an elaborate theory of beauty based on the aesthetics of scales, thought the body heat of the mammals cloying and nauseating, and refused to feed beside them, and this was fine for the mammals, who, led by Monkey, distrusted anyone odd enough to be born in an egg, and dismissed them as lowlifes on the evolutionary scale; they were shoveling down everything — bird food, dog biscuits, and even the thin wafers reserved for the fish.

"Don't touch that!" said Berkeley. "The fish have to eat, too! They can't leave the tanks!"

Monkey, startled by the watchdog, looked at the wafers in his fist thoughtfully for a second, then crammed them into his mouth. "That's their problem."

Deep inside, Berkeley began a rumbling bark, let it build slowly, and by the time it hit the air it was a full-throated growl so frightening that Monkey jumped four, maybe five feet into the air. He threw the wafers at Berkeley. "Okay — okay, give it to 'em! But remember one thing, dog: You're a mammal, too. It's unnatural to take sides against your own kind."

Scornfully, the watchdog turned away, trembling with fury. He snuffled up the wafers in his mouth, carried them to the huge, man-sized tanks, and dropped them in amongst the sea horses, guppies, and jellyfish throbbing like hearts. Goldfish floated toward him, his voice and fins fluttering. He kept a slightly startled expression. "What the hell is going on? Where's Mr. Tilford?"

Berkeley strained to keep his voice steady. "Gone."

"For good?" asked Goldfish. "Berkeley, we heard what the others said. They'll let us starve — "

"No," he said. "I'll protect you."

Goldfish bubbled relief, then looked panicky again. "What if Tilford doesn't come back ever?"

The watchdog let his head hang. The thought seemed too terrible to consider. He said, more to console himself than Goldfish, "It's his Shoppe. He has to come back."

"But suppose he *is* dead, like Monkey says." Goldfish's unblinking, lidless eyes grabbed at Berkeley and refused to release his gaze. "Then it's our Shoppe, right?"

"Eat your dinner."

Goldfish called, "Berkeley, wait — "

But the watchdog was deeply worried now. He returned miserably to the front door. He let fly a long, plaintive howl, his head tilted back like a mountaintop wolf silhouetted by the moon in a Warner Brothers cartoon — he did look like that — his insides hurting with the thought that if Tilford was dead, or indifferent to their problems, that if no one came to rescue them, then they were dead, too. True, there was a great deal of Tilford inside Berkeley, what he remembered from his training as a pup, but this faint sense of procedure and fair play hardly seemed enough to keep order in the Shoppe, maintain the peace, and more important provide for them as the old man had. He'd never looked upon himself as a leader, preferring to attribute his distaste for decision to a rare ability to see all sides. He was no hero like Old Yeller, or the legendary Gellert, and testing his ribs with his teeth, he wondered how much weight he'd lost from worry. Ten pounds? Twenty pounds? He covered both eyes with his black paws, whimpered a little, feeling a failure of nerve, a soft white core of fear like a slug in his stomach. Then he drew breath and, with it, new determination. The owner couldn't be dead. Monkey would never convince him of that. He simply had business elsewhere. And when he returned, he would expect to find the Shoppe as he left it. Maybe even running more smoothly, like an old Swiss watch that he had wound and left ticking. When the watchdog tightened his jaws, they creaked at the hinges, but he tightened them all the same. His eyes narrowed. No evil had visited the Shoppe from outside. He'd seen to that. None, he vowed, would destroy it from within.

But he could not be everywhere at once. The corrosion grew day by day. Cracks, then fissures began to appear, it seemed to Berkeley, everywhere, and in places where he least expected them. Puddles and pyramidal plops were scattered underfoot like traps. Bacterial flies were everywhere. Then came maggots. Hamsters gnawed at electrical cords in the storeroom. Frog fell sick with a genital infection. The fish, though the gentlest of creatures, caused undertow by demanding day-and-night protection, claiming they were handicapped in the competition for food, confined to their tanks, and besides, they were from the most ancient tree; all life came from the sea, they argued, the others owed *them*.

Old blood feuds between beasts erupted, too, grudges so tired you'd have thought them long buried, but not so. The Siamese began to give Berkeley funny looks, and left the room whenever he entered. Berkeley let him be, thinking he'd come to his senses. Instead, he jumped Rabbit when Berkeley wasn't looking, the product of this assault promising a new creature — a cabbit — with jack-rabbit legs and long feline whiskers never seen in the Pet Shoppe before. Rabbit took this badly. In the beginning she sniffed a great deal, and with good reason — rape was a vicious thing — but her grief and pain got out of hand, and soon she was lost in it with no way out, like a child in a dark forest, and began organizing the females of every species to stop cohabiting with the males. Berkeley stood back, afraid to butt in because Rabbit said that it was none of his damned business and he was as bad as all the rest. He pleaded reason, his eyes burnt-out from sleeplessness, with puffy bags beneath them, and when that did no good, he pleaded restraint.

"The storeroom's half-empty," he told Monkey on the fifth day. "If we don't start rationing the food, we'll starve."

"There's always food."

Berkeley didn't like the sound of that. "Where?"

Smiling, Monkey swung his eyes to the fishtanks.

"Don't you go near those goldfish!"

Monkey stood at bay, his eyes tacked hatefully on Berkeley, who ground his teeth, possessed by the sudden, wild desire to bite him, but knowing, finally, that he had the upper hand in the Pet Shoppe, the power. In other words, bigger teeth. As much as he hated to admit it, his only advantage, if he hoped to hold the line, his only trump, if he truly wanted to keep them afloat, was the fact that he outweighed them all. They were afraid of him. Oddly enough, the real validity of his values and viewpoint rested, he realized, on his having the biggest paw. The thought fretted him. For all his idealism, truth was decided in the end by those who could be bloodiest in fang and claw. Yet and still, Monkey had an arrogance that made Berkeley weak in the knees.

"Dog," he said, scratching under one arm, "you got to sleep *some*time."

And so Berkeley did. After hours of standing guard in the storeroom, or trying to console Rabbit, who was now talking of aborting the cabbit, begging her to reconsider, or reassuring the birds, who crowded together in one corner against, they said, threatening moves by the reptiles, or splashing various medicines on Frog, whose sickness had now spread to the iguana — after all this, Berkeley did drop fitfully to sleep by the front door. He slept greedily, dreaming of better days. He twitched and woofed in his sleep, seeing himself schtupping the little French poodle down the street, and it was good, like making love to lightning, she moved so well with him; and then of his puppyhood, when his worst problems were remembering where he'd buried food from Tilford's table, or figuring out how to sneak away from his mother, who told him all dogs had cold noses because they were late coming to the Ark and had to ride next to the rail. His dream cycled on, as all dreams do, with greater and greater clarity from one chamber of vision to the next until he saw, just before waking, the final drawer of dream-work spill open on the owner's return. Splendidly dressed, wearing a bowler hat and carrying a walking stick, sober, with a gentle smile for Berkeley (Berkeley was sure), Tilford threw open the Pet Shoppe door in a blast of wind and burst of preternatural brilliance that rayed the whole room, evaporated every shadow, and brought the squabbling, the conflict of interpretations, mutations, and internecine battles to a halt. No one dared move. They stood frozen like a fish in ice, or a bird caught in the crosswinds, the colorless light behind the owner so blinding it obliterated their outlines, blurred their precious differences, as if each were a rill of the same ancient light somehow imprisoned in form, with being-formed itself the most preposterous of conditions, outrageous, when you thought it through, because it occasioned suffering, meant separation from other forms, and the illusion of identity, but even this ended like a dream within the watchdog's dream, and only he and the owner remained. Reaching down, he stroked Berkeley's head. And at last he said, like God whispering to Samuel: *Well done.* It was all Berkeley had ever wanted. He woofed again, snoring like a sow, and scratched in his sleep; he heard the owner whisper *begun,* which was a pretty strange thing for him to say, even for Tilford, even in a dream. His ears strained forward; *begun,* Tilford said again. And for an instant Berkeley thought he had the tense wrong, intending to say, "Now we can begin," or something prophetically appropriate like that, but suddenly he was awake, and Parrot was flapping his wings and shouting into Berkeley's ear.

"The gun," said Parrot. "Monkey has it."

Berkeley's eyes, still phlegmed by sleep, blearily panned the counter. The room was swimming, full of smoke from a fire in the storeroom. He was short of wind. And, worse, he'd forgotten about the gun, a Smith and Wesson, that Tilford had bought after pet shop owners in Seattle were struck by thieves who specialized in stealing exotic birds. Monkey had it now. Berkeley's water ran down his legs. He'd propped the pistol between the cash register and a display of plastic dog collars, and his wide, yellow grin was frighteningly like that of a general Congress has just given the go-ahead to on a scorched-earth policy.

"Get it!" said Parrot. "You promised to protect us, Berkeley!"

For a few fibrous seconds he stood trembling paw-deep in dung, the odor of decay burning his lungs, but he couldn't come full awake, and still he felt himself to be on the fringe of a dream, his hair moist because dreaming of the French poodle had made him sweat. But the pistol . . . There was no power balance now. He'd been outplayed. No hope unless he took it away. Circling the counter, head low and growling, or trying to work up a decent growl, Berkeley crept to the cash register, his chest pounding, bunched his legs to leap, then sprang, pretending the black explosion of flame and smoke was like television gunfire, though it ripped skin right off his ribs, sent teeth flying down his throat, and blew him back like an empty pelt against Tortoise's cage. He lay still. Now he felt nothing in his legs. Purple blood like that deepest in the body cascaded to the floor from his side, rushing out with each heartbeat, and he lay twitching a little, only seeing now that he'd slept too long. Flames licked along the floor. Fish floated belly up in a dark, unplugged fishtank. The females had torn Siamese to pieces. Speckled lizards were busy sucking baby canaries from their eggs. And in the holy ruin of the Pet Shoppe the tarantula roamed free over the corpses of Frog and Iguana. Beneath him, Berkeley heard the ancient Tortoise stir, clearing a rusty throat clogged from disuse. Only he would survive the spreading fire, given his armor. His eyes burning from the smoke, the watchdog tried to explain his dream before the blaze reached them. "We could have endured, we had enough in common — for Christ's sake, we're *all* animals."

"Indeed," said Tortoise grimly, his eyes like headlights in a shell that echoed cavernously. "Indeed." [1984]

JAMES JOYCE *(1882–1941) was born James Augustine Aloysius Joyce in Rathgar, a suburb of Dublin, during a turbulent era of political change in Ireland. His parents sent him at the age of six to the best Jesuit school, Clongowes Wood College, where he spent three years; but in 1891 his father was no longer able to afford the tuition, and he was withdrawn. During the period of his parents' financial decline, Joyce — a brilliant student — was educated at home and then given free tuition at Belvedere College, where he won prizes for his essays. Shortly after taking his bachelor's degree in 1902 from University College, Dublin, he left Ireland for Paris, where he attended one class at the Collège de Médecine but dropped out because he could not afford the fees. Nearly starving, he remained in Paris and wrote what he called "Epiphanies." These were notebook jottings of overheard conversations or passing observations that he later incorporated into his fiction, thinking that they illuminated in a flash the meaning of a group of apparently unrelated phenomena. In April 1903 Joyce returned to Dublin because his mother was dying. He remained in Ireland for a short time as a teacher, but the following year he went to live abroad again, disillusioned by his home country's political corruption and religious hypocrisy.*

Dubliners (1916), a group of fifteen short stories begun in 1904, was Joyce's attempt to "write a chapter of the moral history" of Ireland. He chose Dublin for the setting because that city seemed to him "the center of paralysis," but he also thought of following the book with another entitled "Provincials." As if to prove his perception of the extent of stifling moral repression in his country, he had great difficulties getting the book published — a struggle lasting nine years. This so angered and frustrated Joyce that he never again lived in Ireland; he settled in Trieste, Zurich, and Paris and wrote the novels that established him as one of the greatest authors of modern times: A Portrait of the Artist as a Young Man *(1916),* Ulysses *(1922), and* Finnegan's Wake *(1939).*

Joyce's stories about the lives of young people, servants, politicians, and the complacent middle class were intended to represent a broad spectrum of Dublin life, not "a collection of tourist impressions" but a penetrating account of the spiritual waste of his times. Today's reader finds it difficult to believe that some stories in Dubliners *could have appeared so scandalous to Joyce's publishers that at one point the plates were destroyed at the printers. "Araby" and "The Dead" suggest the periods of youth, adolescence, and maturity that Joyce included in his book. His technique blends a detached sympathy for his subject with a "scrupulous meanness" of observed detail. Instead of dramatic plots, he structured his stories around "epiphanies" — evanescent moments that reveal "a sudden spiritual manifestation, whether in the vulgarity of speech or of gesture or in a memorable expression of the mind itself."*

RELATED COMMENTARIES: *Richard Ellmann, "A Biographical Perspective on Joyce's 'The Dead,'" page 1414; Frank O'Connor, "Style and Form in Joyce's 'The Dead,'" page 1482.*

Araby

North Richmond Street, being blind, was a quiet street except at the hour when the Christian Brothers' School set the boys free. An uninhabited house of two storeys stood at the blind end, detached from its neighbours in a square ground. The other houses of the street, conscious of decent lives within them, gazed at one another with brown imperturbable faces.

The former tenant of our house, a priest, had died in the back drawing-room. Air, musty from having been long enclosed, hung in all the rooms, and the waste room behind the kitchen was littered with old useless papers. Among these I found a few paper-covered books, the pages of which were curled and damp: *The Abbot*, by Walter Scott, *The Devout Communicant*, and *The Memoirs of Vidocq*. I liked the last best because its leaves were yellow. The wild garden behind the house contained a central apple-tree and a few straggling bushes under one of which I found the late tenant's rusty bicycle-pump. He had been a very charitable priest; in his will he had left all his money to institutions and the furniture of his house to his sister.

When the short days of winter came dusk fell before we had well eaten our dinners. When we met in the street the houses had grown sombre. The space of sky above us was the colour of ever-changing violet and towards it the lamps of the street lifted their feeble lanterns. The cold air stung us and we played till our bodies glowed. Our shouts echoed in the silent street. The career of our play brought us through the dark muddy lanes behind the houses where we ran the gauntlet of the rough tribes from the cottages, to the back doors of the dark dripping gardens where odours arose from the ashpits, to the dark odorous stables where a coachman smoothed and combed the horse or shook music from the buckled harness. When we returned to the street light from the kitchen windows had filled the areas. If my uncle was seen turning the corner we hid in the shadow until we had seen him safely housed. Or if Mangan's sister came out on the doorstep to call her brother in to his tea we watched her from our shadow peer up and down the street. We waited to see whether she would remain or go in and, if she remained, we left our shadow and walked up to Mangan's steps resignedly. She was waiting for us, her figure defined by the light from the half-opened door. Her brother always teased her before he obeyed and I stood by the railings looking at her. Her dress swung as she moved her body and the soft rope of her hair tossed from side to side.

Every morning I lay on the floor in the front parlour watching her door. The blind was pulled down to within an inch of the sash so that I could not be seen. When she came out on the doorstep my heart leaped. I ran to the hall, seized my books, and followed her. I kept her brown figure always in my eye and, when we came near the point at which our ways diverged, I quickened my pace and passed her. This happened morning after morning. I had never spoken to her, except for a few casual words, and yet her name was like a summons to all my foolish blood.

Her image accompanied me even in places the most hostile to romance. On Saturday evenings when my aunt went marketing I had to go to carry some of the parcels. We walked through the flaring streets, jostled by drunken men and bargaining women, amid the curses of labourers, the shrill litanies of shop-boys who stood on guard by the barrel of pigs' cheeks, the nasal chanting of street-singers, who sang a *come-all-you* about O'Donovan Rossa, or a ballad about the troubles in our native land. These noises converged in a single sensation of life for me: I imagined that I bore my chalice safely through a throng of foes. Her name sprang to my lips at moments in strange prayers and praises which I myself did not understand. My eyes were often full of tears (I could not tell why) and at times a flood from my heart seemed to pour itself out into my bosom. I thought little of the future. I did not know whether I would ever speak to her or not or, if I spoke to her, how I could tell her of my confused adoration. But my body was like a harp and her words and gestures were like fingers running upon the wires.

One evening I went into the back drawing-room in which the priest had died. It was a dark rainy evening and there was no sound in the house. Through one of the broken panes I heard the rain impinge upon the earth, the fine incessant needles of water playing in the sodden beds. Some distant lamp or lighted window gleamed below me. I was thankful that I could see so little. All my senses seemed to desire to veil themselves and, feeling that I was about to slip from them, I pressed the palms of my hands together until they trembled, murmuring: *"O love! O love!"* many times.

At last she spoke to me. When she addressed the first words to me I was so confused that I did not know what to answer. She asked me was I going to *Araby*. I forgot whether I answered yes or no. It would be a splendid bazaar, she said she would love to go.

"And why can't you?" I asked.

While she spoke she turned a silver bracelet round and round her wrist. She could not go, she said, because there would be a retreat that week in her convent. Her brother and two other boys were fighting for their caps and I was alone at the railings. She held one of the spikes, bowing her head towards me. The light from the lamp opposite our door caught the white curve of her neck, lit up her hair that rested there and, falling, lit up the hand upon the railing. It fell over one side of her dress and caught the white border of a petticoat, just visible as she stood at ease.

"It's well for you," she said.

"If I go," I said, "I will bring you something."

What innumerable follies laid waste my waking and sleeping thoughts after that evening! I wished to annihilate the tedious intervening days. I chafed against the work of school. At night in my bedroom and by day in the classroom her image came between me and the page I strove to read. The syllables of the word *Araby* were called to me through the silence in which my soul luxuriated and cast an Eastern enchantment over me. I asked for leave to go to the bazaar on Saturday night. My aunt was surprised and hoped it was not some Freemason affair. I answered few questions in class. I watched my master's face pass from amiability to sternness; he hoped I was not beginning to idle. I could not call my wandering thoughts together. I had hardly any patience with the serious work of life which, now that it stood between me and my desire, seemed to me child's play, ugly monotonous child's play.

On Saturday morning I reminded my uncle that I wished to go to the bazaar in the evening. He was fussing at the hallstand, looking for the hat-brush, and answered me curtly:

"Yes, boy, I know."

As he was in the hall I could not go into the front parlour and lie at the window. I left the house in bad humour and walked slowly towards the school. The air was pitilessly raw and already my heart misgave me.

When I came home to dinner my uncle had not yet been home. Still it was early. I sat staring at the clock for some time and, when its ticking began to irritate me, I left the room. I mounted the staircase and gained the upper part of the house. The high cold empty gloomy rooms liberated me and I went from room to room singing. From the front window I saw my companions playing below in the street. Their cries reached me weakened and indistinct and, leaning my forehead against the cool glass, I looked over at the dark house where she lived. I may have stood there for an hour, seeing nothing but the brown-clad figure cast by my imagination, touched discreetly by the lamplight at the curved neck, at the hand upon the railings and at the border below the dress.

When I came downstairs again I found Mrs. Mercer sitting at the fire. She was an old garrulous woman, a pawnbroker's widow, who collected used stamps for some pious purpose. I had to endure the gossip of the tea-table. The meal was prolonged beyond an hour and still my uncle did not come. Mrs. Mercer stood up to go: she was sorry she couldn't wait any longer, but it was after eight o'clock and she did not like to be out late, as the night air was bad for her. When she had gone I began to walk up and down the room, clenching my fists. My aunt said:

"I'm afraid you may put off your bazaar for this night of Our Lord."

At nine o'clock I heard my uncle's latchkey in the halldoor. I heard him talking to himself and heard the hallstand rocking when it had received the weight of his overcoat. I could interpret these signs. When he was midway through his dinner I asked him to give me the money to go to the bazaar. He had forgotten.

"The people are in bed and after their first sleep now," he said.

I did not smile. My aunt said to him energetically:

"Can't you give him the money and let him go? You've kept him late enough as it is."

My uncle said he was very sorry he had forgotten. He said he believed in the old saying: "All work and no play makes Jack a dull boy." He asked me where I was going and, when I had told him a second time he asked me did I know *The Arab's Farewell to his Steed.* When I left the kitchen he was about to recite the opening lines of the piece to my aunt.

I held a florin[1] tightly in my hand as I strode down Buckingham Street towards the station. The sight of the streets thronged with buyers and glaring with gas recalled to me the purpose of my journey. I took my seat in a third-class carriage of a deserted train. After an intolerable delay the train moved out of the station slowly. It crept onward among ruinous houses and over the twinkling river. At Westland Row Station a crowd of people pressed to the carriage doors; but the porters moved them back, saying that it was a special train for the bazaar. I remained alone in the bare carriage. In a few minutes the train drew up beside an improvised wooden platform. I passed out on to the road and saw by the lighted dial of a clock that it was ten minutes to ten. In front of me was a large building which displayed the magical name.

I could not find any sixpenny entrance and, fearing that the bazaar would be closed, I passed in quickly through a turnstile, handing a shilling to a weary-looking man. I found myself in a big hall girdled at half its height by a gallery. Nearly all the stalls were closed and the greater part of the hall was in darkness. I recognised a silence like that which pervades a church after a service. I walked into the centre of the bazaar timidly. A few people were gathered about the stalls which were still open. Before a curtain, over which the words *Café Chantant* were written in coloured lamps, two men were counting money on a salver. I listened to the fall of the coins.

Remembering with difficulty why I had come I went over to one of the stalls and examined porcelain vases and flowered tea-sets. At the door of the stall a young lady was talking and laughing with two young gentlemen. I remarked their English accents and listened vaguely to their conversation.

"O, I never said such a thing!"

"O, but you did!"

"O, but I didn't!"

"Didn't she say that?"

"Yes. I heard her."

"O, there's a . . . fib!"

Observing me the young lady came over and asked me did I wish to buy anything. The tone of her voice was not encouraging; she seemed to have spoken to me out of a sense of duty. I looked humbly at the great jars that stood like eastern guards at either side of the dark entrance to the stall and murmured:

"No, thank you."

The young lady changed the position of one of the vases and went back to the two young men. They began to talk of the same subject. Once or twice the young lady glanced at me over her shoulder.

I lingered before her stall, though I knew my stay was useless, to make my interest in her wares seem the more real. Then I turned away slowly and

---

[1] A silver coin worth two shillings.

walked down the middle of the bazaar. I allowed the two pennies to fall against the sixpence in my pocket. I heard a voice call from one end of the gallery that the light was out. The upper part of the hall was now completely dark.

Gazing up into the darkness I saw myself as a creature driven and derided by vanity; and my eyes burned with anguish and anger.   [1916]

JAMES JOYCE

The Dead

Lily, the caretaker's daughter, was literally run off her feet. Hardly had she brought one gentleman into the little pantry behind the office on the ground floor and helped him off with his overcoat than the wheezy hall-door bell clanged again and she had to scamper along the bare hallway to let in another guest. It was well for her she had not to attend to the ladies also. But Miss Kate and Miss Julia had thought of that and had converted the bathroom upstairs into a ladies' dressing-room. Miss Kate and Miss Julia were there, gossiping and laughing and fussing, walking after each other to the head of the stairs, peering down over the banisters and calling down to Lily to ask her who had come.

It was always a great affair, the Misses Morkan's annual dance. Everybody who knew them came to it, members of the family, old friends of the family, the members of Julia's choir, any of Kate's pupils that were grown up enough and even some of Mary Jane's pupils too. Never once had it fallen flat. For years and years it had gone off in splendid style as long as anyone could remember; ever since Kate and Julia, after the death of their brother Pat, had left the house in Stoney Batter and taken Mary Jane, their only niece, to live with them in the dark gaunt house on Usher's Island, the upper part of which they had rented from Mr Fulham, the corn-factor on the ground floor. That was a good thirty years ago if it was a day. Mary Jane, who was then a little girl in short clothes, was now the main prop of the household for she had the organ in Haddington Road. She had been through the Academy and gave a pupils' concert every year in the upper room of the Antient Concert Rooms. Many of her pupils belonged to better-class families on the Kingstown and Dalkey line. Old as they were, her aunts also did their share. Julia, though she was quite grey, was still the leading soprano in Adam and Eve's, and Kate, being too feeble to go about much, gave music lessons to beginners on the old square piano in the back room. Lily, the caretaker's daughter, did house-maid's work for them. Though their life was modest they believed in eating well; the best of everything: diamond-bone sirloins, three-shilling tea and the best bottled stout. But Lily seldom made a mistake in the orders so that she got on well with her three mistresses. They were fussy, that was all. But the only thing they would not stand was back answers.

Of course they had good reason to be fussy on such a night. And then it was long after ten o'clock and yet there was no sign of Gabriel and his wife. Besides they were dreadfully afraid that Freddy Malins might turn up screwed. They would not wish for worlds that any of Mary Jane's pupils should see him under the influence; and when he was like that it was sometimes very hard to manage him. Freddy Malins always came late but they wondered what could be keeping Gabriel: and that was what brought them every two minutes to the banisters to ask Lily had Gabriel or Freddy come.

— O, Mr Conroy, said Lily to Gabriel when she opened the door for him, Miss Kate and Miss Julia thought you were never coming. Good-night, Mrs Conroy.

— I'll engage they did, said Gabriel, but they forget that my wife here takes three mortal hours to dress herself.

He stood on the mat, scraping the snow from his goloshes, while Lily led his wife to the foot of the stairs and called out:

— Miss Kate, here's Mrs Conroy.

Kate and Julia came toddling down the dark stairs at once. Both of them kissed Gabriel's wife, said she must be perished alive and asked was Gabriel with her.

— Here I am as right as the mail, Aunt Kate! Go on up. I'll follow, called out Gabriel from the dark.

He continued scraping his feet vigorously while the three women went upstairs, laughing, to the ladies' dressing-room. A light fringe of snow lay like a cape on the shoulders of his overcoat and like toecaps on the toes of his goloshes; and, as the buttons of his overcoat slipped with a squeaking noise through the snow-stiffened frieze, a cold fragrant air from out-of-doors escaped from crevices and folds.

— Is it snowing again, Mr Conroy? asked Lily.

She had preceded him into the pantry to help him off with his overcoat. Gabriel smiled at the three syllables she had given his surname and glanced at her. She was a slim, growing girl, pale in complexion and with hay-coloured hair. The gas in the pantry made her look still paler. Gabriel had known her when she was a child and used to sit on the lowest step nursing a rag doll.

— Yes, Lily, he answered, and I think we're in for a night of it.

He looked up at the pantry ceiling, which was shaking with the stamping and shuffling of feet on the floor above, listened for a moment to the piano and then glanced at the girl, who was folding his overcoat carefully at the end of a shelf.

— Tell me, Lily, he said in a friendly tone, do you still go to school?

— O no, sir, she answered. I'm done schooling this year and more.

— O, then, said Gabriel gaily, I suppose we'll be going to your wedding one of these fine days with your young man, eh?

The girl glanced back at him over her shoulder and said with great bitterness:

— The men that is now is only all palaver and what they can get out of you.

Gabriel coloured as if he felt he had made a mistake and, without looking at her, kicked off his goloshes and flicked actively with his muffler at his patent-leather shoes.

He was a stout tallish young man. The high colour of his cheeks pushed upwards even to his forehead where it scattered itself in a few formless patches of pale red; and on his hairless face there scintillated restlessly the polished lenses and the bright gilt rims of the glasses which screened his delicate and restless eyes. His glossy black hair was parted in the middle and brushed in a long curve behind his ears where it curled slightly beneath the groove left by his hat.

When he had flicked lustre into his shoes he stood up and pulled his waistcoat down more tightly on his plump body. Then he took a coin rapidly from his pocket.

— O Lily, he said, thrusting it into her hands, it's Christmas-time, isn't it? Just . . . here's a little. . . .

He walked rapidly towards the door.

— O no, sir! cried the girl, following him. Really, sir, I wouldn't take it.

— Christmas-time! Christmas-time! said Gabriel, almost trotting to the stairs and waving his hand to her in deprecation.

The girl, seeing that he had gained the stairs, called out after him:

— Well, thank you, sir.

He waited outside the drawing-room door until the waltz should finish, listening to the skirts that swept against it and to the shuffling of feet. He was still discomposed by the girl's bitter and sudden retort. It had cast a gloom over him which he tried to dispel by arranging his cuffs and the bows of his tie. Then he took from his waistcoat pocket a little paper and glanced at the headings he had made for his speech. He was undecided about the lines from Robert Browning for he feared they would be above the heads of his hearers. Some quotation that they could recognise from Shakespeare or from the Melodies would be better. The indelicate clacking of the men's heels and the shuffling of their soles reminded him that their grade of culture differed from his. He would only make himself ridiculous by quoting poetry to them which they could not understand. They would think that he was airing his superior education. He would fail with them just as he had failed with the girl in the pantry. He had taken up a wrong tone. His whole speech was a mistake from first to last, an utter failure.

Just then his aunts and his wife came out of the ladies' dressing-room. His aunts were two small plainly dressed old women. Aunt Julia was an inch or so the taller. Her hair, drawn low over the tops of her ears, was grey; and grey also, with darker shadows, was her large flaccid face. Though she was stout in build and stood erect her slow eyes and parted lips gave her the appearance of a woman who did not know where she was or where she was going. Aunt Kate was more vivacious. Her face, healthier than her sister's, was all puckers and creases, like a shrivelled red apple, and her hair, braided in the same old-fashioned way, had not lost its ripe nut colour.

They both kissed Gabriel frankly. He was their favourite nephew, the son of their dead elder sister, Ellen, who had married T. J. Conroy of the Port and Docks.

— Gretta tells me you're not going to take a cab back to Monkstown to-night, Gabriel, said Aunt Kate.

— No, said Gabriel, turning to his wife, we had quite enough of that last year, hadn't we? Don't you remember, Aunt Kate, what a cold Gretta got out of it? Cab windows rattling all the way, and the east wind blowing in after we passed Merrion. Very jolly it was. Gretta caught a dreadful cold.

Aunt Kate frowned severely and nodded her head at every word.

— Quite right, Gabriel, quite right, she said. You can't be too careful.

— But as for Gretta there, said Gabriel, she'd walk home in the snow if she were let.

Mrs Conroy laughed.

— Don't mind him, Aunt Kate, she said. He's really an awful bother, what with green shades for Tom's eyes at night and making him do the dumb-bells, and forcing Eva to eat the stirabout. The poor child! And she simply hates the sight of it! . . . O, but you'll never guess what he makes me wear now!

She broke out into a peal of laughter and glanced at her husband, whose admiring and happy eyes had been wandering from her dress to her face and hair. The two aunts laughed heartily too, for Gabriel's solicitude was a standing joke with them.

— Goloshes! said Mrs Conroy. That's the latest. Whenever it's wet underfoot I must put on my goloshes. To-night even he wanted me to put them on, but I wouldn't. The next thing he'll buy me will be a diving suit.

Gabriel laughed nervously and patted his tie reassuringly while Aunt Kate nearly doubled herself, so heartily did she enjoy the joke. The smile soon faded from Aunt Julia's face and her mirthless eyes were directed towards her nephew's face. After a pause she asked:

— And what are goloshes, Gabriel?

— Goloshes, Julia! exclaimed her sister. Goodness me, don't you know what goloshes are? You wear them over your . . . over your boots, Gretta, isn't it?

— Yes, said Mrs Conroy. Guttapercha things. We both have a pair now. Gabriel says everyone wears them on the continent.

— O, on the continent, murmured Aunt Julia, nodding her head slowly.

Gabriel knitted his brows and said, as if he were slightly angered:

— It's nothing very wonderful but Gretta thinks it very funny because she says the word reminds her of Christy Minstrels.

— But tell me, Gabriel, said Aunt Kate, with brisk tact. Of course, you've seen about the room. Gretta was saying . . .

— O, the room is all right, replied Gabriel. I've taken one in the Gresham.

— To be sure, said Aunt Kate, by far the best thing to do. And the children, Gretta, you're not anxious about them?

— O, for one night, said Mrs Conroy. Besides, Bessie will look after them.

— To be sure, said Aunt Kate again. What a comfort it is to have a girl like that, one you can depend on! There's that Lily, I'm sure I don't know what has come over her lately. She's not the girl she was at all.

Gabriel was about to ask his aunt some questions on this point but she broke off suddenly to gaze after her sister who had wandered down the stairs and was craning her neck over the banisters.

— Now, I ask you, she said, almost testily, where is Julia going? Julia! Julia! Where are you going?

Julia, who had gone halfway down one flight, came back and announced blandly:

— Here's Freddy.

At the same moment a clapping of hands and a final flourish of the pianist told that the waltz had ended. The drawing-room door was opened from within and some couples came out. Aunt Kate drew Gabriel aside hurriedly and whispered into his ear:

— Slip down, Gabriel, like a good fellow and see if he's all right, and don't let him up if he's screwed. I'm sure he's screwed. I'm sure he is.

Gabriel went to the stairs and listened over the banisters. He could hear two persons talking in the pantry. Then he recognised Freddy Malins' laugh. He went down the stairs noisily.

— It's such a relief, said Aunt Kate to Mrs Conroy, that Gabriel is here. I always feel easier in my mind when he's here. . . . Julia, there's Miss Daly and Miss Power will take some refreshment. Thanks for your beautiful waltz, Miss Daly. It made lovely time.

A tall wizen-faced man, with a stiff grizzled moustache and swarthy skin, who was passing out with his partner said:

— And may we have some refreshment, too, Miss Morkan?

— Julia, said Aunt Kate summarily, and here's Mr Browne and Miss Furlong. Take them in, Julia, with Miss Daly and Miss Power.

— I'm the man for the ladies, said Mr Browne, pursing his lips until his moustache bristled and smiling in all his wrinkles. You know, Miss Morkan, the reason they are so fond of me is —

He did not finish his sentence, but, seeing that Aunt Kate was out of earshot, at once led the three young ladies into the back room. The middle of the room was occupied by two square tables placed end to end, and on these Aunt Julia and the caretaker were straightening and smoothing a large cloth. On the sideboard were arrayed dishes and plates, and glasses and bundles of knives and forks and spoons. The top of the closed square piano served also as a sideboard for viands and sweets. At a smaller sideboard in one corner two young men were standing, drinking hop-bitters.

Mr Browne led his charges thither and invited them all, in jest, to some ladies' punch, hot, strong and sweet. As they said they never took anything strong he opened three bottles of lemonade for them. Then he asked one of the young men to move aside, and, taking hold of the decanter, filled out for himself a goodly measure of whisky. The young men eyed him respectfully while he took a trial sip.

— God help me, he said, smiling, it's the doctor's orders.

His wizened face broke into a broader smile, and the three young ladies laughed in musical echo to his pleasantry, swaying their bodies to and fro, with nervous jerks of their shoulders. The boldest said:

— O, now, Mr Browne, I'm sure the doctor never ordered anything of the kind.

Mr Browne took another sip of his whisky and said, with sidling mimicry:

— Well, you see, I'm like the famous Mrs Cassidy, who is reported to have said: *Now, Mary Grimes, if I don't take it, make me take it, for I feel I want it.*

His hot face had leaned forward a little too confidentially and he had assumed a very low Dublin accent so that the young ladies, with one instinct, received his speech in silence. Miss Furlong, who was one of Mary Jane's pupils, asked Miss Daly what was the name of the pretty waltz she had played; and Mr Browne, seeing that he was ignored, turned promptly to the two young men who were more appreciative.

A red-faced young woman, dressed in pansy, came into the room, excitedly clapping her hands and crying:

— Quadrilles! Quadrilles!

Close on her heels came Aunt Kate, crying:

— Two gentlemen and three ladies, Mary Jane!

— O, here's Mr Bergin and Mr Kerrigan, said Mary Jane. Mr Kerrigan, will you take Miss Power? Miss Furlong, may I get you a partner, Mr Bergin. O, that'll just do now.

— Three ladies, Mary Jane, said Aunt Kate.

The two young gentlemen asked the ladies if they might have the pleasure, and Mary Jane turned to Miss Daly.

— O, Miss Daly, you're really awfully good, after playing for the last two dances, but really we're so short of ladies to-night.

— I don't mind in the least, Miss Morkan.

— But I've a nice partner for you, Mr Bartell D'Arcy, the tenor. I'll get him to sing later on. All Dublin is raving about him.

— Lovely voice, lovely voice! said Aunt Kate.

As the piano had twice begun the prelude to the first figure Mary Jane led her recruits quickly from the room. They had hardly gone when Aunt Julia wandered slowly into the room, looking behind her at something.

— What is the matter, Julia? asked Aunt Kate anxiously. Who is it?

Julia, who was carrying in a column of table-napkins, turned to her sister and said, simply, as if the question had surprised her:

— It's only Freddy, Kate, and Gabriel with him.

In fact right behind her Gabriel could be seen piloting Freddy Malins across the landing. The latter, a young man of about forty, was of Gabriel's size and build, with very round shoulders. His face was fleshy and pallid, touched with colour only at the thick hanging lobes of his ears and at the wide wings of his nose. He had coarse features, a blunt nose, a convex and receding brow, tumid and protruded lips. His heavy-lidded eyes and the disorder of his scanty hair made him look sleepy. He was laughing heartily in a high key at a story which he had been telling Gabriel on the stairs and at the same time rubbing the knuckles of his left fist backwards and forwards into his left eye.

— Good-evening, Freddy, said Aunt Julia.

Freddy Malins bade the Misses Morkan good-evening in what seemed an offhand fashion by reason of the habitual catch in his voice and then, seeing that Mr Browne was grinning at him from the sideboard, crossed the room on rather shaky legs and began to repeat in an undertone the story he had just told to Gabriel.

— He's not so bad, is he? said Aunt Kate to Gabriel.

Gabriel's brows were dark but he raised them quickly and answered:

— O no, hardly noticeable.

— Now, isn't he a terrible fellow! she said. And his poor mother made him take the pledge on New Year's Eve. But come on, Gabriel, into the drawing-room.

Before leaving the room with Gabriel she signalled to Mr Browne by frowning and shaking her forefinger in warning to and fro. Mr Browne nodded in answer and, when she had gone, said to Freddy Malins:

— Now, then, Teddy, I'm going to fill you out a good glass of lemonade just to buck you up.

Freddy Malins, who was nearing the climax of his story, waved the offer aside impatiently but Mr Browne, having first called Freddy Malins' attention to a disarray in his dress, filled out and handed him a full glass of lemonade. Freddy Malins' left hand accepted the glass mechanically, his right hand being engaged in the mechanical readjustment of his dress. Mr Browne, whose face was once more wrinkling with mirth, poured out for himself a glass of whisky while Freddy Malins exploded, before he had well reached the climax of his story, in a kink of high-pitched bronchitic laughter and, setting down his untasted and overflowing glass, began to rub the knuckles of his left fist backwards and forwards into his left eye, repeating words of his last phrase as well as his fit of laughter would allow him.

Gabriel could not listen while Mary Jane was playing her Academy piece, full of runs and difficult passages, to the hushed drawing-room. He liked music but the piece she was playing had no melody for him and he doubted whether it had any melody for the other listeners, though they had begged Mary Jane to play something. Four young men, who had come from the refreshment-room to stand in the doorway at the sound of the piano, had gone away quietly in couples after a few minutes. The only persons who seemed to follow the music were Mary Jane herself, her hands racing along the key-board or lifted from it at the pauses like those of a priestess in momentary imprecation, and Aunt Kate standing at her elbow to turn the page.

Gabriel's eyes, irritated by the floor, which glittered with beeswax under the heavy chandelier, wandered to the wall above the piano. A picture of the balcony scene in *Romeo and Juliet* hung there and beside it was a picture of the two murdered princes in the Tower which Aunt Julia had worked in red, blue and brown wools when she was a girl. Probably in the school they had gone to as girls that kind of work had been taught, for one year his mother had worked for him as a birthday present a waistcoat of purple tabinet, with little foxes' heads upon it, lined with brown satin and having round mulberry buttons. It was strange that his mother had had no musical talent though Aunt Kate used to call her the brains carrier of the Morkan family. Both she and Julia had always seemed a little proud of their serious and matronly sister. Her photograph stood before the pierglass. She held an open book on her knees and was pointing out something in it to Constantine who, dressed in a man-o'-war suit, lay at her feet. It was she who had chosen the names for her sons for she was very sensible of the dignity of family life. Thanks to her, Constantine was now senior curate in Balbriggan and, thanks to her, Gabriel himself had taken his degree in the Royal University. A shadow passed over his face as he remembered her sullen opposition to his marriage. Some slighting phrases she had used still rankled in his memory; she had once spoken of Gretta as being country cute and that was not true of Gretta at all. It was Gretta who had nursed her during all her last long illness in their house at Monkstown.

He knew that Mary Jane must be near the end of her piece for she was playing again the opening melody with runs of scales after every bar and while he waited for the end the resentment died down in his heart. The piece ended with a trill of octaves in the treble and a final deep octave in the bass. Great applause greeted Mary Jane as, blushing and rolling up her music nervously, she escaped from the room. The most vigorous clapping came from the four young men in the doorway who had gone away to the refreshment-room at the beginning of the piece but had come back when the piano had stopped.

Lancers were arranged. Gabriel found himself partnered with Miss Ivors. She was a frank-mannered talkative young lady, with a freckled face and prominent brown eyes. She did not wear a low-cut bodice and the large brooch which was fixed in the front of her collar bore on it an Irish device.

When they had taken their places she said abruptly:

— I have a crow to pluck with you.

— With me? said Gabriel.

She nodded her head gravely.

— What is it? asked Gabriel, smiling at her solemn manner.

— Who is G.C.? answered Miss Ivors, turning her eyes upon him.

Gabriel coloured and was about to knit his brows, as if he did not understand, when she said bluntly:

— O, innocent Amy! I have found out that you write for *The Daily Express*. Now, aren't you ashamed of yourself?

— Why should I be ashamed of myself? asked Gabriel, blinking his eyes and trying to smile.

— Well, I'm ashamed of you, said Miss Ivors frankly. To say you'd write for a rag like that. I didn't think you were a West Briton.

A look of perplexity appeared on Gabriel's face. It was true that he wrote a literary column every Wednesday in *The Daily Express*, for which he was paid fifteen shillings. But that did not make him a West Briton surely. The books he received for review were almost more welcome than the paltry cheque. He loved to feel the covers and turn over the pages of newly printed books. Nearly every day when his teaching in the college was ended he used to wander down the quays to the second-hand booksellers, to Hickey's on Bachelor's Walk, to Webb's or Massey's on Aston's Quay, or to O'Clohissey's in the by-street. He did not know how to meet her charge. He wanted to say that literature was above politics. But they were friends of many years' standing and their careers had been parallel, first at the University and then as teachers: he could not risk a grandiose phrase with her. He continued blinking his eyes and trying to smile and murmured lamely that he saw nothing political in writing reviews of books.

When their turn to cross had come he was still perplexed and inattentive. Miss Ivors promptly took his hand in a warm grasp and said in a soft friendly tone:

— Of course, I was only joking. Come, we cross now.

When they were together again she spoke of the University question and Gabriel felt more at ease. A friend of hers had shown her his review of Browning's poems. That was how she had found out the secret: but she liked the review immensely. Then she said suddenly:

— O, Mr Conroy, will you come for an excursion to the Aran Isles this summer? We're going to stay there a whole month. It will be splendid out in the Atlantic. You ought to come. Mr Clancy is coming, and Mr Kilkelly and Kathleen Kearney. It would be splendid for Gretta too if she'd come. She's from Connacht, isn't she?

— Her people are, said Gabriel shortly.

— But you will come, won't you? said Miss Ivors, laying her warm hand eagerly on his arm.

— The fact is, said Gabriel, I have already arranged to go —

— Go where? asked Miss Ivors.

— Well, you know, every year I go for a cycling tour with some fellows and so —

— But where? asked Miss Ivors.

— Well, we usually go to France or Belgium or perhaps Germany, said Gabriel awkwardly.

— And why do you go to France and Belgium, said Miss Ivors, instead of visiting your own land?

— Well, said Gabriel, it's partly to keep in touch with the languages and partly for a change.

— And haven't you your own language to keep in touch with — Irish? asked Miss Ivors.

— Well, said Gabriel, if it comes to that, you know, Irish is not my language.

Their neighbours had turned to listen to the cross-examination. Gabriel glanced right and left nervously and tried to keep his good humour under the ordeal which was making a blush invade his forehead.

— And haven't you your own land to visit, continued Miss Ivors, that you know nothing of, your own people, and your own country?

— O, to tell you the truth, retorted Gabriel suddenly, I'm sick of my own country, sick of it!

— Why? asked Miss Ivors.

Gabriel did not answer for his retort had heated him.

— Why? repeated Miss Ivors.

They had to go visiting together and, as he had not answered her, Miss Ivors said warmly:

— Of course, you've no answer.

Gabriel tried to cover his agitation by taking part in the dance with great energy. He avoided her eyes for he had seen a sour expression on her face. But when they met in the long chain he was surprised to feel his hand firmly pressed. She looked at him from under her brows for a moment quizzically until he smiled. Then, just as the chain was about to start again, she stood on tiptoe and whispered into his ear:

— West Briton!

When the lancers were over Gabriel went away to a remote corner of the room where Freddy Malins' mother was sitting. She was a stout feeble old woman with white hair. Her voice had a catch in it like her son's and she stuttered slightly. She had been told that Freddy had come and that he was nearly all right. Gabriel asked her whether she had had a good crossing. She lived with her married daughter in Glasgow and came to Dublin on a visit once a year. She answered placidly that she had had a beautiful crossing and that the captain had been most attentive to her. She spoke also of the beautiful house her daughter kept in Glasgow, and of all the nice friends they had there. While her tongue rambled on Gabriel tried to banish from his mind all memory of the unpleasant incident with Miss Ivors. Of course the girl or woman, or whatever she was, was an enthusiast but there was a time for all things. Perhaps he ought not to have answered her like that. But she had no right to call him a West Briton before people, even in joke. She had tried to make him ridiculous before people, heckling him and staring at him with her rabbit's eyes.

He saw his wife making her way towards him through the waltzing couples. When she reached him she said into his ear:

— Gabriel, Aunt Kate wants to know won't you carve the goose as usual. Miss Daly will carve the ham and I'll do the pudding.

— All right, said Gabriel.

— She's sending in the younger ones first as soon as this waltz is over so that we'll have the tables to ourselves.

— Were you dancing? asked Gabriel.

— Of course I was. Didn't you see me? What words had you with Molly Ivors?

— No words. why? Did she say so?

— Something like that. I'm trying to get that Mr D'Arcy to sing. He's full of conceit, I think.

— There were no words, said Gabriel moodily, only she wanted me to go for a trip to the west of Ireland and I said I wouldn't.

His wife clasped her hands excitedly and gave a little jump.

— O, do go, Gabriel, she cried. I'd love to see Galway again.

— You can go if you like, said Gabriel coldly.

She looked at him for a moment, then turned to Mrs Malins and said:

— There's a nice husband for you, Mrs Malins.

While she was threading her way back across the room Mrs Malins, without adverting to the interruption, went on to tell Gabriel what beautiful places there were in Scotland and beautiful scenery. Her son-in-law brought them every year to the lakes and they used to go fishing. Her son-in-law was a splendid fisher. One day he caught a fish, a beautiful big big fish, and the man in the hotel boiled it for their dinner.

Gabriel hardly heard what she said. Now that supper was coming near he began to think again about his speech and about the quotation. When he saw Freddy Malins coming across the room to visit his mother Gabriel left the chair free for him and retired into the embrasure of the window. The room had already cleared and from the back room came the clatter of plates and knives. Those who still remained in the drawing-room seemed tired of danc-ing and were conversing quietly in little groups. Gabriel's warm trembling fingers tapped the cold pane of the window. How cool it must be outside! How pleasant it would be to walk out alone, first along by the river and then through the park! The snow would be lying on the branches of the trees and forming a bright cap on the top of the Wellington Monument. How much more pleasant it would be there than at the supper-table!

He ran over the headings of his speech: Irish hospitality, sad memories, the Three Graces, Paris, the quotation from Browning. He repeated to himself a phrase he had written in his review: *One feels that one is listening to a thought-tormented music.* Miss Ivors had praised the review. Was she sincere? Had she really any life of her own behind all her propagandism? There had never been any ill-feeling between them until that night. It unnerved him to think that she would be at the supper-table, looking up at him while he spoke with her critical quizzing eyes. Perhaps she would not be sorry to see him fail in his speech. An idea came into his mind and gave him courage. He would say, alluding to Aunt Kate and Aunt Julia: *Ladies and Gentlemen, the generation which is now on the wane among us may have had its faults but for my part I think it had certain qualities of hospitality, of humour, of humanity, which the new and very serious and hypereducated generation that is growing up around us seems to me to lack.* Very good: that was one for Miss Ivors. What did he care that his aunts were only two ignorant old women?

A murmur in the room attracted his attention. Mr Browne was advanc-ing from the door, gallantly escorting Aunt Julia, who leaned upon his arm, smiling and hanging her head. An irregular musketry of applause escorted her also as far as the piano and then, as Mary Jane seated herself on the stool, and Aunt Julia, no longer smiling, half turned so as to pitch her voice fairly into the room, gradually ceased. Gabriel recognised the prelude. It was that of an old song of Aunt Julia's — *Arrayed for the Bridal*. Her voice, strong and clear in tone, attacked with great spirit the runs which embellish the air and though she sang very rapidly she did not miss even the smallest of the grace notes. To follow the voice, without looking at the singer's face, was to feel and share the excitement of swift and secure flight. Gabriel applauded loudly with all the others at the close of the song and loud applause was borne in from the invisible supper-table. It sounded so genuine that a little colour struggled into Aunt Julia's face as she bent to replace in the music-stand the old leather-bound song-book that had her initials on the cover. Freddy Malins, who had listened with his head perched sideways to hear her better, was still applauding when everyone else had ceased and talking animatedly to his mother who nodded her head gravely and slowly in acquiescence. At last, when he could clap no more, he stood up suddenly and hurried across the room to Aunt Julia whose hand he seized and held in both his hands, shaking it when words failed him or the catch in his voice proved too much for him.

— I was just telling my mother, he said, I never heard you sing so well, never. No, I never heard your voice so good as it is to-night. Now! Would you believe that now? That's the truth. Upon my word and honour that's the truth. I never heard your voice sound so fresh and so . . . so clear and fresh, never.

Aunt Julia smiled broadly and murmured something about compliments as she released her hand from his grasp. Mr Browne extended his open hand towards her and said to those who were near him in the manner of a showman introducing a prodigy to an audience:

— Miss Julia Morkan, my latest discovery!

He was laughing very heartily at this himself when Freddy Malins turned to him and said:

— Well, Browne, if you're serious you might make a worse discovery. All I can say is I never heard her sing half so well as long as I am coming here. And that's the honest truth.

— Neither did I, said Mr Browne. I think her voice has greatly improved.

Aunt Julia shrugged her shoulders and said with meek pride:

— Thirty years ago I hadn't a bad voice as voices go.

— I often told Julia, said Aunt Kate emphatically, that she was simply thrown away in that choir. But she never would be said by me.

She turned as if to appeal to the good sense of the others against a refractory child while Aunt Julia gazed in front of her, a vague smile of reminiscence playing on her face.

— No, continued Aunt Kate, she wouldn't be said or led by anyone, slaving there in that choir night and day, night and day. Six o'clock on Christmas morning! And all for what?

— Well, isn't it for the honour of God, Aunt Kate? asked Mary Jane, twisting round on the piano-stool and smiling.

Aunt Kate turned fiercely on her niece and said:

— I know all about the honour of God, Mary Jane, but I think it's not at all honourable for the pope to turn out the women out of the choirs that have slaved there all their lives and put little whipper-snappers of boys over their heads. I suppose it is for the good of the Church if the pope does it. But it's not just, Mary Jane, and it's not right.

She had worked herself into a passion and would have continued in defence of her sister for it was a sore subject with her but Mary Jane, seeing that all the dancers had come back, intervened pacifically:

— Now, Aunt Kate, you're giving scandal to Mr Browne who is of the other persuasion.

Aunt Kate turned to Mr Browne, who was grinning at this allusion to his religion, and said hastily:

— O, I don't question the pope's being right. I'm only a stupid old woman and I wouldn't presume to do such a thing. But there' such a thing as common everday politeness and gratitude. And if I were in Julia's place I'd tell that Father Healy straight up to his face. . . .

— And besides, Aunt Kate, said Mary Jane, we really are all hungry and when we are hungry we are all very quarrelsome.

— And when we are thirsty we are also quarrelsome, added Mr Browne.

— So that we had better go to supper, said Mary Jane, and finish the discussion afterwards.

On the landing outside the drawing-room Gabriel found his wife and Mary Jane trying to persuade Miss Ivors to stay for supper. But Miss Ivors, who had put on her hat and was buttoning her cloak, would not stay. She did not feel in the least hungry and she had already overstayed her time.

— But only for ten minutes, Molly, said Mrs Conroy. That won't delay you.

— To take a pick itself, said Mary Jane, after all your dancing.

— I really couldn't, said Miss Ivors.

— I am afraid you didn't enjoy yourself at all, said Mary Jane hopelessly.

— Ever so much, I assure you, said Miss Ivors, but you really must let me run off now.

— But how can you get home? asked Mrs Conroy.

— O, it's only two steps up the quay.

Gabriel hesitated a moment and said:

— If you will allow me, Miss Ivors, I'll see you home if you really are obliged to go.

But Miss Ivors broke away from them.

— I won't hear of it, she cried. For goodness sake go in to your suppers and don't mind me. I'm quite well able to take care of myself.

— Well, you're the comical girl, Molly, said Mrs Conroy frankly.

— *Beannacht libh,*[1] cried Miss Ivors, with a laugh, as she ran down the staircase.

Mary Jane gazed after her, a moody puzzled expression on her face, while Mrs Conroy leaned over the banisters to listen for the hall-door. Gabriel

---

[1] "A blessing on you" (Irish — traditional way of saying "farewell").

asked himself was he the cause of her abrupt departure. But she did not seem to be in ill humour: she had gone away laughing. He stared blankly down the staircase.

At that moment Aunt Kate came toddling out of the supper-room, almost wringing her hands in despair.

— Where is Gabriel? she cried. Where on earth is Gabriel? There's everyone waiting in there, stage to let, and nobody to carve the goose!

— Here I am, Aunt Kate! cried Gabriel, with sudden animation, ready to carve a flock of geese, if necessary.

A fat brown goose lay at one end of the table and at the other end, on a bed of creased paper strewn with sprigs of parsley, lay a great ham, stripped of its outer skin and peppered over with crust crumbs, a neat paper frill round its shin and beside this was a round of spiced beef. Between these rival ends ran parallel lines of side-dishes: two little minsters of jelly, red and yellow; a shallow dish full of blocks of blancmange and red jam, a large green leaf-shaped dish with a stalk-shaped handle, on which lay bunches of purple raisins and peeled almonds, a companion dish on which lay a solid rectangle of Smyrna figs, a dish of custard topped with grated nutmeg, a small bowl full of chocolates and sweets wrapped in gold and silver papers and a glass vase in which stood some tall celery stalks. In the centre of the table there stood, as sentries to a fruit-stand which upheld a pyramid of oranges and American apples, two squat old-fashioned decanters of cut glass, one containing port and the other dark sherry. On the closed square piano a pudding in a huge yellow dish lay in waiting and behind it were three squads of bottles of stout and ale and minerals, drawn up according to the colours of their uniforms, the first two black, with brown and red labels, the third and smallest squad white, with transverse green sashes.

Gabriel took his seat boldly at the head of the table and, having looked to the edge of the carver, plunged his fork firmly into the goose. He felt quite at ease now for he was an expert carver and liked nothing better than to find himself at the head of a well-laden table.

— Miss Furlong, what shall I send you? he asked. A wing or a slice of the breast?

— Just a small slice of the breast.

— Miss Higgins, what for you?

— O, anything at all, Mr Conroy.

While Gabriel and Miss Daly exchanged plates of goose and plates of ham and spiced beef Lily went from guest to guest with a dish of hot floury potatoes wrapped in a white napkin. This was Mary Jane's idea and she had also suggested apple sauce for the goose but Aunt Kate had said that plain roast goose without apple sauce had always been good enough for her and she hoped she might never eat worse. Mary Jane waited on her pupils and saw that they got the best slices and Aunt Kate and Aunt Julia opened and carried across from the piano bottles of stout and ale for the gentlemen and bottles of minerals for the ladies. There was a great deal of confusion and laughter and noise, the noise of orders and counter-orders, of knives and forks, of corks and glass-stoppers. Gabriel began to carve second helpings as soon as he had finished the first round without serving himself. Everyone protested loudly so that he compromised by taking a long draught of stout for he had found the carving hot work. Mary Jane settled down quietly to her supper but Aunt Kate and Aunt Julia were still toddling round the table, walking on each other's heels, getting in each other's way and giving each other unheeded orders. Mr Browne begged of them to sit down and eat their suppers and so did Gabriel but they said there was time enough so that, at last, Freddy Malins stood up and, capturing Aunt Kate, plumped her down on her chair amid general laughter.

When everyone had been well served Gabriel said, smiling:

— Now, if anyone wants a little more of what vulgar people call stuffing let him or her speak.

A chorus of voices invited him to begin his own supper and Lily came forward with three potatoes which she had reserved for him.

— Very well, said Gabriel amiably, as he took another preparatory draught, kindly forget my existence, ladies and gentlemen, for a few minutes.

He set to his supper and took no part in the conversation with which the table covered Lily's removal of the plates. The subject of talk was the opera company which was then at the Theatre Royal. Mr Bartell D'Arcy, the tenor, a dark-complexioned young man with a smart moustache, praised very highly the leading contralto of the company but Miss Furlong thought she had a rather vulgar style of production. Freddy Malins said there was a negro chieftain singing in the second part of the Gaiety pantomime who had one of the finest tenor voices he had ever heard.

— Have you heard him? he asked Mr Bartell D'Arcy across the table.

— No, answered Mr Bartell D'Arcy carelessly.

— Because, Freddy Malins explained, now I'd be curious to hear your opinion of him. I think he has a grand voice.

— It takes Teddy to find out the really good things, said Mr Browne familiarly to the table.

— And why couldn't he have a voice too? asked Freddy Malins sharply. Is it because he's only a black?

Nobody answered this question and Mary Jane led the table back to the legitimate opera. One of her pupils had given her a pass for *Mignon*. Of course it was very fine, she said, but it made her think of poor Georgina Burns. Mr Browne could go back farther still, to the old Italian companies that used to come to Dublin — Tietjens, Ilma de Murzka, Campanini, the great Trebelli, Giuglini, Ravelli, Aramburo. Those were the days, he said, when there was something like singing to be heard in Dublin. He told too of how the top gallery of the old Royal used to be packed night after night, of how one night an Italian tenor had sung five encores to *Let Me Like a Soldier Fall*, introducing a high C every time, and of how the gallery boys would sometimes in their enthusiasm unyoke the horses from the carriage of some great *prima donna* and pull her themselves through the streets to her hotel. Why did they never play the grand old operas now, he asked, *Dinorah, Lucrezia Borgia?* Because they could not get the voices to sing them: that was why.

— O, well, said Mr Bartell D'Arcy, I presume there are as good singers to-day as there were then.

— Where are they? asked Mr Browne defiantly.

— In London, Paris, Milan, said Mr Bartell D'Arcy warmly. I suppose Caruso, for example, is quite as good, if not better than any of the men you have mentioned.

— Maybe so, said Mr Browne. But I may tell you I doubt it strongly.

— O, I'd give anything to hear Caruso sing, said Mary Jane.

— For me, said Aunt Kate, who had been picking a bone, there was only one tenor. To please me, I mean. But I suppose none of you ever heard of him.

— Who was he, Miss Morkan? asked Mr Bartell D'Arcy politely.

— His name, said Aunt Kate, was Parkinson. I heard him when he was in his prime and I think he had then the purest tenor voice that was ever put into a man's throat.

— Strange, said Mr Bartell D'Arcy. I never even heard of him.

— Yes, yes, Miss Morkan is right, said Mr Browne. I remember hearing of old Parkinson but he's too far back for me.

— A beautiful pure sweet mellow English tenor, said Aunt Kate with enthusiasm.

Gabriel having finished, the huge pudding was transferred to the table. The clatter of forks and spoons began again. Gabriel's wife served out spoonfuls of the pudding and passed the plates down the table. Midway down they were held up by Mary Jane, who replenished them with raspberry or orange jelly or with blancmange and jam. The pudding was of Aunt Julia's making and she received praises for it from all quarters. She herself said that it was not quite brown enough.

— Well, I hope, Miss Morkan, said Mr Browne, that I'm brown enough for you because, you know, I'm all brown.

All the gentlemen, except Gabriel, ate some of the pudding out of compliment to Aunt Julia. As Gabriel never ate sweets the celery had been left for him. Freddy Malins also took a stalk of celery and ate it with his pudding. He had been told that celery was a capital thing for the blood and he was just then under the doctor's care. Mrs Malins, who had been silent all through the supper, said that her son was going down to Mount Melleray in a week or so. The table then spoke of Mount Melleray, how bracing the air was down there, how hospitable the monks were and how they never asked for a penny-piece from their guests.

— And do you mean to say, asked Mr Browne incredulously, that a chap can go down there and put up there as if it were a hotel and live on the fat of the land and then come away without paying a farthing?

— O, most people give some donation to the monastery when they leave, said Mary Jane.

— I wish we had an institution like that in our Church, said Mr Browne candidly.

He was astonished to hear that the monks never spoke, got up at two in the morning and slept in their coffins. He asked what they did it for.

— That's the rule of the order, said Aunt Kate firmly.

— Yes, but why? asked Mr Browne.

Aunt Kate repeated that it was the rule, that was all. Mr Browne still seemed not to understand. Freddy Malins explained to him, as best he could, that the monks were trying to make up for the sins committed by all the sinners in the outside world. The explanation was not very clear for Mr Browne grinned and said:

— I like that idea very much but wouldn't a comfortable spring bed do them as well as a coffin?

— The coffin, said Mary Jane, is to remind them of their last end.

As the subject had grown lugubrious it was buried in a silence of the table during which Mrs Malins could be heard saying to her neighbour in an indistinct undertone:

— They are very good men, the monks, very pious men.

The raisins and almonds and figs and apples and oranges and chocolates and sweets were now passed about the table and Aunt Julia invited all the guests to have either port or sherry. At first Mr Bartell D'Arcy refused to take either but one of his neighbours nudged him and whispered something to him upon which he allowed his glass to be filled. Gradually as the last glasses were being filled the conversation ceased. A pause followed, broken only by the noise of the wine and by unsettlings of chairs. The Misses Morkan, all three, looked down at the tablecloth. Someone coughed once or twice and then a few gentlemen patted the table gently as a signal for silence. The silence came and Gabriel pushed back his chair and stood up.

The patting at once grew louder in encouragement and then ceased altogether. Gabriel leaned his ten trembling fingers on the tablecloth and smiled nervously at the company. Meeting a row of upturned faces he raised his eyes to the chandelier. The piano was playing a waltz tune and he could hear the skirts sweeping against the drawing-room door. People, perhaps, were standing in the snow on the quay outside, gazing up at the lighted windows and listening to the waltz music. The air was pure there. In the distance lay the park where the trees were weighted with snow. The Wellington Monument wore a gleaming cap of snow that flashed westward over the white field of Fifteen Acres.

He began:

— Ladies and Gentlemen.

— It has fallen to my lot this evening, as in years past, to perform a very pleasing task but a task for which I am afraid my poor powers as a speaker are all too inadequate.

— No, no! said Mr Browne.

— But, however that may be, I can only ask you to-night to take the will for the deed and to lend me your attention for a few moments while I endeavour to express to you in words what my feelings are on this occasion.

— Ladies and Gentlemen. It is not the first time that we have gathered together under this hospitable roof, around this hospitable board. It is not the first time that we have been the recipients — or perhaps, I had better say, the victims — of the hospitality of certain good ladies.

He made a circle in the air with his arm and paused. Everyone laughed or smiled at Aunt Kate and Aunt Julia and Mary Jane who all turned crimson with pleasure. Gabriel went on more boldly:

— I feel more strongly with every recurring year that our country has no tradition which does it so much honour and which it should guard so jealously as that of its hospitality. It is a tradition that is unique as far as my experience goes (and I have visited not a few places abroad) among the modern nations. Some would say, perhaps, that with us it is rather a failing than anything to be boasted of. But granted even that, it is, to my mind, a princely failing, and one that I trust will long be cultivated among us. Of one thing, at least, I am sure. As long as this one roof shelters the good ladies aforesaid — and I wish from my heart it may do so for many and many a long year to come — the tradition of genuine warm-hearted courteous Irish hospitality, which our forefathers have handed down to us and which we in turn must hand down to our descendants, is still alive among us.

A hearty murmur of assent ran round the table. It shot through Gabriel's mind that Miss Ivors was not there and that she had gone away discourteously: and he said with confidence in himself:

— Ladies and Gentlemen.

— A new generation is growing up in our midst, a generation actuated by new ideas and new principles. It is serious and enthusiastic for these new ideas and its enthusiasm, even when it is misdirected, is, I believe, in the main sincere. But we are living in a sceptical and, if I may use the phrase, a thought-tormented age: and sometimes I fear that this new generation, educated or hypereducated as it is, will lack those qualities of humanity, of hospitality, of kindly humour which belonged to an older day. Listening tonight to the names of all those great singers of the past it seemed to me, I must confess, that we were living in a less spacious age. Those days might, without exaggeration, be called spacious days: and if they are gone beyond recall let us hope, at least, that in gatherings such as this we shall still speak of them with pride and affection, still cherish in our hearts the memory of those dead and gone great ones whose fame the world will not willingly let die.

— Hear, hear! said Mr Browne loudly.

— But yet, continued Gabriel, his voice falling into a softer inflection, there are always in gatherings such as this sadder thoughts that will recur to our minds: thoughts of the past, of youth, of changes, of absent faces that we miss here to-night. Our path through life is strewn with many such sad memories: and were we to brood upon them always we could not find the heart to go on bravely with our work among the living. We have all of us living duties and living affections which claim, and rightly claim, our strenuous endeavours.

— Therefore, I will not linger on the past. I will not let any gloomy moralising intrude upon us here to-night. Here we are gathered together for a brief moment from the bustle and rush of our everyday routine. We are met here as friends, in the spirit of good-fellowship, as colleagues, also to a certain extent, in the true spirit of *camaraderie*, and as the guests of — what shall I call them? — the Three Graces of the Dublin musical world.

The table burst into applause and laughter at this sally. Aunt Julia vainly asked each of her neighbours in turn to tell her what Gabriel had said.

— He says we are the Three Graces, Aunt Julia, said Mary Jane.

Aunt Julia did not understand but she looked up, smiling, at Gabriel, who continued in the same vein:

— Ladies and Gentlemen.

— I will not attempt to play to-night the part that Paris played on another occasion. I will not attempt to choose between them. The task would be an invidious one and one beyond my poor powers. For when I view them in turn, whether it be our chief hostess herself, whose good heart, whose too good heart, has become a byword with all who knew her, or her sister, who seems to be gifted with perennial youth and whose singing must have been a surprise and a revelation to us all to-night, or, last but not least, when I consider our youngest hostess, talented, cheerful, hard-working and the best of nieces, I confess, Ladies and Gentlemen, that I do not know to which of them I should award the prize.

Gabriel glanced down at his aunts and, seeing the large smile on Aunt Julia's face and the tears which had risen to Aunt Kate's eyes, hastened to close. He raised his glass of port gallantly, while every member of the company fingered a glass expectantly, and said loudly:

— Let us toast them all three together. Let us drink to their health, wealth, long life, happiness and prosperity and may they long continue to hold the proud and self-won position which they hold in their profession and the position of honour and affection which they hold in our hearts.

All the guests stood up, glass in hand, and, turning towards the three seated ladies, sang in unison, with Mr Browne as leader:

For they are jolly gay fellows,
For they are jolly gay fellows,
For they are jolly gay fellows,
Which nobody can deny.

Aunt Kate was making frank use of her handkerchief and even Aunt Julia seemed moved. Freddy Malins beat time with his pudding-fork and the singers turned towards one another, as if in melodious conference, while they sang, with emphasis:

Unless he tells a lie,
Unless he tells a lie.

Then, turning once more towards their hostesses, they sang:

For they are jolly gay fellows,
For they are jolly gay fellows,
For they are jolly gay fellows,
Which nobody can deny.

The acclamation which followed was taken up beyond the door of the supper-room by many of the other guests and renewed time after time, Freddy Malins acting as officer with his fork on high.

The piercing morning air came into the hall where they were standing so that Aunt Kate said:

— Close the door, somebody. Mrs Malins will get her death of cold.

— Browne is out there, Aunt Kate, said Mary Jane.

— Browne is everywhere, said Aunt Kate, lowering her voice.

Mary Jane laughed at her tone.

— Really, she said archly, he is very attentive.

— He has been laid on here like the gas, said Aunt Kate in the same tone, all during the Christmas.

She laughed herself this time good-humouredly and then added quickly:

— But tell him to come in, Mary Jane, and close the door. I hope to goodness he didn't hear me.

At that moment the hall-door was opened and Mr Browne came in from the doorstep, laughing as if his heart would break. He was dressed in a long green overcoat with mock astrakhan cuffs and collar and wore on his head an oval fur cap. He pointed down the snow-covered quay from where the sound of shrill prolonged whistling was borne in.

— Teddy will have all the cabs in Dublin out, he said.

Gabriel advanced from the little pantry behind the office, struggling into his overcoat and, looking round the hall, said:

— Gretta not down yet?

— She's getting on her things, Gabriel, said Aunt Kate.

— Who's playing up there? asked Gabriel.

— Nobody. They're all gone.

— O no, Aunt Kate, said Mary Jane. Bartell D'Arcy and Miss O'Callaghan aren't gone yet.

— Someone is strumming at the piano, anyhow, said Gabriel.

Mary Jane glanced at Gabriel and Mr Browne and said with a shiver:

— It makes me feel cold to look at you two gentlemen muffled up like that. I wouldn't like to face your journey home at this hour.

— I'd like nothing better this minute, said Mr Browne stoutly, than a rattling fine walk in the country or a fast drive with a good spanking goer between the shafts.

— We used to have a very good horse and trap at home, said Aunt Julia sadly.

— The never-to-be-forgotten Johnny, said Mary Jane, laughing.

Aunt Kate and Gabriel laughed too.

— Why, what was wonderful about Johnny? asked Mr Browne.

— The late lamented Patrick Morkan, our grandfather, that is, explained Gabriel, commonly known in his later years as the old gentleman, was a glue-boiler.

— O, now, Gabriel, said Aunt Kate, laughing, he had a starch mill.

— Well, glue or starch, said Gabriel, the old gentleman had a horse by the name of Johnny. And Johnny used to work in the old gentleman's mill, walking round and round in order to drive the mill. That was all very well; but now comes the tragic part about Johnny. One fine day the old gentleman thought he'd like to drive out with the quality to a military review in the park.

— The Lord have mercy on his soul, said Aunt Kate compassionately.

— Amen, said Gabriel. So the old gentleman, as I said, harnessed Johnny and put on his very best tall hat and his very best stock collar and drove out in grand style from his ancestral mansion somewhere near Back Lane, I think.

Everyone laughed, even Mrs Malins, at Gabriel's manner and Aunt Kate said:

— O now, Gabriel, he didn't live in Back Lane, really. Only the mill was there.

— Out from the mansion of his forefathers, continued Gabriel, he drove with Johnny. And everything went on beautifully until Johnny came in sight of King Billy's statue: and whether he fell in love with the horse King Billy sits on or whether he thought he was back again in the mill, anyhow he began to walk round the statue.

Gabriel paced in a circle round the hall in his goloshes amid the laughter of the others.

— Round and round he went, said Gabriel, and the old gentleman, who was a very pompous old gentleman, was highly indignant. *Go on, sir! What do you mean, sir? Johnny! Johnny! Most extraordinary conduct! Can't understand the horse!*

The peals of laughter which followed Gabriel's imitation of the incident were interrupted by a resounding knock at the hall-door. Mary Jane ran to open it and let in Freddy Malins. Freddy Malins, with his hat well back on his head and his shoulders humped with cold, was puffing and steaming after his exertions.

— I could only get one cab, he said.

— O, we'll find another along the quay, said Gabriel.

— Yes, said Aunt Kate. Better not keep Mrs Malins standing in the draught.

Mrs Malins was helped down the front steps by her son and Mr Browne and, after many manœuvres, hoisted into the cab. Freddy Malins clambered in after her and spent a long time settling her on the seat, Mr Browne helping him with advice. At last she was settled comfortably and Freddy Malins invited Mr Browne into the cab. There was a good deal of confused talk, and then Mr Browne got into the cab. The cabman settled his rug over his knees, and bent down for the address. The confusion grew greater and the cabman was directed differently by Freddy Malins and Mr Browne, each of whom had his head out through a window of the cab. The difficulty was to know where to drop Mr Browne along the route and Aunt Kate, Aunt Julia and Mary Jane helped the discussion from the doorstep with cross-directions and contradictions and abundance of laughter. As for Freddy Malins he was speechless with laughter. He popped his head in and out of the window every moment, to the great danger of his hat, and told his mother how the discussion was progressing till at last Mr Browne shouted to the bewildered cabman above the din of everybody's laughter:

— Do you know Trinity College?

— Yes, sir, said the cabman.

— Well, drive bang up against Trinity College gates, said Mr Browne, and then we'll tell you where to go. You understand now?

— Yes, sir, said the cabman.

— Make like a bird for Trinity college.

— Right, sir, cried the cabman.

The horse was whipped up and the cab rattled off along the quay amid a chorus of laughter and adieus.

Gabriel had not gone to the door with the others. He was in a dark part of the hall gazing up the staircase. A woman was standing near the top of the first flight, in the shadow also. He could not see her face but he could see the terracotta and salmonpink panels of her skirt which the shadow made appear black and white. It was his wife. She was leaning on the banisters, listening to something. Gabriel was surprised at her stillness and strained his ear to listen also. But he could hear little save the noise of laughter and dispute on the front steps, a few chords struck on the piano and a few notes of a man's voice singing.

He stood still in the gloom of the hall, trying to catch the air that the voice was singing and gazing up at his wife. There was grace and mystery in her attitude as if she were a symbol of something. He asked himself what is a woman standing on the stairs in the shadow, listening to distant music, a symbol of. If he were a painter he would paint her in that attitude. Her blue felt hat would show off the bronze of her hair against the darkness and the dark panels of her skirt would show off the light ones. *Distant Music* he would call the picture if he were a painter.

The hall-door closed; and Aunt Kate, Aunt Julia and Mary Jane came down the hall, still laughing.

— Well, isn't Freddy terrible? said Mary Jane. He's really terrible.

Gabriel said nothing but pointed up the stairs towards where his wife was standing. Now that the hall-door was closed the voice and the piano could be heard more clearly. Gabriel held up his hand for them to be silent. The song seemed to be in the old Irish tonality and the singer seemed uncertain both of his words and of his voice. The voice, made plaintive by distance and by the singer's hoarseness, faintly illuminated the cadence of the air with words expressing grief:

> *O, the rain falls on my heavy locks*
> *And the dew wets my skin,*
> *My babe lies cold . . .*

— O, exclaimed Mary Jane. It's Bartell D'Arcy singing and he wouldn't sing all the night. O, I'll get him to sing a song before he goes.

— O do, Mary Jane, said Aunt Kate.

Mary Jane brushed past the others and ran to the staircase but before she reached it the singing stopped and the piano was closed abruptly.

— O, what a pity! she cried. Is he coming down, Gretta?

Gabriel heard his wife answer yes and saw her come down towards them. A few steps behind her were Mr Bartell D'Arcy and Miss O'Callaghan.

— O, Mr D'Arcy, cried Mary Jane, it's downright mean of you to break off like that when we were all in raptures listening to you.

— I have been at him all the evening, said Miss O'Callaghan, and Mrs Conroy too and he told us he had a dreadful cold and couldn't sing.

— O, Mr D'Arcy, said Aunt Kate, now that was a great fib to tell.

— Can't you see that I'm as hoarse as a crow? said Mr D'Arcy roughly.

He went into the pantry hastily and put on his overcoat. The others, taken aback by his rude speech, could find nothing to say. Aunt Kate wrinkled her brows and made signs to the others to drop the subject. Mr D'Arcy stood swathing his neck carefully and frowning.

— It's the weather, said Aunt Julia, after a pause.

— Yes, everybody has colds, said Aunt Kate readily, everybody.

— They say, said Mary Jane, we haven't had snow like it for thirty years; and I read this morning in the newspapers that the snow is general all over Ireland.

— I love the look of snow, said Aunt Julia sadly.

— So do I, said Miss O'Callaghan. I think Christmas is never really Christmas unless we have the snow on the ground.

— But poor Mr D'Arcy doesn't like the snow, said Aunt Kate, smiling.

Mr D'Arcy came from the pantry, fully swathed and buttoned, and in a repentant tone told them the history of the cold. Everyone gave him advice and said it was a great pity and urged him to be very careful of his throat in the night air. Gabriel watched his wife who did not join in the conversation. She was standing right under the dusty fanlight and the flame of the gas lit up the rich bronze of her hair which he had seen her drying at the fire a few days before. She was in the same attitude and seemed unaware of the talk about her. At last she turned towards them and Gabriel saw that there was colour on her cheeks and that her eyes were shining. A sudden tide of joy went leaping out of his heart.

— Mr D'Arcy, she said, what is the name of that song you were singing?

— It's called *The Lass of Aughrim*, said Mr D'Arcy, but I couldn't remember it properly. Why? Do you know it?

— *The Lass of Aughrim*, she repeated. I couldn't think of the name.

— It's a very nice air, said Mary Jane. I'm sorry you were not in voice to-night.

— Now, Mary Jane, said Aunt Kate, don't annoy Mr D'Arcy. I won't have him annoyed.

Seeing that all were ready to start she shepherded them to the door where good-night was said:

— Well, good-night, Aunt Kate, and thanks for the pleasant evening.

— Good-night, Gabriel. Good-night, Gretta!

— Good-night, Aunt Kate, and thanks ever so much. Good-night, Aunt Julia.

— O, good-night, Gretta, I didn't see you.

— Good-night, Mr D'Arcy. Good-night, Miss O'Callaghan.

— Good-night, Miss Morkan.

— Good-night, again.

— Good-night, all. Safe home.

— Good-night. Good-night.

The morning was still dark. A dull yellow light brooded over the houses and the river; and the sky seemed to be descending. It was slushy underfoot; and only streaks and patches of snow lay on the roofs, on the parapets of the quay and on the area railings. The lamps were still burning redly in the murky air and, across the river, the palace of the Four Courts stood out menacingly against the heavy sky.

She was walking on before him with Mr Bartell D'Arcy, her shoes in a brown parcel tucked under one arm and her hands holding her skirt up from the slush. She had no longer any grace of attitude but Gabriel's eyes were still bright with happiness. The blood went bounding along his veins; and the thoughts were rioting through his brain, proud, joyful, tender, valorous.

She was walking on before him so lightly and so erect that he longed to run after her noiselessly, catch her by the shoulders and say something foolish and affectionate into her ear. She seemed to him so frail that he longed to defend her against something and then to be alone with her. Moments of their secret life together burst like stars upon his memory. A heliotrope envelope was lying beside his breakfast-cup and he was caressing it with his hand. Birds were twittering in the ivy and the sunny web of the curtain was shimmering along the floor: he could not eat for happiness. They were standing on the crowded platform and he was placing a ticket inside the warm palm of her glove. He was standing with her in the cold, looking in through a grated window at a man making bottles in a roaring furnace. It was very cold. Her face, fragrant in the cold air, was quite close to his; and suddenly she called out to the man at the furnace.

— Is the fire hot, sir?

But the man could not hear her with the noise of the furnace. It was just as well. He might have answered rudely.

A wave of yet more tender joy escaped from his heart and went coursing in warm flood along his arteries. Like the tender fires of stars moments of their life together, that no one knew of or would ever know of, broke upon and illumined his memory. He longed to recall to her those moments, to make her forget the years of their dull existence together and remember only their moments of ecstasy. For the years, he felt, had not quenched his soul or hers. Their children, his writing, her household cares had not quenched all their souls' tender fire. In one letter that he had written to her then he had said: *Why is it that words like these seem to me so dull and cold? Is it because there is no word tender enough to be your name?*

Like distant music these words that he had written years before were borne towards him from the past. He longed to be alone with her. When the others had gone away, when he and she were in their room in the hotel, then they would be alone together. He would call her softly:

— Gretta!

Perhaps she would not hear at once: she would be undressing. Then something in his voice would strike her. She would turn and look at him. . . .

At the corner of Winetavern Street they met a cab. He was glad of its rattling noise as it saved him from conversation. She was looking out of the window and seemed tired. The others spoke only a few words, pointing out some building or street. The horse galloped along wearily under the murky morning sky, dragging his old rattling box after his heels, and Gabriel was again in a cab with her, galloping to catch the boat, galloping to their honeymoon.

As the cab drove across O'Connell Bridge Miss O'Callaghan said:

— They say you never cross O'Connell Bridge without seeing a white horse.

— I see a white man this time, said Gabriel.

— Where? asked Mr Bartell D'Arcy.

Gabriel pointed to the statue, on which lay patches of snow. Then he nodded familiarly to it and waved his hand.

— Good-night, Dan, he said gaily.

When the cab drew up before the hotel Gabriel jumped out and, in spite of Mr Bartell D'Arcy's protest, paid the driver. He gave the man a shilling over his fare. The man saluted and said:

— A prosperous New Year to you, sir.

— The same to you, said Gabriel cordially.

She leaned for a moment on his arm in getting out of the cab and while standing at the curbstone, bidding the others good-night. She leaned lightly on his arm, as lightly as when she had danced with him a few hours before. He had felt proud and happy then, happy that she was his, proud of her grace and wifely carriage. But now, after the kindling again of so many memories, the first touch of her body, musical and strange and perfumed, sent through him a keen pang of lust. Under cover of her silence he pressed her arm closely to his side; and, as they stood at the hotel door, he felt that they had escaped from their lives and duties, escaped from home and friends and run away together with wild and radiant hearts to a new adventure.

An old man was dozing in a great hooded chair in the hall. He lit a candle in the office and went before them to the stairs. They followed him in silence, their feet falling in soft thuds on the thickly carpeted stairs. She mounted the stairs behind the porter, her head bowed in the ascent, her frail shoulders curved as with a burden, her skirt girt tightly about her. He could have flung his arms about her hips and held her still for his arms were trembling with desire to seize her and only the stress of his nails against the palms of his hands held the wild impulse of his body in check. The porter halted on the stairs to settle his guttering candle. They halted too on the steps below him. In the silence Gabriel could hear the falling of the molten wax into the tray and the thumping of his own heart against his ribs.

The porter led them along a corridor and opened a door. Then he set his unstable candle down on a toilet-table and asked at what hour they were to be called in the morning.

— Eight, said Gabriel.

The porter pointed to the tap of the electric-light and began a muttered apology but Gabriel cut him short.

— We don't want any light. We have enough light from the street. And I say, he added, pointing to the candle, you might remove that handsome article, like a good man.

The porter took up his candle again, but slowly for he was surprised by such a novel idea. Then he mumbled good-night and went out. Gabriel shot the lock to.

A ghostly light from the street lamp lay in a long shaft from one window to the door. Gabriel threw his overcoat and hat on a couch and crossed the room towards the window. He looked down into the street in order that his emotion might calm a little. Then he turned and leaned against a chest of drawers with his back to the light. She had taken off her hat and cloak and was standing before a large swinging mirror, unhooking her waist. Gabriel paused for a few moments, watching her, and then said:

— Gretta!

She turned away from the mirror slowly and walked along the shaft of light towards him. Her face looked so serious and weary that the words would not pass Gabriel's lips. No, it was not the moment yet.

— You look tired, he said.

— I am a little, she answered.

— You don't feel ill or weak?

— No, tired: that's all.

She went on to the window and stood there, looking out. Gabriel waited again and then, fearing that diffidence was about to conquer him, he said abruptly:

— By the way, Gretta!

— What is it?

— You know that poor fellow Malins? he said quickly.

— Yes. What about him?

— Well, poor fellow, he's a decent sort of chap after all, continued Gabriel in a false voice. He gave me back that sovereign I lent him and I didn't expect it really. It's a pity he wouldn't keep away from that Browne, because he's not a bad fellow at heart.

He was trembling now with annoyance. Why did she seem so abstracted? He did not know how he could begin. Was she annoyed, too, about something? If she would only turn to him or come to him of her own accord! To take her as she was would be brutal. No, he must see some ardour in her eyes first. He longed to be master of her strange mood.

— When did you lend him the pound? she asked, after a pause.

Gabriel strove to restrain himself from breaking out into brutal language about the sottish Malins and his pound. He longed to cry to her from his soul, to crush her body against his, to overmaster her. But he said:

— O, at Christmas, when he opened that little Christmas-card shop in Henry Street.

He was in such a fever of rage and desire that he did not hear her come from the window. She stood before him for an instant, looking at him strangely. Then, suddenly raising herself on tiptoe and resting her hands lightly on his shoulders, she kissed him.

— You are a very generous person, Gabriel, she said.

Gabriel, trembling with delight at her sudden kiss and at the quaintness of her phrase, put his hands on her hair and began smoothing it back, scarcely touching it with his fingers. The washing had made it fine and brilliant. His heart was brimming over with happiness. Just when he was wishing for it she had come to him of her own accord. Perhaps her thoughts had been running with his. Perhaps she had felt the impetuous desire that was in him and then the yielding mood had come upon her. Now that she had fallen to him so easily he wondered why he had been so diffident.

He stood, holding her head between his hands. Then, slipping one arm swiftly about her body and drawing her towards him, he said softly:

— Gretta dear, what are you thinking about?

She did not answer nor yield wholly to his arm. He said again, softly:

— Tell me what it is, Gretta. I think I know what is the matter. Do I know?

She did not answer at once. Then she said in an outburst of tears:

— O, I am thinking about that song, *The Lass of Aughrim.*

She broke loose from him and ran to the bed and, throwing her arms across the bed-rail, hid her face. Gabriel stood stock-still for a moment in astonishment and then followed her. As he passed in the way of the cheval-glass he caught sight of himself in full length, his broad, well-filled shirtfront, the face whose expression always puzzled him when he saw it in a mirror and his glimmering gilt-rimmed eyeglasses. He halted a few paces from her and said:

— What about the song? Why does that make you cry?

She raised her head from her arms and dried her eyes with the back of her hand like a child. A kinder note than he had intended went into his voice.

— Why, Gretta? he asked.

— I am thinking about a person long ago who used to sing that song.

— And who was the person long ago? asked Gabriel, smiling.

— It was a person I used to know in Galway when I was living with my grandmother, she said.

The smile passed away from Gabriel's face. A dull anger began to gather again at the back of his mind and the dull fires of his lust began to glow angrily in his veins.

— Someone you were in love with? he asked ironically.

— It was a young boy I used to know, she answered, named Michael Furey. He used to sing that song, *The Lass of Aughrim.* He was very delicate.

Gabriel was silent. He did not wish her to think that he was interested in this delicate boy.

— I can see him so plainly, she said after a moment. Such eyes as he had: big dark eyes! And such an expression in them — an expression!

— O, then, you were in love with him? said Gabriel.

— I used to go out walking with him, she said, when I was in Galway.

A thought flew across Gabriel's mind.

— Perhaps that was why you wanted to go to Galway with that Ivors girl? he said coldly.

She looked at him and asked in surprise:

— What for?

Her eyes made Gabriel feel awkward. He shrugged his shoulders and said:

— How do I know? To see him perhaps.

She looked away from him along the shaft of light towards the window in silence.

— He is dead, she said at length. He died when he was only seventeen. Isn't that a terrible thing to die so young as that?

— What was he? asked Gabriel, still ironically.

— He was in the gasworks, she said.

Gabriel felt humiliated by the failure of his irony and by the evocation of this figure from the dead, a boy in the gasworks. While he had been full of memories of their secret life together, full of tenderness and joy and desire, she had been comparing him in her mind with another. A shameful conscious-ness of his own person assailed him. He saw himself as a ludicrous figure, acting as a pennyboy for his aunts, a nervous well-meaning sentimentalist, orating to vulgarians and idealising his own clownish lusts, the pitiable fatuous fellow he had caught a glimpse of in the mirror. Instinctively he turned his back more to the light lest she might see the shame that burned upon his forehead.

He tried to keep up his tone of cold interrogation but his voice when he spoke was humble and indifferent.

— I suppose you were in love with this Michael Furey, Gretta, he said.

— I was great with him at that time, she said.

Her voice was veiled and sad. Gabriel, feeling now how vain it would be to try to lead her whither he had purposed, caressed one of her hands and said, also sadly:

— And what did he die of so young, Gretta? Consumption, was it?

— I think he died for me, she answered.

A vague terror seized Gabriel at this answer as if, at that hour when he had hoped to triumph, some impalpable and vindictive being was coming against him, gathering forces against him in its vague world. But he shook himself free of it with an effort of reason and continued to caress her hand. He did not question her again for he felt that she would tell him of herself. Her hand was warm and moist: it did not respond to his touch but he continued to caress it just as he had caressed her first letter to him that spring morning.

— It was in the winter, she said, about the beginning of the winter when

I was going to leave my grandmother's and come up here to the convent. And he was ill at the time in his lodgings in Galway and wouldn't be let out and his people in Oughterard were written to. He was in decline, they said, or something like that. I never knew rightly.

She paused for a moment and sighed.

— Poor fellow, she said. He was very fond of me and he was such a gentle boy. We used to go out together, walking, you know, Gabriel, like the way they do in the country. He was going to study singing only for his health. He had a very good voice, poor Michael Furey.

— Well; and then? asked Gabriel.

— And then when it came to the time for me to leave Galway and come up to the convent he was much worse and I wouldn't be let see him so I wrote a letter saying I was going up to Dublin and would be back in the summer and hoping he would be better then.

She paused for a moment to get her voice under control and then went on:

— Then the night before I left I was in my grandmother's house in Nuns' Island, packing up, and I heard gravel thrown up against the window. The window was so wet I couldn't see so I ran downstairs as I was and slipped out the back into the garden and there was the poor fellow at the end of the garden, shivering.

— And did you not tell him to go back? asked Gabriel.

— I implored of him to go home at once and told him he would get his death in the rain. But he said he did not want to live. I can see his eyes as well as well! He was standing at the end of the wall where there was a tree.

— And did he go home? asked Gabriel.

— Yes, he went home. And when I was only a week in the convent he died and he was buried in Oughterard where his people came from. O, the day I heard that, that he was dead!

She stopped, choking with sobs, and, overcome by emotion, flung herself face downward on the bed, sobbing in the quilt. Gabriel held her hand for a moment longer, irresolutely, and then, shy of intruding on her grief, let it fall gently and walked quietly to the window.

She was fast asleep.

Gabriel, leaning on his elbow, looked for a few moments unresentfully on her tangled hair and half-open mouth, listening to her deep-drawn breath. So she had had that romance in her life: a man had died for her sake. It hardly pained him now to think how poor a part he, her husband, had played in her life. He watched her while she slept as though he and she had never lived together as man and wife. His curious eyes rested long upon her face and on her hair: and, as he thought of what she must have been then, in that time of her first girlish beauty, a strange friendly pity for her entered his soul. He did not like to say even to himself that her face was no longer beautiful but he knew that it was no longer the face for which Michael Furey had braved death.

Perhaps she had not told him all the story. His eyes moved to the chair over which she had thrown some of her clothes. A petticoat string dangled to the floor. One boot stood upright, its limp upper fallen down: the fellow of it lay upon its side. He wondered at his riot of emotions of an hour before. From what had it proceeded? From his aunt's supper, from his own foolish speech, from the wine and dancing, the merry-making when saying good-night in the hall, the pleasure of the walk along the river in the snow. Poor Aunt Julia! She, too, would soon be a shade with the shade of Patrick Morkan and his horse. He had caught that haggard look upon her face for a moment when she was singing *Arrayed for the Bridal.* Soon, perhaps, he would be sitting in that same drawing-room, dressed in black, his silk hat on his knees. The blinds would be drawn down and Aunt Kate would be sitting beside him, crying and blowing her nose and telling him how Julia had died. He would cast about his mind for some words that might console her, and would find only lame and useless ones. Yes, yes: that would happen very soon.

The air of the room chilled his shoulders. He stretched himself cautiously along under the sheets and lay down beside his wife. One by one they were all becoming shades. Better pass boldly into that other world, in the full glory of some passion, than fade and wither dismally with age. He thought of how she who lay beside him had locked in her heart for so many years that image of her lover's eyes when he had told her that he did not wish to live.

Generous tears filled Gabriel's eyes. He had never felt like that himself towards any woman but he knew that such a feeling must be love. The tears gathered more thickly in his eyes and in the partial darkness he imagined he saw the form of a young man standing under a dripping tree. Other forms were near. His soul had approached that region where dwell the vast hosts of the dead. He was conscious of, but could not apprehend, their wayward and flickering existence. His own identity was fading out into a grey impalpable world: the solid world itself which these dead had one time reared and lived in was dissolving and dwindling.

A few light taps upon the pane made him turn to the window. It had begun to snow again. He watched sleepily the flakes, silver and dark, falling obliquely against the lamplight. The time had come for him to set out on his journey westward. Yes, the newspapers were right: snow was general all over Ireland. It was falling on every part of the dark central plain, on the treeless hills, falling softly upon the Bog of Allen and, farther westward, softly falling into the dark mutinous Shannon waves. It was falling, too, upon every part of the lonely churchyard on the hill where Michael Furey lay buried. It lay thickly drifted on the crooked crosses and headstones, on the spears of the little gate, on the barren thorns. His soul swooned slowly as he heard the snow falling faintly through the universe and faintly falling, like the descent of their last end, upon all the living and the dead.   [1916]

FRANZ KAFKA *(1883–1924) led a life whose events are simple and sad. He was born into a Jewish family in Prague, and from youth onward he feared his authoritarian father so much that he stuttered in his presence, although he spoke easily with others. In 1906 he received a doctorate in jurisprudence, and for many years he worked a tedious job as a civil service lawyer investigating claims at the state Worker's Accident Insurance Institute. He never married and lived for the most part with his parents, writing fiction at night (he was an insomniac) and publishing only a few slim volumes of stories during his lifetime. Meditation, a collection of sketches, appeared in 1912; The Stoker: A Fragment in 1913; The Metamorphosis in 1915; The Judgment in 1916; In the Penal Colony in 1919; and A Country Doctor in 1920. Only a few of his friends knew that Kafka was also at work on the great novels that were published after his death from tuberculosis: Amerika, The Trial, and The Castle. (He asked his literary executor, Max Brod, to burn these works in manuscript, but Brod refused.) Kafka's despair with his writing, his job, his father, and his life was complete. Like Gustave Flaubert — whom he admired — he used his fiction as a "rock" to which he clung in order not to be drowned in the waves of the world around him. With typical irony, however, he saw the effort as futile: "By scribbling I run ahead of myself in order to catch myself up at the finishing post. I cannot run away from myself."*

In his diaries Kafka recorded his obsession with literature. "What will be my fate as a writer is very simple. My talent for portraying my dreamlike inner life has thrust all other matters into the background." "A Hunger Artist" is one of Kafka's most striking "parables of alienation," as his biographer Ernst Pawel has noted, but the "dreamlike" quality of his imagination is apparent in all Kafka's work.

Kafka is perhaps best known as the author of the waking nightmare "The Metamorphosis," whose remarkable first sentence is one of the most famous in short story literature. The hero of the story, Gregor Samsa (pronounced Zamza*), is the son of philistine, middle-class parents in Prague, as was Kafka, and literary critics have tended to interpret the story as an autobiographical fiction, using the "monstrous insect" as a Freudian symbol that characterizes Kafka's sense of inadequacy before his demanding father. Kafka himself considered psychoanalysis "a helpless error," regarding Freud's theories as very rough pictures that do not do justice to either the details or the essence of life. Perhaps the greatest literary influence on Kafka was Flaubert; both writers used language with ironic precision and without explicit intrusion of their private sentiments. The visionary, nightmarish quality of Kafka's fiction is in striking contrast to its precise and formal style, the clarity of which intensifies the dark richness of the fantasy.*

RELATED COMMENTARIES: *Gustav Janouch, "Kafka's View of 'The Metamorphosis,'" page 1439; Milan Kundera, "Kafka and Modern History," page 1444; Jane Smiley, "Gregor: My Life as a Bug," page 1495; and John Updike, "Kafka and 'The Metamorphosis,'" page 1502.*

FRANZ KAFKA

A Hunger Artist

Translated by Willa and Edwin Muir

During these last decades the interest in professional fasting has mark-edly diminished. It used to pay very well to stage such great performances under one's own management, but today that is quite impossible. We live in a different world now. At one time the whole town took a lively interest in the hunger artist; from day to day of his fast the excitement mounted; every-body wanted to see him at least once a day; there were people who bought season tickets for the last few days and sat from morning till night in front of his small barred cage; even in the nighttime there were visiting hours, when the whole effect was heightened by torch flares; on fine days the cage was set out in the open air, and then it was the children's special treat to see the hunger artist; for their elders he was often just a joke that happened to be in fashion, but the children stood openmouthed, holding each other's hands for greater security, marveling at him as he sat there pallid in black tights, with his ribs sticking out so prominently, not even on a seat but down among straw on the ground, sometimes giving a courteous nod, answering questions with a constrained smile, or perhaps stretching an arm through the bars so that one might feel how thin it was, and then again withdrawing deep into himself, paying no attention to anyone or anything, not even to the all-impor-tant striking of the clock that was the only piece of furniture in his cage, but merely staring into vacancy with half-shut eyes, now and then taking a sip from a tiny glass of water to moisten his lips.

Besides casual onlookers there were also relays of permanent watchers selected by the public, usually butchers, strangely enough, and it was their task to watch the hunger artist day and night, three of them at a time, in case he should have some secret recourse to nourishment. This was nothing but a formality, instituted to reassure the masses, for the initiates knew well enough that during his fast the artist would never in any circumstances, not even under forcible compulsion, swallow the smallest morsel of food; the honor of his profession forbade it. Not every watcher, of course, was capable of under-standing this, there were often groups of night watchers who were very lax in carrying out their duties and deliberately huddled together in a retired corner to play cards with great absorption, obviously intending to give the hunger artist the chance of a little refreshment, which they supposed he could draw from some private hoard. Nothing annoyed the artist more than such watchers; they made him miserable; they made his fast seem unendurable; sometimes he mastered his feebleness sufficiently to sing during their watch for as long as he could keep going, to show them how unjust their suspicions were. But that was of little use; they only wondered at his cleverness in being able to fill his mouth even while singing. Much more to his taste were the watchers who sat close up to the bars, who were not content with the dim night lighting of the hall but focused him in the full glare of the electric pocket torch given them by the impresario. The harsh light did not trouble him at all, in any case he could never sleep properly, and he could always drowse a little, whatever the light, at any hour, even when the hall was thronged with noisy onlookers. He was quite happy at the prospect of spending a sleepless night with such watchers; he was ready to exchange jokes with them, to tell them stories out of his nomadic life, anything at all to keep them awake and demonstrate to them again that he had no eatables in his cage and that he was fasting as not one of them could fast. But his happiest moment was when the morning came and an enormous breakfast was brought them, at his expense, on which they flung themselves with the keen appetite of healthy men after a weary night of wakefulness. Of course there were people who argued that this breakfast was an unfair attempt to bribe the watchers, but that was going rather too far, and when they were invited to take on a night's vigil without a breakfast, merely for the sake of the cause, they made themselves scarce, although they stuck stubbornly to their suspicions.

Such suspicions, anyhow, were a necessary accompaniment to the profession of fasting. No one could possibly watch the hunger artist continuously, day and night, and so no one could produce first-hand evidence that the fast had really been rigorous and continuous; only the artist himself could know that, he was therefore bound to be the sole completely satisfied spectator of his own fast. Yet for other reasons he was never satisfied; it was not perhaps mere fasting that had brought him to such skeleton thinness that many people had regretfully to keep away from his exhibitions, because the sight of him was too much for them, perhaps it was dissatisfaction with himself that had worn him down. For he alone knew, what no other initiate knew, how easy it was to fast. It was the easiest thing in the world. He made no secret of this, yet people did not believe him, at the best they set him down as modest, most of them, however, thought he was out for publicity or else was some kind of cheat who found it easy to fast because he had discovered a way of making it easy, and then had the impudence to admit the fact, more or less. He had to put up with all that, and in the course of time had got used to it, but his inner dissatisfaction always rankled, and never yet, after any term of fasting — this must be granted to his credit — had he left the cage of his own free will. The longest period of fasting was fixed by his impresario at forty days, beyond that term he was not allowed to go, not even in great cities, and there was good reason for it, too. Experience had proved that for about forty days the interest of the public could be stimulated by a steadily increasing pressure of advertisement, but after that the town began to lose interest, sympathetic support began notably to fall off; there were of course local variations as between one town and another or one country and another, but as a general rule forty days marked the limit. So on the fortieth day the flower-bedecked cage was opened, enthusiastic spectators filled the hall, a military band played, two doctors entered the cage to measure the results of the fast, which were announced through a megaphone, and finally two young ladies appeared blissful at having been selected for the honor, to help the hunger artist down the few steps leading to a small table on which was spread a carefully chosen invalid repast. And at this very moment the artist always turned stubborn. True, he would entrust his bony arms to the outstretched helping hands of the ladies bending over him, but stand up he would not. Why stop fasting at this particular moment, after forty days of it? He had held out for a long time, an illimitably long time; why stop now, when he was in his best fasting form, or rather, not yet quite in his best fasting form? Why should he be cheated of the fame he would get for fasting longer, for being not only the record hunger artist of all time, which presumably he was already, but for beating his own record by a performance beyond human imagination, since he felt that there were no limits to his capacity for fasting? His public pretended to admire him so much, why should it have so little patience with him; if he could endure fasting longer, why shouldn't the public endure it? Besides, he was tired, he was comfortable sitting in the straw, and now he was supposed to lift himself to his full height and go down to a meal the very thought of which gave him a nausea that only the presence of the ladies kept him from betraying, and even that with an effort. And he looked up into the eyes of the ladies who were apparently so friendly and in reality so cruel, and shook his head, which felt too heavy on its strengthless neck. But then there happened yet again what always happened. The impresario came forward, without a word — for the band made speech impossible — lifted his arms in the air above the artist, as if inviting Heaven to look down upon its creature here in the straw, this suffering martyr, which indeed he was, although in quite another sense; grasped him around the emaciated waist, with exaggerated caution, so that the frail condition he was in might be appreciated; and committed him to the care of the blenching ladies, not without secretly giving him a shaking so that his legs and body tottered and swayed. The artist now submitted completely; his head lolled on his breast as if it had landed there by chance; his body was hollowed out; his legs in a spasm of self-preservation clung close to each other at the knees, yet scraped on the ground as if it were not really solid ground, as if they were only trying to find solid ground; and the whole weight of his body, a featherweight after all, relapsed onto one of the ladies, who, looking around for help and panting a little — this post of honor was not at all what she had expected it to be — first stretched her neck as far as she could to keep her face at least free from contact with the artist, then finding this impossible, and her more fortunate companion not coming to her aid but merely holding extended in her own trembling hand the little bunch of knucklebones that was the artist's, to the great delight of the spectators burst into tears and had to be replaced by an attendant who had long been stationed in readiness. Then came the food, a little of which the impresario managed to get between the artist's lips, while he sat in a kind of half-fainting trance, to the accompaniment of cheerful patter designed to distract the public's attention from the artist's condition; after that, a toast was drunk to the public, supposedly prompted by a whisper from the artist in the impresario's ear; the band confirmed it with a mighty flourish, the spectators melted away, and no one had any cause to be dissatisfied with the proceedings, no one except the hunger artist himself, he only, as always.

So he lived for many years, with small regular intervals of recuperation, in visible glory, honored by the world, yet in spite of that troubled in spirit, and all the more troubled because no one would take his trouble seriously. What comfort could he possibly need? What more could he possibly wish for? And if some good-natured person, feeling sorry for him, tried to console him by pointing out that his melancholy was probably caused by fasting, it could happen, especially when he had been fasting for some time, that he reacted with an outburst of fury and to the general alarm began to shake the bars of his cage like a wild animal. Yet the impresario had a way of punishing these outbreaks which he rather enjoyed putting into operation. He would apologize publicly for the artist's behavior, which was only to be excused, he admitted, because of the irritability caused by fasting; a condition hardly to be understood by well-fed people; then by natural transition he went on to mention the artist's equally incomprehensible boast that he could fast for much longer than he was doing; he praised the high ambition, the good will, the great self-denial undoubtedly implicit in such a statement; and then quite simply countered it by bringing out photographs, which were also on sale to the public, showing the artist on the fortieth day of a fast lying in bed almost dead from exhaustion. This perversion of the truth, familiar to the artist though it was, always unnerved him afresh and proved too much for him. What was a consequence of the premature ending of his fast was here presented as the cause of it! To fight against this lack of understanding, against a whole world of nonunderstanding, was impossible. Time and again in good faith he stood by the bars listening to the impresario, but as soon as the photographs appeared he always let go and sank with a groan back onto his straw, and the reassured public could once more come close and gaze at him.

A few years later when the witnesses of such scenes called them to mind, they often failed to understand themselves at all. For meanwhile the aforementioned change in public interest had set in; it seemed to happen almost overnight; there may have been profound causes for it, but who was going to bother about that; at any rate the pampered hunger artist suddenly found himself deserted one fine day by the amusement-seekers, who went streaming past him to other more-favored attractions. For the last time the impresario hurried him over half Europe to discover whether the old interest might still survive here and there; all in vain; everywhere, as if by secret agreement, a positive revulsion from professional fasting was in evidence. Of course it could not really have sprung up so suddenly as all that, and many premonitory symptoms which had not been sufficiently remarked or suppressed during the rush and glitter of success now came retrospectively to mind, but it was now too late to take any countermeasures. Fasting would surely come into fashion again at some future date, yet that was no comfort for those living in the present. What, then, was the hunger artist to do? He had been applauded by thousands in his time and could hardly come down to showing himself in a street booth at village fairs, and as for adopting another profession, he was not only too old for that but too fanatically devoted to fasting. So he took leave of the impresario, his partner in an unparalleled career, and hired himself to a large circus; in order to spare his own feelings he avoided reading the conditions of his contract.

A large circus with its enormous traffic in replacing and recruiting men, animals, and apparatus can always find a use for people at any time, even for a hunger artist, provided of course that he does not ask too much, and in this particular case anyhow it was not only the artist who was taken on but his famous and long-known name as well, indeed considering the peculiar nature of his performance, which was not impaired by advancing age, it could not be objected that here was an artist past his prime, no longer at the height of his professional skill, seeking a refuge in some quiet corner of a circus; on the contrary, the hunger artist averred that he could fast as well as ever, which was entirely credible, he even alleged that if he were allowed to fast as he liked and this was at once promised him without more ado, he could astound the world by establishing a record never yet achieved, a statement that certainly provoked a smile among the other professionals, since it left out of account the change in public opinion, which the hunger artist in his zeal conveniently forgot.

He had not, however, actually lost his sense of the real situation and took it as a matter of course that he and his cage should be stationed, not in the middle of the ring as a main attraction, but outside, near the animal cages, on a site that was after all easily accessible. Large and gaily painted placards made a frame for the cage and announced what was to be seen inside it. When the public came thronging out in the intervals to see the animals, they could hardly avoid passing the hunger artist's cage and stopping there for a moment, perhaps they might even have stayed longer had not those pressing behind them in the narrow gangway, who did not understand why they should be held up on their way toward the excitements of the menagerie, made it impossible for anyone to stand gazing quietly for any length of time. And that was the reason why the hunger artist, who had of course been looking forward to these visiting hours as the main achievement of his life, began instead to shrink from them. At first he could hardly wait for the intervals; it was exhilerating to watch the crowds come streaming his way, until only too soon — not even the most obstinate self-deception, clung to almost consciously, could hold out against the fact — the conviction was borne in upon him that these people, most of them, to judge from their actions, again and again, without exception, were all on their way to the menagerie. And the first sight of them from the distance remained the best. For when they reached his cage he was at once deafened by the storm of shouting and abuse that arose from the two contending factions, which renewed themselves continuously, of those who wanted to stop and stare at him — he soon began to dislike them more than the others — not out of real interest but only out of obstinate self-assertiveness, and those who wanted to go straight on to the animals. When the first great rush was past, the stragglers came along, and these, whom nothing could have prevented from stopping to look at him as long as they had breath, raced past with long strides, hardly even glancing at him, in their haste to get to the menagerie in time. And all too rarely did it happen that he had a stroke of luck, when some father of a family fetched up before him with his children, pointed a finger at the hunger artist, and explained at length what the phenomenon meant, telling stories of earlier years when he himself had watched similar but much more thrilling performances, and the children, still rather uncomprehending, since neither inside nor outside school had they been sufficiently prepared for this lesson — what did they care about fasting? — yet showed by the brightness of their intent eyes that new and better times might be coming. Perhaps, said the hunger artist to himself many a time, things would be a little better if his cage were set not quite so near the menagerie. That made it too easy for people to make their choice, to say nothing of what he suffered from the stench of the menagerie, the animals' restlessness by night, the carrying past of raw lumps of flesh for the beasts of prey, the roaring at feeding times, which depressed him continually. But he did not dare to lodge a complaint with the management; after all, he had the animals to thank for the troops of people who passed his cage, among whom there might always be one here and there to take an interest in him, and who could tell where they might seclude him if he called attention to his existence and thereby to the fact that, strictly speaking, he was only an impediment on the way to the menagerie.

A small impediment, to be sure, one that grew steadily less. People grew familiar with the strange idea that they could be expected, in times like these, to take an interest in a hunger artist, and with this familiarity the verdict went out against him. He might fast as much as he could, and he did so; but nothing could save him now, people passed him by. Just try to explain to anyone the art of fasting! Anyone who has no feeling for it cannot be made to understand it. The fine placards grew dirty and illegible, they were torn down; the little notice board telling the number of fast days achieved, which at first was changed carefully every day, had long stayed at the same figure, for after the first few weeks even this small task seemed pointless to the staff; and so the artist simply fasted on and on, as he had once dreamed of doing, and it was no trouble to him, just as he had always foretold, but no one counted the days, no one, not even the artist himself, knew what records he was already breaking and his heart grew heavy. And when once in a while some leisurely passer-by stopped, made merry over the old figure on the board, and spoke of swindling, that was in its way the stupidest lie ever invented by indifference and inborn malice, since it was not the hunger artist who was cheating, he was working honestly, but the world was cheating him of his reward.

Many more days went by, however, and that too came to an end. An overseer's eye fell on the cage one day and he asked the attendants why this perfectly good cage should be left standing there unused with dirty straw inside it; nobody knew, until one man, helped out by the notice board, remembered about the hunger artist. They poked into the straw with sticks and found him in it. "Are you still fasting?" asked the overseer, "when on earth do you mean to stop?" "Forgive me, everybody," whispered the hunger artist; only the overseer, who had his ear to the bars, understood him. "Of course," said the overseer, and tapped his forehead with a finger to let the attendants know what state the man was in, "we forgive you." "I always wanted you to admire my fasting," said the hunger artist. "We do admire it," said the overseer, affably. "But you shouldn't admire it," said the hunger artist. "Well then we don't admire it," said the overseer, "but why shouldn't we admire it?" "Because I have to fast, I can't help it," said the hunger artist. "What a fellow you are," said the overseer, "and why can't you help it?" "Because," said the hunger artist, lifting his head a little and speaking, with his lips pursed, as if for a kiss, right into the overseer's ear, so that no syllable might be lost, "because I couldn't find the food I liked. If I had found it, believe me, I should have made no fuss and stuffed myself like you or anyone else." These were his last words, but in his dimming eyes remained the firm though no longer proud persuasion that he was still continuing to fast.

"Well, clear this out now!" said the overseer, and they buried the hunger artist, straw and all. Into the cage they put a young panther. Even the most insensitive felt it refreshing to see this wild creature leaping around the cage that had so long been dreary. The panther was all right. The food he liked was brought him without hesitation by the attendants; he seemed not even to miss his freedom; his noble body, furnished almost to the bursting point with all that it needed, seemed to carry freedom around with it too; somewhere in his jaws it seemed to lurk; and the joy of life streamed with such ardent passion from his throat that for the onlookers it was not easy to stand the shock of it. But they braced themselves, crowded around the cage, and did not want ever to move away.   [1924]

FRANZ KAFKA

The Metamorphosis

Translated by Willa and Edwin Muir

I

As Gregor Samsa awoke one morning from uneasy dreams he found himself transformed in his bed into a gigantic insect. He was lying on his hard, as it were armor-plated, back and when he lifted his head a little he could see his dome-like brown belly divided into stiff arched segments on top of which the bed quilt could hardly keep in position and was about to slide off completely. His numerous legs, which were pitifully thin compared to the rest of his bulk, waved helplessly before his eyes.

What has happened to me? he thought. It was no dream. His room, a regular human bedroom, only rather too small, lay quiet between the four familiar walls. Above the table on which a collection of cloth samples was unpacked and spread out — Samsa was a commercial traveler — hung the picture which he had recently cut out of an illustrated magazine and put into a pretty gilt frame. It showed a lady, with a fur cap on and a fur stole, sitting upright and holding out to the spectator a huge fur muff into which the whole of her forearm had vanished!

Gregor's eyes turned next to the window, and the overcast sky — one could hear rain drops beating on the window gutter — made him quite melancholy. What about sleeping a little longer and forgetting all this nonsense, he thought, but it could not be done, for he was accustomed to sleep on his right side and in his present condition he could not turn himself over. However violently he forced himself towards his right side he always rolled on to his back again. He tried it at least a hundred times, shutting his eyes to keep from seeing his struggling legs, and only desisted when he began to feel in his side a faint dull ache he had never experienced before.

Oh God, he thought, what an exhausting job I've picked on! Traveling about day in, day out. It's much more irritating work than doing the actual business in the office, and on top of that there's the trouble of constant traveling, of worrying about train connections, the bed and irregular meals, casual acquaintances that are always new and never become intimate friends. The devil take it all! He felt a slight itching up on his belly; slowly pushed himself on his back nearer to the top of the bed so that he could lift his head more easily; identified the itching place which was surrounded by many small white spots the nature of which he could not understand and made to touch it with a leg, but drew the leg back immediately, for the contact made a cold shiver run through him.

He slid down again into his former position. This getting up early, he thought, makes one quite stupid. A man needs his sleep. Other commercials live like harem women. For instance, when I come back to the hotel of a morning to write up the orders I've got, these others are only sitting down to breakfast. Let me just try that with my chief; I'd be sacked on the spot. Anyhow, that might be quite a good thing for me, who can tell? If I didn't have to hold my hand because of my parents I'd have given notice long ago, I'd have gone to the chief and told him exactly what I think of him. That would knock him endways from his desk! It's a queer way of doing, too, this sitting on high at a desk and talking down to employees, especially when they have to come quite near because the chief is hard of hearing. Well, there's still hope; once I've saved enough money to pay back my parents' debts to him — that should take another five or six years — I'll do it without fail. I'll cut myself completely loose then. For the moment, though, I'd better get up, since my train goes at five.

He looked at the alarm clock ticking on the chest. Heavenly Father! he thought. It was half-past six o'clock and the hands were quietly moving on, it was even past the half-hour, it was getting on toward a quarter to seven. Had the alarm clock not gone off? From the bed one could see that it had been properly set for four o'clock; of course it must have gone off. Yes, but was it possible to sleep quietly through that ear-splitting noise? Well, he had not slept quietly, yet apparently all the more soundly for that. But what was he to do now? The next train went at seven o'clock; to catch that he would need to hurry like mad and his samples weren't even packed up, and he himself wasn't feeling particularly fresh and active. And even if he did catch the train he wouldn't avoid a row with the chief, since the firm's porter would have been waiting for the five o'clock train and would have long since reported his failure to turn up. The porter was a creature of the chief's, spineless and stupid. Well, supposing he were to say he was sick? But that would be most unpleasant and would look suspicious, since during his five years' employment he had not been ill once. The chief himself would be sure to come with the sick-insurance doctor, would reproach his parents with their son's laziness and would cut all excuses short by referring to the insurance doctor, who of course regarded all mankind as perfectly healthy malingerers. And would he be so far wrong on this occasion? Gregor really felt quite well, apart from a drowsiness that was utterly superfluous after such a long sleep, and he was even unusually hungry.

As all this was running through his mind at top speed without his being able to decide to leave his bed — the alarm clock had just struck a quarter to seven — there came a cautious tap at the door behind the head of his bed. "Gregor," said a voice — it was his mother's — "it's a quarter to seven. Hadn't you a train to catch?" That gentle voice! Gregor had a shock as he heard his own voice answering hers, unmistakably his own voice, it was true, but with a persistent horrible twittering squeak behind it like an undertone, that left the words in their clear shape only for the first moment and then rose up reverberating round them to destroy their sense, so that one could not be sure one had heard them rightly. Gregor wanted to answer at length and explain everything, but in the circumstances he confined himself to saying: "Yes, yes, thank you, Mother, I'm getting up now." The wooden door between them must have kept the change in his voice from being noticeable outside, for his mother contented herself with this statement and shuffled away. Yet this brief exchange of words had made the other members of the family aware that Gregor was still in the house, as they had not expected, and at one of the side doors his father was already knocking, gently, yet with his fist. "Gregor, Gregor," he called, "what's the matter with you?" And after a little while he called again in a deeper voice: "Gregor! Gregor!" At the other side door his sister was saying in a low, plaintive tone: "Gregor? Aren't you well? Are you needing anything?" He answered them both at once: "I'm just ready," and did his best to make his voice sound as normal as possible by enunciating the words very clearly and leaving long pauses between them. So his father went back to his breakfast, but his sister whispered: "Gregor, open the door, do." However, he was not thinking of opening the door, and felt thankful for the prudent habit he had acquired in traveling of locking all doors during the night, even at home.

His immediate intention was to get up quietly without being disturbed, to put on his clothes and above all eat his breakfast, and only then to consider what else was to be done, since in bed, he was well aware, his meditations would come to no sensible conclusion. He remembered that often enough in bed he had felt small aches and pains, probably caused by awkward postures, which had proved purely imaginary once he got up, and he looked forward eagerly to seeing this morning's delusions gradually fall away. That the change in his voice was nothing but the precursor of a severe chill, a standing ailment of commercial travelers, he had not the least possible doubt.

To get rid of the quilt was quite easy; he had only to inflate himself a little and it fell off by itself. But the next move was difficult, especially because he was so uncommonly broad. He would have needed arms and hands to hoist himself up; instead he had only the numerous little legs which never stopped waving in all directions and which he could not control in the least. When he tried to bend one of them it was the first to stretch itself straight; and did he succeed at last in making it do what he wanted, all the other legs meanwhile waved the more wildly in a high degree of unpleasant agitation. "But what's the use of lying idle in bed," said Gregor to himself.

He thought that he might get out of bed with the lower part of his body first, but this lower part, which he had not yet seen and of which he could form no clear conception, proved too difficult to move; it shifted so slowly; and when finally, almost wild with annoyance, he gathered his forces together and thrust out recklessly, he had miscalculated the direction and bumped heavily against the lower end of the bed, and the stinging pain he felt informed him that precisely this lower part of his body was at the moment probably the most sensitive.

So he tried to get the top part of himself out first, and cautiously moved his head towards the edge of the bed. That proved easy enough, and despite its breadth and mass the bulk of his body at last slowly followed the movement of his head. Still, when he finally got his head free over the edge of the bed he felt too scared to go on advancing, for after all if he let himself fall in this way it would take a miracle to keep his head from being injured. And at all costs he must not lose consciousness now, precisely now; he would rather stay in bed.

But when after a repetition of the same efforts he lay in his former position again, sighing, and watched his little legs struggling against each other more wildly than ever, if that were possible, and saw no way of bringing any order into this arbitrary confusion, he told himself again that it was impossible to stay in bed and that the most sensible course was to risk everything for the smallest hope of getting away from it. At the same time he did not forget meanwhile to remind himself that cool reflection, the coolest possible, was much better than desperate resolves. In such moments he focused his eyes as sharply as possible on the window, but, unfortunately, the prospect of the morning fog, which muffled even the other side of the narrow street, brought him little encouragement and comfort. "Seven o'clock already," he said to himself when the alarm clock chimed again, "seven o'clock already and still such a thick fog." And for a little while he lay quiet, breathing lightly, as if perhaps expecting such complete repose to restore all things to their real and normal condition.

But then he said to himself: "Before it strikes a quarter past seven I must be quite out of this bed, without fail. Anyhow, by that time someone will have come from the office to ask for me, since it opens before seven." And he set himself to rocking his whole body at once in a regular rhythm, with the idea of swinging it out of the bed. If he tipped himself out in that way he could keep his head from injury by lifting it at an acute angle when he fell. His back seemed to be hard and was not likely to suffer from a fall on the carpet. His biggest worry was the loud crash he would not be able to help making, which would probably cause anxiety, if not terror, behind all the doors. Still, he must take the risk.

When he was already half out of the bed — the new method was more a game than an effort, for he needed only to hitch himself across by rocking to and fro — it struck him how simple it would be if he could get help. Two strong people — he thought of his father and the servant girl — would be amply sufficient; they would only have to thrust their arms under his convex back, lever him out of the bed, bend down with their burden and then be patient enough to let him turn himself right over on to the floor, where it was to be hoped his legs would then find their proper function. Well, ignoring the fact that the doors were all locked, ought he really to call for help? In spite of his misery he could not suppress a smile at the very idea of it.

He had got so far that he could barely keep his equilibrium when he rocked himself strongly, and he would have to nerve himself very soon for the final decision since in five minutes' time it would be a quarter past seven — when the front doorbell rang. "That's someone from the office," he said to himself, and grew almost rigid, while his little legs only jigged about all the faster. For a moment everything stayed quiet. "They're not going to open the door," said Gregor to himself, catching at some kind of irrational hope. But then of course the servant girl went as usual to the door with her heavy tread and opened it. Gregor needed only to hear the first good morning of the visitor to know immediately who it was — the chief clerk himself. What a fate, to be condemned to work for a firm where the smallest omission at once gave rise to the gravest suspicion! Were all employees in a body nothing but scoundrels, was there not among them one single loyal devoted man who, had he wasted only an hour or so of the firm's time in a morning, was so tormented by conscience as to be driven out of his mind and actually incapable of leaving his bed? Wouldn't it really have been sufficient to send an apprentice to inquire — if any inquiry were necessary at all — did the chief clerk himself have to come and thus indicate to the entire family, an innocent family, that this suspicious circumstance could be investigated by no one less versed in affairs than himself? And more through the agitation caused by these reflections than through any act of will Gregor swung himself out of bed with all his strength. There was a loud thump, but it was not really a crash. His fall was broken to some extent by the carpet, his back, too, was less stiff then he thought, and so there was merely a dull thud, not so very startling. Only he had not lifted his head carefully enough and had hit it; he turned it and rubbed it on the carpet in pain and irritation.

"That was something falling down in there," said the chief clerk in the next room to the left. Gregor tried to suppose to himself that something like what had happened to him today might some day happen to the chief clerk; one really could not deny that it was possible. But as if in brusque reply to this supposition the chief clerk took a couple of firm steps in the next-door room and his patent leather boots creaked. From the right-hand room his sister was whispering to inform him of the situation: "Gregor, the chief clerk's here." "I know," muttered Gregor to himself; but he didn't dare to make his voice loud enough for his sister to hear it.

"Gregor," said his father now from the left-hand room, "the chief clerk has come and wants to know why you didn't catch the early train. We don't know what to say to him. Besides, he wants to talk to you in person. So open the door, please. He will be good enough to excuse the untidiness of your room." "Good morning, Mr. Samsa," the chief clerk was calling amiably meanwhile. "He's not well," said his mother to the visitor, while his father was still speaking through the door, "he's not well, sir, believe me. What else would make him miss a train! The boy thinks about nothing but his work. It makes me almost cross the way he never goes out in the evenings; he's been here the last eight days and has stayed at home every single evening. He just sits there quietly at the table reading a newspaper or looking through railway timetables. The only amusement he gets is doing fretwork. For instance, he spent two or three evenings cutting out a little picture frame; you would be surprised to see how pretty it is; it's hanging in his room; you'll see it in a minute when Gregor opens the door. I must say I'm glad you've come, sir; we should never have got him to unlock the door by ourselves; he's so obstinate; and I'm sure he's unwell, though he wouldn't have it to be so this morning." "I'm just coming," said Gregor slowly and carefully, not moving an inch for fear of losing one word of the conversation. "I can't think of any other explanation, madam," said the chief clerk, "I hope it's nothing serious. Although on the other hand I must say that we men of business — fortunately or unfortunately — very often simply have to ignore any slight indisposition, since business must be attended to." "Well, can the chief clerk come in now?" asked Gregor's father impatiently, again knocking on the door. "No," said Gregor. In the left-hand room a painful silence followed this refusal, in the right-hand room his sister began to sob.

Why didn't his sister join the others? She was probably newly out of bed and hadn't even begun to put on her clothes yet. Well, why was she crying? Because he wouldn't get up and let the chief clerk in, because he was in danger of losing his job, and because the chief would begin dunning his parents again for the old debts? Surely these were things one didn't need to worry about for the present. Gregor was still at home and not in the least thinking of deserting the family. At the moment, true, he was lying on the carpet and no one who knew the condition he was in could seriously expect him to admit the chief clerk. But for such a small discourtesy, which could plausibly be explained away somehow later on, Gregor could hardly be dismissed on the spot. And it seemed to Gregor that it would be much more sensible to leave him in peace for the present than to trouble him with tears and entreaties. Still, of course, their uncertainty bewildered them all and excused their behavior.

"Mr. Samsa," the chief clerk called now in a louder voice, "what's the matter with you? Here you are, barricading yourself in your room, giving only 'yes' and 'no' for answers, causing your parents a lot of unnecessary trouble and neglecting — I mention this only in passing — neglecting your business duties in an incredible fashion. I am speaking here in the name of your parents and of your chief, and I beg you quite seriously to give me an immediate and precise explanation. You amaze me, you amaze me. I thought you were a quiet, dependable person, and now all at once you seem bent on making a disgraceful exhibition of yourself. The chief did hint to me early this morning a possible explanation for your disappearance — with reference to the cash payments that were entrusted to you recently — but I almost pledged my solemn word of honor that this could not be so. But now that I see how incredibly obstinate you are, I no longer have the slightest desire to take your part at all. And your position in the firm is not so unassailable. I came with the intention of telling you all this in private, but since you are wasting my time so needlessly I don't see why your parents shouldn't hear it too. For some time past your work has been most unsatisfactory; this is not the season of the year for a business boom, of course, we admit that, but a season of the year for doing no business at all, that does not exist, Mr. Samsa, must not exist."

"But, sir," cried Gregor, beside himself and in his agitation forgetting everything else, "I'm just going to open the door this very minute. A slight illness, an attack of giddiness, has kept me from getting up. I'm still lying in bed. But I feel all right again. I'm getting out of bed now. Just give me a moment or two longer! I'm not quite so well as I thought. But I'm all right, really. How a thing like that can suddenly strike one down! Only last night I was quite well, my parents can tell you, or rather I did have a slight presentiment. I must have showed some sign of it. Why didn't I report it at the office! But one always thinks that an indisposition can be got over without staying in the house. Oh sir, do spare my parents! All that you're reproaching me with now has no foundation; no one has ever said a word to me about it. Perhaps you haven't looked at the last orders I sent in. Anyhow, I can still catch the eight o'clock train, I'm much the better for my few hours' rest. Don't let me detain you here, sir; I'll be attending to business very soon, and do be good enough to tell the chief so and to make my excuses to him!"

And while all this was tumbling out pell-mell and Gregor hardly knew what he was saying, he had reached the chest quite easily, perhaps because of the practice he had had in bed, and was now trying to lever himself upright by means of it. He meant actually to open the door, actually to show himself and speak to the chief clerk; he was eager to find out what the others, after all their insistence, would say at the sight of him. If they were horrified then the responsibility was no longer his and he could stay quiet. But if they took it calmly, then he had no reason either to be upset, and could really get to the station for the eight o'clock train if he hurried. At first he slipped down a few times from the polished surface of the chest, but at length with a last heave he stood upright; he paid no more attention to the pains in the lower part of his body, however they smarted. Then he let himself fall against the back of a near-by chair, and clung with his little legs to the edges of it. That brought him into control of himself again and he stopped speaking, for now he could listen to what the chief clerk was saying.

"Did you understand a word of it?" the chief clerk was asking; "surely he can't be trying to make fools of us?" "Oh dear," cried his mother, in tears, "perhaps he's terribly ill and we're tormenting him. Grete! Grete!" she called out then. "Yes, Mother?" called his sister from the other side. They were calling to each other across Gregor's room. "You must go this minute for the doctor. Gregor is ill. Go for the doctor, quick. Did you hear how he was speaking?" "That was no human voice," said the chief clerk in a voice notice-ably low beside the shrillness of the mother's. "Anna! Anna!" his father was calling through the hall to the kitchen, clapping his hands, "get a locksmith at once!" And the two girls were already running through the hall with a swish of skirts — how could his sister have got dressed so quickly? — and were tearing the front door open. There was no sound of its closing again; they had evidently left it open, as one does in houses where some great misfortune has happened.

But Gregor was now much calmer. The words he uttered were no longer understandable, apparently, although they seemed clear enough to him, even clearer than before, perhaps because his ear had grown accustomed to the sound of them. Yet at any rate people now believed that something was wrong with him, and were ready to help him. The positive certainty with which these first measures had been taken comforted him. He felt himself drawn once more into the human circle and hoped for great and remarkable results from both the doctor and the locksmith, without really distinguishing precisely between them. To make his voice as clear as possible for the decisive conver-sation that was now imminent he coughed a little, as quietly as he could, of course, since this noise too might not sound like a human cough for all he was able to judge. In the next room meanwhile there was complete silence. Perhaps his parents were sitting at the table with the chief clerk, whispering, perhaps they were all leaning against the door and listening.

Slowly Gregor pushed the chair towards the door, then let go of it, caught hold of the door for support — the soles at the end of his little legs were somewhat sticky — and rested against it for a moment after his efforts. Then he set himself to turning the key in the lock with his mouth. It seemed, unhappily, that he hadn't really any teeth — what could he grip the key with? — but on the other hand his jaws were certainly very strong; with their help he did manage to set the key in motion, heedless of the fact that he was undoubtedly damaging them somewhere, since a brown fluid issued from his mouth, flowed over the key and dripped on the floor. "Just listen to that," said the chief clerk next door; "he's turning the key." That was a great encouragement to Gregor; but they should all have shouted encouragement to him, his father and mother too: "Go on, Gregor," they should have called out, "keep going, hold on to that key!" And in the belief that they were all following his efforts intently, he clenched his jaws recklessly on the key with all the force at his command. As the turning of the key progressed he circled round the lock, holding on now only with his mouth, pushing on the key, as required, or pulling it down again with all the weight of his body. The louder click of the finally yielding lock literally quickened Gregor. With a deep breath of relief he said to himself: "So I didn't need the locksmith," and laid his head on the handle to open the door wide.

Since he had to pull the door towards him, he was still invisible when it was really wide open. He had to edge himself slowly round the near half of the double door, and to do it very carefully if he was not to fall plump upon his back just on the threshold. He was still carrying out this difficult manoeuvre, with no time to observe anything else, when he heard the chief clerk utter a loud "Oh!" — it sounded like a gust of wind — and now he could see the man, standing as he was nearest to the door, clapping one hand before his open mouth and slowly backing away as if driven by some invisible steady pressure. His mother — in spite of the chief clerk's being there her hair was still undone and sticking up in all directions — first clasped her hands and looked at his father, then took two steps towards Gregor and fell on the floor among her outspread skirts, her face hidden on her breast. His father knotted his fist with a fierce expression on his face as if he meant to knock Gregor back into his room, then looked uncertainly round the living room, covered his eyes with his hands and wept till his great chest heaved.

Gregor did not go now into the living room, but leaned against the inside of the firmly shut wing of the door, so that only half his body was visible and his head above it bending sideways to look at the others. The light had meanwhile strengthened; on the other side of the street one could see clearly a section of the endlessly long, dark gray building opposite — it was a hospital — abruptly punctuated by its row of regular windows; the rain was still falling, but only in large singly discernible and literally singly splashing drops. The breakfast dishes were set out on the table lavishly, for breakfast was the most important meal of the day to Gregor's father, who lingered it out for hours over various newspapers. Right opposite Gregor on the wall hung a photograph of himself on military service, as a lieutenant, hand on sword, a carefree smile on his face, inviting one to respect his uniform and military bearing. The door leading to the hall was open, and one could see that the front door stood open too, showing the landing beyond and the beginning of the stairs going down.

"Well," said Gregor, knowing perfectly that he was the only one who had retained any composure, "I'll put my clothes on at once, pack up my samples and start off. Will you only let me go? You see, sir, I'm not obstinate, and I'm willing to work; traveling is a hard life, but I couldn't live without it. Where are you going, sir? To the office? Yes? Will you give a true account of all this? One can be temporarily incapacitated, but that's just the moment for remembering former services and bearing in mind that later on, when the incapacity has been got over, one will certainly work with all the more industry and concentration. I'm loyally bound to serve the chief, you know that very well. Besides, I have to provide for my parents and my sister. I'm in great difficulties, but I'll get out of them again. Don't make things any worse for me than they are. Stand up for me in the firm. Travelers are not popular there, I know. People think they earn sacks of money and just have a good time. A prejudice there's no particular reason for revising. But you, sir, have a more comprehensive view of affairs than the rest of the staff, yes, let me tell you in confidence, a more comprehensive view than the chief himself, who, being the owner, lets his judgment easily be swayed against one of his employees. And you know very well that the traveler, who is never seen in the office almost the whole year round, can so easily fall a victim to gossip and ill luck and unfounded complaints, which he mostly knows nothing about, except when he comes back exhausted from his rounds, and only then suffers in person from their evil consequences, which he can no longer trace back to the original causes. Sir, sir, don't go away without a word to me to show that you think me in the right at least to some extent!"

But at Gregor's very first words the chief clerk had already backed away and only stared at him with parted lips over one twitching shoulder. And while Gregor was speaking he did not stand still one moment but stole away towards the door, without taking his eyes off Gregor, yet only an inch at a time, as if obeying some secret injunction to leave the room. He was already at the hall, and the suddenness with which he took his last step out of the living room would have made one believe he had burned the sole of his foot. Once in the hall he stretched his right arm before him towards the staircase, as if some supernatural power were waiting there to deliver him.

Gregor perceived that the chief clerk must on no account be allowed to go away in this frame of mind if his position in the firm were not to be endangered to the utmost. His parents did not understand this so well; they had convinced themselves in the course of years that Gregor was settled for life in this firm, and besides they were so occupied with their immediate troubles that all foresight had forsaken them. Yet Gregor had this foresight. The chief clerk must be detained, soothed, persuaded and finally won over; the whole future of Gregor and his family depended on it! If only his sister had been there! She was intelligent; she had begun to cry while Gregor was still lying quietly on his back. And no doubt the chief clerk, so partial to ladies, would have been guided by her; she would have shut the door of the flat and in the hall talked him out of his horror. But she was not there, and Gregor would have to handle the situation himself. And without remembering that he was still unaware what powers of movement he possessed, without even remembering that his words in all possibility, indeed in all likelihood, would again be unintelligible, he let go the wing of the door, pushed himself through the opening, started to walk towards the chief clerk, who was already ridiculously clinging with both hands to the railing on the landing; but immediately, as he was feeling for a support, he fell down with a little cry upon all his numerous legs. Hardly was he down when he experienced for the first time this morning a sense of physical comfort; his legs had firm ground under them; they were completely obedient, as he noted with joy; they even strove to carry him forward in whatever direction he chose; and he was inclined to believe that a final relief from all his sufferings was at hand. But in the same moment as he found himself on the floor, rocking with suppressed eagerness to move, not far from his mother, indeed just in front of her, she, who had seemed so completely crushed, sprang all at once to her feet, her arms and fingers outspread, cried: "Help, for God's sake, help!" bent her head down as if to see Gregor better, yet on the contrary kept backing senselessly away; had quite forgotten that the laden table stood behind her; sat upon it hastily, as if in absence of mind, when she bumped into it; and seemed altogether unaware that the big coffee pot beside her was upset and pouring coffee in a flood over the carpet.

"Mother, Mother," said Gregor in a low voice, and looked up at her. The chief clerk, for the moment, had quite slipped from his mind; instead, he could not resist snapping his jaws together at the sight of the streaming coffee. That made his mother scream again, she fled from the table and fell into the arms of his father, who hastened to catch her. But Gregor had now no time to spare for his parents; the chief clerk was already on the stairs; with his chin on the banisters he was taking one last backward look. Gregor made a spring, to be as sure as possible of overtaking him; the chief clerk must have divined his intention, for he leaped down several steps and vanished; he was still yelling "Ugh!" and it echoed through the whole staircase.

Unfortunately, the flight of the chief clerk seemed completely to upset Gregor's father, who had remained relatively calm until now, for instead of running after the man himself, or at least not hindering Gregor in his pursuit, he seized in his right hand the walking stick which the chief clerk had left behind on a chair, together with a hat and greatcoat, snatched in his left hand a large newspaper from the table and began stamping his feet and flourishing the stick and the newspaper to drive Gregor back into his room. No entreaty of Gregor's availed, indeed no entreaty was even understood, however humbly he bent his head his father only stamped on the floor the more loudly. Behind his father his mother had torn open a window, despite the cold weather, and was leaning far out of it with her face in her hands. A strong draught set in from the street to the staircase, the window curtains blew in, the newspapers on the table fluttered, stray pages whisked over the floor. Pitilessly Gregor's father drove him back, hissing and crying "Shoo!" like a savage. But Gregor was quite unpracticed in walking backwards, it really was a slow business. If he only had a chance to turn round he could get back to his room at once, but he was afraid of exasperating his father by the slowness of such a rotation and at any moment the stick in his father's hand might hit him a fatal blow on the back or on the head. In the end, however, nothing else was left for him to do since to his horror he observed that in moving backwards he could not even control the direction he took; and so, keeping an anxious eye on his father all the time over his shoulder, he began to turn round as quickly as he could, which was in reality very slowly. Perhaps his father noted his good intentions, for he did not interfere except every now and then to help him in the manoeuvre from a distance with the point of the stick. If only he would have stopped making that unbearable hissing noise! It made Gregor quite lose his head. He had turned almost completely round when the hissing noise so distracted him that he even turned a little the wrong way again. But when at last his head was fortunately right in front of the doorway, it appeared that his body was too broad simply to get through the opening. His father, of course, in his present mood was far from thinking of such a thing as opening the other half of the door, to let Gregor have enough space. He had merely the fixed idea of driving Gregor back into his room as quickly as possible. He would never have suffered Gregor to make the circumstantial preparations for standing up on end and perhaps slipping his way through the door. Maybe he was now making more noise than ever to urge Gregor forward, as if no obstacle impeded him; to Gregor, anyhow, the noise in his rear sounded no longer like the voice of one single father; this was really no joke, and Gregor thrust himself — come what might — into the doorway. One side of his body rose up, he was tilted at an angle in the doorway, his flank was quite bruised, horrid blotches stained the white door, soon he was stuck fast and, left to himself, could not have moved at all, his legs on one side fluttered trembling to the air, those on the other were crushed painfully to the floor — when from behind his father gave him a strong push which was literally a deliverance and he flew far into the room, bleeding freely. The door was slammed behind him with the stick, and then at last there was silence.

II

Not until it was twilight did Gregor awake out of a deep sleep, more like a swoon than a sleep. He would certainly have waked up of his own accord not much later, for he felt himself sufficiently rested and well-slept, but it seemed to him as if a fleeting step and a cautious shutting of the door leading into the hall had aroused him. The electric lights in the street cast a pale sheen here and there on the ceiling and the upper surfaces of the furniture, but down below, where he lay, it was dark. Slowly, awkwardly trying out his feelers, which he now first learned to appreciate, he pushed his way to the door to see what had been happening there. His left side felt like one single long, unpleasant tense scar, and he had actually to limp on his two rows of legs. One little leg, moreover, had been severely damaged in the course of that morning's events — it was almost a miracle that only one had been damaged — and trailed uselessly behind him.

He had reached the door before he discovered what had really drawn him to it: the smell of food. For there stood a basin filled with fresh milk in which floated little sops of white bread. He could almost have laughed with joy, since he was now still hungrier than in the morning, and he dipped his head almost over the eyes straight into the milk. But soon in disappointment he withdrew it again; not only did he find it difficult to feed because of his tender left side — and he could only feed with the palpitating collaboration of his whole body — he did not like the milk either, although milk had been his favorite drink and that was certainly why his sister had set it there for him, indeed it was almost with repulsion that he turned away from the basin and crawled back to the middle of the room.

He could see through the crack of the door that the gas was turned on in the living room, but while usually at this time his father made a habit of reading the afternoon newspaper in a loud voice to his mother and occasionally to his sister as well, not a sound was now to be heard. Well, perhaps his father had recently given up this habit of reading aloud, which his sister had mentioned so often in conversation and in her letters. But there was the same silence all around, although the flat was certainly not empty of occupants. "What a quiet life our family has been leading," said Gregor to himself, and as he sat there motionless staring into the darkness he felt great pride in the fact that he had been able to provide such a life for his parents and sister in such a fine flat. But what if all the quiet, the comfort, the contentment were now to end in horror? To keep himself from being lost in such thoughts Gregor took refuge in movement and crawled up and down the room.

Once during the long evening one of the side doors was opened a little and quickly shut again, later the other side door too; someone had apparently wanted to come in and then thought better of it. Gregor now stationed himself immediately before the living room door, determined to persuade any hesitating visitor to come in or at least to discover who it might be; but the door was not opened again and he waited in vain. In the early morning, when the doors were locked, they had all wanted to come in, now that he had opened one door and the other had apparently been opened during the day, no one came in and even the keys were on the other side of the doors.

It was late at night before the gas went out in the living room, and Gregor could easily tell that his parents and his sister had all stayed awake until then, for he could clearly hear the three of them stealing away on tiptoe. No one was likely to visit him, not until the morning, that was certain; so he had plenty of time to meditate at his leisure on how he was to arrange his life afresh. But the lofty, empty room in which he had to lie flat on the floor filled him with an apprehension he could not account for, since it had been his very own room for the past five years — and with a half-unconscious action, not without a slight feeling of shame, he scuttled under the sofa, where he felt comfortable at once, although his back was a little cramped and he could not lift his head up, and his only regret was that his body was too broad to get the whole of it under the sofa.

He stayed there all night, spending the time partly in a light slumber, from which his hunger kept waking him up with a start, and partly in worrying and sketching vague hopes, which all led to the same conclusion, that he must lie low for the present and, by exercising patience, and the utmost consideration, help the family to bear the inconvenience he was bound to cause them in his present condition.

Very early in the morning, it was still almost night, Gregor had the chance to test the strength of his new resolutions, for his sister, nearly fully dressed, opened the door from the hall and peered in. She did not see him at once, yet when she caught sight of him under the sofa — well, he had to be somewhere, he couldn't have flown away, could he? — she was so startled that without being able to help it she slammed the door shut again. But as if regretting her behavior she opened the door again immediately and came in on tiptoe, as if she were visiting an invalid or even a stranger. Gregor had pushed his head forward to the very edge of the sofa and watched her. Would she notice that he had left the milk standing, and not for lack of hunger, and would she bring in some other kind of food more to his taste? If she did not do it of her own accord, he would rather starve than draw her attention to the fact, although he felt a wild impulse to dart out from under the sofa, throw himself at her feet and beg her for something to eat. But his sister at once noticed, with surprise, that the basin was still full, except for a little milk that had been spilt all around it, she lifted it immediately, not with her bare hands, true, but with a cloth and carried it away. Gregor was wildly curious to know what she would bring instead, and made various speculations about it. Yet what she actually did next, in the goodness of her heart, he could never have guessed at. To find out what he liked she brought him a whole selection of food, all set out on an old newspaper. There were old, half-decayed vegetables, bones from last night's supper covered with a white sauce that had thickened; some raisins and almonds; a piece of cheese that Gregor would have called uneatable two days ago; a dry roll of bread, a buttered roll, and a roll both buttered and salted. Besides all that, she set down again the same basin, into which she had poured some water, and which was apparently to be reserved for his exclusive use. And with fine tact, knowing that Gregor would not eat in her presence, she withdrew quickly and even turned the key, to let him understand that he could take his ease as much as he liked. Gregor's legs all whizzed towards the food. His wounds must have healed completely, moreover, for he felt no disability, which amazed him and made him reflect how more than a month ago he had cut one finger a little with a knife and had still suffered pain from the wound only the day before yesterday. Am I less sensitive now? he thought, and sucked greedily at the cheese, which above all the other edibles attracted him at once and strongly. One after another and with tears of satisfaction in his eyes he quickly devoured the cheese, the vegetables and the sauce; the fresh food, on the other hand, had no charms for him, he could not even stand the smell of it and actually dragged away to some little distance the things he could eat. He had long finished his meal and was only lying lazily on the same spot when his sister turned the key slowly as a sign for him to retreat. That roused him at once, although he was nearly asleep, and he hurried under the sofa again. But it took considerable self-control for him to stay under the sofa, even for the short time his sister was in the room, since the large meal had swollen his body somewhat and he was so cramped he could hardly breathe. Slight attacks of breathlessness afflicted him and his eyes were starting a little out of his head as he watched his unsuspecting sister sweeping together with a broom not only the remains of what he had eaten but even the things he had not touched, as if these were now of no use to anyone, and hastily shoveling it all into a bucket, which she covered with a wooden lid and carried away. Hardly had she turned her back when Gregor came from under the sofa and stretched and puffed himself out.

In this manner Gregor was fed, once in the early morning while his parents and the servant girl were still asleep, and a second time after they had all had their midday dinner, for then his parents took a short nap and the servant girl could be sent out on some errand or other by his sister. Not that they would have wanted him to starve, of course, but perhaps they could not have borne to know more about his feeding than from hearsay, perhaps too his sister wanted to spare them such little anxieties wherever possible, since they had quite enough to bear as it was.

Under what pretext the doctor and the locksmith had been got rid of on that first morning Gregor could not discover, for since what he had said was not understood by the others it never struck any of them, not even his sister, that he could understand what they said, and so whenever his sister came into his room he had to content himself with hearing her utter only a sigh now and then and an occasional appeal to the saints. Later on, when she had got a little used to the situation — of course she could never get completely used to it — she sometimes threw out a remark which was kindly meant or could be so interpreted. "Well, he liked his dinner today," she would say when Gregor had made a good clearance of his food; and when he had not eaten, which gradually happened more and more often, she would say almost sadly: "Everything's been left standing again."

But although Gregor could get no news directly, he overheard a lot from the neighboring rooms, and as soon as voices were audible, he would run to the door of the room concerned and press his whole body against it. In the first few days especially there was no conversation that did not refer to him somehow, even if only indirectly. For two whole days there were family consultations at every mealtime about what should be done; but also between meals the same subject was discussed, for there were always at least two members of the family at home, since no one wanted to be alone in the flat and to leave it quite empty was unthinkable. And on the very first of these days the household cook — it was not quite clear what and how much she knew of the situation — went down on her knees to his mother and begged leave to go, and when she departed, a quarter of an hour later, gave thanks for her dismissal with tears in her eyes as if for the greatest benefit that could have been conferred on her, and without any prompting swore a solemn oath that she would never say a single word to anyone about what had happened.

Now Gregor's sister had to cook too, helping her mother; true, the cooking did not amount to much, for they ate scarcely anything. Gregor was always hearing one of the family vainly urging another to eat and getting no answer but: "Thanks, I've had all I want," or something similar. Perhaps they drank nothing either. Time and again his sister kept asking his father if he wouldn't like some beer and offered kindly to go and fetch it herself, and when he made no answer suggested that she could ask the concierge to fetch it, so that he need feel no sense of obligation, but then a round "No" came from his father and no more was said about it.

In the course of that very first day Gregor's father explained the family's financial position and prospects to both his mother and his sister. Now and then he rose from the table to get some voucher or memorandum out of the small safe he had rescued from the collapse of his business five years earlier. One could hear him opening the complicated lock and rustling papers out and shutting it again. This statement made by his father was the first cheerful information Gregor had heard since his imprisonment. He had been of the opinion that nothing at all was left over from his father's business, at least his father had never said anything to the contrary, and of course he had not asked him directly. At the time Gregor's sole desire was to do his utmost to help the family to forget as soon as possible the catastrophe which had overwhelmed the business and thrown them all into a state of complete despair. And so he had set to work with unusual ardor and almost overnight had become a commercial traveler instead of a little clerk, with of course much greater chances of earning money, and his success was immediately translated into good round coin which he could lay on the table for his amazed and happy family. These had been fine times, and they had never recurred, at least not with the same sense of glory, although later on Gregor had earned so much money that he was able to meet the expenses of the whole household and did so. They had simply got used to it, both the family and Gregor; the money was gratefully accepted and gladly given, but there was no special uprush of warm feeling. With his sister alone had he remained intimate, and it was a secret plan of his that she, who loved music, unlike himself, and could play movingly on the violin, should be sent next year to study at the Conservatorium, despite the great expense that would entail, which must be made up in some other way. During his brief visits home the Conservatorium was often mentioned in the talks he had with his sister, but always merely as a beautiful dream which could never come true, and his parents discouraged even these innocent references to it; yet Gregor had made up his mind firmly about it and meant to announce the fact with due solemnity on Christmas Day.

Such were the thoughts, completely futile in his present condition, that went through his head as he stood clinging upright to the door and listening. Sometimes out of sheer weariness he had to give up listening and let his head fall negligently against the door, but he always had to pull himself together again at once, for even the slight sound his head made was audible next door and brought all conversation to a stop. "What can he be doing now?" his father would say after a while, obviously turning towards the door, and only then would the interrupted conversation gradually be set going again.

Gregor was now informed as amply as he could wish — for his father tended to repeat himself in his explanations, partly because it was a long time since he had handled such matters and partly because his mother could not always grasp things at once — that a certain amount of investments, a very small amount it was true, had survived the wreck of their fortunes and had even increased a little because the dividends had not been touched meanwhile. And besides that, the money Gregor brought home every month — he had kept only a few dollars for himself — had never been quite used up and now amounted to a small capital sum. Behind the door Gregor nodded his head eagerly, rejoiced at this evidence of unexpected thrift and foresight. True, he could really have paid off some more of his father's debts to the chief with his extra money, and so brought much nearer the day on which he could quit his job, but doubtless it was better the way his father had arranged it.

Yet this capital was by no means sufficient to let the family live on the interest of it; for one year, perhaps, or at the most two, they could live on the principal, that was all. It was simply a sum that ought not to be touched and should be kept for a rainy day; money for living expenses would have to be earned. Now his father was still hale enough but an old man, and he had done no work for the past five years and could not be expected to do much; during these five years, the first years of leisure in his laborious though unsuccessful life, he had grown rather fat and become sluggish. And Gregor's old mother, how was she to earn a living with her asthma, which troubled her even when she walked through the flat and kept her lying on a sofa every other day panting for breath beside an open window? And was his sister to earn her bread, she who was still a child of seventeen and whose life hitherto had been so pleasant, consisting as it did in dressing herself nicely, sleeping long, helping in the housekeeping, going out to a few modest entertainments and above all playing the violin? At first whenever the need for earning money was mentioned Gregor let go his hold on the door and threw himself down on the cool leather sofa beside it, he felt so hot with shame and grief.

Often he just lay there the long nights through without sleeping at all, scrabbling for hours on the leather. Or he nerved himself to the great effort of pushing an armchair to the window, then crawled up over the window sill and, braced against the chair, leaned against the windowpanes, obviously in some recollection of the sense of freedom that looking out of a window always used to give him. For in reality day by day things that were even a little way off were growing dimmer to his sight; the hospital across the street, which he used to execrate for being all too often before his eyes, was now quite beyond his range of vision, and if he had not known that he lived in Charlotte Street, a quiet street but still a city street, he might have believed that his window gave on a desert waste where gray sky and gray land blended indistinguishably into each other. His quick-witted sister only needed to observe twice that the armchair stood by the window; after that whenever she had tidied the room she always pushed the chair back to the same place at the window and even left the inner casements open.

If he could have spoken to her and thanked her for all she had to do for him, he could have borne her ministrations better; as it was, they oppressed him. She certainly tried to make as light as possible of whatever was disagreeable in her task, and as time went on she succeeded, of course, more and more, but time brought more enlightenment to Gregor too. The very way she came in distressed him. Hardly was she in the room when she rushed to the window, without even taking time to shut the door, careful as she was usually to shield the sight of Gregor's room from the others, and as if she were almost suffocating tore the casements open with hasty fingers, standing then in the open draught for a while even in the bitterest cold and drawing deep breaths. This noisy scurry of hers upset Gregor twice a day; he would crouch trembling under the sofa all the time, knowing quite well that she would certainly have spared him such a disturbance had she found it at all possible to stay in his presence without opening a window.

On one occasion, about a month after Gregor's metamorphosis, when there was surely no reason for her to be still startled at his appearance, she came a little earlier than usual and found him gazing out of the window, quite motionless, and thus well placed to look like a bogey. Gregor would not have been surprised had she not come in at all, for she could not immediately open the window while he was there, but not only did she retreat, she jumped back as if in alarm and banged the door shut; a stranger might well have thought that he had been lying in wait for her there meaning to bite her. Of course he hid himself under the sofa at once, but he had to wait until midday before she came again, and she seemed more ill at ease than usual. This made him realize how repulsive the sight of him still was to her, and that it was bound to go on being repulsive, and what an effort it must cost her not to run away even from the sight of the small portion of his body that stuck out from under the sofa. In order to spare her that, therefore, one day he carried a sheet on his back to the sofa — it cost him four hours' labor — and arranged it there in such a way as to hide him completely, so that even if she were to bend down she could not see him. Had she considered the sheet unnecessary, she would certainly have stripped it off the sofa again, for it was clear enough that this curtaining and confining of himself was not likely to conduce Gregor's comfort, but she left it where it was, and Gregor even fancied that he caught a thankful glance from her eye when he lifted the sheet carefully a very little with his head to see how she was taking the new arrangement.

For the first fortnight his parents could not bring themselves to the point of entering his room, and he often heard them expressing their appreciation of his sister's activities, whereas formerly they had frequently scolded her for being as they thought a somewhat useless daughter. But now, both of them often waited outside the door, his father and his mother, while his sister tidied his room, and as soon as she came out she had to tell them exactly how things were in the room, what Gregor had eaten, how he had conducted himself this time and whether there was not perhaps some slight improvement in his condition. His mother, moreover, began relatively soon to want to visit him, but his father and sister dissuaded her at first with arguments which Gregor listened to very attentively and altogether approved. Later, however, she had to be held back by main force, and when she cried out: "Do let me in to Gregor, he is my unfortunate son! Can't you understand that I must go to him?" Gregor thought that it might be well to have her come in, not every day, of course, but perhaps once a week; she understood things, after all, much better than his sister, who was only a child despite the efforts she was making and had perhaps taken on so difficult a task merely out of childish thoughtlessness.

Gregor's desire to see his mother was soon fulfilled. During the daytime he did not want to show himself at the window, out of consideration for his parents, but he could not crawl very far around the few square yards of floor space he had, nor could he bear lying quietly at rest all during the night, while he was fast losing any interest he had ever taken in food, so that for mere recreation he had formed the habit of crawling crisscross over the walls and ceiling. He especially enjoyed hanging suspended from the ceiling; it was much better than lying on the floor; one could breathe more freely; one's body swung and rocked lightly; and in the almost blissful absorption induced by this suspension it could happen to his own surprise that he let go and fell plump on the floor. Yet he now had his body much better under control than formerly, and even such a big fall did him no harm. His sister at once remarked the new distraction Gregor had found for himself — he left traces behind him of the sticky stuff on his soles wherever he crawled — and she got the idea in her head of giving him as wide a field as possible to crawl in and of removing the pieces of furniture that hindered him, above all the chest of drawers and the writing desk. But that was more than she could manage all by herself; she did not dare ask her father to help her; and as for the servant girl, a young creature of sixteen who had had the courage to stay on after the cook's departure, she could not be asked to help, for she had begged as an especial favor that she might keep the kitchen door locked and open it only on a definite summons; so there was nothing left but to apply to her mother at an hour when her father was out. And the old lady did come, with exclamations of joyful eagerness, which, however, died away at the door of Gregor's room. Gregor's sister, of course, went in first, to see that everything was in order before letting his mother enter. In great haste Gregor pulled the sheet lower and rucked it more in folds so that it really looked as if it had been thrown accidentally over the sofa. And this time he did not peer out from under it; he renounced the pleasure of seeing his mother on this occasion and was only glad that she had come at all. "Come in, he's out of sight," said his sister, obviously leading her mother in by the hand. Gregor could now hear the two women struggling to shift the heavy old chest from its place, and his sister claiming the greater part of the labor for herself, without listening to the admonitions of her mother who feared she might overstrain herself. It took a long time. After at least a quarter of an hour's tugging his mother objected that the chest had better be left where it was, for in the first place it was too heavy and could never be got out before his father came home, and standing in the middle of the room like that it would only hamper Gregor's movements, while in the second place it was not at all certain that removing the furniture would be doing a service to Gregor. She was inclined to think to the contrary; the sight of the naked walls made her own heart heavy, and why shouldn't Gregor have the same feeling, considering that he had been used to his furniture for so long and might feel forlorn without it. "And doesn't it look," she concluded in a low voice — in fact she had been almost whispering all the time as if to avoid letting Gregor, whose exact whereabouts she did not know, hear even the tones of her voice, for she was convinced that he could not understand her words — "doesn't it look as if we were showing him, by taking away his furniture, that we have given up hope of his ever getting better and are just leaving him coldly to himself? I think it would be best to keep his room exactly as it has always been, so that when he comes back to us he will find everything unchanged and be able all the more easily to forget what has happened in between."

On hearing these words from his mother Gregor realized that the lack of all direct human speech for the past two months together with the monotony of family life must have confused his mind, otherwise he could not account for the fact that he had quite earnestly looked forward to having his room emptied of furnishing. Did he really want his warm room, so comfortably fitted with old family furniture, to be turned into a naked den in which he would certainly be able to crawl unhampered in all directions but at the price of shedding simultaneously all recollection of his human background? He had indeed been so near the brink of forgetfulness that only the voice of his mother, which he had not heard for so long, had drawn him back from it. Nothing should be taken out of his room; everything must stay as it was; he could not dispense with the good influence of the furniture on his state of mind; and even if the furniture did hamper him in his senseless crawling round and round, that was no drawback but a great advantage.

Unfortunately his sister was of the contrary opinion; she had grown accustomed, and not without reason, to consider herself an expert in Gregor's affairs as against her parents, and so her mother's advice was now enough to make her determined on the removal not only of the chest and the writing desk, which had been her first intention, but of all the furniture except the indispensable sofa. This determination was not, of course, merely the outcome of childish recalcitrance and of the self-confidence she had recently developed so unexpectedly and at such cost; she had in fact perceived that Gregor needed a lot of space to crawl about in, while on the other hand he never used the furniture at all, so far as could be seen. Another factor might have been also the enthusiastic temperament of an adolescent girl, which seeks to indulge itself on every opportunity and which now tempted Grete to exaggerate the horror of her brother's circumstances in order that she might do all the more for him. In a room where Gregor lorded it all alone over empty walls no one save herself was likely ever to set foot.

And so she was not to be moved from her resolve by her mother who seemed moreover to be ill at ease in Gregor's room and therefore unsure of herself, was soon reduced to silence and helped her daughter as best she could to push the chest outside. Now, Gregor could do without the chest, if need be, but the writing desk he must retain. As soon as the two women had got the chest out of his room, groaning as they pushed it, Gregor stuck his head out from under the sofa to see how he might intervene as kindly and cautiously as possible. But as bad luck would have it, his mother was the first to return, leaving Grete clasping the chest in the room next door where she was trying to shift it all by herself, without of course moving it from the spot. His mother however was not accustomed to the sight of him, it might sicken her and so in alarm Gregor backed quickly to the other end of the sofa, yet could not prevent the sheet from swaying a little in front. That was enough to put her on the alert. She paused, stood still for a moment and then went back to Grete.

Although Gregor kept reassuring himself that nothing out of the way was happening, but only a few bits of furniture were being changed round, he soon had to admit that all this trotting to and fro of the two women, their little ejaculations and the scraping of furniture along the floor affected him like a vast disturbance coming from all sides at once, and however much he tucked in his head and legs and cowered to the very floor he was bound to confess that he would not be able to stand it for long. They were clearing his room out; taking away everything he loved; the chest in which he kept his fret saw and other tools was already dragged off; they were now loosening the writing desk which had almost sunk into the floor, the desk at which he had done all his homework when he was at the commercial academy, at the grammar school before that, and, yes, even at the primary school — he had no more time to waste in weighing the good intentions of the two women, whose existence he had by now almost forgotten, for they were so exhausted that they were laboring in silence and nothing could be heard but the heavy scuffling of their feet.

And so he rushed out — the women were just leaning against the writing desk in the next room to give themselves a breather — and four times changed his direction, since he really did not know what to rescue first, then on the wall opposite, which was already otherwise cleared, he was struck by the picture of the lady muffled in so much fur and quickly crawled up to it and pressed himself to the glass, which was a good surface to hold on to and comforted his hot belly. This picture at least, which was entirely hidden beneath him, was going to be removed by nobody. He turned his head towards the door of the living room so as to observe the women when they came back.

They had not allowed themselves much of a rest and were already coming; Grete had twined her arm round her mother and was almost supporting her. "Well, what shall we take now?" said Grete, looking round. Her eyes met Gregor's from the wall. She kept her composure, presumably because of her mother, bent her head down to her mother, to keep her from looking up, and said, although in a fluttering, unpremeditated voice: "Come, hadn't we better go back to the living room for a moment?" Her intentions were clear enough to Gregor, she wanted to bestow her mother in safety and then chase him down from the wall. Well, just let her try it! He clung to his picture and would not give it up. He would rather fly in Grete's face.

But Grete's words had succeeded in disquieting her mother, who took a step to one side, caught sight of the huge brown mass on the flowered wallpaper, and before she was really conscious that what she saw was Gregor screamed in a loud, hoarse voice: "Oh God, oh God!" fell with outspread arms over the sofa as if giving up and did not move. "Gregor!" cried his sister, shaking her fist and glaring at him. This was the first time she had directly addressed him since his metamorphosis. She ran into the next room for some aromatic essence with which to rouse her mother from her fainting fit. Gregor wanted to help too — there was still time to rescue the picture — but he was stuck fast to the glass and had to tear himself loose; he then ran after his sister into the next room as if he could advise her, as he used to do; but then had to stand helplessly behind her; she meanwhile searched among various small bottles and when she turned round started in alarm at the sight of him; one bottle fell on the floor and broke; a splinter of glass cut Gregor's face and some kind of corrosive medicine splashed him; without pausing a moment longer Grete gathered up all the bottles she could carry and ran to her mother with them; she banged the door shut with her foot. Gregor was now cut off from his mother, who was perhaps nearly dying because of him; he dared not open the door for fear of frightening away his sister, who had to stay with her mother; there was nothing he could do but wait; and harassed by self-reproach and worry he began now to crawl to and fro, over everything, walls, furniture and ceiling, and finally in his despair, when the whole room seemed to be reeling round him, fell down on to the middle of the big table.

A little while elapsed, Gregor was still lying there feebly and all around was quiet, perhaps that was a good omen. Then the doorbell rang. The servant girl was of course locked in her kitchen, and Grete would have to open the door. It was his father. "What's been happening?" were his first words; Grete's face must have told him everything. Grete answered in a muffled voice, apparently hiding her head on his breast: "Mother has been fainting, but she's better now. Gregor's broken loose." "Just what I expected," said his father, "just what I've been telling you, but you women would never listen." It was clear to Gregor that his father had taken the worst interpretation of Grete's all too brief statement and was assuming that Gregor had been guilty of some violent act. Therefore Gregor must now try to propitiate his father, since he had neither time nor means for an explanation. And so he fled to the door of his own room and crouched against it, to let his father see as soon as he came in from the hall that his son had the good intention of getting back into his room immediately and that it was not necessary to drive him there, but that if only the door were opened he would disappear at once.

Yet his father was not in the mood to perceive such fine distinctions. "Ah!" he cried as soon as he appeared, in a tone which sounded at once angry and exultant. Gregor drew his head back from the door and lifted it to look at his father. Truly, this was not the father he had imagined to himself; admittedly he had been too absorbed of late in his new recreation of crawling over the ceiling to take the same interest as before in what was happening elsewhere in the flat, and he ought really to be prepared for some changes. And yet, and yet, could that be his father? The man who used to lie wearily sunk in bed whenever Gregor set out on a business journey; who welcomed him back of an evening lying in a long chair in a dressing gown; who could not really rise to his feet but only lifted his arms in greeting, and on the rare occasions when he did go out with his family, on one or two Sundays a year and on high holidays, walked between Gregor and his mother, who were slow walkers anyhow, even more slowly than they did, muffled in his old greatcoat, shuffling laboriously forward with the help of his crook-handled stick which he set down most cautiously at every step and, whenever he wanted to say anything, nearly always came to a full stop and gathered his escort around him? Now he was standing there in fine shape; dressed in a smart blue uniform with gold buttons, such as bank messengers wear; his strong double chin bulged over the stiff high collar of his jacket; from under his bushy eyebrows his black eyes darted fresh and penetrating glances; his onetime tangled white hair had been combed flat on either side of a shining and carefully exact parting. He pitched his cap, which bore a gold monogram, probably the badge of some bank, in a wide sweep across the whole room on to a sofa and with the tail-ends of his jacket thrown back, his hands in his trouser pockets, advanced with a grim visage towards Gregor. Likely enough he did not himself know what he meant to do; at any rate he lifted his feet uncommonly high, and Gregor was dumbfounded at the enormous size of his shoe soles. But Gregor could not risk standing up to him, aware as he had been from the very first day of his new life that his father believed only the severest measures suitable for dealing with him. And so he ran before his father, stopping when he stopped and scuttling forward again when his father made any kind of move. In this way they circled the room several times without anything decisive happening; indeed the whole operation did not even look like a pursuit because it was carried out so slowly. And so Gregor did not leave the floor, for he feared that his father might take as a piece of peculiar wickedness any excursion of his over the walls or the ceiling. All the same, he could not stay this course much longer, for while his father took one step he had to carry out a whole series of movements. He was already beginning to feel breathless, just as in his former life his lungs had not been very dependable. As he was staggering along, trying to concentrate his energy on running, hardly keeping his eyes open; in his dazed state never even thinking of any other escape than simply going forward; and having almost forgotten that the walls were free to him, which in this room were well provided with finely carved pieces of furniture full of knobs and crevices — suddenly something lightly flung landed close behind him and rolled before him. It was an apple; a second apple followed immediately; Gregor came to a stop in alarm; there was no point in running on, for his father was determined to bombard him. He had filled his pockets with fruit from the dish on the sideboard and was now shying apple after apple, without taking particularly good aim for the moment. The small red apples rolled about the floor as if magnetized and cannoned into each other. An apple thrown without much force grazed Gregor's back and glanced off harmlessly. But another following immediately landed right on his back and sank in; Gregor wanted to drag himself forward, as if this startling, incredible pain could be left behind him: but he felt as if nailed to the spot and flattened himself out in a complete derangement of all his senses. With his last conscious look he saw the door of his room being torn open and his mother rushing out ahead of his screaming sister, in her underbodice, for her daughter had loosened her clothing to let her breathe more freely and recover from her swoon, he saw his mother rushing towards his father, leaving one after another behind her on the floor her loosened petticoats, stumbling over her petticoats straight to his father and embracing him, in complete union with him — but here Gregor's sight began to fail — with her hands clasped round his father's neck as she begged for her son's life.

III

The serious injury done to Gregor, which disabled him for more than a month — the apple went on sticking in his body as a visible reminder, since no one ventured to remove it — seemed to have made even his father recollect that Gregor was a member of the family, despite his present unfortunate and repulsive shape, and ought not to be treated as an enemy, that, on the contrary, family duty required the suppression of disgust and the exercise of patience, nothing but patience.

And although his injury had impaired, probably forever, his power of movement, and for the time being it took him long, long minutes to creep across his room like an old invalid — there was no question now of crawling up the wall — yet in his own opinion he was sufficiently compensated for this worsening of his condition by the fact that towards evening the living-room door, which he used to watch intently for an hour or two beforehand, was always thrown open, so that lying in the darkness of his room, invisible to the family, he could see them all at the lamp-lit table and listen to their talk, by general consent as it were, very different from his earlier eavesdropping.

True, their intercourse lacked the lively character of former times, which he had always called to mind with a certain wistfulness in the small hotel bedrooms where he had been wont to throw himself down, tired out, on damp bedding. They were now mostly very silent. Soon after supper his father would fall asleep in his armchair; his mother and sister would admonish each other to be silent; his mother, bending low over the lamp, stitched at fine sewing for an underwear firm; his sister, who had taken a job as a salesgirl, was learning shorthand and French in the evenings on the chance of bettering herself. Sometimes his father woke up, and as if quite unaware that he had been sleeping said to his mother: "What a lot of sewing you're doing today!" and at once fell asleep again, while the two women exchanged a tired smile.

With a kind of mulishness his father persisted in keeping his uniform on even in the house; his dressing gown hung uselessly on its peg and he slept fully dressed where he sat, as if he were ready for service at any moment and even here only at the beck and call of his superior. As a result, his uniform, which was not brand-new to start with, began to look dirty, despite all the loving care of the mother and sister to keep it clean, and Gregor often spent whole evenings gazing at the many greasy spots on the garment, gleaming with gold buttons always in a high state of polish, in which the old man sat sleeping in extreme discomfort and yet quite peacefully.

As soon as the clock struck ten his mother tried to rouse his father with gentle words and to persuade him after that to get into bed, for sitting there he could not have a proper sleep and that was what he needed most, since he had to go to duty at six. But with the mulishness that had obsessed him since he became a bank messenger he always insisted on staying longer at the table, although he regularly fell asleep again and in the end only with the greatest trouble could be got out of his armchair and into his bed. However insistently Gregor's mother and sister kept urging him with gentle reminders, he would go on slowly shaking his head for a quarter of an hour, keeping his eyes shut, and refuse to get to his feet. The mother plucked at his sleeve, whispering endearments in his ear, the sister left her lessons to come to her mother's help, but Gregor's father was not to be caught. He would only sink down deeper in his chair. Not until the two women hoisted him up by the armpits did he open his eyes and look at them both, one after the other, usually with the remark: "This is a life. This is the peace and quiet of my old age." And leaning on the two of them he would heave himself up, with difficulty, as if he were a great burden to himself, suffer them to lead him as far as the door and then wave them off and go on alone, while the mother abandoned her needlework and the sister her pen in order to run after him and help him farther.

Who could find time, in this overworked and tired-out family, to bother about Gregor more than was absolutely needful? The household was reduced more and more; the servant girl was turned off; a gigantic bony charwoman with white hair flying round her head came in morning and evening to do the rough work; everything else was done by Gregor's mother, as well as great piles of sewing. Even various family ornaments, which his mother and sister used to wear with pride at parties and celebrations, had to be sold, as Gregor discovered of an evening from hearing them all discuss the prices obtained. But what they lamented most was the fact that they could not leave the flat which was much too big for their present circumstances, because they could not think of any way to shift Gregor. Yet Gregor saw well enough that consideration for him was not the main difficulty preventing the removal, for they could have easily shifted him in some suitable box with a few air holes in it; what really kept them from moving into another flat was rather their own complete hopelessness and the belief that they had been singled out for a misfortune such as had never happened to any of their relations or acquaintances. They fulfilled to the uttermost all that the world demands of poor people, the father fetched breakfast for the small clerks in the bank, the mother devoted her energy to making underwear for strangers, the sister trotted to and fro behind the counter at the behest of customers, but more than this they had not the strength to do. And the wound in Gregor's back began to nag at him afresh when his mother and sister, after getting his father into bed, came back again, left their work lying, drew close to each other and sat cheek by cheek; when his mother, pointing towards his room, said: "Shut that door now, Grete," and he was left again in darkness, while next door the women mingled their tears or perhaps sat dry-eyed staring at the table.

Gregor hardly slept at all by night or by day. He was often haunted by the idea that next time the door opened he would take the family's affairs in hand again just as he used to do; once more, after this long interval, there appeared in his thoughts the figures of the chief and the chief clerk, the commercial travelers and the apprentices, the porter who was so dull-witted, two or three friends in other firms, a chambermaid in one of the rural hotels, a sweet and fleeting memory, a cashier in a milliner's shop, whom he had wooed earnestly but too slowly — they all appeared, together with strangers or people he had quite forgotten, but instead of helping him and his family they were one and all unapproachable and he was glad when they vanished. At other times he would not be in the mood to bother about his family, he was only filled with rage at the way they were neglecting him, and although he had no clear idea of what he might care to eat he would make plans for getting into the larder to take the food that was after all his due, even if he were not hungry. His sister no longer took thought to bring him what might especially please him, but in the morning and at noon before she went to business hurriedly pushed into his room with her foot any food that was available, and in the evening cleared it out again with one sweep of the broom, heedless of whether it had been merely tasted, or — as most frequently happened — left untouched. The cleaning of his room, which she now did always in the evenings, could not have been more hastily done. Streaks of dirt stretched along the walls, here and there lay balls of dust and filth. At first Gregor used to station himself in some particularly filthy corner when his sister arrived, in order to reproach her with it, so to speak. But he could have sat there for weeks without getting her to make any improvements; she could see the dirt as well as he did, but she had simply made up her mind to leave it alone. And yet, with a touchiness that was new to her, which seemed anyhow to have infected the whole family, she jealously guarded her claim to be the sole caretaker of Gregor's room. His mother once subjected his room to a thorough cleaning, which was achieved only by means of several buckets of water — all this dampness of course upset Gregor too and he lay widespread, sulky and motionless on the sofa — but she was well punished for it. Hardly had his sister noticed the changed aspect of his room than she rushed in high dudgeon into the living room and, despite the imploringly raised hands of her mother, burst into a storm of weeping, while her parents — her father had of course been startled out of his chair — looked on at first in helpless amazement; then they too began to go into action; the father reproached the mother on his right for not having left the cleaning of Gregor's room to his sister; shrieked at the sister on his left that never again was she to be allowed to clean Gregor's room; while the mother tried to pull the father into his bedroom, since he was beyond himself with agitation; the sister, shaken with sobs, then beat upon the table with her small fists; and Gregor hissed loudly with rage because not one of them thought of shutting the door to spare him such a spectacle and so much noise.

Still, even if the sister, exhausted by her daily work, had grown tired of looking after Gregor as she did formerly, there was no need for his mother's intervention or for Gregor's being neglected at all. The charwoman was there. This old widow, whose strong bony frame had enabled her to survive the worst a long life could offer, by no means recoiled from Gregor. Without being in the least curious she had once by chance opened the door of his room and at the sight of Gregor, who, taken by surprise, began to rush to and fro although no one was chasing him, merely stood there with her arms folded. From that time she never failed to open his door a little for a moment, morning and evening, to have a look at him. At first she even used to call him to her, with words which apparently she took to be friendly, such as: "Come along, then, you old dung beetle!" or "Look at the old dung beetle, then!" To such allocutions Gregor made no answer, but stayed motionless where he was, as if the door had never been opened. Instead of being allowed to disturb him so senselessly whenever the whim took her, she should rather have been ordered to clean out his room daily, that charwoman! Once, early in the morning — heavy rain was lashing on the windowpanes, perhaps a sign that spring was on the way — Gregor was so exasperated when she began addressing him again that he ran at her, as if to attack her, although slowly and feebly enough. But the charwoman instead of showing fright merely lifted high a chair that happened to be beside the door, and as she stood there with her mouth wide open it was clear that she meant to shut it only when she brought the chair down on Gregor's back. "So you're not coming any nearer?" she asked, as Gregor turned away again, and quietly put the chair back into the corner.

Gregor was now eating hardly anything. Only when he happened to pass the food laid out for him did he take a bit of something in his mouth as a pastime, kept it there for an hour at a time and usually spat it out again. At first he thought it was chagrin over the state of his room that prevented him from eating, yet he soon got used to the various changes in his room. It had become a habit in the family to push into his room things there was no room for elsewhere, and there were plenty of these now, since one of the rooms had been let to three lodgers. These serious gentlemen — all three of them with full beards, as Gregor once observed through a crack in the door — had a passion for order, not only in their own room but, since they were now members of the household, in all its arrangements, especially in the kitchen. Superfluous, not to say dirty, objects they could not bear. Besides, they had brought with them most of the furnishings they needed. For this reason many things could be dispensed with that it was no use trying to sell but that should not be thrown away either. All of them found their way into Gregor's room. The ash can likewise and the kitchen garbage can. Anything that was not needed for the moment was simply flung into Gregor's room by the charwoman, who did everything in a hurry; fortunately Gregor usually saw only the object, whatever it was, and the hand that held it. Perhaps she intended to take the things away again as time and opportunity offered, or to collect them until she could throw them all out in a heap, but in fact they just lay wherever she happened to throw them, except when Gregor pushed his way through the junk heap and shifted it somewhat, at first out of necessity, because he had not room enough to crawl, but later with increasing enjoyment, although after such excursions, being sad and weary to death, he would lie motionless for hours. And since the lodgers often ate their supper at home in the common living room, the living room door stayed shut many an evening, yet Gregor reconciled himself quite easily to the shutting of the door, for often enough on evenings when it was opened he had disregarded it entirely and lain in the darkest corner of his room, quite unnoticed by the family. But on one occasion the charwoman left the door open a little and it stayed ajar even when the lodgers came in for supper and the lamp was lit. They set themselves at the top end of the table where formerly Gregor and his father and mother had eaten their meals, unfolded their napkins and took knife and fork in hand. At once his mother appeared in the other doorway with a dish of meat and close behind her his sister with a dish of potatoes piled high. The food steamed with a thick vapor. The lodgers bent over the food set before them as if to scrutinize it before eating, in fact the man in the middle, who seemed to pass for an authority with the other two, cut a piece of meat as it lay on the dish, obviously to discover if it were tender or should be sent back to the kitchen. He showed satisfaction, and Gregor's mother and sister, who had been watching anxiously, breathed freely and began to smile.

The family itself took its meals in the kitchen. Nonetheless, Gregor's father came into the living room before going in to the kitchen and with one prolonged bow, cap in hand, made a round of the table. The lodgers all stood up and murmured something in their beards. When they were alone again they ate their food in almost complete silence. It seemed remarkable to Gregor that among the various noises coming from the table he could always distinguish the sound of their masticating teeth, as if this were a sign to Gregor that one needed teeth in order to eat, and that with toothless jaws even of the finest make one could do nothing. "I'm hungry enough," said Gregor sadly to himself, "but not for that kind of food. How these lodgers are stuffing themselves, and here am I dying of starvation!"

On that very evening — during the whole of his time there Gregor could not remember ever having heard the violin — the sound of violin-playing came from the kitchen. The lodgers had already finished their supper, the one in the middle had brought out a newspaper and given the other two a page apiece, and now they were leaning back at ease reading and smoking. When the violin began to play they pricked up their ears, got to their feet, and went on tiptoe to the hall door where they stood huddled together. Their movements must have been heard in the kitchen, for Gregor's father called out: "Is the violin-playing disturbing you, gentlemen? It can be stopped at once." "On the contrary," said the middle lodger, "could not Fräulein Samsa come and play in this room, beside us, where it is much more convenient and comfortable?" "Oh certainly," cried Gregor's father, as if he were the violin-player. The lodgers came back into the living room and waited. Presently Gregor's father arrived with the music stand, his mother carrying the music and his sister with the violin. His sister quietly made everything ready to start playing; his parents, who had never let rooms before and so had an exaggerated idea of the courtesy due to lodgers, did not venture to sit down on their own chairs; his father leaned against the door, the right hand thrust between two buttons of his livery coat, which was formally buttoned up; but his mother was offered a chair by one of the lodgers and, since she left the chair just where he had happened to put it, sat down in a corner to one side.

Gregor's sister began to play; the father and mother, from either side, intently watched the movements of her hands. Gregor, attracted by the playing, ventured to move forward a little until his head was actually inside the living room. He felt hardly any surprise at his growing lack of consideration for the others; there had been a time when he prided himself on being considerate. And yet just on this occasion he had more reason than ever to hide himself, since owing to the amount of dust which lay thick in his room and rose into the air at the slightest movement, he too was covered with dust; fluff and hair and remnants of food trailed with him, caught on his back and along his sides; his indifference to everything was much too great for him to turn on his back and scrape himself clean on the carpet, as once he had done several times a day. And in spite of his condition, no shame deterred him from advancing a little over the spotless floor of the living room.

To be sure, no one was aware of him. The family was entirely absorbed in the violin-playing; the lodgers, however, who first of all had stationed themselves, hands in pockets, much too close behind the music stand so that they could all have read the music, which must have bothered his sister, had soon retreated to the window, half-whispering with downbent heads, and stayed there while his father turned an anxious eye on them. Indeed, they were making it more than obvious that they had been disappointed in their expectation of hearing good or enjoyable violin-playing, that they had had more than enough of the performance and only out of courtesy suffered a continued disturbance of their peace. From the way they all kept blowing the smoke of their cigars high in the air through nose and mouth one could divine their irritation. And yet Gregor's sister was playing so beautifully. Her face leaned sideways, intently and sadly her eyes followed the notes of music. Gregor crawled a little farther forward and lowered his head to the ground so that it might be possible for his eyes to meet hers. Was he an animal, that music had such an effect upon him? He felt as if the way were opening before him to the unknown nourishment he craved. He was determined to push forward till he reached his sister, to pull at her skirt and so let her know that she was to come into his room with her violin, for no one here appreciated her playing as he would appreciate it. He would never let her out of his room, at least, not so long as he lived; his frightful appearance would become, for the first time, useful to him; he would watch all the doors of his room at once and spit at intruders; but his sister should need no constraint, she should stay with him of her own free will; she should sit beside him on the sofa, bend down her ear to him and hear him confide that he had had the firm intention of sending her to the Conservatorium, and that, but for his mishap, last Christmas — surely Christmas was long past? — he would have announced it to everybody without allowing a single objection. After this confession his sister would be so touched that she would burst into tears, and Gregor would then raise himself to her shoulder and kiss her on the neck, which, now that she went to business, she kept free of any ribbon or collar.

"Mr. Samsa!" cried the middle lodger, to Gregor's father, and pointed, without wasting any more words, at Gregor, now working himself slowly forwards. The violin fell silent, the middle lodger first smiled to his friends with a shake of the head and then looked at Gregor again. Instead of driving Gregor out, his father seemed to think it more needful to begin by soothing down the lodgers, although they were not at all agitated and apparently found Gregor more entertaining than the violin-playing. He hurried toward them and, spreading out his arms, tried to urge them back into their own room and at the same time to block their view of Gregor. They now began to be really a little angry, one could not tell whether because of the old man's behavior or because it had just dawned on them that all unwittingly they had such a neighbor as Gregor next door. They demanded explanations of his father, they waved their arms like him, tugged uneasily at their beards, and only with reluctance backed towards their room. Meanwhile Gregor's sister, who stood there as if lost when her playing was so abruptly broken off, came to life again, pulled herself together all at once after standing for a while holding violin and bow in nervelessly hanging hands and staring at her music, pushed her violin into the lap of her mother, who was still sitting in her chair fighting asthmatically for breath, and ran into the lodgers' room to which they were now being shepherded by her father rather more quickly than before. One could see the pillows and blankets on the beds flying under her accustomed fingers and being laid in order. Before the lodgers had actually reached their room she had finished making the beds and slipped out.

The old man seemed once more to be so possessed by his mulish self-assertiveness that he was forgetting all the respect he should show to his lodgers. He kept driving them on and driving them on until in the very door of the bedroom the middle lodger stamped his foot loudly on the floor and so brought him to a halt. "I beg to announce," said the lodger, lifting one hand and looking also at Gregor's mother and sister, "that because of the disgusting conditions prevailing in this household and family" — here he spat on the floor with emphatic brevity — "I give you notice on the spot. Naturally I won't pay you a penny for the days I have lived here, on the contrary I shall consider bringing an action for damages against you, based on claims — believe me — that will be easily susceptible of proof." He ceased and stared straight in front of him, as if he expected something. In fact his two friends at once rushed into the breach with these words: "And we too give notice on the spot." On that he seized the door-handle and shut the door with a slam.

Gregor's father, groping with his hands, staggered forward and fell into his chair; it looked as if he were stretching himself there for his ordinary evening nap, but the marked jerkings of his head, which was as if uncontrollable, showed that he was far from asleep. Gregor had simply stayed quietly all the time on the spot where the lodgers had espied him. Disappointment at the failure of his plan, perhaps also the weakness arising from extreme hunger, made it impossible for him to move. He feared, with a fair degree of certainty, that at any moment the general tension would discharge itself in a combined attack upon him, and he lay waiting. He did not react even to the noise made by the violin as it fell off his mother's lap from under her trembling fingers and gave out a resonant note.

"My dear parents," said his sister, slapping her hand on the table by way of introduction, "things can't go on like this. Perhaps you don't realize that, but I do. I won't utter my brother's name in the presence of this creature, and so all I say is: we must try to get rid of it. We've tried to look after it and to put up with it as far as is humanly possible, and I don't think anyone could reproach us in the slightest."

"She is more than right," said Gregor's father to himself. His mother, who was still choking for lack of breath, began to cough hollowly into her hand with a wild look in her eyes.

His sister rushed over to her and held her forehead. His father's thoughts seemed to have lost their vagueness at Grete's words, he sat more upright, fingering his service cap that lay among the plates still lying on the table from the lodgers' supper, and from time to time looked at the still form of Gregor.

"We must try to get rid of it," his sister now said explicitly to her father, since her mother was coughing too much to hear a word, "it will be the death of both of you, I can see that coming. When one has to work as hard as we do, all of us, one can't stand this continual torment at home on top of it. At least I can't stand it any longer." And she burst into such a passion of sobbing that her tears dropped on her mother's face, where she wiped them off mechanically.

"My dear," said the old man sympathetically, and with evident understanding, "but what can we do?"

Gregor's sister merely shrugged her shoulders to indicate the feeling of helplessness that had now overmastered her during her weeping fit, in contrast to her former confidence.

"If he could understand us," said her father, half questioningly; Grete, still sobbing, vehemently waved a hand to show how unthinkable that was.

"If he could understand us," repeated the old man, shutting his eyes to consider his daughter's conviction that understanding was impossible, "then perhaps we might come to some agreement with him. But as it is —"

"He must go," cried Gregor's sister. "That's the only solution, Father. You must just try to get rid of the idea that this is Gregor. The fact that we've believed it for so long is the root of all our trouble. But how can it be Gregor? If this were Gregor, he would have realized long ago that human beings can't live with such a creature, and he'd have gone away on his own accord. Then we wouldn't have any brother, but we'd be able to go on living and keep his memory in honor. As it is, this creature persecutes us, drives away our lodgers, obviously wants the whole apartment to himself and would have us all sleep in the gutter. Just look, Father," she shrieked all at once, "he's at it again!" And in an access of panic that was quite incomprehensible to Gregor she even quitted her mother, literally thrusting the chair from her as if she would rather sacrifice her mother than stay so near to Gregor, and rushed behind her father, who also rose up, being simply upset by her agitation, and half-spread his arms out as if to protect her.

Yet Gregor had not the slightest intention of frightening anyone, far less his sister. He had only begun to turn round in order to crawl back to his room, but it was certainly a startling operation to watch, since because of his disabled condition he could not execute the difficult turning movements except by lifting his head and then bracing it against the floor over and over again. He paused and looked round. His good intentions seemed to have been recognized; the alarm had only been momentary. Now they were all watching him in melancholy silence. His mother lay in her chair, her legs stiffly outstretched and pressed together, her eyes almost closing for sheer weariness; his father and his sister were sitting beside each other, his sister's arm around the old man's neck.

Perhaps I can go on turning round now, thought Gregor, and began his labors again. He could not stop himself from panting with the effort, and had to pause now and then to take breath. Nor did anyone harass him, he was left entirely to himself. When he had completed the turn-round he began at once to crawl straight back. He was amazed at the distance separating him from his room and could not understand how in his weak state he had managed to accomplish the same journey so recently, almost without remarking it. Intent on crawling as fast as possible, he barely noticed that not a single word, not an ejaculation from his family, interfered with his progress. Only when he was already in the doorway did he turn his head round, not completely, for his neck muscles were getting stiff, but enough to see that nothing had changed behind him except that his sister had risen to her feet. His last glance fell on his mother, who was not quite overcome by sleep.

Hardly was he well inside his room when the door was hastily pushed shut, bolted, and locked. The sudden noise in his rear startled him so much that his little legs gave beneath him. It was his sister who had shown such haste. She had been standing ready waiting and had made a light spring forward, Gregor had not even heard her coming, and she cried "At last!" to her parents as she turned the key in the lock.

"And what now?" said Gregor to himself, looking round in the darkness. Soon he made the discovery that he was now unable to stir a limb. This did not surprise him, rather it seemed unnatural that he should ever actually have been able to move on these feeble little legs. Otherwise he felt relatively comfortable. True, his whole body was aching, but it seemed that the pain was gradually growing less and would finally pass away. The rotting apple in his back and the inflamed area around it, all covered with soft dust, already hardly troubled him. He thought of his family with tenderness and love. The decision that he must disappear was one that he held to even more strongly than his sister, if that were possible. In this state of vacant and peaceful meditation he remained until the tower clock struck three in the morning. The first broadening of light in the world outside the window entered his consciousness once more. Then his head sank to the floor of its own accord and from his nostrils came the last faint flicker of his breath.

When the charwoman arrived early in the morning — what between her strength and her impatience she slammed all the doors so loudly, never mind how often she had been begged not to do so, that no one in the whole apartment could enjoy any quiet sleep after her arrival — she noticed nothing unusual as she took her customary peep into Gregor's room. She thought he was lying motionless on purpose, pretending to be in the sulks; she credited him with every kind of intelligence. Since she happened to have the long-handled broom in her hand she tried to tickle him up with it from the doorway. When that too produced no reaction she felt provoked and poked at him a little harder, and only when she had pushed him along the floor without meeting any resistance was her attention aroused. It did not take her long to establish the truth of the matter, and her eyes widened, she let out a whistle, yet did not waste much time over it but tore open the door of the Samsas' bedroom and yelled into the darkness at the top of her voice: "Just look at this, it's dead; it's lying here dead and done for!"

Mr. and Mrs. Samsa started up in their double bed and before they realized the nature of the charwoman's announcement had some difficulty in overcoming the shock of it. But then they got out of bed quickly, one on either side, Mr. Samsa throwing a blanket over his shoulders, Mrs. Samsa in nothing but her nightgown; in this array they entered Gregor's room. Meanwhile the door of the living room opened, too, where Grete had been sleeping since the advent of the lodgers; she was completely dressed as if she had not been to bed, which seemed to be confirmed also by the paleness of her face. "Dead?" said Mrs. Samsa, looking questioningly at the charwoman, although she could have investigated for herself, and the fact was obvious enough without investigation. "I should say so," said the charwoman, proving her words by pushing Gregor's corpse a long way to one side with her broomstick. Mrs. Samsa made a movement as if to stop her, but checked it. "Well," said Mr. Samsa, "now thanks be to God." He crossed himself, and the three women followed his example. Grete, whose eyes never left the corpse, said: "Just see how thin he was. It's such a long time since he's eaten anything. The food came out again just as it went in." Indeed, Gregor's body was completely flat and dry, as could only now be seen when it was no longer supported by the legs and nothing prevented one from looking closely at it.

"Come in beside us, Grete, for a little while," said Mrs. Samsa with a tremulous smile, and Grete, not without looking back at the corpse, followed her parents into their bedroom. The charwoman shut the door and opened the window wide. Although it was so early in the morning a certain softness was perceptible in the fresh air. After all, it was already the end of March.

The three lodgers emerged from their room and were surprised to see no breakfast; they had been forgotten. "Where's our breakfast?" said the middle lodger peevishly to the charwoman. But she put her finger to her lips and hastily, without a word, indicated by gestures that they should go into Gregor's room. They did so and stood, their hands in the pockets of their somewhat shabby coats, around Gregor's corpse in the room where it was now fully light.

At that the door of the Samsas' bedroom opened and Mr. Samsa appeared in his uniform, his wife on one arm, his daughter on the other. They all looked a little as if they had been crying; from time to time Grete hid her face on her father's arm.

"Leave my house at once!" said Mr. Samsa, and pointed to the door without disengaging himself from the women. "What do you mean by that?" said the middle lodger, taken somewhat aback, with a feeble smile. The two others put their hands behind them and kept rubbing them together, as if in gleeful expectation of a fine set-to in which they were bound to come off the winners. "I mean just what I say," answered Mr. Samsa, and advanced in a straight line with his two companions towards the lodger. He stood his ground at first quietly, looking at the floor as if his thoughts were taking a new pattern in his head. "Then let us go, by all means," he said, and looked up at Mr. Samsa as if in a sudden access of humility he were expecting some renewed sanction for this decision. Mr. Samsa merely nodded briefly once or twice with meaning eyes. Upon that the lodger really did go with long strides into the hall, his two friends had been listening and had quite stopped rubbing their hands for some moments and now went scuttling after him as if afraid that Mr. Samsa might get into the hall before them and cut them off from their leader. In the hall they all three took their hats from the rack, their sticks from the umbrella stand, bowed in silence and quitted the apartment. With a suspiciousness which proved quite unfounded Mr. Samsa and the two women followed them out to the landing; leaning over the banister they watched the three figures slowly but surely going down the long stairs, vanishing from sight at a certain turn of the staircase on every floor and coming into view again after a moment or so; the more they dwindled, the more the Samsa family's interest in them dwindled, and when a butcher's boy met them and passed them on the stairs coming up proudly with a tray on his head, Mr. Samsa and the two women soon left the landing and as if a burden had been lifted from them went back into their apartment.

They decided to spend this day in resting and going for a stroll; they had not only deserved such a respite from work but absolutely needed it. And so they sat down at the table and wrote three notes of excuse, Mr. Samsa to his board of management, Mrs. Samsa to her employer and Grete to the head of her firm. While they were writing, the charwoman came in to say that she was going now, since her morning's work was finished. At first they only nodded without looking up, but as she kept hovering there they eyed her irritably. "Well?" said Mr. Samsa. The charwoman stood grinning in the doorway as if she had good news to impart to the family but meant not to say a word unless properly questioned. The small ostrich feather standing upright on her hat, which had annoyed Mr. Samsa ever since she was engaged, was waving gaily in all directions. "Well, what is it then?" asked Mrs. Samsa, who obtained more respect from the charwoman than the others. "Oh," said the charwoman, giggling so amiably that she could not at once continue, "just this, you don't need to bother about how to get rid of the thing next door. It's been seen to already." Mrs. Samsa and Grete bent over their letters again, as if preoccupied; Mr. Samsa, who perceived that she was eager to begin describing it all in detail, stopped her with a decisive hand. But since she was not allowed to tell her story, she remembered the great hurry she was in, being obviously deeply huffed: "Bye, everybody," she said, whirling off violently, and departed with a frightful slamming of doors.

"She'll be given notice tonight," said Mr. Samsa, but neither from his wife nor his daughter did he get any answer, for the charwoman seemed to have shattered again the composure they had barely achieved. They rose, went to the window and stayed there, clasping each other tight. Mr. Samsa turned in his chair to look at them and quietly observed them for a little. Then he called out: "Come along, now, do. Let bygones be bygones. And you might have some consideration for me." The two of them complied at once, hastened to him, caressed him and quickly finished their letters.

Then they all three left the apartment together, which was more than they had done for months, and went by tram into the open country outside the town. The tram, in which they were the only passengers, was filled with warm sunshine. Leaning comfortably back in their seats they canvassed their prospects for the future, and it appeared on closer inspection that these were not at all bad, for the jobs they had got, which so far they had never really discussed with each other, were all three admirable and likely to lead to better things later on. The greatest immediate improvement in their condition would of course arise from moving to another house; they wanted to take a smaller and cheaper but also better situated and more easily run apartment than the one they had, which Gregor had selected. While they were thus conversing, it struck both Mr. and Mrs. Samsa, almost at the same moment, as they became aware of their daughter's increasing vivacity, that in spite of all the sorrow of recent times, which had made her cheeks pale, she had bloomed into a pretty girl with a good figure. They grew quieter and half unconsciously exchanged glances of complete agreement, having come to the conclusion that it would soon be time to find a good husband for her. And it was like a confirmation of their new dreams and excellent intentions that at the end of their journey their daughter sprang to her feet first and stretched her young body.   [1915]

JAMAICA KINCAID *(b. 1949) was born and educated in St. Johns, Antigua, in the West Indies. Her father was a carpenter, and her family doted upon her, the only child. Kincaid remembers:*

> *My mother did keep everything I ever wore, and basically until I was quite grown up my past was sort of a museum to me. Clearly, the way I became a writer was that my mother wrote my life for me and told it to me. I can't help but think that it made me interested in the idea of myself as an object. I can't account for the reason I became a writer any other way, because I certainly didn't know writers. And not only that. I thought writing was something that people just didn't do anymore, that went out of fashion, like the bustle. I really didn't read a book that was written in the twentieth century until I was about seventeen and away from home.*

Kincaid left Antigua to study in the United States, but she found college "a dismal failure," so she educated herself. She began writing and published her stories in Rolling Stone, *the* Paris Review, *and* The New Yorker, *where she became a staff writer in 1978. Six years later she published her first book,* At the Bottom of the River, *a collection of stories, which won the Morton Dauwen Zabel Award of the American Academy and Institute of Arts and Letters. In 1985 her book of interrelated stories* Annie John, *about a girl's coming of age in the West Indies, was also much praised. In her autobiographical writing, Kincaid often explores the idea that her deep affection for her family and her native country developed into a conflicting need for separation and independence as she grew up.*

Typically Kincaid writes in a deliberately precise rhythmic style about intense emotions, as in her story "Girl" (1984). Her fiction is free from conventional plots, characters, and dialogue. The critic Suzanne Freeman has recognized that "what Kincaid has to tell me, she tells, with her singsong style, in a series of images that are as sweet and mysterious as the secrets that children whisper in your ear." Although Kincaid is married to an American and lives in New York City, she feels that the British West Indies will continue to be the source for her fiction. "What I really feel about America is that it's given me a place to be myself — but myself as I was formed somewhere else." A Small Place (1989), another book about the West Indies, was described by the novelist Salman Rushdie as "a jeremiad of great clarity and a force that one might have called torrential were the language not so finely controlled." Her latest book, Lucy, *was published in 1990.*

JAMAICA KINCAID

Girl

Wash the white clothes on Monday and put them on the stone heap; wash the color clothes on Tuesday and put them on the clothesline to dry; don't walk barehead in the hot sun; cook pumpkin fritters in very hot sweet oil; soak your little cloths right after you take them off; when buying cotton to make yourself a nice blouse, be sure that it doesn't have gum on it, because that way it won't hold up well after a wash; soak salt fish overnight before you cook it; is it true that you sing benna[1] in Sunday school?; always eat your food in such a way that it won't turn someone else's stomach; on Sundays try to walk like a lady and not like the slut you are so bent on becoming; don't sing benna in Sunday school; you mustn't speak to wharf-rat boys, not even to give directions; don't eat fruits on the street — flies will follow you; *but I don't sing benna on Sundays at all and never in Sunday school;* this is how to sew on a button; this is how to make a button-hole for the button you have just sewed on; this is how to hem a dress when you see the hem coming down and so to prevent yourself from looking like the slut I know you are so bent on becoming; this is how you iron your father's khaki shirt so that it doesn't have a crease; this is how you iron your father's khaki pants so that they don't have a crease; this is how you grow okra — far from the house, because okra tree harbors red ants; when you are growing dasheen, make sure it gets plenty of water or else it makes your throat itch when you are eating it; this is how you sweep a corner; this is how you sweep a whole house; this is how you sweep a yard; this is how you smile to someone you don't like too much; this is how you smile to someone you don't like at all; this is how you smile to someone you like completely; this is how you set a table for tea; this is how you set a table for dinner; this is how you set a table for dinner with an important guest; this is how you set a table for lunch; this is how you set a table for breakfast; this is how to behave in the presence of men who don't know you very well, and this way they won't recognize immediately the slut I have warned you against becoming; be sure to wash every day, even if it is with your own spit; don't squat down to play marbles — you are not a boy, you know; don't pick people's flowers — you might catch something; don't throw stones at blackbirds, because it might not be a blackbird at all; this is how to make a bread pudding; this is how to make doukona;[2] this is how to make pepper pot; this is how to make a good medicine for a cold; this is how to make a good medicine to throw away a child before it even becomes a child; this is how to catch a fish; this is how to throw back a fish you don't

---

[1] Calypso music.

[2] A spicy plantain pudding.

like, and that way something bad won't fall on you; this is how to bully a man; this is how a man bullies you; this is how to love a man, and if this doesn't work there are other ways, and if they don't work don't feel too bad about giving up; this is how to spit up in the air if you feel like it, and this is how to move quick so that it doesn't fall on you; this is how to make ends meet; always squeeze bread to make sure it's fresh; *but what if the baker won't let me feel the bread?;* you mean to say that after all you are really going to be the kind of woman who the baker won't let near the bread?   [1984]

MILAN KUNDERA *(b. 1929) was born in Brno, Czechoslovakia. As a child he intended to become a musician, following the example of his father, Ludvík Kundera, a pianist and pupil of the great Czech composer, Leoš Janáček, but in 1948 Kundera decided this was not his true vocation. Instead he studied scriptwriting and directing at the Prague Academy of Music and Dramatic Arts. After publishing three poetry collections and a play, he felt he discovered his voice as a writer when, at nearly thirty, he wrote the first short stories of the cycle* Laughable Loves. *"The Hitchhiking Game" is from the second of the three volumes of that cycle, published in 1969.*

Like other Czech students of his generation, Kundera had joined the Communist Party — when he was eighteen — but he was expelled from it in 1950, reinstated in 1956, and expelled yet again, after he made a speech to the congress of Czech writers in 1967 advocating greater artistic freedom. When the Soviets invaded the country in 1968, Kundera was charged with being a "counterrevolutionary" and forced to leave his teaching job. In 1975, the Czech government gave him an extended travel visa so that he could live in Paris while retaining his Czech citizenship. Kundera's novels include The Joke *(1969),* Life Is Elsewhere *(1974), and* The Farewell Party *(1976).* The Book of Laughter and Forgetting *(1980) is a collection of interrelated stories, mixing fantasy and nostalgia with brutal realism. In 1985 he published the popular novel* The Unbearable Lightness of Being; *he followed it with* The Art of the Novel *(1989) and* Immortality *(1991).*

Kundera feels that although the drama of politics is often present in his books, his fictional characters are not taking part in any particular politics but acting in more general realms of humor, irony, and imagination. Philip Roth's introduction to the English edition of Laughable Loves *discusses Kundera as a writer finely tuned to the harsh realities of contemporary political power struggles. In "The Hitchhiking Game," Roth noted,*

> *Simply by fooling around and indulging their curiosity, the lovers find they have managed to deepen responsibility as well as passion. . . . What is so often laughable, in the stories of Kundera's Czechoslovakia, is how grimly serious just about everything turns out to be, jokes and games and pleasure included; what's laughable is how terribly little there is to laugh at with any joy.*

RELATED COMMENTARY: *Milan Kundera, "Kafka and Modern History," page 1444.*

MILAN KUNDERA

The Hitchhiking Game

Translated by Suzanne Rappaport

I

The needle on the gas gauge suddenly dipped toward empty and the young driver of the sports car declared that it was maddening how much gas the car ate up. "See that we don't run out of gas again," protested the girl (about twenty-two), and reminded the driver of several places where this had already happened to them. The young man replied that he wasn't worried, because whatever he went through with her had the charm of adventure for him. The girl objected; whenever they had run out of gas on the highway it had, she said, always been an adventure only for her. The young man had hidden and she had had to make ill use of her charms by thumbing a ride and letting herself be driven to the nearest gas station, then thumbing a ride back with a can of gas. The young man asked the girl whether the drivers who had given her a ride had been unpleasant, since she spoke as if her task had been a hardship. She replied (with awkward flirtatiousness) that sometimes they had been *very* pleasant but that it hadn't done her any good as she had been burdened with the can and had had to leave them before she could get anything going. "Pig," said the young man. The girl protested that she wasn't a pig, but that he really was. God knows how many girls stopped him on the highway, when he was driving the car alone! Still driving, the young man put his arm around the girl's shoulders and kissed her gently on the forehead. He knew that she loved him and that she was jealous. Jealousy isn't a pleasant quality, but if it isn't overdone (and if it's combined with modesty), apart from its inconvenience there's even something touching about it. At least that's what the young man thought. Because he was only twenty-eight, it seemed to him that he was old and knew everything that a man could know about women. In the girl sitting beside him he valued precisely what, until now, he had met with least in women: purity.

The needle was already on empty, when to the right the young man caught sight of a sign, announcing that the station was a quarter of a mile ahead. The girl hardly had time to say how relieved she was before the young man was signaling left and driving into a space in front of the pumps. However, he had to stop a little way off, because beside the pumps was a huge gasoline truck with a large metal tank and a bulky hose, which was refilling the pumps. "We'll have to wait," said the young man to the girl and got out of the car. "How long will it take?" he shouted to the man in overalls. "Only a moment," replied the attendant, and the young man said: "I've heard that one before." He wanted to go back and sit in the car, but he saw that the girl had gotten out the other side. "I'll take a little walk in the meantime," she said. "Where to?" the young man asked on purpose, wanting to see the girl's embarrassment. He had known her for a year now but she would still get shy in front of him. He enjoyed her moments of shyness, partly because they distinguished her from the women he'd met before, partly because he was aware of the law of universal transience, which made even his girl's shyness a precious thing to him.

II

The girl really didn't like it when during the trip (the young man would drive for several hours without stopping) she had to ask him to stop for a moment somewhere near a clump of trees. She always got angry when, with feigned surprise, he asked her why he should stop. She knew that her shyness was ridiculous and old-fashioned. Many times at work she had noticed that they laughed at her on account of it and deliberately provoked her. She always got shy in advance at the thought of how she was going to get shy. She often longed to feel free and easy about her body, the way most of the women around her did. She had even invented a special course in self-persuasion: she would repeat to herself that at birth every human being received one out of the millions of available bodies, as one would receive an allotted room out of the millions of rooms in an enormous hotel. Consequently, the body was fortuitous and impersonal, it was only a ready-made, borrowed thing. She would repeat this to herself in different ways, but she could never manage to feel it. This mind-body dualism was alien to her. She was too much one with her body; that is why she always felt such anxiety about it.

She experienced this same anxiety even in her relations with the young man, whom she had known for a year and with whom she was happy, perhaps because he never separated her body from her soul and she could live with him *wholly*. In this unity there was happiness, but right behind the happiness lurked suspicion, and the girl was full of that. For instance, it often occurred to her that the other women (those who weren't anxious) were more attractive and more seductive and that the young man, who did not conceal the fact that he knew this kind of woman well, would someday leave her for a woman like that. (True, the young man declared that he'd had enough of them to last his whole life, but she knew that he was still much younger than he thought.) She wanted him to be completely hers and she to be completely his, but it often seemed to her that the more she tried to give him everything, the more she denied him something: the very thing that a light and superficial love or a flirtation gives to a person. It worried her that she was not able to combine seriousness with lightheartedness.

But now she wasn't worrying and any such thoughts were far from her mind. She felt good. It was the first day of their vacation (of their two-week vacation, about which she had been dreaming for a whole year), the sky was blue (the whole year she had been worrying about whether the sky would really be blue), and he was beside her. At his, "Where to?" she blushed, and left the car without a word. She walked around the gas station, which was situated beside the highway in total isolation, surrounded by fields. About a hundred yards away (in the direction in which they were traveling), a wood began. She set off for it, vanished behind a little bush, and gave herself up to her good mood. (In solitude it was possible for her to get the greatest enjoyment from the presence of the man she loved. If his presence had been continuous, it would have kept on disappearing. Only when alone was she able to *hold on* to it.)

When she came out of the wood onto the highway, the gas station was visible. The large gasoline truck was already pulling out and the sports car moved forward toward the red turret of the pump. The girl walked on along the highway and only at times looked back to see if the sports car was coming. At last she caught sight of it. She stopped and began to wave at it like a hitchhiker waving at a stranger's car. The sports car slowed down and stopped close to the girl. The young man leaned toward the window, rolled it down, smiled, and asked, "Where are you headed, miss?" "Are you going to Bystritsa?" asked the girl, smiling flirtatiously at him. "Yes, please get in," said the young man, opening the door. The girl got in and the car took off.

III

The young man was always glad when his girl friend was gay. This didn't happen too often; she had a quite tiresome job in an unpleasant environment, many hours of overtime without compensatory leisure and, at home, a sick mother. So she often felt tired. She didn't have either particularly good nerves or self-confidence and easily fell into a state of anxiety and fear. For this reason he welcomed every manifestation of her gaiety with the tender solicitude of a foster parent. He smiled at her and said: "I'm lucky today. I've been driving for five years, but I've never given a ride to such a pretty hitchhiker."

The girl was grateful to the young man for every bit of flattery; she wanted to linger for a moment in its warmth and so she said, "You're very good at lying."

"Do I look like a liar?"

"You look like you enjoy lying to women," said the girl, and into her words there crept unawares a touch of the old anxiety, because she really did believe that her young man enjoyed lying to women.

The girl's jealousy often irritated the young man, but this time he could easily overlook it for, after all, her words didn't apply to him but to the unknown driver. And so he just casually inquired, "Does it bother you?"

"If I were going with you, then it would bother me," said the girl and her words contained a subtle, instructive message for the young man; but the end of her sentence applied only to the unknown driver, "but I don't know you, so it doesn't bother me."

"Things about her own man always bother a woman more than things about a stranger" (this was now the young man's subtle, instructive message to the girl), "so seeing that we are strangers, we could get on well together."

The girl purposely didn't want to understand the implied meaning of his message, so she now addressed the unknown driver exclusively:

"What does it matter, since we'll part company in a little while?"

"Why?" asked the young man.

"Well, I'm getting out at Bystritsa."

"And what if I get out with you?"

At those words the girl looked up at him and found that he looked exactly as she imagined him in her most agonizing hours of jealousy. She was alarmed at how he was flattering her and flirting with her (an unknown hitchhiker), and *how becoming it was to him.* Therefore she responded with defiant provocativeness, "What would *you* do with me, I wonder?"

"I wouldn't have to think too hard about what to do with such a beautiful woman," said the young man gallantly and at this moment he was once again speaking far more to his own girl than to the figure of the hitchhiker.

But this flattering sentence made the girl feel as if she had caught him at something, as if she had wheedled a confession out of him with a fraudulent trick. She felt toward him a brief flash of intense hatred and said, "Aren't you rather too sure of yourself?"

The young man looked at the girl. Her defiant face appeared to him to be completely convulsed. He felt sorry for her and longed for her usual, familiar expression (which he used to call childish and simple). He leaned toward her, put his arm around her shoulders, and softly spoke the name with which he usually addressed her and with which he now wanted to stop the game.

But the girl released herself and said: "You're going a bit too fast!"

At this rebuff the young man said: "Excuse me, miss," and looked silently in front of him at the highway.

IV

The girl's pitiful jealousy, however, left her as quickly as it had come over her. After all, she was sensible and knew perfectly well that all this was merely a game. Now it even struck her as a little ridiculous that she had repulsed her man out of a jealous rage. It wouldn't be pleasant for her if he found out why she had done it. Fortunately women have the miraculous ability to change the meaning of their actions after the event. Using this ability, she decided that she had repulsed him not out of anger but so that she could go on with the game, which, with its whimsicality, so well suited the first day of their vacation.

So again she was the hitchhiker, who had just repulsed the overenterprising driver, but only so as to slow down his conquest and make it more exciting. She half turned toward the young man and said caressingly:

"I didn't mean to offend you, mister!"

"Excuse me, I won't touch you again," said the young man.

He was furious with the girl for not listening to him and refusing to be herself when that was what he wanted. And since the girl insisted on continuing in her role, he transferred his anger to the unknown hitchhiker whom she was portraying. And all at once he discovered the character of his own part: he stopped making the gallant remarks with which he had wanted to flatter his girl in a roundabout way, and began to play the tough guy who treats women to the coarser aspects of his masculinity: willfulness, sarcasm, self-assurance.

This role was a complete contradiction of the young man's habitually solicitous approach to the girl. True, before he had met her, he had in fact behaved roughly rather than gently toward women. But he had never resembled a heartless tough guy, because he had never demonstrated either a particularly strong will or ruthlessness. However, if he did not resemble such a man, nonetheless he had *longed* to at one time. Of course it was a quite naive desire, but there it was. Childish desires withstand all the snares of the adult mind and often survive into ripe old age. And this childish desire quickly took advantage of the opportunity to embody itself in the proffered role.

The young man's sarcastic reserve suited the girl very well — it freed her from herself. For she herself was, above all, the epitome of jealousy. The moment she stopped seeing the gallantly seductive young man beside her and saw only his inaccessible face, her jealousy subsided. The girl could forget herself and give herself up to her role.

Her role? What was her role? It was a role out of trashy literature. The hitchhiker stopped the car not to get a ride, but to seduce the man who was driving the car. She was an artful seductress, cleverly knowing how to use her charms. The girl slipped into this silly, romantic part with an ease that astonished her and held her spellbound.

V

There was nothing the young man missed in his life more than light-heartedness. The main road of his life was drawn with implacable precision. His job didn't use up merely eight hours a day, it also infiltrated the remaining time with the compulsory boredom of meetings and home study, and, by means of the attentiveness of his countless male and female colleagues, it infiltrated the wretchedly little time he had left for his private life as well. This private life never remained secret and sometimes even became the subject of gossip and public discussion. Even two weeks' vacation didn't give him a feeling of liberation and adventure; the gray shadow of precise planning lay even here. The scarcity of summer accommodations in our country compelled him to book a room in the Tatras six months in advance, and since for that he needed a recommendation from his office, its omnipresent brain thus did not cease knowing about him even for an instant.

He had become reconciled to all this, yet all the same from time to time the terrible thought of the straight road would overcome him — a road along which he was being pursued, where he was visible to everyone, and from which he could not turn aside. At this moment that thought returned to him. Through an odd and brief conjunction of ideas the figurative road became identified with the real highway along which he was driving — and this led him suddenly to do a crazy thing.

"Where did you say you wanted to go?" he asked the girl.

"To Banska Bystritsa," she replied.

"And what are you going to do there?"

"I have a date there."

"Who with?"

"With a certain gentleman."

The car was just coming to a large crossroads. The driver slowed down so he could read the road signs, then turned off to the right.

"What will happen if you don't arrive for that date?"

"It would be your fault and you would have to take care of me."

"You obviously didn't notice that I turned off in the direction of Nove Zamky."

"Is that true? You've gone crazy!"

"Don't be afraid, I'll take care of you," said the young man.

So they drove and chatted thus — the driver and the hitchhiker who did not know each other.

The game all at once went into a higher gear. The sports car was moving away not only from the imaginary goal of Banska Bystritsa, but also from the real goal, toward which it had been heading in the morning: the Tatras and the room that had been booked. Fiction was suddenly making an assault upon real life. The young man was moving away from himself and from the implacable straight road, from which he had never strayed until now.

"But you said you were going to the Low Tatras!" The girl was surprised.

"I am going, miss, wherever I feel like going. I'm a free man and I do what I want and what it pleases me to do."

VI

When they drove into Nove Zamky it was already getting dark.

The young man had never been here before and it took him a while to orient himself. Several times he stopped the car and asked the passersby directions to the hotel. Several streets had been dug up, so that the drive to the hotel, even though it was quite close by (as all those who had been asked asserted), necessitated so many detours and roundabout routes that it was almost a quarter of an hour before they finally stopped in front of it. The hotel looked unprepossessing, but it was the only one in town and the young man didn't feel like driving on. So he said to the girl, "Wait here," and got out of the car.

Out of the car he was, of course, himself again. And it was upsetting for him to find himself in the evening somewhere completely different from his intended destination — the more so because no one had forced him to do it and as a matter of fact he hadn't even really wanted to. He blamed himself for this piece of folly, but then became reconciled to it. The room in the Tatras could wait until tomorrow and it wouldn't do any harm if they celebrated the first day of their vacation with something unexpected.

He walked through the restaurant — smoky, noisy, and crowded — and asked for the reception desk. They sent him to the back of the lobby near the staircase, where behind a glass panel a superannuated blonde was sitting beneath a board full of keys. With difficulty, he obtained the key to the only room left.

The girl, when she found herself alone, also threw off her role. She didn't feel ill-humored, though, at finding herself in an unexpected town. She was so devoted to the young man that she never had doubts about anything he did, and confidently entrusted every moment of her life to him. On the other hand the idea once again popped into her mind that perhaps — just as she was now doing — other women had waited for her man in his car, those women whom he met on business trips. But surprisingly enough this idea didn't upset her at all now. In fact, she smiled at the thought of how nice it was that today she was this other woman, this irresponsible, indecent other woman, one of those women of whom she was so jealous. It seemed to her that she was cutting them all out, that she had learned how to use their weapons; how to give the young man what until now she had not known how to give him: lightheartedness, shamelessness, and dissoluteness. A curious feeling of satisfaction filled her, because she alone had the ability to be all women and in this way (she alone) could completely captivate her lover and hold his interest.

The young man opened the car door and led the girl into the restaurant. Amid the din, the dirt, and the smoke he found a single, unoccupied table in a corner.

VII

"So how are you going to take care of me now?" asked the girl provocatively.

"What would you like for an aperitif?"

The girl wasn't too fond of alcohol, still she drank a little wine and liked vermouth fairly well. Now, however, she purposely said: "Vodka."

"Fine," said the young man. "I hope you won't get drunk on me."

"And if I do?" said the girl.

The young man did not reply but called over a waiter and ordered two vodkas and two steak dinners. In a moment the waiter brought a tray with two small glasses and placed it in front of them.

The man raised his glass, "To you!"

"Can't you think of a wittier toast?"

Something was beginning to irritate him about the girl's game. Now sitting face to face with her, he realized that it wasn't just the *words* which were turning her into a stranger, but that her *whole persona* had changed, the movements of her body and her facial expression, and that she unpalatably and faithfully resembled that type of woman whom he knew so well and for whom he felt some aversion.

And so (holding his glass in his raised hand), he corrected his toast: "O.K., then I won't drink to you, but to your kind, in which are combined so successfully the better qualities of the animal and the worse aspects of the human being."

"By 'kind' do you mean all women?" asked the girl.

"No, I mean only those who are like you."

"Anyway it doesn't seem very witty to me to compare a woman with an animal."

"O.K.," the young man was still holding his glass aloft, "then I won't drink to your kind, but to your soul. Agreed? To your soul, which lights up when it descends from your head into your belly, and which goes out when it rises back up to your head."

The girl raised her glass. "O.K., to my soul, which descends into my belly."

"I'll correct myself once more," said the young man. "To your belly, into which your soul descends."

"To my belly," said the girl, and her belly (now that they had named it specifically), as it were, responded to the call; she felt every inch of it.

Then the waiter brought their steaks and the young man ordered them another vodka and some water (this time they drank to the girl's breasts), and the conversation continued in this peculiar, frivolous tone. It irritated the young man more and more how *well able* the girl was to become the lascivious miss. If she was able to do it so well, he thought, it meant that she really *was* like that. After all, no alien soul had entered into her from somewhere in space. What she was acting now was she herself; perhaps it was the part of her being which had formerly been locked up and which the pretext of the game had let out of its cage. Perhaps the girl supposed that by means of the game she was *disowning* herself, but wasn't it the other way around? Wasn't she becoming herself only through the game? Wasn't she freeing herself through the game? No, opposite him was not sitting a strange woman in his girl's body; it was his girl, herself, no one else. He looked at her and felt growing aversion toward her.

However, it was not only aversion. The more the girl withdrew from him *psychically*, the more he longed for her *physically*. The alien quality of her soul drew attention to her body, yes, as a matter of fact it turned her body into a body for *him* as if until now it had existed for the young man hidden within clouds of compassion, tenderness, concern, love, and emotion, as if it had been lost in these clouds (yes, as if this body had been lost!). It seemed to the young man that today he was seeing his girl's body for the first time.

After her third vodka and soda the girl got up and said flirtatiously, "Excuse me."

The young man said, "May I ask you where you are going, miss?"

"To piss, if you'll permit me," said the girl and walked off between the tables back toward the plush screen.

VIII

She was pleased with the way she had astounded the young man with this word, which — in spite of all its innocence — he had never heard from her. Nothing seemed to her truer to the character of the woman she was playing than this flirtatious emphasis placed on the word in question. Yes, she was pleased, she was in the best of moods. The game captivated her. It allowed her to feel what she had not felt till now: a *feeling of happy-go-lucky irresponsibility.*

She, who was always uneasy in advance about her every next step, suddenly felt completely relaxed. The alien life in which she had become involved was a life without shame, without biographical specifications, without past or future, without obligations. It was a life that was extraordinarily free. The girl, as a hitchhiker, could do anything, *everything was permitted her.* She could say, do, and feel whatever she liked.

She walked through the room and was aware that people were watching her from all the tables. It was a new sensation, one she didn't recognize: *indecent joy caused by her body.* Until now she had never been able to get rid of the fourteen-year-old girl within herself who was ashamed of her breasts and had the disagreeable feeling that she was indecent, because they stuck out from her body and were visible. Even though she was proud of being pretty and having a good figure, this feeling of pride was always immediately curtailed by shame. She rightly suspected that feminine beauty functioned above all as sexual provocation and she found this distasteful. She longed for her body to relate only to the man she loved. When men stared at her breasts in the street it seemed to her that they were invading a piece of her most secret privacy which should belong only to herself and her lover. But now she was the hitchhiker, the woman without a destiny. In this role she was relieved of the tender bonds of her love and began to be intensely aware of her body. And her body became more aroused the more alien the eyes watching it.

She was walking past the last table when an intoxicated man, wanting to show off his worldliness, addressed her in French: "*Combien, mademoiselle?*"

The girl understood. She thrust out her breasts and fully experienced every movement of her hips, then disappeared behind the screen.

IX

It was a curious game. This curiousness was evidenced, for example, in the fact that the young man, even though he himself was playing the unknown driver remarkably well, did not for a moment stop seeing his girl in the hitchhiker. And it was precisely this that was tormenting. He saw his girl seducing a strange man, and had the bitter privilege of being present, of seeing at close quarters how she looked and of hearing what she said when she was cheating on him (when she had cheated on him, when she would cheat on him). He had the paradoxical honor of being himself the pretext of her unfaithfulness.

This was all the worse because he worshipped rather than loved her. It had always seemed to him that her inward nature was *real* only within the bounds of fidelity and purity, and that beyond these bounds it simply didn't exist. Beyond these bounds she would cease to be herself, as water ceases to be water beyond the boiling point. When he now saw her crossing this horrifying boundary with nonchalant elegance, he was filled with anger.

The girl came back from the rest room and complained: "A guy over there asked me: *Combien, mademoiselle?*"

"You shouldn't be surprised," said the young man, "after all, you look like a whore."

"Do you know that it doesn't bother me in the least?"

"Then you should go with the gentleman!"

"But I have you."

"You can go with him after me. Go and work out something with him."

"I don't find him attractive."

"But in principle you have nothing against it, having several men in one night."

"Why not, if they're good-looking."

"Do you prefer them one after the other or at the same time?"

"Either way," said the girl.

The conversation was proceeding to still greater extremes of rudeness; it shocked the girl slightly but she couldn't protest. Even in a game there lurks a lack of freedom; even a game is a trap for the players. If this had not been a game and they had really been two strangers, the hitchhiker could long ago have taken offense and left. But there's no escape from a game. A team cannot flee from the playing field before the end of the match, chess pieces cannot desert the chessboard: the boundaries of the playing field are fixed. The girl knew that she had to accept whatever form the game might take, just because it was a game. She knew that the more extreme the game became, the more it would be a game and the more obediently she would have to play it. And it was futile to evoke good sense and warn her dazed soul that she must keep her distance from the game and not take it seriously. Just because it was only a game her soul was not afraid, did not oppose the game, and narcotically sank deeper into it.

The young man called the waiter and paid. Then he got up and said to the girl, "We're going."

"Where to?" The girl feigned surprise.

"Don't ask, just come on," said the young man.

"What sort of way is that to talk to me?"

"The way I talk to whores," said the young man.

X

They went up the badly lit staircase. On the landing below the second floor a group of intoxicated men was standing near the rest room. The young man caught hold of the girl from behind so that he was holding her breast with his hand. The men by the rest room saw this and began to call out. The girl wanted to break away, but the young man yelled at her: "Keep still!" The men greeted this with general ribaldry and addressed several dirty remarks to the girl. The young man and the girl reached the second floor. He opened the door of their room and switched on the light.

It was a narrow room with two beds, a small table, a chair, and a washbasin. The young man locked the door and turned to the girl. She was standing facing him in a defiant pose with insolent sensuality in her eyes. He looked at her and tried to discover behind her lascivious expression the familiar features which he loved tenderly. It was as if he were looking at two images through the same lens, at two images superimposed one upon the other with the one showing through the other. These two images showing through each other were telling him that *everything* was in the girl, that her soul was terrifyingly amorphous, that it held faithfulness and unfaithfulness, treachery and innocence, flirtatiousness and chastity. This disorderly jumble seemed disgusting to him, like the variety to be found in a pile of garbage. Both images continued to show through each other and the young man understood that the girl differed only on the surface from other women, but deep down was the same as they: full of all possible thoughts, feelings, and vices, which justified all his secret misgivings and fits of jealousy. The impression that certain outlines delineated her as an individual was only a delusion to which the other person, the one who was looking, was subject — namely himself. It seemed to him that the girl he loved was a creation of his desire, his thoughts, and his faith and that the *real* girl now standing in front of him was hopelessly alien, hopelessly *ambiguous*. He hated her.

"What are you waiting for? Strip," he said.

The girl flirtatiously bent her head and said, "Is it necessary?"

The tone in which she said this seemed to him very familiar; it seemed to him that once long ago some other woman had said this to him, only he no longer knew which one. He longed to humiliate her. Not the hitchhiker, but his own girl. The game merged with life. The game of humiliating the hitchhiker became only a pretext for humiliating his girl. The young man had forgotten that he was playing a game. He simply hated the woman standing in front of him. He stared at her and took a fifty-crown bill from his wallet. He offered it to the girl. "Is that enough?"

The girl took the fifty crowns and said: "You don't think I'm worth much."

The young man said: "You aren't worth more."

The girl nestled up against the young man. "You can't get around me like that! You must try a different approach, you must work a little!"

She put her arms around him and moved her mouth toward his. He put his fingers on her mouth and gently pushed her away. He said: "I only kiss women I love."

"And you don't love me?"

"No."

"Whom do you love?"

"What's that got to do with you? Strip!"

XI

She had never undressed like this before. The shyness, the feeling of inner panic, the dizziness, all that she had always felt when undressing in front of the young man (and she couldn't hide in the darkness), all this was gone. She was standing in front of him self-confident, insolent, bathed in light, and astonished at where she had all of a sudden discovered the gestures, heretofore unknown to her, of a slow, provocative striptease. She took in his glances, slipping off each piece of clothing with a caressing movement and enjoying each individual stage of this exposure.

But then suddenly she was standing in front of him completely naked and at this moment it flashed through her head that now the whole game would end, that, since she had stripped off her clothes, she had also stripped away her dissimulation, and that being naked meant that she was now herself and the young man ought to come up to her now and make a gesture with which he would wipe out everything and after which would follow only their most intimate love-making. So she stood naked in front of the young man and at this moment stopped playing the game. She felt embarrassed and on her face appeared the smile, which really belonged to her — a shy and confused smile.

But the young man didn't come to her and didn't end the game. He didn't notice the familiar smile. He saw before him only the beautiful, alien body of his own girl, whom he hated. Hatred cleansed his sensuality of any sentimental coating. She wanted to come to him, but he said: "Stay where you are, I want to have a good look at you." Now he longed only to treat her like a whore. But the young man had never had a whore and the ideas he had about them came from literature and hearsay. So he turned to these ideas and the first thing he recalled was the image of a woman in black underwear (and black stockings) dancing on the shiny top of a piano. In the little hotel room there was no piano, there was only a small table covered with a linen cloth leaning against the wall. He ordered the girl to climb up on it. The girl made a pleading gesture, but the young man said, "You've been paid."

When she saw the look of unshakable obsession in the young man's eyes, she tried to go on with the game, even though she no longer could and no longer knew how. With tears in her eyes she climbed onto the table. The top was scarcely three feet square and one leg was a little bit shorter than the others so that standing on it the girl felt unsteady.

But the young man was pleased with the naked figure, now towering above him, and the girl's shy insecurity merely inflamed his imperiousness. He wanted to see her body in all positions and from all sides, as he imagined other men had seen it and would see it. He was vulgar and lascivious. He used words that she had never heard from him in her life. She wanted to refuse, she wanted to be released from the game. She called him by his first name, but he immediately yelled at her that she had no right to address him so intimately. And so eventually in confusion and on the verge of tears, she obeyed, and bent forward and squatted according to the young man's wishes, saluted, and then wiggled her hips as she did the Twist for him. During a slightly more violent movement, when the cloth slipped beneath her feet and she nearly fell, the young man caught her and dragged her to the bed.

He had intercourse with her. She was glad that at least now finally the unfortunate game would end and they would again be the two people they had been before and would love each other. She wanted to press her mouth against his. But the young man pushed her head away and repeated that he only kissed women he loved. She burst into loud sobs. But she wasn't even allowed to cry, because the young man's furious passion gradually won over her body, which then silenced the complaint of her soul. On the bed there were soon two bodies in perfect harmony, two sensual bodies, alien to each other. This was exactly what the girl had most dreaded all her life and had scrupulously avoided till now: love-making without emotion or love. She knew that she had crossed the forbidden boundary, but she proceeded across it without objections and as a full participant — only somewhere, far off in a corner of her consciousness, did she feel horror at the thought that she had never known such pleasure, never so much pleasure as at this moment — beyond the boundary.

XII

Then it was all over. The young man got up off the girl and, reaching out for the long cord hanging over the bed, switched off the light. He didn't want to see the girl's face. He knew that the game was over, but didn't feel like returning to their customary relationship. He feared this return. He lay beside the girl in the dark in such a way that their bodies would not touch.

After a moment he heard her sobbing quietly. The girl's hand diffidently, childishly touched his. It touched, withdrew, then touched again, and then a pleading, sobbing voice broke the silence, calling him by his name and saying, "I am me, I am me. . . ."

The young man was silent, he didn't move, and he was aware of the sad emptiness of the girl's assertion, in which the unknown was defined in terms of the same unknown quantity.

And the girl soon passed from sobbing to loud crying and went on endlessly repeating this pitiful tautology: "I am me, I am me, I am me. . . ."

The young man began to call compassion to his aid (he had to call it from afar, because it was nowhere near at hand), so as to be able to calm the girl. There were still thirteen days' vacation before them.   [1969]

DAVID HERBERT LAWRENCE (1885–1930) *was born the son of a coal miner in the industrial town of Eastwood, in Nottinghamshire, England. His mother had been a schoolteacher, and she was frustrated by the hard existence of a coal miner's wife. Through her financial sacrifices, Lawrence was able to complete high school; then he studied to become a teacher. In 1909, shortly after he began teaching in South London, he published his first novel,* The White Peacock, *but he was not established as a major literary figure until the publication of* Sons and Lovers *in 1913. Much of his fiction, like this novel and the story "Odour of Chrysanthemums," is about characters caught between their unsatisfactory relationships with others and their struggle to break free. Lawrence sought an ideal balance or, as he wrote in the novel* Women in Love *(1920), a "star equilibrium," in which two beings are attracted to each other but never lose their individuality. He felt that "no emotion is supreme, or exclusively worth living for. All emotions go to the achieving of a living relationship between a human being and the other human being or creature or thing he becomes purely related to."*

A prolific writer, Lawrence suffered from tuberculosis and spent years wandering in Italy, Australia, Mexico, New Mexico, and southern France, seeking a warm, sunny climate. He also fled to primitive societies to escape the industrialization and commercialism of Western life. A virulent social critic, he was frequently harassed by censorship because his short stories, novels, and poetry were often explicitly sexual and he always challenged conventional moral attitudes. Literature, for Lawrence, had two great functions: providing an emotional experience, and then, if the reader had the courage of his or her own feelings and could live imaginatively, becoming "a mine of practical truth."

Lawrence wrote stories all his life, publishing a first collection, The Prussian Officer, *in 1914; it was followed by four other collections. In 1961 his stories were compiled in a three-volume paperback edition that has gone through numerous reprintings. The style of the early stories is harshly realistic, but Lawrence's depiction of his characters' emotional situations changed in his later work, where he created fantasies like his famous and chilling story "The Rocking-Horse Winner."*

RELATED COMMENTARIES: *Janice H. Harris, "A Psychosocial Explication of Lawrence's 'The Rocking-Horse Winner,'" page 1428; D. H. Lawrence, "The Lust of Hate in Poe's 'The Cask of Amontillado,'" page 1446.*

D. H. LAWRENCE

Odour of Chrysanthemums

I

The small locomotive engine, Number 4, came clanking, stumbling down from Selston with seven full wagons. It appeared round the corner with loud threats of speed, but the colt that it startled from among the gorse, which still flickered indistinctly in the raw afternoon, out-distanced it at a canter. A woman, walking up the railway line to Underwood, drew back into the hedge, held her basket aside, and watched the footplate[1] of the engine advancing. The trucks thumped heavily past, one by one, with slow inevitable movement, as she stood insignificantly trapped between the jolting black wagons and the hedge; then they curved away towards the coppice where the withered oak leaves dropped noiselessly, while the birds, pulling at the scarlet hips beside the track, made off into the dusk that had already crept into the spinney. In the open, the smoke from the engine sank and cleaved to the rough grass. The fields were dreary and forsaken, and in the marshy strip that led to the whimsey, a reedy pit-pond, the fowls had already abandoned their run among the alders, to roost in the tarred fowl-house. The pit-bank loomed up beyond the pond, flames like red sores licking its ashy sides, in the afternoon's stagnant light. Just beyond rose the tapering chimneys and the clumsy black headstocks of Brinsley Colliery. The two wheels were spinning fast up against the sky, and the winding engine rapped out its little spasms. The miners were being turned up.

The engine whistled as it came into the wide bay of railway lines beside the colliery, where rows of trucks stood in harbour.

Miners, single, trailing and in groups, passed like shadows diverging home. At the edge of the ribbed level of sidings squat a low cottage, three steps down from the cinder track. A large bony vine clutched at the house, as if to claw down the tiled roof. Round the bricked yard grew a few wintry primroses. Beyond, the long garden sloped down to a bush-covered brook course. There were some twiggy apple trees, winter-crack trees, and ragged cabbages. Beside the path hung dishevelled pink chrysanthemums, like pink cloths hung on bushes. A woman came stooping out of the felt-covered fowl-house, half-way down the garden. She closed and padlocked the door, then drew herself erect, having brushed some bits from her white apron.

She was a tall woman of imperious mien, handsome, with definite black eyebrows. Her smooth black hair was parted exactly. For a few moments she stood steadily watching the miners as they passed along the railway: then she

---

[1] Platform on early locomotives for the engineer to stand on.

turned towards the brook course. Her face was calm and set, her mouth was closed with disillusionment. After a moment she called:

"John!" There was no answer. She waited, and then said distinctly:

"Where are you?"

"Here!" replied a child's sulky voice from among the bushes. The woman looked piercingly through the dusk.

"Are you at that brook?" she asked sternly.

For answer the child showed himself before the raspberry-canes that rose like whips. He was a small, sturdy boy of five. He stood quite still, defiantly.

"Oh!" said the mother, conciliated. "I thought you were down at that wet brook — and you remember what I told you —"

The boy did not move or answer.

"Come, come on in," she said more gently, "it's getting dark. There's your grandfather's engine coming down the line!"

The lad advanced slowly, with resentful, taciturn movement. He was dressed in trousers and waistcoat of cloth that was too thick and hard for the size of the garments. They were evidently cut down from a man's clothes.

As they went slowly towards the house he tore at the ragged wisps of chrysanthemums and dropped the petals in handfuls among the path.

"Don't do that — it does look nasty," said his mother. He refrained, and she, suddenly pitiful, broke off a twig with three or four wan flowers and held them against her face. When mother and son reached the yard her hand hesitated, and instead of laying the flower aside, she pushed it in her apron-band. The mother and son stood at the foot of the three steps looking across the bay of lines at the passing home of the miners. The trundle of the small train was imminent. Suddenly the engine loomed past the house and came to a stop opposite the gate.

The engine-driver, a short man with round grey beard, leaned out of the cab high above the woman.

"Have you got a cup of tea?" he said in a cheery, hearty fashion.

It was her father. She went in, saying she would mash. Directly, she returned.

"I didn't come to see you on Sunday," began the little grey-bearded man.

"I didn't expect you," said his daughter.

The engine-driver winced; then, reassuming his cheery, airy manner, he said:

"Oh, have you heard then? Well, and what do you think —?"

"I think it is soon enough," she replied.

At her brief censure the little man made an impatient gesture, and said coaxingly, yet with dangerous coldness:

"Well, what's a man to do? It's no sort of life for a man of my years, to sit at my own hearth like a stranger. And if I'm going to marry again it may as well be soon as late — what does it matter to anybody?"

The woman did not reply, but turned and went into the house. The man in the engine-cab stood assertive, till she returned with a cup of tea and a piece of bread and butter on a plate. She went up the steps and stood near the footplate of the hissing engine.

"You needn't 'a' brought me bread an' butter," said her father. "But a cup of tea" — he sipped appreciatively — "it's very nice." He sipped for a moment or two, then: "I hear as Walter's got another bout on," he said.

"When hasn't he?" said the woman bitterly.

"I heerd tell of him in the 'Lord Nelson' braggin' as he was going to spend that b —— afore he went: half a sovereign that was."

"When?" asked the woman.

"A' Sat'day night — I know that's true."

"Very likely," she laughed bitterly. "He gives me twenty-three shillings."

"Aye, it's a nice thing, when a man can do nothing with his money but make a beast of himself!" said the grey-whiskered man. The woman turned her head away. Her father swallowed the last of his tea and handed her the cup.

"Aye," he sighed, wiping his mouth. "It's a settler, it is ——."

He put his hand on the lever. The little engine strained and groaned, and the train rumbled towards the crossing. The woman again looked across the metals. Darkness was settling over the spaces of the railway and trucks: the miners, in grey sombre groups, were still passing home. The winding engine pulsed hurriedly, with brief pauses. Elizabeth Bates looked at the dreary flow of men, then she went indoors. Her husband did not come.

The kitchen was small and full of firelight; red coals piled glowing up the chimney mouth. All the life of the room seemed in the white, warm hearth and the steel fender reflecting the red fire. The cloth was laid for tea; cups glinted in the shadows. At the back, where the lowest stairs protruded into the room, the boy sat struggling with a knife and a piece of white wood. He was almost hidden in the shadow. It was half-past four. They had but to await the father's coming to begin tea. As the mother watched her son's sullen little struggle with the wood, she saw herself in his silence and pertinacity; she saw the father in her child's indifference to all but himself. She seemed to be occupied by her husband. He had probably gone past his home, slunk past his own door, to drink before he came in, while his dinner spoiled and wasted in waiting. She glanced at the clock, then took the potatoes to strain them in the yard. The garden and fields beyond the brook were closed in uncertain darkness. When she rose with the saucepan, leaving the drain steaming into the night behind her, she saw the yellow lamps were lit along the high road that went up the hill away beyond the space of the railway lines and the field.

Then again she watched the men trooping home, fewer now and fewer.

Indoors the fire was sinking and the room was dark red. The woman put her saucepan on the hob, and set a batter-pudding near the mouth of the oven. Then she stood unmoving. Directly, gratefully, came quick young steps to the door. Someone hung on the latch a moment, then a little girl entered and began pulling off her outdoor things, dragging a mass of curls, just ripening from gold to brown, over her eyes with her hat.

Her mother chid her for coming late from school, and said she would have to keep her at home the dark winter days.

"Why, mother, it's hardly a bit dark yet. The lamp's not lighted, and my father's not home."

"No, he isn't. But it's a quarter to five! Did you see anything of him?"

The child became serious. She looked at her mother with large, wistful blue eyes.

"No, mother, I've never seen him. Why? Has he come up an' gone past, to Old Brinsley? He hasn't, mother, 'cos I never saw him."

"He'd watch that," said the mother bitterly, "he'd take care as you didn't see him. But you may depend upon it, he's seated in the 'Prince o' Wales.' He wouldn't be this late."

The girl looked at her mother piteously.

"Let's have our teas, mother, should we?" said she.

The mother called John to table. She opened the door once more and looked out across the darkness of the lines. All was deserted: she could not hear the winding-engines.

"Perhaps," she said to herself, "he's stopped to get some ripping done."

They sat down to tea. John, at the end of the table near the door, was almost lost in the darkness. Their faces were hidden from each other. The girl crouched against the fender slowly moving a thick piece of bread before the fire. The lad, his face a dusky mark on the shadow, sat watching her who was transfigured in the red glow.

"I do think it's beautiful to look in the fire," said the child.

"Do you?" said her mother. "Why?"

"It's so red, and full of little caves —— and it feels so nice, and you can fair smell it."

"It'll want mending directly," replied her mother, "and then if your father comes he'll carry on and say there never is a fire when a man comes home sweating from the pit. A public house is always warm enough."

There was silence till the boy said complainingly: "Make haste, our Annie."

"Well, I am doing! I can't make the fire do it no faster, can I?"

"She keeps wafflin' it about so's to make 'er slow," grumbled the boy.

"Don't have such an evil imagination, child," replied the mother.

Soon the room was busy in the darkness with the crisp sound of crunching. The mother ate very little. She drank her tea determinedly, and sat thinking. When she rose her anger was evident in the stern unbending of her head. She looked at the pudding in the fender and broke out:

"It is a scandalous thing as a man can't even come home to his dinner! If it's crozzled up to a cinder I don't see why I should care. Past his very door he goes to get to a public-house, and here I sit with his dinner waiting for him —"

She went out. As she dropped piece after piece of coal on the red fire, the shadows fell on the walls, till the room was almost in total darkness.

"I canna see," grumbled the invisible John. In spite of herself, the mother laughed.

"You know the way to your mouth," she said. She set the dust-pan outside the door. When she came again like a shadow on the hearth, the lad repeated, complaining sulkily:

"I canna see."

"Good gracious!" cried the mother irritably, "you're as bad as your father if it's a bit dusk!"

Nevertheless, she took a paper spill from a sheaf on the mantelpiece and proceeded to light the lamp that hung from the ceiling in the middle of the room. As she reached up, her figure displayed itself just rounding with maternity.

"Oh, mother ——!" exclaimed the girl.

"What?" said the woman, suspended in the act of putting the lamp-glass over the flame. The copper reflector shone handsomely on her, as she stood with uplifted arm, turning to face her daughter.

"You've got a flower in your apron!" said the child, in a little rapture at this unusual event.

"Goodness me!" exclaimed the woman, relieved. "One would think the house was afire." She replaced the glass and waited a moment before turning up the wick. A pale shadow was seen floating vaguely on the floor.

"Let me smell!" said the child, still rapturously, coming forward and putting her face to her mother's waist.

"Go along, silly!" said the mother, turning up the lamp. The light revealed their suspense so that the woman felt it almost unbearable. Annie was still bending at her waist. Irritably, the mother took the flowers out from her apron-band.

"Oh, mother — don't take them out!" Annie cried, catching her hand and trying to replace the sprig.

"Such nonsense!" said the mother, turning away. The child put the pale chrysanthemums to her lips, murmuring:

"Don't they smell beautiful!"

Her mother gave a short laugh.

"No," she said, "not to me. It was chrysanthemums when I married him, and chrysanthemums when you were born, and the first time they ever brought him home drunk, he'd got brown chrysanthemums in his button-hole."

She looked at the children. Their eyes and their parted lips were wondering. The mother sat rocking in silence for some time. Then she looked at the clock.

"Twenty minutes to six!" In a tone of fine bitter carelessness she continued: "Eh, he'll not come now till they bring him. There he'll stick! But he needn't come rolling in here in his pit-dirt, for *I* won't wash him. He can lie on the floor —— Eh, what a fool I've been, what a fool! And this is what I came here for, to this dirty hole, rats and all, for him to slink past his very door. Twice last week — he's begun now ——"

She silenced herself, and rose to clear the table.

While for an hour or more the children played, subduedly intent, fertile of imagination, united in fear of the mother's wrath, and in dread of their father's home-coming, Mrs. Bates sat in her rocking-chair making a "singlet" of thick cream-coloured flannel, which gave a dull wounded sound as she tore off the grey edge. She worked at her sewing with energy, listening to the children, and her anger wearied itself, lay down to rest, opening its eyes from time to time and steadily watching, its ears raised to listen. Sometimes even her anger quailed and shrank, and the mother suspended her sewing, tracing the footsteps that thudded along the sleepers outside: she would lift her head sharply to bid the children "hush," but she recovered herself in time, and the footsteps went past the gate, and the children were not flung out of their play-world.

But at last Annie sighed, and gave in. She glanced at her wagon of slippers, and loathed the game. She turned plaintively to her mother.

"Mother!" — but she was inarticulate.

John crept out like a frog from under the sofa. His mother glanced up.

"Yes," she said, "just look at those shirt-sleeves!"

The boy held them out to survey them, saying nothing. Then somebody called in a hoarse voice away down the line, and suspense bristled in the room, till two people had gone by outside, talking.

"It is time for bed," said the mother.

"My father hasn't come," wailed Annie plaintively. But her mother was primed with courage.

"Never mind. They'll bring him when he does come — like a log." She meant there would be no scene. "And he may sleep on the floor till he wakes himself. I know he'll not go to work to-morrow after this!"

The children had their hands and faces wiped with a flannel. They were very quiet. When they had put on their night-dresses, they said their prayers, the boy mumbling. The mother looked down at them, at the brown silken bush of intertwining curls in the nape of the girl's neck, at the little black head of the lad, and her heart burst with anger at their father, who caused all three such distress. The children hid their faces in her skirts for comfort.

When Mrs. Bates came down, the room was strangely empty, with a tension of expectancy. She took up her sewing and stitched for some time without raising her head. Meantime her anger was tinged with fear.

II

The clock struck eight and she rose suddenly, dropping her sewing on her chair. She went to the stair-foot door, opened it, listening. Then she went out, locking the door behind her.

Something scuffled in the yard, and she started, though she knew it was only the rats with which the place was over-run. The night was very dark. In the great bay of railway lines, bulked with trucks, there was no trace of light, only away back she could see a few yellow lamps at the pit-top, and the red smear of the burning pit-bank on the night. She hurried along the edge of the track, then, crossing the converging lines, came to the stile by the white gates, whence she emerged on the road. Then the fear which had led her shrank. People were walking up to New Brinsley; she saw the lights in the houses; twenty yards farther on were the broad windows of the "Prince of Wales," very warm and bright, and the loud voices of men could be heard distinctly. What a fool she had been to imagine that anything had happened to him! He was merely drinking over there at the "Prince of Wales." She faltered. She had never yet been to fetch him, and she never would go. So she continued her walk towards the long straggling line of houses, standing back on the highway. She entered a passage between the dwellings.

"Mr. Rigley? — Yes! Did you want him? No, he's not in at this minute."

The raw-boned woman leaned forward from her dark scullery and peered at the other, upon whom fell a dim light through the blind of the kitchen window.

"Is it Mrs. Bates?" she asked in a tone tinged with respect.

"Yes. I wondered if your Master was at home. Mine hasn't come yet."

"'Asn't 'e! Oh, Jack's been 'ome an' 'ad 'is dinner an' gone out. 'E's just gone for 'alf an hour afore bed-time. Did you call at the 'Prince of Wales'?"

"No ——"

"No, you didn't like ——! It's not very nice." The other woman was indulgent. There was an awkward pause. "Jack never said nothink about — about your Master," she said.

"No! — I expect he's stuck in there!"

Elizabeth Bates said this bitterly, and with recklessness. She knew that the woman across the yard was standing at her door listening, but she did not care. As she turned:

"Stop a minute! I'll just go an' ask Jack if 'e knows anythink," said Mrs. Rigley.

"Oh no — I wouldn't like to put ——!"

"Yes, I will, if you'll just step inside an' see as th' childer doesn't come downstairs and set theirselves afire."

Elizabeth Bates, murmuring a remonstrance, stepped inside. The other woman apologised for the state of the room.

The kitchen needed apology. There were little frocks and trousers and childish undergarments on the squab and on the floor, and a litter of playthings everywhere. On the black American cloth of the table were pieces of bread and cake, crusts, slops, and a teapot with cold tea.

"Eh, ours is just as bad," said Elizabeth Bates, looking at the woman, not at the house. Mrs. Rigley put a shawl over her head and hurried out, saying:

"I shanna be a minute."

The other sat, noting with faint disapproval the general untidiness of the room. Then she fell to counting the shoes of various sizes scattered over the floor. There were twelve. She sighed and said to herself: "No wonder!" — glancing at the litter. There came the scratching of two pairs of feet on the yard, and the Rigleys entered. Elizabeth Bates rose. Rigley was a big man, with very large bones. His head looked particularly bony. Across his temple was a blue scar, caused by a wound got in the pit, a wound in which the coal-dust remained blue like tattooing.

"'Asna 'e come whoam yit?" asked the man, without any form of greeting, but with deference and sympathy. "I couldna say wheer he is — 'e's non ower theer!" — he jerked his head to signify the "Prince of Wales."

"'E's 'appen gone up to th' 'Yew,'" said Mrs. Rigley.

There was another pause. Rigley had evidently something to get off his mind:

"Ah left 'im finishin' a stint," he began. "Loose-all 'ad bin gone about ten minutes when we com'n away, an' I shouted: 'Are ter comin', Walt?' an' 'e said: 'Go on, Ah shanna be but a' ef a minnit,' so we com'n ter th' bottom, me an' Bowers, thinkin' as 'e wor just behint, an' 'ud come up i' th' next bantle —— "

He stood perplexed, as if answering a charge of deserting his mate. Elizabeth Bates, now again certain of disaster, hastened to reassure him:

"I expect 'e's gone up to th' 'Yew Tree,' as you say. It' not the first time. I've fretted myself into a fever before now. He'll come home when they carry him."

"Ay, isn't it too bad!" deplored the other woman.

"I'll just step up to Dick's an' see if 'e *is* theer," offered the man, afraid of appearing alarmed, afraid of taking liberties.

"Oh, I wouldn't think of bothering you that far," said Elizabeth Bates, with emphasis, but he knew she was glad of his offer.

As they stumbled up the entry, Elizabeth Bates heard Rigley's wife run across the yard and open her neighbour's door. At this, suddenly all the blood in her body seemed to switch away from her heart.

"Mind!" warned Rigley. "Ah've said many a time as Ah'd fill up them ruts in this entry, sumb'dy 'll be breakin' their legs yit."

She recovered herself and walked quickly along with the miner.

"I don't like leaving the children in bed, and nobody in the house," she said.

"No, you dunna!" he replied courteously. They were soon at the gate of the cottage.

"Well, I shanna be many minnits. Dunna you be frettin' now, 'e'll be all right," said the butty.[2]

"Thank you very much, Mr. Rigley," she replied.

"You're welcome!" he stammered, moving away. "I shanna be many minnits."

The house was quiet. Elizabeth Bates took off her hat and shawl, and rolled back the rug. When she had finished, she sat down. It was a few minutes past nine. She was startled by the rapid chuff of the winding-engine at the pit, and the sharp whirr of the brakes on the rope as it descended. Again she felt the painful sweep of her blood, and she put her hand to her side, saying aloud: "Good gracious! — it's only the nine o'clock deputy going down," rebuking herself.

She sat still listening. Half an hour of this, and she was wearied out.

"What am I working myself up like this for?" she said pitiably to herself, "I s'll only be doing myself some damage."

---

[2] A fellow workman in a colliery.

She took out her sewing again.

At a quarter to ten there were footsteps. One person! She watched for the door to open. It was an elderly woman, in a black bonnet and a black woollen shawl — his mother. She was about sixty years old, pale, with blue eyes, and her face all wrinkled and lamentable. She shut the door and turned to her daughter-in-law peevishly.

"Eh, Lizzie, whatever shall we do, whatever shall we do!" she cried.

Elizabeth drew back a little, sharply.

"What is it, mother?" she said.

The elder woman seated herself on the sofa.

"I don't know, child, I can't tell you!" — she shook her head slowly. Elizabeth sat watching her, anxious and vexed.

"I don't know," replied the grandmother, sighing very deeply. "There's no end to my troubles, there isn't. The things I've gone through, I'm sure it's enough ——!" She wept without wiping her eyes, the tears running.

"But, mother," interrupted Elizabeth, "what do you mean? What is it?"

The grandmother slowly wiped her eyes. The fountains of her tears were stopped by Elizabeth's directness. She wiped her eyes slowly.

"Poor child! Eh, you poor thing!" she moaned. "I don't know what we're going to do, I don't — and you as you are — it's a thing, it is indeed!"

Elizabeth waited.

"Is he dead?" she asked, and at the words her heart swung violently, though she felt a slight flush of shame at the ultimate extravagance of the question. Her words sufficiently frightened the old lady, almost brought her to herself.

"Don't say so, Elizabeth! We'll hope it's not as bad as that; no, may the Lord spare us that, Elizabeth. Jack Rigley came just as I was sittin' down to a glass afore going to bed, an' 'e said: "Appen you'll go down th' line, Mrs. Bates. Walt's had an accident. 'Appen you'll go an' sit wi' 'er till we can get him home.' I hadn't time to ask him a word afore he was gone. An' I put my bonnet on an' come straight down, Lizzie. I thought to myself: 'Eh, that poor blessed child, if anybody should come an' tell her of a sudden, there's no knowing' what'll 'appen to 'er.' You mustn't let it upset you, Lizzie — or you know what to expect. How long is it, six months — or is it five, Lizzie? Ay!" — the old woman shook her head — "time slips on, it slips on! Ay!"

Elizabeth's thoughts were busy elsewhere. If he was killed — would she be able to manage on the little pension and what she could earn? — she counted up rapidly. If he was hurt — they wouldn't take him to the hospital — how tiresome he would be to nurse! — but perhaps she'd be able to get him away from the drink and his hateful ways. She would — while he was ill. The tears offered to come to her eyes at the picture. But what sentimental luxury was this she was beginning? She turned to consider the children. At any rate she was absolutely necessary for them. They were her business.

"Ay!" repeated the old woman, "it seems but a week or two since he brought me his first wages. Ay — he was a good lad, Elizabeth, he was, in his way. I don't know why he got to be such a trouble, I don't. He was a happy lad at home, only full of spirits. But there's no mistake he's been a handful of trouble, he has! I hope the Lord'll spare him to mend his ways. I hope so, I hope so. You've had a sight o' trouble with him, Elizabeth, you have indeed. But he was a jolly enough lad wi' me, he was, I can assure you. I don't know how it is. . . ."

The old woman continued to muse aloud, a monotonous irritating sound, while Elizabeth thought concentratedly, startled once, when she heard the winding-engine chuff quickly, and the brakes skirr with a shriek. Then she heard the engine more slowly, and the brakes made no sound. The old woman did not notice. Elizabeth waited in suspense. The mother-in-law talked, with lapses into silence.

"But he wasn't your son, Lizzie, an' it makes a difference. Whatever he was, I remember him when he was little, an' I learned to understand him and to make allowances. You've got to make allowances for them ——"

It was half-past ten, and the old woman was saying: "But it's trouble from beginning to end; you're never too old for trouble, never too old for that ——" when the gate banged back, and there were heavy feet on the steps.

"I'll go, Lizzie, let me go," cried the old woman, rising. But Elizabeth was at the door. It was a man in pit-clothes.

"They're bringin' 'im, Misses," he said. Elizabeth's heart halted a moment. Then it surged on again, almost suffocating her.

"Is he — is it bad?" she asked.

The man turned away, looking at the darkness:

"The doctor says 'e'd been dead hours. 'E saw 'im i' th' lamp-cabin."

The old woman, who stood just behind Elizabeth, dropped into a chair, and folded her hands, crying: "Oh, my boy, my boy!"

"Hush!" said Elizabeth, with a sharp twitch of a frown. "Be still, mother, don't waken th' children: I wouldn't have them down for anything!"

The old woman moaned softly, rocking herself. The man was drawing away. Elizabeth took a step forward.

"How was it?" she asked.

"Well, I couldn't say for sure," the man replied, very ill at ease. "'E wor finishin' a stint an' th' butties 'ad gone, an' a lot o' stuff come down atop 'n 'im."

"And crushed him?" cried the widow, with a shudder.

"No," said the man, "it fell at th' back of 'im. 'E wor under th' face, an' it niver touched 'im. It shut 'im in. It seems 'e wor smothered."

Elizabeth shrank back. She heard the old woman behind her cry:

"What? — what did 'e say it was?"

The man replied, more loudly: "'E wor smothered!"

Then the old woman wailed aloud, and this relieved Elizabeth.

"Oh, mother," she said, putting her hand on the old woman, "don't waken th' children, don't waken th' children."

She wept a little, unknowing, while the old mother rocked herself and moaned. Elizabeth remembered that they were bringing him home, and she must be ready. "They'll lay him in the parlour," she said to herself, standing a moment pale and perplexed.

Then she lighted a candle and went into the tiny room. The air was cold and damp, but she could not make a fire, there was no fireplace. She set down the candle and looked round. The candlelight glittered on the lustre-glasses, on the two vases that held some of the pink chrysanthemums, and on the dark mahogany. There was a cold, deathly smell of chrysanthemums in the room. Elizabeth stood looking at the flowers. She turned away, and calculated whether there would be room to lay him on the floor, between the couch and the chiffonier. She pushed the chairs aside. There would be room to lay him down and to step round him. Then she fetched the old red tablecloth, and another old cloth, spreading them down to save her bit of carpet. She shivered on leaving the parlour; so, from the dresser drawer she took a clean shirt and put it at the fire to air. All the time her mother-in-law was rocking herself in the chair and moaning.

"You'll have to move from there, mother," said Elizabeth. "They'll be bringing him in. Come in the rocker."

The old mother rose mechanically, and seated herself by the fire, continuing to lament. Elizabeth went into the pantry for another candle, and there, in the little pent-house under the naked tiles, she heard them coming. She stood still in the pantry doorway, listening. She heard them pass the end of the house, and come awkwardly down the three steps, a jumble of shuffling footsteps and muttering voices. The old woman was silent. The men were in the yard.

Then Elizabeth heard Matthews, the manager of the pit, say: "You go in first, Jim. Mind!"

The door came open, and the two women saw a collier backing into the room, holding one end of a stretcher, on which they could see the nailed pit-boots of the dead man. The two carriers halted, the man at the head stooping to the lintel of the door.

"Wheer will you have him?" asked the manager, a short, white-bearded man.

Elizabeth roused herself and came from the pantry carrying the unlighted candle.

"In the parlour," she said.

"In there, Jim!" pointed the manager, and the carriers backed round into the tiny room. The coat with which they had covered the body fell off as they awkwardly turned through the two doorways, and the women saw their man, naked to the waist, lying stripped for work. The old woman began to moan in a low voice of horror.

"Lay th' stretcher at th' side," snapped the manager, "an' put 'im on th' cloths. Mind now, mind! Look you now ——!"

One of the men had knocked off a vase of chrysanthemums. He stared awkwardly, then they set down the stretcher. Elizabeth did not look at her husband. As soon as she could get in the room, she went and picked up the broken vase and the flowers.

"Wait a minute!" she said.

The three men waited in silence while she mopped up the water with a duster.

"Eh, what a job, what a job, to be sure!" the manager was saying, rubbing his brow with trouble and perplexity. "Never knew such a thing in my life, never! He'd no business to ha' been left. I never knew such a thing in my life! Fell over him clean as a whistle, an' shut him in. Not four foot of space, there wasn't — yet it scarce bruised him."

He looked down at the dead man, lying prone, half naked, all grimed with coal-dust.

"'Sphyxiated,' the doctor said. It *is* the most terrible job I've ever known. Seems as if it was done o' purpose. Clean over him, an' shut 'im in, like a mouse-trap" — he made a sharp, descending gesture with his hand.

The colliers standing by jerked aside their heads in hopeless comment.

The horror of the thing bristled upon them all.

Then they heard the girl's voice upstairs calling shrilly: "Mother, mother — who is it? Mother, who is it?"

Elizabeth hurried to the foot of the stairs and opened the door:

"Go to sleep!" she commanded sharply. "What are you shouting about? Go to sleep at once — there's nothing ——"

Then she began to mount the stairs. They could hear her on the boards, and on the plaster floor of the little bedroom. They could hear her distinctly:

"What's the matter now? — what's the matter with you, silly thing?" — her voice was much agitated, with an unreal gentleness.

"I thought it was some men come," said the plaintive voice of the child. "Has he come?"

"Yes, they've brought him. There's nothing to make a fuss about. Go to sleep now, like a good child."

They could hear her voice in the bedroom, they waited whilst she covered the children under the bedclothes.

"Is he drunk?" asked the girl, timidly, faintly.

"No! No — he's not! He — he's asleep."

"Is he asleep downstairs?"

"Yes — and don't make a noise."

There was silence for a moment, then the men heard the frightened child again:

"What's that noise?"

"It's nothing, I tell you, what are you bothering for?"

The noise was the grandmother moaning. She was oblivious of everything, sitting on her chair rocking and moaning. The manager put his hand on her arm and bade her "Sh — sh!!"

The old woman opened her eyes and looked at him. She was shocked by this interruption, and seemed to wonder.

"What time is it?" the plaintive thin voice of the child, sinking back unhappily into sleep, asked this last question.

"Ten o'clock," answered the mother more softly. Then she must have bent down and kissed the children.

Matthews beckoned to the men to come away. They put on their caps and took up the stretcher. Stepping over the body, they tiptoed out of the house. None of them spoke till they were far from the wakeful children.

When Elizabeth came down she found her mother alone on the parlour floor, leaning over the dead man, the tears dropping on him.

"We must lay him out," the wife said. She put on the kettle, then returning knelt at the feet, and began to unfasten the knotted leather laces. The room was clammy and dim with only one candle, so that she had to bend her face almost to the floor. At last she got off the heavy boots and put them away.

"You must help me now," she whispered to the old woman. Together they stripped the man.

When they arose, saw him lying in the naïve dignity of death, the women stood arrested in fear and respect. For a few moments they remained still, looking down, the old mother whimpering. Elizabeth felt counter-manded. She saw him, how utterly inviolable he lay in himself. She had nothing to do with him. She could not accept it. Stooping, she laid her hand on him, in claim. He was still warm, for the mine was hot where he had died. His mother had his face between her hands, and was murmuring incoher-ently. The old tears fell in succession as drops from wet leaves; the mother was not weeping, merely her tears flowed. Elizabeth embraced the body of her husband, with cheek and lips. She seemed to be listening, inquiring, trying to get some connection. But she could not. She was driven away. He was impregnable.

She rose, went into the kitchen, where she poured warm water into a bowl, brought soap and flannel and a soft towel.

"I must wash him," she said.

Then the old mother rose stiffly, and watched Elizabeth as she carefully washed his face, carefully brushing the big blond moustache from his mouth with the flannel. She was afraid with a bottomless fear, so she ministered to him. The old woman, jealous, said:

"Let me wipe him!" — and she kneeled on the other side drying slowly as Elizabeth washed, her big black bonnet sometimes brushing the dark head of her daughter-in-law. They worked thus in silence for a long time. They never forgot it was death, and the touch of the man's dead body gave them strange emotions, different in each of the women; a great dread possessed them both, the mother felt the lie was given to her womb, she was denied; the wife felt the utter isolation of the human soul, the child within her was a weight apart from her.

At last it was finished. He was a man of handsome body, and his face showed no traces of drink. He was blond, full-fleshed, with fine limbs. But he was dead.

"Bless him," whispered his mother, looking always at his face, and speaking out of sheer terror. "Dear lad — bless him!" She spoke in a faint, sibilant ecstasy of fear and mother love.

Elizabeth sank down again to the floor, and put her face against his neck, and trembled and shuddered. But she had to draw away again. He was dead, and her living flesh had no place against his. A great dread and weariness held her: she was so unavailing. Her life was gone like this.

"White as milk he is, clear as a twelve-month baby, bless him, the darling!" the old mother murmured to herself. "Not a mark on him, clear and clean and white, beautiful as ever a child was made," she murmured with pride. Elizabeth kept her face hidden.

"He went peaceful, Lizzie — peaceful as sleep. Isn't he beautiful, the lamb? Ay — he must ha' made his peace, Lizzie. 'Appen he made it all right, Lizzie, shut in there. He'd have time. He wouldn't look like this if he hadn't made his peace. The lamb, the dear lamb. 'Eh, but he had a hearty laugh. I loved to hear it. He had the heartiest laugh, Lizzie, as a lad ——"

Elizabeth looked up. The man's mouth was fallen back, slightly open under the cover of the moustache. The eyes, half shut, did not show glazed in the obscurity. Life with its smoky burning gone from him, had left him apart and utterly alien to her. And she knew what a stranger he was to her. In her womb was ice of fear, because of this separate stranger with whom she had been living as one flesh. Was this what it all meant — utter, intact separateness, obscured by heat of living? In dread she turned her face away. The fact was too deadly. There had been nothing between them, and yet they had come together, exchanging their nakedness repeatedly. Each time he had taken her, they had been two isolated beings, far apart as now. He was no more responsible than she. The child was like ice in her womb. For as she looked at the dead man, her mind, cold and detached, said clearly: "Who am I? What have I been doing? I have been fighting a husband who did not exist. *He* existed all the time. What wrong have I done? What was that I have been living with? There lies the reality, this man." And her soul died in her for fear: she knew she had never seen him, he had never seen her, they had met in the dark and had fought in the dark, not knowing whom they met nor whom they fought. And now she saw, and turned silent in seeing. For she had been wrong. She had said he was something he was not; she had felt familiar with him. Whereas he was apart all the while, living as she never lived, feeling as she never felt.

In fear and shame she looked at his naked body, that she had known falsely. And he was the father of her children. Her soul was torn from her body and stood apart. She looked at his naked body and was ashamed, as if she had denied it. After all, it was itself. It seemed awful to her. She looked at his face, and she turned her own face to the wall. For his look was other than hers, his way was not her way. She had denied him what he was — she saw it now. She had refused him as himself. And this had been her life, and his life. She was grateful to death, which restored the truth. And she knew she was not dead.

And all the while her heart was bursting with grief and pity for him. What had he suffered? What stretch of horror for this helpless man! She was rigid with agony. She had not been able to help him. He had been cruelly injured, this naked man, this other being, and she could make no reparation. There were the children — but the children belonged to life. This dead man had nothing to do with them. He and she were only channels through which life had flowed to issue in the children. She was a mother — but how awful she knew it now to have been a wife. And he, dead now, how awful he must have felt it to be a husband. She felt that in the next world he would be a stranger to her. If they met there, in the beyond, they would only be ashamed of what had been before. The children had come, for some mysterious reason, out of both of them. But the children did not unite them. Now he was dead, she knew how eternally he was apart from her, how eternally he had nothing more to do with her. She saw this episode of her life closed. They had denied each other in life. Now he had withdrawn. An anguish came over her. It was finished then: it had become hopeless between them long before he died. Yet he had been her husband. But how little!

"Have you got his shirt, 'Lizabeth?"

Elizabeth turned without answering, though she strove to weep and behave as her mother-in-law expected. But she could not, she was silenced. She went into the kitchen and returned with the garment.

"It is aired," she said, grasping the cotton shirt here and there to try. She was almost ashamed to handle him; what right had she or anyone to lay hands on him; but her touch was humble on his body. It was hard work to clothe him. He was so heavy and inert. A terrible dread gripped her all the while: that he could be so heavy and utterly inert, unresponsive, apart. The horror of the distance between them was almost too much for her — it was so infinite a gap she must look across.

At last it was finished. They covered him with a sheet and left him lying, with his face bound. And she fastened the door of the little parlour, lest the children should see what was lying there. Then, with peace sunk heavy on her heart, she went about making tidy the kitchen. She knew she submitted to life, which was her immediate master. But from death, her ultimate master, she winced with fear and shame.   [1909]

D. H. L A W R E N C E

The Rocking-Horse Winner

There was a woman who was beautiful, who started with all the advantages, yet she had no luck. She married for love, and the love turned to dust. She had bonny children, yet she felt they had been thrust upon her, and she could not love them. They looked at her coldly, as if they were finding fault with her. And hurriedly she felt she must cover up some fault in herself. Yet what it was that she must cover up she never knew. Nevertheless, when her children were present, she always felt the center of her heart go hard. This troubled her, and in her manner she was all the more gentle and anxious for her children, as if she loved them very much. Only she herself knew that at the center of her heart was a hard little place that could not feel love, no, not for anybody. Everybody else said of her: "She is such a good mother. She adores her children." Only she herself, and her children themselves, knew it was not so. They read it in each other's eyes.

There were a boy and two little girls. They lived in a pleasant house, with a garden, and they had discreet servants, and felt themselves superior to anyone in the neighborhood.

Although they lived in style, they felt always an anxiety in the house. There was never enough money. The mother had a small income, and the father had a small income, but not nearly enough for the social position which they had to keep up. The father went into town to some office. But though he had good prospects, these prospects never materialized. There was always the grinding sense of the shortage of money, though the style was always kept up.

At last the mother said: "I will see if *I* can't make something." But she did not know where to begin. She racked her brains, and tried this thing and the other, but could not find anything successful. The failure made deep lines come into her face. Her children were growing up, they would have to go to school. There must be more money, there must be more money. The father, who was always very handsome and expensive in his tastes, seemed as if he never *would* be able to do anything worth doing. And the mother, who had a great belief in herself, did not succeed any better, and her tastes were just as expensive.

And so the house came to be haunted by the unspoken phrase: *There must be more money! There must be more money!* The children could hear it all the time though nobody said it aloud. They heard it at Christmas, when the expensive and splendid toys filled the nursery. Behind the shining modern rocking horse, behind the smart doll's house, a voice would start whispering: "There *must* be more money! There *must* be more money!" And the children would stop playing, to listen for a moment. They would look into each other's eyes, to see if they had all heard. And each one saw in the eyes of the other two that they too had heard. "There *must* be more money! There *must* be more money!"

It came whispering from the springs of the still-swaying rocking horse, and even the horse, bending his wooden, champing head, heard it. The big doll, sitting so pink and smirking in her new pram, could hear it quite plainly, and seemed to be smirking all the more self-consciously because of it. The foolish puppy, too, that took the place of the teddy bear, he was looking so extraordinarily foolish for no other reason but that he heard the secret whisper all over the house: "There *must* be more money!"

Yet nobody ever said it aloud. The whisper was everywhere, and therefore no one spoke it. Just as no one ever says: "We are breathing!" in spite of the fact that breath is coming and going all the time.

"Mother," said the boy Paul one day, "why don't we keep a car of our own? Why do we always use Uncle's, or else a taxi?"

"Because we're the poor members of the family," said the mother.

"But why *are* we, Mother?"

"Well — I suppose," she said slowly and bitterly, "it's because your father has no luck."

The boy was silent for some time.

"Is luck money, Mother?" he asked rather timidly.

"No, Paul. Not quite. It's what causes you to have money."

"Oh!" said Paul vaguely. "I thought when Uncle Oscar said *filthy lucker*, it meant money."

"*Filthy lucre* does mean money," said the mother. "But it's lucre, not luck."

"Oh!" said the boy. "Then what *is* luck, Mother?"

"It's what causes you to have money. If you're lucky you have money. That's why it's better to be born lucky than rich. If you're rich, you may lose your money. But if you're lucky, you will always get more money."

"Oh! Will you? And is Father not lucky?"

"Very unlucky, I should say," she said bitterly.

The boy watched her with unsure eyes.

"Why?" he asked.

"I don't know. Nobody ever knows why one person is lucky and another unlucky."

"Don't they? Nobody at all? Does *nobody* know?"

"Perhaps God. But He never tells."

"He ought to, then. And aren't you lucky either, Mother?"

"I can't be, if I married an unlucky husband."

"But by yourself, aren't you?"

"I used to think I was, before I married. Now I think I am very unlucky indeed."

"Why?"

"Well — never mind! Perhaps I'm not really," she said.

The child looked at her, to see if she meant it. But he saw, by the lines of her mouth, that she was only trying to hide something from him.

"Well, anyhow," he said stoutly, "I'm a lucky person."

"Why?" said his mother, with a sudden laugh.

He stared at her. He didn't even know why he had said it.

"God told me," he asserted, brazening it out.

"I hope He did, dear!" she said, again with a laugh, but rather bitter.

"He did, Mother!"

"Excellent!" said the mother.

The boy saw she did not believe him; or, rather, that she paid no attention to his assertion. This angered him somewhat, and made him want to compel her attention.

He went off by himself, vaguely, in a childish way, seeking for the clue to "luck." Absorbed, taking no heed of other people, he went about with a sort of stealth, seeking inwardly for luck. He wanted luck, he wanted it, he wanted it. When the two girls were playing dolls in the nursery, he would sit on his big rocking horse, charging madly into space, with a frenzy that made the little girls peer at him uneasily. Wildly the horse careered, the waving dark hair of the boy tossed, his eyes had a strange glare in them. The little girls dared not speak to him.

When he had ridden to the end of his mad little journey, he climbed down and stood in front of his rocking horse, staring fixedly into its lowered face. Its red mouth was slightly open, its big eye was wide and glassy-bright.

Now! he could silently command the snorting steed. Now, take me to where there is luck! Now take me!

And he would slash the horse on the neck with the little whip he had asked Uncle Oscar for. He *knew* the horse could take him to where there was luck, if only he forced it. So he would mount again, and start on his furious ride, hoping at last to get there. He knew he could get there.

"You'll break your horse, Paul!" said the nurse.

"He's always riding like that! I wish he'd leave off!" said his elder sister Joan.

But he only glared down on them in silence. Nurse gave him up. She could make nothing of him. Anyhow he was growing beyond her.

One day his mother and his uncle Oscar came in when he was on one of his furious rides. He did not speak to them.

"Hallo, you young jockey! Riding a winner?" said his uncle.

"Aren't you growing too big for a rocking horse? You're not a very little boy any longer, you know," said his mother.

But Paul only gave a blue glare from his big, rather close-set eyes. He would speak to nobody when he was in full tilt. His mother watched him with an anxious expression on her face.

At last he suddenly stopped forcing his horse into the mechanical gallop, and slid down.

"Well, I got there!" he announced fiercely, his blue eyes still flaring, and his sturdy long legs straddling apart.

"Where did you get to?" asked his mother.

"Where I wanted to go," he flared back at her.

"That's right, son!" said Uncle Oscar. "Don't you stop till you get there. What's the horse's name?"

"He doesn't have a name," said the boy.

"Gets on without all right?" asked the uncle.

"Well, he has different names. He was called Sansovino last week."

"Sansovino, eh? Won the Ascot. How did you know his name?"

"He always talks about horse races with Bassett," said Joan.

The uncle was delighted to find that his small nephew was posted with all the racing news. Bassett, the young gardener, who had been wounded in the left foot in the war and had got his present job through Oscar Cresswell, whose batman he had been, was a perfect blade of the "turf." He lived in the racing events, and the small boy lived with him.

Oscar Cresswell got it all from Bassett.

"Master Paul comes and asks me, so I can't do more than tell him, sir," said Bassett, his face terribly serious, as if he were speaking of religious matters.

"And does he ever put anything on a horse he fancies?"

"Well — I don't want to give him away — he's a young sport, a fine sport, sir. Would you mind asking him himself? He sort of takes a pleasure in it, and perhaps he'd feel I was giving him away, sir, if you don't mind."

Bassett was serious as a church.

The uncle went back to his nephew and took him off for a ride in the car.

"Say, Paul, old man, do you ever put anything on a horse?" the uncle asked.

The boy watched the handsome man closely.

"Why, do you think I oughtn't to?" he parried.

"Not a bit of it! I thought perhaps you might give me a tip for the Lincoln."

The car sped on into the country, going down to Uncle Oscar's place in Hampshire.

"Honor bright?" said the nephew.

"Honor bright, son!" said the uncle.

"Well, then, Daffodil."

"Daffodil! I doubt it, sonny. What about Mirza?"

"I only know the winner," said the boy. "That's Daffodil."

"Daffodil, eh?"

There was a pause. Daffodil was an obscure horse comparatively.

"Uncle!"

"Yes, son?"

"You won't let it go any further, will you? I promised Bassett."

"Bassett be damned, old man! What's he got to do with it?"

"We're partners. We've been partners from the first. Uncle, he lent me my first five shillings, which I lost. I promised him, honor bright, it was only between me and him; only you gave me that ten-shilling note I started winning with, so I thought you were lucky. You won't let it go any further, will you?"

The boy gazed at his uncle from those big, hot, blue eyes, set rather close together. The uncle stirred and laughed uneasily.

"Right you are, son! I'll keep your tip private. Daffodil, eh? How much are you putting on him?"

"All except twenty pounds," said the boy. "I keep that in reserve."

The uncle thought it a good joke.

"You keep twenty pounds in reserve, do you, you young romancer? What are you betting, then?"

"I'm betting three hundred," said the boy gravely. "But it's between you and me, Uncle Oscar! Honor bright?"

The uncle burst into a roar of laughter.

"It's between you and me all right, you young Nat Gould,"[1] he said, laughing. "But where's your three hundred?"

"Bassett keeps it for me. We're partners."

---

[1]Nathaniel Gould (1857–1919), British novelist and sports columnist known best for a series of novels about horse racing.

"You are, are you! And what is Bassett putting on Daffodil?"

"He won't go quite as high as I do, I expect. Perhaps he'll go a hundred and fifty."

"What, pennies?" laughed the uncle.

"Pounds," said the child, with a surprised look at his uncle. "Bassett keeps a bigger reserve than I do."

Between wonder and amusement Uncle Oscar was silent. He pursued the matter no further, but he determined to take his nephew with him to the Lincoln races.

"Now, son," he said, "I'm putting twenty on Mirza, and I'll put five for you on any horse you fancy. What's your pick?"

"Daffodil, Uncle."

"No, not the fiver on Daffodil!"

"I should if it was my own fiver," said the child.

"Good! Good! Right you are! A fiver for me and a fiver for you on Daffodil."

The child had never been to a race meeting before, and his eyes were blue fire. He pursed his mouth tight, and watched. A Frenchman just in front had put his money on Lancelot. Wild with excitement, he flailed his arms up and down, yelling *"Lancelot! Lancelot!"* in his French accent.

Daffodil came in first, Lancelot second, Mirza third. The child, flushed and with eyes blazing, was curiously serene. His uncle brought him four five-pound notes, four to one.

"What am I to do with these?" he cried, waving them before the boy's eyes.

"I suppose we'll talk to Bassett," said the boy. "I expect I have fifteen hundred now; and twenty in reserve; and this twenty."

His uncle studied him for some moments.

"Look here, son!" he said. "You're not serious about Bassett and that fifteen hundred, are you?"

"Yes, I am. But it's between you and me, Uncle. Honor bright!"

"Honor bright all right, son! But I must talk to Bassett."

"If you'd like to be a partner, Uncle, with Bassett and me, we could all be partners. Only, you'd have to promise, honor bright, Uncle, not to let it go beyond us three. Bassett and I are lucky, and you must be lucky, because it was your ten shillings I started winning with. . . ."

Uncle Oscar took both Bassett and Paul into Richmond Park for an afternoon, and there they talked.

"It's like this, you see, sir," Bassett said. "Master Paul would get me talking about racing events, spinning yarns, you know, sir. And he was always keen on knowing if I'd made or if I'd lost. It's about a year since, now, that I put five shillings on Blush of Dawn for him — and we lost. Then the luck turned, with that ten shillings he had from you, that we put on Singhalese. And since then, it's been pretty steady, all things considering. What do you say, Master Paul?"

"We're all right when we're sure," said Paul. "It's when we're not quite sure that we go down."

"Oh, but we're careful then," said Bassett.

"But when are you *sure*?" Uncle Oscar smiled

"It's Master Paul, sir," said Bassett, in a secret, religious voice. "It's as if he had it from heaven. Like Daffodil, now, for the Lincoln. That was as sure as eggs."

"Did you put anything on Daffodil?" asked Oscar Cresswell.

"Yes, sir. I made my bit."

"And my nephew?"

Bassett was obstinately silent, looking at Paul.

"I made twelve hundred, didn't I, Bassett? I told Uncle I was putting three hundred on Daffodil."

"That's right," said Bassett, nodding.

"But where's the money?" asked the uncle.

"I keep it safe locked up, sir. Master Paul he can have it any minute he likes to ask for it."

"What, fifteen hundred pounds?"

"And twenty! And *forty*, that is, with the twenty he made on the course."

"It's amazing!" said the uncle.

"If Master Paul offers you to be partners, sir, I would, if I were you; if you'll excuse me," said Bassett.

Oscar Cresswell thought about it.

"I'll see the money," he said.

They drove home again, and sure enough, Bassett came round to the garden house with fifteen hundred pounds in notes. The twenty pounds reserve was left with Joe Glee, in the Turf Commission deposit.

"You see, it's all right, Uncle, when I'm *sure*! Then we go strong, for all we're worth. Don't we, Bassett?"

"We do that, Master Paul."

"And when are you sure?" said the uncle, laughing.

"Oh, well, sometimes I'm *absolutely* sure, like about Daffodil," said the boy; "and sometimes I have an idea; and sometimes I haven't even an idea, have I, Bassett? Then we're careful, because we mostly go down."

"You do, do you! And when you're sure, like about Daffodil, what makes you sure, sonny?"

"Oh, well, I don't know," said the boy uneasily. "I'm sure, you know, Uncle; that's all."

"It's as if he had it from heaven, sir," Bassett reiterated.

"I should say so!" said the uncle.

But he became a partner. And when the Leger was coming on, Paul was "sure" about Lively Spark, which was a quite inconsiderable horse. The boy insisted on putting a thousand on the horse, Bassett went for five hundred, and Oscar Cresswell two hundred. Lively Spark came in first, and the betting had been ten to one against him. Paul had made ten thousand.

"You see," he said, "I was absolutely sure of him."

Even Oscar Cresswell had cleared two thousand.

"Look here, son," he said, "this sort of thing makes me nervous."

"It needn't, Uncle! Perhaps I shan't be sure again for a long time."

"But what are you going to do with your money?" asked the uncle.

"Of course," said the boy. "I started it for Mother. She said she had no luck, because Father is unlucky, so I thought if *I* was lucky, it might stop whispering."

"What might stop whispering?"

"Our house. I *hate* our house for whispering."

"What does it whisper?"

"Why — why" — the boy fidgeted — "why, I don't know. But it's always short of money, you know, Uncle."

"I know it, son, I know it."

"You know people send Mother writs, don't you, Uncle?"

"I'm afraid I do," said the uncle.

"And then the house whispers, like people laughing at you behind your back. It's awful, that is! I thought if I was lucky. . . ."

"You might stop it," added the uncle.

The boy watched him with big blue eyes, that had an uncanny cold fire in them, and he said never a word.

"Well, then!" said the uncle. "What are we doing?"

"I shouldn't like Mother to know I was lucky," said the boy.

"Why not, son?"

"She'd stop me."

"I don't think she would."

"Oh!" — and the boy writhed in an odd way — "I *don't* want her to know, Uncle."

"All right, son! We'll manage it without her knowing."

They managed it very easily. Paul, at the other's suggestion, handed over five thousand pounds to his uncle, who deposited it with the family lawyer, who was then to inform Paul's mother that a relative had put five thousand pounds into his hands, which sum was to be paid out a thousand pounds at a time, on the mother's birthday, for the next five years.

"So she'll have a birthday present of a thousand pounds for five successive years," said Uncle Oscar. "I hope it won't make it all the harder for her later."

Paul's mother had her birthday in November. The house had been "whispering" worse than ever lately, and, even in spite of his luck, Paul could not bear up against it. He was very anxious to see the effect of the birthday letter, telling his mother about the thousand pounds.

When there were no visitors, Paul now took his meals with his parents, as he was beyond the nursery control. His mother went into town nearly every day. She had discovered that she had an odd knack of sketching furs and dress materials, so she worked secretly in the studio of a friend who was the chief artist for the leading drapers. She drew the figures of ladies in furs and ladies in silk and sequins for the newspaper advertisements. This young woman artist earned several thousand pounds a year, but Paul's mother only made several hundreds, and she was again dissatisfied. She so wanted to be first in something, and she did not succeed, even in making sketches for drapery advertisements.

She was down to breakfast on the morning of her birthday. Paul watched her face as she read her letters. He knew the lawyer's letter. As his mother read it, her face hardened and became more expressionless. Then a cold, determined look came on her mouth. She hid the letter under the pile of others, and said not a word about it.

"Didn't you have anything nice in the post for your birthday, Mother?" said Paul.

"Quite moderately nice," she said, her voice cold and absent.

She went away to town without saying more.

But in the afternoon Uncle Oscar appeared. He said Paul's mother had had a long interview with the lawyer, asking if the whole five thousand could not be advanced at once, as she was in debt.

"What do you think, Uncle?" said the boy.

"I leave it to you, son."

"Oh, let her have it, then! We can get some more with the other," said the boy.

"A bird in the hand is worth two in the bush, laddie!" said Uncle Oscar.

"But I'm sure to *know* for the Grand National; or the Lincolnshire; or else the Derby. I'm sure to know for *one* of them," said Paul.

So Uncle Oscar signed the agreement, and Paul's mother touched the whole five thousand. Then something very curious happened. The voices in the house suddenly went mad, like a chorus of frogs on a spring evening. There were certain new furnishings, and Paul had a tutor. He was *really* going to Eton, his father's school, in the following autumn. There were flowers in the winter, and a blossoming of the luxury Paul's mother had been used to. And yet the voices in the house, behind the sprays of mimosa and almond blossom, and from under the piles of iridescent cushions, simply trilled and screamed in a sort of ecstasy: "There *must* be more money! Oh-h-h; there *must* be more money. Oh, now, now-w! Now-w-w — there *must* be more money! — more than ever! More than ever!"

It frightened Paul terribly. He studied away at his Latin and Greek. But his intense hours were spent with Bassett. The Grand National had gone by; he had not "known," and had lost a hundred pounds. Summer was at hand. He was in agony for the Lincoln. But even for the Lincoln he didn't "know," and he lost fifty pounds. He became wild-eyed and strange, as if something were going to explode in him.

"Let it alone, son! Don't you bother about it!" urged Uncle Oscar. But it was as if the boy couldn't really hear what his uncle was saying.

"I've got to know for the Derby! I've got to know for the Derby!" the child reiterated, his big blue eyes blazing with a sort of madness.

His mother noticed how overwrought he was.

"You'd better go to the seaside. Wouldn't you like to go now to the seaside, instead of waiting? I think you'd better," she said, looking down at him anxiously, her heart curiously heavy because of him.

But the child lifted his uncanny blue eyes. "I couldn't possibly go before the Derby, Mother!" he said. "I couldn't possibly!"

DAVID LEAVITT (b. 1961) *grew up as a "facbrat" in Palo Alto, California, ~ere his father taught at Stanford University. At an early age Leavitt was a sensitive ~erver of the instability of family life around him:*

> *In a community where the divorce rate had reached a record high, and every family seemed to have at least one child in prison, or in a hospital, or dead of an overdose, my parents had never even separated. Still, there were sharp words, often, and a sense of desperate effort and hard, unrewarded labor through it all. . . . Sometimes it seemed to me that we walked around the house opened up and bleeding; yet talking, laughing, smiling, like actors in a horror movie who, during a break in the shooting, simply forget to remove the prop knives from their backs or mop up the imitation blood. In this case the blood was real, though we pretended it wasn't.*

After Leavitt's graduation from Yale University in 1983, he began, as he says, "to lead the sort of life that makes a good biographical note in the back of a literary magazine." He worked an office job in Manhattan and started to publish his stories and articles in The New Yorker, Harper's, *and* Esquire. *In 1984 Leavitt won an O. Henry Prize for his short fiction. That same year his first collection of stories,* Family Dancing, *was nominated for the National Book Critics Circle Award. His first novel,* The Lost Language of Cranes, *appeared in 1987. In 1991 he published another volume of stories,* A Place I've Never Been. *"Braids" is a recent story. While* England Sleeps, *his second novel, was published in 1993.*

Leavitt says he feels himself a member of a new generation "determined to find in their adulthood the stability that eluded them in childhood. Homes, families, marriages claim them, and they know they must make peace with those claims, but they also take as a given the constant possibility that everything will blow up in their faces." Leavitt writes fiction to dramatize his sense of the futility of planning for the future in what he calls "an age of ironic hopelessness . . . . It came to me very early, that ironic and distanced view on things, and it's stayed."

RELATED COMMENTARY: *David Leavitt, "The Way I Live Now," page 1447.*

DAVID LEAVITT

Braids

When I got the invitation to Diana's wedding — elegantly embossed, archaically formal (the ceremony, it stated, would take place at "twelve-thirty o'clock") — the first thing I did was the *TV Guide* crossword puzzle. After that I pondered. I was not so much surprised by Diana getting married as I was by her inviting me. What, I wondered, would motivate a person like Diana to ask her former lover, a woman she had lived with for a year and a

"Why not?" she said, her voice becoming heavy when she was opposed. "Why not? You can still go from the seaside to see the Derby with your uncle Oscar, if that's what you wish. No need for you to wait here. Besides, I think you care too much about these races. It's a bad sign. My family has been a gambling family, and you won't know till you grow up how much damage it has done. But it has done damage. I shall have to send Bassett away, and ask Uncle Oscar not to talk racing to you, unless you promise to be reasonable about it; go away to the seaside and forget it. You're all nerves!"

"I'll do what you like, Mother, so long as you don't send me away till after the Derby," the boy said.

"Send you away from where? Just from this house?"

"Yes," he said, gazing at her.

"Why, you curious child, what makes you care about this house so much, suddenly? I never knew you loved it."

He gazed at her without speaking. He had a secret within a secret, something he had not divulged, even to Bassett or to his uncle Oscar.

But his mother, after standing undecided and a little bit sullen for some moments, said:

"Very well, then! Don't go to the seaside till after the Derby, if you don't wish it. But promise me you won't let your nerves go to pieces. Promise you won't think so much about horse racing and *events*, as you call them!"

"Oh, no," said the boy casually. "I won't think much about them, Mother. You needn't worry. I wouldn't worry, Mother, if I were you."

"If you were me and I were you," said his mother, "I wonder what we *should* do!"

"But you know you needn't worry, Mother, don't you?" the boy repeated.

"I should be awfully glad to know it," she said wearily.

"Oh, well you *can*, you know. I mean, you *ought* to know you needn't worry," he insisted.

"Ought I? Then I'll see about it," she said.

Paul's secret of secrets was his wooden horse, that which had no name. Since he was emancipated from a nurse and a nursery governess, he had had his rocking horse removed to his own bedroom at the top of the house.

"Surely, you're too big for a rocking horse!" his mother had remonstrated.

"Well, you see, Mother, till I can have a *real* horse, I like to have *some* sort of animal about," had been his quaint answer.

"Do you feel he keeps you company?" She laughed.

"Oh, yes! He's very good, he always keeps me company, when I'm there," said Paul.

So the horse, rather shabby, stood in an arrested prance in the boy's bedroom.

The Derby was drawing near, and the boy grew more and more tense. He hardly heard what was spoken to him, he was very frail, and his eyes were really uncanny. His mother had sudden strange seizures of uneasiness about him. Sometimes, for half an hour, she would feel a sudden anxiety about him that was almost anguish. She wanted to rush to him at once, and know he was safe.

Two nights before the Derby, she was at a big party in town, when one of her rushes of anxiety about her boy, her firstborn, gripped her heart till she could hardly speak. She fought with the feeling, might and main, for she believed in common sense. But it was too strong. She had to leave the dance and go downstairs to telephone to the country. The children's nursery governess was terribly surprised and startled at being rung up in the night.

"Are the children all right, Miss Wilmot?"

"Oh, yes, they are quite all right."

"Master Paul? Is he all right?"

"He went to bed as right as a trivet. Shall I run up and look at him?"

"No," said Paul's mother reluctantly. "No! Don't trouble. It's all right. Don't sit up. We shall be home fairly soon." She did not want her son's privacy intruded upon.

"Very good," said the governess.

It was about one o'clock when Paul's mother and father drove up to their house. All was still. Paul's mother went to her room and slipped off her white fur cloak. She had told her maid not to wait up for her. She heard her husband downstairs, mixing a whisky and soda.

And then, because of the strange anxiety at her heart, she stole upstairs to her son's room. Noiselessly she went along the upper corridor. Was there a faint noise? What was it?

She stood, with arrested muscles, outside his door, listening. There was a strange, heavy, and yet not loud noise. Her heart stood still. It was a soundless noise, yet rushing and powerful. Something huge, in violent, hushed motion. What was it? What in God's name was it? She ought to know. She felt that she knew the noise. She knew what it was.

Yet she could not place it. She couldn't say what it was. And on and on it went, like a madness.

Softly, frozen with anxiety and fear, she turned the door handle.

The room was dark. Yet in the space near the window, she heard and saw something plunging to and fro. She gazed in fear and amazement.

Then suddenly she switched on the light, and saw her son, in his green pajamas, madly surging on the rocking horse. The blaze of light suddenly lit him up, as he urged the wooden horse, and lit her up, as she stood, blonde, in her dress of pale green and crystal, in the doorway.

"Paul!" she cried. "Whatever are you doing?"

"It's Malabar!" he screamed, in a powerful, strange voice. "It's Malabar!"

His eyes blazed at her for one strange and senseless second, as he ceased urging his wooden horse. Then he fell with a crash to the ground, and she, all her tormented motherhood flooding upon her, rushed to gather him up.

But he was unconscious, and unconscious he remained, with some brain fever. He talked and tossed, and his mother sat stonily by his side.

"Malabar! It's Malabar! Bassett, Bassett, I *know!* It's Malabar!"

So the child cried, trying to get up and urge the rock[ ] him his inspiration.

"What does he mean by Malabar?" asked the heart-fr[ ]

"I don't know," said the father stonily.

"What does he mean by Malabar?" she asked her broth[ ]

"It's one of the horses running for the Derby," was the an[ ]

And, in spite of himself, Oscar Cresswell spoke to Bassett, put a thousand on Malabar: at fourteen to one.

The third day of the illness was critical: they were waiting for [ ] The boy, with his rather long, curly hair, was tossing ceaselessly on th[ ] He never slept nor regained consciousness, and his eyes were like blue[ ] His mother sat, feeling her heart had gone, turned actually into a ston[ ]

In the evening, Oscar Cresswell did not come, but Bassett se[ ] message, saying could he come up for one moment, just one mome[ ] Paul's mother was very angry at the intrusion, but on second thought s[ ] agreed. The boy was the same. Perhaps Bassett might bring him to con[ ] sciousness.

The gardener, a shortish fellow with a little brown mustache, and sharp little brown eyes, tiptoed into the room, touched his imaginary cap to Paul's mother, and stole to the bedside, staring with glittering, smallish eyes at the tossing, dying child.

"Master Paul!" he whispered. "Master Paul! Malabar came in first all right, a clean win. I did as you told me. You've made over seventy thousand pounds, you have; you've got over eighty thousand. Malabar came in all right, Master Paul."

"Malabar! Malabar! Did I say Malabar, Mother? Did I say Malabar? Do you think I'm lucky, Mother? I knew Malabar, didn't I? Over eighty thousand pounds! I call that lucky, don't you, Mother? Over eighty thousand pounds! I knew, didn't I know I knew? Malabar came in all right. If I ride my horse till I'm sure, then I tell you, Bassett, you can go as high as you like. Did you go for all you were worth, Bassett?"

"I went a thousand on it, Master Paul."

"I never told you, Mother, that if I can ride my horse, and *get there,* then I'm absolutely sure — oh, absolutely! Mother, did I ever tell you? I *am* lucky!"

"No, you never did," said the mother.

But the boy died in the night.

And even as he lay dead, his mother heard her brother's voice saying to her: "My God, Hester, you're eighty-odd thousand to the good, and a poor devil of a son to the bad. But, poor devil, poor devil, he's best gone out of a life where he rides his rocking horse to find a winner."

[1926]

month and whose heart she had suddenly and callously broken, to a celebration of her union with a man? It seems to me that that is asking for trouble.

I decided to call Leonore, who had been a close friend of Diana's and mine during the days when we were together, and who always seemed to have answers. "Leonore, Diana's getting married," I said when she picked up the phone.

"If you ask me," Leonore said, "she's wanted a man since day one. Remember that gay guy she tried to make it with? He said he wanted to change, have kids and all? It's not him, is it?"

I looked at the invitation. "Mark Charles Cadwallader," I said.

"Well, for his sake," Leonore said, "I only hope he knows what he's getting into. As for Miss Diana, her doings are of no interest to me."

"But Leonore," I said, "the question is: should I go to the wedding?" imagining myself, suddenly, in my red T-shirt which said "Baby Butch" (a present from Diana), re-introducing myself to her thin, severe, long-necked mother, Marjorie Winters.

"I think that would depend on the food," Leonore said. You could always count on Leonore for an answer like that. Her advice always meant the same thing. It meant: be an adult and make up your own mind.

After I hung up, I poured myself some coffee and propped the invitation in front of me to look at. For the first few seconds it hadn't even clicked who was getting married. I had read: "Mr and Mrs Humphrey Winters cordially invite you to celebrate the wedding of their daughter, Diana Helaine," and thought: who is Diana Helaine? Then it hit me, because for years, in fact, the whole year and a month, Diana had refused to tell me what her middle initial stood for — positively refused, she said, out of embarrassment, while I tried to imagine what horrors could lie behind that "H" — Hildegard? Hester? Hulga? She was coyly, irritatingly insistent about not letting the secret out, like certain girls who would have nothing to do with me in eighth grade. Now she was making public to the world what she insisted on hiding from me, and it made perfect sense. Diana Helaine, not a different person, is getting married, I thought, and it was true, the fact in and of itself didn't surprise me. During the year and a month, combing the ghost of her once knee-length hair, I couldn't count how many times she'd said, very off-the-cuff, "You know, Ellen, sometimes I think this lesbian life is for the birds. Maybe I should just give it up, get married, and have two point four babies." I'd smile and say, "If you do that, Diana, you can count on my coming to the wedding with a shotgun and shooting myself there in front of everybody." To which, still strumming her hair like a guitar and staring into the mirror, she would respond only with a faint smile, as if she could think of nothing in the world she would enjoy more.

First things first: we were lovers, and I don't mean schoolgirls touching each other in exploratory ways in dormitories after dark. I mean, we lived together, shared tampons and toothpaste, had one bed to sleep in, and for all the world (and ourselves) to see. Diana was in law school in San Francisco, and I had a job at Milpitas State Hospital (I still do). Each day I'd drive an hour and a half there and an hour and a half back, and when I got home Diana would be waiting for me in bed, a fat textbook propped on her lap. We had a couple friends, Leonore and Callie, for instance, and were always invited to things together, and, when she left me, we were even thinking about getting power-of-attorney over one another. I was Diana's first woman lover, though she had had plenty of boyfriends. I had never slept with a boy, but had been making love with girls since early in high school. Which meant that, for me, being a lesbian was just how things were. But for Diana — well, from day one it was adventure, event and episode. For a while we just had long blushing talks over pizza during which she confessed she was "curious." It's ridiculous how many supposedly straight girls come on to you that way — plopping themselves down on your lap and fully expecting you to go through all the hard work of initiating them into Sapphic love out of sheer lust for recruitment. No way, I said. The last thing I need is to play guinea pig, testing ground, only to be left when the fun's over and a new boyfriend shows up on the horizon. But no, Diana said. I mean, yes. I think I *do*. I mean, I think I *am*. At which point she would always have just missed the last bus home and would have to spend the night in my bed, where it was only a matter of time before I had no more defences.

After we became lovers, Diana cut her hair off, and bought me the "Baby Butch" T-shirt. She joined all sorts of groups and organizations, dragged me to unsavory bars, insisted, fiercely, on telling her parents everything. (They did not respond well.) Only in private did she muse over her other options. I think she thought she was rich enough not to have to take any vow or promise all that seriously. Rich people are like that, I have noticed. They think a love affair is like a shared real estate venture they can just buy out of when they get tired of it.

Diana had always said the one reason she definitely wanted to get married was for the presents, so the day before the wedding I took my credit card and went to Nordstrom's, where indeed I found her name in the bridal registry, and was handed a computer printout with her china pattern, silver, stainless, and other assorted requirements. I was already over my spending limit, so I bought her the ultimate — a Cuisinart — which I had wrapped to carry in white crêpe paper with a huge yellow bow. Next came the equally important matter of buying myself a dress for the wedding. It had been maybe five, six years since I'd owned a dress. But buying clothes is like riding a bicycle — it comes back — and soon, remembering age-old advice from my mother on hems and necklines, I had picked out a pretty yellow sundress with a smattering of daisies, and a big, wide-brimmed hat. It was easy.

The invitation had been addressed to Miss Ellen Britchkey and guest, and afterwards, in the parking lot, that made me think about my life — how there was no one in it. And then, as I was driving home from Nordstrom's, for the first time in years I had a seizure of accident panic. I couldn't believe I was travelling at sixty miles an hour, part of a herd of speeding cars which passed and raced each other, coming within five or six inches of collision and death every ten seconds. It astonished me to realize that I drove every day of my life, that every day of my life I risked ending my life, that all I had to do was swerve the wrong way, or look only in the front and not the side mirror, and I might hit another car, or hit a child on the way to a wedding, and have to live the rest of my life with the guilt, or die. Horrified, I headed right, into the slow lane. The slow lane was full of scared women, crawling home alone. It was no surprise to me. I was one with the scared women crawling home alone. After Diana left me, I moved down the peninsula to a miniature house — that is the only way to describe it — two rooms with a roof, and shingles, and big pretty windows. It was my solitude house, my self-indulgence house, my remorse and secret-pleasure house. There I ate take-out Chinese food, read and re-read *Little House on the Prairie*, stayed up late watching re-runs of *Star Trek* and *The Honeymooners*. I lived by my wits, by survival measures. The television was one of those tiny ones, the screen smaller than a human face.

Diana — I only have one picture of her, and it is not a good likeness. In it she wears glasses and has long, long hair, sweeping below the white fringe of the picture, to her knees. She cut all her hair off as an offering to me the day after the first night we made love, and presented it that evening in a box — two neat braids, clipped easily as toenail parings, offered like a dozen roses. I stared at them, the hair still braided, still fresh with the smell of shampoo, and joked that I had bought her a comb, like in *The Gift of the Magi*. She didn't get it. "Don't you see?" she said. "I did it for you — I changed myself for you, as an act of love." I looked at her, her new boyish bangs, her face suddenly so thin-seeming without its frame of yellow hair. She was used to big gestures, to gifts which made an impact.

"Diana," I lied (for I had loved her long hair), "it's the most generous thing anyone's ever done for me." To say she'd done it for me — well, it was a little bit like a mean trick my sister pulled on me one Christmas when we were kids. She had this thing about getting a little tiny tree to put on top of the piano. And I, of course, wanted a great big one, like the Wagner family down the block. And then, about ten days before Christmas, she said, "Ellen, I have an early Christmas present for you," and she handed me a box, inside which were about a hundred miniature Christmas tree ornaments.

I can recognize a present with its own motive.

If I've learned one thing from Diana, it's that there's more to a gift than just giving.

The next day was the day of the wedding, and somehow, without hitting any children, I drove to the hotel in Hillsborough where the ceremony and reception were taking place. A doorman escorted me to a private drawing-room where, nervous about being recognized, I kept the Cuisinart in front of my face as long as I could, until finally an older woman with a carnation over her breast, apparently an aunt or something, said, "May I take that, dear?" and I had to surrender the Cuisinart to a tableful of presents, some of which were hugely and awkwardly wrapped and looked like human heads. I thanked her, suddenly naked in my shame, and sturdied myself to brave the drawing-room where the guests milled. I recognized two or three faces from college, all part of Diana's set — rich, straight, preppy, not the sort I had hung around with at all. And in the distance I saw her very prepared parents, her mother thin and severe-looking as ever in a sleeveless black dress, her streaked hair cut short, like Diana's, her neck and throat nakedly displaying a brilliant jade necklace, while her father, in his tuxedo, talked with some other men and puffed at a cigar. Turning to avoid them, I almost walked right into Walter Bevins, who was Diana's gay best friend, or "hag fag," in college, and we were so relieved to see each other we grabbed a couple of whisky sours and headed to as secluded a corner as we could find. "Boy, am I glad to see a familiar face," Walter said. "Can you believe this? Though I must say, I never doubted Diana would get married in anything less than splendour."

"Me neither," I admitted. "I was just a little surprised that Diana was getting married at all."

"Weren't we all!" Walter said. "But he seems like a nice guy. A lawyer, of course. *Very* cute, a real shame that he's heterosexual, if you ask me. But apparently she loves him and he loves her and that's just fine. Look, there he is."

Walter pointed to a tall, dark man with a moustache and beard who stood in the middle of the drawing-room crowd, shaking hands and laughing with a circle of elderly women. To my horror, his eye caught ours, and he disentangled himself from the old women and walked over to where we were sitting. "Walter," he said. Then he looked at me and said, "Ellen?"

I nodded and smiled.

"Ellen, Ellen," he said, and reached out a hand which, when I took it, lifted me from the safety of my sofa on to my feet. "It is such a pleasure to meet you," he said. "Come with me for a second, I've wanted a chance to talk with you for so long, and once the wedding takes place — who knows?"

I smiled nervously at Walter, who raised a hand in comradeship, and was led by the groom through a door to an ante-chamber, empty except for a card table piled high with bridesmaids' bouquets. "I just want you to know," he said, "how happy Diana and I are that you could make it. She speaks so warmly of you. And I also want you to know, just so there's no tension, Diana's told me everything, and I'm fully accepting of her past."

"Thank you, Mark," I said, horrified that at my age I could already be part of someone's "past." It sounded fake to me, as if lesbianism were just a stage Diana had passed through, and I was some sort of perpetual adolescent, never seeing the adult light of heterosexuality.

"Charlie," Mark said. "I'm called Charlie."

He opened the door and, as we were heading back out into the drawing-room, he said, "Oh, by the way, we've seated you next to the schizophrenic girl. Your being a social worker and all, we figured you wouldn't mind."

"Me?" I said. "Mind? Not at all."

"Thanks. Boy, is Diana going to be thrilled to see you."

Then he was gone into the crowd.

Once back in the drawing-room I searched for Walter, but couldn't seem to find him. I was surrounded on all sides by elderly women with elaborate, peroxided hairdos. Their purses fascinated me. Some were hard as shells and shaped like kidneys, others made out of punctured leather which reminded me of birth control pill dispensers. Suddenly I found myself face to nose with Marjorie Winters, whose eyes visibly bulged upon recognizing me. We had met once, when Diana had brought me home for a weekend, but that was before she had told her mother the nature of our relationship. After Diana came out — well, I believe the exact words were, "I never want that woman in my house again."

"Ellen," Marjorie said now, just as I had imagined she might. "What a surprise." She smiled, whether with contempt or triumph I couldn't tell.

"Well, you know I wouldn't miss Diana's wedding, Mrs. Winters," I said. "And this certainly is a lovely hotel."

She smiled. "Yes, isn't it? Red, look who's here," she said, and motioned over her husband, who for no particular reason except that his name was Humphrey was called Red. He was an amiable, absent-minded man, and he stared at me in earnest, trying to figure out who I was.

"You remember Diana's friend Ellen, from college, don't you?"

"Oh yes," he said. "Of course." Clearly he knew nothing. I believe his wife liked to keep him in a perpetual dark like that, so that he wouldn't be distracted from earning money.

"Ellen's a social worker," Marjorie said, "at the State Hospital at Milpitas. So Diana and I thought it would be a good idea to seat her next to the schizophrenic girl, don't you think?"

I winced in punishment.

"Oh yes," Red said. "Definitely. I imagine they'll have a lot of things to talk about."

A little tinkling bell rang, and Marjorie said, "Oh goodness, that's my cue. Be a dear, and do take care of Natalie," squeezing my hand. Then she was gone. She had won, and she was glorying in her victory. And not for the first time that day, I wondered: why is it that the people who always win always win?

The guests were beginning to move outdoors, to the garden, where the ceremony was taking place. Lost in the crowd, I spied and manoeuvred my way next to Walter. "How's it going, little one?" he said.

"I feel like a piece of shit," I said. I wasn't in the mood to make small talk.

"Well," he said, "that's what weddings are for." We headed through a pair of French doors, then, into a small, beautiful garden, full of blooming roses and wreaths and huge baskets of wisteria and lilies. Handsome, uniformed men — mostly brothers of the groom, I presumed — were helping everyone to their seats. Thinking we were a couple, one of them escorted Walter and me to one of the back rows, along with several other young couples who had brought their babies, and might have to run out to change a diaper or something in the middle of the ceremony.

As soon as everyone was seated the string quartet in the corner began to play something sweet and Chopin-like, and then the procession started — first Diana's sister, who was matron of honour; then the bridesmaids, each arm-in-arm with an usher, each dressed in a different pastel dress which was coordinated perfectly with her bouquet; and then, finally, Diana herself, looking resplendent in her white dress. Everyone gave out little oohs and aahs as she entered, locked tight between her parents. It had been two years since we'd seen each other and, looking at her, I thought I'd cry, I felt like such a piece of nothing, such a worthless piece of garbage without her — she was really that beautiful. Her hair was growing back, which was the worst thing. She had it braided and piled on her head and woven with wild flowers. Her skin was flawless, smooth — skin I'd touched hundreds, thousands of times — and there was an astonishing brightness about her eyes, as if she could see right through everything to its very heart. From the altar, the groom looked on, grinning like an idiot, a proud professor who seemed to be saying, with his teary grin, see, look what I've got, look what chose me. And Diana too, approaching him at the altar, was all bright smiles, all eagerness, no doubt, no regret or hesitation registering in her face, and I wondered what she was thinking now: if she was thinking about her other life, her long committed days and nights as a lesbian.

The music stopped. They stood, back to us, the audience, before the reverent reverend. He began to lecture them solemnly. And then I saw it. It would be like the final episode of *Dynasty*. I saw myself stand up, run to the front of the garden while noises of confusion rose up from the guests, and, before anyone could say anything, do anything, pull out the gun and consummate, right there, all over the grass, my own splendid marriage to vengeance.

But of course I didn't do anything like that. Instead I just sat there with Walter and listened as Diana, love of my life, my lover, my life, repeated the marriage vows, her voice a little trembly, as if to suggest she was just barely holding in her tears. They said their I do's. They exchanged rings. They kissed, and everyone cheered.

At my table in the dining-room were seated Walter, the Winters' maid, Juanita, her son, the schizophrenic girl, and the schizophrenic girl's mother. It was in the darkest, most invisible corner of the room, and I could see it was no accident that Marjorie Winters had gathered us all here — all the misfits and minorities, the kooks and oddities of the wedding. For a minute, sitting down and gazing out at the other tables, which were full of beautiful women and men in tuxedos, I was so mad at Diana I wanted to run back to the present table and reclaim my Cuisinart, which I really couldn't afford to be giving her anyway, and which she certainly didn't deserve. But then I realized that people would probably think I was a thief and call the hotel detective or the police, and I decided not to.

The food, Leonore would have been pleased to know, appeared mediocre. Next to me, the schizophrenic girl stabbed with her knife at a pathetic-looking little bowl of melon balls and greenish strawberries, while her mother looked out exhaustedly, impatiently, at the expanse of the hotel dining-room.

Seeing that the schizophrenic girl had started, Juanita's son, who must have been seven feet tall, began eating as well, but she slapped his hand. Not wanting to embarrass him by staring, I looked at the schizophrenic girl. I knew she was the schizophrenic girl by her glasses — big, ugly red ones from the Seventies, the kind where the temples start at the bottom of the frames — and her bowl-shaped hair cut. Also, I recognized the way she slumped over her fruit salad, as if she was afraid someone might steal it.

"Hello," I said to her.

She didn't say anything. Her mother, dragged back into focus, looked down at her and said, "Oh now, Natalie."

"Hello," Natalie said.

The mother smiled. "Are you with the bride or the groom?" she asked.

"The bride."

"Relation?"

"Friend from college."

"How nice," the mother said. "We're with the groom. Old neighbours. Natalie and Charlie were born the same day in the same hospital, isn't that right, Nat?"

"Yes," Natalie said.

"She's very shy," the mother said to me, and winked.

Across the table Walter was asking Juanita's son if he played basketball. Shyly, in a Jamaican accent, he admitted that he did. His face was as arch and stern as that of his mother, a fat brown woman with the eyes of a prison guard. She smelled very clean, almost antiseptic. I remembered that Diana had once told me how Juanita was her mother's greatest confidante, her best friend, and lying in bed that night, in giggles, we had speculated on whether they might not be lovers.— both secretly aroused, I suppose now, by the thought of Diana's mother sleeping with Juanita, aroused by that earthy ammonia smell, the thought of all that moist dark skin. But it was too late for such games. Across the room, the bride was having her chair pulled out for her by the groom.

"Natalie, are you in school?" I asked.

She continued to stab at her fruit, not really eating it as much as trying to decimate the pieces of melon.

"Tell the lady, Natalie," said her mother.

"Yes."

"Natalie's in a very special school," the mother said.

"I'm a social worker," I said. "I understand about Natalie."

"Oh really, you are?" the mother said, and relief flushed her face. "I'm so glad. It's so painful, having to explain — you know —"

Across the table Walter was trying to get Juanita to reveal the secret location of the honeymoon. "I'm not saying," Juanita said. "Not one word."

"Come on," said Walter. "I won't tell a soul, I swear."

"I'm on TV," Natalie said.

"Oh now," said her mother.

"I am. I'm on *The Facts of Life*. I'm Tootie."

"Now, Natalie, you know you're not."

"And I'm also on *All My Children* during the day. It's a tough life, but I manage."

"Natalie, you know you're not to tell these stories."

"Did someone mention *All My Children*?" asked Juanita's son. Walter too looked interested.

"My lips are forever sealed," Juanita said to no one in particular. "There's no chance no way no one's going to get me to say one word."

Diana and Ellen. Ellen and Diana. When we were together, everything about us seethed. We lived from seizure to seizure. Our fights were glorious, manic, our need to fight like an allergy, something which reddens and irritates the edges of everything and demands release. Once Diana broke the air-conditioner and I wouldn't forgive her. "Leave me alone," I screamed.

"No," she said. "I want to talk about it. Now."

"Well, I don't."

"Why are you punishing me?" Diana said. "It's not my fault."

"I'm not punishing you."

"You are. You're shutting me up when I have something I want to say."

"Damn it, won't you just leave me alone? Can't you leave anything alone?"

"Let me say what I have to say, damn it!"

"What?"

"I didn't break it on purpose! I broke it by accident!"

"Damn it, Diana, leave me the fuck alone! Why don't you just go away?"

"You are so hard!" Diana said, tears in her eyes, and slammed out the door into the bedroom.

After we fought, consumed, crazed, we made love like animals, then crawled about the house for days, cats in a cage, lost in a torpor of lazy carnality. It helped that the air-conditioner was broken. It kept us slick. There was always, between us, heat and itch.

Once, in those most desperate, most remorse-filled days after Diana left, before I moved down the peninsula to my escape-hatch dream house, I made a list which was titled "Reasons I love her."

1) Her hair.
2) Her eyes.
3) Her skin. (Actually, most of her body except maybe her elbows.)
4) The way she talks for the plants when she waters them, saying things like, "Boy was I thirsty, thanks for the drink." (This one was a lie. That habit actually infuriated me.)
5) Her advantages: smart and nice.
6) Her devotion to me, to us as a couple.
7) How much she loved me.
8) Her love for me.
9) How she loves me.

There was less to that list than met the eye. When Diana left me — and it must be stated, here and now, she did so cruelly, callously, and suddenly — she said that the one thing she wanted me to know was that she still considered herself a lesbian. It was only me she was leaving. "Don't think I'm just another straight girl who used you," she insisted, as she gathered all her things into monogrammed suitcases. "I just don't feel we're right for each other. You're a social worker. I'm not good enough for you. Our lives, our ideas about the world — they're just never going to mesh."

Outside, I knew, her mother's station wagon waited in ambush. Still I pleaded. "Diana," I said, "you got me into this thing. You lured me in, pulled me in against my will. You can't leave just like that."

But she was already at the door. "I want you to know," she said, "because of you, I'll be able to say, loud and clear, for the rest of my life, I am a lesbian," and kissed me on the cheek.

In tears I stared at her, astonished that this late in the game she still thought my misery at her departure might be quelled by abstract gestures to sisterhood. Also that she could think me that stupid. I saw through her quaking, frightened face, her little-boy locks.

"You're a liar," I said, and, grateful for the anger, she crumpled up her face, screamed, "Damn you, Ellen," and ran out the door.

As I said, our fights were glorious.

All she left behind were her braids.

Across the dining-room, Diana stood with her new husband, holding a big knife over the wedding cake. Everyone was cheering. The knife sank into the soft white flesh of the cake, came out again thick with silken frosting and crumbs. Diana cut two pieces. Like snakes, their arms intertwined, she and Charlie fed each other.

Then they danced. A high-hipped young woman in sequins got up on the bandstand and sang, "Graduation's almost here my love, teach me tonight."

After the bride and groom had been given their five minutes of single glory on the dance floor, and the parents and grandparents had joined them, I felt a tap on my shoulder. "Care to tango avec moi, my dear?" Walter said.

"Walter," I said. "I'd be delighted."

We got up from the table and moved out on to the floor. I was extremely nervous, sweating through my dress. I hadn't actually spoken to Diana yet, doubted she'd even seen me. Now, not three feet away, she stood, dancing and laughing, Mrs Mark Charles Cadwallader.

I kept my eyes on Walter's lapel. The song continued, ended. The couples broke up. And then, there she was, approaching me, all smiles, all bright eyes. "Ellen," she said, embracing me, and her mother shot us a wrathful glance. "Ellen. Let me look at you."

She looked at me. I looked at her. Close-up, she looked slightly unravelled, her make-up smeared, her eyes red and a little tense. "Come with me to the ladies' room," she said. "My contacts are killing me."

She took my hand and swept me out of the ballroom into the main hotel lobby. Everyone in the lobby stared at us frankly, presuming, I suppose, that she was a runaway bride, and I her maid. But we were only running away to the ladies' room.

"These contacts!" she said once we got there, and opening one eye wide peeled off a small sheath of plastic. "I was worried that you wouldn't. I've felt so bad about you, Ellen, worried about you so much, since — well, since things ended between us. I was hoping this wedding could be a reconciliation for us. That now we could start again. As friends."

She turned away from the lamplit mirror and flashed me a big smile. I just looked up at her.

"Yes," I said. "I'd like that."

Diana removed the other lens and licked it. It seemed to me a highly unorthodox method of cleaning. Then, nervously, she replaced the lens and looked at herself in the mirror. She had let down her guard. Her face looked haggard, and red blusher was streaming off her cheeks.

"I didn't invite Leonore for a reason," she said. "I knew she'd do something to embarrass me, come all dyked out or something. I'm not trying to deny my past, you know. Charlie knows everything. Have you met him?"

"Yes," I said.

"And isn't he a wonderful guy?"

"Yes."

"I have nothing against Leonore. I just believe in subtlety these days. You, I knew I could count on you for some subtlety, some class. Leonore definitely lacks class."

It astonished me, all that wasn't being said. I wanted to mention it all — her promise on the doorstep, the gun, the schizophrenic girl. But there was so much. Too much. Nowhere to begin.

Finished with her ablations, we sat down in parallel toilets. "It is nearly impossible to pee in this damned dress," she said to me through the divider. "I can't wait to get out of it."

"I can imagine," I said.

Then there was a loud spilling noise, and Diana gave out a little sigh of relief. "I've got a terrible bladder infection," she said. "Remember in college how it was such a big status symbol to have a bladder infection because it meant you were having sex? Girls used to come into the dining-hall clutching big jars of cranberry juice and moaning, and the rest of us would look at them a little jealously." She faltered. "Or some of us did," she added. "I guess not you, huh, Ellen?"

"No, I was a lesbian," I said, "and still am, and will be until the day I die." I don't know why I said that, but it shut her up.

For about thirty seconds there was not a sound from the other side of the divider, and then I heard Diana sniffling. I didn't know what to say.

"Christ," Diana said, after a few seconds, and blew her nose. "Christ. Why'd I get married?"

I hesitated. "I'm not sure I'm the person to ask," I said. "Did your mother have anything to do with it?"

"Oh, Ellen," Diana said, "please!" I heard her spinning the toilet paper roll. "Look," she said, "you probably resent me incredibly. You probably think

I'm a sell-out and a fool and that I was a royal bitch to you. You probably think when Charlie does it to me I lie there and pretend I'm feeling something when I'm not. Well, it's not true. Not in the least." She paused. "I was just not prepared to go through my life as a social freak, Ellen," she said. "I want a normal life, just like everybody. I want to go to parties and not have to die inside trying to explain who it is I'm with. Charlie's very good for me in that way, he's very understanding and generous." She blew her nose again. "I'm not denying you were part of my life, that our relationship was a big thing for me," she said. "I'm just saying it's finished. That part's finished."

Defiantly she flushed.

We stood up, pulled up our underpants and stepped out of the toilet booths to face each other. I looked Diana right in the eye, and I noticed her weaken. I saw it. I could have kissed her or something, I knew, and made her even more miserable. But I didn't really see the point.

Afterwards, we walked together out of the ladies' room, back into the ballroom, where we were accosted by huge crowds of elderly women with purses which looked to me like the shellacked sushi in certain Japanese restaurant windows.

"Was it okay?" Walter asked me, taking my arm and leading me back to our table for cake.

"Yes," I said. "Okay." But he could see from my face how utterly miserable I was.

"Don't even try," Juanita said, giggling hysterically to herself as we got back to the table. "You're not getting a word out of me, so don't even begin to ask me questions."

Once I knew a schizophrenic girl. Her name was Holly Reardon and she was my best friend from age five to eight. We played house a lot, and sometimes we played spaceship, crawling together into a cubby-hole behind my parents' sofa bed, then turning off the lights and pretending the living-room was some fantastic planet. We did well with our limited resources. But then money started disappearing, and my mother sat me down one day and asked me if I had noticed the money always disappeared when Holly came to visit. I shook my head vigorously no, refusing to believe her. And then one day my favourite stuffed animal, a dog called Rufus, disappeared, and I didn't tell my mother, and didn't tell my mother, until one day she said to me, "Ellen, what happened to Rufus?" and I started to cry. We never found Rufus. Holly had done something with him. And it wasn't because of me that she went away, my parents assured me, it wasn't because of me that her parents closed up the house and had to move into an apartment. Holly was not well. Years later, when I went to work at the State Hospital, I think somewhere, secretly, I hoped Holly might be there, a patient there, that we might play house and spaceship in the linen closets. But of course she wasn't. Who knows where she is now?

After the wedding I felt so depressed I had ice-cream for dinner. I did several acrostic puzzles. I watched *The Honeymooners* and I watched *Star Trek*.

I watched Sally Jesse Raphael. I watched *The Twilight Zone*. Fortunately it was not one of the boring Western ones, but an episode I liked particularly, about a little girl with a doll which says things like, "My name is Talking Tina and I'm going to kill you." I wished I'd had a doll like that when I was growing up. Next was *Night Gallery*. I almost never watch *Night Gallery*, but when I do it seems I always see the same episode, the one about two people who meet on a road and are filled with a mysterious sense of *déjà vu*, of having met before. It turns out they live in the mind of a writer who has been re-writing the same scene a thousand times. Near the end they rail at their creator to stop tormenting them by summoning them into existence over and over, to suffer over and over. At the risk of mysticism, it seems to me significant that every time I have tuned into *Night Gallery* in my life it is this episode I have seen.

Then there was nothing more good to watch.

I got up, paced around the house, tried not to think about any of it: Holly Reardon, or Natalie, or Diana, or those poor people living in the mind of a writer and getting re-written over and over again. I tried not to think about all the Chinese dinners I wasn't going to be able to have because I'd spent so much money on that Cuisinart for Diana, who probably could afford to buy herself a hundred Cuisinarts if she wanted. I tried not to think about their honeymoon, about what secret, glorious place they were bound for. It was too late for it still to make me mad that the whole world, fired up to stop me and Diana, was in a conspiracy to protect the privacy of the angelic married couple she had leapt into to save herself, to make sure their perfect honeymoon wasn't invaded by crazy lesbian ex-lovers with shotguns and a whole lot of unfinished business on their minds. Unfortunately, any anger I felt, which might have saved me, was counteracted by how incredibly sorry I felt for Diana, how sad she had seemed, weeping in the ladies' room on her wedding day.

I went to the closet and took out Diana's braids. God knows, I hadn't opened the box for years. But now I took it carefully from the shelf and opened it. There were the braids, only a little faded, a little tangled, and of course no longer smelling of shampoo. I lifted one up. I was surprised at how silky the hair felt, even this old. Carefully, to protect myself, I rubbed just a little of it at first against my face. I shuddered. It could have been her.

I went to the bed, carrying the braids with me. I laid them along my chest. I have never had long hair. Now I tried to imagine what it felt like, tried to imagine I was Diana imagining me, a woman she had loved, a woman she had given her hair, a woman who now lay on a bed somewhere, crying, using all the strength she could muster just not to force the braids down her throat. But I knew Diana was on a plane somewhere in the sky, or in a car, or more likely than that, lying in a heart-shaped bed while a man hovered over her, his hands running through her new hair, and that probably all she was thinking was how much better off she was than me, how much richer, and how lucky to have escaped before she was sucked so far in that like me it would be too late ever to get out. Was I so pathetic? Possibly. And possibly Diana was going to be happier for the choice she had made. But I think more likely, lying on that mysterious bed, she was contemplating a whole life of mistakes spinning out from one act of compromise, and realizing she preferred a life of easy mistakes to one which was harder but better. Who was I to criticize? Diana had her tricks, and so did Juanita, and so, for that matter, did that schizophrenic girl stabbing at her melon balls. We all had our little tricks.

I took the braids off myself. I stood up. A few hairs broke loose from the gathered ropes, fell lightly to the floor. They didn't even look like anything; they might have been pieces of straw.   [1988]

URSULA K. LE GUIN (b. 1929) is the daughter of Theodora Kroeber, a writer, and Alfred Louis Kroeber, a pioneering anthropologist at the University of California at Berkeley. From her family background Le Guin acquired a double orientation, humanistic and scientific, that shows in all her writing. She was educated at Radcliffe College and Columbia University, where she completed a master's thesis in medieval romance literature. In 1953 she married the historian Charles Le Guin, with whom she had three children. Although she wrote her first science-fiction story at the age of twelve, she didn't begin publishing until twenty years later. One of her stories, "Semley's Necklace," grew into her first published novel, Rocannon's World (1966). Another story, "Winter's King," introduced the setting she developed for her first major success, the novel The Left Hand of Darkness (1969). These stories and novels, along with Planet of Exile (1966), City of Illusions (1967), The Dispossessed (1974), the novella The Word for World Is Forest (1976), and stories in The Wind's Twelve Quarters (1976), form the Hainish cycle, a series of independent works sharing an imaginary historic background. Le Guin has also published several other fantasy novels and three more story collections.

Although Le Guin's earliest work primarily attracted a devoted audience of science-fiction readers, her later work — especially The Left Hand of Darkness — has wider appeal. In that novel she explored the theme of androgyny on the planet Winter (Gethen), where inhabitants may adopt alternately male and female roles. Le Guin insists on Aristotle's definition of Homo sapiens as social animals, and she shows how difficult it is to think of our fellow humans as people, rather than as men and women.

Le Guin brings to fantasy fiction a wealth of literary scholarship, crediting Leo Tolstoy, Anton Chekhov, and Virginia Woolf (among others) as her primary influences. Most of her stories, like "The Ones Who Walk Away from Omelas," are about reciprocal relationships, illustrating "the sort of golden rule that whatever you touch, touches you." This maxim has scientific backings in ecology and philosophical echoes in Taoism and Zen. Le Guin has said that she works best with what she calls "fortune cookie ideas" suggested by someone else. Through her stories she shows how simple concepts hide a mass of complexity and contradiction that can create anarchy when human beings try to act on them. In 1990 Le Guin published Dancing at the Edge of the World: Thoughts on Words, Women, Places.

RELATED COMMENTARY: Ursula K. Le Guin, "The Scapegoat in Omelas," page 1449.

URSULA K. LE GUIN

The Ones Who Walk Away from Omelas

With a clamor of bells that set the swallows soaring, the Festival of Summer came to the city. Omelas, bright-towered by the sea. The rigging of the boats in harbor sparkled with flags. In the streets between houses with red roofs and painted walls, between old moss-grown gardens and under avenues of trees, past great parks and public buildings, processions moved. Some were decorous: old people in long stiff robes of mauve and grey, grave master workmen, quiet, merry women carrying their babies and chatting as they walked. In other streets the music beat faster, a shimmering of gong and tambourine, and the people went dancing, the procession was a dance. Children dodged in and out, their high calls rising like the swallows' crossing flights over the music and the singing. All the processions wound towards the north side of the city, where on the great water-meadow called the Green Fields boys and girls, naked in the bright air, with mud-stained feet and ankles and long, lithe arms, exercised their restive horses before the race. The horses wore no gear at all but a halter without bit. Their manes were braided with streamers of silver, gold, and green. They flared their nostrils and pranced and boasted to one another; they were vastly excited, the horse being the only animal who has adopted our ceremonies as his own. Far off to the north and west the mountains stood up half encircling Omelas on her bay. The air of morning was so clear that the snow still crowning the Eighteen Peaks burned with white-gold fire across the miles of sunlit air, under the dark blue of the sky. There was just enough wind to make the banners that marked the racecourse snap and flutter now and then. In the silence of the broad green meadows one could hear the music winding through the city streets, farther and nearer and ever approaching, a cheerful faint sweetness of the air that from time to time trembled and gathered together and broke out into the great joyous clanging of the bells.

Joyous! How is one to tell about joy? How describe the citizens of Omelas?

They were not simple folk, you see, though they were happy. But we do not say the words of cheer much any more. All smiles have become archaic. Given a description such as this one tends to make certain assumptions. Given a description such as this one tends to look next for the King, mounted on a splendid stallion and surrounded by his noble knights, or perhaps in a golden litter borne by great-muscled slaves. But there was no king. They did not use swords, or keep slaves. They were not barbarians. I do not know the rules and laws of their society, but I suspect that they were singularly few. As they did without monarchy and slavery, so they also got on without the stock exchange, the advertisement, the secret police, and the bomb. Yet I repeat that these were not simple folk, not dulcet shepherds, noble savages, bland utopians. They were not less complex than us. The trouble is that we have a bad habit, encouraged by pedants and sophisticates, of considering happiness as something rather stupid. Only pain is intellectual, only evil interesting. This is the treason of the artist: a refusal to admit the banality of evil and the terrible boredom of pain. If you can't lick 'em, join 'em. If it hurts, repeat it. But to praise despair is to condemn delight, to embrace violence is to lose hold of everything else. We have almost lost hold; we can no longer describe a happy man, nor make any celebration of joy. How can I tell you about the people of Omelas? They were not naïve and happy children — though their children were, in fact, happy. They were mature, intelligent, passionate adults whose lives were not wretched. O miracle! but I wish I could describe it better. I wish I could convince you. Omelas sounds in my words like a city in a fairy tale, long ago and far away, once upon a time. Perhaps it would be best if you imagined it as your own fancy bids, assuming it will rise to the occasion, for certainly I cannot suit you all. For instance, how about technology? I think that there would be no cars or helicopters in and above the streets; this follows from the fact that the people of Omelas are happy people. Happiness is based on a just discrimination of what is necessary, what is neither necessary nor destructive, and what is destructive. In the middle category, however — that of the unnecessary but undestructive, that of comfort, luxury, exuberance, etc. — they could perfectly well have central heating, subway trains, washing machines, and all kinds of marvelous devices not yet invented here, floating light-sources, fuelless power, a cure for the common cold. Or they could have none of that: it doesn't matter. As you like it. I incline to think that people from towns up and down the coast have been coming in to Omelas during the last days before the Festival on very fast little trains and double-decked trams and that the train station of Omelas is actually the handsomest building in town, though plainer than the magnificent Farmers' Market. But even granted trains, I fear that Omelas so far strikes some of you as goody-goody. Smiles, bells, parades, horses, bleh. If so, please add an orgy. If an orgy would help, don't hesitate. Let us not, however, have temples from which issue beautiful nude priests and priestesses already half in ecstasy and ready to copulate with any man or woman, lover or stranger, who desires union with the deep godhead of the blood, although that was my first idea. But really it would be better not to have any temples in Omelas — at least, not manned temples. Religion yes, clergy no. Surely the beautiful nudes can just wander about, offering themselves like divine soufflés to the hunger of the needy and the rapture of the flesh. Let them join the processions. Let tambourines be struck above the copulations, and the glory of desire be proclaimed upon the gongs, and (a not unimportant point) let the offspring of these delightful rituals be beloved and looked after by all. One thing I know there is none of in Omelas is guilt. But what else should there be? I thought at first there were no drugs, but that is puritanical. For those who like it, the faint insistent sweetness of *drooz* may perfume the ways of the city, *drooz* which first brings a great lightness and brilliance to the mind and limbs, and then after some hours a dreamy languor, and wonderful visions at last of the very arcana and inmost secrets of the Universe, as well as exciting the pleasure of sex beyond all belief; and it is not habit-forming. For more modest tastes I think there ought to be beer. What else, what else belongs in the joyous city? The sense of victory, surely, the celebration of courage. But as we did without clergy, let us do without soldiers. The joy built upon successful slaughter is not the right kind of joy; it will not do; it is fearful and it is trivial. A boundless and generous contentment, a magnanimous triumph felt not against some outer enemy but in communion with the finest and fairest in the souls of all men everywhere and the splendor of the world's summer: this is what swells the hearts of the people of Omelas, and the victory they celebrate is that of life. I really don't think many of them need to take *drooz*.

Most of the processions have reached the Green Fields by now. A marvelous smell of cooking goes forth from the red and blue tents of the provisioners. The faces of small children are amiably sticky; in the benign grey beard of a man a couple of crumbs of rich pastry are entangled. The youths and girls have mounted their horses and are beginning to group around the starting line of the course. An old woman, small, fat, and laughing, is passing out flowers from a basket, and tall young men wear her flowers in their shining hair. A child of nine or ten sits at the edge of the crowd, alone, playing on a wooden flute. People pause to listen, and they smile, but they do not speak to him, for he never ceases playing and never sees them, his dark eyes wholly rapt in the sweet, thin magic of the tune.

He finishes, and slowly lowers his hands holding the wooden flute.

As if that little private silence were the signal, all at once a trumpet sounds from the pavillion near the starting line: imperious, melancholy, piercing. The horses rear on their slender legs, and some of them neigh in answer. Sober-faced, the young riders stroke the horses' necks and soothe them, whispering, "Quiet, quiet, there my beauty, my hope. . . ." They begin to form in rank along the starting line. The crowds along the racecourse are like a field of grass and flowers in the wind. The Festival of Summer has begun.

Do you believe? Do you accept the festival, the city, the joy? No? Then let me describe one more thing.

In a basement under one of the beautiful public buildings of Omelas, or perhaps in the cellar of one of its spacious private homes, there is a room. It has one locked door, and no window. A little light seeps in dustily between cracks in the boards, secondhand from a cobwebbed window somewhere across the cellar. In one corner of the little room a couple of mops, with stiff, clotted, foul-smelling heads, stand near a rusty bucket. The floor is dirt, a little damp to the touch, as cellar dirt usually is. The room is about three paces long and two wide: a mere broom closet or disused tool room. In the room a child is sitting. It could be a boy or a girl. It looks about six, but actually is nearly ten. It is feeble-minded. Perhaps it was born defective, or perhaps it has become imbecile through fear, malnutrition, and neglect. It picks its nose and occasionally fumbles vaguely with its toes or genitals, as it sits hunched in the corner farthest from the bucket and the two mops. It is afraid of the mops. It finds them horrible. It shuts its eyes, but it knows the mops are still standing there; and the door is locked; and nobody will come. The door is always locked; and nobody ever comes, except that sometimes — the child has no understanding of time or interval — sometimes the door rattles terribly and opens, and a person, or several people, are there. One of them may come in and kick the child to make it stand up. The others never come close, but peer in at it with frightened, disgusted eyes. The food bowl and the water jug are hastily filled, the door is locked, the eyes disappear. The people at the door never say anything, but the child, who has not always lived in the tool room, and can remember sunlight and its mother's voice, sometimes speaks. "I will be good," it says. "Please let me out. I will be good!" They never answer. The child used to scream for help at night, and cry a good deal, but now it only makes a kind of whining, "eh-haa, eh-haa," and it speaks less and less often. It is so thin there are no calves to its legs; its belly protrudes; it lives on a half-bowl of corn meal and grease a day. It is naked. Its buttocks and thighs are a mass of festered sores, as it sits in its own excrement continually.

They all know it is there, all the people of Omelas. Some of them have come to see it, others are content merely to know it is there. They all know that it has to be there. Some of them understand why, and some do not, but they all understand that their happiness, the beauty of their city, the tenderness of their friendships, the health of their children, the wisdom of their scholars, the skill of their makers, even the abundance of their harvest and the kindly weathers of their skies, depend wholly on this child's abominable misery.

This is usually explained to children when they are between eight and twelve, whenever they seem capable of understanding; and most of those who come to see the child are young people, though often enough an adult comes, or comes back, to see the child. No matter how well the matter has been explained to them, these young spectators are always shocked and sickened at the sight. They feel disgust, which they had thought themselves superior to. They feel anger, outrage, impotence, despite all the explanations. They would like to do something for the child. But there is nothing they can do. If the child were brought up into the sunlight out of that vile place, if it were cleaned and fed and comforted, that would be a good thing, indeed; but if it were done, in that day and hour all the prosperity and beauty and delight of Omelas would wither and be destroyed. Those are the terms. To exchange all the goodness and grace of every life in Omelas for that single, small improvement: to throw away the happiness of thousands for the chance of the happiness of one: that would be to let guilt within the walls indeed.

The terms are strict and absolute; there may not even be a kind word spoken to the child.

Often the young people go home in tears, or in a tearless rage, when they have seen the child and faced this terrible paradox. They may brood over it for weeks or years. But as time goes on they begin to realize that even if the child could be released, it would not get much good of its freedom: a little vague pleasure of warmth and food, no doubt, but little more. It is too degraded and imbecile to know any real joy. It has been afraid too long ever to be free of fear. Its habits are too uncouth for it to respond to humane treatment. Indeed, after so long it would probably be wretched without walls about it to protect it, and darkness for its eyes, and its own excrement to sit in. Their tears at the bitter injustice dry when they begin to perceive the terrible justice of reality and to accept it. Yet it is their tears and anger, the trying of their generosity and the acceptance of their helplessness, which are perhaps the true source of the splendor of their lives. Theirs is no vapid, irresponsible happiness. They know that they, like the child, are not free. They know compassion. It is the existence of the child, and their knowledge of its existence, that makes possible the nobility of their architecture, the poignancy of their music, the profundity of their science. It is because of the child that they are so gentle with children. They know that if the wretched one were not there snivelling in the dark, the other one, the flute-player, could make no joyful music as the young riders line up in their beauty for the race in the sunlight of the first morning of summer.

Now do you believe in them? Are they not more credible? But there is one more thing to tell, and this is quite incredible.

At times one of the adolescent girls or boys who go to see the child does not go home to weep or rage, does not, in fact, go home at all. Sometimes also a man or woman much older falls silent for a day or two, and then leaves home. These people go out into the street, and walk down the street alone. They keep walking, and walk straight out of the city of Omelas, through the beautiful gates. They keep walking across the farmlands of Omelas. Each one goes alone, youth or girl, man or woman. Night falls; the traveler must pass down village streets, between the houses with yellow-lit windows, and on out into the darkness of the fields. Each alone, they go west or north, towards the mountains. They go on. They leave Omelas, they walk ahead into the darkness, and they do not come back. The place they go towards is a place even less imaginable to most of us than the city of happiness. I cannot describe it at all. It is possible that it does not exist. But they seem to know where they are going, the ones who walk away from Omelas.   [1976]

DORIS LESSING *(b. 1919) was born in Persia (now Iran), where her father managed a bank. When she was five her family moved to a farm in Rhodesia (now Zimbabwe), in an isolated part of Africa that had not been settled before by white people. Lessing left school at the age of fourteen in rebellion against her mother. After a first marriage failed, she married again and had one son. She was a Communist for some years in her twenties, when she "learned a great deal, chiefly about the nature of political power, how groups of people operate." Then in 1949 she left her husband in Rhodesia and came with her son to London, where she has lived as a professional writer ever since, "at first rather poor, but now comfortable."*

Africa remains in Lessing's consciousness as "an inexplicable majestic silence lying just over the border of memory or of thought. Africa gives you the knowledge that man is a small creature, among other creatures, in a large landscape." Her first two books, the novel The Grass Is Singing *(1950) and a volume of short stories,* This Was the Old Chief's Country *(1951), are based on her experiences in Rhodesia. They develop the theme of the exploitation of blacks by white people — although Lessing also considers racial prejudice "only one aspect of the atrophy of the imagination that prevents us from seeing ourselves in every creature that breathes under the sun." She has published many novels, but perhaps the most influential was* The Golden Notebook *(1962), an experimental book exploring the destructive relationships between men and women that mirror the lack of coherence and order in our fragmented, materialistic century.*

Lessing's short stories have often been compared to those of D. H. Lawrence. Like him, she is highly receptive to emotions that surface during the writing of fiction:

> *This question of I, who am I, what different levels there are inside of us, is very relevant to writing, to the process of creative writing about which we know nothing whatsoever. Every writer feels he, she, hits a different level. A certain kind of writing or emotion comes from it. But you don't know who it is who lives there.*

Like Lawrence, Lessing is not always confident of rational solutions to the problems of modern life. In her fiction she goes beyond Lawrence, however, to explore the possibilities for change. Lessing's African Stories *was published in 1981;* The Doris Lessing Reader *appeared in 1989. "Debbie and Julie" is from* The Real Thing, *stories and sketches published in 1992.*

Debbie and Julie

The fat girl in the sky-blue coat again took herself to the mirror. She could not keep away from it. Why did the others not comment on her scarlet cheeks, just like when she got measles, and the way her hair was stuck down with sweat? But they didn't notice her; she thought they did not see her. This was because of Debbie who protected her, so they got nothing out of noticing her.

She knew it was cold outside, for she had opened a window to check. Inside this flat it was, she believed, warm, but the heating in the block was erratic, particularly in bad weather, and then the electric fires were brought out and Debbie swore and complained and said she was going to move. But Julie knew Debbie would not move. She could not: she had fought for this flat to be hers, and people (men) from everywhere — "from all over the world," as Julie would proudly say to herself — knew Debbie was here. And besides, Julie was going to need to think of Debbie here, when she herself got home: remember the bright rackety place where people came and went, some of them frightening, but none threatening her, Julie, because Debbie looked after her.

She was so wet she was afraid she would start squelching. What if the wet came through the coat? Back she went to the bathroom and took off the coat. The dress — Debbie's, like the once smart coat — was now orange instead of yellow, because it was soaked. Julie knew there would be a lot of water at some point, because the paperback Debbie had bought her said so, but she didn't know if she was simply sweating. In the book everything was so tidy and regular, and she had checked the stages she must expect a dozen times. But now she stood surrounded by jars of bath salts and lotions on the shelf that went all around the bathroom, and felt cold water springing from her forehead, hot water running down her legs. She seemed to have pains everywhere, but could not match what she felt with the book.

On went the blue coat again. It was luckily still loose on her, for Debbie was a big girl, and she was small. Back she went to the long mirror in Debbie's room, and what she saw on her face, a look of distracted pain, made her decide it was time to leave. She longed for Debbie, who might after all just turn up. She could not bear to go without seeing her . . . *she had promised!* But she had to, now, at once, and she wrote on a piece of paper she had kept ready just in case. "I am going now. Thanks for everything. Thank you, thank you, thank you. All my love, Julie." Then her home address. She stuck this letter in a sober white envelope into the frame of Debbie's mirror and went into the living room, where a lot of people were lolling about watching the TV. No, not really a lot, four people crammed the little room. No one even looked at her. Then the man she was afraid of, and who had tried to "get" her, took in the fact that she stood there, enormous and smiling foolishly in her blue coat, and gave her the look she always got from him, which said he didn't know why Debbie bothered with her but didn't care. He was a sharp clever man, handsome she supposed, in a flashy Arab way. He was from Lebanon, and she must make allowances because there was a war there. Sitting beside him on the sofa was the girl who took the drugs around for him. She was smart and clever, like him, but blonde shiny, and she looked like a model for cheap clothes. A model was what she said she was, but Julie knew she wasn't. And there were two girls Julie had never seen before, and she supposed they were innocents, as she had been. They looked all giggly and anxious to please, and they were waiting. For Debbie?

Julie went quietly through the room to the landing outside and stood watching for the lift. She checked her carrier bag, ready for a month now, stuffed under her bed. In it was a torch, pieces of string wrapped in a piece of plastic, two pairs of knickers, a cardigan, a thick towel with an old blouse of Debbie's cut open to lie flat inside it and be soft and satiny, and some sanitary pads. The pads were Debbie's. She bled a lot each month. The lift came but Julie had gone back into the flat, full of trouble and worry. She felt ill-prepared, she did not have enough of something, but what could it be? The way she felt told her nothing, except that what was going to happen would be uncontrollable, and until today she had felt in control, and even confident. From shelves in the bathroom she took, almost at random, some guest towels and stuffed them into the carrier. She told herself she was stealing from Debbie, but knew Debbie wouldn't mind. She never did, would only say, "Just take it, love, if you want it." Then she might laugh and say, "Take what you want and *don't* pay for it!" Which was her motto in life, she claimed on every possible occasion. Julie knew better. Debbie could say this as much as she liked, but what she, Julie, had learned from Debbie was, simply, this: what things cost, the value of everything, and of people, of what you did for them, and what they did for you. When she had first come into this flat, brought by Debbie, who had seen her standing like a dummy on the platform at Waterloo at midnight on that first evening she arrived by herself in London, she had been as green as . . . those girls next door, waiting, but not knowing what for. She had been innocent and silly, and what that all boiled down to was that she hadn't known the price of anything. She hadn't known what had to be paid. This was what she had learned from Debbie, even though Debbie had never allowed her to pay for anything, ever.

From the moment she had been seen on the platform five months ago on a muggy, drizzly August evening, she had been learning how ignorant she was. For one thing, it was not only Debbie who had seen her; a lot of other people on the lookout in various parts of the station would have moved in on her like sharks if Debbie hadn't got to her first. Some of these people were baddies and some were goodies, but the kind ones would have sent her straight home.

For the second time she went through the living room and no one looked at her. The Lebanese was smiling and talking in an elderly-brotherly way to the new girls. Well, they had better watch out for themselves.

For the second time she waited for the lift. She seemed quite wrenched with pain. Was it worse? Yes, it was.

In the bitter black street that shone with lights from the lamps and the speeding cars she hauled herself on to a bus. Three stops, and by the time she reached where she wanted, she knew she had cut it too fine. She got off in a sleet shower under a street lamp and saw her blue coat turning dark with wet. Now she was far from being too hot, she was ready to shiver and shake, but could not decide if this was panic. Everything she had planned had seemed so easy, one thing after another, but she had not foreseen that she would stand at a bus stop, afraid to leave the light there, not knowing what the sensations were that wrenched her body. Was she hot? Cold? Nauseous? Hungry? A good thing the weather was so bad, no one was about. She walked boldly through the sleet and turned into a dark and narrow alley where she hurried, because it smelled bad and scared her, then out into a yard full of builders' rubbish and rusty skips. There was a derelict shed at one end. This shed was where she was going, where she had been only three days before to make sure it was still there, had not been pulled down, and that she could get in the door. But now something she had not foreseen. A large dog stood in the door, a great black threatening beast, and it was growling. She could see the gleam of its teeth and eyes. But she knew she had to get into the shed, and quickly. Again water poured hotly down her legs. Her head was swimming. Hot knives carved her back. She found a half brick and flung it at the wall near the dog, who disappeared into the shed growling. This was awful . . . Julie went into the shed, shut the door behind her, with difficulty because it dragged on broken hinges, and switched on the torch. The dog stood against a wall looking at her, but now she could see it would not hurt her. Its tail was sweeping about in the dirt, and it was so thin she could see its ribs under the dirty black shabby fur. Its eyes were bright and frantic. It wanted her to be good to it. She said, "It's all right, it's only me," and went to the corner of the shed away from the dog, where she had spread a folded blanket. The blanket was there, but the dog had been lying on it. She turned the blanket so the clean part inside was on the top. Now, having reached her refuge, she didn't know what to do. She took off her soaking knickers. She put the carrier bag close to the blanket. Afraid someone might see the gleam of light, she switched off the torch, first making sure she knew where it was. She could hear the dog breathing, and the flap-flap of its tail. It was lying down, not far from her. She could smell the wet doggy smell, and she was grateful for that, pleased the dog was there. Now she was in no doubt she had got here just in time, because her whole body was hot and fierce with pain, and she wanted to cry out, but knew she must not. She was groaning, though, and she heard herself: "Debbie, Debbie, Debbie . . ." All those months Debbie had said, "Don't worry about anything, when the time comes I'll see everything's all right." But Debbie had gone off with the new man to Paris, saying she would be back in a week, but had rung from New York to say, "How are you, honey? I'll be back at the weekend." That was three weeks ago. The "honey" had told Julie this man was different from the others, not only because he was an American: Debbie had never called her anything but Julie, wouldn't have dreamed of changing her behaviour for any man, but this "honey" had not been for Julie, but for the man who was listening. "I don't blame her," Julie was muttering now. "She always said she wanted just one man, not Tom and Dick and Harry." But while Julie was making herself think, I don't blame her, she was groaning, "Oh, Debbie, Debbie, why did you leave me?"

Debbie had left her to cope on her own, after providing everything from shelter and food and visits to a doctor, to the clothes and the bright blue coat that had hidden her so well no one had known. Debbie and she joked how little people noticed about other people. "You'd better watch your diet," the Lebanese had said. "Don't you let her" — meaning Debbie — "stuff you with food all the time."

Julie was on all fours on the blanket, her head between her arms, her fists clenched tight, and she was crying. The pain was awful, but that wasn't the worst of it. She felt so alone, so lonely. It occurred to her that having her bottom up in the air was probably not the right thing. She squatted, her back against a cold brick wall, and went on sweating and moaning. She could hear the dog whining, in sympathy, she thought. Water, or was it blood, poured out. She was afraid to switch on the torch to see. She felt the dog sniff at her face and neck, but it went off again. She could see absolutely nothing, it was so dark. Then she felt a rush, as if her insides were pouring out, and she thought, Why didn't the book say there would be all this water all the time? Then she thought, But that's the baby, and put her hand down and under her on the blanket was a wet slippery lump. She felt for the torch and switched it on. The baby was greyish and bloody and its mouth was opening and shutting. Now she was in a panic. Before, she had decided she must wait before cutting the cord, because the paperback said there was no hurry, but she was desperate to get the cord cut, in case the baby died. She found where the cord came out of the baby, a thick twisted rope of flesh, full of life, hot and pulsing in her hand. She found the scissors. She found the string. She cut the birth cord with the scissors, and trembled with fear. Blood everywhere, and the dog had come close and was sitting so near she could touch it. Its eyes were saying, Please, please . . . It was gulping and licking its lips, because of all the blood, when it was so hungry.

"You wait a bit," she said to the poor dog. Now she tied the cord up with the string that had boiled a long time in the saucepan. She was worrying because she was getting something wrong, but couldn't remember what it was. As for boiling the string, what sense did that make, when you saw the filth in this shed. Tramps had used it. The dog . . . other dogs too, probably. For all she knew, other girls had given birth in it. Most sheds were garden sheds, and full of plants in pots, and locked up. She knew, because she had checked so many. Not many places where a girl could give birth to a baby in peace and quiet — or a stray dog find a dry place out of the rain . . . She was getting giggly and silly, she could feel herself losing control. Meanwhile the baby was lying in a pool of bloody water and was mouthing and pulling its face about, and she ought to be doing something. Surely it ought to be crying? It was so slippery. The paperback didn't say anything about the baby being greasy and wet and so slippery she would be afraid to lift it. She pulled out the bundle of towel from the carrier and laid it flat, with the soft pink satin of Debbie's blouse smooth on top. She used both hands to pick the baby up round its middle and felt it squirm, probably because her hands were so cold. Its wriggling strength, its warmth, the life she could feel beating there, astonished and pleased her. Unexpectedly she was full of pleasure and pride. The baby's perfectly all right, she thought, looking in the torchlight at hands, feet . . . what else should she look for? Oh, yes, it was a girl. Was it deformed? The baby had an enormous cunt, a long wrinkled slit. Was that normal? Why didn't the book say?

She folded the baby firmly into the towel, with the bottom of the towel well tucked in over its feet, and only its face showing. Then she picked it up. It began to roar in short angry spasms. And now the panic began again. She had not thought the baby would cry so loudly . . . someone would come . . . what should she do . . . but she couldn't leave the shed because there was a thing called the afterbirth. As she thought this, there was another wet rush, all down her legs, and out plopped a mass of something that looked like liver with the end of the thick red cord coming out of it.

And now she knew what to do. She raised herself from the squatting position, clutching the baby with one arm and using the other hand to push herself up from the floor. She stood shakily by the bloody mess and moved away a few paces with the baby held high up and close against her. At once the dog crawled forward, giving her a desperate look that said, Don't get in my way. It ate up the afterbirth in quick gulps. It hopefully licked the bloody blanket, and briefly lifted its muzzle to look at her, wagging its long dirty tail. Then it went back to its place and sat with its back to the wall, watching. Meanwhile the baby let out short angry cries and kicked hard in its cocoon of towel. Julie thought, Should I just leave the baby here and run for it? No, the dog . . . But as she thought this, the baby stopped and lay quietly looking at her. Well, she wasn't going to look back, she wasn't going to love it.

She had to leave here, and she was a swamp of blood, water, God only knew what.

She took a cautious look. Blood trickled down her legs. And she had actually believed a tampon or two would be enough! She laid the baby down on a clean place on the blanket, keeping an eye on the dog. Its eyes gleamed in the torchlight. She put on a pair of clean knickers and packed in sanitary towels. She tried to tie the guest towels around her waist to make an extra pad, but they were too stiff. Now she picked up the baby, which was just like a papoose and looking around with its blurry little eyes. She took up the carrier bag and then the torch. She said to the dog, "Poor dog, I'm sorry," and went out, making sure the door was open for the dog. She switched off the torch, though the ground was rough and had bricks and bits of wood lying about. She could just see: there were lights in windows high up across the street. The sleet still blew down. She was already shivering. And the baby only had the towel around it . . . She put the bundle of baby under the flap of the now loose coat and went quickly across the uneven ground to the alley, and even through the bad-smelling place and then along the pavement to a telephone box she had made sure would be conveniently close when she was looking for the shed or somewhere safe. There was no one near the telephone box, no one anywhere around. She put the baby down on the floor and walked towards the brilliant lights of the pub at the corner. She did not look back. The pub was crammed and hot and noisy. Now what she was afraid of was that she might smell so strongly of blood someone would notice. She could hardly make her way to the toilet. There she removed her knickers with the pads of sanitary towels, which were already soaked. She used one of the guest towels to wash herself down. She went on soaking the towel in hot water and wringing it out, then wiping herself, watching how the blood at once began trickling on to the clean white skin of her inner thighs. But she could not stay there for ever, washing. She rubbed the same towel, wrung out in hot water, over her sticky head. She combed her hair flat. Well, it wouldn't stay flat for long: being naturally curly it would spring back into its own shape soon. Debbie said it was sweet, like a little girl. She filled her knickers with new pads, put the bloody pads into the container, and went out into the pub. Now there was music from the jukebox, pounding away, and the beat went straight through her, vibrating and making her feel sick. She wanted badly to get away from the music, but she bought a shandy, reaching over the shoulders of men arguing about football to get it. Unremarked, she went to stand near a small window that overlooked the telephone box. She could see the bundle, a small pathetic thing, like folded newspapers or a dropped jersey, on the floor of the box. She had first found the shed, then looked for the telephone box, and then hoped there would be a window somewhere close by, and there was.

She stood by the window for only five minutes or so. Then she saw a young man and a girl go into the telephone box. Through window glass streaked again with sleet, she saw the girl pick up the bundle from the floor, while the young man telephoned. She ought to leave . . . she ought not to stand here . . . but she stayed, watching, while the noise of the pub beat around her. The ambulance came in no time. Two ambulance men. The girl came out of the telephone box with the bundle, and the young man was behind her. The ambulance men took the bundle, first one, then the other, then handed it back to the girl, who got into the ambulance. The young man stood on the pavement, the girl inside waved to him, and he got in to go with them. So the baby was safe. It was done. She had done it. As she went out into the sleety rain she saw the ambulance lights vanish, and her heart plunged into loss and became empty and bitter, in the way she had been determined would not happen. "Debbie," she whispered, the tears running. "Where are you, Debbie?" Not necessarily New York. Or even the States. Canada . . . Mexico . . . the Costa Brava . . . South America . . . The people coming and going in Debbie's flat were always off somewhere, or just back. Rio . . . San Francisco, you name it. And Debbie had said to her, "One day it will be your turn." But now it was Debbie's turn. Why should she ever come back? She wanted to have "just one regular customer." Once she had said, by mistake, "just one man." Julie had heard this, but did not comment. Debbie could be as hard and as jokey as she liked, but she couldn't fool Julie, who knew she was the only person who really understood Debbie.

Now Julie was walking to the Underground, as fast as she could. Her legs were shaky, but she felt all right. All she wanted was to get home. It had been impossible to go home, or even think too much about home where her father (she was sure) would simply throw her out. But now, it was only a question of a few stops on the Underground, and then the train. At the most, an hour and a half.

The Underground train was full of people. They had had a meal after work, or been in a pub. Like Julie! She kept looking at all those faces and thinking, What would you say if you knew? At Waterloo she sat on a bench near an old man with a drinker's face, a tramp. She gave him a pound, but she was thinking of the dog. She did not have to wait long for a train. It was not full. Surely she ought to be tired, or sick or something? Most of all she was hungry. A great plate of steak and eggs, that was what she needed. And Debbie there too, eating opposite her.

A plump fresh-faced girl in a damp sky-blue coat sat upright among the other home-goers, holding a carrier bag that had on it, written red on black, SUSIE'S STYLES! Her eyes shone. Her young fresh fair hair curled all over her head. She vibrated with confidence, with secrets.

At the station she had to decide between a bus and walking home. Not the bus: on it there'd almost certainly be someone she knew, and perhaps even from her school. She didn't want to be looked at yet. The sleet was now a chilly blowy rain, with the sting of ice in it, but it wasn't bad, more of an occasional sharp pattering coming into her face and invigorating her. But she was going to arrive home all wet and pathetic, not at all as she had planned.

When she turned into her street, lights showed behind the curtains in all the windows. No one was out. What was she going to do about that coat, wet through, and, worse, hanging on her? Her mother would notice all that space under the coat and wonder. Three doors from home she glanced around to make sure no one was watching, and stripped off the coat in one fast movement and dropped it into a dustbin. Even in this half dark, lit with dull gleams from a window, she could see blood-stains on the lining. And her dress? The yellow dress was limp and grubby, but the cardigan came down low and hid most of it. This was going to be the dangerous part, all right, and only luck would get her through it. She ran up the steps and rang the bell, smiling, while she clutched the carrier bag so it could hide her front, which was still squashy and fat where the baby had been.

Heavy steps. Her father. The door opened slowly while he fumbled at locks, and she kept the smile going, and her heart beat, and then he stood in front of her large and black with the light behind him, so that her heart went small and weak . . . but then he turned so she could see his face and she thought, That can't be him, that can't be my *father* — for he had shrunk and become grey and ordinary, and . . . *what on earth had she been afraid of?* She could just hear what Debbie would say about him! Why, he was nothing at all. He called out in a sharp barking voice, "Anne, Anne, she's here." He was a man waiting for his wife to take command, crying as he went stumbling down the hall. Julie's mother came fast towards her. She was already crying, and that meant she could not see anything much. She put her arms around Julie and sobbed and said, "Oh, Julie, Julie, why didn't you . . . ? But come in, why, you're soaked." And she pushed and pulled Julie towards, and then into, the living room, where the old man (which is how Julie was seeing him with her new eyes) sat bowed in his chair, tears running down his face.

"She's all right, Len," said Anne, Julie's mother. She let go of her daughter and sat upright in her chair, knees together, feet together, dabbing her cheeks under her eyes, and stared at Len with a look that said, There, I told you so.

"Get her a cup of tea, Anne," said Len. And then, to Julie, but without looking at her, looking at his wife in a heavy awful way that told Julie how full of calamity had been their discussions about her, "Sit down, we aren't going to eat you."

Julie sat on the edge of a chair, but gingerly, because it hurt. It was as if she had been anaesthetized by urgency, but now she was safe, pains and soreness could make themselves felt. She watched her parents weep, their bitter faces full of loss. She saw how they sat, each in a chair well apart from the other, not comforting each other, or holding her, or wanting to hold each other, or to hold her.

"Oh, Julie," said her mother, "oh, *Julie.*"

"Mum, can I have a sandwich?"

"Of course you can. We've had our supper. I'll just . . ."

Julie smiled, she could not help it, and it was a sour little smile. She knew that what had been on those plates was exactly calculated, not a pea or a bit of potato left over. The next proper meal (lunch, tomorrow) would already be on a plate ready to cook, with a plastic film over it, in the fridge. Her mother went off to the kitchen, to work out how to feed Julie, and now Julie was alone with her father, and that wasn't good.

"You mustn't think we are going to ask you awkward questions," said her father, still not looking at her, and Julie knew that her mother had said, "We mustn't ask her any awkward questions. We must wait for her to tell us."

You bloody well ought to ask some questions, Julie was thinking, noting that already the raucous angry irritation her parents always made her feel was back, and strong. And, at the moment, dangerous.

But they had expected her to come back, then? For she had been making things easier for herself by saying, They won't care I'm not there! They probably won't even notice! Now she could see how much they had been grieving for her. How was she going to get herself out of here up to the bathroom? If she could just have a bath! At this point her mother came back with a cup of tea. Julie took it, drank it down at once, though it was too hot, and handed the cup back. She saw her mother had realized she meant it: she needed to eat, was hungry, could drink six cups of tea one after another. "Would you mind if I had a bath, Mum? I won't take a minute. I fell and the street was all slippery. It was sleeting."

She had already got herself to the door, clutching the carrier in front of her.

"You didn't hurt yourself?" enquired her father.

"No, I only slipped, I got all muddy."

"You run along and have a bath, girl," said her mother. "It'll give me time to boil an egg for sandwiches."

Julie ran upstairs. Quick, quick, she mustn't make a big thing of this bath, mustn't stay in it. Her bedroom was just so, all pretty and pink, and her big panda sat on her pillow. She flung off her clothes and waves of a nasty sour smell came up at her. She stuffed them all into the carrier and grabbed from the cupboard her pink-flowered dressing gown. What would Debbie have to say about that? she wondered, and wanted to laugh, thinking of Debbie here, sprawling on her bed with the panda. She found childish pyjamas stuffed into the back of a drawer. What was she going to do for padding? Her knickers showed patches of blood and that meant the pads hadn't been enough. She found some old panties and went into the bathroom with them. The bath filled quickly and there were waves of steam. Careful, she didn't want to faint, and her head was light. She got in and submerged her head. Quick, quick . . . She soaped and rubbed, getting rid of the birth, the dirty shed, the damp dog smell, the blood, all that blood. It was still welling gently out of her, not much but enough to make her careful when she dried herself on the fluffy pink towels her mother changed three times a week. She put on her knickers and packed them with old panties. On went the pyjamas, the pink dressing gown. She combed her hair.

There. It was all gone. Her breasts, she knew from the book, would have milk, but she would put on a tight bra and fill it with cotton wool. She would manage. In this house, her home, they did not see each other naked. Her mother hadn't come in for years when she was having a bath, and she always knocked on the bedroom door. In Debbie's flat people ran about naked or half dressed and Debbie might answer the door in her satin camiknickers, those great breasts of hers lolling about. Debbie often came in when Julie was in the bath to sit on the loo and chat . . . Tears filled Julie's eyes. Oh, no, she certainly must not cry.

She stuffed the bag with the bloody pads and her dirty clothes in it under her bed, well to the back. She would get rid of it all very early in the morning before her parents woke, which they would, at seven o'clock.

She went down the stairs, a good little girl washed and brushed, ready for the night.

In the living room her parents were silent and apart in their two well separated chairs. They had been crying again. Her father was relieved at what he saw when he cautiously took a look at her (as if it had been too painful to see her before), and he said, "It's good to have you home, Julie." His voice broke.

Her mother said, "I've made you some nice sandwiches."

Four thin slices of white bread had been made into two sandwiches and cut diagonally across, the yellow of the egg prettily showing, with sprigs of parsley disposed here and there. Hunger sprang in Julie like a tiger, and she ate ravenously, watching her mother's pitying, embarrassed face. Why, she thinks I've been short of food! Well, that's a good thing, it'll put her off the scent.

Her mother went off to make more food. Would she boil another egg, perhaps?

"Anything'll do, Mum. Jam . . . I'd love some jam on some toast."

She had finished the sandwiches and drunk down the tea long before her mother had returned with a tray, half a loaf of bread, butter, strawberry jam, more tea.

"I don't like to think of you going without food," she said.

"But I didn't, not really," said Julie, remembering all the feasts she had had with Debbie, the pizzas that arrived all hours of the day and the night from almost next door, the Kentucky chicken, the special steak feeds when Debbie got hungry, which was often. In the little kitchen was a bowl from Morocco kept piled with fruit. "You must get enough vitamins," Debbie kept saying, and brought in more grapes, more apples and pears, let alone fruit Julie had never heard of, like pomegranates and pawpaws, which Debbie had learned to like on one of her trips somewhere.

"We aren't going to pester you with questions," said her mother.

"I've been with a girl. Her name is Debbie. She was good to me. I've been all right," said Julie, looking at her mother, and then at her father. *There, don't ask any more questions.*

"A girl?" said her father heavily. He still kept his eyes away from Julie, because when he looked at her the tears started up again.

"Well, I haven't been with a boyfriend," said Julie and could not stop herself from laughing at this ridiculous idea.

They were all laughing with relief, with disbelief . . . they think I've been off with a boy! What were they imagining? Julie contemplated the incident in the school cloakroom with Billy Jayson that so improbably had led to the scene in the shed with the dog. She had joked with Debbie that it would be a virgin birth. "He hardly got it in," she had said. "I didn't think anything had really happened."

Probably Billy had forgotten all about it. Unless he connected her leaving school and running away from home with that scene in the cloakroom? But why should he? It was four months after they had tussled and shoved and giggled, she saying, No no, and he saying, Oh come on, then.

"Are you going back to school?" asked her mother carefully. "The officer came round last week and said you still could. There are two terms left. And you've always been a good girl before this."

"Yes, I'll go back," said Julie. Seven months — she could manage that. She'd be bored, but never mind. And then . . . . This was the moment she should say something more, explain, make up some lies, for they both sat staring at her, their faces full of what they had been feeling for the long five months she had been gone. She knew she was treating them badly, refusing to say anything. Well, she would, but not now, she was suddenly absolutely exhausted. Full of hot tea and food, she felt herself letting go, letting herself slide . . . She began to yawn and could not stop. But they did not suggest she should go to bed, and this was because they simply could not believe they wouldn't get anything more from her.

But there was nothing she could say. She looked at her father, that cautious, greyish, elderly man, sitting heavily in his chair. At her mother, who seemed almost girlish as she sat upright there in her pretty pale blue dress with its nice little collar and the little pearl buttons down the front. Her grey curls were sprightly, and her blue eyes full of wounded and uncomprehending innocence. Julie thought, I wish I could just snuggle up to Mum and she could hold me and I could go to sleep. Surely this must have happened when she was small, but she could not remember it. In this family, they simply did not touch each other.

Full of the clarity of her exhaustion, and because of what she had learned in the last months, she saw her parents and knew that — they cancelled each other out. Debbie would say there was something wrong with their chemistry. They did not disagree. They never raised their voices, or argued. Each day was a pattern of cups of tea, meals, cups of coffee and biscuits, always at exactly the same times, with bedtime as the goal. They seldom went out. They saw very few people, only each other. It was as if they had switched themselves off.

They had been old when she was born, was that the trouble?

At Debbie's people shouted, kissed, hugged, argued, fought, threatened, wept, and screamed.

There were two bedrooms in that flat. Debbie had given her the little one to herself. She was supposed to make herself scarce when Debbie came in with a man, a new one, but not when Derek was there, Debbie's real boyfriend. Derek joked a lot and ordered Julie about. How about making me a cup of tea, getting me a drink, making me some bacon and eggs, what have you been doing with yourself, why don't you get yourself a new hairdo, a new dress? He liked Julie, though she did not like him much. She knew he was not good enough for Debbie.

Soon Debbie would get rid of him. As she had the man who once owned the flat and took a percentage of what she earned. But Debbie had found out something bad about him, had put the screws on, got the flat for herself, worked for herself. Julie had seen this man just once, and he had given her the creeps. "My first love," Debbie joked, and laughed loudly when Julie grimaced. Derek did not give her the creeps, he was just nothing! Ordinary. Boring. But the man Debbie had gone to New York with was a TV producer. He was making a series no one had heard about in England, not good enough to sell here, he said. This man was more like it, but Julie thought Debbie would get rid of him too, when something better came up.

All these thoughts, these judgments, so unlike anything ever said or thought in her own home, went on in Julie's mind quite comfortably, though they wouldn't do for herself. Debbie had to be like this, because of her hard life. This included something bad that Debbie had never talked about, but it was why she had been so good to Julie. Probably, just like Julie, Debbie had stood very late in a railway station, pregnant, her head full of rubbish about how she would get a job, have the baby, bring it up, find a man who would love her and the baby. Or perhaps it had been something else to do with being pregnant and alone. It was not she, Julie, who had earned five months of Debbie's love and protection, it was pregnant Julie, helpless and alone.

Oh, yes, Debbie was fond of her.

Sometimes she spent the night in Debbie's big bed because Debbie could not bear to sleep alone. She got scared, she said. She could not believe that Julie wasn't frightened of the dark. Debbie always crashed straight off to sleep, even when she hadn't been drinking. Then Julie cautiously got up on her elbow and bent over sleeping Debbie, to examine her, try and find out . . . Debbie was a big handsome girl. Her skin was very white, and she had black shiny straight hair, and she made up her lips to be thin and scarlet and curving, just right for the lashing, slashing tongue behind them. When she was asleep her face was smooth and closed, and her lips were ordinary, quite pathetic Julie thought, and there was wear under her eyes. That face showed nothing of why Debbie said to people coming into the flat who might notice Julie the wrong way, "Lay off, do you hear? Lay off, or I'll . . ." And her scarlet lips and her black eyes were nasty, frightening.

But if Debbie woke in the night, she might turn to Julie and draw her into an embrace that told Julie how little she knew about love, about tenderness. Then Julie lay awake, astounded at the revelations this big hot smooth body made, and went on making, even though Debbie was off to sleep again. She never actually "did anything." Julie even waited for "something" to happen. Nothing ever did. Just once Debbie put her hand down to touch the mound of Julie's stomach, but took it quickly away. Julie lay entangled with Debbie, and they were like two cats that have finished washing each other and gone to sleep, and Julie knew how terribly she had been deprived at home, and how empty and sad her parents were. Suppose she said to her mother now, Mum, let me come into your bed tonight, I'm scared, I've missed you . . . She could just see her mother's embarrassed, timid face. "But Julie, you're a big girl now."

Anne and Len slept in twin beds stretched out parallel to each other, the night table between them.

There were tears in Julie's eyes, and she did not know it, but then she did and looked quickly at her mother, then her father, for they must not know she would give anything to cry and cry, and be comforted and held . . . But they weren't looking at her, only at the television. They had switched it on, without her noticing. Now all three of them sat staring at it.

On the screen a woman announcer smiled the special smile that goes with royalty, animals, and children and said, "At eight o'clock this evening a newly born baby girl was found in a telephone box in Islington. She was warmly wrapped and healthy. She weighed seven pounds and three ounces. The nurses have called her Rosie." Hot waves of jealousy went through Julie when she saw how the nurse smiled down at the little face seen briefly by Julie in torchlight, and then again through the sleet outside the shed. "The mother is urged to come forward as she might be in need of urgent medical attention."

It was the late news.

Surely they were going to guess? But why should they? It was hard enough for her to believe that she could sit here in her pretty little dressing gown smelling of bath powder, when she had given birth by herself in a dirty shed with only a dog for company. Four hours ago, that was all!

"Why don't we have a dog, Mum?" asked Julie, knowing what she was going to hear.

"But they are such a nuisance, Julie. And who's going to take it for walks?"

"I will, Mum."

"But you'll have finished school in July, and I don't want the bother of a dog, and I'm sure Len doesn't."

Her father didn't say anything. He leaned forward and turned off the set. The screen went blank.

"I often wonder what Jessie thinks," he remarked, "when she sees something like this on the telly, I mean."

"Oh, leave it, Len," said Anne warningly.

Julie did not really hear this, but then she did: her ears sprang to life, and she knew something extraordinary was about to happen.

"That's why we were so worried about you," said Julie's father, heavy, grief-ridden, reproachful. "It's easy enough to happen, how were we to know you weren't —"

"Len, we agreed we wouldn't ever —"

"What about Auntie Jessie?" asked Julie, trying to take it in. A silence. "Well, what about her, Dad? You can't just leave it like that."

"Len," said Anne wildly.

"Your Auntie Jessie got herself into the family way," said her father, determined to say it, ignoring his wife's face, her distress. His face was saying, Why should she be spared when she's given us such a bad time? "She wasn't much older than you are now." At last he was looking straight at Julie, full of reproach, and his eyes dripped tears all down his face and on to his tie. "It can happen easy enough, can't it?"

"You mean . . . but what happened to the baby? Was it born?"

"Your cousin Freda," said Len, still bitter and obstinate, his accusing eyes on his daughter.

"You mean, Freda is . . . you mean. Auntie Jessie's mum and dad didn't mind?"

"They minded, all right," said Anne. "I remember all that well enough. They wanted the baby adopted, but Jessie stuck it out and had it, and in the end they came around. I still think they were right and Jessie was wrong. She was only seventeen. She never would say who the father was. She was stuck at home with the baby when she should have been out enjoying herself and learning things. She got married when she was a baby herself."

By now Julie was more or less herself again, though she felt as if she'd been on a roller coaster. Above all, what she was thinking was, I've got to get it all out of them now, because I know them, they'll clam up and never talk of it again.

"Didn't Uncle Bob mind?" she asked.

"Not so that he wouldn't marry her, he married her, didn't he, and she had a love child he had to take on," said her father, full of anger and accusations.

"A love child," said Julie derisively, unable to stop herself. But her parents didn't notice.

"That's what they call it, I believe," said her father, all heavy and sarcastic. "Well, that's what can happen, Julie, and you've always been such a sensible girl and that made it worse." And now, unbelievably, this father of hers, whom she had so feared she ran away from home, sat sobbing, covering his face with his hands.

Her mother was weeping, her eyes bright, her cheeks red.

In a moment Julie would be bawling too.

"I'm going to bed," she said, getting up. "Oh, I'm sorry Mum, I'm sorry, Dad, I'm sorry . . ."

"It's all right, Julie," said her mother.

Julie went out of the room and up the stairs and into her room, walking carefully now, because she was so sore. And she felt numbed and confused, because of Aunt Jessica and her cousin Freda. Why, she, Julie, could have . . . she could be sitting here now, with her baby Rosie, they wouldn't have thrown her out.

She didn't know what to think, or to feel . . . She felt . . . she wanted . . . "Oh, Debbie," she cried, but silently, tucked into her little bed, her arms around the panda. "Oh, Debbie, what am I to do?"

She thought, In July, when I've finished school, I am going back, I'm going to run away, I'll go to London and get a job, and I can have my baby. For a few minutes she persuaded herself it was not the silly little girl who had run away who said this, but the Debbie-taught girl who knew what things cost. Then she said to herself, Stop it, stop it, you know better.

She thought of Aunt Jessie's house. She had always enjoyed that house. It occurred to her now that Debbie's place and Aunt Jessie's had a lot in common — noisy, disturbing, exciting. Which was why her parents did not much like going there. But here, a baby here, Rosie with her long wrinkled cunt here . . . Julie was laughing her raucous, derisive laugh, but it was unhappy because she had understood that Rosie her daughter could not come here, because she, Julie, could not stand it.

I'll take Rosie to Debbie's in London, said Julie, in a final futile attempt.

But Debbie had taken in pregnant Julie. *That was what had been paid.*

If Julie brought baby Rosie here, then she would have to stay here. Until she got married. Like Auntie Jessie. Julie thought of Uncle Bob. Now she realized she had always seen him as Auntie Jessie's shadow, not up to much. She had wondered why Auntie Jessie married him. Now she knew.

I've got to get out of here, she thought, I've got to. In July I'll leave. I'll have my O levels. I can get them easily. I'll work hard and get my five O levels. I'll go to London. I know how things are, now. Look, I've lived in Debbie's flat, and I didn't let myself get hurt by them. I was clever, no one knew I was pregnant, only Debbie. I had Rosie by myself in that shed with only a dog to help me, and then I put Rosie in a safe place and now she's all right, and I've come home, and I've managed it all so well they never even guessed. I'm all right.

With her arms around the panda Julie thought, I can do anything I want to do, I've proved that.

And she drifted off to sleep. [1987]

NAGUIB MAHFOUZ *(b. 1911) — his name was anglicized from Abdel Aziz al-Sabilgi — was born in Cairo, Egypt, and educated at the University of Cairo. He published his first story in 1934, the year of his graduation from the university. For the next five years he worked as a journalist while publishing short fiction in magazines. In 1939 his first collection of stories and a novel were both published. That year Mahfouz also took a job as a civil servant in the Ministry of Islamic Affairs to help him support his wife and two daughters. He never depended on his writing for his living. Instead he said that he "spent on literature — on books and paper . . . I was a government employee in the morning and a writer in the evening" until he retired from the civil service in 1971.*

Mahfouz continued to publish novels throughout his life — nearly forty to date — but he didn't turn his attention back to short fiction until 1963. He usually did extensive research for his novels but, as he told an interviewer, he worked more spontaneously on short fiction: "My short stories come straight from the heart." Mahfouz has published fourteen volumes of stories, some of which are considered classics in modern Arabic literature. The Islamic religion is central to his life, but he feels that "excessive concern with religion seems to me a last resort for people who have been exhausted by life."

Despite the sweeping philosophical themes and sense of life's mysterious forces reflected in the often virtuosic handling of time in Mahfouz's fiction, as in "Half a Day," the realistic setting of most of his fiction is inevitably the same small district in the sprawling city of Cairo. His translator Denys Johnson-Davies has noted that Mahfouz's books "are sited in that square mile or so which makes up the districts of Gamaliyya and al-Hussein, an area which includes that vast bazaar known to tourists as Khan al-Khalili, with its numerous mosques, cafes, small shops, and jostling motley of colorful characters."

Mahfouz describes himself as "someone who loves literature." According to Johnson-Davies, Mahfouz was so delighted to see his work in print when he began writing that he was surprised when an editor summoned him to the office of a magazine that had accepted one of his stories and gave him a pound note: "'One gets paid for them as well!' exclaimed the budding writer in disbelief — and it was with the same modest disbelief that, more than half a century later, he received the news of the Nobel Prize."

Naguib Mahfouz

Half a Day

Translated by Denys Johnson-Davies

I proceeded alongside my father, clutching his right hand, running to keep up with the long strides he was taking. All my clothes were new: the black shoes, the green school uniform, and the red tarboosh. My delight in my new clothes, however, was not altogether unmarred, for this was no feast day but the day on which I was to be cast into school for the first time.

My mother stood at the window watching our progress, and I would turn toward her from time to time, as though appealing for help. We walked along a street lined with gardens; on both sides were extensive fields planted with crops, prickly pears, henna trees, and a few date palms.

"Why school?" I challenged my father openly. "I shall never do anything to annoy you."

"I'm not punishing you," he said, laughing. "School's not a punishment. It's the factory that makes useful men out of boys. Don't you want to be like your father and brothers?"

I was not convinced. I did not believe there was really any good to be had in tearing me away from the intimacy of my home and throwing me into this building that stood at the end of the road like some huge, high-walled fortress, exceedingly stern and grim.

When we arrived at the gate we could see the courtyard, vast and crammed full of boys and girls. "Go in by yourself," said my father, "and join them. Put a smile on your face and be a good example to others."

I hesitated and clung to his hand, but he gently pushed me from him. "Be a man," he said. "Today you truly begin life. You will find me waiting for you when it's time to leave."

I took a few steps, then stopped and looked but saw nothing. Then the faces of boys and girls came into view. I did not know a single one of them, and none of them knew me. I felt I was a stranger who had lost his way. But glances of curiosity were directed toward me, and one boy approached and asked, "Who brought you?"

"My father," I whispered.

"My father's dead," he said quite simply.

I did not know what to say. The gate was closed, letting out a pitiable screech. Some of the children burst into tears. The bell rang. A lady came along, followed by a group of men. The men began sorting us into ranks. We were formed into an intricate pattern in the great courtyard surrounded on three sides by high buildings of several floors; from each floor we were overlooked by a long balcony roofed in wood.

"This is your new home," said the woman. "Here too there are mothers and fathers. Here there is everything that is enjoyable and beneficial to knowledge and religion. Dry your tears and face life joyfully."

We submitted to the facts, and this submission brought a sort of contentment. Living beings were drawn to other living beings, and from the first moments my heart made friends with such boys as were to be my friends and fell in love with such girls as I was to be in love with, so that it seemed my misgivings had had no basis. I had never imagined school would have this rich variety. We played all sorts of different games: swings, the vaulting horse, ball games. In the music room we chanted our first songs. We also had our first introduction to language. We saw a globe of the Earth, which revolved and showed the various continents and countries. We started learning the numbers. The story of the Creator of the universe was read to us, we were told of His present world and of His Hereafter, and we heard examples of what He said. We ate delicious food, took a little nap, and woke up to go on with friendship and love, play and learning.

As our path revealed itself to us, however, we did not find it as totally sweet and unclouded as we had presumed. Dust-laden winds and unexpected accidents came about suddenly, so we had to be watchful, at the ready, and very patient. It was not all a matter of playing and fooling around. Rivalries could bring about pain and hatred or give rise to fighting. And while the lady would sometimes smile, she would often scowl and scold. Even more frequently she would resort to physical punishment.

In addition, the time for changing one's mind was over and gone and there was no question of ever returning to the paradise of home. Nothing lay ahead of us but exertion, struggle, and perseverance. Those who were able took advantage of the opportunities for success and happiness that presented themselves amid the worries.

The bell rang announcing the passing of the day and the end of work. The throngs of children rushed toward the gate, which was opened again. I bade farewell to friends and sweethearts and passed through the gate. I peered around but found no trace of my father, who had promised to be there. I stepped aside to wait. When I had waited for a long time without avail, I decided to return home on my own. After I had taken a few steps, a middle-aged man passed by, and I realized at once that I knew him. He came toward me, smiling, and shook me by the hand, saying, "It's a long time since we last met — how are you?"

With a nod of my head, I agreed with him and in turn asked, "And you, how are you?"

"As you can see, not all that good, the Almighty be praised!"

Again he shook me by the hand and went off. I proceeded a few steps, then came to a startled halt. Good Lord! Where was the street lined with gardens? Where had it disappeared to? When did all these vehicles invade it? And when did all these hordes of humanity come to rest upon its surface? How did these hills of refuse come to cover its sides? And where were the fields that bordered it? High buildings had taken over, the street surged with children, and disturbing noises shook the air. At various points stood conjurers showing off their tricks and making snakes appear from baskets. Then there was a band announcing the opening of a circus, with clowns and weight lifters walking in front. A line of trucks carrying central security troops crawled majestically by. The siren of a fire engine shrieked, and it was not clear how the vehicle would cleave its way to reach the blazing fire. A battle raged between a taxi driver and his passenger, while the passenger's wife called out for help and no one answered. Good God! I was in a daze. My head spun. I almost went crazy. How could all this have happened in half a day, between early morning and sunset? I would find the answer at home with my father. But where was my home? I could see only tall buildings and hordes of people. I hastened on to the crossroads between the gardens and Abu Khoda. I had to cross Abu Khoda to reach my house, but the stream of cars would not let up. The fire engine's siren was shrieking at full pitch as it moved at a snail's pace, and I said to myself, "Let the fire take its pleasure in what it consumes." Extremely irritated, I wondered when I would be able to cross. I stood there a long time, until the young lad employed at the ironing shop on the corner came up to me. He stretched out his arm and said gallantly, "Grandpa, let me take you across."   [1989]

BERNARD MALAMUD (1914–1986), *the prominent Jewish American writer, was born in Brooklyn, New York, to Max and Bertha Fidelman Malamud, Russian immigrants who ran a mom-and-pop grocery store. Malamud published his earliest stories in Brooklyn's Erasmus Hall High School literary magazine. In 1936 he graduated from City College in New York; in 1942 he earned his M.A. degree from Columbia University with a thesis on the English novelist Thomas Hardy. While teaching English at Erasmus Hall High School in 1945, Malamud married Ann De Chiara, an Italian American. Throughout his life his stories appeared in a variety of magazines and, like "Black Is My Favorite Color," reflected his interest in minority groups: Jews, Italians, blacks, and others. From 1949 to 1961 Malamud taught English at Oregon State University; then he joined the faculty at Bennington College in Vermont. In his later years he traveled and lectured extensively throughout the world.*

Malamud published two novels, The Natural *(1952) and* The Assistant *(1957), before his first collection of short stories,* The Magic Barrel, *came out in 1958. It won a National Book Award.* Idiots First, *his second collection, appeared in 1963;* Pictures of Fidelman: An Exhibition, *a unit of stories published over twelve years, was issued in 1969.* The Stories of Bernard Malamud *(1983) and* The People and Uncollected Stories *(1989) are his last story collections. He also published five other novels.*

Malamud has said that from the beginning of his career he enjoyed alternating work on novels and short stories.

> *Some writers don't need the short story to launch them into fiction, but I think it is a loss not to attempt to find out whether one can write them. Whatever happens happens quickly. The writer mounts his personal Pegasus, even if it is an absent-minded nag who never made it on the race track; an ascension occurs and the ride begins. The scenery often surprises, and so do some of the people one meets. . . . García Márquez will start a fiction with someone pushing a dream around, or running from one, and before you know it he has peopled a small country. Working alone to create stories, despite serious inconveniences, is not a bad way to live our human loneliness. . . . Art celebrates life and gives us our measure.*

BERNARD MALAMUD

Black Is My Favorite Color

Charity Quietness sits in the toilet eating her two hard-boiled eggs while I'm having my ham sandwich and coffee in the kitchen. That's how it goes, only don't get the idea of ghettoes. If there's a ghetto I'm the one that's in it. She's my cleaning woman from Father Divine and comes in once a week to my small three-room apartment on my day off from the liquor store.

"Peace," she says to me, "Father reached on down and took me right up in Heaven." She's a small person with a flat body, frizzy hair, and a quiet face that the light shines out of, and Mama had such eyes before she died. The first time Charity Quietness came in to clean, a little more than a year and a half, I made the mistake to ask her to sit down at the kitchen table with me and eat her lunch. I was still feeling not so hot after Ornita left, but I'm the kind of man — Nat Lime, forty-four, a bachelor with a daily growing bald spot on the back of my head, and I could lose frankly fifteen pounds — who enjoys company so long as he has it. So she cooked up her two hard-boiled eggs and sat down and took a small bite out of one of them. But after a minute she stopped chewing and she got up and carried the eggs in a cup to the bathroom, and since then she eats there. I said to her more than once, "Okay, Charity Quietness, so have it your way, eat the eggs in the kitchen by yourself and I'll eat when you're done," but she smiles absentminded, and eats in the toilet. It's my fate with colored people.

Although black is still my favorite color you wouldn't know it from my luck except in short quantities, even though I do all right in the liquor store business in Harlem, on Eighth Avenue between 110th and 111th. I speak with respect. A large part of my life I've had dealings with Negro people, most on a business basis but sometimes for friendly reasons with genuine feeling on both sides. I'm drawn to them. At this time of my life I should have one or two good colored friends, but the fault isn't necessarily mine. If they knew what was in my heart toward them, but how can you tell that to anybody nowadays? I've tried more than once but the language of the heart either is a dead language or else nobody understands it the way you speak it. Very few. What I'm saying is, personally for me there's only one human color and that's the color of blood. I like a black person if not because he's black, then because I'm white. It comes to the same thing. If I wasn't white my first choice would be black. I'm satisfied to be white because I have no other choice. Anyway, I got an eye for color. I appreciate. Who wants everybody to be the same? Maybe it's like some kind of a talent. Nat Lime might be a liquor dealer in Harlem, but once in the jungle in New Guinea in the Second World War, I got the idea, when I shot at a running Jap and missed him, that I had some kind of a talent, though maybe it's the kind where you have a good idea now and then, but in the end what do they come to? After all, it's a strange world.

Where Charity Quietness eats her eggs makes me think about Buster Wilson when we were both boys in the Williamsburg section of Brooklyn. There was this long block of run-down dirty frame houses in the middle of a not-so-hot white neighborhood full of pushcarts. The Negro houses looked to me like they had been born and died there, dead not long after the beginning of the world. I lived on the next street. My father was a cutter with arthritis in both hands, big red knuckles and fingers so swollen he didn't cut, and my mother was the one who went to work. She sold paper bags from a second-hand pushcart on Ellery Street. We didn't starve but nobody ate chicken unless we were sick, or the chicken was. This was my first acquaintance with a lot of black people and I used to poke around on their poor block. I think I thought, brother, if there can be like this, what can't there be? I mean I caught an early idea what life was about. Anyway, I met Buster Wilson there. He used to play marbles by himself. I sat on the curb across the street, watching him shoot one marble lefty and the other one righty. The hand that won picked up the marbles. It wasn't so much of a game but he didn't ask me to come over. My idea was to be friendly, only he never encouraged, he discouraged. Why did I pick him out for a friend? Maybe because I had no others then, we were new in the neighborhood, from Manhattan. Also I liked his type. Buster did everything alone. He was a skinny kid and his brothers' clothes hung on him like worn-out potato sacks. He was a beanpole boy, about twelve, and I was then ten. His arms and legs were burnt-out matchsticks. He always wore a brown wool sweater, one arm half unraveled, the other went down to the wrist. His long and narrow head had a white part cut straight in the short woolly hair, maybe with a ruler there, by his father, a barber but too drunk to stay a barber. In those days though I had little myself I was old enough to know who was better off, and the whole block of colored houses made me feel bad in the daylight. But I went there as much as I could because the street was full of life. In the night it looked different, it's hard to tell a cripple in the dark. Sometimes I was afraid to walk by the houses when they were dark and quiet. I was afraid there were people looking at me that I couldn't see. I liked it better when they had parties at night and everybody had a good time. The musicians played their banjos and saxophones and the houses shook with the music and laughing. The young girls, with their pretty dresses and ribbons in their hair, caught me in my throat when I saw them through the windows.

But with the parties came drinking and fights. Sundays were bad days after the Saturday night parties. I remember once that Buster's father, also long and loose, always wearing a dirty gray Homburg hat, chased another black man in the street with a half-inch chisel. The other one, maybe five feet high, lost his shoe and when they wrestled on the ground he was already bleeding through his suit, a thick red blood smearing the sidewalk. I was frightened by the blood and wanted to pour it back in the man who was bleeding from the chisel. On another time Buster's father was playing in a crap game with two big bouncy red dice, in the back of an alley between two middle houses. Then about six men started fist-fighting there, and they ran out of the alley and hit each other in the street. The neighbors, including children, came out and watched, everybody afraid but nobody moving to do anything. I saw the same thing near my store in Harlem, years later, a big crowd watching two men in the street, their breaths hanging in the air on a winter night, murdering each other with switch knives, but nobody moved to call a cop. I didn't either. Anyway, I was just a young kid but I still remember how the cops drove up in a police paddy wagon and broke up the fight by hitting everybody they could hit with big nightsticks. This was in the days before La Guardia. Most of the fighters were knocked out cold, only one or two got away. Buster's father started to run back in his house but a cop ran after him and cracked him on his Homburg hat with a club, right on the front porch. Then the Negro men were lifted up by the cops, one at the arms and the other at the feet, and they heaved them in the paddy wagon. Buster's father hit the back of the wagon and fell, with his nose spouting very red blood, on top of three other men. I personally couldn't stand it, I was scared of the human race so I ran home, but I remember Buster watching without any expression in his eyes. I stole an extra fifteen cents from my mother's pocketbook and I ran back and asked Buster if he wanted to go to the movies, I would pay. This was the first time he talked to me.

So we went more than once to the movies. But we never got to be friends. Maybe because it was a one-way proposition — from me to him. Which includes my invitations to go with me, my (poor mother's) movie money, Hershey chocolate bars, watermelon slices, even my best Nick Carter and Merriwell books that I spent hours picking up in the junk shops, and that he never gave me back. Once, he let me go in his house to get a match so we could smoke some butts we found, but it smelled so heavy, so impossible, I died till I got out of there. What I saw in the way of furniture I won't mention — the best was falling apart in pieces. Maybe we went to the movies all together five or six matinees that spring and in the summertime, but when the shows were over he usually walked home by himself.

"Why don't you wait for me, Buster?" I said. "We're both going in the same direction."

But he was walking ahead and didn't hear me. Anyway he didn't answer.

One day when I wasn't expecting it he hit me in the teeth. I felt like crying but not because of the pain. I spit blood and said, "What did you hit me for? What did I do to you?"

"Because you a Jew bastard. Take your Jew movies and your Jew candy and shove them up your Jew ass."

And he ran away.

I thought to myself how was I to know he didn't like the movies. When I was a man I thought, you can't force it.

Years later, in the prime of my life, I met Mrs. Ornita Harris. She was standing by herself under an open umbrella at the bus stop, crosstown 110th, and I picked up her green glove that she had dropped on the wet sidewalk. It was in the end of November. Before I could ask her was it hers, she grabbed the glove out of my hand, closed her umbrella, and stepped in the bus. I got on right after her. I was annoyed so I said, "If you'll pardon me, Miss, there's no law that you have to say thanks, but at least don't make a criminal out of me."

"Well, I'm sorry," she said, "but I don't like white men trying to do me favors."

I tipped my hat and that was that. In ten minutes I got off the bus but she was already gone.

Who expected to see her again, but I did. She came into my store about a week later for a bottle of Scotch.

"I would offer you a discount," I told her, "but I know you don't like a certain kind of a favor and I'm not looking for a slap in the face."

Then she recognized me and got a little embarrassed.

"I'm sorry I misunderstood you that day."

"So mistakes happen."

The result was she took the discount. I gave her a dollar off.

She used to come in every two weeks for a fifth of Haig & Haig. Sometimes I waited on her, sometimes my helpers, Jimmy or Mason, also colored, but I said to give the discount. They both looked at me but I had nothing to be ashamed. In the spring when she came in we used to talk once in a while. She was a slim woman, dark, but not the most dark, about thirty years I would say, also well built, with a combination nice legs and a good-size bosom that I like. Her face was pretty, with big eyes and high cheekbones, but lips a little thick and nose a little broad. Sometimes she didn't feel like talking, she paid for the bottle, less discount, and walked out. Her eyes were tired and she didn't look to me like a happy woman.

I found out her husband was once a window cleaner on the big buildings, but one day his safety belt broke and he fell fifteen stories. After the funeral she got a job as a manicurist in a Times Square barber shop. I told her I was a bachelor and lived with my mother in a small three-room apartment on West Eighty-third near Broadway. My mother had cancer, and Ornita said she was very sorry.

One night in July we went out together. How that happened I'm still not so sure. I guess I asked her and she didn't say no. Where do you go out with a Negro woman? We went to the Village. We had a good dinner and walked in Washington Square Park. It was a hot night. Nobody was surprised when they saw us, nobody looked at us like we were against the law. If they looked maybe they saw my new lightweight suit that I bought yesterday and my shiny bald spot when we walked under a lamp, also how pretty she was for a man my type. We went in a movie on West Eighth Street. I didn't want to go in but she said she had heard about the picture. I wondered what was in her mind and I thought to myself, whatever is in there it's not a certain white man that I know. All night long we went together like we were chained. After the movie she wouldn't let me take her back to Harlem. When I put her in a taxi she asked me, "Why did we bother?"

For the steak, I thought of saying. Instead I said, "You're worth the bother."

"Thanks anyway."

Kiddo, I thought to myself after the taxi left, you just found out what's what, now the best thing is forget her.

It's easy to say. In August we went out the second time. That was the night she wore a purple dress and I thought to myself, my God, what colors. Who paints that picture paints a masterpiece. Everybody looked at us but I had pleasure. That night when she took off her dress it was in a furnished room I had the sense to rent a few days before. With my sick mother, I couldn't ask her to come to my apartment, and she didn't want me to go home with her where she lived with her brother's family on West 115th near Lenox Avenue. Under her purple dress she wore a black slip, and when she took that off she had white underwear. When she took off the white underwear she was black again. But I know where the next white was, if you want to call it white. And that was the night I think I fell in love with her, the first time in my life, though I have liked one or two girls I used to go with when I was a boy. It was a serious proposition. I'm the kind of a man when I think of love I'm thinking of marriage. I guess that's why I am a bachelor.

That same week I had a holdup in my place, two big men — both black — with revolvers. One got excited when I rang open the cash register so he could take the money, and he hit me over the ear with his gun. I stayed in the hospital a couple of weeks. Otherwise I was insured. Ornita came to see me. She sat on a chair without talking much. Finally I saw she was uncomfortable so I suggested she ought to go home.

"I'm sorry it happened," she said.

"Don't talk like it's your fault."

When I got out of the hospital my mother was dead. She was a wonderful person. My father died when I was thirteen and all by herself she kept the family alive and together. I sat shiva for a week and remembered how she sold paper bags on her pushcart. I remembered her life and what she tried to teach me. Nathan, she said, if you ever forget you are a Jew a goy will remind you. Mama, I said, rest in peace on this subject. But if I do something you don't like, remember, on earth it's harder than where you are. Then when my week of mourning was finished, one night I said, "Ornita, let's get married. We're both honest people and if you love me like I love you it won't be such a bad time. If you don't like New York I'll sell out here and we'll move someplace else. Maybe to San Francisco where nobody knows us. I was there for a week in the Second War and I saw white and colored living together."

"Nat," she answered me, "I like you but I'd be afraid. My husband woulda killed me."

"Your husband is dead."

"Not in my memory."

"In that case I'll wait."

"Do you know what it'd be like — I mean the life we could expect?"

"Ornita," I said, "I'm the kind of a man, if he picks his own way of life he's satisfied."

"What about children? Were you looking forward to half-Jewish polka dots?"

"I was looking forward to children."

"I can't," she said.

Can't is can't. I saw she was afraid and the best thing was not to push. Sometimes when we met she was so nervous that whatever we did she couldn't enjoy it. At the same time I still thought I had a chance. We were together more and more. I got rid of my furnished room and she came to my apartment — I gave away Mama's bed and bought a new one. She stayed with me all day on Sundays. When she wasn't so nervous she was affectionate, and if I know what love is, I had it. We went out a couple of times a week, the same way — usually I met her in Times Square and sent her home in a taxi, but I talked more about marriage and she talked less against it. One night she told me she was still trying to convince herself but she was almost convinced. I took an inventory of my liquor stock so I could put the store up for sale.

Ornita knew what I was doing. One day she quit her job, the next she took it back. She also went away a week to visit her sister in Philadelphia for a little rest. She came back tired but said maybe. Maybe is maybe so I'll wait. The way she said it, it was closer to yes. That was the winter two years ago. When she was in Philadelphia I called up a friend of mine from the army, now a CPA, and told him I would appreciate an invitation for an evening. He knew why. His wife said yes right away. When Ornita came back we went there. The wife made a fine dinner. It wasn't a bad time and they told us to come again. Ornita had a few drinks. She looked relaxed, wonderful. Later, because of a twenty-four-hour taxi strike I had to take her home on the subway. When we got to the 116th Street station she told me to go back on the train, and she would walk the couple of blocks to her house. I didn't like a woman walking alone on the streets at that time of the night. She said she never had any trouble but I insisted nothing doing. I said I would walk to her stoop with her and when she went upstairs I would go to the subway.

On the way there, on 115th in the middle of the block before Lenox, we were stopped by three men — maybe they were boys. One had a black hat with a half-inch brim, one a green cloth hat, and the third wore a black leather cap. The green hat was wearing a short coat and the other two had long ones. It was under a streetlight but the leather cap snapped a six-inch switchblade open in the light.

"What you doin' with this white son of a bitch?" he said to Ornita.

"I'm minding my own business," she answered him, "and I wish you would too."

"Boys," I said, "we're all brothers. I'm a reliable merchant in the neighborhood. This young lady is my dear friend. We don't want any trouble. Please let us pass."

"You talk like a Jew landlord," said the green hat. "Fifty a week for a single room."

"No charge fo' the rats," said the half-inch brim.

"Believe me, I'm no landlord. My store is Nathan's Liquors between Hundred Tenth and Eleventh. I also have two colored clerks, Mason and Jimmy, and they will tell you I pay good wages as well as I give discounts to certain customers."

"Shut your mouth, Jewboy," said the leather cap, and he moved the knife back and forth in front of my coat button. "No more black pussy for you."

"Speak with respect about this lady, please."

I got slapped on my mouth.

"That ain't no lady," said the long face in the half-inch brim, "that's black pussy. She deserve to have evvy bit of her hair shave off. How you like to have evvy bit of your hair shave off, black pussy?"

"Please leave me and this gentleman alone or I'm gonna scream long and loud. That's my house three doors down."

They slapped her. I never heard such a scream. Like her husband was falling fifteen stories.

I hit the one that slapped her and the next I knew I was laying in the gutter with a pain in my head. I thought, good-bye, Nat, they'll stab me for sure, but all they did was take my wallet and run in three directions.

Ornita walked back with me to the subway and she wouldn't let me go home with her again.

"Just get home safely."

She looked terrible. Her face was gray and I still remembered her scream. It was a terrible winter night, very cold February, and it took me an hour and ten minutes to get home. I felt bad for leaving her but what could I do?

We had a date downtown the next night but she didn't show up, the first time.

In the morning I called her in her place of business.

"For God's sake, Ornita, if we got married and moved away we wouldn't have the kind of trouble that we had. We wouldn't come in that neighborhood any more."

"Yes, we would. I have family there and don't want to move anyplace else. The truth of it is I can't marry you, Nat. I got troubles enough of my own."

"I coulda sworn you love me."

"Maybe I do but I can't marry you."

"For God's sake, why?"

"I got enough trouble of my own."

I went that night in a cab to her brother's house to see her. He was a quiet man with a thin mustache. "She gone," he said, "left for a long visit to some close relatives in the South. She said to tell you she appreciate your intentions but didn't think it will work out."

"Thank you kindly," I said.

Don't ask me how I got home.

Once, on Eighth Avenue, a couple of blocks from my store, I saw a blind man with a white cane tapping on the sidewalk. I figured we were going in the same direction so I took his arm.

"I can tell you're white," he said.

A heavy colored woman with a full shopping bag rushed after us.

"Never mind," she said, "I know where he live."

She pushed me with her shoulder and I hurt my leg on the fire hydrant.

That's how it is. I give my heart and they kick me in my teeth.

"Charity Quietness — you hear me? — come out of that goddamn toilet!"   [1963]

KATHERINE MANSFIELD (1888–1923) *was born Kathleen Mansfield Beauchamp in Wellington, New Zealand. In 1903 she persuaded her father, a banker and industrialist, to send her to London to study the cello. After a brief return to New Zealand, she went back to London with a small allowance from her family, deciding to become a writer instead of a musician after meeting D. H. Lawrence and Virginia Woolf. Mansfield's first book of short stories,* In a German Pension, *was published in 1911. In the same year she met the literary critic John Middleton Murry, who became her husband in 1918.* Bliss and Other Stories *(1920) established her reputation and was followed by* The Garden-Party *(1922).*

Mansfield took Anton Chekhov as her model, but after she was stricken with tuberculosis in 1918 she found it difficult to work. In her posthumously published Journal *(1927), she often upbraided herself when she felt too ill to write: "Look at the stories that wait and wait just at the threshold. Why don't I let them in? And their place would be taken by others who are lurking beyond just there — waiting for the chance." Finally she sought a cure for her illness at the Gurdjieff Institute in France, run by the noted Armenian mystic Georges Ivanovitch Gurdjieff, whose methods combined spiritual and physical healing. She died at the institute a few months after her thirty-fourth birthday.*

Eighty-eight of Mansfield's stories have been published (including fifteen left unfinished), and they have had a great influence on the development of the literary form. As did Chekhov and James Joyce, Mansfield simplified plot to intensify its emotional impact, dramatizing small moments to reveal the larger significance in people's lives, or, as Willa Cather observed, approaching "the major forces of life through comparatively trivial incidents." Mansfield developed her own technique of narration in which she transformed a chance incident into a terse psychological drama, as in "The Garden-Party." As would a Symbolist poet, she used concrete images — such as the pear tree in "Bliss" — to convey her characters' feelings, or what she called "the state of the soul." Her stories have affected later writers as powerfully as Chekhov's affected her.

RELATED COMMENTARIES: *Willa Cather, "The Stories of Katherine Mansfield," page 1398; Katherine Mansfield, "Review of Woolf's 'Kew Gardens,'" page 1454.*

KATHERINE MANSFIELD

Bliss

Although Bertha Young was thirty she still had moments like this when she wanted to run instead of walk, to take dancing steps on and off the pavement, to bowl a hoop, to throw something up in the air and catch it again, or to stand still and laugh at — nothing — at nothing, simply.

What can you do if you are thirty and, turning the corner of your own street, you are overcome, suddenly, by a feeling of bliss — absolute bliss! — as though you'd suddenly swallowed a bright piece of that late afternoon sun and it burned in your bosom, sending out a little shower of sparks into every particle, into every finger and toe? . . .

Oh, is there no way you can express it without being "drunk and disorderly"? How idiotic civilization is! Why be given a body if you have to keep it shut up in a case like a rare, rare fiddle?

"No, that about the fiddle is not quite what I mean," she thought, running up the steps and feeling in her bag for the key — she's forgotten it, as usual — and rattling the letter-box. "It's not what I mean, because — — Thank you, Mary" — she went into the hall. "Is nurse back?"

"Yes, M'm."

"And has the fruit come?"

"Yes, M'm. Everything's come."

"Bring the fruit up to the dining-room, will you? I'll arrange it before I go upstairs."

It was dusky in the dining-room and quite chilly. But all the same Bertha threw off her coat; she could not bear the tight clasp of it another moment, and the cold air fell on her arms.

But in her bosom there was still that bright glowing place — that shower of little sparks coming from it. It was almost unbearable. She hardly dared to breathe for fear of fanning it higher, and yet she breathed deeply, deeply. She hardly dared to look into the cold mirror — but she did look, and it gave her back a woman, radiant, with smiling, trembling lips, with big, dark eyes and an air of listening, waiting for something . . . divine to happen . . . that she knew must happen . . . infallibly.

Mary brought in the fruit on a tray and with it a glass bowl, and a blue dish, very lovely, with a strange sheen on it as though it had been dipped in milk.

"Shall I turn on the light, M'm?"

"No, thank you. I can see quite well."

There were tangerines and apples stained with strawberry pink. Some yellow pears, smooth as silk, some white grapes covered with a silver bloom and a big cluster of purple ones. These last she had bought to tone in with the new dining-room carpet. Yes, that did sound rather far-fetched and absurd, but it was really why she had bought them. She had thought in the shop: "I must have some purple ones to bring the carpet up to the table." And it had seemed quite sense at the time.

When she had finished with them and had made two pyramids of these bright round shapes, she stood away from the table to get the effect — and it really was most curious. For the dark table seemed to melt into the dusky light and the glass dish and the blue bowl to float in the air. This, of course in her present mood, was so incredibly beautiful. . . . She began to laugh.

"No, no. I'm getting hysterical." And she seized her bag and coat and ran upstairs to the nursery.

Nurse sat at a low table giving Little B her supper after her bath. The baby had on a white flannel gown and a blue woollen jacket, and her dark, fine hair was brushed up into a funny little peak. She looked up when she saw her mother and began to jump.

"Now, my lovey, eat it up like a good girl," said Nurse, setting her lips in a way that Bertha knew, and that meant she had come into the nursery at another wrong moment.

"Has she been good, Nanny?"

"She's been a little sweet all the afternoon," whispered Nanny. "We went to the park and I sat down on a chair and took her out of the pram and a big dog came along and put his head on my knee and she clutched its ear, tugged it. Oh, you should have seen her."

Bertha wanted to ask if it wasn't rather dangerous to let her clutch at a strange dog's ear. But she did not dare to. She stood watching them, her hands by her side, like the poor little girl in front of the rich little girl with the doll.

The baby looked up at her again, stared, and then smiled so charmingly that Bertha couldn't help crying:

"Oh, Nanny, do let me finish giving her her supper while you put the bath things away."

"Well, M'm, she oughtn't to be changed hands while she's eating," said Nanny, still whispering. "It unsettles her; it's very likely to upset her."

How absurd it was. Why have a baby if it has to be kept — not in a case like a rare, rare fiddle — but in another woman's arms?

"Oh, I must!" said she.

Very offended, Nanny handed her over.

"Now, don't excite her after her supper. You know you do, M'm. And I have such a time with her after!"

Thank heaven! Nanny went out of the room with the bath towels.

"Now I've got you to myself, my little precious," said Bertha, as the baby leaned against her.

She ate delightfully, holding up her lips for the spoon and then waving her hands. Sometimes she wouldn't let the spoon go; and sometimes, just as Bertha had filled it, she waved it away to the four winds.

When the soup was finished Bertha turned round to the fire.

"You're nice — you're very nice!" said she, kissing her warm baby. "I'm fond of you. I like you."

And, indeed, she loved Little B so much — her neck as she bent forward, her exquisite toes as they shone transparent in the firelight — that all her feeling of bliss came back again, and again she didn't know how to express it — what to do with it.

"You're wanted on the telephone," said Nanny, coming back in triumph and seizing *her* Little B.

Down she flew. It was Harry.

"Oh, is that you, Ber? Look here. I'll be late. I'll take a taxi and come along as quickly as I can, but get dinner put back ten minutes — will you? All right?"

"Yes, perfectly. Oh, Harry!"

"Yes?"

What had she to say? She'd nothing to say. She only wanted to get in touch with him for a moment. She couldn't absurdly cry: "Hasn't it been a divine day!"

"What is it?" rapped out the little voice.

"Nothing. *Entendu,*" said Bertha, and hung up the receiver, thinking how more than idiotic civilization was.

They had people coming to dinner. The Norman Knights — a very sound couple — he was about to start a theater, and she was awfully keen on interior decoration, a young man, Eddie Warren, who had just published a little book of poems and whom everybody was asking to dine, and a "find" of Bertha's called Pearl Fulton. What Miss Fulton did, Bertha didn't know. They had met at the club and Bertha had fallen in love with her, as she always did fall in love with beautiful women who had something strange about them.

The provoking thing was that, though they had been about together and met a number of times and really talked, Bertha couldn't yet make her out. Up to a certain point Miss Fulton was rarely, wonderfully frank, but the certain point was there, and beyond that she would not go.

Was there anything beyond it? Harry said "No." Voted her dullish, and "cold like all blond women, with a touch, perhaps, of anæmia of the brain." But Bertha wouldn't agree with him; not yet, at any rate.

"No, the way she has of sitting with her head a little on one side, and smiling, has something behind it, Harry, and I must find out what that something is."

"Most likely it's a good stomach," answered Harry.

He made a point of catching Bertha's heels with replies of that kind . . . "liver frozen, my dear girl," or "pure flatulence," or "kidney disease," . . . and so on. For some strange reason Bertha liked this, and almost admired it in him very much.

She went into the drawing-room and lighted the fire; then, picking up the cushions, one by one, that Mary had disposed so carefully, she threw them back on to the chairs and the couches. That made all the difference; the room came alive at once. As she was about to throw the last one she surprised herself by suddenly hugging it to her, passionately, passionately. But it did not put out the fire in her bosom. Oh, on the contrary!

The windows of the drawing-room opened on to a balcony overlooking the garden. At the far end, against the wall, there was a tall, slender pear tree in fullest, richest bloom; it stood perfect, as though becalmed against the jade-green sky. Bertha couldn't help feeling, even from this distance, that it had not a single bud or a faded petal. Down below, in the garden beds, the red and yellow tulips, heavy with flowers, seemed to lean upon the dusk. A grey cat, dragging its belly, crept across the lawn, and a black one, its shadow, trailed after. The sight of them, so intent and so quick, gave Bertha a curious shiver.

"What creepy things cats are!" she stammered, and she turned away from the window and began walking up and down. . . .

How strong the jonquils smelled in the warm room. Too strong? Oh, no. And yet, as though overcome, she flung down on a couch and pressed her hands to her eyes.

"I'm too happy — too happy!" she murmured.

And she seemed to see on her eyelids the lovely pear tree with its wide open blossoms as a symbol of her own life.

Really — really — she had everything. She was young. Harry and she were as much in love as ever, and they got on together splendidly and were really good pals. She had an adorable baby. They didn't have to worry about money. They had this absolutely satisfactory house and garden. And friends — modern, thrilling friends, writers and painters and poets or people keen on social questions — just the kind of friends they wanted. And then there were books, and there was music, and she had found a wonderful little dressmaker, and they were going abroad in the summer, and their new cook made the most superb omelettes. . . .

"I'm absurd! Absurd!" She sat up; but she felt quite dizzy, quite drunk. It must have been the spring.

Yes, it was the spring. Now she was so tired she could not drag herself upstairs to dress.

A white dress, a string of jade beads, green shoes and stockings. It wasn't intentional. She had thought of this scheme hours before she stood at the drawing-room window.

Her petals rushed softly into the hall, and she kissed Mrs. Norman Knight, who was taking off the most amusing orange coat with a procession of black monkeys round the hem and up the fronts.

". . . Why! Why! Why is the middle-class so stodgy — so utterly without a sense of humor! My dear, it's only a fluke that I am here at all — Norman being the protective fluke. For my darling monkeys so upset the train that it rose to a man and simply ate me with its eyes. Didn't laugh — wasn't amused — that I should have loved. No, just stared — and bored me through and through."

"But the cream of it was," said Norman, pressing a large tortoiseshell-rimmed monocle into his eye, "you don't mind me telling this, Face, do you?" (In their home and among their friends they called each other Face and Mug.) "The cream of it was when she, being full fed, turned to the woman beside her and said: 'Haven't you ever seen a monkey before?'"

"Oh, yes!" Mrs. Norman Knight joined in the laughter. "Wasn't that too absolutely creamy?"

And a funnier thing still was that now her coat was off she did look like a very intelligent monkey — who had even made that yellow silk dress out of scraped banana skins. And her amber earrings; they were like little dangling nuts.

"This is a sad, sad fall!" said Mug, pausing in front of Little B's perambulator. "When the perambulator comes into the hall ——" and he waved the rest of the quotation away.

The bell rang. It was lean, pale Eddie Warren (as usual) in a state of acute distress.

"It *is* the right house, *isn't* it?" he pleaded.

"Oh, I think so — I hope so," said Bertha brightly.

"I have had such a *dreadful* experience with a taxi-man; he was *most* sinister. I couldn't get him to *stop*. The *more* I knocked and called the *faster* he went. And *in* the moonlight this *bizarre* figure with the *flattened* head *crouching* over the *lit-tle* wheel. . . ."

He shuddered, taking off an immense white silk scarf. Bertha noticed that his socks were white, too — most charming.

"But how dreadful!" she cried.

"Yes, it really was," said Eddie, following her into the drawing-room. "I saw myself *driving* through Eternity in a *timeless* taxi."

He knew the Norman Knights. In fact, he was going to write a play for N. K. when the theater scheme came off.

"Well, Warren, how's the play?" said Norman Knight, dropping his monocle and giving his eye a moment in which to rise to the surface before it was screwed down again.

And Mrs. Norman Knight: "Oh, Mr. Warren, what happy socks!"

"I *am* so glad you like them," said he, staring at his feet. "They seem to have got so *much* whiter since the moon rose." And he turned his lean sorrowful young face to Bertha. "There *is* a moon, you know."

She wanted to cry: "I am sure there is — often — often!"

He really was a most attractive person. But so was Face, crouched before the fire in her banana skins, and so was Mug, smoking a cigarette and saying as he flicked the ash: "Why doth the bridegroom tarry?"

"There he is, now."

Bang went the front door open and shut. Harry shouted: "Hullo, you people. Down in five minutes." And they heard him swarm up the stairs. Bertha couldn't help smiling; she knew how he loved doing things at high pressure. What, after all, did an extra five minutes matter? But he would pretend to himself that they mattered beyond measure. And then he would make a great point of coming into the drawing-room, extravagantly cool and collected.

Harry had such a zest for life. Oh, how she appreciated it in him. And his passion for fighting — for seeking in everything that came up against him another test of his power and of his courage — that, too, she understood. Even when it made him just occasionally, to other people, who didn't know him well, a little ridiculous perhaps. . . . For there were moments when he rushed into battle where no battle was. . . . She talked and laughed and positively forgot until he had come in (just as she had imagined) that Pearl Fulton had not turned up.

"I wonder if Miss Fulton has forgotten?"

"I expect so," said Harry. "Is she on the 'phone?"

"Ah! There's a taxi, now." And Bertha smiled with that little air of proprietorship that she always assumed while her women finds were new and mysterious. "She lives in taxis."

"She'll run to fat if she does," said Harry coolly, ringing the bell for dinner. "Frightful danger for blond women."

"Harry — don't," warned Bertha, laughing up at him.

Came another tiny moment, while they waited, laughing and talking, just a trifle too much at their ease, a trifle too unaware. And then Miss Fulton, all in silver, with a silver fillet binding her pale blond hair, came in smiling, her head a little on one side.

"Am I late?"

"No, not at all," said Bertha. "Come along." And she took her arm and they moved into the dining-room.

What was there in the touch of that cool arm that could fan — fan — start blazing — blazing — the fire of bliss that Bertha did not know what to do with?

Miss Fulton did not look at her; but then she seldom did look at people directly. Her heavy eyelids lay upon her eyes and the strange half smile came and went upon her lips as though she lived by listening rather than seeing. But Bertha knew, suddenly, as if the longest, most intimate look had passed between them — as if they had said to each other: "You, too?" — that Pearl Fulton, stirring the beautiful red soup in the grey plate, was feeling just what she was feeling.

And the others? Face and Mug, Eddie and Harry, their spoons rising and falling — dabbing their lips with their napkins, crumbling bread, fiddling with the forks and glasses and talking.

"I met her at the Alpha shore — the weirdest little person. She'd not only cut off her hair, but she seemed to have taken a dreadfully good snip off her legs and arms and her neck and her poor little nose as well."

"Isn't she very *liée*[1] with Michael Oat?"

"The man who wrote *Love in False Teeth*?"

"He wants to write a play for me. One act. One man. Decides to commit suicide. Gives all the reasons why he should and why he shouldn't. And just as he has made up his mind either to do it or not to do it — curtain. Not half a bad idea."

"What's he going to call it — 'Stomach Trouble'?"

"I *think* I've come across the *same* idea in a lit-tle French review, *quite* unknown in England."

No, they didn't share it. They were dears — dears — and she loved having them there, at her table, and giving them delicious food and wine. In fact, she longed to tell them how delightful they were, and what a decorative group they made, how they seemed to set one another off and how they reminded her of a play by Tchekof!

Harry was enjoying his dinner. It was part of his — well, not his nature, exactly, and certainly not his pose — his — something or other — to talk about food and to glory in his "shameless passion for the white flesh of the lobster" and "the green of pistachio ices — green and cold like the eyelids of Egyptian dancers."

---

[1] Linked or connected with; friendly with (the implication being that they are more than just "friends").

When he looked up at her and said: "Bertha, this is a very admirable *soufflée!*" she almost could have wept with child-like pleasure.

Oh, why did she feel so tender toward the whole world tonight? Everything was good — was right. All that happened seemed to fill again her brimming cup of bliss.

And still, in the back of her mind, there was the pear tree. It would be silver now, in the light of poor dear Eddie's moon, silver as Miss Fulton, who sat there turning a tangerine in her slender fingers that were so pale a light seemed to come from them.

What she simply couldn't make out — what was miraculous — was how she should have guessed Miss Fulton's mood so exactly and so instantly. For she never doubted for a moment that she was right, and yet what had she to go on? Less than nothing.

"I believe this does happen very, very rarely between women. Never between men," thought Bertha. "But while I am making coffee in the drawing-room perhaps she will 'give a sign.'"

What she meant by that she did not know, and what would happen after that she could not imagine.

While she thought like this she saw herself talking and laughing. She had to talk because of her desire to laugh.

"I must laugh or die."

But when she noticed Face's funny little habit of tucking something down the front of her bodice — as if she kept a tiny, secret hoard of nuts there, too — Bertha had to dig her nails into her hands — so as not to laugh too much.

It was over at last. And: "Come and see my new coffee machine," said Bertha.

"We only have a new coffee machine once a fortnight," said Harry. Face took her arm this time; Miss Fulton bent her head and followed after.

The fire had died down in the drawing-room to a red, flickering "nest of baby phoenixes," said Face.

"Don't turn up the light for a moment. It is so lovely." And down she crouched by the fire again. She was always cold . . . "without her little red flannel jacket, of course," thought Bertha.

At that moment Miss Fulton "gave the sign."

"Have you a garden?" said the cool, sleepy voice.

This was so exquisite on her part that all Bertha could do was to obey. She crossed the room, pulled the curtains apart, and opened those long windows.

"There!" she breathed.

And the two women stood side by side looking at the slender, flowering tree. Although it was so still it seemed, like the flame of a candle, to stretch up, to point, to quiver in the bright air, to grow taller and taller as they gazed — almost to touch the rim of the round, silver moon.

How long did they stand there? Both, as it were, caught in that circle of unearthly light, understanding each other perfectly, creatures of another world, and wondering what they were to do in this one with all this blissful treasure that burned in their bosoms and dropped, in silver flowers, from their hair and hands?

Forever — for a moment? And did Miss Fulton murmur: "Yes. Just *that*." Or did Bertha dream it?

Then the light was snapped on and Face made the coffee and Harry said: "My dear Mrs. Knight, don't ask me about my baby. I never see her. I shan't feel the slightest interest in her until she has a lover," and Mug took his eye out of the conservatory for a moment and then put it under glass again and Eddie Warren drank his coffee and set down the cup with a face of anguish as though he had drunk and seen the spider.

"What I want to do is to give the young men a show. I believe London is simply teeming with first-chop, unwritten plays. What I want to say to 'em is: 'Here's the theater. Fire ahead.'"

"You know, my dear, I am going to decorate a room for the Jacob Nathans. Oh, I am so tempted to do a fried-fish scheme, with the backs of the chairs shaped like frying pans and lovely chip potatoes embroidered all over the curtains."

"The trouble with our young writing men is that they are still too romantic. You can't put out to sea without being seasick and wanting a basin. Well, why won't they have the courage of those basins?"

"A *dreadful* poem about a *girl* who was *violated* by a begger *without* a nose in a lit-tle wood. . . ."

Miss Fulton sank into the lowest, deepest chair and Harry handed round the cigarettes.

From the way he stood in front of her shaking the silver box and saying abruptly: "Egyptian? Turkish? Virginian? They're all mixed up," Bertha realized that she not only bored him; he really disliked her. And she decided from the way Miss Fulton said: "No, thank you, I won't smoke," that she felt it, too, and was hurt.

"Oh, Harry, don't dislike her. You are quite wrong about her. She's wonderful, wonderful. And, besides, how can you feel so differently about someone who means so much to me? I shall try to tell you when we are in bed tonight what has been happening. What she and I have shared."

At those last words something strange and almost terrifying darted into Bertha's mind. And this something blind and smiling whispered to her: "Soon these people will go. The house will be quiet — quiet. The lights will be out. And you and he will be alone together in the dark room — the warm bed. . . ."

She jumped up from her chair and ran over to the piano.

"What a pity someone does not play!" she cried. "What a pity somebody does not play."

For the first time in her life Bertha Young desired her husband.

Oh, she loved him — she'd been in love with him, of course, in every other way, but just not in that way. And, equally, of course, she'd understood that he was different. They'd discussed it so often. It had worried her dreadfully at first to find that she was so cold, but after a time it had not seemed to matter. They were so frank with each other such good pals. That was the best of being modern.

But now — ardently! ardently! The word ached in her ardent body! Was this what that feeling of bliss had been leading up to? But then — then ——

"My dear," said Mrs. Norman Knight, "you know our shame. We are the victims of time and train. We live in Hampstead. It's been so nice."

"I'll come with you into the hall," said Bertha. "I love having you. But you must not miss the last train. That's so awful, isn't it?"

"Have a whisky, Knight, before you go?" called Harry.

"No, thanks, old chap."

Bertha squeezed his hand for that as she shook it.

"Good night, good-bye," she cried from the top step, feeling that this self of hers was taking leave of them forever.

When she got back into the drawing-room the others were on the move.

". . . Then you can come part of the way in my taxi."

"I shall be *so* thankful *not* to have to face *another* drive *alone* after my *dreadful* experience."

"You can get a taxi at the rank just at the end of the street. You won't have to walk more than a few yards."

"That's comfort. I'll go and put on my coat."

Miss Fulton moved toward the hall and Bertha was following when Harry almost pushed past.

"Let me help you."

Bertha knew that he was repenting his rudeness — she let him go. What a boy he was in some ways — so impulsive — so simple.

And Eddie and she were left by the fire.

"I *wonder* if you have seen Bilks' *new* poem called *Table d'Hôte*," said Eddie softly. "It's *so* wonderful. In the last Anthology. Have you got a copy? I'd *so* like to *show* it to you. It begins with an *incredibly* beautiful line: 'Why Must it Always be Tomato Soup?'"

"Yes," said Bertha. And she moved noiselessly to a table opposite the drawing-room door and Eddie glided noiselessly after her. She picked up the little book and gave it to him; they had not made a sound.

While he looked it up she turned her head toward the hall. And she saw . . . Harry with Miss Fulton's coat in his arms and Miss Fulton with her back turned to him and her head bent. He tossed the coat away, put his hands on her shoulders, and turned her violently to him. His lips said: "I adore you," and Miss Fulton laid her moonbeam fingers on his cheeks and smiled her sleepy smile. Harry's nostrils quivered; his lips curled back in a hideous grin while he whispered: "Tomorrow," and with her eyelids Miss Fulton said: "Yes."

"Here it is," said Eddie. "'Why Must it Always be Tomato Soup?' It's so *deeply* true, don't you feel? Tomato soup is so *dreadfully* eternal."

"If you prefer," said Harry's voice, very loud, from the hall, "I can 'phone you a cab to come to the door."

"Oh, no. It's not necessary," said Miss Fulton, and she came up to Bertha and gave her the slender fingers to hold.

"Good-bye. Thank you so much."

"Good-bye," said Bertha.

Miss Fulton held her hand a moment longer.

"Your lovely pear tree!" she murmured.

And then she was gone, with Eddie following, like the black cat following the grey cat.

"I'll shut up shop," said Harry, extravagantly cool and collected.

"Your lovely pear tree — pear tree — pear tree!"

Bertha simply ran over to the long windows.

"Oh, what is going to happen now?" she cried.

But the pear tree was as lovely as ever and as full of flower and as still.

[1920]

KATHERINE MANSFIELD

The Garden-Party

And after all the weather was ideal. They could not have had a more perfect day for a garden-party if they had ordered it. Windless, warm, the sky without a cloud. Only the blue was veiled with a haze of light gold, as it is sometimes in early summer. The gardener had been up since dawn, mowing the lawns and sweeping them, until the grass and the dark flat rosettes where the daisy plants had been seemed to shine. As for the roses, you could not help feeling they understood that roses are the only flowers that impress people at garden-parties; the only flowers that everybody is certain of knowing. Hundreds, yes, literally hundreds, had come out in a single night; the green bushes bowed down as though they had been visited by archangels.

Breakfast was not yet over before the men came to put up the marquee.

"Where do you want the marquee put, mother?"

"My dear child, it's no use asking me. I'm determined to leave everything to you children this year. Forget I am your mother. Treat me as an honoured guest."

But Meg could not possibly go and supervise the men. She had washed her hair before breakfast, and she sat drinking her coffee in a green turban, with a dark wet curl stamped on each cheek. Jose, the butterfly, always came down in a silk petticoat and a kimono jacket.

"You'll have to go, Laura; you're the artistic one."

Away Laura flew, still holding her piece of bread-and-butter. It's so delicious to have an excuse for eating out of doors, and besides, she loved having to arrange things; she always felt she could do it so much better than anybody else.

Four men in their shirt-sleeves stood grouped together on the garden path. They carried staves covered with rolls of canvas, and they had big tool-bags slung on their backs. They looked impressive. Laura wished now that she had not got the bread-and-butter, but there was nowhere to put it, and she couldn't possibly throw it away. She blushed and tried to look severe and even a little bit short-sighted as she came up to them.

"Good morning," she said, copying her mother's voice. But that sounded so fearfully affected that she was ashamed, and stammered like a little girl, "Oh — er — have you come — is it about the marquee?"

"That's right, miss," said the tallest of the men, a lanky, freckled fellow, and he shifted his tool-bag, knocked back his straw hat and smiled down at her. "That's about it."

His smile was so easy, so friendly that Laura recovered. What nice eyes he had, small, but such dark blue! And now she looked at the others, they were smiling too. "Cheer up, we won't bite," their smile seemed to say. How very nice workmen were! And what a beautiful morning! She mustn't mention the morning; she must be businesslike. The marquee.

"Well, what about the lily-lawn? Would that do?"

And she pointed to the lily-lawn with the hand that didn't hold the bread-and-butter. They turned, they stared in the direction. A little fat chap thrust out his under-lip, and the tall fellow frowned.

"I don't fancy it," said he. "Not conspicuous enough. You see, with a thing like a marquee," and he turned to Laura in his easy way, "you want to put it somewhere where it'll give you a bang slap in the eye, if you follow me."

Laura's upbringing made her wonder for a moment whether it was quite respectful of a workman to talk to her of bangs slap in the eye. But she did quite follow him.

"A corner of the tennis-court," she suggested. "But the band's going to be in one corner."

"H'm, going to have a band, are you?" said another of the workmen. He was pale. He had a haggard look as his dark eyes scanned the tennis-court. What was he thinking?

"Only a very small band," said Laura gently. Perhaps he wouldn't mind so much if the band was quite small. But the tall fellow interrupted.

"Look here, miss, that's the place. Against those trees. Over there. That'll do fine."

Against the karakas. Then the karaka-trees would be hidden. And they were so lovely, with their broad, gleaming leaves, and their clusters of yellow fruit. They were like trees you imagined growing on a desert island, proud, solitary, lifting their leaves and fruits to the sun in a kind of silent splendour. Must they be hidden by a marquee?

They must. Already the men had shouldered their staves and were making for the place. Only the tall fellow was left. He bent down, pinched a sprig of lavender, put his thumb and forefinger to his nose and snuffed up the smell. When Laura saw that gesture she forgot all about the karakas in her wonder at him caring for things like that — caring for the smell of lavender. How many men that she knew would have done such a thing? Oh, how extraordinarily nice workmen were, she thought. Why couldn't she have workmen for friends rather than the silly boys she danced with and who came to Sunday night supper? She would get on much better with men like these.

It's all the fault, she decided, as the tall fellow drew something on the back of an envelope, something that was to be looped up or left to hang, of these absurd class distinctions. Well, for her part, she didn't feel them. Not a bit, not an atom. . . . And now there came the chock-chock of wooden hammers. Some one whistled, some one sang out, "Are you right there, matey?" "Matey!" The friendliness of it, the — the — Just to prove how happy she was, just to show the tall fellow how at home she felt, and how she despised stupid conventions, Laura took a big bite of her bread-and-butter as she stared at the little drawing. She felt just like a work-girl.

"Laura, Laura, where are you? Telephone, Laura!" a voice cried from the house.

"Coming!" Away she skimmed, over the lawn, up the path, up the steps, across the veranda, and into the porch. In the hall her father and Laurie were brushing their hats ready to go to the office.

"I say, Laura," said Laurie very fast, "you might just give a squiz at my coat before this afternoon. See if it wants pressing."

"I will," said she. Suddenly she couldn't stop herself. She ran at Laurie and gave him a small, quick squeeze. "Oh, I do love parties, don't you?" gasped Laura.

"Ra-ther," said Laurie's warm, boyish voice, and he squeezed his sister too, and gave her a gentle push. "Dash off to the telephone, old girl."

The telephone. "Yes, yes; oh yes. Kitty? Good morning, dear. Come to lunch? Do, dear. Delighted of course. It will only be a very scratch meal — just the sandwich crusts and broken meringue-shells and what's left over. Yes, isn't it a perfect morning? Your white? Oh, I certainly should. One moment — hold the line. Mother's calling." And Laura sat back. "What, mother? Can't hear."

Mrs. Sheridan's voice floated down the stairs. "Tell her to wear that sweet hat she had on last Sunday."

"Mother says you're to wear that *sweet* hat you had on last Sunday. Good. One o'clock. Bye-bye."

Laura put back the receiver, flung her arms over her head, took a deep breath, stretched and let them fall. "Huh," she sighed, and the moment after the sigh she sat up quickly. She was still, listening. All the doors in the house seemed to be open. The house was alive with soft, quick steps and running voices. The green baize door that led to the kitchen regions swung open and shut with a muffled thud. And now there came a long, chuckling absurd sound. It was the heavy piano being moved on its stiff castors. But the air! If you stopped to notice, was the air always like this? Little faint winds were playing chase, in at the tops of the windows, out at the doors. And there were two tiny spots of sun, one on the inkpot, one on a silver photograph frame, playing too. Darling little spots. Especially the one on the inkpot lid. It was quite warm. A warm little silver star. She could have kissed it.

The front door bell pealed, and there sounded the rustle of Sadie's print skirt on the stairs. A man's voice murmured; Sadie answered, careless, "I'm sure I don't know. Wait. I'll ask Mrs. Sheridan."

"What is it, Sadie?" Laura came into the hall.

"It's the florist, Miss Laura."

It was, indeed. There, just inside the door, stood a wide, shallow tray full of pots of pink lilies. No other kind. Nothing but lilies — canna lilies, big pink flowers, wide open, radiant, almost frighteningly alive on bright crimson stems.

"O-oh Sadie!" said Laura, and the sound was like a little moan. She crouched down as if to warm herself at that blaze of lilies; she felt they were in her fingers, on her lips, growing in her breast.

"It's some mistake," she said faintly. "Nobody ever ordered so many. Sadie, go and find mother."

But at that moment Mrs. Sheridan joined them.

"It's quite right," she said calmly. "Yes, I ordered them. Aren't they lovely?" She pressed Laura's arm. "I was passing the shop yesterday, and I saw them in the window. And I suddenly thought for once in my life I shall have enough canna lilies. The garden-party will be a good excuse."

"But I thought you said you didn't mean to interfere," said Laura. Sadie had gone. The florist's man was still outside at his van. She put her arm round her mother's neck and gently, very gently, she bit her mother's ear.

"My darling child, you wouldn't like a logical mother, would you? Don't do that. Here's the man."

He carried more lilies still, another whole tray.

"Bank them up, just inside the door, on both sides of the porch, please," said Mrs. Sheridan. "Don't you agree, Laura?"

"Oh, I *do* mother."

In the drawing-room Meg, Jose and good little Hans had at last succeeded in moving the piano.

"Now, if we put this chesterfield against the wall and move everything out of the room except the chairs, don't you think?"

"Quite."

"Hans, move these tables into the smoking-room, and bring a sweeper to take these marks off the carpet and — one moment, Hans —" Jose loved giving orders to the servants, and they loved obeying her. She always made them feel they were taking part in some drama. "Tell mother and Miss Laura to come here at once."

"Very good, Miss Jose."

She turned to Meg. "I want to hear what the piano sounds like, just in case I'm asked to sing this afternoon. Let's try over 'This life is Weary.'"

Pom! Ta-ta-ta *Tee*-ta! The piano burst out so passionately that Jose's face changed. She clasped her hands. She looked mournfully and enigmatically at her mother and Laura as they came in.

This Life is *Wee*-ary,
A Tear — a Sigh.
A Love that *Chan*-ges,
This Life is *Wee*-ary,
A Tear — a Sigh.
A Love that *Chan*-ges,
And then . . . Good-bye!

But at the word "Good-bye," and although the piano sounded more desperate than ever, her face broke into a brilliant, dreadfully unsympathetic smile. "Aren't I in good voice, mummy?" she beamed.

This Life is *Wee*-ary,
Hope comes to Die.
A Dream — a *Wa*-kening.

But now Sadie interrupted them. "What is it, Sadie?"

"If you please, m'm, cook says have you got the flags for the sandwiches?"

"The flags for the sandwiches, Sadie?" echoed Mrs. Sheridan dreamily. And the children knew by her face that she hadn't got them. "Let me see." And she said to Sadie firmly, "Tell cook I'll let her have them in ten minutes."

Sadie went.

"Now, Laura," said her mother quickly. "Come with me into the smoking-room. I've got the names somewhere on the back of an envelope. You'll have to write them out for me. Meg, go upstairs this minute and take that wet thing off your head. Jose, run and finish dressing this instant. Do you hear me, children, or shall I have to tell your father when he comes home to-night? And — and, Jose, pacify cook if you do go into the kitchen, will you? I'm terrified of her this morning."

The envelope was found at last behind the dining-room clock, though how it had got there Mrs. Sheridan could not imagine.

"One of you children must have stolen it out of my bag, because I remember vividly — cream cheese and lemon-curd. Have you done that?"

"Yes."

"Egg and —" Mrs. Sheridan held the envelope away from her. "It looks like mice. It can't be mice, can it?"

"Olive, pet," said Laura, looking over her shoulder.

"Yes, of course, olive. What a horrible combination it sounds. Egg and olive."

They were finished at last, and Laura took them off to the kitchen. She found Jose there pacifying the cook, who did not look at all terrifying.

"I have never seen such exquisite sandwiches," said Jose's rapturous voice. "How many kinds did you say there were, cook? Fifteen?"

"Fifteen, Miss Jose."

"Well, cook, I congratulate you."

Cook swept up crusts with the long sandwich knife, and smiled broadly.

"Godber's has come," announced Sadie, issuing out of the pantry. She had seen the man pass the window.

That meant the cream puffs had come. Godber's were famous for their cream puffs. Nobody ever thought of making them at home.

"Bring them in and put them on the table, my girl," ordered cook.

Sadie brought them in and went back to the door. Of course Laura and Jose were far too grown-up to really care about such things. All the same, they couldn't help agreeing that the puffs looked very attractive. Very. Cook began arranging them, shaking off the extra icing sugar.

"Don't they carry one back to all one's parties?" said Laura.

"I suppose they do," said practical Jose, who never liked to be carried back. "They look beautifully light and feathery, I must say."

"Have one each, my dears," said cook in her comfortable voice. "Yer ma won't know."

Oh, impossible. Fancy cream puffs so soon after breakfast. The very idea made one shudder. All the same, two minutes later Jose and Laura were licking their fingers with that absorbed inward look that only comes from whipped cream.

"Let's go into the garden, out by the back way," suggested Laura. "I want to see how the men are getting on with the marquee. They're such awfully nice men."

But the back door was blocked by cook, Sadie, Godber's man and Hans.

Something had happened.

"Tuk-tuk-tuk," clucked cook like an agitated hen. Sadie had her hand clapped to her cheek as though she had toothache. Hans's face was screwed up in the effort to understand. Only Godber's man seemed to be enjoying himself; it was his story.

"What's the matter? What's happened?"

"There's been a horrible accident," said Cook. "A man killed."

"A man killed! Where? How? When?"

But Godber's man wasn't going to have his story snatched from under his very nose.

"Know those little cottages just below here, miss?" Know them? Of course, she knew them. "Well, there's a young chap living there, name of Scott, a carter. His horse shied at a traction-engine, corner of Hawke Street this morning, and he was thrown out on the back of his head. Killed."

"Dead!" Laura stared at Godber's man.

"Dead when they picked him up," said Godber's man with relish. "They were taking the body home as I come up here." And he said to the cook, "He's left a wife and five little ones."

"Jose, come here." Laura caught hold of her sister's sleeve and dragged her through the kitchen to the other side of the green baize door. There she paused and leaned against it. "Jose!" she said, horrified, "however are we going to stop everything?"

"Stop everything, Laura!" cried Jose in astonishment. "What do you mean?"

"Stop the garden-party, of course." Why did Jose pretend?

But Jose was still more amazed. "Stop the garden-party? My dear Laura, don't be so absurd. Of course we can't do anything of the kind. Nobody expects us to. Don't be so extravagant."

"But we can't possibly have a garden-party with a man dead just outside the front gate."

That really was extravagant, for the little cottages were in a lane to themselves at the very bottom of a steep rise that led up to the house. A broad road ran between. True, they were far too near. They were the greatest possible eyesore, and they had no right to be in that neighbourhood at all. They were little mean dwellings painted a chocolate brown. In the garden patches there was nothing but cabbage stalks, sick hens and tomato cans. The very smoke coming out of their chimneys was poverty-stricken. Little rags and shreds of smoke, so unlike the great silvery plumes that uncurled from the Sheridan's chimneys. Washerwomen lived in the lane and sweeps and a cobbler, and a man whose house-front was studded all over with minute bird-cages. Children swarmed. When the Sheridans were little they were forbidden to set foot there because of the revolting language and of what they might catch. But since they were grown up, Laura and Laurie on their prowls sometimes walked through. It was disgusting and sordid. They came out with a shudder. But still one must go everywhere; one must see everything. So through they went.

"And just think of what the band would sound like to that poor woman," said Laura.

"Oh, Laura!" Jose began to be seriously annoyed. "If you're going to stop a band playing every time some one has an accident, you'll lead a very strenuous life. I'm every bit as sorry about it as you. I feel just as sympathetic." Her eyes hardened. She looked at her sister just as she used to when they were little and fighting together. "You won't bring a drunken workman back to life by being sentimental," she said softly.

"Drunk! Who said he was drunk?" Laura turned furiously on Jose. She said, just as they had used to say on those occasions, "I'm going straight up to tell mother."

"Do, dear," cooed Jose.

"Mother, can I come in your room?" Laura turned the big glass door-knob.

"Of course, child. Why, what's the matter? What's given you such a colour?" And Mrs. Sheridan turned round from her dressing-table. She was trying on a new hat.

"Mother, a man's been killed," began Laura.

"*Not* in the garden?" interrupted her mother.

"No, no!"

"Oh, what a fright you gave me!" Mrs. Sheridan sighed with relief, and took off the big hat and held it on her knees.

"But listen, mother," said Laura. Breathless, half-choking, she told the dreadful story. "Of course, we can't have our party, can we?" she pleaded. "The band and everybody arriving. They'd hear us, mother; they're nearly neighbors!"

To Laura's astonishment her mother behaved just like Jose, it was harder to bear because she seemed amused. She refused to take Laura seriously.

"But, my dear child, use your common sense. It's only by accident we've heard of it. If some one had died there normally — and I can't understand how they keep alive in those poky little holes — we should still be having our party, shouldn't we?"

Laura had to say "yes" to that, but she felt it was all wrong. She sat down on her mother's sofa and pinched the cushion frill.

"Mother, isn't it really terribly heartless of us?" she asked.

"Darling!" Mrs. Sheridan got up and came over to her, carrying the hat. Before Laura could stop her she had popped it on. "My child!" said her mother, "the hat is yours. It's made for you. It's much too young for me. I have never seen you look such a picture. Look at yourself!" And she held up her hand-mirror.

"But, mother," Laura began again. She couldn't look at herself; she turned aside.

This time Mrs. Sheridan lost patience just as Jose had done.

"You are being very absurd, Laura," she said coldly. "People like that don't expect sacrifices from us. And it's not very sympathetic to spoil everybody's enjoyment as you're doing now."

"I don't understand," said Laura, and she walked quickly out of the room into her own bedroom. There, quite by chance, the first thing she saw was this charming girl in the mirror, in her black hat trimmed with gold daisies, and a long black velvet ribbon. Never had she imagined she could look like that. Is mother right? she thought. And now she hoped her mother was right. Am I being extravagant? Perhaps it was extravagant. Just for a moment she had another glimpse of that poor woman and those little children, and the body being carried into the house. But it all seemed blurred, unreal, like a picture in the newspaper. I'll remember it again after the party's over, she decided. And somehow that seemed quite the best plan. . . .

Lunch was over by half-past one. By half-past two they were all ready for the fray. The green-coated band had arrived and was established in a corner of the tennis-court.

"My dear!" trilled Kitty Maitland, "aren't they too like frogs for words? You ought to have arranged them round the pond with the conductor in the middle on a leaf."

Laurie arrived and hailed them on his way to dress. At the sight of him Laura remembered the accident again. She wanted to tell him. If Laurie agreed with the others, then it was bound to be all right. And she followed him into the hall.

"Laurie!"

"Hallo!" He was half-way upstairs, but when he turned round and saw Laura he suddenly puffed out his cheeks and goggled his eyes at her. "My word, Laura; You do look stunning," said Laurie. "What an absolutely topping hat!"

Laura said faintly, "Is it?" and smiled up at Laurie, and didn't tell him after all.

Soon after that people began coming in streams. The band struck up; the hired waiters ran from the house to the marquee. Wherever you looked there were couples strolling, bending to the flowers, greeting, moving on over the lawn. They were like bright birds that had alighted in the Sheridans' garden for this one afternoon, on their way to — where? Ah, what happiness it is to be with people who all are happy, to press hands, press cheeks, smile into eyes.

"Darling Laura, how well you look!"

"What a becoming hat, child!"

"Laura, you look quite Spanish. I've never seen you look so striking."

And Laura, glowing, answered softly, "Have you had tea? Won't you have an ice? The passion-fruit ices really are rather special." She ran to her father and begged him. "Daddy darling, can't the band have something to drink?"

And the perfect afternoon slowly ripened, slowly faded, slowly its petals closed.

"Never a more delightful garden-party . . ." "The greatest success . . ." "Quite the most . . ."

Laura helped her mother with the good-byes. They stood side by side in the porch till it was all over.

"All over, all over, thank heaven," said Mrs. Sheridan. "Round up the others, Laura. Let's go and have some fresh coffee. I'm exhausted. Yes, it's been very successful. But oh, these parties, these parties! Why will you children insist on giving parties!" And they all of them sat down in the deserted marquee.

"Have a sandwich, daddy dear. I wrote the flag."

"Thanks." Mr. Sheridan took a bite and the sandwich was gone. He took another. "I suppose you didn't hear of a beastly accident that happened to-day?" he said.

"My dear," said Mrs. Sheridan, holding up her hand, "we did. It nearly ruined the party. Laura insisted we should put it off."

"Oh, mother!" Laura didn't want to be teased about it.

"It was a horrible affair all the same," said Mr. Sheridan. "The chap was married too. Lived just below in the lane, and leaves a wife and half a dozen kiddies, so they say."

An awkward little silence fell. Mrs. Sheridan fidgeted with her cup. Really, it was very tactless of father . . .

Suddenly she looked up. There on the table were all those sandwiches, cakes, puffs, all uneaten, all going to be wasted. She had one of her brilliant ideas.

"I know," she said. "Let's make up a basket. Let's send that poor creature some of this perfectly good food. At any rate, it will be the greatest treat for the children. Don't you agree? And she's sure to have neighbours calling in and so on. What a point to have it all ready prepared. Laura!" She jumped up. "Get me the big basket out of the stairs cupboard."

"But, mother, do you really think it's a good idea?" said Laura.

Again, how curious, she seemed to be different from them all. To take scraps from their party. Would the poor woman really like that?

"Of course! What's the matter with you to-day? An hour or two ago you were insisting on us being sympathetic, and now —"

Oh, well! Laura ran for the basket. It was filled, it was heaped by her mother.

"Take it yourself, darling," said she. "Run down just as you are. No, wait, take the arum lilies too. People of that class are so impressed by arum lilies."

"The stems will ruin her lace frock," said practical Jose.

So they would. Just in time. "Only the basket, then. And, Laura!" — her mother followed her out of the marquee — "don't on any account —"

"What, mother?"

No, better not put such ideas into the child's head! "Nothing! Run along."

It was just growing dusky as Laura shut their garden gates. A big dog ran by like a shadow. The road gleamed white, and down below in the hollow the little cottages were in deep shade. How quiet it seemed after the afternoon. Here she was going down the hill to somewhere where a man lay dead, and she couldn't realize it. Why couldn't she? She stopped a minute. And it seemed to her that kisses, voices, tinkling spoons, laughter, the smell of crushed grass were somehow inside her. She had no room for anything else. How strange! She looked up at the pale sky, and all she thought was, "Yes, it was the most successful party."

Now the broad road was crossed. The lane began, smoky and dark. Women in shawls and men's tweed caps hurried by. Men hung over the palings; the children played in the doorways. A low hum came from the mean little cottages. In some of them there was a flicker of light, and a shadow, crab-like, moved across the window. Laura bent her head and hurried on. She wished now she had put on a coat. How her frock shone! And the big hat with the velvet streamer — if only it was another hat! Were the people looking at her? They must be. It was a mistake to have come; she knew all along it was a mistake. Should she go back even now?

No, too late. This was the house. It must be. A dark knot of people stood outside. Beside the gate an old, old woman with a crutch sat in a chair, watching. She had her feet on a newspaper. The voices stopped as Laura drew near. The group parted. It was as though she was expected, as though they had known she was coming here.

Laura was terribly nervous. Tossing the velvet ribbon over her shoulder, she said to a woman standing by, "Is this Mrs. Scott's house?" and the woman, smiling queerly, said, "It is, my lass."

Oh, to be away from this! She actually said, "Help me, God," as she walked up the tiny path and knocked. To be away from those staring eyes, or to be covered up in anything, one of those women's shawls even. I'll just leave the basket and go, she decided. I shan't even wait for it to be emptied.

Then the door opened. A little woman in black showed in the gloom.

Laura said, "Are you Mrs. Scott?" But to her horror the woman answered, "Walk in please, miss," and she was shut in the passage.

"No," said Laura, "I don't want to come in. I only want to leave this basket. Mother sent —"

The little woman in the gloomy passage seemed not to have heard her. "Step this way, please, miss," she said in an oily voice, and Laura followed her.

She found herself in a wretched little low kitchen, lighted by a smoky lamp. There was a woman sitting before the fire.

"Em," said the little creature who had let her in. "Em! It's a young lady." She turned to Laura. She said meaningly, "I'm 'er sister, Miss. You'll excuse 'er, won't you?"

"Oh, but of course!" said Laura. "Please, please don't disturb her. I — I only want to leave —"

But at that moment the woman at the fire turned round. Her face, puffed up, red, with swollen eyes and swollen lips, looked terrible. She seemed as though she couldn't understand why Laura was there. What did it mean? Why was this stranger standing in the kitchen with a basket? What was it all about? And the poor face puckered up again.

"All right, my dear," said the other. "I'll thenk the young lady."

And again she began, "You'll excuse her, miss, I'm sure," and her face, swollen too, tried an oily smile.

Laura only wanted to get out, to get away. She was back in the passage. The door opened. She walked straight through into the bedroom, where the dead man was lying.

"You'd like a look at 'im, wouldn't you?" said Em's sister, and she brushed past Laura over to the bed. "Don't be afraid, my lass, —" and now her voice sounded fond and sly, and fondly she drew down the sheet —"'e looks a picture. There's nothing to show. Come along, my dear."

There lay a young man, fast asleep — sleeping so soundly, so deeply, that he was far, far away from them both. Oh, so remote, so peaceful. He was dreaming. Never wake him up again. His head was sunk in the pillow, his eyes were closed; they were blind under the closed eyelids. He was given up to his dream. What did garden-parties and baskets and lace frocks matter to him? He was far from all those things. He was wonderful, beautiful. While they were laughing and while the band was playing, this marvel had come to the lane. Happy . . . happy. . . . All is well, said that sleeping face. This is just as it should be. I am content.

But all the same you had to cry, and she couldn't go out of the room without saying something to him. Laura gave a loud childish sob.

"Forgive my hat," she said.

And this time she didn't wait for Em's sister. She found her way out of the door, down the path, past all those dark people. At the corner of the lane she met Laurie.

He stepped out of the shadow. "Is that you, Laura?"

"Yes."

"Mother was getting anxious. Was it all right?"

"Yes, quite. Oh, Laurie!" She took his arm, she pressed up against him.

"I say, you're not crying, are you?" asked her brother.

Laura shook her head. She was.

Laurie put his arm round her shoulder. "Don't cry," he said in his warm, loving voice. "Was it awful?"

"No," sobbed Laura. "It was simply marvellous. But, Laurie —" She stopped, she looked at her brother. "Isn't life," she stammered, "isn't life —" But what life was she couldn't explain. No matter. He quite understood.

"*Isn't* it, darling?" said Laurie.   [1922]

SAADAT HASAN MANTO (1912–1955), *whom Salman Rushdie has called "the undisputed master of the modern Indian short story," was born into a family of lawyers in what is now the Indian state of Punjab. Uninterested in formal education, he briefly attended the Aligrah Muslim University but left to work as a journalist. In 1936 he moved to Bombay, India's film capital, and began to edit a film magazine and freelanced as a script writer. When British-dominated India was partitioned into the independent countries of India and Pakistan in 1947, Manto's Muslim wife and children migrated to Pakistan. The following year Manto was forced to join them, pressured by the resentment against Muslims expressed by the Hindu staff of the film company that employed him. Manto later described the tumult surrounding him in war-torn Bombay:*

> I found it impossible to decide which of the two countries was now my homeland — India or Pakistan? Who was responsible for the blood which was being so mercilessly shed every day? Where were they going to inter the bones which had been stripped of the flesh of religion by vultures and birds of prey? Now that we were free [of British rule], had subjection ceased to exist? Who would be our slaves? When we were colonial subjects, we could dream of freedom, but now that we were free, what would our dreams be? Were we even free? Thousands of Hindus and Muslims were dying all around us. Why were they dying? All these questions had different answers: the Indian answer, the Pakistani answer, the British answer. Every question had an answer, but when you tried to look for truth, they were no help.

Manto wrote most of his 200 stories while he lived in Pakistan, after he gave up his work at the Indian film studio. As Khalid Hasan, his translator from the Urdu into English, understood about Manto, "He alone of the writers of his time was able to turn the bloody events of 1947 into great literature. He took no sides and wrote with detachment and passion about the brutalities committed by Hindus, Muslims, and Sikhs in the name of religion and nationalism." The story "The Dog of Titwal" is from Manto's collection Kingdom's End and Other Stories *(1987). In its depiction of what Hasan has described as "a world brutalized and turned upside-down by communal blood-letting," Manto evinces a clear-eyed observation of the human character worthy of Chekhov and Maupassant, two short story writers he took as his mentors. A year before his death from alcoholism at the age of forty-two, Manto wrote his own epitaph:*

> Here lies Saadat Hasan Manto. With him lie buried all the arts and mysteries of short story writing. Under tons of earth he lies, wondering if he is a greater short story writer than God.

Saadat Hasan Manto

The Dog of Titwal

Translated by Khalid Hasan

The soldiers had been entrenched in their positions for several weeks, but there was little, if any, fighting, except for the dozen rounds they ritually exchanged every day. The weather was extremely pleasant. The air was heavy with the scent of wild flowers and nature seemed to be following its course, quite unmindful of the soldiers hiding behind rocks and camouflaged by mountain shrubbery. The birds sang as they always had and the flowers were in bloom. Bees buzzed about lazily.

Only when a shot rang out, the birds got startled and took flight, as if a musician had struck a jarring note on his instrument. It was almost the end of September, neither hot nor cold. It seemed as if summer and winter had made their peace. In the blue skies, cotton clouds floated all day like barges on a lake.

The soldiers seemed to be getting tired of this indecisive war where nothing much ever happened. Their positions were quite impregnable. The two hills on which they were placed faced each other and were about the same height, so no one side had an advantage. Down below in the valley, a stream zigzagged furiously on its stony bed like a snake.

The air force was not involved in the combat and neither of the adversaries had heavy guns or mortars. At night, they would light huge fires and hear each others' voices echoing through the hills.

The last round of tea had just been taken. The fire had gone cold. The sky was clear and there was a chill in the air and a sharp, though not unpleasant, smell of pine cones. Most of the soldiers were already asleep, except Jamadar Harnam Singh, who was on night watch. At two o'clock, he woke up Ganda Singh to take over. Then he lay down, but sleep was as far away from his eyes as the stars in the sky. He began to hum a Punjabi folk song:

Buy me a pair of shoes, my lover
A pair of shoes with stars on them
Sell your buffalo, if you have to
But buy me a pair of shoes
With stars on them

It made him feel good and a bit sentimental. He woke up the others one by one. Banta Singh, the youngest of the soldiers, who had a sweet voice, began to sing a lovelorn verse from *Heer Ranjha*, that timeless Punjabi epic of love and tragedy. A deep sadness fell over them. Even the grey hills seemed to have been affected by the melancholy of the song.

This mood was shattered by the barking of a dog. Jamadar Harnam Singh said, "Where has this son of a bitch materialized from?"

The dog barked again. He sounded closer. There was a rustle in the bushes. Banta Singh got up to investigate and came back with an ordinary mongrel in tow. He was wagging his tail. "I found him behind the bushes and he told me his name was Jhun Jhun," Banta Singh announced. Everybody burst out laughing.

The dog went to Harnam Singh who produced a cracker from his kitbag and threw it on the ground. The dog sniffed at it and was about to eat it, when Harnam Singh snatched it away. ". . . Wait, you could be a Pakistani dog."

They laughed. Banta Singh patted the animal and said to Harnam Singh, "Jamadar sahib, Jhun Jhun is an Indian dog."

"Prove your identity," Harnam Singh ordered the dog, who began to wag his tail.

"This is no proof of identity. All dogs can wag their tails," Harnam Singh said.

"He is only a poor refugee," Banta Singh said, playing with his tail.

Harnam Singh produced another cracker from his kitbag. "And all Pakistanis, including dogs, will be shot."

A soldier shouted, "*India Zindabad!*"

The dog, who was about to munch his cracker, stopped dead in his tracks, put his tail between his legs and looked scared. Harnam Singh laughed. "Why are you afraid of your own country? Here, Jhun Jhun, have another cracker."

The morning broke very suddenly, as if someone had switched on a light in a dark room. It spread across the hills and valleys of Titwal, which is what the area was called.

The war had been going on for months, but nobody could be quite sure who was winning it.

Jamadar Harnam Singh surveyed the area with his binoculars. He could see smoke rising from the opposite hill, which meant that, like them, the enemy was busy preparing breakfast.

Subedar Himmat Khan of the Pakistan army gave his huge moustache a twirl and began to study the map of the Titwal sector. Next to him sat his wireless operator who was trying to establish contact with the platoon commander to obtain instructions. A few feet away, the soldier Bashir sat on the ground, his back against a rock and his rifle in front of him. He was humming:

Where did you spend the night, my love, my moon?
Where did you spend the night?

Enjoying himself, he began to sing more loudly, savouring the words. Suddenly, he heard Subedar Himmat Khan scream, "Where did *you* spend the night?"

But this was not addressed to Bashir. It was a dog he was shouting at. He had come to them from nowhere a few days ago, stayed in the camp quite happily and then suddenly disappeared last night. However, he had now returned like a bad coin.

Bashir smiled and began to sing to the dog. "Where did you spend the night, where did you spend the night?" But he only wagged his tail. Subedar Himmat Khan threw a pebble at him. "All he can do is wag his tail, the idiot."

"What has he got around his neck?" Bashir asked. One of the soldiers grabbed the dog and undid his makeshift rope collar. There was a small piece of cardboard tied to it. "What does it say?" the soldier, who could not read, asked.

Bashir stepped forward and with some difficulty was able to decipher the writing. "It says Jhun Jhun."

Subedar Himmat Khan gave his famous moustache another mighty twirl and said, "Perhaps it is a code. Does it say anything else, Bashirey?"

"Yes sir, it says it is an Indian dog."

"What does that mean?" Subedar Himmat Khan asked.

"Perhaps it is a secret," Bashir answered seriously.

"If there is a secret, it is in that word Jhun Jhun," another soldier ventured in a wise guess.

"You may have something there," Subedar Himmat Khan observed.

Dutifully, Bashir read the whole thing again. "Jhun Jhun. This is an Indian dog."

Subedar Himmat Khan picked up the wireless set and spoke to his platoon commander, providing him with a detailed account of the dog's sudden appearance in their position, his equally sudden disappearance the night before and his return that morning. "What are you talking about?" the platoon commander asked.

Subedar Himmat Khan studied the map again. Then he tore up a packet of cigarettes, cut a small piece from it and gave it to Bashir. "Now write on it in Gurmukhi, the language of those Sikhs . . ."

"What should I write?"

"Well . . ."

Bashir had an inspiration. "Shun Shun, yes, that's right. We counter Jhun Jhun with Shun Shun."

"Good," Subedar Himmat Khan said approvingly. "And add: This is a Pakistani dog."

Subedar Himmat Khan personally threaded the piece of paper through the dog's collar and said, "Now go join your family."

He gave him something to eat and then said, "Look here, my friend, no treachery. The punishment for treachery is death."

The dog kept eating his food and wagging his tail. Then Subedar Himmat Khan turned him round to face the Indian position and said, "Go and take this message to the enemy, but come back. These are the orders of your commander."

The dog wagged his tail and moved down the winding hilly track that led into the valley dividing the two hills. Subedar Himmat Khan picked up his rifle and fired in the air.

The Indians were a bit puzzled, as it was somewhat early in the day for that sort of thing. Jamadar Harnam Singh, who in any case was feeling bored, shouted, "Let's give it to them."

The two sides exchanged fire for half an hour, which, of course, was a complete waste of time. Finally, Jamadar Harnam Singh ordered that enough was enough. He combed his long hair, looked at himself in the mirror and asked Banta Singh, "Where has that dog Jhun Jhun gone?"

"Dogs can never digest butter, goes the famous saying," Banta Singh observed philosophically.

Suddenly, the soldier on lookout duty shouted, "There he comes."

"Who?" Jamadar Harnam Singh asked.

"What was his name? Jhun Jhun," the soldier answered.

"What is he doing?" Harnam Singh asked.

"Just coming our way," the soldier replied, peering through his binoculars.

Subedar Harnam Singh snatched them from him. "That's him all right and there's something round his neck. But, wait, that's the Pakistani hill he's coming from, the motherfucker."

He picked up his rifle, aimed, and fired. The bullet hit some rocks close to where the dog was. He stopped.

Subedar Himmat Khan heard the report and looked through his binoculars. The dog had turned round and was running back. "The brave never run away from battle. Go forward and complete your mission," he shouted at the dog. To scare him, he fired in his general direction. Harnam Singh fired at the same time. The bullet passed within inches of the dog, who leapt in the air, flapping his ears. Subedar Himmat Khan fired again, hitting some stones.

It soon became a game between the two soldiers, with the dog running round in circles in a state of great terror. Both Himmat Khan and Harnam Singh were laughing boisterously. The dog began to run towards Harnam Singh, who abused him loudly and fired. The bullet caught him in the leg. He yelped, turned around, and began to run towards Himmat Khan, only to meet more fire, which was only meant to scare him. "Be a brave boy. If you are injured, don't let that stand between you and your duty. Go, go, go," the Pakistani shouted.

The dog turned. One of his legs was now quite useless. He began to drag himself towards Harnam Singh, who picked up his rifle, aimed carefully, and shot him dead.

Subedar Himmat Khan sighed, "The poor bugger has been martyred."

Jamadar Himmat Singh ran his hand over the still-hot barrel of his rifle and muttered, "He died a dog's death." [1949]

BOBBIE ANN MASON *(b. 1942) grew up on a farm outside Mayfield, Kentucky. As a child she loved to read, and her parents always made sure she had books, mostly popular fiction about the Bobbsey Twins and the Nancy Drew mysteries. After majoring in journalism at the University of Kentucky, she took several jobs in New York City with movie magazines, writing articles about Annette Funicello, Troy Donahue, Fabian, and other teen stars. Next she went to graduate school at the University of Connecticut, where she received her Ph.D. in literature with a dissertation on Vladimir Nabokov's* Ada. *This study was later published in paperback as* Nabokov's Garden *(1974).*

After graduate school, Mason wrote The Girl Sleuth: A Feminist Guide to the Bobbsey Twins, Nancy Drew, and Their Sisters *(1975) about her favorite childhood reading; then, in her late thirties, she started writing short stories. In 1980* The New Yorker *published her first story. "It took me a long time to discover my material," she says. "It wasn't a matter of developing writing skills, it was a matter of knowing how to see things. And it took me a very long time to grow up. I'd been writing for a long time, but was never able to see what there was to write about. And I always aspired to things away from home, so it took me a long time to look back at home and realize that that's where the center of my thoughts was." Mason writes about the working-class people of western Kentucky, and her stories have contributed to a renaissance of regional fiction in America, creating a literary style that critics have labeled "shopping mall realism."*

Mason's first collection, Shiloh and Other Stories, *won the 1982 Hemingway Foundation Award. In 1985 reviewers of her novel* In Country *compared her to Ann Beattie and other "writers of her generation who chronicle aimless lives in prose that tends to be as laconic and stripped down as her characters' emotional range." Mason doesn't regard herself as a feminist writer, despite the heroine in her often reprinted story "Shiloh." She feels that she writes about ordinary people*

> who've got a toe-hold in the middle class. They're people who are from the lower class and who've moved up in the world a little. . . . The people I write about — it seems they either want to get away from home, get away from town, see the world, or they want to stay home, and they're afraid to leave, so they accommodate — or it wouldn't occur to them to leave. But I'm interested in that tension between longing to stay and longing to go. And I think that world sets up a lot of frustrations and there are a lot of limits set for people.

Love Life (1989) *is her second collection of stories.*

BOBBIE ANN MASON

Shiloh

Leroy Moffitt's wife, Norma Jean, is working on her pectorals. She lifts three-pound dumbbells to warm up, then progresses to a twenty-pound barbell. Standing with her legs apart, she reminds Leroy of Wonder Woman.

"I'd give anything if I could just get these muscles to where they're real hard," says Norma Jean. "Feel this arm. It's not as hard as the other one."

"That's 'cause you're right-handed," says Leroy, dodging as she swings the barbell in an arc.

"Do you think so?"

"Sure."

Leroy is a truckdriver. He injured his leg in a highway accident four months ago, and his physical therapy, which involves weights and a pulley, prompted Norma Jean to try building herself up. Now she is attending a body-building class. Leroy has been collecting temporary disability since his tractor-trailer jackknifed in Missouri, badly twisting his left leg in its socket. He has a steel pin in his hip. He will probably not be able to drive his rig again. It sits in the backyard, like a gigantic bird that has flown home to roost. Leroy has been home in Kentucky for three months, and his leg is almost healed, but the accident frightened him and he does not want to drive any more long hauls. He is not sure what to do next. In the meantime, he makes things from craft kits. He started by building a miniature log cabin from notched Popsicle sticks. He varnished it and placed it on the TV set, where it remains. It reminds him of a rustic Nativity scene. Then he tried string art (sailing ships on black velvet), a macramé owl kit, a snap-together B–17 Flying Fortress, and a lamp made out of a model truck, with a light fixture screwed on the top of the cab. At first the kits were diversions, something to kill time, but now he is thinking about building a full-scale log house from a kit. It would be considerably cheaper than building a regular house, and besides, Leroy has grown to appreciate how things are put together. He has begun to realize that in all the years he was on the road he never took time to examine anything. He was always flying past scenery.

"They won't let you build a log cabin in any of the new subdivisions," Norma Jean tells him.

"They will if I tell them it's for you," he says, teasing her. Ever since they were married, he has promised Norma Jean he would build her a new home one day. They have always rented, and the house they live in is small and nondescript. It does not even feel like a home, Leroy realizes now.

Norma Jean works at the Rexall drugstore, and she has acquired an amazing amount of information about cosmetics. When she explains to Leroy the three stages of complexion care, involving creams, toners, and moisturizers, he thinks happily of other petroleum products — axle grease, diesel fuel.

This is a connection between him and Norma Jean. Since he has been home, he has felt unusually tender about his wife and guilty over his long absences. But he can't tell what she feels about him. Norma Jean has never complained about his traveling; she has never made hurt remarks, like calling his truck a "widow-maker." He is reasonably certain she has been faithful to him, but he wishes she would celebrate his permanent homecoming more happily. Norma Jean is often startled to find Leroy at home, and he thinks she seems a little disappointed about it. Perhaps he reminds her too much of the early days of their marriage, before he went on the road. They had a child who died as an infant, years ago. They never speak about their memories of Randy, which have almost faded, but now that Leroy is home all the time, they sometimes feel awkward around each other, and Leroy wonders if one of them should mention the child. He has the feeling that they are waking up out of a dream together — that they must create a new marriage, start afresh. They are lucky they are still married. Leroy has read that for most people losing a child destroys the marriage — or else he heard this on *Donahue*. He can't always remember where he learns things anymore.

At Christmas, Leroy bought an electric organ for Norma Jean. She used to play the piano when she was in high school. "It don't leave you," she told him once. "It's like riding a bicycle."

The new instrument had so many keys and buttons that she was bewildered by it at first. She touched the keys tentatively, pushed some buttons, then pecked out "Chopsticks." It came out in an amplified fox-trot rhythm, with marimba sounds.

"It's an orchestra!" she cried.

The organ had a pecan-look finish and eighteen preset chords, with optional flute, violin, trumpet, clarinet, and banjo accompaniments. Norma Jean mastered the organ almost immediately. At first she played Christmas songs. Then she bought *The Sixties Songbook* and learned every tune in it, adding variations to each with the rows of brightly colored buttons.

"I didn't like these old songs back then," she said. "But I have this crazy feeling I missed something."

"You didn't miss a thing," said Leroy.

Leroy likes to lie on the couch and smoke a joint and listen to Norma Jean play "Can't Take My Eyes Off You" and "I'll Be Back." He is back again. After fifteen years on the road, he is finally settling down with the woman he loves. She is still pretty. Her skin is flawless. Her frosted curls resemble pencil trimmings.

Now that Leroy has come home to stay, he notices how much the town has changed. Subdivisions are spreading across western Kentucky like an oil slick. The sign at the edge of town says "Pop: 11,500" — only seven hundred more than it said twenty years before. Leroy can't figure out who is living in all the new houses. The farmers who used to gather around the courthouse square on Saturday afternoons to play checkers and spit tobacco juice have gone. It has been years since Leroy has thought about the farmers, and they have disappeared without his noticing.

Leroy meets a kid named Stevie Hamilton in the parking lot at the new shopping center. While they pretend to be strangers meeting over a stalled car, Stevie tosses an ounce of marijuana under the front seat of Leroy's car. Stevie is wearing orange jogging shoes and a T-shirt that says CHATTAHOOCHE SUPER-RAT. His father is a prominent doctor who lives in one of the expensive subdivisions in a new white-columned brick house that looks like a funeral parlor. In the phone book under his name there is a separate number, with the listing "Teenagers."

"Where do you get this stuff?" asks Leroy. "From your pappy?"

"That's for me to know and you to find out," Stevie says. He is slit-eyed and skinny.

"What else you got?"

"What you interested in?"

"Nothing special. Just wondered."

Leroy used to take speed on the road. Now he has to go slowly. He needs to be mellow. He leans back against the car and says, "I'm aiming to build me a log house, soon as I get time. My wife, though, I don't think she likes the idea."

"Well, let me know when you want me again," Stevie says. He has a cigarette in his cupped palm, as though sheltering it from the wind. He takes a long drag, then stomps it on the asphalt and slouches away.

Stevie's father was two years ahead of Leroy in high school. Leroy is thirty-four. He married Norma Jean when they were both eighteen, and their child Randy was born a few months later, but he died at the age of four months and three days. He would be about Stevie's age now. Norma Jean and Leroy were at the drive-in, watching a double feature (*Dr. Strangelove* and *Lover Come Back*), and the baby was sleeping in the back seat. When the first movie ended, the baby was dead. It was the sudden infant death syndrome. Leroy remembers handing Randy to a nurse at the emergency room, as though he were offering her a large doll as a present. A dead baby feels like a sack of flour. "It just happens sometimes," said the doctor, in what Leroy always recalls as a nonchalant tone. Leroy can hardly remember the child anymore, but he still sees vividly a scene from *Dr. Strangelove* in which the President of the United States was talking in a folksy voice on the hot line to the Soviet premier about the bomber accidentally headed toward Russia. He was in the War Room, and the world map was lit up. Leroy remembers Norma Jean standing catatonically beside him in the hospital and himself thinking: Who is this strange girl? He had forgotten who she was. Now scientists are saying that crib death is caused by a virus. Nobody knows anything, Leroy thinks. The answers are always changing.

When Leroy gets home from the shopping center, Norma Jean's mother, Mabel Beasley, is there. Until this year, Leroy has not realized how much time she spends with Norma Jean. When she visits, she inspects the closets and then the plants, informing Norma Jean when a plant is droopy or yellow. Mabel calls the plants "flowers," although there are never any blooms. She always notices if Norma Jean's laundry is piling up. Mabel is a short, over-weight woman whose tight, brown-dyed curls look more like a wig than the actual wig she sometimes wears. Today she has brought Norma Jean an off-white dust ruffle she made for the bed; Mabel works in a custom-upholstery shop.

"This is the tenth one I made this year," Mabel says. "I got started and couldn't stop."

"It's real pretty," says Norma Jean.

"Now we can hide things under the bed," says Leroy, who gets along with his mother-in-law primarily by joking with her. Mabel has never really forgiven him for disgracing her by getting Norma Jean pregnant. When the baby died, she said that fate was mocking her.

"What's that thing?" Mabel says to Leroy in a loud voice, pointing to a tangle of yarn on a piece of canvas.

Leroy holds it up for Mabel to see. "It's my needlepoint," he explains. "This is a *Star Trek* pillow cover."

"That's what a woman would do," says Mabel. "Great day in the morning!"

"All the big football players on TV do it," he says.

"Why, Leroy, you're always trying to fool me. I don't believe you for one minute. You don't know what to do with yourself — that's the whole trouble. Sewing!"

"I'm aiming to build us a log house," says Leroy. "Soon as my plans come."

"Like *heck* you are," says Norma Jean. She takes Leroy's needlepoint and shoves it into a drawer. "You have to find a job first. Nobody can afford to build now anyway."

Mabel straightens her girdle and says, "I still think before you get tied down y'all ought to take a little run to Shiloh."

"One of these days, Mama," Norma Jean says impatiently.

Mabel is talking about Shiloh, Tennessee. For the past few years, she has been urging Leroy and Norma Jean to visit the Civil War battleground there. Mabel went there on her honeymoon — the only real trip she ever took. Her husband died of a perforated ulcer when Norma Jean was ten, but Mabel, who was accepted into the United Daughters of the Confederacy in 1975, is still preoccupied with going back to Shiloh.

"I've been to kingdom come and back in that truck out yonder," Leroy says to Mabel, "but we never yet set foot in that battleground. Ain't that something? How did I miss it?"

"It's not even that far," Mabel says.

After Mabel leaves, Norma Jean reads to Leroy from a list she has made. "Things you could do," she announces. "You could get a job as a guard at Union Carbide, where they'd let you set on a stool. You could get on at the lumberyard. You could do a little carpenter work, if you want to build so bad. You could —"

"I can't do something where I'd have to stand up all day."

"You ought to try standing up all day behind a cosmetics counter. It's amazing that I have strong feet, coming from two parents that never had strong feet at all." At the moment Norma Jean is holding on to the kitchen counter, raising her knees one at a time as she talks. She is wearing two-pound ankle weights.

"Don't worry," says Leroy. "I'll do something."

"You could truck calves to slaughter for somebody. You wouldn't have to drive any big old truck for that."

"I'm going to build you this house," says Leroy. "I want to make you a real home."

"I don't want to live in any log cabin."

"It's not a cabin. It's a house."

"I don't care. It looks like a cabin."

"You and me together could lift those logs. It's just like lifting weights."

Norma Jean doesn't answer. Under her breath, she is counting. Now she is marching through the kitchen. She is doing goose steps.

Before his accident, when Leroy came home he used to stay in the house with Norma Jean, watching TV in bed and playing cards. She would cook fried chicken, picnic ham, chocolate pie — all his favorites. Now he is home alone much of the time. In the mornings, Norma Jean disappears, leaving a cooling place in the bed. She eats a cereal called Body Buddies, and she leaves the bowl on the table, with the soggy tan balls floating in a milk puddle. He sees things about Norma Jean that he never realized before. When she chops onions, she stares off into a corner, as if she can't bear to look. She puts on her house slippers almost precisely at nine o'clock every evening and nudges her jogging shoes under the couch. She saves bread heels for the birds. Leroy watches the birds at the feeder. He notices the peculiar way goldfinches fly past the window. They close their wings, then fall, then spread their wings to catch and lift themselves. He wonders if they close their eyes when they fall. Norma Jean closes her eyes when they are in bed. She wants the lights turned out. Even then, he is sure she closes her eyes.

He goes for long drives around town. He tends to drive a car rather carelessly. Power steering and an automatic shift make a car feel so small and inconsequential that his body is hardly involved in the driving process. His injured leg stretches out comfortably. Once or twice he has almost hit something, but even the prospect of an accident seems minor in a car. He cruises the new subdivisions, feeling like a criminal rehearsing for a robbery. Norma Jean is probably right about a log house being inappropriate here in the new subdivisions. All the houses look grand and complicated. They depress him.

One day when Leroy comes home from a drive he finds Norma Jean in tears. She is in the kitchen making a potato and mushroom-soup casserole, with grated-cheese topping. She is crying because her mother caught her smoking.

"I didn't hear her coming. I was standing here puffing away pretty as you please," Norma Jean says, wiping her eyes.

"I knew it would happen sooner or later," says Leroy, putting his arm around her.

"She don't know the meaning of the word 'knock,'" says Norma Jean. "It's a wonder she hadn't caught me years ago."

"Think of it this way," Leroy says. "What if she caught me with a joint?"

"You better not let her!" Norma Jean shrieks. "I'm warning you, Leroy Moffitt!"

"I'm just kidding. Here, play me a tune. That'll help you relax."

Norma Jean puts the casserole in the oven and sets the timer. Then she plays a ragtime tune, with horns and banjo, as Leroy lights up a joint and lies on the couch, laughing to himself about Mabel's catching him at it. He thinks of Stevie Hamilton — a doctor's son pushing grass. Everything is funny. The whole town seems crazy and small. He is reminded of Virgil Mathis, a boastful policeman Leroy used to shoot pool with. Virgil recently led a drug bust in a back room at a bowling alley, where he seized ten thousand dollars' worth of marijuana. The newspaper had a picture of him holding up the bags of grass and grinning widely. Right now, Leroy can imagine Virgil breaking down the door and arresting him with a lungful of smoke. Virgil would probably have been alerted to the scene because of all the racket Norma Jean is making. Now she sounds like a hard-rock band. Norma Jean is terrific. When she switches to a Latin-rhythm version of "Sunshine Superman," Leroy hums along. Norma Jean's foot goes up and down, up and down.

"Well, what do you think?" Leroy says, when Norma Jean pauses to search through her music.

"What do I think about what?"

His mind had gone blank. Then he says, "I'll sell my rig and build us a house." That wasn't what he wanted to say. He wanted to know what she thought — what she *really* thought — about them.

"Don't start in on that again," says Norma Jean. She begins playing "Who'll Be the Next in Line?"

Leroy used to tell hitchhikers his whole life story — about his travels, his hometown, the baby. He would end with a question: "Well, what do you think?" It was just a rhetorical question. In time, he had the feeling that he'd been telling the same story over and over to the same hitchhikers. He quit talking to hitchhikers when he realized how his voice sounded — whining and self-pitying, like some teenage-tragedy song. Now Leroy has the sudden impulse to tell Norma Jean about himself, as if he had just met her. They have known each other so long they have forgotten a lot about each other. They could become reacquainted. But when the oven timer goes off and she runs to the kitchen, he forgets why he wants to do this.

The next day, Mabel drops by. It is Saturday and Norma Jean is cleaning. Leroy is studying the plans for his log house, which have finally come in the mail. He has them spread out on the table — big sheets of stiff blue paper, with diagrams and numbers printed in white. While Norma Jean runs the vacuum, Mabel drinks coffee. She sets her coffee cup on a blueprint.

"I'm just waiting for time to pass," she says to Leroy, drumming her fingers on the table.

As soon as Norma Jean switches off the vacuum, Mabel says in a loud voice, "Did you hear about the datsun dog that killed the baby?"

Norma Jean says, "The word is 'dachshund.'"

"They put the dog on trial. It chewed the baby's legs off. The mother was in the next room all the time." She raises her voice. "They thought it was neglect."

Norma Jean is holding her ears. Leroy manages to open the refrigerator and get some Diet Pepsi to offer Mabel. Mabel still has some coffee and she waves away the Pepsi.

"Datsuns are like that," Mabel says. "They're jealous dogs. They'll tear a place to pieces if you don't keep an eye on them."

"You better watch out what you're saying, Mabel," says Leroy.

"Well, facts is facts."

Leroy looks out the window at his rig. It is like a huge piece of furniture gathering dust in the backyard. Pretty soon it will be an antique. He hears the vacuum cleaner. Norma Jean seems to be cleaning the living room rug again.

Later, she says to Leroy, "She just said that about the baby because she caught me smoking. She's trying to pay me back."

"What are you talking about?" Leroy says, nervously shuffling blueprints.

"You know good and well," Norma Jean says. She is sitting in a kitchen chair with her feet up and her arms wrapped around her knees. She looks small and helpless. She says, "The very idea, her bringing up a subject like that! Saying it was neglect."

"She didn't mean that," Leroy says.

"She might not have *thought* she meant it. She always says things like that. You don't know how she goes on."

"But she didn't really mean it. She was just talking."

Leroy opens a king-sized bottle of beer and pours it into two glasses, dividing it carefully. He hands a glass to Norma Jean and she takes it from him mechanically. For a long time, they sit by the kitchen window watching the birds at the feeder.

Something is happening. Norma Jean is going to night school. She has graduated from her six-week body-building course and now she is taking an adult-education course in composition at Paducah Community College. She spends her evenings outlining paragraphs.

"First you have a topic sentence," she explains to Leroy. "Then you divide it up. Your secondary topic has to be connected to your primary topic."

To Leroy, this sounds intimidating. "I never was any good in English," he says.

"It makes a lot of sense."

"What are you doing this for, anyhow?"

She shrugs. "It's something to do." She stands up and lifts her dumbbells a few times.

"Driving a rig, nobody cared about my English."

"I'm not criticizing your English."

Norma Jean used to say, "If I lose ten minutes' sleep, I just drag all day." Now she stays up late, writing compositions. She got a B on her first paper — a how-to theme on soup-based casseroles. Recently Norma Jean has been cooking unusual foods — tacos, lasagna, Bombay chicken. She doesn't play the organ anymore, though her second paper was called "Why Music Is Important to Me." She sits at the kitchen table, concentrating on her outlines, while Leroy plays with his log house plans, practicing with a set of Lincoln Logs. The thought of getting a truckload of notched, numbered logs scares him, and he wants to be prepared. As he and Norma Jean work together at the kitchen table, Leroy has the hopeful thought that they are sharing something, but he knows he is a fool to think this. Norma Jean is miles away. He knows he is going to lose her. Like Mabel, he is just waiting for time to pass.

One day, Mabel is there before Norma Jean gets home from work, and Leroy finds himself confiding in her. Mabel, he realizes, must know Norma Jean better than he does.

"I don't know what's got into that girl," Mabel says. "She used to go to bed with the chickens. Now you say she's up all hours. Plus her a-smoking. I like to died."

"I want to make her this beautiful home," Leroy says, indicating the Lincoln Logs. "I think she even wants it. Maybe she was happier with me gone."

"She don't know what to make of you, coming home like this."

"Is that it?"

Mabel takes the roof off his Lincoln Log cabin. "You couldn't get *me* in a log cabin," she says. "I was raised in one. It's no picnic, let me tell you."

"They're different now," says Leroy.

"I tell you what," Mabel says, smiling oddly at Leroy.

"What?"

"Take her down to Shiloh. Y'all need to get out together, stir a little. Her brain's all balled up over them books."

Leroy can see traces of Norma Jean's features in her mother's face. Mabel's worn face has the texture of crinkled cotton, but suddenly she looks pretty. It occurs to Leroy that Mabel has been hinting all along that she wants them to take her with them to Shiloh.

"Let's all go to Shiloh," he says. "You and me and her. Come Sunday."

Mabel throws up her hand in protest. "Oh, no, not me. Young folks want to be by themselves."

When Norma Jean comes in with groceries, Leroy says excitedly, "Your mama here's been dying to go to Shiloh for thirty-five years. It's about time we went, don't you think?"

"I'm not going to butt in on anybody's second honeymoon," Mabel says.

"Who's going on a honeymoon, for Christ's sake?" Norma Jean says loudly.

"I never raised no daughter of mine to talk that-a-way," Mabel says.

"You ain't seen nothing yet," says Norma Jean. She starts putting away boxes and cans, slamming cabinet doors.

"There's a log cabin at Shiloh," Mabel says. "It was there during the battle. There's bullet holes in it."

"When are you going to *shut up* about Shiloh, Mama?" asks Norma Jean.

"I always thought Shiloh was the prettiest place, so full of history,"

Mabel goes on. "I just hoped y'all could see it once before I die, so you could tell me about it." Later, she whispers to Leroy, "You do what I said. A little change is what she needs."

"Your name means 'the king,'" Norma Jean says to Leroy that evening. He is trying to get her to go to Shiloh, and she is reading a book about another century.

"Well, I reckon I ought to be right proud."

"I guess so."

"Am I still king around here?"

Norma Jean flexes her biceps and feels them for hardness. "I'm not fooling around with anybody, if that's what you mean," she says.

"Would you tell me if you were?"

"I don't know."

"What does *your* name mean?"

"It was Marilyn Monroe's real name."

"No kidding!"

"Norma comes from the Normans. They were invaders," she says. She closes her book and looks hard at Leroy. "I'll go to Shiloh with you if you'll stop staring at me."

On Sunday, Norma Jean packs a picnic and they go to Shiloh. To Leroy's relief, Mabel says she does not want to come with them. Norma Jean drives, and Leroy, sitting beside her, feels like some boring hitchhiker she has picked up. He tries some conversation, but she answers him in monosyllables. At Shiloh, she drives aimlessly through the park, past bluffs and trails and steep ravines. Shiloh is an immense place, and Leroy cannot see it as a battleground. It is not what he expected. He thought it would look like a golf course. Monuments are everywhere, showing through the thick clusters of trees. Norma Jean passes the log cabin Mabel mentioned. It is surrounded by tourists looking for bullet holes.

"That's not the kind of log house I've got in mind," says Leroy apologetically.

"I know *that*."

"This is a pretty place. Your mama was right."

"It's O.K.," says Norma Jean. "Well, we've seen it. I hope she's satisfied."

They burst out laughing together.

At the park museum, a movie on Shiloh is shown every half hour, but they decide that they don't want to see it. They buy a souvenir Confederate flag for Mabel, and then they find a picnic spot near the cemetery. Norma Jean has brought a picnic cooler, with pimiento sandwiches, soft drinks, and Yodels. Leroy eats a sandwich and then smokes a joint, hiding it behind the picnic cooler. Norma Jean has quit smoking altogether. She is picking cake crumbs from the cellophane wrapper, like a fussy bird.

Leroy says, "So the boys in gray ended up in Corinth. The Union soldiers zapped 'em finally. April 7, 1862."

They both know that he doesn't know any history. He is just talking about some of the historical plaques they have read. He feels awkward, like a boy on a date with an older girl. They are still just making conversation.

"Corinth is where Mama eloped to," says Norma Jean.

They sit in silence and stare at the cemetery for the Union dead and, beyond, at a tall cluster of trees. Campers are parked nearby, bumper to bumper, and small children in bright clothing are cavorting and squealing. Norma Jean wads up the cake wrapper and squeezes it tightly in her hand. Without looking at Leroy, she says, "I want to leave you."

Leroy takes a bottle of Coke out of the cooler and flips off the cap. He holds the bottle poised near his mouth but cannot remember to take a drink. Finally he says, "No, you don't."

"Yes, I do."

"I won't let you."

"You can't stop me."

"Don't do me that way."

Leroy knows Norma Jean will have her own way. "Didn't I promise to be home from now on?" he says.

"In some ways, a woman prefers a man who wanders," says Norma Jean. "That sounds crazy, I know."

"You're not crazy."

Leroy remembers to drink from his Coke. Then he says, "Yes, you *are* crazy. You and me could start all over again. Right back at the beginning."

"We *have* started all over again," says Norma Jean. "And this is how it turned out."

"What did I do wrong?"

"Nothing."

"Is this one of those women's lib things?" Leroy asks.

"Don't be funny."

The cemetery, a green slope dotted with white markers, looks like a subdivision site. Leroy is trying to comprehend that his marriage is breaking up, but for some reason he is wondering about white slabs in a graveyard.

"Everything was fine till Mama caught me smoking," says Norma Jean, standing up. "That set something off."

"What are you talking about?"

"She won't leave me alone — *you* won't leave me alone." Norma Jean seems to be crying, but she is looking away from him. "I feel eighteen again. I can't face that all over again." She starts walking away. "No, it *wasn't* fine. I don't know what I'm saying. Forget it."

Leroy takes a lungful of smoke and closes his eyes as Norma Jean's words sink in. He tries to focus on the fact that thirty-five hundred soldiers died on the grounds around him. He can only think of that war as a board game with plastic soldiers. Leroy almost smiles, as he compares the Confederates' daring attack on the Union camps and Virgil Mathis's raid on the bowling alley. General Grant, drunk and furious, shoved the southerners back to Corinth, where Mabel and Jet Beasley were married years later, when Mabel was still thin and good-looking. The next day, Mabel and Jet visited the battleground, and then Norma Jean was born, and then she married Leroy and they had a baby, which they lost, and now Leroy and Norma Jean are here at the same battleground. Leroy knows he is leaving out a lot. He is leaving out the insides of history. History was always just names and dates to him. It occurs to him that building a house out of logs is similarly empty — too simple. And the real inner workings of a marriage, like most of history, have escaped him. Now he sees that building a log house is the dumbest idea he could have had. It was clumsy of him to think Norma Jean would want a log house. It was a crazy idea. He'll have to think of something else, quickly. He will wad the blueprints into tight balls and fling them into the lake. Then he'll get moving again. He opens his eyes. Norma Jean has moved away and is walking through the cemetery, following a serpentine brick path.

Leroy gets up to follow his wife, but his good leg is asleep and his bad leg still hurts him. Norma Jean is far away, walking rapidly toward the bluff by the river, and he tries to hobble toward her. Some children run past him, screaming noisily. Norma Jean has reached the bluff, and she is looking out over the Tennessee River. Now she turns toward Leroy and waves her arms. Is she beckoning to him? She seems to be doing an exercise for her chest muscles. The sky is unusually pale — the color of the dust ruffle Mabel made for their bed.   [1982]

GUY DE MAUPASSANT *(1850–1893) was born in Normandy, the son of a wealthy stockbroker. Unable to accept discipline in school, he joined the army during the Franco-Prussian War of 1870–1871. Then for seven years he apprenticed himself to Gustave Flaubert, a distant relative, who attempted to teach him to write. Maupassant remembered, "I wrote verses, short stories, longer stories, even a wretched play. Nothing survived. The master read everything. Then, the following Sunday at lunch, he developed his criticisms." Flaubert taught Maupassant that talent "is nothing other than a long patience. Work."*

The essence of Flaubert's now famous teaching is that the writer must look at everything to find some aspect of it that no one has yet seen or expressed. "Everything contains some element of the unexplored because we are accustomed to use our eyes only with the memory of what other people before us have thought about the object we are looking at. The least thing has a bit of the unknown about it. Let us find this."

In 1880 Maupassant caused a sensation with the publication of his story "Boule de Suif" ("Ball of Fat"), a dramatic account of prostitution and bourgeois hypocrisy. During the next decade, before his gradual incapacitation and death from syphilis, he published nearly 300 stories. Characterized by compact and dramatic narrative lines, they read as modern short stories, eliminating the moral judgments and the long digressions used by many earlier writers. Along with his younger contemporary Anton Chekhov, Maupassant is responsible for technical advances that moved the short story toward an austerity that has marked it ever since. These two writers influenced nearly everyone who has written short fiction after them. As Joseph Conrad recognized, "Facts, and again facts, are his [Maupassant's] unique concern. That is why he is not always properly understood." Maupassant's lack of sentimentality toward his characters, as in his depiction of the wife in "The Necklace," laid him open to charges of cynicism and hardness. Even if Maupassant's stories display a greater distance from his characters and a less sympathetic irony than Chekhov's, both writers were the most accomplished of narrators, equal in their powers of exact observation and independent judgment and in their supple, practiced knowledge of their craft.

RELATED COMMENTARIES: *Kate Chopin, "How I Stumbled upon Maupassant," page 1407; Guy de Maupassant, "The Writer's Goal," page 1456.*

GUY DE MAUPASSANT

The Necklace

Translated by Marjorie Laurie

She was one of those pretty and charming girls who are sometimes, as if by a mistake of destiny, born in a family of clerks. She had no dowry, no expectations, no means of being known, understood, loved, wedded by any rich and distinguished man; and she let herself be married to a little clerk at the Ministry of Public Instructions.

She dressed plainly because she could not dress well, but she was as unhappy as though she had really fallen from her proper station, since with women there is neither caste nor rank: and beauty, grace, and charm act instead of family and birth. Natural fineness, instinct for what is elegant, suppleness of wit, are the sole hierarchy, and make from women of the people the equals of the very greatest ladies.

She suffered ceaselessly, feeling herself born for all the delicacies and all the luxuries. She suffered from the poverty of her dwelling, from the wretched look of the walls, from the worn-out chairs, from the ugliness of the curtains. All those things, of which another woman of her rank would never even have been conscious, tortured her and made her angry. The sight of the little Breton peasant, who did her humble housework aroused in her regrets which were despairing, and distracted dreams. She thought of the silent antechambers hung with Oriental tapestry, lit by tall bronze candelabra, and of the two great footmen in knee breeches who sleep in the big armchairs, made drowsy by the heavy warmth of the hot-air stove. She thought of the long *salons* fitted up with ancient silk, of the delicate furniture carrying priceless curiosities, and of the coquettish perfumed boudoirs made for talks at five o'clock with intimate friends, with men famous and sought after, whom all women envy and whose attention they all desire.

When she sat down to dinner, before the round table covered with a tablecloth three days old, opposite her husband, who uncovered the soup tureen and declared with an enchanted air, "Ah, the good *pot-au-feu*! I don't know anything better than that," she thought of dainty dinners, of shining silverware, of tapestry which peopled the walls with ancient personages and with strange birds flying in the midst of a fairy forest; and she thought of delicious dishes served on marvelous plates, and of the whispered gallantries which you listen to with a sphinxlike smile, while you are eating the pink flesh of a trout or the wings of a quail.

She had no dresses, no jewels, nothing. And she loved nothing but that; she felt made for that. She would so have liked to please, to be envied, to be charming, to be sought after.

She had a friend, a former schoolmate at the convent, who was rich, and whom she did not like to go and see any more, because she suffered so much when she came back.

But one evening, her husband returned home with a triumphant air, and holding a large envelope in his hand.

"There," said he. "Here is something for you."

She tore the paper sharply, and drew out a printed card which bore these words:

"The Minister of Public Instruction and Mme. Georges Ramponneau request the honor of M. and Mme. Loisel's company at the palace of the Ministry on Monday evening, January eighteenth."

Instead of being delighted, as her husband hoped, she threw the invitation on the table with disdain, murmuring:

"What do you want me to do with that?"

"But, my dear, I thought you would be glad. You never go out, and this is such a fine opportunity. I had awful trouble to get it. Everyone wants to go; it is very select, and they are not giving many invitations to clerks. The whole official world will be there."

She looked at him with an irritated glance, and said, impatiently:

"And what do you want me to put on my back?"

He had not thought of that; he stammered:

"Why, the dress you go to the theater in. It looks very well, to me."

He stopped, distracted, seeing his wife was crying. Two great tears descended slowly from the corners of her eyes toward the corners of her mouth. He stuttered:

"What's the matter? What's the matter?"

But, by violent effort, she had conquered her grief, and she replied, with a calm voice, while she wiped her wet cheeks:

"Nothing. Only I have no dress and therefore I can't go to this ball. Give your card to some colleague whose wife is better equipped than I."

He was in despair. He resumed:

"Come, let us see, Mathilde. How much would it cost, a suitable dress, which you could use on other occasions. Something very simple?"

She reflected several seconds, making her calculations and wondering also what sum she could ask without drawing on herself an immediate refusal and a frightened exclamation from the economical clerk.

Finally, she replied, hesitatingly:

"I don't know exactly, but I think I could manage it with four hundred francs."

He had grown a little pale, because he was laying aside just that amount to buy a gun and treat himself to a little shooting next summer on the plain of Nanterre, with several friends who went to shoot larks down there, of a Sunday.

But he said:

"All right. I will give you four hundred francs. And try to have a pretty dress."

The day of the ball drew near, and Mme. Loisel seemed sad, uneasy, anxious. Her dress was ready, however. Her husband said to her one evening:

"What is the matter? Come, you've been so queer these last three days."

And she answered:

"It annoys me not to have a single jewel, not a single stone, nothing to put on. I shall look like distress. I should almost rather not go at all."

He resumed:

"You might wear natural flowers. It's very stylish at this time of the year. For ten francs you can get two or three magnificent roses."

She was not convinced.

"No; there's nothing more humiliating than to look poor among other women who are rich."

But her husband cried:

"How stupid you are! Go look up your friend Mme. Forestier, and ask her to lend you some jewels. You're quite thick enough with her to do that."

She uttered a cry of joy:

"It's true. I never thought of it."

The next day she went to her friend and told of her distress.

Mme. Forestier went to a wardrobe with a glass door, took out a large jewelbox, brought it back, opened it, and said to Mme. Loisel:

"Choose, choose, my dear."

She saw first of all some bracelets, then a pearl necklace, then a Venetian cross, gold and precious stones of admirable workmanship. She tried on the ornaments before the glass, hesitated, could not make up her mind to part with them, to give them back. She kept asking:

"Haven't you any more?"

"Why, yes. Look. I don't know what you like."

All of a sudden she discovered, in a black satin box, a superb necklace of diamonds, and her heart began to beat with an immoderate desire. Her hands trembled as she took it. She fastened it around her throat, outside her high necked dress, and remained lost in ecstasy at the sight of herself.

Then she asked, hesitating, filled with anguish:

"Can you lend me that, only that?"

"Why, yes, certainly."

She sprang upon the neck of her friend, kissed her passionately, then fled with her treasure.

The day of the ball arrived. Mme. Loisel made a great success. She was prettier than them all, elegant, gracious, smiling, and crazy with joy. All the men looked at her, asked her name, endeavored to be introduced. All the attachés of the Cabinet wanted to waltz with her. She was remarked by the minister himself.

She danced with intoxication, with passion, made drunk by pleasure, forgetting all, in the triumph of her beauty, in the glory of her success, in a sort of cloud of happiness composed of all this homage, of all this admiration, of all these awakened desires, and of that sense of complete victory which is so sweet to a woman's heart.

She went away about four o'clock in the morning. Her husband had been sleeping since midnight, in a little deserted anteroom, with three other gentlemen whose wives were having a good time. He threw over her shoulders the wraps which he had brought, modest wraps of common life, whose poverty contrasted with the elegance of the ball dress. She felt this, and wanted to escape so as not to be remarked by the other women, who were enveloping themselves in costly furs.

Loisel held her back.

"Wait a bit. You will catch cold outside. I will go and call a cab."

But she did not listen to him, and rapidly descended the stairs. When they were in the street they did not find a carriage; and they began to look for one, shouting after the cabmen whom they saw passing by at a distance.

They went down toward the Seine, in despair, shivering with cold. At last they found on the quay one of those ancient noctambulant coupés[1] which, exactly as if they were ashamed to show their misery during the day, are never seen round Paris until after nightfall.

It took them to their door in the Rue des Martyrs, and once more, sadly, they climbed up homeward. All was ended, for her. And as to him, he reflected that he must be at the Ministry at ten o'clock.

She removed the wraps which covered her shoulders before the glass, so as once more to see herself in all her glory. But suddenly she uttered a cry. She no longer had the necklace around her neck!

Her husband, already half undressed, demanded:

"What is the matter with you?"

She turned madly toward him:

"I have — I have — I've lost Mme. Forestier's necklace."

He stood up, distracted.

"What! — how? — impossible!"

And they looked in the folds of her dress, in the folds of her cloak, in her pockets, everywhere. They did not find it.

He asked:

"You're sure you had it on when you left the ball?"

"Yes, I felt it in the vestibule of the palace."

"But if you had lost it in the street we should have heard it fall. It must be in the cab."

"Yes. Probably. Did you take his number?"

"No. And you, didn't you notice it?"

"No."

They looked, thunderstruck, at one another. At last Loisel put on his clothes.

"I shall go back on foot," said he, "over the whole route which we have taken to see if I can find it."

And he went out. She sat waiting on a chair in her ball dress, without strength to go to bed, overwhelmed, without fire, without a thought.

Her husband came back about seven o'clock. He had found nothing.

He went to Police Headquarters, to the newspaper offices, to offer a

---

[1] An enclosed four-wheeled carriage.

reward; he went to the cab companies — everywhere, in fact, whither he was urged by the least suspicion of hope.

She waited all day, in the same condition of mad fear before this terrible calamity.

Loisel returned at night with a hollow, pale face; he had discovered nothing.

"You must write to your friend," said he, "that you have broken the clasp of her necklace and that you are having it mended. That will give us time to turn round."

She wrote at his dictation.

At the end of a week they had lost all hope.

And Loisel, who had aged five years, declared:

"We must consider how to replace that ornament."

The next day they took the box which had contained it, and they went to the jeweler whose name was found within. He consulted his books.

"It was not I, madame, who sold that necklace; I must simply have furnished the case."

Then they went from jeweler to jeweler, searching for a necklace like the other, consulting their memories, sick both of them with chagrin and anguish.

They found, in a shop at the Palais Royal, a string of diamonds which seemed to them exactly like the one they looked for. It was worth forty thousand francs. They could have it for thirty-six.

So they begged the jeweler not to sell it for three days yet. And they made a bargain that he should buy it back for thirty-four thousand francs, in case they found the other one before the end of February.

Loisel possessed eighteen thousand francs which his father had left him. He would borrow the rest.

He did borrow, asking a thousand francs of one, five hundred of another, five louis here, three louis there. He gave notes, took up ruinous obligations, dealt with usurers and all the race of lenders. He compromised all the rest of his life, risked his signature without even knowing if he could meet it; and, frightened by the pains yet to come, by the black misery which was about to fall upon him, by the prospect of all the physical privation and of all the moral tortures which he was to suffer, he went to get the new necklace, putting down upon the merchant's counter thirty-six thousand francs.

When Mme. Loisel took back the necklace, Mme. Forestier said to her, with a chilly manner:

"You should have returned it sooner; I might have needed it."

She did not open the case, as her friend had so much feared. If she had detected the substitution, what would she have thought, what would she have said? Would she not have taken Mme. Loisel for a thief?

Mme. Loisel now knew the horrible existence of the needy. She took her part, moreover, all of a sudden, with heroism. That dreadful debt must be paid. She would pay it. They dismissed their servant; they changed their lodgings; they rented a garret under the roof.

She came to know what heavy housework meant and the odious cares of the kitchen. She washed the dishes, using her rosy nails on the greasy pots and pans. She washed the dirty linen, the shirts, and the dishcloths, which she dried upon a line; she carried the slops down to the street every morning, and carried up the water, stopping for breath at every landing. And, dressed like a woman of the people, she went to the fruiterer, the grocer, the butcher, her basket on her arm, bargaining, insulted, defending her miserable money sou by sou.

Each month they had to meet some notes, renew others, obtain more time.

Her husband worked in the evening making a fair copy of some trades-man's accounts, and late at night he often copied manuscript for five sous a page.

And this life lasted for ten years.

At the end of ten years, they had paid everything, everything, with the rates of usury, and the accumulations of the compound interest.

Mme. Loisel looked old now. She had become the woman of impover-ished households — strong and hard and rough. With frowsy hair, skirts askew, and red hands, she talked loud while washing the floor with great swishes of water. But sometimes, when her husband was at the office, she sat down near the window, and she thought of that gay evening of long ago, of that ball where she had been so beautiful and so fêted.

What would have happened if she had not lost that necklace? Who knows? Who knows? How life is strange and changeful! How little a thing is needed for us to be lost or to be saved!

But, one Sunday, having gone to take a walk in the Champs Elysées to refresh herself from the labor of the week, she suddenly perceived a woman who was leading a child. It was Mme. Forestier, still young, still beautiful, still charming.

Mme. Loisel felt moved. Was she going to speak to her? Yes, certainly. And now that she had paid, she was going to tell her all about it. Why not?

She went up.

"Good-day, Jeanne."

The other, astonished to be familiarly addressed by this plain goodwife, did not recognize her at all, and stammered.

"But — madam! — I do not know — you must be mistaken."

"No. I am Mathilde Loisel."

Her friend uttered a cry.

"Oh, my poor Mathilde! How you are changed!"

"Yes, I have had days hard enough, since I have seen you, days wretched enough — and that because of you!"

"Of me! How so?"

"Do you remember that diamond necklace which you lent me to wear at the ministerial ball?"

"Yes. Well?"

"Well, I lost it."

"What do you mean? You brought it back."

"I brought you back another just like it. And for this we have been ten years paying. You can understand that it was not easy for us, who had nothing. At last it is ended, and I am very glad."

Mme. Forestier had stopped.

"You say that you bought a necklace of diamonds to replace mine?"

"Yes. You never noticed it, then! They were very like."

And she smiled with a joy which was proud and naïve at once.

Mme. Forestier, strongly moved, took her two hands.

"Oh, my poor Mathilde! Why, my necklace was paste. It was worth at most five hundred francs!"   [1884]

HERMAN MELVILLE *(1819–1891) published his first short story in 1853 as "Bartleby, the Scrivener: A Story of Wall Street." Behind him were seven years of writing novels beginning with the burst of creative energy that produced his early books of sea adventure:* Typee *(1846),* Omoo *(1847),* Mardi *(1849),* Redburn *(1849), and* White-Jacket *(1850). All of these were based on his experiences on board ship. Melville had been left in poverty at the age of fifteen when his father went bankrupt, and in 1839 he went to sea as a cabin boy. Two years later he sailed on a whaler bound for the Pacific, but he deserted in the Marquesas Islands and lived for a time with cannibals. Having little formal education, Melville later boasted that "a whale ship was my Yale College and my Harvard." His most ambitious book was* Moby-Dick *(1851), a work of great allegorical complexity heavily indebted to the influence of Nathaniel Hawthorne, Melville's neighbor in the Berkshires at the time he wrote it.* Moby-Dick *was not a commercial success, however, and the novel that followed it,* Pierre *(1852), was dismissed by the critics as incomprehensible trash.*

*It was at this point that Melville turned to the short story. Between 1853 and 1856 he published fifteen sketches and stories and a serialized historical novel, promising the popular magazines that his stories would "contain nothing of any sort to shock the fastidious." But when this work and another novel (*The Confidence Man, *1857) failed to restore his reputation, he ceased trying to support his family by his pen. He moved from his farm in the Berkshires to a house in New York City bought for him by his father-in-law, and worked for more than twenty years as an inspector of customs. He published a few books of poems and wrote a short novel,* Billy Budd, *which critics acclaimed as one of his greatest works when it was published — thirty years after his death.*

Melville stood at the crossroads in the early history of American short fiction. When he began to publish in magazines, Hawthorne and Edgar Allan Poe had already done their best work in the romantic vein of tales and sketches, and the realistic local-color school of short stories had not yet been established. Melville created something new in "Bartleby, the Scrivener," a fully developed, if discursive, short story set in a contemporary social context. It baffled readers of Putnam's Monthly Magazine *in 1853, when it was published in two installments. One reviewer called it "a Poeish tale with an infusion of more natural sentiment." For the rest of his stories, Melville used the conventional form of old-fashioned tales mostly set in remote times or places.*

RELATED COMMENTARIES: *Herman Melville, "Blackness in Hawthorne's 'Young Goodman Brown,'" page 1458; J. Hillis Miller, "A Deconstructive Reading of Melville's 'Bartleby, the Scrivener,'" page 1460.*

Herman Melville

Bartleby, the Scrivener

A Story of Wall Street

I am a rather elderly man. The nature of my avocations, for the last thirty years, has brought me into more than ordinary contact with what would seem an interesting and somewhat singular set of men, of whom, as yet, nothing, that I know of, has ever been written — I mean, the law-copyists, or scriveners. I have known very many of them, professionally and privately, and, if I pleased, could relate divers histories, at which good-natured gentlemen might smile, and sentimental souls might weep. But I waive the biographies of all other scriveners, for a few passages in the life of Bartleby, who was a scrivener, the strangest I ever saw, or heard of. While, of other law-copyists, I might write the complete life, of Bartleby nothing of that sort can be done. I believe that no materials exist, for a full and satisfactory biography of this man. It is an irreparable loss to literature. Bartleby was one of those beings of whom nothing is ascertainable, except from the original sources, and, in his case, those are very small. What my own astonished eyes saw of Bartleby, *that* is all I know of him, except, indeed, one vague report, which will appear in the sequel.

Ere introducing the scrivener, as he first appeared to me, it is fit I make some mention of myself, my *employés*, my business, my chambers, and general surroundings, because some such description is indispensable to an adequate understanding of the chief character about to be presented. Imprimis:[1] I am a man who, from his youth upwards, has been filled with a profound conviction that the easiest way of life is the best. Hence, though I belong to a profession proverbially energetic and nervous, even to turbulence, at times, yet nothing of that sort have I ever suffered to invade my peace. I am one of those unambitious lawyers who never address a jury, or in any way draw down public applause; but, in the cool tranquillity of a snug retreat, do a snug business among rich men's bonds, and mortgages, and title-deeds. All who know me, consider me an eminently *safe* man. The late John Jacob Astor, a personage little given to poetic enthusiasm, had no hesitation in pronouncing my first grand point to be prudence; my next, method. I do not speak it in vanity, but simply record the fact, that I was not unemployed in my profession by the late John Jacob Astor; a name which, I admit, I love to repeat; for it hath a rounded and orbicular sound to it, and rings like unto bullion. I will freely add, that I was not insensible to the late John Jacob Astor's good opinion.

Some time prior to the period at which this little history begins, my

---

[1] In the first place (Latin).

avocations had been largely increased. The good old office, now extinct in the State of New York, of a Master in Chancery, had been conferred upon me. It was not a very arduous office, but very pleasantly remunerative. I seldom lose my temper; much more seldom indulge in dangerous indignation at wrongs and outrages; but I must be permitted to be rash here and declare, that I consider the sudden and violent abrogation of the office of Master in Chancery, by the new Constitution, as a —— premature act; inasmuch as I had counted upon a life-lease of the profits, whereas I only received those of a few short years. But this is by the way.

My chambers were up stairs, at No. — Wall Street. At one end, they looked upon the white wall of the interior of a spacious skylight shaft, penetrating the building from top to bottom.

This view might have been considered rather tame than otherwise, deficient in what landscape painters call "life." But, if so, the view from the other end of my chambers offered, at least, a contrast, if nothing more. In that direction, my windows commanded an unobstructed view of a lofty brick wall, black by age and everlasting shade; which wall required no spy-glass to bring out its lurking beauties, but, for the benefit of all near-sighted spectators, was pushed up to within ten feet of my window-panes. Owing to the great height of the surrounding buildings, and my chambers being on the second floor, the interval between this wall and mine not a little resembled a huge square cistern.

At the period just preceding the advent of Bartleby, I had two persons as copyists in my employment, and a promising lad as an office-boy. First, Turkey; second, Nippers; third, Ginger Nut. These may seem names, the like of which are not usually found in the Directory. In truth, they were nicknames, mutually conferred upon each other by my three clerks, and were deemed expressive of their respective persons or characters. Turkey was a short, pursy Englishman, of about my own age — that is, somewhere not far from sixty. In the morning, one might say, his face was of a fine florid hue, but after twelve o'clock, meridian — his dinner hour — it blazed like a grate full of Christmas coals; and continued blazing — but, as it were, with a gradual wane — till six o'clock, P.M., or thereabouts; after which, I saw no more of the proprietor of the face, which, gaining its meridian with the sun, seemed to set with it, to rise, culminate, and decline the following day, with the like regularity and undiminished glory. There are many singular coincidences I have known in the course of my life, not the least among which was the fact, that, exactly when Turkey displayed his fullest beams from his red and radiant countenance, just then, too, at that critical moment, began the daily period when I considered his business capacities as seriously disturbed for the remainder of the twenty-four hours. Not that he was absolutely idle, or averse to business then; far from it. The difficulty was, he was apt to be altogether too energetic. There was a strange, inflamed, flurried, flighty recklessness of activity about him. He would be incautious in dipping his pen into his inkstand. All his blots upon my documents were dropped there after twelve o'clock, meridian. Indeed, not only would he be reckless, and sadly given to making blots in the afternoon, but, some days, he went further, and was rather noisy. At such times, too, his face flamed with augmented blazonry, as if cannel coal had been heaped on anthracite. He made an unpleasant racket with his chair; spilled his sand-box; in mending his pens, impatiently split them all to pieces, and threw them on the floor in a sudden passion; stood up, and leaned over his table, boxing his papers about in a most indecorous manner, very sad to behold in an elderly man like him. Nevertheless, as he was in many ways a most valuable person to me, and all the time before twelve o'clock, meridian, was the quickest, steadiest creature, too, accomplishing a great deal of work in a style not easily to be matched — for these reasons, I was willing to overlook his eccentricities, though, indeed, occasionally, I remonstrated with him. I did this very gently, however, because, though the civilest, nay, the blandest and most reverential of men in the morning, yet, in the afternoon, he was disposed, upon provocation, to be slightly rash with his tongue — in fact, insolent. Now, valuing his morning services as I did, and resolved not to lose them — yet, at the same time, made uncomfortable by his inflamed ways after twelve o'clock — and being a man of peace, unwilling by my admonitions to call forth unseemly retorts from him, I took upon me, one Saturday noon (he was always worse on Saturdays) to hint to him, very kindly, that, perhaps, now that he was growing old, it might be well to abridge his labors; in short, he need not come to my chambers after twelve o'clock, but, dinner over, had best go home to his lodgings, and rest himself till tea-time. But no; he insisted upon his afternoon devotions. His countenance became intolerably fervid, as he oratorically assured me — gesticulating with a long ruler at the other end of the room — that if his services in the morning were useful, how indispensable, then, in the afternoon?

"With submission, sir," said Turkey, on this occasion, "I consider myself your right-hand man. In the morning I but marshal and deploy my columns; but in the afternoon I put myself at their head, and gallantly charge the foe, thus" — and he made a violent thrust with the ruler.

"But the blots, Turkey," intimated I.

"True; but, with submission, sir, behold these hairs! I am getting old. Surely, sir, a blot or two of a warm afternoon is not to be severely urged against gray hairs. Old age — even if it blot the page — is honorable. With submission, sir, we *both* are getting old."

This appeal to my fellow-feeling was hardly to be resisted. At all events, I saw that go he would not. So, I made up my mind to let him stay, resolving, nevertheless, to see to it that, during the afternoon, he had to do with my less important papers.

Nippers, the second on my list, was a whiskered, sallow, and, upon the whole, rather piratical-looking young man, of about five-and-twenty. I always deemed him the victim of two evil powers — ambition and indigestion. The ambition was evinced by a certain impatience of the duties of a mere copyist, an unwarrantable usurpation of strictly professional affairs such as the original drawing up of legal documents. The indigestion seemed betokened in an occasional nervous testiness and grinning irritability, causing the teeth to audibly grind together over mistakes committed in copying; unnecessary maledictions, hissed, rather than spoken, in the heat of business; and especially by a continual discontent with the height of the table where he worked. Though of a very ingenious mechanical turn, Nippers could never get this table to suit him. He put chips under it, blocks of various sorts, bits of pasteboard, and at last went so far as to attempt an exquisite adjustment, by final pieces of folded blotting paper. But no invention would answer. If, for the sake of easing his back, he brought the table-lid at a sharp angle well up towards his chin, and wrote there like a man using the steep roof of a Dutch house for his desk, then he declared that it stopped the circulation in his arms. If now he lowered the table to his waistbands, and stooped over it in writing, then there was a sore aching in his back. In short, the truth of the matter was, Nippers knew not what he wanted. Or, if he wanted anything, it was to be rid of a scrivener's table altogether. Among the manifestations of his diseased ambition was a fondness he had for receiving visits from certain ambiguous-looking fellows in seedy coats, whom he called his clients. Indeed, I was aware that not only was he, at times, considerable of a ward-politician, but he occasionally did a little business at the justices' courts, and was not unknown on the steps of the Tombs.[2] I have good reason to believe, however, that one individual who called upon him at my chambers, and who, with a grand air, he insisted was his client, was no other than a dun, and the alleged title-deed, a bill. But, with all his failings, and the annoyances he caused me, Nippers, like his compatriot Turkey, was a very useful man to me; wrote a neat, swift hand; and, when he chose, was not deficient in a gentlemanly sort of deportment. Added to this, he always dressed in a gentlemanly sort of way; and so, incidentally, reflected credit upon my chambers. Whereas, with respect to Turkey, I had much ado to keep him from being a reproach to me. His clothes were apt to look oily, and smell of eating-houses. He wore his pantaloons very loose and baggy in summer. His coats were execrable, his hat not to be handled. But while the hat was a thing of indifference to me, inasmuch as his natural civility and deference, as a dependent Englishman, always led him to doff it the moment he entered the room, yet his coat was another matter. Concerning his coats, I reasoned with him; but with no effect. The truth was, I suppose, that a man with so small an income could not afford to sport such a lustrous face and a lustrous coat at one and the same time. As Nippers once observed, Turkey's money went chiefly for red ink. One winter day, I presented Turkey with a highly respectable-looking coat of my own — a padded gray coat, of a most comfortable warmth, and which buttoned straight up from the knee to the neck. I thought Turkey would appreciate the favor, and abate his rashness and obstreperousness of afternoons. But no; I verily believe that buttoning himself up in so downy and blanket-like a coat had a pernicious effect upon him upon the same principle that too much oats are bad for horses. In fact, precisely as a rash, restive horse is said to feel his oats, so Turkey felt his coat. It made him insolent. He was a man whom prosperity harmed.

Though, concerning the self-indulgent habits of Turkey, I had my own

---

[2] A prison in New York City.

private surmises, yet, touching Nippers, I was well persuaded that, whatever might be his faults in other respects, he was, at least, a temperate young man. But, indeed, nature herself seemed to have been his vintner, and, at his birth, charged him so thoroughly with an irritable, brandy-like disposition, that all subsequent potations were needless. When I consider how, amid the stillness of my chambers, Nippers would sometimes impatiently rise from his seat, and stooping over his table, spread his arms wide apart, seize the whole desk, and move it, and jerk it, with a grim, grinding motion on the floor, as if the table were a perverse voluntary agent, intent on thwarting and vexing him, I plainly perceive that, for Nippers, brandy-and-water were altogether superfluous.

It was fortunate for me that, owing to its peculiar cause — indigestion — the irritability and consequent nervousness of Nippers were mainly observable in the morning, while in the afternoon he was comparatively mild. So that, Turkey's paroxysms only coming on about twelve o'clock, I never had to do with their eccentricities at one time. Their fits relieved each other, like guards. When Nippers' was on, Turkey's was off; and *vice versa*. This was a good natural arrangement, under the circumstances.

Ginger Nut, the third on my list, was a lad, some twelve years old. His father was a carman, ambitious of seeing his son on the bench instead of a cart, before he died. So he sent him to my office, as student at law, errand-boy, cleaner, and sweeper, at the rate of one dollar a week. He had a little desk to himself, but he did not use it much. Upon inspection, the drawer exhibited a great array of the shells of various sorts of nuts. Indeed, to this quick-witted youth, the whole noble science of the law was contained in a nutshell. Not the least among the employments of Ginger Nut, as well as one which he discharged with the most alacrity, was his duty as cake and apple purveyor for Turkey and Nippers. Copying lawpapers being proverbially a dry, husky sort of business, my two scriveners were fain to moisten their mouths very often with Spitzenbergs, to be had at the numerous stalls nigh the Custom House and Post Office. Also, they sent Ginger Nut very frequently for that peculiar cake — small, flat, round, and very spicy — after which he had been named by them. Of a cold morning, when business was but dull, Turkey would gobble up scores of these cakes, as if they were mere wafers — indeed, they sell them at the rate of six or eight for a penny — the scrape of his pen blending with the crunching of the crisp particles in his mouth. Of all the fiery afternoon blunders and flurried rashness of Turkey, was his once moistening a ginger-cake between his lips, and clapping it on to a mortgage, for a seal. I came within an ace of dismissing him then. But he mollified me by making an oriental bow, and saying —

"With submission, sir, it was generous of me to find you in stationery on my own account."

Now my original business — that of a conveyancer and title hunter, and drawer-up of recondite documents of all sorts — was considerably increased by receiving the Master's office. There was now great work for scriveners. Not only must I push the clerks already with me, but I must have additional help.

In answer to my advertisement, a motionless young man one morning stood upon my office threshold, the door being open, for it was summer. I can see that figure now — pallidly neat, pitiably respectable, incurably forlorn! It was Bartleby.

After a few words touching his qualifications, I engaged him, glad to have among my corps of copyists a man of so singularly sedate an aspect, which I thought might operate beneficially upon the flighty temper of Turkey, and the fiery one of Nippers.

I should have stated before that ground-glass folding-doors divided my premises into two parts, one of which was occupied by my scriveners, the other by myself. According to my humor, I threw open these doors, or closed them. I resolved to assign Bartleby a corner by the folding-doors, but on my side of them, so as to have this quiet man within easy call, in case any trifling thing was to be done. I placed his desk close up to a small side-window in that part of the room, a window which originally had afforded a lateral view of certain grimy brickyards and bricks, but which, owing to subsequent erections, commanded at present no view at all, though it gave some light. Within three feet of the panes was a wall, and the light came down from far above, between two lofty buildings, as from a very small opening in a dome. Still further to a satisfactory arrangement, I procured a high green folding screen, which might entirely isolate Bartleby from my sight, though not remove him from my voice. And thus, in a manner, privacy and society were conjoined.

At first, Bartleby did an extraordinary quantity of writing. As if long famishing for something to copy, he seemed to gorge himself on my documents. There was no pause for digestion. He ran a day and night line, copying by sunlight and by candle-light. I should have been quite delighted with his application, had he been cheerfully industrious. But he wrote on silently, palely, mechanically.

It is, of course, an indispensable part of a scrivener's business to verify the accuracy of his copy, word by word. Where there are two or more scriveners in an office, they assist each other in this examination, one reading from the copy, the other holding the original. It is a very dull, wearisome, and lethargic affair. I can readily imagine that, to some sanguine temperaments, it would be altogether intolerable. For example, I cannot credit that the mettlesome poet, Byron, would have contentedly sat down with Bartleby to examine a law document of, say five hundred pages, closely written in a crimpy hand.

Now and then, in the haste of business, it had been my habit to assist in comparing some brief document myself, calling Turkey or Nippers for this purpose. One object I had, in placing Bartleby so handy to me behind the screen, was, to avail myself of his services on such trivial occasions. It was on the third day, I think, of his being with me, and before any necessity had arisen for having his own writing examined, that, being much hurried to complete a small affair I had in hand, I abruptly called to Bartleby. In my haste and natural expectancy of instant compliance, I sat with my head bent over the original on my desk, and my right hand sideways, and somewhat nervously extended with the copy, so that, immediately upon emerging from his re-treat, Bartleby might snatch it and proceed to business without the least delay.

In this very attitude did I sit when I called to him, rapidly stating what it was I wanted him to do — namely, to examine a small paper with me. Imagine my surprise, nay, my consternation, when, without moving from his privacy, Bartleby, in a singularly mild, firm voice, replied, "I would prefer not to."

I sat awhile in perfect silence, rallying my stunned faculties. Immediately it occurred to me that my ears had deceived me, or Bartleby had entirely misunderstood my meaning. I repeated my request in the clearest tone I could assume; but in quite as clear a one came the previous reply, "I would prefer not to."

"Prefer not to," echoed I, rising in high excitement, and crossing the room with a stride. "What do you mean? Are you moonstruck? I want you to help me compare this sheet here — take it," and I thrust it towards him.

"I would prefer not to," said he.

I looked at him steadfastly. His face was leanly composed; his gray eye dimly calm. Not a wrinkle of agitation rippled him. Had there been the least uneasiness, anger, impatience, or impertinence in his manner; in other words, had there been anything ordinarily human about him, doubtless I should have violently dismissed him from the premises. But as it was, I should have as soon thought of turning my pale plaster-of-paris bust of Cicero out of doors. I stood gazing at him awhile, as he went on with his own writing, and then reseated myself at my desk. This is very strange, thought I. What had one best do? But my business hurried me. I concluded to forget the matter for the present, reserving it for my future leisure. So, calling Nippers from the other room, the paper was speedily examined.

A few days after this, Bartleby concluded four lengthy documents, being quadruplicates of a week's testimony taken before me in my High Court of Chancery. It became necessary to examine them. It was an important suit, and great accuracy was imperative. Having all things arranged, I called Turkey, Nippers, and Ginger Nut, from the next room, meaning to place the four copies in the hands of my four clerks, while I should read from the original. Accordingly, Turkey, Nippers, and Ginger Nut had taken their seats in a row, each with his document in his hand, when I called to Bartleby to join this interesting group.

"Bartleby! quick, I am waiting."

I heard a slow scrape of his chair legs on the uncarpeted floor, and soon he appeared standing at the entrance of his hermitage.

"What is wanted?" said he, mildly.

"The copies, the copies," said I, hurriedly. "We are going to examine them. There" — and I held towards him the fourth quadruplicate.

"I would prefer not to," he said, and gently disappeared behind the screen.

For a few moments I was turned into a pillar of salt, standing at the head of my seated column of clerks. Recovering myself, I advanced towards the screen, and demanded the reason for such extraordinary conduct.

"*Why* do you refuse?"

"I would prefer not to."

With any other man I should have flown outright into a dreadful passion, scorned all further words, and thrust him ignominiously from my presence. But there was something about Bartleby that not only strangely disarmed me, but, in a wonderful manner, touched and disconcerted me. I began to reason with him.

"These are your own copies we are about to examine. It is labor saving to you, because one examination will answer for your four papers. It is common usage. Every copyist is bound to help examine his copy. Is it not so? Will you not speak? Answer!"

"I prefer not to," he replied in a flute-like tone. It seemed to me that, while I had been addressing him, he carefully revolved every statement that I made; fully comprehended the meaning; could not gainsay the irresistible conclusion; but, at the same time, some paramount consideration prevailed with him to reply as he did.

"You are decided, then, not to comply with my request a request made according to common usage and common sense?"

He briefly gave me to understand, that on that point my judgment was sound. Yes: his decision was irreversible.

It is not seldom the case that, when a man is browbeaten in some unprecedented and violently unreasonable way, he begins to stagger in his own plainest faith. He begins, as it were, vaguely to surmise that, wonderful as it may be, all the justice and all the reason is on the other side. Accordingly, if any disinterested persons are present, he turns to them for some reinforcement for his own faltering mind.

"Turkey," said I, "what do you think of this? Am I not right?"

"With submission, sir," said Turkey, in his blandest tone, "I think that you are."

"Nippers," said I, "what do *you* think of it?"

"I think I should kick him out of the office."

(The reader of nice perceptions will have perceived that, it being morning, Turkey's answer is couched in polite and tranquil terms, but Nippers replies in ill-tempered ones. Or, to repeat a previous sentence, Nippers' ugly mood was on duty, and Turkey's off.)

"Ginger Nut," said I, willing to enlist the smallest suffrage in my behalf, "what do *you* think of it?"

"I think, sir, he's a little *luny*," replied Ginger Nut, with a grin.

"You hear what they say," said I, turning towards the screen, "come forth and do your duty."

But he vouchsafed no reply. I pondered a moment in sore perplexity. But once more business hurried me. I determined again to postpone the consideration of this dilemma to my future leisure. With a little trouble we made out to examine the papers without Bartleby, though at every page or two Turkey deferentially dropped his opinion, that this proceeding was quite out of the common; while Nippers, twitching in his chair with a dyspeptic nervousness, ground out, between his set teeth, occasional hissing maledictions against the stubborn oaf behind the screen. And for his (Nippers') part, this was the first and the last time he would do another man's business without pay.

Meanwhile Bartleby sat in his hermitage, oblivious to everything but his own peculiar business there.

Some days passed, the scrivener being employed upon another lengthy work. His late remarkable conduct led me to regard his ways narrowly. I observed that he never went to dinner; indeed, that he never went anywhere. As yet I had never, of my personal knowledge, known him to be outside of my office. He was a perpetual sentry in the corner. At about eleven o'clock though, in the morning, I noticed that Ginger Nut would advance towards the opening in Bartleby's screen, as if silently beckoned thither by a gesture invisible to me where I sat. The boy would then leave the office, jingling a few pence, and reappear with a handful of ginger-nuts, which he delivered in the hermitage, receiving two of the cakes for his trouble.

He lives, then, on ginger-nuts, thought I; never eats a dinner, properly speaking; he must be a vegetarian, then, but no; he never eats even vegetables, he eats nothing but ginger-nuts. My mind then ran on in reveries concerning the probable effects upon the human constitution of living entirely on ginger-nuts. Ginger-nuts are so called, because they contain ginger as one of their peculiar constituents, and the final flavoring one. Now, what was ginger? A hot, spicy thing. Was Bartleby hot and spicy? Not at all. Ginger, then, had no effect upon Bartleby. Probably he preferred it should have none.

Nothing so aggravates an earnest person as a passive resistance. If the individual so resisted be of a not inhumane temper, and the resisting one perfectly harmless in his passivity, then, in the better moods of the former, he will endeavor charitably to construe to his imagination what proves impossible to be solved by his judgment. Even so, for the most part, I regarded Bartleby and his ways. Poor fellow! thought I, he means no mischief; it is plain he intends no insolence; his aspect sufficiently evinces that his eccentricities are involuntary. He is useful to me. I can get along with him. If I turn him away, the chances are he will fall in with some less indulgent employer, and then he will be rudely treated, and perhaps driven forth miserably to starve. Yes. Here I can cheaply purchase a delicious self-approval. To befriend Bartleby; to humor him in his strange wilfulness, will cost me little or nothing, while I lay up in my soul what will eventually prove a sweet morsel for my conscience. But this mood was not invariable with me. The passiveness of Bartleby sometimes irritated me. I felt strangely goaded on to encounter him in new opposition — to elicit some angry spark from him answerable to my own. But, indeed, I might as well have essayed to strike fire with my knuckles against a bit of Windsor soap. But one afternoon the evil impulse in me mastered me, and the following little scene ensued:

"Bartleby," said I, "when those papers are all copied, I will compare them with you."

"I would prefer not to."

"How? Surely you do not mean to persist in that mulish vagary?"

No answer.

I threw open the folding-doors nearby, and turning upon Turkey and Nippers, exclaimed:

"Bartleby a second time says, he won't examine his papers. What do you think of it, Turkey?"

It was afternoon, be it remembered. Turkey sat glowing like a brass boiler; his bald head steaming; his hands reeling among his blotted papers.

"Think of it?" roared Turkey. "I think I'll just step behind his screen, and black his eyes for him!"

So saying, Turkey rose to his feet and threw his arms into a pugilistic position. He was hurrying away to make good his promise, when I detained him, alarmed at the effect of incautiously rousing Turkey's combativeness after dinner.

"Sit down, Turkey," said I, "and hear what Nippers has to say. What do you think of it, Nippers? Would I not be justified in immediately dismissing Bartleby?"

"Excuse me, that is for you to decide, sir. I think his conduct quite unusual, and, indeed, unjust, as regards Turkey and myself. But it may only be a passing whim."

"Ah," exclaimed I, "you have strangely changed your mind, then — you speak very gently of him now."

"All beer," cried Turkey; "gentleness is effects of beer — Nippers and I dined together to-day. You see how gentle *I* am, sir. Shall I go and black his eyes?"

"You refer to Bartleby, I suppose. No, not to-day, Turkey," I replied; "pray, put up your fists."

I closed the doors, and again advanced towards Bartleby. I felt additional incentives tempting me to my fate. I burned to be rebelled against again. I remembered that Bartleby never left the office.

"Bartleby," said I, "Ginger Nut is away; just step around to the Post Office, won't you?" (it was but a three minutes' walk) "and see if there is anything for me."

"I would prefer not to."

"You *will* not?"

"I *prefer* not."

I staggered to my desk, and sat there in a deep study. My blind inveteracy returned. Was there any other thing in which I could procure myself to be ignominiously repulsed by this lean, penniless wight? my hired clerk? What added thing is there, perfectly reasonable, that he will be sure to refuse to do?

"Bartleby!"

No answer.

"Bartleby," in a louder tone.

No answer.

"Bartleby," I roared.

Like a very ghost, agreeably to the laws of magical invocation, at the third summons, he appeared at the entrance of his hermitage.

"Go to the next room, and tell Nippers to come to me."

"I would prefer not to," he respectfully and slowly said, and mildly disappeared.

"Very good, Bartleby," said I, in a quiet sort of serenely-severe self-possessed tone, intimating the unalterable purpose of some terrible retribution very close at hand. At the moment I half intended something of the kind. But upon the whole, as it was drawing towards my dinner-hour, I thought it best to put on my hat and walk home for the day, suffering much from perplexity and distress of mind.

Shall I acknowledge it? The conclusion of this whole business was, that it soon became a fixed fact of my chambers, that a pale young scrivener, by the name of Bartleby, had a desk there; that he copied for me at the usual rate of four cents a folio (one hundred words); but he was permanently exempt from examining the work done by him, that duty being transferred to Turkey and Nippers, out of compliment, doubtless, to their superior acuteness; moreover, said Bartleby was never, on any account, to be dispatched on the most trivial errand of any sort; and that even if entreated to take upon him such a matter, it was generally understood that he would "prefer not to" — in other words, that he would refuse point blank.

As days passed on, I became considerably reconciled to Bartleby. His steadiness, his freedom from all dissipation, his incessant industry (except when he chose to throw himself into a standing revery behind his screen), his great stillness, his unalterableness of demeanor under all circumstances, made him a valuable acquisition. One prime thing was this — *he was always there* — first in the morning, continually through the day, and the last at night. I had a singular confidence in his honesty. I felt my most precious papers perfectly safe in his hands. Sometimes, to be sure, I could not, for the very soul of me, avoid falling into sudden spasmodic passions with him. For it was exceeding difficult to bear in mind all the time those strange peculiarities, privileges, and unheard-of exemptions, forming the tacit stipulations on Bartleby's part under which he remained in my office. Now and then, in the eagerness of dispatching pressing business, I would inadvertently summon Bartleby, in a short, rapid tone, to put his finger, say, on the incipient tie of a bit of red tape with which I was about compressing some papers. Of course, from behind the screen the usual answer, "I prefer not to," was sure to come; and then, how could a human creature, with the common infirmities of our nature, refrain from bitterly exclaiming upon such perverseness — such unreasonableness? However, every added repulse of this sort which I received only tended to lessen the probability of my repeating the inadvertence.

Here it must be said, that, according to the custom of most legal gentlemen occupying chambers in densely populated law buildings, there were several keys to my door. One was kept by a woman residing in the attic, which person weekly scrubbed and daily swept and dusted my apartments. Another was kept by Turkey for convenience sake. The third I sometimes carried in my own pocket. The fourth I knew not who had.

Now, one Sunday morning I happened to go to Trinity Church, to hear a celebrated preacher, and finding myself rather early on the ground I thought I would walk round to my chambers for a while. Luckily I had my key with me; but upon applying it to the lock, I found it resisted by something inserted from the inside. Quite surprised, I called out; when to my consternation a key was turned from within; and thrusting his lean visage at me, and holding the door ajar, the apparition of Bartleby appeared, in his shirt-sleeves, and otherwise in a strangely tattered *deshabille*, saying quietly that he was sorry, but he was deeply engaged just then, and preferred not admitting me at present. In a brief word or two, he moreover added, that perhaps I had better walk round the block two or three times, and by that time he would probably have concluded his affairs.

Now, the utterly unsurmised appearance of Bartleby, tenanting my law-chambers of a Sunday morning, with his cadaverously gentlemanly *nonchalance*, yet withal firm and self-possessed, had such a strange effect upon me, that incontinently I slunk away from my own door, and did as desired. But not without sundry twinges of impotent rebellion against the mild effrontery of this unaccountable scrivener. Indeed, it was his wonderful mildness chiefly, which not only disarmed me, but unmanned me, as it were. For I consider that one, for the time, is sort of unmanned when he tranquilly permits his hired clerk to dictate to him, and order him away from his own premises. Furthermore, I was full of uneasiness as to what Bartleby could possibly be doing in my office in his shirt-sleeves, and in an otherwise dismantled condition on a Sunday morning. Was anything amiss going on? Nay, that was out of the question. It was not to be thought of for a moment that Bartleby was an immoral person. But what could he be doing there? — copying? Nay again, whatever might be his eccentricities, Bartleby was an eminently decorous person. He would be the last man to sit down to his desk in any state approaching to nudity. Besides, it was Sunday; and there was something about Bartleby that forbade the supposition that he would by any secular occupation violate the proprieties of the day.

Nevertheless, my mind was not pacified; and full of a restless curiosity, at last I returned to the door. Without hindrance I inserted my key, opened it, and entered. Bartleby was not to be seen. I looked round anxiously, peeped behind his screen; but it was very plain that he was gone. Upon more closely examining the place, I surmised that for an indefinite period Bartleby must have ate, dressed, and slept in my office, and that too without plate, mirror, or bed. The cushioned seat of a rickety old sofa in one corner bore the faint impress of a lean, reclining form. Rolled away under his desk, I found a blanket; under the empty grate, a blacking box and brush; on a chair, a tin basin, with soap and a ragged towel; in a newspaper a few crumbs of ginger-nuts and a morsel of cheese. Yes, thought I, it is evident enough that Bartleby has been making his home here, keeping bachelor's hall all by himself. Immediately then the thought came sweeping across me, what miserable friendlessness and loneliness are here revealed! His poverty is great; but his solitude, how horrible! Think of it. Of a Sunday, Wall Street is deserted as Petra;[3] and every night of every day it is an emptiness. This building, too,

---

[3] A city in what is now Jordan, once the center of an Arab kingdom. It was deserted for more than ten centuries, until its rediscovery by explorers in 1812.

which of week-days hums with industry and life, at nightfall echoes with sheer vacancy, and all through Sunday is forlorn. And here Bartleby makes his home; sole spectator of a solitude which he has seen all populous — a sort of innocent and transformed Marius[4] brooding among the ruins of Carthage!

For the first time in my life a feeling of overpowering stinging melancholy seized me. Before, I had never experienced aught but a not unpleasing sadness. The bond of a common humanity now drew me irresistibly to gloom. A fraternal melancholy! For both I and Bartleby were sons of Adam. I remembered the bright silks and sparkling faces I had seen that day, in gala trim, swan-like sailing down the Mississippi of Broadway; and I contrasted them with the pallid copyist, and thought to myself, Ah, happiness courts the light, so we deem the world is gay; but misery hides aloof, so we deem that misery there is none. These sad fancyings — chimeras, doubtless, of a sick and silly brain — led on to other and more special thoughts, concerning the eccentricities of Bartleby. Presentiments of strange discoveries hovered round me. The scrivener's pale form appeared to me laid out, among uncaring strangers, in its shivering winding-sheet.

Suddenly I was attracted by Bartleby's closed desk, the key in open sight left in the lock.

I mean no mischief, seek the gratification of no heartless curiosity, thought I; besides, the desk is mine, and its contents, too, so I will make bold to look within. Everything was methodically arranged, the papers smoothly placed. The pigeon-holes were deep, and removing the files of documents, I groped into their recesses. Presently I felt something there, and dragged it out. It was an old bandanna handkerchief, heavy and knotted. I opened it, and saw it was a saving's bank.

I now recalled all the quiet mysteries which I had noted in the man. I remembered that he never spoke but to answer; that, though at intervals he had considerable time to himself, yet I had never seen him reading — no, not even a newspaper; that for long periods he would stand looking out, at his pale window behind the screen, upon the dead brick wall; I was quite sure he never visited any refectory or eating-house; while his pale face clearly indicated that he never drank beer like Turkey; or tea and coffee even, like other men; that he never went anywhere in particular that I could learn; never went out for a walk, unless, indeed, that was the case at present; that he had declined telling who he was, or whence he came, or whether he had any relatives in the world; that though so thin and pale, he never complained of ill-health. And more than all, I remembered a certain unconscious air of pallid — how shall I call it? — of pallid haughtiness, say, or rather an austere reserve about him, which has positively awed me into my tame compliance with his eccentricities, when I had feared to ask him to do the slightest incidental thing for me, even though I might know, from his long-continued

---

[4] Gaius Marius (157?–86 B.C.), a Roman General, several times elected consul. Marius's greatest military successes came in the Jugurthine War, in Africa. Later, when his opponents gained power and he was banished, he fled to Africa. Carthage was a city in North Africa.

motionlessness, that behind his screen he must be standing in one of those dead-wall reveries of his.

Revolving all these things, and coupling them with the recently discovered fact, that he made my office his constant abiding place and home, and not forgetful of his morbid moodiness; revolving all these things, a prudential feeling began to steal over me. My first emotions had been those of pure melancholy and sincerest pity; but just in proportion as the forlornness of Bartleby grew and grew to my imagination, did that same melancholy merge into fear, that pity into repulsion. So true it is, and so terrible, too, that up to a certain point the thought or sight of misery enlists our best affections; but, in certain special cases, beyond that point it does not. They err who would assert that invariably this is owing to the inherent selfishness of the human heart. It rather proceeds from a certain hopelessness of remedying excessive and organic ill. To a sensitive being, pity is not seldom pain. And when at last it is perceived that such pity cannot lead to effectual succor, common sense bids the soul be rid of it. What I saw that morning persuaded me that the scrivener was the victim of innate and incurable disorder. I might give alms to his body; but his body did not pain him; it was his soul that suffered, and his soul I could not reach.

I did not accomplish the purpose of going to Trinity Church that morning. Somehow, the things I had seen disqualified me for the time from churchgoing. I walked homeward, thinking what I would do with Bartleby. Finally, I resolved upon this — I would put certain calm questions to him the next morning, touching his history, etc., and if he declined to answer them openly and unreservedly (and I supposed he would prefer not), then to give him a twenty dollar bill over and above whatever I might owe him, and tell him his services were no longer required; but that if in any other way I could assist him, I would be happy to do so, especially if he desired to return to his native place, wherever that might be, I would willingly help to defray the expenses. Moreover, if, after reaching home, he found himself at any time in want of aid, a letter from him would be sure of a reply.

The next morning came.

"Bartleby," said I, gently calling to him behind his screen.

No reply.

"Bartleby," said I, in a still gentler tone, "come here; I am not going to ask you to do anything you would prefer not to do — I simply wish to speak to you."

Upon this he noiselessly slid into view.

"Will you tell me, Bartleby, where you were born?"

"I would prefer not to."

"Will you tell me *anything* about yourself?"

"I would prefer not to."

"But what reasonable objection can you have to speak to me? I feel friendly towards you."

He did not look at me while I spoke, but kept his glance fixed upon my bust of Cicero, which, as I then sat, was directly behind me, some six inches above my head.

"What is your answer, Bartleby?" said I, after waiting a considerable time for a reply, during which his countenance remained immovable, only there was the faintest conceivable tremor of the white attenuated mouth.

"At present I prefer to give no answer," he said, and retired into his hermitage.

It was rather weak in me I confess, but his manner, on this occasion, nettled me. Not only did there seem to lurk in it a certain calm disdain, but his perverseness seemed ungrateful, considering the undeniable good usage and indulgence he had received from me.

Again I sat ruminating what I should do. Mortified as I was at his behavior, and resolved as I had been to dismiss him when I entered my office, nevertheless I strangely felt something superstitious knocking at my heart, and forbidding me to carry out my purpose, and denouncing me for a villain if I dared to breathe one bitter word against this forlornest of mankind. At last, familiarly drawing my chair behind his screen, I sat down and said: "Bartleby, never mind, then, about revealing your history; but let me entreat you, as a friend, to comply as far as may be with the usages of this office. Say now, you will help to examine papers tomorrow or next day: in short, say now, that in a day or two you will begin to be a little reasonable: — say so, Bartleby."

"At present I would prefer not to be a little reasonable," was his mildly cadaverous reply.

Just then the folding-doors opened, and Nippers approached. He seemed suffering from an unusually bad night's rest, induced by severer indigestion than common. He overheard those final words of Bartleby.

"*Prefer not*, eh?" gritted Nippers — "I'd *prefer* him, if I were you, sir," addressing me — "I'd *prefer* him; I'd give him preferences, the stubborn mule! What is it, sir, pray, that he *prefers* not to do now?"

Bartleby moved not a limb.

"Mr. Nippers," said I, "I'd prefer that you would withdraw for the present."

Somehow, of late, I had got into the way of involuntarily using this word "prefer" upon all sorts of not exactly suitable occasions. And I trembled to think that my contact with the scrivener had already and seriously affected me in a mental way. And what further and deeper aberration might it not yet produce? This apprehension had not been without efficacy in determining me to summary measures.

As Nippers, looking very sour and sulky, was departing, Turkey blandly and deferentially approached.

"With submission, sir," said he, "yesterday I was thinking about Bartleby here, and I think that if he would but prefer to take a quart of good ale every day, it would do much towards mending him, and enabling him to assist in examining his papers."

"So you have got the word, too," said I, slightly excited.

"With submission, what word, sir?" asked Turkey, respectfully crowding himself into the contracted space behind the screen, and by so doing, making me jostle the scrivener. "What word, sir?"

"I would prefer to be left alone here," said Bartleby, as if offended at being mobbed in his privacy.

"That's the word, Turkey," said I — *"that's* it."

"Oh, *prefer?* oh yes — queer word. I never use it myself. But, sir, as I was saying, if he would but prefer —"

"Turkey," interrupted I, "you will please withdraw."

"Oh certainly, sir, if you prefer that I should."

As he opened the folding-door to retire, Nippers at his desk caught a glimpse of me, and asked whether I would prefer to have a certain paper copied on blue paper or white. He did not in the least roguishly accent the word "prefer." It was plain that it involuntarily rolled from his tongue. I thought to myself, surely I must get rid of a demented man, who already has in some degree turned the tongues, if not the heads of myself and clerks. But I thought it prudent not to break the dismission at once.

The next day I noticed that Bartleby did nothing but stand at his window in his dead-wall revery. Upon asking him why he did not write, he said that he had decided upon doing no more writing.

"Why, how now? what next?" exclaimed I, "do no more writing?"

"No more."

"And what is the reason?"

"Do you not see the reason for yourself?" he indifferently replied.

I looked steadfastly at him, and perceived that his eyes looked dull and glazed. Instantly it occurred to me, that his unexampled diligence in copying by his dim window for the first few weeks of his stay with me might have temporarily impaired his vision.

I was touched. I said something in condolence with him. I hinted that of course he did wisely in abstaining from writing for a while; and urged him to embrace that opportunity of taking wholesome exercise in the open air. This, however, he did not do. A few days after this, my other clerks being absent, and being in a great hurry to dispatch certain letters by the mail, I thought that, having nothing else earthly to do, Bartleby would surely be less inflexible than usual, and carry these letters to the Post Office. But he blankly declined. So, much to my inconvenience, I went myself.

Still added days went by. Whether Bartleby's eyes improved or not, I could not say. To all appearance, I thought they did. But when I asked him if they did he vouchsafed no answer. At all events, he would do no copying. At last, in replying to my urgings, he informed me that he had permanently given up copying.

"What!" exclaimed I; "suppose your eyes should get entirely well — better than ever before — would you not copy then?"

"I have given up copying," he answered, and slid aside.

He remained as ever, a fixture in my chamber. Nay — if that were possible — he became still more of a fixture than before. What was to be done? He would do nothing in the office; why should he stay there? In plain fact, he had now become a millstone to me, not only useless as a necklace, but afflictive to bear. Yet I was sorry for him. I speak less than truth when I say that, on his own account, he occasioned me uneasiness. If he would but have named a single relative or friend, I would instantly have written, and urged their taking the poor fellow away to some convenient retreat. But he seemed alone, absolutely alone in the universe. A bit of wreck in the mid-Atlantic. At length, necessities connected with my business tyrannized over all other considerations. Decently as I could, I told Bartleby that in six days' time he must unconditionally leave the office. I warned him to take measures, in the interval, for procuring some other abode. I offered to assist him in this endeavor, if he himself would but take the first step towards a removal. "And when you finally quit me, Bartleby," added I, "I shall see that you go not away entirely unprovided. Six days from this hour, remember."

At the expiration of that period, I peeped behind the screen, and lo! Bartleby was there.

I buttoned up my coat, balanced myself; advanced slowly towards him, touched his shoulder, and said, "The time has come; you must quit this place; I am sorry for you; here is money; but you must go."

"I would prefer not," he replied, with his back still towards me.

"You *must*."

He remained silent.

Now I had an unbounded confidence in this man's common honesty. He had frequently restored to me sixpences and shillings carelessly dropped upon the floor, for I am apt to be very reckless in such shirt-button affairs. The proceeding, then, which followed will not be deemed extraordinary.

"Bartleby," said I, "I owe you twelve dollars on account; here are thirty-two; the odd twenty are yours — Will you take it?" and I handed the bills towards him.

But he made no motion.

"I will leave them here, then," putting them under a weight on the table. Then taking my hat and cane and going to the door, I tranquilly turned and added — "After you have removed your things from these offices, Bartleby, you will of course lock the door — since every one is now gone for the day but you — and if you please, slip your key underneath the mat, so that I may have it in the morning. I shall not see you again; so good-bye to you. If, hereafter, in your new place of abode, I can be of any service to you, do not fail to advise me by letter. Good-bye, Bartleby, and fare you well."

But he answered not a word; like the last column of some ruined temple, he remained standing mute and solitary in the middle of the otherwise deserted room.

As I walked home in a pensive mood, my vanity got the better of my pity. I could not but highly plume myself on my masterly management in getting rid of Bartleby. Masterly I call it, and such it must appear to any dispassionate thinker. The beauty of my procedure seemed to consist in its perfect quietness. There was no vulgar bullying, no bravado of any sort, no choleric hectoring, and striding to and fro across the apartment, jerking out vehement commands for Bartleby to bundle himself off with his beggarly traps. Nothing of the kind. Without loudly bidding Bartleby depart — as an inferior genius might have done — I *assumed* the ground that depart he must; and upon that assumption built all I had to say. The more I thought over my procedure, the more I was charmed with it. Nevertheless, next morning, upon awakening, I had my doubts — I had somehow slept off the fumes of vanity. One of the coolest and wisest hours a man has, is just after he awakes in the morning. My procedure seemed as sagacious as ever — but only in theory. How it would prove in practice — there was the rub. It was truly a beautiful thought to have assumed Bartleby's departure; but, after all, that assumption was simply my own, and none of Bartleby's. The great point was, not whether I had assumed that he would quit me, but whether he would prefer to do so. He was more a man of preferences than assumptions.

After breakfast, I walked down town, arguing the probabilities *pro* and *con*. One moment I thought it would prove a miserable failure, and Bartleby would be found all alive at my office as usual; the next moment it seemed certain that I should find his chair empty. And so I kept veering about. At the corner of Broadway and Canal Street, I saw quite an excited group of people standing in earnest conversation.

"I'll take odds he doesn't," said a voice as I passed.

"Doesn't go? — done!" said I, "put up your money."

I was instinctively putting my hand in my pocket to produce my own, when I remembered that this was an election day. The words I had overheard bore no reference to Bartleby, but to the success or non-success of some candidate for the mayoralty. In my intent frame of mind, I had, as it were, imagined that all Broadway shared in my excitement, and were debating the same question with me. I passed on, very thankful that the uproar of the street screened my momentary absent-mindedness.

As I had intended, I was earlier than usual at my office door. I stood listening for a moment. All was still. He must be gone. I tried the knob. The door was locked. Yes, my procedure had worked to a charm; he indeed must be vanished. Yet a certain melancholy mixed with this: I was almost sorry for my brilliant success. I was fumbling under the door mat for the key, which Bartleby was to have left there for me, when accidentally my knee knocked against a panel, producing a summoning sound, and in response a voice came to me from within — "Not yet; I am occupied."

It was Bartleby.

I was thunderstruck. For an instant I stood like the man who, pipe in mouth, was killed one cloudless afternoon long ago in Virginia, by summer lightning; at his own warm open window he was killed, and remained leaning out there upon the dreamy afternoon, till someone touched him, when he fell.

"Not gone!" I murmured at last. But again obeying that wondrous ascendancy which the inscrutable scrivener had over me, and from which ascendancy, for all my chafing, I could not completely escape, I slowly went down stairs and out into the street, and while walking round the block, considered what I should next do in this unheard-of perplexity. Turn the man out by an actual thrusting I could not; to drive him away by calling him hard names would not do; calling in the police was an unpleasant idea; and yet, permit him to enjoy his cadaverous triumph over me — this, too, I could not think of. What was to be done? or, if nothing could be done, was there anything further that I could *assume* in the matter? Yes, as before I had prospectively assumed that Bartleby would depart, so now I might retrospectively assume that departed he was. In the legitimate carrying out of this assumption, I might enter my office in a great hurry, and pretending not to see Bartleby at all, walk straight against him as if he were air. Such a proceeding would in a singular degree have the appearance of a home-thrust. It was hardly possible that Bartleby could withstand such an application of the doctrine of assumption. But upon second thoughts the success of the plan seemed rather dubious. I resolved to argue the matter over with him again.

"Bartleby," said I, entering the office, with a quietly severe expression, "I am seriously displeased. I am pained, Bartleby. I had thought better of you. I had imagined you of such a gentlemanly organization, that in any delicate dilemma a slight hint would suffice — in short, an assumption. But it appears I am deceived. Why," I added, unaffectedly starting, "You have not even touched that money yet," pointing to it, just where I had left it the evening previous.

He answered nothing.

"Will you, or will you not, quit me?" I now demanded in a sudden passion, advancing close to him.

"I would prefer *not* to quit you," he replied, gently emphasizing the *not*.

"What earthly right have you to stay here? Do you pay any rent? Do you pay my taxes? Or is this property yours?"

He answered nothing.

"Are you ready to go on and write now? Are your eyes recovered? Could you copy a small paper for me this morning? or help examine a few lines? or step round to the Post Office? In a word, will you do anything at all, to give a coloring to your refusal to depart the premises?"

He silently retired into his hermitage.

I was now in such a state of nervous resentment that I thought it but prudent to check myself at present from further demonstrations. Bartleby and I were alone. I remembered the tragedy of the unfortunate Adams and the still more unfortunate Colt in the solitary office of the latter; and how poor Colt, being dreadfully incensed by Adams, and imprudently permitting himself to get wildly excited, was at unawares hurried into his fatal act an act which certainly no man could possibly deplore more than the actor himself.[5] Often it had occurred to me in my ponderings upon the subject that had that altercation taken place in the public street, or at a private residence, it would not have terminated as it did. It was the circumstance of being alone in a solitary office, up stairs, of a building entirely unhallowed by humanizing domestic associations — an uncarpeted office, doubtless, of a dusty, haggard sort of appearance — this it must have been, which greatly helped to enhance the irritable desperation of the hapless Colt.

But when this old Adam of resentment rose in me and tempted me concerning Bartleby, I grappled him and threw him. How? Why, simply by

---

[5] John C. Colt murdered Samuel Adams in January 1842. Later that year, after his conviction, Colt committed suicide a half-hour before he was to be hanged. The case received wide and sensationalistic press coverage at the time.

recalling the divine injunction: "A new commandment give I unto you, that ye love one another." Yes, this it was that saved me. Aside from higher considerations, charity often operates as a vastly wise and prudent principle — a great safeguard to its possessor. Men have committed murder for jealousy's sake, and anger's sake, and hatred's sake, and selfishness' sake, and spiritual pride's sake; but no man, that ever I heard of, ever committed a diabolical murder for sweet charity's sake. Mere self-interest, then, if no better motive can be enlisted, should, especially with high-tempered men, prompt all beings to charity and philanthropy. At any rate, upon the occasion in question, I strove to drown my exasperated feelings towards the scrivener by benevolently construing his conduct. Poor fellow, poor fellow! thought I, he don't mean anything; and besides, he has seen hard times, and ought to be indulged.

I endeavored, also, immediately to occupy myself, and at the same time to comfort my despondency. I tried to fancy, that in the course of the morning, at such time as might prove agreeable to him, Bartleby, of his own free accord, would emerge from his hermitage and take up some decided line of march in the direction of the door. But no. Half-past twelve o'clock came; Turkey began to glow in the face, overturn his inkstand, and become generally obstreperous; Nippers abated down into quietude and courtesy; Ginger Nut munched his noon apple; and Bartleby remained standing at his window in one of his profoundest dead-wall reveries. Will it be credited? Ought I to acknowledge it? That afternoon I left the office without saying one further word to him.

Some days now passed, during which, at leisure intervals I looked a little into "Edwards[6] on the Will," and "Priestley[7] on Necessity." Under the circumstances, those books induced a salutary feeling. Gradually I slid into the persuasion that these troubles of mine, touching the scrivener, had been all predestined from eternity, and Bartleby was billeted upon me for some mysterious purpose of an all-wise Providence, which it was not for a mere mortal like me to fathom. Yes, Bartleby, stay there behind your screen, thought I; I shall persecute you no more; you are harmless and noiseless as any of these old chairs; in short, I never feel so private as when I know you are here. At last I see it, I feel it; I penetrate to the predestined purpose of my life. I am content. Others may have loftier parts to enact; but my mission in this world, Bartleby, is to furnish you with office-room for such period as you may see fit to remain.

---

[6] Jonathan Edwards, *Freedom of the Will* (1754). Edwards was an important American theologian, a rigidly orthodox Calvinist who believed in the doctrine of predestination and a leader of the Great Awakening, the religious revival that swept the North American colonies in the 1740s.

[7] Joseph Priestley (1733–1803), English scientist and clergyman. Priestly began as a Unitarian but developed his own radical ideas on "natural determinism." As a scientist, he did early experiments with electricity and was one of the first to discover the existence of oxygen. As a political philosopher, he championed the French Revolution — a cause so unpopular in England that he had to flee that country and spend the last decade of his life in the United States.

I believe that this wise and blessed frame of mind would have continued with me, had it not been for the unsolicited and uncharitable remarks obtruded upon me by my professional friends who visited the rooms. But thus it often is, that the constant friction of illiberal minds wears out at last the best resolves of the more generous. Though to be sure, when I reflected upon it, it was not strange that people entering my office should be struck by the peculiar aspect of the unaccountable Bartleby, and so be tempted to throw out some sinister observations concerning him. Sometimes an attorney, having business with me, and calling at my office, and finding no one but the scrivener there, would undertake to obtain some sort of precise information from him touching my whereabouts; but without heeding his idle talk, Bartleby would remain standing immovable in the middle of the room. So after contemplating him in that position for a time, the attorney would depart, no wiser than he came.

Also, when a reference was going on, and the room full of lawyers and witnesses, and business driving fast, some deeply-occupied legal gentleman present, seeing Bartleby wholly unemployed, would request him to run round to his (the legal gentleman's) office and fetch some papers for him. Thereupon, Bartleby would tranquilly decline, and yet remain idle as before. Then the lawyer would give a great stare, and turn to me. And what could I say? At last I was made aware that all through the circle of my professional acquaintance, a whisper of wonder was running round, having reference to the strange creature I kept at my office. This worried me very much. And as the idea came upon me of his possibly turning out a long-lived man, and keeping occupying my chambers, and denying my authority; and perplexing my visitors; and scandalizing my professional reputation; and casting a general gloom over the premises; keeping soul and body together to the last upon his savings (for doubtless he spent but half a dime a day), and in the end perhaps outlive me, and claim possession of my office by right of his perpetual occupancy: as all these dark anticipations crowded upon me more and more, and my friends continually intruded their relentless remarks upon the apparition in my room; a great change was wrought in me. I resolved to gather all my faculties together, and forever rid me of this intolerable incubus.

Ere revolving any complicated project, however, adapted to this end, I first simply suggested to Bartleby the propriety of his permanent departure. In a calm and serious tone, I commended the idea to his careful and mature consideration. But, having taken three days to meditate upon it, he apprised me, that his original determination remained the same; in short, that he still preferred to abide with me.

What shall I do? I now said to myself, buttoning up my coat to the last button. What shall I do? what ought I to do? what does conscience say I *should* do with this man, or, rather, ghost. Rid myself of him, I must; go, he shall. But how? You will not thrust him, the poor, pale, passive mortal you will not thrust such a helpless creature out of your door? you will not dishonor yourself by such cruelty? No, I will not, I cannot do that. Rather would I let him live and die here, and then mason up his remains in the wall. What, then, will you do? For all your coaxing, he will not budge. Bribes he leaves under your own paper-weight on your table; in short, it is quite plain that he prefers to cling to you.

Then something severe, something unusual must be done. What! surely you will not have him collared by a constable, and commit his innocent pallor to the common jail? And upon what ground could you procure such a thing to be done? — a vagrant, is he? What! he a vagrant, a wanderer, who refuses to budge? It is because he will not be a vagrant, then, that you seek to count him *as* a vagrant. That is too absurd. No visible means of support: there I have him. Wrong again: for indubitably he *does* support himself, and that is the only unanswerable proof that any man can show of his possessing the means so to do. No more, then. Since he will not quit me, I must quit him. I will change my offices; I will move elsewhere, and give him fair notice, that if I find him on my new premises I will then proceed against him as a common trespasser.

Acting accordingly, next day I thus addressed him: "I find these chambers too far from the City Hall; the air is unwholesome. In a word, I propose to remove my offices next week, and shall no longer require your services. I tell you this now, in order that you may seek another place."

He made no reply, and nothing more was said.

On the appointed day I engaged carts and men, proceeded to my chambers, and, having but little furniture, everything was removed in a few hours. Throughout, the scrivener remained standing behind the screen, which I directed to be removed the last thing. It was withdrawn; and, being folded up like a huge folio, left him the motionless occupant of a naked room. I stood in the entry watching him a moment, while something from within me upbraided me.

I re-entered, with my hand in my pocket — and — and my heart in my mouth.

"Good-bye, Bartleby; I am going — good-bye, and God some way bless you; and take that," slipping something in his hand. But it dropped upon the floor, and then — strange to say — I tore myself from him whom I had so longed to be rid of.

Established in my new quarters, for a day or two I kept the door locked, started at every footfall in the passages. When I returned to my rooms, after any little absence, I would pause at the threshold for an instant, and attentively listen, ere applying my key. But these fears were needless. Bartleby never came nigh me.

I thought all was going well, when a perturbed-looking stranger visited me, inquiring whether I was the person who had recently occupied rooms at No. — Wall Street.

Full of forebodings, I replied that I was.

"Then, sir," said the stranger, who proved a lawyer, "you are responsible for the man you left there. He refuses to do any copying; he refuses to do anything; he says he prefers not to; and he refuses to quit the premises."

"I am very sorry, sir," said I, with assumed tranquillity, but an inward tremor, "but, really, the man you allude to is nothing to me — he is no relation or apprentice of mine, that you should hold me responsible for him."

"In mercy's name, who is he?"

"I certainly cannot inform you. I know nothing about him. Formerly I employed him as a copyist; but he has done nothing for me now for some time past."

"I shall settle him, then — good morning, sir."

Several days passed, and I heard nothing more; and, though I often felt a charitable prompting to call at the place and see poor Bartleby, yet a certain squeamishness, of I know not what, withheld me.

All is over with him, by this time, thought I, at last, when, through another week, no further intelligence reached me. But, coming to my room the day after, I found several persons waiting at my door in a high state of nervous excitement.

"That's the man here — he comes," cried the foremost one, whom I recognized as the lawyer who had previously called upon me alone.

"You must take him away, sir, at once," cried a portly person among them, advancing upon me, and whom I knew to be the landlord of No. — Wall Street. "These gentlemen, my tenants, cannot stand it any longer; Mr. B ——" pointing to the lawyer, "has turned him out of his room, and he now persists in haunting the building generally, sitting upon the banisters of the stairs by day, and sleeping in the entry by night. Everybody is concerned; clients are leaving the offices; some fears are entertained of a mob; something you must do, and that without delay."

Aghast at this torrent, I fell back before it, and would fain have locked myself in my new quarters. In vain I persisted that Bartleby was nothing to me — no more than to any one else. In vain — I was the last person known to have anything to do with him, and they held me to the terrible account. Fearful, then, of being exposed in the papers (as one person present obscurely threatened), I considered the matter, and, at length, said, that if the lawyer would give me a confidential interview with the scrivener, in his (the lawyer's) own room, I would, that afternoon, strive my best to rid them of the nuisance they complained of.

Going up stairs to my old haunt, there was Bartleby silently sitting upon the banister at the landing.

"What are you doing here, Bartleby?" said I.

"Sitting upon the banister," he mildly replied.

I motioned him into the lawyer's room, who then left us.

"Bartleby," said I, "are you aware that you are the cause of great tribulation to me, by persisting in occupying the entry after being dismissed from the office?"

No answer.

"Now one of two things must take place. Either you must do something, or something must be done to you. Now what sort of business would you like to engage in? Would you like to re-engage in copying for some one?"

"No; I would prefer not to make any change."

"Would you like a clerkship in a dry-goods store?"

"There is too much confinement about that. No, I would not like a clerkship; but I am not particular."

"Too much confinement," I cried, "why, you keep yourself confined all the time!"

"I would prefer not to take a clerkship," he rejoined, as if to settle that little item at once.

"How would a bar-tender's business suit you? There is no trying of the eye-sight in that."

"I would not like it at all; though, as I said before, I am not particular."

His unwonted wordiness inspirited me. I returned to the charge.

"Well, then, would you like to travel through the country collecting bills for the merchants? That would improve your health."

"No, I would prefer to be doing something else."

"How, then, would going as a companion to Europe, to entertain some young gentleman with your conversation — how would that suit you?"

"Not at all. It does not strike me that there is anything definite about that. I like to be stationary. But I am not particular."

"Stationary you shall be, then," I cried, now losing all patience, and, for the first time in all my exasperating connections with him, fairly flying into a passion. "If you do not go away from these premises before night, I shall feel bound — indeed, I *am* bound — to — to — to quit the premises my-self!" I rather absurdly concluded, knowing not with what possible threat to try to frighten his immobility into compliance. Despairing of all further ef-forts, I was precipitately leaving him, when a final thought occurred to me — one which had not been wholly unindulged before.

"Bartleby," said I, in the kindest tone I could assume under such exciting circumstances, "will you go home with me now not to my office, but my dwelling — and remain there till we can conclude upon some convenient arrangement for you at our leisure? Come, let us start now, right away."

"No: at present I would prefer not to make any change at all."

I answered nothing; but, effectually dodging every one by the sudden-ness and rapidity of my flight, rushed from the building, ran up Wall Street towards Broadway, and, jumping into the first omnibus, was soon removed from pursuit. As soon as tranquillity returned, I distinctly perceived that I had now done all that I possibly could, both in respect to the demands of the landlord and his tenants, and with regard to my own desire and sense of duty, to benefit Bartleby, and shield him from rude persecution. I now strove to be entirely care-free and quiescent; and my conscience justified me in the at-tempt; though, indeed, it was not so successful as I could have wished. So fearful was I of being again hunted out by the incensed landlord and his exasperated tenants, that, surrendering my business to Nippers, for a few days, I drove about the upper part of the town and through the suburbs, in my rockaway; crossed over to Jersey City and Hoboken, and paid fugitive visits to Manhattanville and Astoria. In fact, I almost lived in my rockaway for the time.

When again I entered my office, lo, a note from the landlord lay upon the desk. I opened it with trembling hands. It informed me that the writer had sent to the police, and had Bartleby removed to the Tombs as a vagrant. Moreover, since I knew more about him than any one else, he wished me to appear at that place, and make a suitable statement of the facts. These tidings had a conflicting effect upon me. At first I was indignant; but, at last, almost approved. The landlord's energetic, summary disposition, had led him to adopt a procedure which I do not think I would have decided upon myself; and yet, as a last resort, under such peculiar circumstances, it seemed the only plan.

As I afterwards learned, the poor scrivener, when told that he must be conducted to the Tombs, offered not the slightest obstacle, but, in his pale, unmoving way, silently acquiesced.

Some of the compassionate and curious by-standers joined the party; and headed by one of the constables arm-in-arm with Bartleby, the silent procession filed its way through all the noise, and heat, and joy of the roaring thoroughfares at noon.

The same day I received the note, I went to the Tombs, or, to speak more properly, the Halls of Justice. Seeking the right officer, I stated the purpose of my call, and was informed that the individual I described was, indeed, within. I then assured the functionary that Bartleby was a perfectly honest man, and greatly to be compassionated, however unaccountably eccentric. I narrated all I knew, and closed by suggesting the idea of letting him remain in as indulgent confinement as possible, till something less harsh might be done — though, indeed, I hardly knew what. At all events, if nothing else could be decided upon, the alms-house must receive him. I then begged to have an interview.

Being under no disgraceful charge, and quite serene and harmless in all his ways, they had permitted him freely to wander about the prison, and, especially, in the inclosed grass-platted yards thereof. And so I found him there, standing all alone in the quietest of the yards, his face towards a high wall, while all around, from the narrow slits of the jail windows, I thought I saw peering out upon him the eyes of murderers and thieves.

"Bartleby!"

"I know you," he said, without looking round — "and I want nothing to say to you."

"It was not I that brought you here, Bartleby," said I, keenly pained at his implied suspicion. "And to you, this should not be so vile a place. Nothing reproachful attaches to you by being here. And see, it is not so sad a place as one might think. Look, there is the sky, and here is the grass."

"I know where I am," he replied, but would say nothing more, and so I left him.

As I entered the corridor again, a broad meat-like man, in an apron, accosted me, and, jerking his thumb over my shoulder, said "Is that your friend?"

"Yes."

"Does he want to starve? If he does, let him live on the prison fare, that's all."

"Who are you?" asked I, not knowing what to make of such an un-officially speaking person in such a place.

"I am the grub-man. Such gentlemen as have friends here, hire me to provide them with something good to eat."

"Is this so?" said I, turning to the turnkey.

He said it was.

"Well, then," said I, slipping some silver into the grub-man's hands (for so they called him), "I want you to give particular attention to my friend there; let him have the best dinner you can get. And you must be as polite to him as possible."

"Introduce me, will you?" said the grub-man, looking at me with an expression which seemed to say he was all impatience for an opportunity to give a specimen of his breeding.

Thinking it would prove of benefit to the scrivener, I acquiesced; and, asking the grub-man his name, went up with him to Bartleby.

"Bartleby, this is a friend; you will find him very useful to you."

"Your sarvant, sir, your sarvant," said the grub-man, making a low salutation behind his apron. "Hope you find it pleasant here, sir; nice grounds — cool apartments — hope you'll stay with us some time — try to make it agreeable. What will you have for dinner to-day?"

"I prefer not to dine to-day," said Bartleby, turning away. "It would disagree with me; I am unused to dinners." So saying, he slowly moved to the other side of the inclosure, and took up a position fronting the dead-wall.

"How's this?" said the grub-man, addressing me with a stare of astonishment. "He's odd, ain't he?"

"I think he is a little deranged," said I, sadly.

"Deranged? deranged is it? Well, now, upon my word, I thought that friend of yourn was a gentleman forger; they are always pale and genteel-like, them forgers. I can't help pity 'em — can't help it, sir. Did you know Monroe Edwards?" he added, touchingly, and paused. Then, laying his hand piteously on my shoulder, sighed, "he died of consumption at Sing-Sing. So you weren't acquainted with Monroe?"

"No, I was never socially acquainted with any forgers. But I cannot stop longer. Look to my friend yonder. You will not lose by it. I will see you again."

Some few days after this, I again obtained admission to the Tombs, and went through the corridors in quest of Bartleby; but without finding him.

"I saw him coming from his cell not long ago," said a turnkey, "may be he's gone to loiter in the yards."

So I went in that direction.

"Are you looking for the silent man?" said another turnkey, passing me. "Yonder he lies — sleeping in the yard there. 'Tis not twenty minutes since I saw him lie down."

The yard was entirely quiet. It was not accessible to the common prisoners. The surrounding walls, of amazing thickness, kept off all sounds behind them. The Egyptian character of the masonry weighed upon me with its gloom. But a soft imprisoned turf grew under foot. The heart of the eternal pyramids, it seemed, wherein, by some strange magic, through the clefts, grass-seed, dropped by birds, had sprung.

Strangely huddled at the base of the wall, his knees drawn up, and lying on his side, his head touching the cold stones, I saw the wasted Bartleby. But nothing stirred. I paused; then went close up to him; stooped over, and saw that his dim eyes were open; otherwise he seemed profoundly sleeping. Something prompted me to touch him. I felt his hand, when a tingling shiver ran up my arm and down my spine to my feet.

The round face of the grub-man peered upon me now. "His dinner is ready. Won't he dine to-day, either? Or does he live without dining?"

"Lives without dining," said I, and closed the eyes.

"Eh! — He's asleep, ain't he?"

"With kings and counselors,"[8] murmured I.

There would seem little need for proceeding further in this history. Imagination will readily supply the meagre recital of poor Bartleby's interment. But, ere parting with the reader, let me say, that if this little narrative has sufficiently interested him, to awaken curiosity as to who Bartleby was, and what manner of life he led prior to the present narrator's making his acquaintance, I can only reply, that in such curiosity I fully share, but am wholly unable to gratify it. Yet here I hardly know whether I should divulge one little item of rumor, which came to my ear a few months after the scrivener's decease. Upon what basis it rested, I could never ascertain; and hence, how true it is I cannot now tell. But, inasmuch as this vague report has not been without a certain suggestive interest to me, however sad, it may prove the same with some others; and so I will briefly mention it. The report was this: that Bartleby had been a subordinate clerk in the Dead Letter Office at Washington, from which he had been suddenly removed by a change in the administration. When I think over this rumor, hardly can I express the emotions which seize me. Dead letters! does it not sound like dead men? Conceive a man by nature and misfortune prone to a pallid hopelessness, can any business seem more fitted to heighten it than that of continually handling these dead letters, and assorting them for the flames? For by the cart-load they are annually burned. Sometimes from out the folded paper the pale clerk takes a ring — the finger it was meant for, perhaps, moulders in the grave; a bank-note sent in swiftest charity — he whom it would relieve, nor eats nor hungers any more; pardon for those who died despairing; hope for those who died unhoping; good tidings for those who died stifled by unrelieved calamities. On errands of life, these letters speed to death.

Ah, Bartleby! Ah, humanity!   [1853]

---

[8] A reference to Job 3:14. Job, who has lost his family and all his property and been stricken by a terrible disease, wishes he had never been born: "then had I been at rest with kings and counselors of the earth, which built desolate places for themselves."

YUKIO MISHIMA (1925–1970) was the pseudonym of Hiraoka Kimitake, the Japanese author whose works are most translated into English. Born in Tokyo and educated at the aristocratic Peer's School and Tokyo Imperial University, Mishima became a legend in his own time after a spectacular ritual suicide. He was obsessed with the idea that Japan was becoming a decadent Western nation after World War II because it had turned away from the classic samurai tradition, which combined spiritual dedication and the martial arts. A bisexual, Mishima was also a physical fitness addict, and he formed the Shield Society with a small private army. These young men were united in their desire to protect the country from what they envisioned as a threatened leftist uprising.

In 1970 Mishima and four of his followers invaded the headquarters of Japan's Eastern Ground Self-Defense Forces. After capturing the troops on the military base, he stood on a roof and exhorted them to return Japan to the earlier purity of its samurai traditions. The troops jeered him. Recognizing his failure to convince them, Mishima withdrew into a room nearby, knelt on the floor, and stabbed himself in the stomach as a young disciple beheaded him in the ritual of seppuku, reserved for samurai warriors. As the eminent author Marguerite Yourcenar stated in her study of Mishima's life, he was "a martyr of the heroic Japan to which he returned, so to speak, against the tide."

By the time of his death, Mishima was established as one of Japan's leading writers. He began to publish fiction when he was in his twenties, and several of his novels, such as Confessions of a Mask (1949), Temple of the Golden Pavilion (1959), The Sailor Who Fell from Grace with the Sea (1965), and The Sea of Fertility (1975), were translated into English. Short story collections suggesting Mishima's view of the corruption of contemporary Japanese society and the decay of its moral values include Death in Midsummer (1966) and Acts of Worship (1989). "Fountains in the Rain" is an early story about the end of a love affair.

YUKIO MISHIMA

Fountains in the Rain

Translated by John Bester

The boy was tired of walking in the rain dragging the girl, heavy as a sandbag and weeping continually, around with him.

A short while ago, in a tea shop in the Marunouchi Building, he had told her he was leaving her.

The first time in his life that he'd broken with a woman!

It was something he had long dreamed of; it had at last become a reality.

It was for this alone that he had loved her, or pretended to love her; for

935

this alone he had assiduously undermined her defenses; for this alone he'd furiously sought the chance to sleep with her, slept with her — till lo, the preparations were complete and it only remained to pronounce the phrase he had longed just once to pronounce with his own lips, with due authority, like the edict of a king:

"It's time to break it off!"

Those words, the mere enunciation of which would be enough to rend the sky asunder. . . . Those words that he had cherished so passionately even while half-resigned to the impossibility of the fact. . . . That phrase, more heroic, more glorious than any other in the world, which would fly in a straight line through the heavens like an arrow released from its bow. . . . That spell which only the most human of humans, the most manly of men, might utter. . . . In short:

"It's time to break it off!"

All the same, Akio felt a lingering regret that he'd been obliged to say it with such a deplorable lack of clarity, with a rattling noise in the throat, like an asthmatic with a throatful of phlegm, which even a preliminary draft of soda pop through his straw had failed to avert.

At the time, his chief fear had been that the words might not have been heard. He'd have died sooner than be asked what he'd said and have to repeat it. After all, if a goose that for years had longed to lay a golden egg had found it smashed before anyone could see it, would it promptly have laid another?

Fortunately, however, she had heard. She'd heard, and he hadn't had to repeat it, which was a splendid piece of luck. Under his own steam, Akio had crossed the pass over the mountains that he'd gazed at for so long in the distance.

Sure proof that she'd heard had been vouchsafed in a flash, like chewing gum ejected from a vending machine.

The windows were closed because of the rain, so that the voices of the customers talking around them, the clatter of dishes, the ping of the cash register clashed with each other all the more violently, rebounding subtly off the clammy condensation on the inside of the panes to create a single, mind-fuddling commotion.

Akio's muffled words had no sooner reached Masako's ears through the general uproar than her eyes — wide, staring eyes that seemed to be trying to shove her surroundings away from her thin, unprepossessing features — opened still wider. They were no longer eyes so much as an embodiment of disaster, irretrievable disaster. And then, all at once, the tears had burst forth.

There was no business of breaking into sobs; nor did she bawl her head off: the tears simply gushed, expressing nothing, and with a most impressive force.

Akio naturally assumed that waters of such pressure and flow would soon cease. And he marveled at the peppermint freshness of mind with which he contemplated the phenomenon. This was precisely what he had planned, worked to encompass, and brought to reality: a splendid achievement, though admittedly somewhat mechanical.

It was to witness this, he told himself again, that he had made love to Masako: he, who had always been free from the dominance of desire.

And the tearful face of the woman now in front of him — this was reality! A genuine forsaken woman — forsaken by himself, Akio!

Even so, Masako's tears went on for so long with no sign of abating that the boy began to worry about the people around them.

Masako, still wearing her light-colored raincoat, was sitting upright in her chair. The collar of a red blouse showed at the neck of the coat. She looked as though set in her present position, with her hands pressed down on the edge of the table, a tremendous force in both of them.

She stared straight ahead, letting the tears flow unchecked. She made no move to take out a handkerchief to wipe them. Her breath, catching in her thin throat, gave out a regular wheeze like new shoes, and the mouth that with student perverseness she refused to paint turned up disconsolately, quivering continually.

The older customers were looking at them curiously, with stares of a kind calculated to disturb Akio's newfound sense of maturity.

The abundance of Masako's tears was a genuine cause for astonishment. Not for a moment did their volume diminish. Tired of watching, Akio dropped his gaze and looked at the tip of the umbrella he had stood against a chair. The raindrops running from it had formed a small, darkish puddle on the old-fashioned, tile mosaic floor. Even the puddle began to look like Masako's tears to him.

Abruptly, he grabbed the bill and stood up.

The June rains had been falling steadily for three days. As he left the Marunouchi Building and unfurled his umbrella, the girl came silently after him. Since she had no umbrella herself, he had no choice but to let her share his. It reminded him of the way older people, for the benefit of the outside world, went on pretending even after they'd stopped feeling anything. Now he too had acquired the same habit; to share an umbrella with a girl once you'd made the move to break with her was just a gesture for other people's benefit. It was simply being cut-and-dried about things. Yes: to be cut-and-dried (even when it took such subtle forms) suited Akio's nature. . . .

As they wandered along the broad sidewalk in the direction of the Imperial Palace, the problem foremost in his mind was finding somewhere to dump this tearbag he was saddled with.

I wonder — he thought vaguely to himself — if the fountains work even when it's raining?

Why should the idea of fountains have occurred to him? Another few paces, and he realized the physical pun in his own train of thought.

The girl's wet raincoat, which he was touching — remotely, of course, and unfeelingly — in the cramped space beneath the umbrella, had the texture of a reptile. But he bore with it, forcing his mind to follow the pun to its logical conclusion.

Yes: fountains in the rain. He'd bring the fountains and Masako's tears into confrontation. Even Masako would surely find her match there. For one thing, the fountains were the type that used the same water over and over again, so the girl, whose tears all ran to waste, could hardly compete with them. A human being was scarcely a match for a reflex fountain; almost certainly, she'd give up and stop crying. Then he'd be able somehow to get rid of this unwanted baggage. The only question was whether the fountains would be working as usual in the rain.

Akio walked in silence. Masako, still weeping, followed doggedly under the same umbrella. Thus, while it was difficult to shake her off, it was easy to drag her along where he wanted.

What with the rain and the tears, Akio felt as if his whole body was getting wet. It was all right for Masako in her white boots, but his own socks, inside his loafers, felt like thick, wet seaweed around his feet.

There was some time still before the office workers came out, and the sidewalk was deserted. Traversing a pedestrian crossing, they made their way toward Wadakura Bridge, which crossed the palace moat. When they reached the end of the bridge with its old-fashioned wooden railings topped by pointed knobs, they could see on their left a swan floating on the moat in the rain and, to the right, on the other side of the moat, the white tablecloths and red chairs of a hotel dining room, dimly visible through rain-blurred glass. They crossed the bridge. Passing between high stone ramparts, they turned left and emerged in the small garden with the fountains.

Masako, as ever, was crying soundlessly.

Just inside the garden was a large Western-style summer-house. The benches under its roof, which consisted of a kind of blind of fine reeds, were protected to some extent from the rain, so Akio sat down with his umbrella still up and Masako sat down next to him, at an angle, so that all he could see, right in front of his nose, was a shoulder of her white raincoat and her wet hair. The rain on the hair, repelled by the oil on it, looked like a scattering of fine white dew. Still crying, with her eyes wide open, she might almost have been in some kind of coma, and Akio felt an urge to give the hair a tug, to bring her out of it.

She went on crying, endlessly. It was perfectly clear that she was waiting for him to say something, which made it impossible, as a matter of pride, for him to break the silence. It occurred to him that since that one momentous sentence he hadn't spoken a single word.

Not far away, the fountains were throwing up their waters in profusion, but Masako showed no inclination to look at them.

Seen from here, head on, the three fountains, two small and one large, were lined up one behind the other, and the sound, blotted out by the rain, was distant and faint, but the fact that their blurring of spray was not visible at a distance gave the lines of water, dividing up in various directions, a clearly defined look like curved glass tubes.

Not a soul was in sight anywhere. Th lawn on this side of the fountains and the low ornamental hedge were a brilliant green in the rain.

Beyond the garden, though, there was a constant procession of wet truck hoods and bus roofs in red, white, or yellow; the red light of a signal at a crossing was clearly visible, but when it changed to the lower green, the light disappeared in a cloud of spray from the fountains.

The act of sitting down and remaining still and silent aroused an indefinable anger in the boy. With it, amusement at his little joke of a while ago disappeared.

He couldn't have said what he was angry about. Not long before, he had been on a kind of high, but now, suddenly, he was beset with an obscure sense of dissatisfaction. Nor was his inability to dispose of the forever crying Masako the whole extent of the frustration.

Her? I could easily deal with *her* if I cared to, he told himself. I could just shove her in the fountain and do a bunk — and that would be the end of it. The thought restored his earlier elation. No, the only trouble was the absolute frustration he felt at the rain, the tears, the leaden sky that hung like a barrier before him. They pressed down on him on all sides, reducing his freedom to a kind of damp rag.

Angry, the boy gave in to a simple desire to hurt. Nothing would satisfy him now till he had got Masako thoroughly soaked in the rain and given her a good eyeful of the fountains.

Getting up suddenly, he set off running without so much as a glance back; raced on along the gravel path that encircled the fountains outside and a few steps higher than the walk around the fountains themselves; reached a spot that gave a full view of that; and came to a halt.

The girl came running through the rain. Checking herself just as she was about to collide with him, she took a firm grip of the umbrella he was holding up. Damp with tears and rain, her face was pale.

"Where are you going?" she said through her gasps.

Akio was not supposed to reply, yet found himself talking as effortlessly as though he'd been waiting for her to ask this very thing.

"Just look at the fountains. Look! You can cry as much as you like, but you're no match for *them*."

And the two of them tilted the umbrella and, freed from the need to keep their eyes on each other, stared for a while at the three fountains: the central one imposing, the other two slighter, like attendants flanking it on both sides.

Amidst the constant turmoil of the fountains and the pool around them, the streaks of rain falling into the water were almost indistinguishable. Paradoxically, the only sound that struck the ear was the fitful drone of distant cars; the noise of the fountains wove itself so closely into the surrounding air that unless you made an effort to hear you seemed to be enclosed in perfect silence.

First, the water at the bottom bounced in isolated drops off the huge shallow basin of black granite, then ran in a continual drizzle over the black rim.

Another six jets of water, describing far-flung radiating arcs in the air, stood guard around the main column that shot upward from the center of each basin.

This column, if you watched carefully, did not always achieve the same

height. In the almost complete absence of a breeze, the water spouted verti-
cally and undisturbed toward the gray, rainy sky, varying from time to time
in the height of its summit. Occasionally, ragged water would be flung up to
an astonishing height before finally dispersing into droplets and floating to
earth again.

The water near the summit, shadowed by the clouds that were visible
through it, was gray with an admixture of chalky white, almost too powdery-
looking for real water, and a misty spray clung about it, while around the
column played a mass of foam in large white flakes mingling like snow with
the rain.

But Akio was less taken with the three main columns of water than with
the water that shot out in radiating curves all around.

The jets from the big central fountain in particular leaped far above the
marble rim, flinging up their white manes only to dash themselves gallantly
down again onto the surface of the pool. The sight of their untiring rushing
to the four quarters threatened to usurp his attention. Almost before he knew
it, his mind, which till now had been with him in this place, was being taken
over by the water, carried away on its rushing, cast far away. . . .

It was the same when he watched the central column.

At first glance, it seemed as neat, as motionless, as a sculpture fashioned
out of water. Yet watching closely he could see a transparent ghost of movement moving upward from bottom to top. With furious speed it climbed,
steadily filling a slender cylinder of space from base to summit, replacing each
moment what had been lost the moment before, in a kind of perpetual
replenishment. It was plain that at heaven's height it would be finally frustrated; yet the unwaning power that supported unceasing failure was magnificent.

The fountains he had brought the girl to see had ended by completely
fascinating the boy himself. He was still dwelling on their virtues when his
gaze, lifted higher, met the sky from which the all-enveloping rain was falling.

He got rain on his eyelashes.

The sky, hemmed in by dense clouds, hung low over his head; the rain
fell copiously and without cease. The whole scene was filled with rain. The
rain descending on his face was exactly the same as that falling on the roofs
of the red-brick buildings and hotel in the distance. His own almost beardless
face, smooth and shiny, and the rough concrete that floored the deserted room
of one of those buildings were no more than two surfaces exposed, unresist-
ing, to the same rain. From the rain's point of view, his cheeks and the dirty
concrete roof were quite identical.

Immediately, the image of the fountains there before his eyes was wiped
from his mind. Quite suddenly, fountains in the rain seemed to represent no
more than the endless repetition of a stupid and pointless process.

Before long, he had forgotten both his joke of a while ago and the anger
that had followed it, and felt his mind steadily becoming empty.

Empty, save for the falling rain. . . .

Aimlessly, the boy started walking.

"Where are you going?" She fell into step with him as she spoke, this time keeping a firm hold on the handle of the umbrella.

"Where? That's my business, isn't it? I told you quite plainly some time ago, didn't I?"

"What did you tell me?"

He gazed at her in horror, but the rain had washed away the traces of tears from the drenched face, and although the damp, reddened eyes still showed the aftermath of weeping, the voice in which she spoke was no longer shaky.

"What do you mean, 'what'? I told you a while back, didn't I? — that we'd better split up."

Just then, the boy spotted, beyond her profile as it moved through the rain, some crimson azalea bushes blooming, small and grudgingly, here and there on the lawn.

"Really? Did you say that? I didn't hear you." Her voice was normal.

Almost bowled over by shock, the boy managed a few steps further before an answer finally came and he stammered:

"But — in that case, what did you cry for? I don't get it."

She didn't reply immediately. Her wet little hand was still firmly attached to the umbrella handle.

"The tears just came. There wasn't any special reason."

Furious, he wanted to shout something at her, but at the crucial moment it came out as an enormous sneeze.

If I'm not careful I'm going to get a cold, he thought.   [1963]

LORRIE MOORE (b. 1957) *was born in Glen Falls, New York, daughter of an insurance executive and a housewife. After completing her studies at St. Lawrence University and Cornell University, where she earned an M.F.A. in 1982, Moore began teaching at the University of Wisconsin. As an undergraduate she won a* Seventeen *magazine short story contest in 1976, and she has been publishing her fiction in magazines such as* Cosmopolitan, Ms., *and* The New Yorker *ever since. In 1987 her novel* Anagrams *was published.*

Self-Help, Moore's first collection of short stories, appeared in 1985. As the title of the book suggests, several of the humorous stories, like "How to Become a Writer," were narrated in what Moore calls "second person, mock-imperative" voices as she parodied the self-improvement manuals popular with American readers. In the book Moore included sketches to cover various situations — "The Kid's Guide to Divorce," "How to Talk to Your Mother," "How to Be an Other Woman."

Reviewers noted that typically the fictional characters narrating Moore's stories were intelligent people whose self-knowledge only contributed to their sense of distress, so they reacted by attempting to distance themselves from their dilemmas through humor. A character in Moore's second collection, Like Life *(1990), is told, "Everything's a joke with you." She replies, "Nothing's a joke with me. It just all comes out like one." Moore has said that the stories in* Self-Help, *written between 1980 and 1983, were stylistic experiments. She thought,*

> *Let's see what happens when one eliminates the subject, leaves the verb shivering at the start of a clause; what happens when one appropriates the "how-to" form for a fiction, for an irony, for a "how-not-to" . . . the self-help proffered here, then, is perhaps only that of art itself, which, if you agree with Oscar Wilde, is quite useless.*

LORRIE MOORE

How to Become a Writer

First, try to be something, anything, else. A movie star/astronaut. A movie star/missionary. A movie star/kindergarten teacher. President of the World. Fail miserably. It is best if you fail at an early age — say, fourteen. Early, critical disillusionment is necessary so that at fifteen you can write long haiku sequences about thwarted desire. It is a pond, a cherry blossom, a wind brushing against sparrow wing leaving for mountain. Count the syllables. Show it to your mom. She is tough and practical. She has a son in Vietnam and a husband who may be having an affair. She believes in wearing brown because it hides spots. She'll look briefly at your writing, then back up at you with a face blank as a donut. She'll say: "How about emptying the dishwasher?" Look away. Shove the forks in the fork drawer. Accidentally break one of the freebie gas station glasses. This is the required pain and suffering. This is only for starters.

In your high school English class look only at Mr. Killian's face. Decide faces are important. Write a villanelle about pores. Struggle. Write a sonnet. Count the syllables: nine, ten, eleven, thirteen. Decide to experiment with fiction. Here you don't have to count syllables. Write a short story about an elderly man and woman who accidentally shoot each other in the head, the result of an inexplicable malfunction of a shotgun which appears mysteriously in their living room one night. Give it to Mr. Killian as your final project. When you get it back, he has written on it: "Some of your images are quite nice, but you have no sense of plot." When you are home, in the privacy of your own room, faintly scrawl in pencil beneath his black-inked comments: "Plots are for dead people, pore-face."

Take all the babysitting jobs you can get. You are great with kids. They love you. You tell them stories about old people who die idiot deaths. You sing them songs like "Blue Bells of Scotland," which is their favorite. And when they are in their pajamas and have finally stopped pinching each other, when they are fast asleep, you read every sex manual in the house, and wonder how on earth anyone could ever do those things with someone they truly loved. Fall asleep in a chair reading Mr. McMurphy's *Playboy.* When the McMurphys come home, they will tap you on the shoulder, look at the magazine in your lap, and grin. You will want to die. They will ask you if Tracey took her medicine all right. Explain, yes, she did, that you promised her a story if she would take it like a big girl and that seemed to work out just fine. "Oh, marvelous," they will exclaim.

Try to smile proudly.

Apply to college as a child psychology major.

As a child psychology major, you have some electives. You've always liked birds. Sign up for something called "The Ornithological Field Trip." It meets Tuesdays and Thursdays at two. When you arrive at Room 134 on the first day of class, everyone is sitting around a seminar table talking about metaphors. You've heard of these. After a short, excruciating while, raise your hand and say diffidently, "Excuse me, isn't this Birdwatching One-oh-one?" The class stops and turns to look at you. They seem to all have one face — giant and blank as a vandalized clock. Someone with a beard booms out, "No, this is Creative Writing." Say: "Oh — right," as if perhaps you knew all along. Look down at your schedule. Wonder how the hell you ended up here. The computer, apparently, has made an error. You start to get up to leave and then don't. The lines at the registrar this week are huge. Perhaps you should stick with this mistake. Perhaps your creative writing isn't all that bad. Perhaps it is fate. Perhaps this is what your dad meant when he said, "It's the age of computers, Francie, it's the age of computers."

Decide that you like college life. In your dorm you meet many nice people. Some are smarter than you. And some, you notice, are dumber than you. You will continue, unfortunately, to view the world in exactly these terms for the rest of your life.

The assignment this week in creative writing is to narrate a violent happening. Turn in a story about driving with your Uncle Gordon and another one about two old people who are accidentally electrocuted when they go to turn on a badly wired desk lamp. The teacher will hand them back to you with comments: "Much of your writing is smooth and energetic. You have, however, a ludicrous notion of plot." Write another story about a man and a woman who, in the very first paragraph, have their lower torsos accidentally blitzed away by dynamite. In the second paragraph, with the insurance money, they buy a frozen yogurt stand together. There are six more paragraphs. You read the whole thing out loud in class. No one likes it. They say your sense of plot is outrageous and incompetent. After class someone asks you if you are crazy.

Decide that perhaps you should stick to comedies. Start dating someone who is funny, someone who has what in high school you called a "really great sense of humor" and what now your creative writing class calls "self-contempt giving rise to comic form." Write down all of his jokes, but don't tell him you are doing this. Make up anagrams of his old girlfriend's name and name all of your socially handicapped characters with them. Tell him his old girlfriend is in all of your stories and then watch how funny he can be, see what a really great sense of humor he can have.

Your child psychology advisor tells you you are neglecting courses in your major. What you spend the most time on should be what you're majoring in. Say yes, you understand.

In creative writing seminars over the next two years, everyone continues to smoke cigarettes and ask the same things: "But does it work?" "Why should we care about this character?" "Have you earned this cliché?" These seem like important questions.

On days when it is your turn, you look at the class hopefully as they scour your mimeographs for a plot. They look back up at you, drag deeply, and then smile in a sweet sort of way.

You spend too much time slouched and demoralized. Your boyfriend suggests bicycling. Your roommate suggests a new boyfriend. You are said to be self-mutilating and losing weight, but you continue writing. The only happiness you have is writing something new, in the middle of the night, armpits damp, heart pounding, something no one has yet seen. You have only those brief, fragile, untested moments of exhilaration when you know: you are a genius. Understand what you must do. Switch majors. The kids in your nursery project will be disappointed, but you have a calling, an urge, a delusion, an unfortunate habit. You have, as your mother would say, fallen in with a bad crowd.

Why write? Where does writing come from? These are questions to ask yourself. They are like: Where does dust come from? Or: Why is there war? Or: If there's a God, then why is my brother now a cripple?

These are questions that you keep in your wallet, like calling cards. These are questions, your creative writing teacher says, that are good to address in your journals but rarely in your fiction.

The writing professor this fall is stressing the Power of the Imagination. Which means he doesn't want long descriptive stories about your camping trip last July. He wants you to start in a realistic context but then to alter it. Like recombinant DNA. He wants you to let your imagination sail, to let it grow big-bellied in the wind. This is a quote from Shakespeare.

Tell your roommate your great idea, your great exercise of imaginative power: a transformation of Melville to contemporary life. It will be about monomania and the fish-eat-fish world of life insurance in Rochester, New York. The first line will be "Call me Fishmeal," and it will feature a menopausal suburban husband named Richard, who because he is so depressed all the time is called "Mopey Dick" by his witty wife Elaine. Say to your roommate: "Mopey Dick, get it?" Your roommate looks at you, her face blank as a large Kleenex. She comes up to you, like a buddy, and puts an arm around your burdened shoulders. "Listen, Francie," she says, slow as speech therapy. "Let's go out and get a big beer."

The seminar doesn't like this one either. You suspect they are beginning to feel sorry for you. They say: "You have to think about what is happening. Where is the story here?"

The next semester the writing professor is obsessed with writing from personal experience. You must write from what you know, from what has happened to you. He wants death, he wants camping trips. Think about what has happened to you. In three years there have been three things: you lost your virginity; your parents got divorced; and your brother came home from a forest ten miles from the Cambodian border with only half a thigh, a permanent smirk nestled into one corner of his mouth.

About the first you write: "It created a new space, which hurt and cried in a voice that wasn't mine, 'I'm not the same anymore, but I'll be okay.'"

About the second you write an elaborate story of an old married couple who stumble upon an unknown land mine in their kitchen and accidentally blow themselves up. You call it: "For Better or for Liverwurst."

About the last you write nothing. There are no words for this. Your typewriter hums. You can find no words.

At undergraduate cocktail parties, people say, "Oh, you write? What do you write about?" Your roommate, who has consumed too much wine, too little cheese, and no crackers at all, blurts: "Oh, my god, she always writes about her dumb boyfriend."

Later on in life you will learn that writers are merely open, helpless texts with no real understanding of what they have written and therefore must half-believe anything and everything that is said of them. You, however, have not yet reached this stage of literary criticism. You stiffen and say, "I do not," the same way you said it when someone in the fourth grade accused you of really liking oboe lessons and your parents really weren't just making you take them.

Insist you are not very interested in any one subject at all, that you are interested in the music of language, that you are interested in — in — syllables, because they are the atoms of poetry, the cells of the mind, the breath of the soul. Begin to feel woozy. Stare into your plastic wine cup.

"Syllables?" you will hear someone ask, voice trailing off, as they glide slowly toward the reassuring white of the dip.

Begin to wonder what you do write about. Or if you have anything to say. Or if there even is such a thing as a thing to say. Limit these thoughts to no more than ten minutes a day; like sit-ups, they can make you thin.

You will read somewhere that all writing has to do with one's genitals. Don't dwell on this. It will make you nervous.

Your mother will come visit you. She will look at the circles under your eyes and hand you a brown book with a brown briefcase on the cover. It is entitled: *How to Become a Business Executive.* She has also brought the *Names for Baby* encyclopedia you asked for; one of your characters, the aging clown–schoolteacher, needs a new name. Your mother will shake her head and say: "Francie, Francie, remember when you were going to be a child psychology major?"

Say: "Mom, I like to write."

She'll say: "Sure you like to write. Of course. Sure you like to write."

Write a story about a confused music student and title it: "Schubert Was the One with the Glasses, Right?" It's not a big hit, although your roommate likes the part where the two violinists accidentally blow themselves up in a recital room. "I went out with a violinist once," she says, snapping her gum.

Thank god you are taking other courses. You can find sanctuary in nineteenth-century ontological snags and invertebrate courting rituals. Certain globular mollusks have what is called "Sex by the Arm." The male octopus, for instance, loses the end of one arm when placing it inside the female body during intercourse. Marine biologists call it "Seven Heaven." Be glad you know these things. Be glad you are not just a writer. Apply to law school.

From here on in, many things can happen. But the main one will be this: you decide not to go to law school after all, and, instead, you spend a good, big chunk of your adult life telling people how you decided not to go to law school after all. Somehow you end up writing again. Perhaps you go to graduate school. Perhaps you work odd jobs and take writing courses at night. Perhaps you are working on a novel and writing down all the clever remarks and intimate personal confessions you hear during the day. Perhaps you are losing your pals, your acquaintances, your balance.

You have broken up with your boyfriend. You now go out with men who, instead of whispering "I love you," shout: "Do it to me, baby." This is good for your writing.

Sooner or later you have a finished manuscript more or less. People look at it in a vaguely troubled sort of way and say, "I'll bet becoming a writer was always a fantasy of yours, wasn't it?" Your lips dry to salt. Say that of all the fantasies possible in the world, you can't imagine being a writer even making the top twenty. Tell them you were going to be a child psychology major. "I bet," they always sigh, "you'd be great with kids." Scowl fiercely. Tell them you're a walking blade.

Quit classes. Quit jobs. Cash in old savings bonds. Now you have time like warts on your hands. Slowly copy all of your friends' addresses into a new address book.

Vacuum. Chew cough drops. Keep a folder full of fragments.

An eyelid darkening sideways.
World as conspiracy.
Possible plot? A woman gets on a bus.
Suppose you threw a love affair and nobody came?

At home drink a lot of coffee. At Howard Johnson's order the cole slaw. Consider how it looks like the soggy confetti of a map: where you've been, where you're going — "You Are Here," says the red star on the back of the menu.

Occasionally a date with a face blank as a sheet of paper asks you whether writers often become discouraged. Say that sometimes they do and sometimes they do. Say it's a lot like having polio.

"Interesting," smiles your date, and then he looks down at his arm hairs and starts to smooth them, all, always, in the same direction.   [1985]

ES'KIA MPHAHLELE *(b. 1919) was born in Pretoria, South Africa, and educated in church schools, where as a black African he had a more European-oriented education than most white South Africans, since the teachers in the church schools were often English clergymen. Mphahlele (pronounced* em-shay-lay) *attended the University of South Africa and later earned a doctorate at the University of Denver in the United States. He was an English and Afrikaans teacher at Orlando High School in Johannesburg when, in 1947, he published his first book of short stories,* Man Must Live. *Seven hundred copies of this book were distributed by the* African Bookman, *and Mphahlele felt it was "an ecstatic experience" seeing his work in print. At that time only three other previous works of fiction about urban South Africa had been published by black writers. The critic Ursula Barnett recognized that "Mphahlele was the first to portray permanent township dwellers against their own background. [White] Readers had possibly seen 'natives' . . . but had never followed the people . . . into their lives."*

Two more collections of Mphahlele's short fiction were published, The Living and the Dead *(1961) and* In Corner B *(1967), from which "Mrs. Plum" is taken. Then Mphahlele turned his attention to writing novels and autobiographical essays and editing the influential* Journal of New African Literature and the Arts. *In 1987 he became the director of a community education project in Soweto for the Council for Black Education and Research.*

Mphahlele has described "Mrs. Plum," a long story exploring the relationship between a white liberal South African widow and her black maid Karabo, as "the best thing" that he "ever pulled off." Karabo narrates the story, and it is clear from what she says that neither woman thinks of the other as an individual person; instead each is a representative of her race. The tragedy is not only that the society they inhabit is flagrantly unjust, with its migratory labor and pass law restrictions for blacks, but also that because the two women's relationship is based on dissembling, the gulf between them is ultimately unbridgeable.

E S ' K I A   M P H A H L E L E

Mrs. Plum

I

My madam's name was Mrs. Plum. She loved dogs and Africans and said that everyone must follow the law even if it hurt. These were three big things in Madam's life.

I came to work for Mrs. Plum in Greenside, not very far from the centre of Johannesburg, after leaving two white families. The first white people I worked for as a cook and laundry woman were a man and his wife in

Parktown North. They drank too much and always forgot to pay me. After five months I said to myself No. I am going to leave these drunks. So that was it. That day I was as angry as a red-hot iron when it meets water. The second house I cooked and washed for had five children who were badly brought up. This was in Belgravia. Many times they called me You Black Girl and I kept quiet. Because their mother heard them and said nothing. Also I was only new from Phokeng my home, far away near Rustenburg, I wanted to learn and know the white people before I knew how far to go with the others I would work for afterwards. The thing that drove me mad and made me pack and go was a man who came to visit them often. They said he was cousin or something like that. He came to the kitchen many times and tried to make me laugh. He patted me on the buttocks. I told the master. The man did it again and I asked the madam that very day to give me my money and let me go.

These were the first nine months after I had left Phokeng to work in Johannesburg. There were many of us girls and young women from Phokeng, from Zeerust, from Shuping, from Kosten, and many other places who came to work in the cities. So the suburbs were full of blackness. Most of us had already passed Standard Six and so we learned more English where we worked. None of us liked to work for white farmers, because we know too much about them on the farms near our homes. They do not pay well and they are cruel people.

At Easter time so many of us went home for a long weekend to see our people and to eat chicken and sour milk and *morogo* — wild spinach. We also took home sugar and condensed milk and tea and coffee and sweets and custard powder and tinned foods.

It was a home-girl of mine, Chimane, who called me to take a job in Mrs. Plum's house, just next door to where she worked. This is the third year now. I have been quite happy with Mrs. Plum and her daughter Kate. By this I mean that my place as a servant in Greenside is not as bad as that of many others. Chimane too does not complain much. We are paid six pounds a month with free food and free servant's room. No one can ever say that they are well paid, so we go on complaining somehow. Whenever we meet on Thursday afternoons, which is time off for all of us black women in the suburbs, we talk and talk and talk: about our people at home and their letters; about their illnesses; about bad crops; about a sister who wanted a school uniform and books and school fees; about some of our madams and masters who are good, or stingy with money or food, or stupid or full of nonsense, or who kill themselves and each other, or who are dirty — and so many things I cannot count them all.

Thursday afternoons we go to town to look at the shops, to attend a woman's club, to see our boy friends, to go to bioscope some of us. We turn up smart, to show others the clothes we bought from the black men who sell soft goods to servants in the suburbs. We take a number of things and they come round every month for a bit of money until we finish paying. Then we dress the way of many white madams and girls. I think we look really smart. Sometimes we catch the eyes of a white woman looking at us and we laugh and laugh until we nearly drop on the ground because we feel good inside ourselves.

II

What did the girl next door call you? Mrs. Plum asked me the first day I came to her. Jane, I replied. Was there not an African name? I said yes, Karabo. All right, Madam said. We'll call you Karabo, she said. She spoke as if she knew a name is a big thing. I knew so many whites who did not care what they called black people as long as it was all right for their tongue. This pleased me, I mean Mrs. Plum's use of *Karabo;* because the only time I heard the name was when I was home or when my friends spoke to me. Then she showed me what to do: meals, meal times, washing, and where all the things were that I was going to use.

My daughter will be here in the evening, Madam said. She is at school. When the daughter came, she added, she would tell me some of the things she wanted me to do for her every day.

Chimane, my friend next door, had told me about the daughter Kate, how wild she seemed to be, and about Mr. Plum who had killed himself with a gun in a house down the street. They had left the house and come to this one.

Madam is a tall woman. Not slender, not fat. She moves slowly, and speaks slowly. Her face looks very wise, her forehead seems to tell me she has a strong liver: she is not afraid of anything. Her eyes are always swollen at the lower eyelids like a white person who has not slept for many many nights or like a large frog. Perhaps it is because she smokes too much, like wet wood that will not know whether to go up in flames or stop burning. She looks me straight in the eyes when she talks to me, and I know she does this with other people too. At first this made me fear her, now I am used to her. She is not a lazy woman, and she does many things outside, in the city and in the suburbs.

This was the first thing her daughter Kate told me when she came and we met. Don't mind mother, Kate told me. She said, She is sometimes mad with people for very small things. She will soon be all right and speak nicely to you again.

Kate, I like her very much, and she likes me too. She tells me many things a white woman does not tell a black servant. I mean things about what she likes and does not like, what her mother does or does not do, all these. At first I was unhappy and wanted to stop her, but now I do not mind.

Kate looks very much like her mother in the face. I think her shoulders will be just as round and strong-looking. She moves faster than Madam. I asked her why she was still at school when she was so big. She laughed. Then she tried to tell me that the school where she was was for big people, who had finished with lower school. She was learning big things about cooking and food. She can explain better, me I cannot. She came home on weekends.

Since I came to work for Mrs. Plum Kate has been teaching me plenty of cooking. I first learned from her and Madam the word *recipes*. When Kate came home, she found I had read the recipe she left me. So we just cooked straightaway. Kate thinks I am fit to cook in a hotel. Madam thinks so too. Never never! I thought. Cooking in a hotel is like feeding oxen. No one can say thank you to you. After a few months I could cook the Sunday lunch and later I could cook specials for Madam's or Kate's guests.

Madam did not only teach me cooking. She taught me how to look after guests. She praised me when I did very very well; not like the white people I had worked for before. I do not know what runs crooked in the heads of other people. Madam also had classes in the evenings for servants to teach them how to read and write. She and two other women in Greenside taught in a church hall.

As I say, Kate tells me plenty of things about Madam. She says to me she says, My mother goes to meetings many times. I ask her I say, What for? She says to me she says, For your people. I ask her I say, My people are in Phokeng far away. They have got mouths, I say. Why does she want to say something for them? Does she know what my mother and what my father want to say? They can speak when they want to. Kate raises her shoulders and drops them and says, How can I tell you Karabo? I don't say your people — your family only. I mean all the black people in the country. I say Oh! What do the black people want to say? Again she raises her shoulders and drops them, taking a deep breath.

I ask her I say, With whom is she in the meeting?

She says, With other people who think like her.

I ask her I say, Do you say there are people in the world who think the same things?

She nods her head.

I ask, What things?

So that a few of your people should one day be among those who rule this country, get more money for what they do for the white man, and — what did Kate say again? Yes, that Madam and those who think like her also wanted my people who have been to school to choose those who must speak for them in the — I think she said it looks like a *Kgotla* at home who rule the villages.

I say to Kate I say, Oh I see now. I say, Tell me Kate why is Madam always writing on the machine, all the time everyday nearly?

She replies she says, Oh my mother is writing books.

I ask, You mean a book like those? — pointing at the books on the shelves.

Yes, Kate says.

And she told me how Madam wrote books and other things for newspapers and she wrote for the newspapers and magazines to say things for the black people who should be treated well, be paid more money, for the black people who can read and write many things to choose those who want to speak for them.

Kate also told me she said, My mother and other women who think like her put on black belts over their shoulders when they are sad and they want to show the white government they do not like the things being done by whites to blacks. My mother and the others go and stand where the people in government are going to enter or go out of a building.

I ask her I say, Does the government and the white people listen and stop their sins? She says No. But my mother is in another group of white people.

I ask, Do the people of the government give the women tea and cakes? Kate says, Karabo! How stupid; oh!

I say to her I say, Among my people if someone comes and stands in front of my house I tell him to come in and I give him food. You white people are wonderful. But they keep standing there and the government people do not give them anything.

She replies, You mean strange. How many times have I taught you not to say *wonderful* when you mean *strange*! Well, Kate says with a short heart and looking cross and she shouts, Well they do not stand there the whole day to ask for tea and cakes stupid. Oh dear!

Always when Madam finished to read her newspapers she gave them to me to read to help me speak and write better English. When I had read she asked me to tell her some of the things in it. In this way, I did better and better and my mind was opening and opening and I was learning and learning many things about the black people inside and outside the towns which I did not know in the least. When I found words that were too difficult or I did not understand some of the things I asked Madam. She always told me You see this, you see that, eh? with a heart that can carry on a long way. Yes, Madam writes many letters to the papers. She is always sore about the way the white police beat up black people; about the way black people who work for whites are made to sit at the Zoo Lake with their hearts hanging, because the white people say our people are making noise on Sunday after-noon when they want to rest in their houses and gardens; about many ugly things that happen when some white people meet black man on the pavement or street. So Madam writes to the papers to let others know, to ask the government to be kind to us.

In the first year Mrs. Plum wanted me to eat at table with her. It was very hard, one because I was not used to eating at table with a fork and knife, two because I heard of no other kitchen worker who was handled like this. I was afraid. Afraid of everybody, of Madam's guests if they found me doing this. Madam said I must not be silly. I must show that African servants can also eat at table. Number three, I could not eat some of the things I loved very much: meali-meal porridge with sour milk or *morogo*, stamped mealies mixed with butter beans, sour porridge for breakfast and other things. Also, except for morning porridge, our food is nice when you eat with the hand. So nice that it does not stop in the mouth or the throat to greet anyone before it passes smoothly down.

We often had lunch together with Chimane next door and our garden boy — Ha! I must remember never to say *boy* again when I talk about a man. This makes me think of a day during the first few weeks in Mrs. Plum's house. I was talking about Dick her garden man and I said "garden boy." And she says to me she says, Stop talking about a "boy," Karabo. Now listen here, she says, You Africans must learn to speak properly about each other. And she says White people won't talk kindly about you if you look down upon each other.

I say to her I say Madam, I learned the word from the white people I worked for, and all the kitchen maids say "boy."

She replies she says to me, Those are white people who know nothing, just low-class whites. I say to her I say I thought white people know everything.

She said, You'll learn, my girl, and you must start in this house, hear? She left me there thinking, my mind mixed up.

I learned. I grew up.

III

If any woman or girl does not know the Black Crow Club in Bree Street, she does not know anything. I think nearly everything takes place inside and outside that house. It is just where the dirty part of the City begins, with factories and the market. After the market is the place where Indians and Coloured people live. It is also at the Black Crow that the buses turn round and back to the black townships. Noise, noise, noise all the time. There are women who sell hot sweet potatoes and fruit and monkey nuts and boiled eggs in the winter, boiled mealies and the other things in the summer, all these on the pavements. The streets are always full of potato and fruit skins and monkey nut shells. There is always a strong smell of roast pork. I think it is because of Piel's cold storage down Bree Street.

Madam said she knew the black people who work in the Black Crow. She was happy that I was spending my afternoon on Thursday in such a club. You will learn sewing, knitting, she said, and other things that you like. Do you like to dance? I told her I said, Yes, I want to learn. She paid the two shillings fee for me each month.

We waited on the first floor, we the ones who were learning sewing; waiting for the teacher. We talked and laughed about madams and masters, and their children and their dogs and birds and whispered about our boy friends.

Sies![1] My Madam you do not know — *mojuta oa'nete*[2] — a real miser . . .

Jo — jo — jo![3] you should see our new dog. A big thing like this. People! Big in a foolish way . . .

What! Me, I take a master's bitch by the leg, me, and throw it away so that it keeps howling, *tjwe — tjwe! ngo — wu ngo — wu!*[4] I don't play about with them, me . . .

Shame, poor thing! God sees you, true. . . . !

They wanted me to take their dog out for a walk every afternoon and I told them I said it is not my work in other houses the garden man does it.

---

[1] Shame!
[2] Cheap; a real miser.
[3] You, you, you!
[4] He belongs to us.

I just said to myself I said they can go to the chickens. Let them bite their elbow before I take out a dog, I am not so mad yet. . . .

Hei![5] It is not like the child of my white people who keeps a big white rat and you know what? He puts it on his bed when he goes to school. And let the blankets just begin to smell of urine and all the nonsense and they tell me to wash them. *Hei,* people . . . !

Did you hear about Rebone, people? Her Madam put her out, because her master was always tapping her buttocks with his fingers. And yesterday the madam saw the master press Rebone against himself. . . .

Jo — jo — jo! people . . . !

Dirty white man!

No, not dirty. The madam smells too old for him.

Hei! Go and wash your mouth with soap, this girl's mouth is dirty. . . .

Jo, Rebone, daughter of the people! We must help her to find a job before she thinks of going back home.

The teacher came. A woman with strong legs, a strong face, and kind eyes. She had short hair and dressed in a simple but lovely floral frock. She stood well on her legs and hips. She had a black mark between the two top front teeth. She smiled as if we were her children. Our group began with games, and then Lilian Ngoyi took us for sewing. After this she gave a brief talk to all of us from the different classes.

I can never forget the things this woman said and how she put them to us. She told us that the time had passed for black girls and women in the suburbs to be satisfied with working, sending money to our people and going to see them once a year. We were to learn, she said, that the world would never be safe for black people until they were in the government with the power to make laws. The power should be given by the Africans who were more than the whites.

We asked her questions and she answered them with wisdom. I shall put some of them down in my own words as I remember them.

Shall we take the place of the white people in the government?

Some yes. But we shall be more than they as we are more in the country. But also the people of all colours will come together and there are good white men we can choose and there are Africans some white people will choose to be in the government.

There are good madams and masters and bad ones. Should we take the good ones for friends?

A master and a servant can never be friends. Never, so put that out of your head, will you! You are not even sure if the ones you say are good are not like that because they cannot breathe or live without the work of your hands. As long as you need their money, face them with respect. But you must know that many sad things are happening in our country and you, all of you, must always be learning, adding to what you already know, and obey us when we ask you to help us.

---

[5] Hi!

At other times Lilian Ngoyi told us she said, Remember your poor people at home and the way in which the whites are moving them from place to place like sheep and cattle. And at other times again she told us she said, Remember that a hand cannot wash itself, it needs another to do it.

I always thought of Madam when Lilian Ngoyi spoke. I asked myself, What would she say if she knew that I was listening to such words. Words like: A white man is looked after by his black nanny and his mother when he is a baby. When he grows up the white government looks after him, sends him to school, makes it impossible for him to suffer from the great hunger, keeps a job ready and open for him as soon as he wants to leave school. Now Lilian Ngoyi asked she said, How many white people can be born in a white hospital, grow up in white streets, be clothed in lovely cotton, lie on white cushions; how many whites can live all their lives in a fenced place away from people of other colours and then, as men and women learn quickly the correct ways of thinking, learn quickly to ask questions in their minds, big questions that will throw over all the nice things of a white man's life? How many? Very, very few! For those whites who have not begun to ask, it is too late. For those who have begun and are joining us with both feet in our house, we can only say Welcome!

I was learning. I was growing up. Every time I thought of Madam, she became more and more like a dark forest which one fears to enter, and which one will never know. But there were several times when I thought, This woman is easy to understand, she is like all other white women. What else are they teaching you at the Black Crow, Karabo?

I tell her I say, nothing, Madam. I ask her I say Why does Madam ask?

You are changing.

What does Madam mean?

Well, you are changing.

But we are always changing Madam.

And she left me standing in the kitchen. This was a few days after I had told her that I did not want to read more than one white paper a day. The only magazines I wanted to read, I said to her, were those from overseas, if she had them. I told her that white papers had pictures of white people most of the time. They talked mostly about white people and their gardens, dogs, weddings and parties. I asked her if she could buy me a Sunday paper that spoke about my people. Madam bought it for me. I did not think she would do it.

There were mornings when, after hanging the white people's washing on the line Chimane and I stole a little time to stand at the fence and talk. We always stood where we could be hidden by our rooms.

Hei, Karabo, you know what? That was Chimane.

No — what? Before you start, tell me, has Timi come back to you?

Ach, I do not care. He is still angry. But boys are fools, they always come back dragging themselves on their empty bellies. *Hei* you know what?

Yes?

The Thursday past I saw Moruti K. K. I laughed until I dropped on the ground. He is standing in front of the Black Crow. I believe his big stomach was crying from hunger. Now he has a small dog in his armpit, and is standing before a woman selling boiled eggs and — *hei* home-girl! — tripe and intestines are boiling in a pot — oh — the smell! you could fill a hungry belly with it, the way it was good. I think Moruti K. K. is waiting for the woman to buy a boiled egg. I do not know what the woman was still doing. I am standing nearby. The dog keeps wriggling and pushing out its nose, looking at the boiling tripe. Moruti keeps patting it with his free hand, not so? Again the dog wants to spill out of Moruti's hand and it gives a few sounds through the nose. *Hei* man, home-girl! One two three the dog spills out to catch some of the good meat! It misses falling into the hot gravy in which the tripe is swimming I do not know how. Moruti K. K. tries to chase it. It has tumbled on to the woman's eggs and potatoes and all are in the dust. She stands up and goes after K. K. She is shouting to him to pay, not so? Where am I at that time? I am nearly dead with laughter the tears are coming down so far.

I was myself holding tight on the fence so as not to fall through laughing. I held my stomach to keep back a pain in the side.

I ask her I say, Did Moruti K. K. come back to pay for the wasted food?

Yes, he paid.

The dog?

He caught it. That is a good African dog. A dog must look for its own food when it is not time for meals. Not these stupid spoiled angels the whites keep giving tea and biscuits.

Hmm.

Dick our garden man joined us, as he often did. When the story was repeated to him the man nearly rolled on the ground laughing.

He asks who is Reverend K. K.

I say he is the owner of the Black Crow.

Oh!

We reminded each other, Chimane and I, of the round minister. He would come into the club, look at us with a smooth smile on his smooth round face. He would look at each one of us, with that smile on all the time, as if he had forgotten that I was there. Perhaps he had, because as he looked at us, almost stripping us naked with his watery shining eyes — funny — he could have been a farmer looking at his ripe corn, thinking many things.

K. K. often spoke without shame about what he called ripe girls — *mat-jitjana* — with good firm breasts. He said such girls were pure without any nonsense in their heads and bodies. Everybody talked a great deal about him and what they thought he must be doing in his office whenever he called in so-and-so.

The Reverend K. K. did not belong to any church. He baptised, married, and buried people for a fee, who had no church to do such things for them. They said he had been driven out of the Presbyterian Church. He had formed his own, but it did not go far. Then he later came and opened the Black Crow. He knew just how far to go with Lilian Ngoyi. She said although he used his club to teach us things that would help us in life, she could not go on if he was doing any wicked things with the girls in his office. Moruti K. K. feared her, and kept his place.

IV

When I began to tell my story I thought I was going to tell you mostly about Mrs. Plum's two dogs. But I have been talking about people. I think Dick is right when he says What is a dog! And there are so many dogs cats and parrots in Greenside and other places that Mrs. Plum's dogs do not look special. But there was something special in the dog business in Madam's house. The way in which she loved them, maybe.

Monty[6] is a tiny animal with long hair and small black eyes and a face nearly like that of an old woman. The other, Malan, is a bit bigger, with brown and white colours. It has small hair and looks naked by the side of the friend. They sleep in two separate baskets which stay in Madam's bedroom. They are to be washed often and brushed and sprayed and they sleep on pink linen. Monty has a pink ribbon which stays on his neck most of the time. They both carry a cover on their backs. They make me fed up when I see them in their baskets, looking fat, and as if they knew all that was going on everywhere.

It was Dick's work to look after Monty and Malan, to feed them, and to do everything for them. He did this together with garden work and cleaning of the house. He came at the beginning of this year. He just came, as if from nowhere, and Madam gave him the job as she had chased away two before him, she told me. In both cases, she said that they could not look after Monty and Malan.

Dick had a long heart, even although he told me and Chimane that European dogs were stupid, spoiled. He said One day those white people will put ear rings and toe rings and bangles on their dogs. That would be the day he would leave Mrs. Plum. For, he said, he was sure that she would want him to polish the rings and bangles with Brasso.

Although he had a long heart, Madam was still not sure of him. She often went to the dogs after a meal or after a cleaning and said to them Did Dick give you food sweethearts? Or, Did Dick wash you sweethearts? Let me see. And I could see that Dick was blowing up like a balloon with anger. These things called white people! he said to me. Talking to dogs!

I say to him I say, People talk to oxen at home do I not say so?

Yes, he says, but at home do you not know that a man speaks to an ox because he wants to make it pull the plough or the wagon or to stop or to stand still for a person to inspan it. No one simply goes to an ox looking at him with eyes far apart and speaks to it. Let me ask you, do you ever see a person where we come from take a cow and press it to his stomach or his cheek? Tell me!

---

[6] *Monty and Malan* Dr. D. F. Malan, a leading figure of the Dutch Reformed Church and subsequent leader of the Nationalist party, which ushered in the worst phase of apartheid in 1948. Monty may be a reference to British Field Marshall B. L. ("Monty") Montgomery.

And I say to Dick I say, We were talking about an ox, not a cow.

He laughed with his broad mouth until tears came out of his eyes. At a certain point I laughed aloud too.

One day when you have time, Dick says to me, he says, you should look into Madam's bedroom when she has put a notice outside her door.

Dick, what are you saying? I ask.

I do not talk, me. I know deep inside me.

Dick was about our age, I and Chimane. So we always said *moshiman'o*[7] when we spoke about his tricks. Because he was not too big to be a boy to us. He also said to us *Hei, lona banyana kelona* — Hey you girls, you! His large mouth always seemed to be making ready to laugh. I think Madam did not like this. Many times she would say What is there to make you laugh here? Or in the garden she would say This is a flower and when it wants water that is not funny! Or again, if you did more work and stopped trying to water my plants with your smile you would be more useful. Even when Dick did not mean to smile. What Madam did not get tired of saying was, If I left you to look after my dogs without anyone to look after you at the same time you would drown the poor things.

Dick smiled at Mrs. Plum. Dick hurt Mrs. Plum's dogs? Then cows can fly. He was really — really afraid of white people, Dick. I think he tried very hard not to feel afraid. For he was always showing me and Chimane in private how Mrs. Plum walked, and spoke. He took two bowls and pressed them to his chest, speaking softly to them as Madam speaks to Monty and Malan. Or he sat at Madam's table and acted the way she sits when writing. Now and again he looked back over his shoulder, pulled his face long like a horse's making as if he were looking over his glasses while telling me something to do. Then he would sit on one of the armchairs, cross his legs, and act the way Madam drank her tea; he held the cup he was thinking about between his thumb and the pointing finger, only letting their nails meet. And he laughed after every act. He did these things, of course, when Madam was not home. And where was I at such times? Almost flat on my stomach, laughing.

But oh how Dick trembled when Mrs. Plum scolded him! He did his house-cleaning very well. Whatever mistake he made, it was mostly with the dogs; their linen, their food. One white man came into the house one afternoon to tell Madam that Dick had been very careless when taking the dogs out for a walk. His own dog was waiting on Madam's stoop. He repeated that he had been driving down our street; and Dick had let loose Monty and Malan to cross the street. The white man made plenty of noise about this and I think wanted to let Madam know how useful he had been. He kept on saying Just one inch, *just* one inch. It was lucky I put on my brakes quick enough. . . . But your boy kept on smiling — Why? Strange. My boy would only do it twice and only twice and then . . . ! His pass. The man moves his hand like one writing, to mean that he could sign his servant's pass for him

---

[7] This boy.

to go and never come back. When he left, the white man said Come on Rusty, the boy is waiting to clean you. Dogs with names, men without, I thought.

Madam climbed on top of Dick for this, as we say.

Once one of the dogs, I don't know which — Malan or Monty — tore my stocking — brand new, you hear — and tore it with its teeth and paws. When I told Madam about it, my anger as high as my throat, she gave me money to buy another pair. It happened again. This time she said she was not going to give me money because I must also keep my stockings where the two gentlemen would not reach them. Mrs. Plum did not want us ever to say *Voetsek* when we wanted the dogs to go away. Me I said this when they came sniffing at my legs or fingers. I hate it.

In my third year in Mrs. Plum's house, many things happened, most of them all bad for her. There was trouble with Kate; Chimane had big trouble; my heart was twisted by two loves; and Monty and Malan became real dogs for a few days.

Madam had a number of suppers and parties. She invited Africans to some of them. Kate told me the reasons for some of the parties. Like her mother's books when finished, a visitor from across the seas and so on. I did not like the black people who came here to drink and eat. They spoke such difficult English like people who were full of all the books in the world. They looked at me as if I were right down there whom they thought little of — me a black person like them.

One day I heard Kate speak to her mother. She says I don't know why you ask so many Africans to the house. A few will do at a time. She said something about the government which I could not hear well. Madam replies she says to her You know some of them do not meet white people often, so far away in their dark houses. And she says to Kate that they do not come because they want her as a friend but they just want drink for nothing.

I simply felt that I could not be the servant of white people and of blacks at the same time. At my home or in my home I could serve them without a feeing of shame. And now, if they were only coming to drink!

But one of the black men and his sister always came to the kitchen to talk to me. I must have looked unfriendly the first time, for Kate talked to me about it afterwards as she was in the kitchen when they came. I know that at that time I was not easy at all. I was ashamed and I felt that a white person's house was not the place for me to look happy in front of other black people while the white man looked on.

Another time it was easier. The man was alone. I shall never forget that night, as long as I live. He spoke kind words and I felt my heart grow big inside me. It caused me to tremble. There were several other visits. I knew that I loved him, I could never know what he really thought of me, I mean as a woman and he as a man. But I loved him, and I still think of him with a sore heart. Slowly I came to know the pain of it. Because he was a doctor and so full of knowledge and English I could not reach him. So I knew he could not stoop down to see me as someone who wanted him to love me.

Kate turned very wild. Mrs. Plum was very much worried. Suddenly it looked as if she were a new person, with new ways and new everything. I do not know what was wrong or right. She began to play the big gramophone aloud, as if the music were for the whole of Greenside. The music was wild and she twisted her waist all the time, with her mouth half-open. She did the same things in her room. She left the big school and every Saturday night now she went out. When I looked at her face, there was something deep and wild there on it, and when I thought she looked young she looked old, and when I thought she looked old she was young. We were both 22 years of age. I think that I could see the reason why her mother was so worried, why she was suffering.

Worse was to come.

They were now openly screaming at each other. They began in the sitting-room and went upstairs together, speaking fast hot biting words, some of which I did not grasp. One day Madam comes to me and says You know Kate loves an African, you know the doctor who comes to supper here often. She says he loves her too and they will leave the country and marry outside. Tell me, Karabo, what do your people think of this kind of thing between a white woman and a black man? It *cannot* be right is it?

I reply and I say to her We have never seen it happen before where I come from.

That's right, Karabo, it is just madness.

Madam left. She looked like a hunted person.

These white women, I say to myself I say these white women, why do not they love their own men and leave us to love ours!

From that minute I knew that I would never want to speak to Kate. She appeared to me as a thief, as a fox that falls upon a flock of sheep at night. I hated her. To make it worse, he would never be allowed to come to the house again.

Whenever she was home there was silence between us. I no longer wanted to know anything about what she was doing, where or how.

I lay awake for hours on my bed. Lying like that, I seemed to feel parts of my body beat and throb inside me, the way I have seen big machines doing, pounding and pounding and pushing and pulling and pouring some water into one hole which came out at another end. I stretched myself so many times so as to feel tired and sleepy.

When I did sleep, my dreams were full of painful things.

One evening I made up my mind, after putting it off many times. I told my boy-friend that I did not want him any longer. He looked hurt, and that hurt me too. He left.

The thought of the African doctor was still with me and it pained me to know that I should never see him again; unless I met him in the street on a Thursday afternoon. But he had a car. Even if I did meet him by luck, how could I make him see that I loved him? Ach, I do not believe he would even stop to think what kind of woman I am. Part of that winter was a time of longing and burning for me. I say part because there are always things to keep servants busy whose white people go to the sea for the winter.

To tell the truth, winter was the time for servants; not nannies, because they went with their madams so as to look after the children. Those like me stayed behind to look after the house and dogs. In winter so many families went away that the dogs remained the masters and madams. You could see them walk like white people in the streets. Silent but with plenty of power. And when you saw them you knew that they were full of more nonsense and fancies in the house.

There was so little work to do.

One week word was whispered round that a home-boy of ours was going to hold a party in his room on Saturday. I think we all took it for a joke. How could the man be so bold and stupid? The police were always driving about at night looking for black people; and if the whites next door heard the party noise — *oho*! But still, we were full of joy and wanted to go. As for Dick, he opened his big mouth and nearly fainted when he heard of it and that I was really going.

During the day on the big Saturday Kate came.

She seemed a little less wild. But I was not ready to talk to her. I was surprised to hear myself answer her when she said to me Mother says you do not like a marriage between a white girl and a black man, Karabo.

Then she was silent.

She says But I want to help him, Karabo.

I ask her I say You want to help him to do what?

To go higher and higher, to the top.

I knew I wanted to say so much that was boiling in my chest. I could not say it. I thought of Lilian Ngoyi at the Black Crow, what she said to us. But I was mixed up in my head and in my blood.

You still agree with my mother?

All I could say was I said to your mother I had never seen a black man and a white woman marrying, you hear me? What I think about it is my business.

I remembered that I wanted to iron my party dress and so I left her. My mind was full of the party again and I was glad because Kate and the doctor would not worry my peace that day. And the next day the sun would shine for all of us, Kate or no Kate, doctor or no doctor.

The house where our home-boy worked was hidden from the main road by a number of trees. But although we asked a number of questions and counted many fingers of bad luck until we had no more hands for fingers, we put on our best pay-while-you-wear dresses and suits and clothes bought from boys who had stolen them, and went to our home-boy's party. We whispered all the way while we climbed up to the house. Someone who knew told us that the white people next door were away for the winter. Oh, so that is the thing! we said.

We poured into the garden through the back and stood in front of his room laughing quietly. He came from the big house behind us, and were we not struck dumb when he told us to go into the white people's house! Was he mad? We walked in with slow footsteps that seemed to be sniffing at the floor, not sure of anything. Soon we were standing and sitting all over on the nice warm cushions and the heaters were on. Our home-boy turned the lights low. I counted fifteen people inside. We saw how we loved one another's evening dress. The boys were smart too.

Our home-boy's girl-friend Naomi was busy in the kitchen preparing food. He took out glasses and cold drinks — fruit juice, tomato juice, ginger beers, and so many other kinds of soft drinks. It was just too nice. The tarts, the biscuits, the snacks, the cakes, *woo*, that was a party, I tell you. I think I ate more ginger cake than I had ever done in my life. Naomi had baked some of the things. Our home-boy came to me and said I do not want the police to come here and have reason to arrest us, so I am not serving hot drinks, not even beer. There is no law that we cannot have parties, is there? So we can feel free. Our use of this house is the master's business. If I had asked him he would have thought me mad.

I say to him I say, You have a strong liver to do such a thing.

He laughed.

He played pennywhistle music on gramophone records — Miriam Makeba, Dorothy Masuka, and other African singers and players. We danced and the party became more and more noisy and more happy. *Hai,* those girls Miriam and Dorothy, they can sing, I tell you! We ate more and laughed more and told more stories. In the middle of the party, our home-boy called us to listen to what he was going to say. Then he told us how he and a friend of his in Orlando collected money to bet on a horse for the July Handicap in Durban. They did this each year but lost. Now they had won two hundred pounds. We all clapped hands and cheered. Two hundred pounds *woo!*

You should go and sit at home and just eat time, I say to him. He laughs and says You have no understanding not one little bit.

To all of us he says Now my brothers and sisters enjoy yourselves. At home I should slaughter a goat for us to feast and thank our ancestors. But this is town life and we must thank them with tea and cake and all those sweet things. I know some people think I must be so bold that I could be midwife to a lion that is giving birth, but enjoy yourselves and have no fear.

Madam came back looking strong and fresh.

The very week she arrived the police had begun again to search servants' rooms. They were looking for what they called loafers and men without passes who they said were living with friends in the suburbs against the law. Our dog's-meat boys became scarce because of the police. A boy who had a girl-friend in the kitchens, as we say, always told his friends that he was coming for dog's meat when he meant he was visiting his girl. This was because we gave our boy-friends part of the meat the white people bought for the dogs and us.

One night a white and a black policeman entered Mrs. Plum's yard. They said they had come to search. She says no, they cannot. They say Yes, they must do it. She answers No. They forced their way to the back, to Dick's room and mine. Mrs. Plum took the hose that was running in the front garden and quickly went round to the back. I cut across the floor to see what she was going to say to the men. They were talking to Dick, using dirty words. Mrs. Plum did not wait, she just pointed the hose at the two policemen. This seemed to surprise them. They turned round and she pointed it into their faces. Without their seeing me I went to the tap at the corner of the house and opened it more. I could see Dick, like me, was trying to keep down his laughter. They shouted and tried to wave the water away, but she kept the hose pointing at them, now moving it up and down. They turned and ran through the back gate, swearing the while.

That fixes that, Mrs. Plum said.

The next day the morning paper reported it.

They arrived in the afternoon — the two policemen — with another. They pointed out Mrs. Plum and she was led to the police station. They took her away to answer for stopping the police while they were doing their work.

She came back and said she had paid bail.

At the magistrate's court, Madam was told that she had done a bad thing. She would have to pay a fine or else go to prison for fourteen days. She said she would go to jail to show that she felt she was not in the wrong.

Kate came and tried to tell her that she was doing something silly going to jail for a small thing like that. She tells Madam she says This is not even a thing to take to the high court. Pay the money. What is £5?

Madam went to jail.

She looked very sad when she came out. I thought of what Lilian Ngoyi often said to us: You must be ready to go to jail for the things you believe are true and for which you are taken by the police. What did Mrs. Plum really believe about me, Chimane, Dick, and all the other black people? I asked myself. I did not know. But from all those things she was writing for the papers and all those meetings she was going to where white people talked about black people and the way they are treated by the government, from what those white women with black bands over their shoulders were doing standing where a white government man was going to pass, I said to myself I said This woman, *hai,* I do not know she seems to think very much of us black people. But why was she so sad?

Kate came back home to stay after this. She still played the big gramophone loud-loud-loud and twisted her body at her waist until I thought it was going to break. Then I saw a young white man come often to see her. I watched them through the opening near the hinges of the door between the kitchen and the sitting-room where they sat. I saw them kiss each other for a long time. I saw him lift up Kate's dress and her white-white legs begin to tremble, and — oh I am afraid to say more, my heart was beating hard. She called him Jim. I thought it was funny because white people in the shops call black men Jim.

Kate had begun to play with Jim when I met a boy who loved me and I loved. He was much stronger than the one I sent away and I loved him more, much more. The face of the doctor came to my mind often, but it did not hurt me so any more. I stopped looking at Kate and her Jim through openings. We spoke to each other, Kate and I, almost as freely as before but not quite. She and her mother were friends again.

Hallo, Karabo, I heard Chimane call me one morning as I was starching my apron. I answered. I went to the line to hang it. I saw she was standing at the fence, so I knew she had something to tell me. I went to her.

Hallo!

Hallo, Chimane!

O kae?

Ke teng. Wena?

At that moment a woman came out through the back door of the house where Chimane was working.

I have not seen that one before, I say, pointing with my head.

Chimane looked back. Oh, that one. *Hei,* daughter-of-the-people, *Hei,* you have not seen miracles. You know this is Madam's mother-in-law as you see her there. Did I never tell you about her?

No, never.

White people, nonsense. You know what? That poor woman is here now for two days. She has to cook for herself and I cook for the family.

On the same stove?

Yes, She comes after me when I have finished.

She has her own food to cook?

Yes, Karabo. White people have no heart no sense.

What will eat them up if they share their food?

Ask me, just ask me. God! She clapped her hands to show that only God knew, and it was His business, not ours.

Chimane asks me she says, Have you heard from home?

I tell her I say, Oh daughter-of-the-people, more and more deaths. Something is finishing the people at home. My mother has written. She says they are all right, my father too and my sisters, except for the people who have died. Malebo, the one who lived alone in the house I showed you last year, a white house, he is gone. Then teacher Sedimo. He was very thin and looked sick all the time. He taught my sisters not me. His mother-in-law you remember I told you died last year — no, the year before. Mother says also there is a woman she does not think I remember because I last saw her when I was a small girl she passed away in Zeerust she was my mother's greatest friend when they were girls. She would have gone to her burial if it was not because she has swollen feet.

How are the feet?

She says they are still giving her trouble. I ask Chimane, How are your people at Nokaneng? They have not written?

She shook her head.

I could see from her eyes that her mind was on another thing and not her people at that moment.

Wait for me Chimane eh, forgive me, I have scones in the oven, eh! I will just take them out and come back, eh!

When I came back to her Chimane was wiping her eyes. They were wet.

Karabo, you know what?

E — e. I shook my head.

I am heavy with child.

Hau!

There was a moment of silence.

Who is it, Chimane?

Timi. He came back only to give me this.

But he loves you. What does he say have you told him?

I told him yesterday. We met in town.

I remembered I had not seen her at the Black Crow.

Are you sure, Chimane? You have missed a month?

She nodded her head.

Timi himself — he did not use the thing?

I only saw after he finished, that he had not.

Why? What does he say?

He tells me he says I should not worry I can be his wife.

Timi is a good boy, Chimane. How many of these boys with town ways who know too much will even say Yes it is my child?

Hai, Karabo, you are telling me other things now. Do you not see that I have not worked long enough for my people? If I marry now who will look after them when I am the only child?

Hm. I hear your words. It is true. I tried to think of something soothing to say.

Then I say You can talk it over with Timi. You can go home and when the child is born you look after it for three months and when you are married you come to town to work and can put your money together to help the old people while they are looking after the child.

What shall we be eating all the time I am at home? It is not like those days gone past when we had land and our mother could go to the fields until the child was ready to arrive.

The light goes out in my mind and I cannot think of the right answer. How many times have I feared the same thing? Luck and the mercy of the gods that is all I live by. That is all we live by — all of us.

Listen, Karabo. I must be going to make tea for Madam. It will soon strike half-past ten.

I went back to the house. As Madam was not in yet, I threw myself on the divan in the sitting-room. Malan came sniffing at my legs. I put my foot under its fat belly and shoved it up and away from me so that it cried *tjunk — tjunk — tjunk* as it went out. I say to it I say Go and tell your brother what I have done to you and tell him to try it and see what I will do. Tell your grandmother when she comes home too.

When I lifted my eyes he was standing in the kitchen door, Dick. He says to me he says *Hau!* now you have also begun to speak to dogs!

I did not reply I just looked at him, his mouth ever stretched out like the mouth of a bag, and I passed to my room.

I sat on my bed and looked at my face in the mirror. Since the morning I had been feeling as if a black cloud were hanging over me, pressing on my head and shoulders. I do not know how long I sat there. Then I smelled Madam. What was it? Where was she? After a few moments I knew what it was. My perfume and scent. I used the same cosmetics as Mrs. Plum's. I should have been used to it by now. But this morning — why did I smell Mrs. Plum like this? Then, without knowing why, I asked myself I said, Why have I been using the same cosmetics as Madam? I wanted to throw them all out. I stopped. And then I took all the things and threw them into the dustbin. I was going to buy other kinds on Thursday; finished!

I could not sit down. I went out and into the white people's house. I walked through and the smell of the house made me sick and seemed to fill up my throat. I went to the bathroom without knowing why. It was full of the smell of Madam. Dick was cleaning the bath. I stood at the door and looked at him cleaning the dirt out of the bath, dirt from Madam's body. *Sies!* I said aloud. To myself I said, Why cannot people wash the dirt of their own bodies out of the bath? Before Dick knew I was near I went out. Ach, I said again to myself, why should I think about it now when I have been doing their washing for so long and cleaned the bath many times when Dick was ill. I had held worse things from her body times without number. . . .

I went out and stood midway between the house and my room, looking into the next yard. The three-legged grey cat next door came to the fence and our eyes met. I do not know how long we stood like that looking at each other. I was thinking, Why don't you go and look at your grandmother like that? when it turned away and mewed hopping on three legs. Just like someone who feels pity for you.

In my room I looked into the mirror on the chest of drawers. I thought Is this Karabo this?

Thursday came, and the afternoon off. At the Black Crow I did not see Chimane. I wondered about her. In the evening I found a note under my door. It told me if Chimane was not back that evening I should know that she was at 660 3rd Avenue, Alexandra Township. I was not to tell the white people.

I asked Dick if he could not go to Alexandra with me after I had washed the dishes. At first he was unwilling. But I said to him I said, Chimane will not believe that you refused to come with me when she sees me alone. He agreed.

On the bus Dick told me much about his younger sister whom he was helping with money to stay at school until she finished; so that she could become a nurse and a midwife. He was very fond of her, as far as I could find out. He said he prayed always that he should not lose his job, as he had done many times before, after staying a few weeks only at each job; because of this he had to borrow monies from people to pay his sister's school fees, to buy her clothes and books. He spoke of her as if she were his sweetheart. She was clever at school, pretty (she was in the photo Dick had shown me before). She was in Orlando Township. She looked after his old people, although she was only thirteen years of age. He said to me he said Today I still owe many people because I keep losing my job. You must try to stay with Mrs. Plum, I said.

I cannot say that I had all my mind on what Dick was telling me. I was thinking of Chimane: what could she be doing? Why that note?

We found her in bed. In that terrible township where night and day are full of knives and bicycle chains and guns and the barking of hungry dogs and of people in trouble. I even held my heart in my hands. She was in pain and her face, even in the candlelight, was grey. She turned her eyes at me. A fat woman was sitting in a chair. One arm rested on the other and held her chin in its palm. She had hardly opened the door for us after we had shouted our names when she was on her bench again as if there were nothing else to do.

She snorted, as if to let us know that she was going to speak. She said There is your friend. There she is my own-own niece who comes from the womb of my own sister, my sister who was made to spit out my mother's breast to give way for me. Why does she go and do such an evil thing. *Ao!* you young girls of today you do not know children die so fast these days that you have to thank God for sowing a seed in your womb to grow into a child. If she had let the child be born I should have looked after it or my sister would have been so happy to hold a grandchild on her lap, but what does it help? She has allowed a worm to cut the roots, I don't know.

Then I saw that Chimane's aunt was crying. Not once did she mention her niece by her name, so sore her heart must have been. Chimane only moaned.

Her aunt continued to talk, as if she was never going to stop for breath, until her voice seemed to move behind me, not one of the things I was thinking: trying to remember signs, however small, that could tell me more about this moment in a dim little room in a cruel township without street lights, near Chimane. Then I remembered the three-legged cat, its grey-green eyes, its *miau*. What was this shadow that seemed to walk about us but was not coming right in front of us?

I thanked the gods when Chimane came to work at the end of the week. She still looked weak, but that shadow was no longer there. I wondered Chimane had never told me about her aunt before. Even now I did not ask her.

I told her I told her white people that she was ill and had been fetched to Nokaneng by a brother. They would never try to find out. They seldom did, these people. Give them any lie, and it will do. For they seldom believe you whatever you say. And how can a black person work for white people and be afraid to tell them lies. They are always asking the questions, you are always the one to give the answers.

Chimane told me all about it. She had gone to a woman who did these things. Her way was to hold a sharp needle, cover the point with the finger, and guide it into the womb. She then fumbled in the womb until she found the egg and then pierced it. She gave you something to ease the bleeding. But the pain, spirits of our forefathers!

Mrs. Plum and Kate were talking about dogs one evening at dinner. Every time I brought something to table I tried to catch their words. Kate seemed to find it funny, because she laughed aloud. There was a word I could not hear well which began with *sem* — : whatever it was, it was to be for dogs. This I understood by putting a few words together. Mrs. Plum said it was something that was common in the big cities of America, like New York. It was also something Mrs. Plum wanted and Kate laughed at the thought. Then later I was to hear that Monty and Malan could be sure of a nice burial.

Chimane's voice came up to me in my room the next morning, across the fence. When I come out she tells me she said *Hei* child-of-my-father, here is something to tickle your ears. You know what? What? I say. She says, These white people can do things that make the gods angry. More godless people I have not seen. The madam of our house says the people of Greenside want to buy ground where they can bury their dogs. I heard them talk about it in the sitting-room when I was giving them coffee last night. *Hei*, people, let our forefathers come and save us!

Yes, I say, I also heard the madam of our house talk about it with her daughter. I just heard it in pieces. By my mother one day these dogs will sit at table and use knife and fork. These things are to be treated like people now, like children who are never going to grow up.

Chimane sighed and she says *Hela batho*,[8] why do they not give me some of that money they will spend on the ground and on gravestones to buy stockings! I have nothing to put on, by my mother.

Over her shoulder I saw the cat with three legs. I pointed with my head. When Chimane looked back and saw it she said *Hm*, even *they* live like kings. The mother-in-law found it on a chair and the madam said the woman should not drive it away. And there was no other chair, so the woman went to her room.

Hela!

I was going to leave when I remembered what I wanted to tell Chimane. It was that five of us had collected a £1 each to lend her so that she could pay the woman of Alexandra for having done that thing for her. When Chimane's time came to receive money we collected each month and which we took in turns, she would pay us back. We were ten women and each gave £2 at a time. So one waited ten months to receive £20. Chimane thanked us for helping her.

I went to wake up Mrs. Plum as she had asked me. She was sleeping late this morning. I was going to knock at the door when I heard strange noises in the bedroom. What is the matter with Mrs. Plum? I asked myself. Should I call her, in case she is ill? No, the noises were not those of a sick person. They were happy noises but like those a person makes in a dream, the voice full of sleep. I bent a little to peep through the keyhole. What is this? I kept asking myself. Mrs. Plum! Malan! What is she doing this one? Her arm was round Malan's belly and pressing its back against her stomach at the navel, Mrs. Plum's body in a nightdress moving in jerks like someone in fits . . . her leg rising and falling . . . Malan silent like a thing to be owned without any choice it can make to belong to another.

The gods save me! I heard myself saying, the words sounding like wind rushing out of my mouth. So this was what Dick said I would find out for myself!

No one could say where it all started; who talked about it first; whether the police wanted to make a reason for taking people without passes and people living with servants and working in towns or not working at all. But the story rushed through Johannesburg that servants were going to poison the white people's dogs. Because they were too much work for us: that was the reason. We heard that letters were sent to the newspapers by white people asking the police to watch over the dogs to stop any wicked things. Some said

---

[8] Oh gosh, people!

that we the servants were not really bad, we were being made to think of doing these things by evil people in town and in the locations. Others said the police should watch out lest we poison madams and masters because black people did not know right from wrong when they were angry. We were still children at heart, others said. Mrs. Plum said that she had also written to the papers.

Then it was the police came down on the suburbs like locusts on a cornfield. There were lines and lines of men who were arrested hour by hour in the day. They liked this very much, the police. Everybody they took, everybody who was working was asked, Where's the poison eh? Where did you hide it? Who told you to poison the dogs eh? If you tell us we'll leave you to go free, you hear? and so many other things.

Dick kept saying It is wrong this thing they want to do to kill poor dogs. What have these things of God done to be killed for? Is it the dogs that make us carry passes? Is it dogs that make the laws that give us pain? People are just mad they do not know what they want, stupid! But when white police- man spoke to him, Dick trembled and lost his tongue and the things he thought. He just shook his head. A few moments after they had gone through his pockets he still held his arms stretched out, like the man of straw who frightens away birds in a field. Only when I hissed and gave him a sign did he drop his arms. He rushed to a corner of the garden to go on with his work.

Mrs. Plum had put Monty and Malan in the sitting-room, next to her. She looked very much worried. She called me. She asked me she said Karabo, you think Dick is a boy we can trust? I did not know how to answer. I did not know whom she was talking about when she said *we*. Then I said I do not know, Madam. You know! she said. I looked at her. I said I do not know what Madam thinks. She said she did not think anything, that was why she asked. I nearly laughed because she was telling a lie this time and not I.

At another time I should have been angry if she lied to me, perhaps. She and I often told each other lies, as Kate and I also did. Like when she came back from jail, after that day when she turned a hosepipe on two policemen. She said life had been good in jail. And yet I could see she was ashamed to have been there. Not like our black people who are always being put in jail and only look at it as the white man's evil game. Lilian Ngoyi often told us this, and Mrs. Plum showed me how true those words are. I am sure that we have kept to each other by lying to each other.

There was something in Mrs. Plum's face as she was speaking which made me fear her and pity her at the same time. I had seen her when she had come from prison; I had seen her when she was shouting at Kate and the girl left the house; now there was this thing about dog poisoning. But never had I seen her face like this before. The eyes, the nostrils, the lips, the teeth seemed to be full of hate, tired, fixed on doing something bad; and yet there was something on that face that told me she wanted me on her side.

Dick is all right Madam, I found myself saying. She took Malan and Monty in her arms and pressed them to herself, running her hands over their heads. They looked so safe, like a child in a mother's arm.

Mrs. Plum said All right you may go. She said Do not tell anybody what I have asked about Dick eh?

When I told Dick about it, he seemed worried.

It is nothing, I told him.

I had been thinking before that I did not stand with those who wanted to poison the dogs, Dick said. But the police have come out, I do not care what happens to the dumb things, now.

I asked him I said Would you poison them if you were told by someone to do it?

No. But I do not care, he replied.

The police came again and again. They were having a good holiday, everyone could see that. A day later Mrs. Plum told Dick to go because she would not need his work any more.

Dick was almost crying when he left. Is Madam so unsure of me? he asked. I never thought a white person could fear me! And he left.

Chimane shouted from the other yard. She said, *Hei ngoana'rona,*[9] the boers are fire-hot eh!

Mrs. Plum said she would hire a man after the trouble was over.

A letter came from my parents in Phokeng. In it they told me my uncle had passed away. He was my mother's brother. The letter also told me of other deaths. They said I would not remember some, I was sure to know the others. There were also names of sick people.

I went to Mrs. Plum to ask her if I could go home. She asks she says When did he die? I answer I say It is three days, Madam. She says So that they have buried him? I reply Yes Madam. Why do you want to go home then? Because my uncle loved me very much Madam. But what are you going to do there? To take my tears and words of grief to his grave and to my old aunt, Madam. No you cannot go, Karabo. You are working for me you know? Yes, Madam. I, and not your people pay you. I must go Madam, that is how we do it among my people, Madam. She paused. She walked into the kitchen and came out again. If you want to go, Karabo, you must lose the money for the day you will be away. Lose my pay, Madam? Yes, Karabo.

The next day I went to Mrs. Plum and told her I was leaving for Phokeng and was not coming back to her. Could she give me a letter to say that I worked for her. She did, with her lips shut tight. I could feel that something between us was burning like raw chillies. The letter simply said that I had worked for Mrs. Plum for three years. Nothing more. The memory of Dick being sent away was still an open sore in my heart.

The night before the day I left, Chimane came to see me in my room. She had her own story to tell me. Timi, her boy-friend, had left her — for good. Why? Because I killed his baby. Had he not agreed that you should do it? No. Did he show he was worried when you told him you were heavy? He was worried, like me as you saw me, Karabo. Now he says if I kill one I shall eat all his children up when we are married. You think he means what he

---

[9] Child.

says? Yes, Karabo. He says his parents would have been very happy to know that the woman he was going to marry can make his seed grow.

Chimane was crying, softly.

I tried to speak to her, to tell her that if Timi left her just like that, he had not wanted to marry her in the first place. But I could not, no, I could not. All I could say was Do not cry, my sister, do not cry. I gave her my handkerchief.

Kate came back the morning I was leaving, from somewhere very far I cannot remember where. Her mother took no notice of what Kate said asking her to keep me, and I was not interested either.

One hour later I was on the Railway bus to Phokeng. During the early part of the journey I did not feel anything about the Greenside house I had worked in. I was not really myself, my thoughts dancing between Mrs. Plum, my uncle, my parents, and Phokeng, my home. I slept and woke up many times during the bus ride. Right through the ride I seemed to see, sometimes in sleep, sometimes between sleep and waking, a red car passing our bus, then running behind us. Each time I looked out it was not there.

Dreams came and passed. He tells me he says You have killed my seed I wanted my mother to know you are a woman in whom my seed can grow. . . . Before you make the police take you to jail make sure that it is for something big you should go to jail for, otherwise you will come out with a heart and mind that will bleed inside you and poison you. . . .

The bus stopped for a short while, which made me wake up.

The Black Crow, the club women . . . *Hei,* listen! I lie to the madam of our house and I say I had a telegram from my mother telling me she is very very sick. I show her a telegram my sister sent me as if Mother were writing. So I went home for a nice weekend. . . .

The laughter of the women woke me up, just in time for me to stop a line of saliva coming out over my lower lip. The bus was making plenty of dust now as it was running over part of the road they were digging up. I was sure the red car was just behind us, but it was not there when I woke.

Any one of you here who wants to be baptized or has a relative without a church who needs to be can come and see me in the office. . . . A round man with a fat tummy and sharp hungry eyes, a smile that goes a long, long way . . .

The bus was going uphill, heavily and noisily.

I kick a white man's dog, me, or throw it there if it has not been told the black people's law. . . . This is Mister Monty and this is Mister Malan. Now get up you lazy boys and meet Mister Kate. Hold out your hands and say hallo to him. . . . Karabo, bring two glasses there. . . . Wait a bit — What will you chew boys while Mister Kate and I have a drink? Nothing? Sure?

We were now going nicely on a straight tarred road and the trees rushed back. Mister Kate. What nonsense, I thought.

Look Karabo, Madam's dogs are dead. What? Poison. I killed them. She drove me out of a job did she not? For nothing. Now I want her to feel she drove me out for something. I came back when you were in your room and took the things and poisoned them. . . . And you know what? She has buried them in clean pink sheets in the garden. *Ao,* clean clean good sheets. I am going to dig them out and take one sheet do you want the other one? Yes, give me the other one I will send it to my mother. . . . *Hei*, Karabo, see here they come. Monty and Malan. The bloody fools they do not want to stay in their hole. Go back you silly fools. Oh you do not want to move eh? Come here, now I am going to throw you in the big pool. No, Dick! No Dick! no, no! Dick! They cannot speak do not kill things that cannot speak. Madam can speak for them she always does. No! Dick . . . !

I woke up with a jump after I had screamed Dick's name, almost hitting the window. My forehead was full of sweat. The red car also shot out of my sleep and was gone. I remembered a friend of ours who told us how she and the garden man had saved two white sheets in which their white master had buried their two dogs. They went to throw the dogs in a dam.

When I told my parents my story Father says to me he says, So long as you are in good health my child, it is good. The worker dies, work does not. There is always work. I know when I was a boy a strong sound body and a good mind were the biggest things in life. Work was always there, and the lazy man could never say there was no work. But today people see work as something bigger than everything else, bigger than health, because of money.

I reply I say, Those days are gone Papa. I must go back to the city after resting a little to look for work. I must look after you. Today people are too poor to be able to help you.

I knew when I left Greenside that I was going to return to Johannesburg to work. Money was little, but life was full and it was better than sitting in Phokeng and watching the sun rise and set. So I told Chimane to keep her eyes and ears open for a job.

I had been at Phokeng for one week when a red car arrived. Somebody was sitting in front with the driver, a white woman. At once I knew it to be that of Mrs. Plum. The man sitting beside her was showing her the way, for he pointed towards our house in front of which I was sitting. My heart missed a few beats. Both came out of the car. The white woman said Thank you to the man after he had spoken a few words to me.

I did not know what to do and how to look at her as she spoke to me. So I looked at the piece of cloth I was sewing pictures on. There was a tired but soft smile on her face. Then I remembered that she might want to sit. I went inside to fetch a low bench for her. When I remembered it afterwards, the thought came to me that there are things I never think white people can want to do at our homes when they visit for the first time: like sitting, drinking water or entering the house. This is how I thought when the white priest came to see us. One year at Easter Kate drove me home as she was going to the north. In the same way I was at a loss what to do for a few minutes.

Then Mrs. Plum says, I have come to ask you to come back to me, Karabo. Would you like to?

I say I do not know, I must think about it first.

She says, Can you think about it today? I can sleep at the town hotel and come back tomorrow morning, and if you want to you can return with me.

I wanted her to say she was sorry to have sent me away, I did not know how to make her say it because I know white people find it too much for them to say Sorry to a black person. As she was not saying it, I thought of two things to make it hard for her to get me back and maybe even lose me in the end.

I say, You must ask my father first, I do not know, should I call him?

Mrs. Plum says, Yes.

I fetched both Father and Mother. They greeted her while I brought benches. Then I told them what she wanted.

Father asks Mother and Mother asks Father. Father asks me. I say if they agree, I will think about it and tell her the next day.

Father says, It goes by what you feel my child.

I tell Mrs. Plum I say, if you want me to think about it I must know if you will want to put my wages up from £6 because it is too little.

She asks me, How much will you want?

Up by £4.

She looked down for a few moments.

And then I want two weeks at Easter and not just the weekend. I thought if she really wanted me she would want to pay for it. This would also show how sorry she was to lose me.

Mrs. Plum says, I can give you one week. You see you already have something like a rest when I am in Durban in the winter.

I tell her I say I shall think about it.

She left.

The next day she found me packed and ready to return with her. She was very much pleased and looked kinder than I had ever known her. And me, I felt sure of myself, more than I had ever done.

Mrs. Plum says to me, You will not find Monty and Malan.

Oh?

Yes, they were stolen the day after you left. The police have not found them yet. I think they are dead myself.

I thought of Dick . . . my dream. Could he? And she . . . did this woman come to ask me to return because she had lost two animals she loved?

Mrs. Plum says to me she says, You know, I like your people, Karabo, the Africans.

And Dick and Me? I wondered.   [1967]

BHARATI MUKHERJEE (b. 1940) was born in Calcutta, India. As a young girl she lived in London with her parents and sisters, but she returned to India in 1951 and was educated at the universities of Calcutta and Baroda. While studying for her doctorate at the University of Iowa Writers Workshop, she married the novelist Clark Blaise in 1963. For ten years they lived in Canada, where she published two novels, The Tiger's Daughter (1972) and Wife (1975). Mukherjee and her husband then lived for a year in India, an experience that led to their collaboration on the journal Days and Nights in Calcutta (1977). It describes their different impressions of the country — Blaise was fascinated by his introduction to Bengali life and culture, Mukherjee angered by the oppression of women in India.

In 1980 Mukherjee came to live in the United States where she began teaching at the University of Iowa. In Canada she had been conscious of racism: "I was frequently taken for a prostitute or a shoplifter, frequently assumed to be a domestic, praised by astonished auditers that I didn't have a 'singsong' accent. The society itself . . . routinely made crippling assumptions about me, and about my 'kind.'" In the United States, Mukherjee became more optimistic. She has described the note card pinned above her writing desk to give her inspiration. It quotes the showman Liberace, whom she admires as an "American original": "Too much of a good thing is simply wonderful." She feels that her writing has lost the "mordant and self-protected irony" she had adopted from her previous literary model, V. S. Naipaul. Her outlook is more tolerant in The Middleman and Other Stories (1988), the book that established her reputation in this country.

The critic Ann Mandel has understood that in her stories such as "The Management of Grief," Mukherjee is dramatizing the immigrant's "request for recognition — the desire to be 'visible' in honorable ways, to be recognized as a person rather than as an ethnic stereotype." The characters in The Middleman represent America's newest wave of Third World immigrants — Filipino, Salvadoran, Iraqi, Indian. Mukherjee's recent novels are Jasmine (1989) and The Holder of the World (1993).

RELATED COMMENTARY: Bharati Mukherjee, "A Four-Hundred-Year-Old Woman," page 1465.

BHARATI MUKHERJEE

The Management of Grief

A woman I don't know is boiling tea the Indian way in my kitchen. There are a lot of women I don't know in my kitchen, whispering and moving tactfully. They open doors, rummage through the pantry, and try not to ask me where things are kept. They remind me of when my sons were small, on Mother's Day or when Vikram and I were tired, and they would make big, sloppy omelets. I would lie in bed pretending I didn't hear them.

Dr. Sharma, the treasurer of the Indo-Canada Society, pulls me into the hallway. He wants to know if I am worried about money. His wife, who has just come up from the basement with a tray of empty cups and glasses, scolds him. "Don't bother Mrs. Bhave with mundane details." She looks so monstrously pregnant her baby must be days overdue. I tell her she shouldn't be carrying heavy things. "Shaila," she says, smiling, "this is the fifth." Then she grabs a teenager by his shirttails. He slips his Walkman off his head. He has to be one of her four children; they have the same domed and dented foreheads. "What's the official word now?" she demands. The boy slips the headphones back on. "They're acting evasive, Ma. They're saying it could be an accident or a terrorist bomb."

All morning, the boys have been muttering, Sikh bomb, Sikh bomb. The men, not using the word, bow their heads in agreement. Mrs. Sharma touches her forehead at such a word. At least they've stopped talking about space debris and Russian lasers.

Two radios are going in the dining room. They are tuned to different stations. Someone must have brought the radios down from my boys' bedrooms. I haven't gone into their rooms since Kusum came running across the front lawn in her bathrobe. She looked so funny, I was laughing when I opened the door.

The big TV in the den is being whizzed through American networks and cable channels.

"Damn!" some man swears bitterly. "How can these preachers carry on like nothing's happened?" I want to tell him we're not that important. You look at the audience, and at the preacher in his blue robe with his beautiful white hair, the potted palm trees under a blue sky, and you know they care about nothing.

The phone rings and rings. Dr. Sharma's taken charge. "We're with her," he keeps saying. "Yes, yes, the doctor has given calming pills. Yes, yes, pills are having necessary effect." I wonder if pills alone explain this calm. Not peace, just a deadening quiet. I was always controlled, but never repressed. Sound can reach me, but my body is tensed, ready to scream. I hear their voices all around me. I hear my boys and Vikram cry, "Mommy, Shaila!" and their screams insulate me, like headphones.

The woman boiling water tells her story again and again. "I got the news first. My cousin called from Halifax before six A.M., can you imagine? He'd gotten up for prayers and his son was studying for medical exams and heard on a rock channel that something had happened to a plane. They said first it had disappeared from the radar, like a giant eraser just reached out. His father called me, so I said to him, what do you mean, 'something bad'? You mean a hijacking? And he said, *Behn*, there is no confirmation of anything yet, but check with your neighbors because a lot of them must be on that plane. So I called poor Kusum straight-away. I knew Kusum's husband and daughter were booked to go yester-day."

Kusum lives across the street from me. She and Satish had moved in less than a month ago. They said they needed a bigger place. All these people, the Sharmas and friends from the Indo-Canada Society, had been there for the housewarming. Satish and Kusum made tandoori on their big gas grill and even the white neighbors piled their plates high with that luridly red, charred, juicy chicken. Their younger daughter had danced, and even our boys had broken away from the Stanley Cup telecast to put in a reluctant appearance. Everyone took pictures for their albums and for the community newspapers — another of our families had made it big in Toronto — and now I wonder how many of those happy faces are gone. "Why does God give us so much if all along He intends to take it away?" Kusum asks me.

I nod. We sit on carpeted stairs, holding hands like children. "I never once told him that I loved him," I say. I was too much the well-brought-up woman. I was so well brought up I never felt comfortable calling my husband by his first name.

"It's all right," Kusum says. "He knew. My husband knew. They felt it. Modern young girls have to say it because what they feel is fake."

Kusum's daughter Pam runs in with an overnight case. Pam's in her McDonald's uniform. "Mummy! You have to get dressed!" Panic makes her cranky. "A reporter's on his way here."

"Why?"

"You want to talk to him in your bathrobe?" She starts to brush her mother's long hair. She's the daughter who's always in trouble. She dates Canadian boys and hangs out in the mall, shopping for tight sweaters. The younger one, the goody-goody one according to Pam, the one with a voice so sweet that when she sang *bhajans* for Ethiopian relief even a frugal man like my husband wrote out a hundred-dollar check, *she* was on that plane. *She* was going to spend July and August with grandparents because Pam wouldn't go. Pam said she'd rather waitress at McDonald's. "If it's a choice between Bombay and Wonderland, I'm picking Wonderland," she'd said.

"Leave me alone," Kusum yells. "You know what I want to do? If I didn't have to look after you now, I'd hang myself."

Pam's young face goes blotchy with pain. "Thanks," she says, "don't let me stop you."

"Hush," pregnant Mrs. Sharma scolds Pam. "Leave your mother alone. Mr. Sharma will tackle the reporters and fill out the forms. He'll say what has to be said."

Pam stands her ground. "You think I don't know what Mummy's thinking? *Why her?* That's what. That's sick! Mummy wishes my little sister were alive and I were dead."

Kusum's hand in mine is trembly hot. We continue to sit on the stairs.

She calls before she arrives, wondering if there's anything I need. Her name is Judith Templeton and she's an appointee of the provincial government. "Multiculturalism?" I ask, and she says "partially," but that her mandate is bigger. "I've been told you knew many of the people on the flight," she says. "Perhaps if you'd agree to help us reach the others . . . ?"

She gives me time at least to put on tea water and pick up the mess in the front room. I have a few *samosas* from Kusum's housewarming that I could fry up, but then I think, why prolong this visit?

Judith Templeton is much younger than she sounded. She wears a blue suit with a white blouse and a polka-dot tie. Her blond hair is cut short, her only jewelry is pearl-drop earrings. Her briefcase is new and expensive looking, a gleaming cordovan leather. She sits with it across her lap. When she looks out the front windows onto the street, her contact lenses seem to float in front of her light blue eyes.

"What sort of help do you want from me?" I ask. She has refused the tea, out of politeness, but I insist, along with some slightly stale biscuits.

"I have no experience," she admits. "That is, I have an M.S.W. and I've worked in liaison with accident victims, but I mean I have no experience with a tragedy of this scale —"

"Who could?" I ask.

"— and with the complications of culture, language, and customs. Someone mentioned that Mrs. Bhave is a pillar — because you've taken it more calmly."

At this, perhaps, I frown, for she reaches forward, almost to take my hand. "I hope you understand my meaning, Mrs. Bhave. There are hundreds of people in Metro directly affected, like you, and some of them speak no English. There are some widows who've never handled money or gone on a bus, and there are old parents who still haven't eaten or gone outside their bedrooms. Some houses and apartments have been looted. Some wives are still hysterical. Some husbands are in shock and profound depression. We want to help, but our hands are tied in so many ways. We have to distribute money to some people, and there are legal documents — these things can be done. We have interpreters, but we don't always have the human touch, or maybe the right human touch. We don't want to make mistakes, Mrs. Bhave, and that's why we'd like to ask you to help us."

"More mistakes, you mean," I say.

"Police matters are not in my hands," she answers.

"Nothing I can do will make any difference," I say. "We must all grieve in our own way."

"But you are coping very well. All the people said, Mrs. Bhave is the strongest person of all. Perhaps if the others could see you, talk with you, it would help them."

"By the standards of the people you call hysterical, I am behaving very oddly and very badly, Miss Templeton." I want to say to, *I wish I could scream, starve, walk into Lake Ontario, jump from a bridge.* "They would not see me as a model. I do not see myself as a model."

I am a freak. No one who has ever known me would think of me reacting this way. This terrible calm will not go away.

She asks me if she may call again, after I get back from a long trip that we all must make. "Of course," I say. "Feel free to call, anytime."

Four days later, I find Kusum squatting on a rock overlooking a bay in Ireland. It isn't a big rock, but it juts sharply out over water. This is as close as we'll ever get to them. June breezes balloon out her sari and unpin her knee-length hair. She has the bewildered look of a sea creature whom the tides have stranded.

It's been one hundred hours since Kusum came stumbling and screaming across my lawn. Waiting around the hospital, we've heard many stories. The police, the diplomats, they tell us things thinking that we're strong, that knowledge is helpful to the grieving, and maybe it is. Some, I know, prefer ignorance, or their own versions. The plane broke into two, they say. Unconsciousness was instantaneous. No one suffered. My boys must have just finished their breakfasts. They loved eating on planes, they loved the smallness of plates, knives, and forks. Last year they saved the airline salt and pepper shakers. Half an hour more and they would have made it to Heathrow.

Kusum says that we can't escape our fate. She says that all those people — our husbands, my boys, her girl with the nightingale voice, all those Hindus, Christians, Sikhs, Muslims, Parsis, and atheists on that plane — were fated to die together off this beautiful bay. She learned this from a swami in Toronto.

I have my Valium.

Six of us "relatives" — two widows and four widowers — chose to spend the day today by the waters instead of sitting in a hospital room and scanning photographs of the dead. That's what they call us now: relatives. I've looked through twenty-seven photos in two days. They're very kind to us, the Irish are very understanding. Sometimes understanding means freeing a tourist bus for this trip to the bay, so we can pretend to spy our loved ones through the glassiness of waves or in sun-speckled cloud shapes.

I could die here, too, and be content.

"What is that, out there?" She's standing and flapping her hands, and for a moment I see a head shape bobbing in the waves. She's standing in the water, I on the boulder. The tide is low, and a round, black, head-sized rock has just risen from the waves. She returns, her sari end dripping and ruined, and her face is a twisted remnant of hope, the way mine was a hundred hours ago, still laughing but inwardly knowing that nothing but the ultimate tragedy could bring two women together at six o'clock on a Sunday morning. I watch her face sag into blankness.

"That water felt warm, Shaila," she says at length.

"You can't," I say. "We have to wait for our turn to come."

I haven't eaten in four days, haven't brushed my teeth.

"I know," she says. "I tell myself I have no right to grieve. They are in a better place than we are. My swami says depression is a sign of our selfishness."

Maybe I'm selfish. Selfishly I break away from Kusum and run, sandals slapping against stones, to the water's edge. What if my boys aren't lying pinned under the debris? What if they aren't stuck a mile below that innocent blue chop? What if, given the strong currents . . .

Now I've ruined my sari, one of my best. Kusum has joined me, knee deep in water that feels to me like a swimming pool. I could settle in the water, and my husband would take my hand and the boys would slap water in my face just to see me scream.

"Do you remember what good swimmers my boys were, Kusum?"

"I saw the medals," she says.

One of the widowers, Dr. Ranganathan from Montreal, walks out to us, carrying his shoes in one hand. He's an electrical engineer. Someone at the hotel mentioned his work is famous around the world, something about the place where physics and electricity come together. He has lost a huge family, something indescribable. "With some good luck," Dr. Ranganathan suggests to me, "a good swimmer could make it safely to some island. It is quite possible that there may be many, many microscopic islets scattered around."

"You're not just saying that?" I tell Dr. Ranganathan about Vinod, my elder son. Last year he took diving as well.

"It's a parent's duty to hope," he says. "It is foolish to rule out possibilities that have not been tested. I myself have not surrendered hope."

Kusum is sobbing once again. "Dear lady," he says, laying his free hand on her arm, and she calms down.

"Vinod is how old?" he asks me. He's very careful, as we all are. *Is,* not *was.*

"Fourteen. Yesterday he was fourteen. His father and uncle were going to take him down to the Taj and give him a big birthday party. I couldn't go with them because I couldn't get two weeks off from my stupid job in June." I process bills for a travel agent. June is a big travel month.

Dr. Ranganathan whips the pockets of his suit jacket inside out. Squashed roses, in darkening shades of pink, float on the water. He tore the roses off creepers in somebody's garden. He didn't ask anyone if he could pluck the roses, but now there's been an article about it in the local papers. When you see an Indian person, it says, please give them flowers.

"A strong youth of fourteen," he says, "can very likely pull to safety a younger one."

My sons, though four years apart, were very close. Vinod wouldn't let Mithun drown. *Electrical engineering,* I think, foolishly perhaps: this man knows important secrets of the universe, things closed to me. Relief spins me lightheaded. No wonder my boys' photographs haven't turned up in the gallery of photos of the recovered dead. "Such pretty roses," I say.

"My wife loved pink roses. Every Friday I had to bring a bunch home. I used to say, Why? After twenty-odd years of marriage you're still needing proof positive of my love?" He has identified his wife and three of his children. Then others from Montreal, the lucky ones, intact families with no survivors. He chuckles as he wades back to shore. Then he swings around to ask me a question. "Mrs. Bhave, you are wanting to throw in some roses for your loved ones? I have two big ones left."

But I have other things to float: Vinod's pocket calculator; a half-painted model B-52 for my Mithun. They'd want them on their island. And for my husband? For him I let fall into the calm, glassy waters a poem I wrote in the hospital yesterday. Finally he'll know my feelings for him.

"Don't tumble, the rocks are slippery," Dr. Ranganathan cautions. He holds out a hand for me to grab.

Then it's time to get back on the bus, time to rush back to our waiting posts on hospital benches.

Kusum is one of the lucky ones. The lucky ones flew here, identified in multiplicate their loved ones, then will fly to India with the bodies for proper ceremonies. Satish is one of the few males who surfaced. The photos of faces we saw on the walls in an office at Heathrow and here in the hospital are mostly of women. Women have more body fat, a nun said to me matter-of-factly. They float better.

Today I was stopped by a young sailor on the street. He had loaded bodies, he'd gone into the water when — he checks my face for signs of strength — when the sharks were first spotted. I don't blush, and he breaks down. "It's all right," I say. "Thank you." I heard about the sharks from Dr. Ranganathan. In his orderly mind, science brings understanding, it holds no terror. It is the shark's duty. For every deer there is a hunter, for every fish a fisherman.

The Irish are not shy; they rush to me and give me hugs and some are crying. I cannot imagine reactions like that on the streets of Toronto. Just strangers, and I am touched. Some carry flowers with them and give them to any Indian they see.

After lunch, a policeman I have gotten to know quite well catches hold of me. He says he thinks he has a match for Vinod. I explain what a good swimmer Vinod is.

"You want me with you when you look at photos?" Dr. Ranganathan walks ahead of me into the picture gallery. In these matters, he is a scientist, and I am grateful. It is a new perspective. "They have performed miracles," he says. "We are indebted to them."

The first day or two the policemen showed us relatives only one picture at a time; now they're in a hurry, they're eager to lay out the possibles, and even the probables.

The face on the photo is of a boy much like Vinod; the same intelligent eyes, the same thick brows dipping into a V. But this boy's features, even his cheeks, are puffier, wider, mushier.

"No." My gaze is pulled by other pictures. There are five other boys who look like Vinod.

The nun assigned to console me rubs the first picture with a fingertip. "When they've been in the water for a while, love, they look a little heavier."

The bones under the skin are broken, they said on the first day — try to adjust your memories. It's important.

"It's not him. I'm his mother. I'd know."

"I know this one!" Dr. Ranganathan cries out, and suddenly from the back of the gallery. "And this one!" I think he senses that I don't want to find my boys. "They are the Kutty brothers. They were also from Montreal." I don't mean to be crying. On the contrary, I am ecstatic. My suitcase in the hotel is packed heavy with dry clothes for my boys.

The policeman starts to cry. "I am so sorry. I am so sorry, ma'am. I really thought we had a match."

With the nun ahead of us and the policeman behind, we, the unlucky ones without our children's bodies, file out of the makeshift gallery.

From Ireland most of us go on to India. Kusum and I take the same direct flight to Bombay, so I can help her clear customs quickly. But we have to argue with a man in uniform. He has large boils on his face. The boils swell and glow with sweat as we argue with him. He wants Kusum to wait in line and he refuses to take authority because his boss is on a tea break. But Kusum won't let her coffins out of sight, and I shan't desert her though I know that my parents, elderly and diabetic, must be waiting in a stuffy car in a scorching lot.

"You bastard!" I scream at the man with the popping boils. Other passengers press closer. "You think we're smuggling contraband in those coffins!"

Once upon a time we were well-brought-up women; we were dutiful wives who kept our heads veiled, our voices shy and sweet.

In India, I become, once again, an only child of rich, ailing parents. Old friends of the family come to pay their respects. Some are Sikh, and inwardly, involuntarily, I cringe. My parents are progressive people; they do not blame communities for a few individuals.

In Canada it is a different story now.

"Stay longer," my mother pleads. "Canada is a cold place. Why would you want to be by yourself?" I stay.

Three months pass. Then another.

"Vikram wouldn't have wanted you to give up things!" they protest. They call my husband by the name he was born with. In Toronto he'd changed to Vik so the men he worked with at his office would find his name as easy as Rod or Chris. "You know, the dead aren't cut off from us!"

My grandmother, the spoiled daughter of a rich zamindar, shaved her head with rusty razor blades when she was widowed at sixteen. My grandfather died of childhood diabetes when he was nineteen, and she saw herself as the harbinger of bad luck. My mother grew up without parents, raised indifferently by an uncle, while her true mother slept in a hut behind the main estate house and took her food with the servants. She grew up a rationalist. My parents abhor mindless mortification.

The zamindar's daughter kept stubborn faith in Vedic rituals; my parents rebelled. I am trapped between two modes of knowledge. At thirty-six,

I am too old to start over and too young to give up. Like my husband's spirit, I flutter between worlds.

Courting aphasia, we travel. We travel with our phalanx of servants and poor relatives. To hill stations and to beach resorts. We play contract bridge in dusty gymkhana clubs. We ride stubby ponies up crumbly mountain trails. At tea dances, we let ourselves be twirled twice round the ballroom. We hit the holy spots we hadn't made time for before. In Varanasi, Kalighat, Rishikesh, Hardwar, astrologers and palmists seek me out and for a fee offer me cosmic consolations.

Already the widowers among us are being shown new bride candidates. They cannot resist the call of custom, the authority of their parents and older brothers. They must marry; it is the duty of a man to look after a wife. The new wives will be young widows with children, destitute but of good family. They will make loving wives, but the men will shun them. I've had calls from the men over crackling Indian telephone lines. "Save me," they say, these substantial, educated, successful men of forty. "My parents are arranging a marriage for me." In a month they will have buried one family and returned to Canada with a new bride and partial family.

I am comparatively lucky. No one here thinks of arranging a husband for an unlucky widow.

Then, on the third day of the sixth month into this odyssey, in an abandoned temple in a tiny Himalayan village, as I make my offering of flowers and sweetmeats to the god of a tribe of animists, my husband descends to me. He is squatting next to a scrawny sadhu in moth-eaten robes. Vikram wears the vanilla suit he wore the last time I hugged him. The sadhu tosses petals on a butter-fed flame, reciting Sanskrit mantras, and sweeps his face of flies. My husband takes my hands in his.

You're beautiful, he starts. Then, *What are you doing here?*

Shall I stay? I ask. He only smiles, but already the image is fading. *You must finish alone what we started together.* No seaweed wreathes his mouth. He speaks too fast, just as he used to when we were an envied family in our pink split-level. He is gone.

In the windowless altar room, smoky with joss sticks and clarified butter lamps, a sweaty hand gropes for my blouse. I do not shriek. The sadhu arranges his roe. The lamps hiss and sputter out.

When we come out of the temple, my mother says, "Did you feel something weird in there?"

My mother has no patience with ghosts, prophetic dreams, holy men, and cults.

"No," I lie. "Nothing."

But she knows that she's lost me. She knows that in days I shall be leaving.

Kusum's put up her house for sale. She wants to live in an ashram in Hardwar. Moving to Hardwar was her swami's idea. Her swami runs two ashrams, the one in Hardwar and another here in Toronto.

"Don't run away," I tell her.

"I'm not running away," she says. "I'm pursuing inner peace. You think you or that Ranganathan fellow are better off?"

Pam's left for California. She wants to do some modeling, she says. She says when she comes into her share of the insurance money she'll open a yoga-cum-aerobics studio in Hollywood. She sends me postcards so naughty I daren't leave them on the coffee table. Her mother has withdrawn from her and the world.

The rest of us don't lose touch, that's the point. Talk is all we have, says Dr. Ranganathan, who has also resisted his relatives and returned to Montreal and to his job, alone. He says, Whom better to talk with than other relatives? We've been melted down and recast as a new tribe.

He calls me twice a week from Montreal. Every Wednesday night and every Saturday afternoon. He is changing jobs, going to Ottawa. But Ottawa is over a hundred miles away, and he is forced to drive two hundred and twenty miles a day from his home in Montreal. He can't bring himself to sell his house. The house is a temple, he says; the king-sized bed in the master bedroom is a shrine. He sleeps on a folding cot. A devotee.

There are still some hysterical relatives. Judith Templeton's list of those needing help and those who've "accepted" is in nearly perfect balance. Acceptance means you speak of your family in the past tense and you make active plans for moving ahead with your life. There are courses at Seneca and Ryerson we could be taking. Her gleaming leather briefcase is full of college catalogues and lists of cultural societies that need our help. She has done impressive work, I tell her.

"In the textbooks on grief management," she replies — I am her confidante, I realize, one of the few whose grief has not sprung bizarre obsessions — "there are stages to pass through: rejection, depression, acceptance, reconstruction." She has compiled a chart and finds that six months after the tragedy, none of us still rejects reality, but only a handful are reconstructing. "Depressed acceptance" is the plateau we've reached. Remarriage is a major step in reconstruction (though she's a little surprised, even shocked, over *how* quickly some of the men have taken on new families). Selling one's house and changing jobs and cities is healthy.

How to tell Judith Templeton that my family surrounds me, and that like creatures in epics, they've changed shapes? She sees me as calm and accepting but worries that I have no job, no career. My closest friends are worse off than I. I cannot tell her my days, even my nights, are thrilling.

She asks me to help with families she can't reach at all. An elderly couple in Agincourt whose sons were killed just weeks after they had brought their parents over from a village in Punjab. From their names, I know they are Sikh. Judith Templeton and a translator have visited them twice with offers of money for airfare to Ireland, with bank forms, power-of-attorney forms, but they have refused to sign, or to leave their tiny apartment. Their sons' money is frozen in the bank. Their sons' investment apartments have been trashed by tenants, the furnishings sold off. The parents fear that anything they sign or any money they receive will end the company's or the country's obligations to them. They fear they are selling their sons for two airline tickets to a place they've never seen.

The high-rise apartment is a tower of Indians and West Indians, with a sprinkling of Orientals. The nearest bus-stop kiosk is lined with women in saris. Boys practice cricket in the parking lot. Inside the building, even I wince a bit from the ferocity of onion fumes, the distinctive and immediate Indianness of frying ghee, but Judith Templeton maintains a steady flow of information. These poor old people are in imminent danger of losing their place and all their services.

I say to her, "They are Sikh. They will not open up to a Hindu woman." And what I want to add is, as much as I try not to, I stiffen now at the sight of beards and turbans. I remember a time when we all trusted each other in this new country, it was only the new country we worried about.

The two rooms are dark and stuffy. The lights are off, and an oil lamp sputters on the coffee table. The bent old lady has let us in, and her husband is wrapping a white turban over his oiled, hip-length hair. She immediately goes to the kitchen, and I hear the most familiar sound of an Indian home, tap water hitting and filling a teapot.

They have not paid their utility bills, out of fear and inability to write a check. The telephone is gone, electricity and gas and water are soon to follow. They have told Judith their sons will provide. They are good boys, and they have always earned and looked after their parents.

We converse a bit in Hindi. They do not ask about the crash and I wonder if I should bring it up. If they think I am here merely as a translator, then they may feel insulted. There are thousands of Punjabi speakers, Sikhs, in Toronto to do a better job. And so I say to the old lady, "I too have lost my sons, and my husband, in the crash."

Her eyes immediately fill with tears. The man mutters a few words which sound like a blessing. "God provides and God takes away," he says.

I want to say, But only men destroy and give back nothing. "My boys and my husband are not coming back," I say. "We have to understand that."

Now the old woman responds. "But who is to say? Man alone does not decide these things." To this her husband adds his agreement.

Judith asks about the bank papers, the release forms. With a stroke of the pen, they will have a provincial trustee to pay their bills, invest their money, send them a monthly pension.

"Do you know this woman?" I ask them.

The man raises his hand from the table, turns it over, and seems to regard each finger separately before he answers. "This young lady is always coming here, we make tea for her, and she leaves papers for us to sign." His eyes scan a pile of papers in the corner of the room. "Soon we will be out of tea, then will she go away?"

The old lady adds, "I have asked my neighbors and no one else gets *angrezi* visitors. What have we done?"

"It's her job," I try to explain. "The government is worried. Soon you will have no place to stay, no lights, no gas, no water."

"Government will get its money. Tell her not to worry, we are honorable people."

I try to explain the government wishes to give money, not take. He raises his hand. "Let them take," he says. "We are accustomed to that. That is no problem."

"We are strong people," says the wife. "Tell her that."

"Who needs all this machinery?" demands the husband. "It is unhealthy, the bright lights, the cold air on a hot day, the cold food, the four gas rings. God will provide, not government."

"When our boys return," the mother says.

Her husband sucks his teeth. "Enough talk," he says.

Judith breaks in. "Have you convinced them?" The snaps on her cordovan briefcase go off like firecrackers in that quiet apartment. She lays the sheaf of legal papers on the coffee table. "If they can't write their names, an X will do — I've told them that."

Now the old lady has shuffled to the kitchen and soon emerges with a pot of tea and two cups. "I think my bladder will go first on a job like this," Judith says to me, smiling. "If only there was some way of reaching them. Please thank her for the tea. Tell her she's very kind."

I nod in Judith's direction and tell them in Hindi, "She thanks you for the tea. She thinks you are being very hospitable but she doesn't have the slightest idea what it means."

I want to say, Humor her. I want to say, My boys and my husband are with me too, more than ever. I look in the old man's eyes and I can read his stubborn, peasant's message: *I have protected this woman as best I can. She is the only person I have left. Give to me or take from me what you will, but I will not sign for it. I will not pretend that I accept.*

In the car, Judith says, "You see what I'm up against? I'm sure they're lovely people, but their stubbornness and ignorance are driving me crazy. They think signing a paper is signing their sons' death warrants, don't they?"

I am looking out the window. I want to say, *In our culture, it is a parent's duty to hope.*

"Now Shaila, this next woman is a real mess. She cries day and night, and she refuses all medical help. We may have to —"

"Let me out at the subway," I say.

"I beg your pardon?" I can feel those blue eyes staring at me.

It would not be like her to disobey. She merely disapproves, and slows at a corner to let me out. Her voice is plaintive. "Is there anything I said? Anything I did?"

I could answer her suddenly in a dozen ways, but I choose not to. "Shaila? Let's talk about it," I hear, then slam the door.

A wife and mother begins her life in a new country, and that life is cut short. Yet her husband tells her: Complete what we have started. We, who stayed out of politics and came half way around the world to avoid religious and political feuding, have been the first in the New World to die from it. I no longer know what we started, nor how to complete it. I write letters to the editors of local papers and to members of Parliament. Now at least they admit it was a bomb. One MP answers back, with sympathy, but with a challenge. You want to make a difference? Work on a campaign. Work on mine. Politicize the Indian voter.

My husband's old lawyer helps me set up a trust. Vikram was a saver and a careful investor. He had saved the boys' boarding school and college fees. I sell the pink house at four times what we paid for it and take a small apartment downtown. I am looking for a charity to support.

We are deep in the Toronto winter, gray skies, icy pavements. I stay indoors, watching television. I have tried to assess my situation, how best to live my life, to complete what we began so many years ago. Kusum has written me from Hardwar that her life is now serene. She has seen Satish and has heard her daughter sing again. Kusum was on a pilgrimage, passing through a village, when she heard a young girl's voice, singing one of her daughter's favorite *bhajans*. She followed the music through the squalor of a Himalayan village, to a hut where a young girl, an exact replica of her daughter, was fanning coals under the kitchen fire. When she appeared, the girl cried out, "Ma!" and ran away. What did I think of that?

I think I can only envy her.

Pam didn't make it to California, but writes me from Vancouver. She works in a department store, giving makeup hints to Indian and Oriental girls. Dr. Ranganathan has given up his commute, given up his house and job, and accepted an academic position in Texas, where no one knows his story and he has vowed not to tell it. He calls me now once a week.

I wait, I listen and I pray, but Vikram has not returned to me. The voices and the shapes and the nights filled with visions ended abruptly several weeks ago.

I take it as a sign.

One rare, beautiful, sunny day last week, returning from a small errand on Yonge Street, I was walking through the park from the subway to my apartment. I live equidistant from the Ontario Houses of Parliament and the University of Toronto. The day was not cold, but something in the bare trees caught my attention. I looked up from the gravel, into the branches and the clear blue sky beyond. I thought I heard the rustling of larger forms, and I waited a moment for voices. Nothing.

"What?" I asked.

Then as I stood in the path looking north to Queen's Park and west to the university, I heard the voices of my family one last time. *Your time has come,* they said. *Go, be brave.*

I do not know where this voyage I have begun will end. I do not know which direction I will take. I dropped the package on a park bench and started walking.   [1988]

ALICE MUNRO *(b. 1931) grew up on a farm in a rural community near Lake Huron in Ontario, Canada, where her father raised silver foxes. After attending the University of Western Ontario for two years, she married and moved to British Columbia. Munro remembers that she began writing things down when she was about twelve, and at age fifteen she decided she would soon write a great novel: "But I thought perhaps I wasn't ready so I would write a short story in the meantime." She began publishing her stories when she was a university student, but her writing progressed very slowly during the next several years after she remarried and raised a family. "I never intended to be a short story writer," she has explained. "I started writing them because I didn't have time to write anything else — I had three children. And then I got used to writing stories, so I saw my material that way, and now I don't think I'll ever write a novel." In 1968 Munro published her first collection of stories,* Dance of the Happy Shades, *which won the Governor General's Award in Canada. Three years later she published her second book,* Lives of Girls and Women. *Another collection of stories,* Something I've Been Meaning to Tell You, *appeared in 1974, and a series of connected stories titled* Who Do You Think You Are? *was published in 1978, giving Munro her second Governor General's Award. She won her third with* The Progress of Love *in 1987. Her most recent book,* Friend of My Youth, *was published in 1990.*

Almost all Munro's stories are set in southern Ontario, where she grew up and now lives with her second husband. She sees herself as an anachronism, "because I write about places where your roots are and most people don't live that kind of life any more at all. Most writers, probably, the writers who are most in tune with our time, write about places that have no texture because this is where most of us live."

Although Lives of Girls and Women *was published as a novel, Munro first wrote it as a series of stories, which she later revised in a loosely patterned autobiographical structure. Frequently her narrator is a young girl, who notes in great detail what she sees around her, while conveying a poignant sense of her own subjectivity, as in "Walker Brothers Cowboy." Literary critics have observed that Munro's stories about small town life are reminiscent of the fiction of American writers such as Flannery O'Connor and Eudora Welty.*

A L I C E   M U N R O

Walker Brothers Cowboy

After supper my father says, "Want to go down and see if the Lake's still there?" We leave my mother sewing under the dining-room light, making clothes for me against the opening of school. She has ripped up for this purpose an old suit and an old plaid wool dress of hers, and she has to cut and match very cleverly and also make me stand and turn for endless fittings, sweaty, itchy from the hot wool, ungrateful. We leave my brother in bed in the little screened porch at the end of the front verandah, and sometimes he kneels on his bed and presses his face against the screen and calls mournfully, "Bring me an ice cream cone!" but I call back, "You will be asleep," and do not even turn my head.

Then my father and I walk gradually down the long, shabby sort of street, with Silverwoods Ice Cream signs standing on the sidewalk, outside tiny, lighted stores. This is in Tuppertown, an old town on Lake Huron, an old grain port. The street is shaded, in some places, by maple trees whose roots have cracked and heaved the sidewalk and spread out like crocodiles into the bare yards. People are sitting out, men in shirt-sleeves and under-shirts and women in aprons — not people we know but if anybody looks ready to nod and say, "Warm night," my father will nod too and say something the same. Children are still playing. I don't know them either because my mother keeps my brother and me in our own yard, saying he is too young to leave it and I to mind him. I am not so sad to watch their evening games because the games themselves are ragged, dissolving. Children, of their own will, draw apart, separate into islands of two or one under the heavy trees, occupying themselves in such solitary ways as I do all day, planting pebbles in the dirt or writing in it with a stick.

Presently we leave these yards and houses behind, we pass a factory with boarded-up windows, a lumberyard whose high wooden gates are locked for the night. Then the town falls away in a defeated jumble of shreds and small junkyards, the sidewalk gives up and we are walking on a sandy path with burdocks, plantains, humble nameless weeds all around. We enter a vacant lot, a kind of park really, for it is kept clear of junk and there is one bench with a slat missing on the back, a place to sit and look at the water. Which is generally grey in the evening, under a lightly overcast sky, no sunsets, the horizon dim. A very quiet, washing noise on the stones of the beach. Further along, towards the main part of town, there is a stretch of sand, a water slide, floats bobbing around the safe swimming area, a life guard's rickety throne. Also a long dark green building, like a roofed verandah, called the Pavilion, full of farmers and their wives, in stiff good clothes, on Sundays. That is the part of the town we used to know when we lived at Dungannon and came here three or four times a summer, to the Lake. That, and the docks where we would go and look at the grain boats, ancient, rusty, wallowing, making us wonder how they got past the breakwater let alone to Fort William.

Tramps hang around the docks and occasionally on these evenings wander up the dwindling beach and climb the shifting, precarious path boys have made, hanging onto dry bushes, and say something to my father which, being frightened of tramps, I am too alarmed to catch. My father says he is a bit hard up himself. "I'll roll you a cigarette if it's any use to you," he says, and he shakes tobacco out carefully on one of the thin butterfly papers, flicks it with his tongue, seals it, and hands it to the tramp who takes it and walks away. My father also rolls and lights and smokes one cigarette of his own.

He tells me how the Great Lakes came to be. All where Lake Huron is now, he says, used to be flat land, a wide flat plain. Then came the ice, creeping down from the north, pushing deep into the low places. Like *that* — and he shows me his hand with his spread fingers pressing the rock-hard ground where we are sitting. His fingers make hardly any impression at all and he says, "Well, the old ice cap had a lot more power behind it than this hand has." And then the ice went back, shrank back towards the North Pole where it came from, and left its fingers of ice in the deep places it had gouged, and ice turned to lakes and there they were today. They were *new*, as time went. I try to see that plain before me, dinosaurs walking on it, but I am not able even to imagine the shore of the Lake when the Indians were there, before Tuppertown. The tiny share we have of time appalls me, though my father seems to regard it with tranquillity. Even my father, who sometimes seems to me to have been at home in the world as long as it has lasted, has really lived on this earth only a little longer than I have, in terms of all the time there has been to live in. He has not known a time, any more than I, when automobiles and electric lights did not at least exist. He was not alive when this century started. I will be barely alive — old, old — when it ends. I do not like to think of it. I wish the Lake to be always just a lake, with the safe-swimming floats marking it, and the breakwater and the lights of Tuppertown.

My father has a job, selling for Walker Brothers. This is a firm that sells almost entirely in the country, the back country. Sunshine, Boylesbridge, Turnaround — that is all his territory. Not Dungannon where we used to live, Dungannon is too near town and my mother is grateful for that. He sells cough medicine, iron tonic, corn plasters, laxatives, pills for female disorders, mouth wash, shampoo, liniment, salves, lemon and orange and raspberry concentrate for making refreshing drinks, vanilla, food colouring, black and green tea, ginger, cloves and other spices, rat poison. He has a song about it, and these two lines:

And have all linaments and oils,
For everything from corns to boils. . . .

Not a very funny song, in my mother's opinion. A pedlar's song, and that is what he is, a pedlar knocking at backwoods kitchens. Up until last winter we had our own business, a fox farm. My father raised silver foxes and sold their pelts to the people who make them into capes and coats and muffs. Prices fell, my father hung on hoping they would get better next year, and they fell again, and he hung on one more year and one more and finally it was not possible to hang on any more, we owed everything to the feed company. I have heard my mother explain this, several times, to Mrs. Oliphant who is the only neighbour she talks to. (Mrs. Oliphant also has come down in the world, being a schoolteacher who married the janitor.) We poured all we had into it, my mother says, and we came out with nothing. Many people could say the same thing, these days, but my mother has no time for the national calamity, only ours. Fate has flung us onto a street of poor people (it does not matter that we were poor before, that was a different sort of poverty), and the only way to take this, as she sees it, is with dignity, with bitterness, with no reconciliation. No bathroom with a claw-footed tub and a flush toilet is going to comfort her, nor water on tap and sidewalks past the house and milk in bottles, not even the two movie theatres and the Venus Restaurant and Woolworths so marvellous it has live birds singing in its fan-cooled corners and fish as tiny as fingernails, as bright as moons, swimming in its green tanks. My mother does not care.

In the afternoons she often walks to Simon's Grocery and takes me with her to help carry things. She wears a good dress, navy blue with little flowers, sheer, worn over a navy-blue slip. Also a summer hat of white straw, pushed down on the side of the head, and white shoes I have just whitened on a newspaper on the back steps. I have my hair freshly done in long damp curls which the dry air will fortunately soon loosen, a stiff large hair-ribbon on top of my head. This is entirely different from going out after supper with my father. We have not walked past two houses before I feel we have become objects of universal ridicule. Even the dirty words chalked on the sidewalk are laughing at us. My mother does not seem to notice. She walks serenely like a lady shopping, like a *lady* shopping, past the housewives in loose beltless dresses torn under the arms. With me her creation, wretched curls and flaunting hair bow, scrubbed knees and white socks — all I do not want to be. I loathe even my name when she says it in public, in a voice so high, proud, and ringing, deliberately different from the voice of any other mother on the street.

My mother will sometimes carry home, for a treat, a brick of ice cream — pale Neapolitan; and because we have no refrigerator in our house we wake my brother and eat it at once in the dining room, always darkened by the wall of the house next door. I spoon it up tenderly, leaving the chocolate till last, hoping to have some still to eat when my brother's dish is empty. My mother tries then to imitate the conversations we used to have at Dungannon, going back to our earliest, most leisurely days before my brother was born, when she would give me a little tea and a lot of milk in a cup like hers and we would sit out on the step facing the pump, the lilac tree, the fox pens beyond. She is not able to keep from mentioning those days. "Do you remember when we put you in your sled and Major pulled you?" (Major our dog, that we had to leave with neighbours when we moved.) "Do you remember your sandbox outside the kitchen window?" I pretend to remember far less than I do, wary of being trapped into sympathy or any unwanted emotion.

My mother has headaches. She often has to lie down. She lies on my brother's narrow bed in the little screened porch, shaded by heavy branches. "I look up at that tree and I think I am at home," she says.

"What you need," my father tells her, "is some fresh air and a drive in the country." He means for her to go with him, on his Walker Brothers route.

That is not my mother's idea of a drive in the country.

"Can I come?"

"Your mother might want you for trying on clothes."

"I'm beyond sewing this afternoon," my mother says.

"I'll take her then. Take both of them, give you a rest."

What is there about us that people need to be given a rest from? Never mind. I am glad enough to find my brother and make him go to the toilet and get us both into the car, our knees unscrubbed, my hair unringleted. My father brings from the house his two heavy brown suitcases, full of bottles, and sets them on the back seat. He wears a white shirt, brilliant in the sunlight, a tie, light trousers belonging to his summer suit (his other suit is black, for funerals, and belonged to my uncle before he died), and a creamy straw hat. His salesman's outfit, with pencils clipped in the shirt pocket. He goes back once again, probably to say goodbye to my mother, to ask her if she is sure she doesn't want to come, and hear her say, "No. No thanks, I'm better just to lie here with my eyes closed." Then we are backing out of the driveway with the rising hope of adventure, just the little hope that takes you over the bump into the street, the hot air starting to move, turning into a breeze, the houses growing less and less familiar as we follow the short cut my father knows, the quick way out of town. Yet what is there waiting for us all afternoon but hot hours in stricken farmyards, perhaps a stop at a country store and three ice cream cones or bottles of pop, and my father singing? The one he made up about himself has a title — "The Walker Brothers Cowboy" — and it starts out like this:

> Old Ned Fields, he now is dead,
> So I am ridin' the route instead. . . .

Who is Ned Fields? The man he has replaced, surely, and if so he really is dead; yet my father's voice is mournful-jolly, making his death some kind of nonsense, a comic calamity. "Wisht I was back on the Rio Grande, plungin' through the dusky sand." My father sings most of the time while driving the car. Even now, heading out of town, crossing the bridge and taking the sharp turn onto the highway, he is humming something, mumbling a bit of a song to himself, just tuning up, really, getting ready to improvise, for out along the highway we pass the Baptist Camp, the Vacation Bible Camp, and he lets loose:

> Where are the Baptists, where are the Baptists,
> where are all the Baptists today?
> They're down in the water, in Lake Huron water,
> with their sins all a-gittin' washed away.

My brother takes this for straight truth and gets up on his knees trying to see down to the Lake. "I don't see any Baptists," he says accusingly. "Neither do I, son," says my father. "I told you, they're down in the Lake."

No roads paved when we left the highway. We have to roll up the windows because of dust. The land is flat, scorched, empty. Bush lots at the back of the farms hold shade, black pine-shade like pools nobody can ever get to. We bump up a long lane and at the end of it what could look more unwelcoming, more deserted than the tall unpainted farmhouse with grass growing uncut right up to the front door, green blinds down and a door upstairs opening on nothing but air? Many houses have this door, and I have never yet been able to find out why. I ask my father and he says they are for walking in your sleep. *What?* Well if you happen to be walking in your sleep and you want to step outside. I am offended, seeing too late that he is joking, as usual, but my brother says sturdily, "If they did that they would break their necks."

The nineteen-thirties. How much this kind of farmhouse, this kind of afternoon, seem to me to belong to that one decade in time, just as my father's hat does, his bright flared tie, our car with its wide running board (an Essex, and long past its prime). Cars somewhat like it, many older, none dustier, sit in the farmyards. Some are past running and have their doors pulled off, their seats removed for use on porches. No living things to be seen, chickens or cattle. Except dogs. There are dogs, lying in any kind of shade they can find, dreaming, their lean sides rising and sinking rapidly. They get up when my father opens the car door, he has to speak to them. "Nice boy, there's a boy, nice old boy." They quiet down, go back to their shade. He should know how to quiet animals, he has held desperate foxes with tongs around their necks. One gentling voice for the dogs and another, rousing, cheerful, for calling at doors. "Hello there, Missus, it's the Walker Brothers man and what are you out of today?" A door opens, he disappears. Forbidden to follow, forbidden even to leave the car, we can just wait and wonder what he says. Sometimes trying to make my mother laugh he pretends to be himself in a farm kitchen, spreading out his sample case. "Now then, Missus, are you troubled with parasitic life? Your children's scalps, I mean. All those crawly little things we're too polite to mention that show up on the heads of the best of families? Soap alone is useless, kerosene is not too nice a perfume, but I have here —" Or else, "Believe me, sitting and driving all day the way I do I *know* the value of these fine pills. Natural relief. A problem common to old folks, too, once their days of activity are over — How about you, Grandma?" He would wave the imaginary box of pills under my mother's nose and she would laugh finally, unwillingly. "He doesn't say that really, does he?" I said, and she said no of course not, he was too much of a gentleman.

One yard after another, then, the old cars, the pumps, dogs, views of grey barns and falling-down sheds and unturning windmills. The men, if they are working in the fields, are not in any fields that we can see. The children are far away, following dry creek beds or looking for blackberries, or else they are hidden in the house, spying at us through cracks in the blinds. The car seat has grown slick with our sweat. I dare my brother to sound the horn, wanting to do it myself but not wanting to get the blame. He knows better. We play *I Spy*, but it is hard to find many colours. Grey for the barns and sheds and toilets and houses, brown for the yard and fields, black or brown for the dogs. The rusting cars show rainbow patches, in which I strain to pick out purple or green; likewise I peer at doors for shreds of old peeling paint, maroon or yellow. We can't play with letters, which would be better, because my brother is too young to spell. The game disintegrates anyway. He claims my colours are not fair, and wants extra turns.

In one house no door opens, though the car is in the yard. My father knocks and whistles, calls, "Hullo there! Walker Brothers man!" but there is not a stir of reply anywhere. This house has no porch, just a bare, slanting slab of cement on which my father stands. He turns around, searching the barnyard, the barn whose mow must be empty because you can see the sky through it, and finally he bends to pick up his suitcases. Just then a window is opened upstairs, a white pot appears on the sill, is tilted over and its contents splash down the outside wall. The window is not directly above my father's head, so only a stray splash would catch him. He picks up his suitcases with no particular hurry and walks, no longer whistling, to the car. "Do you know what that was?" I say to my brother. "*Pee.*" He laughs and laughs.

My father rolls and lights a cigarette before he starts the car. The window has been slammed down, the blind drawn, we never did see a hand or face. "Pee, pee," sings my brother ecstatically. "Somebody dumped down pee!" "Just don't tell your mother that," my father says. "She isn't liable to see the joke." "Is it in your song?" my brother wants to know. My father says no but he will see what he can do to work it in.

I notice in a little while that we are not turning in any more lanes, though it does not seem to me that we are headed home. "Is this the way to Sunshine?" I ask my father, and he answers, "No ma'am it's not." "Are we still in your territory?" He shakes his head. "We're going *fast*," my brother says approvingly, and in fact we are bouncing along through dry puddle-holes so that all the bottles in the suitcases clink together and gurgle promisingly.

Another lane, a house, also unpainted, dried to silver in the sun.

"I thought we were out of your territory."

"We are."

"Then what are we going in here for?"

"You'll see."

In front of the house a short, sturdy woman is picking up washing, which had been spread on the grass to bleach and dry. When the car stops she stares at it hard for a moment, bends to pick up a couple more towels to add to the bundle under her arm, comes across to us, and says in a flat voice, neither welcoming nor unfriendly, "Have you lost your way?"

My father takes his time getting out of the car. "I don't think so," he says. "I'm the Walker Brothers man."

"George Golley is our Walker Brothers man," the woman says, "and he was out here no more than a week ago. Oh, my Lord God," she says harshly, "it's you."

"It was, the last time I looked in the mirror," my father says. The woman gathers all the towels in front of her and holds on to them tightly, pushing them against her stomach as if it hurt. "Of all the people I never thought to see. And telling me you were the Walker Brothers man."

"I'm sorry if you were looking forward to George Golley," my father says humbly.

"And look at me, I was prepared to clean the hen-house. You'll think that's just an excuse but it's true. I don't go round looking like this every day." She is wearing a farmer's straw hat, through which pricks of sunlight penetrate and float on her face, a loose, dirty print smock, and running shoes. "Who are those in the car, Ben? They're not yours?"

"Well I hope and believe they are," my father says, and tells our names and ages. "Come on, you can get out. This is Nora, Miss Cronin. Nora, you better tell me, is it still Miss, or have you got a husband hiding in the woodshed?"

"If I had a husband that's not where I'd keep him, Ben," she says, and they both laugh, her laugh abrupt and somewhat angry. "You'll think I got no manners, as well as being dressed like a tramp," she says. "Come on in out of the sun. It's cool in the house."

We go across the yard ("Excuse me taking you in this way but I don't think the front door has been opened since Papa's funeral, I'm afraid the hinges might drop off"), up the porch steps, into the kitchen, which really is cool, high ceilinged, the blinds of course down, a simple, clean, threadbare room with waxed worn linoleum, potted geraniums, drinking-pail and dipper, a round table with scrubbed oilcloth. In spite of the cleanness, the wiped and swept surfaces, there is a faint sour smell — maybe of the dishrag or the tin dipper or the oilcloth, or the old lady, because there is one, sitting in an easy chair under the clock shelf. She turns her head slightly in our direction and says, "Nora? Is that company?"

"Blind," says Nora in a quick explaining voice to my father. Then, "You won't guess who it is, Momma. Hear his voice."

My father goes to the front of her chair and bends and says hopefully, "Afternoon, Mrs. Cronin."

"Ben Jordan," says the old lady with no surprise. "You haven't been to see us in the longest time. Have you been out of the country?"

My father and Nora look at each other.

"He's married, Momma," says Nora cheerfully and aggressively. "Married and got two children and here they are." She pulls us forward, makes each of us touch the old lady's dry, cool hand while she says our names in turn. Blind! This is the first blind person I have ever seen close up. Her eyes are closed, the eyelids sunk away down, showing no shape of the eyeball, just hollows. From one hollow comes a drop of silver liquid, a medicine, or a miraculous tear.

"Let me get into a decent dress," Nora says. "Talk to Momma. It's a treat for her. We hardly ever see company, do we Momma?"

"Not many makes it out this road," says the old lady placidly. "And the ones that used to be around here, our old neighbours, some of them have pulled out."

"True everywhere," my father says.

"Where's your wife then?"

"Home. She's not too fond of the hot weather, makes her feel poorly."

"Well." This is a habit of country people, old people, to say "well," meaning, "is that so?" with a little extra politeness and concern.

Nora's dress, when she appears again — stepping heavily on Cuban heels down the stairs in the hall — is flowered more lavishly than anything my mother owns, green and yellow on brown, some sort of floating sheer crepe, leaving her arms bare. Her arms are heavy, and every bit of her skin you can see is covered with little dark freckles like measles. Her hair is short, black, coarse, and curly, her teeth very white and strong. "It's the first time I knew there was such a thing as green poppies," my father says, looking at her dress.

"You would be surprised all the things you never knew," says Nora, sending a smell of cologne far and wide when she moves and displaying a change of voice to go with the dress, something more sociable and youthful. "They're not poppies anyway, they're just flowers. You go and pump me some good cold water and I'll make these children a drink." She gets down from the cupboard a bottle of Walker Brothers Orange syrup.

"You telling me you were the Walkers Brothers man!"

"It's the truth, Nora. You go and look at my sample cases in the car if you don't believe me. I got the territory directly south of here."

"Walker Brothers? Is that a fact? You selling for Walker Brothers?"

"Yes ma'am."

"We always heard you were raising foxes over Dungannon way."

"That's what I was doing, but I kind of run out of luck in that business."

"So where're you living? How long've you been out selling?"

"We moved into Tuppertown. I been at it, oh, two, three months. It keeps the wolf from the door. Keeps him as far away as the back fence."

Nora laughs. "Well I guess you count yourself lucky to have the work. Isabel's husband in Brantford, he was out of work the longest time. I thought if he didn't find something soon I was going to have them all land in here to feed, and I tell you I was hardly looking forward to it. It's all I can manage with me and Momma."

"Isabel married," my father says. "Muriel married too?"

"No, she's teaching school out west. She hasn't been home for five years. I guess she finds something better to do with her holidays. I would if I was her." She gets some snapshots out of the table drawer and starts showing him. "That's Isabel's oldest boy, starting school. That's the baby sitting in her carriage. Isabel and her husband. Muriel. That's her roommate with her. That's a fellow she used to go around with, and his car. He was working in a bank out there. That's her school, it has eight rooms. She teaches Grade Five." My father shakes his head. "I can't think of her any way but when she was going to school, so shy I used to pick her up on the road — I'd be on my way to see you — and she would not say one word, not even agree it was a nice day."

"She's got over that."

"Who are you talking about?" says the old lady.

"Muriel. I said she's got over being shy."

"She was here last summer."

"No Momma that was Isabel. Isabel and her family were here last summer. Muriel's out west."

"I meant Isabel."

Shortly after this the old lady falls asleep, her head on the side, her mouth open. "Excuse her manners," Nora says. "It's old age." She fixes an afghan over her mother and says we can all go into the front room where our talking won't disturb her.

"You two," my father says. "Do you want to go outside and amuse yourselves?"

Amuse ourselves how? Anyway I want to stay. The front room is more interesting than the kitchen, though barer. There is a gramophone and a pump organ and a picture on the wall of Mary, Jesus' mother — I know that much — in shades of bright blue and pink with a spiked band of light around her head. I know that such pictures are found only in the homes of Roman Catholics and so Nora must be one. We have never known any Roman Catholics at all well, never well enough to visit in their houses. I think of what my grandmother and my Aunt Tena, over in Dungannon, used to always say to indicate that somebody was a Catholic. *So-and-so digs with the wrong foot,* they would say. *She digs with the wrong foot.* That was what they would say about Nora.

Nora takes a bottle, half full, out of the top of the organ and pours some of what is in it into the two glasses that she and my father have emptied of the orange drink.

"Keep it in case of sickness?" my father says.

"Not on your life," says Nora. "I'm never sick. I just keep it because I keep it. One bottle does me a fair time, though, because I don't care for drinking alone. Here's luck!" She and my father drink and I know what it is. Whisky. One of the things my mother has told me in our talks together is that my father never drinks whisky. But I see he does. He drinks whisky and he talks of people whose names I have never heard before. But after a while he turns to a familiar incident. He tells about the chamberpot that was emptied out the window. "Picture me there," he says, "hollering my heartiest. *Oh, lady, it's your Walker Brothers man, anybody home?*" He does himself hollering, grinning absurdly, waiting, looking up in pleased expectation, and then — oh, ducking, covering his head with his arms, looking as if he begged for mercy (when he never did anything like that, I was watching), and Nora laughs, almost as hard as my brother did at the time.

"That isn't true! That's not a word true!"

"Oh, indeed it is ma'am. We have our heroes in the ranks of Walker Brothers. I'm glad you think it's funny," he says sombrely.

I ask him shyly, "Sing the song."

"What song? Have you turned into a singer on top of everything else?"

Embarrassed, my father says, "Oh, just this song I made up while I was driving around, it gives me something to do, making up rhymes."

But after some urging he does sing it, looking at Nora with a droll, apologetic expression, and she laughs so much that in places he has to stop and wait for her to get over laughing so he can go on, because she makes him laugh too. Then he does various parts of his salesman's spiel. Nora when she laughs squeezes her large bosom under her folded arms. "You're crazy," she says. "That's all you are." She sees my brother peering into the gramophone and she jumps up and goes over to him. "Here's us sitting enjoying ourselves and not giving you a thought, isn't it terrible?" she says. "You want me to put a record on, don't you? You want to hear a nice record? Can you dance? I bet your sister can, can't she?"

I say no. "A big girl like you and so good-looking and can't dance!" says Nora. "It's high time you learned. I bet you'd make a lovely dancer. Here, I'm going to put on a piece I used to dance to and even your daddy did, in his dancing days. You didn't know your daddy was a dancer, did you? Well, he is a talented man, your daddy!"

She puts down the lid and takes hold of me unexpectedly around the waist, picks up my other hand and starts making me go backwards. "This is the way, now, this is how they dance. Follow me. This foot, see. One and one-two. One and one-two. That's fine, that's lovely, don't look at your feet! Follow me, that's right, see how easy? You're going to be a lovely dancer! One and one-two. One and one-two. Ben, see your daughter dancing!" *Whispering while you cuddle near me. Whispering where no one can hear me. . . .*

Round and round the linoleum, me proud, intent, Nora laughing and moving with great buoyancy, wrapping me in her strange gaiety, her smell of whisky, cologne, and sweat. Under the arms her dress is damp, and little drops form along her upper lip, hang in the soft black hairs at the corners of her mouth. She whirls me around in front of my father — causing me to stumble, for I am by no means so swift a pupil as she pretends — and lets me go, breathless.

"Dance with me, Ben."

"I'm the world's worst dancer, Nora, and you know it."

"I certainly never thought so."

"You would now."

She stands in front of him, arms hanging loose and hopeful, her breasts, which a moment ago embarrassed me with their warmth and bulk, rising and falling under her loose flowered dress, her face shining with the exercise, and delight.

"Ben."

My father drops his head and says quietly, "Not me, Nora."

So she can only go and take the record off. "I can drink alone but I can't dance alone," she says. "Unless I am a whole lot crazier than I think I am."

"Nora," says my father smiling. "You're not crazy."

"Stay for supper."

"Oh, no. We couldn't put you to the trouble."

"It's no trouble. I'd be glad of it."

"And their mother would worry. She'd think I'd turned us over in a ditch."

"Oh, well. Yes."

"We've taken a lot of your time now."

"Time." says Nora bitterly. "Will you come by ever again."

"I will if I can," says my father.

"Bring the children. Bring your wife."

"Yes I will," says my father. "I will if I can."

When she follows us to the car he says, "You come to see us too, Nora. We're right on Grove Street, left-hand side going in, that's north, and two doors this side — east — of Baker Street."

Nora does not repeat these directions. She stands close to the car in her soft, brilliant dress. She touches the fender, making an unintelligible mark in the dust there.

On the way home my father does not buy any ice cream or pop, but he does go into a country store to get a package of licorice, which he shares with us. *She digs with the wrong foot*, I think, and the words seem sad to me as never before, dark, perverse. My father does not say anything to me about not mentioning things at home, but I know, just from the thoughtfulness, the pause when he passes the licorice, that there are things not to be mentioned. The whisky, maybe the dancing. No worry about my brother, he does not notice enough. At most he might remember the blind lady, the picture of Mary.

"Sing," my brother commands my father, but my father says gravely, "I don't know, I seem to be fresh out of songs. You watch the road and let me know if you see any rabbits."

So my father drives and my brother watches the road for rabbits and I feel my father's life flowing back from our car in the last of the afternoon, darkening and turning strange, like a landscape that has an enchantment on it, making it kindly, ordinary, and familiar while you are looking at it, but changing it, once your back is turned, into something you will never know, with all kinds of weathers, and distances you cannot imagine.

When we get closer to Tuppertown the sky becomes gently overcast, as always, nearly always, on summer evenings by the Lake.   [1968]

JOYCE CAROL OATES *(b. 1938) was born in Lockport, New York, one of three children in a Roman Catholic family. She began to put picture stories down on paper even before she could write, and she remembers that her parents "dutifully" supplied her with lined tablets and gave her a typewriter when she was fourteen. In 1956, after Oates graduated from high school, she went on a scholarship to major in English at Syracuse University, but she did not devote most of her time to writing until after she received her M.A. from the University of Wisconsin in 1961. Discovering by chance that one of her stories had been cited in the honor roll of Martha Foley's annual* The Best American Short Stories, *Oates assembled the fourteen stories in her first book,* By the North Gate *(1963). Her career was launched, and as John Updike has speculated, she "was perhaps born a hundred years too late; she needs a lustier audience, a race of Victorian word-eaters to be worthy of her astounding productivity, her tireless gift of self-enthrallment."*

One of our most prolific authors, Oates has published almost seventy books, including over a hundred stories. Recent collections of stories are Raven's Wing *(1986) and* The Assignation *(1988); the same year she published the essays in* (Woman) Writer: Occasions and Opportunities. *Oates also writes poetry and literary criticism, including the volume* New Heaven, New Earth *(1974), analyzing the "visionary experience in literature" as exemplified in the work of Henry James, Virginia Woolf, Franz Kafka, D. H. Lawrence, Flannery O'Connor, and others. As a writer, critic, and professor at Princeton University, she dedicates her life to "promoting and exploring literature. . . . I am not conscious of being in any particular literary tradition, though I share with my contemporaries an intense interest in the formal aspects of writing; each of my books is an experiment of a kind, an investigation of the relationship between a certain consciousness and its formal aesthetic expression."*

The story "Where Are You Going, Where Have You Been?" was first published in Epoch *in 1966; it was included in* The Best American Short Stories *of 1967 and* Prize Stories: The O. Henry Awards 1968, *and was made into a film. Oates has said that this story, based on an article in* Life *magazine about a Tucson, Arizona, murderer, has been "constantly misunderstood by one generation, and intuitively understood by another." She sees the story as dealing with a human being "struggling heroically to define personal identity in the face of incredible opposition, even in the face of death itself." The story "Heat," which recalls Katherine Anne Porter's "He," is from her recent collection* Heat and Other Stories *(1992). Her latest collection is* Haunted: Tales of the Grotesque *(1994).*

RELATED COMMENTARY: *Joyce Carol Oates, "'Smooth Talk': Short Story into Film," page 1477.*

Heat

It was midsummer, the heat rippling above the macadam roads. Cicadas screaming out of the trees and the sky like pewter, glaring.

The days were the same day, like the shallow mud-brown river moving always in the same direction but so slow you couldn't see it. Except for Sunday: church in the morning, then the fat Sunday newspaper, the color comics and newsprint on your fingers.

Rhea and Rhoda Kunkel went flying on their rusted old bicycles, down the long hill toward the railroad yard, Whipple's Ice, the scrubby pastureland where dairy cows grazed. They'd stolen six dollars from their own grandmother who loved them. They were eleven years old, they were identical twins, they basked in their power.

Rhea and Rhoda Kunkel: it was always Rhea-and-Rhoda, never Rhoda-and-Rhea, I couldn't say why. You just wouldn't say the names that way. Not even the teachers at school would say them that way.

We went to see them in the funeral parlor where they were waked, we were made to. The twins in twin caskets, white, smooth, gleaming, perfect as plastic, with white satin lining puckered like the inside of a fancy candy box. And the waxy white lilies, and the smell of talcum powder and perfume. The room was crowded, there was only one way in and out.

Rhea and Rhoda were the same girl, they'd wanted it that way.

Only looking from one to the other could you see they were two.

The heat was gauzy, you had to push your way through like swimming. On their bicycles Rhea and Rhoda flew through it hardly noticing, from their grandmother's place on Main Street to the end of South Main where the paved road turned to gravel leaving town. That was the summer before seventh grade, when they died. Death was coming for them but they didn't know.

They thought the same thoughts sometimes at the same moment, had the same dream and went all day trying to remember it, bringing it back like something you'd be hauling out of the water on a tangled line. We watched them, we were jealous. None of us had a twin. Sometimes they were serious and sometimes, remembering, they shrieked and laughed like they were being killed. They stole things out of desks and lockers but if you caught them they'd hand them right back, it was like a game.

There were three floor fans in the funeral parlor that I could see, tall whirring fans with propellor blades turning fast to keep the warm air moving. Strange little gusts came from all directions making your eyes water. By this time Roger Whipple was arrested, taken into police custody. No one had hurt him. He would never stand trial, he was ruled mentally unfit, he would never be released from confinement.

He died there, in the state psychiatric hospital, years later, and was brought back home to be buried, the body of him I mean. His earthly remains.

Rhea and Rhoda Kunkel were buried in the same cemetery, the First Methodist. The cemetery is just a field behind the church.

In the caskets the dead girls did not look like anyone we knew really. They were placed on their backs with their eyes closed, and their mouths, the way you don't always in life when you're sleeping. Their faces were too small. Every eyelash showed, too perfect. Like angels everyone was saying and it was strange it was *so*. I stared and stared.

What had been done to them, the lower parts of them, didn't show in the caskets.

Roger Whipple worked for his father at Whipple's Ice. In the newspaper it stated he was nineteen, he'd gone to DeWitt Clinton until he was sixteen, my mother's friend Sadie taught there and remembered him from the special education class. A big slow sweet-faced boy with these big hands and feet, thighs like hams. A shy gentle boy with good manners and a hushed voice.

He wasn't simpleminded exactly, like the others in that class. He was watchful, he held back.

Roger Whipple in overalls squatting in the rear of his father's truck, one of his older brothers drove. There would come the sound of the truck in the driveway, the heavy block of ice smelling of cold, ice tongs over his shoulder. He was strong, round-shouldered like an older man. Never staggered or grunted. Never dropped anything. Pale washed-looking eyes lifting out of a big face, a soft mouth wanting to smile. We giggled and looked away. They said he'd never been the kind to hurt even an animal, all the Whipples swore.

Sucking ice, the cold goes straight into your jaws and deep into the bone.

People spoke of them as the Kunkel twins. Mostly nobody tried to tell them apart. Homely corkscrew-twisty girls you wouldn't know would turn up so quiet and solemn and almost beautiful, perfect little dolls' faces with the freckles powdered over, touches of rouge on the cheeks and mouths. I was tempted to whisper to them, kneeling by the coffins. Hey Rhea! Hey Rhoda! Wake *up!*

They had loud slip-sliding voices that were the same voice. They weren't shy. They were always first in line. One behind you and one in front of you and you'd better be wary of some trick. Flamey-orange hair and the bleached-out skin that goes with it, freckles like dirty raindrops splashed on their faces. Sharp green eyes they'd bug out until you begged them to stop.

Places meant to be serious, Rhea and Rhoda had a hard time sitting still. In church, in school, a sideways glance between them could do it. Jamming their knuckles into their mouths, choking back giggles. Sometimes laughing escaped through their fingers like steam hissing. Sometimes it came out like snorting and then none of us could hold back. The worst time was in assembly, the principal up there telling us that Miss Flagler had died, we would all miss her. Tears shining in the woman's eyes behind her goggle-glasses and one of the twins gave a breathless little snort, you could feel it like flames running down the whole row of girls, none of us could hold back.

Sometimes the word "tickle" was enough to get us going, just that word.

I never dreamt about Rhea and Rhoda so strange in their caskets sleeping out in the middle of a room where people could stare at them, shed tears and pray over them. I never dream about actual things, only things I don't know. Places I've never been, people I've never seen. Sometimes the person I am in the dream isn't me. Who it is, I don't know.

Rhea and Rhoda bounced up the drive behind. Whipple's Ice. They were laughing like crazy and didn't mind the potholes jarring their teeth, or the clouds of dust. If they'd had the same dream the night before, the hot sunlight erased it entirely.

When death comes for you you sometimes know and sometimes don't.

Roger Whipple was by himself in the barn, working. Kids went down there to beg him for ice to suck or throw around or they'd tease him, not out of meanness but for something to do. It was slow, the days not changing in the summer, heat sometimes all night long. He was happy with children that age, he was that age himself in his head, sixth grade learning abilities as the newspaper stated though he could add and subtract quickly. Other kinds of arithmetic gave him trouble.

People were saying afterward he'd always been strange. Watchful like he was, those thick soft lips. The Whipples did wrong, to let him run loose.

They said he'd always been a good gentle boy, went to Sunday school and sat still there and never gave anybody any trouble. He collected Bible cards, he hid them away under his mattress for safekeeping. Mr. Whipple started in early, disciplining him the way you might discipline a big dog or a horse. Not letting the creature know he has any power to be himself exactly. Not giving him the opportunity to test his will.

Neighbors said the Whipples worked him like a horse in fact. The older brothers were the most merciless. And why they all wore coveralls, heavy denim and long legs on days so hot, nobody knew. The thermometer above the First Midland Bank read 98°F. on noon of that day, my mother said.

Nights afterward my mother would hug me before I went to bed. Pressing my face hard against her breasts and whispering things I didn't hear, like praying to Jesus to love and protect *her* little girl and keep *her* from harm but I didn't hear, I shut my eyes tight and endured it. Sometimes we prayed together, all of us or just my mother and me kneeling by my bed. Even then I knew she was a good mother, there was this girl she loved as her daughter that was me and loved more than that girl deserved. There was nothing I could do about it.

Mrs. Kunkel would laugh and roll her eyes over the twins. In that house they were "double trouble" — you'd hear it all the time like a joke on the radio that keeps coming back. I wonder did she pray with them too. I wonder would they let her.

In the long night you forget about the day, it's like the other side of the world. Then the sun is there, and the heat. You forget.

We were running through the field behind school, a place where people dumped things sometimes and there was a dead dog there, a collie with beautiful fur but his eyes were gone from the sockets and the maggots had got him where somebody tried to lift him with her foot and when Rhea and Rhoda saw they screamed a single scream and hid their eyes.

They did nice things — gave their friends candy bars, nail polish, some novelty key chains they'd taken from somewhere, movie stars' pictures framed in plastic. In the movies they'd share a box of popcorn not noticing where one or the other of them left off and a girl who wasn't any sister of theirs sat.

Once they made me strip off my clothes where we'd crawled under the Kunkel's veranda. This was a large hollowed-out space where the earth dropped away at one end, you could sit without bumping your head, it was cool and smelled of dirt and stone. Rhea said all of a sudden, Strip! and Rhoda said at once, Strip! — come on! So it happened. They wouldn't let me out unless I took off my clothes, my shirt and shorts, yes and my panties too. Come *on* they said whispering and giggling, they were blocking the way out so I had no choice. I was scared but I was laughing too. This is to show our power over you, they said. But they stripped too just like me.

You have power over others you don't realize until you test it.

Under the Kunkels' veranda we stared at each other but we didn't touch each other. My teeth chattered because what if somebody saw us? Some boy, or Mrs. Kunkel herself? I was scared but I was happy too. Except for our faces, their face and mine, we could all be the same girl.

The Kunkel family lived in one side of a big old clapboard house by the river, you could hear the trucks rattling on the bridge, shifting their noisy gears on the hill. Mrs. Kunkel had eight children, Rhea and Rhoda were the youngest. Our mothers wondered why Mrs. Kunkel had let herself go — she had a moon-shaped pretty face but her hair was frizzed ratty, she must have weighed two hundred pounds, sweated and breathed so hard in the warm weather. They'd known her in school. Mr. Kunkel worked construction for the county. Summer evenings after work he'd be sitting on the veranda drinking beer, flicking cigarette butts out into the yard, you'd be fooled almost thinking they were fireflies. He went barechested in the heat, his upper body dark like stained wood. Flat little purplish nipples inside his chest hair the girls giggled to see. Mr. Kunkel teased us all, he'd mix Rhea and Rhoda up the way he'd mix the rest of us up like it was too much trouble to keep names straight.

Mr. Kunkel was in police custody, he didn't even come to the wake. Mrs. Kunkel was there in rolls of chin fat that glistened with sweat and tears, the makeup on her face was caked and discolored so you were embarrassed to look. It scared me, the way she grabbed me as soon as my parents and I came in. Hugging me against her big balloon breasts sobbing and all the strength went out of me, I couldn't push away.

The police had Mr. Kunkel, for his own good they said. He'd gone to the Whipples, though the murderer had been taken away, saying he would kill anybody he could get his hands on, the old man, the brothers. They were all responsible he said, his little girls were dead. Tear them apart with his bare hands he said but he had a tire iron.

Did it mean anything special, or was it just an accident, Rhea and Rhoda had taken six dollars from their grandmother an hour before? Because death was coming for them, it had to happen one way or another.

If you believe in God you believe that. And if you don't believe in God it's obvious.

Their grandmother lived upstairs over a shoe store downtown, an apartment looking out on Main Street. They'd bicycle down there for something to do and she'd give them grape juice or lemonade and try to keep them a while, a lonely old lady but she was nice, she was always nice to me, it was kind of nasty of Rhea and Rhoda to steal from her but they were like that. One was in the kitchen talking with her and without any plan or anything the other went to use the bathroom then slipped int her bedroom, got the money out of her purse like it was something she did every day of the week, that easy. On the stairs going down to the street Rhoda whispered to Rhea what did you *do?* knowing Rhea had done something she hadn't ought to have done but not knowing what it was or anyway how much money it was. They started in poking each other, trying to hold the giggles back until they were safe away.

On their bicycles they stood high on the pedals, coasting, going down the hill but not using their brakes. *What did you do! Oh what did you do!*

Rhea and Rhoda always said they could never be apart. If one didn't know exactly where the other was that one could die. Or the other could die. Or both.

Once they'd gotten some money from somewhere, they wouldn't say where, and paid for us all to go to the movies. And ice cream afterward too.

You could read the newspaper articles twice through and still not know what he did. Adults talked about it for a long time but not so we could hear. I thought probably he'd used an ice pick. Or maybe I heard somebody guess that who didn't know any more than me.

We liked it that Rhea and Rhoda had been killed, and all the stuff in the paper, and everybody talking about it, but we didn't like it that they were dead, we missed them.

Later, in the tenth grade, the Kaufmann twins moved into our school district. Doris and Diane. But it wasn't the same thing.

Roger Whipple said he didn't remember any of it. Whatever he did, he didn't remember. At first everybody thought he was lying then they had to accept it as true, or true in some way, doctors from the state hospital examined him. He said over and over he hadn't done anything and he didn't remember the twins there that afternoon but he couldn't explain why their bicycles were where they were at the foot of his stairway and he couldn't explain why he'd taken a bath in the middle of the day. The Whipples admitted that wasn't a practice of Roger's or of any of them, ever, a bath in the middle of the day.

Roger Whipple was a clean boy, though. His hands always scrubbed so you actually noticed, swinging the block of ice off the truck and, inside the kitchen, helping to set it in the ice box. They said he'd go crazy if he got bits of straw under his nails from the ice house or inside his clothes. He'd been taught to shave and he shaved every morning without fail, they said the sight of the beard growing in, the scratchy feel of it, seemed to scare him.

A few years later his sister Linda told us how Roger was built like a horse. She was our age, a lot younger than him, she made a gesture toward her crotch so we'd know what she meant. She'd happened to see him a few times she said, by accident.

There he was squatting in the dust laughing, his head lowered watching Rhea and Rhoda circle him on their bicycles. It was a rough game where the twins saw how close they could come to hitting him, brushing him with the bike fenders and he'd lunge out not seeming to notice if his fingers hit the spokes, it was all happening so fast you maybe wouldn't feel pain. Out back of the ice house where the yard blended in with the yard of the old railroad depot next door that wasn't used any more. It was burning hot in the sun, dust rose in clouds behind the girls. Pretty soon they got bored with the game though Roger Whipple even in his heavy overalls wanted to keep going. He was red-faced with all the excitement, he was a boy who loved to laugh and didn't have much chance. Rhea said she was thirsty, she wanted some ice, so Roger Whipple scrambled right up and went to get a big bag of ice cubes! — he hadn't any more sense than that.

They sucked on the ice cubes and fooled around with them. He was panting and lolling his tongue pretending to be a dog and Rhea and Rhoda cried, Here doggie! Here doggie-doggie! tossing ice cubes at Roger Whipple he tried to catch in his mouth. That went on for a while. In the end the twins just dumped the rest of the ice onto the dirt then Roger Whipple was saying he had some secret things that belonged to his brother Eamon he could show them. Hidden under his bed mattress, would they like to see what the things were?

He wasn't one who could tell Rhea from Rhoda or Rhoda from Rhea. There was a way some of us knew, the freckles on Rhea's face were a little darker than Rhoda's. Rhea's eyes were just a little darker than Rhoda's. But you'd have to see the two side by side with no clowning around to know.

Rhea said okay, she'd like to see the secret things. She let her bike fall where she was straddling it.

Roger Whipple said he could only take one of them upstairs to his room at a time, he didn't say why.

Okay said Rhea. Of the Kunkel twins Rhea always had to be first. She'd been born first, she said. Weighed a pound or two more.

Roger Whipple's room was in a strange place — on the second floor of the Whipple house above an unheated storage space that had been added after the main part of the house was built. There was a way of getting to the room from the outside, up a flight of rickety wood stairs. That way Roger could get in and out of his room without going through the rest of the house. People said the Whipples had him live there like some animal, they didn't want him tramping through the house but they denied it. The room had an inside door too.

Roger Whipple weighed about one-hundred ninety pounds that day. In the hospital he swelled up like a balloon, people said, bloated from the drugs, his skin was soft and white as bread dough and his hair fell out. He was an old man when he died aged thirty-one.

Exactly why he died, the Whipples never knew. The hospital just told them his heart had stopped in his sleep.

Rhoda shaded her eyes watching her sister running up the stairs with Roger Whipple behind her and felt the first pinch of fear, that something was wrong, or was going to be wrong. She called after them in a whining voice that she wanted to come along too, she didn't want to wait down there all alone, but Rhea just called back to her to be quiet and wait her turn, so Rhoda waited, kicking at the ice cubes melting in the dirt, and after a while she got restless and shouted up to them — the door was shut, the shade on the window was drawn — saying she was going home, damn them she was sick of waiting she said and she was going home. But nobody came to the door or looked out the window, it was like the place was empty. Wasps had built one of those nests that look like mud in layers under the eaves and the only sound was wasps.

Rhoda bicycled toward the road so anybody who was watching would think she was going home, she was thinking she hated Rhea! hated her damn twin sister! wished she was dead and gone, God damn her! She was going home and the first thing she'd tell their mother was that Rhea had stolen six dollars from Grandma: she had it in her pocket right that moment.

The Whipple house was an old farmhouse they'd tried to modernize by putting on red asphalt siding meant to look like brick. Downstairs the rooms were big and drafty, upstairs they were small, some of them unfinished and with bare floorboards, like Roger Whipple's room which people would afterward say based on what the police said was like an animal's pen, nothing in it but a bed shoved into a corner and some furniture and boxes and things Mrs. Whipple stored there.

Of the Whipples — there were seven in the family still living at home — only Mrs. Whipple and her daughter Iris were home that afternoon. They said they hadn't heard a sound except for kids playing in the back, they swore it.

Rhoda was bent on going home and leaving Rhea behind but at the end of the driveway something made her turn her bicycle wheel back . . . so if you were watching you'd think she was just cruising around for something to do, a red-haired girl with whitish skin and freckles, skinny little body, pedaling fast, then slow, then coasting, then fast again, turning and dipping and criss-crossing her path, talking to herself as if she was angry. She hated Rhea! She was furious at Rhea! But feeling sort of scared too and sickish in the pit of her belly knowing that she and Rhea shouldn't be in two places, something might happen to one of them or to both. Some things you know.

So she pedaled back to the house. Laid her bike down in the dirt next to Rhea's. The bikes were old hand-me-downs, the kickstands were broken. But their daddy had put on new Goodyear tires for them at the start of the summer and he'd oiled them too.

You never would see just one of the twins' bicycles anywhere, you always saw both of them laid down on the ground and facing in the same direction with the pedals in about the same position.

Rhoda peered up at the second floor of the house, the shade drawn over the window, the door still closed. She called out Rhea? Hey Rhea? starting up the stairs making a lot of noise so they'd hear her, pulling on the railing as if to break it the way a boy would. Still she was scared. But making noise like that and feeling so disgusted and mad helped her get stronger, and there was Roger Whipple with the door open staring down at her flush-faced and sweaty as if he was scared too. He seemed to have forgotten her. He was wiping his hands on his overalls. He just stared, a lemony light coming up in his eyes.

Afterward he would say he didn't remember anything — didn't remember anything. Big as a grown man but round-shouldered so it was hard to judge how tall he was, or how old. His straw-colored hair falling in his eyes and his fingers twined together as if he was praying or trying with all his strength to keep his hands still. He didn't remember anything about the twins or anything in his room or in the ice house afterward but he cried a lot, he acted scared and guilty and sorry, they decided he shouldn't be put on trial, there was no point to it.

Mrs. Whipple kept to the house afterward, never went out not even to church or grocery shopping. She died of cancer just before Roger died, she'd loved him she said, she always said none of it had been his fault really, he wasn't the kind of boy even to hurt an animal, he'd loved kittens especially and was a good sweet obedient boy and religious too and whatever happened it must have been because those girls were teasing him, he'd had a lifetime of being teased and taunted by children, his heart broken by all the abuse, and something must have snapped that day, that was all.

The Whipples were the ones, though, who called the police. Mr. Whipple found the girls' bodies back in the ice house hidden under some straw and canvas.

He found them around nine that night, with a flashlight. He knew, he said. The way Roger was acting, and the fact the Kunkel girls were missing, word had gotten out. He knew but he didn't know what he knew or what he would find. Roger taking a bath like that in the middle of the day and washing his hair too and shaving for the second time and not answering when his mother spoke to him, just sitting there staring at the floor as if he was listening to something no one else could hear. He knew, Mr. Whipple said. The hardest minute of his life was in the ice house lifting that canvas to see what was under it.

He took it hard too, he never recovered. He hadn't any choice but to think what a lot of people thought — it had been his fault. He was an old-time Methodist, he took all that seriously, but none of it helped him. Believed Jesus Christ was his personal savior and He never stopped loving Roger or turned His face from him and if Roger did truly repent in his heart he would be saved and they would be reunited in Heaven, all the Whipples reunited. He believed, but none of it helped in his life.

The ice house is still there but boarded up and derelict, the Whipples' ice business ended long ago. Strangers live in the house and the yard is littered with rusting hulks of cars and pickup trucks. Some Whipples live scattered around the country but none in town. The old train depot is still there too.

After I'd been married some years I got involved with this man, I won't say his name, his name is not a name I say, but we would meet back there sometimes, back in that old lot that's all weeds and scrub trees. Wild as kids and on the edge of being drunk. I was crazy for this guy, I mean crazy like I could hardly think of anybody but him or anything but the two of us making love the way we did, with him deep inside me I wanted it never to stop just fuck and fuck and fuck I'd whisper to him and this went on for a long time, two or three years then ended the way these things do and looking back on it I'm not able to recognize that woman as if she was someone not even not-me but a crazy woman I would despise, making so much of such a thing, risking her marriage and her kids finding out and her life being ruined for such a thing, my God. The things people do.

It's like living out a story that has to go on its way.

Behind the ice house in his car I'd think of Rhea and Rhoda and what happened that day upstairs in Roger Whipple's room. And the funeral parlor with the twins like dolls laid out and their eyes like dolls' eyes too that shut when you tilt them back. One night when I wasn't asleep but wasn't awake either I saw my parents standing in the doorway of my bedroom watching me and I knew their thoughts, how they were thinking of Rhea and Rhoda and of me their daughter wondering how they could keep me from harm and there was no clear answer.

In his car in his arms I'd feel my mind drift. After we'd made love or at least after the first time. And I saw Rhoda Kunkel hesitating on the stairs a few steps down from Roger Whipple. I saw her white-faced and scared but deciding to keep going anyway, pushing by Roger Whipple to get inside the room, to find Rhea, she had to brush against him where he was standing as if he meant to block her but not having the nerve exactly to block her and he was smelling of his body and breathing hard but not in imitation of any dog now, not with his tongue flopping and lolling to make them laugh. Rhoda was asking where was Rhea? — she couldn't see well at first in the dark little cubbyhole of a room because the sunshine had been so bright outside.

Roger Whipple said Rhea had gone home. His voice sounded scratchy as if it hadn't been used in some time. She'd gone home he said and Rhoda said right away that Rhea wouldn't go home without her and Roger Whipple came toward her saying yes she did, yes she *did* as if he was getting angry she wouldn't believe him. Rhoda was calling, Rhea? Where are you? Stumbling against something on the floor tangled with the bedclothes.

Behind her was this big boy saying again and again yes she did, yes she *did*, his voice rising but it would never get loud enough so that anyone would hear and come save her.

I wasn't there, but some things you know.   [1991]

JOYCE CAROL OATES

Where Are You Going, Where Have You Been?

For Bob Dylan

Her name was Connie. She was fifteen and she had a quick nervous giggling habit of craning her neck to glance into mirrors, or checking other people's faces to make sure her own was all right. Her mother, who noticed everything and knew everything and who hadn't much reason any longer to look at her own face, always scolded Connie about it. "Stop gawking at yourself, who are you? You think you're so pretty?" she would say. Connie would raise her eyebrows at these familiar complaints and look right through her mother, into a shadowy vision of herself as she was right at that moment: she knew she was pretty and that was everything. Her mother had been pretty once too, if you could believe those old snapshots in the album, but now her looks were gone and that was why she was always after Connie.

"Why don't you keep your room clean like your sister? How've you got your hair fixed — what the hell stinks? Hair spray? You don't see your sister using that junk."

Her sister June was twenty-four and still lived at home. She was a secretary in the high school Connie attended, and if that wasn't bad enough — with her in the same building — she was so plain and chunky and steady that Connie had to hear her praised all the time by her mother and her mother's sisters. June did this, June did that, she saved money and helped clean the house and cooked and Connie couldn't do a thing, her mind was all filled with trashy daydreams. Their father was away at work most of the time and when he came home he wanted supper and he read the newspaper at supper and after supper he went to bed. He didn't bother talking much to them, but around his bent head Connie's mother kept picking at her until Connie wished her mother was dead and she herself was dead and it was all over. "She makes me want to throw up sometimes," she complained to her friends. She had a high, breathless, amused voice which made everything she said a little forced, whether it was sincere or not.

There was one good thing: June went places with girl friends of hers, girls who were just as plain and steady as she, and so when Connie wanted to do that her mother had no objections. The father of Connie's best girl friend drove the girls the three miles to town and left them off at a shopping plaza, so that they could walk through the stores or go to a movie, and when he came to pick them up again at eleven he never bothered to ask what they had done.

They must have been familiar sights, walking around that shopping plaza in their shorts and flat ballerina slippers that always scuffed the sidewalk, with charm bracelets jingling on their thin wrists; they would lean together to whisper and laugh secretly if someone passed by who amused or interested them. Connie had long dark blond hair that drew anyone's eye to it, and she wore part of it pulled up on her head and puffed out and the rest of it she let fall down her back. She wore a pullover jersey blouse that looked one way when she was at home and another way when she was away from home. Everything about her had two sides to it, one for home and one for anywhere that was not home: her walk that could be childlike and bobbing, or languid enough to make anyone think she was hearing music in her head, her mouth which was pale and smirking most of the time, but bright and pink on these evenings out, her laugh which was cynical and drawling at home — "Ha, ha, very funny" — but high-pitched and nervous anywhere else, like the jingling of the charms on her bracelet.

Sometimes they did go shopping or to a movie, but sometimes they went across the highway, ducking fast across the busy road, to a drive-in restaurant where older kids hung out. The restaurant was shaped like a big bottle, though squatter than a real bottle, and on its cap was a revolving figure of a grinning boy who held a hamburger aloft. One night in midsummer they ran across, breathless with daring, and right away someone leaned out a car window and invited them over, but it was just a boy from high school they didn't like. It made them feel good to be able to ignore him. They went up through the maze of parked and cruising cars to the bright-lit, fly-infested restaurant, their faces pleased and expectant as if they were entering a sacred building that loomed out of the night to give them what haven and what blessing they yearned for. They sat at the counter and crossed their legs at the ankles, their thin shoulders rigid with excitement and listened to the music that made everything so good: the music was always in the background like music at a church service, it was something to depend upon.

A boy named Eddie came in to talk with them. He sat backwards on his stool, turning himself jerkily around in semi-circles and then stopping and turning again, and after a while he asked Connie if she would like something to eat. She said she did and so she tapped her friend's arm on her way out — her friend pulled her face up into a brave droll look — and Connie said she would meet her at eleven, across the way. "I just hate to leave her like that," Connie said earnestly, but the boy said that she wouldn't be alone for long. So they went out to his car and on the way Connie couldn't help but let her eyes wander over the windshields and faces all around her, her face gleaming with the joy that had nothing to do with Eddie or even this place; it might have been the music. She drew her shoulders up and sucked in her breath with the pure pleasure of being alive, and just at that moment she happened to glance at a face just a few feet from hers. It was a boy with shaggy black hair, in a convertible jalopy painted gold. He stared at her and then his lips widened into a grin. Connie slit her eyes at him and turned away, but she couldn't help glancing back and there he was still watching her. He wagged a finger and laughed and said, "Gonna get you, baby," and Connie turned away again without Eddie noticing anything.

She spent three hours with him, at the restaurant where they ate hamburgers and drank Cokes in wax cups that were always sweating, and then down an alley a mile or so away, and when he left her off at five to eleven only the movie house was still open at the plaza. Her girl friend was there, talking with a boy. When Connie came up the two girls smiled at each other and Connie said, "How was the movie?" and the girl said, "*You* should know." They rode off with the girl's father, sleepy and pleased, and Connie couldn't help but look at the darkened shopping plaza with its big empty parking lot and its signs that were faded and ghostly now, and over at the drive-in restaurant where cars were still circling tirelessly. She couldn't hear the music at this distance.

Next morning June asked her how the movie was and Connie said, "So-so."

She and that girl and occasionally another girl went out several times a week that way, and the rest of the time Connie spent around the house — it was summer vacation — getting in her mother's way and thinking, dreaming, about the boys she met. But all the boys fell back and dissolved into a single face that was not even a face, but an idea, a feeling, mixed up with the urgent insistent pounding of the music and the humid night air of July. Connie's mother kept dragging her back to the daylight by finding things for her to do or saying suddenly, "What's this about the Pettinger girl?"

And Connie would say nervously, "Oh, her. That dope." She always drew thick clear lines between herself and such girls, and her mother was simple and kindly enough to believe her. Her mother was so simple, Connie thought, that it was maybe cruel to fool her so much. Her mother went scuffling around the house in old bedroom slippers and complained over the telephone to one sister about the other, then the other called up and the two of them complained about the third one. If June's name was mentioned her mother's tone was approving, and if Connie's name was mentioned it was disapproving. This did not really mean she disliked Connie and actually Connie thought that her mother preferred her to June because she was prettier, but the two of them kept up a pretense of exasperation, a sense that they were tugging and struggling over something of little value to either of them. Sometimes, over coffee, they were almost friends, but something would come up — some vexation that was like a fly buzzing suddenly around their heads — and their faces went hard with contempt.

One Sunday Connie got up at eleven — none of them bothered with church — and washed her hair so that it could dry all day long, in the sun. Her parents and sister were going to a barbecue at an aunt's house and Connie said no, she wasn't interested, rolling her eyes, to let mother know just what she thought of it. "Stay home alone then," her mother said sharply. Connie sat out back in a lawn chair and watched them drive away, her father quiet and bald, hunched around so that he could back the car out, her mother with a look that was still angry and not at all softened through the windshield, and in the back seat poor old June all dressed up as if she didn't know what a barbecue was, with all the running yelling kids and the flies. Connie sat with her eyes closed in the sun, dreaming and dazed with the warmth about her as if this were a kind of love, the caresses of love, and her mind slipped over onto thoughts of the boy she had been with the night before and how nice he had been, how sweet it always was, not the way someone like June would suppose but sweet, gentle, the way it was in movies and promised in songs; and when she opened her eyes she hardly knew where she was, the back yard ran off into weeds and a fenceline of trees and behind it the sky was perfectly blue and still. The asbestos "ranch house" that was now three years old startled her — it looked small. She shook her head as if to get awake.

It was too hot. She went inside the house and turned on the radio to drown out the quiet. She sat on the edge of her bed, barefoot, and listened for an hour and a half to a program called XYZ Sunday Jamboree, record after record of hard, fast, shrieking songs she sang along with, interspersed by exclamations from "Bobby King": "An' look here you girls at Napoleon's — Son and Charley want you to pay real close attention to this song coming up!"

And Connie paid close attention herself, bathed in a glow of slow-pulsed joy that seemed to rise mysteriously out of the music itself and lay languidly about the airless little room, breathed in and breathed out with each gentle rise and fall of her chest.

After a while she heard a car coming up the drive. She sat up at once, startled, because it couldn't be her father so soon. The gravel kept crunching all the way in from the road — the driveway was long — and Connie ran to the window. It was a car she didn't know. It was an open jalopy, painted a bright gold that caught the sun opaquely. Her heart began to pound and her fingers snatched at her hair, checking it, and she whispered "Christ. Christ," wondering how bad she looked. The car came to a stop at the side door and the horn sounded four short taps as if this were a signal Connie knew.

She went into the kitchen and approached the door slowly, then hung out the screen door, her bare toes curling down off the step. There were two boys in the car and now she recognized the driver: he had shaggy, shabby black hair that looked crazy as a wig and he was grinning at her.

"I ain't late, am I?" he said.

"Who the hell do you think you are?" Connie said.

"Toldja I'd be out, didn't I?"

"I don't even know who you are."

She spoke sullenly, careful to show no interest or pleasure, and he spoke in a fast bright monotone. Connie looked past him to the other boy, taking her time. He had fair brown hair, with a lock that fell onto his forehead. His sideburns gave him a fierce, embarrassed look, but so far he hadn't even bothered to glance at her. Both boys wore sunglasses. The driver's glasses were metallic and mirrored everything in miniature.

"You wanta come for a ride?" he said.

Connie smirked and let her hair fall loose over one shoulder.

"Don'tcha like my car? New paint job," he said. "Hey."

"What?"

"You're cute."

She pretended to fidget, chasing flies away from the door.

"Don'tcha believe me, or what?" he said.

"Look, I don't even know who you are," Connie said in disgust.

"Hey, Ellie's got a radio, see. Mine's broke down." He lifted his friend's arm and showed her the little transistor the boy was holding, and now Connie began to hear the music. It was the same program that was playing inside the house.

"Bobby King?" she said.

"I listen to him all the time. I think he's great."

"He's kind of great," Connie said reluctantly.

"Listen, that guy's *great*. He knows where the action is."

Connie blushed a little, because the glasses made it impossible for her to see just what this boy was looking at. She couldn't decide if she liked him or if he was just a jerk, and so she dawdled in the doorway and wouldn't come down or go back inside. She said, "What's all that stuff painted on your car?"

"Can'tcha read it?" He opened the door very carefully, as if he was afraid it might fall off. He slid out just as carefully, planting his feet firmly on the ground, the tiny metallic world in his glasses slowing down like gelatine hardening and in the midst of it Connie's bright green blouse. "This here is my name, to begin with," he said. ARNOLD FRIEND was written in tar-like black letters on the side, with a drawing of a round grinning face that reminded Connie of a pumpkin, except it wore sunglasses. "I wanta introduce myself, I'm Arnold Friend and that's my real name and I'm gonna be your friend, honey, and inside the car's Ellie Oscar, he's kinda shy." Ellie brought his transistor up to his shoulder and balanced it there. "Now these numbers are a secret code, honey," Arnold Friend explained. He read off the numbers 33, 19, 17 and raised his eyebrows at her to see what she thought of that, but she didn't think much of it. The left rear fender had been smashed and around it was written, on the gleaming gold background: DONE BY CRAZY WOMAN DRIVER. Connie had to laugh at that. Arnold Friend was pleased at her laughter and looked up at her. "Around the other side's a lot more — you wanta come and see them?"

"No."

"Why not?"

"Why should I?"

"Don'tcha wanta see what's on the car? Don'tcha wanta go for a ride?"

"I don't know."

"Why not?"

"I got things to do."

"Like what?"

"Things."

He laughed as if she had said something funny. He slapped his thighs. He was standing in a strange way, leaning back against the car as if he were balancing himself. He wasn't tall, only an inch or so taller than she would be if she came down to him. Connie liked the way he was dressed, which was the way all of them dressed: tight faded jeans stuffed into black, scuffed boots, a belt that pulled his waist in and showed how lean he was, and a white pull-over shirt that was a little soiled and showed the hard small muscles of his arms and shoulders. He looked as if he probably did hard work, lifting and carrying things. Even his neck looked muscular. And his face was a familiar face, somehow: the jaw and chin and cheeks slightly darkened, because he hadn't shaved for a day or two, and the nose long and hawk-like, sniffing as if she were a treat he was going to gobble up and it was all a joke.

"Connie, you ain't telling the truth. This is your day set aside for a ride with me and you know it," he said, still laughing. The way he straightened and recovered from his fit of laughing showed that it had been all fake.

"How do you know what my name is?" she said suspiciously.

"It's Connie."

"Maybe and maybe not."

"I know my Connie," he said, wagging his finger. Now she remembered him even better, back at the restaurant, and her cheeks warmed at the thought of how she sucked in her breath just at the moment she passed him how she must have looked to him. And he had remembered her. "Ellie and I come out here especially for you," he said. "Ellie can sit in back. How about it?"

"Where?"

"Where what?"

"Where're we going?"

He looked at her. He took off the sunglasses and she saw how pale the skin around his eyes was, like holes that were not in shadow but instead in light. His eyes were like chips of broken glass that catch the light in an amiable way. He smiled. It was as if the idea of going for a ride somewhere, to some place, was a new idea to him.

"Just for a ride, Connie sweetheart."

"I never said my name was Connie," she said.

"But I know what it is. I know your name and all about you, lots of things," Arnold Friend said. He had not moved yet but stood still leaning back against the side of his jalopy. "I took a special interest in you, such a pretty girl, and found out all about you like I know your parents and sister are gone somewheres and I know where and how long they're going to be gone, and I know who you were with last night, and your best friend's name is Betty. Right?"

He spoke in a simple lilting voice, exactly as if he were reciting the words to a song. His smile assured her that everything was fine. In the car Ellie turned up the volume on his radio and did not bother to look around at them.

"Ellie can sit in the back seat," Arnold Friend said. He indicated his friend with a casual jerk of his chin, as if Ellie did not count and she could not bother with him.

"How'd you find out all that stuff?" Connie said.

"Listen? Betty Schultz and Tony Fitch and Jimmy Pettinger and Nancy Pettinger," he said, in a chant. "Raymond Stanley and Bob Hutter —"

"Do you know all those kids?"

"I know everybody."

"Look, you're kidding. You're not from around here."

"Sure."

"But — how come we never saw you before?"

"Sure you saw me before," he said. He looked down at his boots, as if he were a little offended. "You just don't remember."

"I guess I'd remember you," Connie said.

"Yeah?" He looked up at this, beaming. He was pleased. He began to mark time with the music from Ellie's radio, tapping his fists lightly together. Connie looked away from his smile to the car, which was painted so bright it almost hurt her eyes to look at it. She looked at that name, ARNOLD FRIEND. And up at the front fender was an expression that was familiar — MAN THE FLYING SAUCERS. It was an expression kids had used the year before, but didn't use this year. She looked at it for a while as if the words meant something to her that she did not yet know.

"What're you thinking about? Huh?" Arnold Friend demanded. "Not worried about your hair blowing around in the car, are you?"

"No."

"Think I maybe can't drive good?"

"How do I know?"

"You're a hard girl to handle. How come?" he said. "Don't you know I'm your friend? Didn't you see me put my sign in the air when you walked by?"

"What sign?"

"My sign." And he drew an X in the air, leaning out toward her. They were maybe ten feet apart. After his hand fell back to his side the X was still in the air, almost visible. Connie let the screen door close and stood perfectly still inside it, listening to the music from her radio and the boy's blend together. She stared at Arnold Friend. He stood there so stiffly relaxed, pretending to be relaxed, with one hand idly on the door handle as if he were keeping himself up that way and had no intention of ever moving again. She recognized most things about him, the tight jeans that showed his thighs and buttocks and the greasy leather boots and the tight shirt, and even that slippery friendly smile of his, that sleepy dreamy smile that all the boys used to get across ideas they didn't want to put into words. She recognized all this and also the singsong way he talked, slightly mocking, kidding, but serious and a little melancholy, and she recognized the way he tapped one fist against the other in homage to the perpetual music behind him. But all these things did not come together.

She said suddenly, "Hey, how old are you?"

His smile faded. She could see then that he wasn't a kid, he was much older — thirty, maybe more. At this knowledge her heart began to pound faster.

"That's a crazy thing to ask. Can'tcha see I'm your own age?"

"Like hell you are."

"Or maybe a coupla years older, I'm eighteen."

"Eighteen?" she said doubtfully.

He grinned to reassure her and lines appeared at the corners of his mouth. His teeth were big and white. He grinned so broadly his eyes became slits and she saw how thick the lashes were, thick and black as if painted with a black tar-like material. Then he seemed to become embarrassed, abruptly, and looked over his shoulder at Ellie. "*Him*, he's crazy," he said. "Ain't he a riot, he's a nut, a real character." Ellie was still listening to the music. His sunglasses told nothing about what he was thinking. He wore a bright orange shirt unbuttoned halfway to show his chest, which was a pale, bluish chest and not muscular like Arnold Friend's. His shirt collar was turned up all around and the very tips of the collar pointed out past his chin as if they were protecting him. He was pressing the transistor radio up against his ear and sat there in a kind of daze, right in the sun.

"He's kinda strange," Connie said.

"Hey, she says you're kinda strange! Kinda strange!" Arnold Friend cried. He pounded on the car to get Ellie's attention. Ellie turned for the first time and Connie saw with shock that he wasn't a kid either — he had a fair, hairless face, cheeks reddened slightly as if the veins grew too close to the surface of his skin, the face of a forty-year-old baby. Connie felt a wave of dizziness rise in her at this sight and she stared at him as if waiting for something to change the shock of the moment, make it all right again. Ellie's lips kept shaping words, mumbling along with the words blasting his ear.

"Maybe you two better go away," Connie said faintly.

"What? How come?" Arnold Friend cried. "We come out here to take you for a ride. It's Sunday." He had the voice of the man on the radio now. It was the same voice, Connie thought. "Don'tcha know it's Sunday all day and honey, no matter who you were with last night today you're with Arnold Friend and don't you forget it! — Maybe you better step out here," he said, and this last was in a different voice. It was a little flatter, as if the heat was finally getting to him.

"No. I got things to do."

"Hey."

"You two better leave."

"We ain't leaving until you come with us."

"Like hell I am —"

"Connie, don't fool around with me. I mean, I mean, don't fool *around,*" he said, shaking his head. He laughed incredulously. He placed his sunglasses on top of his head, carefully, as if he were indeed wearing a wig, and brought the stems down behind his ears. Connie stared at him, another wave of dizziness and fear rising in her so that for a moment he wasn't even in focus but was just a blur, standing there against his gold car, and she had the idea that he had driven up the driveway all right but had come from nowhere before that and belonged nowhere and that everything about him and even the music that was so familiar to her was only half real.

"If my father comes and sees you —"

"He ain't coming. He's at a barbecue."

"How do you know that?"

"Aunt Tillie's. Right now they're — uh — they're drinking. Sitting around," he said vaguely, squinting as if he were staring all the way to town and over to Aunt Tillie's back yard. Then the vision seemed to clear and he nodded energetically. "Yeah. Sitting around. There's your sister in a blue dress, huh? And high heels, the poor sad bitch — nothing like you, sweetheart! And your mother's helping some fat woman with the corn, they're cleaning the corn — husking the corn —"

"What fat woman?" Connie cried.

"How do I know what fat woman. I don't know every goddamn fat woman in the world!" Arnold Friend laughed.

"Oh, that's Mrs. Hornby. . . . Who invited her?" Connie said. She felt a little light-headed. Her breath was coming quickly.

"She's too fat. I don't like them fat. I like them the way you are, honey," he said, smiling sleepily at her. They stared at each other for a while, through the screen door. He said softly, "Now what you're going to do is this: you're going to come out that door. You're going to sit up front with me and Ellie's going to sit in the back, the hell with Ellie, right? This isn't Ellie's date. You're my date. I'm your lover, honey."

"What? You're crazy —"

"Yes, I'm your lover. You don't know what that is but you will," he said. "I know that too. I know all about you. But look: it's real nice and you couldn't ask for nobody better than me, or more polite. I always keep my word. I'll tell you how it is, I'm always nice at first, the first time. I'll hold you so tight you won't think you have to try to get away or pretend anything because you'll know you can't. And I'll come inside you where it's all secret and you'll give in to me and you'll love me —"

"Shut up! You're crazy!" Connie said. She backed away from the door. She put her hands against her ears as if she'd heard something terrible, something not meant for her. "People don't talk like that, you're crazy," she muttered. Her heart was almost too big now for her chest and its pumping made sweat break out all over her. She looked out to see Arnold Friend pause and then take a step toward the porch lurching. He almost fell. But, like a clever drunken man, he managed to catch his balance. He wobbled in his high boots and grabbed hold of one of the porch posts.

"Honey?" he said. "You still listening?"

"Get the hell out of here!"

"Be nice, honey. Listen."

"I'm going to call the police —"

He wobbled again and out of the side of his mouth came a fast spat curse, an aside not meant for her to hear. But even this "Christ!" sounded forced. Then he began to smile again. She watched this smile come, awkward as if he were smiling from inside a mask. His whole face was a mask, she thought wildly, tanned down onto his throat but then running out as if he had plastered make-up on his face but had forgotten about his throat.

"Honey —? Listen, here's how it is. I always tell the truth and I promise you this: I ain't coming in that house after you."

"You better not! I'm going to call the police if you — if you don't —"

"Honey," he said, talking right through her voice, "honey, I'm not coming in there but you are coming out here. You know why?"

She was panting. The kitchen looked like a place she had never seen before, some room she had run inside but which wasn't good enough, wasn't going to help her. The kitchen window had never had a curtain, after three years, and there were dishes in the sink for her to do — probably — and if you ran your hand across the table you'd probably feel something sticky there.

"You listening, honey? Hey?"

"— going to call the police —"

"Soon as you touch the phone I don't need to keep my promise and can come inside. You won't want that."

She rushed forward and tried to lock the door. Her fingers were shaking. "But why lock it," Arnold Friend said gently, talking right into her face. "It's just a screen door. It's just nothing." One of his boots was at a strange angle, as if his foot wasn't in it. It pointed out to the left, bent at the ankle. "I mean, anybody can break through a screen door and glass and wood and iron or anything else if he needs to, anybody at all and specially Arnold Friend. If the place got lit up with a fire, honey, you'd come running out into my arms, right into my arms and safe at home — like you knew I was your lover and'd stopped fooling around, I don't mind a nice shy girl but I don't like no fooling around." Part of those words were spoken with a slight rhythmic lilt, and Connie somehow recognized them — the echo of a song from last year, about a girl rushing into her boy friend's arms and coming home again —

Connie stood barefoot on the linoleum floor, staring at him. "What do you want?" she whispered.

"I want you," he said.

"What?"

"Seen you that night and thought, that's the one, yes sir. I never needed to look any more."

"But my father's coming back. He's coming to get me. I had to wash my hair first —" She spoke in a dry, rapid voice, hardly raising it for him to hear.

"No, your daddy is not coming and yes, you had to wash your hair and you washed it for me. It's nice and shining and all for me, I thank you, sweetheart," he said, with a mock bow, but again he almost lost his balance. He had to bend and adjust his boots. Evidently his feet did not go all the way down; the boots must have been stuffed with something so that he would seem taller. Connie stared out at him and behind him Ellie in the car, who seemed to be looking off toward Connie's right, into nothing. This Ellie said, pulling the words out of the air one after another as if he were just discovering them, "You want me to pull out the phone?"

"Shut your mouth and keep it shut," Arnold Friend said, his face red from bending over or maybe from embarrassment because Connie had seen his boots. "This ain't none of your business."

"What — what are you doing? What do you want?" Connie said. "If I call the police they'll get you, they'll arrest you —"

"Promise was not to come in unless you touch that phone, and I'll keep that promise," he said. He resumed his erect position and tried to force his shoulders back. He sounded like a hero in a movie, declaring something important. He spoke too loudly and it was as if he were speaking to someone behind Connie. "I ain't made plans for coming in that house where I don't belong but just for you to come out to me, the way you should. Don't you know who I am?"

"You're crazy," she whispered. She backed away from the door but did not want to go into another part of the house, as if this would give him permission to come through the door. "What do you. . . . You're crazy, you. . . ."

"Huh? What're you saying, honey?"

Her eyes darted everywhere in the kitchen. She could not remember what it was, this room.

"This is how it is, honey: you come out and we'll drive away, have a nice ride. But if you don't come out we're gonna wait till your people come home and then they're all going to get it."

"You want that telephone pulled out?" Ellie said. He held the radio away from his ear and grimaced, as if without the radio the air was too much for him.

"I toldja shut up, Ellie." Arnold Friend said, "You're deaf, get a hearing aid, right? Fix yourself up. This little girl's no trouble and's gonna be nice to me, so Ellie keep to yourself, this ain't your date — right? Don't hem in on me. Don't hog. Don't crush. Don't bird dog. Don't trail me," he said in a rapid meaningless voice, as if he were running through all the expressions he'd learned but was no longer sure which one of them was in style, then rushing on to new ones, making them up with his eyes closed, "Don't crawl under my fence, don't squeeze in my chipmunk hole, don't sniff my glue, suck my popsicle, keep your own greasy fingers on yourself!" He shaded his eyes and peered in at Connie, who was backed against the kitchen table. "Don't mind him, honey, he's just a creep. He's a dope. Right? I'm the boy for you and like I said you come out here nice like a lady and give me your hand, and nobody else gets hurt, I mean, your nice old bald-headed daddy and your mummy and your sister in her high heels. Because listen: why bring them in this?"

"Leave me alone," Connie whispered.

"Hey, you know that old woman down the road, the one with the chickens and stuff — you know her?"

"She's dead!"

"Dead? What? You know her?" Arnold Friend said.

"She's dead —"

"Don't you like her?"

"She's dead — she's — she isn't here any more —"

"But don't you like her, I mean, you got something against her? Some grudge or something?" Then his voice dipped as if he were conscious of rudeness. He touched the sunglasses on top of his head as if to make sure they were still there. "Now you be a good girl."

"What are you going to do?"

"Just two things, or maybe three," Arnold Friend said. "But I promise it won't last long and you'll like me that way you get to like people you're close to. You will. It's all over for you here, so come on out. You don't want your people in any trouble, do you?"

She turned and bumped against a chair or something, hurting her leg, but she ran into the back room and picked up the telephone. Something roared in her ear, a tiny roaring, and she was so sick with fear that she could do nothing but listen to it — the telephone was clammy and very heavy and her fingers groped down to the dial but were too weak to touch it. She began to scream into the phone, into the roaring. She cried out, she cried for her mother, she felt her breath start jerking back and forth in her lungs as if it were something Arnold Friend were stabbing her with again and again with no tenderness. A noisy sorrowful wailing rose all about her and she was locked inside it the way she was locked inside this house.

After a while she could hear again. She was sitting on the floor, with her wet back against the wall.

Arnold Friend was saying from the door, "That's a good girl. Put the phone back."

She kicked the phone away from her.

"No, honey. Pick it up. Put it back right."

She picked it up and put it back. The dial tone stopped.

"That's a good girl. Now you come outside."

She was hollow with what had been fear, but what was now just an emptiness. All that screaming had blasted it out of her. She sat, one leg cramped under her, and deep inside her brain was something like a pinpoint of light that kept going and would not let her relax. She thought, I'm not going to see my mother again. She thought, I'm not going to sleep in my bed again. Her bright green blouse was all wet.

Arnold Friend said, in a gentle-loud voice that was like a stage voice. "The place where you came from ain't there any more, and where you had in mind to go is cancelled out. This place you are now — inside your daddy's house — is nothing but a cardboard box I can knock down any time. You know that and always did know it. You hear me?"

She thought, I have got to think. I have to know what to do.

"We'll go out to a nice field, out in the country here where it smells so nice and it's sunny," Arnold Friend said. "I'll have my arms tight around you so you won't need to try to get away and I'll show you what love is like, what it does. The hell with this house! It looks solid all right," he said. He ran a fingernail down the screen and the noise did not make Connie shiver, as it would have the day before. "Now put your hand on your heart, honey. Feel that? That feels solid too but we know better, be nice to me, be sweet like you can because what else is there for a girl like you but to be sweet and pretty and give in? — and get away before her people come back?"

She felt her pounding heart. Her hands seemed to enclose it. She thought for the first time in her life that it was nothing that was hers, that belonged to her, but just a pounding, living thing inside this body that wasn't hers either.

"You don't want them to get hurt," Arnold Friend went on. "Now get up, honey. Get up all by yourself."

She stood.

"Now turn this way. That's right. Come over to me — Ellie, put that away, didn't I tell you? You dope. You miserable creepy dope," Arnold Friend said. His words were not angry but only part of an incantation. The incantation was kindly. "Now come out through the kitchen to me honey and let's see a smile, try it, you're a brave sweet little girl and now they're eating corn and hotdogs cooked to bursting over an outdoor fire, and they don't know one thing about you and never did and honey you're better than them because not one of them would have done this for you."

Connie felt the linoleum under her feet; it was cool. She brushed her hair back out of her eyes. Arnold Friend let go of the post tentatively and opened his arms for her, his elbows pointing up toward each other and his wrist limp, to show that this was an embarrassed embrace and a little mocking, he didn't want to make her self-conscious.

She put out her hand against the screen. She watched herself push the door slowly open as if she were safe back somewhere in the other doorway, watching this body and this head of long hair moving out into the sunlight where Arnold Friend waited.

"My sweet little blue-eyed girl," he said, in a half-sung sigh that had nothing to do with her brown eyes but was taken up just the same by the vast sunlit reaches of the land behind him and on all sides of him, so much land that Connie had never seen before and did not recognize except to know that she was going to it.   [1970]

humped his love for Martha up the hills and through the swamps. In its intransitive form, "to hump" meant "to walk," or "to march," but it implied burdens far beyond the intransitive.

Almost everyone humped photographs. In his wallet, Lieutenant Cross carried two photographs of Martha. The first was a Kodachrome snapshot signed "Love," though he knew better. She stood against a brick wall. Her eyes were gray and neutral, her lips slightly open as she stared straight-on at the camera. At night, sometimes, Lieutenant Cross wondered who had taken the picture, because he knew she had boyfriends, because he loved her so much, and because he could see the shadow of the picture taker spreading out against the brick wall. The second photograph had been clipped from the 1968 Mount Sebastian yearbook. It was an action shot — women's volleyball — and Martha was bent horizontal to the floor, reaching, the palms of her hands in sharp focus, the tongue taut, the expression frank and competitive. There was no visible sweat. She wore white gym shorts. Her legs, he thought, were almost certainly the legs of a virgin, dry and without hair, the left knee cocked and carrying her entire weight, which was just over one hundred pounds. Lieutenant Cross remembered touching that left knee. A dark theater, he remembered, and the movie was *Bonnie and Clyde*, and Martha wore a tweed skirt, and during the final scene, when he touched her knee, she turned and looked at him in a sad, sober way that made him pull his hand back, but he would always remember the feel of the tweed skirt and the knee beneath it and the sound of the gunfire that killed Bonnie and Clyde, how embarrassing it was, how slow and oppressive. He remembered kissing her good night at the dorm door. Right then, he thought, he should've done something brave. He should've carried her up the stairs to her room and tied her to the bed and touched that left knee all night long. He should've risked it. Whenever he looked at the photographs, he thought of new things he should've done.

What they carried was partly a function of rank, partly of field specialty.

As a first lieutenant and platoon leader, Jimmy Cross carried a compass, maps, code books, binoculars, and a .45-caliber pistol that weighed 2.9 pounds fully loaded. He carried a strobe light and the responsibility for the lives of his men.

As an RTO, Mitchell Sanders carried the PRC-25 radio, a killer, twenty-six pounds with its battery.

As a medic, Rat Kiley carried a canvas satchel filled with morphine and plasma and malaria tablets and surgical tape and comic books and all the things a medic must carry, including M&M's for especially bad wounds, for a total weight of nearly twenty pounds.

As a big man, therefore a machine gunner, Henry Dobbins carried the M-60, which weighed twenty-three pounds unloaded, but which was almost always loaded. In addition, Dobbins carried between ten and fifteen pounds of ammunition draped in belts across his chest and shoulders.

As PFCs or Spec 4s, most of them were common grunts and carried the standard M-16 gas-operated assault rifle. The weapon weighed 7.5 pounds unloaded, 8.2 pounds with its full twenty-round magazine. Depending on numerous factors, such as topography and psychology, the riflemen carried anywhere from twelve to twenty magazines, usually in cloth bandoliers, adding on another 8.4 pounds at minimum, fourteen pounds at maximum. When it was available, they also carried M-16 maintenance gear — rods and steel brushes and swabs and tubes of LSA oil — all of which weighed about a pound. Among the grunts, some carried the M-79 grenade launcher, 5.9 pounds unloaded, a reasonably light weapon except for the ammunition, which was heavy. A single round weighed ten ounces. The typical load was twenty-five rounds. But Ted Lavender, who was scared, carried thirty-four rounds when he was shot and killed outside Than Khe, and he went down under an exceptional burden, more than twenty pounds of ammunition, plus the flak jacket and helmet and rations and water and toilet paper and tranquilizers and all the rest, plus the unweighed fear. He was dead weight. There was no twitching or flopping. Kiowa, who saw it happen, said it was like watching a rock fall, or a big sandbag or something — just boom, then down — not like the movies where the dead guy rolls around and does fancy spins and goes ass over teakettle — not like that, Kiowa said, the poor bastard just flat-fuck fell. Boom. Down. Nothing else. It was a bright morning in mid-April. Lieutenant Cross felt the pain. He blamed himself. They stripped off Lavenders' canteens and ammo, all the heavy things, and Rat Kiley said the obvious, the guy's dead, and Mitchell Sanders used his radio to report one U.S. KIA[3] and to request a chopper. Then they wrapped Lavender in his poncho. They carried him out to a dry paddy, established security, and sat smoking the dead man's dope until the chopper came. Lieutenant Cross kept to himself. He pictured Martha's smooth young face, thinking he loved her more than anything, more than his men, and now Ted Lavender was dead because he loved her so much and could not stop thinking about her. When the dust-off arrived, they carried Lavender aboard. Afterward they burned Than Khe. They marched until dusk, then dug their holes, and that night Kiowa kept explaining how you had to be there, how fast it was, how the poor guy just dropped like so much concrete. Boom-down, he said. Like cement.

In addition to the three standard weapons — the M-60, M-16, and M-79 — they carried whatever presented itself, or whatever seemed appropriate as a means of killing or staying alive. They carried catch-as-catch-can. At various times, in various situations, they carried M-14s and CAR-15s and Swedish Ks and grease guns and captured AK-47s and Chi-Coms and RPGs and Simonov carbines and black-market Uzis and .38-caliber Smith & Wesson handguns and 66 mm LAWs and shotguns and silencers and blackjacks and bayonets and C-4 plastic explosives. Lee Strunk carried a slingshot; a weapon of last resort, he called it. Mitchell Sanders carried brass knuckles. Kiowa carried his grandfather's feathered hatchet. Every third or fourth man carried a Claymore antipersonnel mine — 3.5 pounds with its firing device. They all carried

---

[3] Killed in action.

fragmentation grenades — fourteen ounces each. They all carried at least one M-18 colored smoke grenade — twenty-four ounces. Some carried CS or tear-gas grenades. Some carried white-phosphorus grenades. They carried all they could bear, and then some, including a silent awe for the terrible power of the things they carried.

In the first week of April, before Lavender died, Lieutenant Jimmy Cross received a good-luck charm from Martha. It was a simple pebble, an ounce at most. Smooth to the touch, it was a milky-white color with flecks of orange and violet, oval-shaped, like a miniature egg. In the accompanying letter, Martha wrote that she had found the pebble on the Jersey shoreline, precisely where the land touched water at high tide, where things came together but also separated. It was this separate-but-together quality, she wrote, that had inspired her to pick up the pebble and to carry it in her breast pocket for several days, where it seemed weightless, and then to send it through the mail, by air, as a token of her truest feelings for him. Lieutenant Cross found this romantic. But he wondered what her truest feelings were, exactly, and what she meant by separate-but-together. He wondered how the tides and waves had come into play on that afternoon along the Jersey shoreline when Martha saw the pebble and bent down to rescue it from geology. He imagined bare feet. Martha was a poet, with the poet's sensibilities, and her feet would be brown and bare, the toenails unpainted, the eyes chilly and somber like the ocean in March, and though it was painful, he wondered who had been with her that afternoon. He imagined a pair of shadows moving along the strip of sand where things came together but also separated. It was phantom jealousy, he knew, but he couldn't help himself. He loved her so much. On the march, through the hot days of early April, he carried the pebble in his mouth, turning it with his tongue, tasting sea salts and moisture. His mind wandered. He had difficulty keeping his attention on the war. On occasion he would yell at his men to spread out the column, to keep their eyes open, but then he would slip away into daydreams, just pretending, walking barefoot along the Jersey shore, with Martha, carrying nothing. He would feel himself rising. Sun and waves and gentle winds, all love and lightness.

What they carried varied by mission.

When a mission took them to the mountains, they carried mosquito netting, machetes, canvas tarps, and extra bug juice.

If a mission seemed especially hazardous, or if it involved a place they knew to be bad, they carried everything they could. In certain heavily mined AOs,[4] where the land was dense with Toe Poppers and Bouncing Betties, they took turns humping a twenty-eight-pound mine detector. With its head-phones and big sensing plate, the equipment was a stress on the lower back and shoulders, awkward to handle, often useless because of the shrapnel in

---

[4] Areas of operations.

the earth, but they carried it anyway, partly for safety, partly for the illusion of safety.

On ambush, or other night missions, they carried peculiar little odds and ends. Kiowa always took along his New Testament and a pair of moccasins for silence. Dave Jensen carried night-sight vitamins high in carotin. Lee Strunk carried his slingshot; ammo, he claimed, would never be a problem. Rat Kiley carried brandy and M&M's. Until he was shot, Ted Lavender carried the starlight scope, which weighed 6.3 pounds with its aluminum carrying case. Henry Dobbins carried his girlfriend's pantyhose wrapped around his neck as a comforter. They all carried ghosts. When dark came, they would move out single file across the meadows and paddies to their ambush coordinates, where they would quietly set up the Claymores and lie down and spend the night waiting.

Other missions were more complicated and required special equipment. In mid-April, it was their mission to search out and destroy the elaborate tunnel complexes in the Than Khe area south of Chu Lai. To blow the tunnels, they carried one-pound blocks of pentrite high explosives, four blocks to a man, sixty-eight pounds in all. They carried wiring, detonators, and battery-powered clackers. Dave Jensen carried earplugs. Most often, before blowing the tunnels, they were ordered by higher command to search them, which was considered bad news, but by and large they just shrugged and carried out orders. Because he was a big man, Henry Dobbins was excused from tunnel duty. The others would draw numbers. Before Lavender died there were seventeen men in the platoon, and whoever drew the number seventeen would strip off his gear and crawl in head first with a flashlight and Lieutenant Cross's .45-caliber pistol. The rest of them would fan out as security. They would sit down or kneel, not facing the hole, listening to the ground beneath them, imagining cobwebs and ghosts, whatever was down there — the tunnel walls squeezing in — how the flashlight seemed impossibly heavy in the hand and how it was tunnel vision in the very strictest sense, compression in all ways, even time, and how you had to wiggle in — ass and elbows — a swallowed-up feeling — and how you found yourself worrying about odd things — will your flashlight go dead? Do rats carry rabies? If you screamed, how far would the sound carry? Would your buddies hear it? Would they have the courage to drag you out? In some respects, though not many, the waiting was worse than the tunnel itself. Imagination was a killer.

On April 16, when Lee Strunk drew the number seventeen, he laughed and muttered something and went down quickly. The morning was hot and very still. Not good, Kiowa said. He looked at the tunnel opening, then out across a dry paddy toward the village of Than Khe. Nothing moved. No clouds or birds or people. As they waited, the men smoked and drank Kool-Aid, not taking much, feeling sympathy for Lee Strunk but also feeling the luck of the draw. You win some, you lose some, said Mitchell Sanders, and sometimes you settle for a rain check. It was a tired line and no one laughed.

Henry Dobbins ate a tropical chocolate bar. Ted Lavender popped a tranquilizer and went off to pee.

After five minutes, Lieutenant Jimmy Cross moved to the tunnel, leaned down, and examined the darkness. Trouble, he thought — a cave-in maybe. And then suddenly, without willing it, he was thinking about Martha. The stresses and fractures, the quick collapse, the two of them buried alive under all that weight. Dense, crushing love. Kneeling, watching the hole, he tried to concentrate on Lee Strunk and the war, all the dangers, but his love was too much for him, he felt paralyzed, he wanted to sleep inside her lungs and breathe her blood and be smothered. He wanted her to be a virgin and not a virgin, all at once. He wanted to know her. Intimate secrets — why poetry? Why so sad? Why the grayness in her eyes? Why so alone? Not lonely, just alone — riding her bike across campus or sitting off by herself in the cafeteria. Even dancing, she danced alone — and it was the aloneness that filled him with love. He remembered telling her that one evening. How she nodded and looked away. And how, later, when he kissed her, she received the kiss without returning it, her eyes wide open, not afraid, not a virgin's eyes, just flat and uninvolved.

Lieutenant Cross gazed at the tunnel. But he was not there. He was buried with Martha under the white sand at the Jersey shore. They were pressed together, and the pebble in his mouth was her tongue. He was smiling. Vaguely, he was aware of how quiet the day was, the sullen paddies, yet he could not bring himself to worry about matters of security. He was beyond that. He was just a kid at war, in love. He was twenty-two years old. He couldn't help it.

A few moments later Lee Strunk crawled out of the tunnel. He came up grinning, filthy but alive. Lieutenant Cross nodded and closed his eyes while the others clapped Strunk on the back and made jokes about rising from the dead.

Worms, Rat Kiley said. Right out of the grave. Fuckin' zombie.

The men laughed. They all felt great relief.

Spook City, said Mitchell Sanders.

Lee Strunk made a funny ghost sound, a kind of moaning, yet very happy, and right then, when Strunk made that high happy moaning sound, when he went *Ahhooooo*, right then Ted Lavender was shot in the head on his way back from peeing. He lay with his mouth open. The teeth were broken. There was a swollen black bruise under his left eye. The cheekbone was gone. Oh shit, Rat Kiley said, the guy's dead. The guy's dead, he kept saying, which seemed profound — the guy's dead. I mean really.

The things they carried were determined to some extent by superstition. Lieutenant Cross carried his good-luck pebble. Dave Jensen carried a rabbit's foot. Norman Bowker, otherwise a very gentle person, carried a thumb that had been presented to him as a gift by Mitchell Sanders. The thumb was dark brown, rubbery to the touch, and weighed four ounces at most. It had been cut from a VC corpse, a boy of fifteen or sixteen. They'd found him at the bottom of an irrigation ditch, badly burned, flies in his mouth and eyes. The boy wore black shorts and sandals. At the time of his death he had been carrying a pouch of rice, a rifle, and three magazines of ammunition.

You want my opinion, Mitchell Sanders said, there's a definite moral here.

He put his hand on the dead boy's wrist. He was quiet for a time, as if counting a pulse, then he patted the stomach, almost affectionately, and used Kiowa's hunting hatchet to remove the thumb.

Henry Dobbins asked what the moral was.

Moral?

You know. *Moral.*

Sanders wrapped the thumb in toilet paper and handed it across to Norman Bowker. There was no blood. Smiling, he kicked the boy's head, watched the flies scatter, and said, It's like with that old TV show — Paladin. Have gun, will travel.

Henry Dobbins thought about it.

Yeah, well, he finally said. I don't see no moral.

There it *is*, man.

Fuck off.

They carried USO stationery and pencils and pens. They carried Sterno, safety pins, trip flares, signal flares, spools of wire, razor blades, chewing tobacco, liberated joss sticks and statuettes of the smiling Buddha, candles, grease pencils, *The Stars and Stripes,* fingernail clippers, Psy Ops[5] leaflets, bush hats, bolos, and much more. Twice a week, when the resupply choppers came in, they carried hot chow in green Mermite cans and large canvas bags filled with iced beer and soda pop. They carried plastic water containers, each with a two-gallon capacity. Mitchell Sanders carried a set of starched tiger fatigues for special occasions. Henry Dobbins carried Black Flag insecticide. Dave Jensen carried empty sandbags that could be filled at night for added protection. Lee Strunk carried tanning lotion. Some things they carried in common. Taking turns, they carried the big PRC-77 scrambler radio, which weighed thirty pounds with its battery. They shared the weight of memory. They took up what others could no longer bear. Often, they carried each other, the wounded or weak. They carried infections. They carried chess sets, basketballs, Vietnamese-English dictionaries, insignia of rank, Bronze Stars and Purple Hearts, plastic cards imprinted with the Code of Conduct. They carried diseases, among them malaria and dysentery. They carried lice and ringworm and leeches and paddy algae and various rots and molds. They carried the land itself — Vietnam, the place, the soil — a powdery orange-red dust that covered their boots and fatigues and faces. They carried the sky. The whole atmosphere, they carried it, the humidity, the monsoons, the stink of fungus and decay, all of it, they carried gravity. They moved like mules. By

[5]Psychological operations.

daylight they took sniper fire, at night they were mortared, but it was not battle, it was just the endless march, village to village, without purpose, nothing won or lost. They marched for the sake of the march. They plodded along slowly, dumbly, leaning forward against the heat, unthinking, all blood and bone, simple grunts, soldiering with their legs, toiling up the hills and down into the paddies and across the rivers and up again and down, just humping, one step and then the next and then another, but no volition, no will, because it was automatic, it was anatomy, and the war was entirely a matter of posture and carriage, the hump was everything, a kind of inertia, a kind of emptiness, a dullness of desire and intellect and conscience and hope and human sensibility. Their principles were in their feet. Their calculations were biological. They had no sense of strategy or mission. They searched the villages without knowing what to look for, not caring, kicking over jars of rice, frisking children and old men, blowing tunnels, sometimes setting fires and sometimes not, then forming up and moving on to the next village, then other villages, where it would always be the same. They carried their own lives. The pressures were enormous. In the heat of early afternoon, they would remove their helmets and flak jackets, walking bare, which was dangerous but which helped ease the strain. They would often discard things along the route of march. Purely for comfort, they would throw away rations, blow their Claymores and grenades, no matter, because by nightfall the resupply choppers would arrive with more of the same, then a day or two later still more, fresh watermelons and crates of ammunition and sunglasses and woolen sweaters — the resources were stunning — sparklers for the Fourth of July, colored eggs for Easter. It was the great American war chest — the fruits of science, the smokestacks, the canneries, the arsenals at Hartford, the Minnesota forests, the machine shops, the vast fields of corn and wheat — they carried like freight trains; they carried it on their backs and shoulders — and for all the ambiguities of Vietnam, all the mysteries and unknowns, there was at least the single abiding certainty that they would never be at a loss for things to carry.

After the chopper took Lavender away, Lieutenant Jimmy Cross led his men into the village of Than Khe. They burned everything. They shot chickens and dogs, they trashed the village well, they called in artillery and watched the wreckage, then they marched for several hours through the hot afternoon, and then at dusk, while Kiowa explained how Lavender died, Lieutenant Cross found himself trembling.

He tried not to cry. With his entrenching tool, which weighed five pounds, he began digging a hole in the earth.

He felt shame. He hated himself. He had loved Martha more than his men, and as a consequence Lavender was now dead, and this was something he would have to carry like a stone in his stomach for the rest of the war.

All he could do was dig. He used his entrenching tool like an ax, slashing, feeling both love and hate, and then later, when it was full dark, he sat at the bottom of his foxhole and wept. It went on for a long while. In part, he was grieving for Ted Lavender, but mostly it was for Martha, and for himself, because she belonged to another world, which was not quite real, and because she was a junior at Mount Sebastian College in New Jersey, a poet and a virgin and uninvolved, and because he realized she did not love him and never would.

Like cement, Kiowa whispered in the dark. I swear to God — boom-down. Not a word.

I've heard this, said Norman Bowker.

A pisser, you know? Still zipping himself up. Zapped while zipping.

All right, fine. That's enough.

Yeah, but you had to see it, the guy just —

I *heard*, man. Cement. So why not shut the fuck *up?*

Kiowa shook his head sadly and glanced over at the hole where Lieutenant Jimmy Cross sat watching the night. The air was thick and wet. A warm, dense fog had settled over the paddies and there was the stillness that precedes rain.

After a time Kiowa sighed.

One thing for sure, he said. The Lieutenant's in some deep hurt. I mean that crying jag — the way he was carrying on — it wasn't fake or anything, it was real heavy-duty hurt. The man cares.

Sure, Norman Bowker said.

Say what you want, the man does care.

We all got problems.

Not Lavender.

No, I guess not, Bowker said. Do me a favor, though.

Shut up?

That's a smart Indian. Shut up.

Shrugging, Kiowa pulled off his boots. He wanted to say more, just to lighten up his sleep, but instead he opened his New Testament and arranged it beneath his head as a pillow. The fog made things seem hollow and unattached. He tried not to think about Ted Lavender, but then he was thinking how fast it was, no drama, down and dead, and how it was hard to feel anything except surprise. It seemed un-Christian. He wished he could find some great sadness, or even anger, but the emotion wasn't there and he couldn't make it happen. Mostly he felt pleased to be alive. He liked the smell of the New Testament under his cheek, the leather and ink and paper and glue, whatever the chemicals were. He liked hearing the sounds of night. Even his fatigue, it felt fine, the stiff muscles and the prickly awareness of his own body, a floating feeling. He enjoyed not being dead. Lying there, Kiowa admired Lieutenant Jimmy Cross's capacity for grief. He wanted to share the man's pain, he wanted to care as Jimmy Cross cared. And yet when he closed his eyes, all he could think was Boom-down, and all he could feel was the pleasure of having his boots off and the fog curling in around him and the damp soil and the Bible smells and the plush comfort of night.

After a moment Norman Bowker sat up in the dark.

What the hell, he said. You want to talk, *talk*. Tell it to me.

Forget it.

No, man, go on. One thing I hate, it's a silent Indian.

For the most part they carried themselves with poise, a kind of dignity. Now and then, however, there were times of panic, when they squealed or wanted to squeal but couldn't, when they twitched and made moaning sounds and covered their heads and said Dear Jesus and flopped around on the earth and fired their weapons blindly and cringed and sobbed and begged for the noise to stop and went wild and made stupid promises to themselves and to God and to their mothers and fathers, hoping not to die. In different ways, it happened to all of them. Afterward, when the firing ended, they would blink and peek up. They would touch their bodies, feeling shame, then quickly hiding it. They would force themselves to stand. As if in slow motion, frame by frame, the world would take on the old logic — absolute silence, then the wind, then sunlight, then voices. It was the burden of being alive. Awkwardly, the men would reassemble themselves, first in private, then in groups, becoming soldiers again. They would repair the leaks in their eyes. They would check for casualties, call in dust-offs, light cigarettes, try to smile, clear their throats and spit and begin cleaning their weapons. After a time someone would shake his head and say, No lie, I almost shit my pants, and someone else would laugh, which meant it was bad, yes, but the guy had obviously not shit his pants, it wasn't that bad, and in any case nobody would ever do such a thing and then go ahead and talk about it. They would squint into the dense, oppressive sunlight. For a few moments, perhaps, they would fall silent, lighting a joint and tracking its passage from man to man, inhaling, holding in the humiliation. Scary stuff, one of them might say. But then someone else would grin or flick his eyebrows and say, Roger-dodger, almost cut me a new asshole, *almost.*

There were numerous such poses. Some carried themselves with a sort of wistful resignation, others with pride or stiff soldierly discipline or good humor or macho zeal. They were afraid of dying but they were even more afraid to show it.

They found jokes to tell.

They used a hard vocabulary to contain the terrible softness. *Greased*, they'd say. *Offed, lit up, zapped while zipping.* It wasn't cruelty, just stage presence. They were actors and the war came at them in 3-D. When someone died, it wasn't quite dying, because in a curious way it seemed scripted, and because they had their lines mostly memorized, irony mixed with tragedy, and because they called it by other names, as if to encyst and destroy the reality of death itself. They kicked corpses. They cut off thumbs. They talked grunt lingo. They told stories about Ted Lavender's supply of tranquilizers, how the poor guy didn't feel a thing, how incredibly tranquil he was.

There's a moral here, said Mitchell Sanders.

They were waiting for Lavender's chopper, smoking the dead man's dope.

The moral's pretty obvious, Sanders said, and winked. Stay away from drugs. No joke, they'll ruin your day every time.

Cute, said Henry Dobbins.

Mind-blower, get it? Talk about wiggy — nothing left, just blood and brains.

They made themselves laugh.

There it is, they'd say, over and over, as if the repetition itself were an act of poise, a balance between crazy and almost crazy, knowing without going. There it is, which meant be cool, let it ride, because oh yeah, man, you can't change what can't be changed, there it is, there it absolutely and positively and fucking well *is*.

They were tough.

They carried all the emotional baggage of men who might die. Grief, terror, love, longing — these were intangibles, but the intangibles had their own mass and specific gravity, they had tangible weight. They carried shameful memories. They carried the common secret of cowardice barely restrained, the instinct to run or freeze or hide, and in many respects this was the heaviest burden of all, for it could never be put down, it required perfect balance and perfect posture. They carried their reputations. They carried the soldier's greatest fear, which was the fear of blushing. Men killed, and died, because they were embarrassed not to. It was what had brought them to the war in the first place, nothing positive, no dreams of glory or honor, just to avoid the blush of dishonor. They died so as not to die of embarrassment. They crawled into tunnels and walked point and advanced under fire. Each morning, despite the unknowns, they made their legs move. They endured. They kept humping. They did not submit to the obvious alternative, which was simply to close the eyes and fall. So easy, really. Go limp and tumble to the ground and let the muscles unwind and not speak and not budge until your buddies picked you up and lifted you into the chopper that would roar and dip its nose and carry you off to the world. A mere matter of falling, yet no one ever fell. It was not courage, exactly; the object was not valor. Rather, they were too frightened to be cowards.

By and large they carried these things inside, maintaining the masks of composure. They sneered at sick call. They spoke bitterly about guys who had found release by shooting off their own toes or fingers. Pussies, they'd say. Candyasses. It was fierce, mocking talk, with only a trace of envy or awe, but even so, the image played itself out behind their eyes.

They imagined the muzzle against flesh. They imagined the quick, sweet pain, then the evacuation to Japan, then a hospital with warm beds and cute geisha nurses.

They dreamed of freedom birds.

At night, on guard, staring into the dark, they were carried away by jumbo jets. They felt the rush of takeoff. *Gone!* they yelled. And then velocity, wings and engines, a smiling stewardess — but it was more than a plane, it was a real bird, a big sleek silver bird with feathers and talons and high screeching. They were flying. The weights fell off, there was nothing to bear.

They laughed and held on tight, feeling the cold slap of wind and altitude, soaring, thinking *It's over, I'm gone!* — they were naked, they were light and free — it was all lightness, bright and fast and buoyant, light as light, a helium buzz in the brain, a giddy bubbling in the lungs as they were taken up over the clouds and the war, beyond duty, beyond gravity and mortification and global entanglements — *Sin loi!*⁶ they yelled, *I'm sorry, motherfuckers, but I'm out of it, I'm goofed, I'm on a space cruise, I'm gone!* — and it was a restful, disencumbered sensation, just riding the light waves, sailing that big silver freedom bird over the mountains and oceans, over America, over the farms and great sleeping cities and cemeteries and highways and the golden arches of McDonald's. It was flight, a kind of fleeing, a kind of falling, falling higher and higher, spinning off the edge of the earth and beyond the sun and through the vast, silent vacuum where there were no burdens and where everything weighed exactly nothing. *Gone!* they screamed, *I'm sorry but I'm gone!* And so at night, not quite dreaming, they gave themselves over to lightness, they were carried, they were purely borne.

On the morning after Ted Lavender died, First Lieutenant Jimmy Cross crouched at the bottom of his foxhole and burned Martha's letters. Then he burned the two photographs. There was a steady rain falling, which made it difficult, but he used heat tabs and Sterno to build a small fire, screening it with his body, holding the photographs over the tight blue flame with the tips of his fingers.

He realized it was only a gesture. Stupid, he thought. Sentimental, too, but mostly just stupid.

Lavender was dead. You couldn't burn the blame.

Besides, the letters were in his head. And even now, without photographs, Lieutenant Cross could see Martha playing volleyball in her white gym shorts and yellow T-shirt. He could see her moving in the rain.

When the fire died out, Lieutenant Cross pulled his poncho over his shoulders and ate breakfast from a can.

There was no great mystery, he decided.

In those burned letters Martha had never mentioned the war, except to say, Jimmy, take care of yourself. She wasn't involved. She signed the letters "Love," but it wasn't love, and all the fine lines and technicalities did not matter.

The morning came up wet and blurry. Everything seemed part of everything else, the fog and Martha and the deepening rain.

It was a war, after all.

Half smiling, Lieutenant Jimmy Cross took out his maps. He shook his head hard, as if to clear it, then bent forward and began planning the day's march. In ten minutes, or maybe twenty, he would rouse the men and they would pack up and head west, where the maps showed the country to be green and inviting. They would do what they had always done. The rain

---

⁶ "Sorry about that!"

might add some weight, but otherwise it would be one more day layered upon all the other days.

He was realistic about it. There was that new hardness in his stomach.

No more fantasies, he told himself.

Henceforth, when he thought about Martha, it would be only to think that she belonged elsewhere. He would shut down the daydreams. This was not Mount Sebastian, it was another world, where there were no pretty poems or midterm exams, a place where men died because of carelessness and gross stupidity. Kiowa was right. Boom-down, and you were dead, never partly dead.

Briefly, in the rain, Lieutenant Cross saw Martha's gray eyes gazing back at him.

He understood.

It was very sad, he thought. The things men carried inside. The things men did or felt they had to do.

He almost nodded at her, but didn't.

Instead he went back to his maps. He was now determined to perform his duties firmly and without negligence. It wouldn't help Lavender, he knew that, but from this point on he would comport himself as a soldier. He would dispose of his good-luck pebble. Swallow it, maybe, or use Lee Strunk's slingshot, or just drop it along the trail. On the march he would impose strict field discipline. He would be careful to send out flank security, to prevent straggling or bunching up, to keep his troops moving at the proper pace and at the proper interval. He would insist on clean weapons. He would confiscate the remainder of Lavender's dope. Later in the day, perhaps, he would call the men together and speak to them plainly. He would accept the blame for what had happened to Ted Lavender. He would be a man about it. He would look them in the eyes, keeping his chin level, and he would issue the new SOPs in a calm, impersonal tone of voice, an officer's voice, leaving no room for argument or discussion. Commencing immediately, he'd tell them, they would no longer abandon equipment along the route of march. They would police up their acts. They would get their shit together, and keep it together, and maintain it neatly and in good working order.

He would not tolerate laxity. He would show strength, distancing himself.

Among the men there would be grumbling, of course, and maybe worse, because their days would seem longer and their loads heavier, but Lieutenant Cross reminded himself that his obligation was not to be loved but to lead. He would dispense with love; it was not now a factor. And if anyone quarreled or complained, he would simply tighten his lips and arrange his shoulders in the correct command posture. He might give a curt little nod. Or he might not. He might just shrug and say Carry on, then they would saddle up and form into a column and move out toward the villages of Than Khe.   [1986]

FLANNERY O'CONNOR *(1925–1964) was born in Savannah, Georgia, the only child of Roman Catholic parents. When she was thirteen her father was found to have disseminated lupus, an incurable disease in which antibodies in the immune system attack the body's own substances. After her father's death in 1941, O'Connor attended Georgia State College for Women in Milledgeville, where she also published stories and edited the literary magazine. On the strength of these stories, she was awarded a fellowship at the Writers Workshop at the University of Iowa and earned her M.F.A. degree there. Late in 1950 she became ill with what was diagnosed as lupus, and she returned to Milledgeville to start a series of treatments that temporarily arrested the disease. Living with her mother on the family's 500-acre dairy farm, O'Connor began to work again, writing from nine to twelve in the morning and spending the rest of the day resting, reading, writing letters, and raising peacocks.*

O'Connor's first book, Wise Blood, *a complex comic novel attacking the contemporary secularization of religion, was published in 1952. It was followed in 1955 by a collection of stories,* A Good Man Is Hard to Find. *O'Connor was able to see a second novel,* The Violent Bear It Away, *through to publication in 1960, but she died of lupus in 1964, having completed enough stories for a second collection,* Everything That Rises Must Converge *(1965). Her total output of just thirty-one stories, collected in her* Complete Stories, *won the National Book Award for fiction in 1972.*

Despite her illness, O'Connor was never a recluse; she accepted as many lecture invitations as her health would permit. A volume of her lectures and occasional pieces was published in 1969 as Mystery and Manners. *It is a valuable companion to her stories and novels, because she often reflected on her writing and interpreted her fiction. As a devout Roman Catholic, O'Connor was uncompromising in her religious views: "For I am no disbeliever in spiritual purpose and no vague believer. This means that for me the meaning of life is centered in our Redemption by Christ and what I see in the world I see in relation to that." As Joyce Carol Oates recognized in her essay "The Visionary Art of Flannery O'Connor," O'Connor is one of the great religious writers of modern times, unique "in her celebration of the necessity of succumbing to the divine through violence that is immediate and irreparable. There is no mysticism in her work that is only spiritual; it is physical as well." O'Connor's stories, like the three included here, frequently involve family relationships, but they are not meant to be read as realistic fiction, despite her remarkable ear for dialogue. O'Connor said she wrote them as parables, as the epigraph to "A Good Man Is Hard to Find" attests.*

RELATED COMMENTARIES: *See Casebook on Flannery O'Connor, pages 1541–1571, including Flannery O'Connor, "From 'Letters 1954–1955,'" page 1542, "Writing Short Stories," page 1544, "The Element of Suspense in 'A Good Man Is Hard to Find,'" page 1549; V. S. Pritchett, "Flannery O'Connor: Satan Comes to Georgia," page 1552; Robert H. Brinkmeyer, Jr., "Flannery O'Connor and Her Readers," page 1554; Dorothy Tuck McFarland, "On 'Good Country People,'" page 1559; Wayne C. Booth, "A Rhetorical Reading of O'Connor's 'Everything That Rises Must Converge,'" page 1563; Anthony Di Renzo, "A Dialogical Reading of 'Everything That Rises Must Converge,'" page 1567.*

FLANNERY O'CONNOR

Everything That Rises Must Converge

Her doctor had told Julian's mother that she must lose twenty pounds on account of her blood pressure, so on Wednesday nights Julian had to take her downtown on the bus for a reducing class at the Y. The reducing class was designed for working girls over fifty, who weighed from 165 to 200 pounds. His mother was one of the slimmer ones, but she said ladies did not tell their age or weight. She would not ride the buses by herself at night since they had been integrated, and because the reducing class was one of her few pleasures, necessary for her health, and *free*, she said Julian could at least put himself out to take her, considering all she did for him. Julian did not like to consider all she did for him, but every Wednesday night he braced himself and took her.

She was almost ready to go, standing before the hall mirror, putting on her hat, while he, his hands behind him, appeared pinned to the door frame, waiting like Saint Sebastian for the arrows to begin piercing him. The hat was new and had cost her seven dollars and a half. She kept saying, "Maybe I shouldn't have paid that for it. No, I shouldn't have. I'll take it off and return it tomorrow. I shouldn't have bought it."

Julian raised his eyes to heaven. "Yes, you should have bought it," he said. "Put it on and let's go." It was a hideous hat. A purple velvet flap came down on one side of it and stood up on the other; the rest of it was green and looked like a cushion with the stuffing out. He decided it was less comical than jaunty and pathetic. Everything that gave her pleasure was small and depressed him.

She lifted the hat one more time and set it down slowly on top of her head. Two wings of gray hair protruded on either side of her florid face, but her eyes, sky-blue, were as innocent and untouched by experience as they must have been when she was ten. Were it not that she was a widow who had struggled fiercely to feed and clothe and put him through school and who was supporting him still, "until he got on his feet," she might have been a little girl that he had to take to town.

"It's all right, it's all right," he said. "Let's go." He opened the door himself and started down the walk to get her going. The sky was a dying violet and the houses stood out darkly against it, bulbous liver-colored monstrosities of a uniform ugliness though no two were alike. Since this had been a fashionable neighborhood forty years ago, his mother persisted in thinking they did well to have an apartment in it. Each house had a narrow collar of dirt around it in which sat, usually, a grubby child. Julian walked with his hands in his pockets, his head down and thrust forward, and his eyes glazed with the determination to make himself completely numb during the time he would be sacrificed to her pleasure.

The door closed and he turned to find the dumpy figure, surmounted by the atrocious hat, coming toward him. "Well," she said, "you only live once and paying a little more for it, I at least won't meet myself coming and going."

"Some day I'll start making money," Julian said gloomily — he knew he never would — "and you can have one of those jokes whenever you take the fit." But first they would move. He visualized a place where the nearest neighbor would be three miles away on either side.

"I think you're doing fine," she said, drawing on her gloves. "You've only been out of school a year. Rome wasn't built in a day."

She was one of the few members of the Y reducing class who arrived in hat and gloves and who had a son who had been to college. "It takes time," she said, "and the world is in such a mess. This hat looked better on me than any of the others, though when she brought it out I said, 'Take that thing back. I wouldn't have it on my head,' and she said, 'Now wait till you see it on,' and when she put it on me, I said, 'We-ull,' and she said, 'If you ask me, that hat does something for you and you do something for the hat, and besides,' she said, 'with that hat, you won't meet yourself coming and going.'"

Julian thought he could have stood his lot better if she had been selfish, if she had been an old hag who drank and screamed at him. He walked along, saturated in depression, as if in the midst of his martyrdom he had lost his faith. Catching sight of his long, hopeless, irritated face, she stopped suddenly with a grief-stricken look, and pulled back on his arm. "Wait on me," she said. "I'm going back to the house and take this thing off and tomorrow I'm going to return it. I was out of my head. I can pay the gas bill with the seven-fifty."

He caught her arm in a vicious grip. "You are not going to take it back," he said. "I like it."

"Well," she said, "I don't think I ought . . ."

"Shut up and enjoy it," he muttered, more depressed than ever.

"With the world in the mess it's in," she said, "it's a wonder we can enjoy anything. I tell you, the bottom rail is on the top."

Julian sighed.

"Of course," she said, "if you know who you are, you can go anywhere." She said this every time he took her to the reducing class. "Most of them in it are not our kind of people," she said, "but I can be gracious to anybody. I know who I am."

"They don't give a damn for your graciousness," Julian said savagely. "Knowing who you are is good for one generation only. You haven't the foggiest idea where you stand now or who you are."

She stopped and allowed her eyes to flash at him. "I most certainly do know who I am," she said, "and if you don't know who you are, I'm ashamed of you."

"Oh hell," Julian said.

"Your great-grandfather was a former governor of this state," she said. "Your grandfather was a prosperous landowner. Your grandmother was a Godhigh."

"Will you look around you," he said tensely, "and see where you are now?" and he swept his arm jerkily out to indicate the neighborhood, which the growing darkness at least made less dingy.

"You remain what you are," she said. "Your great-grandfather had a plantation and two hundred slaves."

"There are no more slaves," he said irritably.

"They were better off when they were," she said. He groaned to see that she was off on that topic. She rolled onto it every few days like a train on an open track. He knew every stop, every junction, every swamp along the way, and knew the exact point at which her conclusion would roll majestically into the station: "It's ridiculous. It's simply not realistic. They should rise, yes, but on their own side of the fence."

"Let's skip it," Julian said.

"The ones I feel sorry for," she said, "are the ones that are half white. They're tragic."

"Will you skip it?"

"Suppose we were half white. We would certainly have mixed feelings."

"I have mixed feelings now," he groaned.

"Well let's talk about something pleasant," she said. "I remember going to Grandpa's when I was a little girl. Then the house had double stairways that went up to what was really the second floor — all the cooking was done on the first. I used to like to stay down in the kitchen on account of the way the walls smelled. I would sit with my nose pressed against the plaster and take deep breaths. Actually the place belonged to the Godhighs but your grandfather Chestny paid the mortgage and saved it for them. They were in reduced circumstances," she said, "but reduced or not, they never forgot who they were."

"Doubtless that decayed mansion reminded them," Julian muttered. He never spoke of it without contempt or thought of it without longing. He had seen it once when he was a child before it had been sold. The double stairways had rotted and had been torn down. Negroes were living in it. But it remained in his mind as his mother had known it. It appeared in his dreams regularly. He would stand on the wide porch, listening to the rustle of oak leaves, then wander through the high-ceilinged hall into the parlor that opened onto it and gaze at the worn rugs and faded draperies. It occurred to him that it was he, not she, who could have appreciated it. He preferred its threadbare elegance to anything he could name and it was because of it that all the neighborhoods they had lived in had been a torment to him — whereas she had hardly known the difference. She called her insensitivity "being adjustable."

"And I remember the old darky who was my nurse, Caroline. There was no better person in the world. I've always had a great respect for my colored friends," she said. "I'd do anything in the world for them and they'd . . ."

"Will you for God's sake get off that subject?" Julian said. When he got on a bus by himself, he made it a point to sit down beside a Negro, in reparation as it were for his mother's sins.

"You're mighty touchy tonight," she said. "Do you feel all right?"

"Yes I feel all right," he said. "Now lay off."

She pursed her lips. "Well, you certainly are in a vile humor," she observed. "I just won't speak to you at all."

They had reached the bus stop. There was no bus in sight and Julian, his hands still jammed in his pockets and his head thrust forward, scowled down the empty street. The frustration of having to wait on the bus as well as ride on it began to creep up his neck like a hot hand. The presence of his mother was borne in upon him as she gave a pained sigh. He looked at her bleakly. She was holding herself very erect under the preposterous hat, wearing it like a banner of her imaginary dignity. There was in him an evil urge to break her spirit. He suddenly unloosened his tie and pulled it off and put it in his pocket.

She stiffened. "Why must you look like *that* when you take me to town?" she said. "Why must you deliberately embarrass me?"

"If you'll never learn where you are," he said, "you can at least learn where I am."

"You look like a — thug," she said.

"Then I must be one," he murmured.

"I'll just go home," she said. "I will not bother you. If you can't do a little thing like that for me . . ."

Rolling his eyes upward, he put his tie back on. "Restored to my class," he muttered. He thrust his face toward her and hissed, "True culture is in the mind, the *mind*," he said, and tapped his head, "the mind."

"It's in the heart," she said, "and in how you do things and how you do things is because of who you *are*."

"Nobody in the damn bus cares who you are."

"I care who I am," she said icily.

The lighted bus appeared on top of the next hill and as it approached, they moved out into the street to meet it. He put his hand under her elbow and hoisted her up on the creaking step. She entered with a little smile, as if she were going into a drawing room where everyone had been waiting for her. While he put in the tokens, she sat down on one of the broad front seats for three which faced the aisle. A thin woman with protruding teeth and long yellow hair was sitting on the end of it. His mother moved up beside her and left room for Julian beside herself. He sat down and looked at the floor across the aisle where a pair of thin feet in red and white canvas sandals were planted.

His mother immediately began a general conversation meant to attract anyone who felt like talking. "Can it get any hotter?" she said and removed from her purse a folding fan, black with a Japanese scene on it, which she began to flutter before her.

"I reckon it might could," the woman with the protruding teeth said, "but I know for a fact my apartment couldn't get no hotter."

"It must get the afternoon sun," his mother said. She sat forward and looked up and down the bus. It was half filled. Everybody was white. "I see we have the bus to ourselves," she said. Julian cringed.

"For a change," said the woman across the aisle, the owner of the red and white canvas sandals. "I come on one the other day and they were thick as fleas — up front and all through."

"The world is in a mess everywhere," his mother said. "I don't know how we've let it get in this fix."

"What gets my goat is all those boys from good families stealing automobile tires," the woman with the protruding teeth said. "I told my boy, I said you may not be rich but you been raised right and if I ever catch you in any such mess, they can send you on to the reformatory. Be exactly where you belong."

"Training tells," his mother said. "Is your boy in high school?"

"Ninth grade," the woman said.

"My son just finished college last year. He wants to write but he's selling typewriters until he gets started," his mother said.

The woman leaned forward and peered at Julian. He threw her such a malevolent look that she subsided against the seat. On the floor across the aisle there was an abandoned newspaper. He got up and got it and opened it out in front of him. His mother discreetly continued the conversation in a lower tone but the woman across the aisle said in a loud voice, "Well that's nice. Selling typewriters is close to writing. He can go right from one to the other."

"I tell him," his mother said, "that Rome wasn't built in a day."

Behind the newspaper Julian was withdrawing into the inner compartment of his mind where he spent most of his time. This was a kind of mental bubble in which he established himself when he could not bear to be part of what was going on around him. From it he could see out and judge but in it he was safe from any kind of penetration from without. It was the only place where he felt free of the general idiocy of his fellows. His mother had never entered it but from it he could see her with absolute clarity.

The old lady was clever enough and he thought that if she had started from any of the right premises, more might have been expected of her. She lived according to the laws of her own fantasy world, outside of which he had never seen her set foot. The law of it was to sacrifice herself for him after she had first created the necessity to do so by making a mess of things. If he had permitted her sacrifices, it was only because her lack of foresight had made them necessary. All of her life had been a struggle to act like a Chestny without the Chestny goods, and to give him everything she thought a Chestny ought to have; but since, said she, it was fun to struggle, why complain? And when you had won, as she had won, what fun to look back on the hard times! He could not forgive her that she had enjoyed the struggle and that she thought *she* had won.

What she meant when she said she had won was that she had brought him up successfully and had sent him to college and that he had turned out so well — good looking (her teeth had gone unfilled, so that his could be straightened), intelligent (he realized he was too intelligent to be a success), and with a future ahead of him (there was of course no future ahead of him). She excused his gloominess on the grounds that he was still growing up and his radical ideas on his lack of practical experience. She said he didn't yet know a thing about "life," that he hadn't even entered the real world — when already he was as disenchanted with it as a man of fifty.

The further irony of all this was that in spite of her, he had turned out so well. In spite of going to only a third-rate college, he had, on his own initiative, come out with a first-rate education; in spite of growing up dominated by a small mind, he had ended up with a large one; in spite of all her foolish views, he was free of prejudice and unafraid to face facts. Most miraculous of all, instead of being blinded by love for her as she was for him, he had cut himself emotionally free of her and could see her with complete objectivity. He was not dominated by his mother.

The bus stopped with a sudden jerk and shook him from his meditation. A woman from the back lurched forward with little steps and barely escaped falling in his newspaper as she righted herself. She got off and a large Negro got on. Julian kept his paper lowered to watch. It gave him a certain satisfaction to see injustice in daily operation. It confirmed his view that with a few exceptions there was no one worth knowing within a radius of three hundred miles. The Negro was well dressed and carried a briefcase. He looked round and then sat down on the other end of the seat where the woman with the red and white canvas sandals was sitting. He immediately unfolded a newspaper and obscured himself behind it. Julian's mother's elbow at once prodded insistently into his ribs. "Now you see why I won't ride on these buses by myself," she whispered.

The woman with the red and white canvas sandals had risen at the same time the Negro sat down and had gone further back in the bus and taken the seat of the woman who had got off. His mother leaned forward and cast her an approving look.

Julian rose, crossed the aisle, and sat down in the place of the woman with the canvas sandals. From this position, he looked serenely across at his mother. Her face had turned an angry red. He stared at her, making his eyes the eyes of a stranger. He felt his tension suddenly lift as if he had openly declared war on her.

He would have liked to get in conversation with the Negro and to talk with him about art or politics or any subject that would be above the comprehension of those around them, but the man remained entrenched behind his paper. He was either ignoring the change of seating or had never noticed it. There was no way for Julian to convey his sympathy.

His mother kept her eyes fixed reproachfully on his face. The woman with the protruding teeth was looking at him avidly as if he were a type of monster new to her.

"Do you have a light?" he asked the Negro.

Without looking away from his paper, the man reached in his pocket and handed him a packet of matches.

"Thanks," Julian said. For a moment he held the matches foolishly. A NO SMOKING sign looked down upon him from over the door. This alone would not have deterred him; he had no cigarettes. He had quit smoking some months before because he could not afford it. "Sorry," he muttered and handed back the matches. The Negro lowered the paper and gave him an annoyed look. He took the matches and raised the paper again.

His mother continued to gaze at him but she did not take the advantage of his momentary discomfort. Her eyes retained their battered look. Her face seemed to be unnaturally red, as if her blood pressure had risen. Julian allowed no glimmer of sympathy to show on his face. Having got the advantage, he wanted desperately to keep it and carry it through. He would have liked to teach her a lesson that would last her a while, but there seemed no way to continue the point. The Negro refused to come out from behind his paper.

Julian folded his arms and looked stolidly before him, facing her but as if he did not see her, as if he had ceased to recognize her existence. He visualized a scene in which, the bus having reached their stop, he would remain in his seat and when she said, "Aren't you going to get off?" he would look at her as a stranger who had rashly addressed him. The corner they got off on was usually deserted, but it was well lighted and it would not hurt her to walk by herself the four blocks to the Y. He decided to wait until the time came and then decide whether or not he would let her get off by herself. He would have to be at the Y at ten to bring her back, but he could leave her wondering if he was going to show up. There was no reason for her to think she could always depend on him.

He retired again into the high-ceilinged room sparsely settled with large pieces of antique furniture. His soul expanded momentarily but then he became aware of his mother across from him and the vision shriveled. He studied her coldly. Her feet in little pumps dangled like a child's and did not quite reach the floor. She was training on him an exaggerated look of reproach. He felt completely detached from her. At that moment he could with pleasure have slapped her as he would have slapped a particularly obnoxious child in his charge.

He began to imagine various unlikely ways by which he could teach her a lesson. He might make friends with some distinguished Negro professor or lawyer and bring him home to spend the evening. He would be entirely justified but her blood pressure would rise to 300. He could not push her to the extent of making her have a stroke, and moreover, he had never been successful at making any Negro friends. He had tried to strike up an acquaintance on the bus with some of the better types, with ones that looked like professors or ministers or lawyers. One morning he had sat down next to a distinguished-looking dark brown man who had answered his questions with a sonorous solemnity but who had turned out to be an undertaker. Another day he had sat down beside a cigar-smoking Negro with a diamond ring on his finger, but after a few stilted pleasantries, the Negro had rung the buzzer and risen, slipping two lottery tickets into Julian's hand as he climbed over him to leave.

He imagined his mother lying desperately ill and his being able to secure only a Negro doctor for her. He toyed with that idea for a few minutes and then dropped it for a momentary vision of himself participating as a sympathizer in a sit-in demonstration. This was possible but he did not linger with it. Instead, he approached the ultimate horror. He brought home a beautiful suspiciously Negroid woman. Prepare yourself, he said. There is nothing you can do about it. This is the woman I've chosen. She's intelligent, dignified, even good, and she's suffered and she hasn't thought it *fun.* Now persecute us, go ahead and persecute us. Drive her out of here, but remember, you're driving me too. His eyes were narrowed and through the indignation he had generated, he saw his mother across the aisle, purplefaced, shrunken to the dwarf-like proportions of her moral nature, sitting like a mummy beneath the ridiculous banner of her hat.

He was tilted out of his fantasy again as the bus stopped. The door opened with a sucking hiss and out of the dark a large, gaily dressed, sullen-looking colored woman got on with a little boy. The child, who might have been four, had on a short plaid suit and a Tyrolean hat with a blue feather in it. Julian hoped that he would sit down beside him and that the woman would push in beside his mother. He could think of no better arrangement.

As she waited for her tokens, the woman was surveying the seating possibilities — he hoped with the idea of sitting where she was least wanted. There was something familiar-looking about her but Julian could not place what it was. She was a giant of a woman. Her face was set not only to meet opposition but to seek it out. The downward tilt of her large lower lip was like a warning sign: DON'T TAMPER WITH ME. Her bulging figure was encased in a green crepe dress and her feet overflowed in red shoes. She had on a hideous hat. A purple velvet flap came down on one side of it and stood up on the other; the rest of it was green and looked like a cushion with the stuffing out. She carried a mammoth red pocketbook that bulged throughout as if it were stuffed with rocks.

To Julian's disappointment, the little boy climbed up on the empty seat beside his mother. His mother lumped all children, black and white, into the common category, "cute," and she thought little Negroes were on the whole cuter than little white children. She smiled at the little boy as he climbed on the seat.

Meanwhile the woman was bearing down upon the empty seat beside Julian. To his annoyance, she squeezed herself into it. He saw his mother's face change as the woman settled herself next to him and he realized with satisfaction that this was more objectionable to her than it was to him. Her face seemed almost gray and there was a look of dull recognition in her eyes, as if suddenly she had sickened at some awful confrontation. Julian saw that it was because she and the woman had, in a sense, swapped sons. Though his mother would not realize the symbolic significance of this, she would feel it. His amusement showed plainly on his face.

The woman next to him muttered something unintelligible to herself. He was conscious of a kind of bristling next to him, muted growling like that of an angry cat. He could not see anything but the red pocketbook upright on the bulging green thighs. He visualized the woman as she had stood waiting for her tokens — the ponderous figure, rising from the red shoes upward over the solid hips, the mammoth bosom, the haughty face, to the green and purple hat.

His eyes widened.

The vision of the two hats, identical, broke upon him with the radiance of a brilliant sunrise. His face was suddenly lit with joy. He could not believe that Fate had thrust upon his mother such a lesson. He gave a loud chuckle so that she would look at him and see that he saw. She turned her eyes on him slowly. The blue in them seemed to have turned a bruised purple. For a moment he had an uncomfortable sense of her innocence, but it lasted only a second before principle rescued him. Justice entitled him to laugh. His grin hardened until it said to her as plainly as if he were saying aloud: Your punishment exactly fits your pettiness. This should teach you a permanent lesson.

Her eyes shifted to the woman. She seemed unable to bear looking at him and to find the woman preferable. He became conscious again of the bristling presence at his side. The woman was rumbling like a volcano about to become active. His mother's mouth began to twitch slightly at one corner. With a sinking heart, he saw incipient signs of recovery on her face and realized that this was going to strike her suddenly as funny and was going to be no lesson at all. She kept her eyes on the woman and an amused smile came over her face as if the woman were a monkey that had stolen her hat. The little Negro was looking up at her with large fascinated eyes. He had been trying to attract her attention for some time.

"Carver," the woman said suddenly. "Come heah!"

When he saw that the spotlight was on him at last, Carver drew his feet up and turned himself toward Julian's mother and giggled.

"Carver!" the woman said. "You heah me? Come Heah!"

Carver slid down from the seat but remained squatting with his back against the base of it, his head turned slowly around toward Julian's mother, who was smiling at him. The woman reached a hand across the aisle and snatched him to her. He righted himself and hung backwards on her knees, grinning at Julian's mother. "Isn't he cute?" Julian's mother said to the woman with the protruding teeth.

"I reckon he is," the woman said without conviction.

The Negress yanked him upright but he eased out of her grip and shot across the aisle and scrambled, giggling wildly, onto the seat beside his love.

"I think he likes me," Julian's mother said, and smiled at the woman. It was the smile she used when she was being particularly gracious to an inferior. Julian saw everything lost. The lesson had rolled off her like rain on a roof.

The woman stood up and yanked the little boy off the seat as if she were snatching him from contagion. Julian could feel the rage in her at having no weapon like his mother's smile. She gave the child a sharp slap across his leg. He howled once and then thrust his head into her stomach and kicked his feet against her shins. "Behave," she said vehemently.

The bus stopped and the Negro who had been reading the newspaper got off. The woman moved over and set the little boy down with a thump between herself and Julian. She held him firmly by the knee. In a moment he put his hands in front of his face and peeped at Julian's mother through his fingers.

"I see yoooooooo!" she said and put her hand in front of her face and peeped at him.

The woman slapped his hand down. "Quit yo' foolishness," she said, "before I knock the living Jesus out of you!"

Julian was thankful that the next stop was theirs. He reached up and pulled the cord. The woman reached up and pulled it at the same time. Oh my God, he thought. He had the terrible intuition that when they got off the bus together, his mother would open her purse and give the little boy a nickel. The gesture would be as natural to her as breathing. The bus stopped and the woman got up and lunged to the front, dragging the child, who wished to stay on, after her. Julian and his mother got up and followed. As they neared the door, Julian tried to relieve her of her pocketbook.

"No," she murmured, "I want to give the little boy a nickel."

"No!" Julian hissed. "No!"

She smiled down at the child and opened her bag. The bus door opened and the woman picked him up by the arm and descended with him, hanging at her hip. Once in the street she set him down and shook him.

Julian's mother had to close her purse while she got down the bus step but as soon as her feet were on the ground, she opened it again and began to rummage inside. "I can't find but a penny," she whispered, "but it looks like a new one."

"Don't do it!" Julian said fiercely between his teeth. There was a streetlight on the corner and she hurried to get under it so that she could better see into her pocketbook. The woman was heading off rapidly down the street with the child still hanging backward on her hand.

"Oh little boy!" Julian's mother called and took a few quick steps and caught up with them just beyond the lamppost. "Here's a bright new penny for you," and she held out the coin, which shone bronze in the dim light.

The huge woman turned and for a moment stood, her shoulders lifted and her face frozen with frustrated rage, and stared at Julian's mother. Then all at once she seemed to explode like a piece of machinery that had been given one ounce of pressure too much. Julian saw the black fist swing out with the red pocketbook. He shut his eyes and cringed as he heard the woman shout, "He don't take nobody's pennies!" When he opened his eyes, the woman was disappearing down the street with the little boy staring wide-eyed over her shoulder. Julian's mother was sitting on the sidewalk.

"I told you not to do that," Julian said angrily. "I told you not to do that!"

He stood over her for a minute, gritting his teeth. Her legs were stretched out in front of her and her hat was on her lap. He squatted down and looked her in the face. It was totally expressionless. "You got exactly what you deserved," he said. "Now get up."

He picked up her pocketbook and put what had fallen out back in it. He picked the hat up off her lap. The penny caught his eye on the sidewalk and he picked that up and let it drop before her eyes into the purse. Then he stood up and leaned over and held his hands out to pull her up. She remained immobile. He sighed. Rising above them on either side were black apartment buildings, marked with irregular rectangles of light. At the end of the block a man came out of a door and walked off in the opposite direction. "All right," he said, "suppose somebody happens by and wants to know why you're sitting on the sidewalk?"

She took the hand and, breathing hard, pulled heavily up on it and then stood for a moment, swaying slightly as if the spots of light in the darkness were circling around her. Her eyes, shadowed and confused, finally settled on his face. He did not try to conceal his irritation. "I hope this teaches you a lesson," he said. She leaned forward and her eyes raked his face. She seemed trying to determine his identity. Then, as if she found nothing familiar about him, she started off with a headlong movement in the wrong direction.

"Aren't you going to the Y?" he asked.

"Home," she muttered.

"Well, are we walking?"

For answer she kept going. Julian followed along, his hands behind him. He saw no reason to let the lesson she had had go without backing it up with an explanation of its meaning. She might as well be made to understand what had happened to her. "Don't think that was just an uppity Negro woman," he said. "That was the whole colored race which will no longer take your condescending pennies. That was your black double. She can wear the same hat as you, and to be sure," he added gratuitously (because he thought it was funny), "it looked better on her than it did on you. What all this means," he said, "is that the old world is gone. The old manners are obsolete and your graciousness is not worth a damn." He thought bitterly of the house that had been lost for him. "You aren't who you think you are," he said.

She continued to plow ahead, paying no attention to him. Her hair had come undone on one side. She dropped her pocketbook and took no notice. He stopped and picked it up and handed it to her but she did not take it.

"You needn't act as if the world had come to an end," he said, "because it hasn't. From now on you've got to live in a new world and face a few realities for a change. Buck up," he said, "it won't kill you."

She was breathing fast.

"Let's wait on the bus," he said.

"Home," she said thickly.

"I hate to see you behave like this," he said. "Just like a child. I should be able to expect more of you." He decided to stop where he was and make her stop and wait for a bus. "I'm not going any farther," he said, stopping. "We're going on the bus."

She continued to go on as if she had not heard him. He took a few steps and caught her arm and stopped her. He looked into her face and caught his breath. He was looking into a face he had never seen before. "Tell Grandpa to come get me," she said.

He stared, stricken.

"Tell Caroline to come get me," she said.

Stunned, he let her go and she lurched forward again, walking as if one leg were shorter than the other. A tide of darkness seemed to be sweeping her from him. "Mother!" he cried. "Darling, sweetheart, wait!" Crumpling, she fell to the pavement. He dashed forward and fell at her side, crying, "Mamma, Mamma!" He turned her over. Her face was fiercely distorted. One eye, large and staring, moved slightly to the left as if it had become unmoored. The other remained fixed on him, raked his face again, found nothing, and closed.

"Wait here, wait here!" he cried and jumped up and began to run for help toward a cluster of lights he saw in the distance ahead of him. "Help, help!" he shouted, but his voice was thin, scarcely a thread of sound. The lights drifted farther away the faster he ran and his feet moved numbly as if they carried him nowhere. The tide of darkness seemed to sweep him back to her, postponing from moment to moment his entry into the world of guilt and sorrow.

[1965]

FLANNERY O'CONNOR

Good Country People

Besides the neutral expression that she wore when she was alone, Mrs. Freeman had two others, forward and reverse, that she used for all her human dealings. Her forward expression was steady and driving like the advance of a heavy truck. Her eyes never swerved to left or right but turned as the story turned as if they followed a yellow line down the center of it. She seldom used the other expression because it was not often necessary for her to retract a statement, but when she did, her face came to a complete stop, there was an almost imperceptible movement of her black eyes, during which they seemed to be receding, and then the observer would see that Mrs. Freeman, though she might stand there as real as several grain sacks thrown on top of each other, was no longer there in spirit. As for getting anything across to her when this was the case, Mrs. Hopewell had given it up. She might talk her head off. Mrs. Freeman could never be brought to admit herself wrong on any point. She would stand there and if she could be brought to say anything, it was something like, "Well, I wouldn't of said it was and I wouldn't of said it wasn't," or letting her gaze range over the top kitchen shelf where there was an assortment of dusty bottles, she might remark, "I see you ain't ate many of them figs you put up last summer."

They carried on their most important business in the kitchen at breakfast. Every morning Mrs. Hopewell got up at seven o'clock and lit her gas heater and Joy's. Joy was her daughter, a large blonde girl who had an artificial leg. Mrs. Hopewell thought of her as a child though she was thirty-two years old and highly educated. Joy would get up while her mother was eating and lumber into the bathroom and slam the door, and before long, Mrs. Freeman would arrive at the back door. Joy would hear her mother call, "Come on in," and then they would talk a while in low voices that were indistinguishable in the bathroom. By the time Joy came in, they had usually finished the weather report and were on one or the other of Mrs. Freeman's daughters, Glynese or Carramae, Joy called them Glycerin and Caramel. Glynese, a redhead, was eighteen and had many admirers; Carramae, a blonde, was only fifteen but already married and pregnant. She could not keep anything on her stomach. Every morning Mrs. Freeman told Mrs. Hopewell how many times she had vomited since the last report.

Mrs. Hopewell liked to tell people that Glynese and Carramae were two of the finest girls she knew and that Mrs. Freeman was a *lady* and that she was never ashamed to take her anywhere or introduce her to anybody they might meet. Then she would tell how she had happened to hire the Freemans in the first place and how they were a godsend to her and how she had had them four years. The reason for her keeping them so long was that they were not trash. They were good country people. She had telephoned the man whose name they had given as a reference and he had told her that Mr. Freeman was a good farmer but that his wife was the nosiest woman ever to walk the earth. "She's got to be into everything," the man said. "If she don't get there before the dust settles, you can bet she's dead, that's all. She'll want to know all your business. I can stand him real good," he had said, "but me nor my wife neither could have stood that woman one more minute on this place." That had put Mrs. Hopewell off for a few days.

She had hired them in the end because there were no other applicants but she had made up her mind beforehand exactly how she would handle the woman. Since she was the type who had to be into everything, then, Mrs. Hopewell had decided, she would not only let her be into everything, she would *see to it* that she was into everything — she would give her the responsibility of everything, she would put her in charge. Mrs. Hopewell had no bad qualities of her own but she was able to use other people's in such a constructive way that she never felt the lack. She had hired the Freemans and she had kept them four years.

Nothing is perfect. This was one of Mrs. Hopewell's favorite sayings. Another was: that is life! And still another, the most important, was: well, other people have their opinions too. She would make these statements, usually at the table, in a tone of gentle insistence as if no one held them but her, and the large hulking Joy, whose constant outrage had obliterated every expression from her face, would stare just a little to the side of her, her eyes icy blue, with the look of someone who has achieved blindness by an act of will and means to keep it.

When Mrs. Hopewell said to Mrs. Freeman that life was like that, Mrs. Freeman would say, "I always said so myself." Nothing had been arrived at by anyone that had not first been arrived at by her. She was quicker than Mr. Freeman. When Mrs. Hopewell said to her after they had been on the place a while, "You know, you're the wheel behind the wheel," and winked, Mrs.

Freeman had said, "I know it. I've always been quick. It's some that are quicker than others."

"Everybody is different," Mrs. Hopewell said.

"Yes, most people is," Mrs. Freeman said.

"It takes all kinds to make the world."

"I always said it did myself."

The girl was used to this kind of dialogue for breakfast and more of it for dinner; sometimes they had it for supper too. When they had no guest they ate in the kitchen because that was easier. Mrs. Freeman always managed to arrive at some point during the meal and to watch them finish it. She would stand in the doorway if it were summer but in the winter she would stand with one elbow on top of the refrigerator and look down on them, or she would stand by the gas heater, lifting the back of her skirt slightly. Occasionally she would stand against the wall and roll her head from side to side. At no time was she in any hurry to leave. All this was very trying on Mrs. Hopewell but she was a woman of great patience. She realized that nothing is perfect and that in the Freemans she had good country people and that if, in this day and age, you get good country people, you had better hang onto them.

She had had plenty of experience with trash. Before the Freemans she had averaged one tenant family a year. The wives of these farmers were not the kind you would want to be around you for very long. Mrs. Hopewell, who had divorced her husband long ago, needed someone to walk over the fields with her; and when Joy had to be impressed for these services, her remarks were usually so ugly and her face so glum that Mrs. Hopewell would say, "If you can't come pleasantly, I don't want you at all," to which the girl, standing square and rigid-shouldered with her neck thrust slightly forward, would reply, "If you want me, here I am — LIKE I AM."

Mrs. Hopewell excused this attitude because of the leg (which had been shot off in a hunting accident when Joy was ten). It was hard for Mrs. Hopewell to realize that her child was thirty-two now and that for more than twenty years she had had only one leg. She thought of her still as a child because it tore her heart to think instead of the poor stout girl in her thirties who had never danced a step or had any *normal* good times. Her name was really Joy but as soon as she was twenty-one and away from home, she had had it legally changed. Mrs. Hopewell was certain that she had thought and thought until she had hit upon the ugliest name in any language. Then she had gone and had the beautiful name, Joy, changed without telling her mother until after she had done it. Her legal name was Hulga.

When Mrs. Hopewell thought the name, Hulga, she thought of the broad blank hull of a battleship. She would not use it. She continued to call her Joy to which the girl responded but in a purely mechanical way.

Hulga had learned to tolerate Mrs. Freeman who saved her from taking walks with her mother. Even Glynese and Carramae were useful when they occupied attention that might otherwise have been directed at her. At first she had thought she could not stand Mrs. Freeman for she had found that it was not possible to be rude to her. Mrs. Freeman would take on strange resentments and for days together she would be sullen but the source of her displeasure was always obscure; a direct attack, a positive leer, blatant ugliness to her face — these never touched her. And without warning one day, she began calling her Hulga.

She did not call her that in front of Mrs. Hopewell who would have been incensed but when she and the girl happened to be out of the house together, she would say something and add the name Hulga to the end of it, and the big spectacled Joy-Hulga would scowl and redden as if her privacy had been intruded upon. She considered the name her personal affair. She had arrived at it first purely on the basis of its ugly sound and then the full genius of its fitness had struck her. She had a vision of the name working like the ugly sweating Vulcan who stayed in the furnace and to whom, presumably, the goddess had to come when called. She saw it as the name of her highest creative act. One of her major triumphs was that her mother had not been able to turn her dust into Joy, but the greater one was that she had been able to turn it herself into Hulga. However, Mrs. Freeman's relish for using the name only irritated her. It was as if Mrs. Freeman's beady steel-pointed eyes had penetrated far enough behind her face to reach some secret fact. Something about her seemed to fascinate Mrs. Freeman and then one day Hulga realized that it was the artificial leg. Mrs. Freeman had a special fondness for the details of secret infections, hidden deformities, assaults upon children. Of diseases, she preferred the lingering or incurable. Hulga had heard Mrs. Hopewell give her the details of the hunting accident, how the leg had been literally blasted off, how she had never lost consciousness. Mrs. Freeman could listen to it any time as if it had happened an hour ago.

When Hulga stumped into the kitchen in the morning (she could walk without making the awful noise but she made it — Mrs. Hopewell was certain — because it was ugly-sounding), she glanced at them and did not speak. Mrs. Hopewell would be in her red kimono with her hair tied around her head in rags. She would be sitting at the table, finishing her breakfast and Mrs. Freeman would be hanging by her elbow outward from the refrigerator, looking down at the table. Hulga always put her eggs on the stove to boil and then stood over them with her arms folded, and Mrs. Hopewell would look at her — a kind of indirect gaze divided between her and Mrs. Freeman — and would think that it she would only keep herself up a little, she wouldn't be so bad looking. There was nothing wrong with her face that a pleasant expression wouldn't help. Mrs. Hopewell said that people who looked on the bright side of things would be beautiful even if they were not.

Whenever she looked at Joy this way, she could not help but feel that it would have been better if the child had not taken the Ph.D. It had certainly not brought her out any and now that she had it, there was no more excuse for her to go to school again. Mrs. Hopewell thought it was nice for girls to go to school to have a good time but Joy had "gone through." Anyhow, she would not have been strong enough to go again. The doctors had told Mrs. Hopewell that with the best of care, Joy might see forty-five. She had a weak heart. Joy had made it plain that if it had not been for this condition, she would be far from these red hills and good country people. She would be in a university lecturing to people who knew what she was talking about. And Mrs. Hopewell could very well picture her there, looking like a scarecrow and lecturing to more of the same. Here she went about all day in a six-year-old skirt and a yellow sweat shirt with a faded cowboy on a horse embossed on it. She thought this was funny; Mrs. Hopewell thought it was idiotic and showed simply that she was still a child. She was brilliant but she didn't have a grain of sense. It seemed to Mrs. Hopewell that every year she grew less like other people and more like herself — bloated, rude, and squint-eyed. And she said such strange things! To her own mother she had said — without warning, without excuse, standing up in the middle of a meal with her face purple and her mouth half full — "Woman! do you ever look inside? Do you ever look inside and see what you are *not*? God!" she had cried sinking down again and staring at her plate, "Malebranche was right: we are not our own light. We are not our own light!" Mrs. Hopewell had no idea to this day what brought that on. She had only made the remark, hoping Joy would take it in, that a smile never hurt anyone.

The girl had taken the Ph.D. in philosophy and this left Mrs. Hopewell at a complete loss. You could say, "My daughter is a nurse," or "My daughter is a schoolteacher," or even, "My daughter is a chemical engineer." You could not say, "My daughter is a philosopher." That was something that had ended with the Greeks and Romans. All day Joy sat on her neck in a deep chair, reading. Sometimes she went for walks but she didn't like dogs or cats or birds or flowers or nature or nice young men. She looked at nice young men as if she could smell their stupidity.

One day Mrs. Hopewell had picked up one of the books the girl had just put down and opening it at random, she read, "Science, on the other hand, has to assert its soberness and seriousness afresh and declare that it is concerned solely with what-is. Nothing — how can it be for science anything but a horror and a phantasm? If science is right, then one thing stands firm: science wishes to know nothing of nothing. Such is after all the strictly scientific approach to Nothing. We know it by wishing to know nothing of Nothing." These words had been underlined with a blue pencil and they worked on Mrs. Hopewell like some evil incantation in gibberish. She shut the book quickly and went out of the room as if she were having a chill.

This morning when the girl came in, Mrs. Freeman was on Carramae. "She thrown up four times after supper," she said, "and was up twict in the night after three o'clock. Yesterday she didn't do nothing but ramble in the bureau drawer. All she did. Stand up there and see what she could run up on."

"She's got to eat," Mrs. Hopewell muttered, sipping her coffee, while she watched Joy's back at the stove. She was wondering what the child had said to the Bible salesman. She could not imagine what kind of a conversation she could possibly have had with him.

He was a tall gaunt hatless youth who had called yesterday to sell them a Bible. He had appeared at the door, carrying a large black suitcase that weighted him so heavily on one side that he had to brace himself against the door facing. He seemed on the point of collapse but he said in a cheerful voice.

"Good morning, Mrs. Cedars!" and set the suitcase down on the mat. He was not a bad-looking young man though he had on a bright blue suit and yellow socks that were not pulled up far enough. He had prominent face bones and a streak of sticky-looking brown hair falling across his forehead.

"I'm Mrs. Hopewell," she said.

"Oh!" he said, pretending to look puzzled but with his eyes sparkling, "I saw it said 'The Cedars' on the mailbox so I thought you was Mrs. Cedars!" and he burst out in a pleasant laugh. He picked up the satchel and under cover of a pant, he fell forward into her hall. It was rather as if the suitcase had moved first, jerking him after it. "Mrs. Hopewell!" he said and grabbed her hand. "I hope you are well!" and he laughed again and then all at once his face sobered completely. He paused and gave her a straight earnest look and said, "Lady, I've come to speak of serious things."

"Well, come in," she muttered, none too pleased because her dinner was almost ready. He came into the parlor and sat down on the edge of a straight chair and put the suitcase between his feet and glanced around the room as if he were sizing her up by it. Her silver gleamed on the two sideboards; she decided he had never been in a room as elegant as this.

"Mrs. Hopewell," he began, using her name in a way that sounded almost intimate, "I know you believe in Chrustian service."

"Well yes," she murmured.

"I know," he said and paused, looking very wise with his head cocked on one side, "that you're a good woman. Friends have told me."

Mrs. Hopewell never liked to be taken for a fool. "What are you selling?" she asked.

"Bibles," the young man said and his eye raced around the room before he added, "I see you have no family Bible in your parlor, I see that is the one lack you got!"

Mrs. Hopewell could not say, "My daughter is an atheist and won't let me keep the Bible in the parlor." She said, stiffening slightly, "I keep my Bible by my bedside." This was not the truth. It was in the attic somewhere.

"Lady," he said, "the word of God ought to be in the parlor."

"Well, I think that's a matter of taste," she began. "I think . . ."

"Lady," he said, "for a Chrustian, the word of God ought to be in every room in the house besides in his heart. I know you're a Chrustian because I can see it in every line of your face."

She stood up and said, "Well, young man, I don't want to buy a Bible and I smell my dinner burning."

He didn't get up. He began to twist his hands and looking down at them he said softly, "Well lady, I'll tell you the truth — not many people want to buy one nowadays and besides, I know I'm real simple. I don't know how to say a thing but to say it. I'm just a country boy." He glanced up into her unfriendly face. "People like you don't like to fool with country people like me!"

"Why!" she cried, "good country people are the salt of the earth! Besides, we all have different ways of doing, it takes all kinds to make the world go 'round. That's life!"

"You said a mouthful," he said.

"Why, I think there aren't enough good country people in the world!" she said, stirred. "I think that's what's wrong with it!"

His face had brightened. "I didn't inraduce myself," he said. "I'm Manley Pointer from out in the country around Willohobie, not even from a place, just from near a place."

"You wait a minute," she said. "I have to see about my dinner." She went out to the kitchen and found Joy standing near the door where she had been listening.

"Get rid of the salt of the earth," she said, "and let's eat."

Mrs. Hopewell gave her a pained look and turned the heat down under the vegetables. "I can't be rude to anybody," she murmured and went back into the parlor.

He had opened the suitcase and was sitting with a Bible on each knee.

"You might as well put those up," she told him. "I don't want one."

"I appreciate your honesty," he said. "You don't see any more real honest people unless you go way out in the country."

"I know," she said, "real genuine folks!" Through the crack in the door she heard a groan.

"I guess a lot of boys come telling you they're working their way through college," he said, "but I'm not going to tell you that. Somehow," he said, "I don't want to go to college. I want to devote my life to Chrustian service. See," he said, lowering his voice, "I got this heart condition. I may not live long. When you know it's something wrong with you and you may not live long, well then, lady . . ." He paused, with his mouth open, and stared at her.

He and Joy had the same condition! She knew that her eyes were filling with tears but she collected herself quickly and murmured, "Won't you stay for dinner? We'd love to have you!" and was sorry the instant she heard herself say it.

"Yes mam," he said in an abashed voice, "I would sher love to do that!"

Joy had given him one look on being introduced to him and then throughout the meal had not glanced at him again. He had addressed several remarks to her, which she had pretended not to hear. Mrs. Hopewell could not understand deliberate rudeness, although she lived with it, and she felt she had always to overflow with hospitality to make up for Joy's lack of courtesy. She urged him to talk about himself and he did. He said he was the seventh child of twelve and that his father had been crushed under a tree when he himself was eight years old. He had been crushed very badly, in fact, almost cut in two and was practically not recognizable. His mother had got along the best she could by hard working and she had always seen that her children went to Sunday School and that they read the Bible every evening. He was now nineteen years old and he had been selling Bibles for four months. In that time he had sold seventy-seven Bibles and had the promise of two more sales. He wanted to become a missionary because he thought that was the way you could do most for people. "He who losest his life shall find it," he said simply and he was so sincere, so genuine and earnest that

Mrs. Hopewell would not for the world have smiled. He prevented his peas from sliding onto the table by blocking them with a piece of bread which he later cleaned his plate with. She could see Joy observing sidewise how he handled his knife and fork and she saw too that every few minutes, the boy would dart a keen appraising glance at the girl as if he were trying to attract her attention.

After dinner Joy cleared the dishes off the table and disappeared and Mrs. Hopewell was left to talk with him. He told her again about his childhood and his father's accident and about various things that had happened to him. Every five minutes or so she would stifle a yawn. He sat for two hours until finally she told him she must go because she had an appointment in town. He packed his Bibles and thanked her and prepared to leave, but in the doorway he stopped and wrung her hand and said that not on any of his trips had he met a lady as nice as her and he asked if he could come again. She had said she would always be happy to see him.

Joy had been standing in the road, apparently looking at something in the distance, when he came down the steps toward her, bent to the side with his heavy valise. He stopped where she was standing and confronted her directly. Mrs. Hopewell could not hear what he said but she trembled to think what Joy would say to him. She could see that after a minute Joy said something and that then the boy began to speak again, making an excited gesture with his free hand. After a minute Joy said something else at which the boy began to speak once more. Then to her amazement, Mrs. Hopewell saw the two of them walk off together, toward the gate. Joy had walked all the way to the gate with him and Mrs. Hopewell could not imagine what they had said to each other, and she had not yet dared to ask.

Mrs. Freeman was insisting upon her attention. She had moved from the refrigerator to the heater so that Mrs. Hopewell had to turn and face her in order to seem to be listening. "Glynese gone out with Harvey Hill again last night," she said. "She had this sty."

"Hill," Mrs. Hopewell said absently, "is that the one who works in the garage?"

"Nome, he's the one that goes to chiropracter school," Mrs. Freeman said. "She had this sty. Been had it two days. So she says when he brought her in the other night he says, 'Lemme get rid of that sty for you,' and she says, 'How?' and he says, 'You just lay yourself down acrost the seat of that car and I'll show you.' So she done it and he popped her neck. Kept on a-popping it several times until she made him quit. This morning," Mrs. Freeman said, "she ain't got no sty. She ain't got no traces of a sty."

"I never heard of that before," Mrs. Hopewell said.

"He ast her to marry him before the Ordinary," Mrs. Freeman went on, "and she told him she wasn't going to be married in no *office*."

"Well, Glynese is a fine girl," Mrs. Hopewell said. "Glynese and Carramae are both fine girls."

"Carramae said when her and Lyman was married Lyman said it sure felt sacred to him. She said he said he wouldn't take five hundred dollars for being married by a preacher."

"How much would he take?" the girl asked from the stove.

"He said he wouldn't take five hundred dollars," Mrs. Freeman repeated.

"Well we all have work to do," Mrs. Hopewell said.

"Lyman said it just felt more sacred to him," Mrs. Freeman said. "The doctor wants Carramae to eat prunes. Says instead of medicine. Says them cramps is coming from pressure. You know where I think it is?"

"She'll be better in a few weeks," Mrs. Hopewell said.

"In the tube," Mrs. Freeman said. "Else she wouldn't be as sick as she is."

Hulga had cracked her two eggs into a saucer and was bringing them to the table along with a cup of coffee that she had filled too full. She sat down carefully and began to eat, meaning to keep Mrs. Freeman there by questions if for any reason she showed an inclination to leave. She could perceive her mother's eye on her. The first round-about question would be about the Bible salesman and she did not wish to bring it on. "How did he pop her neck?" she asked.

Mrs. Freeman went into a description of how he had popped her neck. She said he owned a '55 Mercury but that Glynese said she would rather marry a man with only a '36 Plymouth who would be married by a preacher. The girl asked what if he had a '32 Plymouth and Mrs. Freeman said what Glynese had said was a '36 Plymouth.

Mrs. Hopewell said there were not many girls with Glynese's common sense. She said what she admired in those girls was their common sense. She said that reminded her that they had had a nice visitor yesterday, a young man selling Bibles. "Lord," she said, "he bored me to death but he was so sincere and genuine I couldn't be rude to him. He was just good country people, you know," she said, " — just the salt of the earth."

"I seen him walk up," Mrs. Freeman said, "and then later — I seen him walk off," and Hulga could feel the slight shift in her voice, the slight insinuation, that he had not walked off alone, had he? Her face remained expressionless but the color rose into her neck and she seemed to swallow it down with the next spoonful of egg. Mrs. Freeman was looking at her as if they had a secret together.

"Well, it takes all kinds of people to make the world go 'round," Mrs. Hopewell said. "It's very good we aren't all alike."

"Some people are more alike than others," Mrs. Freeman said.

Hulga got up and stumped, with about twice the noise that was necessary, into her room and locked the door. She was to meet the Bible salesman at ten o'clock at the gate. She had thought about it half the night. She had started thinking of it as a great joke and then she had begun to see profound implications in it. She had lain in bed imagining dialogues for them that were insane on the surface but that reached below to depths that no Bible salesman would be aware of. Their conversation yesterday had been of this kind.

He had stopped in front of her and had simply stood there. His face was bony and sweaty and bright, with a little pointed nose in the center of it, and his look was different from what it had been at the dinner table. He was gazing at her with open curiosity, with fascination, like a child watching a new fantastic animal at the zoo, and he was breathing as if he had run a great distance to reach her. His gaze seemed somehow familiar but she could not think where she had been regarded with it before. For almost a minute he didn't say anything. Then on what seemed an insuck of breath, he whispered, "You ever ate a chicken that was two days old?"

The girl looked at him stonily. He might have just put this question up for consideration at the meeting of a philosophical association. "Yes," she presently replied as if she had considered it from all angles.

"It must have been mighty small!" he said triumphantly and shook all over with little nervous giggles, getting very red in the face, and subsiding finally into his gaze of complete admiration, while the girl's expression remained exactly the same.

"How old are you?" he asked softly.

She waited some time before she answered. Then in a flat voice she said, "Seventeen."

His smiles came in succession like waves breaking on the surface of a little lake. "I see you got a wooden leg," he said. "I think you're brave. I think you're real sweet."

The girl stood blank and solid and silent.

"Walk to the gate with me," he said. "You're a brave sweet little thing and I liked you the minute I seen you walk in the door."

Hulga began to move forward.

"What's your name?" he asked, smiling down on the top of her head.

"Hulga," she said.

"Hulga," he murmured, "Hulga. Hulga. I never heard of anybody name Hulga before. You're shy, aren't you, Hulga?" he asked.

She nodded, watching his large red hand on the handle of the giant valise.

"I like girls that wear glasses," he said. "I think a lot. I'm not like these people that a serious thought don't ever enter their heads. It's because I may die."

"I may die too," she said suddenly and looked up at him. His eyes were very small and brown, glittering feverishly.

"Listen," he said, "don't you think some people was meant to meet on account of what all they got in common and all? Like they both think serious thoughts and all?" He shifted the valise to his other hand so that the hand nearest her was free. He caught hold of her elbow and shook it a little. "I don't work on Saturday," he said. "I like to walk in the woods and see what Mother Nature is wearing. O'er the hills and far away. Pic-nics and things. Couldn't we go on a pic-nic tomorrow? Say yes, Hulga," he said and gave her a dying look as if he felt his insides about to drop out of him. He had even seemed to sway slightly toward her.

During the night she had imagined that she seduced him. She imagined that the two of them walked on the place until they came to the storage barn beyond the two back fields and there, she imagined, that things came to such a pass that she very easily seduced him and that then, of course, she had to reckon with his remorse. True genius can get an idea across even to an inferior mind. She imagined that she took his remorse in hand and changed it into a deeper understanding of life. She took all his shame away and turned it into something useful.

She set off for the gate at exactly ten o'clock, escaping without drawing Mrs. Hopewell's attention. She didn't take anything to eat, forgetting that food is usually taken on a pic-nic. She wore a pair of slacks and a dirty white shirt, and as an afterthought, she had put some Vapex on the collar of it since she did not own any perfume. When she reached the gate no one was there.

She looked up and down the empty highway and had the furious feeling that she had been tricked, that he had only meant to make her walk to the gate after the idea of him. Then suddenly he stood up, very tall, from behind a bush on the opposite embankment. Smiling, he lifted his hat which was new and wide-brimmed. He had not worn it yesterday and she wondered if he had bought it for the occasion. It was toast-colored with a red and white band around it and was slightly too large for him. He stepped from behind the bush still carrying the black valise. He had on the same suit and the same yellow socks sucked down in his shoes from walking. He crossed the highway and said, "I knew you'd come!"

The girl wondered acidly how he had known this. She pointed to the valise and asked, "Why did you bring your Bibles?"

He took her elbow, smiling down on her as if he could not stop. "You can never tell when you'll need the word of God, Hulga," he said. She had a moment in which she doubted that this was actually happening and then they began to climb the embankment. They went down into the pasture toward the woods. The boy walked lightly by her side, bouncing on his toes. The valise did not seem to be heavy today; he even swung it. They crossed half the pasture without saying anything and then, putting his hand easily on the small of her back, he asked softly, "Where does your wooden leg join on?"

She turned an ugly red and glared at him and for an instant the boy looked abashed. "I didn't mean you no harm," he said. "I only meant you're so brave and all. I guess God takes care of you."

"No," she said, looking forward and walking fast, "I don't even believe in God."

At this he stopped and whistled. "No!" he exclaimed as if he were too astonished to say anything else.

She walked on and in a second he was bouncing at her side, fanning with his hat. "That's very unusual for a girl," he remarked, watching her out of the corner of his eye. When they reached the edge of the wood, he put his hand on her back again and drew her against him without a word and kissed her heavily.

The kiss, which had more pressure than feeling behind it, produced that extra surge of adrenalin in the girl that enables one to carry a packed trunk out of a burning house, but in her, the power went at once to the brain. Even before he released her, her mind, clear and detached and ironic anyway, was regarding him from a great distance, with amusement but with pity. She had never been kissed before and she was pleased to discover that it was an unexceptional experience and all a matter of the mind's control. Some people might enjoy drain water if they were told it was vodka. When the boy, looking expectant but uncertain, pushed her gently away, she turned and walked on, saying nothing as if such business, for her, were common enough.

He came along panting at her side, trying to help her when he saw a root that she might trip over. He caught and held back the long swaying blades of thorn vine until she had passed beyond them. She led the way and he came breathing heavily behind her. Then they came out on a sunlit hillside, sloping softly into another one a little smaller. Beyond, they could see the rusted top of the old barn where the extra hay was stored.

The hill was sprinkled with small pink weeds. "Then you ain't saved?" he asked suddenly, stopping.

The girl smiled. It was the first time she had smiled at him at all. "In my economy," she said, "I'm saved and you are damned but I told you I didn't believe in God."

Nothing seemed to destroy the boy's look of admiration. He gazed at her now as if the fantastic animal at the zoo had put its paw through the bars and given him a loving poke. She thought he looked as if he wanted to kiss her again and she walked on before he had the chance.

"Ain't there somewheres we can sit down sometime?" he murmured, his voice softening toward the end of the sentence.

"In that barn," she said.

They made for it rapidly as if it might slide away like a train. It was a large two-story barn, cool and dark inside. The boy pointed up the ladder that led into the loft and said, "It's too bad we can't go up there."

"Why can't we?" she asked.

"Yer leg," he said reverently.

The girl gave him a contemptuous look and putting both hands on the ladder, she climbed it while he stood below, apparently awestruck. She pulled herself expertly through the opening and then looked down at him and said, "Well, come on if you're coming," and he began to climb the ladder, awkwardly bringing the suitcase with him.

"We won't need the Bible," she observed.

"You never can tell," he said, panting. After he had got into the loft, he was a few seconds catching his breath. She had sat down in a pile of straw. A wide sheath of sunlight, filled with dust particles, slanted over her. She lay back against a bale, her face turned away, looking out the front opening of the barn where hay was thrown from a wagon into the loft. The two pink-speckled hillsides lay back against a dark ridge of woods. The sky was cloudless and cold blue. The boy dropped down by her side and put one arm under her and the other over her and began methodically kissing her face, making little noises like a fish. He did not remove his hat but it was pushed far enough back not to interfere. When her glasses got in his way, he took them off of her and slipped them into his pocket.

The girl at first did not return any of the kisses but presently she began to and after she had put several on his cheek, she reached his lips and remained there, kissing him again and again as if she were trying to draw all the breath out of him. His breath was clear and sweet like a child's and the kisses were sticky like a child's. He mumbled about loving her and about knowing when he first seen her that he loved her, but the mumbling was like the sleepy fretting of a child being put to sleep by his mother. Her mind, throughout this, never stopped or lost itself for a second to her feelings. "You ain't said you loved me none," he whispered finally, pulling back from her. "You got to say that."

She looked away from him off into the hollow sky and then down at a black ridge and then down farther into what appeared to be two green swelling lakes. She didn't realize he had taken her glasses but this landscape could not seem exceptional to her for she seldom paid any close attention to her surroundings.

"You got to say it," he repeated. "You got to say you love me."

She was always careful how she committed herself. "In a sense," she began, "if you use the word loosely, you might say that. But it's not a word I use. I don't have illusions. I'm one of those people who see *through* to nothing."

The boy was frowning. "You got to say it. I said it and you got to say it," he said.

The girl looked at him almost tenderly. "You poor baby," she murmured. "It's just as well you don't understand," and she pulled him by the neck, face-down, against her. "We are all damned," she said, "but some of us have taken off our blindfolds and see that there's nothing to see. It's a kind of salvation."

The boy's astonished eyes looked blankly through the ends of her hair. "Okay," he almost whined, "but do you love me or don'tcher?"

"Yes," she said and added, "in a sense. But I must tell you something. There mustn't be anything dishonest between us." She lifted his head and looked him in the eye. "I am thirty years old," she said. "I have a number of degrees."

The boy's look was irritated but dogged. "I don't care," he said. "I don't care a thing about what all you done. I just want to know if you love me or don'tcher?" and he caught her to him and wildly planted her face with kisses until she said, "Yes, yes."

"Okay then," he said, letting her go. "Prove it."

She smiled, looking dreamily out on the shifty landscape. She had seduced him without even making up her mind to try. "How?" she asked, feeling that he should be delayed a little.

He leaned over and put his lips to her ear. "Show me where your wooden leg joins on," he whispered.

The girl uttered a sharp little cry and her face instantly drained of color. The obscenity of the suggestion was not what shocked her. As a child she had sometimes been subject to feelings of shame but education had removed the last traces of that as a good surgeon scrapes for cancer; she would no more have felt it over what he was asking than she would have believed in his Bible. But she was as sensitive about the artificial leg as a peacock about his tail. No one ever touched it but her. She took care of it as someone else would his soul, in private and almost with her own eyes turned away. "No," she said.

"I known it," he muttered, sitting up. "You're just playing me for a sucker."

"Oh no no!" she cried. "It joins on at the knee. Only at the knee. Why do you want to see it?"

The boy gave her a long penetrating look. "Because," he said, "it's what makes you different. You ain't like anybody else."

She sat staring at him. There was nothing about her face or her round freezing-blue eyes to indicate that this had moved her; but she felt as if her heart had stopped and left her mind to pump her blood. She decided that for the first time in her life she was face to face with real innocence. This boy, with an instinct that came from beyond wisdom, had touched the truth about her. When after a minute, she said in a hoarse high voice, "All right," it was like surrendering to him completely. It was like losing her own life and finding it again, miraculously, in his.

Very gently be began to roll the slack leg up. The artificial limb, in a white sock and brown flat shoe, was bound in a heavy material like canvas and ended in an ugly jointure where it was attached to the stump. The boy's face and his voice were entirely reverent as he uncovered it and said, "Now show me how to take it off and on."

She took it off for him and put it back on again and then he took it off himself, handling it as tenderly as if it were a real one. "See!" he said with a delighted child's face. "Now I can do it myself!"

"Put it back on," she said. She was thinking that she would run away with him and that every night he would take the leg off and every morning put it back on again. "Put it back on," she said.

"Not yet," he murmured, setting it on its foot out of her reach. "Leave it off for a while. You got me instead."

She gave a little cry of alarm but he pushed her down and began to kiss her again. Without the leg she felt entirely dependent on him. Her brain seemed to have stopped thinking altogether and to be about some other function that it was not very good at. Different expressions raced back and forth over her face. Every now and then the boy, his eyes like two steel spikes, would glance behind him where the leg stood. Finally she pushed him off and said, "Put it back on me now."

"Wait," he said. He leaned the other way and pulled the valise toward him and opened it. It had a pale blue spotted lining and there were only two Bibles in it. He took one of these out and opened the cover of it. It was hollow and contained a pocket flask of whiskey, a pack of cards, and a small blue box with printing on it. He laid these out in front of her one at a time in an evenly-spaced row, like one presenting offerings at the shrine of a goddess. He put the blue box in her hand. THIS PRODUCT TO BE USED ONLY FOR THE PREVENTION OF DISEASE, she read, and dropped it. The boy was unscrewing the top of the flask. He stopped and pointed, with a smile, to the deck of cards. It was not an ordinary deck but one with an obscene picture on the back of each card. "Take a swig," he said, offering her the bottle first. He held it in front of her, but like one mesmerized, she did not move.

Her voice when she spoke had an almost pleading sound. "Aren't you," she murmured, "aren't you just good country people?"

The boy cocked his head. He looked as if he were just beginning to understand that she might be trying to insult him. "Yeah," he said, curling his lip slightly, "but it ain't held me back none. I'm as good as you any day in the week."

"Give me my leg," she said.

He pushed it farther away with his foot. "Come on now, let's begin to have us a good time," he said coaxingly. "We ain't got to know one another good yet."

"Give me my leg!" she screamed and tried to lunge for it but he pushed her down easily.

"What's the matter with you all of a sudden?" he asked, frowning as he screwed the top on the flask and put it quickly back inside the Bible. "You just a while ago said you didn't believe in nothing. I thought you was some girl!"

Her face was almost purple. "You're a Christian!" she hissed. "You're a fine Christian! You're just like them all — say one thing and do another. You're a perfect Christian, you're . . ."

The boy's mouth was set angrily. "I hope you don't think," he said in a lofty indignant tone, "that I believe in that crap! I may sell Bibles but I know which end is up and I wasn't born yesterday and I know where I'm going!"

"Give me my leg!" she screeched. He jumped up so quickly that she barely saw him sweep the cards and the blue box into the Bible and throw the Bible into the valise. She saw him grab the leg and then she saw it for an instant slanted forlornly across the inside of the suitcase with a Bible at either side of its opposite ends. He slammed the lid shut and snatched up the valise and swung it down the hole and then stepped through himself.

When all of him had passed but his head, he turned and regarded her with a look that no longer had any admiration in it. "I've gotten a lot of interesting things," he said. "One time I got a woman's glass eye this way. And you needn't to think you'll catch me because Pointer ain't really my name. I use a different name at every house I call at and don't stay nowhere long. And I'll tell you another thing, Hulga," he said, using the name as if he didn't think much of it, "you ain't so smart. I been believing in nothing ever since I was born!" and then the toast-colored hat disappeared down the hole and the girl was left, sitting on the straw in the dusty sunlight. When she turned her churning face toward the opening, she saw his blue figure struggling successfully over the green speckled lake.

Mrs. Hopewell and Mrs. Freeman, who were in the back pasture, digging up onions, saw him emerge a little later from the woods and head across the meadow toward the highway. "Why, that looks like that nice dull young man that tried to sell me a Bible yesterday," Mrs. Hopewell said, squinting. "He must have been selling them to the Negroes back in there. He was so simple," he said, "but I guess the world would be better off if we were all that simple."

Mrs. Freeman's gaze drove forward and just touched him before he disappeared under the hill. Then she returned her attention to the evil-smelling onion shoot she was lifting from the ground. "Some can't be that simple," she said. "I know I never could." [1955]

FLANNERY O'CONNOR

A Good Man Is Hard to Find

The dragon is by the side of the road, watching those who pass. Beware lest he devour you. We go to the Father of Souls, but it is necessary to pass by the dragon.

St. Cyril of Jerusalem

The grandmother didn't want to go to Florida. She wanted to visit some of her connections in east Tennessee and she was seizing at every chance to change Bailey's mind. Bailey was the son she lived with, her only boy. He was sitting on the edge of his chair at the table, bent over the orange sports section of the *Journal*. "Now look here, Bailey," she said, "see here, read this," and she stood with one hand on her thin hip and the other rattling the newspaper at his bald head. "Here this fellow that calls himself The Misfit is aloose from the Federal Pen and headed toward Florida and you read here what it says he did to these people. Just you read it. I wouldn't take my children in any direction with a criminal like that aloose in it. I couldn't answer to my conscience if I did."

Bailey didn't look up from his reading so she wheeled around then and faced the children's mother, a young woman in slacks, whose face was as broad and innocent as a cabbage and was tied around with a green headkerchief that had two points on the top like a rabbit's ears. She was sitting on the sofa, feeding the baby his apricots out of a jar. "The children have been to Florida before," the old lady said. "You all ought to take them somewhere else for a change so they would see different parts of the world and be broad. They never have been to east Tennessee."

The children's mother didn't seem to hear her but the eight-year-old boy, John Wesley, a stocky child with glasses, said, "If you don't want to go to Florida, why dontcha stay at home?" He and the little girl, June Star, were reading the funny papers on the floor.

"She wouldn't stay at home to be queen for a day," June Star said without raising her yellow head.

"Yes and what would you do if this fellow, The Misfit, caught you?" the grandmother asked.

"I'd smack his face," John Wesley said.

"She wouldn't stay at home for a million bucks," June Star said. "Afraid she'd miss something. She has to go everywhere we go."

"All right, Miss," the grandmother said. "Just remember that the next time you want me to curl your hair."

June Star said her hair was naturally curly.

The next morning the grandmother was the first one in the car, ready to go. She had her big black valise that looked like the head of a hippopotamus in one corner, and underneath it she was hiding a basket with Pitty Sing, the cat, in it. She didn't intend for the cat to be left alone in the house for three days because he would miss her too much and she was afraid he might brush against one of the gas burners and accidentally asphyxiate himself. Her son, Bailey, didn't like to arrive at a motel with a cat.

She sat in the middle of the back seat with John Wesley and June Star on either side of her. Bailey and the children's mother and the baby sat in front and they left Atlanta at eight forty-five with the mileage on the car at 55890. The grandmother wrote this down because she thought it would be interesting to say how many miles they had been when they got back. It took them twenty minutes to reach the outskirts of the city.

The old lady settled herself comfortably, removing her white cotton gloves and putting them up with her purse on the shelf in front of the back window. The children's mother still had on slacks and still had her head tied up in a green kerchief, but the grandmother had on a navy blue straw sailor hat with a bunch of white violets on the brim and a navy blue dress with a small white dot in the print. Her collars and cuffs were white organdy trimmed with lace and at her neckline she had pinned a purple spray of cloth violets containing a sachet. In case of an accident, anyone seeing her dead on the highway would know at once that she was a lady.

She said she thought it was going to be a good day for driving, neither too hot nor too cold, and she cautioned Bailey that the speed limit was fifty-five miles an hour and that the patrolmen hid themselves behind billboards and small clumps of trees and sped out after you before you had a chance to slow down. She pointed out interesting details of the scenery: Stone Mountain; the blue granite that in some places came up to both sides of the highway; the brilliant red clay banks slightly streaked with purple; and the various crops that made rows of green lace-work on the ground. The trees were full of silver-white sunlight and the meanest of them sparkled. The children were reading comic magazines and their mother had gone back to sleep.

"Let's go through Georgia fast so we won't have to look at it much," John Wesley said.

"If I were a little boy," said the grandmother, "I wouldn't talk about my native state that way. Tennessee has the mountains and Georgia has the hills."

"Tennessee is just a hillbilly dumping ground," John Wesley said, "and Georgia is a lousy state too."

"You said it," June Star said.

"In my time," said the grandmother, folding her thin veined fingers, "children were more respectful of their native states and their parents and everything else. People did right then. Oh look at the cute little pickaninny!" she said and pointed to a Negro child standing in the door of a shack. "Wouldn't that make a picture, now?" she asked and they all turned and looked at the little Negro out of the back window. He waved.

"He didn't have any britches on," June Star said.

"He probably didn't have any," the grandmother explained. "Little niggers in the country don't have things like we do. If I could paint, I'd paint that picture," she said.

The children exchanged comic books.

The grandmother offered to hold the baby and the children's mother passed him over the front seat to her. She set him on her knee and bounced him and told him about the things they were passing. She rolled her eyes and screwed up her mouth and stuck her leathery thin face into his smooth bland one. Occasionally he gave her a faraway smile. They passed a large cotton field with five or six graves fenced in the middle of it, like a small island. "Look at the graveyard!" the grandmother said, pointing it out. "That was the old family burying ground. That belonged to the plantation."

"Where's the plantation?" John Wesley asked.

"Gone with the Wind," said the grandmother. "Ha. Ha."

When the children finished all the comic books they had brought, they opened the lunch and ate it. The grandmother ate a peanut butter sandwich and an olive and would not let the children throw the box and the paper napkins out the window. When there was nothing else to do they played a game by choosing a cloud and making the other two guess what shape it suggested. John Wesley took one the shape of a cow and June Star guessed a cow and John Wesley said, no, an automobile, and June Star said he didn't play fair, and they began to slap each other over the grandmother.

The grandmother said she would tell them a story if they would keep quiet. When she told a story, she rolled her eyes and waved her head and was very dramatic. She said once when she was a maiden lady she had been courted by a Mr. Edgar Atkins Teagarden from Jasper, Georgia. She said he was a very good-looking man and a gentleman and that he brought her a watermelon every Saturday afternoon with his initials cut in it, E. A. T. Well, one Saturday, she said, Mr. Teagarden brought the watermelon and there was nobody at home and he left it on the front porch and returned in his buggy to Jasper, but she never got the watermelon, she said, because a nigger boy ate it when he saw the initials, E. A. T.! This story tickled John Wesley's funny bone and he giggled and giggled but June Star didn't think it was any good. She said she wouldn't marry a man that just brought her a watermelon on Saturday. The grandmother said she would have done well to marry Mr. Teagarden because he was a gentleman and had bought Coca-Cola stock when it first came out and that he had died only a few years ago, a very wealthy man.

They stopped at The Tower for barbecued sandwiches. The Tower was a part stucco and part wood filling station and dance hall set in a clearing outside of Timothy. A fat man named Red Sammy Butts ran it and there were signs stuck here and there on the building and for miles up and down the highway saying, TRY RED SAMMY'S FAMOUS BARBECUE. NONE LIKE FAMOUS RED SAMMY'S! RED SAM! THE FAT BOY WITH THE HAPPY LAUGH. A VETERAN! RED SAMMY'S YOUR MAN!

Red Sammy was lying on the bare ground outside The Tower with his head under a truck while a gray monkey about a foot high, chained to a small chinaberry tree, chattered nearby. The monkey sprang back into the tree and got on the highest limb as soon as he saw the children jump out of the car and run toward him.

Inside, The Tower was a long dark room with a counter at one end and tables at the other and dancing space in the middle. They all sat down at a board table next to the nickelodeon and Red Sam's wife, a tall burnt-brown woman with hair and eyes lighter than her skin, came and took their order. The children's mother put a dime in the machine and played "The Tennessee Waltz," and the grandmother said that tune always made her want to dance. She asked Bailey if he would like to dance but he only glared at her. He didn't have a naturally sunny disposition like she did and trips made him nervous. The grandmother's brown eyes were very bright. She swayed her head from side to side and pretended she was dancing in her chair. June Star said play something she could tap to so the children's mother put in another dime and played a fast number and June Star stepped out onto the dance floor and did her tap routine.

"Ain't she cute?" Red Sam's wife said, leaning over the counter. "Would you like to come be my little girl?"

"No I certainly wouldn't," June Star said. "I wouldn't live in a broken-down place like this for a million bucks!" and she ran back to the table.

"Ain't she cute?" the woman repeated, stretching her mouth politely.

"Aren't you ashamed?" hissed the grandmother.

Red Sam came in and told his wife to quit lounging on the counter and hurry up with these people's order. His khaki trousers reached just to his hip bones and his stomach hung over them like a sack of meal swaying under his shirt. He came over and sat down at a table nearby and let out a combination sigh and yodel. "You can't win," he said. "You can't win," and he wiped his sweating red face off with a gray handkerchief. "These days you don't know who to trust," he said. "Ain't that the truth?"

"People are certainly not nice like they used to be," said the grandmother.

"Two fellers come in here last week," Red Sammy said, "driving a Chrysler. It was a old beat-up car but it was a good one and these boys looked all right to me. Said they worked at the mill and you know I let them fellers charge the gas they bought? Now why did I do that?"

"Because you're a good man!" the grandmother said at once.

"Yes'm, I suppose so," Red Sam said as if he were struck with this answer.

His wife brought the orders, carrying the five plates all at once without a tray, two in each hand and one balanced on her arm. "It isn't a soul in this green world of God's that you can trust," she said. "And I don't count nobody out of that, not nobody," she repeated, looking at Red Sammy.

"Did you read about that criminal, The Misfit, that's escaped?" asked the grandmother.

"I wouldn't be a bit surprised if he didn't attack this place right here," said the woman. "If he hears about it being here, I wouldn't be none surprised to see him. If he hears it's two cent in the cash register, I wouldn't be a tall surprised if he. . . ."

"That'll do," Red Sam said. "Go bring these people their Co'-Colas," and the woman went off to get the rest of the order.

"A good man is hard to find," Red Sammy said. "Everything is getting terrible. I remember the day you could go off and leave your screen door unlatched. Not no more."

He and the grandmother discussed better times. The old lady said that in her opinion Europe was entirely to blame for the way things were now. She said the way Europe acted you would think we were made of money and Red Sam said it was no use talking about it, she was exactly right. The children ran outside into the white sunlight and looked at the monkey in the lacy chinaberry tree. He was busy catching fleas on himself and biting each one carefully between his teeth as if it were a delicacy.

They drove off again into the hot afternoon. The grandmother took cat naps and woke up every few minutes with her own snoring. Outside of Toombsboro she woke up and recalled an old plantation that she had visited in this neighborhood once when she was a young lady. She said the house had six white columns across the front and that there was an avenue of oaks leading up to it and two little wooden trellis arbors on either side in front where you sat down with your suitor after a stroll in the garden. She recalled exactly which road to turn off to get to it. She knew that Bailey would not be willing to lose any time looking at an old house, but the more she talked about it, the more she wanted to see it once again and find out if the little twin arbors were still standing. "There was a secret panel in this house," she said craftily, not telling the truth but wishing that she were, "and the story went that all the family silver was hidden in it when Sherman came through but it was never found. . . ."

"Hey!" John Wesley said. "Let's go see it! We'll find it! We'll poke all the woodwork and find it! Who lives there? Where do you turn off at? Hey Pop, can't we turn off there?"

"We never have seen a house with a secret panel!" June Star shrieked. "Let's go to the house with the secret panel! Hey Pop, can't we go see the house with the secret panel!"

"It's not far from here, I know," the grandmother said. "It won't take over twenty minutes."

Bailey was looking straight ahead. His jaw was as rigid as a horseshoe. "No." he said.

The children began to yell and scream that they wanted to see the house with the secret panel. John Wesley kicked the back of the front seat and June

Star hung over her mother's shoulder and whined desperately into her ear that they never had any fun even on their vacation, that they could never do what THEY wanted to do. The baby began to scream and John Wesley kicked the back of the seat so hard that his father could feel the blows in his kidney.

"All right!" he shouted and drew the car to a stop at the side of the road. "Will you all shut up? Will you all just shut up for one second? If you don't shut up, we won't go anywhere."

"It would be very educational for them," the grandmother murmured.

"All right," Bailey said, "but get this: this is the only time we're going to stop for anything like this. This is the one and only time."

"The dirt road that you have to turn down is about a mile back," the grandmother directed. "I marked it when we passed."

"A dirt road," Bailey groaned.

After they had turned around and were headed toward the dirt road, the grandmother recalled other points about the house, the beautiful glass over the front doorway and the candle-lamp in the hall. John Wesley said that the secret panel was probably in the fireplace.

"You can't go inside this house," Bailey said. "You don't know who lives there."

"While you all talk to the people in front, I'll run around behind and get in a window," John Wesley suggested.

"We'll all stay in the car," his mother said.

They turned onto the dirt road and the car raced roughly along in a swirl of pink dust. The grandmother recalled the times when there were no paved roads and thirty miles was a day's journey. The dirt road was hilly and there were sudden washes in it and sharp curves on dangerous embankments. All at once they would be on a hill, looking down over the blue tops of trees for miles around, then the next minute, they would be in a red depression with the dust-coated trees looking down on them.

"This place had better turn up in a minute," Bailey said, "or I'm going to turn around."

The road looked as if no one had traveled on it for months.

"It's not much farther," the grandmother said and just as she said it, a horrible thought came to her. The thought was so embarrassing that she turned red in the face and her eyes dilated and her feet jumped up, upsetting her valise in the corner. The instant the valise moved, the newspaper top she had over the basket under it rose with a snarl and Pitty Sing, the cat, sprang onto Bailey's shoulder.

The children were thrown to the floor and their mother, clutching the baby was thrown out the door onto the ground, the old lady was thrown into the front seat. The car turned over once and landed right-side-up in a gulch off the side of the road. Bailey remained in the driver's seat with the cat gray-striped with a broad white face and an orange nose clinging to his neck like a caterpillar.

As soon as the children saw they could move their arms and legs, they scrambled out of the car, shouting, "We've had an ACCIDENT!" The grandmother was curled up under the dashboard, hoping she was injured so that Bailey's wrath would not come down on her all at once. The horrible thought she had before the accident was that the house she had remembered so vividly was not in Georgia but in Tennessee.

Bailey removed the cat from his neck with both hands and flung it out the window against the side of a pine tree. Then he got out of the car and started looking for the children's mother. She was sitting against the side of the red gutted ditch, holding the screaming baby, but she only had a cut down her face and a broken shoulder. "We've had an ACCIDENT!" the children screamed in a frenzy of delight.

"But nobody's killed," June Star said with disappointment as the grandmother limped out of the car, her hat still pinned to her head but the broken front brim standing up at a jaunty angle and the violet spray hanging off the side. They all sat down in the ditch, except the children, to recover from the shock. They were all shaking.

"Maybe a car will come along," said the children's mother hoarsely.

"I believe I have injured an organ," said the grandmother, pressing her side, but no one answered her. Bailey's teeth were clattering. He had on a yellow sport shirt with bright blue parrots designed in it and his face was as yellow as the shirt. The grandmother decided that she would not mention that the house was in Tennessee.

The road was about ten feet above and they could only see the tops of the trees on the other side of it. Behind the ditch they were sitting in there were more woods, tall and dark and deep. In a few minutes they saw a car some distance away on top of a hill, coming slowly as if the occupants were watching them. The grandmother stood up and waved both arms dramatically to attract their attention. The car continued to come on slowly, disappeared around a bend and appeared again, moving even slower, on top of the hill they had gone over. It was a big black battered hearse-like automobile. There were three men in it.

It came to a stop just over them and for some minutes, the driver looked down with a steady expressionless gaze to where they were sitting, and didn't speak. Then he turned his head and muttered something to the other two and they got out. One was a fat boy in black trousers and a red sweat shirt with a silver stallion embossed on the front of it. He moved around on the right side of them and stood staring, his mouth partly open in a kind of loose grin. The other had on khaki pants and a blue striped coat and a gray hat pulled very low, hiding most of his face. He came around slowly on the left side. Neither spoke.

The driver got out of the car and stood by the side of it, looking down at them. He was an older man than the other two. His hair was just beginning to gray and he wore silver-rimmed spectacles that gave him a scholarly look. He had a long creased face and didn't have on any shirt or undershirt. He had on blue jeans that were too tight for him and was holding a black hat and a gun. The two boys also had guns.

"We've had an ACCIDENT!" the children screamed.

The grandmother had the peculiar feeling that the bespectacled man was someone she knew. His face was as familiar to her as if she had known him all her life but she could not recall who he was. He moved away from the car and began to come down the embankment, placing his feet carefully so that he wouldn't slip. He had on tan and white shoes and no socks, and his ankles were red and thin. "Good afternoon," he said. "I see you all had you a little spill."

"We turned over twice!" said the grandmother.

"Oncet," he corrected. "We seen it happen. Try their car and see will it run, Hiram," he said quietly to the boy with the gray hat.

"What you got that gun for?" John Wesley asked. "Whatcha gonna do with that gun?"

"Lady," the man said to the children's mother, "would you mind calling them children to sit down by you? Children make me nervous. I want all you all to sit down right together there where you're at."

"What are you telling US what to do for?" June Star asked.

Behind them the line of woods gaped like a dark open mouth. "Come here," said the mother.

"Look here now," Bailey said suddenly, "we're in a predicament! We're in. . . ."

The grandmother shrieked. She scrambled to her feet and stood staring. "You're The Misfit!" she said. "I recognized you at once!"

"Yes'm," the man said, smiling slightly as if he were pleased in spite of himself to be known, "but it would have been better for all of you, lady, if you hadn't of reckernized me."

Bailey turned his head sharply and said something to his mother that shocked even the children. The old lady began to cry and The Misfit reddened.

"Lady," he said, "don't you get upset. Sometimes a man says things he don't mean. I don't reckon he meant to talk to you thataway."

"You wouldn't shoot a lady, would you?" the grandmother said and removed a clean handkerchief from her cuff and began to slap at her eyes with it.

The Misfit pointed the toe of his shoe into the ground and made a little hole and then covered it up again. "I would hate to have to," he said.

"Listen," the grandmother almost screamed, "I know you're a good man. You don't look a bit like you have common blood. I know you must come from nice people!"

"Yes mam," he said, "finest people in the world." When he smiled he showed a row of strong white teeth. "God never made a finer woman than my mother and my daddy's heart was pure gold," he said. The boy with the red sweat shirt had come around behind them and was standing with his gun at his hip. The Misfit squatted down on the ground. "Watch them children, Bobby Lee," he said. "You know they make me nervous." He looked at the six of them huddled together in front of him and he seemed to be embarrassed as if he couldn't think of anything to say. "Ain't a cloud in the sky," he remarked, looking up at it. "Don't see no sun but don't see no cloud neither."

"Yes, it's a beautiful day," said the grandmother. "Listen," she said, "You shouldn't call yourself The Misfit because I know you're a good man at heart. I can just look at you and tell."

"Hush!" Bailey yelled. "Hush! Everybody shut up and let me handle this!" He was squatting in the position of a runner about to sprint forward but he didn't move.

"I pre-chate that, lady," The Misfit said and drew a little circle in the ground with the butt of his gun.

"It'll take a half a hour to fix this here car," Hiram called, looking over the raised hood of it.

"Well, first you and Bobby Lee get him and that little boy to step over yonder with you." The Misfit said, pointing to Bailey and John Wesley, "The boys want to ast you something," he said to Bailey. "Would you mind stepping back in them woods there with them?"

"Listen," Bailey began, "we're in a terrible predicament! Nobody realizes what this is," and his voice cracked. His eyes were as blue and intense as the parrots in his shirt and he remained perfectly still.

The grandmother reached up to adjust her hat brim as if she were going to the woods with him but it came off in her hand. She stood staring at it and after a second she let it fall to the ground. Hiram pulled Bailey up by the arm as if he were assisting an old man. John Wesley caught hold of his father's hand and Bobby Lee followed. They went off toward the woods and just as they reached the dark edge, Bailey turned and supporting himself against a gray naked pine trunk, he shouted, "I'll be back in a minute, Mamma, wait on me!"

"Come back this instant!" his mother shrilled but they all disappeared into the woods.

"Bailey Boy!" the grandmother called in a tragic voice but she found she was looking at The Misfit squatting on the ground in front of her. "I just know you're a good man," she said desperately. "You're not a bit common!"

"Nome, I ain't a good man," The Misfit said after a second as if he had considered her statement carefully, "but I ain't the worst in the world neither. My daddy said I was a different breed of dog from my brothers and sisters. 'You know,' Daddy said, 'it's some that can live their whole life out without asking about it and it's others has to know why it is, and this boy is one of the latters. He's going to be into everything!'" He put on his black hat and looked up suddenly and then away deep into the woods as if he were embarrassed again. "I'm sorry I don't have on a shirt before you ladies," he said, hunching his shoulders slightly. "We buried our clothes that we had on when we escaped and we're just making do until we can get better. We borrowed these from some folks we met," he explained.

"That's perfectly all right," the grandmother said. "Maybe Bailey has an extra shirt in his suitcase."

"I'll look and see terrectly," The Misfit said.

"Where are they taking him?" the children's mother screamed.

"Daddy was a card himself," The Misfit said. "You couldn't put anything over on him. He never got in trouble with the Authorities though. Just had the knack of handling them."

"You could be honest too if you'd only try," said the grandmother. "Think how wonderful it would be to settle down and live a comfortable life and not have to think about somebody chasing you all the time."

The Misfit kept scratching in the ground with the butt of his gun as if he were thinking about it. "Yes'm, somebody is always after you," he murmured.

The grandmother noticed how thin his shoulder blades were just behind his hat because she was standing up looking down at him. "Do you ever pray?" she asked.

He shook his head. All she saw was the black hat wiggle between his shoulder blades. "Nome," he said.

There was a pistol shot from the woods, followed closely by another. Then silence. The old lady's head jerked around. She could hear the wind move through the tree tops like a long satisfied insuck of breath. "Bailey Boy!" she called.

"I was a gospel singer for a while," The Misfit said. "I been most everything. Been in the arm service, both land and sea, at home and abroad, been twict married, been an undertaker, been with the railroads, plowed Mother Earth, been in a tornado, seen a man burnt alive oncet," and he looked up at the children's mother and the little girl who were sitting close together, their faces white and their eyes glassy; "I even seen a woman flogged," he said.

"Pray, pray," the grandmother began, "pray, pray. . . ."

"I never was a bad boy that I remember of," The Misfit said in an almost dreamy voice, "but somewheres along the line I done something wrong and got sent to the penitentiary. I was buried alive," and he looked up and held her attention to him by a steady stare.

"That's when you should have started to pray," she said. "What did you do to get sent to the penitentiary, that first time?"

"Turn to the right, it was a wall," The Misfit said, looking up again at the cloudless sky. "Turn to the left, it was a wall. Look up it was a ceiling, look down it was a floor. I forgot what I done, lady. I set there and set there, trying to remember what it was I done and I ain't recalled it to this day. Oncet in a while, I would think it was coming to me, but it never come."

"Maybe they put you in by mistake," the old lady said vaguely.

"Nome," he said. "It wasn't no mistake. They had the papers on me."

"You must have stolen something," she said.

The Misfit sneered slightly. "Nobody had nothing I wanted," he said. "It was a head-doctor at the penitentiary said what I had done was kill my daddy but I known that for a lie. My daddy died in nineteen ought nineteen of the epidemic flu and I never had a thing to do with it. He was buried in the Mount Hopewell Baptist churchyard and you can see for yourself."

"If you would pray," the old lady said, "Jesus would help you."

"That's right," The Misfit said.

"Well then, why don't you pray?" she asked trembling with delight suddenly.

"I don't want no hep," he said. "I'm doing all right by myself."

Bobby Lee and Hiram came ambling back from the woods. Bobby Lee was dragging a yellow shirt with bright blue parrots in it.

"Throw me that shirt, Bobby Lee," The Misfit said. The shirt came flying at him and landed on his shoulder and he put it on. The grandmother couldn't name what the shirt reminded her of. "No, lady," The Misfit said while he was buttoning it up, "I found out the crime don't matter. You can do one thing or you can do another, kill a man or take a tire off his car, because sooner or later you're going to forget what it was you done and just be punished for it."

The children's mother had begun to make heaving noises as if she couldn't get her breath. "Lady," he asked, "would you and that little girl like to step off yonder with Bobby Lee and Hiram and join your husband?"

"Yes, thank you," the mother said faintly. Her left arm dangled help-lessly and she was holding the baby, who had gone to sleep, in the other. "Hep that lady up, Hiram," The Misfit said as she struggled to climb out of the ditch, "and Bobby Lee, you hold onto that little girl's hand."

"I don't want to hold hands with him," June Star said. "He reminds me of a pig."

The fat boy blushed and laughed and caught her by the arm and pulled her off into the woods after Hiram and her mother.

Alone with The Misfit, the grandmother found that she had lost her voice. There was not a cloud in the sky nor any sun. There was nothing around her but woods. She wanted to tell him that he must pray. She opened and closed her mouth several times before anything came out. Finally she found herself saying, "Jesus, Jesus," meaning, Jesus will help you, but the way she was saying it, it sounded as if she might be cursing.

"Yes'm," The Misfit said as if he agreed. "Jesus thown everything off balance. It was the same case with Him as with me except He hadn't com-mitted any crime and they could prove I had committed one because they had the papers on me. Of course," he said, "they never shown me my papers. That's why I sign myself now. I said long ago, you get your signature and sign everything you do and keep a copy of it. Then you'll know what you done and you can hold up the crime to the punishment and see do they match and in the end you'll have something to prove you ain't been treated right. I call myself The Misfit," he said, "because I can't make what all I done wrong fit what all I gone through in punishment."

There was a piercing scream from the woods, followed closely by a pistol report. "Does it seem right to you, lady, that one is punished a heap and another ain't punished at all?"

"Jesus!" the old lady cried. "You've got good blood! I know you wouldn't shoot a lady! I know you come from nice people! Pray! Jesus, you ought not to shoot a lady. I'll give you all the money I've got!"

"Lady," The Misfit said, looking beyond her far into the woods, "there never was a body that give the undertaker a tip."

There were two more pistol reports and the grandmother raised her head like a parched old turkey hen crying for water and called, "Bailey Boy, Bailey Boy!" as if her heart would break.

"Jesus was the only One that ever raised the dead," The Misfit continued, "and He shouldn't have done it. He thrown everything off balance. If He did what He said, then it's nothing for you to do but throw away everything and follow Him, and if He didn't, then it's nothing for you to do but enjoy the few minutes you got left the best you can by killing somebody or burning down his house or doing some other meanness to him. No pleasure but meanness," he said and his voice had become almost a snarl.

"Maybe He didn't raise the dead," the old lady mumbled, not knowing what she was saying and feeling so dizzy that she sank down in the ditch with her legs twisted under her.

"I wasn't there so I can't say He didn't," The Misfit said. "I wisht I had of been there," he said, hitting the ground with his fist. "It ain't right I wasn't there because if I had of been there I would of known. Listen lady," he said in a high voice, "if I had of been there I would of known and I wouldn't be like I am now." His voice seemed about to crack and the grandmother's head cleared for an instant. She saw the man's face twisted close to her own as if he were going to cry and she murmured, "Why you're one of my babies. You're one of my own children!" She reached out and touched him on the shoulder. The Misfit sprang back as if a snake had bitten him and shot her three times through the chest. Then he put his gun down on the ground and took off his glasses and began to clean them.

Hiram and Bobby Lee returned from the woods and stood over the ditch, looking down at the grandmother who half sat and half lay in a puddle of blood with her legs crossed under her like a child's and her face smiling up at the cloudless sky.

Without his glasses, The Misfit's eyes were red-rimmed and pale and defenseless-looking. "Take her off and throw her where you thrown the others," he said, picking up the cat that was rubbing itself against his leg.

"She was a talker, wasn't she?" Bobby Lee said, sliding down the ditch with a yodel.

"She would of been a good woman," The Misfit said, "if it had been somebody there to shoot her every minute of her life."

"Some fun!" Bobby Lee said.

"Shut up, Bobby Lee," The Misfit said. "It's no real pleasure in life."

[1955]

FRANK O'CONNOR *was the pseudonym for Michael Francis O'Donovan (1903–1966), who was born in Cork, Ireland. His parents were so poor that he attended school only through the fourth grade, at the Christian Brothers School in Cork. During the Irish struggle for independence from England (1918–1921), he was briefly a member of the Irish Republican Army. For several years thereafter he worked as a librarian in Cork and Dublin; it was at this time that he began using his pseudonym so he would not jeopardize his job as a public official. He had started to write stories as a boy, and for a while he could not decide whether to be a painter or a writer: "I discovered by the time I was sixteen or seventeen that paints cost too much money, so I became a writer because you could be a writer with a pencil and a penny notebook."*

When O'Connor was twenty-eight years old, the Atlantic Monthly *published his story "Guests of the Nation," which he later said was an imitation of Isaac Babel's stories in* Red Cavalry. *His first collection of stories appeared that same year (1931), and from then on he made his living as a writer. During the 1950s he lived in the United States, teaching at Harvard and Northwestern universities and publishing two excellent critical works,* The Mirror in the Roadway *(1956), a study of the modern novel, and* The Lonely Voice *(1963), a history of the short story. O'Connor was a prolific writer, editor, critic, and translator, with almost fifty books to his credit, including fourteen volumes of short stories. He often rewrote his stories several times, even after they were published, so many of them appear in different versions in his various volumes.*

O'Connor's greatest achievement was in the short story. Primarily indebted to Anton Chekhov, he declared himself to be an old-fashioned storyteller, believing that a story should have the sound of a person speaking. This conviction gives his fiction an engaging tone, confirming — as do Chekhov's stories — the author's basic sympathy toward his characters. In praising O'Connor's stories, the noted Irish poet William Butler Yeats said that he was "doing for Ireland what Chekhov did for Russia."

RELATED COMMENTARIES: *Frank O'Connor, "The Nearest Thing to Lyric Poetry Is the Short Story," page 1481; Frank O'Connor, "Style and Form in Joyce's 'The Dead,'" page 1482.*

FRANK O'CONNOR

Guests of the Nation

I

At dusk the big Englishman, Belcher, would shift his long legs out of the ashes and say "Well, chums, what about it?" and Noble or me would say "All right, chum" (for we had picked up some of their curious expressions), and the little Englishman, Hawkins, would light the lamp and bring out the cards. Sometimes Jeremiah Donovan would come up and supervise the game and get excited over Hawkins's cards, which he always played badly, and shout at him as if he was one of our own "Ah, you divil, you, why didn't you play the tray?"

But ordinarily Jeremiah was a sober and contented poor devil like the big Englishman, Belcher, and was looked up to only because he was a fair hand at documents, though he was slow enough even with them. He wore a small cloth hat and big gaiters over his long pants, and you seldom saw him with his hands out of his pockets. He reddened when you talked to him, tilting from toe to heel and back, and looking down all the time at his big farmer's feet. Noble and me used to make fun of his broad accent, because we were from the town.

I couldn't at the time see the point of me and Noble guarding Belcher and Hawkins at all, for it was my belief that you could have planted that pair down anywhere from this to Claregalway and they'd have taken root there like a native weed. I never in my short experience seen two men to take to the country as they did.

They were handed on to us by the Second Battalion when the search for them became too hot, and Noble and myself, being young, took over with a natural feeling of responsibility, but Hawkins made us look like fools when he showed that he knew the country better than we did.

"You're the bloke they calls Bonaparte," he says to me. "Mary Brigid O'Connell told me to ask you what you done with the pair of her brother's socks you borrowed."

For it seemed, as they explained it, that the Second used to have little evenings, and some of the girls of the neighborhood turned in, and, seeing they were such decent chaps, our fellows couldn't leave the two Englishmen out of them. Hawkins learned to dance "The Walls of Limerick," "The Siege of Ennis," and "The Waves of Tory" as well as any of them, though, naturally, he couldn't return the compliment, because our lads at that time did not dance foreign dances on principle.

So whatever privileges Belcher and Hawkins had with the Second they just naturally took with us, and after the first day or two we gave up all pretense of keeping a close eye on them. Not that they could have got far, for they had accents you could cut with a knife and wore khaki tunics and overcoats with civilian pants and boots. But it's my belief that they never had any idea of escaping and were quite content to be where they were.

It was a treat to see how Belcher got off with the old woman of the house where we were staying. She was a great warrant to scold, and cranky even with us, but before ever she had a chance of giving our guests, as I may call them, a lick of her tongue, Belcher had made her his friend for life. She was breaking sticks, and Belcher, who hadn't been more than ten minutes in the house, jumped up from his seat and went over to her.

"Allow me, madam," he says, smiling his queer little smile, "please allow me"; and he takes the bloody hatchet. She was struck too paralytic to speak, and after that, Belcher would be at her heels, carrying a bucket, a basket, or a load of turf, as the case might be. As Noble said, he got into looking before she leapt, and hot water, or any little thing she wanted, Belcher would have it ready for her. For such a huge man (and though I am five foot ten myself I had to look up at him) he had an uncommon shortness or should I say lack? of speech. It took us some time to get used to him, walking in and out, like a ghost, without a word. Especially because Hawkins talked enough for a platoon, it was strange to hear big Belcher with his toes in the ashes come out with a solitary "Excuse me, chum" or "That's right, chum." His one and only passion was cards, and I will say for him that he was a good card-player. He could have fleeced myself and Noble, but whatever we lost to him Hawkins lost to us, and Hawkins played with the money Belcher gave him.

Hawkins lost to us because he had too much old gab, and we probably lost to Belcher for the same reason. Hawkins and Noble would spit at one another about religion into the early hours of the morning, and Hawkins worried the soul out of Noble, whose brother was a priest, with a string of questions that would puzzle a cardinal. To make it worse even in treating of holy subjects, Hawkins had a deplorable tongue. I never in all my career met a man who could mix such a variety of cursing and bad language into an argument. He was a terrible man, and a fright to argue. He never did a stroke of work, and when he had no one else to talk to, he got stuck in the old woman.

He met his match in her, for one day when he tried to get her to complain profanely of the drought, she gave him a great come-down by blaming it entirely on Jupiter Pluvius (a deity neither Hawkins nor I have ever heard of, though Noble said that among the pagans it was believed that he had something to do with the rain). Another day he was swearing at the capitalists for starting the German war when the old lady laid down her iron, puckered up her little crab's mouth, and said: "Mr. Hawkins, you can say what you like about the war, and think you'll deceive me because I'm only a simple poor countrywoman, but I know what started the war. It was the Italian Count that stole the heathen divinity out of the temple in Japan. Believe me, Mr. Hawkins, nothing but sorrow and want can follow the people that disturb the hidden powers."

A queer old girl, all right.

II

We had our tea one evening, and Hawkins lit the lamp and we all sat into cards. Jeremiah Donovan came in too, and sat down and watched us for a while, and it suddenly struck me that he had no great love for the two Englishmen. It came as a great surprise to me, because I hadn't noticed anything about him before.

Late in the evening a really terrible argument blew up between Hawkins and Noble, about capitalists and priests and love of your country.

"The capitalists," says Hawkins with an angry gulp, "pays the priests to tell you about the next world so as you won't notice what the bastards are up to in this."

"Nonsense, man!" says Noble, losing his temper. "Before ever a capitalist was thought of, people believed in the next world."

Hawkins stood up as though he was preaching a sermon.

"Oh, they did, did they?" he says with a sneer. "They believed all the things you believe, isn't that what you mean? And you believe that God created Adam, and Adam created Shem, and Shem created Jehoshophat. You believe all that silly old fairytale about Eve and Eden and the apple. Well, listen to me, chum. If you're entitled to hold a silly belief — like that, I'm entitled to hold my silly belief which is that the first thing your God created was a bleeding capitalist, with morality and Rolls-Royce complete. Am I right, chum?" he says to Belcher.

"You're right, chum," says Belcher with his amused smile, and got up from the table to stretch his long legs into the fire and stroke his moustache. So, seeing that Jeremiah Donovan was going, and that there was no knowing when the argument about religion would be over, I went out with him. We strolled down to the village together, and then he stopped and started blushing and mumbling and saying I ought to be behind, keeping guard on the prisoners. I didn't like the tone he took with me, and anyway I was bored with life in the cottage, so I replied by asking him what the hell we wanted guarding them at all for. I told him I'd talked it over with Noble, and that we'd both rather be out with a fighting column.

"What use are those fellows to us?" says I.

He looked at me in surprise and said: "I thought you knew we were keeping them as hostages."

"Hostages?" I said.

"The enemy have prisoners belonging to us," he says, "and now they're talking of shooting them. If they shoot our prisoners, we'll shoot theirs."

"Shoot them?" I said.

"What else did you think we were keeping them for?" he says.

"Wasn't it very unforeseen of you not to warn Noble and myself of that in the beginning?" I said.

"How was it?" says he. "You might have known it."

"We couldn't know it, Jeremiah Donovan," says I. "How could we when they were on our hands so long?"

"The enemy have our prisoners as long and longer," says he.

"That's not the same thing at all," says I.

"What difference is there?" says he.

I couldn't tell him, because I knew he wouldn't understand. If it was only an old dog that was going to the vet's, you'd try and not get too fond of him, but Jeremiah Donovan wasn't a man that would ever be in danger of that.

"And when is this thing going to be decided?" says I.

"We might hear tonight," he says. "Or tomorrow or the next day at latest. So if it's only hanging round here that's a trouble to you, you'll be free soon enough."

It wasn't the hanging round that was a trouble to me at all by this time. I had worse things to worry about. When I got back to the cottage the argument was still on. Hawkins was holding forth in his best style, maintaining that there was no next world, and Noble was maintaining that there was; but I could see that Hawkins had had the best of it.

"Do you know what, chum?" he was saying with a saucy smile. "I think you're just as big a bleeding unbeliever as I am. You say you believe in the next world, and you know just as much about the next world as I do, which is sweet damn-all. What's heaven? You don't know. Where's heaven? You don't know. You know sweet damn-all! I ask you again, do they wear wings?"

"Very well, then," says Noble, "they do. Is that enough for you? They do wear wings."

"Where do they get them, then? Who makes them? Have they a factory for wings? Have they a sort of store where you hands in your chit and takes your bleeding wings?"

"You're an impossible man to argue with," says Noble. "Now, listen to me —" And they were off again.

It was long after midnight when we locked up and went to bed. As I blew out the candle I told Noble what Jeremiah Donovan was after telling me. Noble took it very quietly. When we'd been in bed about an hour he asked me did I think we ought to tell the Englishmen. I didn't think we should, because it was more than likely that the English wouldn't shoot our men, and even if they did, the brigade officers, who were always up and down with the Second Battalion and knew the Englishmen well, wouldn't be likely to want them plugged. "I think so too," says Noble. "It would be great cruelty to put the wind up them now."

"It was very unforeseen of Jeremiah Donovan anyhow," says I.

It was next morning that we found it so hard to face Belcher and Hawkins. We went about the house all day scarcely saying a word. Belcher didn't seem to notice; he was stretched into the ashes as usual, with his usual look of waiting in quietness for something unforeseen to happen, but Hawkins noticed and put it down to Noble's being beaten in the argument of the night before.

"Why can't you take a discussion in the proper spirit?" he says severely. "You and your Adam and Eve! I'm a Communist, that's what I am. Communist or anarchist, it all comes to much the same thing." And for hours he went round the house, muttering when the fit took him. "Adam and Eve! Adam and Eve! Nothing better to do with their time than picking bleeding apples!"

III

I don't know how we got through that day, but I was very glad when it was over, the tea things were cleared away, and Belcher said in his peaceable way: "Well, chums, what about it?" We sat round the table and Hawkins took out the cards, and just then I heard Jeremiah Donovan's footstep on the path and a dark presentiment crossed my mind. I rose from the table and caught him before he reached the door.

"What do you want?" I asked.

"I want those two solider friends of yours," he says, getting red.

"Is that the way, Jeremiah Donovan?" I asked.

"That's the way. There were four of our lads shot this morning, one of them a boy of sixteen."

"That's bad," I said.

At that moment Noble followed me out, and the three of us walked down the path together, talking in whispers. Feeney, the local intelligence officer, was standing by the gate.

"What are you going to do about it?" I asked Jeremiah Donovan.

"I want you and Noble to get them out; tell them they're being shifted again; that'll be the quietest way."

"Leave me out of that," says Noble under his breath.

Jeremiah Donovan looks at him hard.

"All right," he says. "You and Feeney get a few tools from the shed and dig a hole by the far end of the bog. Bonaparte and myself will be after you. Don't let anyone see you with the tools. I wouldn't like it to go beyond ourselves."

We saw Feeney and Noble go round to the shed and went in ourselves. I left Jeremiah Donovan to do the explanations. He told them that he had orders to send them back to the Second Battalion. Hawkins let out a mouthful of curses, and you could see that though Belcher didn't say anything, he was a bit upset too. The old woman was for having them stay in spite of us, and she didn't stop advising them until Jeremiah Donovan lost his temper and turned on her. He had a nasty temper, I noticed. It was pitch-dark in the cottage by this time, but no one thought of lighting the lamp, and in the darkness the two Englishmen fetched their topcoats and said good-bye to the old woman.

"Just as a man makes a home of a bleeding place, some bastard at headquarters thinks you're too cushy and shunts you off," says Hawkins, shaking her hand.

"A thousand thanks, madam," says Belcher. "A thousand thanks for everything" — as though he'd made it up.

We went round to the back of the house and down towards the bog. It was only then that Jeremiah Donovan told them. He was shaking with excitement.

"There were four of our fellows shot in Cork this morning and now you're to be shot as a reprisal."

"What are you talking about?" snaps Hawkins. "It's bad enough being mucked about as we are without having to put up with your funny jokes."

"It isn't a joke," says Donovan. "I'm sorry, Hawkins, but it's true," and begins on the usual rigmarole about duty and how unpleasant it is.

I never noticed that people who talk a lot about duty find it much of a trouble to them.

"Oh, cut it out!" says Hawkins.

"Ask Bonaparte," says Donovan, seeing that Hawkins isn't taking him seriously. "Isn't it true, Bonaparte?"

"It is," I say, and Hawkins stops.

"Ah, for Christ's sake, chum!"

"I mean it, chum," I say.

"You don't sound as if you mean it."

"If he doesn't mean it, I do," says Donovan, working himself up.

"What have you against me, Jeremiah Donovan?"

"I never said I had anything against you. But why did your people take out four of our prisoners and shoot them in cold blood?"

He took Hawkins by the arm and dragged him on, but it was impossible to make him understand that we were in earnest. I had the Smith and Wesson in my pocket and I kept fingering it and wondering what I'd do if they put up a fight for it or ran, and wishing to God they'd do one or the other. I knew if they did run for it, that I'd never fire on them. Hawkins wanted to know was Noble in it, and when we said yes, he asked us why Noble wanted to plug him. Why did any of us want to plug him? What had he done to us? Weren't we all chums? Didn't we understand him and didn't he understand us? Did we imagine for an instant that he'd shoot us for all the so-and-so officers in the so-and-so British Army?

By this time we'd reached the bog, and I was so sick I couldn't even answer him. We walked along the edge of it in the darkness, and every now and then Hawkins would call a halt and begin all over again, as if he was wound up, about our being chums, and I knew that nothing but the sight of the grave would convince him that we had to do it. And all the time I was hoping that something would happen; that they'd run for it or that Noble would take over the responsibility from me. I had the feeling that it was worse on Noble than on me.

IV

At last we saw the lantern in the distance and made towards it. Noble was carrying it, and Feeney was standing somewhere in the darkness behind him, and the picture of them so still and silent in the bogland brought it home to me that we were in earnest, and banished the last bit of hope I had.

Belcher, on recognizing Noble, said: "Hallo, chum," in his quiet way, but Hawkins flew at him at once, and the argument began all over again, only this time Noble had nothing to say for himself and stood with his head down, holding the lantern between his legs.

It was Jeremiah Donovan who did the answering. For the twentieth time, as though it was haunting his mind, Hawkins asked if anybody thought he'd shoot Noble.

"Yes, you would," says Jeremiah Donovan.

"No, I wouldn't, damn you!"

"You would, because you'd know you'd be shot for not doing it."

"I wouldn't, not if I was to be shot twenty times over. I wouldn't shoot a pal. And Belcher wouldn't — isn't that right, Belcher?"

"That's right, chum, " Belcher said, but more by way of answering the question than of joining in the argument. Belcher sounded as though whatever unforeseen thing he'd always been waiting for had come at last.

"Anyway, who says Noble would be shot if I wasn't? What do you think I'd do if I was in his place, out in the middle of a blasted bog?"

"What would you do?" asks Donovan.

"I'd go with him wherever he was going, of course. Share my last bob with him and stick by him through thick and thin. No one can ever say of me that I let down a pal."

"We had enough of this," says Jeremiah Donovan, cocking his revolver. "Is there any message you want to send?"

"No, there isn't."

"Do you want to say your prayers?"

Hawkins came out with a cold-blooded remark that even shocked me and turned on Noble again.

"Listen to me, Noble," he says. "You and me are chums. You can't come over to my side, so I'll come over to your side. That show you I mean what I say? Give me a rifle and I'll go along with you and the other lads."

Nobody answered him. We knew that was no way out.

"Hear what I'm saying?" he says. "I'm through with it. I'm a deserter or anything else you like. I don't believe in your stuff, but it's no worse than mine. That satisfy you?"

Noble raised his head, but Donovan began to speak and he lowered it again without replying.

"For the last time, have you any messages to send?" says Donovan in a cool, excited sort of voice.

"Shut up, Donovan! You don't understand me, but these lads do. They're not the sort to make a pal and kill a pal. They're not the tools of any capitalist."

I alone of the crowd saw Donovan raise his Webley to the back of Hawkins's neck, and as he did so I shut my eyes and tried to pray. Hawkins had begun to say something else when Donovan fired, and as I opened my eyes at the bang, I saw Hawkins stagger at the knees and lie out flat at Noble's feet, slowly and as quiet as a kid falling asleep, with the lantern-light on his lean legs and bright farmer's boots. We all stood very still, watching him settle out in the last agony.

Then Belcher took out a handkerchief and began to tie it about his own eyes (in our excitement we'd forgotten to do the same for Hawkins), and, seeing it wasn't big enough, turned and asked for the loan of mine. I gave it to him and he knotted the two together and pointed with his foot at Hawkins.

"He's not quite dead," he says. "Better give him another."

Sure enough, Hawkins's left knee is beginning to rise. I bend down and put my gun to his head; then, recollecting myself, I get up again. Belcher understands what's in my mind.

"Give him his first," he says. "I don't mind. Poor bastard, we don't know what's happening to him now."

I knelt and fired. By this time I didn't seem to know what I was doing. Belcher, who was fumbling a bit awkwardly with the handkerchiefs, came out with a laugh as he heard the shot. It was the first time I heard him laugh and it sent a shudder down my back; it sounded so unnatural.

"Poor bugger!" he said quietly. "And last night he was so curious about it all. It's very queer, chums, I always think. Now he knows as much about it as they'll ever let him know, and last night he was all in the dark."

Donovan helped him to tie the handkerchiefs about his eyes. "Thanks, chum," he said. Donovan asked if there were any messages he wanted sent.

"No, chum," he says, "Not for me. If any of you would like to write to Hawkins's mother, you'll find a letter from her in his pocket. He and his mother were great chums. But my missus left me eight years ago. Went away with another fellow and took the kid with her. I like the feeling of a home, as you may have noticed, but I couldn't start again after that."

It was an extraordinary thing, but in those few minutes Belcher said more than in all the weeks before. It was just as if the sound of the shot had started a flood of talk in him and he could go on the whole night like that, quite happily, talking about himself. We stood round like fools now that he couldn't see us any longer. Donovan looked at Noble, and Noble shook his head. Then Donovan raised his Webley, and at that moment Belcher gives his queer laugh again. He may have thought we were talking about him, or perhaps he noticed the same thing I'd noticed and couldn't understand it.

"Excuse me, chums," he says. "I feel I'm talking the hell of a lot, and so silly, about my being so handy about a house and things like that. But this thing came on me suddenly. You'll forgive me, I'm sure."

"You don't want to say a prayer?" asks Donovan.

"No, chum," he says. "I don't think it would help. I'm ready, and you boys want to get it over."

"You understand that we're only doing our duty?" says Donovan.

Belcher's head was raised like a blind man's, so that you could only see his chin and the tip of his nose in the lantern-light.

"I never could make out what duty was myself," he said. "I think you're all good lads, if that's what you mean. I'm not complaining."

Noble, just as if he couldn't bear any more of it, raised his fist at Donovan, and in a flash Donovan raised his gun and fired. The big man went over like a sack of meal, and this time there was no need of a second shot.

I don't remember much about the burying, but that it was worse than all the rest because we had to carry them to the grave. It was all mad lonely with nothing but a patch of lantern-light between ourselves and the dark, and birds hooting and screeching all round, disturbed by the guns. Noble went through Hawkins's belongings to find the letter from his mother, and then joined his hands together. He did the same with Belcher. Then, when we'd filled the grave, we separated from Jeremiah Donovan and Feeney and took our tools back to the shed. All the way we didn't speak a word. The kitchen was dark and cold as we'd left it, and the old woman was sitting over the hearth, saying her beads. We walked past her into the room, and Noble struck a match to light the lamp. She rose quietly and came to the doorway with all her cantankerousness gone.

"What did ye do with them?" she asked in a whisper, and Noble started so that the match went out in his hand.

"What's that?" he asked without turning around.

"I heard ye," she said.

"What did you hear?" asked Noble.

"I heard ye. Do ye think I didn't hear ye, putting the spade back in the houseen?"

Noble struck another match and this time the lamp lit for him.

"Was that what ye did to them?" she asked.

Then, by God, in the very doorway, she fell on her knees and began praying, and after looking at her for a minute or two Noble did the same by the fireplace. I pushed my way out past her and left them at it. I stood at the door, watching the stars and listening to the shrieking of the birds dying out over the bogs. It is so strange what you feel at times like that that you can't describe it. Noble says he saw everything ten times the size, as though there were nothing in the whole world but that little patch of bog with the two Englishmen stiffening into it, but with me it was as if the patch of bog where the Englishmen were was a million miles away, and even Noble and the old woman, mumbling behind me, and the birds and the bloody stars were all far away, and I was somehow very small and very lost and lonely like a child astray in the snow. And anything that happened to me afterwards, I never felt the same about again. [1931, 1954]

BEN OKRI *(b. 1959), author of short stories and novels about the social chaos in his native country of Nigeria, was taken to London as a young child but returned to Nigeria in 1963 at the outbreak of the civil war in Biafra. He was educated in Nigeria and at the University of Essex, England. He recalled that storytelling played an important role in his life when he was a boy in Lagos:*

> We are a people who are massaged by fictions; we grow up in a sea of narratives and myths, the perpetual invention of stories. When I was growing up, you sat with your age mates in the evenings and the elders would come out and tell you stories, if you asked them, or your mother would tell you stories to illustrate a hundred different points, lessons, morals she wanted to get across to you. Or you'd tell stories to one another as a way of making the moonlight more intoxicating, more beautiful. You invented stories; you were encouraged to take existing stories and weave your own variation of them.

Okri's father wanted him to become a lawyer, but Okri insisted on becoming a writer. He wrote hundreds of poems and placed a few articles, as he remembered, about social problems like "excessive rent charged to poor people, vicious landlords, water tanks, bad roads, disease in the ghetto, and so on" in a local newspaper. Then he began to write short fiction about the same subjects, believing that the short story was one of the best forms for learning how to write. One story grew into his first novel, Flowers and Shadows, *published when he was twenty-one. Another novel and two collections of short stories followed, and in 1991 his novel* The Famished Road *won the prestigious British Booker Prize.*

The story "In the Shadow of War," from Okri's second collection, Stars of the New Curfew *(1988), contains the suggestion of surrealist imagery that has led critics to compare his work to the writing of Jorge Luis Borges and the drawings of Hieronymus Bosch. Okri disputes these comparisons, insisting that his stories are realistic representations of life in Nigeria as it is experienced inside the consciousness of the people who live there. He has pointed out that Nigeria contains nearly 300 different tribal groupings of people,*

> which means that you have an incredible diversity of belief systems. I happen to think that human beings are largely composed of the world view that they have inherited; in other words, we see the world through our belief system. . . . So what seems like surrealism or fantastic writing actually is not fantastic writing, it's simply writing about the place in the tone and the spirit of the place.

In the Shadow of War

That afternoon three soldiers came to the village. They scattered the goats and chickens. They went to the palm-front bar and ordered a calabash of palm-wine. They drank amidst the flies.

Omovo watched them from the window as he waited for his father to go out. They both listened to the radio. His father had bought the old Grundig cheaply from a family that had to escape the city when the war broke out. He had covered the radio with a white cloth and made it look like a household fetish. They listened to the news of bombings and air raids in the interior of the country. His father combed his hair, parted it carefully, and slapped some aftershave on his unshaven face. Then he struggled into the shabby coat that he had long outgrown.

Omovo stared out of the window, irritated with his father. At that hour, for the past seven days, a strange woman with a black veil over her head had been going past the house. She went up the village paths, crossed the Express road, and disappeared into the forest. Omovo waited for her to appear.

The main news was over. The radio announcer said an eclipse of the moon was expected that night. Omovo's father wiped the sweat off his face with his palm and said, with some bitterness:

"As if an eclipse will stop this war."

"What is an eclipse?" Omovo asked.

"That's when the world goes dark and strange things happen."

"Like what?"

His father lit a cigarette.

"The dead start to walk about and sing. So don't stay out late, eh."

Omovo nodded.

"Heclipses hate children. They eat them."

Omovo didn't believe him. His father smiled, gave Omovo his ten kobo allowance, and said:

"Turn off the radio. It's bad for a child to listen to news of war."

Omovo turned it off. His father poured a libation at the doorway and then prayed to his ancestors. When he had finished he picked up his briefcase and strutted out briskly. Omovo watched him as he threaded his way up the path to the bus-stop at the main road. When a danfo bus came, and his father went with it, Omovo turned the radio back on. He sat on the window-sill and waited for the woman. The last time he saw her she had glided past with agitated flutters of her yellow smock. The children stopped what they were doing and stared at her. They had said that she had no shadow. They had said that her feet never touched the ground. As she went past, the children began to throw things at her. She didn't flinch, didn't quicken her pace, and didn't look back.

The heat was stupefying. Noises dimmed and lost their edges. The villagers stumbled about their various tasks as if they were sleep-walking. The three soldiers drank palm-wine and played draughts beneath the sun's oppressive glare. Omovo noticed that whenever children went past the bar the soldiers called them, talked to them, and gave them some money. Omovo ran down the stairs and slowly walked past the bar. The soldiers stared at him. On his way back one of them called him.

"What's your name" he asked.

Omovo hesitated, smiled mischievously, and said:

"Heclipse."

The soldier laughed, spraying Omovo's face with spit. He had a face crowded with veins. His companions seemed uninterested. They swiped flies and concentrated on their game. Their guns were on the table. Omovo noticed that they had numbers on them. The man said:

"Did your father give you that name because you have big lips?"

His companions looked at Omovo and laughed. Omovo nodded.

"You are a good boy," the man said. He paused. Then he asked, in a different voice:

"Have you seen that woman who covers her face with a black cloth?"

"No."

The man gave Omovo ten kobo and said:

"She is a spy. She helps our enemies. If you see her come and tell us at once, you hear?"

Omovo refused the money and went back upstairs. He re-positioned himself on the window-sill. The soldiers occasionally looked at him. The heat got to him and soon he fell asleep in a sitting position. The cocks, crowing dispiritedly, woke him up. He could feel the afternoon softening into evening. The soldiers dozed in the bar. The hourly news came on. Omovo listened without comprehension to the day's casualties. The announcer succumbed to the stupor, yawned, apologized, and gave further details of the fighting.

Omovo looked up and saw that the woman had already gone past. The men had left the bar. He saw them weaving between the eaves of the thatch houses, stumbling through the heat-mists. The woman was further up the path. Omovo ran downstairs and followed the men. One of them had taken off his uniform top. The soldier behind had buttocks so big they had begun to split his pants. Omovo followed them across the Express road. When they got into the forest the men stopped following the woman, and took a different route. They seemed to know what they were doing. Omovo hurried to keep the woman in view.

He followed her through the dense vegetation. She wore faded wrappers and a grey shawl, with the black veil covering her face. She had a red basket on her head. He completely forgot to determine if she had a shadow, or whether her feet touched the ground.

He passed unfinished estates, with their flaking ostentatious signboards and their collapsing fences. He passed an empty cement factory: blocks lay crumbled in heaps and the workers' sheds were deserted. He passed a baobab tree, under which was the intact skeleton of a large animal. A snake dropped from a branch and slithered through the undergrowth. In the distance, over the cliff edge, he heard loud music and people singing war slogans above the noise.

He followed the woman till they came to a rough camp on the plain below. Shadowy figures moved about in the half-light of the cave. The woman went to them. The figures surrounded her and touched her and led her into the cave. He heard their weary voices thanking her. When the woman re-appeared she was without the basket. Children with kwashiorkor stomachs and women wearing rags led her half-way up the hill. Then, reluctantly, touching her as if they might not see her again, they went back.

He followed her till they came to a muddied river. She moved as if an invisible force were trying to blow her away. Omovo saw capsized canoes and trailing water-logged clothes on the dark water. He saw floating items of sacrifice: loaves of bread in polythene wrappings, gourds of food, Coca-Cola cans. When he looked at the canoes again they had changed into the shapes of swollen dead animals. He saw outdated currencies on the riverbank. He noticed the terrible smell in the air. Then he heard the sound of heavy breathing from behind him, then someone coughing and spitting. He recognized the voice of one of the soldiers urging the others to move faster. Omovo crouched in the shadow of a tree. The soldiers strode past. Not long afterwards he heard a scream. The men had caught up with the woman. They crowded round her.

"Where are the others?" shouted one of them.

The woman was silent.

"You dis witch! You want to die, eh? Where are they?"

She stayed silent. Her head was bowed. One of the soldiers coughed and spat towards the river.

"Talk! Talk!" he said, slapping her.

The fat soldier tore off her veil and threw it to the ground. She bent down to pick it up and stopped in the attitude of kneeling, her head still bowed. Her head was bald, and disfigured with a deep corrugation. There was a livid gash along the side of her face. The bare-chested soldier pushed her. She fell on her face and lay still. The lights changed over the forest and for the first time Omovo saw that the dead animals on the river were in fact the corpses of grown men. Their bodies were tangled with river-weed and their eyes were bloated. Before he could react, he heard another scream. The woman was getting up, with the veil in her hand. She turned to the fat soldier, drew herself to her fullest height, and spat in his face. Waving the veil in the air, she began to howl dementedly. The two other soldiers backed away. The fat soldier wiped his face and lifted the gun to the level of her stomach. A moment before Omovo heard the shot a violent beating of wings just above him scared him from his hiding place. He ran through the forest screaming. The soldiers tramped after him. He ran through a mist which seemed to have risen from the rocks. As he ran he saw an owl staring at him from a canopy of leaves. He tripped over the roots of a tree and blacked out when his head hit the ground.

When he woke up it was very dark. He waved his fingers in front of his face and saw nothing. Mistaking the darkness for blindness he screamed, thrashed around, and ran into a door. When he recovered from his shock he heard voices outside and the radio crackling on about the war. He found his way to the balcony, full of wonder that his sight had returned. But when he got there he was surprised to find his father sitting on the sunken cane chair, drinking palm-wine with the three soldiers. Omovo rushed to his father and pointed frantically at the three men.

"You must thank them," his father said. "They brought you back from the forest."

Omovo, overcome with delirium, began to tell his father what he had seen. But his father, smiling apologetically at the soldiers, picked up his son and carried him off to bed. [1988]

TILLIE OLSEN (b. 1913) was born in Omaha, Nebraska, the daughter of political refugees from the Russian Czarist repression after the revolution of 1905. Her father was a farmer, packing-house worker, house painter, and jack-of-all-trades; her mother was a factory worker. At the age of fifteen Olsen dropped out of high school to help support her family during the Depression. She was a member of the Young Communist League, involved in the Warehouse Union's labor disputes in Kansas City. At age nineteen she began her first novel, Yonnondio. Four chapters of this book about a poverty-stricken working-class family were completed in the next four years, during which time she married, gave birth to her first child, and was left with the baby by her husband because, as she later wrote in her autobiographical story "I Stand Here Ironing," he "could no longer endure sharing want" with them. In 1934 a section of the first chapter of her novel was published in Partisan Review, but she abandoned the unfinished book in 1937. The year before she had married Jack Olsen, with whom she had three more children; raising the children and working for political causes took up all her time. In the 1940s she was a factory worker, in the 1950s a secretary, and not until 1953, when her youngest daughter started school, could she begin writing again.

That year Olsen enrolled in a class in fiction writing at San Francisco State College. She was awarded a Stanford University creative writing fellowship for 1955 and 1956. During the 1950s she wrote the four stories collected in Tell Me a Riddle, which established her reputation when the book was published as a paperback in 1961. Identified as a champion of the reemerging feminist movement, Olsen wrote a biographical introduction to Rebecca Harding Davis's nineteenth-century proletarian novel, Life in the Iron Mills, published by the Feminist Press in 1972. Two years later, after several grants and creative writing fellowships, she published the still-unfinished Yonnondio. Silences, a collection of essays exploring the different circumstances that obstruct or silence literary creation, appeared in 1978.

As the Canadian author Margaret Atwood has understood about Olsen,

> Few writers have gained such wide respect on such a small body of published work. . . . Among women writers in the United States, "respect" is too pale a word: "reverence" is more like it. This is presumably because women writers, even more than their male counterparts, recognize what a heroic feat it is to have held down a job, raised four children, and still somehow managed to become and to remain a writer.

A radical feminist, Olsen has said that she felt no personal guilt as a single parent over her daughter's predicament, as described in her confessional narrative "I Stand Here Ironing," since "guilt is a word used far too sloppily, to cover up harmful situations in society that must be changed." Her four stories have appeared in more than fifty anthologies and have been translated into many languages. In 1994 she was awarded the Rea Award for the Short Story, a literary prize that honors a living American author who has made "a significant contribution to the short story as an art form."

TILLIE OLSEN

I Stand Here Ironing

I stand here ironing, and what you asked me moves tormented back and forth with the iron.

"I wish you would manage the time to come in and talk with me about your daughter. I'm sure you can help me understand her. She's a youngster who needs help and whom I'm deeply interested in helping."

"Who needs help." . . . Even if I came, what good would it do? You think because I am her mother I have a key, or that in some way you could use me as a key? She has lived for nineteen years. There is all that life that has happened outside of me, beyond me.

And when is there time to remember, to sift, to weigh, to estimate, to total? I will start and there will be an interruption and I will have to gather it all together again. Or I will become engulfed with all I did or did not do, with what should have been and what cannot be helped.

She was a beautiful baby. The first and only one of our five that was beautiful at birth. You do not guess how new and uneasy her tenancy in her now-loveliness. You did not know her all those years she was thought homely, or see her poring over her baby pictures, making me tell her over and over how beautiful she had been — and would be, I would tell her — and was now, to the seeing eye. But the seeing eyes were few or nonexistent. Including mine.

I nursed her. They feel that's important nowadays, I nursed all the children, but with her, with all the fierce rigidity of first motherhood, I did like the books then said. Though her cries battered me to trembling and my breasts ached with swollenness, I waited till the clock decreed.

Why do I put that first? I do not even know if it matters, or if it explains anything.

She was a beautiful baby. She blew shining bubbles of sound. She loved motion, loved light, loved color and music and textures. She would lie on the floor in her blue overalls patting the surface so hard in ecstasy her hands and feet would blur. She was a miracle to me, but when she was eight months old I had to leave her daytimes with the woman downstairs to whom she was no miracle at all, for I worked or looked for work and for Emily's father, who "could no longer endure" (he wrote in his good-bye note) "sharing want with us."

I was nineteen. It was pre-relief, pre-WPA world of the depression. I would start running as soon as I got off the streetcar, running up the stairs, the place smelling sour, and awake or asleep to startle awake, when she saw me she would break into a clogged weeping that could not be comforted, a weeping I can hear yet.

After a while I found a job hashing at night so I could be with her days, and it was better. But it came to where I had to bring her to his family and leave her.

It took a long time to raise the money for her fare back. Then she got chicken pox and I had to wait longer. When she finally came, I hardly knew her, walking quick and nervous like her father, looking like her father, thin, and dressed in a shoddy red that yellowed her skin and glared at the pockmarks. All the baby loveliness gone.

She was two. Old enough for nursery school they said, and I did not know then what I know now — the fatigue of the long day, and the lacerations of group life in the kinds of nurseries that are only parking places for children.

Except that it would have made no difference if I had known. It was the only place there was. It was the only way we could be together, the only way I could hold a job.

And even without knowing, I knew. I knew the teacher that was evil because all these years it has curdled into my memory, the little boy hunched in the corner, her rasp, "why aren't you outside, because Alvin hits you? that's no reason, go out, scaredy." I knew Emily hated it even if she did not clutch and implore "don't go Mommy" like the other children, mornings.

She always had a reason why we should stay home. Momma, you look sick. Momma, I feel sick. Momma, the teachers aren't there today, they're sick. Momma, we can't go, there was a fire last night. Momma, it's a holiday today, no school, they told me.

But never a direct protest, never rebellion. I think of our others in their three-, four-year-oldness — the explosions, the tempers, the denunciations, the demands — and I feel suddenly ill. I put the iron down. What in me demanded that goodness in her? And what was the cost, the cost to her of such goodness?

The old man living in the back once said in his gentle way: "You should smile at Emily more when you look at her." What *was* in my face when I looked at her? I loved her. There were all the acts of love.

It was only with the others I remembered what he said, and it was the face of joy, and not of care or tightness or worry I turned to them — too late for Emily. She does not smile easily, let alone almost always as her brothers and sisters do. Her face is closed and sombre, but when she wants, how fluid. You must have seen it in her pantomimes, you spoke of her rare gift for comedy on the stage that rouses laughter out of the audience so dear they applaud and applaud and do not want to let her go.

Where does it come from, that comedy? There was none of it in her when she came back to me that second time, after I had to send her away again. She had a new daddy now to learn to love, and I think perhaps it was a better time.

Except when we left her alone nights, telling ourselves she was old enough.

"Can't you go some other time, Mommy, like tomorrow?" she would ask. "Will it be just a little while you'll be gone? Do you promise?"

The time we came back, the front door open, the clock on the floor in the hall. She rigid awake. "It wasn't just a little while. I didn't cry. Three times I called you, just three times, and then I ran downstairs to open the door so · you could come faster. The clock talked loud. I threw it away, it scared me what it talked."

She said the clock talked loud again that night I went to the hospital to have Susan. She was delirious with the fever that comes before red measles, but she was fully conscious all the week I was gone and the week after we were home when she could not come near the new baby or me.

She did not get well. She stayed skeleton thin, not wanting to eat, and night after night she had nightmares. She would call for me, and I would rouse from exhaustion to sleepily call back: "You're all right, darling, go to sleep, it's just a dream," and if she still called, in a sterner voice, "now go to sleep, Emily, there's nothing to hurt you." Twice, only twice, when I had to get up for Susan anyhow, I went in to sit with her.

Now when it is too late (as if she would let me hold her and comfort her like I do the others) I get up and go to her at once at her moan or restless stirring. "Are you awake, Emily? Can I get you something?" And the answer is always the same: "No, I'm all right, go back to sleep, Mother."

They persuaded me at the clinic to send her away to a convalescent home in the country where "she can have the kind of food and care you can't manage for her, and you'll be free to concentrate on the new baby." They still send children to that place. I see pictures on the society page of sleek young women planning affairs to raise money for it, or dancing at the affairs, or decorating Easter eggs or filling Christmas stockings for the children.

They never have a picture of the children so I do not know if the girls still wear those gigantic red bows and the ravaged looks on the every other Sunday when parents can come to visit "unless otherwise notified" — as we were notified the first six weeks.

Oh it is a handsome place, green lawns and tall trees and fluted flower beds. High up on the balconies of each cottage the children stand, the girls in their red bows and white dresses, the boys in white suits and giant red ties. The parents stand below shrieking up to be heard and the children shriek down to be heard, and between them the invisible wall "Not To Be Contaminated by Parental Germs or Physical Affection."

There was a tiny girl who always stood hand in hand with Emily. Her parents never came. One visit she was gone. "They moved her to Rose Cottage," Emily shouted in explanation. "They don't like you to love anybody here."

She wrote once a week, the labored writing of a seven-year-old. "I am fine. How is the baby. If I write my leter nicly I will have a star. Love." There never was a star. We wrote every other day, letters she could never hold or keep but only hear read — once. "We simply do not have room for children to keep any personal possessions," they patiently explained when we pieced one Sunday's shrieking together to plead how much it would mean to Emily, who loved so to keep things, to be allowed to keep her letters and cards.

Each visit she looked frailer. "She isn't eating," they told us.

(They had runny eggs for breakfast or mush with lumps, Emily said later, I'd hold it in my mouth and not swallow. Nothing ever tasted good, just when they had chicken.)

It took us eight months to get her released home, and only the fact that she gained back so little of her seven lost pounds convinced the social worker.

I used to try to hold and love her after she came back, but her body would stay stiff, and after a while she'd push away. She ate little. Food sickened her, and I think much of life too. Oh she had physical lightness and brightness, twinkling by on skates, bouncing like a ball up and down up and down over the jump rope, skimming over the hill; but these were momentary.

She fretted about her appearance, thin and dark and foreign-looking at a time when every little girl was supposed to look or thought she should look a chubby blonde replica of Shirley Temple. The doorbell sometimes rang for her, but no one seemed to come and play in the house or to be a best friend. Maybe because we moved so much.

There was a boy she loved painfully through two school semesters. Months later she told me how she had taken pennies from my purse to buy him candy. "Licorice was his favorite and I brought him some every day, but he still liked Jennifer better'n me. Why, Mommy?" The kind of question for which there is no answer.

School was a worry for her. She was not glib or quick in a world where glibness and quickness were easily confused with ability to learn. To her overworked and exasperated teachers she was an overconscientious "slow learner" who kept trying to catch up and was absent entirely too often.

I let her be absent, though sometimes the illness was imaginary. How different from my now-strictness about attendance with the others. I wasn't working. We had a new baby. I was home anyhow. Sometimes, after Susan grew old enough, I would keep her home from school, too, to have them all together.

Mostly Emily had asthma, and her breathing, harsh and labored, would fill the house with a curiously tranquil sound. I would bring the two old dresser mirrors and her boxes of collections to her bed. She would select beads and single earrings, bottle tops and shells, dried flowers and pebbles, old postcards and scraps, all sorts of oddments; then she and Susan would play Kingdom, setting up landscapes and furniture, peopling them with action.

Those were the only times of peaceful companionship between her and Susan. I have edged away from it, that poisonous feeling between them, that terrible balancing of hurts and needs I had to do between the two, and did so badly, those earlier years.

Oh there were conflicts between the others too, each one human, needing, demanding, hurting, taking — but only between Emily and Susan, no, Emily toward Susan that corroding resentment. It seems so obvious on the surface, yet it is not obvious; Susan, the second child, Susan, golden- and curly-haired and chubby, quick and articulate and assured, everything in appearance and manner Emily was not; Susan, not able to resist Emily's precious things, losing or sometimes clumsily breaking them; Susan telling jokes and riddles to company for applause while Emily sat silent (to say to me later: that was *my* riddle, Mother, I told it to Susan); Susan, who for all the five years' difference in age was just a year behind Emily in developing physically.

I am glad for that slow physical development that widened the difference between her and her contemporaries, though she suffered over it. She was too vulnerable for that terrible world of youthful competition, of preening and parading, of constant measuring of yourself against every other, of envy, "If I had that copper hair," "If I had that skin. . . ." She tormented herself enough about not looking like the others, there was enough of unsureness, the having to be conscious of words before you speak, the constant caring — what are they thinking of me? without having it all magnified by the merciless physical drives.

Ronnie is calling. He is wet and I change him. It is rare there is such a cry now. That time of motherhood is almost behind me when the ear is not one's own but must always be racked and listening for the child cry, the child call. We sit for a while and I hold him, looking out over the city spread in charcoal with its soft aisles of light. "*Shoogily*," he breathes and curls closer. I carry him back to bed, asleep. *Shoogily*. A funny word, a family word, inherited from Emily, invented by her to say: *comfort*.

In this and other ways she leaves her seal, I say aloud. And startle at my saying it. What do I mean? What did I start to gather together, to try and make coherent? I was at the terrible, growing years. War years. I do not remember them well. I was working, there were four smaller ones now, there was not time for her. She had to help be a mother, and housekeeper, and shopper. She had to get her seal. Mornings of crisis and near hysteria trying to get lunches packed, hair combed, coats and shoes found, everyone to school or Child Care on time, the baby ready for transportation. And always the paper scribbled on by a smaller one, the book looked at by Susan then mislaid, the homework not done. Running out to that huge school where she was one, she was lost, she was a drop; suffering over the unpreparedness, stammering and unsure in her classes.

There was so little time left at night after the kids were bedded down. She would struggle over books, always eating (it was in those years she developed her enormous appetite that is legendary in our family) and I would be ironing, or preparing food for the next day, or writing V-mail to Bill, or tending the baby. Sometimes, to make me laugh, or out of her despair, she would imitate happenings or types at school.

I think I said once: "Why don't you do something like this in the school amateur show?" One morning she phoned me at work, hardly understandable through the weeping: "Mother, I did it. I won, I won; they gave me first prize; they clapped and clapped and wouldn't let me go."

Now suddenly she was Somebody, and as imprisoned in her difference as she had been in anonymity.

She began to be asked to perform at other high schools, even in colleges, then at city and statewide affairs. The first one we went to, I only recognized her that first moment when thin, shy, she almost drowned herself into the curtains. Then: Was this Emily? The control, the command, the convulsing and deadly clowning, the spell, then the roaring, stamping audience, unwilling to let this rare and precious laughter out of their lives.

Afterwards: You ought to do something about her with a gift like that — but without money or knowing how, what does one do? We have left it all to her, and the gift has so often eddied inside, clogged and clotted, as been used and growing.

She is coming. She runs up the stairs two at a time with her light graceful step, and I know she is happy tonight. Whatever it was that occasioned your call did not happen today.

"Aren't you ever going to finish the ironing, Mother? Whistler painted his mother in a rocker. I'd have to paint mine standing over an ironing board." This is one of her communicative nights and she tells me everything and nothing as she fixes herself a plate of food out of the icebox.

She is so lovely. Why did you want me to come in at all? Why were you concerned? She will find her way.

She starts up the stairs to bed. "Don't get me up with the rest in the morning." "But I thought you were having midterms." "Oh, those," she comes back in, kisses me, and says quite lightly, "in a couple of years when we'll all be atom-dead they won't matter a bit."

She has said it before. She *believes* it. But because I have been dredging the past, and all that compounds a human being is so heavy and meaningful in me, I cannot endure it tonight.

I will never total it all. I will never come in to say: She was a child seldom smiled at. Her father left me before she was a year old. I had to work her first six years when there was work, or I sent her home and to his relatives. There were years she had care she hated. She was dark and thin and foreign-looking in a world where the prestige went to blondeness and curly hair and dimples, she was slow where glibness was prized. She was a child of anxious, not proud, love. We were poor and could not afford for her the soil of easy growth. I was a young mother, I was a distracted mother. There were other children pushing up, demanding. Her younger sister seemed all that she was not. There were years she did not want me to touch her. She kept too much in herself, her life was such she had to keep too much in herself. My wisdom came too late. She has much to her and probably little will come of it. She is a child of her age, of depression, of war, of fear.

Let her be. So all that is in her will not bloom but in how many does it? There is still enough left to live by. Only help her to know — help make it so there is cause for her to know — that she is more than this dress on the ironing board, helpless before the iron.   [1961]

CYNTHIA OZICK *(b. 1928) sees a clear distinction between art and life: "As for life, I don't like it. I notice no 'interplay of life and art.' Life is that which — pressingly, persistently, unfailingly, imperially — interrupts." In Ozick's life there has been a long time between what Grace Paley would call "knowing and telling." Ozick was born in New York City, the daughter of a pharmacist. She received a B.A. from New York University in 1949 and an M.A. from Ohio State University in 1950 with a thesis titled "Parable in Henry James." She didn't publish her first work, the novel* Trust, *until 1966. Three collections of short fiction followed:* The Pagan Rabbi and Other Stories *(1971),* Bloodshed and Three Novellas *(1976), and* Levitation *(1981). In 1989 she published* Metaphor and Memory: Essays *and* The Shawl, *a novella developing the short story included here.*

In her essay "The Lesson of the Master" in Art and Ardor *(1983), Ozick described how as a young writer she was betrayed by Henry James. After college she worshiped literature, seeing herself "a priest at that altar, and that altar was all of my life." She felt that James was trying to teach her a lesson through his fiction, that an aspiring writer ought "to live immaculately, unspoiled by what we mean when we say 'life' — relationship, family mess, distraction, exhaustion, anxiety, above all disappointment." Ozick remembers herself as a nearsighted twenty-two-year old "infected with the commonplace intention of writing a novel" and trying to live "like the elderly bald-headed Henry James." Years later she realized her mistake. To be a writer,*

> one must keep one's psychological distance from the supreme artists. . . . The true Lesson of the Master, then, is, simply, never to venerate what is complete, burnished, whole. . . . never to worship ripe Art or the ripened artist; but instead to seek to be young while young, primitive while primitive, ungainly when ungainly — to look for crudeness and rudeness, to husband one's own stupidity or ungenius.

Yet Ozick also understands that life "interrupts," and the journey to art is beset with difficulties. In her best short fiction, such as the Holocaust story "The Shawl," she accepts the challenge of her craft, writing in a swiftly imagistic style. She admits that "in beginning a story I know nothing at all: surely not where I am going, and hardly at all how to get there."

The Shawl

Stella, cold, cold, the coldness of hell. How they walked on the roads together, Rosa with Magda curled up between sore breasts, Magda wound up in the shawl. Sometimes Stella carried Magda. But she was jealous of Magda. A thin girl of fourteen, too small, with thin breasts of her own, Stella wanted to be wrapped in a shawl, hidden away, asleep, rocked by the march, a baby, a round infant in arms. Magda took Rosa's nipple, and Rosa never stopped walking, a walking cradle. There was not enough milk; sometimes Magda sucked air; then she screamed. Stella was ravenous. Her knees were tumors on sticks, her elbows chicken bones.

Rosa did not feel hunger; she felt light, not like someone walking but like someone in a faint, in trance, arrested in a fit, someone who is already a floating angel, alert and seeing everything, but in the air, not there, not touching the road. As if teetering on the tips of her fingernails. She looked into Magda's face through a gap in the shawl: a squirrel in a nest, safe, no one could reach her inside the little house of the shawl's windings. The face, very round, a pocket mirror of a face: but it was not Rosa's bleak complexion, dark like cholera, it was another kind of face altogether, eyes blue as air, smooth feathers of hair nearly as yellow as the Star sewn into Rosa's coat. You could think she was one of *their* babies.

Rosa, floating, dreamed of giving Magda away in one of the villages. She could leave the line for a minute and push Magda into the hands of any woman on the side of the road. But if she moved out of line they might shoot. And even if she fled the line for half a second and pushed the shawl-bundle at a stranger, would the woman take it? She might be surprised, or afraid; she might drop the shawl, and Magda would fall out and strike her head and die. The little round head. Such a good child, she gave up screaming, and sucked now only for the taste of the drying nipple itself. The neat grip of the tiny gums. One mite of a tooth tip sticking up in the bottom gum, how shining, an elfin tombstone of white marble, gleaming there. Without complaining, Magda relinquished Rosa's teats, first the left, then the right; both were cracked, not a sniff of milk. The duct crevice extinct, a dead volcano, blind eye, chill hole, so Magda took the corner of the shawl and milked it instead. She sucked and sucked, flooding the threads with wetness. The shawl's good flavor, milk of linen.

It was a magic shawl, it could nourish an infant for three days and three nights. Magda did not die, she stayed alive, although very quiet. A peculiar smell, of cinnamon and almonds, lifted out of her mouth. She held her eyes open every moment, forgetting how to blink or nap, and Rosa and sometimes Stella studied their blueness. On the road they raised one burden of a leg after another and studied Magda's face. "Aryan," Stella said, in a voice grown as thin as a string; and Rosa thought how Stella gazed at Magda like a young cannibal. And the time that Stella said "Aryan," it sounded to Rosa as if Stella had really said, "Let us devour her."

But Magda lived to walk. She lived that long, but she did not walk very well, partly because she was only fifteen months old, and partly because the spindles of her legs could not hold up her fat belly. It was fat with air, full and round. Rosa gave almost all her food to Magda, Stella gave nothing; Stella was ravenous, a growing child herself, but not growing much. Stella did not menstruate. Rosa did not menstruate. Rosa was ravenous, but also not; she learned from Magda how to drink the taste of a finger in one's mouth. They were in a place without pity, all pity was annihilated in Rosa, she looked at Stella's bones without pity. She was sure that Stella was waiting for Magda to die so she could put her teeth into the little thighs.

Rosa knew Magda was going to die very soon; she should have been dead already, but she had been buried away deep inside the magic shawl, mistaken there for the shivering mound of Rosa's breasts; Rosa clung to the shawl as if it covered only herself. No one took it away from her. Magda was mute. She never cried. Rosa hid her in the barracks, under the shawl, but she knew that one day someone would inform; or one day someone, not even Stella, would steal Magda to eat her. When Magda began to walk Rosa knew that Magda was going to die very soon, something would happen. She was afraid to fall asleep; she slept with the weight of her thigh on Magda's body; she was afraid she would smother Magda under her thigh. The weight of Rosa was becoming less and less, Rosa and Stella were slowly turning into air.

Magda was quiet, but her eyes were horribly alive, like blue tigers. She watched. Sometimes she laughed — it seemed a laugh, but how could it be? Magda had never seen anyone laugh. Still, Magda laughed at her shawl when the wind blew its corners, the bad wind with pieces of black in it, that made Stella's and Rosa's eyes tear. Magda's eyes were always clear and tearless. She watched like a tiger. She guarded her shawl. No one could touch it; only Rosa could touch it. Stella was not allowed. The shawl was Magda's own baby, her pet, her little sister. She tangled herself up in it and sucked on one of the corners when she wanted to be very still.

Then Stella took the shawl away and made Magda die.

Afterward Stella said: "I was cold."

And afterward she was always cold, always. The cold went into her heart: Rosa saw that Stella's heart was cold. Magda flopped onward with her little pencil legs scribbling this way and that, in search of the shawl; the pencils faltered at the barracks opening, where the light began. Rosa saw and pursued. But already Magda was in the square outside the barracks, in the jolly light. It was the roll-call arena. Every morning Rosa had to conceal Magda under the shawl against a wall of the barracks and go out and stand in the arena with Stella and hundreds of others, sometimes for hours, and Magda, deserted, was quiet under the shawl, sucking on her corner. Every day Magda was silent, and so she did not die. Rosa saw that today Magda was going to die, and at the same time a fearful joy ran in Rosa's two palms, her fingers were on fire, she was astonished, febrile: Magda, in the sunlight, swaying on her pencil legs, was howling. Ever since the drying up of Rosa's nipples, ever since Magda's last scream on the road, Magda had been devoid of any syllable; Magda was a mute. Rosa believed that something had gone wrong with her vocal cords, with her windpipe, with the cave of her larynx; Magda was defective, without a voice; perhaps she was deaf; there might be something amiss with her intelligence; Magda was dumb. Even the laugh that came when the ash-stippled wind made a clown out of Magda's shawl was only the air-blown showing of her teeth. Even when the lice, head lice and body lice, crazed her so that she became as wild as one of the big rats that plundered the barracks at daybreak looking for carrion, she rubbed and scratched and kicked and bit and rolled without a whimper. But now Magda's mouth was spilling a long viscous rope of clamor.

"Maaaa —"

It was the first noise Magda had ever sent out from her throat since the drying up of Rosa's nipples.

"Maaaa . . . aaa!"

Again! Magda was wavering in the perilous sunlight of the arena, scribbling on such pitiful little bent shins. Rosa saw. She saw that Magda was grieving the loss of her shawl, she saw that Magda was going to die. A tide of commands hammered in Rosa's nipples: Fetch, get, bring! But she did not know which to go after first, Magda or the shawl. If she jumped out into the arena to snatch Magda up, the howling would not stop, because Magda would still not have the shawl; but if she ran back into the barracks to find the shawl, and if she found it, and if she came after Magda holding it and shaking it, then she would get Magda back, Magda would put the shawl in her mouth and turn dumb again.

Rosa entered the dark. It was easy to discover the shawl. Stella was heaped under it, asleep in her thin bones. Rosa tore the shawl free and flew — she could fly, she was only air — into the arena. The sunheat murmured of another life, of butterflies in summer. The light was placid, mellow. On the other side of the steel fence, far away, there were green meadows speckled with dandelions and deep-colored violets; beyond them, even farther, inno-cent tiger lilies, tall, lifting their orange bonnets. In the barracks they spoke of "flowers," of "rain": excrement, thick turd-braids, and the slow stinking maroon waterfall that slunk down from the upper bunks, the stink mixed with a bitter fatty floating smoke that greased Rosa's skin. She stood for an instant at the margin of the arena. Sometimes the electricity inside the fence would seem to hum; even Stella said it was only an imagining, but Rosa heard real sounds in the wire: grainy sad voices. The farther she was from the fence, the more clearly the voices crowded at her. The lamenting voices strummed so convincingly, so passionately, it was impossible to suspect them of being phantoms. The voices told her to hold up the shawl, high; the voices told her to shake it, to whip with it, to unfurl it like a flag. Rosa lifted, shook, whipped, unfurled. Far off, very far, Magda leaned across her air-fed belly, reaching out with the rods of her arms. She was high up, elevated, riding someone's shoulder. But the shoulder that carried Magda was not coming toward Rosa and the shawl, it was drifting away, the speck of Magda was moving more and more into the smoky distance. Above the shoulder a helmet glinted. A light tapped the helmet and sparkled it into a goblet. Below the helmet a black body like a domino and a pair of black boots hurled themselves in the direction of the electrified fence. The electric voices began to chatter wildly. "Maamaa, maaamaaa," they all hummed together. How far Magda was from Rosa now, across the whole square, past a dozen barracks, all the way on the other side! She was no bigger than a moth.

All at once Magda was swimming through the air. The whole of Magda traveled through loftiness. She looked like a butterfly touching a silver vine. And the moment Magda's feathered round head and her pencil legs and balloonish belly and zigzag arms splashed against the fence, the steel voices went mad in their growling, urging Rosa to run and run to the spot where Magda had fallen from her flight against the electrified fence; but of course Rosa did not obey them. She only stood, because if she ran they would shoot, and if she tried to pick up the sticks of Magda's body they would shoot, and if she let the wolf's screech ascending now through the ladder of her skeleton break out, they would shoot; so she took Magda's shawl and filled her own mouth with it, stuffed it in and stuffed it in, until she was swallowing up the wolf's screech and tasting the cinnamon and almond depth of Magda's saliva; and Rosa drank Magda's shawl until it dried. [1980]

GRACE PALEY *(b. 1922) was born in New York City. She studied at Hunter College and New York University, and in 1942 she married for the first time. She had two children from that marriage. In the 1950s she turned from writing poetry to short fiction. Her first book of stories,* The Little Disturbances of Man *(1959), established her reputation as a writer with a remarkably supple gift for language. As Susan Sontag later said, "She is that rare kind of writer, a natural with a voice like no one else's — funny, sad, lean, modest, energetic, acute." When this book went out of print in 1965, its reputation survived, strengthened by the infrequent appearances of her new stories in magazines such as the* Atlantic Monthly, Esquire, *the* Noble Savage, Genesis West, *the* New American Review, Ararat, *and* Fiction.

During the 1960s and 1970s Paley was prominent as a nonviolent activist protesting the Vietnam War. She was secretary of the Greenwich Village Peace Center, spent time in jail for her antiwar activities, and visited Hanoi and Moscow as a member of peace delegations, defining herself as a "somewhat combative pacifist and cooperative anarchist." During the World Peace Congress in Moscow in 1973, she condemned the Soviet Union for silencing political dissidents; the congress disassociated itself from her statement. Paley has long been a feminist and active in the antinuclear movement. In 1974 her second volume of stories, Enormous Changes at the Last Minute, *was published — it is a quieter, more openly personal collection of seventeen stories, many of them, such as "A Conversation with My Father," autobiographical. Her third book of stories,* Later the Same Day, *appeared in 1985. In 1988 Paley was designated the first official New York State Author by an act of the state legislature.*

Paley refuses to blame her teaching jobs or her involvements as an activist for her relatively low productivity as a writer. She says she writes "from distress." What she tries to get at in her stories is "a history of everyday life," and her subject matter and prose style are unmistakable. Living in a Manhattan apartment close to the Greenwich Village School (P.S. 41), Little Tony's Unisex Haircutters, the Famous Ray's Pizza, the H & H Fruit and Vegetable Market, and the Jefferson Market Branch of the New York Public Library, Paley observes her neighbors, friends, and family with compassion, humor, and hope. Her spare dissection of her characters is never performed at the expense of sympathy for the human condition. It is likely that, as was true of her Russian counterpart Isaac Babel, her production of stories will be limited. As she puts it, "There is a long time in me between knowing and telling." The Collected Stories of Grace Paley *was published in 1994.*

RELATED COMMENTARY: *Grace Paley, "A Conversation with Ann Charters,"* page 1484.

GRACE PALEY

A Conversation with My Father

My father is eighty-six years old and in bed. His heart, that bloody motor, is equally old and will not do certain jobs any more. It still floods his head with brainy light. But it won't let his legs carry the weight of his body around the house. Despite my metaphors, this muscle failure is not due to his old heart, he says, but to a potassium shortage. Sitting on one pillow, leaning on three, he offers last-minute advice and makes a request.

"I would like you to write a simple story just once more," he says, "the kind de Maupassant wrote, or Chekhov, the kind you used to write. Just recognizable people and then write down what happened to them next."

I say, "Yes, why not? That's possible." I want to please him, though I don't remember writing that way. I *would* like to try to tell such a story, if he means the kind that begins: "There was a woman . . ." followed by plot, the absolute line between two points which I've always despised. Not for literary reasons, but because it takes all hope away. Everyone, real or invented, deserves the open destiny of life.

Finally I thought of a story that had been happening for a couple of years right across the street. I wrote it down, then read it aloud. "Pa," I said, "how about this? Do you mean something like this?"

> Once in my time there was a woman and she had a son. They lived nicely, in a small apartment in Manhattan. This boy at about fifteen became a junkie, which is not unusual in our neighborhood. In order to maintain her close friendship with him, she became a junkie too. She said it was part of the youth culture, with which she felt very much at home. After a while, for a number of reasons, the boy gave it all up and left the city and his mother in disgust. Hopeless and alone, she grieved. We all visit her.

"O.K., Pa, that's it," I said, "an unadorned and miserable tale."

"But that's not what I mean," my father said. "You misunderstood me on purpose. You know there's a lot more to it. You know that. You left everything out. Turgenev wouldn't do that. Chekhov wouldn't do that. There are in fact Russian writers you never heard of, you don't have an inkling of, as good as anyone, who can write a plain ordinary story, who would not leave out what you have left out. I object not to facts but to people sitting in trees talking senselessly, voices from who knows where. . . ."

"Forget that one, Pa, what have I left out now? In this one?"

"Her looks, for instance."

"Oh. Quite handsome, I think. Yes."

"Her hair?"

"Dark, with heavy braids, as though she were a girl or a foreigner."

"What were her parents like, her stock? That she became such a person. It's interesting, you know."

"From out of town. Professional people. The first to be divorced in their county. How's that? Enough?" I asked.

"With you, it's all a joke," he said. "What about the boy's father? Why didn't you mention him? Who was he? Or was the boy born out of wedlock?"

"Yes," I said. "He was born out of wedlock."

"For Godsakes, doesn't anyone in your stories get married? Doesn't anyone have the time to run down to City Hall before they jump into bed?"

"No," I said. "In real life, yes. But in my stories, no."

"Why do you answer me like that?"

"Oh, Pa, this is a simple story about a smart woman who came to N.Y.C. full of interest love trust excitement very up to date, and about her son, what a hard time she had in this world. Married or not, it's of small consequence."

"It is of great consequence," he said.

"O.K.," I said.

"O.K. O.K. yourself," he said, "but listen. I believe you that she's good-looking, but I don't think she was so smart."

"That's true," I said. "Actually that's the trouble with stories. People start out fantastic. You think they're extraordinary, but it turns out as the work goes along, they're just average with a good education. Sometimes the other way around, the person's a kind of dumb innocent, but he outwits you and you can't even think of an ending good enough."

"What do you do then?" he asked. He had been a doctor for a couple of decades and then an artist for a couple of decades and he's still interested in details, craft, technique.

"Well, you just have to let the story lie around till some agreement can be reached between you and the stubborn hero."

"Aren't you talking silly now?" he asked. "Start again," he said. "It so happens I'm not going out this evening. Tell the story again. See what you can do this time."

"O.K.," I said. "But it's not a five-minute job." Second attempt:

> Once, across the street from us, there was a fine handsome woman, our neighbor. She had a son whom she loved because she'd known him since birth (in helpless chubby infancy, and in the wrestling, hugging ages, seven to ten, as well as earlier and later). This boy, when he fell into the fist of adolescence, became a junkie. He was not a hopeless one. He was in fact hopeful, an ideologue and successful converter. With his busy brilliance, he wrote persuasive articles for his high-school newspaper. Seeking a wider audience, using important connections, he drummed into Lower Manhattan newsstand distribution a periodical called *Oh! Golden Horse!*
>
> In order to keep him from feeling guilty (because guilt is the stony heart of nine tenths of all clinically diagnosed cancers in America today, she said), and because she had always believed in giving bad habits room at home where one could keep an eye on them, she too became a junkie. Her kitchen was famous for a while — a center

for intellectual addicts who knew what they were doing. A few felt artistic like Coleridge[1] and others were scientific and revolutionary like Leary.[2] Although she was often high herself, certain good mothering reflexes remained, and she saw to it that there was lots of orange juice around and honey and milk and vitamin pills. However, she never cooked anything but chili, and that no more than once a week. She explained, when we talked to her, seriously, with neighborly concern, that it was her part in the youth culture and she would rather be with the young, it was an honor, than with her own generation.

One week, while nodding through an Antonioni film, this boy was severely jabbed by the elbow of a stern and proselytizing girl, sitting beside him. She offered immediate apricots and nuts for his sugar level, spoke to him sharply, and took him home.

She had heard of him and his work and she herself published, edited, and wrote a competitive journal called *Man Does Live by Bread Alone*. In the organic heat of her continuous presence he could not help but become interested once more in his muscles, his arteries, and nerve connections. In fact he began to love them, treasure them, praise them with funny little songs in *Man Does Live*. . . .

> the fingers of my flesh transcend
> my transcendental soul
> the tightness in my shoulders end
> my teeth have made me whole

To the mouth of his head (that glory of will and determination) he brought hard apples, nuts, wheat germ, and soybean oil. He said to his old friends, From now on, I guess I'll keep my wits about me. I'm going on the natch. He said he was about to begin a spiritual deep-breathing journey. How about you too, Mom? he asked kindly.

His conversion was so radiant, splendid, that neighborhood kids his age began to say that he had never been a real addict at all, only a journalist along for the smell of the story. The mother tried several times to give up what had become without her son and his friends a lonely habit. This effort only brought it to supportable levels. The boy and his girl took their electronic mimeograph and moved to the bushy edge of another borough. They were very strict. They said they would not see her again until she had been off drugs for sixty days.

At home alone in the evening, weeping, the mother read and reread the seven issues of *Oh! Golden Horse!* They seemed to her as truthful as ever. We often crossed the street to visit and console. But if we mentioned any of our children who were at college or in the hospital or dropouts at home, she would cry out, My baby! My baby! and burst into terrible, face-scarring, time-consuming tears. The End.

First my father was silent, then he said, "Number One: You have a nice

---

[1] Samuel Taylor Coleridge (1772–1834), English Romantic poet, who was an opium addict.

[2] Timothy Leary (b. 1920), sometime Harvard professor of psychology and early advocate of the use of LSD.

sense of humor. Number Two: I see you can't tell a plain story. So don't waste time." Then he said sadly, "Number Three: I suppose that means she was alone, she was left like that, his mother. Alone. Probably sick?"

I said, "Yes."

"Poor woman. Poor girl, to be born in a time of fools, to live among fools. The end. The end. You were right to put that down. The end."

I didn't want to argue, but I had to say, "Well, it is not necessarily the end, Pa."

"Yes," he said, "what a tragedy. The end of a person."

"No, Pa," I begged him. "It doesn't have to be. She's only about forty. She could be a hundred different things in this world as time goes on. A teacher or a social worker. An ex-junkie! Sometimes it's better than having a master's in education."

"Jokes," he said. "As a writer that's your main trouble. You don't want to recognize it. Tragedy! Plain tragedy! Historical tragedy! No hope. The end."

"Oh, Pa," I said. "She could change."

"In your own life, too, you have to look it in the face." He took a couple of nitroglycerin. "Turn to five," he said, pointing to the dial on the oxygen tank. He inserted the tubes into his nostrils and breathed deep. He closed his eyes and said, "No."

I had promised the family to always let him have the last word when arguing, but in this case I had a different responsibility. That woman lives across the street. She's my knowledge and my invention. I'm sorry for her. I'm not going to leave her there in that house crying. (Actually neither would Life, which unlike me has no pity.)

Therefore: She did change. Of course her son never came home again. But right now, she's the receptionist in a storefront community clinic in the East Village. Most of the customers are young people, some old friends. The head doctor has said to her, "If we only had three people in this clinic with your experiences. . . ."

"The doctor said that?" My father took the oxygen tubes out of his nostrils and said, "Jokes. Jokes again."

"No, Pa, it could really happen that way, it's a funny world nowadays."

"No," he said. "Truth first. She will slide back. A person must have character. She does not."

"No, Pa," I said. "That's it. She's got a job. Forget it. She's in that storefront working."

"How long will it be?" he asked. "Tragedy! You too. When will you look it in the face?"   [1974]

OCTAVIO PAZ *(b. 1914), the 1990 Nobel Prize–winning Mexican poet and essayist, was born in Mexico City. He has said that he "came from a typical Mexican family," European on his mother's side and Mexican Indian on his father's side, but his father was a distinguished lawyer who took part in the Mexican Revolution and defended Emiliano Zapata, the peasant revolutionary leader advocating agrarian reform. Paz recalled that his "family had been impoverished by the revolution and the civil war. Our house, full of antique furniture, books, and other objects, was gradually crumbling to bits." While still a teenager, Paz began to publish poetry in literary journals. His first book of seven poems,* Rustic Moon, *was published in 1933.*

In 1937 Paz went abroad to attend a congress of antifascist writers in Spain. He also spent a short time in Paris, where he met many surrealist writers. "My experiences in Spain confirmed my revolutionary ardor," he notes, "but at the same time made me mistrust revolutionary theories. This brought me closer to the political attitude of the surrealists" rather than the official social realism doctrines of the communist bureaucracy in the Soviet Union. Back in Mexico City, Paz worked as a journalist supporting the cause of the Spanish Republicans until the German-Soviet pact at the outbreak of World War II made him withdraw from politics. In 1944 Paz received a Guggenheim fellowship that enabled him to live in San Francisco for a year, where he studied the work of a number of American poets, among them e. e. cummings, Wallace Stevens, and William Carlos Williams, who translated Paz's poetry into English. As a poet, Paz felt that "my career wasn't brilliant and my advancement was slow."

The need for financial security led Paz to enter the diplomatic service after publishing a book of essays about Mexican culture, The Labyrinth of Solitude, *in 1956. In the 1960s he was the Mexican ambassador to India, until he resigned in 1968 in protest of his government's use of violence against a student uprising in Mexico City. Since that time Paz has lived for the most part in Mexico when not lecturing at American universities. He has published numerous books of poetry and essays and a few short stories, including the surrealist story "My Life with the Wave," which was included in* Eagle or Sun? *(1970). In the story Paz uses what the critic Jason Wilson has recognized as images that "refer to wholesome, natural archetypes dormant and unconscious [in human beings]. . . . Paz links water symbolism with woman and pre-natal paradise; water is fertility and self-knowledge, and is both creative and destructive."*

Although Paz is primarily a poet and has written little short fiction, he regards "the fragment to be the form that best reflects the ever-changing reality that we live and are." In an essay in Alternating Current *(1973) commenting on the fragmentary nature of contemporary life, Paz defines literature as "metaphors of the world" within a writer: "I've always thought of literature as a language, but by language I mean the plurality of visions in the world."*

OCTAVIO PAZ

My Life with the Wave

Translated by Eliot Weinberger

When I left that sea, a wave moved ahead of the others. She was tall and light. In spite of the shouts of the others who grabbed her by her floating clothes, she clutched my arm and went off with me leaping. I didn't want to say anything to her, because it hurt me to shame her in front of her friends. Besides, the furious stares of the elders paralyzed me. When we got to town, I explained to her that it was impossible, that life in the city was not what she had been able to imagine with the ingenuity of a wave that had never left the sea. She watched me gravely: "No, your decision is made. You can't go back." I tried sweetness, hardness, irony. She cried, screamed, hugged, threatened. I had to apologize.

The next day my troubles began. How could we get on the train without being seen by the conductor, the passengers, the police? Certainly the rules say nothing in respect to the transport of waves on the railroad, but this same reserve was an indication of the severity with which our act would be judged. After much thought I arrived at the station an hour before departure, took my seat, and, when no one was looking, emptied the water tank for the passengers; then, carefully, poured in my friend.

The first incident came about when the children of a nearby couple declared their noisy thirst. I stopped them and promised them refreshments and lemonade. They were at the point of accepting when another thirsty passenger approached. I was about to invite her also, but the stare of her companion stopped me. The lady took a paper cup, approached the tank, and turned the faucet. Her cup was barely half full when I leaped between the woman and my friend. She looked at me astonished. While I apologized, one of the children turned the faucet again. I closed it violently. The lady brought the cup to her lips:

"Agh, this water is salty."

The boy echoed her. Various passengers rose. The husband called the conductor:

"This man put salt in the water."

The conductor called the Inspector:

"So you put substances in the water?"

The Inspector in turn called the police:

"So you poisoned the water?"

The police in turn called the Captain:

"So you're the poisoner?"

The captain called three agents. The agents took me to an empty car amid the stares and whispers of the passengers. At the next station they took me off and pushed and dragged me to the jail. For days no one spoke to me, except during the long interrogations. When I explained my story no one believed me, not even the jailer, who shook his head, saying: "The case is grave, truly grave. You didn't want to poison the children?" One day they brought me before the Magistrate.

"Your case is difficult," he repeated. I will assign you to the Penal Judge."

A year passed. Finally they judged me. As there were no victims, my sentence was light. After a short time, my day of liberty arrived.

The Chief of the Prison called me in:

"Well, now you're free. You were lucky. Lucky there were no victims. But don't do it again, because the next time won't be so short . . ."

And he stared at me with the same grave stare with which everyone watched me.

The same afternoon I took the train and after hours of uncomfortable traveling arrived in Mexico City. I took a cab home. At the door of my apartment I heard laughter and singing. I felt a pain in my chest, like the smack of a wave of surprise when surprise smacks us across the chest: my friend was there, singing and laughing as always.

"How did you get back?"

"Simple: in the train. Someone, after making sure that I was only salt water, poured me in the engine. It was a rough trip: soon I was a white plume of vapor, soon I fell in a fine rain on the machine. I thinned out a lot. I lost many drops."

Her presence changed my life. The house of dark corridors and dusty furniture was filled with air, with sun, with sounds and green and blue reflections, a numerous and happy populace of reverberations and echoes. How many waves is one wave, and how it can make a beach or a rock or jetty out of a wall, a chest, a forehead that it crowns with foam! Even the abandoned corners, the abject corners of dust and debris were touched by her light hands. Everything began to laugh and everywhere shined with teeth. The sun entered the old rooms with pleasure and stayed in my house for hours, abandoning the other houses, the district, the city, the country. And some nights, very late, the scandalized stars watched it sneak from my house.

Love was a game, a perpetual creation. All was beach, sand, a bed of sheets that were always fresh. If I embraced her, she swelled with pride, incredibly tall, like the liquid stalk of a poplar; and soon that thinness flowered into a fountain of white feathers, into a plume of smiles that fell over my head and back and covered me with whiteness. Or she stretched out in front of me, infinite as the horizon, until I too became horizon and silence. Full and sinuous, it enveloped me like music or some giant lips. Her present was a going and coming of caresses, of murmurs, of kisses. Entered in her waters, I was drenched to the socks and in a wink of an eye I found myself up above, at the height of vertigo, mysteriously suspended, to fall like a stone and feel myself gently deposited on the dryness, like a feather. Nothing is comparable to sleeping in those waters, to wake pounded by a thousand happy light lashes, by a thousand assaults that withdrew laughing.

But never did I reach the center of her being. Never did I touch the nakedness of pain and of death. Perhaps it does not exist in waves, that secret site that renders a woman vulnerable and mortal, that electric button where all interlocks, twitches, and straightens out to then swoon. Her sensibility, like that of women, spread in ripples, only they weren't concentric ripples, but rather eccentric, spreading each time farther, until they touched other galaxies. To love her was to extend to remote contacts, to vibrate with far-off stars we never suspected. But her center . . . no, she had no center, just an emptiness as in a whirlwind, that sucked me in and smothered me.

Stretched out side by side, we exchanged confidences, whispers, smiles. Curled up, she fell on my chest and there unfolded like a vegetation of murmurs. She sang in my ear, a little snail. She became humble and transparent, clutching my feet like a small animal, calm water. She was so clear I could read all of her thoughts. Certain nights her skin was covered with phosphorescence and to embrace her was to embrace a piece of night tattooed with fire. But she also became black and bitter. At unexpected hours she roared, moaned, twisted. Her groans woke the neighbors. Upon hearing her, the sea wind would scratch at the door of the house or rave in a loud voice on the roof. Cloudy days irritated her; she broke furniture, said bad words, covered me with insults and green and gray foam. She spit, cried, swore, prophesied. Subject to the moon, to the stars, to the influence of the light of other worlds, she changed her moods and appearance in a way that I thought fantastic, but it was as fatal as the tide.

She began to miss solitude. The house was full of snails and conches, of small sailboats that in her fury she had shipwrecked (together with the others, laden with images, that each night left my forehead and sank in her ferocious or pleasant whirlwinds). How many little treasures were lost in that time! But my boats and the silent song of the snails was not enough. I had to install in the house a colony of fish. I confess that it was not without jealousy that I watched them swimming in my friend, caressing her breasts, sleeping between her legs, adorning her hair with light flashes of color.

Among all those fish there were a few particularly repulsive and ferocious ones, little tigers from the aquarium, with large fixed eyes and jagged and bloodthirsty mouths. I don't know by what aberration my friend delighted in playing with them, shamelessly showing them a preference whose significance I preferred to ignore. She passed long hours confined with those horrible creatures. One day I couldn't stand it any more; I threw open the door and launched after them. Agile and ghostly they escaped my hands while she laughed and pounded me until I fell. I thought I was drowning. And when I was at the point of death, and purple, she deposited me on the bank and began to kiss me, saying I don't know what things. I felt very weak, fatigued, and humiliated. And at the same time her voluptuousness made me close my eyes, because her voice was sweet and she spoke to me of the delicious death of the drowned. When I recovered, I began to fear and hate her.

I had neglected my affairs. Now I began to visit friends and renew old and dear relations. I met an old girlfriend. Making her swear to keep my secret, I told her of my life with the wave. Nothing moves women so much as the possibility of saving a man. My redeemer employed all of her arts, but what could a woman, master of a limited number of souls and bodies, do in front of my friend who was always changing—and always identical to herself in her incessant metamorphoses.

Winter came. The sky turned gray. Fog fell on the city. Frozen drizzle rained. My friend cried every night. During the day she isolated herself, quiet and sinister, stuttering a single syllable, like an old woman who grumbles in a corner. She became cold; to sleep with her was to shiver all night and to feel freeze, little by little, the blood, the bones, the thoughts. She turned deep, impenetrable, restless. I left frequently and my absences were each time more prolonged. She, in her corner howled loudly. With teeth like steel and a corrosive tongue she gnawed the walls, crumbled them. She passed the nights in mourning, reproaching me. She had nightmares, deliriums of the sun, of warm beaches. She dreamt of the pole and of changing into a great block of ice, sailing beneath black skies in nights long as months. She insulted me. She cursed and laughed; filled the house with guffaws and phantoms. She called up the monsters of the depths, blind ones, quick ones, blunt. Charged with electricity, she carbonized all she touched; full of acid, she dissolved whatever she brushed against. Her sweet embraces became knotty cords that strangled me. And her body, greenish and elastic, was an implacable whip that lashed, lashed, lashed. I fled. The horrible fish laughed with ferocious smiles.

There in the mountains, among the tall pines and precipices, I breathed the cold thin air like a thought of liberty. At the end of a month I returned. I had decided. It had been so cold that over the marble of the chimney, next to the extinct fire, I found a statue of ice. I was unmoved by her weary beauty. I put her in a big canvas sack and went out to the streets with the sleeper on my shoulders. In a restaurant in the outskirts I sold her to a waiter friend who immediately began to chop her into little pieces, which he carefully deposited in the buckets where bottles are chilled.   [1949]

EDGAR ALLAN POE (1809–1849), *the son of poor traveling actors, was adopted by the merchant John Allan of Richmond, Virginia, after the death of Poe's mother. He was educated in Virginia and England, served two years in the army as an enlisted man, then entered the military academy at West Point, from which he was expelled after a year. When John Allan disinherited him, Poe turned to writing to earn his living. In 1833 his story "Ms. Found in a Bottle" won a fifty-dollar prize for the best story in a popular Baltimore periodical, and shortly afterward Poe became editor of the* Southern Literary Messenger. *In 1836 he married his cousin Virginia Clemm, who was thirteen years old. Poe's brilliant reviews, poems, and stories attracted wide attention, but the magazine fired him in 1837 because of his unstable temperament. His remaining years were a struggle with poverty, depression, poor health aggravated by addiction to drugs and alcohol, and — after 1847 — grief over the death of his wife. The writer Jorge Luis Borges observed that Poe's life "was short and unhappy, if unhappiness can be short."*

Most of Poe's stories can be divided into two categories: tales of terror, such as "The Cask of Amontillado" (1846) and "The Tell-Tale Heart" (1843), in which unity of effect or a single impression is of the greatest importance, and stories of intellect or reason, analytic tales that are precursors of the modern detective story. When critics accused him of imitating German romantic writers such as Heinrich von Kleist in his monologues of inspired madness, Poe answered, "Terror is not of Germany, but of the soul."

Poe is also important as one of the earliest writers to attempt to formulate an aesthetic theory about the short story form, or the "prose tale," as it was called in his time. His most extensive comments on this subject are in his reviews of Hawthorne's tales for the periodicals Graham's Magazine *in 1842 and* Godey's Lady's Book *in 1847; in these reviews he also described his own philosophy of composition. Poe believed that unity of a "single effect" was the most essential quality of all successful short fiction. He praised Hawthorne for his "invention, creation, imagination, originality" — qualities Poe himself possessed in abundance.*

RELATED COMMENTARIES: *D. H. Lawrence, "The Lust of Hate in Poe's 'The Cask of Amontillado,'" page 1446; Edgar Allan Poe, "The Importance of the Single Effect in a Prose Tale," page 1488.*

EDGAR ALLAN POE

The Cask of Amontillado

The thousand injuries of Fortunato I had borne as I best could; but when he ventured upon insult, I vowed revenge. You, who so well know the nature of my soul, will not suppose, however, that I gave utterance to a threat. *At length* I would be avenged; this was a point definitely settled — but the very definitiveness with which it was resolved precluded the idea of risk. I must not only punish, but punish with impunity. A wrong is unredressed when retribution overtakes its redresser. It is equally unredressed when the avenger fails to make himself felt as such to him who has done the wrong.

It must be understood, that neither by word nor deed had I given Fortunato cause to doubt my good-will. I continued, as was my wont, to smile in his face, and he did not perceive that my smile *now* was at the thought of his immolation.

He had a weak point — this Fortunato — although in other regards he was a man to be respected and even feared. He prided himself on his con-noisseurship in wine. Few Italians have the true virtuoso spirit. For the most part their enthusiasm is adopted to suit the time and opportunity — to prac-tise imposture upon the British and Austrian *millionnaires*. In painting and gemmary Fortunato, like his countrymen, was a quack — but in the matter of old wines he was sincere. In this respect I did not differ from him materially: I was skilful in the Italian vintages myself, and bought largely whenever I could.

It was about dusk, one evening during the supreme madness of the carnival season, that I encountered my friend. He accosted me with excessive warmth, for he had been drinking much. The man wore motley. He had on a tight-fitting parti-striped dress, and his head was surmounted by the conical cap and bells. I was so pleased to see him, that I thought I should never have done wringing his hand.

I said to him: "My dear Fortunato, you are luckily met. How remarkably well you are looking to-day! But I have received a pipe[1] of what passes for Amontillado, and I have my doubts."

"How?" said he. "Amontillado? A pipe? Impossible! And in the middle of the carnival!"

"I have my doubts," I replied; "and I was silly enough to pay the full Amontillado price without consulting you in the matter. You were not to be found, and I was fearful of losing a bargain."

"Amontillado!"

"I have my doubts."

---

[1] A large cask or keg.

"Amontillado!"

"And I must satisfy them."

"Amontillado!"

"As you are engaged, I am on my way to Luchesi. If any one has a critical turn, it is he. He will tell me" —— "

"Luchesi cannot tell Amontillado from Sherry."

"And yet some fools will have it that his taste is a match for your own."

"Come, let us go."

"Whither?"

"To your vaults."

"My friend, no; I will not impose upon your good nature. I perceive you have an engagement. Luchesi ——"

"I have no engagement; — come."

"My friend, no. It is not the engagement, but the severe cold with which I perceive you are afflicted. The vaults are insufferably damp. They are encrusted with nitre."

"Let us go, nevertheless. The cold is merely nothing. Amontillado! You have been imposed upon. And as for Luchesi, he cannot distinguish Sherry from Amontillado."

Thus speaking, Fortunato possessed himself of my arm. Putting on a mask of black silk, and drawing a *roquelaire*[2] closely about my person, I suffered him to hurry me to my palazzo.

There were no attendants at home; they had absconded to make merry in honor of the time. I had told them that I should not return until the morning, and had given them explicit orders not to stir from the house. These orders were sufficient, I well knew, to insure their immediate disappearance, one and all, as soon as my back was turned.

I took from their sconces two flambeaux, and giving one to Fortunato, bowed him through several suites of rooms to the archway that led into the vaults. I passed down a long and winding staircase, requesting him to be cautious as he followed. We came at length to the foot of the descent, and stood together on the damp ground of the catacombs of the Montresors.

The gait of my friend was unsteady, and the bells upon his cap jingled as he strode.

"The pipe?" said he.

"It is farther on," said I; "but observe the white web-work which gleams from these cavern walls."

He turned toward me, and looked into my eyes with two filmy orbs that distilled the rheum of intoxication.

"Nitre?" he asked, at length.

"Nitre," I replied. "How long have you had that cough?"

"Ugh! ugh! ugh! — ugh! ugh! ugh! — ugh! ugh! ugh! — ugh! ugh! ugh! — ugh! ugh! ugh!"

My poor friend found it impossible to reply for many minutes.

---

[2] A short cloak.

"It is nothing," he said, at last.

"Come," I said, with decision, "we will go back; your health is precious. You are rich, respected, admired, beloved; you are happy, as once I was. You are a man to be missed. For me it is no matter. We will go back; you will be ill, and I cannot be responsible. Besides, there is Luchesi ——"

"Enough," he said; "the cough is a mere nothing; it will not kill me. I shall not die of a cough."

"True — true," I replied; "and, indeed, I had no intention of alarming you unnecessarily; but you should use all proper caution. A draught of this Medoc will defend us from the damps."

Here I knocked off the neck of a bottle which I drew from a long row of its fellows that lay upon the mould.

"Drink," I said, presenting him the wine.

He raised it to his lips with a leer. He paused and nodded to me familiarly, while his bells jingled.

"I drink," he said, "to the buried that repose around us."

"And I to your long life."

He again took my arm, and we proceeded.

"These vaults," he said, "are extensive."

"The Montresors," I replied. "were a great and numerous family."

"I forget your arms."

"A huge human foot d'or,[3] in a field azure; the foot crushes a serpent rampant whose fangs are imbedded in the heel."

"And the motto?"

"Nemo me impune lacessit."[4]

"Good!" he said.

The wine sparkled in his eyes and the bells jingled. My own fancy grew warm with the Medoc. We had passed through walls of piled bones, with casks and puncheons intermingling into the inmost recesses of the catacombs. I paused again, and this time I made bold to seize Fortunato by an arm above the elbow.

"The nitre!" I said; "see, it increases. It hangs like moss upon the vaults. We are below the river's bed. The drops of moisture trickle among the bones. Come, we will go back ere it is too late. Your cough ——"

"It is nothing," he said; "let us go on. But first, another draught of the Medoc."

I broke and reached him a flagon of De Grâve. He emptied it at a breath. His eyes flashed with a fierce light. He laughed and threw the bottle upward with a gesticulation I did not understand.

I looked at him in surprise. He repeated the movement — a grotesque one.

"You do not comprehend?" he said.

"Not, I," I replied.

---

[3]Of gold.
[4]"No one wounds me with impunity"; the motto of the royal arms of Scotland.

"Then you are not of the brotherhood."

"How?"

"You are not of the masons."

"Yes, yes," I said; "yes, yes."

"You? Impossible! A mason?"

"A mason," I replied.

"A sign," he said.

"It is this," I answered, producing a trowel from beneath the folds of my *roquelaire*.

"You jest," he exclaimed, recoiling a few paces. "But let us proceed to the Amontillado."

"Be it so," I said, replacing the tool beneath the cloak, and again offering him my arm. He leaned upon it heavily. We continued our route in search of the Amontillado. We passed through a range of low arches, descended, passed on, and descending again, arrived at a deep crypt, in which the foulness of the air caused our flambeaux rather to glow than flame.

At the most remote end of the crypt there appeared another less spacious. Its walls had been lined with human remains, piled to the vault overhead, in the fashion of the great catacombs of Paris. Three sides of this interior crypt were still ornamented in this manner. From the fourth the bones had been thrown down, and lay promiscuously upon the earth, forming at one point a mound of some size. Within the wall thus exposed by the displacing of the bones, we perceived a still interior recess, in depth about four feet, in width three, in height six or seven. It seemed to have been constructed for no especial use within itself, but formed merely the interval between two of the colossal supports of the roof of the catacombs, and was backed by one of their circumscribing walls of solid granite.

It was in vain that Fortunato, uplifting his dull torch, endeavored to pry into the depth of the recess. Its termination the feeble light did not enable us to see.

"Proceed," I said; "herein is the Amontillado. As for Luchesi ——"

"He is an ignoramus," interrupted my friend, as he stepped unsteadily forward, while I followed immediately at his heels. In an instant he had reached the extremity of the niche, and finding his progress arrested by the rock, stood stupidly bewildered. A moment more and I had fettered him to the granite. In its surface were two iron staples, distant from each other about two feet, horizontally. From one of these depended a short chain, from the other a padlock. Throwing the links about his waist, it was but the work of a few seconds to secure it. He was too much astounded to resist. Withdrawing the key I stepped back from the recess.

"Pass your hand," I said, "over the wall; you cannot help feeling the nitre. Indeed it is *very* damp. Once more let me *implore* you to return. No? Then I must positively leave you. But I must first render you all the little attentions in my power."

"The Amontillado!" ejaculated my friend, not yet recovered from his astonishment.

"True," I replied; "the Amontillado."

As I said these words I busied myself among the pile of bones of which I have before spoken. Throwing them aside, I soon uncovered a quantity of building stone and mortar. With these materials and with the aid of my trowel, I began vigorously to wall up the entrance of the niche.

I had scarcely laid the first tier of the masonry when I discovered that the intoxication of Fortunato had in a great measure worn off. The earliest indication I had of this was a low moaning cry from the depth of the recess. It was *not* the cry of a drunken man. There was then a long and obstinate silence. I laid the second tier, and the third, and the fourth; and then I heard the furious vibrations of the chain. The noise lasted for several minutes, during which, that I might hearken to it with the more satisfaction, I ceased my labors and sat down upon the bones. When at last the clanking subsided, I resumed the trowel, and finished without interruption the fifth, the sixth, and the seventh tier. The wall was now nearly upon a level with my breast. I again paused, and holding the flambeaux over the masonwork, threw a few feeble rays upon the figure within.

A succession of loud and shrill screams, bursting suddenly from the throat of the chained form, seemed to thrust me violently back. For a brief moment I hesitated — I trembled. Unsheathing my rapier, I began to grope with it about the recess; but the thought of an instant reassured me. I placed my hand upon the solid fabric of the catacombs, and felt satisfied. I reapproached the wall. I replied to the yells of him who clamored. I reechoed — I aided — I surpassed them in volume and in strength. I did this, and the clamorer grew still.

It was now midnight, and my task was drawing to a close. I had completed the eighth, the ninth, and the tenth tier. I had finished a portion of the last and the eleventh; there remained but a single stone to be fitted and plastered in. I struggled with its weight; I placed it partially in its destined position. But now there came from out the niche a low laugh that erected the hairs upon my head. It was succeeded by a sad voice, which I had difficulty in recognizing as that of the noble Fortunato. The voice said —

"Ha! ha! ha! — he! he! — a very good joke indeed — an excellent jest. We will have many a rich laugh about it at the palazzo — he! he! he! — over our wine — he! he! he!"

"The Amontillado!" I said.

"He! he! he! — he! he! he! — yes, the Amontillado. But is it not getting late? Will not they be awaiting us at the palazzo, the Lady Fortunato and the rest? Let us be gone."

"Yes," I said, "let us be gone."

"*For the love of God, Montresor!*"

"Yes," I said, "for the love of God!"

But to these words I hearkened in vain for a reply. I grew impatient. I called aloud:

"Fortunato!"

No answer. I called again:

"Fortunato!"

No answer still, I thrust a torch through the remaining aperture and let it fall within. There came forth in return only a jingling of the bells. My heart grew sick — on account of the dampness of the catacombs. I hastened to make an end of my labor. I forced the last stone into its position; I plastered it up. Against the new masonry I re-erected the old rampart of bones. For the half of a century no mortal has disturbed them. *In pace requiescat!*   [1846]

EDGAR ALLAN POE

The Tell-Tale Heart

True! — nervous — very, very dreadfully nervous I had been and am; but why *will* you say that I am mad? The disease had sharpened my senses — not destroyed — not dulled them. Above all was the sense of hearing acute. I heard all things in the heaven and in the earth. I heard many things in hell. How, then, am I mad? Hearken! and observe how healthily — how calmly I can tell you the whole story.

It is impossible to say how first the idea entered my brain; but once conceived, it haunted me day and night. Object there was none. Passion there was none. I loved the old man. He had never wronged me. He had never given me insult. For his gold I had no desire. I think it was his eye! yes, it was this! One of his eyes resembled that of a vulture — a pale blue eye, with a film over it. Whenever it fell upon me, my blood ran cold; and so by degrees — very gradually — I made up my mind to take the life of the old man, and thus rid myself of the eye for ever.

Now this is the point. You fancy me mad. Madmen know nothing. But you should have seen *me*. You should have seen how wisely I proceeded — with what caution — with what foresight — with what dissimulation I went to work! I was never kinder to the old man than during the whole week before I killed him. And every night, about midnight, I turned the latch of his door and opened it — oh, so gently! And then, when I had made an opening sufficient for my head, I put in a dark lantern, all closed, closed, so that no light shone out, and then I thrust in my head. Oh, you would have laughed to see how cunningly I thrust it in! I moved it slowly — very, very slowly, so that I might not disturb the old man's sleep. It took me an hour to place my whole head within the opening so far that I could see him as he lay upon his bed. Ha — would a madman have been so wise as this? And then, when my head was well in the room, I undid the lantern cautiously — oh, so cautiously — cautiously (for the hinges creaked) — I undid it just so much that a single thin ray fell upon the vulture eye. And this I did for seven long nights — every night just after midnight — but I found the eye always closed; and so it was impossible to do the work; for it was not the old man who vexed me, but his Evil Eye. And every morning, when the day broke, I went boldly into the chamber, and spoke courageously to him, calling him by name in a hearty tone, and inquiring how he had passed the night. So you see he would have been a very profound old man, indeed, to suspect that every night, just at twelve, I looked in upon him while he slept.

Upon the eighth night I was more than usually cautious in opening the door. A watch's minute hand moves more quickly than did mine. Never before that night had I *felt* the extent of my own powers — of my sagacity. I could scarcely contain my feelings of triumph. To think that there I was, opening the door, little by little, and he not even to dream of my secret deeds or thoughts. I fairly chuckled at the idea; and perhaps he heard me; for he moved on the bed suddenly, as if startled. Now you may think that I drew back — but no. His room was as black as pitch with the thick darkness (for the shutters were close fastened, through fear of robbers), and so I knew that he could not see the opening of the door, and I kept pushing it on steadily, steadily.

I had my head in, and was about to open the lantern, when my thumb slipped upon the tin fastening, and the old man sprang up in the bed, crying out — "Who's there?"

I kept quite still and said nothing. For a whole hour I did not move a muscle, and in the meantime I did not hear him lie down. He was still sitting up in the bed listening; — just as I have done, night after night, hearkening to the death watches in the wall.

Presently I heard a slight groan, and I knew it was the groan of mortal terror. It was not a groan of pain or of grief — oh, no! — it was the low stifled sound that arises from the bottom of the soul when overcharged with awe. I knew the sound well. Many a night, just at midnight, when all the world slept, it has welled up from my own bosom, deepening with its dreadful echo, the terrors that distracted me. I say I knew it well. I knew what the old man felt, and pitied him, although I chuckled at heart. I knew that he had been lying awake ever since the first slight noise, when he had turned in the bed. His fears had been ever since growing upon him. He had been trying to fancy them causeless, but could not. He had been saying to himself — "It is nothing but the wind in the chimney — it is only a mouse crossing the floor," or "it is merely a cricket which has made a single chirp." Yes, he has been trying to comfort himself with these suppositions; but he had found all in vain. *All in vain*; because Death, in approaching him, had stalked with his black shadow before him, and enveloped the victim. And it was the mournful influence of the unperceived shadow that caused him to feel — although he neither saw nor heard — to *feel* the presence of my head within the room.

When I had waited a long time, very patiently, without hearing him lie down, I resolved to open a little — a very, very little crevice in the lantern. So I opened it — you cannot imagine how stealthily, stealthily — until, at length, a single dim ray, like the thread of the spider, shot from out the crevice and full upon the vulture eye.

It was open — wide, wide open — and I grew furious as I gazed upon it. I saw it with perfect distinctness — all a dull blue, with a hideous veil over it that chilled the very marrow in my bones, but I could see nothing else of the old man's face or person: for I had directed the ray as if by instinct, precisely upon the damned spot.

And now have I not told you that what you mistake for madness is but over-acuteness of the senses? — now, I say, there came to my ears a low, dull, quick sound, such as a watch makes when enveloped in cotton. I knew *that* sound well too. It was the beating of the old man's heart. It increased my fury, as the beating of a drum stimulates the soldier into courage.

But even yet I refrained and kept still. I scarcely breathed. I held the lantern motionless. I tried how steadily I could maintain the ray upon the eye. Meantime the hellish tattoo of the heart increased. It grew quicker and quicker, and louder and louder every instant. The old man's terror *must* have been extreme! It grew louder, I say, louder every moment! — do you mark me well? I have told you that I am nervous: so I am. And now at the dead hour of the night, amid the dreadful silence of that old house, so strange a noise as this excited me to uncontrollable terror. Yet, for some minutes longer I refrained and stood still. But the beating grew louder, louder! I thought the heart must burst. And now a new anxiety seized me — the sound would be heard by a neighbor! The old man's hour had come! With a loud yell, I threw open the lantern and leaped into the room. He shrieked once — once only. In an instant I dragged him to the floor, and pulled the heavy bed over him. I then smiled gaily, to find the deed so far done. But, for many minutes, the heart beat on with a muffled sound. This, however, did not vex me; it would not be heard through the wall. At length it ceased. The old man was dead. I removed the bed and examined the corpse. Yes, he was stone, stone dead. I placed my hand upon the heart and held it there many minutes. There was no pulsation. He was stone dead. His eye would trouble me no more.

If still you think me mad, you will think so no longer when I describe the wise precautions I took for the concealment of the body. The night waned, and I worked hastily, but in silence. First of all I dismembered the corpse. I cut off the head and the arms and the legs.

I then took up three planks from the flooring of the chamber, and deposited all between the scantlings. I then replaced the boards so cleverly, so cunningly, that no human eye — not even *his* — could have detected any-thing wrong. There was nothing to wash out — no stain of any kind — no blood-spot whatever. I had been too wary for that. A tub had caught all — ha! ha!

When I had made an end of these labors, it was four o'clock — still dark as midnight. As the bell sounded the hour, there came a knocking at the street door. I went down to open it with a light heart — for what had I *now* to fear? There entered three men, who introduced themselves, with perfect suavity, as officers of the police. A shriek had been heard by a neighbor during the night; suspicion of foul play had been aroused; information had been lodged at the police office, and they (the officers) had been deputed to search the premises.

I smiled — for *what* had I to fear? I bade the gentlemen welcome. The shriek, I said, was my own in a dream. The old man, I mentioned, was absent in the country. I took my visitors all over the house. I bade them search —

search *well*. I led them, at length, to *his* chamber. I showed them his treasures, secure, undisturbed. In the enthusiasm of my confidence, I brought chairs into the room, and desired them *here* to rest from their fatigues, while I myself; in the wild audacity of my perfect triumph, placed my own seat upon the very spot beneath which reposed the corpse of the victim.

The officers were satisfied. My *manner* had convinced them. I was singularly at ease. They sat, and while I answered cheerily, they chatted familiar things. But, ere long, I felt myself getting pale and wished them gone. My head ached, and I fancied a ringing in my ears: but still they sat and still chatted. The ringing became more distinct: — it continued and became more distinct: I talked more freely to get rid of the feeling: but it continued and gained definitiveness — until, at length, I found that the noise was *not* within my ears.

No doubt I now grew *very* pale; — but I talked more fluently, and with a heightened voice. Yet the sound increased — and what could I do? It was *a low, dull, quick sound — much such a sound as a watch makes when enveloped in cotton.* I gasped for breath — and yet the officers heard it not. I talked more quickly — more vehemently; but the noise steadily increased. I arose and argued about trifles, in a high key and with violent gesticulations, but the noise steadily increased. Why *would* they not be gone? I paced the floor to and fro with heavy strides, as if excited to fury by the observation of the men — but the noise steadily increased. Oh God! what *could* I do? I foamed — I raved — I swore! I swung the chair upon which I had been sitting, and grated it upon the boards, but the noise arose over all and continually increased. It grew louder — louder — *louder*! And still the men chatted pleasantly, and smiled. Was it possible they heard not? Almighty God! — no, no! They heard! — they suspected! — they *knew*! — they were making a mockery of my horror! — this I thought, and this I think. But any thing was better than this agony! Any thing was more tolerable than this derision! I could bear those hypocritical smiles no longer! I felt that I must scream or die! — and now — again! — hark! louder! louder! louder! *louder*! —

"Villains!" I shrieked, "dissemble no more! I admit the deed! — tear up the planks! — here, here! — it is the beating of his hideous heart!"   [1843]

KATHERINE ANNE PORTER *(1890–1980) was born Callie Russell Porter in Indian Creek, Texas. When she was only two years old her mother died. Educated at boarding schools and an Ursuline convent, Porter worked briefly as a reporter in Chicago and Denver. As a child she had wanted to be a writer, but it took fifteen years of serious writing before she trusted herself enough as a stylist to approach a publisher. Most of her life during this time was a financial struggle; she spent only 10 percent of her energies on writing, and "the other 90 percent went to keeping my head above water." She nearly lost her life in the influenza epidemic that swept the United States at the end of World War I, and when she recovered she went to Mexico to study Aztec and Mayan art.*

Porter achieved acclaim with her first collection of short stories, Flowering Judas and Other Stories, *in 1930. Her most productive decade as a writer was the 1930s, when she published* Noon Wine *(1937) and* Pale Horse, Pale Rider: Three Short Novels *(1939). She supported herself with lecture tours and teaching jobs at various universities while she worked on her novel* Ship of Fools *(1962), which took over two decades to complete. In 1965 her* Collected Stories *won both the Pulitzer Prize and the National Book Award.*

Porter's style is not so recognizably "southern" as William Faulkner's or Flannery O'Connor's. She was a southerner by tradition and inheritance, but she had thought of herself since childhood as "always restless, always a roving spirit." She was very conscious of her own art as a storyteller, and of the art of fiction in general; she wrote personal essays on Willa Cather, Katherine Mansfield, Flannery O'Connor, Eudora Welty, and Virginia Woolf. Particularly indebted in her best stories to Mansfield, Porter attempted to dramatize a character's state of mind rather than develop a complicated plot. Her analysis of Mansfield's literary practice in the essay "The Art of Katherine Mansfield" can also be applied to a story such as "He":

> *With fine objectivity, she bares a moment of experience, real experience, in the life of some one human being; she states no belief, gives no motives, airs no theories, but simply presents to the reader a situation, a place, and a character, and there it is; and the emotional content is present as implicitly as the germ is in the grain of wheat.*

KATHERINE ANNE PORTER

He

Life was very hard for the Whipples. It was hard to feed all the hungry mouths, it was hard to keep the children in flannels during the winter, short as it was: "God knows what would become of us if we lived north," they would say: keeping them decently clean was hard. "It looks like our luck won't never let up on us," said Mr. Whipple, but Mrs. Whipple was all for taking what was sent and calling it good, anyhow when the neighbors were in earshot. "Don't ever let a soul hear us complain," she kept saying to her husband. She couldn't stand to be pitied. "No, not if it comes to it that we have to live in a wagon and pick cotton around the country," she said, "nobody's going to get a chance to look down on us."

Mrs. Whipple loved her second son, the simple-minded one, better than she loved the other two children put together. She was forever saying so, and when she talked with certain of her neighbors, she would even throw in her husband and her mother for good measure.

"You needn't keep on saying it around," said Mr. Whipple, "you'll make people think nobody else has any feelings about Him but you."

"It's natural for a mother," Mrs. Whipple would remind him. "You know yourself it's more natural for a mother to be that way. People don't expect so much of fathers, some way."

This didn't keep the neighbors from talking plainly among themselves. "A Lord's pure mercy if He should die," they said. "It's the sins of the fathers," they agreed among themselves. "There's bad blood and bad doings somewhere, you can bet on that." This behind the Whipples' back. To their faces everybody said, "He's not so bad off. He'll be all right yet. Look how He grows!"

Mrs. Whipple hated to talk about it, she tried to keep her mind off it, but every time anybody set foot in the house, the subject always came up, and she had to talk about Him first, before she could get on to anything else. It seemed to ease her mind. "I wouldn't have anything happen to Him for all the world, but it just looks like I can't keep Him out of mischief. He's so strong and active, He's always into everything; He was like that since He could walk. It's actually funny sometimes, the way He can do anything; it's laughable to see Him up to His tricks. Emly has more accidents; I'm forever tying up her bruises, and Adna can't fall a foot without cracking a bone. But He can do anything and not get a scratch. The preacher said such a nice thing once when he was here. He said, and I'll remember it to my dying day, 'The innocent walk with God — that's why He don't get hurt.'" Whenever Mrs. Whipple repeated these words, she always felt a warm pool spread in her breast, and the tears would fill her eyes, and then she could talk about something else.

He did grow and He never got hurt. A plank blew off the chicken house and struck Him on the head and He never seemed to know it. He had learned a few words, and after this He forgot them. He didn't whine for food as the other children did, but waited until it was given Him; He ate squatting in the corner, smacking and mumbling. Rolls of fat covered Him like an overcoat, and He could carry twice as much wood and water as Adna. Emly had a cold in the head most of the time — "she takes that after me," said Mrs. Whipple — so in bad weather they gave her the extra blanket off His cot. He never seemed to mind the cold.

Just the same, Mrs. Whipple's life was a torment for fear something might happen to Him. He climbed the peach trees much better than Adna and went skittering along the branches like a monkey, just a regular monkey.

"Oh, Mrs. Whipple, you hadn't ought to let Him do that. He'll lose His balance sometime. He can't rightly know what He's doing."

Mrs. Whipple almost screamed out at the neighbor. "He *does* know what He's doing! He's as able as any other child! Come down out of there, you!" When He finally reached the ground she could hardly keep her hands off Him for acting like that before people, a grin all over His face and her worried sick about Him all the time.

"It's the neighbors," said Mrs. Whipple to her husband. "Oh, I do mortally wish they would keep out of our business. I can't afford to let Him do anything for fear they'll come nosing around about it. Look at the bees, now. Adna can't handle them, they sting him up so; I haven't got time to do everything, and now I don't dare let Him. But if He gets a sting He don't really mind."

"It's just because He ain't got sense enough to be scared of anything," said Mr. Whipple.

"You ought to be ashamed of yourself," said Mrs. Whipple, "talking that way about your own child. Who's to take up for Him if we don't, I'd like to know? He sees a lot that goes on, He listens to things all the time. And anything I tell Him to do He does it. Don't never let anybody hear you say such things. They'd think you favored the other children over Him."

"Well, now I don't, and you know it, and what's the use of getting all worked up about it? You always think the worst of everything. Just let Him alone, He'll get along somehow. He gets plenty to eat and wear, don't He?" Mr. Whipple suddenly felt tired out. "Anyhow, it can't be helped now."

Mrs. Whipple felt tired too, she complained in a tired voice. "What's done can't never be undone, I know that as good as anybody; but He's my child, and I'm not going to have people say anything. I get sick of people coming around saying things all the time."

In the early fall Mrs. Whipple got a letter from her brother saying he and his wife and two children were coming over for a little visit next Sunday week. "Put the big pot in the little one," he wrote at the end. Mrs. Whipple read this part out loud twice, she was so pleased. Her brother was a great one for saying funny things. "We'll just show him that's no joke," she said, "we'll just butcher one of the suckling pigs."

"It's a waste and I don't hold with waste the way we are now," said Mr. Whipple. "That pig'll be worth money by Christmas."

"It's a shame and a pity we can't have a decent meal's vittles once in a while when my own family comes to see us," said Mrs. Whipple. "I'd hate for his wife to go back and say there wasn't a thing in the house to eat. My God, it's better than buying up a great chance of meat in town. There's where you'd spend the money!"

"All right, do it yourself then," said Mr. Whipple. "Christamighty, no wonder we can't get ahead!"

The question was how to get the little pig away from his ma, a great fighter, worse than a Jersey cow. Adna wouldn't try it: "That sow'd rip my insides out all over the pen." "All right, old fraidy," said Mrs. Whipple, "*He's* not scared. Watch *Him* do it." And she laughed as though it was all a good joke and gave Him a little push towards the pen. He sneaked up and snatched the pig right away from the teat and galloped back and was over the fence with the sow raging at His heels. The little black squirming thing was screeching like a baby in a tantrum, stiffening its back and stretching its mouth to the ears. Mrs. Whipple took the pig with her face stiff and sliced its throat with one stroke. When He saw the blood He gave a great jolting breath and ran away. "But He'll forget and eat plenty, just the same," thought Mrs. Whipple. Whenever she was thinking, her lips moved making words. "He'd eat it all if I didn't stop Him. He'd eat up every mouthful from the other two if I'd let Him."

She felt badly about it. He was ten years old now and a third again as large as Adna, who was going on fourteen. "It's a shame, a shame," she kept saying under her breath, "and Adna with so much brains!"

She kept on feeling badly about all sorts of things. In the first place it was the man's work to butcher; the sight of the pig scraped pink and naked made her sick. He was too fat and soft and pitiful-looking. It was simply a shame the way things had to happen. By the time she had finished it up, she almost wished her brother would stay at home.

Early Sunday morning Mrs. Whipple dropped everything to get Him all cleaned up. In an hour He was dirty again, with crawling under fences after a possum, and straddling along the rafters of the barn looking for eggs in the hayloft. "My Lord, look at you now after all my trying! And here's Adna and Emly staying so quiet. I get tired trying to keep you decent. Get off that shirt and put on another, people will say I don't half dress you!" And she boxed Him on the ears, hard. He blinked and blinked and rubbed His head, and His face hurt Mrs. Whipple's feelings. Her knees began to tremble, she had to sit down while she buttoned His shirt. "I'm just all gone before the day starts."

The brother came with his plump healthy wife and two great roaring hungry boys. They had a grand dinner, with the pig roasted to a crackling in the middle of the table, full of dressing, a pickled peach in his mouth and plenty of gravy for the sweet potatoes.

"This looks like prosperity all right," said the brother; "you're going to have to roll me home like I was a barrel when I'm done."

Everybody laughed out loud; it was fine to hear them laughing all at once around the table. Mrs. Whipple felt warm and good about it. "Oh, we've got six more of these; I say it's as little as we can do when you come to see us so seldom."

He wouldn't come into the dining room, and Mrs. Whipple passed it off very well. "He's timider than my other two," she said, "He'll just have to get used to you. There isn't everybody He'll make up with, you know how it is with some children, even cousins." Nobody said anything out of the way.

"Just like my Alty here," said the brother's wife. "I sometimes got to lick him to make him shake hands with his own grandmammy."

So that was over, and Mrs. Whipple loaded up a big plate for Him first, before everybody. "I always say He ain't to be slighted, no matter who else goes without," she said, and carried it to Him herself.

"He can chin Himself on the top of the door," said Emly, helping along.

"That's fine. He's getting along fine," said the brother.

They went away after supper. Mrs. Whipple rounded up the dishes, and sent the children to bed and sat down and unlaced her shoes. "You see?" she said to Mr. Whipple. "That's the way my whole family is. Nice and considerate about everything. No out-of-the-way remarks — they *have* got refinement. I get awfully sick of people's remarks. Wasn't that pig good?"

Mr. Whipple said, "Yes, we're out three hundred pounds of pork, that's all. It's easy to be polite when you come to eat. Who knows what they had in their minds all along?"

"Yes, that's like you," said Mrs. Whipple. "I don't expect anything else from you. You'll be telling me next that my own brother will be saying around that we made Him eat in the kitchen! Oh, my God!" She rocked her head in her hands, a hard pain started in the very middle of her forehead. "Now it's all spoiled, and everything was so nice and easy. All right, you don't like them and you never did — all right, they'll not come here again soon, never you mind! But they *can't* say He wasn't dressed every lick as good as Adna — oh, honest, sometimes I wish I was dead!"

"I wish you'd let up," said Mr. Whipple. "It's bad enough as it is."

It was a hard winter. It seemed to Mrs. Whipple that they hadn't ever known anything but hard times, and now to cap it all a winter like this. The crops were about half of what they had a right to expect; after the cotton was in it didn't do much more than cover the grocery bill. They swapped off one of the plow horses, and got cheated, for the new one died of the heaves. Mrs. Whipple kept thinking all the time it was terrible to have a man you couldn't depend on not to get cheated. They cut down on everything, but Mrs. Whipple kept saying there are things you can't cut down on, and they cost money. It took a lot of warm clothes for Adna and Emly, who walked four miles to school during the three-months session. "He sets around the fire a lot, He won't need so much," said Mr. Whipple. "That's so," said Mrs. Whipple, "and when He does the outdoor chores He can wear your tarpaullion coat. I can't do no better, that's all."

In February He was taken sick, and lay curled up under His blanket looking very blue in the face and acting as if He would choke. Mr. and Mrs. Whipple did everything they could for Him for two days, and then they were scared and sent for the doctor. The doctor told them they must keep Him warm and give Him plenty of milk and eggs. "He isn't as stout as He looks, I'm afraid," said the doctor. "You've got to watch them when they're like that. You must put more cover onto Him, too."

"I just took off His big blanket to wash," said Mrs. Whipple, ashamed. "I can't stand dirt."

"Well, you'd better put it back on the minute it's dry," said the doctor, "or He'll have pneumonia."

Mr. and Mrs. Whipple took a blanket off their own bed and put His cot in by the fire. "They can't say we didn't do everything for Him," she said, "even to sleeping cold ourselves on His account."

When the winter broke He seemed to be well again, but He walked as if His feet hurt Him. He was able to run a cotton planter during the season.

"I got it all fixed up with Jim Ferguson about breeding the cow next time," said Mr. Whipple. "I'll pasture the bull this summer and give Jim some fodder in the fall. That's better than paying out money when you haven't got it."

"I hope you didn't say such a thing before Jim Ferguson," said Mrs. Whipple. "You oughtn't to let him know we're so down as all that."

"Godamighty, that ain't saying we're down. A man is got to look ahead sometimes. He can lead the bull over today. I need Adna on the place."

At first Mrs. Whipple felt easy in her mind about sending Him for the bull. Adna was too jumpy and couldn't be trusted. You've got to be steady around animals. After He was gone she started thinking, and after a while she could hardly bear it any longer. She stood in the lane and watched for Him. It was nearly three miles to go and a hot day, but He oughtn't to be so long about it. She shaded her eyes and stared until colored bubbles floated in her eyeballs. It was just like everything else in life, she must always worry and never know a moment's peace about anything. After a long time she saw Him turn into the side lane, limping. He came on very slowly, leading the big hulk of an animal by a ring in the nose, twirling a little stick in His hand, never looking back or sideways, but coming on like a sleepwalker with His eyes half shut.

Mrs. Whipple was scared sick of bulls; she had heard awful stories about how they followed on quietly enough, and then suddenly pitched on with a bellow and pawed and gored a body to pieces. Any second now that black monster would come down on Him, my God, He'd never have sense enough to run.

She mustn't make a sound nor a move; she mustn't get the bull started. The bull heaved his head aside and horned the air at a fly. Her voice burst out of her in a shriek, and she screamed at Him to come on, for God's sake. He didn't seem to hear her clamor, but kept on twirling His switch and limping on, and the bull lumbered along behind him as gently as a calf. Mrs. Whipple stopped calling and ran towards the house, praying under her breath: "Lord, don't let anything happen to Him. Lord, you *know* people will say we oughtn't to have sent Him. You *know* they'll say we didn't take care of Him. Oh, get Him home, safe home, safe home, and I'll look out for Him better! Amen."

She watched from the window while He led the beast in, and tied him up in the barn. It was no use trying to keep up, Mrs. Whipple couldn't bear another thing. She sat down and rocked and cried with her apron over her head.

From year to year the Whipples were growing poorer and poorer. The place just seemed to run down of itself, no matter how hard they worked. "We're losing our hold," said Mrs. Whipple. "Why can't we do like other people and watch for our best chances? They'll be calling us poor white trash next."

"When I get to be sixteen I'm going to leave," said Adna. "I'm going to get a job in Powell's grocery store. There's money in that. No more farm for me."

"I'm going to be a schoolteacher," said Emly. "But I've got to finish the eighth grade, anyhow. Then I can live in town. I don't see any chances here."

"Emly takes after my family," said Mrs. Whipple. "Ambitious every last one of them, and they don't take second place for anybody."

When fall came Emly got a chance to wait on table in the railroad eating-house in the town near by, and it seemed such a shame not to take it when the wages were good and she could get her food too, that Mrs. Whipple decided to let her take it, and not bother with school until the next session. "You've got plenty of time," she said. "You're young and smart as a whip."

With Adna gone too, Mr. Whipple tried to run the farm with just Him to help. He seemed to get along fine, doing His work and part of Adna's without noticing it. They did well enough until Christmas time, when one morning He slipped on the ice coming up from the barn. Instead of getting up He thrashed round and round, and when Mr. Whipple got to Him, He was having some sort of fit.

They brought Him inside and tried to make Him sit up, but He blubbered and rolled, so they put Him to bed and Mr. Whipple rode to town for the doctor. All the way there and back he worried about where the money was to come from: it sure did look like he had about all the troubles he could carry.

From then on He stayed in bed. His legs swelled up double their size, and the fits kept coming back. After four months, the doctor said, "It's no use, I think you'd better put Him in the County Home for treatment right away. I'll see about it for you. He'll have good care there and be off your hands."

"We don't begrudge Him any care, and I won't let Him out of my sight," said Mrs. Whipple. "I won't have it said I sent my sick child off among strangers."

"I know how you feel," said the doctor. "You can't tell me anything about that, Mrs. Whipple. I've got a boy of my own. But you'd better listen to me. I can't do anything more for Him, that's the truth."

Mr. and Mrs. Whipple talked it over a long time that night after they went to bed. "It's just charity," said Mrs. Whipple, "that's what we've come to, charity! I certainly never looked for this."

"We pay taxes to help support the place just like everybody else," said Mr. Whipple, "and I don't call that taking charity. I think it would be fine to have Him where He'd get the best of everything . . . and besides, I can't keep up with these doctor bills any longer."

"Maybe that's why the doctor wants us to send Him — he's scared he won't get his money," said Mrs. Whipple.

"Don't talk like that," said Mr. Whipple, feeling pretty sick, "or we won't be able to send Him."

"Oh, but we won't keep Him there long," said Mrs. Whipple. "Soon's He's better, we'll bring Him right back home."

"The doctor has told you and told you time and again He can't ever get better, and you might as well stop talking," said Mr. Whipple.

"Doctors don't know everything," said Mrs. Whipple, feeling almost happy. "But anyhow, in the summer Emly can come home for a vacation, and Adna can get down for Sundays: we'll all work together and get on our feet again, and the children will feel they've got a place to come to."

All at once she saw it full summer again, with the garden going fine, and new white roller shades up all over the house, and Adna and Emly home, so full of life, all of them happy together. Oh, it could happen, things would ease up on them.

They didn't talk before Him much, but they never knew just how much He understood. Finally the doctor set the day and a neighbor who owned a double-seated carryall offered to drive them over. The hospital would have sent an ambulance, but Mrs. Whipple couldn't stand to see Him going away looking so sick as all that. They wrapped Him in blankets, and the neighbor and Mr. Whipple lifted Him into the back seat of the carryall beside Mrs. Whipple, who had on her black shirt waist. She couldn't stand to go looking like charity.

"You'll be all right, I guess I'll stay behind," said Mr. Whipple. "It don't look like everybody ought to leave the place at once."

"Besides, it ain't as if He was going to stay forever," said Mrs. Whipple to the neighbor. "This is only for a little while."

They started away, Mrs. Whipple holding to the edges of the blankets to keep Him from sagging sideways. He sat there blinking and blinking. He worked His hands out and began rubbing His nose with His knuckles, and then with the end of the blanket. Mrs. Whipple couldn't believe what she saw; He was scrubbing away big tears that pulled out of the corners of His eyes. He sniveled and made a gulping noise. Mrs. Whipple kept saying, "Oh, honey, you don't feel so bad, do you? You don't feel so bad, do you?" for He seemed to be accusing her of something. Maybe He remembered that time she boxed His ears, maybe He had been scared that day with the bull, maybe He had slept cold and couldn't tell her about it; maybe He knew they were sending Him away for good and all because they were too poor to keep Him. Whatever it was, Mrs. Whipple couldn't bear to think of it. She began to cry, frightfully, and wrapped her arms tight around Him. His head rolled on her shoulder: she had loved Him as much as she possibly could, there were Adna and Emly who had to be thought of too, there was nothing she could do to make up to Him for His life. Oh, what a mortal pity He was ever born.

They came in sight of the hospital, with the neighbor driving very fast, not daring to look behind him.   [1927]

FRANK SARGESON *(1903–1982) was born in Hamilton, New Zealand, and earned a law degree at Auckland University. After graduation he spent a year in Europe before returning to New Zealand to support himself working casual jobs as a laborer while he devoted himself to writing fiction. Unlike his earlier compatriot Katherine Mansfield, Sargeson settled in New Zealand and avoided European or Russian models. Instead he followed the literary example of American writers such as Ernest Hemingway, developing a style of understated, naturalistic short fiction that later established a tradition of social realism in New Zealand literature. In the 1930s Sargeson began to publish his first stories in the radical journal* Tomorrow *reflecting life during the Depression in rural North Island New Zealand. His early collections,* Conversation with My Uncle and Other Sketches *(1936) and* A Man and His Wife *(1940), led to the award of first prize in the New Zealand Centennial Literary Competitions in 1940 and publication of his short fiction in* Penguin New Writing *in 1943–1944. After World War II, Sargeson turned to writing longer works, publishing seven novels and several plays and memoirs before his death.*

The literary historian Vincent O'Sullivan has observed that Sargeson's stories showed other New Zealand writers "that there was a way of listening to the near inarticulate, and writing of it with tough resilience." The geographical isolation, economic hardships, and limited opportunities in New Zealand during the Depression years set the stage for the elemental conflicts played out among Sargeson's fictional characters. As the critic William Broughton recognized,

> *it says much that is disturbing about his country that Sargeson's vision was accepted by a generation of readers as a naturalistic and inherently truthful vision of the experiences of a male working class in New Zealand. Part of this acceptance involved the recognition that Sargeson had an unerring skill with dialogue. His recording of the New Zealand working class vernacular has not been surpassed and has seldom been matched by later writers. The idiomatic speech, with its flattened cadences, its laconic and sometimes wry ironies, and its cautious and limited vocabulary, became intimately associated with his distinctive sketches and stories.*

In a story like "A Great Day," Sargeson dramatizes with great subtlety and precision the result of an unspoken rivalry between two young men. As in a Hemingway story, the understated narrative forces the reader to read between the lines and participate in the story in order to make sense of what the fictional characters cannot allow themselves to articulate about their situation.

A Great Day

It was beginning to get light when Ken knocked on the door of Fred's bach.[1]

Are you up? he said.

Fred called out that he was, and in a moment he opened the door.

Just finished my breakfast, he said. We'd better get moving.

It didn't take long. The bach was right on the edge of the beach, and they got the dinghy on to Ken's back and he carried it down the beach, and Fred followed with the gear. Ken was big enough to make light work of the dinghy but it was all Fred could do to manage the gear. There wasn't much of him and he goddamned the gear every few yards he went.

The tide was well over half-way out, and the sea was absolutely flat without even a ripple breaking on the sand. Except for some seagulls that walked on the sand and made broad-arrow marks where they walked there wasn't a single thing moving. It was so still it wasn't natural. Except for the seagulls you'd have thought the world had died in the night.

Ken eased the dinghy off his shoulders and turned it the right way up, and Fred dropped the anchor and the oars on the sand, and heaved the sugar bag of fishing gear into the dinghy.

I wouldn't mind if I was a big hefty bloke like you, he said.

Well, Ken didn't say anything to that. He sat on the stern of the dinghy and rolled himself a cigarette, and Fred got busy and fixed the oars and rowlocks and tied on the anchor.

Come on, he said, we'll shove off. And with his trousers rolled up he went and tugged at the bow, and with Ken shoving at the stern the dinghy began to float, so Fred hopped in and took the oars, and then Ken hopped in and they were off.

It's going to be a great day, Fred said.

It certainly looked like it. The sun was coming up behind the island they were heading for, and there wasn't a cloud in the sky.

We'll make for the same place as last time, Fred said. You tell me if I don't keep straight. And for a time he rowed hard without sending the dinghy along very fast. The trouble was his short legs, he couldn't get them properly braced against the stern seat. And Ken, busy rolling a supply of cigarettes, didn't watch out where he was going, so when Fred took a look ahead he was heading for the wrong end of the island.

Hey, he said, you take a turn and I'll tell you where to head for.

So they changed places and Ken pulled wonderfully well. For a time it

---

[1] Cabin.

was more a mental shock you got with each jerk of the dinghy. You realised how strong he was. He had only a shirt and a pair of shorts on, and his big body, hard with muscle, must have been over six feet long.

Gee, I wish I had your body, Fred said. It's no wonder the girls chase you. But look at the sort of joker I am.

Well, he wasn't much to look at. There was so little of him. And the old clothes he wore had belonged to someone considerably bigger than he was. And he had on an old hat that came down too far, and would have come down further if it hadn't bent his ears over and sat on them as if they were brackets.

How about a smoke? Fred said.

Sure. Sorry.

And to save him from leaving off rowing Fred reached over and took the tin out of his shirt pocket.

That's the curse of this sustenance,[2] Fred said. A man's liable to be out of smokes before pay-day.

Yes, I suppose he is, Ken said.

It's rotten being out of work, Fred said. Thank the Lord I've got this dinghy. D'you know last year I made over thirty pounds out of fishing?

And how've you done this year?

Not so good. You're the first bloke I've had to go out with me this year that hasn't wanted me to go shares. Gee, you're lucky to be able to go fishing for fun.

It's about time I landed a position, Ken said. I've over a month's holiday.

Yes I know. But you've got money saved up, and it doesn't cost you anything to live when you can live with your auntie. How'd you like to live in that damn bach of mine and pay five bob[3] a week rent? And another thing, you've got education.

It doesn't count for much these days. A man has to take any position he can get.

Yes, but if a man's been to one of those High Schools it makes him different. Not any better, mind you. I'm all for the working class because I'm a worker myself, but an educated bloke has the advantage over a bloke like me. The girls chase him just to mention one thing, specially if he happens to be a big he-man as well.

Ken didn't say anything to that. He just went on pulling, and he got Fred to stick a cigarette in his mouth and light it at the same time as he lit his own. And then Fred lolled back in his seat and watched him, and you could tell that about the only thing they had in common was that they both had cigarettes dangling out of their mouths.

Pull her round a bit with your left, Fred said. And there's no need to bust your boiler.

It's O.K. Ken said.

---

[2] Unemployment compensation.
[3] Shillings.

You've got the strength, Fred said.

I'm certainly no infant.

What good's a man's strength anyway? Say he goes and works in an office?

I hadn't thought of that.

Another thing, he gets old. Fancy you getting old and losing your strength. Wouldn't it be a shame?

Sure, Ken said. Why talk about it?

It sort of fascinates me. You'll die someday, and where'll that big frame of yours be then?

That's an easy one. Pushing up the daisies.

It might as well be now as anytime, mightn't it?

Good Lord, I don't see that.

A man'd forget for good. It'd be just the same as it is out here on a day like this. Only better.

Ken stopped rowing to throw away his cigarette.

My God, he said, you're a queer customer. Am I heading right?

Pull with your left, Fred said. But I'll give you a spell.

It's O.K. Ken said.

And he went on rowing and after a bit Fred emptied the lines out of the sugar bag and began cutting up the bait. And after a bit longer when they were about half-way over to the island he said they'd gone far enough, so Ken shipped his oars and threw the anchor overboard, and they got their lines ready and began to fish.

And by that time it was certainly turning out a great day. The sun was getting hot but there still wasn't any wind, and as the tide had just about stopped running out down the Gulf the dinghy hardly knew which way to pull on the anchor rope. They'd pulled out less than two miles from the shore, but with the sea as it was it might have been anything from none at all up to an infinite number. You couldn't hear a sound or see anything moving. It was another world. The houses on the short didn't belong. Nor the people either.

Wouldn't you like to stay out here for good? Fred said.

Ring off, Ken said. I got a bite.

So did I, but it was only a nibble. Anyhow it's not a good day for fish. It wants to be cloudy.

So I've heard.

I've been thinking, Fred said, it's funny you never learnt to swim.

Oh I don't know. Up to now I've always lived in country towns.

Doesn't it make you feel a bit windy?

On a day like this! Anyhow, you couldn't swim that distance yourself.

Oh couldn't I! You'd be surprised . . . get a bite?

Yes I did.

Same here . . . you'll be settling down here, won't you, Ken?

It depends if I can get a position.

I suppose you'll go on living with your auntie.

That depends too. If I got a good position I might be thinking of getting married.

Gee, that'd be great, wouldn't it?

I got another bite, Ken said.

Same here, I reckon our lines are crossed.

So they pulled in their lines and they were crossed sure enough, but Ken had hooked the smallest snapper you ever saw.

He's no good, Fred said. And he worked the fish off the hook and held it in his hand. They're pretty little chaps, aren't they? he said. Look at his colours.

Let him go, Ken said.

Poor little beggar, Fred said. I bet he wonders what's struck him. He's trying to get his breath. Funny isn't it, when there's plenty of air about? It's like Douglas Credit.

Oh for God's sake, Ken said.

I bet in less than five minutes he forgets about how he was nearly suffocated, Fred said, and he threw the fish back. And it lay bewildered for a second on the surface, then it flipped its tail and was gone. It was comical in its way and they both laughed.

They always do that, Fred said. But don't you wish you could swim like him?

Ken didn't say anything to that and they put fresh bait on their hooks and tried again, but there were only nibbles. They could bring nothing to the surface.

I'll tell you what, Fred said, those nibbles might be old men snapper only they won't take a decent bite at bait like this.

And he explained that off the end of the island there was a reef where they could get plenty of big mussels. It would be just nice with the tide out as it was. The reef wouldn't be uncovered, it never was, but you could stand on it in water up to your knees and pull up the mussels. And if you cut the inside out of a big mussel you only had to hang it on your hook for an old man snapper to go for it with one big bite.

It's a fair way, Ken said.

It doesn't matter, Fred said. We've got oceans of time. And he climbed past Ken to pull up the anchor, and Ken pulled in the lines, and then Fred insisted on rowing and they started for the end of the island.

And by that time the tide had begun to run in up the Gulf and there was a light wind blowing up against the tide, so that the sea, almost without your noticing it, was showing signs of coming up a bit rough. And the queer thing was that with the movement the effect of another world was destroyed. You seemed a part of the real world of houses and people once more. Yet with the sea beginning to get choppy the land looked a long way off.

Going back, Ken said, we'll be pulling against the wind.

Yes, Fred said, but the tide'll be a help. Anyhow, what's it matter when a man's out with a big hefty bloke like you?

Nor did he seem to be in too much of a hurry to get to his reef. He kept resting on his oars to roll cigarettes, and when Ken said something about it he said they had oceans of time.

You're in no hurry to get back, he said, Mary'll keep.

Well, Ken didn't say anything to that.

Mary's a great kid, Fred said.

Sure, Ken said. Mary's one of the best.

I've known Mary for years, Fred said.

Yes, Ken said. So I've gathered.

I suppose you have. Up to a while ago Mary and I used to be great cobbers.

I'll give you a spell, Ken said.

But Fred said it was O.K.

Mary's got a bit of education too, he said. Only when her old man died the family was hard up so she had to go into service. It was lucky she got a good place at your auntie's. Gee, I've been round there and had tea sometimes when your auntie's been out, and oh boy is the tucker any good!

Look here, Ken said, at this rate we'll never get to that reef.

Oh yes we will, Fred said, and he pulled a bit harder. If only a man hadn't lost his job, he said.

I admit it must be tough, Ken said.

And then Fred stood up and took a look back at the shore.

I thought there might be somebody else coming out, he said, but there isn't. So thank God for that. And he said that he couldn't stand anybody hanging around when he was fishing. By the way, he said, I forgot to do this before. And he stuffed pieces of cotton-wool into his ears. If the spray gets in my ears it gives me the earache, he said.

Then he really did settle down to his rowing, and with the sea more or less following them it wasn't long before they were off the end of the island.

Nobody lived on the island. There were a few holiday baches but they were empty now that it was well on into the autumn. Nor from this end could you see any landing places, and with the wind blowing up more and more it wasn't too pleasant to watch the sea running up the rocks. And Fred had to spend a bit of time manoeuvering around before he found his reef.

It was several hundred yards out with deep water all around, and it seemed to be quite flat. If the sea had been calm it might have been covered to a depth of about a foot with the tide as it was. But with the sea chopping across it wasn't exactly an easy matter to stand there. At one moment the water was down past your knees, and the next moment you had to steady yourself while it came up round your thighs. And it was uncanny to stand there, because with the deep water all round you seemed to have discovered a way of standing up out in the sea.

Anyhow, Fred took off his coat and rolled up his sleeves and his trousers as far as they'd go, and then he hopped out and got Ken to do the same and keep hold of the dinghy. Then he steadied himself and began dipping his hands down and pulling up mussels and throwing them back into the dinghy, and he worked at a mad pace as though he hadn't a moment to lose. It seemed only a minute or so before he was quite out of breath.

It's tough work, he said. You can see what a weak joker I am.

I'll give you a spell, Ken said, only keep hold of the boat.

Well, Fred held the dinghy, and by the way he was breathing and the look of his face you'd have thought he was going to die. But Ken had other matters to think about, he was steadying himself and dipping his hands down more than a yard away, and Fred managed to pull himself together and shove off the dinghy and hop in. And if you'd been sitting in the stern as he pulled away you'd have seen that he had his eyes shut. Nor did he open them except when he took a look ahead to see where he was going, and with the cotton-wool in his ears it was difficult for him to hear.

So for a long time he rowed like that against seas that were getting bigger and bigger, but about half-way back to the shore he took a spell. He changed over to the other side of the seat, so he didn't have to sit facing the island, and he just sat there keeping the dinghy straight on. Then when he felt that he had collected all his strength he stood up and capsized the dinghy. It took a bit of doing but he did it.

And after that, taking it easy, he started on his long swim for the shore.

[1940]

LESLIE MARMON SILKO (b. 1948), a Laguna Pueblo Native American, was born and grew up in New Mexico. She was educated at Board of Indian Affairs schools in Laguna, a Catholic school in Albuquerque, and the University of New Mexico, where she received her B.A. in English in 1969. After teaching at various colleges, she became a professor of English at the University of Arizona at Tucson. Silko's first novel, Ceremony (1977), is regarded as one of the most important books in modern Native American literature. In it she forged a connection between the shared past of the tribe and the individual life of a native American returning home after World War II. Silko has received a National Endowment for the Arts fellowship, a Pushcart Prize, and a three-year grant from the MacArthur Foundation, which enabled her to take time off from teaching and become "a little less beholden to the everyday world."

Storyteller (1981), a collection of tribal folktales, family anecdotes, photographs by her grandfather, and her own poems and stories, is Silko's personal anthology of the Laguna Pueblo culture. "Lullaby," "Storyteller," and "Yellow Woman" are from that collection. "Lullaby" and "Storyteller" are about the injustices suffered by southwestern and Alaskan Native Americans at the mercy of the exploitative Anglo-American society engulfing them. "Yellow Woman" illustrates Silko's skill in retelling a traditional Native American legend in a realistic contemporary context that confirms its emotional truth and makes it accessible to a larger audience.

Tales about a "ka'tsina" mountain spirit who seduces the Yellow Woman away from her husband and family were first told to the fictional heroine by her grandfather. The Yellow Woman in the traditional captivity narratives can be interpreted in several ways — as a girl who runs off with men outside the tribe, as a raped and kidnapped married woman, as a spirit, as a fertility archetype. In creating fiction, Silko works with all the implied meanings of the old legends; she has said that she writes "because I like seeing how I can translate [a] sort of feeling or flavor or sense of a story that's told and heard onto the page." Her most recent books are The Almanac of the Dead (1991) and Sacred Water (1993).

RELATED COMMENTARIES: See Casebook on Leslie Marmon Silko, pages 1572–1595, including Leslie Marmon Silko, "Language and Literature from a Pueblo Indian Perspective," page 1573; Kim Barnes, "An Interview with Leslie Marmon Silko," page 1578; Cochiti Pueblo Story, "Sun Steals Yellow Woman," page 1585; Paula Gunn Allen, "Whirlwind Man Steals Yellow Woman," page 1586; Jim Ruppert, "Storytelling: The Fiction of Leslie Silko," page 1587; Linda L. Danielson, "A Feminist Reading of 'Storyteller': Grandmother Spider's Web," page 1590.

LESLIE MARMON SILKO

Lullaby

The sun had gone down but the snow in the wind gave off its own light. It came in thick tufts like new wool — washed before the weaver spins it. Ayah reached out for it like her own babies had, and she smiled when she remembered how she had laughed at them. She was an old woman now, and her life had become memories. She sat down with her back against the wide cottonwood tree, feeling the rough bark on her back bones; she faced east and listened to the wind and snow sing a high-pitched Yeibechei song. Out of the wind she felt warmer, and she could watch the wide fluffy snow fill in her tracks, steadily, until the direction she had come from was gone. By the light of the snow she could see the dark outline of the big arroyo a few feet away. She was sitting on the edge of Cebolleta Creek, where in the springtime the thin cows would graze on grass already chewed flat to the ground. In the wide deep creek bed where only a trickle of water flowed in the summer, the skinny cows would wander, looking for new grass along winding paths splashed with manure.

Ayah pulled the old Army blanket over her head like a shawl. Jimmie's blanket — the one he had sent to her. That was a long time ago and the green wool was faded, and it was unraveling on the edges. She did not want to think about Jimmie. So she thought about the weaving and the way her mother had done it. On the tall wooden loom set into the sand under a tamarack tree for shade. She could see it clearly. She had been only a little girl when her grandma gave her the wooden combs to pull the twigs and burrs from the raw, freshly washed wool. And while she combed the wool, her grandma sat beside her, spinning a silvery strand of yarn around the smooth cedar spindle. Her mother worked at the loom with yarns dyed bright yellow and red and gold. She watched them dye the yarn in boiling black pots full of beeweed petals, juniper berries, and sage. The blankets her mother made were soft and woven so tight that rain rolled off them like birds' feathers. Ayah remembered sleeping warm on cold windy nights, wrapped in her mother's blankets on the hogan's sandy floor.

The snow drifted now, with the northwest wind hurling it in gusts. It drifted up around her black overshoes — old ones with little metal buckles. She smiled at the snow which was trying to cover her little by little. She could remember when they had no black rubber overshoes; only the high buckskin leggings that they wrapped over their elkhide moccasins. If the snow was dry or frozen, a person could walk all day and not get wet; and in the evenings the beams of the ceiling would hang with lengths of pale buckskin leggings, drying out slowly.

She felt peaceful remembering. She didn't feel cold any more. Jimmie's blanket seemed warmer than it had ever been. And she could remember the morning he was born. She could remember whispering to her mother, who was sleeping on the other side of the hogan, to tell her it was time now. She did not want to wake the others. The second time she called to her, her mother stood up and pulled on her shoes; she knew. They walked to the old stone hogan together, Ayah walking a step behind her mother. She waited alone, learning the rhythms of the pains while her mother went to call the old woman to help them. The morning was already warm even before dawn and Ayah smelled the bee flowers blooming and the young willow growing at the springs. She could remember that so clearly, but his birth merged into the births of the other children and to her it became all the same birth. They named him for the summer morning and in English they called him Jimmie.

It wasn't like Jimmie died. He just never came back, and one day a dark blue sedan with white writing on its doors pulled up in front of the boxcar shack where the rancher let the Indians live. A man in a khaki uniform trimmed in gold gave them a yellow piece of paper and told them that Jimmie was dead. He said the Army would try to get the body back and then it would be shipped to them; but it wasn't likely because the helicopter had burned after it crashed. All of this was told to Chato because he could understand English. She stood inside the doorway holding the baby while Chato listened. Chato spoke English like a white man and he spoke Spanish too. He was taller than the white man and he stood straighter too. Chato didn't explain why; he just told the military man they could keep the body if they found it. The white man looked bewildered; he nodded his head and he left. Then Chato looked at her and shook his head, and then he told her, "Jimmie isn't coming home anymore," and when he spoke, he used the words to speak of the dead. She didn't cry then, but she hurt inside with anger. And she mourned him as the years passed, when a horse fell with Chato and broke his leg, and the white rancher told them he wouldn't pay Chato until he could work again. She mourned Jimmie because he would have worked for his father then; he would have saddled the big bay horse and ridden the fence lines each day, with wire cutters and heavy gloves, fixing the breaks in the barbed wire and putting the stray cattle back inside again.

She mourned him after the white doctors came to take Danny and Ella away. She was at the shack alone that day they came. It was back in the days before they hired Navajo women to go with them as interpreters. She recognized one of the doctors. She had seen him at the children's clinic at Cañoncito about a month ago. They were wearing khaki uniforms and they waved papers at her and a black ball-point pen, trying to make her understand their English words. She was frightened by the way they looked at the children, like the lizard watches the fly. Danny was swinging on the tire swing on the elm tree behind the rancher's house, and Ella was toddling around the front door, dragging the broomstick horse Chato made for her. Ayah could see they wanted her to sign the papers, and Chato had taught her to sign her name. It was something she was proud of. She only wanted them to go, and to take their eyes away from her children.

She took the pen from the man without looking at his face and she signed the papers in three different places he pointed to. She stared at the ground by their feet and waited for them to leave. But they stood there and began to point and gesture at the children. Danny stopped swinging. Ayah could see his fear. She moved suddenly and grabbed Ella into her arms; the child squirmed, trying to get back to her toys. Ayah ran with the baby toward Danny; she screamed for him to run and then she grabbed him around his chest and carried him too. She ran south into the foothills of juniper trees and black lava rock. Behind her she heard the doctors running, but they had been taken by surprise, and as the hills became steeper and the cholla cactus were thicker, they stopped. When she reached the top of the hill, she stopped to listen in case they were circling around her. But in a few minutes she heard a car engine start and they drove away. The children had been too surprised to cry while she ran with them. Danny was shaking and Ella's little fingers were gripping Ayah's blouse.

She stayed up in the hills for the rest of the day, sitting on a black lava boulder in the sunshine where she could see for miles all around her. The sky was light blue and cloudless, and it was warm for late April. The sun warmth relaxed her and took the fear and anger away. She lay back on the rock and watched the sky. It seemed to her that she could walk into the sky, stepping through clouds endlessly. Danny played with little pebbles and stones, pretending they were birds' eggs and then little rabbits. Ella sat at her feet and dropped fistfuls of dirt into the breeze, watching the dust and particles of sand intently. Ayah watched a hawk soar high above them, dark wings gliding; hunting or only watching, she did not know. The hawk was patient and he circled all afternoon before he disappeared around the high volcanic peak the Mexicans called Guadalupe.

Late in the afternoon, Ayah looked down at the gray boxcar shack with the paint all peeled from the wood; the stove pipe on the roof was rusted and crooked. The fire she had built that morning in the oil drum stove had burned out. Ella was asleep in her lap now and Danny sat close to her, complaining that he was hungry; he asked when they would go to the house. "We will stay up here until your father comes," she told him, "because those white men were chasing us." The boy remembered then and he nodded at her silently.

If Jimmie had been there he could have read those papers and explained to her what they said. Ayah would have known then, never to sign them. The doctors came back the next day and they brought a BIA[1] policeman with them. They told Chato they had her signature and that was all they needed. Except for the kids. She listened to Chato sullenly; she hated him when he told her it was the old woman who died in the winter, spitting blood; it was her old grandma who had given the children this disease. "They don't spit blood" she said coldly. "The whites lie." She held Ella and Danny close to her, ready to run to the hills again. "I want a medicine man first," she said to Chato, not

---

[1] Bureau of Indian Affairs.

looking at him. He shook his head. "It's too late now. The policeman is with them. You signed the paper." His voice was gentle.

It was worse than if they had died: to lose the children and to know that somewhere, in a place called Colorado, in a place full of sick and dying strangers, her children were without her. There had been babies that died soon after they were born, and one that died before he could walk. She had carried them herself, up to the boulders and great pieces of the cliff that long ago crashed down from Long Mesa; she laid them in the crevices of sandstone and buried them in fine brown sand with round quartz pebbles that washed down the hills in the rain. She had endured it because they had been with her. But she could not bear this pain. She did not sleep for a long time after they took her children. She stayed on the hill where they had fled the first time, and she slept rolled up in the blanket Jimmie had sent her. She carried the pain in her belly and it was fed by everything she saw: the blue sky of their last day together and the dust and pebbles they played with; the swing in the elm tree and the broomstick horse choked life from her. The pain filled her stomach and there was no room for food or for her lungs to fill with air. The air and the food would have been theirs.

She hated Chato, not because he let the policeman and doctors put the screaming children in the government car, but because he had taught her to sign her name. Because it was like the old ones always told her about learning their language or any of their ways: it endangered you. She slept alone on the hill until the middle of November when the first snows came. Then she made a bed for herself where the children had slept. She did not lie down beside Chato again until many years later, when he was sick and shivering and only her body could keep him warm. The illness came after the white rancher told Chato he was too old to work for him anymore, and Chato and his old woman should be out of the shack by the next afternoon because the rancher had hired new people to work there. That had satisfied her. To see how the white man repaid Chato's years of loyalty and work. All of Chato's fine-sounding English talk didn't change things.

It snowed steadily and the luminous light from the snow gradually diminished into the darkness. Somewhere in Cebolleta a dog barked and other village dogs joined with it. Ayah looked in the direction she had come, from the bar where Chato was buying the wine. Sometimes he told her to go on ahead and wait; and then he never came. And when she finally went back looking for him, she would find him passed out at the bottom of the wooden steps to Azzie's Bar. All the wine would be gone and most of the money too, from the pale blue check that came to them once a month in a government envelope. It was then that she would look at his face and his hands, scarred by ropes and the barbed wire of all those years, and she would think, this man is a stranger; for forty years she had smiled at him and cooked his food, but he remained a stranger. She stood up again, with the snow almost to her knees, and she walked back to find Chato.

It was hard to walk in the deep snow and she felt the air burn in her lungs. She stopped a short distance from the bar to rest and readjust the blanket. But this time he wasn't waiting for her on the bottom step with his old Stetson hat pulled down and his shoulders hunched up in his long wool overcoat.

She was careful not to slip on the wooden steps. When she pushed the door open, warm air and cigarette smoke hit her face. She looked around slowly and deliberately, in every corner, in every dark place that the old man might find to sleep. The bar owner didn't like Indians in there, especially Navajos, but he let Chato come in because he could talk Spanish like he was one of them. The men at the bar stared at her, and the bartender saw that she left the door open wide. Snowflakes were flying inside like moths and melting into a puddle on the oiled wood floor. He motioned to her to close the door, but she did not see him. She held herself straight and walked across the room slowly, searching the room with every step. The snow in her hair melted and she could feel it on her forehead. At the far corner of the room, she saw red flames at the mica window of the old stove door; she looked behind the stove just to make sure. The bar got quiet except for the Spanish polka music playing on the jukebox. She stood by the stove and shook the snow from her blanket and held it near the stove to dry. The wet wool smell reminded her of new-born goats in early March, brought inside to warm near the fire. She felt calm.

In past years they would have told her to get out. But her hair was white now and her face was wrinkled. They looked at her like she was a spider crawling slowly across the room. They were afraid; she could feel the fear. She looked at their faces steadily. They reminded her of the first time the white people brought her children back to her that winter. Danny had been shy and hid behind the thin white woman who brought them. And the baby had not known her until Ayah took her into her arms, and then Ella had nuzzled close to her as she had when she was nursing. The blonde woman was nervous and kept looking at a dainty gold watch on her wrist. She sat on the bench near the small window and watched the dark snow clouds gather around the mountains; she was worrying about the unpaved road. She was frightened by what she saw inside too: the strips of venison drying on a rope across the ceiling and the children jabbering excitedly in a language she did not know. So they stayed for only a few hours. Ayah watched the government car disappear down the road and she knew they were already being weaned from these lava hills and from this sky. The last time they came was in early June, and Ella stared at her the way the men in the bar were now staring. Ayah did not try to pick her up; she smiled at her instead and spoke cheerfully to Danny. When he tried to answer her, he could not seem to remember and he spoke English words with the Navajo. But he gave her a scrap of paper that he had found somewhere and carried in his pocket; it was folded in half, and he shyly looked up at her and said it was a bird. She asked Chato if they were home for good this time. He spoke to the white woman and she shook her head. "How much longer?" he asked, and she said she didn't know; but Chato saw how she stared at the boxcar shack. Ayah turned away then. She did not say good-bye.

She felt satisfied that the men in the bar feared her. Maybe it was her face and the way she held her mouth with teeth clenched tight, like there was nothing anyone could do to her now. She walked north down the road, searching for the old man. She did this because she had the blanket, and there would be no place for him except with her and the blanket in the old adobe barn near the arroyo. They always slept there when they came to Cebolleta. If the money and the wine were gone, she would be relieved because then they could go home again; back to the old hogan with a dirt roof and rock walls where she herself had been born. And the next day the old man could go back to the few sheep they still had, to follow along behind them, guiding them, into dry sandy arroyos where sparse grass grew. She knew he did not like walking behind old ewes when for so many years he rode big quarter-horses and worked with cattle. But she wasn't sorry for him; he should have known all along what would happen.

There had not been enough rain for their garden in five years; and that was when Chato finally hitched a ride into the town and brought back brown boxes of rice and sugar and big tin cans of welfare peaches. After that, at the first of the month they went to Cebolleta to ask the postmaster for the check; and then Chato would go to the bar and cash it. They did this as they planted the garden every May, not because anything would survive the summer dust, but because it was time to do this. The journey passed the days that smelled silent and dry like the caves above the canyon with yellow painted buffaloes on their walls.

He was walking along the pavement when she found him. He did not stop or turn around when he heard her behind him. She walked beside him and she noticed how slowly he moved now. He smelled strong of woodsmoke and urine. Lately he had been forgetting. Sometimes he called her by his sister's name and she had been gone for a long time. Once she had found him wandering on the road to the white man's ranch, and she asked him why he was going that way; he laughed at her and said, "You know they can't run that ranch without me," and he walked on determined, limping on the leg that had been crushed many years before. Now he looked at her curiously, as if for the first time, but he kept shuffling along, moving slowly along the side of the highway. His gray hair had grown long and spread out on the shoulders of the long overcoat. He wore the old felt hat pulled down over his ears. His boots were worn out at the toes and he had stuffed pieces of an old red shirt in the holes. The rags made his feet look like little animals up to their ears in snow. She laughed at his feet; the snow muffled the sound of her laugh. He stopped and looked at her again. The wind had quit blowing and the snow was falling straight down; the southeast sky was beginning to clear and Ayah could see a star.

"Let's rest awhile," she said to him. They walked away from the road and up the slope to the giant boulders that had tumbled down from the red sandrock mesa throughout the centuries of rainstorms and earth tremors. In a place where the boulders shut out the wind, they sat down with their backs against the rock. She offered half of the blanket to him and they sat wrapped together.

The storm passed swiftly. The clouds moved east. They were massive and full, crowding together across the sky. She watched them with the feeling of horses — steely blue-gray horses startled across the sky. The powerful haunches pushed into the distances and the tail hairs streamed white mist behind them. The sky cleared. Ayah saw that there was nothing between her and the stars. The light was crystalline. There was no shimmer, no distortion through earth haze. She breathed the clarity of the night sky; she smelled the purity of the half moon and the stars. He was lying on his side with his knees pulled up near his belly for warmth. His eyes were closed now, and in the light from the stars and the moon, he looked young again.

She could see it descend out of the night sky: an icy stillness from the edge of the thin moon. She recognized the freezing. It came gradually, sinking snowflake by snowflake until the crust was heavy and deep. It had the strength of the stars in Orion, and its journey was endless. Ayah knew that with the wine he would sleep. He would not feel it. She tucked the blanket around him, remembering how it was when Ella had been with her; and she felt the rush so big inside her heart for the babies. And she sang the only song she knew to sing for babies. She could not remember if she had ever sung it to her children, but she knew that her grandmother had sung it and her mother had sung it:

> The earth is your mother,
>   she holds you.
> The sky is your father,
>   he protects you.
> Sleep,
> sleep.
> Rainbow is your sister,
>   she loves you.
> The winds are your brothers,
>   they sing to you.
> Sleep,
> sleep.
> We are together always
> We are together always
> There never was a time
> when this
> was not so.

[1981]

LESLIE MARMON SILKO

Storyteller

I

Every day the sun came up a little lower on the horizon, moving more slowly until one day she got excited and started calling the jailer. She realized she had been sitting there for many hours, yet the sun had not moved from the center of the sky. The color of the sky had not been good lately; it had been pale blue, almost white, even when there were no clouds. She told herself it wasn't a good sign for the sky to be indistinguishable from the river ice, frozen solid and white against the earth. The tundra rose up behind the river but all the boundaries between the river and hills and sky were lost in the density of the pale ice.

She yelled again, this time some English words which came randomly into her mouth, probably swear words she'd heard from the oil drilling crews last winter. The jailer was an Eskimo, but he would not speak Yupik to her. She had watched people in the other cells; when they spoke to him in Yupik he ignored them until they spoke English.

He came and stared at her. She didn't know if he understood what she was telling him until he glanced behind her at the small high window. He looked at the sun, and turned and walked away. She could hear the buckles on his heavy snowmobile boots jingle as he walked to the front of the building.

It was like the other buildings that white people, the Gussucks,[1] brought with them: BIA[2] and school buildings, portable buildings that arrived sliced in halves, on barges coming up the river. Squares of metal paneling bulged out with the layers of insulation stuffed inside. She had asked once what it was and someone told her it was to keep out the cold. She had not laughed then, but she did now. She walked over to the small double-pane window and she laughed out loud. They thought they could keep out the cold with stringy yellow waddling. Look at the sun. It wasn't moving; it was frozen, caught in the middle of the sky. Look at the sky, solid as the river with ice which had trapped the sun. It had not moved for a long time; in a few more hours it would be weak, and heavy frost would begin to appear on the edges and spread across the face of the sun like a mask. Its light was pale yellow, worn thin by the winter.

She could see people walking down the snow-packed roads, their breath steaming out from their parka hoods, faces hidden and protected by deep ruffs of fur. There were no cars or snowmobiles that day so she calculated it

---

[1] White people.
[2] Bureau of Indian Affairs.

was fifty below zero, the temperature which silenced their machines. The metal froze; it split and shattered. Oil hardened and moving parts jammed solidly. She had seen it happen to their big yellow machines and the giant drill last winter when they came to drill their test holes. The cold stopped them, and they were helpless against it.

Her village was many miles upriver from this town, but in her mind she could see it clearly. Their house was not near the village houses. It stood alone on the bank upriver from the village. Snow had drifted to the eaves of the roof on the north side, but on the west side, by the door, the path was almost clear. She had nailed scraps of red tin over the logs last summer. She had done it for the bright red color, not for added warmth the way the village people had done. This final winter had been coming down even then; there had been signs of its approach for many years.

II

She went because she was curious about the big school where the Government sent all the other girls and boys. She had not played much with the village children while she was growing up because they were afraid of the old man, and they ran when her grandmother came. She went because she was tired of being alone with the old woman whose body had been stiffening for as long as the girl could remember. Her knees and knuckles were swollen grotesquely, and the pain had squeezed the brown skin of her face tight against the bones; it left her eyes hard like river stone. The girl asked once, what it was that did this to her body, and the old woman had raised up from sewing a sealskin boot, and stared at her.

"The joints," the old woman said in a low voice, whispering like wind across the roof, "the joints are swollen with anger."

Sometimes she did not answer and only stared at the girl. Each year she spoke less and less, but the old man talked more — all night sometimes, not to anyone but himself; in a soft deliberate voice, he told stories, moving his smooth brown hands above the blankets he had not fished or hunted with the other men for many years although he was not crippled or sick. He stayed in his bed, smelling like dry fish and urine, telling stories all winter; and when warm weather came, he went to his place on the river bank. He sat with a long willow stick, poking at the smoldering moss he burned against the insects while he continued with the stories.

The trouble was that she had not recognized the warnings in time. She did not see what the Gussuck school would do to her until she walked into the dormitory and realized that the old man had not been lying about the place. She thought he had been trying to scare her as he used to when she was very small and her grandmother was outside cutting up fish. She hadn't believed what he told her about the school because she knew he wanted to keep her there in the log house with him. She knew what he wanted.

The dormitory matron pulled down her underpants and whipped her with a leather belt because she refused to speak English.

"Those backwards village people," the matron said, because she was an

Eskimo who had worked for the BIA a long time, "they kept this one until she was too big to learn." The other girls whispered in English. They knew how to work the showers, and they washed and curled their hair at night. They ate Gussuck food. She laid on her bed and imagined what her grandmother might be sewing, and what the old man was eating in his bed. When summer came, they sent her home.

The way her grandmother had hugged her before she left for school had been a warning too, because the old woman had not hugged or touched her for many years. Not like the old man, whose hands were always hunting, like ravens circling lazily in the sky, ready to touch her. She was not surprised when the priest and the old man met her at the landing strip, to say that the old lady was gone. The priest asked her where she would like to stay. He referred to the old man as her grandfather, but she did not bother to correct him. She had already been thinking about it; if she went with the priest, he would send her away to a school. But the old man was different. She knew he wouldn't send her back to school. She knew he wanted to keep her.

III

He told her one time that she would get too old for him faster than he got too old for her; but again she had not believed him because sometimes he lied. He had lied about what he would do with her if she came into his bed. But as the years passed, she realized what he said was true. She was restless and strong. She had no patience with the old man who had never changed his slow smooth motions under the blankets.

The old man was in his bed for the winter; he did not leave it except to use the slop bucket in the corner. He was dozing with his mouth open slightly; his lips quivered and sometimes they moved like he was telling a story even while he dreamed. She pulled on the sealskin boots, the mukluks with the bright red flannel linings her grandmother had sewn for her, and she tied the braided red yarn tassels around her ankles over the gray wool pants. She zipped the wolfskin parka. Her grandmother had worn it for many years, but the old man said that before she died, she instructed him to bury her in an old black sweater, and to give the parka to the girl. The wolf pelts were creamy colored and silver, almost white in some places, and when the old lady had walked across the tundra in the winter, she disappeared into the snow.

She walked toward the village, breaking her own path through the deep snow. A team of sled dogs tied outside a house at the edge of the village leaped against their chains to bark at her. She kept walking, watching the dusky sky for the first evening stars. It was warm and the dogs were alert. When it got cold again, the dogs would lie curled and still, too drowsy from the cold to bark or pull at the chains. She laughed loudly because it made them howl and snarl. Once the old man had seen her tease the dogs and he shook his head. "So that's the kind of woman you are," he said, "in the wintertime the two of us are no different from those dogs. We wait in the cold for someone to bring us a few dry fish."

She laughed out loud again, and kept walking. She was thinking about the Gussuck oil drillers. They were strange; they watched her when she walked near their machines. She wondered what they looked like underneath their quilted goosedown trousers; she wanted to know how they moved. They would be something different from the old man.

The old man screamed at her. He shook her shoulders so violently that her head bumped against the log wall. "I smelled it!" he yelled, "as soon as I woke up! I am sure of it now. You can't fool me!" His thin legs were shaking inside the baggy wool trousers; he stumbled over her boots in his bare feet. His toe nails were long and yellow like bird claws; she had seen a gray crane last summer fighting another in the shallow water on the edge of the river. She laughed out loud and pulled her shoulder out of his grip. He stood in front of her. He was breathing hard and shaking; he looked weak. He would probably die next winter.

"I'm warning you," he said, "I'm warning you." He crawled into his bunk then, and reached under the old soiled feather pillow for a piece of dry fish. He lay back on the pillow, staring at the ceiling and chewed dry strips of salmon. "I don't know what the old woman told you," he said, "but there will be trouble." He looked over to see if she was listening. His face suddenly relaxed into a smile, his dark slanty eyes were lost in wrinkles of brown skin. "I could tell you, but you are too good for warnings now. I can smell what you did all night with the Gussucks."

She did not understand why they came there, because the village was small and so far upriver that even some Eskimos who had been away to school would not come back. They stayed downriver in the town. They said the village was too quiet. They were used to the town where the boarding school was located, with electric lights and running water. After all those years away at school, they had forgotten how to set nets in the river and where to hunt seals in the fall. Those who left did not say it, but their confidence had been destroyed. When she asked the old man why the Gussucks bothered to come to the village, his narrow eyes got bright with excitement.

"They only come when there is something to steal. The fur animals are too difficult for them to get now, and the seals and fish are hard to find. Now they come for oil deep in the earth. But this is the last time for them." His breathing was wheezy and fast; his hands gestured at the sky. "It is approaching. As it comes, ice will push across the sky." His eyes were open wide and he stared at the low ceiling rafters for hours without blinking. She remembered all this clearly because he began the story that day, the story he told from that time on. It began with a giant bear which he described muscle by muscle, from the curve of the ivory claws to the whorls of hair at the top of the massive skull. And for eight days he did not sleep, but talked continuously of the giant bear whose color was pale blue glacier ice.

IV

The snow was dirty and worn down in a path to the door. On either side of the path, the snow was higher than her head. In front of the door there were jagged yellow stains melted into the snow where men had urinated. She stopped in the entry way and kicked the snow off her boots. The room was dim; a kerosene lantern by the cash register was burning low. The long wooden shelves were jammed with cans of beans and potted meats. On the bottom shelf a jar of mayonnaise was broken open, leaking oily white clots on the floor. There was no one in the room except the yellowish dog sleeping in front of the long glass display case. A reflection made it appear to be lying on the knives and ammunition inside the case. Gussucks kept dogs inside their houses with them; they did not seem to mind the odors which seeped out of the dogs. "They tell us we are dirty for the food we eat — raw fish and fermented meat. But we do not live with dogs," the old man once said. She heard voices in the back room, and the sound of bottles set down hard on tables.

They were always confident. The first year they waited for the ice to break up on the river, and then they brought their big yellow machines up river on barges. They planned to drill their test holes during the summer to avoid the freezing. But the imprints and graves of their machines were still there, on the edge of the tundra above the river, where the summer mud had swallowed them before they ever left sight of the river. The village people had gathered to watch the white men, and to laugh as they drove the giant machines, one by one, off the steel ramp into the bogs; as if sheer numbers of vehicles would somehow make the tundra solid. But the old man said they behaved like desperate people, and they would come back again. When the tundra was frozen solid, they returned.

Village women did not even look through the door to the back room. The priest had warned them. The storeman was watching her because he didn't let Eskimos or Indians sit down at the tables in the back room. But she knew he couldn't throw her out if one of his Gussuck customers invited her to sit with him. She walked across the room. They stared at her, but she had the feeling she was walking for someone else, not herself, so their eyes did not matter. The red-haired man pulled out a chair and motioned for her to sit down. She looked back at the storeman while the red-haired man poured her a glass of red sweet wine. She wanted to laugh at the storeman the way she laughed at the dogs, straining against their chains, howling at her.

The red-haired man kept talking to the other Gussucks sitting around the table, but he slid one hand off the top of the table to her thigh. She looked over at the storeman to see if he was still watching her. She laughed out loud at him and the red-haired man stopped talking and turned to her. He asked if she wanted to go. She nodded and stood up.

Someone in the village had been telling him things about her, he said as they walked down the road to his trailer. She understood that much of what he was saying, but the rest she did not hear. The whine of the big generators at the construction camp sucked away the sound of his words. But English was of no concern to her anymore, and neither was anything the Christians in the village might say about her or the old man. She smiled at the effect of the subzero air on the electric lights around the trailers; they did not shine. They left only flat yellow holes in the darkness.

It took him a long time to get ready, even after she had undressed for him. She waited in the bed with the blankets pulled close, watching him. He adjusted the thermostat and lit candles in the room, turning out the electric lights. He searched through a stack of record albums until he found the right one. She was not sure about the last thing he did: he taped something on the wall behind the bed where he could see it while he laid on top of her. He was shriveled and white from the cold; he pushed against her body for warmth. He guided her hands to his thighs; he was shivering.

She had returned a last time because she wanted to know what it was he stuck on the wall above the bed. After he finished each time, he reached up and pulled it loose, folding it carefully so that she could not see it. But this time she was ready; she waited for his fast breathing and sudden collapse on top of her. She slid out from under him and stood up beside the bed. She looked at the picture while she got dressed. He did not raise his face from the pillow, and she thought she heard teeth rattling together as she left the room.

She heard the old man move when she came in. After the Gussuck's trailer, the log house felt cool. It smelled like dry fish and cured meat. The room was dark except for the blinking yellow flame in the mica window of the oil stove. She squatted in front of the stove and watched the flames for a long time before she walked to the bed where her grandmother had slept. The bed was covered with a mound of rags and fur scraps the old woman had saved. She reached into the mound until she felt something cold and solid wrapped in a wool blanket. She pushed her fingers around it until she felt smooth stone. Long ago, before the Gussucks came, they had burned whale oil in the big stone lamp which made light and heat as well. The old woman had saved everything they would need when the time came.

In the morning, the old man pulled a piece of dry caribou meat from under the blankets and offered it to her. While she was gone, men from the village had brought a bundle of dry meat. She chewed it slowly, thinking about the way they still came from the village to take care of the old man and his stories. But she had a story now, about the red-haired Gussuck. The old man knew what she was thinking, and his smile made his face seem more round than it was.

"Well," he said, "what was it?"

"A woman with a big dog on top of her."

He laughed softly to himself and walked over to the water barrel. He dipped the tin cup into the water.

"It doesn't surprise me," he said.

V

"Grandma," she said, "there was something red in the grass that morning. I remember." She had not asked about her parents before. The old woman stopped splitting the fish bellies open for the willow drying racks. Her jaw muscles pulled so tightly against her skull, the girl thought the old woman would not be able to speak.

"They bought a tin can full of it from the storeman. Late at night. He told them it was alcohol safe to drink. They traded a rifle for it." The old woman's voice sounded like each word stole strength from her. "It made no difference about the rifle. That year the Gussuck boats had come, firing big guns at the walrus and seals. There was nothing left to hunt after that anyway. So," the old lady said, in a low soft voice the girl had not heard for a long time, "I didn't say anything to them when they left that night."

"Right over there," she said, pointing at the fallen poles, half buried in the river sand and tall grass, "in the summer shelter. The sun was high half the night then. Early in the morning when it was still low, the policeman came around. I told the interpreter to tell him that the storeman had poisoned them." She made outlines in the air in front of her, showing how their bodies laid twisted on the sand; telling the story was like laboring to walk through deep snow; sweat shone in the white hair around her forehead. "I told the priest too, after he came. I told him the storeman lied." She turned away from the girl. She held her mouth even tighter, set solidly, not in sorrow or anger, but against the pain, which was all that remained. "I never believed," she said, "not much anyway. I wasn't surprised when the priest did nothing."

The wind came off the river and folded the tall grass into itself like river waves. She could feel the silence the story left, and she wanted to have the old woman go on.

"I heard sounds that night, grandma. Sounds like someone was singing. It was light outside. I could see something red on the ground." The old woman did not answer her; she moved to the tub full of fish on the ground beside the work bench. She stabbed her knife into the belly of a whitefish and lifted it onto the bench. "The Gussuck storeman left the village right after that," the old woman said as she pulled the entrails from the fish, "otherwise, I could tell you more." The old woman's voice flowed with the wind blowing off the river; they never spoke of it again.

When the willows got their leaves and the grass grew tall along the river banks and around the sloughs, she walked early in the morning. While the sun was still low on the horizon, she listened to the wind off the river; its sound was like the voice that day long ago. In the distance, she could hear the engines of the machinery the oil drillers had left the winter before, but she did not go near the village or the store. The sun never left the sky and the summer became the same long day, with only the winds to fan the sun into brightness or allow it to slip into twilight.

She sat beside the old man at his place on the river bank. She poked the smoky fire for him, and felt herself growing wide and thin in the sun as if she had been split from belly to throat and strung on the willow pole in preparation for the winter to come. The old man did not speak anymore. When men from the village brought him fresh fish he hid them deep in the river grass where it was cool. After he went inside, she split the fish open and spread them to dry on the willow frame the way the old woman had done. Inside, he dozed and talked to himself. He had talked all winter, softly and incessantly about the giant polar bear stalking a long man across Bering Sea ice. After all the months the old man had been telling the story, the bear was within a hundred feet of the man; but the ice fog had closed in on them now and the man could only smell the sharp ammonia odor of the bear, and hear the edge of the snow crust crack under the giant paws.

One night she listened to the old man tell the story all night in his sleep, describing each crystal of ice and the slightly different sounds they made under each paw; first the left and then the right paw, then the hind feet. Her grandmother was there suddenly, a shadow around the stove. She spoke in her low wind voice and the girl was afraid to sit up to hear more clearly. Maybe what she said had been to the old man because he stopped telling the story and began to snore softly the way he had long ago when the old woman had scolded him for telling his stories while others in the house were trying to sleep. But the last words she heard clearly: "It will take a long time, but the story must be told. There must not be any lies." She pulled the blanket up around her chin, slowly, so that her movements would not be seen. She thought her grandmother was talking about the old man's bear story; she did not know about the other story then.

She left the old man wheezing and snoring in his bed. She walked through river grass glistening with frost; the bright green summer color was already fading. She watched the sun move across the sky, already lower on the horizon, already moving away from the village. She stopped by the fallen poles of the summer shelter where her parents had died. Frost glittered on the river sand too; in a few more weeks there would be snow. The predawn light would be the color of an old woman. An old woman sky full of snow. There had been something red lying on the ground the morning they died. She looked for it again, pushing aside the grass with her foot. She knelt in the sand and looked under the fallen structure for some trace of it. When she found it, she would know what the old woman had never told her. She squatted down close to the gray poles and leaned her back against them. The wind made her shiver.

The summer rain had washed the mud from between the logs; the sod blocks stacked as high as her belly next to the log walls had lost their square-cut shape and had grown into soft mounts of tundra moss and stiff-bladed grass bending with clusters of seed bristles. She looked at the north-west, in the direction of the Bering Sea. The cold would come down from there to find narrow slits in the mud, rainwater holes in the outer layer of sod which protected the log house. The dark green tundra stretched away flat and continuous. Somewhere the sea and the land met; she knew by their dark green colors there were no boundaries between them. That was how the cold would come: when the boundaries were gone the polar ice would range across the land into the sky. She watched the horizon for a long time. She would stand in that place on the north side of the house and she would keep watch on the northwest horizon, and eventually she would see it come. She would watch for its approach in the stars, and hear it come with the wind. These preparations were unfamiliar, but gradually she recognized them as she did her own footprints in the snow.

She emptied the slop jar beside his bed twice a day and kept the barrel full of water melted from river ice. He did not recognize her anymore, and when he spoke to her, he called her by her grandmother's name and talked about people and events from long ago, before he went back to telling the story. The giant bear was creeping across the new snow on its belly, close enough now that the man could hear the rasp of its breathing. On and on in a soft singing voice, the old man caressed the story, repeating the words again and again like gentle strokes.

The sky was gray like a river crane's egg; its density curved into the thin crust of frost already covering the land. She looked at the bright red color of the tin against the ground and the sky and she told the village men to bring the pieces for the old man and her. To drill the test holes in the tundra, the Gussucks had used hundreds of barrels of fuel. The village people split open the empty barrels that were abandoned on the river bank, and pounded the red tin into flat sheets. The village people were using the strips of tin to mend walls and roofs for winter. But she nailed it on the log walls for its color. When she finished, she walked away with the hammer in her hand, not turning around until she was far away, on the ridge above the river banks, and then she looked back. She felt a chill when she saw how the sky and the land were already losing their boundaries, already becoming lost in each other. But the red tin penetrated the think white color of earth and sky; it defined the boundaries like a wound revealing the ribs and heart of a great caribou about to bolt and be lost to the hunter forever. That night the wind howled and when she scratched a hole through the heavy frost on the inside of the window, she could see nothing but the impenetrable white; whether it was blowing snow or snow that had drifted as high as the house, she did not know.

It had come down suddenly, and she stood with her back to the wind looking at the river, its smoky water clotted with ice. The wind had blown the snow over the frozen river, hiding thin blue streaks where fast water ran under ice translucent and fragile as memory. But she could see shadows of boundaries, outlines of paths which were slender branches of solidity reaching out from the earth. She spent days walking on the river, watching the colors of ice that would safely hold her, kicking the heel of her boot into the snow crust, listening for a solid sound. When she could feel the paths through the soles of her feet, she went to the middle of the river where the fast gray water churned under a thin pane of ice. She looked back. On the river bank in the distance she could see the red tin nailed to the log house, something now swallowed up by the heavy white belly of the sky or caught in the folds of the frozen earth. It was time.

The wolverine fur around the hood of her parka was white with the frost from her breathing. The warmth inside the store melted it, and she felt tiny drops of water on her face. The storeman came in from the back room. She unzipped the parka and stood by the oil stove. She didn't look at him, but stared instead at the yellowish dog, covered with scabs of matted hair, sleeping in front of the stove. She thought of the Gussuck's picture, taped on the wall above the bed and she laughed out loud. The sound of her laughter was piercing; the yellow dog jumped to its feet and the hair bristled down its back. The storeman was watching her. She wanted to laugh again because he didn't know about the ice. He did not know that it was prowling the earth, or that it had already pushed its way into the sky to seize the sun. She sat down in the chair by the stove and shook her long hair loose. He was like a dog tied up all winter, watching while the others got fed. He remembered how she had gone with the oil drillers, and his blue eyes moved like flies crawling over her body. He held his thin pale lips like he wanted to spit on her. He hated the people because they had something of value, the old man said, something which the Gussucks could never have. They thought they could take it, suck it out of the earth or cut it from the mountains; but they were fools.

There was a matted hunk of dog hair on the floor by her foot. She thought of the yellow insulation coming unstuffed: their defense against the freezing going to pieces as it advanced on them. The ice was crouching on the northwest horizon like the old man's bear. She laughed out loud again. The sun would be down now; it was time.

The first time he spoke to her, she did not hear what he said, so she did not answer or even look up at him. He spoke to her again but his words were only noises coming from his pale mouth, trembling now as his anger began to unravel. He jerked her up and the chair fell over behind her. His arms were shaking and she could feel his hands tense up, pulling the edges of the parka tighter. He raised his fist to hit her, his thin body quivering with rage; but the fist collapsed with the desire he had for the valuable things, which, the old man had rightly said, was the only reason they came. She could hear his heart pounding as he held her close and arched his hips against her, groaning and breathing in spasms. She twisted away from him and ducked under his arms.

She ran with a mitten over her mouth, breathing through the fur to protect her lungs from the freezing air. She could hear him running behind her, his heavy breathing, the occasional sound of metal jingling against metal. But he ran without his parka or mittens, breathing the frozen air; its fire squeezed the lungs against the ribs and it was enough that he could not catch her near his store. On the river bank he realized how far he was from his stove, and the wads of yellow stuffing that held off the cold. But the girl was not able to run very fast through the deep drifts at the edge of the river. The twilight was luminous and he could still see clearly for a long distance; he knew he could catch her so he kept running.

When he neared the middle of the river she looked over her shoulder. He was not following her tracks; he went straight across the ice, running the shortest distance to reach her. He was close then; his face was twisted and scarlet from exertion and the cold. There was satisfaction in his eyes; he was sure he could outrun her.

She was familiar with the river, down to the instant the ice flexed into hairline fractures, and the cracking bone-sliver sounds gathered momentum with the opening ice until the sound of the churning gray water was set free. She stopped and turned to the sound of the river and the rattle of swirling ice fragments where he fell through. She pulled off a mitten and zipped the parka to her throat. She was conscious then of her own rapid breathing.

She moved slowly, kicking the ice ahead with the heal of her boot, feeling for sinews of ice to hold her. She looked ahead and all around herself; in the twilight, the dense white sky had merged into the flat snow-covered tundra. In the frantic running she had lost her place on the river. She stood still. The east bank of the river was lost in the sky; the boundaries had been swallowed by the freezing white. And then, in the distance, she saw something red, and suddenly it was as she had remembered it all those years.

VI

She sat on her bed and while she waited, she listened to the old man. The man had found a small jagged knoll on the ice. He pulled his beaver fur cap off his head; the fur inside it steamed with his body heat and sweat. He left it upside down on the ice for the great bear to stalk, and he waited downwind on top of the ice knoll; he was holding the jade knife.

She thought she could see the end of his story in the way he wheezed out the words; but still he reached into his cache of dry fish and dribbled water into his mouth from the tin cup. All night she listened to him describe each breath the man took, each motion of the bear's head as it tried to catch the sound of the man's breathing, and tested the wind for his scent.

The state trooper asked her questions, and the woman who cleaned house for the priest translated them into Yupik. They wanted to know what happened to the storeman, the Gussack who had been seen running after her down the road onto the river late last evening. He had not come back, and the Gussuck boss in Anchorage was concerned about him. She did not answer for a long time because the old man suddenly sat up in his bed and began to talk excitedly, looking at all of them — the trooper in his dark glasses and the housekeeper in the corduroy parka. He kept saying, "The story! The story! Eh-ya! The great bear! The hunter!"

They asked her again, what happened to the man from the Northern Commercial store. "He lied to them. He told them it was safe to drink. But I will not lie." She stood up and put on the gray wolfskin parka. "I killed him," she said, "but I don't lie."

The attorney came back again, and the jailer slid open the steel doors and opened the cell to let him in. He motioned for the jailer to stay to translate for him. She laughed when she saw how the jailer would be forced by this Gussuck to speak Yupik to her. She liked the Gussuck attorney for that, and for the thinning hair on his head. He was very tall, and she liked to think about the exposure of his head to the freezing; she wondered if he would feel the ice descending from the sky before the others did. He wanted to know why she told the state trooper she had killed the storeman. Some village children had seen it happen, he said, and it was an accident. "That's all you have to say to the judge: it was an accident." He kept repeating it over and over again to her, slowly in a loud but gentle voice: "It was an accident. He was running after you and he fell through the ice. That's all you have to say in court. That's all. And they will let you go home. Back to your village." The jailer translated the words sullenly, staring down at the floor. She shook her head. "I will not change the story, not even to escape this place and go home. I intended that he die. The story must be told as it is." The attorney exhaled loudly; his eyes looked tired. "Tell her that she could not have killed him that way. He was a white man. He ran after her without a parka or mittens. She could not have planned that." He paused and turned toward the cell door. "Tell her I will do all I can for her. I will explain to the judge that her mind is confused." She laughed out loud when the jailer translated what the attorney said. The Gussucks did not understand the story; they could not see the way it must be told, year after year as the old man had done, without lapse or silence.

She looked out the window at the frozen white sky. The sun had finally broken loose from the ice but it moved like a wounded caribou running on strength which only dying animals find, leaping and running on bullet-shattered lungs. Its light was weak and pale; it pushed dimly through the clouds. She turned and faced the Gussuck attorney.

"It began a long time ago," she intoned steadily, "in the summertime. Early in the morning, I remember, something red in the tall river grass. . . ."

The day after the old man died, men from the village came. She was sitting on the edge of her bed, across from the woman the trooper hired to watch her. They came into the room slowly and listened to her. At the foot of her bed they left a king salmon that had been split open wide and dried last summer. But she did not pause or hesitate; she went on with the story, and she never stopped, not even when the woman got up to close the door behind the village men.

The old man would not change the story even when he knew the end was approaching. Lies could not stop what was coming. He thrashed around on the bed, pulling the blankets loose, knocking bundles of dried fish and meat on the floor. The man had been on the ice for many hours. The freezing winds on the ice knoll had numbed his hands in the mittens, and the cold had exhausted him. He felt a single muscle tremor in his hand that he could not suppress, and the jade knife fell; it shattered on the ice, and the blue glacier bear turned slowly to face him.   [1975]

LESLIE MARMON SILKO

Yellow Woman

I

My thigh clung to his with dampness, and I watched the sun rising up through the tamaracks and willows. The small brown water birds came to the river and hopped across the mud, leaving brown scratches in the alkali-white crust. They bathed in the river silently. I could hear the water, almost at our feet where the narrow fast channel bubbled and washed green ragged moss and fern leaves. I looked at him beside me, rolled in the red blanket on the white river sand. I cleaned the sand out of the cracks between my toes, squinting because the sun was above the willow trees. I looked at him for the last time, sleeping on the white river sand.

I felt hungry and followed the river south the way we had come the afternoon before, following our footprints that were already blurred by the lizard tracks and bug trails. The horses were still lying down, and the black one whinnied when he saw me but he did not get up — maybe it was because the corral was made out of thick cedar branches and the horses had not yet felt the sun like I had. I tried to look beyond the pale red mesas to the pueblo. I knew it was there, even if I could not see it, on the sand rock hill above the river, the same river that moved past me now and had reflected the moon last night.

The horse felt warm underneath me. He shook his head and pawed the sand. The bay whinnied and leaned against the gate trying to follow, and I remembered him asleep in the red blanket beside the river. I slid off the horse and tied him close to the other horse. I walked north with the river again, and the white sand broke loose in footprints over footprints.

"Wake up."

He moved in the blanket and turned his face to me with his eyes still closed. I knelt down to touch him.

"I'm leaving."

He smiled now, eyes still closed. "You are coming with me, remember?" He sat up now with his bare dark chest and belly in the sun.

"Where?"

"To my place."

"And will I come back?"

He pulled his pants on. I walked away from him, feeling him behind me and smelling the willows.

"Yellow Woman," he said.

I turned to face him. "Who are you?" I asked.

He laughed and knelt on the low, sandy bank, washing his face in the river. "Last night you guessed my name, and you knew why I had come."

1157

I stared past him at the shallow moving water and tried to remember the night, but I could only see the moon in the water and remember his warmth around me.

"But I only said that you were him and that I was Yellow Woman — I'm not really her — I have my own name and I come from the pueblo on the other side of the mesa. Your name is Silva and you are a stranger I met by the river yesterday afternoon."

He laughed softly. "What happened yesterday has nothing to do with what you will do today, Yellow Woman."

"I know — that's what I'm saying — the old stories about the ka'tsina spirit[1] and Yellow Woman can't mean us."

My old grandpa liked to tell those stories best. There is one about Badger and Coyote who went hunting and were gone all day, and when the sun was going down they found a house. There was a girl living there alone, and she had light hair and eyes and she told them that they could sleep with her. Coyote wanted to be with her all night so he sent Badger into a prairie-dog hole, telling him he thought he saw something in it. As soon as Badger crawled in, Coyote blocked up the entrance with rocks and hurried back to Yellow Woman.

"Come here," he said gently.

He touched my neck and I moved close to him to feel his breathing and to hear his heart. I was wondering if Yellow Woman had known who she was — if she knew that she would become part of the stories. Maybe she'd had another name that her husband and relatives called her so that only the ka'tsina from the north and the storytellers would know her as Yellow Woman. But I didn't go on; I felt him all around me, pushing me down into the white river sand.

Yellow Woman went away with the spirit from the north and lived with him and his relatives. She was gone for a long time, but then one day she came back and she brought twin boys.

"Do you know the story?"

"What story?" He smiled and pulled me close to him as he said this. I was afraid lying there on the red blanket. All I could know was the way he felt, warm, damp, his body beside me. This is the way it happens in the stories, I was thinking, with no thought beyond the moment she meets the ka'tsina spirit and they go.

"I don't have to go. What they tell in stories was real only then, back in time immemorial, like they say."

He stood up and pointed at my clothes tangled in the blanket. "Let's go," he said.

I walked beside him, breathing hard because he walked fast, his hand around my wrist. I had stopped trying to pull away from him, because his hand felt cool and the sun was high, drying the river bed into alkali. I will see someone, eventually I will see someone, and then I will be certain that he

---

[1] A mountain spirit of the Pueblo Indians.

is only a man — some man from nearby — and I will be sure that I am not Yellow Woman. Because she is from out of time past and I live now and I've been to school and there are highways and pickup trucks that Yellow Woman never saw.

It was an easy ride north on horseback. I watched the change from the cottonwood trees along the river to the junipers that brushed past us in the foothills, and finally there were only piñons, and when I looked up at the rim of the mountain plateau I could see pine trees growing on the edge. Once I stopped to look down, but the pale sandstone had disappeared and the river was gone and the dark lava hills were all around. He touched my hand, not speaking, but always singing softly a mountain song and looking into my eyes.

I felt hungry and wondered what they were doing at home now — my mother, my grandmother, my husband, and the baby. Cooking breakfast, saying. "Where did she go? — maybe kidnapped," and Al going to the tribal police with the details: "She went walking along the river."

The house was made with black lava rock and red mud. It was high above the spreading miles of arroyos and long mesas. I smelled a mountain smell of pitch and buck brush. I stood there beside the black horse, looking down on the small, dim country we had passed, and I shivered.

"Yellow Woman, come inside where's it's warm."

II

He lit a fire in the stove. It was an old stove with a round belly and an enamel coffeepot on top. There was only the stove, some faded Navajo blankets, and a bedroll and cardboard box. The floor was made of smooth adobe plaster, and there was one small window facing east. He pointed at the box.

"There's some potatoes and the frying pan." He sat on the floor with his arms around his knees pulling them close to his chest and he watched me fry the potatoes. I didn't mind him watching me because he was always watching me — he had been watching me since I came upon him sitting on the river bank trimming leaves from a willow twig with his knife. We ate from the pan and he wiped the grease from his fingers on his Levis.

"Have you brought women here before?" He smiled and kept chewing, so I said, "Do you always use the same tricks?"

"What tricks?" He looked at me like he didn't understand.

"The story about being a ka'tsina from the mountains. The story about Yellow Woman."

Silva was silent; his face was calm.

"I don't believe it. Those stories couldn't happen now," I said.

He shook his head and said softly, "But someday they will talk about us, and they will say, 'Those two lived long ago when things like that happened.'"

He stood up and went out. I ate the rest of the potatoes and thought about things — about the noise the stove was making and the sound of the mountain wind outside. I remembered yesterday and the day before, and then I went outside.

I walked past the corral to the edge where the narrow trail cut through the black rim rock. I was standing in the sky with nothing around me but the wind that came down from the blue mountain peak behind me. I could see faint mountain images in the distance miles across the vast spread of mesas and valleys and plains. I wondered who was over there to feel the mountain wind on those sheer blue edges — who walks on the pine needles in those blue mountains.

"Can you see the pueblo?" Silva was standing behind me.

I shook my head. "We're too far away."

"From here I can see the world." He stepped out on the edge. "The Navajo reservation begins over there." He pointed to the east. "The Pueblo boundaries are over here." He looked below us to the south, where the narrow trail seemed to come from. "The Texans have their ranches over there, starting with that valley, the Concho Valley. The Mexicans run some cattle over there too."

"Do you ever work for them?"

"I steal from them," Silva answered. The sun was dropping behind us and shadows were filling the land below. I turned away from the edge that dropped forever into the valleys below.

"I'm cold," I said; "I'm going inside." I started wondering about this man who could speak the Pueblo language so well but who lived on a mountain and rustled cattle. I decided that this man Silva must be Navajo, because Pueblo men didn't do things like that.

"You must be a Navajo."

Silva shook his head gently. "Little Yellow Woman," he said, "you never give up, do you? I have told you who I am. The Navajo people know me, too." He knelt down and unrolled the bedroll and spread the extra blankets out on a piece of canvas. The sun was down, and the only light in the house came from outside — the dim orange light from sundown.

I stood there and waited for him to crawl under the blankets.

"What are you waiting for?" he said, and I lay down beside him. He undressed me slowly like the night before beside the river — kissing my face gently and running his hands up and down my belly and legs. He took off my pants and then he laughed.

"Why are you laughing?"

"You are breathing so hard."

I pulled away from him and turned my back to him.

He pulled me around and pinned me down with his arms and chest. "You don't understand, do you, little Yellow Woman? You will do what I want."

And again he was all around me with his skin slippery against mine, and I was afraid because I understood that his strength could hurt me. I lay underneath him and I knew that he could destroy me. But later, while he slept beside me, I touched his face and I had a feeling — the kind of feeling for him that overcame me that morning along the river. I kissed him on the forehead and he reached out for me.

When I woke up in the morning he was gone. It gave me a strange feeling because for a long time I sat there on the blankets and looked around the little house for some object of his — some proof that he had been there or maybe that he was coming back. Only the blankets and the cardboard box remained. The .30–30[2] that had been leaning in the corner was gone, and so was the knife I had used the night before. He was gone, and I had my chance to go now. But first I had to eat, because I knew it would be a long walk home.

I found some dried apricots in the cardboard box, and I sat down on a rock at the edge of the plateau rim. There was no wind and the sun warmed me. I was surrounded by silence. I drowsed with apricots in my mouth, and I didn't believe that there were highways or railroads or cattle to steal.

When I woke up, I stared down at my feet in the black mountain dirt. Little black ants were swarming over the pine needles around my foot. They must have smelled the apricots. I thought about my family far below me. They would be wondering about me, because this had never happened to me before. The tribal police would file a report. But if old Grandpa weren't dead he would tell them what happened — he would laugh and say, "Stolen by a ka'tsina, a mountain spirit. She'll come home — they usually do." There are enough of them to handle things. My mother and grandmother will raise the baby like they raised me. Al will find someone else, and they will go on like before, except that there will be a story about the day I disappeared while I was walking along the rver. Silva had come for me; he said he had. I did not decide to go. I just went. Moonflowers blossom in the sand hills before dawn, just as I followed him. That's what I was thinking as I wandered along the trail through the pine trees.

It was noon when I got back. When I saw the stone house I remembered that I had meant to go home. But that didn't seem important any more, maybe because there were little blue flowers growing in the meadow behind the stone house and the gray squirrels were playing in the pines next to the house. The horses were standing in the corral, and there was a beef carcass hanging on the shady side of a big pine in front of the house. Flies buzzed around the clotted blood that hung from the carcass. Silva was washing his hands in a bucket full of water. He must have heard me coming because he spoke to me without turning to face me.

"I've been waiting for you."

"I went walking in the big pine trees."

I looked into the bucket full of bloody water with brown-and-white animal hairs floating in it. Silva stood there letting his hand drip, examining me intently.

"Are you coming with me?"

"Where?" I asked him.

---

[2] A rifle.

"To sell the meat in Marquez."

"If you're sure it's O.K."

"I wouldn't ask you if it wasn't," he answered.

He sloshed the water around in the bucket before he dumped it out and set the bucket upside down near the door. I followed him to the corral and watched him saddle the horses. Even beside the horses he looked tall, and I asked him again if he wasn't Navajo. He didn't say anything; he just shook his head and kept cinching up the saddle.

"But Navajos are tall."

"Get on the horse," he said, "and let's go."

The last thing he did before we started down the steep trail was to grab the .30–30 from the corner. He slid the rifle into the scabbard that hung from his saddle.

"Do they ever try to catch you?" I asked

"They don't know who I am."

"Then why did you bring the rifle?"

"Because we are going to Marquez where the Mexicans live."

III

The trail leveled out on a narrow ridge that was steep on both sides like an animal spine. On one side I could see where the trail went around the rocky gray hills and disappeared into the southeast where the pale sandrock mesas stood in the distance near my home. On the other side was a trail that went west, and as I looked far into the distance I thought I saw the little town. But Silva said no, that I was looking in the wrong place, that I just thought I saw houses. After that I quit looking off into the distance; it was hot and the wildflowers were closing up their deep-yellow petals. Only the waxy cactus flowers bloomed in the bright sun, and I saw every color that a cactus blossom can be; the white ones and the red ones were still buds, but the purple and the yellow were blossoms, open full and the most beautiful of all.

Silva saw him before I did. The white man was riding a big gray horse, coming up the trail toward us. He was traveling fast and the gray horse's feet sent rocks rolling off the trail into the dry tumbleweeds. Silva motioned for me to stop and we watched the white man. He didn't see us right away, but finally his horse whinnied at our horses and he stopped. He looked at us briefly before he loped the gray horse across the three hundred yards that separated us. He stopped his horse in front of Silva, and his young fat face was shadowed by the brim of his hat. He didn't look mad, but his small, pale eyes moved from the blood-soaked gunny sacks hanging from my saddle to Silva's face and then back to my face.

"Where did you get the fresh meat?" the white man asked.

"I've been hunting," Silva said, and when he shifted his weight in the saddle the leather creaked.

"The hell you have, Indian. You've been rustling cattle. We've been looking for the thief for a long time."

The rancher was fat, and sweat began to soak through his white cowboy shirt and the wet cloth stuck to the thick rolls of belly fat. He almost seemed to be panting from the exertion of talking, and he smelled rancid, maybe because Silva scared him.

Silva turned to me and smiled. "Go back up the mountain, Yellow Woman."

The white man got angry when he heard Silva speak in a language he couldn't understand. "Don't try anything, Indian. Just keep riding to Marquez. We'll call the state police from there."

The rancher must have been unarmed because he was very frightened and if he had a gun he would have pulled it out then. I turned my horse around and the rancher yelled, "Stop!" I looked at Silva for an instant and there was something ancient and dark — something I could feel in my stomach — in his eyes, and when I glanced at his hand I saw his finger on the trigger of the .30–30 that was still in the saddle scabbard. I slapped my horse across the flank and the sacks of raw meat swung against my knees as the horse leaped up the trail. It was hard to keep my balance, and once I thought I felt the saddle slipping backward; it was because of this that I could not look back.

I didn't stop until I reached the ridge where the trail forked. The horse was breathing deep gasps and there was a dark film of sweat on its neck. I looked down in the direction I had come from, but I couldn't see the place. I waited. The wind came up and pushed warm air past me. I looked up at the sky, pale blue and full of thin clouds and fading vapor trails left by jets.

I think four shots were fired — I remember hearing four hollow explosions that reminded me of deer hunting. There could have been more shots after that, but I couldn't have heard them because my horse was running again and the loose rocks were making too much noise as they scattered around his feet.

Horses have a hard time running downhill, but I went that way instead of uphill to the mountain because I thought it was safer. I felt better with the horse running southeast past the round gray hills that were covered with cedar trees and black lava rock. When I got to the plain in the distance I could seen the dark green patches of tamaracks that grew along the river; and beyond the river I could see the beginning of the pale sandrock mesas. I stopped the horse and looked back to see if anyone was coming; then I got off the horse and turned the horse around, wondering if it would go back to its corral under the pines on the mountain. It looked back at me for a moment and then plucked a mouthful of green tumbleweeds before it trotted back up the trail with its ears pointed forward, carrying its head daintily to one side to avoid stepping on the dragging reins. When the horse disappeared over the last hill, the gunny sacks full of meat were still swinging and bouncing.

IV

I walked toward the river on a wood-hauler's road that I knew would eventually lead to the paved road. I was thinking about waiting beside the road for someone to drive by, but by the time I got to the pavement I had decided it wasn't very far to walk if I followed the river back the way Silva and I had come.

The river water tasted good, and I sat in the shade under a cluster of silvery willows. I thought about Silva, and I felt sad at leaving him; still, there was something strange about him, and I tried to figure it out all the way back home.

I came back to the place on the river bank where he had been sitting the first time I saw him. The green willow leaves that he had trimmed from the branch were still lying there, wilted in the sand. I saw the leaves and I wanted to go back to him — to kiss him and to touch him — but the mountains were too far away now. And I told myself, because I believe it, he will come back sometime and be waiting again by the river.

I followed the path up from the river into the village. The sun was getting low, and I could smell supper cooking when I got to the screen door of my house. I could hear their voices inside — my mother was telling my grandmother how to fix the Jell-O and my husband, Al, was playing with the baby. I decided to tell them that some Navajo had kidnapped me, but I was sorry that old Grandpa wasn't alive to hear my story because it was the Yellow Woman stories he liked to tell best. [1974]

Isaac Bashevis Singer (1904–1991) *was born in Radzymin, Poland. After his education at a rabbinical seminary in Warsaw, he worked as a proofreader and translator before emigrating to the United States in 1935. Settling in New York City, he made his living as a journalist for the* Jewish Daily Forward, *a Yiddish-language paper. He also wrote autobiographical sketches, short stories, and novels in Yiddish for many years. In 1950 his writing became available to a wider audience when he began to publish it in English translations, starting with the realistic historical chronicle* The Family Moskat. *Singer's first collection of short stories,* Gimpel the Fool and Other Stories *(translated by the noted American novelist Saul Bellow and others), appeared in 1957, and during the 1960s and 1970s he alternated novels with books of short fiction. A prolific writer, Singer has also published three volumes of autobiographical reminiscences. In 1978 he was awarded the Nobel Prize for Literature. His* Collected Stories *appeared in 1981.*

In all his work Singer explores the traditions of Jewish life, past and present, expressing his fascination with the history of his people: "I was born with the feeling that I am part of an unlikely adventure, something that couldn't have happened, but happened all the same." In the best of his short stories, as in "The Spinoza of Market Street," he dramatizes multiple levels of human existence, both physical and spiritual, and the ambiguous nature of life itself, capable as it is of many interpretations.

Singer has said that in his short stories he is interested in writing about people who are "obsessed by some mania or fixed idea, and everything turns around this idea. . . . Since we don't know really what reality is, whatever we are obsessed with becomes our reality." His stories are always based on a realistically observed setting, however, since "a miracle must be invented among realism, because, if it's one miracle after the other and there's no realism, the miracle itself becomes nothing." All great literature begins in realism, according to Singer, who with great clear-sightedness puts the events of our everyday existence in the category of the marvelous too. "Once a man brought me a story which began with a cut-off head which spoke. And I said to the man, 'Isn't it miracle enough that a head which is not chopped off can talk?'"

ISAAC BASHEVIS SINGER

The Spinoza of Market Street

Translated by Martha Glicklich and Cecil Hemley

I

Dr. Nahum Fischelson paced back and forth in his garret room in Market Street, Warsaw. Dr. Fischelson was a short, hunched man with a grayish beard, and was quite bald except for a few wisps of hair remaining at the nape of the neck. His nose was as crooked as a beak and his eyes were large, dark, and fluttering like those of some huge bird. It was a hot summer evening, but

Dr. Fischelson wore a black coat which reached to his knees, and he had on a stiff collar and a bow tie. From the door he paced slowly to the dormer window set high in the slanting room and back again. One had to mount several steps to look out. A candle in a brass holder was burning on the table and a variety of insects buzzed around the flame. Now and again one of the creatures would fly too close to the fire and sear its wings, or one would ignite and glow on the wick for an instant. At such moments Dr. Fischelson grimaced. His wrinkled face would twitch and beneath his disheveled mustache he would bite his lips. Finally he took a handkerchief from his pocket and waved it at the insects.

"Away from there, fools and imbeciles," he scolded. "You won't get warm here; you'll only burn yourself."

The insects scattered but a second later returned and once more circled the trembling flame. Dr. Fischelson wiped the sweat from his wrinkled forehead and sighed, "Like men they desire nothing but the pleasure of the moment." On the table lay an open book written in Latin, and on its broad-margined pages were notes and comments printed in small letters by Dr. Fischelson. The book was Spinoza's *Ethics* and Dr. Fischelson had been studying it for the last thirty years. He knew every proposition, every proof, every corollary, every note by heart. When he wanted to find a particular passage, he generally opened to the place immediately without having to search for it. But, nevertheless, he continued to study the *Ethics* for hours every day with a magnifying glass in his bony hand, murmuring and nodding his head in agreement. The truth was that the more Dr. Fischelson studied, the more puzzling sentences, unclear passages, and cryptic remarks he found. Each sentence contained hints unfathomed by any of the students of Spinoza. Actually the philosopher had anticipated all of the criticisms of pure reason made by Kant and his followers. Dr. Fischelson was writing a commentary on the *Ethics*. He had drawers full of notes and drafts, but it didn't seem that he would ever be able to complete his work. The stomach ailment which had plagued him for years was growing worse from day to day. Now he would get pains in his stomach after only a few mouthfuls of oatmeal. "God in Heaven, it's difficult, very difficult," he would say to himself, using the same intonation as had his father, the late Rabbi of Tishevitz. "It's very, very hard."

Dr. Fischelson was not afraid of dying. To begin with, he was no longer a young man. Secondly, it is stated in the fourth part of the *Ethics* that "a free man thinks of nothing less than of death and his wisdom is a meditation not of death, but of life." Thirdly, it is also said that "the human mind cannot be absolutely destroyed with the human body but there is some part of it that remains eternal." And yet Dr. Fischelson's ulcer (or perhaps it was a cancer) continued to bother him. His tongue was always coated. He belched frequently and emitted a different foul-smelling gas each time. He suffered from heartburn and cramps. At times he felt like vomiting and at other times he was hungry for garlic, onions, and fried foods. He had long ago discarded the medicines prescribed for him by the doctors and had sought his own remedies. He found it beneficial to take grated radish after meals and lie on his bed, belly down, with his head hanging over the side. But these home remedies offered only temporary relief. Some of the doctors he consulted insisted there was nothing the matter with him. "It's just nerves," they told him. "You could live to be a hundred."

But on this particular hot summer night, Dr. Fischelson felt his strength ebbing. His knees were shaky, his pulse weak. He sat down to read and his vision blurred. The letters on the page turned from green to gold. The lines became waved and jumped over each other, leaving white gaps as if the text had disappeared in some mysterious way. The heat was unbearable, flowing down directly from the tin roof; Dr. Fischelson felt he was inside of an oven. Several times he climbed the four steps to the window and thrust his head out into the cool of the evening breeze. He would remain in that position for so long his knees would become wobbly. "Oh it's a fine breeze," he would murmur, "really delightful," and he would recall that according to Spinoza, morality and happiness were identical, and that the most moral deed a man could perform was to indulge in some pleasure which was not contrary to reason.

II

Dr. Fischelson standing on the top step at the window and looking out, could see into two worlds. Above him were the heavens, thickly strewn with stars. Dr. Fischelson had never seriously studied astronomy but he could differentiate between the planets, those bodies which like the earth, revolve around the sun, and the fixed stars, themselves distant suns, whose light reaches us a hundred or even a thousand years later. He recognized the constellations which mark the path of the earth in space and that nebulous sash, the Milky Way. Dr. Fischelson owned a small telescope he had bought in Switzerland where he had studied and he particularly enjoyed looking at the moon through it. He could clearly make out on the moon's surface the volcanoes bathed in sunlight and the dark, shadowy craters. He never wearied of gazing at those cracks and crevasses. To him they seemed both near and distant, both substantial and insubstantial. Now and then he would see a shooting star trace a wide arc across the sky and disappear, leaving a fiery trail behind it. Dr. Fischelson would know then that a meteorite had reached our atmosphere, and perhaps some unburned fragment of it had fallen into the ocean or had landed in the desert or perhaps even in some inhabited region. Slowly the stars which had appeared from behind Dr. Fischelson's roof rose until they were shining above the house across the street. Yes, when Dr. Fischelson looked up into the heavens, he became aware of that infinite extension which is, according to Spinoza, one of God's attributes. It comforted Dr. Fischelson to think that although he was only a weak, puny man, a changing mode of the absolutely infinite Substance, he was nevertheless a part of the cosmos, made of the same matter as the celestial bodies; to the extent that he was a part of the Godhead, he knew he could not be destroyed. In such moments, Dr. Fischelson experienced the *Amor dei Intellectualis* which is, according to the philosopher of Amsterdam, the highest perfection of the mind. Dr. Fischelson breathed deeply, lifted his head as high as his stiff collar permitted and actually felt he was whirling in company with the earth, the sun, the stars of the Milky Way, and the infinite host of galaxies known only to infinite thought. His legs became light and weightless and he grasped the window frame with both hands as if afraid he would lose his footing and fly out into eternity.

When Dr. Fischelson tired of observing the sky, his glance dropped to Market Street below. He could see a long strip extending from Yanash's market to Iron Street with the gas lamps lining it merged into a string of fiery dots. Smoke was issuing from the chimneys on the black, tin roofs; the bakers were heating their ovens, and here and there sparks mingled with the black smoke. The street never looked so noisy and crowded as on a summer evening. Thieves, prostitutes, gamblers, and fences loafed in the square which looked from above like a pretzel covered with poppy seeds. The young men laughed coarsely and the girls shrieked. A peddler with a keg of lemonade on his back pierced the general din with his intermittent cries. A watermelon vendor shouted in a savage voice, and the long knife which he used for cutting the fruit dripped with the blood-like juice. Now and again the street became even more agitated. Fire engines, their heavy wheels clanging, sped by; they were drawn by sturdy black horses which had to be tightly curbed to prevent them from running wild. Next came an ambulance, its siren screaming. Then some thugs had a fight among themselves and the police had to be called. A passerby was robbed and ran about shouting for help. Some wagons loaded with firewood sought to get through into the courtyards where the bakeries were located but the horses could not lift the wheels over the steep curbs and the drivers berated the animals and lashed them with their whips. Sparks rose from the clanging hoofs. It was now long after seven, which was the prescribed closing time for stores, but actually business had only begun. Customers were led in stealthily through back doors. The Russian policemen on the street, having been paid off, noticed nothing of this. Merchants continued to hawk their wares, each seeking to outshout the others.

"Gold, gold, gold," a woman who dealt in rotten oranges shrieked.

"Sugar, sugar, sugar," croaked a dealer of overripe plums.

"Heads, heads, heads," a boy who sold fishheads roared.

Through the window of a Hasidic study house across the way, Dr. Fischelson could see boys with long sidelocks swaying over holy volumes, grimacing and studying aloud in sing-song voices. Butchers, porters, and fruit dealers were drinking beer in the tavern below. Vapor drifted from the tavern's open door like steam from a bathhouse, and there was the sound of loud music. Outside of the tavern, streetwalkers snatched at drunken soldiers and at workers on their way home from the factories. Some of the men carried bundles of wood on their shoulders, reminding Dr. Fischelson of the wicked who are condemned to kindle their own fires in Hell. Husky record players poured out their raspings through open windows. The liturgy of the high holidays alternated with vulgar vaudeville songs.

Dr. Fischelson peered into the half-lit bedlam and cocked his ears. He knew that the behavior of this rabble was the very antithesis of reason. These people were immersed in the vainest of passions, were drunk with emotions, and, according to Spinoza, emotion was never good. Instead of the pleasure they ran after, all they succeeded in obtaining was disease and prison, shame and the suffering that resulted from ignorance. Even the cats which loitered on the roofs here seemed more savage and passionate than those in other parts of the town. They caterwauled with the voices of women in labor, and like demons scampered up walls and leaped onto eaves and balconies. One of the toms paused at Dr. Fischelson's window and let out a howl which made Dr. Fischelson shudder. The doctor stepped from the window and, picking up a broom, brandished it in front of the black beast's glowing, green eyes. "Scat, begone, you ignorant savage!" — and he rapped the broom handle against the roof until the tom ran off.

III

When Dr. Fischelson had returned to Warsaw from Zurich, where he had studied philosophy, a great future had been predicted for him. His friends had known that he was writing an important book on Spinoza. A Jewish Polish journal had invited him to be a contributor; he had been a frequent guest at several wealthy households and he had been made head librarian at the Warsaw synagogue. Although even then he had been considered an old bachelor, the matchmakers had proposed several rich girls for him. But Dr. Fischelson had not taken advantage of these opportunities. He had wanted to be as independent as Spinoza himself. And he had been. But because of his heretical ideas he had come into conflict with the rabbi and had had to resign his post as librarian. For years after that, he had supported himself by giving private lessons in Hebrew and German. Then, when he had become sick, the Berlin Jewish community had voted him a subsidy of five hundred marks a year. This had been made possible through the intervention of the famous Dr. Hildesheimer with whom he corresponded about philosophy. In order to get by on so small a pension, Dr. Fischelson had moved into the attic room and had begun cooking his own meals on a kerosene stove. He had a cupboard which had many drawers, and each drawer was labeled with the food it contained — buckwheat, rice, barley, onions, carrots, potatoes, mushrooms. Once a week Dr. Fischelson put on his wide-brimmed black hat, took a basket in one hand and Spinoza's *Ethics* in the other, and went off to the market for his provisions. While he was waiting to be served, he would open the *Ethics.* The merchants knew him and would motion him to their stalls.

"A fine piece of cheese, Doctor — just melts in your mouth."

"Fresh mushrooms, Doctor, straight from the woods."

"Make way for the doctor, ladies," the butcher would shout. "Please don't block the entrance."

During the early years of his sickness, Dr. Fischelson had still gone in the evening to a café which was frequented by Hebrew teachers and other intellectuals. It had been his habit to sit there and play chess while drinking a half a glass of black coffee. Sometimes he would stop at the bookstores on Holy Cross Street where all sorts of old books and magazines could be purchased cheap. On one occasion a former pupil of his had arranged to meet him at a restaurant one evening. When Dr. Fischelson arrived, he had been surprised to find a group of friends and admirers who forced him to sit at the head of the table while they made speeches about him. But these were things that had happened long ago. Now people were no longer interested in him. He had isolated himself completely and had become a forgotten man. The events of 1905 when the boys of Market Street had begun to organize strikes, throw bombs at police stations, and shoot strike breakers so that the stores were closed even on weekdays had greatly increased his isolation. He began to despise everything associated with the modern Jew — Zionism, socialism, anarchism. The young men in question seemed to him nothing but an ignorant rabble intent on destroying society, society without which no reasonable existence was possible. He still read a Hebrew magazine occasionally, but he felt contempt for modern Hebrew, which had no roots in the Bible or the Mishnah. The spelling of Polish words had changed also. Dr. Fischelson concluded that even the so-called spiritual men had abandoned reason and were doing their utmost to pander to the mob. Now and again he still visited a library and browsed through some of the modern histories of philosophy, but he found that the professors did not understand Spinoza, quoted him incorrectly, attributed their own muddled ideas to the philosopher. Although Dr. Fischelson was well aware that anger was an emotion unworthy of those who walk the path of reason, he would become furious, and would quickly close the book and push it from him. "Idiots," he would mutter, "asses, upstarts." And he would vow never again to look at modern philosophy.

IV

Every three months a special mailman who only delivered money orders brought Dr. Fischelson eighty rubles. He expected his quarterly allotment at the beginning of July but as day after day passed and the tall man with the blond mustache and the shiny buttons did not appear, the doctor grew anxious. He had scarcely a groschen left. Who knows — possibly the Berlin community had rescinded his subsidy; perhaps Dr. Hildesheimer had died, God forbid; the post office might have made a mistake. Every event has its cause, Dr. Fischelson knew. All was determined, all necessary, and a man of reason had no right to worry. Nevertheless, worry invaded his brain, and buzzed about like the flies. If the worst came to the worst, it occurred to him, he could commit suicide, but then he remembered that Spinoza did not approve of suicide and compared those who took their own lives to the insane.

One day when Dr. Fischelson went out to a store to purchase a composition book, he heard people talking about war. In Serbia somewhere, an Austrian prince had been shot and the Austrians had delivered an ultimatum to the Serbs. The owner of the store, a young man with a yellow beard and shifty yellow eyes, announced, "We are about to have a small war," and he advised Dr. Fischelson to store up food because in the near future there was likely to be a shortage.

Everything happened so quickly. Dr. Fischelson had not even decided whether it was worthwhile to spend four groschen on a newspaper, and already posters had been hung up announcing mobilization. Men were to be seen walking on the street with round, metal tags on their lapels, a sign that they were being drafted. They were followed by their crying wives. One Monday when Dr. Fischelson descended to the street to buy some food with his last kopecks, he found the stores closed. The owners and their wives stood outside and explained that merchandise was unobtainable. But certain special customers were pulled to one side and let in through back doors. On the street all was confusion. Policemen with swords unsheathed could be seen riding on horseback. A large crowd had gathered around the tavern where, at the command of the czar, the tavern's stock of whiskey was being poured into the gutter.

Dr. Fischelson went to his old café. Perhaps he would find some acquaintances there who would advise him. But he did not come across a single person he knew. He decided, then, to visit the rabbi of the synagogue where he had once been librarian, but the sexton with the six-sided skullcap informed him that the rabbi and his family had gone off to the spas. Dr. Fischelson had other old friends in town but he found no one at home. His feet ached from so much walking; black and green spots appeared before his eyes and he felt faint. He stopped and waited for the giddiness to pass. The passers-by jostled him. A dark-eyed high-school girl tried to give him a coin. Although the war had just started, soldiers eight abreast were marching in full battle dress — the men were covered with dust and were sunburnt. Canteens were strapped to their sides and they wore rows of bullets across their chests. The bayonets on their rifles gleamed with a cold, green light. They sang with mournful voices. Along with the men came cannons, each pulled by eight horses; their blind muzzles breathed gloomy terror. Dr. Fischelson felt nauseous. His stomach ached; his intestines seemed about to turn themselves inside out. Cold sweat appeared on his face.

"I'm dying," he thought. "This is the end." Nevertheless, he did manage to drag himself home where he lay down on the iron cot and remained, panting and gasping. He must have dozed off because he imagined that he was in his home town, Tishevitz. He had a sore throat and his mother was busy wrapping a stocking stuffed with hot salt around his neck. He could hear talk going on in the house; something about a candle and about how a frog had bitten him. He wanted to go out into the street but they wouldn't let him because a Catholic procession was passing by. Men in long robes, holding double-edged axes in their hands, were intoning in Latin as they sprinkled holy water. Crosses gleamed; sacred pictures waved in the air. There was an odor of incense and corpses. Suddenly the sky turned a burning red and the whole world started to burn. Bells were ringing; people rushed madly about. Flocks of birds flew overhead, screeching. Dr. Fischelson awoke with a start. His body was covered with sweat and his throat was now actually sore. He tried to meditate about his extraordinary dream, to find its rational connection with what was happening to him and to comprehend it *sub specie eternitatis*, but none of it made sense. "Alas, the brain is a receptacle for nonsense," Dr. Fischelson thought. "This earth belongs to the mad."

And he once more closed his eyes; once more he dozed; once more he dreamed.

V

The eternal laws, apparently, had not yet ordained Dr. Fischelson's end.

There was a door to the left of Dr. Fischelson's attic room which opened off a dark corridor, cluttered with boxes and baskets, in which the odor of fried onions and laundry soap was always present. Behind this door lived a spinster whom the neighbors called Black Dobbe. Dobbe was tall and lean, and as black as a baker's shovel. She had a broken nose and there was a mustache on her upper lip. She spoke with the hoarse voice of a man and she wore men's shoes. For years Black Dobbe had sold bread, rolls, and bagels which she had bought from the baker at the gate of the house. But one day she and the baker had quarreled and she had moved her business to the marketplace and now she dealt in what were called "wrinklers," which was a synonym for cracked eggs. Black Dobbe had no luck with men. Twice she had been engaged to baker's apprentices but in both instances they had returned the engagement contract to her. Some time afterwards she had received an engagement contract from an old man, a glazier who claimed that he was divorced, but it had later come to light that he still had a wife. Black Dobbe had a cousin in America, a shoemaker, and repeatedly she boasted that this cousin was sending her passage, but she remained in Warsaw. She was constantly being teased by the women who would say, "There's no hope for you, Dobbe. You're fated to die an old maid." Dobbe also answered, "I don't intend to be a slave for any man. Let them all rot."

That afternoon Dobbe received a letter from America. Generally she would go to Leizer the tailor and have him read it to her. However, that day Leizer was out and so Dobbe thought of Dr. Fischelson, whom the other tenants considered a convert since he never went to prayer. She knocked on the door of the doctor's room but there was no answer. "The heretic is probably out," Dobbe thought but, nevertheless, she knocked once more, and this time the door moved slightly. She pushed her way in and stood there frightened. Dr. Fischelson lay fully clothed on his bed; his face was as yellow as wax; his Adam's apple stuck out prominently; his beard pointed upward. Dobbe screamed; she was certain that he was dead, but — no — his body moved. Dobbe picked up a glass which stood on the table, ran into the corridor, filled the glass with water from the faucet, hurried back, and threw the water into the face of the unconscious man. Dr. Fischelson shook his head and opened his eyes.

"What's wrong with you?" Dobbe asked. "Are you sick?"

"Thank you very much. No."

"Have you a family? I'll call them."

"No family," Dr. Fischelson said.

Dobbe wanted to fetch the barber from across the street but Dr. Fischelson signified that he didn't wish the barber's assistance. Since Dobbe was not going to the market that day, no "wrinklers" being available, she decided to do a good deed. She assisted the sick man to get off the bed and smoothed down the blanket. Then she undressed Dr. Fischelson and prepared some soup for him on the kerosene stove. The sun never entered Dobbe's room, but here squares of sunlight shimmered on the faded walls. The floor was painted red. Over the bed hung a picture of a man who was wearing a broad frill around his neck and had long hair. "Such an old fellow and yet he keeps his place so nice and clean," Dobbe thought approvingly. Dr. Fischelson asked for the *Ethics*, and she gave it to him disapprovingly. She was certain it was a Gentile prayer book. Then she began bustling about, brought in a pail of water, swept the floor. Dr. Fischelson ate; after he had finished, he was much stronger and Dobbe asked him to read her the letter.

He read it slowly, the paper trembling in his hands. It came from New York, from Dobbe's cousin. Once more he wrote that he was about to send her a "really important letter" and a ticket to America. By now, Dobbe knew the story by heart and she helped the old man decipher her cousin's scrawl. "He's lying," Dobbe said. "He forgot about me a long time ago." In the evening, Dobbe came again. A candle in a brass holder was burning on the chair next to the bed. Reddish shadows trembled on the walls and ceiling. Dr. Fischelson sat propped up in bed, reading a book. The candle threw a golden light on his forehead which seemed as if cleft in two. A bird had flown in through the window and was perched on the table. For a moment Dobbe was frightened. This man made her think of witches, of black mirrors and corpses wandering around at night and terrifying women. Nevertheless, she took a few steps toward him and inquired, "How are you? Any better?"

"A little, thank you."

"Are you really a convert?" she asked although she wasn't quite sure what the word meant.

"Me, a convert? No, I'm a Jew like any other Jew," Dr. Fischelson answered.

The doctor's assurances made Dobbe feel more at home. She found the bottle of kerosene and lit the stove, and after that she fetched a glass of milk from her room and began cooking kasha. Dr. Fischelson continued to study the *Ethics*, but that evening he could make no sense of the theorems and proofs with their many references to axioms and definitions and other theorems. With trembling hand he raised the book to his eyes and read, "The idea of each modification of the human body does not involve adequate knowledge of the human body itself . . . The idea of the idea of each modification of the human mind does not involve adequate knowledge of the human mind."

VI

Dr. Fischelson was certain he would die any day now. He made out his will, leaving all of his books and manuscripts to the synagogue library. His clothing and furniture would go to Dobbe since she had taken care of him. But death did not come. Rather his health improved. Dobbe returned to her business in the market, but she visited the old man several times a day, prepared soup for him, left him a glass of tea, and told him news of the war. The Germans had occupied Kalish, Bendin, and Cestechow, and they were marching on Warsaw. People said that on a quiet morning one could hear the rumblings of the cannon. Dobbe reported that the casualties were heavy. "They're falling like flies," she said. "What a terrible misfortune for the women."

She couldn't explain why, but the old man's attic room attracted her. She liked to remove the gold-rimmed books from the bookcase, dust them, and then air them on the windowsill. She would climb the few steps to the window and look out through the telescope. She also enjoyed talking to Dr. Fischelson. He told her about Switzerland, where he had studied, of the great cities he had passed through, of the high mounains that were covered with snow even in the summer. His father had been a rabbi, he said, and before he, Dr. Fischelson, had become a student, he had attended a yeshiva. She asked him how many languages he knew and it turned out that he could speak and write Hebrew, Russian, German, and French, in addition to Yiddish. He also knew Latin. Dobbe was astonished that such an educated man should live in an attic room on Market Street. But what amazed her most of all was that although he had the title "Doctor," he couldn't write prescriptions. "Why don't you become a real doctor?" she would ask him. "I am a doctor," he would answer. "I'm just not a physician." "What kind of a doctor?" "A doctor of philosophy." Although she had no idea of what this meant, she felt it must be very important. "Oh, my blessed mother," she would say, "where did you get such a brain?"

Then one evening after Dobbe had given him his crackers and his glass of tea with milk, he began questioning her about where she came from, who her parents were, and why she had not married. Dobbe was surprised. No one had ever asked her such questions. She told him her story in a quiet voice and stayed until eleven o'clock. Her father had been a porter at the kosher butcher shops. Her mother had plucked chickens in the slaughterhouse. The family had lived in a cellar at No. 19 Market Street. When she had been ten, she had become a maid. The man she had worked for had been a fence who bought stolen goods from thieves on the square. Dobbe had had a brother who had gone into the Russian army and had never returned. Her sister had married a coachman in Praga and had died in childbirth. Dobbe told of the battles between the underworld and the revolutionaries in 1905, of blind Itche and his gang and how they collected protection money from the stores, of the thugs who attacked young boys and girls out on Saturday afternoon strolls if they were not paid money for security. She also spoke of the pimps who drove about in carriages and abducted women to be sold in Buenos Aires. Dobbe swore that some men had even sought to inveigle her into a brothel, but that she had run away. She complained of a thousand evils done to her. She had been robbed; her boy friend had been stolen; a competitor had once poured a pint of kerosene into her basket of bagels; her own cousin, the shoemaker, had cheated her out of a hundred rubles before he had left for America. Dr. Fischelson listened to her attentively. He asked her questions, shook his head, and grunted.

"Well, do you believe in God?" he finally asked her.

"I don't know," she answered. "Do you?"

"Yes, I believe."

"Then why don't you go to synagogue?" she asked.

"God is everywhere," he replied. "In the synagogue. In the marketplace. In this very room. We ourselves are parts of God."

"Don't say such things," Dobbe asked. "You frighten me."

She left the room and Dr. Fischelson was certain she had gone to bed. But he wondered why she had not said good night. "I probably drove her away with my philosophy," he thought. The very next moment he heard her footsteps. She came in carrying a pile of clothing like a peddler.

"I wanted to show you these," she said. "They're my trousseau." And she began to spread out, on the chair, dresses — woolen, silk, velvet. Taking each dress up in turn, she held it to her body. She gave him an account of every item in her trousseau — underwear, shoes, stockings.

"I'm not wasteful," she said. "I'm a saver. I have enough money to go to America."

Then she was silent and her face turned brick-red. She looked at Dr. Fischelson out of the corner of her eyes, timidly, inquisitively. Dr. Fischelson's body suddenly began to shake as if he had the chills. He said, "Very nice, beautiful things." His brow furrowed and he pulled at his beard with two fingers. A sad smile appeared on his toothless mouth and his large fluttering eyes, gazing into the distance through the attic window, also smiled sadly.

VII

The day that Black Dobbe came to the rabbi's chambers and announced that she was to marry Dr. Fischelson, the rabbi's wife thought she had gone mad. But the news had already reached Leizer the tailor, and had spread to the bakery, as well as to other shops. There were those who thought that the "old maid" was very lucky; the doctor, they said, had a vast hoard of money. But there were others who took the view that he was a run-down degenerate who would give her syphilis. Although Dr. Fischelson had insisted that the wedding be a small, quiet one, a host of guests assembled in the rabbi's rooms. The baker's apprentices who generally went about barefoot, and in their underwear, with paper bags on the tops of their heads, now put on light-colored suits, straw hats, yellow shoes, gaudy ties, and they brought with them huge cakes and pans filled with cookies. They had even managed to find a bottle of vodka although liquor was forbidden in wartime. When the bride and groom entered the rabbi's chamber, a murmur arose from the crowd. The women could not believe their eyes. The woman that they saw was not the one they had known. Dobbe wore a wide-brimmed hat which was amply adorned with cherries, grapes, and plumes, and the dress that she had on was of white silk and was equipped with a train; on her feet were high-heeled shoes, gold in color, and from her thin neck hung a string of imitation pearls. Nor was this all: her fingers sparkled with rings and glittering stones. Her face was veiled. She looked almost like one of those rich brides which were married in the Vienna Hall. The bakers' apprentices whistled mockingly. As for Dr. Fischelson, he was wearing his black coat and broad-toed shoes. He was scarcely able to walk; he was leaning on Dobbe. When he saw the crowd from the doorway, he became frightened and began to retreat, but Dobbe's former employer approached him saying, "Come in, come in, bridegroom. Don't be bashful. We are all brethren now."

The ceremony proceeded according to the law. The rabbi, in a worn satin gaberdine, wrote the marriage contract and then had the bride and groom touch his handkerchief as a token of agreement; the rabbi wiped the point of the pen on his skullcap. Several porters who had been called from the street to make up the quorum supported the canopy. Dr. Fischelson put on a white robe as a reminder of the day of his death and Dobbe walked around him seven times as custom required. The light from the braided candles flickered on the walls. The shadows wavered. Having poured wine into a goblet, the rabbi chanted the benedictions in a sad melody. Dobbe uttered only a single cry. As for the other women, they took out their lace handkerchiefs and stood with them in their hands, grimacing. When the bakers' boys began to whisper wisecracks to each other, the rabbi put a finger to his lips and murmured, *"Eh nu oh,"* as a sign that talking was forbidden. The moment came to slip the wedding ring on the bride's finger, but the bridegroom's hand started to tremble and he had trouble locating Dobbe's index finger. The next thing, according to custom, was the smashing of the glass, but though Dr. Fischelson kicked the goblet several times, it remained unbroken. The girls lowered their heads, pinched each other gleefully, and giggled. Finally one of the apprentices struck the goblet with his heel and it shattered. Even the rabbi could not restrain a smile. After the ceremony the guests drank vodka and ate cookies. Dobbe's former employer came up to Dr. Fischelson and said, *"Mazel tov,* bridegroom. Your luck should be as good as your wife." "Thank you, thank you," Dr. Fischelson murmured, "but I don't look forward to any luck." He was anxious to return as quickly as possible to his attic room. He felt a pressure in his stomach and his chest ached. His face had become greenish. Dobbe had suddenly become angry. She pulled back her veil and called out to the crowd, "What are you laughing at? This isn't a show." And without picking up the cushion cover in which the gifts were wrapped, she returned with her husband to their rooms on the fifth floor.

Dr. Fischelson lay down on the freshly made bed in his room and began reading the *Ethics*. Dobbe had gone back to her own room. The doctor had explained to her that he was an old man, that he was sick and without strength. He had promised her nothing. Nevertheless she returned wearing a silk nightgown, slippers with pompoms, and with her hair hanging down over her shoulders. There was a smile on her face, and she was bashful and hesitant. Dr. Fischelson trembled and the *Ethics* dropped from his hands. The candle went out. Dobbe groped for Dr. Fischelson in the dark and kissed his mouth. "My dear husband," she whispered to him, *"Mazel tov."*

What happened that night could be called a miracle. If Dr. Fischelson hadn't been convinced that every occurrence is in accordance with the laws of nature, he would have thought that Black Dobbe had bewitched him.

Powers long dormant awakened in him. Although he had had only a sip of the benediction wine, he was as if intoxicated. He kissed Dobbe and spoke to her of love. Long-forgotten quotations from Klopstock, Lessing, Goethe, rose to his lips. The pressures and aches stopped. He embraced Dobbe, pressed her to himself, was again a man as in his youth. Dobbe was faint with delight; crying, she murmured things to him in a Warsaw slang which he did not understand. Later, Dr. Fischelson slipped off into the deep sleep young men know. He dreamed that he was in Switzerland and that he was climbing mountains — running, falling, flying. At dawn he opened his eyes; it seemed to him that someone had blown into his ears. Dobbe was snoring. Dr. Fischelson quietly got out of bed. In his long nightshirt he approached the window, walked up the steps and looked out in wonder. Market Street was asleep, breathing with a deep stillness. The gas lamps were flickering. The black shutters on the stores were fastened with iron bars. A cool breeze was blowing. Dr. Fischelson looked up at the sky. The black arch was thickly sown with stars — there were green, red, yellow, blue stars; there were large ones and small ones, winking and steady ones. There were those that were clustered in dense groups and those that were alone. In the higher sphere, apparently, little notice was taken of the fact that a certain Dr. Fischelson had in his declining days married someone called Black Dobbe. Seen from above even the Great War was nothing but a temporary play of the modes. The myriads of fixed stars continued to travel their destined courses in unbounded space. The comets, planets, satellites, asteroids kept circling these shining centers. Worlds were born and died in cosmic upheavals. In the chaos of nebulae, primeval matter was being formed. Now and again a star tore loose, and swept across the sky, leaving behind it a fiery streak. It was the month of August when there were showers of meteors. Yes, the divine substance was extended and had neither beginning nor end; it was absolute, indivisible, eternal, without duration, infinite in its attributes. Its waves and bubbles danced in the universal cauldron, seething with change, following the unbroken chain of causes and effects, and he, Dr. Fischelson, with his unavoidable fate, was part of this. The doctor closed his eyelids and allowed the breeze to cool the sweat on his forehead and stir the hair of his beard. He breathed deeply of the midnight air, supported his shaky hands on the windowsill and murmured, "Divine Spinoza, forgive me. I have become a fool."   [1961]

JANE SMILEY (b. 1949) was born in Los Angeles and educated at Vassar College and the University of Iowa, where she earned her doctorate in 1978. The author of several books of fiction, she published her first novel, Barn Blind, in 1980. In 1987 appeared her first collection of short fiction, The Age of Grief, which included the story "Long Distance." Smiley's novel about the rural midwest, A Thousand Acres, won the 1991 National Book Critics Circle Award and a Pulitzer Prize.

Primarily regarding herself as a novelist, Smiley told interviewer Suzanne Berne that she thought of the short story as "a couple of separate ideas coming into juxtaposition with one another . . . it's akin to having three or four interesting objects on your desk and you move them around until you can see some relationship among them." In most of her fiction she explores the theme of familial relationships, sometimes writing from a male family member's point of view, as in "Long Distance."

Smiley is fascinated with the subject of the family because she feels that

> what has happened in the twentieth century is that all the forms of systematic thought about society and culture have failed. They have proved themselves to be brutal and ineffective. Right now writers are trying to come up with some other system for thinking about individuals as social beings and society as formed of individuals. Clearly the immediate form between the individual and society is the family.

As an eloquent chronicler of family love who has thought long and hard on her subject, Smiley believes that its mainspring is "discipline. A way of maintaining order, for the sake of others, for the future." She is currently a professor of English at Iowa State University.

RELATED COMMENTARY: Jane Smiley, "Gregor: My Life as a Bug," page 1495.

JANE SMILEY

Long Distance

Kirby Christianson is standing under the shower, fiddling with the hot-water spigot and thinking four apparently simultaneous thoughts: that there is never enough hot water in this apartment, that there was always plenty of hot water in Japan, that Mieko will be here in four days, and that he is unable to control Mieko's expectations of him in any way. The thoughts of Mieko are accompanied by a feeling of anxiety as strong as the sensation of the hot water, and he would like the water to flow through him and wash it away. He turns from the shower head and bends backward, so that the stream can pour over his face.

When he shuts off the shower, the phone is ringing. A sense that it has been ringing for a long time — can a mechanical noise have a quality of desperation? — propels him naked and dripping into the living room. He picks up the phone and his caller, as he has suspected, is Mieko. Perhaps he is psychic; perhaps this is only a coincidence; or perhaps no one else has called him in the past week or so.

The connection has a crystalline clarity that tricks him into not allowing for the satellite delay. He is already annoyed after the first hello. Mieko's voice is sharp, high, very Japanese, although she speaks superb English. He says, "Hello, Mieko," and he *sounds* annoyed, as if she calls him too much, although she has only called once to give him her airline information and once to change it. Uncannily attuned to the nuances of his voice, she says, "Oh, Kirby," and falls silent.

Now there will be a flurry of tedious apologies, on both sides. He is tempted to hang up on her, call her back, and blame his telephone — faulty American technology. But he can't be certain that she is at home. So he says, "Hello, Mieko? Hello, Mieko? Hello, Mieko?" more and more loudly, as if her voice were fading. His strategy works. She shouts, "Can you hear me, Kirby? I can hear you, Kirby."

He holds the phone away from his ear. He says, "That's better. Yes, I can hear you now."

"Kirby, I cannot come. I cannot go through with my plan. My father has lung cancer, we learned this morning."

He has never met the father, has seen the mother and the sister only from a distance, at a department store.

"Can you hear me, Kirby?"

"Yes, Mieko. I don't know what to say."

"You don't have to say anything. I have said to my mother that I am happy to stay with her. She is considerably relieved."

"Can you come later, in the spring?"

"My lie was that this Melville seminar I was supposed to attend would be offered just this one time, which was why I had to go now."

"I'm sorry."

"I know that I am only giving up pleasure. I know that my father might die."

As she says this, Kirby is looking out his front window at the snowy roof of the house across the street, and he understands at once from the hopeless tone of her voice that to give up the pleasure that Mieko has promised herself is harder than to die. He understands that in his whole life he has never given up a pleasure that he cherished as much as Mieko cherished this one. He understands that in a just universe the father would rather die alone than steal such a pleasure from his daughter. All these thoughts occur simultaneously and are accompanied by a lifting of the anxiety he felt in the shower. She isn't coming. She is never coming. He is off the hook. He says, "But it's hard for you to give it up, Mieko. It is for me, too. I'm sorry."

The sympathetic tones in his voice wreck her self-control, and she begins to weep. In the five months that Kirby knew Mieko in Japan, and in the calls between them since, she has never shed a tear, hardly ever let herself be caught in a low moment, but now she weeps with absolute abandon, in long, heaving sobs, saying, "Oh, oh, oh," every so often. Once, the sounds fade, as if she has put down the phone, but he does not dare hang up, does not even dare move the phone from one ear to the other. This attentive listening is what he owes to her grief, isn't it? If she had come and he had disappointed her, as he would have, this is how she would have wept in solitude after swallowing her disappointment in front of him. But this is her father's doing, not his. He can give her a little company after all. He presses the phone so hard to his ear that it hurts. The weeping goes on for a long time and he is afraid to speak and interfere with what will certainly be her only opportunity to give way to her feelings. She gives one final wailing "Ohhh" and then begins to cough and choke. Finally she quiets, and then sighs. After a moment of silence, she says, "Kirby, you should not have listened."

"How could I hang up?"

"A Japanese man would have."

"You sound better, if you are back to comparing me with Japanese men."

"I am going to hang up now, Kirby. I am sorry not to come. Good-bye."

"Don't hang up."

"Good-bye."

"Mieko?"

"Good-bye, Kirby."

"Call me! Call me again!" He is not sure that she hears him. He looks at the phone and then puts it on the cradle.

Two hours later he is on the highway. This is, after all, two days before Christmas, and he is on his way to spend the holidays with his two brothers and their wives and children, whom he hasn't seen in years. He has thought little about this visit, beyond buying a few presents. Mieko's coming loomed, imposing and problematic. They had planned to drive out west together — she paid an extra fare so that she could land in Minneapolis and return from San Francisco — and he had looked forward to seeing the mountains again. They had made reservations on a bus that carries tourists into Yellowstone National Park in the winter, to look at the smoky geysers and the wildlife and the snow. The trip would have seemed very American to her. Buffalo and men in cowboy boots and hats. But it seemed very Japanese to him — deep snow, dark pines, sharp mountains.

The storm rolls in suddenly, the way it sometimes does on I-35 in Iowa, startling him out of every thought except alertness. Snow swirls everywhere, blotting out the road, the other cars, sometimes even his own front end. The white of his headlights reflects back to him, so that he seems to be driving into a wall. He can hardly force himself to maintain thirty-five miles an hour, although he knows he must. To stop would be to invite a rear-end collision. And the shoulder of the road is invisible. Only the white line, just beside the left front corner of the car, reveals itself intermittently as the wind blows the snow off the pavement. He ejects the tape he is playing and turns on the radio, to the state weather station. He notices that his hand is shaking. He could be killed. The utter blankness of the snowy whirl gives him a way of imagining what it would be like to be dead. He doesn't like the feeling.

He remembers reading two winters ago about an elderly woman whose son dropped her off at her apartment. She discovered that she had forgotten her key, and with the wind-chill factor at eighty below zero, she froze before she got to the manager's office. The winter before that a kid who broke his legs in a snowmobile accident crawled three miles to the nearest farmhouse, no gloves, only a feed cap on his head.

Twenty below, thirty below — the papers always make a big deal of the temperature. Including wind chill, seventy, a hundred below. Kirby carries a flashlight, a down sleeping bag, a sweat shirt that reads UNIVERSITY OF NEBRASKA, gloves and mittens. His car has new tires, front-wheel drive, and plenty of antifreeze. He has a thermos of coffee. But the horror stories roll through his mind anyway. A family without boots or mittens struggles two miles to a McDonald's through high winds, blowing snow, thirty below. *Why would they travel in that weather?* Kirby always thinks when he reads the papers, but of course they do. He does. Always has.

A gust takes the car, just for a second, and Kirby grips the wheel more tightly. The same gust twists the enveloping snow aloft and reveals the Clear Lake rest stop. Kirby is tempted to stop, tempted not to. He has, after all, never died before, and he has driven through worse than this. He passes the rest stop. Lots of cars are huddled there; but then, lots of cars are still on the highway. Maybe the storm is letting up.

As soon as he is past the rest stop, he thinks of Mieko, her weeping. She might never weep like that again, even if she heard of his death. The connection in her mind between the two of them, the connection that she allowed to stretch into the future despite all his admonitions and all her resolutions, is broken now. Her weeping has the sound of its breaking. And if he died here, in the next ten minutes, how would she learn of it? His brothers wouldn't contact her, not even if she were still coming, because they didn't know she had planned to come. And if she were ever to call him back, she would get only a disconnect message and would assume that he had moved. He can think of no way that she could hear of his death, even though no one would care more than she would. These thoughts fill him with self-pity, but at least they drive out the catalogue of horror: station wagon skids into bridge abutment, two people killed, two paralyzed from the neck down, mother survives unharmed, walks to nearby farmhouse. Kirby weighs the boredom and good fellowship he will encounter sitting out the storm at a truck stop against possible tragedy. Fewer cars are on the road, more are scattered on the median strip. Inertia carries him onward. He is almost to Minnesota, after all, where they really know how to take care of the roads. He will stop at the tourist center and ask about conditions.

But he drives past the tourist center by mistake, lost in thought. He decides to stop in Faribault. But by then the snow seems to be tapering off.

Considering the distance he has traveled, Minneapolis isn't far now. He checks the odometer. Only fifty miles or so. An hour and a half away, at this speed. His mind eases over the numbers with customary superhighway confidence, but at once he imagines himself reduced to walking, walking in this storm, with only a flashlight, a thermos of coffee, a University of Nebraska sweat shirt — and the distance swells to infinity. Were he reduced to his own body, his own power, it might be too far to walk just to find a telephone.

For comfort he calls up images of Japan and southern China, something he often does. These images are the one tangible gift of his travels. So many human eyes have looked upon every scene there for so many eons that every sight has an arranged quality: a flowering branch in the foreground, a precipitous mountainside in the background, a small bridge between. A path, with two women in red kimonos, that winds up a hillside. A white room with pearly rice-paper walls and a futon on the mat-covered floor, branches of cherry blossoms in a vase in the corner. They seem like postcards, but they are scenes he has actually looked upon: on a three-day trip out of Hong Kong into southern China, with some other teachers from his school on a trip to Kyoto, and at Akira's house. Akira was a fellow teacher at his school who befriended him. His house had four rooms, two Japanese style and two Western style.

He remembers, of course, other scenes of Japan — acres of buses, faces staring at his Westernness, the polite but bored rows of students in his classroom — when he is trying to decide whether to go back there. But these are not fixed, have no power; they are just memories, like memories of bars in Lincoln or the pig houses on his grandfather's farm.

And so, he survives the storm. He pulls into the driveway of Harold's new house, one he has not seen, though it is in a neighborhood he remembers from junior high school. The storm is over. Harold has his snowblower out and is making a path from the driveway to his front door. With the noise and because his back is turned, he is unaware of Kirby's arrival. Kirby stops the car, stretches, and looks at his watch. Seven hours for a four-hour trip. Kirby lifts his shoulders and rotates his head, but does not beep his horn just yet. The fact is that he has frightened himself with the blinding snow, the miles of slick and featureless landscape, thoughts of Japan, and the thousands and thousands of miles between here and there. His car might be a marble that has rolled, only by luck, into a safe corner. He presses his fingers against his eyes and stills his breathing.

Harold turns around, grins, and shuts off the snowblower. It is a Harold identical to the Harold that Kirby has always known. Same bright snowflake ski hat, same bright ski clothing. Harold has spent his whole life skiing and ski-jumping. His bushy beard grows up to the hollows of his eyes, and when he leans into the car his mustache is, as always, crusted with ice.

"Hey!" he says. He backs away, and Kirby opens the car door.

"Made it!" Kirby says. That is all he will say about the trip. The last thing he wants to do is start a discussion about near misses. Compared with some of Harold's near misses, this is nothing. In fact, near misses on the highway aren't worth mentioning unless a lot of damage has been done to the car. Kirby knows of near misses that Harold has never dared to describe to anyone besides him, because they show a pure stupidity that even Harold has the sense to be ashamed of.

At dinner, over sweet and savory Nordic fare that Kirby is used to but doesn't much like, the people around the table, his relatives, waver in the smoky candlelight, and Kirby imagines that he can feel the heat of the flames on his face. The other people at the table seem unfamiliar. Leanne, Harold's wife, he has seen only once, at their wedding. She is handsome and self-possessed-looking, but she sits at the corner of the table, like a guest in her own house. Eric sits at the head, and Mary Beth, his wife, jumps up and down to replenish the food. This assumption of primogeniture is a peculiarity of Eric's that has always annoyed Kirby, but even aside from that they have never gotten along. Eric does his best — earnest handshake and smile each time they meet, two newsy letters every year, pictures of the children (known between Harold and Kirby as "the little victims"). Eric has a Ph.D. from Columbia in American history, but he does not teach. He writes for a conservative think tank, articles that appear on the op-ed pages of newspapers and in the think tank's own publications. He specializes in "the family." Kirby and Harold have made countless jokes at Eric's expense. Kirby knows that more will be made this trip, if only in the form of conspiratorial looks, rolling eyes. Eric's hobby — Mary Beth's, too, for they share everything — is developing each nuance of his Norwegian heritage into a fully realized ostentation. Mary Beth is always busy, usually baking. That's all Kirby knows about her, and all he cares to know.

Across the table Anna, their older daughter, pale, blue-eyed, cool, seems to be staring at him, but Kirby can hardly see her. He is thinking about Mieko. Kirby looks at his watch. It is very early morning in Osaka. She is probably about to wake up. Her disappointment will have receded hardly a particle, will suck her down as soon as she thuds into consciousness. "Oh, oh, oh": he can hear her cries as clearly as if they were still vibrating in the air. He is amazed at having heard such a thing, and he looks carefully at the women around the table. Mieko would be too eager to please here, always looking after Mary Beth and Leanne, trying to divine how she might be helpful. Finally, Mary Beth would speak to her with just a hint of sharpness, and Mieko would be crushed. Her eyes would seek Kirby's for reassurance, and he would have none to give. She would be too little, smaller even than Anna, and her voice would be too high and quick. These thoughts give him such pain that he stares for relief at Kristin, Eric's youngest, age three, who is humming over her dinner. She is round-faced and paunchy, with dark hair cut straight across her forehead and straight around her collar. From time to time she and Leanne exchange merry glances.

Harold is beside him; that, at least, is familiar and good, and it touches Kirby with a pleasant sense of expectation, as if Harold, at any moment, might pass him a comic book or a stick of gum. In fact, Harold does pass him something — an icy cold beer, which cuts the sweetness of the food and seems to adjust all the figures around the table so that they stop wavering.

Of course his eyes open well before daylight, but he dares not move. He is sharing a room with Harold the younger, Eric's son, whose bed is between his and the door. He worries that if he gets up he will stumble around and crash into walls and wake Harold. The digits on the clock beside Harold's bed read 5:37, but when Kirby is quiet he can hear movement elsewhere in the house. When he closes his eyes the footsteps present themselves as a needle and thread, stitching a line through his thoughts. He has just been driving. His arms ache from gripping the wheel. The car slides diagonally across the road, toward the median. It slides and slides, through streams of cars, toward a familiar exit, the Marshalltown exit, off to the left, upward. His eyes open again. The door of the room is open, and Anna is looking in. After a moment she turns and goes away. It is 6:02. Sometime later Leanne passes with Isaac, the baby, in her arms.

Kirby cannot bear to get up and face his brothers and their families. As always, despair presents itself aesthetically. The image of Harold and Leanne's living room, matching plaid wing chairs and couch, a triple row of wooden pegs by the maple front door, seems to Kirby the image of the interior of a coffin. The idea of spending five years, ten years, a lifetime, with such furniture makes him gasp. But his own apartment, armchair facing the television, which sits on a spindly coffee table, is worse. Mary Beth and Eric's place, where he has been twice, is the worst, because it's pretentious; they have antique wooden trunks and high-backed benches painted blue with stenciled flowers in red and white. Everything, everything, they own is blue and white, or white with blue, and Nordic primitive. Now even the Japanese images he calls up are painful. The pearly white Japanese-style room in Akira's house was bitterly cold in the winter, and he spent one night there only half-sleeping, his thighs drawn to his chest, the perimeters of the bed too cold even to touch. His head throbbing, Kirby lies pinned to the bed by impossibility. He literally can't summon up a room, a stick of furniture, that he can bear to think of. Harold the younger rolls over and groans, turning his twelve-year-old face toward Kirby's. His mouth opens and he breathes noisily. It is 6:27.

At breakfast, Leanne sets a bowl of raisin bran before him, and he is struck by the elasticity of her motion. She smiles, so cool and kind that Kirby is suddenly daunted. Ten minutes later, when Anna enters the kitchen in her bathrobe, yawning, he recalls, suddenly, her appearance in the doorway to his room. Fifth grade. Only fifth grade. He can see that now, but the night before, and in the predawn darkness, she had seemed older, more threatening, the way girls get at fourteen and fifteen. "Cereal, sweetie?" Leanne says, and Anna nods, scratching. She sits down without a word and focuses on the back of the Cheerios box. Kirby decides that he was dreaming and puts the incident out of his mind; but, "sweetie" — he would like for Leanne to call him that.

Harold, of course, is at his store, managing the Christmas rush, and the house is less festive in his absence. Eric has sequestered himself in Leanne's sewing room, with his computer, and as soon as Anna stands up from breakfast, Mary Beth begins to arrange the day's kitchen schedule. Kirby rinses his cup and goes into the living room. It is nine in the morning, and the day stretches before him, empty. He walks through the plaid living room to the window, where he regards the outdoor thermometer. It reads four degrees below zero. Moments later it is five degrees below zero. Moments after that he is standing beside Harold's bar, pouring himself a glass of bourbon. He has already drunk it when Anna appears in the doorway, dressed now, and staring at him again. She makes him think of Mieko again — though the child is blond and self-contained, she is Mieko's size. Last evening, when he was thinking of Mieko, he was looking at Anna. He says, attempting jovial warmth, "Good morning, Anna. Why do you keep staring at me?"

She is startled. "I don't. I was looking at the bookshelves."

"But you stared at me last night, at dinner. And you came to the door of my room early this morning. I know because I was awake."

"No, I didn't." But then she softens, and says with eager curiosity, "Are you a socialist?"

While Kirby is trying not to laugh, he hears Mary Beth sing from the kitchen. "Anna? Your brother is going sledding. You want to go?"

Anna turns away before Kirby can answer and mounts the stairs. A "No!" floats, glassy and definite, from the second floor.

Kirby sits down in one of the plaid armchairs the gazes at an arrangement of greenery and shiny red balls and candles that sits on a table behind the couch. He gazes and gazes, contemplating the notion of Eric and Mary Beth discussing his politics and his life. He is offended. He knows that if he were to get up and do something he would stop being offended, but he gets up only to pour himself another drink. It is nearly ten. Books are around everywhere, and Kirby picks one up.

People keep opening doors and coming in, having been elsewhere. Harold comes home for lunch, Leanne and Isaac return from the grocery store and the hardware store, Harold the younger stomps in, covered with snow from sledding, eats a sandwich, and stomps out again. Eric opens the study door, takes a turn through the house, goes back into the study again. He does this three times, each time failing to speak to Kirby, who is sitting quietly. Perhaps he does not see him. He is an old man, Kirby thinks, and his ass has spread considerably in the past four years; he is thirty-six going on fifty-round-shouldered, wearing slacks rather than jeans. What a jerk.

But then Kirby's bad mood twists into him, and he lets his head drop on the back of his chair. What is a man? Kirby thinks. What is a man, what is a man? It is someone, Eric would say, who votes, owns property, has a wife, worries. It is someone, Harold would say, who can chop wood all day and fuck all night, who can lift his twenty-five-pound son above his head on the palm of his hand.

After lunch the men have all vanished again, even Isaac, who is taking a nap. In various rooms the women do things. They make no noise. Harold's house is the house of a wealthy man, Kirby realizes. It is large enough to be silent and neat most of the time, the sort of house Kirby will never own. It is Harold and Eric who are alike now. Only Kirby's being does not extend past his fingertips and toes to family, real estate, reputation.

Sometime in the afternoon, when Kirby is still sitting quietly and his part of the room is shadowed by the movement of the sun to the other side of the house, Kristin comes in from the kitchen, goes straight to the sofa, pulls off one of the cushions, and begins to jump repeatedly from the cushion to the floor. When he says, "Kristen, what are you doing?" she is not startled. She says, "Jumping."

"Do you like to jump?"

She says, "It's a beautiful thing to do," in her matter-of-fact, deep, three-year-old voice. Kirby can't believe she knows what she is saying. She jumps three or four more times and then runs out again.

At dinner she is tired and tiresome. When Eric tells her to eat a bite of her meat (ham cooked with apricots), she looks him right in the face and says, "No."

"One bite," he says. "I mean it."

"No. I mean it." She looks up at him. He puts his napkin on the table and pushes back his chair. In a moment he has swept her through the doorway and up the stairs. She is screaming. A door slams and the screaming is muffled. When he comes down and seats himself, carefully laying his napkin over his slacks, Anna says, "It's her body."

The table quiets. Eric says, "What?"

"It's her body."

"What does that mean?"

"She should have control over her own body. Food. Other stuff. I don't know." She has started strong but weakens in the face of her father's glare. Eric inhales sharply, and Kirby cannot restrain himself. He says, "How can you disagree with that? It sounds self-evident to me."

"Does it? The child is three years old. How can she have control over her own body when she doesn't know anything about it? Does she go out without a coat if it's twenty below zero? Does she eat only cookies for three days? Does she wear a diaper until she's five? This is one of those phrases they are using these days. They all mean the same thing."

"What do they mean?" As Kirby speaks, Leanne and Mary Beth look up, no doubt wishing that he had a wife or a girl friend here to restrain him. Harold looks up, too. He is grinning.

Eric shifts in his chair, uncomfortable, Kirby suddenly realizes, at being predictably stuffy once again. Eric says, "It's Christmas. Let's enjoy it."

Harold says, "Principles are principles, any day of the year."

Eric takes the bait and lets himself say, "The family is constituted for a purpose, which is the sometimes difficult socialization of children. For a certain period of their lives others control them. In early childhood others control their bodies. They are taught to control themselves. Even Freud says that the young barbarian has to be taught to relinquish his feces, sometimes by force."

"Good Lord, Eric," Leanne says.

Eric is red in the face. "Authority is a principle I believe in." He looks around the table and then at Anna, openly angry that she has gotten him into this. Across Anna's face flits a look that Kirby has seen before, has seen on Mieko's face, a combination of self-doubt and resentment molded into composure.

"Patriarchy is what you mean," Kirby says, realizing from the tone of his own voice that rage has replaced sympathy and, moreover, is about to get the better of him.

"Why not? It works."

"For some people, at a great cost. Why should daughters be sacrificed to the whims of the father?" He should stop now. He doesn't. "Just because he put his dick somewhere once or twice." The result of too many bourbons too early in the day.

"In my opinion —" Eric seems not to notice the vulgarity, but Harold, beside Kirby, snorts with pleasure.

"I don't want to talk about this," Leanne says. Kirby blushes and falls silent, knowing that he has offended her. It is one of those long holiday meals, and by the time they get up from the table, Kirby feels as if he has been sitting in a dim, candlelit corner most of his life.

There is another ritual — the Christmas Eve unwrapping of presents — and by that time Kirby realizes that he is actively intoxicated and had better watch his tone of voice and his movements. Anna hands out the gifts with a kind of rude bashfulness, and Kirby is surprised at the richness of the array: from Harold he has gotten a cotton turtleneck and a wool sweater, in bright, stylish colors; from Leanne a pair of very fancy gloves; from Isaac three pairs of Ragg wool socks; from Eric's family, as a group, a blue terry-cloth robe and sheepskin slippers. When they open his gifts, he is curious to see what the wrappings reveal: he has bought it all so long before. Almost everything is some gadget available in Japan but not yet in the States. Everyone peers and oohs and aahs. It gives Kirby a headache and a sense of his eyeballs expanding and contracting. Tomorrow night he will be on his way home again, and though he cannot bear to stay here, after all, he cannot bear to leave either.

He drifts toward the stairs, intending to go to bed, but Harold looms before him, grinning and commanding. "Your brain needs some oxygen, brother," he says. Then they are putting on their parkas, and then they are outside, in a cold so sharp that Kirby's nose, the only exposed part of him, stings. Harold strides down the driveway, slightly ahead of him, and Kirby expects him to speak, either for or against Eric, but he doesn't. He only walks. The deep snow is so solidly frozen that it squeaks beneath their boots. The only thing Harold says the whole time they are walking is, "Twenty-two below, not counting the wind chill. Feels good, doesn't it?"

"Feels dangerous," Kirby says.

"It is," Harold says.

The neighborhood is brightly decorated, and the colored lights have their effect on Kirby. For the first time in three Christmases he feels a touch of the mystery that he thinks of as the Christmas spirit. Or maybe it is love for Harold.

Back at the house, everyone has gone to bed except Leanne and Mary Beth, who are drying dishes and putting them away. They are also, Kirby realizes — after Harold strides through the kitchen and up the stairs — arguing, although with smiles and in polite tones. Kirby goes to a cabinet and lingers over getting himself a glass for milk. Mary Beth says, "Kristen will make the connection. She's old enough."

"I can't believe that."

"She saw all the presents being handed out and unwrapped. And Anna will certainly make the connection."

"Anna surely doesn't believe in Santa Claus anymore."

"Unofficially, probably not."

"It's Isaac's first Christmas," Leanne says. "He'll like all the wrappings."

"I wish you'd thought of that before you wrapped the family presents and his Santa presents in the same paper."

"That's a point, too. They're his presents. I don't think Kristin will notice them."

"If they're the only wrapped presents, she will. She notices everything."

Now Leanne turns and gazes at Mary Beth, her hands on her hips. A long silence follows. Leanne flicks a glance at Kirby, who pretends not to notice. Finally she says, "All right, Mary Beth. I'll unwrap them."

"Thank you," Mary Beth says. "I'll finish this, if you want." Kirby goes out of the kitchen and up to his bedroom. The light is already off, and Harold the younger is on his back, snoring.

When he gets up an hour later, too drunk to sleep, Kirby sees Leanne arranging the last of Santa's gifts under the tree. She turns the flash of her glance upon him as he passes through the living room to the kitchen. "Mmm," he says, uncomfortable, "can't sleep."

"Want some cocoa? I always make some before I go to bed."

He stops. "Yeah. Why not? Am I mistaken, or have you been up since about six a.m.?"

"About that. But I'm always wired at midnight, no matter what."

He follows her into the kitchen, remembering now that they have never conversed and wishing that he had stayed in bed. He has drunk himself stupid. Whatever words he has in him have to be summoned from very far down. He sits at the table. After a minute he puts his chin in his hand. After a long, blank, rather pleasant time, the cocoa is before him, marshmallow and all. He looks at it. When Leanne speaks, Kirby is startled, as if he had forgotten that she was there.

"Tired?" she says.

"Too much to drink."

"I noticed."

"I don't have anything more to say about it."

"I'm not asking."

He takes a sip of his cocoa. He says, "Do you all see much of Eric and family?"

"They came last Christmas. He came by himself in the summer. To a conference on the future of the family."

"And so you have to put up with him, right?"

"Harold has a three-day limit. I don't care."

"I noticed you unwrapped all Isaac's presents."

She shrugs, picks at the sole of her boot. She yawns without covering her mouth, and then says, "Oh, I'm sorry." She smiles warmly, looking right at him. "I am crazy about Kristin. Crazy enough to not chance messing up Christmas for her."

"Today she told me that jumping off a cushion was a beautiful thing to do."

Leanne smiles. "Yesterday she said that it was wonderful of me to give her a napkin. You know, I don't agree with Eric about that body stuff. I think they naturally do what is healthy for them. Somebody did an experiment with one-year-olds, gave them a range of foods to choose from, and they always chose a balanced diet. They also want to be toilet trained sooner or later. I think it's weird the way Eric thinks that every little thing is learned rather than realized."

"That's a nice phrase." He turns his cup handle so that it points away and then back in his direction. Finally he says, "Can I tell you about something?"

"Sure."

"Yesterday a friend of mine called me from Japan, a woman, to say that she couldn't come visit me. Her father has cancer. She had planned to arrive here the day after tomorrow, and we were going to take a trip out west. It isn't important, exactly. I don't know."

Leanne is silent but attentive, picking at the sole of her boot. Now that he has mentioned it, the memory of Mieko's anguish returns to him like a glaring light or a thundering noise, so enormous that he is nearly robbed of the power to speak. He pushes it out. "She can't come now, ever. She probably won't ever call or write me again. And really, this has saved her. She had all sorts of expectations that I couldn't have . . . well, wouldn't have fulfilled, and if she had come she would have been permanently compromised."

"Did you have some kind of affair when you were there?"

"For a few months. She's very pretty. I think she's the prettiest woman I've ever seen. She teaches mathematics at the school where I was teaching. After I had been with Mieko for a few weeks, I realized that no one, maybe in her whole adult life, had asked her how she was, or had put his arm around her shoulders, or had taken care of her in any way. The slightest affection was like a drug she couldn't get enough of."

"What did you feel?"

"I liked her. I really did. I was happy to see her when she came by. But she longed for me more than I have ever longed for anything."

"You were glad to leave."

"I was glad to leave."

"So what's the problem?"

"When she called yesterday, she broke down completely. I listened. I thought it was the least I could do, but now I think that she is compromised. Japanese people are very private. It scares me how much I must have embarrassed her. I look back on the spring and the summer and yesterday's call, and I see that, one by one, I broke down every single one of her strengths, everything she had equipped herself with to live in a Japanese way. I was so careful for a year and a half. I didn't date Japanese women, and I was very distant — but when I was so lonely, and she was so pretty, and I thought, well, she's twenty-seven, and she lives in this sophisticated city, Osaka. But mostly I was lonely."

Leanne gazes across the table in that way of hers, calm and considering. Finally she says, "Eric comes in for a lot of criticism around here. His style's all wrong, for one thing. And he drives Harold the younger and Anna crazy. But I've noticed something about him. He never tries to get something for nothing. I admire that."

Now Kirby looks around the room, at the plants on the windowsill, the hoarfrost on the windowpanes, the fluorescent light harsh on the stainless-steel sink, and it seems to him that all at once, now that he realizes it, his life and Mieko's have taken their final form. She is nearly too old to marry, and by the end of her father's cancer and his life she will be much too old. And himself. Himself. Leanne's cool remark has revealed his permanent smallness. He looks at his hands, first his knuckles, then his palms. He says, "It seems so dramatic to say that I will never get over this."

"Does it? To me it seems like saying that what people do is important." And though he looks at her intently, seeking some sort of pardon, she says nothing more, only picks at her boot for a moment or two, and then gets up and puts their cups in the sink. He follows her out of the kitchen, through the living room. She turns out all the lights, so that the house is utterly dark. At the bottom of the stairs, unable to see anything, he stumbles and puts his hand on her arm. She takes it, in a grasp that is dry and cool, and guides it to the banister. Then, soft and fleeting, he feels a disembodied kiss on his cheek.   [1987]

SUSAN SONTAG *(b. 1933), cultural critic and woman of letters, was born in New York City, earned her undergraduate degree at the University of California at Berkeley and the University of Chicago, and received her graduate degrees in English and philosophy from Harvard University. She taught in various colleges until the mid-1960s, when she began to write full-time. The collection* Against Interpretation and Other Essays *(1966), especially the article "Notes on Camp," which defends "camp" art as a legitimate form because "there exists a good taste of bad taste," established her reputation.* Illness as Metaphor *(1978) develops the argument that society uses physical illnesses such as tuberculosis and cancer to project a sense of its own inadequacies and irrational fears. Sontag wrote this book after her own successful bout with cancer.* Styles of Radical Will *(1969),* On Photography *(1977), and* A Susan Sontag Reader *(1982) helped strengthen her reputation, as the critic Hilton Kramer has written, for possessing "an unfailing faculty for dividing intellectual opinion and inspiring a sense of outrage, consternation, and betrayal among the many readers" who disagree with her. In addition to her works of nonfiction, Sontag has published several novels — most recently* The Volcano Lover *(1992) — and screenplays, and a collection of experimental short stories,* I, Etcetera *(1991).*

Sontag's fiction is fueled by her pleasure in using her mind to invent characters and situations. She admits to thinking "that the model of writing as self-expression is much too crude. If I thought that what I'm doing when I write is expressing myself, I'd junk my typewriter. . . . Writing is a much more complicated activity than that." Stories such as "The Way We Live Now" illustrate her belief that "artists are spokesmen of what in our sensibility is changing, and they choose among a number of possible different ways of rendering experience."

Sontag's way of "rendering experience" resulted in one of the first American stories about AIDS, published in the November 24, 1986, issue of The New Yorker *magazine, three years before her book* AIDS and Its Metaphors. *The writer David Leavitt has described his experience of reading "The Way We Live Now" and the strong effect the story had on him.*

RELATED COMMENTARY: *David Leavitt, "The Way I Live Now," page 1447.*

S U S A N   S O N T A G

The Way We Live Now

At first he was just losing weight, he felt only a little ill, Max said to Ellen, and he didn't call for an appointment with his doctor, according to Greg, because he was managing to keep on working at more or less the same rhythm, but he did stop smoking, Tanya pointed out, which suggests he was frightened, but also that he wanted, even more than he knew, to be healthy, or healthier, or maybe just to gain back a few pounds, said Orson, for he told her, Tanya went on, that he expected to be climbing the walls (isn't that what people say?) and found, to his surprise, that he didn't miss cigarettes at all and reveled in the sensation of his lung's being ache-free for the first time in years. But did he have a good doctor, Stephen wanted to know, since it would have been crazy not to go for a checkup after the pressure was off and he was back from the conference in Helsinki, even if by then he was feeling better. And he said, to Frank, that he would go, even though he was indeed frightened, as he admitted to Jan, but who wouldn't be frightened now, though, odd as that might seem, he hadn't been worrying until recently, he avowed to Quentin, it was only in the last six months that he had the metallic taste of panic in his mouth, because becoming seriously ill was something that happened to other people, a normal delusion, he observed to Paolo, if one was thirty-eight and had never had a serious illness; he wasn't, as Jan confirmed, a hypochondriac. Of course, it was hard not to worry, everyone was worried, but it wouldn't do to panic, because, as Max pointed out to Quentin, there wasn't anything one could do except wait and hope, wait and start being careful, be careful, and hope. And even if one did prove to be ill, one shouldn't give up, they had new treatments that promised an arrest of the disease's inexorable course, research was progressing. It seemed that everyone was in touch with everyone else several times a week, checking in, I've never spent so many hours at a time on the phone, Stephen said to Kate, and when I'm exhausted after the two or three calls made to me, giving me the latest, instead of switching off the phone to give myself a respite I tap out the number of another friend or acquaintance, to pass on the news. I'm not sure I can afford to think so much about it, Ellen said, and I suspect my own motives, there's something morbid I'm getting used to, getting excited by, this must be like what people felt in London during the Blitz. As far as I know, I'm not at risk, but you never know, said Aileen. This thing is totally unprecedented, said Frank. But don't you think he ought to see a doctor, Stephen insisted. Listen, said Orson, you can't force people to take care of themselves, and what makes you think the worst, he could be just run down, people still do get ordinary illnesses, awful ones, why are you assuming it has to be that. But all I want to be sure, said Stephen, is that he understands the options, because most people don't, that's why they won't see a doctor or have the test, they think there's nothing one can do. But is there anything one can do, he said to Tanya (according to Greg), I mean what do I gain if I go to the doctor; if I'm really ill, he's reported to have said, I'll find out soon enough.

And when he was in the hospital, his spirits seemed to lighten, according to Donny. He seemed more cheerful than he had been in the last months, Ursula said, and the bad news seemed to come almost as a relief, according to Ira, as a truly unexpected blow, according to Quentin, but you'd hardly expect him to have said the same thing to all his friends, because his relation to Ira was so different from his relation to Quentin (this according to Quentin, who was proud of their friendship), and perhaps he thought Quentin wouldn't be undone by seeing him weep, but Ira insisted that couldn't be the reason he behaved so differently with each, and that maybe he was feeling less shocked, mobilizing his strength to fight for his life, at the moment he saw Ira but overcome by feelings of hopelessness when Quentin arrived with flowers, because anyway the flowers threw him into a bad mood, as Quentin told Kate, since the hospital room was choked with flowers, you couldn't have crammed another flower into that room, but surely you're exaggerating, Kate said, smiling, everybody likes flowers. Well, who wouldn't exaggerate at a time like this, Quentin said sharply. Don't you think this is an exaggeration. Of course I do, said Kate gently, I was only teasing, I mean I didn't mean to tease. I know that, Quentin said, with tears in his eyes, and Kate hugged him and said well, when I go this evening I guess I won't bring flowers, what does he want, and Quentin said, according to Max, what he likes best is chocolate. Is there anything else, asked Kate, I mean like chocolate but not chocolate. Licorice, said Quentin, blowing his nose. And besides that. Aren't you exaggerating now, Quentin said, smiling. Right, said Kate, so if I want to bring him a whole raft of stuff, besides chocolate and licorice, what else. Jelly beans, Quentin said.

He didn't want to be alone, according to Paolo, and lots of people came in the first week, and the Jamaican nurse said there were other patients on the floor who would be glad to have the surplus flowers, and people weren't afraid to visit, it wasn't like the old days, as Kate pointed out to Aileen, they're not even segregated in the hospital anymore, as Hilda observed, there's nothing on the door of his room warning visitors of the possibility of contagion, as there was a few years ago; in fact, he's in a double room and, as he told Orson, the old guy on the far side of the curtain (who's clearly on the way out, said Stephen) doesn't even have the disease, so, as Kate went on, you really should go and see him, he'd be happy to see you, he likes having people visit, you aren't not going because you're afraid, are you. Of course not, Aileen said, but I don't know what to say, I think I'll feel awkward, which he's bound to notice, and that will make him feel worse, so I won't be doing him any good, will I. But he won't notice anything, Kate said, patting Aileen's hand, it's not like that, it's not the way you imagine, he's not judging people or wondering about their motives, he's just happy to see his friends. But I never was really a friend of his, Aileen said, you're a friend, he's always liked you, you told me he talks about Nora with you, I know he likes me, he's even attracted to me, but he respects you. But, according to Wesley, the reason Aileen was so stingy with her visits was that she could never have him to herself, there were always others there already and by the time they left still others had arrived, she'd been in love with him for years, and I can understand, said Donny, that Aileen should feel bitter that if there could have been a woman friend he did more than occasionally bed, a woman he really loved, and my God, Victor said, who had known him in those years, he was crazy about Nora, what a heart-rending couple they were, two surly angels, then it couldn't have been she.

And when some of the friends, the ones who came every day, waylaid the doctor in the corridor, Stephen was the one who asked the most informed questions, who'd been keeping up not just with the stories that appeared several times a week in the *Times* (which Greg confessed to have stopped reading, unable to stand it anymore) but with articles in the medical journals published here and in England and France, and who knew socially one of the principal doctors in Paris who was doing some much-publicized research on the disease, but his doctor said little more than that the pneumonia was not life-threatening, the fever was subsiding, of course he was still weak but he was responding well to the antibiotics, that he'd have to complete his stay in the hospital, which entailed a minimum of twenty-one days on the IV, before she could start him on the new drug, for she was optimistic about the possibility of getting him into the protocol; and when Victor said that if he had so much trouble eating (he'd say to everyone when they coaxed him to eat some of the hospital meals, that food didn't taste right, that he had a funny metallic taste in his mouth) it couldn't be good that friends were bringing him all that chocolate, the doctor just smiled and said that in these cases the patient's morale was also an important factor, and if chocolate made him feel better she saw no harm in it, which worried Stephen, as Stephen said later to Donny, because they wanted to believe in the promises and taboos of today's high-tech medicine but here this reassuringly curt and silver-haired specialist in the disease, someone quoted frequently in the papers, was talking like some oldfangled country GP who tells the family that tea with honey or chicken soup may do as much for the patient as penicillin, which might mean, as Max said, that they were just going through the motions of treating him, that they were not sure about what to do, or rather, as Xavier interjected, that they didn't know what the hell they were doing, that the truth, the real truth, as Hilda said, upping the ante, was that they didn't, the doctors, really have any hope.

   Oh, no, said Lewis, I can't stand it, wait a minute, I can't believe it, are you sure, I mean are they sure, have they done all the tests, it's getting so when the phone rings I'm scared to answer because I think it will be someone telling me someone else is ill; but did Lewis really not know until yesterday, Robert said testily, I find that hard to believe, everybody is talking about it, it seems impossible that someone wouldn't have called Lewis; and perhaps Lewis did know, was for some reason pretending not to know already, because, Jan recalled, didn't Lewis say something months ago to Greg, and not only to Greg, about his not looking well, losing weight, and being worried about him and wishing he'd see a doctor, so it couldn't come as a total surprise. Well, everybody is worried about everybody now, said Betsy, that seems to be the way we live, the way we live now. And, after all, they were once very close, doesn't Lewis still have the keys to his apartment, you know the way you let someone keep the keys after you've broken up, only a little because you hope the person might just saunter in, drunk or high, late some evening, but mainly because it's wise to have a few sets of keys strewn around town, if you live alone, at the top of a former commerical building that, pretentious as it is, will never acquire a doorman or even a resident superintendent, someone whom you can call on for the keys late one night if you find you've lost yours or have locked yourself out. Who else has keys, Tanya inquired, I was thinking somebody might drop by tomorrow before coming to the hospital and bring some treasures, because the other day, Ira said, he was complaining about how dreary the hospital room was, and how it was like being locked up in a motel room, which got everybody started telling funny stories about motel rooms they'd known, and at Ursula's story, about the Luxury Budget Inn in Schenectady, there was an uproar of laughter around his bed, while he watched them in silence, eyes bright with fever, all the while, as Victor recalled, gobbling that damned chocolate. But, according to Jan, whom Lewis's keys enabled to tour the swank of his bachelor lair with an eye to bringing over some art consolation to brighten up the hospital room, the Byzantine icon wasn't on the wall over his bed, and that was a puzzle until Orson remembered that he'd recounted without seeming upset (this disputed by Greg) that the boy he'd recently gotten rid of had stolen it, along with four of the *maki-e* lacquer boxes, as if these were objects as easy to sell on the street as a TV or a stereo. But he's always been very generous, Kate said quietly, and though he loves beautiful things isn't really attached to them, to things, as Orson said, which is unusual in a collector, as Frank commented, and when Kate shuddered and tears sprang to her eyes and Orson inquired anxiously if he, Orson, had said something wrong, she pointed out that they'd begun talking about him in a retrospective mode, summing up what he was like, what made them fond of him, as if he were finished, completed, already a part of the past.

Perhaps he was getting tired of having so many visitors, said Robert, who was, as Ellen couldn't help mentioning, someone who had come only twice and was probably looking for a reason not to be in regular attendance, but there could be no doubt, according to Ursula, that his spirits had dipped, not that there was any discouraging news from the doctors, and he seemed now to prefer being alone a few hours of the day; and he told Donny that he'd begun keeping a diary for the first time in his life, because he wanted to record the course of his mental reactions to this astonishing turn of events, to do something parallel to what the doctors were doing, who came every morning and conferred at his bedside about his body, and that perhaps it wasn't so important what he wrote in it, which amounted, as he said wryly to Quentin, to little more than the usual banalities about terror and amazement that this was happening to him, to him also, plus the usual remorseful assessments of his past life, his pardonable superficialities, capped by resolves to live better, more deeply, more in touch with his work and his friends, and not to care so passionately about what people thought of him, interspersed with admonitions to himself that in this situation his will to live counted more than anything else and that if he really wanted to live, and trusted life, and liked himself well enough (down, ol' debbil Thanatos!), he *would* live, he would be an exception; but perhaps all this, as Quentin ruminated, talking on the phone to Kate, wasn't the point, the point was that by the very keeping of the diary he was accumulating something to reread one day, slyly staking out his claim to a future time, in which the diary would be an object, a relic, in which he might not actually reread it, because he would want to have put this ordeal behind him, but the diary would be there in the drawer of his stupendous Majorelle desk, and he could already, he did actually say to Quentin one late sunny afternoon, propped up in the hospital bed, with the stain of chocolate framing one corner of a heartbreaking smile, see himself in the penthouse, the October sun streaming through those clear windows instead of this streaked one, and the diary, the pathetic diary, safe inside the drawer.

It doesn't matter about the treatment's side effects, Stephen said (when talking to Max), I don't know why you're so worried about that, every strong treatment has some dangerous side effects, it's inevitable, you mean otherwise the treatment wouldn't be effective, Hilda interjected, and anyway, Stephen went on doggedly, just because there *are* side effects it doesn't mean he has to get them, or all of them, each one, or even some of them. That's just a list of all the possible things that could go wrong, because the doctors have to cover themselves, so they make up a worst-case scenario, but isn't what's happening to him, and to so many other people, Tanya interrupted, a worst-case scenario, a catastrophe no one could have imagined, it's too cruel, and isn't everything a side effect, quipped Ira, even *we* are all side effects, but we're not bad side effects, Frank said, he likes having his friends around, and we're helping each other, too; because his illness sticks us all in the same glue, mused Xavier, and, whatever the jealousies and grievances from the past that have made us wary and cranky with each other, when something like this happens (the sky is falling, the sky is falling!) you understand what's really important. I agree, Chicken Little, he is reported to have said. But don't you think, Quentin observed to Max, that being as close to him as we are, making time to drop by the hospital every day, is a way of our trying to define ourselves more firmly and irrevocably as the well, those who aren't ill, who aren't going to fall ill, as if what's happened to him couldn't happen to us, when in fact the chances are that before long one of us will end up where he is, which is probably what he felt when he was one of the cohort visiting Zack in the spring (you never knew Zack, did you?), and, according to Clarice, Zack's widow, he didn't come very often, he said he hated hospitals, and didn't feel he was doing Zack any good, that Zack would see on his face how uncomfortable he was. Oh, he was one of those, Aileen said. A coward. Like me.

And after he was sent home from the hospital, and Quentin had volunteered to move in and was cooking meals and taking telephone messages and keeping the mother in Mississippi informed, well, mainly keeping her from flying to New York and heaping her grief on her son and confusing the household routine with her oppressive ministrations, he was able to work an hour or two in his study, on days he didn't insist on going out, for a meal or a movie, which tired him. He seemed optimistic, Kate thought, his appetite was good, and what he said, Orson reported, was that he agreed when

Stephen advised him that the main thing was to keep in shape, he was a fighter, right, he wouldn't be who he was if he weren't, and was he ready for the big fight, Stephen asked rhetorically (as Max told it to Donny), and he said you bet, and Stephen added it could be a lot worse, you could have gotten the disease two years ago, but now so many scientists are working on it, the American team and the French team, everyone bucking for that Nobel Prize a few years down the road, that all you have to do is stay healthy for another year or two and then there will be good treatment. Yes, he said, Stephen said, my timing is good. And Betsy, who had been climbing on and rolling off macrobiotic diets for a decade, came up with a Japanese specialist she wanted him to see but thank God, Donny reported, he'd had the sense to refuse, but he did agree to see Victor's visualization therapist, although what could one possibly visualize, said Hilda, when the point of visualizing disease was to see it as an entity with contours, borders, here rather than there, something limited, something you were the host of, in the sense that you could disinvite the disease, while this was so total; or would be, Max said. But the main thing, said Greg, was to see that he didn't go the macrobiotic route, which might be harmless for plump Betsy but could only be devastating for him, lean as he'd always been, with all the cigarettes and other appetite-suppressing chemicals he'd been welcoming into his body for years; and now was hardly the time, as Stephen pointed out, to be worried about cleaning up his act, and eliminating the chemical additives and other pollutants that we're all blithely or not so blithely feasting on, blithely since we're healthy, healthy as we can be; so far, Ira said. Meat and potatoes is what I'd be happy to see him eating, Ursula said wistfully. And spaghetti and clam sauce, Greg added. And thick cholesterol-rich omelets with smoked mozzarella, suggested Yvonne, who had flown from London for the weekend to see him. Chocolate cake, said Frank. Maybe not chocolate cake, Ursula said, he's already eating so much chocolate.

And when, not right away but still only three weeks later, he was accepted into the protocol for the new drug, which took considerable behind-the-scenes lobbying with the doctors, he talked less about being ill, according to Donny, which seemed like a good sign, Kate felt, a sign that he was not feeling like a victim, feeling not that he *had* a disease but, rather, was living *with* a disease (that was the right cliché, wasn't it?), a more hospitable arrangement, said Jan, a kind of cohabitation which implied that it was something temporary, that it could be terminated, but terminated how, said Hilda, and when you say hospitable, Jan, I hear hospital. And it was encouraging, Stephen insisted, that from the start, at least from the time he was finally persuaded to make the telephone call to his doctor, he was willing to say the name of the disease, pronounce it often and easily, as if it were just another word, like boy or gallery or cigarette or money or deal, as in no big deal, Paolo interjected, because, as Stephen continued, to utter the name is a sign of health, a sign that one has accepted being who one is, mortal, vulnerable, not exempt, not an exception after all, it's a sign that one is willing, truly willing, to fight for one's life. And we must say the name, too, and often, Tanya added, we mustn't lag behind him in honesty, or let him feel that, the effort of honesty having been made, it's something done with and he can go on to other things. One is so much better prepared to help him, Wesley replied. In a way he's fortunate, said Yvonne, who had taken care of a problem at the New York store and was flying back to London this evening, sure, fortunate, said Wesley, no one is shunning him, Yvonne went on, no one's afraid to hug him or kiss him lightly on the mouth, in London we are, as usual, a few years behind you, people I know, people who would seem to be not even remotely at risk, are just terrified, but I'm impressed by how cool and rational you all are; you find us cool, asked Quentin. But I have to say, he's reported to have said, I'm terrified, I find it very hard to read (and you know how he loves to read, said Greg; yes, reading is his television, said Paolo) or to think, but I don't feel hysterical. I feel quite hysterical, Lewis said to Yvonne. But you're able to *do* something for him, that's wonderful, how I wish I could stay longer, Yvonne answered, it's rather beautiful, I can't help thinking, this utopia of friendship you've assembled around him (this pathetic utopia, said Kate), so that the disease, Yvonne concluded, is not, anymore, out there. Yes, don't you think we're more at home here, with him, with the disease, said Tanya, because the imagined disease is so much worse than the reality of him, whom we all love, each in our fashion, having it. I know for me his getting it has quite demystified the disease, said Jan, I don't feel afraid, spooked, as I did before he became ill, when it was only news about remote acquaintances, whom I never saw again after they became ill. But you know you're not going to come down with the disease, Quentin said, to which Ellen replied, on her behalf, that's not the point, and possibly untrue, my gynecologist says that everyone is at risk, everyone who has a sexual life, because sexuality is a chain that links each of us to many others, unknown others, and now the great chain of being has become a chain of death as well. It's not the same for you, Quentin insisted, it's not the same for you as it is for me or Lewis or Frank or Paolo or Max, I'm more and more frightened, and I have every reason to be. I don't think about whether I'm at risk or not, said Hilda, I know that I was afraid to know someone with the disease, afraid of what I'd see, what I'd feel, and after the first day I came to the hospital I felt so relieved. I'll never feel that way, that fear, again; he doesn't seem different from me. He's not, Quentin said.

According to Lewis, he talked more often about those who visited more often, which is natural, said Betsy, I think he's even keeping a tally. And among those who came or checked in by phone every day, the inner circle as it were, those who were getting more points, there was still a further competition, which was what was getting on Betsy's nerves, she confessed to Jan; there's always that vulgar jockeying for position around the bedside of the gravely ill, and though we all feel suffused with virtue at our loyalty to him (speak for yourself, said Jan), to the extent that we're carving time out of every day, or almost every day, though some of us are dropping out, as Xavier pointed out, aren't we getting at least as much out of this as he is. Are we, said Jan. We're rivals for a sign from him of special pleasure over a visit, each stretching for the brass ring of his favor, wanting to feel the most wanted, the true nearest and dearest, which is inevitable with someone who doesn't have a spouse and children or an official in-house lover, hierarchies that no one would dare contest, Betsy went on, so we are the family he's founded, without meaning to, without official titles and ranks (we, we, snarled Quentin); and is it so clear, though some of us, Lewis and Quentin and Tanya and Paolo, among others, are ex-lovers and all of us more or less than friends, which one of us he prefers, Victor said (now it's us, raged Quentin), because sometimes I think he looks forward more to seeing Aileen, who has visited only three times, twice at the hospital and once since he's been home, than he does you or me; but, according to Tanya, after being very disappointed that Aileen hadn't come, now he was angry, while, according to Xavier, he was not really hurt but touchingly passive, accepting Aileen's absence as something he somehow deserved. But he's happy to have people around, said Lewis; he says when he doesn't have company he gets very sleepy, he sleeps (according to Quentin), and then perks up when someone arrives, it's important that he not feel ever alone. But, said Victor, there's one person he hasn't heard from, whom he'd probably like to hear from more than most of us; but she didn't just vanish, even right after she broke away from him, and he knows exactly where she lives now, said Kate, he told me he put in a call to her last Christmas Eve, and she said it's nice to hear from you and Merry Christmas, and he was shattered, according to Orson, and furious and disdainful, according to Ellen (what do you expect of her, said Wesley, she was burned out), but Kate wondered if maybe he hadn't phoned Nora in the middle of a sleepless night, what's the time difference, and Quentin said no, I don't think so, I think he wouldn't want her to know.

And when he was feeling even better and had regained the pounds he'd shed right away in the hospital, though the refrigerator started to fill up with organic wheat germ and grapefruit and skimmed milk (he's worried about his cholesterol count, Stephen lamented), and told Quentin he could manage by himself now, and did, he started asking everyone who visited how he looked, and everyone said he looked great, so much better than a few weeks ago, which didn't jibe with what anyone had told him at that time; but then it was getting harder and harder to know how he looked, to answer such a question honestly when among themselves they wanted to be honest, both for honesty's sake and (as Donny thought) to prepare for the worst, because he'd been looking like *this* for so long, at least it seemed so long, that it was as if he'd always been like this, how did he look before, but it was only a few months, and those words, pale and wan looking and fragile, hadn't they always applied? And one Thursday Ellen, meeting Lewis at the door of the building, said, as they rode up together in the elevator, how is he *really*? But you see how he is, Lewis said tartly, he's fine, he's perfectly healthy, and Ellen understood that of course Lewis didn't think he was perfectly healthy but that he wasn't worse, and that was true, but wasn't it, well, almost heartless to talk like that. Seems inoffensive to me, Quentin said, but I know what you mean, I remember once talking to Frank, somebody, after all, who has volunteered to do five hours a week of office work at the Crisis Center (I know, said Ellen), and Frank was going on about this guy, diagnosed almost a year ago, and so much further along, who'd been complaining to Frank on the phone about the indifference of some doctor, and had gotten quite abusive about the doctor, and Frank was saying there was no reason to be so upset, the implication being that *he*, Frank, wouldn't behave so irrationally, and I said, barely able to control my scorn, but Frank, Frank, he has every reason to be upset, he's dying, and Frank said, said according to Quentin, oh, I don't like to think about it that way.

And it was while he was still home, recuperating, getting his weekly treatment, still not able to do much work, he complained, but, according to Quentin, up and about most of the time and turning up at the office several days a week, that bad news came about two remote acquaintances, one in Houston and one in Paris, news that was intercepted by Quentin on the ground that it could only depress him, but Stephen contended that it was wrong to lie to him, it was so important for him to live in the truth; that had been one of his first victories, that he was candid, that he was even willing to crack jokes about the disease, but Ellen said it wasn't good to give him this end-of-the-world feeling, too many people were getting ill, it was becoming such a common destiny that maybe some of the will to fight for his life would be drained out of him if it seemed to be as natural as, well, death. Oh, Hilda said, who didn't know personally either the one in Houston or the one in Paris, but knew *of* the one in Paris, a pianist who specialized in twentieth-centurly Czech and Polish music, I have his records, he's such a valuable person, and, when Kate glared at her, continued defensively, I know every life is equally sacred, but that *is* a thought, another thought, I mean, all these valuable people who aren't going to have their normal four score as it is now, these people aren't going to be replaced, and it's such a loss to the culture. But this isn't going to go on forever, Wesley said, it can't, they're bound to come up with something (they, they, muttered Stephen), but did you ever think, Greg said, that if some people don't die, I mean even if they can keep them alive (they, they, muttered Kate), they continue to be carriers, and that means, if you have a conscience, that you can never make love, make love fully, as you'd been wont — wantonly, Ira said — to do. But it's better than dying, said Frank. And in all his talk about the future, when he allowed himself to be hopeful, according to Quentin, he never mentioned the prospect that even if he didn't die, if he were so fortunate as to be among the first generation of the disease's survivors, never mentioned, Kate confirmed, that whatever happened it was over, the way he had lived until now, but, according to Ira, he did think about it, the end of bravado, the end of folly, the end of trusting life, the end of taking life for granted, and of treating life as something that, samurai-like, he thought himself ready to throw away lightly, impudently; and Kate recalled, sighing, a brief exchange she'd insisted on having as long as two years ago, huddling on a banquette covered with steel-gray industrial carpet on an upper level of The Prophet and toking up for their next foray onto the dance floor: she'd said hesitantly, for it felt foolish asking a prince of debauchery to, well, take it easy, and she wasn't keen on playing big sister, a role, as Hilda confirmed, he inspired in many women, are you being careful, honey, you know what I mean. And he replied, Kate went on, no, I'm not, listen, I can't, I just can't, sex is too important to me, always has been (he started talking like that, according to Victor, after Nora left him), and if I get it, well, I get it. But he wouldn't talk like that now, would he, said Greg; he must feel awfully foolish now, said Betsy, like someone who went on smoking, saying I can't give up cigarettes, but when the bad X-ray is taken even the most besotted nicotine addict can stop on a dime. But sex isn't like cigarettes, is it, said Frank, and, besides, what good does it do to remember that he was reckless, said Lewis angrily, the appalling thing is that you just have to be unlucky once, and wouldn't he feel even worse if he'd stopped three years ago and had come down with it anyway, since one of the most terrifying features of the disease is that you don't know when you contracted it, it could have been ten years ago, because surely this disease has existed for years and years, long before it was recognized; that is, named. Who knows how long (I think a lot about that, said Max) and who knows (I know what you're going to say, Stephen interrupted) how many are going to get it.

I'm feeling fine, he's reported to have said whenever someone asked him how he was, which was almost always the first question anyone asked. Or: I'm feeling better, how are you? But he said other things, too, I'm playing leapfrog with myself, he is reported to have said, according to Victor. And: There must be a way to get something positive out of this situation, he's reported to have said to Kate. How American of him, said Paolo. Well, said Betsy, you know the old American adage: When you've got a lemon, make lemonade. The one thing I'm sure I couldn't take, Jan said he said to her, is becoming disfigured, but Stephen hastened to point out the disease doesn't take that form very often anymore, its profile is mutating, and, in conversation with Ellen, wheeled up words like blood-brain barrier; I never thought there was a barrier *there*, said Jan. But he mustn't know about Max, Ellen said, that would really depress him, please don't tell him, he'll have to know, Quentin said grimly, and he'll be furious not to have been told. But there's time for that, when they take Max off the respirator, said Ellen; but isn't it incredible, Frank said, Max was fine, not feeling ill at all, and then to wake up with a fever of a hundred and five, unable to breathe, but that's the way it often starts, with absolutely no warning, Stephen said, the disease has so many forms. And when, after another week had gone by, he asked Quentin where Max was, he didn't question Quentin's account of a spree in the Bahamas, but then the number of people who visited regularly was thinning out, partly because the old feuds that had been put aside through the first hospitalization and the return home had resurfaced, and the flickering enmity between Lewis and Frank exploded, even though Kate did her best to mediate between them, and also because he himself had done something to loosen the bonds of love that united the friends around him, by seeming to take them all for granted, as if it were perfectly normal for so many people to carve out so much time and attention for him, visit him every few days, talk about him incessantly on the phone with each other; but, according to Paolo, it wasn't that he was less grateful, it was just something he was getting used to, the visits. It had become, with time, a more ordinary kind of situation, a kind of ongoing party, first at the hospital and now since he was home, barely on his feet again, it being clear, said Robert, that I'm on the B list; but Kate said, that's absurd, there's no list; and Victor said, but there is, only it's not he, it's Quentin who's drawing it up. He wants to see us, we're helping him, we have to do it the way he wants, he fell down yesterday on the way to the bathroom, he mustn't be told about Max (but he already knew, according to Donny), it's getting worse.

When I was home, he is reported to have said, I was afraid to sleep, as I was dropping off each night it felt like just that, as if I were falling down a black hole, to sleep felt like giving in to death, I slept every night with the light on; but here, in the hospital, I'm less afraid. And to Quentin he said, one morning, the fear rips through me, it tears me open; and, to Ira, it presses me together, squeezes me toward myself. Fear gives everything its hue, its high. I feel so, I don't know how to say it, exalted, he said to Quentin. Calamity is an amazing high, too. Sometimes I feel *so* well, so powerful, it's as if I could jump out of my skin. Am I going crazy, or what? Is it all this attention and coddling I'm getting from everybody, like a child's dream of being loved? Is it the drugs? I know it sounds crazy but sometimes I think this is a *fantastic* experience, he said shyly; but there was also the bad taste in the mouth, the pressure in the head and at the back of the neck, the red, bleeding gums, the painful, if pink-lobed, breathing, and his ivory pallor, color of white chocolate. Among those who wept when told over the phone that he was back in the hospital were Kate and Stephen (who'd been called by Quentin), and Ellen, Victor, Aileen, and Lewis (who were called by Kate), and Xavier and Ursula (who were called by Stephen). Among those who didn't weep were Hilda, who said that she'd just learned that her seventy-five-year-old aunt was dying of the disease, which she'd contracted from a transfusion given during her successful double bypass of five years ago, and Frank and Donny and Betsy, but this didn't mean, according to Tanya, that they weren't moved and appalled, and Quentin thought they might not be coming soon to the hospital but would send presents; the room, he was in a private room this time, was filling up with flowers, and plants, and books, and tapes. The high tide of barely suppressed acrimony of the last weeks at home subsided into the routines of hospital visiting, though more than a few resented Quentin's having charge of the visiting book (but it was Quentin who had the idea, Lewis pointed out); now, to insure a steady stream of visitors, preferably no more than two at a time (this, the rule in all hospitals, wasn't enforced here, at least on this floor; whether out of kindness or inefficiency, no one could decide), Quentin had to be called first, to get one's time slot, there was no more casual dropping by. And his mother could no longer be prevented from taking a plane and installing herself in a hotel near the hospital; but he seemed to mind her daily presence less than expected, Quentin said; said Ellen it's we who mind, do you suppose she'll stay long. It was easier to be generous with each other visiting him here in the hospital, as Donny pointed out, than at home, where one minded never being alone with him; coming here, in our twos and twos, there's no doubt about what our role is, how we should be, collective, funny, distracting, undemanding, light, it's important to be light, for in all this dread there is gaiety, too, as the poet said, said Kate. (His eyes, his glittering eyes, said Lewis.) His eyes looked dull, extinguished, Wesley said to Xavier, but Betsy said his face, not just his eyes, looked soulful, warm; whatever is there, said Kate, I've never been so aware of his eyes; and Stephen said, I'm afraid of what my eyes show, the way I watch him, with too much intensity, or a phony kind of casualness, said Victor. And, unlike at home, he was clean-shaven each morning, at whatever hour they visited him; his curly hair was always combed; but he complained that the nurses had changed since he was here the last time, and that he didn't like the change, he wanted everyone to be the same. The room was furnished now with some of his personal effects (odd word for one's things, said Ellen), and Tanya brought drawings and a letter from her nine-year-old dyslexic son, who was writing now, since she'd purchased a computer; and Donny brought champagne and some helium balloons, which were anchored to the foot of his bed; tell me about something that's going on, he said, waking up from a nap to find Donny and Kate at the side of his bed, beaming at him; tell me a story, he said wistfully, said Donny, who couldn't think of anything to say; *you're* the story, Kate said. And Xavier brought an eighteenth-century Guatemalan wooden statue of Saint Sebastian with upcast eyes and open mouth, and when Tanya said what's that, a tribute to eros past, Xavier said where I come from Sebastian is venerated as a protector against pestilence. Pestilence symbolized by arrows? Symbolized by arrows. All people remember is the body of a beautiful youth bound to a tree, pierced by arrows (of which he always seems oblivious, Tanya interjected), people forget that the story continues, Xavier continued, that when the Christian women came to bury the martyr they found him still alive and nursed him back to health. And he said, according to Stephen, I didn't know Saint Sebastian didn't die. It's undeniable, isn't it, said Kate on the phone to Stephen, the fascination of the dying. It makes me ashamed. We're learning how to die, said Hilda, I'm not ready to learn, said Aileen; and Lewis, who was coming straight from the other hospital, the hospital where Max was still being kept in ICU, met Tanya getting out of the elevator on the tenth floor, and as they walked together down the shiny corridor past the open doors, averting their eyes from the other patients sunk in their beds, with tubes in their noses, irradiated by the bluish light from the television sets, the thing I can't bear to think about, Tanya said to Lewis, is someone dying with the TV on.

He has that strange, unnerving detachment now, said Ellen, that's what upsets me, even though it makes it easier to be with him. Sometimes he was querulous. I can't stand them coming in here taking my blood every morning, what are they doing with all that blood, he is reported to have said; but where was his anger, Jan wondered. Mostly he was lovely to be with, always saying how are *you*, how are you feeling. He's so sweet now, said Aileen. He's so nice, said Tanya. (Nice, nice, groaned Paolo.) At first he was very ill, but he was rallying, according to Stephen's best information, there was no fear of his not recovering this time, and the doctor spoke of his being discharged from the hospital in another ten days if all went well, and the mother was persuaded to fly back to Mississippi, and Quentin was readying the penthouse for his return. And he was still writing his diary, not showing it to anyone, though Tanya, first to arrive one late-winter morning, and finding him dozing, peeked, and was horrified, according to Greg, not by anything she read but by a progressive change in his handwriting: in the recent pages, it was becoming spidery, less legible, and some lines of script wandered and tilted about the page. I was thinking, Ursula said to Quentin, that the difference between a story and a painting or photograph is that in a story you can write, He's still alive. But in a painting or a photo you can't show "still." You can just show him being alive. He's still alive, Stephen said.   [1986]

JOHN STEINBECK (1902–1968) *was born in Salinas and raised near Monterey in the fertile farm country of the Salinas Valley in California, the locale for his story "The Chrysanthemums." His mother was a former schoolteacher; his father was the county treasurer. In high school Steinbeck wrote for the school newspaper and was president of his class. He enjoyed literature from an early age and read novels by Gustave Flaubert, Fyodor Dostoevsky, and Thomas Hardy in the family library. Enrolled at Stanford University as an English major, Steinbeck dropped out before graduating and worked at odd jobs — fruit picker, caretaker, laboratory assistant — while he practiced writing fiction. Several times he took short-term jobs with the Spreckels Sugar Company and gained a perspective on labor problems, which he would later describe in his novels.*

In 1929 Steinbeck began his literary career by publishing Cup of Gold, *a fictionalized biography of Henry Morgan, the seventeenth-century Welsh pirate. His next book,* The Pastures of Heaven *(1932), is a collection of short stories about the people in a farm community in California. The critic Brian Barbour has stated that Steinbeck realized early in his career that the short story form was not congenial to his talents. He needed the more expansive form of the novel to give his characters a chance for what he considered real growth. In 1936 Steinbeck wrote* In Dubious Battle, *his first major political novel. He then published four more novels and another book of short fiction before his greatest work,* The Grapes of Wrath *(1939). This book, about a family from the Dust Bowl who emigrate to California and struggle to make a living despite agricultural exploitation, won Steinbeck the Pulitzer Prize. Among his many other successful novels are* East of Eden *(1952) and* The Winter of Our Discontent *(1961). He received the Nobel Prize for Literature in 1962.*

One of the most accomplished popular novelists in the United States, Steinbeck excelled — as did Ernest Hemingway — in the creation of exciting conflicts, convincing dialogue, and recognizable characters to dramatize his philosophy of life. Although his production of short stories was relatively slight, his work is often anthologized because of his clear, realistic treatment of social themes as his characters struggle to forge meaningful lives. "The Chrysanthemums" echoes the D. H. Lawrence story "Odour of Chrysanthemums" in its concerns with sexual roles and the difficulty of striking a balance between self-interest and the needs of others. Steinbeck's biographer, Jackson J. Benson, also commented that the excellence of "The Chrysanthemums" lies in "its delicate, indirect handling of a woman's emotions . . . [especially] the difficulty of the woman in finding a creative significant role in a male-dominated society."

JOHN STEINBECK

The Chrysanthemums

The high grey-flannel fog of winter closed off the Salinas Valley from the sky and from all the rest of the world. On every side it sat like a lid on the mountains and made of the great valley a closed pot. On the broad, level land floor the gang plows bit deep and left the black earth shining like metal where the shares had cut. On the foothill ranches across the Salinas River, the yellow stubble fields seemed to be bathed in pale cold sunshine, but there was no sunshine in the valley now in December. The thick willow scrub along the river flamed with sharp and positive yellow leaves.

It was a time of quiet and of waiting. The air was cold and tender. A light wind blew up from the southwest so that the farmers were mildly hopeful of a good rain before long; but fog and rain do not go together.

Across the river, on Henry Allen's foothill ranch there was little work to be done, for the hay was cut and stored and the orchards were plowed up to receive the rain deeply when it should come. The cattle on the higher slopes were becoming shaggy and rough-coated.

Elisa Allen, working in her flower garden, looked down across the yard and saw Henry, her husband, talking to two men in business suits. The three of them stood by the tractor shed, each man with one foot on the side of the little Fordson. They smoked cigarettes and studied the machine as they talked.

Elisa watched them for a moment and then went back to her work. She was thirty-five. Her face was lean and strong and her eyes were as clear as water. Her figure looked blocked and heavy in her gardening costume, a man's black hat pulled low down over her eyes, clod-hopper shoes, a figured print dress almost completely covered by a big corduroy apron with four big pockets to hold the snips, the trowel and scratcher, the seeds, and the knife she worked with. She wore heavy leather gloves to protect her hands while she worked.

She was cutting down the old year's chrysanthemum stalks with a pair of short and powerful scissors. She looked down toward the men by the tractor shed now and then. Her face was eager and mature and handsome; even her work with the scissors was overeager, overpowerful. The chrysanthemum stems seemed too small and easy for her energy.

She brushed a cloud of hair out of her eyes with the back of her glove, and left a smudge of earth on her cheek in doing it. Behind her stood the neat white farm house with red geraniums close-banked around it as high as the windows. It was a hard-swept looking little house with hard-polished windows, and a clean mud-mat on the front steps.

Elisa cast another glance toward the tractor shed. The strangers were getting into their Ford coupe. She took off a glove and put her strong fingers down into the forest of new green chrysanthemum sprouts that were growing around the old roots. She spread the leaves and looked down among the close-growing stems. No aphids were there, no sowbugs or snails or cutworms. Her terrier fingers destroyed such pests before they could get started.

Elisa started at the sound of her husband's voice. He had come near quietly, and he leaned over the wire fence that protected her flower garden from cattle and dogs and chickens.

"At it again," he said. "You've got a strong new crop coming."

Elisa straightened her back and pulled on the gardening glove again. "Yes. They'll be strong this coming year." In her tone and on her face there was a little smugness.

"You've got a gift with things," Henry observed. "Some of those yellow chrysanthemums you had this year were ten inches across. I wish you'd work out in the orchard and raise some apples that big."

Her eyes sharpened. "Maybe I could do it, too. I've a gift with things, all right. My mother had it. She could stick anything in the ground and make it grow. She said it was having planters' hands that knew how to do it."

"Well, it sure works with flowers," he said.

"Henry, who were those men you were talking to?"

"Why, sure, that's what I came to tell you. They were from the Western Meat Company. I sold thirty head of three-year-old steers. Got nearly my own price, too."

"Good," she said. "Good for you."

"And I thought," he continued, "I thought how it's Saturday afternoon, and we might go into Salinas for dinner at a restaurant, and then to a picture show — to celebrate, you see."

"Good," she repeated. "Oh, yes. That will be good."

Henry put on his joking tone. "There's fights tonight. How'd you like to go to the fights?"

"Oh, no," she said breathlessly. "No, I wouldn't like fights."

"Just fooling, Elisa. We'll go to a movie. Let's see. It's two now. I'm going to take Scotty and bring down those steers from the hill. It'll take us maybe two hours. We'll go in town about five and have dinner at the Cominos Hotel. Like that?"

"Of course I'll like it. It's good to eat away from home."

"All right, then. I'll go get up a couple of horses."

She said, "I'll have plenty of time to transplant some of these sets, I guess."

She heard her husband calling Scotty down by the barn. And a little later she saw the two men ride up the pale yellow hillside in search of the steers.

There was a little square sandy bed kept for rooting the chrysanthemums. With her trowel she turned the soil over and over, and smoothed it and patted it firm. Then she dug ten parallel trenches to receive the sets. Back at the chrysanthemum bed she pulled out the little crisp shoots, trimmed off the leaves at each one with her scissors, and laid it on a small orderly pile.

A squeak of wheels and plod of hoofs came from the road. Elisa looked up. The country road ran along the dense bank of willows and cottonwoods that bordered the river, and up this road came a curious vehicle, curiously drawn. It was an old spring-wagon, with a round canvas top on it like the corner of a prairie schooner. It was drawn by an old bay horse and a little grey-and-white burro. A big stubble-bearded man sat between the cover flaps and drove the crawling team. Underneath the wagon, between the hind wheels, a lean and rangy mongrel dog walked sedately. Words were painted on the canvas, in clumsy, crooked letters. "Pots, pans, knives, sisors, lawn mores, Fixed." Two rows of articles, and the triumphantly definitive "Fixed" below. The black paint had run down in little sharp points beneath each letter.

Elisa, squatting on the ground, watched to see the crazy, loose-jointed wagon pass by. But it didn't pass. It turned into the farm road in front of her house, crooked old wheels skirling and squeaking. The rangy dog darted from between the wheels and ran ahead. Instantly the two ranch shepherds flew out at him. Then all three stopped, and with stiff and quivering tails, with taut straight legs, with ambassadorial dignity, they slowly circled, sniffing daintily. The caravan pulled up to Elisa's wire fence and stopped. Now the newcomer dog, feeling outnumbered, lowered his tail and retired under the wagon with raised hackles and bared teeth.

The man on the seat called out, "That's a bad dog in a fight when he gets started."

Elisa laughed. "I see he is. How soon does he generally get started?"

The man caught up her laughter and echoed it heartily. "Sometimes not for weeks and weeks," he said. He climbed stiffly down, over the wheel. The horse and the donkey dropped like unwatered flowers.

Elisa saw that he was a very big man. Although his hair and beard were greying, he did not look old. His worn black suit was wrinkled and spotted with grease. The laughter had disappeared from his face and eyes the moment his laughing voice ceased. His eyes were dark, and they were full of the brooding that gets in the eyes of teamsters and of sailors. The calloused hands he rested on the wire fence were cracked, and every crack was a black line. He took off his battered hat.

"I'm off my general road, ma'am," he said. "Does this dirt road cut over across the river to the Los Angeles highway?"

Elisa stood up and shoved the thick scissors in her apron pocket. "Well, yes, it does, but it winds around and then fords the river. I don't think your team could pull through the sand."

He replied with some asperity, "It might surprise you what them beasts can pull through."

"When they get started?" she asked.

He smiled for a second. "Yes. When they get started."

"Well," said Elisa, "I think you'll save time if you go back to the Salinas road and pick up the highway there."

He drew a big finger down the chicken wire and made it sing. "I ain't in any hurry, ma'am. I go from Seattle to San Diego and back every year. Takes all my time. About six months each way. I aim to follow nice weather."

Elisa took off her gloves and stuffed them in the apron pocket with the scissors. She touched the under edge of her man's hat, searching for fugitive hairs. "That sounds like a nice kind of a way to live," she said.

He leaned confidentially over the fence. "Maybe you noticed the writing on my wagon. I mend pots and sharpen knives and scissors. You got any of them things to do?"

"Oh, no," she said, quickly. "Nothing like that." Her eyes hardened with resistance.

"Scissors is the worst thing," he explained. "Most people just ruin scissors trying to sharpen 'em, but I know how. I got a special tool. It's a little bobbit kind of thing, and patented. But it sure does the trick."

"No. My scissors are all sharp."

"All right, then. Take a pot," he continued earnestly, "a bent pot, or a pot with a hole. I can make it like new so you don't have to buy no new ones. That's a savings for you."

"No," she said shortly. "I tell you I have nothing like that for you to do."

His face fell to an exaggerated sadness. His voice took on a whining undertone. "I ain't had a thing to do today. Maybe I won't have no supper tonight. You see I'm off my regular road. I know folks on the highway clear from Seattle to San Diego. They save their things for me to sharpen up because they know I do it so good and save them money."

"I'm sorry," Elisa said irritably. "I haven't anything for you to do."

His eyes left her face and fell to searching the ground. They roamed about until they came to the chrysanthemum bed where she had been working. "What's them plants, ma'am?"

The irritation and resistance melted from Elisa's face. "Oh, those are chrysanthemums, giant whites and yellows. I raise them every year, bigger than anybody around here."

"Kind of a long-stemmed flower? Looks like a quick puff of colored smoke?" he asked.

"That's it. What a nice way to describe them."

"They smell kind of nasty till you get used to them," he said.

"It's a good bitter smell," she retorted, "not nasty at all."

He changed his tone quickly, "I like the smell myself."

"I had ten-inch-blooms this year," she said.

The man leaned farther over the fence. "Look, I know a lady down the road a piece, has got the nicest garden you ever seen. Got nearly every kind of flower but no chrysanthemums. Last time I was mending a copper-bottom washtub for her (that's a hard job but I do it good), she said to me, 'If you ever run acrost some nice chrysanthemums I wish you'd try to get me a few seeds.' That's what she told me."

Elisa's eyes grew alert and eager. "She couldn't have known much about chrysanthemums. You *can* raise them from seed, but it's much easier to root the little sprouts you see there."

"Oh," he said. "I s'pose I can't take none to her, then."

"Why yes you can," Elisa cried. "I can put some in damp sand, and you can carry them right along with you. They'll take root in the pot if you keep them damp. And then she can transplant them."

"She'd sure like to have some, ma'am. You say they're nice ones?"

"Beautiful," she said. "Oh, beautiful." Her eyes shone. She tore off the battered hat and shook out her dark pretty hair. "I'll put them in a flower pot, and you can take them right with you. Come into the yard."

While the man came through the picket gate Elisa ran excitedly along the geranium-bordered path to the back of the house. And she returned carrying a big red flower pot. The gloves were forgotten now. She kneeled on the ground by the starting bed and dug up the sandy soil with her fingers and scooped it into the bright new flower pot. Then she picked up the little pile of shoots she had prepared. With her strong fingers she pressed them into the sand and tamped around them with her knuckles. The man stood over her. "I'll tell you what to do," she said. "You remember so you can tell the lady."

"Yes, I'll try to remember."

"Well, look. These will take root in about a month. Then she must set them out, about a foot apart in good rich earth like this, see?" She lifted a handful of dark soil for him to look at. "They'll grow fast and tall. Now remember this: In July tell her to cut them down, about eight inches from the ground."

"Before they bloom?" he asked.

"Yes, before they bloom." Her face was tight with eagerness. "They'll grow right up again. About the last of September the buds will start."

She stopped and seemed perplexed. "It's the budding that takes the most care," she said hesitantly. "I don't know how to tell you." She looked deep into his eyes, searchingly. Her mouth opened a little, and she seemed to be listening. "I'll try to tell you," she said. "Did you ever hear of planting hands?"

"Can't say I have, ma'am."

"Well, I can only tell you what it feels like. It's when you're picking off the buds you don't want. Everything goes right down into your fingertips. You watch your fingers work. They do it themselves. You can feel how it is. They pick and pick the buds. They never make a mistake. They're with the plant. Do you see? Your fingers and the plant. You can feel that, right up your arm. They know. They never make a mistake. You can feel it. When you're like that you can't do anything wrong. Do you see that? Can you understand that?"

She was kneeling on the ground looking up at him. Her breast swelled passionately.

The man's eyes narrowed. He looked away self-consciously. "Maybe I know," he said. "Sometimes in the night in the wagon there — "

Elisa's voice grew husky. She broke in on him, "I've never lived as you do, but I know what you mean. When the night is dark — why, the stars are sharp-pointed, and there's quiet. Why, you rise up and up! Every pointed star gets driven into your body. It's like that. Hot and sharp and — lovely."

Kneeling there, her hand went out toward his legs in the greasy black trousers. Her hesitant fingers almost touched the cloth. Then her hand dropped to the ground. She crouched low like a fawning dog.

He said, "It's nice, just like you say. Only when you don't have no dinner, it ain't."

She stood up then, very straight, and her face was ashamed. She held the flower pot out to him and placed it gently in his arms. "Here. Put it in your wagon, on the seat, where you can watch it. Maybe I can find something for you to do."

At the back of the house she dug in the can pile and found two old and battered aluminum saucepans. She carried them back and gave them to him. "Here, maybe you can fix these."

His manner changed. He became professional. "Good as new I can fix them." At the back of his wagon he set a little anvil, and out of an oily tool box dug a small machine hammer. Elisa came through the gate to watch him while he pounded out the dents in the kettles. His mouth grew sure and knowing. At a difficult part of the work he sucked his underlip.

"You sleep right in the wagon?" Elisa asked.

"Right in the wagon, ma'am. Rain or shine I'm dry as a cow in there."

"It must be nice," she said. "It must be very nice. I wish women could do such things."

"It ain't the right kind of a life for a woman."

Her upper lip raised a little, showing her teeth. "How do you know? How can you tell?" she said.

"I don't know, ma'am," he protested. "Of course I don't know. Now here's your kettles, done. You don't have to buy no new ones."

"How much?"

"Oh, fifty cents'll do. I keep my prices down and my work good. That's why I have all them satisfied customers up and down the highway."

Elisa brought him a fifty-cent piece from the house and dropped it in his hand. "You might be surprised to have a rival some time. I can sharpen scissors, too. And I can beat the dents out of little pots. I could show you what a woman might do."

He put his hammer back in the oily box and shoved the little anvil out of sight. "It would be a lonely life for a woman, ma'am, and a scarey life, too, with animals creeping under the wagon all night." He climbed over the singletree, steadying himself with a hand on the burro's white rump. He settled himself in the seat, picked up the lines. "Thank you kindly, ma'am," he said. "I'll do like you told me; I'll go back and catch the Salinas road."

"Mind," she called, "if you're long in getting there, keep the sand damp."

"Sand, ma'am? . . . Sand? Oh, sure. You mean around the chrysanthemums. Sure I will." He clucked his tongue. The beasts leaned luxuriously into their collars. The mongrel dog took his place between the back wheels. The wagon turned and crawled out the entrance road and back the way it had come, along the river.

Elisa stood in front of her wire fence watching the slow progress of the caravan. Her shoulders were straight, her head thrown back, her eyes half-closed, so that the scene came vaguely into them. Her lips moved silently, forming the words "Good-bye — good-bye." Then she whispered, "That's a bright direction. There's a glowing there." The sound of her whisper startled her. She shook herself free and looked about to see whether anyone had been listening. Only the dogs had heard. They lifted their heads toward her from their sleeping in the dust, and then stretched out their chins and settled asleep again. Elisa turned and ran hurriedly into the house.

In the kitchen she reached behind the stove and felt the water tank. It was full of hot water from the noonday cooking. In the bathroom she tore off her soiled clothes and flung them into the corner. And then she scrubbed herself with a little block of pumice, legs and thighs, loins and chest and arms, until her skin was scratched and red. When she had dried herself she stood in front of a mirror in her bedroom and looked at her body. She tightened her stomach and threw out her chest. She turned and looked over her shoulder at her back.

After a while she began to dress, slowly. She put on her newest under-clothing and her nicest stockings and the dress which was the symbol of her prettiness. She worked carefully on her hair, penciled her eyebrows and rouged her lips.

Before she was finished she heard the little thunder of hoofs and the shouts of Henry and his helper as they drove the red steers into the corral. She heard the gate bang shut and set herself for Henry's arrival.

His step sounded on the porch. He entered the house calling, "Elisa, where are you?"

"In my room, dressing. I'm not ready. There's hot water for your bath. Hurry up. It's getting late."

When she heard him splashing in the tub, Elisa laid his dark suit on the bed, and shirt and socks and tie beside it. She stood his polished shoes on the floor beside the bed. Then she went to the porch and sat primly and stiffly down. She looked toward the river road where the willow-line was still yellow with frosted leaves so that under the high grey fog they seemed a thin band of sunshine. This was the only color in the grey afternoon. She sat unmoving for a long time. Her eyes blinked rarely.

Henry came banging out of the door, shoving his tie inside his vest as he came. Elisa stiffened and her face grew tight. Henry stopped short and looked at her. "Why — why, Elisa. You look so nice!"

"Nice? You think I look nice? What do you mean by 'nice'?"

Henry blundered on. "I don't know. I mean you look different, strong and happy."

"I am strong? Yes, strong. What do you mean 'strong'?"

He looked bewildered. "You're playing some kind of a game," he said helplessly. "It's a kind of a play. You look strong enough to break a calf over your knee, happy enough to eat it like a watermelon."

For a second she lost her rigidity. "Henry! Don't talk like that. You didn't know what you said." She grew complete again. "I'm strong," she boasted, "I never knew before how strong."

Henry looked down toward the tractor shed, and when he brought his eyes back to her, they were his own again. "I'll get out the car. You can put on your coat while I'm starting."

Elisa went into the house. She heard him drive to the gate and idle down his motor, and then she took a long time to put on her hat. She pulled it here and pressed it there. When Henry turned the motor off she slipped into her coat and went out.

The little roadster bounced along on the dirt road by the river, raising the birds and driving the rabbits into the brush. Two cranes flapped heavily over the willow-line and dropped into the river-bed.

Far ahead on the road Elisa saw a dark speck. She knew.

She tried not to look as they passed it, but her eyes would not obey. She whispered to herself sadly, "He might have thrown them off the road. That wouldn't have been much trouble, not very much. But he kept the pot," she explained. "He had to keep the pot. That's why he couldn't get them off the road."

The roadster turned a bend and she saw the caravan ahead. She swung full around toward her husband so she could not see the little covered wagon and the mismatched team as the car passed them.

In a moment it was over. The thing was done. She did not look back.

She said loudly, to be heard above the motor. "It will be good, tonight, a good dinner."

"Now you're changed again," Henry complained. He took one hand from the wheel and patted her knee. "I ought to take you in to dinner oftener. It would be good for both of us. We get so heavy out on the ranch."

"Henry," she asked, "could we have wine at dinner?"

"Sure we could. Say! That will be fine."

She was silent for a while; then she said, "Henry, at those prize fights, do the men hurt each other very much?"

"Sometimes a little, not often. Why?"

"Well, I've read how they break noses, and blood runs down their chests. I've read how the fighting gloves get heavy and soggy with blood."

He looked around at her. "What's the matter, Elisa? I didn't know you read things like that." He brought the car to a stop, then turned to the right over the Salinas River bridge.

"Do any women ever go to the fights?" she asked.

"Oh, sure, some. What's the matter Elisa? Do you want to go? I don't think you'd like it, but I'll take you if you really want to go."

She relaxed limply in the seat. "Oh, no. No. I don't want to go. I'm sure I don't." Her face was turned away from him. "It will be enough if we can have wine. It will be plenty." She turned up her coat collar so he could not see that she was crying weakly — like an old woman.   [1938]

AMY TAN (*b. 1952*) *was born in Oakland, California. Her father was educated as an engineer in Beijing; her mother left China in 1949, just before the communist revolution. Tan remembers that as a child she felt like an American girl trapped in a Chinese body: "There was shame and self-hate. There is this myth that America is a melting pot, but what happens in assimilation is that we end up deliberately choosing the American things — hot dogs and apple pie — and ignoring the Chinese offerings."*

After her father's death, Tan and her mother lived in Switzerland, where she attended high school. "I was a novelty," she recalls. "There were so few Asians in Europe that everywhere I went people stared. Europeans asked me out. I had never been asked out in America." After attending a small college in Oregon, she worked for IBM as a writer of computer manuals. In 1984 Tan and her mother visited China and met her relatives; there she made the important discovery, as she has said, that "I belonged to my family and my family belonged to China." A year later, back in San Francisco, Tan read Louise Erdrich's Love Medicine *and was so impressed by the power of its interlocking stories about another cultural minority, American Indians, that she began to write short stories herself. One of them was published in a little magazine read by a literary agent in San Diego, who urged Tan to outline a book about the conflicts between different cultures and generations of Chinese mothers and daughters in America. After her agent negotiated a $50,000 advance from Putnam's, Tan worked full-time on the first draft of her book* The Joy Luck Club *(1989) and finished it in four months.*

"Two Kinds" is an excerpt from that novel. At first Tan thought her book contract was "all a token minority thing. I thought they had to fill a quota since there weren't many Chinese Americans writing." But her book was a best-seller and was nominated for a National Book Award. As the novelist Valerie Miner has recognized, Tan's special gifts are her storytelling ability and her "remarkable ear for dialogue and dialect, representing the choppy English of the mother and the sloppy California vernacular of the daughter with a sensitive authenticity." At the heart of Tan's book is the tough bond between mother and daughter. "I'm my own person," the daughter says. "How can she be her own person," the mother answers. "When did I give her up?" Tan has also published another novel, The Kitchen God's Wife *(1992), and a children's book,* The Moon Lady *(1992).*

Two Kinds

My mother believed you could be anything you wanted to be in America. You could open a restaurant. You could work for the government and get good retirement. You could buy a house with almost no money down. You could become rich. You could become instantly famous.

"Of course you can be prodigy, too," my mother told me when I was nine. "You can be best anything. What does Auntie Lindo know? Her daughter, she is only best tricky."

America was where all my mother's hopes lay. She had come here in 1949 after losing everything in China: her mother and father, her family home, her first husband, and two daughters, twin baby girls. But she never looked back with regret. There were so many ways for things to get better.

We didn't immediately pick the right kind of prodigy. At first my mother thought I could be a Chinese Shirley Temple. We'd watch Shirley's old movies on TV as though they were training films. My mother would poke my arm and say, "*Ni kan*" — You watch. And I would see Shirley tapping her feet, or singing a sailor song, or pursing her lips into a very round O while saying, "Oh my goodness."

"*Ni kan*," said my mother as Shirley's eyes flooded with tears. "You already know how. Don't need talent for crying!"

Soon after my mother got this idea about Shirley Temple, she took me to a beauty training school in the Mission district and put me in the hands of a student who could barely hold the scissors without shaking. Instead of getting big fat curls, I emerged with an uneven mass of crinkly black fuzz. My mother dragged me off to the bathroom and tried to wet down my hair.

"You look like Negro Chinese," she lamented, as if I had done this on purpose.

The instructor of the beauty training school had to lop off these soggy clumps to make my hair even again. "Peter Pan is very popular these days," the instructor assured my mother. I now had hair the length of a boy's, with straight-across bangs that hung at a slant two inches above my eyebrows. I liked the haircut and it made me actually look forward to my future fame.

In fact, in the beginning, I was just as excited as my mother, maybe even more so. I pictured this prodigy part of me as many different images, trying each one on for size. I was a dainty ballerina girl standing by the curtains, waiting to hear the right music that would send me floating on my tiptoes. I was like the Christ child lifted out of the straw manger, crying with holy indignity. I was Cinderella stepping from her pumpkin carriage with sparkly cartoon music filling the air.

In all of my imaginings, I was filled with a sense that I would soon become *perfect*. My mother and father would adore me. I would be beyond reproach. I would never feel the need to sulk for anything.

But sometimes the prodigy in me became impatient. "If you don't hurry up and get me out of here, I'm disappearing for good," it warned. "And then you'll always be nothing."

Every night after dinner, my mother and I would sit at the Formica kitchen table. She would present new tests, taking her examples from stories of amazing children she had read in *Ripley's Believe It or Not,* or *Good Housekeeping, Reader's Digest,* and a dozen other magazines she kept in a pile in our bathroom. My mother got these magazines from people whose houses she cleaned. And since she cleaned many houses each week, we had a great assortment. She would look through them all, searching for stories about remarkable children.

The first night she brought out a story about a three-year-old boy who knew the capitals of all the states and even most of the European countries. A teacher was quoted as saying the little boy could also pronounce the names of the foreign cities correctly.

"What's the capital of Finland?" my mother asked me, looking at the magazine story.

All I knew was the capital of California, because Sacramento was the name of the street we lived on in Chinatown. "Nairobi!" I guessed, saying the most foreign word I could think of. She checked to see if that was possibly one way to pronounce "Helsinki" before showing me the answer.

The tests got harder — multiplying numbers in my head, finding the queen of hearts in a deck of cards, trying to stand on my head without using my hands, predicting the daily temperatures in Los Angeles, New York, and London.

One night I had to look at a page from the Bible for three minutes and then report everything I could remember. "Now Jehoshaphat had riches and honor in abundance and . . . that's all I remember, Ma," I said.

And after seeing my mother's disappointed face once again, something inside of me began to die. I hated the tests, the raised hopes and failed expectations. Before going to bed that night, I looked in the mirror above the bathroom sink and when I saw only my face staring back — and that it would always be this ordinary face — I began to cry. Such a sad, ugly girl! I made high-pitched noises like a crazed animal, trying to scratch out the face in the mirror.

And then I saw what seemed to be the prodigy side of me — because I had never seen that face before. I looked at my reflection, blinking so I could see more clearly. The girl staring back at me was angry, powerful. This girl and I were the same. I had new thoughts, willful thoughts, or rather thoughts filled with lots of won'ts. I won't let her change me, I promised myself. I won't be what I'm not.

So now on nights when my mother presented her tests, I performed listlessly, my head propped on one arm. I pretended to be bored. And I was. I got so bored I started counting the bellows of the foghorns out on the bay while my mother drilled me in other areas. The sound was comforting and reminded me of the cow jumping over the moon. And the next day, I played a game with myself, seeing if my mother would give up on me before eight bellows. After a while I usually counted only one, maybe two bellows at most. At last she was beginning to give up hope.

Two or three months had gone by without any mention of my being a prodigy again. And then one day my mother was watching *The Ed Sullivan Show* on TV. The TV was old and the sound kept shorting out. Every time my mother got halfway up from the sofa to adjust the set, the sound would go back on and Ed would be talking. As soon as she sat down, Ed would go silent again. She got up, the TV broke into loud piano music. She sat down. Silence. Up and down, back and forth, quiet and loud. It was like a stiff embraceless dance between her and the TV set. Finally she stood by the set with her hand on the sound dial.

She seemed entranced by the music, a little frenzied piano piece with this mesmerizing quality, sort of quick passages and then teasing lilting ones before it returned to the quick playful parts.

"*Ni kan*," my mother said, calling me over with hurried hand gestures. "Look here."

I could see why my mother was fascinated by the music. It was being pounded out by a little Chinese girl, about nine years old, with a Peter Pan haircut. The girl had the sauciness of a Shirley Temple. She was proudly modest like a proper Chinese child. And she also did this fancy sweep of a curtsy, so that the fluffy skirt of her white dress cascaded slowly to the floor like the petals of a large carnation.

In spite of these warning signs, I wasn't worried. Our family had no piano and we couldn't afford to buy one, let alone reams of sheet music and piano lessons. So I could be generous in my comments when my mother bad-mouthed the little girl on TV.

"Play note right, but doesn't sound good! No singing sound," complained my mother.

"What are you picking on her for?" I said carelessly. "She's pretty good. Maybe she's not the best, but she's trying hard." I knew almost immediately I would be sorry I said that.

"Just like you," she said. "Not the best. Because you not trying." She gave a little huff as she let go of the sound dial and sat down on the sofa.

The little Chinese girl sat down also to play an encore of "Anitra's Dance" by Grieg. I remember the song, because later on I had to learn how to play it.

Three days after watching *The Ed Sullivan Show*, my mother told me what my schedule would be for piano lessons and piano practice. She had talked to Mr. Chong, who lived on the first floor of our apartment building. Mr. Chong was a retired piano teacher and my mother had traded house-cleaning services for weekly lessons and a piano for me to practice on every day, two hours a day, from four until six.

When my mother told me this, I felt as though I had been sent to hell. I whined and then kicked my foot a little when I couldn't stand it anymore.

"Why don't you like me the way I am? I'm *not* a genius! I can't play the piano. And even if I could, I wouldn't go on TV if you paid me a million dollars!" I cried.

My mother slapped me. "Who ask you be genius?" she shouted. "Only ask you be your best. For you sake. You think I want you be genius? Hnnh! What for! Who ask you!"

"So ungrateful," I heard her mutter in Chinese. "If she had as much talent as she has temper, she would be famous now."

Mr. Chong, whom I secretly nicknamed Old Chong, was very strange, always tapping his fingers to the silent music of an invisible orchestra. He looked ancient in my eyes. He had lost most of the hair on top of his head and he wore thick glasses and had eyes that always looked tired and sleepy. But he must have been younger than I thought, since he lived with his mother and was not yet married.

I met Old Lady Chong once and that was enough. She had this peculiar smell like a baby that had done something in its pants. And her fingers felt like a dead person's, like an old peach I once found in the back of the refrigerator; the skin just slid off the meat when I picked it up.

I soon found out why Old Chong had retired from teaching piano. He was deaf. "Like Beethoven!" he shouted to me. "We're both listening only in our head!" And he would start to conduct his frantic silent sonatas.

Our lessons went like this. He would open the book and point to different things, explaining their purpose: "Key! Treble! Bass! No sharps or flats! So this is C major! Listen now and play after me!"

And then he would play the C scale a few times, a simple chord, and then, as if inspired by an old, unreachable itch, he gradually added more notes and running trills and a pounding bass until the music was really something quite grand.

I would play after him, the simple scale, the simple chord, and then I just played some nonsense that sounded like a cat running up and down on top of garbage cans. Old Chong smiled and applauded and then said, "Very good! But now you must learn to keep time!"

So that's how I discovered that Old Chong's eyes were too slow to keep up with the wrong notes I was playing. He went through the motions in half-time. To help me keep rhythm, he stood behind me, pushing down on my right shoulder for every beat. He balanced pennies on top of my wrists so I would keep them still as I slowly played scales and arpeggios. He had me curve my hand around an apple and keep that shape when playing chords. He marched stiffly to show me how to make each finger dance up and down, staccato like an obedient little soldier.

He taught me all these things, and that was how I also learned I could be lazy and get away with mistakes, lots of mistakes. If I hit the wrong notes because I hadn't practiced enough, I never corrected myself. I just kept playing in rhythm. And Old Chong kept conducting his own private reverie.

So maybe I never really gave myself a fair chance. I did pick up the basics pretty quickly, and I might have become a good pianist at that young age. But I was so determined not to try, not to be anybody different that I learned to play only the most ear-splitting preludes, the most discordant hymns.

Over the next year, I practiced like this, dutifully in my own way. And then one day I heard my mother and her friend Lindo Jong both talking in a loud bragging tone of voice so others could hear. It was after church, and I was leaning against the brick wall wearing a dress with stiff white petticoats. Auntie Lindo's daughter, Waverly, who was about my age, was standing farther down the wall about five feet away. We had grown up together and shared all the closeness of two sisters squabbling over crayons and dolls. In other words, for the most part, we hated each other. I thought she was snotty. Waverly Jong had gained a certain amount of fame as "Chinatown's Littlest Chinese Chess Champion."

"She bring home too many trophy," lamented Auntie Lindo that Sunday. "All day she play chess. All day I have no time do nothing but dust off her winnings." She threw a scolding look at Waverly, who pretended not to see her.

"You lucky you don't have this problem," said Auntie Lindo with a sigh to my mother.

And my mother squared her shoulders and bragged: "Our problem worser than yours. If we ask Jing-mei wash dish, she hear nothing but music. It's like you can't stop this natural talent."

And right then, I was determined to put a stop to her foolish pride.

A few weeks later, Old Chong and my mother conspired to have me play in a talent show which would be held in the church hall. By then, my parents had saved up enough to buy me a secondhand piano, a black Wurlitzer spinet with a scarred bench. It was the showpiece of our living room.

For the talent show, I was to play a piece called "Pleading Child" from Schumann's *Scenes from Childhood*. It was a simple, moody piece that sounded more difficult than it was. I was supposed to memorize the whole thing, playing the repeat parts twice to make the piece sound longer. But I dawdled over it, playing a few bars and then cheating, looking up to see what notes followed. I never really listened to what I was playing. I daydreamed about being somewhere else, about being someone else.

The part I liked to practice best was the fancy curtsy: right foot out, touch the rose on the carpet with a pointed foot, sweep to the side, left leg bends, look up and smile.

My parents invited all the couples from the Joy Luck Club to witness my debut. Auntie Lindo and Uncle Tin were there. Waverly and her two older brothers had also come. The first two rows were filled with children both younger and older than I was. The littlest ones got to go first. They recited simple nursery rhymes, squawked out tunes on miniature violins, twirled Hula Hoops, pranced in pink ballet tutus, and when they bowed or curtsied, the audience would sigh in unison, "Awww," and then clap enthusiastically.

When my turn came, I was very confident. I remember my childish excitement. It was as if I knew, without a doubt, that the prodigy side of me really did exist. I had no fear whatsoever, no nervousness. I remember thinking to myself, This is it! This is it! I looked out over the audience, at my mother's blank face, my father's yawn, Auntie Lindo's stiff-lipped smile, Waverly's sulky expression. I had on a white dress layered with sheets of lace, and a pink bow in my Peter Pan haircut. As I sat down I envisioned people jumping to their feet and Ed Sullivan rushing up to introduce me to everyone on TV.

And I started to play. It was so beautiful. I was so caught up in how lovely I looked that at first I didn't worry how I would sound. So it was a surprise to me when I hit the first wrong note and I realized something didn't sound quite right. And then I hit another and another followed that. A chill started at the top of my head and began to trickle down. Yet I couldn't stop playing, as though my hands were bewitched. I kept thinking my fingers would adjust themselves back, like a train switching to the right track. I played this strange jumble through two repeats, the sour notes staying with me all the way to the end.

When I stood up, I discovered my legs were shaking. Maybe I had just been nervous and the audience, like Old Chong, had seen me go through the right motions and had not heard anything wrong at all. I swept my right foot out, went down on my knee, looked up and smiled. The room was quiet, except for Old Chong, who was beaming and shouting, "Bravo! Bravo! Well done!" But then I saw my mother's face, her stricken face. The audience clapped weakly, and as I walked back to my chair, with my whole face quivering as I tried not to cry, I heard a little boy whisper loudly to his mother, "That was awful," and the mother whispered back, "Well, she certainly tried."

And now I realized how many people were in the audience, the whole world it seemed. I was aware of eyes burning into my back. I felt the shame of my mother and father as they sat stiffly throughout the rest of the show.

We could have escaped during intermission. Pride and some strange sense of honor must have anchored my parents to their chairs. And so we watched it all: the eighteen-year-old boy with a fake mustache who did a magic show and juggled flaming hoops while riding a unicycle. The breasted girl with white makeup who sang from *Madama Butterfly* and got honorable mention. And the eleven-year-old boy who won first prize playing a tricky violin song that sounded like a busy bee.

After the show, the Hsus, the Jongs, and the St. Clairs from the Joy Luck Club came up to my mother and father.

"Lots of talented kids," Auntie Lindo said vaguely, smiling broadly.

"That was somethin' else," said my father, and I wondered if he was referring to me in a humorous way, or whether he even remembered what I had done.

Waverly looked at me and shrugged her shoulders. "You aren't a genius like me," she said matter-of-factly. And if I hadn't felt so bad, I would have pulled her braids and punched her stomach.

But my mother's expression was what devastated me: a quiet, blank look that said she had lost everything. I felt the same way, and it seemed as if everybody were now coming up, like gawkers at the scene of an accident, to see what parts were actually missing. When we got on the bus to go home, my father was humming the busy-bee tune and my mother was silent. I kept thinking she wanted to wait until we got home before shouting at me. But when my father unlocked the door to our apartment, my mother walked in and then went to the back, into the bedroom. No accusations. No blame. And in a way, I felt disappointed. I had been waiting for her to start shouting, so I could shout back and cry and blame her for all my misery.

I assumed my talent-show fiasco meant I never had to play the piano again. But two days later, after school, my mother came out of the kitchen and saw me watching TV.

"Four clock," she reminded me as if it were any other day. I was stunned, as though she were asking me to go through the talent-show torture again. I wedged myself more tightly in front of the TV.

"Turn off TV," she called from the kitchen five minutes later.

I didn't budge. And then I decided. I didn't have to do what my mother said anymore. I wasn't her slave. This wasn't China. I had listened to her before and look what happened. She was the stupid one.

She came out from the kitchen and stood in the arched entryway of the living room. "Four clock," she said once again, louder.

"I'm not going to play anymore," I said nonchalantly. "Why should I? I'm not a genius."

She walked over and stood in front of the TV. I saw her chest was heaving up and down in an angry way.

"No!" I said, and I now felt stronger, as if my true self had finally emerged. So this was what had been inside me all along.

"No! I won't!" I screamed.

She yanked me by the arm, pulled me off the floor, snapped off the TV. She was frighteningly strong, half pulling, half carrying me toward the piano as I kicked the throw rugs under my feet. She lifted me up and onto the hard bench. I was sobbing by now, looking at her bitterly. Her chest was heaving even more and her mouth was open, smiling crazily as if she were pleased I was crying.

"You want me to be someone that I'm not!" I sobbed. "I'll never be the kind of daughter you want me to be!"

"Only two kinds of daughters," she shouted in Chinese. "Those who are obedient and those who follow their own mind! Only one kind of daughter can live in this house. Obedient daughter!"

"Then I wish I wasn't your daughter. I wish you weren't my mother," I shouted. As I said these things I got scared. I felt like worms and toads and slimy things were crawling out of my chest, but it also felt good, as if this awful side of me had surfaced, at last.

"Too late change this," said my mother shrilly.

And I could sense her anger rising to its breaking point. I wanted to see it spill over. And that's when I remembered the babies she had lost in China, the ones we never talked about. "Then I wish I'd never been born!" I shouted. "I wish I were dead! Like them."

It was as if I had said the magic words, Alakazam! — and her face went blank, her mouth closed, her arms went slack, and she backed out of the room, stunned, as if she were blowing away like a small brown leaf, thin, brittle, lifeless.

It was not the only disappointment my mother felt in me. In the years that followed, I failed her so many times, each time asserting my own will, my right to fall short of expectations. I didn't get straight As. I didn't become class president. I didn't get into Stanford. I dropped out of college.

For unlike my mother, I did not believe I could be anything I wanted to be. I could only be me.

And for all those years, we never talked about the disaster at the recital or my terrible accusations afterward at the piano bench. All that remained unchecked, like a betrayal that was now unspeakable. So I never found a way to ask her why she had hoped for something so large that failure was inevitable.

And even worse, I never asked her what frightened me the most: Why had she given up hope?

For after our struggle at the piano, she never mentioned my playing again. The lessons stopped, the lid to the piano was closed, shutting out the dust, my misery, and her dreams.

So she surprised me. A few years ago, she offered to give me the piano, for my thirtieth birthday. I had not played in all those years. I saw the offer as a sign of forgiveness, a tremendous burden removed.

"Are you sure?" I asked shyly. "I mean, won't you and Dad miss it?"

"No, this your piano," she said firmly. "Always your piano. You only one can play."

"Well, I probably can't play anymore," I said. "It's been years."

"You pick up fast," said my mother, as if she knew this was certain. "You have natural talent. You could been genius if you want to."

"No I couldn't."

"You just not trying," said my mother. And she was neither angry nor sad. She said it as if to announce a fact that could never be disproved. "Take it," she said.

But I didn't at first. It was enough that she had offered it to me. And after that, every time I saw it in my parents' living room, standing in front of the bay windows, it made me feel proud, as if it were a shiny trophy I had won back.

Last week I sent a tuner over to my parents' apartment and had the piano reconditioned, for purely sentimental reasons. My mother had died a few months before and I had been getting things in order for my father, a little bit at a time. I put the jewelry in special silk pouches. The sweaters she had knitted in yellow, pink, bright orange — all the colors I hated — I put those in moth-proof boxes. I found some old Chinese silk dresses, the kind with little slits up the sides. I rubbed the old silk against my skin, then wrapped them in tissue and decided to take them home with me.

After I had the piano tuned, I opened the lid and touched the keys. It sounded even richer than I remembered. Really, it was a very good piano. Inside the bench were the same exercise notes with handwritten scales, the same secondhand music books with their covers held together with yellow tape.

I opened up the Schumann book to the dark little piece I had played at the recital. It was on the left-hand side of the page, "Pleading Child." It looked more difficult than I remembered. I played a few bars, surprised at how easily the notes came back to me.

And for the first time, or so it seemed, I noticed the piece on the right-hand side. It was called "Perfectly Contented." I tried to play this one as well. It had a lighter melody but the same flowing rhythm and turned out to be quite easy. "Pleading Child" was shorter but slower; "Perfectly Contented" was longer but faster. And after I played them both a few times, I realized they were two halves of the same song.   [1989]

JAMES THURBER *(1894–1961), the humorist, was born in Columbus, Ohio. When he was a boy he lost an eye, which kept him from military service in World War I. After his graduation from Ohio State University, he worked as a newspaper reporter in Columbus and New York and lived in Paris. He came back to New York in 1926 to submit his humorous sketches to a new magazine,* The New Yorker. *He also served a short time as its managing editor, and the magazine printed his cartoons, fables, stories, and essays for the rest of his life. Among Thurber's many books are* Fables for Our Time *(1940),* My World — And Welcome to It *(1942),* The Thurber Carnival *(1945), and* Thurber Country *(1953).*

Thurber said he began to write as a young man in "a rather curious style . . . tight journalese laced with heavy doses of Henry James." But his contact with E. B. White and Harold Ross at The New Yorker *taught him to value clarity above all else. After he matured as a writer he reflected on why James's way of writing no longer worked for him: "James is like — well, I had a bulldog once who used to drag rails around, enormous ones. . . . Once he brought home a chest of drawers — without the drawers in it. Found it on an ash-heap. Well, he'd start to get these things in the garden gate, everything finely balanced, you see, and then crash, he'd come up against the gate posts. He'd get it through finally, but I had that feeling in some of James's novels: that he was trying to get that rail through a gate not wide enough for it."*

In discussing how he wrote stories, Thurber once quoted a definition of the difference between English and American humor: "The English treat the commonplace as if it were remarkable and the Americans treat the remarkable as if it were commonplace." His best stories, such as "The Secret Life of Walter Mitty," venture into fantasy while treating the remarkable as commonplace. He felt at home in the short story, never wanting to write a longer work, yet he recognized that there could also be serious elements in his fiction. "In anything funny you write that isn't close to serious you've missed something along the line." To Thurber, humor was "emotional chaos remembered in tranquility," and although the chaos provoked the immediate comic response, the power of ordered remembering gave the incident its deeper meaning. His best fiction and drawings were inspired by his comic view of the perennial battle of the sexes, in which intimidating women try to keep the upper hand over shy, trapped little men like the gentle Waterbury shopper Walter Mitty.

JAMES THURBER

The Secret Life of Walter Mitty

"**W**e're going through!" The Commander's voice was like thin ice breaking. He wore his full-dress uniform, with the heavily braided white cap pulled down rakishly over one cold gray eye. "We can't make it, sir. It's spoiling for a hurricane, if you ask me." "I'm not asking you, Lieutenant Berg," said the Commander. "Throw on the power lights! Rev her up to 8,500! We're going through!" The pounding of the cylinders increased: ta-pocketa-pocketa-pocketa-*pocketa-pocketa*. The Commander stared at the ice forming on the pilot window. He walked over and twisted a row of complicated dials. "Switch on No. 8 auxiliary!" he shouted. "Switch on No. 8 auxiliary!" repeated Lieutenant Berg. "Full strength in No. 3 turret!" shouted the Commander. "Full strength in No. 3 turret!" The crew, bending to their various tasks in the huge, hurtling eight-engined Navy hydroplane, looked at each other and grinned. "The Old Man'll get us through," they said to one another. "The Old Man ain't afraid of Hell!" . . .

"Not so fast! You're driving too fast!" said Mrs. Mitty. "What are you driving so fast for?"

"Hmm?" said Walter Mitty. He looked at his wife, in the seat beside him, with shocked astonishment. She seemed grossly unfamiliar, like a strange woman who had yelled at him in a crowd. "You were up to fifty-five," she said. "You know I don't like to go more than forty. You were up to fifty-five." Walter Mitty drove on toward Waterbury in silence, the roaring of the SN202 through the worst storm in twenty years of Navy flying fading in the remote, intimate airways of his mind. "You're tensed up again," said Mrs. Mitty. "It's one of your days. I wish you'd let Dr. Renshaw look you over."

Walter Mitty stopped the car in front of the building where his wife went to have her hair done. "Remember to get those overshoes while I'm having my hair done," she said. "I don't need overshoes," said Mitty. She put her mirror back into her bag. "We've been all through that," she said, getting out of the car. "You're not a young man any longer." He raced the engine a little. "Why don't you wear your gloves? Have you lost your gloves?" Walter Mitty reached in a pocket and brought out the gloves. He put them on, but after she had turned and gone into the building and he had driven on to a red light, he took them off again. "Pick it up, brother!" snapped a cop as the light changed, and Mitty hastily pulled on his gloves and lurched ahead. He drove around the streets aimlessly for a time, and then he drove past the hospital on his way to the parking lot.

. . . "It's the millionaire banker, Wellington McMillan," said the pretty nurse. "Yes?" said Walter Mitty, removing his gloves slowly. "Who has the case?" "Dr. Renshaw and Dr. Benbow, but there are two specialists here, Dr. Remington from New York and Dr. Pritchard-Mitford from London. He flew over." A door opened down a long, cool corridor and Dr. Renshaw came out. He looked distraught and haggard. "Hello, Mitty," he said. "We're having the devil's own time with McMillan, the millionaire banker and close personal friend of Roosevelt. Obstreosis of the ductal tract. Tertiary. Wish you'd take a look at him." "Glad to," said Mitty.

In the operating room there were whispered introductions: "Dr. Remington, Dr. Mitty, Mr. Pritchard-Mitford, Dr. Mitty." "I've read your book on streptothricosis," said Pritchard-Mitford, shaking hands. "A brilliant performance, sir." "Thank you," said Walter Mitty. "Didn't know you were in the States, Mitty," grumbled Remington. "Coals to Newcastle, bring Mitford and me up here for a tertiary." "You are very kind," said Mitty. A huge, complicated machine, connected to the operating table, with many tubes and wires, began at this moment to go pocketa-pocketa-pocketa. "The new anesthetizer is giving way!" shouted an interne. "There is no one in the East who knows how to fix it!" "Quiet, man!" said Mitty, in a low, cool voice. He sprang to the machine, which was now going pocketa-pocketa-queep-pocketa-queep. He began fingering delicately a row of glistening dials. "Give me a fountain pen!" he snapped. Someone handed him a fountain pen. He pulled a faulty piston out of the machine and inserted the pen in its place. "That will hold for ten minutes," he said. "Get on with the operation." A nurse hurried over and whispered to Renshaw, and Mitty saw the man turn pale. "Coreopsis has set in," said Renshaw nervously. "If you would take over, Mitty?" Mitty looked at him and at the craven figure of Benbow, who drank, and at the grave, uncertain faces of the two great specialists. "If you wish," he said. They slipped a white gown on him; he adjusted a mask and drew on thin gloves; nurses handed him shining. . . .

"Back it up, Mac! Look out for that Buick!" Walter Mitty jammed on the brakes. "Wrong lane, Mac," said the parking-lot attendant, looking at Mitty closely. "Gee. Yeh," muttered Mitty. He began cautiously to back out of the lane marked "Exit Only." "Leave her sit there," said the attendant. "I'll put her away." Mitty got out of the car. "Hey, better leave the key." "Oh," said Mitty, handing the man the ignition key. The attendant vaulted into the car, backed it up with insolent skill, and put it where it belonged.

They're so damn cocky, thought Walter Mitty, walking along Main Street; they think they know everything. Once he had tried to take his chains off, outside New Milford, and he had got them wound around the axles. A man had had to come out in a wrecking car and unwind them, a young, grinning garageman. Since then Mrs. Mitty always made him drive to the garage to have the chains taken off. The next time, he thought, I'll wear my right arm in a sling; they won't grin at me then. I'll have my right arm in a sling and they'll see I couldn't possibly take the chains off myself. He kicked at the slush on the sidewalk. "Overshoes," he said to himself, and he began looking for a shoe store.

When he came out into the street again, with the overshoes in a box under his arm, Walter Mitty began to wonder what the other thing was his wife had told him to get. She had told him, twice, before they set out from their house for Waterbury. In a way he hated these weekly trips to town —

he was always getting something wrong. Kleenex, he thought, Squibb's, razor blades? No. Toothpaste, toothbrush, bicarbonate, carborundum, initiative and referendum? He gave it up. But she would remember it. "Where's the what's-its-name?" she would ask. "Don't tell me you forgot the what's-its-name." A newsboy went by shouting something about the Waterbury trial.

. . . "Perhaps this will refresh your memory." The District Attorney suddenly thrust a heavy automatic at the quiet figure on the witness stand. "Have you ever seen this before?" Walter Mitty took the gun and examined it expertly. "This is my Webley-Vickers 50.80," he said calmly. An excited buzz ran around the courtroom. The Judge rapped for order. "You are a crack shot with any sort of firearms, I believe?" said the District Attorney, insinuatingly. "Objection!" shouted Mitty's attorney. "We have shown that the defendant could not have fired the shot. We have shown that he wore his right arm in a sling on the night of the fourteenth of July." Walter Mitty raised his hand briefly and the bickering attorneys were stilled. "With any known make of gun," he said evenly, "I could have killed Gregory Fitzhurst at three hundred feet *with my left hand.*" Pandemonium broke loose in the courtroom. A woman's scream rose above the bedlam and suddenly a lovely, dark-haired girl was in Walter Mitty's arms. The District Attorney struck at her savagely. Without rising from his chair, Mitty let the man have it on the point of the chin. "You miserable cur!" . . .

"Puppy biscuit," said Walter Mitty. He stopped walking and the buildings of Waterbury rose up out of the misty courtroom and surrounded him again. A woman who was passing laughed. "He said 'Puppy biscuit,'" she said to her companion. "That man said 'Puppy biscuit' to himself." Walter Mitty hurried on. He went into an A. & P., not the first one he came to but a smaller one farther up the street. "I want some biscuit for small, young dogs," he said to the clerk. "Any special brand, sir?" The greatest pistol shot in the world thought a moment. "It says 'Puppies Bark for It' on the box," said Walter Mitty.

His wife would be through at the hairdresser's in fifteen minutes, Mitty saw in looking at his watch, unless they had trouble drying it; sometimes they had trouble drying it. She didn't like to get to the hotel first; she would want him to be there waiting for her as usual. He found a big leather chair in the lobby, facing a window, and he put the overshoes and the puppy biscuit on the floor beside it. He picked up an old copy of *Liberty* and sank down into the chair. "Can Germany Conquer the World through the Air?" Walter Mitty looked at the pictures of bombing planes and of ruined streets.

. . . "The cannonading has got the wind up in young Raleigh, sir," said the sergeant. Captain Mitty looked up at him through tousled hair. "Get him to bed," he said wearily. "With the others. I'll fly alone." "But you can't, sir," said the sergeant anxiously. "It takes two men to handle that bomber and the Archies are pounding hell out of the air. Von Richtman's circus is between here and Saulier." "Somebody's got to get that ammunition dump." said Mitty. "I'm going over. Spot of brandy?" He poured a drink for the sergeant and one for himself. War thundered and whined around the dugout and battered at the door. There was a rending of wood and splinters flew through the room. "A bit of a near thing," said Captain Mitty carelessly. "The box barrage is closing in," said the sergeant. "We only live once, Sergeant," said Mitty, with his faint, fleeting smile. "Or do we?" He poured another brandy and tossed it off. "I never see a man could hold his brandy like you, sir," said the sergeant. "Begging your pardon, sir." Captain Mitty stood up and strapped on his huge Webley-Vickers automatic. "It's forty kilometers through hell, sir," said the sergeant. Mitty finished one last brandy. "After all," he said softly, "what isn't?" The pounding of the cannon increased; there was the rat-tat-tatting of machine guns, and from somewhere came the menacing pocket-pocketa-pocketa of the new flame-throwers. Walter Mitty walked to the door of the dugout humming "Auprès de Ma Blonde." He turned and waved to the sergeant. "Cheerio!" he said. . . .

Something struck his shoulder. "I've been looking all over this hotel for you," said Mrs. Mitty. "Why do you have to hide in this old chair? How did you expect me to find you?" "Things close in," said Walter Mitty vaguely. "What?" Mrs. Mitty said. "Did you get the what's-its-name? The puppy biscuit? What's in that box?" "Overshoes," said Mitty. "Couldn't you have put them on in the store?" "I was thinking," said Walter Mitty. "Does it ever occur to you that I am sometimes thinking?" She looked at him. "I'm going to take your temperature when I get you home," she said.

They went out through the revolving doors that made a faintly derisive whistling sound when you pushed them. It was two blocks to the parking lot. At the drugstore on the corner she said, "Wait here for me. I forgot something. I won't be a minute." She was more than a minute. Walter Mitty lighted a cigarette. It began to rain, rain with sleet in it. He stood up against the wall of the drugstore, smoking. . . . He put his shoulders back and his heels together. "To hell with the handkerchief," said Walter Mitty scornfully. He took one last drag on his cigarette and snapped it away. Then with that faint, fleeting smile playing about his lips, he faced the firing squad; erect and motionless, proud and disdainful, Walter Mitty the Undefeated, inscrutable to the last. [1942]

Tatyana Nikitichna Tolstaya (b. 1951), the great-grandniece of Leo Tolstoy and the granddaughter of the Soviet writer Alexei Tolstoy, would have become a successful writer on the basis of her literary talent even without her distinguished ancestors. Tolstaya was born in Leningrad and earned a degree from Leningrad University in 1974. She then moved to Moscow and worked for several years at a publishing house. In 1983 her first volume of short fiction appeared, but she gained wide recognition as a writer three years later with the publication of a long story, "Peters," in the Russian literary journal Novyi mir (New World).

In 1987 Tolstaya's second collection of stories was published in Russia and sold out its copies immediately. The next year she was writer-in-residence at the University of Richmond, Virginia, and she has continued to teach at American universities since that time. Her first collection of short fiction in English, On the Golden Porch, was published in 1989 and secured her an international reputation. "Night," which recalls Katherine Anne Porter's "He," is from her most recent book, Sleepwalker in a Fog (1991), a collection of eight stories.

Many of Tolstaya's stories dramatize situations familiar to all readers, where children and elderly people are at the mercy of callous people who do not understand them. As the critic Michael Meyer has noted, Tolstaya's "sensuous style explores the inner lives of her characters, who are defined by their perceptions and emotions rather than by national borders."

TATYANA TOLSTAYA

Night

In the mornings Alexei Petrovich's mama yawns loud and long: hurrah, onward, a new morning gushes in through the window; the cactuses shine, the curtains quiver; the gates of the nighttime realm have slammed shut; dragons, mushrooms, and frightening dwarfs have plunged below the earth once again, life triumphs, the heralds blow their horns: a new day! a new day! Da-da-da da da-daa!

Mamochka combs her thinning hair oh so quickly with her hands, throws her bluish legs over the high bed frame — let them hang for a moment and think: all day they'll have to drag around the 135 kilos that Mamochka has accumulated in the course of eighty years.

Alexei Petrovich opened his eyes: Sleep slips serenely from his body; everything is forgotten, the last crow flies off into the gloom; the nocturnal guests, gathering their ghostly, ambiguous props, have interrupted the play until next time. A breeze sweetly fans Alexei Petrovich's bald spot, the newly grown bristle on his cheeks pricks his palm. Isn't it time to get up? Mamochka will give the order. Mamochka is so big, loud, and spacious, and Alexei Petrovich is so little. Mamochka knows everything, can do everything, gets in everywhere. Mamochka is all powerful. Whatever she says, goes. And he —is a late child, a little bundle, nature's blunder, a soap sliver, a weed intended for burning that accidentally wormed its way in among its healthy brethren when the Sower generously scattered the full-blooded seeds of life about the earth.

Can I get up already, or is it early? Don't squawk. Mamochka is carrying out her morning ritual: She honks into a handkerchief, pulls her stockings, sticking and prickling, onto the columns of her legs, fastens them under her swollen knees with little rings of white rubber. She hoists a linen frame with fifteen buttons onto her monstrous breast; buttoning it in the back is probably hard. The gray chignon is reattached at Mamochka's zenith; shaken from a clean nighttime glass, her freshened teeth flutter. Mamochka's facade will be concealed under a white, pleated dickey, and, hiding the seams on the back, the insides out, napes, back stairs, and emergency exits — a sturdy dark blue jacket will cover the whole majestic building. The palace has been erected.

Everything you do is good, Mamochka. Everything's right.

Everyone is already awake in the apartment, everyone's stirring, all the Men and Women have started talking. They slam doors, burble water, jingle on the other side of the wall. The morning ship has left the slip, it cuts through the blue water, the sails fill with wind, the well-dressed travelers, laughing, exchange remarks with one another on the deck. What shores lie ahead? Mamochka is at the wheel, Mamochka is on the captain's bridge, from the crow's nest Mamochka looks onto the shining ripples.

"Alexei, get up! Shave, brush your teeth, wash your ears. Take a clean towel. Put the cap back on the toothpaste. Don't forget to flush. And don't touch anything in there, you hear me?"

All right, all right, Mamochka. How right everything you say is. How much sense everything immediately makes, how open the horizons become, how reliable a voyage with an experienced pilot. The old colored maps are unrolled, the route is drawn in with a red dotted line, all the dangers are marked with bright, clear pictures: there's the dread lion, and on this shore — a rhinoceros; here a whale spouts a toylike fountain, and over there — is the most dangerous creature, the big-eyed, big-tailed Sea Girl, slippery, malicious, alluring.

Alexei Petrovich will wash up, put himself together; Mamochka will come and check whether he messed anything, or else the neighbors will yell again; and then it's food time. What did Mamochka make today? To get to the bathroom you have to go through the kitchen. Old ladies grumble at the hot stove, they're stewing poison in pots, they add the roots of terrible plants, follow Alexei Petrovich with bad looks. Mamochka! don't let them hurt me!

Dripped a little on the floor. Oh no.

There's already a crowd in the hallway: the Men and Women are leaving, noisily checking for their keys, coin purses.

The corner door with opaque glass is wide open; on the threshold stands that brazen Sea Girl, smirking. She winks at Alexei Petrovich; she's all tilted; she puffs Tobacco, her Leg is stuck out, her nets laid — don't you want to be caught, eh? But Mamochka's to the rescue, she's already racing like a locomotive, her red wheels pound, she whistles, out of the way!

"Shameless hussy! Get out of here, I say! Not enough for you . . . have to have a sick man as well! . . ."

"Ga-ga-ga!" The Sea Girl isn't afraid.

Dart — and into the room. Saved. Yu-u-ck. Women — are terrifying. It isn't clear what they're here for, but they're very unsettling. They walk by — smelling like they do . . . and they have — Legs. There are lots of them on the street, and in every house, in this one, and that one, and that one, behind every door, they've hidden, they're doing something, bending, rummaging around, giggling into their fists; they know something and they won't tell Alexei Petrovich. He'll sit down at the table and think about Women. Once Mamochka took him with her out of town, to the beach; there were lots of them there. There was one . . . a wavy sort of fairy . . . like a little dog . . . Alexei Petrovich liked her. He went up close and looked at her.

"Well, what are you staring at?" shouted the fairy. "Get out of here, you retard!"

Mamochka came in with a bubbling pot. He looked in. There were the pink weenies of sausages. He was glad. Mamochka sets the table, moves, wipes up. The knife pops out of his fingers, strikes the oilcloth somewhere to the side.

"In your hands, take the sausage in your hands."

Ah, Mamochka, guiding star! Heart of gold! You'll fix everything. Wise, you'll unravel all the tangles, you'll destroy all the back alleys, all the labyrinths of this incomprehensible, unnavigable world with your powerful hand, you'll sweep away all the walls — here's an even, leveled plaza. Boldly take one more step. Farther on — wind-fallen trees.

Alexei Petrovich has his own world — in his head, the real one. Everything's allowed there. But this one, outside — is bad, wrong. And it's very hard to remember what's good and what's bad. They've set up and agreed upon written Rules that are awfully complicated. They've learned them, their memory is good. But it's hard for him to live by someone else's Rules.

Mamochka poured coffee. Coffee has a Smell. You drink it — and the smell goes over to you. Why aren't you allowed to make your lips into a tube, cross your eyes to look at your mouth, and smell yourself? Let Mamochka turn her back.

"Alexei, behave yourself!"

After breakfast they cleaned the table, set out the glue, cardboard, scissors, tied a napkin around Alexei Petrovich: he's going to glue boxes. When he's done a hundred of them—they'll take them to the pharmacy. They'll get some money. Alexei Petrovich loves these boxes, he doesn't like to part with them. He wants to hide them on the sly, save at least some for himself, but Mamochka watches carefully and takes them away.

And then other people carry them out of the pharmacy, eat little white balls from them, and they tear up the boxes and throw them away. They throw them right in the trash bin, even worse, in their apartments, in the kitchen, in the trash he saw a ripped-up, dirtied box with a cigarette butt inside. A fearful black rage then filled Alexei Petrovich, his eyes flashed, he foamed at the mouth, forgot words, fiery spots flashed in front of his eyes, he could have strangled, torn them to pieces. Who did this? Who dared do this? Come on out, why don't you! He rolled up his sleeves: Where is he? Mamochka ran over, calmed him down, led the enraged Alexei Petrovich off, took away the knife, tore the hammer from his convulsed fingers. The Men and Women were afraid and sat quietly, hidden in their rooms.

The sun has moved to another window. Alexei Petrovich has finished his work. Mamochka fell asleep in the chair, she's snoring, her cheeks gurgle, she whistles: pssshhew-ew-ew . . . Alexei Petrovich oh so quietly takes two boxes, ca-arefully, on tip-tip-tippy-toes — goes to his bed, ca-aarefully, carefully puts them under his pillow. At night he'll take them out and sniff them. How the glue smells! Soft, sour, muffled, like the letter *F*.

Mamochka woke up, it's time to take a walk. Down the stairs, only not in the elevator — you can't close Alexei Petrovich up in the elevator: he'll begin to flail and squeal like a rabbit; why don't you understand? — they're pulling, pulling on my legs, dragging them down.

Mamochka floats ahead, nods at acquaintances. Today we'll deliver the boxes: unpleasant. Alexei Petrovich deliberately drags his feet: he doesn't want to go to the pharmacy.

"Alexei, don't stick out your tongue!"

The dawn has fallen behind the tall buildings. The gold windowpanes burn right under the roof. Special people live there, not the same kind as us: they fly like white doves, flitting from balcony to balcony. A smooth, feathery breast, human face — if a bird like that roosts on your railings, tilts its head and starts to coo and bill — you'll look into its eyes, forget human speech, and start clucking in bird language, you'll jump along the iron poles with fuzzy little legs.

Under the horizon, under the bowl of the earth, giant wheels have started turning, monstrous conveyer belts are winding, toothed gears are pulling the sun down and the moon up. The day is tired, it has folded its white wings, flies westward, big, in loose clothes, it waves a sleeve, releases stars, blesses the people walking on the chilling earth: good-bye, good-bye, I'll come again tomorrow.

They're selling ice cream on the corner. He'd really like some ice cream. Men and Women — but especially Women — stick money into the square window and get a frosty, crunchy goblet. They laugh; they throw the round, sticky papers on the ground or stick them on the wall, they open their mouths wide, lick the sweet, needlelike cold with red tongues.

"Mamochka, ice cream!"

"You're not allowed. You have a sore throat."

If he mustn't, he mustn't. But he really, really wants some. It's awful how much he wants some. If he had one of those monies, like other Men and Women have, one of the silvery, shiny ones; or a little yellow piece of paper that smells like bread — they also take those at the square windows. Ooh, ooh, ooh, how he wants ice cream, they're all allowed, they all get ice cream.

"Alexei, don't twist your head around!"

Mamochka knows best. I'm going to listen to Mamochka. Only she knows the safe path through the thickets of the world. But if Mamochka turned away . . . Pushkin Square.

"Mamochka, Pushkin — is he a writer?"

"A writer."

"I'm going to be a writer too."

"Of course you will. If you want to — you will."

And why not? He wants to, so he will be. He'll get some paper, a pencil, and he'll be a writer. There, that's decided. He'll be a writer. That's fine.

In the evenings Mamochka sits in a spacious armchair, pushes her glasses down on her nose, and reads thickly:

> *"A pall the storm casts on the sky,*
> *And whirls the twisting snow,*
> *First like a beast she'll howl and cry,*
> *Then like a child sob soft and low."*

Alexei Petrovich really loves this. He laughs heartily, baring his yellow teeth; happy, he stamps his foot.

> *"First like a beast she'll howl and cry,*
> *Then like a child sob soft and low."*

The words get to the end — and turn around, get to the end again — and turn around again.

> *"Apall thus tormacas tson thus ky,*
> *An dwhirls thet wistings no!*
> *First likab eastsheel howland cry,*
> *Then likach ild sobs off tandlow!"*

Very good. This is how she'll howl: oo-oooooo!

Shhh, sshhh, Alexei, calm down!

The sky is all sprinkled with stars. Alexei Petrovich knows them: little shining beads, hanging all by themselves in the black emptiness. When Alexei Petrovich lies in bed and wants to go to sleep, his legs start growing on their own, down, down, and his head grows up, up, to the black dome, up, and sways like the top of a tree in a storm, while the stars scrape his skull like sand. And the second Alexei Petrovich, inside, keeps shrinking and shrinking, compressing, he disappears in a poppy seed, in a sharp needle tip, in a microbe, in nothingness, and if he's not stopped, he'll vanish there completely. But the outside, giant Alexei Petrovich sways like a pine log mast, grows, scratches his bald spot against the night dome, doesn't allow the little one to disappear into a dot. And these two Alexei Petroviches are one and the same. And this makes sense, this is right.

At home Mamochka undresses, demolishes her daytime corpus, puts on a red robe, becomes simpler, warmer, more comprehensible. Alexei Petrovich wants Mamochka to pick him up. What nonsense! Mamochka goes out into the kitchen. It seems like she's been gone an awful long time. Alexei Petrovich checked whether the boxes were still there, sniffed the oilcloth, took a chance, and went out into the hall. The corner door, where the guests of the Sea Girl giggle at night, was cracked open. A white bed was visible. Where's Mamochka? Maybe she's in there? Alexei Petrovich peeped in the crack cautiously. No one. Maybe Mamochka hid in the closet? Should he go in? The room is empty. On the Sea Girl's table — an open tin can, bread, a nibbled pickle. And — a little piece of yellow paper and silver circles. Money! Take the money, run downstairs along the dark staircase, into the labyrinth of streets, look for the square window, and they'll give him a sweet cold cup.

Alexei Petrovich grabs, jingles, knocks things over, runs, slams the door, breaths loud and fast, trips. The street. It's dark. Which way? That way? Or this way? What's in his fist? Money! Someone else's money! The money shows through his hairy fist. Stick his hand in his pocket. No, it'll show through anyway. Someone else's money! He took someone else's money! Passersby turn around, whisper to one another: "He took someone else's money!" People press to the windows, shoving each other: Let me look. Where is he? There he is! He has money! Aha! You took it, did you? Alexei Petrovich runs in the dark. Clink clink clink clink—the coins in his pocket. The whole city has spilled out onto the street. The shutters are thrown open. Hands point from every window, eyes shine, long red tongues stick out: "He took the money!" Let out the dogs. The fire engines blare, the hoses uncoil: Where is he? Over there! After him! Crazed, Alexei Petrovich rushes about. Throw it away, tear it from his hands, away, away, there it is, there it is! With his foot! Stamp on it with his foot! Traaaammmpple it! That's it. . . . There. . . . It's not breathing. It's quiet. It's died out. He wiped his face. There. Now where? Night. There's a smell. Where's Mamochka? Night. In the entryways wolves stand in black columns: they're waiting. I'll walk backward. I'll trick them. Good. It's stifling. I'll unbutton. I'll unbutton everything. Good. Now? Women with Legs walked by. They turned around. Snorted. So that's the way it is? Whaaaat? Me? I'm a wolf! I walk backward!!! Aha, scared are you? I'll catch up with you, I'll pounce, we'll see just what these Legs of yours are! He rushed at them. A cry. A-a-a-a! A blow. Don't hit! A blow. Men smell of Tobacco, they hit you in the stomach, the teeth! Don't! Forget it, leave him alone — don't you see? . . . Let's go.

Alexei Petrovich leans against a drainpipe, spits something black, whines. Little one, so little, alone, you got lost on the street, you came into this world by mistake. Get out of here, it's not for you! Alexei Petrovich cries with a loud howl, raising his disfigured face to the stars.

Mamochka, Mamochka, where are you? Mamochka, the road is black, the voices are silent, the paths lead into a deep swamp. Mamochka, your child is crying, dying, your only one, beloved, long-awaited, long-suffered. . . .

Mamochka is running, Mamochka is gasping, she stretches out her hands, shouts, grabs, presses him to her breast, feels him all over, kisses him. Mamochka is sobbing — she's found him, found him!

Mamochka leads Alexei Petrovich by the reins into a warm den, into a soft nest, under a white wing.

The swollen face is washed. Alexei Petrovich snuffles at the table, a napkin tied round him.

"Do you want a soft-boiled egg? Soft-boiled, a runny one?"

Alexei Petrovich nods his head: Yes, I want one. The grandfather clock ticks. It's peaceful. Delicious hot milk, soft, like the letter *N*. Something clears inside his head. That's right, he wanted to be . . .

"Mamochka, give me paper and a pencil! Quick! I'm going to be a writer!"

"Lord almighty! My poor baby! Why on earth . . . Well, now, don't cry, calm down, I'll give you some; just wait, you have to blow your nose."

White paper, a sharp pencil. Quickly, quickly, while he hasn't forgotten! He knows everything, he has understood the world, understood the Rules, grasped the laws of connection of millions of snatches and of odd bits and pieces! Lightning strikes Alexei Petrovich's brain! He frets, he grumbles, grabs a piece of paper, pushes the glasses aside with his elbow, and, surprised at his own joyful renewal, hurriedly writes the newly acquired truth in big letters: "Night. Night. Night. Night. Night. Night. Night. Night. Night. Night . . ."   [1991]

Leo Tolstoy (1828–1910) *is generally considered the greatest Russian writer of prose fiction. Born on his parents' estate in the province of Tula, he spent his years at the university drinking and gambling like many other noblemen, but in his twenties he joined the Russian army and began writing sketches of military life. After he left the army and traveled in Europe, he settled down to writing. He produced his two great novels,* War and Peace *and* Anna Karenina, *in 1869 and 1877 respectively. As Tolstoy grew older, he began to be dissatisfied with literature, reaching the conclusion that art is ungodly because it is founded on imagination. Vladimir Nabokov described Tolstoy's obsession thus: "Somehow, the process of seeking the Truth seemed more important to him than the easy, vivid, brilliant discovery of the illusion of truth through the medium of his artistic genius." In his eighties Tolstoy decided that by living comfortably on his country estate he was betraying his ideal of simple, saintly existence, so he wandered away from his home, heading for a monastery. He died in the waiting room of a little railway station, refusing to let his wife come near him.*

In "The Soul of the Artist" (1896), an essay about Guy de Maupassant, Tolstoy wrote:

> *The cement which binds together every work of art into a whole and thereby produces the effect of lifelike illusion, is not the unity of persons and places, but that of the author's independent moral relation to the subject. . . . Therefore, a writer who has not a clear, definite, and fresh view of the universe, and especially a writer who does not even consider this necessary, cannot produce a work of art. He may write much and beautifully, but a work of art will not result.*

The chief theme of Tolstoy's writing, as in his great story "The Death of Ivan Ilych" (1886), is that the only certain happiness is to live for others. This helps to explain the tragedy of Ivan Ilych, who just before his death realizes that he has not lived as he should have. The story took Tolstoy two years to finish. In its first version, it was told in the first person by a colleague, who was given the diary Ivan Ilych kept during his fatal illness. The narrator begins, "It is impossible, absolutely impossible, to live as I have lived, and as we all live. I realized that as a result of the death of an acquaintance of mine, Ivan Ilych, and of the diary he left behind." Finally Tolstoy told the story in the third person, without using the diary.

RELATED COMMENTARY: Leo Tolstoy, "Chekhov's Intent in 'The Darling,'" page 1497.

LEO TOLSTOY

The Death of Ivan Ilych

Translated by Louise and Aylmer Maude

I

During an interval in the Melvinski trial in the large building of the Law Courts, the members and public prosecutor met in Ivan Egorovich Shebek's private room, where the conversation turned on the celebrated Krasovski case. Fëdor Vasilievich warmly maintained that it was not subject to their jurisdiction, Ivan Egorovich maintained the contrary, while Peter Ivanovich, not having entered into the discussion at the start, took no part in it but looked through the *Gazette* which had just been handed in.

"Gentlemen," he said, "Ivan Ilych has died!"

"You don't say so!"

"Here, read it yourself," replied Peter Ivanovich, handing Fëdor Vasilievich the paper still damp from the press. Surrounded by a black border were the words: "Praskovya Fëdorovna Golovina, with profound sorrow, informs relatives and friends of the demise of her beloved husband Ivan Ilych Golovin, Member of the Court of Justice, which occurred on February the 4th of this year 1882. The funeral will take place on Friday at one o'clock in the afternoon."

Ivan Ilych had been a colleague of the gentlemen present and was liked by them all. He had been ill for some weeks with an illness said to be incurable. His post had been kept open for him, but there had been conjectures that in case of his death Alexeev might receive his appointment, and that either Vinnikov or Shtabel would succeed Alexeev. So on receiving the news of Ivan Ilych's death the first thought of each of the gentlemen in that private room was of the changes and promotions it might occasion among themselves or their acquaintances.

"I shall be sure to get Shtabel's place or Vinnikov's," thought Fëdor Vasilievich. "I was promised that long ago, and the promotion means an extra eight hundred rubles a year for me besides the allowance."

"Now I must apply for my brother-in-law's transfer from Kaluga," thought Peter Ivanovich. "My wife will be very glad, and then she won't be able to say that I never do anything for her relations."

"I thought he would never leave his bed again," said Peter Ivanovich aloud. "It's very sad."

"But what really was the matter with him?"

"The doctors couldn't say — at least they could, but each of them said something different. When last I saw him I thought he was getting better."

"And I haven't been to see him since the holidays. I always meant to go."

"Had he any property?"

"I think his wife had a little — but something quite trifling."

"We shall have to go to see her, but they live so terribly far away."

"Far away from you, you mean. Everything's far away from your place."

"You see, he never can forgive my living on the other side of the river," said Peter Ivanovich, smiling at Shebek. Then, still talking of the distances between different parts of the city, they returned to the Court.

Besides considerations as to the possible transfers and promotions likely to result from Ivan Ilych's death, the mere fact of the death of a near acquaintance aroused, as usual, in all who heard of it the complacent feeling that, "it is he who is dead and not I."

Each one thought or felt, "Well, he's dead but I'm alive!" But the more intimate of Ivan Ilych's acquaintances, his so-called friends, could not help thinking also that they would now have to fulfill the very tiresome demands of propriety by attending the funeral service and paying a visit of condolence to the widow.

Fëdor Vasilievich and Peter Ivanovich had been his nearest acquaintances. Peter Ivanovich had studied law with Ivan Ilych and had considered himself to be under obligations to him.

Having told his wife at dinner-time of Ivan Ilych's death and of his conjecture that it might be possible to get her brother transferred to their circuit, Peter Ivanovich sacrificed his usual nap, put on his evening clothes, and drove to Ivan Ilych's house.

At the entrance stood a carriage and two cabs. Leaning against the wall in the hall downstairs near the cloak-stand was a coffin-lid covered with cloth of gold, ornamented with gold cord and tassels, that had been polished up with metal powder. Two ladies in black were taking off their fur cloaks. Peter Ivanovich recognized one of them as Ivan Ilych's sister, but the other was a stranger to him. His colleague Schwartz was just coming downstairs, but on seeing Peter Ivanovich enter he stopped and winked at him, as if to say: "Ivan Ilych has made a mess of things — not like you and me."

Schwartz's face, with his Piccadilly whiskers and his slim figure in evening dress, had as usual an air of elegant solemnity which contrasted with the playfulness of his character and had a special piquancy here, or so it seemed to Peter Ivanovich.

Peter Ivanovich allowed the ladies to precede him and slowly followed them upstairs. Schwartz did not come down but remained where he was, and Peter Ivanovich understood that he wanted to arrange where they should play bridge that evening. The ladies went upstairs to the widow's room, and Schwartz, with seriously compressed lips but a playful look in his eyes, indicated by a twist of his eyebrows the room to the right where the body lay.

Peter Ivanovich, like everyone else on such occasions, entered feeling uncertain what he would have to do. All he knew was that at such times it is always safe to cross oneself. But he was not quite sure whether one should make obeisances while doing so. He therefore adopted a middle course. On entering the room he began crossing himself and made a slight movement resembling a bow. At the same time, as far as the motion of his head and arm allowed, he surveyed the room. Two young men — apparently nephews, one of whom was a high-school pupil — were leaving the room, crossing themselves as they did so. An old woman was standing motionless, and a lady with strangely arched eyebrows was saying something to her in a whisper. A vigorous, resolute Church Reader, in a frock-coat, was reading something in a loud voice with an expression that precluded any contradiction. The butler's assistant, Gerasim, stepping lightly in front of Peter Ivanovich, was strewing something on the floor. Noticing this, Peter Ivanovich was immediately aware of a faint odor of a decomposing body.

The last time he had called on Ivan Ilych, Peter Ivanovich had seen Gerasim in the study. Ivan Ilych had been particularly fond of him and he was performing the duty of a sick nurse.

Peter Ivanovich continued to make the sign of the cross, slightly inclining his head in an intermediate direction between the coffin, the Reader, and the icons on the table in a corner of the room. Afterwards, when it seemed to him that this movement of his arm in crossing himself had gone on too long, he stopped and began to look at the corpse.

The dead man lay, as dead men always lie, in a specially heavy way, his rigid limbs sunk in the soft cushions of the coffin, with the head forever bowed on the pillow. His yellow waxen brow with bald patches over his sunken temples was thrust up in the way peculiar to the dead, the protruding nose seeming to press on the upper lip. He was much changed and had grown even thinner since Peter Ivanovich had last seen him, but, as is always the case with the dead, his face was handsomer and above all more dignified than when he was alive. The expression on the face said that what was necessary had been accomplished, and accomplished rightly. Besides this there was in that expression a reproach and a warning to the living. This warning seemed to Peter Ivanovich out of place, or at least not applicable to him. He felt a certain discomfort and so he hurriedly crossed himself once more and turned and went out the door — too hurriedly and too regardless of propriety, as he himself was aware.

Schwartz was waiting for him in the adjoining room with legs spread wide apart and both hands toying with his top-hat behind his back. The mere sight of that playful, well-groomed, and elegant figure refreshed Peter Ivanovich. He felt that Schwartz was above all these happenings and would not surrender to any depressing influences. His very look said that this incident of a church service for Ivan Ilych could not be a sufficient reason for infringing the order of the session — in other words, that it would certainly not prevent his unwrapping a new pack of cards and shuffling them that evening while a footman placed four fresh candles on the table: in fact, that there was no reason for supposing that this incident would hinder their spending the evening agreeably. Indeed he said this in a whisper as Peter Ivanovich passed him, proposing that they should meet for a game at Fëdor Vasilievich's. But apparently Peter Ivanovich was not destined to play bridge that evening. Praskovya Fëdorovna (a short, fat woman who despite all efforts to the contrary had continued to broaden steadily from her shoulders downwards and who had the same extraordinarily arched eyebrows as the lady who had been standing by the coffin), dressed all in black, her head covered with lace, came out of her own room with some other ladies, conducted them to the room where the dead body lay, and said: "The service will begin immediately. Please go in."

Schwartz, making an indefinite bow, stood still, evidently neither accepting nor declining this invitation. Praskovya Fëdorovna, recognizing Peter Ivanovich, sighed, went close up to him, took his hand, and said: "I know you were a true friend to Ivan Ilych . . ." and looked at him awaiting some suitable response. And Peter Ivanovich knew that, just as it had been the right thing to cross himself in that room, so what he had to do here was to press her hand, sigh, and say, "Believe me. . . ." So he did all this and as he did it felt that the desired result had been achieved: that both he and she were touched.

"Come with me. I want to speak to you before it begins," said the widow. "Give me your arm."

Peter Ivanovich gave her his arm and they went to the inner rooms, passing Schwartz, who winked at Peter Ivanovich compassionately.

"That does for our bridge! Don't object if we find another player. Perhaps you can cut in when you do escape," said his playful look.

Peter Ivanovich sighed still more deeply and despondently, and Praskovya Fëdorovna pressed his arm gratefully. When they reached the drawing-room, upholstered in pink cretonne and lighted by a dim lamp, they sat down at the table — she on a sofa and Peter Ivanovich on a low pouffe, the springs of which yielded spasmodically under his weight. Praskovya Fëdorovna had been on the point of warning him to take another seat, but felt that such a warning was out of keeping with her present condition and so changed her mind. As he sat down on the pouffe Peter Ivanovich recalled how Ivan Ilych had arranged this room and had consulted him regarding this pink cretonne with green leaves. The whole room was full of furniture and knick-knacks, and on her way to the sofa the lace of the widow's black shawl caught on the carved edge of the table. Peter Ivanovich rose to detach it, and the springs of the pouffe, relieved of his weight, rose also and gave him a push. The widow began detaching her shawl herself, and Peter Ivanovich again sat down, suppressing the rebellious springs of the pouffe under him. But the widow had not quite freed herself and Peter Ivanovich got up again, and again the pouffe rebelled and even creaked. When this was all over she took out a clean cambric handkerchief and began to weep. The episode with the shawl and the struggle with the pouffe had cooled Peter Ivanovich's emotions and he sat there with a sullen look on his face. This awkward situation was interrupted by Sokolov, Ivan Ilych's butler, who came to report that the plot in the cemetery that Praskovya Fëdorovna had chosen would cost two hundred rubles. She stopped weeping and, looking at Peter Ivanovich with the air of a victim, remarked in French that it was very hard for her. Peter

Ivanovich made a silent gesture signifying his full conviction that it must indeed be so.

"Please smoke," she said in a magnanimous yet crushed voice, and turned to discuss with Sokolov the price of the plot for the grave.

Peter Ivanovich while lighting his cigarette heard her inquiring very circumstantially into the price of different plots in the cemetery and finally decided which she would take. When that was done she gave instructions about engaging the choir. Sokolov then left the room.

"I look after everything myself," she told Peter Ivanovich, shifting the albums that lay on the table; and noticing that the table was endangered by his cigarette-ash, she immediately passed him an ashtray, saying as she did so: "I consider it an affectation to say that my grief prevents my attending to practical affairs. On the contrary, if anything can — I won't say console me, but — distract me, it is seeing to everything concerning him." She again took out her handkerchief as if preparing to cry, but suddenly, as if mastering her feeling, she shook herself and began to speak calmly. "But there is something I want to talk to you about."

Peter Ivanovich bowed, keeping control of the springs of the pouffe, which immediately began quivering under him.

"He suffered terribly the last few days."

"Did he?" said Peter Ivanovich.

"Oh, terribly! He screamed unceasingly, not for minutes but for hours. For the last three days he screamed incessantly. It was unendurable. I cannot understand how I bore it; you could hear him three rooms off. Oh, what I have suffered!"

"Is it possible that he was conscious all that time?" asked Peter Ivanovich.

"Yes," she whispered. "To the last moment. He took leave of us a quarter of an hour before he died, and asked us to take Vasya away."

The thought of the sufferings of this man he had known so intimately, first as a merry little boy, then as a school-mate, and later as a grown-up colleague, suddenly struck Peter Ivanovich with horror, despite an unpleasant consciousness of his own and this woman's dissimulation. He again saw that brow, and that nose pressing down on the lip, and felt afraid for himself.

"Three days of frightful suffering and then death! Why, that might suddenly, at any time, happen to me," he thought, and for a moment felt terrified. But — he did not himself know how — the customary reflection at once occurred to him that this had happened to Ivan Ilych and not to him, and that it should not and could not happen to him, and that to think that it could would be yielding to depression which he ought not to do, as Schwartz's expression plainly showed. After which reflection Peter Ivanovich felt reassured, and began to ask with interest about the details of Ivan Ilych's death, as though death was an accident natural to Ivan Ilych but certainly not to himself.

After many details of the really dreadful physical sufferings Ivan Ilych had endured (which details he learnt only from the effect those sufferings had produced on Praskoyva Fëdorovna's nerves) the widow apparently found it necessary to get to business.

"Oh, Peter Ivanovich, how hard is it! How terribly, terribly hard!" and she again began to weep.

Peter Ivanovich sighed and waited for her to finish blowing her nose. When she had done so he said, "Believe me . . ." and she again began talking and brought out what was evidently her chief concern with him — namely, to question him as to how she could obtain a grant of money from the government on the occasion of her husband's death. She made it appear that she was asking Peter Ivanovich's advice about her pension, but he soon saw that she already knew about that to the minutest detail, more even than he did himself. She knew how much could be got out of the government in consequence of her husband's death, but wanted to find out whether she could not possibly extract something more. Peter Ivanovich tried to think of some means of doing so, but after reflecting for a while and, out of propriety, condemning the government for its niggardliness, he said he thought that nothing more could be got. Then she sighed and evidently began to devise means of getting rid of her visitor. Noticing this, he put out his cigarette, rose, pressed her hand, and went out into the anteroom.

In the dining-room where the clock stood that Ivan Ilych had liked so much and had bought at an antique shop, Peter Ivanovich met a priest and a few acquaintances who had come to attend the service, and he recognized Ivan Ilych's daughter, a handsome young woman. She was in black and her slim figure appeared slimmer than ever. She had a gloomy, determined, almost angry expression, and bowed to Peter Ivanovich as though he were in some way to blame. Behind her, with the same offended look, stood a wealthy young man, an examining magistrate, whom Peter Ivanovich also knew and who was her fiancé, as he had heard. He bowed mournfully to them and was about to pass into the death-chamber, when from under the stairs appeared the figure of Ivan Ilych's schoolboy son, who was extremely like his father. He seemed a little Ivan Ilych, such as Peter Ivanovich remembered when they studied law together. His tear-stained eyes had in them the look that is seen in the eyes of boys of thirteen or fourteen who are not pure-minded. When he saw Peter Ivanovich he scowled morosely and shamefacedly. Peter Ivanovich nodded to him and entered the death-chamber. The service began: candles, groans, incense, tears, and sobs. Peter Ivanovich stood looking gloomily down at his feet. He did not look once at the dead man, did not yield to any depressing influence, and was one of the first to leave the room. There was no one in the anteroom, but Gerasim darted out of the dead man's room, rummaged with his strong hands among the fur coats to find Peter Ivanovich's, and helped him on with it.

"Well, friend Gerasim," said Peter Ivanovich, so as to say something. "It's a sad affair, isn't it?"

"It's God's will. We shall all come to it some day," said Gerasim, displaying his teeth — the even, white teeth of a healthy peasant — and, like a man in the thick of urgent work, he briskly opened the front door, called the coachman, helped Peter Ivanovich into the sledge, and sprang back to the porch as if in readiness for what he had to do next.

Peter Ivanovich found the fresh air particularly pleasant after the smell of incense, the dead body, and carbolic acid.

"Where to, sir?" asked the coachman.

"It's not too late even now. . . . I'll call round on Fëdor Vasilievich."

He accordingly drove there and found them just finishing the first rubber, so that it was quite convenient for him to cut in.

II

Ivan Ilych's life had been most simple and most ordinary and therefore most terrible.

He had been a member of the Court of Justice, and died at the age of forty-five. His father had been an official who after serving in various ministries and departments in Petersburg had made the sort of career which brings men to positions from which by reason of their long service they cannot be dismissed, though they were obviously unfit to hold any responsible position, and for whom therefore posts are specially created, which though fictitious carry salaries of from six to ten thousand rubles that are not fictitious, and in receipt of which they live on to a great age.

Such was the Privy Councillor and superfluous member of various superfluous institutions, Ilya Epimovich Golovin.

He had three sons, of whom Ivan Ilych was the second. The eldest son was following in his father's footsteps only in another department, and was already approaching that stage in the service at which a similar sinecure would be reached. The third son was a failure. He had ruined his prospects in a number of positions and was now serving in the railway department. His father and brothers, and still more their wives, not merely disliked meeting him, but avoided remembering his existence unless compelled to do so. His sister had married Baron Greff, a Petersburg official of her father's type. Ivan Ilych was *le phénix de la famille*[1] as people said. He was neither as cold and formal as his elder brother nor as wild as the younger, but was a happy mean between them — an intelligent, polished, lively, and agreeable man. He had studied with his younger brother at the School of Law, but the latter had failed to complete the course and was expelled when he was in the fifth class. Ivan Ilych finished the course well. Even when he was at the School of Law he was just what he remained for the rest of his life: a capable, cheerful, good-natured, and sociable man, though strict in the fulfillment of what he considered to be his duty: and he considered his duty to be what was so considered by those in authority. Neither as a boy nor as a man was he a toady, but from early youth was by nature attracted to people of high station as a fly is drawn to the light, assimilating their ways and views of life and establishing friendly

---

[1] The pride of the family. (Unless otherwise indicated, all foreign phrases are in French — often the everyday language of middle-class and upper-class Russians of Tolstoy's time.)

relations with them. All the enthusiasms of childhood and youth passed without leaving much trace on him; he succumbed to sensuality, to vanity, and latterly among the highest classes to liberalism, but always within limits which his instinct unfailingly indicated to him as correct.

At school he had done things which had formerly seemed to him very horrid and made him feel disgusted with himself when he did them; but when later on he saw that such actions were done by people of good position and that they did not regard them as wrong, he was able not exactly to regard them as right, but to forget about them entirely or not be at all troubled at remembering them.

Having graduated from the School of Law and qualified for the tenth rank of the civil service, and having received money from his father for his equipment, Ivan Ilych ordered himself clothes as Scharmer's, the fashionable tailor, hung a medallion inscribed *respice finem*[2] on his watch-chain, took leave of his professor and the prince who was patron of the school, had a farewell dinner with his comrades at Donon's first-class restaurant, and with his new and fashionable portmanteau, linen, clothes, shaving and other toilet appliances, and a traveling rug, all purchased at the best shops, he set off for one of the provinces where, through his father's influence, he had been attached to the Governor as an official for special service.

In the province Ivan Ilych soon arranged as easy and agreeable a position for himself as he had had at the School of Law. He performed his official tasks, made his career, and at the same time amused himself pleasantly and decorously. Occasionally he paid official visits to country districts, where he behaved with dignity both to his superiors and inferiors, and performed the duties entrusted to him, which related chiefly to the sectarians,[3] with an exactness and incorruptible honesty of which he could not but feel proud.

In official matters, despite his youth and taste for frivolous gaiety, he was exceedingly reserved, punctilious, and even severe; but in society he was often amusing and witty, and always good-natured, correct in his manner, and *bon enfant*,[4] as the governor and his wife — with whom he was like one of the family — used to say of him.

In the province he had an affair with a lady who made advances to the elegant young lawyer, and there was also a milliner; and there were carousals with aides-de-camp who visited the district, and after-supper visits to a certain outlying street of doubtful reputation; and there was too some obsequiousness to his chief and even to his chief's wife, but all this was done with such a tone of good breeding that no hard names could be applied to it. It all came under the heading of the French saying: *"Il faut que jeunesse se passe."*[5] It was all done with clean hands, in clean linen, with French phrases, and above all among people of the best society and consequently with the approval of people of rank.

---

[2] "Consider your end," that is, your death (Latin).
[3] "Old Believers," dissenters from the Orthodox Church.
[4] One of the boys (literally, "a good child").
[5] "Youth will have its day."

So Ivan Ilych served for five years and then came a change in his official life. The new and reformed judicial institutions were introduced, and new men were needed. Ivan Ilych became such a new man. He was offered the post of examining magistrate, and he accepted it though the post was in another province and obliged him to give up the connections he had formed and to make new ones. His friends met to give him a send-off; they had a group-photograph taken and presented him with a silver cigarette-case, and he set off to his new post.

As examining magistrate Ivan Ilych was just as *comme il faut*[6] and decorous a man, inspiring general respect and capable of separating his official duties from his private life, as he had been when acting as an official on special service. His duties now as examining magistrate were far more interesting and attractive than before. In his former position it had been pleasant to wear an undress uniform made by Scharmer, and to pass through the crowd of petitioners and officials who were timorously awaiting an audience with the governor, and who envied him as with free and easy gait he went straight into his chief's private room to have a cup of tea and a cigarette with him. But not many people had then been directly dependent on him — only police officials and the sectarians when he went on special missions — and he liked to treat them politely, almost as comrades, as if he were letting them feel that he who had the power to crush them was treating them in this simple, friendly way. There were then but few such people. But now, as an examining magistrate, Ivan Ilych felt that everyone without exception, even the most important and self-satisfied, was in his power, and that he need only write a few words on a sheet of paper with a certain heading, and this or that important, self-satisfied person would be brought before him in the role of an accused person or a witness, and if he did not choose to allow him to sit down, would have to stand before him and answer his questions. Ivan Ilych never abused his power; he tried on the contrary to soften its expression, but the consciousness of it and of the possibility of softening its effect, supplied the chief interest and attraction of his office. In his work itself, especially in his examinations, he very soon acquired a method of eliminating all considerations irrelevant to the legal aspect of the case, and reducing even the most complicated case to a form in which it would be presented on paper only in its externals, completely excluding his personal opinion of the matter, while above all observing every prescribed formality. The work was new and Ivan Ilych was one of the first men to apply the new Code of 1864.[7]

On taking up the post of examining magistrate in a new town, he made new acquaintances and connections, placed himself on a new footing, and assumed a somewhat different tone. He took up an attitude of rather dignified aloofness towards the provincial authorities, but picked out the best circle of legal gentlemen and wealthy gentry living in the town and assumed a tone of slight dissatisfaction with the government, of moderate liberalism, and of

---

[6]Proper (literally, "as it should be").

[7]The emancipation of the serfs in 1861 was followed by a thorough all-round reform of judicial proceedings. [Translators' note]

enlightened citizenship. At the same time, without at all altering the elegance of his toilet, he ceased shaving his chin and allowed his beard to grow as it pleased.

Ivan Ilych settled down very pleasantly in this new town. The society there, which inclined towards opposition to the Governor, was friendly, his salary was larger, and he began to play *vint*,[8] which he found added not a little to the pleasure of life, for he had a capacity for cards, played good-humoredly, and calculated rapidly and astutely, so that he usually won.

After living there for two years he met his future wife, Praskovya Fëdorovna Mikhel, who was the most attractive, clever, and brilliant girl of the set in which he moved, and among other amusements and relaxations from his labors as examining magistrate, Ivan Ilych established light and playful relations with her.

While he had been an official on special service he had been accustomed to dance, but now as an examining magistrate it was exceptional for him to do so. If he danced now, he did it as if to show that though he served under the reformed order of things, and had reached the fifth official rank, yet when it came to dancing he could do it better than most people. So at the end of an evening he sometimes danced with Praskovya Fëdorovna, and it was chiefly during these dances that he captivated her. She fell in love with him. Ivan Ilych had at first no definite intention of marrying, but when the girl fell in love with him he said to himself: "Really, why shouldn't I marry?"

Praskovya Fëdorovna came of a good family, was not bad looking, and had some little property. Ivan Ilych might have aspired to a more brilliant match, but even this was good. He had his salary, and she, he hoped, would have an equal income. She was well connected, and was a sweet, pretty, and thoroughly correct young woman. To say that Ivan Ilych married because he fell in love with Praskovya Fëdorovna and found that she sympathized with his views of life would be as incorrect as to say that he married because his social circle approved of the match. He was swayed by both these considerations: the marriage gave him personal satisfaction, and at the same time it was considered the right thing by the most highly placed of his associates.

So Ivan Ilych got married.

The preparations for marriage and the beginning of married life, with its conjugal caresses, the new furniture, new crockery, and new linen, were very pleasant until his wife became pregnant — so that Ivan Ilych had begun to think that marriage would not impair the easy, agreeable, gay, and always decorous character of his life, approved of by society and regarded by himself as natural, but would even improve it. But from the first months of his wife's pregnancy, something new, unpleasant, depressing, and unseemly, and from which there was no way of escape, unexpectedly showed itself.

His wife, without any reason — *de gaieté de coeur*[9] as Ivan Ilych expressed

---

[8] A form of bridge. [Translators' note]
[9] From sheer exuberance (literally, "from happiness of heart").

it to himself — began to disturb the pleasure and propriety of their life. She began to be jealous without any cause, expected him to devote his whole attention to her, found fault with everything, and made coarse and ill-mannered scenes.

At first Ivan Ilych hoped to escape from the unpleasantness of this state of affairs by the same easy and decorous relation to life that had served him heretofore: he tried to ignore his wife's disagreeable moods, continued to live in his usual easy and pleasant way, invited friends to his house for a game of cards, and also tried going out to his club or spending his evenings with friends. But one day his wife began upbraiding him so vigorously, using such coarse words, and continued to abuse him every time he did not fulfil her demands, so resolutely and with such evident determination not to give way till he submitted — that is, till he stayed at home and was bored just as she was — that he became alarmed. He now realized that matrimony — at any rate with Praskovya Fëdorovna — was not always conducive to the pleasures and amenities of life, but on the contrary often infringed both comfort and propriety, and that he must therefore entrench himself against such infringement. And Ivan Ilych began to seek for means of doing so. His official duties were the one thing that imposed upon Praskovya Fëdorovna, and by means of his official work and the duties attached to it he began struggling with his wife to secure his own independence.

With the birth of their child, the attempts to feed it and the various failures in doing so, and with the real and imaginary illnesses of mother and child, in which Ivan Ilych's sympathy was demanded but about which he understood nothing, the need of securing for himself an existence outside his family life became still more imperative.

As his wife grew more irritable and exacting and Ivan Ilych transferred the center of gravity of his life more and more to his official work so did he grow to like his work better and became more ambitious than before.

Very soon, within a year of his wedding, Ivan Ilych had realized that marriage, though it may add some comforts to life, is in fact a very intricate and difficult affair towards which in order to perform one's duty, that is, to lead a decorous life approved of by society, one must adopt a definite attitude just as towards one's official duties.

And Ivan Ilych evolved such an attitude towards married life. He only required of it those conveniences — dinner at home, housewife, and bed — which it could give him, and above all that propriety of external forms required by public opinion. For the rest he looked for light-hearted pleasure and propriety, and was very thankful when he found them, but if he met with antagonism and querulousness he at once retired into his separate fenced-off world of official duties, where he found satisfaction.

Ivan Ilych was esteemed a good official, and after three years was made Assistant Public Prosecutor. His new duties, their importance, the possibility of indicting and imprisoning anyone he chose, the publicity his speeches received, and the success he had in all these things made his work still more attractive.

More children came. His wife became more and more querulous and ill-tempered, but the attitude Ivan Ilych had adopted towards his home life rendered him almost impervious to her grumbling.

After seven years' service in that town he was transferred to another province as Public Prosecutor. They moved, but were short of money and his wife did not like the place they moved to. Though the salary was higher the cost of living was greater, besides which two of their children died and family life became still more unpleasant for him.

Praskovya Fëdorovna blamed her husband for every inconvenience they encountered in their new home. Most of the conversations between husband and wife, especially as to the children's education, led to topics which recalled former disputes, and those disputes were apt to flare up again at any moment. There remained only those rare periods of amorousness which still came to them at times but did not last long. These were islets at which they anchored for a while and then again set out upon that ocean of veiled hostility which showed itself in their aloofness from one another. This aloofness might have grieved Ivan Ilych had he considered that it ought not to exist, but he now regarded the position as normal, and even made it the goal at which he aimed in family life. His aim was to free himself more and more from those unpleasantnesses and to give them a semblance of harmlessness and propriety. He attained this by spending less and less time with his family, and when obliged to be at home he tried to safeguard his position by the presence of outsiders. The chief thing however was that he had his official duties. The whole interest of his life now centered in the official world and that interest absorbed him. The consciousness of his power, being able to ruin anybody he wished to ruin, the importance, even the external dignity of his entry into court, or meetings with his subordinates, his success with superiors and inferiors, and above all his masterly handling of cases, of which he was conscious — all this gave him pleasure and filled his life, together with chats with his colleagues, dinners, and bridge. So that on the whole Ivan Ilych's life continued to flow as he considered it should do — pleasantly and properly.

So things continued for another seven years. His eldest daughter was already sixteen, another child had died, and only one son was left, a schoolboy and a subject of dissension. Ivan Ilych wanted to put him in the School of Law, but to spite him Praskovya Fëdorovna entered him at the High School. The daughter had been educated at home and had turned out well: the boy did not learn badly either.

III

So Ivan Ilych lived for seventeen years after his marriage. He was already a Public Prosecutor of long standing, and had declined several proposed transfers while awaiting a more desirable post, when an unanticipated and unpleasant occurrence quite upset the peaceful course of his life. He was expecting to be offered the post of presiding judge in a University town, but Happe somehow came to the front and obtained the appointment instead. Ivan Ilych became irritable, reproached Happe, and quarreled both with him and with his immediate superiors — who became colder to him and again passed him over when other appointments were made.

This was in 1880, the hardest year of Ivan Ilych's life. It was then that it became evident on the one hand that his salary was insufficient for them to live on, and on the other that he had been forgotten, and not only this, but that what was for him the greatest and most cruel injustice appeared to others a quite ordinary occurrence. Even his father did not consider it his duty to help him. Ivan Ilych felt himself abandoned by everyone, and that they regarded his position with a salary of 3,500 rubbles as quite normal and even fortunate. He alone knew that with the consciousness of the injustices done him, with his wife's incessant nagging, and with the debts he had contracted by living beyond his means, his position was far from normal.

In order to save money that summer he obtained leave of absence and went with his wife to live in the country at her brother's place.

In the country, without his work, he experienced *ennui* for the first time in his life, and not only *ennui* but intolerable depression, and he decided that it was impossible to go on living like that, and that it was necessary to take energetic measures.

Having passed a sleepless night pacing up and down the veranda, he decided to go to Petersburg and bestir himself, in order to punish those who had failed to appreciate him and to get transferred to another ministry.

Next day, despite many protests from his wife and her brother, he started for Petersburg with the sole object of obtaining a post with a salary of five thousand rubles a year. He was no longer bent on any particular department, or tendency, or kind of activity. All he now wanted was an appointment to another post with a salary of five thousand rubles, either in the administration, in the banks, with the railways, in one of the Empress Marya's Institutions,[10] or even in the customs — but it had to carry with it a salary of five thousand rubles and be in a ministry other than that in which they had failed to appreciate him.

And this quest of Ivan Ilych's was crowned with remarkable and unexpected success. At Kursk an acquaintance of his, F. I. Ilyin, got into the first-class carriage, sat down beside Ivan Ilych, and told him of a telegram just received by the Governor of Kursk announcing that a change was about to take place in the ministry: Peter Ivanovich was to be superseded by Ivan Semënovich.

The proposed change, apart from its significance for Russia, had a special significance for Ivan Ilych, because by bringing forward a new man, Peter Petrovich, and consequently his friend Zachar Ivanovich, it was highly favorable for Ivan Ilych, since Zachar Ivanovich was a friend and colleague of his.

In Moscow this news was confirmed, and on reaching Petersburg Ivan Ilych found Zachar Ivanovich and received a definite promise of an appointment in his former department of Justice.

---

[10]Orphanages founded by the wife of Czar Paul I, who ruled from 1796 to 1801.

A week later he telegraphed to his wife: "Zachar in Miller's place. I shall receive appointment on presentation of report."

Thanks to this change of personnel, Ivan Ilych had unexpectedly obtained an appointment in his former ministry which placed him two stages above his former colleagues besides giving him five thousand rubles salary and three thousand five hundred rubles for expenses connected with his removal. All his ill humor towards his former enemies and the whole department vanished, and Ivan Ilych was completely happy.

He returned to the country more cheerful and contented than he had been for a long time. Praskovya Fëdorovna also cheered up and a truce was arranged between them. Ivan Ilych told of how he had been fêted by everybody in Petersburg, how all those who had been his enemies were put to shame and now fawned on him, how envious they were of his appointment, and how much everybody in Petersburg had liked him.

Praskovya Fëdorovna listened to all this and appeared to believe it. She did not contradict anything, but only made plans for their life in the town to which they were going. Ivan Ilych saw with delight that these plans were his plans, that he and his wife agreed, and that, after a stumble, his life was regaining its due and natural character of pleasant lightheartedness and decorum.

Ivan Ilych had come back for a short time only, for he had to take up his new duties on the 10th of September. Moreover, he needed time to settle into the new place, to move all his belongings from the province, and to buy and order many additional things: in a word, to make such arrangements as he had resolved on, which were almost exactly what Praskovya Fëdorovna too had decided on.

Now that everything had happened so fortunately, and that he and his wife were at one in their aims and moreover saw so little of one another, they got on together better than they had done since the first years of marriage. Ivan Ilych had thought of taking his family away with him at once, but the insistence of his wife's brother and her sister-in-law, who had suddenly become particularly amiable and friendly to him and his family, induced him to depart alone.

So he departed, and the cheerful state of mind induced by his success and by the harmony between his wife and himself, the one intensifying the other, did not leave him. He found a delightful house, just the thing both he and his wife had dreamt of. Spacious, lofty reception rooms in the old style, a convenient and dignified study, rooms for his wife and daughter, a study for his son — it might have been specially built for them. Ivan Ilych himself superintended the arrangements, chose the wallpapers, supplemented the furniture (preferably with antiques which he considered particularly *comme il faut*), and supervised the upholstering. Everything progressed and progressed and approached the ideal he had set himself: even when things were only half completed they exceeded his expectations. He saw what a refined and elegant character, free from vulgarity, it would all have when it was ready. On falling asleep he pictured to himself how the reception-room would look. Looking at the yet unfinished drawing-room he could see the fireplace, the screen, the what-not, the little chairs dotted here and there, the dishes and plates on the walls, and the bronzes, as they would be when everything was in place. He was pleased by the thought of how his wife and daughter, who shared his taste in this matter, would be impressed by it. They were certainly not expecting as much. He had been particularly successful in finding, and buying cheaply, antiques which gave a particularly aristocratic character to the whole place. But in his letters he intentionally understated everything in order to be able to surprise them. All this so absorbed him that his new duties — though he liked his official work — interested him less than he had expected. Sometimes he even had moments of absent-mindedness during the Court Sessions, and would consider whether he should have straight or curved cornices for his curtains. He was so interested in it all that he often did things himself, rearranging the furniture, or rehanging the curtains. Once when mounting a step-ladder to show the upholsterer, who did not understand, how he wanted the hangings draped, he made a false step and slipped, but being a strong and agile man he clung on and only knocked his side against the knob of the window frame. The bruised place was painful but the pain soon passed, and he felt particularly bright and well just then. He wrote: "I feel fifteen years younger." He thought he would have everything ready by September, but it dragged on till mid-October. But the result was charming not only in his eyes but to everyone who saw it.

In reality it was just what is usually seen in the houses of people of moderate means who want to appear rich, and therefore succeed only in resembling others like themselves: there were damasks, dark wood, plants, rugs, and dull and polished bronzes — all the things people of a certain class have in order to resemble other people of that class. His house was so like the others that it would never have been noticed, but to him it all seemed to be quite exceptional. He was very happy when he met his family at the station and brought them to the newly furnished house all lit up, where a footman in a white tie opened the door into the hall decorated with plants, and when they went on into the drawing room, and the study uttering exclamations of delight. He conducted them everywhere, drank in their praises eagerly, and beamed with pleasure. At tea that evening, when Praskovya Fëdorovna among other things asked him about his fall, he laughed and showed them how he had gone flying and had frightened the upholsterer.

"It's a good thing I'm a bit of an athlete. Another man might have been killed, but I merely knocked myself, just here; it hurts when it's touched, but it's passing off already — it's only a bruise."

So they began living in their new home — in which, as always happens, when they got thoroughly settled in they found they were just one room short — and with the increased income, which as always was just a little (some five hundred rubles) too little, but it was all very nice.

Things went particularly well at first, before everything was finally arranged and while something had still to be done: this thing bought, that thing ordered, another thing moved, and something else adjusted. Though there were some disputes between husband and wife, they were both so well satisfied and had so much to do that it all passed off without any serious quarrels. When nothing was left to arrange it became rather dull and something seemed to be lacking, but they were then making acquaintances, forming habits, and life was growing fuller.

Ivan Ilych spent his mornings at the law court and came home to dinner, and at first he was generally in a good humor, though he occasionally became irritable just on account of his house. (Every spot on the tablecloth or the upholstery, and every broken windowblind string, irritated him. He had devoted so much trouble to arranging it all that every disturbance of it distressed him.) But on the whole his life ran its course as he believed life should do: easily, pleasantly, and decorously.

He got up at nine, drank his coffee, read the paper, and then put on his undress uniform and went to the law courts. There the harness in which he worked had already been stretched to fit him and he donned it without a hitch: petitioners, inquiries at the chancery, the chancery itself, and the sittings public and administrative. In all this the thing was to exclude everything fresh and vital, which always disturbs the regular course of official business, and to admit only official relations with people, and then only on official grounds. A man would come, for instance, wanting some information. Ivan Ilych, as one in whose sphere the matter did not lie, would have nothing to do with him: but if the man had some business with him in his official capacity, something that could be expressed on officially stamped paper, he would do everything, positively everything he could within the limits of such relations, and in doing so would maintain the semblance of friendly human relations, that is, would observe the courtesies of life. As soon as the official relations ended, so did everything else. Ivan Ilych possessed this capacity to separate his real life from the offical side of affairs and not mix the two, in the highest degree, and by long practice and natural aptitude had brought it to such a pitch that sometimes, in the manner of a virtuoso, he would even allow himself to let the human and official relations mingle. He let himself do this just because he felt that he could at any time he chose resume the strictly official attitude again and drop the human relation. And he did it all easily, pleasantly, correctly, and even artistically. In the intervals between the sessions he smoked, drank tea, chatted a little about politics, a little about general topics, a little about cards, but most of all about official appointments. Tired, but with the feelings of a virtuoso — one of the first violins who has played his part in an orchestra with precision — he would return home to find that his wife and daughter had been out paying calls, or had a visitor, and that his son had been to school, had done his homework with his tutor, and was duly learning what is taught at High Schools. Everything was as it should be. After dinner, if they had no visitors, Ivan Ilych sometimes read a book that was being much discussed at the time, and in the evening settled down to work, that is, read official papers, compared the depositions of witnesses, and noted paragraphs of the Code applying to them. This was neither dull nor amusing. It was dull when he might have been playing bridge, but if no bridge was available it was at any rate better than doing nothing or sitting with his wife. Ivan Ilych's chief pleasure was giving little dinners to which he invited men and women of good social position, and just as his drawing-room resembled all other drawing-rooms so did his enjoyable little parties resemble all other such parties.

Once they even gave a dance. Ivan Ilych enjoyed it and everything went off well, except that it led to a violent quarrel with his wife about the cakes and sweets. Praskovya Fëdorovna had made her own plans, but Ivan Ilych insisted on getting everything from an expensive confectioner and ordered too many cakes, and the quarrel occurred because some of those cakes were left over and the confectioner's bill came to forty-five rubles. It was a great and disagreeable quarrel. Praskovya Fëdorovna called him "a fool and an imbecile," and he clutched at his head and made angry allusions to divorce.

But the dance itself had been enjoyable. The best people were there, and Ivan Ilych had danced with Princess Trufonova, a sister of the distinguished founder of the Society "Bear My Burden."

The pleasures connected with his work were pleasures of ambition; his social pleasures were those of vanity; but Ivan Ilych's greatest pleasure was playing bridge. He acknowledged that whatever disagreeable incident happened in his life, the pleasure that beamed like a ray of light about everything else was to sit down to bridge with good players, not noisy partners, and of course to four-handed bridge (with five players it was annoying to have to stand out, though one pretended not to mind), to play a clever and serious game (when the cards allowed it), and then to have supper and drink a glass of wine. After a game of bridge, especially if he had won a little (to win a large sum was unpleasant), Ivan Ilych went to bed in specially good humor.

So they lived. They formed a circle of acquaintances among the best people and were visited by people of importance and by young folk. In their views as to their acquaintances, husband, wife, and daughter were entirely agreed, and tacitly and unanimously kept at arm's length and shook off the various shabby friends and relations who, with much show of affection, gushed into the drawing-room with its Japanese plates on the walls. Soon these shabby friends ceased to obtrude themselves and only the best people remained in the Golovins' set.

Young men made up to Lisa, and Petrishchev, an examining magistrate and Dmitri Ivanovich Petrishchev's son and sole heir, began to be so attentive to her that Ivan Ilych had already spoken to Praskovya Fëdorovna about it, and considered whether they should not arrange a party for them, or get up some private theatricals.

So they lived, and all went well, without change, and life flowed pleasantly.

IV

They were all in good health. It could not be called ill health if Ivan Ilych sometimes said that he had a queer taste in his mouth and felt some discomfort in his left side.

But this discomfort increased and, though not exactly painful, grew into a sense of pressure in his side accompanied by ill humor. And his irritability became worse and worse and began to mar the agreeable, easy, and correct life that had established itself in the Golovin family. Quarrels between husband and wife became more and more frequent, and soon the ease and amenity disappeared and even the decorum was barely maintained. Scenes again became frequent, and very few of those islets remained on which husband and wife could meet without explosion. Praskovya Fëdorovna now had good reason to say that her husband's temper was trying. With characteristic exaggeration she said he had always had a dreadful temper, and that it had needed all her good nature to put up with it for twenty years. It was true that now the quarrels were started by him. His bursts of temper always came just before dinner, often just as he began to eat his soup. Sometimes he noticed that a plate or dish was chipped, or the food was not right, or his son put his elbow on the table, or his daughter's hair was not done as he liked it, and for all this he blamed Praskovya Fëdorovna. At first she retorted and said disagreeable things to him, but once or twice he fell into such a rage at the beginning of dinner that she realized it was due to some physical derangement brought on by taking food, and so she restrained herself and did not answer, but only hurried to get the dinner over. She regarded this self-restraint as highly praiseworthy. Having come to the conclusion that her husband had a dreadful temper and made her life miserable, she began to feel sorry for herself, and the more she pitied herself the more she hated her husband. She began to wish he would die; yet she did not want him to die because then his salary would cease. And this irritated her against him still more. She considered herself dreadfully unhappy just because not even his death could save her, and though she concealed her exasperation, that hidden exasperation of hers increased his irritation also.

After one scene in which Ivan Ilych had been particularly unfair and after which he had said in explanation that he certainly was irritable but that it was due to his not being well, she said that if he was ill it should be attended to, and insisted on his going to see a celebrated doctor.

He went. Everything took place as he had expected and as it always does. There was the usual waiting and the important air assumed by the doctor, with which he was so familiar (resembling that which he himself assumed in court), and the sounding and listening, and the questions which called for answers that were foregone conclusions and were evidently unnecessary, and the look of importance which implied that "if only you put yourself in our hands we will arrange everything — we know indubitably how it has to be done, always in the same way for everybody alike." It was all just as it was in the law courts. The doctor put on just the same air towards him as he himself put on towards an accused person.

The doctor said that so-and-so indicated that there was so-and-so inside the patient, but if the investigation of so-and-so did not confirm this, then he must assume that and that. If he assumed that and that, then . . . and so on. To Ivan Ilych only one question was important: was his case serious or not? But the doctor ignored that inappropriate question. From his point of view it was not the one under consideration, the real question was to decide between a floating kidney, chronic catarrh, or appendicitis. It was not a question of Ivan Ilych's life or death, but one between a floating kidney it, but will follow the treatment seriously till summer, and then we shall see. From now there must be no more of this wavering!" This was easy to say but impossible to carry out. The pain in his side oppressed him and seemed to grow worse and more incessant, while the taste in his mouth grew stranger and stranger. It seemed to him that his breath had a digusting smell, and he was conscious of a loss of appetite and strength. There was no deceiving himself: something terrible, new, and more important than anything before in his life, was taking place within him of which he alone was aware. Those about him did not understand or would not understand it, but thought everything in the world was going on as usual. That tormented Ivan Ilych more than anything. He saw that his household, especially his wife and daughter who were in a perfect whirl of visiting, did not understand anything of it and were annoyed that he was so depressed and so exacting, as if he were to blame for it. Though they tried to disguise it he saw that he was an obstacle in their path, and that his wife had adopted a definite line in regard to his illness and kept to it regardless of anything he said or did. Her attitude was this: "You know," she would say to her friends, "Ivan Ilych can't do as other people do, and keep to the treatment prescribed for him. One day he'll take his drops and keep strictly to his diet and go to bed in good time, but the next day unless I watch him he'll suddenly forget his medicine, eat sturgeon — which is forbidden — and sit up playing cards till one o'clock in the morning."

"Oh, come, when was that?" Ivan Ilych would ask in vexation. "Only once at Peter Ivanovich's."

"And yesterday with Shebek."

"Well, even if I hadn't stayed up, this pain would have kept me awake."

"Be that as it may you'll never get well like that, but will always make us wretched."

Praskovya Fëdorovna's attitude to Ivan Ilych's illness, as she expressed it both to others and to him, was that it was his own fault and was another of the annoyances he caused her. Ivan Ilych felt that this opinion escaped her involuntarily — but that did not make it easier for him.

At the law courts too, Ivan Ilych noticed, or thought he noticed, a strange attitude towards himself. It sometimes seemed to him that people were watching him inquisitively as a man whose place might soon be vacant. Then again, his friends would suddenly begin to chaff him in a friendly way about his low spirits, as if the awful, horrible, and unheard-of thing that was going on within him, incessantly gnawing at him and irresistibly drawing him away, was a very agreeable subject for jests. Schwartz in particular irritated him by his jocularity, vivacity, and *savoir-faire*, which reminded him of what he himself had been ten years ago.

Friends came to make up a set and they sat down to cards. They dealt, bending the new cards to soften them, and he sorted the diamonds in his hand and found he had seven. His partner said "No trumps" and supported him with two diamonds. What more could be wished for? It ought to be jolly and lively. They would make a grand slam. But suddenly Ivan Ilych was conscious of that gnawing pain, that taste in his mouth, and it seemed ridiculous that in such circumstances he should be pleased to make a grand slam.

He looked at his partner Mikhail Mikhaylovich, who rapped the table with his strong hand and instead of snatching up the tricks pushed the cards courteously and indulgently towards Ivan Ilych that he might have the pleasure of gathering them up without the trouble of stretching out his hand for them. "Does he think I am too weak to stretch out my arm?" thought Ivan Ilych, and forgetting what he was doing he over-trumped his partner, missing the grand slam by three tricks. And what was more awful of all was that he saw how upset Mikhail Mikhaylovich was about it but did not himself care. And it was dreadful to realize why he did not care.

They all saw that he was suffering and said: "We can stop if you are tired. Take a rest." Lie down? No, he was not at all tired, and he finished the rubber. All were gloomy and silent. Ivan Ilych felt that he had diffused this gloom over them and could not dispel it. They had supper and went away, and Ivan Ilych was left alone with the consciousness that his life was poisoned and was poisoning the lives of others, and that this poison did not weaken but penetrated more and more deeply into his whole being.

With this consciousness, and with physical pain besides the terror, he must go to bed, often to lie awake the greater part of the night. Next morning he had to get up again, dress, go to the law courts, speak, and write; or if he did not go out, spend at home those twenty-four hours a day each of which was a torture. And he had to live thus all alone on the brink of an abyss, with no one who understood or pitied him.

V

So one month passed and then another. Just before the New Year his brother-in-law came to town and stayed at their house. Ivan Ilych was at the law courts and Praskovya Fëdorovna had gone shopping. When Ivan Ilych came home and entered his study he found his brother-in-law there — a healthy, florid man — unpacking his portmanteau himself. He raised his head on hearing Ivan Ilych's footsteps and looked up at him for a moment without a word. That stare told Ivan Ilych everything. His brother-in-law opened his mouth to utter an exclamation of surprise but checked himself, and that action confirmed it all.

"I have changed, eh?"

"Yes, there is a change."

And after that, try as he would to get his brother-in-law to return to the subject of his looks, the latter would say nothing about it. Praskovya Fëdorovna came home and her brother went out to her. Ivan Ilych locked the door and began to examine himself in the glass, first full face, then in profile. He took up a portrait of himself taken with his wife, and compared it with what he saw in the glass. The change in him was immense. Then he bared his arms to the elbow, looked at them, drew the sleeves down again, sat down on an ottoman, and grew blacker than night.

"No, no, this won't do!" he said to himself, and jumped up, went to the table, took up some law papers and began to read them, but could not continue. He unlocked the door and went into the reception-room. The door leading to the drawing room was shut. He approached it on tiptoe and listened.

"No, you are exaggerating!" Praskovya Fëdorovna was saying.

"Exaggerating! Don't you see it? Why, he's a dead man! Look at his eyes — there's no light in them. But what is it that is wrong with him?"

"No one knows. Nikolaevich said something, but I don't know what. And Leshchetitsky[11] said quite the contrary. . . ."

Ivan Ilych walked away, went to his own room, lay down, and began musing: "The kidney, a floating kidney." He recalled all the doctors had told him of how it detached itself and swayed about. And by an effort of imagination he tried to catch that kidney and arrest it and support it. So little was needed for this, it seemed to him. "No, I'll go to see Peter Ivanovich again." He rang, ordered the carriage, and got ready to go.

"Where are you going, Jean?" asked his wife, with a specially sad and exceptionally kind look.

This exceptionally kind look irritated him. He looked morosely at her.

"I must go to see Peter Ivanovich."[12]

He went to see Peter Ivanovich, and together they went to see his friend, the doctor. He was in, and Ivan Ilych had a long talk with him.

Reviewing the anatomical and physiological details of what in the doctor's opinion was going on inside him, he understood it all.

There was something, a small thing, in the vermiform appendix. It might all come right. Only stimulate the energy of one organ and check the activity of another, then absorption would take place and everything would come right. He got home rather late for dinner, ate his dinner, and conversed cheerfully, but could not for a long time bring himself to go back to work in his room. At last, however, he went to his study and did what was necessary, but the consciousness that he had put something aside — an important, intimate matter which he would revert to when his work was done — never left him. When he had finished his work he remembered that this intimate matter was the thought of his vermiform appendix. But he did not give himself up to it, and went to the drawing-room for tea. There were callers there, including the examining magistrate who was a desirable match for his daughter, and they were conversing, playing the piano, and singing. Ivan Ilych, as Praskovya Fëdorovna remarked, spent that evening more cheerfully than usual, but he never for a moment forgot that he had postponed the important matter of the appendix. At eleven o'clock he said good-night and went to his bedroom. Since his illness he had slept alone in a small room next to his study. He undressed and took up a novel by Zola,[13] but instead of reading it he fell into thought, and in his imagination that desired improvement in the vermiform appendix occurred. There were

---

[11] Two doctors, the latter a celebrated specialist. [Translators' note]
[12] That was the friend whose friend was a doctor. [Translators' note]
[13] Émile Zola (1840–1902), French novelist.

the absorption and evacuation and the re-establishment of normal activity. "Yes, that's it!" he said to himself. "One need only assist nature, that's all." He remembered his medicine, rose, took it, and lay down on his back watching for the beneficent action of the medicine and for it to lessen the pain. "I need only take it regularly and avoid all injurious influences. I am already feeling better, much better." He began touching his side: it was not painful to the touch. "There, I really don't feel it. It's much better already." He put out the light and turned on his side. . . . "The appendix is getting better, absorption is occurring." Suddenly he felt the old, familiar, dull, gnawing pain, stubborn and serious. There was the same familiar loathsome taste in his mouth. His heart sank and he felt dazed. "My God! My God!" he muttered. "Again, again! and it will never cease." And suddenly the matter presented itself in a quite different aspect. "Vermiform appendix! Kidney!" he said to himself. "It's not a question of appendix or kidney, but of life and . . . death. Yes, life was there and now it is going, going and I cannot stop it. Yes. Why deceive myself? Isn't it obvious to everyone but me that I'm dying, and that it's only a question of weeks, days . . . it may happen this moment. There was light and now there is darkness. I was here and now I'm going there! Where?" A chill came over him, his breathing ceased, and he felt only the throbbing of his heart.

"When I am not, what will there be? There will be nothing. Then where shall I be when I am no more? Can this be dying? No, I don't want to!" He jumped up and tried to light the candle, felt for it with trembling hands, dropped candle and candlestick on the floor, and fell back on his pillow.

"What's the use? It makes no difference," he said to himself, staring with wide-open eyes into the darkness. "Death. Yes, death. And none of them know or wish to know it, and they have no pity for me. Now they are playing." (He heard through the door the distant sound of a song and its accompaniment.) "It's all the same to them, but they will die too! Fools! I first, and they later, but it will be the same for them. And now they are merry . . . the beasts!"

Anger choked him and he was agonizingly, unbearably miserable. "It is impossible that all men have been doomed to suffer this awful horror!" He raised himself.

"Something must be wrong. I must calm myself — must think it all over from the beginning." And he again began thinking. "Yes, the beginning of my illness: I knocked my side, but I was still quite well that day and the next. It hurt a little, then rather more. I saw the doctors, then followed despondency and anguish, more doctors, and I drew nearer to the abyss. My strength grew less and I kept coming nearer and nearer, and now I have wasted away and there is no light in my eyes. I think of the appendix — but this is death! I think of mending the appendix, and all the while here is death! Can it really be death?" Again terror seized him and he gasped for breath. He leant down and began feeling for the matches, pressing with his elbow on the stand beside the bed. It was in his way and hurt him, he grew furious with it, pressed on it still harder, and upset it. Breathless and in despair he fell on his back, expecting death to come immediately.

Meanwhile the visitors were leaving. Praskovya Fëdorovna was seeing them off. She heard something fall and came in.

"What has happened?"

"Nothing. I knocked it over accidentally."

She went out and returned with a candle. He lay there panting heavily, like a man who has run a thousand yards, and stared upwards at her with a fixed look.

"What is it, Jean?"

"No . . . no . . . thing. I upset it." ("Why speak of it? She won't understand," he thought.)

And in truth she did not understand. She picked up the stand, lit his candle, and hurried away to see another visitor off. When she came back he still lay on his back, looking upwards.

"What is it? Do you feel worse?"

"Yes."

She shook her head and sat down.

"Do you know, Jean, I think we must ask Leshchetitsky to come and see you here."

This meant calling in the famous specialist, regardless of expense. He smiled malignantly and said "No." She remained a little longer and then went up to him and kissed his forehead.

While she was kissing him he hated her from the bottom of his soul and with difficulty refrained from pushing her away.

"Good-night. Please God you'll sleep."

"Yes."

VI

Ivan Ilych saw that he was dying, and he was in continual despair.

In the depth of his heart he knew he was dying, but not only was he not accustomed to the thought, he simply did not and could not grasp it.

The syllogism he had learnt from Kiezewetter's Logic:[14] "Caius is a man, men are mortal, therefore Caius is mortal," had always seemed to him correct as applied to Caius, but certainly not as applied to himself. That Caius — man in the abstract — was mortal, was perfectly correct, but he was not Caius, not an abstract man, but a creature quite, quite separate from all others. He had been little Vanya, with a mama and a papa, with Mitya and Volodya, with the toys, a coachman and a nurse, afterwards with Katenka and with all the joys, griefs, and delights of childhood, boyhood, and youth. What did Caius know of the smell of that striped leather ball Vanya had been so fond of? Had Caius kissed his mother's hand like that, and did the silk of her dress rustle so for Caius? Had he rioted like that at school when the pastry was bad? Had Caius

---

[14] Klaus Kiezewetter (1766–1819), *The Outline of Logic According to Kantian Principles*, a popular text in Russia, based on the teachings of German philosopher Immanuel Kant (1722–1804).

been in love like that? Could Caius preside at a session as he did? "Caius really was mortal, and it was right for him to die; but for me, little Vanya, Ivan Ilych, with all my thoughts and emotions, it's altogether a different matter. It cannot be that I ought to die. That would be too terrible."

Such was his feeling.

"If I had to die like Caius I should have known it was so. An inner voice would have told me so, but there was nothing of the sort in me and I and all my friends felt that our case was quite different from that of Caius. And now here it is!" he said to himself. "It can't be. It's impossible! But here it is. How is this? How is one to understand it?"

He could not understand it, and tried to drive this false, incorrect, morbid thought away and to replace it by other proper and healthy thoughts. But that thought, and not the thought only but the reality itself, seemed to come and confront him.

And to replace that thought he called up a succession of others, hoping to find in them some support. He tried to get back into the former current of thoughts that had once screened the thought of death from him. But strange to say, all that formerly shut off, hidden, and destroyed, his consciousness of death, no longer had that effect. Ivan Ilych now spent most of his time in attempting to re-establish that old current. He would say to himself: "I will take up my duites again — after all I used to live by them." And banishing all doubts he would go to the law courts, enter into conversation with his colleagues, and sit carelessly as was his wont, scanning the crowd with a thoughtful look and leaning both his emaciated arms on the arms of his oak chair; bending over as usual to a colleague and drawing his papers nearer he would interchange whispers with him, and then suddenly raising his eyes and sitting erect would pronounce certain words and open the proceedings. But suddenly in the midst of those proceedings the pain in his side, regardless of the stage the proceedings had reached, would begin its own gnawing work. Ivan Ilych would turn his attention to it and try to drive the thought of it away, but without success. *It* would come and stand before him and look at him, and he would be petrified and the light would die out of his eyes, and he would again begin asking himself whether *It* alone was true. And his colleagues and subordinates would see with surprise and distress that he, the brilliant and subtle judge, was becoming confused and making mistakes. He would shake himself, try to pull himself together, manage somehow to bring the sitting to a close, and return home with the sorrowful consciousness that his judicial labors could not as formerly hide from him what he wanted them to hide, and could not deliver him from *It*. And what was worst of all was that *It* drew his attention to itself not in order to make him take some action but only that he should look at *It*, look it straight in the face: look at it and without doing anything, suffer inexpressibly.

And to save himself from this condition Ivan Ilych looked for consolations — new screens — and new screens were found and for a while seemed to save him, but then they immediately fell to pieces or rather became transparent, as if *It* penetrated them and nothing could veil *It*.

In these latter days he would go into the drawing-room he had arranged

— that drawing-room where he had fallen and for the sake of which (how bitterly ridiculous it seemed) he had sacrificed his life — for he knew that his illness originated with that knock. He would enter and see that something had scratched the polished table. He would look for the cause of this and find that it was the bronze ornamentation of an album, that had got bent. He would take up the expensive album which he had lovingly arranged, and feel vexed with his daughter and her friends for their untidiness — for the album was torn here and there and some of the photographs turned upside down. He would put it carefully in order and bend the ornamentation back into position. Then it would occur to him to place all those things in another corner of the room, near the plants. He could call the footman, but his daughter or wife would come to help him. They would not agree, and his wife would contradict him, and he would dispute and grow angry. But that was all right, for then he did not think about *It*. *It* was invisible.

But then, when he was moving something himself, his wife would say: "Let the servants do it. You will hurt yourself again." And suddenly *It* would flash through the screen and he would see it. It was just a flash, and he hoped it would disappear, but he would involuntarily pay attention to his side. "Its sits there as before, gnawing just the same!" And he could no longer forget *It*, but could distinctly see it looking at him from behind the flowers. "What is it all for?"

"It really is so! I lost my life over that curtain as I might have done when storming a fort. Is that possible? How terrible and how stupid. It can't be true! It can't, but it is."

He would go to his study, lie down, and again be alone with *It*: face to face with *It*. And nothing could be done with *It* except to look at it and shudder.

VII

How it happened it is impossible to say because it came about step by step, unnoticed, but in the third month of Ivan Ilych's illness, his wife, his daughter, his son, his acquaintances, the doctors, the servants, and above all he himself, were aware that the whole interest he had for other people was whether he would soon vacate his place, and at last release the living from the discomfort caused by his presence and be himself released from his sufferings.

He slept less and less. He was given opium and hypodermic injections of morphine, but this did not relieve him. The dull depression he experienced in a somnolent condition at first gave him a little relief, but only as something new, afterwards it became as distressing as the pain itself or even more so.

Special foods were prepared for him by the doctors' orders, but all those foods became increasingly distasteful and disgusting to him.

For his excretions also special arrangements had to be made, and this was a torment to him every time — a torment from the uncleanliness, the unseemliness, and the smell, and from knowing that another person had to take part in it.

But just through this most unpleasant matter, Ivan Ilych obtained comfort. Gerasim, the butler's young assistant, always came in to carrry the things out. Gerasim was a clean, fresh peasant lad, grown stout on town food and always cheerful and bright. At first the sight of him, in his clean Russian peasant costume, engaged on that disgusting task embarrassed Ivan Ilych.

Once when he got up from the commode too weak to draw up his trousers, he dropped into a soft armchair and looked with horror at his bare, enfeebled thighs with the muscles so sharply marked on them.

Gerasim with a firm light tread, his heavy boots emitting a pleasant smell of tar and fresh winter air, came in wearing a clean Hessian apron, the sleeves of his print shirt tucked up over his strong bare young arms; and refraining from looking at his sick master out of consideration for his feelings, and restraining the joy of life that beamed from his face, he went up to the commode.

"Gerasim!" said Ivan Ilych in a weak voice.

Gerasim started, evidently afraid he might have committed some blunder, and with a rapid movement turned his fresh, kind, simply young face which just showed the first downy signs of a beard.

"Yes, sir?"

"That must be very unpleasant for you. You must forgive me. I am helpless."

"Oh, why, sir," and Gerasim's eyes beamed and he showed his glistening white teeth, "what's a little trouble? It's a case of illness with you, sir."

And his deft strong hands did their accustomed task, and he went out of the room stepping lightly. Five minutes later he as lightly returned.

Ivan Ilych was still sitting in the same position in the armchair.

"Gerasim," he said when the latter had replaced the freshly-washed utensil. "Please come here and help me." Gerasim went up to him. "Lift me up. It is hard for me to get up, and I have sent Dmitri away."

Gerasim went up to him, grasped his master with his strong arms deftly but gently, in the same way that he stepped — lifted him, supported him with one hand, and with the other drew up his trousers and would have set him down again, but Ivan Ilych asked to be led to the sofa. Gerasim, without an effort and without apparent pressure, led him, almost lifting him, to the sofa and placed him on it.

"Thank you. How easily and well you do it all!"

Gerasim smiled again and turned to leave the room. But Ivan Ilych felt his presence such a comfort that he did not want to let him go.

"One thing more, please move up that chair. No, the other one — under my feet. It is easier for me when my feet are raised."

Gerasim brought the chair, set it down gently in place, and raised Ivan Ilych's legs on to it. It seemed to Ivan Ilych that he felt better while Gerasim was holding up his legs.

"It's better when my legs are higher," he said. "Place that cushion under them."

Gerasim did so. He again lifted the legs and placed them, and again

Ivan Ilych felt better while Gerasim held his legs. When he set them down Ivan Ilych fancied he felt worse.

"Gerasim," he said. "Are you busy now?"

"Not at all, sir," said Gerasim, who had learnt from the townsfolk how to speak to gentlefolk.

"What have you still to do?"

"What have I to do? I've done everything except chopping the logs for tomorrow."

"Then hold my legs up a bit higher, can you?"

"Of course I can. Why not?" And Gerasim raised his master's legs higher and Ivan Ilych thought that in that position he did not feel any pain at all.

"And how about the logs?"

"Don't trouble about that, sir. There's plenty of time."

Ivan Ilych told Gerasim to sit down and hold his legs, and began to talk to him. And strange to say it seemed to him that he felt better while Gerasim held his legs up.

After that Ivan Ilych would sometimes call Gerasim and get him to hold his legs on his shoulders, and he liked talking to him. Gerasim did it all easily, willingly, simply, and with a good nature that touched Ivan Ilych. Health, strength, and vitality in other people were offensive to him, but Gerasim's strength and vitality did not mortify but soothed him.

What tormented Ivan Ilych most was the deception, the lie, which for some reason they all accepted, that he was not dying but was simply ill, and that he only need keep quiet and undergo a treatment and then something very good would result. He however knew that do what they would nothing would come of it, only still more agonizing suffering and death. This deception tortured him — their not wishing to admit what they all knew and what he knew, but wanting to lie to him concerning his terrible condition, and wishing and forcing him to participate in that lie. Those lies — lies enacted over him on the eve of his death and destined to degrade this awful, solemn act to the level of their visitings, their curtains, their sturgeon for dinner — were a terrible agony for Ivan Ilych. And strangely enough, many times when they were going through their antics over him he had been within a hair-breadth of calling out to them: "Stop lying! You know and I know that I am dying. Then at least stop lying about it!" But he had never had the spirit to do it. The awful, terrible act of his dying was, he could see, reduced by those about him to the level of a casual, unpleasant, and almost indecorous incident (as if someone entered a drawing-room diffusing an unpleasant odor) and this was done by that very decorum which he had served all his life long. He saw that no one felt for him, because no one even wished to grasp his position. Only Gerasim recognized it and pitied him. And so Ivan Ilych felt at ease only with him. He felt comforted when Gerasim supported his legs (sometimes all night long) and refused to go to bed, saying, "Don't you worry, Ivan Ilych. I'll get sleep enough later on," or when he suddenly became familiar and exclaimed: "If you weren't sick it would be another matter, but as it is, why should I grudge a little trouble?" Gerasim alone did not lie; everything showed that he alone understood the facts of the case and did not consider it necessary to disguise them, but simply felt sorry for his emaciated and enfeebled master. Once when Ivan Ilych was sending him away he even said straight out: "We shall all of us die, so why should I grudge a little trouble?" — expressing the fact that he did not think his work burdensome, because he was doing it for a dying man and hoped someone would do the same for him when his time came.

Apart from this lying, or because of it, what most tormented Ivan Ilych was that no one pitied him as he wished to be pitied. At certain moments after prolonged suffering he wished most of all (though he would have been ashamed to confess it) for someone to pity him as a sick child is pitied. He longed to be petted and comforted. He knew he was an important functionary, that he had a beard turning grey, and that therefore what he longed for was impossible, but still he longed for it. And in Gerasim's attitude towards him there was something akin to what he wished for, and so that attitude comforted him. Ivan Ilych wanted to weep, wanted to be petted and cried over, and then his colleague Shebek would come, and instead of weeping and being petted, Ivan Ilych would assume a serious, severe, and profound air, and by force of habit would express his opinion on a decision of the Court of Cassation and would stubbornly insist on that view. This falsity around him and within him did more than anything else to poison his last days.

VIII

It was morning. He knew it was morning because Gerasim had gone, and Peter the footman had come and put out the candles, drawn back one of the curtains, and begun quietly to tidy up. Whether it was morning or evening, Friday or Sunday, made no difference, it was all just the same: the gnawing, unmitigated, agonizing pain, never ceasing for an instant, the consciousness of life inexorably waning but not yet extinguished, the approach of that ever dreaded and hateful Death which was the only reality, and always the same falsity. What were days, weeks, hours, in such a case?

"Will you have some tea, sir?"

"He wants things to be regular, and wishes the gentlefolk to drink tea in the morning," thought Ivan Ilych, and only said "No."

"Wouldn't you like to move onto the sofa, sir?"

"He wants to tidy up the room, and I'm in the way. I am uncleanliness and disorder," he thought, and said only:

"No, leave me alone."

The man went on bustling about. Ivan Ilych stretched out his hand. Peter came up, ready to help.

"What is it, sir?"

"My watch."

Peter took the watch which was close at hand and gave it to his master.

"Half-past eight. Are they up?"

"No, sir, except Vasily Ivanich" (the son) "who has gone to school.

Praskovya Fëdorovna ordered me to wake her if you asked for her. Shall I do so?"

"No, there's no need to." "Perhaps I'd better have some tea," he thought, and added aloud: "Yes, bring me some tea."

Peter went to the door, but Ivan Ilych dreaded being left alone. "How can I keep him here? Oh yes, my medicine." "Peter, give me my medicine." "Why not? Perhaps it may still do me some good." He took a spoonful and swallowed it. "No, it won't help. It's all tomfoolery, all deception," he decided as soon as he became aware of the familiar, sickly, hopeless taste. "No, I can't believe in it any longer. But the pain, why this pain? If it would only cease just for a moment!" And he moaned. Peter turned towards him. "It's all right. Go and fetch me some tea."

Peter went out. Left alone Ivan Ilych groaned not so much with pain, terrible though that was, as from mental anguish. Always and for ever the same, always these endless days and nights. If only it would come quicker! If only *what* would come quicker? Death, darkness? . . . No, no! Anything rather than death!

When Peter returned with the tea on a tray, Ivan Ilych stared at him for a time in perplexity, not realizing who and what he was. Peter was disconcerted by that look and his embarrassment brought Ivan Ilych to himself.

"Oh, tea! All right, put it down. Only help me to wash and put on a clean shirt."

And Ivan Ilych began to wash. With pauses for rest, he washed his hands and then his face, cleaned his teeth, brushed his hair, and looked in the glass. He was terrified by what he saw, especially by the limp way in which his hair clung to his pallid forehead.

While his shirt was being changed he knew that he would be still more frightened at the sight of his body, so he avoided looking at it. Finally he was ready. He drew on a dressing gown, wrapped himself in a plaid, and sat down in the armchair to take his tea. For a moment he felt refreshed, but as soon as he began to drink the tea he was again aware of the same taste, and the pain also returned. He finished it with an effort, and then lay down stretching out his legs, and dismissed Peter.

Always the same. Now a spark of hope flashes up, then a sea of despair rages, and always pain; always pain, always despair, and always the same. When alone he had a dreadful and distressing desire to call someone, but he knew beforehand that with others present it would be still worse. "Another dose of morphine — to lose consciousness. I will tell him, the doctor, that he must think of something else. It's impossible, impossible, to go on like this."

An hour and another pass like that. But now there is a ring at the door bell. Perhaps it's the doctor? It is. He comes in fresh, hearty, plump, and cheerful, with that look on his face that seems to say: "There now, you're in a panic about something, but we'll arrange it all for you directly!" The doctor knows this expression is out of place here, but he has put it on once for all and can't take it off — like a man who has put on a frock-coat in the morning to pay a round of calls.

The doctor rubs his hands vigorously and reassuringly.

"Brr! How cold it is! There's such a sharp frost; just let me warm myself!" he says, as if it were only a matter of waiting till he was warm, and then he would put everything right.

"Well now, how are you?"

Ivan Ilych feels that the doctor would like to say: "Well, how are our affairs?" but that even he feels that this would not do, and says instead: "What sort of a night have you had?"

Ivan Ilych looks at him as much as to say: "Are you really never ashamed of lying?" But the doctor does not wish to understand this question, and Ivan Ilych says: "Just as terrible as ever. The pain never leaves me and never subsides. If only something. . . ."

"Yes, you sick people are always like that. . . . There, now I think I am warm enough. Even Praskovya Fëdorovna, who is so particular, could find no fault with my temperature. Well, now I can say good-morning," and the doctor presses his patient's hand.

Then, dropping his former playfulness, he begins with a most serious face to examine the patient, feeling his pulse and taking his temperature, and then begins the sounding and auscultation.

Ivan Ilych knows quite well and definitely that all this is nonsense and pure deception, but when the doctor, getting down on his knee, leans over him, putting his ear first higher then lower, and performs various gymnastic movements over him with a significant expression on his face, Ivan Ilych submits to it all as he used to submit to the speeches of the lawyers, though he knew very well that they were all lying and why they were lying.

The doctor, kneeling on the sofa, is still sounding him when Praskovya Fëdorovna's silk dress rustles at the door and she is heard scolding Peter for not having let her know of the doctor's arrival.

She comes in, kisses her husband, and at once proceeds to prove that she has been up a long time already, and only owing to a misunderstanding failed to be there when the doctor arrived.

Ivan Ilych looks at her, scans her all over, sets against her the whiteness and plumpness and cleanness of her hands and neck, the gloss of her hair, and the sparkle of her vivacious eyes. He hates her with his whole soul. And the thrill of hatred he feels for her makes him suffer from her touch.

Her attitude towards him and his disease is still the same. Just as the doctor had adopted a certain relation to his patient which he could not abandon, so had she formed one towards him — that he was not doing something he ought to do and was himself to blame, and that she reproached him lovingly for this — and she could not now change that attitude.

"You see he doesn't listen to me and doesn't take his medicine at the proper time. And above all he lies in a position that is no doubt bad for him — with his legs up."

She described how he made Gerasim hold his legs up.

The doctor smiled with a contemptuous affability that said: "What's to be done? These sick people do have foolish fancies of that kind, but we must forgive them."

When the examination was over the doctor looked at his watch, and then Praskovya Fëdorovna announced to Ivan Ilych that it was of course as he pleased, but she had sent today for a celebrated specialist who would examine him and have a consultation with Michael Danilovich (their regular doctor).

"Please don't raise any objections. I am doing this for my own sake," she said ironically, letting it be felt that she was doing it all for his sake and only said this to leave him no right to refuse. He remained silent, knitting his brows. He felt that he was so surrounded and involved in a mesh of falsity that it was hard to unravel anything.

Everything she did for him was entirely for her own sake, and she told him she was doing for herself what she actually was doing for herself, as if that was so incredible that he must understand the opposite.

At half-past eleven the celebrated specialist arrived. Again the sounding began and the significant conversations in his presence and in another room, about the kidneys and the appendix, and the questions and answers, with such an air of importance that again, instead of the real question of life and death which now alone confronted him, the question arose of the kidney and appendix which were not behaving as they ought to and would now be attacked by Michael Danilovich and the specialist and forced to amend their ways.

The celebrated specialist took leave of him with a serious though not hopeless look, and in reply to the timid question Ivan Ilych, with eyes glistening with fear and hope, put to him as to whether there was a chance of recovery, said that he could not vouch for it but there was a possibility. The look of hope with which Ivan Ilych watched the doctor out was so pathetic that Praskovya Fëdorovna, seeing it, even wept as she left the room to hand the doctor his fee.

The gleam of hope kindled by the doctor's encouragement did not last long. The same room, the same pictures, curtains, wallpaper, medicine bottles, were all there, and the same aching suffering body, and Ivan Ilych began to moan. They gave him a subcutaneous injection and he sank into oblivion.

It was twilight when he came to. They brought him his dinner and he swallowed some beef tea with difficulty, and then everything was the same again and night was coming on.

After dinner, at seven o'clock, Praskovya Fëdorovna came into the room in evening dress, her full bosom pushed up by her corset, and with traces of powder on her face. She had reminded him in the morning that they were going to the theater. Sarah Bernhardt was visiting the town and they had a box, which he had insisted on their taking. Now he had forgotten about it and her toilet offended him, but he concealed his vexation when he remembered that he had himself insisted on their securing a box and going because it would be an instructive and aesthetic pleasure for the children.

Praskovya Fëdorovna came in, self-satisfied but yet with a rather guilty air. She sat down and asked how he was, but, as he saw, only for the sake of asking and not in order to learn about it, knowing that there was nothing to learn — and then went on to what she really wanted to say: that she would not on any account have gone but that the box had been taken and Helen and their daughter were going, as well as Petrishchev (the examining magistrate, their daughter's fiancé) and that it was out of the question to let them go alone; but that she would have much preferred to sit with him for a while; and he must be sure to follow the doctor's orders while she was away.

"Oh, and Fëdor Petrovich" (the fiancé) "would like to come in. May he? And Lisa?"

"All right."

Their daughter came in in full evening dress, her fresh young flesh exposed (making a show of that very flesh which in his own case caused so much suffering), strong, healthy, evidently in love, and impatient with illness, suffering, and death, because they interfered with her happiness.

Fëdor Petrovich came in too, in evening dress, his hair curled *à la Capoul*,[15] a tight stiff collar round his long sinewy neck, an enormous white shirt-front and narrow black trousers tightly stretched over his strong thighs. He had one white glove tightly drawn on, and was holding his opera hat in his hand.

Following him the schoolboy crept in unnoticed, in a new uniform, poor little fellow, and wearing gloves. Terribly dark shadows showed under his eyes, the meaning of which Ivan Ilych knew well.

His son had always seemed pathetic to him, and now it was dreadful to see the boy's frightened look of pity. It seemed to Ivan Ilych that Vasya was the only one besides Gerasim who understood and pitied him.

They all sat down and again asked how he was. A silence followed. Lisa asked her mother about the opera-glasses, and there was an altercation between mother and daughter as to who had taken them and where they had been put. This occasioned some unpleasantness.

Fëdor Petrovich inquired of Ivan Ilych whether he had ever seen Sarah Bernhardt. Ivan Ilych did not at first catch the question, but then replied: "No, have you seen her before?"

"Yes, in *Adrienne Lecouvreur*."[16]

Praskovya Fëdorovna mentioned some rôles in which Sarah Bernhardt was particularly good. Her daughter disagreed. Conversation sprang up as to the elegance and realism of her acting — the sort of conversation that is always repeated and is always the same.

In the midst of the conversation Fëdor Petrovich glanced at Ivan Ilych and became silent. The others also looked at him and grew silent. Ivan Ilych was staring with glittering eyes straight before him, evidently indignant with them. This had to be rectified, but it was impossible to do so. The silence had to be broken, but for a time no one dared to break it and they all became afraid that the conventional deception would suddenly become obvious and the truth become plain to all. Lisa was the first to pluck up courage and break that silence, but by trying to hide what everybody was feeling, she betrayed it.

---

[15] An elaborate hair styling for men. Capoul was a famous French singer.
[16] Comedy by French playwrights Eugène Scribe and Ernest Legouvé.

"Well, if we are going it's time to start," she said, looking at her watch, a present from her father, and with a faint and significant smile at Fëdor Petrovich relating to something known only to them. She got up with a rustle of her dress.

They all rose, said good-night, and went away.

When they had gone it seemed to Ivan Ilych that he felt better; the falsity had gone with them. But the pain remained — that same pain and that same fear that made everything monotonously alike, nothing harder and nothing easier. Everything was worse.

Again minute followed minute and hour followed hour. Everything remained the same and there was no cessation. And the inevitable end of it all became more and more terrible.

"Yes, send Gerasim here," he replied to a question Peter asked.

IX

His wife returned late at night. She came in on tiptoe, but he heard her, opened his eyes, and made haste to close them again. She wished to send Gerasim away and to sit with him herself, but he opened his eyes and said: "No, go away."

"Are you in great pain?"

"Always the same."

"Take some opium."

He agreed and took some. She went away.

Till about three in the morning he was in a state of stupefied misery. It seemed to him that he and his pain were being thrust into a narrow, deep black sack, but though they were pushed further and further in they could not be pushed to the bottom. And this, terrible enough in itself, was accompanied by suffering. He was frightened yet wanted to fall through the sack, he struggled but yet co-operated. And suddenly he broke through, fell, and regained consciousness. Gerasim was sitting at the foot of the bed dozing quietly and patiently, while he himself lay with his emaciated stockinged legs resting on Gerasim's shoulders; the same shaded candle was there and the same unceasing pain.

"Go away, Gerasim," he whispered.

"It's all right, sir. I'll stay a while."

"No. Go away."

He removed his legs from Gerasim's shoulders, turned sideways onto his arm, and felt sorry for himself. He only waited till Gerasim had gone into the next room and then restrained himself no longer but wept like a child. He wept on account of his helplessness, his terrible loneliness, the cruelty of man, the cruelty of God, and the absence of God.

"Why hast Thou done all this? Why hast Thou brought me here? Why, why dost Thou torment me so terribly?"

He did not expect an answer and yet wept because there was no answer and could be none. The pain again grew more acute, but he did not stir and did not call. He said to himself: "Go on! Strike me! But what is it for? What have I done to Thee? What is it for?"

Then he grew quiet and not only ceased weeping but even held his breath and became all attention. It was as though he were listening not to an audible voice but to the voice of his soul, to the current of thoughts arising within him.

"What is it you want?" was the first clear conception capable of expression in words, that he heard.

"What do you want? What do you want?" he repeated to himself.

"What do I want? To live and not to suffer," he answered.

And again he listened with such concentrated attention that even his pain did not distract him.

"To live? How?" asked his inner voice.

"Why, to live as I used to — well and pleasantly."

"As you lived before, well and pleasantly?" the voice repeated.

And in imagination he began to recall the best moments of his pleasant life. But strange to say none of those best moments of his pleasant life now seemed at all what they had then seemed — none of them except the first recollections of childhood. There, in childhood, there had been something really pleasant with which it would be possible to live if it could return. But the child who had experienced that happiness existed no longer, it was like a reminiscence of somebody else.

As soon as the period began which had produced the present Ivan Ilych, all that had then seemed joys now melted before his sight and turned into something trivial and often nasty.

And the further he departed from childhood and the nearer he came to the present the more worthless and doubtful were the joys. This began with the School of Law. A little that was really good was still found there — there was lightheartedness, friendship, and hope. But in the upper classes there had already been fewer of such good moments. Then during the first years of his official career, when he was in the service of the Governor, some pleasant moments again occurred: they were the memories of love for a woman. Then all became confused and there was still less of what was good; later on again there was still less that was good, and the further he went the less there was. His marriage, a mere accident, then the disenchantment that followed it, his wife's bad breath and the sensuality and hypocrisy: then the deadly official life and those preoccupations about money, a year of it, and two, and ten, and twenty, and always the same thing. And the longer it lasted the more deadly it became. "It is as if I had been going downhill while I imagined I was going up. And that is really what it was. I was going up in public opinion, but to the same extent life was ebbing away from me. And now it is all done and there is only death."

"Then what does it mean? Why? It can't be that life is so senseless and horrible. But if it really has been so horrible and senseless, why must I die and die in agony? There is something wrong!"

"Maybe I did not live as I ought to have done," it suddenly occurred to him. "But how could that be, when I did everything properly?" he replied, and immediately dismissed from his mind this, the sole solution of all the riddles of life and death, as something quite impossible.

"Then what do you want now? To live? Live how? Live as you lived in the law courts when the usher proclaimed 'The judge is coming!' The judge is coming, the judge!" he repeated to himself. "Here he is, the judge. But I am not guilty!" he exclaimed angrily. "What is it for?" And he ceased crying, but turning his face to the wall continued to ponder on the same question: Why, and for what purpose, is there all this horror? But however much he pondered he found no answer. And whenever the thought occurred to him, as it often did, that it all resulted from his not having lived as he ought to have done, he at once recalled the correctness of his whole life and dismissed so strange an idea.

X

Another fortnight passed. Ivan Ilych now no longer left his sofa. He would not lie in bed but lay on the sofa, facing the wall nearly all the time. He suffered ever the same unceasing agonies and in his loneliness pondered always on the same insoluble question: "What is this? Can it be that it is Death?" And the inner voice answered: "Yes, it is Death."

"Why these sufferings?" And the voice answered, "For no reason — they just are so." Beyond and besides this there was nothing.

From the very beginning of his illness, ever since he had first been to see the doctor, Ivan Ilych's life had been divided between two contrary and alternating moods: now it was despair and the expectation of this uncomprehended and terrible death, and now hope and an intently interested observation of the functioning of his organs. Now before his eyes there was only a kidney or an intestine that temporarily evaded its duty, and now only that incomprehensible and dreadful death from which it was impossible to escape.

These two states of mind had alternated from the very beginning of his illness, but the further it progressed the more doubtful and fantastic became the conception of the kidney, and the more real the sense of impending death.

He had but to call to mind what he had been three months before and what he was now, to call to mind with what regularity he had been going downhill, for every possibility of hope to be shattered.

Latterly during that loneliness in which he found himself as he lay facing the back of the sofa, a loneliness in the midst of a populous town and surrounded by numerous acquaintances and relations but that yet could not have been more complete anywhere — either at the bottom of the sea or under the earth — during that terrible loneliness Ivan Ilych had lived only in memories of the past. Pictures of his past rose before him one after another. They always began with what was nearest in time and then went back to what was most remote — to his childhood — and rested there. If he thought of the stewed prunes that had been offered him that day, his mind went back to the raw shrivelled French plums of his childhood, their peculiar flavor and the flow of saliva when he sucked their stones, and along with the memory of that taste came a whole series of memories of those days: his nurse, his brother, and their toys. "No, I mustn't think of that. . . . It is too painful," Ivan Ilych said to himself, and brought himself back to the present — to the button on the back of the sofa and the creases in its morocco. "Morocco is expensive, but it does not wear well: there had been a quarrel about it. It was a different kind of quarrel and a different kind of morocco that time when we tore father's portfolio and were punished, and mama brought us some tarts. . . ." And again his thoughts dwelt on his childhood, and again it was painful and he tried to banish them and fix his mind on something else.

Then again together with that chain of memories another series passed through his mind — of how his illness had progressed and grown worse. There also the further back he looked the more life there had been. There had been more of what was good in life and more of life itself. The two merged together. "Just as the pain went on getting worse and worse, so my life grew worse and worse," he thought. "There is one bright spot there at the back, at the beginning of life, and afterwards all becomes blacker and blacker and proceeds more and more rapidly — in inverse ratio to the square of the distance from death," thought Ivan Ilych. And the example of a stone falling downwards with increasing velocity entered his mind. Life, a series of increasing sufferings, flies further and further towards its end — the most terrible suffering. "I am flying. . . ." He shuddered, shifted himself, and tried to resist, but was already aware that resistance was impossible, and again with eyes weary of gazing but unable to cease seeing what was before them, he stared at the back of the sofa and waited — awaiting that dreadful fall and shock and destruction.

"Resistance is impossible!" he said to himself. "If I could only understand what it is all for! But that too is impossible. An explanation would be possible if it could be said that I have not lived as I ought to. But it is impossible to say that," and he remembered all the legality, correctitude, and propriety of his life. "That at any rate can certainly not be admitted," he thought, and his lips smiled ironically as if someone could see that smile and be taken in by it. "There is no explanation! Agony, death. . . . What for?"

XI

Another two weeks went by in this way and during that fortnight an event occurred that Ivan Ilych and his wife had desired. Petrishchev formally proposed. It happened in the evening. The next day Praskovya Fëdorovna came into her husband's room considering how best to inform him of it, but that very night there had been a fresh change for the worse in his condition. She found him still lying on the sofa but in a different position. He lay on his back, groaning and staring fixedly straight in front of him.

She began to remind him of his medicines, but he turned his eyes towards her with such a look that she did not finish what she was saying; so great an animosity, to her in particular, did that look express.

"For Christ's sake let me die in peace!" he said.

She would have gone away, but just then their daughter came in and went up to say good morning. He looked at her as he had done at his wife, and in reply to her inquiry about his health said dryly that he would soon free them all of himself. They were both silent and after sitting with him for a while went away.

"Is it our fault?" Lisa said to her mother. "It's as if we were to blame! I am sorry for papa, but why should we be tortured?"

The doctor came at his usual time. Ivan Ilych answered "Yes" and "No," never taking his angry eyes from him, and at last said: "You know you can do nothing for me, so leave me alone."

"We can ease your sufferings."

"You can't even do that. Let me be."

The doctor went into the drawing-room and told Praskovya Fëdorovna that the case was very serious and that the only resource left was opium to allay her husband's sufferings, which must be terrible.

It was true, as the doctor said, that Ivan Ilych's physical sufferings were terrible, but worse than the physical sufferings were his mental sufferings, which were his chief torture.

His mental sufferings were due to the fact that that night, as he looked at Gerasim's sleepy, good-natured face with its prominent cheek-bones, the question suddenly occurred to him: "What if my whole life has really been wrong?"

It occurred to him that what had appeared perfectly impossible before, namely that he had not spent his life as he should have done, might after all be true. It occurred to him that his scarcely perceptible attempts to struggle against what was considered good by the most highly placed people, those scarcely noticeable impulses which he had immediately suppressed, might have been the real thing, and all the rest false. And his professional duties and the whole arrangement of his life and of his family, and all his social and official interests, might all have been false. He tried to defend all those things to himself and suddenly felt the weakness of what he was defending. There was nothing to defend.

"But if that is so," he said to himself, "and I am leaving this life with the consciousness that I have lost all that was given me and it is impossible to rectify it — what then?"

He lay on his back and began to pass his life in review in quite a new way. In the morning when he saw first his footman, then his wife, then his daughter, and then the doctor, their every word and movement confirmed to him the awful truth that had been revealed to him during the night. In them he saw himself — all that for which he had lived — and saw clearly that it was not real at all, but a terrible and huge deception which had hidden both life and death. This consciousness intensified his physical suffering tenfold. He groaned and tossed about, and pulled at his clothing which choked and stifled him. And he hated them on that account.

He was given a large dose of opium and became unconscious, but at noon his sufferings began again. He drove everybody away and tossed from side to side.

His wife came to him and said:

"Jean, my dear, do this for me. It can't do any harm and often helps. Healthy people often do it."

He opened his eyes wide.

"What? Take communion? Why? It's unnecessary! However. . . ."

She began to cry.

"Yes, do, my dear. I'll send for our priest. He is such a nice man."

"All right. Very well," he muttered.

When the priest came and heard his confession, Ivan Ilych was softened and seemed to feel a relief from his doubts and consequently from his sufferings, and for a moment there came a ray of hope. He again began to think of the vermiform appendix and the possibility of correcting it. He received the sacrament with tears in his eyes.

When they laid him down again afterwards he felt a moment's ease, and the hope that he might live awoke in him again. He began to think of the operation that had been suggested to him. "To live! I want to live!" he said to himself.

His wife came in to congratulate him after his communion, and when uttering the usual conventional words she added:

"You feel better, don't you?"

Without looking at her he said "Yes."

Her dress, her figure, the expression of her face, the tone of her voice, all revealed the same thing. "This is wrong, it is not as it should be. All you have lived for and still live for is falsehood and deception, hiding life and death from you." And as soon as he admitted that thought, his hatred and his agonizing physical suffering again sprang up, and with that suffering a consciousness of the unavoidable, approaching end. And to this was added a new sensation of grinding shooting pain and a feeling of suffocation.

The expression of his face when he uttered that "yes" was dreadful. Having uttered it, he looked her straight in the eyes, turned on his face with a rapidity extraordinary in his weak state and shouted:

"Go away! Go away and leave me alone!"

XII

From that moment the screaming began that continued for three days, and was so terrible that one could not hear it through two closed doors without horror. At the moment he answered his wife he realized that he was lost, that there was no return, that the end had come, the very end, and his doubts were still unsolved and remained doubts.

"Oh! Oh! Oh!" he cried in various intonations. He had begun by screaming "I won't!" and continued screaming on the letter *O*.

For three whole days, during which time did not exist for him, he struggled in that black sack into which he was being thrust by an invisible, resistless force. He struggled as a man condemned to death struggles in the hands of the executioner, knowing that he cannot save himself. And every moment he felt that despite all his efforts he was drawing nearer and nearer to what terrified him. He felt that his agony was due to his being thrust into that black hole and still more to his not being able to get right into it. He was hindered from getting into it by his conviction that his life had been a good one. That very justification of his life held him fast and prevented his moving forward, and it caused him most torment of all.

Suddenly some force struck him in the chest and side, making it still harder to breathe, and he fell through the hole and there at the bottom was a light. What had happened to him was like the sensation one sometimes experiences in a railway carriage when one thinks one is going backwards while one is really going forwards and suddenly becomes aware of the real direction.

"Yes, it was all not the right thing," he said to himself, "but that's no matter. It can be done. But what *is* the right thing?" he asked himself, and suddenly grew quiet.

This occurred at the end of the third day, two hours before his death. Just then his schoolboy son had crept softly in and gone up to the bedside. The dying man was still screaming desperately and waving his arms. His hand fell on the boy's head, and the boy caught it, pressed it to his lips, and began to cry.

At that very moment Ivan Ilych fell through and caught sight of the light, and it was revealed to him that though his life had not been what it should have been, this could still be rectified. He asked himself, "What *is* the right thing?" and grew still, listening. Then he felt that someone was kissing his hand. He opened his eyes, looked at his son, and felt sorry for him. His wife came up to him and he glanced at her. She was gazing at him open-mouthed, with undried tears on her nose and cheek and a despairing look on her face. He felt sorry for her too.

"Yes, I am making them wretched," he thought. "They are sorry, but it will be better for them when I die." He wished to say this but had not the strength to utter it. "Besides, why speak? I must act," he thought. With a look at his wife he indicated his son and said: "Take him away . . . sorry for him . . . sorry for you too. . . ." He tried to add, "forgive me," but said "forgo" and waved his hand, knowing that He whose understanding mattered would understand.

And suddenly it grew clear to him that what had been oppressing him and would not leave him was all dropping away at once from two sides, from ten sides, and from all sides. He was sorry for them, he must act so as not to hurt them: release them and free himself from these sufferings. "How good and how simple!" he thought. "And the pain?" he asked himself. "What had become of it? Where are you, pain?"

He turned his attention to it.

"Yes, here it is. Well, what of it? Let the pain be."

"And death . . . where is it?"

He sought his former accustomed fear of death and did not find it. "Where is it? What death?" There was no fear because there was no death.

In place of death there was light.

"So that's what it is!" he suddenly exclaimed aloud. "What joy!"

To him all this happened in a single instant, and the meaning of that instant did not change. For those present his agony continued for another two hours. Something rattled in his throat, his emaciated body twitched, then the gasping and rattle became less and less frequent.

"It is finished!" said someone near him.

He heard these words and repeated them in his soul.

"Death is finished," he said to himself. "It is no more!"

He drew in a breath, stopped in the midst of a sigh, stretched out, and died.   [1886]

JOHN UPDIKE *(b. 1932) was born in Shillington, Pennsylvania, an only child. His father taught algebra in a local high school, and his mother wrote short stories and novels. His mother's consciousness of a special destiny, combined with his family's meager income — they lived with his mother's parents for the first thirteen years of Updike's life — made him "both arrogant and shy" as a teenager. He wrote stories, drew cartoons, and clowned for the approval of his peers. After getting straight A's in high school, he went to Harvard University on a full scholarship, studying English and graduating summa cum laude in 1954. He spent a year at Oxford on a fellowship, then joined the staff of* The New Yorker. *In 1959 Updike published both his first book of short fiction,* The Same Door, *and his first novel,* The Poorhouse Fair. *That year he also moved from New York City to a coastal town in Massachusetts, where he has lived most of the time since.*

In the 1960s, 1970s, and early 1980s, Updike continued to alternate novels and collections of stories, adding occasional volumes of verse, collections of essays, and one play. His novels include Rabbit, Run *(1960),* Couples *(1968),* Rabbit Redux *(1971), and* Marry Me *(1976).* Rabbit Is Rich *(1981), continuing the story of Harry "Rabbit" Angstrom, a suburban Pennsylvanian whom Updike has traced through adolescence, marriage, fatherhood, and middle age, won virtually every major American literary award for the year it appeared; Updike concluded the series with* Rabbit at Rest *(1991). Updike's collections of stories include* Pigeon Feathers *(1962),* Museums and Women *(1972), and* Problems and Other Stories *(1981). In 1983 Updike won the National Book Critics Circle Award for his collection of essays and criticism* Hugging the Shore. *In 1989 he published his memoirs,* Self-Consciousness. *His novel* Brazil *appeared in 1994.*

Updike has said he is indebted to J. D. Salinger's stories for the literary form he adopted to describe the painful experience of adolescence: "I learned a lot from Salinger's short stories; he did remove the short narrative from the wise-guy, slice-of-life stories of the thirties and forties. Like most innovative artists, he made new room for shapelessness, for life as it is lived." Updike writes realistic narrative, believing that "fiction is a tissue of lies that refreshes and informs our sense of actuality. Reality is — chemically, atomically, biologically — a fabric of microscopic accuracies." His fiction, such as the story "A & P," concentrates on these "microscopic accuracies," tiny details of characterization and setting brilliantly described.

RELATED COMMENTARY: *John Updike, "Kafka and 'The Metamorphosis,'" page 1502.*

JOHN UPDIKE

A & P

In walks these three girls in nothing but bathing suits. I'm in the third checkout slot, with my back to the door, so I don't see them until they're over by the bread. The one that caught my eye first was the one in the plaid green two-piece. She was a chunky kid, with a good tan and a sweet broad soft-looking can with those two crescents of white just under it, where the sun never seems to hit, at the top of the backs of her legs. I stood there with my hand on a box of HiHo crackers trying to remember if I rang it up or not. I ring it up again and the customer starts giving me hell. She's one of these cash-register-watchers, a witch about fifty with rouge on her cheekbones and no eyebrows, and I know it made her day to trip me up. She'd been watching cash registers for fifty years and probably never seen a mistake before.

By the time I got her feathers smoothed and her goodies into a bag — she gives me a little snort in passing, if she'd been born at the right time they would have burned her over in Salem — by the time I get her on her way the girls had circled around the bread and were coming back, without a pushcart, back way along the counters, in the aisle between the checkouts and the Special bins. They didn't even have shoes on. There was this chunky one, with the two-piece — it was bright green and the seams on the bra were still sharp and her belly was still pretty pale so I guessed she just got it (the suit) — there was this one, with one of those chubby berry-faces, the lips all bunched together under her nose, this one, and a tall one, with black hair that hadn't quite frizzed right, and one of these sunburns right across under the eyes, and a chin that was too long — you know, the kind of girl other girls think is very "striking" and "attractive" but never quite makes it, as they very well know, which is why they like her so much — and then the third one, that wasn't quite so tall. She was the queen. She kind of led them, the other two peeking around and making their shoulders round. She didn't look around, not this queen, she just walked straight on slowly, on these long white prima-donna legs. She came down a little hard on her heels, as if she didn't walk in her bare feet that much, putting down her heels and then letting the weight move along to her toes as if she was testing the floor with every step, putting a little deliberate extra action into it. You never know for sure how girls' minds work (do you really think it's a mind in there or just a little buzz like a bee in a glass jar?) but you got the idea she had talked the other two into coming in here with her, and now she was showing them how to do it, walk slow and hold yourself straight.

She had on a kind of dirty-pink — beige maybe, I don't know — bathing suit with a little nubble all over it, and what got me, the straps were down. They were off her shoulders looped loose around the cool tops of her arms, and I guess as a result the suit had slipped a little on her, so all around the top of the cloth there was this shining rim. If it hadn't been there you wouldn't have known there could have been anything whiter than those shoulders. With the straps pushed off, there was nothing between the top of the suit and the top of her head except just *her,* this clean bare plane of the top of her chest down from the shoulder bones like a dented sheet of metal tilted in the light. I mean, it was more than pretty.

She had sort of oaky hair that the sun and salt had bleached, done up in a bun that was unravelling, and a kind of prim face. Walking into the A & P with your straps down, I suppose it's the only kind of face you *can* have. She held her head so high her neck, coming up out of those white shoulders, looked kind of stretched, but I didn't mind. The longer her neck was, the more of her there was.

She must have felt in the corner of her eye me and over my shoulder Stokesie in the second slot watching, but she didn't tip. Not this queen. She kept her eyes moving across the racks, and stopped, and turned so slow it made my stomach rub the inside of my apron, and buzzed to the other two, who kind of huddled against her for relief, and then they all three of them went up the cat-and-dog-food-breakfast-cereal-macaroni-rice-raisins-seasonings-spreads-spaghetti-soft-drinks-crackers-and-cookies aisle. From the third slot I look straight up this aisle to the meat counter, and I watched them all the way. The fat one with the tan sort of fumbled with the cookies, but on second thought she put the package back. The sheep pushing their carts down the aisle — the girls were walking against the usual traffic (not that we have one-way signs or anything) — were pretty hilarious. You could see them, when Queenie's white shoulders dawned on them, kind of jerk, or hop, or hiccup, but their eyes snapped back to their own baskets and on they pushed. I bet you could set off dynamite in an A & P and the people would by and large keep reaching and checking oatmeal off their lists and muttering "Let me see, there was a third thing, began with A, asparagus, no, ah, yes, applesauce!" or whatever it is they do mutter. But there was no doubt, this jiggled them. A few houseslaves in pin curlers even looked around after pushing their carts past to make sure what they had seen was correct.

You know, it's one thing to have a girl in a bathing suit down on the beach, where what with the glare nobody can look at each other much anyway, and another thing in the cool of the A & P, under the fluorescent lights, against all those stacked packages, with her feet paddling along naked over our checkboard green-and-cream rubber-tile floor.

"Oh Daddy," Stokesie said beside me. "I feel so faint."

"Darling," I said. "Hold me tight." Stokesie's married, with two babies chalked up on his fuselage already, but as far as I can tell that's the only difference. He's twenty-two, and I was nineteen this April.

"Is it done?" he asks, the responsible married man finding his voice. I forgot to say he thinks he's going to be manager some sunny day, maybe in 1990 when it's called the Great Alexandrov and Petrooshki Tea Company or something.

What he meant was, our town is five miles from a beach, with a big summer colony out on the Point, but we're right in the middle of town, and the women generally put on a shirt or shorts or something before they get out of the car into the street. And anyway these are usually women with six children and varicose veins mapping their legs and nobody, including them, could care less. As I say, we're right in the middle of town, and if you stand at our front doors you can see two banks and the Congregational church and the newspaper store and three real-estate offices and about twenty-seven old freeloaders tearing up Central Street because the sewer broke again. It's not as if we're on the Cape; we're north of Boston and there's people in this town haven't seen the ocean for twenty years.

The girls had reached the meat counter and were asking McMahon something. He pointed, they pointed, and they shuffled out of sight behind a pyramid of Diet Delight peaches. All that was left for us to see was old McMahon patting his mouth and looking after them sizing up their joints. Poor kids, I began to feel sorry for them, they couldn't help it.

Now here comes the sad part of the story, at least my family says it's sad, but I don't think it's so sad myself. The store's pretty empty, it being Thursday afternoon, so there was nothing much to do except lean on the register and wait for the girls to show up again. The whole store was like a pinball machine and I didn't know which tunnel they'd come out of. After a while they come around out of the far aisle, around the light bulbs, records at discount of the Caribbean Six or Tony Martin Sings or some such gunk you wonder they waste the wax on, sixpacks of candy bars, and plastic toys done up in cellophane that fall apart when a kid looks at them anyway. Around they come, Queenie still leading the way, and holding a little gray jar in her hand. Slots Three through Seven are unmanned and I could see her wondering between Stokes and me, but Stokesie with his usual luck draws an old party in baggy gray pants who stumbles up with four giant cans of pineapple juice (what do these bums *do* with all that pineapple juice? I've often asked myself) so the girls come to me. Queenie puts down the jar and I take it into my fingers icy cold. Kingfish Fancy Herring Snacks in Pure Sour Cream: 49¢. Now her hands are empty, not a ring or a bracelet, bare as God made them, and I wonder where the money's coming from. Still with that prim look she lifts a folded dollar bill out of the hollow at the center of her nubbled pink top. The jar went heavy in my hand. Really, I thought that was so cute.

Then everybody's luck begins to run out. Lengel comes in from haggling with a truck full of cabbages on the lot and is about to scuttle into that door marked MANAGER behind which he hides all day when the girls touch his eye. Lengel's pretty dreary, teaches Sunday school and the rest, but he doesn't miss that much. He comes over and says, "Girls, this isn't the beach."

Queenie blushes, though maybe it's just a brush of sunburn I was noticing for the first time, now that she was so close. "My mother asked me to pick up a jar of herring snacks." Her voice kind of startled me, the way voices do when you see the people first, coming out so flat and dumb yet kind of tony, too, the way it ticked over "pick up" and "snacks." All of a sudden I slid right down her voice into her living room. Her father and the other men were standing around in ice-cream coats and bow ties and the women were in sandals picking up herring snacks on toothpicks off a big glass plate and they were all holding drinks the color of water with olives and sprigs of mint in them. When my parents have somebody over they get lemonade and if it's a real racy affair Schlitz in tall glasses with "They'll Do It Every Time" cartoons stencilled on.

"That's all right," Lengel said. "But this isn't the beach." His repeating this struck me as funny, as if it had just occurred to him, and he had been thinking all these years the A & P was a great big sand dune and he was the head lifeguard. He didn't like my smiling — as I say he doesn't miss much — but he concentrates on giving the girls that sad Sunday-school-superintendent stare.

Queenie's blush is no sunburn now, and the plump one in plaid, that I liked better from the back — a really sweet can — pipes up, "We weren't doing any shopping. We just came in for the one thing."

"That makes no difference," Lengel tells her, and I could see from the way his eyes went that he hadn't noticed she was wearing a two-piece before. "We want you decently dressed when you come in here."

"We *are* decent," Queenie says suddenly, her lower lip pushing, getting sore now that she remembers her place, a place from which the crowd that runs the A & P must look pretty crummy. Fancy Herring Snacks flashed in her very blue eyes.

"Girls, I don't want to argue with you. After this come in here with your shoulders covered. It's our policy." He turns his back. That's policy for you. Policy is what the kingpins want. What the others want is juvenile delinquency.

All this while, the customers had been showing up with their carts but, you know, sheep, seeing a scene, they had all bunched up on Stokesie, who shook open a paper bag as gently as peeling a peach, not wanting to miss a word. I could feel in the silence everybody getting nervous, most of all Lengel, who asks me, "Sammy, have you rung up their purchase?"

I thought and said "No" but it wasn't about that I was thinking. I go through the punches, 4, 9, GROC, TOT — it's more complicated than you think, and after you do it often enough, it begins to make a little song, that you hear words to, in my case "Hello (*bing*) there, you (*gung*) hap-py *pee*-pul (*splat*)!" — the *splat* being the drawer flying out. I uncrease the bill, tenderly as you may imagine, it just having come from between the two smoothest scoops of vanilla I had ever known were there, and pass a half and a penny into her narrow pink palm, and nestle the herrings in a bag and twist its neck and hand it over, all the time thinking.

The girls, and who'd blame them, are in a hurry to get out, so I say "I quit" to Lengel enough for them to hear, hoping they'll stop and watch me, their unsuspected hero. They keep right on going, into the electric eye; the door flies open and they flicker across the lot to their car, Queenie and Plaid and Big Tall Goony-Goony (not that as raw material she was so bad), leaving me with Lengel and a kink in his eyebrow.

"Did you say something, Sammy?"

"I said I quit."

"I thought you did."

"You didn't have to embarrass them."

"It was they who were embarrassing us."

I started to say something that came out "Fiddle-de-doo." It's a saying of my grandmother's, and I know she would have been pleased.

"I don't think you know what you're saying," Lengel said.

"I know you don't," I said. "But I do." I pull the bow at the back of my apron and start shrugging it off my shoulders. A couple customers that had been heading for my slot begin to knock against each other, like scared pigs in a chute.

Lengel sighs and begins to look very patient and old and gray. He's been a friend of my parents for years. "Sammy, you don't want to do this to your Mom and Dad," he tells me. It's true, I don't. But it seems to me that once you begin a gesture it's fatal not to go through with it. I fold the apron, "Sammy" stitched in red on the pocket, and put it on the counter, and drop the bow tie on top of it. The bow tie is theirs, if you've ever wondered. "You'll feel this for the rest of your life," Lengel says, and I know that's true, too, but remembering how he made that pretty girl blush makes me so scrunchy inside I punch the No Sale tab and the machine whirs "pee-pul" and the drawer splats out. One advantage to this scene taking place in summer, I can follow this up with a clean exit, there's no fumbling around getting your coat and galoshes, I just saunter into the electric eye in my white shirt that my mother ironed the night before, and the door heaves itself open, and outside the sunshine is skating around on the asphalt.

I look around for my girls, but they're gone, of course. There wasn't anybody but some young married screaming with her children about some candy they didn't get by the door of a powder-blue Falcon station wagon. Looking back in the big windows, over the bags of peat moss and aluminum lawn furniture stacked on the pavement, I could see Lengel in my place in the slot, checking the sheep through. His face was dark gray and his back stiff, as if he'd just had an injection of iron, and my stomach kind of fell as I felt how hard the world was going to be to me hereafter.   [1961]

ALICE WALKER (b. 1944) was the eighth and youngest child of Willie Lee and Minnie Lou Grant Walker, sharecroppers in Eatonton, Georgia. Walker did well in school, encouraged by her teachers and her mother, whose stories she loved as "a walking history of our community." For two years, Walker attended Spelman College in Atlanta, the oldest college for black women in the United States. Then she studied at Sarah Lawrence College in New York, where she began her writing career by publishing a book of poetry, Once (1968). Since that time Walker has published several collections of poetry, novels, volumes of short stories, and Living by the Word (1988), a book of essays. Her best-known novel, The Color Purple (1982), won the American Book Award and the Pulitzer Prize and has been made into a motion picture. Recent books are The Temple of My Familiar (1989) and Possessing the Secret of Joy (1992).

Walker's books show her commitment to the idea of radical social change. She was active in the civil rights movement in Mississippi, where she met and married a civil rights lawyer from whom she separated after the birth of their daughter. In confronting the painful struggle of black people's history, Walker asserts that the creativity of black women, the extent to which they are permitted to express themselves, is a measure of the health of the entire American society. She calls herself a "womanist," her term for a black feminist. In her definition, "womanism" is perferable to "feminism" because, as she has said,

> Part of our tradition as black women is that we are universalists. Black children, yellow children, red children, brown children, that is the black woman's normal, day-to-day relationship. In my family alone, we are about four different colors. When a black woman looks at the world, it is so different . . . when I look at the people in Iran they look like kinfolk. When I look at the people in Cuba, they look like my uncles and nieces.

Walker credits many writers for influencing her prose style in her short fiction. Virginia Woolf, Zora Neale Hurston, and Gabriel García Márquez seem to Walker to be "like musicians; at one with their cultures and their historical subconscious." Her two books of stories show a clear progression of theme. The women of In Love and Trouble (1973) struggle against social injustice almost in spite of themselves, as does the title character in "Roselily," from that collection; the heroines of You Can't Keep a Good Woman Down (1981) consciously challenge conventions. Walker has said, "Writing really helps you heal yourself. I think if you write long enough, you will be a healthy person. That is, if you write what you need to write, as opposed to what will make money, or what will make fame."

RELATED COMMENTARY: Alice Walker, "Zora Neale Hurston: A Cautionary Tale and a Partisan View," page 1505.

Roselily

Dearly Beloved

She dreams; dragging herself across the world. A small girl in her mother's white robe and veil, knee raised waist high through a bowl of quicksand soup. The man who stands beside her is against this standing on the front porch of her house, being married to the sound of cars whizzing by on highway 61.

we are gathered here

Like cotton to be weighed. Her fingers at the last minute busily removing dry leaves and twigs. Aware it is a superficial sweep. She knows he blames Mississippi for the respectful way the men turn their heads up in the yard, the women stand waiting and knowledgeable, their children held from mischief by teachings from the wrong God. He glares beyond them to the occupants of the cars, white faces glued to promises beyond a country wedding, noses thrust forward like dogs on a track. For him they usurp the wedding.

in the sight of God

Yes, open house. That is what country black folks like. She dreams she does not already have three children. A squeeze around the flowers in her hands chokes off three and four and five years of breath. Instantly she is ashamed and frightened in her superstition. She looks for the first time at the preacher, forces humility into her eyes, as if she believes he is, in fact, a man of God. She can imagine God, a small black boy, timidly pulling the preacher's coattail.

to join this man and this woman

She thinks of ropes, chains, handcuffs, his religion. His place of worship. Where she will be required to sit apart with covered head. In Chicago, a word she hears when thinking of smoke, from his description of what a cinder was, which they never had in Panther Burn. She sees hovering over the heads of the clean neighbors in her front yard black specks falling, clinging, from the sky. But in Chicago. Respect, a chance to build. Her children at last from underneath the detrimental wheel. A chance to be on top. What a relief, she thinks. What a vision, a view, from up so high.

in holy matrimony.

Her fourth child she gave away to the child's father who had some money. Certainly a good job. Had gone to Harvard. Was a good man but weak because good language meant so much to him he could not live with Roselily. Could not abide TV in the living room, five beds in three rooms, no Bach except from four to six on Sunday afternoons. No chess at all. She does not forget to worry about her son among his father's people. She wonders if the New England climate will agree with him. If he will ever come down to Mississippi, as his father did, to try to right the country's wrongs. She wonders if he will be stronger than his father. His father cried off and on throughout her pregnancy. Went to skin and bones. Suffered nightmares, retching and falling out of bed. Tried to kill himself. Later told his wife he found the right baby through friends. Vouched for, the sterling qualities that would make up his character.

It is not her nature to blame. Still, she is not entirely thankful. She supposes New England, the North, to be quite different from what she knows. It seems right somehow to her that people who move there to live return home completely changed. She thinks of the air, the smoke, the cinders. Imagines cinders big as hailstones; heavy, weighing on the people. Wonders how this pressure finds it way into the veins, roping the springs of laughter.

If there's anybody here that knows a reason why

But of course they know no reason why beyond what they daily have come to know. She thinks of the man who will be her husband, feels shut away from him because of the stiff severity of his plain black suit. His religion. A lifetime of black and white. Of veils. Covered head. It is as if her children are already gone from her. Not dead, but exalted on a pedestal, a stalk that has no roots. She wonders how to make new roots. It is beyond her. She wonders what one does with memories in a brand-new life. This had seemed easy, until she thought of it. "The reasons why . . . the people who" . . . she thinks, and does not wonder where the thought is from.

these two should not be joined

She thinks of her mother, who is dead. Dead, but still her mother. Joined. This is confusing. Of her father. A gray old man who sold wild mink, rabbit, fox skins to Sears, Roebuck. He stands in the yard, like a man waiting for a train. Her young sisters stand behind her in smooth green dresses, with flowers in their hands and hair. They giggle, she feels, at the absurdity of the wedding. They are ready for something new. She thinks the man beside her should marry one of them. She feels old. Yoked. An arm seems to reach out from behind her and snatch her backward. She thinks of cemeteries and the long sleep of grandparents mingling in the dirt. She believes that she believes in ghosts. In the soil giving back what it takes.

together

In the city. He sees her in a new way. This she knows, and is grateful. But is it new enough? She cannot always be a bride and virgin, wearing robes and veil. Even now her body itches to be free of satin and voile, organdy and lily of the valley. Memories crash against her. Memories of being bare to the sun. She wonders what it will be like. Not to have to go to a job. Not to work in a sewing plant. Not to worry about learning to sew straight seams in workingmen's overalls, jeans, and dress pants. Her place will be in the home, he has said, repeatedly, promising her rest she had prayed for. But now she wonders. When she is rested, what will she do? They will make babies — she thinks practically about her fine brown body, his strong black one. They will be inevitable. Her hands will be full. Full of what? Babies. She is not comforted.

let him speak

She wishes she had asked him to explain more of what he meant. But she was impatient. Impatient to be done with sewing. With doing everything for three children, alone. Impatient to leave the girls she had known since childhood, their children growing up, their husbands hanging around her, already old, seedy. Nothing about them that she wanted, or needed. The fathers of her children driving by, waving, not waving; reminders of times she would just as soon forget. Impatient to see the South Side, where they would live and build and be respectable and respected and free. Her husband would free her. A romantic hush. Proposal. Promises. A new life! Respectable, reclaimed, renewed. Free! In robe and veil.

or forever hold

She does not even know if she loves him. She loves his sobriety. His refusal to sing just because he knows the tune. She loves his pride. His blackness and his gray car. She loves his understanding of her *condition*. She thinks she loves the effort he will make to redo her into what he truly wants. His love of her makes her completely conscious of how unloved she was before. This is something; though it makes her unbearably sad. Melancholy. She blinks her eyes. Remembers she is finally being married, like other girls. Like other girls, women? Something strains upward behind her eyes. She thinks of the something as a rat trapped, concerned, scurrying to and fro in her head, peering through the windows of her eyes. She wants to live for once. But doesn't know quite what that means. Wonders if she has ever done it. If she ever will. The preacher is odious to her. She wants to strike him out of the way, out of her light, with the back of her hand. It seems to her he has always been standing in front of her, barring her way.

his peace.

The rest she does not hear. She feels a kiss, passionate, rousing, within the general pandemonium. Cars drive up blowing their horns. Firecrackers go off. Dogs come from under the house and begin to yelp and bark. Her husband's hand is like the clasp of an iron gate. People congratulate. Her children press against her. They look with awe and distaste mixed with hope at their new father. He stands curiously apart, in spite of the people crowding about to grasp his free hand. He smiles at them all but his eyes are as if turned inward. He knows they cannot understand that he is not a Christian. He will not explain himself. He feels different, he looks it. The old women thought he was like one of their sons except that he had somehow got away from them. Still a son, not a son. Changed.

She thinks how it will be later in the night in the silvery gray car. How they will spin through the darkness of Mississippi and in the morning be in Chicago, Illinois. She thinks of Lincoln, the president. That is all she knows about the place. She feels ignorant, *wrong*, backward. She presses her worried fingers into his palm. He is standing in front of her. In the crush of well-wishing people, he does not look back.   [1973]

EUDORA WELTY *(b. 1909) was born in Jackson, Mississippi, where she has spent nearly her whole life. She has a predominately tranquil view of the South, so her stories and novels provide a strong contrast to the turbulent fiction of William Faulkner and Richard Wright, who also wrote about Mississippi. Welty grew up as one of three children in a close-knit family living two blocks from the state capitol. Her father was the president of an insurance company, and her mother was a thrifty housewife who kept a Jersey cow in a little pasture behind the backyard. An insatiable reader as a child, Welty began writing spontaneously and continued, without any particular encouragement or any plan to be a writer, during her years in college. In her midtwenties she started to publish stories in the* Southern Review, *but she credits the persistence of her New York literary agent with helping her get a story published in the* Atlantic Monthly *in 1941. This event led directly to the publication of her first book of stories,* A Curtain of Green, *the same year.*

During World War II Welty was a staff member of the New York Times Book Review *while she lived at home with her mother and continued to write short fiction. Another collection was published in 1943 as* The Wide Net and Other Stories. *After leaving her newspaper work, she turned a short story into her first novel,* Delta Wedding *(1946), on the advice of her agent. She has produced several other story collections over the years. Her novel* The Optimist's Daughter *won the Pulitzer Prize in 1972. In 1980* The Collected Stories of Eudora Welty *appeared, forty-one stories in all. Welty is also a fine critic of the short story. Her essays and reviews of the work of writers such as Anton Chekhov, Willa Cather, Katherine Anne Porter, Virginia Woolf, and Isak Dinesen, as well as some comments on her own work, were collected in* The Eye of the Story *(1977). Eight years later the book* Conversations with Eudora Welty *was a best-seller.*

In the preface to her collected stories, Welty stated,

> I have been told, both in approval and in accusation, that I seem to love all my characters. What I do in writing of any character is to try to enter into the mind, heart, and skin of a human being who is not myself. Whether this happens to be a man or a woman, old or young, with skin black or white, the primary challenge lies in making the jump itself. It is the act of a writer's imagination that I set most high.

Although her fiction contains occasional sharp glances at southern people, as in "Why I Live at the P.O.," her usual manner is a calm celebration of her characters' minor victories, as in "A Worn Path."

RELATED COMMENTARIES: *Eudora Welty, "Is Phoenix Jackson's Grandson Really Dead?" page 1507; Eudora Welty, "Plot and Character in Chekhov's 'The Darling,'" page 1510; Eudora Welty, "Reality in Chekhov's Stories," page 1512.*

EUDORA WELTY

Why I Live at the P.O.

I was getting along fine with Mama, Papa-Daddy, and Uncle Rondo until my sister Stella-Rondo just separated from her husband and came back home again. Mr. Whitaker! Of course I went with Mr. Whitaker first, when he first appeared here in China Grove, taking "Pose Yourself" photos, and Stella-Rondo broke us up. Told him I was one-sided. Bigger on one side than the other, which is a deliberate, calculated falsehood: I'm the same. Stella-Rondo is exactly twelve months to the day younger than I am and for that reason she's spoiled.

She's always had anything in the world she wanted and then she'd throw it away. Papa-Daddy gave her this gorgeous Add-a-Pearl necklace when she was eight years old and she threw it away playing baseball when she was nine, with only two pearls.

So as soon as she got married and moved away from home the first thing she did was separate! From Mr. Whitaker! This photographer with the popeyes she said she trusted. Came home from one of those towns up in Illinois and to our complete surprise brought this child of two.

Mama said she like to make her drop dead for a second. "Here you had this marvelous blonde child and never so much as wrote your mother a word about it," says Mama. "I'm thoroughly ashamed of you." But of course she wasn't.

Stella-Rondo just calmly takes off this *hat*, I wish you could see it. She says, "Why, Mama, Shirley-T.'s adopted, I can prove it."

"How?" says Mama, but all I says was, "H'm!" There I was over the hot stove, trying to stretch two chickens over five people and a completely unexpected child into the bargain, without one moment's notice.

"What do you mean — 'H'm!'?" says Stella-Rondo, and Mama says, "I heard that, Sister."

I said that oh, I didn't mean a thing, only that whoever Shirley-T. was, she was the spit-image of Papa-Daddy if he'd cut off his beard, which of course he'd never do in the world. Papa-Daddy's Mama's papa and sulks.

Stella-Rondo got furious! She said, "Sister, I don't need to tell you you got a lot of nerve and always did have and I'll thank you to make no future reference to my adopted child whatsoever."

"Very well," I said. "Very well, very well. Of course I noticed at once she looks like Mr. Whitaker's side too. That frown. She looks like a cross between Mr. Whitaker and Papa-Daddy."

"Well, all I can say is she isn't."

"She looks exactly like Shirley Temple to me," says Mama, but Shirley-T. just ran away from her.

So the first thing Stella-Rondo did at the table was turn Papa-Daddy against me.

"Papa-Daddy," she says. He was trying to cut up his meat. "Papa-Daddy!" I was taken completely by surprise. Papa-Daddy is about a million years old and's got this long-long beard. "Papa-Daddy, Sister says she fails to understand why you don't cut off your beard."

So Papa-Daddy l-a-y-s down his knife and fork! He's real rich. Mama says he is, he says he isn't. So he says, "Have I heard correctly? You don't understand why I don't cut off my beard?"

"Why," I says, "Papa-Daddy, of course I understand, I did not say any such of a thing, the idea!"

He says, "Hussy!"

I says, "Papa-Daddy, you know I wouldn't any more want you to cut off your beard than the man in the moon. It was the farthest thing from my mind! Stella-Rondo sat there and made that up while she was eating breast of chicken."

But he says, "So the postmistress fails to understand why I don't cut off my beard. Which job I got you through my influence with the government. 'Bird's nest' — is that what you call it?"

Not that it isn't the next to smallest P.O. in the entire state of Mississippi.

I says, "Oh, Papa-Daddy," I says, "I didn't say any such of a thing, I never dreamed it was a bird's nest, I have always been grateful though this is the next to smallest P.O. in the state of Mississippi, and I do not enjoy being referred to as a hussy by my own grandfather."

But Stella-Rondo says, "Yes, you did say it too. Anybody in the world could of heard you, that had ears."

"Stop right there," says Mama, looking at *me.*

So I pulled my napkin straight back through the napkin ring and left the table.

As soon as I was out of the room Mama says, "Call her back, or she'll starve to death," but Papa-Daddy says, "This is the beard I started growing on the Coast when I was fifteen years old." He would of gone on till nightfall if Shirley-T. hadn't lost the Milky Way she ate in Cairo.[1]

So Papa-Daddy says, "I am going out and lie in the hammock, and you can all sit here and remember my words: I'll never cut off my beard as long as I live, even one inch, and I don't appreciate it in you at all." Passed right by me in the hall and went straight out and got in the hammock.

It would be a holiday. It wasn't five minutes before Uncle Rondo suddenly appeared in the hall in one of Stella-Rondo's flesh-colored kimonos, all cut on the bias, like something Mr. Whitaker probably thought was gorgeous.

"Uncle Rondo!" I says. "I didn't know who that was! Where are you going?"

"Sister," he says, "get out of my way, I'm poisoned."

"If you're poisoned stay away from Papa-Daddy," I says. "Keep out of

---

[1] Cairo, Illinois.

the hammock. Papa-Daddy will certainly beat you on the head if you come within forty miles of him. He thinks I deliberately said he ought to cut off his beard after he got me the P.O., and I've told him and told him and told him, and he acts like he just don't hear me. Papa-Daddy must of gone stone deaf."

"He picked a fine day to do it then," says Uncle Rondo, and before you could say "Jack Robinson" flew out in the yard.

What he'd really done, he'd drunk another bottle of that prescription. He does it every single Fourth of July as sure as shooting, and it's horribly expensive. Then he falls over in the hammock and snores. So he insisted on zigzagging right on out to the hammock, looking like a half-wit.

Papa-Daddy woke up with this horrible yell and right there without moving an inch he tried to turn Uncle Rondo against me. I heard every word he said. Oh, he told Uncle Rondo I didn't learn to read till I was eight years old and he didn't see how in the world I ever got the mail put up at the P.O., much less read it all, and he said if Uncle Rondo could only fathom the lengths he had gone to get me that job! And he said on the other hand he thought Stella-Rondo had a brilliant mind and deserved credit for getting out of town. All the time he was just lying there swinging as pretty as you please and looping out his beard, and poor Uncle Rondo was *pleading* with him to slow down the hammock, it was making him as dizzy as a witch to watch it. But that's what Papa-Daddy likes about a hammock. So Uncle Rondo was too dizzy to get turned against me for the time being. He's Mama's only brother and is a good case of a one-track mind. Ask anybody. A certified pharmacist.

Just then I heard Stella-Rondo raising the upstairs window. While she was married she got this peculiar idea that it's cooler with the windows shut and locked. So she has to raise the window before she can make a soul hear her outdoors.

So she raises the window and says, "*Oh!*" You would have thought she was mortally wounded.

Uncle Rondo and Papa-Daddy didn't even look up, but kept right on with what they were doing. I had to laugh.

I flew up the stairs and threw the door open! I says, "What in the wide world's the matter, Stella-Rondo? You mortally wounded?"

"No," she says, "I am not mortally wounded but I wish you would do me the favor of looking out that window there and telling me what you see."

So I shade my eyes and look out the window.

"I see the front yard," I says.

"Don't you see any human beings?" she says.

"I see Uncle Rondo trying to run Papa-Daddy out of the hammock," I says. "Nothing more. Naturally, it's so suffocating-hot in the house, with all the windows shut and locked, everybody who cares to stay in their right mind will have to go out and get in the hammock before the Fourth of July is over."

"Don't you notice anything different about Uncle Rondo?" asks Stella-Rondo.

"Why, no, except he's got on some terrible-looking flesh-colored contraption I wouldn't be found dead in, is all I can see," I says.

"Never mind, you won't be found dead in it, because it happens to be part of my trousseau, and Mr. Whitaker took several dozen photographs of me in it," says Stella-Rondo. "What on earth could Uncle Rondo *mean* by wearing part of my trousseau out in the broad open daylight without saying so much as 'Kiss my foot,' *knowing* I only got home this morning after my separation and hung my negligee up on the bathroom door, just as nervous as I could be?"

"I'm sure I don't know, and what do you expect me to do about it?" I says. "Jump out the window?"

"No, I expect nothing of the kind. I simply declare that Uncle Rondo looks like a fool in it, that's all," she says. "It makes me sick to my stomach."

"Well, he looks as good as he can," I says. "As good as anybody in reason could." I stood up for Uncle Rondo, please remember. And I said to Stella-Rondo, "I think I would do well not to criticize so freely if I were you and came home with a two-year-old child I had never said a word about, and no explanation whatever about my separation."

"I asked you the instant I entered this house not to refer one more time to my adopted child, and you gave me your word of honor you would not," was all Stella-Rondo would say, and started pulling out every one of her eyebrows with some cheap Kress[2] tweezers.

So I merely slammed the door behind me and went down and made some green-tomato pickle. Somebody had to do it. Of course Mama had turned both the niggers loose; she always said no earthly power could hold one anyway on the Fourth of July, so she wouldn't even try. It turned out that Jaypan fell in the lake and came within a very narrow limit of drowning.

So Mama trots in. Lifts up the lid and says, "H'm! Not very good for your Uncle Rondo in his precarious condition, I must say. Or poor little adopted Shirley-T. Shame on you!"

That made me tired. I says, "Well, Stella-Rondo had better thank her lucky stars it was her instead of me came trotting in with that very peculiar-looking child. Now if it had been me that trotted in from Illinois and brought a peculiar-looking child of two, I shudder to think of the reception I'd of got, much less controlled the diet of an entire family."

"But you must remember, Sister, that you were never married to Mr. Whitaker in the first place and didn't go up to Illinois to live," says Mama, shaking a spoon in my face. "If you had I would of been just as overjoyed to see you and your little adopted girl as I was to see Stella-Rondo, when you wound up with your separation and came on back home."

"You would not," I says.

"Don't contradict me, I would," says Mama.

But I said she couldn't convince me though she talked till she was blue in the face. Then I said, "Besides, you know as well as I do that that child is not adopted."

---

[2]Store brand from the Kress Company chain of variety stores.

"She most certainly is adopted," says Mama, stiff as a poker.

I says, "Why, Mama, Stella-Rondo had her just as sure as anything in this world, and just too stuck up to admit it."

"Why, Sister," said Mama. "Here I thought we were going to have a pleasant Fourth of July, and you start right out not believing a word your own baby sister tells you!"

"Just like Cousin Annie Flo. Went to her grave denying the facts of life," I remind Mama.

"I told you if you ever mentioned Annie Flo's name I'd slap your face," says Mama, and slaps my face.

"All right, you wait and see," I says.

"I," says Mama, "I prefer to take my children's word for anything when it's humanly possible." You ought to see Mama, she weighs two hundred pounds and has real tiny feet.

Just then something perfectly horrible occurred to me.

"Mama," I says, "can that child talk?" I simply had to whisper! "Mama, I wonder if that child can be — you know — in any way? Do you realize," I says, "that she hasn't spoken one single, solitary word to a human being up to this minute? This is the way she looks," I says, and I looked like this.

Well, Mama and I just stood there and stared at each other. It was horrible!

"I remember well that Joe Whitaker frequently drank like a fish," says Mama. "I believed to my soul he drank *chemicals*." And without another word she marches to the foot of the stairs and calls Stella-Rondo.

"Stella-Rondo? O-o-o-o-o! Stella-Rondo!"

"What?" says Stella-Rondo from upstairs. Not even the grace to get up off the bed.

"Can that child of yours talk?" asks Mama.

Stella-Rondo says, "Can she what?"

"Talk! Talk!" says Mama. "Burdyburdyburdyburdy!"

So Stella-Rondo yells back, "Who says she can't talk?"

"Sister says so," says Mama.

"You didn't have to tell me, I know whose word of honor don't mean a thing in this house," says Stella-Rondo.

And in a minute the loudest Yankee voice I ever heard in my life yells out, "OE'm Pop-OE the Sailor-r-r Ma-a-an!" and then somebody jumps up and down in the upstairs hall. In another second the house would of fallen down.

"Not only talks, she can tap-dance!" calls Stella-Rondo. "Which is more than some people I won't name can do."

"Why, the little precious darling thing!" Mama says, so surprised. "Just as smart as she can be!" Starts talking baby talk right there. Then she turns on me. "Sister, you ought to be thoroughly ashamed! Run upstairs this instant and apologize to Stella-Rondo and Shirley-T."

"Apologize for what?" I says. "I merely wondered if the child was normal, that's all. Now that she's proved she is, why, I have nothing further to say."

But Mama just turned on her heel and flew out, furious. She ran right upstairs and hugged the baby. She believed it was adopted. Stella-Rondo hadn't done a thing but turn her against me from upstairs while I stood there helpless over the hot stove. So that made Mama, Papa-Daddy, and the baby all on Stella-Rondo's side.

Next, Uncle Rondo.

I must say that Uncle Rondo has been marvelous to me at various times in the past and I was completely unprepared to be made to jump out of my skin, the way it turned out. Once Stella-Rondo did something perfectly horrible to him — broke a chain letter from Flanders Field[3] — and he took the radio back he had given her and gave it to me. Stella-Rondo was furious! For six months we all had to call her Stella instead of Stella-Rondo, or she wouldn't answer. I always thought Uncle Rondo had all the brains of the entire family. Another time he sent me to Mammoth Cave,[4] with all expenses paid.

But this would be the day he was drinking that prescription, the Fourth of July.

So at supper Stella-Rondo speaks up and says she thinks Uncle Rondo ought to try to eat a little something. So finally Uncle Rondo said he would try a little cold biscuits and ketchup, but that was all. So *she* brought it to him.

"Do you think it wise to disport with ketchup in Stella-Rondo's flesh-colored kimono?" I says. Trying to be considerate! If Stella-Rondo couldn't watch out for her trousseau, somebody had to.

"Any objections?" asks Uncle Rondo, just about to pour out all the ketchup.

"Don't mind what she says, Uncle Rondo," says Stella-Rondo. "Sister has been devoting this solid afternoon to sneering out my bedroom window at the way you look."

"What's that?" says Uncle Rondo. Uncle Rondo has got the most terrible temper in the world. Anything is liable to make him tear the house down if it comes at the wrong time.

So Stella-Rondo says, "Sister says, 'Uncle Rondo certainly does look like a fool in that pink kimono!'"

Do you remember who it was really said that?

Uncle Rondo spills out all the ketchup and jumps out of his chair and tears off the kimono and throws it down on the dirty floor and puts his foot on it. It had to be sent all the way to Jackson to the cleaners and repleated.

"So that's your opinion of your Uncle Rondo, is it?" he says. "I look like a fool, do I? Well, that's the last straw. A whole day in this house with nothing to do, and then to hear you come out with a remark like that behind my back!"

"I didn't say any such of a thing, Uncle Rondo," I says, "and I'm not saying who did, either. Why, I think you look all right. Just try to take care of

---

[3] American military cemetery in Belgium dating from World War I.
[4] Mammoth Cave, Kentucky, a network of natural underground caverns.

yourself and not talk and eat at the same time," I says. "I think you better go lie down."

"Lie down my foot," says Uncle Rondo. I ought to of known by that he was fixing to do something perfectly horrible.

So he didn't do anything that night in the precarious state he was in — just played Casino with Mama and Stella-Rondo and Shirley-T. and gave Shirley-T. a nickel with a head on both sides. It tickled her nearly to death, and she called him "Papa." But at 6:30 A.M. the next morning, he threw a whole five-cent package of some unsold one-inch firecrackers from the store as hard as he could into my bedroom and they every one went off. Not one bad one in the string. Anybody else, there'd be one that wouldn't go off.

Well, I'm just terribly susceptible to noise of any kind, the doctor has always told me I was the most sensitive person he had ever seen in his whole life, and I was simply prostrated. I couldn't eat! People tell me they heard it as far as the cemetery, and old Aunt Jep Patterson, that had been holding her own so good, thought it was Judgment Day and she was going to meet her whole family. It's usually so quiet here.

And I'll tell you it didn't take me any longer than a minute to make up my mind what to do. There I was with the whole entire house on Stella-Rondo's side and turned against me. If I have anything at all I have pride.

So I just decided I'd go straight down to the P.O. There's plenty of room there in the back, I says to myself.

Well! I made no bones about letting the family catch on to what I was up to. I didn't try to conceal it.

The first thing they knew, I marched in where they were all playing Old Maid and pulled the electric oscillating fan out by the plug, and everything got real hot. Next I snatched the pillow I'd done the needlepoint on right off the davenport from behind Papa-Daddy. He went "Ugh!" I beat Stella-Rondo up the stairs and finally found my charm bracelet in her bureau drawer under a picture of Nelson Eddy.[5]

"So that's the way the land lies," says Uncle Rondo. There he was, piecing on the ham. "Well, Sister, I'll be glad to donate my army cot if you got any place to set it up, providing you'll leave right this minute and let me get some peace." Uncle Rondo was in France.

"Thank you kindly for the cot and 'peace' is hardly the word I would select if I had to resort to firecrackers at 6:30 A.M. in a young girl's bedroom," I says back to him. "And as to where I intend to go, you seem to forget my position as postmistress of China Grove, Mississippi," I says. "I've always got the P.O."

Well, that made them all sit up and take notice.

I went out front and started digging up some four-o'clocks to plant around the P.O.

"Ah-ah-ah!" says Mama, raising the window. "Those happen to be my

---

[5] Nelson Eddy (1901–1967), singer in many Hollywood musical films of the 1930s.

1298 *Eudora Welty*

four-o'clocks. Everything planted in that star is mine. I've never known you to make anything grow in your life."

"Very well," I says. "But I take the fern. Even you, Mama, can't stand there and deny that I'm the one watered that fern. And I happen to know where I can send in a box top and get a packet of one thousand mixed seeds, no two the same kind, free."

"Oh, where?" Mama wants to know.

But I says, "Too late. You 'tend to your house, and I'll 'tend to mine. You hear things like that all the time if you know how to listen to the radio. Perfectly marvelous offers. Get anything you want free."

So I hope to tell you I marched in and got that radio, and they could of all bit a nail in two, especially Stella-Rondo, that it used to belong to, and she well knew she couldn't get it back, I'd sue for it like a shot. And I very politely took the sewing-machine motor I helped pay the most on to give Mama for Christmas back in 1929, and a good big calendar, with the first-aid remedies on it. The thermometer and the Hawaiian ukulele certainly were rightfully mine, and I stood on the step-ladder and got all my watermelon-rind preserves and every fruit and vegetable I'd put up, every jar. Then I began to pull the tacks out of the bluebird wall vases on the archway to the dining room.

"Who told you you could have those, Miss Priss?" says Mama, fanning as hard as she could.

"I bought 'em and I'll keep track of 'em," I says. "I'll tack 'em up one on each side the post-office window, and you can see 'em when you come to ask me for your mail, if you're so dead to see 'em."

"Not I! I'll never darken the door to that post office again if I live to be a hundred," Mama says. "Ungrateful child! After all the money we spent on you at the Normal."[6]

"Me either," says Stella-Rondo. "You can just let my mail lie there and *rot*, for all I care. I'll never come and relieve you of a single, solitary piece."

"I should worry," I says. "And who you think's going to sit down and write you all those big fat letters and postcards, by the way? Mr. Whitaker? Just because he was the only man ever dropped down in China Grove and you got him — unfairly — is he going to sit down and write you a lengthy correspondence after you come home giving no rhyme nor reason whatsoever for your separation and no explanation for the presence of that child? I may not have your brilliant mind, but I fail to see it."

So Mama says, "Sister, I've told you a thousand times that Stella-Rondo simply got homesick, and this child is far too big to be hers," and she says, "Now, why don't you just sit down and play Casino?"

Then Shirley-T. sticks out her tongue at me in this perfectly horrible way. She has no more manners than the man in the moon. I told her she was going to cross her eyes like that some day and they'd stick.

"It's too late to stop me now," I says. "You should have tried that

---

[6] A two-year school for teacher training.

yesterday. I'm going to the P.O. and the only way you can possibly see me is to visit me there."

So Papa-Daddy says, "You'll never catch me setting foot in that post office, even if I should take a notion into my head to write a letter some place." He says, "I won't have you reachin' out of that little old window with a pair of shears and cuttin' off any beard of mine. I'm too smart for you!"

"We all are," says Stella-Rondo.

But I said, "If you're so smart, where's Mr. Whitaker?"

So then Uncle Rondo says, "I'll thank you from now on to stop reading all the orders I get on postcards and telling everybody in China Grove what you think is the matter with them," but I says, "I draw my own conclusions and will continue in the future to draw them." I says, "If people want to write their inmost secrets on penny postcards, there's nothing in the wide world you can do about it, Uncle Rondo."

"And if you think we'll ever *write* another postcard you're sadly mistaken," says Mama.

"Cutting off your nose to spite your face then," I says. "But if you're all determined to have no more to do with the U.S. mail, think of this: What will Stella-Rondo do now, if she wants to tell Mr. Whitaker to come after her?"

"Wah!" says Stella-Rondo. I knew she'd cry. She had a conniption fit right there in the kitchen.

"It will be interesting to see how long she holds out," I says. "And now — I am leaving."

"Good-bye," says Uncle Rondo.

"Oh, I declare," says Mama, "to think that a family of mine should quarrel on the Fourth of July, or the day after, over Stella-Rondo leaving old Mr. Whitaker and having the sweetest little adopted child! It looks like we'd all be glad!"

"Wah!" says Stella-Rondo, and has a fresh conniption fit.

"*He* left *her* — you mark my words," I says. "That's Mr. Whitaker. I know Mr. Whitaker. After all, I knew him first. I said from the beginning he'd up and leave her. I foretold every single thing that's happened."

"Where did he go?" asks Mama.

"Probably to the North Pole, if he knows what's good for him," I says.

But Stella-Rondo just bawled and wouldn't say another word. She flew to her room and slammed the door.

"Now look what you've gone and done, Sister," says Mama. "You go apologize."

"I haven't got time, I'm leaving," I says.

"Well, what are you waiting around for?" asks Uncle Rondo.

So I just picked up the kitchen clock and marched off, without saying "Kiss my foot," or anything, and never did tell Stella-Rondo good-bye.

There was a nigger girl going along on a little wagon right in front.

"Nigger girl," I says, "come help me haul these things down the hill, I'm going to live in the post office."

Took her nine trips in her express wagon. Uncle Rondo came out on the porch and threw her a nickel.

And that's the last I've laid eyes on any of my family or my family laid eyes on me for five solid days and nights. Stella-Rondo may be telling the most horrible tales in the world about Mr. Whitaker, but I haven't heard them. As I tell everybody, I draw my own conclusions.

But oh, I like it here. It's ideal, as I've been saying. You see, I've got everything cater-cornered, the way I like it. Hear the radio? All the war news. Radio, sewing machine, book ends, ironing board and that great big piano lamp — peace, that's what I like. Butter-bean vines planted all along the front where the strings are.

Of course, there's not much mail. My family are naturally the main people in China Grove, and if they prefer to vanish from the face of the earth, for all the mail they get or the mail they write, why, I'm not going to open my mouth. Some of the folks here in town are taking up for me and some turned against me. I know which is which. There are always people who will quit buying stamps just to get on the right side of Papa-Daddy.

But here I am, and here I'll stay. I want the world to know I'm happy.

And if Stella-Rondo should come to me this minute, on bended knees, and *attempt* to explain the incidents of her life with Mr. Whitaker, I'd simply put my fingers in both my ears and refuse to listen.   [1941]

EUDORA WELTY

A Worn Path

It was December — a bright frozen day in the early morning. Far out in the country there was an old Negro woman with her head tied in a red rag, coming along a path through the pinewoods. Her name was Phoenix Jackson. She was very old and small and she walked slowly in the dark pine shadows, moving a little from side to side in her steps, with the balanced heaviness and lightness of a pendulum in a grandfather clock. She carried a thin, small cane made from an umbrella, and with this she kept tapping the frozen earth in front of her. This made a grave and persistent noise in the still air, that seemed meditative like the chirping of a solitary little bird.

She wore a dark striped dress reaching down to her shoe tops, and an equally long apron of bleached sugar sacks, with a full pocket: all neat and tidy, but every time she took a step she might have fallen over her shoelaces, which dragged from her unlaced shoes. She looked straight ahead. Her eyes were blue with age. Her skin had a pattern all its own of numberless branching wrinkles and as though a whole little tree stood in the middle of her forehead, but a golden color ran underneath, and the two knobs of her cheeks were illumined by a yellow burning under the dark. Under the red rag her hair came down on her neck in the frailest of ringlets, still black, and with an odor like copper.

Now and then there was a quivering in the thicket. Old Phoenix said, "Out of my way, all you foxes, owls, beetles, jack rabbits, coons and wild animals! . . . Keep out from under these feet, little bobwhites. . . . Keep the big wild hogs out of my path. Don't let none of those come running my direction. I got a long way." Under her small black-freckled hand her cane, limber as a buggy whip, would switch at the brush as if to rouse up any hiding things.

On she went. The woods were deep and still. The sun made the pine needles almost too bright to look at, up where the wind rocked. The cones dropped as light as feathers. Down in the hollow was the mourning dove — it was not too late for him.

The path ran up a hill. "Seem like there is chains about my feet, time I get this far," she said, in the voice of argument old people keep to use with themselves. "Something always take a hold of me on this hill — pleads I should stay."

After she got to the top she turned and gave a full, severe look behind her where she had come. "Up through pines," she said at length. "Now down through oaks."

Her eyes opened their widest, and she started down gently. But before she got to the bottom of the hill a bush caught her dress.

Her fingers were busy and intent, but her skirts were full and long, so that before she could pull them free in one place they were caught in another. It was not possible to allow the dress to tear. "I in the thorny bush," she said. "Thorns, you doing your appointed work. Never want to let folks pass, no sir. Old eyes thought you was a pretty little *green* bush."

Finally, trembling all over, she stood free, and after a moment dared to stoop for her cane.

"Sun so high!" she cried, leaning back and looking, while the thick tears went over her eyes. "The time getting all gone here."

At the foot of this hill was a place where a log was laid across the creek.

"Now comes the trial," said Phoenix.

Putting her right foot out, she mounted the log and shut her eyes. Lifting her skirt, leveling her cane fiercely before her, like a festival figure in some parade, she began to march across. Then she opened her eyes and she was safe on the other side.

"I wasn't as old as I thought," she said.

But she sat down to rest. She spread her skirts on the bank around her and folded her hands over her knees. Up above her was a tree in a pearly cloud of mistletoe. She did not dare to close her eyes, and when a little boy brought her a plate with a slice of marble-cake on it she spoke to him. "That would be acceptable," she said. But when she went to take it there was just her own hand in the air.

So she left that tree, and had to go through a barbed-wire fence. There she had to creep and crawl, spreading her knees and stretching her fingers like a baby trying to climb the steps. But she talked loudly to herself: she could not let her dress be torn now, so late in the day, and she could not pay for having her arm or her leg sawed off if she got caught fast where she was.

At last she was safe through the fence and risen up out in the clearing. Big dead trees, like black men with one arm, were standing in the purple stalks of the withered cotton field. There sat a buzzard.

"Who you watching?"

In the furrow she made her way along.

"Glad this not the season for bulls," she said, looking sideways, "and the good Lord made his snakes to curl up and sleep in the winter. A pleasure I don't see no two-headed snake coming around that tree, where it come once. It took a while to get by him, back in the summer."

She passed through the old cotton and went into a field of dead corn. It whispered and shook and was taller than her head. "Through the maze now," she said, for there was no path.

Then there was something tall, black, and skinny there, moving before her.

At first she took it for a man. It could have been a man dancing in the field. But she stood still and listened, and it did not make a sound. It was as silent as a ghost.

"Ghost," she said sharply, "who be you the ghost of? For I have heard of nary death close by."

But there was no answer — only the ragged dancing in the wind.

She shut her eyes, reached out her hand, and touched a sleeve. She found a coat and inside that an emptiness, cold as ice.

"You scarecrow," she said. Her face lighted. "I ought to be shut up for good," she said with laughter. "My senses is gone. I too old. I the oldest people I ever know. Dance, old scarecrow," she said, "while I dancing with you."

She kicked her foot over the furrow, and with mouth drawn down, shook her head once or twice in a little strutting way. Some husks blew down and whirled in streamers about her skirts.

Then she went on, parting her way from side to side with the cane, through the whispering field. At last she came to the end, to a wagon track where the silver grass blew between the red ruts. The quail were walking around like pullets, seeming all dainty and unseen.

"Walk pretty," she said. "This the easy place. This the easy going."

She followed the track, swaying through the quiet bare fields, through the little strings of trees silver in their dead leaves, past cabins silver from weather, with the doors and windows boarded shut, all like old women under a spell sitting there. "I walking in their sleep," she said, nodding her head vigorously.

In a ravine she went where a spring was silently flowing through a hollow log. Old Phoenix bent and drank. "Sweet-gum makes the water sweet," she said, and drank more. "Nobody know who made this well, for it was here when I was born."

The track crossed a swampy part where the moss hung as white as lace from every limb. "Sleep on, alligators, and blow your bubbles." Then the track went into the road.

Deep, deep the road went down between the high green-colored banks. Overhead the live-oaks met, and it was as dark as a cave.

A black dog with a lolling tongue came up out of the weeds by the ditch. She was meditating, and not ready, and when he came at her she only hit him a little with her cane. Over she went in the ditch, like a little puff of milkweed.

Down there, her senses drifted away. A dream visited her, and she reached her hand up, but nothing reached down and gave her a pull. So she lay there and presently went to talking. "Old woman," she said to herself, "that black dog come up out of the weeds to stall you off, and now there he sitting on his fine tail, smiling at you."

A white man finally came along and found her — a hunter, a young man, with his dog on a chain.

"Well, Granny!" he laughed. "What are you doing there?"

"Lying on my back like a June-bug waiting to be turned over, mister," she said, reaching up her hand.

He lifted her up, gave her a swing in the air, and set her down. "Anything broken, Granny?"

"No sir, them old dead weeds is springy enough," said Phoenix, when she had got her breath. "I thank you for your trouble."

"Where do you live, Granny?" he asked, while the two dogs were growling at each other.

"Away back yonder, sir, behind the ridge. You can't even see it from here."

"On your way home?"

"No sir, I going to town."

"Why, that's too far! That's as far as I walk when I come out myself, and I get something for my trouble." He patted the stuffed bag he carried, and there hung down a little closed claw. It was one of the bobwhites, with its beak hooked bitterly to show it was dead. "Now you go on home, Granny!"

"I bound to go to town, mister," said Phoenix. "The time come around."

He gave another laugh, filling the whole landscape. "I know you old colored people! Wouldn't miss going to town to see Santa Claus!"

But something held old Phoenix very still. The deep lines in her face went into a fierce and different radiation. Without warning, she had seen with her own eyes a flashing nickel fall out of the man's pocket onto the ground.

"How old are you, Granny?" he was saying.

"There is no telling, mister," she said, "no telling."

Then she gave a little cry and clapped her hands and said, "Git on away from here, dog! Look! Look at that dog!" She laughed as if in admiration. "He ain't scared of nobody. He a big black dog." She whispered, "Sic him!"

"Watch me get rid of that cur," said the man. "Sic him, Pete! Sic him!"

Phoenix heard the dogs fighting, and heard the man running and throwing sticks. She even heard a gunshot. But she was slowly bending forward by that time, further and further forward, the lid stretched down over her eyes, as if she were doing this in her sleep. Her chin was lowered almost to her knees. The yellow palm of her hand came out from the fold of her apron. Her fingers slid down and along the ground under the piece of money with the grace and care they would have in lifting an egg from under a setting hen. Then she slowly straightened up, she stood erect, and the nickel was in her apron pocket. A bird flew by. Her lips moved. "God watching me the whole time. I come to stealing."

The man came back, and his own dog panted about them. "Well, I scared him off that time," he said, and then he laughed and lifted his gun and pointed it at Phoenix.

She stood straight and faced him.

"Doesn't the gun scare you?" he said, still pointing it.

"No, sir, I seen plenty go off closer by, in my day, and for less than what I done," she said, holding utterly still.

He smiled, and shouldered the gun. "Well, Granny," he said, "you must be a hundred years old, and scared of nothing. I'd give you a dime if I had any money with me. But you take my advice and stay home, and nothing will happen to you."

"I bound to go on my way, mister," said Phoenix. She inclined her head in the red rag. Then they went in different directions, but she could hear the gun shooting again and again over the hill.

She walked on. The shadows hung from the oak trees to the road like curtains. Then she smelled wood-smoke, and smelled the river, and she saw a steeple and the cabins on their steep steps. Dozens of little black children whirled around her. There ahead was Natchez shining. Bells were ringing. She walked on.

In the paved city it was Christmas time. There were red and green electric lights strung and crisscrossed everywhere, and all turned on in the daytime. Old Phoenix would have been lost if she had not distrusted her eyesight and depended on her feet to know where to take her.

She paused quietly on the sidewalk where people were passing by. A lady came along in the crowd, carrying an armful of red-, green-, and silver-wrapped presents; she gave off perfume like the red roses in hot summer, and Phoenix stopped her.

"Please, missy, will you lace up my shoe?" She held up her foot.

"What do you want, Grandma?"

"See my shoe," said Phoenix. "Do all right for out in the country, but wouldn't look right to go in a big building."

"Stand still then, Grandma," said the lady. She put her packages down on the sidewalk beside her and laced and tied both shoes tightly.

"Can't lace 'em with a cane," said Phoenix. "Thank you, missy. I doesn't mind asking a nice lady to tie up my shoe, when I gets out on the street."

Moving slowly and from side to side, she went into the big building, and into a tower of steps, where she walked up and around and around until her feet knew to stop.

She entered a door, and there she saw nailed up on the wall the document that had been stamped with the gold seal and framed in the gold frame, which matched the dream that was hung up in her head.

"Here I be," she said. There was a fixed and ceremonial stiffness over her body.

"A charity case, I suppose," said an attendant who sat at the desk before her.

But Phoenix only looked above her head. There was sweat on her face, the wrinkles in her skin shone like a bright net.

"Speak up, Grandma," the woman said. "What's your name? We must have your history, you know. Have you been here before? What seems to be the trouble with you?"

Old Phoenix only gave a twitch to her face as if a fly were bothering her.

"Are you deaf?" cried the attendant.

But then the nurse came in.

"Oh, that's just old Aunt Phoenix," she said. "She doesn't come for herself — she has a little grandson. She makes these trips just as regular as clockwork. She lives away back off the Old Natchez Trace." She bent down. "Well, Aunt Phoenix, why don't you just take a seat? We won't keep you standing after your long trip." She pointed.

The old woman sat down, bolt upright in the chair.

"Now, how is the boy?" asked the nurse.

Old Phoenix did not speak.

"I said, how is the boy?"

But Phoenix only waited and stared straight ahead, her face very solemn and withdrawn into rigidity.

"Is his throat any better?" asked the nurse. "Aunt Phoenix, don't you hear me? Is your grandson's throat any better since the last time you came for the medicine?"

With her hands on her knees, the old woman waited, silent, erect and motionless, just as if she were in armor.

"You mustn't take up our time this way, Aunt Phoenix," the nurse said. "Tell us quickly about your grandson, and get it over. He isn't dead, is he?"

At last there came a flicker and then a flame of comprehension across her face, and she spoke.

"My grandson. It was my memory had left me. There I sat and forgot why I made my long trip."

"Forgot?" The nurse frowned. "After you came so far?"

Then Phoenix was like an old woman begging a dignified forgiveness for waking up frightened in the night. "I never did go to school, I was too old at the Surrender," she said in a soft voice. "I'm an old woman without an education. It was my memory fail me. My little grandson, he is just the same, and I forgot it in the coming."

"Throat never heals, does it?" said the nurse, speaking in a loud, sure voice to old Phoenix. By now she had a card with something written on it, a little list. "Yes. Swallowed lye. When was it? — January — two, three years ago —"

Phoenix spoke unasked now. "No, missy, he not dead, he just the same. Every little while his throat began to close up again, and he not able to swallow. He not get his breath. He not able to help himself. So the time come around, and I go on another trip for the soothing medicine."

"All right. The doctor said as long as you came to get it, you could have it," said the nurse. "But it's an obstinate case."

"My little grandson, he sit up there in the house all wrapped up, waiting by himself," Phoenix went on. "We is the only two left in the world. He suffer and it don't seem to put him back at all. He got a sweet look. He going to last. He wear a little patch quilt and peep out holding his mouth open like a little bird. I remembers so plain now. I not going to forget him again, no, the whole enduring time. I could tell him from all the others in creation."

"All right." The nurse was trying to hush her now. She brought her a bottle of medicine. "Charity," she said, making a check mark in a book.

Old Phoenix held the bottle close to her eyes, and then carefully put it into her pocket.

"I thank you," she said.

"It's Christmas time, Grandma," said the attendant. "Could I give you a few pennies out of my purse?"

"Five pennies is a nickel," said Phoenix stiffly.

"Here's a nickel," said the attendant.

Phoenix rose carefully and held out her hand. She received the nickel and then fished the other nickel out of her pocket and laid it beside the new one. She stared at her palm closely, with her head on one side.

Then she gave a tap with her cane on the floor.

"This is what come to me to do," she said. "I going to the store and buy my child a little windmill they sells, made out of paper. He going to find it hard to believe there such a thing in the world. I'll march myself back where he waiting, holding it straight up in this hand."

She lifted her free hand, gave a little nod, turned around, and walked out of the doctor's office. Then her slow step began on the stairs, going down.

[1941]

EDITH WHARTON *(1862–1937) was born into a wealthy family in New York City. She later wrote, "My little-girl life, safe, guarded, monotonous, was cradled in the only world about which, according to Goethe [the German poet], it is impossible to write poetry. The small society into which I was born was 'good' in the most prosaic sense of the term, and its only interest, for the generality of readers, lies in the fact of its sudden and total extinction." She was raised by governesses and tutors in the family homes in Paris, New York City, and Newport, Rhode Island. At an early age she decided to become a writer, and when she was only thirteen she disregarded Goethe and published, at her own expense, a collection of verse.*

After her marriage in 1885, Wharton began to write stories for popular magazines. Her first collection of stories, The Greater Inclination *(1899), was followed by books of fiction almost every year for more than a quarter of a century, a total of eleven collections of stories and sixteen novels. She lived most of her life in Paris, but her periodic visits to her country estate in the Berkshires, near Lenox, Massachusetts, helped her write with authority about life in America. Her best works include the early novel* The House of Mirth *(1905);* Ethan Frome *(1911), a laconically powerful New England tragedy; and* The Age of Innocence *(1920), a novel about old New York society. As a rule, Wharton's conventional novels of manners develop characterizations; her short stories, more satiric, emphasize plots. In both forms her point of view is always poised, her prose style elegant and tightly controlled.*

One of Wharton's good friends was another expatriate and keen observer of the society they knew so well, Henry James. James, who also visited her in the Berkshires, had a profound influence on her writing, encouraging her to set a high standard. Like James, Wharton enjoyed defining her artistic methods as a storyteller. In 1925 she published The Writing of Fiction, *where in analyzing the French and Russian contributions to the short-story form, she recognized that "instead of a loose web spread over the surface of life they have made it, at its best, a shaft driven straight into the heart of human experience." Her story "Roman Fever" (1936) has an ending that may strike the reader as "a shaft driven straight into the heart," but every detail in the realistic depiction of the characters and their situation is a carefully placed signpost pointing to the dramatic disclosure in the last sentence.*

RELATED COMMENTARY: *Edith Wharton, "Every Subject Must Contain within Itself Its Own Dimensions," page 1514.*

EDITH WHARTON

Roman Fever

I

From the table at which they had been lunching two American ladies of ripe but well-cared-for middle age moved across the lofty terrace of the Roman restaurant and, leaning on its parapet, looked first at each other, and then down on the outspread glories of the Palatine and the Forum, with the same expression of vague but benevolent approval.

As they leaned there a girlish voice echoed up gaily from the stairs leading to the court below. "Well, come along, then," it cried, not to them but to an invisible companion, "and let's leave the young things to their knitting" and a voice as fresh laughed back: "Oh, look here, Babs, not actually *knitting* —" "Well, I mean figuratively," rejoined the first. "After all, we haven't left our poor parents much else to do . . . ." and at that point the turn of the stairs engulfed the dialogue.

The two ladies looked at each other again, this time with a tinge of smiling embarrassment, and the smaller and paler one shook her head and colored slightly.

"Barbara!" she murmured, sending an unheard rebuke after the mocking voice in the stairway.

The other lady, who was fuller, and higher in color, with a small determined nose supported by vigorous black eyebrows, gave a good-humored laugh. "That's what our daughters think of us!"

Her companion replied by a deprecating gesture. "Not of us individually. We must remember that. It's just the collective modern idea of Mothers. And you see — " Half guiltily she drew from her handsomely mounted black hand-bag a twist of crimson silk run through by two fine knitting needles. "One never knows," she murmured. "The new system has certainly given us a good deal of time to kill; and sometimes I get tired just looking — even at this." Her gesture was now addressed to the stupendous scene at their feet.

The dark lady laughed again, and they both relapsed upon the view, contemplating it in silence, with a sort of diffused serenity which might have been borrowed from the spring effulgence of the Roman skies. The luncheon-hour was long past, and the two had their end of the vast terrace to themselves. At its opposite extremity a few groups, detained by a lingering look at the outspread city, were gathering up guide-books and fumbling for tips. The last of them scattered, and the two ladies were alone on the air-washed height.

"Well, I don't see why we shouldn't just stay here," said Mrs. Slade, the lady of the high color and energetic brows. Two derelict basket-chairs stood near, and she pushed them into the angle of the parapet, and settled herself in one, her gaze upon the Palatine. "After all, it's still the most beautiful view in the world."

"It always will be, to me," assented her friend Mrs. Ansley, with so slight a stress on the "me" that Mrs. Slade, though she noticed it, wondered if it were not merely accidental, like the random underlinings of old-fashioned letter-writers.

"Grace Ansley was always old-fashioned," she thought; and added aloud, with a retrospective smile: "It's a view we've both been familiar with for a good many years. When we first met here we were younger than our girls are now. You remember?"

"Oh, yes, I remember," murmured Mrs. Ansley, with the same undefinable stress — "There's that head-waiter wondering," she interpolated. She was evidently far less sure than her companion of herself and of her rights in the world.

"I'll cure him of wondering," said Mrs. Slade, stretching her hand toward a bag as discreetly opulent-looking as Mrs. Ansley's. Signing to the head-waiter, she explained that she and her friend were old lovers of Rome, and would like to spend the end of the afternoon looking down on the view — that is, if it did not disturb the service? The head-waiter, bowing over her gratuity, assured her that the ladies were most welcome, and would be still more so if they would condescend to remain for dinner. A full moon night, they would remember. . . .

Mrs. Slade's black brows drew together, as though references to the moon were out-of-place and even unwelcome. But she smiled away her frown as the head-waiter retreated. "Well, why not? We might do worse. There's no knowing, I suppose, when the girls will be back. Do you even know back from *where?* I don't!"

Mrs. Ansley again colored slightly. "I think those young Italian aviators we met at the Embassy invited them to fly to Tarquinia for tea. I suppose they'll want to wait and fly back by moonlight."

"Moonlight — moonlight! What a part it still plays. Do you suppose they're as sentimental as we were?"

"I've come to the conclusion that I don't in the least know what they are," said Mrs. Ansley. "And perhaps we didn't know much more about each other."

"No; perhaps we didn't."

Her friend gave her a shy glance. "I never should have supposed you were sentimental, Alida."

"Well, perhaps I wasn't." Mrs. Slade drew her lids together in retrospect; and for a few moments the two ladies, who had been intimate since childhood, reflected how little they knew each other. Each one, of course, had a label ready to attach to the other's name; Mrs. Delphin Slade, for instance, would have told herself, or any one who asked her, that Mrs. Horace Ansley, twenty-five years ago, had been exquisitely lovely — no, you wouldn't believe it, would you? . . . though, of course, still charming, distinguished. . . . Well, as a girl she had been exquisite; far more beautiful than her daughter Barbara, though certainly Babs, according to the new standards at any rate, was more effective — had more *edge,* as they say. Funny where she got it, with those two nullities as parents. Yes; Horace Ansley was — well, just the duplicate of his wife. Museum specimens of old New York. Good-looking, irreproachable, exemplary. Mrs. Slade and Mrs. Ansley had lived opposite each other — actually as well as figuratively — for years. When the drawing-room curtains in No. 20 East 73rd Street were renewed, No. 23, across the way, was always aware of it. And of all the movings, buyings, travels, anniversaries, illnesses — the tame chronicle of an estimable pair. Little of it escaped Mrs. Slade. But she had grown bored with it by the time her husband made his big *coup* in Wall Street, and when they bought in upper Park Avenue had already begun to think: "I'd rather live opposite a speakeasy for a change; at least one might see it raided." The idea of seeing Grace raided was so amusing that (before the move) she launched it at a woman's lunch. It made a hit, and went the rounds — she sometimes wondered if it had crossed the street, and reached Mrs. Ansley. She hoped not, but didn't much mind. Those were the days when respectability was at a discount, and it did the irreproachable no harm to laugh at them a little.

A few years later, and not many months apart, both ladies lost their husbands. There was an appropriate exchange of wreaths and condolences, and a brief renewal of intimacy in the half-shadow of their mourning; and now, after another interval, they had run across each other in Rome, at the same hotel, each of them the modest appendage of a salient daughter. The similarity of their lot had again drawn them together, lending itself to mild jokes, and the mutual confession that, if in old days it must have been tiring to "keep up" with daughters, it was now, at times, a little dull not to.

No doubt, Mrs. Slade reflected, she felt her unemployment more than poor Grace ever would. It was a big drop from being the wife of Delphin Slade to being his widow. She had always regarded herself (with a certain conjugal pride) as his equal in social gifts, as contributing her full share to the making of the exceptional couple they were: but the difference after his death was irremediable. As the wife of the famous corporation lawyer, always with an international case or two on hand, every day brought its exciting and unexpected obligation: the impromptu entertaining of eminent colleagues from abroad, the hurried dashes on legal business to London, Paris or Rome, where the entertaining was so handsomely reciprocated; the amusement of hearing in her wake: "What, that handsome woman with the good clothes and the eyes is Mrs. Slade — *the* Slade's wife? Really? Generally the wives of celebrities are such frumps."

Yes; being *the* Slade's widow was a dullish business after that. In living up to such a husband all her faculties had been engaged; now she had only her daughter to live up to, for the son who seemed to have inherited his father's gifts had died suddenly in boyhood. She had fought through that agony because her husband was there, to be helped and to help; now, after the father's death, the thought of the boy had become unbearable. There was nothing left but to mother her daughter; and dear Jenny was such a perfect daughter that she needed no excessive mothering. "Now with Babs Ansley I don't know that I *should* be so quiet," Mrs. Slade sometimes half-enviously reflected; but Jenny, who was younger than her brilliant friend, was that rare accident, an extremely pretty girl who somehow made youth and prettiness seem as safe as their absence. It was all perplexing — and to Mrs. Slade a little boring. She wished that Jenny would fall in love — with the wrong man, even; that she might have to be watched, out-manœuvred, rescued. And instead, it was Jenny who watched her mother, kept her out of draughts, made sure that she had taken her tonic. . . .

Mrs. Ansley was much less articulate than her friend, and her mental portrait of Mrs. Slade was slighter, and drawn with fainter touches. "Alida Slade's awfully brilliant; but not as brilliant as she thinks," would have summed it up; though she would have added, for the enlightenment of strangers, that Mrs. Slade had been an extremely dashing girl; much more so than her daughter, who was pretty, of course, and clever in a way, but had none of her mother's — well, "vividness," some one had once called it. Mrs. Ansley would take up current words like this, and cite them in quotation marks, as unheard-of audacities. No; Jenny was not like her mother. Sometimes Mrs. Ansley thought Alida Slade was disappointed; on the whole she had had a sad life. Full of failures and mistakes; Mrs. Ansley had always been rather sorry for her. . . .

So these two ladies visualized each other, each through the wrong end of her little telescope.

II

For a long time they continued to sit side by side without speaking. It seemed as though, to both, there was a relief in laying down their somewhat futile activities in the presence of the vast Memento Mori which faced them. Mrs. Slade sat quite still, her eyes fixed on the golden slope of the Palace of the Caesars, and after a while Mrs. Ansley ceased to fidget with her bag, and she too sank into meditation. Like many intimate friends, the two ladies had never before had occasion to be silent together, and Mrs. Ansley was slightly embarrassed by what seemed, after so many years, a new stage in their intimacy, and one with which she did not yet know how to deal.

Suddenly the air was full of that deep clangor of bells which periodically covers Rome with a roof of silver. Mrs. Slade glanced at her wristwatch. "Five o'clock already," she said, as though surprised.

Mrs. Ansley suggested interrogatively: "There's bridge at the Embassy at five." For a long time Mrs. Slade did not answer. She appeared to be lost in contemplation, and Mrs. Ansley thought the remark had escaped her. But after a while she said, as if speaking out of a dream: "Bridge, did you say? Not unless you want to. . . . But I don't think I will, you know."

"Oh, no," Mrs. Ansley hastened to assure her. "I don't care to at all. It's so lovely here; and so full of old memories, as you say." She settled herself in her chair, and almost furtively drew forth her knitting. Mrs. Slade took sideway note of this activity, but her own beautifully cared-for hands remained motionless on her knee.

"I was just thinking," she said slowly, "what different things Rome stands for to each generation of travelers. To our grandmothers, Roman fever; to our mothers, sentimental danger — how we used to be guarded! — to our daughters, no more dangers than the middle of Main Street. They don't know it — but how much they're missing!"

The long golden light was beginning to pale, and Mrs. Ansley lifted her knitting a little closer to her eyes. "Yes; how we were guarded!"

"I always used to think," Mrs. Slade continued, "that our mothers had a much more difficult job than our grandmothers. When Roman fever stalked the streets it must have been comparatively easy to gather in the girls at the danger hour; but when you and I were young, with such beauty calling us, and the spice of disobedience thrown in, and no worse risk than catching cold during the cool hour after sunset, the mothers used to be put to it to keep us in — didn't they?"

She turned again toward Mrs. Ansley, but the latter had reached a delicate point in her knitting. "One, two, three — slip two; yes, they must have been," she assented, without looking up.

Mrs. Slade's eyes rested on her with a deepened attention. "She can knit — in the face of *this!* How like her. . . ."

Mrs. Slade leaned back, brooding, her eyes ranging from the ruins which faced her to the long green hollow of the Forum, the fading glow of the church fronts beyond it, and the outlying immensity of the Colosseum. Suddenly she thought: "It's all very well to say that our girls have done away with sentiment and moonlight. But if Babs Ansley isn't out to catch that young aviator — the one who's a Marchese — then I don't know anything. And Jenny has no chance beside her. I know that too. I wonder if that's why Grace Ansley likes the two girls to go everywhere together? My poor Jenny as a foil — !" Mrs. Slade gave a hardly audible laugh, and at the sound Mrs. Ansley dropped her knitting.

"Yes — ?"

"I — oh, nothing. I was only thinking how your Babs carries everything before her. That Campolieri boy is one of the best matches in Rome. Don't look so innocent, my dear — you know he is. And I was wondering, ever so respectfully, you understand . . . wondering how two such exemplary characters as you and Horace had managed to produce anything quite so dynamic." Mrs. Slade laughed again, with a touch of asperity.

Mrs. Ansley's hands lay inert across her needles. She looked straight out at the great accumulated wreckage of passion and splendor at her feet. But her small profile was almost expressionless. At length she said: "I think you overrate Babs, my dear."

Mrs. Slade's tone grew easier. "No; I don't. I appreciate her. And perhaps envy you. Oh, my girl's perfect; if I were a chronic invalid I'd — well, I think I'd rather be in Jenny's hands. There must be times . . . but there! I always wanted a brilliant daughter . . . and never quite understood why I got an angel instead."

Mrs. Ansley echoed her laugh in a faint murmur. "Babs is an angel too."

"Of course — of course! But she's got rainbow wings. Well, they're wandering by the sea with their young men; and here we sit . . . and it all brings back the past a little too acutely."

Mrs. Ansley had resumed her knitting. One might almost have imagined (if one had known her less well, Mrs. Slade reflected) that, for her also, too many memories rose from the lengthening shadows of those august ruins. But no; she was simply absorbed in her work. What was there for her to worry about? She knew that Babs would almost certainly come back engaged to the extremely eligible Campolieri. "And she'll sell the New York house, and settle down near them in Rome, and never be in their way . . . she's much too tactful. But she'll have an excellent cook, and just the right people in for bridge and cocktails . . . and a perfectly peaceful old age among her grandchildren."

Mrs. Slade broke off this prophetic flight with a recoil of self-disgust. There was no one of whom she had less right to think unkindly than of Grace Ansley. Would she never cure herself of envying her? Perhaps she had begun too long ago.

She stood up and leaned against the parapet, filling her troubled eyes with the tranquilizing magic of the hour. But instead of tranquilizing her the sight seemed to increase her exasperation. Her gaze turned toward the Colosseum. Already its golden flank was drowned in purple shadow, and above it the sky curved crystal clear, without light or color. It was the moment when afternoon and evening hang balanced in mid-heaven.

Mrs. Slade turned back and laid her hand on her friend's arm. The gesture was so abrupt that Mrs. Ansley looked up, startled.

"The sun's set. You're not afraid, my dear?"

"Afraid — ?"

"Of Roman fever or pneumonia? I remember how ill you were that winter. As a girl you had a very delicate throat, hadn't you?"

"Oh, we're all right up here. Down below, in the Forum, it does get deathly cold, all of a sudden . . . but not here."

"Ah, of course you know because you had to be so careful." Mrs. Slade turned back to the parapet. She thought: "I must make one more effort not to hate her." Aloud she said: "Whenever I look at the Forum from up here I remember that story about a great-aunt of yours, wasn't she? A dreadfully wicked great-aunt?"

"Oh yes; Great-aunt Harriet. The one who was supposed to have sent her young sister out to the Forum after sunset to gather a night-blooming flower for her album. All our great-aunts and grandmothers used to have albums of dried flowers."

Mrs. Slade nodded. "But she really sent her because they were in love with the same man —"

"Well, that was the family tradition. They said Aunt Harriet confessed it years afterward. At any rate, the poor little sister caught the fever and died. Mother used to frighten us with the story when we were children."

"And you frightened *me* with it, that winter when you and I were here as girls. The winter I was engaged to Delphin."

Mrs. Ansley gave a faint laugh. "Oh, did I? Really frightened you? I don't believe you're easily frightened."

"Not often; but I was then. I was easily frightened because I was too happy. I wonder if you know what that means?"

"I — yes. . . ." Mrs. Ansley faltered.

"Well, I suppose that was why the story of your wicked aunt made such an impression on me. And I thought: 'There's no more Roman fever, but the Forum is deathly cold after sunset — especially after a hot day. And the Colosseum's even colder and damper.'"

"The Colosseum — ?"

"Yes. It wasn't easy to get in, after the gates were locked for the night. Far from easy. Still, in those days it could be managed; it was managed, often. Lovers met there who couldn't meet elsewhere. You knew that?"

"I — I daresay. I don't remember."

"You don't remember? You don't remember going to visit some ruins or other one evening, just after dark, and catching a bad chill? You were supposed to have gone to see the moon rise. People always said that expedition was what caused your illness."

There was a moment's silence; then Mrs. Ansley rejoined: "Did they? It was all so long ago."

"Yes. And you got well again — so it didn't matter. But I suppose it struck your friend — the reason given for your illness, I mean — because everybody knew you were so prudent on account of your throat, and your mother took such care of you. . . . You *had* been out late sight-seeing, hadn't you, that night?"

"Perhaps I had. The most prudent girls aren't always prudent. What made you think of it now?"

Mrs. Slade seemed to have no answer ready. But after a moment she broke out: "Because I simply can't bear it any longer — "

Mrs. Ansley lifted her head quickly. Her eyes were wide and very pale. "Can't bear what?"

"Why — your not knowing that I've always known why you went."

"Why I went — ?"

"Yes. You think I'm bluffing, don't you? Well, you went to meet the man I was engaged to — and I can repeat every word of the letter that took you there."

While Mrs. Slade spoke Mrs. Ansley had risen unsteadily to her feet. Her bag, her knitting and gloves, slid in a panic-stricken heap to the ground. She looked at Mrs. Slade as though she were looking at a ghost.

"No, no — don't," she faltered out.

"Why not? Listen, if you don't believe me. 'My one darling, things can't go on like this. I must see you alone. Come to the Colosseum immediately after dark tomorrow. There will be somebody to let you in. No one whom you need fear will suspect' — but perhaps you've forgotten what the letter said?"

Mrs. Ansley met the challenge with an unexpected composure. Steadying herself against the chair she looked at her friend, and replied: "No; I know it by heart too."

"And the signature? 'Only *your* D.S.' Was that it? I'm right, am I? That was the letter that took you out that evening after dark?"

Mrs. Ansley was still looking at her. It seemed to Mrs. Slade that a slow struggle was going on behind the voluntarily controlled mask of her small quiet face. "I shouldn't have thought she had herself so well in hand," Mrs. Slade reflected, almost resentfully. But at this moment Mrs. Ansley spoke, "I don't know how you knew. I burnt that letter at once."

"Yes; you would, naturally — you're so prudent!" The sneer was open now. "And if you burnt the letter you're wondering how on earth I know what was in it. That's it, isn't it?"

Mrs. Slade waited, but Mrs. Ansley did not speak.

"Well, my dear, I know what was in that letter because I wrote it!"

"You wrote it?"

"Yes."

The two women stood for a minute staring at each other in the last golden light. Then Mrs. Ansley dropped back into her chair. "Oh," she murmured, and covered her face with her hands.

Mrs. Slade waited nervously for another word or movement. None came, and at length she broke out: "I horrify you."

Mrs. Ansley's hands dropped to her knee. The face they uncovered was streaked with tears. "I wasn't thinking of you. I was thinking — it was the only letter I ever had from him!"

"And I wrote it. Yes; I wrote it! But I was the girl he was engaged to. Did you happen to remember that?"

Mrs. Ansley's head dropped again. "I'm not trying to excuse myself. . . . I remembered. . . ."

"And still you went?"

"Still I went."

Mrs. Slade stood looking down on the small bowed figure at her side. The flame of her wrath had already sunk, and she wondered why she had ever thought there would be any satisfaction in inflicting so purposeless a wound on her friend. But she had to justify herself.

"You do understand? I'd found out — and I hated you, hated you. I knew you were in love with Delphin — and I was afraid; afraid of you, of your quiet ways, your sweetness . . . your . . . well, I wanted you out of the way, that's all. Just for a few weeks; just till I was sure of him. So in a blind fury I wrote that letter. . . . I don't know why I'm telling you now."

"I suppose," said Mrs. Ansley slowly, "it's because you've always gone on hating me."

"Perhaps. Or because I wanted to get the whole thing off my mind." She paused. "I'm glad you destroyed the letter. Of course I never thought you'd die."

Mrs. Ansley relapsed into silence, and Mrs. Slade, leaning above her, was conscious of a strange sense of isolation, of being cut off from the warm current of human communion. "You think me a monster!"

"I don't know. . . . It was the only letter I had, and you say he didn't write it?"

"Ah, how you care for him still!"

"I cared for that memory," said Mrs. Ansley.

Mrs. Slade continued to look down on her. She seemed physically reduced by the blow — as if, when she got up, the wind might scatter her like a puff of dust. Mrs. Slade's jealousy suddenly leapt up again at the sight. All these years the woman had been living on that letter. How she must have loved him, to treasure the mere memory of its ashes! The letter of the man her friend was engaged to. Wasn't it she who was the monster?

"You tried your best to get him away from me, didn't you? But you failed; and I kept him. That's all."

"Yes. That's all."

"I wish now I hadn't told you. I'd no idea you'd feel about it as you do; I thought you'd be amused. It all happened so long ago, as you say; and you must do me the justice to remember that I had no reason to think you'd ever taken it seriously. How could I, when you were married to Horace Ansley two months afterward? As soon as you could get out of bed your mother rushed you off to Florence and married you. People were rather surprised — they wondered at its being done so quickly; but I thought I knew. I had an idea you did it out of *pique* — to be able to say you'd got ahead of Delphin and me. Girls have such silly reasons for doing the most serious things. And your marrying so soon convinced me that you'd never really cared."

"Yes. I suppose it would," Mrs. Ansley assented.

The clear heaven overhead was emptied of all its gold. Dusk spread over it, abruptly darkening the Seven Hills. Here and there lights began to twinkle through the foliage at their feet. Steps were coming and going on the deserted terrace — waiters looking out of the doorway at the head of the stairs, then reappearing with trays and napkins and flasks of wine. Tables were moved, chairs straightened. A feeble string of electric lights flickered out. Some vases of faded flowers were carried away, and brought back replenished. A stout lady in a dust-coat suddenly appeared, asking in broken Italian if any one had seen the elastic band which held together her tattered Baedeker. She poked with her stick under the table at which she had lunched, the waiters assisting.

The corner where Mrs. Slade and Mrs. Ansley sat was still shadowy and deserted. For a long time neither of them spoke. At length Mrs. Slade began again: "I suppose I did it as a sort of joke —"

"A joke?"

"Well, girls are ferocious sometimes, you know. Girls in love especially. And I remember laughing to myself all that evening at the idea that you were waiting around there in the dark, dodging out of sight, listening for every sound, trying to get in — Of course I was upset when I heard you were so ill afterward."

Mrs. Ansley had not moved for a long time. But now she turned slowly toward her companion. "But I didn't wait. He'd arranged everything. He was there. We were let in at once," she said.

Mrs. Slade sprang up from her leaning position. "Delphin there? They let you in? — Ah, now you're lying!" she burst out with violence.

Mrs. Ansley's voice grew clearer, and full of surprise. "But of course he was there. Naturally he came —"

"Came? How did he know he'd find you there? You must be raving!"

Mrs. Ansley hesitated, as though reflecting. "But I answered the letter. I told him I'd be there. So he came."

Mrs. Slade flung her hands up to her face. "Oh, God — you answered! I never thought of your answering. . . ."

"It's odd you never thought of it, if you wrote the letter."

"Yes. I was blind with rage."

Mrs. Ansley rose, and drew her fur scarf about her. "It is cold here. We'd better go. . . . I'm sorry for you," she said as she clasped the fur about her throat.

The unexpected words sent a pang through Mrs. Slade. "Yes; we'd better go." She gathered up her bag and cloak. "I don't know why you should be sorry for me," she muttered.

Mrs. Ansley stood looking away from her toward the dusky secret mass of the Colosseum. "Well — because I didn't have to wait that night."

Mrs. Slade gave an unquiet laugh. "Yes; I was beaten there. But I oughtn't to begrudge it to you, I suppose. At the end of all these years. After all, I had everything; I had him for twenty-five years. And you had nothing but that one letter that he didn't write."

Mrs. Ansley was again silent. At length she turned toward the door of the terrace. She took a step, and turned back, facing her companion.

"I had Barbara," she said, and began to move ahead of Mrs. Slade toward the stairway. [1936]

JOHN EDGAR WIDEMAN (*b. 1941*) *was born in Washington, D.C., and grew up in the Homewood section of Pittsburgh, Pennsylvania, an inner-city ghetto he has written about frequently in his fiction. At the University of Pennsylvania, Wideman was both a star athlete and a brilliant scholar: He earned All-Ivy honors in basketball as well as a place in the Philadelphia Big Five Basketball Hall of Fame, and he was one of two African Americans to receive a Rhodes scholarship in 1963, the year he graduated. Wideman spent the next three years at Oxford University studying English literature and followed this experience with a year at the University of Iowa Writers Workshop as a Kent fellow. After teaching at the University of Wyoming, he is now a professor of English at the University of Massachusetts, Amherst.*

Wideman published his first novels in the 1960s and followed them with two volumes of short stories in the 1980s, Damballah *(1981) and* Fever *(1989), in addition to several other books. In 1990 his novel* Philadelphia Fire *won the American Book Award and the PEN/Faulkner Prize for fiction.* All Stories Are True: The Collected Stories of John Edgar Wideman, *thirty-five stories in all, appeared in 1992. "The Beginning of Homewood" is an early story included in* Damballah. *It explores a theme Wideman had introduced in his novels* A Glance Away *(1967) and* Hiding Place *(1981), and later developed in his nonfiction memoir* Brothers and Keepers *(1984), which the* New York Times *listed as one of the ten best books of the year.*

Wideman's theme is our failure to understand one another, as evidenced by Wideman's alienation from his brother Robby, the "you" in the autobiographical story "The Beginning of Homewood." Robby stayed in the Homewood ghetto, became a criminal, and went to jail instead of getting an education like his brother and leaving the impoverished black community. As the critic James W. Coleman recognized, what distinguishes Wideman's writing about this theme is his

> insistence that talented, successful black people act responsibly toward family and community after they have achieved success. . . . Wideman has been moving toward fictional forms and approaches that incorporate what he has learned from his formal training in Western universities and what he has been learning from his studies of black culture. Wideman's continuing aim has been to make his fiction more substantive, more meaningful, by giving it a much stronger black voice.

JOHN EDGAR WIDEMAN

The Beginning of Homewood

I have just finished reading a story which began as a letter to you. A letter I began writing on a Greek island two years ago, but never finished, never sent, a letter which became part of the story I haven't finished either. Rereading makes it very clear that something is wrong with the story. I understand now that part of what's wrong is the fact that I never finished the letter to you. The letter remains inside the story, buried, bleeding through when I read. What's wrong is the fact that I never finished the letter, never sent it and it is buried now in a place only I can see. Because the letter was meant for you. I began by trying to say some things to you, but they never got sent, never reached you so there is something wrong about the story nothing can fix.

In a way the story came before the letter. The story concerned the beginning of Homewood and a woman, a black woman who in 1859 was approximately eighteen years old. She was the property of a prosperous farmer who employed slave labor to cultivate the land he owned near Cumberland, Maryland. I wanted to tell the story of the woman's escape, her five-hundred-mile flight through hostile, dangerous territory and her final resettlement in Homewood, a happy ending or beginning from our point of view since this woman turns out to be Great-great-great-grandmother Sybela Owens. The idea of the story had been on my mind for years, ever since I'd heard Aunt May tell it the night of Grandpa's funeral. For some reason being in Europe again sharpened the need to get it down on paper. Maybe the trip to the concentration camp at Dachau, maybe the legend I'd heard about Delos, an island sacred to Apollo where no one was allowed to be born or to die, maybe the meals alone in restaurants where no one else was speaking English, maybe the Greek word *helidone* which means swallows and sounds like a perfect poem about birds, maybe all of that had something to do with sharpening the need. Anyway I was sitting in a cafe scribbling messages on postcards. Halfway through the stack I got tired of trying to be cute and funny and realized the only person I needed to write was you. So I started a letter in my notebook. And that's when the first words of Sybela Owens's story said themselves. Five or six sentences addressed to you and then the story took over.

Aunt May's voice got me started on the story. Sitting in a cafe, staring out at the gray sky and gray sea, and mad because it was my last morning on the island and I'd been hoping for blue skies and sunshine, sitting there trying to figure out why I was on a Greek island and why you were six thousand miles away in prison and what all that meant and what I could say to you about it, I heard Aunt May's voice. She was singing Lord reach down and touch me. I heard the old church rocking through the cries of sea birds.

Lord reach down and touch me, the Gospel Chorus of Homewood African Methodist Episcopal Zion Church singing, *Touch me with Thy holy grace* because *Lord if you would touch me, Thy touch would save me from sin.* And Aunt May was right there singing with them. You know how she is. Trying to outsing everybody with the congregation harmonizes with the Gospel Chorus. She had on one of those funny little hats like she wears with all the flowers and a veil. I could hear her singing and I could feel her getting ready to shout. In a minute she'd be up and out in the aisle shaking everything on her old bones she could shake, carrying on till the ushers came and steadied her and helped her back to her seat. I could see the little hat she keeps centered just right on top of her head no matter how hard the spirit shakes her. And see her eyes rolling to the ceiling, that yellow ceiling sanctified by the sweat of Deacon Barclay and the Men's Auxiliary when they put up the scaffolds and climb with buckets of Lysol and water and hearts pumping each year a little less strongly up there in the thin air to scrub the grit from the plaster so it shines like a window to let God's light in and let the prayers of the Saints out.

That's when the story, or meditation I had wanted to decorate with the trappings of a story began. At least the simple part of it. The part concerning the runaway and her dash for freedom, the story I had been trying to tell for years. Its theme was to be the urge for freedom, the resolve of the runaway to live free or die. An old, simple story, but because the heroine was Great-great-great-grandmother Sybela Owens, I felt the need to tell it again.

What was not simple was the crime of this female runaway set against your crime. What was not simple was my need to tell Sybela's story so it connected with yours. One was root and the other branch but I was too close to you and she was too far away and there was the matter of guilt, of responsibility, I couldn't tell either story without implicating myself.

This woman, this Sybela Owens our ancestor, bore the surname of her first owner and the Christian name, Sybela, which was probably a corruption of Sybil, a priestess pledged to Apollo. The Sybil of Greek myth could see the future but her power was also a curse because like the black woman tagged with her name centuries later, Sybil was a prisoner. A jealous magician had transformed the Greek Sybil into a bird, caged her and robbed her of speech. She possessed only a song and became a bauble, a plaything in a gilded cage set out to entertain dinner guests in the wizard's palace. This was to be her role for eternity, except that once, addressed by a seer who heard a hauntingly human expressiveness in her song, she managed to reply, "My name is Sybil and I wish to die."

On the plantation Sybela Owens was called Belle. Called that by some because it was customary for slaves to disregard the cumbersome, ironic names bestowed by whites, and rechristen one another in a secret, second language, a language whose forms and words gave substance to the captives' need to see themselves as human beings. Called Belle by others because it was convenient and the woman answered to it. Called Belle by a few because these older slaves remembered another black woman, an African who had lived with a cage on her shoulders for twenty years and the cage had a little tinkling bell attached to it so you knew when she was coming and naturally they had started calling her Bell, in derision at first, mocking her pride, her futile stubbornness on a point most of the women had conceded long before, a point which peopled the plantation with babies as various in hue as the many colors of Joseph's coat, then Belle because she had not broken, Mother Belle finally because she was martyr and saint, walking among them with the horrible contraption on her shoulders but unwavering, straight and tall as the day the iron cage had been fitted to her body; her pride their pride, her resistance a reminder not of the other women's fall, but of the shame of those who had undone them. Called Belle because they saw in this beautiful Sybela a striking resemblance, a reincarnation almost of the queenly, untouchable one who had been sent to suffer with them.

Every morning the slaves were awakened by the blast of a conch shell. Blowing the conch horn would have been a black man's job. To be up before everybody else while the sky was still dark and the grass chilly with dew. A black man would have to do it. And do it to the others who hated to hear him as much as he hated the cold walk in his bare feet to the little rise where he was expected to be every morning and every morning like he was some kind of goddamn rooster stand there and blast away on the conch till other feet started shuffling in the rows of dark huts.

Sybela would have heard the conch shell a thousand mornings. Strangely, the first morning of her freedom when she heard nothing but bird cries and the rasp of crickets, she missed the horn. The three or four dresses in which she had cocooned herself unfurl as she rolls away from Charlie Bell's hard back. She shivers as a draft runs up between her clothes and her skin, breaking the seal of heat. She stares at the horizon while the sky drifts grayly across the mirror of her eyes. In the rifts between the dark hills, mist smolders dense and white as drifted snow; the absolute stillness is still and more absolute because of the ground noise of birds and insects. She rises to a sitting position and lifts her arm from the rags beneath which her children sleep and hugs the mantle of her entire wardrobe closer to her body. In the quiet moments of that first morning of freedom she misses the moaning horn and hates the white man, her lover, her liberator, her children's father sleeping beside her.

Charlie Bell had stolen her, her and the two children, stolen them from his own father when he learned the old man intended to include them in a lot of slaves sold to a speculator. She had no warning. Just his knock, impatient, preemptive as it always was when he decided to take her from her sleep. Using no more words than he did when he demanded her body, he made it clear what he wanted. In a few minutes all that was useful and portable was gleaned from the hut, the children roused, every piece of clothing layered on their backs and then all of them rushing into the night, into the woods bordering the northern end of the plantation. He pushed them without words, a rage in his grunts, in his hands, rage she felt aimed at her and the frightened children though it was the forest he tore at and cursed. The dark woods responded to his attack with one of their own: branches whipped at the runaways' faces, roots snarled their feet, dry wood snapped loud enough to wake the dead.

It began, like most things between them, in silence, at night. After an hour or so they had to carry the children. Charlie Bell lifted Maggie who was older and heavier than her brother, and Sybela draped Thomas in the sling across her chest not because she conceded anything to the man's strength but because when she bowed into the darkness she reached for the sobs of fear and exhaustion she knew the man could not quiet. Maggie would cling to Charlie Bell, the plunge through the forest would become a game as she burrowed her head into his shoulder. She would be riding a horse and the jostling gallop, the fury of the man's heartbeat would lull her to sleep. But the boy was frightened more by the white man than the crashing forest. Thomas was not much more than a baby but he would scramble along on his thin, bowlegs till he dropped. Never complaining, Thomas would pick himself up a hundred times and not even notice the shrieks of invisible animals, but he could not abide the man's presence, the man's anger, and he whined until Sybela pressed him to sleep against her body.

The first morning of her freedom she looked quickly away from the white man, forgetting the knife-thrust of hatred as she listened to the complaints of her body and surveyed the place where exhaustion had forced them to drop. Charlie Bell must know where they are going. She had heard stories of runaways traveling for weeks in a great circle that brought them back to the very spot where they had begun their escape. The man must know. All white men seemed to know the magic that connected the plantation to the rest of the world, a world which for her was no more than a handful of words she had heard others use. The words *New Orleans, Canada, Philadelphia, Cumberland* were impossible for her to say. Except silently to herself, sifting them through her mind the way old heathen Orion was always fingering the filthy string of beads he wore around his neck. She did not hear the conch shell and realized for the first time in her life she was alone. In spite of the children still tied to her with strings that twisted deep inside her belly, in spite of the man, she knew she could just walk away from all of them, walk away even if the price was heavy drops of her blood dripping at every step because she was nowhere and no one was watching and the earth could swallow her or the gray sky press down like a gigantic pillow and snuff out her life, her breath, the way Charlie Bell had tried once, and it would be nobody but her dead, nobody knowing her death just like nobody heard in the silence of this morning her thoughts; and that was the thing she would not walk away from, the drone of her voice speaking to itself, monotonous and everlasting as cricket hum. She could not leave it, or bury it and cry over it; she was nothing but that sound, and the sound was alone.

I wanted to dwell on Sybela's first free morning but the chant of the Gospel Chorus wouldn't let me sit still. *Lord, reach down and touch me.* The chorus wailing and then Reba Love Jackson soloing. I heard May singing and heard Mother Bess telling what she remembers and what she had heard about Sybela Owens. I was thinking the way Aunt May talks. I heard her laughter, her amens, and *can I get a witness,* her digressions within digressions, the webs she spins and brushes away with her hands. Her stories exist because of their parts and each part is a story worth telling, worth examining to find the stories it contains. What seems to ramble begins to cohere when the listener understands the process, understands that the voice seeks to recover everything, but the voice proclaims *nothing is lost,* that the listener is not passive but lives like everything else within the story. Somebody shouts *Tell the truth.* You shout too. May is preaching and dances out between the shiny, butt-rubbed, wooden pews doing what she's been doing since the first morning somebody said *Freedom.* Freedom.

One of the last times I saw you, you were in chains. Not like Isaac Hayes when he mounts the stage for a concert or poses for an album cover, not those flaunted, ironic, who's-shucking-who gold chains draped over his ten-thou-sand-dollar-a-night brown body but the real thing, old-time leg irons and wrist shackles and twenty pounds of iron dragged through the marbled corridors of the county courthouse in Fort Collins, the Colorado town where they'd finally caught up with you and your cut buddy Ruchell. I waited outside the courtroom for a glimpse of you, for a chance to catch your eye and raise my clenched fist high enough for you and everybody else to see. I heard a detective say: "These are a couple of mean ones. Spades from back East. Bad dudes. Wanted in Pennsylvania for Murder One."

You and Ruchell were shackled together. In your striped prison issue coveralls you were the stars everyone had been awaiting. People murmured and pointed and stared and the sea of faces parted for your passage. In the eyes of the other green-coveralled prisoners waiting to be arraigned there was a particular attentiveness and awe, a humility almost as they came face to face with you — the Big Time. Your hair was nappy and shot straight out of the tops of your heads. Made you look a foot taller. Leg irons forced you to shuffle; your upper bodies swayed to make up for the drag of the iron. Neither of you had shaved. Neither looked down at the gaggle of deputies shooing back the crowd. The two of you could have been a million miles away discussing Coltrane or pussy. Everything about your faces disclaimed the accident that was happening to your bodies. The slept-in, too small coveralls, the steel bracelets, the rattling pimp-strut shuffle through the marbled hall-way some other black prisoner had freshly mopped. You were intent on one another, smiling, nodding, whispering inside a glass cage. I thought of your ambition to be an entertainer. Admired the performance you were giving them.

Bad dudes, Mean nigger men. Killers.

If they had captured Great-great-great-grandmother Sybela Owens, they would have made a spectacle of her return to the plantation, just as they paraded you, costumed, fettered through the halls. Because they had not allowed you soap or combs or mirrors or razors, you looked as if you had been hiding for days in the bush, bringing some of its wildness with you into the clean halls of justice. She too, if they had caught her, would have returned part wild thing. Her long hair matted, her nails ragged and caked with mud, her skirts in tatters, the raw smell of the woods soaked into her clothes and skin. She would have struggled to walk unbowed behind the horses, at the end of the rope depending from her wrists to saddle horn. Her eyes would have been fixed in the middle distance, beyond the slumped backs of the sleepy riders, above the broken line of slave row cabins the hunting party finally reached. Her shoes would be gone, her wrists bloody. There would be dark splotches across her back where the coarse homespun cloth has fused with her flesh. The shame she will never speak of, more bearable now than it will ever be because now it is a fiery pain in her groin blotting out the humiliation she will remember and have to deal with once the pain has subsided. A funky, dirty black woman, caught and humbled, marched through the slave quarters like the prize of war she is, like the pawn she is in the grand scheme of the knights on horseback. But her eyes are on the moon. Like yours. I ask myself again *why not me,* why is it the two of you skewered and displayed like she would have been if she hadn't kept running. Ask myself if I would have committed the crime of running away or if I would have stayed and tried to make the best of a hopeless situation. Ask if you really had any choice, if anything had changed in the years between her crime and yours. Could you have run away without committing a crime? Were there names other than "outlaw" to call you, were there words other than "crime" to define your choice?

Mother Bess is down off Bruston Hill now. She talks about you and asks about you and says God give her strength she's crossing that river and coming over to see you. She talks about Sybela Owens. May saw Sybela Owens too. May was staring at the tall, straight trees behind the house when she felt eyes on her, eyes which had burrowed right down into the place where she was daydreaming. May let her own eyes slowly find the ones watching her. Cautiously she lowered her gaze down past the tall trees, the slant of the roof, the rhythmed silhouette of gray shingles and boards, down past the scarred post supporting the porch roof, the knobby uprights of the rocking chair's back, stopping finally at the old woman who sat dark and closed as a fist. Sybela Owens's ancient eyes blinked in the bright sunlight but did not waver; they had waited patiently as if they had all the time in the world for May to reach them. Then it was May's turn to wait. She quieted everything inside herself as the old eyes shushed her and patted her and said her name in a way she had never heard it said before. *May.* The eyes never left her, but after an instant which seemed forever, May was released. Sybela Owens's eyes never left her but they had fallen asleep again. Among the million brown wrinkles and folds in the old woman's face were two invisible shutters which slid down over her eyes. They were in place again and though May could not see through them, she understood that Grandmother Owens could still look out.

"And let me tell you all something. That's right. You all listen up because I'm gon tell you what you ain't never heard. That's right. And you heard it from May and May be long gone but you all remember where you heard it. Yes indeed. About Grandmother Owens now. She had power. A freeing kind of power. I heard them say it and you might hear somebody say it and think that's just old people talking or them old time down home tales don't nobody believe no more but you listen to me and hear me tell it like it was because I was there, me, May, and I wasn't nothing but a child in knickers but I had sense enough to know it when I felt it, sense enough to let the power touch me, yes Lawd, reach down and touch me, and I felt it from my nappy head down to my dirty toes, felt it even though I was a child, felt it raising me up from scratching at my backside and playing in dirt. Grandmother Owens touched me and I felt it. Felt all the life running out me and something new filling me up at the same time. Just as clear as a bell I heard her say my name. And say so many other things there ain't no words for but they all rushing in so fast felt my whole self moving out the way to make room. Thought her power gon bust me wide open. Bust me clean open and I be running down off that hill like melting snow."

And Mother Bess said, Tell the truth. Said. Yes. Yes. And May kept on telling.

"That's all. Ain't no more. Old as she was and young as I was, she let me feel the power. And I'm a witness. That's what I am now. Your Aunt May's a witness. I'm telling you it happened and I don't know much else about Grandmother Owens except what I been told cause that's the only time I seen her. Just before they brought her down off Bruston Hill. Didn't last a month they say. Took her down off that hill and she was dead in a month, a month after they carried her down. Strong enough to fight when they came for her. But she let them take her. Know she let them cause if she set her mind on not moving, nobody on God's green earth could budge that woman a inch. Because she had the power. I'm a witness. Had it still as sure as she sitting in that rocking chair in petticoats and a black cape and a long black dress. Sun hot as fire and she never sweat one bit. Had it and touched me with it. And changed my life. Yes she did. Told me to live free all this time and be a witness all this time. And told me come a day her generations fill this city and need to know the truth.

"Yes, Lawd. Everybody talking about heaven ain't going there. Hmmph. And everybody talking about freedom ain't been free and never gon be. If the Lord set a burden on you so heavy you can't move nothing but one thumb, you better believe what I'm telling you, the wiggling of that one thumb make you the freest thing in the world. Grandmother Owens now. She suffered in Egypt. She suffered under them cruel pharaohs. Told her when to jump and when to spit and beat her unmerciful she didn't jump or spit fast enough to suit em. That's what it was all about. Evil pharaohs and Hebrews who was God's chosen people, chosen to suffer and get hard like iron in a fire. Now youall see people just like I do, see them every day strutting round here in them fancy clothes or riding them big cars and they don't know they's still jumping and spitting when they told. They don't know it. Too ignorant to know it. Hmmph. And tell you *gwan out my face, nigger,* you try and tell them something. But it be the same. Pharaohs and Hebrew children. Cept some few like Grandmother Owens get up one morning and gone. Run a hundred miles a day with little children on her back, her and that white man Charlie Bell and them babies run by night and sleep by day, crisscrossing rivers and forests full of alligators and wolves. Now that's something, ain't it? Grandmother

Owens wasn't hardly no more than a child. Hardly old as Shirley sitting there but she got up one bright morning and heard the freedom trumpet and lit out not knowing a thing but she was gon keep running till she free. . . ."

On the first night of her first day of freedom after the children had finally fallen asleep under her arm and Charlie Bell's restless tossing had quieted to the grunting and twitching of a hound dog dreaming of a hunt, and the stars and insects reigned absolute in the darkness, Sybela thought she saw a star fall and remembered the old story about a night when all of heaven had seemed to come unstuck and hundreds of stars plummeted from the sky and you couldn't hear the rooster or the conch horn next morning for the prayers rising from the cabins. Niggers took the fiery night for a sign of Judgment Day coming. And the story said didn't nobody go to work that morning and didn't none the white folks come round and say a mumbling word neither. She believed she saw the star go, let go like a leaf does a tree, then tumble not like a leaf but with a stone's dead heaviness through water. But the dark waters of the sky closed up without a ripple so she couldn't be sure whether she saw a star fall or not. The swift turning of her eye loosed one of the tears brimming there and it slanted coolly and hotly down her cheek and she didn't know its source any more than she understood why one star tumbled and the other didn't and after she dug the back of her hand into both eyepits and her eyes were bone dry again she couldn't be sure if there had been a tear any more than she could be sure the flicker of motion crossing a corner of her eye had been an actual star's dying.

"They some the first settle here in Homewood. On Hamilton Avenue where Albion comes in. Trolley cars used to be on Hamilton but Charlie and Sybela Owens come here long before that. Most the city still be what you call Northside now. Old Allegheny then. Wasn't but a few families this side the river and hardly none at all out this way when Grandmother Owens come. Brought two children from slavery and had eighteen more that lived after they got here. Most born up on Bruston Hill after the other white men let Charlie know they didn't want one of their kind living with no black woman so Charlie he up and moved. Way up on Bruston Hill where nobody round trying to mind his business. Stead of killing them busybodies he took Grandmother Owens up there and that's the start of Homewood. Children and grandchildren coming down off that hill and settling. Then other Negroes and every other kind of people moving here because the life was good and everybody welcome. They say the land Charlie owned on Hamilton was fixed. After he left, nothing grow or prosper there. They say Grandmother Owens cursed it and Charlie warned all them white folks not to touch his land. He said he would go to keep peace but nobody better not set a foot on the land he left behind. That spiteful piece of property been the downfall of so many I done forgot half the troubles come to people try to live there. You all remember where that crazy woman lived what strangled her babies and slit her own throat and where they built that fancy Jehovah Witness church over on Hamilton that burnt to the ground. That's the land. Lot's still empty cept for ashes and black stones and that's where Grandmother Owens first lived. What goes round comes round, yes it does, now."

And Mother Bess said Preach. Said Tell the truth.

Sybela's story could end here but it doesn't. I still hear May's voice:

"It hurts me. Hurts me to my heart. I remembers the babies. How beautiful they were. Then somebody tells me this one's dead, or that one's dying or Rashad going to court today or they gave Tommy Life. And I remembers the babies. Holding them. Seeing them once or twice a year at somebody's wedding, somebody's funeral or maybe at the Westinghouse picnic. Sitting on a bench at Kennywood Park watching the merry-go-round and listening to the music and a brown-skinned boy walk by with his arm around a little gal's shoulder and he grin at me all sheepish or turn his head real quick like he don't know the funny looking old lady on the bench, and I know he's one of the babies and remember the last time I saw him and how I patted his nappy head and said *My, my, you sure are getting big* or *My, my, you're grown now, a big man now,* and remember him peeking at me with the same sheepish grin and don't you know that's what I remembers when I hear he's robbed a store or been sent to prison or run off from some girl he's left with a baby, or comes around on Westinghouse picnic day at Kennywood Park to ask me for some ride money or to show me his family, his babies and let me hold them a minute."

My story could end here, now. Sybela Owens is long dead, rocking on the porch in her black cape like the sea taxis on their anchors when the water is too mean for the journey to Delos. Great-great-great-grandmother Owens is meeting May's eyes, gazing through the child to the shadowy generations, to storms which will tilt the earth on its axis. The old woman watches her children fall like stars from the night sky, each one perfect, each one a billion years in the making, each one dug from her womb so the black heavens are crisscrossed infinitely by the filaments of her bright pain which no matter how thinly stretched are unbreakable and connect her with her progeny and each point of light to every other. The vision blinds her. She sighs and crosses her wrists under the ruins of her bosom.

It could end here or there but I have one more thing to tell you. The Supreme Court has decided to hear a case in which a group of inmates are arguing that they had a right to attempt an escape from prison because conditions in the prison constituted cruel and unusual punishment and thereby violated the prisoners' human rights. It's a bitch, ain't it? The Court has a chance to say yes, a chance to author its version of the Emancipation Proclamation. The Court could set your crime against Sybela's, the price of our freedom against yours. The Court could ask why you are where you are, and why the rest of us are here.

So the struggle doesn't ever end. Her story, your story, the connections. But now the story, or pieces of story are inside this letter and it's addressed to you and I'll send it and that seems better than the way it was before. For now. Hold on.   [1981]

CHRISTA WOLF (b. 1929), one of the foremost novelists and essayists who lived in East Germany and documented life in the German Democratic Republic, was born in Landsberg and moved in 1945 to Gammelin in the eastern part of Germany. From 1949 to 1953 she studied literature, or what she called "the snares of theory," in Jena and Leipzig, married and had two daughters, and then worked for nearly a decade in the organization of the German Writers' Union and as an editor and anthologist. She began to live in East Berlin as a freelance writer in 1962, publishing several prize-winning novels and books of essays over the next thirty years. The first of her books to be published in English, The Quest for Christa T (1970), was allowed only a limited sale in the original German edition in East Germany; her later book about the nuclear disaster at Chernobyl, Accident: A Day's News (1989), won the Scholl Prize for Literature in West Germany, where it was a best-seller.

In Grace Paley's introduction to Wolf's The Author's Dimension: Selected Essays (1993), Paley described her first meeting with Wolf in East Berlin a dozen years before, and her awareness that Wolf "was needed — an experience most American writers don't have too often. The country was poor but lively with direction, socialist direction, newness happening all around her among the ruins, idealism, and a way to turn away from a shameful national past." Wolf herself has written that "after the war, we had to learn to live under the eyes of nations that shuddered at our name." The story "Exchanging Glances," from What Remains and Other Stories (1993), is an autobiographical story describing the evacuation before the Germans surrendered to the Americans on the Day of Liberation, May 5, 1945.

As political repression intensified in East Germany, Wolf was censored for her criticism of the patriarchy. In Cassandra: A Novel and Four Essays (1984), she expressed her fear of a coming holocaust resulting from what she saw as a trivialization of women's role in society. Wolf has never lost her taste for controversy nor her belief that the writer's function is to produce "opposition literature." As she wrote perceptively after the recent disappearance of both the Berlin Wall and the East German nation, the "politicians, economic managers, and party officials need a fatherland to carry on their enterprises. There is no motherland in sight, no more than before."

CHRISTA WOLF

Exchanging Glances

Translated by Heike Schwarzbauer and Rick Jabvarian

1

I've forgotten what my grandmother was wearing the time that nasty word "Asia" got her back on her feet. Why she of all people should be the first to come to mind I can't say; during her lifetime she was never pushy. I remember all her dresses: the brown one with the crocheted collar, which she wore on Christmas and all family birthdays, her black silk blouse, the checkered apron, and the knitted black mottled sweater she wore on winter days while sitting by the stove perusing the *Landsberg Gazette*. Yet for this trip she had nothing suitable to wear — and this is not just my memory playing tricks with me. Her little button-up boots were useful, though. They hung suspended at the ends of her too short, slightly crooked legs, always two centimeters above the floor, even when she was sitting on the edge of an air-raid cot, even when the floor was nothing but hard earth, as it was on that April day I have chosen to recall here. The bomber squadrons which now passed overhead during broad daylight on their way to Berlin were already out of earshot. Someone had pushed open the door of the air-raid shelter, and in the bright triangle of sunlight at the entrance, three steps from the dangling button-up boots of my grandmother, stood a pair of knee-high black military boots, and in them an SS officer, whose blond brain had registered every single word my grandmother had uttered during the long air-raid alarm: "No, no, I'm not budging from here, I don't care if they kill me, one old woman more or less won't matter." "What?" said the SS officer. "Tired of living? You'd rather fall into the hands of those Asian hordes? Don't you know that the Russians lop women's breasts right off?"

That brought my grandmother wheezing to her feet. "Oh God," she said, "what has humanity done to deserve this?" "Are you starting up again!" bellowed my grandfather. Now I can see them clearly, walking into the courtyard and taking up their positions alongside our handcart: Grandmother in her fine black coat, on her head the light and dark brown striped kerchief which my children still wore when they had a sore throat. She leans with her right hand against the back cross beam of the handcart. Grandfather, wearing a cap with earflaps and a herringbone jacket, is posted next to the drawbar. Time is short, the night is drawing near, closing in along with the enemy, albeit from different directions: night from the west and the enemy from the east. In the south, where they meet and where lies the small town of Nauen, flames rage against the sky. We imagine we can decipher the fiery script; the writing on the sky seems clear and spells out: Go west.

But first we must search for my mother. She is forever disappearing when it's time to move on; she wants to go back and must go on. On occasion, both urges are equally strong. At such moments, she invents pretexts and runs away, saying, I'll hang myself; and my brother and I, still dwelling in the realm where such words are taken literally, run into the small forest where my mother has no business being, nor do we wish to have any business there; we catch each other gazing at the treetops, we avoid looking at each other, voicing unutterable speculations is impossible anyway. We also keep silent when my mother, who is getting bonier and thinner with each passing week, comes up from the village, throws a small sack of flour on the handcart, and reproaches us: What did you think you were doing running around and making everyone crazy with worry? And who's going to get the farmers to cough up some food if not me?

She hitches herself to the front of the cart, my brother and I push from behind, the sky provides eerie fireworks, and once again I hear that delicate sound as the humdrum train *Reality* veers off the tracks and races crazily out of control right into the wildest "unreality," and I am shaken with laughter, the impropriety of which I find deeply offensive.

The only thing is, I can't convince anyone that I'm not laughing at us, God forbid, us settled, proper, respectable people in the two-story house next to the poplar tree, us colorful peep-show people in the vinegar pot; Mannikin, mannikin, timpe te / Flounder, flounder in the sea / My old Missis Ilsebill / Will not have it as I will. But none of us had wanted to become emperor, or Pope for that matter, and most certainly not God. One was quite content selling flour and butter fat and sour pickles and malt coffee in the store downstairs, the other to learn English vocabulary at the table with the black oilcloth and glance from time to time at the town and the river, which lay there quite still and in their proper places and never awakened in me the desire to leave them. With unwavering determination my little brother put together ever-new odd constructions with his Erector set and then insisted on setting them in one senseless motion or another with the aid of twine and wheels, while upstairs in her kitchen, my grandmother made the kind of home fries with onions and marjoram which disappeared from the face of the earth when she died, and my grandfather hung the tar wire up on the window lock, took off his blue cobbler's apron, and cut a dozen fine notches into each crust of bread on the wooden cutting board at the kitchen table, so that his toothless gums could chew it.

No, I don't know why they put us in the vinegar pot, and I don't know for the life of me why that makes me laugh, even though my uncle asks me suspiciously time and again from his place at the head of the second handcart in our tiny caravan: I'd like to know what's so funny here. Even though I understand how disappointed someone must be that the fear of being laughed at doesn't even subside once one has finally been promoted to a position of confidentiality in one's firm. Even though I would have liked to do with the favor of assuring him that I was laughing at myself, I was a bad liar and I distinctly felt that I was absent, although any one of those figures leaning against the wind in the darkness could easily have been mistaken for me. You can't see yourself when you're lost within yourself, but I saw all of us just as I see us today, as if someone had lifted me out of my shell and set me down next to it with the command: Take a good look!

That's what I did, but I didn't like what I saw.

I saw us straying from the country road, groping about in the darkness on side paths, and, finally, coming upon a tree-lined road leading toward a gate, a secluded estate, and a crooked, slightly shaky man who was limping to the stables in the middle of the night. He was not given to wondering at anything and so addressed the desperate, exhausted little troop in his particular, indifferent manner: Well, folks, Sodom and Gomorrah? Never mind. There's always room in the smallest cabin for a happy, loving couple.

The man is not so bright, my mother said uneasily, as we followed Kalle across the courtyard, and my grandfather, who never said much, declared with satisfaction, He is pretty crazy in his head. And so he was. Kalle called my grandfather boss, he who had held no higher rank in his lifetime than that of private in the Kaiser's infantry regiment, cobbler's apprentice under Herr Lebüse in Bromberg, and signalman for the German Reich in the administrative district of Frankfurt (Oder). Boss, said Kalle, it's best if you take that cubbyhole back there in the corner. He then disappeared, whistling, "One more drop for the road. Oh, just one more drop for the road . . ." But the people sleeping in the bunk beds had already downed their ration of tea for the night, and the inevitable liverwurst sandwiches had been handed out as well, judging from the smell. I tried to block my nose with my arm while sleeping. My grandfather, who was almost deaf, began saying his prayers at full volume as he did every night, but when he reached "and forgive us our trespasses," my grandmother shouted into his ear that he was disturbing the others, whereupon they started quarreling. Everyone throughout the hall could hear them, whereas up until then their old creaky wooden beds had been their only witness, along with the black framed likeness of an angel with the inscription: "Even when hope's last anchor pulls away, do not despair!"

Kalle woke us at daybreak. "I 'spect you'll be knowin' how to man a horse 'n' buggy?" he asked my uncle. "Because Herr Volk, what is the owner hereabouts, wants to move on with bag and baggage, but who'll drive the oxcart with the feed bags?" "Me," said my uncle, and he stood fast, even when my aunt nagged repeatedly that oxen were dangerous animals and why should he risk his hide for strangers . . . "Shut your mouth!" he snapped. "And how else are you gonna get all your junk away from here?" We were all allowed to climb aboard and our handcart was lashed to the rear stanchion. "Fine and dandy," said Kalle, "just don't think that the oxen will be quicker than your handcart." Herr Volk showed up in person to hire his new coachman with a handshake; he wore a hunting hat, a loden coat, and knickerbockers. And Frau Volk came to bestow a kind and cultured word on the women who now, in one way or another, numbered among her domestics, but I didn't like her because she called me by my first name without asking and allowed her dachshund bitch, Suzie, to sniff at our legs, which presumably reeked of liverwurst sandwiches. My aunt could see now that these were high-class people; my uncle wouldn't have gone into service with some nobody anyway. Then the shooting began right behind us and we headed off at a quick pace. God takes care of his own, said my grandmother.

The night before, however, I had dreamed for the last time that recurring child's dream: I'm not my parents' child at all, the babies got mixed up and I belong to the shopkeeper Rambow in Friedrichstadt, who is much too clever to openly claim his rights, although he has seen through it all and has measures in reserve, so that I'm ultimately forced to stay out of the street where he lies in wait for me in the doorway of his shop, lollipops in hand. That night in my dream, I had been able to tell him point-blank that I had lost all fear of him, even the memory of that fear of him, that his power over me was at an end, and from then on, I would come to his shop every day and pick up two bars of chocolate. Rambow the shopkeeper had meekly accepted my conditions.

He was finished, without a doubt, for he was no longer needed. The babies hadn't been mixed up, but I was no longer myself either. I would never forget when the stranger who had taken hold of me since and did with me as he pleased had entered me. It was on that cold January morning, when I was hurrying out of my town toward Küstrin on board a truck, greatly surprised at how gray indeed was that town in which I had always found all the light and all the colors I needed. Then someone inside me said slowly and clearly, You'll never see this again.

My horror was indescribable. The sentence was irreversible. All I could do was keep that which I knew to myself, truthfully and faithfully; watch the ebb and flow of rumors and hopes swell and fall; carry on for the time being, which I owed the others, to say what they wanted me to say. But the stranger in me ate at my insides and grew, and possibly he would soon refuse to obey in my stead. Already he had begun to nudge me from time to time, and the others were casting sidelong glances in my direction. Now she's laughing again. If we only knew what at.

2

This is supposed to be a report on *liberation*, the hour of liberation, and I thought, Nothing is easier than that. That hour has been clearly focused in my mind's eye all these years, it has lain ready and waiting, fully completed in my memory. And even if there have been reasons to let it lie until now, twenty-five years should surely have erased, or at least faded, those reasons. I need only say the word and the machine will start running, and everything will appear on the paper as if of its own accord — a series of accurate, highly defined pictures. Against all expectations, I got caught up in the question of what clothes my grandmother was wearing on the road, at which point I happened upon that stranger who, one day, had turned me into herself and now has become yet another, pronouncing other sentences, and ultimately I must accept that the series of images will not add up to anything, memory is not a photo album, and liberation depends not only on a date and the coincidental movements of the Allied troops but also on certain difficult and prolonged movements within oneself. And while time may erase reasons, it also continuously creates new ones, rendering rather more difficult the selection of one particular hour; the need arises to specify what one has been liberated from, and if one is conscientious, perhaps to what purpose as well. Which brings to mind the passing of a childhood fear, the shopkeeper Rambow, who surely was a respectable man, and so one searches for a new approach, which only succeeds in bringing one a little closer and no more. The passing of my fear of low-flying fighter planes. You made your bed, now lie in it, as Kalle would say if he were still alive, but I assume he is dead, like so many of the cast of characters (yes, death erases reasons).

Dead like Wilhelm Grund, the foreman, after the strafers shot him in the belly. That's how I saw my first corpse at the age of sixteen; rather late for those years, I must say. (I can't count the infant I handed in a stiff bundle from a truck to a refugee woman; I didn't see him, I only heard his mother scream and ran away.) Chance had it that Wilhelm Grund was lying there instead of me, for pure chance alone had occupied my uncle with a sick horse in the barn that morning, so that we weren't ahead of the others heading toward the country road alongside Grund's oxcart as usual. Here, I had to say to myself, was also where we should have been, and not where it was safe, although we could hear the gunfire, and the fifteen horses were wild with fear. I have been afraid of horses ever since. But what I have feared even more ever since that moment are the faces of people forced to see what no person should have to see. The young farmhand Gerhard Grund had such a face as he burst through the barn door, managed a few steps, and then collapsed: Herr Volk, what have they done to my father!

He was my age. His father lay in the dust at the side of the road next to his oxen, eyes staring upward, one could say heavenward if one absolutely insisted. I saw that nothing could lower that gaze, not his wife's wailing or the whining of his three other children. This time around, they forgot to tell us that this was not a sight for us children. "Quick," said Herr Volk. "We've got to get out of here." They would have grabbed me the same way they grabbed the corpse by the shoulders and legs and dragged him to the edge of the woods. Just as the tarpaulins from the granary of the estate served as his coffin, so would they have served any of us, myself included. I, too, would have gone to the grave without words and without song, just like Wilhelm Grund the farmhand. Their wailing would have followed me down, and then they would have pushed on like us, because we couldn't stay. For a long time they would have had no desire to speak, just as we remained silent, and then they would have had to ask themselves what they could do to stay alive themselves, and they would have torn off large birch branches, just as we did now, and covered the handcarts with them, as if the foreign pilots would let themselves be fooled by a little wandering birch grove. Everything, everything would be like now, only I would no longer be one of them. And the difference which was everything to me meant hardly anything to most of the others here. Gerhard Grund was already sitting in his father's seat and drove the oxen forward with his very whip, and Herr Volk nodded to him: "Good boy. Your father died a soldier's death."

I didn't really believe this. It wasn't the way a soldier's death had been described in the textbooks and newspapers, and I told that authority with whom I was continuously in touch and whom I labeled with the name of God — albeit against my own scruples and reservations — that, in my opinion, a man and father of four children did not deserve an end such as this. War is war, said Herr Volk, and certainly it was and had to be, yet I claimed that this deviated from the ideal of death for Führer and Reich, and I didn't ask whom my mother meant when she hugged Frau Grund and said aloud, "Damn them. Those damned criminals."

Since I happened to be on guard at the time, it was my job to report by whistle signal the next series of attacks, two American fighters. Just as I had figured, the birch grove came to a halt clearly visible from afar and easy prey on the desolate country road. Everything that had legs jumped out of the handcarts and threw itself in the ditch, myself included. The only difference was that this time around I did not bury my head in the sand but lay on my back and continued eating my sandwich. I did not want to die and I certainly was not up to defying death and I knew fear better than I cared to.

But one does not die twice in one day. I wanted to see the one who dared shoot at me, for I had the odd idea that in every plane there sat a few individual people. First I saw the white stars under the wings, but then, as they broke away for a new approach, the helmet-covered heads of the pilots and, finally, even the naked white spots of their faces. Prisoners I had seen, but this was the attacking enemy face to face; I knew that I was supposed to hate him and it seemed unnatural that I found myself wondering for the space of a second whether they were having fun with whatever they were doing. They soon stopped, though.

When we got back to the wagons, one of our oxen, the one they called Heinrich, sank to its knees. Blood spurted from its throat. My uncle and grandfather unharnessed it. My grandfather, who had stood alongside the dead Wilhelm Grund without uttering a word, now hurled curses from his toothless mouth. "The innocent creature," he said hoarsely. "These bastards, damned, confounded dogs, every one of them." I was afraid he might begin to cry and hoped he would get everything off his chest by cursing. I forced myself to look at the animal for an entire minute. It couldn't be reproach that I detected in its gaze, so why did I feel guilty? Herr Volk handed his hunting rifle to my uncle and pointed to a spot behind the ox's ear. We were sent away. At the sound of the shot, I looked back. The ox dropped heavily onto its side. All evening the women were occupied with cooking the meat. By the time we sat in the straw eating the broth, it was already dark. Kalle, who had bitterly complained about being hungry, greedily slurped from his bowl, wiped his mouth on his sleeve, and begin to sing croakingly with content-ment, "All dogs bite, all dogs bite, but only hot dogs get bitten . . ." "To hell with you, you crazy fella," my grandfather went at him furiously. Kalle let himself drop onto the straw and stuck his head under his jacket.

3

One need not be afraid when everyone else is afraid. To know this is certainly liberating, but liberation was still to come, and I want to record what today's memory is prepared to yield on the subject. It was the morning of the fifth of May, a beautiful day, and once more panic broke out when we heard that we were encircled by Soviet armored tank troops. Then word came down: By forced march to Schwerin, where the Americans are, and anyone who was still capable of asking himself questions would have had to find it quite strange how everyone was surging forward toward that enemy which had been after our lives for days now. Of all that was now still possible I found nothing desirable, or even bearable, for that matter, but the world stubbornly refused to end and we were not prepared to cope after a messed-up end of the world. Therefore I understood the horrific words uttered by one woman when told that the miracle weapon longed for by the Führer could only exterminate everyone, both the enemy and the Germans. Let them go ahead and use it, is what she said.

We moved past the last houses of the village along a sandy road. A soldier was washing up at a pump next to a red Mecklenburg farmhouse. He stood there, legs apart, with the sleeves of his white undershift rolled up, and called out to us, "The Führer is dead," the same way one says, "Nice weather today." I was more stunned at his tone of voice than at the realization that the man was speaking the truth.

I trudged on alongside our cart, heard the coachmen's hoarse shouts, the groaning of the exhausted horses, saw the small fires by the side of the road wherein smoldered the papers of the officers of the Wehrmacht, saw heaps of guns and antitank grenade launchers sprouting ghostlike from the ditches, saw typewriters, suitcases, radios, and all manner of precious war equipment senselessly lining our way, and could not help recalling the sound of that sentence over and over again, which, instead of being one everyday sentence among others, should, I felt, have echoed frightfully between Heaven and earth.

Then came the paper. The street was suddenly flooded with paper; they were still throwing it out of the Wehrmacht vehicles in wild anger — forms, induction orders, files, proceedings, documents from the headquarters of a military district, banal routine letters as well as secret commando affairs, and the statistics of the dead fallen from doubly secured safes, whose contents piqued no one's curiosity now that they lay thrown at our feet. As if there were something repulsive about the paper trash, I did not stoop to pick up a page either, which I felt sorry about later. I did, however, catch the canned food which a truck driver threw to me. The swing of his arm reminded me of the movement, often performed, with which, in the summer of '39, I had thrown cigarette packs onto the dusty convoys which rolled eastward past our house, day and night. In the six-year interim I had stopped being a child; summer was coming again, but I had no idea how I would spend it.

The supply convoy of a Wehrmacht unit had been abandoned by its escort on a side road. All those who passed by took as much as they could carry. The order of the column dissolved, many were beside themselves, where before out of fear, now out of greed. Only Kalle laughed, dragging a large block of butter to our cart, clapping his hands, and shouting happily, "Well, I'll be damned! Look at them getting all worked up!"

Then we saw the prisoners from the concentration camp. The rumor that the Oranienburgers were being driven right behind us had haunted us like a ghost. The suspicion that we were fleeing from them as well did not occur to me back then. They stood at the edge of the forest and gazed questioningly at us. We could have given them a sign that the air was clear, but nobody did. Cautiously, they approached the street. They looked different from all the people I had seen up to then, and I wasn't surprised that we automatically shrank back from them. But it betrayed us, this shrinking back, it showed that, in spite of what we protested to each other and ourselves, we knew. All we unhappy ones who had been driven away from all our possessions, from our farms and our manors, from our shops and musty bedrooms and brightly polished parlors with the picture of the Führer on the wall — we knew: these people, who had been declared animals and who were now slowly coming toward us to take revenge — we had dropped them. Now the ragged would put on our clothes and stick their bloody feet in our shoes, now the starved would seize hold of the flour and the sausage we had just snatched. And to my horror I felt, It is just, and I was horrified to feel that it was just, and knew for a fraction of a second that we were guilty. I forgot it again.

The prisoners pounced not on the bread but on the guns by the side of the road. They loaded up on ammunition, crossed the road without paying any attention to us, struggled up the opposite slope, and mounted sentry there. Silently, they looked down at us. I couldn't bear looking at them. Why don't they scream, I thought, or shoot into the air, or shoot at us, goddamnit! But they stood there peacefully, I saw that some of them were reeling and could barely bring themselves to hold their guns and stand up. Perhaps they had been praying for this moment day and night. I couldn't help them and they couldn't help me; I didn't understand them and I didn't need them, and everything about them was completely foreign to me.

There came a call from the front that everybody except the drivers should dismount. This was an order. A deep breath went through the convoy, for this could mean only one thing: the final steps toward freedom lay ahead. Before we could move on, the Polish drivers jumped off, coiled the reins around the stanchion of the wagon, put the whip on the seat, formed a small squad, and set about going back, eastward. Herr Volk, immediately turning a bluish-red color, blocked their way. At first he spoke quietly to them, but soon he began to scream. Conspiracy, foul play, refusal to work, he shouted. That's when I saw a Polish migrant worker push aside a German estate farmer. Now the world had truly turned topsy-turvy, only Herr Volk hadn't noticed yet; he automatically reached for his whip, but his lash was stopped in midair, someone was holding his arm, the whip dropped to the ground and the Poles walked on. His hand pressed against his heart, Herr Volk leaned heavily against the cart and let himself be comforted by his thin-lipped wife and the silly dachshund Suzie, while Kalle railed at him from above, shouting, Bastard, bastard. The French people, who stayed with us, called out greetings to the departing Poles, who understood those greetings no more than I did, but understood their sound, and so did I, and it hurt being so strictly excluded from their shouting, waving, and the tossing of their caps, from their joy and their language. But it had to be that way. The world consisted of the victors and the defeated. The former were free to express their emotions. The latter — us — had to lock them inside ourselves from now on. The enemy should not see us weak.

There he was, by the way. I would have preferred a fire-breathing dragon to this light Jeep with its gum-chewing driver and the three casual officers who, out of bottomless condescension, had not even uncovered their holsters. I tried to make an expressionless face and look right through them, and told myself that their unconstrained laughter, their clean uniforms, their indifferent glances, the whole damned victor's pose had probably been ordered for our special humiliation.

The people around me began to hide watches and rings. I, too, took my watch off my wrist and carelessly put it in my coat pocket. The guard at the end of the line, a lanky, hulking man beneath an impossible steel helmet, which had made us burst out laughing whenever we saw it in the newsreels, pointed out with one hand to the few people carrying arms where to throw their weapons, while his other hand frisked us civilians with a few firm, routine police motions. Petrified with indignation but secretly proud that they believed me capable of carrying a weapon, I let myself be searched. At which point my overworked sentry routinely asked, "Your watch?" So he wanted my watch, the victor, but he didn't get it, for I succeeded in fooling him with the statement that the other one, "your comrade," his brother officer, had already pocketed it. I escaped unscathed as far as the watch was concerned, at which point my heightened sense of hearing signaled once more the rising sound of an airplane engine. Despite the fact that this was no longer any of my business, I kept an eye on its approach route out of habit and threw myself to the ground by reflex as it swooped down; once more the horrid dark shadow flitting quickly across grass and trees, once more the atrocious sound of bullets pounding into soil. Still? I thought to myself in astonishment, realizing that one can get used to the feeling of being out of danger in a second. With malicious glee I saw American artillerymen bringing an American gun into position and firing it at an American plane, which hurriedly zoomed up and disappeared beyond the forest.

Now, one should be capable of saying how it felt when it became quiet. I stayed put for a while behind the tree. I believe I didn't care about the fact that, from that minute on, possibly no bomb or MG shrapnel would ever again be dropped down on me. I wasn't curious as to what would happen now. I didn't know what use there was for a dragon once it stops breathing fire. I had no idea how the horned Siegfried is supposed to act if the dragon asks him for his watch rather than gobbling him up, hair and hide. I didn't feel like watching how Herr Siegfried and Herr Dragon would get along as private citizens. And I certainly didn't feel like going to the Americans in the occupied mansions for every bucket of water, and I most definitely didn't feel like entering into a fight with black-haired Lieutenant Davidson from Ohio, at the end of which I saw myself obliged to declare that now my pride absolutely demanded that I hate him.

And I felt even less up to the talk with the concentration-camp prisoner who sat with us by the fire at night wearing a pair of bent wire-frame spectacles and mentioned in passing the word "Communism" as if it were a permitted, household word such as "hatred" or "war" or "extermination." No. And least of all did I feel like knowing about the sadness and the dismay which were in his voice when he asked us, "Where, then, have you lived all these years?"

I didn't feel up to liberation. I was lying under my tree, all was quiet. I was lost and I reflected that I wanted to make a note of the branches against that very beautiful May sky. Then my lanky, off-duty sergeant came up the slope, a squealing German girl hanging on each arm. All three moved in the direction of the mansion, and finally I had a reason to turn away a little and cry.   [1993]

TOBIAS WOLFF *(b. 1945) began his recent best-selling memoir by writing, "My first stepfather used to say that what I didn't know would fill a book. Well, here it is." A compassionate sense of paradox and irony permeates his writing, as in the story "Say Yes," adding an emotional color to the transparently clear prose of his narratives.*

Born in Birmingham, Alabama, Wolff followed his mother to the Pacific Northwest when his parents divorced. It is this period in his life that is the subject of his memoir This Boy's Life *(1989). After being expelled from prep school, he served in the U.S. Army in Vietnam in 1964–1968. Then he studied at Oxford University and Stanford University, where in 1975–1976 he received a Wallace Stegner fellowship in creative writing. Two National Endowment for the Arts fellowships followed, along with a Mary Roberts Rinehart grant, an Arizona Council on the Arts fellowship, a Guggenheim fellowship, three O. Henry short story prizes, and the P.E.N./Faulkner Award for Fiction for* The Barracks Thief *(1984), a novella about his army experience. Wolff's first book was a collection of short stories,* In the Garden of the North American Martyrs *(1981).* Back in the World, *a second collection of stories, was published in 1985.*

Wolff credits several writers as influences on his fiction: Ernest Hemingway, Anton Chekhov, Paul Bowles, Sherwood Anderson, John Cheever, Flannery O'Connor, and Raymond Carver — "the list has no end so I'd better stop here." He prefers writing short stories to novels because "when I write a short story, I feel like I'm somehow cooperating with the story; when I try to work in longer forms, I feel like I'm beating them into existence. I feel a kind of clumsiness that I don't feel when I'm writing short stories." Wolff regards writing as an "essentially optimistic art," because

> *the very act of writing assumes, to begin with, that someone cares to hear what you have to say. It assumes that people share, that people can be reached, that people can be touched and even in some cases changed. . . . So many of the things in our world tend to lead us to despair. It seems to me that the final symptom of despair is silence, and that storytelling is one of the sustaining arts; it's one of the affirming arts. . . . A writer may have a certain pessimism in his outlook, but the very act of being a writer seems to me to be an optimistic act.*

Tobias Wolff

Say Yes

They were doing the dishes, his wife washing while he dried. He'd washed the night before. Unlike most men he knew, he really pitched in on the housework. A few months earlier he'd overheard a friend of his wife's congratulate her on having such a considerate husband, and he thought, *I try.* Helping out with the dishes was a way of showing how considerate he was.

They talked about different things and somehow got on the subject of whether white people should marry black people. He said that all things considered, he thought it was a bad idea.

"Why?" she asked.

Sometimes his wife got this look where she pinched her brows together and bit her lower lip and stared down at something. When he saw her like this he knew he should keep his mouth shut, but he never did. Actually it made him talk more. She had that look now.

"Why?" she asked again, and stood there with her hand inside a bowl, not washing it but just holding it above the water.

"Listen," he said, "I went to school with blacks, and I've worked with blacks and lived on the same street with blacks, and we've always gotten along just fine. I don't need you coming along now and implying that I'm a racist."

"I didn't imply anything," she said, and began washing the bowl again, turning it around in her hand as though she were shaping it. "I just don't see what's wrong with a white person marrying a black person, that's all."

"They don't come from the same culture as we do. Listen to them sometime — they even have their own language. That's okay with me, I *like* hearing them talk" — he did; for some reason it always made him feel happy — "but it's different. A person from their culture and a person from our culture could never really *know* each other."

"Like you know me?" his wife asked.

"Yes. Like I know you."

"But if they love each other," she said. She was washing faster now, not looking at him.

Oh boy, he thought. He said, "Don't take my word for it. Look at the statistics. Most of those marriages break up."

"Statistics." She was piling dishes on the drainboard at a terrific rate, just swiping at them with the cloth. Many of them were greasy, and there were flecks of food between the tines of the forks. "All right," she said, "what about foreigners? I suppose you think the same thing about two foreigners getting married."

"Yes," he said, "as a matter of fact I do. How can you understand someone who comes from a completely different background?"

"Different," said his wife. "Not the same, like us."

"Yes, different," he snapped, angry with her for resorting to this trick of repeating his words so that they sounded crass, or hypocritical. "These are dirty," he said, and dumped all the silverware back into the sink.

The water had gone flat and gray. She stared down at it, her lips pressed tight together, then plunged her hands under the surface. "Oh!" she cried, and jumped back. She took her right hand by the wrist and held it up. Her thumb was bleeding.

"Ann, don't move," he said. "Stay right there." He ran upstairs to the bathroom and rummaged in the medicine chest for alcohol, cotton, and a Band-Aid. When he came back down she was leaning against the refrigerator with her eyes closed, still holding her hand. He took the hand and dabbed at her thumb with the cotton. The bleeding had stopped. He squeezed it to see how deep the wound was and a single drop of blood welled up, trembling and bright, and fell to the floor. Over the thumb she stared at him accusingly. "It's shallow," he said. "Tomorrow you won't even know it's there." He hoped that she appreciated how quickly he had come to her aid. He'd acted out of concern for her, with no thought of getting anything in return, but now the thought occurred to him that it would be a nice gesture on her part not to start up that conversation again, as he was tired of it. "I'll finish up here," he said. "You go and relax."

"That's okay," she said. "I'll dry."

He began to wash the silverware again, giving a lot of attention to the forks.

"So," she said, "you wouldn't have married me if I'd been black."

"For Christ's sake, Ann!"

"Well, that's what you said, didn't you?"

"No, I did not. The whole question is ridiculous. If you had been black we probably wouldn't even have met. You would have had your friends and I would have had mine. The only black girl I ever really knew was my partner in the debating club, and I was already going out with you by then."

"But if we had met, and I'd been black?"

"Then you probably would have been going out with a black guy." He picked up the rinsing nozzle and sprayed the silverware. The water was so hot that the metal darkened to pale blue, then turned silver again.

"Let's say I wasn't," she said. "Let's say I am black and unattached and we meet and fall in love."

He glanced over at her. She was watching him and her eyes were bright. "Look," he said, taking a reasonable tone, "this is stupid. If you were black you wouldn't be you." As he said this he realized it was absolutely true. There was no possible way of arguing with the fact that she would not be herself if she were black. So he said it again: "If you were black you wouldn't be you."

"I know," she said, "but let's just say."

He took a deep breath. He had won the argument but he still felt cornered. "Say what?" he asked.

"That I'm black, but still me, and we fall in love. Will you marry me?"

He thought about it.

"Well?" she said, and stepped close to him. Her eyes were even brighter. "Will you marry me?"

"I'm thinking," he said.

"You won't, I can tell. You're going to say no."

"Let's not move too fast on this," he said. "There are lots of things to consider. We don't want to do something we would regret for the rest of our lives."

"No more considering. Yes or no."

"Since you put it that way —"

"Yes or no."

"Jesus, Ann. All right. No."

She said, "Thank you," and walked from the kitchen into the living room. A moment later he heard her turning the pages of a magazine. He knew that she was too angry to be actually reading it, but she didn't snap through the pages the way he would have done. She turned them slowly, as if she were studying every word. She was demonstrating her indifference to him, and it had the effect he knew she wanted it to have. It hurt him.

He had no choice but to demonstrate his indifference to her. Quietly, thoroughly, he washed the rest of the dishes. Then he dried them and put them away. He wiped the counters and the stove and scoured the linoleum where the drop of blood had fallen. While he was at it, he decided, he might as well mop the whole floor. When he was done the kitchen looked new, the way it looked when they were first shown the house, before they had ever lived here.

He picked up the garbage pail and went outside. The night was clear and he could see a few stars to the west, where the lights of the town didn't blur them out. On El Camino the traffic was steady and light, peaceful as a river. He felt ashamed that he had let his wife get him into a fight. In another thirty years or so they would both be dead. What would all that stuff matter then? He thought of the years they had spent together, and how close they were, and how well they knew each other, and his throat tightened so that he could hardly breathe. His face and neck began to tingle. Warmth flooded his chest. He stood there for a while, enjoying these sensations, then picked up the pail and went out the back gate.

The two mutts from down the street had pulled over the garbage can again. One of them was rolling around on his back and the other had something in her mouth. Growling, she tossed it into the air, leaped up and caught it, growled again and whipped her head from side to side. When they saw him coming they trotted away with short, mincing steps. Normally he would heave rocks at them, but this time he let them go.

The house was dark when he came back inside. She was in the bathroom. He stood outside the door and called her name. He heard bottles clinking, but she didn't answer him. "Ann, I'm really sorry," he said. "I'll make it up to you, I promise."

"How?" she asked.

He wasn't expecting this. But from a sound in her voice, a level and definite note that was strange to him, he knew that he had to come up with the right answer. He leaned against the door. "I'll marry you," he whispered.

"We'll see," she said. "Go on to bed. I'll be out in a minute."

He undressed and got under the covers. Finally he heard the bathroom door open and close.

"Turn off the light," she said from the hallway.

"What?"

"Turn off the light."

He reached over and pulled the chain on the bedside lamp. The room went dark. "All right," he said. He lay there, but nothing happened. "All right," he said again. Then he heard a movement across the room. He sat up, but he couldn't see a thing. The room was silent. His heart pounded the way it had on their first night together the way it still did when he woke at a noise in the darkness and waited to hear it again — the sound of someone moving through the house, a stranger. [1985]

VIRGINIA WOOLF (1882–1941) *is best known as a novelist, critic, and essayist; she published only one book of short stories, early in her career. The daughter of Sir Leslie Stephen, a scholar and editor of the monumental* Dictionary of National Biography, *she was educated at home in her father's library, keenly aware that if she had been born a boy, she would have gone on to Cambridge or Oxford. Later, guided by this sense of injustice, she wrote two feminist works,* A Room of One's Own *(1929) and* Three Guineas *(1938). In frail health all her life, she married the journalist Leonard Woolf in 1912, and they lived in Bloomsbury, the fashionably bohemian section of London. Her first novel,* The Voyage Out, *was published in 1915. Two years later the Woolfs set two stories by "L. and V. Woolf" on an old handpress and published them under the imprint of the Hogarth Press. The little pamphlet was so successful that their press became a thriving enterprise, publishing the work of authors such as Katherine Mansfield and T. S. Eliot. In 1921 the Hogarth Press published* Monday or Tuesday, *Woolf's collection of short stories, and the following year — sustained by the freedom of having her own printing press — she began to publish the unconventional novels that made her reputation:* Jacob's Room *(1922),* Mrs. Dalloway *(1925),* To the Lighthouse *(1927), and* The Waves *(1931).*

Dissatisfied with realistic fiction, Woolf explored the psychological nature of consciousness. She believed that beneath the appearance of change and disorder that marks daily life is a timeless reality that becomes apparent only during pure "moments of being," when the self is transcended and the individual consciousness becomes an undifferentiated part of a greater whole. For Woolf, the description of the immediate flow of her characters' thoughts and feelings, as in "Kew Gardens," was more important than the realistic depiction of their physical behavior. Some readers, including her good friend E. M. Forster, wondered whether she hadn't gone too far: "She does not tell a story or weave a plot — can she create character?"

Throughout her life, Woolf wrote short stories to relax between the arduous bouts of work on her novels, usually sketching a story out in rough form, then putting the draft away in a drawer. She felt that in her fiction she revealed "some order" about the world, "a token of some real thing behind appearances; and I make it real by putting it into words." If an editor asked her for a short story, she would take out a sketch and rewrite it several times. She discussed with her husband the possibility of republishing Monday or Tuesday *with her later stories, and after her suicide, Leonard Woolf saw this book through to publication as* A Haunted House and Other Stories *(1953).*

RELATED COMMENTARY: *Katherine Mansfield, "Review of Woolf's 'Kew Gardens,'" page 1454.*

VIRGINIA WOOLF

Kew Gardens

From the oval-shaped flower-bed there rose perhaps a hundred stalks spreading into heart-shaped or tongue-shaped leaves half way up and unfurling at the tip red or blue or yellow petals marked with spots of colour raised upon the surface; and from the red, blue, or yellow gloom of the throat emerged a straight bar, rough with gold dust and slightly clubbed at the end. The petals were voluminous enough to be stirred by the summer breeze, and when they moved, the red, blue, and yellow lights passed one over the other, staining an inch of the brown earth beneath with a spot of the most intricate colour. The light fell either upon the smooth grey back of a pebble, or the shell of a snail with its brown circular veins, or, falling into a raindrop, it expanded with such intensity of red, blue, and yellow the thin walls of water that one expected them to burst and disappear. Instead, the drop was left in a second silver grey once more, and the light now settled upon the flesh of a leaf, revealing the branching thread of fibre beneath the surface, and again it moved on and spread its illumination in the vast green spaces beneath the dome of the heart-shaped and tongue-shaped leaves. Then the breeze stirred rather more briskly overhead and the colour was flashed into the air above, into the eyes of the men and women who walk in Kew Gardens in July.

The figures of these men and women straggled past the flower-bed with a curiously irregular movement not unlike that of the white and blue butterflies who crossed the turf in zig-zag flights from bed to bed. The man was about six inches in front of the woman, strolling carelessly, while she bore on with greater purpose, only turning her head now and then to see that the children were not too far behind. The man kept this distance in front of the woman purposely, though perhaps unconsciously, for he wanted to go on with his thoughts.

"Fifteen years ago I came here with Lily," he thought. "We sat somewhere over there by a lake, and I begged her to marry me all through the hot afternoon. How the dragon-fly kept circling round us: how clearly I see the dragon-fly and her shoe with the square silver buckle at the toe. All the time I spoke I saw her shoe and when it moved impatiently I knew without looking up what she was going to say: the whole of her seemed to be in her shoe. And my love, my desire, were in the dragon-fly; for some reason I thought that if it settled there, on that leaf, the broad one with the red flower in the middle of it, if the dragon-fly settled on the leaf she would say 'Yes' at once. But the dragon-fly went round and round: it never settled anywhere — of course not, happily not, or I shouldn't be walking here with Eleanor and the children — Tell me, Eleanor, d'you ever think of the past?"

"Why do you ask, Simon?"

"Because I've been thinking of the past. I've been thinking of Lily, the woman I might have married . . . Well, why are you silent? Do you mind my thinking of the past?"

"Why should I mind, Simon? Doesn't one always think of the past, in a garden with men and women lying under the trees? Aren't they one's past, all that remains of it, those men and women, those ghosts lying under the trees, . . . one's happiness, one's reality?"

"For me, a square silver shoe-buckle and a dragon-fly —"

"For me, a kiss. Imagine six little girls sitting before their easels twenty years ago, down by the side of a lake, painting the water-lilies, the first red water-lilies I'd ever seen. And suddenly a kiss, there on the back of my neck. And my hand shook all the afternoon so that I couldn't paint. I took out my watch and marked the hour when I would allow myself to think of the kiss for five minutes only — it was so precious — the kiss of an old grey-haired woman with a wart on her nose, the mother of all my kisses all my life. Come Caroline, come Hubert."

They walked on past the flower-bed, now walking four abreast, and soon diminished in size among the trees and looked half transparent as the sunlight and shade swam over their backs in large trembling irregular patches.

In the oval flower-bed the snail, whose shell had been stained red, blue, and yellow for the space of two minutes or so, now appeared to be moving very slightly in its shell, and next began to labour over the crumbs of loose earth which broke away and rolled down as it passed over them. It appeared to have a definite goal in front of it, differing in this respect from the singular high-stepping angular green insect who attempted to cross in front of it, and waited for a second with its antennae trembling as if in deliberation, and then stepped off as rapidly and strangely in the opposite direction. Brown cliffs with deep green lakes in the hollows, flat blade-like trees that waved from root to tip, round boulders of grey stone, vast crumpled surfaces of a thin crackling texture — all these objects lay across the snail's progress between one stalk and another to his goal. Before he had decided whether to circumvent the arched tent of a dead leaf or to breast it there came past the bed the feet of other human beings.

This time they were both men. The younger of the two wore an expression of perhaps unnatural calm; he raised his eyes and fixed them very steadily in front of him while his companion spoke, and directly his companion had done speaking he looked on the ground again and sometimes opened his lips only after a long pause and sometimes did not open them at all. The elder man had a curiously uneven and shaky method of walking, jerking his hand forward and throwing up his head abruptly, rather in the manner of an impatient carriage horse tired of waiting outside a house; but in the man these gestures were irresolute and pointless. He talked almost incessantly; he smiled to himself and again began to talk, as if the smile had been an answer. He was talking about spirits — the spirits of the dead, who, according to him, were even now telling him all sorts of odd things about their experiences in Heaven.

"Heaven was known to the ancients as Thessaly, William, and now, with this war, the spirit matter is rolling between the hills like thunder." He paused, seemed to listen, smiled, jerked his head, and continued: —

"You have a small electric battery and a piece of rubber to insulate the wire — isolate? — insulate? — well, we'll skip the details, no good going into details that wouldn't be understood — and in short the little machine stands in any convenient position by the head of the bed, we will say, on a neat mahogany stand. All arrangements being properly fixed by workmen under my direction, the widow applies her ear and summons the spirit by sign as agreed. Women! Widows! Women in black —"

Here he seemed to have caught sight of a woman's dress in the distance, which in the shade looked a purple black. He took off his hat, placed his hand upon his heart, and hurried towards her muttering and gesticulating feverishly. But William caught him by the sleeve and touched a flower with the tip of his walking-stick in order to divert the old man's attention. After looking at it for a moment in some confusion the old man bent his ear to it and seemed to answer a voice speaking from it, for he began talking about the forests of Uruguay which he had visited hundreds of years ago in company with the most beautiful young woman in Europe. He could be heard murmuring about forests of Uruguay blanketed with the wax petals of tropical roses, nightingales, sea beaches, mermaids, and women drowned at sea, as he suffered himself to be moved on by William, upon whose face the look of stoical patience grew slowly deeper and deeper.

Following his steps so closely as to be slightly puzzled by his gestures came two elderly women of the lower middle class, one stout and ponderous, the other rosy-cheeked and nimble. Like most people of their station they were frankly fascinated by any signs of eccentricity betokening a disordered brain, especially in the well-to-do; but they were too far off to be certain whether the gestures were merely eccentric or genuinely mad. After they had scrutinised the old man's back in silence for a moment and given each other a queer, sly look, they went on energetically piecing together their very complicated dialogue:

"Nell, Bert, Lot, Cess, Phil, Pa, he says, I says, she says, I says, I says, I says —"

"My Bert, Sis, Bill, Grandad, the old man, sugar,

Sugar, flour, kippers, greens
Sugar, sugar, sugar."

The ponderous woman looked through the pattern of falling words at the flowers standing cool, firm, and upright in the earth, with a curious expression. She saw them as a sleeper waking from a heavy sleep sees a brass candlestick reflecting the light in an unfamiliar way, and closes his eyes and opens them, and seeing the brass candlestick again, finally starts broad awake and stares at the candlestick with all his powers. So the heavy woman came to a standstill opposite the oval-shaped flower-bed, and ceased even to pretend to listen to what the other woman was saying. She stood there letting the words fall over her, swaying the top part of her body slowly backwards and forwards, looking at the flowers. Then she suggested that they should find a seat and have their tea.

The snail had now considered every possible method of reaching his goal without going round the dead leaf or climbing over it. Let alone the effort needed for climbing a leaf, he was doubtful whether the thin texture which vibrated with such an alarming crackle when touched even by the tip of his horns would bear his weight; and this determined him finally to creep beneath it, for there was a point where the leaf curved high enough from the ground to admit him. He had just inserted his head in the opening and was taking stock of the high brown roof and was getting used to the cool brown light when two other people came past outside on the turf. This time they were both young, a young man and a young woman. They were both in the prime of youth, or even in that season which precedes the prime of youth, the season before the smooth pink folds of the flower have burst their gummy case, when the wings of the butterfly, though fully grown, are motionless in the sun.

"Lucky it isn't Friday," he observed.

"Why? D'you believe in luck?"

"They make you pay sixpence on Friday."

"What's sixpence anyway? Isn't it worth sixpence?"

"What's 'it' — what do you mean by 'it'?"

"O anything — I mean — you know what I mean."

Long pauses came between each of these remarks: they were uttered in toneless and monotonous voices. The couple stood still on the edge of the flower-bed, and together pressed the end of her parasol deep down into the soft earth. The action and the fact that his hand rested on the top of hers expressed their feelings in a strange way, as these short insignificant words also expressed something, words with short wings for their heavy body of meaning, inadequate to carry them far and thus alighting awkwardly upon the very common objects that surrounded them and were to their inexperienced touch so massive: but who knows (so they thought as they pressed the parasol into the earth) what precipices aren't concealed in them, or what slopes of ice don't shine in the sun on the other side? Who knows? Who has ever seen this before? Even when she wondered what sort of tea they gave you at Kew, he felt that something loomed up behind her words, and stood vast and solid behind them; and the mist very slowly rose and uncovered — O Heavens, — what were those shapes? — little white tables, and waitresses who looked first at her and then at him; and there was a bill that he would pay with a real two shilling piece, and it was real, all real, he assured himself, fingering the coin in his pocket, real to everyone except to him and to her; even to him it began to seem real; and then — but it was too exciting to stand and think any longer, and he pulled the parasol out of the earth with a jerk and was impatient to find the place where one had tea with other people, like other people.

"Come along Trissie; it's time we had our tea."

"Wherever *does* one have one's tea?" she asked with the oddest thrill of excitement in her voice, looking vaguely round and letting herself be drawn on down the grass path, trailing her parasol, turning her head this way and that way, forgetting her tea, wishing to go down there and then down there, remembering orchids and cranes among wild flowers, a Chinese pagoda and a crimson-crested bird; but he bore her on.

Thus one couple after another with much the same irregular and aimless movement passed the flower-bed and were enveloped in layer after layer of green-glue vapour, in which at first their bodies had substance and a dash of colour, but later both substance and colour dissolved in the green-blue atmosphere. How hot it was! So hot that even the thrush chose to hop, like a mechanical bird, in the shadow of the flowers, with long pauses between one movement and the next; instead of rambling vaguely the white butterflies danced one above another, making with their white shifting flakes the outline of a shattered marble column above the tallest flowers; the glass roofs of the palm house shone as if a whole market full of shiny green umbrellas had opened in the sun; and in the drone of the aeroplane the voice of the summer sky murmured its fierce soul. Yellow and black, pink and snow white, shapes of all these colours, men, women, and children, were spotted for a second upon the horizon, and then, seeing the breadth of yellow that lay upon the grass, they wavered and sought shade beneath the trees, dissolving like drops of water in the yellow and green atmosphere, staining it faintly with red and blue. It seemed as if all gross and heavy bodies had sunk down in the heat motionless and lay huddled upon the ground, but their voices went wavering from them as if they were flames lolling from the thick waxen bodies of candles. Voices, yes, voices, wordless voices, breaking the silence suddenly with such depth of contentment, such passion of desire, or, in the voices of children, such freshness of surprise; breaking the silence? But there was no silence; all the time the motor omnibuses were turning their wheels and changing their gear; like a vast nest of Chinese boxes all of wrought steel turning ceaselessly one within another the city murmured; on the top of which the voices cried aloud and the petals of myriads of flowers flashed their colours into the air. [1919]

RICHARD WRIGHT *(1908–1960) was born on a plantation near Natchez, Mississippi, the son of a farmhand and a country schoolteacher. His home life was disrupted when his father deserted the family, and Wright later said it was only through reading that he managed to keep himself alive. As soon as he could he moved north, to Memphis, Chicago, and then to New York City, where he became involved in radical politics. He was a member of the Communist Party from 1932 to 1944. In the 1930s he worked as a reporter for* New Masses, *a correspondent for the Harlem bureau of the* Daily Worker, *and an editor for* New Challenge, *a left-wing magazine that published his "Blueprint for Negro Writing," an effort to bridge the gap between Marxism and black nationalism, in 1938. He was also then writing the stories that appeared in* Uncle Tom's Children *(1938), which won first prize in a contest for writers in the Federal Writers' Project during the Depression. Wright's early fiction was strongly influenced by Ernest Hemingway's way of writing stories, but Wright also set himself the problem of how to use a modernist style to write about social issues:*

> Practically all of us, young writers, were influenced by Ernest Hemingway. We liked the simple, direct way in which he wrote, but a great many of us wanted to write about social problems. The question came up: How could we write about social problems and use a simple style? Hemingway's style is so concentrated on naturalistic detail that there is no room for social comment. One boy said that one way was to dig deeper into the character and try to get something that will live. I decided to try it.

The result was the five stories published in Uncle Tom's Children. *Next Wright turned to his first novel,* Native Son *(1940), an American classic dramatizing a brutal story of racial conflict. This was followed by* Black Boy *(1945), a brilliant autobiography written when he was not yet forty. The next year he left the United States to spend the last fourteen years of his life in Paris, feeling himself alienated from American values. In 1960, the year Wright died, he gathered for publication his second book of short stories,* Eight Men, *made up of fiction that had appeared over the years in magazines and anthologies, including "The Man Who Was Almost a Man," written in the 1930s.*

Telling stories from a realistic view of his own experience, Wright experimented with literary techniques in all his fiction. His short stories dramatize the same themes as his novels and are equally experimental. "The Man Who Was Almost a Man" weaves the black farm boy's speech so skillfully with standard English narration that most readers are unaware of the effect of the deliberate juxtaposition, but this technique brings us closer to the boy's world while making an implicit social comment about his exclusion from the exploitative white society engulfing him.

RELATED COMMENTARY: *Richard Wright, "Reading Fiction," page 1516.*

RICHARD WRIGHT

The Man Who Was Almost a Man

Dave struck out across the fields, looking homeward through paling light. Whut's the use talkin wid em niggers in the field? Anyhow, his mother was putting supper on the table. Them niggers can't understan nothing. One of these days he was going to get a gun and practice shooting, then they couldn't talk to him as though he were a little boy. He slowed, looking at the ground. Shucks, Ah ain scareda them even ef they are biggern me! Aw, Ah know whut Ahma do. Ahm going by ol Joe's sto n git that Sears Roebuck catlog n look at them guns. Mebbe Ma will lemme buy one when she gits mah pay from ol man Hawkins. Ahma beg her t gimme some money. Ahm ol ernough to hava gun. Ahm seventeen. Almost a man. He strode, feeling his long loose-jointed limbs. Shucks, a man oughta hava little gun aftah he done worked hard all day.

He came in sight of Joe's store. A yellow lantern glowed on the front porch. He mounted steps and went through the screen door, hearing it bang behind him. There was a strong smell of coal oil and mackerel fish. He felt very confident until he saw fat Joe walk in through the rear door, then his courage began to ooze.

"Howdy, Dave! Whutcha want?"

"How yuh, Mistah Joe? Aw, Ah don wanna buy nothing. Ah jus wanted t see ef yuhd lemme look at tha catlog erwhile."

"Sure! You wanna see it here?"

"Nawsuh. Ah wants t take it home wid me. Ah'll bring it back termorrow when Ah come in from the fiels."

"You plannin on buying something?"

"Yessuh."

"Your ma lettin you have your own money now?"

"Shucks. Mistah Joe, Ahm gittin t be a man like anybody else!"

Joe laughed and wiped his greasy white face with a red bandanna.

"Whut you plannin on buyin?"

Dave looked at the floor, scratched his head, scratched his thigh, and smiled. Then he looked up shyly.

"Ah'll tell yuh, Mistah Joe, ef yuh promise yuh won't tell."

"I promise."

"Waal, Ahma buy a gun."

"A gun? What you want with a gun?"

"Ah wanna keep it."

"You ain't nothing but a boy. You don't need a gun."

"Aw, lemme have the catlog, Mistah Joe. Ah'll bring it back."

Joe walked through the rear door. Dave was elated. He looked around at barrels of sugar and flour. He heard Joe coming back. He craned his neck to see if he were bringing the book. Yeah, he's got it. Gawddog, he's got it!

"Here, but be sure you bring it back. It's the only one I got."

"Sho, Mistah Joe."

"Say, if you wanna buy a gun, why don't you buy one from me? I gotta gun to sell."

"Will it shoot?"

"Sure it'll shoot."

"Whut kind is it?"

"Oh, it's kinda old . . . a left-hand Wheeler. A pistol. A big one."

"Is it got bullets in it?"

"It's loaded."

"Kin Ah see it?"

"Where's your money?"

"What yuh wan fer it?"

"I'll let you have it for two dollars."

"Just two dollahs? Shucks, Ah could buy tha when Ah git mah pay."

"I'll have it here when you want it."

"Awright, suh. Ah be in fer it."

He went through the door, hearing it slam again behind him. Ahma git some money from Ma n buy me a gun! Only two dollahs! He tucked the thick catalogue under his arm and hurried.

"Where yuh been, boy?" His mother held a steaming dish of black-eyed peas.

"Aw, Ma, Ah jus stopped down the road t talk wid the boys."

"Yuh know bettah t keep suppah waitin."

He sat down, resting the catalogue on the edge of the table.

"Yuh git up from there and git to the well n wash yosef! Ah ain feedin no hogs in mah house!"

She grabbed his shoulder and pushed him. He stumbled out of the room, then came back to get the catalogue.

"Whut this?"

"Aw, Ma, it's jusa catlog."

"Who yuh git it from?"

"From Joe, down at the sto."

"Waal, thas good. We kin use it in the outhouse."

"Naw, Ma." He grabbed for it. "Gimme ma catlog, Ma."

She held onto it and glared at him.

"Quit hollerin at me! Whut's wrong wid yuh? Yuh crazy?"

"But Ma, please. It ain mine! It's Joe's! He tol me t bring it back t im termorrow."

She gave up the book. He stumbled down the back steps, hugging the thick book under his arm. When he had splashed water on his face and hands, he groped back to the kitchen and fumbled in a corner for the towel. He bumped into a chair; it clattered to the floor. The catalogue sprawled at his feet. When he had dried his eyes he snatched up the book and held it again under his arm. His mother stood watching him.

"Now, ef yuh gonna act a fool over that ol book, Ah'll take it n burn it up."

"Naw, Ma, please."

"Waal, set down n be still!"

He sat down and drew the oil lamp close. He thumbed page after page, unaware of the food his mother set on the table. His father came in. Then his small brother.

"Whutcha got there, Dave?" his father asked.

"Jusa catlog," he answered, not looking up.

"Yeah, here they is!" His eyes glowed at blue-and-black revolvers. He glanced up, feeling sudden guilt. His father was watching him. He eased the book under the table and rested it on his knees. After the blessing was asked, he ate. He scooped up peas and swallowed fat meat without chewing. Buttermilk helped to wash it down. He did not want to mention money before his father. He would do much better by cornering his mother when she was alone. He looked at his father uneasily out of the edge of his eye.

"Boy, how come yuh don quit foolin wid tha book n eat yo suppah?"

"Yessuh."

"How you n ol man Hawkins gitten erlong?"

"Suh?"

"Can't yuh hear? Why don yuh lissen? Ah ast yu how wuz yuh n ol man Hawkins gittin erlong?"

"Oh, swell, Pa. Ah plows mo lan than anybody over there."

"Waal, yuh oughta keep you mind on whut yuh doin."

"Yessuh."

He poured his plate full of molasses and sopped it up slowly with a chunk of cornbread. When his father and brother had left the kitchen, he still sat and looked again at the guns in the catalogue, longing to muster courage enough to present his case to his mother. Lawd, ef Ah only had tha pretty one! He could almost feel the slickness of the weapon with his fingers. If he had a gun like that he would polish it and keep it shining so it would never rust. N Ah'd keep it loaded, by Gawd!

"Ma?" His voice was hesitant.

"Hunh?"

"Ol man Hawkins give yuh mah money yit?"

"Yeah, but ain no usa yuh thinking bout throwin nona it erway. Ahm keeping tha money sos yuh kin have cloes t go to school this winter."

He rose and went to her side with the open catalogue in his palms. She was washing dishes, her head bent low over a pan. Shyly he raised the book. When he spoke, his voice was husky, faint.

"Ma, Gawd knows Ah wans one of these."

"One of whut?" she asked, not raising her eyes.

"One of these," he said again, not daring even to point. She glanced up at the page, then at him with wide eyes.

"Nigger, is yuh gone plumb crazy?"

"Aw, Ma — "

"Git outta here! Don yuh talk t me bout no gun! Yuh a fool!"

"Ma, Ah kin buy one fer two dollahs."

"Not ef Ah knows it, yuh ain!"

"But yuh promised me one — "

"Ah don care what Ah promised! Yuh ain nothing but a boy yit!"

"Ma, ef yuh lemme buy one Ah'll *never* ast yuh fer nothing no mo."

"Ah tol yuh t git outta here! Yuh ain gonna toucha penny of tha money fer no gun! Thas how come Ah has Mistah Hawkins t pay yo wages t me, cause Ah knows yuh ain got no sense."

"But, Ma, we needa gun. Pa ain got no gun. We needa gun in the house. Yuh kin never tell whut might happen."

"Now don yuh try to maka fool outta me, boy! Ef we did hava gun, yuh wouldn't have it!"

He laid the catalogue down and slipped his arm around her waist.

"Aw, Ma, Ah done worked hard alla summer n ain ast yuh fer nothing, is Ah, now?"

"Thas whut yuh spose t do!"

"But Ma, Ah wans a gun. Yuh kin lemme have two dollahs outta mah money. Please, Ma. I kin give it to Pa. . . . Please, Ma! Ah loves yuh, Ma."

When she spoke her voice came soft and low.

"What yu wan wida gun, Dave? Yuh don need no gun. Yuh'll git in trouble. N ef yo pa jus thought Ah let yuh have money t buy a gun he'd hava fit."

"Ah'll hide it, Ma. It ain but two dollahs."

"Lawd, chil, whut's wrong wid yuh?"

"Ain nothin wrong. Ma. Ahm almos a man now. Ah wans a gun."

"Who gonna sell yuh a gun?"

"Ol Joe at the sto."

"N it don cos but two dollahs?"

"Thas all, Ma. Jus two dollahs. Please, Ma."

She was stacking the plates away; her hands moved slowly, reflectively. Dave kept an anxious silence. Finally, she turned to him.

"Ah'll let yuh git tha gun ef yuh promise me one thing."

"What's tha, Ma?"

"Yuh bring it straight back t me, yuh hear? It be fer Pa."

"Yessum! Lemme go now, Ma."

She stooped, turned slightly to one side, raised the hem of her dress, rolled down the top of her stocking, and came up with a slender wad of bills.

"Here," she said. "Lawd knows yuh don need no gun. But yer pa does. Yuh bring it right back t me, yuh hear? Ahma put it up. Now ef yuh don, Ahma have yuh pa lick yuh so hard yuh won fergit it."

"Yessum."

He took the money, ran down the steps, and across the yard.

"Dave! Yuuuuuh Daaaaave!"

He heard, but he was not going to stop now. "Now, Lawd!"

The first movement he made the following morning was to reach under his pillow for the gun. In the gray light of dawn he held it loosely, feeling a sense of power. Could kill a man with a gun like this. Kill anybody, black or white. And if he were holding his gun in his hand, nobody could run over him; they would have to respect him. It was a big gun, with a long barrel and a heavy handle. He raised and lowered it in his hand, marveling at its weight.

He had not come straight home with it as his mother had asked; instead he had stayed out in the fields, holding the weapon in his hand, aiming it now and then at some imaginary foe. But he had not fired it; he had been afraid that his father might hear. Also he was not sure he knew how to fire it.

To avoid surrendering the pistol he had not come into the house until he knew that they were all asleep. When his mother had tiptoed to his bedside late that night and demanded the gun, he had first played possum; then he had told her that the gun was hidden outdoors, that he would bring it to her in the morning. Now he lay turning it slowly in his hands. He broke it, took out the cartridges, felt them, and then put them back.

He slid out of bed, got a long strip of old flannel from a trunk, wrapped the gun in it, and tied it to his naked thigh while it was still loaded. He did not go in to breakfast. Even though it was not yet daylight, he started for Jim Hawkins' plantation. Just as the sun was rising he reached the barns where the mules and plows were kept.

"Hey! That you, Dave?"

He turned. Jim Hawkins stood eying him suspiciously.

"What're yuh doing here so early?"

"Ah didn't know Ah wuz gittin up so early, Mistah Hawkins. Ah was fixin t hitch up ol Jenny n take her t the fiels."

"Good. Since you're so early, how about plowing that stretch down by the woods?"

"Suits me, Mistah Hawkins."

"O.K. Go to it!"

He hitched Jenny to a plow and started across the fields. Hot dog! This was just what he wanted. If he could get down by the woods, he could shoot his gun and nobody would hear. He walked behind the plow, hearing the traces creaking, feeling the gun tied tight to his thigh.

When he reached the woods, he plowed two whole rows before he decided to take out the gun. Finally, he stopped, looked in all directions, then untied the gun and held it in his hand. He turned to the mule and smiled.

"Know whut this is, Jenny? Naw, yuh wouldn know! Yuhs jusa ol mule! Anyhow, this is a gun, n it kin shoot, by Gawd!"

He held the gun at arm's length. Whut t hell, Ahma shoot this thing! He looked at Jenny again.

"Lissen here, Jenny! When Ah pull this ol trigger, Ah don wan yuh t run n acka fool now!"

Jenny stood with head down, her short ears pricked straight. Dave walked off about twenty feet, held the gun far out from him at arm's length, and turned his head. Hell, he told himself, Ah ain afraid. The gun felt loose in his fingers; he waved it wildly for a moment. The he shut his eyes and tightened his forefinger. Bloom! A report half deafened him and he thought his right hand was torn from his arm. He heard Jenny whinnying and galloping over the field, and he found himself on his knees, squeezing his fingers hard between his legs. His hand was numb; he jammed it into his mouth, trying to warm it, trying to stop the pain. The gun lay at his feet. He did not quite know what had happened. He stood up and stared at the gun as though it were a living thing. He gritted his teeth and kicked the gun. Yuh almos broke mah arm! He turned to look for Jenny; she was far over the fields, tossing her head and kicking wildly.

"Hol on there, ol mule!"

When he caught up with her she stood trembling, walling her big white eyes at him. The plow was far away; the traces had broken. Then Dave stopped short, looking, not believing. Jenny was bleeding. Her left side was red and wet with blood. He went closer. Lawd, have mercy! Wondah did Ah shoot this mule? He grabbed for Jenny's mane. She flinched, snorted, whirled, tossing her head.

"Hol on now! Hol on."

Then he saw the hole in Jenny's side, right between the ribs. It was round, wet, red. A crimson stream streaked down the front leg, flowing fast. Good Gawd! Ah wuzn't shootin at tha mule. He felt panic. He knew he had to stop that blood, or Jenny would bleed to death. He had never seen so much blood in all his life. He chased the mule for half a mile, trying to catch her. Finally she stopped, breathing hard, stumpy tail half arched. He caught her mane and led her back to where the plow and gun lay. Then he stopped and grabbed handfuls of damp black earth and tried to plug the bullet hole. Jenny shuddered, whinnied, and broke from him.

"Hol on! Hol on now!"

He tried to plug it again, but blood came anyhow. His fingers were hot and sticky. He rubbed dirt into his palms, trying to dry them. Then again he attempted to plug the bullet hole, but Jenny shied away, kicking her heels high. He stood helpless. He had to do something. He ran at Jenny; she dodged him. He watched a red stream of blood flow down Jenny's leg and form a bright pool at her feet.

"Jenny . . . Jenny," he called weakly.

His lips trembled. She's bleeding t death! He looked in the direction of home, wanting to go back, wanting to get help. But he saw the pistol lying in the damp black clay. He had a queer feeling that if he only did something, this would not be; Jenny would not be there bleeding to death.

When he went to her this time, she did not move. She stood with sleepy, dreamy eyes; and when he touched her she gave a low-pitched whinny and knelt to the ground, her front knees slopping in blood.

"Jenny . . . Jenny . . ." he whispered.

For a long time she held her neck erect; then her head sank, slowly. Her ribs swelled with a mighty heave and she went over.

Dave's stomach felt empty, very empty. He picked up the gun and held it gingerly between his thumb and forefinger. He buried it at the foot of a tree. He took a stick to cover the pool of blood with dirt — but what was the use? There was Jenny lying with her mouth open and her eyes walled and glassy. He could not tell Jim Hawkins he had shot his mule. But he had to tell something. Yeah, Ah'll tell em Jenny started gittin wil n fell on the joint of the plow. . . . But that would hardly happen to a mule. He walked across the field slowly, head down.

It was sunset. Two of Jim Hawkins' men were over near the edge of the woods digging a hole in which to bury Jenny. Dave was surrounded by a knot of people, all of whom were looking down at the dead mule.

"I don't see how in the world it happened," said Jim Hawkins for the tenth time.

The crowd parted and Dave's mother, father, and small brother pushed into the center.

"Where Dave?" his mother called.

"There he is," said Jim Hawkins.

His mother grabbed him.

"Whut happened, Dave? Whut yuh done?"

"Nothin."

"C mon, boy, talk," his father said.

Dave took a deep breath and told the story he knew nobody believed.

"Waal," he drawled. "Ah brung ol Jenny down here sos Ah could do mah plowin. Ah plowed bout two rows, just like yuh see." He stopped and pointed at the long rows of upturned earth. "Then somethin musta been wrong wid ol Jenny. She wouldn ack right a-tall. She started snortin n kickin her heels. Ah tried t hol her, but she pulled erway, rearin n goin in. Then when the point of the plow was stickin up in the air, she swung erroun n twisted herself back on it. . . . She stuck herself n started t bleed. N fo Ah could do anything, she wuz dead."

"Did you ever hear of anything like that in all your life?" asked Jim Hawkins.

There were white and black standing in the crowd. They murmured. Dave's mother came close to him and looked hard into his face. "Tell the truth, Dave," she said.

"Looks like a bullet hole to me," said one man.

"Dave, whut yuh do wid the gun?" his mother asked.

The crowd surged in, looking at him. He jammed his hands into his pockets, shook his head slowly from left to right, and backed away. His eyes were wide and painful.

"Did he hava gun?" asked Jim Hawkins.

"By Gawd, Ah tol yuh tha wuz a gun wound," said a man, slapping his thigh.

His father caught his shoulders and shook him till his teeth rattled.

"Tell whut happened, yuh rascal! Tell whut. . . ."

Dave looked at Jenny's stiff legs and began to cry.

"Whut yuh do wid tha gun?" his mother asked.

"What wuz he doin wida gun?" his father asked.

"Come on and tell the truth," said Hawkins. "Ain't nobody going to hurt you. . . ."

His mother crowded close to him.

"Did yuh shoot tha mule, Dave?"

Dave cried, seeing blurred white and black faces.

"Ahh ddinn gggo tt sshooot hher. . . . Ah ssswear ffo Gawd Ahh ddin. . . . Ah wuz a-tryin t sssee ef the old gggun would sshoot —"

"Where yuh git the gun from?" his father asked.

"Ah got it from Joe, at the sto."

"Where yuh git the money?"

"Ma give it t me."

"He kept worryin me, Bob. Ah had t. Ah tol im t bring the gun right back t me. . . . It was fer yuh, the gun."

"But how yuh happen to shoot that mule?" asked Jim Hawkins.

"Ah wuzn shootin at the mule, Mistah Hawkins. The gun jumped when Ah pulled the trigger. . . . N fo Ah knowed anythin Jenny was there a-bleedin."

Somebody in the crowd laughed. Jim Hawkins walked close to Dave and looked into his face.

"Well, looks like you have bought you a mule, Dave."

"Ah swear fo Gawd, Ah didn go t kill the mule, Mistah Hawkins!"

"But you killed her!"

All the crowd was laughing now. They stood on tiptoe and poked heads over one another's shoulders.

"Well, boy, looks like yuh done bought a dead mule! Hahaha!"

"Ain tha ershame."

"Hohohohoho."

Dave stood, head down, twisting his feet in the dirt.

"Well, you needn't worry about it, Bob," said Jim Hawkins to Dave's father. "Just let the boy keep on working and pay me two dollars a month."

"Whut yuh wan fer yo mule, Mistah Hawkins?"

Jim Hawkins screwed up his eyes.

"Fifty dollars."

"Whut yuh do wid tha gun?" Dave's father demanded.

Dave said nothing.

"Yuh wan me t take a tree n beat yuh till yuh talk!"

"Nawsuh!"

"Whut yuh do wid it?"

"Ah throwed it erway."

"Where?"

"Ah . . . Ah throwed it in the creek."

"Waal, c mon home. N firs thing in the mawnin git to tha creek n fin tha gun."

"Yessuh."

"Whut yuh pay fer it?"

"Two dollahs."

"Take tha gun n git yo money back n carry it to Mistah Hawkins, yuh hear? N don fergit Ahma lam you black bottom good fer this! Now march yosef on home, suh!"

Dave turned and walked slowly. He heard people laughing. Dave glared, his eyes welling with tears. Hot anger bubbled in him. Then he swallowed and stumbled on.

That night Dave did not sleep. He was glad that he had gotten out of killing the mule so easily, but he was hurt. Something hot seemed to turn over inside him each time he remembered how they had laughed. He tossed on his bed, feeling his hard pillow. *N Pa says he's gonna beat me. . . .* He remembered other beatings, and his back quivered. *Naw, naw, Ah sho don wan im t beat me tha way no mo. Dam em all! Nobody ever gave him anything. All he did was work. They treat me like a mule, n then they beat me.* He gritted his teeth. *N Ma had t tell on me.*

Well, if he had to, he would take old man Hawkins that two dollars. But that meant selling the gun. And he wanted to keep that gun. Fifty dollars for a dead mule.

He turned over, thinking how he had fired the gun. He had an itch to fire it again. *Ef other men kin shoota gun, by Gawd, Ah kin!* He was still, listening. *Mebbe they all sleepin now.* The house was still. He heard the soft breathing of his brother. *Yes, now!* He would go down and get that gun and see if he could fire it! He eased out of bed and slipped into overalls.

The moon was bright. He ran almost all the way to the edge of the woods. He stumbled over the ground, looking for the spot where he had buried the gun. *Yeah, here it is.* Like a hungry dog scratching for a bone, he pawed it up. He puffed his black cheeks and blew dirt from the trigger and barrel. He broke it and found four cartridges unshot. He looked around; the fields were filled with silence and moonlight. He clutched the gun stiff and hard in his fingers. But, as soon as he wanted to pull the trigger, he shut his eyes and turned his head. *Naw, Ah can't shoot wid mah eyes closed n mah head turned.* With effort he held his eyes open; then he squeezed. *Blooooom!* He was stiff, not breathing. The gun was still in his hands. Dammit, he'd done it! He fired again. *Blooooom!* He smiled. *Bloooom! Blooooom! Click, click.* There! It was empty. If anybody could shoot a gun, he could. He put the gun into his hip pocket and started across the fields.

When he reached the top of a ridge he stood straight and proud in the moonlight, looking at Jim Hawkins' big white house, feeling the gun sagging in his pocket. *Lawd, ef Ah had just one mo bullet Ah'd taka shot at tha house. Ah'd like t scare ol man Hawkins jusa little. . . . Jusa enough t let im know Dave Saunders is a man.*

To his left the road curved, running to the tracks of the Illinois Central. He jerked his head, listening. From far off came a faint *hooooof-hooooof; hooooof-hooooof. . . .* He stood rigid. *Two dollahs a mont. Les see now. . . . Tha means it'll take bout two years. Shucks! Ah'll be dam!*

He started down the road, toward the tracks. Yeah, here she comes! He stood beside the track and held himself stiffly. Here she comes, erroun the ben. . . . C mon, yuh slow poke! C mon! He had his hand on his gun; something quivered in his stomach. Then the train thundered past, the gray and brown box cars rumbling and clinking. He gripped the gun tightly; then he jerked his hand out of his pocket. Ah betcha Bill wouldn't do it! Ah betcha. . . . The cars slid past, steel grinding upon steel. Ahm ridin yuh ternight, so hep me Gawd! He was hot all over. He hesitated just a moment; then he grabbed, pulled atop of a car, and lay flat. He felt his pocket; the gun was still there. Ahead the long rails were glinting in the moonlight, stretching away, away to somewhere, somewhere where he could be a man. . . . [1961]

HISAYE YAMAMOTO *(b. 1921) was born in Redondo Beach, California, the child of Japanese immigrants. She studied languages at Compton Junior College, but in 1942, after the Japanese bombed Pearl Harbor and anti-Japanese feeling ran high on the West Coast, she and her family — like 110,000 other people of Japanese ancestry — were forceably interned in a relocation camp until the end of the war. Yamamoto had begun to write while a teenager, and in the concentration camp she worked as a reporter and a columnist for the camp newspaper, the* Poston [Arizona] Chronicle. *After the war she and her family moved to Los Angeles, where for three years she wrote for the African American weekly newspaper, the* Los Angeles Tribune.

In 1948 Yamamoto began to publish her fiction in journals like the Kenyon Review *and* Arizona Quarterly. *The next year she received a John Hay Whitney Foundation Opportunity Fellowship, which gave her more time for her writing. In the 1950s she continued to publish short stories while she wrote for the* Catholic Worker, *attracted to its pacifist ideals. Several of her stories were included in Martha Foley's annual lists of "Distinctive Short Stories," and in 1986 she received the American Book Award for Lifetime Achievement from the Before Columbus Foundation. Yamamoto's short fiction was collected in* Seventeen Syllables and Other Stories *(1989), and in 1991 two of her narratives about girlhood in a southern California Japanese-American prewar rural community, "Seventeen Syllables" and "Yoneko's Earthquake," were the basis of a film produced for PBS's American Playhouse series.*

Yamamoto has said that "the Japanese tradition has had a great influence on my writing since my parents brought it with them from Japan and how could they not help but transmit it to us? I even wonder if I would have been a writer at all without this tradition to go by, since most of the stories seem to deal with this interaction of the Japanese tradition with the American experience." "The Eskimo Connection" is a recent story.

HISAYE YAMAMOTO

The Eskimo Connection

In the late winter of 1975 Emiko Toyama was really surprised when she got a letter from a young Eskimo. It seemed he'd come across a reprinted poem of hers that he'd read in an Asian American publication that was several years old and as a fellow Asian American had taken a chance and written her in care of the magazine.

The surprise was two-fold when Alden Ryan Walunga, for that was his name, identified himself as a prisoner-patient at a federal penitentiary in the midwest. A Yupik, he was only twenty-three years old, young enough to be one of her children. She wondered whether she should write back. What commonality was there between a probably embittered young man and an aging Nisei widow in Los Angeles with several children, three still at home, whose main avocation was not writing poetry but babysitting the grandchildren? He had enclosed with his letter a photocopied prison weekly containing an essay of his and he asked for a "critique."

More reason not to reply. The article was brief but remarkably confused. It was a passionate cry against the despoiling of his native land which somehow turned into a sermon repeating the Biblical prophecy that such an evil was only part of the wholesale corruption to precede the return of Christ, so it was like he didn't know whether to laugh or cry. And the language was imprecise, not enough to set her teeth on edge as sometimes happened, but almost.

Emiko had begun learning rather early to soft-pedal her critical instincts. As a young woman in camp, she had hung out sometimes with people who wrote and painted and she knew what vulnerable psyches resided in creative critters. And it wasn't just them, either. She had a relative who had stopped writing letters for years because, among other things, her husband and daughter had once laughed at her syntax. And Emiko herself had once been actually pummeled by a dear friend whose poem she had made light of. This friend had stopped writing poems for years. People ought to be more callous, she knew, they ought to be more determined. But, alas, most egos were covered with the thinnest of egg-shells.

And then to tamper with words written with feeling was to destroy the feeling, usually.

Nevertheless, against her own better judgment, she wrote a careful note telling Alden Ryan Walunga as tactfully as possible that the essay was eminently worth writing but that the message might be made stronger, clearer, with a revision of language here and there. She encouraged him with the observation that certainly, a strong voice was needed to speak up on behalf of the Eskimo.

He took it very gracefully, but he mentioned that he had studied two semesters at the University of Alaska and that his mother was wondering whether it was all right to send on his Air Force text of Robert Penn Warren's *Modern Rhetoric*. As the sporadic exchange of letters continued, she pieced together enough to learn that he was the third of seven children with two older sisters and four younger brothers, which he attributed to the Eskimo need for survival; that he was being treated for depression (he mentioned massive doses of thorazine); that he attended meetings of Alcoholics Anonymous there at the prison; that he had come to Christ with such fervor that he considered the study of His Word the main preoccupation of his life.

To this end, he had already paraphrased four Pauline epistles using Strong's *Exhaustive Concordance of the Bible* (with Greek dictionary) and he mentioned his greed for other resources like Josephus' historical works as well as the treatises on Biblical psychology and demonology. He wrote that he was frustrated by prison rules which allowed only one book at a time to be borrowed once a month from area libraries. In one letter he said his next borrowing would be a dictionary on the Bible, more "elaborate" than the one he already had.

He also read other things: Victor Hugo's *The Hunchback of Notre Dame*, Fyodor Dostoevsky's *The Brothers Karamazov*, N. Scott Momaday's *House Made of Dawn*, and he asked whether she had read any of Yukio Mishima whom he described as "a Japanese writer who famously and traditionally committed suicide with a sword." He also recommended Peter Freuchen's *Book of the Eskimo* and a Stanford University study of the Alaskan native, as being accurate depictions of his people.

Emiko tried to send him an Asian American literary magazine on one occasion and was taken aback when it was returned to her with a form letter stipulating that she must get permission from the prison chaplain before submitting such materials. So she sent the magazine to the chaplain's office and received a polite note saying that although an exception had been made and the magazine given to the prisoner, the chaplain's office was authorized to pass on religious materials only and other literature should be sent in care of the education department.

She felt something like a cold hand touch her when she received these official notices — that was what being in prison was, was it, the relinquishment of every liberty that those on the outside took for granted?

But Alden Ryan Walunga seemed to be an exuberant spirit even under these stifling conditions. The whole first page of his letter would be taken up with the salutation, thusly:

> DEAR EMIKO!
>
>   EMIKO!
>
>   EMIKO!

before the actual letter began on page two. Once, staring at the first page, she was amused to see that with the addition of one letter, she could write him back:

> DEAR ESKIMO!
>
>   ESKIMO!
>
>   ESKIMO!

but she decided it would be rather childish and desisted.

In one letter he wrote that a poem he had submitted a couple of years before to a New York magazine called *A.D.* had been accepted for publication. He had been called to the chaplain's office to be shown a $50 check, with the warning that all literary submissions had to first be officially approved. She wrote to congratulate him.

Then, for awhile, there was no word from Alden Ryan Walunga, but Emiko, trying as usual to cope with the needs of her brood, scarcely noticed. Her husband's insurance was adequate if she managed shrewdly, but it was always something — dentist, doctor, marijuana, living together without marriage, distressing report cards, flu, filling out unwieldy applications for college grants, keeping up with the seasonal needs of the yard, a new roof or water heater that had to be squeezed in somehow. Besides these routine cares, something else was in the air, something insidious and seemingly contagious: most of her friends, neighbors, and relatives seemed to be getting divorced, many of them after twenty-five years of marriage or more! If Mits had not died, would they too be undergoing such trauma?

So, when after some months Alden Ryan Walunga resumed corresponding with a somewhat apologetic note explaining that he had been through some kind of spiritual crisis involving "deception," implying a self-delusion, so that he was now back to square one, she answered him with, "So what else is new?" or words to that effect. Without going into detail, she mentioned the discombobulations taking place in her neck of the woods. He wrote back that such upheavals were to be expected, of course, since pandemonium had been prophesied, and he stressed the importance of holding fast to the Lord Jesus Christ.

Alden Ryan Walunga never mentioned the reason for his incarceration and Emiko never asked. If he did not wish to reveal the nature of his crime, she did not wish to know it, but in the back of her mind she decided that he was in prison for forgery. This was because years ago she had an apartment neighbor who had twice been in prison for forgery and he was among her pleasanter memories: he played Bach on the piano but he seemed to be one of the innocents of the world, living about a foot off the ground. She especially remembered him, with his bushy grey hair and horn-rimmed glasses, because of two occasions when he had asked her to remove a sliver from his hand. Both times, when she returned with a needle which she sterilized with the flame of a match, he had begun whimpering and cringing. The first time she had laughed out loud, thinking he was kidding, until she saw that his tears and cries were real. He had actually been terrified!

Besides, Emiko was not sure that prisons were the answer to crime. It was a known fact, was it not, that prisons, as most of them were now constituted, rarely rehabilitated? Not only was she against capital punishment, she was also against prisons, even though, pinned down in an argument, she admitted that there must be some system to temporarily segregate those who persisted in preying on others. She agreed with the wise man who had called for a society "in which it is easier to be good."

She remembered the horror of the year before, the mousetrapping and cooking alive of five young men and women who had gotten disillusioned with the establishment and taken matters into their own hands. She could not forget the extravagantly leaping fire which came across almost real on the peacock screen — so real that you could almost hear them screaming. And then to hear the mayor of the city afterwards proclaiming that it was only "morally right" to reimburse those in the neighborhood whose homes had been damaged. She had never been able to get his definition of morality out of her mind.

In February of 1976 there came a belated and elegant valentine card with the news that he was being transferred to McNeil Island Penitentiary via Terminal Island and Lompoc, and he wondered whether Emiko was anywhere in the environs of either stopping-off place. He thanked her for the snapshots of her family she had dug up and sent at his request. Bogged down by another family crisis, she wrote that she would not be able to go and meet him. But she felt guilty. "That which I should have done, I did not do," chanted a small voice in the back of her mind.

If Alden was disappointed, he did not mention it. His first letter from McNeil Island contained an appreciation of the place:

> It is beauty that I am after in my writing. There is lots of beauty in McNeil. Today I was a little depressed as I had allowed my mind to stray away from Jesus Christ and that attitude chain-reacted to a sin that reinforced the negative feelings. After supper I isolated myself in the sloping green lawn and layed down, closed eyes.
>
> The sun made itself felt as the cumulus clouds departed. A gentle breeze swept across. Somewhere, where there was a small sandy beach, the surfs ran back and forth, lazily, back and forth sweeping. The air's odor reminded me of home quiescently and of my love, Ophelia. God was soothing me, telling me that I am His child and he forgives. I fell asleep, and relaxed. He massaged my soul. Alleluia!

There were two publications there, he said, *Newsbuoy*, a weekly inmate paper, and *Smoke Talk*, "a quarterly for us American Indians." He had attended an American Indian Alcoholic Seminar and Transactional Analysis seminar given by the Pacific Institute. He had become a member of AA, he added, and was "enjoying the spiritual aspect of it":

> We had an AA banquet where I danced with the brave ladies recovering from the evil of that (heinous) drug. In the brotherhood of American Indians we will be having our pow wow this coming 26th. The sun rises for us and the bell tolls for us; what else can they do?

Then life took one of those odd turns, so that Emiko felt that she was being given a second chance — maybe she and her correspondent were destined to meet after all. The only son of her childhood friend, Mary, was getting married to a girl in Seattle and Mary Fukuda insisted that Emiko go along with her and her husband. The matter was settled, she said, they were footing the bill for the plane and hotel. So Emiko wrote to McNeil and asked Alden if she might be able to see him.

She found out that she would have to get permission first from his Case Manager, so she wrote for the proper form, filled it out, and sent it back. She had not received permission by the day of departure — they left the city gratefully in the midst of a heat wave — but she did not worry too much about it. Once in Seattle, she figured, it would be a simple matter to reach the proper authorities and explain her mission. Surely, since she had already asked to be put on Alden's visitors list, and since she was coming all the way from Los Angeles, permission would be forthcoming

Despite a soft drizzle, the early July wedding was grand, and Emiko was swept up in the before-and-after festivities for a time. The Fukudas were staying on for a few days to take in the sights and Emiko, it was agreed, would try to get over to Steilacoom from where she could take the prison boat over. The Fukuda's son had a friend working at McNeil, so she was referred to him for assistance. In like Flynn, she thought, with such help.

But for some reason, permission was denied. Was his crime so terrible then? Or was it merely some prison protocol that had to be observed? Emiko was crestfallen but she joined the Fukudas in their sight-seeing and managed to enjoy the rest of her stay in the Northwest. She phoned home only once to make sure all was peaceful there, and as she told the Fukudas, she got the impression that the kids didn't care if she ever got back. (Years later, she was to find out that her younger daughter, rebelling at last against her sister's authoritarianism, had dragged her all the way around the house by her long hair.)

When she arrived home, the waiting pile of mail contained the letter from the penitentiary informing her that she had been placed on Alden Ryan Walunga's visitors list. Thanks a lot, she thought, knowing she would probably never have occasion to go to Seattle again.

But she read the regulations out of curiosity. Steilacoom, the paper said, was thirteen miles southwest of Tacoma, and there was a free twenty-minute ride on the prison boat to McNeil Island. An inmate was permitted only four visits a month and female visitors were "requested to be careful of the attire they wear to the institution," with "skin-tight leotards and stretch pants, short miniskirts and lowcut dresses considered improper in the prison setting." Well, she would have to bear that in mind. No bikinis, either, she supposed.

No one was to alight from the boat until a bell rang to give permission. One could buy a $1.00 meal ticket for a box lunch (available all visiting days) to be eaten with the man being visited; vending machines and soft drinks were available in the visiting room. No food (such as cakes that might contain hacksaws or hashish brownies, Emiko interpolated) was allowed to be brought in by visitors, no article allowed to be exchanged. Pictures could be shown with permission from the Visiting Room Officer; hobby craft might be given to visitors in the visiting room with the prior approval of the Hobby Shop Officer.

A handshake and embraces were permitted before and after the visit only; "during the visit you may have no physical contact"; visits could be terminated at any time if the Visiting Room Officer detected any untoward behavior; inmates might take one sealed package of cigarettes if they wanted because they would not be allowed to carry any cigarettes from the visiting room.

Alden must have been inured to disappointment; he did not dwell on her failure to visit. He only wrote that he was happy to have her on his visitors list. Besides, he had applied for and received a Basic Educational Opportunity Grant, so he was looking forward to taking classes from Tacoma Community College in the fall. Also, armed with a course in Greek New Testament Grammar from Moody Bible Institute, he was continuing his attack on the Greek original in order to make his own translation of the Gospels.

He also sent her a short story he had written, titled "The Coffin of 1974."

Emiko found the story disturbing. It was afflicted with the same dichotomous anguish as that first essay of his that she had read:

> Snowbirds ran through the air, rapidly singing the Bering Sea
> Spring song in the thin and white air, landing upon the melting and

softening snow, very wild, almost invisible as they blended with the snow and exposed gravel of earth, and then suddenly they would be driven by some unfelt wind to find another place to seek out stone fly meals, flies who had long hibernated and were trying to restore the littleness of their lives.

Quietly the snowbirds were alerted as they sensed the approaching crunches on the tundra snow. Their heads became uneasy and loose, as if they were unscrewing them off. Their wings rose momentarily to flap but were doubtfully lowered back. They were getting confused. They were getting scared. Their ancestor snowbirds had transmitted them a traditional wariness against homo sapiens, especially against little Eskimo boys, fat parkas on with overflowing fur outlining their faces, armed with slingshots.

The coffin, borne by "six dark people," was heavy because the deceased had gained 27 pounds in prison:

The sky was inky blue. The silent clouds hardly moved and seemed to refuse to move. The Bering Sea was belligerently nervous with three-foot size ripples in response to a current that was breaking up and enclosing the island with ice floes and icebergs. The breeze was tranquil and smelled of raw and recent butcher of brown walruses. The village houses appeared wet and were wooden and light brown, some with tarpaper and some with peeling and peeling white paint, and most with chimneys lazily exhaling silver smoke, but all with that glassy wet, relaxing and tired countenance. Most also had bloodied melting Bering Sea Spring snow, because the walrus spoil of the day.

The tiny black and white eyes of the little snowbirds united their focus to the approaching mystery but their little warm hearts had ceased their tachycardia. In fact, they were lining up in a file as if in response to a military and folk-hero who was honoring them a pass.

The mother was grieving for her oldest son. He was the one in the coffin. And if Emiko read the story correctly, it was the oldest son who, with a twenty-two Remington magnum rifle, had killed both his uncle (his mother's youngest brother) and a girl relative. The girl relative had also been raped.

There was a lot of blood in the story, both walrus and human. But there was, all of a sudden, a happy ending. The oldest son had not died, after all. He was reborn in Christ, a new man, washed clean of his sins! Alleluia!

Emiko was stunned by the story. Was this, then, Alden's story?

But she merely sent it back to him with the "corrections, suggestions, and remarks" for which he had asked, praising the poetry of the stark landscape with the snowbirds.

The last communication she got from Alden had a regular stamp on the envelope, unlike the previous envelopes with the printed prison frank. He wrote from the Seattle City Jail, where he had been transferred for his own protection after telling the authorities what he had seen of a homosexual rape at the prison. He did not much care for the Seattle City Jail with the constant sounds of traffic and sirens rising day and night from the street way down below. He expressed distaste for "the occupants of a neighboring cell, a bunch of black and white homosexuals" whose "demonic malaria becomes active in pretentious talk and behavior . . . the pitiful perverts are even called by their feminine nicknames by the officers."

But he reported gladsome news, too. He had been recommended for a transfer to Alaska! That was around September. Wallowing in the mire of modern family life, Emiko did not answer Alden until just before Christmas, when she wrote him a brief note in a greeting card. She had managed, meanwhile, to send him another Asian American literary magazine on the assumption that she would no longer have to go through all the red tape as before.

The card was returned by the jail, stamped Unclaimed. But the magazine may have reached its destination, for although it was never acknowledged, neither was it returned. Emiko liked to think that Alden still kept it somewhere among his prison mementos even though paroled. He was probably very busy spreading the Word of God there in that isolated settlement overlooking the Bering Sea.

Or, if not paroled, there would be frequent visits there in the Alaska prison from his mother, his sisters and brothers, from his beloved Ophelia, and Lord knows whom else. There would be piles of studying to do, lots of poems, stories and essays to write.

Either way, Emiko — holding fast to the Lord Jesus Christ and refusing to consider any other alternatives — imagined he was probably much too busy back there on his home ground to continue to be the pen pal of some old woman way down there in California. [1983]

PART TWO

COMMENTARIES

The next part of this book consists of critical comments on the short story form and on various individual stories. In the preface to his story collection *Twice-told Tales*, Nathaniel Hawthorne wrote that a writer "would have reason to be ashamed if he could not criticize his own work as fairly as another man's, and — though it is little his business, and perhaps still less his interest — he can hardly resist a temptation to achieve something of the sort. If writers were allowed to do so, and would perform the task with perfect sincerity and unreserve, their opinions of their own productions would often be more valuable and instructive than the works themselves." Although Hawthorne was not entirely serious in this last statement, there is some truth in what he said. Writers' attitudes about creating short fiction can often clarify their work, place their stories in a larger context of literary history, and shed light on the creative process.

Reading literary criticism can also help stimulate your response to the stories. "Criticism is not literature, and the pleasure of criticism is not the pleasure of literature," observed the noted teacher and critic Lionel Trilling. "But experience suggests that the two pleasures go together, and the pleasure of criticism makes literature and its pleasure the more readily accessible."

The commentaries in this section are arranged alphabetically by author. The headnotes to the stories in Part One of the anthology refer you to the related commentaries in this and the next part of the book.

CHINUA ACHEBE *delivered "An Image of Africa: Racism in Conrad's* Heart of Darkness" *as a public lecture at the University of Massachusetts, Amherst, in 1974. It was later included in his book* Hopes and Impediments: Selected Essays *(1988). In his preface to that book, Achebe notes that the great African American W. E. B. Du Bois wrote in* The Souls of Black Folk *that "the problem of the Twentieth Century is the problem of the colour line." Achebe points out that Du Bois wrote that sentence in 1903, only one year later than Conrad wrote* Heart of Darkness. *Achebe continues, "This chronology is of the utmost importance. Therefore the defence sometimes proffered: that Conrad should not be judged by the standards of later times; that racism had not become an issue in the world when he wrote his famous African novel, will have to clarify whose world it is talking about."*

CHINUA ACHEBE

An Image of Africa: Conrad's Heart of Darkness

*H*eart of Darkness projects the image of Africa as "the other world," the antithesis of Europe and therefore of civilization, a place where man's vaunted intelligence and refinement are finally mocked by triumphant bestiality. The book opens on the River Thames, tranquil, resting peacefully "at the decline of day after ages of good service done to the race that peopled its banks." But the actual story will take place on the River Congo, the very antithesis of the Thames. The River Congo is quite decidedly not a River Emeritus. It has rendered no service and enjoys no old-age pension. We are told that "going up that river was like travelling back to the earliest beginning of the world."

Is Conrad saying then that these two rivers are very different, one good, the other bad? Yes, but that is not the real point. It is not the differentness that worries Conrad but the lurking hint of kinship, of common ancestry. For the Thames too "has been one of the dark places of the earth." It conquered its darkness, of course, and is now in daylight and at peace. But if it were to visit its primordial relative, the Congo, it would run the terrible risk of hearing grotesque echoes of its own forgotten darkness, and falling victim to an avenging recrudescence of the mindless frenzy of the first beginnings.

These suggestive echoes comprise Conrad's famed evocation of the African atmosphere in Heart of Darkness. In the final consideration, his method amounts to no more than a steady, ponderous, fake-ritualistic repetition of two antithetical sentences, one about silence and the other about frenzy. We can inspect samples of this: (a) "It was the stillness of an implacable force brooding over an inscrutable intention" and (b) "The steamer toiled along slowly on the edge of a black and incomprehensible frenzy." Of course, there is a judicious change of adjective from time to time, so that instead of "inscrutable," for example, you might have "unspeakable," even plain "mysterious," etc., etc.

The eagle-eyed English critic F. R. Leavis drew attention long ago to Conrad's "adjectival insistence upon inexpressible and incomprehensible mystery." That insistence must not be dismissed lightly, as many Conrad critics have tended to do, as a mere stylistic flaw; for it raises serious questions of artistic good faith. When a writer while pretending to record scenes, incidents, and their impact is in reality engaged in inducing hypnotic stupor in his readers through a bombardment of emotive words and other forms of trickery, much more has to be at stake than stylistic felicity. Generally, normal readers are well armed to detect and resist such underhand activity. But Conrad chose his subject well — one which was guaranteed not to put him in conflict with the psychological predisposition of his readers or raise the need for him to contend with their resistance. He chose the role of purveyor of comforting myths.

The most interesting and revealing passages in *Heart of Darkness* are, however, about people. I must crave the indulgence of my reader to quote almost a whole page from about the middle of the story when representatives of Europe in a steamer going down the Congo encounter the denizens of Africa:

> We were wanderers on a prehistoric earth, on an earth that wore the aspect of an unknown planet. We could have fancied ourselves the first of men taking possession of an accursed inheritance, to be subdued at the cost of profound anguish and of excessive toil. But suddenly, as we struggled round a bend, there would be a glimpse of rush walls, of peaked grass-roofs, a burst of yells, a whirl of black limbs, a mass of hands clapping, of feet stamping, of bodies swaying, of eyes rolling, under the droop of heavy and motionless foliage. The steamer toiled along slowly on the edge of the black and incomprehensible frenzy. The prehistoric man was cursing us, praying to us, welcoming us — who could tell? We were cut off from the comprehension of our surroundings; we glided past like phantoms, wondering and secretly appalled, as sane men would be before an enthusiastic outbreak in a madhouse. We could not understand because we were too far and could not remember because we were travelling in the night of first ages, of those ages that are gone, leaving hardly a sign — and no memories.
>
> The earth seemed unearthly. We are accustomed to look upon the shackled form of a conquered monster, but there — there you could look at a thing monstrous and free. It was unearthly, and the men were — No, they were not inhuman. Well, you know, that was the worst of it — this suspicion of their not being inhuman. It would come slowly to one. They howled and leaped, and spun, and made horrid faces; but what thrilled you was just the thought of their humanity — like yours — the thought of your remote kinship with

this wild and passionate uproar. Ugly. Yes, it was ugly enough; but if you were man enough you would admit to yourself that there was in you just the faintest trace of a response to the terrible frankness of that noise, a dim suspicion of there being a meaning in it which you — you so remote from the night of first ages — could comprehend.

Herein lies the meaning of *Heart of Darkness* and the fascination it holds over the Western mind: "What thrilled you was just the thought of their humanity — like yours. . . . Ugly."

Having shown us Africa in the mass, Conrad then zeros in, half a page later, on a specific example, giving us one of his rare descriptions of an African who is not just limbs or rolling eyes:

> And between whiles I had to look after the savage who was fireman. He was an improved specimen; he could fire up a vertical boiler. He was there below me, and, upon my word, to look at him was as edifying as seeing a dog in a parody of breeches and a feather hat, walking on his hind legs. A few months of training had done for that really fine chap. He squinted at the steam gauge and at the water gauge with an evident effort of intrepidity — and he had filed his teeth, too, the poor devil, and the wool of his pate shaved into queer patterns, and three ornamental scars on each of his cheeks. He ought to have been clapping his hands and stamping his feet on the bank, instead of which he was hard at work, a thrall to strange witchcraft, full of improving knowledge.

As everybody knows, Conrad is a romantic on the side. He might not exactly admire savages clapping their hands and stamping their feet but they have at least the merit of being in their place, unlike this dog in a parody of breeches. For Conrad, things being in their place is of the utmost importance.

"Fine fellows — cannibals — in their place," he tells us pointedly. Tragedy begins when things leave their accustomed place, like Europe leaving its safe stronghold between the policeman and the baker to take a peep into the heart of darkness.

Before the story takes us into the Congo basin proper we are given this nice little vignette as an example of things in their place:

> Now and then a boat from the shore gave one a momentary contact with reality. It was paddled by black fellows. You could see from afar the white of their eyeballs glistening. They shouted, sang; their bodies streamed with perspiration; they had faces like grotesque masks — these chaps; but they had bone, muscle, a wild vitality, an intense energy of movement, that was as natural and true as the surf along their coast. They wanted no excuse for being there. They were a great comfort to look at.

Towards the end of the story Conrad lavishes a whole page quite unexpectedly on an African woman who has obviously been some kind of mistress to Mr. Kurtz and now presides (if I may be permitted a little liberty) like a formidable mystery over the inexorable imminence of his departure: "She was savage and superb, wild-eyed and magnificent. . . . She stood looking at us without a stir and like the wilderness itself, with an air of brooding over an inscrutable purpose."

This Amazon is drawn in considerable detail, albeit of a predictable nature, for two reasons. First, she is in her place and so can win Conrad's special brand of approval; and second, she fulfils a structural requirement of the story; a savage counterpart to the refined, European woman who will step forth to end the story: "She came forward, all in black with a pale head, floating toward me in the dusk. She was in mourning. . . . She took both my hands in hers and murmured, 'I had heard you were coming.'. . . She had a mature capacity for fidelity, for belief, for suffering."

The difference in the attitude of the novelist to these two women is conveyed in too many direct and subtle ways to need elaboration. But perhaps the most significant difference is the one implied in the author's bestowal of human expression to the one and the withholding of it from the other. It is clearly not part of Conrad's purpose to confer language on the "rudimentary souls" of Africa. In place of speech they made "a violent babble of uncouth sounds." They "exchanged short grunting phrases" even among themselves. But most of the time they were too busy with their frenzy. There are two occasions in the book, however, when Conrad departs somewhat from his practice and confers speech, even English speech, on the savages. The first occurs when cannibalism gets the better of them: "'Catch 'im,' he snapped, with a bloodshot widening of his eyes and a flash of sharp white teeth — 'catch 'im. Give 'im to us.' 'To you, eh?' I asked; 'what would you do with them?' 'Eat 'im!' he said curtly."

The other occasion was the famous announcement: "Mistah Kurtz — he dead."

At first sight these instances might be mistaken for unexpected acts of generosity from Conrad. In reality they constitute some of his best assaults. In the case of the cannibals the incomprehensible grunts that had thus far served them for speech suddenly proved inadequate for Conrad's purpose of letting the European glimpse the unspeakable craving in their hearts. Weighing the necessity for consistency in the portrayal of the dumb brutes against the sensational advantages of securing their conviction by clear, unambiguous evidence issuing out of their own mouths, Conrad chose the latter. As for the announcement of Mr. Kurtz's death by the "insolent black head in the doorway," what better or more appropriate *finis* could be written to the horror story of that wayward child of civilization who willfully had given his soul to the powers of darkness and "taken a high seat amongst the devils of the land" than the proclamation of his physical death by the forces he had joined?

It might be contended, of course, that the attitude to the African in *Heart of Darkness* is not Conrad's but that of his fictional narrator, Marlow, and that far from endorsing it Conrad might indeed be holding it up to irony and criticism. Certainly, Conrad appears to go to considerable pains to set up layers of insulation between himself and the moral universe of his story. He has, for example, a narrator behind a narrator. The primary narrator is Marlow, but his account is given to us through the filter of a second, shadowy person. But if Conrad's intention is to draw a *cordon sanitaire* between himself and the moral and psychological *malaise* of his narrator, his care seems to me totally wasted because he neglects to hint, clearly and adequately, at an alternative frame of reference by which we may judge the actions and opinions of his characters. It would not have been beyond Conrad's power to make that provision if he had thought it necessary. Conrad seems to me to approve of Marlow, with only minor reservations — a fact reinforced by the similarities between their two careers.

Marlow comes through to us not only as a witness of truth, but one holding those advanced and humane views appropriate to the English liberal tradition which required all Englishmen of decency to be deeply shocked by atrocities in Bulgaria or the Congo of King Leopold of the Belgians or wherever.

Thus, Marlow is able to toss out such bleeding-heart sentiments as these:

> They were all dying slowly — it was very clear. They were not enemies, they were not criminals, they were nothing earthly now — nothing but black shadows of disease and starvation, lying confusedly in the greenish gloom. Brought from all the recesses of the coast in all the legality of time contracts, lost in uncongenial surroundings, fed on unfamiliar food, they sickened, became inefficient, and were then allowed to crawl away and rest.

The kind of liberalism espoused here by Marlow/Conrad touched all the best minds of the age in England, Europe, and America. It took different forms in the minds of different people but almost always managed to sidestep the ultimate question of equality between white people and black people. That extraordinary missionary Albert Schweitzer, who sacrificed brilliant careers in music and theology in Europe for a life of service to Africans in much the same area as Conrad writes about, epitomizes the ambivalence. In a comment which has often been quoted Schweitzer says: "The African is indeed my brother but my junior brother." And so he proceeded to build a hospital appropriate to the needs of junior brothers with standards of hygiene reminiscent of medical practice in the days before the germ theory of disease came into being. Naturally he became a sensation in Europe and America. Pilgrims flocked, and I believe still flock even after he has passed on, to witness the prodigious miracle in Lambaréné, on the edge of the primeval forest.

Conrad's liberalism would not take him quite as far as Schweitzer's, though. He would not use the word "brother" however qualified; the farthest he would go was "kinship." When Marlow's African helmsman falls down with a spear in his heart he gives his white master one final disquieting look: "And the intimate profundity of that look he gave me when he received his hurt remains to this day in my memory — like a claim of distant kinship affirmed in a supreme moment."

It is important to note that Conrad, careful as ever with his words, is concerned not so much about "distant kinship" as about someone *laying a claim* on it. The black man lays a claim on the white man which is well-nigh intolerable. It is the laying of this claim which frightens and at the same time fascinates Conrad, "the thought of their humanity — like yours. . . . Ugly."

The point of my observations should be quite clear by now, namely that Joseph Conrad was a thoroughgoing racist. That this simple truth is glossed over in criticisms of his work is due to the fact that white racism against Africa is such a normal way of thinking that its manifestations go completely unremarked. Students of *Heart of Darkness* will often tell you that Conrad is concerned not so much with Africa as with the deterioration of one European mind caused by solitude and sickness. They will point out to you that Conrad is, if anything, less charitable to the Europeans in the story than he is to the natives, that the point of the story is to ridicule Europe's civilizing mission in Africa. A Conrad student informed me in Scotland that Africa is merely a setting for the disintegration of the mind of Mr. Kurtz.

Which is partly the point. Africa as setting and backdrop which eliminates the African as human factor. Africa as a metaphysical battlefield devoid of all recognizable humanity, into which the wandering European enters at his peril. Can nobody see the preposterous and perverse arrogance in thus reducing Africa to the role of props for the break-up of one petty European mind? But that is not even the point. The real question is the dehumanization of Africa and Africans which this age-long attitude has fostered and continues to foster in the world. And the question is whether a novel which celebrates this dehumanization, which depersonalizes a portion of the human race, can be called a great work of art. My answer is: No, it cannot. 　　　　[1974]

SHERWOOD ANDERSON *commented on his practice of writing short stories in his autobiography,* A Story Teller's Story, *published in 1924. This book was his first attempt to write his memoirs and authenticate his "legend" — an impoverished childhood, a revolt against business life, and an entrance into the avant-garde literary circles of Chicago, New Orleans, and New York. He was more concerned with the meaning than with the facts of his life. In his rejection of the "plot" story (a story emphasizing plot over character, setting, or theme), which he considered contrived fiction, he became a strong influence on many subsequent writers of short stories and revitalized the American short story tradition.*

SHERWOOD ANDERSON

Form, Not Plot, in the Short Story

For such men as myself you must understand there is always a great difficulty about telling the tale after the scent has been picked up. . . . Having, from a conversation overheard or in some other way, got the tone of a tale, I was like a woman who has just become impregnated. Something was growing inside me. At night when I lay in my bed I could feel the heels of the tale kicking against the walls of my body. Often as I lay thus every word of the tale came to me quite clearly but when I got out of bed to write it down the words would not come.

I had constantly to seek in roads new to me. Other men had felt what I had felt, had seen what I had seen — how had they met the difficulties I faced? My father when he told his tales walked up and down the room before his audience. He pushed out little experimental sentences and watched his audience narrowly. There was a dull-eyed old farmer sitting in a corner of the room. Father had his eyes on the fellow. "I'll get him," he said to himself. He watched the farmer's eyes. When the experimental sentence he had tried did not get anywhere he tried another and kept trying. Besides words he had — to help the telling of his tales — the advantage of being able to act out those parts for which he could find no words. He could frown, shake his fists, smile, let a look of pain or annoyance drift over his face.

These were his advantages that I had to give up if I was to write my tales rather than tell them and how often I had cursed my fate.

How significant words had become to me! At about this time an American woman living in Paris, Miss Gertrude Stein, had published a book called *Tender Buttons* and it had come into my hands. How it had excited me! Here was something purely experimental and dealing in words separated from sense — in the ordinary meaning of the word sense — an approach I was sure the poets must often be compelled to make. Was it an approach that would help me? I decided to try it.

A year or two before the time of which I am now writing an American painter, Mr. Felix Russman, had taken me one day into his workshop to show me his colors. He laid them out on a table before me and then his wife called him out of the room and he stayed for half an hour. It had been one of the most exciting moments of my life. I shifted the little pans of color about, laid one color against another. I walked away and came near. Suddenly there had flashed into my consciousness, for perhaps the first time in my life, the secret inner world of the painters. Before that time I had wondered often enough why certain paintings, done by the old masters, and hung in our Chicago Art Institute, had so strange an effect upon me. Now I thought I knew. The true painter revealed all of himself in every stroke of his brush. Titian made one feel so utterly the splendor of himself; from Fra Angelico and Sandro Botticelli there came such a deep human tenderness that on some days it fairly brought tears to the eyes; in a most dreadful way and in spite of all his skill Bouguereau gave away his own inner nastiness while Leonardo made one feel all of the grandeur of his mind just as Balzac[1] had made his readers feel the universality and wonder of his mind.

Very well then, the words used by the tale-teller were as the colors used by the painter. Form was another matter. It grew out of the materials of the tale and the teller's reaction to them. It was the tale trying to take form that kicked about inside the tale-teller at night when he wanted to sleep.

And words were something else. Words were the surfaces, the clothes of the tale. I thought I had begun to get something a little clearer now. I had smiled to myself a little at the sudden realization of how little native American words had been used by American story-writers. When most American writers wanted to be very American they went in for slang. Surely we American scribblers had paid long and hard for the English blood in our veins. The English had got their books into our schools, their ideas of correct forms of expression were firmly fixed in our minds. Words as commonly used in our writing were in reality an army that marched in a certain array and the generals in command of the army were still English. One saw the words as marching, always just so — in books — and came to think of them so — in books.

But when one told a tale to a group of advertising men sitting in a barroom in Chicago or to a group of laborers by a factory door in Indiana one instinctively disbanded the army. There were moments then for what have always been called by our correct writers "unprintable words." One got now and then a certain effect by a bit of profanity. One dropped instinctively into the vocabulary of the men about, was compelled to do so to get the full effect sought for the tale. Was the tale he was telling not just the tale of a man named Smoky Pete and how he caught his foot in the trap set for himself? — or perhaps one was giving them the Mama Geigans story. The devil. What had the words of such a tale to do with Thackeray[2] or Fielding?[3] Did the men to whom one told the tale not know a dozen Smoky Petes and Mama Geigans? Had one ventured into the classic English models for tale-telling at that moment there would have been a roar. "What the devil! Don't you go high-toning us!"

And it was sure one did not always seek a laugh from his audience. Sometimes one wanted to move the audience, make them squirm with sympathy. Perhaps one wanted to throw an altogether new light on a tale the audience already knew.

Would the common words of our daily speech in shops and offices do the trick? Surely the Americans among whom one sat talking had felt everything the Greeks had felt, everything the English felt? Deaths came to them,

---

[1] Honoré de Balzac (1799–1850), French novelist, one of the earliest realists.
[2] William Makepeace Thackeray (1811–1863), English novelist.
[3] Henry Fielding (1707–1754), one of the first English novelists.

the tricks of fate assailed their lives. I was certain none of them lived felt or talked as the average American novel made them live feel and talk and as for the plot short stories of the magazines — those bastard children of de Maupassant, Poe, and O. Henry[4] — it was certain there were no plot short stories ever lived in any life I had known anything about.   [1924]

MARGARET ATWOOD *wrote "Reading Blind" as an introduction to* The Best American Short Stories 1989, *a volume she edited with Shannon Ravenel. The* Best American Short Stories *series was started in 1915, but since 1978 the publisher, Houghton Mifflin, has invited a different writer to edit it every year, hoping that a variety of viewpoints could be expressed in each book. Out of a total of two thousand stories published in 1989, Atwood's job was to pick twenty. She found herself asking some tough questions: "What would be my criteria, if any? How would I be able to tell the best from the merely better? How would I know?" This essay is her attempt to answer these questions.*

M A R G A R E T   A T W O O D

Reading Blind

Whenever I'm asked to talk about what constitutes a "good" story, or what makes one well-written story "better" than another, I begin to feel very uncomfortable. Once you start making lists or devising rules for stories, or for any other kind of writing, some writer will be sure to happen along and casually break every abstract rule you or anyone else has ever thought up, and take your breath away in the process. The word *should* is a dangerous one to use when speaking of writing. It's a kind of challenge to the deviousness and inventiveness and audacity and perversity of the creative spirit. Sooner or later, anyone who has been too free with it will be liable to end up wearing it like a dunce's cap. We don't judge good stories by the application to them of some set of external measurements, as we judge giant pumpkins at the Fall Fair. We judge them by the way they strike us. And that will depend on a great many subjective imponderables, which we lump together under the general heading of taste. . . .

---

[4]O. Henry, pseudonym of William Sydney Porter (1862–1910), famous American author of short stories with elaborate plots and often "trick" endings.

I've spoken of "the voice of the story," which has become a sort of catchall phrase; but by it I intend something more specific: a speaking voice, like the singing voice in music, that moves not across space, across the page, but through time. Surely every written story is, in the final analysis, a score for voice. Those little black marks on the page mean nothing without their retranslation into sound. Even when we read silently, we read with the ear, unless we are reading bank statements.

Perhaps, by abolishing the Victorian practice of family reading and by removing from our school curricula those old standbys, the set memory piece and the recitation, we've deprived both writers and readers of something essential to stories. We've led them to believe that prose comes in visual blocks, not in rhythms and cadences; that its texture should be flat because a page is flat; that written emotion should not be immediate, like a drumbeat, but more remote, like a painted landscape: something to be contemplated. But understatement can be overdone, plainsong can get too plain. When I asked a group of young writers, earlier this year, how many of them ever read their own work aloud, not one of them said she did.

I'm not arguing for the abolition of the eye, merely for the reinstatement of the voice, and for an appreciation of the way it carries the listener along with it at the pace of the story. (Incidentally, reading aloud disallows cheating; when you're reading aloud, you can't skip ahead.)

Our first stories come to us through the air. We hear voices.

Children in oral societies grow up within a web of stories; but so do all children. We listen before we can read. Some of our listening is more like listening in, to the calamitous or seductive voices of the adult world, on the radio or the television or in our daily lives. Often it's an overhearing of things we aren't supposed to hear, eavesdropping on scandalous gossip or family secrets. From all these scraps of voices, from the whispers and shouts that surround us, even from the ominous silences, the unfilled gaps in meaning, we patch together for ourselves an order of events, a plot or plots; these, then, are the things that happen, these are the people they happen to, this is the forbidden knowledge.

We have all been little pitchers with big ears, shooed out of the kitchen when the unspoken is being spoken, and we have probably all been tale-bearers, blurters at the dinner table, unwitting violators of adult rules of censorship. Perhaps this is what writers are: those who never kicked the habit. We remained tale-bearers. We learned to keep our eyes open, but not to keep our mouths shut.

If we're lucky, we may also be given stories meant for our ears, stories intended for us. These may be children's Bible stories, tidied up and simplified and with the vicious bits left out. They may be fairy tales, similarly sugared, although if we are very lucky it will be the straight stuff in both instances, with the slaughters, thunderbolts, and red-hot shoes left in. In any case, these tales will have deliberate, molded shapes, unlike the stories we have patched together for ourselves. They will contain mountains, deserts, talking donkeys, dragons; and, unlike the kitchen stories, they will have definite endings. We are likely to accept these stories as being on the same level of reality as the kitchen stories. It's only when we are older that we are taught to regard one kind of story as real and the other kind as mere invention. This is about the same time we're taught to believe that dentists are useful, and writers are not.

Traditionally, both the kitchen gossips and the readers-out-loud have been mothers or grandmothers, native languages have been mother tongues, and the kinds of stories that are told to children have been called nursery tales or old wives' tales. It struck me as no great coincidence when I learned recently that, when a great number of prominent writers were asked to write about the family member who had had the greatest influence on their literary careers, almost all of them, male as well as female, had picked their mothers. Perhaps this reflects the extent to which North American children have been deprived of their grandfathers, those other great repositories of story; perhaps it will come to change if men come to share in early child care, and we will have old husbands' tales. But as things are, language, including the language of our earliest-learned stories, is a verbal matrix, not a verbal patrix. . . .

Two kinds of stories we first encounter — the shaped tale, the overheard impromptu narrative we piece together — form our idea of what a story is and color the expectations we bring to stories later. Perhaps it's from the collisions between these two kinds of stories — what is often called "real life" (and which writers greedily think of as their "material") and what is sometimes dismissed as "mere literature" or "the kinds of things that happen only in stories" — that original and living writing is generated. A writer with nothing but a formal sense will produce dead work, but so will one whose only excuse for what is on the page is that it really happened. Anyone who has been trapped in a bus beside a nonstop talker graced with no narrative skill or sense of timing can testify to that. Or, as Raymond Chandler[1] says in "The Simple Art of Murder": "All language begins with speech, and the speech of common men at that, but when it develops to the point of becoming a literary medium it only looks like speech."

Expressing yourself is not nearly enough. You must express the story. . . .

Perhaps all I want from a good story is what children want when they listen to tales both told and overheard — which turns out to be a good deal.

They want their attention held, and so do I. I always read to the end, out of some puritanical, and adult, sense of duty owed; but if I start to fidget and skip pages, and wonder if conscience demands I go back and read the middle, it's a sign that the story has lost me, or I have lost it.

They want to feel they are in safe hands, that they can trust the teller. With children this may mean simply that they know the speaker will not betray them by closing the book in the middle, or mixing up the heroes and

---

[1] Raymond Chandler (1888–1959), American novelist and screenwriter whose work featured the popular fictional detective Philip Marlowe.

the villains. With adult readers it's more complicated than that, and involves many dimensions, but there's the same element of keeping faith. Faith must be kept with the language — even if the story is funny, its language must be taken seriously — with the concrete details of locale, mannerism, clothing; with the shape of the story itself. A good story may tease, as long as this activity is foreplay and not used as an end in itself. If there's a promise held out, it must be honored. Whatever is hidden behind the curtain must be revealed at last, and it must be at one and the same time completely unexpected and inevitable. It's in this last respect that the story (as distinct from the novel) comes closest to resembling two of its oral predecessors, the riddle and the joke. Both, or all three, require the same mystifying buildup, the same surprising twist, the same impeccable sense of timing. If we guess the riddle at once, or if we can't guess it because the answer makes no sense — if we see the joke coming, or if the point is lost because the teller gets it muddled — there is failure. Stories can fail in the same way.

But anyone who has ever told, or tried to tell, a story to children will know that there is one thing without which none of the rest is any good. Young children have little sense of dutifulness or of delaying anticipation. They are longing to hear a story, but only if you are longing to tell one. They will not put up with your lassitude or boredom: If you want their full attention, you must give them yours. You must hold them with your glittering eye or suffer the pinches and whispering. You need the Ancient Mariner[2] element, the Scheherazade[3] element: a sense of urgency. *This is the story I must tell; this is the story you must hear.*

Urgency does not mean frenzy. The story can be a quiet story, a story about dismay or missed chances or a wordless revelation. But it must be urgently told. It must be told with as much intentness as if the teller's life depended on it. And, if you are a writer, so it does, because your life as the writer of each particular story is only as long, and as good, as the story itself. Most of those who hear it or read it will never know you, but they will know the story. Their act of listening is its reincarnation. . . .

From listening to the stories of others, we learn to tell our own.

[1989]

JAMES BALDWIN *wrote this account of how he became a writer in his book* Notes of a Native Son *(1955). He admitted that "the most difficult (and most rewarding) thing in my life has been the fact that I was born a Negro and was forced, therefore, to effect some kind of truce with this reality." As his biographer Louis H. Pratt has understood, this "truce" forced Baldwin "into an open confrontation with*

---

[2] In "The Rime of the Ancient Mariner," by Samuel Taylor Coleridge (1772–1834), the Ancient Mariner's "glittering eye" and supernatural tale enthrall his listener.
[3] Wily narrator of *Thousand and One Nights* who uses her stories to entertain her husband, the Sultan, to keep him from killing her.

his experience, enabling him to make an honest assessment of his past. . . . Baldwin the artist has been liberated because he has found a way to use his past and to transform those experiences resulting therefrom into art."

JAMES BALDWIN

Autobiographical Notes

I was born in Harlem thirty-one years ago. I began plotting novels at about the time I learned to read. The story of my childhood is the usual bleak fantasy, and we can dismiss it with the unrestrained observation that I certainly would not consider living it again. In those days my mother was given to the exasperating and mysterious habit of having babies. As they were born, I took them over with one hand and held a book with the other. The children probably suffered, though they have since been kind enough to deny it, and in this way I read *Uncle Tom's Cabin* and *A Tale of Two Cities* over and over and over again; in this way, in fact, I read just about everything I could get my hands on — except the Bible, probably because it was the only book I was encouraged to read. I must also confess that I wrote — a great deal — and my first professional triumph, in any case, the first effort of mine to be seen in print, occurred at the age of twelve or thereabouts, when a short story I had written about the Spanish revolution won some sort of prize in an extremely short-lived church newspaper. I remember the story was censored by the lady editor, though I don't remember why, and I was outraged.

Also wrote plays, and songs, for one of which I received a letter of congratulations from Mayor La Guardia, and poetry, about which the less said, the better. My mother was delighted by all these goings-on, but my father wasn't; he wanted me to be a preacher. When I was fourteen I became a preacher, and when I was seventeen I stopped. Very shortly thereafter I left home. For God knows how long I struggled with the world of commerce and industry — I guess they would say they struggled with *me* — and when I was about twenty-one I had enough done of a novel to get a Saxton Fellowship. When I was twenty-two the fellowship was over, the novel turned out to be unsalable, and I started waiting on tables in a Village[1] restaurant and writing book reviews — mostly, as it turned out, about the Negro problem, concerning which the color of my skin made me automatically an expert. Did another book, in company with photographer Theodore Pelatowski, about the store-front churches in Harlem. This book met exactly the same fate as my first —

---

[1] Greenwich Village, New York City.

fellowship, but no sale. (It was a Rosenwald Fellowship.) By the time I was twenty-four I had decided to stop reviewing books about the Negro problem — which, by this time, was only slightly less horrible in print than it was in life — and I packed my bags and went to France, where I finished, God knows how, *Go Tell It on the Mountain.*

Any writer, I suppose, feels that the world into which he was born is nothing less than a conspiracy against the cultivation of his talent — which attitude certainly has a great deal to support it. On the other hand, it is only because the world looks on his talent with such a frightening indifference that the artist is compelled to make his talent important. So that any writer, looking back over even so short a span of time as I am here forced to assess, finds that the things which hurt him and the things which helped him cannot be divorced from each other; he could be helped in a certain way only because he was hurt in a certain way; and his help is simply to be enabled to move from one conundrum to the next — one is tempted to say that he moves from one disaster to the next. When one begins looking for influences one finds them by the score. I haven't thought much about my own, not enough anyway; I hazard that the King James Bible, the rhetoric of the store-front church, something ironic and violent and perpetually understated in Negro speech — and something of Dickens' love for bravura — have something to do with me today; but I wouldn't stake my life on it. Likewise, innumerable people have helped me in many ways; but finally, I suppose, the most difficult (and most rewarding) thing in my life has been the fact that I was born a Negro and was forced, therefore, to effect some kind of truce with this reality. (Truce, by the way, is the best one can hope for.)

One of the difficulties about being a Negro writer (and this is not special pleading, since I don't mean to suggest that he has it worse than anybody else) is that the Negro problem is written about so widely. The bookshelves groan under the weight of information, and everyone therefore considers himself informed. And this information, furthermore, operates usually (generally, popularly) to reinforce traditional attitudes. Of traditional attitudes there are only two — For or Against — and I, personally, find it difficult to say which attitude has caused me the most pain. I am perfectly aware that the change from ill-will to good-will, however motivated, however imperfect, however expressed, is better than no change at all.

But it is part of the business of the writer — as I see it — to examine attitudes, to go beneath the surface, to tap the source. From this point of view the Negro problem is nearly inaccessible. It is not only written about so widely; it is written about so badly. It is quite possible to say that the price a Negro pays for becoming articulate is to find himself, at length, with nothing to be articulate about. ("You taught me the language," says Caliban to Prospero,[2] "and my profit on't is I know how to curse.") Consider: The tremendous social activity that this problem generates imposes on whites and

---

[2] In Shakespeare's *The Tempest,* the monster Caliban is a servant of the magician Prospero.

Negroes alike the necessity of looking forward, of working to bring about a better day. This is fine, it keeps the waters troubled; it is all, indeed, that has made possible the Negro's progress. Nevertheless, social affairs are not generally speaking the writer's prime concern, whether they ought to be or not; it is absolutely necessary that he establish between himself and these affairs a distance that will allow, at least, for clarity, so that before he can look forward in any meaningful sense, he must first be allowed to take a long look back. In the context of the Negro problem neither whites nor blacks, for excellent reasons of their own, have the faintest desire to look back; but I think that the past is all that makes the present coherent, and further, that the past will remain horrible for exactly as long as we refuse to assess it honestly.

I know, in any case, that the most crucial time in my own development came when I was forced to recognize that I was a kind of bastard of the West; when I followed the line of my past I did not find myself in Europe but in Africa. And this meant that in some subtle way, in a really profound way, I brought to Shakespeare, Bach, Rembrandt, to the stones of Paris, to the cathedral at Chartres, and to the Empire State Building, a special attitude. These were not really my creations, they did not contain my history; I might search in them in vain forever for any reflection of myself. I was an interloper; this was not my heritage. At the same time I had no other heritage which I could possibly hope to use — I had certainly been unfitted for the jungle or the tribe. I would have to appropriate these white centuries, I would have to make them mine — I would have to accept my special attitude, my special place in this scheme — otherwise I would have no place in *any* scheme. What was the most difficult was the fact that I was forced to admit something I had always hidden from myself, which the American Negro has had to hide from himself as the price of his public progress; that I hated and feared white people. This did not mean that I loved black people; on the contrary, I despised them, possibly because they failed to produce Rembrandt. In effect, I hated and feared the world. And this meant, not only that I thus gave the world an altogether murderous power over me, but also that in such a self-destroying limbo I could never hope to write.

One writes out of one thing only — one's own experience. Everything depends on how relentlessly one forces from this experience the last drop, sweet or bitter, it can possibly give. This is the only real concern of the artist, to recreate out of the disorder of life that order which is art. The difficulty then, for me, of being a Negro writer was the fact that I was, in effect, prohibited from examining my own experience too closely by the tremendous demands and the very real dangers of my social situation.

I don't think the dilemma outlined above is uncommon. I do think, since writers work in the disastrously explicit medium of language, that it goes a little way towards explaining why, out of the enormous resources of Negro speech and life, and despite the example of Negro music, prose written by Negroes has been generally speaking so pallid and so harsh. I have not written about being a Negro at such length because I expect that to be my only subject, but only because it was the gate I had to unlock before I could hope to write about anything else. I don't think that the Negro problem in

America can be even discussed coherently without bearing in mind its context; its context being the history, traditions, customs, the moral assumptions and preoccupations of the country; in short, the general social fabric. Appearances to the contrary, no one in America escapes its effects and everyone in America bears some responsibility for it. I believe this the more firmly because it is the overwhelming tendency to speak of this problem as though it were a thing apart. But in the work of Faulkner, in the general attitude and certain specific passages in Robert Penn Warren,[3] and, most significantly, in the advent of Ralph Ellison, one sees the beginnings — at least — of a more genuinely penetrating search. Mr. Ellison, by the way, is the first Negro novelist I have ever read to utilize in language, and brilliantly, some of the ambiguity and irony of Negro life.

About my interests: I don't know if I have any, unless the morbid desire to own a sixteen-millimeter camera and make experimental movies can be so classified. Otherwise, I love to eat and drink — it's my melancholy conviction that I've scarcely ever had enough to eat (this is because it's *impossible* to eat enough if you're worried about the next meal) — and I love to argue with people who do not disagree with me too profoundly, and I love to laugh. I do *not* like bohemia, or bohemians, I do not like people whose principal aim is pleasure, and I do not like people who are *earnest* about anything. I don't like people who like me because I'm a Negro; neither do I like people who find in the same accident grounds for contempt. I love America more than any other country in the world, and, exactly for this reason, I insist on the right to criticize her perpetually. I think all theories are suspect, that the finest principles may have to be modified, or may even be pulverized by the demands of life, and that one must find, therefore, one's own moral center and move through the world hoping that this center will guide one aright. I consider that I have many responsibilities, but none greater than this: to last, as Hemingway says, and get my work done.

I want to be an honest man and a good writer. [1955]

ROBERT BONE *is a folklore critic who is a professor of English at Teachers College, Columbia University. His book* Down Home: Origins of the Afro-American Short Story *(1975) is a pioneering effort to study the fiction of Paul Laurence Dunbar, Charles Chesnutt, Jean Toomer, Zora Neale Hurston, Claude McKay, Langston Hughes, and Arna Bontemps. As the epigraph for his volume, Bone quotes Isak Dinesen: "All sorrows can be borne if you put them into a story."*

---

[3] Robert Penn Warren (1905–1989), American novelist, poet, and critic.

ROBERT BONE

A Folkloric Analysis of Hurston's Spunk and The Gilded Six-Bits

Guilty for having left the folk community in order to pursue her personal ambitions, Hurston seeks atonement through her art. She is determined to avoid stagnation by transcending her milieu, but equally determined to give voice to that milieu, to become its spokesman. The result is her bardic fiction, written in the local-color vein.

Two of these local-color stories, "Spunk" and "Sweat," are closely related to the Brer Rabbit tales. In their central polarities between the cruel and powerful and the weak and oppressed, echoes of the master-slave relationship are unmistakable. Like the animal fables from which they are descended, these tales are exercises in the art of masking. The secret theme of "Spunk" is the violation of black womanhood. . . . The racial implications are effectively disguised by an all-black cast of characters, but the emotional marrow of these tales is a sublimated racial anger.

"Spunk" (*Opportunity*, June 1925) is concerned with two varieties of courage or definitions of manhood. Spunk Banks is a giant of a man who carries off his neighbor's wife and defies him to redress the injury. Joe Kanty, the aggrieved husband, hesitates to challenge his tormentor, but taunted by the village men, he attacks him from behind, only to be shot to death. The men function as a chorus, observing and commenting on the action. At the outset Spunk wins their admiration through his fearlessness, while Joe is despised for his apparent cowardice. In the end, however, a villager proclaims that "Joe was a braver man than Spunk." Amid the derisive shouts of his audience he explains that it requires a greater courage for the weaker to attack the stronger man.

Behind the two antagonists loom the archetypal figures of Brer Rabbit and Brer Bear. Joe Kanty, as his name suggests, would be helpless in an open test of strength; his only hope lies in a surprise attack. The story thus endorses the survival values of subterfuge and treachery, up to and including an assault from behind. Two conflicting codes, one "honorable" or Anglo-Saxon, the other "cowardly" or Negro, are juxtaposed. The story repudiates conventional morality and affirms the outlaw code imposed upon the black man by his social subjugation. Hurston thus invokes the ancient wisdom of the folktale to reconcile the frontier virtues of courage and manliness with the brutal facts of caste.

"The Gilded Six-Bits" (*Story*, August 1933) is Hurston's principal achievement in the short-story form. The tale inaugurates the second and most creative phase of her career, which followed her return to Eatonville in

1932. She now was a mature woman: her ambivalent feelings toward the folk community had been resolved; her adolescent impulse to escape it, mastered. Her curiosity to witness something of the larger world had been appeased, and she was ready to accept her destiny. That destiny, she now perceived, was to embrace her folk experience and give it form. The fruit of self-acceptance was a burst of creativity, beginning with the present story and extending through three novels.

The story is concerned with a crisis in the lives of Joe and Missie May. They have been happily married for a year when Slemmons, an urbanized Negro from Chicago, opens an ice-cream parlor in Eatonville. Dazzled by his fancy clothes and city ways, Missie May forgets herself and takes him as a lover. Joe discovers the deception and drives Slemmons off, but it is many months before he can forgive his thoroughly remorseful wife. Structurally speaking, the woman functions as a pivot between two value systems: the one urban and "sophisticated," the other rural and elemental. At first she chooses falsely, but in the end the deep and abiding values of the countryside prevail.

"The Gilded Six-Bits" is essentially a drama of sin and redemption, a symbolic reenactment of the Fall. As the story opens, Joe and Missie May frolic in prelapsarian innocence. Their pastoral surroundings and simple way of life constitute a Paradise where "all, everything was right." Into this happy Eden comes the Tempter, Slemmons, who proffers not an apple but a ten-dollar gold piece suspended from his watch chain. That the gold should prove to be illusory is Hurston's bitter comment on the Great Migration. Through Slemmons the city is exposed as a repository of false values.

The shallowness of urban culture is conveyed through Slemmons' attitude toward time. In the modern world of progress and improvement, of which the ice-cream parlor is an emblem, time is a commodity. The capitalist ethos, with its obligation to convert time into money, is symbolized by Slemmons' golden watch charm. But the peasant world of Joe and Missie May responds to natural rather than artificial rhythms: "Finally the sun's tide crept upon the shore of night and drowned its hours." In this world, time has a moral and theological rather than economic significance. It is primarily a healing force, repairing the breach that guilt has opened in the human soul.

"The Gilded Six-Bits" thus reveals the central core of Hurston's values. In this story, written in the depths of the Depression, she attacks the acquisitive society from a standpoint not unlike that of the Southern Agrarians. For the first time her social conservatism, inherited from Booker Washington by way of Eatonville, finds in pastoral an appropriate dramatic form. At the same time that her values coalesce, her narrative voice assumes a new authority. A mature style emerges whose metaphors, drawn from folk speech, function as a celebration of agrarian ideals. Having discovered her subject and mastered her idiom, she turns to those longer works of fiction where, for the most part, her achievement as a writer lies.   [1975]

JORGE LUIS BORGES *was interviewed by Roberto Alifano in 1981–1983, and their dialogues were published as* Twenty-four Conversations with Borges *(1984). Alifano's method was simplicity itself: Putting on his tape recorder, he initiated a subject and Borges "willingly and eloquently would answer. He never set any restrictions." Thus, forty cassette tapes were recorded, Borges always a fund of imaginative ideas expressed in "spontaneous yet elegant" language, discoursing on topics such as North American literature, Nathaniel Hawthorne, the detective story, and the tango.*

JORGE LUIS BORGES

The Labyrinth in The Garden of Forking Paths

Translated by Roberto Alifano

Alifano: Borges, I would like to talk with you about [an image which seems] to obsess you and which you repeat throughout your work. I am referring to labyrinths. . . . How did labyrinths enter your literary work; what fascinates you about them?

Borges: Well, I discovered the labyrinth in a book published in France by Garnier that my father had in his library. The book had a very odd engraving that took a whole page and showed a building that resembled an amphitheater. I remember that it had cracks and seemed tall, taller than the cypresses and the men that stood around it. My eyesight was not perfect — I was very myopic — but I thought that if I used a magnifying glass, I would be able to see a minotaur within the building. That labyrinth was, besides, a symbol of bewilderment, a symbol of being lost in life. I believe that all of us, at one time or another, have felt that we are lost, and I saw in the labyrinth the symbol of that condition. Since then, I have held that vision of the labyrinth.

Alifano: Borges, what has always intrigued me about labyrinths is not that people get lost within them, but rather that they are constructions intentionally made to confound us. Don't you think that this concept is odd?

Borges: Yes, it is a very odd idea, the idea of envisioning a builder of labyrinths, the idea of an architect of labyrinths is indeed odd. It is the idea of the father of Icarus, Daedalus, who was the first builder of a labyrinth — the labyrinth of Crete. There is also Joyce's conception, if we are looking for a more literary figure. I have always been puzzled by the labyrinth. It is a very strange idea, an idea which has never left me.

Alifano: Various forms of labyrinths appear in your stories. Labyrinths placed in time, like the one of "The Garden of Forking Paths," where you tell about a lost labyrinth.

Borges: Ah, yes, I do speak of a lost labyrinth in it. Now, a lost labyrinth seems to me to be something magical, and it is because a labyrinth is a place where one loses oneself, a place (in my story) that in turn is lost in time. The idea of a labyrinth which disappears, of a lost labyrinth, is twice as magical. That story is a tale which I imagined to be multiplied or forked in various directions. In that story the reader is presented with all the events leading to the execution of a crime whose intention the reader does not understand. I dedicated that story to Victoria Ocampo. . . .

Alifano: Do you conceive the image of losing ourselves in a labyrinth as a pessimistic view of the future of mankind?

Borges: No, I don't. I believe that in the idea of the labyrinth there is also hope, or salvation; if we were positively sure the universe is a labyrinth, we would feel secure. But it may not be a labyrinth. In the labyrinth there is a center: That terrible center is the minotaur. However, we don't know if the universe has a center; perhaps it doesn't. Consequently, it is probable that the universe is not a labyrinth but simply chaos, and if that is so, we are indeed lost.

Alifano: Yes, if it didn't have a center, it wouldn't be a cosmos but chaos. Do you believe that the universe may have a secret center?

Borges: I don't see why not. It is easy to conceive that it has a center, one that can be terrible, or demonic, or divine. I believe that if we think in those terms unconsciously we are thinking of the labyrinth. That is, if we believe there is a center, somehow we are saved. If that center exists, life is coherent. There are events which surely lead us to think that the universe is a coherent structure. Think, for example, of the rotation of the planets, the seasons of the year, the different stages in our lives. All that leads us to believe that there is a labyrinth, that there is an order, that there is a secret center of the universe, as you have suggested, that there is a great architect who conceived it. But it also leads us to think that it may be irrational, that logic cannot be applied to it, that the universe is unexplainable to us, to mankind — and *that* in itself is a terrifying idea.

Alifano: All those aspects of the labyrinth fascinated you then?

Borges: Yes, all of them. But I have also been attracted by the very word *labyrinth*, which is a beautiful word. It derives from the Greek *labyrinthos*, which initially denotes the shafts and corridors of a mine and that now denotes that strange construction especially built so that people would get lost. Now the English word *maze* is not as enchanting or powerful as the Spanish word *laberinto*. *Maze* also denotes a dance, in which the dancers weave a sort of labyrinth in space and time. Then we find *amazement, to be amazed, to be unamazed,* but I believe that *labyrinth* is the essential word, and it is the one I am drawn to.   [1983]

PETER BROOKS *teaches at Yale University, where he is Tripp Professor of the Humanities and chairman of the French Department. This analysis of Jorge Luis Borges's "The Garden of Forking Paths" is from Brooks's book* Reading for the Plot: Design and Intention in Narrative *(1984). A skilled exponent of narrative theory, Brooks defines plot as "the design and intention of narrative, what shapes a story and gives it a certain direction or intent of meaning." He acknowledges that "plot is so basic to our experience of reading, and indeed to our very articulation of experience in general, that criticism has often passed it over in silence, as too obvious to bear discussion. Yet the obvious can often be the most interesting, as well as the most difficult, to talk about."*

PETER BROOKS

A Narratological Analysis of Borges's The Garden of Forking Paths

Other experimental novelists of our time, perhaps especially in North and South America, have worked more specifically with the parody of traditional plot, developing in part the model furnished by Joyce's use of Homeric plot. John Barth, for instance, constructs *The Sot-Weed Factor* on an elaborate parodic resurrection of eighteenth-century plotting (in the manner of Fielding[1]), very much including plot as machination and conspiracy, which in its modern context is made to seem both an obsolete system of meaning and a paradigm of our desire for epic adventure and its coherent fulfillment. The remarkable energy of Barth's fiction comes in part from the exuberance of his pastiches of past forms: Repeating with ludic variation the outmoded forms gives the narrative its motor force. And one could say similar things about Thomas Pynchon or Julio Cortázar or Manuel Puig or Carlos Fuentes: Fuentes indeed in the novella *Aura* pulls off the tour-de-force of a narrative that proceeds chronologically backward, from death to birth, both parodying traditional forms and showing us something about how we always decoded such forms, from the end.

Such texts have been called metafictions or, more soberly, critical fictions, in that they reflect upon traditional novelistic devices in a highly self-conscious way and use them only in quotation marks, so to speak. This is, of course, not new in the history of the novel. One could argue with some plausibility that the novel as genre incorporates the antinovel — its critical

---

[1] Henry Fielding (1707–1754), English playwright and novelist known for his parodic style.

reflection — from the earliest stages of its history: certainly in *Don Quixote*, perhaps even in the earlier picaresque; and surely from Flaubert onward into Modernism, the self-reflexive ironies of the novelistic enterprise have been a major preoccupation. The difference of the postmodern is, I think, one of degree: a greater explicitness in the abandonment of mimetic claims, a more overt staging of narrative's arbitrariness and lack of authority, a more open playfulness about fictionality. The most exemplary of all the instances one could cite here might well be Jorges Luis Borges, who notes in his preface to *Ficciones* that rather than write books, or commentaries on existing books, he has preferred to write glosses on imaginary books, presenting in each case a problem in the nature of fictions reduced to essential outline.

One Borges story speaks directly to some of the issues of plot that have concerned us. "The Garden of Forking Paths" is in some manner a framed tale. Its outer and ostensible action concerns the need of one Yu Tsun, German-employed spy in Britain, to communicate to his chief in Germany the name of the town (in Belgium) where there is a new British air base, so the Germans can bomb it — before Yu Tsun's voice is silenced by Captain Richard Madden, who is hot in pursuit. How can Yu Tsun make the "report" of his revolver heard in Germany in the minutes left to him? The answer lies in the telephone book, a text that — rather like the Musgrave ritual — will prove capable of a metonymic unpacking that will provide a plot: Shooting the one person with the surname "Albert" listed in the telephone book will, by the instant publicity of the murder, its perpetrator, and its victim, transmit the name of the town — Albert — to Germany. Catching the train to Ashgrove just before Richard Madden arrives at the station — and thus gaining forty minutes in which to perform his crime and send its message — Yu Tsun has defined a problem in space and time, in metaphor (one thing substituted for another), and metonymy (the slippage from one name, or its referent, to another).

At the core of Borges's tale stands the *mise-en-abyme*[2] of this problem, the labyrinth-novel known as *The Garden of Forking Paths*, written by Yu Tsun's ancestor Ts'ui Pên, reconstructed and translated by the sinologist Stephen Albert. This maze of a novel undertakes to represent, not a single plot — following a protagonist through that career defined and delimited by the choices he makes, leading to an outcome — but all possible plots: In "The Garden of Forking Paths," there are no roads not taken, since all can be taken, with wholly different outcomes. The novel — which Yu Tsun has always considered "an indeterminate heap of contradictory drafts" — is in fact a utopia of plotting, creating all possible futures and holding them all in the present, allowing all possible, even contradictory, outcomes to occur. As such, it is "an enormous riddle, or parable, whose theme is time" — the one problem that is never mentioned in its text. As Stephen Albert continues his exposition: "*The Garden of Forking Paths* is an incomplete, but not false, image of the universe as Ts'ui Pên conceived it. In contrast to Newton and Schopen-

---

[2] Story within a story (French).

hauer, your ancestor did not believe in a uniform, absolute time. He believed in an infinite series of time, in a growing, dizzying net of divergent, convergent, and parallel times." Thus the future always exists as one potential present, even as an accomplished past, and when Yu Tsun shoots Stephen Albert, he realizes his earlier maxim: *"The author of an atrocious undertaking ought to imagine that he has already accomplished it, ought to impose upon himself a future as irrevocable as the past."* Yet this dastardly future of treachery and murder (which will entail Yu Tsun's execution as well) is "merely" an escape from the labyrinth, which remains unaffected, which indeed deconstructs this outcome as simply one contingency, a possible *fabula*³ produced by a truly infinite *sjužet*.⁴ Forking paths and crossroads — such as the one where Oedipus unwittingly, yet predictably, killed his father, Laius — are both random and determined. The labyrinth is ultimately that of narrative literature, which is ever replaying time, subverting and perverting it, in order to claim that it is not simply "time lost," always in the knowledge that this loss is the very condition of the meanings that narrative claims to relate.   [1984]

ITALO **CALVINO** *believed that six qualities defined the universal laws of good narrative that future generations of writers and readers would recognize: lightness, quickness, exactitude, visibility, multiplicity, and consistency. In* Six Memos for the Next Millennium *(1992), Calvino stated, "My confidence in the future of literature consists in the knowledge that there are things that only literature can give us, by means specific to it." In this excerpt, he discusses the quality of quickness in good storytelling.*

---

³ A term used by Russian formalist critics to denote the basic events that make up a narrative.

⁴ A term used by Russian formalist critics to describe how the basic events are manipulated or arranged to create a narrative.

ITALO CALVINO

On "Quickness" in Narrative

Translated by Patrick Creagh

I do not wish to say that quickness is a value in itself. Narrative time can also be delaying, cyclic, or motionless. In any case, a story is an operation carried out on the length of time involved, an enchantment that acts on the passing of time, either contracting or dilating it. Sicilian storytellers use the formula "lu cuntu nun mette tempu" (time takes no time in a story) when they want to leave out links or indicate gaps of months or even years. The technique of oral narration in the popular tradition follows functional criteria. It leaves out unnecessary details but stresses repetition: for example, when the tale consists of a series of the same obstacles to be overcome by different people. A child's pleasure in listening to stories lies partly in waiting for things he expects to be repeated: situations, phrases, formulas. Just as in poems and songs the rhymes help to create the rhythm, so in prose narrative there are events that rhyme. The Charlemagne legend is highly effective narrative because it is a series of events that echo each other as rhymes do in a poem.

If during a certain period of my career as a writer I was attracted by folktales and fairytales, this was not the result of loyalty to an ethnic tradition (seeing that my roots are planted in an entirely modern and cosmopolitan Italy), nor the result of nostalgia for things I read as a child (in my family, a child could read only educational books, particularly those with some scientific basis). It was rather because of my interest in style and structure, in the economy, rhythm, and hard logic with which they are told. In working on my transcription of Italian folktales as recorded by scholars of the last century, I found most enjoyment when the original text was extremely laconic. This I tried to convey, respecting the conciseness and at the same time trying to obtain the greatest possible narrative force. See, for instance, number 57 in *Italian Folktales (Fiabe italiane)*:

> A king fell ill and was told by his doctors "Majesty, if you want to get well, you'll have to obtain one of the ogre's feathers. That will not be easy, since the ogre eats every human he sees."
> The king passed the word on to everybody, but no one was willing to go to the ogre. Then he asked one of his most loyal and courageous attendants, who said, "I will go."
> The man was shown the road and told, "On a mountaintop are seven caves, in one of which lives the ogre."
> The man set out and walked until dark, when he stopped at an inn . . .[1]

---

[1] "The Feathered Ogre," translated by George Martin, from *Italian Folktales* (New York: Harcourt Brace Jovanovich, 1956, 1980).

Not a word is said about what illness the king was suffering from, or why on earth an ogre should have feathers, or what those caves were like. But everything mentioned has a necessary function in the plot. The very first characteristic of a folktale is economy of expression. The most outlandish adventures are recounted with an eye fixed on the bare essentials. There is always a battle against time, against the obstacles that prevent or delay the fulfillment of a desire or the repossession of something cherished but lost. Or time can stop altogether, as in the castle of Sleeping Beauty. To bring this about, Charles Perrault has only to write: "Les broches mêmes qui étaient au feu toutes pleines de perdrix et de faisans s'endormirent, et le feu aussi. Tout cela se fit en un moment; les Fées n'étaient pas longues à leur besogne" (Even the spits on the fire, all laden with partridges and pheasants, went to sleep, and the fire along with them. All this happened in a moment: the fairies were not long at their work).

The relativity of time is the subject of a folktale known almost everywhere: a journey to another world is made by someone who thinks it has lasted only a few hours, though when he returns, his village is unrecognizable because years and years have gone by. In early American literature, of course, this was the theme of Washington Irving's "Rip Van Winkle," which acquired the status of a foundation myth for your ever-changing society.

This motif can also be interpreted as an allegory of narrative time and the way in which it cannot be measured against real time. And the same significance can be seen in the reverse operation, in the expanding of time by the internal proliferations from one story to another, which is a feature of oriental storytelling. Scheherazade tells a story in which someone tells a story in which someone tells a story, and so forth. The art that enables Scheherazade to save her life every night consists of knowing how to join one story to another, breaking off at just the right moment — two ways of manipulating the continuity and discontinuity of time. It is a secret of rhythm, a way of capturing time that we can recognize from the very beginning: in the epic by means of the metrical effects of the verse, in prose narrative by those effects that make us eager to know what comes next.

Everybody knows the discomfort felt when someone sets out to tell a joke without being good at it and gets everything wrong, by which I mean, above all, the links and the rhythms. This feeling is evoked in one of Boccaccio's novellas (VI.1), which is in fact devoted to the art of storytelling.

A jovial company of ladies and gentlemen, guests of a Florentine lady in her country house, go for an after-lunch outing to another pleasant place in the neighborhood. To cheer them on their way, one of the men offers to tell a story.

> "Mistress Oretta, if you please, I shall carry you a great part of the way we have to go on horseback, with one of the best stories in the world." "Sir," she replied, "I pray you to do so; that will be most agreeable." Hearing this, master cavalier, who perhaps fared no better with sword at side than with tale on tongue, began his story, which was indeed a very fine one. But what with his repeating of the same

word three or four or six times over, his recapitulations, his "I didn't say that right," his erring in putting one name for another, he spoiled it dreadfully. Also his delivery was very poor, quite out of keeping with the circumstances and the quality of his persons. Mistress Oretta, hearing him, was many times taken with a sweat and a sinking of the heart, as if she were sick and about to die. At last, unable to endure the torment any longer and seeing that the gentleman was entangled in a maze of his own making, she said pleasantly: "Sir, this horse of yours has too hard a trot, and I pray you to set me on my feet again."

The novella is a horse, a means of transport with its own pace, a trot or a gallop according to the distance and the ground it has to travel over; but the speed Boccaccio is talking about is a mental speed. The listed defects of the clumsy storyteller are above all offenses against rhythm, as well as being defects of style, because he does not use the expressions appropriate either to the characters or to the events. In other words, even correctness of style is a question of quick adjustment, of agility of both thought and expression. . . .

[1992]

WILLA CATHER read the fiction of other writers with a shrewd and discriminating eye. In the volume On Writing *(1949), a collection of her critical essays on literature as art, she analyzed the stories of Sarah Orne Jewett and Katherine Mansfield, among other authors. Cather essentially wrote in praise of the simplest spirit in human beings. There is no theory about the art of fiction in her discussion but instead "a vision as level and wide as the landscapes and skyscapes of the West," where she grew up.*

WILLA CATHER

The Stories of Katherine Mansfield

Every writer and critic of discernment who looked into Katherine Mansfield's first volume of short stories must have felt that here was a very individual talent. At this particular time few writers care much about their medium except as a means for expressing ideas. But in Katherine Mansfield one recognized virtuosity, a love for the medium she had chosen.

The qualities of a second-rate writer can easily be defined, but a first-rate writer can only be experienced. It is just the thing in him which escapes analysis that makes him first-rate. One can catalogue all the qualities that he shares with other writers, but the thing that is his very own, his timbre, this cannot be defined or explained any more than the quality of a beautiful speaking voice can be.

It was usually Miss Mansfield's way to approach the major forces of life through comparatively trivial incidents. She chose a small reflector to throw a luminous streak out into the shadowy realm of personal relationships. I feel that personal relationships, especially the uncatalogued ones, the seemingly unimportant ones, interested her most. To my thinking, she never measured herself up so fully as in the two remarkable stories about an English family in New Zealand, "Prelude" and "At the Bay."

I doubt whether any contemporary writer has made one feel more keenly the many kinds of personal relationships which exist in an everyday "happy family" who are merely going on living their daily lives, with no crises or shocks or bewildering complications to try them. Yet every individual in that household (even the children) is clinging passionately to his individual soul, is in terror of losing it in the general family flavour. As in most families, the mere struggle to have anything of one's own, to be one's self at all, creates an element of strain which keeps everybody almost at the breaking-point.

One realizes that even in harmonious families there is this double life: the group life, which is the one we can observe in our neighbour's household, and, underneath, another — secret and passionate and intense — which is the real life that stamps the faces and gives character to the voices of our friends. Always in his mind each member of these social units is escaping, running away, trying to break the net which circumstances and his own affections have woven about him. One realizes that human relationships are the tragic necessity of human life; that they can never be wholly satisfactory, that every ego is half the time greedily seeking them, and half the time pulling away from them. In those simple relationships of loving husband and wife, affectionate sisters, children and grandmother, there are innumerable shades of sweetness and anguish which make up the pattern of our lives day by day, though they are not down in the list of subjects from which the conventional novelist works.

Katherine Mansfield's peculiar gift lay in her interpretation of these secret accords and antipathies which lie hidden under our everyday behavior, and which more than any outward events make our lives happy or unhappy. Had she lived, her development would have gone on in this direction more than in any other. When she touches this New Zealand family and those faraway memories ever so lightly, as in "The Doll's House," there is a magic one does not find in the other stories, fine as some of them are. With this theme the very letters on the page become alive. She communicates vastly more than she actually writes. One goes back and runs through the pages to find the text which made one know certain things about Linda or Burnell or Beryl, and the text is not there — but something was there, all the same — is there, though no typesetter will ever set it. It is this overtone, which is too fine for the printing press and comes through without it, that makes one know that this writer had something of the gift which is one of the rarest things in writing, and quite the most precious. That she had not the happiness of developing her powers to the full is sad enough. She wrote the truth from Fontainebleau a few weeks before she died: *"The old mechanism isn't mine any longer, and I can't control the new."* She had lived through the first stage, had outgrown her young art, so that it seemed false to her in comparison with the new light that was breaking within. The "new mechanism," big enough to convey the new knowledge, she had not the bodily strength to set in motion.

Katherine Mansfield's published *Journal* begins in 1914 and ends in 1922, some months before her death. It is the record of a long struggle with illness, made more cruel by lack of money and by the physical hardships that war conditions brought about in England and France. At the age of twenty-two (when most young people have a secret conviction that they are immortal), she was already ill in a Bavarian *pension*. From the time when she left New Zealand and came back to England to make her own way, there was never an interval in which she did not have to drive herself beyond her strength. She never reached the stage when she could work with a relaxed elbow. In her story "Prelude," when the family are moving, and the storeman lifts the little girl into the dray and tucks her up, he says: "Easy does it." She knew this, long afterward, but she never had a chance to put that method into practice. In all her earlier stories there is something fierce about her attack, as if she took up a new tale in the spirit of overcoming it. "Do or die" is the mood, — indeed, she must have faced that alternative more than once: a girl come back to make her living in London, without health or money or influential friends, — with no assets but talent and pride.

In her volume of stories entitled *Bliss*, published in 1920 (most of them had been written some years before and had appeared in periodicals), she throws down her glove, utters her little challenge in the high language which she knew better than did most of her readers:

> But I tell you, my lord fool, out of this nettle, danger, we pluck this flower, safety.

A fine attitude, youthful and fiery: out of all the difficulties of life and art we will snatch *something*. No one was ever less afraid of the nettle; she was defrauded unfairly of the physical vigour which seems the natural accompaniment of a high and daring spirit.

At thirteen Katherine Mansfield made the long voyage to England with her grandmother, to go to school in London. At eighteen she returned to her own family in Wellington, New Zealand. It was then the struggle against circumstances began. She afterward burned all her early diaries, but it is those I should have liked to read. Exile may be easy to bear for those who have lived their lives. But at eighteen, after four years of London, to be thrown back into a prosperous commercial colony at the end of the world was starvation. There is no homesickness and no hunger so unbearable. Many a young artist would sell his future, all his chances, simply to get back to the world where other people are doing the only things that, to his inexperience, seem worth doing at all.

Years afterward, when Katherine Mansfield had begun to do her best work but was rapidly sinking in vitality, her homesickness stretched all the other way — backwards, for New Zealand and that same crude Wellington. Unpromising as it was for her purpose, she felt that it was the only territory she could claim, in the deepest sense, as her own. The *Journal* tells us how often she went back to it in her sleep. She recounts these dreams at some length: but the entry which makes one realize that homesickness most keenly is a short one, made in Cornwall in 1918:

> *June 20th.* The twentieth of June 1918.
> C'est de la misère.
> Non, pas ça exactement. Il y a quelque chose — une profonde malaise me suive comme un ombre.
> Oh, why write bad French? Why write at all? 11,500 miles are so many — too many by 11,499 3/4 for me.

Eleven thousand five hundred miles is the distance from England to New Zealand.

By this, 1918, she had served her apprenticeship. She had gone through a succession of enthusiasms for this master and that, formed friendships with some of the young writers of her own time. But the person who had freed her from the self-consciousness and affections of the experimenting young writer, and had brought her to her realest self, was not one of her literary friends but, quite simply, her own brother.

He came over in 1915 to serve as an officer. He was younger than she, and she had not seen him for six years. After a short visit with her in London he went to the front, and a few weeks later was killed in action. But he had brought to his sister the New Zealand of their childhood, and out of those memories her best stories were to grow. For the remaining seven years of her life (she died just under thirty-five) her brother seems to have been almost constantly in her mind. A great change comes over her feelings about art; what it is, and why it is. When she prays to become "humble," it is probably the slightly showy quality in the early stories that she begs to be delivered from — and forgiven for. The *Journal* from 1918 on is a record of a readjustment to life, a changing sense of its deepest realities. One of the entries in 1919 recounts a dream in which her brother, "Chummie," came back to her:

> I hear his hat and stick thrown on to the hall-table. He runs up the stairs, three at a time. "Hullo, darling!" But I can't move — I can't move. He puts his arm round me, holding me tightly, and we kiss — a long, firm, family kiss. And the kiss means: We are of the same blood; we have absolute confidence in each other; we love; all is well; nothing can ever come between us.

In the same year she writes:

> Now it is May 1919. Six o'clock. I am sitting in my own room thinking of Mother: I want to cry. But my thoughts are beautiful and full of gaiety. I think of *our* house, *our* garden, *us* children — the lawn, the

gate and Mother coming in. "Children! Children!" I really only ask for time to write it all.

But she did not find too late the things she cared for most. She could not have written that group of New Zealand stories when she first came to London. There had to be a long period of writing for writing's sake. The spontaneous untutored outpouring of personal feeling does not go very far in art. It is only the practiced hand that can make the natural gesture, — and the practiced hand has often to grope its way. She tells us that she made four false starts on "At the Bay," and when she finished the story it took her nearly a month to recover.

The *Journal*, painful though it is to read, is not the story of utter defeat. She had not, as she said, the physical strength to write what she now knew were, to her, the most important things in life. But she had found them, she possessed them, her mind fed on them. On them, and on the language of her greatest poet. (She read Shakespeare continually, when she was too ill to leave her bed.) The inexhaustible richness of that language seems to have been like a powerful cordial, warmed her when bodily nourishment failed her.

Among the stories she left unfinished there is one of singular beauty, written in the autumn of 1922, a few months before her death, the last piece of work she did. She called it "Six Years After": Linda and Burnell grown old, and the boy six years dead. It has the same powerful slightness which distinguishes the other New Zealand stories, and an even deeper tenderness.

Of the first of the New Zealand stories, "Prelude," Miss Mansfield wrote an answer to the inquiries of an intimate friend:

> This is about as much as I can say about it. You know, if the truth were known, I have a perfect passion for the island where I was born. Well, in the early morning there I always remember feeling that this little island has dipped back into the dark blue sea during the night only to rise again at gleam of day, all hung with bright spangles and glittering drops. (When you ran over the dewy grass you positively felt that your feet tasted salt.) I tried to catch that moment — with something of its sparkle and its flavour. And just as on those mornings white milky mists rise and uncover some beauty, then smother it again and then again disclose it, I tried to lift that mist from my people and let them be seen and then to hide them again. . . . It's so difficult to describe all this and it sounds perhaps over-ambitious and vain.

An unpretentious but very suggestive statement of how an artist sets to work, and of the hazy sort of thing that almost surely lies behind and directs interesting or beautiful design. And not with the slighter talents only. Tolstoy himself, one knows from the different lives and letters, went to work in very much the same way. The long novels, as well as the short tales, grew out of little family dramas, personal intolerances and predilections, — promptings not apparent to the casual reader and incomprehensible to the commercial novel-maker.   [1949]

JOHN CHEEVER *wrote this article for the October 30, 1978, issue of* Newsweek. *He was newsworthy at that time because he had just published a collection of short fiction,* The Stories of John Cheever, *which had become a best-seller. Cheever humorously refers to his early financial struggles in the article, but in Susan Cheever's book about her father, she remembers that he was often deeply frustrated by how little he earned from* The New Yorker: *"The money they paid him just wasn't enough to live on — even in the years when we children were in public schools and the family in a rented house." The second part of the* Newsweek *article almost becomes a story about Cheever's suburban neighborhood. Evidently there was nothing in the contemporary scene that he couldn't turn into a narrative.*

JOHN CHEEVER

Why I Write Short Stories

To publish a definitive collection of short stories in one's late 60s seems to me, as an American writer, a traditional and a dignified occasion, eclipsed in no way by the fact that a great many of the stories in my current collection were written in my underwear.

This is not to say that I was ever a Bohemian. Hardly a man is now alive who can remember when Harold Ross edited *The New Yorker* magazine, but I am one of these. The Ross editorial queries were genuinely eccentric. In one short story of mine, I invented a character who returned home from work and changed his clothes before dinner. Ross wrote on the galley margin, "Eh? What's this? Cheever looks to me like a one-suiter." He was so right. At the space rates he paid, I could afford exactly one suit. In the mornings, I dressed in this and took the elevator to a windowless room in the basement where I worked. Here I hung my suit on a hanger, wrote until nightfall when I dressed and returned to our apartment. A great many of my stories were written in boxer shorts.

A collection of short stories appears like a lemon in the current fiction list, which is indeed a garden of love, erotic horseplay, and lewd and ancient family history; but so long as we are possessed by experience that is distinguished by its intensity and its episodic nature, we will have the short story in our literature, and without a literature we will, of course, perish. It was F. R. Leavis who said that literature is the first distinction of a civilized man.

Who reads short stories? one is asked, and I like to think that they are read by men and women in the dentist's office, waiting to be called to the chair; they are read on transcontinental plane trips instead of watching a banal and vulgar film spin out the time between our coasts; they are read by discerning and well-informed men and women who seem to feel that narrative fiction can contribute to our understanding of one another and the sometimes bewildering world around us.

The novel, in all its greatness, demands at least some passing notice of the classical unities, preserving that mysterious link between esthetics and moral fitness; but to have this unyielding antiquity exclude the newness in our ways of life would be regrettable. This newness is known to some of us through "Star Wars," to some of us through the melancholy that follows a fielder's error in the late innings of a ball game. In the pursuit of this newness, contemporary painting seems to have lost the language of the landscape, the still-life, and — most important — the nude. Modern music has been separated from those rhythms and tonalities that are most deeply ingrained in our memories, but literature still possesses the narrative — the story — and one would defend this with one's life.

In the short stories of my esteemed colleagues — and in a few of my own — I find those rented summer houses, those one-night love affairs, and those lost key rings that confound traditional esthetics. We are not a nomadic people, but there is more than a hint of this spirit of our great country — and the short story is the literature of the nomad.

I like to think that the view of a suburban street that I imagine from my window would appeal to a wanderer or to someone familiar with loneliness. Here is a profoundly moving display of nostalgia, vision, and love, none of it more than 30 years old, including most of the trees. Here are white columns from the manorial South, brick and timber walls from Elizabethan England, saltbox houses from our great maritime past, and flat-roofed echoes of Frank Lloyd Wright and his vision of a day when we would all enjoy solar heating, serene and commodious interiors, and peace on earth.

The lots are $1\frac{1}{2}$ acres, flowers and vegetables grow in the yards, and here and there one finds, instead of tomatoes, robust stands of cannabis with its feathery leaf. Here, in this victorious domesticity, the principle crop is a hazardous drug. And what do I see hanging in the Hartshores' clothes-yard but enough seasoning marijuana to stone a regiment.

Is forgetfulness some part of the mysteriousness of life? If I speak to Mr. Hartshore about his cannabis crop, will he tell me that the greatness of Chinese civilization stood foursquare on the fantasies of opium? But it is not I who will speak to Mr. Hartshore. I will be Charlie Dilworth, a very abstemious man who lives in the house next door. He has a No Smoking sign on his front lawn, and his passionate feelings about marijuana have been intelligently channeled into a sort of reverse blackmail.

I hear them litigating late one Saturday afternoon when I have come back from playing touch football with my sons. The light is going. It is autumn. Charlie's voice is loud and clear and can be heard by anyone interested. "You keep your dogs off my lawn, you cook your steaks in the house, you keep your record player down, you keep your swimming-pool filter off in the evenings, and you keep your window shades drawn. Otherwise, I'll report your drug crop to the police and with my wife's uncle sitting as judge this month you'll get at least six months in the can for criminal possession."

They part. Night falls. Here and there a housewife, apprehending the first frost, takes in her house plants while from an Elizabethan, a Nantucket, and a Frank Lloyd Wright chimney comes the marvelous fragrance of wood smoke. You can't put this scene in a novel. [1978]

ANTON CHEKHOV *described his theories of literature and his practice as a storyteller in countless letters to his family and friends. He was not a systematic critic, and he did not necessarily follow his own advice to other writers. Brevity and concentration on a few essentials of scene and character were the essence of his technique, but he was not always as drastically laconic in his stories as his letters suggest. What is consistently clear in his advice to other writers is his own untiring compassion and his desire to speak honestly in his efforts to help them. He wrote in his notebook, "Man will only become better when you make him see what he is like."*

These letters are to his older brother, his publisher, and a younger author whose work he admired.

ANTON CHEKHOV

Technique in Writing the Short Story

Translated by Constance Garnett

FROM A LETTER TO ALEXANDER P. CHEKHOV

In my opinion a true description of Nature should be very brief and have a character of relevance. Commonplaces such as, "the setting sun bathing in the waves of the darkening sea, poured its purple gold, etc." — "the swallows flying over the surface of the water twittered merrily" — such commonplaces one ought to abandon. In descriptions of Nature one ought to seize upon the little particulars, grouping them in such a way that, in reading, when you shut your eyes, you get a picture.

For instance, you will get the full effect of a moonlight night if you write that on the mill-dam a little glowing star-point flashed from the neck of a broken bottle, and the round, black shadow of a dog, or a wolf, emerged and ran, etc. Nature becomes animated if you are not squeamish about employing comparisons of her phenomena with ordinary human activities, etc.

In the sphere of psychology, details are also the thing. God preserve us from commonplaces. Best of all is it to avoid depicting the hero's state of mind; you ought to try to make it clear from the hero's actions. It is not necessary to portray many characters. The center of gravity should be in two persons: him and her.   [1886]

FROM A LETTER TO ALEKSEY S. SUVORIN

You abuse me for objectivity, calling it indifference to good and evil, lack of ideals and ideas, and so on. You would have me, when I describe horse-thieves, say: "Stealing horses is an evil." But that has been known for ages without my saying so. Let the jury judge them; it's my job simply to show what sort of people they are. I write: You are dealing with horse-thieves, so let me tell you that they are not beggars but well-fed people, that they are people of a special cult, and that horse-stealing is not simply theft but a passion. Of course it would be pleasant to combine art with a sermon, but for me personally it is extremely difficult and almost impossible, owing to the conditions of technique. You see, to depict horse-thieves in seven hundred lines I must all the time speak and think in their tone and feel in their spirit, otherwise, if I introduce subjectivity, the image becomes blurred and the story will not be as compact as all short stories ought to be. When I write, I reckon entirely upon the reader to add for himself the subjective elements that are lacking in the story.   [1890]

FROM A LETTER TO MAXIM GORKY

More advice: when reading the proofs, cross out a host of terms qualifying nouns and verbs. You have so many such terms that the reader's mind finds it a task to concentrate on them, and he soon grows tired. You understand it at once when I say, "The man sat on the grass"; you understand it because it is clear and makes no demands on the attention. On the other hand, it is not easily understood, and it is difficult for the mind, if I write, "A tall, narrow-chested, middle-sized man, with a red beard, sat on the green grass, already trampled by pedestrians, sat silently, shyly, and timidly looked about him." That is not immediately grasped by the mind, whereas good writing should be grasped at once — in a second.   [1899]

KATE CHOPIN *made a number of translations, mostly of stories by Guy de Maupassant, and she published several essays on literature in St. Louis periodicals. She wrote about the influence of Maupassant on her fiction in response to an invitation from the editor of the* Atlantic Monthly *in 1896. He returned her first version of the essay, however, advising her to "set forth the matter directly." Her revised version was later included in the magazine with the title "In the Confidence of a Story-Teller," but the section describing how she first encountered Maupassant's tales and the impression they made on her was dropped, perhaps because she spoke so enthusiastically about the French writer's escape "from tradition and authority." This portion of the essay is reprinted from the manuscript included in Volume 2 of* The Complete Works of Kate Chopin *(1969).*

K A T E   C H O P I N

How I Stumbled upon Maupassant

About eight years ago there fell accidentally into my hands a volume of Maupassant's tales. These were new to me. I had been in the woods, in the fields, groping around; looking for something big, satisfying, convincing, and finding nothing but — myself; a something neither big nor satisfying but wholly convincing. It was at this period of my emerging from the vast solitude in which I had been making my own acquaintance, that I stumbled upon Maupassant. I read his stories and marvelled at them. Here was life, not fiction; for where were the plots, the old fashioned mechanism and stage trapping that in a vague, unthinking way I had fancied were essential to the art of story making? Here was a man who had escaped from tradition and authority, who had entered into himself and looked out upon life through his own being and with his own eyes; and who, in a direct and simple way, told us what he saw. When a man does this, he gives us the best that he can; something valuable for it is genuine and spontaneous. He gives us his impressions. Someone told me the other day that Maupassant had gone out of fashion. I was not grieved to hear it. He has never seemed to me to belong to the multitude, but rather to the individual. He is not one whom we gather in crowds to listen to — whom we follow in procession — with beating of brass instruments. He does not move us to throw ourselves into the throng — having the integral of an unthinking whole to shout his praise. I even like to think that he appeals to me alone. You probably like to think that he reaches you exclusively. A whole multitude may be secretly nourishing the belief in regard to him for all I know. Someway I like to cherish the delusion that he has spoken to no one else so directly, so intimately as he does to me. He did not say, as another might have done, "do you see these are charming stories of mine? take them into your closet — study them closely — mark their combination — observe the method, the manner of their putting together — and if ever you are moved to write stories you can do no better than to imitate."

[1896]

STEPHEN CRANE *wrote about the wreck of the* Commodore *in the article* "Stephen Crane's Own Story" *in the* New York Press *on January 7, 1897. At that time arms and provisions were being smuggled from Florida to Cuba to aid the insurrection against Spanish rule. Crane boarded the* Commodore *in Jacksonville on December 31, 1896. The ship was loaded with a cargo of rifles and ammunition. As the scholar Olov W. Fryckstedt explained, Crane "looked forward to a long period of unknown adventures and exciting dangers in the Cuban mountains. But during the night of January 1 the ship foundered fifteen miles off the coast of Florida after a mysterious explosion in the engine room." The first part of Crane's newspaper story describes the loading of the ship, the peril of sandbars, the explosion in the engine room, and the lowering of the lifeboats. Then, with the ship's "whistle of despair," it became clear to everyone on board that the situation was hopeless. The bustling action before the shipwreck is the substance of Crane's newspaper report; his thirty desperate hours afterward in the 10-foot dinghy became the story of "The Open Boat."*

STEPHEN CRANE

The Sinking of the Commodore

A WHISTLE OF DESPAIR

Now the whistle of the *Commodore* had been turned loose, and if there ever was a voice of despair and death, it was in the voice of this whistle. It had gained a new tone. It was as if its throat was already choked by the water, and this cry on the sea at night, with a wind blowing the spray over the ship, and the waves roaring over the bow, and swirling white along the decks, was to each of us probably a song of man's end.

It was now that the first mate showed a sign of losing his grip. To us who were trying in all stages of competence and experience to launch the lifeboat he raged in all terms of fiery satire and hammerlike abuse. But the boat moved at last and swung down toward the water.

Afterward, when I went aft, I saw the captain standing, with his arm in a sling, holding on to a stay with his one good hand and directing the launching of the boat. He gave me a five-gallon jug of water to hold, and asked me what I was going to do. I told him what I thought was about the proper thing, and he told me then that the cook had the same idea, and ordered me to go forward and be ready to launch the ten-foot dinghy.

IN THE TEN-FOOT DINGHY

I remember well that he turned then to swear at a colored stoker who was prowling around, done up in life preservers until he looked like a feather bed. I went forward with my five-gallon jug of water, and when the captain came we launched the dinghy, and they put me over the side to fend her off from the ship with an oar.

They handed me down the water jug, and then the cook came into the boat, and we sat there in the darkness, wondering why, by all our hopes of future happiness, the captain was so long in coming over to the side and ordering us away from the doomed ship.

The captain was waiting for the other boat to go. Finally he hailed in the darkness: "Are you all right, Mr. Graines?"

The first mate answered: "All right, sir."

"Shove off, then," cried the captain.

The captain was just about to swing over the rail when a dark form came forward and a voice said, "Captain, I go with you."

The captain answered: "Yes, Billy; get in."

HIGGINS LAST TO LEAVE SHIP

It was Billy Higgins, the oiler. Billy dropped into the boat and a moment later the captain followed, bringing with him an end of about forty yards of lead line. The other end was attached to the rail of the ship.

As we swung back to leeward the captain said: "Boys, we will stay right near the ship till she goes down."

This cheerful information, of course, filled us all with glee. The line kept us headed properly into the wind, and as we rode over the monstrous waves we saw upon each rise the swaying lights of the dying *Commodore*.

When came the gray shade of dawn, the form of the *Commodore* grew slowly clear to us as our little ten-foot boat rose over each swell. She was floating with such an air of buoyancy that we laughed when we had time, and said, "What a gag it would be on those other fellows if she didn't sink at all."

But later we saw men aboard of her, and later still they began to hail us.

HELPING THEIR MATES

I had forgot to mention that previously we had loosened the end of the lead line and dropped much further to leeward. The men on board were a mystery to us, of course, as we had seen all the boats leave the ship. We rowed back to the ship, but did not approach too near, because we were four men in a ten-foot boat, and we knew that the touch of a hand on our gunwale would assuredly swamp us.

The first mate cried out from the ship that the third boat had foundered alongside. He cried that they had made rafts, and wished us to tow them.

The captain said, "All right."

Their rafts were floating astern. "Jump in!" cried the captain, but there was a singular and most harrowing hesitation. There were five white men and two negroes. This scene in the gray light of morning impressed one as would a view into some place where ghosts move slowly. These seven men on the stern of the sinking *Commodore* were silent. Save the words of the mate to the captain there was no talk. Here was death, but here also was a most singular and indefinable kind of fortitude.

Four men, I remember, clambered over the railing and stood there watching the cold, steely sheen of the sweeping waves.

"Jump," cried the captain again.

The old chief engineer first obeyed the order. He landed on the outside raft and the captain told him how to grip the raft and he obeyed as promptly and as docilely as a scholar in riding school.

THE MATE'S MAD PLUNGE

A stoker followed him, and then the first mate threw his hands over his head and plunged into the sea. He had no life belt and for my part, even when he did this horrible thing, I somehow felt that I could see in the expression of his hands, and in the very toss of his head, as he leaped thus to death, that it was rage, rage, rage unspeakable that was in his heart at the time.

And then I saw Tom Smith, the man who was going to quit filibustering after this expedition, jump to a raft and turn his face toward us. On board the *Commodore* three men strode, still in silence and with their faces turned toward us. One man had his arms folded and was leaning against the deckhouse. His feet were crossed, so that the toe of his left foot pointed downward. There they stood gazing at us, and neither from the deck nor from the rafts was a voice raised. Still was there this silence.

TRIED TO TOW THE RAFTS

The colored stoker on the first raft threw us a line and we began to tow. Of course, we perfectly understood the absolute impossibility of any such thing; our dinghy was within six inches of the water's edge, there was an enormous sea running, and I knew that under the circumstances a tugboat would have no light task in moving these rafts.

But we tried it, and would have continued to try it indefinitely, but that something critical came to pass. I was at an oar and so faced the rafts. The cook controlled the line. Suddenly the boat began to go backward and then we saw this negro on the first raft pulling on the line hand over hand and drawing us to him.

He had turned into a demon. He was wild — wild as a tiger. He was crouched on this raft and ready to spring. Every muscle of him seemed to be turned into an elastic spring. His eyes were almost white. His face was the face of a lost man reaching upward, and we knew that the weight of his hand on our gunwale doomed us.

THE COMMODORE SINKS

The cook let go of the line. We rowed around to see if we could not get a line from the chief engineer, and all this time, mind you, there were no shrieks, no groans, but silence, silence and silence, and then the *Commodore* sank.

She lurched to windward, then swung afar back, righted and dove into the sea, and the rafts were suddenly swallowed by this frightful maw of the ocean. And then by the men on the ten-foot dinghy were words said that were still not words — something far beyond words.

The lighthouse of Mosquito Inlet stuck up above the horizon like the point of a pin. We turned our dinghy toward the shore.

The history of life in an open boat for thirty hours would no doubt be instructive for the young, but none is to be told here and now. For my part I would prefer to tell the story at once, because from it would shine the splendid manhood of Captain Edward Murphy and of William Higgins, the oiler, but let it suffice at this time to say that when we were swamped in the surf and making the best of our way toward the shore the captain gave orders amid the wildness of the breakers as clearly as if he had been on the quarter deck of a battleship.

John Kitchell of Daytona came running down the beach, and as he ran the air was filled with clothes. If he had pulled a single lever and undressed, even as the fire horses harness, he could not seem to me to have stripped with more speed. He dashed into the water and dragged the cook. Then he went after the captain, but the captain sent him to me, and then it was that he saw Billy Higgins lying with his forehead on sand that was clear of the water, and he was dead.   [1897]

RALPH ELLISON *gave an interview for the "Art of Fiction" series of the* Paris Review *that was reprinted in his volume of essays,* Shadow and Act *(1964). In the introduction to that book he said that what is basic to the fiction writer's confrontation with the world is "converting experience into symbolic action. Good fiction is made of that which is real, and reality is difficult to come by. So much of it depends upon the individual's willingness to discover his true self, upon his defining himself — for the time being at least — against his background."*

RALPH ELLISON

The Influence of Folklore on Battle Royal

Interviewer: Can you give us an example of the use of folklore in your own novel?

Ellison: Well, there are certain themes, symbols, and images which are based on folk material. For example, there is the old saying amongst Negroes: If you're black, stay back; if you're brown, stick around; if you're white, you're right. And there is the joke Negroes tell on themselves about their being so black they can't be seen in the dark. In my book this sort of thing was merged with the meanings which blackness and light have long had in Western mythology: evil and goodness, ignorance and knowledge, and so on. In my novel the narrator's development is one through blackness to light; that is, from ignorance to enlightenment: invisibility to visibility. He leaves the South and goes North; this, as you will notice in reading Negro folktales, is always the road to freedom — the movement upward. You have the same thing again when he leaves his underground cave for the open.

It took me a long time to learn how to adapt such examples of myth into my work — also ritual. The use of ritual is equally a vital part of the creative process. I learned a few things from Eliot, Joyce, and Hemingway, but not how to adapt them. When I started writing, I knew that in both *The Waste Land*[1] and *Ulysses*[2] ancient myth and ritual were used to give form and significance to the material; but it took me a few years to realize that the myths and rites which we find functioning in our everyday lives could be used in the same way. In my first attempt at a novel — which I was unable to complete — I began by trying to manipulate the simple structural unities of *beginning, middle,* and *end,* but when I attempted to deal with the psychological strata — the images, symbols, and emotional configurations — of the experience at hand, I discovered that the unities were simply cool points of stability on which one could suspend the narrative line — but beneath the surface of apparently rational human relationships there seethed a chaos before which I was helpless. People rationalize what they shun or are incapable of dealing with; these superstitions and their rationalizations become ritual as they govern behavior. The rituals become social forms, and it is one of the functions of the artist to recognize them and raise them to the level of art.

I don't know whether I'm getting this over or not. Let's put it this way: Take the "Battle Royal" passage in my novel, where the boys are blindfolded and forced to fight each other for the amusement of the white observers. This

---

[1] Long, extremely influential poem (1922) by T. S. Eliot (1888–1965).
[2] Experimental novel (1922) by James Joyce (1882–1941).

is a vital part of behavior pattern in the South, which both Negroes and whites thoughtlessly accept. It is a ritual in preservation of caste lines, a keeping of taboo to appease the gods and ward off bad luck. It is also the initiation ritual to which all greenhorns are subjected. This passage which states what Negroes will see I did not have to invent; the patterns were already there in society, so that all I had to do was present them in a broader context of meaning. In any society there are many rituals of situation which, for the most part, go unquestioned. They can be simple or elaborate, but they are the connective tissue between the work of art and the audience.

Interviewer: Do you think a reader unacquainted with this folklore can properly understand your work?

Ellison: Yes, I think so. It's like jazz; there's no inherent problem which prohibits understanding but the assumptions brought to it. We don't all dig Shakespeare uniformly, or even *Little Red Riding Hood.* The understanding of art depends finally upon one's willingness to extend one's humanity and one's knowledge of human life. I noticed, incidentally, that the Germans, having no special caste assumptions concerning American Negroes, dealt with my work simply as a novel. I think Americans will come to view it that way in twenty years — if it's around that long.

Interviewer: Don't you think it will be?

Ellison: I doubt it. It's not an important novel. I failed of eloquence, and many of the immediate issues are rapidly fading away. If it does last, it will be simply because there are things going on in its depth that are of more permanent interest than on its surface. I hope so, anyway.   [1964]

RICHARD ELLMANN *was the author of prize-winning biographies of the Irish writers James Joyce and Oscar Wilde. As a biographer Ellmann seemed to have possessed an encyclopedic knowledge of his subject, yet his grasp of the facts of literary production was balanced by his brilliant use of these facts to suggest his sensitive perception of how the creative process functioned in an author's life. Instead of emphasizing biographical details in his discussion of "The Dead," Ellmann perceptively used the story to illuminate a stage of Joyce's development as an artist. This excerpt is from Ellmann's* James Joyce: New and Revised Edition *(1982).*

RICHARD ELLMANN

A Biographical Perspective on Joyce's The Dead

And now Gabriel and Gretta go to the Hotel Gresham, Gabriel fired by his living wife and Gretta drained by the memory of her dead lover. He learns for the first time of the young man in Galway, whose name Joyce has deftly altered from Sonny or Michael Bodkin to Michael Furey. The new name implies, like the contrast of the militant Michael and the amiable Gabriel, that violent passion is in her Galway past, not in her Dublin present. Gabriel tries to cut Michael Furey down. "What was he?" he asks, confident that his own profession of language teacher (which of course he shared with Joyce) is superior; but she replies, "He was in the gasworks," as if this profession was as good as any other. Then Gabriel tries again, "And what did he die of so young, Gretta? Consumption, was it?" He hopes to register the usual expressions of pity, but Gretta silences and terrifies him by her answer, "I think he died for me."[1] Since Joyce has already made clear that Michael Furey was tubercular, this answer of Gretta has a fine ambiguity. It asserts the egoism of passion, and unconsciously defies Gabriel's reasonable question.

Now Gabriel begins to succumb to his wife's dead lover, and becomes a pilgrim to emotional intensities outside of his own experience. From a biographical point of view, these final pages compose one of Joyce's several tributes to his wife's artless integrity. Nora Barnacle, in spite of her defects of education, was independent, unself-conscious, instinctively right. Gabriel acknowledges the same coherence in his own wife, and he recognizes in the west of Ireland, in Michael Furey, a passion he has himself always lacked. "Better pass boldly into the other world, in the full glory of some passion, than fade and wither dismally with age," Joyce makes Gabriel think. Then comes that strange sentence in the final paragraph: "The time had come for him to set out on his journey westward." The cliché runs that journeys westward are towards death, but the west has taken on a special meaning in the story. Gretta Conroy's west is the place where life has been lived simply and passionately. The context and phrasing of the sentence suggest that Gabriel is on the edge of sleep, and half-consciously accepts what he has hitherto scorned, the possibility of an actual trip to Connaught. What the

---

[1] Adaline Glasheen has discovered here an echo of Yeats's nationalistic play, *Cathleen ni Houlihan* (1902), where the old woman who symbolizes Ireland sings a song of "yellow-haired Donough that was hanged in Galway." When she is asked, "What was it brought him to his death?" she replies, "He died for love of me; many a man has died for love of me." [Ellmann's note]

sentence affirms, at last, on the level of feeling, is the west, the primitive, untutored, impulsive country from which Gabriel had felt himself alienated before; in the story, the west is paradoxically linked also with the past and the dead. It is like Aunt Julia Morkan who, though ignorant, old, grey-skinned, and stupefied, seizes in her song at the party "the excitement of swift and secure flight."

The tone of the sentence, "The time had come for him to set out on his journey westward," is somewhat resigned. It suggests a concession, a relinquishment, and Gabriel is conceding and relinquishing a good deal — his sense of the importance of civilized thinking, of continental tastes, of all those tepid but nice distinctions on which he has prided himself. The bubble of his self-possession is pricked; he no longer possesses himself, and not to possess oneself is in a way a kind of death. It is a self-abandonment not unlike Furey's, and through Gabriel's mind runs the imagery of Calvary. He imagines the snow on the cemetery at Oughterard, lying "thickly drifted on the crooked crosses and headstones, on the spears of the little gate, on the barren thorns." He thinks of Michael Furey who, Gretta has said, died for her, and envies him his sacrifice for another kind of love than Christ's. To some extent Gabriel too is dying for her, in giving up what he had most valued in himself, all that holds him apart from the simpler people at the party. He feels close to Gretta through sympathy if not through love; now they are both past youth, beauty, and passion; he feels close also to her dead lover, another lamb burnt on her altar, though she too is burnt now; he feels no resentment, only pity. In his own sacrifice of himself he is conscious of a melancholy unity between the living and the dead.

Gabriel, who has been sick of his own country, finds himself drawn inevitably into a silent tribute to it of much more consequence than his spoken tribute to the party. He has had illusions of the rightness of a way of life that should be outside of Ireland; but through this experience with his wife he grants a kind of bondage, of acceptance, even of admiration to a part of the country and a way of life that are most Irish. Ireland is shown to be stronger, more intense than he. At the end of *A Portrait of the Artist*, too, Stephen Dedalus, who has been so resolutely opposed to nationalism, makes a similar concession when he interprets his departure from Ireland as an attempt to forge a conscience for his race. . . .

That Joyce at the age of twenty-five and -six should have written this story ought not to seem odd. Young writers reach their greatest eloquence in dwelling upon the horrors of middle age and what follows it. But beyond this proclivity which he shared with others, Joyce had a special reason for writing the story of "The Dead" in 1906 and 1907. In his own mind he had thoroughly justified his flight from Ireland, but he had not decided the question of where he would fly *to*. In Trieste and Rome he had learned what he had unlearned in Dublin, to be a Dubliner. As he had written his brother from Rome with some astonishment, he felt humiliated when anyone attacked his "impoverished country." "The Dead" is his first song of exile.   [1982]

WILLIAM FAULKNER *was writer-in-residence at the University of Virginia in 1957 and 1958. During that time he encouraged students to ask questions about his writing. He answered more than 2,000 queries on everything from spelling to the nature of man, including a series of questions about "A Rose for Emily" addressed to him at different interviews by students of Frederick Gwynn and Joseph Blotner. These professors later edited the book* Faulkner in the University *(1959), in which the following excerpt first appeared.*

WILLIAM FAULKNER

The Meaning of A Rose for Emily

Interviewer: What is the meaning of the title "A Rose for Emily"?

Faulkner: Oh, it's simply the poor woman had had no life at all. Her father had kept her more or less locked up and then she had a lover who was about to quit her, she had to murder him. It was just "A Rose for Emily" — that's all.

Interviewer: I was wondering, one of your short stories, "A Rose for Emily," what ever inspired you to write this story . . . ?"

Faulkner: That to me was another sad and tragic manifestation of man's condition in which he dreams and hopes, in which he is in conflict with himself or with his environment or with others. In this case there was the young girl with a young girl's normal aspirations to find love and then a husband and a family, who was brow-beaten and kept down by her father, a selfish man who didn't want her to leave home because he wanted a house-keeper, and it was a natural instinct of — repressed which — you can't repress it — you can mash it down but it comes up somewhere else and very likely in a tragic form, and that was simply another manifestation of man's injustice to man, of the poor tragic human being struggling with its own heart, with others, with its environment, for the simple things which all human beings want. In that case it was a young girl that just wanted to be loved and to love and to have a husband and a family.

Interviewer: And that purely came from your imagination?

Faulkner: Well, the story did but the condition is there. It exists. I didn't invent that condition, I didn't invent the fact that young girls dream of someone to love and children and a home, but the story of what her own particular tragedy was was invented, yes. . . .

Interviewer: Sir, it has been argued that "A Rose for Emily" is a criticism of the North, and others have argued saying that it is a criticism of the South. Now, could this story, shall we say, be more properly classified as a criticism of the times?

Faulkner: Now that I don't know, because I was simply trying to write about people. The writer uses environment — what he knows — and if there's a symbolism in which the lover represented the North and the woman who murdered him represents the South, I don't say that's not valid and not there, but it was no intention of the writer to say, Now let's see, I'm going to write a piece in which I will use a symbolism for the North and another symbol for the South, that he was simply writing about people, a story which he thought was tragic and true, because it came out of the human heart, the human aspiration, the human — the conflict of conscience with glands, with the Old Adam. It was a conflict not between the North and the South so much as between, well you might say, God and Satan.

Interviewer: Sir, just a little more on that thing. You say it's a conflict between God and Satan. Well, I don't quite understand what you mean. Who is — did one represent the ——

Faulkner: The conflict was in Miss Emily, that she knew that you do not murder people. She had been trained that you do not take a lover. You marry, you don't take a lover. She had broken all the laws of her tradition, her background, and she had finally broken the law of God too, which says you do not take human life. And she knew she was doing wrong, and that's why her own life was wrecked. Instead of murdering one lover, and then to go and take another and when she used him up to murder him, she was expiating her crime.

Interviewer: Was the "Rose for Emily" an idea or a character? Just how did you go about it?

Faulkner: That came from a picture of the strand of hair on the pillow. It was a ghost story. Simply a picture of a strand of hair on the pillow in the abandoned house. [1959]

MAVIS GALLANT *developed her ideas about "What Is Style?" in her* Paris Notebooks *published in 1985. There she admitted that she was unable to analyze the style of her own short fiction because she was too close to it: "The manner of writing, the thread spun out of the story itself, may with time have grown instinctive. I know that the thread must hold from beginning to end, and that I would like to be invisible."*

MAVIS GALLANT

What Is Style?

I do not reread my own work unless I have to; I fancy no writer does. The reason why, probably, is that during the making of the story every line has been read and rewritten and read again to the point of glut. . . . Leaving aside the one analysis closed to me, of my own writing, let me say what style is *not*: it is not a last-minute addition to prose, a charming and universal slipcover, a coat of paint used to mask the failings of a structure. Style is inseparable from structure, part of the conformation of whatever the author has to say. What he says — this is what fiction is about — is that something is taking place and that nothing lasts. Against the sustained tick of a watch, fiction takes the measure of a life, a season, a look exchanged, the turning point, desire as brief as a dream, the grief and terror that after childhood we cease to express. The lie, the look, the grief are without permanence. The watch continues to tick where the story stops.

A loose, a wavering, a slipshod, an affected, a false way of transmitting even a fragment of this leaves the reader suspicious: What is this too elaborate or too simple language hiding? What is the author trying to disguise? Probably he doesn't know. He has shown the works of the watch instead of its message. He may be untalented, just as he may be a gifted author who for some deeply private reason (doubt, panic, the pressures of a life unsuited to writing) has taken to rearranging the works in increasingly meaningless patterns. All this is to say that content, meaning, intention and form must make up a whole, and must above all have a reason to be.

There are rules of style. By applying them doggedly any literate, ambitious and determined person should be able to write like Somerset Maugham. Maugham was conscious of his limitations and deserves appreciation on that account: "I knew that I had no lyrical quality, I had a small vocabulary . . . I had little gift for metaphors; the original or striking simile seldom occurred to me. Poetic flights and the great imaginative sweep were beyond my powers." He decided, sensibly, to write "as well as my natural defects allowed" and to aim at "lucidity, simplicity and euphony." The chance that some other indispensable quality had been overlooked must have been blanketed by a lifetime of celebrity. Now, of course, first principles are there to be heeded or, at the least, considered with care; but no guided tour of literature, no commitment to the right formula or to good taste (which is changeable anyway), can provide, let alone supplant, the inborn vitality and tension of living prose.

Like every other form of art, literature is no more and nothing less than a matter of life and death. The only question worth asking about a story — or a poem, or a piece of sculpture, or a new concert hall — is, "Is it dead or alive?" If a work of the imagination needs to be coaxed into life, it is better scrapped and forgotten. Working to rule, trying to make a barely breathing work of fiction simpler and more lucid and more euphonious merely injects into the desperate author's voice a tone of suppressed hysteria, the result of what E. M. Forster called "confusing order with orders." And then, how reliable are the rules? Listen to Pablo Picasso's rejection of a fellow-artist: "He looks up at the sky and says, 'Ah, the sky is blue,' and he paints a blue sky. Then he takes another look and says, 'The sky is mauve, too,' and he adds some mauve. The next time he looks he notices a trace of pink, and he adds a little pink." It sounds a proper mess, but Picasso was talking about Pierre Bonnard. As soon as we learn the names, the blues, mauves and pinks acquire a meaning, a reason to be. Picasso was right, but only in theory. In the end, everything depends on the artist himself.

Style in writing, as in painting, is the author's thumbprint, his mark. I do not mean that it establishes him as finer or greater than other writers, though that can happen too. I am thinking now of prose style as a writer's armorial bearings, his name and address. In a privately printed and libellous pamphlet, Colette's first husband, Willy, who had fraudulently signed her early novels, tried to prove she had gone on to plagiarize and plunder different things he had written. As evidence he offered random sentences from work he was supposed to have influenced or inspired. Colette's manner, robust and personal, seems to leap from the page. Willy believed he had taught Colette "everything," and it may have been true — "everything," that is, except her instinct for language, her talent for perceiving the movement of life and a faculty for describing it. He was bound to have influenced her writing; it couldn't be helped. But by the time he chose to print a broadside on the subject, his influence had been absorbed, transmuted and — most humbling for the teacher — had left no visible trace.

There is no such a thing as a writer who has escaped being influenced. I have never heard a professional writer of any quality or standing talk about "pure" style, or say he would not read this or that for fear of corrupting or affecting his own; but I have heard it from would-be writers and amateurs. Corruption — if that is the word — sets in from the moment a child learns to speak and to hear language used and misused. A young person who does not read, and read widely, will never write anything — at least, nothing of inter-est. From time to time, in France, a novel is published purporting to come from a shepherd whose only influence has been the baaing of lambs on some God-forsaken slope of the Pyrenees. His artless and untampered-with mode of expression arouses the hope that there will be many more like him, but as a rule he is never heard from again. For "influences" I would be inclined to substitute "acquisitions." What they consist of, and amount to, are affected by taste and environment, preferences and upbringing (even, and sometimes particularly, where the latter has been rejected), instinctive selection. The beginning writer has to choose, tear to pieces, spit out, chew up and assimilate as naturally as a young animal — as naturally and as ruthlessly. Style cannot be copied, except by the untalented. It is, finally, the distillation of a lifetime of reading and listening, of selection and rejection. But if it is not a true voice, it is nothing.   [1985]

SANDRA M. GILBERT AND SUSAN GUBAR *present a feminist reading of Charlotte Perkins Gilman's "The Yellow Wallpaper" in* The Madwoman in the Attic: The Woman Writer and the Nineteenth-Century Literary Imagination *(1979). In this book they argue that a recognizable literary tradition existed in English and American literature in which the female imagination had demonstrated "the anxiety of authorship." According to Gilbert and Gubar, "Images of enclosure and escape, fantasies in which maddened doubles functioned as asocial surrogates for docile selves . . . such patterns reoccurred throughout this tradition, along with obsessive depictions of diseases like anorexia, agoraphobia, and claustrophobia." Gilman's story is securely within this tradition of the "literature of confinement," in which a woman writer, trapped by the patriarchal society, tries to struggle free "through strategic redefinitions of self, art, and society."*

SANDRA M. GILBERT AND SUSAN GUBAR

A Feminist Reading of Gilman's The Yellow Wallpaper

As if to comment on the unity of all these points — on, that is, the anxiety-inducing connections between what women writers tend to see as their parallel confinements in texts, houses, and maternal female bodies — Charlotte Perkins Gilman brought them all together in 1890 in a striking story of female confinement and escape, a paradigmatic tale which (like *Jane Eyre*) seems to tell *the* story that all literary women would tell if they could speak their "speechless woe." "The Yellow Wallpaper," which Gilman herself called "a description of a case of nervous breakdown," recounts in the first person the experiences of a woman who is evidently suffering from a severe post-partum psychosis. Her husband, a censorious and paternalistic physician, is treating her according to methods by which S. Weir Mitchell, a famous "nerve specialist," treated Gilman herself for a similar problem. He has confined her to a large garret room in an "ancestral hall" he has rented, and he has forbidden her to touch pen to paper until she is well again, for he feels, says the narrator, "that with my imaginative power and habit of story-making, a nervous weakness like mine is sure to lead to all manner of excited fancies, and that I ought to use my will and good sense to check the tendency."

The cure, of course, is worse than the disease, for the sick woman's mental condition deteriorates rapidly. "I think sometimes that if I were only well enough to write a little it would relieve the press of ideas and rest me," she remarks, but literally confined in a room she thinks is a one-time nursery because it has "rings and things" in the walls, she is literally locked away from creativity. The "rings and things," although reminiscent of children's gymnastic equipment, are really the paraphernalia of confinement, like the gate at the head of the stairs, instruments that definitively indicate her imprisonment. Even more tormenting, however, is the room's wallpaper: a sulphurous yellow paper, torn off in spots, and patterned with "lame uncertain curves" that "plunge off at outrageous angles" and "destroy themselves in unheard of contradictions." Ancient, smoldering, "unclean" as the oppressive structures of the society in which she finds herself, this paper surrounds the narrator like an inexplicable text, censorious and overwhelming as her physician husband, haunting as the "hereditary estate" in which she is trying to survive. Inevitably she studies its suicidal implications — and inevitably, because of her "imaginative power and habit of story-making," she revises it, projecting her own passion for escape into its otherwise incomprehensible hieroglyphics. "This wall-paper," she decides, at a key point in her story,

> has a kind of sub-pattern in a different shade, a particularly irritating one, for you can only see it in certain lights, and not clearly then.
> But in the places where it isn't faded and where the sun is just so — I can see a strange, provoking, formless sort of figure, that seems to skulk about behind that silly and conspicuous front design.

As time passes, this figure concealed behind what corresponds (in terms of what we have been discussing) to the facade of the patriarchal text becomes clearer and clearer. By moonlight the pattern of the wallpaper "becomes bars! The outside pattern I mean, and the woman behind it is as plain as can be." And eventually, as the narrator sinks more deeply into what the world calls madness, the terrifying implications of both the paper and the figure imprisoned behind the paper begin to permeate — that is, to *haunt* — the rented ancestral mansion in which she and her husband are immured. The "yellow smell" of the paper "creeps all over the house," drenching every room in its subtle aroma of decay. And the woman creeps too — through the house, in the house, and out of the house, in the garden and "on that long road under the trees." Sometimes, indeed, the narrator confesses, "I think there are a great many women" both behind the paper and creeping in the garden, "and sometimes only one, and she crawls around fast, and her crawling shakes [the paper] all over. . . . And she is all the time trying to climb through. But nobody could climb through that pattern — it strangles so; I think that is why it has so many heads."

Eventually it becomes obvious to both reader and narrator that the figure creeping through and behind the wallpaper is both the narrator and the narrator's double. By the end of the story, moreover, the narrator has enabled this double to escape from her textual/architectural confinement: "I pulled and she shook, I shook and she pulled, and before morning we had peeled off yards of that paper." Is the message of the tale's conclusion mere madness? Certainly the righteous Doctor John — whose name links him to the anti-hero of Charlotte Brontë's *Villette* — has been temporarily defeated, or at least momentarily stunned. "Now why should that man have fainted?"

the narrator ironically asks as she creeps around her attic. But John's unmasculine swoon of surprise is the least of the triumphs Gilman imagines for her madwoman. More significant are the madwoman's own imaginings and creations, mirages of health and freedom with which her author endows her like a fairy godmother showering gold on a sleeping heroine. The woman from behind the wallpaper creeps away, for instance, creeps fast and far on the long road, in broad daylight. "I have watched her sometimes away off in the open country," says the narrator, "creeping as fast as a cloud shadow in a high wind."

Indistinct and yet rapid, barely perceptible but inexorable, the progress of that cloud shadow is not unlike the progress of nineteenth-century literary women out of the texts defined by patriarchal poetics into the open spaces of their own authority. That such an escape from the numb world behind the patterned walls of the text was a flight from disease into health was quite clear to Gilman herself. When "The Yellow Wallpaper" was published she sent it to Weir Mitchell whose strictures had kept her from attempting the pen during her own breakdown, thereby aggravating her illness, and she was delighted to learn, years later, that "he had changed his treatment of nervous prostration since reading" her story. "If that is a fact," she declared, "I have not lived in vain." Because she was a rebellious feminist besides being a medical iconoclast, we can be sure that Gilman did not think of this triumph of hers in narrowly therapeutic terms. Because she knew, with Emily Dickinson, that "Infection in the sentence breeds," she knew that the cure for female despair must be spiritual as well as physical, aesthetic as well as social. What "The Yellow Wallpaper" shows she knew, too, is that even when a supposedly "mad" woman has been sentenced to imprisonment in the "infected" house of her own body, she may discover that, as Sylvia Plath[1] was to put it seventy years later, she has "a self to recover, a queen."   [1979]

CHARLOTTE PERKINS GILMAN *wrote her autobiography,* The Living of Charlotte Perkins Gilman *(1935), in the last years of her life. Her intelligence and strength of character are evident in this work, as is her modesty after a long career as an eminent American feminist. Her straightforward description of her mental breakdown nearly fifty years earlier is in marked contrast to the obsessive fantasy of her story "The Yellow Wallpaper," written shortly after her illness.*

---

[1]Sylvia Plath (1932–1963), American poet.

CHARLOTTE PERKINS GILMAN

Undergoing the Cure for Nervous Prostration

This was a worse horror than before, for now I saw the stark fact — that I was well while away and sick while at home — a heartening prospect! Soon ensued the same utter prostration, the unbearable inner misery, the ceaseless tears. A new tonic had been invented, Essence of Oats, which was given me, and did some good for a time. I pulled up enough to do a little painting that fall, but soon slipped down again and stayed down. An old friend of my mother's, dear Mrs. Diman, was so grieved at this condition that she gave me a hundred dollars and urged me to go away somewhere and get cured.

At that time the greatest nerve specialist in the country was Dr. S. W. Mitchell of Philadelphia. Through the kindness of a friend of Mr. Stetson's living in that city, I went to him and took "the rest cure"; went with the utmost confidence, prefacing the visit with a long letter giving "the history of the case" in a way a modern psychologist would have appreciated. Dr. Mitchell only thought it proved self-conceit. He had a prejudice against the Beechers. "I've had two women of your blood here already," he told me scornfully. This eminent physician was well versed in two kinds of nervous prostration; that of the business man exhausted from too much work, and the society woman exhausted from too much play. The kind I had was evidently behind him. But he did reassure me on one point — there was no dementia, he said, only hysteria.

I was put to bed and kept there. I was fed, bathed, rubbed, and responded with the vigorous body of twenty-six. As far as he could see there was nothing the matter with me, so after a month of this agreeable treatment he sent me home, with this prescription:

> Live as domestic a life as possible. Have your child with you all the time. (Be it remarked that if I did but dress the baby it left me shaking and crying — certainly far from a healthy companionship for her, to say nothing of the effect on me.) Lie down an hour after each meal. Have but two hours' intellectual life a day. And never touch pen, brush, or pencil as long as you live.

I went home, followed those directions rigidly for months, and came perilously near to losing my mind. The mental agony grew so unbearable that I would sit blankly moving my head from side to side — to get out from under the pain. Not physical pain, not the least "headache" even, just mental torment, and so heavy in its nightmare gloom that it seemed real enough to dodge.

I made a rag baby, hung it on a doorknob, and played with it. I would crawl into remote closets and under beds — to hide from the grinding pressure of that profound distress. . . .

Finally, in the fall of '87, in a moment of clear vision, we agreed to separate, to get a divorce. There was no quarrel, no blame for either one, never an unkind word between us, unbroken mutual affection — but it seemed plain that if I went crazy, it would do my husband no good, and be a deadly injury to my child.

What this meant to the young artist, the devoted husband, the loving father, was so bitter a grief and loss that nothing would have justified breaking the marriage save this worse loss which threatened. It was not a choice between going and staying, but between going, sane, and staying, insane. If I had been of the slightest use to him or to the child, I would have "stuck it," as the English say. But this progressive weakening of the mind made a horror unnecessary to face; better for that dear child to have separated parents than a lunatic mother.

We had been married four years and more. This miserable condition of mind, this darkness, feebleness, and gloom, had begun in those difficult years of courtship, had grown rapidly worse after marriage, and was now threatening utter loss; whereas I had repeated proof that the moment I left home I began to recover. It seemed right to give up a mistaken marriage.

Our mistake was mutual. If I had been stronger and wiser I should never have been persuaded into it. Our suffering was mutual too, his unbroken devotion, his manifold cares and labors in tending a sick wife, his adoring pride in the best of babies, all coming to naught, ending in utter failure — we sympathized with each other but faced a bitter necessity. The separation must come as soon as possible, the divorce must wait for conditions.

If this decision could have been reached sooner it would have been much better for me, the lasting mental injury would have been less. Such recovery as I have made in forty years, and the work accomplished, seem to show that the fear of insanity was not fulfilled, but the effects of nerve bankruptcy remain to this day. So much of my many failures, of misplay and misunderstanding and "queerness" is due to this lasting weakness, and kind friends so unfailingly refuse to allow for it, to believe it, that I am now going to some length in stating the case.

[1935]

NADINE GORDIMER *wrote "The Flash of Fireflies" as a representative from South Africa in the International Short Story Symposium conducted by the* Kenyon Review *in 1968. Gordimer's essay analyzing the connection between the social and aesthetic implications of this literary form became well known for its definition of a short story as "the flash of fireflies." In 1992 Gordimer developed her ideas further in a UNESCO conference on "African Fiction on the Threshold of the 21st Century," when she quoted Albert Camus, Gabriel García Márquez and Agostinho Neto in her comments on how to transform social structures and stimulate African literature.*

Albert Camus wrote, "One either serves the whole of man or one does not serve him at all. And if man needs bread and justice, he also needs pure beauty, which is the bread of his heart." . . . Gabriel García Márquez wrote, "The best way a writer can serve a revolution is to write as well as he can." . . . Neto (remember his words: "If writing is one of the conditions of your being alive, you create that condition"). . . . Bread, justice, and the bread of the heart — which is the beauty of literature: these are all our business in Africa's twenty-first century.

NADINE GORDIMER

The Flash of Fireflies

Why is it that while the death of the novel is good for post-mortem at least once a year, the short story lives on unmolested? It cannot be because — to borrow their own jargon — literary critics regard it as merely a minor art form. Most of them, if pressed, would express the view that it is a highly specialized and skilful form, closer to poetry, etc. But they would have to be pressed; otherwise they wouldn't bother to discuss it at all. When Chekhov crops up, it is as a playwright, and Katherine Mansfield is a period personality from the Lady Chatterley set. Yet no one suggests that we are practicing a dead art form. And, like a child suffering from healthy neglect, the short story survives.

"To say that no one now much likes novels is to exaggerate very little. The large public which used to find pleasure in prose fictions prefer movies, television, journalism, and books of 'fact,'" Gore Vidal wrote recently (*Encounter*, December 1967). If the cinema and television have taken over so much of the novel's territory, just as photography forced painting into wastelands which may or may not be made to bloom, hasn't the short story been overrun, too? This symposium is shoptalk and it would seem unnecessary for us to go over the old definitions of where and how the short story differs from the novel, but the answer to the question must lie somewhere here. Both novel and story use the same material: human experience. Both have the same aim: to communicate it. Both use the same medium: the written word. There is a general and recurrent dissatisfaction with the novel as a means of netting ultimate reality — another term for the quality of human life — and inevitably there is even a tendency to blame the tools: words have become hopelessly blunted by overuse, dinned to death by admen, and, above all, debased by political creeds that have twisted and changed their meaning. Various ways out have been sought. In England, a return to classicism in technique and a turning to the exoticism of sexual aberration and physical and mental abnormality as an extension of human experience and therefore of subject matter;

in Germany and America, a splendid abandon in making a virtue of the vice of the novel's inherent clumsiness by stuffing it not with nineteenth-century horsehair narrative but twentieth-century anecdotal-analytical plastic foam; in France, the "laboratory novel" struggling to get away from the anthropocentric curse of the form and the illusion of depth of the psychological novel, and landing up very much where Virginia Woolf was, years ago, staring at the mark on the wall. Burroughs[1] has invented the reader-participation novel. For the diseased word, George Steiner has even suggested silence.

If the short story is alive while the novel is dead, the reason must lie in approach and method. The short story, as a form and as a *kind of creative vision*, must be better equipped to attempt the capture of ultimate reality at a time when (whichever way you choose to see it) we are drawing nearer to the mystery of life or are losing ourselves in a bellowing wilderness of mirrors, as the nature of that reality becomes more fully understood or more bewilderingly concealed by the discoveries of science and the proliferation of communication media outside the printed word.

Certainly the short story always has been more flexible and open to experiment than the novel. Short-story writers always have been subject at the same time to both a stricter technical discipline and a wider freedom than the novelist. Short-story writers have known — and solved by nature of their choice of form — what novelists seem to have discovered in despair only now: the strongest convention of the novel, prolonged coherence of tone, to which even the most experimental of novels must conform unless it is to fall apart, is false to the nature of whatever can be grasped of human reality. How shall I put it? Each of us has a thousand lives and a novel gives a character only one. *For the sake of the form.* The novelist may juggle about with chronology and throw narrative overboard; all the time his characters have the reader by the hand, there is a consistency of relationship throughout the experience that cannot and does not convey the quality of human life, where contact is more like the flash of fireflies, in and out, now here, now there, in darkness. Short-story writers see by the light of the flash; theirs is the art of the only thing one can be sure of — the present moment. Ideally, they have learned to do without explanation of what went before, and what happens beyond this point. How the characters will appear, think, behave, comprehend, tomorrow or at any other time in their lives, is irrelevant. A discrete moment of truth is aimed at — not *the* moment of truth, because the short story does not deal in cumulatives.

The problem of how best to take hold of ultimate reality, from the technical to stylistic point of view, is one that the short-story writer is accustomed to solving specifically in relation to an area — event, mental state, mood, appearance — which is heightenedly manifest in a single situation. Take fantasy for an example. Writers are becoming more and more aware of the waviness of the line that separates fantasy from the so-called rational in human perception. It is recognized that fantasy is no more than a shift in

---

[1] William Burroughs (b. 1914), author of *Naked Lunch* and other experimental novels.

angle; to put it another way, the rational is simply another, the most obvious, kind of fantasy. Writers turn to the less obvious fantasy as a wider lens on ultimate reality. But this fantasy is something that changes, merges, emerges, disappears as a pattern does viewed through the bottom of a glass. It is true for the moment when one looks down through the glass; but the same vision does not transform everything one sees, consistently throughout one's whole consciousness. Fantasy in the hands of short-story writers is so much more successful than when in the hands of novelists because it is necessary for it to hold good only for the brief illumination of the situation it dominates. In the series of developing situations of the novel the sustainment of the tone of fantasy becomes a high-pitched ringing in the reader's ears. How many fantasy novels achieve what they set out to do: convey the shift and change, to and fro, beneath, above, and around the world of appearances? The short story recognizes that full comprehension of a particular kind in the reader, like full apprehension of a particular kind in the writer, is something of limited duration. The short story is a fragmented and restless form, a matter of hit or miss, and it is perhaps for this reason that it suits modern consciousness — which seems best expressed as flashes of fearful insight alternating with near-hypnotic states of indifference.

These are technical and stylistic considerations. Marxist criticism sees the survival of an art form in relation to social change. What about the socio-political implications of the short story's survival? George Lukács has said that the novel is a bourgeois art form whose enjoyment presupposes leisure and privacy. It implies the living room, the armchair, the table lamp; just as epic implies the illiterates round the tribal story-teller, and Shakespeare implies the two audiences — that of the people and that of the court — of a feudal age. From this point of view the novel marks the apogee of an exclusive, individualist culture; the nearest it ever got to a popular art form (in the sense of bringing people together in direct participation in an intellectually stimulating experience) was the nineteenth-century custom of reading novels aloud to the family. Here again it would seem that the short story shares the same disadvantages as the novel. It is an art form solitary in communication; yet another sign of the increasing loneliness and isolation of the individual in a competitive society. You cannot enjoy the experience of a short story unless you have certain minimum conditions of privacy in which to read it; and these conditions are those of middle-class life. But of course a short story, by reason of its length and its *completeness*, totally contained in the brief time you give to it, depends less than the novel upon the classic conditions of middle-class life, and perhaps corresponds to the breakup of that life which is taking place. In that case, although the story may outlive the novel, it may become obsolete when the period of disintegration is replaced by new social forms and the art forms that express them. One doesn't have to embrace the dreariness of conventional "social realism" in literature to grant this. That our age is threshing about desperately for a way out of individual human isolation, and that our present art forms are not adequate to it, it is obvious to see in all the tatty dressing-up games, from McLuhan's theories to pop art, in which we seek a substitute for them.   [1968]

JANICE HUBBARD HARRIS *wrote* The Short Fiction of D. H. Lawrence *(1984) after the scholar Mark Spilka pointed out to her in the late 1960s that there was no critical literature on Lawrence's stories. "Where were the analyses of that lively body of fiction capable, as Julian Moynahan says, of bringing light back into the eyes of the reader exhausted by* The Plumed Serpent *or fainting amid the incremental repetitions of* The Rainbow?" *Her critical approach to the stories incorporates several modes — biographical, psychological, sociological, feminist. Comparing Lawrence with his contemporaries James Joyce, Katherine Mansfield, and Virginia Woolf, Harris concludes that "Lawrence is clearly the leader in range, sheer quantity of masterpieces, and, something harder to define, in stretching the conventions of the [short story] genre to include a variety of new possibilities."*

JANICE H. HARRIS

A Psychosocial Explication of Lawrence's The Rocking-Horse Winner

"The Rocking-Horse Winner" opens with the distant, singsong voice of a fairy tale: "There was a woman who was beautiful, who started with all the advantages, yet she had no luck." So begins an ancient tale. A brave young boy is challenged by his true love. He rides off into a dreamland where he struggles and succeeds at attaining secret knowledge. He brings the secret knowledge back and with it wins treasure houses of gold, giving all to his love. Undercutting this fairy tale, however, is another, which forms a grotesque shadow, a nightmare counter to the wish fulfillment narrative. The "true love" of the brave young boy is his cold-hearted mother. The quest he has embarked on is hopeless, for every success brings a new and greater trial. Like the exhausted and terrified daughter in Rumplestiltskin, this son is perpetually set the task of spinning more gold. In this tale, no magical dwarf comes to the child's aid; the boy finally spins himself out, dropping dead on his journey, his eyes turned to stone. Like all good fairy tales, this one has several complementary levels of reference: social, familial, psychological.

On the social level, the tale reads as a satire on the equation of money, love, luck, and happiness. The target of the satire, the mother, cannot be happy without an unending flow of cold, sure cash. As she sees it, luck and lucre are the same thing. Yearning for some response and real affection from her, Paul adds the term "love," making a solid, tragic construction. Quite simply, the tale concludes that these equations are deadly. The mother, representing a society run on a money ethic, has given the younger generation a murderous education.

On a familial level, the tale dramatizes an idea implied as early as *Sons and Lovers* but overtly stated only in a late autobiographical fragment and these last tales. The idea is that mothers shape their sons into the desirable opposite of their husbands. Whatever they are powerless to prevent or alter in their mates, mothers will seek to prevent or alter in their sons. In "The Rocking-Horse Winner," the woman cannot alter her husband's ineffectuality. She herself tries to be effective in the world of commerce and money, but she fails, partly because of the lack of opportunities available to her. So she turns unconsciously to her son. In this reading, Paul's death owes less to the specific character of his mother's demands and more to the strength of those demands. He dies — cannot live, cannot grow and flourish — partly because he is too good a son, and she is a woman with unbounded desires and no way to work directly toward their gratification. In *Sons and Lovers,* the young son kills, literally and figuratively, the paralyzed and paralyzing mother. The alternative pattern, which Lawrence felt to be common among the men of his generation, is played out in "The Rocking-Horse Winner."

But the tale acts out still another nexus of meaning, one implied in both the satire on a society governed by a money ethic and in the dramatization of a mother devourer. On this level, the hobbyhorse comes more to the fore. . . . This lonely, preadolescent boy continually retreats to his own room where, in great secrecy, he mounts his play horse and rides himself into a trancelike ecstasy. His action and the result it brings powerfully echo Lawrence's description of masturbation, physical and psychic, in his essay "Pornography and Obscenity." Discussing censorship, Lawrence praises art that inspires genuine sexual arousal, that invites union with the other, whether the "other" is another person, an idea, a landscape, the sun. Obscene art is essentially solipsistic; it arouses the desire to turn inward, to chafe, to ride the self in an endless and futile circle of self-stimulation, analysis, gratification. In masturbation, there is no reciprocity, no exchange between self and other. Applying Lawrence's indictment of masturbation to Paul's situation, we see that Paul has been taught to ride himself, that is, his hobbyhorse or obsessions, obsessions he inherited from his mother. . . .

If one takes these three levels of reference and seeks out their complementarity, one sees the rich logic of the tale. The money ethic, the devouring of sons by mothers, and the preference for masturbation are parallel in cause and result. All develop and respect only the kind of knowledge that will increase one's capacity to control. For example, like any money-maker, Paul learns about the horses only to manipulate his earnings — money and love. Paul's mother, in a variation on the theme, does not bother to learn anything about her son because she does not perceive him as useful to her. Further, Paul mounts his hobbyhorse, his surrogate sexual partner, only as a way of fulfilling his own narrowly defined program for success and happiness. In no case is the object that is to be known — horse, son, sexual partner — seen to have a life of its own, an otherness to be appreciated rather than manipulated, a furtherness that can give the knower a glimpse into all that is beyond him or her. In addition, the resolution of each nexus of meaning carries the same ironic denouement: The quest for absolute control leads to the loss of control.

The mother's house, which she wants to be luxurious and proper, is haunted by crass whispers. She and her son, striving to control love and fortune, are compulsive, obsessed; Paul dies and thereby loses all chance for the very human love and contact he sought. The mother loses the very means by which her fortune was assured.   [1984]

ZORA NEALE HURSTON *continued throughout her life to make what the critic Mary Helen Washington called "unorthodox and paradoxical assertions on racial issues." Often conveyed with great wit and style, Hurston's views were always passionately held, as in her essay "What White Publishers Won't Print," first published in* Negro Digest *in April 1950.*

ZORA NEALE HURSTON

What White Publishers Won't Print

I have been amazed by the Anglo-Saxon's lack of curiosity about the internal lives and emotions of the Negroes, and for that matter, any non-Anglo-Saxon peoples within our borders, above the class of unskilled labor.

This lack of interest is much more important than it seems at first glance. It is even more important at this time than it was in the past. The internal affairs of the nation have bearings on the international stress and strain, and this gap in the national literature now has tremendous weight in world affairs. National coherence and solidarity is implicit in a thorough understanding of the various groups within a nation, and this lack of knowledge about the internal emotions and behavior of the minorities cannot fail to bar our understanding. Man, like all the other animals, fears and is repelled by that which he does not understand, and mere difference is apt to connote something malign.

The fact that there is no demand for incisive and full-dress stories around Negroes above the servant class is indicative of something of vast importance to this nation. This blank is NOT filled by the fiction built around upper-class Negroes exploiting the race problem. Rather, it tends to point it up. A college-bred Negro still is not a person like other folks, but an interesting problem, more or less. It calls to mind a story of slavery time. In this story, a master with more intellectual curiosity than usual, set out to see how much he could teach a particularly bright slave of his. When he had gotten him up to higher mathematics and to be a fluent reader of Latin, he called in a neighbor to show off his brilliant slave, and to argue that Negroes had brains just like the slave-owners had, and given the same opportunities, would turn out the same.

The visiting master of slaves looked and listened, tried to trap the literate slave in Algebra and Latin, and failing to do so in both, turned to his neighbor and said:

"Yes, he certainly knows his higher mathematics, and he can read Latin better than many white men I know, but I cannot bring myself to believe that he understands a thing that he is doing. It is all an aping of our culture. All on the outside. You are crazy if you think that it has changed him inside in the least. Turn him loose, and he will revert at once to the jungle. He is still a savage, and no amount of translating Virgil and Ovid is going to change him. In fact, all you have done is to turn a useful savage into a dangerous beast."

That was in slavery time, yes, and we have come a long, long way since then, but the troubling thing is that there are still too many who refuse to believe in the ingestion and digestion of western culture as yet. Hence the lack of literature about the higher emotions and love life of upper-class Negroes and the minorities in general.

Publishers and producers are cool to the idea. Now, do not leap to the conclusion that editors and producers constitute a special class of unbelievers. That is far from true. Publishing houses and theatrical promoters are in business to make money. They will sponsor anything that they believe will sell. They shy away from romantic stories about Negroes and Jews because they feel that they know the public indifference to such works, unless the story or play involves racial tension. It can then be offered as a study in Sociology, with the romantic side subdued. They know the scepticism in general about the complicated emotions in the minorities. The average American just cannot conceive of it, and would be apt to reject the notion, and publishers and producers take the stand that they are not in business to educate, but to make money. Sympathetic as they might be, they cannot afford to be crusaders.

In proof of this, you can note various publishers and producers edging forward a little, and ready to go even further when the trial balloons show that the public is ready for it. This public lack of interest is the nut of the matter.

The question naturally arises as to the why of this indifference, not to say scepticism, to the internal life of educated minorities.

The answer lies in what we may call the AMERICAN MUSEUM OF UN-NATURAL HISTORY. This is an intangible built on folk belief. It is assumed that all non-Anglo-Saxons are uncomplicated stereotypes. Everybody knows all about them. They are lay figures mounted in the museum where all may take them in at a glance. They are made of bent wires without insides at all. So how could anybody write a book about the nonexistent?

The American Indian is a contraption of copper wires in an eternal war-bonnet, with no equipment for laughter, expressionless face, and that says "How" when spoken to. His only activity is treachery leading us to massacres. Who is so dumb as not to know all about Indians, even if they have never seen one, nor talked with anyone who ever knew one?

The American Negro exhibit is a group of two. Both of these mechanical toys are built so that their feet eternally shuffle, and their eyes pop and roll. Shuffling feet and those popping, rolling eyes denote the Negro and no characterization is genuine without this monotony. One is seated on a stump picking away on his banjo and singing and laughing. The other is a most amoral character before a share-cropper's shack mumbling about injustice. Doing this makes him out to be a Negro "intellectual." It is as simple as all that.

The whole museum is dedicated to the convenient "typical." In there is the "typical" Oriental, Jew, Yankee, Westerner, Southerner, Latin, and even out-of-favor Nordics like the German. The Englishman "I say old chappie," and the gesticulating Frenchman. The least observant American can know all at a glance. However, the public willingly accepts the untypical in Nordics, but feels cheated if the untypical is portrayed in others. The author of *Scarlet Sister Mary* complained to me that her neighbors objected to her book on the grounds that she had the characters thinking, "and everybody know that Nigras don't think."

But for the national welfare, it is urgent to realize that the minorities do think, and think about something other than the race problem. That they are very human and internally, according to natural endowment, are just like everybody else. So long as this is not conceived, there must remain that feeling of unsurmountable difference, and difference to the average man means something bad. If people were made right, they would be just like him.

The trouble with the purely problem arguments is that they leave too much unknown. Argue all you will or may about injustice, but as long as the majority cannot conceive of a Negro or a Jew feeling and reacting inside just as they do, the majority will keep right on believing that people who do not feel like them cannot possibly feel as they do, and conform to the established pattern. It is well known that there must be a body of waived matter, let us say, things accepted and taken for granted by all in a community before there can be that commonality of feeling. The usual phrase is having things in common. Until this is thoroughly established in respect to Negroes in America, as well as of other minorities, it will remain impossible for the majority to conceive of a Negro experiencing a deep and abiding love and not just the passion of sex. That a great mass of Negroes can be stirred by the pageants of Spring and Fall; the extravaganza of summer, and the majesty of winter. That they can and do experience discovery of the numerous subtle faces as a foundation for a great and selfless love, and the diverse nuances that go to destroy that love as with others. As it is now, this capacity, this evidence of high and complicated emotions, is ruled out. Hence the lack of interest in a romance uncomplicated by the race struggle has so little appeal.

This insistence on defeat in a story where upper-class Negroes are portrayed, perhaps says something from the subconscious of the majority. Involved in western culture, the hero or the heroine, or both, must appear frustrated and go down to defeat, somehow. Our literature reeks with it. Is it the same as saying, "You can translate Virgil, and fumble with the differential calculus, but can you really comprehend it? Can you cope with our subtleties?"

That brings us to the folklore of "reversion to type." This curious doctrine has such wide acceptance that it is tragic. One has only to examine the huge literature on it to be convinced. No matter how high we may *seem* to climb, put us under strain and we revert to type, that is, to the bush. Under a superficial layer of western culture, the jungle drums throb in our veins.

This ridiculous notion makes it possible for that majority who accept it to conceive of even a man like the suave and scholarly Dr. Charles S. Johnson to hide a black cat's bone on his person, and indulge in a midnight voodoo ceremony, complete with leopard skin and drums if threatened with the loss of the presidency of Fisk University, or the love of his wife. "Under the skin . . . better to deal with them in business, etc., but otherwise keep them at a safe distance and under control. I tell you, Carl Van Vechten, think as you like, but they are just not like us."

The extent and extravagance of this notion reaches the ultimate in nonsense in the widespread belief that the Chinese have bizarre genitals, because of that eye-fold that makes their eyes seem to slant. In spite of the fact that no biology has ever mentioned any such difference in reproductive organs makes no matter. Millions of people believe it. "Did you know that a Chinese has . . ." Consequently, their quiet contemplative manner is interpreted as a sign of slyness and a treacherous inclination.

But the opening wedge for better understanding has been thrust into the crack. Though many Negroes denounced Carl Van Vechten's *Nigger Heaven* because of the title, and without ever reading it, the book, written in the deepest sincerity, revealed Negroes of wealth and culture to the white public. It created curiosity even when it aroused scepticism. It made folks want to know. Worth Tuttle Hedden's *The Other Room* has definitely widened the opening. Neither of these well-written works take a romance of upper-class Negro life as the central theme, but the atmosphere and the background is there. These works should be followed up by some incisive and intimate stories from the inside.

The realistic story around a Negro insurance official, dentist, general practitioner, undertaker, and the like would be most revealing. Thinly disguised fiction around the well-known Negro names is not the answer, either. The "exceptional" as well as the Ol' Man Rivers has been exploited all out of context already. Everybody is already resigned to the "exceptional" Negro, and willing to be entertained by the "quaint." To grasp the penetration of western civilization in a minority, it is necessary to know how the average behaves and lives. Books that deal with people like in Sinclair Lewis' *Main Street* is the necessary metier. For various reasons, the average, struggling, non-morbid Negro is the best-kept secret in America. His revelation to the public is the thing needed to do away with that feeling of difference which inspires fear and which ever expresses itself in dislike.

It is inevitable that this knowledge will destroy many illusions and romantic traditions which America probably likes to have around. But then, we have no record of anybody sinking into a lingering death on finding out that there was no Santa Claus. The old world will take it in its stride. The realization that Negroes are no better nor no worse, and at times just as boring as everybody else, will hardly kill off the population of the nation.

Outside of racial attitudes, there is still another reason why this literature should exist. Literature and other arts are supposed to hold up the mirror to nature. With only the fractional "exceptional" and the "quaint" portrayed, a true picture of Negro life in America cannot be. A great principle of national art has been violated.

These are the things that publishers and producers, as the accredited representatives of the American people, have not as yet taken into consideration sufficiently. Let there be light! [1950]

SHIRLEY JACKSON *wrote this "biography of a story" in 1960 as a lecture to be delivered before reading "The Lottery" to college audiences. After her death it was included in* Come Along with Me *(1968), edited by her husband, Stanley Edgar Hyman. The lecture also contained extensive quotations from letters she had received from readers who took the story literally. These so disgusted Jackson that she promised her listeners at the conclusion of her talk, "I am out of the lottery business for good."*

S H I R L E Y   J A C K S O N

The Morning of June 28, 1948, and The Lottery

On the morning of June 28, 1948, I walked down to the post office in our little Vermont town to pick up the mail. I was quite casual about it, as I recall — I opened the box, took out a couple of bills and a letter or two, talked to the postmaster for a few minutes, and left, never supposing that it was the last time for months that I was to pick up the mail without an active feeling of panic. By the next week I had had to change my mailbox to the largest one in the post office, and casual conversation with the postmaster was out of the question, because he wasn't speaking to me. June 28, 1948, was the day *The New Yorker* came out with a story of mine in it. It was not my first published story, nor my last, but I have been assured over and over that if it had been the only story I ever wrote or published, there would be people who would not forget my name.

I had written the story three weeks before, on a bright June morning when summer seemed to have come at last, with blue skies and warm sun and no heavenly signs to warn me that my morning's work was anything but just another story. The idea had come to me while I was pushing my daughter up the hill in her stroller — it was, as I say, a warm morning, and the hill was steep, and beside my daughter the stroller held the day's groceries — and perhaps the effort of that last fifty yards up the hill put an edge to the story; at any rate, I had the idea fairly clearly in my mind when I put my daughter in her playpen and the frozen vegetables in the refrigerator, and, writing the story, I found that it went quickly and easily, moving from beginning to end without pause. As a matter of fact, when I read it over later I decided that except for one or two minor corrections, it needed no changes, and the story I finally typed up and sent off to my agent the next day was almost word for word the original draft. This, as any writer of stories can tell you, is not a usual thing. All I know is that when I came to read the story over I felt strongly that I didn't want to fuss with it. I didn't think it was perfect, but I didn't want to fuss with it. It was, I thought, a serious, straightforward story, and I was pleased and a little surprised at the ease with which it had been written; I was reasonably proud of it, and hoped that my agent would sell it to some magazine and I would have the gratification of seeing it in print.

My agent did not care for the story, but — as she said in her note at the time — her job was to sell it, not to like it. She sent it at once to *The New Yorker*, and about a week after the story had been written I received a telephone call from the fiction editor of *The New Yorker*; it was quite clear that he did not really care for the story, either, but *The New Yorker* was going to buy it. He asked for one change — that the date mentioned in the story be changed to coincide with the date of the issue of the magazine in which the story would appear, and I said of course. He then asked, hesitantly, if I had any particular interpretation of my own for the story; Mr. Harold Ross, then the editor of *The New Yorker*, was not altogether sure that he understood the story, and wondered if I cared to enlarge upon its meaning. I said no. Mr. Ross, he said, thought that the story might be puzzling to some people, and in case anyone telephoned the magazine, as sometimes happened, or wrote in asking about the story, was there anything in particular I wanted them to say? No, I said, nothing in particular; it was just a story I wrote.

I had no more preparation than that. I went on picking up the mail every morning, pushing my daughter up and down the hill in her stroller, anticipating pleasurably the check from *The New Yorker*, and shopping for groceries. The weather stayed nice and it looked as though it was going to be a good summer. Then, on June 28, *The New Yorker* came out with my story.

Things began mildly enough with a note from a friend at *The New Yorker*: "Your story has kicked up quite a fuss around the office," he wrote. I was flattered; it's nice to think that your friends notice what you write. Later that day there was a call from one of the magazine's editors; they had had a couple of people phone in about my story, he said, and was there anything I particularly wanted him to say if there were any more calls? No, I said, nothing particular; anything he chose to say was perfectly all right with me; it was just a story.

I was further puzzled by a cryptic note from another friend: "Heard a man talking about a story of yours on the bus this morning," she wrote. "Very exciting. I wanted to tell him I knew the author, but after I heard what he was saying I decided I'd better not."

One of the most terrifying aspects of publishing stories and books is the realization that they are going to be read, and read by strangers. I had never fully realized this before, although I had of course in my imagination dwelt lovingly upon the thought of the millions and millions of people who were going to be uplifted and enriched and delighted by the stories I wrote. It had simply never occurred to me that these millions and millions of people might be so far from being uplifted that they would sit down and write me letters I was downright scared to open; of the three-hundred-odd letters that I received that summer I can count only thirteen that spoke kindly to me, and they were mostly from friends. Even my mother scolded me: "Dad and I did not care at all for your story in *The New Yorker*," she wrote sternly, "it does seem, dear, that this gloomy kind of story is what all you young people think about these days. Why don't you write something to cheer people up?"

By mid-July I had begun to perceive that I was very lucky indeed to be safely in Vermont, where no one in our small town had ever heard of *The New Yorker*, much less read my story. Millions of people, and my mother, had taken a pronounced dislike to me.

The magazine kept no track of telephone calls, but all letters addressed to me care of the magazine were forwarded directly to me for answering, and all letters addressed to the magazine — some of them addressed to Harold Ross personally; these were the most vehement — were answered at the magazine and then the letters were sent me in great batches, along with carbons of the answers written at the magazine. I have all the letters still, and if they could be considered to give any accurate cross section of the reading public, or the reading public of *The New Yorker*, or even the reading public of one issue of *The New Yorker*, I would stop writing now.

Judging from these letters, people who read stories are gullible, rude, frequently illiterate, and horribly afraid of being laughed at. Many of the writers were positive that *The New Yorker* was going to ridicule them in print, and the most cautious letters were headed, in capital letters: NOT FOR PUBLI-CATION or PLEASE DO NOT PRINT THIS LETTER, or, at best, THIS LETTER MAY BE PUBLISHED AT YOUR USUAL RATES OF PAYMENT. Anonymous letters, of which there were a few, were destroyed. *The New Yorker* never published any comment of any kind about the story in the magazine, but did issue one publicity release saying that the story had received more mail than any piece of fiction they had ever published; this was after the newspapers had gotten into the act, in midsummer, with a front-page story in the San Francisco *Chronicle* begging to know what the story meant, and a series of columns in New York and Chicago papers pointing out that *New Yorker* subscriptions were being canceled right and left.

Curiously, there are three main themes which dominate the letters of that first summer — three themes which might be identified as bewilderment, speculation, and plain old-fashioned abuse. In the years since then, during which the story has been anthologized, dramatized, televised, and even — in one completely mystifying transformation — made into a ballet, the tenor of letters I receive has changed. I am addressed more politely, as a rule, and the letters largely confine themselves to questions like what does this story mean? The general tone of the early letters, however, was a kind of wide-eyed, shocked innocence. People at first were not so much concerned with what the story meant; what they wanted to know was where these lotteries were held, and whether they could go there and watch.   [1968]

HENRY JAMES *kept a record of his works-in-progress in notebooks for more than thirty years; his comments, often written hastily, were for his own eyes. After completing his last great novel,* The Golden Bowl (1904), *he wrote elaborate prefaces for the twenty-four volumes in the New York Edition of his works, published in 1907–1909. This explanation of "The Beast in the Jungle" was included in the preface for a collection of ten short stories in a volume in that series.*

HENRY JAMES

The Subject of The Beast in the Jungle

The subject of this elaborated fantasy ["The Beast in the Jungle"] — which, I must add, I hold a successful thing only as its motive may seem to the reader to stand out sharp — can't quite have belonged to the immemorial company of such solicitations; though in spite of this I meet it, in ten lines of an old notebook, but as a recorded conceit and an accomplished fact. Another poor sensitive gentleman . . . — my attested predilection for poor sensitive gentlemen almost embarrasses me as I march! — was to have been, after a strange fashion and from the threshold of his career, condemned to keep counting with the unreasoned prevision of some extraordinary fate; the conviction, lodged in his brain, part and parcel of his imagination from far back, that experience would be marked for him, and whether for good or for ill, by some rare distinction, some incalculable violence or unprecedented stroke. So I seemed to see him start in life — under the so mixed star of the extreme of apprehension and the extreme of confidence; all to the logical, the quite inevitable effect of the complication aforesaid: his having to wait and wait for the right recognition; none of the mere usual and normal human adventures, whether delights or disconcertments, appearing to conform to the great type of his fortune. So it is that he's depicted. No gathering appearance, no descried or interpreted promise or portent, affects his superstitious soul either as a damnation deep enough (if damnation be in question) for his appointed *quality* of consciousness, or as a translation into bliss sublime enough (on *that* hypothesis) to fill, in vulgar parlance, the bill. Therefore as each item of experience comes, with its possibilities, into view, he can but dismiss it under this sterilising habit of the failure to find it good enough and thence to appropriate it.

His one desire remains of course to meet his fate, or at least to divine it, to see it as intelligible, to learn it, in a word; but none of its harbingers, pretended or supposed, speak his ear in the true voice; they wait their moment at his door only to pass on unheeded, and the years ebb while he holds his breath and stays his hand and — from the dread not less of imputed pride than of imputed pusillanimity — stifles his distinguished secret. He perforce lets everything go — leaving all the while his general presumption disguised and his general abstention unexplained; since he's ridden by the idea of what things may lead to, since they mostly always lead to human communities, wider or intenser, of experience, and since, above all, in his uncertainty, he mustn't compromise others. Like the blinded seeker in the old-fashioned game he "burns," on occasion, as with the sense of the hidden thing near — only to deviate again however into the chill; the chill that indeed settles on him as the striking of his hour is deferred. His career thus resolves itself into a great negative adventure, my report of which presents, for its centre, the fine case that has caused him most tormentedly to "burn," and then most unprofitably to stray. He is afraid to recognise what he incidentally misses, since what his high belief amounts to is not that he shall have felt and vibrated less than any one else, but that he shall have felt and vibrated more; which no acknowledgement of the minor loss must conflict with. Such a course of existence naturally involves a climax — the final flash of the light under which he reads his lifelong riddle and sees his conviction proved. He has indeed been marked and indeed suffered his fortune — which is precisely to have been the man in the world to whom nothing whatever was to happen. My picture leaves him overwhelmed — at last he has understood; though in thus disengaging my treated theme for the reader's benefit I seem to acknowledge that this more detached witness may not successfully have done so. I certainly grant that any felt merit in the thing must all depend on the clearness and charm with which the subject just noted expresses itself.   [1908]

GUSTAV JANOUCH *published his recollections of Franz Kafka in* Conversations with Kafka (1953). *Janouch's father was employed by the Workers' Accident Insurance Institute with Kafka, and he introduced his son to Kafka in 1920 because they were both "scribblers." Janouch was only seventeen at the time, and very impressionable. Having read* The Metamorphosis, *he was disappointed by his first sight of Kafka: "'So this is the creator of the mysterious bug, Samsa,' I said to myself, disillusioned to see before me a simple, well-mannered man." But when their conversation was over that day — after Kafka had told Janouch that he wrote at night* *because daytime was a "great enchantment . . . it distracts from the darkness within"* — *Janouch asked himself, "Is he not himself the unfortunate bug in* The Metamorphosis?" *Their acquaintance ripened into a friendship, which lasted until Kafka's death in 1924.*

GUSTAV JANOUCH

Kafka's View of **The Metamorphosis**

Translated by Goronwy Rees

I spent my first week's wages on having Kafka's three stories — *The Metamorphosis, The Judgement,* and *The Stoker* — bound in a dark brown leather volume, with the name *Franz Kafka* elegantly tooled in gold lettering.

The book lay in the brief-case on my knee as I told Kafka about the warehouse-cinema. [Janouch was a pianist at the cinema.] Then I proudly took the volume out of the case and gave it across the desk to Kafka.

"What is this?" he asked in astonishment.

"It's my first week's wages."

"Isn't that a waste?"

Kafka's eyelids fluttered. His lips were sharply drawn in. For a few seconds he contemplated the name in the gold lettering, hastily thumbed through the pages of the book and — with obvious embarrassment — placed it before me on the desk. I was about to ask why the book offended him, when he began to cough. He took a handkerchief from his pocket, held it to his mouth, replaced it when the attack was over, stood up and went to the small washstand behind his desk and washed his hands, then said as he dried them: "You overrate me. Your trust oppresses me."

He sat himself at his desk and said, with his hands to his temples: "I am no burning bush. I am not a flame."

I interrupted him. "You shouldn't say that. It's not just. To me, for example, you are fire, warmth, and light."

"No, no!" he contradicted me, shaking his head. "You are wrong. My scribbling does not deserve a leather binding. It's only my own personal spectre of horror. It oughtn't to be printed at all. It should be burned and destroyed. It is without meaning."

I became furious. "Who told you that?" I was forced to contradict him — "How can you say such a thing? Can you see into the future? What you are saying to me is entirely your subjective feeling. Perhaps your scribbling, as you call it, will tomorrow represent a significant voice in the world. Who can tell today?"

I drew a deep breath.

Kafka stared at the desk. At the corners of his mouth were two short, sharp lines of shadow.

I was ashamed of my outburst, so I said quietly, in a low, explanatory tone: "Do you remember what you said to me about the Picasso exhibition?"

Kafka looked at me without understanding.

I continued: "You said that art is a mirror which — like a clock running fast — foretells the future. Perhaps your writing is, in today's *Cinema of the Blind,* only a mirror of tomorrow."

"Please, don't go on," said Kafka fretfully, and covered his eyes with both hands.

I apologized. "Please forgive me, I didn't mean to upset you. I'm stupid."

"No, no — you're not that!" Without removing his hands, he rocked his whole body to and fro. "You are right. You are certainly right. Probably that's why I can't finish anything. I am afraid of the truth. But can one do otherwise?" He took his hands away from his eyes, placed his clenched fists on the table, and said in a low, suppressed voice: "One must be silent, if one can't give any help. No one, through his own lack of hope, should make the condition of the patient worse. For that reason, all my scribbling is to be destroyed. I am no light. I have merely lost my way among my own thorns. I'm a dead end."

Kafka leaned backwards. His hands slipped lifelessly from the table. He closed his eyes.

"I don't believe it," I said with utter conviction, yet added appeasingly: "And even if it were true, it would be worthwhile to display the dead end to people."

Kafka merely shook his head slowly. "No, no . . . I am weak and tired."

"You should give up your work here," I said gently, to relax the tension which I felt between us.

Kafka nodded. "Yes, I should. I wanted to creep away behind this office desk, but it only increased my weakness. It's become —," Kafka looked at me with an indescribably painful smile, "— a cinema of the blind."

Then he closed his eyes again.

I was glad at this moment there was a knock on the door behind me.

[1953]

SARAH ORNE JEWETT *wrote "Looking Back on Girlhood" for the* Youth's Companion *magazine. It was published in the issue of January 7, 1892, near the end of her long career as a writer (she published at least 146 stories between 1868 and 1904). Jewett's reminiscence of how she became a writer is marked by the same sympathy for others and love of her native landscape that permeates her local-color fiction. As the critic Richard Cary has noted, her lucid and unassuming prose style conveys her "marked regard for the significance of the ordinary."*

SARAH ORNE JEWETT

Looking Back on Girlhood

In giving this brief account of my childhood, or, to speak exactly, of the surroundings which have affected the course of my work as a writer, my first thought flies back to those who taught me to observe, and to know the deep pleasures of simple things; and to be interested in the lives of people about me.

With its high hills and pine forests, and all its ponds and brooks and distant mountain views, there are few such delightful country towns in New England as the one where I was born. Being one of the oldest colonial settlements, it is full of interesting traditions and relics of the early inhabitants, both Indians and Englishmen. Two large rivers join just below the village at the head of tidewater, and these, with the great inflow from the sea, make a magnificent stream, bordered on its seaward course now by high-wooded banks of dark pines and hemlocks, and again by lovely green fields that slope gently to long lines of willows at the water's edge.

There is never-ending pleasure in making one's self familiar with such a region. One may travel at home in a most literal sense, and be always learning history, geography, botany, or biography — whatever one chooses.

I have had a good deal of journeying in my life, and taken great delight in it, but I have never taken greater delight than in my rides and drives and tramps and voyages within the borders of my native town. There is always something fresh, something to be traced or discovered, something particularly to be remembered. One grows rich in memories and associations.

I believe that we should know our native towns much better than most of us do, and never let ourselves be strangers at home. Particularly when one's native place is so really interesting as my own [Berwick, Maine]! . . .

My grandfather died in my eleventh year, and presently the Civil War began.

From that time the simple village life was at an end. Its provincial character was fading out; shipping was at a disadvantage, and there were no more bronzed sea-captains coming to dine and talk about their voyages, no more bags of filberts or oranges for the children, or great red jars of olives; but in these childish years I had come in contact with many delightful men and women of real individuality and breadth of character, who had fought the battle of life to good advantage, and sometimes against great odds.

In these days I was given to long, childish illnesses, and it must be honestly confessed, to instant drooping if ever I were shut up in school. I had apparently not the slightest desire for learning, but my father was always ready to let me be his companion in long drives about the country.

In my grandfather's business household, my father, unconscious of tonnage and timber measurement, of the markets of the Windward Islands or the Mediterranean ports, had taken to his book, as old people said, and gone to college and begun that devotion to the study of medicine which only ended with his life.

I have tried already to give some idea of my father's character in my story of *The Country Doctor,* but all that is inadequate to the gifts and character of the man himself. He gave me my first and best knowledge of books by his own delight and dependence upon them, and ruled my early attempts at writing by the severity and simplicity of his own good taste.

"Don't try to write *about* people and things, tell them just as they are!"

How often my young ears heard these words without comprehending them! But while I was too young and thoughtless to share in an enthusiasm for Sterne[1] or Fielding,[2] and Smollett[3] or Don Quixote,[4] my mother and grand-mother were leading me into the pleasant ways of *Pride and Prejudice,*[5] and *The Scenes of Clerical Life,*[6] and the delightful stories of Mrs. Oliphant.[7]

The old house was well provided with leather-bound books of a deeply serious nature, but in my youthful appetite for knowledge, I could even in the driest find something vital, and in the more entertaining I was completely lost.

My father had inherited from his father an amazing knowledge of human nature, and from his mother's French ancestry, that peculiarly French trait, called *gaieté de cœur.*[8] Through all the heavy responsibilities and anxieties of his busy professional life, this kept him young at heart and cheerful. His visits to his patients were often made perfectly delightful and refreshing to them by his kind heart, and the charm of his personality.

I knew many of the patients whom he used to visit in lonely inland farms, or on the seacoast in York and Wells. I used to follow him about silently, like an undemanding little dog, content to follow at his heels.

I had no consciousness of watching or listening, or indeed of any special interest in the country interiors. In fact, when the time came that my own world of imaginations was more real to me than any other, I was sometimes

---

[1] Laurence Sterne (1713–1768), English novelist best known for his humorous nine-volume series, *The Life and Opinions of Tristram Shandy.*

[2] Henry Fielding (1707–1754), English playwright and novelist known for his parodic style.

[3] Tobias George Smollett (1721–1771), Scottish novelist.

[4] Bewildered knight and main character of Miguel de Cervantes' satiric novel, *Don Quixote* (1615).

[5] *Pride and Prejudice* (1813), novel by the English writer Jane Austen (1775–1817) that, by its treatment of an ordinary family with ordinary problems, influenced the modern English novel.

[6] *The Scenes of Clerical Life* (1885), book of fictional sketches by Victorian novelist George Eliot [Mary Ann Evans]. Eliot (1819–1880) developed the method of psychological analysis widely used in modern fiction.

[7] Margaret Oliphant (1828–1897), prolific Victorian novelist, historical writer, and bi-ographer known for her sympathetic depictions of rural life.

[8] Lightheartedness (in French literally, gaiety of heart).

perplexed at my father's directing my attention to certain points of interest in the character or surroundings of our acquaintances.

I cannot help believing that he recognized, long before I did myself, in what direction the current of purpose in my life was setting. Now, as I write my sketches of country life, I remember again and again the wise things he said, and the sights he made me see. He was only impatient with affectation and insincerity.

I may have inherited something of my father's and grandfather's knowledge of human nature, but my father never lost a chance of trying to teach me to observe. I owe a great deal to his patience with a heedless little girl given far more to dreams than to accuracy, and with perhaps too little natural sympathy for the dreams of others.

The quiet village life, the dull routine of farming or mill life, early became interesting to me. I was taught to find everything that an imaginative child could ask, in the simple scenes close at hand.

I say these things eagerly, because I long to impress upon every boy and girl this truth: that it is not one's surroundings that can help or hinder — it is having a growing purpose in one's life to make the most of whatever is in one's reach.

If you have but a few good books, learn those to the very heart of them. Don't for one moment believe that if you had different surroundings and opportunities you would find the upward path any easier to climb. One condition is like another, if you have not the determination and the power to grow in yourself.

I was still a child when I began to write down the things I was thinking about, but at first I always made rhymes and found prose so difficult that a school composition was a terror to me, and I do not remember ever writing one that was worth anything. But in course of time rhymes themselves became difficult and prose more and more enticing, and I began my work in life, most happy in finding that I was to write of those country characters and rural landscapes to which I myself belonged, and which I had been taught to love with all my heart.

I was between nineteen and twenty when my first sketch was accepted by Mr. Howells[9] for the *Atlantic.* I already counted myself as by no means a new contributor to one or two other magazines — *Young Folks* and *The Riverside* — but I had no literary friends "at court."

I was very shy about speaking of my work at home, and even sent it to the magazine under an assumed name, and then was timid about asking the postmistress for those mysterious and exciting editorial letters which she announced upon the post office list as if I were a stranger in the town.

[1892]

---

[9] William Dean Howells (1837–1920), American novelist and editor.

MILAN KUNDERA *reflected on Kafka's fiction in* The Art of the Novel *(1986), where he defined the adjective "Kafkan" in several different ways. Believing that a comic element was inherent to the meaning of the word, Kundera stated that a Kafkan character (perhaps like Gregor Samsa or the Hunger Artist) "is trapped in the joke of his own life like a fish in a bowl; he doesn't think it funny. Indeed, a joke is a joke only if you're outside the bowl; by contrast, the Kafkan takes us inside, into the guts of a joke, into the horror of the comic."*

MILAN KUNDERA

Kafka and Modern History

Translated by Linda Asher and David Bellos

There are tendencies in modern history that produce the Kafkaesque quality in the broad social dimension: the progressive concentration of power, tending to deify itself [make itself godlike]; the bureaucratization of social activity that turns all institutions into boundless labyrinths; and the resulting depersonalization of the individual.

Totalitarian states, as extreme concentrations of these tendencies, have brought out the close relationship between Kafka's novels and real life. But . . . in fact, the society we call democratic is also familiar with the process that bureaucratizes and depersonalizes; the entire planet has become a theater of this process. . . .

Why was Kafka the first novelist to grasp these tendencies, which appeared on History's stage so clearly and brutally only after his death? Mystifications and legends aside, there is no significant trace anywhere of Franz Kafka's political interests; in that sense, he is different from all his Prague friends, from Max Brod, Franz Werfel, Egon Erwin Kisch, and from all the avantgardes that, claiming to know the direction of History, indulged in conjuring up the face of the future.

So how is it that not their works but those of their solitary, introverted companion, immersed in his own life and his art, are recognized today as a sociopolitical prophecy, and are for that very reason banned in a large part of the world?

I pondered this mystery one day after witnessing a little scene in the home of an old friend of mine. The woman in question had been arrested in 1951 during the Stalinist trials in Prague, and convicted of crimes she hadn't committed. Hundreds of Communists were in the same situation at the time. All their lives they had entirely identified themselves with their Party. When it suddenly became their prosecutor, they agreed, like Joseph K., "to examine their whole lives, their entire past, down to the smallest details" to find the hidden offense and, in the end, to confess to imaginary crimes. My friend managed to save her own life because she had the extraordinary courage to refuse to undertake — as her comrades did, as the poet A. did — the "search for her offense." Refusing to assist her persecutors, she became unusable for the final show trial. So instead of being hanged she got away with life imprisonment. After fourteen years, she was completely rehabilitated and released.

The woman had a one-year-old child when she was arrested. On release from prison, she thus rejoined her fifteen-year-old son and had the joy of sharing her humble solitude with him from then on. That she became passionately attached to the boy is entirely comprehensible. One day I went to see them — by then her son was twenty-five. The mother, hurt and angry, was crying. The cause was utterly trivial: the son had overslept or something like that. I asked the mother: "Why get so upset over such a trifle? Is it worth crying about? Aren't you overdoing it?"

It was the son who answered for his mother: "No, my mother's not overdoing it. My mother is a splendid, brave woman. She resisted when everyone else cracked. She wants me to become a real man. It's true, all I did was oversleep, but what my mother reproached me for is something much deeper. It's my attitude. My selfish attitude. I want to become what my mother wants me to be. And with you as a witness, I promise her I will."

What the party never managed to do to the mother, the mother had managed to do to her son. She had forced him to identify with an absurd accusation, to "seek his offense," to make a public confession. I looked on, dumbfounded, at this Stalinist minitrial, and I understood all at once that the psychological mechanisms that function in great (apparently incredible and inhuman) historical events are the same as those that regulate private (quite ordinary and very human) situations. [1988]

DAVID **HERBERT LAWRENCE** *published* Studies in Classic American Literature *in 1923. It includes his responses to the writings of Poe, Hawthorne, Melville, and the poet Walt Whitman, among others. As an Englishman, Lawrence read American authors for their contribution to the cultural life of the Western world, and not merely as writers of children's books, which he said was how most European readers viewed American authors at the time. Lawrence's judgments are often startling, sometimes extreme, but never dull. They reflect the moral passion exhibited in the rest of his work, especially his abhorrence of possessive love.*

D. H. LAWRENCE

The Lust of Hate in Poe's The Cask of Amontillado

The best [of Poe's] tales all have the same burden. Hate is as inordinate as love, and as slowly consuming, as secret, as underground, as subtle. All this underground vault business in Poe only symbolizes that which takes place *beneath* the consciousness. On top, all is fair-spoken. Beneath, there is the awful murderous extremity of burying alive. Fortunato, in "The Cask of Amontillado," is buried alive out of perfect hatred, as the lady Madeline of Usher[1] is buried alive out of love. The lust of hate is the inordinate desire to consume and unspeakably possess the soul of the hated one, just as the lust of love is the desire to possess, or to be possessed by, the beloved, utterly. But in either case the result is the dissolution of both souls, each losing itself in transgressing its own bounds.

The lust of Montresor is to devour utterly the soul of Fortunato. It would be no use killing him outright. If a man is killed outright his soul remains integral, free to return into the bosom of some beloved, where it can enact itself. In walling-up his enemy in the vault, Montresor seeks to bring about the indescribable capitulation of the man's soul, so that he, the victor, can possess himself of the very being of the vanquished. Perhaps this can actually be done. Perhaps, in the attempt, the victor breaks the bonds of his own identity, and collapses into nothingness, or into the infinite. Becomes a monster. [1923]

DAVID LEAVITT *published his article "The Way I Live Now" in the* New York Times *on July 9, 1989. It is an unusually candid account of how contemporary literature continues to offer the reader "a possibility of catharsis" in troubled times. Leavitt experienced this intense psychological release after reading Susan Sontag's story, "The Way We Live Now." Aristotle described the experience of catharsis in his* Poetics *two thousand years ago.*

---

[1] In Poe's story "The Fall of the House of Usher."

DAVID LEAVITT

The Way I Live Now

It used to be that when people asked me why I hadn't written about AIDS, I'd get angry. Because I had published a book of short stories and a novel that dealt with the themes of homosexuality and illness, I suppose they assumed the subject would come naturally to me. So what? I'd shout back. I'm not obligated to write about *anything*. Only if and when I was inspired to write about AIDS would I write about it.

But the truth was that AIDS scared me so much I wanted to block it out of my mind. When AIDS came up in a conversation, I'd change the subject; when a frightening headline leaped out at me from the pages of the news-paper, I'd hurriedly skim the article, and, once assured that it described no symptoms I could claim to be suffering from myself, turn the page. Only later, when people I was close to started to get sick, and I met writers who, in the panicked wake of diagnosis, didn't have the luxury of waiting for "inspiration," did I recognize the extent to which I was masking denial with self-righteousness.

I will always remember the mid-1980s, in New York City, as a time when the streets were filled with an almost palpable sense of mourning and panic. The office of the Gay Men's Health Crisis, or G.M.H.C., was a somber, silent place; it was no surprise to me that friends who did volunteer work there often mysteriously overslept the mornings they were supposed to go. The G.M.H.C.'s gray-carpeted hallways had a funereal hush that seemed the calm obverse of the dread sweeping the city: men anxiously prodding their necks for swollen lymph glands, or craning to examine mysterious pimples in the mirror. Everyone knew what the signs were, but no one knew exactly what they meant.

Then, somewhere near the end of that long corridor of anxiety, I read Susan Sontag's story "The Way We Live Now" in *The New Yorker*, and felt a sense of enormous and long-withheld release. Up to that point, reading fiction about AIDS had seemed to me akin to being shown a brick wall somewhere in the distance and then, at full speed, being hurled into it. Sontag, however, had written a story that transcended horror and grief, and which was there-fore redemptive, if not of AIDS itself, then at least of the processes by which people cope with it. The story was told from the multiple points of view of the many friends of a man with AIDS; its long sentences swirled madly around the never-named disease, just as the characters — dozens of them — swirled around their suffering friend, arguing, comforting, annoying each other, giving each other their anxieties, their metaphors, their lies.

"The Way We Live Now" succeeded, for me, primarily because it offered a possibility of catharsis, and at that time, catharsis was something we all badly needed. Particularly in the early years of the epidemic, a diagnosis of

AIDS carried with it a crushing burden of guilt; the knowledge that the transmission of the virus could have been avoided if one had skipped a particular sexual encounter proved to some people almost as unbearable as the sudden, distinct possibility of death, and as a result, both the sick and the "worried well" were forever rooting through their sexual histories in an obsessive effort to determine when or if they'd been infected. As Sontag would later point out in her book, *AIDS and Its Metaphors,* there was an intimate link between the mythology of the disease and a mythology of sex as something dirty, low, and indulgent; AIDS was like the "Roman Fever" of Edith Wharton's famous short story, an illness that marked the girls who suffered from it as having made the mistake of "going to the Coliseum" with Italian men.

What "The Way We Live Now" did so beautifully was to place the small tragedy of each HIV transmission into the larger context of the history of human interaction. In the age of AIDS, Sontag wrote, "the great chain of being has become a chain of death as well." And by reminding the reader that the "chain" of sexuality through which the virus had been spread was still the chain of life, Sontag managed to lift, at least partially, the moral onus of AIDS.

"The Way We Live Now" made me feel less alone in my dread, and therefore brave enough to read more. What I learned, as I read, was that of the people who were writing about AIDS regularly, some cared deeply about those who were sick, while others didn't care at all. And if anything distinguished the worthy writing about AIDS from the worthless, the discourse from the cant, it was the simple question of whether the author cared.

[1989]

URSULA K. LE GUIN *published* The Wind's Twelve Quarters, *the collection of short fiction in which "Those Who Walk Away from Omelas" appeared, in 1975. The stories in this book form a disturbing group, posing questions that stay with the reader long after each story is finished. In her commentary Le Guin describes the source for the idea of her story.*

URSULA K. LE GUIN

The Scapegoat in Omelas

The central idea of this psychomyth, the scapegoat, turns up in Dostoyevsky's *Brothers Karamazov,* and several people have asked me, rather suspiciously, why I gave the credit to William James. The fact is, I haven't been able to re-read Dostoyevsky, much as I loved him, since I was twenty-five, and I'd simply forgotten he used the idea. But when I met it in James's "The Moral Philosopher and the Moral Life," it was with a shock of recognition. Here is how James puts it:

> Or if the hypothesis were offered us of a world in which Messrs.
> Fourier's and Bellamy's and Morris's utopias should all be outdone,
> and millions kept permanently happy on the one simple condition
> that a certain lost soul on the far-off edge of things should lead a life
> of lonely torment, what except a specific and independent sort of
> emotion can it be which would make us immediately feel, even
> though an impulse arose within us to clutch at the happiness so
> offered, how hideous a thing would be its enjoyment when deliber-
> ately accepted as the fruit of such a bargain?

The dilemma of the American conscience can hardly be better stated. Dostoyevsky was a great artist, and a radical one, but his early social radicalism reversed itself, leaving him a violent reactionary. Whereas the American James, who seems so mild, so naïvely gentlemanly — look how he says "us," assuming all his readers are so decent as himself — was, and remained, and remains, a genuinely radical thinker. Directly after the "lost soul" passage he goes on,

> All the higher, more penetrating ideals are revolutionary. They present
> themselves far less in the guise of effects of past experience than in
> that of probable causes of future experience, factors to which the
> environment and the lessons it has so far taught us must learn to
> bend.

The application of those two sentences to this story, and to science fiction, and to all thinking about the future, is quite direct. Ideals as "the probable causes of future experience" — that is a subtle and an exhilarating remark!

Of course I didn't read James and sit down and say, Now I'll write a story about that "lost soul." It seldom works that simply. I sat down and started a story, just because I felt like it, with nothing but the word "Omelas" in mind. It came from a road sign: Salem (Oregon) backwards. Don't you read road signs backwards? POTS, WOLS nerdlihc. Ocsicnarf Nas . . . Salem equals schelomo equals salaam equals Peace. Melas. O melas. Omelas. Homme hélas. "Where *do* you get your ideas from, Ms. Le Guin?" From forgetting Dostoyevsky and reading road signs backwards, naturally. Where else?

[1975]

SIMON O. LESSER *presented an uncommonly poetic view of academic literary criticism in his book* Fiction and the Unconscious *(1957). He began by stating, "A book is a dream to which one attempts to give substance in the recalcitrant materials to which one is limited when awake." "The recalcitrant materials" of his literary study were the evidence he assembled to analyze what he regarded as our "apparently insatiable appetite for fiction." Indebted to psychoanalytic theory, he gave special attention, as in this reading of Nathaniel Hawthorne's tale, "to the characteristics that make it possible for fiction to give us pleasure and satisfaction even when it deals with events and problems which might arouse painful reactions if treated in other forms of discourse or experienced in life itself." His explanation was that in many cases, "the appeal of a story depends largely on things grasped below the threshold of awareness."*

SIMON O. LESSER

A Psychological Reading of Hawthorne's My Kinsman, Major Molineux

As soon as we look at "My Kinsman, Major Molineux" more closely, we discover that it is only in part a story of baffled search: Robin is never so intent on finding his illustrious relative as he believes he is and as it appears. The story even tells us why this is so. To some extent we understand from the very beginning; the explanations offered serve basically to remind us of things we have experienced ourselves.

As Robin walks into the town, it will be remembered, he realizes that he should probably have asked the ferryman how to get to the home of Major Molineux. Today we have scientific evidence for what Hawthorne, and we, understand intuitively, the significance of such forgetting. Earlier in the same paragraph we have been told something equally significant. Robin walks into the town "with as light a step as if his day's journey had not already exceeded thirty miles, and with as eager an eye as if he were entering London city, instead of the little metropolis of a New England colony." This though he has momentarily lost sight of the reason for his visit! As early as this we begin to suspect that the town attracts the youth for reasons which have nothing whatever to do with finding his influential relative. The intimation does not surprise us. Robin is eighteen. The ferryman has surmised that this is his first visit to town. In a general way we understand why his eye is "eager."

Robin makes his first inquiry for his kinsman with reasonable alacrity. But a considerable time appears to elapse before his second inquiry, at the tavern, and he is evidently spurred to enter it as much by the odor of food, which reminds him of his own hunger, as by any zeal to find the Major.

After his rebuff at the tavern it perhaps seems reasonable enough that Robin should drop his inquiries and simply walk through the streets looking for Major Molineux. If our critical faculties were not already somewhat re-laxed, however, it might occur to us at once that this is a singularly inefficient way of looking for anyone. And Robin does not pursue his impractical plan with any ardor. He stares at the young men he encounters with as much interest as at the old ones; though he notices the jaunty gait of others, he never increases his pace; and there are many pauses "to examine the gorgeous display of goods in the shop windows."

Nor does his lack of success make him impatient. Only the approach of the elderly gentleman he had first accosted causes him to abandon his plan and turn down a side street. He is now so tired and hungry that he *considers* demanding guidance from the first solitary passerby he encounters. But while this resolution is, as Hawthorne puts it, "gaining strength," what he actually does is enter "a street of mean appearance, on either side of which a row of ill-built houses was straggling toward the harbor." It is of the utmost importance that Robin continues his "researches" on this less respectable street, although no one is visible along its entire extent. If we were not by now so completely immersed in the concealed story which is unfolding itself, we might begin to wonder consciously whether Robin is seriously searching for his kinsman.

The encounters with women which follow explain the attraction of the street. They show that unconsciously Robin is searching for sexual adventure. The strength of his desire is almost pathetically betrayed by his half-willing-ness to believe the cock-and-bull story of the pretty young "housekeeper." Here, if not before, we identify one of the specific forces which is inhibiting Robin in his search for his kinsman: He would like a greater measure of sexual freedom than it is reasonable to suppose he would enjoy in the home of a colonial official.

The encounter with the watchman furnishes additional evidence of Robin's ambivalence. The youth could scarcely hope to find a better person of whom to ask directions. It is likely that he is also held back in this case by guilt about what he has just been doing, but the ease with which he has permitted himself to be diverted from his search is probably one of the sources of that guilt.

After further wandering Robin finally detains the passerby who tells him that the Major will pass that very spot within the hour. In talking with the kindly gentleman who joins him to await the arrival of the Major, Robin is unable to restrain himself from boasting of his shrewdness and grown-upness. These boasts help us to understand another of the forces which has been holding him back: He wants to succeed through his own efforts and his own merit. His departure from home has evidently caused him to dream of achieving economic as well as sexual independence. When at the end of the story the gentleman suggests that Robin may decide to stay in town and may prosper without the help of his kinsman, he is simply giving expression to the youth's unvoiced but readily discernible desire.

The gentleman has an opportunity to observe how halfhearted Robin is about finding his kinsman. When the sounds of the approaching procession become more clearly audible, the youth comes to the conclusion that some kind of "prodigious merry-making" is going forward and suggests that he and his new-found friend step around the corner, to a point where he thinks everyone is hastening, and partake of their share of the fun. He has to be reminded by his companion that he is searching for his kinsman, who is supposed to pass by the place where they now are in a very short time. With insight and artistry Hawthorne spreads the evidence of Robin's irresoluteness of purpose from the very beginning of the story to the moment of Major Molineux's appearance; but so subtle is the evidence, so smoothly does it fit into the surface flow of the narrative, that its significance never obtrudes itself on our attention.

By this point in the story, furthermore, we unconsciously understand Robin's vacillation more completely than I have been able to suggest. We see that, unbeknown to himself, the youth has good reasons for *not* wanting to find Major Molineux: When he finds him, he will have to resubmit to the kind of authority from which, temporarily at least, he has just escaped. At some deep level the Major appears anything but a potential benefactor; he symbol-izes just those aspects of the father from which the youth so urgently desires to be free. As an elderly relative of the father and an authority figure, he may be confused with the father. In any case, however undeservedly, he has now become the target of all the hostile and rebellious feelings which were origi-nally directed against the father.

Hawthorne tells us these things, it is interesting to note, by means of just the kind of unconscious manifestations which twentieth century psychol-ogy has found so significant. While Robin sits on the steps of the church, fighting his desire to sleep, he has a fantasy in which he imagines that his kinsman is already dead! And his very next thought is of his father's house-hold. He wonders how "that evening of ambiguity and weariness" has been spent at home, and has a second fantasy of such hallucinatory vividness that he wonders if he is "here or there." Nor is this an idle question. His father and Major Molineux are so inextricably linked in his mind that in a sense the drama in which he is involved is being played out "there" — at home — as well as in the town where bodily he happens to be.

The climax of this drama, so puzzling to the conscious intellect, is immediately comprehensible to that portion of the mind which has been following the hidden course of developments. It is comprehensible although Hawthorne describes Robin's feelings, as is right, in vague terms. Robin never understands those feelings and the reader would find it disturbing if they were too plainly labeled.

The feelings would probably never have secured open expression except under circumstances as out of the ordinary as those the story describes. But now everything conspires not simply to permit but to encourage Robin to give in to tendencies which as we know he was finding it difficult to control. To everyone present Major Molineux is overtly what he is to the youth on some dark and secret level — a symbol of restraint and unwelcome authority. He is this even to the elderly gentleman, the watchman, the man by his side — people whose disapproval of the crowd's behavior might have had a powerful effect upon him. Without a voice being raised in protest, the crowd is acting out the youth's repressed impulses and in effect urging him to act on them also. The joy the crowd takes in asserting its strength and the reappearance of the lady of the scarlet petticoat provide him with incentives for letting himself go.

And so Robin makes common cause with the crowd. He laughs — he laughs louder than anyone else. So long as he himself did not know how he would act he had reason to fear the crowd, and the relief he feels at the easing of the immediate situation is one of the sources of his laughter. But his decision resolves still deeper and more vexing conflicts. The relief he feels that he can vent his hostility for his kinsman and abandon his search for him is the ultimate source of his "riotous mirth." It is fueled by energy which until then was being expended in repression and inner conflict.

Although Hawthorne uses figurative language which may keep his meaning from being consciously noted, he is at pains to let us know that murderous hate underlies the merriment of the crowd of which Robin becomes a part. When the laughter momentarily dies down, the procession resumes its march.

> On they went, like fiends that throng in mockery around some dead potentate, mighty no more, but majestic still in his agony. On they went, in counterfeited pomp, in senseless uproar, in frenzied merriment, trampling all on an old man's heart.

Symbolically and to some extent actually the crowd has carried out the fantasy Robin had on the steps of the church.

To the conscious mind "My Kinsman, Major Molineux" is a story of an ambitious youth's thwarted search for an influential relative he wants to find. To the unconscious, it is a story of the youth's hostile and rebellious feelings for the relative — and for the father — and his wish to be free of adult domination. To the conscious mind it is a story of a search which was unsuccessful because of external difficulties. To the unconscious — like *Hamlet*, with which it has more than one point in common — it is a story of a young man caught up in an enterprise for which he has no stomach and debarred from succeeding in it by internal inhibitions.

From one point of view the unacknowledged forces playing upon the apparently simple and candid central character of "My Kinsman, Major Molineux" are deeply abhorrent. Our sympathy for the character should tell us, however, that there is another side to the matter. The tendencies which assert themselves in Robin exist in all men. What he is doing, unwittingly but flamboyantly, is something which every young man does and must do, however gradually, prudently, and inconspicuously: He is destroying an image of paternal authority so that, freed from its restraining influence, he can begin life as an adult.   [1957]

KATHERINE MANSFIELD *reviewed Virginia Woolf's story "Kew Gardens" in the* Athenaeum *on June 13, 1919. As the literary historian Clare Hanson has noted, Mansfield might have suggested an idea for this story to Woolf in a letter two years before, describing a garden with people engaged in "conversation, their slow pacing — their glances as they pass one another — the pauses as the flowers 'come in' as it were." In her favorable review of Woolf's story, Mansfield stressed the elements she regarded most highly in short fiction: She preferred atmosphere to action, and she valued the language of the story as much as the subject of the narrative. She believed that atmosphere and language together give short fiction an ethical dimension. According to Hanson, Mansfield was following Anton Chekhov in this conviction: "While she did not suggest that the artist should in any crude sense set out to preach or prove a point, she did believe that the 'true' artist's work would make an ethical impression, and that it was the duty of the critic to register this impression and measure its depth and quality."*

K ATHERINE M ANSFIELD

Review of Woolf's Kew Gardens

If it were not a matter to sigh over, it would be almost amusing to remember how short a time has passed since Samuel Butler[1] advised the budding author to keep a note-book. What would be the author's reply to such counsel nowadays but an amused smile: "I keep nothing else!" True; but if we remember rightly, Samuel Butler goes a little further; he suggests that the note-book should be kept in the pocket, and that is what the budding author finds intolerably hard. Up till now he has been so busy growing and

---

[1]Samuel Butler (1835–1902), Victorian essayist and autobiographical novelist.

blowing that his masterpieces still are unwritten, but there are the public waiting, gaping. Hasn't he anything to offer before they wander elsewhere? Can't he startle their attention by sheer roughness and crudeness and general slapdashery? Out comes the note-book and the deed is done. And since they find its contents absolutely thrilling and satisfying, is it to be wondered at that the risk of producing anything bigger, more solid, and more positive — is not taken? The note-books of young writers are their laurels; they prefer to rest on them. It is here that one begins to sigh, for it is here that the young author begins to swell and to demand that, since he has chosen to make his note-books his All, they shall be regarded as of the first importance, read with a deadly seriousness and acclaimed as a kind of new Art — the art of not taking pains, of never wondering why it was one fell in love with this or that, but contenting oneself with the public's dreary interest in promiscuity.

Perhaps that is why one feels that Mrs Virginia Woolf's story belongs to another age. It is so far removed from the note-book literature of our day, so exquisite an example of love at second sight. She begins where the others leave off, entering Kew Gardens, as it were, alone and at her leisure when their little first screams of excitement have died away and they have rushed afield to some new brilliant joy. It is strange how conscious one is, from the first paragraph, of this sense of leisure: Her story is bathed in it as if it were a light, still and lovely, heightening the importance of everything, and filling all that is within her vision with that vivid, disturbing beauty that haunts the air the last moment before sunset or the first moment after dawn. Poise — yes, poise. Anything may happen; her world is on tiptoe.

This is her theme. In Kew Gardens there was a flower-bed full of red and blue and yellow flowers. Through the hot July afternoon men and women "straggled past the flower-bed with a curiously irregular movement not unlike that of the white and blue butterflies who crossed the turf in zig-zag flights from bed to bed," paused for a moment, were "caught" in its dazzling net, and then moved on again and were lost. The mysterious intricate life of the flower-bed goes on untouched by these odd creatures. A little wind moves, stirring the petals so that their colours shake on to the brown earth, grey of a pebble, shell of a snail, a raindrop, a leaf, and for a moment the secret life is half-revealed; then a wind blows again, and the colours flash in the air and there are only leaves and flowers. . . .

It happens so often — or so seldom — in life, as we move among the trees, up and down the known and unknown paths, across the lawns and into the shade and out again, that something — for no reason that we can discover — gives us pause. Why is it that, thinking back upon that July afternoon, we see so distinctly that flower-bed? We must have passed myriads of flowers that day; why do these particular ones return? It is true, we stopped in front of them, and talked a little and then moved on. But though we weren't conscious of it at the time, something was happening — something . . .

But it would seem that the author, with her wise smile, is as indifferent as the flowers to these odd creatures and their ways. The tiny rich minute life of a snail — how she describes it! the angular high-stepping green insect — how passionate is her concern for him! Fascinated and credulous, we believe these things are all her concern until suddenly with a gesture she shows us the flower-bed, growing, expanding in the heat and light, filling a whole world.   [1919]

GUY DE MAUPASSANT *wrote an analysis of how he created fiction in the lengthy preface to his novel* Pierre and Jean *in 1888. In this excerpt he analyzes his intent as a writer and presents his view of realism. Maupassant wanted to clarify the point that no fiction can be called "realistic," if that term means a mirror image of life. Henry James later wrote that Maupassant's preface contains many insights into the nature of literature, including an important distinction between different kinds of fiction. James realized that Maupassant's "readers must be grateful to him for such a passage as that in which he remarks that whereas the public at large very legitimately says to a writer, 'Console me, amuse me, terrify me, make me cry, make me dream, or make me think,' what the sincere critic says is, 'Make me something fine in the form that shall suit you best, according to your temperament.' This seems to me to put into a nutshell the whole question of the different classes of fiction. . . . There are simply as many different kinds as there are persons practising the art, for if a picture, a tale, or a novel be a direct impression of life (and that surely constitutes its interest and value), the impression will vary according to the plate [temperament] that takes it, the particular structure and mixture of the recipient."*

GUY DE MAUPASSANT

The Writer's Goal

Translated by Mallay Charters

[T]he serious writer's] goal is not to tell us a story, to entertain or to move us, but to make us think and to make us understand the deep and hidden meaning of events. By virtue of having seen and meditated, he views the universe, objects, facts, and human beings in a certain way which is personal, the result of combining his observations and reflections. It is this personal view of the world that he tries to communicate to us by reproducing it in fiction. To move us, as he has been moved himself by the spectacle of life, he must reproduce it before our eyes with a scrupulous accuracy. He should compose his work so adroitly, and with such dissimulation and apparent simplicity, that it is impossible to uncover its plan or to perceive his intentions.

Instead of fabricating an adventure and spinning it out in a way that keeps it interesting until the end, the writer will pick up his characters at a certain point of their existence and carry them, by natural transitions, to the following period. He will show how minds are modified under the influence of environmental circumstances, and how sentiments and passions are developed. In this fashion, he will show our loves, our hates, our struggles in all kinds of social conditions; and how social interests, financial interests, political interests, and personal interests all compete with each other.

The writer's cleverness with his plot will thus consist not in the use of sentiment or charm, in an engaging beginning or an emotional catastrophe, but in the adroit grouping of small constant facts from which the reader will grasp a definitive sense of the work. . . . [The author] should know how to eliminate, among the minute and innumerable daily occurrences, all those which are useless to him. He must emphasize those which would have escaped the notice of less clear-sighted observers, which give the story its effect and value as fiction. . . .

A writer would find it impossible to describe everything in life, because he would need at least a volume a day to list the multitude of unimportant incidents filling up our hours.

Some selectivity is required — which is the first blow to the "entire truth" theory [of realistic literature].

Life, moreover, is composed of the most unpredictable, disparate, and contradictory elements. It is brutal, inconsequential, and disconnected, full of inexplicable, illogical, catastrophes.

This is why the writer, having selected a theme, will take from this chaotic life, encumbered with hazards and trivialities, only the details useful to his subject and omit all the others.

One example out of a thousand: The number of people in the world who die every day in accidents is considerable. But can we drop a roof tile on a main character's head, or throw him under the wheels of a car, in the middle of a narrative, under the pretext that it is necessary to have an accident?

Life can leave everything the same as it was. Or it can speed up some events and drag out others. Literature, on the other hand, presents cleverly orchestrated events and concealed transitions, essential incidents highlighted by the writer's skill alone. In giving every detail its exact degree of shading in accordance with its importance, the author produces the profound impression of the particular truth he wishes to point out.

To make things seem real on the page consists in giving the complete *illusion* of reality, following the logical order of facts, and not servilely transcribing the pell-mell succession of chronological events in life.

I conclude from this analysis that writers who call themselves realists should more accurately call themselves illusionists.

How childish, moreover, to believe in an absolute reality, since we each carry a personal one in our thoughts and in our senses. Our eyes, our ears, our sense of smell and taste create as many truths as there are individuals. Our minds, diversely impressed by the reception of the senses' information, comprehend, analyze, and judge as if each of us belonged to a separate race.

Thus each of us makes, individually, a personal illusion of the world. It may be a poetic, sentimental, joyful, melancholy, sordid, or dismal one, according to our nature. The writer's goal is to reproduce this illusion of life faithfully, using all the literary techniques at his disposal.   [1888]

HERMAN MELVILLE *wrote an eloquent essay on Nathaniel Hawthorne's volume of short stories,* Mosses from an Old Manse *for the New York periodical the* Literary World *in August 1850. Unlike Edgar Allan Poe in his review of Hawthorne's short fiction, Melville did not use the opportunity to theorize about the form of the short story. Instead he conveyed his enthusiasm for Hawthorne's tragic vision, what Melville saw as the "great power of blackness" in Hawthorne's writing that derived "its force from its appeals to that Calvinistic sense of Innate Depravity and Original Sin." This was the aspect of Hawthorne's work that seemed most congenial to Melville's own genius while he continued work that summer on his novel-in-progress,* Moby-Dick.

HERMAN MELVILLE

Blackness in Hawthorne's Young Goodman Brown

It is curious, how a man may travel along a country road, and yet miss the grandest or sweetest of prospects, by reason of an intervening hedge so like all other hedges as in no way to hint of the wide landscape beyond. So has it been with me concerning the enchanting landscape in the soul of this Hawthorne, this most excellent Man of Mosses. His Old Manse has been written now four years, but I never read it till a day or two since. I had seen it in the bookstores — heard of it often — even had it recommended to me by a tasteful friend, as a rare, quiet book, perhaps too deserving of popularity to be popular. But there are so many books called "excellent" and so much unpopular merit, that amid the thick stir of other things, the hint of my taste ful friend was disregarded; and for four years the Mosses on the Old Manse never refreshed me with their perennial green. It may be, however, that all this while, the book, like wine, was only improving in flavor and body. . . .

But it is the least part of genius that attracts admiration. Where Haw-thorne is known, he seems to be deemed a pleasant writer, with a pleasant style — a sequestered, harmless man, from whom any deep and weighty thing would hardly be anticipated: a man who means no meanings. But there is no man, in whom humor and love, like mountain peaks, soar to such a rapt height, as to receive the irradiations of the upper skies; there is no man in whom humor and love are developed in that high form called genius — no such man can exist without also possessing, as the indispensable complement of these, a great, deep intellect, which drops down into the universe like a plummet. Or, love and humor are only the eyes, through which such an intellect views this world. The great beauty in such a mind is but the product of its strength. . . .

For spite of all the Indian-summer sunlight on the hither side of Haw-thorne's soul, the other side — like the dark half of the physical sphere — is shrouded in a blackness, ten times black. But this darkness but gives more effect to the ever-moving dawn, that forever advances through it, and circum-navigates his world. Whether Hawthorne has simply availed himself of this mystical blackness as a means to the wondrous effects he makes it to produce in his lights and shades; or whether there really lurks in him, perhaps un-known to himself, a touch of Puritanic gloom — this I cannot altogether tell. Certain it is, however, that this great power of blackness in him derives its force from its appeals to that Calvinistic sense of Innate Depravity and Origi-nal Sin, from whose visitations, in some shape or other, no deeply thinking mind is always and wholly free. For, in certain moods, no man can weigh this world, without throwing in something, somehow like Original Sin, to strike the uneven balance. . . .

But with whatever motive, playful or profound, Nathaniel Hawthorne has chosen to entitle his pieces in the manner he has, it is certain that some of them are directly calculated to deceive — egregiously deceive — the su-perficial skimmer of pages. To be downright and candid once more, let me cheerfully say that two of these titles did dolefully dupe no less an eagle-eyed reader than myself; and that, too, after I had been impressed with a sense of the great depth and breadth of this American man. "Who in the name of thunder" (as the country people say in this neighborhood), "who in the name of thunder," would anticipate any marvel in a piece entitled "Young Good-man Brown"? You would of course suppose that it was a simple little tale, intended as a supplement to "Goody Two-Shoes." Whereas it is deep as Dante; nor can you finish it, without addressing the author in his own words: "It is yours to penetrate, in every bosom, the deep mystery of sin." And with Young Goodman, too, in allegorical pursuit of his Puritan wife, you cry out in your anguish,

> "Faith!" shouted Goodman Brown, in a voice of agony and desperation; and the echoes of the forest mocked him, crying — "Faith! Faith!" as if bewildered wretches were seeking her, all through the wilderness.

Now this same piece, entitled "Young Goodman Brown," is one of the two that I had not at all read yesterday; and I allude to it now, because it is, in itself, such a strong positive illustration of that blackness in Hawthorne which I had assumed from the mere occasional shadows of it, as revealed in several of the other sketches. But had I previously perused "Young Goodman Brown," I should have been at no pains to draw the conclusion which I came to at a time when I was ignorant that the book contained one such direct and unqualified manifestation of it.   [1850]

J. HILLIS MILLER *analyzed the effect of what he called "Bartleby's celebrated immobility" in the critical study* Versions of Pygmalion *(1990). Miller was intent on examining "strange and unaccountable" versions of the Pygmalion myth in European literature; each story he discussed "contains a character who does something like falling in love with a statue." In Miller's view, a story like "Bartleby, the Scrivener" was an occasion for "the act of personification essential to all storytelling and storyreading."*

J. HILLIS MILLER

A Deconstructive Reading of Melville's Bartleby, the Scrivener

After the failure of all these strategies for getting rid of Bartleby, the narrator tries another. In part through charity but in part through the notion that it is his fate to have Bartleby permanently in his chambers, he decides to try to live with Bartleby, to take him as a permanent fixture in his office. The narrator looks into two quite different books that deny man free will in determining his life, "Edwards on the Will" and "Priestly on Necessity." For Jonathan Edwards man does not have free will because everything he does is predestined by God. For Joseph Priestly, on the other hand, man is bound within the chains of a universal material necessity. Everything happens through physical causality, and therefore everything happens as it must happen, as it has been certain through all time to happen. In either case Bartleby's presence in the narrator's rooms is something predestined:

> Gradually I slid into the persuasion that these troubles of mine touch-
> ing the scrivener, had been all predestined from eternity, and Bar-
> tleby was billeted upon me for some mysterious purpose of an

all-wise Providence, which it was not for a mere mortal like me to fathom. Yes, Bartleby, stay there behind your screen, thought I; I shall persecute you no more; you are harmless and noiseless as any of these old chairs; in short, I never feel so private as when I know you are here. At last I see it, I feel it; I penetrate to the predestinated purpose of my life. I am content. Others may have loftier parts to enact; but my mission in this world, Bartleby, is to furnish you with office-room for such period as you may see fit to remain.

This strategy fails too, when the narrator's clients and associates let him know that Bartleby's presence in his offices is scandalizing his professional reputation. It is then that the narrator, who is nothing if not logical, conceives his strangest way of dealing with Bartleby. Since Bartleby will not budge, he himself will leave. The immobility of Bartleby turns the narrator into a nomad: "No more then. Since he will not quit me, I must quit him. I will change my offices; I will move elsewhere."

When the new tenants and the landlord of his old premises come to charge the narrator with responsibility for the nuisance Bartleby is causing, "haunting the building generally, sitting upon the banisters of the stairs by day, and sleeping in the entry by night," the narrator tries first a new strategy of saying he is in no way related to Bartleby or responsible for him. But it is no use: "I was the last person known to have anything to do with him, and they held me to the terrible account."

The narrator then meets Bartleby once more face to face. He offers to set him up in a respectable position, as a clerk in a dry-goods store, a bartender, a bill collector, or a companion for young gentlemen traveling to Europe. To all these ludicrous suggestions Bartleby replies that he is not particular, but he would prefer to remain "stationary." The narrator then, and finally, offers to take Bartleby home with him, like a stray cat, and give him refuge there. This meets with the same reply. The narrator flees the building and becomes truly a vagrant, wandering for days here and there in his rockaway.

The narrator's life and work seem to have been permanently broken by the irruption of Bartleby. It is not he but his old landlord who deals effectively with the situation. He has Bartleby "removed to the Tombs as a vagrant." This is just what the more intellectually consequent narrator has not been able to bring himself to do, not just because Bartleby is not, strictly speaking, a vagrant and not just because doing such violence to Bartleby would disobey the law of charity, but because he cannot respond with violence to a resistance that has been purely passive and has thereby "disarmed" or "unmanned" any decisive action: "Turn the man out by an actual thrusting I could not; to drive him away by calling him hard names would not do; calling in the police was an unpleasant idea . . . You will not thrust him, the poor, pale, passive mortal, — you will not thrust such a helpless creature out of your door? you will not dishonor yourself by such cruelty? No, I will not, I cannot do that."

Even after the police have been called in and society has placed Bartleby where he belongs, the narrator continues to be haunted by a sense of unfulfilled responsibility. He visits him in the Tombs, the prison so called because it was in the Egyptian Revival style of architecture, but also no doubt in response to a deeper sense of kinship between incarceration and death: "The Eygptian character of the masonry weighed upon me with its gloom. But a soft imprisoned turf grew under foot. The heart of the eternal pyramids, it seemed, wherein, by some strange magic, through the clefts, grass-seed, dropped by birds, had sprung." Bartleby is appropriately placed in the Tombs since, if the prison courtyard where Bartleby dies is green life in the midst of death, Bartleby has been death in the midst of life. In the Tombs the narrator makes his last unsuccessful attempt to deal with Bartleby in a rational manner, to reincorporate him into ordinary life. He "narrates" to the prison authorities, as he says, "all I knew" about Bartleby, telling them Bartleby does not really belong there but must stay "till something less harsh might be done — though indeed I hardly knew what." He yields at last to the accounting for Bartleby that had been used by Ginger Nut: "I think, sir, he's a little *luny*." The narrator now tells the "grub-man" in the prison, Mr. Cutlets, "I think he is a little deranged." One powerful means society has for dealing with someone who does not fit any ordinary social category is to declare him insane.

Mr. Cutlets has his own curious and by no means insignificant way of placing Bartleby. He thinks Bartleby must be a forger. "Deranged? deranged is it? Well now, upon my word, I thought that friend of yourn was a gentleman forger; they are always pale and genteel-like, them forgers. I can't help pity 'em — can't help it, sir. Did you know Monroe Edwards?" To which the narrator answers, "No, I was never socially acquainted with any forgers." In a way Mr. Cutlets has got Bartleby right, since forgery involves the exact copying of someone else's handwriting in order to make a false document that functions performatively as if it were genuine. Bartleby is a species of forger in reverse. He copies documents all right, but he does this in such a way as to deprive them of their power to make anything happen. On the other hand, when the narrator has copied documents checked, corrected, and made functional, he is himself performing an act of forgery. He may not be socially acquainted with any forgers, but he is in a manner of speaking one himself.

The arrangement he makes with Mr. Cutlets to feed Bartleby in prison is the narrator's last attempt to reincorporate Bartleby into society. There is much emphasis on eating in the story, on what the narrator's different employees eat and drink and on how little Bartleby eats, apparently nothing at all in prison: "'I prefer not to dine to-day,' said Bartleby, turning away. 'It would disagree with me; I am unused to dinners.' So saying he slowly moved to the other side of the inclosure, and took up a position fronting the dead-wall." Eating is one of the basic ways to share our common humanity. This Bartleby refuses, or rather he says he would prefer not to share in the ritual of eating. To refuse that is in the end deadly. Bartleby's death makes him what he has been all along, a bit of death in the midst of life.

It is entirely appropriate that the narrator's account of Bartleby should end with Bartleby's death, not because any biography should end with the death of the biographee but because in death Bartleby becomes what he has always already been. As I have said, his "I would prefer not to" is strangely oriented toward the future. It opens the future, but a future of perpetual not-yet. It can only come as death, and death is that which can never be present. There, at the end, the narrator finds the corpse of Bartleby, "strangely huddled at the base of the wall, his knees drawn up, and lying on his side, his head touching the cold stones." In an earlier version, the "Bartleby" fragment in the Melville family papers in the Gansevoort-Lansing Collection at the New York Public Library, Bartleby is found by the narrator lying in a white-washed room with his head against a tombstone: "It was clean, well-lighted and scrupulously white washed. The head-stone was standing up against the wall, and stretched on a blanket at its base, his head touching the cold marble and his feet upon the threshold lay the wasted form of Bartleby."

The corpse of Bartleby is not the presence of Bartleby. It is his eternal absence. In death he becomes what he has always been, a cadaver who "lives without dining," as the narrator says to the grub-man. Bartleby returns at death, in the final version of the story, to a fetal position. He is the incursion into life of that unattainable realm somewhere before birth and after death. But the word "realm" is misleading. What Bartleby brings is not a realm in the sense of place we might go. It is the otherness that all along haunts or inhabits life from the inside. This otherness can by no method, such as the long series of techniques the narrator tries, be accounted for, narrated, rationalized, or in any other way reassimilated into ordinary life, though it is a permanent part of that ordinary life. Bartleby is the alien that may neither be thrust out the door nor domesticated, brought into the family, given citizenship papers. Bartleby is the invasion of death into life, but not death as something from outside life. He is death as the other side of life or the cohabitant with life. "Death," nevertheless, is not the proper name for this ghostly companion of life, as if it were an allegorical meaning identified at last. Nor is "Death" its generic or common name. "Death" is a catachresis for what can never be named properly.

The narrator's last method of attempting to deal with Bartleby is his narration, going all the way from "I am a rather elderly man" to "Ah Bartleby! Ah humanity!" This narration is explicitly said to be written down and addressed to a "reader." It repeats for a more indeterminate reader, that is, for whoever happens to read it, the quasi-legal deposition he has made before the proper officer of "the Tombs, or to speak more properly, the Halls of Justice." If the narrator can encompass Bartleby with words, if he can do justice to him, he may simultaneously have accounted for him, naturalized him after all, and freed himself from his unfulfilled obligation. He will have made an adequate response to the demand Bartleby has made on him. The narrator, that is, may have justified himself while doing justice to Bartleby.

This is impossible because Bartleby cannot be identified. His story cannot be told. But the reader at the end knows better just why this is so, since we have watched the narrator try one by one a whole series of strategies for accounting for someone and has seen them one by one fail. This failure leaves Bartleby still imperturbably bringing everything to a halt or indefinitely postponing everything with his "I would prefer not to." The narrator's account is not so much an account as an apology for his failure to give an adequate account.

The narrator's writing is also an attempt at a reading, a failed attempt to read Bartleby. In this sense it is the first in a long line of attempts to read Bartleby the scrivener, though the narrator's successors do this by trying to read the text written by Melville, "Bartleby, the Scrivener." Just as Bartleby by his immovable presence in the narrator's office has demanded to be read and accounted for by him, so Melville's strange story demands to be read and accounted for. Nor have readers failed to respond to the demand. A large secondary literature has grown up around "Bartleby," remarkable for its multiplicity and diversity. All claim in one way or another to have identified Bartleby and to have accounted for him, to have done him justice. They tend to exemplify that function of policing or putting things in their place which is entrusted by our society to literary studies as one realm among many of the academic forms of accounting or accounting for. In the case of the essays on "Bartleby" this accounting often takes one or the other of two main forms, as Warminski has observed. These forms could be put under the aegis of the two-pronged last paragraph of the story — "Ah Bartleby! Ah humanity!" — or they might be said to fly in the face either of Bartleby's "But I am not particular" or of the manifest failure of the narrator's attempt to draw close to Bartleby by way of "the bond of a common humanity." Many of the essays try to explain Bartleby either by making him an example of some universal type, for example "existential man," or by finding some particular original or explanatory context for him, for example one of Melville's acquaintances who worked in a law office, or some aspect of nineteenth-century capitalism in America. But Bartleby is neither general nor particular: he is neutral. As such, he disables reading by any of these strategies, any attempt to put "Bartleby the Scrivener" in its place by answering the question, "In mercy's name, who is he?"

No doubt my own reading also claims to have identified Bartleby, in this case by defining him as the neutral in-between that haunts all thinking and living by dialectical opposition. All readings of the story, including my own, are more ways to call in the police. They are ways of trying to put Bartleby in his place, to convey him where we want to put him, to make sense of him, even if it is an accounting that defines him as the nonsense that inhabits all sense-making. All readings attempt in one way or another to fulfill what the narrator has tried and failed to do: to tell Bartleby's story in a way that will allow us to assimilate him and the story into the vast archives of rationalization that make up the secondary literature of our profession. We are institutionalized to do that work of policing for our society. None of these techniques of assimilation works any better than any of the narrator's meth-ods, and we remain haunted by Bartleby, but haunted also by "Bartleby, the Scrivener: A Story of Wall-Street." I claim, however, that my accounting succeeds where the others fail by showing (though that is not quite the right word) why it is that "accounting for" in any of its usual senses cannot work, either for the story or for the character the story poses.   [1990]

BHARATI MUKHERJEE *wrote "A Four-Hundred-Year-Old Woman" for volume two of Janet Sternburg's* The Writer on Her Work *(1991). In the essay Mukherjee analyzed how the experience of leaving India to make her home and career in America has shaped her view of herself as a writer.*

BHARATI MUKHERJEE

A Four-Hundred-Year-Old Woman

I was born into a class that did not live in its native language. I was born into a city that feared its future, and trained me for emigration. I attended a school run by Irish nuns, who regarded our walled-off school compound in Calcutta as a corner (forever green and tropical) of England. My "country" — called in Bengali *desh,* and suggesting more a homeland than a nation of which one is a citizen — I have never seen. It is the ancestral home of my father and is now in Bangladesh. Nevertheless, I speak his dialect of Bengali, and think of myself as "belonging" to Faridpur, the tiny green-gold village that was his birthplace. I was born into a religion that placed me, a Brahmin, at the top of its hierarchy while condemning me, as a woman, to a role of subservience. The larger political entity to which I gave my first allegiance — India — was not even a sovereign nation when I was born.

My horoscope, cast by a neighborhood astrologer when I was a week-old infant, predicted that I would be a writer, that I would win some prizes, that I would cross "the black waters" of oceans and make my home among aliens. Brought up in a culture that places its faith in horoscopes, it never occurred to me to doubt it. The astrologer meant to offer me a melancholy future; to be destined to leave India was to be banished from the sources of true culture. The nuns at school, on the other hand, insinuated that India had long outlived its glories, and that if we wanted to be educated, modern women and make something of our lives, we'd better hit the trail westward. All my girlhood, I straddled the seesaw of contradictions. *Bilayat,* meaning the scary, unknown "abroad," was both boom time and desperate loss.

I have found my way to the United States after many transit stops. The unglimpsed phantom Faridpur and the all too real Manhattan have merged as "desh." I am an American. I am an American writer, in the American mainstream, trying to extend it. This is a vitally important statement for me — I am not an Indian writer, not an exile, not an expatriate. I am an immigrant; my investment is in the American reality, not the Indian. I look on ghettoization — whether as a Bengali in India or as a hyphenated Indo-American in North America — as a temptation to be surmounted.

It took me ten painful years, from the early seventies to the early eighties, to overthrow the smothering tyranny of nostalgia. The remaining struggle for me is to make the American readership, meaning the editorial and publishing industries as well, acknowledge the same fact. (As the reception of such films as *Gandhi* and *A Passage to India* as well as *The Far Pavillions* and *The Jewel in the Crown* shows, nostalgia is a two-way street. Americans can feel nostalgic for a world they never knew.) The foreign-born, the exotically raised Third World immigrant with non-Western religions and non-European languages and appearance, can be as American as any steerage passenger from Ireland, Italy, or the Russian Pale. As I have written in another context (a review article in *The Nation* on books by Studs Terkel and Al Santoli), we are probably only a few years away from a Korean *What Makes Choon-li Run?* or a Hmong *Call It Sleep*. In other words, my literary agenda begins by acknowledging that America has transformed *me*. It does not end until I show how I (and the hundreds of thousands like me) have transformed America.

The agenda is simply stated, but in the long run revolutionary. Make the familiar exotic; the exotic familiar.

I have had to create an audience. I cannot rely on shorthand references to my community, my religion, my class, my region, or my old school tie. I've had to sensitize editors as well as readers to the richness of the lives I'm writing about. The most moving form of praise I receive from readers can be summed up in three words: *I never knew*. Meaning, I see these people (call them Indians, Filipinos, Koreans, Chinese) around me all the time and I never knew they had an inner life. I never knew they schemed and cheated, suffered, felt so strongly, cared so passionately. When even the forms of praise are so rudimentary, the writer knows she has an inexhaustible fictional population to enumerate. Perhaps even a mission, to appropriate a good colonial word.

I have been blessed with an enormity of material. I can be Chekhovian and Tolstoyan — with melancholy and philosophical perspectives on the breaking of hearts as well as the fall of civilizations — and I can be a brash and raucous homesteader, Huck Finn and Woman Warrior, on the unclaimed plains of American literature. My material, reduced to jacket-flap copy, is the rapid and dramatic transformation of the United States since the early 1970s. Within that perceived perimeter, however, I hope to wring surprises.

Yet (I am a writer much given to "yet") my imaginative home is also in the tales told by my mother and grandmother, the world of the Hindu epics. For all the hope and energy I have placed in the process of immigration and accommodation — I'm a person who couldn't ride a public bus when she first arrived, and now I'm someone who watches tractor pulls on obscure cable channels — there are parts of me that remain Indian, parts that slide against the masks of newer selves. The form that my stories and novels take inevitably reflects the resources of Indian mythology — shape-changing, miracles, godly perspectives. My characters can, I hope, transcend the straitjacket of simple psychologizing. The people I write about are culturally and politically several hundred years old: consider the history they have witnessed (colonialism, technology, education, liberation, civil war, uprooting). They have shed old identities, taken on new ones, and learned to hide the scars. They may sell you newspapers, or clean your offices at night.

Writers (especially American writers, weaned on the luxury of affluence and freedom) often disavow the notion of a "literary duty" or "political consciousness," citing the all-too-frequent examples of writers ruined by their shrill commitments. Glibness abounds on both sides of the argument, but finally I have to side with my "Third World" compatriots: I do have a duty, beyond telling a good story or drawing a convincing character. My duty is to give voice to continents, but also to redefine the nature of *American* and what makes an American. In the process, work like mine and dozens like it will open up the canon of American literature.

It has not been an easy transition, from graduate student to citizen, from natural-born expatriate to the hurly-burly of immigration. My husband (Clark Blaise) and I spent fifteen years in his *desh* of Canada, and Canada was a country that discouraged the very process of assimilation. Eventually, it also discouraged the very presence of "Pakis" in its midst, and in 1980, a low point in our lives, we left, gave up our tenured, full-professor lives for the free-lancing life in the United States.

We were living in Iowa City in 1983 when Emory University called me to be writer-in-residence for the winter semester. My name, apparently, had been suggested to them by an old friend. I hadn't published a book in six years (two earlier novels, *The Tiger's Daughter* and *Wife*, as well as our joint nonfiction study, *Days and Nights in Calcutta*, were out of print) but somehow Emory didn't hold it against me.

Atlanta turned out to be the luckiest writing break of my life. For one of those mysterious reasons, stories that had been gathering in me suddenly exploded. I wrote nearly all the stories in *Darkness* (Penguin, 1985) in those three months. I finally had a glimpse of my true material, and that is immigration. In other words, transformation — not preservation. I saw myself and my own experience refracted through a dozen separate lives. Clark, who remained in Iowa City until our younger son finished high school, sent me newspaper accounts, and I turned them into stories. Indian friends in Atlanta took me to dinners and table gossip became stories. Suddenly, I had begun appropriating the American language. My stories were about the hurly-burly of the unsettled magma between two worlds.

Eventually — inevitably — we made our way to New York. My next batch of stories (*The Middleman and Other Stories*, Grove, 1988) appropriate the American language in ways that are personally most satisfying to me (one Chicago reviewer likened it to Nabokov's *Lolita*), and my characters are now as likely to be American as immigrant, and Chinese, Filipino, or Middle Eastern as much as Indian. That book has enjoyed widespread support both critically and commercially, and empowered me to write a new novel, *Jasmine*, and to contract for a major work, historical in nature, that nevertheless incorporates a much earlier version of my basic theme, due for completion in the next three years. *Days and Nights in Calcutta* is being made into a feature film.

My theme is the making of new Americans. Wherever I travel in the (very) Old World, I find "Americans" in the making, whether or not they ever make it to these shores. I see them as dreamers and conquerors, not afraid of transforming themselves, not afraid of abandoning some of their principles along the way. In *Jasmine,* my "American" is born in a Punjabi village, marries at fourteen, and is widowed at sixteen. Nevertheless, she is an American and will enter the book as an Iowa banker's wife.

Ancestral habits of mind can be constricting; they also confer one's individuality. I know I can appropriate the American language, but I can never be a minimalist. I have too many stories to tell. I am aware of myself as a four-hundred-year-old woman, born in the captivity of a colonial, preindustrial oral culture and living now as a contemporary New Yorker.

My image of artistic structure and artistic excellence is the Moghul miniature painting with its crazy foreshortening of vanishing point, its insistence that everything happens simultaneously, bound only by shape and color. In the miniature paintings of India, there are a dozen separate foci, the most complicated stories can be rendered on a grain of rice, the corners are as elaborated as the centers. There is a sense of the interpenetration of all things. In the Moghul miniature of my life, there would be women investigating their bodies with mirrors, but they would be doing it on a distant balcony under fans wielded by bored serving girls; there would be a small girl listening to a bent old woman; there would be a white man eating popcorn and watching a baseball game; there would be cocktail parties and cornfields and a village set among rice paddies and skyscrapers. In a sense, I wrote that story, "Courtly Vision," at the end of *Darkness.* And in a dozen other ways I'm writing it today, and I will be writing, in the Moghul style, till I get it right. [1991]

VLADIMIR NABOKOV *delivered lectures on Russian literature to his classes at Cornell University from 1948 to 1958. Forced to leave his native country at the age of twenty to escape what he called "the bloated octopus of the state" after the Russian Revolution, he took with him a passionate love for his homeland and for the "fiery, fanciful, free" literature of prerevolutionary Russia. For Nabokov, the great Russian writers of the nineteenth century (he began his lecture series with Nikolai Gogol) were more than artists: They were the last free voices in Russia for whom the government did not dictate absolute limits of imagination.*

VLADIMIR NABOKOV

Gogol's Genius in The Overcoat

Gogol was a strange creature, but genius is always strange; it is only your healthy second-rater who seems to the grateful reader to be a wise old friend, nicely developing the reader's own notions of life. Great literature skirts the irrational. *Hamlet* is the wild dream of a neurotic scholar. Gogol's *The Overcoat* is a grotesque and grim nightmare making black holes in the dim pattern of life. The superficial reader of that story will merely see in it the heavy frolics of an extravagant buffoon; the solemn reader will take for granted that Gogol's prime intention was to denounce the horrors of Russian bureaucracy. But neither the person who wants a good laugh, nor the person who craves for books "that make one think" will understand what *The Overcoat* is really about. Give me the creative reader; this is a tale for him.

Steady Pushkin,[1] matter-of-fact Tolstoy, restrained Chekhov have all had their moments of irrational insight which simultaneously blurred the sentence and disclosed a secret meaning worth the sudden focal shift. But with Gogol this shifting is the very basis of his art, so that whenever he tried to write in the round hand of literary tradition and to treat rational ideas in a logical way, he lost all trace of talent. When, as in his immortal *The Overcoat*, he really let himself go and pottered happily on the brink of his private abyss, he became the greatest artist that Russia has yet produced.

The sudden slanting of the rational plane of life may be accomplished of course in many ways, and every great writer has his own method. With Gogol it was a combination of two movements: a jerk and a glide. Imagine a trap-door that opens under your feet with absurd suddenness, and a lyrical gust that sweeps you up and then lets you fall with a bump into the next traphole. The absurd was Gogol's favorite muse — but when I say "the absurd," I do not mean the quaint or the comic. The absurd has as many shades and degrees as the tragic has, and moreover, in Gogol's case, it borders upon the latter. It would be wrong to assert that Gogol placed his characters in absurd situations. You cannot place a man in an absurd situation if the whole world he lives in is absurd; you cannot do this if you mean by "absurd" something provoking a chuckle or a shrug. But if you mean the pathetic, the human condition, if you mean all such things that in less weird worlds are linked up with the loftiest aspirations, the deepest sufferings, the strongest passions — then of course the necessary breach is there, and a pathetic human, lost in the midst of Gogol's nightmarish, irresponsible world would be "absurd," by a kind of secondary contrast.

---

[1] Aleksandr Pushkin (1799–1837), considered by many (including Nabokov) the greatest Russian poet. Nabokov translated his novel in verse, *Eugene Onegin*, into English. For introductions to Anton Chekhov and Leo Tolstoy, see pages 279 and 1236.

On the lid of the tailor's snuff-box there was "the portrait of a General; I do not know what general because the tailor's thumb has made a hole in the general's face and a square of paper has been gummed over the hole." Thus with the absurdity of Akaky Akakievich Bashmachkin. We did not expect that, amid the whirling masks, one mask would turn out to be a real face, or at least the place where that face ought to be. The essence of mankind is irrationally derived from the chaos of fakes which form Gogol's world. Akaky Akakievich, the hero of *The Overcoat*, is absurd *because* he is pathetic, *because* he is human, and *because* he has been engendered by those very forces which seem to be in such contrast to him.

He is not merely human and pathetic. He is something more, just as the background is not mere burlesque. Somewhere behind the obvious contrast there is a subtle genetic link. His being discloses the same quiver and shimmer as does the dream world to which he belongs. The allusions to something else behind the crudely painted screens, are so artistically combined with the superficial texture of the narration that civic-minded Russians have missed them completely. But a creative reading of Gogol's story reveals that here and there is the most innocent descriptive passage, this or that word, sometimes a mere adverb or a preposition, for instance the word "even" or "almost," is inserted in such a way as to make the harmless sentence explode in a wild display of nightmare fireworks; or else the passage that had started in a rambling colloquial manner all of a sudden leaves the tracks and swerves into the irrational where it really belongs; or again, quite as suddenly, a door bursts open and a mighty wave of foaming poetry rushes in only to dissolve in bathos,[2] or to turn into its own parody, or to be checked by the sentence breaking and reverting to a conjuror's patter, that patter which is such a feature of Gogol's style. It gives one the sensation of something ludicrous and at the same time stellar, lurking constantly around the corner — and one likes to recall that the difference between the comic side of things, and their cosmic side, depends upon one sibilant.

So what is that queer world, glimpses of which we keep catching through the gaps of the harmless looking sentences? It is in a way the *real* one but it looks wildly absurd to us, accustomed as we are to the stage setting that screens it. It is from these glimpses that the main character of *The Overcoat*, the meek little clerk, is formed, so that he embodies the spirit of that secret but real world which breaks through Gogol's style. He is, that meek little clerk, a ghost, a visitor from some tragic depths who by chance happened to assume the disguise of a petty official. Russian progressive critics sensed in him the image of the underdog and the whole story impressed them as a social protest. But it is something much more than that. The gaps and black holes in the texture of Gogol's style imply flaws in the texture of life itself. Something is very wrong and all men are mild lunatics engaged in pursuits that seem to them very important while an absurdly logical force keeps them at their futile jobs — this is the real "message" of the story. In this world of

---

[2]One source has defined *bathos* as "pathos [the evoking of sympathy, sorrow, or pity] so overdone that it evokes laughter rather than pity."

utter futility, of futile humility and futile domination, the highest degree that passion, desire, creative urge can attain is a new cloak which both tailors and customers adore on their knees. I am not speaking of the moral point or the moral lesson. There can be no moral lesson in such a world because there are no pupils and no teachers: this world *is* and it excludes everything that might destroy it, so that any improvement, any struggle, any moral purpose or endeavor, are as utterly impossible as changing the course of a star. It is Gogol's world and as such wholly different from Tolstoy's world, or Pushkin's, or Chekhov's, or my own. But after reading Gogol one's eyes may become gogolized and one is apt to see bits of his world in the most unexpected places. I have visited many countries, and something like Akaky Akakievich's overcoat has been the passionate dream of this or that chance acquaintance who never had heard about Gogol.   [1981]

VLADIMIR NABOKOV *was a skillful guide to fiction in his* Lectures on Russian Literature. *As this excerpt from his analysis of Anton Chekhov's stories shows, he blended wit, irreverence, and critical insight in his summary of the intricacies of plot and character, illuminating the artistic achievements of the author. Nabokov felt that Chekhov's books are "sad books for humorous people" — that is, only a reader with a sense of humor can really appreciate their sadness. Chekhov's subtle humor pervades the grayness of the lives he created, flickering through his prose style: "He did it," said Nabokov, "by keeping all his words in the same dim light and of the same exact tint of gray, a tint between the color of an old fence and that of a low cloud."*

VLADIMIR NABOKOV

A Reading of Chekhov's The Lady with the Little Dog

Chekhov comes into the story "The Lady with the Little Dog" without knocking. There is no dilly-dallying. The very first paragraph reveals the main character, the young fair-haired lady followed by her white Spitz dog on the waterfront of a Crimean resort, Yalta, on the Black Sea. And immediately after, the male character Gurov appears. His wife, whom he has left with the children in Moscow, is vividly depicted: her solid frame, her thick black eyebrows, and the way she has of calling herself "a woman who thinks." One notes the magic of the trifles the author collects — the wife's manner of dropping a certain mute letter in spelling and her calling her husband by the longest and fullest form of his name, both traits in combination with the impressive dignity of her beetle-browed face and rigid poise forming exactly the necessary impression. A hard woman with the strong feminist and social ideas of her time, but one whom her husband finds in his heart of hearts to be narrow, dull-minded, and devoid of grace. The natural transition is to Gurov's constant unfaithfulness to her, to his general attitude toward women — "that inferior race" is what he calls them, but without that inferior race he could not exist. It is hinted that these Russian romances were not altogether as light-winged as in the Paris of Maupassant. Complications and problems are unavoidable with those decent hesitating people of Moscow who are slow heavy starters but plunge into tedious difficulties when once they start going.

Then with the same neat and direct method of attack, with the bridging formula "and so . . ." (or perhaps still better rendered in English by that "Now" which begins a new paragraph in straightforward fairy tales), we slide back to the lady with the dog. Everything about her, even the way her hair was done, told him that she was bored. The spirit of adventure — though he realized perfectly well that his attitude toward a lone woman in a fashionable sea town was based on vulgar stories, generally false — this spirit of adventure prompts him to call the little dog, which thus becomes a link between her and him. They are both in a public restaurant.

> He beckoned invitingly to the Spitz, and when the dog approached him, shook his finger at it. The Spitz growled; Gurov threatened it again.
> The lady glanced at him and at once dropped her eyes.
> "He doesn't bite," she said and blushed.
> "May I give him a bone?" he asked; and when she nodded he inquired affably, "Have you been in Yalta long?"
> "About five days."

They talk. The author has hinted already that Gurov was witty in the company of women; and instead of having the reader take it for granted (you know the old method of describing the talk as "brilliant" but giving no samples of the conversation), Chekhov makes him joke in a really attractive, winning way. "Bored, are you? An average citizen lives in . . . (here Chekhov lists the names of beautifully chosen, super-provincial towns) and is not bored, but when he arrives here on his vacation it is all boredom and dust. One could think he came from Granada" (a name particularly appealing to the Russian imagination). The rest of their talk, for which this sidelight is richly sufficient, is conveyed indirectly. Now comes a first glimpse of Chekhov's own system of suggesting atmosphere by the most concise details of nature, "the sea was of a warm lilac hue with a golden path for the moon"; whoever has lived in Yalta knows how exactly this conveys the impression of a summer evening there. This first movement of the story ends with Gurov alone in his hotel room thinking of her as he goes to sleep and imagining her delicate weak-looking neck and her pretty gray eyes. It is to be noted that only now, through the medium of the hero's imagination, does Chekhov give a visible and definite form to the lady, features that fit perfectly with her listless manner and expression of boredom already known to us.

> Getting into bed he recalled that she had been a schoolgirl only recently, doing lessons like his own daughter; he thought how much timidity and angularity there was still in her laugh and her manner of talking with a stranger. It must have been the first time in her life that she was alone in a setting in which she was followed, looked at, and spoken to for one secret purpose alone, which she could hardly fail to guess. He thought of her slim, delicate throat, her lovely gray eyes.
>
> "There's something pathetic about her, though," he thought, and dropped off.

The next movement (each of the four diminutive chapters or movements of which the story is composed is not more than four or five pages long), the next movement starts a week later with Gurov going to the pavilion and bringing the lady iced lemonade on a hot windy day, with the dust flying; and then in the evening when the sirocco subsides, they go on the pier to watch the incoming steamer. "The lady lost her lorgnette in the crowd," Chekhov notes shortly, and this being so casually worded, without any direct influence on the story — just a passing statement — somehow fits in with that helpless pathos already alluded to.

Then in her hotel room her awkwardness and tender angularity are delicately conveyed. They have become lovers. She was now sitting with her long hair hanging down on both sides of her face in the dejected pose of a sinner in some old picture. There was a watermelon on the table. Gurov cut himself a piece and began to eat unhurriedly. This realistic touch is again a typical Chekhov device.

She tells him about her existence in the remote town she comes from and Gurov is slightly bored by her naiveté, confusion, and tears. It is only now that we learn her husband's name: von Dideritz — probably of German descent.

They roam about Yalta in the early morning mist.

> At Oreanda they sat on a bench not far from the church, looked down at the sea, and were silent. Yalta was barely visible through the morning mist; white clouds rested motionlessly on the mountaintops. The leaves did not stir on the trees, the crickets chirped, and the monotonous muffled sound of the sea that rose from below spoke of the peace, the eternal sleep awaiting us. So it rumbled below when there was no Yalta, no Oreanda here; so it rumbles now, and it will rumble as indifferently and hollowly when we are no more. . . . Sitting beside a young woman who in the dawn seemed so lovely, Gurov, soothed and spellbound by these magical surroundings — the sea, the mountains, the clouds, the wide sky — thought how everything is really beautiful in this world when one reflects: everything except what we think or do ourselves when we forget the higher aims of life and our own human dignity.

A man strolled up to them — probably a watchman — looked at them and walked away. And this detail, too, seemed so mysterious and beautiful. They saw a steamer arrive from Feodosia, its lights extinguished in the glow of dawn.

"There is dew on the grass," said Anna Sergeievna, after a silence.

"Yes, it's time to go home."

Then several days pass and then she has to go back to her home town.

"'Time for me, too, to go North,' thought Gurov as he returned after seeing her off." And there the chapter ends.

The third movement plunges us straight into Gurov's life in Moscow. The richness of a gay Russian winter, his family affairs, the dinners at clubs and restaurants, all this is swiftly and vividly suggested. Then a page is devoted to a queer thing that has happened to him: he cannot forget the lady with the little dog. He has many friends, but the curious longing he has for talking about his adventure finds no outlet. When he happens to speak in a very general way of love and women, nobody guesses what he means, and only his wife moves her dark eyebrows and says: "Stop that fatuous posing; it does not suit you."

And now comes what in Chekhov's quiet stories may be called the climax. There is something that your average citizen calls romance and something he calls prose — though both are the meat of poetry for the artist. Such a contrast has already been hinted at by the slice of watermelon which Gurov crunched in a Yalta hotel room at a most romantic moment, sitting heavily and munching away. This contrast is beautifully followed up when at last Gurov blurts out to a friend late at night as they come out of the club: If you knew what a delightful woman I met in Yalta! His friend, a bureaucratic civil servant, got into his sleigh, the horses moved, but suddenly he turned and called back to Gurov. Yes? asked Gurov, evidently expecting some reaction to what he had just mentioned. By the way, said the man, you were quite right. That fish at the club was decidedly smelly.

This is a natural transition to the description of Gurov's new mood, his feeling that he lives among savages where cards and food are life. His family, his bank, the whole trend of his existence, everything seems futile, dull, and senseless. About Christmas he tells his wife he is going on a business trip to St. Petersburg, instead of which he travels to the remote Volga town where the lady lives.

Critics of Chekhov in the good old days when the mania for the civic problem flourished in Russia were incensed with his way of describing what they considered to be trivial unnecessary matters instead of thoroughly examining and solving the problems of bourgeois marriage. For as soon as Gurov arrives in the early hours to that town and takes the best room at the local hotel, Chekhov, instead of describing his mood or intensifying his difficult moral position, gives what is artistic in the highest sense of the word: he notes the gray carpet, made of military cloth, and the inkstand, also gray with dust, with a horesman whose hand waves a hat and whose head is gone. That is all: it is nothing but it is everything in authentic literature. A feature in the same line is the phonetic transformation which the hotel porter imposes on the German name von Dideritz. Having learned the address Gurov goes there and looks at the house. Opposite was a long gray fence with nails sticking out. An unescapable fence, Gurov says to himself, and here we get the concluding note in the rhythm of drabness and grayness already suggested by the carpet, the inkstand, the illiterate accent of the porter. The unexpected little turns and the lightness of the touches are what places Chekhov, above all Russian writers of fiction, on the level of Gogol and Tolstoy.

Presently he saw an old servant coming out with the familiar little white dog. He wanted to call it (by a kind of conditional reflex), but suddenly his heart began beating fast and in his excitement he could not remember the dog's name — another delightful touch. Later on he decides to go to the local theatre, where for the first time the operetta *The Geisha* is being given. In sixty words Checkov paints a complete picture of a provincial theatre, not forgetting the town-governor who modestly hid in his box behind a plush curtain so that only his hands were visible. Then the lady appeared. And he realized quite clearly that now in the whole world there was none nearer and dearer and more important to him than this slight woman, lost in a small-town crowd, a woman perfectly unremarkable, with a vulgar lorgnette in her hand. He saw her husband and remembered her qualifying him as a flunkey — he distinctly resembled one.

A remarkably fine scene follows when Gurov manages to talk to her, and then their mad swift walk up all kinds of staircases and corridors, and down again, and up again, amid people in the various uniforms of provincial officials. Neither does Chekhov forget "two schoolboys who smoked on the stairs and looked down at him and her."

"You must leave," Anna Sergeievna went on in a whisper. "Do you hear, Dmitri Dmitrich? I will come and see you in Moscow. I have never been happy; I am unhappy now, and I never, never shall be happy, never! So don't make me suffer still more! I swear I'll come to Moscow. But now let us part. My dear, good, precious one, let us part!"

She pressed his hand and walked rapidly downstairs, turning to look round at him, and from her eyes he could see that she really was unhappy. Gurov stood for a while, listening, then when all grew quiet, he found his coat and left the theatre.

The fourth and last little chapter gives the atmosphere of their secret meetings in Moscow. As soon as she would arrive she used to send a red-capped messenger to Gurov. One day he was on his way to her and his daughter was with him. She was going to school, in the same direction as he. Big damp snowflakes were slowly coming down.

The thermometer, Gurov was saying to his daughter, shows a few degrees above freezing point (actually 37° above, Fahrenheit), but nevertheless snow is falling. The explanation is that this warmth applies only to the surface of the earth, while in the higher layers of the atmosphere the temperature is quite different.

And as he spoke and walked, he kept thinking that not a soul knew or would ever know about these secret meetings.

What puzzled him was that all the false part of his life, his bank, his club, his conversations, his social obligations — all this happened openly, while the real and interesting part was hidden.

> He had two lives, an open one, seen and known by all who needed to know of it, full of conventional truth and conventional falsehood, exactly like the lives of his friends and acquaintances; and another life that went on in secret. And through some strange, perhaps accidental, combination of circumstances, everything that was of interest and importance to him, everything that was essential to him, everything about which he felt sincerely and did not deceive himself, everything that constituted the core of his life, was going on concealed from others; while all that was false, the shell in which he hid to cover the truth — his work at the bank for instance, his discussions at the club, his references to the "inferior race," his appearances at anniversary celebrations with his wife — all that went on in the open. Judging others by himself, he did not believe what he saw, and always fancied that every man led his real, most interesting life under cover of secrecy as under cover of night. The personal life of every individual is based on secrecy, and perhaps it is partly for that reason that civilized man is so nervously anxious that personal privacy should be respected.

The final scene is full of that pathos which has been suggested in the very beginning. They meet, she sobs, they feel that they are the closest of couples, the tenderest of friends, and he sees that his hair is getting a little gray and knows that only death will end their love.

> The shoulders on which his hands rested were warm and quivering. He felt compassion for this life, still so warm and lovely, but probably already about to begin to fade and wither like his own. Why did she love him so much? He always seemed to women different from what he was, and they loved in him not himself, but the man whom their imagination had created and whom they had been eagerly seeking all their lives; and afterwards, when they saw their mistake, they loved him nevertheless. And not one of them had been happy with him. In the past he had met women, come together with them, parted from them, but he had never once loved; it was anything you please, but not love. And only now when his head was gray he had fallen in love, really, truly — for the first time in his life.

They talk, they discuss their position, how to get rid of the necessity of this sordid secrecy, how to be together always. They find no solution and in the typical Chekhov way the tale fades out with no definite full-stop but with the natural motion of life.

> And it seemed as though in a little while the solution would be found, and then a new and glorious life would begin; and it was clear

to both of them that the end was still far off, and that what was to be most complicated and difficult for them was only just beginning.

All the traditional rules of story telling have been broken in this wonderful short story of twenty pages or so. There is no problem, no regular climax, no point at the end. And it is one of the greatest stories ever written.

[1981]

JOYCE CAROL OATES *discussed a film based on one of her short stories in her book* (Woman) Writer: Occasions and Opportunities *(1989). In her preface she compared the "erratic and wayward" process of using her unconscious to write imaginative fiction with the "fully conscious writing in which communication is the primary intention" in the creation of an essay. Writing about test driving a Ferrari Testarossa sports car and interviewing the prize fighter Mike Tyson were two of her other topics in this essay collection, where she hoped "Not the writer but the subject is the subject."*

J O Y C E   C A R O L   O A T E S

Smooth Talk: *Short Story into Film*

Some years ago in the American Southwest there surfaced a tabloid psychopath known as "The Pied Piper of Tucson." I have forgotten his name, but his specialty was the seduction and occasional murder of teen-aged girls. He may or may not have had actual accomplices, but his bizarre activities were known among a circle of teenagers in the Tucson area; for some reason they kept his secret, deliberately did not inform parents or police. It was this fact, not the fact of the mass murderer himself, that struck me at the time. And this was a pre-Manson time, early or mid-1960s.

The Pied Piper mimicked teenagers in their talk, dress, and behavior, but he was not a teenager — he was a man in his early thirties. Rather short, he stuffed rags in his leather boots to give himself height. (And sometimes walked unsteadily as a consequence: did none among his admiring constituency notice?) He charmed his victims as charismatic psychopaths have always charmed their victims, to the bewilderment of others who fancy themselves free of all lunatic attractions. The Pied Piper of Tucson: a trashy dream, a tabloid archetype, sheer artifice, comedy, cartoon — surrounded, however improbably, and finally tragically, by real people. You think that, if you look twice, he won't be there. But there he is.

I don't remember any longer where I first read about this Pied Piper — very likely in *Life* Magazine. I do recall deliberately not reading the full article because I didn't want to be distracted by too much detail. It was not after all the mass murderer himself who intrigued me, but the disturbing fact that a number of teenagers — from "good" families — aided and abetted his crimes. This is the sort of thing authorities and responsible citizens invariably call "inexplicable" because they can't find explanations for it. *They* would not have fallen under this maniac's spell, after all.

An early draft of my short story "Where Are You Going, Where Have You Been?" — from which the film *Smooth Talk* was adapted by Joyce Chopra and Tom Cole — had the rather too explicit title "Death and the Maiden." It was cast in a mode of fiction to which I am still partial — indeed, every third or fourth story of mine is probably in this mode — "realistic allegory," it might be called. It is Hawthornean, romantic, shading into parable. Like the medieval German engraving from which my title was taken, the story was minutely detailed yet clearly an allegory of the fatal attractions of death (or the devil). An innocent young girl is seduced by way of her own vanity; she mistakes death for erotic romance of a particularly American/trashy sort.

In subsequent drafts the story changed its tone, its focus, its language, its title. It became "Where Are You Going, Where Have You Been?" Written at a time when the author was intrigued by the music of Bob Dylan, particularly the hauntingly elegiac song "It's All Over Now, Baby Blue," it was dedicated to Bob Dylan. The charismatic mass murderer drops into the background and his innocent victim, a fifteen-year-old, moves into the foreground. She becomes the true protagonist of the tale, courting and being courted by her fate, a self-styled 1950s pop figure, alternately absurd and winning. There is no suggestion in the published story that "Arnold Friend" has seduced and murdered other young girls, or even that he necessarily intends to murder Connie. Is his interest "merely" sexual? (Nor is there anything about the complicity of other teenagers. I saved that yet more provocative note for a current story, "Testimony.") Connie is shallow, vain, silly, hopeful, doomed — but capable nonetheless of an unexpected gesture of heroism at the story's end. Her smooth-talking seducer, who cannot lie, promises her that her family will be unharmed if she gives herself to him; and so she does. The story ends abruptly at the point of her "crossing over." We don't know the nature of her sacrifice, only that she is generous enough to make it.

In adapting a narrative so spare and thematically foreshortened as "Where Are You Going, Where Have You Been?" film director Joyce Chopra and screenwriter Tom Cole were required to do a good deal of filling in, expanding, inventing. Connie's story becomes lavishly, and lovingly, textured; she is not an allegorical figure so much as a "typical" teen-aged girl (if Laura Dern, spectacularly good-looking, can be so defined). Joyce Chopra, who has done documentary films on contemporary teenage culture and, yet more authoritatively, has an adolescent daughter of her own, creates in *Smooth Talk* a vivid and absolutely believable world for Connie to inhabit. Or worlds: as in the original story there is Connie-at-home, and there is Connie-with-her-friends. Two fifteen-year-old girls, two finely honed styles, two voices, sometimes but not often overlapping. It is one of the marvelous visual features of the film that we *see* Connie and her friends transform themselves, once they are safely free of parental observation. The girls claim their true identities in the neighborhood shopping mall. What freedom, what joy!

Smooth Talk is, in a way, as much Connie's mother's story as it is Connie's; its center of gravity, its emotional nexus, is frequently with the mother — warmly and convincingly played by Mary Kay Place. (Though the mother's sexual jealousy of her daughter is slighted in the film.) Connie's ambiguous relationship with her affable, somewhat mysterious father (well played by Levon Helm) is an excellent touch: I had thought, subsequent to the story's publication, that I should have built up the father, suggesting, as subtly as I could, an attraction there paralleling the attraction Connie feels for her seducer, Arnold Friend. And Arnold Friend himself — "A. Friend" as he says — is played with appropriately overdone sexual swagger by Treat Williams, who is perfect for the part; and just the right age. We see that Arnold Friend isn't a teenager even as Connie, mesmerized by his presumed charm, does not seem to *see* him at all. What is so difficult to accomplish in prose — nudging the reader to look over the protagonist's shoulder, so to speak — is accomplished with enviable ease in film.

Treat Williams as Arnold Friend is supreme in his very awfulness, as, surely, the original Pied Piper of Tucson must have been. (Though no one involved in the film knew about the original source.) Mr. Williams flawlessly impersonates Arnold Friend as Arnold Friend impersonates — is it James Dean? James Dean regarding himself in mirrors, doing James Dean impersonations? That Connie's fate is so trashy is in fact her fate.

What is outstanding in Joyce Chopra's *Smooth Talk* is its visual freshness, its sense of motion and life; the attentive intelligence the director has brought to the semi-secret world of the American adolescent — shopping mall flirtations, drive-in restaurant romances, highway hitchhiking, the fascination of rock music played very, very loud. (James Taylor's music for the film is wonderfully appropriate. We hear it as Connie hears it; it is the music of her spiritual being.) Also outstanding, as I have indicated, and numerous critics have noted, are the acting performances. Laura Dern is so dazzlingly right as "my" Connie that I may come to think I modeled the fictitious girl on her, in the way that writers frequently delude themselves about motions of causality.

My difficulties with *Smooth Talk* have primarily to do with my chronic hesitation — about seeing/hearing work of mine abstracted from its contexture of language. All writers know that language is their subject; quirky word choices, patterns of rhythm, enigmatic pauses, punctuation marks. Where the quick scanner sees "quick" writing, the writer conceals nine tenths of the iceberg. Of course we all have "real" subjects, and we will fight to the death to defend those subjects, but beneath the tale-telling it is the tale-telling that grips us so very fiercely. The writer works in a single dimension, the director works in three. I assume they are professionals to their fingertips; authorities in their medium as I am an authority (if I am) in mine. I would fiercely defend the placement of a semicolon in one of my novels but I would probably have deferred in the end to Joyce Chopra's decision to reverse the story's conclusion, turn it upside down, in a sense, so that the film ends not with death, not with a sleepwalker's crossing over to her fate, but upon a scene of reconciliation, rejuvenation.

A girl's loss of virginity, bittersweet but not necessarily tragic. Not today. A girl's coming-of-age that involves her succumbing to, but then rejecting, the "trashy dreams" of her pop teenage culture. "Where Are You Going, Where Have You Been?" defines itself as allegorical in its conclusion: Death and Death's chariot (a funky souped-up convertible) have come for the Maiden. Awakening is, in the story's final lines, moving out into the sunlight where Arnold Friend waits:

> "My sweet little blue-eyed girl," he said in a half-sung sigh that had nothing to do with [Connie's] brown eyes but was taken up just the same by the vast sunlit reaches of the land behind him and on all sides of him — so much land that Connie had never seen before and did not recognize except to know that she was going to it.

— a conclusion impossible to transfigure into film.   [1989]

FRANK O'CONNOR *was a skilled teacher of the short story, and his comments on the literary form can be as irreverent as they are profound. In this interview in the* Paris Review, *reprinted from the first volume of* Writers at Work, *collections of interviews from that journal which appeared in 1958, O'Connor compared himself with Guy de Maupassant and then went on to discuss his own practice as a writer. His analysis of the history of the short story appeared in more extended form in his book* The Lonely Voice, *published in 1963.*

FRANK O'CONNOR

The Nearest Thing to Lyric Poetry Is the Short Story

Interviewer: Why do you prefer the short story for your medium?

O'Connor: Because it's the nearest thing I know to lyric poetry — I wrote lyric poetry for a long time, then discovered that God had not intended me to be a lyric poet, and the nearest thing to that is the short story. A novel actually requires far more logic and far more knowledge of circumstances, whereas a short story can have the sort of detachment from circumstances that lyric poetry has. . . .

Interviewer: What about working habits? How do you start a story?

O'Connor: "Get black on white" used to be Maupassant's advice — that's what I always do. I don't give a hoot what the writing's like, I write any sort of rubbish which will cover the main outlines of the story, then I can begin to see it. When I write, when I draft a story, I never think of writing nice sentences about, "It was a nice August evening when Elizabeth Jane Moriarty was coming down the road." I just write roughly what happened, and then I'm able to see what the construction looks like. It's the design of the story which to me is most important, the thing that tells you there's a bad gap in the narrative here and you really ought to fill that up in some way or another. I'm always looking at the design of the story, not the treatment. Yesterday I was finishing off a piece about my friend A. E. Coppard, the greatest of all the English storytellers, who died about a fortnight ago. I was describing the way Coppard must have written these stories, going around with a notebook, recording what the lighting looked like, what that house looked like, and all the time using metaphor to suggest it to himself, "The road looked like a mad serpent going up the hill," or something of the kind, and "She said so-and-so, and the man in the pub said something else." After he had written them all out, he must have got the outline of his story, and he'd start working in all the details. Now, I could never do that at all. I've got to see what these people did, first of all, and *then* I start thinking of whether it was a nice August evening or a spring evening. I have to wait for the theme before I can do anything.

Interviewer: Do you rewrite?

O'Connor: Endlessly, endlessly, endlessly. And keep on rewriting, and after it's published, and then after it's published in book form, I usually rewrite it again. I've rewritten versions of most of my early stories and one of these days, God help, I'll publish these as well.

Interviewer: Do you keep notes as a source of supply for future stories?

O'Connor: Just notes of themes. If somebody tells me a good story, I'll write it down in my four lines; that is the secret of the theme. If you make the subject of a story twelve or fourteen lines, that's a treatment. You've already committed yourself to the sort of character, the sort of surroundings, and the moment you've committed yourself, the story is already written. It has ceased to be fluid, you can't design it any longer, you can't model it. So I always confine myself to my four lines. If it won't go into four, that means you haven't reduced it to its ultimate simplicity, reduced it to the fable.

[1958]

FRANK O'CONNOR *analyzed the stories in James Joyce's* Dubliners *in a chapter entitled "Work in Progress" in his 1963 study of the short story,* The Lonely Voice. *O'Connor addressed himself to the question of why Joyce gave up writing stories after* Dubliners; *he understood that "it is as difficult to think of a real storyteller, like Chekhov, who had experienced the thrill of the completed masterpiece, giving up short stories forever as it is to think of Keats giving up lyric poetry." The answer, for O'Connor, can be found by comparing the formal differences between the stories at the beginning of* Dubliners *and "The Dead" at the end. This is where his analysis begins.*

FRANK O'CONNOR

Style and Form in Joyce's **The Dead**

"The Dead," Joyce's last story, is entirely different from all the others. It is also immensely more complicated, and it is not always easy to see what any particular episode represents, though it is only too easy to see that it represents something. The scene is the annual dance of the Misses Morkan, old music teachers on Usher's Island, and ostensibly it is no more than a report of what happened at it, except at the end, when Gabriel Conroy and his wife Gretta return to their hotel room. There she breaks down and tells him of a youthful and innocent love affair between herself and a boy of seventeen in Galway, who had caught his death of cold from standing under her bedroom window. But this final scene is irrelevant only in appearance, for in effect it is the real story, and everything that has led up to it has been simply an enormously expanded introduction, a series of themes all of which find their climax in the hotel bedroom.

The setting of the story in a warm, vivacious lighted house in the midst of night and snow is an image of life itself, but every incident, almost every speech, has a crack in it through which we perceive the presence of death all about us, as when Gabriel says that Gretta "takes three *mortal* hours to dress herself," and the aunts say that she must be "perished alive" — an Irishism that ingeniously suggests both life and death. Several times the warmth and gaiety give rise to the idea of love and marriage, but each time it is knocked dead by phrase or incident. At the very opening of the story Gabriel suggests to the servant girl, Lily, that they will soon be attending her wedding, but she retorts savagely that "the men that is now is only all palaver and what they can get out of you," the major theme of the story, for all grace is with the dead: The younger generation have not the generosity of the two old sisters, the younger singers (Caruso, for instance!) cannot sing as well as some long dead English tenor. Gabriel's aunt actually sings "Arrayed for the Bridal," but she is only an old woman who has been dismissed from her position in the local church choir.

Gabriel himself is fired by passion for his wife, but when they return to their hotel bedroom the electric light has failed, and his passion is also extinguished when she tells him the story of her love for a dead boy. Whether it is Gabriel's quarrel with Miss Ivors, who wants him to spend his summer holiday patriotically in the West of Ireland (where his wife and the young man had met), the discussion of Cistercian monks who are supposed to sleep in their coffins, "to remind them of their last end," or the reminiscences of old singers and old relatives, everything pushes Gabriel toward that ultimate dissolution of identity in which real things disappear from about us, and we are as alone as we shall be on our deathbeds.

But it is easy enough to see from "The Dead" why Joyce gave up storytelling. One of his main passions — the elaboration of style and form — had taken control, and the short story is too tightly knit to permit expansion like this. And — what is much more important — it is quite clear from "The Dead" that he had already begun to lose sight of the submerged population that was his original subject. There are little touches of it here and there, as in the sketches of Freddy Malins and his mother — the old lady who finds everything "beautiful" — "beautiful crossing," "beautiful house," "beautiful scenery," "beautiful fish" — but Gabriel does not belong to it, nor does Gretta nor Miss Ivors. They are not characters but personalities, and Joyce would never again be able to deal with characters, people whose identity is determined by their circumstances. His own escape to Trieste, with its enlargement of his own sense of identity, had caused them to fade from his mind or — to put it more precisely — had caused them to reappear in entirely different guises. This is something that is always liable to happen to the provincial storyteller when you put him into a cosmopolitan atmosphere.   [1963]

GRACE PALEY *talked with Ann Charters about her experiences as a short story writer during lunch in her Greenwich Village apartment on a snowy day in February 1986. On the wall above the kitchen table hung an oil painting, a still life of vegetables painted by her father after his retirement from medicine. Paley mentions her father's interest in art in her story "A Conversation with My Father."*

GRACE PALEY

A Conversation with Ann Charters

Charters: Some literary critics think that short stories are more closely related to poetry than to the novel. Would you agree?

Paley: I would say that stories are closer to poetry than they are to the novel because first they are shorter, and second they are more concentrated, more economical, and that kind of economy, the pulling together of all the information and making leaps across the information, is really close to poetry. By leaps I mean thought leaps and feeling leaps. Also, when short stories are working right, you pay more attention to language than most novelists do.

Charters: Poe said unity was an essential factor of short stories. Do you have any ideas about this in your own work?

Paley: I suppose there has to be some kind of unity, but that's true in a novel too. It seems to me that unity is form. Form is really the vessel in which the story or poem or novel exists. The reason I don't have an answer for you is that there's really no telling — sometimes I like to start a story with one thing and end it with another. I don't know where the unity is in that case. I see the word *unity* meaning that something has to be whole, even if it ends in an open way.

Charters: You mean, as you wrote in "A Conversation with My Father," that "everyone, real or invented, deserves the open destiny of life."

Paley: Yes.

Charters: You started writing poetry before short stories, and the language of your fiction is often as compressed and metaphorical as the language of poetry. Can you describe the process of how you learned to write?

Paley: Let me put it this way: I went to school to poetry — that was where I learned how to write. People learn to write by doing various things. I suppose I also wrote a lot of letters, since it was the time of the Second World War. But apart from that I wrote poems, that's what I wrote. I thought about language a lot. That was important to me. That was my teacher. My fiction teacher was poetry.

Charters: What poets did you read when you were learning how to write?

Paley: I just read all the poets. If there was an anthology of poets, I read every single one. I knew all the Victorians. I read the Imagists. At a certain point I fell in love with the Englishmen who came to America — Christopher Isherwood, Stephen Spender, and W. H. Auden. I thought Auden was the greatest. And I loved the poetry of Dylan Thomas. Yeats meant a lot to me. I paid attention to all of them and listened to all of them. Some of them must have gotten into my ear. That's not up to me to say. That's for the reader to say. The reader of my stories will tell me, "This is whom you're influenced by," but I can't say that. I feel I was influenced by everybody.

Charters: Why did you stop writing poetry and start writing stories? What did the form of the short story offer you that the poem didn't?

Paley: First of all, I began to think of certain subject matter, women's lives specifically, and what was happening around me. I was in my thirties, which I guess is the time people start to notice these things, women's and men's lives and what their relationship is. I knew lots of women with small kids, and I was developing very close relationships with a variety of women. All sorts of things began to worry me, and I began to think about them a lot. I couldn't deal with any of this subject matter in poetry; I just didn't know how. I didn't have the technique. Other people can, but I didn't want to write poems saying "I feel this" and "I feel that." That was the last thing I wanted to do.

I can give you a definition that can be proven wrong in many ways, but for me it was that in writing poetry I wanted to talk to the world, I wanted to address the world, so to speak. But writing stories, I wanted to get the world to explain itself to me, to speak to me. And for me that was the essential difference between writing poetry and stories, and it still is, in many ways. So I had to get that world to talk to me. I had to reach out to it, a very different thing than writing poems. I had to reach out to the world and get it to tell me what it was all about, because I didn't understand it. I just didn't understand. Also, I'd always been very interested in people and told funny stories, and I didn't have any room for doing that in poems, again because of my own self. My poems were too literary, that's the real reason.

Charters: What do you mean, you had to get the world to tell you what it was all about?

Paley: In the first story I ever wrote, "The Contest," I did exactly what I just told you — I got this guy to talk. That's what I did. I had a certain guy in mind. In fact, I stuck pretty close to my notion of what he was, and the story was about a contest he had told me about. The second story I wrote was about Aunt Rose in "Goodbye and Good Luck." That began with my husband's aunt visiting us, and saying exactly the sentence I used to start the story: "I was popular in certain circles." But the rest has nothing to do with her life at all. She looked at us, this aunt of his, and she felt we didn't appreciate her, so she looked at us and she said to us, "Listen," she said. "I was popular in certain circles." That statement really began that particular story. That story was about lots of older women I knew who didn't get married, and I was thinking about them. These are two examples of how I began, how I got to my own voice by hearing and using all these other voices.

Charters: I suppose "A Conversation with My Father" isn't typical of your work, because the story you make up for him isn't what he wants, the old-fashioned Chekhov or Maupassant story, and it's not really one of your "voice" stories either, is it?

Paley: No. I'm just trying to oblige him.

Charters: So that may be one of the jokes of the story?

Paley: It could be, but I never thought of it that way. I think it's a good story. People have found it useful in literature classes, which I think is funny, but nice.

Charters: Did you make up the plot of "A Conversation with My Father," or did it actually happen when you were visiting him before he died?

Paley: My father was eighty-six years old and in bed. I spent a lot of time with him. He was an artist, and he painted pictures after he retired from being a doctor. I visited him at least once a week, and we were very close. We would have discussions. I never wrote a story for him about this neighbor, but he did say to me once, "Why can't you write a regular story, for God's sake?" something like that. So that particular story is both about literature and about that particular discussion, but it's also about generational differences, about different ways of looking at life. What my father thought could be done in the world was due to his own history. What I thought could be done in the world was different, not because I was a more open person, because he was also a very open person, but because I lived in a particularly open time, the late 1960s. The story I wrote for him was about all these druggies. It was made up, but it was certainly true. I could point out people on my block whose kids became junkies. Many of them have recovered from being junkies and are in good shape now.

Charters: Did you know any mothers in Greenwich Village who became junkies to keep their kids company?

Paley: Sure. It was a very open neighborhood then, with lots of freedom. But my father was born into a very different time. He was born in Czarist Russia and came over to America when he was twenty and worked hard and studied medicine and had a profession.

Charters: When you were growing up did you read the writers your father admired — Maupassant and Chekhov?

Paley: Actually, he had never mentioned Maupassant to me before. He did mention him in that conversation. He did read a lot, he loved Chekhov. And when he came to this country, he taught himself English by reading Dickens.

Charters: So the idea for the story came to you when he mentioned Maupassant?

Paley: Well, not really. He had just read my story "Faith in a Tree," and there are a lot of voices coming from all over in that story. And so he asked me, "What is this? All those voices? Voices from who knows where?" He wasn't actually that heavy. But when I wrote about our conversation it became a fiction, and it's different from what really happened.

Charters: It must have been fun for you to make up the two versions of the story about your neighbor in "A Conversation with My Father."

Paley: I enjoyed writing that story. Some stories you don't enjoy, because they're very hard. I didn't write it right off, but I enjoyed it.

Charters: How many days did it take you to write?

Paley: There's no such thing as days with me when I write a story. More like months. I write it and I write slow, and then I rewrite, and then I put it away, and then I take it out again. It's tedious in some respects. But that's the way it works.

Charters: When do you decide it's finished?

Paley: When I've gone over it and I can't think of another thing to change.

Charters: I was looking over your book *Enormous Changes at the Last Minute,* which is where "A Conversation with My Father" appears, and I noticed you've placed it between two very dark stories, "The Little Girl," about a runaway in the Village who commits suicide after she's raped, and "The Immigrant Story," about the starvation of the young children in a Jewish family in Poland before the mother emigrates to America. I assume you did this for a reason. When you put a collection of short fiction together, how do you order the stories?

Paley: I always have something in mind. I like to put one or two at the beginning that will be readable immediately, and then I just work it out. I like to mix the long and the short, and the serious and the funny ones. But I did put those two dark stories around "A Conversation with My Father" to show him I could look tragedy in the face. Remember he asks me at the end of the story, "When will you look it in the face?"

Charters: Was that one of the things he actually said to you when you visited him?

Paley: Well, he did tend to say that I wouldn't look things in the face. That things were hard, and I wasn't looking at it. I didn't see certain problems with my kids when they were small, and he was in some degree right. In "The Immigrant Story" a man tells me, "You have a rotten rosy temperament." But then she says, "Rosiness is not a worse windowpane than gloomy gray when viewing the world." They're both just prisms to look through.

Charters: Is that what you still believe?

Paley: Well, I do believe it, but I also believe that things are bad.

Charters: A theme that some students find when reading "A Conversation with My Father" is that one of the things you don't want to look in the face that your father is trying to prepare you for is his own death. Were you conscious of that when you wrote the story?

Paley: No.

Charters: Can you see that theme in it now?

Paley: No. But maybe you're right. As I said, that's not up to me to say. Maybe the reader of a particular story knows better than the writer what it means. But I know I wasn't thinking about that when I wrote it. I wasn't thinking of his death at all. I was thinking of him being sick and trying not to get him excited.   [1986]

EDGAR ALLAN POE *was one of the earliest writers to discuss the aesthetic qualities of the short story as a distinct prose narrative form. In his day literary criticism was still a new field, lacking a terminology and developed concepts. His two long reviews praising the tales of Nathaniel Hawthorne were published in* Graham's Magazine *in 1842 and* Godey's Lady's Book *in 1847; they are pioneering examples of the analytic literary essay. The following excerpt is taken from the 1842 piece, in which Poe amplifies his theory of the short story and his views on the nature of originality in literature.*

E D G A R   A L L A N   P O E

The Importance of the Single Effect in a Prose Tale

But it is of [Hawthorne's] tales that we desire principally to speak. The tale proper, in our opinion, affords unquestionably the fairest field for the exercise of the loftiest talent, which can be afforded by the wide domains of mere prose. Were we bidden to say how the highest genius could be most advantageously employed for the best display of its own powers, we should answer, without hesitation — in the composition of a rhymed poem, not to exceed in length what might be perused in an hour. Within this limit alone can the highest order of true poetry exist. We need only here say, upon this topic, that, in almost all classes of composition, the unity of effect or impression is a point of the greatest importance. It is clear, moreover, that this unity cannot be thoroughly preserved in productions whose perusal cannot be completed at one sitting. We may continue the reading of a prose composition, from the very nature of prose itself, much longer than we can persevere, to any good purpose, in the perusal of a poem. This latter, if truly fulfilling the demands of the poetic sentiment, induces an exaltation of the soul which cannot be long sustained. All high excitements are necessarily transient. Thus a long poem is a paradox. And, without unity of impression, the deepest effects cannot be brought about. Epics were the offspring of an imperfect sense of Art, and their reign is no more. A poem *too* brief may produce a vivid, but never an intense or enduring impression. Without a certain continuity of effort — without a certain duration or repetition of purpose — the soul is never deeply moved. There must be the dropping of the water upon the rock. . . .

Were we called upon, however, to designate that class of composition which, next to such a poem as we have suggested, should best fulfill the demands of high genius — should offer it the most advantageous field of exertion — we should unhesitatingly speak of the prose tale, as Mr.

Hawthorne has here exemplified it. We allude to the short prose narrative, requiring from a half-hour to one or two hours in its perusal. The ordinary novel is objectionable, from its length, for reasons already stated in substance. As it cannot be read at one sitting, it deprives itself, of course, of the immense force derivable from *totality*. Worldly interests intervening during the pauses of perusal, modify, annul, or counteract, in a greater or less degree, the impressions of the book. But simple cessation in reading would, of itself, be sufficient to destroy the true unity. In the brief tale, however, the author is enabled to carry out the fullness of his intention, be it what it may. During the hour of perusal the soul of the reader is at the writer's control. There are no external or extrinsic influences — resulting from weariness or interruption.

A skillful literary artist has constructed a tale. If wise, he has not fashioned his thoughts to accommodate his incidents; but having conceived, with deliberate care, a certain unique or single *effect* to be wrought out, he then invents such incidents — he then combines such events as may best aid him in establishing this preconceived effect. If his very initial sentence tend not to the outbringing of this effect, then he has failed in his first step. In the whole composition there should be no word written, of which the tendency, direct or indirect, is not to the one pre-established design. And by such means, with such care and skill, a picture is at length painted which leaves in the mind of him who contemplates it with a kindred art, a sense of the fullest satisfaction. The idea of the tale has been presented unblemished, because undisturbed; and this is an end unattainable by the novel. Undue brevity is just as exceptionable here as in the poem; but undue length is yet more to be avoided.

We have said that the tale has a point of superiority even over the poem. In fact, while the *rhythm* of this latter is an essential aid in the development of the poem's highest idea — the idea of the Beautiful — the artificialities of this rhythm are an inseparable bar to the development of all points of thought or expression which have their basis in *Truth*. But Truth is often, and in very great degree, the aim of the tale. Some of the finest tales are tales of ratiocination. Thus the field of this species of composition, if not in so elevated a region of the mountain of Mind, is a tableland of far vaster extent than the domain of the mere poem. Its products are never so rich, but infinitely more numerous, and more appreciable by the mass of mankind. The writer of the prose tale, in short, may bring to his theme a vast variety of modes or reflections of thought and expression — (the ratiocinative, for example, the sarcastic, or the humorous) which are not only antagonistical to the nature of the poem, but absolutely forbidden by one of its most peculiar and indispensable adjuncts; we allude, of course, to rhythm. It may be added, here, *par parenthèse*, that the author who aims at the purely beautiful in a prose tale is laboring at a great disadvantage. For Beauty can be better treated in the poem. Not so with terror, or passion, or horror, or a multitude of such other points. . . .

Of Mr. Hawthorne's "Tales" we would say, emphatically, that they belong to the highest region of Art — an Art subservient to genius of a very lofty order. We have supposed, with good reason for so supposing, that he had been thrust into his present position by one of the impudent cliques which beset our literature, and whose pretensions it is our full purpose to expose at the earliest opportunity; but we have been most agreeably mistaken. We know of few compositions which the critic can more honestly commend than these "Twice-Told Tales." As Americans, we feel proud of the book.

Mr. Hawthorne's distinctive trait is invention, creation, imagination, originality — a trait which, in the literature of fiction, is positively worth all the rest. But the nature of the originality, so far as regards its manifestation in letters, is but imperfectly understood. The inventive or original mind as frequently displays itself in novelty of *tone* as in novelty of matter. Mr. Hawthorne is original in *all* points.

It would be a matter of some difficulty to designate the best of these tales; we repeat that, without exception, they are beautiful . . . In the way of objection we have scarcely a word to say of these tales. There is, perhaps, a somewhat too general or prevalent *tone* — a tone of melancholy and mysticism. The subjects are insufficiently varied. There is not so much of *versatility* evinced as we might well be warranted in expecting from the high powers of Mr. Hawthorne. But beyond these trivial exceptions we have really none to make. The style is purity itself. Force abounds. High imagination gleams from every page. Mr. Hawthorne is a man of the truest genius. . . .   [1842]

EVE KOSOFSKY SEDGWICK *wrote her essay "The Beast in the Closet: James and the Writing of Homosexual Panic" for Ruth Yeazell's edition of* Sex, Politics, and Science in the Nineteenth-Century Novel *(1986). It was recently reprinted in the noted feminist historian Elaine Showalter's collection of essays,* Speaking of Gender *(1989). As Showalter has explained, gender as a category of literary analysis has followed hard on the heels of the development of feminist criticism in the 1980s: "Within the Anglo-American feminist discourse, the term 'gender' has been used for the past several years to stand for the social, cultural, and psychological meaning imposed upon biological sexual identity; indeed, the problematization of gender relations, according to theorist Jane Flax, is 'the single most important advance in feminist theory.'"*

EVE KOSOFSKY SEDGWICK

The Beast in the Closet: A Gender Critic Reads James's The Beast in the Jungle

The conventional view of the story, emphasizing May Bartram's interest in liberating, unmediatedly, Marcher's heterosexual possibilities, would see her as unsuccessful in doing so until too late — until the true revelation that comes, however, only after her death. If what needs to be liberated is in the first place Marcher's potential for homosexual desire, however, the trajectory of the story must be seen as far bleaker. I hypothesize that what May Bartram would have liked for Marcher, the narrative she wished to nurture for him, would have been a progress from a vexed and gaping self-ignorance around his homosexual possibilities to a self-knowledge of them that would have freed him to find and enjoy a sexuality of whatever sort emerged. What she sees happen to Marcher, instead, is the "progress" that the culture more insistently enforces: the progress from a vexed and gaping self-ignorance around his homosexual possibilities, to a completed and rationalized and wholly concealed and accepted one. The moment of Marcher's full incorporation of his erotic self-ignorance is the moment at which the imperatives of the culture cease to enforce him, and he becomes instead the enforcer of the culture.

Section 4 of the story marks the moment at which May Bartram realizes that, far from helping dissolve Marcher's closet, she has instead and irremediably been permitting him to reinforce it. It is in this section and the next, too, that it becomes explicit in the story that Marcher's fate, what was to have happened to him and did happen, involves a change in him from being the suffering object of a Law or judgment (of a doom in the original sense of the word) to being the embodiment of that Law.

If the transition I am describing is, in certain respects, familiarly Oedipal, the structuring metaphor behind its description here seems to be oddly alimentative. The question that haunts Marcher in these sections is whether what he has thought of as the secret of his future may not be, after all, in the past; and the question of passing, of who is passing through what or what is passing through whom, of what residue remains to *be* passed, is the form in which he compulsively poses his riddle. Is the beast eating him, or is he eating the beast? "It hasn't passed you by," May Bartram tells him. "It has done its office. It has made you its own." "It's past. It's behind," she finally tells him, to which he replies, "*Nothing,* for me, is past; nothing *will* pass till I pass myself, which I pray my stars may be as soon as possible. Say, however, . . . that I've eaten my cake, as you contend, to the last crumb — how can the thing I've never felt at all be the thing I was marked out to feel?" What May Bartram sees, that Marcher does not, is that the process of incorporating — of embodying — the Law of masculine self-ignorance, is the one that has the least in the world to do with feeling. To gape at and, rebelliously, be forced to swallow the Law is to feel; but to have it finally stick to one's ribs, become however incongruously a part of one's own organism, is then to perfect at the same moment a new hard-won insentience of it and an assumption of (or subsumption by) an identification with it. May Bartram answers Marcher's question, "You take your 'feelings' for granted. You were to suffer your fate. That was not necessarily to know it." Marcher's fate is to cease to suffer fate, and, instead, to become it. May Bartram's fate, with the "slow fine shudder" that climaxes her ultimate appeal to Marcher, is herself to swallow this huge, bitter bolus with which *she* can have *no* deep identification, and to die of it — of what is, to her, knowledge, not power. "So on her lips would the law itself have sounded." Or, tasted.

To end a reading of May Bartram with her death, to end with her silenced forever in that ultimate closet, "her" tomb that represents (to Marcher) *his fate* . . . it leaves us in danger of figuring May Bartram, or more generally the woman in heterosexuality, as only the exact, heroic supplement to the murderous enforcements of male homophobic/homosocial self-ignorance. "The Fox," Emily Dickinson wrote, "fits the Hound." It would be only too easy to describe May Bartram as the fox that most irreducibly fits this particular hound. She seems the woman (don't we all know them?) who has not only the most delicate nose for but the most potent attraction toward men who are at crises of homosexual panic . . . — Though for that matter, won't most women admit that an arousing nimbus, an excessively refluent and dangerous maelstrom of eroticism, somehow attends men in general at such moments, even otherwise boring men?

If one is to avoid the Barrie-ism of describing May Bartram in terms that reduce her perfectly to the residue-less sacrifice John Marcher makes in his Beast, it might be by inquiring into the difference of the paths of her own desire. What does she want — not for him, but for herself — from their relationship? What does she actually get? To speak less equivocally from my own eros and experience, there is a particular relation to truth and authority that a mapping of male homosexual panic offers to a woman in the emotional vicinity. The fact that male heterosexual entitlement in (at least modern Anglo-American) culture depends on a perfected but always friable self-ignorance in men as to the significance of their desire for other men, means that it is always open to women to know something that it is much more dangerous for any nonhomosexual-identified man to know. The ground of May Bartram's and John Marcher's relationship from the first is that she has the advantage of him, cognitively: she remembers, as he does not, where and when and with whom they have met before, and most of all she remembers his "secret" from a decade ago while he forgets having told it to her. This differential of knowledge affords her a "slight irony," an "advantage" — but one that he can at the same time use to his own profit as "the buried treasure of her knowledge," "this little hoard." As their relationship continues, the sense of power and of a marked, rather free-floating irony about May Bartram becomes stronger and stronger, even in proportion to Marcher's accelerating progress toward self-ignorance and toward a blindly selfish expropriation of her emotional labor. Both the care and the creativity of her investment in him, the imaginative reach of her fostering his homosexual potential as a route back to his truer perception of herself, are forms of gender-political resilience in her as well as of love. They are forms of excitement, too, of real though insufficient power, and of pleasure.

In the last scene of the "The Beast in the Jungle," John Marcher becomes, in this reading, not the finally self-knowing man who is capable of heterosexual love, but the irredeemably self-ignorant man who embodies and enforces heterosexual compulsion. In this reading, that is to say, May Bartram's prophecy to Marcher that "You'll never know now" is *a true one*.

Importantly for the homosexual plot, too, the final scene is also the only one in the entire story that reveals or tests the affective quality of Marcher's perception of another man. "The shock of the face" — this is, in the last scene, the beginning of what Marcher ultimately considers "the most extraordinary thing that had happened to him." At the beginning of Marcher's confrontation with this male figure at the cemetery, the erotic possibilities of the connection between the men appear to be all open. The man, whose "mute assault" Marcher feels "so deep down that he winced at the steady thrust," in mourning profoundly over "a grave apparently fresh," but (perhaps only to Marcher's closet-sharpened suspicions?) a slightest potential of Whitmanian cruisiness seems at first to tinge the air, as well.

> His pace was slow, so that — and all the more as there was a kind of hunger in his look — the two men were for a minute directly confronted. Marcher knew him at once for one of the deeply stricken . . . nothing lived but the deep ravage of the features he showed. He *showed* them — that was the point; he was moved, as he passed, by some impulse that was either a signal for sympathy or, more possibly, a challenge to an opposed sorrow. He might already have been aware of our friend. . . . What Marcher was at all events conscious of was in the first place that the image of scarred passion presented to him was conscious too — of something that profaned the air; and in the second that, roused, startled, shocked, he was yet the next moment looking after it, as it went, with envy.

The path traveled by Marcher's desire in this brief and cryptic non-encounter reenacts a classic trajectory of male entitlement. Marcher begins with the possibility of *desire for* the man, in response to the man's open "hunger" ("which," afterward, "still flared for him like a smoky torch"). Deflecting that desire under a fear of profanation, he then replaces it with envy, with an *identification with* the man in that man's (baffled) desire for some other, female, dead object. "The stranger passed, but the raw glare of his grief remained, making our friend wonder in pity what wrong, what wound it expressed, what injury not to be healed. What had the man *had*, to make him by the loss of it so bleed and yet live?"

What had the man *had*? The loss by which a man *so bleeds and yet lives* is, is it not, supposed to be the castratory one of the phallus figured as mother, the inevitability of whose sacrifice ushers sons into the status of fathers and into the control (read both ways) of the Law. What is strikingly open in the ending of "The Beast in the Jungle" is how central to that process is man's desire for man — and the denial of that desire. The imperative that there *be* a male figure to take this place is the clearer in that, at an earlier climactic moment, in a female "shock of the face," May Bartram has presented to Marcher her own face, in a conscious revelation that was far more clearly of desire.

> It had become suddenly, from her movement and attitude, beautiful and vivid to him that she had something more to give him; her wasted face delicately shone with it — it glittered almost as with the white lustre of silver in her expression. She was right, incontestably, for what he saw in her face was the truth, and strangely, without consequence, while their talk of it as dreadful was still in the air, she appeared to present it as inordinately soft. This, prompting bewilderment, made him but gape the more gratefully for her revelation, so that they continued for some minutes silent, her face shining at him, her contact imponderably pressing, and his stare all kind but all expectant. The end, none the less, was that what he had expected failed to come to him.

To the shock of the female face, Marcher is not phobic but simply numb. It is only by turning his desire for the male face into an envious identification with male loss that Marcher finally comes into *any* relation to a woman — and then it is a relation through one dead woman (the other man's) to another dead woman of his own. That is to say, it is the relation of *compulsory* heterosexuality.

When Lytton Strachey's[1] claim to be a conscientious objector was being examined, he was asked what he would do if a German were to try to rape his sister. "I should," he is said to have replied, "try and interpose my own body." Not the gay self-knowledge but the heterosexual, self-ignorant acting out of just this fantasy ends "The Beast in the Jungle." To face the gaze of the Beast would have been, for Marcher, to dissolve it. To face the "kind of hunger in the look" of the grieving man — to explore at all into the sharper lambencies of that encounter — would have been to dissolve the closet. Marcher, instead, to the very end, turns his back — re-creating a double scenario of homosexual compulsion and heterosexual compulsion. "He saw the Jungle of his life and saw the lurking Beast; then, while he looked, perceived it, as by a stir of the air, rise, huge and hideous, for the leap that was to settle him. His eyes darkened — it was close; and, instinctively turning, in his hallucination, to avoid it, he flung himself, face down, on the tomb."   [1986]

---

[1]Lytton Strachey (1880–1932), English biographer.

JANE SMILEY *prefaced her view of "Gregor: My Life as a Bug," published in* Harper's Magazine *in August 1992, with three sentences summarizing the events of Kafka's story "The Metamorphosis."*

JANE SMILEY

Gregor: My Life as a Bug

After some strenuous months of adjusting to and caring for the "giant dung beetle" that has unaccountably replaced their son, Gregor, the Samsa family have gone away to the country, to get some fresh air and plan for the future. The lodgers who precipitated the crisis are gone, as is the cleaning lady who has been "looking after" Gregor for the last few weeks. Gregor himself, much desiccated and weakened, but alive, has been carried out to the dustheap to ponder his metamorphosis.

All day, though sunk deeply in the stupor of profound physical weakness, Gregor had sensed the light beyond his eyelids, woven into his dreams, as it were, in the form of an uneasy awareness that soon he would wake up, that soon, all too soon, he wouldn't be able to avoid that, but it was only at dusk that he actually did rise to consciousness, and beheld the now familiar sight of his domed belly and his numerous helpless little legs glinting in the roseate shafts of sunlight that lengthened from the west down the otherwise dreary stretch of alley that ran behind the row of apartment houses.

The cleaning lady, practical and straightforward in her way, had not been much of a diagnostician and even less of an entomologist — what could she know, without education? — but the Samsas had willingly, perhaps even eagerly, accepted her certification of Gregor's death. Gregor had, too (had he not?), so disheartened was he by his sister's revulsion (you couldn't hide such a thing, a physical reaction like that, that much was crystal clear). Nor could you, Gregor reflected, die by wishing to. All too often, you had to wake up and live on. Make the best of things. Focus on the little physical pleasures of moving and eating and feeling a bit of a breeze and try to get through the rest.

With practiced ease, but somewhat slowed by lingering weakness, Gregor rolled from his back to his thorax, and lifted himself on legs that trembled but held. The dust and dirt that the cleaning lady had thrown out with him shifted and slid off his shining shell. His long feet sank into the dust, but it wasn't that hard to pull himself upward, nibbling a rind of cheese and a stale bit of cake and a brown apple core as he went. Slowly — it didn't matter; by himself, with none of that sense of anxiety that his parents and sister had communicated to him for the last months, he could move as he wished. And in the dark, too. The sunset had faded and a warm redolent breeze came to his proboscis. He got to the apex of the dustheap and remembered an advertising slogan he had seen once for a sleeping nostrum — "Knit up the ravelled sleave of care! — with Levy's Sleeping Draught! You'll feel better in the morning!" And he did feel better, no two ways about that. Now when he thought of his sister's reaction, well, it was her problem. Clearly, out here in the alley, he had problems of his own.

He smelled, as much as saw, the delicious odor of some rotting meat — mutton, it was — but when he stepped toward it, he toppled alarmingly forward, and then, unable to catch his balance, fell farther forward until he found himself rolling head over tail down the other side of the dustheap. He did manage to pick up the bit of mutton as he went, but only at the cost of painfully wrenching his back plates. Then he rolled out onto the cobblestones, and that was unpleasant, too — bruising his head and sides, making him ache all over, in fact. But the mutton was delicious. The thing was just to enjoy it, enjoy it at his leisure, the way they had never let him do during his whole life. And he did — he relished it bite by bite, concentrating, forgetting the pain, focusing on the pleasure.

The cobblestones were big as well as hard — how did people walk on these cobblestones? — they were like hills! What were the town's engineers thinking of, building streets like this — surely people would complain. You had to walk between them, along the seams, if you wanted to get anywhere. Gregor shook himself, and then made his way slowly, exploring with his feelers. It was a puzzle indeed, how the town had changed this way, and then he passed a large metal cavern, dark but square-shaped and raised off the stone — clearly not a door, looking more than anything like a drainpipe, but so extraordinarily large! Gregor marveled.

And then he realized. He was not nearly so large himself as they had made him out to be. Well, that was typical of them, the way they had always magnified problems. Any little change was monstrous to them. They were fearful people. He had known that, especially his mother, and his father wasn't any better, even though he hid his fear with anger. But it was hard, living at home, not to react the way they expected you to react. Well, now that was his sister's concern, too.

He skittered with great speed and grace between the cobblestones, stopping to drink from a puddle. Cool, refreshing. The sleep and food had perked him right up.

The thing was, they weren't bad people, he could see that. They did their best, given their fears, given how housebound they were — his own fears, too, why not admit that? He had expected them to change, but he hadn't really had the guts to *make* them change. It had all stayed more or less the same — everything unspoken, everything dictated by habit and duty. What did it matter, really, whether he was serving them, as he had when he was working, or they were serving him? Just the same tangle of anxiety and pressure and obligation and tedium. Sure, love was somewhere in there, but you had to get away to find it.

A silver light swelled over the cobblestones, and Gregor looked up to see the moon, calm and full as a plate, pause over his alley. He hadn't seen it in months, since before his "metamorphosis." It was different now, though, not flat but full of facets like a giant diamond. He lifted his back pair of legs and gave a triumphant buzz of joy. Sure the world held dangers, but hell, so what? What was that compared to setting out? Compared to the actual, authentic, bona fide transformation that lay ahead of him now?

Gregor looked up at the building. Perhaps those were his family's windows, just lighting up there on the third floor, as they returned from wherever they had been. He hoped they felt better. He wanted only good things for them, after all. He gazed for a moment, then raised his proboscis in a single salute. He was off now, down the alley to the street, and to many streets beyond. He stretched his young body, and headed down the road between the cobblestones.   [1992]

LEO TOLSTOY *wrote his commentary on "The Darling" a year after his friend Anton Chekhov's death as a way of protesting what Tolstoy considered an unfair caricature of a simple, good-hearted woman, the central character in the story. That Tolstoy experienced such a strong emotional affinity with Chekhov's fictional heroine that he felt compelled to defend her is a striking testimony to Chekhov's power as a short story writer and to Tolstoy's obsessive concern with morality. Tolstoy's argument is essentially based on the point of view of the patriarch. Chekhov's point of view in the story is much more subtle. His narrative has prompted other, very different interpretations, as evidenced by Eudora Welty's reading (see p. 1510).*

LEO TOLSTOY

Chekhov's Intent in The Darling

Translated by Constance Garnett

There is a story of profound meaning in the Book of Numbers which tells how Balak, the King of the Moabites, sent for the prophet Balaam to curse the Israelites who were on his borders. Balak promised Balaam many gifts for this service, and Balaam, tempted, went to Balak, and went with him up the mountain, where an altar was prepared with calves and sheep sacrificed in readiness for the curse. Balak waited for the curse, but instead of cursing, Balaam blessed the people of Israel.

And Balak said unto Balaam, What hast thou done unto me? I took thee to curse mine enemies, and, behold, thou hast blessed them altogether.

And he answered and said, Must I not take heed to speak that which the Lord hath put in my mouth?

And Balak said unto him, Come, I pray thee, with me into another place . . . and curse me them from thence.

But again, instead of cursing, Balaam blessed. And so it was the third time also.

And Balak's anger was kindled against Balaam, and he smote his hands together: And Balak said unto Balaam, I called thee to curse my enemies, and, behold, thou hast altogether blessed them these three times.

Therefore now flee thee to thy place: I thought to promote thee unto great honour; but, lo, the Lord hast kept thee back from honour.

And so Balaam departed without having received the gifts, because, instead of cursing, he had blessed the enemies of Balak. [Numbers 23: 11–13; 24:10–11]

What happened to Balaam often happens to real poets and artists. Tempted by Balak's gifts, popularity, or by false preconceived ideas, the poet does not see the angel barring his way, though the ass sees him, and he means to curse, and yet, behold, he blesses.

This is just what happened to the true poet and artist Chekhov when he wrote this charming story "The Darling."

The author evidently means to mock at the pitiful creature — as he judges her with his intellect, but not with his heart — the Darling, who after first sharing Kukin's anxiety about his theater, then throwing herself into the interests of the timber trade, then under the influence of the veterinary surgeon regarding the campaign against the foot and mouth disease as the most important matter in the world, is finally engrossed in the grammatical questions and the interests of the little schoolboy in the big cap. Kukin's surname is absurd, even his illness and the telegram announcing his death, the timber merchant with his respectability, the veterinary surgeon, even the boy — all are absurd, but the soul of the Darling, with her faculty of devoting herself with her whole being to any one she loves, is not absurd, but marvelous and holy.

I believe that while he was writing "The Darling," the author had in his mind, though not in his heart, a vague image of a new woman; of her equality with man; of a woman mentally developed, learned, working independently for the good of society as well as, if not better than, a man; of the woman who has raised and upholds the woman question; and in writing "The Darling" he wanted to show what woman ought not to be. The Balak of public opinion bade Chekhov curse the weak, submissive undeveloped woman devoted to man; and Chekhov went up the mountain, and the calves and sheep were laid upon the altar, but when he began to speak, the poet blessed what he had come to curse. In spite of its exquisite gay humor, I at least cannot read without tears some passages of this wonderful story. I am touched by the description of her complete devotion and love for Kukin and all that he cares for, and for the timber merchant and for the veterinary surgeon, and even more of her sufferings when she is left alone and has no one to love; and finally the account of how with all the strength of womanly, motherly feelings (of which she has no experience in her own life) she devotes herself with boundless love to the future man, the schoolboy in the big cap.

The author makes her love the absurd Kukin, the insignificant timber merchant, and the unpleasant veterinary surgeon, but love is no less sacred whether its object is a Kukin or a Spinoza, a Pascal, or a Schiller,[1] and whether the objects of it change as rapidly as with the Darling, or whether the object of it remains the same throughout the whole life.

Some time ago I happened to read in the *Novoe Vremya* an excellent article upon woman. The author has in this article expressed a remarkably clever and profound idea about woman. "Women," he says, "are trying to show us they can do everything we men can do. I don't contest it; I am prepared to admit women can do everything men can do, and possibly better than men; but the trouble is that men cannot do anything faintly approaching to what women can do."

Yes, that is undoubtedly true, and it is true not only with regard to birth, nurture, and early education of children. Men cannot do that highest, best work which brings man nearest to God — the work of love, and complete devotion to the loved object, which good women have done, do, and will do so well and so naturally. What would become of the world, what would become of us men if women had not that faculty and did not exercise it? We could get on without women doctors, women telegraph clerks, women lawyers, women scientists, women writers, but life would be a sorry affair without mothers, helpers, friends, comforters, who love in men the best in them, and imperceptibly instill, evoke, and support it. There would have been no Magdalen with Christ, no Claire with St. Francis; there would have been no wives of the Dekabrists[2] in Siberia; there would not have been among the Duhobors[3] those wives who, instead of holding their husbands back, supported them in their martyrdom for truth; there would not have been those thousands and thousands of unknown women — the best of all, as the unknown always are — the comforters of the drunken, the weak, and the dissolute, who, more than any, need the comfort of love. That love, whether devoted to a Kukin or to Christ, is the chief, grand, unique strength of woman.

What an amazing misunderstanding it is — all this so-called woman question, which, as every vulgar idea is bound to do, has taken possession of the majority of women, and even of men.

---

[1] Baruch Spinoza (1632–1677), Dutch philosopher; Blaise Pascal (1623–1662), French scientist and philosopher; Johann Christoph Friedrich von Schiller (1759–1805), German poet, playwright, and critic.

[2] Members of the unsuccessful December 1825 uprising against Czar Nicholas I.

[3] Members of the Christian sect that advocated following inner spirituality instead of church or government doctrine.

"Woman longs to improve herself" — what can be more legitimate and just than that?

But a woman's work is from her very vocation different from man's, and so the ideal of feminine perfection cannot be the same as the ideal of masculine perfection. Let us admit that we do not know what that ideal is; it is quite certain in any case that it is not the ideal of masculine perfection. And yet it is to the attainment of that masculine ideal that the whole and the absurd and evil activity of the fashionable woman movement, which is such a stumbling-block to woman, is directed.

I am afraid that Chekhov was under the influence of that misunderstanding when he wrote "The Darling."

He, like Balaam, intended to curse, but the god of poetry forbade him, and commanded him to bless. And he did bless, and unconsciously clothed this sweet creature in such an exquisite radiance that she will always remain a type of what a woman can be in order to be happy herself, and to make the happiness of those with whom destiny throws her.

What makes the story so excellent is that the effect is unintentional.

I learned to ride a bicycle in a hall large enough to drill a division of soldiers. At the other end of the hall a lady was learning. I thought I must be careful to avoid getting into her way, and began looking at her. And as I looked at her I began unconsciously getting nearer and nearer to her, and in spite of the fact that, noticing the danger, she hastened to retreat, I rode down upon her and knocked her down — that is, I did the very opposite of what I wanted to do, simply because I concentrated my attention upon her.

The same thing has happened to Chekhov, but in an inverse sense: He wanted to knock the Darling down, and concentrating upon her the close attention of the poet, he raised her up.   [1905]

LIONEL TRILLING *was an eminent critic, biographer, novelist, and professor of literature at Columbia University, one of the influential group of New York intellectuals after World War II who insisted on America's cultural continuity with the European tradition. Trilling championed "the idea of the adversary culture" in the work of the Modernist writers he admired, such as Joseph Conrad, D. H. Lawrence, James Joyce, and Frank Kafka. His essay "On the Teaching of Modern Literature" in* Beyond Culture *(1965) is based on his lectures at Columbia, where he taught* Heart of Darkness *by analyzing Conrad's "discovery and canonization of the primal, non-ethical energies." Trilling's interpretation as a culture critic can be contrasted with the perspective of African writer Chinua Achebe on Conrad's story (see p. 1373).*

LIONEL TRILLING

The Greatness of Conrad's Heart of Darkness

Whether or not Joseph Conrad read either Blake[1] or Nietzsche[2] I do not know, but his *Heart of Darkness* follows in their line. This very great work has never lacked for the admiration it deserves, and it has been given a kind of canonical place in the legend of modern literature by Eliot's[3] having it so clearly in mind when he wrote *The Waste Land* and his having taken from it the epigraph to "The Hollow Men." But no one, to my knowledge, has ever confronted in an explicit way its strange and terrible message of ambivalence toward the life of civilization. Consider that its protagonist, Kurtz, is a progressive and a liberal and that he is the highly respected representative of a society which would have us believe it is benign, although in fact it is vicious. Consider too that he is a practitioner of several arts, a painter, a writer, a musician, and into the bargain a political orator. He is at once the most idealistic and the most practically successful of all the agents of the Belgian exploitation of the Congo. Everybody knows the truth about him which Marlow discovers — that Kurtz's success is the result of a terrible ascendancy he has gained over the natives of his distant station, an ascendancy which is derived from his presumed magical or divine powers, that he has exercised his rule with an extreme of cruelty, that he has given himself to unnamable acts of lust. This is the world of the darker pages of *The Golden Bough*.[4] It is one of the great points of Conrad's story that Marlow speaks of the primitive life of the jungle not as being noble or charming or even free but as being base and sordid — and for *that* reason compelling: He himself feels quite overtly its dreadful attraction. It is to this devilish baseness that Kurtz has yielded himself, and yet Marlow, although he does indeed treat him with hostile irony, does not find it possible to suppose that Kurtz is anything but a hero of the spirit. For me it is still ambiguous whether Kurtz's famous deathbed cry, "The horror! The horror!" refers to the approach of death or to his experience of savage life. Whichever it is, to Marlow the fact that Kurtz could utter this cry at the point of death, while Marlow himself, when death threatens him, can know it only as a weary grayness, marks the difference between the ordinary man and a hero of the spirit. Is this not the essence of the modern belief about the nature of the artist, the man who goes

---

[1] William Blake (1757–1827), English Romantic poet.

[2] Friedrich Wilhelm Nietzsche (1844–1900), German philosopher.

[3] T. S. Eliot (1888–1965), American-born English poet and critic and author of *The Waste Land* (1922).

[4] A study of magic and religion (1911) written by the Scottish anthropologist Sir James George Frazer (1854–1941).

down into that hell which is the historical beginning of the human soul, a beginning not outgrown but established in humanity as we know it now, preferring the reality of this hell to the bland lies of the civilization that has overlaid it?   [1965]

JOHN UPDIKE *wrote a foreword to* The Complete Stories of Franz Kafka *in 1983. Updike begins his essay by quoting "He," one of Kafka's aphorisms: "All that he does seems to him, it is true, extraordinarily new, but also, because of the incredible spate of new things, extraordinarily amateurish, indeed scarcely tolerable, incapable of becoming history, breaking short the chain of the generations, cutting off for the first time at its most profound source the music of the world, which before him could at least be divined. Sometimes in his arrogance he has more anxiety for the world than for himself." Updike has great sympathy for Kafka and has written about him with considerable perception.*

JOHN UPDIKE

Kafka and The Metamorphosis

The century since Franz Kafka was born has been marked by the idea of "modernism" — a self-consciousness new among centuries, a consciousness of being new. Sixty years after his death, Kafka epitomizes one aspect of this modern mind-set: a sensation of anxiety and shame whose center cannot be located and therefore cannot be placated; a sense of an infinite difficulty within things, impeding every step; a sensitivity acute beyond usefulness, as if the nervous system, flayed of its old hide of social usage and religious belief, must record every touch as pain. In Kafka's peculiar and highly original case this dreadful quality is mixed with immense tenderness, oddly good humor, and a certain severe and reassuring formality. The combination makes him an artist; but rarely can an artist have struggled against greater inner resistance and more sincere diffidence as to the worth of his art. . . .

Kafka dated his own maturity as a writer from the long night of September 22nd–23rd, 1912, in which he wrote "The Judgment" at a single eight-hour sitting. He confided to his diary that morning, "Only *in this way* can writing be done, only with such coherence, with such a complete opening out of the body and the soul." Yet the story is not quite free of the undeclared neurotic elements that twist the earlier work; the connection between the engagement and the father seems obscure, and the old man's fury illogical.

But in staring at, with his hero Georg, "the bogey conjured up by his father," Kafka broke through to a great cavern of stored emotion. He loved this story, and among friends praised — he who deprecated almost everything from his own pen — its *Zweifellosigkeit*, its "indubitableness." Soon after its composition, he wrote, in a few weeks, "The Metamorphosis," an indubitable masterpiece. It begins with a fantastic premise, whereas in "The Judgment" events become fantastic. This premise — the gigantic insect — established in the first sentence, "The Metamorphosis" unfolds with a beautiful naturalness and a classic economy. It takes place in three acts: three times the metamorphosed Gregor Samsa ventures out of his room, with tumultuous results. The members of his family — rather simpler than Kafka's own, which had three sisters — dispose themselves around the central horror with a touching, as well as an amusing, plausibility. The father's fury, roused in defense of the fragile mother, stems directly from the action and inflicts a psychic wound gruesomely objectified in the rotting apple Gregor carries in his back; the evolutions of the sister, Grete, from shock to distasteful ministration to a certain sulky possessiveness and finally to exasperated indifference are beautifully sketched, with not a stroke too much. The terrible but terribly human tale ends with Grete's own metamorphosis, into a comely young woman. This great story resembles a great story of the nineteenth century, Tolstoy's "The Death of Ivan Ilyich"; in both, a hitherto normal man lies hideously, suddenly stricken in the midst of a family whose irritated, banal daily existence flows around him. The abyss within life is revealed, but also life itself.

What kind of insect is Gregor? Popular belief has him a cockroach, which would be appropriate for a city apartment; and the creature's retiring nature and sleazy dietary preferences would seem to conform. But, as Vladimir Nabokov, who knew his entomology, pointed out in his lectures upon "The Metamorphosis" at Cornell University, Gregor is too broad and convex to be a cockroach. The charwoman calls him a "dung beetle" (*Mistkäfer*) but, Nabokov said, "it is obvious that the good woman is adding the epithet only to be friendly." Kafka's Eduard Raban of "Wedding Preparations" daydreams, walking along, "As I lie in bed I assume the shape of a big beetle, a stag beetle or a cockchafer, I think." Gregor Samsa, awaking, sees "numerous legs, which were pitifully thin compared to the rest of his bulk." If "numerous" is more than six, he must be a centipede — not an insect at all. From evidence in the story he is brown in color and about as long as the distance between a doorknob and the floor; he is broader than half a door. He has a voice at first, "but with a persistent horrible twittering squeak behind it like an undertone," which disappears as the story progresses. His jaws don't work as ours do but he has eyelids, nostrils, and a neck. He is, in short, impossible to picture except when the author wants to evoke his appearance, to bump the reader up against some astounding, poignant new aspect of Gregor's embodiment. The strange physical discomfort noted in the earlier work is here given its perfect allegorical envelope. A wonderful moment comes when Gregor, having been painfully striving to achieve human postures, drops to his feet:

Hardly was he down when he experienced for the first time this morning a sense of physical discomfort; his legs had firm ground under them; they were completely obedient, as he noted with joy; they even strove to carry him forward in whatever direction he chose; and he was inclined to believe that a final relief from all his sufferings was at hand.

When "The Metamorphosis" was to be published as a book in 1915, Kafka, fearful that the cover illustrator "might want to draw the insect itself," wrote the publisher, "Not that, please not that! . . . The insect itself cannot be depicted. It cannot even be shown from a distance." He suggested instead a scene of the family in the apartment with a locked door, or a door open and giving on darkness. Any theatrical or cinematic version of the story must founder on this point of external representation: A concrete image of the insect would be too distracting and shut off sympathy; such a version would lack the very heart of comedy and pathos which beats in the unsteady area between objective and subjective, where Gregor's insect and human selves swayingly struggle. Still half-asleep, he notes his extraordinary condition yet persists in remembering and trying to fulfill his duties as a travelling salesman and the mainstay of this household. Later, relegated by the family to the shadows of a room turned storage closet, he responds to violin music and creeps forward, covered with dust and trailing remnants of food, to claim his sister's love. Such scenes could not be done except with words. In this age that lives and dies by the visual, "The Metamorphosis" stands as a narrative absolutely literary, able to exist only where language and the mind's hazy wealth of imagery intersect.

"The Metamorphosis" stands also as a gateway to the world Kafka created after it. His themes and manner were now all in place. His mastery of official pomposity — the dialect of documents and men talking business — shows itself here for the first time, in the speeches of the chief clerk. Music will again be felt, by mice and dogs, as an overwhelming emanation in Kafka's later fables — a theme whose other side is the extreme sensitivity to noise, and the longing for unblemished silence, that Kafka shared with his hero in "The Burrow." Gregor's death scene, and Kafka's death wish, return in "A Hunger Artist" — the saddest, I think, of Kafka's stories, written by a dying man who was increasingly less sanguine (his correspondence reveals) about dying. The sweeping nature of the hunger artist's abstention is made plain by the opposing symbol of the panther who replaces him in his cage: "the joy of life streamed with such ardent passion from his throat that for the onlookers it was not easy to stand the shock of it." In 1920 Milena Jesenská wrote to Brod: "Frank cannot live. Frank does not have the capacity for living. . . . He is absolutely incapable of living, just as he is incapable of getting drunk. He possesses not the slightest refuge. For that reason he is exposed to all those things against which we are protected. He is like a naked man among a multitude who are dressed." After Gregor Samsa's incarnation, Kafka showed a fondness for naked heroes — animals who have complicated and even pedantic confessions to make but who also are distinguished by some keenly observed bestial traits — the ape of "A Report to an Academy" befouls himself and his fur jumps with fleas; the dog of "Investigations" recalls his young days when, very puppylike, "I believed that great things were going on around me of which I was the leader and to which I must lend my voice, things which must be wretchedly thrown aside if I did not run for them and wag my tail for them"; the mouse folk of "Josephine the Singer" pipe and multiply and are pervaded by an "unexpended, ineradicable childishness"; and the untaxonomic inhabitant of "The Burrow" represents the animal in all of us, his cheerful consumption of "small fry" existentially yoked to a terror of being consumed himself. An uncanny empathy broods above these zoömorphs, and invests them with more of their creator's soul than all but a few human characters receive. So a child, cowed and bored by the world of human adults, makes companions of pets and toy animals.   [1983]

ALICE WALKER *wrote about Zora Neale Hurston in her collection* In Search of Our Mothers' Gardens: Womanist Prose *(1983). There she also looked at Flannery O'Connor, Langston Hughes, Jean Toomer, and other writers from what she called her "womanist" perspective as a radical black woman. To clarify the meaning of her term, Walker added that "womanist is to feminist as purple is to lavender."*

A L I C E   W A L K E R

Zora Neale Hurston: A Cautionary Tale and a Partisan View

During the early and middle years of her career Zora was a cultural revolutionary simply because she was always herself. Her work, so vigorous among the rather pallid productions of many of her contemporaries, comes from the essence of black folk life. During her later life she became frightened of the life she had always dared bravely before. Her work too became reactionary, static, shockingly misguided and timid. (This is especially true of her last novel, *Seraphs on the Sewannee,* which is not even about black people, which is no crime, but *is* about white people for whom it is impossible to care, which is.)

A series of misfortunes battered Zora's spirit and her health. And she was broke.

Being broke made all the difference.

Without money of one's own in a capitalist society, there is no such thing as independence. This is one of the clearest lessons of Zora's life, and why I consider the telling of her life "a cautionary tale." We must learn from it what we can.

Without money, an illness, even a simple one, can undermine the will. Without money, getting into a hospital is problematic and getting out without money to pay for the treatment is nearly impossible. Without money, one becomes dependent on other people, who are likely to be — even in their kindness — erratic in their support and despotic in their expectations of return. Zora was forced to rely, like Tennessee Williams's Blanche, "on the kindness of strangers." Can anything be more dangerous, if the strangers are forever in control? Zora, who worked so hard, was never able to make a living from her work.

She did not complain about not having money. She was not the type. (Several months ago I received a long letter from one of Zora's nieces, a bright ten-year-old, who explained to me that her aunt was so proud that the only way the family could guess she was ill or without funds was by realizing they had no idea where she was. Therefore, none of the family attended either Zora's sickbed or her funeral.) Those of us who have had "grants and fellowships from 'white folks'" know this aid is extended in precisely the way welfare is extended in Mississippi. One is asked, *curtly*, more often than not: How much do you need *just to survive?* Then one is — if fortunate — given a third of that. What is amazing is that Zora, who became an orphan at nine, a runaway at fourteen, a maid and manicurist (because of necessity and not from love of the work) before she was twenty — with one dress — managed to become Zora Neale Hurston, author and anthropologist, at all.

For me, the most unfortunate thing Zora ever wrote is her autobiography. After the first several chapters, it rings false. One begins to hear the voice of someone whose life required the assistance of too many transitory "friends." A Taoist proverb states that *to act sincerely with the insincere is dangerous.* (A mistake blacks as a group have tended to make in America.) And so we have Zora sincerely offering gratitude and kind words to people one knows she could not have respected. But this unctuousness, so out of character for Zora, is also a result of dependency, a sign of her powerlessness, her inability to pay back her debts with anything but words. They must have been bitter ones for her. In her dependency, it should be remembered, Zora was not alone — because it is quite true that America does not support or honor us as human beings, let alone as blacks, women, and artists. We have taken help where it was offered because we are committed to what we do and to the survival of our work. Zora was committed to the survival of her people's cultural heritage as well.

In my mind, Zora Neale Hurston, Billie Holiday, and Bessie Smith form a sort of unholy trinity. Zora *belongs* in the tradition of black women singers, rather than among "the literati," at least to me. There were the extreme highs and lows of her life, her undaunted pursuit of adventure, passionate emotional and sexual experience, and her love of freedom. Like Billie and Bessie she followed her own road, believed in her own gods, pursued her own dreams, and refused to separate herself from "common" people. It would have been nice if the three of them had had one another to turn to, in times of need. I close my eyes and imagine them: Bessie would be in charge of all the money; Zora would keep Billie's masochistic tendencies in check and prevent her from singing embarrassing anything-for-a-man songs, thereby preventing Billie's heroin addiction. In return, Billie could be, along with Bessie, the family that Zora felt she never had.

We are a people. A people do not throw their geniuses away. And if they are thrown away, it is our duty *as artists and as witnesses for the future* to collect them again for the sake of our children, and, if necessary, bone by bone.

[1979]

EUDORA WELTY *included this discussion of her story "The Worn Path" in her book* The Eye of the Story *(1977). It appeared in the section "On Writing," along with her most extensive essays on the art of short fiction — essays that take up general topics such as place and time in fiction, and the art of reading and writing stories. Her reviews of the work of Isak Dinesen, Ralph Ellison, William Faulkner, and Virginia Woolf from the* New York Times *are also included in this collection.*

E U D O R A   W E L T Y

Is Phoenix Jackson's Grandson Really Dead?

A story writer is more than happy to be read by students; the fact that these serious readers think and feel something in response to his work he finds life-giving. At the same time he may not always be able to reply to their specific questions in kind. I wondered if it might clarify something, for both the questioners and myself, if I set down a general reply to the question that comes to me most often in the mail, from both students and their teachers, after some classroom discussion. The unrivaled favorite is this: "Is Phoenix Jackson's grandson really *dead?*"

It refers to a short story I wrote years ago called "A Worn Path," which tells of a day's journey an old woman makes on foot from deep in the country into town and into a doctor's office on behalf of her little grandson; he is at home, periodically ill, and periodically she comes for his medicine; they give it to her as usual, she receives it and starts the journey back.

I had not meant to mystify readers by withholding any fact; it is not a writer's business to tease. The story is told through Phoenix's mind as she undertakes her errand. As the author at one with the character as I tell it, I must assume that the boy is alive. As the reader, you are free to think as you like, of course: The story invites you to believe that no matter what happens, Phoenix for as long as she is able to walk and can hold to her purpose will make her journey. The *possibility* that she would keep on even if he were dead is there in her devotion and its single-minded, single-track errand. Certainly the *artistic* truth, which should be good enough for the fact, lies in Phoenix's own answer to that question. When the nurse asks, "He isn't dead, is he?" she speaks for herself: "He still the same. He going to last."

The grandchild is the incentive. But it is the journey, the going of the errand, that is the story, and the question is not whether the grandchild is in reality alive or dead. It doesn't affect the outcome of the story or its meaning from start to finish. But it is not the question itself that has struck me as much as the idea, almost without exception implied in the asking, that for Phoenix's grandson to be dead would somehow make the story "better."

It's *all right*, I want to say to the students who write to me, for things to be what they appear to be, and for words to mean what they say. It's all right, too, for words and appearances to mean more than one thing — ambiguity is a fact of life. A fiction writer's responsibility covers not only what he presents as the facts of a given story but what he chooses to stir up as their implications; in the end, these implications, too, become facts, in the larger, fictional sense. But it is not all right, not in good faith, for things *not* to mean what they say.

The grandson's plight was real and it made the truth of the story, which is the story of an errand of love carried out. If the child no longer lived, the truth would persist in the "wornness" of the path. But his being dead can't increase the truth of the story, can't affect it one way or the other. I think I signal this, because the end of the story has been reached before old Phoenix gets home again: she simply starts back. To the question "Is the grandson really dead?" I could reply that it doesn't make any difference. I could also say that I did not make him up in order to let him play a trick on Phoenix. But my best answer would be: "*Phoenix* is alive."

The origin of a story is sometimes a trustworthy clue to the author — or can provide him with the clue — to its key image; maybe in this case it will do the same for the reader. One day I saw a solitary old woman like Phoenix. She was walking; I saw her, at middle distance, in a winter country landscape, and watched her slowly make her way across my line of vision. That sight of her made me write the story. I invented an errand for her, but that only seemed a living part of the figure she was herself: What errand other than for someone else could be making her go? And her going was the first thing, her persisting in her landscape was the real thing, and the first and the real were what I wanted and worked to keep. I brought her up close enough, by imagination, to describe her face, make her present to the eyes, but the full-length figure moving across the winter fields was the indelible one and the image to keep, and the perspective extending into the vanishing distance the true one to hold in mind.

I invented for my character, as I wrote, some passing adventures —

some dreams and harassments and a small triumph or two, some jolts to her pride, some flights of fancy to console her, one or two encounters to scare her, a moment that gave her cause to feel ashamed, a moment to dance and preen — for it had to be a *journey,* and all these things belonged to that, parts of life's uncertainty.

A narrative line is in its deeper sense, of course, the tracing out of a meaning, and the real continuity of a story lies in this probing forward. The real dramatic force of a story depends on the strength of the emotion that has set it going. The emotional value is the measure of the reach of the story. What gives any such content to "A Worn Path" is not its circumstances but its *subject:* the deep-grained habit of love.

What I hoped would come clear was that in the whole surround of this story, the world it threads through, the only certain thing at all is the worn path. The habit of love cuts through confusion and stumbles or contrives its way out of difficulty, it remembers the way even when it forgets, for a dumfounded moment, its reason for being. The path is the thing that matters.

Her victory — old Phoenix's — is when she sees the diploma in the doctor's office, when she finds "nailed up on the wall the document that had been stamped with the gold seal and framed in the gold frame, which matched the dream that was hung up in her head." The return with the medicine is just a matter of retracing her own footsteps. It is the part of the journey, and of the story, that can now go without saying.

In the matter of function, old Phoenix's way might even do as a sort of parallel to your way of work if you are a writer of stories. The way to get there is the all-important, all-absorbing problem, and this problem is your reason for undertaking the story. Your only guide, too, is your sureness about your subject, about what this subject is. Like Phoenix, you work all your life to find your way, through all the obstructions and the false appearances and the upsets you may have brought on yourself, to reach a meaning — using inventions of your imagination, perhaps helped out by your dreams and bits of good luck. And finally too, like Phoenix, you have to assume that what you are working in aid of is life, not death.

But you would make the trip anyway — wouldn't you? — just on hope.

[1977]

EUDORA WELTY *included her statement on Anton Chekhov's "The Darling" in her book* The Eye of the Story (1977). *In her brief reading she analyzes the elements of plot ("aware of its clear open stress, the variations all springing from Chekhov's boundless and minute perception of character"), character motivation ("maternalism: for there it is most naturally innocent of anything but formless, thoughtless, blameless embracing; the true innocence is in never perceiving"), and theme ("Protest to the darlings of this world will always be [delivered] — out of inward and silent rebellion alone").*

EUDORA WELTY

Plot and Character in Chekhov's The Darling

Clearly, the fact that stories have plots in common is of no more account than that many people have blue eyes. Plots are, indeed, what the story writer sees with, and so do we as we read. The plot is the Why. Why? is asked and replied to at various depths; the fishes in the sea are bigger the deeper we go. To learn that character is a more awe-inspiring fish and (in a short story, though not, I think, in a novel) one some degrees deeper down than situation, we have only to read Chekhov. What constitutes the reality of his characters is what they reveal to us. And the possibility that they may indeed reveal everything is what makes fictional characters differ so greatly from us in real life; yet isn't it strange that they don't really *seem* to differ? This is one clue to the extraordinary magnitude of character in fiction. Characters in the plot connect us with the vastness of our secret life, which is endlessly explorable. This is their role. What happens to them is what they have been put here to show.

In his story "The Darling," the darling's first husband, the theater manager, dies suddenly *because* of the darling's sweet passivity; this is the causality of fiction. In everyday or real life he might have held on to his health for years. But under Chekhov's hand he is living and dying in dependence on, and in revelation of, Olenka's character. He can only last a page and a half. Only by force of the story's circumstance is he here at all; Olenka took him up to begin with because he lived next door. . . . Kukin proposes and they are married. . . . And when Kukin dies, Olenka's cry of heartbreak is this: "Vanitchka, my precious, my darling! Why did I ever meet you! Why did I know you and love you! Your poor brokenhearted Olenka is all alone without you!"

With variations the pattern is repeated, and we are made to feel it as plot, aware of its clear open stress, the variations all springing from Chekhov's boundless and minute perception of character. The timber-merchant, another neighbor, is the one who walks home from the funeral with Olenka. The outcome follows tenderly, is only natural. After three days, he calls. "He did not stay long, only about ten minutes, and he did not say much, but when he left, Olenka loved him — loved him so much that she lay awake all night in a perfect fever."

Olenka and Pustovalov get along very well together when they are married. . . . Even in her dreams Olenka is in the timber business, dreaming of "perfect mountains of planks and boards," and cries out in her sleep, so that Pustovalov says to her tenderly, "Olenka, what's the matter, darling? Cross yourself!" But the timber merchant inevitably goes out in the timber yard one day without his cap on; he catches cold and dies, to leave Olenka a widow once more. "I've nobody, now you've left me, my darling," she sobs after the funeral. "How can I live without you?"

And the timber merchant is succeeded by a veterinary surgeon — who gets transferred to Siberia. But the plot is not repetition — it is direction. The love which Olenka bears to whatever is nearest her reaches its final and, we discover, its truest mold in maternalism: For there it is most naturally innocent of anything but formless, thoughtless, blameless *embracing*; the true innocence is in never perceiving. Only mother love could endure in a pursuit of such blind regard, caring so little for the reality of either life involved so long as love wraps them together, Chekhov tells us — unpretentiously, as he tells everything, and with the simplest of concluding episodes. Olenka's character is seen purely then for what it is: limpid reflection, mindless and purposeless regard, love that falls like the sun and rain on all alike, vacant when there is nothing to reflect.

We know this because, before her final chance to love, Olenka is shown to us truly alone:

> [She] got thinner and plainer; and when people met her in the street they did not look at her as they used to, and did not smile to her; evidently her best years were over and left behind, and now a new sort of life had begun for her, which did not bear thinking about. . . . And what was worst of all, she had no opinions of any sort. She saw the objects about her and understood what she saw, but could not form any opinions about them, and did not know what to talk about. And how awful it is not to have any opinions! She wanted a love that would absorb her whole being, her whole soul and reason — that would give her ideas and an object in her life, and would warm her old blood.

The answer is Sasha, the ten-year-old son of the veterinary surgeon, an unexpected blessing from Siberia — a schoolchild. The veterinarian has another wife now, but this no longer matters. "Olenka, with arms akimbo, walked about the yard giving directions. Her face was beaming, and she was brisk and alert, as though she had waked from a long sleep. . . ." "An island is a piece of land entirely surrounded by water," Sasha reads aloud. "'An island is a piece of land,' she repeated, and this was the first opinion to which she gave utterance with positive conviction, after so many years of silence and dearth of ideas." She would follow Sasha halfway to school, until he told her to go back. She would go to bed thinking blissfully of Sasha, "who lay sound asleep in the next room, sometimes crying out in his sleep, 'I'll give it to you! Get away! Shut up!'"

The darling herself *is* the story; all else is sacrificed to her; deaths and departures are perfunctory and to be expected. The last words of the story are the child's and a protest, but they are delivered in his sleep, as indeed protest to the darlings of this world will always be — out of inward and silent rebellion alone, as this master makes plain.   [1977]

EUDORA WELTY *analyzed the topic of reality in Chekhov's short fiction in* The Eye of the Story *(1979), when she discussed what she called "the revolution brought about by the gentle Chekhov to the short story." Welty realized that "by removing the formal plot he did not leave the story structureless; he endowed it with another kind of structure — one which embodied the principle of growth." She felt that at the heart of Chekhov's method was his respect for each individual's own view of reality: "He is not trying to teach us, through his characters; he only asks us to understand them."*

E U D O R A   W E L T Y

Reality in Chekhov's Stories

Chekhov [is] the least self-obtrusive of story writers. It is the story he's written that has gained a self — a clear, unself-conscious identity, vigorous, purposeful, ongoing. This freeing of the form came from the deeps of his temperament, we might suppose. The abhorrence he felt toward coercion in human affairs must have had its own part in clearing away the confines of arbitrary plot, manipulated characters. As the grandson of a serf, who had "squeezed the slave out of himself drop by drop," Chekhov knew all the better what it meant to make himself free as an artist.

Thus he dared to make himself free to enter the body, spirit, mind and heart of a character, and free of any crippling wish to use him as a spokesman for himself, or as a moral example, or as a scapegoat. In the writing of his stories he conscientiously yielded only to the authority of his feeling for human beings as human beings.

And no human being is out of bounds to Chekhov. No state of health or stage of consciousness or time of life could have appeared strange to him. As a storyteller he is within any character he invents — a woman in her seventh month of pregnancy, an aged learned man suffering from insomnia and "strange and inappropriate thoughts," even a little dog being trained for a music-hall act, who "grew so used to the word 'talent,' that every time her master pronounced it, she jumped up as if it had been her name."

Neither did he hesitate to deal with any subject he wished. Chekhov wrote of sex with honesty and lack of fuss, as he wrote of all human experience. As always, it is a character's feelings that give it its meaning. Much ahead of his time, and perhaps of ours, in "The Duel" he treated with candor and seriousness a young woman of compelling sexuality. "The Lady with the Pet Dog" is a compassionate study of a cynical middle-aged man surprised when, almost against his will and against his belief, his sexual worldliness turns into the honesty and difficulty of belated love.

Chekhov's candor, which was natural to him, was more than a revulsion against lying and hypocrisy. It was a tool in his work. His candor was exploratory and painstaking — he might have used it as the doctor in him would know how, treating the need for truth between human beings as an emergency. . . .

The depth of Chekhov's feeling for man is the very element out of which his stories spring, out of which they continue to draw their life. The reader who, like the present one, must rely on translations should not venture to speak in close particular about sentences, perhaps. But it seems plain enough to be a fundamental fact of Chekhov's work that the passion is not in the sentence but in the whole.

Passion does not burst from him as a storm, with a storm's threat — driving winds and bolts of lightning, crashes of thunder; it is more like a climate, prevailing, all-enfolding. "The Lady with the Pet Dog" is pervaded with a gentleness that can be ominous as thunder, and a grace that can strike you to the heart; it is a love story concluding with these words: " . . . and it was clear to both of them that the end was still far off, and that what was to be most complicated and difficult for them was only just beginning."

It is a story firmly restrained, whose mood is not broken from first to last; nothing is placed in full direct glare. There is, rather, a quiet shimmering from within, and then the emergence of that last sentence, which is not a summation but a prophecy, and which long after the story ends goes on pulsing light into the mind.

The stories leave no havoc on the surface. Their reach, even their nature, might be reflected on the seismograph; they run close to the nerve of our inner lives.

They don't date. They could not have been written outside the time and place of their origin — they are a living part of both. If there are certain similarities in Chekhov's times and ours that strike us when we read him, the significance is other than historical. Though no two centuries are very much like each other, some hours, perhaps, are; moments are; critical moments nearly always are. Emotions are the same. We are the same. The man, not the day, is the lasting phenomenon.

In the whole population of Chekhov's characters, every single one, the least, the smallest, the youngest, the most obscure, has its clear identity. No life is too brief or too inconsequential for him to be inattentive to its own reality.

[1979]

EDITH WHARTON *included "Telling a Short Story" in her book* The Writing of Fiction *(1925), from which this excerpt is taken. Her disciplined attempt to state a theory of narrative form was modeled on the example of her mentor, Henry James. She took as the epigraph of her book a quotation from the early English poet Thomas Traherne: "Order the beauty even of Beauty is." Concerned with defining the difference between the short story and longer forms of prose narrative, Wharton was herself an accomplished writer of both.*

EDITH WHARTON

Every Subject Must Contain within Itself Its Own Dimensions

It is sometimes said that a "good subject" for a short story should always be capable of being expanded into a novel.

The principle may be defendable in special cases; but it is certainly a misleading one on which to build any general theory. Every "subject" (in the novelist's sense of the term) must necessarily contain within itself its own dimensions; and one of the fiction-writer's essential gifts is that of discerning whether the subject which presents itself to him, asking for incarnation, is suited to the proportions of a short story or of a novel. If it appears to be adapted to both the chances are that it is inadequate to either.

It would be as great a mistake, however, to try to base a hard-and-fast theory on the denial of the rule as on its assertion. Instances of short stories made out of subjects that could have been expanded into a novel, and that are yet typical short stories and not mere stunted novels, will occur to every-one. General rules in art are useful chiefly as a lamp in a mine, or a handrail down a black stairway; they are necessary for the sake of the guidance they give, but it is a mistake, once they are formulated, to be too much in awe of them.

There are at least two reasons why a subject should find expression in novel-form rather than as a tale; but neither is based on the number of what may be conveniently called incidents, or external happenings, which the narrative contains. There are novels of action which might be condensed into short stories without the loss of their distinguishing qualities. The marks of the subject requiring a longer development are, first, the gradual unfolding of the inner life of its characters, and secondly the need of producing in the reader's mind the sense of the lapse of time. Outward events of the most varied and exciting nature may without loss of probability be crowded into a few hours, but moral dramas usually have their roots deep in the soul, their rise far back in time; and the suddenest-seeming clash in which they culminate should be led up to step by step if it is to explain and justify itself.

There are cases, indeed, when the short story may make use of the moral drama at its culmination. If the incident dealt with be one which a single retrospective flash sufficiently lights up, it is qualified for use as a short story; but if the subject be so complex, and its successive phases so interesting, as to justify elaboration, the lapse of time must necessarily be suggested, and the novel-form becomes appropriate.

The effect of compactness and instantaneity sought in the short story is attained mainly by the observance of two "unities" — the old traditional one of time, and that other, more modern and complex, which requires that any rapidly enacted episode shall be seen through only one pair of eyes. . . .

One thing more is needful for the ultimate effect of probability; and that is, never to let the character who serves as reflector record anything not naturally within his register. It should be the story-teller's first care to choose this reflecting mind deliberately, as one would choose a building-site, or decide upon the orientation of one's house, and when this is done, to live inside the mind chosen, trying to feel, see and react exactly as the latter would, no more, no less, and, above all, no otherwise. Only thus can the writer avoid attributing incongruities of thought and metaphor to his chosen interpreter.

[1925]

RICHARD WRIGHT *took an epigraph from the Book of Job for his autobiography,* Black Boy *(1945): "They meet with darkness in the daytime/And they grope at noonday as in the night." After describing being brutalized by poverty and emotional deprivation in his early childhood, Wright recalled his first encounter with literature. A schoolteacher told him the story of Bluebeard and his seven wives. Wright was electrified by what he heard. The "whispered story of deception and murder had been the first experience of my life that had elicited from me a total emotional response. . . . I had tasted what to me was life, and I would have more of it, somehow, someway."*

RICHARD WRIGHT

Reading Fiction

I was now running more away from something than toward something. But that did not matter to me. My mood was: I've got to get away; I can't stay here.

But what was it that always made me feel that way? From where in this southern darkness had I caught a sense of freedom? Why was it that I was able to act upon vaguely felt notions? What was it that made me feel things deeply enough for me to try to order my life by my feelings? The external world of whites and blacks, which was the only world that I had ever known, surely had not evoked in me any belief in myself. The people I had met had advised and demanded submission. What, then, was I after? How dare I consider my feelings superior to the gross environment that sought to claim me?

It had been only through books — at best, no more than vicarious cultural transfusions — that I had managed to keep myself alive in a negatively vital way. Whenever my environment had failed to support or nourish me, I had clutched at books; consequently, my belief in books had risen more out of a sense of desperation than from any abiding conviction of their ultimate value. In a peculiar sense, life had trapped me in a realm of emotional rejection; I had not embraced insurgency through open choice. Existing emotionally on the sheer, thin margin of southern culture, I had felt that nothing short of life itself hung upon each of my actions and decisions; and I had grown used to change, to movement, to making many adjustments.

In the main, my hope was merely a kind of self-defence, a conviction that if I did not leave I would perish, either because of possible violence of others against me, or because of my possible violence against them. The substance of my hope was formless and devoid of any real sense of direction, for in my southern living I had seen no looming landmark by which I could, in a positive sense, guide my daily actions. The shocks of southern living had rendered my personality tender and swollen, tense and volatile, and my flight was more a shunning of external and internal dangers than an attempt to embrace what I felt I wanted.

It had been my accidental reading of fiction and literary criticism that had evoked in me vague glimpses of life's possibilities. Of course, I had never seen or met the men who wrote the books I read, and the kind of world in which they lived was as alien to me as the moon. But what enabled me to overcome my chronic distrust was that these books — written by men like Dreiser, Masters, Mencken, Anderson, and Lewis[1] — seemed defensively critical of

---

[1] Theodore Dreiser (1871–1945), Edgar Lee Masters (1869–1950), Henry Louis Mencken (1880–1956), Sherwood Anderson (1876–1941), and Sinclair Lewis (1885–1951) were important American writers during the first half of the twentieth century.

the straitened American environment. These writers seemed to feel that America could be shaped nearer to the hearts of those who lived in it. And it was out of these novels and stories and articles, out of the emotional impact of imaginative constructions of heroic or tragic deeds, that I felt touching my face a tinge of warmth from an unseen light; and in my leaving I was groping toward that invisible light, always trying to keep my face so set and turned that I would not lose the hope of its faint promise, using it as my justification for action.

The white South said that it knew "niggers," and I was what the white South called a "nigger." Well, the white South had never known me — never known what I thought, what I felt. The white South said that I had a "place" in life. Well, I had never felt my "place"; or, rather, my deepest instincts had always made me reject the "place" to which the white South had assigned me. It had never occurred to me that I was in any way an inferior being. And no word that I had ever heard fall from the lips of southern white men had ever made me really doubt the worth of my own humanity.   [1945]

CASEBOOKS

CASEBOOKS

This section of the anthology assembles background material for in-depth studies of three major writers of short fiction. Raymond Carver, Flannery O'Connor, and Leslie Marmon Silko are each represented in Part One with three stories. Gathered here to help you understand their achievement as storytellers is a variety of commentary about their work by the writers themselves in different literary forms ranging from poetry to informal letters and formal essays, along with a variety of approaches to their stories taken by recent critics. Each casebook begins with the author's commentary, followed by important literary sources (for Carver and Silko) and relevant criticism.

CASEBOOK 1

RAYMOND CARVER

Raymond Carver offers a clear example of how a contemporary author has responded to the work of earlier short story writers to follow a line of thought that links him with his predecessors. Carver has credited the influence of Ernest Hemingway and John Gardner on his work, but he paid his most extensive tribute to Anton Chekhov by creating the story "Errand" (p. 235) about Chekhov's death, after reading Henri Troyat's biography of Chekhov. Carver believed that Chekhov was the greatest short story writer who ever lived; he was impressed by the sheer number of Chekhov's stories and by what Carver called "the awesome frequency with which he produced masterpieces, stories . . . that lay bare our emotions in ways only true art can accomplish." Carver also responded to Chekhov's dedication to the craft of writing by commenting that Chekhov once scolded another writer: "Your laziness stands out between the lines of every story. You don't work on your sentences. You must, you know. That's what makes art." Also in this section Carver's editor Tom Jenks recalls Carver's explanation of the origin of "Cathedral" (p. 224), and the critic Arthur Saltzman analyzes "What We Talk About When We Talk About Love" (p. 243).

On Writing

Back in the mid-1960s, I found I was having trouble concentrating my attention on long narrative fiction. For a time I experienced difficulty in trying to read it as well as in attempting to write it. My attention span had gone out on me; I no longer had the patience to try to write novels. It's an involved story, too tedious to talk about here. But I know it has much to do now with why I write poems and short stories. Get in, get out. Don't linger. Go on. It could be that I lost any great ambitions at about the same time, in my late twenties. If I did, I think it was good it happened. Ambition and a little luck are good things for a writer to have going for him. Too much ambition and bad luck, or no luck at all, can be killing. There has to be talent.

Some writers have a bunch of talent; I don't know any writers who are without it. But a unique and exact way of looking at things, and finding the right context for expressing that way of looking, that's something else. *The World According to Garp* is, of course, the marvelous world according to John Irving. There is another world according to Flannery O'Connor, and others according to William Faulkner and Ernest Hemingway. There are worlds according to Cheever, Updike, Singer, Stanley Elkin, Ann Beattie, Cynthia Ozick, Donald Barthelme, Mary Robison, William Kittredge, Barry Hannah, Ursula K. Le Guin. Every great or even every very good writer makes the world over according to his own specifications.

It's akin to style, what I'm talking about, but it isn't style alone. It is the writer's particular and unmistakable signature on everything he writes. It is his world and no other. This is one of the things that distinguishes one writer from another. Not talent. There's plenty of that around. But a writer who has some special way of looking at things and who gives artistic expression to that way of looking: that writer may be around for a time.

Isak Dinesen said that she wrote a little every day, without hope and without despair. Someday I'll put that on a three-by-five card and tape it to the wall beside my desk. I have some three-by-five cards on the wall now. "Fundamental accuracy of statement is the ONE sole morality of writing." Ezra Pound. It is not everything by ANY means, but if a writer has "fundamental accuracy of statement" going for him, he's at least on the right track.

I have a three-by-five up there with this fragment of a sentence from a story by Chekhov: ". . . and suddenly everything became clear to him." I find these words filled with wonder and possibility. I love their simple clarity, and the hint of revelation that's implied. There is mystery, too. What has been unclear before? Why is it just now becoming clear? What's happened? Most of all — what now? There are consequences as a result of such sudden awakenings. I feel a sharp sense of relief — and anticipation.

I overheard the writer Geoffrey Wolff say "No cheap tricks" to a group of writing students. That should go on a three-by-five card. I'd amend it a little to "No tricks." Period. I hate tricks. At the first sign of a trick or a gimmick in a piece of fiction, a cheap trick or even an elaborate trick, I tend to look for cover. Tricks are ultimately boring, and I get bored easily, which may go along with my not having much of an attention span. But extremely clever chi-chi writing, or just plain tomfoolery writing, puts me to sleep. Writers don't need tricks or gimmicks or even necessarily need to be the smartest fellows on the block. At the risk of appearing foolish, a writer sometimes needs to be able to just stand and gape at this or that thing — a sunset or an old shoe — in absolute and simple amazement.

Some months back, in the *New York Times Book Review,* John Barth said that ten years ago most of the students in his fiction writing seminar were interested in "formal innovation," and this no longer seems to be the case. He's a little worried that writers are going to start writing mom-and-pop novels in the 1980s. He worries that experimentation may be on the way out, along with liberalism. I get a little nervous if I find myself within earshot of somber discussions about "formal innovation" in fiction writing. Too often "experimentation" is a license to be careless, silly, or imitative in the writing. Even worse, a license to try to brutalize or alienate the reader. Too often such writing gives us no news of the world, or else describes a desert landscape and that's all — a few dunes and lizards here and there, but no people; a place uninhabited by anything recognizably human, a place of interest only to a few scientific specialists.

It should be noted that real experiment in fiction is original, hard-earned and cause for rejoicing. But someone else's way of looking at things — Barthelme's, for instance — should not be chased after by other writers. It won't work. There is only one Barthelme, and for another writer to try to appropriate Barthelme's peculiar sensibility or mise en scène under the rubric of innovation is for that writer to mess around with chaos and disaster and, worse, self-deception. The real experimenters have to Make It New, as Pound urged, and in the process have to find things out for themselves. But if writers haven't taken leave of their senses, they also want to stay in touch with us, they want to carry news from their world to ours.

It's possible, in a poem or a short story, to write about commonplace things and objects using commonplace but precise language, and to endow those things — a chair, a window curtain, a fork, a stone, a woman's earring — with immense, even startling power. It is possible to write a line of seemingly innocuous dialogue and have it send a chill along the reader's spine — the source of artistic delight, as Nabokov would have it. That's the kind of writing that most interests me. I hate sloppy or haphazard writing whether it flies under the banner of experimentation or else is just clumsily rendered realism. In Isaac Babel's wonderful short story, "Guy de Maupassant," the narrator has this to say about the writing of fiction: "No iron can pierce the heart with such force as a period put just at the right place." This too ought to go on a three-by-five.

Evan Connell said once that he knew he was finished with a short story when he found himself going through it and taking out commas and then going through the story again and putting commas back in the same places. I like that way of working on something. I respect that kind of care for what is being done. That's all we have, finally, the words, and they had better be the right ones, with the punctuation in the right places so that they can best say what they are meant to say. If the words are heavy with the writer's own unbridled emotions, or if they are imprecise and inaccurate for some other reason — if the words are in any way blurred — the reader's eyes will slide right over them and nothing will be achieved. The reader's own artistic sense will simply not be engaged. Henry James called this sort of hapless writing "weak specification."

I have friends who've told me they had to hurry a book because they needed the money, their editor or their wife was leaning on them or leaving them — something, some apology for the writing not being very good. "It would have been better if I'd taken the time." I was dumbfounded when I heard a novelist friend say this. I still am, if I think about it, which I don't. It's none of my business. But if the writing can't be made as good as it is within us to make it, then why do it? In the end, the satisfaction of having done our best, and the proof of that labor, is the one thing we can take into the grave. I wanted to say to my friend, for heaven's sake go do something else. There have to be easier and maybe more honest ways to try and earn a living. Or else just do it to the best of your abilities, your talents, and then don't justify or make excuses. Don't complain, don't explain.

In an essay called, simply enough, "Writing Short Stories," Flannery O'Connor talks about writing as an act of discovery. O'Connor says she most often did not know where she was going when she sat down to work on a short story. She says she doubts that many writers know where they are going when they begin something. She uses "Good Country People" as an example of how she put together a short story whose ending she could not even guess at until she was nearly there:

> When I started writing that story, I didn't know there was going to be a Ph.D. with a wooden leg in it. I merely found myself one morning writing a description of two women I knew something about, and before I realized it, I had equipped one of them with a daughter with a wooden leg. I brought in the Bible salesman, but I had no idea what I was going to do with him. I didn't know he was going to steal that wooden leg until ten or twelve lines before he did it, but when I found out that this was what was going to happen, I realized it was inevitable.

When I read this some years ago it came as a shock that she, or anyone for that matter, wrote stories in this fashion. I thought this was my uncomfortable secret, and I was a little uneasy with it. For sure I thought this way of working on a short story somehow revealed my own shortcomings. I remember being tremendously heartened by reading what she had to say on the subject.

I once sat down to write what turned out to be a pretty good story, though only the first sentence of the story had offered itself to me when I began it. For several days I'd been going around with this sentence in my head: "He was running the vacuum cleaner when the telephone rang." I knew a story was there and that it wanted telling. I felt it in my bones, that a story belonged with that beginning, if I could just have the time to write it. I found the time, an entire day — twelve, fifteen hours even — if I wanted to make use of it. I did, and I sat down in the morning and wrote the first sentence, and other sentences promptly began to attach themselves. I made the story just as I'd make a poem; one line and then the next, and the next. Pretty soon I could see a story, and I knew it was my story, the one I'd been wanting to write.

I like it when there is some feeling of threat or sense of menace in short stories. I think a little menace is fine to have in a story. For one thing, it's good for the circulation. There has to be tension, a sense that something is imminent, that certain things are in relentless motion, or else, most often, there simply won't be a story. What creates tension in a piece of fiction is partly the way the concrete words are linked together to make up the visible action of the story. But it's also the things that are left out, that are implied, the landscape just under the smooth (but sometimes broken and unsettled) surface of things.

V. S. Pritchett's definition of a short story is "something glimpsed from the corner of the eye, in passing." Notice the "glimpse" part of this. First the glimpse. Then the glimpse given life, turned into something that illuminates the moment and may, if we're lucky — that word again — have even further-ranging consequences and meaning. The short story writer's task is to invest the glimpse with all that is in his power. He'll bring his intelligence and literary skill to bear (his talent), his sense of proportion and sense of the fitness of things: of how things out there really are and how he sees those things — like no one else sees them. And this is done through the use of clear and specific language, language used so as to bring to life the details that will light up the story for the reader. For the details to be concrete and convey meaning, the language must be accurate and precisely given. The words can be so precise they may even sound flat, but they can still carry; if used right, they can hit all the notes.   [1981]

RAYMOND CARVER

Creative Writing 101

A long time ago — it was the summer of 1958 — my wife and I and our two baby children moved from Yakima, Washington, to a little town outside of Chico, California. There we found an old house and paid twenty-five dollars a month rent. In order to finance this move, I'd had to borrow a hundred and twenty-five dollars from a druggist I'd delivered prescriptions for, a man named Bill Barton.

This is by way of saying that in those days my wife and I were stone broke. We had to eke out a living, but the plan was that I would take classes at what was then called Chico State College. But for as far back as I can remember, long before we moved to California in search of a different life and our slice of the American pie, I'd wanted to be a writer. I wanted to write, and I wanted to write anything — fiction, of course, but also poetry, plays, scripts, articles for *Sports Afield*, *True*, *Argosy*, and *Rogue* (some of the magazines I was then reading), pieces for the local newspaper — anything that involved putting words together to make something coherent and of interest to someone besides myself. But at the time of our move, I felt in my bones I had to get some education in order to go along with being a writer. I put a very high premium on education then — much higher in those days than now, I'm sure, but that's because I'm older and have an education. Understand that nobody in my family had ever gone to college or for that matter had got beyond the mandatory eighth grade in high school. I didn't know *anything*, but I knew I didn't know anything.

So along with this desire to get an education, I had this very strong desire to write; it was a desire so strong that, with the encouragement I was given in college, and the insight acquired, I kept on writing long after "good sense" and the "cold facts" — the "realities" of my life told me, time and again, that I ought to quit, stop the dreaming, quietly go ahead and do something else.

That fall at Chico State I enrolled in classes that most freshman students have to take, but I enrolled as well for something called Creative Writing 101. This course was going to be taught by a new faculty member named John Gardner, who was already surrounded by a bit of mystery and romance. It was said that he'd taught previously at Oberlin College but had left there for some reason that wasn't made clear. One student said Gardner had been fired — students, like everyone else, thrive on rumor and intrigue — and another student said Gardner had simply quit after some kind of flap. Someone else said his teaching load at Oberlin, four or five classes of freshman English each semester, had been too heavy and that he couldn't find time to write. For it was said that Gardner was a real, that is to say a practicing, writer — someone who had written novels and short stories. In any case, he was going to teach CW 101 at Chico State, and I signed up.

I was excited about taking a course from a real writer. I'd never laid eyes on a writer before, and I was in awe. But where were these novels and short stories, I wanted to know. Well, nothing had been published yet. It was said that he couldn't get his work published and that he carried it around with him in boxes. (After I became his student, I was to see those boxes of manuscript. Gardner had become aware of my difficulty in finding a place to work. He knew I had a young family and cramped quarters at home. He offered me the key to his office. I see that gift now as a turning point. It was a gift not made casually, and I took it, I think, as a kind of mandate — for that's what it was. I spent part of every Saturday and Sunday in his office, which is where he kept the boxes of manuscript. The boxes were stacked up on the floor beside the desk. *Nickel Mountain*, grease-pencilled on one of the boxes, is the only title I recall. But it was in his office, within sight of his unpublished books, that I undertook my first serious attempts at writing.) . . .

For short story writers in his class, the requirement was one story, ten to fifteen pages in length. For people who wanted to write a novel — I think there must have been one or two of these souls — a chapter of around twenty pages, along with an outline of the rest. The kicker was that this one short story, or the chapter of the novel, might have to be revised ten times in the course of the semester for Gardner to be satisfied with it. It was a basic tenet of his that a writer found what he wanted to say in the ongoing process of seeing what he'd said. And this seeing, or seeing more clearly, came about through revision. He *believed* in revision, endless revision; it was something very close to his heart and something he felt was vital for writers, at whatever stage of their development. And he never seemed to lose patience rereading a student story, even though he might have seen it in five previous incarnations.

I think his idea of a short story in 1958 was still pretty much his idea of a short story in 1982; it was something that had a recognizable beginning, middle, and an end to it. Once in a while he'd go to the blackboard and draw a diagram to illustrate a point he wanted to make about rising or falling emotion in a story — peaks, valleys, plateaus, resolution, *denouement*, things like that. Try as I might, I couldn't muster a great deal of interest or really understand this side of things, the stuff he put on the blackboard. But what I did understand was the way he would comment on a student story that was undergoing class discussion. Gardner might wonder aloud about the author's reasons for writing a story about a crippled person, say, and leaving out the fact of the character's crippledness until the very end of the story. "So you think it's a good idea not to let the reader know this man is crippled until the last sentence?" His tone of voice conveyed his disapproval, and it didn't take more than an instant for everyone in class, including the author of the story, to see that it wasn't a good stategy to use. Any strategy that kept important and necessary information away from the reader in the hope of overcoming him by surprise at the end of the story was cheating.

In class he was always referring to writers whose names I was not familiar with. Or if I knew their names, I'd never read the work. . . . He talked about James Joyce and Flaubert and Isak Dinesen as if they lived just down the road, in Yuba City. He said, "I'm here to tell you who to read as well as teach you how to write." I'd leave class in a daze and make straight for the library to find books by these writers he was talking about.

Hemingway and Faulkner were the reigning authors in those days. But altogether I'd probably read at the most two or three books by these fellows. Anyway, they were so well-known and so much talked about, they couldn't be all that good, could they? I remember Gardner telling me, "Read all the Faulkner you can get your hands on, and then read all of Hemingway to clean the Faulkner out of your system."

He introduced us to the "little" or literary periodicals by bringing a box of these magazines to class one day and passing them around so that we could acquaint ourselves with their names, see what they looked like and what they felt like to hold in the hand. He told us that this was where most of the best fiction in the country and just about all of the poetry was appearing. Fiction, poetry, literary essays, book reviews of recent books, criticism of *living* authors *by* living authors. I felt wild with discovery in those days.

For the seven or eight of us who were in his class, he ordered heavy black binders and told us we should keep our written work in these. He kept his own work in such binders, he said, and of course that settled it for us. We carried our stories in those binders and felt we were special, exclusive, singled out from others. And so we were.

I don't know how Gardner might have been with other students when it came time to have conferences with them about their work. I suspect he gave everybody a good amount of attention. But it was and still is my impression that during that period he took my stories more seriously, read them closer and more carefully, than I had any right to expect. I was completely unprepared for the kind of criticism I received from him. Before our conference he would have marked up my story, crossing out unacceptable sentences, phrases, individual words, even some of the punctuation; and he gave me to understand that these deletions were not negotiable. In other cases he would bracket sentences, phrases, or individual words, and these were items we'd talk about, these cases were negotiable. And he wouldn't hesitate to add something to what I'd written — a word here and there, or else a few words, maybe a sentence that would make clear what I was trying to say. We'd discuss commas in my story as if nothing else in the world mattered more at that moment — and, indeed, it did not. He was always looking to find something to praise. When there was a sentence, a line of dialogue, or a narrative passage that he liked, something that he thought "worked" and moved the story along in some pleasant or unexpected way, he'd write "Nice" in the margin, or else "Good!" And seeing these comments, my heart would lift.

It was close, line-by-line criticism he was giving me, and the reasons behind the criticism, why something ought to be this way instead of that; and it was invaluable to me in my development as a writer. After this kind of detailed talk about the text, we'd talk about the larger concerns of the story, the "problem" it was trying to throw light on, the conflict it was trying to grapple with, and how the story might or might not fit into the grand scheme of story writing. It was his conviction that if the words in the story were blurred because of the author's insensitivity, carelessness, or sentimentality, then the story suffered from a tremendous handicap. But there was something even worse and something that must be avoided at all costs: if the words and the sentiments were dishonest, the author was faking it, writing about things he didn't care about or believe in, then nobody could ever care anything about it.

A writer's values and craft. This is what the man taught and what he stood for, and this is what I've kept by me in the years since that brief but all-important time.   [1983]

RAYMOND CARVER

The Ashtray

> You could write a story about this ashtray, for example, and a man and a woman. But the man and woman are always the two poles of your story. The North Pole and the South. Every story has these two poles — *he* and *she*.
>
> *A. P. Chekhov*

They're alone at the kitchen table in her friend's
apartment. They'll be alone for another hour, and then
her friend will be back. Outside, it's raining —
the rain coming down like needles, melting last week's
snow. They're smoking and using the ashtray . . . Maybe
just one of them is smoking . . . *He's* smoking! Never
mind. Anyway, the ashtray is filling up with
cigarettes and ashes.

She's ready to break into tears at any minute.
To plead with him, in fact, though she's proud
and has never asked for anything in her life.
He sees what's coming, recognizes the signs —
a catch in her voice as she brings her fingers
to her locket, the one her mother left her.
He pushes back his chair, gets up, goes over to
the window . . . He wishes it were tomorrow and he
were at the races. He wishes he was out walking,
using his umbrella . . . He strokes his mustache
and wishes he were anywhere except here. But
he doesn't have any choice in the matter. He's got

to put a good face on this for everybody's sake.
God knows, he never meant for things to come to
this. But it's sink or swim now. A wrong
move and he stands to lose her friend, too.
Her breathing slows. She watches him but
doesn't say anything. She knows, or thinks she
knows, where this is leading. She passes a hand
over her eyes, leans forward and puts her head
in her hands. She's done this a few times
before, but has no idea it's something
that drives him wild. He looks away and grinds
his teeth. He lights a cigarette, shakes out
the match, stands a minute longer at the window.

Then walks back to the table and sits
down with a sigh. He drops the match in the ashtray.
She reaches for his hand, and he lets her
take it. Why not? Where's the harm?
Let her. His mind's made up. She covers his
fingers with kisses, tears fall onto his wrist.

He draws on his cigarette and looks at her
as a man would look indifferently on
a cloud, a tree, or a field of oats at sunset.
He narrows his eyes against the smoke. From time
to time he uses the ashtray as he waits
for her to finish weeping.   [1984]

RAYMOND CARVER

On Errand

In early 1987 an editor at E. P. Dutton sent me a copy of the newly published Henri Troyat biography, *Chekhov*. Immediately upon the book's arrival, I put aside what I was doing and started reading. I seem to recall reading the book pretty much straight through, able, at the time, to devote entire afternoons and evenings to it.

On the third or fourth day, nearing the end of the book, I came to the little passage where Chekhov's doctor — a Badenweiler physician by the name of Dr Schwöhrer, who attended Chekhov during his last days — is summoned by Olga Knipper Chekhov to the dying writer's bedside in the early morning hours of July 2, 1904. It is clear that Chekhov has only a little while to live. Without any comment on the matter, Troyat tells his readers that this Dr Schwöhrer ordered up a bottle of champagne. Nobody had asked for champagne, of course; he just took it upon himself to do it. But this little piece of human business struck me as an extraordinary action. Before I really knew what I was going to do with it, or how I was going to proceed, I felt I had been launched into a short story of my own then and there. I wrote a few lines and then a page or two more. How did Dr Schwöhrer go about ordering champagne and at that late hour at this hotel in Germany? How was it delivered to the room and by whom, etc.? What was the protocol involved when the champagne arrived? Then I stopped and went ahead to finish reading the biography.

But just as soon as I'd finished the book I once again turned my attention back to Dr Schwöhrer and that business of the champagne. I was seriously interested in what I was doing. But what *was* I doing? The only thing that was clear to me was that I thought I saw an opportunity to pay homage — if I could bring it off, do it rightly and honorably — to Chekhov, the writer who has meant so much to me for such a long time.

I tried out ten or twelve openings to the piece, first one beginning and then another, but nothing felt right. Gradually I began to move the story away from those final moments back to the occasion of Chekhov's first public hemorrhage from tuberculosis, something that occurred in a restaurant in Moscow in the company of his friend and publisher, Suvorin. Then came the hospitalization and the scene with Tolstoy, the trip with Olga to Badenweiler, the brief period of time there in the hotel together before the end, the young bellman who makes two important appearances in the Chekhov suite and, at the end, the mortician who, like the bellman, isn't to be found in the biographical account.

The story was a hard one to write, given the factual basis of the material. I couldn't stray from what had happened, nor did I want to. As much as anything, I needed to figure out how to breathe life into actions that were merely suggested or not given moment in the biographical telling. And, finally, I saw that I needed to set my imagination free and simply invent within the confines of the story. I knew as I was writing this story that it was a good deal different from anything I'd ever done before. I'm pleased, and grateful, that it seems to have come together. [1988]

Carver's widow, Tess Gallagher, has described her "personal connection" to the composition of "Errand" in a film about Raymond Carver, "To Write and Keep Kind."

Ray had been through many, many drafts, and he said, "I just don't know how to get out of this story." I had seen a draft or two by then and was empathizing with his waiter character. I said, "That waiter is going to be looking down, and he's going to see the cork that has popped out of the champagne. I think the ending is involved with his response to the cork. He's going to bend down to get that cork, and we're going to know something from that gesture, that action."

Henri Troyat

From Chekhov

Translated by Michael Henry Heim

. . . The friends who came to see [Chekhov] found him stretched out on a daybed wearing a dressing gown. He would apologize to them for the informality of his attire and force himself to make jokes and appear interested in everything, but they were all struck by his hollow cheeks, waxen complexion, and dilated pupils. Dr. Rossolimo observed that like all tubercular patients he spoke of the disease with an almost reckless indifference. With his burning hands and flushed cheeks could he really believe in a cure?

One evening Chekhov was reminiscing happily with the writer Gilyarovsky, one of the first to encourage him to write, when Gilyarovsky mentioned he had recently returned from a visit to the steppe. All at once Chekhov grew pensive: "Oh, the steppe, the steppe! What a lucky man you are! That's where the poetry is." And he closed his eyes, smiled a childlike smile, and let his head drop onto the pillow. "I am certain he dreamed of the steppe," Gilyarovsky wrote.

Towards the end of the month Chekhov's temperature went down and he felt strong enough to get out of bed. On May 31 he announced triumphantly to his sister: "Just think. Today for the first time I put on shoes and a coat [. . .] and for the first time went out for a ride." Now there was nothing to hold him back from the journey Dr. Taube had counseled. On June 3, 1904, Anton and Olga took the train for Berlin.

Although he had left Moscow in a morbid mood, Chekhov perked up at once in Berlin. A change of place always did him good. From a comfortable room at the Hotel Savoy ("the best in Berlin") he wrote Maria letter after optimistic letter: his appetite had improved; he was putting a bit of flesh on his bones; his diarrhea had subsided; his legs no longer ached; in fact, he was on his feet all day, "running around Berlin," raiding the shops, riding through the Tiergarten. It was the first time he had ever been out of Russia with Olga, and he felt all the closer to her for their being "stranded" in a foreign city; he enjoyed discovering a new world and discussing new impressions with her. He claimed jestingly that he had not seen a single good-looking woman and that German women dressed "abominably." Yet, as he admitted to Maria, "people live a comfortable existence, the food is good, life is not expensive, [. . .] the streets are clean, order reigns." In his optimism he even made plans to spend some time at the Italian lakes and return to Yalta in August via Constantinople.

Chekhov's confidence in the future was not shared by Dr. Karl Ewald, the specialist Dr. Taube had recommended. After giving Chekhov a careful examination, Dr. Ewald spread his arms in a gesture of helplessness and left without a word. The message was obvious. "It was cruel of him, of course," Dr. Altschuler later wrote, "but Ewald's attitude may be explained by the fact that he did not understand how anyone could have permitted a man so ill to undertake so long a journey — and for what?" After an interview with Chekhov the Berlin correspondent for *Russian News* reported to his editor: "I am of the opinion that Chekhov's days are numbered. He seemed mortally ill: he was terribly thin, coughed all the time, gasped for breath at the slightest movement, and was running a high temperature."

The same journalist saw the Chekhovs off at the Potsdam station, where after three days in Berlin they took the train for Badenweiler in the Black Forest. "He had trouble making his way up the small staircase at the station," he wrote, "and sat down for several minutes to catch his breath. But as the train began to pull out, he disregarded my plea and leaned out of the window to nod good-bye."

Badenweiler is a spa on the western edge of the Black Forest not far from Basel, a clean, calm, unexciting little town that seemed to Chekhov made for convalescence. Olga and he spent their first two days there in a boarding-house, then moved into a private house that took in guests. The large, well-kept garden, all gravel paths and flower beds, afforded a beautiful view of the mountains. Chekhov spent the entire day — from morning until seven in the evening — seated or reclining in a comfortable chair. In Badenweiler the sun did not burn, he wrote to his sister, it caressed the skin. The spa physician, a Dr. Schwöhrer, proved perfectly competent and easy to get on with. Besides absolute rest he prescribed a diet of cocoa, oatmeal drenched in butter, and strawberry tea ("to aid the patient's sleep"). And while Chekhov could not help grumbling about Schwöhrer's "quackery," he boasted to Maria that he was growing stronger fast. On June 13 he went so far as to write to his mother: "My health is improving, and it's likely I'll be completely cured in a week." Olga was hopeful enough to leave him on his own and go to Basel to have her teeth examined.

After a week of euphoria, however, Chekhov once more gave way to anxiety, boredom, and the need for change. "I can't get used to this German peace and quiet," he wrote to Maria. "There's not a sound inside or out except when a band with no talent strikes up at seven in the morning and noon. There's not a drop of talent, not a drop of good taste anywhere to be seen, only great quantities of order and honesty. There's a good deal more talent in Russia, to say nothing of Italy or France." Now Dr. Schwöhrer seemed wanting too: "The same stupid cocoa, the same oatmeal." Since there was no question of their leaving Badenweiler, however, they left the house they had been staying at for the Hotel Sommer, the best the spa had to offer. Chekhov would sit out on the balcony of his room for hours, watching people enter and leave the post office across the road. Or he would plan journeys, perusing timetables and requesting information on departure dates for boats en route to Odessa from Trieste or Marseilles.

Then Badenweiler was hit by a heat wave. Chekhov, his lungs half destroyed, suffered horribly. "It's caught me unawares," he wrote to Maria, "and since all I have with me is winter clothes, I'm suffocating and dream of getting out of here." In this letter, the last Chekhov ever wrote, he gives in to despair for the first time: "The food is very tasty, but it doesn't do me much good. My stomach keeps getting upset. I can't eat the kind of butter they have here. Apparently my stomach is ruined beyond all hope. About the only remedy for it is to fast, in other words, to refrain from eating entirely, and that's that. And the only remedy for short-windedness is to keep perfectly still." His letter to her crossed one of hers to him saying that since he was doing so well she and their brother Ivan had decided to go on a short tour of the Caucasus. "So take care of yourself, dear Antosha. Try to cough less and eat more. Gather your strength and come home."

On June 29 Chekhov had a sudden violent attack and Schwöhrer had to give him both morphine and oxygen, but his pulse returned to normal and he had a peaceful night. The respite was short-lived; next day he had a new attack. Two correspondents from the Russian press rushed to Badenweiler and wired back alarming reports on the state of Chekhov's health. Chekhov, meanwhile, soon over the second attack and perfectly lucid and calm, instructed his bank in Berlin to make all payments in his wife's name. When Olga asked him the reason for his concern, he replied evasively, "It's nothing really. Just in case . . ."

On July 1 he seemed to feel better and the correspondents' reports were more optimistic: his heart was doing well, the day had passed uneventfully. Towards evening he insisted that Olga, who had not left his bedside for three days, should take a walk in the hotel grounds. When she returned, she lay down on a narrow couch near the bed. He scolded her for looking so sad. To cheer her up, he started improvising a story. It took place in a fashionable watering place where the guests were all "well-fed bankers" and "rosy-cheeked English and American tourists." Every day they would work up an appetite by going on a hike, and every evening they would rush back to the hotel dreaming of the delicious meal awaiting them. One day they returned to learn that the chef had decamped and they would have no dinner. At this point Chekhov began to describe how each of the hungry gourmets reacted to the disaster. For all her anguish Olga could not help laughing.

Although the heat was still oppressive, Chekhov soon fell asleep. His breath came in spurts, but his face was calm. Then at half past twelve he sat up in bed and called for a doctor. It was the first time Olga had ever heard him do so. Suddenly she felt very much alone in their large German hotel where everyone was asleep for the night. After a moment of indecision she recalled that there were two Russian students in the room next door. She ran and woke them, and one of them immediately rushed off to fetch Dr. Schwöhrer. "I can still hear the sound of the gravel under his shoes in the silence of that stifling July night," she later wrote.

Fever had made Chekhov delirious. He went on about a sailor or asked about the Japanese, his eyes shining. But when Olga tried to place an ice bag on his chest, he suddenly regained consciousness and said, "Don't put ice on an empty stomach."

The windows were wide open, but he could not stop panting; his temples were bathed in sweat. Dr. Schwöhrer arrived at two o'clock. When

Chekhov saw him, he sat up, leaned back against the pillows, and, in a final reflex of courtesy, mustered his weak German and said, *"Ich sterbe."*[1] Schwöhrer immediately gave him a camphor injection, but his heart failed to react. He was about to send for an oxygen pillow when Chekhov, lucid to the end, protested in a broken voice, "What's the use? Before it arrives, I'll be a corpse." So Dr. Schwöhrer sent for a bottle of champagne.

When it came, Chekhov took a glass and, turning to Olga, said with a smile, "It's been so long since I've had champagne." He emptied the glass slowly and lay down on his left side. A few moments later he stopped breathing. He had passed from life to death with characteristic simplicity.

It was July 2, 1904, three o'clock in the morning. A large black-winged moth had flown in through the window and was banging wildly against the lamp. The muffled sound soon grew maddeningly distracting. Dr. Schwöhrer withdrew after a few words of consolation. All at once there was a joyous explosion: the cork had popped out of the champagne bottle and foam was fizzing out after it. The moth found its way out of the window and disappeared into the sultry night. Silence returned. When day broke at last, Olga was still sitting and staring into her husband's face. It was peaceful, smiling, knowing. "There were no human voices, no everyday sounds," she wrote. "There was only beauty, peace, and the grandeur of death." [1987]

T O M   J E N K S

The Origin of Cathedral

I first met Ray Carver in New York in early September 1984 at a publishing dinner to launch Gary Fisketjon's Vintage Contemporary paperback series. Many of the new VC authors and their friends were there: Richard Ford, Toby Wolff, Jay McInerney, Tom McGuane, Jim Crumley, and Ralph Beer — a distinctly male crowd, and what struck me most was that, as we geared up to move to a nightclub, Ray, amid teasing about running off somewhere to see a woman, put himself in a taxi and headed for his hotel room alone. By the ginger way he got himself into the cab and laughingly ducked the barbs all around him, there was no doubt he meant to keep himself out of trouble.

But he was fair game for the friendly taunts that followed him into the cab. We were witnessing the Good Ray, but we all knew about the Bad Ray, the one who used to be Lord Misrule himself.

---

[1] "I am dying."

Reformed, Ray was fast becoming the most famous short story writer in the world, and the facts of his life were well known, partly because they were often the stuff of his writing and because fame brings a peculiar public intimacy.

At the time, I was an editor of *Esquire* and had made Ray's acquaintance through the mail and on the phone. I had published some of his work and knew him somewhat, and as I watched him slip away in the cab, I imagined him going back to his hotel room (it was early yet — ten o'clock) and telephoning Tess Gallagher at their home in Syracuse. Each evening they set aside the hours beyond ten o'clock to spend with each other. He *was*, in a sense, running off to see a woman.

A year and a half later, I visited them in Syracuse. During the days, Ray and I read stories for a book we were working on and at night we watched TV. One night, we were watching a PBS version of *Wuthering Heights*, and Ray began to tell about another night of TV: the night the blind man for whom Tess once worked had come to visit. Tess told her side, too — how Ray was uneasy about the man's visit, uncomfortable with his blindness and his familiarity with Tess, a mild jealousy rising in Ray. Their evening was slow and tedious, and ended with the three of them watching PBS, just as we were. But on the night the blind man was visiting, Tess had fallen asleep, and then a program about cathedrals came on. The blind man had no idea what a cathedral looked like, and, in the end, Ray sat on the floor with him, holding his hands, drawing a cathedral so the blind man could sense the miracle of the shape.

Ray had written this story and titled it "Cathedral." Tess, who with Ray's encouragement had recently begun writing stories, had her own version, titled "The Harvest." She gave me a copy, humorously telling Ray, "Watch out, I'm nipping at your heels." Their good-natured competition and openness was rare in my experience of writers, many of whom are cagey about the intimate, personal connections in their work. . . .   [1993]

ARTHUR M. SALTZMAN

A Reading of What We Talk About When We Talk About Love

The volume's title story extends the theme of the heart's perpetual commotion by updating and burlesquing Plato's *Symposium*. "What We Talk About When We Talk About Love" also features the most expansive conversationalists in this collection: Mel and Terri, both of whom are married for the second time and both sporting scars from their first marriages, and Nick (the narrator) and Laura, newlyweds who are still in the throes of a mutual romantic trance. Mel and Terri carry on the bulk of the gin-induced discussion of love, whereas Nick and Laura are more equivocal and seem content to placate their friends or to reassure one another with intimate gestures.

Mel and Terri propose divergent definitions of "real love." A cardiologist who once spent five years studying in a seminary, Mel contends that love is a spiritual phenomenon whose pinnacle was and continues to be the chivalric code. Terri, on the other hand, argues that the brutality of her first husband, Ed, displayed the formidableness of his passion for her. As the conversation gains momentum, contradictions surface in their testimonies. Mel, the self-proclaimed spiritual scientist, confesses his daydreams about murdering his first wife that parallel Terri's grotesque tales of her relationship with Ed. Meanwhile, Terri grows increasingly anxious about redeeming her volatile past, even at the expense of offending her present husband: "'He did love me though, Mel. Grant me that,' Terri said. 'That's all I'm asking. He didn't love me the way you love me. I'm not saying that. But he loved me. You can grant me that, can't you?'"

The greatest obstacle to any ideal of love turns out to be the transitoriness of love. After all, both Mel and Terri had vowed allegiance to their original partners, so what is there to prevent the same deterioration from happening again? Ironically, the "saving grace" of love is its elasticity — one can move one from divorce or tragedy and love anew — but this is further evidence against love's absolute status and hollows out current protestations of devotion. In other words, love's transient nature could be either its vindication or its vanquishment — the source of its preciousness or its untrustworthiness. Consequently, the very situation that the four friends occupy as they conduct their leisurely talking and drinking around the dinner table is shown to have the same fragile charms as the subject at hand:

> The afternoon sun was like a presence in this room, the spacious light
> of ease and generosity. We could have been anywhere, somewhere
> enchanted. We raised our glasses again and grinned at each other like
> children who had agreed on something forbidden.

The relative articulateness of these characters by no means enables them to reach a satisfactory conclusion, and as a result Mel suggests that "it ought to make us feel ashamed when we talk like we know what we're talking about when we talk about love." In this way, Mel echoes Pausanias' declaration in *The Symposium*: "I do not think, Phaidros, that the rules were properly laid down, I mean that we should just simply belaud Love. For if Love were one, that would do, but really he is not one; since he is not one, it is more proper to say first which we are to praise."

Mel's crowning point regarding the spiritual core of love recalls Holly's envious vision of the dignified intimacy of the old people she encountered in "Gazebo." Mel relates how, after a terrible automobile accident, an old man and woman lay barely alive in their hospital beds; they were completely covered by casts and bandages. However, despite his horrible injuries, the husband was primarily depressed because he could not see his wife through the tiny eyeholes in his bandages. By this time Mel has grown rather drunk and profane, and his testiness toward Terri belies his argument. So, too, is his chivalric hero, the medieval knight, tarnished by the admission that he often suffocated in his armor; moreover, his protective gear was also a measure of his inaccessibility. Finally, when Mel fantasizes about arriving in the guise of a beekeeper (helmeted, anonymous, and padded from head to toe) at the house of his first wife in order to release a swarm of bees, he modernizes and disqualifies the knight's noble image.

Nick and Laura come close to embodying a simple yet profound enjoyment of one another's company, but when Nick ostentatiously kisses Laura's hand, Mel and Terri find it more amusing than tender. They all toast to "true love," but Terri's gentle admonishment to Laura — "Wait awhile" — suggests that time misses no one in its assault on affection. Rating the quality of the consolation that remains at the end of the story depends upon to what extent the elusive, unpredictable, hazardous process of love compensates for the skewering of the romantic ideal (upon which the discussants cannot agree anyway). In the darkened room, silent save for "the human noise we sat there making," perhaps these moments together, deeply imbued with shared sensibilities, make up for the antagonisms, the regrets, the flirtations, the spilled gin.   [1988]

FLANNERY O'CONNOR

Flannery O'Connor provides the unusual example of a writer who shared her own interpretation of her short stories with her readers. While acknowledging that there is usually more than one way to read a story, she also stated that there was only one way she could possibly have written it. O'Connor's discussion of her story "A Good Man Is Hard to Find" (p. 1063) can be read alongside the interpretations of "Good Country People" (p. 1048) and "Everything That Rises Must Converge" (p. 1037) by academic critics Dorothy Tuck McFarland, Wayne C. Booth, and Anthony Di Renzo. The noted English short story writer and critic V. S. Pritchett gives his overview of O'Connor's literary achievement, and Robert H. Brinkmeyer, Jr., considers the relationship between O'Connor and her readers.

FLANNERY O'CONNOR

From Letters 1954–1955

To Sally Fitzgerald

26 Dec 54

. . . **I** have finally got off the ms. for my collection [*A Good Man Is Hard to Find*] and it is scheduled to appear in May. Without yr kind permission I have taken the liberty of dedicating (grand verb) it to you and Robert. This is because you all are my adopted kin and if I dedicated it to any of my blood kin they would think they had to go into hiding. Nine stories about original sin, with my compliments.

I have been invited to go to Greensboro to the Women's College in March to be on an arts panel. That is where Brother Randall Jarrell holds forth. I accepted but I am not looking forward to it. Can you fancy me hung in conversation with the likes of him?

When I had lunch with Giroux [O'Connor's editor] in Atlanta he told me about Cal's escapade in Cincinnati. It seems [Cal] convinced everybody it was Elizabeth who was going crazy . . . Toward the end he gave a lecture at the university that was almost pure gibberish. I guess nobody noticed, thinking it was the new criticism . . .

I just got a check for $200 for the 2nd prize in the O. Henry book this year. My ex-mentor Paul Engle does the selecting. Jean Stafford got the first one.

I am walking with a cane these days which gives me a great air of distinction. The scientist tells me this has nothing to do with the lupus but is rheumatism. I would not believe it except that the dose of ACTH has not been increased. Besides which I now feel it makes very little difference what you call it. As the niggers say, I have the misery.

I am reading everything I can of Romano Guardini's [Italian priest and theologian]. Have you become acquainted with his work? A book called *The Lord* of his is very fine.

To Elizabeth McKee

13 January 1955

The carbon of "An Exile in the East" is enclosed, but I don't know if you realize or not that this is a rewritten version of "The Geranium" originally printed in *Accent*. *Accent* didn't pay me for it and it is rather much changed, but I enclose both stories so [the editor] can see what she's doing. I don't want to go to the penitentiary for selling a story twice (but if I do I would like to get a good price for the story).

To Robert Giroux

22 January 55

Nothing has been said about a picture for the jacket of this collection *but if you have to have one,* I would be much obliged if you could use the enclosed so that I won't have to have a new picture made. This is a self-portrait with a pheasant cock, that I painted in 1953; however, I think it will do justice to the subject for some time to come.

26 February 55

I have just written a story called "Good Country People" that Allen and Caroline [Tate?] both say is the best thing I have written and should be in this collection. I told them I thought it was too late, but anyhow I am writing now to ask if it is. It is really a story that would set the whole collection on its feet. It is 27 pages and if you can eliminate the one called "A Stroke of Good Fortune," and the other called "An Afternoon in the Woods," this one would fit the available space nicely. Also I remember you said it would be good to have one that had never been published before. I could send it to you at once *on being wired.* Please let me know.

Giroux wired O'Connor that every effort would be made to include the story. After he had read it, he wrote suggesting that an appearance by the mother and Mrs. Freeman at the end might improve it. Flannery recognized the value of the suggestion and added the sentences that are now a part of the story.

7 March 55

I like the suggestion about the ending of "Good Country People" and enclose a dozen or so lines that can be added on to *the present end.* I enclose them in case you can get them put on before I get the proofs. I am mighty wary of making changes on proofs . . .

To Sally and Robert Fitzgerald

1 April 55

We are wondering if #6 is here yet or due to arrive momentarily. Let us hear and if you need any names, I'll be glad to cable you a rich collection. I have just got back from Greensboro where I said nothing intelligent the whole time, but enjoyed myself. Mr. Randall Jarrell, wife and stepdaughters I met and et dinner with. I must say I was shocked at what a very kind man he is — that is the last impression I expected to have of him. I also met Peter Taylor, who is more like folks. Mrs. Jarrell is writing a novel. You get the impression the two stepdaughters may be at it too and maybe the dog. Mr. Jarrell has a beard and looks like Mephistopheles (sp?) only fatter. Mrs. Jarrell is very friendly & sunkist.

The Easter rabbit is bringing my mother a three-quarter ton truck.

I trust Giroux will be sending you a copy of the book soon. I wrote a very hot story at the last minute called "Good Country People": so now there are ten.

While I was in NC I heard somebody recite a barroom ballad. I don't remember anything but the end but beinst you all are poets I will give it to you as it is mighty deathless:

> "They stacked the stiffs outside the door.
> They made, I reckon, a cord or more."

I call that real poetry.

I have put the cane up and am walking on my own very well. Let us hear. Regards to children.   [1955]

FLANNERY O'CONNOR

Writing Short Stories

. . . Perhaps the central question to be considered in any discussion of the short story is what do we mean by short. Being short does not mean being slight. A short story should be long in depth and should give us an experience of meaning. I have an aunt who thinks that nothing happens in a story unless somebody gets married or shot at the end of it. I wrote a story about a tramp who marries an old woman's idiot daughter in order to acquire the old woman's automobile. After the marriage, he takes the daughter off on a wedding trip in the automobile and abandons her in an eating place and drives on by himself. Now that is a complete story. There is nothing more relating to the mystery of that man's personality that could be shown through that particular dramatization. But I've never been able to convince my aunt that it's a complete story. She wants to know what happened to the idiot daughter after that.

Not long ago that story was adapted for a television play, and the adapter, knowing his business, had the tramp have a change of heart and go back and pick up the idiot daughter and the two of them ride away, grinning madly. My aunt believes that the story is complete at last, but I have other sentiments about it — which are not suitable for public utterance. When you write a story, you only have to write one story, but there will always be people who will refuse to read the story you have written.

And this naturally brings up the awful question of what kind of a reader you are writing for when you write fiction. Perhaps we each think we have a personal solution for this problem. For my own part, I have a very high opinion of the art of fiction and a very low opinion of what is called the "average" reader. I tell myself that I can't escape him, that this is the personality I am supposed to keep awake, but that at the same time, I am also supposed to provide the intelligent reader with the deeper experience that he looks for in fiction. Now actually, both of these readers are just aspects of the writer's own personality, and in the last analysis, the only reader he can know anything about is himself. We all write at our own level of understanding, but it is the peculiar characteristic of fiction that its literal surface can be made to yield entertainment on an obvious physical plane to one sort of reader while the selfsame surface can be made to yield meaning to the person equipped to experience it there.

Meaning is what keeps the short story from being short. I prefer to talk about the meaning in a story rather than the theme of a story. People talk about the theme of a story as if the theme were like the string that a sack of chicken feed is tied with. They think that if you can pick out the theme, the way you pick the right thread in the chicken-feed sack, you can rip the story open and feed the chickens. But this is not the way meaning works in fiction.

When you can state the theme of a story, when you can separate it from the story itself, then you can be sure the story is not a very good one. The meaning of a story has to be embodied in it, has to be made concrete in it. A story is a way to say something that can't be said any other way, and it takes every word in the story to say what the meaning is. You tell a story because a statement would be inadequate. When anybody asks what a story is about, the only proper thing is to tell him to read the story. The meaning of fiction is not abstract meaning but experienced meaning, and the purpose of making statements about the meaning of a story is only to help you to experience that meaning more fully.

Fiction is an art that calls for the strictest attention to the real — whether the writer is writing a naturalistic story or a fantasy. I mean that we always begin with what is or with what has an eminent possibility of truth about it. Even when one writes a fantasy, reality is the proper basis of it. A thing is fantastic because it is so real, so real that it is fantastic. Graham Greene has said that he can't write, "I stood over a bottomless pit," because that couldn't be true, or "Running down the stairs I jumped into a taxi," because that couldn't be true either. But Elizabeth Bowen can write about one of her characters that "she snatched at her hair as if she heard something in it," because that is eminently possible.

I would even go so far as to say that the person writing a fantasy has to be even more strictly attentive to the concrete detail than someone writing in a naturalistic vein — because the greater the story's strain on the credulity, the more convincing the properties in it have to be.

A good example of this is a story called "The Metamorphosis" by Franz Kafka. This is a story about a man who wakes up one morning to find that he has turned into a cockroach overnight, while not discarding his human nature. The rest of the story concerns his life and feelings and eventual death as an insect with human nature, and this situation is accepted by the reader because the concrete detail of the story is absolutely convincing. The fact is that this story describes the dual nature of man in such a realistic fashion that it is almost unbearable. The truth is not distorted here, but rather, a certain distortion is used to get at the truth. If we admit, as we must, that appearance is not the same thing as reality, then we must give the artist the liberty to make certain rearrangements of nature if these will lead to greater depths of vision. The artist himself always has to remember that what he is rearranging *is* nature, and that he has to know it and be able to describe it accurately in order to have the authority to rearrange it at all.

The peculiar problem of the short-story writer is how to make the action he describes reveal as much of the mystery of existence as possible. He has only a short space to do it in and he can't do it by statement. He has to do it by showing, not by saying, and by showing the concrete — so that his problem is really how to make the concrete work double time for him.

In good fiction, certain of the details will tend to accumulate meaning from the action of the story itself, and when this happens they become symbolic in the way they work. I once wrote a story called "Good Country People," in which a lady Ph.D. has her wooden leg stolen by a Bible salesman whom she has tried to seduce. Now I'll admit that, paraphrased in this way, the situation is simply a low joke. The average reader is pleased to observe anybody's wooden leg being stolen. But without ceasing to appeal to him and without making any statements of high intention, this story does manage to operate at another level of experience, by letting the wooden leg accumulate meaning. Early in the story, we're presented with the fact that the Ph.D. is spiritually as well as physically crippled. She believes in nothing but her own belief in nothing, and we perceive that there is a wooden part of her soul that corresponds to her wooden leg. Now of course this is never stated. The fiction writer states as little as possible. The reader makes this connection from things he is shown. He may not even know that he makes the connection, but the connection is there nevertheless and it has its effect on him. As the story goes on, the wooden leg continues to accumulate meaning. The reader learns how the girl feels about her leg, how her mother feels about it, and how the country woman on the place feels about it; and finally, by the time the Bible salesman comes along, the leg has accumulated so much meaning that it is, as the saying goes, loaded. And when the Bible salesman steals it, the reader realizes that he has taken away part of the girl's personality and has revealed her deeper affliction to her for the first time.

If you want to say that the wooden leg is a symbol, you can say that. But it is a wooden leg first, and as a wooden leg it is absolutely necessary to the story. It has its place on the literal level of the story, but it operates in depth as well as on the surface. It increases the story in every direction, and this is essentially the way a story escapes being short.

Now a little might be said about the way in which this happens. I wouldn't want you to think that in that story I sat down and said, "I am now going to write a story about a Ph.D. with a wooden leg, using the wooden leg as a symbol for another kind of affliction." I doubt myself if many writers know what they are going to do when they start out. When I started writing that story, I didn't know there was going to be a Ph.D. with a wooden leg in it. I merely found myself one morning writing a description of two women that I knew something about, and before I realized it, I had equipped one of them with a daughter with a wooden leg. As the story progressed, I brought in the Bible salesman, but I had no idea what I was going to do with him. I didn't know he was going to steal that wooden leg until ten or twelve lines before he did it, but when I found out that this was what was going to happen, I realized that it was inevitable. This is a story that produces a shock for the reader, and I think one reason for this is that it produced a shock for the writer.

Now despite the fact that this story came about in this seemingly mindless fashion, it is a story that almost no rewriting was done on. It is a story that was under control throughout the writing of it, and it might be asked how this kind of control comes about, since it is not entirely conscious.

I think the answer to this is what Maritain[1] calls "the habit of art." It is a fact that fiction writing is something in which the whole personality takes part — the conscious as well as the unconscious mind. Art is the habit of the artist; and habits have to be rooted deep in the whole personality. They have to be cultivated like any other habit, over a long period of time, by experience; and teaching any kind of writing is largely a matter of helping the student develop the habit of art. I think this is more than just a discipline, although it is that; I think it is a way of looking at the created world and of using the senses so as to make them find as much meaning as possible in things.

Now I am not so naïve as to suppose that most people come to writers' conferences in order to hear what kind of vision is necessary to write stories that will become a permanent part of our literature. Even if you do wish to hear this, your greatest concerns are immediately practical. You want to know how you can actually write a good story, and further, how you can tell when you've done it; and so you want to know what the form of a short story is, as if the form were something that existed outside of each story and could be applied or imposed on the material. Of course, the more you write, the more you will realize that the form is organic, that it is something that grows out of the material, that the form of each story is unique. A story that is any good can't be reduced, it can only be expanded. A story is good when you continue to see more and more in it, and when it continues to escape you. In fiction two and two is always more than four.

The only way, I think, to learn to write short stories is to write them, and then to try to discover what you have done. The time to think of technique is when you've actually got the story in front of you. The teacher can help the student by looking at his individual work and trying to help him decide if he has written a complete story, one in which the action fully illuminates the meaning.

Perhaps the most profitable thing I can do is to tell you about some of the general observations I made about these seven stories I read of yours. All of these observations will not fit any one of the stories exactly, but they are points nevertheless that it won't hurt anyone interested in writing to think about.

The first thing that any professional writer is conscious of in reading

---

[1] Jacques Maritain (1882–1973), French philosopher and critic.

anything is, naturally, the use of language. Now the use of language in these stories was such that, with one exception, it would be difficult to distinguish one story from another. While I can recall running into several clichés, I can't remember one image or one metaphor from the seven stories. I don't mean there weren't images in them; I just mean that there weren't any that were effective enough to take away with you.

In connection with this, I made another observation that startled me considerably. With the exception of one story, there was practically no use made of the local idiom. Now this is a Southern Writers' Conference. All the addresses on these stories were from Georgia or Tennessee, yet there was no distinctive sense of Southern life in them. A few place-names were dropped, Savannah or Atlanta or Jacksonville, but these could just as easily have been changed to Pittsburgh or Passaic without calling for any other alteration in the story. The characters spoke as if they had never heard any kind of language except what came out of a television set. This indicates that something is way out of focus.

There are two qualities that make fiction. One is the sense of mystery and the other is the sense of manners. You get the manners from the texture of existence that surrounds you. The great advantage of being a Southern writer is that we don't have to go anywhere to look for manners; bad or good, we've got them in abundance. We in the South live in a society that is rich in contradiction, rich in irony, rich in contrast, and particularly rich in its speech. And yet here are six stories by Southerners in which almost no use is made of the gifts of the region.

Of course the reason for this may be that you have seen these gifts abused so often that you have become self-conscious about using them. There is nothing worse than the writer who doesn't *use* the gifts of the region, but wallows in them. Everything becomes so Southern that it's sickening, so local that it is unintelligble, so literally reproduced that it conveys nothing. The general gets lost in the particular instead of being shown through it.

However, when the life that actually surrounds us is totally ignored, when our patterns of speech are absolutely overlooked, then something is out of kilter. The writer should then ask himself if he is not reaching out for a kind of life that is artificial to him.

An idiom characterizes a society, and when you ignore the idiom, you are very likely ignoring the whole social fabric that could make a meaningful character. You can't cut characters off from their society and say much about them as individuals. You can't say anything meaningful about the mystery of a personality unless you put that personality in a believable and significant social context. And the best way to do this is through the character's own language. When the old lady in one of Andrew Lytle's stories says contemptuously that she has a mule that is older than Birmingham, we get in that one sentence a sense of a society and its history. A great deal of the Southern writers' work is done for him before he begins, because our history lives in our talk. In one of Eudora Welty's stories a character says, "Where I come from, we use fox for yard dogs and owls for chickens, but we sing true." Now there is a whole book in that one sentence; and when the people of your section can talk like that, and you ignore it, you're just not taking advantage of what's yours. The sound of our talk is too definite to be discarded with impunity, and if the writer tries to get rid of it, he is liable to destroy the better part of his creative power.

Another thing I observed about these stories is that most of them don't go very far inside a character, don't reveal very much of the character. I don't mean that they don't enter the character's mind, but they simply don't show that he has a personality. Again this goes back partly to speech. These characters have no distinctive speech to reveal themselves with; and sometimes they have no really distinctive features. You feel in the end that no personality is revealed because no personality is there. In most good stories it is the character's personality that creates the action of the story. In most of these stories, I feel that the writer has thought of some action and then scrounged up a character to perform it. You will usually be more successful if you start the other way around. If you start with a real personality, a real character, then something is bound to happen; and you don't have to know what before you begin. In fact it may be better if you don't know what before you begin. You ought to be able to discover something from your stories. If you don't, probably nobody else will.   [1961]

FLANNERY O'CONNOR

The Element of Suspense in **A Good Man Is Hard to Find**

A story really isn't any good unless it successfully resists paraphrase, unless it hangs on and expands in the mind. Properly, you analyze to enjoy, but it's equally true that to analyze with any discrimination, you have to have enjoyed already, and I think that the best reason to hear a story read is that it should stimulate that primary enjoyment.

I don't have any pretensions to being an Aeschylus or Sophocles and providing you in this story with a cathartic experience out of your mythic background, though this story I'm going to read certainly calls up a good deal of the South's mythic background, and it should elicit from you a degree of pity and terror, even though its way of being serious is a comic one. I do think, though, that like the Greeks you should know what is going to happen in this story so that any element of suspense in it will be transferred from its surface to its interior.

I would be most happy if you had already read it, happier still if you knew it well, but since experience has taught me to keep my expectations along these lines modest, I'll tell you that this is the story of a family of six which, on its way driving to Florida, gets wiped out by an escaped convict who calls himself the Misfit. The family is made up of the Grandmother and her son, Bailey, and his children, John Wesley and June Star and the baby, and there is also the cat and the children's mother. The cat is named Pitty Sing, and the Grandmother is taking him with them, hidden in a basket.

Now I think it behooves me to try to establish with you the basis on which reason operates in this story. Much of my fiction takes its character from a reasonable use of the unreasonable, though the reasonableness of my use of it may not always be apparent. The assumptions that underlie this use of it, however, are those of the central Christian mysteries. These are assumptions to which a large part of the modern audience takes exception. About this I can only say that there are perhaps other ways than my own in which this story could be read, but none other by which it could have been written. Belief, in my own case anyway, is the engine that makes perception operate.

The heroine of this story, the Grandmother, is in the most significant position life offers the Christian. She is facing death. And to all appearances she, like the rest of us, is not too well prepared for it. She would like to see the event postponed. Indefinitely.

I've talked to a number of teachers who use this story in class and who tell their students that the Grandmother is evil, that in fact, she's a witch, even down to the cat. One of these teachers told me that his students, and particularly his southern students, resisted this interpretation with a certain bemused vigor, and he didn't understand why. I had to tell him that they resisted it because they all had grandmothers or great-aunts just like her at home, and they knew, from personal experience, that the old lady lacked comprehension, but that she had a good heart. The southerner is usually tolerant of those weaknesses that proceed from innocence, and he knows that a taste for self-preservation can be readily combined with the missionary spirit.

This same teacher was telling his students that morally the Misfit was several cuts above the Grandmother. He had a really sentimental attachment to the Misfit. But then a prophet gone wrong is almost always more interesting than your grandmother, and you have to let people take their pleasures where they find them.

It is true that the old lady is a hypocritical old soul; her wits are no match for the Misfit's, nor is her capacity for grace equal to his; yet I think the unprejudiced reader will feel that the Grandmother has a special kind of triumph in this story which instinctively we do not allow to someone altogether bad.

I often ask myself what makes a story work, and what makes it hold up as a story, and I have decided that it is probably some action, some gesture of a character that is unlike any other in the story, one which indicates where the real heart of the story lies. This would have to be an action or a gesture which was both totally right and totally unexpected; it would have to be one that was both in character and beyond character; it would have to suggest both the world and eternity. The action or gesture I'm talking about would have to be on the anagogical level, that is, the level which has to do with the Divine life and our participation in it. It would be a gesture that transcended any neat allegory that might have been intended or any pat moral categories a reader could make. It would be a gesture which somehow made contact with mystery.

There is a point in this story where such a gesture occurs. The Grandmother is at last alone, facing the Misfit. Her head clears for an instant and she realizes, even in her limited way, that she is responsible for the man before her and joined to him by ties of kinship which have their roots deep in the mystery she has been merely prattling about so far. And at this point, she does the right thing, she makes the right gesture.

I find that students are often puzzled by what she says and does here, but I think myself that if I took out this gesture and what she says with it, I would have no story. What was left would not be worth your attention. Our age not only does not have a very sharp eye for the almost imperceptible intrusions of grace, it no longer has much feeling for the nature of the violences which precede and follow them. The devil's greatest wile, Baudelaire has said, is to convince us that he does not exist.

I suppose the reasons for the use of so much violence in modern fiction will differ with each writer who uses it, but in my own stories I have found that violence is strangely capable of returning my characters to reality and preparing them to accept their moment of grace. Their heads are so hard that almost nothing else will do the work. This idea, that reality is something to which we must be returned at considerable cost, is one which is seldom understood by the casual reader, but it is one which is implicit in the Christian view of the world.

I don't want to equate the Misfit with the devil. I prefer to think that, however unlikely this may seem, the old lady's gesture, like the mustard-seed, will grow to be a great crow-filled tree in the Misfit's heart, and will be enough of a pain to him there to turn him into the prophet he was meant to become. But that's another story.

This story has been called grotesque, but I prefer to call it literal. A good story is literal in the same sense that a child's drawing is literal. When a child draws, he doesn't intend to distort but to set down exactly what he sees, and as his gaze is direct, he sees the lines that create motion. Now the lines of motion that interest the writer are usually invisible. They are lines of spiritual motion. And in this story you should be on the lookout for such things as the action of grace in the Grandmother's soul, and not for the dead bodies.

We hear many complaints about the prevalence of violence in modern fiction, and it is always assumed that this violence is a bad thing and meant to be an end in itself. With the serious writer, violence is never an end in itself. It is the extreme situation that best reveals what we are essentially, and I believe these are times when writers are more interested in what we are essentially than in the tenor of our daily lives. Violence is a force which can be used for good or evil, and among other things taken by it is the kingdom of heaven. But regardless of what can be taken by it, the man in the violent situation reveals those qualities least dispensable in his personality, those qualities which are all he will have to take into eternity with him; and since the characters in this story are all on the verge of eternity, it is appropriate to think of what they take with them. In any case, I hope that if you consider these points in connection with the story, you will come to see it as something more than an account of a family murdered on the way to Florida.   [1969]

V. S. PRITCHETT

Flannery O'Connor: Satan Comes to Georgia

All the characters in the very powerful stories of Flannery O'Connor — *Everything That Rises Must Converge* — are exposed: That is to say they are plain human beings in whose fractured lives the writer has discovered an uncouth relationship with the lasting myths and the violent passions of human life. The people are rooted in their scene, but as weeds are rooted. It would be fashionable to call her stories Gothic: They certainly have the curious inner strain of fable — replacing the social interest which is a distinguishing quality of the American novel. (She herself was an invalid most of her life and died in her native Georgia in 1964 at the age of thirty-eight.) The Southern writers have sometimes tended to pure freakishness or have concentrated on the eccentricities of a decaying social life: But this rotting and tragic order has thrown up strong, if theatrical, themes. Flannery O'Connor was born too late to be affected by the romantic and nostalgic legend of the tragic South: The grotesque for its own sake means nothing to her. It is a norm. . . .

The passions are just beneath the stagnant surface in Flannery O'Connor's stories. She was an old Catholic, not a convert, in the South of the poor white of the Bible Belt and this gave her a critical skirmishing power. But the symbolism of religion, rather than the acrimonies of sectarian dispute, fed her violent imagination — the violence is itself oddly early Protestant — as if she had seen embers of the burning Bible-fed imagery in the minds of her own characters. The symbols are always ominous: At sunset a wood may be idyllic, but also look blood-sodden. They usually precede an act of violence which will introduce the character at the end of the story "into the world of guilt and sorrow." This is her ground as a fabulist or moralist. We are left with an illusion shattered, with the chilly task of facing our hatreds. . . . The essence of Flannery O'Connor's vision is that she sees terror as a purification — unwanted, of course: it is never the sadomasochist's intended indulgence. The moment of purification may actually destroy; it will certainly show someone changed.

Symbolism has been fatal to many writers: It offers a quick return of unearned meaning. . . . But . . . whenever one detects a symbol, one is impressed by Flannery O'Connor's use of it: It is concrete and native to the text. Take the title story of the book: a middle-aged widow, dressed up in an awful new hat, is seen going with her son to a slimming class in order to get her high blood pressure down. She is a "Southern lady" in reduced circumstances and now, bitterly but helplessly opposed to Negro integration, she sticks to her dignity. "If you know who you are, you can go anywhere. . . . I can be gracious to anybody. I know who I am." This is true, in a way, but it is also a cliché, as her son tells her while they travel on the integrated local bus. Here a disturbing figure appears: a Negro woman with her child. She had on a hideous hat. A purple flap came down on one side of it and stood up on the other; the rest of it was green like a cushion with the stuffing out. The hat is exactly a replica of the white woman's hat. To her son this is comical; it ought to teach his silly mother a lesson in racialism. The Negro woman's child sees the joke too. The white woman becomes gracious to the child and prepares to do a terrible, gracious thing: to give the little child a bright new penny. When they all get off the bus she does this. The huge Negro woman, seeming "to explode like a piece of machinery that had been given one ounce of pressure too much," knocks the white woman down. Her son, who has hated his mother for years, sees a reality kill his mother and his own guilt.

Many of the stories are variations of the theme of the widowed mother who has emasculated her son; or the widower who is tragically unaware of what he is doing to his child. In one instance, a widower destroys his grandchild. These stories are not arguments; they are not case histories or indignation meetings. They are selected for the claustrophobic violence which will purify but destroy. The characters are engaged in a struggle for personal power which they usually misunderstand. . . .

If these stories are antihumanist propaganda one does not notice it until afterwards. Like all Gothic writers, Flannery O'Connor has a deep sense of the Devil or rather of the multiplicity of devils, though not in any conventional religious sense. To the poor-white Gospellers, Satan has become Literature. For her the devils are forces which appear in living shape: the stray bull which kills the old farming widow whose sons let her down; the criminal child who is proud of being an irredeemable destroyer because he has been called a child of Satan, and looks forward, eagerly — it is his right — to an eternity in the flames of hell which he takes to be literal fire; the delinquent girl who has been taught by psychiatrists to regard her vice as an illness sees this as an emancipating distinction. The author is not playing the easy game of paradox which is commonly a tiresome element in the novels of Catholic converts: For her, the role of the diabolic is to destroy pride in a misconceived virtue.

A short story ought to be faultless without being mechanical. The wrong word, a misplaced paragraph, an inadequate phrase or a convenient explanation, start fatal leaks in this kind of writing which is formally very close to poetry. That closeness must be totally sustained. There are no faults of craftsmanship in Flannery O'Connor's stories. She writes a plain style: She has a remarkable ear for the talk of the poor whites, for the received ideas of the educated; and she creates emotion and the essence of people by vivid images. . . . Flannery O'Connor is at pains to make us know intimately the lives of these poor white and struggling small-town people. They are there as they live, not in the interest of their ignorant normality, but in the interest of their exposure to forces in themselves that they do not yet understand. Satan, they will discover, is not just a word. He has legs — and those legs are their own.

[1980]

R O B E R T   H .   B R I N K M E Y E R ,   J R .

Flannery O'Connor and Her Readers

As her letters and essays clearly indicate, O'Connor was very much concerned with her reading audience. Her comments on her audience and how it affected her as an artist, however, were not entirely consistent, and it seems clear that O'Connor was of two minds on the subject.[1] One part of O'Connor downplayed the significance of the audience, saying that artists should be concerned with one thing — their art — and that they bear no responsibility to the audience. By this line of thinking writers concentrate on making their fiction — the characters and their worlds — come alive, and they make sure that the story works as a story and not as a medium for expressing an abstract statement. The meaning of a piece of fiction, O'Connor insisted, was the entire experience one has with it and was not a statement imposed on it that could then later be extracted and held up as its "message." Such thinking was central to the advice she wrote (December 11, 1956) to A. about writing fiction. O'Connor wrote that a writer should merely "start simply with a character or anything that you can make come alive." She continued, "When you have a character he will create his own situation and his situation will suggest some kind of resolution as you get into it. Wouldn't it be better to discover a meaning in what you write than to impose one?" (*HB*, 188).

Behind O'Connor's thinking is the thought of Saint Thomas Aquinas, whom O'Connor frequently cites. For Aquinas a work of art is, as O'Connor points out in "Catholic Novelists and Their Readers," "a good in itself," being "wholly concerned with the good of that which is made." As such, it "glorifies

---

[1] The most extensive discussion of O'Connor's interpretation of her audience is in Carol Shloss, *Flannery O'Connor's Dark Comedies: The Limits of Inference* (Baton Rouge, 1980). [Brinkmeyer's note]

God because it reflects God," and writers have no cause to put their work to any other end; such endeavors only undermine the integrity of the vision and sully the purity of the art. Modern writers, O'Connor says in this same essay, by and large fail to heed Aquinas's lesson and instead wrench their art to make it fit utilitarian ends. For her, in contrast, "the artist has his hands full and does his duty if he attends to his art. He can safely leave the evangelizing to the evangelists" (*MM*, 171, 173, 171).

Catholic writers, in O'Connor's eyes, were particularly prone to distort their fiction for utilitarian purposes — to make it do something rather than be something. Particularly disturbing to her were those writers, in part goaded by the Catholic press, who wrote in pious language about the pieties of the Church. O'Connor's attitude toward this type of fiction was sharp: "As for the fiction," she wrote (February 19, 1956) to John Lynch, "the motto of the Catholic press should be: We guarantee to corrupt nothing but your taste" (*HB*, 138). In ignoring the realities of the here and now outside the Church, such fiction was for O'Connor little more than religious propaganda, the stuff one expects to find in the vestibules of churches but not in bookstores. These writers, she believed, were too concerned with presenting the Church in a favorable light and tending to their readership's spiritual needs; O'Connor's answer to them was that in writing fiction the Catholic writer "does not decide what would be good for the Christian body and proceed to deliver it" (*MM*, 183). Instead, as we have seen O'Connor stressing, writers must work within the limitations of their vocation to create the best story — not tract — possible. "The writer is only free when he can tell the reader to go jump in the lake," O'Connor said in one of her interviews, stressing the artist's independence from the audience. She added that though the writer of course wants to communicate a personal vision, "whether [the reader] likes it or not is no concern of the writer" (*CFO*, 39).

If in this way O'Connor downplayed the significance of the audience, she also frequently said something quite different. She argued that the audience played a crucial role in artistic creation and that writers always had to be aware of, and to take account of, their audience. She spoke of this connection in "Catholic Novelists and Their Readers," saying that "it takes readers as well as writers to make literature," and she added in "The Catholic Novelist in the Protestant South" that "it is what writer, character, and reader share that makes it possible to write fiction at all." Elsewhere (in "Novelist and Believer") O'Connor wrote that fiction was ultimately an attempt at communication; successful writing, she added, was not merely a rendering of the artist's vision but a rendering of it in such a way that the reader could understand it. "The novelist doesn't write to express himself, he doesn't write simply to render a vision he believes true, rather he renders his vision so it can be transferred, as nearly whole as possible, to his reader," she wrote. "You can safely ignore the reader's taste, but you can't ignore his nature, you can't ignore his limited patience. Your problem is going to be difficult in direct proportion as your beliefs depart from his." She echoes this observation in "Some Aspects of the Grotesque in Southern Fiction," saying that the writer's vision "has to be transmitted and that the limitations and blind spots of his audience will very definitely affect the way he is able to show what he sees" (*MM*, 182, 204–205, 162, 47).

When speaking of her own audience, O'Connor almost always stressed the great distance she felt between herself and her readers and pointed to the ways this gulf pressured and limited her as a writer. She believed that she and other American Catholic writers lacked a significant and responsive audience, and that this situation stifled imaginative growth and artistic expression. O'Connor found several reasons for this development. Central to the Catholic writer's plight, O'Connor believed, was the fact that in America Catholic writers lacked a distinctive social and cultural heritage based on religious identity. In "The Catholic Novelist in the Protestant South" she asserts that "the writer whose themes are religious particularly needs a region where these themes find a response in the life of the people." She then adds: "The American Catholic is short on places that reflect his particular religious life and his particular problems. This country isn't exactly cut in his image." She goes on to say that even in areas where there are large numbers of Catholics, Catholic life there lacks "the significant features that result in a high degree of regional self-consciousness" and so offers the Catholic writer few "exploitable benefits." O'Connor's analysis of Catholic writers continues: "They have no great geographical extent, they have no particularly significant history, certainly no history of defeat; they have no real peasant class, and no cultural unity of the kind you find in the South." She adds that Catholics usually "blend almost imperceptively into the general materialistic background." This lack of a strong cultural tradition and a supportive audience greatly burdens Catholic writers, impoverishing their imaginative life and art. "If the Catholic faith were central to life in America, Catholic fiction would fare better, but the Church is not central to this society." O'Connor continues. "The things that bind us together as Catholics are known only to ourselves. A secular society understands us less and less. It becomes more and more difficult in America to make belief believable" (*MM*, 200, 201).

These final words point to the second reason American Catholics lack a supportive audience: The larger society they write from and to is overwhelmingly secular and materialistic, money based rather than religious based. O'Connor, as we saw in the first chapter, was well aware of the trends in modern social and intellectual thought that since the Enlightenment have been validating and valorizing the human consciousness and rationality while undermining and reducing the significance of the religious. In a letter (October 19, 1958) to T. R. Spivey, O'Connor wrote that by and large people in today's society have "no sense of the power of God that could produce the Incarnation and the Resurrection. They are all so busy explaining away the virgin birth and such things, reducing everything to human proportions that in time they lose even the sense of the human itself, what they were aiming to reduce everything to" (*HB*, 300). Because moderns lacked a faith in transcendent values and order, O'Connor, as she said in "Some Aspects of the Grotesque in Southern Fiction," saw the age as one "which doubts both fact and value, which is swept this way and that by momentary convictions"

(*MM*, 49). O'Connor found such relativism particularly disturbing, and this in part explains her strong attraction to the fundamentalist imperative that defines all values according to the simple — but total — choice of being for either Christ or the Devil.

Given these trends and developments, O'Connor saw her own position, as well as that of almost all American Catholic writers, as being particularly precarious in terms of communicating with her readership. O'Connor frequently asserted in her letters that she could consistently count on only a handful of informed readers — an assertion largely borne out by the number of vicious and misinformed readings her work received, particularly early on — and that she had to make these readers go a long way in her life as an author. O'Connor knew hers was not the type of fiction that most Catholic readers yearned to read — not, in other words, fiction that was thoroughly positive and that went out of its way to celebrate the life of the Church. She characterized the general Catholic reader as unthinking, and she said that this reader "is so busy looking for something that fits his needs, and shows him in the best possible light, that he will find suspect anything that doesn't serve such purpose" (*MM*, 182). Elsewhere, in a letter (May 4, 1963) to Sister Mariella Gable, she wrote that those Catholic readers who demand that the writer make Christianity look desirable are asking the writer to describe Christianity's essence and not what the writer actually sees. "Ideal Christianity doesn't exist, because anything the human being touches, even Christian truth, he deforms slightly in his own image," she wrote, adding a bit later that the tendency of the Catholic readers she had been discussing "is always toward the abstract and therefore toward allegory, thinness, and ultimately what they are looking for is apologetic fiction. The best of them think: make it look desirable because it is desirable. And the rest of them think: make it look desirable so I won't look like a fool for holding it" (*HB*, 516). Such readers would find little to like in O'Connor's fiction and in all likelihood would see it as a good deal more than suspect — subversive, probably.

O'Connor of course felt an even greater distance from what she saw as the thoroughly secular and unbelieving general reader, the reader to whom she claimed primarily wrote. In "The Catholic Novelists and Their Readers" she said that Catholic readers make a great mistake in supposing that Catholic writers write exclusively for them. "Occasionally this may happen," she wrote, "but generally it is not happening today" (*MM*, 185), and O'Connor made it clear elsewhere that it was not happening in her fiction. To A., O'Connor wrote (August 2, 1955) of the audience she perceived, saying that "one of the awful things about writing when you are a Christian is that for you the ultimate reality is the Incarnation, the present reality is the Incarnation, and nobody believes in the Incarnation; that is, nobody in your audience. My audience are the people who think God is dead. At least these are the people I am conscious of writing for" (*HB*, 92). Trying to bridge this gap between believing author and unbelieving audience was a terrible burden for O'Connor, and one that haunted her throughout her career. In a review of Caroline Gordon's *The Malefactors*, O'Connor wrote that "making grace believable to the contemporary reader is the almost insurmountable problem of the novelist who writes from the standpoint of Christian orthodoxy," an observation that speaks crucially to O'Connor's own situation in communicating with her audience (*PG*, 16).

O'Connor further perceived her audience as making demands that she was not prepared to meet — ever. She complained in "Some Aspects of the Grotesque in Southern Fiction" that her freedom as a writer was always under pressure, since everywhere "the novelist is asked to be the handmaid of his age." She wrote, "Whenever the public is heard from, it is heard demanding a literature which is balanced and which will somehow heal the ravages of our time." This literature, she said elsewhere in this essay, was based on what she called "a realism of fact" — a realism that associated "the only legitimate material for long fiction with the movement of social forces, with the typical, with the fidelity to the way things look and happen in normal life." Such realism, she added, limited both the scope of the imaginative vision of artists and their fiction. As O'Connor noted here and elsewhere, her own fiction was written with a realism of an altogether different sort — a realism that sought not to mirror the typical but to reveal the spiritual. To this end, she says in "Novelist and Believer," the writer "is bound by the reasonable possibilities, not the probabilities of his culture" (*MM*, 46, 39, 165).

If the overall critical environment established its own orthodoxy for fiction, O'Connor also saw general readers establishing their own expectations and demands for what they should experience in the act of reading. She characterized the general readers as being "tired," of wanting what she called at one point "Instant Uplift" — that is, wanting to have their spirits raised in an act of easy compassion and sentiment. This demand for uplift and the redemptive act, O'Connor notes in "Some Aspects of the Grotesque in Southern Fiction," is a characteristic human need, and one that both the storyteller and the listener find particularly compelling in narrative. What bothers O'Connor is not that the reader seeks this motion in fiction but that the reader "has forgotten the cost of it." She explains that the modern reader's "sense of evil is diluted or lacking altogether, and so he has forgotten the price of restoration. When he reads a novel, he wants either his senses tormented or his spirits raised. He wants to be transported, instantly, either to mock damnation or a mock innocence." To underscore the risks the writer takes in ignoring such readers, O'Connor writes in this same essay that there are those who "say that the serious writer doesn't have to bother about the tired reader, but he does, because they are all tired. One old lady who wants her heart uplifted wouldn't be so bad, but you multiply her two hundred and fifty thousand times and what you get is a book club" (*MM*, 165, 48–49). . . .

[1989]

Abbreviations

Abbreviations of works by Flannery O'Connor commonly cited in the text refer to the following editions:

CFO   *Conversations with Flannery O'Connor.* Edited by Rosemary M. Magee. Jackson, Miss., 1987.

HB   *The Habit of Being: Letters.* Edited by Sally Fitzgerald. New York, 1969.

MM   *Mystery and Manners: Occasional Prose.* Edited by Sally Fitzgerald and Robert Fitzgerald. New York, 1969.

PG   *The Presence of Grace and Other Book Reviews by Flannery O'Connor.* Compiled by Leo J. Zuber. Edited by Carter W. Martin. Athens, Ga., 1983.

DOROTHY TUCK MCFARLAND

On Good Country People

"Good Country People," the penultimate story in the collection, is something of a comic variation on "A Good Man Is Hard To Find." As the grandmother of the title story thinks of herself as a good Christian woman who believes in all the conventional platitudes, Hulga Hopewell, the Ph.D. in philosophy who is the protagonist of "Good Country People," thinks of herself as a good nihilist who energetically disbelieves in all the conventional platitudes. In their titles both stories implicitly ask the reader to consider what are good men or good people. And in both stories O'Connor uses conventional language for comic and ironic purposes, emphasizing the meaninglessness of the platitudes in the mouths of her characters, and at the same time using their words to sound the main themes of the story. For instance, Hulga's mother, Mrs. Hopewell, characteristically strings together remarks like "Everybody is different. . . . It takes all kinds to make the world. . . . Nothing is perfect." Nevertheless, she actually tolerates differences and imperfections very poorly. Two of the themes in the story grow out of the characters' attitudes toward uniqueness ("everybody is different") and imperfection.

Mrs. Hopewell and her tenant's wife, Mrs. Freeman, embody contrasting ways of looking at the world that provide the frame for the story. Whereas Mrs. Hopewell is determined always to put a smiling face on things and never look beneath the surface, the gimlet-eyed Mrs. Freeman has a fondness for hidden things: "the details of secret infections, hidden deformities, assaults upon children." She is obsessed with the physical demands and ills of the body, and in her conversation about her two daughters she dwells on the details of two major aspects of their physical being: their sexuality and their ailments. One daughter, Glynese, is being courted by several admirers, one of whom is going to chiropractor school and who cures her of a sty by popping her neck. The other daughter, Carramae, is pregnant and unable to "keep anything on her stomach."

Mrs. Hopewell's daughter, Hulga, is antagonized by her mother's platitudinous optimism to the extent that her face has come to wear a look of constant outrage that "obliterated every other expression." She finds Mrs. Freeman tolerable only on the ground that Mrs. Freeman diverts some of her mother's attention from her; otherwise, she is uncomfortable with Mrs. Freeman's fascination with the secrets of the body.

Hulga has rejected the physical world and the life of the body in preference for the life of the mind: "She didn't like dogs or cats or birds or flowers or nature or nice young men. She looked at nice young men as if she could smell their stupidity." Her rejection of the physical world stems from her awareness of its liability to imperfection. Hulga's own imperfection is gross — she lost a leg when she was ten — but O'Connor obviously intended her to be a figure of all mankind, which suffers from the imperfections of the human condition. Hulga insists on calling attention to her physical imperfection and refuses to try to improve her appearance. However, this defensive insistence that she be accepted "LIKE I AM" does not indicate that *she* has really accepted what she is; rather, it suggests that she is trying to insulate herself against the pain of difference and imperfection.

Hulga's choice of her name reflects her response to her condition. Named Joy by her mother, she could not tolerate the incongruity between the idea of joy and her knowledge that she was "dust." She therefore chose to emphasize her deformity and ugliness by assuming an ugly name — Hulga — and a rude manner, and closed herself to joy for the sake of affirming the truth about herself. The persona she creates with the name Hulga is a blind, stony, armored creature. To her mother, the name Hulga suggests the "broad blank hull of a battleship." Hulga herself is described as being "square and rigid-shouldered," and as standing "blank and solid and silent" Her face is characteristically expressionless, and her "icy blue" eyes have the "look of someone who has achieved blindness by an act of will and means to keep it." Though she believes the self she has created is her true self, this imagery suggests that her willful blindness prevents her from seeing the true nature of the human condition as much as does her mother's insistence on always looking "at the bright side of things."

Though she has rejected joy for herself, Hulga has not given up on the possibility of love, and this secret desire is her one area of vulnerability. However, she thinks the persona she has created through her name is a means of making herself invulnerable, so that she can command and control love from a position of strength. She envisions her name working "like the ugly sweating Vulcan who stayed in the furance and to whom the goddess [of love] had to come when called."

When an apparently naive country boy appears selling Bibles, Hulga feels that he offers no threat to her and allows herself to respond to his open admiration. Despite her utter inexperience (she has never been kissed) she decides to demonstrate her command of love by seducing him. She reinforces her image of herself as a woman of intellectual superiority and worldly wisdom by imagining that the simple Bible salesman, once seduced, will suffer from remorse, whereupon she will take away his shame and "transform it into something useful."

However, the Bible salesman's simplicity seduces her. Having climbed with her into the loft of an isolated barn, the Bible salesman gets Hulga to declare (with some reservations) that she loves him. He then demands that she prove it by showing him where her wooden leg joins on. At first shocked by his proposal, Hulga resists until he tells her why: "because [the wooden leg is] what makes you different." She feels that the Bible salesman, "with an instinct that came from beyond wisdom, had touched the truth about her." She comes to the conclusion that for the first time in her life she has encountered true innocence. She is so moved by her perception of his innocence that she lets down her defenses and allows her hidden vulnerability to emerge.

This area of vulnerability O'Connor equates with Hulga's soul and symbolizes it by her wooden leg: "she was as sensitive about the artificial leg as a peacock about his tail. No one ever touched it but her. She took care of it as someone else would his soul, in private and almost with her own eyes turned away." The leg is also, as the Bible salesman cannily recognized, what makes her different — a difference which, up to now, she has worn defensively and defiantly. Now, for the first time in the story, she accepts her difference, and allows herself to be touched in what is symbolically her soul. Accepting herself, she can surrender herself, and having surrendered herself she finds herself again, in the classic progression of love. When she allows the Bible salesman to remove her leg, "it was like surrendering to him completely. It was like losing her own life and finding it again, miraculously, in his."

Significantly, she surrenders to love in a scene in which her physical grotesqueness is not only emphasized but becomes the very means of love's expression and fulfillment. Though this scene of the Bible salesman removing Hulga's wooden leg is objectively ludicrous (and O'Connor's handling of it is full of irony), Hulga herself is, for the first time, completely without irony. The boy seems to her to be "entirely reverent" as he approaches the leg, and his removal of it is clearly the psychological and emotional equivalent to Hulga of the act of love: "She was thinking that she would run away with him and that every night he would take the leg off and every morning put it back on again."

Hulga's surrender to love also makes her vulnerable to a revelation of her own blindness. She had been convinced that she can see and that others cannot, and that she knows the truth. "Woman!" she had once shouted at her mother, enraged at Mrs. Hopewell's habit of blandly papering over ugliness with smiles. "Do you ever look inside . . . and see what you are *not*?" As a philosopher, Hulga is professionally concerned with truth. She is convinced that she has no illusions, that she has seen through appearances to the nothing that is beneath. "Some of us," she informs the Bible salesman, "have taken off our blindfolds and see that there's nothing to see." And she is utterly convinced of the truth of her assessment of the Bible salesman's innocence.

The Bible salesman, however, is anything but an innocent. Having put Hulga's leg out of her reach, he takes out of his suitcase a hollowed-out Bible containing a flask of whiskey, a deck of pornographic playing cards, and a packet of contraceptives. In response to Hulga's evident dismay, he replies, "What's the matter with you all of a sudden? . . . You just a while ago said you didn't believe in nothing. I thought you was some girl!" When he sees that he will get no farther with her, he snatches up her wooden leg, thrusts it into his suitcase, and disappears down the ladder of the barn loft.

The Bible salesman's thoroughgoing nihilism shows up Hulga's claim to believe in nothing as a superficial intellectual posture. Both his actions and his words devastate her assumption of intellectual superiority: "he turned and regarded her with a look that no longer had any admiration in it. . . . 'And I'll tell you another thing, Hulga,' he said, using the name as if he didn't think much of it, 'you ain't so smart. I been believing in nothing ever since I was born!'"

Hulga is left stranded, her previously stony face "churning" with emotion. But the Bible salesman's destruction of her illusions and her defenses (like the destruction of conventional order that resulted from the grandmother's encounter with The Misfit) may be, for Hulga, the means of her salvation. That the Bible salesman might be a kind of savior is suggested in the description of Hulga's final glimpse of him. Looking out the window of the barn loft, she sees him making his way across the pasture. O'Connor implicitly compares him to Christ walking on the water; to Hulga's blurred vision (the Bible salesman has also taken her glasses), he seems to be "struggling successfully over the green speckled lake."

The actual or implied references to Christ in *A Good Man Is Hard to Find* are numerous. The climactic moment in the title story comes about after The Misfit expresses his intense concern over the question of whether or not Jesus raised the dead. . . . The Bible salesman in "Good Country People" is implicitly compared to Christ.

Christ, as Simeon prophesied in St. Luke's gospel, is a "sign that will be contradicted," a sign of the presence of God in the world that, to many, will not seem to be a sign of God at all — will seem, rather, its opposite. The unexpected and often grotesque and incongruous ways in which O'Connor felt Christ to be present in the world is, I think, the real subject of this collection. Not only is the image of Christ suggested in unlikely places or associated with unlikely characters; but in style as well the stories embody contradiction and incongruity — in the double point of view, in the mixture of comedy and horror, in the pervasive tone of emotional flatness and irony, on the one hand, and the intimations of depth and serious meaning on the other. Thematically and stylistically, the centrality of Christ — of that which we experience as contradictory — provides *A Good Man Is Hard to Find* with a unity that makes it more than simply a random collection of stories. . . . I would add another gloss on the meaning of the title: the good man is so hard to find because he appears in such unlikely guises, because he is hidden in irony and contradiction. [1976]

WAYNE C. BOOTH *was George M. Pullman Distinguished Service Professor of English at the University of Chicago. As a literary critic his concern has been exploring the ways in which works of fiction act on the reader in different modes of persuasion. Among his many studies are* The Rhetoric of Fiction *(1983),* The Company We Keep: An Ethics of Fiction *(1988), and* The Rhetoric of Irony *(1974), from which this reading of Flannery O'Connor's "Everything That Rises Must Converge" is taken.*

WAYNE C. BOOTH

A Rhetorical Reading of O'Connor's Everything That Rises Must Converge

This is an extremely complex story, not only in its ironic undercuttings but in its affirmations. No reading of it can be considered adequate unless it somehow relates the curious title to the various attempts to "rise" and to the failures to "converge." In the web of inference that we must create to see the story whole, our running translation of Julian's judgments into alternative judgments is only one strand. But once we have discerned that strand clearly, the rest of the story gives few difficulties.

Since Julian's is the only mind offering us opinions (except for a few observations and metaphors from the narrator, most notably the final sentence), we must sooner or later decide how far we can trust him. It is not hard to see that he is unreliable about many things. "He never spoke of it without contempt or thought of it without longing" — what kind of man is it, we ask, who always belies his true feelings? His life is full of such contradictions, showing that in his own way he is as far out of touch with reality as he takes his mother to be. His radical self-deception is perhaps clearest in the long fantasy that begins when he "withdraws into the inner compartment of his mind where he spent most of his time." No one could misread his own character more thoroughly than Julian does in thinking that he has "turned out so well," that he has a "first rate education," that he has a "large" mind, that he is "free of prejudice and unafraid to face facts" — remember, this is the boy who "did not like to consider all she did for him" and who can take pride in having "cut himself emotionally free of her." The closer we look at the disharmonies among his various opinions and actions, the more vigorously we must work in reconstructing the terrible lost young man we see behind his self-defensive rhetoric. His childish efforts to hurt his mother begin in a comic light, as he poses like a martyr and does everything he possibly can to spoil her one pleasant time of the week. But the comedy slowly gives place to pathos and horror as he runs over in his mind the possible tortures he might subject her to, then enjoys her humiliation about the duplicate hat, and finally — so wrapped up in his own petty bitterness and futility that he cannot see what is in front of his eyes — shouts irony-laden insults at the stricken woman. "You aren't who you think you are," he says, summarizing himself as much as his mother. "You've got to live in the new world and face a few realities for a change. Buck up, it won't kill you." It *is* killing her, and *he* is the one who must now begin to "face a few realities for a change."

These disharmonies are simple and clear. But the reconstruction of what "the realities" are — of what Julian must face — is not so easy. It is obviously not to be found in the "unreal," absurdly "innocent" world of the class-bound mother, nor in the equally unreal and absurd but vicious world of Julian. One kind of unmistakable reality is found in the irreducible, often harsh details of the life that Julian and his mother encounter but cannot see because of the abstractions that blur their vision. The mother does not see real "Negroes," for example, only the stereotypes that her childhood has provided her with. But Julian does not see real people either; instead he sees only the stereotypes that his liberal opinions dictate. Similarly, neither of them can see the other: Julian cannot see his mother for what she is; she cannot see what a miserable failure she has helped to create in him.

Our question then becomes: is there some ordering of values that for this story constitutes an alternative reality, one that in a sense judges everything the characters do? Our knowledge that Flannery O'Connor was known as a devout Catholic, or even that she herself talked about her stories in religious terms, can only alert us to one possible direction of interpretation. She might, after all, write one story that was entirely different from the others; for all I know, independently of my reading, she could have written this one before being converted, or after losing her faith. Even the most detailed knowledge about the author's life and statements of purpose can only alert me to certain possibilities; I must finally ask what kinds of clues the story itself provides to aid in the task of reconstructing a world of values that contrast with Julian's inanities.

The curious title is itself a kind of warning that seems to be spoken, as it were, in a special tone of voice. It simply does not harmonize easily with most of the surface, and indeed at first hardly makes sense at all. Does everything that "rises" in the story "converge"? Hardly. The black characters are "rising," but in spite of the liberal platitudes of Julian, there is no sign in the story that in their rising they will converge with the whites or with each other; one must thus ask whether or in what limited sense they are rising at all. Julian's liberal abstractions lead him to expect all Negroes to want his sympathy and interest, and to conform to his stereotyped demand that they "rise" to "talk on subjects that would be *above* the comprehension of those around him." But they insist on dwelling in a totally inaccessible world.

Julian has been "rising," too, as he obtains what he likes to think was a "first-class education." But his sense of elevation has, obviously, separated him not only from his mother but from all of his roots, without providing him with any other allegiances that could possibly support the claim of the title. What, then, can the title mean? It does not help us much to learn that it comes from the works of Teilhard de Chardin, the Catholic priest whose scientific and theological speculations earned him the accusation of heresy.

Is there any genuine change in the story that could be considered a "rising"? There is one, indeed, if we take seriously the change in Julian produced by the catastrophe. Julian is not just nasty and petty throughout the story; he is totally absorbed in his own ego. In contrast to his mother, who is "innocent," he is corrupt. Her desire is not to do ill in the world, but good, and only the limitations of what Julian calls her "fantasy world" betray her. But Julian, as we discover him behind his rationalizations, is actually malevolent, totally incapable of "converging" with the interests of any other person. His thoughts run constantly on his hatred of the world and his desire to "justify" himself in ways that he knows will hurt his mother deeply. "He would be entirely justified [in bringing home a Negro wife] but her blood pressure would rise to 300. He could not push her to the extent of making her have a stroke, and moreover, he had never been successful at making any Negro friends."

Throughout his absurd but vicious fantasies there thus run clues that prepare us for his discovery at the end. "For a moment he had an uncomfortable sense of her *innocence,* but it lasted only a second before *principle* rescued him. *Justice* entitled him to laugh." Dimly aware of her "innocence," passionately devoted to proving his own "principles" and obtaining "justice," he can be touched only by the greatest of disasters. Having never once been genuinely touched by any trouble, having in fact used his mother and her innocence as a shield against knowledge of himself, he is at last "stricken," "stunned." The change in him is as startling as the physical change produced in her by the stroke which he has helped to induce: "Darling, sweetheart, wait!" He is "crumpled," crushed into letting his defenses down and trying, too late, to call to his mother in love.

It would probably be a mistake to see anything strongly affirmative in this final dropping of all his egotistical defenses and crying "Mamma, mamma." He has not risen very far, but as he watches her destruction, falls at her side, and then runs for help, there has been, at last, a "convergence," a meeting of two human wills, that *might* presage his genuine "entry into the world of guilt and sorrow." For the Julian we have known throughout the story to experience either genuine guilt or sorrow would be a "rise" indeed, a rise based on the final convergence. The honest nightmare of his nothingness moving into "nowhere" in the final paragraph is thus a great improvement — in the light of this view of reality we now share with the implied author — over the "mental bubble" in which he established himself, where "he was safe from any kind of penetration from without." In his bubble he had been able to "see her with absolute clarity," or so he thought. Now, at the end, his bubble has been penetrated; he is swept by a "tide of darkness," and we are led to feel that he is for the first time in a position from which some sort of genuine human life is conceivable.

Whether this interpretation is sound or not, it certainly is never stated. Except for the ending, most of the words report Julian's misguided thoughts without open correction, and they must consequently be reconstructed. But they are not translated into a message.

There is perhaps no absolute need to go further than this. Readers of many different faiths and anti-faiths can presumably participate in this story of punishment and discovery, without pushing toward any special meaning for words like sin, innocence, faith, realities, guilt, and sorrow. But those of us who have read many of Flannery O'Connor's stories and studied her life will be unable to resist seeing Julian's final problematic redemption as presented in a religious light, even a specifically Roman Catholic light. Once the story is reread from this point of view, many additional ironies accumulate, ranging from Julian's name and his saintly posings at the beginning to the gratuitousness of grace at the end. But Flannery O'Connor was eager to write stories that were not mere allegories; as she intended, this story can be experienced by anyone who catches the essential contrast among the three systems of norms, Julian's, his mother's, and the cluster of traditional, conventional values we share with the author. Though it may seem thinner to those for whom Julian's self-absorption and cruelty are judged in secular terms than for a Catholic who sees him as in mortal sin, the structure of experience will be the same for both: Everyone will be forced to reject all or most of what the words seem to say. At every point we must decide on one out of many possible reconstructions, on the basis of a set of unshakable but silent beliefs that we are expected to share (however fleetingly) with the author. No one who fails to discern and feel some sympathy for these beliefs — only a few of them specifically Roman Catholic — is likely to make very much of the story.

For readers who do see behind Julian's absurd and egotistical words, the energy devoted to the act of seeing will of course increase the emotional effect and thus their estimate of the story's worth. This will not necessarily lead them to agree with me that it is a first-class story. But if they like it at all, the force of their liking will have been strengthened by the active engagement with the ironies.　　　　　　　　　　　　　　　　　　　　　　　　　　　　　　　[1974]

Anthony Di Renzo

A Dialogical Reading of Everything That Rises Must Converge

Bakhtin's[1] carnivalesque reading of history, of course, owes much to Marx, but such a view is far older. It harkens back to medieval folklore, to Lady Fortune and her wheel, and to the towering sarcasm and grotesque imagery of the Old Testament prophets. It is also one of the dominant themes of Flannery O'Connor's fiction, particularly *Everything That Rises Must Converge*. John Desmond's *Risen Sons: Flannery O'Connor's Vision of History* persuasively argues that O'Connor's late work wrestles specifically with the problem of historical change. Although the problem of history is a favorite subject among the other writers of the Southern Renaissance, O'Connor's work radically differs from theirs in tone and technique. Her older contemporaries use history as myth, a timeless matrix to which they can return in memory to shape and give meaning to their material. They are tragedians, elegists, poets. The chaos of history can be transcended by, sublimated into, the stillness of art — the Grecian urn that Faulkner's Ike McCaslin claims is the repository of the heart's secret truth.

O'Connor's attitude toward and depiction of history in *Everything That Rises Must Converge* is the opposite of Ike McCaslin's. She makes no attempt to transcend or sublimate its chaos. She is not a tragedian, an elegist, or a poet but a tumbler, a juggler, a contortionist. Her wildly comical stories focus on the timeliness of the present, not the timelessness of the past, and read prophetic signs into contemporary events and crises. O'Connor does not believe one can, or should, mentally return to the past to interpret one's life. Such a strategy is a dangerous and ludicrous form of solipsism, a dreamlike monologue denying all dialogue with the exterior world. Yet there is no escape from the present in *Everything That Rises Must Converge*. The world is a pitiless carnival that destroys people's most cherished illusions about the past. Mrs. Chestny's memories of her mansion and her black nanny, Tanner's dream of the old fishing hole explode in the faces of these characters like trick cigars. Rather than allowing her grotesques to slip into a nostalgic coma, which would mentally preserve their individual identities, O'Connor forces

---

[1] Mikhail Bakhtin (1895–1975) was a Russian literary critic who emphasized the primacy of language, rather than class or economics, in effecting historical change. In Bakhtin's theory, different "discourses" (languages specific to particular individuals, social groups, or cultures) compete in dialogue with each other, seeking power and control. Bakhtin saw the tumultuous medieval carnival as a place where unruly, rebellious, popular discourses were free to engage in dialogue with — and often undermine — the official "monologic" discourse of those in power, the Church and King.

them to lose themselves completely and physically in the violent flux of the present. The experience, more often than not, kills them.

Facing the historical present, however, was almost as painful for O'Connor as it is for her characters. The grotesqueness of much of the death-dealing satire in *Everything That Rises Must Converge* is an expression of the author's own ambivalent fascination with the great crisis that disrupted the South in the late fifties and early sixties: the rise of the civil rights movement. The grotesqueness of O'Connor's satire, however, can also be seen as a product of that crisis. Indeed, there is a direct correlation in her work between the processes of satire and the processes of history. Satire, according to Leon Guilhamet, transforms and mutates the established literary genres of the past to ironically comment on the present. A socially conscious art form, often dealing with crisis and breakdown, satire is parasitic in its approach, destabilizing in its effect: "The apparent instability of satire . . . is a normative condition by which the host genres are deformed or restructured to compose the satire. But even in this restructuring those host genres do not lose their internal defining traits. What they do lose is their dominant and defining relationship to the overall literary structure. Instead of dominating, the host genre plays a subordinate role in relation to the other generic strategies and to a deforming ironic pattern."

The grotesqueness of satire, in other words, is the grotesqueness of transition. The past is being "de-formed," is in the process of being "subsumed" by an "emerging" structure, a new way of seeing and speaking. History in *Everything That Rises Must Converge* works the same way, exhibits the same dynamics, particularly in the collection's more surrealistic stories about race relations. O'Connor depicts history as an ironic, darkly funny force that mutates forms; but these forms are social rather than literary: customs, morals, manners, values. Like satire, history de-forms the pattern of the past, subsumes it to an emerging gestalt so that new faces, new voices can be seen and heard. This "struggle" between an old way of life "stubbornly resisting" the new way of life "about to be born" is the poetics of the grotesque, which Bakhtin associates with "the crisis of change." That crisis breaks up a hitherto unchallenged, monolithic way of defining and articulating the world and paves the way for dramatic dialogue. Instead of one voice, there are many voices, contesting and redefining the truth. Alice Walker's conversation with her mother in her essay "Beyond the Peacock" has a direct bearing on our discussion of O'Connor. Mother and daughter sit in a Georgia diner discussing Southern letters:

> "One day I was invited to speak at a gathering of Mississippi librarians and before I could get started, one of the authorities on Mississippi history and literature got up and said she really *did* think Southerners wrote so well because 'we' lost the war. She was white, of course, but half the librarians in the room were black."
>
> "I bet she was real old," says my mother. "They're the only ones still worrying over that war."
>
> "So I got up and said no, 'we' didn't lose the war. '*You* all' lost the war. And you all's loss was our gain."

"Those old ones will just have to die out," says my mother.

"Well," I say, "I believe that the truth about any subject only comes when all the sides of the story are put together, and all their different meanings make one new one. Each writer writes the missing parts to the other writer's story. And the whole story is what I'm after."

"Well, I doubt if you can ever get the *true* missing parts of anything away from the white folks," my mother says softly, so as not to offend the waitress who is mopping up a nearby table; "they've sat on the truth so long by now they've mashed the life out of it."

The boldness, wit, and ferocity in this dialogue can help us to understand the peculiar tonal problems of *Everything That Rises Must Converge*. Readers have often been troubled by the ambivalence of O'Connor's narrator in this collection. She seems simultaneously to approve of and protest her characters' punishing deaths, to mock and to mourn them. It's as if there were not one narrator for these stories but two, engaged in a heated debate. O'Connor's wavering narrative tone recalls the dying Tanner's wavering vision in "Judgement Day." During his last moments, Tanner tries to keep two faces in focus — one pale, one dark. These faces are the two masks of O'Connor's Janus-like narrator: one black, one white. They represent the two sides, the two alternate interpretations of one of the major conflicts in *Everything That Rises Must Converge*: racial integration. Four of the nine stories in the collection deal directly or indirectly with this issue, and they are as eccentric as they are original. We are puzzled by O'Connor's technique. No matter how tragic the content of these stories, her style remains grotesquely comical. There are two explanations for this deliberate disjunction between form and content. The first is religious. For O'Connor, words like *integration* and *segregation*, *union* and *secession* have a universal as well as a local meaning. They take on a mythic dimension, a biblical concern with people's right relationship with God and with each other. Since O'Connor deliberately places the social tragedy of her white characters — the destruction of their pride, privilege, and heritage — against the cosmic background of Christian comedy — her characters' moral obligation to see that they and their black neighbors are equal in the eyes of God — she dissociates herself partly from their suffering and humiliation, never allows them to take center stage. This dissociation produces a certain alienation in the reader, provides the necessary distance for O'Connor's comedy.

The second explanation for the deliberate disjunction between form and content in O'Connor's work has more to do with history than religion, is closer in spirit to Brecht than to the Bible. The open-endedness of *Everything That Rises Must Converge* corresponds with the open-endedness of historical crisis and change. Alice Walker's retort to the white librarian about the Civil War — "You all's loss was our gain" — could serve as an epigraph to O'Connor's collection. Her stories queerly illustrate the simultaneous losses and gains of social conflict. As her white characters are decentered and disempowered, her black characters replace them and begin to assert themselves. Although we partly see this process through the eyes of O'Connor's middle-class whites, she prevents us from completely identifying with them.

Consequently, we interpret their individual destruction as part of a larger historical pattern. Seen against this larger pattern, their lives and death cease to be tragic, because what is tragic for them may not be tragic for others. O'Connor's narrator is acutely aware of this dichotomy, hence her ambivalent depiction of death and violence in "Everything That Rises Must Converge." The narrator clearly sympathizes with Mrs. Chestny, trying to maintain her self-identity under a "preposterous hat," the "banner" of her "imaginary dignity." But she also sympathizes with the enormous black woman who attacks her, who cannot stomach the condescension of a silly white woman giving her son "a bright new penny." These contradictory sympathies converge in Mrs. Chestny's stroke. Her death is both heartbreaking and grotesque. She falls apart before our eyes like a mechanical doll with a ruptured mainspring:

> She continued to plow ahead, paying no attention to [Julian]. Her hair had come undone on the side. She dropped her pocketbook and took no notice. He stooped and picked it up and handed it to her but she did not take it. . . .
>
> She was breathing fast.
>
> Let's wait on the bus," he said.
>
> "Home," she said thickly. . . .
>
> She continued to go as if she had not heard him. He took a few steps and caught her arm and stopped her. He looked into her face and caught his breath. He was looking into a face he had never seen before. "Tell Grandpa to come get me," she said.
>
> He stared, stricken.
>
> "Tell Caroline [her black nanny] to get me," she said.
>
> Stunned, he let her go and she lurched forward again, walking as if one leg were shorter than the other. A tide of darkness seemed to be sweeping her from him. "Mother!" he cried. "Darling, sweetheart, wait!" Crumpling, she fell to the pavement. He dashed forward and fell at her side, crying, "Mamma, Mamma!" He turned her over. Her face was fiercely distorted. One eye, large and staring, moved slightly to the left as if it had become unmoored. The other remained fixed on him, raked his face again, found nothing and closed.

In some ways, Julian's position — for all its snideness and shallowness — has been validated by the story: an old world is "gone," an old set of manners "obsolete," and Mrs. Chestny's graciousness "is not worth a damn." The black woman who wallops her is not "an uppity Negro woman" but "the whole colored race" who will no longer endure Mrs. Chestny's kind of institutional condescension. Competing with this position, however, is another point of view, one which longs for the manners and gentility of the old dispensation — just as Julian can pine away for the lost Chestny mansion while attacking his mother's narrowmindedness. "He never spoke of [the antebellum estate] without contempt or thought of it without longing," the narrator reports. This compelling blend of contempt and longing that exists in O'Connor's double-minded narrator perfectly expresses the peculiar schizophrenia created by historical change. As time and circumstance in

Everything That Rises Must Converge destroy the last vestige of the old white South, we hear a chorus of contradictory voices: "Drop dead! Don't go! Good riddance! What a loss!" The more monologic narrative world in the fiction of Allen Tate — where many opinions about race relations are entertained but few from the point of view of blacks — has become a crazy dialogue in the fiction of O'Connor. Blacks subversively speak for themselves in her world — in action if not always in words — and a more integrated picture of the South is presented, one which by necessity is unromantic and demythified. Alice Walker is a fervent admirer of O'Connor's grotesquely heightened realism: "It was for her description of white women that I appreciated her work at first, because when she set her pen to them not a whiff of magnolia hovered in the air (and the tree itself might never have been planted), and yes, I could say, yes, these white folks without the magnolia (who are indifferent to the tree's existence), and these black folks without melons and superior racial patience, these are like the Southerners I know."

O'Connor eschews the mythopoeic aesthetic of modernism, which sometimes characterizes the art of the Southern Renaissance. She has no use of the self-contained or the self-enchanted. Rather, her grotesque fiction is open-ended and disenchanted, based on the repartee of comedy, the slapstick exchange of farce. Her characters do not apostrophize a legendary past, do not speak in monologues or soliloquies. Overwhelmed by a banal present, they speak instead in fragments and clichés, verbally undermining each other. O'Connor's talent best expresses itself through the stream of history, not the stream of consciousness; the rush and tumble of action and dialogue, not the stillness of repose and meditation. Her narrator is not a hypnotically individualized voice — the virtuosos, orators, and tall-tale tellers we find in Faulkner — but a collective, a transcript of chatter from a crowded, tense, integrated bus. All loftiness and clarity disappear in a confusion of japes, growls, jokes, and squabbles. It is like a market, a carnival of noise.

The strange multiplicity of voices in O'Connor's fiction explains its fascinating polyphony. Now tender, now harsh, now engaged, now detached, it forms a humorously intricate counterpoint of emotions and reactions. O'Connor's narrator is no tragic soloist, but has the many voices of a comic opera ensemble — hence the briskness and flippancy of her fiction, its constantly shifting tone. The reader is trundled about in a high-powered clown cart, and amid the noise and confusion, even the most tragic things become funny. Flannery O'Connor's South is no less awful than William Faulkner's but she does not take it as seriously. Many of her stories, in fact, parody and trivialize the tragic themes of Faulkner's great novels. The threat of miscegenation, the ultimate abomination in *Absalom, Absalom!*, which causes Henry Sutpen to shoot Charles Bon, becomes something to snicker at in "Everything That Rises Must Converge," Julian's childish fantasy of raising his mother's blood pressure: "He imagined . . . the ultimate horror. He brought home a beautiful suspiciously Negroid woman. Prepare yourself, he said. There is nothing you can do about it. This is the woman I've chosen. She's intelligent, dignified, even good, and she's suffered and she hasn't thought it *fun*. Now persecute us, go ahead and persecute us." . . .   [1993]

CASEBOOK 3

LESLIE MARMON SILKO

Leslie Marmon Silko, as the critic Sven Birkerts has recognized in American Energies, *weaves together in her writing the "naturalistic narrative modes [of the European literary tradition] with the more startling mythopoeia of the indigenous storytelling tradition" she grew up with in her Native American tribe. This casebook begins with Silko's discussion of language and literature through a Pueblo Indian perspective, edited from an oral presentation in which Silko said that she deliberately spoke informally because she intended what she said to be heard, not read. Then, in an interview with Kim Barnes, Silko discusses her view of her audience and her background growing up in a matriarchal society. Two versions of a tribal story from scholars studying the Native American oral tradition may be compared with Silko's retelling of the legend in "Yellow Woman" (p. 1157). "Sun Steals Yellow Woman" is a Cochiti Pueblo tale collected by anthropologist Ruth Benedict and "Whirlwind Man Steals Yellow Woman" is a retelling of the story by poet and professor of literature Paula Gunn Allen. Finally, the literary critic Jim Ruppert considers Silko's reinterpretation of "Yellow Woman," and Linda L. Danielson gives a feminist reading of "Storyteller" (p. 1145) and "Lullaby" (p. 1138).*

LESLIE MARMON SILKO

Language and Literature from a Pueblo Indian Perspective

Where I come from, the words that are most highly valued are those which are spoken from the heart, unpremeditated and unrehearsed. Among the Pueblo people, a written speech or statement is highly suspect because the true feelings of the speaker remain hidden as he reads words that are detached from the occasion and the audience. I have intentionally not written a formal paper to read to this session because of this and because I want you to hear and to experience English in a nontraditional structure, a structure that follows patterns from the oral tradition. For those of you accustomed to a structure that moves from point A to point B to point C, this presentation may be somewhat difficult to follow because the structure of Pueblo expression resembles something like a spider's web — with many little threads radiating from a center, crisscrossing each other. As with the web, the structure will emerge as it is made and you must simply listen and trust, as the Pueblo people do, that meaning will be made.

I suppose the task that I have today is a formidable one because basically I come here to ask you, at least for a while, to set aside a number of basic approaches that you have been using and probably will continue to use in approaching the study of English or the study of language; first of all, I come to ask you to see language from the Pueblo perspective, which is a perspective that is very much concerned with including the whole of creation and the whole of history and time. And so we very seldom talk about breaking language down into words. As I will continue to relate to you, even the use of a specific language is less important than the one thing — which is the "telling," or the storytelling. And so, as Simon Ortiz has written, if you approach a Pueblo person and want to talk words or, worse than that, to break down an individual word into its components, ofttimes you will just get a blank stare, because we don't think of words as being isolated from the speaker, which, of course, is one element of the oral tradition. Moreover, we don't think of words as being alone: Words are always with other words, and the other words are almost always in a story of some sort.

Today I have brought a number of examples of stories in English because I would like to get around to the question that has been raised, or the topic that has come along here, which is what changes we Pueblo writers

---

This "essay" is an edited transcript of an oral presentation. The "author" deliberately did not read from a prepared paper so that the audience could experience firsthand one dimension of the oral tradition — non-linear structure. Her remarks were intended to be heard, not read.

might make with English as a language for literature. But at the same time I would like to explain the importance of storytelling and how it relates to a Pueblo theory of language.

So first I would like to go back to the Pueblo Creation story. The reason I go back to that story is because it is an all-inclusive story of creation and how life began. Tséitsínako, Thought Woman, by thinking of her sisters, and together with her sisters, thought of everything which is, and this world was created. And the belief was that everything in this world was a part of the original creation, and that the people at home realized that far away there were others — other human beings. There is even a section of the story which is a prophesy — which describes the origin of the European race, the African, and also remembers the Asian origins.

Starting out with this story, with this attitude which includes all things, I would like to point out that the reason the people are more concerned with story and communication and less with a particular language is in part an outgrowth of the area [pointing to a map] where we find oursleves. Among the twenty Pueblos there are at least six distinct languages, and possibly seven. Some of the linguists argue — and I don't set myself up to be a linguist at all — about the number of distinct languages. But certainly Zuni is all alone, and Hopi is all alone, and from mesa to mesa there are subtle differences in language — very great differences. I think that this might be the reason that what particular language was being used wasn't as important as what a speaker was trying to say. And this, I think, is reflected and stems or grows out of a particular view of the story — that is, that language *is* story. At Laguna many words have stories which make them. So when one is telling a story, and one is using words to tell the story, each word that one is speaking has a story of its own too. Often the speakers or tellers go into the stories of the words they are using to tell one story so that you get stories within stories, so to speak. This structure becomes very apparent in the storytelling, and what I would like to show you later on by reading some pieces that I brought is that this structure also informs the writing and the stories which are currently coming from Pueblo people. I think what is essential in this sense of story, and story within story, and the idea that one story is only the beginning of many stories, and the sense that stories never truly end. I would like to propose that these views of structure and the dynamics of storytelling are some of the contributions which Native American cultures bring to the English language or at least to literature in the English language.

First of all, a lot of people think of storytelling as something that is done at bedtime — that it is something that is done for small children. When I use the term "storytelling," I include a far wider range of telling activity. I also do not limit storytelling to simply old stories, but to again go back to the original view of creation, which sees that it is all part of a whole; we do not differentiate or fragment stories and experiences. In the beginning, Tséitsínako, Thought Woman, thought of all these things, and all of these things are held together as one holds many things together in a single thought.

So in the telling (and today you will hear a few of the dimensions of this telling) first of all, as was pointed out earlier, the storytelling always includes the audience and the listeners, and, in fact, a great deal of the story is believed to be inside the listener, and the storyteller's role is to draw the story out of the listeners. This kind of shared experience grows out of a strong community base. The storytelling goes on and continues from generation to generation.

The Origin story functions basically as a maker of our identity — with the story we know who we are. We are the Lagunas. This is where we came from. We came this way. We came by this place. And so from the time you are very young, you hear these stories, so that when you go out into the wider world, when one asks who you are, or where are you from, you immediately know: We are the people who came down from the north. We are the people of these stories. It continues down into clans so that you are not just talking about Laguna Pueblo people, you are talking about your own clan. Within the clans there are stories which identify the clan.

In the Creation story, Antelope says that he will help knock a hole in the earth so that the people can come up, out into the next world. Antelope tries and tries, and he uses his hooves and is unable to break through; and it is then that Badger says, "Let me help you." And Badger very patiently uses his claws and digs a way through, bringing the people into the world. When the Badger clan people think of themselves, or when the Antelope people think of themselves, it is as people who are of *this* story, and this is *our* place, and we fit into the very beginning when the people first came, before we began our journey south.

So you can move, then, from the idea of one's identity as a tribal person into clan identity. Then we begin to get to the extended family, and this is where we begin to get a kind of story coming into play which some people might see as a different kind of story, though Pueblo people do not. Anthropologists and ethnologists have, for a long time, differentiated the types of oral language they find in the Pueblos. They tended to rule out all but the old and sacred and traditional stories and were not interested in family stories and the family's account of itself. But these family stories are just as important as the other stories — the older stories. These family stories are given equal recognition. There is no definite, pre-set pattern for the way one will hear the stories of one's own family, but it is a very critical part of one's childhood, and it continues on throughout one's life. You will hear stories of importance to the family — sometimes wonderful stories — stories about the time a maternal uncle got the biggest deer that was ever seen and brought back from the mountains. And so one's sense of who the family is, and who you are, will then extend from that — "I am from the family of my uncle who brought in this wonderful deer, and it was a wonderful hunt" — so you have this sort of building or sense of identity.

There are also other stories, stories about the time when another uncle, perhaps, did something that wasn't really acceptable. In other words, this process of keeping track, of telling, is an all-inclusive process which begins to create a total picture. So it is very important that you know all of the stories — both positive and not so positive — about one's own family. The reason that it is very important to keep track of all the stories in one's own family is because you are liable to hear a story from somebody else who is perhaps an enemy of the family, and you are liable to hear a version which has been changed, a version which makes your family sound disreputable — something that will taint the honor of the family. But if you have already heard the story, you know your family's version of what *really* happened that night, so when somebody else is mentioning it, you will have a version of the story to counterbalance it. Even when there is no way around it — old Uncle Pete did a terrible thing — by knowing the stories that come out of other families, by keeping very close watch, listening constantly to learn the stories about other families, one is in a sense able to deal with terrible sorts of things that might happen within one's own family. When a member of one's own family does something that cannot be excused, one always knows stories about similar things which happened in other families. And it is not done maliciously. I think it is very important to realize this. Keeping track of all the stories within the community gives a certain distance, a useful perspective which brings incidents down to a level we can deal with. If others have done it before, it cannot be so terrible. If others have endured, so can we.

The stories are always bringing us together, keeping this whole together, keeping this family together, keeping this clan together. "Don't go away, don't isolate yourself, but come here, because we have all had these kinds of experiences" — this is what the people are saying to you when they tell you these other stories. And so there is this constant pulling together to resist what seems to me to be a basic part of human nature: When some violent emotional experience takes place, people get the urge to run off and hide or separate themselves from others. And of course, if we do that, we are not only talking about endangering the group, we are also talking about the individual or the individual family never being able to recover or to survive. Inherent in this belief is the feeling that one does not recover or get well by one's self, but it is together that we look after each other and take care of each other.

In the storytelling, then, we see this process of bringing people together, and it works not only on the family level, but also on the level of the individual. Of course, the whole Pueblo concept of the individual is a little bit different from the usual Western concept of the individual. But one of the beauties of the storytelling is that when something happens to an individual, many people will come to you and take you aside, or maybe a couple of people will come and talk to you. These are occasions of storytelling. These occasions of storytelling are continuous; they are a way of life.

Storytelling lies at the heart of the Pueblo people, and so when someone comes in and says, "When did they tell the stories, or what time of day does the storytelling take place?" that is a ridiculous question. The storytelling goes on constantly — as some old grandmother puts on the shoes of a little child and tells the child the story of a little girl who didn't wear her shoes. At the same time somebody comes into the house for coffee to talk with an adolescent boy who has just been into a lot of trouble, to reassure him that *he* got into that kind of trouble, or somebody else's son got into that kind of trouble too. You have this constant ongoing process, working on many different levels.

One of the stories I like to bring up about helping the individual in crisis is a recent story, and I want to remind you that we make no distinctions between the stories — whether they are history, whether they are fact, whether they are gossip — these distinctions are not useful when we are talking about this particular experience with language. Anyway, there was a young man who, when he came back from the war in Vietnam, had saved up his Army pay and bought a beautiful red Volkswagen Beetle. He was very proud of it, and one night drove up to a place right across the reservation line. It is a very notorious place for many reasons, but one of the more notorious things about the place is a deep arroyo behind the place. This is the King's Bar. So he ran in to pick up a cold six-pack to take home, but he didn't put on his emergency brake. And his little red Volkswagen rolled back into the arroyo and was all smashed up. He felt very bad about it, but within a few days everybody had come to him and told him stories about other people who had lost cars to that arroyo. And probably the story that made him feel the best was about the time that George Day's station wagon, with his mother-in-law and kids in the back, rolled into that arroyo. So everybody was saying, "Well, at least your mother-in-law and kids weren't in the car when it rolled in," and you can't argue with that kind of story. He felt better then because he wasn't alone anymore. He and his smashed-up Volkswagen were now joined with all the other stories of cars that fell into that arroyo.

There are a great many parallels between Pueblo experiences and the remarks that have been made about South Africa and the Caribbean countries — similarities in experiences so far as language is concerned. More specifically, with the experience of English being imposed upon the people. The Pueblo people, of course, have seen intruders come and intruders go. The first they watched come were the Spaniards; while the Spaniards were there, things had to be conducted in Spanish. But as the old stories say, if you wait long enough, they'll go. And sure enough, they went. Then another bunch came in. And old stories say, well, if you wait around long enough, not so much that they'll go, but at least their ways will go. One wonders now, when you see what's happening to technocratic-industrial culture, now that we've used up most of the sources of energy, you think perhaps the old people are right.

But anyhow, our experience with English has been different because the Bureau of Indian Affairs schools were so terrible that we never heard of Shakespeare. There was Dick and Jane, and I can remember reading that the robins were heading south for winter, but I knew that all winter the robins were around Laguna. It took me a long time to figure out what was going on. I worried for quite a while about the robins because they didn't leave in the winter, not realizing that the textbooks were written in Boston. The big textbook companies are up here in Boston and *their* robins do go south in the winter. But this freed us and encouraged us to stay with our narratives. Whatever literature we received at school (which was damn little), at home the storytelling, the special regard for telling and bringing together through the telling, was going on constantly. It has continued, and so we have a great body of classical oral literature, both in the narratives and in the chants and songs.

As the old people say, "If you can remember the stories, you will be all right. Just remember the stories." And, of course, usually when they say that to you, when you are young, you wonder what in the world they mean. But when I returned — I had been away from Laguna Pueblo for a couple of years, well more than a couple of years after college and so forth — I returned to Laguna and I went to Laguna-Acoma high school to visit an English class, and I was wondering how the telling was continuing, because Laguna Pueblo, as the anthropologists have said, is one of the more acculturated pueblos. So I walked into this high school English class and there they were sitting, these very beautiful Laguna and Acoma kids. But I knew that out in their lockers they had cassette tape recorders, and I knew that at home they had stereos, and they were listening to Kiss and Led Zeppelin and all those other things. I was almost afraid, but I had to ask — I had with me a book of short fiction (it's called *The Man to Send Rain Clouds* [New York: Viking Press, 1974]), and among the stories of other Native American writers, it has stories that I have written and Simon Ortiz has written. And there is one particular story in the book about the killing of a state policeman in New Mexico by three Acoma Pueblo men. It was an act that was committed in the early fifties. I was afraid to ask, but I had to. I looked at the class and I said, "How many of you heard this story before you read it in the book?" And I was prepared to hear this crushing truth that indeed the anthropologists were right about the old traditions dying out. But it was amazing, you know, almost all but one or two students raised their hands. They had heard that story, just as Simon and I had heard it, when we were young. That was my first indication that storytelling continues on. About half of them had heard it in English, about half of them had heard it in Laguna. I think again, getting back to one of the original statements, that if you begin to look at the core of the importance of the language and how it fits in with the culture, it is the *story* and the feeling of the story which matters more than what language it's told in.   [1979]

KIM BARNES

An Interview with Leslie Marmon Silko

KB: The first question I want to ask you is, who do you consider to be your audience? Who are you writing for?

LS: I've never thought too much about an audience per se. When I first started writing, I wasn't sure that anyone would want to read or listen to the work that I did. I didn't think about it at first. In a way, it's good not to think about an audience. If you start thinking about the audience, it can inhibit what you do. When I was younger, there was concern about what will Grandma think, or what will Mama say or something like this, and that in a sense is being concerned about audience and can really inhibit a writer. Initially, I guess I assumed that I wouldn't have to worry about an audience because there would not be an audience. I didn't think about it, and I didn't even worry too much about what Mama would think or what Grandma would think or what Uncle So-and-So would think or what the people would think because at first I didn't think that I would ever have to worry that they would see what I had written. Now, I'm working on this new novel which is long and complex to the point of being foolhardy. Who knows, a polite way would be to call it an ambitious project. But I'm so caught up in trying to see if I can make it happen. It's sort of a personal challenge, and again I'm not thinking about an audience. I've been quoted in other interviews as saying that I want this novel to be a novel that, when you shop at a Safeway store, it will be in the little wire racks at the check-out station and that I don't want to write something that the MLA [Modern Language Association] will want. I want something that will horrify the people at the MLA. Mostly, I'm teasing, but in another way I'm not. I'm sad to see that so little serious fiction gets out into the world. I was amazed that Umberto Eco's *The Name of the Rose* and Mark Helprin's book *Winter's Tale* made it to the wire racks at the check-out stands in the United States. So I'm probably only part-way serious when I say that I don't think about an audience.

KB: So you didn't write a book like *Storyteller* for a particularly white or Indian audience.

LS: I don't think about Indian and white. What I wanted to do was clarify the interrelationship between the stories I had heard and my sense of story-telling and language that had been given to me by the old folks, the people back home. I gave examples of what I heard as best I could remember, and how I developed these elements into prose, into fiction and into poetry, moving from what was basically an oral tradition into a written tradition. The way I figured it, there would be some Native American people who would be interested in it and some Laguna Pueblo people who would be interested in it. There might be other people who are working out of a different cultural tradition but still working with oral material and working in their own art to bring the two together who would be interested. The book is for people who are interested in that relationship between the spoken and the written.

KB: Do you consider yourself a storyteller in a traditional sense?

LS: No, not at all. My friend Mei-mei Berssenbrugge, the poet, spent some time at Laguna Pueblo a few years ago, and she sat in on a kind of a session. I hesitate to call it a storytelling session because they're real sponta-neous. It was at my uncle's house, and my uncle's wife Anita and her two sisters were there and some other people. It was in the evening and everyone was feeling jolly and talking. We might have started out with some kind of notorious incident that had happened recently, and pretty soon Mei-mei was sitting there listening to the way people would relate something that hap-pened, and we'd all laugh and then one of Anita's sister's would say, "Well, you remember the time," then the other sister would take over. When the whole session was over, we all went back over to my grandma's house where Mei-mei and I were staying, and Mei-mei said, "They really have a way of telling these stories and incidents and kind of playing off one another." She was really impressed, and I said, "See, I'm not in that class at all." I suppose if I didn't have the outlook of the writer, I might get better at storytelling, but I always say that I'm not good at giving off-the-cuff presentations. Oh, sometimes I have a fine moment. If you really want to hear people who can get rolling in telling, you have to go down to Laguna and kind of fall into the right situation, right feelings and right time.

KB: Was a storyteller a spiritual leader? Was he or she someone who was born into or inherited that role?

LS: It's not like that at all. There is a period of time at the winter solstice when people get together for four days and four nights, and they re-tell all the stories connected with the emergence and the migration of the People. There are people who have to learn and remember those stories and people who have to participate in that telling and re-telling once a year. Those people would probably be designated persons, but they would not be specially designated in any kind of ceremonial or religious way. They wouldn't be called storytellers; they would be called ceremonial religious leaders. The key to understanding storytellers and storytelling at Laguna Pueblo is to realize that you grow up not just being aware of narrative and making a story or seeing a story in what happens to you and what goes on around you all the time, but just being appreciative and delighted in narrative exchanges. When you meet somebody at a post office, he or she says, "How are you, how are you doing?" At Laguna, people will stand there and they'll tell you how they are doing. At Laguna, it's a way of interacting. It isn't like there's only one storyteller designated. That's not it at all. It's a whole way of being. When I say "storytelling," I don't just mean sitting down and telling a once-upon-a-time kind of story. I mean a whole way of seeing yourself, the people around you, your life, the place of your life in the bigger context, not just in terms of nature and location, but in terms of what has gone on before, what's happened to other people. So it's a whole way of being, but there are some people who are willing to be funnier or better storytellers than others, and some people because they are older or they remember better, have a larger repertoire of the *humma-hah* stories. It's not at all like the Irish idea of the bard or the chosen one.

KB: Why are you writing these stories? Are you trying to put the oral tradition in a more stable or lasting form? Do you think anything is lost in the writing down of these stories?

LS: Well, no, I'm not trying to save them, I'm not trying to put them in a stable or lasting form. I write them down because I like seeing how I can translate this sort of feeling or flavor or sense of a story that's told and heard onto the page. Obviously, some things will be lost because you're going from one medium to another. And I use *translate* in the broadest sense. I don't mean translate from the Laguna Pueblo language to English, I mean the feeling or the sense that language is being used orally. So I play with the page and things that you could do on the page, and repetitions. When you have an audience, when you're telling a story and people are listening, there's repetition of crucial points. That's something that on the printed page looks really crummy and is redundant and useless, but in the actual telling is necessary. So I play around with the page by using different kinds of spacing or indentations or even italics so that the reader can sense, say, that the tone of the voice has changed. If you were hearing a story, the speed would increase at certain points. I want to see how much I can make the page communicate those nuances and shifts to the reader. I'm intrigued with that. I recognize the inherent problem; there's no way that hearing a story and reading a story are the same thing; but that doesn't mean that everyone should throw up his hands and say it can't be done or say that what's done on the page isn't catching some of those senses. When I read off the page and read some of the *humma-hah* stories that I wrote down or go through some of the Aunt Susie material, then of course, I think it's more persuasive. In a way, that's not fair; because I'm reading it out loud, I've gone back again. But I think there are some instances where I've been successful so that the reader has a sense of how it might sound if I were reading it to him or her.

KB: In a work like *Storyteller*, are you actually creating something, or are you simply re-telling a myth?

LS: Every time a story is told, and this is one of the beauties of the oral tradition, each telling is a new and unique story, even if it's repeated word for word by the same teller sitting in the same chair. I work to try to help the reader have the sense of how it would sound if the reader could be hearing it. That's original. And no matter how carefully I remember, memory gets all mixed together with imagination. It does for everybody. But I don't change the spirit or the mood or the tone of the story. For some stories, I could just hear Aunt Susie's voice reverberating. The challenge was to get it down so you could have a sense of my Aunt Susie's sound and what it was like. Earlier you said something about writing the stories down in some way that they would be saved. Nobody saves stories. Writing down a story, even tape-recording stories, doesn't save them in the sense of saving their life within a community. Stories stay alive within the community like the Laguna Pueblo community because the stories have a life of their own. The life of the story is not something that any individual person can save and certainly not someone writing it down or recording it on tape or video. That's a nice little idea, and in some places where they've had these kind of archival materials, younger people can go and see or listen to certain stories. But if for whatever reasons the community no longer has a place for a story or a story no longer has a life within that particular period, that doesn't mean that the story no longer has life; that's something that no single person can decide. The old folks at Laguna would say, "If it's important, you'll remember it." If it's really important, if it really has a kind of substance that reaches to the heart of the community life and what's gone before and what's gone later, it will be remembered. And if it's not remembered, the people no longer wanted it, or it no longer had its place in the community.

People outside the community are often horrified to hear some old-timer say, "No, I won't tell my stories to the tape recorder. No, I won't put them on video tape. If these younger folks don't listen and remember from me, then maybe these stories are meant to end with me." It's very tough-minded. It flies in the face of all the anthropologists and people who get moist-eyed over what a good turn they're doing for the Native American communities by getting down these stories. I tend to align myself with the tougher-minded people. The folks at home will say, "If it's important, if it has relevance, it will stay regardless of whether it's on video tape, taped, or written down." It's only the western Europeans who have this inflated pompous notion that every word, everything that's said or done is real important, and it's got to live on and on forever. And only Americans think that America, which has barely been around 200 years, which is a joke, what a short period of time, only Americans think that we'll just continue on. It takes a tremendous amount of stupid blind self-love to think that your civilization or your culture will continue on, when all you have to do is look at history and see that civilizations and people a lot better than people building the MX have disappeared. . . .

KB: In *Ceremony*, you write about a man's experience. Do you feel like you were going outside of your experience in doing this? Is the Native American male's experience much different from the female's?

LS: Well, I don't know if it is or not since I never was a Native American male, you know. But what I do believe is that again, on that deep, deep level, that deep level where we're moved to fear, sorrow, loss, joy, camaraderie, on that deep level, men and women are the same, just like all human beings are. The way the heart pushes in the chest feels the same, whether a woman or a man is experiencing terror. What would trigger it will differ. A woman walking alone at night can be terrified by the sound of other footsteps; it wouldn't necessarily terrify a man, unless an hour before some guys had said, "Look buddy, we're going to get you." Then I think the same physiological response would be there. In *Ceremony*, the male character was dealing with grief and loss and rage and a kind of sickness at heart and loneliness; I have great faith that my consciousness and experience on that level of feeling is true for him.

People have noticed that I write about men and what they did and how they hung out together and so on. That's more complex. In Laguna Pueblo, little girls aren't kept with the women, and little boys aren't kept with the men. Children sort of range freely, and men and women range freely. The division of labor at Laguna Pueblo, especially when I was growing up, was much more flexible. Whoever was strong enough and ready to do a certain task would do it.

I had this omnivorous appetite for watching people do things. And I watched how my great-grandmother got down on her knees even when she was old and feeble, but I also watched how men built things. Nobody shooed me away, no one told me girls couldn't watch men build a shed. In the Pueblo, men don't go off as much. It's not like your middle-America, white middle-class man who goes off to work, and work is far away from where the women and children are. In the Pueblo, the men are around. There's all kinds of stuff going on, and people are very busy. I spent a lot of time listening and watching men from the time I was a little girl. And I think that more people, women and men, could write about one another if there wasn't this kind of segregation of the sexes that we have in America. Men can handle writing about women only insofar as they are getting them into or out of bed. But, you know, that isn't because it can't be done, that isn't because only men know what men do, that's because in this particular stupid, great middle-America society, men and women really don't know very much about one another. But that doesn't mean that it is inherent and that it has to be. That's just this one particular place in time.

KB: I find the yellow woman Kochininako, particularly interesting. Do you see the myths concerning her as having arisen from the need for escape on the part of the women from a kind of social and sexual domination?

LS: No, not at all. The need for that kind of escape is the need of a woman in middle-America, a white Anglo, the WASP woman. In the Pueblo, the lineage of the child is traced through the mother, so it's a matrilineal system. The houses are the property of the woman, not the man. The land is generally passed down through the female side because the houses belong to the women. One of my early memories was when our house needed to be replastered with the traditional adobe and mud plaster. It was a crew of women who came and plastered the house. Why? The women own the houses so the women maintain what they own. The kinds of things that cause white upper-middle-class women to flee the home for awhile to escape or get away from domination and powerlessness and inferior status, *vis-a-vis* the husband, and the male, those kinds of forces are not operating, they're not operating at all. What's operating in those stories of Kochininako is this attraction, this passion, this connection between the human world and the animal and spirit worlds. Buffalo Man is a buffalo, and he can be in the form of a buffalo, but there is this link, and the link is sealed with sexual intimacy, which is emblematic of that joining of two worlds. At the end of the story, the people have been starving, and the buffalo says, "We will give up our spirits, we will come and die for these people because we are related to them. Kochininako is our sister-in-law." She's a . . . what do you call it in anthropology or sociology, one who shatters the cultural paradigms or steps through or steps out. She does that because there's a real overpowering sexual attraction that's felt. The attraction is symbolized by or typified by the kind of sexual power that draws her to the buffalo man, but the power which draws her to Buffalo Man is actually the human, the link, the animal and human world, those two being drawn together. It's that power that's really operating, and the sexual nature of it is just a metaphor for that power. So that's what's going on there. It doesn't have anything to do with, "Things are really bad at home, so I think I'll run off for awhile." That's not what it's about.

KB: I wanted to ask you a question about the mother figures in some of your work. I was trying to look for a word to describe them. I couldn't quite come up with it. Ambivalent is the wrong word, but you never know quite how to feel about them. For instance, in the very first story in *Storyteller*, the little girl wants corn to eat, and she drowns herself in the lake because her mother won't give it to her. And there's the mother in *Ceremony* . . .

LS: And then the aunt and the mother's sister. I know what you're talking about. People, women especially, ask me about that and men too. It's a real tough one. The story about the little girl who ran away, that's a story which is very clear in *Storyteller*. It's a story that Aunt Susie liked to tell. In a matrilineal society, in a matriarchy, and especially in this particular matriarchy, the women, as I've already said, control the houses, the lineage of the children, and a lot of the decisions about marriages and so forth. In a sense, the women have called the shots pretty much in the world of relationships and the everyday world. While the Pueblo women were kind of running the show, buying and selling sheep, and of course the Navajos are the same way too, the women making many of the business decisions, the Pueblo men would be taking care of ceremonial matters or maybe out hunting. Although there have been a few Laguna women who were great hunters also. So the female, the mother, is a real powerful person, and she's much more the authority figure. It's a kind of reversal. Your dad is the one who's the soft-touch, and it's the mother's brother who reprimands you. If you're really out of hand and she can't deal with you, it will be your mother's brother, not your father, she goes to. When a man marries, he goes to his wife's house or household or whatever, and his position is one you can feel more of an alliance with . . . more of an alliance with the father because he, in some ways, has less power in that household. So when you have a story like that one, that explains it. But then, how do you explain Tao's mother who is kind of a lost and unfortunate figure, or how do we explain Aunti? And people have talked about how my male characters have vulnerability and all kinds of complexities and the women . . . they're not as vulnerable. You have to have some vulnerability in a character for readers to be able to establish some kind of link with them. So why don't we see that in my female characters? We have to go back, I suppose, to the women I grew up with. I grew up with women who were really strong, women with a great deal of power, let us say, within the family. And I think about that, and I try to think about my mother: is there something about the way she and I have gotten along, or how we related to one another? But, just remember what the position of the father and the mother would be in Pueblo society. If someone was going to thwart you or frighten you, it would tend to be a woman; you see it coming from your mother, or sent by your mother. . . .   [1986]

Sun Steals Yellow Woman

Collected by Ruth Benedict

At old Cochiti (Tiputse) lived a man and his wife. His name was Stilina (dance shells). His wife went for water and Sun came and stole her. Her husband didn't know where she had gone. He mourned for her and tried to follow her tracks. He was lying in a muddy place and something crawled on his neck and spoke to him. It was Spider Woman. She said, "What are you doing here?" "I'm mourning for my wife who was stolen from me." "Don't think of her, my son, and keep wondering where your wife is. Your wife is where the sun comes up. There are two roads to that place, a new and an old. Don't follow the new road; take the old. On the new road a dangerous person will kill you. So go the old road."

He started on his journey. When he came to the two roads, he wondered why Spider Woman had said not to go by the good road, so he took the new road. He came to the house of Whirlwind Man. He was out hunting, only his mother was at home. She set out food for her guest. He was still eating, when he heard Whirlwind Man coming. He came in. They fought. The mother tried to separate them, but Shell Man killed Whirlwind Man. His mother was frightened. She said, "Hurry, hurry, press his stomach. See if you can make him alive again." Then Shell Man pressed him, and he came to life. Then his mother said to her son, "Don't fight with this man any more, my son. It is because of Shell Man that you are alive again." She put food out again.

Whirlwind Man said to Shell Man, "I will take you where you wish to go." So he took him where Sun rises. Whirlwind Man picked him up and took him to the top of the high cliffs where his wife was. Whirlwind Man said to Shell Man, "Go over yonder, you will find her alone. Sun is out hunting." He went into Sun's house, and he found his wife grinding. She was frightened. "How did you get here, my husband? Nobody comes here, it is too dangerous." "I've come to get you. Before Sun comes home from hunting I will take you back." She got ready. They went out before Sun came home. When they got where Whirlwind was waiting, he started homeward with them.

Sun came home and the woman was gone. He shot an arrow after them but it fell to one side. They were safe, no man can harm a woman while she is carrying his child. They reached Whirlwind Man's house. "We have to go on to our home," they said. They came to their own house. While they were coming along the road, Sun shot another arrow. Shell Man cried, "Hurry up, we must go faster, the man who stole you is coming after us!" Sun was shooting. When they got to Tiputse, Sun was right behind them, but the woman was safe. Sun said to Yellow Woman, "You shall have a child and he shall be chief of this people." [1936]

PAULA GUNN ALLEN

Whirlwind Man Steals Yellow Woman

Kochinnenako, Yellow Woman, was grinding corn one day with her three sisters. They looked into the water jars and saw that they were empty. They said, "We need some water." Kochinnenako said she would go, and taking the jars made her way across the mesa and went down to the spring. She climbed the rockhewn stairs to the spring that lay in a deep pool of shade. As she knelt to dip the gourd dipper into the cool shadowed water, she heard someone coming down the steps. She looked up and saw Whirlwind Man. He said, "Gutwatzi, Kochinnenako. Are you here?"

"Da'waa'e," she said, dipping water calmly into the four jars beside her. She didn't look at him.

"Put down the dipper," he said. "I want you to come with me."

"I am filling these jars with water as you can see," she said. "My sisters and I are grinding corn, and they are waiting for me."

"No," Whirlwind Man said. "You must come and go with me. If you won't come, well, I'll have to kill you." He showed her his knife.

Kochinnenako put the dipper down carefully. "All right," she said. "I guess I'll go with you." She got up. She went with Whirlwind Man to the other side of the world where he lived with his mother, who greeted her like his wife.

The jars stayed, tall and fat and cool in the deep shade by the shadowed spring.

That was one story. She knew they laughed about Kochinnenako. Brought her up when some woman was missing for awhile. Said she ran off with a Navajo, or maybe with a mountain spirit, "Like Kochinnenako." Maybe the name had become synonymous with "whore" at Guadalupe. Ephanie knew that Yellow was the color of woman, ritual color of faces painted in death, or for some of the dances. But there was a tone of dismissal, or derision there that she couldn't quite pin down, there anyway. No one told how Kochinnenako went with Whirlwind Man because she was forced. Said, "Then Whirlwind Man raped Kochinnenako." Rather, the story was that his mother had greeted Yellow Woman, and made her at home in their way. And that when Kochinnenako wanted to return home, had agreed, asking only that she wait while the old woman prepared gifts for Kochinnenako's sisters.

Ephanie wondered if Yellow Woman so long ago had known what was happening to her. If she could remember it or if she thought maybe she had dreamed it. If they laughed at her, or threw her out when she returned. She wondered if Kochinnenako cried. [1983]

JIM RUPPERT

Storytelling: The Fiction of Leslie Silko

Leslie Silko as a contemporary writer and a Laguna brings a new perception to the effort to topple [the boundaries of fiction], or rather an old one, older than American Literature. Her short fiction and her novel *Ceremony* are illuminated by the assumption that the story has a greater, truer reality than the objective reality of the world around us. In the story reality, the seeming simplicity and reality of objective actions are reinterpreted and woven into a larger scheme through which the actions take on a new and deeper meaning and their place in a mythic pattern emerges. The characters and the readers must believe as much as the author that the world exists in story which gives objective reality its meaning, or they are lost. Although the story may be stretched over eons, although it may move slowly and our understanding of it come only with great difficulty, we can understand it; we can enter into the story reality. Despite the hardships and the violent wrenchings of perspective required to do this, the attempt is necessary because it is only through entry into the story reality that each character is given his/her identity and perhaps ultimately so are we, the readers.

The "Yellow Woman" is an excellent example of the larger, all-encompassing reality of the story through which individual objective actions are reinterpreted and given new meaning. The contemporary girl by the river is incorporated into the traditional mythic Laguna story. In the Laguna story, Yellow Woman is near the river where she is surprised by a mountain spirit. The mountain spirit seduces her, and they go through a series of interesting adventures before she returns home, rather reluctantly to her husband and relatives. The original Yellow Woman of the Laguna tale is aware of the inevitability of her actions; it has been ordained since time immemorial. In Silko's story, a young girl is seduced by the river and swept away by someone who says he is a mountain spirit. She feels that an old Laguna story is patterning the encounter. The girl becomes confused and uncertain about her identity; is she the person she always thought she was, the one living in an objective mundane reality, or is she becoming Yellow Woman of the stories? She struggles to affirm that she is a girl with her own name and a family, to establish time boundaries and boundaries between objective reality and myths. "I don't have to go," she says to the man. "What they tell in stories was real only then, back in time immemorial, like they say." As she goes off with the mountain spirit man, she cries that if only she might see someone who knew her, who could place her in the objective reality, she would be sure of her identity. "I will see someone, and then I will be certain that he is only a man — some man from nearby — and I will be sure I am not Yellow Woman." But the reality of the story triumphs and following the Laguna story, she runs off with the man. She is seduced into the story and goes off into the mountains where time seems to matter little and where she sees the larger pattern. When she leaves her husband, a new meaning is given it, and on the mountain she sees the larger patterns of living: in her own words, she can see "the world."

The girl's merging into the story seems to occur in part because it is ordained (a fortuitous collection of particulars), but more important the girl projects the proper psychic framework of a balanced being, while she is wondering if Yellow Woman herself had a sense of a separate identity or knew she was to become a story. The girl at this time is able to live totally in the present, in the story flow. "This is the way it happens in the stories, I was thinking with no thought beyond the moment she meets the Ka'tsina spirit and they go." At this time, the girl is thinking about her identity, not about the past or the future, for identity, as all existentialists know, reveals a child of the present moment. As if understanding the girl's thoughts and anticipation of her words, the mountain spirit man says, "What happened yesterday has nothing to do with what you will do today, Yellow Woman." Her description of her departure emphasizes the power of the story and her non-willful entering into it. "They [the girl's family] will go on like before, except there will be a story about the day I disappeared while I was walking along the river. Silva had come for me; he said he had. I did not decide to go. I just went. Moonflowers blossom in the sand hills before dawn, just as I followed him." When she finally returns home, according to the traditional story pattern, she speaks of "my story" and wishes that old grandpa was still alive because, as a storyteller, he would understand the identity the story gave her. In an interview in *Suntracks*, Silko explains this function of stories in oral traditions.

> That's how you know, that's how you belong, that's how you know you belong, if the stories incorporate you into them. There have to be stories. It's stories that make this a community. People tell those stories about you and your family or about others and they begin to create your identity. In a sense, you are told who you are, or you know who you are by the stories that are told about you. . . .

In "Storyteller" the reality of the story and the individual's identity are woven together into one story reality that patterns all others. The girl's revenge, the bear's revenge on the hunter, and the land's revenge on the Gussucks lose their separateness and merge at the end of the story. In the beginning, the girl is ignorant of her identity. The old storyteller begins a long story of the hunter and the bear designed to explain and ease the approach of the "final winter" and the killing cold. As the girl outlines her own story, she listens more closely to the old man's story. They seem to coincide. She knows that the larger story, the one of the coming of the final winter, of the final retribution, will soon be completed.

> Somewhere the sea and land met; she knew by their dark green colors there would be no boundaries between them. That was how the cold would come: when the boundaries were gone, the polar ice would range across the land into the sky.

Just as the land and sky will lose their boundaries, so too the girl loses the boundaries between objective reality and the story, between the present flow of the story and ideas of the past and future — all will be the story. When she runs out on the ice, she enters the story reality of no boundaries. She has no identity and doesn't know where she is. Finally, she recognizes the red tin, part of the story of her parents. Before this recognition, the story could have ended incorrectly, but now she is guided by the story pattern and no longer confused by the dissolution of the boundaries. She is saved, and the store-keeper dies. After this, she has an identity, not only that of storyteller in the community, but also an identity created by the all-inclusive story of the destruction of the Gussucks.

What I think we see in Silko's short fiction is that the story has a greater reality than objective reality, and that this story reality can be entered by placing ourselves in proximity to the story and acting with no thought beyond the moment so as to enter the story. In story reality, we assume an identity meaningful not only for ourselves, but also for the community that lives through the story. . . .

It may be commonplace to say that Silko's work attempts to introduce dimensions of oral literature into written literature, and seeks a unification of the two in a new reality or a better explanation of the ordinary one, but her work at once stands out from modern fiction because of it and blends with it.

Of course, modern writers have injected and explored the mythic dimension in their works, but normally it has been in the creation of personal myths as with Yeats, the reemergence of mythic patterns as structural aides to meaning as in Joyce and Lawrence, or the exposé and potential salvation of a disintegrated culture as with Eliot. In the development of contemporary fiction, "self-conscious" fiction struggles to incorporate the consciousness of the writer writing the story into the story, thus creating a myth of the writer. The result is that fiction and reality merge into one sphere. Silko, while having a different mission in inviting the story reality into what appears to be a non-story world, picks up the thrust of contemporary art toward an understanding of performance. The telling of the story creates a reality that merges with the non-story reality. The storyteller functions as a catalyst and an intersection for the merger of story reality and objective reality. The performance of the story becomes part of the story and though we do not feel the presence of Silko herself, the result is the same — a vision of the world as a unity of fiction and reality. . . . This is in effect a self-consciousness of oral literature. The story is being performed, and created. It is the material for future legends and the archetype for future tellings; the world and the story have been welded together.   [1981]

L I N D A   L .   D A N I E L S O N

A Feminist Reading of Storyteller: *Grandmother Spider's Web*

Over the last twenty years, the general development of scholarship about women's lives and art parallels an unprecedented flowering of creative writing by American Indian women. But in view of these parallel developments, American Indian women have shown little interest in the feminist movement, and conversely mainstream feminist scholarship has paid strikingly little attention to the writing of American Indian women.

Leslie Silko's *Storyteller* (1981), a product of this literary florescence, has remained virtually undiscussed as a whole by critics of any stamp. With its emphasis on women tradition bearers, female deities, and its woman author's personal perspective, *Storyteller* seems to ask for a feminist critical treatment.

But feminism is not all one thing, and an Anglocentric feminism will not get us far with *Storyteller* or any other text by an American Indian woman writer. Rather . . . a tribal cultural awareness joined with a feminist sensitivity to the non-linear, harmonious, achronological, and inclusive field modes of perception will engender a tribally informed feminist critical perspective that can correct a skew introduced by both male and Anglocentric bias in the study of American Indian life and literature. What is more, such a perspective may provide what no other critical approach has — a unified and coherent interpretation of *Storyteller*.

Certainly, some mainstream feminist social concerns link Indian women with white women and with other women of color. In her essay, "Honoring the Vision of 'Changing Woman'" (1984), Rayna Green outlines some of these universal women's issues: wages, social services, reproductive rights, and large questions of peace, equality, and political power. But, as Kate Shanley Vangen points out [in *A Gathering of Spirit*], despite Indian women's concern with key issues of the majority women's movement, "equality *per se* may have a different meaning for Indian women and Indian people. That difference begins with personal and tribal sovereignty — the right to be legally recognized as peoples empowered to determine our own destiny."

A tribally informed feminism pays attention to cultural differences as well as to similarities of world view. Such a feminism, for example, acknowledges that roles and stereotypes of women within Laguna society are not those of white society. The power relations between Indian men and women are not the same as power relations between white women and men; white male-dominated institutions oppress both tribal men and women. Furthermore, both Indian men and women writers express in their work perceptual patterns and cultural values that stand in marked contrast to much of what is valorized by the white male schools of critical thought. The work of both

Indian and white feminist editors and literary critics is essential to this understanding. In addition, feminist cultural scholars' responses to oral tradition, to Indian culture, and to men's cultural scholarship provide a fresh background against which to understand the literary works.

Several lines of inquiry among mainstream feminist literary critics can be usefully applied to the work of Indian women writers. For example, feminist scholars have challenged the institutional bases of literature within the critical establishment to demonstrate how our concept of "literature" has excluded and misread women's work.

Particularly applicable to Silko's *Storyteller* are feminist critical strategies to reclaim as legitimate literary subjects, women's experience and female mythic power. Sandra M. Gilbert sees this strategy as a matter of *re-vision*, seeing anew: "When I say we must redo our history, therefore, I mean we must review, reimagine, rethink, rewrite, revise, and reinterpret the events and documents that constitute it" [*Feminist Criticism*].

Silko's *Storyteller* represents just such a re-vision of the world from her vantage point as a Laguna Indian woman. In fact, understanding her re-vision and reinterpretation of personal and tribal memory leads us past the easy impulse to call *Storyteller* a collage, a family album, or pastiche, or into a conception of its unity and significance as a literary work. In seeing anew, Silko expresses a deeply unified view of the world, reclaiming as central to her craft the tribe, the significance of ordinary women's and men's lives, and the set of values arising from the female power of the primary Keresan deities.

Clearly Silko's first loyalty is to family and tribe rather than to womanness. But we need to understand that, for a tribal woman, concern with the lives and dignity of the men of her tribe may well constitute a feminist stance. Much more than tribal men, the male-dominated Euro-American world view and its institutions have been the oppressive forces that Silko must resist. Sometimes white women participate in the racism of that Euro-American world. Equally, sometimes tribal men absorb and embody the colonizers' posture of male superiority, perhaps in an unconscious effort to ameliorate the pain of their own oppression. But both men and women are victims of oppression by male-dominated institutions. *Storyteller*, like most writing by American Indian women, creatively resists that oppression.

Silko presents a highly personal view of tribal ways and at the same time a tribal slant on her personal memories, richly fed by the foremothers and forefathers whose words inspire *Storyteller*. Through the book she reclaims both personal and tribal traditions about men and women, animals and holy people, community and creativity. Silko is concerned with how humans fit into the cosmos, and the relationship between Creators and Destroyers engages her to the exclusion of any battle between the sexes. She pays constant attention to fair credit and representation for both men and women as active and responsible beings. While Silko maintains solidarity with tribal men (and deer and bears and Coyotes), she insists on the priority of female creator-gods, an idea that had been subverted through the tribe's colonial experience. In so doing, Silko insists on both a woman-centered traditionality and a personal independence of vision that constitutes such a reimagining as Gilbert recommends in order to know one's self and culture uncolonized.

Reclaiming identity, be it personal, sexual, or cultural, says Alicia Ostriker [in *Stealing the Language*], involves "a vigorous and varied invasion of the sanctuaries of existing language," one of which is certainly literature and its established forms. Ostriker continues, "Where women write strongly as women, it is clear that their intention is to subvert and transform the life and literature they inherit." As a product of Bureau of Indian Affairs (B.I.A.) schools and mainstream American university education, Silko has inherited Euro-American traditions about what constitutes a book and conventions about how one speaks as an author. But like many other contemporary women and tribal men writers, Silko subverts and transforms these inherited traditions, appropriating the making of books to her own purposes. *Storyteller* as physical object generally follows the conventions: the front cover, title page, and back cover blurb contain all the usual communications between publisher and book buyer. Silko's name appears as author. But past the title page she reclaims the interior of the book for her own purposes. There are no numbered divisions or chapters within *Storyteller.* The book is not a novel, not an autobiography. Lee Marmon's photo may stand next to Silko's poetic retelling of a traditional myth; nearby may be a letter to poet James Wright.

Inside the book Silko simply denies individual authorship. Self-effacement is not the usual author's stance in mainstream Euro-American literary practice. Taking such a stance, Silko reclaims authority as a storyteller who speaks for the community. It is the same authority expressed in the prefatory poem of her novel *Ceremony* when Thought-Woman, the Spider, "is sitting in her room / thinking of a story now / I'm telling you the story / she is thinking." The myths and stories have come to Silko through specific others, whom she credits: Aunt Susie Marmon, Great-Grandmother Maria Anaya Marmon, Aunt Alice Little, Grandma Lillie, Grandpa Hank Marmon, her father Lee Marmon, her friend and fellow writer Simon Ortiz. Among these, incidentally, the grandmothers are the primary sources instead of the unconsulted, as in so much anthropological fieldwork. At some points, Silko credits the "they say" of common oral tradition. "Traditionally," she says, "everyone from the youngest child to the oldest person, was expected to listen and to be able to recall or tell a portion, if only a small detail, from a narrative account or story. Thus the remembering and retelling were a communal process" [*Antaeus*, 1986]. Silko's self-effacement in her writing suggests the traditional artist's lack of self-focus and declares her grounding in the values of Pueblo culture, at the same time that it expresses her faith in the creativity of the community.

This creative community, moreover, consists of listeners as well as artists or tellers. Silko says, "A great deal of the story is believed to be inside the listener, and the storyteller's role is to draw the story out of the listeners." But Silko is, after all, not a simple village artisan free of influence from the outside world. In adopting the written English literary tradition as her expressive vehicle, she moves into an artistic world that is shaped largely by white men and is not prepared to deal sympathetically with Indians of either sex nor with women of any color. So in effacing her own authorship, crediting the community, mixing once-sacrosanct genres, and abjuring linear structure — in short, by denying the standards and customs of white male-dominated literary criticism — Silko reclaims the making of books from the white male critical establishment.

Furthermore, Silko defies the usual white notions of the proper literary Indian. Jarold Ramsey warns that the ethnographic perspective in literary scholarship tends tacitly "to deny the imaginative freedom of the writer" by imposing "a kind of *classicism* on 'authentic' Indian literary materials and relegating everything else (assimilations, adaptations, and so on) to the status of impure curiosities unworthy of serious attention" [*College English* 41, October 1979]. Silko insists on a community (primarily of modern women as tradition bearers), on forms such as village gossip, and on an idea of individuality that does not fit most literary or cultural scholars' expectations. The title story of the work is set not in her own Laguna pueblo, but among the Inuit of Alaska. Silko preserves Aunt Susie's language, an educated English including words like *precipitous* and *accessible*. Besides the right to their own language, she emphasizes the storytellers' right to say, "The way I heard it was . . . ," and she extends these rights to herself as she both adapts traditional stories to her own ends and recreates specific tellers' versions.

While Silko reclaims her individual and tribal identity from white male-dominated American scholarship, she has also reclaimed the centrality of female power and female artistic expression within Keresan culture. [In *The Sacred Hoop*] Paula Gunn Allen points to Keresan culture, with its female creator-figures, as "the last extreme mother-right people on earth," in which male leaders hold temporal power within the village through the agency of I'atyik'u or Corn Mother; these caciques are therefore referred to as *Mother*. But the fact remains that these are men exercising temporal power, and that women have generally been subservient to male authority, even though mythic power does reside in the female. . . .

Though Silko has apparently had no encounters with tribal authority over *Storyteller*, she and her grandmothers before her, judging from the work of Parsons and Franz Boas at least, were either subverting male control of tribal discourse or subverting portrayals of women in white anthropological documents.

Having in the very making of *Storyteller* asserted independence of both post-colonial tribal politics and white scholarly traditions, Silko uses structural, thematic, imagistic, and metacommunicative tools to reclaim a whole and woman-centered cosmos. In this nurturant and balanced community, both men and women can live and understand their relationship to relatives, storytelling, witchery, rain, deer, coyotes, and other inhabitants of the world. . . .

The central character in "Storyteller" uses narrative to maintain the integrity of self and culture in opposition to the pressures of white culture. She experiments with white culture, satisfying her curiosity about both school and sex. But when she leaves school to return to the village, "English was of no concern to her anymore, and neither was anything the Christians in the village might say about her or the old man."

The old man is not, as the local Catholic priest supposes, her grandfather. And the interpersonal politics of her sexual relationship with the old man are disturbing, especially at the moment when he screams at her and shakes her violently for having engaged in sex with the white man. But she always seems to choose freely in her relationship with the old man. Besides, the real significance of her sexuality with the old man may be to suggest her absorption into her culture. This, for Silko, overrides the implied oppressiveness of the relationship. Indeed, a similar putting on of old ways is suggested when she wears her grandmother's clothing: "She zipped the wolfskin parka. Her grandmother had worn it for many years, but the old man said that before she died, she had instructed him to bury her in an old black sweater and to give the parka to the girl." But the principal induction into the tradition comes as she learns the manner and reason for storytelling from the old man, and the subject of her own story, beginning with the death of her parents, from her grandmother.

Taking on the bodies and the stories of the old people, she comes to understand what the old man means: "It will take a long time, but the stories must be told. There must not be any lies." She insists on the integrity of her own story; in revenge for her parents' death after an opportunistic storekeeper had apparently sold them canned heat as drinking alcohol, she had lured the present storekeeper onto the weak river ice, where he had chased her and fallen through to his death. In her jail cell her liberal white attorney makes excuses for her. She couldn't possibly have planned it; her mind was confused. She insists, "I intended that he die. The story must be told as it is."

Through the contrast between the Anglo interpretation of the story and the girl's version, Silko is warning non-Indian readers to beware of the limits of their cultural system. Kate Shanley Vangen [in *Coyote Was Here*] cautions that readers often take delight in exoticism and fail to own up to the politics operative in the way we derive meaning from reading. In *Storyteller*, the white discursive system, suggests Vangen, does not allow people to think certain thoughts. The white characters — whether oil field workers, priests, educators, or functionaries of the Law — are all unable to accept who the protagonist is or what she says. Her curious, active sexuality causes them to try either to use or reform her. The lawyer cannot accept that she may have with justification actively planned the death of the storekeeper. Vangen suggests that if some legal functionary finally does believe her, the system will want to punish her for murder or have her hospitalized. The story teaches readers something about their part in the transaction. Grandmother Spider sometimes teaches through her bite. The lessons are disturbing but no less necessary.

Web imagery reinforces the structural statement in the story "Lullaby" as the old Navaho woman, Ayah, spins the narrative of the end of her and her husband's lives. One could see her as a victim. Her children have been taken by white people who "know best." Her husband's loyalty to an employer has been rewarded by callous dismissal and eviction. The husband, Chato, is evidently drinking himself into discouraged oblivion. But the structural context of the spider web, combined with the story's imagery, associates Ayah with Spider Woman, and thus with control over the making of her life.

Throughout the story Ayah is literally wrapped in the web of a foreign weaver — a faded, ravelled U.S. Army blanket sent to her by a son who died while in the service. But she remembers from her childhood the women who wove: "And while she combed the wool, her grandma sat beside her, spinning the silvery strand of yarn around the smooth cedar spindle. Her mother worked at the loom with yarns dyed bright yellow and red and gold." At the end of a long day's reminiscence, Ayah walks to Cebolleta to hunt for Chato at Azzie's bar. She stays long enough to shake the snow off her blanket and dry herself. "In past years," Silko writes, "they would have told her to get out. But her hair was white now and her face was wrinkled. They looked at her like she was a spider crawling slowly across the room." This is not a lowly or contemptible spider. What the bar customers fear is mythic power.

When Ayah finds Chato, he is in pitiful condition, wandering in mind and body. She looks at him with the objectivity and compassion of Grandmother Spider, and as they settle down for the night in an old adobe barn, she sings a lullaby that she knows from her own mother and grandmother:

> The earth is your mother,
> she holds you.
> The sky is your father,
> he protects you.

When she puts the Army blanket around Chato, knowing that he will freeze to death — and most likely she will too — she becomes like Grandmother Spider, appropriating the foreign web, using it as the mythic Spider so often does to carry someone away from a bad situation and to protect one who needs it. Both Ayah as memory maker and Silko as image maker create this protective web. . . . Balance, community, and creativity are all. Silko claims from her tribal woman's traditions, her nurturant woman-centered mythology, and her woman's experience that this is so.

A feminist reading of *Storyteller* does not give us a gynocratic manifesto. Here female strength does not imply liberation from the men of one's own tribe. Men's traditions dealing with transitoriness, change, and extinction complement women's nurturant traditions of continuance; the relationship is not adversarial as in the white feminist view of Euro-American culture. What we find in *Storyteller* is a woman's vision of her life and the traditions that nourish her. Silko reinvents those traditions so as to reclaim women's power that has been lost or reduced through colonialism: power over her body and her life, over a language not designed to carry her messages, over mythic stories adapted to serve male and colonial authority, even over the nature of authorship itself. *Storyteller* speaks into being the creative community of Thought Woman and Grandmother Spider.   [1988]

PART FOUR

APPENDICES

APPENDICES

A BRIEF HISTORY
OF THE SHORT STORY

The history of storytelling extends far back to a time long before the invention of the printing press. Stories have such a long history, and their forms are so diverse, that anyone attempting to investigate their earliest development in close detail would be taking on a herculean task. For thousands of years this genre could hardly be described as an entity cohesive enough to "evolve." A brief chronological survey, however, may help readers gain a perspective on the human miracle that is the modern literary form.

In their broadest categories, stories can be intended and accepted as *factual* — examples include histories or narratives of real battles, victories, happenings, and so forth — or *fictional*, stories made up to entertain or instruct the listener. Early fictional narratives are what interest us here. Margaret Atwood, in "Reading Blind," has analyzed some essential characteristics of good storytelling. The first tales we know of are those of the oral tradition, the creation myths of tribal peoples who were trying to explain how things got started.

Literary scholars believe that the next important stage in the evolution of storytelling was the period of the beast fables, stories in which animals are shown acting like humans in order to teach a moral lesson. The fables of the Greek slave Aesop (620?–560? B.C.) are still well known, and the beast fable form is even used occasionally by modern writers.

Another very early form of the story is the religious parable, a short and pithy story with a moral twist, such as the parable of the wise and foolish virgins in the New Testament. These stories, as well as passages of narrative in the Old Testament such as the description of the creation of the universe in Genesis or the story of Samson in Judges, were not intended as fiction, which is a word derived from Latin that means "something shaped, molded, or devised."

In the classical and postclassical literature of Greece and Rome, brief tales were often included in larger narrative collections, such as the *Satyricon* of Petronius in the first century A.D. and the *Metamorphoses* of Apuleius in the second century. These stories, along with fiction from Asian cultures, which was brought to Europe from the East by various means, became part of the reservoir of traditional material for later storytellers. An example of the tortuous path taken by such works is the *Panchatantra*. Its original Sanskrit form dates back at least to the early sixth century. In a variety of translations it spread through Europe in the Middle Ages. Finally, according to the editor Frank Edgerton, it was translated by Thomas North into English in 1570 from "an Italian version of a Latin version of a Hebrew version of an Arabic version of a [lost] Pahlavi [middle Iranian] version of some [lost] Sanskrit version of the original *Panchatantra*."

In the medieval period in Europe, short narratives were most commonly written in verse, whether they were heroic episodes such as the *Battle of Maldon* or low-life comic tales of French origin called *fabliaux*. Prose was usually reserved for devotional and instructive pieces until the fourteenth century. Around that time paper was introduced instead of parchment, and then secular tales in both prose and verse became popular, most notably the short prose tales of the Italian writer Giovanni Boccaccio (1313–1375). His best-known book is the *Decameron*, a series of one hundred tales told by seven ladies and three gentlemen who fled the plague that devastated Florence in 1348. In the same century, the Englishman Geoffrey Chaucer (d. 1400) wrote the *Canterbury Tales*, a collection of religious and secular tales, some derived from Boccaccio. Most of Chaucer's stories were narrated in verse.

The *Canterbury Tales* include several different short fictional genres such as the religious parable, the romance, and the fabliau. While Chaucer's collection exhibits remarkable stylistic polish and variety, a common theme is the unresolved relation between art and morality. The medieval distrust of purely imaginative literature extends far back in European culture, appearing in Plato's philosophy as well as in many other sources.

Boccaccio and Chaucer took great care to assure their readers that their stories would give both pleasure and moral instruction. The "moral behind the story" was a guarantee that the tales were more than mere entertainment. In the thirteenth century, the Christian theologian St. Thomas Aquinas cautioned against what he called "secular eloquence." Aquinas said, "He who strives principally after eloquence does not intend that men should admire what he says, but strives rather to gain their admiration for himself. Eloquence, however, is commendable when the speaker has no desire to display himself but wishes only to benefit his listeners." Imaginative stories were distrusted because they could be too entertaining. Five hundred years ago the first book ever printed was a collection of *exempla*, short prose narratives meant to serve as the basis for instruction by clergy, illustrating what an early writer called "excellent Lessons of Morality."

The medieval distrust of stories as entertainment took hundreds of years to overcome. Most of the Renaissance storytellers in Italy, England, France, and Spain are part of the Boccaccian tradition and include a structure of moral and religious values in their narratives. Through the centuries writers in different countries drew from the tales of preceding collections, so that by 1795, according to the scholar Roger Paulin, "the claim of a given story to be unusual or extraordinary, original or authentic, often did not stand up to very close scrutiny."

It wasn't until the eighteenth century, after secularization had gathered force in Europe, that fictional narratives were given the opportunity to evolve into forms we recognize as closer relations of modern stories and novels. These prose forms developed in periodicals popular with European readers from the emerging middle class, who had the education and the leisure time to enjoy them. The new periodicals printed a variety of prose — character sketches, satires, gothic tales, rogue stories, simple adventure stories, and sentimental sketches with predictable moral outcomes in which the hero or heroine is rewarded and the villain is punished. In France, Voltaire also composed his philosophical tales in the mideighteenth century, and his contemporaries Denis Diderot and the Marquis de Sade wrote stories to illustrate their theories of morality and psychology. These authors used satire to convey their views of the debasement of morality in conventional fiction, and the falsification of reality in many traditional tales. The older tradition had played itself out, and a new era of storytelling was about to begin.

The periodicals, with a rapidly growing number of readers, became a market for professional writers of stories. This literary form was also shaped and given vitality by the spirit of its age, the romantic period in European literature. At that time originality and imagination were valued above all other qualities in writing. This was in contrast to the emphasis on tradition and reason that shaped the attitude of eighteenth-century, neoclassical writers. In short fiction from the early years of the new periodicals, there is also a fascination with psychology and with unusual or eccentric behavior. Horror stories and criminal stories became popular, and gradually narratives opened up, as Paulin has stated, "to take in more moral and social awareness, satire, and the realm of the fancy and romantic imagination."

The mostly anonymous early writers for periodicals are not credited with inventing what is known today as the short story, even if their writing prepared the way for it. Most historians of this genre agree that the short story did not appear until the nineteenth century, almost a hundred years after the novel began to flourish as a literary form. Then a different kind of short fictional narrative emerged, an original prose work in which every word chosen in the structure of the plot, and every detail of description and characterization, contributed to a unified impression.

German writers were the first to experiment and develop this new form into original, imaginative narratives that resemble what we call short stories. Johann Wolfgang von Goethe (1749–1832) wrote some short prose fiction, but he composed his stories in collections or included them in his novels. His contemporary Ludwig Tieck (1773–1853), a reader of English gothic tales and the fantastic novels of Laurence Sterne (1713–1768), was more of an innovator.

Tieck was a slick popular writer for magazines, and he experimented with stories he called "novelle," which blend fantasy and reality in ways that influenced his contemporaries, especially the German writers E. T. A. Hoffmann (1776–1822) and Heinrich von Kleist (1777–1811).

Kleist presented events as more logically connected than in Tieck's and Hoffmann's stories, but even Kleist's fiction plays with the notion that a tale doesn't always have to follow a rational pattern or allow for a moral explanation. Probably the most famous German writers from the early nineteenth century are the brothers Grimm. They assembled a collection of "Childhood and Household Tales" from folk material; it was soon translated throughout the world. In our century the Danish writer Isak Dinesen revitalized some of these early Germanic forms of short fiction containing supernatural elements, as in her fairy story "The Sailor-Boy's Tale." In recent years the early French and German fairy tales have also been reimagined as gothic fiction or metafiction by Angela Carter, and the Italian fairy tales have been edited by Italo Calvino.

More than 150 years ago, the writer Washington Irving (1783–1859) read the German authors and was inspired to create Americanized versions of European folktales. Irving's *Sketch Book* (1819–1820) contains "Rip Van Winkle" and "The Legend of Sleepy Hollow," two of the earliest short stories in the United States. In 1827 Irving's contemporary Walter Scott (1771–1832) published the first modern short story in England, "The Two Drovers." Irving's tales had an enormous influence on the next generation of writers in America. He handled fictional narrative in a relaxed, predominantly descriptive and discursive manner, saying, "I consider a story merely as a frame on which to sketch my materials."

Shortly afterward, the young writers Nathaniel Hawthorne and Edgar Allan Poe began contributing fiction to magazines. They chose typically romantic subjects, writing about colorful or extraordinary individuals living in remote times and places, but they structured their narratives differently from how Irving did. They used more dramatic compression in developing their plots and revealing their characters. Most literary historians credit them as the first American writers to create a considerable number of successful short stories.

Hawthorne never explained fully how he wrote his stories, but Poe published his theories about short fiction in his book reviews. He did not insist that a short story be written any certain way. Instead, he stressed the concept that power and unity could be achieved in works of short fiction. This idea was a novelty in Poe's time, when the short story was not a highly regarded literary form.

Most critics regard Edgar Allan Poe and Nikolai Gogol as the two greatest and most influential writers of short fiction during the romantic era. Their stories, together with the moral fiction of Hawthorne, are more properly called "tales," the label the writers themselves gave to their magazine work. The tale, according to the scholar Northrop Frye's definition, is closer to the prose romance than to the novel. In the tale the author makes no attempt to delineate the characters as real people. Instead, they are stylized figures who "expand into psychological archetypes."

Herman Melville's "Bartleby, the Scrivener," by contrast, is more of a story. Melville subtitled it "A Story of Wall Street." He was acutely aware of the fickle literary tastes of his readers, and in "Bartleby, the Scrivener," his first published story, which appeared in 1853, he consciously created a humorous surface that he hoped would have popular appeal while concealing the serious meanings. The attorney who narrates the story of Bartleby is not a psychological abstraction, as is Hawthorne's Goodman Brown or Poe's Montresor. Melville gave us so many realistic details about the lawyer's life that we get a strong sense of his perplexity in the face of his mysterious scrivener's stubborn will.

Bartleby is also one of the "little men" who Frank O'Connor theorized is the true subject of the short story, a character originating in a "submerged population group." O'Connor argued that Melville's scrivener, and Gogol's even earlier Russian clerk in "The Overcoat," were the progenitors of fictional offspring who would later emerge in scores of stories by important writers of short fiction, including Sherwood Anderson, Anton Chekhov, and James Joyce. They would also create, in O'Connor's words, "outlawed figures wandering about the fringes of society, superimposed sometimes on symbolic figures whom they caricature and echo — Christ, Socrates, Moses."

The midnineteenth century was a time of great transition in literature as the earlier mode of romanticism slowly gave way to realism. If the tale is a close relation of the early prose romance, then the short story is akin to the later realist novel. Instead of being, as Frye has said, "idealized by revery" as in a romance, characters in a novel (and in short stories) wear recognizable social masks and reflect an everyday reality.

Gustave Flaubert's and Leo Tolstoy's fiction illustrates this realist mode. In their stories the characters are products of a highly developed society, and their fictive world is a mirror of the actual world of men and women at the time. Realist authors usually refrain from commenting at great length on their characters' psychology. Instead, their psychology is manifested in things said and done by the characters themselves. While romantic writers are interested in subjective states of awareness per se, realist writers are likely to be more concerned with the social causes and consequences of those states. They put greater emphasis on the particular physical circumstances in which they place their characters.

In America around the time of the Civil War, the popular magazine tale slowly gave way to the more realistic story. This is when local-color stories, set in particular regions (for example, New England, the Midwest, the South), emerged. Kate Chopin and Sarah Orne Jewett are two of the important writers of stories in this idiom.

In the 1890s Ambrose Bierce developed the macabre world of Poe's fantasy vision, writing short stories with a realistic surface that explore the workings of the protagonist's mind. Sometimes — as in "An Occurrence at Owl Creek Bridge" — Bierce ventured close to the stream-of-consciousness technique developed by later modernist writers. Bierce's fiction combines elements of romanticism, realism, and modernism. Trying to fit his stories into a neat historical category illustrates the impossibility of presenting the history of the short story as a smooth, linear evolution.

The realists Willa Cather, Stephen Crane, Henry James, and Edith Wharton were America's most distinguished short story authors at the end of the century. But European influences were also strong. In 1893, in his introduction to Hamlin Garland's story collection *Main-Travelled Roads*, William Dean Howells wrote that magazine fiction was so popular in America that finally "the hour of the short story in book form has struck." To account for what he called the "material prosperity" of short fiction, Howells credited — among other factors — "the vogue that Maupassant's tales in the original or in versions have enjoyed."

Two Europeans, the Frenchman Guy de Maupassant and the Russian Anton Chekhov, were the most influential writers of short fiction at the end of the nineteenth century. They brought remarkable innovations to the content and form of the short story. Both wrote realistic fiction, and both are considered modern writers because of the content of their stories. They insisted on focusing on the particular here-and-now quality of ordinary human existence rather than proselytizing for any particular religious, philosophical, or political system of belief.

As Kate Chopin realized, Maupassant was a writer "who had escaped from tradition and authority, who had entered into himself and looked out upon life through his own being and with his own eyes; and who, in a direct and simple way, told us what he saw." This is reminiscent of Chekhov's statement about his own difficult process of squeezing "the slave out of himself" in order to become a decent human being and an honest writer.

In Maupassant's short stories plots are tightly organized and usually conclude with a decisive action. Details of the characters' appearance and behavior are sharply etched into the narrative, as if their physicality were especially important to the skeptical materialist Maupassant. In Chekhov's stories, by contrast, plots include less decisive action. They are subordinate to sympathetic dramatization of the characters' psychology and mood. The writer Sean O'Faolain has labeled Maupassant "the relentless realist" and Chekhov "the persistent moralist" to distinguish further between them.

Experimental writers of the next generation were primarily influenced by Chekhov, developing his less sharply detailed, more subtly impressionistic atmosphere in their work. These were the modernist writers in the early years of the twentieth century, who challenged the conventions of the dominant literature and culture. In Europe this group included Isaac Babel, Joseph Conrad, James Joyce, Franz Kafka, D. H. Lawrence, Katherine Mansfield, and Virginia Woolf. Influenced profoundly by both Chekhov and Maupassant were the American modernists, including Sherwood Anderson, William Faulkner, Ernest Hemingway, Katherine Anne Porter, and Richard Wright.

The modernist writers explored the concept of an interiorized plot. As Mansfield said, "If we are not to look for [external] facts and events . . . we must be sure of finding these central points of significance transferred to the endeavors and emotions of the characters portrayed." Joyce's *Dubliners*, fifteen stories begun in 1904 and published in 1916, was one of the landmarks of this period.

Rather than constructing his stories around a dramatic climax in the action, Joyce heightened the climactic moment of self-realization that he found in Chekhov's stories. He coined a special literary term, *epiphany* (a "showing forth"), for this inner revelation. Such often painful flashes of recognition illuminate Joyce's fluid narratives, for instance, the boy's realization at the end of "Araby": "Gazing up into the darkness I saw myself as a creature driven and derided by vanity; and my eyes burned with anguish and anger." The critic Ian Reid has pointed out that the significant revelation in modernist stories may sometimes be only for perceptive readers, not for the fictional character. Gregor Samsa's consciousness is but a dimly flickering spark at the conclusion of Kafka's "The Metamorphosis," and he expires still trapped inside his suffocating transformation.

Since the end of the modernist period, authors have explored a variety of patterns of short narrative fiction. Most writers of popular magazine fiction favor old-fashioned closed plots, dramatizing a single, unified incident with a decisive conclusion. But we now enjoy a great diversity of periodicals — mass-circulation specialty magazines, little magazines, highbrow magazines, and regional magazines. Authors of "quality fiction" for these periodicals, such as Ann Beattie and Tobias Wolff in *The New Yorker*, for example, or Louise Erdrich and Alice Walker in *Ms.* magazine, often favor short stories dramatizing less conclusive action, which does not rise to any momentous peak. These writers invite close thematic scrutiny from attentive readers because their stories seem to lack both the certain meaning of earlier realist stories and the consistent subjective point of view of the nineteenth-century romantic tales.

Literary critics distinguish between two types of stories being written today: "traditional stories," descending from Poe and Maupassant, which are plotted and closed (like the work of Paul Bowles, Bessie Head, and Eudora Welty, among many others in this anthology), and "modern stories," descending from Chekhov and Joyce, which are less plotted and more open (like the work of John Barth, Jamaica Kincaid, and Grace Paley, among others). The same writer may use either traditional or modern structures in different works, depending on the material. The short story is so flexible that it may well be ideally suited, as Nadine Gordimer has said, to "convey the quality of human life, where contact is more like the flash of fireflies, in and out, now here, now there, in darkness. Short story writers see by the light of the flash; theirs is the art of the only thing one can be sure of — the present moment."

Fiction by contemporary writers is so close to us that it is better examined on a thematic or aesthetic spectrum, as the critic Susan Lohafer has suggested in her book *Coming to Terms with the Short Story*. She even pokes fun at the conventional historical survey of the short story in introductory literature courses at American colleges and universities:

> As the result of undergraduate survey courses, there are many people who can tell you how the form developed; how it emerged from the sleepy hollows of Washington Irving; took on the moral and arabesque shapes of Hawthorne and Poe; how it stretched socially and

regionally to James and Jewett; how it spoke the vernacular in Calaveras County, turned naturalistic in an open boat, reached deep into the psyche in Winesburg, in Babylon, and, of course, In Our Time; how it branched out southern and suburban and ethnic and far.

In one great sweep, Lohafer surveys the contribution of our earliest writers and then alludes to well-known stories by Mark Twain ("Calaveras County") and Stephen Crane ("open boat"). Next comes a reference to three great short story writers publishing after World War I who "reached deep into the psyche" — Sherwood Anderson ("Winesburg"), F. Scott Fitzgerald ("Babylon"), and Ernest Hemingway (his earliest story collection, *In Our Time*). These authors revitalized the American short story by writing in what Anderson called "the common words of our daily speech" to tell stories that often featured characters outside mainstream society. In their best work the three authors suggested implicitly more than they stated explicitly.

After these American modernist writers redefined the possibilities of the short story, there was a proliferation of short story writers during and after the 1930s who developed the literary form even further. "How it branched out southern" refers to the fiction of William Faulkner, Flannery O'Connor, Katherine Anne Porter, Eudora Welty, and Richard Wright; "suburban" refers to the stories from the 1940s and 1950s by John Cheever and Shirley Jackson, as well as to more recent "suburban" fiction by Ann Beattie, Joyce Carol Oates, and John Updike. "Ethnic" refers to the stories from the 1960s to the present by Jack Agueros, James Baldwin, Sandra Cisneros, Bernard Malamud, Leslie Marmon Silko, Isaac Bashevis Singer, Amy Tan, Alice Walker, and John Edgar Wideman, among many others who write from the perspective of minority cultures in the United States. "And far" refers to writers like Woody Allen, John Barth, Donald Barthelme, T. Coraghessan Boyle, and Lorrie Moore, inventors of ironic parodies, self-reflexive metafictions, collages, and other language experiments that offer a sometimes difficult but often dazzling postmodernist spectrum of contemporary short fiction. However brief Lohafer's summary, her conclusion is helpful: Once readers have a solid context for the evolution of the short story form, the guideline of its historical development may be less important than the quality of the individual voices of contemporary authors.

In recent years the short story has been alive and well in the hands of writers in every country of the world, from Isabel Allende, Jorge Luis Borges, Gabriel García Márquez, and Octavio Paz, in Latin America, to Chinua Achebe, Nadine Gordimer, Bessie Head, and Es'Kia Mphahlele in Africa; Naguib Mahfouz in the Middle East; Saadat Hasan Manto in Pakistan; and Yukio Mishima in Japan. In Europe and North America, the tradition continues with a rich diversity of literary forms and styles as new generations of writers come of age. The flood of new magazine fiction often carries with it stories of real literary distinction. The significant differences among contemporary short stories are not historical or geographical but are in the attitudes toward life that govern an author's sense of reality, and the literary techniques of expression that these attitudes call forth.

As John Cheever realized, "So long as we are possessed by experience that is distinguished by its intensity and its episodic nature, we will have the short story in our literature." The history of the short story is open-ended, as befits a mature and vigorous literary form. The ideal reader is also open to new writing, ready to be enchanted by the magic of each writer's imagination, revealed in his or her engagement with the short story.

For reference and further reading, see Walter Allen, *The Short Story in English* (1981); W. M. Aycock; ed., *The Teller and the Tale* (1982); H. E. Bates, *The Modern Short Story* (1972); John Bayley, *The Short Story: Henry James to Elizabeth Bowen* (1988); Peter Brooks, *Reading for the Plot* (1984); Daniel Burke, *Beyond Interpretation: Studies in the Modern Short Story* (1991); Eugene Current-Garcia (with W. R. Patrick), *What Is the Short Story?* (1961); Frank Edgerton, *The Panchatantra* (1965); Hans Eichner, *Four German Writers* (1964); Norman Friedman, *Form and Meaning in Fiction* (1975); Clare Hanson, *Short Stories and Short Fictions* (1985); Dominic Head, *The Modernist Short Story* (1992); M. J. Hoffman and P. D. Murphy, eds., *Essentials of the Theory of Fiction* (1988); Susan Lohafer, *Coming to Terms with the Short Story* (1985); Susan Lohafer and J. E. Clarey, eds., *Short Story Theory at a Crossroads* (1989); Charles E. May, ed., *Short Story Theories* (1976); Heather McClave, ed., *Women Writers of the Short Story* (1980); Frank O'Connor, *The Lonely Voice* (1963); Sean O'Faolain, *The Short Story* (1951); Roger Paulin, *The Brief Compass: The Nineteenth-Century German Novelle* (1985); T. G. Pavel, *Fictional Worlds* (1986); Ian Reid, *The Short Story* (1977); Danforth Ross, *The American Short Story* (1961); Robert Scholes and Robert Kellogg, *The Nature of Narrative* (1966); Valerie Shaw, *The Short Story* (1983); Michael Stephens, *The Dramaturgy of Style: Voice in Short Fiction* (1986); Peter O. Stummer, ed., *The Story Must Be Told: Short Narrative Prose* (1986); Gordon Weaver, ed., *The American Short Story, 1945–1980* (1983); and Alfred Weber and Walter F. Greiner, *Short-Story-Theorien 1573–1973* (1977).

THE ELEMENTS
OF FICTION

PLOT

Since the short story is defined as a prose narrative usually involving one connected episode or a sequence of related events, the element of plot is basic to this literary form. *Plot* is the sequence of events in a story and their relation to one another. Usually they are related by causation, and their meaning lies in this relation.

Many readers who enjoy short stories have pondered the question, Why is a short story short? There seem to be various reasons, but two are fundamental. Often the material that the writer takes for his or her story is in itself restricted, consisting of one incident or a closely related sequence of events. Or, if the material is broader, the story may be short because the writer has compressed it.

Literary critics have made an important distinction between the object of representation in a narrative (the events or action of the story that the writer is referring to) and the written story itself (the way the author uses words to present the action). The critic Norman Friedman has suggested that "a short story may be short not because its action is inherently small, but rather because the author has chosen — in working with an episode or plot — to omit certain of its parts. In other words, an action may be large in size and still be short in the telling because not all of it is there."

A short story can cover the events of a brief episode, as does Grace Paley's "A Conversation with My Father," or encompass action that takes years to conclude, as in Leo Tolstoy's "The Death of Ivan Ilych." Usually stories that are static, where little change occurs, are relatively short (as

Paley's), while more dynamic actions, covering a longer time and involving the characters' changes from one state to another, are longer (as Tolstoy's). Yet the narrative possibilities are endless. The writer may omit or condense complex episodes to intensify their dramatic effect (Isaac Babel's "My First Goose") or expand a single incident to make a relatively long story (John Barth's "Lost in the Funhouse").

Regardless, the short story usually has an end orientation — the outcome of the action or the conclusion of the plot — inherent in its opening paragraphs, what Poe called the "single effect." The storyteller must stay within the limits of this "single effect" established early on in the narrative. The novelist may conclude a single episode long before the end of a novel and then pick up the thread of another narrative, or interpret an event from another angle in a different character's point of view, chaining episode to episode and character to character so that each casts light on the others. But a story stops earlier. Its narrative dramatizes a single effect complete unto itself, even if a writer may conceive of it in the larger framework of a story cycle, such as Sherwood Anderson's *Winesburg, Ohio*, James Joyce's *Dubliners*, or Louise Erdrich's *Love Medicine*.

The plot of a short story usually involves a conflict or struggle between opposing forces. The discerning reader can see it develop in a pattern during the course of the narration, whether its events proceed chronologically or are rearranged with flashbacks, as in Ambrose Bierce's "An Occurrence at Owl Creek Bridge." Even if a plot lacks a momentous peak in the action, it always includes the basic pattern of a beginning, a middle, and an end.

In most stories the beginning sets up the problem or conflict; the middle is where the author introduces various complications that prolong suspense and make the struggle more meaningful; and the end resolves the conflict to a greater or lesser degree. In successful stories the writer shapes these stages into a complex structure that impresses the reader with its balance and proportion.

The first part of the plot, called the *exposition*, introduces characters, scene, time, and situation. The particular pattern varies from story to story, of course, and from author to author. Nathaniel Hawthorne began "Young Goodman Brown," for example, with only a few short paragraphs of exposition, the leave-taking between Goodman Brown and his young wife, Faith. Herman Melville devoted pages to exposition in his much longer story "Bartleby, the Scrivener," describing the lawyer, his two eccentric copyists, and his office boy before introducing the title character.

The second part of the plot is called the *rising action*, the dramatization of events that complicate the situation and gradually intensify the conflict. In "Young Goodman Brown" the rising action is twofold. Goodman Brown's walk through the forest with the devil, when he meets Goody Cloyse and then hides to spy on the minister and the deacon, is the beginning of the rising action. It leads to the scene when Goodman Brown looks to heaven, hears a young woman's lamentations, and sees a pink ribbon flutter through the air and catch on the branch of a tree. After this, he shouts "My Faith is gone!" and the reader is told that he has become "the chief horror of the scene."

Then the narration proceeds to a further development of the rising action, which takes the reader to the *climax* of the plot or *turning point* of the story, its emotional high point. Goodman Brown speeds through the forest and joins the devil's congregation inside the ring of fire formed by the four burning pines. He stands beside his wife and prepares to participate in an unholy communion, the scene "beneath the canopy of fire" that Hawthorne illuminated with brilliant descriptive power. There Goodman Brown summons the courage to beseech his wife to "resist the wicked one"; this is the climax of the plot. The pace of the narration breaks off dramatically at this point. In a single sentence Hawthorne then shows us Goodman Brown alone "amid calm night and solitude."

Now begins the fourth stage of the narration, called the *falling action*, where the problem or conflict presented in the earlier sections proceeds toward resolution. This last section of the plot, and the *conclusion* which follows in the final paragraph, is comparatively brief in this story, balancing the short exposition at the beginning. Nevertheless, in these last parts of the story, Hawthorne was careful to bring the sequence of related events to an end.

A story's ending often contains an element of surprise, just as the other stages of narration engage the reader's curiosity, heighten suspense, and prolong the expectation of a satisfying conclusion. There is little surprise in finding Goodman Brown "a distrustful, if not a desperate man" after his fearful night in the forest, but Hawthorne gave the story a final unexpected twist in the last sentence describing the funeral. Goodman Brown's survivors "carved no hopeful verse upon his tombstone, for his dying hour was gloom." Hawthorne's continuation of the narrative to a point in time beyond his main character's death places the individual conflict dramatized in the story in a larger moral context and reveals to the reader a deeper perception of the situation, a more subtle reflection of what life is like.

Plot can work in several ways. It can be an outgrowth of a character's personality or will, as in Young Goodman Brown's insistence on his meeting with the devil or in Montresor's insane scheme of revenge against Fortunato in Edgar Allan Poe's "The Cask of Amontillado." It can be propelled by an apparent accident of fate, as when two mustachioed thieves appear out of nowhere on a winter night in Nikolai Gogol's "The Overcoat" and steal Akaky Akakievich's new overcoat right off his back. It can be controlled by the setting, as in Stephen Crane's "The Open Boat." Most often the plots of stories can be understood as the interaction of character with circumstances: for example, in F. Scott Fitzgerald's "Babylon Revisited" and Gustave Flaubert's "A Simple Heart."

Plot does not emerge just through the description of events in the story. It can also be carried forward in dialogue, as when Hawthorne introduced the characters, the time, and the situation through the conversation between Goodman Brown and his wife in the beginning of the story. Readers also respond to *foreshadowing* and *dramatic irony* as the plot moves along, anticipating a turn of events which may or may not go along with our expectations. In the opening of Flannery O'Connor's "A Good Man Is Hard to Find," we can visualize the grandmother beginning the car trip dressed in navy blue trimmed with white organdy and lace and a sachet of cloth violets so that "in case of an accident, anyone seeing her dead on the highway would know at once that she was a lady." Later in the story we learn that although she survives the car accident, being dressed so neatly doesn't save her from being killed by the Misfit after she pleads with him, "I know you wouldn't shoot a lady!"

Regardless of the author's method of narration, the goal is the same: The writer of short stories must *show* the reader what is important through the dramatic action of the plot and the other elements of the story, and not just explicitly *tell* the reader what to think. Invention, not preaching, enchants the reader. Hawthorne dramatized his own final judgment of Goodman Brown by inventing the detail of his tombstone, not by concluding with an explicit, solemn pronouncement about the necessity of keeping faith in human nature alive. The illusion of reality must always be sustained by the plot. Until the end of the story, events should continue to unfold with the easy forward movement of an apparently endless silk handkerchief drawn from a skillful magician's coat sleeve.

CHARACTER

The action of the plot is performed by the *characters* in the story, the people who make something happen or produce an effect. And not always just people. Various authors have experimented with trees, chairs, and shoes as characters or with animals, such as the German shepherd and the monkey in Charles Johnson's "Menagerie." But when we say *character*, we usually mean a person. With a plot we do not just ask, What next? We also ask, Why?

The answer is usually found in the characters, who are plausible if we can understand their actions. The characters themselves don't always have a conscious awareness of why they act the way they do, or — if they have an awareness — it isn't always accurate. Yet there always *are* reasons, and the reader may discover them before the characters do. The reader instinctively wants to connect the events of a story by more than their simple chronological sequence. Assuming a relation between the events and the characters makes the story seem coherent.

How are the characters in a short story to be understood? Any discussion of character tends to drift sooner or later into a value judgment, since our principles of definition and evaluation for fictional characters are based on the ones we use for real people, controversial and confused as they may be for most of us. The important distinction to remember is that we are reading about *fictional* characters in a short story, not real ones.

We are on firmer ground in literary discussions when we analyze the writer's method of characterization as well as the character's personality. We know that Montresor is a murderer in Poe's "The Cask of Amontillado," but pigeonholing his character does not bring us very close to understanding the miracle of horror that Poe accomplished in the story. We can approach it more readily by relishing the language Poe used in dialogue and description to show us the specific mental processes of his main character as he proceeds with his obsessive plan to avenge his honor.

In all successful fiction characters come alive as individuals. They must materialize on the page through the accumulation of details about their appearance, actions, and responses, as seen, heard, and felt physical realities. Hawthorne told us little about the physical appearance of Goodman Brown except that he is young and newly married. We do not even know his first name — "Goodman" was used by the Puritans as a title of respect for those below the rank of gentleman. We know more about his wife — her name is Faith, she is pretty and affectionate, and she wears pink ribbons on her cap.

The lack of physical details about him makes Goodman Brown less than flesh and blood to most readers. He remains an abstraction in a moral allegory. Thus Hawthorne was able to reveal more clearly the figure of a man on trial for his belief in good and evil. As we are caught up in reading the story, Goodman Brown's actions as a fictional "person" provoke our curiosity and his responses arouse our alarm. If he continues to interest us after we have finished reading the story, it is because we are fascinated, as Hawthorne was, with moral dilemma that the narrative dramatizes.

Characters are sometimes called *round* or *flat*. For characters in a story to emerge as round, the reader must feel the play and pull of their actions and responses to situations. If the reader sees the characters as capable of alternatives, then the characters become more real, or round. Characters can also be called *dynamic* or *static*. Ivan Ilych in Leo Tolstoy's story "The Death of Ivan Ilych" is both round (he has a multifaceted personality as presented in the story) and dynamic (he changes). His wife is both flat and static, or so we think from her brief appearances.

Each writer of short fiction puts his or her own emphasis on character. An attentive reader can perceive that Anton Chekhov and Jorge Luis Borges, for example, did not develop characters in the same way. Chekhov, a great nineteenth-century realist, placed highest emphasis on character, believing that it determines our fate. Borges, a contemporary teller of philosophical tales, believed that our subjective nature makes it impossible for us to understand the essential riddle of human action, so he made plot more important than character.

Different fictional worlds make different demands on the reader, who realizes that the importance given to characterization by various storytellers is an indication of their vision of life. Regardless of the emphasis on character, what is most important is the truth of the fictional character, flat or round, dynamic or static. Avoiding *sentimentality* (emotional overindulgence) and *stereotyping* (generalized, oversimplified judgment) in the creation of characters, the writer must be able to suggest enough complexity to engage the reader's emotions or the story will not be a success.

SETTING

Setting is the place and time of the story. To set the scene, the writer attempts to create in the reader's visual imagination the illusion of a solid world in which the story takes place. With a few deft strokes in the opening paragraph of "Young Goodman Brown," Hawthorne sketched a street in Salem village during Puritan times, but the mass of details about the physical landscape are not given to us until Goodman Brown enters the forest. Then Hawthorne painted a gloomy growth of "innumerable trunks and . . . thick boughs overhead" that serves as the main scene for his character's troubled journey. Sometimes the setting is merely the backdrop for the action, as while Goodman Brown talks with Faith in the first scene; at other times it is central to the action, as it becomes when Goodman Brown enters the forest.

When the writer locates the narrative in a physical setting, the reader is moved along step by step toward acceptance of the fiction. The *external* reality of the setting is always an appearance, an illusion, a mirage of language as insubstantial as a shimmering oasis in a desert or a Puritan wilderness evoked in 1835 on the page of a young author's manuscript. Yet this invented setting is essential if the reader is to be given the opportunity to glimpse a truth about *internal* life from the characters and the plot. When Goodman Brown enters the dark, tangled world of the seventeenth-century forest surrounding Salem village, the reader may perceive that he really enters the dreary, dark world of his own mind, which has brought him to exchange the companionship of his young wife for the dubious attractions of the devil.

The setting of a story furnishes the location for its world of feeling, the different emotional associations awakened in the reader's mind by a dark New England forest in a Hawthorne story or a dank burial crypt in a Poe story. A sense of place is essential if readers are to begin to engage themselves in the fictional characters' situations.

Place helps make the characters seem real, but, to be most effective, the setting must also have a dramatic use. It must be shown, or at least felt, to affect character or plot. The gloom of the forest increases the doubt in Goodman Brown's mind that he has taken the right path. The mound of piled bones outside the granite niche where Montresor entombs his victim suggests the death awaiting Fortunato. Imagining the details of setting in the creation of stories, writers must exert their talents to make the reader see only the fictional world that emerges on the printed page, under the illusion that while the story unfolds, it is the real world itself.

POINT OF VIEW

As a specific literary term, *point of view* refers to the way the story is told. In giving an account of the events in a story, the author must decide whether to employ a *first-person narrator*, using the pronoun "I," or a *third-person narrator*, using the pronouns "he," "she," and "they." (The second-person narrator, "you," is rarely used, since a forced identification of the reader with the fictional world is usually difficult to maintain successfully.) If the chosen point of view is not right for the complete dramatic ordering of the subject, the narrative will not reveal all its possibilities to the writer, and the pattern of the story will be incomplete. If Hawthorne had chosen to tell his story from the point of view of Goodman Brown, for example, using the first-person narrator to describe how an evening in the forest with the devil ruined his life forever, it is likely that the story would have struck the reader as the gloomy ruminations of a religious fanatic. It would also necessarily have ended with Goodman Brown's death, and its larger meaning would not have emerged so explicitly.

The most frequently used ways of telling stories fall into two major categories:

First-person narrator (narrator a participant in the story)

    a. A major character
    b. A minor character

Third-person narrator (narrator a nonparticipant in the story)

    a. Omniscient — seeing into the minds of all characters
    b. Limited omniscient — seeing into one or, infrequently, two characters' minds
    c. Objective — seeing into none of the characters' minds.

First-Person Narrator

When the narrator is one of the characters in the story, he or she can be either a major or a minor character in the action. Poe's "The Cask of Amontillado" presents the narrator as the central character. By contrast, Joseph Conrad's "Heart of Darkness" is a frame story that begins with first-person narration by a character so minor that he exists mostly to introduce the person who will proceed to narrate the story.

The first-person narrator can move freely within the fictional world, and he or she can approach other fictional characters as closely as one human being can approach another, but the narrator has no way of understanding these characters except by observation of what they say and do. By making his narrator a major character in the action, Poe intensified the impact of Montresor's insane behavior, showing us his apparent imperviousness to the horror of what he is doing.

The authority of a first-person narrator is limited, although it is immediate and compelling as far as it goes. He or she is an eyewitness. The first-person narrator can also summarize less important events or back off from the immediate scene and meditate on its significance, since he or she is usually telling a story that happened in the past. But his or her meditations, like Montresor's, are not always trustworthy.

The biased report of the first-person narrator must have a dramatic significance in the story, since there is often a discrepancy between the way he or she sees characters and events and the reader's sense of what really happened. At the end of "The Cask of Amontillado," Montresor says that his heart "grew sick — on account of the dampness of the catacombs." The reader may perceive the truth differently and feel that Montresor has at least subconsciously realized the horror of what he has just done to Fortunato.

In "Bartleby, the Scrivener," Melville also chose an eyewitness to tell his story. The lawyer tells us he is sympathetic to Bartleby, but his incessant self-congratulation in his description of his tolerant treatment of the scrivener may cause some readers to mistrust him. Thus the narrator of the story becomes another screen around Bartleby, blocking our view as effectively as the "high green folding screen" he places around his employee in his office. Later the lawyer's suggestions to Bartleby that he seek other employment by working as a bartender or entertaining a young gentleman with his conversation are so ludicrously inappropriate that they serve to heighten our sense of the mysterious nature of the scrivener's behavior. Bartleby's four quiet words "I prefer not to" reverberate against the constant stream of the lawyer's well-intentioned but self-important explanations. The story would read very differently if Melville had let Bartleby narrate it.

Third-Person Narrator

The *omniscient* point of view of third-person narration is most clearly apparent in fairy tales beginning "Once upon a time," when the teller knows everything there is to know about all the characters, both inside and out — what they think and feel as well as what they do. In the hands of a master such as Hawthorne, a feeling for the complexity of human life emerges through the controlling authority of the omniscient narrator. This is achieved by a continual shifting of focus from the close view to a larger perspective. When this type of narration is used by a writer who is also a genius at the realistic rendering of experience, as is Tolstoy in "The Death of Ivan Ilych," the powerful combination of the author's great imaginative ability and moral genius invests the various characters and scenes with such reality that we accept them without question.

Limited omniscient narration is usually confined to revealing the thoughts of one character. This method was first developed in fiction by Gustave Flaubert, who exchanged the distancing of "once upon a time" (with its implied moral view) for an interior, more subjective view of characters and event. Flaubert's story "A Simple Heart" is an example of limited omniscient narration. Its narrator also sticks to *impartial* (not judgmental) *omniscience*; he tells the story without really evaluating or commenting on the actions, which speak for themselves.

Henry James formulated another theory about limited omniscient narration. He referred to certain characters in his stories as the *central intelligence.* Stories told by this method of narration are not always about a single central character. They do, however, involve a character, placed at the center of the story's action, through whose "intelligence" the author registers and evaluates everything that happens, including what happens to and within the character. In this kind of story, such as James Joyce's "The Dead," this character's psyche is the stage for the drama. Having established this single evaluating intelligence, the writer may range over the whole cast of characters and dramatize their views of the action. These will, however, always be perceived through or measured against the thoughts and feelings of the central intelligence, who may not understand what is going on at the time but will finally perceive the truth. In "The Dead" the central character, Gabriel Conroy, sees himself as a very different man at the end of the story from the man he imagined himself at the beginning. The actual drama of the story is not the events described but rather Gabriel's growth in moral awareness.

The stories of Stephen Crane are another variant of the limited omniscient point of view. The narration may at any given moment in a Crane story reveal a different character's perceptions and feelings. In "The Open Boat" Crane rendered the sensations of the various participants in the shipwreck, constantly changing point of view to borrow the eyes, ears, and tactile senses of all four men in the boat. If the war correspondent has the last word, it is because the author found him the best person to say what the pattern of the story required at that point.

Objective narration presents what appears to be a detached perspective on the characters and the plot of a story. Setting, action, and dialogue are laid out on the page without the narrator's comments or the characters' reflection. When Conrad said that Maupassant was interested in using only *facts* to tell his story, Conrad was implying that Maupassant was attempting objective narration. Maupassant himself insisted on his "personal view" as a writer and his selectivity presenting "the illusion of reality." For example, Maupassant's "personal view" included a snobbish disdain for the social-climbing wife from a modest background in "The Necklace," apparent in his choice of words in the first page of the story.

Hemingway is an example of an author attempting a more rigorous use of objective narration. In "Hills Like White Elephants," the reader must supply the interpretation for the characters' tense dialogue. This technique often forces the reader to read between the lines and participate more fully in the story in order to make sense of what the fictional characters cannot allow themselves to feel or say about their situation.

Narration can be classified into further subcategories — for example, stream-of-consciousness first- or third-person narrator — but the different ways of telling stories available to writers are always more flexible than rigid categories imply. Franz Kafka, who used Gregor Samsa as his central intelligence through most of "The Metamorphosis," continued the story well beyond Gregor's death. Awareness of the pattern of narration helps the reader become sensitive to the construct of language that is the story. The way the story is written is an essential part of what it is saying. As a creation of the writer, the narrative voice is always part of the "lie" of fiction, not always identical with the voice of the writer telling the story. Good readers remember Lawrence's dictim: Trust the tale, not the teller.

STYLE AND VOICE

Style is the characteristic way an author uses language to create short fiction. On its most basic level, style is the result of the writer's habitual use of certain rhetorical patterns, including sentence length and complexity, word choice and placement, and punctuation. In addition to the verbal patterns of literary style, *voice* is an essential element of all good fiction. Voice is the total effect of the author's rhetorical and stylistic choices. It can be flat, as in Margaret Atwood's "Happy Endings," to suggest the narrator's psychological exhaustion. Or voice can be exuberant, as in Toni Cade Bambara's "The Lesson," suggesting the naiveté of the young narrator.

The way that authors use language to tell a story conveys the quality of their mind to the reader. As we follow the story on the page we seem to hear the narration as well as understand it. Eudora Welty once said that "my own words, when I am at work on a story, I hear too as they go, in the same voice that I hear when I read in books. When I write and the sound of it comes back to my ears, then I act to make my changes. I have always trusted this voice." From the reader's initial encounter with the first words on the page, the voice of the storyteller is the agent that evokes the imaginary landscape of fiction and conveys part of the story's meaning. For example, D. H. Lawrence's fairy-tale tone at the beginning of "The Rocking-Horse Winner" prepares the reader for the strange, otherworldly events as the story progresses.

An author's choice of tone in a narrative conveys his or her unstated attitudes toward the story. The dry restraint in Hawthorne's comment about Goodman Brown's "excellent resolve" as he turns the corner by the meetinghouse and enters the forest is an example of the way tone contributes to Hawthorne's dignified, lofty prose style. A subtle irony, drawing attention to the differences between what is said in the omniscient point of view of the storyteller and what Hawthorne really thought, helped him keep an emotional distance from his characters suitable to the level of abstraction he created in the narrative. In contrast, Sherwood Anderson used everyday speech and more understated irony to set up a feeling of intimacy with the reader. This narrative voice suggests a sympathy for the characters in the realistic stories about frustrated, small-town lives, as in "Death in the Woods."

Be careful in judging the tone of stories that have been translated from foreign languages. It is nearly impossible for a translation to capture the exact tone of the original language, even if it renders most other details of the story accurately.

SYMBOLISM AND ALLEGORY

A literary symbol can be anything in a story's setting, plot, or characterization that suggests an abstract meaning to the reader in addition to its literal significance. Consider the pear tree in bloom outside the window in Katherine Mansfield's "Bliss." Literally full of fragile pear blossoms, the tree is an abstract symbol of the awakening sexuality of the young wife in the story, suggesting her innocence and purity. That her husband's mistress also responds to the beauty of the pear tree deepens the irony of Mansfield's story.

The total context of a story often suggests a symbolic as well as literal reading of the narrative. After closing the anthology and thinking about a story you've just read, you may be struck by the way some elements of the story suggest deeper meaning by eliciting your emotional responses.

Charlotte Perkins Gilman used the claustrophobic setting of her story "The Yellow Wallpaper" to help her reverse and subvert her readers' traditional associations about marriage. Instead of being a conventional symbol of home — safety, comfort, and refuge — the house in the story becomes a symbol of the wife's imprisonment and degradation.

Symbols are not always interpreted the same way by different readers. Faith's pink ribbons in "Young Goodman Brown" may symbolize her youth and innocence to one reader, and her femininity and coquettishness to another. Faith is such an abstract character that either interpretation is possible. Regardless of how the symbol of the pink ribbons is interpreted, they are experienced as a dominant image in the somber landscape of Hawthorne's fiction. Some readers may even see them as an example of Hawthorne's exploration of the ambiguous nature of signs, similar to the ambiguous nature of Goodman Brown's night in the forest. Symbols are more eloquent as specific images — visual ideas — than any paraphrase, unifying the story and suggesting infinitely more than they state.

A story becomes an *allegory* when all the characters, places, things, and events represent symbolic qualities, and their interactions are meant to reveal a moral truth. Whereas symbolism results from the multiple meanings inherent in a good story, allegory tends to have a fixed meaning. Hawthorne's "Young Goodman Brown" and Shirley Jackson's "The Lottery" seem to exist more on the abstract, symbolic level of moral allegory than as realistic fiction in most readers' imaginations. Kafka's genius in describing Gregor's internal state in "The Metamorphosis" is so extraordinary that we read the details of the fantasy story quite literally; to many readers its allegorical meaning as a fable of alienation seems more restrictive and less compelling than Kafka's painful dramatization of Gregor's life after he wakes up and finds himself transformed into a monstrous insect.

THEME

Theme is a generalization about the meaning of a story. While the plot of a story can be summarized by saying what happened in the action (a young Puritan husband loses his faith in God and humankind after attending a witches' coven), the theme is an even more general statement of the meaning of the story (losing faith can destroy a person's life). It is often difficult for readers to find words to describe what a story means. Sometimes, after many futile minutes of trying to "boil down" a story to a one-sentence essence, the words that come irresistibly to mind are the ones written in another context by the American poet Archibald MacLeish: "A poem should not mean / But be."

What makes the statement of a theme so difficult is that the theme must be true to any and all of the specific details in the narrative. This is the test to apply to a theme, once it has been stated. Finding a summary of the plot or a statement of the theme does not mean that you understand a story and so can skip reading it, however. The theme or meaning of any good story is inseparable from the language of the complete narrative. In fact, the way the writer fleshes out a dramatic structure to embody the theme is, in the final sense, the most important achievement of the story, infinitely more significant than the bare theme standing alone in its unconvincing nakedness on a sheet of notebook paper. A reader who does not know this should try to re-create a story from memory after writing a one-sentence summary of its theme.

Some readers tend to look for moral judgments about life when they think about the meaning of a story, but literature does not demand that they do. It is possible that an interesting, well-constructed story also contains a meaning with moral implications, as Hawthorne's "Young Goodman Brown" does. It is equally possible that an interesting, well-constructed story is without a moral, existing as a complete and satisfactory aesthetic pattern in itself, such as Poe's "The Cask of Amontillado." Ultimately, all great literature makes a statement beyond morality. The innate impulse to tell a story does not necessarily originate in a moral sense or a conscience. It probably arises from the mysterious and inexplicable human urge to communicate and to create, to provide a personal expression in the way the author presents her or his sense of what life is like in a narrative form.

The storyteller says, "Let me tell you how it is," and our interest as readers is always in what the story can show us about human experience. Theme is an abstract formulation of that truth, the author's vision of the meaning of life. Anton Chekhov's theme in "The Lady with the Pet Dog," for instance, is better rendered not as a moral injunction (do not commit adultery) but as a statement of a deep truth (love is a serious business). The same theme emerges from scores of other stories. We can understand the limitations of theme as a substitute for the work of art, but our attempt to state the theme is not necessarily foolish or misleading. Often it can help us understand the story better.

Most writers do not like to tell what their stories are "about." Even when they do, as Flannery O'Connor did in her explanation of the theme of "A Good Man Is Hard to Find" or as William Faulkner did in "A Rose for Emily," some readers agree intellectually but not emotionally with the writer's interpretation. O'Connor said she understood that her story might be read in different ways by different people, but she could have written it only with the one meaning she had in mind. She also insisted that a story is not the sum total of its theme or abstract meaning but rather what she called its "experienced" meaning: "A story is a way to say something that can't be said any other way, and it takes every word in the story to say what the meaning is. . . . When anybody asks what a story is about, the only proper thing is to tell him to read the story."

Theme comes last in a discussion of the elements of fiction because all the other elements must be accounted for in determining it. The structure and theme of a story are fused like the body and soul of a reader; their interaction creates a living pattern. While the various actions of the plot must strike the reader as realistic and inevitable, the complete truth that it reveals is in essence indefinable and untranslatable outside the story. Trying to arrive at the theme of a story teaches us that no statement of it can be final, except that magical entity, the story itself. As Leo Tolstoy once told a friend:

> The most important thing in a work of art is that it should have a kind
> of focus, i.e., there should be some place where all the rays meet or
> from which they issue. *And this focus must not be able to be completely
> explained in words.* This indeed is one of the significant facts about a
> true work of art — that its content in its entirety can be expressed only
> by itself.

APPENDIX 3

WRITING ABOUT SHORT STORIES

In writing about literature, you clarify your relationship to what you have read. This relationship goes beyond a basic emotional response to the story, whether you enjoyed it or not. You write to reveal what Ernest Hemingway referred to as "the measure of what you brought to the reading." As soon as you ask the smallest question about the meaning or structure of a story and try to answer it, you are beginning a critical inquiry that involves your intellect as well as your emotions. This activity is called the interpretation of the text. What makes it valuable is that it reveals to you and to others how you respond to the stories after they have entertained, instructed, and perhaps enchanted you. Now it is your turn to explain their effect on you, and to analyze how they did it. Once you have asked yourself what there is about a story that gives you pleasure — the style, the form, the meaning — you have begun to discover "the measure of what you brought to the reading." Keeping a journal in which you record your responses to the stories you read is often the first stage of the process of writing about short fiction. The next stage is to communicate your ideas to someone else. Turning yourself from a reader into a writer takes time, but if you understand the various steps involved, the process becomes much easier.

KEEPING A SHORT STORY JOURNAL

In her essay "On Keeping a Notebook," Joan Didion put her finger on the reason why writers keep a record of their experience: "We forget all too soon the things we thought we could never forget. . . . Keeping in touch is what notebooks are all about." If you keep a section of your notebook for recording your impressions after reading the stories assigned in class, you will find that writing down your responses soon after you've finished a story helps you to remember what you thought about it. This journal also ensures that you will set aside the time necessary to put your reactions into words, which always involves gathering your thoughts and finding the language to express them adequately. Your journal is a relatively painless first step in the journey of transforming yourself from a reader into a writer.

Some students prefer to record their responses systematically, taking each of the different elements of fiction as separate categories and recording separate impressions of the story's characterization, setting, plot, style, and so forth after finishing each narrative. Other students proceed less analytically and write a running commentary of observations and comments as they read the story. Regardless of how you proceed, you should jot down quotations from the story to illustrate your observations and include queries if something in the story puzzled you in your first reading. You can go back to these questions and answer them after you've read the story a second time or discussed them in class. These reading notes can help you review for an exam, but they are also a primary resource when you begin to write an assigned essay about what you have read.

WRITING THE PAPER

An essay about literature can take various forms and be various lengths, depending on the nature of the assignment. Whether you are writing an essay of only a few paragraphs or a research paper of several thousand words, the basic requirement is always the same. You must keep in mind that an essay on short stories (or on any subject, for that matter) is a type of expository writing, and *expository* means "serving to clarify, set forth, or explain in detail" an idea about the subject. Writing about literature helps you clarify your ideas. If you want your essay to communicate these ideas clearly to a reader, you must understand that it always requires two things to be effective: a strong thesis sentence or central idea about your topic, and an adequate development of your thesis sentence. How you organize your paper will depend on the way you choose to develop your central idea. The three principal ways of organizing essays about short stories — explication, analysis, and comparison and contrast — will be taken up after a discussion of ways to find a thesis sentence.

Getting Ideas for Your Topic and Thesis Sentence

Most effective short papers (about 500 words) usually treat one aspect of the story: its theme, characterization, setting, point of view, or literary style. These are some of the possible *topics* for your paper, the general subject you are going to write about. Usually your first response to a story is a jumble of impressions that do not separate themselves into neat categories of *topics* and *thesis sentences*. You must sort through these impressions to select a topic on which to concentrate in order to get ideas for your thesis sentence.

Before you can start your essay, you should feel that you understand the story thoroughly as a whole. Read it again to remind yourself of the passages that strike you with particular force. Underline the words and sentences you consider significant — or, even better, make a list in your notebook of what seems important while you are rereading the story. These can be outstanding descriptions of the characters or settings, passages of meaningful dialogue, details showing the way the author builds toward the story's climax, or hints that foreshadow the conclusion. To stimulate ideas about topics, you may want to jot down answers to the following questions about the elements of the story as you reread it.

Plot. Does the plot depend on chance or coincidence, or does it grow out of the personalities of the characters? Are any later incidents foreshadowed early in the story? Are the episodes presented in chronological order? If not, why not? Does the climax indicate a change in a situation or a change in a character? How dramatic is this change? Or is there no change at all?

Character. Are the characters believable? Are they stereotypes? Do they suggest real people, or abstract qualities? Is there one protagonist or are there several? Does the story have an antagonist? How does the author tell you about the main character — through description of physical appearance, actions, thoughts, and emotions, or through contrast with a minor character? Does the main character change in the course of the story? If so, how? Why?

Setting. How does the setting influence the plot and the characters? Does it help to suggest or develop the meaning of the story?

Point of View. How does the point of view shape the theme? Would the story change if told from a different viewpoint? In first-person narration, can you trust the narrator?

Style. Is the author's prose style primarily literal or figurative? Can you find examples of irony in dialogue or narrative passages? If dialect or colloquial speech is used, what is its effect? Does the author call attention to the way he or she uses words, or is the literary style inconspicuous?

Theme. Does the story's title help explain its meaning? Can you find a suggestion of the theme in specific passages or dialogue or description? Are certain symbols or repetitions of images important in revealing the author's intent in the story, what Poe would call "the single effect"?

Now put the text aside and look over the notes in your journal. Can you see any pattern in them? You may find that you have been most impressed by the way the author developed characterizations, for example. Then you will have a possible topic for your paper. Certainly if you have a choice, you should pick whatever appeals to you the most in the story and concentrate on it.

If you still cannot come up with a topic, ask for help in your next class. Perhaps your instructor will suggest something: "Why don't you discuss the way Hawthorne used irony in 'Young Goodman Brown'?" Often the class will be assigned one topic to write about. Some students think assigned topics make writing more difficult; others find they make it easier to begin to write.

A topic, however, is not the same as a thesis sentence. A topic is a general subject (for example, the character of Goodman Brown). A thesis sentence, by contrast, makes a statement about a topic; it is usually the result of thinking about the topic and narrowing it down to focus on some relationship of the topic to the story as a whole. A good thesis sentence has two important functions. First, it suggests a way for you to write about the story. Second, it makes clear to your reader the approach you have taken toward the topic. To *write* critically about short fiction, you must *think* critically about it. You start with an interpretation of the entire story and then show how some particular aspect of it contributes to what you think is its overall pattern and meaning.

Narrowing Ideas to a Thesis

A thesis sentence states the central idea you will develop in your paper. It should be easy for the reader of your essay to recognize — even if it's sometimes hard for you to formulate. A thesis sentence is a complete sentence that points the way you will take to clarify your interpretation of the story. In Hawthorne's story, for example, you might decide to write about the character of Goodman Brown (*topic*). You interpret the story to be a warning about the danger of losing religious faith (*theme*). If you think about the way your topic relates to the theme, your analysis might lead you to the idea that Goodman Brown lost his religious faith through the sin of pride. This thought process narrows the topic into a thesis, which you can state as the sentence "The story 'Young Goodman Brown' shows how a man can lose his religious faith through the sin of pride."

The test of a good thesis sentence is whether your *subject* ("The story 'Young Goodman Brown'") is followed by a clearly focused *predicate* ("shows how a man can lose his religious faith through the sin of pride"). What you want is a statement of an idea that you can then develop in your essay.

Finding a thesis sentence is often the biggest stumbling block for writers of expository prose. How do you know if your idea is worth developing in a paper? Generally speaking, a thesis will work if it expresses a specific idea about the story that you *want* to develop. If you are not interested to begin with, or do not like the story you are writing about, you probably will not write effectively, but you almost always write better about an idea if it is sharply focused.

Sometimes the thesis sentence occurs to you while you are thinking about the story; then you can jot it down as a fully formed idea right away. Other times you may find that you are unable to formulate any definite idea about the story until you start to write. No single procedure works for all writers at all times. You might begin writing with a trial thesis in mind, putting down rough ideas or a string of sentences as you think about the general topic you have chosen. Or you might decide to go back to the notes you took in your journal while reading the story and try to organize them into a simple outline about your topic, looking for connections between things that might suggest a direction to take in a trial essay and then hoping a thesis sentence will emerge while you free-associate with paper and pencil in hand. You might also get an idea for a thesis sentence by talking about the story with a friend.

Whatever way you start, do not settle for anything quick and facile. "Hawthorne's use of irony in 'Young Goodman Brown' is interesting" is much too general to be helpful to you in writing a good essay. Keep thinking or scribbling away at your first rough draft until you find an idea that gives you a specific direction to take in your paper. "Hawthorne's use of irony in 'Young Goodman Brown' suggests his judgment of the Puritan moral code" is a thesis sentence that has a clearly focused predicate. It states a definite relationship of the topic to the meaning of the thesis you want to explore. Then you know you are on your way to writing a good essay.

Writing and Revising

If you begin the first paragraph of your essay with a strong thesis sentence, your ideas will usually flow in writing and revising the paper. You will often discover further possibilities for refining your thesis while using it to interpret the text. That is one reason you should allow plenty of time to complete a writing assignment. It's an unusual first draft in which the central idea is developed coherently and fully enough to be turned in as a finished paper. Revision often stimulates further thought, sharpening and strengthening the development of your thesis. In the process of writing, you will come to understand the story more fully as your thesis takes you closer to its meaning.

Try not to become discouraged about writing by visualizing some distant final product — a well-organized essay, neatly typed on clean, white paper, shimmering on the page in what looks like pristine perfection. Remember that it took time to get that way. Your essay originated in half-formed, often confused thoughts that had to be coaxed to arrange themselves into coherent paragraphs linked by what only much later appear to be inevitable transitions. More often than not, the 500 words you might think are a perfect essay when you turn in your final paper will be the end result — if you took enough time in writing — of winnowing down 1,000 or more words from your rough drafts. You must amplify and clarify your thesis, editing your sentences and paragraphs so that each one relates coherently to your central idea. Then your essay will express your insights about the story so clearly that they can be understood as you intended.

At the beginning, it is best to forget about the end result and give all your thought and effort to the *process* of writing. If you find it useful, make an outline and try to follow it, but this practice varies with different writers. Some find it valuable to organize their notes about the story into a formal outline, whereas others prefer to make a rough sketch of the steps they plan to follow in developing their central idea. You may find that you do not want to use an outline at all, although in general it can help to keep you from straying too far from the point you are trying to make. Remember, too, that there is no fixed rule about the number of drafts or the amount of revision necessary before you have a finished essay. Every essay changes from the first rough draft through various revisions; an essay is often gone over several times in the days or weeks between getting the assignment and bringing the finished paper to class. In the various stages of writing, different aspects of the central idea often reveal themselves and are integrated into the paper, depending on your degree of concentration and involvement in the assignment. Even if you scrap sentences or whole paragraphs that do not relate to your final discussion, you have not wasted your time, because your early efforts to put your thoughts down on paper bring you to the point where you have better insights.

You will probably have to rewrite your opening paragraph many times to tailor your thesis sentence to the final shape your ideas have taken. Some writers just sketch in the first paragraph and go back to polish it when the rest of the essay is finished. Often you will want to amplify and refine your thesis sentence, dividing it into several sentences in your introductory remarks. Then it becomes a *thesis statement*, rather than a single sentence.

Developing the Thesis

While it is possible to write many different kinds of papers about short fiction, most college instructors assign students the task of interpreting the text. The literary items used in the headnotes on each writer in this anthology and defined in the Glossary (pages 1645–1654) can help you find a vocabulary to express your ideas. You cannot write intelligently about any subject without using the special terminology of that subject, whether it is English, economics, psychology, or engineering. At the same time, dropping the terms in your paper the way a person might drop names at a party will not impress your readers. Understand what the terms mean so you can use them to think and write critically about the elements of a story when you begin to interpret the text in the light of your central idea.

You will usually develop your thesis statement in the body of your essay by following one or more of the three common methods of writing about literature: *explication, analysis,* and *comparison and contrast.*

TYPES OF LITERARY PAPERS

Explication

The word *explication* is derived from a Latin word that means "unfolding." When you explicate a text, you unfold its meaning in an essay, proceeding carefully to interpret it passage by passage, sometimes even line by line or word by word. A good explication concentrates on details, quoting the text of the story to bring them to the attention of a reader who might have missed them approaching the story from a different perspective. An entire story is usually too long to explicate completely — the explication would be far longer than the story — so you will usually select a short passage or section that relates to the idea you are developing. Often this short section is a key scene, a crucial conversation, or an opening or closing paragraph where the implications of the text can be revealed to develop the central idea of your essay.

Although explication does not concern itself with the author's life or times, his or her historical period may determine the definitions of words or the meaning of concepts that appear in the passage being interpreted. If the story is a century or more old, the meanings of some words may have changed. The explication is supposed to reveal what the author might have meant when he or she wrote the story, not assuming conscious intentions, but explicating possibilities. For older stories, you will have to do a little research if the passage chosen for explication contains words whose meanings have changed. The *Oxford English Dictionary*, available in the reference section of your college library, will give you the meaning of a word in a particular era. The philosophical, religious, scientific, or political beliefs of the author, or of the author's age, may also enter into your interpretation of the text. The main emphasis in explication, however, is on the meaning of the words — both *denotative* and *connotative* — and the way those words affect the reader.

The following student paper is an example of how explication is used to develop a central idea in an essay.

Whether you accept the student's interpretation of the scene with the pink ribbon or not, it is a good example of the use of explication to show a way to read the text that develops the central idea of an essay. The thesis statement is clearly presented in the opening paragraph, so the reader knows what the essay will be about. At first the student approached the explication with the idea that Goodman Brown's essential weakness was his pride in trusting his senses more than his faith in God. The student felt from the start that the entire scene with the ribbon was a trick played on the protagonist. Rereading the story, he found evidence in Hawthorne's words to support this interpretation. Then, in writing the essay, he developed this thesis a step further, concluding the paper with two sentences about the "short step from believing in the devil to being taken in by him." This is an example of how the writing process itself can clarify and develop ideas. Just be sure the ideas are closely related, so your reader can follow you. Do not get sidetracked or introduce a new topic.

Quotation of passages from the story is always more effective than a simple summary of events. Giving a plot summary is a common error of inexperienced essay writers. Most stories are so short that the reader remembers them without a summary. Some instructors assign plot summaries as writing exercises, but they should not be confused with interpretive essays. An essay is organized according to logic, not simply the sequence of the plot. Give evidence that develops your thesis statement logically by quoting from the text. Explication — at its simplest, a quotation followed by your interpretation of the words — should develop an *idea* about the story,

The Devil's Tricks in "Young Goodman Brown"

Use quotes for titles of stories.

Hawthorne's "Young Goodman Brown" is the story of a man whose life is ruined because of the sin of pride, which makes him lose his faith in God. Goodman Brown agrees to meet the devil in the forest, and his faith is destroyed when he sees a pink ribbon fluttering to earth. He believes this ribbon could only have fallen from his beloved wife's cap. It is this scene in the story that reveals his weakness. His pride makes him trust the evidence of his own senses more than his faith in God.

Start with general thesis sentence.

Narrow the thesis to show specific direction your paper will take.

Hawthorne begins the scene in which Goodman Brown loses his faith by leaving him without other characters around him for the first time in the story. Alone with his soul, he has only himself to depend on. The devil has abandoned him in the middle of the dark woods with the maple staff that became a witch's broomstick when it was borrowed by Goody Cloyse earlier in the evening. Thus the reader has already seen the devil's tricks.

Transition: Repeat key words of thesis.

Suggest background of scene before you begin explication.

Other black magic is in store for Goodman Brown. Gazing upward "into the deep arch of the firmament," he lifts his hands to pray. The word "firmament," with its biblical connotations, suggests that Goodman Brown has set his mind on God. He has scarcely begun his prayer, however, when his concentration is broken: "a cloud, though no wind was stirring, hurried across the zenith and hid the brightening stars." The devil's magic show has begun, although Goodman Brown is not aware of it.

Start to quote from the story. Do not set off short quote.

He accepts the appearance of the "black mass" of the cloud overhead and forgets his prayer, listening instead to a "<u>confused</u> and <u>doubtful</u> sound of voices. . . . The next moment, so <u>indistinct</u> were the sounds, he doubted whether he had heard aught. . . ." The adjectives and verbs I have underlined in Hawthorne's description suggest the lack of substance in what Goodman Brown hears and sees; he is, after all, standing under a dark cloud. The next moment he believes he hears the voice "of a young woman, uttering lamentations, yet with an <u>uncertain</u> sorrow, and entreating for some favor, which, <u>perhaps</u>, it would grieve her to obtain;

Main section of the explication: Text quoted in the order it appears.

OK to use "I"; italics are not in original.

and all the <u>unseen</u> multitude, both saints and sinners, <u>seemed</u> to encourage her onward."

At this point Goodman Brown believes not only that he hears the voice of a young woman, but also that the woman is his wife, Faith. By now he is completely deluded. When he shouts his wife's name he is mocked by the ghosts he senses around him: "The <u>echoes</u> of the forest mocked him crying, 'Faith! Faith!' <u>as if</u> bewildered wretches were seeking her all through the wilderness." Here Hawthorne has built his description out of thin air. The <u>echoes</u> of Goodman Brown's voice sound <u>as if</u> bewildered, which is certainly ironic, since he himself is <u>truly</u> bewildered here.

Good active verbs.

Paragraph concludes with a strong idea about Hawthorne's use of irony in the scene.

Goodman Brown's temptation leads to his fall in the next paragraph, when "the dark cloud swept away, leaving the clear and silent sky above Goodman Brown. But something fluttered lightly down through the air and caught on the branch of a tree. The young man seized it, and <u>beheld</u> a pink ribbon." Hawthorne's language has changed, becoming simple and stark. It suggests the physicality of what it describes. Goodman Brown might have doubted the evidence of his eyes and ears if he stopped to reflect on what he had been shown in the "clear and silent sky" above his head, but before he could reflect, the devil gave him what he took to be something tangible to hold onto, something that looks like a pink ribbon.

Good insight into change in language.

Thoughtful analysis of character's motivation.

On the evidence of what he sees as a ribbon, Goodman Brown jumps to the conclusion that Faith has joined in the worship of the devil. He surrenders his trust in God forever. He becomes a victim of his own pride, believing in the evidence of his own senses more than in God. As a Puritan, Goodman Brown believes in the devil as much as he believes in God. Hawthorne might be suggesting that his belief contributed to his downfall. The story shows that it is but a short step from believing in the devil to being taken in by him.

End explication; start conclusion, tying back to thesis.

Conclusion goes one step further, to a wider implication of the thesis (logically connected).

which is the reason you were asked to write your interpretation in the first place.

Analysis

An *analysis* of a story is the result of the process of separating it into its parts in order to study the whole. Analysis is commonly applied in thinking about almost any complex subject. When you are asked to analyze a story, you must break it down into various parts and then usually select a single aspect for close study. If you are writing a short essay, try to keep the topic small enough to handle in a few paragraphs. Often what you are analyzing is one of the elements of fiction, an aspect of style, characterization, setting, or symbolism, for example.

While explication deals with a specific section of the text, analysis can range further, discussing details throughout the narrative that are related to your thesis. It is not possible to analyze every word of an entire story, any more than you would attempt to explicate an entire work. You may begin with a general idea, or arrive at one by thinking about some smaller detail in the story that catches your attention.

Perhaps you begin by noticing the path through the forest as you read "Young Goodman Brown." When you stop to think about it later, you realize that Hawthorne's various descriptions of this path contribute to the pattern of the story. You sense a connection of the path with the effect of "blackness" you feel building up in the narrative. This single detail of the setting can suggest a central idea that you might want to investigate. You could write, for example, about the path the protagonist takes on his walk through the forest and analyze the way its use in the different sections of the narrative develops what Melville called Hawthorne's "power of blackness."

Regardless of where you start to think analytically — with the whole or with one of its parts — you will usually begin to write an essay that is developed by analysis by moving from a general thesis statement to the particular part of the story being analyzed. The essay "The Path toward Evil" is an example of how a student has analyzed "Young Goodman Brown" by following Hawthorne's references to the path through the forest.

Here the thesis sentence opens the essay, and the analysis follows from it. The student separated the story into various parts, analyzing the way the path figured in it at each stage of narration. You will notice that explication also plays a role in this essay. Even when analysis is your chosen method of developing your central idea, you should quote examples from the story to support your main points. Each time you use a quotation, comment on it to integrate it smoothly into your discussion.

Comparison and Contrast

If you were to write about two of the Hawthorne stories in this anthology, or to develop an idea about any two stories, you would probably use comparison and contrast. When using the technique of comparison, you place

The Path toward Evil

The path's purpose in "Young Goodman Brown" is to show that "evil is the nature of mankind," which is the dominant theme of Hawthorne's story. It is a very dark theme, as Herman Melville realized in his 1850 review of Hawthorne's <u>Mosses from an Old Manse</u>. Satan has been with the Puritans since they came to America. The "dreary . . . narrow" path Goodman Brown follows through the gloomy forest is proof that human beings have frequently walked with the devil in the new land. Goodman Brown's journey on the path makes him realize there are two kinds of evil: social and personal. He meets social evil first, and is confused by it. Then he meets the "blackness" that is the evil within himself, and he is totally destroyed.

When he begins to walk on the path with the devil, Goodman Brown is too innocent to understand what he hears. He does not realize that the religious intolerance of the early Puritan settlers is wrong. So his companion, the devil, enlightens him further, telling him about present-day corruption in the community. The church deacons have drunk the communion wine, and the lawyers "are firm supporters of my interest." Now Goodman Brown is horrified because he understands the meaning of the devil's remarks. He takes the first step along the path from innocence to disillusionment when he recognizes hypocrisy in the respected village elders.

He proceeds a step further when he sees his own catechism teacher, the deacon, and the minister on the forest path, too. He does not understand what they are doing there. He asks himself, "Whither, then, could these holy men be journeying so deep into the heathen wilderness?" While Goodman Brown now recognizes social evil, he does not understand it. He must go further along the path to discover his own evil nature.

Goodman Brown finds the answer to his question in the story's climax. The path takes him and the "holy men" to the same destination. After he has come to believe that his wife is about to become one of the devil's accomplices, he

Thesis sentence, supported by evidence from supplementary reading.

Analysis narrows thesis and points to direction of paper's development.

Analysis is coherent — organized from beginning of story to end.

Quote from story to illustrate idea.

Good transition: One step leads to another.

Quote evidence for assertion.

End of first part (social evil).

Begin second part (personal evil).

runs desperately down the path, which "grew wilder and drearier and more faintly traced, and vanished at length, leaving him in the heart of the dark wilderness, still rushing onward with the instinct that guides mortal man to evil." Although the trail is a path toward evil, it is, paradoxically, his last connection with the familiar Puritan life that has sustained him. When it stops, he is lost.

Good comment on the quote — relates it to central idea.

The path terminates in the forest clearing, with its altar dedicated to the worship of Satan. Here he learns "to behold the whole earth one stain of guilt, one mighty blood spot." There are no paths out of the wilderness now for Goodman Brown. The whole earth is bathed in blood, with no firm ground upon which to fix a path that will lead him safely home. Overwhelmed by his visions in the forest, he is a lost soul. He has realized his own evil nature.

Evidence to support the analysis of the personal evil in Goodman Brown.

As Hawthorne knew, the Puritan settlers of Salem felt the forest was evil. They had to make paths in order to live in it. They would have died of exposure if left alone in the woods, and they needed paths to other nearby settlements. To journey alone in the forest was, as Goodman Brown learned, to leave the clearly defined, if hypocritical, moral path of the established religious community and so to invite damnation. Hawthorne dramatized his dark theme of man's essentially evil nature by showing Goodman Brown's fate. He leaves the apparently straight and narrow path of the religious settlement for the twisting, crooked path of the forest. It is a dark journey of his soul to meet "the deep mystery" of original sin.

Begin conclusion: Historical background relates to particular details of the story.

Restatement of thesis.

the two stories side by side and comment on their similarities. In contrasting two stories, you point out their differences. Most of the time you will use both methods, since no two stories are exactly the same. It is always more meaningful to compare and contrast two stories that have something in common than two that are unrelated. As you work on your essay you will find that if there are no important similarities in the stories, your discussion will be as strained and pointless as an attempt to link closely any two dissimilar objects, whether mismatched stories or apples and oranges.

You can also compare and contrast two or more elements within a single story. For example, in Poe's "The Cask of Amontillado," you could discuss the character of Montresor as he sees himself and as he is viewed by the reader, or the differences between the two characters, Fortunato and

The Single Effect in
Hawthorne's "Young Goodman Brown"
and Poe's "The Cask of Amontillado"

In addition to writing short fiction, Edgar Allan Poe published literary criticism, in which he explained his own
standards for prose tales. Poe stated that the primary goal
in creating works in this literary genre should be the development of a "certain . . . single effect." According to Poe,
an author invents such incidents in the story as will establish this "preconceived effect." Poe introduced this theory
in one of his reviews of a collection of Nathaniel Hawthorne's tales. The theory was conceived by Poe and based
on the work of Hawthorne; so the stories of both men emphasize the creation of such a "single effect."

> *General background information on topic.*
>
> *Summary of most important facts about topic.*
>
> *Topic narrowed to thesis sentence.*

Hawthorne's "Young Goodman Brown" and Poe's "The
Cask of Amontillado' show each author's use of the method
of "single effect." Poe's story examines the psychological
processes in a madman's plot for revenge, and Hawthorne's
story describes a man's fall from innocence, but both tales
are constructed similarly. The action of both stories features a single character. Both stories are unified by a central theme. Every word, phrase, and image used by the
author moves the theme closer to complete development.
Neither story is realistic--that is, the events described are
not plausible as real-life experiences. When Goodman
Brown walks with a flesh-and-blood devil, for example, it is
immediately clear that the story is a fantasy, because flesh-
and-blood devils did not exist in Puritan Salem. A similar
world of fantasy operates in "The Cask of Amontillado."
The ease with which the narrator is able to lead Fortunato
to his death is not true to life as we know it.

> *Important similarities.*
>
> *Single protagonist.*
>
> *Central theme.*
>
> *Not realistic.*
>
> *Specific examples.*

Both stories feature a single character, and both emphasize a unity of single effect in developing their themes, but
there are some fundamental differences between the stories.
The first is created by the nature of the two literary forms
the authors use. Hawthorne was writing a moral allegory.
Every aspect of the story symbolizes something else. Goodman Brown's wife, for example, is the embodiment of morality and simple faith; even her name, "Faith," contributes to

> *Begin analyzing differences.*
>
> *Hawthorne's form.*
>
> *Good example.*

this symbolic meaning. The story would have a different effect if she were named "Gertrude." Poe was writing a psychological fantasy. Fortunato is shown dressed in a cap similar to one that would be worn by a court jester. By calling attention to his outfit, the narrator, Montresor, adds to the degradation of Fortunato, which is part of the aim of his plan for revenge. Poe's fantasy is based on human emotions, while Hawthorne's allegory is based on intellect.

Contrast with Poe's form.

Summarize differences.

There is another major difference in the style of the two stories. Poe said that the first sentence of any tale should bring out the effect on which the rest depends. Although Poe set up the rules, Hawthorne did not keep to them. The opening sentence of "Young Goodman Brown" is in no hurry: "Young Goodman Brown came forth at sunset into the street at Salem village; but put his head back, after crossing the threshold, to exchange a parting kiss with his young wife." Goodman Brown is going on a journey, but the nature of the journey--which is central to the theme--is not clear. The concise opening of Poe's tale, however, reveals the theme: "The thousand injuries of Fortunato I had borne as I best could; but when he ventured upon insult, I vowed revenge." This sentence leaves no doubt in the reader's mind about the meaning of the story. The narrator declares that revenge is foremost in his mind, and the action that follows develops the idea of a character obsessed by the desire for revenge.

Another feature of Poe's theory related to another difference in the stories.

Quote to give evidence of difference.

Contrast with Hawthorne.

Both Poe and Hawthorne were artists deeply interested in creating works of fiction. Despite their differences of form and literary style, both created unified stories based on a "single effect," as shown in the two classic tales "Young Goodman Brown" and "The Cask of Amontillado."

Concluding summary clear, but a little brief.

Montresor. If your topic calls for you to use the method of comparison and contrast to elucidate your central idea, it is usually smoother to mingle your treatment of the two stories or elements as you go along than to write the first half of your paper about one and the second half about the other. The result of such a fifty-fifty split is rarely a unified essay; rather, it tends to give the impression of two separate commentaries flimsily linked together.

In the example of a paper whose thesis is developed by the method of comparison and contrast, the student shaped the first paragraph to conclude with the central idea, serving as an introduction to the comparison and contrast of the two stories. The stories' similarities were discussed in the next paragraph, and their differences analyzed in the rest of the paper. Throughout, elements of both stories were compared and contrasted side by side, sometimes with general analytic comments, at other times with explication and interpretation of the text. The technique of comparison and contrast is also a way to analyze stories. Specific quotations from the texts always help the reader get a clearer idea of the general points you are making in your analysis.

Writing about the Context and the Stories

In addition to developing an idea about short fiction by explication, analysis, or comparison and contrast — all methods primarily involving a close reading of the text — there are other ways to write about short stories. The *context* of short fiction is important as well as the text, as the headnotes to each author's work in this anthology have stressed. The context of literature is usually defined as the biographical and historical background of the work. Literature does not exist in a vacuum. Created by a human being at some particular time in history, it is intended to speak to other human beings about ideas that have human relevance. Any critical method that clarifies the meaning and the pattern of a short story is valuable, and often literary critics use more than one method in their approach to a text, as you can see from Janice H. Harris's psychosocial analysis of D. H. Lawrence's "The Rocking-Horse Winner" in the Commentary section (page 1428).

A paper on the context of a story is also an expository essay based on the development of a central idea or thesis statement. Usually this kind of critical essay develops the thesis of the paper by suggesting the connection of *cause and effect*. That is to say, you maintain that the story has characteristics that originate from causes or sources in the author's background — personal life, historical period, or literary influences. For example, you can use Kate Chopin's statement on her discovery of Maupassant's stories (on page 1407) to show something about her own method of writing short fiction. To establish this connection between the life and work of a writer, you could also analyze or explicate a Chopin story, or compare one of her stories with one of Maupassant's. The amount of time you spend on the context or the text of the story will depend on the emphasis you wish to make in your paper. You have already read two student essays that briefly mention the context of the stories, referring in one case to Melville's recognition of the power of blackness in Hawthorne's short fiction and in the other to Poe's theory of the single effect (pages 1631 and 1633).

You have probably written papers about literature in a biographical context. A favorite high school term paper project is to assign the student an author to write about, requiring library research into his or her life or historical period. If you wrote this kind of a paper, you may have organized your material chronologically, tracing the life of your author and briefly describing his or her most important literary works, often with no clearly defined thesis in mind. In writing an essay based on a unified central idea, by contrast, you must ask yourself how knowing the facts of an author's life can help you understand that author's story. You should never assume a connection between a writer's life and the literary work. A story can reflect the life of the man or woman who wrote it, but there are often disparities between the work of fiction and the realities of the life that are as important as the connections you can draw between them. If you plan to give a biographical analysis of Melville's "Bartleby, the Scrivener," for example, showing how it illustrates Melville's own decision to stop earning his living as a writer, you must remember that he wrote the story in 1853, several years before he decided to give up writing fiction for a popular audience. In 1853, Bartleby's "I would prefer not to" was not yet Melville's conscious choice. This particular biographical reading of the story will not take you very far in your interpretation of its psychological, sociological, or philosophical complexities.

A biographical approach to literature requires at least as much care as textual criticism of the story, care in discovering and presenting the facts of an author's life and in using a sensitive interpretation of them to show relevant connections between a writer and a story. Writers often employ their own experience as the basis for their fiction, as F. Scott Fitzgerald did in "Babylon Revisited." Your task as a critic is to show how an awareness of Fitzgerald's experiences in Paris helps you to understand the story. Richard Ellmann's biographical perspective on James Joyce's "The Dead" in the Commentary section (page 1414) is a masterful example of the application of this particular critical strategy.

You will usually be proceeding on firmer ground when you combine biographical facts with a discussion of an author's thematic or aesthetic intentions in writing fiction, and then relate this material to specific stories. Here again, be cautious. Statements by writers about how and why they created short stories are not necessarily the same as what a given story may show. Use your judgment carefully. Poe wrote model stories based on his theory of the "single effect," but Anton Chekhov did not always follow his own advice about how to write fiction. In "The Lady with the Pet Dog" (page 289) he wrote beautifully about the physical setting of Yalta, instead of restricting himself to the barest description, as he advised another writer to do in his letters (page 1405).

The contexts supplied by the writers themselves in the commentaries on the short story form and on particular stories included in this anthology are meant to stimulate ideas for your essays. They give the historical and biographical backgrounds of some of the stories. These excerpts can furnish a perspective from which you may view the individual stories, as did the students who used the quotations of Melville and Poe in two of the sample essays here. Or you can write about the commentaries as a subject in themselves, part of the wider context of short story literature. You can report on the entire books they came from (Frank O'Connor's study of the short story form, for example, or Eudora Welty's *The Eye of the Story*), if they are available in your college library.

Other Perspectives

Material from other classes can also be used in papers about short stories. If you major in history or psychology, for example, you can investigate the way stories are sometimes read to give valuable historical or psychological information about the world they describe. You are not limited to writing about remote times when considering essays that take this approach. Joyce Carol Oates's story "Where Are You Going, Where Have You Been?" is about modern teenage life. A paper about it could investigate the connection between Oates's fantasy and psychological theories about adolescence in contemporary America. Characters in literature are often used in psychological and sociological textbooks to illustrate pathological symptoms or complexes. Sociology textbooks, for example, cite Oates's fictional characters as representing current tendencies toward *anomie,* a condition in which normative standards of conduct have weakened or disappeared. It is possible in writing about literature to illustrate philosophical, historical, sociological, or psychological material you are familiar with through your work in other college courses.

Finally, you can argue a particular ideological point of view in writing about literature. Being aware of different critical approaches may lead you to think about stories in ways you might never have considered. If you look up critical articles on the stories in the Commentary section of this anthology or in your college library, you will find that academic critics usually write about literature using a particular strategy. The more traditional approaches before 1970 tended to be formalist or biographical and historical (and occasionally Marxist). In the past twenty years more innovative contemporary theory has been developed by feminist, gender, reader-response, and deconstructionist critics, among others.

At times the background of the author can suggest an ideological approach: Richard Wright was a communist, Tillie Olsen is a feminist, Flannery O'Connor was a Catholic, and so forth. At other times an ideology held by the student but not necessarily by the author can lead to a fresh reading of a story. Depending on what you as a reader bring to "The Metamorphosis," for example, there is a "Freudian Kafka, an existentialist Kafka, a Catholic Kafka, a Marxist Kafka, a Zionist Kafka," and so forth, as suggested by the critic Hans Eichner.

Proceed with your literary analysis according to your ideology with great care, realizing that you might become insensitive to nuances of meaning other than those you are predisposed to find in a doctrinaire interpretation of the text. (The Commentary section of this anthology includes examples of different critical approaches, including deconstructionist, historical, folkloric, rhetorical, biographical, feminist, psychological, and gender criticism.) At the same time an ideological approach can illuminate aspects of a story that are valid and relevant for contemporary readers. A feminist interpretation of "Young Goodman Brown," for example, must not take the story literally, because Hawthorne wrote it as a moral allegory, but a feminist could use the story to argue provocatively about implied sexual stereotyping in Hawthorne's characterization of women.

Arguments about the interpretation of literature are acceptable so long as they are supported by evidence from the text. Writers do not intend their readers to worship literature like priests at an altar. Take courage, and try to express your own point of view. In the Commentary section, Leo Tolstoy's attempt to read his own philosophy into Anton Chekhov's "The Darling" (page 1497) and Chinua Achebe's spirited critique of Joseph Conrad's "Heart of Darkness" (page 1373) are two examples of iconoclastic but well-presented interpretations of great short stories. Literary critics and scholars are now examining and revising the canon of accepted masterpieces as changes in society and the influence of new critical theory alter our expectations of what we look for in literature. Interpretations of great works change, as we enlarge and redefine the canon to reflect our hopes for an improved society and a more enlightened community of readers.

You misread stories if you think of them as absolute, perfect, final statements far removed from the commonplaces of life. They need the reader's involvement to come alive as imaginative literature. As Raymond Carver said, "Good fiction is partly a bringing of the news from one world to another. That end is good in and of itself, I think. . . . [Reading] just has to be there for the fierce pleasure we take in doing it, and the different kind of pleasure that's taken in reading something that's durable and made to last, as well as beautiful in and of itself." Through their aesthetic patterns, stories show us what life is like. What they are ultimately saying, in their affirmation of life and human creativity, is — in the words of Henry James — "Live! Live!"

SOME COMMON PROBLEMS IN WRITING ABOUT STORIES

Interpret, don't summarize. Summarizing the plot in an essay is not the same as developing insights into a story's pattern and meaning. Occasionally you can summarize the plot in a sentence if you are making a transition from one part of your paper to another, but keep in mind that the reader of your paper is usually your teacher, who has already read the story and will get the impression that you do not know much about what you are doing if you ramble on about the plot.

Write about how you read the story. Try to express your own ideas *through* the text. If you find yourself summarizing the story in more than a couple of sentences, it is probably because you did not organize your essay around a strong thesis. Your impressions and ideas are the measure of your encounter with literature. Writing about stories encourages your clarification of these ideas. Be sure to state your central idea in a sentence in your paper. It does not matter where it appears, although if you include it in your opening paragraph it will help you keep to the point in your discussion.

Woman as Victim in "Young Goodman Brown"

A feminist reader can accuse Hawthorne of portraying his female characters not as powerful individuals but rather as gullible victims. In "Young Goodman Brown," the women characters are clearly powerless to prevent the eventual destruction of the protagonist, Goodman Brown.

Introduction to thesis statement.

While Hawthorne never intended any of the characters in his moral allegory to be read realistically (their names clearly indicate that they function on an abstract, symbolic level of meaning in the story), his attitude toward women as weak and pitiful creatures is apparent in every scene in which they appear. In the exposition of the story, Goodman Brown is kissing his Faith good-bye. It is no coincidence that he then begins his journey to the forest, where he loses his faith in humankind. Faith is described as sweet and pretty. The pinkness of her cap ribbons blatantly advertises her youth and innocence. When she pleads with her husband to remain home with her, he speaks to her as if she were a small child and bids her say her bedtime prayers. Then, to add insult to injury, Hawthorne describes her as "peeping" (not looking) after him with a dependent, "melancholy air," as if she were incapable of spending a night alone. This marriage is plainly not one of equals. Goodman Brown seems more like a father than like a newlywed husband in this scene. "Poor little Faith!" he thinks, the diminutive "little" emphasizing his attitude that a wife is someone to be looked after, not listened to.

Narrow thesis.

Begin analysis.

Quote and interpretation.

Even when "sweet" Faith is surrounded by the unholy coven later in the story, she is not portrayed as being evil. She utters lamentations "with an uncertain sorrow." Has this married woman no mind of her own? Doesn't she, like her husband, have to agree to come to this meeting on her own? Instead, she is portrayed as an innocent victim, which makes sense on an allegorical level, but hardly does credit to women in general.

Repetition of central idea.

Finally, at the end of the story, when Goodman Brown is busy living out his life in gloomy thought, Faith's happy nature has absolutely no power to combat his cynicism.

More evidence.

How could she be happy to live the rest of her life with such a man? Hawthorne never explained how Faith reacted to her husband's changed outlook after his night in the forest. Are we to believe that she merely accepted his change, docile as ever?

Analysis of minor characters.

Two other women appear in the story--Goody Cloyse and Goodman Brown's mother--but neither is portrayed as powerful or worthy of more than brief consideration. Goody Cloyse was shown to be so frail that she has to enlist the help of a male (the devil) to get to the meeting. Goodman Brown's mother, who "threw out her hand to warn him back" at the witches' coven, has no more power over him than poor little Faith. These three women nourish the brief portion of this earthly life that Goodman Brown enjoyed, but are unable to save his blind masculine soul in the end. Taking the longer view, who were the true victims--the women in the story or Goodman Brown?

Conclusion.

Avoid long personal anecdotes. Writing on the basis of your personal experience can result in a fine memoir, but such an essay is usually not about the literature you were asked to discuss. You may want to introduce an analysis of D. H. Lawrence's "The Rocking-Horse Winner" with a short anecdote about a relevant experience you had as a child with a rocking horse, but make sure your anecdote goes on for only a few sentences before you connect it explicitly with your central idea about Lawrence's story.

Use the text to check your interpretation. Opinions about literature can be wrong. Do not insist on ideas that will not fit the details of the story. You may stumble on a central idea for your paper with an intuitive leap or a hunch about the story's meaning, but be sure the specific details of the story support your interpretation. The student who had an intuition that Goodman Brown was being tricked by the devil in the scene with the pink ribbon went back to Hawthorne's words for evidence to support his theory (see page 1628). You may decide that Hawthorne's story is a heavily veiled nineteenth-century treatment of a wife's infidelity and her husband's resulting nervous breakdown, but can you prove it by quoting from the text? "Whatever I discover in the story is right for me," you may say, but that will not take you very far when writing a paper for an English class. Stories are tough, tangible constructions of language, not shifting tea leaves in the bottom of an empty cup into which you can project whatever meaning you like.

Make good use of quotations. You must quote from the story to give evidence of your interpretation. Usually a sentence should introduce and follow each quotation, linking it to the idea being developed in your paper. In the comparison and contrast essay on page 1633, for example, the student discussed the opening sentences of the Hawthorne and Poe tales to make a point about the differences. Each time she quoted, she introduced the quotation and followed it by a comment of her own to explain how the quotation related to her main idea. Never drop quotations into the body of your essay without a comment.

Be careful not to quote too much. Use only those passages that are relevant to your discussion. Overquoting can weaken an essay, easily turning it into a string of short quotations choppily connected by a few insufficient words from you. Be sure to make it clear to the reader why the passage you are quoting is important.

When the quotation is short (four lines or less), it should be enclosed in quotation marks and included within the regular text, as you have seen in the sample essays. When typing a quotation longer than four lines, separate it from the preceding typewritten line with double space. Then indent ten spaces, *omit quotation marks*, and type with a double spacing (unless your instructor tells you differently). If you had a reason to include the opening paragraph of "Young Goodman Brown" in your essay, for example, you would type it like this:

> Young Goodman Brown came forth at sunset into the street
> at Salem village; but put his head back, after crossing the
> threshold, to exchange a parting kiss with his young wife. And
> Faith, as the wife was aptly named, thrust her own pretty head
> into the street, letting the wind play with the pink
> ribbons of her cap while she called to Goodman Brown.

In a shorter passage in which you use a quotation within a quotation, such as a line of dialogue inside an excerpt from a story, use double and single quotation marks: "The echoes of the forest mocked him, crying, 'Faith! Faith!' as if bewildered wretches were seeking her all through the wilderness."

If you wish to leave out words in a quoted passage, use ellipsis points, that is, three periods (or four periods if the omitted material includes the end of a sentence): "And Faith . . . thrust her own pretty head into the street. . . ."

Always quote the exact wording, punctuation, and capitalization of the original text. If you underline words in a quotation for emphasis, say that you have done so, as the writer of the first student paper did in his explication of Hawthorne's text (see page 1628).

If you find an error, for example a misspelled word in a quotation, indicate that the error is in the original by inserting *sic*, a Latin word meaning "thus," in brackets after the error itself.

Last but not least, punctuate sentences that appear in quotation marks correctly. Commas and periods always belong *inside* the quotation marks, whether or not they appeared in the original text. Semicolons, question marks, colons, and exclamation points, however, belong *outside* the quotation marks, unless they are part of the quoted material.

Avoid plagiarism. Any material you borrow from other sources and include in your paper must be documented. If you present someone else's material (other than factual information) as if it were your own, you may be open to the charge of plagiarism. Even with factual information, if you use the exact wording of a source, you must indicate that it is a quotation. To be on the safe side, it is always better to footnote your original source, or give credit by working into your essay the name of the author and the title of the work in which you found the material you borrowed.

The one exception of this principle is information that is considered *common knowledge.* Common knowledge is material that is repeated in a number of sources, so that it is difficult to tell what the original source might have been. Such items as the basic biographical facts about an author or information about the publication of specific stories do not need footnoting, unless you quote someone's exact words at length in your essay.

Know when and how to document your sources. Include the name of the author and the page number in a parenthetical citation or in the text itself:

> In Richard J. Jacobson's study, we learn that Hawthorne feared
> the artist might become "insulated from the common business of
> life" (27).

If you cite from more than one book by an author, mention the title in the text, or include a shortened form of the title in the citation:

> We learn that Hawthorne feared the artist might become
> "insulated from the common business of life" (Jacobson,
> Hawthorne's Conception 27).

If your instructor asks you to use footnotes or endnotes, instead of parenthetical citation, you may place notes at the bottom of the page on which the reference appears, or they may be gathered together on a separate *notes* page at the end of your essay. When you footnote a source, indent the first line of each footnote five spaces before listing the author's first and last name; the title of the book; the city of publication, publisher, and date in parentheses; and the page number cited:

> [1]Richard J. Jacobson, Hawthorne's Conception of the
> Creative Process (Cambridge, MA: Harvard UP, 1965) 27.

Instructions for basic documentation form for different sources — books, magazines, encyclopedias, and so on — appear in every handbook and guide to writing college papers. They may also be found in various manuals of style and style sheets that should be available in the reference section of your college library.

GUIDELINES: HOW TO WRITE AN ESSAY ABOUT SHORT STORIES

1. DO NOT WAIT UNTIL THE LAST MINUTE TO START. Allow plenty of time to write and revise.

2. BE SURE YOU HAVE A CLEAR IDEA OF WHAT YOU WANT TO SAY ABOUT THE STORY. Can you state this idea as a sharply focused thesis sentence? Remember that all expository writing serves to clarify, set forth, or explain in detail an idea about a topic.

3. READ THE STORY OVER AGAIN, checking the notes in your journal and taking notes that will help you amplify your central idea. It might help at this point to assemble a short outline, to stake out the ground you intend your essay to cover. Look for an approach that is distinctive enough to be worth your time and effort, yet manageable enough to be handled in a paper of the length you are assigned.

4. DECIDE HOW YOU WANT TO PROCEED TO DEVELOP YOUR THESIS. Will you use explication, analysis, or comparison and contrast? Is it appropriate to show a cause in an author's life or times and its effect on the work? If you have notes from your reading or research, assemble and number them in the order you intend to use them to develop your central idea.

5. WRITE A ROUGH DRAFT OF YOUR ESSAY. Be sure to state your central idea as a thesis sentence somewhere — depending on how you organize your discussion of the story. If you are using an outline, try to follow it, but allow yourself the possibility of discovering something new that you did not know you had to say about the story while you are writing. If you have taken notes or jotted down quotations from your reading, try to introduce such material smoothly into your discussion. Remember that the heart of literary criticism is good quotation. Brief, accurate examples from the text that illustrate the points you are trying to make about your thesis are essential in writing about stories.

6. ALLOW SOME TIME TO PASS BEFORE YOU LOOK OVER YOUR ROUGH DRAFT — AT LEAST A DAY. THEN MAKE AT LEAST ONE THOROUGH REVISION BEFORE YOU COPY OR TYPE A FINISHED DRAFT OF YOUR PAPER. Some students find they need several revisions before they are satisfied with what they have written. When you review your rough draft, concentrate and read critically. Remember that Isaac Babel would sometimes write 100 drafts of a story before he was satisfied. Let your words stimulate a flow of ideas about your topic; this will lead you to find more ways to illustrate your thesis or develop your train of thought. Fill out paragraphs that seem thin. Be sure transitions between paragraphs are smooth and quotations are integrated into the discussion. If you sense that your sentences are wordy, try to be more concise. Eliminate repetition. Be sure your general organization is coherent and your discussion proceeds in a clear, logical order.

7. CHECK OVER YOUR PAPER ONE LAST TIME to make sure you have always used complete sentences and correct spelling and punctuation. Avoid sentence fragments and exclamation points, unless they are part of a quotation.

8. TYPE THE PAPER OR WRITE IT NEATLY IN ITS FINAL FORM. If your instructor requires some particular style for class papers, such as extra-wide margins or triple spacing, follow those instructions. Use $8^1/_2$-by-11-inch paper. Type if you can, double spacing between lines. If you write by hand, use ink and write on only one side of each piece of paper. Leave generous margins at the top, bottom, and sides. Number the pages, beginning with the number 2 (not the word *two*) in the upper-right-hand corner of the second page. (Your title on the first page will indicate that it is the first page.) Clip or staple your pages together in the upper-left-hand corner. Be sure your name, your instructor's name, your class and section number, and the date appear on your paper.

9. READ YOUR ESSAY OVER ONE LAST TIME FOR TYPOGRAPHICAL ERRORS. Make legible corrections in ink. Have you put quotation marks around titles of short stories ("A Rose for Emily") and underlined the titles of books (<u>Collected Stories of William Faulkner</u>)? Have you placed commas and periods *within* quotation marks in the titles and quotations that appear in your essay? Have you inadvertently left out any words or sentences when you went from the rough draft to the final version of your essay?

10. FINALLY, MAKE A COPY OF YOUR PAPER — A CARBON OR A PHOTO-COPY — BEFORE YOU HAND IT IN, AND KEEP IT. It is a good idea to save your notes and rough drafts as well, in case the accuracy of a quotation or the originality of your work is called into question.

What do you do after you hand in your paper? You have probably spent so much time on it, thinking, organizing, writing, and rewriting, that you feel you may never want to read it again. The act of writing the essay will have clarified your thinking about the story, so you carry with you the intangible benefit of something learned in the writing process. Returning to your essay in the future might have one final benefit: Your paper will refresh your memory, reminding you of what you did not know you knew, about both yourself and the short story.

APPENDIX 4

GLOSSARY OF
LITERARY TERMS

ABSTRACT LANGUAGE Language that describes ideas or qualities rather than specific, observable people, places, and things, which are described in CONCRETE LANGUAGE.

ACTION At its simplest, the thing or things that happen in a story's PLOT — what the CHARACTERS do and what is done to them. A story may have more than one action (a plot and one or more SUBPLOTS), but a successful short story usually has one identifiable central action.

ALLEGORY A narrative in which CHARACTERS, places, things, and events represent general qualities and their interactions are meant to reveal a general or abstract truth. Such characters, places, things, and events thus often function as SYMBOLS of the concepts or ideas referred to.

ALLUSION An implied or indirect reference to something with which the reader is supposed to be familiar.

AMBIGUITY A situation expressed in such a way as to admit more than one possible interpretation; also, the way of expressing such a situation. Many short story writers intend some element of their work to be ambiguous, but careless or sloppy writing often creates unintentional ambiguity, or *vagueness*.

ANECDOTE A brief, unified NARRATION of one incident or EPISODE, often humorous and often based on an actual event. Some very good short stories may consist of nothing more than an anecdote; others may be made up of several anecdotes strung together, or may use one or more anecdotes as a way of advancing the PLOT or developing a CHARACTER.

ANTAGONIST A CHARACTER in some stories who is in real or imagined opposition to the PROTAGONIST or HERO. The CONFLICT between these characters makes up the ACTION, or PLOT, of the story. It is usually resolved in some way, but it need not be.

ANTICLIMAX An unexpected, insignificant RESOLUTION to a narrative, sometimes appearing in the place of a CLIMAX, sometimes after a true climax.
Many anticlimaxes are the unintended result of inept writing, but often
— especially in MODERN works — they are used intentionally to indicate the randomness, futility, or boredom of human life and action.

ANTI-STORY An experimental short story that attempts to convey OBJECTIVE
reality by avoiding what its authors consider the false CONVENTIONS of
PLOT, CHARACTER, and THEME, relying instead on seemingly uninter-
preted and unarranged fragments of direct experience and language.

ATMOSPHERE The MOOD, feeling, or quality of life in a story as conveyed by
the author's choices of language and organization in describing the
SETTING in which the speech and activity of the CHARACTERS takes place.
The atmosphere in which an author makes characters appear and events
occur is often important in determining the TONE of the work.

CENTRAL INTELLIGENCE A CHARACTER (often but not always the NARRATOR)
through whose perception the author observes the ACTION of a story
and whose perspective thus shapes the reader's view of that action. The
term was coined by Henry James, who felt, essentially, that the true
subject matter of FICTION is the effect of the action on the understanding
of this central intelligence.

CHARACTER Any person who plays a part in a narrative. Characters may be
FLAT — simple, one-dimensional, unsurprising, and usually unchanging or *static* — or ROUND — complex, full, described in detail, often contradictory, and usually *dynamic*, i.e., changing in some way during the
story. The main character in the story can usually be labeled the PRO-
TAGONIST or HERO; he or she is often in CONFLICT with some other
character, an ANTAGONIST. Other characters who affect the ACTION
slightly or only indirectly may be called *minor* characters; but, depending on the intention or the skill of the author, the main characters need
not be round, nor the minor characters flat. Minor characters are often
as full and complex as major characters, or fuller.

CLIMAX The turning point or point of highest interest in a narrative; the
point at which the most important part of the ACTION takes place and
the final outcome or RESOLUTION of the PLOT becomes inevitable. Leading up to the climax is the RISING ACTION of the story; after the climax,
the FALLING ACTION takes the reader to the DENOUEMENT or conclusion,
in which the results of the climactic action are presented.

COINCIDENCE An event or situation that arises for no apparent reason and
with little or no preparation, and then has a significant effect on the
working out of the PLOT or the lives of one or more of the CHARACTERS
in a work; a chance happening that has an important consequence or
result; an accident of fate.

COMPLICATION The introduction and development of a CONFLICT between
CHARACTERS or between a character and his or her situation. A complication moves the PLOT forward by exciting the reader's expectation that
the conflict so introduced must lead to a CLIMAX and reach some ultimate RESOLUTION as a result.

COMPRESSION The use of few or short words, sentences, or paragraphs, or
of very brief descriptions of CHARACTERS and SETTINGS and narrations
of incidents, to tell a story as clearly and simply as possible; in general,
an economical use of language.

CONCRETE LANGUAGE Language that describes or portrays specific, observable persons, places, and things rather than general ideas or qualities, which are described in ABSTRACT LANGUAGE.

CONFLICT The opposition presented to the main CHARACTER (or PROTAGONIST) of a narrative by another character (an ANTAGONIST), by events or situations, by fate, or by some aspect of the protagonist's own personality or nature. The conflict is introduced by means of a COMPLICATION that sets in motion the RISING ACTION, usually toward a CLIMAX and eventual RESOLUTION.

CONNOTATION The meaning of a word (or words) that is implied or suggested by the specific associations the word calls to mind and by the TONE in which it is used, as opposed to its literal meaning or denotation.

CONVENTION A traditional or commonly accepted technique of writing or device used in writing, often an unbelievable device that the reader agrees to believe — such as, for example, the fact that a FIRST-PERSON NARRATOR is addressing the reader in a friendly and intimate manner.

CONVENTIONAL Following or observing CONVENTIONS; often used in a derogatory manner to indicate a certain overreliance on such conventions and thus a lack of originality or failure of imagination on the part of the writer.

CRISIS The turning point in a narrative; the point at which the ACTION reaches its CLIMAX and its RESOLUTION becomes inevitable.

DECONSTRUCTION A critical approach investigating the unstable properties of language, especially the destabilization of single definitions of meaning and the defamiliarization of literary CONVENTIONS. In the words of one critic, deconstruction is "not a dismantling of the structure of a text, but a demonstration that it has already dismantled itself."

DENOUEMENT The conclusion of an ACTION or PLOT, in which the FALLING ACTION is brought to a close and the outcome or outcomes of the CLIMAX are presented to the reader; from a French word meaning "the untying of a knot."

DESCRIPTION The use of language to present the features of a person, place, or thing.

DIALOGUE The written presentation of words spoken by CHARACTERS in a narrative; used to introduce the CONFLICT, give some impressions of the lives and personalities of the characters who are speaking, and advance the ACTION to its CLIMAX and RESOLUTION.

DICTION The choice and arrangement of specific words and types of words to tell a story. A writer's diction is an important element of STYLE, and has a significant effect on the meaning of a story: The same ACTION will leave a different impression on the reader when it is narrated in street slang, in the simple, precise language of an old schoolteacher, or in the professional jargon of a lawyer or a social scientist.

DIDACTIC A term used to describe a narrative or other work of art that is presented in order to teach a specific lesson, convey a MORAL, or inspire and provide a model for proper behavior.

DISTANCE An author's or a NARRATOR's spatial or temporal — and hence emotional — removal or aloofness from the ACTION of a narrative, and hence from its CHARACTERS.

DRAMATIC IRONY The reader's awareness of a discrepancy between a CHARACTER's perception of his or her own situation or activities, or of their consequences, and the true nature of that situation or those consequences.

EPIGRAPH A quotation an author places at the beginning of a literary work that often suggests its THEME.

EPIPHANY A "showing forth" or sudden revelation of the true nature of a CHARACTER or situation through a specific event — a word, gesture, or other action — that causes the reader to see the significance of that character or situation in a new light. The term was first popularized in modern literature by James Joyce.

EPISODE A specific, usually very brief incident, often complete in itself and usually narrated at once and as a whole (as in an ANECDOTE). A story may consist of the NARRATION of one episode, or of several episodes strung together and united by a common SETTING or common CHARACTERS or proceeding toward a single CLIMAX and RESOLUTION; the latter kind of story is referred to as an *episodic* narrative.

EXPLICATION The act of explaining or interpreting the meaning of a text.

EXPOSITION The presentation of background information that a reader must be aware of, especially of situations that exist and events that have occurred before the ACTION of a story begins.

FABLE A very short, often humorous narrative told to present a MORAL. A fable's CHARACTERS are often animals, and particular animals have CONVENTIONAL associations with specific abstract qualities or values — the fox represents wiliness, the ant industry, and the lion nobility, for example. Leo Tolstoy said that "the bad fable has a moral, while the good fable is a moral."

FAIRY TALE A story or FANTASY that appeals to our sense of the marvelous, in which we suspend disbelief and let our subconscious patterns of wish fulfillment express themselves through magical occurrences, characters, or objects.

FALLING ACTION The events of a narrative that follow the CLIMAX and resolve the CONFLICT that reached its highest point in that climax before bringing the story to its conclusion or DENOUEMENT.

FANTASY A narrative or events in a narrative that have no possible existence in reality and could not have occurred in a real world; used sometimes to amuse or delight readers, sometimes to comment on or illustrate by contrast some aspect of reality, and sometimes, as in a FABLE, to present a clear MORAL that will not be complicated or diminished by the untidiness or inconsistency of reality, or as in a FAIRY TALE, to express patterns of wish fulfillment.

FICTION A narrative drawn from an author's imagination, made up of an ACTION or PLOT of imagined events involving imagined CHARACTERS in imagined or imaginatively reconstructed SETTINGS; lies told with the tolerance, consent, and even complicity of the listener or reader.

FIGURATIVE LANGUAGE The use of a word or a group of words that is literally inaccurate to describe or define a person, event, or thing vividly by calling forth the sensations or responses that person, event, or thing evokes. Such language often takes the form of METAPHORS, in which one thing is equated with another, or of SIMILES, in which one thing is compared to another by using *like, as,* or some other such connecting word.

FIRST-PERSON NARRATION The telling of a story by a person who was involved in or directly observed the ACTION narrated. Such a NARRATOR refers to himself or herself as *I* and becomes a CHARACTER in the story, with his or her understanding shaping the reader's perception of the events and characters.

FLASHBACK A technique of EXPOSITION in which the flow of events in a narrative is interrupted to present to the reader an earlier incident or situation that has a bearing on the story or its CHARACTERS.

FLAT CHARACTER A simple, one-dimensional, usually unchanging CHARACTER who shows none of the human depth, complexity, and contrariness of a ROUND CHARACTER or of most real people.

FOLKTALE A narrative that comes out of the tradition — usually the oral tradition — of a specific culture, and is used to communicate that culture's beliefs, values, history, and MYTHS from generation to generation.

FORESHADOWING The introduction of specific words, IMAGES, or events into a narrative to suggest or anticipate later events that are central to the ACTION and its RESOLUTION.

FORMALISM A critical approach that stresses the self-contained and self-referential nature of a work of art. Formalism took root in the 1920s and 1930s, flourished in the "New Criticism" of the 1940s and 1950s, and is still influential today. Formalists promote close reading, focusing on internal patterns of language and meaning within a text and excluding "external" considerations such as the author's biography, social history, or the reader's personal idiosyncratic response.

FRAME STORY A story within a story; a narrative told within the framework of another fictional setting and situation.

GENRE A type of literary work, such as SHORT STORY, NOVEL, essay, play, or poem. The term may also be used to classify literature within a type, such as science-fiction stories or detective novels.

HERO/HEROINE The PROTAGONIST of a story or other narrative; the main CHARACTER, whose CONFLICT is presented and resolved in the ACTION or PLOT. Traditionally, *heroine* has been used to refer to a female hero, but *hero* may be, and is more and more being, used to refer to a protagonist of either sex.

IMAGE A word or group of words used to give a CONCRETE representation, either literal or FIGURATIVE, of a sensory experience or an object that is perceived by the senses.

IMAGERY The use of IMAGES, especially of a consistent pattern of related images — often FIGURATIVE ones — to convey an overall sensory impression.

IMPARTIAL OMNISCIENCE The telling of a story by a THIRD-PERSON NARRATOR whose OMNISCIENCE does not allow for any evaluation or judgment of the CHARACTERS and their activities.

IMPRESSIONISM A way of writing in which an author presents CHARACTERS and events in a highly subjective and personal light, freely admitting an authorial POINT OF VIEW and effectively denying any claim to OBJECTIVITY or disinterestedness; after the style of the French impressionist painters of the late years of the nineteenth century, who sought to free painting from the REALISTIC, representational CONVENTIONS of the day.

IRONY The reader's or audience's awareness of a reality that differs from the reality the CHARACTERS perceive (DRAMATIC IRONY) or the literal meaning of the author's words (VERBAL IRONY).

LIMITED OMNISCIENCE The ability of a THIRD-PERSON NARRATOR to tell the reader directly about any events that have occurred, are occurring, or will occur in the PLOT of a story, and about the thoughts and feelings of one particular CHARACTER, or a few characters; distinguished from simple OMNISCIENCE, whereby such a NARRATOR can tell the reader directly about the thoughts and feelings of any character.

MAGICAL REALISM Fiction that interweaves REALISTIC and FANTASTIC details, juxtaposing the marvelous with the ordinary, as in the stories of Jorge Luis Borges and Gabriel García Márquez.

METAFICTION Stories about language and the process of writing, exemplified by the work of John Barth, Jorge Luis Borges, Italo Calvino, and Julio Cortázar, among many others.

METAPHOR An implied comparison of two different things that is achieved by a FIGURATIVE verbal equation of those things. "Love is a rose," "War is hell," and "The exam was a killer" are all metaphors, intended not to define the first terms mentioned but to attribute certain qualities to the thing being discussed.

MINIMALISM A literary style exemplifying economy and restraint, as seen in the stories of Donald Barthelme and Raymond Carver. Some of Ernest Hemingway's stories, such as "Hills Like White Elephants," could be considered pioneering works of minimalism in American literature.

MODERNISM A label loosely applied to the work of certain writers of the late nineteenth and early twentieth centuries who investigated the structure and texture of literature and challenged its CONVENTIONS.

MOOD The ATMOSPHERE that is created by the author's choice of details and the words with which to present them.

MORAL The lesson to be drawn from a story, especially from a FABLE or (in this sense the word is often used disparagingly) from a heavily DIDACTIC story.

MOTIVATION The external forces (SETTING, circumstance) and internal forces (personality, temperament, morality, intelligence) that compel a CHARACTER to act as he or she does in a narrative.

MYTH A traditional story, often a FOLKTALE arising out of a culture's oral tradition and involving gods or superhumanly heroic figures, that is used to explain the way things are and the way things happen, and to transmit the culture's values and beliefs from generation to generation.

NARRATION The dramatic telling of the events that make up the ACTION or PLOT of a story. FIRST-PERSON NARRATION is the telling of a story by a NARRATOR who participated in or directly observed the events being recounted and who is thus a CHARACTER in the story, identifying himself or herself as *I*. THIRD-PERSON NARRATION is the telling of a story by a detached, almost always anonymous voice who refers to the characters as *he, she,* and *they*. A third-person narrator may or may not be OMNISCIENT.

NARRATIVE A sequence of events, often (but not always) unified and connected in storytelling.

NARRATOR The teller of a story; usually either a CHARACTER who participates in the story's ACTION (see FIRST-PERSON NARRATION) or a detached, anonymous observer who may or may not present himself or herself as OMNISCIENT of the story's action from the beginning (see THIRD-PERSON NARRATION).

NATURALISM An extreme form of REALISM in which authors present their work as a scientific observation of a world in which people's acts are strictly determined by their nature and the nature of their surroundings.

NOVEL A long fictional prose narrative.

NOVELLA A short novel; a work of prose FICTION whose length falls somewhere between that of a SHORT STORY and that of a NOVEL; sometimes (though infrequently today) referred to as a *novelette*. Different critics have attempted to specify different standards of length for a novella or short novel — some saying 15,000 to 50,000 words, others 50 to 125 ordinary book pages — but there is no universal agreement on such a standard.

OBJECTIVITY An attempt by an author to remove himself or herself from any personal involvement with the CHARACTERS and ACTIONS of a story, to tell the story without bias and without expressing any personal opinions or making any personal judgments of the characters.

OMNISCIENCE Literally, "all-knowingness"; the ability of an author or a NARRATOR (usually a THIRD-PERSON NARRATOR) to tell the reader directly about any events that have occurred, are occurring, or will occur in the PLOT of a story, and about the thoughts and feelings of any CHARACTER.

PACE The rate at which the ACTION of a story progresses. Pace may be affected by varying the lengths of words, sentences, and paragraphs, by COMPRESSING or expanding the NARRATION of certain incidents or EPISODES, or by introducing and repeating certain key words and formulaic phrases.

PARABLE A narrative, usually short, that is told to answer a difficult moral question or teach a moral truth; often a form of ALLEGORY, because each person, event, or thing in the parable represents a literally unrelated person, event, thing, or quality that is involved in the moral dilemma being examined.

PARODY A humorous imitation of another, usually serious, work or type of work, in which the parodist adopts the quirks of STYLE or the CONVENTIONS of the work or works being imitated and uses them in extreme and ridiculous ways, or applies them to a comically inappropriate subject matter.

PATHOS The quality in a work that evokes sorrow or pity. Inappropriate pathos, or a too-frequent resorting to pathetic effects, can reduce a work to SENTIMENTALITY or *bathos*.

PERSONA The fictional mask or voice an author may adopt to tell a story.

PLOT The series of events in a narrative that form the ACTION, in which a CHARACTER or characters face an internal or external CONFLICT that propels the story to a CLIMAX and an ultimate RESOLUTION.

POINT OF VIEW The perspective from which an author lets the reader view the ACTION of a narrative; thus, the choice of who tells the story. In FIRST-PERSON NARRATION the NARRATOR tells a story he or she took part in or observed directly; such a narrator usually knows only what has been explicitly revealed, or what he or she has been able to deduce from that. In THIRD-PERSON NARRATION the narrator is not directly involved in the story and so views it from a certain DISTANCE. Such a narrator may be OMNISCIENT about the CHARACTERS and their actions and MOTIVATIONS, or his or her knowledge may be LIMITED to what one or a few characters know, or even to the plainly observable speeches and acts of the characters.

PROTAGONIST The main CHARACTER of a narrative; its HERO. The ACTION of the story is usually the presentation and RESOLUTION of some internal or external CONFLICT of the protagonist; if the conflict is with another major character, that character may be called the ANTAGONIST.

REALISM The telling of a story in a manner that is faithful to the reader's experience of real life, limiting events in the PLOT to things that might actually happen and CHARACTERS to people who might actually exist.

RESOLUTION The FALLING ACTION of a narrative, in which the CONFLICT, set in motion during the RISING ACTION and reaching its high point in the CLIMAX, is settled, or at least significantly altered, and the story moves swiftly toward its conclusion or DENOUEMENT.

REVERSAL Any turnabout in the fortunes of a CHARACTER, especially of the PROTAGONIST.

RISING ACTION The event or events that present and develop the CONFLICT whose dramatization is the story's ACTION; the COMPLICATION (or set of complications) that leads up to the CLIMAX.

ROMANTICISM A literary movement that flourished in the nineteenth century, valuing individuality, imagination, and the truth revealed in nature.

ROUND CHARACTER A full, complex, multidimensional CHARACTER whose personality reveals some of the richness and contradictoriness we are accustomed to observing in actual people, rather than the transparent obviousness of a FLAT CHARACTER.

SATIRE A work that ridicules some aspect of human behavior by portraying it at its most extreme; distinguished from PARODY, which burlesques the STYLE or content of another *work* or type of work.

SENTIMENTALITY An overreliance on emotional effect or PATHOS so great as to strain the reader's willingness to believe; also referred to as *bathos*.

SETTING The place and time in which a story's ACTION takes place; also, in a broader sense, the culture and the ways of life of the CHARACTERS and the shared beliefs and assumptions that guide their lives.

SHORT STORY A short fictional prose NARRATIVE. The term is often applied to any work of narrative prose FICTION shorter than a NOVEL. Edgar Allan Poe said the story's distinguishing factors were that it possesses aesthetic unity and can be read in one sitting. The trouble with that definition, as the writer William Saroyan once pointed out, is that some people can sit longer than others. See the discussion of this term in the Introduction and in the Elements of Fiction.

SIMILE A FIGURATIVE comparison of one thing to another, especially to one that is not usually thought of as similar. The comparison is achieved by using connecting words such as *like* or *as*. An old country song says, "Life is like a mountain railway," and then goes on to describe the narrow, tortuous paths people must follow in dealing with life's moral dilemmas, and the steep fall that awaits those who are not careful. The simile makes possible this figurative comparison of two such dissimilar things as *life*, a very large abstraction, and *mountain railway*, a very specific and seemingly unrelated object.

SKETCH A relaxed, static, predominantly descriptive literary composition often close to an essay in form.

STEREOTYPE A generalized, oversimplified CHARACTER (often a STOCK CHAR-

ACTER) whose thoughts and actions are excessively predictable because they are used so frequently that they have become CONVENTIONAL.

STOCK CHARACTERS CONVENTIONAL CHARACTERS who appear in numerous works, especially in works of the same type, and behave in predictable ways. Examples include the cruel stepmother in fairy tales, or the hard-boiled detective in certain mystery stories.

STORY An account of an incident or a series of events, either factual or invented.

STREAM OF CONSCIOUSNESS The narrative technique by which an author attempts to capture the flow of a CHARACTER's thoughts, often in a series of separate and apparently unrelated passages that unite to give an IMPRESSIONISTIC view of reality as seen by that character.

STRUCTURALISM A critical approach that developed contemporaneously with FORMALISM, similarly stressing attention to the formal elements of texts but regarding them as manifestations of a larger series of cultural codes and conventions that govern responses to works of art (and indeed all other human artifacts). Structuralist criticism studies categories of thought and finds them embedded in language itself — or, more precisely, in the relations among the constituent parts of language.

STYLE The habitual manner of expression of an author. An author's style is the product of choices, made consciously or unconsciously, about elements such as vocabulary, organization, DICTION, IMAGERY, PACE, and even certain recurring THEMES or subjects.

SUBPLOT A minor PLOT, often involving one or more secondary CHARACTERS, that may add a COMPLICATION to the ACTION of a narrative or may reinforce that action or provide an enlightening contrast to it or a welcome relief from its tension.

SURREALISM A way of writing that involves the presentation of a super-real, dreamlike world where CONVENTIONS are upended and rationality is dispensed with. The spontaneous creations of the unconscious are depicted in a surrealistic work through FANTASY and incongruous IMAGERY.

SUSPENSE The anxious uncertainty an author creates in a reader about the outcome of a story's ACTION. Suspense is often resolved when the action reaches a CLIMAX, after which the RESOLUTION is more or less inevitable.

SYMBOL A person, event, or thing that stands for or represents by association some other, usually broader, idea or range of ideas, in addition to maintaining its own literal meaning.

TALE An early form of the SHORT STORY, usually involving remote places and times, and events leading to a dramatic, conclusive ending.

TALL TALE A TALE or SHORT STORY based on a consciously ludicrous distortion.

THEME The central, unifying point or idea that is made concrete, developed, and explored in the ACTION and the IMAGERY of a work of fiction.

THIRD-PERSON NARRATION The telling of a story by a detached, usually anonymous NARRATOR, a voice who refers to all the characters as *he, she,* and *they.* Such a narrator may view the story with full OMNISCIENCE, which may or may not be IMPARTIAL OMNISCIENCE; or he or she may have only LIMITED OMNISCIENCE, seeing through the eyes of only one or a few CHARACTERS.

TONE The expression of the author's attitude toward his or her subject matter — the CHARACTERS, their SETTING, and the ACTION they undertake or undergo. Tone is revealed in the author's DICTION, IMAGERY, organization, vocabulary, and various other choices that contribute to the making of a STYLE.

UNITY The relation of all parts of a work to one central or organizing principle that forms them into a complete and coherent whole.

UNRELIABLE NARRATOR A fictional CHARACTER telling the story whose knowledge or judgment about events and other characters is so flawed as to make him or her a misleading guide to the author's intentions.

VERBAL IRONY The reader's awareness of a discrepancy between the real meaning of the situation being presented and the literal meaning of the author's words in presenting it.

VERISIMILITUDE The use of certain lifelike details to give an imaginative narrative work the semblance of reality or actuality.

VOICE A term referring to the specific manner chosen by the author to tell the story. Voice encompasses elements of POINT OF VIEW and literary STYLE (TONE, DICTION, etc.).

YARN An elaborated ANECDOTE or series of anecdotes narrated in colloquial language.

CHRONOLOGICAL LISTING
OF AUTHORS AND STORIES

Nathaniel Hawthorne (1804–1864)
My Kinsman, Major Molineux (1832)
Young Goodman Brown (1835)

Nikolai Gogol (1809–1852)
The Overcoat (1840)

Edgar Allan Poe (1809–1849)
The Tell-Tale Heart (1843)
The Cask of Amontillado (1846)

Herman Melville (1819–1891)
Bartleby, the Scrivener (1853)

Gustave Flaubert (1821–1880)
A Simple Heart (1877)

Leo Tolstoy (1828–1910)
The Death of Ivan Ilych (1886)

Ambrose Bierce (1842–1914?)
An Occurrence at Owl Creek Bridge
  (1891)

Henry James (1843–1916)
The Beast in the Jungle (1903)

Sarah Orne Jewett (1849–1909)
A White Heron (1886)

Guy de Maupassant (1850–1893)
The Necklace (1884)

Kate Chopin (1851–1904)
Désirée's Baby (1892)
The Story of an Hour (1894)

Joseph Conrad (1857–1924)
Heart of Darkness (1902)

Charles Chesnutt (1858–1932)
The Sheriff's Children (1899)

Anton Chekhov (1860–1904)
The Darling (1899)
The Lady with the Pet Dog (1899)

Charlotte Perkins Gilman (1860–1935)
The Yellow Wallpaper (1892)

Edith Wharton (1862–1937)
Roman Fever (1936)

Stephen Crane (1871–1900)
The Open Boat (1897)

Willa Cather (1873–1947)
Paul's Case (1905)

Acknowledgments (continued from p. iv)

Jack Agueros. "Dominoes" from *Dominoes & Other Stories from the Puerto Rican* by Jack Agueros. Curbstone Press, 1993. Copyright © 1993 by Jack Agueros. Distributed by InBook. Used with permission of Curbstone Press.

Paula Gunn Allen. "Whirlwind Man Steals Yellow Woman" from *Spider Woman's Grand-daughters* by Paula Gunn Allen. Copyright © 1989 by Paula Gunn Allen. Reprinted by permission of Beacon Press.

Woody Allen. "The Kugelmass Episode" from *Side Effects* by Woody Allen. Copyright © 1977 by Woody Allen. Reprinted by permission of Random House, Inc.

Isabel Allende. "And of Clay Are We Created" from *The Stories of Eva Luna* by Isabel Allende, trans. from the Spanish by Margaret Sayers Peden. Copyright © 1989 by Isabel Allende. English translation copyright © 1991 by Macmillan Publishing Company. Reprinted by permission of Atheneum Publishers, an imprint of Macmillan Publishing Company and Lester & Orphen Dennys.

Sherwood Anderson. "Death in the Woods." Copyright 1926 by The American Mercury, Inc. and renewed © 1953 by Eleanor Copenhaver Anderson. "Form, Not Plot, in the Short Story" copyright 1924 by B. W. Huebsch, Inc. and renewed © 1952 by Eleanor Copenhaver Anderson. Reprinted by permission of Harold Ober Associates Incorporated. "Hands" from *Winesburg, Ohio* by Sherwood Anderson. Copyright 1919 and renewed © 1947 by Eleanor Copenhaver Anderson. Reprinted by permission of Viking Penguin, a division of Penguin Books USA, Inc.

Margaret Atwood. "Happy Endings" from an anthology in Canada titled *Murder in the Dark*, published by Coach House Press and from an anthology in the United States titled *Murder in the Dark and Simple Murders*, published by Nan A. Talese Books, Bantam Doubleday and Dell. Copyright © 1983 by Margaret Atwood. Reprinted by permission of the author.

Isaac Babel. "My First Goose" from *The Collected Stories of Isaac Babel* by Isaac Babel. Copyright © 1955 by S. G. Phillips, Inc. Reprinted by permission of S. G. Phillips, Inc.

James Baldwin. "Sonny's Blues" was originally published in *The Partisan Review*, later collected in *Going to Meet the Man* by James Baldwin. Copyright © 1957 by James Baldwin and renewed © 1985 by James Baldwin. Reprinted by permission of the James Baldwin Estate. "Autobiographical Notes" from *Notes of a Native Son* by James Baldwin. Copyright © 1955 and renewed © 1983 by James Baldwin. Reprinted by permission of Beacon Press.

Toni Cade Bambara. "The Lesson" from *Gorilla, My Love* by Toni Cade Bambara. Copyright © 1972 by Toni Cade Bambara. Reprinted by permission of Random House, Inc.

Kim Barnes. "An Interview with Leslie Marmon Silko" from *The Journal of Ethnic Studies* 13 (Winter 1986). Copyright © 1986 by The Journal of Ethnic Studies. Reprinted with permission from the Western Washington University Bureau for Faculty Research.

John Barth. "Lost in the Funhouse" from *Lost in the Funhouse* by John Barth. Copyright © 1967 by The Atlantic Monthly Company. Used by permission of Doubleday, a division of Bantam Doubleday Dell Publishing Group, Inc.

Donald Barthelme. "The Indian Uprising" from *Unspeakable Practices, Unnatural Acts* by Donald Barthelme. Copyright © 1968 by Donald Barthelme. Reprinted by permission of Wylie, Aitken & Stone, Inc.

Ann Beattie. "Janus" from *Where You'll Find Me* by Ann Beattie. Copyright © 1986 by Irony and Pity, Inc. Reprinted by permission of Simon & Schuster, Inc.

Ruth Benedict. "Sun Steals Whirlwind Woman" from *Spider Woman's Granddaughters* by Paula Gunn Allen. Copyright © 1989 by Paula Gunn Allen. Reprinted by permission of Beacon Press.

Amy Bloom. "Silver Water" from *Come to Me* by Amy Bloom. Copyright © 1993 by Amy Bloom. Reprinted by permission of HarperCollins Publishers, Inc.

Robert Bone, "A Folkloric Analysis of Hurston's 'Spunk'" from *Down Home* by Robert Bone. Copyright © 1988 by Columbia University Press. Reprinted by permission of Columbia University Press.

Wayne C. Booth. "A Rhetorical Reading of O'Connor's 'Everything That Rises Must Converge'" from *A Rhetoric of Irony* by Wayne C. Booth. Copyright © 1974 by the University of Chicago. Reprinted by permission of the University of Chicago Press.

Jorge Luis Borges. "The Garden of Forking Paths" from *Labyrinths* by Jorge Luis Borges. Copyright © 1962, 1964 by New Directions Publishing Corp. Reprinted by permission of New Directions Publishing Corp. "The Labyrinth in 'The Garden of Forking Paths'" from *Twenty-four Conversations with Borges* by Robert Alifano. Reprinted by permission of Lascaux Publishers.

Tadeusz Borowski. "This Way for the Gas, Ladies and Gentlemen" from *This Way for the Gas, Ladies and Gentlemen* by Tadeusz Borowski, trans. Barbara Vedder. Copyright 1959 by Maria Borowski. Translation copyright © 1967 by Penguin Books Ltd. Reprinted by permission of Viking Penguin, a division of Penguin Books USA, Inc. and Penguin Books Ltd.

Paul Bowles. "The Eye" from *Midnight Mass* by Paul Bowles. Copyright © 1981 by Paul Bowles. Reprinted by permission of Black Sparrow Press.

Kay Boyle. "Black Boy" from *Fifty Stories* by Kay Boyle. Copyright © 1980 by Kay Boyle. Reprinted by permission of New Directions Publishing Corp.

T. Coraghessan Boyle. "Stones in My Passway, Hellhound on My Trail" from *Greasy Lake and Other Stories* by T. Coraghessan Boyle. Copyright © 1979 by T. Coraghessan Boyle. Reprinted by permission of Viking Penguin, a division of Penguin Books USA, Inc.

Robert H. Brinkmeyer, Jr. "Flannery O'Connor and Her Readers" from *The Art and Vision of Flannery O'Connor* by Robert H. Brinkmeyer, Jr. Copyright © 1989 by Louisiana State University Press. Used with permission.

Peter Brooks. "A Narratological Analysis of Borges's 'The Garden of Forking Paths'" from *Reading for the Plot* by Peter Brooks. Copyright © 1984 by Peter Brooks. Reprinted by permission of Alfred A. Knopf, Inc.

Robert Olen Butler. "A Good Scent from a Strange Mountain" from *A Good Scent from a Strange Mountain* by Robert Olen Butler. Copyright © 1992 by Robert Olen Butler. Reprinted by permission of Henry Holt and Company, Inc.

Italo Calvino. "The Feathered Ogre" from *Italian Folktales: Selected and Retold by Italo Calvino,* trans. George Martin. Copyright © 1956 by Giulio Einaudi editore, s.p.a. English translation copyright © 1980 by Harcourt Brace & Company. Reprinted by permission of Harcourt Brace & Company. "On 'Quickness' in Narrative" from *Six Memos for the Next Millenium* by Italo Calvino, trans. Patrick Creagh. English translation © 1992 by Patrick Creagh. Reprinted by permission of Jonathan Cape Ltd.

Albert Camus. "The Guest" from *Exile and the Kingdom* by Albert Camus. Copyright © 1957, 1958 by Alfred A. Knopf, Inc. Reprinted by permission of Alfred A. Knopf, Inc.

Angela Carter. "The Erl-King" from *The Bloody Chamber and Other Adult Tales* by Angela Carter. Copyright © 1979 by Angela Carter. Reprinted by permission of HarperCollins Publishers, Inc. and Rogers, Coleridge and White.

Raymond Carver, "Cathedral" from *Cathedral* by Raymond Carver. Copyright © 1981, 1982, 1983 by Raymond Carver. "On Errand" from *No Heroics, Please* by Raymond Carver. Copyright © 1992 by Alfred A. Knopf, Inc. "What We Talk About When We Talk About Love" from *What We Talk About When We Talk About Love* by Raymond Carver. Copyright © 1981 by Raymond Carver. Reprinted by permission of Alfred A. Knopf, Inc. "Errand" from *Where I'm Calling From* by Raymond Carver. Copyright © 1988 by Raymond Carver. Used by permission of Grove/Atlantic, Inc. "The Ashtray" from *Where Water Comes Together with Other Water* by Raymond Carver. Copyright © 1984 by Raymond Carver. Reprinted by permission of International Creative Management, Inc. "Creative Writing 101" from the Foreword to *On Becoming a Novelist* by John Gardner. Copyright © 1983 by the Estate of John Gardner. Reprinted by permission of HarperCollins Publishers, Inc. "On Writing" from the February 15, 1981 edition of *The New York Times.* Copyright © 1981 by The New York Times Company. Reprinted by permission of the Estate of Raymond Carver.

Willa Cather. "The Stories of Katherine Mansfield" from *Willa Cather on Writing* by Willa Cather. Copyright © 1949 by the Executors of the Estate of Willa Cather. Reprinted by permission of Alfred A. Knopf, Inc.

John Cheever. "The Swimmer" from *The Stories of John Cheever* by John Cheever. Copyright © 1964 by John Cheever. Reprinted by permission of Alfred A. Knopf, Inc. Excerpt from *Why I Write Short Stories* by John Cheever copyright © 1978 by John Cheever. Reprinted by permission of Wylie, Aitken & Stone, Inc. First appeared in *Newsweek.*

Anton Chekhov. "The Darling" from *Tales of Chekhov Volume 1: The Darling and Other Stories,* originally published by the Ecco Press in 1984. Copyright © 1916, 1944, 1972 by Macmillan Company. Reprinted by permission. "The Lady with the Pet Dog" from *The Portable Chekhov,* edited and translated by Avrahm Yarmolinsky. Copyright 1947, 1968 by The Viking Press, Inc. Copyright © 1975 by Avrahm Yarmolinsky. Reprinted by permission of the publisher, Viking Penguin, a division of Penguin Books USA, Inc.

Sandra Cisneros. "Little Miracles, Kept Promises" from *Woman Hollering Creek* by Sandra Cisneros. Copyright © 1991 by Sandra Cisneros. Published in the United States by Vintage Books, a division of Random House, Inc., New York, and simultaneously in Canada by Random House of Canada Limited, Toronto. Originally published in hardcover by Random House, Inc., New York, in 1991. Reprinted by permission of Susan Bergholz Literary Services, New York.

Julio Cortázar. "Axolotl" from *Blow-Up and Other Stories* by Julio Cortázar. Copyright © 1967 by Julio Cortázar. Reprinted by permission of Random House, Inc.

Linda Danielson. "A Feminist Reading of 'Storyteller'" from *Journal of the Southwest* (Autumn 1988). Copyright © 1988 by Journal of the Southwest. Reprinted by permission of the Journal of the Southwest.

Isak Dinesen. "The Sailor-Boy's Tale" from *Winter's Tales* by Isak Dinesen. Copyright © 1942 by Random House, Inc. and renewed 1970 by Johan Philip Thomas Ingerslev c/o The Rungstedlund Foundation. Reprinted by permission of Pantheon Books, a division of Random House, Inc. and The Rungstedlund Foundation.

Anthony Di Renzo. "A Dialogical Reading of 'Everything That Rises Must Converge,'" originally titled "The Last Laugh and the Liberty of December" from *American Gargoyles: Flannery O'Connor and the Medieval Grotesque* by Anthony Di Renzo. Copyright © 1993 by the Board of Trustees, Southern Illinois University. Reprinted by permission of Southern Illinois University Press and the author.

Ralph Ellison. "Battle Royal" from *Invisible Man* by Ralph Ellison. Copyright © 1948 by Ralph Ellison. Reprinted by permission of Random House, Inc. "King of the Bingo Game" by Ralph Ellison. Copyright © 1944 by Ralph Ellison. "The Influence of Folklore on 'Battle Royal'" from *Shadow and Act* by Ralph Ellison. Copyright © 1964 by Ralph Ellison. Reprinted by permission of William Morris Agency, Inc., on behalf of the author.

Richard Ellman. "A Biographical Perspective on Joyce's 'The Dead'" from *James Joyce: New and Revised Edition* by Richard Ellman. Copyright © 1959, 1982 by Richard Ellman. Reprinted by permission of Oxford University Press, Inc.

Louise Erdrich. "The Red Convertible" from *Love Medicine* by Louise Erdrich. Copyright © 1984 by Louise Erdrich. Reprinted by permission of Henry Holt and Company, Inc.

William Faulkner, "A Rose for Emily" from *Collected Stories of William Faulkner* by William Faulkner. Copyright © 1930 and renewed 1958 by William Faulkner. Reprinted by permission of Random House, Inc. "That Evening Sun" from *Collected Stories of William Faulkner* by William Faulkner. Copyright © 1931 and renewed 1959 by William Faulkner. "The Meaning of 'A Rose for Emily'" from *Faulkner in the University*, eds. Gwynn and Blotner. Copyright © 1959 by The University Press of Virginia. Reprinted by permission of The University Press of Virginia.

F. Scott Fitzgerald. "Babylon Revisited" from *Taps at Reveille* by F. Scott Fitzgerald. Copyright © 1931 by The Curtis Publishing Company and renewed © 1959 by Frances Scott Fitzgerald. Reprinted by permission of Charles Scribner's Sons, an imprint of Macmillan Publishing Company.

Gustave Flaubert. "A Simple Heart" from *Three Tales* by Gustave Flaubert, trans. Robert Baldick. Copyright 1961 by Robert Baldick. Reprinted by permission of Penguin Books Ltd.

Mavis Gallant. "1933" from *Across the Bridge* by Mavis Gallant. Copyright © 1993 by Mavis Gallant. Reprinted by permission of Random House, Inc. "What Is Style?" from *Paris Notebooks* by Mavis Gallant. Copyright © 1955 by Mavis Gallant. Reprinted by permission from Georges Borschardt, Inc.

Gabriel García Márquez. "A Very Old Man with Enormous Wings" from *Leaf Storm and Other Stories* by Gabriel García Márquez. Copyright © 1971 by Gabriel García Márquez. Reprinted by permission of HarperCollins Publishers, Inc.

John Gardner. Excerpt from "What Writers Do," from *Antæus* 40/41 (Winter/Spring 1991). Copyright © 1991 by John Gardner. Reprinted by permission of Ecco Press.

Sandra M. Gilbert and Susan Gubar. "A Feminist Reading of Gilman's 'The Yellow Wallpaper'" from *Madwoman in the Attic* by Sandra M. Gilbert and Susan Gubar. Copyright © 1979 by Yale University Press. Reprinted by permission of Yale University Press.

Nikolai Gogol. "The Overcoat" from *The Overcoat and Other Stories* by Nikolai Gogol, trans. Constance Garnett and trans. revised Leonard J. Kent. Reprinted by permission of Chatto & Windus for the Estate of Constance Garnett, A. P. Watt, Ltd., and Leonard J. Kent.

Nadine Gordimer. "Town and Country Lovers" from *A Soldier's Embrace* by Nadine Gordimer. Copyright © 1975 by Nadine Gordimer. Reprinted by permission of Viking Penguin, a division of Penguin Books USA, Inc. "The Flash of Fireflies" from *The Kenyon Review,* Fall 1968. Originally titled "South Africa." Copyright © 1968 by Kenyon College. Reprinted by permission of The Kenyon Review and the author.

Janice H. Harris. "A Psychological Explication of Lawrence's 'The Rocking-Horse Winner'" from *The Short Fiction of D. H. Lawrence* by Janice Hubbard Harris. Copyright © 1984 by Rutgers, the State University. Reprinted by permission of Rutgers University Press.

Bessie Head. "Life" from *Collectors of Treasures* by Bessie Head. Reprinted by permission of Heinemann Publishers (Oxford) Ltd.

Ernest Hemingway. "Hills Like White Elephants" from *Men Without Women* by Ernest Hemingway. Copyright 1927 by Charles Scribner's Sons and renewed © 1955 Ernest Hemingway. Reprinted by permission of Charles Scribner's Sons, an imprint of Macmillan Publishing Company.

Zora Neale Hurston. "Spunk" and "The Gilded Six-Bits" from Spunk: *The Selected Stories of Zora Neale Hurston.* Copyright © 1985 by The Zora Neale Hurston Estate. "What White Publishers Won't Print" from *I Love Myself When I Am Laughing* by Zora Neale Hurston. Copyright © 1979 by Zora Neale Hurston. Reprinted by permission of Lucy A. Hurston.

Shirley Jackson. "The Lottery" from *The Lottery* by Shirley Jackson. Copyright © 1948, 1949 by Shirley Jackson and renewed © 1976, 1977 by Laurence Hyman, Barry Hyman, Mrs. Sarah Webster, and Mrs. Joanne Schnurer. Reprinted by permission of Farrar, Straus & Giroux, Inc. "The Morning of June 28, 1948" originally titled "Biography of a Story" from *Come Along with Me* by Shirley Jackson. Copyright 1948, 1952, © 1960 by Shirley Jackson. Reprinted by permission of Viking Penguin, a division of Penguin Books USA, Inc.

Gustav Janouch. "Kafka's View of 'The Metamorphosis,'" from *Conversations with Kafka* by Gustav Janouch. Copyright © 1968 by S. Fischer Verlag GMBH Frankfurt-am-Main. Reprinted by permission of New Directions Publishing Corp. and Joan Daves Agency.

Tom Jenks. "The Origin of 'Cathedral'" from *Remembering Ray: A Composite Biography of Raymond Carver,* eds. W. L. Stull and M. P. Caroll. Copyright © 1993 by W. L. Stull and M. P. Caroll. Reprinted by permission of Capra Press.

Charles Johnson. "Menagerie: A Child's Fable" from *The Sorcerer's Apprentice* by Charles Johnson. Copyright © 1984 by Charles Johnson. Reprinted by permission of Atheneum Publishers, an imprint of Macmillan Publishing Company.

Franz Kafka. "The Hunger Artist" and "The Metamorphosis" copyright © 1948 and renewed 1976 by Schoecken Books, Inc. Reprinted by permission of Schoecken Books, a division of Random House, Inc.

Jamaica Kincaid. "Girl" from *At the Bottom of the River* by Jamaica Kincaid. Copyright © 1978, 1983 by Jamaica Kincaid. Reprinted by permission of Farrar, Straus & Giroux, Inc.

Milan Kundera. "The Hitchhiking Game" from *Laughable Loves* by Milan Kundera. Copyright © 1974 by Alfred A. Knopf, Inc. Reprinted by permission of Alfred A. Knopf, Inc. "Kafka and Modern History" originally titled "Somewhere Behind" from *The Art of the Novel* by Milan Kundera, trans. Linda Asher and David Bellos. Copyright © 1988 by Grove Press, Inc. Used by permission of Grove/Atlantic, Inc.

D. H. Lawrence. "Odour of Chrysanthemums" and "The Rocking-Horse Winner" from *Complete Short Stories of D. H. Lawrence* by D. H. Lawrence. Copyright 1933 by the Estate of D. H. Lawrence and renewed © 1961 by Angelo Ravagli and C. M. Weeley, Executors of the Estate of Freida Lawrence. "The Lust of Hate in Poe's 'The Cask of Amontillado,'" originally titled "Edgar Allan Poe" from *Studies in Classic American Literature* by D. H. Lawrence. Copyright 1923 by Thomas Seltzer, Inc. and renewed 1950 by Freida Lawrence. Copyright © 1961 by The Estate of the late Mrs. Freida Lawrence. Reprinted by permission of Viking Penguin, a division of Penguin Books USA, Inc.

David Leavitt. "Braids" from *Soho Square* by David Leavitt. Copyright © 1988 by David Leavitt. "The Way I Live Now" first appeared in the July 9, 1989 edition of *The New York Times.* Copyright © 1989 by David Leavitt. Reprinted by permission of Wylie, Aitken & Stone, Inc.

Ursula K. Le Guin. "The Ones Who Walk Away from Omelas" copyright © 1973, 1975 by Ursula K. Le Guin. Introductory note © 1975 by Ursula K. Le Guin. Reprinted by permission of the author and her agent, Virginia Kidd.

Simon O. Lesser. "A Psychological Reading of Hawthorne's 'My Kinsman, Major Molineux'" from "The Image of My Father" in *Partisan Review,* Vol. 22, No. 3, 1955. Reprinted by permission of the author.

Doris Lessing. "Debbie and Julie" from *The Real Thing* by Doris Lessing. Copyright © 1987, 1988, 1989, 1990, 1991, 1992 by Doris Lessing. Reprinted by permission of HarperCollins Publishers, Inc.

Naguib Mahfouz. "Half a Day" from *The Time and the Place and Other Stories* by Naguib Mahfouz. Copyright © 1991 by the American University in Cairo Press. Used by permission of Doubleday, a division of Bantam Doubleday Dell Publishing Group, Inc.

Bernard Malamud. "Black Is My Favorite Color" from *Idiots First* by Bernard Malamud. Copyright © 1963 by Bernard Malamud. Reprinted by permission of Farrar, Straus & Giroux, Inc.

Katherine Mansfield. "Bliss" and "The Garden-Party" from *The Short Stories of Katherine Mansfield.* Copyright © 1920 by Alfred A. Knopf, Inc. and renewed 1948 by J. Middleton Murry. Reprinted by permission of Alfred A. Knopf, Inc.

Saadat Hasan Manto. "The Dog of Titwal" from *Kingdom's End* by Saadat Hasan Manto. Copyright © 1989 by Saadat Hasan Manto. Reprinted by permission of Penguin Books Ltd.

Bobbie Ann Mason. "Shiloh" from *Shiloh and Other Stories* by Bobbie Ann Mason. Copyright © 1982 by Bobbie Ann Mason. Reprinted by permission of HarperCollins Publishers, Inc.

Dorothy Tuck McFarland. "On 'Good Country People'" from *Flannery O'Connor* by Dorothy Tuck McFarland. Copyright © 1976 by Dorothy Tuck McFarland. Reprinted by permission of the author.

J. Hillis Miller. "A Deconstructive Reading of Melville's 'Bartleby, the Scrivener'" is reprinted by permission of the publishers from *Versions of Pygmalion* by J. Hillis Miller. Copyright © 1990 by the President and Fellows of Harvard College, Cambridge, Mass.: Harvard University Press.

Yukio Mishima. "Fountains in the Rain" from *Acts of Worship* by Yukio Mishima, trans. John Bester. Copyright © 1989 by Kodansha International Ltd. Reprinted by permission. All rights reserved.

Lorrie Moore. "How to Become a Writer" from *Self-Help* by Lorrie Moore. Copyright © 1985 by M. L. Moore. Reprinted by permission of Alfred A. Knopf, Inc.

Es'Kia Mphahlele. "Mrs. Plum" from *Renewal Time* by Es'Kia Mphahlele. Copyright © 1990 by Es'Kia Mphahlele. Reprinted by permission of Readers International.

Bharati Mukherjee. "The Management of Grief" from *The Middleman and Other Stories.* Copyright © 1988 by Bharati Mukherjee. Used by permission of Grove/Atlantic, Inc. "A 400-Year-Old Woman" from *The Writer on Her Work, vol. 2,* ed. Janet Sternburg. Copyright © 1991 by Janet Sternburg. Reprinted by permission of Brandt & Brandt Literary Agents.

Alice Munro. "Walker Brothers Cowboy" from *Dance of the Happy Shades* by Alice Munro. Copyright © 1968 by Alice Munro. Published by McGraw-Hill Ryerson Limited. Reprinted by arrangement with the Virginia Barber Literary Agency and McGraw-Hill Ryerson Limited. All rights reserved.

Vladimir Nabokov. "Gogol's Genius in 'The Overcoat'" from *Nikolai Gogol* by Vladimir Nabokov. Copyright © 1944 by New Directions Publishing Corp. and renewed © 1971 by Vladimir Nabokov. Reprinted by permission of Smith/Skolnik Literary Management. "A Reading of Chekhov's 'The Lady with the Little Dog'" from *Lectures on Literature* by Vladimir Nabokov. Copyright © 1981 by The Estate of Vladimir Nabokov. Reprinted by permission of Harcourt Brace & Company.

Joyce Carol Oates. "Heat" from the 1991 edition of the *Paris Review.* Copyright © 1991 by The Ontario Review, Inc. "Where Are You Going, Where Have You Been?" from *The Wheel of Love and Other Stories* by Joyce Carol Oates. Copyright © 1970 by Joyce Carol Oates. Reprinted by permission of John Hawkins & Associates, Inc. "Smooth Talk: Short Story into Film" from *Woman Writer: Occasions and Opportunities* by Joyce Carol Oates. Copyright © 1988 by The Ontario Review. Reprinted by permission of Dutton Signet, a division of Penguin Books USA, Inc.

Tim O'Brien. "The Things They Carried" from the August 1986 edition of *Esquire.* Copyright © 1986 by Tim O'Brien. Reprinted by permission of International Creative Management, Inc.

Flannery O'Connor. "Good Country People" from *A Good Man Is Hard to Find and Other Stories* by Flannery O'Connor. Copyright © 1953 by Flannery O'Connor and renewed

© 1983 by Regina O'Connor. "A Good Man Is Hard to Find" from *A Good Man Is Hard to Find and Other Stories* by Flannery O'Connor. Copyright © 1955 by Flannery O'Connor and renewed © 1981 by Regina O'Connor. Reprinted by permission of Harcourt Brace & Company. "The Element of Suspense in 'A Good Man Is Hard to Find,'" excerpted from "On Her Own Work," and excerpt from "Writing Short Stories" from *Mystery and Manners* by Flannery O'Connor. Copyright © 1969 by the Estate of Mary Flannery O'Connor. "Everything That Rises Must Converge" from *Everything That Rises Must Converge* by Flannery O'Connor. Copyright © 1965 by the Estate of Mary Flannery O'Connor. "Letters 1955," excerpted from *Habit of Being* by Flannery O'Connor. Copyright © 1979 by Regina O'Connor. Reprinted by permission of Farrar, Straus & Giroux, Inc.

Frank O'Connor, "Guests of the Nation" from *Collected Stories* by Frank O'Connor. Copyright © 1981 by Harriet O'Donovan Sheehy, Executrix of the Estate of Frank O'Connor. Reprinted by permission of Alfred A. Knopf, Inc. and by arrangement with the Estate of Frank O'Connor, c/o Joan Daves Agency as agent for the proprietor. "Style and Form in Joyce's 'The Dead'" from *The Lonely Voice* by Frank O'Connor. Copyright © 1963 by Frank O'Connor. Reprinted by arrangement with the Estate of Frank O'Connor, c/o Joan Daves Agency as agent for the proprietor. "The Nearest Thing to Epic Poetry Is the Short Story" originally titled "Frank O'Connor" from *Writers at Work, First Series*, ed. Malcolm Cowley. Copyright © 1957, 1958 by the *Paris Review* and renewed © 1985 by Malcolm Cowley. Copyright © 1986 by the *Paris Review*. Reprinted by permission of Viking Penguin, a division of Penguin Books USA, Inc. and by arrangement with the Estate of Frank O'Connor, c/o Joan Daves Agency as agent for the proprietor.

Ben Okri. "In the Shadow of War" from *Stars of the New Curfew* by Ben Okri. Copyright © 1988 by Ben Okri. Reprinted by permission of Viking Penguin, a division of Penguin Books USA.

Tillie Olsen. "I Stand Here Ironing" from *Tell Me a Riddle* by Tillie Olsen. Copyright © 1956, 1957, 1960, 1961 by Tillie Olsen. Used by permission of Delacorte Press/Seymour Lawrence, a division of Bantam Doubleday Dell Publishing Group, Inc.

Cynthia Ozick. "The Shawl" from *The Shawl* by Cynthia Ozick. Copyright © 1980, 1983 by Cynthia Ozick. Reprinted by permission of Alfred A. Knopf, Inc.

Grace Paley. "A Conversation with My Father" from *Enormous Changes at the Last Minute* by Grace Paley. Copyright © 1974 by Grace Paley. Reprinted by permission of Farrar, Straus & Giroux, Inc.

Octavio Paz. "My Life with the Wave" from *Eagle or Sun?* by Octavio Paz, trans. Eliot Weinberger. Copyright © 1976 by New Directions Publishing Corp. Reprinted by permission of New Directions Publishing Corp.

Katherine A. Porter. "He" from *Flowering Judas and Other Stories* by Katherine A. Porter. Copyright 1930 and renewed © 1958 by Katherine A. Porter. Reprinted by permission of Harcourt Brace & Company.

V. S. Pritchett. "Flannery O'Connor: Satan Comes to Georgia" from *The Tale Bearers* by V. S. Pritchett. Copyright © 1980 by V. S. Pritchett. Reprinted by permission of Random House, Inc. and Sterling Lord Literistic.

Jim Ruppert. "Story-Telling: The Fiction of Leslie Marmon Silko" from *The Journal of Ethnic Studies* 9 (Spring 1981). Copyright © 1981 by The Journal of Ethnic Studies. Reprinted with permission from the Western Washington University Bureau for Faculty Research.

Arthur M. Saltzman. "A Reading of 'What We Talk About When We Talk About Love'" from *Understanding Raymond Carver* by Arthur M. Saltzman. Copyright © 1988 by the University of South Carolina. Reprinted by permission of the University of South Carolina Press.

Frank Sargeson. "A Great Day" from *Memoirs of a Peon* by Frank Sargeson. Copyright © 1983 by Frank Sargeson. Reprinted by permission of Heinemann Publishers (New Zealand) Ltd.

Eve Kosofky Sedgwick. "The Beast in the Closet" originally appeared in *Sex, Politics, and Science in the Nineteenth-Century Novel*, ed. Ruth Yeazell. Copyright © 1991 by The Johns Hopkins University Press. Reprinted by permission of The Johns Hopkins University Press.

Leslie Marmon Silko. "Lullaby," "Storyteller," and "Yellow Woman" from *Storyteller* by Leslie Marmon Silko. Copyright © 1981 by Leslie Marmon Silko. Reprinted from *Storyteller* by Leslie Marmon Silko, published by Seaver Books, New York, New York. Reprinted with permission. "Language and Literature from a Pueblo Indian's Perspective" from *English Literature: Opening Up the Canon,* eds. Leslie A. Fiedler and Houston A. Baker, Jr. Copyright © 1979 by Leslie Marmon Silko. Reprinted by permission of The Johns Hopkins University Press.

Isaac Bashevis Singer. "The Spinoza of Market Street" from *The Spinoza of Market Street* by Isaac Bashevis Singer. Copyright © 1961 and renewed © 1989 by Isaac Bashevis Singer. Reprinted by permission of Farrar, Straus & Giroux, Inc.

Jane Smiley. "Long Distance" from *The Age of Grief* by Jane Smiley. Copyright © 1977, 1981, 1984, 1986, 1987 by Jane Smiley. Reprinted by permission of Alfred A. Knopf, Inc. "Gregor: My Life as a Bug" from *Harper's Magazine* "Forum." Copyright © 1992 by *Harper's Magazine.* All rights reserved. Reprinted from the August issue by special permission.

Susan Sontag. "The Way We Live Now" by Susan Sontag. Copyright © 1986 by Susan Sontag. Reprinted by permission of Farrar, Straus & Giroux, Inc.

John Steinbeck. "The Chrysanthemums" from *The Long Valley* by John Steinbeck. Copyright 1937 and renewed © 1965 by John Steinbeck. Reprinted by permission of Viking Penguin, a division of Penguin Books USA, Inc.

Amy Tan. "Two Kinds" from *The Joy Luck Club* by Amy Tan. Copyright © 1989 by Amy Tan. Reprinted by permission of G. P. Putnam's Sons.

James Thurber. "The Secret Life of Walter Mitty" from *My World—And Welcome to It* by James Thurber, published by Harcourt Brace & Company, Inc. Copyright © 1942 by James Thurber and renewed © 1970 by Helen Thurber and Rosemary A. Thurber. Reprinted by permission of Rosemary A. Thurber.

Tatyana Tolstaya. "Night" from *Sleepwalker in a Fog* by Tatyana Tolstaya. Copyright © 1992 by Tatyana Tolstaya. Reprinted by permission of Alfred A. Knopf, Inc.

Leo Tolstoy. "Chekhov's Intent in 'The Darling'" from *Tales of Chekhov Volume 1: The Darling and Other Stories,* originally published by the Ecco Press in 1984. Copyright © 1916, 1944, 1972 by Macmillan Company. Reprinted by permission.

Lionel Trilling. "The Greatness of Conrad's 'Heart of Darkness'" from "On the Teaching of Modern Literature" in *Beyond Culture.* Copyright © 1965 by Lionel Trilling. Reprinted by permission of Harcourt Brace & Company.

Henri Troyat. Excerpt from *Chekhov* by Henri Troyat, trans. Michael Henry Heim. Translation copyright © 1986 by E. P. Dutton. Reprinted by permission of Dutton Signet, a division of Penguin Books USA, Inc.

John Updike. "A & P" from *Pigeon Feathers and Other Stories* by John Updike. Copyright © 1962 by John Updike. Reprinted by permission of Alfred A. Knopf, Inc.

Alice Walker. "Roselily" from *In Love & Trouble: Stories of Black Women* by Alice Walker. Copyright © 1972 by Alice Walker. Reprinted by permission of Harcourt Brace & Company. "Zora Neale Hurston: A Cautionary Tale and a Partisan View" from *In Search of Our Mothers' Gardens* by Alice Walker. Copyright © 1983 by Alice Walker. Reprinted by permission from the University of Illinois Press.

Eudora Welty. "Why I Live at the P.O." and "A Worn Path" from *A Curtain of Green and Other Stories* by Eudora Welty. Copyright 1941 and renewed © 1969 by Eudora Welty. Reprinted by permission of Harcourt Brace & Company. "Is Phoenix Jackson's Grandson Really Dead?" and "Plot and Character in Chekhov's 'The Darling,'" originally titled "Reality in Chekhov's Stories" from *The Eye of the Story* by Eudora Welty. Copyright © 1974 by Eudora Welty. Reprinted by permission of Random House, Inc.

Edith Wharton. "Roman Fever" from *Roman Fever and Other Stories* by Edith Wharton. Copyright 1934 by Liberty Magazine and renewed © 1962 by William R. Tyler. "Every Subject Must Contain within Itself Its Own Dimensions" from *The Writing of Fiction* by Edith Wharton. Copyright 1925 by Charles Scribner's Sons and renewed © 1953 by Frederic R. King. Reprinted by permission of Charles Scribner's Sons, an imprint of Macmillan Publishing Company.

John Edgar Wideman. "The Beginning of Homewood" from *All Stories Are True* by John Edgar Wideman. Copyright © 1992 by John Edgar Wideman. Reprinted by permission of Pantheon Books, a division of Random House, Inc.

Christa Wolf. "Exchanging Glances" from *What Remains and Other Stories* by Christa Wolf, trans. Heike Schwarzbauer and Rick Takvorian. Copyright © 1993 by Farrar, Straus & Giroux, Inc. Reprinted by permission of Farrar, Straus & Giroux, Inc.

Tobias Wolff. "Say Yes" from *Back in the World* by Tobias Wolff. Copyright © 1981 by Tobias Wolff. Reprinted by permission of International Creative Management, Inc.

Virginia Woolf. "Kew Garden" from *A Haunted House and Other Stories* by Virginia Woolf.